NO PLAN B

Lee Child
and
Andrew Child

bantam

TRANSWORLD PUBLISHERS
Penguin Random House, One Embassy Gardens,
8 Viaduct Gardens, London SW11 7BW
www.penguin.co.uk

Transworld is part of the Penguin Random House group of companies
whose addresses can be found at global.penguinrandomhouse.com

Penguin
Random House
UK

First published in Great Britain in 2022 by Bantam
an imprint of Transworld Publishers

A CIP catalogue record for this book
is available from the British Library.

ISBNs 9781787633759 (cased)
9781787633766 (tpb)

Typeset in 11.25/15.75 pt Century Old Style by Jouve (UK), Milton Keynes
Printed and bound in Great Britain by Clays Ltd, Elcograf S.p.A.

The authorized representative in the EEA is Penguin Random House Ireland,
Morrison Chambers, 32 Nassau Street, Dublin D02 YH68.

Penguin Random House is committed to a sustainable
future for our business, our readers and our planet. This book
is made from Forest Stewardship Council® certified paper.

For everyone we have lost too soon

ONE

The meeting was held in a room with no windows.

The room was rectangular and it had no windows because it had no external walls. It was contained within a larger, square room. And the square room was contained within an even larger octagonal room. Together this nest of rooms formed the command hub of Unit S2 at the Minerva Correctional Facility in Winson, Mississippi. Along with its sister segregation unit, S1, it was the most secure place in the complex. It was laid out with walls like the concentric rings of a medieval castle. Designed to be impregnable. From the outside, even if attacked by the most determined rescuers. And from the inside, even during the most extreme riot.

The safety aspect was welcome but the reason the hub had been chosen for this meeting was its seclusion. The opportunity it offered for complete secrecy. Because the rest of Unit S2 was vacant. There were no guards. No admin staff.

1

And none of its hundred and twenty isolation cells were in use. They weren't needed. Not with the way the prison was run under its current management. The progressive approach was a cause of great pride. And great PR.

There were six men in the room, and this was the third covert meeting they'd held there in the last week. The men were spread out around a long, narrow table and there were two spare chairs pushed back against a blank, white wall. The furniture was made of bright blue polycarbonate. Each piece was cast in a single mould, leaving no joins or seams. The shape and material made the items hard to break. The colour made it hard to conceal any parts that did somehow get smashed off. It was practical. But not very comfortable. And all left over from the previous administration.

Three of the men were wearing suits. Bruno Hix, Minerva's Chief Executive and joint founder, at the head of the table. Damon Brockman, Chief Operating Officer and the other joint founder, to Hix's right. And Curtis Riverdale, the prison's warden, next to Brockman. The man next to Riverdale, the last one on that side of the table, was wearing a uniform. He was Rod Moseley, Chief of the Winson Police Department. On the opposite side, to Hix's left, were two guys in their late twenties. Both were wearing black T-shirts and jeans. One had a broken nose and two black eyes and a forehead full of angry purple bruises. The other had his left arm in a sling. Both were trying to avoid the other men's eyes.

'So is there a problem or not?' Brockman shrugged his shoulders. 'Can anyone say for sure that there is? No. Therefore we should go ahead as planned. There's too much at stake to start running from shadows.'

'No.' Riverdale shook his head. 'If there *might be* a

problem, that means there is a problem, the way I see things. Safety first. We should—'

'We should find out for sure,' Moseley said. 'Make an informed decision. The key is, did the guy look in the envelope? That's what we need to know.'

No one spoke.

'Well?' Moseley stretched his leg out under the table and kicked the guy with the sling. 'Wake up. Answer the question.'

'Give me a break.' The guy stifled a yawn. 'We had to drive all night to get to Colorado. And all night again to get back here.'

'Cry me a river.' Moseley prodded the guy with his foot. 'Just tell us. Did he look?'

The guy stared at the wall. 'We don't know.'

'Looking in the envelope isn't definitive,' Riverdale said. 'If he did look, we need to know if he understood what he saw. And what he plans to do about it.'

'Whether the guy looked is irrelevant,' Brockman said. 'So what if he did? Nothing in there gives the slightest clue to what's going on.'

Riverdale shook his head. 'It mentions ten a.m. on Friday. Very clearly. The time, the date, the place.'

'So what?' Brockman raised his hands. 'Friday's an occasion for joy and celebration. There's nothing remotely suspicious about it.'

'But the photograph was in there.' Riverdale jabbed the air with his finger in time with each syllable. 'Eight by ten. Impossible to miss.'

'And again, that means nothing.' Brockman threw himself back in his chair. 'Not unless the guy actually comes here. If he shows up on Friday. And even then we'd be OK. We chose very carefully.'

'We didn't. How could we? We only had nine to pick from.'

A smile flashed across Moseley's face. 'Ironic, isn't it? That the one we picked really is innocent.'

'I wouldn't call it ironic.' Riverdale scowled. 'And there weren't nine. There were only five. The others had family. That ruled them out.'

'Nine?' Brockman said. 'Five? Whatever. The number doesn't matter. Only the outcome matters. And the outcome is good enough. Even if the guy shows up, how close would he get? He'd be a hundred feet away, at least.'

'He doesn't have to show up. He could see it on TV. Online. Read about it in the newspapers.'

'The warden has a point,' Moseley said. 'Maybe it would be better not to draw so much attention this time. Maybe we should cancel the media. We could float some BS about respecting the inmates' privacy, or something.'

'No need.' Brockman shook his head. 'You think this guy has a television? A computer? A subscription to the *New York Times*? He's destitute, for goodness' sake. Stop looking for trouble. There isn't any.'

Hix tapped his fingertips on the tabletop. 'Media exposure is good for the brand. We always publicize. We always have. If we change now, we would only attract more attention. Make people think something is wrong. But I do think we need to know. Did he look?' Hix turned to the guys in the T-shirts. 'Best guess. No wrong answer. The chips fell where they fell. We understand that. Just tell us what you believe.'

The guy with the broken nose took a deep breath through his mouth. 'I think he looked.'

'You think?' Hix said. 'But you're not sure.'

'Not one hundred per cent.'

'OK. Where was the envelope?'

'In the bag.'

'Where was the bag?'

'On the ground.'

'You put it down?'

'I needed my hands free.'

'Where was it when the car arrived?' Hix said.

The guy with the sling said, 'On the ground.'

'In the same place?'

'How could we know? I wasn't there when Robert put it down. Robert wasn't conscious when I picked it up.'

Hix paused for a moment. 'OK. How long was the guy alone with the bag?'

'We don't know. Can't have been long. A couple of minutes, max.'

'So it's possible he looked,' Hix said. 'Glanced, anyway.'

'Right,' the guy with the broken nose said. 'And the bag was ripped, remember. How did that happen? And why? We didn't do it.'

Brockman leaned forward. 'It was a crazy scene, from what you told us. Wreckage everywhere. Total chaos. The bag probably got ripped by accident. It doesn't sound like some major clue. And the other two haven't reported that he looked.'

The guy with the sling said, 'They haven't reported at all. We don't know where they are.'

Brockman said, 'Must still be on their way back. Phone problems, probably. But if there was anything to worry about they would have found a way to let us know.'

'And the guy didn't mention anything about it to the police,' Moseley said. 'I've talked to the lieutenant over there a couple times. That has to mean something.'

'I still think he looked,' the guy with the broken nose said.

5

'We should pull the plug,' Riverdale said.

'That's the dumbest thing I ever heard,' Brockman said. 'We didn't set the date. We didn't pick the time. The judge did when he signed the release order. You know that. We pull some bullshit delaying tactic, we wind up ass-deep in inspectors. You know where that would land us. We might as well shoot ourselves in the head, right here, right now.'

Riverdale scowled. 'I'm not saying we delay. I'm saying we go back to the original plan. The switch was always a mistake.'

'That would solve Friday's problem. If there is one. But then we'd have no way out of the bigger jam we're in. Carpenter's situation.'

'I said from the start, the solution to that is simple. A bullet in the back of his head. I'll do it myself if you're too squeamish.'

'You know what that would cost? How much business we would lose?'

'We'll lose a lot more than money if this guy joins the dots.'

'How could he do that?'

'He could come down here. You said so yourself. He could dig around. He was a military cop. It's in his blood.'

'It's years since the guy was an MP,' Moseley said. 'That's what the lieutenant told me.'

Hix tapped the tabletop. 'What else do we know?'

'Not much. He has no driver's licence. No employment history, according to the IRS. Not since he left the army. No social media presence. No recent photographs exist. He's a hobo now. It's kind of sad, but that's the bottom line. Doesn't sound like much to worry about.'

Brockman said, 'Hobo or millionaire, what kind of crazy person would travel halfway across the country because he read a few documents and saw an innocuous picture?'

'Speculate all you want, but this still worries me,' Riverdale said. 'Each time we met, we thought we had the problem contained. Each time, we were wrong. What if we're wrong again now?'

'We weren't wrong.' Brockman slammed his palm into the table. 'We handled each situation as it came up. Ninety-nine per cent.'

'Ninety-nine. Not one hundred.'

'Life isn't perfect. Sometimes there's broken glass to sweep up. Which we've done. We found out there was a leak. We plugged it, the way we all agreed to. We found out about the missing envelope. We retrieved it, the way we all agreed to.'

'And now this strange guy has looked in the envelope.'

'He may have. We don't know. But you have to admit, it's unlikely. He didn't tell the cops. We know that. And he didn't tell the FBI or the Bureau of Prisons. We would know that. So say he figured everything out from a couple of seconds alone with the envelope. Why keep the knowledge to himself? What's he going to do with it? Blackmail us? And you think he's somehow going to schlep twelve hundred miles before Friday? Come on.'

'Gentlemen!' Hix tapped the tabletop again. 'Enough. All right. Here's my decision. We can't know if the guy looked in the envelope. It seems unlikely, so we shouldn't panic. Particularly given the consequences. But at the same time it pays to be cautious. He's easily recognizable, yes?'

The guy with the broken nose nodded. 'For sure. You can't miss him. Six five. Two hundred and fifty pounds. Scruffy.'

'He's banged up pretty good, remember,' the guy with the sling said. 'I took care of that.'

'You should have killed him,' Brockman said.

'I thought I had.'

7

'You should have made sure.'

'How? *Make it look like an accident.* Those were our orders for the other two. I figured they applied to this guy as well. Hard to sell that story if I put a bullet in his brain.'

'Enough!' Hix waited for silence. 'Here's the plan. We'll mount surveillance. Round the clock. Starting now, through Saturday. If he sets one toe in our town, we'll be waiting. And here, we don't have to worry about how anything looks.'

TWO

Jack Reacher arrived in Gerrardsville, Colorado, mid-morning on a Monday, two days before the Minerva guys met in secret for the third time. He had hitched a ride in a truck that was delivering alfalfa bales to a farm south of the town, so he covered the final mile on foot. It was a pleasant walk. The weather was warm, but not hot. Tufts of cloud drifted across the wide blue sky. The mile-high air was thin and clear. As far as he could see, the land was flat and green and fertile. Watering gantries marked the boundaries of endless fields and between them stalks and leaves of all sizes and shades stretched up toward the sun. To the left the horizon was dominated by a line of mountains. They jutted straight out of the ground, no gentle build-up, no smooth foothills, and their peaks, capped with snow, cut into the atmosphere like the teeth of a saw.

Reacher continued until he came to the town's main drag. It carried on for about a half-mile, and there was only one block on either side before the stores and offices gave way to the residential streets. The commercial buildings were a uniform size. They were two storeys high and they all had similar designs. They were all a similar age, too – late nineteenth century, based on the dates carved into some of the lintels – which gave the place a kind of time-capsule feel. A time when craftsmanship was still valued. That was clear. The facades were all made from stone or marble or granite. The woodwork around the doors and windows was intricately carved and lavishly picked out with gold leaf. And every aspect was flawlessly maintained. Reacher appreciated what he saw. But he wasn't in town to admire its architecture. He was there to visit its museum.

The previous day Reacher had picked up a newspaper someone had abandoned in a diner. He found an article about a dentist and a metal detector. The gadget had been given to the guy as a retirement gift. Some kind of an in-joke based on his reputation for finding fillings done by other dentists in new patients' teeth and insisting on replacing them. Anyway, to occupy his sudden leisure time the guy reinvented himself as an amateur archaeologist. He'd long been obsessed by the Civil War so he set out to visit a whole series of battle sites. Big and small. Famous and obscure. And at Pea Ridge, Arkansas, he found a bunch of artillery fragments and other artefacts. These got rolled into a travelling exhibition about the evolution of Union tactics, which caught Reacher's eye. Gerrardsville was one of the venues for the display. And as he was only a few miles away while the show was still open, he figured he'd take a look.

Reacher had a cup of coffee at a café he happened to walk past and got to the museum before lunchtime. He stayed until it closed. When he had to be shooed out by one of the curators. Her name was Alexandra. Reacher struck up a conversation with her about the exhibit. The subject turned to the kind of restaurants there were in the town, and they wound up going for a burger together. Alexandra picked a scruffy kind of place. It had rough wooden tabletops. Long benches. Creaky floorboards. Old LP covers were tacked up all over the walls. But the food came fast. The plates were piled high. The prices were low. Reacher liked everything about it.

While they ate the subject changed to music and they wound up at a bar together. It was small. Intimate. Dark. A blues band was playing. Mainly Magic Slim covers with a handful of Howlin' Wolf songs sprinkled through. Reacher approved. Alexandra ordered a couple of beers and as they drank the subject changed again. It led them in a whole different direction this time. And all the way to Alexandra's apartment.

Her apartment was above a store near the main intersection in the town. It was a small place. The style was minimalist. It didn't have much in the way of furniture. Or decor. But it did have a fridge, so they had another beer. It had a CD player, so they listened to some more music. It had a bedroom. And once they reached it, there wasn't much need for more of anything else.

THREE

The museum didn't open the next day until ten a.m. so Reacher and Alexandra stayed in bed until the last possible minute.

They stayed in bed, but they didn't spend all their time sleeping. Alexandra knew she was cutting it fine but she took a quick shower anyway. She felt it was wise after their recent level of activity. Reacher made coffee. Then she kissed him goodbye and hurried away to her chosen slice of the past. Reacher took a more leisurely shower then made his way down the stairs and out on to the sidewalk. He was thinking about his more immediate future. He paused to gaze at the mountains for a moment. Then he saw a woman walking toward them. She was on the other side of the street, heading west, almost at the intersection. The *Don't Walk* sign was lit up. A guy was standing on the opposite corner, waiting for it for change. And a bus was heading north, about to pass between them.

*

The bus driver only saw movement.

Not much more than a blur. Low and to her right. A spherical object. Swinging down and around through a quarter of a perfect circle. Like a melon had somehow been attached to the end of a rope, she told the mandatory counsellor the following day. Only it wasn't a melon. It was a head. A human head. It was female. Inches from the windshield. There. Bright and pale in the sunlight, like it already belonged to a ghost. Then gone. But not because the driver had imagined it. Not because it was an illusion, like she prayed for it to be. Because it continued on its arc. All the way to the ground. In front of the bus.

Then under it.

The driver veered hard to the left. She threw all her weight on to the brake. No hesitation. No panic. She was well trained. She had years of experience. But she was still too late. She heard the tyres squeal. Heard her passengers scream. And felt the impact. Through the steering wheel. Just a slight, muted ripple running around the hard plastic rim. Less of a jolt than if she'd driven through a deep pothole. Or hit a log. But then, asphalt doesn't have bones that crush and shatter. Wood doesn't have organs that rupture and bleed.

The driver shut her eyes and willed herself not to vomit. She knew the kind of scene that would be waiting for her on the street. She'd been an unwilling partner in a stranger's suicide once before. It was an occupational hazard.

The guy on the opposite corner saw a lot more.

He saw the bus heading north. He saw a woman arrive at the south-east corner of the intersection. He had an unobstructed view. He was close enough to be credible. In his statement he said the woman looked nervous. Twitchy. He

13

saw her check her watch. At first he figured she was in a hurry. He thought she was going to try to run across the street before the bus got too close. But she didn't. She stopped. She stood and squirmed and fidgeted until the bus was almost alongside her. Until there was no chance for it to slow or swerve.

Then she dived under its wheels.

The woman dived. The guy was certain about that. She didn't trip. She didn't fall. It was a deliberate act. He could tell from the timing. The way her body accelerated. The curve it moved through. The precise aim. There was no way it could have been an accident. She had done it on purpose. He could see no other explanation.

Reacher was the only one who saw the whole picture.

He was about fifty feet from the intersection. His outlook was also unobstructed but he had a wider angle of view. He saw the woman and the guy waiting to cross in opposite directions. And he saw a third person. A man. Around five foot ten. Wiry-looking. Wearing a grey hoodie and jeans. On the same side as the woman. Eight feet away from her. A foot back from the kerb. Standing completely still.

The guy had picked his spot carefully. That was clear. He was in the general vicinity of the crosswalk so he didn't attract attention the way someone loitering aimlessly might. He was far enough away from the woman that he didn't appear to be connected to her in any way. But he was close enough that when the bus approached he only needed to take a couple of steps to reach her side. His movement was smooth. Fluid. He was more like a shadow than a physical presence. The woman didn't notice him appear next to her. She didn't notice his foot snake around in front of her ankles.

14

The guy planted his hand between the woman's shoulder blades and pushed. It was a small motion. Economical. Not dramatic. Not something most observers would notice. But sufficient for the guy's purpose. That was for sure. There was no danger of the woman stumbling forward and bouncing off the front of the bus. No danger she might get away with broken bones and a concussion. The guy's foot took care of that. It stopped the woman from moving her own feet. It made sure she pivoted, ankles stationary, arms flailing. And it guaranteed she slammed horizontally on to the ground.

The impact knocked the breath out of the woman's body. Her last breath. Because half a second later the bus's front wheel crushed her abdomen as flat as a folded newspaper.

FOUR

The bus came to rest at an angle from the kerb like it had been stolen by a drunk and then abandoned when the prank lost its gloss. The front end was partly blocking the intersection. Reacher saw the route number on the electronic panel above its entry door switch to a written message: CALL POLICE. He also saw the dead woman's legs. They were jutting out from under the bus, about halfway between its front and rear wheels. One of her sneakers had fallen off. The guy who had pushed her took a black trash bag from the back pocket of his jeans. He shook it open. Crouched down next to her bare foot. Stretched an arm under the bus. Snagged something and pulled it out. Reacher realized it was the woman's purse. The guy slipped it into the trash bag. Stood up. Adjusted his hood. And strolled away, heading south, disappearing from sight.

Reacher ran across the street, diagonally, toward the bus. The sidewalk was starting to fill up. People were spilling out of

16

the shops and cafés and offices to gawp at the body. A man in a suit had stopped his car and climbed out to get a better look. But no one was paying any attention to the guy in the hoodie. He was melting away through the fringe of the crowd. Reacher barrelled through the spectators, shoving people aside, knocking one of them on his ass. The guy in the hoodie cleared the last of the onlookers. He picked up his pace. Reacher kept going, pushing harder. He barged between one final couple and broke back into a run. The guy was sixty feet ahead now. Reacher closed the gap to fifty feet. Forty-five. Then the guy heard the footsteps chasing him. He glanced over his shoulder. Saw Reacher bearing down on him. He started to run, still clutching the trash bag in one hand. He slipped his other hand up inside his hood. Jabbed at a device that was jammed into his right ear. Barked out a couple of sentences. Then veered off into an alleyway that stretched away to his left.

Reacher kept running until he was a couple of feet from the mouth of the alley. Then he stopped. He listened. He heard nothing so he knelt down, crept forward and peered around the corner. He figured if the guy had a gun he'd be looking for a target at head height. If he had a knife he'd be winding up for a lunge to the gut. But Reacher didn't encounter any threat. There was no response at all. So he got back to his feet and took a step forward.

The alley was the cleanest he had ever been in. The walls of the adjoining buildings were pale brick. They looked neat and even. There was no graffiti. None of the first-floor windows were broken. The fire escapes looked freshly painted. There were dumpsters lined up on both sides. They were evenly spaced out. Some were green. Some were blue. All had lids. None were overflowing, and there was no trash blowing around on the ground.

The guy was thirty feet away. His back was against the left-hand wall. He was standing completely still and the trash bag was on the ground at his feet. Reacher moved toward him. He closed the gap to twenty feet. Then the guy lifted the hem of his hoodie. A black, boxy pistol was sticking out of his waistband.

The guy said, 'Hold it. That's close enough.'

Reacher kept moving. He closed the gap to ten feet.

The guy's hand hovered over the grip of his pistol. He said, 'Stop. Keep your hands where I can see them. There's no need for anyone to get hurt. We just need to talk.'

Reacher closed the gap to four feet. Then he said, 'Anyone else.'

'What?' the guy said.

'Someone already got hurt. The woman you pushed. Was there a need for that?'

The guy's mouth opened and closed but no words came out.

Reacher said, 'Down on the ground. Fingers laced behind your head.'

The guy didn't respond.

'Maybe there is no need for anyone else to get hurt,' Reacher said. 'And by *anyone*, I mean *you*. It all depends on what you do next.'

The guy went for his gun. He was fast. But not fast enough. Reacher grabbed the guy's wrist and whipped it away to his right, spinning him around so he was facing the wall.

'Stop.' The guy's voice was suddenly shrill. 'Wait. What are you doing?'

'I'm going to see how you like it,' Reacher said. 'There's no bus. But there are bricks. They'll have to do.'

Reacher let go of the guy's wrist. Moved his hand up.

18

Planted it between the guy's shoulder blades. And pushed. It was a huge motion. Savage. Wild. Way more than sufficient. The guy tried to save himself but he had no chance. The force was overwhelming. He smashed into the wall, face first, and flopped on to the ground like the bones in his legs had dissolved. Blood was sluicing down from the gashes in his forehead. His nose was broken. There was a serious chance he could suffocate. Or drown.

Neither of those outcomes would have worried Reacher too much.

FIVE

Reacher's plan had been to scoop the guy up and carry him back to the bus. That way he'd be ready for when the police arrived. But when he retrieved the trash bag, he paused. The woman's purse was inside. And something in her purse was worth killing for. Reacher had been an investigator in the army for thirteen years. Old habits die hard. And he couldn't hear any sirens yet. He knew he had a little time.

Reacher picked up the fallen gun and tucked it into his waistband. Then he wrestled the guy into the recovery position at the foot of the wall and started with his pockets. There was nothing with a name or an address, as Reacher expected, but the guy did have a bunch of keys. Reacher selected the sharpest one and used it to hack a pair of rough, broad strips from around the top of the trash bag. He wrapped the strips around his hands and took out the purse. It was eighteen inches square, made from some kind of faux leather, tan

20

colour, with a long narrow shoulder strap as well as regular handles. One side was speckled with blood. The opening was secured with a zipper. Reacher unfastened it. He rummaged inside. The first thing he pulled out was the woman's wallet. It held a Mississippi driver's licence with the name Angela St. Vrain and an address in a town called Winson. There were three dollars in singles. A wad of receipts from a supermarket and a drugstore. And a photograph of Angela with a little girl. Maybe three years old. The family resemblance was clear. Mother and daughter. Reacher had no doubt.

Reacher set the wallet on the ground and delved back into the purse. He pulled out a laminated card on a pale blue lanyard. A work ID. It showed that Angela was a prison employee of some kind. At a place called the Minerva Correctional Facility, which was also in Winson, Mississippi. He found a hairbrush and a bunch of make-up and other personal items. A key ring, with three keys on it. And an envelope. It was regular Manila style. Letter size. But it was addressed to someone else. Another resident of Winson, Mississippi called Danny Peel. And it had been opened.

The envelope contained one black-and-white photograph – a mugshot dated sixteen years ago – and a stack of papers. The photograph was of a young adult male. His face was drawn and pinched and he had a smattering of close-cropped hair. A recent cut, Reacher thought, based on the pale skin shining through the stubble. He was also drawn to the kid's eyes. They were set close together, and they were wide open, looking half frightened, half confused. And the kid had another unusual feature. One of his earlobes was missing. His left. It looked like it had been sliced off. Its edge was straight and raw and a scar was visible on his neck, running around the back of his head. Done with a straight razor,

Reacher thought. Someone must have slashed at the kid, going for his throat, and the kid must have twisted and hunched and pulled away. Not fast enough to avoid getting cut. But fast enough to not get killed. Which was something, Reacher thought. Maybe.

The papers broke down into two groups. The first set was marked Mississippi Department of Corrections and it began the life story of a guy called Anton Begovic. Of his adult life, anyway. It told how Begovic had gotten in trouble at eighteen. He was implicated in a burglary. A bunch of other offences were linked to him. The weight of the charges grew until he wound up behind bars. An apparently inevitable progression. And things only got worse for him in prison. Within three years he was in solitary. He stayed there for the next seven. But with the second set of papers Begovic's life turned around.

The change coincided with the prison being taken over by Minerva Correctional. Angela's employer. Begovic was returned to the general population. His behaviour improved. The prison company sponsored an appeal. A PI turned up a deathbed confession from an ex-con who admitted to the offences that had been pinned on Begovic. The detective who put the case together was found to have killed himself a decade ago, neck deep in gambling debt. And a judge ordered Begovic's release. It was imminent. According to the final record, he was going to be set free at ten a.m. that coming Friday.

Reacher slid the photo and the documents back into the envelope. He put the envelope back into the purse and loaded up Angela's other possessions. He zipped the purse closed and dropped it into the trash bag. Then he unwound the plastic strips from his hands and jammed them into his pocket.

He was thinking about the contents of the envelope. The tragic tale of a wrongly convicted man. He wondered what it had to do with Angela. Which made him think of another tragic tale. One that was just beginning. For the little girl in the wallet photo. Angela's daughter. Who would now have to grow up without a mother.

SIX

A car nosed into the entrance to the alley. A black sedan. It was shiny. Sleek. A BMW. Reacher could tell from the blue-and-white emblem on its hood. It was supposed to represent sky and clouds. Reacher had read about it somewhere. That it harked back to the company's roots as an aero engine manufacturer. He had no idea which model it was, though. He was no kind of a car guy.

The BMW crept forward. The driver was also wearing a grey hoodie. He slowed to a stop, lowered his window, and said, 'Hands where I can see them. Then step away.'

Reacher didn't move.

The driver shifted into neutral and revved the engine. He floored the gas pedal twice, three times, then waited for the angry sound to subside. 'I said, step away.'

Reacher stayed still.

The car was ten feet from Reacher and eight feet from the wall. The unconscious guy was on the ground, six inches from Reacher's heels. Presumably he was the driver's buddy. Which would be why the driver wanted Reacher to move. To avoid harming both of them.

Reacher stayed still.

The car crept forward. The driver pulled on the wheel. He kept going, inching across until the gap between Reacher and the front fender was down to four feet. Then he straightened up and hit the gas. The car surged ahead. The driver held the wheel with his right hand. He worked the door handle with his left. He pushed the door all the way open and kept it there like he was a knight on horseback trying to bludgeon his opponent with his shield. Trying to knock him down. Or back him away from his safe position, at least.

Reacher didn't back away. Instead he took a step forward. Toward the car. He raised his knee and drove the ball of his foot into the door. He put all his strength into the kick. All his weight. He connected with the centre of the panel. The metal skin warped and shrieked and deformed. The door slammed shut. The car fizzed past Reacher then swerved away to the right. The driver fought the wheel. He braked, hard, but he was a moment too late. The front right corner of the car slammed into a dumpster on the other side of the alley. Its headlight shattered. The driver slammed into reverse and hit the gas again. He tugged on the wheel. The car slewed around then straightened. Its back left corner was lined up with Reacher's legs. The guy on the ground would be fine. He would be safely beneath the car's rear overhang. But Reacher wouldn't escape. Not at that angle. He'd be crushed against the wall.

Reacher dived toward the mouth of the alley, rolled over once and scrambled back to his feet. The car hit the wall.

25

More glass broke. Shards showered down over the unconscious guy's chest and abdomen. But they weren't sharp enough to cut through his clothes. And the impact wasn't sufficient to immobilize the car.

The driver had stayed in his seat throughout. That was understandable. Avoiding a fist fight was a smart move. But he'd made no attempt to shoot. Reacher figured he must have wanted whatever happened to look like an accident. That would be a little suspicious, given how close they were to the place where the bus had crushed Angela St. Vrain. But a lot less suspicious than leaving a body with a fatal gunshot wound.

Reacher was under no such constraint. He drew the gun he'd taken from the guy on the ground and stepped around the car. He was going for a shot through the passenger window. The driver saw what was happening and lurched forward, straight down the centre of the alley. Reacher fired three shots at the rear window instead. The first turned the glass into a dense mesh of opaque crystals. The second knocked the whole mass on to the car's back seat. The third hit something inside. Reacher was sure about that. But he couldn't tell if it was the driver. Or the head restraint. Or some other random component.

The car stopped. It paused for a moment. Then its one remaining reverse light came on. Its tyres squealed. It sped backward. Reacher fired three more shots. All of them hit the driver's seat. But the car kept on coming. Straight at Reacher. No sign of slowing. No sign of swerving. The driver must have been hunkered down low. Maybe halfway into the footwell, if he was small enough. Reacher figured the guy was using the backup camera to see where to steer. He raised the gun, wondering where the lens would be. Then he pushed the thought away. There was no time. He feinted left

26

then darted to his right. He wanted another try for the passenger window. It was close. A couple more seconds and he'd have a clear shot. Then he would finish the guy. That was for damn sure.

The driver swerved hard right. Reacher was penned in by the wall on one side. He'd be hit by the car if he moved the other way. Or if he went forward. Or if he went back.

The car was moving fast. The rear wing was inches away.

There was nowhere for Reacher to go.

Except up. If he timed it just right.

Reacher jammed the gun into his waistband. Waited another fraction of a second. Then sprang on to the car's trunk and kicked down. Hard. With both legs. He threw his arms above his head for extra lift. His fingertips brushed metal. Rough, cold iron. Part of one of the fire escapes. A rung on its lowest section. Folded into its dormant, horizontal position, like a set of monkey bars in a gym. He grabbed hold. Gripped tight. And swung his legs up to clear the roof of the car.

Reacher almost made it. The top of the empty rear window frame caught his toecaps. He felt an almighty jolt. It slammed through his ankles and his knees and up his body and along his arms and his hands and his fingers. Which loosened. A little. But Reacher didn't let go. He tightened his grip. He watched the car's hood pass beneath him. He straightened his legs, ready to drop down and spin around and take another shot. Through the windshield this time. Straight into the front section of the cabin. Where the driver would have nowhere to hide.

Reacher heard a sound. Above him. It was metal, grating and groaning and tearing. There was a *bang*. Sharp and loud like another gunshot. There was a second noise. A third.

27

From the ironwork. Something was being pulled apart. Maybe because of Reacher's weight. Maybe because of his weight multiplied by the impact with the car. Or maybe because the equipment wasn't as well maintained as it appeared from the ground. Maybe the coats of shiny paint concealed all kinds of structural defects. But whatever the reason, the struts connecting the ladder and the gangway to the framework on the next level were failing. The whole section vibrated. It shook. It started to tilt outward, away from the building. Ten degrees. Fifteen. It stabilized for a moment. It settled. But in a new position. It was canted downward now. At an angle the anchor points had never been designed to support. They started to pull free. They screeched and juddered and pulled their sockets right out of the brittle tuck pointing.

Reacher saw what was happening. He let go of the rung. His feet hit the ground. He took half a step. And a twisted mass of iron landed right on top of him.

SEVEN

For the first fifteen years of his life Jed Starmer didn't give much thought to the concept of the law.

He was aware that laws existed. He understood that they somehow shaped and controlled the world around him, but only in an invisible, abstract sense, like gravity or magnetism. He knew that there were consequences if you broke them. Penalties. Punishments. All kinds of unpleasant outcomes. He had seen huddles of people in orange jump-suits at the side of the highway being forced to pick up trash. He had listened to his foster parents' warnings about juvenile hall. And jail. And ultimately Hell. But still, none of that struck much of a chord. It didn't seem relevant to his life. He wasn't about to rob a bank. Or steal a car. He didn't even cut school very often. There were other things for him to worry about. Far more urgent things, like not being kicked out of the house and forced to live on the street. And how to avoid getting stabbed or shot any time he wanted to go anywhere.

Jed's perspective changed completely on his fifteenth birthday. That was two weeks and two days ago. It was a Sunday so while his foster parents were at church Jed took the bus five miles, deep into South Central LA, where he had been told never to go. He walked the last two hundred yards, along the cracked sidewalk, trying not to look scared, staring straight down, desperate to avoid eye contact with anyone who might be watching. He made it to the short set of worn stone steps that led to his birth mother's apartment building. Scurried to the top. Pushed the door. The lock was broken, as it had been each time he'd snuck over there in the last couple of years, so he stepped into the hallway and started straight up the stairs. Two flights. Then along to the end of the corridor. He knew there was no point trying the buzzer so he knocked. He waited. And he hoped. That his mother would be there. That she would be sober. And that even if she didn't remember what day it was, she would at least remember him.

It turned out Jed's mother did remember. The day, and the person. She was perfectly lucid. She was even dressed. She opened the door, cigarette in hand, and led the way through the blue haze to the apartment's main room. The shades were closed. There was junk everywhere. Clothes. Shoes. Purses. Books. Magazines. CDs. Letters. Bills. All heaped up in vague piles like some half-hearted attempt at organization had been made by someone completely unfamiliar with the concept. She stopped in the centre of the mess for a moment, sighed, then gestured toward the couch. Jed squeezed by and took a seat on one corner. She sat at the opposite end and crushed out her cigarette in an ashtray on the side table next to her. It was already overflowing. A river of ash cascaded on to the carpet. She sighed again then turned to face Jed. She said she'd been expecting him. She hadn't gotten him a present, obviously, but she was glad he had come because there was something she needed to tell him. Two things, in fact.

The first thing was that she was sick. She had pancreatic cancer. Stage four. Jed didn't have a strong grasp of human biology. He didn't know what the pancreas did. He wasn't sure what the number signified. But he gleaned through his mother's tears that the gist was bad. It meant she didn't have long left to live. Months, possibly. Maybe weeks. Certainly not longer.

The second thing Jed's mother told him was the truth about his father. Or what she believed to be the truth, at least.

The first piece of information made Jed feel guilty. It was an unexpected response. He had observed over the years that people generally got upset when they learned close relatives were on the verge of dying. But after the news had sunk in he realized he wasn't sad. He wasn't miserable. He was relieved. Which he knew was wrong. But he couldn't help it. It was like he had been swimming against the tide his whole life with a weight tied around his waist. Caused by worry. The constant fear that the police would show up at the house. With news about his mother. That she had overdosed. Or had been murdered. Or had been found dead and festering in some filthy squat. That he would have to go and identify her body. Or even worse, that she would show up herself, on the doorstep. In who knew what kind of a state. His foster parents disapproved of his mother. Strongly. They made that clear. At every opportunity. The last thing he needed was more guilt by association. But now he could stop worrying. He knew how his mother's story was going to end. And when. The rope was about to be cut. He could swim free at last.

*

31

The second thing Jed learned had a different kind of effect. His mother's words worked like a light shining into a corner of his past that had previously been hidden. They picked out the dots that joined his life to the law. Showed him a connection he hadn't seen before. Something very personal. A link that had shaped his entire existence. It left him with a whole new respect. A determination to never break the law himself. To break the cycle, instead. To not let history repeat itself.

Jed's resolve lasted for exactly two weeks. Then it was lifted to a whole new level. Because of the time he spent online while his foster parents were out at that week's Sunday service. First, he ran a Google search based on the story his mother had told him about his father on his birthday. The results led him to an article on a news site. A long, complex account of events that unfolded over many years. Jed read it carefully. He noted every detail. Every discrepancy. And when he finished he felt like a searchlight had been switched on in his head. A million watts of blinding revelation. His mother's version seemed ridiculously pale in comparison. Like she had illuminated the important parts with a candle. Or a glow-worm. She had missed the crux entirely. Now Jed didn't just see the power of the law. He also saw the danger it brought.

The light from Jed's new knowledge didn't just spill back toward his past. It also shone forward, showing him what he needed to do. And where he needed to go. Which was away from his foster home, for a start. Then away from California altogether.

Jed took two days to plan. To do his research. To build up his courage. Which explained why, at the same time Reacher stepped into the alley in Gerrardsville, Colorado, Jed was standing in front of a dresser in his foster parents' bedroom.

The top drawer was open. His foster mother's tired, stretched underwear was pushed to one side. The wad of twenty-dollar bills was exposed. And Jed was in a quandary. He needed the money. Badly. But he didn't want to steal it. He was desperate not to break the law. So he was trying to convince himself that taking it wouldn't count as stealing. Not if the money was already stolen. Which in a way, he figured it was. It had been provided by the state to pay for his food and shelter. His, and the other three foster kids he lived with. And yet the cash was there, unspent, while they wore clothes that were too small and went to bed hungry each night.

The bottom line was that Jed didn't want to commit a crime. But neither did he want to starve. Or have to hitch a ride across more than half the country. Because regardless of what he wanted, three things were certain. He had a long way to go. Not much time to get there. And he could not afford to be late.

EIGHT

Reacher's ears were ringing when he came around. There was a sharp pain in his head. The weight of the metal on his chest made it hard to breathe. It took him a moment to figure out what was pinning him to the ground. Then another five minutes of shoving and heaving and scrabbling before he was able to wriggle free.

A small crowd had gathered at the mouth of the alley. Reacher recognized some of the people. They had been gawping at the bus after it crushed Angela St. Vrain. The excitement out there must have died down. They must have gambled that the action in the alley would be more interesting. They were certainly more interested in watching than getting involved. It was only when Reacher had almost extracted himself that a couple of the younger men stepped forward and tried to take his arms.

Reacher pushed them away.

One of them said, 'You OK, buddy?'

Reacher said nothing.

'Because we thought we heard gunshots.' The guy shrugged. 'Guess it must have been the metal breaking.'

Reacher took several deep gulps of air while he waited for the crowd to disperse, then got busy checking the alley around him. There were tyre marks on the pavement. Paint transfer in a couple of spots on the walls. A big dent in the nearest dumpster. A scattering of broken glass here and there. But no gun. No guys in hoodies. No car. No trash bag. No purse. And no envelope.

The emergency services were out in force by the time Reacher made his way back to the street. The traffic in all directions had been stopped by four pairs of patrol cars, formed up in Vs with their light bars popping and flashing. A tent had been set up over the area at the side of the bus where Angela St. Vrain's body had been. More to protect the scene from TV crews in helicopters and journalists with long lenses than the weather, Reacher thought. It's not like there was any great mystery about what killed the woman. The *who* was a different story, though. And so was the *why*.

Reacher saw four uniformed officers canvassing the last stragglers in the crowd. He kept on looking until he spotted a guy in a suit emerge from the far side of the bus. The guy was wearing nitrile gloves and he had a small black notebook in his left hand. Reacher thought it said something about the level of crime in the town if they sent a detective to what would seem like a routine traffic accident in many places. He wasn't complaining, though. It saved him the time it would take to find the station house.

Reacher figured the detective would be in his early thirties. He looked to be six feet even and was clearly in good

35

shape. His hair was buzzed short. His suit pants had a razor-sharp crease down the front and back. His shirt was freshly ironed. His tie was neatly knotted. And his shoes gleamed like mirrors.

The guy felt Reacher looking at him so he walked over and held out his hand. 'Detective Harewood. Can I help you?'

Reacher laid out what he had seen at the intersection and what had happened subsequently in the alley. He took it slow and broke the information into manageable chunks. Harewood wrote it all down in his book. He didn't skip anything. He didn't summarize. And he didn't waste any time with undue questions about Reacher's address or occupation.

When they were done with the formalities Reacher took Harewood's card and promised to call if he remembered any further details. Then he walked away. He was confident the case was in good hands. He considered looking for a ride out of town but came down against it. His head hurt. His body was stiff and sore. He decided a good night's sleep was preferable. It would help him heal. And there was something else. The guys in hoodies might come back. They would have to replace their vehicle, obviously. And they'd probably want to hand off the envelope. Or secure it somewhere. But then they might be worried about the witness they left behind. They might want to do something about that.

Reacher certainly hoped they would try.

The town wasn't big. Reacher spent the afternoon staying as visible as possible. He alternated between quartering the streets, looking in store windows, jaywalking and sitting outside cafés drinking coffee. It started out as a pleasant way to kill time. The central district was dotted with pedestrian areas and trees and places to hang out. The local population seemed to be a mix of students and new parents with babies in strollers and hipsters and young professional types in exaggeratedly casual suits. But the longer Reacher kept the search going, the more frustrated he got. He had to face facts. If he was the worm, he was attracting no fish. So he bagged the proposition and headed south, out of town, toward a pair of hotels he remembered from when he'd arrived the day before.

Reacher was wrong.

He realized before he had covered two blocks. He was being watched. Someone had their eyes on him. He could feel it. A chill spread up from the base of his neck. A primal response. A warning mechanism hard-wired into his lizard brain. Finely tuned. Highly reliable. Never to be ignored.

Reacher stopped outside the next store he came to. It sold fancy chocolates in brightly coloured packages. He stood and looked at the window. Not at the display of old tins and giant heaps of truffles. At the reflection of the street.

A black truck with raised suspension and chrome wheels went by. There was no one in the passenger seat. Its driver paid Reacher no attention. Next to pass was a silver Jeep with a pair of kayaks on the roof and red mud sprayed up the side. Its driver was only looking at the back of the black truck. Then came a white sedan. A Toyota Corolla.

Reacher felt a flicker of recognition. He couldn't be certain he'd seen this particular car before. Corollas are popular vehicles. Then it rolled up closer to him. The chill in his neck grew more intense. He could see the guy in the passenger seat. Mid-twenties. Wiry. Cropped hair. Blue T-shirt. He could have been the clone of the guy who had pushed Angela St. Vrain under the bus, only his face was still intact. And he was looking at Reacher. That was for sure. He stared as the car drove past, glanced down at his phone, then turned to peer over his shoulder.

Reacher started walking again. The Corolla took a right at the end of the next block. Reacher pictured it taking the next right. And the next. He estimated the time that would take. Then he crossed the street. That gave him an excuse to look the opposite way without signalling his suspicion. The Corolla was waiting at the previous intersection. Reacher kept going. Not rushing. Not dawdling. Not doing anything to highlight the fact that he was aware of the car following him. Then he turned into the next alley he came to. It was similar to the one he had chased the guy into after the murder. It was clean. Tidy. There was a line of dumpsters. Fire escapes that looked to be sound. But one big difference. A scaffolding tower was set up against the left-hand building where a section of gutter was missing from the base of its roof.

The Corolla had not gone by.

Reacher pressed his back against the wall and edged toward the sidewalk. He saw the nose of a white car stopped at the side of the road, far enough from the mouth of the alley not to be conspicuous. He moved along the wall the opposite way, toward the scaffolding. The metal poles were all fixed together with brackets and bolts. They were rock solid. There was no way to remove any. Not quickly. Not without tools. So he tried the wooden planks that formed the lower platform. The central one was loose. He prised it up. Pulled it out. Carried it toward the street. The car was still almost opposite. Reacher hoped the guys who were looking for him were impatient. He hoped they would get bored waiting for him to come out. Decide to force the issue. Swoop into the alley, like the guy in the BMW had done earlier. Because then he would step forward and ram the plank through the windshield. Hit the driver in the chest. Crush his ribs. Or maybe catch him in the head. Take it clean off his shoulders. Leaving Reacher and the guy in the passenger seat with some time alone.

The Corolla didn't move.

Ten minutes passed. Twenty. Half an hour.

The Corolla didn't move.

Reacher was a patient man. He could out-wait anybody. It was a skill he'd learned during his years in the army. A skill he had honed in the years since then. But he was also realistic. He knew some things never happen, however long you wait for them. The guy in the Corolla had looked at his phone. So he had a picture, or at least a description. That must have come from the guys Reacher had encountered earlier. They might have outlined what happened. Or the four might have gotten together for a debrief. The current pair might have seen the result with their own eyes. They could be cautious. They could be smart enough to hold out for somewhere safer to make their move.

Or somewhere they thought would be safer.

That was fine with Reacher. He was a patient man. He carried the plank back to the scaffolding and slid it into place. Then he stepped out on to the sidewalk and continued on his way.

One of the hotels on the outskirts of the town looked pretty new. It was part of a chain. And therefore anonymous, which usually appealed to Reacher. The other place was on the opposite side of the main street. It must have dated back to the 1930s. The building was long and low with a flat roof. The external walls were rendered and painted pink. It had twelve rooms, each with a number on its door in a mirrored art deco frame. The office was at the end further from town. A pole rose from its roof. At the top there was a cartoon figure. A pineapple in a dress, picked out in yellow and turquoise neon. It had a wild grin on its face. Reacher wasn't sure if it looked friendly or demonic.

Reacher came down in favour of The Pineapple. In his experience, small independent places were better suited to his needs. They were less likely to fuss about expired IDs or to insist on credit cards for payment. He headed for the office and found himself surrounded by mirrors and neon and art deco shapes. The reception desk was covered with them too. A guy appeared from somewhere in the back corner. He was thin. Unhealthily so, with patchy grey hair which made it tough to guess how old he was. His shirt was covered with pictures of parrots and palm trees. His turquoise shorts were baggy on his shrivelled hips and their brightness made his pasty legs look almost blue.

The skinny guy offered Reacher a room for sixty dollars. Reacher countered with eighty dollars in cash for a room with no one on either side. The guy happily agreed. He pocketed the extra twenty and handed Reacher the key to room twelve followed by a dog-eared ledger and a pen for him to sign in with. Reacher scrawled a name and a signature then walked the length of the building and let himself into his room. There was a bed. A closet. A chair. A bathroom. Standard motel fare. The fruit theme didn't extend to the inside of the building. It was a little scruffy in places, but Reacher didn't mind. He kept the light on for ten minutes then switched it off and crossed to the bed.

NINE

*T*icket *first*, Jed Starmer thought, *then something to eat.*

Not that Jed was any kind of an expert traveller. This was only going to be the second time he'd left Los Angeles County since his mother brought him there when he was a baby. Now he was leaving for good and so far he wasn't enjoying the experience. He'd had to pack, which was a problem because he didn't have a suitcase or a duffel. He didn't want to steal one from his foster parents or the other kids he lived with and there was nowhere in his neighbourhood that sold them. So he did the only thing he could think of. He opened up his school backpack and dumped all the institutional crap into the trash. He replaced it with clothes. Just the basics, snatched at random from his closet, as many as would fit. He grabbed his toothbrush from the bathroom, more or less as an afterthought, and jammed it in his pocket. Then he took a final look around the house. He had hated the building the moment he first set foot through the door. He had been miserable pretty much every minute he had spent there. Now it seemed like the most welcoming place in the world.

Now that he was never going to see it again.

Next up was an issue with the bus that Jed needed to catch. It didn't show up when it was supposed to. Which wasn't a concern in terms of time. Jed had built plenty of slack into his schedule. It was a question of exposure. Jed's foster mother got off work early on Tuesdays. She drove home down the street where the bus stop was located. Jed was standing there alone. He was totally exposed. There was no way she could miss him. And if she caught him there with a pocket full of her cash, he would have hell to pay.

Ten minutes ticked by. Twenty. There was no sign of any public transport. No sign of his foster mother. Another five minutes crept past. It couldn't be long until she appeared. She had to be close. Jed couldn't keep still. He started looking around for bolt-holes. Anywhere he could hide if he saw her coming. Then the bus wheezed into sight. It dawdled along the street and ground to a halt next to him. He had severe reservations about its state of maintenance but he couldn't afford to wait for the next one. Not without inviting disaster. So he climbed on board, paid his fare, then hustled to the back and tried not to draw attention to himself through the long, stop-start trek to 7th and Decatur.

Jed jumped down directly across the street from the Greyhound station. He was glad he was no further away. He didn't like the feel of the neighbourhood. Not at all. It was only a couple of blocks from the old Skid Row. He had heard stories. Seen movies. Some guys were hanging around on the sidewalk. A dozen of them. They were skinny. Half of them were smoking. All of them were watching him. Like jackals, he thought. Or hyenas. Like he was their prey. There was another bunch of guys in the parking lot out front of the station. They looked a little older. But no more welcoming. Jed lowered his gaze. He snaked his way around both groups and followed the signs to the terminal entrance.

Things got better once Jed was inside. The terminal building was spacious and bright. There were people standing in line for the ticket counter and others were sitting and sprawling on the rows of blue wire seats, but no one was paying him undue attention. He skirted around the edge of the room and made for the array of self-serve machines. The one he picked was slow. Its screen was smeared with some kind of oily residue but he still managed to navigate the menus and pick his destination and class of service. He took ten twenty-dollar bills from the wad he'd taken from his foster home and fed them, one by one, into the cash receptacle. He supplemented them with four quarters of his own. Started to panic when the machine seemed to freeze. Then relaxed when his ticket nosed its way out of its slot.

Jed ignored the vending machines and moved straight across to the food counter. He studied the menu. He was starving. He wanted everything on it. This was going to be his first meal as an independent citizen and he felt like he deserved a major splurge. The place had the same kind of choices as a McDonald's, as far as he could remember. It was a while since he'd had fast food. His foster mother didn't like him eating it. Or she didn't like paying for it. He wasn't sure which. But either way, it didn't matter. He didn't have to worry about her preferences any more. But he did have to think about his cash reserve.

In the end Jed had taken the entire stash from his foster

mother's drawer. He had come to the conclusion that it would be illogical not to. Either he was entitled to the money, so it would be stupid to leave any behind. Or he was stealing it, in which case he was dooming himself anyway. After paying for the ticket he had three hundred dollars left. Accommodation for that night wouldn't be a problem. Or for the next. He would be on the bus. He would sleep there. He had no choice. But he would need somewhere to stay on Thursday night. A hotel room, maybe, or a bed and breakfast. Those were probably expensive. He would need food and drink along the way. And he would need onward transportation on Friday morning. Quite a long distance. He wasn't sure what form that was going to take, yet. He hoped he could find some random driver going the same way and pay him for a ride. If not, he would have to take a cab. Either way it would cost. Probably a lot. So he decided to be sensible. He ordered a burger and fries, and a bottle of water for the road. He paid with a ten-dollar bill of his own. Slipped his ticket into one back pocket. Slid the rest of his money into the other. And waited for his food to come out.

It took Jed five minutes to finish eating. Then he spent twenty minutes watching the scrolling subtitles on a pair of silent TVs on the wall. One was showing news. The other was showing sports. He wasn't much interested in either. He just wanted something to do until half an hour before his bus was due to leave. He figured thirty minutes would be about right to find its departure point and be on board early enough to get a good seat. When the time came he dumped his tray on a rack next to an overflowing trash can and then made a quick pit stop in the bathroom. When he came out again he saw a guy, standing by the wall, waving. Jed recognized him.

44

The guy had been behind him in line at the food counter. He'd also eaten alone, a couple of tables to the side. Jed was about to walk by when he realized the guy wasn't trying to attract some other stranger's attention. He was waving specifically at him.

At first Jed thought they were about the same age, but when the guy moved closer it was clear he was older. Maybe twenty or twenty-one. He was thin and tanned and he had a mess of blond hair that looked crunchy with salt, like a surfer's.

'Hey, buddy.' The guy held out his hand. He was holding something. A bus ticket. 'This is yours. You dropped it.'

That couldn't be true. Jed had put his ticket away carefully. He was sure about that. He patted his pocket to confirm. And his heart stopped. His pocket was empty. His ticket was gone. He checked the other side. For his money. All his cash . . . which was still there. He was OK. There was no problem. But it was still a moment before he could breathe again.

The blond guy glanced at Jed's ticket. 'Route 1454? Cool. Same as me.'

'Thank you for finding it.' Jed took the ticket. His hand was shaking. 'Can't believe I dropped it.'

'No problem. Weird shit happens sometimes. So, you going to Dallas too?'

Jed shook his head. 'Got a transfer there.'

'Going further?'

Jed nodded. 'Jackson, Mississippi.'

'That's a long way. You visiting family?'

'I don't have any family.'

'Really? None?'

Jed thought about an honest answer. He didn't want to lie.

45

But neither did he want to get into the specifics. Not with a stranger. Not then. So he said, 'Nope. Just me.'

'No parents?'

'Never knew my dad. My mom – cancer.'

'That's harsh, man. No brothers or sisters? Uncles or aunts?'

'Nope.'

'So who's meeting you when you get wherever you're going?'

'No one. Why?'

'Just seems like you got dealt a tough hand, man, if you're all alone in the world. I'm sorry about that.'

Jed shrugged. 'You get used to it.'

'Tell you what – let's ride together. At least as far as Texas. Keep each other company.'

Jed shrugged again. 'OK. If you want.'

'This your first time riding the 'hound?'

Jed nodded.

The blond guy put his arm around Jed's shoulder, pulled him close and dropped his voice to a whisper. 'I'm going to ask you something. It's real important, so listen up. Your bag? The little backpack thing you got going on? You got anything valuable in there? Laptop? Tablet? Nintendo?'

'No. I don't have anything like that.'

'That's good. Real good. The road's not a safe place. But all the same, never let your bag out of your sight. Don't leave it anywhere. Don't let the driver put it in the hold. And keep an arm through the straps when you sleep. You got me?'

'Sure.'

'Good. Now I need to syphon the python. You go ahead. Through the doors, turn left. All the way to the end. Pier sixteen. Get us a pair of seats. Midway between the wheels, if you can. That's the most comfortable. I'll catch up in a minute.'

Jed found the correct bus, climbed in, showed the driver his ticket and made his way down the aisle. More than half the seats were already taken. Everyone on board was older than Jed. Some by three or four years. Some by sixty or seventy. Some people were travelling alone. Some were in pairs. Some were in groups. Many of them had headphones on. Some had pillows. A few were wrapped in blankets. Most had things to occupy themselves with, like books or phones or computers. Jed suddenly felt horribly unprepared. He wanted to turn around. Jump off the bus. Run back to his foster home. Pretend that he had never tried to leave. Forget everything his birth mother had told him. But instead he forced himself into the first empty pair of seats he came to. He shuffled across to the window. Hauled his bag on to his lap. Hugged it to his chest. And focused on the thrum of the engine. The hiss of the ventilation. The murmur of the conversations going on all around him. The smell of disinfectant and other people's food. He told himself that everything was going to be OK. Just as long as he could pull himself together before the blond guy showed up. He didn't need to be any more embarrassed than he already was.

Two minutes before departure time the door at the front of the bus hissed shut. Jed started to rise up in his seat. He was about to call out to the driver. To tell him a passenger was missing. That they had to wait. But he didn't make a sound. He stopped moving. Slid back down. And shifted his bag to the space next to him. Dallas was more than thirty-six hours away. He didn't even know the blond guy's name. He wasn't some kind of lifelong companion. He was grateful to have gotten his ticket back. But he didn't need a day and a half of questions and opinions and dumb-ass advice being shoved down his throat before he switched to the next bus. He was happy to be on his own.

Until ten a.m. on Friday, anyway.

Whether he would be alone after that was a whole other question.

TEN

The lock's mechanism clicked and whirred. Reacher's door swung open. A quadrant of light unfurled across the garish carpet. Two men crept inside. Both mid-twenties. Both holding guns. One eased the door back into place in its frame. They stood still for a moment. Then they started toward the bed. It was only semi-visible. The glow filtering through the thin drapes was pale. But the shape beneath the covers was tall. It was broad. It was what they were expecting.

The men separated, one either side of the mattress. They continued to the head of the bed. It was a warm night but the comforter was pulled all the way up over the pillows. The guy nearer the window shrugged, then prodded what he estimated would be Reacher's shoulder with the muzzle of his gun.

He got no response.

He poked again. Harder. He said, 'Hey. Wake up.'

The ceiling light flicked on. The guys spun around. They

49

saw Reacher at the other end of the room. He opened the door and stepped outside. Then he darted to the side and pressed his back against the external wall.

The guys ran after Reacher. The first one's leading foot touched the ground outside and Reacher smashed him in the face with his forearm. The guy's nose shattered. His neck snapped back. He collapsed through the doorway, piled into his buddy's chest and knocked him down. Reacher scooped up the guy's gun and followed him inside.

The first guy wasn't moving. The second had rolled on to his side and was scrabbling to retrieve his gun from where he'd dropped it when he fell. Reacher stamped on his hand. The guy screamed and curled up into a ball. Reacher grabbed the first guy by the arm, pulled him into the room and closed the door.

There was a bang on the wall. A man's voice yelled, 'Hey. Room Twelve. Keep it down.'

Reacher waited for the second guy to go quiet then said, 'Get up. Sit in the chair if you want. We can be civilized about this.'

The guy scuttled back on his heels and his butt and his good hand until his shoulders were touching the wall.

Reacher said, 'I met a couple of your friends today. Here, in town. In an alley. Where are they now?'

The guy didn't respond.

Reacher said, 'Why did one of them kill a woman this morning? Push her under a bus?'

The guy didn't answer.

Reacher stepped in close and stamped on the guy's other hand. He screamed again, louder, and rolled on to his other side.

There was another bang on the wall. A man's voice yelled, 'Room Twelve. Be quiet. Last warning.'

Reacher waited for the guy to uncurl himself a little then said, 'Who do you work for?'

The guy shook his head.

Reacher stamped on the guy's right knee. He screamed, long and loud.

Reacher said, 'I can go on all night. Can you? The other two. Where are they?'

The guy said, 'They left town.'

'Where are they going?'

'Home. Winson, Mississippi.'

'Why did you stay?'

'We were told to find you.'

'Why?'

'Find out what you know.'

'About?'

The light filtering through the drapes switched from dull grey to pulsing red and blue. Reacher peered out of the window. There were two police cars in the parking lot. One outside his room. One at the far end. An officer was already on foot, heading for the office. To talk to the clerk. To check on numbers and dispositions. And to get a pass key. None of those things would take long. Reacher figured he had sixty seconds at best. He hauled the first guy up on to his feet and turned him so that his back was to the door. He punched the side of the guy's head and let him fall to the floor again. He grabbed the second guy. Pulled him away from the wall. Smashed the back of his head into the floor. Pinched one of his ear lobes to make sure he was unconscious. Dragged him forward until his feet were almost touching the first guy's. They were lying like the hands of a clock at close to three p.m. He wiped his prints off the first guy's gun and tossed it on to the floor. Went into the bathroom. Opened the window. And climbed out.

51

The area at the back of the hotel was not promising. There was a small pool and a bunch of white plastic lounging chairs, all surrounded by a rickety wooden fence. It was eight feet tall. Ancient. No way would it take his weight. The only way out was through the office, and a pair of cops would be coming the other way any second. Two at the front. Two at the back. That was the obvious way to do it. He was trapped. And there was nowhere to hide. Not at ground level, anyway.

Reacher moved back to his bathroom window and lifted one foot on to the sill. He pushed up and grabbed the edge of the roof. Pulled with his arms. Scrambled over the lip. Rolled to the centre. And lay completely still. He heard footsteps on both sides of the building. They were close. The ones at the front stopped moving. Someone thumped on the door.

'Gerrardsville Police Department. Open up.'

The officers at the rear were poking around the pool furniture. One of them took a chair and set it next to the fence. He climbed up and looked over and quartered the area on the far side with his flashlight. Then he jumped down and called, 'Clear.'

Reacher heard the whirr of the lock and then a thump as the door to his room hit one of the unconscious guy's heels. There was a pause, the door closed, then he heard the cop's voice through the bathroom window. It sounded like he was on his radio.

'We have two male suspects, non-responsive. Two guns secured at the scene.'

A second voice said, 'Looks like they got into it over something. Got into it pretty good. No ID. No smell of booze. Better send a bus right away.'

The first voice came back, quieter. 'They can stay in the

hospital overnight. The detective can question them in the morning, if he wants to. We better seal this place, just in case.'

Reacher lay on the roof and watched an ambulance arrive. A pair of paramedics rolled the two guys out on gurneys, loaded them up and drove off. The cops left a couple of minutes later. Reacher stayed where he was for another hour, until he was satisfied that there were no cops lurking and no nosy guests snooping around. Then he climbed down and walked to the office. A couple was leaving as he went in. They looked young. Flushed. Happy. And a little bit furtive.

The same guy was at the counter, wearing the same ridiculous clothes and looking just as sickly and malnourished. He saw Reacher and said, 'You're OK?'

Reacher said, 'I'm fine. Why?'

'The cops let you out already?'

'They never took me in. I went for a walk. Came back and found my door sealed up with crime scene tape. What's that all about?'

'It wasn't my fault. Two guys came. Made me give them a pass key.'

'Then you dialled 911?'

'I guess the guy in Eleven did that. He's a real asshole.'

'I told you I didn't want any neighbours.'

The guy pulled a twenty-dollar bill from his pocket and handed it to Reacher. 'He comes here all the time. With his girlfriend. She's also an asshole. That's their favourite room. He insisted. I'm sorry.'

Reacher handed the twenty back. 'Give me another room. No one either side. And this time, no excuses.'

ELEVEN

*F*ind a job you love and you'll never work a day in your
life.

That's what Lev Emerson was told by his father,
years ago, when he was still in high school. It wasn't an original concept. It wasn't the result of radical new thinking. But
nonetheless, the advice was sound. Old Mr Emerson had followed it himself. He had died happy at the age of seventy-four,
at his workbench, after a lifetime making ladies' hats in the
corner of a little workshop in Brooklyn. Lev Emerson walked
the same talk. Just as enthusiastically. Although it led him
down a path his father could never have anticipated.

On the face of it, Lev Emerson owned and operated a fire
safety business out of a pair of nondescript warehouses on
the south side of Chicago. It was a legitimate corporation. It
was in good standing with the state of Illinois. It had articles
of association. Shareholders. Executive officers. Employees. Accounts with all kinds of recognizable brand-name

54

suppliers. It had plenty of customers, most of whom were satisfied. It paid taxes. It sponsored a local kids' softball team. And it provided cover for certain other materials that Emerson had to have shipped in from a handful of less well-known sources.

The bulk of the corporation's reported income came from sprinkler installations and alarm systems. There was no shortage of co-ops and condo buildings in Chicagoland, as well as offices and industrial premises. New ones were constantly going up. Old ones were always getting refurbished. The pickings were rich for an outfit like Emerson's. And it didn't hurt that the rules and regulations changed so frequently. Something that was up to code one year could be condemned as dangerous the next. And again a couple of years after that. Hidden interests were served. The way things had always been in the Windy City. Pockets got lined. Companies got busy. Plenty of them. Including Emerson's. Corporate clients were its bread and butter. But that didn't mean it turned its back on the little guys. Emerson insisted on offering a full range of services to the safety-conscious homeowner, too. That helped to broaden the customer base, which was good from a business point of view. And the steady flow of station wagons and minivans through the parking lot added to an impression of banal normality. Which was good for another reason.

Emerson's name might have been over the door, but he had nothing to do with the banal, normal side of the business. For that he hired people who knew what they were doing. Who could be trusted to keep their fingers out of the register. And he left them to get on with it. Partly because he was naturally a good delegator. Partly because he had no interest in sprinklers and alarms or anything else that helped to prevent fires. But mostly because his time was fully occupied elsewhere. He had a parallel operation to run.

The thing he loved to do.

The jobs Emerson carried out personally fell into two categories. Those that looked like accidents. And those that didn't. The job he was just finishing would not look like an accident. That was for damn sure. It would be a thing of beauty. Unmistakably deliberate. Impossible to trace back to Emerson. Or his client. Unambiguous in its meaning. And with a signature that was distinct and unique. That way, if the recipient was sufficiently stupid or obtuse, the message could be repeated and the connection would be clear.

Emerson knew it was a stretch to say he was still actively finishing the job. The work was essentially complete. There was nothing more he needed to do. Or that he could do. His continued presence would not affect the outcome in any way. He could have been hundreds of miles away and it would have made no difference. Four of his guys already were. They were heading back to base, driving a pair of anonymous white panel vans, preparing to clean their equipment and resupply for their next project. He could have gone with them. That would have been the prudent thing to do. But he stayed. He wanted to watch. He needed to watch.

Prudence be damned.

The thing he loved to do.

Emerson was on the Talmadge Memorial Bridge in Georgia, nearly two hundred feet above the Savannah River, midway between the mainland and Hutchinson Island. The strip of land that split the waterway that separated Georgia from South Carolina. He was standing, not driving. Leaning with

56

his forearms against the lip of the concrete sidewall on the westbound side. Graeber, his right-hand man, was next to him. He was also leaning on the wall. His pose was exactly the same, but he was just a little shorter. A little younger. A little less obsessed.

Pedestrians weren't encouraged on the bridge. There was no sidewalk. No bike lane. But back during the planning stage the architects had been fearful of vehicles breaking down or crashing into one another. The city couldn't afford for a major artery to get blocked. Even for a short time. In either direction. So they provided a generous shoulder. One on each side. Deliberately adequate to keep the traffic flowing in emergencies. Unintentionally wide enough for suitably motivated individuals to walk or run or ride at other times. And coincidentally perfect for two out-of-towners to hang out and enjoy the late-evening view.

If Emerson had been a regular sightseer he would have been looking in the other direction. Behind him. Toward the old city. To the leafy squares and cobbled streets and ginger-bread houses and domed municipal halls. A rich slice of history all wrapped up in golden light and reflected back off the swirling night-time Savannah water. But Emerson had no interest in the tourist stuff. He didn't care about the city's colonial roots or how closely the layout resembled the founder's original scheme. His focus was on the industrial section. The port area, ahead of him. A sprawling mess of gas storage tanks and container facilities and warehouses that littered the west bank of the river. He was concentrating on one building in particular. A storage unit. A large one, with white metal walls and a white metal roof.

Emerson knew that aside from a crude office nibbled out from one corner the building had no internal walls. He knew that most of its volume was filled with sealed wooden crates. He had been told they contained kids' dolls, imported from China without the correct paperwork. He believed the part about the paperwork. But he figured the last thing he would find in the crates would be kids' dolls. From China or anywhere else. But he didn't care. He'd been given a detailed chemical analysis of the alleged dolls' components and a sample crate, fully packed, identical to the ones in the unit, for him to test. Which he did. Thoroughly. Though he didn't look inside. He wasn't one for taking unnecessary risks. There are some things it's safer not to know.

Emerson's knowledge of the building and its contents wasn't all theoretical. The previous two days had been spent on close observation. First, to gauge its security measures. And second, to ensure that the place was unoccupied, as stipulated. The first was a practical thing. The second, business. If the body count went up, so did his price. It was a basic principle. He wasn't in the game for the money, but he was the best, and that had to be recognized. That was only fair. Plus he had a wife at home. And a son. The kid was in his twenties now, but he was still a liability. Financially speaking. Emerson had all kinds of expenses to take care of. Cars. Food. Clothes. Medical bills. More than a quarter of a million dollars in the last year alone. And one day soon there would be college to pay for. If the kid ever got his act together. Life didn't come cheap for Lev Emerson.

After forty-eight hours Emerson concluded that there was no reason to abort and no cause to demand more money so that morning, before sunrise, the implementation phase had begun. First the alarms were disabled. Intruder, smoke, and temperature. The sprinklers were deactivated. Equipment was brought in. So were the chemicals, formulated specifically for this job, safe in their special containers. Cables were laid. Control mechanisms were installed. Measurements were taken. Calculations were carried out. Predictions were made regarding airflow and heat gain. Holes were cut at strategic positions in the walls and the roof. Crates were moved to optimize circulation. The calculations were repeated. They were checked, and checked again. More adjustments were made. And finally, when Emerson was happy, the site was evacuated. His creation was set and primed and activated. The doors were closed and locked for the final time. The panel vans departed. Emerson and Graeber grabbed a bite to eat and prepared for showtime.

The thing he loved to do.

Graeber nudged Emerson's arm. The first whisper of smoke had curled into view. It was rising hesitantly through one of the new gashes in the storage unit's roof. Still delicate. Pale. Insubstantial. A hint of what was in store. A promise. Emerson felt a flutter in his chest. He was like a music lover hearing the first gentle notes of a favourite symphony. The anticipation was exquisite. Almost too much to bear. The plume thickened. Darkened. Began to twist and twirl and dance. It climbed faster and spread and . . .

Emerson's phone rang. Which shouldn't have been possible. He wrenched it from his pocket and glared at the screen. It said, *Home calling*. Which meant his wife. Who should have known better. He'd outlined the timetable to her, like he always did. He'd been clear. And she knew not to interrupt him during the finale of a job. So he jabbed the button to reject the call. Shoved the phone back into his pocket. Turned back to the storage unit, which now had smoke billowing from five vents. Tried to control his breathing. And waited for the flames.

Thirty seconds later Graeber's phone rang. He checked it, then stepped away and answered. He spoke for more than five minutes. When he returned to Emerson's side his face was pale. His hands were trembling. But Emerson didn't notice. He only had eyes for the inferno. The storage unit's roof was gone, now. Its walls were buckled and warped. The flames writhed and flailed and tormented the sky. The dark void was now bursting with colour, vivid and bright, fluid and alive. Fire trucks were approaching. Racing closer. There was a whole convoy. At least half a dozen. They were using their lights and sirens. Emerson smiled. They shouldn't have left their firehouse. They were pointless. Impotent. They had more chance of blowing out the sun than dousing the fruits of his labour. Any time in the next few hours, anyway.

Graeber lifted his hand. He stretched out, slowly, like he was pushing away a heavy, invisible object. He reached Emerson's arm. Took hold of his sleeve. Gave it a cautious tug.

Emerson ignored him.

Graeber tugged again, harder. 'Boss. You need to call home.'

Emerson didn't turn his head. 'Later.'

Graeber said, 'No. Now. I'm sorry. But trust me. It can't wait.'

'What can't?'

'It's about Kyle. Your son.'

'What's he done now?'

'Boss, I'm so sorry. Kyle is dead. He died an hour ago.'

TWELVE

The Greyhound bus was alive with sound.

The fat tyres thrummed on the blacktop and thumped over every crack and pothole. The ventilation system murmured and sighed. Conflicting bass rhythms escaped from several passengers' headphones. Some of the younger guys laughed out loud at shows they were watching on their tablets and phones. Some of the older ones talked. A couple argued. A few snored and grunted and groaned. Normally an unaccustomed racket like that would have kept Jed Starmer awake. He liked quiet at night, aside from the usual sirens and background traffic noise that filtered through his window and into his bedroom. But the craziness of the last few days had taken its toll. Its sudden absence merged with the darkness and the soft swaying motion. It pulled him down into the depths of sleep. Its hold was so strong that it took a couple of minutes after the driver switched on the bright interior lights for him to surface. By then the bus was stationary, lined up next to another one just like it, and the rest of the passengers were standing and stretching and fussing with their luggage or shuffling up and down in the aisle.

Jed had pulled his backpack on to his lap at some point after the bus left its previous stop in Blythe, California. He was hunched over it, resting his head on its top flap, hugging it tight like a giant teddy bear. He straightened up and pushed the bag on to the seat next him, not wanting to look like a little kid. Then he peered out of his window. He saw a sign on the side of the depot building in the distance. It was covered with mountain silhouettes and cartoon cacti and it said *Welcome to Phoenix, Arizona* in English and Spanish. He checked the time. It was ten after two. The early hours of Wednesday morning. Which meant they were ten minutes ahead of schedule. Their stop would be stretched to an hour and a half. It would be the only significant break they got before El Paso, Texas, which they wouldn't reach until lunchtime. Jed thought about getting out of the bus for a while. Finding something to eat. Stretching his legs. But he decided against it. He only had three hundred dollars left. He had some big expenses coming up. And his whole body felt drained. He doubted he could drag himself out of his seat. So he stayed where he was. Leaned back. Closed his eyes. And made sure not to cuddle his backpack again.

He didn't want to look like a kid.

Back in LA, Jed's foster mother had not slept.

She had gone to bed at her regular time but she was too angry to get any rest. Too angry, and too busy listening for Jed's furtive footsteps. She figured he was out somewhere, carousing with friends. Or worse, with a girl. He must have

62

thought he could break his curfew and do who knew what kind of immoral things without anyone noticing. That he could sneak back home in the middle of the night and act like nothing had happened.

He was wrong.

She was going to show him exactly how wrong.

She spent hours lying still and writing sermons in her head. Rehearsing the lectures she would give him. The admonishments. The punishments. She was practically exhausted by all the thinking when her morning alarm went off. By then the time and her tiredness were turning her anger into worry. Jed still wasn't back. It wasn't like him to stay out all night. She started to think about calling the local hospitals. Maybe the police. Then her worry morphed into full-blown fear. She went to get dressed and found her emergency fund was gone. But twenty-dollar bills don't just disappear. They must have been taken. She checked Jed's closet. Some of his clothes were missing. A strange selection, not what she would have picked if she were taking a trip, but there were definitely gaps. And to seal the deal, when she looked in the bathroom, Jed's toothbrush was gone.

Jed had run away with her money. There was no other explanation. The ungrateful, thieving brat.

Jed's foster mother abandoned the process of getting ready for work. She fetched the phone. Called her boss. Said she was too sick to come in that day. Then she dialled 911 and had a different kind of conversation.

Jed had been desperate not to break the law. To avoid the police coming after him. It hadn't dawned on him there were other reasons for that to happen. He'd been too focused on chasing his new goal. On starting his new life.

*

Lev Emerson hadn't slept much that night, either.

He had spent fourteen hours in his car, with Graeber, blasting north from Georgia through Tennessee and Kentucky and Indiana and then across the corner of Illinois until they reached the outskirts of Chicago. They had split the driving, which was good for safety. But not good for Emerson's state of mind. He had called his wife when he was still on the bridge in Savannah, watching the fire he had set. Her voice had been distant and mechanical, the way a dead person sounds in a dream. She had told him about Kyle. Their son. His rehabilitation had been going so well. Until suddenly it wasn't. That afternoon. His body just shut down. First his liver, of course. Then one system after another. A cascade of total catastrophic failures. She had called the doctor right away, but it was already too late. Nothing could be done. Kyle had shrivelled and shrunk and slipped away right in front of her. She had been powerless to stop him.

Kyle was only twenty-two. It wasn't right. Not after everything they'd done to help him. Not after the amount of money they'd spent.

While Emerson was behind the wheel he had other things to focus on. Not crashing. Not getting pulled over with the needle north of a hundred and twenty. Straightening that kind of thing out can cause serious delays. But when Graeber was driving Emerson found it harder to control his emotions. His wife's words echoed in his head. Memories of his son crowded in after them. Along with the regrets. So many regrets. And so much reluctance to face the scene he knew must await him at home.

Graeber's car was parked in Emerson's garage. He had left it there when they set off for Georgia. Emerson had driven the last leg so he hit the remote, waited for the door to clank

64

up and out of the way and pulled in alongside it. Graeber reached for the door handle but before he got out he turned to his boss. 'What do you want us to do?'

Emerson thought for a moment. About the things he would have to handle when he went inside the house. How long they would take. Then he said, 'Call Shevchenko. He owes us, big time. Tell him we need a plane. Today. And maybe a chopper, tomorrow or the next day. Then meet me at the warehouse. In two hours. Bring the others. And pack a bag.'

'Where are we going?'

'To find the people who sold the thing that killed my son.'

THIRTEEN

Jack Reacher slept lightly in his replacement room. He woke himself at nine a.m. He showered. He got dressed. And he had just folded his toothbrush, ready to leave, when there was a heavy knock at his door.

'Jack Reacher? This is Detective Harewood, Gerrardsville PD. Are you in there? We need to talk.'

Reacher opened the door and let the detective in. Harewood glanced around the space. He waited for Reacher to sit on the bed and then took the only chair. It was a fluffy turquoise thing with a loose arm and it wasn't at all comfortable. Harewood fidgeted in vain for a moment then put a file he'd been carrying down on the floor.

He said, 'You should get a cellphone.'

Reacher said, 'Why?'

'So that people can call you.'

'Like who?'

'Like me.'

'You likely to do that often?'

Harewood paused. 'No. But that's not the point. You're a hard man to find. It would have been easier if I could have called you. Asked you where you were.'

'But you did find me.'

'Eventually. I called all the hotels in town and asked if they had a guy named Reacher registered. Of course they all said no. So I figured you were using an alias. I remembered you told me you came to town to see the exhibition about Pea Ridge. So I called all the hotels back. Asked for a guest named Samuel Curtis. The victorious general from the battle. And boom. Here you are.'

'I'm impressed. You should be a detective.'

Harewood smiled, but without any humour. 'About that. It's why I wanted to talk to you. I wanted to let you know that the case – the woman killed by the bus – has been closed.'

Reacher thought about the two men he'd seen being wheeled away on gurneys the night before. They'd been in bad shape. Maybe the beating they'd taken had made them open to a deal. He said, 'You caught the guys?'

'It's been ruled a suicide.'

Reacher said nothing.

Harewood closed his eyes and shook his head. 'Look, I know what you told me. About the guy in the hoodie. How he pushed the woman. I believe you. But here's the problem. Another witness came forward. He swears he saw the woman dive in front of the bus. Deliberately dive.'

'He's wrong.'

'I believe you. But this other guy? He's . . . respectable.'

'And I'm not?'

'I didn't say that. My lieutenant—'

67

'This *witness* is wrong. Or he's lying. Maybe he's in on it. Or maybe he was paid off.'

Harewood shook his head. 'He's a solid citizen. He's lived right here in town his whole life. Has a house. A wife. A job. Doesn't gamble. Doesn't drink or use drugs. Isn't in debt. Never even got a parking ticket.'

'Other witnesses, then? Passengers on the bus. Someone must have seen something.'

'One passenger thinks she saw the woman jump. But she wasn't wearing her glasses so she's not much use either way. And another passenger saw you. Fleeing the scene. Which is one reason why my lieutenant—'

'Is there a note?'

Harewood paused. 'She left one at her home. In Mississippi. On her kitchen table. We got prints from the ME, pulled her ID and asked the local PD to check her house. They found it right away.'

'Was the note typed?'

'No. It was handwritten. And signed. No red flags there.'

'What makes you think it's genuine?'

Harewood retrieved his file, took out two sheets of paper and handed them to Reacher. 'The first is her most recent job application. The company she works – worked – for makes all their candidates fill in these forms by hand. Supposedly that reveals all kinds of hidden stuff about people's personalities. Helps to weed out sociopaths and other undesirable characters. The second is her note.'

Reacher started with the job form. He didn't have much experience with employment paperwork but what he read struck him as generic and banal. The first box was headed *Please state your reasons for seeking this position.* Angela's writing was large and rounded and a little childish. She had claimed she wanted to help people. To build on the skills she had developed in previous roles. To make a contribution to the community at large. There was nothing to suggest she had been a stand-out candidate. Or that she was looking to work in a prison. It could have been an application for work as a dog warden. Or at a candy store.

The second sheet had no structure. No questions to answer or information to provide. It had started life as a regular piece of blank paper. The kind that gets used in printers and copiers in homes and offices all over the country. All over the world. Pumped out of giant factories by the million. Used and filed and forgotten. Or thrown away. Or shredded. Only this one had not wound up as something ordinary. Something trivial. The words began about an eighth of the way down, close to the edge. *If you're reading this, I'm sorry, but it's because I'm dead* . . .

Reacher compared the samples. The way the letters were formed. The size and the shape and the spacing. The punctuation. The phrasing. He factored in the passage of time. The effect of stress. He was no expert, but he had to admit they did look like the work of the same person. He tucked the note back under the form where he wouldn't have to look at it any more, passed both pages to Harewood and said, 'OK. Motive?'

'A love affair gone bad.'

'How do you figure?'

'Angela was an admin assistant at a prison. When we notified the local PD they contacted her work. It's a private company. They have the right to monitor their employees' personal email. It's a security thing. Built into their contracts. Most people don't know it's there. Or they forget about it. So their IT guy pulled up her account. Standard procedure in the event of a sudden death. He found a message chain going

69

back a few weeks. Evidently Angela wanted to rekindle an old flame. With an old boyfriend who lived near here. A guy named Roth. They set a rendezvous for Tuesday. Yesterday. She implied in her last email that if it didn't work out, she didn't want to live any more. A little passive-aggressive, if you ask me.'

'*Lived* near here?'

'What?'

'You said the boyfriend *lived*.'

Harewood nodded. 'Roth's DOA. He had a heart attack.'

'When?'

'Monday night. Late. Maybe around midnight.'

'So this guy Roth died less than twelve hours before Angela was killed. You buy that as a coincidence?'

Harewood shrugged.

Reacher said, 'Who found the body?'

'His ex-wife.'

'Where?'

'At his apartment. Yesterday morning. He was a big guy. As in ripped. Not fat. He had a home gym. He'd been working out. Which he did regularly. And then, *bang*. Game over. Just like that.'

'Steroids? Or whatever the latest thing is?'

'No indication of any.'

'Why was his ex-wife at his apartment?'

'For breakfast.'

'Is that normal?'

'For them, yes, apparently.'

'How did she get inside?'

'She has a key.'

'Sounds cosy.'

'I guess.'

'Maybe the ex was trying to get back into the picture. Found out about this reunion. Got jealous.'

Harewood shook his head. 'I don't think so. They'd been divorced ten years. She moved to the apartment next door when they split. Neighbours said they got on like brother and sister. Any kind of spark fizzled out years ago. There was no bad blood.'

'Had Roth had other relationships?'

Harewood shrugged.

Reacher said, 'Did the ex know about his relationship with Angela?'

'We didn't ask her about it. We had no reason to. Roth's body was found before Angela got killed. We didn't know anything about her until we pulled her out from under that bus.'

'So the ex didn't confirm the rendezvous?'

'No. That's not to say she didn't know about it. But we already verified it another way.'

Harewood thumbed through his file, pulled out another piece of paper and set it on the edge of the bed. Reacher wasn't familiar with the format but he guessed it was a transcript of the emails that the Minerva IT guys had come up with. It was certainly made up of alternating messages between two people. He assumed they were Angela and Roth but the names weren't shown in a way he could decipher. There were just bunches of letters and numbers with @ signs in the middle and .coms at the end. There were vertical lines at the left of the page, starting at the top of each separate message and running all the way down to the end of the last one. Each successive line was one space to the right so that the lowest message was all squashed up into less than half the width of the page. It was the oldest, from Angela. She had been putting out feelers about getting back together. Reacher could sense her excitement. Her trepidation. The newest message, at the top, written on Sunday morning, was also from Angela. The tone was flat. She sounded depressed. The tentative hope had faded away. All that was left was an under-current of despair. Plus, a bunch of hints that she couldn't carry on alone. Just as Harewood had reported.

Reacher put the paper down. 'If Angela came here to meet Roth, where is her purse? Her car?'

Harewood took the paper and slipped it back into his file. 'Her purse was in her car. Her car was in a parking lot. The first one you come to if you're coming in from the east. Like she would have done.'

'I saw the guy take her purse. They must have dumped it in her car. Was there an envelope inside it?'

Harewood checked his notes. 'No. There was a wallet. Keys. Some personal stuff. But no correspondence. Why?'

'Never mind. How do you account for the blood?'

'What blood?'

'On her purse. There was blood spatter all over one side of it.'

'There's no record of that. What makes you think so?'

'I saw it.'

'How? Blood wouldn't stand out against black leather.'

'The purse was tan. And it wasn't leather.'

Harewood checked his notes again. 'It was leather. And it was black.'

'They must have switched it. Replaced it with a sanitized one.'

'Can you prove that?'

'What about her kid?'

'How do you know she had a kid?'

'Lucky guess.'

Harewood shook his head. 'She made arrangements with a neighbour. A woman who often watched her.'

'Permanent arrangements? With money attached? Adoption papers? Favourite toys?'

Harewood shrugged. 'I only have what the officers in Mississippi passed along. They seem satisfied.'

'And the BMW?'

Harewood shook his head. 'That's another problem. The plates you gave me are registered to a Dodge Caravan in Oklahoma City. The owner was at work yesterday. He has a receipt from a parking garage. Time-stamped, with pictures of the vehicle arriving and leaving.'

'OK. Where are the shell casings? I put six rounds into that car.'

'CSU swept the alley. Twice. It was clean. No trace of any brass.'

'So test my hands for GSR.'

'Which would prove what? That you fired a gun? Not necessarily a gun that fired missing rounds at a missing car.'

'What about the fire escape? There's no hiding that.'

'It collapsed. Sure. But there's no proof *why*.'

'What about—'

'Listen, Reacher. I've already asked all these questions. And I've been told to stop. In no uncertain terms. The file is closed. I just came to let you know the situation. As a courtesy.'

'Then I guess we're done here. You know where the door is.'

Harewood didn't move.

Reacher waited thirty seconds then stood up and dropped his room key on to the bed. 'Do me a favour. Leave that at reception on your way out.'

Harewood said, 'Wait. I came to . . . Well, I didn't just come as a courtesy.'

Reacher sat back down.

'To be completely honest, my lieutenant wants you out of the jurisdiction. He thinks you're trouble.'

'So you're here to drag me across the county line?'

'No. I'm not here at all. Not officially.'

'I figured. Showing evidence to a potential suspect – that can't be SOP around here.'

'No.' Harewood looked down at the floor. 'The lieutenant would have my ass for that.'

'So why did you do it?'

'I ran your record. The 110th. The special investigators. Your old unit. In the army.'

'What about it?'

'Look, I'm new to this gig.'

'And?'

'I don't have anyone else to ask.'

'Ask what?'

'If you were me, what would you do?'

'About what?'

'My lieutenant has ordered me to drop this case. I think he's wrong. I want to keep working it. Should I do that?'

'You're talking about going against your chain of command.'

'Yes, sir. I'm clear about that.'

Reacher paused. 'Marine Corps?'

'How did you know?'

'My father was a Marine. I know the signs.'

'So? What should I do?'

'Your lieutenant – is he a crook? Is he running a cover-up of some kind?'

'I don't think so. I think the guy's just lazy. He's been given a result tied up in ribbons. He doesn't want to untie them and see what's really inside the box. He doesn't want to do the work.'

'What's Roth's ex's name?'

'Hannah Hampton.'

'His address?'

'I'll write it for you.'

'Good. Then this is what you should do. Go back to work. Business as usual. Say nothing more about this.'

'I'm not asking you to work the case for me.'

'I know.'

'You shouldn't get involved.'

'I'm already involved.'

'You should get uninvolved.'

'A woman was murdered. Someone has to do something about that.'

'We will do something. The Police Department.'

'Will you? With your lazy lieutenant?'

Harewood looked at the ground.

'Give me that address. Then keep your head down. I'll be in touch.'

FOURTEEN

Factor in the fittings and fixtures, add on the value of the art that covers the walls, and the Minerva Reception Center in Winson cost more per square foot than any corporate headquarters in the state of Mississippi. That was a soundbite Bruno Hix loved to throw around. Especially to the press. It may even have been true. Hix didn't care. He wasn't a detail man. He was all about creating the right impression. Building the centre was the first thing Minerva did after it bought the prison and the brief Hix gave the architects was simple: Make sure the place reeks of money.

The reception centre was near the entrance to the site, on the opposite side to the secure units. The building was a single storey high, faced in pale stone and shaped like a V. Partly so that it would fit in the available space, which was limited. But mainly so that its windows, which were on its inner face only, did not have a view of the cell blocks and exercise yards. Its conference room took up one whole wing. Hix hustled through the maze of fenced-in walkways that criss-crossed the complex the minute the covert meeting in S2's hub wrapped up, but he still failed to get to it on time. When he burst through the double doors, a little pink and out of breath, six faces were already staring back at him. Three on one side of the long alder table. Two on the other. And one all the way at the far end. They were journalists, there to be briefed about the event planned for Friday. Plus whatever else Hix chose to spoon-feed them while they were his captive audience.

Hix waited for Damon Brockman, Minerva's other co-founder, to take a seat and dismissed the guard who'd been keeping an eye on the visitors. Then he got the ball rolling the way he always did. He stood at the head of the table, stretched out his arms like a TV evangelist and said, 'Tell me the truth. Does this room feel like it's part of a prison?'

Five of the journalists obediently shook their heads. Only the guy at the far end didn't respond.

Hix smiled and moved on to some history. His own, and Brockman's. He talked about how they met three decades ago as rookie wardens at a state facility in Lubbock, Texas. How horrified they had been at the conditions. The lack of resources. The dehumanizing treatment they witnessed. He threw in a little philosophy. Some Foucault. Some Bentham. And he pulled it all together to explain the foundation of Minerva Correctional. Named for the ancient goddess of wisdom and justice, among other things. Committed to seeing inmates for what they were: people. People who had made mistakes, for sure. Who had made bad choices. But who still had potential. Who could make a positive contribution. Who could have a future, given the right kind of environment and support. He described the vocational programmes the company ran. The diet and exercise initiatives they had introduced.

The proactive health screening they provided at all five of their locations. He backed up his examples with statistics. Some may even have been accurate. He claimed dramatic increases in post-release employment rates. A profound drop in recidivism. And he finished by tying everything back to Friday. The jewel in Minerva's crown. The sponsored appeal scheme for well-behaved inmates who could credibly claim to be victims of miscarried justice.

Hix paused to give his concluding point some extra emphasis, then rested his palms on the table, leaned forward, and said, 'Questions?'

Hix always got asked about a bunch of mundane details. The identity of his investors. Recruitment. Employment practices. Visitation rights. Violence. The presence of gangs. He figured there would be something about the environment and the impact of Minerva's operations, too. That had become a hot potato of late. And there could be some wild cards. Spicier issues, which may or may not come up, depending on the feistiness of the audience. Issues like the morality of profiting from other people's incarceration. Whether enough was being done to prevent the sexual abuse of vulnerable inmates. Evidence of racial bias among the guards. Things that required a little more thought and finesse.

Within a quarter of an hour the five journalists sitting close to Hix had ticked all the usual boxes. Hix had tried to make it sound like he had never heard their types of question before. Like he was interested in them. He gave what he thought would be his final answer and was about to wind the session up when the sixth journalist sprang into life. The one at the far end of the table. He was the youngest of the group. He had a round, plump face, straggly blond hair and was dressed in faded clothes from an army surplus store. Like a wannabe Che Guevara in need of a hat and a dye job, Hix thought. And some focus. Until that point the guy had shown little interest in anything going on around him. He had shown little sign of being awake.

'The death rate in Minerva's prisons is shocking,' the guy said. 'Why is it so high?'

Hix glanced down at Brockman and paused for a moment. Then he wet his lips and said, 'The mortality rate at our centres is not high. What makes you think otherwise?'

Brockman slipped his phone out of his pocket. He held it low down, next to his leg, so no one could see him tap out a message with his thumb.

The Guevara guy said, 'I have my sources.'

'Which you can't reveal?' Hix said.

'Correct.'

Hix smiled. 'You're fishing, aren't you, my friend? Well, you're casting your hook in the wrong pond. The health and life expectancy of our inmates is significantly better than at comparable institutions. And that's not down to chance. Or luck. It's thanks to our unique, progressive, humanitarian policies. If fate leads you down the unfortunate path to incarceration, a Minerva facility is where you want to end up. There's no question about that.'

'You're saying your death rate isn't sky high?'

'That's exactly what I'm saying.'

'You have the data to back it up?'

'Of course.'

'Then why don't you publish it?'

'To what end? There's nothing to see.'

'You should publish it anyway. For transparency.'

'We publish everything we're required to by state and federal law.'

79

'Which is a fraction of what state and federal facilities have to publish.'

Hix shrugged. 'We don't make the law. We just comply with it. Scrupulously.'

'You're using it as a smokescreen. You have a serious drug problem in your jails and you're trying to hide it. Whenever an inmate overdoses and has to go to the hospital, you pass it off as some kind of preventative measure coming from your so-called humanitarianism. You've gotten good at hiding the truth about the ones who recover. But when they die? That's where the real story is, right?'

'Wrong. Look, can I hand on heart say there won't be a single drug taken in any of our facilities today? No. We live in the real world. I'm not naive. But when it comes to drugs, just like everything else, Minerva is streets ahead of every other operator in helping and protecting our inmates. The idea that addicts are dying in droves in our care is ridiculous.'

'Prove it. Show us the data.'

'I—'

There was a hard rap on the door behind Hix and the guard who had been watching the group came back into the room. He said, 'I'm sorry to interrupt, sir, but there's a phone call for you.'

'Tell whoever it is I'll call them back. I'm busy here.'

'It's the governor, sir.'

'Oh. What does he want?'

'He didn't say. Just that it was urgent.'

'OK. I guess I shouldn't keep him waiting, then. Could you help these good folks find their way to the exit?'

The guard nodded. 'Happy to.'

Hix turned back to the journalists. 'I'm sorry, but we're going to have to draw a line at this point. Which is a shame because I was really enjoying the debate. My friend at the end of the table, I'll get you those mortality numbers. Assuming our legal guys give me the green light. We have to be careful about privileged information, SEC regulations, things like that. And I'll also have a word with one of our inmates. See if he'll talk to you. When Minerva took this place over the guy had something going on with one of his eyes. Damon and I had seen the same thing with a prisoner years ago, when we were working for a different corrections provider. That company wouldn't bring in a doctor because of the cost. They didn't provide insurance. The condition got worse and worse, and long story short, the prisoner was left completely blind. The same would have happened to our guy, only we got him proactive treatment. Now he's an artist. He paints watercolours. Some of them are on display in a gallery in Jackson. He can give you the real scoop on our humanitarian policies. With no dead junkies involved. I guarantee.'

Hix shook each journalist's hand and when the last one had filed out of the room he flopped down into the seat at the head of the table. 'Bad moment, back there. High death rates? That was a little too close to home.'

'Who is that kid?' Brockman said. 'I like him. Great way to trace drug deaths. We should try it on those assholes at Curtis Correctional. Dig up some dirt. Hit them right when their contract is up in Kansas.'

'We have more urgent issues. That kid needs to be watched. Twenty-four seven, until he leaves town.'

'No need. He's no danger to us. He knows nothing. Like you said, he was fishing.'

'He's no danger yet. But we can't have him poking around. Asking questions. Not if he's looking for drugs.'

'So what if he's looking for drugs? He won't find any. None he can connect to us, anyway.'

'You're missing the point. Drugs don't appear out of thin air. They have to be smuggled. And we can't have anyone watching for packages getting taken into the prison. Or more importantly, out.'

Brockman thought for a moment. 'You're right. Leave it with me. I'll have the guy watched. And discouraged, if necessary.'

'Good. But this leads us to something else. The guy from Colorado. Who might have looked in the envelope. I had thought it would be safe to wait and see if he showed up in town.'

'He won't.'

'He might. And if he does, I don't want there to be any chance of him crossing paths with the journalist kid. Or of us having to deal with the guy and the journalist getting wind of it.'

'You're worrying over nothing.'

'I'm keeping us safe. And protecting our investment. So we're going to make a change to the plan.'

'We're not cancelling the ceremony. Or doing it behind closed doors. Don't listen to Riverdale. That guy—'

'I'm not worried about the publicity. I want it. And it can't hurt us. Worst case? The guy sees a video or reads a report that has a picture with it. After the event it's too late for him to make any waves. The danger is if he shows up. Causes a scene in real time. Gets that nosy kid all fired up. So this is what we're going to do. We're going to push the cordon further out. Figure out how the guy might try to get here. He's homeless, after all. That has to limit his options. So we'll identify any potential approach routes and post our people at strategic locations.'

'Can't hurt, I suppose. But I still don't think he'll come.'

'Assume he will. The question is, how? He doesn't have a car. He can't rent one because he doesn't have a licence.'

'He could steal one.'

'That's possible. What else?'

'Someone he knows could drive him. Or he could hitch a ride with a stranger.'

'Possible. What else?'

'He could go old school. Take the bus. If he could afford a ticket. There's a Greyhound station in Jackson. That must be the closest.'

'He could do that, I guess. At a pinch. Time would be tight if he hasn't already set off. What else?'

Brockman was quiet for a moment. 'That's all I got.'

'OK. So here's what I need you to do. Put two men on the Greyhound station in Jackson. Have them check every bus that comes in from anywhere west of here. Also put two men at the truck stop on 20. If the guy tries to hitch a ride, what are the chances of finding one driver going all the way from Colorado to Winson? Zero. He'll need to get multiple rides. The final pick-up would have to be quite a distance away. Everyone knows better than to stop for hitchhikers near a prison. Put two more men at the intersection with 61, in case he tries his luck there instead. And two more where there's construction on 87, halfway from Jackson. In case the guy stole a car or got a ride with a friend. It's down to one lane, right there. And it's slow. Easy to see who's driving. Or being driven.'

'That's a lot of manpower.'

'There's a lot at stake.'

'What about the prison? And Angela's house? Do we still watch them?'

'Of course. There's no guarantee the guy won't slip through.'

'That's even more manpower.'

'We don't have a choice. Pull a couple of guards out of each unit. Minerva people only. No legacy grunts. Cancel days off and double enough other shifts to pick up the slack. And find the biggest man we've got. Hold him in reserve. The idiots we sent to Colorado as well. If anyone calls in a sighting, have them check it. If the ID is positive, dispatch them. Make sure the guy is properly neutralized this time.'

'If they get there fast enough. And if our guys spot him. They're going to be stretched pretty thin.'

'I have an idea about that. Some insurance, in case he does somehow get through. Something that'll throw him off the scent. I'll take care of it while you handle the other logistics.'

'Understood. And I'll tell Moseley to send out extra patrols. And make sure all his units have this Reacher guy's description.'

'OK. But I want the cops on a watching brief only. We need to handle this ourselves. No official record. And Damon? Double-check everything. Triple-check it. Make sure every-one is at the top of their game. You know what will happen if anything gets screwed up on Friday.'

FIFTEEN

S am Roth's apartment building looked just like all the others on its block. Two storeys. Stone-fronted. Solid but plain. Nice but ordinary. There was nothing to suggest a man had died there within the last thirty-six hours.

Maybe from natural causes.

Maybe not.

Detective Harewood said Roth's death was caused by a heart attack. There was nothing suspicious about that. People die from heart disease all the time. Nearly 700,000 people every year in the United States. More than the population of Vermont. More than one every forty-six seconds.

If heart disease had been the only factor, Reacher might not have been so sceptical. If Roth had not been fit and accustomed to exercise. If Harewood's lieutenant had not been lazy. If Roth had not died hours before he was due to meet Angela St. Vrain. If Angela had not been murdered . . .

Too many *if*s, Reacher thought. And too few answers.

*

The buildings fronted on to a wide, leafy street but the entrances were around the back on a strip that was too small to be called a road but too nice to be called an alley. It was neatly paved. Clean and tidy. There were trees and shrubs. Most of the homes had sun terraces or decks on that side. Roth's building had two terraces, covered for shade, with a pair of doors between them. Both were painted blue. The same shade of navy. There was a parking space on each side. Both were occupied. One by a truck, all red paint and chrome and black glass. The other by a small hatchback. It was silver and sleek and a thick cable snaked from a flap on its rear wing to a box on the wall by the left-hand door.

Roth's apartment was on the right, according to the address Harewood had provided. Reacher knocked on the door to the left. He almost hoped no one would answer. Breaking the news that somebody's loved one was dead was a miserable job. Reacher knew from experience. He knew that suggesting somebody's loved one might have been murdered was almost as bad.

The door jerked open after two long minutes. A woman stood in the entrance. She was wearing three-quarter-length white pants and a plain blue T-shirt. She had nothing on her feet. Her hair was blond, streaked with a little grey, maybe shoulder length. She had it pulled back and tied in a ponytail with a plain elastic band. Her face was ghostly pale except for the deep red circles under her eyes. Reacher figured she would be in her mid-forties, although the circumstances made it hard to judge.

The woman took a moment to size Reacher up then said, 'Sam's not here. He's . . .'

'I know,' Reacher said. 'I'm not looking for Sam. I need to talk to you.'

86

The woman looked blank. 'About Sam. You see, something happened and, Sam, he's . . .'

'It's OK. I know about Sam. Are you Hannah? Hannah Hampton?'

The woman blinked, then nodded. 'Who are you?'

'My name's Reacher.'

'What do you want?'

'Do you know a woman called Angela St. Vrain?'

'Angela? Oh God. I should tell her about Sam.'

'You do know her?'

'Know her? Knew her? Haven't seen her for years. She moved to Mississippi. Oh God, Danny. I should tell him, too.'

'Danny?'

'Danny Peel. He moved out there, too. He got Angela her job.'

'Did Sam know Angela?'

'Of course. They worked together. A few years ago. Sam was her boss. More of a mentor, really.'

'Did Sam know Danny?'

Hannah nodded.

Reacher said, 'Did they keep in touch?'

'Danny, not so much. Angela, off and on. She sometimes reaches out to Sam for advice. With work, mainly. Why all these questions?'

'Had Sam and Angela been in touch recently?'

Hannah paused. 'Over the weekend. She sent him some stuff on email.'

'Work stuff? Or personal?'

'Work.'

'Did Sam say what it was?'

'Some dumb accounting thing. Angela didn't know what to do about it. She was in a state. She was often in a state. Sam

87

shouldn't have gotten involved this time. I said to him, tell her to figure it out for herself. He had more than enough on his plate. But no. That was Sam. He would never turn his back on a friend.'

'What kind of accounting thing?'

'I don't know. Something about a number that didn't add up. Sam didn't go into detail.' Hannah was silent for a moment. 'Wait. What's all this about? You're starting to freak me out. What's going on with Angela? And what's it to you? Tell me or I'm done answering questions.'

Reacher paused. 'Hannah, I have some news. About Angela. It's not good news. Is there somewhere we could sit?'

Hannah took a step back. 'Who are you again?'

'My name's Reacher. Do you remember Detective Harewood? You spoke with him yesterday after you found Sam. I'm sure he left you a card. Call him. He'll vouch for me.'

The door closed, and two minutes later it opened again. Hannah gestured for Reacher to come inside. He followed her into the apartment's main living space. There was a lounge area, all pale wood furniture with soft-coloured fabrics, plus a couple of low bookcases and a small TV in the corner. Then an oval glass dining table surrounded by white leather chairs. And a kitchen at the far end, tucked away behind a breakfast bar. There were two high stools next to it. Hannah made her way across and perched on one. Reacher followed and took the other.

Hannah rested her elbow on the countertop. 'You're going to tell me Angela's dead, too.'

Reacher said, 'How did you know?'

'Detective Harewood told me you used to be a cop. In the army. Well, a cop shows up at your door? He asks about someone, then says he has bad news? Doesn't take a genius. What happened to her?'

'She got hit by a bus.'

'Seriously?'

Reacher nodded.

'I'm sorry. That's awful. Was it an accident?'

'No.'

'Wait. Was it . . . She didn't . . .'

'Jump? No.'

'She was murdered? That's terrible. I told her not to move to Mississippi. People are crazy there, you know.'

'It happened right here. In Gerrardsville.'

'No. I don't believe it. When?'

'Yesterday.'

'What was Angela doing in Gerrardsville, yesterday?'

'The police think she came to see Sam.'

'Why? He was helping her with that accounting thing, but on the phone. And on email. There was no need for her to come all this way.'

'The police think there was something between them.'

'What, like romantically?'

Reacher nodded.

Hannah shook her head. 'Not a chance.'

'Are you sure?'

'A thousand per cent. See, one, if Sam was interested in someone, he'd tell me. And two, if he was looking for romance, you'd be more his cup of tea than Angela.'

'Was that common knowledge?'

'He worked in a prison. He started when he was eighteen. Thirty years ago that wasn't the kind of thing you broadcast. Not in that environment, anyway.'

'Is that why you got divorced?'

89

'It's why we got married. Things were different back then. For both of us. We worked together. Kind of. He was a corrections officer. I worked for a charity that helps ex-cons adjust to normal life. Still do, on a casual basis. So it made sense. But gradually attitudes changed. They improved. Or so we thought.'

'I hear you. But here's the strange thing. I saw a bunch of emails between Sam and Angela. They went back weeks. And they wound up by setting a meeting for yesterday.'

Angela straightened up. 'You hacked into Sam's email?'

'No. I saw printouts. They came from Angela's employer.'

Hannah thought for a moment. 'Sam wasn't scheduled to work yesterday. He mentioned he was planning to go out. If Angela was in town, it's conceivable they were going to meet. But not to hook up. Trust me.'

'So what about the emails I saw?'

'Could someone have impersonated Sam, online, to lure Angela here? If they wanted to kill her? Paedophiles do that kind of thing all the time. With kids, anyway. And Angela already knew Sam. She trusted him. It would be easier to use his identity to trick her than to invent a new one.'

'Good in theory, but no. Angela initiated everything. Said she wanted to rekindle an old flame.'

'But there wasn't any old flame. There couldn't have been.'

'Maybe the accounting thing they were dealing with was more serious than Sam let on. Maybe they set up a meeting to talk about it. Maybe Angela was going to bring some documents for him to see. Or some other kind of evidence. But someone found out. Decided to stop them. And replaced the genuine emails between them with fake ones.'

'Who would do that?'

'A co-worker with light fingers. A boss paying bribes. A supplier ripping off Angela's employer. Plenty of candidates.'

'OK.' Hannah shrugged. 'But I don't know about planting fake emails. Why would anyone go to the trouble? Why not just delete the real ones?'

'To cover their asses. The last fake email from Angela hinted that if Sam didn't take her back, she would kill herself. The guy who killed her made it look like she jumped under that bus. Add those things together and the police have no reason to dig any deeper.'

'If Sam hadn't had his heart attack, he'd have gone to meet Angela. Waited around for a while. And when she didn't show, and he was told she'd killed herself, what would he have done? Figured the stress of the whole thing had gotten too much for her? Maybe.'

'Hannah, did you notice anyone hanging around here recently? Anyone you didn't recognize? On Sunday? Maybe Monday? Maybe in a car?'

'Wait. I'm still thinking through your idea. It might have flown. Worth a shot, I guess. As long as Sam bought Angela's death as suicide. That's the key because he wouldn't have seen whatever evidence she was bringing. And he wouldn't have known about the bogus emails because they wouldn't have shown up on his computer. They couldn't have, or he'd have been, like, *what the hell?*'

'The bogus emails couldn't have shown up, but what about the real ones? What would have happened to those?'

'They'll still be on his computer, I guess.'

'You have a key to his apartment?'

'Sure. Why?'

Reacher stood up. 'I need to see that computer. Right now.'

SIXTEEN

Hannah's hand was shaking when she tried to get the key into the lock on Roth's door.

She said, 'I'm sorry. This is the first time I've been here since . . .'

Reacher said, 'It's OK. You don't have to come inside.'

'No.' Hannah closed her eyes for a moment. She took a deep breath. 'I'm doing this. For Sam. If his friend was murdered, he wouldn't want people to think it was suicide. Angela has – had – a kid. And Sam was a prison guard. He wouldn't want a murderer to go free.'

The main room of Roth's apartment was laid out the same as Hannah's. It had the same kind of furniture, maybe a decade older, a little more tired, with fewer colours. There was no TV and the top of one of the bookcases was filled with a line of framed photographs. Reacher could smell incense coming from somewhere, and right away the sense of trespass he always felt when he had to search a dead person's home started to creep up his spine.

Hannah started toward an archway at the side of the kitchen area but paused when she drew level with the bookcase. She looked down at the photographs. They were all of her. There was a whole series. She was wearing the same gi in each one. In the first picture she had a white belt. By the last, the belt was brown. Hannah stretched out and flipped each photo in turn face down. She said, 'I can't believe he kept those. He knew I hated them.' She sniffed and wiped a tear from her cheek.

Reacher said, 'Do you still train?'

Hannah shook her head. 'Not much. I haven't graded since I moved next door. I only started as a way for Sam and me to go to the gym together. Working out is so boring. He was always nagging me to step it up again.'

Another tear welled up in the corner of Hannah's eye. She blinked it away and began to move again. Through the archway. It led to a dog-legged staircase which opened on to a corridor with three more doors. The first one was open a crack. Hannah pushed it the rest of the way and stepped into Roth's bedroom. It was a small space. Tidy. Impersonal. The bed was made. There was no clothing strewn around. No shoes on the floor. No pictures on the walls. Just a book on the nightstand and a glass of water. The blinds were drawn. There were mirrors on the closet doors, which were closed. And in the far corner there was a small desk. It was made of metal and wood and looked like it could fold down when not in use. There was no chair.

'Not much of an office space.' Hannah took a silver laptop computer from the desk and sat down on the bed. 'The other room's full of his weights and workout stuff. That was more important to him.'

Hannah opened the computer and started tapping away on the keyboard and dragging her finger up and down on a little shiny rectangle below it. After a couple of minutes she turned the screen so that Reacher could see.

She said, 'This is weird. There are no emails from Angela. Plenty from other people. Even a bunch of spam he never got rid of. But none from her. Not even from years ago. None in his inbox. None in any of his folders. And none in the trash. Which is extra weird because Sam had his mail set to keep deleted messages in the trash for a week. I just checked.'

'Are there any emails from Danny Peel?'

Hannah tapped and swiped and clicked for another minute, then nodded her head. 'A few. Mostly from before Danny moved.'

'So what happened to the messages from Angela?'

'Sam must have found a way to permanently delete them. Instantly. I just can't see why he'd do that.'

'Could an expert recover them?'

'Maybe. I don't know.'

'Can you tell if it was definitely Sam who deleted them?'

'No one else had access to his computer. He never takes it anywhere. It's a laptop, but he only bought it because it's small. Not to carry around.'

'Could they be deleted remotely?'

'I don't know. I'm no expert. They could probably be wiped off the central server remotely, I guess. But after he downloaded them? Maybe some high-level hacker could do it. Probably not a regular person.'

'Have you noticed anyone hanging around the building, the last few days? Any cars you didn't recognize?'

'Why are you asking that again? You think someone broke in here after Sam died and wiped his computer?'

Reacher said nothing.

'Oh.' Hannah slowly closed the computer. 'No. You think he was murdered? Like Angela was? No way.'

'Angela was murdered on her way to meet him. In secret. Probably with some critical evidence to show him. Even if Sam believed it was suicide, he had still seen Angela's emails. He knew something was going on. He knew what kind of material she was bringing. That paints a pretty big target on his back.'

'No. It was totally natural causes. I saw him, remember. I found him.'

'Heart attacks can be faked. There are drugs. Chemicals.'

'Not in this case. Because you know the really sad thing? When I saw him, I wasn't even surprised.'

'I heard he was in good health. *Ripped*, Harewood said.'

'He worked out a lot, yes. Too much, actually. It's how he dealt with stress. But healthy? Not so much.'

'Sam was stressed?'

'He had a stressful job.'

'He had that job for thirty years.'

'The stress had gotten worse.'

'How?'

'I don't know.'

'New boss? Staff cuts? Some kind of disciplinary situation?'

'None of those things. He was just . . . having trouble. He didn't say anything, but I know him. Knew him. Knew the signs. He wasn't eating properly. He wasn't sleeping. He was working out too much. Pushing himself too hard. I should have done more to help him. He was a heart attack waiting to happen and I knew it.'

'So he was stressed. More than usual. But how did that cause Angela's emails to disappear?'

'Maybe that was done remotely, like you said.' Hannah was silent for a moment, then she frowned. 'Wait. Sam had dinner at my place, Monday night. I was trying to get him to eat more. It didn't work. He just picked at his food then rushed off home. To work out. Again. What else would he be doing these days? I wasn't happy, but I gave him a goodnight kiss, like I always do. At the door. And across the way I kind of think I might have seen a car. Yes. I remember thinking it must be an Uber waiting for someone, but that it was weird because its lights were off.'

'What colour was it?'

'Something dark. Black, I think.'

'Make? Model?'

'I'm not sure. I couldn't see too well because of Sam's truck.'

Reacher thought for a moment. It hadn't rained that morning. The previous day had been dry, too. But Monday night was an unknown quantity. It had been fine earlier in the day, when he walked into town. But he had spent the evening with Alexandra. At her apartment. The weather was the last thing he was paying attention to. Still, if a vehicle had been parked for any length of time it could have left a trace of some kind. It was worth a look. So Reacher said, 'Come on. Show me where the car was waiting.'

The sun was high when Reacher followed Hannah outside. It was warm and bright and the air was sweet from all the plants growing in pots and urns outside the buildings. There were hardly any shadows. And the ground was bone dry. It was dusty. There were no footprints. No tyre tracks. There was no possibility of any.

Hannah continued toward the opposite wall. She stopped below a spot where a pipe emerged from the brickwork. It was plastic, maybe three inches in diameter, and it ran vertically down before burrowing into the dirt. A drain, Reacher guessed. From a laundry room, or a kitchen or bathroom.

Hannah said, 'The car was right here. By this pipework. On this side. So it was facing away from Sam's door. If anyone was in it, they couldn't have been watching his place.'

Reacher caught up with her. He was thinking, *cars have mirrors*. And the guy who had pushed Angela was experienced. As was his buddy, the driver. As were the two guys Reacher had encountered at The Pineapple. So they would all understand the value of discretion. Reacher was about to mention that when he noticed something about the ground near Hannah's feet. There was a patch that was a little darker than the rest. Not much. Just a fraction of a shade. But discernible. It started at the base of the pipe and fanned out in a semicircle, close to three feet in diameter, fading as it went. There must have been a leak from the drain. Just a gradual one. Not enough to turn the dirt to mud. Not foul-smelling or full of chemicals. Nothing to warrant an urgent repair.

Reacher crouched down and took a closer look at the damp section of earth. It was basically flat, though not entirely smooth. The surface had been disturbed. Probably by grit and gravel blown in the wind. But along with the natural scrapes and scratches Reacher could see a strip made up of more regular shapes. Faint, but definitely there. A tread pattern. From a tyre. It was wide, like the kind a high-performance sedan would have.

'Could you get a picture of that?' Reacher pointed at the track.

Hannah pulled out her phone and fired off half a dozen photographs. 'You really think someone was watching us?'

'Too early to say.'

Hannah suddenly shivered, despite the sun. 'God, I saw them. Their car, anyway. And if they were . . . then they . . . poor Sam.'

'You should stay somewhere else for a few nights. Have you got family near by? Friends?'

'No. It's just me. I'll check into a hotel.'

'Make it one in another town.'

'This is all too much.' Hannah sighed. 'No. It's not. I'll be OK. I guess I better grab some things. What are you going to do?'

'Talk to Harewood. Have him send some technicians down here.'

Hannah took a step toward her apartment then stopped again. 'Damn it. Look at that.'

'What?'

'Sam's mailbox.' Hannah pointed to a mailbox on a post next to Sam's parking space. It was a simple affair, corrugated steel, pressed into shape and painted red just like his truck.

'What about it?'

'It's not shut properly.'

Hannah was right. The mailbox's flap was open a fraction.

'Sam hated that.' Hannah marched across to the box. 'He liked it closed all the way. He was always chewing out the mail carrier if he didn't do it right.' Hannah gave the front of the mailbox a hefty slap with her palm and its lid clicked into place. Then she grabbed it and pulled it open again. 'Better see what's been delivered, I guess. Could be something urgent.'

98

Hannah reached inside and pulled out a single piece of paper. It had no envelope and it was folded into thirds. Hannah glanced at Reacher then unfolded the page. She straightened it. Read it. Then her mouth sagged open and the paper slipped from her fingers and fluttered to the ground. Reacher scooped it up. He saw that it wasn't addressed. It wasn't signed. There were just two lines of printed words:

Wiles Park. 1 p.m. Wednesday. The bench under the tree. Bring the proof.

Disobey and your next-door neighbour will be in hospital by sundown.

Reacher handed the paper back to Hannah and said, 'Where's Wiles Park?'

'Near the centre of town.' Hannah's voice was quiet and hollow. 'Fifteen minutes away, maybe. If you hurry.'

The note said one p.m. The clock in Reacher's head told him that only left ten minutes' leeway.

Harewood and his technicians would have to wait.

SEVENTEEN

The sky gradually brightened and the Greyhound bus continued to thump and rumble its way east. It crossed the rest of Arizona, cut the corner of New Mexico and dropped diagonally down into Texas. With every mile Jed Starmer grew more accustomed to its sounds. He became less likely to be disturbed. But also less tired due to all his hours of sleep, so one effect balanced out the other, meaning that it took him around the same length of time to wake up when the bus stopped in El Paso as it had done in Phoenix.

Jed drifted to the surface, looked around and located the depot sign. He checked his watch. They were bang on schedule. So they would be in El Paso for an hour and five minutes. It was lunchtime and he wouldn't get another decent break until they got to Dallas in the early hours of the next morning. Which meant it made sense to get out and find some food. He was starving, but he felt more energetic than the last time he woke up. He slid across on to the seat next to the aisle. Some of the other passengers were already outside, wandering about. He waited for an elderly couple to shuffle by then stood up and started toward the door. Then he stopped again. He didn't have his backpack. It hadn't been on his lap. He hadn't been hugging it. He hadn't wanted to look like a little kid. So he'd put it on the seat, next to him. Before he fell asleep. But now it wasn't on the seat. It wasn't on the floor. It wasn't in the luggage rack. It was nowhere. It was gone.

Jed remembered the guy in the bus station in LA. The surfer-looking dude who had found his ticket when he dropped it. The guy had warned him. Told him to hang on to his bag. To keep his arm through the strap when he slept. He should have listened. He should have . . .

Jed spotted the backpack. It was outside the bus. A guy was carrying it. He was moving quickly, along the concourse between the piers. He was almost at the depot exit. Jed started to rush down the aisle but almost at once he had to slow down. Nearly to a standstill. The old couple was in the way. Dawdling. Creeping along. It was like they were experimenting to see how slowly it was possible for human beings to move without their feet fusing with the floor. Jed hovered along behind them until they reached the door. They climbed down. Jed jumped out. He ran to the exit. There was no sign of the guy with his backpack. Then Jed caught a glimpse of him. Through a car window. A cab. The guy was reclining in the back seat. He was cradling the backpack. Its top flap was pressing against the glass.

The cab was twenty yards away. Jed ran toward it. He waved. He yelled. The cab accelerated. Jed jumped. He screamed. He kept on running. But the cab just moved faster and faster until it was gone from Jed's sight.

Jed was left on the sidewalk, doubled over, out of breath. He was alone in a strange town, hundreds of miles from the only place he had ever thought of as home. All his worldly goods were gone. His dream of a new life was shattered. Tears blurred his vision. He slid his hand into his front pocket. His fingers searched for coins. If he could find a quarter he could call his foster mother. Beg her to come and get him. To take him back. To save him.

Jed could call.

Whether his foster mother would answer was a whole other question.

Graeber and the other four guys had been waiting for an hour by the time Emerson arrived at the warehouse in Chicago. The four guys were surprised. It wasn't like Emerson to be late. But these were not normal times. Graeber had laid out some of the background for them. Not everything. Emerson was a private kind of guy. He wouldn't want his family's dirty laundry washed in public. And Graeber was ambitious. He didn't want to erode his privileged position in the organization so he stuck to the basics. Just enough to keep the others from asking too many questions. Or getting nervous and walking out.

Emerson's wife had been crazier than he'd expected when he got home. She had screamed at him the moment he walked through the door. She had wailed and pounded on his chest. She had flung things. She had blamed him for what had happened to Kyle. For the fact that the treatment had failed. Which didn't seem fair to Emerson. Not fair at all. He hadn't poured the booze down Kyle's throat. He hadn't rolled his joints or filled his syringes with who knew what. All he had done was try to get the kid better. At huge expense. And not a little personal risk.

102

It had taken all Emerson's strength to stay patient while his wife raged. To try to understand what was going on. And to wait for her Xanax to finally kick in.

Emerson sat at the head of the battered old table and took a moment to compose himself. Then he said, 'Guys, thank you for being here. First up, you should know that this is not business as usual. It's not professional. It's personal. To me. So if anyone wants to sit this one out, you can leave. No hard feelings. No repercussions. I guarantee.'

No one moved.

'Excellent.' Emerson nodded his head. 'So here's the plan, such as it is. We have two known points of contact with these assholes. First, we know who their front man is. Graeber and I will pay him a visit. See if we can't loosen his tongue. Persuade him to share more details of their operation. Second, there's their ship, twelve miles and an inch off the Jersey coast. It's not going anywhere. It can't. Their top guys will probably stay on board. They'll think they're safe there, and it's where they keep all their equipment and supplies. Which suits us fine, for now. As long as none of them sneaks away. So the rest of you, I want you to head over there. A friend is providing a plane. Take a basic dry kit. There's no need for finesse with this job. Then start by setting up surveillance from the shore. There's only one little boat that goes back and forth. If anyone tries to leave, intercept them. If they're customers, let them go. Maybe shake them up a little first. Make sure they know to never come back. If they're anything other than customers, put them on ice. And there's no need to be gentle. Just make sure they're still alive when I get there.'

*

103

Wiles Park was badly named, Reacher thought. It should have been called Wiles Square. Because that's what it was. A square. It was a nice one. An effort had been made to turn it into a place that people would want to visit. That was clear. It was surrounded by cute stores and cafés and restaurants with fancy outdoor seating. There was a fountain in the middle, probably modelled on something from a French chateau, running at a quarter capacity, probably due to a problem with the water supply. There were all kinds of brightly coloured flowers planted between tiny hedges that were cut into intricate geometric shapes. And there were benches. They were made of polished concrete and set out in a wide circle, like the numbers on a clock face. There were twelve of them. But only one was near a tree, as specified by the note in Roth's mailbox.

Reacher picked up a coffee in a to-go cup from the least pretentious-looking café on the perimeter and strolled across to the bench by the tree. He got there at ten to one. He sat down, right in the middle, and waited.

At five to one a guy stepped out from behind the fountain. He was broad, about six two, and he was wearing jeans and a white Rolling Stones T-shirt. His hair was buzzed short and he had on a pair of black, sporty sunglasses. He halved the distance to Reacher's bench, paused, scowled, then came right up close.

The guy said, 'Move.'

Reacher held up his left hand and wiggled his fingers. 'Like this?'

The guy's frown deepened. 'Get off the bench, jackass.'

'Why? Is it yours?'

'I need it. Now.'

104

'There are eleven other benches. Use one of those.'

'I need this one. I won't tell you again. Move.'

Reacher stayed still. He said nothing.

The guy leaned in closer. 'Did you not hear me?'

'I heard you just fine. You said you weren't going to ask me to move again. I figured you changed your mind. If you have one.'

'You better watch your words. You're starting to make me mad.'

'And if I don't? What are you going to do about it?'

The guy turned away. His hands bunched into fists, then relaxed again. He took a deep breath. Then he turned back to face Reacher. 'Look. I'm meeting someone here, at this particular bench. In about a minute's time. It's very important. So I'd appreciate it if you would just move to another one.'

Reacher said, 'You're meeting Sam Roth.'

The guy's scowl returned. 'How did you know?'

'Because you're not meeting Roth. Not any more. You're meeting me.'

'The hell? What's going on here?'

'Change of negotiating stance.' Reacher patted the smooth concrete by his side. 'Sit down. Let's talk. See if we can find a solution everyone can live with.'

'You got the printout?'

'It's near by. I can get it. If we can agree on terms.'

The guy hesitated for a moment, then slowly turned and lowered himself down on to the bench. He perched right on the very edge of the slab, as far away from Reacher as he could get. He said, 'We need to see it. Make sure Roth changed the rota the way we told him to.'

Reacher caught movement over by the fountain. Another

105

guy emerged from behind it. He was about the same height as the guy who was now sitting. He looked a little heavier. He had the same sunglasses and similar clothes, except his shirt was plain and it had sleeves. He took one step forward then stopped and mimed an exaggerated shrug of his shoulders. The first guy shrugged too then beckoned for him to come closer.

The new guy marched across and stopped in front of the bench. His face was red and a vein was bulging on his forehead. He glared at his buddy and said, 'What are you doing with this bozo? We have business to attend to.'

The first guy said, 'Relax. Sit down. He's here in Roth's place.'

The new guy stayed on his feet. 'The hell he is. That wasn't the deal.'

Reacher said, 'The deal's changed. You want the rota rewritten?'

'You know we do.'

'Mr Roth is no longer convinced that altering the rota is necessary. It's up to you to change my mind.'

'Are you nuts?' the new guy said.

'I wouldn't say so. Mildly eccentric, maybe. But who am I to judge?' Reacher patted the concrete on his other side. 'Sit.'

'If you're not nuts, then Roth must be.' The new guy sat. 'If what we have gets out, he's finished. His career's over. He knows that.'

'What you have is bogus.'

'So what? It's credible. There's no way he doesn't get investigated off the back of it. And it doesn't matter what they find. Something. Nothing. Whatever. Shit sticks. His career will be down the toilet.'

'Maybe he doesn't care about that. Maybe he's ready for a new challenge.'

'He cares.'

'Does he?'

'You're bluffing.'

'Am I?'

'Anyway,' the first guy joined in. 'We have insurance. In case he's too stupid to cooperate.'

Reacher said, 'The threat you made against his ex-wife?'

The first guy nodded. 'Accidents happen. Houses catch on fire. So do electric cars. With their owners inside, sometimes.'

Reacher said, 'I'm not a fan of assholes who threaten innocent people. I should break your legs for that.'

The guy puffed himself up. 'Or we could break yours.'

Reacher said, 'Could you?'

A witness would have said the guy fell off the bench. Just flopped sideways, hit the ground and lay there motionless, legs bent, arms by his side. Like when he was sitting, only rotated through ninety degrees. They would have said Reacher didn't move. Or that if he did it was only due to some kind of twitch. Nothing deliberate. Just a momentary spasm in his left arm.

Reacher turned to the new guy. 'The negotiating phase is over. You're not getting the rota changed. You're not going to release the dirt you made up on Roth. And you're not going to lay a finger on Hannah Hampton. Are you clear about that?'

The vein on the guy's forehead started throbbing again. 'I don't know what your plans are, buddy, but you better cancel them. You better leave town. And fast.'

'I was already planning to leave town. But I know someone who lives here. Who works in the Police Department. We were both in the service. If any lies come out about Roth, he'll tell me. If anything happens to Ms Hampton, he'll tell me. I'll come back. I'll find you. And you will have the worst day of your life.'

A witness would have said a very strange thing happened next. The new guy fell off the bench as well. He also flopped sideways and wound up inert on the ground, like a mirror image of his buddy. And again they would have said Reacher didn't move. Not deliberately. Although he did seem to have another spasm.

In his right arm, this time.

EIGHTEEN

J ed Starmer stood at the edge of the sidewalk and pulled a handful of change out of his pocket. He had three quarters plus a bunch of smaller coins. They added up to more than two dollars. But Jed didn't care about the total. What counted was that he could make a call. He could get himself out of the mess he had landed in. Or at least try.

Jed figured there would be some payphones at the Greyhound station so he turned and started to make his way back there. He moved quickly at first, then slowed down and started to look around. He had been so focused on chasing the cab which the guy who had stolen his backpack had taken that he hadn't paid any attention to his surroundings. The street he was on was long and flat. The Greyhound station was far ahead, on the right. Closer, opposite him on his left, there was a weird-looking building. It was pale yellow with smooth, rounded walls. It was tall. It had no windows and its top was cut off at a steep angle. The high side was nearest him and the roof fell away sharply toward the back. It made him think of a cake, or a hat a bishop might wear in a sci-fi movie.

Around the base of the building there was a ring of sculptures. They were made of steel, all curved, interlocking shapes, gleaming in the sunshine like flames. Or scimitar blades. They reminded Jed of a place back in LA. Some kind of a fancy concert hall. He'd never been inside it, but the exterior fascinated him. It was made of shiny metal, too, and the whole surface was twisted and warped like it was melting. Like a localized apocalypse was taking place. Or a scene from a fever dream. Or a sign he was going crazy. He had always found it a little menacing. Like so much in his home town.

If LA still was his home town.

A set of steps ran up to a concourse that separated the round building from a similar, shorter, wider one. Jed climbed up. He paused at the top then walked around to the far side. There was a low wall, presumably to stop pedestrians from falling down on to the street below. Jed perched on the edge. He lined up his coins on the rough concrete surface. Then he took away all of them except the quarters. Three metal circles. Dull with age. Scuffed from use. Innocuous, everyday items. But with the power to shape his future.

Jed had to decide. He could put the coins back in his pocket. Or he could feed them into a phone.

He could go forward. Or back.

Grab a new life. Or settle for his old one.

At the same time Jed was wondering what to do with the quarters a police car pulled on to the forecourt at the side of the Greyhound station. Two officers climbed out. They both

110

had a copy of a photograph in their hands. One officer made her way inside the terminal building. She covered the whole area, showing the picture to all the passengers who were eating or loitering around or returning from the restrooms. The other officer stayed outside. He focused on the line of buses. He was looking for one vehicle in particular. The one that had recently come in from LA.

At the same time the officers were arriving at the Greyhound station in El Paso, Texas, a car was rolling to a halt at the side of the street next to Wiles Park in Gerrardsville, Colorado. A poverty-spec Dodge Charger. Detective Harewood set his dome light flashing on the dash, slid out and walked across to the only bench in the square that was near a tree. He stood for a moment and looked at Reacher. Then he shifted his gaze to the two guys who were still on the ground. They were still motionless.

Harewood said, 'What happened?'

Reacher drained the last of his coffee and set the cup down on the bench. 'They collapsed. Spontaneously.'

'Seriously?'

'They were up to no good. The strain must have gotten too much.'

'And you just happened to be here when it did?'

Reacher took a piece of paper from his pocket and handed it to Harewood. 'They left this in Sam Roth's mailbox.'

'You should have called me. Let me handle it.'

'I figured they could be connected to Angela St. Vrain.'

'Were they?'

'No.'

Harewood checked his watch. 'Did you call them an ambulance, at least?'

Reacher shook his head. 'I tried for a garbage truck. No luck. Apparently it's not trash day.'

Harewood took out his phone and speed-dialled a number. He told someone at his office to arrange medical assistance and a uniformed escort to remain with the guys at the hospital. Then he sat down and said, 'So what kind of *no good* were these guys up to?'

'Trying to blackmail Roth. His ex-wife said he'd been under extra stress at work recently. This explains why.'

'What did they want?'

'To get the staff rota rewritten a particular way. Probably to help them smuggle stuff into the prison they worked at. Possibly to help break someone out.'

'Damn. What did they have on Roth?'

'Nothing real. Just some trumped-up nonsense. They admitted that. But enough to cause trouble for Roth. If he'd stayed alive.'

'I'll figure it out.'

'I'm sure you will.'

'I'll make sense of it one way or another, but level with me. Are you telling the truth?'

'About what?'

'Did you really think these guys had something to do with Angela? Or did you just find the note and come over here looking for trouble? Because I don't see the connection.'

'Turned out there wasn't a connection. Their scheme was local. Completely separate. But here's what I was thinking. The fact is Angela wasn't linked to Roth romantically. He was her former boss. She'd gone to him for help.'

'With what?'

'Some accounting thing at her work. They'd been communicating via email. That's another fact. Now for the speculation.

I think Angela came to Gerrardsville to show Roth something. Some evidence relating to whatever kind of wrongdoing she had uncovered. I think whoever had her killed found this out, but only after she had left Mississippi. Hence staging her accident here. Where they knew she would be. And when.'

'That would account for the timing and location.' Harewood pointed to the ground on either side. 'But not why you thought these guys could be involved.'

'Stopping Angela from showing the evidence to Roth wasn't enough. They needed to recover it. Whatever it was. Hence stealing Angela's purse.'

'How could they be sure the evidence was in Angela's purse?'

Reacher didn't answer.

A frown spread across Harewood's face. 'They could have thought Angela mailed it to Roth before she left home.'

'That would have been the smart move. A package is safer in the US Mail than in a purse. Especially when you have a couple of killers on your tail.'

'And you thought that was *the proof* demanded in the note?'

'I hoped it was. Because then we could have captured a couple of foot soldiers. Worked our way up the food chain. And it would have meant that Roth's death was an accident.'

Harewood was silent for a moment. 'You only try to black-mail someone you think is still alive. Not someone you know you already killed. I guess even without the evidence Angela was bringing Roth knew too much.'

'That's how I see it.'

'I'll get on to the ME. Ask her to run tests for everything known to man that can induce a heart attack.'

'Send some computer guys to Roth's apartment as well. Someone wiped all the emails between him and Angela off

113

his laptop. The real ones. The ones Angela's employer found were fake.'

'Will do.'

'And check the area behind Roth's building for tyre tracks. His ex-wife thinks she saw a car waiting there on Monday night, before he died.'

Harewood shook his head.

'What? You don't believe her?'

'It's not that. I'm just thinking, my lieutenant was pissed about me wanting to investigate one death as a homicide. Now I'll have to tell him we have two.'

'Here's something to soften the blow. You can tell him I'm leaving town.'

'You are? When?'

Reacher stood up. 'Right now.'

'Why? Are you done?'

Reacher smiled. 'I'm just getting started.'

Jed Starmer had sat on the wall long enough for the sun to move and cast the three quarters next to him into deep shadow. He checked his watch. The bus was due to leave in ten minutes. He couldn't delay any longer. It was decision time.

Forward? Or back?

Get on board? Or make a call?

Jed didn't know which he should do. Panic rose in his throat. He felt it choking him. He couldn't breathe. But only for a moment. He swallowed the fear back down. He had already come a long way. On his own. Without needing any stuff. If he kept going he would only be alone for another couple of days. Not even another forty-eight hours. He could manage that long without a change of clothes. Losing his backpack was a setback. But it wasn't a catastrophe. It was no reason to give up. He still had his toothbrush. And he still had three hundred dollars.

Jed stood up. He snatched up the coins and dropped them into his pocket. The only thing he didn't have was time. He had been planning to buy some food. He was starving, but his meal was going to have to wait. Which in a way he could take as a bonus. He could conserve his cash for a little longer. Until he reached Dallas. He could last until then without eating. He was used to be being hungry. That was one thing he could thank his foster mother for.

Jed hurried down the steps and ran the rest of the way back to the Greyhound station. He scurried through the terminal building, weaving his way around the knots of slow-moving passengers, but he stopped before he reached the exit to the concourse. He had spotted a vending machine. It was by the far wall. Next to the payphones. The day was hot. Hotter than he was used to. He had been rushing around in the sun. And the machine was full of all kinds of drinks.

Going without food was one thing. But water was different. He had read that not having enough could mess up your health. Damage your internal organs. Cause lasting harm. He didn't want to start his new life all weak and sickly. But neither did he want to miss the bus. The doors closed a little before departure time. He had seen that happen in LA, a hundred years ago. Or actually yesterday. He checked his watch. Decided it was worth the risk. Pulled the handful of change out of his pocket. Jammed the coins into the slot, one after another, and watched the total on the digital display creep up to the required amount. Then he grabbed the bottle from the delivery chute and raced to the bus.

Jed dashed up the stairs and the bus's door hissed closed

before he was three feet along the aisle. He took the same seat as before. Leaned against the window. And suddenly felt exposed without his backpack. Vulnerable. He craved the way it had felt on his lap. He would have given anything to hug it tight, just then. Whether it made him look like a kid or not.

'Hey, buddy!'

Jed jumped. Someone had flopped into the seat next to him. A guy, a little scruffy, maybe eighteen. Jed recognized him. He had been on board all the way from LA. Sitting near the back. Jed had thought he was part of a group. Now he wasn't sure.

The guy said, 'So. What's happening?'

Jed said, 'Nothing.'

The guy leaned in close. 'You in trouble?'

'Me? No. Why?'

'Are the police looking for you?'

Jed felt like a steel belt had closed around his chest. His heart started to race. 'The police? Of course not. Why would they be?'

'It's OK. You can tell me. It's why you didn't get back on until the last moment, right? You were waiting for them to leave.'

'The police were here? On the bus?'

The guy nodded.

'I didn't know that. I was just . . . slow.'

'Right.' The guy winked. '*Slow.* I'm with you.'

'OK, maybe they were here. But they're not looking for me.'

'Are you sure? Because the cop had a photo. It was old. Four or five years at least. But it sure looked like you. I guess no one else twigged. They just switched the driver and I bet all these old biddies are half blind, but I could see it.'

116

Jed swallowed hard. 'What did you say?'

'Don't worry.' The guy slapped Jed's shoulder. 'I said I hadn't seen you.'

'Thank you.' Jed could finally let out a breath.

'No problem.' The guy paused. 'Hey, I have an idea. Maybe you could buy me breakfast? When we get to Dallas?'

'Buy you breakfast?' Jed thought about his cash supply. He was in no rush to spend any more than absolutely necessary. Then he thought about how easy it would be for the guy to dial 911. He probably had a cellphone. And even if he didn't there were seven more stops before they would reach Dallas. In places where there would be payphones. He forced a smile and said, 'Sure. I'd be happy to.'

'Cool.' The guy swung back into the aisle and headed for his own seat. 'Travelling for hours makes me hungry. See you later . . .'

NINETEEN

Twelve hundred miles away, in Winson, Mississippi, it was time for Curtis Riverdale to get busy.

Riverdale was an anomaly within the Minerva corporation. An outlier. He was unusual because he was in his post when the prison got taken over. Minerva's standard procedure was to sideline the existing warden when a new site was bought. Shift him into some kind of impotent, figurehead position. Wait for the boredom and humiliation to eat away at him until he found a job somewhere else. And if he tried to stick it out, fire him, hot on the heels of a third of his staff.

The process had gotten under way as usual. A bunch of new guards had been drafted in. Proven *Minerva people* from the company's other facilities. Tailor-made to slot in place of the guys who'd just been discarded. The new warden was installed at the same time. A tall, skinny forty-year-old who dressed like a banker and spoke like a radio host. He did all the usual new-boss things to prove he could walk and talk at the same time. But he didn't settle in Winson. He kept getting sick. He spent more time in the hospital than at work. After six months he couldn't take it any more. He quit. And during the new guy's many absences Riverdale took the opportunity to step back up. He proved himself invaluable. Adaptable. Discreet. Able to fit into Minerva's mode of operation in a way Hix had never seen in a warden his company had inherited.

Some correctional corporations treat the business of incarceration as if they were supermarkets. They take a kind of *pile 'em high, sell 'em cheap* approach. But Minerva wasn't like that. Right from the start Hix and Brockman had a different view of what they did. They saw themselves as being more like prospectors in the Old West. Their goal was the same. To sort the gold from the dirt. Only they didn't use shovels and buckets and sieves. They had a system. One they had devised themselves. They had refined it. Improved it. And they used it to sift the constant stream of inmates sent by the states they had contracts with.

The process started with the freshly convicted. The *new fish*. Lawyers evaluated their cases. Accountants reviewed their finances. Genealogists traced their family trees. Then aptitude tests were administered. Inmates with certain skills and talents were identified. Psychologists were brought in to assess their personalities. The suitable ones were selected. The rest were sent to the doctors along with the other prisoners. A whole bunch of screening procedures were carried out. Treatments were prescribed wherever necessary. And after each individual was fully scrutinized and categorized, it was decided which facility to send them to.

The first category of prisoner had the potential for their convictions to be quashed, either for PR or for profit. They were distributed evenly throughout Minerva's sites. The second had no special potential. This was the largest group by far. The corporation's bread and butter. Dull, but necessary. Most of its members went to Minerva's older prisons but some were brought to Winson for appearances' sake. The third category was smaller. More interesting. All its members came to Winson. And the fourth category was smaller still. It wasn't interesting, exactly. But it was lucrative. Often there was only one person in it on any given day. Sometimes there were two. Sometimes there were none at all.

That afternoon there was a single prisoner in the fourth category. He was housed all alone in Unit S1. The segregation unit that was still selectively operational. So that was where Riverdale started his rounds. He had arrangements to make. Personnel to organize. Processing. Packaging. Distribution. There was a whole complex operation to keep on the rails.

That was assuming everything went according to plan on Friday. If not, the place would be mothballed. Indefinitely. And a lot of Minerva staff would find themselves on their way to other prisons. Where they would wind up on the other side of the bars.

Jack Reacher left Gerrardsville, Colorado, on foot, the same way he had arrived two days earlier.

As he walked, Reacher thought about the best way to get to his destination. Winson, Mississippi. He had never heard of the place before he saw it printed on Angela St. Vrain's driver's licence. He had been planning on a detour to Gerrardsville's library to learn more about it, but while they were still on the bench in Wiles Park Detective Harewood had taken out his phone. Pulled up a map. Of sorts. An indistinct multicoloured tangle of roads and other features on a small, scratched screen. But enough to show Reacher the general location of the town. It was on the very edge of the state, no more than a dot, nestled into a C-shaped curve on the east bank of the Mississippi River.

Finding his way to Winson would not be a problem. Reacher was more worried about how long the journey would take. He had two dead bodies on his mind. At least one killer was on the loose. With at least one accomplice. On a trail that was getting colder by the minute. He had plenty of energy. He had cash in his pocket. But not much time.

The mountains were to his right, sawing away at the clear blue sky. The sun was turning pink and starting to dip down toward their highest peaks. It was still warm, but Reacher's shadow was growing longer, dancing and skipping across the rough, bleached blacktop at his side. The air was still. It was quiet. No cars had gone by since he had crossed the town boundary. No vans. No trucks. Normally Reacher would have enjoyed the solitude. But not that day. It only added to his growing impatience.

Reacher picked up his pace and after thirty seconds he heard a sound behind him. A truck's motor. A large diesel, rattling and clattering like a freight train. He looked around and saw a pickup barrelling toward him. It was red. It had black glass and lots of chrome. Reacher had seen it before. He stopped walking, stepped to the edge of the road and let it catch up to him.

The truck braked abruptly to a halt, rocked on its springs for a moment, then the passenger window buzzed down. Hannah Hampton was in the driver's seat. Her right hand was on the steering wheel. She smiled and looked at Reacher and said, 'Open the door.'

Reacher worked the handle and swung the door as far as its hinges allowed it to go.

The smile disappeared from Hannah's face. She brought her left hand up from the gap between her thigh and the driver's door. She was holding a gun. A short, squat, black pistol. It was an inch wide with a three-inch barrel. Less than six inches, total length. A SIG P365, Reacher thought. He had never fired one. Never even handled one. The whole sub-compact thing had gotten popular after his time in the army was over, fuelled by the concealed carry craze. But he had read about that particular model. He knew it was no joke.

Hannah pointed the gun at the centre of Reacher's chest and said, 'Stay there. Stand still.'

A repeat customer. The holy grail of any business. Not someone to be questioned or doubted or turned away.

Lev Emerson was counting on the guys he was after to be running their organization like a business. Albeit not a regular one. He didn't know its name. It didn't advertise. It didn't have a logo, as far as he was aware. No website. No bank details for online payments. No app. No social media presence. Just a front man. And a ship. The last, floating resort of the desperate. The place people had to go when they couldn't get what they needed anywhere else.

Emerson had paid the front man in cash the last time he had gotten involved. The only time. To get his son Kyle on to the ship. Kyle had certainly been desperate. But he hadn't got what he needed. He got something that killed him, instead.

Emerson had paid a lot of cash, the last time. It was a mistake he wouldn't make again. Any kind of further involvement

122

with these guys would be a mistake. But if the front man took the bait, he would be the one making the error. That was for damn sure. Him. The people he worked for. And, most importantly, the people who supplied them. The ultimate source of the poison that had killed Kyle. Because Emerson didn't want to just cut off a limb. He wanted to slay the whole beast. To incinerate every cell in its body.

If the front man took the bait.

Emerson took a breath and hit *send*. His laptop made a *whoosh* sound. His message disappeared from its screen. He pictured it as a stream of 1s and 0s, bouncing around the internet. Pinging from one untraceable server to another, all around the world. Maybe reaching its destination. Maybe not. Maybe being read. Maybe not. Maybe convincing the front man. Appealing to his greed. Bypassing any hint of suspicion about why such a recent customer should be getting back in the market.

Or maybe not.

Jack Reacher had lost count of the number of people who had pointed guns at him over the years. Often the person with their finger on the trigger was angry. Sometimes they were scared. Or determined. Or elated. Or relieved. Occasionally they were calm and professional. But Hannah Hampton had an expression on her face that Reacher had never seen in that kind of situation before. She looked embarrassed.

She said, 'I'm sorry. Ninety-nine per cent of me thinks I'm wrong. That I'm crazy. But I have to know for sure.'

Reacher said, 'Know what?'

'Why you showed up at Sam's door.'

'I told you why.'

'You told me a story. How do I know it's true?'

'You talked to Detective Harewood. He confirmed it.'

Hannah shook her head. 'He confirmed *what* you were doing. Looking into Angela's murder. Not *why*.'

'I'm helping him out.'

'Why?'

'Angela was murdered. So was Sam. Someone should do something about that.'

'Yes. The detective should. It's his job. And he has the whole Police Department to back him up. Why does he need your help?'

'He's facing some . . . institutional obstacles.'

'Such as?'

'That doesn't matter. The only thing that matters is whether you want Sam's killer to go free. If you don't, you need to put the gun down.'

'What if it's not that simple?'

'It is that simple.'

Hannah paused, but she didn't lower the gun. 'Here's my problem. There's a little voice at the back of my head and it won't shut up. It keeps saying you were the only one who knew Angela was murdered. You were the only one who knew Sam didn't have a heart attack. You were the only one who suggested Angela sent Sam some secret evidence. You were the only one who went looking for it.'

'That's why Harewood needs my help.'

'Unless there's another explanation.'

'There isn't.'

'If you had found the evidence at Sam's apartment, or in his mailbox, what would you have done?'

'Given it to Harewood.'

'But would you, though? That's the real question.'

'You think I was trying to get it for myself?'

124

'That's a possibility. You have to admit it. You have no legal standing here. No official role.'

'So you also think I killed Angela? And Sam? That's the bottom line, right?'

Reacher kept his eyes on Hannah's trigger finger. Her knuckle gleamed white. But it didn't flex. Not yet.

Hannah said, 'You know an awful lot about how Angela and Sam died. And why.'

'I don't know nearly enough about that. But what I have learned, I've told Harewood. Because I am helping him. Call him. Ask if that's true.'

'If you're helping, why are you leaving town? Did you find the evidence?' Hannah looked at Reacher. It dawned on her that he had no bag. No case. No bulging pockets. 'Did you destroy it?'

'No.'

'So why are you leaving?'

'Because I *didn't* find it. I need to look somewhere else.'

'Where?'

'Winson, Mississippi.'

'Where Angela lived?'

'Where she worked. Where she found the problem that led to all this.'

Hannah was silent for a moment. 'You're going to find out who killed Sam?'

'I'm going to try.'

'You promise?'

'You have my word.'

'Does that mean anything?'

Reacher nodded.

Hannah said, 'If you find the guy who killed Sam? What will you do?'

'Give him the chance to surrender.'

'And if he doesn't take it?'

'That'll be his problem.'

Hannah lowered the gun. 'OK. I believe you. I think. And I do want Sam's killer caught. So how can I help?'

'You can give me a ride to Denver. There's a Greyhound station there.'

Lev Emerson's message did make its way to the front man. It reached him almost immediately. And it found him in a trusting frame of mind. Or a greedy one. Emerson wasn't sure which. And he didn't care either way. Because the guy replied. No hesitation. No delay. It was nothing fancy. Just a time. A location. And a date.

Emerson sent his confirmation. The meeting was locked in. For the following day. At ten a.m.

Emerson looked across the table at Graeber. He said, 'Fetch a barrel. A big one. We have some mixing to do.'

TWENTY

C urtis Riverdale spent more than an hour in Unit S1. He checked that everything would be ready for Friday afternoon. The equipment. The right people, with the right specialized skills. And he verified the arrangements for transport. That was the part that worried him the most. It made him nervous because it wasn't under his direct control. In his gut he would have liked to run the whole operation. The entire show, from soup to nuts. But in his head he understood the value of compartmentalization. It was better all round if no one at Minerva knew where the packages they sent out were going to end up. And it was better still if the guys who dealt with the final customers had no idea where the merchandise came from. The last thing Riverdale wanted was for the mess to land on Minerva's doorstep if anyone down the line wound up with a bad outcome.

When Riverdale was finally satisfied he left S1 and started toward the first of the three general population units. The one that housed the most interesting inmates. He set out at speed but when he was halfway along the fenced-in walkway that connected the buildings he paused for a moment. He had realized something. If everything went according to plan on Friday it would be the first time a prisoner had moved from one category to another. It would be the first time. And, he hoped, the last. All it did was increase the risk they ran. For no good reason. And in Riverdale's opinion unnecessary risks should always be avoided.

Some people within the Minerva corporation misinterpreted Riverdale's attitude. Damon Brockman was one of them. He took it as a sign that Riverdale was timid. Cautious. Even cowardly. He didn't see that Riverdale was just a survivor. He was on to a good thing at Winson. He had worked hard for the opportunities his job offered him. And he was ready and willing to defend his position. To do whatever was necessary to save his skin.

If Brockman had been quicker, he could have gotten a different perspective on the whole situation. He could have talked to the warden he had brought in to replace Riverdale. If only the new guy had paid more attention to the food that was brought to him from the prison kitchen. To its subtle, extra layer of flavour.

The food that was brought to him exclusively by members of Riverdale's *Old Guard*.

Hannah Hampton drove fast. She was aggressive. But plenty of other drivers around her on I-25 were faster. And crazier. They were constantly zipping past her on both sides. Cutting in front. Crowding close up behind. Reacher saw trucks abandoned in the median, facing the wrong way. Cars sitting on the shoulder with their fronts and rears stoved in. There were even a couple of SUVs in the fields next to the highway. One was upside down, on its roof.

Hannah saw Reacher looking at the wrecks. She said, 'Must have rained recently. People down here don't know how to drive in the rain.'

Reacher said, 'It's not raining now.'

Hannah shrugged. 'I've been thinking about this place you're going. Winson. It sounds pretty small. Off the beaten track. Do you think you can get all the way there on a Greyhound?'

'Probably not. But I'll get close.'

'What will you do then?'

'Don't know yet. I'll figure something out.'

Hannah hit her turn signal and pulled across to the right. A sign said the route to central Denver was coming up in a mile. Hannah slowed down, ready for the exit curve. Then she switched her foot on to the gas and swerved back on to the highway.

'Screw it,' she said. 'Forget the bus. I'm taking you all the way to Mississippi.'

Reacher looked at her. 'You sure? It must be twelve hundred miles.'

'So what? This is Sam's truck. The tank's full. He paid for the diesel. He wouldn't want it to be wasted.'

'Burning up a dead guy's fuel doesn't seem like the best of reasons.'

'It's not the only reason. I've got to leave town for a while, anyway. You told me that. Winson's as good a place to go as anywhere. Probably. When we get there I can go see Danny Peel. Tell him about Sam in person. That's got to be better than breaking the news on the phone. And I can check that Angela's kid is OK.'

'Do you know the neighbour she left the kid with?'

129

'No. But Danny will.'

Reacher thought about the envelope he had seen in Angela's purse. The one that disappeared right after she was killed. It was addressed to this Danny Peel. He would need to talk to the guy about it. Find out how Angela came to have it. And what was so important about it. Taking someone along who knew Danny might help. It might make him more open to talk. Speed up the trust-building phase of the conversation. Make the whole process more efficient. And potentially a lot less messy.

'OK then,' Reacher said. 'Thank you.'

'My pleasure.' Hannah looked across at him for a second. 'But tell me one thing. I'm curious. Your luggage. What happened to it?'

'Nothing.'

'Come on. You can tell me.'

'Nothing happened.'

'Really? Because here's what I think. You got to town. Met a woman. Spent the night. Maybe a few nights. You pissed her off somehow. Or you overstayed your welcome. Wouldn't leave, despite all the hints she dropped. So she lost patience and trashed your stuff. Cut it up. Or set it on fire. Yes. Tell me she burned it. Please. Let that be it.'

'OK. A woman burned it.'

'Really?'

'No.'

'Then where's all your stuff?'

'Right here. In my pocket.'

'What can you possibly fit in your pocket?'

'Everything I need.'

'Everything?'

'Everything. For now.'

*

130

Bruno Hix and Damon Brockman were operating on the assumption that there were four categories of prisoner at Winson. That's what they expected because that's what they had mandated. What they didn't realize was that there were actually five.

The fifth category was in fact the oldest. It pre-dated Minerva's ownership of Winson by several years. It had not been defined by professionals. No doctors were involved in the process. No psychologists. No accountants. Certainly no lawyers. Its members had always been identified by Curtis Riverdale, personally. He relied on his decades of experience. His natural ability to read people. To spot certain things, however well hidden. Things like extreme desperation. Or exceptional greed. Things that would cause an inmate to arrange for his wife, or occasionally his sister, to come to the prison whenever Riverdale told him to. And then to wait, penned in on the secure side of the glass divider, while one of the Old Guard escorted the woman to his office. Where he put his own personal spin on the concept of the conjugal visit.

Sometimes, if Riverdale felt like spicing things up a little, he had the prisoner brought up too. He had him cuffed to a steel bar he'd had attached to the wall in the corridor for that specific purpose. And he left his door open. Just a crack. Not so wide that the prisoner could see into the room. But enough to make sure the sounds from inside weren't muffled in any way.

Riverdale had a visit lined up for that evening. With the wife of a new fish. He was looking forward to it. If she lived up to his expectations, he was thinking of having her brought back on Friday afternoon. To celebrate Winson's return to business as usual.

Assuming everything went according to plan.

*

The further Hannah Hampton drove, the less she spoke.

She had started out pretty talkative after deciding not to drop Reacher off at the Greyhound station. She wanted to know all about him. To understand what kind of guy would walk away from the army and wander around the country with no job. No home to return to. No definite destination. No luggage. She asked him about his childhood. His parents. His brother. How he felt when each of them had died. How he had been affected by growing up on military bases all around the world. She was fascinated by his life as an army cop. She wanted to know about the best case he had investigated. The worst. About any that still haunted him. Why he had left the service. And how he felt about being cast adrift after putting his life on the line for other people for thirteen years.

Reacher was happy to answer. His replies were mostly factual. They were mostly positive. He had come to terms with anything negative in his life years ago. The conversation ticked along. The tyres thumped and rumbled over the joints and gaps in the road. Hannah's phone directed them on to I-70. The highway stretched away in front of them. The mountains grew smaller in the rear window, then finally disappeared into the distant haze. Hannah continued due east until they were well clear of Denver then cut across on the diagonal, almost to the edge of the state. Then they turned again. Straight to the south this time. They plunged across the narrow strip that stretched out sideways from Oklahoma. And kept going, deeper and deeper into Texas.

The conversation began to dry up after Hannah raised the subject of relationships. Reacher turned the questions back toward her and she deflected by talking about her marriage to Sam Roth. He sounded like a nice guy. Hannah had

132

endless anecdotes about him. About their life, together but not together. Some of her memories were tender. Some were funny. Some were wild, from way back in the day. As Hannah reminisced her voice changed. It grew quieter. She spoke more slowly. Eventually a tear ran down her cheek. Just one. She wiped it away and glanced across at Reacher with a look that said, *Your turn*.

Reacher said nothing.

TWENTY-ONE

D amon Brockman was not the kind of guy who readily changed his mind.

When he first heard that someone might have looked in the envelope Angela St. Vrain ran off to Colorado with he didn't see a problem. He still didn't. But neither was he the kind of guy who exposed himself to unnecessary criticism. In his experience there was only one thing worse than something going wrong on his watch. That was getting the blame for it going wrong. And the only thing worse than getting the blame was when someone had previously warned you of the danger. Publicly. When they could say, *I told you so*. Especially when that person was effectively your boss. When they could punish you for it. When they could hit you for it in the pocket. So even though Brockman still thought the chances of Reacher showing up and causing trouble in Winson were close to zero, he decided to act as if the danger was real.

First, he brought forward the time that the sentries were due to be in position. Bruno Hix had asked for them to be posted by six a.m., Thursday. Brockman changed that to three a.m.

Second, he added an extra pair of sentries. Hix had asked for two guys to cover the Greyhound station in Jackson. Brockman put a couple more at the stop that the local bus from Jackson to Winson left from. Plenty of people who visited the prison used that service, which made it the kind of thing anyone new to the area without their own transport might latch on to.

Third, he went into *what if* mode. Hix had already tried to cover every possibility, but Brockman wanted to narrow the odds. To back one horse rather than spread his bets across the whole field. He asked himself, what would he do if he had to get across the country with very few resources? The answer was obvious. He would steal a car. That would be quick and easy. It would be nicer and more comfortable than the Greyhound bus. And it would be safer than hitching a ride. There were all kinds of crazy people out there, preying on the broke and the homeless. He knew that for a fact. Minerva made a bunch of money out of confining them after they got caught.

The only danger involved with stealing a car was that unless you lucked out in some unexpected way the owner would notice the vehicle was missing. They would dial 911. And if the police caught you it would be game over, right there and then. So, to mitigate the risk you would need to switch plates. You could steal some alternatives. Which came with dangers of its own. So it would be better to clone a set. Or to have some random fake ones made. Which would be difficult for a person with limited means.

135

Brockman started to feel better. Car theft was the best option, but it was likely to be off the table for Reacher. Then he started to feel worse. He thought of Curtis Riverdale, of all people. Of something he had said. About Reacher being a former military cop. Some kind of a crack investigator. Reacher had witnessed Angela St. Vrain's *accident*. He had spoken to the police in the town. Maybe he had caught the local news. He could have latched on to Sam Roth's death. He could have joined the dots.

There was no danger of Reacher finding any evidence that led back to Minerva. Brockman was sure about that. But there was another problem. Dead men can't report car thefts.

Brockman took out his phone and hit the speed dial for Rod Moseley. The Chief of the local Police Department.

Moseley answered on the first ring. 'What now? Tell me you have good news for a change.'

Brockman said, 'It's about Sam Roth. The guy we offed in Colorado. We need to know the make and model of his vehicle.'

Hannah Hampton and Reacher had been in Sam Roth's truck for approaching seven hours.

For nearly six of those hours neither of them had spoken. Hannah was focused on the driving. It was a useful distraction for her. She was struggling to keep a lid on her grief. That was clear. At the same time Reacher was focused on nothing in particular. He had tipped his seat back a little. His eyes were closed. He was playing music in his head. There was nothing he could do to make the truck go faster. He couldn't bring their destination any closer. So listening to a few of his favourite bands was the most pleasant way he could think of to pass the time.

Hannah nudged Reacher, and when he opened his eyes she pointed to a sign at the side of the road. It gave the name of a town neither of them had heard of before. Behind it the land was as flat as a board for as far as they could see. It looked dull and brown in the setting sun. A few sparse bushes poked through a crust of scrubby scorched grass. There were a couple of stunted trees. A set of power lines was running dead straight toward the horizon. Above them the cloud was grey and it was stretched thin, like there wasn't quite enough to cover the massive expanse of sky.

Hannah said, 'Time to call it a day?'

They were still heading due south so Reacher figured they hadn't gotten as far as Amarillo yet. That wasn't necessarily a problem. The sign listed the nearby town's amenities. They seemed adequate. Apparently everything came in pairs. There were two gas stations. Two diners. And two hotels. Hannah took the turn-off and a quarter of a mile after the intersection she pulled on to the first gas station's forecourt. She went inside to use the restroom. Reacher pulled the truck up to the nearest pump and filled it with diesel. He went inside to pay and when he came out Hannah was back in the driver's seat. He climbed in and she steered across the street to the first hotel. She parked in a spot at the edge of the lot, midway between the hotel and the first diner. There were only two other cars in sight so they figured competition for rooms wasn't going to be an issue. Food seemed like a more urgent priority.

The diner was set up to look like an old-world cattle station. It had rustic shingles on the roof. The walls were covered with fake logs. There were branding irons hanging from rusty pegs along with all kinds of antique tools Reacher didn't know the purpose of. Inside, the floor was covered with sawdust. The tables and chairs were made of wood. The chairs had leather seat covers the same colour as the saddles in the paintings of cowboys on the walls. The tabletops were criss-crossed with burn marks and pocks and dents. They looked ancient, but even so Reacher suspected the damage had been done in a factory rather than by decades of genuine use.

There were no other customers in the place so a waitress with grey hair and a pink gingham dress gestured for them to pick where they wanted to sit. They took the table in the far corner. Reacher liked it because it let him keep an eye on the entrance as well as the corridor leading to the restrooms. The waitress handed them a couple of menus and left them to make their selections. That didn't take long. There wasn't a great deal of choice. Steak lovers were well catered for. Everyone else was pretty much out of luck.

Hannah and Reacher ordered their food. They waited in silence for it to come. Hannah's appetite for conversation had well and truly dried up. Reacher didn't have anything new to say, either. Ten minutes crawled by and then the waitress dropped off their meals. Big heaps of meat and potatoes with no vegetables in sight. Reacher was happy. Hannah, less so. She nibbled half-heartedly at the edge of her steak. Managed to swallow a couple of fries. Then pushed her plate away.

'I'm sorry.' Hannah stood up. 'I don't mean to be a party-pooper, but I'm bushed. I can't keep my eyes open. I'm going to check in next door. Get some sleep. See you by the truck in the morning?'

Reacher said, 'Sure. Six a.m., sound about right?'

'Works for me. Goodnight.'

Reacher grabbed a newspaper from a holder made of horse-shoes on the wall near the door and read it while he finished his dinner. He ate the untouched food on Hannah's plate. Polished off his coffee, followed by a refill. Then he left sufficient cash to cover both meals and a tip and headed outside.

Four of the stops on the Greyhound route between El Paso and Dallas were brief. Just long enough for new passengers to join the bus or existing ones to get off. Three of the stops were longer. Twenty minutes. Or twenty-five. Sufficient for anyone who was stiff or hungry to stretch their legs or go and get some food.

Jed Starmer didn't leave his seat during any of the stops, long or short. Because he had something on his mind. The police. Officers had shown up in El Paso. With a picture of him. Only one person in the world could have supplied that picture. So only one person could have called 911. His foster mother. She had reported him missing. Or she had reported him as a thief. She was worried about him. Or she was mad at him. Jed knew which option his money was on. And he also knew that the reason didn't matter. The only question that counted was what the police would do next. They could assume that if he wasn't on the bus in El Paso, then the route was a dead end. In which case he was safe. For a while, at least. Or they could keep on looking for him, all the way down the line. All the way to his final destination. In which case he was doomed.

Jed didn't know what the police would do. And the uncertainty was eating him alive. Every time the bus came to a standstill Jed panicked. Even if it was just at an intersection. Even if it was just because of other late-night traffic. Jed pictured the door swinging open. He imagined a cop bounding up the steps. Making his way down the aisle. Shining his flashlight in every passenger's face. Asleep or awake.

Comparing everyone with his photograph. Which was old. His appearance had changed in the last four or five years. He supposed. He hoped. But he wasn't even kidding himself. The guy at the back of the bus had spotted the resemblance. There was no way the police would miss it. They were trained for that kind of thing. He would be identified. Grabbed up. Dragged off the bus. And taken back to LA. To his foster mother. Or to jail.

The bus stopped properly seven times. Seven times the door opened. Three times someone climbed on board. But every time they turned out to be passengers. Not cops. Which meant the cops were no longer looking for him.

Or that they would be there, waiting, when the bus stopped in Dallas.

Lev Emerson's alarm went off at two forty-five a.m., Thursday morning.

It played the theme from Handel's 'Fireworks' music. Loudly. Emerson shut off the sound. He lay still for a moment, in the dark, gathering his thoughts. He was on a couch in the corner of his office in his warehouse in Chicago. He felt at home with the smell of the rough, battered leather. With how the worn surface of the cushion felt against his cheek. He had slept there many, many times over the years. But not for any of the typical reasons married men spent nights away from their beds. It wasn't because of a row he'd had with his wife. He wasn't drunk. He didn't reek of another woman's perfume. He wasn't there to take drugs or watch porn. He was there because of the nature of his work.

When someone with a regular job had an appointment in a faraway town, early in the morning, they could travel the night before. Stay the night in a convenient hotel. Eat a hearty

breakfast and show up at their meeting bright-eyed and rar-
ing to go. But that wasn't an option for Emerson. Not if he
had to take the tools of his trade with him. They weren't
things he could fly with. They had to be transported by road.
In one of his special panel vans. And he didn't like the idea of
leaving one of those vans in a public parking lot. Where an
idiot could crash into it. Or try to steal it. Or take too close an
interest in its contents. Which meant he had to carefully calculate his travel time. Set his alarm. And get up whenever it
was necessary to leave, however early the hour.

As his business took off Emerson had brought people on
board to handle the bulk of the early departures. People he
trusted. But he wasn't above doing the heavy lifting himself.
Particularly when the job was personal. And given that his
guys were currently in New Jersey, watching a ship moored
twelve miles out to sea, he didn't have any option. It was
down to him. And Graeber, who was asleep in the next-door
storeroom. Emerson rolled off the couch. He crossed to his
workbench and fired up his little Nespresso machine. He figured they both could use a good hit of caffeine before they
got on the road.

Jed Starmer had never been to Dallas before, but when he
saw the cluster of sharp, shiny buildings in the distance, plus
one that looked like a golf ball on a stick, he knew he must be
close.

Jed stared out of the bus window. He was on high alert,
scanning the area for blue and red lights. For police cruisers.
For detectives' cars. For officers patrolling on foot. For anyone who might be looking for him. He saw storefronts.
Offices. Bars and restaurants. Hotels. Federal buildings. A
wide pedestrian plaza. A memorial to a dead president. Some

homeless guys, bedded down at the side of the street. But no one connected to law enforcement. As far as he could tell.

So either the cops weren't coming for him. Or they would be lying in wait at the Greyhound station.

Jed felt like the bus took a week to meander its way through the city. He jumped at every vehicle he saw. And at every pedestrian who was still out on the street. No one paid any attention to him. All the same, Jed hunkered down in his seat when the driver made the final turn into the depot. The last thing he saw was a sign for something called the Texas Prison Shuttle. He had never heard of anything like it and the idea made him sad. He could be on his way to prison himself, soon, and if he did wind up behind bars he knew no one would be coming to visit him. There could be convenient transport available, or not. It wouldn't make any difference.

The driver pulled into his designated slot, braked gently to a stop and switched on the interior lights. Some passengers grunted and groaned and pulled blankets and coats over their faces. Others got to their feet and stretched. Then they stepped into the aisle and made for the door. Jed stayed where he was. If he could have wished himself invisible, that's what he would have done. Instead he had to make do with keeping his head down and peering through the gap between the seats in front of him. He focused on the front of the bus. At the top of the steps. To see if anyone got on. No one did. No new passengers. And no police. Not straight away. But there was an hour and five minutes until his connecting bus was due to leave. That was plenty of time for a whole squad of them to show up.

'Hey, buddy.' The guy from the back of the bus dropped

into the seat next to Jed. 'Thanks for waiting. You hungry? Come on. Time for that breakfast you promised me.'

Jed paused at the entrance of the depot and peered inside. The space was a large rectangle with grey tiles on the floor and a ceiling that was high in the centre and low around the edges. The amenities were clustered around the sides, in the lower section. One wall was taken up by the ticket counter, which was closed at that time of the morning. There was a line of self-serve ticket machines. A group of vending machines full of snacks and drinks. Rows of red plastic seats, with people sleeping on some of them. Then there was the section Jed's new friend was interested in. The food concessions. There were two of them. One only sold pizza. The other had a full range of fast-food options.

There were no cops in sight. Yet.

Jed was intending to just get a small snack. He wanted to spend as little time out in the open as possible. And to spend as little money as he could get away with. He still had some major expenses coming up. He knew that. But then he read the menu at the fast-food counter. He smelled the bacon. And the sausages. And the fries. And all his good intentions evaporated. He hadn't eaten since LA. He was so hungry his legs were trembling. He just couldn't help himself. He ordered the Belly Buster Deluxe, which contained pretty much everything it's possible to cook in oil, plus extra onion rings and a Coke. The guy from the back of the bus asked for the same combination. The clerk grunted some instructions to a cook who was hanging around behind her then shuffled across to the register. She hit a few keys and barked out the total. Jed had already done the math in his head. He'd already worked out how much he would have

143

left after factoring in the tax and leaving the smallest acceptable tip.

It was less than he would have liked, but he figured he could live with it.

Jed reached into his back pocket. He felt for his roll of cash. But his fingers touched nothing but lint and fraying seams. His pocket was empty. He checked his other pockets. All of them. He came up with nothing but a few coins and his toothbrush. His money was gone. All of it. He stood still for a moment, trying to make sense of what was happening. Then his knees gave way. He flopped back. His head hit the ground. The lights above him turned into fiery multi-pointed stars. They spun and danced and twirled. Then everything in his world went dark.

TWENTY-TWO

Reacher woke himself up at a quarter past five, Thursday morning. He took a shower. Got dressed. And was outside the hotel by ten to six.

Reacher was outside, as agreed. Hannah Hampton was not. And neither was Sam Roth's truck.

Reacher considered going back inside and asking the guy behind the reception counter what time Hannah had checked out. Then he thought better of it. There was no point. Whether she had left five minutes or five hours before him, he wouldn't be able to catch up to her without a vehicle. And even if he could, he wouldn't. This was a volunteer-only operation. If Hannah was having second thoughts, it was better she didn't come along. It would be a mistake to take her.

There were no vehicles at the gas station on the other side of the street so Reacher started to walk. The highway was only a quarter of a mile away. He figured he could hitch a ride when he got to the intersection. There was usually plenty of

145

truck traffic early in the morning, before the roads got too busy. He hoped there would be at least one driver who could use some company. Who was looking for a little gas money. Or a little conversation to help him stay awake after a long night at the wheel.

The sun was starting to rise but the landscape looked no more inviting than it had the evening before. It was still flat. Still parched and brown. Still featureless. Reacher figured he must have covered a couple of hundred yards but the scene was so vast and so uniform it was like he hadn't moved at all. He pressed on, a little faster. Then he stopped. He heard a sound behind him. An engine. A diesel. Rattling and clanking like a train.

Hannah Hampton pulled up at the side of the road and buzzed down the passenger window.

She said, 'What's going on? Why did you leave without me?'

Reacher said, 'I figured you left without me.'

Hannah checked her watch. 'But it's not six yet. We said we'd meet at six.'

Reacher shrugged. 'Old habits. On time is late where I'm from. Anyway, where did you go? This isn't much of a place for an early-morning joyride.'

'To get coffee.' Hannah pointed at two giant to-go mugs that were jammed into holders in the centre console. 'I thought you liked it. The machine wasn't cleaned in the station across the street. The morning guy was late. He hadn't gotten to it yet. So I had to drive to the other place. It's, like, a mile away. Was I wrong?'

'Absolutely not.' Reacher opened the door and climbed in. 'I do like coffee. And it makes for a much better greeting than last time you picked me up. That's for sure.'

*

146

Jed Starmer woke up a couple of hours later than Reacher. He was on a Greyhound bus. But not the one that had brought him from LA. A different one. Heading east, approaching the border between Texas and Louisiana.

If Jed had been left to himself he might not have made it on to that bus. He had no recollection of getting up off the floor at the depot in Dallas. He just remembered finding himself on a plastic chair, propped up against a table. The guy from the back of the previous bus was sitting opposite him. Between them there were two trays, loaded with food. Belly Buster Deluxes, with extra onion rings and giant cups of Coke. Exactly what they had ordered. Exactly what he was trying to pay for when he realized his money was missing. He thought he must have been mistaken. He thought he must still have it. Relief flooded through him. He slid his hand into his pocket. He needed to touch the cash. To be sure it was there. But his pocket was just as empty as before. He was so confused.

The other guy said, 'If you're wondering about the food, I paid for it.'

'Oh.' Jed was struggling to keep his thoughts straight. 'Thank you. I guess.'

The guy was staring at Jed. His expression wasn't friendly. 'Tell me something. And don't lie. Are you scamming me?'

'What? No. Wait. I don't understand.'

'You say you'll pay. You order the food. Then you stick me with the check.'

'Not deliberately.'

'The whole collapsing thing? You should get an Oscar for that.'

'I don't know what you mean.'

'You really thought you had the money?'

147

'I do have the money. I did have. Now it's gone.'

'How much did you have?'

'Three hundred dollars.'

'In what? Tens? Twenties? Fifties?'

'Twenties.'

The guy shook his head. 'So quite a roll. When did you last have it?'

Jed thought for a moment. 'In El Paso. I got some water. No. Wait. That was from a machine. I used coins. It must have been in LA. On Tuesday. I bought my ticket and a burger.'

'Did you pull out the whole roll? Or just what you needed?'

Jed shrugged. 'The whole roll, I guess.'

'You put what you didn't spend in your pocket?'

'Right.'

'Did anyone see which pocket you put it in?'

'I don't know. Probably. The bus station was pretty busy.'

'Did anyone come close to you? Bump into you? Come into contact in any other way?'

'No. Wait. Yes. The guy who found my ticket. I dropped it and . . . oh.'

'*Oh* is right. So. This guy. Did you talk to him? Did he ask you any questions?'

'We chatted a little, I guess. He said he was getting on my bus. But then he didn't. Now I know why.'

'Did you tell him where you were going?'

'Not exactly. I was pretty vague. Why?'

'Doesn't matter. Now come on. Eat. Before this mess goes cold.'

The other guy cleared his plate then waited for Jed to catch up.

He said, 'Good. Now we should get you to the hospital. Get

you checked out. You whacked your head pretty good when you fell.'

'No.' Jed checked his watch. 'No time. My next bus goes in ten minutes. And anyway, I'm fine.'

'You should call 911, at least. Report the guy in LA.'

Jed shook his head.

'You need to report him. To stop him from ripping anyone else off.'

'There's no point. It's too late. He'll be long gone.'

'You're scared to call the police, aren't you? You're trying to avoid them. How come?'

'I'm not scared. I'm just short of time.'

'You're in some kind of trouble.'

'I told you. I'm not.'

'Then what's the problem? Are you a runaway? Is that it?'

Jed shook his head again. 'No. I'm not running away from anything. I'm just . . . relocating.'

'Really? Where to? How? Where's your stuff? What are you going to do when you get there?'

'I don't know.' Those were good questions, Jed thought. Although only two things really mattered. Where he was going to sleep that night after he got off the bus. And how he was going to finish his journey the next morning. The same two problems he'd faced all along. They were a little more difficult now that he had no money. But he would figure something out. There were people sleeping on the seats near him. He wasn't thrilled at the idea, but he could do the same at the depot in Jackson. It wouldn't kill him for one night. Then he remembered the sign he had seen outside. For the prison shuttle. If they had those in Texas, surely there would be something similar in Mississippi. That could

149

be his salvation. If he could somehow persuade the driver to let him get on board. He looked up and tried to smile. 'Don't worry. I'll be OK.'

'Well, good luck. You're a brave kid.' The guy looked at Jed for a moment then pulled two ten-dollar bills out of his pocket and slid them across the table. 'Here. This is all I can spare. Take it. Just don't let anyone steal it from you this time.'

Hannah Hampton's phone guided them due south until they passed Amarillo, then the highway shifted a little to the east. They would head diagonally across the state until they got to Dallas, Reacher figured. Then it would be a straight shot all the way to Mississippi. A few more stops for diesel and coffee. A few more hours to play music in his head. Unless Hannah decided she wanted to talk again. Either way was fine with him. He tipped his seat back a little further, closed his eyes and settled in for the ride. There wasn't much he could do while they were on the road. But when they got to their destination, he was pretty sure that was going to change. And that was also fine with him.

Lev Emerson's contact had picked a coffee shop in St. Louis, Missouri, for their meeting. The same city as their first rendezvous. A different venue. But the same line of thinking. Somewhere public. Noisy. Hard for anyone to eavesdrop or to record their conversation. And hard for Emerson to do the guy any physical harm without being seen by dozens of witnesses. The guy was cautious. That was clear. But he had overlooked one detail. Last time they met, Emerson didn't know what the guy looked like. He had no option but to wait for him inside, as agreed. But recognizing him was no longer a problem. Which is why Emerson decided to ambush him outside.

When you work with the range of chemicals involved in Emerson's line of business, getting your hands on a little chloroform is child's play. Before he left Chicago Emerson soaked a rag with the stuff and stowed it in a Ziploc bag. He timed the drive so that he and Graeber arrived at the strip mall where the coffee shop was located an hour early. He parked right by the entrance to the parking lot. Watched every car that pulled in. Spotted his contact roll up in a silver Mercedes. Backed out and followed the guy to the other side of the lot. Reversed into the space next to his, passenger side facing him. Graeber jumped out. He was holding a dog-eared road atlas. He stopped the guy and asked him for directions to an industrial park on the outskirts of the city. Emerson slipped out on the other side. He was holding the rag. He looped around the back of the van. Opened one of the doors. Stepped up behind the guy. Clamped the rag over his nose and mouth. And took the guy's weight as he sagged so that he didn't hit the ground. Graeber squeezed between them. He climbed into the van's cargo space. Emerson humped the guy's unconscious body around to the doorway. Graeber grabbed it by the shoulders. Emerson took its ankles. Together they dragged the guy inside. Then Emerson slammed the door and took a quick glance around the parking lot. The whole operation had taken nine seconds. No one had seen a thing.

Damon Brockman walked into Bruno Hix's office and sat down on one of the visitors' chairs that were lined up in front of the big wooden desk.

He said, 'I just took a very interesting call. Remember Lawrence Osborn?'

Hix put down his pen. 'Pepper-spray Larry? Sure. Good guy. Came with us from Kansas City, then had to retire early. Asthma, right?'

'Right. Well, guess who just knocked on Larry's door?'

'Tell me.'

'That kid. The journalist who had a bee in his bonnet about drug deaths.'

'Why's he bothering Larry?'

'Seems he's going after everyone we fired when we took this place over. Figures some of them might have loyalty deficits. Might be willing to spill some beans.'

'None of those guys know anything.'

'Right.'

'And we didn't fire Larry.'

'The kid doesn't know that.'

Hix drummed his fingers on his desk for a moment. 'I don't like this. If the kid's hunting down our ex-employees, who knows what other kinds of digging he's doing. I don't want him here tomorrow. He's too inquisitive. Too much of a pain in the ass. It's time to get rid of him.'

Brockman smiled. 'Agreed. And I know an easy way to do it.'

'How?'

'Larry told the kid he might be able to get some dirt on us, but he needed time to think. He said he'd get in touch if he wanted to go forward. Then he called me to give us the heads-up. See how we wanted him to play it. So, here's what I'm thinking. We have Larry contact the kid. Send him on a wild-goose chase.'

'Like where? And to do what?'

Brockman shrugged. 'Somewhere far away. I don't know.

San Francisco. Key West. The details don't matter. We can make something up. It just has to be urgent. So the kid leaves town tonight. Tomorrow morning at the latest.'

Hix picked up his pen and twirled it between his fingers. 'OK. I like it. Let's do it. Just make it something convincing.'

TWENTY-THREE

The only promise Lev Emerson had to make was that he wouldn't burn the building down.

That was the opposite of the kind of condition Emerson usually signed up to but in the circumstances it made sense. He needed access to some premises. Something secluded. Where no one would hear anything. Or see anything. Or smell anything. Somewhere that was robust. Industrial. He was in a strange city. And he was in a hurry. So he had called the client he had just done the job for in Savannah. The guy owned a vintage warehouse in St. Louis. It was vacant, near the river, with no active businesses close by. Emerson already knew about the place. He remembered it because the guy had once hired him to torch a neighbour's property.

When Emerson's contact came around from the chloroform he was lying flat on his back. He was naked. And he was in the middle of a cold concrete floor. He could smell a slight hint of gasoline. He could see walls in the distance. Made of brick. They looked ancient. A pale, chalky coating was flaking off them. The ceiling was high above him. It was stained from water leaks, and it was supported by rusty metal beams.

The guy's arms and legs were stretched out to his sides. He tried to move them, but he couldn't. Because his wrists and ankles were cable-tied to six-inch stubs of steel that were sprouting from the ground. There were rows and rows of them. They were all that was left of the giant sets of shelves that had been removed and melted down when the storage business which had inhabited the building had been abandoned. The guy pulled with all his might. The plastic strips dug into his skin but the metal stubs didn't even flex.

Emerson was standing on one side of the guy. Graeber was on the other. Near the guy's feet there was a large plastic barrel. And lying on the barrel there was a ladle. The kind they use in restaurants to serve out bowls of soup.

Emerson crouched down and waited for the guy to turn his head and look at him. Then he said, 'Let's not beat around the bush. I know about you. I obviously know about your ship. So the purpose of today is for you to fill in the remaining blank.'

The guy's throat was dry. He managed to say, 'What blank?'

Emerson said, 'I want to know who your supplier is.'

The guy's eyes stretched wide. 'I don't know. I can't tell you.'

Emerson straightened up and crossed to the barrel. He took the ladle in one hand. Removed the lid with the other. Scooped out a big dollop of thick, cream-coloured gel. Crossed back to the guy. And poured the gel all over the guy's genitals.

155

The guy screamed and bucked and thrashed around. 'Stop! What are you doing? What is that stuff?'

Emerson said, 'I could tell you its chemical name, but it wouldn't mean anything to you. Have you seen *Apocalypse Now?*'

'What? Why?'

'Because the name you'll know it by is napalm.'

'No. Seriously? What the . . .'

'It's my own version. Better than the military kind. The key is not skimping on the benzene. The original formula only burns for a few seconds. Mine stays alight for ten minutes. Think about that. Do you feel how it's sticking to your skin?'

The guy wriggled and bounced and tried to fling the gel away from his body. It was heavy, like glue. A little came off but the bulk remained stubbornly attached.

Emerson took a box of matches from his pocket. 'So. Tell me. Where does your organization get its inventory from?'

The guy stopped moving. He was struggling for breath. 'We have a few sources. We get different things from different places.'

'Start with what you got for my son. Where did it come from?'

'I don't know. Honestly. I only have a contact. I tell him what we need. If he can get it, he does. I don't know who he works for. That's the way the system is set up. For security. Just like he doesn't know who I work for.'

'His name?'

'Carpenter. That's what he told me. It might not be his real name.'

'Contact information?'

'It's in my phone. I'll give it to you. But listen. This is the truth. Four weeks ago, Carpenter dropped out of sight. He

156

might have quit. The FBI might have gotten to him. I don't know. But if you can't reach him, don't think I was lying to you.'

Graeber picked the guy's pants up off the floor and pulled a phone out of one of the pockets. He said, 'Passcode?'

The guy reeled off a series of numbers.

Graeber hit a few keys then said, 'Carpenter? You have a picture of him. Is this a joke?'

The guy said, 'He didn't know. It was in case I ever needed leverage. It's redundant now, anyway.'

Emerson said, 'Who cares about a picture if the guy's disappeared? How do we get around him?'

The guy said, 'You can't. He was my only contact.'

'So how are you placing your orders?'

'We're not. We can't. Not until a replacement gets in touch. We're using alternative suppliers right now.'

'How did you pay Carpenter?'

'Cash, at first. Recently, bitcoin. It's untraceable.'

'Who collects the merchandise? Where from?'

The guy missed a beat. 'I don't know where from.'

'So you do know who.'

The guy didn't answer.

Emerson took a match out of the box.

'OK! We use a transport guy. Out of Vicksburg, Mississippi. His name's Lafferty. He's a one-man band. A specialist.'

'Address?'

'In my phone.'

'Good. Now, is there anything else you want to tell us?'

'No. Nothing. I've told you everything. More than I should have done. So please, let me go.'

'First things first. The shipment that went to my son. You arranged that? You were a link in that chain?'

157

The guy closed his eyes and nodded. Just a very slight motion.

Emerson said, 'Let me hear it.'

The guy opened his eyes again and said, 'Yes. I arranged it. Can I go now? If it's a refund you want, I can make that happen. I'm the only one who can.'

Emerson took a ladleful of gel and poured it on the guy's stomach. He took another and poured it on his chest. Graeber put the lid back on the barrel and rolled it to the exit. Then Emerson struck a match.

'A refund?' Emerson said. 'No. But you can go. Like my son had to go when you were done with him. Only you get to go quicker. And with maybe a little more pain.'

The Greyhound bus Jed Starmer was riding reached the depot in Jackson, Mississippi, at a little after one fifteen p.m., Thursday. That was more than forty hours after he left LA. Four people watched it arrive. Two of them were waiting for that bus, specifically. The other two were keeping an eye on everything that came in from the west.

The second pair normally worked at the Minerva facility in Winson. They had been at the station since three a.m. On a special assignment. They were bored. They were tired. And they were suspicious. Of the other two guys. Their attention had been drawn to them the moment they walked on to the covered concourse. They were young. Late teens, or early twenties at the most. They were wearing bright, short-sleeved shirts, unbuttoned, over dirty white undershirts. They had shorts on. No socks. One had sandals. The other had tennis shoes, old and creased, with no laces. Both had long, messed-up, crusty hair. One was blond. The other dark. Neither had shaved recently. Neither was a picture of respectability. That was for sure. But it was their body language that was the real red flag. Their constant fidgeting. The tension in their arms and legs and necks that they couldn't quite suppress.

Corrections officers live or die by their instincts. Their ability to spot trouble before it happens. There's no alternative given that there are times when they're outnumbered two hundred to one. Things can go south fast. Once they start, there's no stopping them. Not without blood getting spilled. So if the Minerva guys had been on duty at the prison and the scruffy kids had been inmates they would have moved on them immediately. No hesitation. They'd have tossed them back in their cells and kept them locked away until they uncovered whatever it was they were up to. However long it took. But out here, in the free world, there was nothing the Minerva guys could do.

Except watch.

Every couple of minutes the blond kid pulled out his phone and stared at its screen.

One of the Minerva guys nudged his partner. 'See that?'

'He's looking at a photo,' the other guy said. 'I can't see who it's of. Can you?'

The first guy shook his head. 'The angle's wrong. I can make out a silhouette. That's all. But you know what it means? They're not here for anyone they know. They're looking for a stranger.'

The second guy was silent for a moment. 'We're here. They're here. What are the odds?'

'If they're looking for the same guy we are, they're not here to stop him. Look at the size of them. You heard what he did to Robert and Dave in Colorado?'

'So they're here to help him. He'll need a ride. Assuming they're looking for the same guy.'

159

'Which is excellent news.'

'How so?'

'Brockman sends us for one guy. We give him three. There has to be a bonus for that.'

'And if they're up to something else, these kids?'

The first guy shrugged. 'Then it's not our problem.'

Jed was the last passenger to get off the bus. He had thought the front of the station looked inviting. It was all curved canopies and neon signs like an old-time movie theatre. It was a different story around back, where the loading and unloading took place. The area was covered. It was dark and full of shadows. Jed had a bad feeling about the place. He didn't want to set foot in it. He stayed where he was, pressed back in his seat, pretending he wasn't there, until the driver stood up and glared at him. Then he had no choice. He accepted the inevitable. He slunk along the aisle and climbed slowly down the steps.

It was clear to the Minerva guys that Reacher wasn't on the bus. Just like he hadn't been on the previous forty-seven buses they had watched arrive. Which meant they were going to have wait even longer. Watch at least one more. The only question was whether they would be doing that alone. Or whether the two kids they had their eyes on would hang around, too. The kids hadn't shown any interest in any of the passengers who had streamed away.

Until Jed appeared.

Jed glanced around, got his bearings and hurried toward the pair of swinging doors that led to the inside of the station. The blond kid checked his phone again. Then he started moving. He closed in on Jed. He came up behind him and grabbed his left arm. He stuck out his right index finger

160

and jabbed it into Jed's kidney. He leaned down and whispered something into Jed's ear. Then they both veered away to the left. Toward the exit to the street. The dark-haired kid was already there. He checked both directions. He beckoned for them to keep moving. Then all three disappeared from view.

TWENTY-FOUR

Some people pick hotels more or less at random. Other people are more careful. They take all kinds of different factors into account. The price. The location. The amenities. The ambience. The discretion of the staff, depending on what they're planning to do while they're there. And who they're planning to do it with.

Emerson and Graeber paid a great deal of attention to their choice of hotel in St. Louis, that Thursday. But for them only one thing mattered. It was all about the parking lot. It had to be large. And it had to be shaped in such a way that at least some of the spaces were positioned well away from the main building. Graeber spent a good half-hour with his phone after they left the warehouse. He used a few different review sites until he found a place he thought was suitable. Then he switched to his favourite mapping app and pinched and zoomed and swiped until he had double-checked it from all angles. It looked promising on the screen. But when they arrived on site they figured that half of the lot must have been sold since the satellite pictures they had seen were taken. Now the section they had been interested in was surrounded by contractors' hoardings emblazoned with computer simulations of a new office building.

Emerson and Graeber moved on to their second choice of hotel. The parking lot was smaller, but it was early enough in the day for plenty of spaces to be vacant. Graeber pulled the van into the most isolated of them and Emerson walked across to reception. He booked one room. He paid for the whole night but he knew they would be leaving at half past one in the morning. That would give them time to get to Vicksburg, Mississippi, and still have an hour for surveillance before the delivery guy they'd learned about showed up for work. The schedule left them with twelve hours to fill. Emerson figured they should use it to get some rest. They'd had an early start. A long drive from Chicago. Followed by a busy morning. So they would split the time into four shifts. Then take turns, one of them in the room and one in the van. The room would be more comfortable. But the van was more important. Its contents were too valuable to be left unattended. And they would be too hard to explain away if anyone in authority found them.

The car was old. It was some kind of station wagon. It was long and green and there were fake wood panels attached to the sides. The kid with the dark hair opened one of the rear doors. The blond kid moved his hand to the centre of Jed's back. He shoved. Hard. Jed tried to stop himself but his fingers skidded across the dusty paintwork and he wound up face down in the footwell. The blond kid slammed the door. He turned to his buddy. His hand was raised for a

163

high-five. Which he never received. Because his buddy was lying on his back on the sidewalk. Unconscious. One of the Minerva guys was standing over him. He had a smile on his face.

The other Minerva guy said, 'Want to tell me what's going on here?'

The blond kid's mouth drooped open, but he didn't speak.

The Minerva guy took a pistol from the waistband of his jeans. 'This is what you need to understand. I'm a law enforcement officer. I witnessed you attempting to kidnap a minor. I shoot you, I get a medal. So if you have anything close to an innocent explanation, now's the time.'

The kid didn't respond.

The Minerva guy checked his watch. There were eight minutes before the next bus was due. Which was annoying. This could be the only action he would see all day. He would have preferred to draw things out a little. Have some fun. Instead he frowned and said, 'Show me your phone.'

The kid didn't move.

The Minerva guy pressed the muzzle of his gun against the kid's sternum. He reached into the kid's pocket and helped himself to the phone. He glanced at it and said, 'Passcode?'

The kid stayed silent.

The Minerva guy said, 'OK. This phone's old. A fingerprint will unlock it. Hold out your hand.'

The kid didn't move.

The Minerva guy said, 'Let's recap. Passcode, or fingerprint?'

The kid didn't answer.

'OK,' the Minerva guy said. 'I'll go with your fingerprint. You know your finger doesn't need to be attached to the rest of you for it to work, right? Or your thumb? Or whatever you used to set it up? Maybe I'll have to snap off all your fingers, one at a time.'

The kid's eyes opened wide and he blurted out a string of six numbers. The Minerva guy entered them into the phone then opened its photo library. It was full of pictures of people surfing and drinking beer and hanging out on beaches, plus one shot of someone's ass. There was nothing that seemed relevant so the guy switched to the phone's messages app. Straight away a different picture filled the screen. It was of Jed Starmer. At the Greyhound station in LA. Taken on Tuesday afternoon. The guy clicked and swiped and saw that the picture had been sent from a California number. There was a note attached to it. A route number. And an arrival time. He handed the phone to his partner, then said to the kid, 'How much?'

The kid's eyes opened even wider. 'I haven't got any money. But I can get some. I'll pay you whatever you want.'

The Minerva guy slapped the kid in the face. Open-handed, but still hard enough to knock him over sideways, into the gutter. Then the guy reached down, grabbed the kid by the undershirt and hauled him back on to his feet. 'How much will you get for snatching the boy?'

'Oh. Nothing. Nada. Honest.'

'Bullshit.'

'It's true.'

'Then why did you snatch him?'

'We had to. We don't have any choice.'

'Everyone has a choice.'

'We don't. We're working it off. There's a debt we owe.'

'Oh yeah? Who do you owe? What for?'

'A guy we met. He gave us some drugs. A lot of drugs. We were supposed to sell them. But they got stolen. And we didn't have any money to pay him back.'

'Who's the guy?'

'I don't know his real name.'

'Where is he?'

'New Orleans.'

'So now you supply him with runaways?'

The kid looked down and nodded.

The Minerva guy said, 'You have someone at the Grey-hound station in – where? LA?'

The kid said, 'He moves around. LA. San Fran. Austin, Texas, one time.'

'He buddies up to lonely-looking boys? Finds out where they're going? Makes sure no one's going to miss them?'

The kid nodded.

'How many times?'

'This is the fourth.'

'How many more?'

The kid shrugged. 'He said he'd tell us when it was enough.'

The Minerva guy checked his watch again, then pulled a plasticuff from his back pocket. 'Turn around. Hands out behind you.'

'What are you going to do?'

'Call 911. You're looking at a lot of jail time, pal. Hopefully in the place where I work. I'll make sure you get a real good welcome.'

'No. Wait. Please. Can't we—'

The guy spun the kid around and secured his wrists. Then he pushed him toward his partner and opened the back door of the car. He said, 'We better check the boy's OK. Make sure you're not in any more trouble.'

Only he couldn't check on anyone. Because the back of the car was empty. The opposite door was open. And Jed was gone.

TWENTY-FIVE

The same time Jed Starmer was exiting the dusty station wagon, Hannah Hampton and Jack Reacher were leaving Louisiana and entering the state of Mississippi. They were at the midpoint of the Vicksburg Bridge, a hundred feet above the river, on I-20, heading east. As they had been for the last five and a half hours, not including stops for diesel and coffee.

Reacher was driving. He wasn't thrilled about that. He certainly hadn't volunteered. Being driven suited his temperament much better. Anyone else on the road who looked into Sam Roth's truck during the first four hundred miles they covered that day would have said Hannah's companion was pretty much comatose. He was lying back in his seat, not moving. Except for his eyes, which just flickered open every now and again. And that was only so he could get a fix on their current position. At first their surroundings were flat and featureless with nothing to see apart from an occasional water tower or utilitarian metal shed at the edge of the arrow-straight road. Then a few trees and bushes appeared between the scrubby fields. The land began to gently rise in a few places and fall away in others. After they passed Dallas the sky became a little bluer. The grass a little greener. The stands of roadside trees thickened up after they crossed into Louisiana. The farmland grew more lush and fertile. Reacher was enjoying the slow-motion, magic-lantern impression of the landscape as it steadily unspooled outside his window. He would have been happy to file the snapshots away in his memory and save his energy for whatever was waiting for him in Winson. When he would no longer be a passenger. But when Hannah handed him the keys after they stopped at a rest area, he figured it would be rude to refuse. And unsafe. There were dark circles under her eyes. Her shoulders were sagging. She struggled to heave the truck's massive door open against a sudden gust of wind, and she was fast asleep before they made it back on to the highway.

Another bridge spanned the river a stone's throw away to the north. An older one. It was all solid piles and cantilevered girders with giant rivets and flags flying from the highest points. Reacher recognized it. He had been shown pictures of it, and the river flowing beneath it, when he was a kid in a classroom on a military base on the other side of the world. Before the bridge they were crossing that day was even built. But not in a lesson about engineering, or geography. The idea was that the children were supposed to chant *one Mississippi, two Mississippi* to help them measure out the seconds. Reacher couldn't understand why. Even at that young age he was able to keep track of time in his head. So he ignored the official topic and focused on the bridge. It looked solid. Purposeful. Dependable. The way a properly designed structure

168

should be. It only carried trains, now. And it was a little worse for wear. Its paint was peeling. Its iron skeleton was streaked with rust. But it was still standing. Still functional. It had once been revered. Now it was surplus to requirements. That was a story Reacher knew well.

A hundred yards beyond the end of the bridge Reacher saw a sign for a truck stop. It claimed to be the largest in Mississippi. Reacher hoped that was true. And he hoped it reflected the scope of the facilities, not just the size of the parking lot. It was time for him to get a change of clothes, and none of the previous places they visited had any in his size.

Hannah woke up when Reacher switched off the engine. The sleep had left her feeling brighter so they walked across the parking lot together, toward the main building. It was shaped like a bow tie. The entrance led into a square, central section that contained the restrooms, and showers for the truck drivers. The triangular area on the left was set up as a food court, with chairs and tables clustered in the centre and three different outlets spread out around the edges. There was a pizza restaurant on one of the angled sides. A place selling fried chicken on the other. And a burger joint which took up the whole of the base. The store filled the entire area to the right, with shelves and racks and display cases scattered about in no discernible order.

Hannah went through the doors first and started toward the bathrooms, but Reacher took her elbow and steered her into the store.

Hannah said, 'What, you can't pick out a pair of pants on your own?'

Reacher checked over his shoulder and said, 'You have a phone?'

'Of course. You want to call someone?'

169

'Does it take pictures?'

'Of course. All phones do these days.'

'Do you hold it up to your eye, like a camera?'

Hannah laughed. 'You hold it out in front. You see the image on the whole screen. Much better than a tiny viewfinder. Why?'

'There's a guy by the counter of the chicken place. He's lurking around like he's waiting for an order to come out. But he was actually watching the entrance. And he did something with his phone. He held it out in front and moved it, like he was tracking me with it when we came in.'

'Move your arm to the side, just an inch?' Hannah peered through the gap between Reacher's bicep and his torso. 'White guy, buzzed hair, T-shirt, jeans?'

Reacher nodded.

'He's still there. Another guy's with him. They look like gym buddies. He still has his phone in his hand. He keeps staring at it, like he's waiting for a message. Maybe they're supposed to be meeting someone? Who's running late for some reason and hasn't gotten in touch to let them know?'

Reacher shook his head. 'He didn't raise the phone until he saw me. Then he pointed it right at me.'

'Are you sure? You really think he took your picture? Why would he do that?'

'I don't know.' Reacher turned around. 'Let's ask him.'

Reacher walked up to the guy with the phone and said, 'Next time, call my agent.'

Wrinkles creased the guy's forehead. He said, 'The hell are you talking about?'

'You want to take my picture, you need permission.'

The guy couldn't help glancing down at his phone. 'I didn't take your picture.'

'I think you did.'

'OK, smartass. So what if I—' The guy's phone made a sound like someone tapping a wine glass with the blunt edge of a knife. He checked its screen. Nodded to his buddy. Then he lifted the hem of his shirt a couple of inches. A black pistol was tucked into his jeans. A Beretta. It wasn't new. The hatching on its grip was scuffed and worn. 'All right, Mr Reacher. Enough of this bullshit. Let's finish this conversation outside.'

The implied threat with the gun was ridiculous. It might as well have been a piece of lettuce. There was no way the guy was about to start shooting. Not there. Not with all the security cameras that were watching him. The dozens of witnesses. The likelihood of collateral damage that would buy him a life sentence, or worse, if anyone died. And in any case, if he was stupid enough to try to draw the pistol he would be unconscious before the barrel cleared his waistband. His buddy would be, too. Reacher half hoped the guy would try it. He had energy to burn after all the hours spent cooped up in the truck. But he knew it would be better to wait until they were somewhere more private so he decided to play along. He stepped back and said, 'After you.'

The guy with the gun shook his head and gestured for Reacher to move first. Reacher started toward the exit. Hannah followed. Then the guy fell in behind them, alongside his partner, and gave directions to the rear of the building. They passed between the long outside wall of the store and a parking area for buses. Eleven vehicles were lined up in their

171

oversized bays but there were no passengers milling around. No drivers. The building was at the edge of the site so there was nothing behind it. No road. No parked cars. No people. Just a strip of cracked pavement between the wall and a fence. The fence was made out of broad wooden slats. It was solid. There were no gaps. No knot holes. It was ten feet high. No one could see over it. No one could see through it. There were no windows on that side of the building. There were no doors. So there were no security cameras. And the walls of the food court and the store angled outwards from the bathroom block. That left a trapezium-shaped area that was totally secluded. No one would see what happened there. No one would call 911. No one would give statements to the police. No one would ever testify in court.

Reacher could see what was coming next. He knew one of the guys behind him was armed. It was safe to assume the other guy would be, too. So they would try to back him and Hannah up against the bathroom block wall. That was clear. Then all the guys would have to do was stay back, and stay awake. Their plan could be to shoot Hannah. Or Reacher. Or both. To kill them. Immobilize them. Or just hold them until reinforcements arrived. But whatever the intention, it would be game over, right there.

Reacher took a half-step to his right then stopped dead. Hannah was alongside him before she realized he wasn't moving any more. She stopped too. Reacher leaned down and whispered, 'Stay behind me. Don't let the guy get a clear shot at you.'

Hannah whispered back, 'Which guy? There are two of them.'

Reacher said, 'Not for long.'

*

172

Reacher heard a voice from behind him. It was the guy who'd been giving the directions. The one who was definitely armed. He said, 'Keep going. No one told you to stand still.'

The guy was close. Closer than when they left the building. Reacher could tell from the sound of his voice. The guy must have taken a couple of extra steps after Reacher stopped, just like Hannah had done. Reacher gauged the distance between them. He pictured the guy's height. Subtracted a couple of inches. Shifted his weight on to the ball of his left foot. Then threw himself backward. He snapped into a fast, clockwise turn, twisting at the waist to add momentum and extending his right arm. He clenched his fist. It traced a wide arc like the head of a sledgehammer. One wielded by a two-hundred-and-fifty-pound maniac. The guy saw the danger. He started to duck. He fumbled for his gun. But he was too slow. The side of Reacher's fist slammed into his temple and felled him like a dead tree in a hurricane.

The second guy jumped back. He lifted his shirt and scrabbled for his own gun. Another Beretta. Reacher matched his movement. He stepped in close, stretched out his left hand and pinned the guy's wrist against his abdomen. He took the guy's weapon. Then shoved him in the chest and sent him staggering away, too far to try to snatch the gun back.

Reacher said, 'Your friend took my picture. Why?'

The guy didn't answer.

Reacher said, 'You wanted to finish the conversation outside. We're outside. So converse.'

The guy shook his head.

Reacher raised the gun. 'Try this instead. You picked this particular spot. No witnesses. No cameras. Why was that?'

The guy held out his hands, palms up. 'I don't know anything. If you're going to shoot me, just get it over with.'

'You're wrong,' Reacher said. 'You do know some things. You know my name.'

'Oh. Yeah. OK.'

'You know you were sent out here to look for me.'

'I guess.'

'So you know who sent you.'

The guy shook his head.

'You know. Who was it?'

The guy didn't answer.

Reacher prodded the body on the ground with his toe.

The guy closed his eyes for a moment. 'Our boss sent us.'

'Name?'

'Mr Brockman.'

'Organization?'

'Minerva Correctional.'

'You work at the prison in Winson?'

The guy nodded.

Reacher said, 'How did Brockman know I'd be here?'

'He didn't. He sent guys to a bunch of places. Just in case.'

'How many guys?'

'I don't know. Eight? Ten? It wasn't like a regular team briefing. We got given our orders in pairs. Word filtered out between us later.'

'Which places?'

'I only know one place for sure. The Greyhound station in Jackson. One of the guys who got sent there is my brother-in-law. He called me. A few minutes ago. They just caught a couple of punks trying to kidnap a homeless kid who'd come in from California. Said he wanted to see if we were having any fun like that. Which was horseshit. Really he wanted to break my balls because he knew we would be totally bored.'

174

'Guess his call was a little premature. What were you supposed to do if you saw me?'

'Verify your ID.'

'And then?'

'Stop you.'

'From doing what?'

'Getting to Winson.'

'Why?'

'So you couldn't cause any trouble.'

'Why would I cause trouble in Winson?'

The guy shrugged. 'Mr Brockman said you were crazy. Crazy people do crazy things.'

'You had to verify my ID. How?'

'We sent your picture to some guys who know what you look like.'

'Which guys?'

'A couple of co-workers.'

'How would they recognize me?'

'Your paths crossed a couple of days ago. In some town in Colorado.'

Reacher smiled. 'I see. Where are these guys?'

'In Winson. I guess. They're still out sick.'

'I'll make sure to drop by their houses while I'm in town. Maybe bring them some grapes. Now. Brockman. Is he a good boss?'

'I guess.'

'Is he a nice guy?'

'If he likes you.'

'Right. I saw what happens to people he doesn't like. In Colorado. So here's what I'm going to do. I will go to Winson. I will cause some trouble for Mr Brockman. Maybe a little more than he's expecting. And when I'm done I'll make sure he knows how much you helped me.'

'No. Please. Don't do that. He'll kill me.'

'Sorry. My mind's made up. Unless . . .'

'Unless what? What do you want? Money? 'Cause that's no problem. I can get you—'

'Not money. Information. There's something weird going on with the accounting at Minerva. I want to know what.'

The guy's eyes stretched wide. 'Accounting? I don't know anything about that. How would I?'

Reacher looked at the guy for a long moment. Over the years he had gotten pretty good at sensing when people were telling the truth. Normally he encouraged that kind of response. But on this occasion he was disappointed to be given an honest answer. It meant the guy was no more use to him. So he punched him in the face and watched him crumple and collapse on to the ground.

'Was that necessary?' Hannah was standing with her hands on her hips. 'He was no threat. You'd already taken his gun.'

Reacher said, 'What about the backup piece in his ankle holster? And the knife in his sock?'

'He has another gun? And a knife?'

'He might have. You wait to find out, you'll be the one who winds up on the ground. And you won't be getting up again. These guys are working with the people who killed Sam. Who killed Angela. And they didn't bring us out here for coffee and cakes.'

Hannah was quiet for more than a minute, then she moved closer to the first guy Reacher had knocked down. 'Is this one dead?'

Reacher shrugged. 'Could have broken his neck, I guess.'

176

'Don't you care?'

'Would you care if you stepped on a cockroach?'

'He's not a cockroach.'

'No. He's worse. He's human. He had a choice.'

'You know something? You're right.' Hannah took another step then kicked the guy in the ribs. 'He did choose this. He chose to help the people who murdered Sam. Not just killed him. *Killed* could be an accident. They took Sam's life on purpose. For some sort of gain. They're assholes. I hate them. I think we should get every last one of them.'

'You'll get no argument from me.'

'Good. So what do we do next?'

TWENTY-SIX

It was a question of balance.

The question arose because the spectators at the next day's ceremony would be divided into two groups. Those who showed up in person. And those who would watch remotely. On TV. Or online. The problem was how to look good to both sets of people. If he remained too static, he would appear stiff and wooden to the live crowd. But if he was too animated, he would come across as a maniac on the screen. The cameras would have to jerk around to keep him in the frame. It would look like he was having a fit. No one told him to his face – everyone said his speech was a triumph – but that's what Bruno Hix believed had happened the last time an innocent man was released. Because he had gotten carried away. He had been feeding off the energy from his audience. Lapping it up. He had overindulged. Like with any great feast it felt good in the moment. But the

178

aftermath was no fun at all. And thanks to the likes of You-Tube, the aftermath would live for ever online.

The solution lay in better preparation. Hix knew that. He had already memorized his words. He was going to knock the content right out of the park. He had no doubt about that. He just needed to work on the delivery. To make sure he hit both targets simultaneously. The real and the virtual. That would be no mean feat. So he had devised a new system. A combination of old technology and new. He had started by getting the prison's maintenance crew to install giant mirrors on one wall of the conference room. He had them build a mock-up of the stage at the opposite end. Then he had two small video cameras delivered. They were designed for people who did active sports. Things like skiing and mountain biking and kayaking. Hix didn't care about how shockproof they were. He wasn't interested in their underwater performance. But there was one feature he figured would be essential. They were voice activated. So he set one on a regular tripod by his side and aimed it at the mirror to capture the kind of distant view the crowd would get. He set the other on a mini tripod sitting right on his lectern. It was pointing straight at his face. Cropped in tight, the way the news guys would do it. His plan was to give the command to record, which would set both cameras going simultaneously. Run through his speech, several times, with different expressions and gestures and degrees of movement. Then he would play the footage back, both feeds side by side on his computer screen, and settle on the best combination.

Hix had blocked out two hours in his diary. He had told his assistant that unless the prison went on lockdown he was not to be disturbed. He climbed up on to the practice stage. He switched on the cameras. He was about to begin the recording. Then the conference room door swung open.

Hix turned and yelled, 'What?'

Damon Brockman stepped into the room. He stayed well away from the stage and said, 'You were right.'

Hix said, 'Of course I was right.' He looked back into the lens of the lectern camera, opened his mouth, then paused. 'Right about what?'

'The drifter from Colorado. Reacher. He was trying to come here.'

'Was?'

'The guys at the truck stop on 20 are all over him.'

'They stopped him?'

'They got a positive ID.'

'So they saw him. I'm asking, did they stop him?'

'They've been on radio silence since they sent his picture. Probably busy keeping him on ice. I've sent Harold up there to help them.'

'Harold?'

'Harold Keane. The guys call him Tiny. You'd recognize him if you saw him. He's been with us ten years. We brought him over here from Atlanta. He's six foot six. Three hundred pounds. All muscle. He won silver in America's Strongest Man two years running when he worked for the Georgia state system.'

'Only silver?'

'Bruno, do me a favour. Don't ever say that to his face.'

'He has a short fuse? Good. But it'll take him a while to get up there. Send the guys from the Megamart as well. The intersection with 61 is way closer.'

'Will do.'

180

'And you can stand the guys down from the Greyhound station in Jackson. No point leaving them there now.'

'I'll text them. Let them know. What about the guys at the construction site on 87?'

'Leave them for now. Just in case. Until we know for sure that Reacher's safely under wraps.'

'Understood.'

'Good. Send the messages. Then why don't you come back? Watch me rehearse for tomorrow?'

'You know, I'd love to. But I'm slammed with other stuff. There's all kinds of craziness going on right now. So sadly I'll just have to go ahead and pass on that very tempting offer.'

The next thing Reacher did was to check whether the first guy he had hit was still alive.

The guy was. He had a pulse. It was fast and faint, but it was there. Reacher didn't care either way on an emotional level. It was purely a practical matter. He needed to know if he had trash to dispose of or an opponent to keep off the field.

Reacher collected the unconscious guys' Berettas. He found their phones, smashed them against the ground with his heel and threw the remains over the fence. Then he and Hannah searched the guys' pockets. They didn't yield any surprises. They each had a wallet with a single ATM card, a driver's licence and a Minerva Correctional ID. One had forty dollars in twenties. The other had sixty. Reacher kept the cash. He still had new clothes to pay for. He also took a car key. It had a Mercury logo on its chunky plastic body and a remote fob on its ring.

Next Reacher pulled off the guys' boots. He tossed them over the fence. He removed the guys' jeans and T-shirts. He tossed them over the fence, too. Then he peeled off the guys' socks. They were thick. Heavy-duty. The kind people wore for hiking and other kinds of vigorous sport. They were slightly damp. Reacher tried to ignore that and tested one for strength. He pulled it to see if it would stretch. Or snap. It gave a little, but it didn't break. He figured they would slow the guys down if nothing else, so he used the socks to secure their ankles and tie their wrists behind their backs. Then he dragged the guys across to the base of the wall for maximum concealment. He was ready to leave them there when a different thought crossed his mind.

He said, 'Hannah? Come with me for a minute?'

Reacher led the way to the parking area at the side of the building. One of the buses had departed, leaving ten others in a tidy row. There were still no passengers in sight. No drivers. No other passers-by. Reacher asked Hannah to keep a lookout then he tried the handles on the nearest bus's luggage compartment hatches. There were three on each side, low down, beneath the windows. All of them were locked. He tried the next bus. All of its hatches were locked, too. It was the same thing with the third bus. But the fourth bus was older. It had come all the way from British Columbia, Canada, according to its licence plates. The first of its hatches was not secured. It pivoted out and up with no effort at all. Reacher left it open. He hurried back to the space behind the building. Picked up the first unconscious guy. Swung him on to his shoulder. Carried him to the bus. Posted him through the hatch and into the cargo hold. He fetched the second guy. Dumped him in the hold next to his buddy. Then he closed the hatch. He pressed his knee against it. Pulled the handle out. And twisted it back and forth until the mechanism failed and it came off in his hand. He did the same to the other five hatch handles. Threw them over the fence. And led the way back to the entrance to the building.

Reacher went into the bathroom to wash his hands. Then he moved on to the store. There was a basic selection of work clothes in the section that catered for truck drivers so he picked out the one pair of pants that looked long enough, a T-shirt, some underwear, and because he'd been to Mississippi before, a light rain jacket. He found a road atlas of the state. Grabbed two large cups of coffee. Paid for everything with the money he'd taken from the Minerva guys. Then he went outside and caught up with Hannah at the truck.

Hannah was happy to take her drink, but she was surprised when Reacher climbed into the passenger seat and set a paper map down on the centre console between them.

She said, 'Why did you waste your money on that? My phone will give us directions. Anywhere we want to go. Right to the front door.'

'This isn't for directions.' Reacher opened the atlas to the page that showed the truck stop. It was near the western border of the state – the river – and roughly halfway between the Gulf to the south and Tennessee to the north. Jackson was to the east, roughly a third of the way to Alabama. Winson was to the south-west, nestling in a deep oxbow on the edge of the riverbank. 'That Minerva guy said that ten people had been sent to watch for me. He said they're deployed in pairs, so that means there are five ambush sites. We know two of them. Where we are now, and the Greyhound station in Jackson. We need to figure out where the other three could be.'

'OK. Well, clearly they anticipated we'd be coming in on 20. But they couldn't have been sure we'd hit the truck stop. Not unless they knew about your strange wardrobe arrangement. Without that we would have kept going, then turned south here. On to 61.' Hannah pointed at a line on the map. 'Somewhere further along there would be the next logical place to try and catch us.'

'No. They would try at the intersection. They can't know you're taking me the whole way to Winson. They'll assume that if I'm on the road I either stole a car or I'm hitching rides. If I stole a car, that's where I'd turn. If someone had picked me up further west and was continuing to Jackson or Meridian, or even Tuscaloosa or Birmingham, that's where they would let me out. So it's where I'd hang around, looking for my next pick-up.'

'Makes sense.' Hannah took a pen from her purse and circled the spot where 61 crossed 20. 'That's potential ambush site number three. Now, if we'd taken the more central route from Colorado through Kansas and Missouri, we'd have wound up coming down 55 into Jackson. Then we'd have come west again. And there's only one route into Winson, wherever you're coming from. They'll put their backstop somewhere on that road.'

Reacher picked up the map, studied it closely for a moment, then set it back down and pointed to a spot near the town boundary. 'There. Look at the contours. It only rises a hundred feet but it's the steepest hill for about a hundred miles. Enough to slow down any trucks, and the rest of the traffic along with them. Slow-moving vehicles are easier to see into. And they're easier to stop.'

Hannah circled the place Reacher had indicated. 'Number four, done. Where's five going to be?'

184

'Jackson.'

'You think? Would they put another team there? They already have the Greyhound station covered.'

'Right. But what if I came in by train? Or got a ride there? How would I get the rest of the way to Winson? There's bound to be a shuttle, or a local bus service. Probably owned by Minerva. Just like they probably own the hotels near the prison.'

'They can do that?'

'Of course. Why only profit off the prisoners when you can make money from their visitors too?'

'You're so cynical.' Hannah stopped with the pen poised above the map. 'But I guess you're right. So where in Jackson would this bus be?'

'Doesn't matter. I'm not going to Jackson. It's too far out of my way. I'll just take care of the intersection and the hilltop for now.'

'*Take care of*? Don't you mean *avoid*?'

Reacher shook his head. 'Basic tactics. If you have the opportunity to degrade the enemy's capability, you take it.'

'Oh. We're going to *degrade* their *capability*? Awesome. I'm up for that. Just tell me what you need me to do.'

'Find a hotel. For tonight.'

'OK. In Winson? For when we're done with the degrading?'

Reacher shook his head. 'No. There's something I want you to think about. I want you to consider going somewhere else. On your own. For a couple of days.'

'The hell I will. I'm going wherever you go. You can't make me drive you all this way then dump me. Talk about a dick move.'

'I didn't make you. I'm not dumping you. But we have new information now. We should be smart. Act accordingly.'

185

'What new information?'

'We've lost the element of surprise. Minerva know I'm coming. They know my name. They have my description. They now have a current photograph. Their people are competent. They're out in force, looking for me. Sticking with me now will expose you to a higher level of risk. Much higher.'

'OK. The risk is higher now. I get that. But you know what? I can take any level of risk I damn well want. You don't get to decide that for me.'

'I'm not deciding. I'm advising. Your goal is to get the people who killed – murdered – Sam. You can't do that if they murder you first. So why don't I go ahead, like an advance party. Get the lie of the land. Sweep out any low-level operatives I find skulking around. Then when the risk is lower, I'll call. You'll join me. And we'll get to the heart of the thing together.'

Hannah was silent for a moment. 'You say the risk is higher. But here's what I don't understand. If we're right, the Minerva guys killed Angela because she uncovered something fishy in the accounts. They killed Sam because Angela told him what she found. So why are they coming after you? What's the connection? What aren't you telling me?'

Reacher paused for a moment, then he talked Hannah through what had happened in Gerrardsville after he witnessed Angela getting pushed in front of the bus. He told her about chasing the guy in the hoodie into the alley. Taking Angela's purse from him. Looking inside. Finding the envelope. The guy's partner showing up in the stolen BMW. And how they got away when the fire escape collapsed.

Hannah punched Reacher in the shoulder. 'Why keep all that a secret? I've gone way out on a limb for you. I don't deserve to be kept in the dark.'

Reacher shrugged. 'Suppose those guys show up in the hospital some time soon. Or at the morgue.'

Hannah was silent for a moment. 'Fair, I guess. I can see why you wouldn't want to advertise a grudge against them. But that's not the key point here. You hurt a couple of Minerva's guys. Maybe saw some incriminating evidence. That's reason for them to come after you. Not the other way around. So why are they expecting you? What else are you holding back?'

'Nothing.'

'You swear?'

Reacher nodded.

'OK,' Hannah said. 'Maybe they know you connected them to the murders?'

Reacher shook his head. 'I told the Gerrardsville police that Angela didn't kill herself, but I hadn't factored Minerva in back then. And the police ignored me, anyway. Angela's file is closed. So is Sam's.'

'Then it has to be about Angela's purse. The Minerva guys took it, so there had to be something important inside.'

'Maybe. Maybe not. They might have thought something important was. They might have hoped. Doesn't mean it was there.'

'Tell me again what was in her purse?'

Reacher listed everything he had seen.

'Could anything have been sewn into the lining?'

'I was a military cop. I know where people hide things.'

'So we're back to the envelope. Tell me about that again.'

'It held a file on a guy called Anton Begovic. Wrongly convicted, due for release tomorrow. Minerva sponsored his appeal.'

'Those jackasses.'

'There's something wrong with setting an innocent man free?'

'No. Of course not. It's just – Minerva. With them everything's about PR. Their head dude is a guy called Bruno Hix. He's notorious. He doesn't take a dump without bringing in an image consultant to exploit it. I bet they got some lawyer who owed them a favour to do the appeal work for free. Then they'll stage a huge hullaballoo and make it look like the whole corporation is run by saints and angels and it'll cost them nothing. Sam was always suspicious of them.'

'Why?'

'If something sounds too good to be true, then it isn't true. That's what he always said. Like with their wages. They pay twenty-five per cent above the industry average, across the board. They make sure everyone knows about it. Then they make sure no one gets any overtime.'

'Where did—'

'Wait! I have an idea. What if this Begovic guy isn't really innocent? What if he paid Minerva to help fix the appeal? Or his family did? Minerva could have tried to wash the money through the books. Not very well. And Angela could have smelled a rat.'

'If there is dirty money, why would they let it anywhere near the business? Why not take it in cash?'

Hannah shook her head. 'See, that's the kind of question you only ask if you've never bought a house. Or a car. Or a spare pair of pants. A big heap of cash is the biggest red flag there is. You'd have the IRS so far up your ass you'd see them when you brush your teeth. No. I think I'm on to something. And you clearly shouldn't be let out on your own. So here's the deal. I'm coming with you. But while you're busy *degrading the enemy* or whatever, I'll hang back at the hotel. I'll dig into Begovic's background. Find out all about his conviction. His appeal. What it was based on. Why it took so long. I'll maybe talk to some of Sam's contacts. Tap into the industry scuttlebutt. Find the real story.'

TWENTY-SEVEN

Five words were ringing in Jed Starmer's ears as he crouched between a pair of dumpsters in an alley on the other side of the Greyhound station: *I'm a law enforcement officer.*

The guy's voice had been a little muffled from where he lay on the floor of the car, but Jed was sure about what he heard. Although he wasn't sure what kind of officer the guy was. He hadn't been wearing a uniform. Neither had his partner. So Jed figured they must be detectives. Or FBI agents. Something high up. Important. But he wasn't too concerned about which organization they belonged to. Or what rank they held. He was just glad they had shown up when they did. He had no idea what the scruffy guys had wanted with him, but it didn't take a clairvoyant to see it wasn't going to be anything good.

Jed was glad the officers had shown up, but at the same time he was horrified. Because it meant they must have been looking for him. That was certainly what it sounded like from the exchanges he overheard. The guy from his first bus must have called them. After they finished their breakfast in Dallas. He'd kept nagging Jed about going to the police. When Jed refused, the guy must have taken matters into his own hands. Which meant Jed would have to change his plans. He had been intending to sleep on the seats in the Greyhound station that night and then make his way to Winson the next morning. He couldn't risk staying in town now. Not in a public place. Not somewhere out in the open. He had no option. He had to leave. Immediately.

Reacher left the atlas, one of the captured Berettas and the last dregs of his coffee in the truck with Hannah and walked back to the main building to change his clothes. After that his plan was simple. He was going to find the next pair of Minerva guys at the nearby intersection and give them exactly what they wanted.

For a moment, at least.

He figured that the guys would be looking for him in a car, or at the side of the road as he tried to hitch a ride. If they spotted him in a car, things could get complicated. They wouldn't be able to stop him right away because of the whole identification rigmarole. They would have to take his photograph, send it off to the guys who had seen him in Colorado and wait for their response. So they would have two choices. They could follow his car and intercept it if his ID was confirmed. Or they could stay put and send the intel to the guys who would be stationed at the outskirts of Winson. Neither of those options appealed to Reacher. Forcing a car off a highway at speed in heavy traffic is dangerous. There's plenty of scope for injuries. Maybe fatalities. Maybe involving other vehicles with innocent drivers and passengers. And if the guys passed the information along the chain, that would be no immediate help either. Reacher would be miles away by then, out of contact, and it would only make his life more difficult when he arrived in the town. So the smart move was to stand where the guys would be hoping to see him, stick out his thumb and hope no regular motorists were on the lookout for company.

From above, the intersection looked like a capital 'A', rotated by forty-five degrees, with a curved crossbar. One side was I-20, which swung a little north of east after clearing the river. The other side was US-61, which branched off and ran to the south. The crossbar was made up of the ramps joining 20 east to 61 south, and 61 north to 20 west. The other significant part of the picture was the space beneath the crossbar. It was taken up by a giant store. Reacher couldn't tell from the map which chain it belonged to or what sort of products it sold. And he didn't much care. The only thing that mattered to him was that it had a convenient parking lot.

The plan was simple. Hannah would pull over on the shoulder just before the east/south ramp. Reacher would get out of the truck. Hannah would continue on 20 toward Jackson, in case anyone was already watching. She would leave the highway at the next intersection and loop around to the giant store. She would wait in the parking lot. The Minerva guys would spot Reacher. They would try to photograph him and detain him, either on the shoulder or in a vehicle. They would have the same kind of success as their buddies at the truck stop had done. And when they were unconscious and immobilized, Reacher would climb down the side of the ramp, make his way to the store and rendezvous with Hannah.

The plan was simple. But it went off the rails before it even got started.

Reacher dumped his old clothes in the trash and walked back to the truck. He opened the passenger door, but he didn't get in. Because someone was in his seat. A guy, late twenties, wearing some kind of European soccer jersey, jeans and motorcycle boots. His hair was buzzed at the sides and a little longer at the top. He had a goatee. And he was holding a gun. In his left hand. A desert-tan-coloured Sig P320. His grip was steady and he was aiming at the centre of Reacher's chest.

Reacher grabbed the guy's wrist and pulled until his forearm was clear of the truck's door frame. He forced it back against the pillar between the windows. Twisted, so the gun was pointing at the ground. Then he slammed the door. He threw all his weight behind it. The guy screamed. The gun fell. It clattered against the truck's running board and skittered away under the next parked car. Reacher felt the guy's wrist go limp. He heard the bones crack and splinter. Then he snatched the door open again. The guy's head was lolling back against the seat. Beads of sweat had sprung out all over his face. His skin looked almost green. Reacher pulled back his right arm. Closed his fist. The guy's throat was exposed. One punch was all it would take.

A voice said, 'Stop.' It was coming from the back seat. Another guy was there. The same kind of age and build as the one with the broken arm. He had a plain black T-shirt on. His head was completely shaved. He was behind Hannah. Leaning forward. And pressing the muzzle of a revolver into the base of her skull.

Hannah was sitting up so straight it was like she was trying to levitate. Her arms were stretched out in front. She was gripping the steering wheel with both hands. Her knuckles were bone white. She was staring straight ahead and her face was twisted into the kind of scowl you'd expect from a parent who found her teenage kids hosting an orgy in her living room.

The gun looked tiny in the guy's hand. It was a Ruger LCR. A .22. Probably the guy's ankle piece, Reacher thought. It wouldn't be much use at distance. You wouldn't choose it as a primary weapon. But at close quarters it would be more than adequate. And in that situation it would be ideal. If the guy got his angle right, there was a good chance the round wouldn't break out through the top of Hannah's skull. It would just bounce around inside her head, pulping her brain, until its energy was dissipated and it came to rest in the resulting mush. Which meant her blood and cerebral jelly wouldn't be sprayed across the windshield for anyone to see. And if the bullet did emerge it certainly wouldn't have enough force left to pierce the truck's steel roof. It was as discreet an option as the guy could hope for. Although with his buddy's life on the line he might not care too much about attracting attention.

Reacher opened his hand and lowered his arm.

'Good decision,' the guy said. 'Now, we're looking for two of our friends. This young lady told me you could help us find them.'

Reacher said, 'You have friends?'

'This is no time for jokes.'

'Who's joking?'

'Tell me where they are.'

'How would I know?'

The guy pulled something out from under his left thigh. He held it up for Reacher to see. It was the Beretta he had left in the truck when he went to change.

The guy said, 'Stop wasting time. Tell me where they are.'

A vehicle rumbled past the rear of the truck. Reacher took a glance. It was a bus. The old one from British Columbia. There were no passengers on board. Only the driver. Reacher hoped he was taking it all the way to Canada. Or given the sudden shift in his mood, straight to a scrapyard. One that wouldn't check it too thoroughly before dumping it in the crusher.

Reacher said, 'They're not far away.'

'Tell me where.'

'I'll show you.'

'Tell me.'

'You'd believe me?'

The guy took a moment to think. 'OK. Are you wearing a belt?'

Reacher nodded.

'Take it off. Give it to me.'

Reacher didn't move.

The guy increased the pressure on the gun. It dug deeper into Hannah's skin. She clenched her teeth but couldn't hold back a long, low whimper.

Reacher slipped his belt through the loops in his pants and held it out in the gap between the truck's front seats. The guy kept the gun pressed against Hannah's skull and stretched out with his left hand. He grabbed the belt, then bit it between his teeth, near the buckle. He fed the free end through. Took up the slack until he had a circle about twelve inches across. Then he pulled the gun away and flipped the belt over Hannah's head and yanked it tight around her neck and the metal stalks of the seat rest. She didn't make another sound but her scowl grew even more fearsome.

'Pep?' the guy said to his buddy in the passenger seat. 'Can you move?'

Pep nodded. 'Think so.'

'Good. Come over here. To my door.'

Pep slid out of the truck and crept around to its rear. He was clutching his left arm to his chest and moving like he had the mother of all hangovers. He made it to the far side. The guy holding the belt slid across. Pep climbed in behind Hannah and slumped back in the seat. He looked like he was about to be sick.

'Sit forward,' the guy holding the belt said. 'All the way. Get your ass right on the edge.'

Pep shuffled to the front of the seat. The guy took Pep's right hand and tied the belt around his wrist so that his palm was flat against the back of the driver's seat, just below the nape of Hannah's neck.

The guy patted Pep between the shoulders then slid the rest of the way across to the passenger side, opened the door and climbed down next to Reacher. He nodded toward Pep and Hannah and said, 'Do I need to draw you a diagram?'

Reacher shook his head.

'Good. Now pick up the SIG Pep dropped. Finger and thumb through the trigger guard. Pass it to me.'

Reacher fished the gun out from under the neighbouring car and handed it to the guy.

'OK.' The guy tucked the gun into the back of his pants and made sure his shirt was covering it. 'Show me where my friends are. And you better make it quick, for the woman's sake.'

Reacher led the way back toward the main building, and as he walked he tried to picture the remote fob on the key ring he had taken after searching the first pair of Minerva guys. He remembered it had four buttons. The lower two were coloured.

One was red. It looked like it had something to do with the alarm. One was blue. It was for opening the trunk. The others were black. They had little white padlock symbols on them. The symbols were faint. They were worn almost all the way off, but Reacher thought the lock on the top-left button was shown as closed.

Reacher slid his hand into his pocket and felt for the fob. He found the top-right button and pressed it with his thumb. He looked around the lot, hoping to see a parked car's turn signals flash.

Nothing happened.

The guy walking behind him said, 'Hey. What are you doing?'

'Keeping my pants from falling down.'

The guy grunted like he wasn't convinced.

They kept on walking. Reacher kept on pressing the unlock button. No lights flashed. They were almost at the entrance to the building. Reacher figured the car must be somewhere else in the lot so he would have to take the guy around the back of the building. Do the job in two stages. He knew for sure the car wasn't over to the right because that was where the buses parked. So he rolled the dice one last time. Headed toward the left. Pressed the unlock button again. And saw a pair of orange lights give a long, slow blink.

The car the lights belonged to was in the final row, in front of the fence that continued along the perimeter of the site. There was an empty space on both sides. But it was a false alarm. A coincidence. It was the wrong kind of car. A Ford Crown Victoria. Reacher had seen hundreds of them during his time in the army. And hundreds more after he left. Although this one was much cleaner than most he had come across. Its paintwork was immaculate. Dark blue, almost

197

black. Shiny, like it had recently been polished. It had strange wheels. A weird grille at the front. Dark tints on the windows. It seemed more like someone's personal vehicle than a detective's car or a cab. So Reacher looked at it more closely. He saw there was a Mercury logo where the blue oval should be. He didn't understand why, but he had never been much of a car guy. And he didn't waste time speculating. He just slid his thumb across to the lock button on the fob. He pressed it. The car's flashers blinked again. Just as lazily. Reacher figured it was unlikely to be a coincidence a second time.

Reacher said, 'This way.' He changed course and made for the rear of the car. It was almost against the fence. Its owner had backed in, ready for a quick exit if necessary. Reacher waited for the guy to catch up then took the keys out of his pocket. He hit the trunk button. The lid unlocked itself but only swung up a couple of inches.

The guy said, 'Do you think I'm new? I'm not opening that.'

Reacher said, 'No problem. I'll do it. You don't need to get any closer. Just one question, first. You work for Minerva?'

'Just hit my ten-year anniversary. Where are my friends? They better not be in that trunk.'

'You were sent here to look for me?'

'We were sent to the intersection. Got moved here when the other guys spotted you. What's in the trunk? Where are my friends?'

'You had guys here. You had some at the Greyhound station. Where else?'

'No idea. Wasn't told, didn't ask. Now, enough talking. Show me what's in the trunk.'

'You're right. Talking's not getting us anywhere. It's time to—'

Reacher butted the guy in the face. He didn't pull his head

back very far. He didn't want to telegraph what was coming. That meant sacrificing some power, so Reacher had to rely on his height and his neck muscles. It wasn't the hardest blow he'd ever delivered. But it was hard enough. It sent the guy reeling back, still on his feet but already unconscious. He smashed into the fence. Teetered for a moment. Reacher stepped in close. He caught the guy before he hit the ground. Dragged him the last few feet to the car. Lifted the trunk lid the rest of the way. Bundled the guy inside. Then slammed it shut. Unlocked the doors and climbed in behind the wheel.

TWENTY-EIGHT

Bruno Hix started his speech three times.

He started. But he couldn't finish. He couldn't get beyond the first couple of lines. He was too distracted. All he could think about was the truck stop. He couldn't help wondering what was happening up there. He'd sent four guys to take care of one drifter. That should have been a walk in the park. But there'd been no confirmation. No status reports. No news of any kind. And the drifter had already made fools out of the men he'd sent to Colorado.

Hix jumped down from the stage. He left the room and hurried along the corridor to the far end of the building's other wing. To Brockman's office. The door was closed. Hix didn't knock. He just opened it and walked in. For a moment he thought Brockman wasn't there. The desk chair was empty. The armchair was empty. Then he saw that Brockman was stretched out on the couch by the window. An abandoned coffee mug was on the floor by his side.

Hix folded his arms. 'Busy, huh?'

Brockman opened his eyes. He sat up. 'Very. I'm strategizing.'

'No news?'

'Actually, yes. There is. Good news. One of my previous strategies has borne fruit, big time. We know how Reacher got to Mississippi so fast. He took a pickup belonging to Sam Roth. The guy Angela St. Vrain was on her way to see. He's dead, obviously, so no one reported it stolen. The guys we moved over from the intersection located it in the truck stop parking lot.'

'They found a truck?'

'Correct.'

'Who cares about a truck? Where's Reacher?'

'He must still be there.'

'Must be? You don't know?'

'The truck's still there. So Reacher must be, too. What's he going to do – walk the rest of the way? So, Bruno – chill. Our guys are there. They're staking it out. We'll hear the moment they have him.'

'Call them. Right now. Put them on speaker.'

'You need to take a valium.' Brockman took out his phone and dialled a number. It rang. And rang. And rang. Until it tripped through to voicemail. Brockman hung up without leaving a message. He dialled another number. That call ended up with voicemail, too. Brockman forced a smile. 'There's nothing to worry about. They must have their phones on silent. To avoid giving their positions away. They're being professional. That's a good thing.'

'Try the other two.'

Brockman dialled again. This time there was no ringtone. The call went straight to voicemail. The same thing happened

201

with the fourth number he tried. 'Their batteries are prob- ably flat. They've been there since three a.m., remember.'

'Something's wrong.'

'Everything's fine. Give it time. Be patient.'

'Did you order the guys back from Jackson?'

'Yes. Right after I left your office.'

'Call them again. Divert them to the truck stop as well.'

'Really? We need seven guys there?'

'We have four there already. Maybe five by now. Have they got the job done?'

Brockman called the guys who'd been at the Greyhound station and passed on Hix's instructions. He hung up. Put his phone away. Waited for Hix to leave. Then pulled his phone back out and dialled another number. He'd forgotten about the guys he had sent to watch the local bus stop. There was no reason to leave them in Jackson any longer. Which was a shame. Brockman could claim some kudos from connecting Reacher with Roth's truck. But he could have claimed a whole lot more if he'd caught Reacher in a trap that Hix hadn't even thought to set.

Reacher backed the Mercury into the space next to Sam Roth's truck. He was hoping that Pep would recognize it and think his buddy was coming to relieve him. Or that it was just some random person's car, on their way to use the facilities in the main building. Anything really, as long as he didn't take it as a threat. As long he didn't start strangling Hannah with the belt.

As long as he hadn't already strangled her.

Reacher jumped out of the car. He pulled the handle on the truck's rear door. It was locked. He couldn't see inside because of the tint on the window. He couldn't see what state

Pep was in. Or what state Hannah was in. He tried the driver's door. It was locked as well. He banged on the glass. Nothing happened. Hannah didn't release the lock.

She didn't. Or she couldn't.

Reacher took the Beretta from his waistband. He flipped it around so he was holding it by the barrel. Then he smashed the butt against the glass in the rear door like it was a hammer. He hit the window hard, low down in the corner at its weakest spot. The glass instantly formed into an opaque mesh of crystals. Reacher gave it a shove. It sagged. But it didn't give all the way. The film that caused the tint was too tough. And it extended too far. It went all the way up and sideways into the frame, and all the way down into the body of the door. Reacher slammed it with the heel of his hand. One side came free. He hit it again. The top and the other side loosened up. Then he hit it again and the whole sheet bent back. It curled and drooped like it was moving in slow motion. It bowed and crept down until it covered the inside surface of the door.

Pep glared out at Reacher through the empty window frame. His skin was even greener than before. His face was sweatier. And he was pulling on the belt with all his strength. Hannah was trying to claw it away from her throat. Her head was thrashing from side to side, but she was making no noise. She was getting no air. Reacher stretched his arm into the truck and punched Pep in the side of the head. Hard. He flopped over sideways and rolled into the footwell. He didn't move. He was out cold. He could no longer deliberately pull the belt. But it was still tied to his wrist. His weight was still keeping it taut.

Hannah still couldn't breathe.

Reacher scrabbled for the handle on the inside of the door,

but he couldn't get to it. The sheet of glass and tinting film was in the way. It was hanging down too far, like a shield. He tried to tear it off. But he couldn't. The film was too strong. So he grabbed the edge and pulled it up. He took hold of the opposite edge with his other hand. Forced the sides together until the sheet and his hands would fit through the frame. He wrestled it down, out of the way. Stretched his arm back in. Released the lock and opened the door.

Reacher hauled Pep upright and pushed him forward. Hannah coughed and spluttered and wheezed as the tension on the belt finally eased. She wriggled her fingers between it and her skin. Loosened it a little further. She sucked in a desperate, gasping breath. Reacher worked at the knot. It had been pulled tight by all the struggling. Pep's arm was still a dead weight. It took another thirty seconds to get it free, then Reacher slipped the loose end through the buckle.

Hannah flopped forward against the steering wheel. She groped for the door handle. Found it. Slid out. Collapsed on to the Mercury's trunk. She lay on her back. Stared at the sky. And breathed.

The atmosphere was foul. It was full of diesel and gasoline fumes from all the traffic in the parking lot and on the highway. Normally Hannah would be repulsed by it. She had grown up with the clear mountain air in Gerrardsville. But in that moment, she couldn't imagine how anything could taste sweeter.

Something told Jed Starmer to stop.

He had spent ten minutes hiding in the alley after he was done running from the scruffy guys' car. It had taken him that long to get his breath back. And to figure out what his next move should be. It was one thing to decide to leave town. But it was another to work out how. He had been hoping to get the rest of the way to Winson on a prison shuttle, but that was only because of the sign he'd seen in Texas. He didn't know for sure they had them in Mississippi. The sign had been in the Greyhound station in Dallas. He hadn't seen one in the station here, in Jackson. But he hadn't had the chance to look, because of the scruffy guys. And he couldn't go back now. The officers might have returned. They might be there, lying in wait for him. He didn't have a phone with internet access so he couldn't google the information. He couldn't risk wandering about at random. He might be spotted. But he could go old school. He remembered running past a stand of payphones, two blocks back. And he still had a few coins in his pocket.

First Jed called directory assistance. Then he called the Minerva facility in Winson. He told the receptionist he was an inmate's relative and he wanted to come visit but didn't know how to get to the prison. He asked if there was a shuttle service from Jackson. The receptionist said there wasn't. Not a dedicated one. Which was why most visitors used the local bus. She gave Jed the address of the stop. She even told him the departure times.

The bus was due to leave in four minutes. Jed had gotten close enough to hear the engine. It was rumbling steadily away, just around the corner. He'd had to run the last quarter-mile to give himself a chance of catching it. The next one wasn't due for another hour. He didn't want to be exposed on the street for that long. But a sudden thought had struck him. Officers had been at the Greyhound station. On the lookout for him. Detectives, or agents, or whatever they were. Which meant there could be more of them at the bus

205

stop. He could run right into them. There would be no way to avoid getting caught. It would be as bad as giving himself up.

Jed stopped. He was almost at the intersection. Then a guy on a bike ran straight into him. Some kind of a messenger. He had a satchel slung over his shoulder and he had been riding on the sidewalk. The impact sent Jed staggering forward. Past the end of the building. The force spun him around. The side of his foot caught in a gap between two paving slabs. He lost his balance. He fell. Rolled over. Came to a halt straddling the kerb. Half on the sidewalk. Half in the gutter. And fully in view of everyone at the bus stop.

People were staring at Jed. Maybe half a dozen. He didn't get a good look at them. And he didn't lie sprawling on the ground long enough to count heads. He just scrambled to his feet and darted back into the lee of the building, out of their sight.

The messenger had propped his bike against the wall. He was standing next to it, watching and waiting. As soon as Jed was in range he shoved him in the chest. He said, 'Idiot. Look where you're going. You could have got me killed.' Then he shoved Jed again and disappeared through a revolving glass door and into the last building on the block.

Jed thought about the people he had seen on the next street. Maybe they were only waiting to get on the bus. Or maybe they were watching it. Or maybe just a pair of them was. A pair of detectives. Or agents. Jed turned to run. And stopped himself again. He had nowhere to go. No other means of transport. The bus was his only shot at leaving town. He'd be crazy not to take it, if it was safe.

If.

Jed had to know for sure. So he crept back to the end of the building. He ducked down. Peered around the corner. And saw two guys. One was slipping a phone into his pocket. The guy gestured to his partner. To start moving. Which they did, straight away. Straight toward Jed.

The guys were both around six feet tall. They were broad. Strong-looking. Their hair was buzzed short. They were wearing jeans and T-shirts and suit coats. Just like the officers at the Greyhound station. They were the same height. The same build. They had the same menacing aura. They were yards away. And they were closing fast.

Jed knew he was finished. He had seen what the other officers had done to the scruffy guys. One had been unconscious within a split second. The other had gotten a gun jammed in his chest. Jed didn't want either of those things to happen to him. But he also knew he could never get away. Not on foot. The officers would be faster than him. And they would be trained to catch people. Plus, they could call for backup. Maybe dogs. Maybe air support. Jed sagged against the wall. He had come so far. He had gotten so close. Then his hand brushed against something. The front wheel of the messenger's bike.

The bike was right there. Next to him. It wasn't locked. That seemed like a sign he should take it. Jed wasn't a thief. He didn't want to steal it. But he also didn't want to get caught. And the messenger had behaved like a total asshole. So Jed decided it would be OK to just borrow the bike. Given the circumstances. Just for a little while. As short a time as possible. Then he could find a way to return it. Bike riding was not something Jed enjoyed. But it had to be better than anything those guys would do if they got their hands on him.

TWENTY-NINE

R eacher was half expecting the truck to be gone when he got back from dumping the Mercury. He left it in the corner on the far side of the lot, tucked in at the side of a donation box for a clothing charity that didn't look like it saw much action. Then he strolled back. He wanted Hannah to have plenty of time to think. To weigh up her options. She had been through a lot in the last couple of days. Finding Sam Roth's body. Learning that he had been murdered. Hearing that Angela St. Vrain had also been murdered. Almost getting murdered herself. Reacher wouldn't have blamed her if she'd jumped into the driver's seat the moment he was out of sight, headed for the highway and put as many miles between them as humanly possible.

The truck was still there. Hannah was standing next to it. A small red suitcase was at her side. A stripey tote bag was attached to its handle and she had her purse slung over her shoulder.

She said, 'We need to talk.'

Reacher said, 'No need to explain. Thanks for staying to say goodbye. And thanks for all your help.'

'What are you talking about? You think those assholes scared me off? Screw them. I was already all in. That goes double now they laid hands on me. No. We need to talk about Sam's truck. We can't use it any more.'

'Is it damaged?'

'Apart from the window, no. That's not the problem. Those guys? Who jumped me? They recognized it somehow. They were walking by, in a hurry, heading for the building, and suddenly they stopped. I saw them checking the licence plate. Then before I twigged what was happening the doors were open and they were inside, shoving their guns in my face. But the point is they must have connected you to Sam. And if they knew to look out for his truck, their buddies will too. At the next ambush. We'll never get through. We need to get a replacement vehicle.'

'You have a point, but our options are limited here. The guys who jumped you must have come in a vehicle. We could find it. Take it. But there's a good chance their buddies would recognize it, too. So there would be no benefit. Or we could steal a car from the parking lot, but it would be reported in minutes. Then we would be worse off. We might not make it to the next ambush at all.'

'Taking people's cars? Stealing other ones?' Hannah smiled and shook her head. 'I was thinking about something less extreme. More legal. We should get a rental car. There must be a bunch of depots in Jackson. Or if we don't want to schlep all that way, we could get one dropped off here. That would be more expensive, but a lot more convenient.'

'How long would that take?'

Hannah pulled her phone out of her purse. 'I'll see who has a car available. Then we can figure out the quickest option.' The screen lit up and her phone unlocked itself. 'And there's something else. When I was waiting for you to change, before those guys showed up, I checked the map to see what the rest of the route to Winson was like. And look.' She held out the phone so that Reacher could see the screen. 'See that red line? It means stationary traffic. I googled it and it turns out that's because of a construction zone. The road's down to a single lane. So this is where the ambush will be. Not the hill you found on the paper map. This is a much better place. We'll be stationary. So we'll be a sitting duck. There's no way they could miss us. Not in a recognizable vehicle. And there's no other route we could take.'

Reacher thought for a moment. 'Does Google say what kind of traffic management they have there? Lights? A guy with a stop/go board?'

'Google didn't. But I also found a couple of online message boards for inmates' families. There's a lot of talk about the problems people have when they go visit. One woman mentioned they're using a pilot vehicle. You know the kind of thing? Usually a pickup with a big illuminated sign in the load bed. It shuttles back and forth. Drivers have to wait until it comes and follow it to the other end. This woman said the driver was a jackass. She claimed he dawdled along extra slow and let the lines back up so much she missed half her visiting time.'

Reacher said, 'Can your phone show the view from a satellite?'

'Sure.' Hannah hit a button at the corner of the screen and flipped it around for Reacher to see. 'It's not a live feed, you know. You're not going to see the pilot vehicle moving around.'

'Don't need to.' Reacher studied the phone for a moment. 'I just need to see the terrain.' He nodded. 'We can make this work for us. We could get a rental car, but it would be better to use the truck. We can get a replacement vehicle delivered to the hotel later, if you want.'

'Sticking with the truck for now is the best way? You're sure?'

'One hundred per cent.'

'It's not about the cost? Because I'm happy to pay.'

'It's not the cost. Trust me.'

Hannah pointed to the truck's rear door. 'What about the window? We can't drive with it in that state.'

'Duct tape will fix it.'

'Duct tape?'

'You can fix anything with duct tape.'

'Are you serious?'

'Absolutely. Look – the tinting film is holding on to all the glass. All we need is something to secure it around the frame. Duct tape.'

'And do you have any? In your extensive selection of luggage, maybe? Because oddly enough, it's not something I carry in my purse.'

'They sell it in the store here. I saw it earlier.'

'Oh. Good. I guess.'

'I'll go grab some. And some emergency road flares. We're going to need those, too.'

'We are? Why?'

'We're going to do some traffic management of our own.'

*

211

Bruno Hix was back on his practice stage. The cameras were running. And this time he made it to the end of his speech in one take. *Pretty good*, he thought. *But could be better.*

Hix had just started his second run-through when the conference room door opened. It was Brockman.

Hix said, 'What now?'

Brockman was silent for a moment. Then he shook his head and said, 'You were right again.'

'About what, this time?'

'The truck stop. Something is wrong up there.'

'Explain.'

'Harold just called. He arrived and there was no sign of our other guys. He looked in all the places it would be logical for them to use on a stake-out. Nada. So he cast his net wider. He checked the parking lot. He cruised up and down every aisle. In the corner, the furthest one away from the building, by some charity donation thing, he found Nick's car. His Marauder. His pride and joy. Harold took a closer look. The doors were unlocked and the keys were on the driver's seat. He thought it looked low at the back. So he popped the trunk. And he was right.'

'Nick was in there? Hell and damnation. Was he alone? Or with whoever he was partnered up with? Steve, wasn't it? Were they alive? Or dead?'

'They were alive. But it wasn't Nick and Steve. Get this. It was Pep and Tony. The guys we sent over from the intersection.'

'How did they get in Nick's trunk?'

'No idea.'

'Where are Nick and Steve?'

'No idea. There was no sign of them anywhere.'

'What about the truck Pep found? The one Reacher was using.'

'It was gone. Harold thought he saw a red truck leaving when he arrived, but he couldn't be sure it was the same one.'

Hix was silent for a moment. 'OK. No point worrying about what's already happened. Call the guys at the construction zone. Give them the description of Reacher's truck. Make sure they know the plates.'

Brockman said, 'Already done.'

'Call them again. Make sure they know what they're dealing with. Tell Harold to get down there. And the guys from the Greyhound station. This Reacher's a menace. I don't want him in my town. Not tomorrow.'

Jed Starmer could finally see the appeal of riding a bike. He had never had the chance to do it very much in the past. He'd never owned one of his own. His foster parents would never have allowed it. So one day, a few months back, he'd badgered a friend into teaching him how to do it. The experience had not been much fun. Jed found that steering in a straight line was next to impossible. He wobbled all over the place. Hit every crack in the pavement. Every pothole. Bumped into a parked car. Fell off four times. Hurt his knee. And his elbow. And his chin. The other kids on the street all laughed at him. He was relieved when it was time to return the bike and limp his way back home. But that afternoon in Jackson, on the messenger's bike, everything was different. At first he only had one thing on his mind. Getting away from the officers who were closing in on him. He didn't worry about staying on two wheels or hurting himself or whether he looked ridiculous. He just raced down the sidewalk, bounced down off the kerb, and swooped and dodged between the cars and trucks that were grinding their way through the choked city streets. He kept going for ten minutes. Fifteen. Then something dawned on him. He was free and clear.

Jed pulled over to the side of the street. He needed to find somewhere to leave the bike where it would be safe. Then, if he could just recall the name of the messenger service he had seen on the guy's bag when they collided, he could find a phone number. He could call and tell someone where the owner would find the bike.

Jed had never intended to keep the bike for long. But he had not anticipated how useful it would be. Or how fun. And he did still have another problem. He had to get to Winson. He couldn't take the bus. He didn't have enough money for a cab. And he couldn't risk standing around in plain sight, trying to hitch a ride. The bike was the obvious answer.

Jed's notes were lost. They had been in his backpack. But he figured he had about fifty miles to go. Sixty at the most. The bike was fast. Easy to pedal. It would only take what, a couple of hours? Maybe three? He could call the messenger service when he arrived in the town. The guy would have to travel a little further to retrieve his bike, but that was too bad. He shouldn't have been such an asshole. Really, he was lucky it was Jed he had encountered. Anyone else would have kept the bike. Or sold it. Jed had no doubt about that. Not after having his backpack stolen. And all his money.

THIRTY

Hannah pulled the truck over on to the shoulder when the GPS in her phone said they were half a mile from the start of the construction zone. Reacher opened the passenger door and climbed out. Hannah had the pack of emergency flares on her lap, ready to go. She grabbed her purse from the back seat and took out her gun. The little SIG Reacher had first seen outside Gerrardsville when they began their journey together. She tucked it into a gap at the side of the driver's seat, then felt Reacher watching her.

Hannah turned and looked at him. 'Any other assholes try anything, I'll be ready. No one's going to sneak up on me. Not again.'

Reacher said, 'You had much practice with that?'

'Hell, yes. Been shooting my whole life. It was the one thing about me my daddy didn't hate.'

'You didn't get along?'

'We did. When I was a little kid.'

'Your mom?'

'Died when I was eight.'

'Sorry to hear that.'

'Not your fault. No one's fault. Guess it's no one's fault my daddy was a bigoted asshole, either, but hey. You play the hand you're dealt. And he did teach me to shoot, which is how I got close to Sam. He worked at the prison. I worked with the parolees. In our free time we'd hang out at the range. So not all bad in the end.'

It would normally take Reacher no more than five minutes to cover half a mile on foot. That afternoon he agreed with Hannah to give it twenty. The road was lined with trees, but it wasn't clear on her phone's screen how dense they were. The only certainty was that the land beyond them was flat and open. There was no other cover, so Reacher wanted to be able to move slowly and smoothly. To stop where necessary. And he wanted to be in position in plenty of time.

Reacher covered the ground in fifteen minutes. The dirt was damp in places and patches of ankle-high grass and weeds made the cuffs of his pants wet and soggy. A rich, musty smell rose up wherever he disturbed the surface. The trees were scattered and patchy and more than a dozen times he had to pause to make sure he wouldn't be seen by passing vehicles. There were individual ones heading west, toward Winson, spread out at random intervals. And little convoys, packed close together, heading east.

Reacher stayed behind the treeline until he was level with the spot where the road got cut down to one lane. He found a shallow depression, maybe left by a dried-up stream, maybe by an abandoned irrigation system. He lay down in it, pressed himself into the ground and settled in to watch. Twelve cars were waiting behind a line that had been painted on the blacktop near a sign warning drivers not to proceed unless they were escorted by the pilot vehicle. A guy was making his way along the shoulder, heading toward the end of the row. He was wearing jeans, a grey T-shirt and black boots. He was carrying a clipboard and he had a yellow safety helmet on his head. He leaned down and looked into each vehicle he passed, checking any passengers. Another guy, a similar height but with a white helmet, was keeping pace on the other side of the vehicles, checking their drivers. The props weren't fooling anyone, Reacher thought. These guys were obviously the next Minerva crew. The only question was whether they were just being thorough or if they hadn't been told about Roth's truck. Reacher smiled to himself. Maybe they did know about it. But if they didn't, they soon would.

The area between Reacher and the road had been flattened and a square section of grass had been replaced with gravel. It was covered with tyre tracks. There were multiple sets. They partially overlapped and all of them entered the space at almost the same spot. The top right-hand corner, from Reacher's perspective. They followed the same loop around, near the edge, and led back out on to the asphalt to Reacher's left, still all together. An SUV was parked in the centre of the rough circle the tracks formed, perpendicular to the road, with its rear facing Reacher. A Ford Explorer. It was burgundy with gold pinstripes and chunky tyres with white letters on the sidewalls. It looked old, but shiny and well cared for.

At the far side of the road, on the shoulder, there was a porta-potty with faded blue-and-white plastic walls. Next to it

217

there was a grey metal box the size of a shipping container. Reacher figured it would be an equipment store. Next to that there was a dump trailer. It was loaded pretty full with tree branches and a net was strung over the top to stop its contents falling or getting blown out. The name, number and web address of the hire company was stencilled on the side.

There was only one thing missing from the scene. Construction workers. There was no sign of any activity at all behind the long line of traffic cones.

Reacher heard the drone of engines approaching from his right and thirty seconds later the pilot vehicle appeared. A line of cars was following in its wake like ducklings trailing their mother. The pilot turned on to the gravel square. It looped around the Explorer, adding another set of tyre tracks, and came to a stop at the side of the road. The cars it had been escorting swung back into their own lane and continued heading east. The pilot pulled out. It was facing west now. It paused, then set off and the waiting cars began to follow.

The guys in the jeans and T-shirts walked back and stopped by the line on the asphalt. They waited, but no more cars appeared from the east. Reacher saw them exchange glances, shrug and cross to the Explorer. They tossed their helmets and clipboards on to the back seat and climbed in the front. They had been at the site for a long time. They felt they deserved a break.

They weren't going to get one.

Reacher heard another engine approaching. A big diesel, coming from his left. The guys in the Explorer picked it up twenty seconds later. They climbed out. Opened the back doors. Started to reach for their props. Then they saw what kind of vehicle was making the sound. A red pickup truck. It had black glass and lots of chrome. It slowed, then stopped in front of the warning sign. The guys checked its licence plate. Then they started moving toward it. They fanned out, one on each side, and paused when they were ten feet away. Each of them had pulled a gun from his waistband.

Reacher got to his feet and started to creep forward.

The guy on the driver's side of the truck yelled, 'All right. Good job getting this far. But your luck's run out. This is the end of the line. Get out, slowly, hands where I can see them.'

There was no response from inside the truck.

Reacher moved a little further.

The guy yelled, 'Do as I tell you and no one will get hurt. We just want to talk. So come on. Get out.'

The truck's doors stayed closed.

Reacher kept moving.

The guy yelled, 'Last chance. Get out or get shot.'

A noise came from the back of the truck. A piercing electronic shriek. It lasted two seconds. Then there was a whirring sound. Then a clunk. The truck's tailgate had opened. The guys raised their guns. They started moving toward it, slowly, trying to stay silent. They made it halfway along the side of the load bed. Three quarters. Then all the way to the back. They paused. They glanced at each other. The guy on the driver's side held up three fingers. He folded one down. He folded the second. Then the third. Both guys took another step. A big one, on the diagonal. Their guns were raised. They were pointing directly into the load bed.

The truck started moving. It accelerated hard. The pedal must have been all the way to the floor. Its rear wheels spun and skittered and kicked up handfuls of grit. The sharp fragments flew through the air like shrapnel. The guys turned and bent and covered their faces. It was an instinctive reaction. But it only lasted for a second. They straightened up and raised their guns and started firing at the truck. Its tailgate was closing again. The guy on the passenger side hit it with one round. The guy on the driver's side was going for the tyres. He did some damage to the blacktop, but nothing else. They each squeezed off another couple of shots, then the guy on the passenger side started running toward the Explorer.

'Come on,' the guy yelled. 'He can't get far.'

The other guy followed him. They jumped inside. The guy behind the wheel pulled out his keys. He jammed one into the ignition. But he didn't fire up the engine.

Reacher was sitting in the centre of the rear seat. Both his arms were stretched out. He had the captured SIG in his left hand. The Beretta in his right. He pressed the muzzles against the back of both guys' heads and said, 'Open the windows.'

The driver turned his key one notch clockwise and buzzed both front windows all the way down.

Reacher said, 'Throw out your guns.'

The guys did as they were told.

Reacher said, 'Do you know who I am?'

Both guys nodded.

'Then you know you need to cooperate. I want some infor-mation. Give it to me, then you can go.'

The driver said, 'We can't. We don't know anything.'

'You work for Minerva?'

The driver nodded.

'Is anyone else looking for me between here and Winson?'

Neither of the guys answered.

Reacher pulled the guns back. He slid the SIG between his knees. Then he leaned through the gap between the front seats and punched the passenger just next to his ear. The guy's head snapped sideways. It smashed into the window, bounced back a few inches, then the guy slumped face first into the dashboard.

Reacher raised the Beretta again. 'Hands on the wheel. Move, and I'll blow your head off. Do you understand?'

The driver grabbed the wheel. His hands were in the ten-to-two position and his knuckles were white like a nervous teenager's before his first lesson.

Reacher said, 'Do you know what I just did?'

'You knocked out Wade.'

'I gave you plausible deniability.'

The driver didn't react.

'Plausible deniability,' Reacher said. 'It means you can do something, then say you didn't and no one can prove otherwise. Like, you can answer my questions.'

The guy didn't respond.

'You can tell me what I need to know. No one will ever find out. Then you can drive away. Lie low for a couple of days. Claim you escaped. Or I could break your arms and legs and throw you in the nearest dumpster. Your choice.'

The guy glanced to his right, but he didn't speak.

Reacher said, 'The cavalry isn't coming. Think about it. How many lanes are open?'

'One.'

'What just drove that way?'

'The truck you stole.'

'Correct. So it's going to meet the pilot vehicle, head on. The person driving it is stubborn like you wouldn't believe. No way is she going to back up again. It's going to take hours to sort that mess out.'

The guy glanced to his left.

221

'No one can get through that way, either. We covered all the bases. It's just you and me. And you have a decision to make.'

The guy was silent for another moment, then he said, 'What do you want to know?'

'Has Brockman got anyone else looking for me between here and Winson?'

'How would I know? Brockman doesn't share his plans with me.'

'Brockman's a smart man, I guess. Relatively speaking. So what did he share?'

'A picture of you. An old one. A description of the truck you stole. And its licence plate.'

'What were your orders?'

'To stop you getting to Winson.'

'Why doesn't Brockman want me to get to Winson?'

'He didn't say.'

'What's happening there in the next couple of days?'

'Nothing special. Some con's getting released tomorrow. There'll be speeches. Some celebrating. It happens a few times every year. The shine's wearing off, to be honest. People are getting used to it now.'

'What else?'

The guy shrugged. 'Nothing.'

'OK. You did the right thing. Start it up. You can go now.'

The guy paused for a moment, frozen. Then his hand shot out. He grabbed the key. Turned it, and the heavy old motor spluttered into life.

'One other thing before you get on your way,' Reacher said. 'See that trailer, over on the far shoulder?'

The guy nodded.

Reacher said, 'Pull up next to it.'

The guy shifted into drive, released the brake, looped around to the opposite shoulder and eased to a stop.

Reacher said, 'Get out for a moment. There's something I need you to do. You can leave the engine running.'

The guy opened his door and climbed down. Reacher did the same and led the way around to the passenger side.

Reacher said, 'See the net that's holding down all the junk? Peel back one corner.'

The guy fiddled with the nearest cleat and released part of the net.

Reacher said, 'Pull out some of those branches at the top. And the bushes. Clear some space.'

The guy grabbed a few of the bigger pieces and dumped them on the ground.

Reacher said, 'Good. Now get your buddy out of the car. Put him in the space you made.'

The guy said, 'Put him in the trailer?'

'Right. We have to make this look realistic. Brockman won't believe you escaped otherwise. He'll think you helped me. That's not what you want to happen. Believe me.'

The guy was still for moment. His mouth was gaping slightly. Then he shrugged and opened the passenger door. He pushed his buddy back in the seat. His head lolled to the side. The guy grabbed his wrists. Hauled him out. Swung him on to his shoulder. Manoeuvred him to the end of the trailer. Set him down on the spoil from the construction work. Then he took hold of the net and started to pull it back into place.

'Wait,' Reacher said. 'I need to borrow your phone for a second.'

The guy shrugged, then took his phone out of his pocket, entered a code to unlock its screen and held it out. Reacher took it and set it on the ground.

He said, 'One more question. The guys Brockman sent to the Greyhound station had to watch out for me on every bus that arrived. All kinds of people would have been milling around. Places like that get pretty chaotic. That's a tall order. The guys at the truck stop had to keep an eye on hundreds of people, coming and going. That's a real challenge. The guys at the intersection didn't know if I would be hitching a ride or already in a car, speeding past. That's like two tasks in one, and neither of them is easy. But you? All you had to do was look through a window. Why do you think you were chosen for that particular job?'

'No idea.'

'No?'

Reacher punched the guy in the solar plexus. That doubled him over forward. Then Reacher drove his knee up into the guy's face. That stood him up again, unconscious, with his arms flailing helplessly at his sides. Reacher shoved the guy's chest and folded him back the other way. He was left with his torso lying on top of the trailer. Reacher grabbed his ankles, lifted, twisted, and dropped him next to his buddy. He threw the branches back in to cover them. Fixed the net in place. Then he picked up the guy's phone and dialled the number for the hire company.

A woman answered after three rings. 'Reed Plant Partners. How can I help?'

Reacher said, 'I'm with the crew doing construction out on 87. We have one of your trailers. Could you confirm when it's scheduled for return?'

Computer keys rattled then the woman's voice came back on the line. 'You have it booked through the end of next month.'

'Can we return it early?'

'It's a fixed-term contract. There are no refunds for early returns.'

'We're not looking for a refund. We just need it off site.'

'Understood. You can bring it back whenever you like. You just have to pay until the date you signed up for.'

'Could you send someone to collect it?'

'There'd be an extra charge.'

'That's fine.'

'I could get someone out on Monday.'

'How about this afternoon?'

'All our guys are busy today.'

'Look, I'm in a bind here. My boss really wants that trailer gone. If there's any way you could swing it, I'd be grateful.'

The woman didn't respond.

Reacher said, 'If there's an extra-extra charge, that would be fine too. As in the kind that doesn't show up on an invoice.'

The woman was silent for a moment longer, then she said, 'It'll cost you a hundred bucks. Cash. Have it ready.'

THIRTY-ONE

Patience is a virtue, Reacher's father used to say. If he was right, then the drivers heading away from Winson that afternoon must have been a really despicable bunch.

Hannah's job had been to block the single-lane stretch of road in the construction zone. She had done it well. She had steered hard right on to the shoulder, reversed toward the line of cones, then swung back and forward four times until the truck was pretty much perpendicular. Her positioning was perfect. The truck's nose was covering three quarters of the shoulder. She hadn't left enough space for anyone to squeeze around the rear. And she'd picked the ideal spot. A giant machine for tearing up the asphalt was parked on the other side so there was no future in anyone trying to move the cones.

Hannah had been stationary for two minutes when the next convoy came into view. The pilot led it closer. And closer.

226

And he didn't slow down. Hannah panicked for a moment. She thought the guy wasn't going to stop. She had a vision of the vehicles ploughing into the side of the truck. One after another. Blow after blow. The truck rolling over. Her getting crushed. Or burned alive. Or both.

The pilot must not have been concentrating. He had driven up and down that stretch of road hundreds of times since the construction project started. He had never come across any kind of obstruction. He had never expected to. So he noticed the truck late. But in time. Just. He threw all his weight on the brake. His wheels locked. His tyres slid on the gravel. But he stopped with maybe a yard to spare.

The vehicles behind the pilot all braked too. None of them collided. A couple honked their horns as if that would help. One driver pulled past the rest and tried to swing around the front of Hannah's truck. He left the shoulder and started to bump across the rough strip of scrubland at the side of the road. He thought he was home and dry. He flipped Hannah off. Then his wheel hit a rut. His truck shuddered to a stop. It listed down toward one corner. There was only one explanation. Its axle was broken. And given the age and the condition of the vehicle, its next stop was most likely going to be the scrapyard.

The driver jumped out and marched up to Hannah's door. He tugged on the handle. It was locked so he started yelling at the window. Flecks of spittle sprayed all over the glass. Other drivers climbed down and joined him. Ten more of them. That was everyone except the pilot. He stayed in his cab and dialled 911. He figured that was his civic duty. And with that done he felt free to sit back and let the chips fall where they may.

By the time Reacher arrived there were four drivers behind

Hannah's truck. They were trying to shove it out of their way and getting nowhere. There were three drivers on one side, baying and screaming, and four on the other.

'Enough.' Reacher stopped six feet from the rear of the truck. 'Be quiet. Get back in your vehicles.'

The guy from the stranded truck said, 'No way. This asshole's blocking the road. My rig's messed up because of him. He's got to pay.'

'Really? Because this is my truck. It's here because I told the driver to block the road. If you have a problem with that, then you have a problem with me.'

Reacher looked at each driver, one at a time. Calmly. Levelly. Right in the eyes. Most of them started to edge away. A couple stayed still. The guy from the stranded truck stepped forward. 'You know what? I do have a problem. My vehicle is totalled. If that's on you, then you better put your hand in your pocket.'

The drivers who had been moving all immediately stopped.

Reacher gestured to the stricken truck. It looked like it was trying to bury itself in the ground. 'That thing?'

The guy nodded.

'Sorry, pal. I used my last quarter in a payphone, last week. You're SOL.'

The guy swung at Reacher's head with a wild right hook. Reacher leaned back and watched the fist sail harmlessly past. The guy's shoulders twisted around and he wound up horribly off balance. All his weight was on his left leg. Reacher swept it out from under him. The guy pitched forward. He fell almost horizontally. Hit the dirt with his face. Tried to get up. But Reacher put his foot between his shoulder blades, pushed him back down and held him in place.

Reacher said, 'Guys, use your heads. You want to get going.

228

I want to get going. But none of us can go anywhere while you're hanging around like some lame-ass mob.'

No one spoke. No one moved. For a moment. Then a driver at the back of the crowd turned and slunk away. The guy who had been next to him followed. A couple more began to move. Then another couple, until all the drivers were shuffling toward their vehicles, grumbling and muttering and shaking their heads. Reacher leaned down and rolled the guy on the ground on to his front. He grabbed his shirt and hoisted him on to his feet. The guy scowled but stayed silent. Reacher shoved him into the lee of the truck where no one could see what would happen next.

Reacher said, 'Is your truck really a write-off?'

The guy scowled. 'I think so. I felt the suspension go.'

'How much is it worth?'

'Five grand.'

'How much in US dollars, here on planet Earth?'

'A grand. Maybe.'

Reacher pulled out his roll of cash, peeled off five hundred dollars and handed them to the guy. 'Here's half. The other half is on you. Consider this a learning experience. Use better judgement in future. If you had stayed on the road and shown a little patience, your truck would still be running.'

Jed Starmer finally admitted that he'd been right the first time. Riding a bike was a total pain in the ass.

It was a pain in the ass. The calves. The thighs. The back. The shoulders. The neck. In pretty much every part of his body. Jed had never been so uncomfortable in his entire life. All he could think was, *People do this for fun? What the hell is wrong with them?*

Everything had been fine while Jed was in the city of

Jackson. The streets were level. There was plenty of traffic so the vehicles had to move slowly. The drivers seemed used to bikes weaving around them. And Jed had to pay attention to finding his way. He remembered that there was only one road to Winson. He didn't have a map so he had to watch out extra carefully for signs. Twice he thought he was lost. But he kept on going and pretty soon the buildings grew smaller and further apart. The trees became taller and closer together. The fields stretched out beyond them. Jed raised his head and looked around. He thought his new surroundings were nice.

At first.

More things changed than the view as Jed rode deeper into the countryside. There were fewer vehicles, but the ones that were around drove much faster. They passed closer to him. He nearly got knocked off the bike half a dozen times. The nervousness from his first lesson came flooding back. And he kept coming to uphill stretches of road. It felt like massive weights were attached to his wheels. Every push on the pedals was a hundred times harder than on the flat. The sun was dipping low, but the air was still hot. Jed was sweating. He was thirsty. He was hungry. He hadn't eaten for more than twelve hours. His head was feeling light. His legs were soft and rubbery. He was praying for a nice long downward slope. For a few minutes when gravity could do the work. When he could rest. When he could pick up a little speed and the wind would rush by and cool his body.

Jed slogged his way around another bend. Looked up. And found himself at the foot of the tallest mountain he had ever seen.

The road into Winson was long and straight and lined with trees. The soft afternoon sunshine filtered through the leaves and cast a web of dappled shadows all along the faded black-top. It was the kind of image Reacher had seen in Sunday newspaper articles about places parents should take their kids for picnics on school vacations. It looked idyllic. There was nothing to indicate that a town lay ahead.

Or a prison.

Or the people who had murdered Angela St. Vrain and Sam Roth.

A couple of miles beyond the sign announcing the town boundary the trees thinned and buildings began to appear. Mainly houses. Mainly single-storey ones, spread apart from each other but standing near to the street. Most of them had wooden sides with dirty white paint that was peeling in handfuls. Plenty had roofs that looked like they were one decent storm away from getting blown completely off.

'I read about this place last night in the hotel before I went to sleep,' Hannah said. 'It has a crazy history. Originally it was a Native American settlement. The French drove them out in, like, 1720. The British took the place from the French. The Spanish moved in when the British quit after the Revolutionary War. They were supposed to be on our side but they didn't want to hand the town over so we took it from them. It thrived while all the trade was centred on the river. There are rumours of a second town, like a shadow, at the bottom of the cliff. Stories of caves and liquor and whores and stolen gold and smuggled jewels. Even if any of that was true, it's all gone now. Blown up, or flooded. Then the river trade faded and the railroads and industry took over. Paper mills, mainly, because of all the trees that grow here. Now the industry's gone too. Which is why there are so many old houses, I guess. And why so many of them are about to fall down.'

Hannah drove in silence for a while, and as they came closer to the town they saw the standard of maintenance improve. The size of the homes increased. They grew closer together. The balance shifted to mainly two-storey properties. Most were still white, but their paint was fresh and bright. Some were blue. Some were yellow. Many had shutters. Most had porches running their full width. Some had verandas with solid columns and ornate wooden railings. The sidewalks that passed them were wide and there were tall, mature trees forming a border with the road.

In the town itself wood construction gave way to brick. There were still plenty of balconies and verandas but with spindly supports and ornate iron railings painted gloss black. It felt like a small-scale copy of New Orleans, Reacher thought. The roofs were mainly flat. The windows were larger, some were square, some had curved tops. There were lots of alleyways. There was parking down both sides of all the streets. Half the spaces were empty. Reacher saw a couple of cafés. A few bars. A small church, built of brick with clumsy stained glass. It looked like it had recently been rebuilt, but on a budget. There was a range of businesses. A pawn shop with guns and guitars hanging two deep in the window. An insurance agent. A tyre bay. A handful of small bed and breakfasts. A fishmonger. A cellphone store. A body shop.

Hannah and Reacher drove around for half an hour. They started at Main Street and quartered the blocks on either side until they had a good sense of the place. Finally they stopped outside a coffee shop. Hannah went in and grabbed two large cups to go. She climbed back into the truck, handed a cup to Reacher and said, 'Hotel?'

Reacher shook his head. 'Prison first. Then food. Then the hotel.'

THIRTY-TWO

J ed Starmer was sitting at the side of the road. The messenger's bike was lying on the shoulder, to his left, where it had fallen after he jumped off.

Jed stared at the bike and sighed. He hadn't really jumped off. He had intended to. He had tried to. But his legs weren't working the way they usually did. So he had pretty much fallen off, if he was honest. Staggered, maybe, or stumbled, if he wanted to put a positive spin on it.

The thing he couldn't put a positive spin on lay to his right. The mountain. Or really, the hill. Or the slope. He had used the minutes he'd been sitting there to rein in his imagination. He wasn't facing Mount Everest. Or the Eiger. Or Kilimanjaro. The rise was probably no more than a hundred feet. But whether it was a hundred or thirty thousand, it made no difference. There was no way Jed could ride up it. He wouldn't even be able to push the bike to the top, the way his legs were shaking. He would just have to sit where he was.

Probably for the rest of his life, since no one was going to come and help him.

Reacher figured that the prison was Winson's equivalent of a portrait in the attic. It was ugly. Unattractive. Hidden away to the west of the town. If it was any further away it would be in the river. But it was what kept the town alive. What made it vibrant. That was clear. There was no other industry to speak of. No other sources of employment. Nothing else to keep the local bakers and launderettes and plumbers and electricians busy on any kind of substantial scale.

The prison site was shaped like a 'D'. The curved side was formed by the riverbank. Beyond it was a seventy-foot drop straight into deep, dirty, fast-flowing water. A fence ran ten feet back from the edge. It had two layers. They were twenty feet high with rolls of razor wire strung along the top. There were floodlights on stout metal poles. And cameras in protective cages. There was a fifteen-foot gap between layers, and another fence ran along the centre line. It was ten feet high, and it had no wire.

The fences continued in the same way along the straight side of the site. The side facing the town. There were four watchtowers level with the outer layer of wire. And three entrances. One was in the centre. It led into a building. It was single-storey, built of brick, with double doors, which were closed, and a video intercom on the door frame. That would be the visitors' entrance, Reacher thought. The staff probably used it, too. The other entrances were at the far ends. They had full-height gates rather than doors. And no signs. One was probably used for supplies. The other would be for shipping in fresh inmates.

Inside the fence, on the river side of the site, there were

five buildings in a line. They were shaped like 'X's. Reacher guessed they would be the cell blocks. The rest of the space was filled with twelve other buildings and three exercise areas. The buildings were all different sizes. They were plain and utilitarian. They could have been factories or warehouses if it weren't for the razor wire and watchtowers that surrounded them. The exercise areas were all the same size, but they were physically separate. Presumably to keep the different categories of prisoners isolated in their own allocated spaces.

The buildings and exercise areas were joined by walkways. The walls and roofs were made of wire mesh. Even from a distance Reacher could see it was thick. Substantial. Anyone would need serious tools to stand a chance of getting through it. Outside, around the buildings and between the walkways, there were some patches of grass. A surprising number, Reacher thought, for such a grim institution. There were squares. Rectangles. Ovals. And twenty feet from the base of each watchtower there was a brick-lined triangle.

The grass was well cared for. It was trimmed short. Edged neatly. And probably fed or fertilized, given the way its deep green stood out against the pale walls of the buildings and the grey blur of the wire mesh. The only other structure inside the fence was newer. It was V-shaped and shoehorned in behind the security building. It was styled like some kind of corporate headquarters and there was a three-dimensional Minerva logo on a plinth, rotating, out front. Reacher figured if any prisoners got loose that would be the first thing to get destroyed.

He said, 'Did you read anything about riots happening here recently?'

Hannah said, 'Nothing official. But on one of the message boards a woman was complaining about her husband getting

235

hurt by a guard. It was during a brawl in the exercise yard. Thirty or forty guys were involved, but her husband was the only one the guard laid into. She complained, and got told her husband had been trying to escape. They said they'd let it slide, but if she made trouble about his injuries he'd wind up getting his sentence extended.'

'Have there been any successful escapes?'

'I don't think so. I didn't come across anything, anyway.'

Reacher was not surprised. The place looked well put together. According to what he'd read in the file he found in Angela St. Vrain's purse, it had been built by the state. Those guys knew what they were doing when it came to locking people up. Reacher had some experience of prisons himself. He had been a military cop. He had put plenty of people inside them. Visited suspects to take statements. Caught inmates who had broken out. Grilled them to find out how. He had even been locked up himself, a couple of times.

The first precaution Reacher noticed was also the simplest. The perimeter was protected by a fence, not a wall. That meant the guards could see everyone who approached any part of the place. They could see if anyone was carrying equipment to break in with or items to throw over. And there were red triangles attached to the fences. They were spaced out at fifteen-foot intervals and they ranged from two to six feet above the ground. Reacher was too far away to read the writing, but the symbol of a stick figure flying backward after getting zapped carried a clear enough message. The fences were electrified. The outer ones would only be powerful enough to knock a person on their ass. That would serve as a warning. It would be the inner fence, all small and innocuous, sandwiched between the ones with the wire on top, that would carry the lethal voltage.

Reacher would bet there were vibration sensors in the ground that would trip if anyone got too close to the fence. Alarms that would trigger if the voltage in the fences dropped. Dogs that would be released if the power failed or got sabotaged. The entrances would all be secured. The one for visitors and staff would be like an airport, with X-ray machines and metal detectors. The vehicle gates would have an airlock arrangement so that the trucks and vans could be held between the layers of fence on their way in or out. Inside the buildings the service ducts would be too narrow for anyone to crawl in or climb up. They would have movement sensors and mesh screens, anyway. The doors and gates in the secure areas would all be centrally controlled, with no keypads for inmates to learn or guess the codes for, like you see in the movies. And if all else failed, there were the watchtowers. Two would be sufficient. The prison had four. A guard in each one with a rifle could cover the whole interior of the stockade plus five hundred feet beyond the perimeter, assuming an adequate level of equipment and training.

The area in front of the prison was laid out in a semicircle. There were swathes of grass and neat, colourful flowerbeds all following the same curve. They looked incongruous, like a bizarre attempt to copy the formal gardens of a European chateau. The only things missing were the fountains. But Reacher knew the real purpose was not aesthetic. It was to maintain a clear field of fire from the two central towers in the event of a breakout. Or an attempt to break in.

There was a broad paved strip around the outside of the semicircle. It was wide enough for vehicles to park in. The left was the staff area. It was half full. Mainly with pickups. Older American models. Some were not in great shape. There were a few sedans sprinkled among them. Mainly domestic, from the cheaper end of the range. Then, at the far side, separated by half a dozen empty spaces, there were three newer vehicles. A Dodge Ram in silver with chrome wheels and a shiny treadplate toolchest slung across its load bed. A BMW sedan, larger than the one Reacher had encountered in Colorado, but also black. Its licence plate read MC1. And a Mercedes, in white, with MC2 on its plate.

The visitors' parking was to the right. There was only one car in that whole area. A VW Bug. It was metallic green. It had two soft tyres. Its running board was hanging off on one side. It wasn't clear if it had been parked or abandoned.

Hannah opened the driver's door and turned to Reacher. 'You ready? We've been here too long. We should go.'

Reacher nodded and climbed in alongside her. There was nothing more to see. But he was left thinking that he knew how an epidemiologist must feel after staring at a sample from a patient with a baffling new disease. On the surface everything looked normal, but he knew there was something wrong. He just didn't know what. Yet.

Bruno Hix was sitting at his desk. He was staring at his computer screen. And his own face was staring back.

The image was magnified. Hix's mouth was gaping open. His eyes were half shut. He looked drunk. Or demented. Or worse, ugly. Hix stamped his foot. Getting two video streams to play side by side was harder than he'd expected. One at a time was fine. But both together, he just couldn't figure out. He had called the prison's IT expert, but the guy had already quit for the day. He was at home, preparing dinner for his cats. He was supposedly coming back, but he was taking his sweet time. A person could crawl faster. Hix was not happy.

He needed to have a word with Riverdale. It was time for some staff changes. And soon.

Hix's office door opened. Slowly.

Hix turned and said, 'Where the . . .'

He saw Brockman framed in the doorway.

'Oh,' Hix said. 'It's you. Is there news?'

Brockman nodded.

Hix said, 'Good news?'

Brockman said, 'Just news.'

'Let's hear it.'

'Harold called. He got to the construction site. Our guys were not there.'

'They deserted their post? What happened? Were they threatened? Bribed?'

'They just disappeared. Brad's Explorer was there, parked in exactly the same place Harold saw it earlier. But there was no sign of Brad or Wade.'

'So what happened?'

'No idea. Harold spoke to the driver of the pilot vehicle. He said there had been a weird incident. He said he was heading east, as usual, and he came across a truck blocking the road. He didn't see the plate, but it was the same model as the one Reacher stole. The same colour.'

'Did he see Reacher?'

'It sounds like it. Here's what Harold said happened. The pilot stopped, assuming the truck was trying to turn around for some reason. He figured it would get out of the way, sooner or later. But the other drivers got antsy. They surrounded the truck. Tried to push it. And got nowhere, naturally. It was just some crazy mass-hysteria thing. They were still trying when a huge guy showed up from the opposite side.'

'Reacher?'

'Well, he chased these other drivers away. Ten of them. And he kicked another guy's ass, apparently. Draw your own conclusion. Then he got in the truck and drove off.'

'What did Harold do?'

'He figured Brad and Wade had gotten knocked out and the guy was dumping them like he'd done with Pep and Tony at the truck stop. The roadblock was for cover. So Harold searched for them. He found nothing. But he's still trying.'

'So we still don't know where our guys are?'

'No.'

'And Reacher?'

'We don't know where he is either.'

'Well, obviously, he got past the roadblock. He could be in town any time. He could already be here. Call Harold. Tell him to come back. Right now.'

'What about Brad and Wade?'

'What about them? They had one job. They failed. We're better off without them.'

Hannah had been using her phone to do some more research while Reacher was scoping out the prison. About food, this time. The next thing on their agenda.

She had found the place people said sold the best burgers in town. She suggested they should head straight there, get some carry-out and take it to their hotel. That wasn't an approach Reacher favoured. He preferred to show up and see how a place looked for himself. He appreciated a good diner. And he was totally opposed to anything that smacked of running and hiding. Reacher was wired to move toward danger. To confront it. To defeat it, or die trying. It was baked into his DNA. But he could tell that Hannah was approaching her limit. She knew people were looking for them. The same group of people who had tried to kill her. It was reasonable for her to want to get off the street. To be out of sight as quickly as possible. It would have been cruel to force her to do otherwise, so Reacher didn't argue.

The burger place was four blocks north of Main Street in a building that used to be a gas station. Its original pumps were still there, now repurposed as decorations with neon lights. The forecourt had been turned into a parking area. The tables were in the main building behind large, curved windows and under an extravagant gull-wing roof.

The drive-through counter was where the old night-service window had been. Hannah pulled up next to it. She ordered, paid and had a paper sack full of food in her hand inside three minutes. She had gotten one burger with a single patty, mushrooms and truffle aioli for herself and two doubles with American cheese and nothing green for Reacher. She waited another minute for their two large coffees to come out then moved toward the exit. She entered the hotel's address into the map on her phone and a robot voice told her to *proceed to the route*. Reacher didn't find that advice helpful.

Once they were back on Main Street the phone directed them to the east, away from the centre of town. The hotel was near the river, to the north. It wasn't far as the crow flies, but a ridge of trees meant there was no direct route. The sun was low in the sky. Dense branches overhead cut the available daylight further. The road was quiet. They didn't see another vehicle for five minutes. Then a car appeared. It came closer and the shape of a lightbar solidified on its roof. It passed them. Its roof bar lit up. The narrow corridor between the trees started to pulse with red and blue. Then the car turned and sped back toward the truck.

241

Hannah said, 'Oh, please, no. What now? What do we do?'

Reacher said, 'There's nothing to worry about. We haven't done anything wrong.'

'We haven't? Those six guys you beat up might tell a different story.'

'They're not here. And they're in no position to call 911. Trust me. This is just routine bullshit. It's going to be fine.'

'What if it isn't?'

Reacher said nothing.

Hannah pulled the truck over to the side of the road. The police car tucked in behind with its lights still flashing. The cop stayed inside for a couple more minutes. Reacher didn't know if he was checking something, calling for reinforcements, or just trying to play mind games. He didn't care which, as long the cop didn't keep it up for too long. He didn't want his burgers to get cold.

The cop finally climbed out and approached the driver's window. He lifted his hand. The knuckle of his middle finger was extended, ready to knock, but Hannah buzzed the window down before he made contact with the glass.

The cop said, 'Good afternoon, s— miss. Do you know why I pulled you over?'

Hannah shook her head. 'I have no idea. I wasn't speeding.' She glanced across at Reacher. 'I haven't done anything wrong.'

'You're driving a vehicle registered to an individual who, according to official records, is currently deceased.'

'Currently? Are you expecting that to change?'

The cop took a deep breath. 'I'll put this plainly. Why are you driving a dead man's truck?'

'The dead man was my ex-husband. We were close. I had

242

permission. I'm on his insurance. And I'm due to inherit the truck as soon as his will is read.'

'Your name, miss?'

'Hannah Hampton-Roth.'

'ID?'

'In my purse. OK if I get it?'

'Go ahead.'

Hannah took her purse from the back seat, rummaged in it for a moment and pulled out her wallet. She opened it, then passed her driver's licence to the cop.

The cop studied the licence for a moment then said, 'Registration? Insurance?'

Hannah leaned across to the passenger side, opened the glovebox and took out a clear plastic pocket. The documents were inside. She straightened and handed it out of the window.

The cop said, 'Wait here.' Then he walked back to his car.

Hannah stretched for the keys to switch the engine off, but Reacher took her hand.

He said, 'Leave it running. If the cop has his gun drawn when he gets back out, floor it. Same applies if another police cruiser shows up. Or anything that could be an unmarked car.'

The cop stayed in his car for five long minutes then returned to Hannah's window. His gun was still in its holster. He handed the documents and the licence back and said, 'You're a long way from home, miss. What brings you to Winson?'

Hannah tucked the licence back into her wallet and handed the plastic pocket to Reacher. 'My ex-husband has – had – friends here. I need to let them know that Sam has passed. That's better done in person than on the phone or email, don't you think?'

'Who were his friends?'

'Angela St. Vrain. Danny Peel. They worked with Sam before Angela and Danny moved out here.'

'Will you be staying with one of them tonight?'

'No. We'll go to a hotel.'

'Which one?'

'We're—'

'Still working on that,' Reacher said.

The cop said, 'You didn't think to make a reservation before you left Colorado?'

Reacher said, 'No.'

'What if you'd come all this way and the hotels were all full?'

'Is that a common problem here?'

The cop was silent for moment then he nodded toward the rear of the truck. 'What happened to your window?'

Hannah sighed. 'Some asshole kids tried to break in.'

'When?'

'Earlier this afternoon. At the rest area, on 20.'

'Kids did this?'

'That's right.'

'Did they steal anything?'

'They saw us walking back after we used the bathrooms and they ran.'

'Did you file a police report?'

'I didn't think there was any point. We didn't get a good look at the kids. I wouldn't have been able to give much of a description.'

'And your tailgate?'

'What about it?'

'It has a bullet hole. Someone take a shot at you?'

Hannah shook head. 'At us? No. Sam, my ex, he was a keen

marksman. He was at a range outside of town one day last week and a newbie had an accidental discharge in the parking lot when he was getting his gun out of his vehicle safe.'

'Did Sam file a report?'

'He figured there was no need. It was an accident. No one got hurt. The guy paid for the damage. If that was wrong, you can't blame Sam. It's up to the club to make sure the rules are followed.'

'What's the name of the club?'

'I don't know. I never went. Sam just called it "the Gun Club". He was a corrections officer. A lot of his co-workers are members, too. It's owned by a retired cop. I'm sure he did the right thing.'

The cop thought for a moment. Then he said, 'All right. You can go. But you need to turn the truck around.'

'Thank you. But why?'

'You need somewhere to stay. The best hotel around here is the Winson Garden. It's easy to find. Follow signs for the prison, then take a left on to Mole Street. I'll follow. Make sure you don't get lost.'

No one was going to come and help him. He had to face reality. So Jed Starmer forced himself on to his feet. He couldn't stay where he was. He was too visible. At least two officers had been searching for him in Jackson. Pretty soon they would accept he had given them the slip. They would have no choice. Then they would have only one place left to look. Jed's final destination. Winson. Which could only be reached via the road he was currently loitering right next to.

Jed still had no idea how he was going to get to the summit. He could barely stand. He felt like someone had stolen his leg bones and replaced them with modelling clay. His stomach was hurting. He couldn't look at any object without the thing's edges blurring and its colours twisting and dancing like it was on fire. He was a hot mess. He knew that. And he knew one other thing. He had come too far to be defeated by a hill.

Jed figured he had a couple of factors on his side. Time. And trees. There were more than twelve hours before he had to be in Winson. All he needed was rest. And someplace where he couldn't be seen from the road. He hobbled across to the bike, which was still lying on its side. Heaved it up on to its wheels. Pushed it over to the long grass at the edge of the shoulder. Set it down. Took another couple of steps. And stopped.

Jed needed rest. But he also needed to be safe. He was heading into a forest. There could be wolves lurking around. Maybe alligators. Maybe coyotes. Maybe in giant, blood-thirsty packs. Jed didn't know what kinds of predators they had in Mississippi. And he didn't want to find out the hard way. So he was going to have to pick his refuge with extra care.

THIRTY-THREE

Hannah was the one with a credit card so she took care of the check-in process at the Winson Garden. Reacher was the one with the suspicious nature so he kept watch over the parking lot. The cop was the one with the orders to observe the stranger so he parked where he had a good view of the hotel's entrance. Where he could make sure the stranger and his unexpected companion did go in. And didn't come back out.

When she was done with the form filling and the bill paying Hannah wheeled her suitcase across the reception area and handed a key card in a little cardboard wallet to Reacher. He took it and slipped it into his back pocket. Almost immediately a phone rang on the counter behind them.

The desk clerk answered it after one ring. 'Winson Garden, Winson's premier guest accommodation. How may I be of assistance today?' He listened for a moment then said in a much quieter voice, almost a whisper, 'Yes, officer. The woman did. The name on her card is Hannah Hampton. Her home address is in Gerrardsville, Colorado. She paid for two people. Two rooms. One night.' Then he nodded to no one in particular and dropped the receiver back into its cradle.

Reacher could feel the desk clerk staring at him. He could practically hear what the guy was thinking. He was wondering why the police were interested in these particular guests. Whether he would have a story to tell in the morning. And whether there would be any kind of a mess to clear up.

It took the Minerva IT guy ten seconds to get Bruno Hix's computer display set up the way he wanted it.

The guy had been forced to leave his cats to eat their dinner alone. He had been made to come back to the prison on his own time. And he had still brought his A game. No one could have solved the problem more quickly or efficiently. That was for sure. So he couldn't understand why the big boss seemed even more annoyed when the job was finished than he had been at the start.

The guy was part offended, part confused. He had done a great job, which wasn't appreciated, but he must also have committed some kind of appalling faux pas. Hix's attitude made that obvious. The problem was he had no idea what he'd done that was so bad. He started to summon the courage to ask Hix what the problem was but before he could speak one of his mother's favourite expressions started to echo in his head: *When you're in a hole, stop digging.* He figured that meant the smart move would be to get out of the office before he made things any worse, so he muttered a vague apology and hurried to the door. He pulled it open, glanced back at Hix and almost blundered straight into Damon Brockman, who was heading the opposite way.

248

Brockman waited for the IT guy to scurry off down the corridor then said, 'Good news. We just dodged a bullet.'

Hix switched off his computer monitor and said, 'We did? How?'

'Our guys not intercepting Reacher at the truck stop? Or at the construction zone? That was a blessing in disguise. Turns out Reacher's not working alone. He has a partner. A woman. If our guys had put Reacher on ice the way we told them to we wouldn't know anything about her. She'd still be out there, invisible, free to do who knows what tomorrow.'

'How did you find out?'

'One of Moseley's guys spotted the truck Reacher was using. Just outside of town. He pulled it over, expecting to find Reacher on his own, but a woman was driving. Reacher was in the passenger seat.'

'The cop found Reacher? Where is he now?'

'At the Winson Garden. With the woman.'

'You sure?'

Brockman nodded. 'The cop directed them there. Followed them. Confirmed they checked in.'

Hix drummed his fingers on the desktop, then said, 'What about this woman? Who is she? What do we know about her?'

'The cop got her ID. Her name's Hannah Hampton. She's Sam Roth's ex-wife. She told the cop they were still close. Before he died. That she had permission to use his truck.'

Hix got up, crossed to the window and looked out through the fence toward the curved parking lot. 'I don't get it. We thought Reacher was only involved because of some fluky chance encounter.'

'Right.'

'We bought into the idea he just happened to be in

Gerrardsville. Saw what happened to Angela St. Vrain. Stuck his nose in where it wasn't wanted.'

'That is what happened.'

'Then how come he's hooked up with Sam Roth's widow? That can't be a coincidence.'

Brockman shrugged. 'Reacher stuck his nose in a bit deeper. That's all. He heard about Roth's death. He decided it didn't pass the smell test. So he started to dig. It's natural he would talk to Roth's widow. Especially given that she found the body.'

'What if there's another explanation? We didn't know Roth was close to his ex. It didn't cross my mind. All the divorced people I know hate their exes. I certainly do. I'd happily grind both of mine into hamburger meat and feed them to the dogs if I could get away with it.'

'I know you would. But what does it matter who Roth was close to?'

'People confide in the people they're close to. What if Roth told his ex what Angela had told him? What if the three of them figured out what's going to happen tomorrow? They would know they couldn't go to the police. So maybe they hired Reacher. He could have been in Gerrardsville specifically to meet them. Not because of some random chance. Our whole theory could be way off the mark.'

'I don't see it. Why would they hire Reacher? How would they know about him? And how would they get hold of him? The guy's a drifter.'

'Is he? Maybe he just wants people to think that. As cover. He's a retired cop. Lots of those guys set up as private detectives when they turn in their badges.'

'He was an MP. Not a regular cop.'

'So what? Same skill set. And he's capable. That's clear. Ask the guys we sent after him.'

Brockman shrugged. 'OK. Say you're right. He came here because the woman hired him. What difference does it make?'

'The difference is that we now have two people to take care of.'

'Which is no biggie. We know exactly where they both are. The only question is whether to stick Harold and the boys on them in their rooms while they sleep or wait till the morning and jump them when they come outside.'

'Do it in their rooms. As soon as possible. Have the bodies brought out on gurneys, in case there are any other guests snooping around.'

'I'll set it up with Harold.'

'Good. And in the meantime, who's watching the hotel?'

'The cop.'

'Too obvious. Send one of our guys.'

'We haven't got anyone. Only the guys we sent to Jackson, and they've been working since three a.m. We need them to back Harold up tonight. Better for them to grab some rest. Come back fresh.'

'If Reacher sees a patrol car out front he'll know something's up. He'll—'

'If Reacher was watching he'd have seen the patrol car leave. I had Moseley send his guy back and tell him to stay out of sight. On the street.'

'Send him back? He left?'

'Only for a minute. He's supposed to be on patrol. He started to go back out. Reported to Moseley. Moseley called me. I took care of it.'

'You sure?'

Brockman nodded. 'Moseley had his guy check with the hotel when he got back on station. The clerk confirmed he saw Reacher and the woman heading to the elevators. He was certain they hadn't come down. He swore he would have noticed if they'd come back through reception. He knew the police were interested in them after the first phone call so he was extra vigilant.'

'OK. Just make sure Harold knows he has two targets now. And tell him to take the insurance with him. The envelope. He needs to make sure it's somewhere Reacher will find it if he comes out on top.'

'Harold won't like that. He'll think it shows you don't have faith in him.'

'Why would I give a rat's ass what Harold thinks? Tell him anyway.'

'You'd give more than a rat's ass if you'd seen the size of him. He's not the kind of guy you want mad at you. Whether you're the CEO or not.'

Reacher had waited for the police car to pull a wide, lazy turn and disappear toward the centre of town. Then he started along the corridor that led to the elevators and the guest rooms. Hannah followed, still towing her suitcase. They passed the elevators and continued to the end of the corridor. To the emergency exit. A sign said the door was alarmed. Reacher was annoyed by that. An inanimate object couldn't experience trepidation. It was a ridiculous proposition. And if the claim was meant as a warning, that didn't work either. The hotel's owners wanted to keep costs to a minimum. The desk clerk's ill-fitting uniform made that clear. So did the generic prints on the walls. The coarse carpet on the floor.

252

The flimsy handles on the bedroom doors. The kinds of people who were satisfied with such low-level junk wouldn't want to get fined for false alarms. There was too much risk that a drunken guest would take a wrong turn and blunder into the latch. Or a smoker would sneak out for a crafty cigarette. Or someone would want to get outside without being seen. Someone like Reacher or Hannah.

Reacher pushed the release bar. The door swung open. No lights flashed. No klaxons sounded.

If you don't want a thing to come back and bite you in the ass, do it yourself.

That was a principle Curtis Riverdale had lived by his whole career. It meant more hours with his sleeves rolled up, for sure, but it had been worthwhile. It had always served him well. In the past. But that afternoon, for the first time in his life, he wasn't sure if it would be enough.

Riverdale had made the arrangements for the next day's ceremony himself, as usual. He had lined up the outdoor seating. The temporary fences. The podium for the TV cameras. Refreshments for the journalists. The stage, for Bruno Hix to strut and preen. A tent to shroud the prison's entrance, for security. Fierce-looking guards to be seen in the watchtowers. And the protesters. He was sure not to forget about them.

Riverdale had covered all the bases. He had double-checked everything, personally. But something else was worrying him. He'd just gotten word from his old buddy Rod Moseley, the Chief of Police. Reacher had made it all the way to the town. Reacher was a wild card. A factor Riverdale could not control. And a lack of control was kryptonite to a guy whose whole world was shaped by rules and procedures and timetables. Plus fences and cell blocks and steel bars.

Riverdale's fingers moved subconsciously to his chest. They traced the outline of an object beneath his undershirt. A key. It hung from a chain he wore around his neck. The chain was fine enough to be discreet but it was made from high-tensile steel. It wasn't ornate. It wasn't a piece of jewellery. Nor was the key. Which was for a padlock. The strongest, most secure, most weatherproof kind available anywhere in the world.

Riverdale still hoped that the ceremony would be a success. That it would garner more kudos for the company. More business, down the line. And another special visit from the new inmate's pretty wife, the same day. But if it wasn't, if the whole thing went sideways, he was ready. He would disappear. No one would ever find him. And Hix and Brockman and everyone who sneered at his sense of caution? They could burn for all he cared.

THIRTY-FOUR

J ed Starmer didn't know what he was looking for. Not exactly. He figured he was in the countryside so there might be a farm nearby. With a barn. Or a stable. Or a shed. He didn't care if there were horses in it. Or cows. Or sacks of gross animal food. Or strange, spiky machines. Just as long as it had walls. And a roof. And a door, which he could close. Where he would be safe. Just until he got his strength back.

Each step he took was harder than the one before. The trees were scattered around at random. They were close together so he had to weave his way between them. The undergrowth was thick and tangled. It constantly snagged his feet and ankles and made him stumble and almost fall. The earth was damp. It had a heavy, musty smell. Jed didn't like it. It seemed dirty to him. Rotten. He imagined himself collapsing and the soil closing around him, engulfing his body, holding him for ever as he slowly decomposed. He tried to go faster and some kind of insect scuttled away from under a decaying leaf. It was all legs and pincers and creepy antennae. He began to think he was worrying about the wrong size of animal. Then he heard a noise, behind him. It sounded like a growl. He forced himself to keep moving. He had come too far to get eaten by some weird creature in a miserable, stinking wood.

Jed squeezed between two more trees and emerged on to a track. It was wide enough for a vehicle to drive on and there were tyre marks on the ground. They were broad and deep. The kind that are made by something heavy. Jed paused to get his bearings. He figured he'd been heading on a diagonal since he dumped the bike, and the track ran at a right angle from the road. So he could go left and wind up more or less where he started, which was familiar, but exposed. Or he could go right. Deeper into the forest. Where he'd be hidden. But where he might be in other kinds of danger.

It occurred to Jed that the track must go somewhere specific. That was the whole point of tracks. People don't cut them through the woods with no purpose in mind. Vehicles don't drive around on them aimlessly. And the place the track led to might have some buildings. Some shelter. Which had to be better than where he was. Or the side of the road.

Jed went right.

He walked for what felt like ten miles but he knew must only be a couple of hundred yards. There was no sign of any buildings. Nothing man-made. Not even a treehouse. At least the track was easy to walk along. Jed stayed to the left and counted his steps. He tried to build up a rhythm. Then he picked up a sound. Something different from earlier. Not an animal. Jed was relieved. He thought it might be wind in the leaves but discarded that theory. The air was too still. He realized it was water. He looked further ahead and saw that the track came to an end at the side of a pond. A large one. Almost a small lake. Some unseen stream must feed it in a last act of independence before falling away and getting consumed by the raging Mississippi.

It was all Jed could do to not fling himself to the ground. The track must just be to support a bunch of recreational bullshit. People wanting to swim or kayak. Or fish. That thought gave rise to another. It made Jed wonder if he could catch something to eat. His stomach was a constant knot of pain. Even a tiny minnow would be welcome. Then he pushed the idea away. He had no rods or lines or hooks or whatever it was people used to snag fish. But maybe he could take a drink. If the water was fresh. If there was nothing rotting in it. Nothing that would poison him. He had seen TV shows where survivalists got all kinds of gross diseases from sipping bad water. He was scared to try. But he was also thirsty. Desperate for fluids in a way he hadn't known was possible. He took a step toward the bank. He figured it couldn't hurt to investigate a little. He took another step and through a gap in the leaves he caught sight of something unnatural. Artificial. Something with a right angle.

The right angle was the corner of a metal box, three feet by three feet by six feet. It was painted dull olive-green. A colour Jed associated with the army. There were military-style letters stencilled on the side as well, in white. They read *WINSON COUNTY VOLUNTEER FIRE DEPARTMENT*. And below, in a smaller size: *AUTHORIZED USERS ONLY*. The lid was held in place by a hasp and eye. There was no padlock. Jed unhooked it and lifted the lid. It folded all the way back so he didn't have to hold it up. Inside, to the left, there was some kind of machine mounted inside a scuffed red tubular frame. It had a handle like Jed had seen on lawn-mowers, presumably to make it start. Coiled up in the space next to it there was a long flexible hose, three inches in diameter, with a mesh cage and a styrofoam float at one end. There were two cans of gas. Two plastic containers full of pink liquid with labels attached with tables specifying how much to add to tanks of water to create fire-inhibiting foam. There was a box of flashlight batteries, but no flashlights. And two shrink packs of bottled water. Thirty-six bottles per pack.

Jed was not an authorized user. And he wasn't a thief. But he was thirsty. He was close to full-on dehydration. Which was dangerous. And the point of fire departments is to save people. To help people in distress. So Jed grabbed the bottle at the nearest corner of the top pack. He pulled and twisted until it came free. Poured the water down his throat in one unbroken stream. Then he took another bottle. He drank that one more slowly, but finished it, too. He dropped the empties in the corner of the box. Removed the pack of batteries. The containers of foam mixture. The gas cans. And the hose. He tried to move the machine, but it was too heavy so he left it where it was. Then he climbed inside. Pulled the lid down, with the empty bottles sandwiched against the lip of the box's long side. That way he had some fresh air but could quickly pull them out if any animals came by.

If any firefighters came and saw their supplies scattered around, that would take more explaining. Jed figured he'd find a way to deal with that, somehow. He'd come too far to worry about *what if*s.

Up in St. Louis, at their second-choice hotel, it was almost time for Lev Emerson and Graeber to swap places again.

It was close to six hours since Emerson had checked in.

Half their rest time was gone. Emerson had spent the first shift in the room, lying on the bed, fully dressed, with the drapes closed. Then he had switched to the back of the van. It was still parked at the far side of the parking lot.

Emerson preferred the van. But not for comfort or facilities. That was for sure. It had no bathroom. No TV. No coffee machine. No air conditioning, back in the load space. Just three cushions lined up on the floor. They were from the first couch that Emerson and his wife had bought together. It was delivered the month after they got married. He had salvaged them when his house got redecorated more than two decades ago. They fitted the space like they were designed for it but their battered leather covers were worn almost all the way through. Their stuffing was wearing thin. Emerson could feel the van's metal floor if he shifted position too quickly. But the van was familiar. He liked the smell of the chemicals. The outline of the tools that were silhouetted in the light from the one-way glass in the rear doors. The way that the space calmed him. Allowed him to control his thoughts.

In the hotel room Emerson was besieged by memories of Kyle. He could hear his son's voice. See his face. How he'd been as an adult. As a kid. He relived snippets of birthday parties. Trips they'd taken. Random moments of everyday life that hadn't seemed significant at the time but now were more valuable than anything in the universe. In the van Emerson could focus on his work. His art. He could remember everything from his first job, burning down a hot-tub factory in Gary, Indiana, to the scene in the warehouse that morning.

Emerson mopped his forehead then sent a text to Graeber. He told him he could keep the room. He preferred to stay in

259

the van. Where he could picture the fate of the distributor they were going to meet in Vicksburg. The next link in the chain that would lead to the people ultimately responsible for Kyle's death. He didn't know how many links there would be. How hard it would be to loosen each tongue in turn. But he did know one thing. However long it took, he would never stop. Not until he got justice for his son.

The problem wasn't so much that the original owners of the Riverside Lodge had built their hotel in the wrong place. It was that they had built it at the wrong time. They had broken ground when Winson's economy was fuelled by more than just the prison. When people still came to the area to explore its natural beauty, not just spend a few minutes talking to a family member or a friend through a sheet of perforated perspex. Hence its position high on the bank of the Mississippi. It had uninterrupted views to the north and the south. And to Louisiana away to the west, so far across the water that it looked like another country. Those first investors thought their clientele would never dry up as they got funnelled past within touching distance by the local roads. Then the interstate came along and syphoned the passing traffic far away to the east.

The Lodge was made up of three distinct sections. A central core, two storeys high, housing the reception area, the bar, restaurant, function rooms and admin facilities. Plus a wing on either side containing the guest rooms. The roofs were flat and the structure was built of brick. There were three colours. A dark band around the base of the building. Pale yellow for the bulk of the walls. And regular vertical strips of white. The architects had insisted on those. They were a nod to the columns that stood out front of all the finest

260

buildings in the region. The other main feature was a porte cochère which jutted out from above the main entrance. It had been designed to protect guests from the sun or the rain when they climbed out of their cars, but it no longer looked very welcoming. Or very safe. In its current state it looked more likely to injure anyone who ventured beneath it. Maybe from falling masonry. Maybe from total collapse.

Hannah stopped the truck in the centre of the Lodge's parking lot and wiped her chin with a paper napkin. She had eaten her burger as she drove from the Winson Garden. She had been hoping to get to it before it went completely cold, but that ship had long sailed. It had been nasty and rubbery and congealed. That didn't stop her from finishing it, though. Or Reacher from ploughing through both of his.

Hannah said, 'This is not how the place looked on the website when I booked. They're taking some major liberties with their advertising. Want me to find us somewhere else to stay?'

Reacher said, 'No. It'll do just fine.'

Hannah looked around the lot. There were three cars close together near the hotel entrance. Generic domestic sedans. Neutral colours. Probably rentals. And an ancient VW microbus away to the right near a blue metal storage container like the one they'd seen at the construction zone. It wasn't clear if the bus was still capable of moving. Hannah said, 'There can't be many guests.'

'That's a good thing.'

'You sure? It isn't usually a good sign.'

'Today's not a usual day.'

'I guess.' Hannah took her foot off the brake, looped around and slotted the truck into the gap on the far side of the container. 'This won't fool anyone who's searching for us, but

261

there's no point advertising where we are, right?' She took off her seatbelt, reached for the door handle, then paused. 'But here's what I don't get. The cop who stopped us wasn't on the level, was he? He was expecting you to be driving. On your own. That was obvious. He was surprised when he saw me. He stammered, then he was all over my ID, and he didn't even ask your name. And the idea that the DMV has updated Sam's records already? Give me a break. So given that the cop was bent, why didn't he shoot us? Or at least arrest us?'

'Ever heard the expression *A fish rots from the head*?'

'No. I hate fish. What have they got to do with the cops?'

'The way I see it, there's bound to be plenty of contact between the police and the prison. Escape drills. Visitors getting caught smuggling. Relatives causing a nuisance in the town. So there'll be plenty of opportunity for Minerva to get its hooks into someone. Makes sense to go for someone high up. With authority. Influence. The beat cops will just have orders to be on the lookout. For me. For the truck. To report anything they see.'

'You think our guy will report that he saw us go to the Winson Garden?'

'I'm counting on it.'

THIRTY-FIVE

The reception area at the Riverside Lodge had a double-height domed ceiling painted to look like a blue sky with a few fleeting clouds. A chandelier hung down from its highest point. It was suspended directly over the centre of a compass motif that was laid into the floor with black-and-white tile and gold dividers. The counter was made of mahogany. It was so shiny it almost glowed after decades of being polished by maids and getting rubbed by guests checking in and out. Reacher knew the hotel must be involved with computers since Hannah had made their reservation online, but none were visible. There was just a thick ledger, bound in green leather. An old-school telephone made of Bakelite with a brown braided cable. And a brass bell to summon attention when no one was waiting to help.

Reacher tapped the plunger on top of the bell and a moment later a guy scurried out from a back room. He looked like he was maybe twenty-five. He had blond hair, a little long but

263

swept back in a neat, tidy style. He was wearing a grey suit. The creases in the pants were razor sharp. His shirt was pressed and his tie was properly knotted.

The guy said, 'How can I assist you this evening?'

Reacher said, 'I need two rooms.'

'Do you have a reservation?'

'No. This is a spur-of-the-moment thing.'

'Let me see what I can do.' The guy opened the ledger and took a fountain pen from his jacket pocket. 'How many nights?'

'Let's start with one. We'll add more if we need them.'

'No problem. Our standard rate is eighty-five dollars per night, per room.'

'Let's say a hundred dollars, cash, for rooms well away from your other guests.'

The guy glanced left, then right. 'We only have three other guests, presently. They're all at the near end of the south wing. How about the two rooms at the far end? You won't even know the others are there.'

'How about the north wing? Is it empty?'

'It is, but I wouldn't recommend it. The refurbishment pro- gramme hasn't been completed yet.'

'Doesn't matter to me.'

'To be honest, the refurb hasn't actually started. The rooms are a bit of a mess.'

'Are they infested? Is there a health hazard of any kind?'

'No. They're functional. Just a little on the scruffy side.'

'You could say the same about me.' Reacher glanced at the sign on the wall which directed guests to the two wings. It showed that rooms 101 through 124 were to the north. 'Give me 112. My friend will take 114. Assuming they're adjacent?'

The guy nodded. 'They are. Can I have your names?'

'Ambrose Burnside. Nat Kimball.'

The guy took the cap off his pen, but Reacher leaned across and closed the ledger.

Reacher said, 'A hundred and ten dollars per night. You pocket the extra and save yourself the trouble of writing anything down.'

The guy said, 'Sorry. Can't do that.'

'There's no such word as *can't*. You have a simple choice. Pocket fifty dollars for doing absolutely nothing. Or – you don't want to know about the alternative. Trust me. Be sensible. Take the money.'

The guy was still for a moment. Then he put the cap back on his pen. 'It's a hundred and ten every night, if you stay longer. Per room. In cash. To me only. None of my co-workers get to hear about this.'

Reacher counted out two hundred and twenty dollars and placed the cash on the counter. The guy scooped it up and slipped it into his back pocket. Then he took two white plastic rectangles out of a drawer. 'One key each?'

Reacher shook his head. 'Two.'

The guy shrugged and pulled out another pair. He poked some buttons on a little machine that was tucked almost out of sight on a low shelf and fed each card in turn into a slot. Then he slid the cards into a pair of cardboard wallets and handed them to Reacher. 'Breakfast's from six till eight. Enjoy your stay.'

Reacher led the way down the north corridor. Hannah followed, towing her suitcase. The even numbers were on the left. The odd numbers were on the right. Halfway along they passed room 112, then stopped outside 114. Reacher handed one cardboard wallet to Hannah. He opened the other and took out both keys. He put them in one back pocket and slid the wallet into the other, where the keys to the room at the Winson Garden still were.

Hannah worked the lock on her door and said, 'I'm going to call Danny Peel. See if he can meet us in the morning before he goes to work.'

Reacher said, 'Good idea. And Hannah – do me one favour. Don't unpack just yet.'

'Why not? You getting fussy about the state of the decor after all?'

'I'll be back in a minute. I'll explain then.'

Reacher walked back to reception, tapped the bell and waited for the smart-looking guy to reappear. Then he laid one of the key cards down on the counter.

He said, 'This one doesn't work. Can you reprogramme it?'

The guy said, 'Did you put it next to your cellphone? Or your credit cards?'

'No.'

'Oh. Well, what about the other one?'

'It worked fine. I went into my room. Then I put it down and came out to speak to my friend. I figured I could get back in with this one, but no luck.'

'Weird.' The guy picked up the card. 'No problem, though. I can fix it right away.'

Reacher said, 'Room 121.'

The guy worked the buttons on the little machine, dipped the key into the slot, and handed it back. Reacher slipped it into his pocket. Then the guy said, 'Wait a minute. You're in 112. I remember because your friend is next door. One one four.'

Reacher nodded. 'Correct. One one two.'

266

'You said 121.'

'I'm good with numbers. I know exactly what I said.'

'Well, whatever you said, I programmed it for 121. My mistake, I guess. You better let me have it back. Do it over.'

Reacher shrugged, pulled out the other card and gave it to the guy. The guy worked the machine again and handed the card back.

The guy said, 'I'm really sorry about that. Stupid of me.'

Reacher said, 'No problem. Same digits. Easy to mix them up. Forget it even happened.'

The hands on the alarm clock crept around to one thirty Friday morning. Bruno Hix was in bed. He had been there for hours. But he hadn't gotten a moment of sleep. He had just lain there, staring at the ceiling, thinking about the stranger who had invaded his town. First, he had thought about the operation to take care of the guy. And his female companion. Harold and the others were going to hit them in their rooms at the hotel. But that had been due to happen at one a.m. Another half-hour had passed. It should have been a simple procedure. He should have heard something. Confirmation that the problem had been eliminated. Unless . . .

Hix's phone rang. He snatched it up from the nightstand. The display showed Brockman's number. Hix hit the answer key. 'Tell me we got them.'

Brockman said, 'It's better than that. Getting stopped by that cop must have spooked them. They've gone.'

'What do you mean, *gone*?'

'They're not in their rooms at the Winson Garden. The beds haven't been touched. And their truck's not in the lot. They must have sneaked away, somehow.'

'They must be staying somewhere else.'

'Not in Winson. They did have a reservation at the Riverside Lodge, pre-paid, in Hannah Hampton's name, but they didn't show up. We called all the B&Bs in town and they're not at any of them. We checked their names and descriptions. They're nowhere. They're history. They're no longer a problem.'

Hix dropped the phone on the pillow and closed his eyes. He breathed freely for the first time that night. He felt his heart rate slow down. He began to drift toward sleep. Then he sat up. He was wide awake again. He grabbed his phone and hit the key to call Brockman back.

Hix said, 'The Riverside Lodge. Where Reacher and the woman made a reservation but didn't show. Did you ask about walk-ins? Anyone paying cash?'

Brockman said, 'No. Why would I? We know they didn't – damn.'

'The penny drops. It's the perfect misdirect. Or almost perfect, given they're dealing with me, not you. Find the clerk who was working yesterday evening. They were probably bribed. Or threatened. Or both. Go to their house. Loosen their tongue. And if Reacher is at the Lodge, send Harold and the guys. Immediately. I don't want this dragging on any longer.'

'I'm on it. And if you think about it, this is good news. If Reacher is at the Riverside Lodge after pulling those kinds of shenanigans, the asshole will think he's safe. Harold's job will be a lot easier.'

By the time the LED display on the van's dashboard blinked around to one thirty a.m. Lev Emerson was sitting in the driver's seat, in the hotel parking lot up in St. Louis, waiting. Behind him in the load space the three old cushions were strapped away in their dedicated space. There was no danger of them getting thrown around in traffic, knocking over chemicals or damaging equipment. Two minutes later Graeber hauled open the passenger door. He had known his boss would want to drive, despite the lack of sleep, so he had taken the time to scare up a large mug of extra-strong coffee. Caffeine and conversation. Enough to keep them on the road all the way to Vicksburg, Mississippi. He hoped.

An hour later, at two thirty a.m., six men walked through the main entrance of the Riverside Lodge, just outside Winson. First was the clerk who had helped Reacher the previous evening. His feet were bare. He was wearing blue-and-white striped pyjamas and his blond hair was sticking out in all kinds of crazy directions. He was followed by the two Minerva guys who had been sent to Colorado. Next came the two guys who had been keeping watch at the Greyhound station in Jackson. The guy who brought up the rear looked like he was as broad as any two of the others. He was six feet six tall. A good three hundred pounds. His chest and biceps were so big that his arms couldn't hang straight down at his sides. He had no neck. His head was shaved. His eyes were small, mean dots that sank beneath the sharp cliff of his forehead. He had a tattoo on his right forearm that once said *Harold & Molly 4ever* in a heart, pierced by an arrow. A cut-price attempt at laser removal had left it reading something more like *larol oily leve*, in an apple.

Harold barged to the front of the group and shoved the kid in the pyjamas toward the mahogany counter. The kid

269

scuttled around behind it and took a key card from its drawer. He prodded some buttons on the programming machine, dipped the card in the slot and held it out. His hand was shaking. He said, 'One one two.' Harold snatched the card and the kid programmed another. He said, 'One one four.' Harold took it too and stared at the cards for a moment. Then he punched the kid in the face.

The kid's body hit the floor and slid until his head was pressed against the side wall. Harold and the other four guys didn't give him a second glance. They started moving immediately, crossed the deserted reception area and made their way down the north corridor. One of them continued to room 114. Hannah's room. The others lined up behind Harold outside 112. Reacher's room.

Harold held up three fingers.

Then two.

Then one.

At two thirty a.m. Jed Starmer was fast asleep. He was curled up in the Winson Volunteer Fire Department's equipment locker at the side of the pond in the woods. The fresh air had taken its toll. So had the physical exertion. And the stress. He was absolutely out for the count.

Jed had no idea that a bobcat had wandered past half an hour earlier. And before that a black bear had been sniffing around. It had been interested in the coil of hose. The gas cans. The containers of foam. But most of all it had been intrigued by the scent escaping from the gap between the sides and the lid. The bear was easily capable of lifting the lid. It could have opened the box even if the latch had been fastened. It was inches away. It was hungry. It was curious. Then the wind changed. The bear turned around. It headed back down the track toward a spot where some teenagers had parked the evening before. They had drunk beer. Eaten burgers. Tossed the wrappers into the undergrowth. And without realizing it, they had saved Jed from the fright of his life.

THIRTY-SIX

H arold touched the key card against the pad on the door to room 112. The mechanism gave a soft click and a small light changed from red to green. Harold slammed down on the handle, shoved the door and charged into the room like the corridor was on fire. Three guys followed him. The other opened the door to room 114. He was slower with the key. Less violent. More cautious as he stepped inside.

Room 112 followed a standard hotel layout. There was a simple closet to the left, open, with a rail and a shelf above. There was a bathroom opposite it. The room opened up beyond that with a bed and an armchair to the right. Both were loaded with too many pillows. There was a painting of a riverboat on the wall above the headboard. A window straight ahead covered with garish curtains. A desk to the left that did double duty as a dressing table. A mirror on the wall above it. And a carpet which was threadbare in the places that saw the heaviest traffic.

Harold lumbered around to the bed and stopped. It was empty. He tapped the guy who was following him on the shoulder and pointed to the floor. The guy ducked down and lifted the bed skirt. He peered underneath, then stood back up and shook his head. Harold pointed to the bathroom. The guy nearest to it pulled back his right fist and pushed the door with his left hand. He reached inside. Flicked on the light. Took a half-step. Another. Then went all the way in and checked behind the shower curtain that hung in front of the tub.

The guy came out of the bathroom and said, 'It's empty. Reacher's gone. Maybe he was never here.'

Room 114 was a mirror image of 112. Its furnishings were equally gaudy. Its fabric was equally worn. One difference was the quality of its air. Instead of smelling mouldy and stale it felt fresh but a little damp. The drapes were pulled aside and the window was open. The Minerva guy – one of the pair from the Greyhound station – picked up on that. He paused just inside the doorway. He was thinking about cockroaches getting in. And wondering if it was a sign that the woman had fled. Or if it was part of a trap. Or if the woman was just a fresh-air fiend. He'd had a girlfriend once who swore she couldn't sleep with the bedroom windows closed.

The guy started to move again. He crept forward. He drew level with the bathroom door. Reacher was waiting inside. He stepped into the doorway and punched the guy in the side of the head. The blow sent him staggering sideways across the entryway. He hit the wall on the far side and his skull left a new dent in the plaster. His arms windmilled around and knocked the hangers off the rail, sending them rattling across the floor.

The guys in room 112 heard the noises. They turned in unison and stared at the connecting wall.

Harold said, 'It's Reacher. He's next door. With the widow. Get him.'

The guys rushed into the corridor. They ran to the door to 114. And stopped. The door was closed and they didn't have a key.

Reacher climbed out of the window. He jumped down and landed on a strip of grass at the edge of the parking lot.

The other Minerva guy from the Greyhound station hammered on the door. He got no response.

Reacher hurried across to the window to room 112. It was unlatched. He had seen to that, earlier.

Harold pushed the three guys aside and slammed the door to room 114 with his palm. The half above the handle flexed an inch but the lock didn't give way.

Reacher opened the window, hauled himself up and climbed inside.

Harold stepped back. He lifted his right leg and drove the sole of his foot into the door at the side of the handle. The architrave shattered. The door whipped open. It slammed into the unconscious guy's feet and bounced back into its place in the ragged frame.

Reacher crossed the room. He opened the door a crack and peered out into the corridor.

Harold barged 114's door with his shoulder and shoved the unconscious guy's legs far enough aside to make a gap he could squeeze through.

Reacher stepped out into the corridor. He said, 'Looking for me?'

The nearest guy turned around. The one who'd been driving the BMW in Colorado. Reacher was already moving toward him. He drove the heel of his right hand into the guy's chin. The guy's head snapped back. His feet left the ground

274

and he slammed down on his back like a roll of carpet. The next guy in line had to jump to the side and press himself against the wall to avoid getting flattened. It was the guy who had killed Angela St. Vrain. Reacher swivelled at the waist and buried his left fist in his solar plexus. The guy doubled over. He bent at the waist. His body was momentarily horizontal. Reacher brought the side of his right fist down on to the back of his head like a club. The guy's knees buckled and he collapsed across his buddy's back in an X shape with his forehead pressed against the wall. The third guy took a glance at what was happening and began to run. Away from Reacher, along the corridor, toward an emergency exit at the far end. Reacher hurdled the tangled bodies and chased after him. But the Minerva guy was lighter. He was faster. And he was desperate. There was nothing Reacher could do. It was a race he had no chance of winning.

A door on the right-hand side of the corridor swung open. The last but one. Room 121. Hannah stepped out. She turned to face the running guy. Her feet were apart, planted securely on the ground. She was holding her SIG out in front, steadily, in a two-handed grip.

She said, 'Stop.' The tone of her voice made it clear she was serious.

The guy slowed, raised his hands, and stopped. Then he lunged for the gun. Hannah pulled it aside, out of his reach. She kicked him in the crotch. Hard. He doubled over. He was gagging. A scream was cut off in his throat. Hannah kneed him in the face. He fell back. He was sprawling and struggling, but still moving. For another split second. Then Reacher caught up and kicked him in the head.

Hannah switched the gun to her right hand, crouched

down and checked the guy's neck for a pulse. There was a sound from down the corridor. It was Harold. He had wrestled the door to room 114 open again. He stepped out. He was so broad he seemed to fill the entire space between the walls. Hannah straightened up and stood next to Reacher. For a moment no one spoke.

Harold broke the silence. He said, 'Drop the gun, little girl. Let's talk.'

Hannah raised the gun and switched back to a two-handed grip. She said, 'No. And let's not.'

Harold took a long step forward.

Hannah said, 'Stop.'

Harold's face twisted into a mean, cruel grin. He took another step.

Hannah said, 'I'm not kidding. Stop.'

Harold took another step.

Hannah took a breath, held it, aimed at Harold's centre mass and pulled her trigger. The noise was devastating. The spent cartridge hit the wall and fizzed down on to the carpet by Reacher's foot. Harold staggered back. He fell. And lay still.

Hannah stepped forward, already leaning down to check Harold for signs of life. Reacher grabbed her arm and pulled her back.

'Let go.' Hannah tried to wriggle free. 'I need to know if—'

Harold sat up. His face was twisted with fury. His shirt was ripped. Metal glinted through the hole in the fabric. He was wearing a ballistic vest. The fibres had flexed like a soccer net stopping a well-struck ball. The surface had distorted. The bullet had pancaked. But the structure had done its job. The bullet had not gotten through.

Reacher had a rule for that kind of situation. Your enemy gets knocked down, they do not get back up. You finish them, there and then. No mercy. No hesitation. But Hannah's intervention had slowed him down. Cost him a second. And that was enough for Harold to haul himself the rest of the way up.

Harold's feet were spread wide. His knuckles were practically brushing the sides of the corridor. His arms and legs were as long as Reacher's. Maybe longer. Which was a problem. It took away one of Reacher's regular advantages. In a fight he could normally stay out of harm's way and still be able to inflict massive damage. But there was no way to hit Harold without the risk of getting hit in return. Of taking some serious punishment. That wasn't a prospect Reacher was keen on. It would reduce his efficiency. Lower his odds of success.

Harold shifted his stance and squared up like some old-school bruiser. It was like he had read Reacher's mind. A mean smile spread across his face. His fists were like sledge-hammers. Weight was on his side. If he could land one blow it would be game over, and he knew it.

Reacher knew it, too. But he also knew there are times when a needle is more effective than a hammer.

'Careful,' Reacher said. 'Don't let your knuckles drag on the ground.'

Harold's eyes narrowed.

'They won't let you in the hospital if you hurt yourself. They'll send you to a vet. Lock you in a zoo afterwards. Or a circus.'

Harold charged forward. He launched an immense right hook. The motion was smooth. Practised. Reacher had no doubt that if Harold's fist made contact with his skull the result would be devastating. But he was expecting it. He snapped his body back from the waist. Just far enough. Harold's fist zipped past his nose. It kept moving. And made contact with the wall. It shattered the surface and smashed through the lattice of wooden slats that supported the plaster. Harold yelled and wrenched his arm, but his hand would not come free. It was stuck like a fish on a barbed hook.

Reacher danced in close and threw a punch of his own. It was vicious. Brutal. It caught Harold right by his ear. It rocked his head to the side. It would have knocked anyone else down. They'd have been unconscious. For a long time. Maybe for ever. But Harold shook his head. Spat out some blood. And grinned.

Reacher switched targets. He stamped down on the side of Harold's knee. Then he drove the heel of his hand into Harold's captive arm, just above the elbow. The joint bent the wrong way. Bone dislocated. Tendons stretched. Ligaments tore. Harold roared with pain. And anger. He grabbed his trapped forearm with his free hand and twisted and heaved with all his might. The wooden strips gave way. Their jagged ends tore his wrist and palm and the back of his hand. His arm flailed around. It was floppy and out of control. And it was spraying rivers of blood. His nails brushed Reacher's cheek. One broke his skin.

Harold took a step forward then stopped and howled with pain. His knee was too damaged. It couldn't take his weight. His right arm was hanging, useless. So he reached around with his left hand and pulled a gun from his waistband.

He started to raise it.

Reacher was already moving. He was running at Harold. Accelerating as fast as he could. But space was restricted. There was little room for manoeuvre. Reacher figured he had one chance. He needed momentum. He needed focus.

So he charged in, leaned forward and ploughed into Harold. His right shoulder drilled into the exact spot Hannah's bullet had hit. Where he knew Harold's ribs would be bruised. Where he hoped they would be broken.

Harold crashed down, flat on his back. He dropped the gun. He howled. He thrashed his legs. Flailed his arms. Reacher moved in, looking for a part of Harold to punch. Or kick. Or stomp. Harold kept on squirming and wriggling. He denied Reacher a target. Then he sat up, fast, like he was exercising at the gym. He lunged and wrapped his good arm around Reacher's thighs. Slid his hand lower and clamped his forearm across the back of Reacher's knees. He flung himself back down, straining and tugging with all his might.

Reacher's knees jackknifed. There was nothing he could do to avoid getting pulled down. He knew that. So he didn't fight gravity. He didn't resist. Instead he aimed, and planted both knees square in the centre of Harold's chest.

Maybe Harold's ribcage had been damaged by the gunshot. Maybe it had been weakened by Reacher's shoulder charge. Maybe he just had porous bones. But whatever the reason, Harold's sternum collapsed. His lungs were crushed flat. So was his heart. His liver. And a bunch of other organs. His body gave one last spasmodic twitch. His head lolled to the side. And then he was still.

Bruno Hix was still awake. He had done everything he could think of to get to sleep. Herbal tea. Whisky. Meditation. Nothing had worked. He felt the anger building inside himself. His big speech was hours away. He didn't want black circles under his eyes because he was short of rest. He didn't want to fluff his lines because he was too tired to concentrate.

Hix stared at the ceiling and pictured himself at the beach

on a tropical island. He'd read somewhere about relaxation techniques and this one was supposed to help. He took it a step further. Imagined what kind of drink he would have in his hand. Maybe a pina colada. Maybe a daiquiri. He was still trying to decide when his peace was shattered by his phone. It was a text. From Brockman.

'Friends' located. H & co on scene. Only a matter of time . . .

That was it. Everything was going to be OK after all. Harold would take care of Reacher. The guy's luck had to run out some time. And if this wasn't the time, if Harold failed, it wouldn't matter. Not now contact had been made. They could fall back on the insurance. Hix had arranged it himself, therefore he didn't have to worry. He was confident it would work if it was needed.

Hix was confident. In the insurance, itself. The note was completely credible. He had put a lot of thought into it. He wasn't worried about whether Reacher would believe it. But for Reacher to believe it he would have to read it. And for him to read it he would have to find it. If he defeated Harold. And Brockman had hinted that Harold might refuse to take it due to some ridiculous sense of pride. Hix pictured the envelope abandoned at Harold's house. Left in the vehicle. Tossed in the trash. Then he got a hold of himself. Forced nice images of the beach back into his head. There was no need to borrow trouble. His plan was elegant. Sophisticated. There was no way the universe would let it get torpedoed by some petulant meathead.

THIRTY-SEVEN

Reacher was worried about the gunshot. The noise it had made. Someone was certain to have heard. The night clerk. Or the other guests in the south wing. One of them was bound to call 911. Maybe they all would. Maybe they already had. One way or another the police would soon be showing up. And Reacher did not want to be around when they got there. The stealthy approach hadn't worked. Now whoever was pulling the strings would have an emergency call and a dead body to work with. A perfect excuse to send in a couple more goons, guns blazing, no questions asked.

Winson was not a New York or a Chicago. It wasn't even a Jackson. Reacher doubted the cops would be on patrol twenty-four seven. Any presence was likely to be confined to the station house at that time of night. The best case would be one guy. Low down the pecking order. Alone with a pot of stewed coffee and a box of stale doughnuts. Someone who would have to call for assistance and wait for another officer to arrive before responding. The worst case would be that a pair of old hands were on duty. Trusted guys. Ready to roll at a moment's notice. Ready to do whatever their boss told them to.

Reacher always planned for the worst. The town wasn't far away. There would be no traffic. The cops would be local. They would know the road, and they would drive fast. He figured he and Hannah had nine minutes to get clear of the hotel.

Hannah was kneeling down near Harold's head. She had checked his neck for a pulse after Reacher climbed off him. She hadn't found one. But she had discovered her legs would no longer work. She was unable to stand up. When the week began she had never seen a dead body. Now she had been up close and personal with two. And this one she felt partially responsible for. Blood was leaking from its crushed chest and oozing toward her knees. She was starting to get mesmerized by it.

Reacher helped Hannah to her feet and guided her back to room 121. He asked her to get her things together. Quickly. And while she packed he went out to the corridor. He took a pillowcase from the bed and filled it with the contents of the Minerva guys' pockets. Their guns. Phones. Wallets. Keys.

Reacher and Hannah made it down the corridor and into reception. They had six minutes left to get clear. Plenty of time. Then Reacher noticed a pair of bare feet. Someone was on the floor, behind the counter. He detoured to investigate. It was the kid who had checked them in. He was in his pyjamas. Alive, but unconscious.

Reacher crossed back to Hannah and they continued to

the parking lot. The three rental cars were still lined up on the south side of the porte cochère. The VW bus had moved closer on the north side. Two other vehicles had arrived and were parked next to it. A Dodge Neon and a Ram panel van. The Dodge had lived a hard life. That was clear. It had dents in its front wings, mud sprayed around its wheel arches, a crack running the whole width of its windshield and a couple of deep gouges in its front fender. The van was dark blue. It was spotless. It had no livery or logo, but it looked like the kind of thing a company would use to ferry stock and supplies between different sites.

They had five minutes left to get clear.

Reacher pointed at the vehicles and said, 'See how they're lined up? One guy came here directly in the van. The others went to the clerk's house. Roused him. And made him drive back in his VW because there would be no room in the car. Which could help us. Wait here a minute.'

Reacher went back inside and crossed to the counter. He checked the kid's pyjamas. Found a key on a rabbit's-foot fob. He fished a wallet out of the pillowcase. Took out all the cash and slipped it into the kid's pocket. Then he tore a page out of the ledger, grabbed a pen off the shelf, and wrote: *Will return the bus. Don't report it stolen. More $ to come. Ambrose Burnside.*

They had three minutes left.

Reacher hurried outside and tossed the key to Hannah. He said, 'The cops will be looking for Sam's truck. See if you can get the VW to start. Better to use it instead.' Then he looped around to the rear of the van. Its door was unlocked. The walls and floor of the cargo area had been boarded up with plywood to protect the paint. Two gurneys were stacked on one another at the right-hand side. They were folded down

283

and secured with elastic straps. Next to them was a black plastic trash bag. Reacher looked inside. It was full of medics' uniforms. There was nothing he could use so Reacher moved on to the front of the vehicle. He went to the passenger side and opened the glovebox. There were two pieces of paper inside. The insurance and registration documents. Reacher checked the details. He was hoping for a corporate name he hadn't seen before. A new thread to pull in whatever illegitimate financial tapestry Angela St. Vrain had been talking to Sam Roth about. But Reacher was out of luck. The papers listed the vehicle's owner as the Minerva Correctional Corporation, with an address in Delaware. Reacher immediately thought, *Tax avoidance*, but he couldn't see a connection to murder.

Two minutes left.

Reacher heard the VW rattle into life. He scanned the rest of the van's cab. It was clean and empty. Then he stepped back to slam the door and spotted something white peeking out from under the passenger seat. It was the corner of an envelope. It must have slipped off the dashboard while the van was moving and slid back there. Reacher fished it out. It was a standard letter size. Thin, like it only had a single piece of paper inside. And it was addressed to Danny Peel. The same name that had been on the envelope in Angela St. Vrain's purse. The same address. But different handwriting. Reacher was confident about that.

Bruno Hix was already the world's greatest living chat-show host, but the extravaganza that was about to go live was destined to cement his status as an all-time legend of broadcasting. It was going to feature the most stars ever interviewed in a single event. It would be the most expensive eight hours of television ever made. It was being filmed in the middle of the Mediterranean, on the deck of his yacht. The audience was already in place. A thousand people divided between less luxurious ships, moored on all four sides. He had a drink in his hand. The cameras were rolling. But his guests hadn't showed up. And somehow he was naked. His hair was falling out. His skin—

Hix's phone rang. His eyes snapped open. He was sweating. He threw back the comforter and lay for a moment, trying to control his breathing. Then he answered the call. It was Brockman again.

Hix said, 'Talk to me.'

The line was silent for a moment. Then Brockman said, 'He's on the loose again.'

'Who? Reacher?'

'Yes.'

'And the woman?'

'Her too.'

'Harold screwed up?'

'Harold's dead. Reacher literally crushed him.'

'Harold. Second best again. Maybe we should put that on his gravestone. What about our other guys?'

'They're hurt. But alive.'

'Where did Reacher go?'

'They don't know. Moseley's guys are searching for him.'

'OK. Keep me posted.'

'Bruno? I've been thinking. About tomorrow. I hate to say this. You know I've been against making any changes, right from the start. But maybe the others were right. With Reacher running around out there, maybe the full ceremony isn't the smart way to go. Maybe it's time we switched to Plan B.'

'We don't have a Plan B. We've never needed one.'

'Maybe it's time to think of one. We can't postpone because of the court order, but the ceremony isn't important. Getting our guy released on time is all that matters. We could put out a statement. Say he was too traumatized to go through with the publicity.'

'The release is the top priority, for sure. But we don't want to throw the baby out with the bathwater. The ceremony is very important. You can't buy that kind of good press. And you're forgetting the insurance. That will take care of Reacher. He'll be miles away at ten a.m. And if he comes back, it'll be too late for him to do anything.'

'Will it work?'

Hix reached out and took a second cellphone from his nightstand. A cheap, simple one. He checked its battery. He checked it had signal. 'Of course it will. We'll have confirmation soon. Nine o'clock. Nine fifteen at the latest.'

The VW was less conspicuous than Roth's truck, but it would still stand out in such a small town. People might know it belonged to the kid from the hotel. The police probably would. Reacher bet they'd pulled him over plenty of times. The way the bus stank of weed, it was pretty much probable cause on wheels. Plus, its reliability was unknown. Reacher didn't want faulty components or a lack of maintenance to do the cops' work for them and leave him and Hannah stranded at the side of the road. So they decided to lie low for the remainder of the night. They headed to a place near the foot of the hill outside the town. Reacher remembered seeing a track leading away into a thick grove of trees. At the time he figured it could be a firebreak, or to provide access for forestry equipment. Either way, it would give them good cover until the morning.

Hannah took her hand off the wheel and picked the envelope up from the dashboard for the third time since they left the hotel. 'How do you think they got a letter addressed to Danny? Maybe he took it to work, meaning to deal with it, and dropped it? Someone found it and was planning to deliver it to his house?'

Reacher said, 'Let's ask him about it in the morning. What time are we seeing him?'

'Nothing's set. I couldn't get a hold of him. He's an early riser so I'll try again first thing. And if he doesn't answer we can always just show up and surprise him.'

The VW was fitted out with a bed and a kitchen and a table and a couch. Reacher appreciated the ingenuity that had gone into the design. And the thoroughness. Every tiny space had been used. But there was no getting away from the fact that the space was tiny. Reacher decided it would be better to let Hannah have it to herself, so he dug through the cupboards until he found a bunch of old blankets. He took one. Spread it on the ground. And lay down under the stars.

There were two words on Reacher's mind as he got ready to sleep. *Brockman*. And *lockdown*. Brockman was a name he'd heard more than once. The guy from Minerva who had sent out all the thugs. Reacher wanted to find him. Kick down his door in the middle of the night. See how he liked it. And see what he knew about whatever it was that Angela St. Vrain had stumbled across.

The problem was that Brockman might not know anything. If Minerva people started getting attacked in their homes it could trigger panic. And lockdown is the default panic response of people who run prisons. It's in their DNA.

So he would have to be patient. They had two leads to follow. Danny Peel, and the release ceremony. He would see what came of those. If nothing productive was uncovered, then he would go after Brockman. And whoever else was involved, until he got some satisfactory answers.

THIRTY-EIGHT

Hannah woke Reacher at a minute after seven thirty a.m. She shook his shoulder and said, 'Danny's still not answering his phone. I'm getting worried. I think we should go to his place. Right now.'

The directions to Danny's house were already teed up on Hannah's phone. Its electronic voice ordered them back to the road, then right, which was the way to Winson. It took Hannah a couple of minutes to get the VW facing the right way. The track was narrow. The steering was heavy. The clutch was stiff. She sawed back and forward, bumping and lurching across the rough surface, until she got a straight shot forward. She picked up a little speed. Reached the mouth of the track. And almost hit a pedestrian. A kid. He looked like he was in his mid-teens. He was pushing some kind of fancy bike up the hill. Very slowly. It was like a contest. Like the bike was trying to pull him back down. The smart money would be on the bike, Reacher thought.

The kid stopped. He was startled by the ancient bus suddenly appearing out of the trees. He stared through the windshield for a moment. Then he toppled backward and the bike landed on top of him.

Hannah jumped out and rushed up to the kid. 'Oh my goodness. I'm so sorry. Are you OK?'

The kid didn't answer.

Hannah pulled the bike off him. 'Are you hurt? Did you hit your head?'

'I'm fine.' The kid rolled on to all fours, struggled to his feet and took hold of the handlebars. 'Give me that. I need to get going.'

'Where to? What's the hurry? Do you have any water? Do your parents know you're here?'

'I've got to get to Winson. I can't be late.'

'Just sit for a moment. Rest. Get your breath back at least.'

'There's no time.'

'You're in no state to walk, let alone ride.' Hannah snatched the handlebars. 'We're going part of your way. Come on. There's a rack at the back. Put the bike on there. We'll give you a ride.'

The bus purred up the hill. The bike rattled and bounced on the rack. The kid sat on the couch at the back of the cabin, stiff and anxious.

Hannah adjusted her mirror so that she could see him without turning around.

She said, 'What's your name?'

The kid said, 'Jed. Jed Starmer.'

'Well, Jed, why's it so important you get to Winson this morning?'

'Something's happening. I can't be late. I've come too far to miss it.'

'What's happening? Where?'

'Someone's getting released from the prison.' Jed took a breath. 'My dad.'

Reacher said, 'I read about that. Anton Begovic?'

Jed nodded. 'He was never married to my mom. That's why we have different last names.'

'Does he know you're coming?'

'He doesn't know I exist.'

The bus crested the hill and Hannah's phone announced they had a left turn coming up in a half-mile.

Reacher said, 'Where did you travel from?'

Jed said, 'LA.'

'On the bike the whole way?'

'On the bus. The Greyhound. I just rode the bike from Jackson.'

'You brought the bike with you?'

'I kind of borrowed it.'

Hannah sighed. Reacher said nothing.

Jed said, 'I didn't steal it. You don't understand. I had everything planned. I was supposed to stay in a hotel, then get a taxi, but all my stuff got stolen, and my money got stolen, and two creepy guys tried to kidnap me, and some cops came, and—'

Reacher said, 'It's OK. No one's accusing you of anything.'

'This is important. I'm not a thief, OK? The guy riding the bike was an asshole. He rode into me, and he pushed me, and he yelled at me. Then he left it right there. On the sidewalk.

291

Unlocked. I had no choice. I'll give it back when I'm done. I swear.'

Hannah said, 'Sounds like you've had an awful time. You lost everything?'

'Pretty much. All I've got left is my toothbrush. I had it in my pocket.'

'What about your mom? Could she not help? Would you like me to call her?'

'You can't. She – pancreatic cancer. It came on quick.'

'I'm sorry.'

Reacher said, 'What's your plan when you get to the prison?'

Jed shrugged. 'Meet my dad, I guess.'

'How? They have some kind of big shindig planned. Press. TV. The whole nine yards. You won't be able to just stroll up and say, *Hi, I'm your kid.*'

Jed shrugged again. 'I've come this far. I'll figure something out.'

They came to the intersection and the phone insisted they should turn. Winson was straight on, so Hannah pulled over to the side of the road. She said, 'It's flat from here. You should be OK on the bike. I'll help you get it off the rack.'

Jed opened the door. 'I can get it. Thanks for the ride.'

Hannah said, 'Hold on a sec. We need to talk real quick.'

'What about?'

'If I'm understanding this right, you're about to meet your dad for the first time. That's a huge thing. For both of you. It needs to handled just right because it's going to have an impact on the whole of the rest of your lives.'

Jed didn't respond.

Hannah said, 'Have you ever met anyone who's been in prison before?'

Jed said, 'No.'

'I have. A lot of times. I work with a charity that helps people when they get out. The next few months are going to be very hard on your dad. Even if he hated it, even if he didn't deserve to be there, he'll be totally used to life in an institution. The outside world is completely different. It's like he's going to be dumped in a strange country where he doesn't speak the language or understand the customs. It'll be daunting for him. It'll be frightening. He'll be overwhelmed with all the changes, and one thing he's really going to struggle with is surprises. He could react . . . in a way he wouldn't be happy about, looking back.'

'What are you saying? That I shouldn't meet my own dad? Because—'

'Not at all. Meeting you, getting to know you, that'll be the best thing that ever happens to him. But finding out he has a kid, on top of all the other changes he's going to be facing, that's a huge deal. It's a transition that has to be handled carefully. Slowly. And today – release day – might not be the best time.'

'But he doesn't know I was even born. He doesn't know to look for me. If we don't connect today he'll disappear again. I'll never find him.'

'That's not how it works.' Hannah rummaged in her purse, pulled out a card and handed it to Jed. 'Here's what I suggest you do. Go to the ceremony outside the prison. See your dad get his freedom back. That's a big deal. It's obviously important to you, since you came all this way. And it'll mean the world to him that you did. But give him a day or two. Then get in touch. Call me when you're ready.

293

I know how the system works. I can help you find where he's staying.'

'What am I going to do for a day or two? In Winson? I have no money. Nothing to eat. Nowhere to sleep.'

Reacher fished another wallet out of the pillowcase and took the cash from it. There was two hundred and forty dollars. He passed it to Jed. 'Hannah's right. You should listen to her. You're at a crossroads in your life. It's important you choose the right way to go.'

Jed wrestled the bike down from the rack at the rear of the bus, climbed on and pedalled straight ahead toward Winson. Hannah pressed the clutch down, then let it back up again without touching the gearstick.

She said, 'This is a bad situation. I'm worried about that kid.'

Reacher said, 'You're right. He's terrible on that bike. We should have made him walk.'

'I'm not talking about road safety. It's the whole deal with Begovic getting released. Minerva will arrange support for him. It's all a big PR stunt so Hix will make sure it's done right. He won't want stories in the press about Begovic killing himself or committing some crime just to get locked up again. But Jed? Who's going to look out for him? If it's true that his mom is dead, he's got no one. I've seen this before. I know how it will play out. The poor kid's setting himself up to fail.'

The phone prompted them to *proceed to the route* so Hannah took the left turn. Then the phone had them swing away to the south and skirt around the centre of the town. The road was surrounded by trees. They were tall and mature, but there were no buildings for more than half a mile. Then they came to one house. It was huge. It was gleaming white. Four columns supported a porch and a balcony which jutted out at the centre. Further balconies ran the whole width on two levels on either side. The place was the size of a hotel and it was surrounded by a wall with a fancy iron gate. A driveway wrapped around an oval patch of grass with flowers and shrubs and a raised fountain. A car was parked between the fountain and the steps leading up to the front door. A BMW sedan. It was large and black. Reacher recognized it. The day before it had been in the curved lot outside the prison.

They continued for another three quarters of a mile then turned to the west. The trees thinned out and houses began to appear on both sides of the street. The homes grew closer and larger and more uniform until the phone said their destination was a hundred feet ahead, on the left. That would place Danny's house on the final lot before a smaller road peeled away to the south. But there was a problem. That lot was empty.

Hannah pulled over at the side of the street and they saw that the lot wasn't completely empty. There was a stand-alone garage in the far corner, with a short drive leading to the side road. There was a mailbox mounted on a skinny metal pole. It had originally been red but its paint had faded over the years, leaving it pink, like a flamingo. And the main portion of the lot hadn't been empty long. It was full of ash. Black and grey and uneven, heaped up in some places, sagging down in others, with the scorched remnants of a brick fireplace in the approximate centre.

Reacher climbed out of the VW. He could smell smoke. Hannah joined him on the sidewalk. She was blinking rapidly and her mouth was open, but she didn't speak. Reacher figured there wasn't much to say. A minute later a man approached them from the next-door house. He would be in his sixties, tall, thin, with silver hair, a plaid shirt and jeans that looked like they were in danger of falling down.

'Morning,' the guy said. 'You folks new to the neighbourhood?'

Reacher said, 'What happened here?'

'There was a fire.'

Reacher caught an echo of his mother's voice. *Ask a stupid question, get a stupid answer.* He said, 'Really? When?'

'Last Saturday. Early in the morning.'

'How did it start?'

'The guy who owned the place was smoking a cigarette. That's what I heard. He woke up, lit his first of the day, then fell back to sleep.'

'Was his name Danny Peel, the owner?'

The guy nodded.

Reacher said, 'Where is he now?'

'We cremated him, Wednesday. Kind of ironic, given the way he went, but those were his wishes. There wasn't much of a crowd. Just me and a couple of people from his work.'

'From the prison?'

The guy nodded again.

'Did people he worked with come by his house often?'

'There was one woman. Don't know her name.'

'Anyone else?'

'He was a quiet kind of a guy. Didn't seem to socialize much. Not at home, anyway.'

'Was anyone at his house on Saturday? Before the fire?'

'I doubt it. Like I said, it was early. And if anyone had been staying overnight, wouldn't they have found more bodies?'

'Did you see anyone in the neighbourhood? Anyone who isn't normally here. Or any unusual vehicles?'

296

'No.'

'Did you notice if any of his windows were open that morning?'

'No. I went out to get the mail. Then I heard the sirens. I didn't see anything. Why all the questions? You're not a cop. Are you from the insurance company?'

'Me? No. I'm just naturally curious.'

THIRTY-NINE

Hannah crossed the street without saying a word. She climbed back into the VW, rested her elbows on the steering wheel and held her head in her hands. Reacher decided to take a look around. He didn't expect to find much. The fire hadn't left much trace of anything, but old habits die hard. He was curious. And he wanted to give Hannah some time to herself.

There had been a lawn between the house and the street, but the grass had been torn up by the firefighters' boots and jagged channels had been cut through the dirt by the run-off water they'd used to extinguish the flames. They couldn't have gotten there very quickly, Reacher thought. There was so little of the structure left. It was like someone had judged things very carefully. Too late to save any of Danny Peel's house. But in time to stop the flames spreading to anyone else's. He picked his way across the rough ground until he was close to what would have been the outer wall. He wondered where the door had been. The kitchen. The bedroom. He could believe the fire had started there. And maybe that a cigarette had been involved. But not that it was an accident. He'd been around the block too many times to swallow that kind of a story.

Reacher looked inside the mailbox. There were four envelopes. All junk. Presumably delivered before the fire. Then he moved on to the garage. It had two roll-up vehicle doors leading to the side street and a personnel door that would have faced the house. He tried the handle. It was locked. The door didn't seem too stout so he leaned his shoulder against it and shoved. The tongue of the lock gouged a little strip out of the frame and it opened easily. Reacher stepped inside. There was a car in each bay. Both were Chevrolets. The closer one was a sedan, probably less than five years old. It was small and white and practical. The other was a Corvette Stingray, maybe from the 1960s. It was long and green and – presumably, if you were a car guy – fun. A wooden workbench stretched the whole width of the garage, against the far wall. Above it there were pegboards that were covered with tools. Domestic ones to the left, like chisels and mallets and saws. Things for working on cars to the right, like spanners and wrenches and hammers. There was also a journal hanging from a hook, and a pen on a chain like they used to have in banks. Reacher looked in the journal. It was full of entries going back five years, neatly written in blue ink, giving details of all the jobs Danny had completed on the Stingray. He had done work on the brakes. Rust in the subframe. Water leaks. Electrical problems. A whole bunch of things, some large, some small, all faithfully recorded. He had been a meticulous guy. That was clear.

*

Reacher got back into the VW's passenger seat. Hannah lifted her head and looked at him. Her eyes were red.

She said, 'So, what now?'

Reacher picked up the envelope he'd found in the van at the Riverside Lodge and held it out to her. 'We open this. It might throw some light on what happened to Danny. And Sam. And Angela. I doubt the Minerva guys had it by chance.'

Hannah was silent for a moment. 'OK. I guess. But I can't. You do it.'

Reacher tore open the envelope. There was a note inside, handwritten in neat, tidy script, on a piece of paper with a company letterhead. The company was a firm of accountants called Moon, Douglas, and Flynn in Hattiesburg, Mississippi. The note was short. It read:

Danny,

I have what you asked for. What you have seen so far is just the tip of the iceberg. I can give you enough to sink the whole ship. Meet me at 11.30 a.m., this Friday, Coal Creek Coffee, corner table, downtown Hattiesburg.

Alan.

PS – pls call to confirm you're coming. I have arrangements to make. Use my cell, not the office number. 399-307-1968.

Reacher handed the page to Hannah. She read it then dropped the paper on to the dashboard in front of her.

She said, 'I don't get it. Is this the same thing Angela went to Sam about? The accounting thing? I can't see the connection.

300

But it would be weird if there were two separate things going on at the same time.'

Reacher said, 'It's the same thing. Remember the information I told you about from Angela's purse? About Begovic's release? It was in an envelope addressed to Danny.'

'How did she come to have it?'

'I was planning on asking Danny.'

'So Danny was corresponding with some Deep Throat-type person. He must have gotten Angela involved. Which got her killed. And indirectly got Sam killed. Oh, boy. Poor Danny. He would have been devastated.'

'It wasn't Danny's fault. He uncovered a crime, apparently. He didn't commit one.'

'Someone did. Someone at Minerva. The same people who set all those goons on us. We need to sink their ship. We need this blockbuster evidence. Whatever it is. Assuming this Alan guy checks out.'

Hannah pulled out her phone and started tapping and swiping. A couple of minutes later she held it up so that Reacher could see the screen.

She said, 'OK. Well, the company's real. It exists. The address, website, social media, logo – everything matches. There's a list of partners. There's one called Alan. Alan McInnes. And get this. They mention Minerva as one of their top clients. What do you think?'

Reacher said, 'Dial the number.'

Hannah entered the digits and hit *Call* plus the button for the speaker. A man answered after three rings.

He said, 'McInnes. Who's this?'

Reacher said, 'Danny Peel. I got your note. I'll see you at Coal Creek, 11.30.'

'Wait. I'm not sure it's safe.'

'Want to pick another venue? Name it.'

'Not the venue. You. How do I know you're Danny?'

'How else would I know your number?'

'I don't know. OK. What's your middle name?'

Reacher looked at Hannah. She shook her head. He said, 'I don't have one.'

'Where did you live before you moved to Winson?'

'Gerrardsville, Colorado.'

'Name of your last boss before you went to work at Minerva?'

'Sam Roth.'

'OK.' There was a moment's silence. 'I'll meet you. But come alone. And don't be late.'

Bruno Hix ended the call. He was sitting in his kitchen, in his pyjamas. He didn't like to be at the prison too early on release days. There was always some kind of last-minute logistical snafu and he couldn't risk encountering anything that would put him in a bad mood before his speech. He took a sip of coffee, switched to his regular phone and called Brockman.

'No Plan B,' he said. 'It's confirmed. Reacher will be nowhere near the ceremony.'

Brockman said, 'Fantastic news. But Bruno – you're sure?'

'Positive. I got it straight from the horse's mouth.'

Hannah tried to pull a U-turn in the street but the old VW's steering was so heavy and slow to respond she bumped up on to the opposite sidewalk and almost clipped Danny Peel's mailbox. She backed up a couple of yards, hauled on the wheel with all her strength, dropped down on to the street and started to build a little speed. The bus mustered all the acceleration of a slug.

Reacher looked back at the mailbox. He said, 'Stop.'

Hannah coasted to the side of the road. Reacher climbed out, walked back and opened the mailbox lid. The junk was still there. Four envelopes, all loose. Also in the box was an elastic band. The kind mail carriers use to hold all the correspondence for the same address together. Someone had removed it and set the separate letters free.

Reacher cut across the muddy lot toward the garage. He let himself in and picked up the maintenance log Danny had kept for the Stingray. He flicked through until he found a number of specific characters. Two capitals. The rest lower case. Then he walked back to the VW, climbed in and said, 'We're not going to Hattiesburg.'

FORTY

The coffee was strong, but it still couldn't keep Lev Emerson awake long enough to reach the state line. He had no choice but to let Graeber drive for a while. He was counting on only napping for a couple of hours, just until he got his second wind, but when he woke up five hours had passed. The van was parked outside a square brick building, four miles north of Vicksburg, Mississippi. The building was the last in a line of three in a paved compound a stone's throw from the river. It was surrounded by trees and a rusty chain-link fence. There was a single-width gate, which hadn't been locked. Each building had two entrances. A vehicle door to the left, tall and wide enough for a van or small truck. And a personnel door to the right. Each had four windows in its second floor, square and dark beneath their crumbling concrete lintels.

Graeber waited for Emerson to get his bearings, then said, 'Morning, boss.'

Emerson grunted and checked his mug for any last dregs of coffee.

Graeber said, 'The other two buildings are deserted. This one doesn't look much better, but the locks are new. They're solid. It's in use.'

'Any sign of the guy?'

'Not yet.'

Emerson checked his watch. It was eight thirty. He grunted again, a little louder this time.

Twenty minutes later a car appeared at the gate. A huge, wallowing Cadillac coupe from the 1970s. It was burgundy. Its paint was shiny. It was well cared for. A guy climbed out. He could have been the same age as the car. He was a little under six feet tall, stocky, with a round face and brown curly hair. He was wearing a brown leather jacket and jeans. He shoved the gate open. Drove through. Closed the gate. Continued to the last building in line and swung in next to Emerson's van.

Emerson worked on the principle that if something wasn't broken there was no need to fix it. He waited for Graeber to jump out with a clipboard in his hand, approach the guy from the Cadillac and say he needed a quote to get a special consignment delivered. Then Emerson slipped out through the passenger door, looped around the back of the van and clamped a rag soaked in chloroform over the guy's mouth and nose. He didn't hold it in place as long as he had done in St. Louis, the day before. They didn't have to move the guy very far. They just wanted to keep him compliant while they got set up. And because no one could notice what they were doing there was no need for subtlety. So they let him fall to the ground when the chemical had done its job and dragged him toward the building.

305

Graeber took the keys from the guy's pocket and found the one he needed to open the vehicle door. There were two vans inside. Both were black. One was a few years old and displayed the kinds of dents and scuffs that accrue during a life spent earning a living. The other looked almost unused. The first was empty. The second had an air-conditioning unit on its roof and its cargo area was fitted out with full-length roll-out racks on both sides.

The far end of the space was set up as a mechanical bay. There were three giant toolboxes on wheels along the wall. Oil stains on the floor. And a hoist attached to a girder on the ceiling with chains hanging down for removing engines. The cogs looked seized and rusty, like they hadn't seen much action for many years.

Graeber reversed both vans out into the courtyard and then watched the guy from the Cadillac while they waited for him to regain consciousness. Emerson searched the office, which was walled off in the remaining quarter of the building's ground floor. He found all the usual administrative stuff. A calendar on the wall. A computer on the desk. Paperwork and stationery items in the drawers. But nothing that gave any insights into the confidential side of the guy's business. The only thing of interest was a pod-style coffee machine on a low filing cabinet. Emerson used it to make a mug for himself and another for Graeber.

When the Cadillac guy woke up he was naked. He was on tiptoes in a pool of congealed oil. His arms were above his head, cable-tied to the chains from the engine hoist. A barrel he had never seen before was standing in front of him, just too far away to kick. There was a ladle on top of it. The kind they use in restaurants. The guy was silent for a moment. He stayed still. Confusion creased his face. Then anger took over. He yelled. He yanked on the chains. He tugged them from side to side. He kicked out in all directions. But all he did was hurt his wrists and skin the balls of his feet.

Emerson heard the racket and came through from the office. He waited for the guy to settle down, then said, 'You've probably figured this out for yourself by now, but we're not interested in you delivering anything for us.'

The guy's eyes opened wide. 'What are you interested in?'

'Deliveries you made in the past.' Emerson opened the phone he had taken from the guy in St. Louis and called up the photograph of Carpenter. He held it out for the guy to see. 'Specifically, deliveries you made for this man.'

'What about them? I picked up a container. Usually just one. Took it to a place in New Jersey.'

'Where did you pick up these containers?'

'It varied. One of five locations. I got told which one the day before. They're all within an hour of here.'

'You knew what was in the containers?'

'No.'

'Don't lie to me.'

'I didn't know. I didn't ask. They didn't tell. But I'm not stupid. I guess I had a good idea.'

'Good. Now, Carpenter. How do I find him?'

'I don't know.'

Emerson opened the barrel, took a ladleful of its contents and poured it on the floor about eighteen inches from the guy's feet.

The guy wriggled his toes further away. 'What's that?'

'Something to focus your mind.' Emerson took out a box of matches, struck one and lit the little creamy puddle on fire. 'Another name for it is napalm.'

307

He took another ladleful from the barrel and stepped toward the guy. The guy started to hop on the toes of one foot. His other leg was raised, ready to kick if he got the chance. Emerson flung the gel. It landed and spread out across the guy's crotch and thighs.

The guy screamed.

'What?' Emerson said. 'I haven't lit it yet. Tell me how to find Carpenter.'

'You can't find him. No one can. He disappeared, like, a month ago. I tried to reach him myself, but I couldn't. He's gone. History. No more.'

'Other contacts in his organization?'

'He was the only one. It was a security thing.'

'That's a shame. It means you're no use to me. You're just a piece of annoying trash. And we all know the most environmentally friendly way to dispose of trash.' Emerson took out another match.

'Wait! Listen. Three weeks ago, maybe four, a new guy came on the scene. He only interacted remotely, and he said he represented a different supplier, but I think it was the same one.'

'Why?'

'The guy already knew the kind of bona fides I would want. They came through real quick. It was the same product. The same containers. The same destination. There've been two pick-ups so far. Both places the old organization used. A third pick-up is scheduled, and that's at another place they used. You tell me – coincidence?'

'This is just dawning on you now? You weren't suspicious before?'

'Why would I care? I figured they must have a reason for this new name. New identity. Maybe someone was muscling in. Maybe they'd had quality issues in the past. Needed a fresh start. As long as there was regular work, good money and no feds, I was happy.'

'The third pick-up that's scheduled. When is it?'

'Today.'

'Time? Place?'

'One p.m. Abandoned paper mill ten miles south-east of a no-bit little town called Winson.'

'Any specific procedures or protocols when you show up?'

'I just drive in and wait. Another van comes in. Their guys open my doors, slide in the container, and off we all go. Two minutes, and I don't even have to get out of the van.'

'You use the new-looking one?'

The guy nodded.

Emerson said, 'The plans for the day have changed. We're going in your place.'

'OK. That's cool. What do you want me to do? Lie low for a while? Leave town for a couple of months? I can do that. And I can forget your faces. Anyone asks, you were never here. We never met. OK?'

Emerson crossed to the tool chests and rummaged through their drawers until he found a tray with three-inch sides. The kind of thing mechanics use to catch oil when they drain an engine. He said, 'There's something else you need to know. One of the consignments you transported for Carpenter was destined for my son.'

'So your kid got what he needed? That's a good thing, right? Demand has to be met somehow. But if this is about the price you paid that's not down to me. So how about this? I donate my fee. To him. To you. To whoever you want.'

Emerson plunged the tray into the barrel and pulled it out, full. 'You think the price was high?'

'I don't know the price. I was just thinking aloud.'

'I'll tell you the price my son paid.' Emerson darted forward and dumped the gel from the tray on the floor around the guy's feet. 'He paid with his life.'

'No. Please. Stop. Your son died? That's horrible. I'm sorry. But it's not my fault.'

'I think it is.' Emerson struck another match. 'And I think it's fair you pay the same.'

Hannah kept her foot on the brake and the gearstick in neutral. 'How can it be a trick? The company checked out. The letter's genuine. If you don't show up, the guy who sent it could get spooked. He seemed twitchy enough already. We may never get another chance to meet him. To find out what Danny discovered. Which could be our only link to whoever killed Sam.'

Reacher said, 'Have you still got the company information on your phone?'

Hannah nodded.

Reacher said, 'Call the switchboard. Ask for Alan McInnes.'

Hannah shrugged, but she did as Reacher asked.

The switchboard operator said, 'I'm sorry. Mr McInnes isn't in the office at present. Would you like his voicemail? But I should just let you know, Mr McInnes is in Australia this week at a conference so it could be a while before he can respond.'

Hannah hung up the call. She said, 'How did you know?'

Jed Starmer wanted the bike to be safe until it was time to return it to the messenger, so he lifted it over a little stone wall at the side of the road, a hundred yards short of the prison, and covered the rest of the ground on foot.

Jed had never seen a place like the prison before. He didn't like it. Not one bit. The metal fence with its rolls of razor wire scared him. He imagined being trapped behind it. He imagined the guards in the watchtowers shooting at him. The cameras panning from side to side on their poles, tracking him if he tried to run. The floodlights shining on him if he tried to hide. He shivered, despite the warmth of the morning sun.

Jed threaded his way through a bunch of folding chairs and wandered across to a temporary fence. It had been set up with a semicircle of sawhorses around the edge of the curved road that bulged out from the front of the prison. He picked a spot in line with a little outdoor stage. He guessed that was where the action would be. It was to the side of a building he thought might be the prison's main entrance. It was hard to be sure because a kind of tent had been set up around it. On the other side of the stage there was a car. A BMW. Black, and very shiny. It was the only vehicle he could see. It was facing a platform with two TV cameras on it. A large one on a tripod and a small one which someone had set on the floor. The only other people who were around were wearing uniforms. They were grey with yellow trim and peaked caps, like the private cops Jed had once seen at a mall.

Jed was tired and his mind started to drift. He thought about his dad. Inside the prison. Stuck there for years, even though he had done nothing wrong. Desperate to get out. Jed couldn't imagine how awful that would feel. How badly it could mess a person up. He began to wonder if the woman in the old VW had been right. Maybe it was a mistake to just show up.

Reacher said, 'I found a book in the garage where Danny kept records of car things. The handwriting was the same as the address on the envelope I saw in Angela's purse.'

311

Hannah said, 'So Danny sent that letter to himself?'

Reacher nodded.

'Why?'

'To keep it safe. He found something out that he shouldn't have. He realized he was in danger. Maybe he went to the police and picked up the same vibe you did, yesterday. Anyway, he figured if the package was in the mail no one could find it. And take it. I bet it was a constant, recurring thing. Every time it was delivered I bet he mailed it straight back out.'

'Then one day he gave it to Angela? Why change his routine?'

'He didn't give it to her. She found it.'

'Where?'

'In Danny's mailbox. On Saturday morning. She heard about the fire and came by when he didn't answer his phone. I looked, myself, just now. There's some junk mail, loose, and an elastic band. The whole bunch came bundled together. Someone separated it. Took something. I thought it was Minerva, taking the letter we just opened. I was wrong. It was Angela.'

'Why would Angela look in Danny's mailbox?'

'The same reason you looked in Sam's. A friend was gone. She was checking to see if there was anything important that needed to be handled. She recognized his handwriting. Figured there was something fishy. Maybe he'd mentioned finding something out to her, before. Maybe she made the connection herself. We'll never know.'

Hannah was quiet for a moment. Then she said, 'The timing fits, I guess. She got the envelope Saturday morning. Emailed Sam Saturday afternoon. Left Winson Sunday, because she needed to find someone to watch her kid. It was maybe latish in the day when she got on the road. And because she was one person, travelling on her own with no one to share the driving, she needed an extra overnight stop. Which got her to Gerrardsville Tuesday morning.'

Reacher nodded. 'It fits.'

'And someone from Minerva knew you looked in the envelope Angela had before they got it back. They tried to stop you getting here. They failed. So they used another envelope addressed to Danny to trick you into leaving again. They probably figured if you looked in one, you'd look in another.'

'It almost worked.'

'That part's fine. But here's what I don't get. The first envelope was full of stuff about this Begovic guy's successful appeal. Which appears to be legit. Now, Angela told Sam the thing she was into had to do with accounting. What's the connection between accounting and Begovic?'

'I don't know. Yet.'

'Maybe we should try and figure that out instead of going to the ceremony.'

'I'm going to the ceremony. You don't have to.'

'What could we possibly learn there? And it could be dangerous. Minerva people are bound to recognize us.'

'That would be dangerous. For them.'

'How about this? We could watch it online. Minerva has its own YouTube channel. There's no need to go in person.'

'There is.'

'What?'

'Someone tried very hard to stop me.'

FORTY-ONE

Reacher counted thirty-nine people outside the prison, aside from Hannah and himself.

He knew why eleven of them were there. Jed Starmer had come to see his dad get released. The two camera operators and six security guards were getting paid. Bruno Hix, who had introduced himself as Minerva's founder and CEO, was enjoying the sound of his own voice. And Damon Brockman, who also claimed to be a founder, was standing on the stage looking smug. Reacher was less sure about the other twenty-eight. He couldn't understand what kind of carrot or stick would make it worth the waste of their time.

Things livened up a little with just over ten minutes on the clock. Hix had been waffling about percentages and quoting philosophers, one minute waving his arms like he worked in an auction house, the next standing stiff and still like someone was shoving a stick up his ass. Then he stopped talking mid-statistic. An old pickup truck trundled into sight behind the crowd. Six people were perched in its load bed. The driver honked his horn and the nearest spectators moved out of the way. For a moment it looked set to make a run at the barrier. Reacher moved alongside Jed Starmer in case there was trouble. Then the truck stopped. The six guys jumped down. They produced placards that were covered with slogans about justice and profit. One showed a cartoon with Lady Justice's scales weighed down with dollar bills. A guy raised a bullhorn. He started yelling demands that the prison should close. The crowd didn't like that. The mood turned ugly. Jeering broke out. The protesters were getting shoved and jostled. The security guards ran over to the fence, nightsticks drawn.

Hix jumped down from the stage, microphone in hand, and strode across to the fence. He said, 'Stop. Let the people speak.'

The guy with the bullhorn took the microphone. He was silent for a moment, then mumbled his way through a litany of complaints and accusations.

Hix nodded and pulled a series of concerned expressions, then he took the microphone back and the sound immediately became clearer and louder. He said, 'My young friends, I'm glad you came here today. I'm glad—' Hix locked eyes with Reacher and suddenly he couldn't find his voice. He stuttered and spluttered for a moment, then tore his gaze away. 'I'm glad you care about fairness and humanity. If you were outside another correctional corporation's facility, there's a very good chance you'd be right. But here, I'm glad to say you're wrong. Minerva cares for the health of those who reside within our walls. Minerva cares for safety. For education. For unlocking potential. And' – Hix turned and dashed back to the stage – 'we care about righting wrongs wherever we find them. But don't just take my word for it. Ladies and gentlemen, I give you Anton Begovic.'

A flap in the tent that was covering the prison entrance opened and a man stepped out. He was wearing a dark suit and a tie and his hair looked freshly cut. He stood for a moment, blinking in the sunlight. Then Brockman, who had done nothing up to that point, jumped down, took the guy's arm and helped him on to the stage.

The guy took the microphone and stepped forward. 'Thank you all for being here. Thank you, Mr Hix. Thank you, Mr Brockman. And most of all, thank you to the Minerva corporation and everyone who is associated with it. When others wanted to lock me up, they fought to set me free. I am truly grateful, and I swear with you all as my witnesses that I will make the most of every second that has been given back to me.'

The guy waved, then Hix and Brockman shepherded him off the other side of the stage and into the BMW.

Jed ducked and tried to scramble under the barrier.

Reacher grabbed him, pulled him back and wrapped an arm around his chest.

Jed wriggled and squirmed. 'Let me go. I need to get to my dad. He's not messed up. You guys are wrong.'

'I can't let you go, Jed,' Reacher said. 'Because that man is not your dad.'

Lev Emerson had stood at the entrance to the workshop just north of Vicksburg and watched the flames curl and flutter. He had watched the body twitch and twist. Brighter and faster then softer and gentler until the corner with the chains hanging from the ceiling was dull and limp and ordinary once more. He crossed the courtyard to where Graeber was waiting after stowing the barrel and checking his mapping apps for an abandoned paper mill near the town of Winson.

They drove in convoy, Graeber in front in the shiny black van that was expected at the paper mill, Emerson behind in his shabby white workhorse. They took a short jog east then settled in on a steady southbound heading until they hit the outskirts of Jackson. Then Graeber pulled into a gas station. When they were both done topping off their tanks Graeber pointed to a diner at the side of the site. It was nothing fancy. Just a long, low brick building with a flat roof and a neon sign promising good food.

'What do you think?' Graeber said. 'Want to grab a bite? Some coffee? We have plenty of time.'

Emerson looked the place over. There were a dozen open parking spots outside its windows. It would be no problem to keep an eye on the white van. He said, 'Sure. Why not?'

The inside of the diner was as simple and functional as the outside. There were ten four-tops, split into two lines of five. Plain furniture. A grey lino floor, scratched in places. A serving counter with two coffee machines. A clock on the wall. A framed map of the state. And a TV. A large one. It was the only newish thing in the place. It was tuned to a local news channel. The sound was off, but words summarizing the action were scrolling across a plain band at the bottom of the screen.

Emerson was facing the windows. He was glancing at a menu, wondering what to eat, when Graeber grabbed his forearm.

Graeber said, 'The TV. Look.'

The screen was filled with the scene from outside the

prison in Winson. A guy in a suit with a brand-new haircut was standing on a stage, speaking into a microphone. The text said, *Exoneree Anton Begovic released from custody following successful appeal thanks Minerva Corporation. Minerva CEO Bruno Hix said . . .*

'Begovic?' Emerson pulled out the stolen phone, opened it to Carpenter's picture and held it up.

Graeber said, 'Or Carpenter. It's the same guy. No doubt about it.'

The camera followed the guy in the suit as a couple of other men guided him into a waiting BMW. The car eased forward, slowly, because of the crowd.

Emerson said, 'Look at the plate. MC1. Contact Fassbender. He owes us a favour. Tell him to find out who owns that car. Like, yesterday.'

An accounting thing, Angela had told Sam. Reacher had expected something complicated. Something that would require training and qualifications to unravel. But it turned out to be the simplest discrepancy in the book. *One too many.* One prisoner. One breakfast. One lunch. One dinner . . .

Jed jumped into the back of the VW and said, 'How can you be so sure that wasn't my dad? You've never met him.'

'I saw his photo from the day he was arrested.'

'People change,' Hannah said. She pulled an exaggerated, fake shiver. 'If you saw a picture of me from sixteen years ago . . .'

Reacher said, 'Part of the real Anton Begovic's ear is missing. Ears don't grow back. That's why the photo in the envelope in Angela's purse was so critical. Without it we would never have known the wrong guy just got released.'

318

Hannah sped up a little. 'Who did get released?'

'Someone who needed a new ID. We'll find out if we can catch up to Hix.'

'What if Hix doesn't go home?'

'I think he will. He wasn't expecting us to be at the ceremony, so he wasn't expecting to run. He'll either hole up, or grab some supplies for the road.'

'And if you're wrong?'

'I'll call Detective Harewood. Have him bring in the FBI.'

Jed said, 'Stop talking about this Hix guy. I don't care about him. I only care about my dad.'

'We need to find Hix so we can find out what happened to your dad.'

'What happened? Nothing happened. He's in prison. Still locked up.'

Reacher didn't reply. Neither did Hannah.

Jed said, 'Where else could he be? The wrong guy came out. My dad must still be inside.'

Reacher said, 'The wrong guy came out. That's all we know for sure.'

'The guy took my dad's name.' Jed started to cry. 'You can't have two people with the same name. My dad's dead. Isn't he? That's what you're not saying. He's dead and I never even got to meet him.'

Hannah cruised slowly past the big white house. The BMW was back in the same spot as it had been that morning.

'Thank goodness. He's there.' Hannah pulled over to the grass verge at the side of the road. 'But what can we do now? You can't buzz the intercom and ask Hix to let you in. I bet the gates are too strong to smash through. They probably have sensors that go off if you climb them. There's broken

319

glass cemented on the top of the walls. And I bet there are sensors in the ground on the other side.'

'Back up, close to the wall.' Reacher took a gun from the pillowcase. The desert-tan SIG P320 he'd captured from the second pair of guys at the truck stop on I-20. 'Jed, look in the bottom drawer. I need five blankets. And the cushion from the couch.'

Reacher tied two of the blankets corner to diagonal corner to maximize their combined length. He rolled them to form a makeshift rope, coiled it, and slung it around his neck. Then he tied the other three blankets together the same way. He secured one end to the VW's rear fender and climbed on to its roof. Hannah passed him the cushion. He set it down on the glass that was fixed into the top of the wall. He laid the blanket over the cushion and lowered it slowly to make sure it didn't touch the ground on the far side. He stepped on to the wall and stood with his feet on the narrow strip of brick without any shards. Checked that the blankets hung down far enough to grab if he needed to climb back out. Then he looked around. There was a clear band of grass, four feet wide, at the base of the wall. That's where the sensors would be buried. Beyond the grass, running the length of the property, there was a swathe of trees twenty feet deep. Reacher aimed for a gap between two of the thinner ones. He jumped, threw himself forward, rolled and pushed himself up into a crouch. He listened. There were no alarms. No bells. No dogs.

Reacher straightened up and moved behind the treeline until he got to a point where he could approach the house on a diagonal, toward one corner. That way there would be no windows directly facing him. He crawled forward until he

320

was at the limit of his cover. Then he lay for five minutes, completely still, observing.

There was a sound, behind him and to the left. A twig snapping. Reacher hustled back then got up and ran toward the source of the noise. He rounded a tree. And found a man. He was sitting at the base of the trunk, hugging his knees to his chest. He peered up at Reacher and whispered, 'Please don't hurt me. Please don't hurt me. Please don't hurt me.'

Reacher kept his voice low. 'I'm not going to hurt you. Who are you?'

The guy straightened a little and when Reacher could see more of him he thought he looked like a young Che Guevara. The guy said, 'My name's Maurice. You?'

'Reacher. What are you doing here?'

'I'd rather not say.'

'You work for Hix? Or anyone at Minerva?'

'Hell, no.'

'You going to call the police, or do anything stupid?'

'The police are the last people I'd call. And could I do anything more stupid than get stuck in this damn yard?'

'OK then. Nice meeting you.' Reacher turned and started back toward the house.

'Wait. Hix is home. So's his number two. And some other guy.'

Reacher ignored him and kept moving.

Maurice scurried after Reacher. 'Wait. Please. I have to ask you. Are you working on a story? Because if you are—'

Reacher said, 'Are you a journalist?'

Maurice nodded.

'I'm not. I'm not going to steal your thunder. So stay here. Lie low. Keep quiet. Don't attract any attention. Somebody's life is at stake.'

'Somebody? Lots of people.'

'What do you mean by that?'

'You're here because of the drugs, right? That's why you're going after Hix. What happened? Did you lose a family member? A friend? In a Minerva prison?'

Reacher grabbed Maurice's arm and dragged him back, deeper into the trees. 'Tell me what you know. All of it. Now. The nutshell version.'

'It's like this. Minerva's an octopus, right? An evil one. On the surface all progressive and enlightened. But the truth? Tentacles everywhere. They cherry-pick inmates. Put them to work. All kinds of ways. Including refining drugs. They do it in their disused separation units. Supply their own populations. Which is why their death rate is so high. They deny it, but it's true. And they've expanded. They supply other markets now, too.'

Drugs made sense, Reacher thought. All prisons have a problem with them. Maybe Minerva saw it as an opportunity. It could be big business. And guys involved in that trade are the kind who find themselves needing new identities from time to time. He said, 'Where's your proof?'

'Death rates. I've got that documented. Nothing else. Yet.'

'I'm going to visit with Hix, right now. The subject may come up. Anything concrete I find, it's all yours.'

FORTY-TWO

Reacher left the cover of the trees and approached the house from the south-east. Toward the rear corner. He climbed up on to the porch railing and wrapped his left arm around the column that supported the balcony. He used his right hand to slip the coiled-up blankets from around his neck. He held one end and swung the rest of the length in an arc. Once. Twice. Then as it neared the top of its third rotation he snapped it in toward the house and straight back out, like a lion tamer with an oversized whip. The tip curled around the column and dropped straight down the other side. Reacher caught it with his left hand. He brought his hands close and gripped both strands together. He shifted the soles of his feet on to the face of the column. Moved his left hand up and pulled. Took a step vertically with his right foot. Moved his right hand. Stepped with his left foot. He kept going until he could grab the upper rail, then he hauled himself up and over and rolled on to the balcony.

Reacher got to his feet. He stood still and listened. He heard nothing.

Along the side of the house a row of glass doors led out to the balcony. There were four. Maybe from bedrooms. They were all closed, and inside white drapes were drawn across them. For privacy. Or to combat the heat.

Reacher moved around to the back of the house. The balcony boards were solid. His feet made no noise. He looked down into the yard. It was an even space, fifty feet square, carved out from the trees and covered with grass. Hix must have been getting ready for a party. There was a bar to the left with a line of silver buckets for ice, tables with trays of plastic cups, and two giant trash cans done up to look like Greek urns. In the centre of the lawn a space had been covered to make a temporary dance floor. And there was a stage to the right with a drum kit, microphone stands and a lighting gantry extending across its whole width.

Reacher continued around the balcony until he found what he was looking for. A sash window with frosted glass. A bathroom. He took out his ATM card and pushed it up into the jamb between the upper and lower panes. He worked it from side to side until the latch eased around and disengaged. He lifted the lower section an inch and looked inside. He saw a tub. A sink. A toilet. But no people. He opened the window the rest of the way and climbed through. He crossed to the door. Opened it a crack. Saw no one. He carried on to the landing. It was a broad U-shape with an ornate rail around the open side, like an internal version of the balcony. The hallway was below. The stairs were at the far end. Voices were echoing up from the ground floor. Three men. They sounded familiar. And they sounded angry.

*

Reacher crept down the stairs. He kept to one side, where the treads were least likely to creak. Made it to the hallway and crossed to the first door to the right. The men were yelling on the other side. Reacher recognized the voices from the ceremony at the prison.

Brockman said, 'It's your fault. If you hadn't lost your nerve and hidden away like a scared little kid, we—'

'You're blowing everything out of proportion.' It was the guy who had emerged from the tent, pretending to be Begovic. 'I was scared, sure. I'm not an idiot. But I was still working. Our contacts are re-established. Deliveries resume this afternoon. I got better rates from two of our customers. There's no shortage of demand out there. And we have all the supply we could ever need. The only question is, how much money do we want to make?'

'But Reacher saw you.'

'So?'

'And he saw the photograph. He knows you're not Begovic.'

'Hasn't the photo been destroyed?'

'Yes.'

'The fingerprint record replaced?'

'Yes.'

'And there's no DNA on file for Begovic. So there's no way to prove I'm not him. You should have talked to me at the start. I would have told you. There's no danger. Especially since the real Begovic will be boxed up within the hour. By tomorrow he'll be in small pieces. There's nothing Reacher or anyone else can do to stop that.'

Reacher opened the door and walked through. He found himself in a kitchen. It had recently been renovated. The surfaces were all marble and pale wood and stainless steel. Three guys were sitting on tall stools at a breakfast bar. They all spun around.

Brockman stood up. 'Reacher? The hell are you doing here?'

Reacher closed the gap between them in two strides and punched Brockman in the face. He fell back, slammed into the counter and slid on to the floor between his two buddies.

Reacher turned to the guy who was posing as Begovic. He said, 'You. Real name?'

The guy climbed down off the stool. He said, 'Bite me.'

'Unusual. I bet you had a tough time at school.' Reacher punched him in the gut. The guy doubled over. Reacher slammed his elbow down into the back of his head and the guy's legs folded and he hit the floor, face first.

Reacher turned to Hix.

Hix stayed on his stool. His phone was in his hand. He said, 'Don't look at me. I'm not telling you a thing.'

Hix jabbed the phone three times. Reacher took it from him. There were three digits on the display: 911. But there was no call in progress. Reacher dropped the phone and crushed it with his heel. Then he walked around the counter to the business side of the kitchen. He opened the drawers in turn until he found one with utensils in it. He took out a knife. A small one. Its blade was only three inches long. But it was sharp. Designed for delicate work. Peeling. Mincing. Dicing. Reacher held it up for Hix to see. He said, 'I watched you on the stage this morning. You looked like you were having fun. Like you loved the attention. The cameras. So tell me this: Will the cameras still love you if I slice your nose off and make you eat it?'

*

326

Reacher was inside the big white house for fewer than ten minutes. When he came out he was carrying a prison ID on a lanyard and a car key. He crossed to Hix's BMW and opened the driver's door. He leaned in and hit a button up on the ceiling near the rear-view mirror. The gates started to swing back over the driveway. He called to Maurice and told him to come out from his hiding place in the trees. Then he walked to the end of the driveway and called to Hannah. He told her to retrieve the cushion from the wall and the blanket that was tied to the fender and bring the VW around to the front of the house.

Hannah parked at the bottom of the stairs leading to the front door. Jed had moved to the passenger seat. Maurice was standing nervously near the VW's rear hood.

'OK,' Reacher said. 'Here's the deal. Jed – your father is alive. I will try to keep him that way, but I'm not going to lie. He's short of time, and he's in a lot of trouble. So no promises. Hannah – I need you to take Jed to the Riverside Lodge. Get a room. Use the name J. P. Slough. Pay cash. Call Detective Harewood. We do need him to get the feds involved. Tell him to start here, at the house. If I'm not at the hotel in two hours, leave town. Don't come back. Maurice – you were half right. Something is killing Minerva inmates. Maybe outsiders, too. But it's not drugs.'

Reacher took the pillowcase and went back to the BMW. By the time he had figured out which switches and toggles to press and push to get the seat adjusted so he could fit behind the wheel Hannah had slid into the passenger seat.

She said, 'You're trying to dump me again. That's a nasty habit.'

Reacher said, 'I'm not dumping you. You just can't come with me this time. It's a one-person job. And I need you to

327

keep an eye on Jed. If things go south, if his dad doesn't make it, he's going to need a lot of help.'

'His dad's really still alive?'

'I believe so.'

'Where?'

'In the prison.'

'Who's the imposter?'

'A guy who goes by Carpenter. Might not be his real name. He's a middleman between Minerva and the clients they supply. He sold a guy out in Paraguay ten years ago. Expected him to die in jail. He didn't. He's back in the States and he's looking to get even. Minerva couldn't wash their hands of Carpenter because they need his contacts. So Carpenter needed a new ID. They took advantage of Begovic's pardon to make the switch. Carpenter was scared so he hid in the prison until the ceremony. Danny Peel noticed the discrepancy in the numbers. He dug. Joined the dots. Told Angela, who told Sam. The rest you know.'

'Where are the Minerva guys now? Hix and Brockman and Carpenter?'

'In the house. The kitchen.'

'We can't leave them unguarded.'

'They're not going anywhere.'

'Under their own steam, perhaps. But what if some of their other guys come looking for them?'

'That's why we need Harewood to bring the FBI.'

'What if they get rescued before the feds show up?'

'That's a risk we'll have to run. I can't stay and watch them. I have to get to Begovic.'

'I'll watch them. I'm not going to run and hide and leave them with the front door open. They killed Sam. I'm not going anywhere until they're in custody. It's my decision. My risk to run. And I have my SIG. I'm not afraid to use it. You saw that last night.'

Reacher said nothing.

Hannah said, 'This other guy who's lurking around. Is he a revolutionary or something? Or does he just have bad dress sense?'

'His name's Maurice. He's a journalist. He seems harmless.'

'He can babysit Jed, then.'

'I guess.'

'Jed was right. They are going to kill his dad. And I don't see how you can stop them.'

'I have an idea.'

'The guy's in a prison cell. You can't break him out. You do know that? Sam studied the ways people try to escape. You need months to plan. To observe. To find sloppiness in the guards' routines. Faulty equipment. Building failures. Staff who are vulnerable because they're getting divorced or they drink or use drugs or gamble or are in debt. You need luck. And even then ninety-nine per cent of attempts fail.'

'My odds are little better than that.'

'Really? What makes you think so?'

'Harold wasn't wearing a wedding ring. And I saw four neat triangles of grass.'

Reacher parked the BMW on Harold's driveway. His house was small and shabby. It was a single-storey with peeling paint, windows caked in dirt, a minimal porch and a scruffy weed-filled yard. Reacher started with the mailbox. It was about set to overflow. He didn't pay much attention to the kinds of letters that were in there. He just took an elastic band from the first bundle he found and moved on to the back door. It wasn't hard to figure out which key to use from the collection in the pillowcase. It was the most scratched one. Reacher let himself in, crossed the kitchen quickly and followed the corridor until he found Harold's bedroom. He opened the closet. There was only one suit hanging there. It was black. A white formal shirt was on a hanger next to it. And rolled up in a drawer, a tie. Also black. Funeral attire, Reacher thought. But that didn't bother him. It would be fine for what he needed. He changed into Harold's clothes and put his own things in the pillowcase. Then he moved on to the garage.

There was theoretically room in it for three cars, but two of the bays were taken up by weightlifting equipment. There were pictures on the wall of Harold in weird spandex outfits grappling with all kinds of heavy objects. Tractors. Tyres. Farm animals. A wheel of cheese. Reacher had questions. The third vehicle bay was empty. There were oil stains on the floor. The remains of a paint spill. Dried-up residue from other fluid leaks. But no logbook. No meticulous records had been kept. Probably no meaningful maintenance had ever taken place in there. Reacher crossed to the tiny worktable. He took a knife. A screwdriver. A hammer. And a roll of duct tape.

When he was back in the car Reacher took all the remaining cash out of the wallets in the pillowcase. He rolled it up, secured it with the elastic band he had taken and put it in his pocket. He emptied everything out of the pillowcase except for the tools and the SIG. Slung the lanyard with the ID on it around his neck. And drove to the prison.

The little crowd had disappeared. So had the security guards and the camera operators. The only people left outside the prison were the contractors, who were strolling around, shifting the chairs and stacking the dismantled pieces of fence. The tent was still obscuring the entrance, though it was less rigid than it had been. Its roof was sagging and its sides were billowing in the breeze. The surface of the stage had been removed. It was piled up in the back of a truck that was sitting next to the exposed framework. Reacher parked next to the truck. He climbed out of the BMW and started to march around and stare at the contractors like a boss. The contractors looked away and pretended they hadn't seen him.

Reacher made his way to the entrance, leaned down like he was inspecting something and gently set the roll of money on its side, next to the fence. Then he strolled back toward the BMW. When he was close he turned to the nearest trio of contractors.

'Hey!' Reacher yelled. 'You three. Stop loafing around. Get that tent taken down. We've got visitors coming soon. How are they supposed to get to the entrance?'

The contractors grumbled and muttered and drifted away to do as they'd been told. Reacher took the pillowcase from the car and carried it to the truck by the stage. He opened the door and put it on the passenger seat. Then he stood back and watched the contractors. He waited. After a couple of minutes one of them noticed the wad of cash. He stepped closer to it. He leaned down to pick it up. But his greed and surprise had overridden his memory. He'd gotten too close to the fence. The sensors under the ground detected his footsteps. They fired off instant signals to the security computers in the control room. A klaxon sounded. Red lights flashed. All the floodlights in the complex came on at once. And all the nearby cameras rotated on their posts to give the operators the clearest possible view of the cause of the problem.

*

331

Reacher jumped in behind the wheel of the truck, fired it up and backed across to a spot near the fence at the foot of the closest watchtower. He grabbed the pillowcase. Gripped it in his teeth. Scrambled on to the truck's roof. Stretched up and took hold of the railing at the top of the tower's half-wall. He pushed with his legs. Pulled with his arms. Poured himself head first over the railing. And was met by no one. There was no guard in the tower. No one with a gun or a uniform was in sight.

Reacher peered over the tower wall on the prison side of the fence. The grass triangle was below him, ahead around sixty degrees. It looked as green and lush as it had done from the outside. From the higher elevation he could see the bricks surrounding it were painted red. A sign for people to keep away from it. Because of its purpose. It was a pit for guards to fire warning shots into. Its ground was soft. It was absorbent. It posed no danger of ricochets. There had been at least one riot recently. Hannah had told him about it. But there was no bullet damage in the neatly manicured grass. Therefore the towers were no longer used, except as window-dressing when Hix was staging a publicity stunt. The heavy lifting in the world of surveillance was done by electronics now. Cameras and sensors. Reacher smiled to himself. It was like they used to say in the army. Sometimes there's no substitute for the Eyeball, Human, Mark One.

FORTY-THREE

The watchtowers were no longer regularly used, but they were still connected to the meshed-in walkways that criss-crossed the prison site. Reacher climbed down the ladder and started toward the building that housed the control centre. He knew where it was because he had made Hix draw a diagram.

Reacher passed through five doors along the way. They were all secured. Hix's ID card opened all of them. The final one was the control centre itself. Beyond that point the doors were designated operational, not administrative. That meant they could only be operated remotely. Which was the whole point of Reacher's visit.

There were two people on duty when Reacher entered the control room. Both men. Both in their late fifties. Both with enough miles on the clock to make sound decisions in times of stress. That was the theory. A hypothesis based more on the likelihood of escape attempts and riots than a one-man incursion. Even an incursion by one man who could do as much damage on his own as a medium-size riot. But either way the theory held water. Reacher gave the guys instructions. They followed to the letter without argument. They didn't even baulk when Reacher locked them in the storage cupboard and broke the key in the outside of the lock.

Reacher checked the display on the access control panel. It was rudimentary, but easy to interpret. The symbols representing all the doors between the control centre and the segregation unit S1 were green. The other doors were all red. That was what he wanted to see so Reacher took the hammer from the pillowcase and smashed the controls. Then he smashed all the CCTV monitors. There was no way he would be able to disable all the cameras on his route. Not easily. And not quickly. But there was no sense in leaving any potential relief crew with the ability to use any of them.

There were five more doors to pass through before Reacher would get to Begovic's cell. The first two were in sections of the mesh walkway. Reacher was completely exposed while he was in there. He was in the heart of enemy territory. Massively outnumbered. Completely outgunned. If either of the doors didn't open, he would have a serious problem. Or if there was some anti-infiltration system he was unaware of, ready to kick in and trap him. Or a backup control panel. Or an automatic reset procedure. He knew there were all kinds of ways he might not leave the place alive.

Reacher approached the first door slowly. Calmly. He stretched out a hand. Pushed. The door swung open. So did the second. The third led from the mesh walkway to a covered corridor. A smaller space. Completely enclosed. He would be like a rat caught in a drainpipe if the doors froze. The third opened. So did the fourth, which led into the segregation unit itself. Reacher was at the centre of the cross, on the ground floor. Above him were the three rooms that formed the unit's command hub. In the middle of each wall a door led to one of the cell wings. Reacher needed the west wing. He identified the door. The fifth. He pushed. It opened.

Reacher paused and looked at each cell door in turn. There were sixteen. Fifteen of these were always unlocked because the wing was not officially in commission. It was only being used for under-the-table projects. Hix had sworn that Begovic would be the only person locked up in there. But if he had tucked a couple of tame psychopaths away in the place, Hix might have thought it was a lie he could get away with.

Reacher listened. He picked up the sound of someone moving. Two people. In the first cell on his right, W1. Hix had described it as a transport preparation area. The door was standing open an inch. Reacher pushed it the rest of the way. Inside there was an operating table. A metal trolley covered with surgical tools. A cabinet full of drugs. Two drip stands. A heart monitor. A person-sized metal box with a 12V car-style battery at one end to power the system that controlled its internal temperature, like a futuristic travel coffin. A defibrillator mounted on the wall. And two men wearing scrubs.

One of the men grabbed a scalpel from the trolley and lunged at Reacher. Straight forward. Going for Reacher's gut. But with no power. No venom. The guy was no knife fighter. That was for sure. Reacher knocked his arm aside, continued to spin, building momentum, and punched the guy just below his ear. The force hurled him across the operating table and into the narrow gap next to the wall.

Reacher turned to the other guy. He was standing with his

hands up. He said, 'Don't hurt me. I won't cause you any trouble. I'll do anything you want.'

'You're getting ready to *prepare* Begovic?'

'I guess. They don't tell us names.'

'You're going to chop him up?'

'God, no. The buyer does that. We send the bodies out whole.'

'Who's the buyer?'

'I don't know.'

Reacher stepped closer.

The guy said, 'I swear. It's way above my pay grade. But there's a rumour. This one's going to our biggest customer. They work out of a ship. Off the Jersey coast. In international waters. Where there are no regulations.'

'So the guys on the ship cut him up. And do what? Store his body parts until they're needed?'

'Eventually. He'll stay alive while only non-essential organs are harvested. You know. Corneas. One kidney. Skin. Some kinds of bone. The big joints. And blood. Blood replenishes itself so it makes sense to keep him alive as long as possible.'

'How much are all those things worth?'

'They use everything, once he's dead. Eight hundred thousand dollars, maybe.'

'You send people to this place. People who are alive when they leave here.'

'It's my job. I just do what I'm told.'

Reacher felt the bile rising from his stomach so he stepped forward, butted the guy in the face and went back out into the corridor.

Cells W2, W4 and W6 were empty. So was W3. W5 showed signs of recent use. There was a regular twin bed with a pale blue comforter and a TV perched on a footlocker by the far wall. The room smelled vaguely of pizza and Chinese food. It was where Carpenter had been hiding out before taking Begovic's place at the release ceremony. W7 was empty. And Begovic himself was in W8. He was on the bed when Reacher opened the door, lying absolutely still. For a moment Reacher thought he was dead. That the whole enterprise had been a trap. Then Begovic blinked.

'Anton?' Reacher kept his voice quiet. 'My name's Reacher. I'm here to help you. To get you out. We have to get moving now. Can you stand up?'

Begovic didn't move. He didn't speak.

So not dead, Reacher thought. Just catatonic. Which was understandable. The guy had been wrongly locked up for years. Promised his freedom. Then bundled back into solitary. Reacher felt some sympathy. But he could also feel the seconds ticking away. 'Begovic!' he said. 'On your feet. Face front. Forward, march.'

Begovic stood and moved to the door. Reacher scanned the room for sentimental possessions but he couldn't see any likely candidates so he eased Begovic out into the corridor. Then toward the door at the centre of the unit. They were halfway there when the lights went out. There was total darkness for six long seconds. Reacher heard two metallic bangs. One behind him. One in front. Begovic's breathing grew louder. Quicker. Shallower. Then there was a deep *clunk* and the light returned, only at about half the brightness.

'What happened?' Begovic's voice was soft and low.

'Main power went out,' Reacher said. 'It switched to the backup generators.'

'OK.' Begovic started moving again.

Not OK, Reacher thought. *Not in the same hemisphere as OK.* But he didn't say anything until he got to the door. There was no point raising the alarm if he was mistaken. Which he wasn't. It was just as he feared.

The door was now locked.

FORTY-FOUR

Emerson and Graeber found the place they were looking for outside Winson with no difficulty. Graeber was driving the black van that was expected at the rendezvous. Emerson was driving the white one. They continued for a quarter of a mile after they spotted the premises then pulled over to the side of the road to figure out their next move.

They were in good time. The area was secluded. The layout looked straightforward. The only issue either of them could see was gaining entry. The site wasn't the most secure they had ever encountered, but they were used to working in deserted buildings. Here they would be dealing with at least one person. Maybe more. And they needed to take supplies in with them. The barrel, in particular. Which meant getting the gate open. And doing it quietly.

The best scenario either of them could come up with was that the guy they were looking to surprise was already there.

If he was, they could let the chloroform do its work then make as much noise as necessary with the gate. They could dynamite the damn thing if they wanted to.

They spent two more minutes kicking around their options then settled on a plan. A simple one, which was the kind Emerson liked best. They would leave the vehicles where they were for the moment. Take the lightweight stepladder, a tarp and a rope from the white van. Climb the wall. Recce all the buildings in the compound. Bring the chloroform. And hope they would get lucky.

'What happened?' Begovic said again.

Reacher knew, but he didn't want to get into the details. He remembered hearing all about it from a tech-minded corporal he had met at Leavenworth years ago when he was there for a prisoner transfer. The guy had explained that prison doors aren't naturally open with the ability to be locked if required. It's the other way around. Their natural state is to be locked, and they can be made to open if required. They work by having two competing magnets. One permanent. One electro. The permanent magnet is fixed into the wall. It naturally pulls a steel bar along a shielded channel in the door and into a socket in the frame, locking it. If the electromagnet receives current it activates, and because it's set up to be stronger than the permanent magnet it pulls the steel bar the opposite way, out of the socket in the frame, unlocking it.

The system has two advantages. Doors can easily be locked or unlocked remotely. It's just a question of applying or denying current to the electromagnet. And if the power is cut for any reason, even for an instant, the system fails-safe and the doors automatically revert to locked.

Someone had figured out that Reacher had set all the doors on his route to be open. They couldn't lock them with the usual controls because Reacher had trashed them with a hammer. So they cut the power. The backup circuits were kept deliberately isolated from the locks. Reacher couldn't help admiring the simplicity of the solution. He also couldn't hide from the depth of the trouble he was in. Trapped in a place designed by experts to be escape-proof. The only possible way out was to restore current to the electromagnet in the door. Which was categorically impossible from where he was.

Unless . . .

The experts who designed the prison had not counted on one of the cells being filled with medical equipment. Reacher did a mental inventory of what he had seen in W1. He figured there might just be a chance, if his high-school physics had stood the test of time. He spun Begovic around and told him to follow.

Reacher grabbed the roll of tissue off the weird one-piece, unbreakable stainless-steel toilet/basin/mirror assembly in the corner of the cell. He handed it to Begovic and said, 'I need you to take all the paper off this. I just want the cardboard tube from the inside. OK?'

Begovic said, 'Sure.' He grabbed the roll, poked one index finger up into the centre and started to pull.

Reacher said, 'Stay here a minute. I'll be back.' He hurried into cell W3, took the hammer out of the pillowcase, stretched up and used the claw to rip the metal conduit carrying the lighting circuit off the ceiling. He tore the wiring free and repeated the process in W5 and W7. He returned to W1 and found Begovic had the cardboard tube ready. Reacher took the knife from the pillowcase and cut a slit into the insulation

341

at the end of the first length of wire he'd harvested. He gripped the plastic between one thumb and finger, and the copper between the other thumb and finger. He pulled them in opposite directions and the shiny copper emerged like a snake shedding its skin. He repeated the process with the other lengths of wire and ended up with three six-foot strands which he joined together into one long piece by twisting the joints between his teeth.

'OK,' Reacher said. 'Hold out the tube. Grip it tight. Don't let it spin.'

Reacher wound the copper around the cardboard again and again, up and down, back and forth, until he had a tight, thick coil with a six-inch tail at each end. He took the defibrillator off the wall. He bound one copper tail to each paddle with duct tape. Led the way out into the corridor and up to the door. Flipped the switch on the defibrillator that said *Charge*. Waited for the light to turn from red to green. Turned the dial to the maximum discharge setting. Gripped the insulated handles that were attached to the paddles. Held the coil up to the doorframe on the side opposite the hinges, roughly halfway up. Then he turned to Begovic and said, 'OK. When you're ready, hit the *shock* button.'

Begovic said, 'Ready.' He stretched out a bony finger and jabbed the red disc.

There was a flash like a bolt of lightning. A buzz like a fuse box overloading. A sudden whiff of burning cardboard and scorched paint. And a soft thud when the coil hit the floor after the copper tails melted away.

Reacher said, 'OK. Let's hope we just fried ourselves a magnet.' He went to W1 and returned a moment later carrying the 12V battery from the body-sized box. 'One way to find out.' There was metal conduit on the wall leading away from the frame on the hinge side of the door. Reacher used the claw of the hammer to tear it free. He pulled out about three feet of cable, doubled it over the knife blade and sliced through. He trimmed back the insulation. Separated the two strands until the ends of the wire were far enough apart to reach the battery's poles. He made contact with the positive. Then the negative. Then he listened. He imagined he could hear the steel rod obeying the electromotive force and sliding slowly along its tube inside the door. Pulling clear of the frame. He held the wires in place for twenty seconds. Thirty. Then he dropped them and stood up.

He grabbed the pillowcase and turned to Begovic. 'That's it. It worked. Or it didn't.'

It had worked. Reacher pushed the door. It swung back. And he came face to face with three men. Two guards with AR-15 rifles. And a pasty-faced guy in a suit.

FORTY-FIVE

Reacher grabbed the stock of the nearer guard's gun and pushed it up toward the ceiling. He kicked the second guard in the balls. Butted the nearer guard in the face. And kicked the second guard in the head before he could crawl away.

Begovic ran to the door that led to the exit corridor. It was locked.

The guy in the suit didn't move. He said, 'You must be Reacher. Hell of an entrance.'

Reacher collected the rifles and slung them over his shoulder. 'Who are you?'

The guy didn't reply.

Begovic said, 'His name's Riverdale. The warden. He's a complete asshole.'

Reacher said, 'Riverdale? OK. Time to redeem yourself. These doors need to open.'

Riverdale stayed silent for a moment. Then he said, 'No

problem. I can do that. You just need to do one thing for me first.'

Reacher said nothing.

Riverdale pointed at Begovic. 'Kill him. Blow his head off. Then you can walk out of here.'

Reacher shook his head. 'I can see why you don't want him walking around, free. But that doesn't work for me.'

Riverdale said, 'This is one of those *the good of the many versus the good of the few* things. Shoot him, that's one dead person. If you don't shoot him, I can't let you take him with you. That's a given. So the doors will stay locked until more of my guys arrive.'

'Have you got any more guys?'

'Plenty more. They'll kill both of you. You'll probably manage to kill me before you bleed out. So that's three dead people. Three dead is worse than one. It's three times as bad. That's ethics 101. So I'm asking you. Do the moral thing. Hell, even Begovic probably sees the logic.'

Begovic said, 'Screw the logic.'

Reacher said, 'Logic. No logic. It still doesn't work for me.'

Riverdale said, 'OK. I'll sweeten the pot. Kill him. We both walk. I give you a million dollars, cash. I hear you're broke. This is your chance to live like a prince.'

'I have everything I need. Everything I want. Which makes me better off than any prince. So no dice.'

'Look around, Reacher. Look at this place. Do you really want to die here? Today?'

'Everyone has to die someday. Someplace.'

'But here? Now?'

'I don't see that happening. Not unless a random meteorite lands on us.'

'No? So what's your proposal.'

345

'Open the doors. Watch us walk out.'

'Be serious.'

'Open the doors. Shoot yourself in the head. Don't watch us walk out.'

Riverdale was silent for a moment, then he said, 'Are you married, Reacher?'

Reacher said, 'No.'

'You ever been married?'

'No.'

'Girlfriend? Significant other?'

'No.'

'OK. Given you're homeless and destitute, I'm guessing you don't get much action. So I have an idea. Might tip the scales.' Riverdale took out his phone and speed-dialled a number. When the call was answered he said, 'Reacher's neutralized. I need to get back to my office. Turn the power back on and unlock the doors between S1 and there.'

Nothing happened for twenty seconds. Then there were simultaneous clicks from all sides of the room and the lights stepped up a level.

Riverdale started toward the exit door. He said, 'Come with me.'

Reacher and Begovic followed through the covered corridor. The rat trap, as Reacher already thought of it. He was expecting guards to burst through the door behind them at any second. Or for Riverdale to hit the floor at some predetermined signal and bullets to tear into them from the front. They covered half the distance. Three quarters. Took a left at the end. And finally made it into the next building. Riverdale led the way up a flight of concrete steps. He said, 'This is the original admin block. Everyone else has moved to Hix's new, fancy building. But not me.'

The steps opened on to a dingy corridor. It smelled vaguely of stewed cabbage and stagnant drains. There were windows on one side looking down over two of the exercise yards. And six office doors on the other side. At the far end a metal bar was fixed to the wall. Reacher figured it would be for cuffing people to, although it was in a very illogical place.

Riverdale ushered Reacher and Begovic down the length of the corridor and into the last office. The floor was bare concrete. There were fluorescent tubes in cages on the ceiling. Framed pictures of motorcycles on the walls. A couch against the far wall, covered in gold-coloured velour. And a metal desk in the centre of the room. Riverdale walked across to it and unlocked the top drawer. He took out a tablet computer, activated it with his thumbprint, opened a file of photographs and handed it to Reacher. He said, 'Take a look.'

Reacher scrolled through the pictures. They were all of women. The youngest would still be in her teens. The oldest, maybe in her sixties. They were all naked. And the pictures had all been taken in that room.

Riverdale said, 'Take your time. Pick your favourite. I can have her here within an hour. You can do what you want to her. For as long as you want.'

Reacher said, 'What's in it for you?'

'I get Begovic.'

'And then?'

'You can go. Free as a bird.'

'How?'

'Same way you got in, I guess. Whatever that was.'

'You know how I got in. You figured it out from the doors I

347

opened. You think I'm crazy? I'm not going back the same way.'

'OK. If I can guarantee you a safe way out, do we have a deal?'

'What kind of safe way?'

Riverdale loosened his tie, unfastened his top button and fished a key on a chain out from under his shirt. 'This opens a gate. A private one. Nobody knows about it but me.'

'Where?'

'Far wall of the warehouse. Brings you out on the safe side of the fence. Takes you to a path cut in the riverbank. All the way down to one of the old caves. It's been used since this whole area was French. Pirates. Smugglers. Bootleggers. Now me. I've got stores in there. Food. A boat. An inflatable.'

'Bullshit.'

'It's true. I was here when the prison was built. Added a few extras of my own. Had a feeling a day like this would come. When someone had to leave in a hurry. Thought it would be me, but hey.'

Reacher nodded. 'One more question, then we can shake hands. What time is Begovic due to be collected?'

'Why?'

'I have a thirst for knowledge.'

Riverdale shrugged. 'Twenty-five minutes from now, give or take.'

Reacher held out his right hand. Riverdale stepped closer to take it. Then Reacher drove the side of the tablet into Riverdale's throat with his left. Riverdale's larynx collapsed. He fell backward and landed in a sprawl on the couch. He couldn't breathe. He couldn't scream. He clawed at his neck. Tears streamed from his eyes. Reacher hurled the tablet on to the ground and stomped it into fragments. He crossed to the desk and rummaged through the open drawer. Took out a twelve-inch ruler. Moved back and grabbed Riverdale by the shoulders. Flipped him over. Pinned him to the couch with his knee. Slid the ruler between the back of Riverdale's neck and the steel chain that held the key. And started to turn.

. The chain cut into Riverdale's skin. Blood dribbled on to the couch. Reacher turned the ruler again. The chain bit deeper. Blood poured over the fabric faster than it could soak in. Reacher turned the ruler again. And again. And again. The chain cut Riverdale's flesh. It tore his crushed windpipe. And finally sliced through his carotid. Blood sprayed right up the back of the couch and on to the wall. Reacher tilted River-dale's head a few degrees, pushed his neck down into the cushion and held him there until his heart had nothing left to pump.

Reacher stood and looked at Begovic. He said, 'What? I took a rational dislike to the guy. He got what he deserved.'

Begovic didn't reply.

Reacher said, 'You OK with what just happened?'

'Nothing happened.' Begovic's face was blank. 'I didn't see a thing.'

Reacher nodded and started for the door. 'Come on. Time to go.'

Begovic didn't move. 'What about the key? The secret exit?'

Reacher said, 'We're not using it.'

'Why not?'

'Either it doesn't exist, or it's booby-trapped.'

'How do you know?'

'It's a universal principle. If something seems too good to be true, it is too good to be true.'

'I guess.' Begovic took one step, then stopped again. 'I wish I'd understood that sixteen years ago.'

'What happened sixteen years ago?'

'I got arrested. The first time.'

Reacher stayed quiet.

Begovic said, 'I met a girl. Wanted to buy her a ring. But I didn't have any money. So a guy loaned me some. More than I needed. A friend of my dead uncle.'

'The money was dirty.'

'Right. But that wasn't the problem. I didn't get caught. He kept one of the bills with my prints on it. Said he'd tell the police I was passing forgeries unless I did something for him. And it was easy, so I thought, *Why not?*'

'What did he want you to do?'

'Go certain places. Certain times. Where people would see me. That was all.'

'You were his patsy in waiting. When he felt the heat, he framed you.'

'Right. Then I got in more trouble. Most of that was on me. But it started with him.'

'I'm sorry.'

'Don't be. Not your fault. Just tell me, how are we going to get out if we can't use the key?'

'I have an idea. But we could use a diversion, first.'

Reacher smashed the square of glass with his elbow and jabbed the button that lay behind it. A klaxon spooled up and began to wail. Red lights started to flash. Reacher joined Begovic at the window and they looked down at the exercise yards. Inmates started to appear from two of the units. A and B. Slowly at first. The men looked tentative. Uncertain. Then the streams of bodies grew faster. More boisterous. The yards started to fill up. Inmates jostled and pushed. Guards appeared in the watchtowers. One had a bullhorn as well as a rifle. He started to call out instructions. They were muffled. Indistinct. Whatever he was saying, the prisoners took no notice.

Reacher turned to Begovic. 'Why is no one coming out of C Block?'

Begovic shrugged. 'Don't know.'

'Is the block in use?'

'Think so. It was before I went back in solitary. Used to see guys from there in the chow hall. Doubt they closed it down since then. Why would they? Where would everyone go?'

Reacher thought about his conversation with Maurice, the journalist, outside Hix's house. About drugs. Maurice's theory that Minerva was making them. Then supplying them to the captive population. Reacher had dismissed the idea when he found out about the organ trading. Now he was reconsidering. Maybe this wasn't an either/or situation. Maybe Minerva was greedy enough to do both. He said, 'These guys from C Block. Do you remember anything about them?'

'I guess. They were kind of cliquey. Sat together, mostly. Didn't talk to the other prisoners. Seemed friendlier with the guards.'

Reacher led the way back down the concrete stairs and then along a bunch of corridors and walkways. It was a trial-and-error process. Three times they came to doors that wouldn't open. The fire alarm created a wider accessible zone than usual between the custodial units and the exercise yards, but that didn't extend to the perimeter of the prison. Its border wasn't predictable. Reacher and Begovic had to thread their way back and forth, sometimes doubling back from

351

blockages, sometimes looping around obstacles. Reacher expected to run into a guard at every doorway. Around every bend. But in that respect the diversion was working. Everyone's attention was focused on the exercise yards. And Reacher didn't have to worry about the cameras. There hadn't been time for the monitors to be fixed. So after five long minutes, and a route only a drunk, crazy crow would fly, Reacher and Begovic wound up at the entrance to C Block.

The door to the hub was standing open. It was wedged by a cinder block. Reacher led the way inside. The basic layout was the same as in the segregation unit. There was a square, central space with wings running perpendicular to each wall. The door to each one was open. The sound of voices and movement and activity was spilling out like they were in the foyer of an office or a workshop. The air was heavy with solvents and the hint of smoke.

Reacher started with the west wing. It was like the offspring of an art studio and a dormitory. There were six beds evenly spaced between areas full of easels covered with canvases. More were hanging on the walls. There were metal shelves overflowing with paint pots and jars of thinner and packs of brushes. Extra lights had been fixed on the ceiling. They were fitted with some kind of blue bulbs so that the whole space felt like it was bathed in daylight even though there were no windows. There were six guys in there. They had faded, stained aprons over their prison uniforms. They were all busy. One was working on a copy of a Monet. Two on Van Goghs. One on a Mondrian. One on a Picasso. One was flinging rough daubs of paint all over a long, rectangular canvas that was stretched out on the floor. None of them paid any attention to Reacher or Begovic.

The north wing was the domain of four guys who were

352

working on documents. Two with computers. Two by hand. Reacher looked over one of the manual guy's shoulders. There were two pieces of paper in front of him. They were the same size. One was filled with writing. It was someone's will. It painstakingly set out the names of people who were going to get a bunch of cash and jewellery and cars and a collection of antique shotguns. The second page was half full. The script looked identical. It listed the same items. The same quantities. The same values. But the names of the people who were set to inherit were different. A woman who wasn't mentioned at all in the first document was set to clean up with the second.

Reacher said, 'Could you write a letter in someone else's handwriting?'

The guy with the pen said, 'Sure. Whose?'

'What if it was a suicide note?'

''Course. Those are easy. No technical terms. Not too long. Not often, anyway.'

The east wing was full of sculptors and jewellers. Three guys were chipping away at blocks of marble. One had clay up to his elbows. One was welding giant girders together. One was hollowing out a tree trunk. Five were melting yellow and white metals in dented crucibles and adding stones of all kinds of colours to make rings and bracelets and pendants. There were posters on the wall showing enlarged versions of signature pieces by Tiffany and Cartier and Bulgari. Some of the trinkets on the guys' workbenches were pretty much indistinguishable to Reacher's eye.

The south wing was home to six guys with computers. They were sitting on threadbare office chairs staring at screens perched on beaten-up, rickety desks and rattling away at cordless keyboards. Three of them were virtually

353

inert, like robots, with just their fingers and eyes showing signs of life. The others were almost dancing in their seats, like concert pianists or seventies rock musicians.

Reacher tapped one of the animated guys on the shoulder. He said, 'Would you have a problem hacking into someone's email?'

The guy stopped fidgeting and said, 'Yeah. Huge problem. I only do it, like, fifty times a day.'

'You could read someone's messages?'

'Read them. Alter them. Delete them. Copy them. Whatever you want.'

FORTY-SIX

The clock in Reacher's head told him it was time to leave. He grabbed Begovic and led the way out of C Block. He was still convinced they would cross paths with a guard. Or a squad of guards called back on duty to deal with the ruckus that had resulted from the fire alarm. But again the unrest served their purpose. They made it to Unit S1 undetected.

The two guys who had been backing Riverdale's play were still on the floor. They were still unconscious. Reacher dragged them through the door he had disabled and shoved them into the preparation cell. He gave each another kick in the head to make sure they wouldn't make an unwelcome appearance any time soon. He did the same to the pair of medics he'd left there earlier. He removed the magazine and dumped one of the rifles on the operating table. Checked the tan SIG. Then he went back out into the hub.

Reacher unslung the other rifle from his shoulder and said

to Begovic, 'Put your hands behind your back like they're tied. Look at the floor. Play along with whatever I say.'

A minute later the door to the unit's south wing swung open. Two guys came through. They had a heavy-duty gurney. One was pushing. One was pulling. The guy in the lead said, 'What's the story here? Why—'

The guy stopped talking. He was looking at Reacher. He couldn't understand why someone he didn't recognize was there. Apparently in authority. Who wasn't part of the programme. He glanced across to Begovic. He couldn't understand why the prisoner was standing upright. Why he was still conscious. Why he wasn't boxed up, ready for transport. The guy's brain struggled for a second. It was trying to fit all the pieces together. Then it quit the puzzle. It didn't matter what the exact picture was. Because whatever shape it took, something was wrong. That was obvious. So he let go of the gurney and his hand darted toward his pocket.

Reacher didn't know if the guy was going for a gun or a phone. He didn't wait to find out. He stepped forward and spun the rifle around as he moved. Then he drove the flat end of its stock into the bridge of the guy's nose. The guy collapsed on to the gurney then rolled off its side. He crashed down on to the floor and lay still, face down, with blood pooling steadily around his head.

'Don't move.' Reacher reversed the rifle and pointed it at the guy who'd been pushing the gurney. 'You can show us the way out. Or I can take you to one of the exercise yards. There are about a hundred guys there who would make you very welcome. That's for sure. OK. You have five seconds to decide.'

Self-preservation won the day. Reacher and Begovic followed the guy through the unit's south wing. The cell doors were all open. There was no sound from inside any of them. Just the squeaking of three pairs of shoes on the concrete floor. A door was set into the wall at the far end. It was made of steel. Painted grey. It looked new. Shiny. The guy who was in the lead held his ID card up to a white plastic square set into the frame. The lock clicked and the guy pushed the door open. It led to a covered walkway. It was narrower than the other ones Reacher had been through. There were no lines painted on the ground. It had solid corrugated metal in place of open mesh. The air was hot and stale. It ran straight for thirty yards. There was a dog-leg to the left. Then it ran straight for another forty yards. There was another grey steel door at the end, which opened into a kind of large shed. There were floor-to-ceiling shelves on two sides. They were full of janitorial supplies and prison uniforms and cans of dried food. A van was parked in the centre. It was dark blue and shiny, like the one Reacher had seen outside the Riverside Lodge. It had been backed into the space. In front of it, in the middle of the opposite wall, there was a roll-up vehicle door. No other people were in sight. Reacher looked through the driver's window. The keys were in the ignition.

Reacher said, 'What opens the exit door?'

The guy said, 'There's a remote clipped to the visor. Hit the button, the door rolls up. Approach the gate in the inner fence. It'll open. Pull forward toward the gate in the outer fence. The inner one will close on its own. Then flash your headlights three times. The guy in the booth will let you out.'

'Flash the headlights. Really?'

'That's the signal.'

Reacher saw that the guy wouldn't meet his eye. So he opened the van's rear door and said, 'Get in. You're riding with Begovic. When we're clear of here I'll come and let you out. But first I'll knock on the bulkhead. If the door opens and Begovic hasn't heard a knock, he's going to shoot out one of your kneecaps.'

The guy shook his head and took a step back. 'Wait. You don't flash your lights. You don't do anything. Just approach the outer gate. The officer in the booth has orders to let this van in or out, any time, no record, no search. Don't worry. You won't be penned in for long.'

Penned in. Two words Reacher did not like the sound of. Not when they applied to him.

Reacher didn't make the guard get in the back of the van. Because Reacher didn't know Begovic well enough. He couldn't predict how Begovic would stand up to the pressure. If he got flustered or showed signs of panic there was too much danger that the guard would go for the gun. He could make a noise. Alert whoever was on duty in the booth. Begovic could wind up taking a stray bullet. Or a deliberate one. So Reacher took a different approach. He knocked the guy out, rolled his body on to the bottom shelf at the side of the room and piled a bunch of baled-up orange jumpsuits in front of it.

The van's engine started at the first turn of the key. The exit door opened at the first press of the remote. The gate in the inner fence rolled aside the moment the van approached. It slid back into place the second the van was through. Then nothing more happened. The outer gate stayed where it was. It was completely still. Inert. Like it was welded shut. Or it was just another fixed panel in the fence. The electrified fence. That was on their left. On their right. And now effectively in front and behind. There was no way forward. No way back. Nowhere to go even if they abandoned the vehicle.

The outer gate didn't move.

Reacher looked at the booth. He couldn't see inside. The glass was mirrored. Maybe no one was there. Maybe the fire alarm protocol required the guard to assist with the evacuation on the other side of the prison. Or maybe the guard was still at his post, waiting for some kind of signal. Something Reacher didn't know about. Something he had to do or the guard would raise the alarm. Reinforcements would come from behind, Reacher thought. Through the warehouse. Heavily armed. He checked the mirror. The roll-up door was still closed. For the moment.

The outer gate didn't move.

Reacher's foot was on the brake. He was thinking about shifting it to the gas pedal. There was no point trying to smash through the gate. It would be too strong. Designed to stop a much heavier vehicle. With a run-up. Not from a standing start. Reacher had no doubt about that. But he figured he could cause a dent. Get some of the truck's metal in contact with the mesh or the frame. Then he could open the van's back door. The cargo space was fitted with shelves. He had seen them when he was getting Begovic situated. He could tear a couple out. Use them to connect the rear of the van to the inner fence. Maybe cause a short circuit. Maybe kill the power for long enough to climb over. If he could find something to cover the razor wire.

The outer gate didn't move.

Reacher looked down. There were mats on the floor. In both footwells. They were made of rubber. Heavy duty. Made to protect the vehicle's floor from boots soaked with Mississippi rain. And thick enough to save a person from getting cut to ribbons. Maybe. There was only one way to find out. Reacher started to lift his foot. Then he stopped. And pressed down again for a moment.

The outer gate twitched. It shuddered. Then it lurched to the side.

Begovic switched from the cargo area to the passenger seat when they were a safe distance from the prison, but he didn't say a word on the rest of the drive to Bruno Hix's home. He pressed himself back against his seat and stayed completely still, apart from his eyes, which were constantly flicking from one side to the other. Reacher didn't speak either. He didn't want to tell Begovic there was a kid waiting for him at the house until they were close. He didn't want to give him the chance to think about it too much. To freak out. But at the same time Reacher didn't feel right making meaningless small talk when he was holding back such a significant piece of information. The further he drove, the less sure he felt about the choice he'd made. Then all of a sudden he was very glad he'd made no mention of Begovic's kid.

There were two vans parked outside Hix's house. One was white with Illinois plates. It looked to be a few years old. It showed plenty of signs of having lived a hard life and it was sitting at the side of the road. The other van was black. It had Mississippi plates. It looked new. Shiny. It was in great shape. All the way from its rear fender to its windshield. But its wings and hood and nose were ruined. Someone had used it to ram Hix's gates. Hard. It had shoved them open maybe four feet.

Reacher pulled over behind the white van. He told Begovic to stay put even if he heard noises from the house. He climbed out. He had the tan SIG in his hand. He checked both other vehicles' cabs and cargo areas. There were no people. Then he made his way through the gap in the gates, across the drive, past the VW and up the steps.

*

360

The front door was open. Reacher peered into the hallway. He could see no one. He could hear nothing. He crept inside. Headed left, toward the kitchen. Where he had left Hix and Brockman and Carpenter, tied up and immobile.

The room was empty.

Reacher didn't care too much about the Minerva guys. But he was worried about Hannah and Jed. He could see two possibilities. Whoever had arrived in the vans had a third vehicle which they used to abduct everyone from the house. Or everyone, including the hostiles, was still in the house or on the grounds.

Reacher favoured the second option. The first would involve a very large vehicle. It would need to hold a minimum of eight people. And it made no sense to abandon the white van. It looked serviceable and the back was crammed with all kinds of specialized tools and equipment.

There was a sound in the next room. A creak. It was quiet. It happened just once. But Reacher had definitely heard something. He crept to the door. Listened. Heard nothing else. Took hold of the handle. Jerked the door open. And jumped back to avoid getting hit by a guy who tumbled on to the floor at his feet.

It was Maurice. The journalist.

Reacher said, 'The hell are you doing in there?'

Maurice said, 'Hiding. Waiting for you. What took you so long?'

'Where are the others? Hannah? The kid?'

'Out back. I think.'

'You think?'

'I think they all are.'

'All?'

'Hannah. The kid. Hix and Brockman. Carpenter. And two new guys.'

'From Minerva?'

'No. They weren't here to rescue anyone. Definitely not. It was like they were looking for Carpenter. Like he was their target.'

'Why did they leave you?'

'They didn't know about me. I was in the laundry room. I went in there hoping it was a pantry. I was starving.'

'They didn't search?'

'I was hiding. I'm good at it. I've had plenty of practice.'

'So did you see what happened? Or only hear?'

'I saw some. They didn't search immediately. They came crashing in. Hannah went for her gun. But they were too fast.'

'Are they armed?'

'One guy, the younger one, he had a gun. The older one had a kind of flask and a cloth. He kicked Hannah's gun away then shoved the cloth in her face. She fell down. Jed tried to rush the guy. He kind of bounced off and the guy grabbed him and shoved the cloth in his face and he fell down too. Then they searched. I only listened after that.'

'What did they want with Carpenter?'

'One of them, the older one I think, because he had this tone like he was in charge, he started questioning him. It was kind of weird. He said Carpenter had sold some liver that was bad and it had killed his son. He wanted to know where it came from. If Hix and Brockman were involved.'

'What did Carpenter say?'

'Nothing. He wouldn't answer. The older guy said that was no problem. He had something better to loosen his tongue. Then I guess he used whatever was on the cloth to knock them out. I heard some thuds, then a bunch of slipping and scuffling. Five times. I guess they dragged everyone out back.'

'Why out back?'

'Because I didn't hear any vehicles and they weren't at the front. I looked. To be honest, I was going to run. Then I remembered you were coming back. Figured I should stay and warn you.'

'You did the right thing.' Reacher started toward the door.

'There's one thing I don't get.' Maurice stayed where he was. 'These guys want revenge for this fatal poisoning. What's that got to do with Minerva? There are no animals at their prisons. The company doesn't own any farms. Where are they getting the livers from?'

'It wasn't food poisoning that killed this guy's kid.' Reacher grabbed the door handle. 'And the liver didn't come from an animal. Not one with four legs.'

Reacher crossed the hallway, ran up the stairs and went into the centre room at the rear of the house. It was a bedroom. It had a polished wood floor. Sleek, pale furniture. And three tall windows covered by white curtains, all closed, which hung down to the floor. Reacher crossed to the centre window and peered around the edge of the curtain. He was looking through a glass door, across the balcony and down on to the big square of grass he had seen when he first broke into the house. The difference now was the people who were there. Hix, Brockman and Carpenter. Naked. Hanging by their wrists from the lighting gantry over the stage. Immobile. Hannah and Jed, on the grass to the right of the stage. Face down. Dressed. Also immobile. And two guys Reacher hadn't seen before. They were ladling some kind of gel out of a large barrel and slopping it into ice troughs they'd taken from the bar.

Reacher ran back down the stairs, through the front door and around to the rear of the building. He stepped up on to the porch. The new guys set the third trough down on the edge of the stage. They were standing on either side of the barrel. They heard the footsteps. Spun around. Pulled out guns. And aimed at Reacher.

The older guy said, 'Drop the weapon. Then get on the ground. Face down.'

The breeze was blowing directly toward Reacher. Past the two guys. Past their barrel.

Reacher said, 'Not going to happen. I have no quarrel with you. I'm here for the woman and the kid. They come with me. The idiots you strung up? Do what you want with them.'

The guy shook his head. 'The woman and the kid are going nowhere. They saw us.'

Reacher was picking up a faint smell. Something familiar. He said, 'They caught a glimpse at best. They're no threat.'

'Doesn't matter. They can put us at the scene. So can you.'

Gasoline, mainly, Reacher thought. And benzene. And something else. Then he made the connection. The combination of ingredients. He looked at the barrel. It was almost empty. Almost. But not quite. He said, 'Not my problem. I'm taking my friends and I'm leaving.'

'You're in no position to be telling us what's going to happen.'

Reacher said, 'I'm in the perfect position.' Then he fired. At the barrel. The bullet pierced the plastic and the remaining napalm ignited instantly. The sides buckled. The shockwave knocked both the guys over. And a tongue of orange flame engulfed the younger one. He screamed and writhed and squeezed off one unaimed round before he lost his grip on his gun.

Reacher jumped down from the porch, stepped forward and shot the younger guy in the head. The older guy was on his back. He wasn't moving. He had escaped the flames completely. But there was a red stain on his shirt. Low down on the left side of his abdomen. It was wet. And it was growing. His buddy's bullet had passed right through him.

The guy rolled over and forced himself on to his hands and knees. He tried to crawl toward the stage. Reacher stepped across and blocked his path.

'Move.' The guy's voice was somewhere between a croak and a whisper.

Reacher stayed still.

The guy nodded toward Carpenter. 'Him. Got to make him talk.'

Reacher said, 'You're going to bleed to death.'

'He killed my son. He has a supplier. I need a name.'

'Your son got a transplant?'

The guy nodded, then slumped down on to his side. 'His liver was toast. He went to rehab after rehab. Nothing stuck. The regular doctors wouldn't help. So I found a clinic. On a ship. They put in a new liver. But it was bad. Kyle died.'

Reacher said, 'The other guys you strung up. They're his suppliers. They run a prison. Find inmates no one will miss and sell them for their organs to be harvested.'

The guy raised his head. 'That true?'

Reacher nodded.

The guy said, 'Help me then. Shoot them.'

'No.'

'Why not? You shot Graeber. My friend.'

'That guy? He was on fire. It was a kindness. I'll make sure the prison operation gets closed down. Permanently. But I'm not going to kill anyone in cold blood.'

'Please. For my son. His name was Kyle Emerson. He was twenty-two.'

'No.'

The guy struggled back on to his hands and knees and crawled another yard.

Reacher picked up a shirt from a pile of clothes at the side of the stage. He held it out and said, 'Keep going and you'll bleed out. Stop, press this against the wound, call 911, maybe you'll have a chance.'

The guy kept on crawling. He made it to the front of the stage. Stretched up. One hand scrabbled for grip on the wooden surface. The other grabbed the rim of an ice trough. The guy tried to haul himself up but only managed to pull the trough off the stage. It was full of cream-coloured gel. The gel flooded across his chest. It flowed down to the front of his pants and mingled with the blood that had soaked into the material. He fell back. Rolled over. Clawed his way on to his knees. Straightened his back. Pulled a box of matches out of his pocket and turned to look at Reacher.

'Now I'm glad you didn't shoot these assholes.' The guy took out a match. 'Now they'll get what they deserve.'

The guy struck the match. A flame flared at its tip. He seemed mesmerized by it for a moment. Then his knees buckled. He toppled backward again. He dropped the match. It landed on his stomach. It was still alight.

Reacher jumped away. It was an instinctive response. A reaction to fire that was baked deep into the back of his brain. Impossible to resist. He felt the heat on his face and arms. Heard a *crump* sound. Thought he heard the guy laugh. Thought he could see him smile. Then he raised the SIG and shot him between the eyes.

The guy's body lay still. The flames danced on.

Reacher heard two sets of footsteps approaching. Both were cautious. And they were separate. Maurice appeared on the porch first. Then Begovic. Maurice stood still. Begovic jumped down and headed toward the stage. Toward his former captors. Then he changed course. He crossed to where Jed was lying and stood and looked down at the kid.

Maurice said quietly, 'Are they dead?'

Reacher pointed to the burnt-up guys. 'Those two are. The others are drugged. They'll be fine.'

'Should we cut the Minerva guys down?'

Reacher shook his head. 'Not yet. There's one more person hiding in the woodwork. Maybe more than one. We need these guys as bait.'

FORTY-SEVEN

Reacher carried Hannah through the gap in the gates and laid her down in the back of the van he'd taken from the prison. Begovic followed and placed Jed next to her. Maurice trailed along at the rear. He didn't want to be left alone in the yard with the dead bodies.

Reacher closed the van's doors and turned to Begovic. 'Can you drive?'

Begovic said, 'I guess. I used to be able to. But that was sixteen years ago.'

'The principle hasn't changed.' Reacher held out the keys. 'Go half a mile up the road. Then pull over and stay there until I join you.'

Reacher waited until the van was moving then asked Maurice for his phone. He dialled 911. The emergency operator answered after two rings.

Reacher said, 'I need the police. And if you can do it, a

368

priest. A guy's had an accident in his yard. His name's Bruno Hix. He keeps talking about something bad he got involved in. Says he wants to make a confession.'

The operator said, 'Sir, what's the address where the accident happened?'

Reacher read the details from a plaque on the wall at the side of Hix's gates.

'Your name, sir?'

'Chivington. John.'

'OK, sir. I can't help you with the priest. But I will send the police. And the paramedics. Hang in there. Help will be with you shortly.'

Reacher ended the call and handed the phone back to Maurice.

Maurice said, 'What now? Should I stay? Or go?'

'That's up to you. Are you only interested in Minerva? Or do you have time for an exposé on dirty cops?'

One police car arrived, seven minutes later. A Dodge Charger. Brand new. Unmarked. It had a dome light flashing on the dash and it was moving fast. It slid to a stop at the side of the black van that had its nose embedded in Hix's gate. The driver's door opened. An officer jumped out. He was pushing sixty. His uniform was crisp. It was neatly pressed, but it was tight around his gut. He drew his gun and hurried toward the house.

The cop skirted the building and stepped out on to the back porch. He glanced at the two burnt corpses. Emerson's was still smouldering. Then he jumped down, hurried across the grass and hauled himself up on to the stage. Hix was starting to regain consciousness. The cop slapped Hix's face. Over and over. A flurry of short, sharp blows. He said, 'Bruno, what the hell happened? Who called 911?'

369

Hix didn't answer. He couldn't.

'Who are these dead guys? How come you're all strung up like this? Where the hell are your clothes?'

Hix managed to blink.

'Are there any more of them? Any who are alive?'

Hix grunted.

The cop lowered his voice. 'Bruno, what did you tell them?'

Hix tried to shrug. He failed.

'Focus. Come on. Concentrate. This is important. What do they know?'

Hix shook his head.

'Do they know anything?'

Hix's voice came out harsh, but quiet. 'They know everything.'

The cop stepped back. He sighed. 'Thanks for being honest, my friend. We had quite the run. I'm sorry it couldn't go on longer. But all good things come to an end.' He slipped his gun into its holster. Took a pair of latex gloves from his pocket. Pulled them on. Leaned down and lifted the cuff of his pants. Unsnapped the strap on his ankle holster. Slid out a small silver revolver, straightened up and held it to Hix's temple. 'I'll make this quick.'

'Stop.' Reacher stood and stepped out from behind the bar. He was holding the SIG. It was levelled on the cop's centre mass.

The cop raised his hands and stepped back.

'Throw the gun off the stage.'

The cop did as he was told.

'Now the other one.'

The cop tossed his official piece.

Maurice emerged from the other side of the bar. He was holding out his phone. He crept forward until he was close

370

enough to read the cop's name badge. 'Chief Moseley, congratulations. What a performance. When you're in jail and I've won the Pulitzer I'm going to post it online. It's a masterclass in self-incrimination. I might have to pixelate parts of Mr Hix, though. I don't want to turn it into a comedy number.'

The smartly dressed kid at the Riverside Lodge was so happy to get his hands on the key to his VW he told Reacher he could have as many rooms in the north wing of the hotel as he liked, for as long as he liked. Reacher said he'd take four, for one night. And that this time he only needed one key for his room.

Maurice had stayed at Hix's to wait for the FBI, then he was planning a trip to DC. Hannah and Begovic stayed at the hotel. Reacher took Jed on a quick trip into town in Sam Roth's truck. They made two stops. The first was at a drugstore. Reacher went in alone. The second was at the burger place in the old gas station. Jed asked for a double with nothing green, just like Reacher, and he had finished it before they got back to the Lodge's parking lot.

The following morning Reacher took Jed for another drive. They collected the bike Jed had been using from its hiding place and brought it to the Lodge. The messenger from Jackson was waiting in the parking lot when they got back. Jed climbed out. The messenger lifted the bike down from the truck's load bed and started to inspect every inch.

The guy said, 'This is a disaster. You've scratched the paint. Crushed the saddle. Deformed the forks. Buckled the rims. It's worthless now. It's ruined. You little asshole.'

Jed said, 'I did my best to look after it. I'm sorry if there's any damage.'

'What use is sorry?' The messenger shoved Jed in the chest. 'You miserable piece of—'

Reacher got out of the truck.

The messenger grabbed the handlebars and scurried across to a station wagon that was parked by the porte cochère. 'Hey, buddy, just a misunderstanding. Thanks for returning it. Guess I'll be leaving now.' He fed the bike in through the tailgate and hurried around to the driver's seat. He started the engine and lurched backward, then changed direction and sped away toward the exit.

Reacher and Jed stood together until the car disappeared from sight. Then Reacher handed Jed a small paper bag from the drugstore. Jed opened it. He pulled out a folding tooth-brush.

Reacher said, 'For the next time you take the Greyhound. Fits better in your pocket than the regular kind.'

Jed said, 'Thank you.'

'Good luck with your dad. I hope you guys work it out.'

'We're going to Colorado. Hannah said we can stay in Sam's house until Dad gets a job.'

'Sam's house is nice. I bet you guys will be happy.'

'Are you coming to Gerrardsville, too?'

'Me? No.'

'Why not? You said it's nice.'

'It is nice. But I've been there before. It's time for some-where new.'

ABOUT THE AUTHORS

Lee Child is one of the world's leading thriller writers. He was born in Coventry, raised in Birmingham, and now lives in New York. It is said one of his novels featuring his hero Jack Reacher is sold somewhere in the world every nine seconds. His books consistently achieve the number one slot on bestseller lists around the world and have sold over one hundred million copies. Lee is the recipient of many awards, including Author of the Year at the 2019 British Book Awards. He was appointed CBE in the 2019 Queen's Birthday Honours.

Andrew Child is the author of nine thrillers written under the name Andrew Grant. He is the younger brother of Lee Child. Born in Birmingham, he lives in Wyoming with his wife, the novelist Tasha Alexander.

Find out more about the Jack Reacher books at www.JackReacher.com

- Take the book selector quiz

- Enter competitions

- Read and listen to extracts

- Find out more about the authors

- Discover Reacher coffee, music and more . . .

PLUS sign up for the monthly Jack Reacher newsletter to get all the latest news delivered direct to your inbox.

For up-to-the-minute news about Lee & Andrew Child find us on Facebook

 /JackReacherOfficial

 /LeeChildOfficial

and discover Jack Reacher books on Twitter

 /LeeChildReacher

WHITAKER'S CONCISE
2021

AN

Almanack

For the Year of Our Lord

2021

ESTABLISHED 1868

BY

JOSEPH WHITAKER, FSA

CONTAINING AN ACCOUNT OF THE

ASTRONOMICAL AND OTHER PHENOMENA

AND

A vast Amount of INFORMATION respecting the
GOVERNMENT, FINANCES, POPULATION,
COMMERCE, and GENERAL STATISTICS of
the various Nations of the WORLD
with an INDEX containing
nearly 7,500
References

OXFORD
RIVERSIDE HOUSE, OSNEY MEADE
OXFORD OX2 0ES

The traditional design of the title page for Whitaker's Almanack which has appeared in each edition since 1868

REBELLION

Published 2021 by Rebellion Publishing Ltd
Riverside House, Osney Mead, Oxford, OX2 0ES, UK

ISBN: 978-1-7810-8979-8

Rebellion Publishing Ltd does not have any control over, or responsibility for, any third-party
websites referred to or in this book. All internet addresses given in this book were correct at the
time of going to press. The contributors and publisher regret any inconvenience caused if addresses have
changed or sites have ceased to exist, but can accept no responsibility for any such changes

This publication contains opinions and ideas of the contributors. It is intended for informational
and educational purposes only. The reader should seek the services of a competent professional
for expert assistance or professional advice. Reference to any organization, publication or
website does not constitute or imply an endorsement by the contributors or the publisher. The
contributors and the publisher specifically disclaim any and all liability arising directly or
indirectly from the use or application of any information contained in this publication

A CIP catalogue record for this book is available from the British Library

Typeset by DLxml, a division of RefineCatch Limited, Bungay, Suffolk
Printed and bound in Italy by L.E.G.O. S.p.A.

To find out more about our publications visit www.rebellionpublishing.com

WHITAKER'S CONCISE
2021

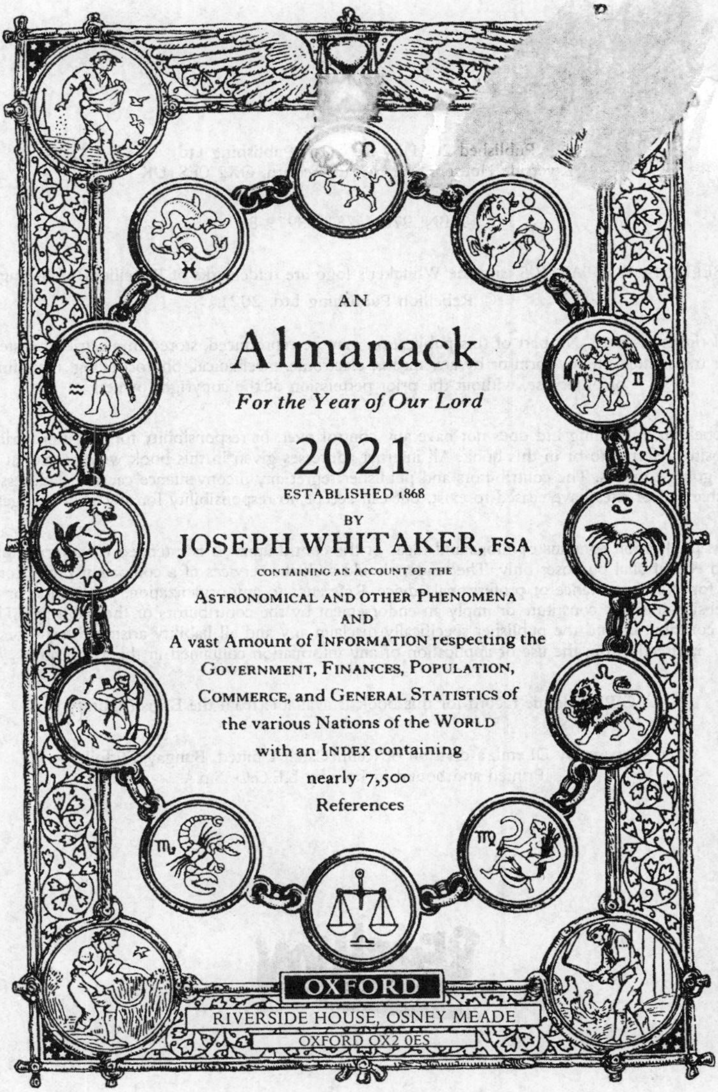

AN

Almanack

For the Year of Our Lord

2021

ESTABLISHED 1868

BY

JOSEPH WHITAKER, FSA

CONTAINING AN ACCOUNT OF THE

ASTRONOMICAL AND OTHER PHENOMENA

AND

A vast Amount of INFORMATION respecting the

GOVERNMENT, FINANCES, POPULATION,

COMMERCE, and GENERAL STATISTICS of

the various Nations of the WORLD

with an INDEX containing

nearly 7,500

References

OXFORD
RIVERSIDE HOUSE, OSNEY MEADE
OXFORD OX2 0ES

The traditional design of the title page for Whitaker's Almanack which has appeared in each edition since 1868

Published 2021 by Rebellion Publishing Ltd
Riverside House, Osney Mead, Oxford, OX2 0ES, UK

ISBN: 978-1-7810-8979-8

Rebellion Publishing Ltd does not have any control over, or responsibility for, any third-party
websites referred to or in this book. All internet addresses given in this book were correct at the
time of going to press. The contributors and publisher regret any inconvenience caused if addresses have
changed or sites have ceased to exist, but can accept no responsibility for any such changes

This publication contains opinions and ideas of the contributors. It is intended for informational
and educational purposes only. The reader should seek the services of a competent professional
for expert assistance or professional advice. Reference to any organization, publication or
website does not constitute or imply an endorsement by the contributors or the publisher. The
contributors and the publisher specifically disclaim any and all liability arising directly or
indirectly from the use or application of any information contained in this publication

A CIP catalogue record for this book is available from the British Library

Typeset by DLxml, a division of RefineCatch Limited, Bungay, Suffolk
Printed and bound in Italy by L.E.G.O. S.p.A.

To find out more about our publications visit www.rebellionpublishing.com

Lists and data underpin our modern information-driven society more than ever. It is refreshing to know that a positive, mild obsession with collecting facts is an ancient phenomenon, and the rise of the printed Almanack, in all its glorious forms before the digital revolution, is an expression of that human drive.

When we first heard that *Whitaker's* was going to cease publication, I was both sad, and intrigued that it was still even going. I had bought copies on many occasions over the years because I felt the contents might come in useful sometime. They have always done so for me, usually when I least expect it, and often to solve a dinner table discussion.

The idea of actually acquiring the book came a few days later when I realised that this beloved tome of things was valuable for its content, but also an important cultural icon. I felt that keeping it in print would be worth the investment of time, money and editorial effort.

At the time of going to press on *Whitaker's Concise 2021*, the UK was once again in lockdown due to COVID-19, with the now-steady rollout of vaccines providing hope for tens of millions of people across the country, and indeed the world. Acquiring and producing a new edition of this wonderful tome presented its own unique challenges over the last year, from building a new team of editors, learning new processes and catching up on time lost between publishers. It would, perhaps, have been easy to miss this year, but the continuity of such a legendary resource in these difficult times, beset as we are by the rise of fake news, 'alternative facts' and conspiracy theories, has never been more vital. While there are sections of the book that are, regretfully, not updated this year, and a few that are missing due to the pressures of the pandemic, we are delighted that a huge amount of the book has been updated as usual. In particular, I would like to mention The Year 2019–20 section, and the many excellent articles on our arts, culture and heritage, as well as politics.

I hope those that buy it and flick through the pages occasionally find it valuable, as might future historians doggedly researching for details in a world whose digital databases have somehow been erased or are now inaccessible.

Jason Kingsley OBE
CEO, Rebellion
www.rebellionpublishing.com

COVER PHOTOGRAPHS

Main image: The Queen confers the honour of knighthood on Captain Sir Thomas Moore at Windsor Castle, on 17 July 2020 © Getty Images

Top, from left to right:
1. Jordan Henderson holds the Premier League Trophy aloft as Liverpool FC celebrate winning the league following their Premier League match against Chelsea FC at Anfield, Liverpool on 22 July 2020 © Getty Images
2. UK in lockdown due to the COVID-19 pandemic at Chessington, England on 30 March 2020 © Getty Images
3. Boris Johnson leaves Downing Street for Prime Minister's Questions a day after announcing new coronavirus restrictions, on 23 September 2020 © Getty Images
4. Artist's depiction of the COVID-19 coronavirus, by Radoslav Zilinsky © Getty Images

SOURCES
Whitaker's was compiled with the assistance of HM Revenue and Customs and the Press Association. Crown copyright material is reproduced with the permission of the Controller of Her Majesty's Stationery Office.

EDITORIAL STAFF
Chief Executive Officer: Jason Kingsley OBE
Chief Technical Officer: Chris Kingsley OBE
Head of Publishing: Ben Smith
Publishing Manager: Beth Lewis
Senior Commissioning Editor: Michael Rowley
Editors and Contributors: Kristen Mankosa; Dr Adam McKie
In-House Designer: Sam Gratton

Thanks to David Francis, Bridette Ledgerwood, Bryce Payton, Donna Scott, Paul Simpson and Kate Townshend. Thanks also to Ruth Northey.

CONTRIBUTORS (where not listed)
Sheridan Williams FRAS, Dr John Savage, John Flannery (Astronomy); Stephen Kershaw (Peerage); Anthea Lipsett (Education); Clive Longhurst (Insurance); Chris Priestley, John Huxley (Legal Notes, England & Wales); Richard McMeeken (Legal Notes, Scotland); and Sarah Perkins (Taxation).
Geomagnetism and Space Weather data supplied by Dr Susan Macmillan of the British Geological Survey.

THE YEAR 2021

THE YEAR 2021

CHRONOLOGICAL CYCLES AND ERAS

Dominical Letter	C
Epact	16
Golden Number (Lunar Cycle)	VIII
Julian Period	6734
Roman Indiction	14
Solar Cycle	14

	Beginning
*Muslim year AH 1442	19/20 Aug 2020
Japanese year Reiwa 3	1 Jan
Roman year 2774 AUC	14 Jan
Regnal year 70	6 Feb
Chinese year of the Ox	12 Feb
Sikh new year	14 Mar
Indian (Saka) year 1943	22 Mar
Hindu new year (Chaitra)	12 Apr
*Jewish year AM 5782	7 Sep

* Year begins at sunset on the previous day

RELIGIOUS CALENDARS

CHRISTIAN

Epiphany	6 Jan
Presentation of Christ in the Temple	2 Feb
Ash Wednesday	17 Feb
The Annunciation	25 Mar
Palm Sunday	28 Mar
Maundy Thursday	1 Apr
Good Friday	2 Apr
Easter Day (western churches)	4 Apr
Easter Day (Eastern Orthodox)	2 May
Rogation Sunday	9 May
Ascension Day	13 May
Pentecost (Whit Sunday)	23 May
Trinity Sunday	30 May
Corpus Christi	3 Jun
All Saints' Day	1 Nov
Advent Sunday	28 Nov
Christmas Day	25 Dec

HINDU

Makar Sankranti	14 Jan
Vasant Panchami (Sarasvati Puja)	16 Feb
Shivaratri	11 Mar
Holi	29 Mar
Chaitra (Spring new year)	12 Apr
Rama Navami	21 Apr
Raksha Bandhan	22 Aug
Krishna Janmashtami	30 Aug
Ganesh Chaturthi, first day	10 Sep
Navratri festival (Durga Puja), first day	7 Oct
Dussehra	14 Oct
Diwali (New Year festival of lights), first day	4 Nov

JEWISH

Purim	26 Feb
Pesach (Passover), first day	28 Mar
Shavuot (Feast of Weeks), first day	17 May
Rosh Hashanah (Jewish new year)	7 Sep
Yom Kippur (Day of Atonement)	16 Sep
Sukkot (Feast of Tabernacles), first day	21 Sep
Hanukkah (Festival of Lights), first day	28 Nov

MUSLIM†

Al-Hijra (Muslim new year)	20 Aug 2020
Ashura	29 Aug 2020
Ramadan, first day	13 April
Eid-ul-Fitr	13 May
Hajj, first day	17 Jul
Eid-ul-Adha	20 Jul

SIKH

Birthday of Guru Gobind Singh Ji	5 Jan
1 Chet (Sikh new year)	14 Mar
‡Hola Mohalla	29 Mar
Vaisakhi	14 Apr
Martyrdom of Guru Arjan Dev Ji	16 Jun
‡Birthday of Guru Nanak Dev Ji	19 Nov
Martyrdom of Guru Tegh Bahdur Ji	24 Nov

† The Islamic calendar is lunar so religious dates may vary by one or two days locally and according to when the new Moon is first seen
‡ Currently celebrated according to the lunar, rather than Nanakshahi, calendar, so the date varies annually

CIVIL CALENDAR

Duchess of Cambridge's birthday	9 Jan
Countess of Wessex's birthday	20 Jan
Accession of the Queen	6 Feb
Duke of York's birthday	19 Feb
St David's Day	1 Mar
Commonwealth Day	8 Mar
Earl of Wessex's birthday	10 Mar
St Patrick's Day	17 Mar
Birthday of the Queen	21 Apr
St George's Day	23 Apr
Coronation Day	2 Jun
Duke of Edinburgh's birthday	10 Jun
The Queen's Official Birthday	12 Jun
Duke of Cambridge's birthday	21 Jun
Duchess of Cornwall's birthday	17 Jul
Princess Royal's birthday	15 Aug
Lord Mayor's Day	13 Nov
Remembrance Sunday	14 Nov
Prince of Wales' birthday	14 Nov
Wedding Day of the Queen	20 Nov
St Andrew's Day	30 Nov

LEGAL CALENDAR

LAW TERMS

Hilary Term	11 Jan to 31 Mar
Easter Term	13 Apr to 28 May
Trinity Term	8 Jun to 30 Jul
Michaelmas Term	1 Oct to 21 Dec

QUARTER DAYS	TERM DAYS *(Scotland)*
(England, Wales & Northern Ireland)	
Lady – 25 Mar	Candlemas – 28 Feb
Midsummer – 24 Jun	Whitsunday – 28 May
Michaelmas – 29 Sep	Lammas – 28 Aug
Christmas – 25 Dec	Martinmas – 28 Nov

2021

JANUARY						
Sunday		3	10	17	24	31
Monday		4	11	18	25	
Tuesday		5	12	19	26	
Wednesday		6	13	20	27	
Thursday		7	14	21	28	
Friday	1	8	15	22	29	
Saturday	2	9	16	23	30	

FEBRUARY					
Sunday		7	14	21	28
Monday	1	8	15	22	
Tuesday	2	9	16	23	
Wednesday	3	10	17	24	
Thursday	4	11	18	25	
Friday	5	12	19	26	
Saturday	6	13	20	27	

MARCH						
Sunday		7	14	21	28	
Monday	1	8	15	22	29	
Tuesday	2	9	16	23	30	
Wednesday	3	10	17	24	31	
Thursday	4	11	18	25		
Friday	5	12	19	26		
Saturday	6	13	20	27		

APRIL					
Sunday		4	11	18	25
Monday		5	12	19	26
Tuesday		6	13	20	27
Wednesday		7	14	21	28
Thursday	1	8	15	22	29
Friday	2	9	16	23	30
Saturday	3	10	17	24	

MAY						
Sunday		2	9	16	23	30
Monday		3	10	17	24	31
Tuesday		4	11	18	25	
Wednesday		5	12	19	26	
Thursday		6	13	20	27	
Friday		7	14	21	28	
Saturday	1	8	15	22	29	

JUNE					
Sunday		6	13	20	27
Monday		7	14	21	28
Tuesday	1	8	15	22	29
Wednesday	2	9	16	23	30
Thursday	3	10	17	24	
Friday	4	11	18	25	
Saturday	5	12	19	26	

JULY					
Sunday		4	11	18	25
Monday		5	12	19	26
Tuesday		6	13	20	27
Wednesday		7	14	21	28
Thursday	1	8	15	22	29
Friday	2	9	16	23	30
Saturday	3	10	17	24	31

AUGUST						
Sunday	1	8	15	22	29	
Monday	2	9	16	23	30	
Tuesday	3	10	17	24	31	
Wednesday	4	11	18	25		
Thursday	5	12	19	26		
Friday	6	13	20	27		
Saturday	7	14	21	28		

SEPTEMBER					
Sunday		5	12	19	26
Monday		6	13	20	27
Tuesday		7	14	21	28
Wednesday	1	8	15	22	29
Thursday	2	9	16	23	30
Friday	3	10	17	24	
Saturday	4	11	18	25	

OCTOBER						
Sunday		3	10	17	24	31
Monday		4	11	18	25	
Tuesday		5	12	19	26	
Wednesday		6	13	20	27	
Thursday		7	14	21	28	
Friday	1	8	15	22	29	
Saturday	2	9	16	23	30	

NOVEMBER					
Sunday		7	14	21	28
Monday	1	8	15	22	29
Tuesday	2	9	16	23	30
Wednesday	3	10	17	24	
Thursday	4	11	18	25	
Friday	5	12	19	26	
Saturday	6	13	20	27	

DECEMBER						
Sunday		5	12	19	26	
Monday		6	13	20	27	
Tuesday		7	14	21	28	
Wednesday	1	8	15	22	29	
Thursday	2	9	16	23	30	
Friday	3	10	17	24	31	
Saturday	4	11	18	25		

PUBLIC HOLIDAYS	England and Wales	Scotland	Northern Ireland
New Year	1 January†	1, 4† January	1 January†
St Patrick's Day	—	—	17 March
*Good Friday	2 April	2 April	2 April
Easter Monday	5 April	—	5 April
Early May	3 May†	3 May	3 May†
Spring	31 May	31 May†	31 May
Battle of the Boyne	—	—	12 July‡
Summer	30 August	2 August	30 August
St Andrew's Day	—	30 November§	—
*Christmas	27, 28 December	27†, 28 December	27, 28 December

* In England, Wales and Northern Ireland, Christmas Day and Good Friday are common law holidays

† Subject to royal proclamation

‡ Subject to proclamation by the Secretary of State for Northern Ireland

§ The St Andrew's Day Holiday (Scotland) Bill was approved by parliament on 29 November 2006; it does not oblige employers to change their existing pattern of holidays but provides the legal framework in which the St Andrew's Day bank holiday could be substituted for an existing local holiday from another date in the year

Note: In the Channel Islands, Liberation Day is a bank and public holiday

2022

JANUARY

Sunday		2	9	16 25 30
Monday		3	10	17 26 31
Tuesday		4	11	18 27
Wednesday		5	12	19 26
Thursday		6	13	20 27
Friday		7	14	21 28
Saturday	1	8	15	22 29

FEBRUARY

Sunday		6	13 20 27
Monday		7	14 21 28
Tuesday	1	8	15 22
Wednesday	2	9	16 23
Thursday	3	10	17 24
Friday	4	11	18 25
Saturday	5	12	19 26

MARCH

Sunday		6	13 20 27
Monday		7	14 21 28
Tuesday	1	8	15 22 29
Wednesday	2	9	16 23 30
Thursday	3	10	17 24 31
Friday	4	11	18 25
Saturday	5	12	19 26

APRIL

Sunday		3	10 17 24
Monday		4	11 18 25
Tuesday		5	12 19 26
Wednesday		6	13 20 27
Thursday		7	14 21 28
Friday	1	8	15 22 29
Saturday	2	9	16 23 30

MAY

Sunday	1	8	15 22 29
Monday	2	9	16 23 30
Tuesday	3	10	17 24 31
Wednesday	4	11	18 25
Thursday	5	12	19 26
Friday	6	13	20 27
Saturday	7	14	21 28

JUNE

Sunday		5	12 19 26
Monday		6	13 20 27
Tuesday		7	14 21 28
Wednesday	1	8	15 22 29
Thursday	2	9	16 23 30
Friday	3	10	17 24
Saturday	4	11	18 25

JULY

Sunday		3	10 17 25
Monday		4	11 18 26
Tuesday		5	12 19 27
Wednesday		6	13 20 28
Thursday		7	14 21 29
Friday	1	8	15 23 30
Saturday	2	9	16 24 31

AUGUST

Sunday		7	14 21 28
Monday	1	8	15 22 29
Tuesday	2	9	16 23 30
Wednesday	3	10	17 24 31
Thursday	4	11	18 25
Friday	5	12	19 26
Saturday	6	13	20 27

SEPTEMBER

Sunday		4	11 18 25
Monday		5	12 19 26
Tuesday		6	13 20 27
Wednesday		7	14 21 28
Thursday	1	8	15 22 29
Friday	2	9	16 23 30
Saturday	3	10	17 24

OCTOBER

Sunday		2	9	16 23 30
Monday		3	10	17 24 31
Tuesday		4	11	18 25
Wednesday		5	12	19 26
Thursday		6	13	20 27
Friday		7	14	21 28
Saturday	1	8	15	22 29

NOVEMBER

Sunday		6	13 20 27
Monday		7	14 21 28
Tuesday	1	8	15 22 29
Wednesday	2	9	16 23 30
Thursday	3	10	17 24
Friday	4	11	18 25
Saturday	5	12	19 26

DECEMBER

Sunday		4	11 18 25
Monday		5	12 19 26
Tuesday		6	13 20 27
Wednesday		7	14 21 28
Thursday	1	8	15 22 29
Friday	2	9	16 23 30
Saturday	3	10	17 24 31

PUBLIC HOLIDAYS	England and Wales	Scotland	Northern Ireland
New Year	1 January†	1, 4† January	1 January†
St Patrick's Day	—	—	17 March
*Good Friday	15 April	15 April	15 April
Easter Monday	18 April	—	18 April
Early May	2 May†	2 May	2 May†
Spring	2 June	2 June†	2 June
Battle of the Boyne	—	—	12 July‡
Summer	30 August	2 August	30 August
St Andrew's Day	—	30 November§	—
*Christmas	26, 27 December	26†, 27 December	26, 27 December

* In England, Wales and Northern Ireland, Christmas Day and Good Friday are common law holidays
† Subject to royal proclamation
‡ Subject to proclamation by the Secretary of State for Northern Ireland
§ The St Andrew's Day Holiday (Scotland) Bill was approved by parliament on 29 November 2006; it does not oblige employers to change their existing pattern of holidays but provides the legal framework in which the St Andrew's Day bank holiday could be substituted for an existing local holiday from another date in the year
Note: In the Channel Islands, Liberation Day is a bank and public holiday

FORTHCOMING EVENTS

Due to the impact of the coronavirus pandemic, the format and dates of many of these events may change.

JANUARY 2021

14–24	London Short Film Festival (online)
15–2 Feb	Celtic Connections Music Festival (online only)
20–31	London Art Fair, Business Design Centre (online only)
29–31	RSPB Big Garden Birdwatch

FEBRUARY

2	World Wetlands Day
3– 21	Leicester Comedy Festival (online)

MARCH

3	World Wildlife Day
4	World Book Day
5–14	Belfast Children's Festival
8	International Women's Day
21	World Poetry Day
26–11 Apr	Ideal Home Show, Olympia, London

APRIL

11	British Academy Film Awards, Royal Opera House, London
22	Earth Day
25	Academy Awards, Los Angeles

MAY

8–16	Stratford-upon-Avon Literary Festival
18–23	RHS Chelsea Flower Show, Royal Hospital, London
20–29 August	Glyndebourne Festival
27–6 June	Hay Festival of Literature and the Arts, Hay-on-Wye
29–30	Bath Festival

JUNE

12	Trooping the Colour, Horse Guards Parade, London
17–20	Isle of Wight Festival
17–20	Royal Highland Show, Edinburgh
Late June	Glastonbury Festival of Contemporary Performing Arts, Somerset
26	Pride Parade, London
29–1 July	London Book Fair, Olympia, London

JULY

2–9	Cheltenham Music Festival
6–11	RHS Hampton Court Palace Flower Show, Surrey
15–18	Crufts Dog Show, NEC, Birmingham
16–18	Tolpuddle Martyrs Festival, Dorset
17–24	The Welsh Proms, St David's Hall, Cardiff
Mid Jul–11 Sep	BBC Promenade Concerts, Royal Albert Hall, London
21–25	RHS Flower Show, Tatton Park, Cheshire
22–25	WOMAD Festival, Charlton Park, Wiltshire
24–31	Three Choirs Festival, Worcester
29–1 Aug	Cambridge Folk Festival
31–7 Aug	National Eisteddfod of Wales, Ceredigion County

AUGUST

6–28	Edinburgh Military Tattoo, Edinburgh Castle
6–29	Edinburgh International Festival
7–8	Brighton Pride, Brighton and Hove
29–30	Notting Hill Carnival, London

SEPTEMBER

3–7 Nov	Blackpool Illuminations, Blackpool Promenade
4	Braemar Royal Highland Gathering, Aberdeenshire
8	International Literacy Day
12–15	TUC Annual Congress
Mid–Late Sept	Liberal Democrat Party Conference
25–29	Labour Party Conference
Sep–Oct	Conservative Party Conference

OCTOBER

13–17	Frieze Art Fair, Regent's Park, London
Mid Oct	Booker Prize Awards
Mid Oct	BFI London Film Festival

NOVEMBER

13	Lord Mayor's Procession and Show, City of London
Mid Nov	CBI Annual Conference

SPORTS EVENTS

JANUARY 2021

9–24 Bowls: World Indoor Bowls Championships, Hopton-on-Sea
10–17 Snooker: Masters, Marshall Arena, Milton Keynes
14–26 Cricket: England tour Sri Lanka, two-Test series

FEBRUARY

6–20 Mar Rugby Union: Six Nations Championship, Europe
5–8 March Cricket: England tour India, four-Test series
7 American Football: Super Bowl 55, Tampa, Florida, USA
10–22 Tennis: Australian Open, Melbourne

MARCH

16–19 Horse Racing: Cheltenham Festival
27 Gymnastics: World Cup, Birmingham

APRIL

1–3 Oct Baseball: Major League Baseball Season
4 Rowing: The Boat Race, Putney to Mortlake, London
8–10 Horse Racing: Grand National, Aintree, Liverpool
10–11 Golf: Masters, Augusta, Georgia, USA
17–3 May Snooker: World Championship, Crucible Theatre, Sheffield
25 Football: EFL Cup final, Wembley Stadium, London
30–1 May Horse Racing: Kentucky Derby, Louisville, Kentucky, USA

MAY

5–9 Equestrian: Badminton Horse Trials, Badminton
8 Football: Scottish Cup Final, Hampden Park, Glasgow
10–23 Aquatics: European Championships, Budapest, Hungary
12–16 Equestrian: Royal Windsor Horse Show, Home Park, Windsor
15 Football: FA Cup Final, Wembley Stadium, London
16 Football: Women's Champions League Final, Gamla Ullevi, Gothenburg, Sweden
20–23 Formula 1: Monaco Grand Prix, Monte Carlo
20–23 Golf: US PGA Championship, Ocean Course, Kiawah Island, South Carolina
22 Football: Women's FA Cup Final, Wembley Stadium, London
22 Rugby Union: European Challenge Cup Final & European Champions Cup Final, Stade de Marseille, France
23–6 Jun Tennis: French Open, Paris
26 Football: UEFA Europa League Final, Stadion Miejski, Gdansk, Poland
28 Motor Racing: Indianapolis 500, Indiana, USA
29 Football: UEFA Champions League Final, Atatürk Olympic Stadium, Istanbul, Turkey

JUNE

4–5 Horse Racing: The Derby, Epsom Downs, Surrey
11–11 Jul Football: UEFA Euro 2020
15–19 Horse Racing: Royal Ascot, Berkshire
17–20 Golf: US Open, Torrey Pines Golf Course, San Diego, California
26–18 Jul Cycling: Tour de France
28–11 Jul Tennis: Wimbledon Championships, All England Lawn Tennis Club, London
29–4 Jul Rowing: Henley Royal Regatta, Henley-on-Thames

JULY

13 Athletics: Diamond League Anniversary Games, London Stadium
15–18 Golf: Open Championship, Royal St Georges, Kent
17 Rugby League: Challenge Cup Final, Wembley Stadium, London
18 Formula 1: British Grand Prix, Silverstone, Northamptonshire
23–8 Aug XXXII Summer Olympic Games, Tokyo, Japan
Late Jul–Aug Cricket: The Hundred, England

AUGUST

4–14 Sep Cricket: India tour England, five-Test series
19–22 Golf: Women's British Open, Carnoustie, Angus, Scotland
24–5 Sep Athletics: Summer Paralympic Games, Tokyo, Japan
30–12 Sep Tennis: US Open, New York

SEPTEMBER

Early Sep–Late Dec American Football: NFL Season
2–5 Equestrian: Burghley Horse Trials, Stamford, Lincolnshire
12 Athletics: Great North Run, Newcastle
18–16 Oct Rugby Union: Women's Rugby World Cup, New Zealand
24–26 Golf: 43rd Ryder Cup, Whistling Straits, Wisconsen, USA
27–1 Oct Cricket: Bob Willis Trophy Final, Lord's, London

OCTOBER

3 Athletics: London Marathon
9 Rugby League: Super League Grand Final, Old Trafford, Manchester
13–17 Cycling: UCI Track Cycling World Championships, Ashgabat, Turkmenistan
18–15 Nov Cricket: ICC T20 Men's World Cup, India
23–27 Nov Rugby League: Rugby League World Cup, England
Late Oct–Early Nov Baseball: World Series

NOVEMBER

1 Athletics: New York City Marathon, New York, USA
14–21 Tennis: ATP World Tour Finals, Pala Alpitour, Turin
22–28 Tennis: Davis Cup Finals, Madrid, Spain
23–5 Dec Snooker: UK Championship, Barbican Centre, York
Late Nov–Jan 2022 Cricket: The Ashes, Australia, five-Test series

CENTENARIES

2020

1520
7 Jun	A summit between England and France began in the Field of the Cloth of Gold
30 Sep	Suleiman the Magnificent succeeded his father Selim I as Ottoman Sultan
21 Oct	The islands of St Pierre and Miquelon were discovered by explorer Joao Alvares Fagundes
28 Nov	Ferdinand Magellan and his fleet became the first Europeans to sail into the Pacific Ocean

1620
16 May	William Adams, navigator, died
7 Aug	Johannes Kepler's mother was arrested for witchcraft
8 Nov	Catholic forces were victorious in the Battle of White Mountain (Thirty Years' War 1618–48)
11 Nov	The *Mayflower* anchored at Cape Cod
31 Oct	John Evelyn, writer, born

1720
10 Feb	Edmond Halley was appointed the second Astronomer Royal at the Greenwich Observatory
17 Feb	The War of the Quadruple Alliance ended with the Treaty of The Hague
6 Mar	Pieter van Bloemen, Flemish painter, died
6 Apr	The South Sea bill was passed in the House of Lords
25 May	The ship *Grand-Saint-Antoine* arrived in Marseille, bringing Europe's last major plague outbreak, which killed around 100,000
15 Nov	Female pirates Anne Bonny and Mary Read are captured in Jamaica along with Captain 'Calico Jack' Rackham and his crew
29 Dec	Theatre Royal Haymarket, then called the 'Hay Market', opens with the play *La Fille à la Mode*

1820
17 Jan	Anne Brontë, novelist and poet, born
29 Jan	King George IV ascended to the throne on the death of his father George III, ending the English Regency
30 Jan	Captain Edward Bransfield became the first person to sight the Antarctic mainland
10 Mar	The Royal Astronomical Society was founded in London
15 Mar	Maine became the 23rd state of the Union, following the Missouri Compromise
11 May	HMS *Beagle,* the ship that carried Charles Darwin on his scientific voyage, was launched
12 May	Florence Nightingale, social reformer and statistician, born
26 Jul	Union Bridge, crossing the River Tweed between England and Scotland, opened
1 Aug	The second half of the Regent's Canal in London, from Camden to Limehouse, was completed
28 Nov	Friedrich Engels, German political philosopher, born

1920
2 Jan	Isaac Asimov, American writer and biochemist, born
10 Jan	The Covenant of the League of Nations came into force
16 Jan	Alcohol Prohibition came into effect nationwide in the USA
23 Jan	Queen Wilhelmina of the Netherlands refused to extradite former German Kaiser Wilhelm II
2 Feb	Soviet Russia recognised the independence of the Republic of Estonia in the Treaty of Tartu
16 May	Joan of Arc (Jeanne d'Arc) was canonised by Pope Benedict XV
21 May	Mexican President Venustiano Carranza was executed by army generals
4 Jun	The Allied Powers defined the borders of the Kingdom of Hungary at the Treaty of Trianon
12 Jul	Soviet Russia recognised the sovereignty of Lithuania
10 Aug	The Treaty of Sèvres abolished the Ottoman Empire
11 Aug	Soviet Russia recognised Latvia's independence in the Treaty of Riga
14 Aug	The Games of the VII Olympiad opened in Antwerp, Belgium
16 Aug	Charles Bukowski, American writer, born
18 Aug	The 19th Amendment to the US Constitution was ratified, granting American women the right to vote
1 Sep	Greater Lebanon was declared a state under the French Mandate for Syria and the Lebanon
29 Sep	Peter D. Mitchell, Nobel Prize winning biochemist, born
2 Nov	Warren G. Harding was elected President of the USA
10 Dec	The Nobel Peace Prize was awarded to US president Woodrow Wilson

2021

1521
3 Jan	Pope Leo X excommunicated the German priest Martin Luther from the Roman Catholic church
28 Jan	Charles V, Holy Roman Emperor, opened the Diet of Worms
17 Mar	Portuguese navigator Ferdinand Magellan reached the Philippines
20 Apr	Zhengde, 11th Emperor of the Ming dynasty, died
23 Apr	Royalists defeated the *comuneros* at the Battle at Villalar
27 Apr	Portuguese navigator Ferdinand Magellan killed by Filipino natives
25 May	The Edict of Worms, outlawing Martin Luther, was issued
13 Aug	The Battle of Tenochtitlan ended with the capture of Cuauhtemoc, last Aztec Emperor
1 Dec	Takeda Shingen, Japanese warlord, born
13 Dec	King Manuel I of Portugal, died

1621
28 Jan	Pope Paul V, persecutor of Galileo, died
9 Feb	Alessandro Ludovisi was elected as Pope Gregory XV
31 Mar	King Philip of Spain (III) and Portugal (II), died
5 Apr	The *Mayflower* set sail from Plymouth, USA on its return voyage to England
3 May	Francis Bacon was accused of bribery
8 Jun	Anne de Xainctonge, founder of the first non-cloistered women's religious community, died
9 Oct	The Ottoman Empire and the Polish-Lithuanian Commonwealth signed the Treaty of Khotyn

1721

19 Mar	Pope Clement XI, died
3 Apr	Robert Walpole was appointed First Lord of the Treasury; *de facto* first prime minister of Great Britain
8 May	Michelangelo dei Conti was elected Pope Innocent XIII
30 Aug	Russia and Sweden signed the Treaty of Nystad, ending the Great Northern War
2 Nov	Tsar Peter I declared Emperor of All Russia
29 Dec	Madame De Pompadour, mistress of King Louis XV of France, born

1821

23 Feb	John Keats, English Romantic poet, died
5 May	Napoleon Bonaparte, military leader and Emperor of France, died
19 Jul	George IV was crowned king of the United Kingdom of Great Britain and Ireland
5 Aug	Bellingshausen's Russian Antarctic expedition, arrived back in Kronstadt
24 Aug	The Treaty of Córdoba was signed by Mexican and Spanish officials
15 Sep	Guatemala enacted the Act of Independence of Central America

1921

4 Feb	Betty Friedan, American feminist and author of *The Feminine Mystique,* born
17 Mar	Dr Marie Stopes opened Britain's first birth control clinic in London
19 Mar	Tommy Cooper, British comedian, born
7 June	The Parliament of Northern Ireland sat for the first time
23 Jul	The Communist Party of China was founded
29 Jul	Adolf Hitler assumed the leadership of the National Socialist German Workers' Party
31 Oct	The Fédération Sportive Féminine Internationale was formed
9 Nov	Benito Mussolini formed the National Fascist Party in Italy
23 Nov	US president Warren G. Harding signed the Willis-Campbell Act, prohibiting the medical prescription of beer or liquor
6 Dec	Anglo-Irish Treaty was signed, marking the end of the Irish War of Independence

2022

1322

14 Oct	King Edward II of England was defeated by Robert the Bruce of Scotland at the Battle of Old Byland

1422

31 Aug	King Henry V died while in France. Henry VI became King of England, aged nine months

1522

6 Sep	Spanish carrack *Nao Victoria* became the first ship to circumnavigate the world
21 Sep	Martin Luther published a translation of the New Testament in German
22 Oct	An earthquake destroyed the original capital of Vila Franca do Campo on Sao Miguel Island

1622

20 May	Osman II, Sultan of the Ottoman Empire, was murdered by his Janissaries
6 Sep	A fleet of Spanish treasure ships sank off the Florida Keys; discovered in 1985, it was later declared the most valuable shipwreck in the world

1722

10 Feb	Notorious pirate Bartholomew 'Black Bart' Roberts was killed off the coast of West Africa
5 Apr	Dutch explorer Jacob Roggeveen became the first European to discover Easter Island, subsequently naming it
27 Sep	Samuel Adams, Founding Father of the United States, born
20 Dec	Kangxi, Emperor of the Qing dynasty, died after a 61-year reign

1822

1 Jan	The Greek Constitution was adopted by the First National Assembly at Epidaurus during the Greek War of Independence
16 Feb	Sir Francis Galton, English polymath, born
25 Apr	Monrovia in Liberia was founded by the American Colonization Society with the aim of sending black American slaves 'back to Africa'
27 Apr	Ulysses S. Grant, 18th US President, born
8 Jul	Percy Shelley, English Romantic poet, died
20 Jul	Gregor Mendel, Czech geneticist, born
7 Sep	Brazil declared its independence from Portugal
27 Sep	French scholar Jean-François Champollion announced he had deciphered Egyptian hieroglyphs using the Rosetta Stone
1 Dec	Pedro I was crowned the first Emperor of Brazil
27 Dec	Louis Pasteur, French microbiologist and chemist, born

1922

5 Jan	Sir Ernest Shackleton, Anglo-Irish explorer, died
2 Feb	*Ulysses* by Irish author James Joyce was published
15 Feb	The inaugural session of the Permanent Court of International Justice was held at The Hague
28 Feb	Britain ended its protectorate over Egypt through a Unilateral Declaration of Independence, nominally granting independence
18 Mar	Mahatma Gandhi was sentenced to six years in prison for sedition in British India
3 Apr	Joseph Stalin was appointed General Secretary of the Communist Party of the Soviet Union
24 Jun	Walther Rathenau, German Foreign Minister and architect of the Treaty of Rapallo, was assassinated by right-wing militants
20 Jul	The German protectorate of Togoland was formally divided into French Togoland and British Togoland
18 Oct	The BBC was formed, and began broadcasting on 14 November
31 Oct	King Victor Emmanuel III appointed Benito Mussolini, leader of the National Fascist Party, as Prime Minister of Italy following the March on Rome
1 Nov	The Ottoman Empire was dissolved, and the sultanate was abolished
4 Nov	British archaeologist Howard Carter's crew discovered the entrance to Pharaoh Tutankhamun's tomb in the Valley of the Kings
18 Nov	Marcel Proust, French author, died
6 Dec	The Irish Free State officially came into existence
30 Dec	The Union of Soviet Socialist Republics was formed

THE UNITED KINGDOM

THE UK IN FIGURES

The United Kingdom comprises Great Britain (England, Wales and Scotland) and Northern Ireland. The Isle of Man and the Channel Islands are Crown dependencies with their own legislative systems and are not part of the UK.

ABBREVIATIONS
ONS   Office for National Statistics
NISRA   Northern Ireland Statistics and Research Agency

All data is for the UK unless otherwise stated.

AREA OF THE UNITED KINGDOM

	Sq. km	Sq. miles
United Kingdom	243,122	93,870
England	130,280	50,301
Wales	20,733	8,005
Scotland	77,958	30,100
Northern Ireland	14,150	5,463

Source: ONS (Crown copyright)

POPULATION

The first official census of population in England, Wales and Scotland was taken in 1801 and a census has been taken every ten years since, except in 1941 when there was no census because of the Second World War. The last official census in the UK was taken on 27 March 2011.

The first official census of population in Ireland was taken in 1841. However, all figures given below refer only to the area which is now Northern Ireland. Figures for Northern Ireland in 1921 and 1931 are estimates based on the censuses taken in 1926 and 1937 respectively.

Estimates of the population of England before 1801, calculated from the number of baptisms, burials and marriages, are:

1570	4,160,221	1670	5,773,646
1600	4,811,718	1700	6,045,008
1630	5,600,517	1750	6,517,035

Further details are available on the ONS website (W www.ons.gov.uk).

CENSUS RESULTS (THOUSANDS)

	United Kingdom			England and Wales			Scotland			Northern Ireland		
	Total	Male	Female	Total	Male	Female	Total	Male	Female	Total	Male	Female
1801	–	–	–	8,893	4,255	4,638	1,608	739	869	–	–	–
1811	13,368	6,368	7,000	10,165	4,874	5,291	1,806	826	980	–	–	–
1821	15,472	7,498	7,974	12,000	5,850	6,150	2,092	983	1,109	–	–	–
1831	17,835	8,647	9,188	13,897	6,771	7,126	2,364	1,114	1,250	–	–	–
1841	20,183	9,819	10,364	15,914	7,778	8,137	2,620	1,242	1,378	1,649	800	849
1851	22,259	10,855	11,404	17,928	8,781	9,146	2,889	1,376	1,513	1,443	698	745
1861	24,525	11,894	12,631	20,066	9,776	10,290	3,062	1,450	1,612	1,396	668	728
1871	27,431	13,309	14,122	22,712	11,059	11,653	3,360	1,603	1,757	1,359	647	712
1881	31,015	15,060	15,955	25,974	12,640	13,335	3,736	1,799	1,936	1,305	621	684
1891	34,264	16,593	17,671	29,003	14,060	14,942	4,026	1,943	2,083	1,236	590	646
1901	38,237	18,492	19,745	32,528	15,729	16,799	4,472	2,174	2,298	1,237	590	647
1911	42,082	20,357	21,725	36,070	17,446	18,625	4,761	2,309	2,452	1,251	603	648
1921	44,027	21,033	22,994	37,887	18,075	19,811	4,882	2,348	2,535	1,258	610	648
1931	46,038	22,060	23,978	39,952	19,133	20,819	4,843	2,326	2,517	1,243	601	642
1951	50,225	24,118	26,107	43,758	21,016	22,742	5,096	2,434	2,662	1,371	668	703
1961	52,709	25,481	27,228	46,105	22,304	23,801	5,179	2,483	2,697	1,425	694	731
1971	55,515	26,952	28,562	48,750	23,683	25,067	5,229	2,515	2,714	1,536	755	781
1981	55,848	27,104	28,742	49,155	23,873	25,281	5,131	2,466	2,664	*1,533	750	783
1991	56,467	27,344	29,123	49,890	24,182	25,707	4,999	2,392	2,607	1,578	769	809
2001	58,789	28,581	30,208	52,042	25,327	26,715	5,062	2,432	2,630	1,685	821	864
2011	63,182	31,028	32,153	56,076	27,574	28,502	5,295	2,567	2,728	1,810	887	923

* Figure includes 44,500 non-enumerated persons

ISLANDS

	Isle of Man			Jersey			Guernsey		
	Total	Male	Female	Total	Male	Female	Total	Male	Female
1901	54,752	25,496	29,256	52,576	23,940	28,636	40,446	19,652	20,794
1921	60,284	27,329	32,955	49,701	22,438	27,263	38,315	18,246	20,069
1951	55,123	25,749	29,464	57,296	27,282	30,014	43,652	21,221	22,431
1971	56,289	26,461	29,828	72,532	35,423	37,109	51,458	24,792	26,666
1991	69,788	33,693	36,095	84,082	40,862	43,220	58,867	28,297	30,570
2001	76,315	37,372	38,943	87,186	42,485	44,701	59,807	29,138	30,669
2006	80,058	39,523	40,535	–	–	–	–	–	–
2011	84,497	41,971	42,526	97,857	48,296	49,561	62,915	31,025	31,890

Source: Guernsey Annual Publication Bulletin, Isle of Man Government, States of Jersey Statistics Unit

RESIDENT POPULATION

ACTUAL AND PROJECTED BY COUNTRY
people, thousands

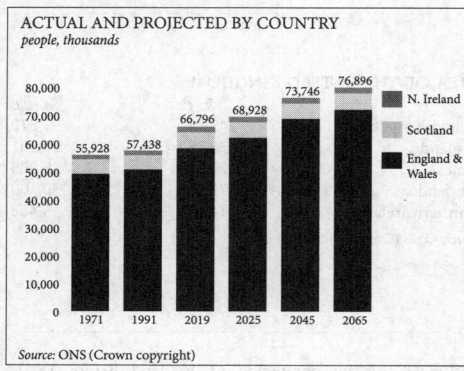

Source: ONS (Crown copyright)

PROJECTED AGE DISTRIBUTION, 2019 AND 2065
percentage

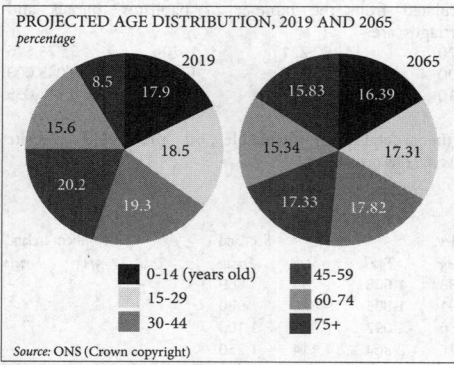

Source: ONS (Crown copyright)

NON-UK BORN RESIDENTS BY COUNTRY OF BIRTH
thousands

	2004	2019
India	94	863
Poland	505	813
Pakistan	285	546
Romania	–	427
Republic of Ireland	453	359
Germany	276	290
Bangladesh	–	260
South Africa	181	251
Italy	228	234
China	152	217

Source: ONS (Crown Copyright)

BY AGE AND SEX (UK), 2018
people, thousands

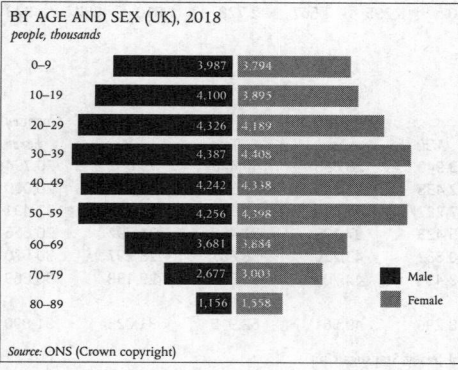

Source: ONS (Crown copyright)

ASYLUM

NATIONALITIES APPLYING FOR UK ASYLUM
in the year ending June

Top 5 Nationalities	2019	2020
1) Iran	4,900	5,169
2) Albania	3,559	3,630
3) Iraq	4,198	3,478
4) Pakistan	2,520	2,172
5) Eritrea	2,294	1,850

Source: Home Office, National Statistics: Asylum

BIRTHS

	Live births 2018	Birth rate 2018*
United Kingdom	731,213	11.0
England and Wales	657,076	11.1
Scotland	51,308	9.4
Northern Ireland	22,829	12.1

* Live births per 1,000 population
Source: ONS (Crown copyright)

FERTILITY RATES
Total fertility rate is the average number of children which would be born to a woman if she experienced the age-specific fertility rates of the period in question throughout her child-bearing life span. The figures for the years 1960–2 are estimates.

	1960–2	2000	2018
United Kingdom	3.07	1.62	1.68
England and Wales	2.77	1.65	1.70
Scotland	2.98	1.48	1.42
Northern Ireland	3.47	1.75	1.85

Source: General Register Office for Scotland, NISRA, ONS (Crown copyright)

MATERNITY RATES FOR ENGLAND AND WALES 2019

	All maternities*	Singleton	All multiple	Twins	Triplets
All ages	633,086	623,430	9,656†	9,513	137
>20	17,683	17,568	115	115	0
20–24	86,260	85,405	855	849	5
25–29	172,301	170,033	2,268	2,242	25
30–34	207,331	204,033	3,298	3,259	39
35–39	120,559	118,216	2,298	2,258	38
40-44	26,700	26,042	658	641	16
45+	2,228	2,065	163	148	14

* Includes stillbirths
† Total includes live maternities of quads and above
Source: ONS (Crown copyright)

TOP TEN BABY NAMES (ENGLAND AND WALES)

	1904 Girls	1904 Boys	2019 Girls	2019 Boys
1	Mary	William	Olivia	Oliver
2	Florence	John	Amelia	George
3	Doris	George	Ilsa	Noah
4	Edith	Thomas	Ava	Arthur
5	Dorothy	Arthur	Mia	Harry
6	Anne	James	Isabella	Leo
7	Margaret	Charles	Sophia	Muhammad
8	Alice	Frederick	Grace	Jack
9	Elizabeth	Albert	Lily	Charlie
10	Elsie	Ernest	Freya	Oscar

Source: ONS (Crown copyright)

LIVE BIRTHS (ENGLAND AND WALES)
by age of mother

Year	under 20	20-29	30-39	40+	All ages
1949	31,850	446,198	224,759	27,711	730,518
1959	46,067	462,643	220,736	19,055	748,501
1969	81,659	527,393	173,238	15,248	797,538
1979	59,143	415,311	157,058	6,516	638,028
1989	55,543	428,061	194,785	9,336	687,725
1999	48,375	292,653	266,592	14,252	621,872
2009	43,243	330,141	305,888	26,976	706,248
2019	17,720	260,700	332,314	29,618	640,370

Source: ONS (Crown copyright)

MARRIAGE AND DIVORCE

	Marriages 2016–17	Divorces 2016–17
England and Wales	249,793	101,669
Scotland	28,440	7,938
Northern Ireland	8,306	2,089

Source: NISRA, ONS (Crown copyright), Scottish Government

LEGAL ABORTIONS

	2005	2018
England and Wales	186,416	200,608
Scotland	12,665	13,286

Source: Department of Health, NHS Scotland

DEATHS

INFANT MORTALITY RATE 2017*

United Kingdom	3.9
England and Wales	3.9
Scotland	3.2
Northern Ireland	4.2

* Deaths of infants under one year of age per 1,000 live births
Source: NISRA, ONS (Crown copyright), Scottish Government

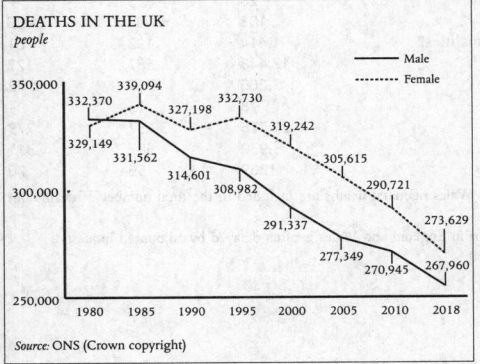

DEATHS IN THE UK
people
— Male
-------- Female

332,370, 339,094, 327,198, 332,730, 319,242, 305,615, 290,721, 273,629
329,149, 331,562, 314,601, 308,982, 291,337, 277,349, 270,945, 267,960

Source: ONS (Crown copyright)

EMPLOYMENT

MEDIAN FULL-TIME GROSS ANNUAL EARNINGS BY REGION (£)

Region	2005	2018
UK	22,888	29,574
England	23,280	29,005
North East	20,263	26,297
North West	21,777	27,315
Yorkshire and the Humber	21,506	26,894
East Midlands	21,494	26,749
West Midlands	21,447	27,716
East	22,883	29,128
London	29,882	38,826
South East	24,229	30,826
South West	21,279	27,969
Wales	20,634	26,346
Scotland	21,312	29,274
Northern Ireland	20,060	27,006

Source: ONS (Crown Copyright)

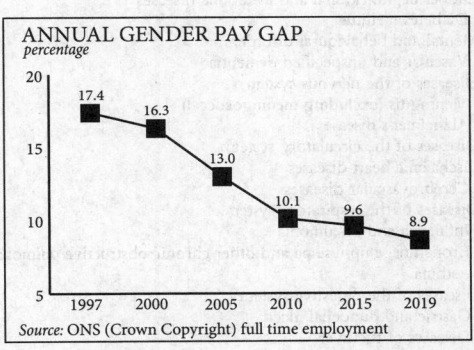

ANNUAL GENDER PAY GAP
percentage

17.4 (1997), 16.3 (2000), 13.0 (2005), 10.1 (2010), 9.6 (2015), 8.9 (2019)

Source: ONS (Crown Copyright) full time employment

OVERSEAS VISITS TO THE UK

Year	Visits (thousands)	Spending (£m)
1980	12,419	2,961
1985	14,450	5,442
1990	18,017	7,748
1995	23,538	11,762
2000	25,207	12,806
2005	29,970	14,247
2010	29,804	16,714
2011	30,798	17,998
2012	31,085	18,640
2013	32,689	21,259
2014	34,380	21,851
2015	36,115	22,072
2016	37,610	22,544
2017	39,214	24.507
2018	37,905	22,897
2019	40,900	28,400

DEATHS BY CAUSE, 2017

	England and Wales	Scotland	N. Ireland
Total deaths	533,253	57,883	16,036
Deaths from natural causes	512,027	54,731	15,757
Certain infectious and parasitic diseases	5,368	686	212
Intestinal infectious diseases	1,259	128	24
Respiratory and other tuberculosis	153	10	3
Meningococcal infection	49	1	2
Viral hepatitis	179	28	3
Human immunodeficiency virus (HIV)	162	6	3
Neoplasms	149,652	16,558	4,581
Malignant neoplasms	146,269	16,207	4,960
Malignant neoplasm of trachea, bronchus and lung	30,131	4,069	1,058
Malignant melanoma of skin	2,106	185	71
Malignant neoplasm of breast	10,219	954	317
Malignant neoplasm of cervix uteri	730	105	19
Malignant neoplasm of prostate	10,755	986	301
Leukaemia	4,315	387	319
Diseases of the blood and blood-forming organs and certain disorders involving the immune mechanism	1,099	98	40
Endocrine, nutritional and metabolic diseases	8,435	1,330	345
Diabetes mellitus	6,046	1,016	230
Mental and behavioural disorders	50,765	4,591	1,457
Vascular and unspecified dementia	49,657	4,161	1,317
Diseases of the nervous system	33,051	3,976	1,063
Meningitis (excluding meningococcal)	154	19	3
Alzheimer's disease	17,984	2,388	583
Diseases of the circulatory system	133,511	15,114	3,780
Ischaemic heart diseases	57,923	6,727	1,825
Cerebrovascular diseases	31,713	3,927	988
Diseases of the respiratory system	73,455	136	1,973
Influenza and Pneumonia	27,635	3,535	742
Bronchitis, emphysema and other chronic obstructive pulmonary diseases	28,597	3,449	1,845
Asthma	1,320	106	38
Diseases of the digestive system	25,627	3,134	800
Gastric and duodenal ulcer	1,866	121	31
Diseases of the liver	8,450	1,063	186
Diseases of the skin and subcutaneous tissue	2,132	188	25
Diseases of the musculo-skeletal system and connective tissue	3,751	388	122
Osteoporosis	810	70	13
Diseases of the genitourinary system	9,106	957	282
Complications of pregnancy, childbirth and the puerperium	26	5	–
Certain conditions originating in the perinatal period	188	98	35
Congenital malformations, deformations and chromosomal abnormalities*	1,414	192	81
Symptoms, signs and abnormal findings not classified elsewhere	12,448	587	127
Senility	7,666	227	42
Sudden infant death syndrome	78	15	–
Deaths from external causes	21,226	3,152	773
Suicide and intentional self-harm	3,930	587	311
Assault	†269	56	20

* Excludes neonatal deaths (those at age under 28 days): for England and Wales neonatal deaths are included in the total number of deaths but excluded from the cause figures

† This will not be a true figure as registration of homicide and assault deaths in England and Wales is often delayed by adjourned inquests

Source: General Register Office for Scotland, NISRA, ONS (Crown copyright)

THE NATIONAL FLAG

The national flag of the United Kingdom is the Union Flag, generally known as the Union Jack.

The Union Flag is a combination of the cross of St George, patron saint of England, the cross of St Andrew, patron saint of Scotland and the cross of St Patrick, patron saint of Ireland.

Cross of St George: cross Gules in a field Argent (red cross on a white ground)

Cross of St Andrew: saltire Argent in a field Azure (white diagonal cross on a blue ground)

Cross of St Patrick: saltire Gules in a field Argent (red diagonal cross on a white ground)

A flag combining the cross of St George and the cross of St Andrew was first introduced by royal decree in 1606 following the conjoining of the English and Scottish crowns in 1603. In 1707 this flag became the flag of Great Britain after the parliaments of the two kingdoms were united. The cross of St Patrick was added in 1801 after the union of Great Britain and Ireland.

FLYING THE UNION FLAG

The correct orientation of the Union Flag when flying is with the broader diagonal band of white uppermost in the hoist (ie near the pole) and the narrower diagonal band of white uppermost in the fly (ie furthest from the pole).

The flying of the Union Flag on government buildings is decided by the Department for Digital Culture, Media and Sport (DCMS) at the Queen's command. There is no formal definition of a government building but it is generally accepted to mean a building owned or used by the Crown and/or predominantly occupied or used by civil servants or the Armed Forces.

The Scottish or Welsh governments are responsible for drawing up their own flag-flying guidance for their buildings. In Northern Ireland, the flying of flags is constrained by The Flags Regulations (Northern Ireland) 2000 and the Police Emblems and Flag Regulations (Northern Ireland) 2002. Individuals, local authorities and other organisations may fly the Union Flag whenever they wish, subject to compliance with any local planning requirement.

FLAGS AT HALF-MAST

Flags are flown at half-mast (ie two-thirds up between the top and bottom of the flagstaff) on the following occasions:
- from the announcement of the death of the sovereign until the funeral
- the death or funeral of a member of the royal family*
- the funerals of foreign rulers*
- the funerals of prime ministers and ex-prime ministers of the UK*
- the funerals of first ministers and ex-first ministers of Scotland, Wales and Northern Ireland (unless otherwise commanded by the sovereign, this only applies to flags in their respective countries)*
- other occasions by special command from the Queen

* By special command from the Queen in each case

DAYS FOR FLYING FLAGS

On 25 March 2008 the DCMS announced that UK government departments in England, Scotland and Wales may fly the Union Flag on their buildings whenever they choose and not just on the designated days listed below. In addition, on the patron saints' days of Scotland and Wales, the appropriate national flag may be flown alongside the Union Flag on UK government buildings in the wider Whitehall area. When flying on designated days flags are hoisted from 8am to sunset.

Duchess of Cambridge's birthday	9 Jan
Countess of Wessex's birthday	20 Jan
Accession of the Queen	6 Feb
Duke of York's birthday	19 Feb
St David's Day (in Wales only)*	1 Mar
Earl of Wessex's birthday	10 Mar
Commonwealth Day (2021)	8 Mar
St Patrick's Day (in Northern Ireland only)†	17 Mar
The Queen's birthday	21 Apr
St George's Day (in England only)*	23 Apr
Europe Day†	9 May
Coronation Day	2 Jun
The Queen's official birthday (2021)	21 Jun
Duke of Edinburgh's birthday	10 Jun
Duke of Cambridge's birthday	21 Jun
Duchess of Cornwall's birthday	17 Jul
Princess Royal's birthday	15 Aug
Remembrance Day (2021)	7 Nov
Prince of Wales' birthday	14 Nov
Wedding Day of the Queen	20 Nov
St Andrew's Day (in Scotland only)*	30 Nov

Opening of parliament by the Queen‡
Prorogation of parliament by the Queen‡

* The appropriate national flag, or the European flag, may be flown in addition to the Union Flag (where there are two or more flagpoles), but not in a superior position
† Only the Union Flag should be flown
‡ Only in the Greater London area, whether or not the Queen performs the ceremony in person

THE ROYAL STANDARD

The Royal Standard comprises four quarterings – two for England (three lions passant), one for Scotland* (a lion rampant) and one for Ireland (a harp).

The Royal Standard is flown when the Queen is in residence at a royal palace, on transport being used by the Queen for official journeys and from Victoria Tower when the Queen attends parliament. It may also be flown on any building (excluding ecclesiastical buildings) during a visit by the Queen. If the Queen is to be present in a building, advice on flag flying can be obtained from the DCMS.

The Royal Standard is never flown at half-mast, even after the death of the sovereign, as the new monarch immediately succeeds to the throne.

* In Scotland a version with two Scottish quarterings is used

THE ROYAL FAMILY

THE SOVEREIGN

ELIZABETH II, by the Grace of God, of the United Kingdom of Great Britain and Northern Ireland and of her other Realms and Territories Queen, Head of the Commonwealth, Defender of the Faith
Her Majesty Elizabeth Alexandra Mary of Windsor, elder daughter of King George VI and of HM Queen Elizabeth the Queen Mother
Born 21 April 1926, at 17 Bruton Street, London W1
Ascended the throne 6 February 1952
Crowned 2 June 1953, at Westminster Abbey
Married 20 November 1947, in Westminster Abbey, HRH the Prince Philip, Duke of Edinburgh
Official residences Buckingham Palace, London SW1A 1AA; Windsor Castle, Berks; Palace of Holyroodhouse, Edinburgh
Private residences Sandringham, Norfolk; Balmoral Castle, Aberdeenshire

HUSBAND OF THE QUEEN

HRH THE PRINCE PHILIP, DUKE OF EDINBURGH, KG, KT, OM, GCVO, GBE, Royal Victorian Chain, AK, QSO, PC, Ranger of Windsor Park
Born 10 June 1921, son of Prince and Princess Andrew of Greece and Denmark, naturalised a British subject 1947, created Duke of Edinburgh, Earl of Merioneth and Baron Greenwich 1947

CHILDREN OF THE QUEEN

HRH THE PRINCE OF WALES (Prince Charles Philip Arthur George), KG, KT, GCB, OM and Great Master of the Order of the Bath, AK, QSO, PC, ADC(P)
Born 14 November 1948, created Prince of Wales and Earl of Chester 1958, succeeded as Duke of Cornwall, Duke of Rothesay, Earl of Carrick and Baron Renfrew, Lord of the Isles and Great Steward of Scotland 1952
Married (1) 29 July 1981 Lady Diana Frances Spencer (Diana, Princess of Wales (1961–97), youngest daughter of the 8th Earl Spencer and the Hon. Mrs Shand Kydd), marriage dissolved 1996; (2) 9 April 2005 Mrs Camilla Rosemary Parker Bowles, now HRH the Duchess of Cornwall, GCVO, PC (*born* 17 July 1947, daughter of Major Bruce Shand and the Hon. Mrs Rosalind Shand)
Residences Clarence House, London SW1A 1BA; Highgrove, Doughton, Tetbury, Glos GL8 8TN; Birkhall, Ballater, Aberdeenshire
Issue
1. HRH the Duke of Cambridge (Prince William Arthur Philip Louis), KG, KT, PC *born* 21 June 1982, *created* Duke of Cambridge, Earl of Strathearn and Baron Carrickfergus 2011 *married* 29 April 2011 Catherine Elizabeth Middleton, now HRH the Duchess of Cambridge, GCVO (*born* 9 January 1982, elder daughter of Michael and Carole Middleton), and has issue, HRH Prince George of Cambridge (Prince George Alexander Louis), *born* 22 July 2013; HRH Princess Charlotte of Cambridge (Princess Charlotte Elizabeth Diana), *born* 2 May 2015; HRH Prince

Louis of Cambridge (Prince Louis Arthur Charles), *born* 23 April 2018 *Residences* Kensington Palace, London W8 4PU; Anmer Hall, Norfolk PE31 6RW
2. HRH the Duke of Sussex (Prince Henry Charles Albert David), KCVO *born* 15 September 1984, *created* Duke of Sussex, Earl of Dumbarton and Baron Kilkeel 2018 *married* 19 May 2018 (Rachel) Meghan Markle, now HRH the Duchess of Sussex (*born* 4 August 1981, daughter of Thomas Markle and Doria Ragland), and has issue, Archie Harrison Mountbatten-Windsor, *born* 6 May 2019 *Residence* Frogmore Cottage, Home Park, Windsor, Berks SL4 2JG

HRH THE PRINCESS ROYAL (Princess Anne Elizabeth Alice Louise), KG, KT, GCVO
Born 15 August 1950, declared the Princess Royal 1987
Married (1) 14 November 1973 Captain Mark Anthony Peter Phillips, CVO (*born* 22 September 1948); marriage dissolved 1992; (2) 12 December 1992 Vice-Adm. Sir Timothy James Hamilton Laurence, KCVO, CB, ADC (P) (*born* 1 March 1955)
Residence Gatcombe Park, Minchinhampton, Glos GL6 9AT
Issue
1. Peter Mark Andrew Phillips, *born* 15 November 1977, *married* 17 May 2008 Autumn Patricia Kelly, and has issue, Savannah Phillips, *born* 29 December 2010; Isla Elizabeth Phillips, *born* 29 March 2012
2. Zara Anne Elizabeth Tindall, MBE, *born* 15 May 1981, *married* 30 July 2011 Michael James Tindall, MBE, and has issue, Mia Grace Tindall, *born* 17 January 2014; Lena Elizabeth Tindall, *born* 18 June 2018

HRH THE DUKE OF YORK (Prince Andrew Albert Christian Edward), KG, GCVO, ADC(P)
Born 19 February 1960, created Duke of York, Earl of Inverness and Baron Killyleagh 1986
Married 23 July 1986 Sarah Margaret Ferguson, now Sarah, Duchess of York (*born* 15 October 1959, younger daughter of Major Ronald Ferguson and Mrs Hector Barrantes), marriage dissolved 1996
Residence Royal Lodge, Windsor Great Park, Berks
Issue
1. HRH Princess Beatrice of York (Princess Beatrice Elizabeth Mary), *born* 8 August 1988
2. HRH Princess Eugenie of York (Princess Eugenie Victoria Helena), *born* 23 March 1990, *married* 12 October 2018 Jack Christopher Stamp Brooksbank

HRH THE EARL OF WESSEX (Prince Edward Antony Richard Louis), KG, GCVO, ADC(P)
Born 10 March 1964, created Earl of Wessex, Viscount Severn 1999 and Earl of Forfar 2019
Married 19 June 1999 Sophie Helen Rhys-Jones, now HRH the Countess of Wessex, GCVO (*born* 20 January 1965, daughter of Mr and Mrs Christopher Rhys-Jones)
Residence Bagshot Park, Bagshot, Surrey GU19 5HS
Issue
1. Lady Louise Mountbatten-Windsor (Louise Alice Elizabeth Mary Mountbatten-Windsor), *born* 8 November 2003
2. Viscount Severn (James Alexander Philip Theo Mountbatten-Windsor), *born* 17 December 2007

NEPHEW AND NIECE OF THE QUEEN

Children of HRH the Princess Margaret, Countess of Snowdon and the Earl of Snowdon (*see* House of Windsor):
EARL OF SNOWDON (DAVID ALBERT CHARLES ARMSTRONG-JONES), *born* 3 November 1961, *married* 8 October 1993 Hon. Serena Alleyne Stanhope, and has issue, Viscount Linley (Charles Patrick Inigo Armstrong-Jones), *born* 1 July 1999; Lady Margarita Armstrong-Jones (Margarita Elizabeth Alleyne Armstrong-Jones), *born* 14 May 2002
LADY SARAH CHATTO (Sarah Frances Elizabeth), *born* 1 May 1964, *married* 14 July 1994 Daniel Chatto, and has issue, Samuel David Benedict Chatto, *born* 28 July 1996; Arthur Robert Nathaniel Chatto, *born* 5 February 1999

COUSINS OF THE QUEEN

Child of HRH the Duke of Gloucester and HRH Princess Alice, Duchess of Gloucester (*see* House of Windsor):
HRH THE DUKE OF GLOUCESTER (Prince Richard Alexander Walter George), KG, GCVO, Grand Prior of the Order of St John of Jerusalem
Born 26 August 1944
Married 8 July 1972 Birgitte Eva van Deurs, now HRH the Duchess of Gloucester, GCVO (*born* 20 June 1946, daughter of Asger Henriksen and Vivian van Deurs)
Residence Kensington Palace, London W8 4PU
Issue
1. Earl of Ulster (Alexander Patrick Gregers Richard), *born* 24 October 1974 *married* 22 June 2002 Dr Claire Alexandra Booth, and has issue, Lord Culloden (Xan Richard Anders), *born* 12 March 2007; Lady Cosima Windsor (Cosima Rose Alexandra), *born* 20 May 2010
2. Lady Davina Windsor (Davina Elizabeth Alice Benedikte), *born* 19 November 1977 *married* 31 July 2004 Gary Christie Lewis (marriage dissolved 2018), and has issue, Senna Kowhai Lewis, *born* 22 June 2010; Tane Mahuta Lewis, *born* 25 May 2012
3. Lady Rose Gilman (Rose Victoria Birgitte Louise), *born* 1 March 1980 *married* 19 July 2008 George Edward Gilman, and has issue, Lyla Beatrix Christabel Gilman, *born* 30 May 2010; Rufus Gilman, *born* 2 November 2012

Children of HRH the Duke of Kent and Princess Marina, Duchess of Kent (*see* House of Windsor):
HRH THE DUKE OF KENT (Prince Edward George Nicholas Paul Patrick), KG, GCMG, GCVO, ADC(P)
Born 9 October 1935
Married 8 June 1961 Katharine Lucy Mary Worsley, now HRH the Duchess of Kent, GCVO (*born* 22 February 1933, daughter of Sir William Worsley, Bt.)
Residence Wren House, Palace Green, London W8 4PY
Issue
1. Earl of St Andrews (George Philip Nicholas), *born* 26 June 1962, *married* 9 January 1988 Sylvana Tomaselli, and has

issue, Lord Downpatrick (Edward Edmund Maximilian George), *born* 2 December 1988; Lady Marina-Charlotte Windsor (Marina-Charlotte Alexandra Katharine Helen), *born* 30 September 1992; Lady Amelia Windsor (Amelia Sophia Theodora Mary Margaret), *born* 24 August 1995
2. Lady Helen Taylor (Helen Marina Lucy), *born* 28 April 1964, *married* 18 July 1992 Timothy Verner Taylor, and has issue, Columbus George Donald Taylor, *born* 6 August 1994; Cassius Edward Taylor, *born* 26 December 1996; Eloise Olivia Katharine Taylor, *born* 3 March 2003; Estella Olga Elizabeth Taylor, *born* 21 December 2004
3. Lord Nicholas Windsor (Nicholas Charles Edward Jonathan), *born* 25 July 1970, *married* 4 November 2006 Princess Paola Doimi de Lupis Frankopan Subic Zrinski, and has issue, Albert Louis Philip Edward Windsor, *born* 22 September 2007; Leopold Ernest Augustus Guelph Windsor, *born* 8 September 2009; Louis Arthur Nicholas Felix Windsor, *born* 27 May 2014

HRH PRINCESS ALEXANDRA, THE HON. LADY OGILVY (Princess Alexandra Helen Elizabeth Olga Christabel), KG, GCVO
Born 25 December 1936
Married 24 April 1963 the Rt. Hon. Sir Angus Ogilvy, KCVO (1928–2004), second son of 12th Earl of Airlie
Residence Thatched House Lodge, Richmond Park, Surrey TW10 5HP
Issue
1. James Robert Bruce Ogilvy, *born* 29 February 1964, *married* 30 July 1988 Julia Rawlinson, and has issue, Flora Alexandra Ogilvy, *born* 15 December 1994; Alexander Charles Ogilvy, *born* 12 November 1996
2. Marina Victoria Alexandra Ogilvy, *born* 31 July 1966, *married* 2 February 1990 Paul Julian Mowatt (marriage dissolved 1997), and has issue, Zenouska May Mowatt, *born* 26 May 1990; Christian Alexander Mowatt, *born* 4 June 1993

HRH PRINCE MICHAEL OF KENT (Prince Michael George Charles Franklin), GCVO
Born 4 July 1942
Married 30 June 1978 Baroness Marie-Christine Agnes Hedwig Ida von Reibnitz, now HRH Princess Michael of Kent (*born* 15 January 1945, daughter of Baron Gunther von Reibnitz)
Residence Kensington Palace, London W8 4PU
Issue
1. Lord Frederick Windsor (Frederick Michael George David Louis), *born* 6 April 1979, *married* 12 September 2009 Sophie Winkleman, and has issue, Maud Elizabeth Daphne Marina Windsor, *born* 15 August 2013; Isabella Alexandra May Windsor, *born* 16 January 2016
2. Lady Gabriella Kingston (Gabriella Marina Alexandra Ophelia), *born* 23 April 1981, *married* 18 May 2019 Thomas Kingston

ORDER OF SUCCESSION

The Succession to the Crown Act 2013 received royal assent on 25 April 2013 and made provision for the order of succession to the Crown not to be dependent on gender and for those members of the royal family married to a Roman Catholic to retain the right of succession to the throne. The provisions of the Act came into force on 26 March 2015, following its ratification by all 16 Realms of the Commonwealth.

On the Act's commencement HRH Prince Michael of Kent and the Earl of St Andrews were restored to the succession. In addition, all male members of the royal family born after 28 October 2011 no longer precede any elder female siblings; and their place in the order of succession changed accordingly.

The following list includes all living descendants of the sons of King George V eligible to succeed to the Crown under the current legislation. Lord Nicholas Windsor, Lord Downpatrick and Lady Marina-Charlotte Windsor renounced their rights to the throne on converting to Roman Catholicism in 2001, 2003 and 2008 respectively. Their children remain in succession provided that they are in communion with the Church of England.

1	HRH the Prince of Wales	31	Lady Davina Windsor
2	HRH the Duke of Cambridge	32	Senna Lewis
3	HRH Prince George of Cambridge	33	Tane Lewis
4	HRH Princess Charlotte of Cambridge	34	Lady Rose Gilman
5	HRH Prince Louis of Cambridge	35	Lyla Gilman
6	HRH the Duke of Sussex	36	Rufus Gilman
7	Archie Mountbatten-Windsor	37	HRH the Duke of Kent
8	HRH the Duke of York	38	Earl of St Andrews
9	HRH Princess Beatrice of York, Mrs Edoardo Mapelli	39	Lady Amelia Windsor
10	HRH Princess Eugenie, Mrs Jack Brooksbank	40	Albert Windsor
11	HRH the Earl of Wessex	41	Leopold Windsor
12	Viscount Severn	42	Louis Windsor
13	Lady Louise Mountbatten-Windsor	43	Lady Helen Taylor
14	HRH the Princess Royal	44	Columbus Taylor
15	Peter Phillips	45	Cassius Taylor
16	Savannah Phillips	46	Eloise Taylor
17	Isla Phillips	47	Estella Taylor
18	Zara Tindall	48	HRH Prince Michael of Kent
19	Mia Tindall	49	Lord Frederick Windsor
20	Lena Tindall	50	Maud Windsor
21	Earl of Snowdon	51	Isabella Windsor
22	Viscount Linley	52	Lady Gabriella Kingston
23	Lady Margarita Armstrong-Jones	53	HRH Princess Alexandra, the Hon. Lady Ogilvy
24	Lady Sarah Chatto	54	James Ogilvy
25	Samuel Chatto	55	Alexander Ogilvy
26	Arthur Chatto	56	Flora Vesterberg
27	HRH the Duke of Gloucester	57	Marina Ogilvy
28	Earl of Ulster	58	Christian Mowatt
29	Lord Culloden	59	Zenouska Mowatt
30	Lady Cosima Windsor		

THE ROYAL HOUSEHOLD

The PRIVATE SECRETARY is responsible for:
• informing and advising the Queen on constitutional, governmental and political matters in the UK, her other Realms and the wider Commonwealth, including communications with the prime minister and government departments
• organising the Queen's domestic and overseas official programme
• the Queen's speeches, messages, patronage, photographs, portraits and official presents
• communications in connection with the role of the royal family
• dealing with correspondence to the Queen from members of the public
• royal travel policy
• coordinating and initiating research to support engagements by members of the royal family

The DIRECTOR OF ROYAL COMMUNICATIONS is in charge of Buckingham Palace's communications office and reports to the Private Secretary. The director is responsible for:
• developing communications strategies to enhance the public understanding of the role of the monarchy
• briefing the British and international media on the role and duties of the Queen and issues relating to the royal family
• responding to media enquiries
• arranging media facilities in the UK and overseas to support royal functions and engagements
• the management of the royal website

The Private Secretary is keeper of the royal archives and is responsible for the care of the records of the sovereign and the royal household from previous reigns, preserved in the royal archives at Windsor. As keeper, it is the Private Secretary's responsibility to ensure the proper management of the records of the present reign with a view to their transfer to the archives as and when appropriate. The Private Secretary is an *ex officio* trustee of the Royal Collection Trust.

The KEEPER OF THE PRIVY PURSE AND TREASURER TO THE QUEEN is responsible for:
• the Sovereign Grant, which is the money paid from the government's Consolidated Fund to meet official expenditure relating to the Queen's duties as Head of State and Head of the Commonwealth and is provided by the government in return for the net surplus from the Crown Estate and other hereditary revenues (*see also* Royal Finances)
• through the Director of Human Resources, the planning and management of personnel policy across the royal household, the allocation of employee and pensioner housing and the administration of all its pension schemes and private estates employees
• information systems and telecommunications
• property services at occupied royal palaces in England, comprising Buckingham Palace, St James's Palace, Clarence House, Marlborough House Mews, the residential and office areas of Kensington Palace, Windsor Castle and buildings in the Home and Great Parks of Windsor and Hampton Court Mews and Paddocks
• delivery of all official and approved travel operations
• audit services
• health and safety; insurance matters
• the Privy Purse, which is mainly financed by the net income of the Duchy of Lancaster, and meets both official and private expenditure incurred by the Queen

• liaison with other members of the royal family and their households on financial matters
• the Queen's private estates at Sandringham and Balmoral, the Queen's Racing Establishment and the Royal Studs and liaison with the Ascot Authority
• the Home Park at Windsor and liaison with the Crown Estate Commissioners concerning the Home Park and the Great Park at Windsor
• the Royal Philatelic Collection
• administrative aspects of the Military Knights of Windsor
• administration of the Royal Victorian Order, of which the Keeper of the Privy Purse is secretary, Long and Faithful Service Medals, and the Queen's cups, medals and prizes, and policy on commemorative medals

The Keeper of the Privy Purse is also responsible for the Royal Mews, assisted by the CROWN EQUERRY, who has day-to-day responsibility for:
• the provision of carriage processions for the state opening of parliament, state visits, Trooping of the Colour, Royal Ascot, the Garter Ceremony, the Thistle Service, the presentation of credentials to the Queen by incoming foreign ambassadors and high commissioners, and other state and ceremonial occasions
• the provision of chauffeur-driven cars
• coordinating travel arrangements by road in respect of the royal household
• supervision and administration of the Royal Mews at Buckingham Palace, Windsor Castle, Hampton Court and the Palace of Holyroodhouse

The Keeper of the Privy Purse is one of three royal trustees (in respect of his responsibilities for the Sovereign Grant) and is Receiver-General of the Duchy of Lancaster and a member of the Duchy's Council.

The Keeper of the Privy Purse has overall responsibility for the DIRECTOR OF OPERATIONS, ROYAL TRAVEL, who is responsible for the provision of travel arrangements by air and rail and is also an *ex officio* trustee of the Royal Collection Trust.

The DIRECTOR OF THE PROPERTY SECTION has day-to-day responsibility for the royal household's property section:
• fire and health and safety
• repairs and refurbishment of buildings and new building work
• utilities and telecommunications
• putting up stages, tents and other work in connection with ceremonial occasions, garden parties and other official functions

The property section is also responsible, on a sub-contract basis from the DCMS, for the maintenance of Marlborough House (which is occupied by the Commonwealth Secretariat).

The MASTER OF THE HOUSEHOLD is responsible for:
• delivering the majority of the official and private entertaining in the Queen's annual programme across all the occupied palaces and residences in the UK when required
• periodic support for entertaining by all other members of the royal family
• furnishings and internal decorative refurbishment of all the occupied palaces in the UK in conjunction with the Director, Royal Collection Trust
• all operational, domestic and kitchen staff in the royal household

The COMPTROLLER, LORD CHAMBERLAIN'S OFFICE is responsible for:

- the organisation of all ceremonial engagements, including state visits to the Queen in the UK, royal weddings and funerals, the state opening of parliament, Guards of Honour at Buckingham Palace, investitures, and the Garter and Thistle ceremonies
- garden parties at Buckingham Palace and the Palace of Holyroodhouse
- the Crown Jewels, which are part of the Royal Collection, when they are in use on state occasions
- coordination of the arrangements for the Queen to be represented at funerals and memorial services and at the arrival and departure of visiting heads of state
- advising on matters of precedence, style and titles, dress, flying of flags, gun salutes, mourning and other ceremonial issues
- supervising the applications for Royal Warrants of Appointment
- advising on the commercial use of royal emblems and contemporary royal photographs
- the ecclesiastical household, the medical household, the bodyguards and certain ceremonial appointments such as Gentlemen Ushers and Pages of Honour
- the Lords in Waiting, who represent the Queen on various occasions and escort visiting heads of state during incoming state visits
- the Queen's bargemaster and watermen and the Queen's swans
- the Royal Almonry and Royal Maundy Service

The Comptroller also has overall responsibility for the MARSHAL OF THE DIPLOMATIC CORPS, who is responsible for the relationship between the royal household and the Diplomatic Heads of Mission in London; and the SECRETARY OF THE CENTRAL CHANCERY OF THE ORDERS OF KNIGHTHOOD, who administers the Orders of Chivalry, makes arrangements for investitures and the distribution of insignia, and ensures the proper public notification of awards through *The London Gazette*.

The DIRECTOR, ROYAL COLLECTION TRUST is responsible for:
- the administration and custodial control of the Royal Collection in all royal residences
- the care, display, conservation and restoration of items in the collection
- initiating and assisting research into the collection and publishing catalogues and books on the collection
- making the collection accessible to the public and educating and informing the public about the collection

The Royal Collection, which contains a large number of works of art, is held by the Queen as sovereign in trust for her successors and the nation and is not owned by her as an individual. The administration, conservation and presentation of the Royal Collection are funded by the Royal Collection Trust solely from income from visitors to Windsor Castle, Buckingham Palace and the Palace of Holyroodhouse. The Royal Collection Trust is chaired by the Prince of Wales. The Lord Chamberlain, the Private Secretary and the Keeper of the Privy Purse are *ex officio* trustees and there are three external trustees appointed by the Queen.

The Director, Royal Collection Trust is also at present the SURVEYOR OF THE QUEEN'S WORKS OF ART, responsible for paintings, miniatures and works of art on paper, including the watercolours, prints and drawings in the Print Room at Windsor Castle, and for the books, manuscripts, coins, medals and insignia in the Royal Library. Royal Collection Enterprises Limited is the trading subsidiary of the Royal Collection Trust. The company, whose chair is the Keeper of the Privy Purse, is responsible for:

- managing access by the public to Windsor Castle (including Frogmore House), Buckingham Palace (including the Royal Mews and the Queen's Gallery) and the Palace of Holyroodhouse (including the Queen's Gallery)
- running shops at each location
- managing the images and intellectual property rights of the Royal Collection

The Director, Royal Collection Trust is also an *ex officio* trustee of Historic Royal Palaces.

PRIVATE SECRETARIES

THE QUEEN
Office: Buckingham Palace, London SW1A 1AA **T** 020-7930 4832
Private Secretary to The Queen, Rt. Hon. Sir Edward Young, KCVO

PRINCE PHILIP, THE DUKE OF EDINBURGH
Office: Buckingham Palace, London SW1A 1AA **T** 020-7930 4832
Private Secretary, Brig. Archie Miller-Bakewell

THE PRINCE OF WALES AND THE DUCHESS OF CORNWALL
Office: Clarence House, London SW1A 1BA **T** 020-7930 4832
Principal Private Secretary, Clive Alderton, CVO

THE DUKE AND DUCHESS OF CAMBRIDGE
Office: Kensington Palace, Palace Green, London W8 4PU
T 020-7930 4832
Private Secretary to the Duke of Cambridge, Simon Case, CVO
Private Secretary to the Duchess of Cambridge, Catherine Quinn

THE DUKE AND DUCHESS OF SUSSEX
Office, Kensington Palace, Palace Green, London W8 4PU
T 020-7930 4832
Private Secretary to the Duke and Duchess of Sussex, Fiona Mcilwham

THE DUKE OF YORK
Office: Buckingham Palace, London SW1A 1AA **T** 020-7024 4227
Private Secretary, Amanda Thirsk, LVO

THE EARL AND COUNTESS OF WESSEX
Office: Bagshot Park, Surrey GU19 5PL **T** 01276-707040
Private Secretary, Capt. Andy Aspden, RN

THE PRINCESS ROYAL
Office: Buckingham Palace, London SW1A 1AA **T** 020-7024 4199
Private Secretary, Charles Davies, MVO

THE DUKE AND DUCHESS OF GLOUCESTER
Office: Kensington Palace, London W8 4PU **T** 020-7368 1000
Private Secretary, Lt.-Col. Alastair Todd

THE DUKE OF KENT
Office: York House, St James's Palace, London SW1A 1BQ
T 020-7930 4872
Private Secretary, Nicholas Turnbull, MBE, QGM

PRINCE AND PRINCESS MICHAEL OF KENT
Office: Kensington Palace, London W8 4PU
W www.princemichael.org.uk
Private Secretary, Camilla Rogers

PRINCESS ALEXANDRA, THE HON. LADY OGILVY
Office: Buckingham Palace, London SW1A 1AA
T 020-7024 4270
Private Secretary, Diane Duke, LVO

SENIOR MANAGEMENT OF THE ROYAL HOUSEHOLD

Lord Chamberlain, Earl Peel, GCVO, PC

HEADS OF DEPARTMENT

Private Secretary to The Queen, Rt. Hon. Edward Young, CVO
Keeper of the Privy Purse, Sir Michael Stevens, KCVO
Master of the Household, Vice-Adm. Tony Johnstone-Burt, CB, OBE
Comptroller, Lord Chamberlain's Office, Lt.-Col. Michael Vernon
Director of the Royal Collection, Tim Knox

NON-EXECUTIVE MEMBERS

Private Secretary to the Duke of Edinburgh, Brig. Archie Miller-Bakewell
Principal Private Secretary to the Prince of Wales and the Duchess of Cornwall, Clive Alderton, LVO

ASTRONOMER ROYAL

The post of Astronomer Royal dates back to 1675, when astronomy had many practical applications in navigation. Today the post is largely honorary, although the Astronomer Royal is expected to be available for consultation on scientific matters for as long as the holder remains a professional astronomer. The Astronomer Royal receives a stipend of £100 a year and is a member of the royal household.

Astronomer Royal, Lord Rees of Ludlow, OM, *apptd* 1995

MASTER OF THE QUEEN'S MUSIC

The office of Master of the Queen's Music is an honour conferred on a musician of great distinction. The office was first created in 1626, when the master was responsible for the court musicians. Since the reign of King George V, the position has had no fixed duties, although the Master may choose to produce compositions to mark royal or state occasions. The Master of the Queen's Music is paid an annual stipend of £15,000. In 2004 the length of appointment was changed from life tenure to a ten-year term.

Master of the Queen's Music, Judith Weir, CBE, *apptd* 2014

POET LAUREATE

The post of Poet Laureate was officially established when John Dryden was appointed by royal warrant as Poet Laureate and Historiographer Royal in 1668. The post is attached to the royal household and was originally conferred on the holder for life; in 1999 the length of appointment was changed to a ten-year term. It is customary for the Poet Laureate to write verse to mark events of national importance. The postholder currently receives an honorarium of £5,750 a year.

The Poet Laureate, Simon Armitage, *apptd* 2019

ROYAL FINANCES

Dating back to the late 17th century the Civil List was originally used by the sovereign to supplement hereditary revenues for paying the salaries of judges, ambassadors and other government officers as well as the expenses of the royal household. In 1760, on the accession of George III, it was decided that the Civil List would be provided by parliament to cover all relevant expenditure in return for the king surrendering the hereditary revenues of the Crown. At that time parliament undertook to pay the salaries of judges, ambassadors etc. In 1831 parliament agreed also to meet the costs of the royal palaces in return for a reduction in the Civil List.

Until 1 April 2012 the Civil List met the central staff costs and running expenses of the Queen's official household. Annual grants-in-aid provided for the maintenance of the occupied royal palaces (*see* Royal Household for a list of occupied palaces) and royal travel.

THE SOVEREIGN GRANT

Under the Sovereign Grant Act 2011, which came into force on 1 April 2012, the funding previously provided by the Civil List and the grants-in-aid was consolidated in the Sovereign Grant. It is provided by HM Treasury from public funds in exchange for the surrender by the Queen of the revenue of the Crown Estate.

For 2016–17 the Sovereign Grant was calculated based on 15 per cent of the income account net surplus of the Crown Estate for the financial year two years previous. From 2017–18 this increased to 25 per cent, providing for a Sovereign Grant of £82.2m in 2018–19. The additional grant generated (£32.9m in 2018–19) will be used to fund the reservicing of Buckingham Palace over a ten-year period.

Official core expenditure met by the Sovereign Grant in 2018–19 amounted to £49.6m. Royal travel accounted for £4.6m of the expenditure and property maintenance for £23.7m. The excess of core expenditure over core Sovereign Grant of £0.3m was transferred from the Sovereign Grant reserve.

The legislative requirement is for Sovereign Grant accounts to be audited by the Comptroller and Auditor-General, scrutinised by the National Audit Office, and submitted to parliament annually. They are subjected to the same scrutiny as for any other government department. The annual report for the year to 31 March 2019 was published in June 2019.

£m	2017–18	2018–19
Sovereign Grant	76.1	82.2
Core	45.7	49.3
Buckingham Palace	30.4	32.9
Transfer (to)/ from the reserve	(28.7)	(15.2)
Core	(2.4)	0.3
Buckingham Palace	(26.3)	(15.5)
Net Expenditure	47.4	67.0

PARLIAMENTARY ANNUITIES

The Civil List acts provided for other members of the royal family to receive annuities from government funds to meet the expenses of carrying out their official duties. Since 1993 these annuities the Queen reimbursed HM Treasury for all of them except those paid to the late Queen Elizabeth the Queen Mother and the Duke of Edinburgh. The Sovereign Grant Act 2011 repealed all parliamentary annuities paid to the royal family, with the exception of that paid to the Duke of Edinburgh (£359,000 in 2018–19). This is now paid directly from the Consolidated Fund.

THE PRIVY PURSE

The funds received by the Privy Purse pay for official expenses incurred by the Queen as head of state and for some of the Queen's private expenditure. The revenues of the Duchy of Lancaster are the principal source of income for the privy purse. The revenues of the Duchy were retained by George III in 1760 when the hereditary revenues were surrendered. The Duchy Council reports to the Chancellor of the Duchy of Lancaster, who is accountable directly to the sovereign rather than to parliament. However the chancellor does answer parliamentary questions on matters relating to the Duchy's responsibilities.

THE DUCHY OF LANCASTER, 1 Lancaster Place, London WC2E 7ED **W** www.duchyoflancaster.co.uk

Chancellor of the Duchy of Lancaster, Rt. Hon. Michael Gove, MP, *apptd* 2019

Chair of the Council, Sir Alan Reid, GCVO
Chief Executive and Clerk, Nathan Thompson
Receiver-General, Sir Michael Stevens, KCVO
Attorney-General, Robert Miles, QC

PERSONAL INCOME

The Queen's personal income derives mostly from investments, and is used to meet private expenditure.

PRINCE OF WALES' FUNDING

The Duchy Estate was created in 1337 by Edward III for his son Prince Edward (the Black Prince) who became the Duke of Cornwall. The Duchy's primary function is to provide an income from its assets for the Prince of Wales. Under a 1337 charter, confirmed by subsequent legislation, the Prince of Wales is not entitled to the proceeds or profit on the sale of Duchy assets but only to the annual income which is generated. The Duchy is responsible for the sustainable and commercial management of its properties, investment portfolio and 55,120 hectares of land, based mostly in the south-west of England. The Prince of Wales also uses a proportion of his Duchy income to meet the cost of his official public duties and the public, charitable and private activities of the Duchess of Cornwall, the Duke and Duchess of Cambridge and the Duke and Duchess of Sussex.

THE DUCHY OF CORNWALL, 10 Buckingham Gate, London SW1E 6LA **T** 020-7834 7346 **W** www.duchyofcornwall.org

Lord Warden of the Stannaries, Sir Nicholas Bacon, Bt., OBE
Receiver-General, Hon. Sir James Leigh-Pemberton, CVO
Attorney-General, Jonathan Crow, QC
Secretary and Keeper of the Records, Alastair Martin

TAXATION

The sovereign is not legally liable to pay income tax or capital gains tax, but since 6 April 1993 has paid both on a voluntary basis. The main provisions for the Queen and the Prince of Wales to pay tax are set out in a Memorandum of Understanding on Royal Taxation presented to parliament on 11 February 1993. The Queen pays income and capital gains tax in respect of her private income and assets, and on the proportion of the income and capital gains of the Privy Purse used for private purposes. Inheritance tax will be paid on the Queen's assets, except for those which pass to the next sovereign, whether automatically or by gift or bequest. The Prince of Wales pays income tax on income from the Duchy of Cornwall used for private purposes.

ROYAL SALUTES

ENGLAND

The basic royal salute is 21 rounds with an extra 20 rounds fired at Hyde Park because it is a royal park. At the Tower of London 62 rounds are fired on royal anniversaries (21 plus a further 20 because the Tower is a royal palace and a further 21 'for the City of London') and 41 on other occasions. When the Queen's official birthday coincides with the Duke of Edinburgh's birthday, 124 rounds are fired from the Tower (62 rounds for each birthday). Gun salutes occur on the following royal anniversaries:

• Accession Day
• The Queen's birthday
• Coronation Day
• Duke of Edinburgh's birthday
• The Queen's Official Birthday
• The Prince of Wales' birthday
• State opening of parliament

Gun salutes also occur when parliament is prorogued by the sovereign, on royal births and when a visiting head of state meets the sovereign in London, Windsor or Edinburgh.

In London, salutes are fired at Hyde Park and the Tower of London although on some occasions (state visits, state opening of parliament and the Queen's birthday parade) Green Park is used instead of Hyde Park. Other military saluting stations in England are at Colchester, Dover, Plymouth, Woolwich and York.

Constable of the Royal Palace and Fortress of London, Gen. Lord Houghton of Richmond, GCB, CBE

Lieutenant of the Tower of London, Lt.-Gen. Sir Simon Mayall, KBE, CB

Master Gunner within The Tower, Col. Hon. Mark Vincent, MBE

Resident Governor and Keeper of the Jewel House, Col. Richard Harrold, CVO, OBE

Master Gunner of St James's Park, Lt.-Gen. Sir Andrew Gregory, KBE, CB

MILITARY RANKS AND TITLES

THE QUEEN

ARMY

Colonel-in-Chief
The Life Guards; The Blues and Royals (Royal Horse Guards and 1st Dragoons); The Royal Scots Dragoon Guards (Carabiniers and Greys); The Royal Lancers (Queen Elizabeths' Own); The Royal Tank Regiment; Corps of Royal Engineers; Grenadier Guards; Coldstream Guards; Scots Guards; Irish Guards; Welsh Guards; The Royal Regiment of Scotland; The Duke of Lancaster's Regiment (King's, Lancashire and Border); The Royal Welsh; Adjutant General's Corps; The Governor General's Horse Guards (of Canada); The King's Own Calgary Regiment (Royal Canadian Armoured Corps); Canadian Forces Military Engineering Branch; Le Royal 22e Regiment; The Governor General's Foot Guards; The Canadian Grenadier Guards; The Stormont, Dundas and Glengarry Highlanders; Le Régiment de la Chaudière; The Royal New Brunswick Regiment; The North Shore (New Brunswick) Regiment; 48th Highlanders of Canada; The Argyll and Sutherland Highlanders of Canada (Princess Louise's); The Calgary Highlanders; Royal Australian Engineers; Royal Australian Infantry Corps; Royal Australian Army Ordnance Corps; Royal Australian Army Nursing Corps; The Corps of Royal New Zealand Engineers; Royal New Zealand Infantry Regiment

Affiliated Colonel-in-Chief
The Queen's Gurkha Engineers

Captain-General
Royal Regiment of Artillery; The Honourable Artillery Company; Combined Cadet Force; Royal Regiment of Canadian Artillery; Royal Regiment of Australian Artillery; Royal Regiment of New Zealand Artillery; Royal New Zealand Armoured Corps

Royal Colonel
Balaklava Company, 5th Battalion The Royal Regiment of Scotland

Patron
Royal Army Chaplains' Department

ROYAL AIR FORCE

Air Commodore-in-Chief
Royal Auxiliary Air Force; Royal Air Force Regiment; Air Reserve (of Canada); Royal Australian Air Force Reserve; Territorial Air Force (of New Zealand)

Commandant-in-Chief
RAF College, Cranwell

Royal Honorary Air Commodore
RAF Marham; 603 (City of Edinburgh) Squadron Royal Auxiliary Air Force

TRI-SERVICE

Colonel-in-Chief
The Canadian Armed Forces Legal Branch

PRINCE PHILIP, DUKE OF EDINBURGH

ROYAL NAVY

Lord High Admiral of the United Kingdom
Admiral of the Fleet
Admiral of the Fleet, Royal Australian Navy
Admiral of the Fleet, Royal New Zealand Navy
Admiral, Royal Canadian Navy
Admiral, Royal Canadian Sea Cadets

ARMY

Field Marshal
Field Marshal, Australian Military Forces
Field Marshal, New Zealand Army
General, Royal Canadian Army
Colonel-in-Chief
The Queen's Royal Hussars (Queen's Own and Royal Irish); The Rifles; Corps of Royal Electrical and Mechanical Engineers; Intelligence Corps; Army Cadet Force Association; The Royal Canadian Regiment; The Royal Hamilton Light Infantry (Wentworth Regiment of Canada); The Cameron Highlanders of Ottawa; The Queen's Own Cameron Highlanders of Canada; The Seaforth Highlanders of Canada; The Royal Canadian Army Cadets; The Royal Australian Corps of Electrical and Mechanical Engineers; The Australian Army Cadet Corps

Royal Colonel
The Highlanders, 4th Battalion The Royal Regiment of Scotland

Honorary Colonel
The Trinidad and Tobago Regiment

Member
Honourable Artillery Company

ROYAL AIR FORCE

Marshal of the Royal Air Force
Marshal of the Royal Australian Air Force
Marshal of the Royal New Zealand Air Force
General, Royal Canadian Air Force
Air Commodore-in-Chief
Royal Canadian Air Cadets
Honorary Air Commodore
RAF Northolt

THE PRINCE OF WALES

ROYAL NAVY

Admiral of the Fleet
Admiral of the Fleet, Royal New Zealand Navy
Vice-Admiral
Royal Canadian Navy
Commodore-in-Chief
HM Naval Base Plymouth; Fleet Atlantic, Royal Canadian Navy
Honorary Commodore-in-Chief
Aircraft Carriers

ARMY

Field Marshal
Field Marshal, New Zealand Army
Lieutenant-General
Canadian Army
Colonel-in-Chief
The Royal Dragoon Guards; The Parachute Regiment; The Royal Gurkha Rifles; Army Air Corps; The Royal Canadian Dragoons; Lord Strathcona's Horse (Royal Canadians); The Royal Regiment of Canada; Royal Winnipeg Rifles; Royal Australian Armoured Corps; The Royal Pacific Islands Regiment; 1st The Queen's Dragoon Guards; The Black Watch (Royal Highland Regiment) of Canada; The Toronto Scottish Regiment (Queen Elizabeth The Queen Mother's Own); The Mercian Regiment; 2nd Battalion The Irish Regiment of Canada

Royal Colonel
The Black Watch, 3rd Battalion The Royal Regiment of Scotland; 51st Highland, 7th Battalion The Royal Regiment of Scotland

Colonel
 The Welsh Guards
Royal Honorary Colonel
 The Queen's Own Yeomanry

ROYAL AIR FORCE
Marshal of the RAF
Marshal of the Royal New Zealand Air Force
Lieutenant-General
 Royal Canadian Air Force
Honorary Air Commodore
 RAF Valley
Colonel-in-Chief
 Air Reserve Canada

THE DUCHESS OF CORNWALL

ROYAL NAVY
Commodore-in-Chief
 Royal Naval Medical Services; Naval Chaplaincy Services
Lady Sponsor
 HMS *Astute;* HMS *Prince of Wales*

ARMY
Colonel-in-Chief
 Queen's Own Rifles of Canada; Royal Australian Corps of Military Police
Royal Colonel
 4th Battalion The Rifles

ROYAL AIR FORCE
Honorary Air Commodore
 RAF Halton; RAF Leeming

THE DUKE OF CAMBRIDGE

ROYAL NAVY
Lieutenant Commander
Commodore-in-Chief
 Scotland Command; Submarines Command

ARMY
Colonel
 Irish Guards
Major
 The Blues and Royals (Royal Horse Guards and 1st Dragoons)

ROYAL AIR FORCE
Squadron Leader
Honorary Air Commandant
 RAF Coningsby

THE DUCHESS OF CAMBRIDGE

ROYAL AIR FORCE
Honorary Air Commandant
 Air Cadets

THE DUKE OF SUSSEX

ROYAL NAVY
Lieutenant-Commander
Commodore-in-Chief
 Small Ships and Diving Command

ROYAL MARINES
Captain-General

ARMY
Major
 The Blues and Royals (Royal Horse Guards and 1st Dragoons)

ROYAL AIR FORCE
Squadron Leader
Honorary Air Commandant
 RAF Honington

THE DUKE OF YORK

ROYAL NAVY
Vice-Admiral
Commodore-in-Chief
 Fleet Air Arm
Admiral of the Sea Cadets Corps

ARMY
Colonel-in-Chief
 The Royal Irish Regiment (27th (Inniskilling), 83rd, 87th and The Ulster Defence Regiment); The Yorkshire Regiment (14th/15th, 19th and 33rd/76th Foot); Small Arms School Corps; The Queen's York Rangers (First Americans); Royal New Zealand Army Logistics Regiment; The Royal Highland Fusiliers of Canada; The Princess Louise Fusiliers (Canada)
Deputy Colonel-in-Chief
 The Royal Lancers (Queen Elizabeths' Own)
Colonel
 Grenadier Guards
Royal Colonel
 The Royal Highland Fusiliers, 2nd Battalion The Royal Regiment of Scotland

ROYAL AIR FORCE
Honorary Air Commodore
 RAF Lossiemouth

THE EARL OF WESSEX

ROYAL NAVY
Commodore-in-Chief
 Royal Fleet Auxiliary
Patron
 Royal Fleet Auxiliary Association

ARMY
Colonel-in-Chief
 Hastings and Prince Edward Regiment; Saskatchewan Dragoons; Prince Edward Island Regiment
Royal Colonel
 2nd Battalion, The Rifles
Royal Honorary Colonel
 Royal Wessex Yeomanry; The London Regiment

ROYAL AIR FORCE
Honorary Air Commodore
 RAF Waddington

THE COUNTESS OF WESSEX

ARMY
Colonel-in-Chief
 Corps of Army Music; Queen Alexandra's Royal Army Nursing Corps; The Lincoln and Welland Regiment; South Alberta Light Horse Regiment
Royal Colonel
 5th Battalion, The Rifles
Patron
 Queen Alexandra's Royal Army Nursing Corps Association

ROYAL AIR FORCE
Honorary Air Commodore
 RAF Wittering

ROYAL NAVY
Sponsor
   HMS *Daring*

THE PRINCESS ROYAL

ROYAL NAVY
Admiral (Chief Commandant for Women in the Royal Navy)
Commodore-in-Chief
   HM Naval Base Portsmouth; Fleet Pacific Royal Canadian
   Navy

ARMY
Colonel-in-Chief
   The King's Royal Hussars; Royal Corps of Signals; Royal
   Logistic Corps; The Royal Army Veterinary Corps; 8th
   Canadian Hussars (Princess Louise's); Royal Newfoundland
   Regiment; Canadian Forces Communications and
   Electronics Branch; The Grey and Simcoe Foresters; The
   Royal Regina Rifles; Royal Canadian Medical Service;
   Royal Canadian Hussars; Royal Australian Corps of Signals;
   Royal Australian Corps of Transport; Royal New Zealand
   Corps of Signals; Royal New Zealand Nursing Corps
Affiliated Colonel-in-Chief
   The Queen's Gurkha Signals; The Queen's Own Gurkha
   Transport Regiment
Royal Colonel
   1st Battalion (Royal Scots Borderers), The Royal Regiment
   of Scotland; 6th Battalion (52nd Lowland Volunteers), The
   Royal Regiment of Scotland
Colonel
   The Blues and Royals (Royal Horse Guards and 1st
   Dragoons)
Honorary Colonel
   University of London Officers' Training Corps; City of
   Edinburgh Universities Officers' Training Corps
Commandant-in-Chief
   First Aid Nursing Yeomanry (Princess Royal's Volunteer
   Corps)

ROYAL AIR FORCE
Honorary Air Commodore
   RAF Brize Norton; University of London Air Squadron

THE DUKE OF GLOUCESTER

ARMY
Colonel-in-Chief
   The Royal Anglian Regiment; Royal Army Medical Corps;
   Royal New Zealand Army Medical Corps
Deputy Colonel-in-Chief
   The Royal Logistic Corps
Royal Colonel
   6th Battalion, The Rifles
Royal Honorary Colonel
   Royal Monmouthshire Royal Engineers (Militia)

ROYAL AIR FORCE
Honorary Air Marshal
Honorary Air Commodore
   RAF Odiham; No. 501 (County of Gloucester) Logistic
   Support Squadron

THE DUCHESS OF GLOUCESTER

ARMY
Colonel-in-Chief
   Royal Army Dental Corps; Royal Australian Army
   Educational Corps; Royal New Zealand Army Educational
   Corps; Royal Canadian Dental Corps; The Royal Bermuda
   Regiment

Deputy Colonel-in-Chief
   Adjutant General's Corps
Royal Colonel
   7th Battalion, The Rifles
Vice-Patron
   Adjutant General's Corps Regimental Association
Patron
   Royal Army Educational Corps Association; Army Families
   Federation

THE DUKE OF KENT

ARMY
Field Marshal
Colonel-in-Chief
   The Royal Regiment of Fusiliers; Lorne Scots (Peel, Dufferin
   and Hamilton Regiment)
Deputy Colonel-in-Chief
   The Royal Scots Dragoon Guards (Carabiniers and Greys)
Royal Colonel
   1st Battalion The Rifles
Colonel
   Scots Guards

ROYAL AIR FORCE
Honorary Air Chief Marshal

THE DUCHESS OF KENT

ARMY
Honorary Major-General
Deputy Colonel-in-Chief
   The Royal Dragoon Guards; Adjutant General's Corps; The
   Royal Logistic Corps

PRINCE MICHAEL OF KENT

ROYAL NAVY
Honorary Vice-Admiral of the Royal Naval Reserves
Commodore-in-Chief of the Maritime Reserves

ARMY
Colonel-in-Chief
   Essex and Kent Scottish Regiment (Ontario)
Royal Honorary Colonel
   Honourable Artillery Company
Senior Colonel
   King's Royal Hussars

ROYAL AIR FORCE
Honorary Air Marshal
   RAF Benson

PRINCESS ALEXANDRA, THE HON. LADY OGILVY

ROYAL NAVY
Patron
   Queen Alexandra's Royal Naval Nursing Service

ARMY
Colonel-in-Chief
   The Canadian Scottish Regiment (Princess Mary's)
Deputy Colonel-in-Chief
   The Royal Lancers
Royal Colonel
   3rd Battalion The Rifles
Royal Honorary Colonel
   The Royal Yeomanry

ROYAL AIR FORCE
Patron and Air Chief Commandant
   Princess Mary's RAF Nursing Service

KINGS AND QUEENS

ENGLISH KINGS AND QUEENS 927–1603

HOUSES OF CERDIC AND DENMARK

927–939 ÆTHELSTAN
Son of Edward the Elder, by Ecgwynn, and grandson of Alfred *acceded* to Wessex and Mercia *c*.924, established direct rule over Northumbria 927, effectively creating the Kingdom of England *reigned* 15 years

939–946 EDMUND I
born 921, son of Edward the Elder, by Eadgifu *married* (1) Ælfgifu (2) Æthelflæd *killed* aged 25 *reigned* 6 years

946–955 EADRED
Son of Edward the Elder, by Eadgifu *reigned* 9 years

955–959 EADWIG
born before 943, son of Edmund and Ælfgifu *married* Ælfgifu *reigned* 3 years

959–975 EDGAR I
born 943, son of Edmund and Ælfgifu *married* (1) Æthelflæd (2) Wulfthryth (3) Ælfthryth *died* aged 32 *reigned* 15 years

975–978 EDWARD I (the Martyr)
born c.962, son of Edgar and Æthelflæd *assassinated* aged *c*.16 *reigned* 2 years

978–1016 ÆTHELRED (the Unready)
born 968/969, son of Edgar and Ælfthryth *married* (1) Ælfgifu (2) Emma, daughter of Richard I, Count of Normandy, 1013–14 dispossessed of kingdom by Swegn Forkbeard (King of Denmark 987–1014) *died* aged *c*.47, *reigned* 38 years

1016 EDMUND II (Ironside)
(Apr–Nov) *born* before 993, son of Æthelred and Ælfgifu *married* Ealdgyth *died* aged over 23 *reigned* 7 months

1016–1035 CNUT (Canute)
born c.995, son of Swegn Forkbeard, King of Denmark, and Gunhild *married* (1) Ælfgifu (2) Emma, widow of Æthelred the Unready. Gained submission of West Saxons 1015, Northumbrians 1016, Mercia 1016, King of all England after Edmund's death, King of Denmark 1019–35, King of Norway 1028–35 *died* aged *c*.40 *reigned* 19 years

1035–1040 HAROLD I (Harefoot)
born 1016/17, son of Cnut and Ælfgifu *married* Ælfgifu 1035 recognised as regent for himself and his brother Harthacnut; 1037 recognised as king *died* aged *c*.23 *reigned* 4 years

1040–1042 HARTHACNUT (Harthacanute)
born c.1018, son of Cnut and Emma. Titular king of Denmark from 1028, acknowledged King of England 1035–7 with Harold I as regent; effective king after Harold's death *died* aged *c*.24 *reigned* 2 years

1042–1066 EDWARD II (the Confessor)
born between 1002 and 1005, son of Æthelred the Unready and Emma *married* Eadgyth, daughter of Godwine, Earl of Wessex *died* aged over 60 *reigned* 23 years

1066 HAROLD II (Godwinesson)
(Jan–Oct) *born c*.1020, son of Godwine, Earl of Wessex, and Gytha *married* (1) Eadgyth (2) Ealdgyth *killed* in battle aged *c*.46 *reigned* 10 months

THE HOUSE OF NORMANDY

1066–1087 WILLIAM I (the Conqueror)
born 1027/8, son of Robert I, Duke of Normandy; obtained the Crown by conquest *married* Matilda, daughter of Baldwin, Count of Flanders *died* aged *c*.60, *reigned* 20 years

1087–1100 WILLIAM II (Rufus)
born between 1056 and 1060, third son of William I; succeeded his father in England only *killed* aged *c*.40 *reigned* 12 years

1100–1135 HENRY I (Beauclerk)
born 1068, fourth son of William I *married* (1) Edith or Matilda, daughter of Malcolm III of Scotland (2) Adela, daughter of Godfrey, Count of Louvain *died* aged 67 *reigned* 35 years

1135–1154 STEPHEN
born not later than 1100, third son of Adela, daughter of William I, and Stephen, Count of Blois *married* Matilda, daughter of Eustace, Count of Boulogne. Feb–Nov 1141 held captive by adherents of Matilda, daughter of Henry I, who contested the Crown until 1153 *died* aged over 53 *reigned* 18 years

THE HOUSE OF ANJOU (PLANTAGENETS)

1154–1189 HENRY II (Curtmantle)
born 1133, son of Matilda, daughter of Henry I, and Geoffrey, Count of Anjou *married* Eleanor, daughter of William, Duke of Aquitaine, and divorced queen of Louis VII of France *died* aged 56 *reigned* 34 years

1189–1199 RICHARD I (Coeur de Lion)
born 1157, third son of Henry II *married* Berengaria, daughter of Sancho VI, King of Navarre *died* aged 42 *reigned* 9 years

1199–1216 JOHN (Lackland)
born 1167, fifth son of Henry II *married* (1) Isabella or Avisa, daughter of William, Earl of Gloucester (divorced) (2) Isabella, daughter of Aymer, Count of Angoulême *died* aged 48 *reigned* 17 years

1216–1272 HENRY III
born 1207, son of John and Isabella of Angoulême *married* Eleanor, daughter of Raymond, Count of Provence *died* aged 65 *reigned* 56 years

1272–1307 EDWARD I (Longshanks)
born 1239, eldest son of Henry III *married* (1) Eleanor, daughter of Ferdinand III, King of Castile (2) Margaret, daughter of Philip III of France *died* aged 68 *reigned* 34 years

1307–1327 EDWARD II
born 1284, eldest surviving son of Edward I and Eleanor *married* Isabella, daughter of Philip IV of France *deposed* Jan 1327 *killed* Sep 1327 aged 43 *reigned* 19 years

1327–1377 EDWARD III
born 1312, eldest son of Edward II *married* Philippa, daughter of William, Count of Hainault *died* aged 64 *reigned* 50 years

1377–1399 RICHARD II
born 1367, son of Edward (the Black Prince), eldest son of Edward III *married* (1) Anne, daughter of Emperor Charles IV (2) Isabelle, daughter of Charles VI of France *deposed* Sep 1399 *killed* Feb 1400 aged 33 *reigned* 22 years

THE HOUSE OF LANCASTER

1399–1413　HENRY IV
born 1366, son of John of Gaunt, fourth son of Edward III, and Blanche, daughter of Henry, Duke of Lancaster *married* (1) Mary, daughter of Humphrey, Earl of Hereford (2) Joan, daughter of Charles, King of Navarre, and widow of John, Duke of Brittany *died* aged *c*.47 *reigned* 13 years

1413–1422　HENRY V
born 1387, eldest surviving son of Henry IV and Mary *married* Catherine, daughter of Charles VI of France *died* aged 34 *reigned* 9 years

1422–1471　HENRY VI
born 1421, son of Henry V *married* Margaret, daughter of René, Duke of Anjou and Count of Provence *deposed* Mar 1461 *restored* Oct 1470 *deposed* Apr 1471 *killed* May 1471 aged 49 *reigned* 39 years

THE HOUSE OF YORK

1461–1483　EDWARD IV
born 1442, eldest son of Richard of York (grandson of Edmund, fifth son of Edward III; and son of Anne, great-granddaughter of Lionel, third son of Edward III) *married* Elizabeth Woodville, daughter of Richard, Lord Rivers, and widow of Sir John Grey *acceded* Mar 1461 *deposed* Oct 1470 *restored* Apr 1471 *died* aged 40 *reigned* 21 years

1483　EDWARD V
(Apr–Jun)　*born* 1470, eldest son of Edward IV *deposed* Jun 1483, *died* probably Jul–Sep 1483, aged 12 *reigned* 2 months

1483–1485　RICHARD III
born 1452, fourth son of Richard of York *married* Anne Neville, daughter of Richard, Earl of Warwick, and widow of Edward, Prince of Wales, son of Henry VI *killed* in battle aged 32 *reigned* 2 years

THE HOUSE OF TUDOR

1485–1509　HENRY VII
born 1457, son of Margaret Beaufort (great-granddaughter of John of Gaunt, fourth son of Edward III) and Edmund Tudor, Earl of Richmond *married* Elizabeth, daughter of Edward IV *died* aged 52 *reigned* 23 years

1509–1547　HENRY VIII
born 1491, second son of Henry VII *married* (1) Catherine, daughter of Ferdinand II, King of Aragon, and widow of his elder brother Arthur (divorced) (2) Anne, daughter of Sir Thomas Boleyn (executed) (3) Jane, daughter of Sir John Seymour (died in childbirth) (4) Anne, daughter of John, Duke of Cleves (divorced) (5) Catherine Howard, niece of the Duke of Norfolk (executed) (6) Catherine, daughter of Sir Thomas Parr and widow of Lord Latimer *died* aged 55 *reigned* 37 years

1547–1553　EDWARD VI
born 1537, son of Henry VIII and Jane Seymour *died* aged 15 *reigned* 6 years

1553
*(6/10–
19 Jul)　**JANE**
born 1537, daughter of Frances (daughter of Mary Tudor, the younger daughter of Henry VII) and Henry Grey, Duke of Suffolk *married* Lord Guildford Dudley, son of the Duke of Northumberland *deposed* Jul 1553 *executed* Feb 1554 aged 16 *reigned* 13/9 days

1553–1558　MARY I
born 1516, daughter of Henry VIII and Catherine of Aragon *married* Philip II of Spain *died* aged 42 *reigned* 5 years

1558–1603　ELIZABETH I
born 1533, daughter of Henry VIII and Anne Boleyn *died* aged 69 *reigned* 44 years

* Depending on whether the date of her predecessor's death (6 July) or that of her official proclamation as Queen (10 July) is taken as the beginning of her reign

BRITISH KINGS AND QUEENS SINCE 1603

THE HOUSE OF STUART

1603–1625　JAMES I (VI OF SCOTLAND)
born 1566, son of Mary, Queen of Scots (granddaughter of Margaret Tudor, elder daughter of Henry VII), and Henry Stewart, Lord Darnley *married* Anne, daughter of Frederick II of Denmark *died* aged 58 *reigned* 22 years

1625–1649　CHARLES I
born 1600, second son of James I *married* Henrietta Maria, daughter of Henry IV of France *executed* 1649 aged 48 *reigned* 23 years

INTERREGNUM 1649–1660

1649–1653　Government by a council of state
1653–1658　Oliver Cromwell, Lord Protector
1658–1659　Richard Cromwell, Lord Protector

1660–1685　CHARLES II
born 1630, eldest son of Charles I *married* Catherine, daughter of John of Portugal *died* aged 54 *reigned* 24 years

1685–1688　JAMES II (VII OF SCOTLAND)
born 1633, second son of Charles I *married* (1) Lady Anne Hyde, daughter of Edward, Earl of Clarendon (2) Mary, daughter of Alphonso, Duke of Modena. Reign ended with flight from kingdom Dec 1688 *died* 1701 aged 67 *reigned* 3 years

INTERREGNUM 11 Dec 1688 to 12 Feb 1689

1689–1702　WILLIAM III
born 1650, son of William II, Prince of Orange, and Mary Stuart, daughter of Charles I *married* Mary, elder daughter of James II *died* aged 51 *reigned* 13 years

and
1689–1694　MARY II
born 1662, elder daughter of James II and Anne *died* aged 32 *reigned* 5 years

1702–1714　ANNE
born 1665, younger daughter of James II and Anne *married* Prince George of Denmark, son of Frederick III of Denmark *died* aged 49 *reigned* 12 years

THE HOUSE OF HANOVER

1714–1727 GEORGE I (Elector of Hanover)
born 1660, son of Sophia (daughter of
Frederick, Elector Palatine, and Elizabeth
Stuart, daughter of James I) and Ernest
Augustus, Elector of Hanover *married* Sophia
Dorothea, daughter of George William, Duke
of Lüneburg-Celle *died* aged 67 *reigned* 12
years

1727–1760 GEORGE II
born 1683, son of George I *married* Caroline,
daughter of John Frederick, Margrave of
Brandenburg-Anspach *died* aged 76 *reigned* 33
years

1760–1820 GEORGE III
born 1738, son of Frederick, eldest son of
George II *married* Charlotte, daughter of
Charles Louis, Duke of Mecklenburg-Strelitz
died aged 81 *reigned* 59 years

REGENCY 1811–1820
Prince of Wales regent owing to the insanity of George III

1820–1830 GEORGE IV
born 1762, eldest son of George III *married*
Caroline, daughter of Charles, Duke of
Brunswick-Wolfenbüttel *died* aged 67 *reigned*
10 years

1830–1837 WILLIAM IV
born 1765, third son of George III *married*
Adelaide, daughter of George, Duke of Saxe-
Meiningen *died* aged 71 *reigned* 7 years

1837–1901 VICTORIA
born 1819, daughter of Edward, fourth son of
George III *married* Prince Albert of Saxe-
Coburg and Gotha *died* aged 81 *reigned* 63
years

THE HOUSE OF SAXE-COBURG AND GOTHA

1901–1910 EDWARD VII
born 1841, eldest son of Victoria and Albert
married Alexandra, daughter of Christian IX of
Denmark *died* aged 68 *reigned* 9 years

THE HOUSE OF WINDSOR

1910–1936 GEORGE V
born 1865, second son of Edward VII *married*
Victoria Mary, daughter of Francis, Duke of
Teck *died* aged 70 *reigned* 25 years

1936 EDWARD VIII
(20 Jan–11 *born* 1894, eldest son of George V *married*
Dec) (1937) Mrs Wallis Simpson *abdicated* 1936 *died*
1972 aged 77 *reigned* 10 months

1936–1952 GEORGE VI
born 1895, second son of George V *married*
Lady Elizabeth Bowes-Lyon, daughter of 14th
Earl of Strathmore and Kinghorne *died* aged
56 *reigned* 15 years

1952– ELIZABETH II
born 1926, elder daughter of George VI
married Philip, son of Prince Andrew of Greece

KINGS AND QUEENS OF SCOTS 1016–1603

1016–1034 MALCOLM II
born c.954, son of Kenneth II *acceded* to Alba
1005, secured Lothian c.1016, obtained
Strathclyde for his grandson Duncan c.1016,
thus reigning over an area approximately the
same as that governed by later rulers of
Scotland *died* aged c.80 *reigned* 18 years

THE HOUSE OF ATHOLL

1034–1040 DUNCAN I
son of Bethoc, daughter of Malcolm II, and
Crinan, Mormaer of Atholl *married* a cousin of
Siward, Earl of Northumbria *reigned* 5 years

1040–1057 MACBETH
born c.1005, son of a daughter of Malcolm II
and Finlaec, Mormaer of Moray *married*
Gruoch, granddaughter of Kenneth III *killed*
aged c.52 *reigned* 17 years

1057–1058 LULACH
(Aug–Mar) *born* c.1032, son of Gillacomgan, Mormaer of
Moray, and Gruoch (and stepson of Macbeth)
died aged c.26 *reigned* 7 months

1058–1093 MALCOLM III (Canmore)
born c.1031, elder son of Duncan I *married*
(1) Ingibiorg (2) Margaret (St Margaret),
granddaughter of Edmund II of England *killed*
in battle aged c.62 *reigned* 35 years

1093–1097 DONALD III BÁN
born c.1033, second son of Duncan I *deposed*
May 1094 *restored* Nov 1094 *deposed* Oct
1097 *reigned* 3 years

1094 DUNCAN II
(May–Nov) *born* c.1060, elder son of Malcolm III and
Ingibiorg *married* Octreda of Dunbar *killed*
aged c.34 *reigned* 6 months

1097–1107 EDGAR
born c.1074, second son of Malcolm III and
Margaret *died* aged c.32 *reigned* 9 years

1107–1124 ALEXANDER I (the Fierce)
born c.1077, fifth son of Malcolm III and
Margaret *married* Sybilla, illegitimate daughter
of Henry I of England *died* aged c.47 *reigned*
17 years

1124–1153 DAVID I (the Saint)
born c.1085, sixth son of Malcolm III and
Margaret *married* Matilda, daughter of
Waltheof, Earl of Huntingdon *died* aged c.68
reigned 29 years

1153–1165 MALCOLM IV (the Maiden)
born c.1141, son of Henry, Earl of
Huntingdon, second son of David I *died* aged
c.24 *reigned* 12 years

1165–1214 WILLIAM I (the Lion)
born c.1142, brother of Malcolm IV *married*
Ermengarde, daughter of Richard, Viscount of
Beaumont *died* aged c.72 *reigned* 49 years

1214–1249 ALEXANDER II
born 1198, son of William I *married* (1) Joan,
daughter of John, King of England (2) Marie,
daughter of Ingelram de Coucy *died* aged 50
reigned 34 years

1249–1286 ALEXANDER III
born 1241, son of Alexander II and Marie
married (1) Margaret, daughter of Henry III of
England (2) Yolande, daughter of the Count of
Dreux *killed* accidentally aged 44 *reigned* 36
years

1286–1290 MARGARET (the Maid of Norway)
born 1283, daughter of Margaret (daughter of
Alexander III) and Eric II of Norway *died* aged
7 *reigned* 4 years

FIRST INTERREGNUM 1290–1292
Throne disputed by 13 competitors. Crown awarded to John
Balliol by adjudication of Edward I of England

THE HOUSE OF BALLIOL

1292–1296   JOHN (Balliol)
born c.1250, son of Dervorguilla, great-great-granddaughter of David I, and John de Balliol married Isabella, daughter of John, Earl of Surrey abdicated 1296 died 1313 aged c.63 reigned 3 years

SECOND INTERREGNUM 1296–1306

Edward I of England declared John Balliol to have forfeited the throne for contumacy in 1296 and took the government of Scotland into his own hands

THE HOUSE OF BRUCE

1306–1329   ROBERT I (Bruce)
born 1274, son of Robert Bruce and Marjorie, Countess of Carrick, and great-grandson of the second daughter of David, Earl of Huntingdon, brother of William I married (1) Isabella, daughter of Donald, Earl of Mar (2) Elizabeth, daughter of Richard, Earl of Ulster died aged 54 reigned 23 years

1329–1371   DAVID II
born 1324, son of Robert I and Elizabeth married (1) Joanna, daughter of Edward II of England (2) Margaret Drummond, widow of Sir John Logie (divorced) died aged 46 reigned 41 years

1332   Edward Balliol, son of John Balliol
(Sep–Dec)

1333–1336   Edward Balliol

THE HOUSE OF STEWART

1371–1390   ROBERT II (Stewart)
born 1316, son of Marjorie (daughter of Robert I) and Walter, High Steward of Scotland married (1) Elizabeth, daughter of Sir Robert Mure of Rowallan (2) Euphemia, daughter of Hugh, Earl of Ross died aged 74 reigned 19 years

1390–1406   ROBERT III
born c.1337, son of Robert II and Elizabeth married Annabella, daughter of Sir John Drummond of Stobhall died aged c.69 reigned 16 years

1406–1437   JAMES I
born 1394, son of Robert III married Joan Beaufort, daughter of John, Earl of Somerset assassinated aged 42 reigned 30 years

1437–1460   JAMES II
born 1430, son of James I married Mary, daughter of Arnold, Duke of Gueldres killed accidentally aged 29 reigned 23 years

1460–1488   JAMES III
born 1452, son of James II married Margaret, daughter of Christian I of Denmark assassinated aged 36 reigned 27 years

1488–1513   JAMES IV
born 1473, son of James III married Margaret Tudor, daughter of Henry VII of England killed in battle aged 40 reigned 25 years

1513–1542   JAMES V
born 1512, son of James IV married (1) Madeleine, daughter of Francis I of France (2) Mary of Lorraine, daughter of the Duc de Guise died aged 30 reigned 29 years

1542–1567   MARY
born 1542, daughter of James V and Mary married (1) the Dauphin, afterwards Francis II of France (2) Henry Stewart, Lord Darnley (3) James Hepburn, Earl of Bothwell abdicated 1567, prisoner in England from 1568, executed 1587 reigned 24 years

1567–1625   JAMES VI (and I of England)
born 1566, son of Mary, Queen of Scots, and Henry, Lord Darnley acceded 1567 to the Scottish throne reigned 58 years succeeded 1603 to the English throne, so joining the English and Scottish crowns in one person. The two kingdoms remained distinct until 1707 when the parliaments of the kingdoms became conjoined

WELSH SOVEREIGNS AND PRINCES

Wales was ruled by sovereign princes from the earliest times until the death of Llywelyn in 1282. The first English Prince of Wales was the son of Edward I, who was born in Caernarvon town on 25 April 1284. According to a discredited legend, he was presented to the Welsh chieftains as their prince, in fulfilment of a promise that they should have a prince who 'could not speak a word of English' and should be native born. This son, who afterwards became Edward II, was created 'Prince of Wales and Earl of Chester' at the Lincoln Parliament on 7 February 1301.

The title Prince of Wales is borne after individual conferment and is not inherited at birth, though some Princes have been declared and styled Prince of Wales but never formally so created (s.). The title was conferred on Prince Charles by the Queen on 26 July 1958. He was invested at Caernarvon on 1 July 1969.

INDEPENDENT PRINCES AD 844 TO 1282

844–878	Rhodri the Great
878–916	Anarawd, son of Rhodri
916–950	Hywel Dda, the Good
950–979	Iago ab Idwal (or Ieuaf)
979–985	Hywel ab Ieuaf, the Bad
985–986	Cadwallon, his brother
986–999	Maredudd ab Owain ap Hywel Dda
999–1005	Cynan ap Hywel ab Ieuaf
1005–1018	Aeddan ap Blegywyrd
1018–1023	Llywelyn ap Seisyll
1023–1039	Iago ab Idwal ap Meurig
1039–1063	Gruffydd ap Llywelyn ap Seisyll
1063–1075	Bleddyn ap Cynfyn
1075–1081	Trahaern ap Caradog
1081–1137	Gruffydd ap Cynan ab Iago
1137–1170	Owain Gwynedd
1170–1194	Dafydd ab Owain Gwynedd
1194–1240	Llywelyn Fawr, the Great
1240–1246	Dafydd ap Llywelyn
1246–1282	Llywelyn ap Gruffydd ap Llywelyn

ENGLISH PRINCES SINCE 1301

1301	Edward (Edward II)
1343	Edward the Black Prince, son of Edward III
1376	Richard (Richard II), son of the Black Prince
1399	Henry of Monmouth (Henry V)
1454	Edward of Westminster, son of Henry VI
1471	Edward of Westminster (Edward V)
1483	Edward, son of Richard III (d. 1484)
1489	Arthur Tudor, son of Henry VII
1504	Henry Tudor (Henry VIII)
1610	Henry Stuart, son of James I (d. 1612)
1616	Charles Stuart (Charles I)
c.1638 (s.)	Charles Stuart (Charles II)
1688 (s.)	James Francis Edward Stuart (The Old Pretender), son of James II (d. 1766)
1714	George Augustus (George II)
1729	Frederick Lewis, son of George II (d. 1751)
1751	George William Frederick (George III)
1762	George Augustus Frederick (George IV)
1841	Albert Edward (Edward VII)
1901	George (George V)
1910	Edward (Edward VIII)
1958	Charles, son of Elizabeth II

PRINCESSES ROYAL

The style Princess Royal is conferred at the sovereign's discretion on his or her eldest daughter. It is an honorary title, held for life, and cannot be inherited or passed on. It was first conferred on Princess Mary, daughter of Charles I, in approximately 1642.

c.1642	Princess Mary (1631–60), daughter of Charles I
1727	Princess Anne (1709–59), daughter of George II
1766	Princess Charlotte (1766–1828), daughter of George III
1840	Princess Victoria (1840–1901), daughter of Victoria
1905	Princess Louise (1867–1931), daughter of Edward VII
1932	Princess Mary (1897–1965), daughter of George V
1987	Princess Anne (b. 1950), daughter of Elizabeth II

DESCENDANTS OF QUEEN VICTORIA

I. HRH Princess Victoria Adelaide Mary Louisa, Princess Royal (1840–1901) *m* Friedrich III (1831–88), later German Emperor

II. HRH Prince Albert Edward (HM KING EDWARD VII) (1841–1910) *succeeded* 22 Jan 1901 *m* HRH Princess Alexandra of Denmark (1844–1925)

III. HRH Princess Alice Maud Mary (1843–78) *m* Prince Ludwig (1837–92), later Grand Duke of Hesse

IV. HRH Prince Alfred Ernest Albert, Duke of Edinburgh (1844–1900) *succeeded* as Duke of Saxe-Coburg and Gotha 1893 *m* Grand Duchess Marie Alexandrovna of Russia (1853–1920)

---

1. HIM Wilhelm II (1859–1941), later German Emperor *m* (1) Princess Augusta Victoria of Schleswig-Holstein-Sonderburg-Augustenburg (1858–1921) (2) Princess Hermine of Reuss (1887–1947). *Issue* Wilhelm (1882–1951); Eitel-Friedrich (1883–1942); Adalbert (1884–1948); August Wilhelm (1887–1949); Oskar (1888–1958); Joachim (1890–1920); Viktoria Luise (1892–1980)

2. Charlotte (1860–1919) *m* Bernhard, Duke of Saxe-Meiningen (1851–1928). *Issue* Feodora (1879–1945)

3. Heinrich (1862–1929) *m* Princess Irene of Hesse (*see* III.3). *Issue* Waldemar (1889–1945); Sigismund (1896–1978); Heinrich (1900–4)

---

1. Albert Victor, Duke of Clarence and Avondale (1864–92)

2. George (HM KING GEORGE V) (1865–1936) (*see* House of Windsor)

3. Louise (1867–1931), later Princess Royal *m* 1st Duke of Fife (1849–1912). *Issue* Alexandra (1891–1959); Maud (1893–1945)

4. Victoria (1868–1935)

5. Maud (1869–1938) *m* Prince Carl of Denmark (1872–1957), later King Haakon VII of Norway. *Issue* Olav V (1903–91)

6. Alexander (6–7 Apr 1871)

---

1. Victoria (1863–1950) *m* Prince Louis of Battenberg (1854–1921), later 1st Marquess of Milford Haven. *Issue* Alice (1885–1969); Louise (1889–1965); George (1892–1938); Louis (1900–79)

2. Elizabeth (1864–1918) *m* Grand Duke Sergius of Russia (1857–1905)

3. Irene (1866–1953) *m* Prince Heinrich of Prussia (*see* I.3)

4. Ernst Ludwig (1868–1937), Grand Duke of Hesse, *m* (1) Princess Victoria Melita of Saxe-Coburg (see IV.3) (2) Princess Eleonore of Solms-Hohensolms-Lich (1871–1937). *Issue* Elizabeth (1895–1903); George (1906–37); Ludwig (1908–68)

5. Frederick William (1870–3)

6. Alix (Tsaritsa of Russia) (1872–1918) *m* Nicholas II, Tsar of All the Russias (1868–1918). *Issue* Olga (1895–1918); Tatiana (1897–1918); Marie (1899–1918); Anastasia (1901–18); Alexis (1904–18)

7. Marie (1874–8)

---

4. Sigismund (1864–6)

5. Victoria (1866–1929) *m* (1) Prince Adolf of Schaumburg-Lippe (1859–1916) (2) Alexander Zubkov (1900–36)

6. Waldemar (1868–79)

7. Sophie (1870–1932) *m* Constantine I (1868–1923), later King of the Hellenes. *Issue* George II (1890–1947); Alexander I (1893–1920); Helena (1896–1982); Paul I (1901–64); Irene (1904–74); Katherine (1913–2007)

8. Margarethe (1872–1954) *m* Prince Friedrich Karl of Hesse (1868–1940). *Issue* Friedrich Wilhelm (1893–1916); Maximilian (1894–1914); Philipp (1896–1980); Wolfgang (1896–1989); Richard (1901–69); Christoph (1901–43)

QUEEN VICTORIA (Alexandrina Victoria) (1819–1901) *succeeded* 20 Jun 1837 *m* (Francis) Albert Augustus Charles Emmanuel, Duke of Saxony, Prince of Saxe-Coburg and Gotha (HRH Albert, Prince Consort) (1819–61)

VI. HRH Princess Louise Caroline Alberta (1848–1939) *m* Marquess of Lorne (1845–1914), later 9th Duke of Argyll

VII. HRH Prince Arthur William Patrick Albert, Duke of Connaught (1850–1942) *m* Princess Louisa of Prussia (1860–1917)

VIII. HRH Prince Leopold George Duncan Albert, Duke of Albany (1853–84) *m* Princess Helena of Waldeck (1861–1922)

IX. HRH Princess Beatrice Mary Victoria Feodore (1857–1944) *m* Prince Henry of Battenberg (1858–96)

1. Alfred, Prince of Saxe-Coburg (1874–99)

2. Marie (1875–1938) *m* Ferdinand (1865–1927), later King of Roumania. *Issue* Carol II (1893–1953); Elisabeth (1894–1956); Marie (1900–61); Nicolas (1903–78); Ileana (1909–91); Mircea (1913–16)

3. Victoria Melita (1876–1936) *m* (1) Grand Duke Ernst Ludwig of Hesse (*see* III.4) (2) Grand Duke Kirill of Russia (1876–1938). *Issue* Marie (1907–51); Kira (1909–67); Vladimir (1917–92)

4. Alexandra (1878–1942) *m* Ernst, Prince of Hohenlohe Langenburg (1863–1950). *Issue* Gottfried (1897–1960); Maria (1899–1967); Alexandra (1901–63); Irma (1902–86)

5. Beatrice (1884–1966) *m* Alfonso of Orleans, Infante of Spain (1886–1975). *Issue* Alvaro (1910–97); Alonso (1912–36); Ataulfo (1913–74)

1. Margaret (1882–1920) *m* Crown Prince Gustaf Adolf (1882–1973), later King of Sweden. *Issue* Gustaf Adolf (1906–47); Sigvard (1907–2002); Ingrid (1910–2000); Bertil (1912–97); Count Carl Bernadotte (1916–2012)

2. Arthur (1883–1938) *m* HH Duchess of Fife (1891–1959). *Issue* Alastair Arthur (1914–43)

3. (Victoria) Patricia (1886–1974) *m* Adm. Hon. Sir Alexander Ramsay (1881–1972). *Issue* Alexander (1919–2000)

1. Alice (1883–1981) *m* Prince Alexander of Teck (1874–1957), later 1st Earl of Athlone. *Issue* May (1906–94); Rupert (1907–28); Maurice (Mar–Sep 1910)

2. Charles Edward (1884–1954), Duke of Albany until title suspended 1917, Duke of Saxe-Coburg-Gotha *m* Princess Victoria Adelheid of Schleswig-Holstein-Sonderburg-Glücksburg (1885–1970). *Issue* Johann Leopold (1906–72); Sibylla (1908–72); Dietmar Hubertus (1909–43); Caroline (1912–83); Friedrich Josias (1918–98)

1. Alexander, 1st Marquess of Carisbrooke (1886–1960) *m* Lady Irene Denison (1890–1956). *Issue* Iris (1920–82)

2. Victoria Eugénie (1887–1969) *m* Alfonso XIII, King of Spain (1886–1941). *Issue* Alfonso (1907–38); Jaime (1908–75); Beatriz (1909–2002); Maria (1911–96); Juan (1913–93); Gonzalo (1914–34)

3. Maj. Lord Leopold Mountbatten (1889–1922)

4. Maurice (1891–1914)

V. HRH Princess Helena Augusta Victoria (1846–1923) *m* Prince Christian of Schleswig-Holstein-Sonderburg-Augustenburg (1831–1917)

1. Christian Victor (1867–1900)

2. Albert (1869–1931), later Duke of Schleswig-Holstein

3. Helena (1870–1948)

4. Marie Louise (1872–1956), *m* Prince Aribert of Anhalt (1864–1933)

5. Harold (12–20 May 1876)

THE HOUSE OF WINDSOR

King George V assumed by royal proclamation (17 July 1917) for his House and family, as well as for all descendants in the male line of Queen Victoria who are subjects of these realms, the name of Windsor.

KING GEORGE V

(George Frederick Ernest Albert), second son of King Edward VII *born* 3 June 1865 *married* 6 July 1893 HSH Princess Victoria Mary Augusta Louise Olga Pauline Claudine Agnes of Teck (Queen Mary *born* 26 May 1867 *died* 24 March 1953) *succeeded* to the throne 6 May 1910 *died* 20 January 1936. *Issue*

1. HRH PRINCE EDWARD Albert Christian George Andrew Patrick David *born* 23 June 1894 *succeeded* to the throne as King Edward VIII, 20 January 1936 *abdicated* 11 December 1936 *created* Duke of Windsor 1937 *married* 3 June 1937 Mrs Wallis Simpson (Her Grace The Duchess of Windsor *born* 19 June 1896 *died* 24 April 1986) *died* 28 May 1972

2. HRH PRINCE ALBERT Frederick Arthur George *born* 14 December 1895 *created* Duke of York 1920 *married* 26 April 1923 Lady Elizabeth Bowes-Lyon, youngest daughter of the 14th Earl of Strathmore and Kinghorne (HM Queen Elizabeth the Queen Mother *born* 4 August 1900 *died* 30 March 2002) *succeeded* to the throne as King George VI, 11 December 1936 *died* 6 February 1952. *Issue*
   (1) HRH Princess Elizabeth Alexandra Mary *succeeded* to the throne as Queen Elizabeth II, 6 February 1952 (*see* Royal Family)
   (2) HRH Princess Margaret Rose (later HRH The Princess Margaret, Countess of Snowdon) *born* 21 August 1930 *married* 6 May 1960 Antony Charles Robert Armstrong-Jones, GCVO *created* Earl of Snowdon 1961 (1930–2017), *marriage dissolved* 1978, *died* 9 February 2002, having had issue (*see* Royal Family)

3. HRH PRINCESS (Victoria Alexandra Alice) MARY *born* 25 April 1897 *created* Princess Royal 1932 *married* 28 February 1922 Viscount Lascelles, later the 6th Earl of Harewood (1882–1947) *died* 28 March 1965. *Issue:*

(1) George Henry Hubert Lascelles, 7th Earl of Harewood, KBE *born* 7 February 1923 *died* 11 July 2011 *married* (1) 1949 Maria (Marion) Stein (marriage dissolved 1967) *issue* *(a)* David Henry George, 8th Earl of Harewood *born* 1950 *(b)* James Edward *born* 1953 *(c)* (Robert) Jeremy Hugh *born* 1955 (2) 1967 Patricia Tuckwell *issue* *(d)* Mark Hubert *born* 1964
(2) Gerald David Lascelles *born* 21 August 1924 *died* 27 February 1998 *married* (1) 1952 Angela Dowding (marriage dissolved 1978) *issue* *(a)* Henry Ulick *born* 1953 (2) 1978 Elizabeth Collingwood (Elizabeth Colvin) *issue* *(b)* Martin David *born* 1962

4. HRH PRINCE HENRY William Frederick Albert *born* 31 March 1900 *created* Duke of Gloucester, Earl of Ulster and Baron Culloden 1928 *married* 6 November 1935 Lady Alice Christabel Montagu-Douglas-Scott, daughter of the 7th Duke of Buccleuch and Queensberry (HRH Princess Alice, Duchess of Gloucester *born* 25 December 1901 *died* 29 October 2004) *died* 10 June 1974. *Issue*
   (1) HRH Prince William Henry Andrew Frederick *born* 18 December 1941 accidentally *killed* 28 August 1972
   (2) HRH Prince Richard Alexander Walter George (HRH The Duke of Gloucester, *see* Royal Family)

5. HRH PRINCE GEORGE Edward Alexander Edmund *born* 20 December 1902 *created* Duke of Kent, Earl of St Andrews and Baron Downpatrick 1934 *married* 29 November 1934 HRH Princess Marina of Greece and Denmark (*born* 30 November 1906 *died* 27 August 1968) *killed* on active service 25 August 1942. *Issue*
   (1) HRH Prince Edward George Nicholas Paul Patrick (HRH The Duke of Kent, *see* Royal Family)
   (2) HRH Princess Alexandra Helen Elizabeth Olga Christabel (HRH Princess Alexandra, the Hon. Lady Ogilvy, *see* Royal Family)
   (3) HRH Prince Michael George Charles Franklin (HRH Prince Michael of Kent, *see* Royal Family)

6. HRH PRINCE JOHN Charles Francis *born* 12 July 1905 *died* 18 January 1919

PRECEDENCE

ENGLAND AND WALES

The Sovereign
The Prince Philip, Duke of Edinburgh
The Prince of Wales
The Sovereign's younger sons
The Sovereign's grandsons
The Sovereign's cousins
Archbishop of Canterbury
Lord High Chancellor
Archbishop of York
The Prime Minister
Lord President of the Council
Speaker of the House of Commons
Speaker of the House of Lords
President of the Supreme Court
Lord Chief Justice of England and
  Wales
Lord Privy Seal
Ambassadors and High Commissioners
Lord Great Chamberlain
Earl Marshal
Lord Steward of the Household
Lord Chamberlain of the Household
Master of the Horse
Dukes, according to their patent of
  creation:
  1. of England
  2. of Scotland
  3. of Great Britain
  4. of Ireland
  5. those created since the Union
Eldest sons of Dukes of the Blood
  Royal
Ministers, Envoys, and other important
  overseas visitors
Marquesses, according to their patent
  of creation:
  1. of England
  2. of Scotland
  3. of Great Britain
  4. of Ireland
  5. those created since the Union
Dukes' eldest sons
Earls, according to their patent of
  creation:
  1. of England
  2. of Scotland
  3. of Great Britain
  4. of Ireland
  5. those created since the Union
Younger sons of Dukes of Blood
  Royal

Marquesses' eldest sons
Dukes' younger sons
Viscounts, according to their patent of
  creation:
  1. of England
  2. of Scotland
  3. of Great Britain
  4. of Ireland
  5. those created since the Union
Earls' eldest sons
Marquesses' younger sons
Bishop of London
Bishop of Durham
Bishop of Winchester
Other English Diocesan Bishops,
  according to seniority of
  consecration
Retired Church of England Diocesan
  Bishops, according to seniority of
  consecration
Suffragan Bishops, according to
  seniority of consecration
Secretaries of State, if of the degree of
  a Baron
Barons, according to their patent of
  creation:
  1. of England
  2. of Scotland (Lords of Parliament)
  3. of Great Britain
  4. of Ireland
  5. those created since the Union,
  including Life Barons
Master of the Rolls
Deputy President of the Supreme
  Court
Justices of the Supreme Court,
  according to seniority of
  appointment
Treasurer of the Household
Comptroller of the Household
Vice-Chamberlain of the Household
Secretaries of State under the degree of
  Baron
Viscounts' eldest sons
Earls' younger sons
Barons' eldest sons
Knights of the Garter
Privy Counsellors
Chancellor of the Order of the Garter
Chancellor of the Exchequer
Chancellor of the Duchy of Lancaster
President of the Queen's Bench
  Division
President of the Family Division

Chancellor of the High Court
Lord Justices of Appeal, according to
  seniority of appointment
Judges of the High Court, according to
  seniority of appointment
Viscounts' younger sons
Barons' younger sons
Sons of Life Peers
Baronets, according to date of patent
Knights of the Thistle
Knights Grand Cross of the Bath
Knights Grand Cross of St Michael
  and St George
Knights Grand Cross of the Royal
  Victorian Order
Knights Grand Cross of the British
  Empire
Knights Commanders of the Bath
Knights Commanders of St Michael
  and St George
Knights Commanders of the Royal
  Victorian Order
Knights Commanders of the British
  Empire
Knights Bachelor
Circuit Judges, according to priority
  and order of their respective
  appointments
Master of the Court of Protection
Companions of the Bath
Companions of St Michael and St
  George
Commanders of the Royal Victorian
  Order
Commanders of the British Empire
Companions of the Distinguished
  Service Order
Lieutenants of the Royal Victorian
  Order
Officers of the British Empire
Companions of the Imperial Service
  Order
Eldest sons of younger sons of peers
Baronets' eldest sons
Eldest sons of knights, in the same
  order as their fathers
Members of the Royal Victorian Order
Members of the British Empire
Baronets' younger sons
Knights' younger sons, in the same
  order as their fathers
Esquires
Gentlemen

WOMEN

Women take the same rank as their husbands or as their brothers; but the daughter of a peer marrying a commoner retains her title as Lady or Honourable. Daughters of peers rank next immediately after the wives of their elder brothers, and before their younger brothers' wives. Daughters of peers marrying peers of a lower degree take the same order of precedence as that of their husbands; thus the daughter of a Duke marrying a Baron becomes of the rank of Baroness only, while her sisters married to commoners retain their rank and take precedence over the Baroness. Merely official rank on the husband's part does not give any similar precedence to the wife.

Peeresses in their own right take the same precedence as peers of the same rank, ie from their date of creation.

SCOTLAND

The Sovereign
The Prince Philip, Duke of Edinburgh
The Lord High Commissioner to the
   General Assembly of the Church of
   Scotland (while that assembly is
   sitting)
The Duke of Rothesay (eldest son of
   the Sovereign)
The Sovereign's younger sons
The Sovereign's grandsons
The Sovereign's nephews
Lord-Lieutenants
Lord Provosts, during their term of
   office*
Sheriffs Principal, during their term of
   office and within the bounds of
   their respective sheriffdoms
Lord Chancellor of Great Britain
Moderator of the General Assembly of
   the Church of Scotland
Keeper of the Great Seal of Scotland
   (the First Minister)
Presiding Officer
The Secretary of State for Scotland
Hereditary High Constable of Scotland
Hereditary Master of the Household in
   Scotland
Dukes, as in England
Eldest sons of Dukes of the Blood
   Royal

Marquesses, as in England
Dukes' eldest sons
Earls, as in England
Younger sons of Dukes of Blood
   Royal
Marquesses' eldest sons
Dukes' younger sons
Lord Justice General
Lord Clerk Register
Lord Advocate
The Advocate General
Lord Justice Clerk
Viscounts, as in England
Earls' eldest sons
Marquesses' younger sons
Lords of Parliament or Barons, as in
   England
Eldest sons of Viscounts
Earls' younger sons
Eldest sons of Lords of Parliament or
   Barons
Knights and Ladies of the Garter
Knights and Ladies of the Thistle
Privy Counsellors
Senators of the College of Justice
   (Lords of Session)
Viscounts' younger sons
Younger sons of Lords of Parliament
   or Barons
Baronets
Knights and Dames Grand Cross of
   orders, as in England

Knights and Dames Commanders of
   orders, as in England
Solicitor-General for Scotland
Lord Lyon King of Arms
Sheriffs Principal, when not within
   own county
Knights Bachelor
Sheriffs
Companions of Orders, as in England
Commanders of the Royal Victorian
   Order
Commanders of the British Empire
Lieutenants of the Royal Victorian
   Order
Companions of the Distinguished
   Service Order
Officers of the British Empire
Companions of the Imperial Service
   Order
Eldest sons of younger sons of peers
Eldest sons of baronets
Eldest sons of knights, as in England
Members of the Royal Victorian Order
Members of the British Empire
Baronets' younger sons
Knights' younger sons
Queen's Counsel
Esquires
Gentlemen

* The Lord Provosts of Aberdeen, Dundee,
Edinburgh and Glasgow are Lord-Lieutenants
for these cities *ex officio* and take precedence as
such

THE PEERAGE

ABBREVIATIONS AND SYMBOLS

S.	Scottish title	§	life peer disqualified from sitting in the House of Lords as a member of the judiciary
I.	Irish title		
**	hereditary peer remaining in the House of Lords	ℂ	life peer who has resigned permanently from the House of Lords
°	there is no 'of' in the title		
b.	born	E.	life peer expelled for absenteeism under section 2 of the House of Lords Reform Act 2014 (*see* below)
s.	succeeded		
m.	married		
c.p.	civil partnership	F_	represents forename
w.	widower or widow	S_	represents surname
M.	minor	†	heir not ascertained at time of going to press
cr.	created	‡	title not ascertained at time of going to press

A full entry in italic type indicates that the recipient of a life peerage died within a year of it being conferred. The name is included in our list for one year for purposes of record.

The rules which govern the creation and succession of peerages are extremely complicated. There are, technically, five separate peerages, the Peerage of England, of Scotland, of Ireland, of Great Britain, and of the United Kingdom. The Peerage of Great Britain dates from 1707 when an Act of Union combined the two kingdoms of England and Scotland and separate peerages were discontinued. The Peerage of the United Kingdom dates from 1801 when Great Britain and Ireland were combined under an Act of Union. Some Scottish peers have received additional peerages of Great Britain or of the UK since 1707, and some Irish peers additional peerages of the UK since 1801.

The Peerage of Ireland was not entirely discontinued from 1801 but holders of Irish peerages, whether pre-dating or created subsequent to the Union of 1801, were not entitled to sit in the House of Lords if they had no additional English, Scottish, Great Britain or UK peerage. However, they were eligible for election to the House of Commons and to vote in parliamentary elections. An Irish peer holding a peerage of a lower grade which enabled him to sit in the House of Lords was introduced there by the title which enabled him to sit, though for all other purposes he was known by his higher title.

In the Peerage of Scotland there is no rank of Baron; the equivalent rank is Lord of Parliament, abbreviated to 'Lord' (the female equivalent is 'Lady').

All peers of England, Scotland, Great Britain or the UK who were 21 years or over, and of British, Irish or Commonwealth nationality were entitled to sit in the House of Lords until the House of Lords Act 1999, when hereditary peers lost the right to sit. However, section two of the act provided an exception for 90 hereditary peers plus the holders of the office of Earl Marshal and Lord Great Chamberlain to remain as members of the House of Lords for their lifetime or pending further reform. Of the 90 hereditary peers, 75 were elected by the hereditary peers in their political party, or Crossbench grouping, and the remaining 15 by the whole house. Until 7 November 2002 any vacancy arising due to the death of one of the 90 excepted hereditary peers was filled by the runner-up to the original election. From 7 November 2002 any vacancy due to a death – or, from 2014, a permanent retirement – has been filled by holding a by-election. By-elections are conducted in accordance with arrangements made by the Clerk of the Parliaments and have to take place within three months of a vacancy occurring. If the vacancy is among the 75, only the excepted hereditary peers in the relevant party or Crossbench grouping are entitled to vote. If

the vacancy is among the other 15, the whole house is entitled to vote.

In the list below, peers currently holding one of the 92 hereditary places in the House of Lords are indicated by **.

HEREDITARY WOMEN PEERS

Most hereditary peerages pass on death to the nearest male heir, but there are exceptions, and several are held by women.

A woman peer in her own right retains her title after marriage, and if her husband's rank is the superior she is designated by the two titles jointly, the inferior one second. Her hereditary claim still holds good in spite of any marriage whether higher or lower. No rank held by a woman can confer any title or even precedence upon her husband but the rank of a hereditary woman peer in her own right is inherited by her eldest son (or in some cases daughter).

After the Peerage Act 1963, hereditary women peers in their own right were entitled to sit in the House of Lords, subject to the same qualifications as men, until the House of Lords Act 1999.

LIFE PEERS

From 1876 to 2009 non-hereditary or life peerages were conferred on certain eminent judges to enable the judicial functions of the House of Lords to be carried out. These lords were known as Lords of Appeal in Ordinary or law lords. The judicial role of the House of Lords as the highest appeal court in the UK ended on 30 July 2009 and since 1 October 2009, under the Constitutional Reform Act 2005, any peer who holds a senior judicial office is disqualified from sitting in the House of Lords until they retire from that office. In the list of life peerages which follows, members of the judiciary who are currently disqualified from sitting and voting in the House of Lords until retirement, are marked by a '§'.

Under the Constitutional Reform and Governance Act 2010, five peers permanently resigned from the House of Lords.

Since 1958 life peerages have been conferred upon distinguished men and women from all walks of life, giving them seats in the House of Lords in the degree of Baron or Baroness. They are addressed in the same way as hereditary lords and barons, and their children have similar courtesy titles.

HOUSE OF LORDS REFORM ACT 2014

The House of Lords Reform Act 2014 makes provision for a member of the House of Lords who is a peer to retire or resign by giving notice in writing to the Clerk of the Parliaments. Resignations may not be rescinded. A number of life peers and elected hereditary peers have already retired permanently under this provision. The Act also makes provision for the expulsion of peers who do not attend the House of Lords for an entire parliamentary session which is longer than six months (indicated by an 'E.' in the following list). Peers on leave of absence or subject to a suspension or disqualification which results in absenteeism for an entire session will not be expelled. The House can also resolve that a peer should not be expelled by reason of special circumstances.

All life peers who have resigned permanently from the House of Lords are indicated by a '℄' in the following list.

PEERAGES EXTINCT SINCE SEPTEMBER 2020
BARONY: Greenhill (cr. 1950)
LIFE PEERAGES: Armstrong of Ilminster (cr. 1988); Bramall (cr. 1987); Chalfont (cr. 1964); Eden of Winton (cr. 1983); Feldman (cr. 1996); Garel-Jones (cr. 1997); Gordon of Strathblane (cr. 1997); Graham of Edmonton (cr. 1983); Hutton (cr. 1997); Lester of Herne Hill (cr. 1993); Maclennan of Rogart (cr. 2001); Maddock (cr. Mawhinney (cr. 2005); May of Oxford (cr. 2001); Nicholls of Birkenhead (cr. 1994); O'Neill of Clackmannan (cr. 2005); Renton of Mount Harry (cr. 1997); Sheldon (cr. 2001); Tombs (cr. 1990); Williams of Elvel (cr. 1985); Wright of Richmond (cr. 1994)

DISCLAIMER OF PEERAGES
The Peerage Act 1963 enables peers to disclaim their peerages for life. Peers alive in 1963 could disclaim within twelve months after the passing of the act (31 July 1963); a person subsequently succeeding to a peerage may disclaim within 12 months (one month if an MP) after the date of succession, or of reaching 21, if later. The disclaimer is irrevocable but does not affect the descent of the peerage after the disclaimant's death, and children of a disclaimed peer may, if they wish, retain their precedence and any courtesy titles and styles borne as children of a peer. The disclaimer

permitted the disclaimant to sit in the House of Commons if elected as an MP. As the House of Lords Act 1999 removed the automatic right of hereditary peers to sit in the House of Lords, they are now entitled to sit in the House of Commons without having to disclaim their titles.

The following peerages are currently disclaimed:
EARLDOM: Selkirk (1994)
BARONIES: Sanderson of Ayot (1971); Silkin (2002)
PEERS WHO ARE MINORS (ie under 21 years of age)
EARLDOM: St Germans (b. 2004)

FORMS OF ADDRESS
Forms of address are given under the style for each individual rank of the peerage. Both formal and social forms of address are given where usage differs; nowadays, the social form is generally preferred to the formal, which increasingly is used only for official documents and on very formal occasions.

ROLL OF THE PEERAGE

Crown Office, House of Lords, London SW1A 0PW
T 020-7219 4687 E hereditary.claims@gmail.com

The Roll of the Peerage is kept at the Crown Office and maintained by the Registrar and Assistant Registrar of the Peerage in accordance with the terms of a 2004 royal warrant. The roll records the names of all living life peers and hereditary peers who have proved their succession to the satisfaction of the Lord Chancellor. The Roll of the Peerage is maintained in addition to the Clerk of the Parliaments' register of hereditary peers eligible to stand for election in House of Lords' by-elections.

A person whose name is not entered on the Roll of the Peerage can not be addressed or mentioned by the title of a peer in any official document.

Registrar, Mrs Ceri King

HEREDITARY PEERS

PEERS OF THE BLOOD ROYAL

Style, His Royal Highness the Duke of _/His Royal Highness the Earl of_/His Royal Highness the Lord_
Style of address (formal) May it please your Royal Highness; *(informal)* Sir

Created	Title, order of succession, name, etc	Heir
	Dukes	
1947	*Edinburgh (1st)*, HRH the Prince Philip, Duke of Edinburgh	The Prince of Wales *
1337	*Cornwall*, HRH the Prince of Wales, s. 1952	‡
1398 S.	*Rothesay*, HRH the Prince of Wales, s. 1952	‡
2011	*Cambridge (1st)*, HRH Prince William of Wales	HRH Prince George of Cambridge
2018	*Sussex (1st)*, HRH Prince Henry of Wales	Archie Mountbatten-Windsor
1986	*York (1st)*, Prince Andrew, HRH the Duke of York	None
1928	*Gloucester (2nd)*, Prince Richard, HRH the Duke of Gloucester, s. 1974	Earl of Ulster
1934	*Kent (2nd)*, Prince Edward, HRH the Duke of Kent, s. 1942	Earl of St Andrews
	Earl	
1999	*Wessex (1st) and Forfar (1st) (2019)*, Prince Edward, HRH the Earl of Wessex	Viscount Severn

* In June 1999 Buckingham Palace announced that the current Earl of Wessex will be granted the Dukedom of Edinburgh when the title reverts to the Crown. The title will only revert to the Crown on both the death of the current Duke of Edinburgh and the Prince of Wales' succession as king
‡ The title is held by the sovereign's eldest son from the moment of his birth or the sovereign's accession

DUKES

Coronet, Eight strawberry leaves

Style, His Grace the Duke of _
Envelope (formal), His Grace the Duke of _; *(social),* The Duke of _. *Letter (formal),* My Lord Duke; *(social),* Dear Duke. *Spoken (formal),* Your Grace; *(social),* Duke
Wife's style, Her Grace the Duchess of _
Envelope (formal), Her Grace the Duchess of _; *(social),* The Duchess of _. *Letter (formal),* Dear Madam; *(social),* Dear Duchess. *Spoken,* Duchess
Eldest son's style, Takes his father's second title as a courtesy title (*see* Courtesy Titles)
Younger sons' style, 'Lord' before forename (F_) and surname (S_)
Envelope, Lord F_ S_. *Letter (formal),* My Lord; *(social),* Dear Lord F_. *Spoken (formal),* My Lord; *(social),* Lord F_
Daughters' style, 'Lady' before forename (F_) and surname (S_)
Envelope, Lady F_ S_. *Letter (formal),* Dear Madam; *(social),* Dear Lady F_. *Spoken,* Lady F_

Created	Title, order of succession, name, etc	Heir
1868 I.	*Abercorn (5th),* James Hamilton, KG, *b.* 1934, *s.* 1979, *w.*	Marquess of Hamilton, *b.* 1969
1701 S.	*Argyll (13th),* Torquhil Ian Campbell, *b.* 1968, *s.* 2001, *m.*	Marquess of Lorne, *b.* 2004
1703 S.	*Atholl (12th),* Bruce George Ronald Murray, *b.* 1960, *s.* 2012, *m.*	Marquis of Tullibardine, *b.* 1985
1682	*Beaufort (12th),* Henry John Fitzroy Somerset, *b.* 1952, *s.* 2017, *m.*	Marquess of Worcester, *b.* 1989
1694	*Bedford (15th),* Andrew Ian Henry Russell, *b.* 1962, *s.* 2003, *m.*	Marquess of Tavistock, *b.* 2005
1663 S.	*Buccleuch (10th) and Queensberry (12th) (S. 1684),* Richard Walter John Montagu Douglas Scott, KT, KBE, *b.* 1954, *s.* 2007, *m.*	Earl of Dalkeith, *b.* 1984
1694	*Devonshire (12th),* Peregrine Andrew Morny Cavendish, KCVO, CBE, *b.* 1944, *s.* 2004, *m.*	Earl of Burlington, *b.* 1969
1900	*Fife (4th),* David Charles Carnegie, *b.* 1961, *s.* 2015, *m.*	Earl of Southesk, *b.* 1989
1675	*Grafton (12th),* Henry Oliver Charles FitzRoy, *b.* 1978, *s.* 2011, *m.*	Earl of Euston, *b.* 2012
1643 S.	*Hamilton (16th) and Brandon (13th) (1711),* Alexander Douglas Douglas-Hamilton, *b.* 1978, *s.* 2010, *m. Premier Peer of Scotland*	Marquess of Douglas and Clydesdale, *b.* 2012
1766 I.	*Leinster (9th),* Maurice FitzGerald, *b.* 1948, *s.* 2004, *m. Premier Duke, Marquess and Earl of Ireland*	Edward F., *b.* 1988
1719	*Manchester (13th),* Alexander Charles David Drogo Montagu, *b.* 1962, *s.* 2002, *m.*	Lord Kimble W. D. M., *b.* 1964
1702	*Marlborough (12th),* Charles James Spencer-Churchill, *b.* 1955, *s.* 2014, *m.*	Marquess of Blandford, *b.* 1992
1707 S. **	*Montrose (8th),* James Graham, *b.* 1935, *s.* 1992, *w.*	Marquis of Graham, *b.* 1973
1483 **	*Norfolk (18th),* Edward William Fitzalan-Howard, *b.* 1956, *s.* 2002, *m. Premier Duke and Earl Marshal*	Earl of Arundel and Surrey, *b.* 1987
1766	*Northumberland (12th),* Ralph George Algernon Percy, *b.* 1956, *s.* 1995, *m.*	Earl Percy, *b.* 1984
1675	*Richmond (11th), Gordon (6th) (1876) and Lennox (11th) (S. 1675),* Charles Henry Gordon Lennox, *b.* 1955, *s.* 2017, *m.*	Earl of March and Kinrara, *b.* 1994
1707 S.	*Roxburghe (11th),* Charles Robert George Innes-Ker, *b.* 1981, *s.* 2019 *Premier Baronet of Scotland*	Lord Edward A. G. I.-K., *b.* 1984
1703	*Rutland (11th),* David Charles Robert Manners, *b.* 1959, *s.* 1999, *m.*	Marquess of Granby, *b.* 1999
1684	*St Albans (14th),* Murray de Vere Beauclerk, *b.* 1939, *s.* 1988, *m.*	Earl of Burford, *b.* 1965
1547 **	*Somerset (19th),* John Michael Edward Seymour, *b.* 1952, *s.* 1984, *m.*	Lord Seymour, *b.* 1982
1833	*Sutherland (7th),* Francis Ronald Egerton, *b.* 1940, *s.* 2000, *m.*	Marquess of Stafford, *b.* 1975
1814 **	*Wellington (9th),* Arthur Charles Valerian Wellesley, OBE, *b.* 1945, *s.* 2014, *m.*	Earl of Mornington, *b.* 1978
1874	*Westminster (7th) and 9th Marquess of Westminster (1831),* Hugh Richard Louis Grosvenor, *b.* 1991, *s.* 2016	To Marquessate only, Earl of Wilton (*see* that title)

MARQUESSES

Coronet, Four strawberry leaves alternating with four silver balls

Style, The Most Hon. the Marquess (of) _ . In Scotland the spelling 'Marquis' is preferred for pre-Union creations
Envelope (formal), The Most Hon. the Marquess of _; *(social),* The Marquess of _. *Letter (formal),* My Lord; *(social),* Dear Lord _.
Spoken (formal), My Lord; *(social),* Lord _
Wife's style, The Most Hon. the Marchioness (of) _
Envelope (formal), The Most Hon. the Marchioness of _; *(social),* The Marchioness of _. *Letter (formal),* Madam; *(social),* Dear
Lady _. *Spoken,* Lady _
Eldest son's style, Takes his father's second title as a courtesy title (*see* Courtesy Titles)
Younger sons' style, 'Lord' before forename and surname, as for Duke's younger sons
Daughters' style, 'Lady' before forename and surname, as for Duke's daughter

Created	Title, order of succession, name, etc	Heir
1915	Aberdeen and Temair (8th), George Ian Alastair Gordon, b. 1983, s. 2020, m.	Earl of Haddo, b. 2012
1876	Abergavenny (6th) and 10th Earl of Abergavenny (1784), Christopher George Charles Nevill, b. 1955, s. 2000, m.	To Earldom only, David M. R. N., b. 1941
1821	Ailesbury (8th), Michael Sidney Cedric Brudenell-Bruce, b. 1926, s. 1974	Earl of Cardigan, b. 1952
1831	Ailsa (9th), David Thomas Kennedy, b. 1958, s. 2015, m.	Earl of Cassilis, b. 1995
1815	Anglesey (8th), Charles Alexander Vaughan Paget, b. 1950, s. 2013, m.	Earl of Uxbridge, b. 1986
1789	Bath (8th), Ceawlin Henry Laszlo Thynn, b. 1974, s. 2020, m.	Viscount Weymouth, b. 2014
1826	Bristol (8th), Frederick William Augustus Hervey, b. 1979, s. 1999, m.	Timothy H. H., b. 1960
1796	Bute (7th), John Colum Crichton-Stuart, b. 1958, s. 1993, m.	Earl of Dumfries, b. 1989
1812 °	Camden (6th), David George Edward Henry Pratt, b. 1930, s. 1983	Earl of Brecknock, b. 1965
1815 **	Cholmondeley (7th), David George Philip Cholmondeley, KCVO, b. 1960, s. 1990, m. Lord Great Chamberlain	Earl of Rocksavage, b. 2009
1816 I. °	Conyngham (8th), Henry Vivian Pierpoint Conyngham, b. 1951, s. 2009, m.	Earl of Mount Charles, b. 1975
1791 I.	Donegall (8th), Arthur Patrick Chichester, b. 1952, s. 2007, m.	Earl of Belfast, b. 1990
1789 I.	Downshire (9th), (Arthur Francis) Nicholas Wills Hill, b. 1959, s. 2003, m.	Earl of Hillsborough, b. 1996
1801 I.	Ely (9th), Charles John Tottenham, b. 1943, s. 2006, m.	Lord Timothy C. T., b. 1948
1801	Exeter (8th), (William) Michael Anthony Cecil, b. 1935, s. 1988, m.	Lord Burghley, b. 1970
1800 I.	Headfort (7th), Thomas Michael Ronald Christopher Taylour, b. 1959, s. 2005, w.	Earl of Bective, b. 1989
1793	Hertford (9th), Henry Jocelyn Seymour, b. 1958, s. 1997, m.	Earl of Yarmouth, b. 1993
1599 S.	Huntly (13th), Granville Charles Gomer Gordon, b. 1944, s. 1987, m. Premier Marquess of Scotland	Earl of Aboyne, b. 1973
1784	Lansdowne (9th), Charles Maurice Mercer Nairne Petty-Fitzmaurice, LVO, b. 1941, s. 1999, m.	Earl of Kerry, b. 1970
1902	Linlithgow (4th), Adrian John Charles Hope, b. 1946, s. 1987	Earl of Hopetoun, b. 1969
1816 I.	Londonderry (10th), Frederick Aubrey Vane-Tempest-Stewart, b. 1972, s. 2012	Lord Reginald A. V.-T.-S., b. 1977
1701 S.	Lothian (13th) and Baron Kerr of Monteviot (life peerage, 2010), Michael Andrew Foster Jude Kerr (Michael Ancram), PC, QC, b. 1945, s. 2004, m.	Lord Ralph W. F. J. K., b. 1957
1917	Milford Haven (4th), George Ivar Louis Mountbatten, b. 1961, s. 1970, m.	Earl of Medina, b. 1991
1838	Normanby (5th), Constantine Edmund Walter Phipps, b. 1954, s. 1994, m.	Earl of Mulgrave, b. 1994
1812	Northampton (7th), Spencer Douglas David Compton, b. 1946, s. 1978, m.	Earl Compton, b. 1973
1682 S.	Queensberry (12th), David Harrington Angus Douglas, b. 1929, s. 1954, m.	Viscount Drumlanrig, b. 1967
1926	Reading (4th), Simon Charles Henry Rufus Isaacs, b. 1942, s. 1980, m.	Viscount Erleigh, b. 1986
1789	Salisbury (7th) and Baron Gascoyne-Cecil (life peerage, 1999), Robert Michael James Gascoyne-Cecil, KG, KCVO, PC, b. 1946, s. 2003, m.	Viscount Cranborne, b. 1970
1800 I.	Sligo (12th), Sebastian Ulick Browne, b. 1964, s. 2014, m.	Earl of Altamont, b. 1988
1787 °	Townshend (8th), Charles George Townshend, b. 1945, s. 2010, m.	Viscount Raynham, b. 1977
1694 S.	Tweeddale (14th), Charles David Montagu Hay, b. 1947, s. 2005	(Lord) Alistair J. M. H., b. 1955
1789 I.	Waterford (9th), Henry Nicholas de la Poer Beresford, b. 1958, s. 2015, m.	Earl of Tyrone, b. 1987
1551	Winchester (18th), Nigel George Paulet, b. 1941, s. 1968, m. Premier Marquess of England	Earl of Wiltshire, b. 1969
1892	Zetland (4th), Lawrence Mark Dundas, b. 1937, s. 1989, m.	Earl of Ronaldshay, b. 1965

EARLS

Coronet, Eight silver balls on stalks alternating with eight gold strawberry leaves

Style, The Rt. Hon. the Earl (of) _

Envelope (formal), The Rt. Hon. the Earl (of) _; *(social),* The Earl (of) _. *Letter (formal),* My Lord; *(social),* Dear Lord _. *Spoken (formal),* My Lord; *(social),* Lord _.

Wife's style, The Rt. Hon. the Countess (of) _

Envelope (formal), The Rt. Hon. the Countess (of) _; *(social),* The Countess (of) _. *Letter (formal),* Madam; *(social),* Lady _. *Spoken (formal),* Madam; *(social),* Lady _.

Eldest son's style, Takes his father's second title as a courtesy title (*see* Courtesy Titles)

Younger sons' style, 'The Hon.' before forename and surname, as for Baron's children

Daughters' style, 'Lady' before forename and surname, as for Duke's daughter

Created	Title, order of succession, name, etc	Heir
1639 S.	*Airlie (13th),* David George Coke Patrick Ogilvy, KT, GCVO, PC, Royal Victorian Chain, *b.* 1926, *s.* 1968, *m.*	Lord Ogilvy, *b.* 1958
1696	*Albemarle (10th),* Rufus Arnold Alexis Keppel, *b.* 1965, *s.* 1979	Viscount Bury, *b.* 2003
1952 °	*Alexander of Tunis (2nd),* Shane William Desmond Alexander, *b.* 1935, *s.* 1969, *m.*	Hon. Brian J. A., CMG, *b.* 1939
1662 S.	*Annandale and Hartfell (11th),* Patrick Andrew Wentworth Hope Johnstone, *b.* 1941, *s.* 1983, *m.* claim established 1985	Lord Johnstone, *b.* 1971
1789 I. °	*Annesley (12th),* Michael Robert Annesley, *b.* 1933, *s.* 2011, *w.*	Viscount Glerawly, *b.* 1957
1785 I.	*Antrim (9th),* Alexander Randal Mark McDonnell, *b.* 1935, *s.* 1977, *m.*	Viscount Dunluce, *b.* 1967
1762 I. **	*Arran (9th) and 5th UK Baron Sudley (1884),* Arthur Desmond Colquhoun Gore, *b.* 1938, *s.* 1983, *m.*	To Earldom only, William H. G., *b.* 1950
1955 ° **	*Attlee (3rd),* John Richard Attlee, *b.* 1956, *s.* 1991, *m.*	None
1714	*Aylesford (12th),* Charles Heneage Finch-Knightley, *b.* 1947, *s.* 2008, *m.*	Lord Guernsey, *b.* 1985
1937 °	*Baldwin of Bewdley (4th),* Edward Alfred Alexander Baldwin, *b.* 1938, *s.* 1976, *m.*	Viscount Corvedale, *b.* 1973
1922	*Balfour (5th),* Roderick Francis Arthur Balfour, *b.* 1948, *s.* 2003, *m.*	Charles G. Y. B., *b.* 1951
1772 °	*Bathurst (9th),* Allen Christopher Bertram Bathurst, *b.* 1961, *s.* 2011, *m.*	Lord Apsley, *b.* 1990
1919 °	*Beatty (3rd),* David Beatty, *b.* 1946, *s.* 1972	Viscount Borodale, *b.* 1973
1797 I.	*Belmore (8th),* John Armar Lowry-Corry, *b.* 1951, *s.* 1960, *m.*	Viscount Corry, *b.* 1985
1739 I.	*Bessborough (12th),* Myles Fitzhugh Longfield Ponsonby, *b.* 1941, *s.* 2002, *m.*	Viscount Duncannon, *b.* 1974
1815	*Bradford (7th),* Richard Thomas Orlando Bridgeman, *b.* 1947, *s.* 1981, *m.*	Viscount Newport, *b.* 1980
1469 S.	*Buchan (17th),* Malcolm Harry Erskine, *b.* 1930, *s.* 1984, *m.*	Lord Cardross, *b.* 1960
1746	*Buckinghamshire (10th),* (George) Miles Hobart-Hampden, *b.* 1944, *s.* 1983, *m.*	Sir John V. Hobart, Bt., *b.* 1945
1800 °	*Cadogan (8th),* Charles Gerald John Cadogan, KBE, *b.* 1937, *s.* 1997, *m.*	Viscount Chelsea, *b.* 1966
1878 °	*Cairns (6th),* Simon Dallas Cairns, CVO, CBE, *b.* 1939, *s.* 1989, *m.*	Viscount Garmoyle, *b.* 1965
1455 S. **	*Caithness (20th),* Malcolm Ian Sinclair, PC, *b.* 1948, *s.* 1965	Lord Berriedale, *b.* 1981
1800 I.	*Caledon (7th),* Nicholas James Alexander, KCVO, *b.* 1955, *s.* 1980, *m.*	Viscount Alexander, *b.* 1990
1661	*Carlisle (13th),* George William Beaumont Howard, *b.* 1949, *s.* 1994	Hon. Philip C. W. H., *b.* 1963
1793	*Carnarvon (8th),* George Reginald Oliver Molyneux Herbert, *b.* 1956, *s.* 2001, *m.*	Lord Porchester, *b.* 1992
1748 I.	*Carrick (11th),* Arion Thomas Piers Hamilton Butler, *b.* 1975, *s.* 2008, *m.*	Hon. Piers E. T. L. B., *b.* 1979
1800 I.°	*Castle Stewart (8th),* Arthur Patrick Avondale Stuart, *b.* 1928, *s.* 1961, *m.*	Viscount Stuart, *b.* 1953
1814 ° **	*Cathcart (7th),* Charles Alan Andrew Cathcart, *b.* 1952, *s.* 1999, *m.*	Lord Greenock, *b.* 1986
1647 I.	*Cavan (13th),* Roger Cavan Lambart, *b.* 1944, *s.* 1988 (claim to the peerage not yet established)	Cavan C. E. L., *b.* 1957
1827 °	*Cawdor (7th),* Colin Robert Vaughan Campbell, *b.* 1962, *s.* 1993, *m.*	Viscount Emlyn, *b.* 1998
1801	*Chichester (9th),* John Nicholas Pelham, *b.* 1944, *s.* 1944, *m.*	Richard A. H. P., *b.* 1952
1803 I. **	*Clancarty (9th),* Nicholas Power Richard Le Poer Trench, *b.* 1952, *s.* 1995, *m.*	None
1776 I.	*Clanwilliam (8th),* Patrick James Meade, *b.* 1960, *s.* 2009, *m.*	Lord Gillford, *b.* 1998
1776	*Clarendon (8th),* George Edward Laurence Villiers, *b.* 1976, *s.* 2009, *m.*	Lord Hyde, *b.* 2008
1620 I. **	*Cork and Orrery (15th),* John Richard Boyle, *b.* 1945, *s.* 2003, *m.*	Viscount Dungarvan, *b.* 1978
1850	*Cottenham (9th),* Mark John Henry Pepys, *b.* 1983, *s.* 2000, *m.*	Viscount Crowhurst, *b.* 2020
1762 I. **	*Courtown (9th),* James Patrick Montagu Burgoyne Winthrop Stopford, *b.* 1954, *s.* 1975, *m.*	Viscount Stopford, *b.* 1988
1697	*Coventry (13th),* George William Coventry, *b.* 1939, *s.* 2004, *m.*	David D. S. C., *b.* 1973

1857 °	*Cowley (8th)*, Garret Graham Wellesley, *b.* 1965, *s.* 2016, *m.*	Viscount Dangan, *b.* 1991
1892	*Cranbrook (5th)*, Gathorne Gathorne-Hardy, *b.* 1933, *s.* 1978, *m.*	Lord Medway, *b.* 1968
1801	*Craven (9th)*, Benjamin Robert Joseph Craven, *b.* 1989, *s.* 1990	Rupert J. E. C., *b.* 1926
1398 S.	*Crawford (29th) and Balcarres (12th) (S. 1651) and Baron Balniel (life peerage, 1974)*, Robert Alexander Lindsay, KT, GCVO, PC, *b.* 1927, *s.* 1975, *m.* *Premier Earl on Union Roll*	Lord Balniel, *b.* 1958
1861	*Cromartie (5th)*, John Ruaridh Blunt Grant Mackenzie, *b.* 1948, *s.* 1989, *m.*	Viscount Tarbat, *b.* 1987
1901	*Cromer (4th)*, Evelyn Rowland Esmond Baring, *b.* 1946, *s.* 1991, *m.*	Viscount Errington, *b.* 1994
1633 S.	*Dalhousie (17th)*, James Hubert Ramsay, *b.* 1948, *s.* 1999, *m. Lord Steward*	Lord Ramsay, *b.* 1981
1725 I.	*Darnley (12th)*, Ivo Donald Stuart Bligh, *b.* 1968, *s.* 2017, *m.*	Lord Clifton, *b.* 1999
1711	*Dartmouth (10th)*, William Legge, *b.* 1949, *s.* 1997, *m.*	Hon. Rupert L., *b.* 1951
1761 °	*De La Warr (11th)*, William Herbrand Sackville, *b.* 1948, *s.* 1988, *m.*	Lord Buckhurst, *b.* 1979
1622	*Denbigh (12th) and Desmond (11th) (I. 1622)*, Alexander Stephen Rudolph Feilding, *b.* 1970, *s.* 1995, *m.*	Viscount Feilding, *b.* 2005
1485	*Derby (19th)*, Edward Richard William Stanley, *b.* 1962, *s.* 1994, *m.*	Lord Stanley, *b.* 1998
1553 **	*Devon (19th)*, Charles Peregrine Courtenay, *b.* 1975, *s.* 2015, *m.*	Lord Courtenay, *b.* 2009
1800 I.	*Donoughmore (8th)*, Richard Michael John Hely-Hutchinson, *b.* 1927, *s.* 1981, *m.*	Viscount Suirdale, *b.* 1952
1661 I.	*Drogheda (12th)*, Henry Dermot Ponsonby Moore, *b.* 1937, *s.* 1989, *m.*	Viscount Moore, *b.* 1983
1837	*Ducie (7th)*, David Leslie Moreton, *b.* 1951, *s.* 1991, *m.*	Lord Moreton, *b.* 1981
1860	*Dudley (5th)*, William Humble David Jeremy Ward, *b.* 1947, *s.* 2013	Hon. Leander G. D. W., *b.* 1971
1660 S. **	*Dundee (12th)*, Alexander Henry Scrymgeour, *b.* 1949, *s.* 1983, *w.*	Lord Scrymgeour, *b.* 1982
1669 S.	*Dundonald (15th)*, Iain Alexander Douglas Blair Cochrane, *b.* 1961, *s.* 1986	Lord Cochrane, *b.* 1991
1686 S.	*Dunmore (12th)*, Malcolm Kenneth Murray, *b.* 1946, *s.* 1995, *w.*	Hon. Geoffrey C. M., *b.* 1949
1833	*Durham (7th)*, Edward Richard Lambton, *b.* 1961, *s.* 2006, *m.*	Viscount Lambton, *b.* 1985
1643 S.	*Dysart (13th)*, John Peter Grant of Rothiemurchus, *b.* 1946, *s.* 2011, *m.*	Lord Huntingtower, *b.* 1977
1837	*Effingham (7th)*, David Mowbray Algernon Howard, *b.* 1939, *s.* 1996, *m.*	Lord Howard of Effingham, *b.* 1971
1507 S.	*Eglinton (19th) and Winton (10th) (S. 1600)*, Hugh Archibald William Montgomerie, *b.* 1966, *s.* 2018, *m.*	Lord Montgomerie, *b.* 2007
1821	*Eldon (6th)*, John Francis Thomas Marie Joseph Columba Fidelis Scott, *b.* 1962, *s.* 2017, *m.*	Viscount Encombe, *b.* 1996
1633 S.	*Elgin (11th) and Kincardine (15th) (S. 1647)*, Andrew Douglas Alexander Thomas Bruce, KT, *b.* 1924, *s.* 1968, *m.*	Lord Bruce, *b.* 1961
1789 I.	*Enniskillen (7th)*, Andrew John Galbraith Cole, *b.* 1942, *s.* 1989, *m.*	Berkeley A. C., *b.* 1949
1789 I.	*Erne (7th)*, John Henry Michael Ninian Crichton, *b.* 1971, *s.* 2016, *m.*	Charles D. B. C., *b.* 1953
1452 S. **	*Erroll (24th)*, Merlin Sereld Victor Gilbert Hay, *b.* 1948, *s.* 1978, *w.* *Hereditary Lord High Constable and Knight Marischal of Scotland*	Lord Hay, *b.* 1984
1661	*Essex (11th)*, Frederick Paul de Vere Capell, *b.* 1944, *s.* 2005	William J. C., *b.* 1952
1711 °	*Ferrers (14th)*, Robert William Saswalo Shirley, *b.* 1952, *s.* 2012, *m.*	Viscount Tamworth, *b.* 1984
1789 °	*Fortescue (8th)*, Charles Hugh Richard Fortescue, *b.* 1951, *s.* 1993, *m.*	John A. F. F., *b.* 1955
1841	*Gainsborough (6th)*, Anthony Baptist Noel, *b.* 1950, *s.* 2009, *m.*	Viscount Campden, *b.* 1977
1623 S.	*Galloway (14th)*, Andrew Clyde Stewart, *b.* 1949, *s.* 2020, *m.*	Lord Garlies, *b.* 1980
1703 S.**	*Glasgow (10th)*, Patrick Robin Archibald Boyle, *b.* 1939, *s.* 1984, *m.*	Viscount of Kelburn, *b.* 1978
1806 I.	*Gosford (7th)*, Charles David Nicholas Alexander John Sparrow Acheson, *b.* 1942, *s.* 1966, *m.*	Nicholas H. C. A., *b.* 1947
1945	*Gowrie (2nd)*, Alexander Patrick Greysteil Hore Ruthven, PC, *b.* 1939, *s.* 1955, *m.*	Viscount Ruthven of Canberra, *b.* 1964
1684 I.	*Granard (10th)*, Peter Arthur Edward Hastings Forbes, *b.* 1957, *s.* 1992, *m.*	Viscount Forbes, *b.* 1981
1833 °	*Granville (6th)*, Granville George Fergus Leveson-Gower, *b.* 1959, *s.* 1996, *m.*	Lord Leveson, *b.* 1999
1806 °	*Grey (7th)*, Philip Kent Grey, *b.* 1940, *s.* 2013, *m.*	Viscount Howick, *b.* 1968
1752	*Guilford (10th)*, Piers Edward Brownlow North, *b.* 1971, *s.* 1999, *m.*	Lord North, *b.* 2002
1619 S.	*Haddington (14th)*, George Edmund Baldred Baillie-Hamilton, *b.* 1985, *s.* 2016	Thomas R. Hamilton-Baillie, *b.* 1948
1919 °	*Haig (3rd)*, Alexander Douglas Derrick Haig, *b.* 1961, *s.* 2009, *m.*	None
1944	*Halifax (3rd)*, Charles Edward Peter Neil Wood, *b.* 1944, *s.* 1980, *m.*	Lord Irwin, *b.* 1977
1754	*Hardwicke (10th)*, Joseph Philip Sebastian Yorke, *b.* 1971, *s.* 1974, *m.*	Viscount Royston, *b.* 2009
1812	*Harewood (8th)*, David Henry George Lascelles, *b.* 1950, *s.* 2011, *m.*	Viscount Lascelles, *b.* 1980
1742	*Harrington (12th)*, Charles Henry Leicester Stanhope, *b.* 1945, *s.* 2009, *m.*	Viscount Petersham, *b.* 1967
1809	*Harrowby (8th)*, Dudley Adrian Conroy Ryder, *b.* 1951, *s.* 2007, *m.*	Viscount Sandon, *b.* 1981°
1605 S. **	*Home (15th)*, David Alexander Cospatrick Douglas-Home, KT, CVO, CBE, *b.* 1943, *s.* 1995, *m.*	Lord Dunglass, *b.* 1987
1821 ° **	*Howe (7th)*, Frederick Richard Penn Curzon, PC, *b.* 1951, *s.* 1984, *m.*	Viscount Curzon, *b.* 1994
1529	*Huntingdon (17th)*, William Edward Robin Hood Hastings-Bass, LVO, *b.* 1948, *s.* 1990	Hon. John P. R. H. H.-B., *b.* 1954
1885	*Iddesleigh (5th)*, John Stafford Northcote, *b.* 1957, *s.* 2004, *m.*	Viscount St Cyres, *b.* 1985
1756	*Ilchester (10th)*, Robin Maurice Fox-Strangways, *b.* 1942, *s.* 2006, *m.*	Paul A. F-S., *b.* 1950
1929	*Inchcape (4th)*, (Kenneth) Peter (Lyle) Mackay, *b.* 1943, *s.* 1994, *m.*	Viscount Glenapp, *b.* 1979
1919	*Iveagh (4th)*, Arthur Edward Rory Guinness, *b.* 1969, *s.* 1992, *m.*	Viscount Elveden, *b.* 2003
1925 °	*Jellicoe (3rd)*, Patrick John Bernard Jellicoe, *b.* 1950, *s.* 2007	Hon. Nicholas C. J., *b.* 1953

1697	*Jersey (10th)*, George Francis William Child Villiers, *b.* 1976, *s.* 1998, *m.*	Viscount Villiers, *b.* 2015
1822 I.	*Kilmorey (6th)*, Sir Richard Francis Needham, PC, *b.* 1942, *s.* 1977, *m.* (Does not use title)	Viscount Newry and Mourne, *b.* 1966
1866	*Kimberley (5th)*, John Armine Wodehouse, *b.* 1951, *s.* 2002, *m.*	Lord Wodehouse, *b.* 1978
1768 I.	*Kingston (12th)*, Robert Charles Henry King-Tenison, *b.* 1969, *s.* 2002	Viscount Kingsborough, *b.* 2000
1633 S. **	*Kinnoull (16th)*, Charles William Harley Hay, *b.* 1962, *s.* 2013, *m.*	Viscount Dupplin, *b.* 2011
1677 S.	*Kintore (14th)*, James William Falconer Keith, *b.* 1976, *s.* 2004, *m.*	Lord Inverurie, *b.* 2010
1624 S.	*Lauderdale (18th)*, Ian Maitland, *b.* 1937, *s.* 2008, *w.*	Viscount Maitland, *b.* 1965
1837	*Leicester (8th)*, Thomas Edward Coke, *b.* 1965, *s.* 2015, *m.*	Viscount Coke, *b.* 2003
1641 S.	*Leven (15th) and Melville (14th) (S. 1690)*, Alexander Ian Leslie Melville, *b.* 1984, *s.* 2012	Hon. Archibald R. L. M., *b.* 1957
1831	*Lichfield (6th)*, Thomas William Robert Hugh Anson, *b.* 1978, *s.* 2005, *m.*	Viscount Anson, *b.* 2011
1803 I.	*Limerick (7th)*, Edmund Christopher Pery, *b.* 1963, *s.* 2003, *m.*	Viscount Pery, *b.* 1991
1572	*Lincoln (19th)*, Robert Edward Fiennes-Clinton, *b.* 1972, *s.* 2001	Hon. William J. Howson, *b.* 1980
1633 S. **	*Lindsay (16th)*, James Randolph Lindesay-Bethune, *b.* 1955, *s.* 1989, *m.*	Viscount Garnock, *b.* 1990
1626	*Lindsey (14th) and Abingdon (9th) (1682)*, Richard Henry Rupert Bertie, *b.* 1931, *s.* 1963, *m.*	Lord Norreys, *b.* 1958
1776 I.	*Lisburne (9th)*, David John Francis Malet Vaughan, *b.* 1945, *s.* 2014, *m.*	Hon. Michael J. W. M. V., *b.* 1948
1822 I.**	*Listowel (6th)*, Francis Michael Hare, *b.* 1964, *s.* 1997	Hon. Timothy P. H., *b.* 1966
1905 **	*Liverpool (5th)*, Edward Peter Bertram Savile Foljambe, *b.* 1944, *s.* 1969, *m.*	Viscount Hawkesbury, *b.* 1972
1945 °	*Lloyd George of Dwyfor (4th)*, David Richard Owen Lloyd George, *b.* 1951, *s.* 2010, *m.*	Viscount Gwynedd, *b.* 1986
1785 I.	*Longford (8th)*, Thomas Frank Dermot Pakenham, *b.* 1933, *s.* 2001, *m.* (Does not use title)	Edward M. P., *b.* 1970
1807	*Lonsdale (8th)*, Hugh Clayton Lowther, *b.* 1949, *s.* 2006, *m.*	Hon. William J. L., *b.* 1957
1633 S.	*Loudoun (15th)*, Simon Michael Abney-Hastings, *b.* 1974, *s.* 2012	Hon. Marcus W. A.-H., *b.* 1981
1795 I.	*Lucan (8th)*, George Charles Bingham, *b.* 1967, *s.* 2016, *m.*	Lord Bingham, *b.* 2019
1880 **	*Lytton (5th)*, John Peter Michael Scawen Lytton, *b.* 1950, *s.* 1985, *m.*	Viscount Knebworth, *b.* 1989
1721	*Macclesfield (9th)*, Richard Timothy George Mansfield Parker, *b.* 1943, *s.* 1992, *m.*	Hon. J. David G. P., *b.* 1945
1800	*Malmesbury (7th)*, James Carleton Harris, *b.* 1946, *s.* 2000, *m.*	Viscount FitzHarris, *b.* 1970
1776	*Mansfield (8th) and Mansfield (9th) (1792)*, Alexander David Mungo Murray, *b.* 1956, *s.* 2015, *m.*	Viscount Stormont, *b.* 1988
1565 S.	*Mar (14th) and Kellie (16th) (S. 1616) and Baron Erskine of Alloa Tower (life peerage, 2000)*, James Thorne Erskine, *b.* 1949, *s.* 1994, *m.*	Hon. Alexander D. E., *b.* 1952
1785 I.	*Mayo (11th)*, Charles Diarmuidh John Bourke, *b.* 1953, *s.* 2006, *m.*	Lord Naas, *b.* 1985
1627 I.	*Meath (15th)*, John Anthony Brabazon, *b.* 1941, *s.* 1998, *m.*	Lord Ardee, *b.* 1977
1766 I.	*Mexborough (8th)*, John Christopher George Savile, *b.* 1931, *s.* 1980, *m.*	Viscount Pollington, *b.* 1959
1813	*Minto (7th)*, Gilbert Timothy George Lariston Elliot-Murray-Kynynmound, *b.* 1953, *s.* 2005, *m.*	Viscount Melgund, *b.* 1984
1562 S.	*Moray (21st)*, John Douglas Stuart, *b.* 1966, *s.* 2011, *m.*	Lord Doune, *b.* 2002
1815	*Morley (7th)*, Mark Lionel Parker, *b.* 1956, *s.* 2015, *m.*	Edward G. P., *b.* 1967
1458 S.	*Morton (22nd)*, John Stewart Sholto Douglas, *b.* 1952, *s.* 2016, *m.*	Lord Aberdour, *b.* 1986
1789	*Mount Edgcumbe (8th)*, Robert Charles Edgcumbe, *b.* 1939, *s.* 1982, *m.*	Piers V. E., *b.* 1946
1947 °	*Mountbatten of Burma (3rd)*, Norton Louis Philip Knatchbull, *b.* 1947, *s.* 2017, *m.*	Lord Brabourne, *b.* 1981
1805 °	*Nelson (10th)*, Simon John Horatio Nelson, *b.* 1971, *s.* 2009, *m.*	Viscount Merton, *b.* 2010
1660 S.	*Newburgh (12th)*, Don Filippo Giambattista Camillo Francesco Aldo Maria Rospigliosi, *b.* 1942, *s.* 1986, *m.*	Princess Donna Benedetta F. M. R., *b.* 1974
1827 I.	*Norbury (7th)*, Richard James Graham-Toler, *b.* 1967, *s.* 2000	None
1806 I.	*Normanton (7th)*, James Shaun Christian Welbore Ellis Agar, *b.* 1982, *s.* 2019, *m.*	Viscount Somerton, *b.* 2016
1647 S.	*Northesk (15th)*, Patrick Charles Carnegy, *b.* 1940, *s.* 2010, *m.*	Hon. Colin D. C., *b.* 1942
1801	*Onslow (8th)*, Rupert Charles William Bullard Onslow, *b.* 1967, *s.* 2011, *m.*	Anthony E. E. O., *b.* 1955
1696 S.	*Orkney (9th)*, (Oliver) Peter St John, *b.* 1938, *s.* 1998, *m.*	Viscount Kirkwall, *b.* 1969
1328 I.	*Ormonde and Ossory (I. 1527)*, The 25th/18th Earl (7th Marquess) died in 1988	†Viscount Mountgarret *b.* 1961 (*see* that title)
1925 **	*Oxford and Asquith (3rd)*, Raymond Benedict Bartholomew Michael Asquith, OBE, *b.* 1952, *s.* 2011, *m.*	Viscount Asquith, *b.* 1979
1929 ° **	*Peel (3rd)*, William James Robert Peel, GCVO, PC, *b.* 1947, *s.* 1969, *m.* Lord Chamberlain	Viscount Clanfield, *b.* 1976
1551	*Pembroke (18th) and Montgomery (15th) (1605)*, William Alexander Sidney Herbert, *b.* 1978, *s.* 2003, *m.*	Lord Herbert, *b.* 2012
1605 S.	*Perth (18th)*, John Eric Drummond, *b.* 1935, *s.* 2002, *m.*	Viscount Strathallan, *b.* 1965
1905	*Plymouth (4th)*, Ivor Edward Other Windsor-Clive, *b.* 1951, *s.* 2018, *m.*	Viscount Windsor, *b.* 1981
1785 I.	*Portarlington (7th)*, George Lionel Yuill Seymour Dawson-Damer, *b.* 1938, *s.* 1959, *m.*	Viscount Carlow, *b.* 1965
1689	*Portland (12th)*, Count Timothy Charles Robert Noel Bentinck, MBE, *b.* 1953, *s.* 1997, *m.*	Viscount Woodstock, *b.* 1984
1743	*Portsmouth (10th)*, Quentin Gerard Carew Wallop, *b.* 1954, *s.* 1984, *m.*	Viscount Lymington, *b.* 1981
1804	*Powis (8th)*, John George Herbert, *b.* 1952, *s.* 1993, *m.*	Viscount Clive, *b.* 1979

1765	*Radnor (9th),* William Pleydell-Bouverie, *b.* 1955, *s.* 2008, *m.*	Viscount Folkestone, *b.* 1999
1831 I.	*Ranfurly (8th),* Edward John Knox, *b.* 1957, *s.* 2018, *m.*	Viscount Northland, *b.* 1994
1771 I.	*Roden (10th),* Robert John Jocelyn, *b.* 1938, *s.* 1993, *m.*	Viscount Jocelyn, *b.* 1989
1801	*Romney (8th),* Julian Charles Marsham, *b.* 1948, *s.* 2004, *m.*	Viscount Marsham, *b.* 1977
1703 S.	*Rosebery (7th),* Neil Archibald Primrose, *b.* 1929, *s.* 1974, *m.*	Lord Dalmeny, *b.* 1967
1806 I.	*Rosse (7th),* William Brendan Parsons, *b.* 1936, *s.* 1979, *m.*	Lord Oxmantown, *b.* 1969
1801 **	*Rosslyn (7th),* Peter St Clair-Erskine, CVO, QPM, *b.* 1958, *s.* 1977, *m.*	Lord Loughborough, *b.* 1986
1457 S.	*Rothes (22nd),* James Malcolm David Leslie, *b.* 1958, *s.* 2005	Hon. Alexander J. L., *b.* 1962
1861 °	*Russell (7th),* John Francis Russell, *b.* 1971, *s.* 2014, *m.*	None
1915 °	*St Aldwyn (3rd),* Michael Henry Hicks Beach, *b.* 1950, *s.* 1992, *m.*	Hon. David S. H. B., *b.* 1955
1815 M.	*St Germans (11th),* Albert Charger Eliot, *b.* 2004, *s.* 2016	Hon. Louis R. E., *b.* 1968
1660 **	*Sandwich (11th),* John Edward Hollister Montagu, *b.* 1943, *s.* 1995, *m.*	Viscount Hinchingbrooke, *b.* 1969
1690	*Scarbrough (13th),* Richard Osbert Lumley, *b.* 1973, *s.* 2004, *m.*	Hon. Thomas H. L., *b.* 1980
1701 S.	*Seafield (13th),* Ian Derek Francis Ogilvie-Grant, *b.* 1939, *s.* 1969, *m.*	Viscount Reidhaven, *b.* 1963
1882	*Selborne (4th),* John Roundell Palmer, GBE, *b.* 1940, *s.* 1971, *m.*	Viscount Wolmer, *b.* 1971
1646 S.	*Selkirk (11th),* Disclaimed for life 1994 (*see* Lord Selkirk of Douglas, Life Peers)	Master of Selkirk, *b.* 1978
1672	*Shaftesbury (12th),* Nicholas Edmund Anthony Ashley-Cooper, *b.* 1979, *s.* 2005, *m.*	Lord Ashley, *b.* 2011
1756 I.	*Shannon (10th),* Richard Henry John Boyle, *b.* 1960, *s.* 2013	Robert F. B., *b.* 1930
1442 **	*Shrewsbury and Waterford (22nd) (I. 1446),* Charles Henry John Benedict Crofton Chetwynd Chetwynd-Talbot, *b.* 1952, *s.* 1980, *m. Premier Earl of England and Ireland*	Viscount Ingestre, *b.* 1978
1961	*Snowdon (2nd),* David Albert Charles Armstrong-Jones, *b.* 1961, *s.* 2017	Viscount Linley, *b.* 1999
1765 °	*Spencer (9th),* Charles Edward Maurice Spencer, *b.* 1964, *s.* 1992, *m.*	Viscount Althorp, *b.* 1994
1703 S.**	*Stair (14th),* John David James Dalrymple, *b.* 1961, *s.* 1996, *m.*	Viscount Dalrymple, *b.* 2008
1984	*Stockton (2nd),* Alexander Daniel Alan Macmillan, *b.* 1943, *s.* 1986	Viscount Macmillan of Ovenden, *b.* 1974
1821	*Stradbroke (6th),* Robert Keith Rous, *b.* 1937, *s.* 1983, *m.*	Viscount Dunwich, *b.* 1961
1847	*Strafford (9th),* William Robert Byng, *b.* 1964, *s.* 2016, *m.*	Viscount Enfield, *b.* 1998
1606 S.	*Strathmore and Kinghorne (19th) (S. 1677),* Simon Patrick Bowes Lyon, *b.* 1986, *s.* 2016	Hon. John F. B. L., *b.* 1988
1603	*Suffolk (21st) and Berkshire (14th) (1626),* Michael John James George Robert Howard, *b.* 1935, *s.* 1941, *m.*	Viscount Andover, *b.* 1974
1235	*Sutherland (25th),* Alastair Charles St Clair Sutherland, *b.* 1947, *s.* 2019, *m.*	Lord Strathnaver, *b.* 1981
1955	*Swinton (3rd),* Nicholas John Cunliffe-Lister, *b.* 1939, *s.* 2006, *m.*	Lord Masham, *b.* 1970
1714	*Tankerville (10th),* Peter Grey Bennet, *b.* 1956, *s.* 1980	Adrian G. B., *b.* 1958
1822 °	*Temple of Stowe (9th),* James Grenville Temple-Gore-Langton, *b.* 1955, *s.* 2013, *m.*	Hon. Robert C. T.-G.-L., *b.* 1957
1815	*Verulam (7th),* John Duncan Grimston, *b.* 1951, *s.* 1973, *m.*	Viscount Grimston, *b.* 1978
1729 °	*Waldegrave (13th),* James Sherbrooke Waldegrave, *b.* 1940, *s.* 1995	Viscount Chewton, *b.* 1986
1759	*Warwick (9th) and Brooke (9th) (1746),* Guy David Greville, *b.* 1957, *s.* 1996, *m.*	Lord Brooke, *b.* 1982
1633 S.	*Wemyss (13th) and March (9th) (S. 1697),* James Donald Charteris, *b.* 1948, *s.* 2008, *m.*	Lord Elcho, *b.* 1984
1621 I.	*Westmeath (13th),* William Anthony Nugent, *b.* 1928, *s.* 1971, *m.*	Sean C. W. N., *b.* 1965
1624	*Westmorland (16th),* Anthony David Francis Henry Fane, *b.* 1951, *s.* 1993, *m.*	Hon. Harry St C. F., *b.* 1953
1876	*Wharncliffe (5th),* Richard Alan Montagu Stuart Wortley, *b.* 1953, *s.* 1987, *m.*	Viscount Carlton, *b.* 1980
1801	*Wilton (8th),* Francis Egerton Grosvenor, *b.* 1934, *s.* 1999, *w.*	Viscount Grey de Wilton, *b.* 1959
1628	*Winchilsea (17th) and Nottingham (12th) (1681),* Daniel James Hatfield Finch Hatton, *b.* 1967, *s.* 1999, *m.*	Viscount Maidstone, *b.* 1998
1766 I. °	*Winterton (8th),* (Donald) David Turnour, *b.* 1943, *s.* 1991, *m.*	Robert C. T., *b.* 1950
1956	*Woolton (3rd),* Simon Frederick Marquis, *b.* 1958, *s.* 1969, *m.*	None
1837	*Yarborough (8th),* Charles John Pelham, *b.* 1963, *s.* 1991, *m.*	Lord Worsley, *b.* 1990

COUNTESSES IN THEIR OWN RIGHT

Style, The Rt. Hon. the Countess (of) _

Envelope (formal), The Rt. Hon. the Countess (of) _; *(social),* The Countess (of) _. *Letter (formal),* Madam; *(social),* Lady _. *Spoken (formal),* Madam; *(social),* Lady _.

Husband, Untitled

Children's style, As for children of an Earl

In Scotland, the heir to a Countess may be styled 'The Master/Mistress of _ (title of peer)'

Created	Title, order of succession, name, etc	Heir
c.1115 S.	Mar (31st), Margaret of Mar, b. 1940, s. 1975, m. Premier Earldom of Scotland	Mistress of Mar, b. 1963

VISCOUNTS

Coronet, Sixteen silver balls

Style, The Rt. Hon. the Viscount _

Envelope (formal), The Rt. Hon. the Viscount _; *(social),* The Viscount _. *Letter (formal),* My Lord; *(social),* Dear Lord _. *Spoken,* Lord _.

Wife's style, The Rt. Hon. the Viscountess _

Envelope (formal), The Rt. Hon. the Viscountess _; *(social),* The Viscountess _. *Letter (formal),* Madam; *(social),* Dear Lady _. *Spoken,* Lady _.

Children's style, 'The Hon.' before forename and surname, as for Baron's children

In Scotland, the heir to a Viscount may be styled 'The Master/Mistress of _ (title of peer)'

Created	Title, order of succession, name, etc	Heir
1945	Addison (4th), William Matthew Wand Addison, b. 1945, s. 1992, m.	Hon. Paul W. A., b. 1973
1919	Allenby (4th), Henry Jaffray Hynman Allenby, b. 1968, s. 2014, m.	Hon. Harry M. E. A., b. 2000
1911	Allendale (4th), Wentworth Peter Ismay Beaumont, b. 1948, s. 2002, m.	Hon. Wentworth A. I. B., b. 1979
1642 S.	of Arbuthnott (17th), John Keith Oxley Arbuthnott, b. 1950, s. 2012, m.	Master of Arbuthnott, b. 1977
1751 I.	Ashbrook (11th), Michael Llowarch Warburton Flower, b. 1935, s. 1995, m.	Hon. Rowland F. W. F., b. 1975
1917 **	Astor (4th), William Waldorf Astor, b. 1951, s. 1966, m.	Hon. William W. A., b. 1979
1781 I.	Bangor (8th), William Maxwell David Ward, b. 1948, s. 1993, m.	Hon. E. Nicholas W., b. 1953
1925	Bearsted (5th), Nicholas Alan Samuel, b. 1950, s. 1996, m.	Hon. Harry R. S., b. 1988
1963	Blakenham (3rd), Caspar John Hare, b. 1972, s. 2018, m.	Hon. Inigo H., b. c.2006
1935	Bledisloe (4th), Rupert Edward Ludlow Bathurst, b. 1964, s. 2009, m.	Hon. Benjamin R. L. B., b. 2004
1712	Bolingbroke (9th) and St John (10th) (1716), Nicholas Alexander Mowbray St John, b. 1974, s. 2011, m.	German A. St J., b. 1980
1960	Boyd of Merton (2nd), Simon Donald Rupert Neville Lennox-Boyd, b. 1939, s. 1983, m.	Hon. Benjamin A. L.-B., b. 1964
1717 I.	Boyne (11th), Gustavus Michael Stucley Hamilton-Russell, b. 1965, s. 1995, m.	Hon. Gustavus A. E. H.-R., b. 1999
1929	Brentford (4th), Crispin William Joynson-Hicks, b. 1933, s. 1983, m.	Hon. Paul W. J.-H., MBE, b. 1971
1929 **	Bridgeman (3rd), Robin John Orlando Bridgeman, b. 1930, s. 1982, m.	Hon. Luke R. O. B., b. 1971
1868	Bridport (4th) and 7th Duke, Bronte in Sicily, 1799, Alexander Nelson Hood, b. 1948, s. 1969	Hon. Peregrine A. N. H., b. 1974
1952 **	Brookeborough (3rd), Alan Henry Brooke, KG, b. 1952, s. 1987, m.	Hon. Christopher A. B., b. 1954
1933	Buckmaster (4th), Adrian Charles Buckmaster, b. 1949, s. 2007, m.	Hon. Andrew N. B., b. 1980
1939	Caldecote (3rd), Piers James Hampden Inskip, b. 1947, s. 1999, m.	Hon. Thomas J. H. I., b. 1985
1941	Camrose (5th), Jonathan William Berry, b. 1970, s. 2016, m.	Hon. Hugo W. B., b. 2000
1954	Chandos (3rd) and Baron Lyttelton of Aldershot (life peerage, 2000), Thomas Orlando Lyttelton, b. 1953, s. 1980, m.	Hon. Oliver A. L., b. 1986
1665 I.	Charlemont (15th), John Dodd Caulfeild, b. 1966, s. 2001, m.	Hon. Shane A. C., b. 1996

1921	*Chelmsford (4th)*, Frederic Corin Piers Thesiger, *b.* 1962, *s.* 1999, *m.* — Hon. Frederic T., *b.* 2006
1717 I.	*Chetwynd (11th)*, Adam Douglas Chetwynd, *b.* 1969, *s.* 2015, *m.* — Hon. Connor A. C., *b.* 2001
1911	*Chilston (4th)*, Alastair George Akers-Douglas, *b.* 1946, *s.* 1982, *m.* — Hon. Oliver I. A.-D., *b.* 1973
1718	*Cobham (12th)*, Christopher Charles Lyttelton, *b.* 1947, *s.* 2006, *m.* — Hon. Oliver C. L., *b.* 1976
1902 **	*Colville of Culross (5th)*, Charles Mark Townshend Colville, *b.* 1959, *s.* 2010 — Master of Colville, *b.* 1961
1826	*Combermere (6th)*, Thomas Robert Wellington Stapleton-Cotton, *b.* 1969, *s.* 2000, *m.* — Hon. Laszlo M. W. S.-C., *b.* 2010
1917	*Cowdray (4th)*, Michael Orlando Weetman Pearson, *b.* 1944, *s.* 1995, *m.* — Hon. Peregrine J. D. P., *b.* 1994
1927 **	*Craigavon (3rd)*, Janric Fraser Craig, *b.* 1944, *s.* 1974 — None
1943	*Daventry (4th)*, James Edward FitzRoy Newdegate, *b.* 1960, *s.* 2000, *m.* — Hon. Humphrey J. F. N., *b.* 1995
1937	*Davidson (4th)*, John Nicolas Alexander Davidson, *b.* 1971, *s.* 2020, *m..* — None
1956	*De L'Isle (2nd)*, Philip John Algernon Sidney, CVO, MBE, *b.* 1945, *s.* 1991, *m.* — Hon. Philip W. E. S., *b.* 1985
1776 I.	*de Vesci (7th)*, Thomas Eustace Vesey, *b.* 1955, *s.* 1983 — Hon. Oliver I. V., *b.* 1991
1917	*Devonport (3rd)*, Terence Kearley, *b.* 1944, *s.* 1973, *m.* — Chester D. H. K., *b.* 1932
1964	*Dilhorne (2nd)*, John Mervyn Manningham-Buller, *b.* 1932, *s.* 1980, *m.* — Hon. James E. M.-B., *b.* 1956
1622 I.	*Dillon (22nd)*, Henry Benedict Charles Dillon, *b.* 1973, *s.* 1982, *m.* — Hon. Francis C. R. D., *b.* 2013
1785 I.	*Doneraile (10th)*, Richard Allen St Leger, *b.* 1946, *s.* 1983, *m.* — Hon. Nathaniel W. R. St J. St L., *b.* 1971
1680 I.	*Downe (12th)*, Richard Henry Dawnay, *b.* 1967, *s.* 2002 — Thomas P. D., *b.* 1978
1959	*Dunrossil (3rd)*, Andrew William Reginald Morrison, *b.* 1953, *s.* 2000, *m.* — Hon. Callum A. B. M., *b.* 1994
1964 **	*Eccles (2nd)*, John Dawson Eccles, CBE, *b.* 1931, *s.* 1999, *m.* — Hon. William D. E., *b.* 1960
1897	*Esher (4th)*, Christopher Lionel Baliol Brett, *b.* 1936, *s.* 2004, *m.* — Hon. Matthew C. A. B., *b.* 1963
1816	*Exmouth (10th)*, Paul Edward Pellew, *b.* 1940, *s.* 1970 — Hon. Edward F. P., *b.* 1978
1620 S.**	*of Falkland (15th)*, Lucius Edward William Plantagenet Cary, *b.* 1935, *s.* 1984, *m. Premier Scottish Viscount on the Roll* — Master of Falkland, *b.* 1963
1720	*Falmouth (9th)*, George Hugh Boscawen, *b.* 1919, *s.* 1962, *w.* — Hon. Evelyn A. H. B., *b.* 1955
1720 I.	*Gage (8th)*, (Henry) Nicolas Gage, *b.* 1934, *s.* 1993, *m.* — Hon. Henry W. G., *b.* 1975
1727 I.	*Galway (13th)*, John Philip Monckton, *b.* 1952, *s.* 2017, *m.* — Alan S. M., *b.* 1934
1478 I.	*Gormanston (17th)*, Jenico Nicholas Dudley Preston, *b.* 1939, *s.* 1940, *m. Premier Viscount of Ireland* — Hon. Jenico F. T. P., *b.* 1974
1816 I.	*Gort (9th)*, Foley Robert Standish Prendergast Vereker, *b.* 1951, *s.* 1995, *m.* — Hon. Robert F. P. V., *b.* 1993
1900 **	*Goschen (4th)*, Giles John Harry Goschen, *b.* 1965, *s.* 1977, *m.* — Hon. Alexander J. E. G., *b.* 2001
1849	*Gough (5th)*, Shane Hugh Maryon Gough, *b.* 1941, *s.* 1951 — None
1929	*Hailsham (3rd) and Baron Hailsham of Kettlethorpe (life peerage, 2015)*, Douglas Martin Hogg, PC, QC, *b.* 1945, *s.* 2001, *m.* — Hon. Quintin J. N. M. H., *b.* 1973
1891	*Hambleden (5th)*, William Henry Bernard Smith, *b.* 1955, *s.* 2012, *m.* — Hon. Bernardo J. S., *b.* 1957
1884	*Hampden (7th)*, Francis Anthony Brand, *b.* 1970, *s.* 2008, *m.* — Hon. Lucian A. B., *b.* 2005
1936 **	*Hanworth (3rd)*, David Stephen Geoffrey Pollock, *b.* 1946, *s.* 1996, *m.* — Harold W. C. P., *b.* 1988
1791 I.	*Harberton (11th)*, Henry Robert Pomeroy, *b.* 1958, *s.* 2004, *m.* — Hon. Patrick C. P., *b.* 1995
1846	*Hardinge (8th)*, Thomas Henry de Montarville Hardinge, *b.* 1993, *s.* 2014 — Hon. Jamie A. D. H., *b.* 1996
1791 I.	*Hawarden (9th)*, (Robert) Connan Wyndham Leslie Maude, *b.* 1961, *s.* 1991, *m.* — Hon. Varian J. C. E. M., *b.* 1997
1960	*Head (2nd)*, Richard Antony Head, *b.* 1937, *s.* 1983, *m.* — Hon. Henry J. H., *b.* 1980
1550	*Hereford (19th)*, Charles Robin de Bohun Devereux, *b.* 1975, *s.* 2004, *m. Premier Viscount of England* — Hon. Henry W. de B. D., *b.* 2015
1842	*Hill (9th)*, Peter David Raymond Charles Clegg-Hill, *b.* 1945, *s.* 2003, *m.* — Hon. Michael C. D. C.-H., *b.* 1988
1796	*Hood (8th)*, Henry Lyttelton Alexander Hood, *b.* 1958, *s.* 1999, *m.* — Hon. Archibald L. S. H., *b.* 1993
1945	*Kemsley (3rd)*, Richard Gomer Berry, *b.* 1951, *s.* 1999, *m.* — Hon. Luke G. B., *b.* 1998
1911	*Knollys (3rd)*, David Francis Dudley Knollys, *b.* 1931, *s.* 1966, *m.* — Hon. Patrick N. M. K., *b.* 1962
1895	*Knutsford (6th)*, Michael Holland-Hibbert, *b.* 1926, *s.* 1986, *w.* — Hon. Henry T. H.-H., *b.* 1959
1954	*Leathers (3rd)*, Christopher Graeme Leathers, *b.* 1941, *s.* 1996, *m.* — Hon. James F. L., *b.* 1969
1781 I.	*Lifford (9th)*, (Edward) James Wingfield Hewitt, *b.* 1949, *s.* 1987, *m.* — Hon. James T. W. H., *b.* 1979
1921	*Long (5th)*, James Richard Long, *b.* 1960, *s.* 2017 — None
1957	*Mackintosh of Halifax (3rd)*, (John) Clive Mackintosh, *b.* 1958, *s.* 1980, *m.* — Hon. Thomas H. G. M., *b.* 1985
1955	*Malvern (3rd)*, Ashley Kevin Godfrey Huggins, *b.* 1949, *s.* 1978 — Hon. M. James H., *b.* 1928
1945	*Marchwood (3rd)*, David George Staveley Penny, *b.* 1936, *s.* 1979, *m.* — Hon. Peter G. W. P., *b.* 1965
1942	*Margesson (3rd)*, Richard Francis David Margesson, *b.* 1960, *s.* 2014, *m.* — None
1660 I.	*Massereene (14th) and Ferrard (7th) (I. 1797)*, John David Clotworthy Whyte-Melville Foster Skeffington, *b.* 1940, *s.* 1992, *m.* — Hon. Charles J. C. W.-M. F. S., *b.* 1973
1802	*Melville (10th)*, Robert Henry Kirkpatrick Dundas, *b.* 1984, *s.* 2011, *m.* — Hon. Max D. H. M. D., *b.* 2018
1916	*Mersey (5th) and 14th Lord Nairne (S. 1681)*, Edward John Hallam Bigham, *b.* 1966, *s.* 2006, *m.* — Hon. David E. H. B., *b.* 1938 (to Viscountcy); Mistress of Nairne, *b.* 2003 (to Lordship of Nairne)
1717 I.	*Midleton (12th)*, Alan Henry Brodrick, *b.* 1949, *s.* 1988, *m.* — Hon. Ashley R. B., *b.* 1980
1962	*Mills (3rd)*, Christopher Philip Roger Mills, *b.* 1956, *s.* 1988, *m.* — None
1716 I.	*Molesworth (12th)*, Robert Bysse Kelham Molesworth, *b.* 1959, *s.* 1997 — Hon. William J. C. M., *b.* 1960
1801 I.	*Monck (7th)*, Charles Stanley Monck, *b.* 1953, *s.* 1982 (Does not use title) — Hon. George S. M., *b.* 1957

1957	*Monckton of Brenchley (3rd)*, Christopher Walter Monckton, *b.* 1952, *s.* 2006, *m.*	Hon. Timothy D. R. M., *b.* 1955
1946	*Montgomery of Alamein (3rd)*, Henry David Montgomery, *b.* 1954, *s.* 2020, *w.*	None
1550 I.	*Mountgarret (18th)*, Piers James Richard Butler, *b.* 1961, *s.* 2004, *m.*	Hon. Theo O. S. B., *b.* 2015
1952	*Norwich (3rd)*, Jason Charles Duff Bede Cooper, *b.* 1959, *s.* 2018	None
1651 S.	*of Oxfuird (14th)*, Ian Arthur Alexander Makgill, *b.* 1969, *s.* 2003, *m.*	Master of Oxfuird, *b.* 2012
1873	*Portman (10th)*, Christopher Edward Berkeley Portman, *b.* 1958, *s.* 1999, *m.*	Hon. Luke O. B. P., *b.* 1984
1743 I.	*Powerscourt (11th) and 5th UK Baron Powerscourt (1885)*, Mervyn Anthony Wingfield, *b.* 1963, *s.* 2015, *m.*	To Viscountcy only, Richard D. N. W., *b.* 1966
1900 **	*Ridley (5th)*, Matthew White Ridley, *b.* 1958, *s.* 2012, *m.*	Hon. Matthew W. R., *b.* 1993
1960	*Rochdale (3rd)*, Jonathan Hugo Durival Kemp, *b.* 1961, *s.* 2015, *m.*	George T. K., *b.* 2001
1919	*Rothermere (4th)*, (Harold) Jonathan Esmond Vere Harmsworth, *b.* 1967, *s.* 1998, *m.*	Hon. Vere R. J. H. H., *b.* 1994
1937	*Runciman of Doxford (3rd)*, Walter Garrison (Garry) Runciman, CBE, *b.* 1934, *s.* 1989, *m.*	Hon. David W. R., *b.* 1967
1918	*St Davids (4th)*, Rhodri Colwyn Philipps, *b.* 1966, *s.* 2009, *m.*	Hon. Roland A. J. E. P., *b.* 1970
1801	*St Vincent (8th)*, Edward Robert James Jervis, *b.* 1951, *s.* 2006, *m.*	Hon. James R. A. J., *b.* 1982
1937	*Samuel (5th)*, Jonathan Herbert Samuel, *b.* 1965, *s.* 2014, *m.*	Hon. Benjamin A. S., *b.* 1983
1911	*Scarsdale (4th)*, Peter Ghislain Nathaniel Curzon, *b.* 1949, *s.* 2000, *m.*	Hon. David J. N. C., *b.* 1958
1905	*Selby (6th)*, Christopher Rolf Thomas Gully, *b.* 1993, *s.* 2001	Hon. (James) Edward H. G. G., *b.* 1945
1805	*Sidmouth (8th)*, Jeremy Francis Addington, *b.* 1947, *s.* 2005, *w.*	Hon. John A., *b.* 1990
1940 **	*Simon (3rd)*, Jan David Simon, *b.* 1940, *s.* 1993, *m.*	None
1960	*Slim (3rd)*, Mark William Rawdon Slim, *b.* 1960, *s.* 2019, *m.*	Hon. Rufus W. R. S., *b.* 1995
1954	*Soulbury (4th)*, Oliver Peter Ramsbotham, *b.* 1943, *s.* 2010, *m.*	Hon. Edward H. R., *b.* 1966
1776 I.	*Southwell (8th)*, Richard Andrew Pyers Southwell, *b.* 1956, *s.* 2020, *m.*	Hon. Charles A. J. S., *b.* 1962
1942	*Stansgate (3rd)*, Stephen Michael Wedgwood Benn, *b.* 1951, *s.* 2014, *m.*	Hon. Daniel J. W. B., *b.* 1991
1959	*Stuart of Findhorn (3rd)*, Dominic Stuart, *b.* 1948, *s.* 1999	Hon. Andrew M. S., *b.* 1957
1957	*Tenby (3rd)*, William Lloyd George, *b.* 1927, *s.* 1983, *m.*	Hon. Timothy H. G. L. G., *b.* 1962
1952 **	*Thurso (3rd)*, John Archibald Sinclair, PC, *b.* 1953, *s.* 1995, *m.*	Hon. James A. R. S., *b.* 1984
1721	*Torrington (11th)*, Timothy Howard St George Byng, *b.* 1943, *s.* 1961, *m.*	Colin H. Cranmer-Byng, *b.* 1960
1936 **	*Trenchard (3rd)*, Hugh Trenchard, *b.* 1951, *s.* 1987, *m.*	Hon. Alexander T. T., *b.* 1978
1921 **	*Ullswater (2nd)*, Nicholas James Christopher Lowther, LVO, PC, *b.* 1942, *s.* 1949, *m.*	Hon. Benjamin J. L., *b.* 1975
1642 I.	*Valentia (16th)*, Francis William Dighton Annesley, *b.* 1959, *s.* 2005, *m.*	Hon. Peter J. A., *b.* 1967
1952 **	*Waverley (3rd)*, John Desmond Forbes Anderson, *b.* 1949, *s.* 1990, *m.*	Hon. Forbes A. R. A., *b.* 1996
1938	*Weir (3rd)*, William Kenneth James Weir, *b.* 1933, *s.* 1975, *m.*	Hon. James W. H. W., *b.* 1965
1918	*Wimborne (4th)*, Ivor Mervyn Vigors Guest, *b.* 1968, *s.* 1993, *m.*	Hon. Ivor N. G. I. G., *b.* 2016
1923 **	*Younger of Leckie (5th)*, James Edward George Younger, *b.* 1955, *s.* 2003, *m.*	Hon. Alexander W. G. Y., *b.* 1993

BARONS/LORDS

Coronet, Six silver balls

Style, The Rt. Hon. the Lord _
    Envelope (formal), The Rt. Hon. Lord _; *(social)*, The Lord _. *Letter (formal)*, My Lord; *(social)*, Dear Lord _. *Spoken*, Lord _.
In the Peerage of Scotland there is no rank of Baron; the equivalent rank is Lord of Parliament and Scottish peers should always be styled 'Lord', never 'Baron'.

Wife's style, The Rt. Hon. the Lady _
Envelope (formal), The Rt. Hon. Lady _; *(social)*, The Lady _. *Letter (formal)*, My Lady; *(social)*, Dear Lady _. *Spoken*, Lady _
Children's style, 'The Hon.' before forename (F_) and surname (S_)
Envelope, The Hon. F_ S_. *Letter*, Dear Mr/Miss/Mrs S_. *Spoken*, Mr/Miss/Mrs S_
In Scotland, the heir to a Lord may be styled 'The Master/Mistress of _ (title of peer)'

Created	Title, order of succession, name, etc	Heir
1911	*Aberconway (4th)*, (Henry) Charles McLaren, *b.* 1948, *s.* 2003, *m.*	Hon. Charles S. M., *b.* 1984
1873 **	*Aberdare (5th)*, Alastair John Lyndhurst Bruce, *b.* 1947, *s.* 2005, *m.*	Hon. Hector M. N. B., *b.* 1974
1835	*Abinger (9th)*, James Harry Scarlett, *b.* 1959, *s.* 2002, *m.*	Hon. Peter R. S., *b.* 1961

1869	*Acton (5th)*, John Charles Ferdinand Harold Lyon-Dalberg-Acton, *b.* 1966, *s.* 2010, *m.*	Hon. Robert P. L.-D.-A., *b.* 1946
1887 **	*Addington (6th)*, Dominic Bryce Hubbard, *b.* 1963, *s.* 1982, *m.*	Hon. Michael W. L. H., *b.* 1965
1896	*Aldenham (6th) and Hunsdon of Hunsdon (4th) (1923)*, Vicary Tyser Gibbs, *b.* 1948, *s.* 1986, *m.*	Hon. Humphrey W. F. G., *b.* 1989
1962	*Aldington (2nd)*, Charles Harold Stuart Low, *b.* 1948, *s.* 2000, *m.*	Hon. Philip T. A. L., *b.* 1990
1945	*Altrincham (4th)*, (Edward) Sebastian Grigg, *b.* 1965, *s.* 2020, *m.*	Hon. Edward L. D. de M. G., *b.* 1995
1929	*Alvingham (3rd)*, Robert Richard Guy Yerburgh, *b.* 1956, *s.* 1956, *m.*	Hon. Robert W. G. Y., *b.* 1971
1892	*Amherst of Hackney (5th)*, Hugh William Amherst Cecil, *b.* 1968, *s.* 2009, *m.*	Hon. Jack W. A. C., *b.* 2001
1881	*Ampthill (5th)*, David Whitney Erskine Russell, *b.* 1947, *s.* 2011, *m.*	Hon. Anthony J. M. R., *b.* 1952
1947	*Amwell (3rd)*, Keith Norman Montague, *b.* 1943, *s.* 1990, *m.*	Hon. Ian K. M., *b.* 1973
1863	*Annaly (6th)*, Luke Richard White, *b.* 1954, *s.* 1990	Hon. Luke H. W., *b.* 1990
1885	*Ashbourne (5th)*, Edward Charles d'Olier Gibson, *b.* 1967, *s.* 2020	Hon. Edward A. G., *b.* 2002
1835	*Ashburton (8th)*, Mark Francis Robert Baring, *b.* 1958, *s.* 2020, *m.*	Hon. Frederick C. F. B., *b.* 1990
1892	*Ashcombe (5th)*, Mark Edward Cubitt, *b.* 1964, *s.* 2013, *m.*	Hon. Richard R. A. C., *b.* 1995
1911 **	*Ashton of Hyde (4th)*, Thomas Henry Ashton, PC, *b.* 1958, *s.* 2008, *m.*	Hon. John E. A., *b.* 1966
1800 I.	*Ashtown (8th)*, Roderick Nigel Godolphin Trench, *b.* 1944, *s.* 2010, *m.*	Hon. Timothy R. H. T., *b.* 1968
1956 **	*Astor of Hever (3rd)*, John Jacob Astor, PC, *b.* 1946, *s.* 1984, *m.*	Hon. Charles G. J. A., *b.* 1990
1789 I.	*Auckland (10th) and Auckland (10th) (1793)*, Robert Ian Burnard Eden, *b.* 1962, *s.* 1997, *m.*	Henry V. E., *b.* 1958
1313	*Audley*, Barony in abeyance between three co-heiresses since 1997	
1900	*Avebury (5th)*, Lyulph Ambrose Lubbock, *b.* 1954, *s.* 2016, *m.*	Hon. Alexander L. R. L., *b.* 1985
1718 I.	*Aylmer (14th)*, (Anthony) Julian Aylmer, *b.* 1951, *s.* 2006, *m.*	Hon. Michael H. A., *b.* 1991
1929	*Baden-Powell (4th)*, David Michael Baden-Powell, *b.* 1940, *s.* 2019, *m.*	Hon. David R. B.-P., *b.* 1971
1780	*Bagot (10th)*, (Charles Hugh) Shaun Bagot, *b.* 1944, *s.* 2001, *m.*	Julian W. D'A. B., *b.* 1943
1953	*Baillieu (3rd)*, James William Latham Baillieu, *b.* 1950, *s.* 1973, *m.*	Hon. Robert L. B., *b.* 1979
1924	*Banbury of Southam (3rd)*, Charles William Banbury, *b.* 1953, *s.* 1981, *m.*	None
1698	*Barnard (12th)*, Henry Francis Cecil Vane, *b.* 1959, *s.* 2016, *m.*	Hon. William H. C. V., *b.* 2005
1887	*Basing (6th)*, Stuart Anthony Whitfield Sclater-Booth, *b.* 1969, *s.* 2007	Hon. Luke W. S.-B., *b.* 2000
1917	*Beaverbrook (3rd)*, Maxwell William Humphrey Aitken, *b.* 1951, *s.* 1985, *m.*	Hon. Maxwell F. A., *b.* 1977
1647 S.	*Belhaven and Stenton (13th)*, Robert Anthony Carmichael Hamilton, *b.* 1927, *s.* 1961, *m.*	Master of Belhaven, *b.* 1953
1848 I.	*Bellew (8th)*, Bryan Edward Bellew, *b.* 1943, *s.* 2010, *m.*	Hon. Anthony R. B. B., *b.* 1972
1856	*Belper (5th)*, Richard Henry Strutt, *b.* 1941, *s.* 1999, *w.*	Hon. Michael H. S., *b.* 1969
1421	*Berkeley (18th) and Gueterbock (life peerage, 2000)*, Anthony Fitzhardinge Gueterbock, OBE, *b.* 1939, *s.* 1992, *m.*	Hon. Thomas F. G., *b.* 1969
1922 **	*Bethell (5th)*, James Nicholas Bethell, *b.* 1967, *s.* 2007, *m.*	Hon. Jacob N. D. B., *b.* 2006
1938	*Bicester (5th)*, Charles James Vivian Smith, *b.* 1963, *s.* 2016, *m.*	Hon. Milo L. V. S., *b.* 2007
1903	*Biddulph (5th)*, (Anthony) Nicholas Colin Maitland Biddulph, *b.* 1959, *s.* 1988	Hon. Robert J. M. B., *b.* 1994
1958	*Birkett (3rd)*, Thomas Birkett, *b.* 1982, *s.* 2015, *m.*	None
1907	*Blyth (5th)*, James Audley Ian Blyth, *b.* 1970, *s.* 2009, *m.*	Hon. Hugo A. J. B., *b.* 2006
1797	*Bolton (8th)*, Harry Algar Nigel Orde-Powlett, *b.* 1954, *s.* 2001, *w.*	Hon. Thomas P. A. O.-P., MC, *b.* 1979
1452 S.	*Borthwick (24th)*, John Hugh Borthwick, *b.* 1940, *s.* 1996, *m.*	Hon. James H. A. B. of Glengelt, *b.* 1940
1922 **	*Borwick (5th)*, (Geoffrey Robert) James Borwick, *b.* 1955, *s.* 2007, *m.*	Hon. Edwin D. W. B., *b.* 1984
1761	*Boston (11th)*, George William Eustace Boteler Irby, *b.* 1971, *s.* 2007, *m.*	Hon. Thomas W. G. B. I., *b.* 1999
1942 **	*Brabazon of Tara (3rd)*, Ivon Anthony Moore-Brabazon, PC, *b.* 1946, *s.* 1974, *m.*	Hon. Benjamin R. M.-B., *b.* 1983
1925	*Bradbury (3rd)*, John Bradbury, *b.* 1940, *s.* 1994, *m.*	Hon. John T. B., *b.* 1973
1962	*Brain (3rd)*, Michael Cottrell Brain, *b.* 1928, *s.* 2014, *m.*	Hon. Thomas R. B., *b.* 1965
1938	*Brassey of Apethorpe (4th)*, Edward Brassey, *b.* 1964, *s.* 2015, *m.*	Hon. Christian B., *b.* 2003
1788	*Braybrooke (11th)*, Richard Ralph Neville, *b.* 1977, *s.* 2017, *m.*	Hon. Edward A. N., *b.* 2015
1957	*Bridges (3rd)*, Mark Thomas Bridges, KCVO, *b.* 1954, *s.* 2017, *m.*	Hon. Nicholas E. B., *b.* 1956
1945	*Broadbridge (5th)*, Air Vice-Marshal Richard John Martin Broadbridge, CB, *b.* 1959, *s.* 2020, *m.*	Hon. Mark A. B., *b.* 1983
1933	*Brocket (3rd)*, Charles Ronald George Nall-Cain, *b.* 1952, *s.* 1967, *m.*	Hon. Alexander C. C. N.-C., *b.* 1984
1860 **	*Brougham and Vaux (5th)*, Michael John Brougham, CBE, *b.* 1938, *s.* 1967	Hon. Charles W. B., *b.* 1971
1776	*Brownlow (7th)*, Edward John Peregrine Cust, *b.* 1936, *s.* 1978, *m.*	Hon. Peregrine E. Q. C., *b.* 1974
1942	*Bruntisfield (3rd)*, Michael John Victor Warrender, *b.* 1949, *s.* 2007, *m.*	Hon. John M. P. C. W., *b.* 1996
1950	*Burden (4th)*, Fraser William Elsworth Burden, *b.* 1964, *s.* 2000	Hon. Ian S. B., *b.* 1967
1529	*Burgh (8th)*, (Alexander) Gregory Disney Leith, *b.* 1958, *s.* 2001, *m.*	Hon. Alexander J. S. L., *b.* 1986
1903	*Burnham (7th)*, Harry Frederick Alan Lawson, *b.* 1968, *s.* 2005	None
1897	*Burton (4th)*, Evan Michael Ronald Baillie, *b.* 1949, *s.* 2013, *m.*	Hon. James E. B., *b.* 1975
1643	*Byron (13th)*, Robert James Byron, *b.* 1950, *s.* 1989, *m.*	Hon. Charles R. G. B., *b.* 1990
1937	*Cadman (3rd)*, John Anthony Cadman, *b.* 1938, *s.* 1966, *m.*	Hon. Nicholas A. J. C., *b.* 1977
1945	*Calverley (3rd)*, Charles Rodney Muff, *b.* 1946, *s.* 1971, *m.*	Hon. Jonathan E. Brown, *b.* 1975

1383	*Camoys (7th),* (Ralph) Thomas Campion George Sherman Stonor, GCVO, PC, *b.* 1940, *s.* 1976, *m.*	Hon. R. William R. T. S., *b.* 1974
1715 I.	*Carbery (12th),* Michael Peter Evans-Freke, *b.* 1942, *s.* 2012, *m.*	Hon. Dominic R. C. E.-F., *b.* 1969
1834 I.	*Carew (7th) and Carew (7th) (1838),* Patrick Thomas Conolly-Carew, *b.* 1938, *s.* 1994, *m.*	Hon. William P. C.-C., *b.* 1973
1916	*Carnock (5th),* Adam Nicolson, *b.* 1957, *s.* 2008, *m.*	Hon. Thomas N., *b.* 1984
1796 I.**	*Carrington (7th) and Carrington (7th) (1797),* Rupert Francis John Carington, *b.* 1948, *s.* 2018, *m.*	Hon. Robert C., *b.* 1990
1812 I.	*Castlemaine (8th),* Roland Thomas John Handcock, MBE, *b.* 1943, *s.* 1973, *m.*	Hon. Ronan M. E. H., *b.* 1989
1936	*Catto (3rd),* Innes Gordon Catto, *b.* 1950, *s.* 2001, *m.*	Hon. Alexander G. C., *b.* 1952
1918	*Cawley (4th),* John Francis Cawley, *b.* 1946, *s.* 2001, *m.*	Hon. William R. H. C., *b.* 1981
1858	*Chesham (7th),* Charles Gray Compton Cavendish, *b.* 1974, *s.* 2009, *m.*	Hon. Oliver N. B. C., *b.* 2007
1945	*Chetwode (2nd),* Philip Chetwode, *b.* 1937, *s.* 1950, *m.*	Hon. Roger C., *b.* 1968
1945	*Chorley (3rd),* Nicholas Rupert Debenham Chorley, *b.* 1966, *s.* 2016, *m.*	Hon. Patrick A. C. C., *b.* 2000
1815	*Churchill (7th),* Michael Richard de Charriere Spencer, *b.* 1960, *s.* 2020, *m.*	Hon. David A. de C. S., *b.* 1970
1858	*Churston (5th),* John Francis Yarde-Buller, *b.* 1934, *s.* 1991, *m.*	Hon. Benjamin F. A. Y.-B., *b.* 1974
1800 I.	*Clanmorris (8th),* Simon John Ward Bingham, *b.* 1937, *s.* 1988, *m.*	Robert D. de B. B., *b.* 1942
1672	*Clifford of Chudleigh (14th),* Thomas Hugh Clifford, *b.* 1948, *s.* 1988, *m.*	Hon. Alexander T. H. C., *b.* 1985
1299	*Clinton (22nd),* Gerard Nevile Mark Fane Trefusis, *b.* 1934, *s.* 1965, *m.*	Hon. Charles P. R. F. T., *b.* 1962
1955	*Clitheroe (2nd),* Ralph John Assheton, *b.* 1929, *s.* 1984, *m.*	Hon. Ralph C. A., *b.* 1962
1919	*Clwyd (4th),* (John) Murray Roberts, *b.* 1971, *s.* 2006, *m.*	Hon. John D. R., *b.* 2006
1948	*Clydesmuir (3rd),* David Ronald Colville, *b.* 1949, *s.* 1996, *m.*	Hon. Richard C., *b.* 1980
1960	*Cobbold (2nd),* David Antony Fromanteel Lytton Cobbold, *b.* 1937, *s.* 1987, *m.*	Hon. Henry F. L. C., *b.* 1962
1919	*Cochrane of Cults (5th),* Thomas Hunter Vere Cochrane, *b.* 1957, *s.* 2017, *m.*	Hon. Michael C. N. C., OBE, *b.* 1959
1954	*Coleraine (3rd),* James Peter Bonar Law, *b.* 1975, *s.* 2020	Hon. Andrew B. L., *b.* 1933
1873	*Coleridge (5th),* William Duke Coleridge, *b.* 1937, *s.* 1984, *w.*	Hon. James D. C., *b.* 1967
1946 **	*Colgrain (4th),* Alastair Colin Leckie Campbell, *b.* 1951, *s.* 2008, *m.*	Hon. Thomas C. D. C., *b.* 1984
1917 **	*Colwyn (3rd),* (Ian) Anthony Hamilton-Smith, CBE, *b.* 1942, *s.* 1966, *m.*	Hon. Craig P. H.-S., *b.* 1968
1956	*Colyton (2nd),* Alisdair John Munro Hopkinson, *b.* 1958, *s.* 1996, *m.*	Hon. James P. M. H., *b.* 1983
1841	*Congleton (9th),* John Patrick Christian Parnell, *b.* 1959, *s.* 2015, *m.*	Hon. Christopher J. E. P., *b.* 1987
1927	*Cornwallis (4th),* Fiennes Wykeham Jeremy Cornwallis, *b.* 1946, *s.* 2010, *m.*	Hon. Fiennes A. W. M. C., *b.* 1987
1874	*Cottesloe (6th),* Thomas Francis Henry Fremantle, *b.* 1966, *s.* 2018	Hon. Edward W. F., *b.* 1961
1929	*Craigmyle (4th),* Thomas Columba Shaw, *b.* 1960, *s.* 1998, *m.*	Hon. Alexander F. S., *b.* 1988
1899	*Cranworth (3rd),* Philip Bertram Gurdon, *b.* 1940, *s.* 1964, *m.*	Hon. Sacha W. R. G., *b.* 1970
1959 **	*Crathorne (2nd),* Charles James Dugdale, KCVO, *b.* 1939, *s.* 1977, *w.*	Hon. Thomas A. J. D., *b.* 1977
1892	*Crawshaw (5th),* David Gerald Brooks, *b.* 1934, *s.* 1997, *m.*	Hon. John P. B., *b.* 1938
1940	*Croft (3rd),* Bernard William Henry Page Croft, *b.* 1949, *s.* 1997, *m.*	None
1797 I.	*Crofton (8th),* Edward Harry Piers Crofton, *b.* 1988, *s.* 2007	Hon. Charles M. G. C., *b.* 1988
1375 **	*Cromwell (7th),* Godfrey John Bewicke-Copley, *b.* 1960, *s.* 1982, *m.*	Hon. David G. B.-C., *b.* 1997
1947	*Crook (3rd),* Robert Douglas Edwin Crook, *b.* 1955, *s.* 2001, *m.*	Hon. Matthew R. C., *b.* 1990
1920	*Cullen of Ashbourne (4th),* Michael John Cokayne, *b.* 1950, *s.* 2016, *m.*	None
1914	*Cunliffe (3rd),* Roger Cunliffe, *b.* 1932, *s.* 1963, *m.*	Hon. Henry C., *b.* 1962
1332	*Darcy de Knayth (19th),* Caspar David Ingrams, *b.* 1962, *s.* 2008	Hon. Thomas R. I., *b.* 1999
1927	*Daresbury (4th),* Peter Gilbert Greenall, *b.* 1953, *s.* 1996, *m.*	Hon. Thomas E. G., *b.* 1984
1924	*Darling (3rd),* (Robert) Julian Henry Darling, *b.* 1944, *s.* 2003, *m.*	Hon. Robert J. C. D., *b.* 1972
1946	*Darwen (4th),* David Paul Cedric Davies, *b.* 1962, *s.* 2011, *m.*	Hon. Oscar K. D., *b.* 1996
1932	*Davies (3rd),* David Davies, *b.* 1940, *s.* 1944, *w.*	Hon. David D. D., *b.* 1975
1812 I.	*Decies (7th),* Marcus Hugh Tristram de la Poer Beresford, *b.* 1948, *s.* 1992, *m.*	Hon. Robert M. D. de la P. B., *b.* 1988
1299	*de Clifford (28th),* Miles Edward Southwell Russell, *b.* 1966, *s.* 2018, *m.*	Hon. Edward S. R., *b.* 1998
1851	*De Freyne (8th),* Fulke Charles Arthur John French, *b.* 1957, *s.* 2009, *m.*	Hon. Alexander J. C. F., *b.* 1988
1821	*Delamere (5th),* Hugh George Cholmondeley, *b.* 1934, *s.* 1979, *m.*	Hugh D. C., *b.* 1998
1838 **	*de Mauley (7th),* Rupert Charles Ponsonby, TD, *b.* 1957, *s.* 2002, *m.*	Ashley G. P., *b.* 1959
1937 **	*Denham (2nd),* Bertram Stanley Mitford Bowyer, KBE, PC, *b.* 1927, *s.* 1948, *m.*	Hon. Richard G. G. B., *b.* 1959
1834	*Denman (6th),* Richard Thomas Stewart Denman, *b.* 1946, *s.* 2012, *m.*	Hon. Robert J. D., *b.* 1995
1887	*De Ramsey (4th),* John Ailwyn Fellowes, *b.* 1942, *s.* 1993, *m.*	Hon. Freddie J. F., *b.* 1978
1264	*de Ros (28th),* Peter Trevor Maxwell, *b.* 1958, *s.* 1983, *m. Premier Baron of England*	Hon. Finbar J. M., *b.* 1988
1881	*Derwent (5th),* Robin Evelyn Leo Vanden-Bempde-Johnstone, LVO, *b.* 1930, *s.* 1986, *m.*	Hon. Francis P. H. V.-B.-J., *b.* 1965
1831	*de Saumarez (7th),* Eric Douglas Saumarez, *b.* 1956, *s.* 1991, *m.*	Hon. Victor T. S., *b.* 1956
1910	*de Villiers (4th),* Alexander Charles de Villiers, *b.* 1940, *s.* 2001, *m.*	None
1930	*Dickinson (3rd),* Martin Hyett Dickinson, *b.* 1961, *s.* 2019, *m.*	Hon. Andrew D., *b.* 1963
1620 I.	*Digby (13th) and Digby (6th) (1765),* Henry Noel Kenelm Digby, *b.* 1954, *s.* 2018, *m.*	Hon. Edward St V. K. D., *b.* 1985
1615	*Dormer (18th),* William Robert Dormer, *b.* 1960, *s.* 2016, *m.*	Hon. Hugo E. G. D., *b.* 1995

1943	*Dowding (3rd)*, Piers Hugh Tremenheere Dowding, *b.* 1948, *s.* 1992, *m.*	Hon. Mark D. J. D., *b.* 1949
1439	*Dudley (15th)*, Jim Anthony Hill Wallace, *b.* 1930, *s.* 2002, *m.*	Hon. Jeremy W. G. W., *b.* 1964
1800 I.	*Dufferin and Clandeboye (11th)*, John Francis Blackwood, *b.* 1944, *s.* 1991, *m.* (claim to the peerage not yet established)	Hon. Francis S. B., *b.* 1979
1929	*Dulverton (3rd)*, (Gilbert) Michael Hamilton Wills, *b.* 1944, *s.* 1992, *m.*	Hon. Robert A. H. W., *b.* 1983
1800 I.	*Dunalley (7th)*, Henry Francis Cornelius Prittie, *b.* 1948, *s.* 1992, *m.*	Hon. Joel H. P., *b.* 1981
1324 I.	*Dunboyne (30th)*, Richard Pierce Theobald Butler, *b.* 1983, *s.* 2013, *m.*	Hon. Caspian F. B., *b.* 2020
1892	*Dunleath (6th)*, Brian Henry Mulholland, *b.* 1950, *s.* 1997, *m.*	Hon. Andrew H. M., *b.* 1981
1439 I.	*Dunsany (21st)*, Randal Plunkett, *b.* 1983, *s.* 2011	Hon. Oliver P., *b.* 1985
1780	*Dynevor (10th)*, Hugo Griffith Uryan Rhys, *b.* 1966, *s.* 2008	Robert D. A. R., *b.* 1963
1963	*Egremont (2nd) and Leconfield (7th) (1859)*, John Max Henry Scawen Wyndham, *b.* 1948, *s.* 1972, *m.*	Hon. George R. V. W., *b.* 1983
1643 S.	*Elibank (15th)*, Robert Francis Alan Erskine-Murray, *b.* 1964, *s.* 2017, *m.*	Hon. Timothy A. E. E.-M., *b.* 1967
1802	*Ellenborough (9th)*, Rupert Edward Henry Law, *b.* 1955, *s.* 2013, *m.*	Hon. James R. T. L., *b.* 1983
1509 S.	*Elphinstone (19th) and Elphinstone (5th) (1885)*, Alexander Mountstuart Elphinstone, *b.* 1980, *s.* 1994, *m.*	Master of Elphinstone, *b.* 2011
1934 **	*Elton (2nd)*, Rodney Elton, TD, *b.* 1930, *s.* 1973, *m.*	Hon. Edward P. E., *b.* 1966
1627 S. **	*Fairfax of Cameron (14th)*, Nicholas John Albert Fairfax, *b.* 1956, *s.* 1964, *m.*	Hon. Edward N. T. F., *b.* 1984
1961	*Fairhaven (3rd)*, Ailwyn Henry George Broughton, *b.* 1936, *s.* 1973, *m.*	Maj. Hon. James H. A. B., *b.* 1963
1916	*Faringdon (3rd)*, Charles Michael Henderson, KCVO, *b.* 1937, *s.* 1977, *m.*	Hon. James H. H., *b.* 1961
1756 I.	*Farnham (13th)*, Simon Kenlis Maxwell, *b.* 1933, *s.* 2001, *w.*	Hon. Robin S. M., *b.* 1965
1856 I.	*Fermoy (6th)*, Maurice Burke Roche, *b.* 1967, *s.* 1984, *m.*	Hon. E. Hugh B. R., *b.* 1972
1826	*Feversham (7th)*, Jasper Orlando Slingsby Duncombe, *b.* 1968, *s.* 2009, *m.*	Hon. Orlando B. D., *b.* 2009
1798 I.	*ffrench (8th)*, Robuck John Peter Charles Mario ffrench, *b.* 1956, *s.* 1986, *m.*	None
1909	*Fisher (4th)*, Patrick Vavasseur Fisher, *b.* 1953, *s.* 2012, *m.*	Hon. Benjamin C. V. F., *b.* 1986
1295	*Fitzwalter (22nd)*, Julian Brook Plumptre, *b.* 1952, *s.* 2004, *m.*	Hon. Edward B. P., *b.* 1989
1776	*Foley (9th)*, Thomas Henry Foley, *b.* 1961, *s.* 2012	Rupert T. F., *b.* 1970
1445 S.	*Forbes (23rd)*, Malcolm Nigel Forbes, *b.* 1946, *s.* 2013, *m. Premier Lord of Scotland*	Master of Forbes, *b.* 2010
1821	*Forester (9th)*, Charles Richard George Weld-Forester, *b.* 1975, *s.* 2004, *m.*	Hon. Brook G. P. W.-F., *b.* 2014
1922	*Forres (4th)*, Alastair Stephen Grant Williamson, *b.* 1946, *s.* 1978, *m.*	Hon. George A. M. W., *b.* 1972
1917	*Forteviot (4th)*, John James Evelyn Dewar, *b.* 1938, *s.* 1993, *w.*	Hon. Alexander J. E. D., *b.* 1971
1951 **	*Freyberg (3rd)*, Valerian Bernard Freyberg, *b.* 1970, *s.* 1993, *m.*	Hon. Joseph J. F., *b.* 2007
1917	*Gainford (3rd)*, George Pease, *b.* 1926, *s.* 2013, *w.*	Hon. Adrian C. P., *b.* 1960
1818 I.	*Garvagh (6th)*, Spencer George Stratford de Redcliffe Canning, *b.* 1953, *s.* 2013, *m.*	Hon. Stratford G. E. de R. C., *b.* 1990
1942 **	*Geddes (3rd)*, Euan Michael Ross Geddes, *b.* 1937, *s.* 1975, *m.*	Hon. James G. N. G., *b.* 1969
1876	*Gerard (5th)*, Anthony Robert Hugo Gerard, *b.* 1949, *s.* 1992	Hon. Rupert B. C. G., *b.* 1981
1824	*Gifford (6th)*, Anthony Maurice Gifford, QC, *b.* 1940, *s.* 1961, *m.*	Hon. Thomas A. G., *b.* 1967
1917	*Gisborough (3rd)*, Thomas Richard John Long Chaloner, *b.* 1927, *s.* 1951, *m.*	Hon. T. Peregrine L. C., *b.* 1961
1899	*Glanusk (5th)*, Christopher Russell Bailey, TD, *b.* 1942, *s.* 1997, *m.*	Hon. Charles H. B., *b.* 1976
1918 **	*Glenarthur (4th)*, Simon Mark Arthur, *b.* 1944, *s.* 1976, *m.*	Hon. Edward A. A., *b.* 1973
1911	*Glenconner (4th)*, Cody Charles Edward Tennant, *b.* 1994, *s.* 2010	Euan L. T., *b.* 1983
1964	*Glendevon (3rd)*, Jonathan Charles Hope, *b.* 1952, *s.* 2009	None
1922	*Glendyne (4th)*, John Nivison, *b.* 1960, *s.* 2008	None
1939	*Glentoran (3rd)*, (Thomas) Robin (Valerian) Dixon, CBE, *b.* 1935, *s.* 1995, *m.*	Hon. Daniel G. D., *b.* 1959
1909	*Gorell (5th)*, John Picton Gorell Barnes, *b.* 1959, *s.* 2007, *m.*	Hon. Oliver G. B., *b.* 1993
1953 **	*Grantchester (3rd)*, Christopher John Suenson-Taylor, *b.* 1951, *s.* 1995, *m.*	Hon. Jesse D. S.-T., *b.* 1977
1782	*Grantley (8th)*, Richard William Brinsley Norton, *b.* 1956, *s.* 1995	Hon. Francis J. H. N., *b.* 1960
1794 I.	*Graves (10th)*, Timothy Evelyn Graves, *b.* 1960, *s.* 2002, *m.*	None
1445 S.	*Gray (23rd)*, Andrew Godfrey Diarmid Stuart Campbell-Gray, *b.* 1964, *s.* 2003, *m.*	Master of Gray, *b.* 1996
1927 **	*Greenway (4th)*, Ambrose Charles Drexel Greenway, *b.* 1941, *s.* 1975, *m.*	Nicholas W. P. G., *b.* 1988
1902	*Grenfell (3rd) and Grenfell of Kilvey (life peerage, 2000)*, Julian Pascoe Francis St Leger Grenfell, *b.* 1935, *s.* 1976, *m.*	Richard A. St L. G., *b.* 1966
1944	*Gretton (4th)*, John Lysander Gretton, *b.* 1975, *s.* 1989, *m.*	Hon. John F. B. G., *b.* 2008
1397	*Grey of Codnor (6th)*, Richard Henry Cornwall-Legh, *b.* 1936, *s.* 1996, *m.*	Hon. Richard S. C. C.-L., *b.* 1976
1955	*Gridley (3rd)*, Richard David Arnold Gridley, *b.* 1956, *s.* 1996, *m.*	Peter A. C. G., *b.* 1940
1964	*Grimston of Westbury (3rd)*, Robert John Sylvester Grimston, *b.* 1951, *s.* 2003, *m.*	Hon. Gerald C. W. G., *b.* 1953
1886	*Grimthorpe (5th)*, Edward John Beckett, *b.* 1954, *s.* 2003, *m.*	Hon. Harry M. B., *b.* 1993
1945	*Hacking (3rd)*, Douglas David Hacking, *b.* 1938, *s.* 1971, *m.*	Hon. Douglas F. H., *b.* 1968
1950	*Haden-Guest (5th)*, Christopher Haden-Guest, *b.* 1948, *s.* 1996, *m.*	Hon. Nicholas H.-G., *b.* 1951
1886	*Hamilton of Dalzell (5th)*, Gavin Goulburn Hamilton, *b.* 1968, *s.* 2006, *m.*	Hon. Francis A. J. G. H., *b.* 2009
1874	*Hampton (7th)*, John Humphrey Arnott Pakington, *b.* 1964, *s.* 2003, *m.*	Hon. Charles R. C. P., *b.* 2005
1939	*Hankey (3rd)*, Donald Robin Alers Hankey, *b.* 1938, *s.* 1996, *m.*	Hon. Alexander M. A. H., *b.* 1947

1958	*Harding of Petherton (3rd)*, William Allan John Harding, *b.* 1969, *s.* 2016, *m.*	Hon. Angus J. E. H., *b.* 2001
1910	*Hardinge of Penshurst (4th)*, Julian Alexander Hardinge, *b.* 1945, *s.* 1997, *m.*	Hon. Hugh F. H., *b.* 1948
1876	*Harlech (7th)*, Jasset David Cody Ormsby-Gore, *b.* 1986, *s.* 2016	None
1939	*Harmsworth (3rd)*, Thomas Harold Raymond Harmsworth, *b.* 1939, *s.* 1990, *m.*	Hon. Dominic M. E. H., *b.* 1973
1815	*Harris (8th)*, Anthony Harris, *b.* 1942, *s.* 1996, *w.*	Rear-Adm. Michael G. T. H., *b.* 1941
1954	*Harvey of Tasburgh (3rd)*, Charles John Giuseppe Harvey, *b.* 1951, *s.* 2010, *m.*	Hon. John C. G. H., *b.* 1993
1295	*Hastings (23rd)*, Delaval Thomas Harold Astley, *b.* 1960, *s.* 2007, *m.*	Hon. Jacob A. A., *b.* 1991
1835	*Hatherton (8th)*, Edward Charles Littleton, *b.* 1950, *s.* 1985, *m.*	Hon. Thomas E. L., *b.* 1977
1776	*Hawke (12th)*, William Martin Theodore Hawke, *b.* 1995, *s.* 2009	None
1927	*Hayter (4th)*, George William Michael Chubb, *b.* 1943, *s.* 2003, *m.*	Hon. Thomas F. F. C., *b.* 1986
1945	*Hazlerigg (3rd)*, Arthur Grey Hazlerigg, *b.* 1951, *s.* 2002, *m.*	Hon. Arthur W. G. H., *b.* 1987
1943	*Hemingford (3rd)*, (Dennis) Nicholas Herbert, *b.* 1934, *s.* 1982, *w.*	Hon. Christopher D. C. H., *b.* 1973
1906	*Hemphill (6th)*, Charles Andrew Martyn Martyn-Hemphill, *b.* 1954, *s.* 2012, *m.*	Hon. Richard P. L. M.-H., *b.* 1990
1799 I. **	*Henley (8th) and Northington (6th) (1885)*, Oliver Michael Robert Eden, PC, *b.* 1953, *s.* 1977, *m.*	Hon. John W. O. E., *b.* 1988
1800 I.	*Henniker (9th) and Hartismere (6th) (1866)*, Mark Ian Philip Chandos Henniker-Major, *b.* 1947, *s.* 2004	Hon. Edward G. M. H.-M., *b.* 1985
1461	*Herbert (19th)*, David John Seyfried Herbert, *b.* 1952, *s.* 2002, *m.* Title called out of abeyance 2002	Hon. Oliver R. S. H., *b.* 1976
1935	*Hesketh (3rd)*, Thomas Alexander Fermor-Hesketh, KBE, PC, *b.* 1950, *s.* 1955, *m.*	Hon. Frederick H. F.-H., *b.* 1988
1828	*Heytesbury (7th)*, James William Holmes à Court, *b.* 1967, *s.* 2004, *w.*	Peter M. H. H. à. C., *b.* 1968
1886	*Hindlip (6th)*, Charles Henry Allsopp, *b.* 1940, *s.* 1993, *w.*	Hon. Henry W. A., *b.* 1973
1950	*Hives (3rd)*, Matthew Peter Hives, *b.* 1971, *s.* 1997, *m.*	Robert G. H., *b.* 1953
1912	*Hollenden (4th)*, Ian Hampden Hope-Morley, *b.* 1946, *s.* 1999, *m.*	Hon. Edward H.-M., *b.* 1981
1897	*Holm Patrick (4th)*, Hans James David Hamilton, *b.* 1955, *s.* 1991, *m.*	Hon. Ion H. J. H., *b.* 1956
1797 I.	*Hotham (8th)*, Henry Durand Hotham, *b.* 1940, *s.* 1967, *m.*	Hon. William B. H., *b.* 1972
1881	*Hothfield (6th)*, Anthony Charles Sackville Tufton, *b.* 1939, *s.* 1991, *m.*	Hon. William S. T., *b.* 1977
1930	*Howard of Penrith (3rd)*, Philip Esme Howard, *b.* 1945, *s.* 1999, *m.*	Hon. Thomas P. H., *b.* 1974
1960	*Howick of Glendale (2nd)*, Charles Evelyn Baring, *b.* 1937, *s.* 1973, *m.*	Hon. David E. C. B., *b.* 1975
1796 I.	*Huntingfield (7th)*, Joshua Charles Vanneck, *b.* 1954, *s.* 1994, *w.*	Hon. Gerard C. A. V., *b.* 1985
1866 **	*Hylton (5th)*, Raymond Hervey Jolliffe, *b.* 1932, *s.* 1967, *m.*	Hon. William H. M. J., *b.* 1967
1933	*Iliffe (3rd)*, Robert Peter Richard Iliffe, *b.* 1944, *s.* 1996, *m.*	Hon. Edward R. I., *b.* 1968
1543 I.	*Inchiquin (18th)*, Conor Myles John O'Brien, *b.* 1943, *s.* 1982, *m.*	Conor J. A. O'B., *b.* 1952
1962	*Inchyra (3rd)*, Christian James Charles Hoyer Millar, *b.* 1962, *s.* 2011, *m.*	Hon. Jake C. R. M., *b.* 1996
1964 **	*Inglewood (2nd)*, (William) Richard Fletcher-Vane, *b.* 1951, *s.* 1989, *m.*	Hon. Henry W. F. F.-V., *b.* 1990
1919	*Inverforth (4th)*, Andrew Peter Weir, *b.* 1966, *s.* 1982, *m.*	Hon. Benjamin A. W., *b.* 1997
1941	*Ironside (3rd)*, Charles Edmund Grenville Ironside, *b.* 1956, *s.* 2020, *m.*	Hon. Frederick T. G. I., *b.* 1991
1952	*Jeffreys (3rd)*, Christopher Henry Mark Jeffreys, *b.* 1957, *s.* 1986, *m.*	Hon. Arthur M. H. J., *b.* 1989
1906	*Joicey (5th)*, James Michael Joicey, *b.* 1953, *s.* 1993, *m.*	Hon. William J. J., *b.* 1990
1937	*Kenilworth (4th)*, (John) Randle Siddeley, *b.* 1954, *s.* 1981, *m.*	Hon. William R. J. S., *b.* 1992
1935	*Kennet (3rd)*, William Aldus Thoby Young, *b.* 1957, *s.* 2009	Hon. Archibald W. K. Y., *b.* 1992
1776 I.	*Kensington (9th) and Kensington (6th) (1886)*, William Owen Edwardes, *b.* 1964, *s.* 2018, *m.*	Hon. William F. I. E., *b.* 1993
1951	*Kenswood (3rd)*, Michael Christopher Whitfield, *b.* 1955, *s.* 2016, *m.*	Hon. Anthony J. W., *b.* 1957
1788	*Kenyon (7th)*, Lloyd Nicholas Tyrell-Kenyon, *b.* 1972, *s.* 2019	Hon. Alexander S. T.-K., *b.* 1975
1947	*Kershaw (4th)*, Edward John Kershaw, *b.* 1936, *s.* 1962, *m.*	Hon. John C. E. K., *b.* 1971
1943	*Keyes (3rd)*, Charles William Packe Keyes, *b.* 1951, *s.* 2005, *m.*	Hon. (Leopold R.) J. K., *b.* 1956
1909	*Kilbracken (4th)*, Christopher John Godley, *b.* 1945, *s.* 2006, *m.*	Hon. James J. G., *b.* 1972
1900	*Killanin (4th)*, (George) Redmond Fitzpatrick Morris, *b.* 1947, *s.* 1999, *m.*	Hon. Luke M. G. M., *b.* 1975
1943	*Killearn (3rd)*, Victor Miles George Aldous Lampson, *b.* 1941, *s.* 1996, *m.*	Hon. Miles H. M. L., *b.* 1977
1789 I.	*Kilmaine (8th)*, John Francis Sandford Browne, *b.* 1983, *s.* 2013	Mark Caulfield-Browne, *b.* 1966
1831	*Kilmarnock (8th)*, Dr Robin Jordan Boyd, *b.* 1941, *s.* 2009, *m.*	Hon. Simon J. B., *b.* 1978
1941	*Kindersley (4th)*, Rupert John Molesworth Kindersley, *b.* 1955, *s.* 2013, *m.*	Hon. Frederick H. M. K., *b.* 1987
1223 I.	*Kingsale (36th)*, Nevinson Mark de Courcy, *b.* 1958, *s.* 2005 *Premier Baron of Ireland*	Joseph K. C. de C., *b.* 1955
1902	*Kinross (5th)*, Christopher Patrick Balfour, *b.* 1949, *s.* 1985, *m.*	Hon. Alan I. B., *b.* 1978
1951	*Kirkwood (3rd)*, David Harvie Kirkwood, PHD, *b.* 1931, *s.* 1970, *m.*	Hon. James S. K., *b.* 1937
1800 I.	*Langford (10th)*, Owain Grenville Rowley-Conwy, *b.* 1958, *s.* 2017, *m.*	Hon. Thomas A. R.-C., *b.* 1987
1942	*Latham (2nd)*, Dominic Charles Latham, *b.* 1954, *s.* 1970	Anthony M. L., *b.* 1954
1431	*Latymer (9th)*, Crispin James Alan Nevill Money-Coutts, *b.* 1955, *s.* 2003, *m.*	Hon. Drummond W. T. M.-C., *b.* 1986
1869	*Lawrence (5th)*, David John Downer Lawrence, *b.* 1937, *s.* 1968	None
1947	*Layton (4th)*, Jonathan Francis Layton, *b.* 1942, *s.* 2018, *m.*	Hon. Jeremy S. L., *b.* 1978
1839	*Leigh (6th)*, Christopher Dudley Piers Leigh, *b.* 1960, *s.* 2003	Hon. Rupert D. L., *b.* 1994

1962	*Leighton of St Mellons (3rd)*, Robert William Henry Leighton Seager, *b.* 1955, *s.* 1998, *m.*	Hon. Simon J. L. S., *b.* 1957
1797	*Lilford (8th)*, Mark Vernon Powys, *b.* 1975, *s.* 2005, *m.*	Michael J. P., *b.* 1934
1945	*Lindsay of Birker (3rd)*, James Francis Lindsay, *b.* 1945, *s.* 1994, *m.*	Alexander S. L., *b.* 1940
1758 I.	*Lisle (9th)*, (John) Nicholas Geoffrey Lysaght, *b.* 1960, *s.* 2003	Hon. David J. L., *b.* 1963
1850	*Londesborough (9th)*, Richard John Denison, *b.* 1959, *s.* 1968, *m.*	Hon. James F. D., *b.* 1990
1541 I.	*Louth (17th)*, Jonathan Oliver Plunkett, *b.* 1952, *s.* 2013	Hon. Matthew O. P., *b.* 1982
1458 S.	*Lovat (16th) and Lovat (5th) (1837)*, Simon Christopher Joseph Fraser, *b.* 1977, *s.* 1995, *m.*	Hon. Jack H. F., *b.* 1984
1946	*Lucas of Chilworth (3rd)*, Simon William Lucas, *b.* 1957, *s.* 2001, *m.*	Hon. John R. M. L., *b.* 1995
1663 **	*Lucas (11th) and Dingwall (8th) (S. 1609)*, Ralph Matthew Palmer, *b.* 1951, *s.* 1991, *m.*	Hon. Lewis E. P., *b.* 1987
1929	*Luke (4th)*, Ian James St John Lawson Johnston, *b.* 1963, *s.* 2016, *m.*	Hon. Samuel A. J. St J. L. J., *b.* 2000
1859	*Lyveden (8th)*, Colin Ronald Vernon, *b.* 1967, *s.* 2017, *m.*	Hon. Robert H. V., *b.* 1942
1959	*MacAndrew (3rd)*, Christopher Anthony Colin MacAndrew, *b.* 1945, *s.* 1989	Hon. Oliver C. J. M., *b.* 1983
1776 I.	*Macdonald (8th)*, Godfrey James Macdonald of Macdonald, *b.* 1947, *s.* 1970, *m.*	Hon. Godfrey E. H. T. M., *b.* 1982
1937	*McGowan (4th)*, Harry John Charles McGowan, *b.* 1971, *s.* 2003, *m.*	Hon. Dominic J. W. M., *b.* 1951
1922	*Maclay (3rd)*, Joseph Paton Maclay, *b.* 1942, *s.* 1969, *m.*	Hon. Joseph P. M., *b.* 1977
1955	*McNair (3rd)*, Duncan James McNair, *b.* 1947, *s.* 1989, *m.*	Hon. William S. A. M., *b.* 1958
1951	*Macpherson of Drumochter (3rd)*, James Anthony Macpherson, *b.* 1979, *s.* 2008, *m.*	Hon. Daniel T. M., *b.* 2013
1937 **	*Mancroft (3rd)*, Benjamin Lloyd Stormont Mancroft, *b.* 1957, *s.* 1987, *m.*	Hon. Arthur L. S. M., *b.* 1995
1807	*Manners (6th)*, John Hugh Robert Manners, *b.* 1956, *s.* 2008, *m.*	Hon. John A. D. M., *b.* 2011
1922	*Manton (4th)*, Miles Ronald Marcus Watson, *b.* 1958, *s.* 2003, *m.*	Hon. Thomas N. C. D. W., *b.* 1985
1908	*Marchamley (4th)*, William Francis Whiteley, *b.* 1968, *s.* 1994, *m.*	Hon. Leon W., *b.* 2004
1965	*Margadale (3rd)*, Alastair John Morrison, *b.* 1958, *s.* 2003, *m.*	Hon. Declan J. M., *b.* 1993
1961	*Marks of Broughton (3rd)*, Simon Richard Marks, *b.* 1950, *s.* 1998, *m.*	Hon. Michael M., *b.* 1989
1964	*Martonmere (2nd)*, John Stephen Robinson, *b.* 1963, *s.* 1989, *m.*	Hon. James I. R., *b.* 2003
1776 I.	*Massy (10th)*, David Hamon Somerset Massy, *b.* 1947, *s.* 1995	Hon. John H. S. M., *b.* 1950
1935	*May (4th)*, Jasper Bertram St John May, *b.* 1965, *s.* 2006, *m.*	None
1925	*Merrivale (4th)*, Derek John Philip Duke, *b.* 1948, *s.* 2007, *m.*	Hon. Thomas D., *b.* 1980
1911	*Merthyr (5th)*, David Trevor Lewis, *b.* 1977, *s.* 2015, *m.*	Hon. Peter H. L., *b.* 1937
1919	*Meston (3rd)*, James Meston, QC, *b.* 1950, *s.* 1984, *m.*	Hon. Thomas J. D. M., *b.* 1977
1838	*Methuen (8th)*, James Paul Archibald Methuen-Campbell, *b.* 1952, *s.* 2014	Thomas R. M. M.-C., *b.* 1977
1711	*Middleton (13th)*, Michael Charles James Willoughby, *b.* 1948, *s.* 2011, *m.*	Hon. James W. M. W., *b.* 1976
1939	*Milford (4th)*, Guy Wogan Philipps, QC, *b.* 1961, *s.* 1999, *m.*	Hon. Archie S. P., *b.* 1997
1933	*Milne (3rd)*, George Alexander Milne, *b.* 1941, *s.* 2005	Hon. Iain C. L. M., *b.* 1949
1951	*Milner of Leeds (3rd)*, Richard James Milner, *b.* 1959, *s.* 2003, *m.*	None
1947	*Milverton (2nd)*, Revd Fraser Arthur Richard Richards, *b.* 1930, *s.* 1978, *w.*	Hon. Michael H. R., *b.* 1936
1873	*Moncreiff (6th)*, Rhoderick Harry Wellwood Moncreiff, *b.* 1954, *s.* 2002, *m.*	Hon. Harry J. W. M., *b.* 1986
1884	*Monk Bretton (3rd)*, John Charles Dodson, *b.* 1924, *s.* 1933, *m.*	Hon. Christopher M. D., *b.* 1958
1885	*Monkswell (6th)*, James Adrian Collier, *b.* 1977, *s.* 2020	Hon. Robert W. G. C., *b.* 1979
1728	*Monson (12th)*, Nicholas John Monson, *b.* 1955, *s.* 2011, *m.*	Hon. Andrew A. J. M., *b.* 1959
1885	*Montagu of Beaulieu (4th)*, Ralph Douglas-Scott-Montagu, *b.* 1961, *s.* 2015, *m.*	Hon. Jonathan D. D.-S.-M., *b.* 1975
1839	*Monteagle of Brandon (7th)*, Charles James Spring Rice, *b.* 1953, *s.* 2013, *m.*	Hon. Michael S. R., *b.* 1935
1943	*Moran (3rd)*, James McMoran Wilson, *b.* 1952, *s.* 2014, *m.*	Hon. David A. M. W., *b.* 1990
1918	*Morris (4th)*, Thomas Anthony Salmon Morris, *b.* 1982, *s.* 2011	Hon. John M. M., *b.* 1983
1950	*Morris of Kenwood (3rd)*, Jonathan David Morris, *b.* 1968, *s.* 2004, *m.*	Hon. Benjamin J. M., *b.* 1998
1831	*Mostyn (7th)*, Gregory Philip Roger Lloyd-Mostyn, *b.* 1984, *s.* 2011	Roger H. L.-M., *b.* 1941
1933	*Mottistone (6th)*, Christopher David Peter Seely, *b.* 1974, *s.* 2013	Hon. Richard W. A. S., *b.* 1988
1945 **	*Mountevans (4th)*, Jeffrey Richard de Corban Evans, *b.* 1948, *s.* 2014, *m.*	Hon. Alexander R. A. E., *b.* 1975
1283	*Mowbray (27th), Segrave (28th) (1295) and Stourton (24th) (1448)*, Edward William Stephen Stourton, *b.* 1953, *s.* 2006, *m.*	Hon. James C. P. S., *b.* 1991
1932	*Moyne (3rd)*, Jonathan Bryan Guinness, *b.* 1930, *s.* 1992, *m.*	Hon. Valentine G. B. G., *b.* 1959
1929 **	*Moynihan (4th)*, Colin Berkeley Moynihan, *b.* 1955, *s.* 1997	Hon. Nicholas E. B. M., *b.* 1994
1781 I.	*Muskerry (9th)*, Robert Fitzmaurice Deane, *b.* 1948, *s.* 1988, *m.*	Hon. Jonathan F. D., *b.* 1986
1627 S.	*Napier (15th) and Ettrick (6th) (1872)*, Francis David Charles Napier, *b.* 1962, *s.* 2012, *m.*	Master of Napier, *b.* 1996
1868	*Napier of Magdala (6th)*, Robert Alan Napier, *b.* 1940, *s.* 1987, *m.*	Hon. James R. N., *b.* 1966
1940	*Nathan (3rd)*, Rupert Harry Bernard Nathan, *b.* 1957, *s.* 2007, *m.*	Hon. Alasdair H. St J. N., *b.* 1999
1960	*Nelson of Stafford (4th)*, Alistair William Henry Nelson, *b.* 1973, *s.* 2006, *m.*	Hon. James J. N., *b.* 1947
1959	*Netherthorpe (3rd)*, James Frederick Turner, *b.* 1964, *s.* 1982, *m.*	Hon. Andrew J. E. T., *b.* 1993
1946	*Newall (2nd)*, Francis Storer Eaton Newall, *b.* 1930, *s.* 1963, *m.*	Hon. Richard H. E. N., *b.* 1961
1776 I.	*Newborough (8th)*, Robert Vaughan Wynn, *b.* 1949, *s.* 1998, *m.*	Antony C. V. W., *b.* 1949
1892	*Newton (5th)*, Richard Thomas Legh, *b.* 1950, *s.* 1992, *m.*	Hon. Piers R. L., *b.* 1979

1930	*Noel-Buxton (4th)*, Charles Connal Noel-Buxton, *b.* 1975, *s.* 2013	Hon. Simon C. N.-B., *b.* 1943
1957	*Norrie (2nd)*, (George) Willoughby Moke Norrie, *b.* 1936, *s.* 1977, *m.*	Hon. Mark W. J. N., *b.* 1972
1884	*Northbourne (6th)*, Charles Walter Henri James, *b.* 1960, *s.* 2019, *m.*	Hon. Christopher W. J., *b.* 1988
1866 **	*Northbrook (6th)*, Francis Thomas Baring, *b.* 1954, *s.* 1990, *m.*	To the Baronetcy, Peter B., *b.* 1939
1878	*Norton (8th)*, James Nigel Arden Adderley, *b.* 1947, *s.* 1993, *m.*	Hon. Edward J. A. A., *b.* 1982
1906	*Nunburnholme (6th)*, Stephen Charles Yanath Wilson, *b.* 1973, *s.* 2000, *m.*	Hon. Charles T. C. W., *b.* 2002
1950	*Ogmore (4th)*, Tudor David Rees-Williams, *b.* 1991, *s.* 2004,	Hon. Dylane R.-W., *b.* 1994
1870	*O'Hagan (4th)*, Charles Towneley Strachey, *b.* 1945, *s.* 1961, *m.*	Hon. Richard T. S., *b.* 1950
1868	*O'Neill (4th)*, Raymond Arthur Clanaboy O'Neill, KCVO, TD, *b.* 1933, *s.* 1944, *w.*	Hon. Shane S. C. O'N., *b.* 1965
1836 I.	*Oranmore and Browne (5th) and Mereworth (3rd) (1926)*, Dominick Geoffrey Thomas Browne, *b.* 1929, *s.* 2002	Shaun D. B., *b.* 1964
1933 **	*Palmer (4th)*, Adrian Bailie Nottage Palmer, *b.* 1951, *s.* 1990	Hon. Hugo B. R. P., *b.* 1980
1914	*Parmoor (5th)*, Michael Leonard Seddon Cripps, *b.* 1942, *s.* 2008, *m.*	Hon. Henry W. A. C., *b.* 1976
1937	*Pender (4th)*, Henry John Richard Denison-Pender, *b.* 1968, *s.* 2016, *m.*	Hon. Miles J. C. D.-P., *b.* 2000
1866	*Penrhyn (7th)*, Simon Douglas-Pennant, *b.* 1938, *s.* 2003, *m.*	Hon. Edward S. D.-P., *b.* 1966
1603	*Petre (18th)*, John Patrick Lionel Petre, KCVO, *b.* 1942, *s.* 1989, *m.*	Hon. Dominic W. P., *b.* 1966
1918	*Phillimore (5th)*, Francis Stephen Phillimore, *b.* 1944, *s.* 1994, *m.*	Hon. Tristan A. S. P., *b.* 1977
1945	*Piercy (3rd)*, James William Piercy, *b.* 1946, *s.* 1981	Hon. Mark E. P. P., *b.* 1953
1827	*Plunket (9th)*, Tyrone Shaun Terence Plunket, *b.* 1966, *s.* 2013, *m.*	Hon. Rory P. R. P., *b.* 2001
1831	*Poltimore (7th)*, Mark Coplestone Bampfylde, *b.* 1957, *s.* 1978, *m.*	Hon. Henry A. W. B., *b.* 1985
1690 S.	*Polwarth (11th)*, Andrew Walter Hepburne-Scott, *b.* 1947, *s.* 2005, *m.*	Master of Polwarth, *b.* 1973
1930	*Ponsonby of Shulbrede (4th) and Ponsonby of Roehampton (life peerage, 2000)*, Frederick Matthew Thomas Ponsonby, *b.* 1958, *s.* 1990, *m.*	Hon. Cameron J. J. P., *b.* 1995
1958	*Poole (2nd)*, David Charles Poole, *b.* 1945, *s.* 1993, *m.*	Hon. Oliver J. P., *b.* 1972
1852	*Raglan (6th)*, Geoffrey Somerset, *b.* 1932, *s.* 2010, *w.*	Inigo A. F. S., *b.* 2004
1932	*Rankeillour (5th)*, Michael Richard Hope, *b.* 1940, *s.* 2005, *w.*	Hon. James F. H., *b.* 1968
1953	*Rathcavan (3rd)*, Hugh Detmar Torrens O'Neill, *b.* 1939, *s.* 1994, *m.*	Hon. François H. N. O'N., *b.* 1984
1916	*Rathcreedan (3rd)*, Christopher John Norton, *b.* 1949, *s.* 1990, *m.*	Hon. Adam G. N., *b.* 1952
1868 I.	*Rathdonnell (5th)*, Thomas Benjamin McClintock-Bunbury, *b.* 1938, *s.* 1959, *m.*	Hon. William L. M.-B., *b.* 1966
1911**	*Ravensdale (4th)*, Daniel Nicholas Mosley, *b.* 1982, *s.* 2017, *m.*	Hon. Alexander L. M., *b.* 2012
1821	*Ravensworth (9th)*, Thomas Arthur Hamish Liddell, *b.* 1954, *s.* 2004, *m.*	Hon. Henry A. T. L., *b.* 1987
1821	*Rayleigh (6th)*, John Gerald Strutt, *b.* 1960, *s.* 1988, *m.*	Hon. John F. S., *b.* 1993
1937	*Rea (4th)*, Matthew James Rea, *b.* 1956, *s.* 1981, *m.*	Hon. Daniel W. R., *b.* 1958
1628 S.**	*Reay (15th)*, Aeneas Simon Mackay, *b.* 1965, *s.* 2013, *m.*	Master of Reay, *b.* 2010
1902	*Redesdale (6th) and Mitford (life peerage, 2000)*, Rupert Bertram Mitford, *b.* 1967, *s.* 1991, *m.*	Hon. Bertram D. M., *b.* 2000
1940	*Reith (3rd)*, James Harry John Reith, *b.* 1971, *s.* 2016, *m.*	Hon. Harry J. J. R., *b.* 2006
1928	*Remnant (3rd)*, James Wogan Remnant, CVO, *b.* 1930, *s.* 1967, *m.*	Hon. Philip J. R., CBE, *b.* 1954
1806 I.	*Rendlesham (9th)*, Charles William Brooke Thellusson, *b.* 1954, *s.* 1999, *m.*	James H. T., *b.* 1961
1933	*Rennell (4th)*, James Roderick David Tremayne Rodd, *b.* 1978, *s.* 2006	None
1964	*Renwick (3rd)*, Robert James Renwick, *b.* 1966, *s.* 2020	Hon. Michael D. R., *b.* 1968
1885	*Revelstoke (7th)*, Alexander Rupert Baring, *b.* 1970, *s.* 2012	Hon. Thomas J. B., *b.* 1971
1905	*Ritchie of Dundee (6th)*, Charles Rupert Rendall Ritchie, *b.* 1958, *s.* 2008, *m.*	Hon. Sebastian R., *b.* 2004
1935	*Riverdale (3rd)*, Anthony Robert Balfour, *b.* 1960, *s.* 1998	Arthur M. B., *b.* 1938
1961	*Robertson of Oakridge (3rd)*, William Brian Elworthy Robertson, *b.* 1975, *s.* 2009	None
1938	*Roborough (4th)*, Massey John Henry Lopes, *b.* 1969, *s.* 2015, *m.*	Hon. Henry M. P. L., *b.* 1997
1931	*Rochester (3rd)*, David Charles Lamb, *b.* 1944, *s.* 2017, *m.*	Hon. Daniel L., *b.* 1971
1934	*Rockley (4th)*, Anthony Robert Cecil, *b.* 1961, *s.* 2011, *m.*	Hon. William E. C., *b.* 1996
1782	*Rodney (11th)*, John George Brydges Rodney, *b.* 1999, *s.* 2011	Nicholas S. H. R., *b.* 1947
1651 S.	*Rollo (14th) and Dunning (5th) (1869)*, David Eric Howard Rollo, *b.* 1943, *s.* 1997, *m.*	Master of Rollo, *b.* 1972
1959	*Rootes (3rd)*, Nicholas Geoffrey Rootes, *b.* 1951, *s.* 1992, *m.*	William B. R., *b.* 1944
1796 I.	*Rossmore (7th) and Rossmore (6th) (1838)*, William Warner Westenra, *b.* 1931, *s.* 1958, *m.*	Hon. Benedict W. W., *b.* 1983
1939 **	*Rotherwick (3rd)*, (Herbert) Robin Cayzer, *b.* 1954, *s.* 1996, *m.*	Hon. H. Robin C., *b.* 1989
1885	*Rothschild (4th)*, (Nathaniel Charles) Jacob Rothschild, OM, GBE, CVO, *b.* 1936, *s.* 1990, *w.*	Hon. Nathaniel P. V. J. R., *b.* 1971
1911	*Rowallan (4th)*, John Polson Cameron Corbett, *b.* 1947, *s.* 1993, *m.*	Hon. Jason W. P. C. C., *b.* 1972
1947	*Rugby (3rd)*, Robert Charles Maffey, *b.* 1951, *s.* 1990, *m.*	Hon. Timothy J. H. M., *b.* 1975
1919 **	*Russell of Liverpool (3rd)*, Simon Gordon Jared Russell, *b.* 1952, *s.* 1981, *m.*	Hon. Edward C. S. R., *b.* 1985
1876	*Sackville (7th)*, Robert Bertrand Sackville-West, *b.* 1958, *s.* 2004, *m.*	Hon. Arthur G. S.-W., *b.* 2000
1964	*St Helens (2nd)*, Richard Francis Hughes-Young, *b.* 1945, *s.* 1980, *w.*	Hon. Henry T. H.-Y., *b.* 1986
1559 **	*St John of Bletso (21st)*, Anthony Tudor St John, *b.* 1957, *s.* 1978, *m.*	Hon. Oliver B. St J., *b.* 1995
1887	*St Levan (5th)*, James Piers Southwell St Aubyn, *b.* 1950, *s.* 2013, *m.*	Hon. Hugh J. St A., *b.* 1983
1885	*St Oswald (6th)*, Charles Rowland Andrew Winn, *b.* 1959, *s.* 1999, *m.*	Hon. Rowland C. S. H. W., *b.* 1986

1960	*Sanderson of Ayot (2nd)*, Alan Lindsay Sanderson, *b.* 1931, *s.* 1971, *m.* Disclaimed for life 1971.	Hon. Michael S., *b.* 1959
1945	*Sandford (3rd)*, James John Mowbray Edmondson, *b.* 1949, *s.* 2009, *w.*	Hon. Devon J. E., *b.* 1986
1871	*Sandhurst (6th)*, Guy Rhys John Mansfield, QC, *b.* 1949, *s.* 2002, *m.*	Hon. Edward J. M., *b.* 1982
1888	*Savile (4th)*, John Anthony Thornhill Lumley-Savile, *b.* 1947, *s.* 2008, *m.*	Hon. James G. A. L.-S., *b.* 1975
1447	*Saye and Sele (21st)*, Nathaniel Thomas Allen Fiennes, *b.* 1920, *s.* 1968, *m.*	Hon. Martin G. F., *b.* 1961
1826	*Seaford (6th)*, Colin Humphrey Felton Ellis, *b.* 1946, *s.* 1999, *m.*	Hon. Benjamin F. T. Ellis-Goodbody, *b.* 1976
1932 **	*Selsdon (3rd)*, Malcolm McEacharn Mitchell-Thomson, *b.* 1937, *s.* 1963, *m.*	Hon. Callum M. M. M.-T., *b.* 1969
1489 S.	*Sempill (21st)*, James William Stuart Whitemore Sempill, *b.* 1949, *s.* 1995, *m.*	Master of Sempill, *b.* 1979
1916	*Shaughnessy (5th)*, Charles George Patrick Shaughnessy, *b.* 1955, *s.* 2007, *m.*	David J. B. S., *b.* 1957
1946	*Shepherd (3rd)*, Graeme George Shepherd, *b.* 1949, *s.* 2001, *m.*	Hon. Patrick M. S., *b.* 1980
1964	*Sherfield (3rd)*, Dwight William Makins, *b.* 1951, *s.* 2006, *m.*	None
1902	*Shuttleworth (5th)*, Charles Geoffrey Nicholas Kay-Shuttleworth, KG, KCVO, *b.* 1948, *s.* 1975, *m.*	Hon. Thomas E. K.-S., *b.* 1976
1950	*Silkin (3rd)*, Christopher Lewis Silkin, *b.* 1947, *s.* 2001. Disclaimed for life 2002.	Rory L. S., *b.* 1954
1963	*Silsoe (3rd)*, Simon Rupert Trustram Eve, *b.* 1966, *s.* 2005	Hon. Peter N. T. E., OBE, *b.* 1930
1947	*Simon of Wythenshawe (3rd)*, Matthew Simon, *b.* 1955, *s.* 2002, *w.* In dormancy since 2016 when the 3rd baron officially reassigned his gender.	Michael B. S., *b.* 1970
1449 S.	*Sinclair (18th)*, Matthew Murray Kennedy St Clair, *b.* 1968, *s.* 2004, *m.*	Master of Sinclair, *b.* 2007
1957	*Sinclair of Cleeve (3rd)*, John Lawrence Robert Sinclair, *b.* 1953, *s.* 1985, *m.*	None
1919	*Sinha (6th)*, Arup Kumar Sinha, *b.* 1966, *s.* 1999, *m.*	Hon. Dilip K. S., *b.* 1967
1828	*Skelmersdale (8th)*, Andrew Bootle-Wilbraham, *b.* 1977, *s.* 2018, *m.*	Hon. Daniel P. B.-W., *b.* 2007
1916	*Somerleyton (4th)*, Hugh Francis Saville Crossley, *b.* 1971, *s.* 2012, *m.*	Hon. John de B. T. S. C., *b.* 2010
1784	*Somers (9th)*, Philip Sebastian Somers Cocks, *b.* 1948, *s.* 1995	Jonathan B. C., *b.* 1985
1780	*Southampton (7th)*, Edward Charles FitzRoy, *b.* 1955, *s.* 2015, *m.*	Hon. Charles E. M. F., *b.* 1983
1959	*Spens (4th)*, Patrick Nathaniel George Spens, *b.* 1968, *s.* 2001	Hon. Peter L. S., *b.* 2000
1640	*Stafford (15th)*, Francis Melfort William Fitzherbert, *b.* 1954, *s.* 1986, *m.*	Hon. Benjamin J. B. F., *b.* 1983
1938	*Stamp (4th)*, Trevor Charles Bosworth Stamp, MD, *b.* 1935, *s.* 1987	Hon. Nicholas C. T. S., *b.* 1978
1839	*Stanley of Alderley (9th)*, Sheffield (9th) (I. 1738) and Eddisbury (8th) (1848), Richard Oliver Stanley, *b.* 1956, *s.* 2013, *m.*	Hon. Charles E. S., *b.* 1960
1318	*Strabolgi (12th)*, Andrew David Whitley Kenworthy, *b.* 1967, *s.* 2010, *m.*	Hon. Joel B. K., *b.* 2004
1628	*Strange (17th)*, Adam Humphrey Drummond of Megginch, *b.* 1953, *s.* 2005, *m.*	Hon. John A. H. D. of M., *b.* 1992
1955	*Strathalmond (3rd)*, William Roberton Fraser, *b.* 1947, *s.* 1976, *m.*	Hon. William G. F., *b.* 1976
1936	*Strathcarron (3rd)*, Ian David Patrick Macpherson, *b.* 1949, *s.* 2006, *m.*	Hon. Rory D. A. M., *b.* 1982
1955 **	*Strathclyde (2nd)*, Thomas Galloway Dunlop du Roy de Blicquy Galbraith, CH, PC, *b.* 1960, *s.* 1985, *m.*	Hon. Charles W. du R. de B. G., *b.* 1962
1900	*Strathcona and Mount Royal (5th)*, Donald Alexander Smith Howard, *b.* 1961, *s.* 2018, *m.*	Hon. Donald A. R. H., *b.* 1994
1836	*Stratheden (7th) and Campbell (7th) (1841)*, David Anthony Campbell, *b.* 1963, *s.* 2011, *m.*	None
1884	*Strathspey (6th)*, James Patrick Trevor Grant of Grant, *b.* 1943, *s.* 1992	Hon. Michael P. F. G., *b.* 1953
1838	*Sudeley (7th)*, Merlin Charles Sainthill Hanbury-Tracy, *b.* 1939, *s.* 1941, *m.*	Nicholas E. J. H.-T., *b.* 1959
1786	*Suffield (13th)*, John Edward Richard Harbord-Hamond, *b.* 1956, *s.* 2016, *m.*	Hon. Sam C. A. H.-H., *b.* 1989
1893	*Swansea (5th)*, Richard Anthony Hussey Vivian, *b.* 1957, *s.* 2005, *m.*	Hon. James H. H. V., *b.* 1999
1907	*Swaythling (5th)*, Charles Edgar Samuel Montagu, *b.* 1954, *s.* 1998, *m.*	Rupert A. S. M., *b.* 1965
1919 **	*Swinfen (3rd)*, Roger Mynors Swinfen Eady, MBE, *b.* 1938, *s.* 1977, *m.*	Hon. Charles R. P. S. E., *b.* 1971
1831 I.	*Talbot of Malahide (11th)*, Richard John Tennant Arundell, *b.* 1957, *s.* 2016, *m.*	Hon. John R. A., *b.* 1998
1946	*Tedder (3rd)*, Robin John Tedder, *b.* 1955, *s.* 1994, *m.*	Hon. Benjamin J. T., *b.* 1985
1884	*Tennyson (6th)*, David Harold Alexander Tennyson, *b.* 1960, *s.* 2006	Alan J. D. T., *b.* 1965
1918	*Terrington (6th)*, Christopher Richard James Woodhouse, MB, *b.* 1946, *s.* 2001, *m.*	Hon. Jack H. L. W., *b.* 1978
1940	*Teviot (2nd)*, Charles John Kerr, *b.* 1934, *s.* 1968, *m.*	Hon. Charles R. K., *b.* 1971
1616	*Teynham (20th)*, John Christopher Ingham Roper-Curzon, *b.* 1928, *s.* 1972, *m.*	Hon. David J. H. I. R.-C., *b.* 1965
1964	*Thomson of Fleet (3rd)*, David Kenneth Roy Thomson, *b.* 1957, *s.* 2006	Hon. Benjamin J. L. T., *b.* 2006
1792 **	*Thurlow (9th)*, Roualeyn Robert Hovell-Thurlow-Cumming-Bruce, *b.* 1952, *s.* 2013, *m.*	Hon. Nicholas E. H.-T.-C.-B., *b.* 1986
1876	*Tollemache (5th)*, Timothy John Edward Tollemache, KCVO, *b.* 1939, *s.* 1975, *m.*	Hon. Edward J. H. T., *b.* 1976
1564 S.	*Torphichen (15th)*, James Andrew Douglas Sandilands, *b.* 1946, *s.* 1975, *m.*	Robert P. S., *b.* 1950
1947 **	*Trefgarne (2nd)*, David Garro Trefgarne, PC, *b.* 1941, *s.* 1960, *m.*	Hon. George G. T., *b.* 1970
1921 **	*Trevethin (and Oaksey (3rd) (1947)*, Patrick John Tristram Lawrence, QC, *b.* 1960, *s.* 2012, *m.*	Hon. Oliver J. T. L., *b.* 1990
1880	*Trevor (5th)*, Marke Charles Hill-Trevor, *b.* 1970, *s.* 1997	Hon. Iain R. H.-T., *b.* 1971
1461 I.	*Trimlestown (21st)*, Raymond Charles Barnewall, *b.* 1930, *s.* 1997	None

1940	*Tryon (4th)*, Charles George Barrington Tryon, *b.* 1976, *s.* 2018, *m.*	Hon. Guy A. G. T., *b.* 2015
1935	*Tweedsmuir (4th)*, John William de l'Aigle (Toby) Buchan, *b.* 1950, *s.* 2008, *m.*	Hon. John A. G. B., *b.* 1986
1523 **	*Vaux of Harrowden (12th)*, Richard Hubert Gordon Gilbey, *b.* 1965, *s.* 2014, *m.*	Hon. Alexander J. C. G., *b.* 2000
1800 I.	*Ventry (8th)*, Andrew Wesley Daubeny de Moleyns, *b.* 1943, *s.* 1987, *m.*	Hon. Francis W. D. de M., *b.* 1965
1762	*Vernon (11th)*, Anthony William Vernon-Harcourt, *b.* 1939, *s.* 2000, *m.*	Hon. Simon A. V.-H., *b.* 1969
1922	*Vestey (3rd)*, Samuel George Armstrong Vestey, GCVO, *b.* 1941, *s.* 1954, *m.*	Hon. William G. V., *b.* 1983
1841	*Vivian (7th)*, Charles Crespigny Hussey Vivian, *b.* 1966, *s.* 2004	Thomas C. B. V., *b.* 1971
1934	*Wakehurst (3rd)*, (John) Christopher Loder, *b.* 1925, *s.* 1970, *m.*	Hon. Timothy W. L., *b.* 1958
1723	*Walpole (10th) and Walpole of Wolterton (8th) (1756)*, Robert Horatio Walpole, *b.* 1938, *s.* 1989, *m.*	Hon. Jonathan R. H. W., *b.* 1967
1780	*Walsingham (9th)*, John de Grey, MC, *b.* 1925, *s.* 1965, *w.*	Hon. Robert de G., *b.* 1969
1792 I.	*Waterpark (8th)*, Roderick Alexander Cavendish, *b.* 1959, *s.* 2013, *m.*	Hon. Luke F. C., *b.* 1990
1942	*Wedgwood (5th)*, Antony John Wedgwood, *b.* 1944, *s.* 2014, *m.*	Hon. Josiah T. A. W., *b.* 1978
1861	*Westbury (6th)*, Richard Nicholas Bethell, MBE, *b.* 1950, *s.* 2001, *m.*	Hon. Richard A. D. B., *b.* 1986
1944	*Westwood (4th)*, (William) Fergus Westwood, *b.* 1972, *s.* 2019	Hon. Alistair C. W., *b.* 1974
1544/5	*Wharton (12th)*, Myles Christopher David Robertson, *b.* 1964, *s.* 2000, *m.*	Hon. Meghan Z. M. R., *b.* 2006
1935	*Wigram (3rd)*, Andrew Francis Clive Wigram, MVO, *b.* 1949, *s.* 2017, *m.*	Hon. Harry R. C. W., *b.* 1977
1491 **	*Willoughby de Broke (21st)*, Leopold David Verney, *b.* 1938, *s.* 1986, *m.*	Hon. Rupert G. V., *b.* 1966
1937	*Windlesham (4th)*, James Rupert Hennessy, *b.* 1968, *s.* 2010, *m.*	Hon. George R. J. H., *b.* 2006
1951	*Wise (3rd)*, Christopher John Clayton Wise, *b.* 1949, *s.* 2012, *m.*	Hon. Thomas C. C. W., *b.* 1989
1869	*Wolverton (8th)*, Miles John Glyn, *b.* 1966, *s.* 2011	Jonathan C. G., *b.* 1990
1928	*Wraxall (4th)*, Antony Hubert Gibbs, *b.* 1958, *s.* 2017, *m.*	Hon. Orlando H. G., *b.* 1995
1915	*Wrenbury (4th)*, William Edward Buckley, *b.* 1966, *s.* 2014, *m.*	Arthur B. B., *b.* 1967
1838	*Wrottesley (6th)*, Clifton Hugh Lancelot de Verdon Wrottesley, *b.* 1968, *s.* 1977, *m.*	Hon. Victor E. F. de V. W., *b.* 2004
1829	*Wynford (9th)*, John Philip Robert Best, *b.* 1950, *s.* 2002, *m.*	Hon. Harry R. F. B., *b.* 1987
1308	*Zouche (18th)*, James Assheton Frankland, *b.* 1943, *s.* 1965, *m.*	Hon. William T. A. F., *b.* 1984

BARONESSES/LADIES IN THEIR OWN RIGHT

Style, The Rt. Hon. the Lady _ , *or* The Rt. Hon. the Baroness _ , according to her preference. Either style may be used, except in the case of Scottish titles (indicated by S.), which are not baronies and whose holders are always addressed as Lady.

Envelope, may be addressed in same way as a Baron's wife or, if she prefers *(formal)*, The Rt. Hon. the Baroness _; *(social)*, The Baroness _. Otherwise as for a Baron's wife

Husband, Untitled

Children's style, As for children of a Baron

In Scotland, the heir to a Lady may be styled 'The Master/Mistress of _ (title of peer)'

Created	*Title, order of succession, name, etc*	*Heir*
1664	*Arlington (11th)*, Jennifer Jane Forwood, *b.* 1939, *s.* 1999, *w.* Title called out of abeyance 1999	Hon. Patrick J. D. F., *b.* 1967
1607	*Balfour of Burleigh (9th)*, Victoria Bruce, *b.* 1973, *s.* 2019, *m.*	Hon. Laetitia B., *b.* 2007
1455	*Berners (16th)*, Pamela Vivien Kirkham, *b.* 1929, *s.* 1995, *w.* Title called out of abeyance 1995	Hon. Rupert W. T. K., *b.* 1953
1529	*Braye (8th)*, Mary Penelope Aubrey-Fletcher, *b.* 1941, *s.* 1985, *m.*	Linda K. C. Fothergill, *b.* 1930
1321	*Dacre (29th)*, Emily Beamish, *b.* 1983, *s.* 2014, *m.*	Three co-heiresses
1283	*Fauconberg (10th) and Conyers (16th) (1509)*, Baronies in abeyance between two co-heiresses since 2013	
1490 S.	*Herries of Terregles (16th)*, (Theresa) Jane Kerr, Marchioness of Lothian, *b.* 1945, *s.* 2017, *m.*	Lady Clare T. Hurd, *b.* 1979
1597	*Howard de Walden (10th)*, Mary Hazel Caridwen Czernin, *b.* 1935, *s.* 2004, *w.* Title called out of abeyance 2004	Hon. Peter J. J. C., *b.* 1966
1602 S.	*Kinloss (13th)*, Teresa Mary Nugent Freeman-Grenville, *b.* 1957, *s.* 2012	Mistress of Kinloss, *b.* 1960
1445 S.	*Saltoun (20th)*, Flora Marjory Fraser, *b.* 1930, *s.* 1979, *w.*	Hon. Katharine I. M. I. F., *b.* 1957
1313	*Willoughby de Eresby (27th)*, (Nancy) Jane Marie Heathcote-Drummond-Willoughby, *b.* 1934, *s.* 1983	Two co-heirs

LIFE PEERS

Style, The Rt. Hon. the Lord _ /The Rt. Hon. the Lady _ , *or*
The Rt. Hon. the Baroness _ , according to her preference
Envelope (formal), The Rt. Hon. Lord _/Lady_/Baroness_;
(social), The Lord _/Lady_/Baroness_ *Letter (formal),* My
Lord/Lady; *(social),* Dear Lord/Lady _. *Spoken,* Lord/
Lady _
Wife's style, The Rt. Hon. the Lady _
Husband, Untitled
Children's style, 'The Hon.' before forename (F_) and surname
(S_)
Envelope, The Hon. F_ S_. *Letter,* Dear Mr/Miss/Mrs S_.
Spoken, Mr/Miss/Mrs S_

KEY
* Hereditary peer who has been granted a life peerage. For
further details, please refer to the Hereditary Peers section.
For example, life peer *Balniel* can be found under his
hereditary title *Earl of Crawford and Balcarres*
§ Members of the Judiciary currently disqualified from sitting
or voting in the House of Lords until they retire from that
office. For further information *see* Law Courts and Offices
‡ Title not confirmed at time of going to press
℃ Peer who has permanently resigned from the House of
Lords
E. Peer who has been expelled for absenteeism, under
section 2 of the House of Lords Reform Act 2014, for
failing to attend a sitting of the House during a session
lasting six months or longer *see* The Peerage, introduction

A full entry in italic type indicates that the recipient of a life
peerage died within a year of it being conferred. The
name is included in our list for one year for purposes of
record.

NEW LIFE PEERAGES
Since December 2019

Ian Christopher Austin; Rt. Hon. Gavin Laurence Barwell; Sir
Henry Campbell Bellingham; Natalie Louise Bennett;
Christine Blower; Sir Ian Terence Botham, OBE; David Ellis
Brownlow, CVO; Harold Mark Carter, CB; Dame Louise
Casey, DBE, CB; Zameer Mohammed Choudrey, CBE;
Kathryn Sloan Clark; Rt. Hon. Kenneth Harry Clarke, CH,
QC; Sir (Nigel) Kim Darroch, KCMG; Brinley Howard
Davies; (Henry) Byron Davies; Rt. Hon. Ruth Elizabeth
Davidson, MSP; Rt. Hon. Nigel Alexander Dodds, OBE; Rt.
Hon. Frank Field; Claire Regina Fox; David George Hamilton
Frost, CMG; Lorraine Fullbrook; Rt. Hon. (Frank) Zac(harias)
Robin Goldsmith; Stephen John Greenhalgh; Sir Gerald
Edgar Grimstone, CVO; Rt. Hon. Dame Heather Carol
Hallett, DBE; Rt. Hon. Philip Hammond; Susan Mary
Hayman; John Hendy, QC; Rt. Hon. Nicholas Le Quesne
Herbert, CBE; Catharine Letitia Hoey; Ruth Elizabeth Hunt;
Rt. Hon. Joseph Edmund Johnson; Rt. Hon. (John) Mark
Lancaster, TD, VR; Evgeny Alexandrovich Lebedev; Rt. Hon.
Sir Patrick Alan McLoughlin, CH; John Mann; Neil Francis
Jeremy Mendoza; Rt. Hon. Nicola Ann Morgan; Charles
Hilary Moore; Dame Helena Louise Morrissey, DBE; Daniel
Michael Gerald Moylan; Stephen Graeme Parkinson; Joanna
Carolyn Penn; Raminder Singh Ranger, CBE; Margaret Mary
Ritchie; Elizabeth Jenny Rosemary Sanderson Aamer Ahmad
Sarfraz; Sir Mark Philip Sedwill, KCMG; Andrew Michael
Gordon Sharpe, OBE; Dame Nemat (Minouche) Talaat
Shafik, DBE; Prem Nath Sikka; Michael Alan Spencer; Keith
Douglas Stewart, QC; Rt. Hon. Gisela Stuart; Sir Edward
Julian Udny-Lister; Rt. Hon. Edward Henry Butler Vaizey;

Veronica Judith Colleton Wadley, CBE; James Stephen
Wharton; Deborah Ann Wilcox; John Zak Woodcock;
Anthony J. Woodley; Sir Simon Andrew Woolley

CREATED UNDER THE APPELLATE JURISDICTION ACT 1876 (AS AMENDED)

BARONS

Created	
2004	*Brown of Eaton-under-Heywood,* Simon Denis Brown, PC, *b.* 1937, *m.*
2004	℃*Carswell,* Robert Douglas Carswell, PC, *b.* 1934, *m.*
2009	*Collins of Mapesbury,* Lawrence Antony Collins, PC, *b.* 1941, *m.*
1995	*Hoffmann,* Leonard Hubert Hoffmann, PC, *b.* 1934, *m.*
2009	*Kerr of Tonaghmore,* Brian Francis Kerr, PC, *b.* 1948, *m.*
1993	℃*Lloyd of Berwick,* Anthony John Leslie Lloyd, PC, *b.,* 1929, *m.*
2005	*Mance,* Jonathan Hugh Mance, PC, *b.* 1943, *m.*
1998	℃*Millett,* Peter Julian Millett, PC, *b.* 1932, *m.*
2007	*Neuberger of Abbotsbury,* David Edmond Neuberger, PC, *b.* 1948, *m.*
1999	*Phillips of Worth Matravers,* Nicholas Addison Phillips, KG, PC, *b.* 1938, *m.*
1997	*Saville of Newdigate,* Mark Oliver Saville, PC, *b.* 1936, *m.*
2000	℃*Scott of Foscote,* Richard Rashleigh Folliott Scott, PC, *b.* 1934, *m.*
2003	*Walker of Gestingthorpe,* Robert Walker, PC, *b.* 1938, *m.*
1992	*Woolf,* Harry Kenneth Woolf, CH, PC, *b.* 1933, *m.*

BARONESSES
2004	*Hale of Richmond,* Brenda Marjorie Hale, DBE, PC, *b.* 1945, *w.*

CREATED UNDER THE LIFE PEERAGES ACT 1958

BARONS

Created	
2001	*Adebowale,* Victor Olufemi Adebowale, CBE, *b.* 1962
2005	*Adonis,* Andrew Adonis, PC, *b.* 1963, *m.*
2017	*Agnew of Oulton,* Theodore Thomas More Agnew, *b.* 1961, *m.*
2011	*Ahmad of Wimbledon,* Tariq Mahmood Ahmad, *b.* 1968, *m.*
1998	*Ahmed,* Nazir Ahmed, *b.* 1957, *m.*
1996	*Alderdice,* John Thomas Alderdice, *b.* 1955, *m.*
2010	*Allan of Hallam,* Richard Beecroft Allan, *b.* 1966
2013	*Allen of Kensington,* Charles Lamb Allen, CBE, *b.* 1957
1998	*Alli,* Waheed Alli, *b.* 1964
2004	*Alliance,* David Alliance, CBE, *b.* 1932
1997	*Alton of Liverpool,* David Patrick Paul Alton, *b.* 1951, *m.*
2018	*Anderson of Ipswich,* David William Kinloch Anderson, KBE, QC, *b.* 1961, *m.*
2005	*Anderson of Swansea,* Donald Anderson, PC, *b.* 1939, *m.*
2015	*Arbuthnot of Edrom,* James Norwich Arbuthnot, PC, *b.* 1952, *m.*
1992	*Archer of Weston-super-Mare,* Jeffrey Howard Archer, *b.* 1940, *m.*
2000	℃*Ashcroft,* Michael Anthony Ashcroft, KCMG, PC, *b.* 1946, *m.*
2020	*Austin,* Ian Christopher Austin, *b.* 1965
1998	*Bach,* William Stephen Goulden Bach, *b.* 1946, *m.*
1997	*Baker of Dorking,* Kenneth Wilfred Baker, CH, PC, *b.* 1934, *m.*

2013   Balfe, Richard Andrew Balfe, b. 1944, m.

1974   ℭ*Balniel, The Earl of Crawford and Balcarres, KT, GCVO, PC, b. 1927, m. (see Hereditary Peers)

2013   Bamford, Anthony Paul Bamford, b. 1945, m.

2015   Barker of Battle, Gregory Leonard George Barker, PC, b. 1966

2019   Barwell, Gavin Laurence Barwell, PC, b. 1972, m.

1997   Bassam of Brighton, (John) Steven Bassam, PC, b. 1953

2008   Bates, Michael Walton Bates, PC, b. 1961, m.

2010   Beecham, Jeremy Hugh Beecham, b. 1944, m.

2015   Beith, Alan James Beith, PC, b. 1943, w.

2020   ‡Bellingham, Henry Campbell Bellingham, b. 1955, m.

2013   Berkeley of Knighton, Michael Fitzhardinge Berkeley, CBE, b. 1948, m.

2001   Best, Richard Stuart Best, OBE, b. 1945, m.

2007   Bew, Prof. Paul Anthony Elliott Bew, b. 1950, m.

2001   Bhatia, Amirali Alibhai Bhatia, OBE, b. 1932, m.

2010   Bichard, Michael George Bichard, KCB, b. 1947, m.

2006   Bilimoria, Karan Faridoon Bilimoria, CBE, b. 1961, m.

2015   Bird, John Anthony Bird, MBE, b. 1946, m.

2000   Birt, John Francis Hodgess Birt, b. 1944, m.

2010   Black of Brentwood, Guy Vaughan Black, b. 1964, m.

2001   Black of Crossharbour, Conrad Moffat Black, b. 1944, m.

1997   Blackwell, Norman Roy Blackwell, b. 1952, m.

2010   Blair of Boughton, Ian Warwick Blair, QPM, b. 1953, m.

2011   Blencathra, David John Maclean, PC, b. 1953

2015   Blunkett, David Blunkett, PC, b. 1947, m.

1995   ℭBlyth of Rowington, James Blyth, b. 1940, m.

2010   Boateng, Paul Yaw Boateng, PC, b. 1951, m.

2010   Boswell of Aynho, Timothy Eric Boswell, b. 1942, m.

2020   Botham, Ian Terence Botham, OBE, b. 1955, m.

2013   Bourne of Aberystwyth, Nicholas Henry Bourne, b. 1952

1996   Bowness, Peter Spencer Bowness, CBE, b. 1943, m.

2003   Boyce, Michael Boyce, KG, GCB, OBE, b. 1943, w.

2006   §Boyd of Duncansby, Colin David Boyd, PC, b. 1953, m.

2006   Bradley, Keith John Charles Bradley, PC, b. 1950, m.

1999   Bradshaw, William Peter Bradshaw, b. 1936, m.

1998   Bragg, Melvyn Bragg, CH, b. 1939, m.

2000   Brennan, Daniel Joseph Brennan, QC, b. 1942, m.

2015   Bridges of Headley, James George Robert Bridges, MBE, b. 1970, m.

2004   Broers, Prof. Alec (Nigel) Broers, b. 1938, m.

1997   Brooke of Alverthorpe, Clive Brooke, b. 1942, m.

2001   ℭBrooke of Sutton Mandeville, Peter Leonard Brooke, CH, PC, b. 1934, m.

1998   ℭBrookman, David Keith Brookman, b. 1937, m.

2006   Browne of Belmont, Wallace Hamilton Browne, b. 1947

2010   Browne of Ladyton, Desmond Henry Browne, PC, b. 1952

2001   Browne of Madingley, Edmund John Phillip Browne, b. 1948

2019   Brownlow of Shurlock Row, David Ellis Brownlow, CVO, b. 1963

2015   Bruce of Bennachie, Malcolm Gray Bruce, b. 1944, m.

2006   Burnett, John Patrick Aubone Burnett, b. 1945, m.

2017   §Burnett of Maldon, Ian Duncan Burnett, PC, b. 1958, m. Lord Chief Justice of England and Wales

1998   Burns, Terence Burns, GCB, b. 1944, m.

1998   Butler of Brockwell, (Frederick Edward) Robin Butler, KG, GCB, CVO, PC, b. 1938, m.

2016   Caine, Jonathan Michael Caine, b. 1966

2014   Callanan, Martin John Callanan, b. 1961, m.

2004   Cameron of Dillington, Ewen (James Hanning) Cameron, b. 1949, m.

1984   ℭCameron of Lochbroom, Kenneth John Cameron, PC, b. 1931, m.

2015   Campbell of Pittenweem, (Walter) Menzies Campbell, CH, CBE, PC, QC, b. 1941, m.

2001   Campbell-Savours, Dale Norman Campbell-Savours, b. 1943, m.

2002   Carey of Clifton, Rt. Revd George Leonard Carey, PC, Royal Victorian Chain, b. 1935, m.

1999   Carlile of Berriew, Alexander Charles Carlile, CBE, QC, b. 1948, m.

2013   Carrington of Fulham, Matthew Hadrian Marshall Carrington, b. 1947, m.

2008   Carter of Barnes, Stephen Andrew Carter, CBE, b. 1964, m.

2004   Carter of Coles, Patrick Robert Carter, b. 1946, m.

2019   Carter of Haslemere, Harold Mark Carter, CB

2014   Cashman, Michael Maurice Cashman, CBE, b. 1950

1990   Cavendish of Furness, (Richard) Hugh Cavendish, b. 1941, m.

1996   Chadlington, Peter Selwyn Gummer, b. 1942, m.

2017   Chartres, Rt. Revd Richard John Carew Chartres, GCVO, PC, b. 1947, m.

2005   Chidgey, David William George Chidgey, b. 1942, m.

2019   Choudrey, Zameer Mohammed Choudrey, CBE, b. 1958, m.

1998   Christopher, Anthony Martin Grosvenor Christopher, CBE, b. 1925, m.

2001   Clark of Windermere, David George Clark, PC, PHD, b. 1939, m.

1998   Clarke of Hampstead, Anthony James Clarke, CBE, b. 1932, m.

2020   Clarke of Nottingham, Kenneth Harry Clarke, CH, PC, QC, b. 1940, w.

2009   ℭClarke of Stone-Cum-Ebony, Anthony Peter Clarke, PC, b. 1943, m.

1998   Clement-Jones, Timothy Francis Clement-Jones, CBE, b. 1949, m.

1990   ℭClinton-Davis, Stanley Clinton Clinton-Davis, PC, b. 1928, m.

2000   Coe, Sebastian Newbold Coe, CH, KBE, b. 1956, m.

2011   Collins of Highbury, Raymond Edward Harry Collins, b. 1954, m.

2001   ℭCondon, Paul Leslie Condon, QPM, b. 1947, m.

2014   Cooper of Windrush, Andrew Timothy Cooper, b. 1963, m.

1997   ℭCope of Berkeley, John Ambrose Cope, PC, b. 1937, m.

2010   Cormack, Patrick Thomas Cormack, b. 1939, m.

2006   Cotter, Brian Joseph Michael Cotter, b. 1938, m.

1991   Craig of Radley, David Brownrigg Craig, GCB, OBE, b. 1929, w.

2006   Crisp, (Edmund) Nigel (Ramsay) Crisp, KCB, b. 1952, m.

2003   ℭCullen of Whitekirk, William Douglas Cullen, KT, PC, b. 1935, m.

2005   Cunningham of Felling, John Anderson Cunningham, PC, b. 1939, m.

1996   Currie of Marylebone, David Anthony Currie, b. 1946, m.

2011   Curry of Kirkharle, Donald Thomas Younger Curry, CBE, b. 1944, m.

2011   Dannatt, (Francis) Richard Dannatt, GCB, CBE, MC, b. 1950, m.

2015   ℭDarling of Roulanish, Alistair Maclean Darling, PC, b. 1953, m.

2019   ‡Darroch of Kew, (Nigel) Kim Darroch, KCMG, b. 1954, m.

2007   Darzi of Denham, Ara Warkes Darzi, OM, KBE, PC, b. 1960, m.

2006   Davidson of Glen Clova, Neil Forbes Davidson, QC, b. 1950, m.

2009   Davies of Abersoch, Evan Mervyn Davies, CBE, b. 1952, m.

2020	*Davies of Brixton*, Brinley Howard Davies, *b.* 1944
2019	*Davies of Gower*, (Henry) Byron Davies, *b.* 1952
1997	*Davies of Oldham*, Bryan Davies, PC, *b.* 1939, *m.*
2010	*Davies of Stamford*, John Quentin Davies, *b.* 1944, *m.*
2006	*Dear*, Geoffrey (James) Dear, QPM, *b.* 1937, *m.*
2010	*Deben*, John Selwyn Gummer, PC, *b.* 1939, *m.*
2012	*Deighton*, Paul Clive Deighton, KBE, *b.* 1956, *m.*
1991	*Desai*, Prof. Meghnad Jagdishchandra Desai, PHD, *b.* 1940, *m.*
1997	*Dholakia*, Navnit Dholakia, OBE, PC, *b.* 1937, *m.*
1993	*Dixon-Smith*, Robert William Dixon-Smith, *b.* 1934, *m.*
2010	*Dobbs*, Michael John Dobbs, *b.* 1948, *m.*
2020	*Dodds*, Nigel Alexander Dodds, OBE, PC, *b.* 1958, *m.*
1985	*Donoughue*, Bernard Donoughue, DPHIL, *b.* 1934, *m.*
2004	*Drayson*, Paul Rudd Drayson, PC, *b.* 1960, *m.*
1994	*Dubs*, Alfred Dubs, *b.* 1932, *m.*
2017	*Duncan of Springbank*, Ian James Duncan, *b.* 1973, *c.p.*
2015	*Dunlop*, Andrew James Dunlop, *b.* 1959, *m.*
2004	*Dykes*, Hugh John Maxwell Dykes, *b.* 1939
1995	*Eames*, Rt. Revd Robert Henry Alexander Eames, OM, PHD, *b.* 1937, *m.*
1992	*Eatwell*, John Leonard Eatwell, PHD, *b.* 1945, *m.*
2011	€*Edmiston*, Robert Norman Edmiston, *b.* 1946, *m.*
1999	*Elder*, Thomas Murray Elder, *b.* 1950
1992	*Elis-Thomas*, Dafydd Elis Elis-Thomas, PC, *b.* 1946, *m.*
1981	€*Elystan-Morgan*, Dafydd Elystan Elystan-Morgan, *b.* 1932, *w.*
2011	*Empey*, Reginald Norman Morgan Empey, OBE, *b.* 1947, *m.*
2000	€*Erskine of Alloa Tower*, Earl of Mar and Kellie, *b.* 1949, *m.* (*see* Hereditary Peers)
1998	*Evans of Watford*, David Charles Evans, *b.* 1942, *m.*
2014	*Evans of Weardale*, Jonathan Douglas Evans, KCB, *b.* 1958
1997	*Falconer of Thoroton*, Charles Leslie Falconer, PC, QC, *b.* 1951, *m.*
2014	*Farmer*, Michael Stahel Farmer, *b.* 1944, *m.*
1999	*Faulkner of Worcester*, Richard Oliver Faulkner, *b.* 1946, *m.*
2010	*Faulks*, Edward Peter Lawless Faulks, QC, *b.* 1950, *m.*
2001	€*Fearn*, Ronald Cyril Fearn, OBE, *b.* 1931, *m.*
2010	*Feldman of Elstree*, Andrew Simon Feldman, PC, *b.* 1966, *m.*
1999	*Fellowes*, Robert Fellowes, GCB, GCVO, PC, *b.* 1941, *m.*
2011	*Fellowes of West Stafford*, Julian Alexander Fellowes, *b.* 1949, *m.*
2020	*Field of Birkenhead*, Frank Field, PC, *b.* 1942
1999	*Filkin*, David Geoffrey Nigel Filkin, CBE, *b.* 1944, *m.*
2011	*Fink*, Stanley Fink, *b.* 1957, *m.*
2013	*Finkelstein*, Daniel William Finkelstein, OBE, *b.* 1962, *m.*
2011	*Flight*, Howard Emerson Flight, *b.* 1948, *m.*
1999	*Forsyth of Drumlean*, Michael Bruce Forsyth, PC, *b.* 1954, *m.*
2015	*Foster of Bath*, Donald Michael Ellison Foster, PC, *b.* 1947, *m.*
1999	€*Foster of Thames Bank*, Norman Robert Foster, OM, *b.* 1935, *m.*
2005	*Foulkes of Cumnock*, George Foulkes, PC, *b.* 1942, *m.*
2001	*Fowler*, (Peter) Norman Fowler, PC, *b.* 1938, *m. Lord Speaker*
2014	*Fox*, Christopher Francis Fox, *b.* 1957, *m.*
2011	*Framlingham*, Michael Nicholson Lord, *b.* 1938, *m.*
2016	*Fraser of Corriegarth*, (Alexander) Andrew (Macdonell) Fraser, *b.* 1946, *m.*
1997	€*Freeman*, Roger Norman Freeman, PC, *b.* 1942, *m.*
2020	*Frost*, David George Hamilton Frost, CMG, *b.* 1965
2009	*Freud*, David Anthony Freud, PC, *b.* 1950, *m.*
2016	*Gadhia*, Jitesh Kishorekumar Gadhia, *b.* 1970, *m.*
2010	*Gardiner of Kimble*, John Gardiner, *b.* 1956, *m.*
2018	*Garnier*, Edward Henry Garnier, PC, QC, *b.* 1952, *m.*
1999	€*Gascoyne-Cecil*, The Marquess of Salisbury, KG, KCVO, PC, *b.* 1946, *m.* (*see* Hereditary Peers)
2017	*Geidt*, Christopher Edward Wollaston MacKenzie Geidt, GCB, GCVO, OBE, PC, *b.* 1961, *m.*
2010	*German*, Michael James German, OBE, *b.* 1945, *m.*
2004	*Giddens*, Prof. Anthony Giddens, *b.* 1938, *m.*
2015	*Gilbert of Panteg*, Stephen Gilbert, *b.* 1963
2011	*Glasman*, Maurice Mark Glasman, *b.* 1961, *m.*
2011	*Glendonbrook*, Michael David Bishop, CBE, *b.* 1942
2014	*Goddard of Stockport*, David Goddard, *b.* 1952
2011	*Gold*, David Laurence Gold, *b.* 1951, *m.*
1999	*Goldsmith*, Peter Henry Goldsmith, PC, QC, *b.* 1950, *m.*
2020	*Goldsmith of Richmond Park*, (Frank) Zac(harias) Robin Goldsmith, PC, *b.* 1975, *m.*
2005	*Goodlad*, Alastair Robertson Goodlad, KCMG, PC, *b.* 1943, *m.*
1999	*Grabiner*, Anthony Stephen Grabiner, QC, *b.* 1945, *m.*
2011	*Grade of Yarmouth*, Michael Ian Grade, CBE, *b.* 1943, *m.*
2000	*Greaves*, Anthony Robert Greaves, *b.* 1942, *m.*
2014	*Green of Deddington*, Andrew Fleming Green, KCMG, *b.* 1941, *m.*
2010	*Green of Hurstpierpoint*, Stephen Keith Green, *b.* 1948, *m.*
2020	*Greenhalgh*, Stephen John Greenhalgh, *b.* 1967, *m.*
2000	€*Grenfell of Kilvey*, Lord Grenfell, *b.* 1935, *m.* (*see* Hereditary Peers)
2004	*Griffiths of Burry Port*, Revd Dr Leslie John Griffiths, *b.* 1942, *m.*
1991	*Griffiths of Fforestfach*, Brian Griffiths, *b.* 1941, *m.*
2020	*Grimstone of Boscobel*, Gerald Edgar Grimstone, CVO, *b.* 1949
2001	*Grocott*, Bruce Joseph Grocott, PC, *b.* 1940, *m.*
2000	*Gueterbock*, Lord Berkeley, OBE, *b.* 1939, *m.* (*see* Hereditary Peers)
2000	€*Guthrie of Craigiebank*, Charles Ronald Llewelyn Guthrie, GCB, GCVO, OBE, *b.* 1938, *m.*
2015	*Hague of Richmond*, William Jefferson Hague, PC, *b.* 1961, *m.*
2015	*Hailsham of Kettlethorpe*, Viscount Hailsham, PC, QC, *b.* 1945, *m.* (*see* Hereditary Peers)
2015	*Hain*, Peter Gerald Hain, PC, *b.* 1950, *m.*
2010	*Hall of Birkenhead*, Anthony William Hall, CBE, *b.* 1951, *m.*
2007	*Hameed*, Dr Khalid Hameed, CBE, *b.* 1941, *m.*
2005	*Hamilton of Epsom*, Archibald Gavin Hamilton, PC, *b.* 1941, *m.*
2020	*Hammond*, Philip Hammond, PC, *b.* 1955, *m.*
2001	*Hannay of Chiswick*, David Hugh Alexander Hannay, GCMG, CH, *b.* 1935, *w.*
1998	*Hanningfield*, Paul Edward Winston White, *b.* 1940
1997	€*Hardie*, Andrew Rutherford Hardie, PC, QC, *b.* 1946, *m.*
2006	*Harries of Pentregarth*, Rt. Revd Richard Douglas Harries, *b.* 1936, *m.*
1998	*Harris of Haringey*, (Jonathan) Toby Harris, *b.* 1953, *m.*
1996	*Harris of Peckham*, Philip Charles Harris, *b.* 1942, *m.*
1999	*Harrison*, Lyndon Henry Arthur Harrison, *b.* 1947, *m.*
2018	*Haselhurst*, Alan Gordon Barraclough Haselhurst, PC, *b.* 1937, *m.*
1993	*Haskel*, Simon Haskel, *b.* 1934, *m.*
1998	*Haskins*, Christopher Robin Haskins, *b.* 1937, *m.*
2005	*Hastings of Scarisbrick*, Michael John Hastings, CBE, *b.* 1958, *m.*

1997   ℭ*Hattersley,* Roy Sidney George Hattersley, PC, *b.* 1932, *m.*

2013   *Haughey,* William Haughey, OBE, *b.* 1956, *m.*

2004   *Haworth,* Alan Robert Haworth, *b.* 1948, *m.*

2014   *Hay of Ballyore,* William Alexander Hay, *b.* 1950, *m.*

2015   *Hayward,* Robert Antony Hayward, OBE, *b.* 1949

2019   *Hendy,* John Hendy, QC, *b.* 1948

2010   *Hennessy of Nympsfield,* Prof. Peter John Hennessy, *b.* 1947, *m.*

2020   *Herbert of South Downs,* Nicholas Le Quesne Herbert, CBE, PC, *b.* 1963, cp.

2001   *Heseltine,* Michael Ray Dibdin Heseltine, CH, PC, *b.* 1933, *m.*

2018   *Heywood of Whitehall, Jeremy John Heywood, GCB, CVO, b. 1961, m., d. 2018*

1997   ℭ*Higgins,* Terence Langley Higgins, KBE, PC, *b.* 1928, *m.*

2010   *Hill of Oareford,* Jonathan Hopkin Hill, CBE, PC, *b.* 1960, *m.*

2000   *Hodgson of Astley Abbotts,* Robin Granville Hodgson, CBE, *b.* 1942, *m.*

2017   *Hogan-Howe,* Bernard Hogan-Howe, QPM, *b.* 1957, *m.*

1991   *Hollick,* Clive Richard Hollick, *b.* 1945, *m.*

2013   *Holmes of Richmond,* Christopher Holmes, MBE, *b.* 1971

1995   *Hope of Craighead,* (James Arthur) David Hope, KT, PC, *b.* 1938, *m.*

2005   ℭ*Hope of Thornes,* Rt. Revd David Michael Hope, KCVO, PC, *b.* 1940

2013   *Horam,* John Rhodes Horam, *b.* 1939, *m.*

2017   *Houghton of Richmond,* John Nicholas Reynolds Houghton, GCB, CBE, *b.* 1954, *m.*

2010   *Howard of Lympne,* Michael Howard, CH, PC, QC, *b.* 1941, *m.*

2004   *Howard of Rising,* Greville Patrick Charles Howard, *b.* 1941, *m.*

2005   *Howarth of Newport,* Alan Thomas Howarth, CBE, PC, *b.* 1944

1997   *Howell of Guildford,* David Arthur Russell Howell, PC, *b.* 1936, *m.*

1997   *Hoyle,* (Eric) Douglas Harvey Hoyle, *b.* 1930, *w.*

1997   *Hughes of Woodside,* Robert Hughes, *b.* 1932, *m.*

2000   *Hunt of Chesterton,* Julian Charles Roland Hunt, CB, *b.* 1941, *m.*

1997   *Hunt of Kings Heath,* Philip Alexander Hunt, OBE, PC, *b.* 1949, *m.*

1997   *Hunt of Wirral,* David James Fletcher Hunt, MBE, PC, *b.* 1942, *m.*

1997   ℭ*Hurd of Westwell,* Douglas Richard Hurd, CH, CBE, PC, *b.* 1930, *w.*

2011   *Hussain,* Qurban Hussain, *b.* 1956, *m.*

2010   *Hutton of Furness,* John Matthew Patrick Hutton, PC, *b.* 1955, *m.*

1997   ℭ*Inge,* Peter Anthony Inge, KG, GCB, PC, *b.* 1935, *w.*

1987   *Irvine of Lairg,* Alexander Andrew Mackay Irvine, PC, QC, *b.* 1940, *m.*

2006   *James of Blackheath,* David Noel James, CBE, *b.* 1937, *m.*

2007   *Janvrin,* Robin Berry Janvrin, GCB, GCVO, PC, *b.* 1946, *m.*

2006   *Jay of Ewelme,* Michael (Hastings) Jay, GCMG, *b.* 1946, *m.*

2020   *Johnson of Marylebone,* Joseph Edmund Johnson, PC, *b.* 1971, *m.*

2001   *Jones,* (Stephen) Barry Jones, PC, *b.* 1937, *m.*

2007   ℭ*Jones of Birmingham,* Digby Marritt Jones, *b.* 1955, *m.*

2005   *Jones of Cheltenham,* Nigel David Jones, *b.* 1948, *m.*

1997   *Jopling,* (Thomas) Michael Jopling, PC, *b.* 1930, *m.*

2000   *Jordan,* William Brian Jordan, CBE, *b.* 1936, *m.*

1991   *Judd,* Frank Ashcroft Judd, *b.* 1935, *m.*

2008   *Judge,* Igor Judge, PC, *b.* 1941, *m.*

2010   *Kakkar,* Prof. Ajay Kumar Kakkar, PC, *b.* 1964, *m.*

2004   *Kalms,* Harold Stanley Kalms, *b.* 1931, *m.*

2015   *Keen of Elie,* Richard Sanderson Keen, PC, QC, *b.* 1954, *m.*

2010   *Kennedy of Southwark,* Roy Francis Kennedy, *b.* 1962, *m.*

2004   *Kerr of Kinlochard,* John (Olav) Kerr, GCMG, *b.* 1942, *m.*

2010   **Kerr of Monteviot,* Marquess of Lothian (Michael Ancram), PC, QC, *b.* 1945, *m.* (*see* Hereditary Peers)

2015   *Kerslake,* Robert Walter Kerslake, *b.* 1955, *m.*

2011   *Kestenbaum,* Jonathan Andrew Kestenbaum, *b.* 1959, *m.*

2001   *Kilclooney,* John David Taylor, PC (NI), *b.* 1937, *m.*

2001   *King of Bridgwater,* Thomas Jeremy King, CH, PC, *b.* 1933, *m.*

2013   *King of Lothbury,* Mervyn Allister King, KG, GBE, *b.* 1948

2005   *Kinnock,* Neil Gordon Kinnock, PC, *b.* 1942, *m.*

1999   *Kirkham,* Graham Kirkham, *b.* 1944, *m.*

1975   ℭ*Kirkhill,* John Farquharson Smith, *b.* 1930, *m.*

2016   *Kirkhope of Harrogate,* Timothy John Robert Kirkhope, *b.* 1945, *m.*

2005   ℭ*Kirkwood of Kirkhope,* Archibald Johnstone Kirkwood, *b.* 1946, *m.*

2010   *Knight of Weymouth,* James Philip Knight, PC, *b.* 1965, *m.*

2007   *Krebs,* Prof. John (Richard) Krebs, FRS, *b.* 1945, *m.*

2004   ℭ*Laidlaw,* Irvine Alan Stewart Laidlaw, *b.* 1942, *m.*

1998   *Laming,* (William) Herbert Laming, CBE, PC, *b.* 1936, *w.*

1998   *Lamont of Lerwick,* Norman Stewart Hughson Lamont, PC, *b.* 1942

2020   *Lancaster of Kimbolton,* (John) Mark Lancaster, TD, VR, PC, *b.* 1970, *m.*

1997   *Lang of Monkton,* Ian Bruce Lang, PC, *b.* 1940, *m.*

2015   *Lansley,* Andrew David Lansley, CBE, PC, *b.* 1956, *m.*

1992   *Lawson of Blaby,* Nigel Lawson, PC, *b.* 1932

2000   *Layard,* Peter Richard Grenville Layard, *b.* 1934, *m.*

1999   *Lea of Crondall,* David Edward Lea, OBE, *b.* 1937

2020   ‡*Lebedev,* Evgeny Alexandrovich Lebedev, *b.* 1980

2006   *Lee of Trafford,* John Robert Louis Lee, *b.* 1942, *m.*

2013   *Leigh of Hurley,* Howard Darryl Leigh, *b.* 1959, *m.*

2004   *Leitch,* Alexander Park Leitch, *b.* 1947, *m.*

2014   *Lennie,* Christopher John Lennie, *b.* 1953, *m.*

1997   *Levene of Portsoken,* Peter Keith Levene, KBE, *b.* 1941, *m.*

1997   *Levy,* Michael Abraham Levy, *b.* 1944, *m.*

2010   *Lexden,* Alistair Basil Cooke, OBE, *b.* 1945

2010   *Liddle,* Roger John Liddle, *b.* 1947, *m.*

2018   *Lilley,* Peter Bruce Lilley, PC, *b.* 1943, *m.*

2010   *Lingfield,* Robert George Alexander Balchin, *b.* 1942, *m.*

1999   *Lipsey,* David Lawrence Lipsey, *b.* 1948, *m.*

2020   ‡*Lister,* Edward Julian Udny-Lister, *b.* 1949, *m.*

2014   *Lisvane,* Robert James Rogers, KCB, *b.* 1950, *m.*

2015   *Livermore,* Spencer Elliot Livermore, *b.* 1975

2013   *Livingston of Parkhead,* Ian Paul Livingston, *b.* 1964, *m.*

2016   *Llewellyn of Steep,* Edward David Gerard Llewellyn, OBE, PC, *b.* 1965, *m.*

1997   ℭ*Lloyd-Webber,* Andrew Lloyd Webber, *b.* 1948, *m.*

2011   *Loomba,* Rajinder Paul Loomba, CBE, *b.* 1943, *m.*

2006   *Low of Dalston,* Prof. Colin MacKenzie Low, CBE, *b.* 1942, *m.*

2000   ℭ*Luce,* Richard Napier Luce, KG, GCVO, PC, *b.* 1936, *m.*

2015   *Lupton,* James Roger Crompton Lupton, CBE, *b.* 1955, *m.*

2000   **Lyttelton of Aldershot,* The Viscount Chandos, *b.* 1953, *m.* (*see* Hereditary Peers)

2010   *McAvoy*, Thomas McLaughlin McAvoy, PC, *b.* 1943, *m.*

1989   *McColl of Dulwich*, Ian McColl, CBE, FRCS, FRCSE, *b.* 1933, *w.*

2010   *McConnell of Glenscorrodale*, Dr Jack Wilson McConnell, PC, *b.* 1960, *m.*

2018   *McCrea of Magherafelt and Cookstown*, Revd Dr (Robert Thomas) William McCrea, *b.* 1948, *m.*

2020   *McLoughlin*, Patrick Alan McLoughlin, CH, PC, *b.* 1957, *m.*

2010   *Macdonald of River Glaven*, Kenneth Donald John Macdonald, QC, *b.* 1953, *m.*

1998   ℂ*Macdonald of Tradeston*, Angus John Macdonald, CBE, PC, *b.* 1940, *m.*

2010   *McFall of Alcluith*, John Francis McFall, PC, *b.* 1944, *m.*

1991   ℂ*Macfarlane of Bearsden*, Norman Somerville Macfarlane, KT, FRSE, *b.* 1926, *m.*

2001   ℂ*MacGregor of Pulham Market*, John Roddick Russell MacGregor, CBE, PC, *b.* 1937, *m.*

2016   *McInnes of Kilwinning*, Mark McInnes, CBE, *b.* 1976

1979   *Mackay of Clashfern*, James Peter Hymers Mackay, KT, PC, FRSE, *b.* 1927, *m.*

1999   *MacKenzie of Culkein*, Hector Uisdean MacKenzie, *b.* 1940

1998   *Mackenzie of Framwellgate*, Brian Mackenzie, OBE, *b.* 1943, *m.*

2004   *McKenzie of Luton*, William David McKenzie, *b.* 1946, *m.*

1996   ℂ*MacLaurin of Knebworth*, Ian Charter MacLaurin, *b.* 1937, *m.*

1995   *McNally*, Tom McNally, PC, *b.* 1943, *m.*

2018   *McNicol of West Kilbride*, Iain Mackenzie McNicol, *b.* 1969, *m.*

2016   *Macpherson of Earl's Court*, Nicholas Ian Macpherson, GCB, *b.* 1959, *m.*

2011   *Magan of Castletown*, George Morgan Magan, *b.* 1945, *m.*

2001   *Maginnis of Drumglass*, Kenneth Wiggins Maginnis, *b.* 1938, *m.*

2015   *Mair*, Prof. Robert James Mair, CBE, PHD, FRS, *b.* 1950, *m.*

2007   *Malloch-Brown*, George Mark Malloch Brown, KCMG, PC, *b.* 1953, *m.*

2008   *Mandelson*, Peter Benjamin Mandelson, PC, *b.* 1953

2019   *Mann*, John Mann, *b.* 1960, *m.*

2011   *Marks of Henley-on-Thames*, Jonathan Clive Marks, QC, *b.* 1952, *m.*

2006   *Marland*, Jonathan Peter Marland, *b.* 1956

1991   *Marlesford*, Mark Shuldham Schreiber, *b.* 1931, *m.*

2015   *Maude of Horsham*, Francis Anthony Aylmer Maude, TD, PC, *b.* 1953, *m.*

2007   *Mawson*, Revd Andrew Mawson, OBE, *b.* 1954, *m.*

2004   *Maxton*, John Alston Maxton, *b.* 1936, *m.*

2013   *Mendelsohn*, Jonathan Neil Mendelsohn, *b.* 1966, *m.*

2020   *Mendoza*, Neil Francis Jeremy Mendoza, *b.* 1959, *m.*

2000   *Mitchell*, Parry Andrew Mitchell, *b.* 1943, *m.*

2000   *Mitford, Lord Redesdale. *b.* 1967, *m.* (*see* Hereditary Peers)

2008   ℂ*Mogg*, John (Frederick) Mogg, KCMG, *b.* 1943, *m.*

2010   *Monks*, John Stephen Monks, *b.* 1945, *m.*

2005   *Moonie*, Dr Lewis George Moonie, *b.* 1947, *m.*

2020   *Moore of Etchingham*, Charles Hilary Moore, *b.* 1956, *m.*

2000   *Morgan*, Kenneth Owen Morgan, *b.* 1934, *m.*

2001   *Morris of Aberavon*, John Morris, KG, PC, QC, *b.* 1931, *m.*

2006   ℂ*Morris of Handsworth*, William Manuel Morris, *b.* 1938, *w.*

2006   *Morrow*, Maurice George Morrow, *b.* 1948, *m.*

2020   *Moylan*, Daniel Michael Gerald Moylan, *b.* 1956

2015   *Murphy of Torfaen*, Paul Peter Murphy, PC, *b.* 1948

2008   *Myners*, Paul Myners, CBE, *b.* 1948, *m.*

1997   *Naseby*, Michael Wolfgang Laurence Morris, PC, *b.* 1936, *m.*

2013   *Nash*, John Alfred Stoddard Nash, *b.* 1949, *m.*

1997   *Newby*, Richard Mark Newby, OBE, PC, *b.* 1953, *m.*

1994   ℂ*Nickson*, David Wigley Nickson, KBE, FRSE, *b.* 1929, *m.*

1998   *Norton of Louth*, Philip Norton, *b.* 1951

2000   *Oakeshott of Seagrove Bay*, Matthew Alan Oakeshott, *b.* 1947, *m.*

2015   *Oates*, Jonathan Oates, *b.* 1969, *c.p.*

2012   *O'Donnell*, Augustine Thomas (Gus) O'Donnell, GCB, *b.* 1952, *m.*

2015   *O'Neill of Gatley*, Terence James O'Neill, *b.* 1957, *m.*

2015   *O'Shaughnessy*, James Richard O'Shaughnessy, *b.* 1976, *m.*

2001   ℂ*Ouseley*, Herman George Ouseley, *b.* 1945, *m.*

1992   *Owen*, David Anthony Llewellyn Owen, CH, PC, *b.* 1938, *m.*

1999   *Oxburgh*, Ernest Ronald Oxburgh, KBE, FRS, PHD, *b.* 1934, *m.*

2013   *Paddick*, Brian Leonard Paddick, *b.* 1958, *m.*

2011   *Palmer of Childs Hill*, Monroe Edward Palmer, OBE, *b.* 1938, *m.*

1991   ℂ*Palumbo*, Peter Garth Palumbo, *b.* 1935, *m.*

2013   *Palumbo of Southwark*, James Rudolph Palumbo, *b.* 1963

2008   *Pannick*, David Philip Pannick, QC, *b.* 1956, *m.*

2000   *Parekh*, Bhikhu Chhotalal Parekh, *b.* 1935, *m.*

2019   *Parkinson of Whitley Bay*, Stephen Graeme Parkinson, *b.* 1983

1999   *Patel*, Narendra Babubhai Patel, KT, *b.* 1938, *m.*

2006   *Patel of Bradford*, Prof. Kamlesh Kumar Patel, OBE, *b.* 1960, *m.*

1997   *Patten*, John Haggitt Charles Patten, PC, *b.* 1945, *m.*

2005   *Patten of Barnes*, Christopher Francis Patten, CH, PC, *b.* 1944, *m.*

1996   *Paul*, Swraj Paul, PC, *b.* 1931, *m.*

1990   *Pearson of Rannoch*, Malcolm Everard MacLaren Pearson, *b.* 1942, *m.*

2001   *Pendry*, Thomas Pendry, PC, *b.* 1934, *m.*

1998   ℂ*Phillips of Sudbury*, Andrew Wyndham Phillips, OBE, *b.* 1939, *m.*

2018   *Pickles*, Eric (Jack) Pickles, PC, *b.* 1952, *m.*

1992   *Plant of Highfield*, Prof. Raymond Plant, PHD, *b.* 1945, *m.*

1987   ℂ*Plumb*, (Charles) Henry Plumb, *b.* 1925, *w.*

2015   *Polak*, Stuart Polak, CBE, *b.* 1961

2000   *Ponsonby of Roehampton*, Lord Ponsonby of Shulbrede, *b.* 1958, *m.* (*see* Hereditary Peers)

2010   *Popat*, Dolar Amarshi Popat, *b.* 1953, *m.*

2015   *Porter of Spalding*, Gary Andrew Porter, CBE, *b.* 1960, *m.*

2000   *Powell of Bayswater*, Charles David Powell, KCMG, *b.* 1941, *m.*

2010   *Prescott*, John Leslie Prescott, *b.* 1938, *m.*

2016   *Price*, Mark Ian Price, CVO, *b.* 1961, *m.*

2015   *Prior of Brampton*, David Gifford Leathes Prior, *b.* 1954, *m.*

2013   *Purvis of Tweed*, Jeremy Purvis, *b.* 1974

1997   *Puttnam*, David Terence Puttnam, CBE, *b.* 1941, *m.*

2001   *Radice*, Giles Heneage Radice, PC, *b.* 1936, *m.*

2005   *Ramsbotham*, David John Ramsbotham, GCB, CBE, *b.* 1934, *m.*

2004   *Rana*, Dr Diljit Singh Rana, MBE, *b.* 1938

2018   *Randall of Uxbridge*, (Alexander) John Randall, PC, *b.* 1955, *m.*

2019   *Ranger*, Raminder Singh Ranger, CBE, *b.* 1947

1997   *Razzall*, (Edward) Timothy Razzall, CBE, *b.* 1943

2019 §*Reed,* Robert John Reed, PC, *b.* 1956, *m.* President of the Supreme Court

2005 *Rees of Ludlow,* Prof. Martin John Rees, OM, *b.* 1942, *m.*

2010 *Reid of Cardowan,* Dr John Reid, PC, *b.* 1947, *m.*

1991 *Renfrew of Kaimsthorn,* (Andrew) Colin Renfrew, FBA, *b.* 1937, *m.*

1999 *Rennard,* Christopher John Rennard, MBE, *b.* 1960, *m.*

1997 ₵*Renwick of Clifton,* Robin William Renwick, KCMG, *b.* 1937, *m.*

2010 *Ribeiro,* Bernard Francisco Ribeiro, CBE, *b.* 1944, *m.*

2014 *Richards of Herstmonceux,* David Julian Richards, GCB, CBE, DSO, *b.* 1952, *m.*

2016 *Ricketts,* Peter (Forbes) Ricketts, GCMG, GCVO, *b.* 1952, *m.*

2010 *Risby,* Richard John Grenville Spring, *b.* 1946

2015 *Robathan,* Andrew Robathan, PC, *b.* 1951, *m.*

2004 *Roberts of Llandudno,* Revd John Roger Roberts, *b.* 1935, *w.*

1999 *Robertson of Port Ellen,* George Islay MacNeill Robertson, KT, GCMG, PC, *b.* 1946, *m.*

1992 *Rodgers of Quarry Bank,* William Thomas Rodgers, PC, *b.* 1928, *w.*

1999 *Rogan,* Dennis Robert David Rogan, *b.* 1942, *m.*

1996 *Rogers of Riverside,* Richard George Rogers, CH, RA, RIBA, *b.* 1933, *m.*

2001 *Rooker,* Jeffrey William Rooker, PC, *b.* 1941, *m.*

2014 *Rose of Monewden,* Stuart Alan Ransom Rose, *b.* 1949

2004 *Rosser,* Richard Andrew Rosser, *b.* 1944, *m.*

2006 *Rowe-Beddoe,* David (Sydney) Rowe-Beddoe, *b.* 1937, *m.*

2004 *Rowlands,* Edward Rowlands, CBE, *b.* 1940, *w.*

1997 *Ryder of Wensum,* Richard Andrew Ryder, OBE, PC, *b.* 1949, *m.*

1996 *Saatchi,* Maurice Saatchi, *b.* 1946, *w.*

2009 *Sacks,* Chief Rabbi Dr Jonathan Henry Sacks, *b.* 1948, *m.*

1989 *Sainsbury of Preston Candover,* John Davan Sainsbury, KG, *b.* 1927, *m.*

1997 *Sainsbury of Turville,* David John Sainsbury, *b.* 1940, *m.*

1985 ₵*Sanderson of Bowden,* Charles Russell Sanderson, *b.* 1933, *m.*

2020 *Sarfraz,* Aamer Ahmad Sarfraz, *b.* 1982

2010 *Sassoon,* James Meyer Sassoon, *b.* 1955, *m.*

1998 *Sawyer,* Lawrence (Tom) Sawyer, *b.* 1943

2014 *Scriven,* Paul James Scriven, *b.* 1966

2020 *Sedwill,* Mark Philip Sedwill, KCMG, *b.* 1964, *m.*

1997 *Selkirk of Douglas,* James Alexander Douglas-Hamilton, PC, QC, *b.* 1942, *m.*

1996 ₵*Sewel,* John Buttifant Sewel, CBE, *b.* 1946

2010 *Sharkey,* John Kevin Sharkey, *b.* 1947, *m.*

1999 ₵*Sharman,* Colin Morven Sharman, OBE, *b.* 1943, *m.*

1994 ₵*Shaw of Northstead,* Michael Norman Shaw, *b.* 1920, *m.*

2006 *Sheikh,* Mohamed Iltaf Sheikh, *b.* 1941, *m.*

2013 *Sherbourne of Didsbury,* Stephen Ashley Sherbourne, CBE, *b.* 1945

2015 *Shinkwin,* Kevin Joseph Maximilian Shinkwin, *b.* 1971

2010 *Shipley,* John Warren Shipley, OBE, *b.* 1946, *m.*

2020 *Sharpe of Epsom,* Andrew Michael Gordon Sharpe, OBE, *b.* 1962

2000 *Shutt of Greetland,* David Trevor Shutt, OBE, PC, *b.* 1942, *m.*

2020 *Sikka,* Prem Nath Sikka, *b.* 1951, *m.*

1997 ₵*Simon of Highbury,* David Alec Gwyn Simon, CBE, *b.* 1939, *m.*

1997 ₵*Simpson of Dunkeld,* George Simpson, *b.* 1942, *m.*

2011 *Singh of Wimbledon,* Indarjit Singh, CBE, *b.* 1932, *m.*

1991 *Skidelsky,* Robert Jacob Alexander Skidelsky, DPHIL, *b.* 1939, *m.*

1997 ₵*Smith of Clifton,* Trevor Arthur Smith, *b.* 1937, *m.*

2005 *Smith of Finsbury,* Christopher Robert Smith, PC, *b.* 1951

2015 *Smith of Hindhead,* Philip Roland Smith, CBE, *b.* 1966

2008 *Smith of Kelvin,* Robert (Haldane) Smith, KT, CH, *b.* 1944, *m.*

1999 *Smith of Leigh,* Peter Richard Charles Smith, *b.* 1945, *m.*

2004 *Snape,* Peter Charles Snape, *b.* 1942, *m.*

2005 *Soley,* Clive Stafford Soley, *b.* 1939

2020 *Spencer,* Michael Alan Spencer, *b.* 1955, *m.*

1997 ₵*Steel of Aikwood,* David Martin Scott Steel, KT, KBE, PC, *b.* 1938, *m.*

2011 *Stephen,* Nicol Ross Stephen, *b.* 1960, *m.*

1991 *Sterling of Plaistow,* Jeffrey Maurice Sterling, GCVO, CBE, *b.* 1934, *m.*

2007 *Stern of Brentford,* Nicholas Herbert Stern, CH, *b.* 1946, *m.*

2005 *Stevens of Kirkwhelpington,* John Arthur Stevens, QPM, *b.* 1942, *m.*

1987 *Stevens of Ludgate,* David Robert Stevens, *b.* 1936, *m.*

2010 *Stevenson of Balmacara,* Robert Wilfrid Stevenson, *b.* 1947, *m.*

1999 *Stevenson of Coddenham,* Henry Dennistoun Stevenson, CBE, *b.* 1945, *m.*

2020 ‡*Stewart,* Keith Douglas Stewart, QC, *b.* 1964, *m.*

2011 *Stirrup,* Graham Eric Stirrup, KG, GCB, AFC, *b.* 1949, *m.*

1983 *Stoddart of Swindon,* David Leonard Stoddart, *b.* 1926, *m.*

1997 *Stone of Blackheath,* Andrew Zelig Stone, *b.* 1942, *m.*

2011 *Stoneham of Droxford,* Benjamin Russell Mackintosh Stoneham, *b.* 1948, *m.*

2011 *Storey,* Michael John Storey, CBE, *b.* 1949, *m.*

2011 *Strasburger,* Paul Cline Strasburger, *b.* 1946, *m.*

2015 *Stunell,* Robert Andrew Stunell, OBE, PC, *b.* 1942, *m.*

2009 *Sugar,* Alan Michael Sugar, *b.* 1947, *m.*

2014 *Suri,* Ranbir Singh Suri, *b.* 1935

1971 ₵*Tanlaw,* Simon Brooke Mackay, *b.* 1934, *m.*

1996 *Taverne,* Dick Taverne, QC, *b.* 1928, *m.*

2010 *Taylor of Goss Moor,* Matthew Owen John Taylor, *b.* 1963, *m.*

2006 *Taylor of Holbeach,* John Derek Taylor, CBE, PC, *b.* 1943, *m.*

1996 *Taylor of Warwick,* John David Beckett Taylor, *b.* 1952, *m.*

1992 *Tebbit,* Norman Beresford Tebbit, CH, PC, *b.* 1931, *m.*

2006 *Teverson,* Robin Teverson, *b.* 1952, *m.*

2013 *Thomas of Cwmgiedd,* Roger John Laugharne Thomas, PC, *b.* 1947, *m.*

1996 *Thomas of Gresford,* Donald Martin Thomas, OBE, QC, *b.* 1937, *m.*

1998 *Tomlinson,* John Edward Tomlinson, *b.* 1939, *m.*

1994 *Tope,* Graham Norman Tope, CBE, *b.* 1943, *m.*

2010 *Touhig,* James Donnelly Touhig, PC, *b.* 1947, *m.*

2012 *Trees,* Alexander John Trees, PHD, *b.* 1946, *m.*

2004 *Triesman,* David Maxim Triesman, *b.* 1943, *m.*

2006 *Trimble,* William David Trimble, PC, *b.* 1944, *m.*

2010 *True,* Nicholas Edward True, CBE, *b.* 1951, *m.*

2004 *Truscott,* Dr Peter Derek Truscott, *b.* 1959, *m.*

1993 *Tugendhat,* Christopher Samuel Tugendhat, *b.* 1937, *m.*

2004 *Tunnicliffe,* Denis Tunnicliffe, CBE, *b.* 1943, *m.*

2000 *Turnberg,* Leslie Arnold Turnberg, MD, *b.* 1934, *m.*

2005 *Turnbull,* Andrew Turnbull, KCB, CVO, PC, *b.* 1945, *m.*

2005 *Turner of Ecchinswell,* (Jonathan) Adair Turner, *b.* 1955, *m.*

2005 *Tyler,* Paul Archer Tyler, CBE, PC, *b.* 1941, *m.*

2018 *Tyrie,* Andrew Guy Tyrie, PC, *b.* 1957

2020   *Vaizey of Didcot*, Edward Henry Butler Vaizey, PC, *b.* 1968, *m.*

2004   *Vallance of Tummel*, Iain (David Thomas) Vallance, *b.* 1943, *w.*

2013   *Verjee*, Rumi Verjee, CBE, *b.* 1957

1985   *Vinson*, Nigel Vinson, LVO, *b.* 1931, *m.*

1992   *Wakeham*, John Wakeham, PC, *b.* 1932, *m.*

1999   *Waldegrave of North Hill*, William Arthur Waldegrave, PC, *b.* 1946, *m.*

2007   *Walker of Aldringham*, Michael John Dawson Walker, GCB, CMG, CBE, *b.* 1944, *m.*

1995   *Wallace of Saltaire*, William John Lawrence Wallace, PC, PHD, *b.* 1941, *m.*

2007   *Wallace of Tankerness*, James Robert Wallace, PC, QC, *b.* 1954, *m.*

2020   *Woodcock*, John Zak Woodcock, *b.* 1978

1998   *Warner*, Norman Reginald Warner, PC, *b.* 1940, *m.*

2011   *Wasserman*, Gordon Joshua Wasserman, *b.* 1938 *m.*

1997   *Watson of Invergowrie*, Michael Goodall Watson, *b.* 1949, *m.*

1999   *Watson of Richmond*, Alan John Watson, CBE, *b.* 1941, *m.*

2015   *Watts*, David Leonard Watts, *b.* 1951, *m.*

2010   *Wei*, Nathanael Ming-Yan Wei, *b.* 1977, *m.*

2007   *West of Spithead*, Alan William John West, GCB, DSC, PC, *b.* 1948, *m.*

2020   *Wharton of Yarm*, James Stephen Wharton, *b.* 1984

2013   *Whitby*, Michael John Whitby, *b.* 1948, *m.*

1996   *Whitty*, John Lawrence (Larry) Whitty, PC, *b.* 1943, *m.*

2011   *Wigley*, Dafydd Wynne Wigley, PC, *b.* 1943, *m.*

2015   *Willetts*, David Lindsay Willetts, PC, *b.* 1956, *m.*

2013   ℭ*Williams of Oystermouth*, Rt. Revd Rowan Douglas Williams, PC, Royal Victorian Chain, DPHIL, *b.* 1950, *m.*

2010   *Willis of Knaresborough*, George Philip Willis, *b.* 1941, *m.*

2010   *Wills*, Michael David Wills, PC, *b.* 1952, *m.*

2002   *Wilson of Dinton*, Richard Thomas James Wilson, GCB, *b.* 1942, *m.*

1992   *Wilson of Tillyorn*, David Clive Wilson, KT, GCMG, PHD, *b.* 1935, *m.*

1995   *Winston*, Robert Maurice Lipson Winston, FRCOG, *b.* 1940, *m.*

2010   *Wolfson of Aspley Guise*, Simon Adam Wolfson, *b.* 1967, *m.*

1991   E. *Wolfson of Sunningdale*, David Wolfson, *b.* 1935, *m.*

2011   *Wood of Anfield*, Stewart Martin Wood, *b.* 1968, *m.*

2020   ‡*Woodley*, Anthony J. Woodley, *b.* 1948, *m.*

2019   *Woolley of Woodford*, Simon Andrew Woolley, *b.* 1962

1999   ℭ*Woolmer of Leeds*, Kenneth John Woolmer, *b.* 1940, *m.*

2013   *Wrigglesworth*, Ian William Wrigglesworth, *b.* 1939, *m.*

2015   *Young of Cookham*, George Samuel Knatchbull Young, CH, PC, *b.* 1941, *m.*

1984   *Young of Graffham*, David Ivor Young, CH, PC, *b.* 1932, *m.*

2004   *Young of Norwood Green*, Anthony (Ian) Young, *b.* 1942, *m.*

BARONESSES

Created

2005   *Adams of Craigielea*, Katherine Patricia Irene Adams, *b.* 1947, *w.*

2007   *Afshar*, Prof. Haleh Afshar, OBE, *b.* 1944, *m.*

2015   *Altmann*, Dr Rosalind Miriam Altmann, CBE, *b.* 1956, *m.*

1997   *Amos*, Valerie Ann Amos, CH, PC, *b.* 1954

2000   *Andrews*, Elizabeth Kay Andrews, OBE, *b.* 1943

1996   *Anelay of St Johns*, Joyce Anne Anelay, DBE, PC, *b.* 1947, *m.*

2010   *Armstrong of Hill Top*, Hilary Jane Armstrong, PC, *b.* 1945, *m.*

1999   *Ashton of Upholland*, Catherine Margaret Ashton, GCMG, PC, *b.* 1956, *m.*

2011   *Bakewell*, Joan Dawson Bakewell, DBE, *b.* 1933

2013   *Bakewell of Hardington Mandeville*, Catherine Mary Bakewell, MBE, *b.* 1949, *m.*

1999   *Barker*, Elizabeth Jean Barker, *b.* 1961, *m.*

2018   *Barran*, Diana Francesca Caroline Barran, MBE, *b.* 1959, *m.*

2010   *Benjamin*, Floella Karen Yunies Benjamin, DBE, *b.* 1949, *m.*

2019   *Bennett of Manor Castle*, Natalie Louise Bennett, *b.*1966

2011   *Berridge*, Elizabeth Rose Berridge, *b.* 1972

2016   *Bertin*, Gabrielle Louise Bertin, *b.* 1978, *m.*

2000   *Billingham*, Angela Theodora Billingham, DPHIL, *b.* 1939, *w.*

1987   *Blackstone*, Tessa Ann Vosper Blackstone, PC, PHD, *b.* 1942

2019   *Blackwood of North Oxford*, Nicola Claire Blackwood, *b.* 1979, *m.*

1999   ℭ*Blood*, May Blood, MBE, *b.* 1938

2016   *Bloomfield of Hinton Waldrist*, Olivia Caroline Bloomfield, *b.* 1960, *m.*

2019   *Blower*, Christine Blower, *b.* 1951

2004   *Bonham-Carter of Yarnbury*, Jane Bonham Carter, *b.* 1957, *w.*

2000   *Boothroyd*, Betty Boothroyd, OM, PC, *b.* 1929

2005   *Bottomley of Nettlestone*, Virginia Hilda Brunette Maxwell Bottomley, PC, *b.* 1948, *m.*

2015   *Bowles of Berkhamsted*, Sharon Margaret Bowles, *b.* 1953, *m.*

2018   *Boycott*, Rosel Marie Boycott, MBE, *b.* 1951, *m.*

2014   *Brady*, Karren Rita Brady, CBE, *b.* 1969, *m.*

2011   *Brinton*, Sarah Virginia Brinton, *b.* 1955, *m.*

2015   *Brown of Cambridge*, Prof. Julia Elizabeth King, DBE, PHD, FRENG, *b.* 1954, *m.*

2010   *Browning*, Angela Frances Browning, *b.* 1946, *m.*

2018   *Bryan of Partick*, Pauline Christina Bryan, *b.* 1950

2018   *Bull*, Deborah Clare Bull, CBE, *b.* 1963

2015   *Burt of Solihull*, Lorely Jane Burt, *b.* 1954, *m.*

1998   *Buscombe*, Peta Jane Buscombe, *b.* 1954, *m.*

2006   *Butler-Sloss*, (Ann) Elizabeth (Oldfield) Butler-Sloss, GBE, PC, *b.* 1933, *m.*

1996   ℭ*Byford*, Hazel Byford, DBE, *b.* 1941, *w.*

2008   *Campbell of Loughborough*, Susan Catherine Campbell, DBE, *b.* 1948

2007   *Campbell of Surbiton*, Jane Susan Campbell, DBE, *b.* 1959, *m.*

2020   ‡*Casey*, Louise Casey, DBE, CB, *b.* 1965

2016   *Cavendish of Little Venice*, Hilary Camilla Cavendish, *b.* 1968, *m.*

2016   *Chakrabarti*, Sharmishta Chakrabarti, PC, CBE, *b.* 1969

1992   *Chalker of Wallasey*, Lynda Chalker, PC, *b.* 1942

2014   *Chisholm of Owlpen*, Caroline Elizabeth (Carlyn) Chisholm, *b.* 1951, *m.*

2005   *Clark of Calton*, Dr Lynda Margaret Clark, PC, *b.* 1949

2020   *Clark*, Kathryn Sloan Clark, *b.* 1967

2000   *Cohen of Pimlico*, Janet Cohen, *b.* 1940, *m.*

2005   *Corston*, Jean Ann Corston, PC, *b.* 1942, *w.*

2007   *Coussins*, Jean Coussins, *b.* 1950, *m.*

2016   *Couttie*, Philippa Marion Roe, *b.* 1962, *m.*

1982   *Cox*, Caroline Anne Cox, *b.* 1937, *w.*

1998   *Crawley*, Christine Mary Crawley, *b.* 1950, *m.*

1990   *Cumberlege*, Julia Frances Cumberlege, CBE, *b.* 1943, *m.*

2020   ‡*Davidson*, Ruth Elizabeth Davidson, PC, MSP, *b.* 1978, *m.*

2005	*Deech,* Ruth Lynn Deech, DBE, *b.* 1943, *m.*
2010	*Donaghy,* Rita Margaret Donaghy, CBE, *b.* 1944, *m.*
2010	*Doocey,* Elizabeth Deirdre Doocey, OBE, *b.* 1948, *m.*
2010	*Drake,* Jean Lesley Patricia Drake, CBE, *b.* 1948, *m.*
2004	*D'Souza,* Dr Frances Gertrude Claire D'Souza, CMG, PC, *b.* 1944, *m.*
1990	ℂ*Dunn,* Lydia Selina Dunn, DBE, *b.* 1940, *m.*
2010	*Eaton,* Ellen Margaret Eaton, DBE, *b.* 1942, *m.*
1990	*Eccles of Moulton,* Diana Catherine Eccles, *b.* 1933, *m.*
1997	ℂ*Emerton,* Audrey Caroline Emerton, DBE, *b.* 1935
2014	*Evans of Bowes Park,* Natalie Jessica Evans, PC, *b.* 1975, *m.*
2017	*Fairhead,* Rona Alison Fairhead, CBE, *b.* 1961, *m.*
2004	*Falkner of Margravine,* Kishwer Falkner, *b.* 1955, *m.*
2015	*Fall,* Catherine Susan Fall, *b.* 1967, *m.*
2015	*Featherstone,* Lynne Choona Featherstone, PC, *b.* 1951
2001	*Finlay of Llandaff,* Ilora Gillian Finlay, *b.* 1949, *m.*
2015	*Finn,* Simone Jari Finn, *b.* 1968, *m.*
1990	*Flather,* Shreela Flather, *b.* 1934, *w.*
2020	*Fleet,* Veronica Judith Colleton Wadley, CBE, *b.* 1952, *m.*
1997	*Fookes,* Janet Evelyn Fookes, DBE, *b.* 1936
2006	*Ford,* Margaret Anne Ford, OBE, *b.* 1957, *m.*
2020	*Fox of Buckley,* Claire Regina Fox, *b.* 1960
2005	*Fritchie,* Irene Tordoff Fritchie, DBE, *b.* 1942, *w.*
2020	*Fullbrook,* Lorraine Fullbrook, *b.* 1959, *m.*
1999	*Gale,* Anita Gale, *b.* 1940
2007	*Garden of Frognal,* Susan Elizabeth Garden, PC, *b.* 1944, *w.*
1981	*Gardner of Parkes,* (Rachel) Trixie (Anne) Gardner, *b.* 1927, *w.*
2013	*Goldie,* Annabel MacNicholl Goldie, *b.* 1950
2001	*Golding,* Llinos Golding, *b.* 1933, *w.*
1998	*Goudie,* Mary Teresa Goudie, *b.* 1946, *m.*
1993	ℂ*Gould of Potternewton,* Joyce Brenda Gould, *b.* 1932, *m.*
2001	*Greenfield,* Susan Adele Greenfield, CBE, *b.* 1950
2000	*Greengross,* Sally Ralea Greengross, OBE, *b.* 1935, *w.*
2013	*Grender,* Rosalind Mary Grender, MBE, *b.* 1962, *m.*
2010	*Grey-Thompson,* Tanni Carys Davina Grey-Thompson, DBE, *b.* 1969, *m.*
2019	*Hallett,* Heather Carol Hallett, DBE, PC, *b.* 1949, *m.*
1991	*Hamwee,* Sally Rachel Hamwee, *b.* 1947
1999	ℂ*Hanham,* Joan Brownlow Hanham, CBE, *b.* 1939, *m.*
2014	*Harding of Winscombe,* Diana Mary (Dido) Harding, *b.* 1967, *m.*
1999	*Harris of Richmond,* Angela Felicity Harris, *b.* 1944, *m.*
1996	*Hayman,* Helene Valerie Hayman, GBE, PC, *b.* 1949, *m.*
2020	*Hayman of Ullock,* Susan Mary Hayman, *b.* 1962, *m.*
2010	*Hayter of Kentish Town,* Dr Dianne Hayter, *b.* 1949, *m.*
2010	*Healy of Primrose Hill,* Anna Healy, *b.* 1955, *m.*
2014	*Helic,* Arminka Helic, *b.* 1968
2004	*Henig,* Ruth Beatrice Henig, CBE, *b.* 1943, *m.*
1991	*Hilton of Eggardon,* Jennifer Hilton, QPM, *b.* 1936
2013	*Hodgson of Abinger,* Fiona Ferelith Hodgson, CBE, *b.* 1954, *m.*
2020	*Hoey,* Catharine Letitia Hoey, *b.* 1946
1995	*Hogg,* Sarah Elizabeth Mary Hogg, *b.* 1946, *m.*
2010	*Hollins,* Prof. Sheila Clare Hollins, *b.* 1946, *m.*
1985	*Hooper,* Gloria Dorothy Hooper, CMG, *b.* 1939
2001	*Howarth of Breckland,* Valerie Georgina Howarth, OBE, *b.* 1940
2001	ℂ*Howe of Idlicote,* Elspeth Rosamond Morton Howe, CBE, *b.* 1932, *w.*
1999	ℂ*Howells of St Davids,* Rosalind Patricia-Anne Howells, OBE, *b.* 1931, *m.*
2010	*Hughes of Stretford,* Beverley Hughes, PC, *b.* 1950, *m.*
2013	*Humphreys,* Christine Mary Humphreys, *b.* 1947
2019	*Hunt of Bethnal Green,* Ruth Elizabeth Hunt, *b.*1980
2010	*Hussein-Ece,* Meral Hussein Ece, OBE, *b.* 1953
2014	*Janke,* Barbara Lilian Janke, *b.* 1947, *m.*
1992	*Jay of Paddington,* Margaret Ann Jay, PC, *b.* 1939, *m.*
2011	*Jenkin of Kennington,* Anne Caroline Jenkin, *b.* 1955, *m.*
2010	*Jolly,* Judith Anne Jolly, *b.* 1951, *m.*
2013	*Jones of Moulsecoomb,* Jennifer Helen Jones, *b.* 1949
2006	*Jones of Whitchurch,* Margaret Beryl Jones, *b.* 1955
2013	*Kennedy of Cradley,* Alicia Pamela Kennedy, *b.* 1969, *m.*
1997	*Kennedy of the Shaws,* Helena Ann Kennedy, QC, *b.* 1950, *m.*
2012	*Kidron,* Beeban Tania Kidron, OBE, *b.* 1961, *m.*
2011	*King of Bow,* Oona Tamsyn King, *b.* 1967, *m.*
2006	*Kingsmill,* Denise Patricia Byrne Kingsmill, CBE, *b.* 1947, *m.*
2009	*Kinnock of Holyhead,* Glenys Elizabeth Kinnock, *b.* 1944, *m.*
1997	ℂ*Knight of Collingtree,* (Joan Christabel) Jill Knight, DBE, *b.* 1927, *w.*
2010	*Kramer,* Susan Veronica Kramer, PC, *b.* 1950, *w.*
2013	*Lane-Fox of Soho,* Martha Lane Fox, CBE, *b.* 1973
2013	*Lawrence of Clarendon,* Doreen Delceita Lawrence, OBE, *b.* 1952
2010	*Liddell of Coatdyke,* Helen Lawrie Liddell, PC, *b.* 1950, *m.*
1997	ℂ*Linklater of Butterstone,* Veronica Linklater, *b.* 1943, *m.*
2011	*Lister of Burtersett,* Margot Ruth Aline Lister, CBE, *b.* 1949
1997	*Ludford,* Sarah Ann Ludford, *b.* 1951, *m.*
2004	*McDonagh,* Margaret Josephine McDonagh, *b.* 1961
2015	*McGregor-Smith,* Ruby McGregor-Smith, CBE, *b.* 1963, *m.*
1999	*McIntosh of Hudnall,* Genista Mary McIntosh, *b.* 1946
2015	*McIntosh of Pickering,* Anne Caroline Ballingall McIntosh, *b.* 1954, *m.*
1991	*Mallalieu,* Ann Mallalieu, QC, *b.* 1945
2008	*Manningham-Buller,* Elizabeth (Lydia) Manningham-Buller, LG, DCB, *b.* 1948, *m.*
2013	*Manzoor,* Zahida Parveen Manzoor, CBE, *b.* 1958, *m.*
1970	*Masham of Ilton,* Susan Lilian Primrose Cunliffe-Lister, *b.* 1935, *w.*
1999	*Massey of Darwen,* Doreen Elizabeth Massey, *b.* 1938, *m.*
2006	*Meacher,* Molly Christine Meacher, *b.* 1940, *m.*
2018	*Meyer,* Catherine Irene Jacqueline Meyer, CBE, *b.* 1953, *m.*
1998	*Miller of Chilthorne Domer,* Susan Elizabeth Miller, *b.* 1954, *m.*
2014	*Mobarik,* Nosheena Shaheen Mobarik, CBE, MEP, *b.* 1957, *m.*
2015	*Mone,* Michelle Georgina Mone, OBE, *b.* 1971
2020	*Morgan of Cotes,* Nicola Ann Morgan, PC, *b.* 1972, *m.*
2004	*Morgan of Drefelin,* Delyth Jane Morgan, *b.* 1961, *m.*
2011	*Morgan of Ely,* Mair Eluned Morgan, *b.* 1967, *m.*
2001	*Morgan of Huyton,* Sally Morgan, *b.* 1959, *m.*
2004	*Morris of Bolton,* Patricia Morris, OBE, *b.* 1953, *m.*
2005	*Morris of Yardley,* Estelle Morris, PC, *b.* 1952
2020	*Morrissey,* Helena Louise Morrissey, DBE, *b.* 1966, *m.*
2004	*Murphy,* Elaine Murphy, *b.* 1947, *m.*
2004	*Neuberger,* Rabbi Julia (Babette Sarah) Neuberger, DBE, *b.* 1950, *m.*
2007	*Neville-Jones,* (Lilian) Pauline Neville-Jones, DCMG, PC, *b.* 1939
2013	*Neville-Rolfe,* Lucy Jeanne Neville-Rolfe, DBE, CMG, *b.* 1953, *m.*
2010	*Newlove,* Helen Margaret Newlove, *b.* 1961, *w.*
1997	*Nicholson of Winterbourne,* Emma Harriet Nicholson, *b.* 1941, *w.*
2000	*Noakes,* Sheila Valerie Masters, DBE, *b.* 1949, *m.*
2000	*Northover,* Lindsay Patricia Granshaw, PC, *b.* 1954
2010	*Nye,* Susan Nye, *b.* 1955, *m.*
1991	*O'Cathain,* Detta O'Cathain, OBE, *b.* 1938, *w.*

2009   *O'Loan,* Nuala Patricia O'Loan, DBE, *b.* 1951, *m.*

1999   *O'Neill of Bengarve,* Onora Sylvia O'Neill, CH, CBE, FRS, FBA, *b.* 1941

1989   ⟪*Oppenheim-Barnes,* Sally Oppenheim-Barnes, PC, *b.* 1930, *w.*

2018   *Osamor,* Martha Otito Osamor, *b.* 1940, *w.*

2006   ⟪*Paisley of St George's,* Eileen Emily Paisley, *b.* 1931, *w.*

2010   *Parminter,* Kathryn Jane Parminter, *b.* 1964, *m.*

2019   *Penn,* Joanna Carolyn Penn, *b.* 1985

1991   ⟪*Perry of Southwark,* Pauline Perry, *b.* 1931, *w.*

2015   *Pidding,* Emma Samantha Pidding, CBE, *b.* 1966

2014   *Pinnock,* Kathryn Mary Pinnock, *b.* 1946, *m.*

1997   *Pitkeathley,* Jill Elizabeth Pitkeathley, OBE, *b.* 1940, *m.*

1999   *Prashar,* Usha Kumari Prashar, CBE, PC, *b.* 1948, *m.*

2015   *Primarolo,* Dawn Primarolo, DBE, PC, *b.* 1954, *m.*

2004   *Prosser,* Margaret Theresa Prosser, OBE, *b.* 1937

2006   *Quin,* Joyce Gwendoline Quin, PC, *b.* 1944

1996   *Ramsay of Cartvale,* Margaret Mildred (Meta) Ramsay, *b.* 1936

2011   *Randerson,* Jennifer Elizabeth Randerson, *b.* 1948, *m.*

1994   *Rawlings,* Patricia Elizabeth Rawlings, *b.* 1939

2014   *Rebuck,* Gail Ruth Rebuck, DBE, *b.* 1952, *w.*

2015   *Redfern,* Elizabeth Marie Redfern, *b.* 1947, *w.*

1998   ⟪*Richardson of Calow,* Kathleen Margaret Richardson, OBE, *b.* 1938, *m.*

2019   *Ritchie of Downpatrick,* Margaret Mary Ritchie, *b.* 1958

2015   *Rock,* Kate Harriet Alexandra Rock, *b.* 1968, *m.*

2004   *Royall of Blaisdon,* Janet Anne Royall, PC, *b.* 1955, *m.*

2019   *Sanderson of Welton,* Elizabeth Jenny Rosemary Sanderson, *b.*1971

2018   *Sater,* Amanda Jacqueline Sater, *b.* 1960, *m.*

1997   *Scotland of Asthal,* Patricia Janet Scotland, PC, QC, *b.* 1955, *m.*

2015   *Scott of Bybrook,* Jane Antoinette Scott, OBE, *b.* 1947, *m.*

2000   *Scott of Needham Market,* Rosalind Carol Scott, *b.* 1957, *m.*

1991   *Seccombe,* Joan Anna Dalziel Seccombe, DBE, *b.* 1930, *w.*

2010   *Shackleton of Belgravia,* Fiona Sara Shackleton, LVO, *b.* 1956, *m.*

2020   *Shafik,* Nemat (Minouche) Talaat Shafik, DBE, *b.* 1962, *m.*

1998   ⟪*Sharp of Guildford,* Margaret Lucy Sharp, *b.* 1938, *m.*

1973   ⟪*Sharples,* Pamela Sharples, *b.* 1923, *w.*

2015   *Sheehan,* Shaista Ahmad Sheehan, *b.* 1959, *m.*

2005   *Shephard of Northwold,* Gillian Patricia Shephard, PC, *b.* 1940, *m.*

2010   *Sherlock,* Maeve Christina Mary Sherlock, OBE, *b.* 1960

2014   *Shields,* Joanna Shields, OBE, *b.* 1962, *m.*

2010   *Smith of Basildon,* Angela Evans Smith, PC, *b.* 1959, *m.*

1995   *Smith of Gilmorehill,* Elizabeth Margaret Smith, *b.* 1940, *w.*

2014   *Smith of Newnham,* Dr Julie Elizabeth Smith, *b.* 1969

2010   *Stedman-Scott,* Deborah Stedman-Scott, OBE, *b.* 1955, *c.p.*

1999   *Stern,* Vivien Helen Stern, CBE, *b.* 1941

2020   *Stuart of Edgbaston,* Gisela Stuart, PC, *b.* 1955, *w.*

2011   *Stowell of Beeston,* Tina Wendy Stowell, MBE, PC, *b.* 1967

2015   *Stroud,* Philippa Claire Stroud, *b.* 1965, *m.*

2016   *Sugg,* Elizabeth Grace Sugg, CBE, *b.* 1977

2013   *Suttie,* Alison Mary Suttie, *b.* 1968

1996   *Symons of Vernham Dean,* Elizabeth Conway Symons, PC, *b.* 1951, *w.*

2005   *Taylor of Bolton,* Winifred Ann Taylor, PC, *b.* 1947, *m.*

1994   **E.** *Thomas of Walliswood,* Susan Petronella Thomas, OBE, *b.* 1935, *w.*

2006   *Thomas of Winchester,* Celia Marjorie Thomas, MBE, *b.* 1945

2015   *Thornhill,* Dorothy Thornhill, MBE, *b.* 1955, *m.*

1998   *Thornton,* (Dorothea) Glenys Thornton, *b.* 1952, *m.*

2005   *Tonge,* Dr Jennifer Louise Tonge, *b.* 1941, *m.*

2011   *Tyler of Enfield,* Claire Tyler, *b.* 1957

1998   *Uddin,* Manzila Pola Uddin, *b.* 1959, *m.*

2007   *Vadera,* Shriti Vadera, PC, *b.* 1962

2005   *Valentine,* Josephine Clare Valentine, *b.* 1958, *m.*

2016   *Vere of Norbiton,* Charlotte Sarah Emily Vere, *b.* 1969

2006   *Verma,* Sandip Verma, *b.* 1959, *m.*

2000   *Walmsley,* Joan Margaret Walmsley, *b.* 1943, *m.*

2007   *Warsi,* Sayeeda Hussain Warsi, PC, *b.* 1971, *m.*

1999   *Warwick of Undercliffe,* Diana Mary Warwick, *b.* 1945, *m.*

2015   *Watkins of Tavistock,* Mary Jane Watkins, PHD, *b.* 1955, *m.*

2010   *Wheatcroft,* Patience Jane Wheatcroft, *b.* 1951, *m.*

2010   *Wheeler,* Margaret Eileen Joyce Wheeler, MBE, *b.* 1949

1999   *Whitaker,* Janet Alison Whitaker, *b.* 1936, *w.*

1996   *Wilcox,* Judith Ann Wilcox, *b.* 1940, *w.*

2019   *Wilcox of Newport,* Deborah Ann Wilcox, *b.* 1969

1999   ⟪*Wilkins,* Rosalie Catherine Wilkins, *b.* 1946

1993   ⟪*Williams of Crosby,* Shirley Vivien Teresa Brittain Williams, CH, PC, *b.* 1930, *w.*

2013   *Williams of Trafford,* Susan Frances Maria Williams, *b.* 1967, *m.*

2014   *Wolf of Dulwich,* Alison Margaret Wolf, CBE, *b.* 1949, *m.*

2011   *Worthington,* Bryony Katherine Worthington, *b.* 1971, *m.*

2017   *Wyld,* Laura Lee Wyld, *b.* 1978, *m.*

2004   *Young of Hornsey,* Prof. Margaret Omolola Young, OBE, *b.* 1951, *m.*

1997   *Young of Old Scone,* Barbara Scott Young, *b.* 1948

COURTESY TITLES

The heir apparent to a Duke, Marquess or Earl uses the highest of his father's other titles as a courtesy title. For example, the Marquess of Blandford is heir to the Dukedom of Marlborough, and Viscount Amberley to the Earldom of Russell. Titles of second heirs (when in use) are also given, and the courtesy title of the father of a second heir is indicated by * eg Earl of Mornington, eldest son of *Marquess of Douro.

The holder of a courtesy title is not styled 'the Most Hon.' or 'the Rt. Hon.', and in correspondence 'the' is omitted before the title. The heir apparent to a Scottish title may use the title 'Master'.

MARQUESSES

Blandford – *Marlborough, D.*
Douglas and Clydesdale – *Hamilton and Brandon, D.*
Graham – *Montrose, D.*
Granby – *Rutland, D.*
*Hamilton – *Abercorn, D.*
Lorne – *Argyll, D.*
Stafford – *Sutherland, D.*
Tavistock – *Bedford, D.*
Tullibardine – *Atholl, D.*
Worcester – *Beaufort, D.*

EARLS

*Aboyne – *Huntly, M.*
Altamont – *Sligo, M.*
Arundel and Surrey – *Norfolk, D.*
Bective – *Headfort, M.*
Belfast – *Donegall, M.*
Brecknock – *Camden, M.*
*Burford – *St Albans, D.*
*Burlington – *Devonshire, D.*
*Cardigan – *Ailesbury, M.*
Cassilis – *Ailsa, M.*
Compton – *Northampton, M.*
Dalkeith – *Buccleuch and Queensberry, D.*
Dumfries – *Bute, M.*
Euston – *Grafton, D.*
Haddo – *Aberdeen and Temair, M.*
Hillsborough – *Downshire, M.*
*Hopetoun – *Linlithgow, M.*
*Kerry – *Lansdowne, M.*
March and Kinrara – *Richmond, Gordon and Lennox, D.*
Medina – *Milford Haven, M.*
*Mornington – *Wellington, D.*
*Mount Charles – *Conyngham, M.*
Mulgrave – *Normanby, M.*
Percy – *Northumberland, D.*
Rocksavage – *Cholmondeley, M.*
Ronaldshay – *Zetland, M.*
*St Andrews – *Kent, D.*
Southesk – *Fife, D.*
Tyrone – *Waterford, M.*
*Ulster – *Gloucester, D.*
Uxbridge – *Anglesey, M.*
*Wiltshire – *Winchester, M.*
Yarmouth – *Hertford, M.*

VISCOUNTS

Aithrie – *Hopetoun, E.*
Alexander – *Caledon, E.*

Althorp – *Spencer, E.*
Andover – *Suffolk and Berkshire, E.*
Anson – *Lichfield, E.*
Asquith – *Oxford and Asquith, E.*
Borodale – *Beatty, E.*
Bury – *Albemarle, E.*
Calne and Calston – *Kerry, E.*
Campden – *Gainsborough, E.*
Carlow – *Portarlington, E.*
Carlton – *Wharncliffe, E.*
Chelsea – *Cadogan, E.*
Chewton – *Waldegrave, E.*
Clanfield – *Peel, E.*
Clive – *Powis, E.*
Coke – *Leicester, E.*
Corry – *Belmore, E.*
Corvedale – *Baldwin of Bewdley, E.*
Cranborne – *Salisbury, M.*
Crowhurst – *Cottenham, E.*
Curzon – *Howe, E.*
Dalrymple – *Stair, E.*
Dangan – *Cowley, E.*
Drumlanrig – *Queensberry, M.*
Duncannon – *Bessborough, E.*
Dungarvan – *Cork and Orrery, E.*
Dunluce – *Antrim, E.*
Dunwich – *Stradbroke, E.*
Dupplin – *Kinnoull, E.*
Elveden – *Iveagh, E.*
Emlyn – *Cawdor, E.*
Encombe – *Eldon, E.*
Enfield – *Strafford, E.*
Erleigh – *Reading, M.*
Errington – *Cromer, E.*
Feilding – *Denbigh and Desmond, E.*
FitzHarris – *Malmesbury, E.*
Folkestone – *Radnor, E.*
Forbes – *Granard, E.*
Garmoyle – *Cairns, E.*
Garnock – *Lindsay, E.*
Glenapp – *Inchcape, E.*
Glerawly – *Annesley, E.*
Grey de Wilton – *Wilton, E.*
Grimston – *Verulam, E.*
Gwynedd – *Lloyd George of Dwyfor, E.*
Hawkesbury – *Liverpool, E.*
Hinchingbrooke – *Sandwich, E.*
Howick – *Grey, E.*
Ikerrin – *Carrick, E.*
Ingestre – *Shrewsbury and Waterford, E.*
Jocelyn – *Roden, E.*

Kelburn – *Glasgow, E.*
Kingsborough – *Kingston, E.*
Kirkwall – *Orkney, E.*
Knebworth – *Lytton, E.*
Lambton – *Durham, E.*
Lascelles – *Harewood, E.*
Linley – *Snowdon, E.*
Lymington – *Portsmouth, E.*
Macmillan of Ovenden – *Stockton, E.*
Maidstone – *Winchilsea and Nottingham, E.*
Maitland – *Lauderdale, E.*
Marsham – *Romney, E.*
Melgund – *Minto, E.*
Merton – *Nelson, E.*
Moore – *Drogheda, E.*
Newport – *Bradford, E.*
Newry and Mourne – *Kilmorey, E.*
Northland – *Ranfurly, E.*
Pery – *Limerick, E.*
Petersham – *Harrington, E.*
Pollington – *Mexborough, E.*
Raynham – *Townshend, M.*
Reidhaven – *Seafield, E.*
Royston – *Hardwicke, E.*
Ruthven of Canberra – *Gowrie, E.*
St Cyres – *Iddesleigh, E.*
Sandon – *Harrowby, E.*
Savernake – *Cardigan, E.*
Severn – *Wessex, E.*
Slane – *Mount Charles, M.*
Somerton – *Normanton, E.*
Stopford – *Courtown, E.*
Stormont – *Mansfield and Mansfield, E.*
Strabane – *Hamilton, M.*
Strathallan – *Perth, E.*
Stuart – *Castle Stewart, E.*
Suirdale – *Donoughmore, E.*
Tamworth – *Ferrers, E.*
Tarbat – *Cromartie, E.*
Villiers – *Jersey, E.*
Wellesley – *Mornington, E.*
Weymouth – *Bath, M.*
Windsor – *Plymouth, E.*
Wolmer – *Selborne, E.*
Woodstock – *Portland, E.*

BARONS (LORDS)

Aberdour – *Morton, E.*
Apsley – *Bathurst, E.*
Ardee – *Meath, E.*
Ashley – *Shaftesbury, E.*
Balniel – *Crawford and Balcarres, E.*
Berriedale – *Caithness, E.*

Bingham – *Lucan, E.*
Brabourne – *Mountbatten of Burma, E.*
Brooke – *Warwick and Brooke, E.*
Bruce – *Elgin and Kincardine, E.*
Buckhurst – *De La Warr, E.*
Burghley – *Exeter, M.*
Cardross – *Buchan, E.*
Cavendish – *Burlington, E.*
Clifton – *Darnley, E.*
Cochrane – *Dundonald, E.*
Courtenay – *Devon, E.*
Culloden – * *Ulster, E.*
Dalmeny – *Rosebery, E.*
Doune – *Moray, E.*
Downpatrick – *St Andrews, E.*
Dunglass – *Home, E.*
Elcho – *Wemyss and March, E.*
Garlies – *Galloway, E.*
Gillford – *Clanwilliam, E.*
Greenock – *Cathcart, E.*
Guernsey – *Aylesford, E.*
Hay – *Erroll, E.*
Herbert – *Pembroke and Montgomery, E.*
Howard of Effingham – *Effingham, E.*
Huntingtower – *Dysart, E.*
Hyde – *Clarendon, E.*
Inverurie – *Kintore, E.*
Irwin – *Halifax, E.*
Johnstone – *Annandale and Hartfell, E.*
Leveson – *Granville, E.*
Loughborough – *Rosslyn, E.*
Masham – *Swinton, E.*
Medway – *Cranbrook, E.*
Montgomerie – *Eglinton and Winton, E.*
Moreton – *Ducie, E.*
Naas – *Mayo, E.*
Norreys – *Lindsey and Abingdon, E.*
North – *Guilford, E.*
Ogilvy – *Airlie, E.*
Oxmantown – *Rosse, E.*
Porchester – *Carnarvon, E.*
Ramsay – *Dalhousie, E.*
St John – *Wiltshire, E.*
Scrymgeour – *Dundee, E.*
Seymour – *Somerset, D.*
Stanley – *Derby, E.*
Strathavon – *Aboyne, E.*
Strathnaver – *Sutherland, E.*
Vere of Hanworth – *Burford, E.*
Wodehouse – *Kimberley, E.*
Worsley – *Yarborough, E.*

PEERS' SURNAMES

The following symbols indicate the rank of the peer holding each title:

C. Countess
D. Duke
E. Earl
M. Marquess
V. Viscount
* Life Peer

Where no designation is given, the title is that of a hereditary Baron or Baroness.

Abney-Hastings — Loudoun, E.
Acheson — Gosford, E.
Adams — A. of Craigielea*
Adderley — Norton
Addington — Sidmouth, V.
Agar — Normanton, E.
Agnew — A. of Oulton*
Ahmad — A. of Wimbledon*
Aitken — Beaverbrook
Akers-Douglas — Chilston, V.
Alexander — A. of Tunis, E.
Alexander — Caledon, E.
Allan — A. of Hallam*
Allen — A. of Kensington*
Allsopp — Hindlip
Alton — A. of Liverpool*
Anderson — A. of Ipswich*
Anderson — A. of Swansea*
Anderson — Waverley, V.
Anelay — A. of St Johns*
Annesley — Valentia, V.
Anson — Lichfield, E.
Arbuthnot — A. of Edrom*
Archer — A. of Weston-super-Mare*
Armstrong — A. of Hill Top*
Armstrong-Jones — Snowdon, E.
Arthur — Glenarthur
Arundell — Talbot of Malahide
Ashley-Cooper — Shaftesbury, E.
Ashton — A. of Hyde
Ashton — A. of Upholland*
Asquith — Oxford and Asquith, E.
Assheton — Clitheroe
Astley — Hastings
Astor — A. of Hever
Aubrey-Fletcher — Braye
Austin — A. of Dudley*
Bailey — Glanusk
Baillie — Burton
Baillie Hamilton — Haddington, E.
Baker — B. of Dorking*
Bakewell — B. of Hardington Mandeville*
Balchin — Lingfield*
Baldwin — B. of Bewdley, E.
Balfour — Kinross
Balfour — Riverdale
Bampfylde — Poltimore

Banbury — B. of Southam
Baring — Ashburton
Baring — Cromer, E.
Baring — Howick of Glendale
Baring — Northbrook
Baring — Revelstoke
Barker — B. of Battle*
Barnes — Gorell
Barnewall — Trimlestown
Bassam — B. of Brighton*
Bathurst — Bledisloe, V.
Beamish — Dacre
Beauclerk — St Albans, D.
Beaumont — Allendale, V.
Beckett — Grimthorpe
Benn — Stansgate, V.
Bennet — Tankerville, E.
Bennett — B. of Manor Castle*
Bentinck — Portland, E.
Beresford — Decies
Beresford — Waterford, M.
Berkeley — B. of Knighton*
Berry — Camrose, V.
Berry — Kemsley, V.
Bertie — Lindsey and Abingdon, E.
Best — Wynford
Bethell — Westbury
Bewicke-Copley — Cromwell
Bigham — Mersey, V.
Bingham — Clanmorris
Bingham — Lucan, E.
Bishop — Glendonbrook*
Black — B. of Brentwood*
Black — B. of Crossharbour*
Blackwood — B. of North Oxford*
Blackwood — Dufferin and Clandeboye
Blair — B. of Boughton*
Bligh — Darnley, E.
Bloomfield — B. of Hinton Waldrist*
Blyth — B. of Rowington*
Bonham Carter — B.-C. of Yarnbury*
Bootle-Wilbraham — Skelmersdale
Boscawen — Falmouth, V.
Boswell — B. of Aynho*
Bottomley — B. of Nettlestone*
Bourke — Mayo, E.
Bourne — B. of Aberystwyth*
Bowes Lyon — Strathmore and Kinghorne, E.
Bowles — B. of Berkhamsted*
Bowyer — Denham
Boyd — B. of Duncansby*
Boyd — Kilmarnock
Boyle — Cork and Orrery, E.
Boyle — Glasgow, E.
Boyle — Shannon, E.
Brabazon — Meath, E.
Brand — Hampden, V.
Brassey — B. of Apethorpe
Bryan — B. of Partick*

Brett — Esher, V.
Bridgeman — Bradford, E.
Brodrick — Midleton, V.
Brooke — B. of Alverthorpe*
Brooke — B. of Sutton Mandeville*
Brooke — Brookeborough, V.
Brooks — Crawshaw
Brougham — Brougham and Vaux
Broughton — Fairhaven
Brown — B. of Eaton-under-Heywood*
Browne — B. of Belmont*
Browne — B. of Ladyton*
Browne — B. of Madingley*
Browne — Kilmaine
Browne — Oranmore and Browne
Browne — Sligo, M.
Brownlow — B. of Shurlock Row*
Bruce — Aberdare
Bruce — Balfour of Burleigh
Bruce — B. of Bennachie*
Bruce — Elgin and Kincardine, E.
Brudenell-Bruce — Ailesbury, M.
Buchan — Tweedsmuir
Buckley — Wrenbury
Burnett — B. of Maldon*
Burt — B. of Solihull*
Butler — B. of Brockwell*
Butler — Carrick, E.
Butler — Dunboyne
Butler — Mountgarret, V.
Byng — Strafford, E.
Byng — Torrington, V.
Cameron — C. of Dillington*
Cameron — C. of Lochbroom*
Campbell — Argyll, D.
Campbell — C. of Loughborough*
Campbell — C. of Pittenweem*
Campbell — C. of Surbiton*
Campbell — Cawdor, E.
Campbell — Colgrain
Campbell — Stratheden and Campbell
Campbell-Gray — Gray
Canning — Garvagh
Capell — Essex, E.
Carey — C. of Clifton*
Carington — Carrington
Carlisle — C. of Berriew*
Carnegie — Fife, D.
Carnegy — Northesk, E.
Carrington — C. of Fulham*
Carter — C. of Barnes*
Carter — C. of Coles*
Carter — C. of Haslemere*
Cary — Falkland, V.
Caulfeild — Charlemont, V.
Cavendish — C. of Furness*
Cavendish — C. of Little Venice*

Cavendish — Chesham
Cavendish — Devonshire, D.
Cavendish — Waterpark
Cayzer — Rotherwick
Cecil — Amherst of Hackney
Cecil — Exeter, M.
Cecil — Rockley
Chalker — C. of Wallasey*
Chaloner — Gisborough
Charteris — Wemyss and March, E.
Chetwynd-Talbot — Shrewsbury and Waterford, E.
Chichester — Donegall, M.
Child Villiers — Jersey, E.
Chisholm — C. of Owlpen*
Cholmondeley — Delamere
Chubb — Hayter
Clark — C. of Calton*
Clark — C. of Kilwinning*
Clarke — C. of Hampstead*
Clarke — C. of Nottingham*
Clarke — C. of Stone-Cum-Ebony*
Clegg-Hill — Hill, V.
Clifford — C. of Chudleigh
Cochrane — C. of Cults
Cochrane — Dundonald, E.
Cocks — Somers
Cohen — C. of Pimlico*
Cokayne — Cullen of Ashbourne
Coke — Leicester, E.
Cole — Enniskillen, E.
Collier — Monkswell
Collins — C. of Highbury*
Collins — C. of Mapesbury*
Colville — Clydesmuir
Colville — C. of Culross, V.
Compton — Northampton, M.
Conolly-Carew — Carew
Cooke — Lexden*
Cooper — C. of Windrush*
Cooper — Norwich, V.
Cope — C. of Berkeley*
Corbett — Rowallan
Cornwall-Legh — Grey of Codnor
Courtenay — Devon, E.
Craig — C. of Radley*
Craig — Craigavon, V.
Crichton — Erne, E.
Crichton-Stuart — Bute, M.
Cripps — Parmoor
Crossley — Somerleyton
Cubitt — Ashcombe
Cunliffe-Lister — Masham of Ilton*
Cunliffe-Lister — Swinton, E.
Cunningham — C. of Felling*
Currie — C. of Marylebone*
Curry — C. of Kirkharle*
Curzon — Howe, E.
Curzon — Scarsdale, V.
Cust — Brownlow
Czernin — Howard de Walden
Dalrymple — Stair, E.

Windsor – *Kent, D.*	Wolfson – *W. of Sunningdale*★	Wright – *W. of Richmond*★	Young – *Kennet*
Windsor-Clive – *Plymouth, E.*	Wood – *Halifax, E.*	Wyndham – *Egremont and*	Young – *Y. of Cookham*★
Wingfield – *Powerscourt, V.*	Wood – *W. of Anfield*★	*Leconfield*	Young – *Y. of Graffham*★
Winn – *St Oswald*	Woodcock – *Walney*★	Wynn – *Newborough*	Young – *Y. of Hornsey*★
Wodehouse – *Kimberley, E.*	Woodhouse – *Terrington*	Yarde-Buller – *Churston*	Young – *Y. of Norwood Green*★
Wolf – *W. of Dulwich*★	Woolley – *W. of Woodford*★	Yerburgh – *Alvingham*	Young – *Y. of Old Scone*★
Wolfson – *W. of Aspley Guise*★	Woolmer – *W. of Leeds*★	Yorke – *Hardwicke, E.*	Younger – *Y. of Leckie, V.*

LORDS SPIRITUAL

The Lords Spiritual are the Archbishops of Canterbury and York and 24 other diocesan bishops of the Church of England. The Bishops of London, Durham and Winchester always have seats in the House of Lords; the other 21 seats were previously filled by the remaining diocesan bishops in order of seniority. However, the Lords Spiritual (Women) Act 2015 provides for vacancies among the remaining 21 places to be filled by any female diocesan bishop in office at the time and, only if there is no female diocesan bishop without a seat, by the longest serving male diocesan bishop. The provision will remain in place for ten years from 2015, equivalent to two fixed-term parliaments. At the end of this period, the provision under the Act will end and the previous arrangements under which vacancies are filled according to length of service as a diocesan bishop will be restored.

The Bishop of Sodor and Man and the Bishop of Gibraltar in Europe are not eligible to sit in the House of Lords.

ARCHBISHOPS

Style, The Most Revd and Rt. Hon. the Lord Archbishop of_
Addressed as Archbishop *or* Your Grace

INTRODUCED TO HOUSE OF LORDS

2012   *Canterbury* (105th), Justin Portal Welby, PC, *b.* 1956, *m., cons.* 2011, *elected* 2011, *trans.* 2013

2006   *York* (98th), Stephen Geoffrey Cottrell, PC, *b.* 1958, *m., cons.* 2004, *elected* 2010, *trans.* 2020

BISHOPS

Style, The Rt. Revd the Lord/Lady Bishop of _
Addressed as Bishop *or* My Lord/Lady
elected date of confirmation as diocesan bishop

INTRODUCED TO HOUSE OF LORDS
as at December 2020

2010   *Birmingham* (9th), David Andrew Urquhart, KCMG, *b.* 1952, *cons.* 2000, *elected* 2006

2012   *Worcester* (113th), John Geoffrey Inge, PHD, *b.* 1955, *m., cons.* 2003, *elected* 2007

2012   *Winchester* (97th), Timothy John Dakin, *b.* 1958, *m., elected* 2011, *cons.* 2012

2013   *Coventry* (9th), Christopher John Cocksworth, PHD, *b.* 1959, *m., cons.* 2008, *elected* 2008

2013   *Oxford* (44th), Stephen John Lindsey Croft, PHD, *b.* 1957, *m., cons.* 2009, *elected* 2009, *trans.* 2016

2013   *Carlisle* (66th), James William Scobie Newcome, *b.* 1953, *m., cons.* 2002, *elected* 2009

2013   *St Albans* (10th), Alan Gregory Clayton Smith, PHD, *b.* 1957, *cons.* 2001, *elected* 2009

2014   *Peterborough* (38th), Donald Spargo Allister, *b.* 1952, *m., cons.* 2010, *elected* 2010

2014   *Portsmouth* (9th), Christopher Richard James Foster, *b.* 1953, *m., cons.* 2001, *elected* 2010

2014   *Chelmsford* (10th), Stephen Geoffrey Cottrell, *b.* 1958, *m., cons.* 2004, *elected* 2010

2014   *Rochester* (107th), James Henry Langstaff, *b.* 1956, *m., cons.* 2004, *elected* 2010

2014   *Ely* (69th), Stephen David Conway, *b.* 1957, *cons.* 2006, *elected* 2010

2014   *Southwark* (10th), Christopher Thomas James Chessun, *b.* 1956, *cons.* 2005, *elected* 2011

2014   *Durham* (74th), Paul Roger Butler, *b.* 1955, *m., cons.* 2004, *elected* 2009, *trans.* 2014

2015   *Leeds* (1st), Nicholas Baines, *b.* 1957, *m., cons.* 2003, *elected* 2011, *trans.* 2014

2015   *Salisbury* (78th), Nicholas Roderick Holtam, *b.* 1954, *m., cons.* 2011, *elected* 2011

2015   *Gloucester* (41st), Rachel Treweek, *b.* 1963, *m., cons.* 2015, *elected* 2015

2016   *Newcastle* (12th), Christine Elizabeth Hardman, *b.* 1951, *m., cons.* 2015, *elected* 2015

2017   *Lincoln* (72nd), Christopher Lowson, *b.* 1953, *m., cons.* 2011, *elected* 2011

2018   *Chichester* (103rd), Martin Clive Warner, PHD, *b.* 1958, *cons.* 2010, *elected* 2012

2018   *Bristol* (56th), Vivienne Frances Faull, *b.* 1955, *m., cons.* 2018, *elected* 2018

2018   *London* (133rd), Dame Sarah Elisabeth Mullally, DBE, PC, *b.* 1952, *m., cons.* 2015, *elected* 2018

2019   *Derby* (8th), Elizabeth Jane Holden Lane, *b.* 1966, *m., cons.* 2015, *elected* 2019

2020   *Blackburn* (9th), Julian Tudor Henderson, *b.* 1954, *m., cons.* 2013, *elected* 2013

2020   *Manchester* (12th), David Stuart Walker, *b.* 1957, *m., cons.* 2000, *elected* 2013

BISHOPS AWAITING SEATS, in order of seniority
as at December 2020
Bath and Wells (79th), Peter Hancock, *b.* 1955, *m., cons.* 2010, *elected* 2014
Exeter (71st), Robert Ronald Atwell, *b.* 1954, *cons.* 2008, *elected* 2014
Liverpool (8th), Paul Bayes, *b.* 1953, *m., cons.* 2010, *elected* 2014
Hereford (106th), Richard Charles Jackson, *b.* 1961, *m., cons.* 2014, *elected* 2019
Guildford (10th), Andrew John Watson, *b.* 1961, *m., cons.* 2008, *elected* 2014
St Edmundsbury and Ipswich (11th), Martin Alan Seeley, *b.* 1954, *m., cons.* 2015, *elected* 2015
Southwell and Nottingham (12th), Paul Gavin Williams, *b.* 1968, *m., cons.* 2009, *elected* 2015
Leicester (7th), Martyn James Snow, *b.* 1968, *m., cons.* 2013, *elected* 2016
Lichfield (99th), Michael Geoffrey Ipgrave, OBE, PHD, *b.* 1958, *m., cons.* 2012, *elected* 2016
Sheffield (8th), Peter Jonathan Wilcox, DPHIL, *b.* 1961, *m., cons.* 2017, *elected* 2017
Truro (16th), Philip Ian Mountstephen, *b.* 1959, *m., cons.* 2018, *elected* 2018
Norwich (72nd), Graham Barham Usher, *b.* 1970, *m., cons.* 2014, *elected* 2019
Chester (41st), Mark Simon Austin Tanner, *b.* 1970, *m., cons.* 2016, *elected* 2020
Chelmsford, vacant

ORDERS OF CHIVALRY

THE MOST NOBLE ORDER OF THE GARTER (1348)

KG
Ribbon, Blue
Motto, Honi soit qui mal y pense (*Shame on him who thinks evil of it*)

The number of Knights and Ladies Companion is limited to 24

SOVEREIGN OF THE ORDER
The Queen

LADIES OF THE ORDER
HRH The Princess Royal, 1994
HRH Princess Alexandra, The Hon. Lady Ogilvy, 2003

ROYAL KNIGHTS
HRH The Prince Philip, Duke of Edinburgh, 1947
HRH The Prince of Wales, 1958
HRH The Duke of Kent, 1985
HRH The Duke of Gloucester, 1997
HRH The Duke of York, 2006
HRH The Earl of Wessex, 2006
HRH The Duke of Cambridge, 2008

EXTRA KNIGHTS COMPANION AND LADIES
HM The Queen of Denmark, 1979
HM The King of Sweden, 1983
HM King Juan Carlos, 1988
HRH Princess Beatrix of the Netherlands, 1989
HIM, Akihito, Emperor Emeritus of Japan, 1998
HM The King of Norway, 2001
HM The King of Spain, 2017
HM The King of the Netherlands, 2018

KNIGHTS AND LADIES COMPANION
Lord Sainsbury of Preston Candover, 1992
Sir Timothy Colman, 1996
Duke of Abercorn, 1999
Lord Inge, 2001
Sir Anthony Acland, 2001
Lord Butler of Brockwell, 2003
Lord Morris of Aberavon, 2003
Sir John Major, 2005
Lord Luce, 2008
Sir Thomas Dunne, 2008
Lord Phillips of Worth Matravers, 2011
Lord Boyce, 2011
Lord Stirrup, 2013
Baroness Manningham-Buller, 2014
Lord King of Lothbury, 2014
Lord Shuttleworth, 2016
Sir David Brewer, 2016
Viscount Brookeborough, 2018
Dame Mary Fagan, 2018
Marquess of Salisbury, 2019
Dame Mary Peters, 2019

Prelate, Bishop of Winchester
Chancellor, Duke of Abercorn, KG
Register, Dean of Windsor, KCVO
Garter King of Arms, Thomas Woodcock, CVO
Lady Usher of the Black Rod, Sarah Clarke, OBE
Secretary, Patric Dickinson, LVO

THE MOST ANCIENT AND MOST NOBLE ORDER OF THE THISTLE (REVIVED 1687)

KT
Ribbon, Green
Motto, Nemo me impune lacessit (*No one provokes me with impunity*)

The number of Knights and Ladies of the Thistle is limited to 16

SOVEREIGN OF THE ORDER
The Queen

ROYAL KNIGHTS
HRH The Prince Philip, Duke of Edinburgh, 1952
HRH The Prince of Wales, Duke of Rothesay, 1977
HRH The Duke of Cambridge, Earl of Strathearn, 2012

ROYAL LADY OF THE ORDER
HRH The Princess Royal, 2000

KNIGHTS AND LADIES
Earl of Elgin and Kincardine, 1981
Earl of Airlie, 1985
Earl of Crawford and Balcarres, 1996
Lord Macfarlane of Bearsden, 1996
Lord Mackay of Clashfern, 1997
Lord Wilson of Tillyorn, 2000
Lord Steel of Aikwood, 2004
Lord Robertson of Port Ellen, 2004
Lord Cullen of Whitekirk, 2007
Lord Hope of Craighead, 2009
Lord Patel, 2009
Earl of Home, 2013
Lord Smith of Kelvin, 2013
Duke of Buccleuch and Queensberry, 2017
Sir Ian Wood, 2018

Chancellor, Earl of Airlie, KT, GCVO, PC
Dean, Very Revd Prof. David Fergusson, OBE
Secretary, Mrs Christopher Roads, LVO
Lord Lyon King of Arms, Dr Joseph Morrow, CBE, QC
Gentleman Usher of the Green Rod, Rear-Adm. Christopher Layman, CB, DSO, LVO

THE MOST HONOURABLE ORDER OF THE BATH (1725)

GCB   GCB *Civil*
Military

GCB   Knight (or Dame) Grand Cross
KCB   Knight Commander
DCB   Dame Commander
CB   Companion

Ribbon, Crimson
Motto, Tria juncta in uno (*Three joined in one*)

Remodelled 1815, and enlarged many times since. The order is divided into civil and military divisions. Women became eligible for the order from 1 January 1971.

THE SOVEREIGN

GREAT MASTER AND FIRST OR PRINCIPAL KNIGHT GRAND CROSS
HRH The Prince of Wales, KG, KT, GCB, OM

Dean of the Order, Dean of Westminster
King of Arms, Air Chief Marshal Sir Stephen Dalton, GCB
Registrar and Secretary, Rear-Adm. Iain Henderson, CB, CBE

Genealogist, Thomas Woodcock, CVO
Gentleman Usher of the Scarlet Rod, Maj.-Gen. James Gordon, CB, CBE
Deputy Secretary, Secretary of the Central Chancery of the Orders of Knighthood
Chancery, Central Chancery of the Orders of Knighthood, St James's Palace, London SW1A 1BH

THE ORDER OF MERIT (1902)

OM *Military*   OM *Civil*

OM
Ribbon, Blue and crimson

This order is designed as a special distinction for eminent men and women without conferring a knighthood upon them. The order is limited in numbers to 24, with the addition of foreign honorary members.

THE SOVEREIGN
HRH The Prince Philip, Duke of Edinburgh, 1968
Lord Foster of Thames Bank, 1997
Prof. Sir Roger Penrose, 2000
Sir Tom Stoppard, 2000
HRH The Prince of Wales, 2002
Lord Rothschild, 2002
Sir David Attenborough, 2005
Baroness Boothroyd, 2005
Sir Timothy Berners-Lee, 2007
Lord Eames, 2007
Lord Rees of Ludlow, 2007
Rt. Hon. Jean Chrétien, QC, 2009
Robert Neil MacGregor, 2010
Hon. John Howard, 2011
David Hockney, 2011
Sir Simon Rattle, 2013
Prof. Sir Magdi Yacoub, 2013
Lord Darzi of Denham, 2016
Prof. Dame Ann Dowling, 2016
Sir James Dyson, 2016

Secretary and Registrar, Lord Fellowes, GCB, GCVO, PC, QSO

Chancery, Central Chancery of the Orders of Knighthood, St James's Palace, London SW1A 1BH

THE MOST DISTINGUISHED ORDER OF ST MICHAEL AND ST GEORGE (1818)

GCMG   KCMG

GCMG Knight (or Dame) Grand Cross
KCMG Knight Commander
DCMG Dame Commander
CMG   Companion

Ribbon, Saxon blue, with scarlet centre
Motto, Auspicium melioris aevi (*Token of a better age*)

THE SOVEREIGN

GRAND MASTER
HRH The Duke of Kent, KG, GCMG, GCVO, ADC

Prelate, Rt. Revd David Urquhart, KCMG
Chancellor, Lord Robertson of Port Ellen, KT, GCMG, PC
Secretary, Permanent Under-Secretary of State at the Foreign and Commonwealth Office and Head of the Diplomatic Service
Registrar, Sir David Manning, GCMG, KCVO
King of Arms, Baroness Ashton of Upholland, GCMG, PC
Lady Usher of the Blue Rod, Dame DeAnne Julius, DCMG, CBE
Dean, Dean of St James's
Deputy Secretary, Secretary of the Central Chancery of the Orders of Knighthood
Hon. Genealogist, Timothy Duke

Chancery, Central Chancery of the Orders of Knighthood, St James's Palace, London SW1A 1BH

THE IMPERIAL ORDER OF THE CROWN OF INDIA (1877) FOR LADIES

CI

Badge, the royal cipher of Queen Victoria in jewels within an oval, surmounted by an heraldic crown and attached to a bow of light blue watered ribbon, edged white

The honour does not confer any rank or title upon the recipient

No conferments have been made since 1947

HM The Queen, 1947

THE ROYAL VICTORIAN ORDER (1896)

GCVO   KCVO

GCVO Knight or Dame Grand Cross
KCVO Knight Commander
DCVO Dame Commander
CVO   Commander
LVO   Lieutenant
MVO   Member

Ribbon, Blue, with red and white edges

Motto, Victoria

THE SOVEREIGN

GRAND MASTER
HRH The Princess Royal, KG, KT, GCVO, QSO

Chancellor, Lord Chamberlain
Secretary, Keeper of the Privy Purse
Registrar, Secretary of the Central Chancery of the Orders of Knighthood
Chaplain, Chaplain of the Queen's Chapel of the Savoy
Hon. Genealogist, David White

THE MOST EXCELLENT ORDER OF THE BRITISH EMPIRE (1917)

GBE   KBE

The order was divided into military and civil divisions in December 1918

GBE Knight or Dame Grand Cross
KBE Knight Commander
DBE Dame Commander
CBE Commander
OBE Officer
MBE Member

Ribbon, Rose pink edged with pearl grey with vertical pearl stripe in centre (military division); without vertical pearl stripe (civil division)
Motto, For God and the Empire

THE SOVEREIGN

GRAND MASTER
HRH The Prince Philip, Duke of Edinburgh, KG, KT, OM, GCVO, GBE, PC

Prelate, Bishop of London
King of Arms, Lt.-Gen. Sir Robert
    Fulton, KBE
Registrar, Secretary of the Central
    Chancery of the Orders of
    Knighthood
Secretary, Secretary of the Cabinet and
    Head of the Home Civil Service
Dean, Dean of St Paul's
Lady Usher of the Purple Rod, Dame
    Amelia Fawcett, DBE, CVO

Chancery, Central Chancery of the Orders
    of Knighthood, St James's Palace,
    London SW1A 1BH

ORDER OF THE COMPANIONS OF HONOUR (1917)

CH

Ribbon, Carmine, with gold edges

This order consists of one class only
and carries with it no title. The number
of awards is limited to 65 (excluding
honorary members).

Amos, Baroness, 2016
Anthony, John, 1981
Attenborough, Sir David, 1995
Atwood, Margaret, 2018
Baker, Dame Janet, 1993
Baker of Dorking, Lord, 1992
Birtwistle, Sir Harrison, 2000
Bragg, Lord, 2017
Brook, Peter, 1998
Brooke of Sutton Mandeville, Lord,
    1992
Campbell of Pittenweem, Lord, 2013
Clarke, of Nottingham, Lord, 2014
Coe, Lord, 2012
De Chastelain, Gen. John, 1998
Dench, Dame Judi, 2005
Elder, Sir Mark, 2017
Elton, Sir John, 2020
Eyre, Sir Richard, 2016
Fraser, Lady Antonia, 2017
Glennie, Dame Evelyn, 2016
Grey, Dame Beryl, 2017
Hannay of Chiswick, Lord, 2003
Henderson, Prof. Richard, 2018
Heseltine, Lord, 1997

Higgs, Prof. Peter, 2012
Hockney, David, 1997
Howard of Lympne, Lord, 2011
Hurd of Westwell, Lord, 1995
Jeffreys, Sir Alec, 2016
King of Bridgwater, Lord, 1992
Lovelock, Prof. James, 2002
McCartney, Sir Paul, 2017
McKellen, Sir Ian Murray, 2007
McKenzie, Prof. Dan Peter, 2003
McLoughlin, Lord, 2019
MacMillan, Prof. Margaret, 2017
Major, Sir John, 1998
O'Neill of Bengarve, Baroness, 2013
Osborne, George, 2016
Owen, Lord, 1994
Patten of Barnes, Lord, 1998
Peters, Dame Mary, 2014
Riley, Bridget, 1998
Rogers of Riverside, Lord, 2008
Rowling, Joanne, 2017
Serota, Sir Nicholas, 2013
Shirley, Dame Stephanie, 2017
Smith, Delia, 2017
Smith, Dame Margaret (Maggie), 2014
Smith of Kelvin, Lord, 2016
Smith, Sir Paul, 2020
Somare, Sir Michael, 1978
Stern of Brentford, Lord, 2017
Strathclyde, Lord, 2013
Strong, Sir Roy, 2015
Te Kanawa, Dame Kiri, 2018
Tebbit, Lord, 1987
Thomas, Sir Keith, 2020
Williams of Crosby, Baroness, 2016
Woolf, Lord, 2015
Young of Cookham, Lord, 2012
Young of Graffham, Lord, 2014
Honorary Members, Bernard Haitink,
    2002; Prof. Amartya Sen, 2000;
    Most Revd Desmond Tutu, 2015
Secretary and Registrar, Secretary of the
    Central Chancery of the Orders of
    Knighthood

THE DISTINGUISHED SERVICE ORDER (1886)

DSO

Ribbon, Red, with blue edges

Bestowed in recognition of especial
services in action of commissioned
officers in the Navy, Army and Royal

Air Force and (since 1942) Mercantile
Marine. The members are Companions
only. A bar may be awarded for any
additional act of service.

THE IMPERIAL SERVICE ORDER (1902)

ISO

Ribbon, Crimson, with blue centre

Appointment as companion of this
order is open to members of the civil
services whose eligibility is determined
by the grade they hold. The order
consists of the sovereign and
companions to a number not exceeding
1,900, of whom 1,300 may belong to
the home civil services and 600 to
overseas civil services. The then prime
minister announced in March 1993
that he would make no further
recommendations for appointments to
the order.

Secretary, Head of the Home Civil
    Service
Registrar, Secretary of the Central
    Chancery of the Orders of
    Knighthood

THE ROYAL VICTORIAN CHAIN (1902)

It confers no precedence on its holders

HM The Queen

HM The Queen of Denmark,
    3501974
HM The King of Sweden, 1975
HRH Princess Beatrix of the
    Netherlands, 1982
Gen. Antonio Eanes, 1985
HM King Juan Carlos, 1986
HM The King of Norway, 1994
Earl of Airlie, 1997
Rt. Revd and Rt. Hon. Lord Carey of
    Clifton, 2002
HRH Prince Philip, Duke of
    Edinburgh, 2007
Rt. Revd and Rt. Hon. Lord Williams
    of Oystermouth, 2012

BARONETAGE AND KNIGHTAGE

BARONETS

Style, 'Sir' before forename and surname, followed by 'Bt.'
 Envelope, Sir F_ S_, Bt. *Letter (formal)*, Dear Sir; *(social)*, Dear
 Sir F_. *Spoken*, Sir F_
Wife's style, 'Lady' followed by surname
 Envelope, Lady S_. *Letter (formal)*, Dear Madam; *(social)*, Dear
 Lady S_. *Spoken*, Lady S_
Style of Baronetess, 'Dame' before forename and surname,
 followed by 'Btss.' (*see also* Dames)

There are five different creations of baronetcies: Baronets of
England (creations dating from 1611); Baronets of Ireland
(creations dating from 1619); Baronets of Scotland or Nova
Scotia (creations dating from 1625); Baronets of Great Britain
(creations after the Act of Union 1707 which combined the
kingdoms of England and Scotland); and Baronets of the
United Kingdom (creations after the union of Great Britain and
Ireland in 1801).

*Badge of
Baronets
of the UK*

*Badge of
Baronets of
Nova Scotia*

*Badge of
Ulster*

The patent of creation limits the destination of a baronetcy,
usually to male descendants of the first baronet. In some cases,
however, special remainders have allowed baronetcies to pass,
in the absence of sons, to another relative. In the case of
baronetcies of Scotland or Nova Scotia, a special remainder of
'heirs male and of tailzie' allows the baronetcy to descend to
heirs general, including women. There are four existing
Scottish baronetcies with such a remainder.

The Official Roll of the Baronetage is kept at the Crown
Office and maintained by the Registrar and Assistant
Registrar of the Baronetage. Anyone who considers that he or
she is entitled to be entered on the roll may apply through the
Crown Office to prove their succession. Every person
succeeding to a baronetcy must exhibit proofs of succession to
the Lord Chancellor. A person whose name is not entered on
the official roll will not be addressed or mentioned by the title
of baronet or baronetess in any official document, nor will he
or she be accorded precedence as a baronet or baronetess.

The Standing Council of the Baronetage, established in
1898 as the Honourable Society of the Baronetage, is
responsible for maintaining the interests of the Baronetage
and for publishing the Official Roll of the Baronetage as
established by royal warrant in 1910 (**W** www.baronetage.org/
official-roll-of-the-baronets).

OFFICIAL ROLL OF THE BARONETAGE, Crown Office,
 House of Lords, London SW1A 0PW **T** 020-7219 4687
 E hereditary.claims@gmail.com
 Registrar, Mrs Ceri King

KNIGHTS

Style, 'Sir' before forename and surname, followed by
 appropriate post-nominal initials if a Knight Grand Cross
 or Knight Commander
 Envelope, Sir F_ S_. *Letter (formal)*, Dear Sir; *(social)*, Dear Sir
 F_. *Spoken*, Sir F_
Wife's style, 'Lady' followed by surname
 Envelope, Lady S_. *Letter (formal)*, Dear Madam; *(social)*, Dear
 Lady S_. *Spoken*, Lady S_

The prefix 'Sir' is not used by knights who are clerics of the
Church of England, who do not receive the accolade. Their
wives are entitled to precedence as the wife of a knight but not
to the style of 'Lady'.

ORDERS OF KNIGHTHOOD

Knight Grand Cross and Knight Commander are the higher
classes of the Orders of Chivalry (*see* Orders of Chivalry).
Honorary knighthoods of these orders may be conferred on
men who are citizens of countries of which the Queen is not
head of state. As a rule, the prefix 'Sir' is not used by honorary
knights.

KNIGHTS BACHELOR

The Knights Bachelor do not constitute a royal order, but
comprise the surviving representation of the ancient state
orders of knighthood. The Register of Knights Bachelor,
instituted by James I in the 17th century, lapsed, and in 1908
a voluntary association under the title of the Society of
Knights (now the Imperial Society of Knights Bachelor) was
formed with the primary objectives of continuing the various
registers dating from 1257 and obtaining the uniform
registration of every created Knight Bachelor. In 1926 a
design for a badge to be worn by Knights Bachelor was
approved and adopted; in 1974 a neck badge and miniature
were added.

THE IMPERIAL SOCIETY OF KNIGHTS BACHELOR,
 Magnesia House, 6 Playhouse Yard, London EC4V 5EX
 Knight Principal, Rt. Hon. Sir Gary Hickinbottom
 Prelate, Rt. Revd and Rt. Hon. Dame Sarah Mullally, DBE
 Registrar, Sir Michael Hirst
 Hon. Treasurer, Sir Clive Thompson
 Clerk to the Council, Col. Simon Doughty

LIST OF BARONETS AND KNIGHTS

as at 31 December 2020
†   Not registered on the Official Roll of the Baronetage
( )   The date of creation of the baronetcy is given in parentheses
I   Baronet of Ireland
NS   Baronet of Nova Scotia
S   Baronet of Scotland

A full entry in italic type indicates that the recipient of a knighthood died within a year of the honour being conferred. The name is included in our list for one year for purposes of record. Peers are not included in this list.

A-B

Aaronson, Sir Michael John, Kt., CBE
†Abdy, Sir Robert Etienne Eric, Bt. (1850)
Abed, *Dr* Sir Fazle Hasan, KCMG
Abel, Sir Christopher Charles, Kt.
Acher, Sir Gerald, Kt., CBE, LVO
Ackroyd, Sir Timothy Robert Whyte, Bt. (1956)
Acland, Sir Antony Arthur, KG, GCMG, GCVO
Acland, *Lt.-Col.* Sir (Christopher) Guy (Dyke), Bt. (1890), LVO
Acland, Sir Dominic Dyke, Bt. (1678)
Adams, Sir Geoffrey Doyne, KCMG
Adams, Sir William James, KCMG
Adjaye, Sir David Frank, Kt., OBE
Adsetts, Sir William Norman, Kt., OBE
Adye, Sir John Anthony, KCMG
Aga Khan IV, HH Prince Karim, KBE
Agnew, Sir Crispin Hamlyn, Bt. (S. 1629)
Agnew, Sir George Anthony, Bt. (1895)
Agnew, Sir Rudolph Ion Joseph, Kt.
Agnew-Somerville, Sir James Lockett Charles, Bt. (1957)
Ah Koy, Sir James Michael, KBE
Aikens, *Rt. Hon.* Sir Richard John Pearson, Kt.
Ainslie, Sir Charles Benedict, Kt., CBE
†Ainsworth, Sir Anthony Thomas Hugh, Bt. (1917)
Aird, Sir (George) John, Bt. (1901)
Airy, *Maj.-Gen.* Sir Christopher John, KCVO, CBE
Aitchison, Sir Charles Walter de Lancey, Bt. (1938)
Ajegbo, Sir Keith Onyema, Kt., OBE
Akenhead, *Hon.* Sir Robert, Kt.
Akers-Jones, Sir David, KBE, CMG
Alberti, *Prof.* Sir Kurt George Matthew Mayer, Kt.
Albu, Sir George, Bt. (1912)
Alcock, *Air Chief Marshal* Sir (Robert James) Michael, GCB, KBE
Aldridge, Sir Rodney Malcolm, Kt., OBE
Alexander, *Rt. Hon.* Sir Daniel (Grian), Kt.
Alexander, Sir Douglas, Bt. (1921)
Alexander, Sir Edward Samuel, Bt. (1945)
Alghanim, Sir Kutayba Yusuf, KCMG

Allan, *Hon.* Sir Alexander Claud Stuart, KCB
Allen, Sir Errol Newton Fitzrose, KCMG
Allen, *Prof.* Sir Geoffrey, Kt., PHD, FRS
Allen, Sir Mark John Spurgeon, Kt., CMG
Allen, *Hon.* Sir Peter Austin Philip Jermyn, Kt.
Allen, Sir Thomas Boaz, Kt., CBE
Allen, *Hon.* Sir William Clifford, KCMG
Allen, Sir William Guilford, Kt.
Alleyne, Sir George Allanmoore Ogarren, Kt.
Alleyne, *Revd* John Olpherts Campbell, Bt. (1769)
Allinson, Sir (Walter) Leonard, KCVO, CMG
Allison, *Air Chief Marshal* Sir John Shakespeare, KCB, CBE
Alston, Sir Richard John William, Kt.,CBE
Altman, Sir Paul Bernard, Kt.
Amess, Sir David Anthony Andrew, Kt.
Amet, *Hon.* Sir Arnold Karibone, Kt.
Amory, Sir Ian Heathcoat, Bt. (1874)
Anderson, *Dr* Sir James Iain Walker, Kt., CBE
Anderson, Sir John Anthony, KBE
Anderson, Sir Leith Reinsford Steven, Kt., CBE
Anderson, *Prof.* Sir Roy Malcolm, Kt.
Anderson, *Air Marshal* Sir Timothy Michael, KCB, DSO
Anderson, Sir (William) Eric Kinloch, KT
Anderton, Sir (Cyril) James, Kt., CBE, QPM
Andrew, Sir Robert John, KCB
Andrew, Sir Warwick, Kt.
Andrews, Sir Ian Charles Franklin, Kt., CBE, TD
Angest, Sir Henry, Kt.
Annesley, Sir Hugh Norman, Kt., QPM
Anson, Sir John, KCB
Anson, Sir Philip Roland, Bt. (1831)
Anstruther, Sir Sebastian Paten Campbell, Bt. (S. 1694 and S. 1700)
Anstruther-Gough-Calthorpe, Sir Euan Hamilton, Bt. (1929)

Antrobus, Sir Edward Philip, Bt. (1815)
Appleyard, Sir Leonard Vincent, KCMG
Arbib, Sir Martyn, Kt.
Arbuthnot, Sir Keith Robert Charles, Bt. (1823)
Arbuthnot, Sir William Reierson, Bt. (1964)
Arbuthnott, *Prof.* Sir John Peebles, Kt., PHD, FRSE
†Archdale, Sir Nicholas Edward, Bt. (1928)
Arculus, Sir Thomas David Guy, Kt.
Armitage, *Air Chief Marshal* Sir Michael John, KCB, CBE
Armitt, Sir John Alexander, Kt., CBE
Armour, *Prof.* Sir James, Kt., CBE
Armstrong, Sir Christopher John Edmund Stuart, Bt. (1841), MBE
Armstrong, Sir Richard, Kt., CBE
Armytage, Sir John Martin, Bt. (1738)
Arnold, *Hon.* Sir Richard David, Kt.
Arnold, Sir Thomas Richard, Kt.
Arnott, Sir Alexander John Maxwell, Bt. (1896)
†Arthur, Sir Benjamin Nathan, Bt. (1841)
Arthur, *Lt.-Gen.* Sir (John) Norman Stewart, KCB, CVO
Arthur, Sir Michael Anthony, KCMG
Arulkumaran, *Prof.* Sir Sabaratnam, Kt.
Asbridge, Sir Jonathan Elliott, Kt.
Ash, *Prof.* Sir Eric Albert, Kt., CBE, FRS, FRENG
Ashburnham, Sir James Fleetwood, Bt. (1661)
Ashworth, *Dr* Sir John Michael, Kt.
Aske, Sir Robert John Bingham, Bt. (1922)
Askew, Sir Bryan, Kt.
Asquith, *Hon.* Sir Dominic Anthony Gerard, KCMG
Astill, *Hon.* Sir Michael John, Kt.
Astley-Cooper, Sir Alexander Paston, Bt. (1821)
Astwood, *Hon.* Sir James Rufus, KBE
Atha, *Air Marshal* Sir Stuart David, KBE, CB, DSO
Atkins, *Rt. Hon.* Sir Robert James, Kt.
Atkinson, Sir William Samuel, Kt.
Atopare, Sir Sailas, GCMG
Attenborough, Sir David Frederick, Kt., OM, CH, CVO, CBE, FRS

Aubrey-Fletcher, Sir Henry Egerton, Bt. (1782), KCVO

Audland, Sir Christopher John, KCMG

Augier, *Prof.* Sir Fitzroy Richard, Kt.

Auld, *Rt. Hon.* Sir Robin Ernest, Kt.

Austen-Smith, *Air Marshal* Sir Roy David, KBE, CB, CVO, DFC

Austin, Sir Peter John, Bt. (1894)

Austin, *Air Marshal* Sir Roger Mark, KCB, AFC

Avei, Sir Moi, KBE

Ayaz, *Dr* Sir Iftikhar Ahmad, KBE

Ayckbourn, Sir Alan, Kt., CBE

Aykroyd, Sir Henry Robert George, Bt. (1920)

Aykroyd, Sir James Alexander Frederic, Bt. (1929)

Aylmer, Sir Richard John, Bt. (I. 1622)

Aylward, *Prof.* Sir Mansel, Kt., CB

Aynsley-Green, *Prof.* Sir Albert, Kt.

Bacha, Sir Bhinod, Kt., CMG

Backhouse, Sir Alfred James Stott, Bt. (1901)

Bacon, Sir Nicholas Hickman Ponsonby, Bt., OBE (1611 and 1627), *Premier Baronet of England*

Baddeley, Sir John Wolsey Beresford, Bt. (1922)

Badge, Sir Peter Gilmour Noto, Kt.

Bagge, Sir (John) Jeremy Picton, Bt. (1867)

Baggott, Sir Matthew David, Kt., CBE, QPM

Bagnall, *Air Chief Marshal* Sir Anthony, GBE, KCB

Bai, Sir Brown, KBE

Bailey, Sir Alan Marshall, KCB

Bailey, Sir Brian Harry, Kt., OBE

Bailey, Sir John Bilsland, KCB

Bailey, Sir John Richard, Bt. (1919)

Bailhache, Sir Philip Martin, Kt.

Bailhache, Sir William, Kt.

Baillie, Sir Adrian Louis, Bt. (1823)

Bain, *Prof.* Sir George Sayers, Kt.

Baird, Sir Charles William Stuart, Bt. (1809)

Baird, Sir James Andrew Gardiner, Bt. (S. 1695)

Baird, *Air Marshal* Sir John Alexander, KBE

Baird, *Vice-Adm.* Sir Thomas Henry Eustace, KCB

Baker, *Hon.* Sir Andrew William, Kt.

Baker, Sir Bryan William, Kt.

Baker, *Hon.* Sir Jeremy Russell, Kt.

Baker, *Prof.* Sir John Hamilton, Kt., QC

Baker, Sir John William, Kt., CBE

Baker, *Rt. Hon.* Sir Jonathan Leslie, Kt.

Baker, *Rt. Hon.* Sir (Thomas) Scott (Gillespie), Kt.

Balasubramanian, *Prof.* Sir Shankar, Kt.

Baldry, Sir Antony Brian, Kt.

Baldwin, *Prof.* Sir Jack Edward, Kt., FRS

Ball, Sir Christopher John Elinger, Kt.

Ball, *Prof.* Sir John Macleod, Kt.

Ball, Sir Richard Bentley, Bt. (1911)

Ballantyne, *Dr* Sir Frederick Nathaniel, GCMG

Band, *Adm.* Sir Jonathon, GCB

Banham, Sir John Michael Middlecott, Kt.

Bannerman, Sir David Gordon, Bt. (S. 1682), OBE

Barber, Sir Brendan, Kt.

Barber, Sir Michael Bayldon, Kt.

Barber, Sir (Thomas) David, Bt. (1960)

Barclay, Sir David Rowat, Kt.

Barclay, Sir Frederick Hugh, Kt.

Barclay, Sir Robert Colraine, Bt. (S. 1668)

Baring, Sir John Francis, Bt. (1911)

Barker, *Hon.* Sir (Richard) Ian, Kt.

Barling, *Hon.* Sir Gerald Edward, Kt.

Barlow, Sir Christopher Hilaro, Bt. (1803)

Barlow, Sir Frank, Kt., CBE

Barlow, Sir James Alan, Bt. (1902)

Barlow, Sir John Kemp, Bt. (1907)

Barnes, Sir (James) David (Francis), Kt., CBE

Barnett, *Hon.* Sir Michael Lancelot Patrick, Kt.

Barnett, *Prof.* Sir Richard Robert, Kt.

Barnewall, Sir Peter Joseph, Bt. (I. 1623)

†Barran, Sir John Ruthven, Bt. (1895)

Barrett, Sir Stephen Jeremy, KCMG

†Barrett-Lennard, Sir Peter John, Bt. (1801)

†Barrington, Sir Benjamin, Bt. (1831)

Barrington-Ward, *Rt. Revd* Simon, KCMG

Barron, *Rt. Hon.* Sir Kevin, Kt.

Barrons, *Gen.* Sir Richard, KCB, CBE, ADC

Barrow, Sir Anthony John Grenfell, Bt. (1835)

Barrow, Sir Timothy Earle, KCMG, LVO, MBE

Barry, Sir (Lawrence) Edward (Anthony Tress), Bt. (1899)

Barter, Sir Peter Leslie Charles, Kt., OBE

†Bartlett, Sir Andrew Alan, Bt. (1913)

Barttelot, *Col.* Sir Brian Walter de Stopham, Bt. (1875), OBE

Bate, *Prof.* Sir Andrew Jonathan, Kt., CBE

Bates, Sir James Geoffrey, Bt. (1880)

Bates, Sir Richard Dawson Hoult, Bt. (1937)

Batho, Sir Peter Ghislain, Bt. (1928)

Bathurst, *Admiral of the Fleet* Sir (David) Benjamin, GCB

Battishill, Sir Anthony Michael William, GCB

Baulcombe, *Prof.* Sir David Charles, Kt., FRS

Baxendell, Sir Peter Brian, Kt., CBE, FRENG

Bayley, Sir Hugh Nigel Edward, Kt.

Bayne, Sir Nicholas Peter, KCMG

Baynes, Sir Christopher Rory, Bt. (1801)

Bazalgette, Sir Peter Lytton, Kt.

Bazley, Sir Thomas John Sebastian, Bt. (1869)

Beache, *Hon.* Sir Vincent Ian, KCMG

Beale, *Lt.-Gen.* Sir Peter John, KBE, FRCP

Beamish, Sir Adrian John, KCMG

Beamish, Sir David Richard, KCB

Bean, *Dr* Sir Charles Richard, Kt.

Bean, *Rt. Hon.* Sir David Michael, Kt.

Bear, Sir Michael David, Kt.

Beatson, *Rt. Hon.* Sir Jack, Kt.

Beaumont, Sir William Blackledge, Kt., CBE

Beavis, *Air Chief Marshal* Sir Michael Gordon, KCB, CBE, AFC

Beck, Sir Edgar Philip, Kt.

Beckett, Sir Richard Gervase, Bt. (1921), QC

Beckett, *Lt.-Gen.* Sir Thomas Anthony, KCB, CBE

Beckwith, Sir John Lionel, Kt., CBE

Beddington, *Prof.* Sir John Rex, Kt., CMG

†Beecham, Sir Robert Adrian, Bt. (1914)

Beevor, Sir Antony James, Kt.

Beevor, Sir Thomas Hugh Cunliffe, Bt. (1784)

Behan, Sir David, Kt., CBE

Beldam, *Rt. Hon.* Sir (Alexander) Roy (Asplan), Kt.

Belgrave, *HE* Sir Elliott Fitzroy, GCMG

Bell, Sir David Charles Maurice, Kt.

Bell, Sir David Robert, KCB

Bell, *Prof.* Sir John Irving, GBE

Bell, Sir John Lowthian, Bt. (1885)

Bell, *Prof.* Sir Peter Robert Frank, Kt.

Bell, *Hon.* Sir Rodger, Kt.

Bellamy, *Hon.* Sir Christopher William, Kt.

Bellingham, Sir Henry Campbell, Kt.

†Bellingham, Sir William Alexander Noel Henry, Bt. (1796)

Bender, Sir Brian Geoffrey, KCB

Benjamin, Sir George William John, Kt., CBE

Benn, Sir (James) Jonathan, Bt. (1914)

Bennett, *Air Vice-Marshal* Sir Erik Peter, KBE, CB

Bennett, *Hon.* Sir Hugh Peter Derwyn, Kt.

Bennett, *Gen.* Sir Phillip Harvey, KBE, DSO

Bennett, Sir Ronald Wilfrid Murdoch, Bt. (1929)

Benson, Sir Christopher John, Kt.

Benton-Jones, Sir James Peter Martin, Bt. (1919)

Beresford, Sir (Alexander) Paul, Kt.

Beresford-Peirse, Sir Henry Njers de la Poer, Bt. (1814)

Berghuser, *Hon.* Sir Eric, Kt., MBE

Beringer, *Prof.* Sir John Evelyn, Kt., CBE

Berman, Sir Franklin Delow, KCMG

Bernard, Sir Dallas Edmund, Bt. (1954)

Berners-Lee, Sir Timothy John, OM, KBE, FRS

Berney, Sir Julian Reedham Stuart, Bt. (1620)

Bernstein, Sir Howard, Kt.

Berragan, *Lt.-Gen.* Sir Gerald William, KBE, CB

Berridge, *Prof.* Sir Michael John, Kt., FRS

Berriman, Sir David, Kt.

Berry, *Prof.* Sir Colin Leonard, Kt., FRCPATH

Berry, *Prof.* Sir Michael Victor, Kt., FRS

Berthoud, Sir Martin Seymour, KCVO, CMG

Berwick, *Prof.* Sir George Thomas, Kt., CBE

Besley, *Prof.* Sir Timothy John, Kt., CBE

Best-Shaw, Sir Thomas Joshua, Bt. (1665)

Bethel, Sir Baltron Benjamin, KCMG

Bethlehem, Sir Daniel, KCMG

Bett, Sir Michael, Kt., CBE

Bettison, Sir Norman George, Kt., QPM

Bevan, Sir James David, KCMG

Bevan, Sir Martyn Evan Evans, Bt. (1958)

Bevan, Sir Nicolas, Kt., CB

Beverley, *Lt.-Gen.* Sir Henry York La Roche, KCB, OBE, RM

Bhadeshia, *Prof.* Sir Harshad Kumar Dharamshi, Kt., FRS

Bibby, Sir Michael James, Bt. (1959)

Biddulph, Sir Ian D'Olier, Bt. (1664)

Biggam, Sir Robin Adair, Kt.

Bilas, Sir Angmai Simon, Kt., OBE

Bill, *Lt.-Gen.* Sir David Robert, KCB

Billière, *Gen.* Sir Peter Edgar de la Cour de la, KCB, KBE, DSO, MC

Bindman, Sir Geoffrey Lionel, Kt.

Bingham, *Hon.* Sir Eardley Max, Kt.

Birch, Sir John Allan, KCVO, CMG

Birch, Sir Roger, Kt., CBE, QPM

Bird, *Prof.* Sir Adrian Peter, Kt., CBE, FRS, FRSE

Bird, Sir Richard Geoffrey Chapman, Bt. (1922)

Birkett, Sir Peter, Kt.

Birkin, Sir John Christian William, Bt. (1905)

Birkin, Sir (John) Derek, Kt., TD

Birkmyre, Sir James, Bt. (1921)

Birrell, Sir James Drake, Kt.

Birss, *Hon.* Sir Colin Ian, Kt.

Birt, Sir Michael, Kt.

Birtwistle, Sir Harrison, Kt., CH

Bischoff, Sir Winfried Franz Wilhelm, Kt.

Black, *Prof.* Sir Nicholas Andrew, Kt.

Black, Sir Robert David, Bt. (1922)

Blackburn, *Vice-Adm.* Sir David Anthony James, KCVO, CB

Blackburne, *Hon.* Sir William Anthony, Kt.

Blackett, Sir Hugh Francis, Bt. (1673)

Blackham, *Vice-Adm.* Sir Jeremy Joe, KCB

Blackman, Sir Frank Milton, KCVO, OBE

Blair, Sir Patrick David Hunter, Bt. (1786)

Blair, *Hon.* Sir William James Lynton, Kt.

†Blake, Sir Charles Valentine Bruce, Bt. (I. 1622)

Blake, Sir Francis Michael, Bt. (1907)

Blake, *Hon.* Sir Nicholas John Gorrod, Kt.

Blake, Sir Peter Thomas, Kt., CBE

Blake, Sir Quentin Saxby, Kt., CBE

Blakemore, *Prof.* Sir Colin Brian, Kt., FRS

Blaker, Sir John, Bt. (1919)

Blakiston, Sir Ferguson Arthur James, Bt. (1763)

Blanch, Sir Malcolm, KCVO

Bland, *Lt.-Col.* Sir Simon Claud Michael, KCVO

Blank, Sir Maurice Victor, Kt.

Blatchford, Sir Ian Craig, Kt.

Blatherwick, Sir David Elliott Spiby, KCMG, OBE

Blavatnik, Sir Leonard, Kt.

Blennerhassett, Sir (Marmaduke) Adrian Francis William, Bt. (1809)

Blewitt, *Maj.* Sir Shane Gabriel Basil, GCVO

Blofeld, *Hon.* Sir John Christopher Calthorpe, Kt.

Blois, Sir Charles Nicholas Gervase, Bt. (1686)

Blomefield, Sir Thomas Charles Peregrine, Bt. (1807)

Bloom, *Prof.* Sir Stephen Robert, Kt.

Bloomfield, Sir Kenneth Percy, KCB

Blundell, *Prof.* Sir Richard William, Kt., CBE, FBA

Blundell, Sir Thomas Leon, Kt., FRS

†Blunden, Sir Hubert Chisholm, Bt. (I. 1766)

Blunt, Sir David Richard Reginald Harvey, Bt. (1720)

Blyth, Sir Charles (Chay), Kt., CBE, BEM

Boardman, *Prof.* Sir John, Kt., FSA, FBA

Bodey, *Hon.* Sir David Roderick Lessiter, Kt.

Bodmer, Sir Walter Fred, Kt., PHD, FRS

Bogan, Sir Nagora, KBE

Bogle, Sir Nigel, Kt.

Boileau, Sir Nicolas Edmond George, Bt. (1838)

Boleat, Sir Mark John, Kt.

Boles, Sir Richard Fortescue, Bt. (1922)

Bollom, *Air Marshal* Sir Simon John, KBE, CB

Bona, Sir Kina, KBE

Bonallack, Sir Michael Francis, Kt., OBE

Bond, Sir John Reginald Hartnell, Kt.

Bond, *Prof.* Sir Michael Richard, Kt., FRCPSYCH, FRCPGLAS, FRCSE

Bone, *Prof.* Sir (James) Drummond, Kt., FRSE

Bone, Sir Roger Bridgland, KCMG

Bonfield, Sir Peter Leahy, Kt., CBE, FRENG

Bonham, Sir George Martin Antony, Bt. (1852)

Bonington, Sir Christian John Storey, Kt., CVO, CBE

Bonsor, Sir Nicholas Cosmo, Bt. (1925)

Boord, Sir Andrew Richard, Bt. (1896)

Boorman, *Lt.-Gen.* Sir Derek, KCB

Booth, Sir Clive, Kt.

Booth, Sir Douglas Allen, Bt. (1916)

Boothby, Sir Brooke Charles, Bt. (1660)

Bore, Sir Albert, Kt.

Boreel, Sir Stephan Gerard, Bt. (1645)

Borthwick, Sir Antony Thomas, Bt. (1908)

Borysiewicz, *Prof.* Sir Leszek Krzysztof, Kt.

Boseto, *Revd* Leslie Tanaboe, KBE

Bosher, Sir Robin, Kt.

Bossano, *Hon.* Sir Joseph John, KCMG

Bossom, Sir Bruce Charles, Bt. (1953)

Boswell, *Lt.-Gen.* Sir Alexander Crawford Simpson, KCB, CBE

Botham, Sir Ian Terence, Kt., OBE

Bottomley, Sir Peter James, Kt.

Bottoms, *Prof.* Sir Anthony Edward, Kt.

Boughey, Sir John George Fletcher, Bt. (1798)

Boulton, Sir John Gibson, Bt. (1944)

Bouraga, Sir Phillip, KBE

Bourn, Sir John Bryant, KCB

Bourne, Sir Matthew Christopher, Kt., OBE

Bowater, Sir Euan David Vansittart, Bt. (1939)

†Bowater, Sir Michael Patrick, Bt. (1914)

Bowden, Sir Andrew, Kt., MBE

Bowden, Sir Nicholas Richard, Bt. (1915)

Bowen, Sir Barry Manfield, KCMG

Bowen, Sir Geoffrey Fraser, Kt.

Bowen, Sir George Edward Michael, Bt. (1921)

Bowes Lyon, Sir Simon Alexander, KCVO

Bowlby, Sir Richard Peregrine Longstaff, Bt. (1923)

Bowman, Sir Charles Edward Beck, Kt.

Bowman, Sir Edwin Geoffrey, KCB

Bowman, Sir Jeffery Haverstock, Kt.

Bowness, Sir Alan, Kt., CBE

Bowyer-Smyth, Sir Thomas Weyland, Bt. (1661)

Boyce, Sir Graham Hugh, KCMG

Boyce, Sir Robert Charles Leslie, Bt. (1952)

Boycott, Sir Geoffrey, Kt., OBE

Boyd, Sir Alexander Walter, Bt. (1916)

Boyd, *Prof.* Sir Ian Lamont, Kt., FRSE
Boyd, Sir John Dixon Iklé, KCMG
Boyd, Sir Michael, Kt.
Boyd, *Prof.* Sir Robert David Hugh, Kt.
Boyd-Carpenter, Sir (Marsom) Henry, KCVO
Boyd-Carpenter, *Lt.-Gen. Hon.* Sir Thomas Patrick John, KBE
Boyle, *Prof.* Sir Roger Michael, Kt., CBE
Boyle, Sir Simon Hugh Patrick, KCVO
Boyle, Sir Stephen Gurney, Bt. (1904)
Bracewell-Smith, Sir Charles, Bt. (1947)
Bradford, Sir Edward Alexander Slade, Bt. (1902)
Bradshaw, *Lt.-Gen.* Sir Adrian, KCB, OBE
Brady, Sir Graham Stuart, Kt.
Brady, *Prof.* Sir John Michael, Kt., FRS
Brailsford, Sir David John, Kt., CBE
Braithwaite, Sir Rodric Quentin, GCMG
Bramley, *Prof.* Sir Paul Anthony, Kt.
Branagh, Sir Kenneth Charles, Kt.
Branson, Sir Richard Charles Nicholas, Kt.
Bratza, *Hon.* Sir Nicolas Dušan, Kt.
Brazier, Sir Julian William Hendy, Kt., TD
Breckenridge, *Prof.* Sir Alasdair Muir, Kt., CBE
Brennan, *Hon.* Sir (Francis) Gerard, KBE
Brenton, Sir Anthony Russell, KCMG
Brewer, Sir David William, KG, CMG, CVO
Brierley, Sir Ronald Alfred, Kt.
Briggs, *Rt. Hon.* Sir Michael Townley Featherstone, Kt. (Lord Briggs of Westbourne)
Brighouse, *Prof.* Sir Timothy Robert Peter, Kt.
Bright, Sir Graham Frank James, Kt.
Bright, Sir Keith, Kt.
Brigstocke, *Adm.* Sir John Richard, KCB
†Brinckman, Sir Theodore Jonathan, Bt. (1831)
†Brisco, Sir Campbell Howard, Bt. (1782)
Briscoe, Sir Brian Anthony, Kt.
Briscoe, Sir John Geoffrey James, Bt. (1910)
Bristow, Sir Laurence Stanley Charles, KCMG
Brittan, Sir Samuel, Kt.
Britton, Sir Paul John James, Kt., CB
†Broadbent, Sir Andrew George, Bt. (1893)
Broadbent, Sir Richard John, KCB
Brocklebank, Sir Aubrey Thomas, Bt. (1885)
†Brodie, Sir Benjamin David Ross, Bt. (1834)

Bromhead, Sir John Desmond Gonville, Bt. (1806)
†Bromley, Sir Charles Howard, Bt. (1757)
Bromley, Sir Michael Roger, KBE
Bromley-Davenport, Sir William Arthur, KCVO
Brook, *Prof.* Sir Richard John, Kt., OBE
Brooke, Sir Alistair Weston, Bt. (1919)
Brooke, Sir Francis George Windham, Bt. (1903)
Brooke, Sir Richard Christopher, Bt. (1662)
Brooke, Sir Rodney George, Kt., CBE
Brooking, Sir Trevor David, Kt., CBE
Brooksbank, Sir (Edward) Nicholas, Bt. (1919)
†Broughton, Sir David Delves, Bt. (1661)
Broughton, Sir Martin Faulkner, Kt.
Broun, Sir Wayne Hercules, Bt. (S. 1686)
Brown, Sir (Austen) Patrick, KCB
Brown, *Adm.* Sir Brian Thomas, KCB, CBE
Brown, Sir David, Kt.
Brown, Sir Ewan, Kt., CBE
Brown, Sir George Francis Richmond, Bt. (1863)
Brown, Sir Mervyn, KCMG, OBE
Brown, Sir Peter Randolph, Kt.
Brown, *Rt. Hon.* Sir Stephen, GBE
Brown, Sir Stephen David Reid, KCVO
†Brownrigg, Sir Michael (Gawen), Bt. (1816)
Browse, *Prof.* Sir Norman Leslie, Kt., MD, FRCS
Bruce, Sir (Francis) Michael Ian, Bt. (s. 1628)
Bruce-Clifton, Sir Hervey Hamish Peter, Bt. (1804)
Bruce-Gardner, Sir Edmund Thomas Peter, Bt. (1945)
Brunner, Sir Hugo Laurence Joseph, KCVO
Brunner, Sir Nicholas Felix Minturn, Bt. (1895)
†Brunton, Sir James Lauder, Bt. (1908)
Bryan, *Hon.* Sir Simon James, Kt.
Bryant, *Air Chief Marshal* Sir Simon, KCB, CBE, ADC
Brydon, Sir Donald Hood, Kt., CBE
Bubb, Sir Stephen John Limrick, Kt.
Buchan-Hepburn, Sir John Alastair Trant Kidd, Bt. (1815)
Buchanan, Sir Andrew George, Bt. (1878), KCVO
Buchanan-Jardine, Sir John Christopher Rupert, Bt. (1885)
Buckland, Sir Ross, Kt.
Buckley, *Dr* Sir George William, Kt.
Buckley, Sir Michael Sidney, Kt.
Buckley, *Lt.-Cdr.* Sir (Peter) Richard, KCVO

Buckley, *Hon.* Sir Roger John, Kt.
Bucknall, *Lt.-Gen.* Sir James Jeffrey Corfield, KCB, CBE
†Buckworth-Herne-Soame, Sir Richard John, Bt. (1697)
Budd, Sir Alan Peter, GBE
Budd, Sir Colin Richard, KCMG
Buffini, Sir Damon Marcus, Kt.
Bull, Sir George Jeffrey, Kt.
†Bull, Sir Stephen Louis, Bt. (1922)
Bullock, Sir Stephen Michael, Kt.
Bultin, Sir Bato, Kt., MBE
Bunbury, Sir Michael William, Bt. (1681), KCVO
Bunyard, Sir Robert Sidney, Kt., CBE, QPM
†Burbidge, Sir John Peter, Bt. (1916)
Burden, Sir Anthony Thomas, Kt., QPM
Burdett, Sir Crispin Peter, Bt. (1665)
Burgen, Sir Arnold Stanley Vincent, Kt., FRS
Burgess, Sir (Joseph) Stuart, Kt., CBE, PHD, FRSC
Burgess, *Prof.* Sir Robert George, Kt.
Burke, Sir James Stanley Gilbert, Bt. (I. 1797)
Burke, Sir (Thomas) Kerry, Kt.
Burn, *Prof.* Sir John, Kt.
Burnell-Nugent, *Vice-Adm.* Sir James Michael, KCB, CBE, ADC
Burnett, Sir Charles David, Bt. (1913)
Burney, Sir Nigel Dennistoun, Bt. (1921)
Burns, *Dr* Sir Henry, Kt.
Burns, Sir (Robert) Andrew, KCMG
Burns, *Rt. Hon.* Sir Simon Hugh McGuigan, Kt.
Burnton, *Rt. Hon.* Sir Stanley Jeffrey, Kt.
Burrell, Sir Charles Raymond, Bt. (1774)
Burridge, *Air Chief Marshal* Sir Brian Kevin, KCB, CBE, ADC
Burton, *Lt.-Gen.* Sir Edmund Fortescue Gerard, KBE
Burton, Sir Graham Stuart, KCMG
Burton, *Hon.* Sir Michael John, GBE
Burton, Sir Michael St Edmund, KCVO, CMG
Butcher, Sir Christopher John, Kt.
Butler, *Dr* Sir David Edgeworth, Kt., CBE
Butler, Sir Percy James, Kt., CBE
Butler, Sir Reginald Richard Michael, Bt. (1922)
Butler, Sir Richard Pierce, Bt. (I. 1628)
Butterfield, *Hon.* Sir Alexander Neil Logie, Kt.
Butterfill, Sir John Valentine, Kt.
Buxton, Sir Crispin Charles Gerard, Bt. (1840)
Buxton, *Rt. Hon.* Sir Richard Joseph, Kt.
Buzzard, Sir Anthony Farquhar, Bt. (1929)

Byatt, Sir Ian Charles Rayner, Kt.
Byron, *Rt. Hon.* Sir Charles Michael
Dennis, Kt.

C-F

Cable, *Rt. Hon.* Sir (John) Vincent, Kt.,
PHD
†Cable-Alexander, Sir Patrick
Desmond William, Bt. (1809)
Cadbury, Sir (Nicholas) Dominic, Kt.
Cadogan, *Prof.* Sir John Ivan George,
Kt., CBE, FRS, FRSE
Cahn, Sir Albert Jonas, Bt. (1934)
Cahn, Sir Andrew Thomas, KCMG
Caine, Sir Michael (Maurice
Micklewhite), Kt., CBE
Caines, Sir John, KCB
Cairns, *Very Revd* John Ballantyne,
KCVO
Caldwell, Sir Edward George, KCB
Callaghan, Sir William Henry, Kt.
Callan, Sir Ivan Roy, KCVO, CMG
Callender, Sir Colin Nigel, Kt., CBE
Callman, *His Hon.* Sir Clive Vernon,
Kt.
Calman, *Prof.* Sir Kenneth Charles,
KCB, MD, FRCP, FRCS, FRSE
Calne, *Prof.* Sir Roy Yorke, Kt., FRS
Calvert-Smith, Sir David, Kt., QC
Cameron, Sir Hugh Roy Graham, Kt.,
QPM
Campbell, *Rt. Hon* Sir Alan, Kt.
Campbell, *Prof.* Sir Colin Murray, Kt.
Campbell, Sir Ian Tofts, Kt., CBE,
VRD
Campbell, Sir James Alexander Moffat
Bain, Bt. (S. 1668)
Campbell, Sir John Park, Kt., OBE
Campbell, Sir Lachlan Philip Kemeys,
Bt. (1815)
Campbell, Sir Louis Auchinbreck, Bt.
(S. 1628)
Campbell, *Dr* Sir Philip Henry
Montgomery, Kt.
Campbell, Sir Roderick Duncan
Hamilton, Bt. (1831)
Campbell, *Dr* Sir Simon Fraser, Kt.,
CBE
Campbell, *Rt. Hon.* Sir William
Anthony, Kt.
†Campbell-Orde, Sir John Simon
Arthur, Bt. (1790)
Cannadine, *Prof.* Sir David Nicholas,
Kt.
Capewell, *Lt.-Gen.* Sir David Andrew,
KCB, OBE, RM
Carden, Sir Christopher Robert, Bt.
(1887)
†Carden, Sir John Craven, Bt. (I.
1787)
Carew, Sir Rivers Verain, Bt. (1661)
Carey, Sir de Vic Graham, Kt.
Carleton-Smith, *Gen.* Sir Mark
Alexander Popham, KCB, CBE,
ADC
Carleton-Smith, *Maj.-Gen.* Sir Michael
Edward, Kt., CBE
Carlisle, Sir James Beethoven, GCMG
Carlisle, Sir John Michael, Kt.

Carlisle, Sir Kenneth Melville, Kt.
Carnegie, Sir Roderick Howard, Kt.
Carnwath, *Rt. Hon.* Sir Robert John
Anderson, Kt., CVO (Lord
Carnwath of Notting Hill)
Carr, Sir Roger Martyn, Kt.
Carrick, Sir Roger John, KCMG, LVO
Carrington, Sir Nigel Martyn, Kt.
Carruthers, Sir Ian James, Kt., OBE
Carsberg, *Prof.* Sir Bryan Victor, Kt.
Carter, Sir Andrew Nicholas, Kt., OBE
Carter, Sir David Anthony, Kt.
Carter, *Prof.* Sir David Craig, Kt.,
FRCSE, FRCSGLAS, FRCPE
Carter, Sir Edward Charles, KCMG
Carter, Sir John Gordon Thomas, Kt.
Carter, *Gen.* Sir Nicholas Patrick, GCB,
CBE, DSO, ADC
Cartledge, Sir Bryan George, KCMG
Caruna, *Hon.* Sir Peter Richard,
KCMG, QC
†Cary, Sir Nicolas Robert Hugh, Bt.
(1955)
Cash, Sir Andrew John, Kt., OBE
Cash, Sir William Nigel Paul, Kt.
Cass, Sir Geoffrey Arthur, Kt.
Cassel, Sir Timothy Felix Harold, Bt.
(1920)
Cassidi, *Adm.* Sir (Arthur) Desmond,
GCB
Castell, Sir William Martin, Kt.
Catto, *Prof.* Sir Graeme Robertson
Dawson, Kt.
Caulfield, *Prof.* Sir Mark Jonathan, Kt.
Cavanagh, *Hon.* Sir John, Kt.
Cave, Sir George Charles, Bt. (1896)
Cave-Browne-Cave, Sir John Robert
Charles, Bt. (1641)
Cayley, Sir Digby William David, Bt.
(1661)
Cazalet, *Hon.* Sir Edward Stephen, Kt.
Cenac, *HE* Sir (Emmanuel) Neville,
GCMG
Chadwick, *Rt. Hon.* Sir John Murray,
Kt.
Chadwick, Sir Joshua Kenneth Burton,
Bt. (1935)
Chadwyck-Healey, Sir Charles
Edward, Bt. (1919)
Chakrabarti, Sir Sumantra, KCB
Chalmers, Sir Iain Geoffrey, Kt.
Chalmers, Sir Neil Robert, Kt.
Chalstrey, Sir (Leonard) John, Kt., MD,
FRCS
Chamberlain, *Hon.* Sir Martin Daniel,
Kt.
Chan, *Rt. Hon.* Sir Julius, GCMG, KBE
Chan, Sir Thomas Kok, Kt., OBE
Chance, Sir John Sebastian, Bt. (1900)
Chandler, Sir Colin Michael, Kt.
Chantler, *Prof.* Sir Cyril, GBE, MD,
FRCP
Chaplin, Sir Malcolm Hilbery, Kt.,
CBE
Chapman, Sir David Robert
Macgowan, Bt. (1958)
Chapman, Sir Frank, Kt.
Chapman, Sir George Alan, Kt.

Chapple, *Field Marshal* Sir John Lyon,
GCB, CBE
Charles, *Hon.* Sir Arthur William
Hessin, Kt.
Charlton, Sir Robert (Bobby), Kt.,
CBE
Charnley, Sir (William) John, Kt., CB,
FRENG
Chastanet, Sir Michael Thomas,
KCMG, OBE
†Chaytor, Sir Bruce Gordon, Bt.
(1831)
Checketts, *Sqn. Ldr.* Sir David John,
KCVO
Checkland, Sir Michael, Kt.
Cheshire, Sir Ian Michael, Kt.
Cheshire, *Air Chief Marshal* Sir John
Anthony, KBE, CB
Chessells, Sir Arthur David (Tim), Kt.
†Chetwynd, Sir Peter James Talbot,
Bt. (1795)
Cheyne, Sir Patrick John Lister, Bt.
(1908)
Chichester, Sir James Henry Edward,
Bt. (1641)
Chilcot, *Rt. Hon.* Sir John Anthony,
GCB
Chilcott, Sir Dominick John, KCMG
Child, Sir (Coles John) Jeremy, Bt.
(1919)
Chinn, Sir Trevor Edwin, Kt., CVO
†Chinubhai, Sir Prashant, Bt. (1913)
Chipperfield, *Prof.* Sir David Alan, Kt.,
CBE
Chipperfield, Sir Geoffrey Howes,
KCB
Chisholm, Sir John Alexander
Raymond, Kt., FRENG
†Chitty, Sir Andrew Edward Willes,
Bt. (1924)
Cholmeley, Sir Hugh John Frederick
Sebastian, Bt. (1806)
Chope, Sir Christopher Robert, Kt.,
OBE
Choudhury, *Hon.* Sir Akhlaq Ur-
Rahman, Kt.
Chow, Sir Chung Kong, Kt.
Chow, Sir Henry Francis, Kt., OBE
Christopher, Sir Duncan Robin
Carmichael, KBE, CMG
Chung, Sir Sze-yuen, GBE, FRENG
Clark, *Prof.* Sir Christopher Munro, Kt.
Clark, Sir Francis Drake, Bt. (1886)
Clark, Sir Jonathan George, Bt. (1917)
Clark, Sir Terence Joseph, KBE, CMG,
CVO
Clark, Sir Timothy Charles, KBE
Clarke, Sir Charles Lawrence
Somerset, Bt. (1831)
Clarke, *Rt. Hon.* Sir Christopher Simon
Courtenay Stephenson, Kt.
Clarke, *Hon.* Sir David Clive, Kt.
Clarke, Sir Jonathan Dennis, Kt.
Clarke, Sir Paul Robert Virgo, KCVO
Clarke, Sir Rupert Grant Alexander,
Bt. (1882)
Clary, *Prof.* Sir David Charles, Kt.
Clay, Sir Edward, KCMG
Clay, Sir Richard Henry, Bt. (1841)

Clayton, Sir David Robert, Bt. (1732)

Cleobury, *Dr* Sir Stephen John, Kt., CBE

Cleaver, Sir Anthony Brian, Kt.

Clegg, *Rt. Hon.* Sir Nicholas William Peter, Kt.

Clementi, Sir David Cecil, Kt.

Clerk, Sir Robert Maxwell, Bt. (S. 1679), OBE

Clerke, Sir Francis Ludlow Longueville, Bt. (1660)

Clifford, Sir Roger Joseph, Bt. (1887)

Clifford, Sir Timothy Peter Plint, Kt.

Clifton-Brown, Sir Geoffrey Robert, Kt.

Coates, Sir Anthony Robert Milnes, Bt. (1911)

Coates, Sir David Frederick Charlton, Bt. (1921)

†Coats, Sir Alexander James Stuart, Bt. (1905)

Cobb, *Hon.* Sir Stephen William Scott, Kt.

Cochrane, Sir (Henry) Marc (Sursock), Bt. (1903)

†Cockburn, Sir Charles Christopher, Bt. (S. 1671)

Cockburn-Campbell, Sir Alexander Thomas, Bt. (1821)

Cockell, Sir Merrick, Kt.

Cockshaw, Sir Alan, Kt., FRENG

Codrington, Sir Christopher George Wayne, Bt. (1876)

Codrington, Sir Giles Peter, Bt. (1721)

Codron, Sir Michael Victor, Kt., CBE

Coghill, Sir Patrick Kendal Farley, Bt. (1778)

Coghlin, *Rt. Hon.* Sir Patrick, Kt.

Cohen, Sir Ivor Harold, Kt., CBE, TD

Cohen, *Hon.* Sir Jonathan Lionel, Kt.

Cohen, *Prof.* Sir Philip, Kt., PHD, FRS

Cohen, Sir Robert Paul, Kt., CBE

Cohen, Sir Ronald, Kt.

Cole, Sir (Robert) William, Kt.

Coleman, Sir Robert John, KCMG

Coleridge, *Hon.* Sir Paul James Duke, Kt.

Coles, Sir (Arthur) John, GCMG

Coles, Sir Jonathan Andrew, Kt.

Colfox, Sir Philip John, Bt. (1939)

Collas, Sir Richard John, Kt.

Collett, Sir Ian Seymour, Bt. (1934)

Collier, Sir Paul, Kt., CBE

Collins, Sir Alan Stanley, KCVO, CMG

Collins, *Hon.* Sir Andrew David, Kt.

Collins, Sir Bryan Thomas Alfred, Kt., OBE, QFSM

Collins, *Dr* Sir David John, Kt., CBE

Collins, Sir John Alexander, Kt.

Collins, Sir Kenneth Darlingston, Kt.

Collins, *Dr* Sir Kevan Arthur, Kt.

Collins, *Prof.* Sir Rory Edwards, Kt.

Collyear, Sir John Gowen, Kt.

Colman, Sir Michael Jeremiah, Bt. (1907)

Colman, Sir Timothy, KG

Colquhoun of Luss, Sir Rory Malcolm, Bt. (1786)

Colt, Sir Edward William Dutton, Bt. (1694)

Colthurst, Sir Charles St John, Bt. (I. 1744)

Colton, *Hon.* Sir Adrian George Patrick, Kt.

Conant, Sir John Ernest Michael, Bt. (1954)

Conner, *Rt Revd* David John, KCVO

Connery, Sir Sean, Kt.

Connolly, Sir William (Billy), Kt., CBE

Connor, Sir William Joseph, Kt.

Conran, Sir Terence Orby, Kt., CH

Cons, *Hon.* Sir Derek, Kt.

Constantinou, Sir Kosta George, Kt., OBE

Constantinou, Sir Theophilus George, Kt., CBE

Conway, *Prof.* Sir Gordon Richard, KCMG, FRS

Cook, Sir Alastair Nathan, Kt., CBE

Cook, Sir Andrew, Kt., CBE

Cook, Sir Christopher Wymondham Rayner Herbert, Bt. (1886)

Cook, *Prof.* Sir Peter Frederic Chester, Kt.

Cooke, *Hon.* Sir Jeremy Lionel, Kt.

Cooke, *Prof.* Sir Ronald Urwick, Kt.

Cooke-Yarborough, Sir Anthony Edmund, Bt. (1661)

Cooksey, Sir David James Scott, GBE

Cooper, *Prof.* Sir Cary Lynn, Kt., CBE

Cooper, *Gen.* Sir George Leslie Conroy, GCB, MC

Cooper, Sir Richard Adrian, Bt. (1905)

Cooper, Sir Robert Francis, KCMG, MVO

Cooper, *Maj.-Gen.* Sir Simon Christie, GCVO

Cooper, Sir William Daniel Charles, Bt. (1863)

Coote, Sir Nicholas Patrick, Bt. (I. 1621), *Premier Baronet of Ireland*

Corbett, *Maj.-Gen.* Sir Robert John Swan, KCVO, CB

Corder, Vice-Adm. Sir Ian Fergus, KBE, CB

Cordy-Simpson, *Lt.-Gen.* Sir Roderick Alexander, KBE, CB

Corness, Sir Colin Ross, Kt.

Corry, Sir James Michael, Bt. (1885)

Cory, Sir (Clinton Charles) Donald, Bt. (1919)

Cory-Wright, Sir Richard Michael, Bt. (1903)

Cossons, Sir Neil, Kt., OBE

Cotter, Sir Patrick Laurence Delaval, Bt. (I. 1763)

Cotterell, Sir Henry Richard Geers, Bt. (1805), OBE

†Cotts, Sir Richard Crichton Mitchell, Bt. (1921)

Coulson, *Rt. Hon.* Sir Peter David William, Kt.

Couper, Sir James George, Bt. (1841)

Courtenay, Sir Thomas Daniel, Kt.

Cousins, *Air Chief Marshal* Sir David, KCB, AFC

Coville, *Air Marshal* Sir Christopher Charles Cotton, KCB

Cowan, *Gen.* Sir Samuel, KCB, CBE

Coward, *Lt.-Gen.* Sir Gary Robert, KBE, CB, OBE

Coward, *Vice-Adm.* Sir John Francis, KCB, DSO

Cowdery, Sir Clive, Kt.

Cowley, *Prof.* Sir Steven Charles, Kt., FRS, FRENG

Cowper-Coles, Sir Sherard Louis, KCMG, LVO

Cox, Sir Alan George, Kt., CBE

Cox, *Prof.* Sir David Roxbee, Kt.

Cox, Sir George Edwin, Kt.

Craft, *Prof.* Sir Alan William, Kt.

Cragg, *Prof.* Sir Anthony Douglas, Kt., CBE

Cragnolini, Sir Luciano, Kt.

Craig-Cooper, Sir (Frederick Howard) Michael, Kt., CBE, TD

Craig-Martin, Sir Michael, Kt., CBE

Crane, *Prof.* Sir Peter Robert, Kt.

Cranston, *Hon.* Sir Ross Frederick, Kt.

Craufurd, Sir Robert James, Bt. (1781)

Crausby, Sir David Anthony, Kt.

Craven, Sir John Anthony, Kt.

Craven, Sir Philip Lee, Kt., MBE

Crawford, *Prof.* Sir Frederick William, Kt., FRENG

Crawford, Sir Robert William Kenneth, Kt., CBE

Crawley-Boevey, Sir Thomas Michael Blake, Bt. (1784)

Cresswell, *Hon.* Sir Peter John, Kt.

Crew, Sir (Michael) Edward, Kt., QPM

Crewe, *Prof.* Sir Ivor Martin, Kt.

Crisp, Sir John Charles, Bt. (1913)

Critchett, Sir Charles George Montague, Bt. (1908)

Crittin, *Hon.* Sir John Luke, KBE

Croft, Sir Owen Glendower, Bt. (1671)

Croft, Sir Thomas Stephen Hutton, Bt. (1818)

Crofton, Sir Edward Morgan, Bt. (1801)

Crofton, Sir William Robert Malby, Bt. (1838)

Crombie, Sir Alexander, Kt.

Crompton, Sir Dan, Kt., CBE, QPM

Cropper, Sir James Anthony, KCVO

Crosby, Sir Lynton Keith, Kt.

Crossley, Sir Sloan Nicholas, Bt. (1909)

Crowe, Sir Brian Lee, KCMG

Cruickshank, Sir Donald Gordon, Kt.

Cubie, *Dr* Sir Andrew, Kt., CBE

Cubitt, Sir Hugh Guy, Kt., CBE

Cubitt, *Maj.-Gen.* Sir William George, KCVO, CBE

Cullen, Sir (Edward) John, Kt., FRENG

Culme-Seymour, Sir Michael Patrick, Bt. (1809)

Culpin, Sir Robert Paul, Kt.

Cummins, Sir Michael John Austin, Kt.

Cunliffe, *Prof.* Sir Barrington, Kt., CBE

Cunliffe, Sir David Ellis, Bt. (1759)

Cunliffe, Sir Jonathan Stephen, Kt., CB

Cunliffe-Owen, Sir Hugo Dudley, Bt. (1920)

Cunningham, *Lt.-Gen.* Sir Hugh Patrick, KBE

Cunningham, *Prof.* Sir John, KCVO

Cunningham, Sir Roger Keith, Kt., CBE

Cunningham, Sir Thomas Anthony, Kt.

Cunynghame, Sir Andrew David Francis, Bt. (S. 1702)

Curran, *Prof.* Sir Paul James, Kt.

Curtain, Sir Michael, KBE

Curtice, *Prof.* Sir John Kevin, Kt., FBA, FRSE

Curtis, Sir Barry John, Kt.

Curtis, Sir Edward Philip, Bt. (1802)

Curtis, *Hon.* Sir Richard Herbert, Kt.

Cuschieri, *Prof.* Sir Alfred, Kt.

Cyrus, *Dr* Sir Arthur Cecil, KCMG, OBE

Dain, Sir David John Michael, KCVO

Dales, Sir Richard Nigel, KCVO

Dalglish, Sir Kenneth, Kt., MBE

Dalrymple-Hay, Sir Malcolm John Robert, Bt. (1798)

†Dalrymple-White, Sir Jan Hew, Bt. (1926)

Dalton, Sir David Nigel, Kt.

Dalton, *Vice-Adm.* Sir Geoffrey Thomas James Oliver, GCB

Dalton, Sir Richard John, KCMG

Dalton, *Air Chief Marshal* Sir Stephen Gary George, GCB

Dalyell, Sir Gordon Wheatley, Bt. (NS 1685)

Dancer, Sir Eric, KCVO, CBE

Daniel, Sir John Sagar, Kt., DSC

Darell, Sir Guy Jeffrey Adair, Bt. (1795)

Darrington, Sir Michael John, Kt.

Dasgupta, *Prof.* Sir Partha Sarathi, Kt.

Dashwood, *Prof.* Sir (Arthur) Alan, KCMG, CBE, QC

Dashwood, Sir Edward John Francis, Bt. (1707), *Premier Baronet of Great Britain*

Dashwood, Sir Frederick George Mahon, Bt. (1684)

Daunt, Sir Timothy Lewis Achilles, KCMG

Davey, *Rt. Hon.* Sir Edward Jonathan, Kt.

Davidson, Sir Martin Stuart, KCMG

Davies, *Prof.* Sir David Evan Naughton, Kt., CBE, FRS, FRENG

Davies, Sir David John, Kt.

Davies, Sir Frank John, Kt., CBE

Davies, *Prof.* Sir Graeme John, Kt., FRENG

Davies, Sir John Howard, Kt.

Davies, Sir John Michael, KCB

Davies, Sir Raymond Douglas, Kt.

Davies, Sir Rhys Everson, Kt., QC

Davis, Sir Andrew Frank, Kt., CBE

Davis, Sir Crispin Henry Lamert, Kt.

Davis, Sir Ian Edward Lamert, Kt.

†Davis, Sir Richard Charles, Bt. (1946)

Davis, Sir Michael Lawrence, Kt.

Davis, *Rt. Hon.* Sir Nigel Anthony Lamert, Kt.

Davis, Sir Peter John, Kt.

Davis, *Hon.* Sir William Easthope, Kt.

Davis-Goff, Sir Robert (William), Bt. (1905)

Davson, Sir George Trenchard Simon, Bt. (1927)

Dawanincura, Sir John Norbert, Kt., OBE

Dawbarn, Sir Simon Yelverton, KCVO, CMG

Dawson, *Hon.* Sir Daryl Michael, KBE, CB

Dawson, Sir Nicholas Anthony Trevor, Bt. (1920)

Day, Sir Barry Stuart, Kt., OBE

Day, *Air Chief Marshal* Sir John Romney, KCB, OBE, ADC

Day, Sir Jonathan Stephen, Kt., CBE

Day, Sir (Judson) Graham, Kt.

Day, Sir Michael John, Kt., OBE

Day, Sir Simon James, Kt.

Day-Lewis, Sir Daniel Michael Blake, Kt.

Deane, *Hon.* Sir William Patrick, KBE

Dearlove, Sir Richard Billing, KCMG, OBE

Deaton, *Prof.* Sir Angus Stewart, Kt.

†Debenham, Sir Thomas Adam, Bt. (1931)

Deegan, Sir Michael, Kt., CBE

Deeny, *Rt. Hon.* Sir Donnell Justin Patrick, Kt.

De Haan, Sir Roger Michael, Kt., CBE

De Halpert, *Rear-Adm.* Sir Jeremy Michael, KCVO, CB

de Hoghton, Sir (Richard) Bernard (Cuthbert), Bt. (1611)

†de la Rue, Sir Edward Walter Henry, Bt. (1898)

Dellow, Sir John Albert, Kt., CBE

Delves, *Lt.-Gen.* Sir Cedric Norman George, KBE

Denison-Smith, *Lt.-Gen.* Sir Anthony Arthur, KBE

Denny, Sir Charles Alistair Maurice, Bt. (1913)

Denny, Sir Piers Anthony de Waltham, Bt. (I. 1782)

Desmond, Sir Denis Fitzgerald, KCVO, CBE

de Trafford, Sir John Humphrey, Bt. (1841)

Devane, Sir Ciaran Gearoid, Kt.

Deverell, *Lt.-Gen.* Sir Christopher Michael, KCB, MBE

Deverell, *Gen.* Sir John Freegard, KCB, OBE

Devereux, Sir Robert, KCB

De Ville, Sir Harold Godfrey Oscar, Kt., CBE

Devine, *Prof.* Sir Thomas Martin, Kt., OBE, FRSE

Devitt, Sir James Hugh Thomas, Bt. (1916)

Dewey, Sir Rupert Grahame, Bt. (1917)

De Witt, Sir Ronald Wayne, Kt.

Diamond, *Prof.* Sir Ian David, Kt., FRSE

Dick-Lauder, Sir Piers Robert, Bt. (S. 1690)

Dilke, Revd Charles John Wentworth, Bt. (1862)

Dilley, Sir Philip Graham, Kt.

Dillon, Sir Andrew Patrick, Kt., CBE

Dillwyn-Venables-Llewelyn, Sir John Michael, Bt. (1890)

Dilnot, Sir Andrew William, Kt., CBE

Dingemans, *Hon.* Sir James Michael, Kt.

Dion, Sir Leo, KBE

Dixon, Sir Jeremy, Kt.

Dixon, Sir Jonathan Mark, Bt. (1919)

Dixon, *Dr* Sir Michael, Kt.

Dixon, Sir Peter John Bellett, Kt.

Djanogly, Sir Harry Ari Simon, Kt., CBE

Dobson, *Vice-Adm.* Sir David Stuart, KBE

Dollery, Sir Colin Terence, Kt.

Don-Wauchope, Sir Roger (Hamilton), Bt. (S. 1667)

Donaldson, *Rt. Hon.* Sir Jeffrey Mark, Kt.

Donaldson, *Prof.* Sir Liam Joseph, Kt.

Donaldson, *Prof.* Sir Simon Kirwan, Kt.

Donnelly, Sir Joseph Brian, KBE, CMG

Donnelly, Sir Martin Eugene, KCB, CMG

Donnelly, *Prof.* Sir Peter James, Kt.

Donohoe, Sir Brian Harold, Kt.

Dorfman, Sir Lloyd, Kt., CBE

Dorman, Sir Philip Henry Keppel, Bt. (1923)

Douglas, *Prof.* Sir Neil James, Kt.

Douglas, *Hon.* Sir Roger Owen, Kt.

Dove, *Hon.* Sir Ian William, Kt.

Dowell, Sir Anthony James, Kt., CBE

Dowling, Sir Robert, Kt.

Downes, *Prof.* Sir Charles Peter, Kt., OBE, FRSE

Downey, Sir Gordon Stanley, KCB

Doyle, Sir Reginald Derek Henry, Kt., CBE

D'Oyly, Sir Hadley Gregory, Bt. (1663)

Drewry, *Lt.-Gen.* Sir Christopher Francis, KCB, CBE

Dryden, Sir John Stephen Gyles, Bt. (1733 and 1795)

Duberly, Sir Archibald Hugh, KCVO, CBE

Duckworth, Sir James Edward Dyce, Bt. (1909)

du Cros, Sir Julian Claude Arthur Mallet, Bt. (1916)

Dudley-Williams, Sir Alastair Edgcumbe James, Bt. (1964)

Duff, *Prof.* Sir Gordon William, Kt.

Duff-Gordon, Sir Andrew Cosmo Lewis, Bt. (1813)

Duffell, *Lt.-Gen.* Sir Peter Royson, KCB, CBE, MC

Duffy, Sir (Albert) (Edward) Patrick, Kt., PHD

Dugdale, Sir (William) Matthew Stratford, Bt. (1936)

Duggin, Sir Thomas Joseph, Kt.

Dunbar, Sir Edward Horace, Bt. (S. 1700)

Dunbar, Sir James Michael, Bt. (S. 1694)

Dunbar, Sir Robert Drummond Cospatrick, Bt. (S. 1698)

Dunbar of Hempriggs, Sir Richard Francis, Bt. (S. 1706)

Dunbar-Nasmith, *Prof.* Sir James Duncan, Kt., CBE

Duncan, *Rt. Hon.* Sir Alan James Carter, KCMG

Duncan, Sir James Blair, Kt.

Dunford, *Dr* Sir John Ernest, Kt., OBE

Dunlop, Sir Thomas, Bt. (1916)

Dunne, Sir Martin, KCVO

Dunne, Sir Thomas Raymond, KG, KCVO

Dunning, Sir Simon William Patrick, Bt. (1930)

Dunnington-Jefferson, Sir John Alexander, Bt. (1958)

Dunstone, Sir Charles William, Kt., CVO

Dunt, *Vice-Adm.* Sir John Hugh, KCB

†Duntze, Sir Daniel Evans, Bt. (1774)

Dupre, Sir Tumun, Kt., MBE

Durand, Sir Edward Alan Christopher David Percy, Bt. (1892)

Durie, Sir David Robert Campbell, KCMG

Durrant, Sir David Alexander, Bt. (1784)

Duthie, Sir Robert Grieve (Robin), Kt., CBE

Dutton, *Lt.-Gen.* Sir James Benjamin, KCB, CBE

Dwyer, Sir Joseph Anthony, Kt.

†Dyer-Bennet, Sir David, Bt. (1678)

Dyke, Sir David William Hart, Bt. (1677)

Dymock, *Vice-Adm.* Sir Anthony Knox, KBE, CB

Dyson, Sir James, Kt., OM, CBE

Dyson, *Rt. Hon.* Sir John Anthony, Kt. (Lord Dyson)

Eadie, Sir James Raymond, Kt., QC

Eady, *Hon.* Sir David, Kt.

Eardley-Wilmot, Sir Benjamin John Assheton, Bt. (1821)

Earle, Sir (Hardman) George (Algernon), Bt. (1869)

Eastwood, *Prof.* Sir David Stephen, Kt.

Eaton, *Adm.* Sir Kenneth John, GBE, KCB

Ebdon, *Prof.* Sir Leslie Colin, Kt., CBE

Ebrahim, Sir (Mahomed) Currimbhoy, Bt. (1910)

Eddington, Sir Roderick Ian, Kt.

Eden, *Hon.* Sir Robert Frederick Calvert, Bt. (E 1672 and 1776)

Eder, *Hon.* Sir Henry Bernard, Kt.

Edis, *Hon.* Sir Andrew Jeremy Coulter, Kt.

Edge, *Capt.* Sir (Philip) Malcolm, KCVO

†Edge, Sir William, Bt. (1937)

Edmonstone, Sir Archibald Bruce Charles, Bt. (1774)

Edward, *Rt. Hon.* Sir David Alexander Ogilvy, KCMG

Edwardes, Sir Michael Owen, Kt.

Edwards, Sir Christopher John Churchill, Bt. (1866)

Edwards, *Prof.* Sir Christopher Richard Watkin, Kt.

Edwards, Sir Gareth Owen, Kt., CBE

Edwards, Sir Llewellyn Roy, Kt.

Edwards, *Prof.* Sir Michael, OBE

Edwards, Sir Robert Paul, Kt.

†Edwards-Moss, Sir David John, Bt. (1868)

Edwards-Stuart, *Hon.* Sir Antony James Cobham, Kt.

Egan, Sir John Leopold, Kt.

Egerton, Sir William de Malpas, Bt. (1617)

Ehrman, Sir William Geoffrey, KCMG

Elder, Sir Mark Philip, Kt., CH, CBE

Eldon, Sir Stewart Graham, KCMG, OBE

Elias, *Rt. Hon.* Sir Patrick, Kt.

Eliott of Stobs, Sir Rodney Gilbert Charles, Bt. (S. 1666)

Elliott, Sir David Murray, KCMG, CB

Elliott, Sir Ivo Antony Moritz, Bt. (1917)

Elliott, *Prof.* Sir John Huxtable, Kt., FBA

Ellis, Sir Vernon James, Kt.

Ellwood, Sir Peter Brian, Kt., CBE

Elphinston, Sir Alexander, Bt. (S. 1701)

Elphinstone, Sir John Howard Main, Bt. (1816)

Elton, Sir Arnold, Kt., CBE

Elton, Sir Charles Abraham Grierson, Bt. (1717)

Elvidge, Sir John, KCB

Elwes, *Dr* Sir Henry William, KCVO

Elwes, Sir Jeremy Vernon, Kt., CBE

Elwood, Sir Brian George Conway, Kt., CBE

Elworthy, *Air Cdre Hon.* Sir Timothy Charles, KCVO, CBE

Enderby, *Prof.* Sir John Edwin, Kt. CBE, FRS

English, Sir Terence Alexander Hawthorne, KBE, FRCS

Ennals, Sir Paul Martin, Kt., CBE

Epstein, *Prof.* Sir (Michael) Anthony, Kt., CBE, FRS

Errington, Sir Robin Davenport, Bt. (1963)

Erskine, Sir (Thomas) Peter Neil, Bt. (1821)

Erskine-Hill, Sir Alexander Roger, Bt. (1945)

Esmonde, Sir Thomas Francis Grattan, Bt. (I. 1629)

†Esplen, Sir William John Harry, Bt. (1921)

Esquivel, *Rt. Hon.* Sir Manuel, KCMG

Essenhigh, *Adm.* Sir Nigel Richard, GCB

Etherington, Sir Stuart James, Kt.

Etherton, *Rt. Hon.* Sir Terence Michael Elkan Barnet, Kt.

Evans, *Rt. Hon.* Sir Anthony Howell Meurig, Kt., RD

Evans, *Prof.* Sir Christopher Thomas, Kt., OBE

Evans, *Air Chief Marshal* Sir David George, GCB, CBE

Evans, *Hon.* Sir David Roderick, Kt.

Evans, Sir Harold Matthew, Kt.

Evans, Sir John Stanley, Kt., QPM

Evans, Sir Malcolm David, KCMG, OBE

Evans, *Prof.* Sir Martin John, Kt., FRS

Evans, Sir Richard Harry, Kt., CBE

Evans, *Prof.* Sir Richard John, Kt.

Evans, Sir Robert, Kt., CBE, FRENG

Evans-Lombe, *Hon.* Sir Edward Christopher, Kt.

†Evans-Tipping, Sir David Gwynne, Bt. (1913)

Evennett, *Rt. Hon.* Sir David Anthony, Kt.

Everard, Sir Henry Peter Charles, Bt. (1911)

Everard, *Lt.-Gen.* Sir James Rupert, KCB, CBE

Everington, *Dr* Sir Anthony Herbert, Kt., OBE

Every, Sir Henry John Michael, Bt. (1641)

Ewart, Sir William Michael, Bt. (1887)

Eyre, Sir Richard Charles Hastings, Kt., CH, CBE

†Fagge, Sir John Christopher Frederick, Bt. (1660)

Fahy, Sir Peter, Kt., QPM

Fairbairn, Sir Robert William, Bt. (1869)

Fairlie-Cuninghame, Sir Robert Henry, Bt. (S. 1630)

Fairweather, Sir Patrick Stanislaus, KCMG

Faldo, Sir Nicholas Alexander, Kt., MBE

†Falkiner, Sir Benjamin Simon Patrick, Bt. (I. 1778)

Fall, Sir Brian James Proetel, GCVO, KCMG

Fallon, *Rt. Hon.* Sir Michael Cathel, KCB

Fancourt, *Hon.* Sir Timothy Miles, Kt.

Fang, *Prof.* Sir Harry, Kt., CBE

Farah, Sir Mohamed (Mo) Muktar Jama, Kt., CBE

Fareed, Sir Djamil Sheik, Kt.

Farmer, Sir Thomas, Kt., CVO, CBE

Farquhar, Sir Michael Fitzroy Henry, Bt. (1796)

Farr, Sir Charles Blandford, Kt., CMG, OBE

Farrar, *Prof.* Sir Jeremy James, Kt., OBE

Farrell, Sir Terence, Kt., CBE

Farrer, Sir (Charles) Matthew, GCVO

Farrington, Sir Henry William, Bt. (1818)

Faull, Sir Jonathan Michael Howard, KCMG

Fay, Sir (Humphrey) Michael Gerard, Kt.

Feachem, *Prof.* Sir Richard George Andrew, KBE

Fean, Sir Thomas Vincent, KCVO

Feilden, Sir Henry Rudyard, Bt. (1846)

Feldmann, *Prof.* Sir Marc, Kt.

Fell, Sir David, KCB

Fender, Sir Brian Edward Frederick, Kt., CMG, PHD

Fenwick, Sir Leonard Raymond, Kt., CBE

Fergus, Sir Howard Archibald, KBE

Ferguson, *Prof.* Sir Michael Anthony John, Kt., CBE, FRS

Ferguson-Davie, Sir Michael, Bt. (1847)

Fergusson, *Rt. Hon.* Sir Alexander Charles Onslow, Kt.

Fergusson of Kilkerran, Sir Charles, Bt. (S. 1703)

Fersht, *Prof.* Sir Alan Roy, Kt., FRS

ffolkes, Sir Robert Francis Alexander, Bt. (1774), OBE

Field, Sir Malcolm David, Kt.

Field, *Hon.* Sir Richard Alan, Kt.

Fielding, Sir Leslie, KCMG

Fields, Sir Allan Clifford, KCMG

Fiennes, Sir Ranulph Twisleton-Wykeham, Bt. (1916), OBE

Figgis, Sir Anthony St John Howard, KCVO, CMG

Finlay, Sir David Ronald James Bell, Bt. (1964)

Finlayson, Sir Garet Orlando, KCMG, OBE

Fish, *Prof.* Sir David Royden, Kt.

†Fison, *Sir* Charles William, Bt. (1905)

Fittall, Sir William Robert, Kt.

FitzGerald, Sir Adrian James Andrew Denis, Bt. (1880)

†Fitzgerald, Sir Andrew Peter, Bt. (1903)

FitzHerbert, Sir Richard Ranulph, Bt. (1784)

Fitzpatrick, *Air Marshal* Sir John Bernard, KBE, CB

Flanagan, Sir Ronald, GBE, QPM

Flaux, *Rt. Hon.* Sir Julian Martin, Kt.

Flint, Sir Douglas Jardine, Kt., CBE

Floud, *Prof.* Sir Roderick Castle, Kt.

Floyd, *Rt. Hon.* Sir Christopher David, Kt.

Floyd, Sir Giles Henry Charles, Bt. (1816)

Foley, *Lt.-Gen.* Sir John Paul, KCB, OBE, MC

Follett, *Prof.* Sir Brian Keith, Kt., FRS

†Forbes of Craigievar, Sir Andrew Iain Ochoncar, Bt. (S. 1630)

Forbes, *Adm.* Sir Ian Andrew, KCB, CBE

Forbes, Sir James Thomas Stewart, Bt. (1823)

Forbes, *Vice-Adm.* Sir John Morrison, KCB

Forbes, *Hon.* Sir Thayne John, Kt.

Forbes Adam, Sir Nigel Colin, Bt. (1917)

Forbes-Leith, Sir George Ian David, Bt. (1923)

Ford, *Lt.-Col.* Sir Andrew Charles, KCVO

Ford, Sir Andrew Russell, Bt. (1929)

Forestier-Walker, Sir Michael Leolin, Bt. (1835)

Forrest, *Prof.* Sir (Andrew) Patrick (McEwen), Kt.

Forte, *Hon.* Sir Rocco John Vincent, Kt.

Forwood, *Hon.* Sir Nicholas James, Kt., QC

Foskett, *Hon.* Sir David Robert, Kt.

Foster, Sir Andrew William, Kt.

Foster, *Prof.* Sir Christopher David, Kt.

Foster, Sir Saxby Gregory, Bt. (1930)

Foulkes, Sir Arthur Alexander, GCMG

Fountain, *Hon.* Sir Cyril Stanley Smith, Kt.

Fowke, Sir David Frederick Gustavus, Bt. (1814)

Fowler, Sir (Edward) Michael Coulson, Kt.

Fox, Sir Ashley, Kt.

Fox, Sir Christopher, Kt., QPM

Fox, Sir Paul Leonard, Kt., CBE

Francis, Sir Horace William Alexander, Kt., CBE, FRENG

Francis, *Hon.* Sir Peter Nicholas, Kt.

Francis, Sir Robert Anthony, Kt., QC

Frank, Sir Robert Andrew, Bt. (1920)

†Fraser, Sir Benjamin James, Bt. (1943)

Fraser, Sir Charles Annand, KCVO

Fraser, Sir James Murdo, KBE

Fraser, *Hon.* Sir Peter Donald, Kt.

Fraser, Sir Simon James, GCMG

Frayling, *Prof.* Sir Christopher John, Kt.

Frederick, Sir Christopher St John, Bt. (1723)

Freedman, *Hon.* Sir (Benjamin) Clive, Kt.

Freedman, *Rt. Hon. Prof.* Sir Lawrence David, KCMG, CBE

†Freeman, Sir James Robin, Bt. (1945)

French, *Air Marshal* Sir Joseph Charles, KCB, CBE

Frere, *Vice-Adm.* Sir Richard Tobias, KCB

Friend, *Prof.* Sir Richard Henry, Kt.

Froggatt, Sir Peter, Kt.

Fry, Sir Graham Holbrook, KCMG

Fry, *Lt.-Gen.* Sir Robert Allan, KCB, CBE

Fry, *Dr* Sir Roger Gordon, Kt., CBE

Fulford, *Rt. Hon.* Sir Adrian Bruce, Kt.

Fuller, Sir James Henry Fleetwood, Bt. (1910)

Fulton, *Lt.-Gen.* Sir Robert Henry Gervase, KBE

Furness, Sir Stephen Roberts, Bt. (1913)

G-I

Gage, *Rt. Hon.* Sir William Marcus, Kt, QC

Gains, Sir John Christopher, Kt.

Gainsford, Sir Ian Derek, Kt.

Gale, *Rt. Hon.* Sir Roger James, Kt.

Galsworthy, Sir Anthony Charles, KCMG

Galway, Sir James, Kt., OBE

Gamble, Sir David Hugh Norman, Bt. (1897)

Gambon, Sir Michael John, Kt., CBE

Gammell, Sir William Benjamin Bowring, Kt.

Gardiner, Sir John Eliot, Kt., CBE

Gardner, *Prof.* Sir Richard Lavenham, Kt.

Gardner, Sir Roy Alan, Kt.

Garland, *Hon.* Sir Patrick Neville, Kt.

Garland, *Hon.* Sir Ransley Victor, KBE

Garland, *Dr* Sir Trevor, KBE

Garnett, *Adm.* Sir Ian David Graham, KCB

Garnham, *Hon.* Sir Neil Stephen, Kt.

Garnier, *Rear-Adm.* Sir John, KCVO, CBE

Garrard, Sir David Eardley, Kt.

Garrett, Sir Anthony Peter, Kt., CBE

Garrick, Sir Ronald, Kt., CBE, FRENG

Garthwaite, Sir (William) Mark (Charles), Bt. (1919)

Garwood, *Air Marshal* Sir Richard Frank, KBE, CB, DFC

Gass, Sir Simon Lawrance, KCMG, CVO

Geim, *Prof.* Sir Andre Konstantin, Kt.

Geno, Sir Makena Viora, KBE

Gent, Sir Christopher Charles, Kt.

George, *Prof.* Sir Charles Frederick, Kt., MD, FRCP

Gerken, *Vice-Adm.* Sir Robert William Frank, KCB, CBE

Gershon, Sir Peter Oliver, Kt., CBE

Gethin, Sir Richard Joseph St Lawrence, Bt. (I. 1665)

Gibb, Sir Barry Alan Crompton, Kt., CBE

Gibb, Sir Robbie Paul, Kt.

Gibbings, Sir Peter Walter, Kt.

Gibbons, Sir William Edward Doran, Bt. (1752)

Gibbs, *Hon.* Sir Richard John Hedley, Kt.

†Gibson, *Revd* Christopher Herbert, Bt. (1931)

Gibson, Sir Ian, Kt., CBE

Gibson, Sir Kenneth Archibald, Kt.

Gibson, *Rt. Hon.* Sir Peter Leslie, Kt.

Gibson-Craig-Carmichael, Sir David Peter William, Bt. (S. 1702 and 1831)

Gieve, Sir Edward John Watson, KCB

Giffard, Sir (Charles) Sydney (Rycroft), KCMG

Gifford, Sir Michael Roger, Kt.

Gilbert, *Air Chief Marshal* Sir Joseph Alfred, KCB, CBE

Gilbey, Sir Walter Gavin, Bt. (1893)

Gill, Sir Robin Denys, KCVO

Gillam, Sir Patrick John, Kt.

Gillen, *Hon.* Sir John de Winter, Kt.

Gillett, Sir Nicholas Danvers Penrose, Bt. (1959)

Gillinson, Sir Clive Daniel, Kt., CBE

Gilmore, *Prof.* Sir Ian Thomas, Kt.

Gilmour, *Hon.* Sir David Robert, Bt. (1926)

Gilmour, Sir John Nicholas, Bt. (1897)

Gina, Sir Lloyd Maepeza, KBE

Giordano, Sir Richard Vincent, KBE

Girolami, Sir Paul, Kt.

Girvan, *Rt. Hon.* Sir (Frederick) Paul, Kt.

Gladstone, Sir Charles Angus, Bt. (1846)

Glean, Sir Carlyle Arnold, GCMG

Globe, *Hon.* Sir Henry Brian, Kt.

Glover, Sir Victor Joseph Patrick, Kt.

Glyn, Sir Richard Lindsay, Bt. (1759 and 1800)

Gobbo, Sir James Augustine, Kt., AC

Godfray, *Prof.* Sir Hugh Charles Jonathan, Kt., CBE

Goldberg, *Prof.* Sir David Paul Brandes, Kt.

Goldring, *Rt. Hon.* Sir John Bernard, Kt.

Gomersall, Sir Stephen John, KCMG

Gonsalves-Sabola, *Hon.* Sir Joaquim Claudino, Kt.

Gooch, Sir Arthur Brian Sherlock Heywood, Bt. (1746)

Gooch, Sir Miles Peter, Bt. (1866)

Good, Sir John James Griffen, Kt., CBE

Goodall, *Air Marshal* Sir Roderick Harvey, KBE, CB, AFC

Goode, *Prof.* Sir Royston Miles, Kt., CBE, QC

Goodenough, Sir Anthony Michael, KCMG

Goodenough, Sir William McLernon, Bt. (1943)

Goodhart, Sir Robert Anthony Gordon, Bt. (1911)

Goodison, Sir Nicholas Proctor, Kt.

Goodson, Sir Alan Reginald, Bt. (1922)

Goodwin, Sir Frederick, KBE

Goold, Sir George William, Bt. (1801)

Goose, *Hon.* Sir Julian Nicholas, Kt.

Gordon, Sir Donald, Kt.

Gordon, Sir Gerald Henry, Kt., CBE, QC

Gordon, Sir Robert James, Bt. (S. 1706)

Gordon-Cumming, Sir Alexander Alastair Penrose, Bt. (1804)

Gore, Sir Hugh Frederick Corbet, Bt. (I. 1622)

Gore-Booth, Sir Josslyn Henry Robert, Bt. (I. 1760)

Goring, Sir William Burton Nigel, Bt. (1678)

Gormley, Sir Antony Mark David, Kt., OBE

Gormley, Sir Paul Brendan, KCMG, MBE

Goschen, Sir (Edward) Alexander, Bt. (1916)

Gosling, Sir (Frederick) Donald, KCVO

Goss, *Hon.* Sir James Richard William, Kt.

Goulden, Sir (Peter) John, GCMG

†Goulding, Sir (William) Lingard Walter, Bt. (1904)

Gourlay, Sir Simon Alexander, Kt.

Gowans, Sir James Learmonth, Kt., CBE, FRCP, FRS

Gowers, *Prof.* Sir William Timothy, Kt.

Gozney, Sir Richard Hugh Turton, KCMG

Graaff, Sir De Villiers, Bt. (1911)

Graham, Sir Alexander Michael, GBE

Graham, Sir Andrew John Noble, Bt. (1906)

Graham, Sir James Bellingham, Bt. (1662)

Graham, Sir James Fergus Surtees, Bt. (1783)

Graham, Sir James Thompson, Kt., CMG

Graham, Sir John Alistair, Kt.

Graham, Sir John Moodie, Bt. (1964)

Graham, Sir Peter, KCB, QC

Graham, *Lt.-Gen.* Sir Peter Walter, KCB, CBE

†Graham, Sir Ralph Stuart, Bt. (1629)

Graham-Moon, Sir Peter Wilfred Giles, Bt. (1855)

Graham-Smith, *Prof.* Sir Francis, Kt.

Grainge, Sir Lucian Charles, Kt., CBE

Grange, Sir Kenneth Henry, Kt., CBE

Grant, Sir Archibald, Bt. (S. 1705)

Grant, *Dr* Sir David, Kt., CBE

Grant, Sir Ian David, Kt., CBE

Grant, Sir John Douglas Kelso, KCMG

Grant, *Prof.* Sir Malcolm John, Kt., CBE

Grant, Sir Mark Justin Lyall, GCMG

Grant, Sir Patrick Alexander Benedict, Bt. (S. 1688)

Grant, Sir Paul Joseph Patrick, Kt.

Grant, *Lt.-Gen.* Sir Scott Carnegie, KCB

Grant-Suttie, Sir James Edward, Bt. (S. 1702)

Granville-Chapman, *Gen.* Sir Timothy John, GBE, KCB, ADC

Grattan-Bellew, Sir Henry Charles, Bt. (1838)

Gray, Sir Bernard Peter, Kt.

Gray, *Hon.* Sir Charles Anthony St John, Kt.

Gray, Sir Charles Ireland, Kt., CBE

Gray, *Prof.* Sir Denis John Pereira, Kt., OBE, FRCGP

Gray, *Dr* Sir John Armstrong Muir, Kt., CBE

Gray, Sir Robert McDowall (Robin), Kt.

Gray, Sir William Hume, Bt. (1917)

Graydon, *Air Chief Marshal* Sir Michael James, GCB, CBE

Grayson, Sir Jeremy Brian Vincent Harrington, Bt. (1922)

Greaves, *Prof.* Sir Melvyn Francis, Kt.

Green, Sir Allan David, KCB, QC

Green, Sir David John Mark, Kt., CB, QC

Green, Sir Edward Patrick Lycett, Bt. (1886)

Green, Sir Gregory David, KCMG

Green, *Hon.* Sir Guy Stephen Montague, KBE

Green, *Prof.* Sir Malcolm, Kt.

Green, *Rt. Hon.* Sir Nicholas Nigel, Kt.

Green, Sir Philip Green, Kt.

Green-Price, Sir Robert John, Bt. (1874)

Greenaway, *Prof.* Sir David, Kt.

Greenaway, Sir Thomas Edward Burdick, Bt. (1933)

Greener, Sir Anthony Armitage, Kt.

Greenstock, Sir Jeremy Quentin, GCMG

Greenwell, Sir Edward Bernard, Bt. (1906)

Greenwood, *Prof.* Sir Brian Mellor, Kt., CBE

Greenwood, *Prof.* Sir Christopher John, GBE, CMG

Gregory, *Lt.-Gen.* Sir Andrew Richard, KBE, CB

Gregory, *Prof.* Sir Michael John, Kt., CBE

Gregson, *Prof.* Sir Peter John Kt., FRENG

Grey, Sir Anthony Dysart, Bt. (1814)

Grice, Sir Paul Edward, Kt.

Griffiths, Sir Michael, Kt.

Grigson, *Hon.* Sir Geoffrey Douglas, Kt.

Grimshaw, Sir Nicholas Thomas, Kt., CBE

Grimstone, Sir Gerald Edgar, Kt.

Grimwade, Sir Andrew Sheppard, Kt., CBE

Grose, *Vice-Adm.* Sir Alan, KBE

Gross, *Rt. Hon.* Sir Peter Henry, Kt.

Grossart, Sir Angus McFarlane McLeod, Kt., CBE

Grotrian, Sir Philip Christian Brent, Bt. (1934)

†Grove, Sir Charles Gerald, Bt. (1874)

Grundy, Sir Mark, Kt.

Guinness, Sir John Ralph Sidney, Kt., CB

Guinness, Sir Kenelm Edward Lee, Bt. (1867)

Guise, Sir Christopher James, Bt. (1783)

Gull, Sir Rupert William Cameron, Bt. (1872)

†Gunning, Sir John Robert, Bt. (1778)

Gunston, Sir John Wellesley, Bt. (1938)

Gurdon, *Prof.* Sir John Bertrand, Kt., DPHIL, FRS

Guthrie, Sir Malcolm Connop, Bt. (1936)

Habgood, Sir Anthony John, Kt.

Haddacks, *Vice-Adm.* Sir Paul Kenneth, KCB

Haddon-Cave, *Rt. Hon.* Sir Charles Anthony, Kt.

Hadlee, Sir Richard John, Kt., MBE

Hagart-Alexander, Sir Claud, Bt. (1886)

Haines, *Prof.* Sir Andrew Paul, Kt.

Haji-Ioannou, Sir Stelios, Kt.

Halberg, Sir Murray Gordon, Kt., MBE

Hall, *Dr* Sir Andrew James, Kt.

Hall, Sir David Bernard, Bt. (1919)

Hall, Sir David Christopher, Bt. (1923)

Hall, *Prof.* Sir David Michael Baldock, Kt.

Hall, Sir Ernest, Kt., OBE

Hall, Sir Geoffrey, Kt.

Hall, Sir Graham Joseph, Kt.

Hall, Sir Iain Robert, Kt.

Hall, Sir John, Kt.

Hall, Sir John Douglas Hoste, Bt. (S. 1687)

Hall, HE *Prof.* Sir Kenneth Octavius, GCMG

Hall, Sir Peter Edward, KBE, CMG

Hall, *Revd* Wesley Winfield, Kt.

Hall, Sir William Joseph, KCVO

Halliday, *Prof.* Sir Alexander Norman, Kt., FRS

Haloute, Sir Assad John, Kt.

Halpern, Sir Ralph Mark, Kt.

Halsey, *Revd* John Walter Brooke, Bt. (1920)

Halstead, Sir Ronald, Kt., CBE

Ham, *Prof.* Sir Christopher John, Kt., CBE

Hamblen, *Rt. Hon.* Sir Nicholas Archibald, Kt.

Hambling, Sir Herbert Peter Hugh, Bt. (1924)

Hamilton, Sir Andrew Caradoc, Bt. (S. 1646)

Hamilton, Sir David, Kt.

Hamilton, Sir George Ernest Craythorne, Kt., QPM

Hamilton, Sir Nigel, KCB

†Hamilton-Dalrymple, Sir Hew Richard, Bt. (S. 1698)

Hamilton-Spencer-Smith, Sir John, Bt. (1804)

Hammick, Sir Jeremy Charles, Bt. (1834)

Hammond, Sir Anthony Hilgrove, KCB, QC

Hampel, Sir Ronald Claus, Kt.

Hampson, Sir Stuart, Kt., CVO

Hampton, Sir (Leslie) Geoffrey, Kt.

Hampton, Sir Philip Roy, Kt.

Hanham, Sir William John Edward, Bt. (1667)

Hankes-Drielsma, Sir Claude Dunbar, KCVO

Hanley, *Rt. Hon.* Sir Jeremy James, KCMG

Hanmer, Sir Wyndham Richard Guy, Bt. (1774)

Hannam, Sir John Gordon, Kt.

Hanson, Sir (Charles) Rupert (Patrick), Bt. (1918)

Harcourt-Smith, *Air Chief Marshal* Sir David, GBE, KCB, DFC

Hardie Boys, *Rt. Hon.* Sir Michael, GCMG

Harding, *Marshal of the Royal Air Force* Sir Peter Robin, GCB

Hardy, Sir David William, Kt.

Hardy, Sir James Gilbert, Kt., OBE

Hare, Sir David, Kt., FRSL

Hare, Sir Nicholas Patrick, Bt. (1818)

Haren, *Dr* Sir Patrick Hugh, Kt.

Harford, Sir Mark John, Bt. (1934)

Harington, Sir David Richard, Bt. (1611)

Harkness, *Very Revd* James, KCVO, CB, OBE

Harley, *Gen.* Sir Alexander George Hamilton, KBE, CB

Harman, *Hon.* Sir Jeremiah LeRoy, Kt.

Harman, Sir John Andrew, Kt.

Harmsworth, Sir Hildebrand Harold, Bt. (1922)

Harper, *Air Marshal* Sir Christopher Nigel, KBE

Harper, Sir Ewan William, Kt., CBE

Harper, *Prof.* Sir Peter Stanley, Kt., CBE

Harris, Sir Christopher John Ashford, Bt. (1932)

Harris, *Air Marshal* Sir John Hulme, KCB, CBE

Harris, *Prof.* Sir Martin Best, Kt., CBE

Harris, Sir Michael Frank, Kt.

Harris, Sir Thomas George, KBE, CMG

Harrison, *Prof.* Sir Brian Howard, Kt.

Harrison, Sir David, Kt., CBE, FRENG

†Harrison, Sir Edwin Michael Harwood, Bt. (1961)

Harrison, *Hon.* Sir Michael Guy Vicat, Kt.

†Harrison, Sir John Wyndham Fowler, Bt. (1922)

Harrop, Sir Peter John, KCB

Hart, *Hon.* Sir Anthony Ronald, Kt.

Hart, Sir Graham Allan, KCB

Hartwell, Sir (Francis) Anthony Charles Peter, Bt. (1805)

Harvey, Sir Charles Richard Musgrave, Bt. (1933)

Harvey, Sir Nicholas Barton, Kt.

Harvie, Sir John Smith, Kt., CBE

Harvie-Watt, Sir James, Bt. (1945)

Harwood, Sir Ronald, Kt., CBE

Haslam, *Prof.* Sir David Antony, Kt., CBE

Hastie, *Cdre* Sir Robert Cameron, KCVO, CBE, RD

Hastings, Sir Max Macdonald, Kt.

Hastings, *Dr* Sir William George, Kt., CBE

Hatter, Sir Maurice, Kt.

Havelock-Allan, Sir (Anthony) Mark David, Bt. (1858), QC

Hawkes, Sir John Garry, Kt., CBE

Hawkhead, Sir Anthony Gerard, Kt., CBE

Hawkins, Sir Richard Caesar, Bt. (1778)

Hawley, Sir James Appleton, KCVO, TD

Haworth, Sir Christopher, Bt. (1911)

†Hay, Sir Ronald Frederick Hamilton, Bt. (S. 1703)

Hayden, *Hon.* Sir Anthony Paul, Kt.

Hayes, Sir Brian, Kt., CBE, QPM

Hayes, Sir Brian David, GCB

Hayes, *Rt. Hon.* Sir John Henry, Kt., CBE

Hayman-Joyce, *Lt.-Gen.* Sir Robert John, KCB, CBE

Hayter, Sir Paul David Grenville, KCB, LVO

Hazlewood, Sir Frederick Asa, KCMG

Head, Sir Patrick, Kt.

Head, Sir Richard Douglas Somerville, Bt. (1838)

Heald, *Rt. Hon.* Sir Oliver, Kt.

Heap, Sir Peter William, KCMG

Heap, *Prof.* Sir Robert Brian, Kt., CBE, FRS

Hearne, Sir Graham James, Kt., CBE

Heathcote, Sir Simon Robert Mark, Bt. (1733), OBE

†Heathcote, Sir Timothy Gilbert, Bt. (1733)

Heaton, Sir Richard, KCB

Heber-Percy, Sir Algernon Eustace Hugh, KCVO

Hedley, *Hon.* Sir Mark, Kt.

Hegarty, Sir John Kevin, Kt.

Heiser, Sir Terence Michael, GCB

Helfgott, Sir Ben, Kt., MBE

Heller, Sir Michael Aron, Kt.

Hempleman-Adams, *Dr* Sir David Kim, KCVO, OBE

Henderson, *Rt Hon.* Sir Launcelot Dinadin James, Kt.

Henderson, *Maj.* Sir Richard Yates, KCVO

Hendrick, Sir Mark, Kt.

Hendry, *Prof.* Sir David Forbes, Kt.

Hendy, Sir Peter Gerard, Kt., CBE

Hennessy, Sir James Patrick Ivan, KBE, CMG

†Henniker, Sir Adrian Chandos, Bt. (1813)

Henniker-Heaton, Sir Yvo Robert, Bt. (1912)

Henriques, *Hon.* Sir Richard Henry Quixano, Kt.

Henry, Sir Lenworth George, Kt., CBE

†Henry, Sir Patrick Denis, Bt. (1923)

Henshaw, Sir David George, Kt.

Herbecq, Sir John Edward, KCB

Heron, Sir Conrad Frederick, KCB, OBE

†Heron-Maxwell, Sir Nigel Mellor, Bt. (S. 1683)

Hervey, Sir Roger Blaise Ramsay, KCVO, CMG

Hervey-Bathurst, Sir Frederick William John, Bt. (1818)

Heseltine, *Rt. Hon.* Sir William Frederick Payne, GCB, GCVO

Hewetson, Sir Christopher Raynor, Kt., TD

Hewett, Sir Richard Mark John, Bt. (1813)

Hewitt, Sir (Cyrus) Lenox (Simson), Kt., OBE

Hewitt, Sir Nicholas Charles Joseph, Bt. (1921)

Heygate, Sir Richard John Gage, Bt. (1831)

Heywood, Sir Peter, Bt. (1838)

Hickey, Sir John Tongri, Kt., CBE

Hickinbottom, *Rt. Hon.* Sir Gary Robert, Kt.

Hickman, Sir (Richard) Glenn, Bt. (1903)

Hicks, Sir Robert, Kt.

Hielscher, Sir Leo Arthur, Kt.

Higgins, Sir David Hartmann, Kt.

Higgins, *Rt. Hon.* Sir Malachy Joseph, Kt.

Hildyard, *Hon.* Sir Robert Henry Thoroton, Kt.

Hill, *Rt. Revd Dr* Christopher John, KCVO

Hill, Sir James Frederick, Bt. (1917), OBE

Hill, Sir John Alfred Rowley, Bt. (I. 1779)

Hill, *Vice-Adm.* Sir Robert Charles Finch, KBE, FRENG

Hill-Norton, *Vice-Adm. Hon.* Sir Nicholas John, KCB

Hill-Wood, Sir Samuel Thomas, Bt. (1921)

Hillhouse, Sir (Robert) Russell, KCB

Hillier, *Air Marshal* Sir Stephen John, KCB, CBE, DFC

Hills, Sir John Robert, Kt., CBE

Hilly, Sir Francis Billy, KCMG

Hine, *Air Chief Marshal* Sir Patrick Bardon, GCB, GBE

Hintze, Sir Michael, Kt.

Hirsch, *Prof.* Sir Peter Bernhard, Kt., PHD, FRS

Hirst, Sir Michael William, Kt.

Hitchens, Sir Timothy Mark, KCVO, CMG

Hoare, *Prof.* Sir Charles Anthony Richard, Kt., FRS

Hoare, Sir Charles James, Bt. (I. 1784)

Hoare, Sir David John, Bt. (1786)

Hobart, Sir John Vere, Bt. (1914)

Hobbs, *Maj.-Gen.* Sir Michael Frederick, KCVO, CBE

Hobhouse, Sir Charles John Spinney, Bt. (1812)

†Hodge, Sir Andrew Rowland, Bt. (1921)

Hodge, Sir James William, KCVO, CMG

Hodgkinson, Sir Michael Stewart, Kt.

Hodson, Sir Michael Robin Adderley, Bt. (I. 1789)

Hogg, Sir Christopher Anthony, Kt.

Hogg, Sir Piers Michael James, Bt. (1846)

Hohn, Sir Christopher, KCMG

Holcroft, Sir Charles Anthony Culcheth, Bt. (1921)

Holden, Sir John David, Bt. (1919)

Holden, Sir Michael Peter, Bt. (1893)

†Holder, Sir Nigel John Charles, Bt. (1898)

Holderness, Sir Martin William, Bt. (1920)

Holdgate, Sir Martin Wyatt, Kt., CB, PHD

Holgate, *Hon.* Sir David John, Kt.

Holland, *Hon.* Sir Christopher John, Kt.

Holland, Sir John Anthony, Kt.

Hollingbery, Sir George Michael Edward, KCMG

Holm, Sir Ian (Holm Cuthbert), Kt., CBE

Holman, *Hon.* Sir Edward James, Kt.

Holman, *Prof.* Sir John Stranger, Kt.

Holmes, Sir John Eaton, GCVO, KBE, CMG

Holroyd, Sir Michael De Courcy Fraser, Kt., CBE

Holroyde, *Rt. Hon.* Sir Timothy Victor, Kt.

Home, Sir William Dundas, Bt. (S. 1671)

Honywood, Sir Filmer Courtenay William, Bt. (1660)

†Hood, Sir John Joseph Harold, Bt. (1922)

Hooper, *Rt. Hon.* Sir Anthony, Kt.

Hope, Sir Alexander Archibald Douglas, Bt. (S. 1628), OBE

Hope-Dunbar, Sir David, Bt. (S. 1664)

Hopkin, *Prof.* Sir Deian Rhys, Kt.

Hopkin, Sir Royston Oliver, KCMG

Hopkins, Sir Anthony Philip, Kt., CBE

Hopkins, Sir Michael John, Kt., CBE, RA, RIBA

Hopwood, *Prof.* Sir David Alan, Kt., FRS

Hordern, *Rt. Hon.* Sir Peter Maudslay, Kt.

Horlick, *Vice-Adm.* Sir Edwin John, KBE, FRENG

Horlick, Sir James Cunliffe William, Bt. (1914)

Horn-Smith, Sir Julian Michael, Kt.

Horne, Sir Alan Gray Antony, Bt. (1929)

Horner, *Hon.* Sir Thomas Mark, Kt.

Horsbrugh-Porter, Sir Andrew Alexander Marshall, Bt. (1902)

Horsfall, Sir Edward John Wright, Bt. (1909)

Hort, Sir Andrew Edwin Fenton, Bt. (1767)

Hosker, Sir Gerald Albery, KCB, QC

Hoskins, *Prof.* Sir Brian John, Kt., CBE, FRS

Hoskyns, Sir Robin Chevallier, Bt. (1676)

Hotung, Sir Joseph Edward, Kt.

Hough, *Prof.* Sir James, Kt., OBE

Houghton, Sir John Theodore, Kt., CBE, FRS

Houghton, Sir Stephen Geoffrey, Kt., CBE

Houldsworth, Sir Richard Thomas Reginald, Bt. (1887)

Hourston, Sir Gordon Minto, Kt.

Housden, Sir Peter James, KCB

House, Sir Stephen, Kt., QPM

Houssemayne du Boulay, Sir Roger William, KCVO, CMG

Houstoun-Boswall, Sir (Thomas) Alford, Bt. (1836)

Howard, Sir David Howarth Seymour, Bt. (1955)

Howard, *Dr* Sir Laurence, KCVO, OBE

Howard, *Prof.* Sir Michael Eliot, Kt., OM, CH, CBE, MC

Howard-Lawson, Sir John Philip, Bt. (1841)

Howarth, *Rt. Hon.* Sir George Edward, Kt.

Howarth, Sir (James) Gerald Douglas, Kt.

Howells, Sir Eric Waldo Benjamin, Kt., CBE

Howes, Sir Christopher Kingston, KCVO, CB

Howlett, *Gen.* Sir Geoffrey Hugh Whitby, KBE, MC

Hoy, Sir Christopher Andrew, Kt., MBE

Hoyle, *Rt. Hon.* Sir Lindsay Harvey, Kt.

Huddleston, *Hon.* Sir Ian William, Kt.

Hudson, Sir Mark, KCVO

Hughes, *Rt. Hon.* Sir Anthony Philip Gilson, Kt. (Lord Hughes of Ombersley)

Hughes, *Rt. Hon.* Sir Simon Henry Ward, Kt.

Hughes, Sir Thomas Collingwood, Bt. (1773), OBE

Hughes-Hallett, Sir Thomas Michael Sydney, Kt.

Hughes-Morgan, Sir (Ian) Parry David, Bt. (1925)

Hull, *Prof.* Sir David, Kt.

Hulme, Sir Philip William, Kt.

Hulse, Sir Edward Jeremy Westrow, Bt. (1739)

Hum, Sir Christopher Owen, KCMG

Humphreys, *Prof.* Sir Colin John, Kt., CBE

Hunt, *Dr* Sir Richard Timothy, Kt.

Hunte, *Hon. Dr* Sir Julian Robert, KCMG, OBE

Hunter, Sir Alistair John, KCMG

Hunter, *Prof.* Sir Laurence Colvin, Kt., CBE, FRSE

Hunter, *Dr* Sir Philip John, Kt., CBE

Hunter, Sir Thomas Blane, Kt.

Huntington-Whiteley, Sir Leopold Maurice, Bt. (1918)

Hurn, Sir (Francis) Roger, Kt.

Hurst, Sir Geoffrey Charles, Kt., MBE

Husbands, *Prof.* Sir Christopher Roy, Kt.

†Hutchison, Sir James Colville, Bt. (1956)

Hutchison, *Rt. Hon.* Sir Michael, Kt.

Hutchison, Sir Robert, Bt. (1939)
Hutt, Sir Dexter Walter, Kt.
Hytner, Sir Nicholas, Kt.
Iacobescu, Sir George, Kt., CBE
Ibbotson, *Vice-Adm.* Sir Richard Jeffrey, KBE, CB, DSC
Ife, *Prof.* Sir Barry William, Kt., CBE
Imbert-Terry, Sir Michael Edward Stanley, Bt. (1917)
Imray, Sir Colin Henry, KBE, CMG
Ingham, Sir Bernard, Kt.
Ingilby, Sir Thomas Colvin William, Bt. (1866)
Inglis, Sir William St Clair, Bt. (S. 1687)
†Inglis of Glencorse, Sir Ian Richard, Bt. (S. 1703)
Ingram, Sir James Herbert Charles, Bt. (1893)
Innes, Sir Alastair Charles Deverell, Bt. (NS 1686)
Innes of Edingight, Sir Malcolm Rognvald, KCVO
Innes, Sir Peter Alexander Berowald, Bt. (S. 1628)
Insall, Sir Donald William, Kt., CBE
Ipatas, *Hon.* Sir Peter, KBE
Irving, *Prof.* Sir Miles Horsfall, Kt., MD, FRCS, FRCSE
Irwin, *Lt.-Gen.* Sir Alistair Stuart Hastings, KCB, CBE
Irwin, *Rt. Hon.* Sir Stephen John, Kt.
Isaacs, Sir Jeremy Israel, Kt.
Isham, Sir Norman Murray Crawford, Bt. (1627), OBE
Ishiguro, Sir Kazuo, Kt., OBE
Italeli, *HE* Sir Iakoba Taeia, GCMG
Ive, Sir Jonathan Paul, KBE
Ivory, Sir Brian Gammell, Kt., CBE

J-L

Jack, Sir Malcolm Roy, KCB
Jack, *Hon.* Sir Raymond Evan, Kt.
Jackling, Sir Roger Tustin, KCB, CBE
Jackson, Sir Barry Trevor, Kt.
Jackson, Sir Kenneth Joseph, Kt.
Jackson, *Gen.* Sir Michael David, GCB, CBE
†Jackson, Sir Neil Keith, Bt. (1815)
Jackson, Sir Nicholas Fane St George, Bt. (1913)
Jackson, *Rt. Hon.* Sir Peter Arthur Brian, Kt.
Jackson, *Rt. Hon.* Sir Rupert Matthew, Kt.
Jackson, Sir Thomas Saint Felix, Bt. (1902)
Jackson, Sir (William) Roland Cedric, Bt. (1869)
Jacob, *Rt. Hon.* Sir Robert Raphael Hayim (Robin), Kt.
Jacobi, Sir Derek George, Kt., CBE
Jacobs, Sir Cecil Albert, Kt., CBE
Jacobs, *Rt. Hon.* Sir Francis Geoffrey, KCMG, QC
Jacobs, *Dr* Sir Michael Graham, Kt.
Jacobs, *Hon.* Sir Richard David, Kt.
Jacomb, Sir Martin Wakefield, Kt.
Jaffray, Sir William Otho, Bt. (1892)

Jagger, Sir Michael Philip, Kt.
James, Sir Jeffrey Russell, KBE
James, Sir John Nigel Courtenay, KCVO, CBE
Jameson, *Brig.* Sir Melville Stewart, KCVO, CBE
Jardine, Sir Andrew Colin Douglas, Bt. (1916)
Jardine of Applegirth, Sir William Murray, Bt. (S. 1672)
Jarman, *Prof.* Sir Brian, Kt., OBE
Jarratt, Sir Alexander Anthony, Kt., CB
Jay, *Hon.* Sir Robert Maurice, Kt.
Jeewoolall, Sir Ramesh, Kt.
Jeffery, Sir Thomas Baird, Kt., CB
Jeffrey, Sir William Alexander, KCB
Jeffreys, *Prof.* Sir Alec John, Kt., CH, FRS
Jeffries, *Hon.* Sir John Francis, Kt.
Jehangir, Sir Cowasji, Bt. (1908)
Jejeebhoy, Sir Jamsetjee, Bt. (1857)
Jenkin, *Hon.* Sir Bernard Christison, Kt.
Jenkins, Sir Brian Garton, GBE
Jenkins, Sir James Christopher, KCB, QC
Jenkins, Sir John, KCMG, LVO
Jenkins, *Dr* Sir Karl William Pamp, Kt., CBE
Jenkins, Sir Michael Nicholas Howard, Kt., OBE
Jenkins, Sir Simon, Kt.
Jenkinson, Sir John Banks, Bt. (1661)
Jenks, Sir (Richard) Peter, Bt. (1932)
Jenner, *Air Marshal* Sir Timothy Ivo, KCB
Jennings, Sir John Southwood, Kt., CBE, FRSE
Jennings, Sir Peter Neville Wake, Kt., CVO
Jephcott, Sir David Welbourn, Bt. (1962)
Jessel, Sir Charles John, Bt. (1883)
Jewkes, Sir Gordon Wesley, KCMG
Jewson, Sir Richard Wilson, KCVO
Job, Sir Peter James Denton, Kt.
John, Sir David Glyndwr, KCMG
John, Sir Elton Hercules (Reginald Kenneth Dwight), Kt., CBE
Johns, *Vice-Adm.* Sir Adrian James, KCB, CBE, ADC
Johns, *Air Chief Marshal* Sir Richard Edward, GCB, KCVO, CBE
Johnson, Sir Colpoys Guy, Bt. (1755)
Johnson, *Gen.* Sir Garry Dene, KCB, OBE, MC
Johnson, *Hon.* Sir Jeremy Charles, Kt.
†Johnson, Sir Patrick Eliot, Bt. (1818)
Johnson, *Hon.* Sir Robert Lionel, Kt.
Johnson-Ferguson, Sir Mark Edward, Bt. (1906)
Johnston, *Lt.-Gen.* Sir Maurice Robert, KCB, CVO, OBE
Johnston, Sir Thomas Alexander, Bt. (S. 1626)
Johnston, Sir William Ian Ridley, Kt., CBE, QPM
Johnstone, *Vice-Adm.* Sir Clive Charles Carruthers, KBE, CB

Johnstone, Sir Geoffrey Adams Dinwiddie, KCMG
Johnstone, Sir (George) Richard Douglas, Bt. (S. 1700)
Johnstone, Sir (John) Raymond, Kt., CBE
Jolliffe, Sir Anthony Stuart, GBE
Jolly, Sir Arthur Richard, KCMG
Jonas, Sir John Peter, Kt., CBE
Jones, Sir Alan Jeffrey, Kt.
Jones, Sir Bryn Terfel, Kt., CBE
Jones, Sir Clive William, KCMG, CBE
Jones, Sir David Charles, Kt., CBE
Jones, Sir Derek William, KCB
Jones, Sir Harry George, Kt., CBE
Jones, *Rt. Revd* James Stuart, KBE
Jones, Sir John Francis, Kt.
Jones, Sir Kenneth Lloyd, Kt., QPM
Jones, Sir Lyndon, Kt.
Jones, Sir Mark Ellis Powell, Kt.
Jones, *Vice-Adm.* Sir Philip Andrew, KCB
Jones, Sir Richard Anthony Lloyd, KCB
Jones, Sir Robert Edward, Kt.
Jones, Sir Roger Spencer, Kt., OBE
†Joseph, *Hon.* Sir James Samuel, Bt. (1943)
Jowell, *Prof.* Sir Jeffrey Lionel, KCMG, QC
Jowitt, *Hon.* Sir Edwin Frank, Kt.
Jugnauth, *Rt. Hon.* Sir Anerood, KCMG
Jungius, *Vice-Adm.* Sir James George, KBE
Kaberry, *Hon.* Sir Christopher Donald, Bt. (1960)
Kabui, Sir Frank Utu Ofagioro, GCMG, OBE
Kadoorie, *Hon.* Sir Michael David, Kt.
Kakaraya, Sir Pato, KBE
Kamit, Sir Leonard Wilson, Kt., CBE
Kapoor, Sir Anish Mikhail, Kt., CBE
Kaputin, Sir John Rumet, KBE, CMG
Kavali, Sir Thomas, Kt., OBE
Kay, *Rt. Hon.* Sir Maurice Ralph, Kt.
Kay, Sir Nicholas Peter, KCMG
Kaye, Sir Paul Henry Gordon, Bt. (1923)
Keane, Sir John Charles, Bt. (1801)
Kearney, *Hon.* Sir William John Francis, Kt., CBE
Keegan, *Dr* Sir Donal Arthur John, KCVO, OBE
Keehan, *Hon.* Sir Michael Joseph, Kt.
Keene, *Rt. Hon.* Sir David Wolfe, Kt.
Keenlyside, Sir Simon John, Kt., CBE
Keith, *Hon.* Sir Brian Richard, Kt.
Keith, *Rt. Hon.* Sir Kenneth, KBE
†Kellett, Sir Stanley Charles, Bt. (1801)
Kelly, Sir Christopher William, KCB
Kelly, Sir David Robert Corbett, Kt., CBE
Kemakeza, Sir Allan, Kt.
Kemball, *Air Marshal* Sir (Richard) John, KCB, CBE
Kemp-Welch, Sir John, Kt.
Kendall, Sir Peter Ashley, Kt.

Kennaway, Sir John-Michael, Bt. (1791)

†Kennedy, Sir George Matthew Rae, Bt. (1836)

Kennedy, *Hon.* Sir Ian Alexander, Kt.

Kennedy, *Prof.* Sir Ian McColl, Kt.

Kennedy, *Rt. Hon.* Sir Paul Joseph Morrow, Kt.

Kenny, Sir Anthony John Patrick, Kt., DPHIL, DLITT, FBA

Kenny, Sir Paul Stephen, Kt.

Kentridge, Sir Sydney Woolf, KCMG, QC

Kenyon, Sir Nicholas Roger, Kt., CBE

Keogh, *Prof.* Sir Bruce Edward, KBE

Kere, *Dr* Sir Nathan, KCMG

Kerr, *Adm.* Sir John Beverley, GCB

Kerr, Sir Ronald James, Kt., CBE

Kerr, *Hon.* Sir Timothy Julian, Kt.

Kershaw, *Prof.* Sir Ian, Kt.

Keswick, Sir Henry Neville Lindley, Kt.

Keswick, Sir John Chippendale Lindley, Kt.

Kevau, *Prof.* Sir Isi Henao, Kt., CBE

Khaw, *Prof.* Sir Peng Tee, Kt.

Kikau, *Ratu* Sir Jone Latianara, KBE

Kimber, Sir Rupert Edward Watkin, Bt. (1904)

King, *Prof.* Sir David Anthony, Kt., FRS

King, Sir James Henry Rupert, Bt. (1888)

King, Sir Julian Beresford, KCVO, CMG

King, *Hon.* Sir Timothy Roger Alan, Kt.

King, Sir Wayne Alexander, Bt. (1815)

Kingman, *Prof.* Sir John Frank Charles, Kt., FRS

Kingman, Sir John Oliver Frank, KCB

Kingsley, Sir Ben, Kt.

Kinloch, Sir David, Bt. (S. 1686)

Kinloch, Sir David Oliphant, Bt. (1873)

Kipalan, Sir Albert, Kt.

Kirch, Sir David Roderick, KBE

Kirkpatrick, Sir Ivone Elliott, Bt. (S. 1685)

Kiszely, *Lt.-Gen.* Sir John Panton, KCB, MC

Kitchin, *Rt. Hon.* Sir David James Tyson, Kt. (Lord Kitchin)

Kitson, *Gen.* Sir Frank Edward, GBE, KCB, MC

Kleinwort, Sir Richard Drake, Bt. (1909)

Klenerman, *Prof.* Sir David, Kt., FRS

Knight, *Rt. Hon.* Sir Gregory, Kt.

Knight, Sir Kenneth John, Kt., CBE, QFSM

Knight, *Air Chief Marshal* Sir Michael William Patrick, KCB, AFC

Knight, *Prof.* Sir Peter, Kt.

Knill, Sir Thomas John Pugin Bartholomew, Bt. (1893)

Knowles, Sir Charles Francis, Bt. (1765)

Knowles, *Hon.* Sir Julian Bernard, Kt.

Knowles, Sir Nigel Graham, Kt.

Knowles, *Hon.* Sir Robin St John, Kt.

Knox, Sir David Laidlaw, Kt.

Knox-Johnston, Sir William Robert Patrick (Sir Robin), Kt., CBE, RD

Koraea, Sir Thomas, Kt.

Kornberg, *Prof.* Sir Hans Leo, Kt., DSc, SCD, PHD, FRS

Korowi, Sir Wiwa, GCMG

Kulukundis, Sir Elias George (Eddie), Kt., OBE

Kulunga, Sir Toami, Kt., OBE, QPM

Kumar, Sir Harpal Singh, Kt.

Kwok-Po Li, *Dr* Sir David, Kt., OBE

Lachmann, *Prof.* Sir Peter Julius, Kt.

Lacon, Sir Edmund Richard Vere, Bt. (1818)

Lacy, Sir Patrick Brian Finucane, Bt. (1921)

Laing, Sir (John) Martin (Kirby), Kt., CBE

Lake, Sir Edward Geoffrey, Bt. (1711)

Lakin, Sir Richard Anthony, Bt. (1909)

Lamb, Sir Albert Thomas, KBE, CMG, DFC

Lamb, *Lt.-Gen.* Sir Graeme Cameron Maxwell, KBE, CMG, DSO

Lamb, *Rt. Hon.* Sir Norman Peter, Kt.

Lambert, *Vice-Adm.* Sir Paul, KCB

†Lambert, Sir Peter John Biddulph, Bt. (1711)

Lambert, Sir Richard Peter, Kt.

Lampl, Sir Peter, Kt., OBE

Lamport, Sir Stephen Mark Jeffrey, GCVO

Lancashire, Sir Steve, Kt.

Landau, Sir Dennis Marcus, Kt.

Lander, Sir Stephen James, KCB

Lane, Prof. Sir David Philip, Kt.

Lane, *Hon.* Sir Peter Richard, Kt.

Langham, Sir John Stephen, Bt. (1660)

Langlands, Sir Robert Alan, Kt.

Langley, *Hon.* Sir Gordon Julian Hugh, Kt.

Langrishe, Sir James Hercules, Bt. (I. 1777)

Langstaff, *Hon.* Sir Brian Frederick James, Kt.

Lankester, Sir Timothy Patrick, KCB

Lapli, Sir John Ini, GCMG

Lapthorne, Sir Richard Douglas, Kt., CBE

Large, Sir Andrew McLeod Brooks, Kt.

Latasi, *Rt. Hon.* Sir Kamuta, KCMG, OBE

Latham, *Rt. Hon.* Sir David Nicholas Ramsey, Kt.

Latham, Sir Richard Thomas Paul, Bt. (1919)

Laughton, Sir Anthony Seymour, Kt.

Laurence, *Vice-Adm.* Sir Timothy James Hamilton, KCVO, CB, ADC

Laurie, Sir Andrew Ronald Emilius, Bt. (1834)

Lavender, *Hon.* Sir Nicholas, Kt.

†Lawrence, Sir Aubrey Lyttelton Simon, Bt. (1867)

Lawrence, Sir Clive Wyndham, Bt. (1906)

Lawrence, Sir Edmund Wickham, GCMG, OBE

Lawrence, Sir Henry Peter, Bt. (1858)

Lawrence, Sir Ivan John, Kt., QC

Lawrence-Jones, Sir Christopher, Bt. (1831)

Laws, *Rt. Hon.* Sir John Grant McKenzie, Kt.

Laws, Sir Stephen Charles, KCB

Lawson, Sir Charles John Patrick, Bt. (1900)

Lawson, *Gen.* Sir Richard George, KCB, DSO, OBE

Lawson-Tancred, Sir Andrew Peter, Bt. (1662)

Lawton, *Prof.* Sir John Hartley, Kt., CBE, FRS

Layard, *Adm.* Sir Michael Henry Gordon, KCB, CBE

Lea, Sir Thomas William, Bt. (1892)

Leahy, Sir Daniel Joseph, Kt.

Leahy, Sir Terence Patrick, Kt.

Learmont, *Gen.* Sir John Hartley, KCB, CBE

Leaver, Sir Christopher, GBE

Lechler, *Prof.* Sir Robert Ian, Kt.

Lechmere, Sir Nicholas Anthony Hungerford, Bt. (1818)

†Leeds, Sir John Charles Hildyard, Bt. (1812)

Lees, Sir Christopher James, Bt. (1897), TD

Lees, Sir David Bryan, Kt.

Lees, Sir Thomas Harcourt Ivor, Bt. (1804)

Lees, Sir (William) Antony Clare, Bt. (1937)

Leese, Sir Richard Charles, Kt., CBE

Leeson, *Air Marshal* Sir Kevin James, KCB, CBE

le Fleming, Sir David Kelland, Bt. (1705)

Legard, Sir Charles Thomas, Bt. (1660)

Legg, Sir Thomas Stuart, KCB, QC

Leggatt, *Rt. Hon.* Sir Andrew Peter, Kt.

Leggatt, *Rt. Hon.* Sir George Andrew Midsomer, Kt.

Leggett, *Prof.* Sir Anthony James, KBE

Le Grand, *Prof.* Sir Julian Ernest, Kt.

Leigh, *Rt. Hon.* Sir Edward Julian Egerton, Kt.

Leigh, Sir Geoffrey Norman, Kt.

Leigh, *Dr* Sir Michael, KCMG

Leigh, Sir Richard Henry, Bt. (1918)

Leigh-Pemberton, Sir James Henry, Kt., CVO

Leighton, Sir John Mark Nicholas, Kt.

Leighton, Sir Michael John Bryan, Bt. (1693)

†Leith-Buchanan, Sir Scott Kelly, Bt. (1775)

Le Marchant, Sir Piers Alfred, Bt. (1841)

Lennox-Boyd, *Hon.* Sir Mark Alexander, Kt.

Leon, Sir John Ronald, Bt. (1911)

Lepani, Sir Charles Watson, KBE

†Leslie, Sir Shaun Rudolph Christopher, Bt. (1876)

Lester, Sir James Theodore, Kt.

Lethbridge, Sir Thomas Periam Hector Noel, Bt. (1804)

Letwin, *Rt. Hon.* Sir Oliver, Kt.

Lever, Sir Jeremy Frederick, KCMG, QC

Lever, Sir Paul, KCMG

Lever, Sir (Tresham) Christopher Arthur Lindsay, Bt. (1911)

Leveson, *Rt. Hon.* Sir Brian Henry, Kt.

Levi, Sir Wasangula Noel, Kt., CBE

Levinge, Sir Richard George Robin, Bt. (I. 1704)

Lewinton, Sir Christopher, Kt.

Lewis, *Hon.* Sir Clive Buckland, Kt.

Lewis, Sir David Thomas Rowell, Kt.

Lewis, Sir John Anthony, Kt., OBE

Lewis, Sir John Henry James, Kt., OBE

Lewis, Sir Leigh Warren, KCB

Lewis, Sir Martyn John Dudley, Kt., CBE

Lewis, Sir Terence Murray, Kt., OBE, GM, QPM

Lewison, *Rt. Hon.* Sir Kim Martin Jordan, Kt.

Ley, Sir Christopher Ian, Bt. (1905)

Li, Sir Ka-Shing, KBE

Lickiss, Sir Michael Gillam, Kt.

Lidington, *Rt. Hon.* Sir David Roy, KCB, CBE

Liddington, Sir Bruce, Kt.

Lightman, *Hon.* Sir Gavin Anthony, Kt.

Lighton, Sir Thomas Hamilton, Bt. (I. 1791)

Likierman, *Prof.* Sir John Andrew, Kt.

Lilleyman, *Prof.* Sir John Stuart, Kt.

Lindblom, *Rt. Hon.* Sir Keith John, Kt.

†Lindsay, Sir James Martin Evelyn, Bt. (1962)

Lindsay, *Hon.* Sir John Edmund Frederic, Kt.

†Lindsay-Hogg, Sir Michael Edward, Bt. (1905)

Lipton, Sir Stuart Anthony, Kt.

Lipworth, Sir (Maurice) Sydney, Kt.

Lister, *Vice-Adm.* Sir Simon Robert, KCB, OBE

Lister-Kaye, Sir John Phillip Lister, Bt. (1812), OBE

Lithgow, Sir William James, Bt. (1925)

Llewellyn, Sir Roderic Victor, Bt. (1922)

Llewellyn-Smith, *Prof.* Sir Christopher Hubert, Kt.

Lloyd, *Prof.* Sir Geoffrey Ernest Richard, Kt., FBA

Lloyd, Sir Nicholas Markley, Kt.

Lloyd, *Rt. Hon.* Sir Peter Robert Cable, Kt.

Lloyd, Sir Richard Ernest Butler, Bt. (1960)

Lloyd, *Rt. Hon.* Sir Timothy Andrew Wigram, Kt.

Lloyd-Edwards, *Capt.* Sir Norman, KCVO, RD

Lloyd Jones, *Rt. Hon.* Sir David, Kt. (Lord Lloyd-Jones)

Loader, Air Marshal Sir Clive Robert, KCB, OBE

Lobban, Sir Iain Robert, KCMG, CB

Lockett, Sir Michael Vernon, KCVO

Lockhead, Sir Moir, Kt., OBE

Loder, Sir Edmund Jeune, Bt. (1887)

Logan, Sir David Brian Carleton, KCMG

Long, Sir Richard Julian, Kt., CBE

Longley, *Hon.* Sir Hartman Godfrey, Kt.

Longmore, *Rt. Hon.* Sir Andrew Centlivres, Kt.

Lorimer, *Lt.-Gen.* Sir John Gordon, KCB, MBE, DSO

Lorimer, Sir (Thomas) Desmond, Kt.

Los, *Hon.* Sir Kubulan, Kt., CBE

Loughran, Sir Gerald Finbar, KCB

Lourdenadin, Sir Ninian Mogan, KCMG, KBE

Lovegrove, Sir Stephen Augustus, KCB

Lovestone, *Prof.* Sir Simon, Kt.

Lovill, Sir John Roger, Kt., CBE

Low, *Dr* Sir John Menzies, Kt., CBE

Lowa, *Rt. Revd* Sir Samson, KBE

Lowcock, Sir Mark Andrew, KCB

Lowe, Sir Frank Budge, Kt.

Lowe, Sir Philip Martin, KCMG

Lowe, Sir Thomas William Gordon, Bt. (1918), QC

Lowson, Sir Ian Patrick, Bt. (1951)

†Lowther, Sir Patrick William, Bt. (1824)

Lowy, Sir Frank, Kt.

Loyd, Sir Julian St John, KCVO

Lu, Sir Tseng Chi, Kt.

Lucas, *Prof.* Sir Colin Renshaw, Kt.

†Lucas, Sir Thomas Edward, Bt. (1887)

Lucas-Tooth, Sir (Hugh) John, Bt. (1920)

Luff, Sir Peter James, Kt.

Lumsden, Sir David James, Kt.

Lushington, Sir John Richard Castleman, Bt. (1791)

Lyall Grant, Sir Mark Justin, KCMG

Lyle, Sir Gavin Archibald, Bt. (1929)

Lynch-Blosse, *Capt.* Sir Richard Hely, Bt. (I. 1622)

Lynch-Robinson, Sir Dominick Christopher, Bt. (1920)

Lyne, *Rt. Hon.* Sir Roderic Michael John, KBE, CMG

Lyons, Sir John, Kt.

Lyons, Sir Michael Thomas, Kt.

M-O

McAlinden, *Hon.* Sir Gerald Joseph, Kt.

McAllister, Sir Ian Gerald, Kt., CBE

McAlpine, Sir Andrew William, Bt. (1918)

McCamley, Sir Graham Edward, KBE

McCanny, *Prof.* Sir John Vincent, Kt., CBE

McCarthy, Sir Callum, Kt.

McCartney, *Rt. Hon.* Sir Ian, Kt.

McCartney, Sir (James) Paul, Kt., CH, MBE

†Macartney, Sir John Ralph, Bt. (I. 1799)

McClement, *Vice-Admiral* Sir Timothy Pentreath, KCB, OBE

Macleod, Sir Iain, KCMG

McCloskey, *Hon.* Sir John Bernard, Kt.

McColl, Sir Colin Hugh Verel, KCMG

McColl, *Gen.* Sir John Chalmers, KCB, CBE, DSO

McCollum, *Rt. Hon.* Sir William, Kt.

McCombe, *Rt. Hon.* Sir Richard George Bramwell, Kt.

McConnell, Sir Robert Shean, Bt. (1900)

†McCowan, Sir David James Cargill, Bt. (1934)

McCoy, Sir Anthony Peter, Kt., OBE

McCullin, Sir Donald, Kt., CBE

MacCulloch, *Prof.* Sir Diarmaid Ninian John, Kt.

McCulloch, *Rt. Revd* Nigel Simeon, KCVO

MacDermott, *Rt. Hon.* Sir John Clarke, Kt.

Macdonald, Sir Alasdair Uist, Kt., CBE

MacDonald, *Hon.* Sir Alistair William Orchard, Kt.

Macdonald of Sleat, Sir Ian Godfrey Bosville, Bt. (S. 1625)

McDonald, *Prof.* Sir James, Kt.

Macdonald, Sir Kenneth Carmichael, KCB

McDonald, Sir Simon Gerard, KCMG, KCVO

McDonald, Sir Trevor, Kt., OBE

McDowell, Sir Eric Wallace, Kt., CBE

MacDuff, *Hon.* Sir Alistair Geoffrey, Kt.

Mace, *Lt.-Gen.* Sir John Airth, KBE, CB

McEwen, Sir John Roderick Hugh, Bt. (1953)

MacFadyen, *Air Marshal* Sir Ian David, KCVO, CB, OBE

†McFarland, Sir Anthony Basil Scott, Bt. (1914)

MacFarlane, *Prof.* Sir Alistair George James, Kt., CBE, FRS

McFarlane, *Rt. Hon.* Sir Andrew Ewart, Kt.

Macfarlane, Sir (David) Neil, Kt.

McGeechan, Sir Ian Robert, Kt., OBE

McGrath, Sir Harvey Andrew, Kt.

†Macgregor, Sir Ian Grant, Bt. (1828)

MacGregor of MacGregor, Sir Malcolm Gregor Charles, Bt. (1795)

McGrigor, Sir James Angus Rhoderick Neil, Bt. (1831)

McIntosh, Sir Neil William David, Kt., CBE

McIntyre, Sir Donald Conroy, Kt., CBE

McIntyre, Sir Meredith Alister, Kt.

Mackay, *Hon.* Sir Colin Crichton, Kt.

MacKay, Sir Francis Henry, Kt.

McKay, Sir Neil Stuart, Kt., CB

McKay, Sir William Robert, KCB

Mackay-Dick, *Maj.-Gen.* Sir Iain Charles, KCVO, MBE

Mackechnie, Sir Alistair John, Kt.

McKellen, Sir Ian Murray, Kt., CH, CBE

†Mackenzie, Sir (James William) Guy, Bt. (1890)

Mackenzie, *Gen.* Sir Jeremy John George, GCB, OBE

†Mackenzie, Sir Peter Douglas, Bt. (S. 1673)

†Mackenzie, Sir Roderick McQuhae, Bt. (S. 1703)

Mackeson, Sir Rupert Henry, Bt. (1954)

Mackey, Sir Craig Thomas, Kt., QPM

Mackey, Sir James, Kt.

McKibbin, *Dr* Sir Malcolm, KCB

McKillop, Sir Thomas Fulton Wilson, Kt.

McKinnon, *Rt. Hon.* Sir Donald Charles, GCVO

McKinnon, *Hon.* Sir Stuart Neil, Kt.

Mackintosh, Sir Cameron Anthony, Kt.

Mackworth, Sir Alan Keith, Bt. (1776)

McLaughlin, Sir Richard, Kt.

Maclean of Dunconnel, Sir Charles Edward, Bt. (1957)

Maclean, *Hon.* Sir Lachlan Hector Charles, Bt., (NS 1631), CVO

Maclean, Sir Murdo, Kt.

†McLeod, Sir James Roderick Charles, Bt. (1925)

MacLeod, *Hon.* Sir (John) Maxwell Norman, Bt. (1924)

Macleod, Sir (Nathaniel William) Hamish, KBE

McLintock, Sir Michael William, Bt. (1934)

McLoughlin, Sir Francis, Kt., CBE

McLoughlin, *Rt. Hon.* Sir Patrick Allen, Kt., CH

Maclure, Sir John Robert Spencer, Bt. (1898)

McMahon, Sir Brian Patrick, Bt. (1817)

McMahon, Sir Christopher William, Kt.

McMaster, Sir Brian John, Kt., CBE

McMichael, *Prof.* Sir Andrew James, Kt., FRS

MacMillan, *Very Revd* Gilleasbuig Iain, KCVO

McMillan, Sir Iain Macleod, Kt., CBE

Macmillan, *Dr* Sir James Loy, Kt., CBE

MacMillan, *Lt.-Gen.* Sir John Richard Alexander, KCB, CBE

McMurtry, Sir David, Kt., CBE

Macnaghten, Sir Malcolm Francis, Bt. (1836)

McNair-Wilson, Sir Patrick Michael Ernest David, Kt.

McNulty, Sir (Robert William) Roy, Kt., CBE

MacPhail, Sir Bruce Dugald, Kt.

Macpherson of Cluny, *Hon.* Sir William Alan, Kt., TD

MacRae, Sir (Alastair) Christopher (Donald Summerhayes), KCMG

Macready, Sir Charles Nevil, Bt. (1923)

Mactaggart, Sir John Auld, Bt. (1938)

McVicar, Sir David, Kt.

McWilliam, Sir Michael Douglas, KCMG

McWilliams, Sir Francis, GBE

Madden, Sir Charles Jonathan, Bt. (1919)

Madden, Sir David Christopher Andrew, KCMG

Madejski, Sir John Robert, Kt., OBE

Madel, Sir (William) David, Kt.

Magee, Sir Ian Bernard Vaughan, Kt., CB

Magnus, Sir Laurence Henry Philip, Bt. (1917)

Maguire, *Hon.* Sir Paul Richard, Kt.

Mahon, Sir William Walter, Bt. (1819), LVO

Mahoney, Sir Paul John, KCMG

Maiden, Sir Colin James, Kt., DPHIL

Maini, *Prof.* Sir Ravinder Nath, Kt.

Maino, Sir Charles, KBE

†Maitland, Sir Charles Alexander, Bt. (1818)

Major, *Rt. Hon.* Sir John, KG, CH

Malbon, *Vice-Adm.* Sir Fabian Michael, KBE

Malcolm, Sir Alexander James Elton, Bt. (S. 1665), OBE

Malcolm, *Dr* Noel Robert, Kt., FBA

Males, *Rt. Hon.* Sir Stephen Martin, Kt.

Malet, Sir Harry Douglas St Lo, Bt. (1791)

Mallaby, Sir Christopher Leslie George, GCMG, GCVO

Mallick, *Prof.* Sir Netar Prakash, Kt.

Mallinson, Sir William James, Bt. (1935)

Malpas, Sir Robert, Kt., CBE

Mander, Sir (Charles) Nicholas, Bt. (1911)

Mann, *Hon.* Sir George Anthony, Kt.

Mann, Sir Rupert Edward, Bt. (1905)

Manning, Sir David Geoffrey, GCMG, KCVO

Mano, Sir Koitaga, Kt., MBE

Mans, *Lt.-Gen.* Sir Mark Francis Noel, KCB, CBE

Mansel, Sir Philip, Bt. (1622)

Manuella, Sir Tulaga, GCMG, MBE

Mara, Sir Nambuga, KBE

Margetson, Sir John William Denys, KCMG

Margetts, Sir Robert John, Kt., CBE

Markesinis, *Prof.* Sir Basil Spyridonos, Kt., QC

Markham, *Prof.* Sir Alexander Fred, Kt.

Markham, Sir (Arthur) David, Bt. (1911)

Marling, Sir Charles William Somerset, Bt. (1882)

Marmot, Prof. Sir Michael Gideon, Kt.

Marr, Sir Leslie Lynn, Bt. (1919)

Marsden, Sir Jonathan Mark, KCVO

†Marsden, Sir Tadgh Orlando Denton, Bt. (1924)

Marshall, Sir Paul, Kt.

Marshall, Sir Peter Harold Reginald, KCMG

Marshall, *Prof. Emeritus* Sir Woodville Kemble, Kt.

Marsters, *HE* Sir Tom John, KBE

Martin, Sir Clive Haydon, Kt., OBE

Martin, Sir Gregory Michael Gerard, Kt.

Martin, *Prof.* Sir Laurence Woodward, Kt.

Masefield, Sir Charles Beech Gordon, Kt.

Mason, *Hon.* Sir Anthony Frank, KBE

Mason, *Prof.* Sir David Kean, Kt., CBE

Mason, Sir Peter James, KBE

Mason, *Prof.* Sir Ronald, KCB, FRS

Massey, *Vice-Adm.* Sir Alan, KCB, CBE, ADC

Matane, HE Sir Paulias Nguna, GCMG, OBE

Matheson of Matheson, Sir Alexander Fergus, Bt. (1882), LVO

Mathews, *Vice-Adm.* Sir Andrew David Hugh, KCB

Mathewson, Sir George Ross, Kt., CBE, PHD, FRSE

Matthews, Sir Terence Hedley, Kt., OBE

Maughan, Sir Deryck, Kt.

Mawer, Sir Philip John Courtney, Kt.

Maxwell, Sir Michael Eustace George, Bt. (S. 1681)

Maxwell Macdonald (formerly Stirling-Maxwell), Sir John Ronald, Bt. (NS 1682)

Maxwell-Scott, Sir Dominic James, Bt. (1642)

May, *Rt. Hon.* Sir Anthony Tristram Kenneth, Kt.

Mayall, *Lt.-Gen.* Sir Simon Vincent, KBE, CB

Mayfield, Sir Andrew Charles, Kt.

Meadow, *Prof.* Sir (Samuel) Roy, Kt., FRCP, FRCPE

Meale, Sir Joseph Alan, Kt.

Medlycott, Sir Mervyn Tregonwell, Bt. (1808)

Meeran, *His Hon.* Sir Goolam Hoosen Kader, Kt.

Meldrum, Sir Graham, Kt., CBE, QFSM

Melhuish, Sir Michael Ramsay, KBE, CMG

Mellars, *Prof.* Sir Paul Anthony, Kt., FBA

Mellon, Sir James, KCMG

Melmoth, Sir Graham John, Kt.

Melville, *Prof.* Sir David, Kt., CBE

Melville-Ross, Sir Timothy David, Kt., CBE

Merifield, Sir Anthony James, KCVO, CB

Messenger, *Gen.* Sir Gordon Kenneth, KCB, DSO, OBE

Metcalf, *Prof.* Sir David Harry, Kt., CBE

†Meyer, Sir (Anthony) Ashley Frank, Bt. (1910)

Meyer, Sir Christopher John Rome, KCMG

†Meyrick, Sir Timothy Thomas Charlton, Bt. (1880)

Miakwe, Hon. Sir Akepa, KBE

Michael, Sir Duncan, Kt.

Michael, Dr Sir Jonathan, Kt.

Michael, Sir Peter Colin, Kt., CBE

Michels, Sir David Michael Charles, Kt.

Middleton, Sir John Maxwell, Kt.

Middleton, Sir Peter Edward, GCB

Miers, Sir (Henry) David Alastair Capel, KBE, CMG

Milbank, Sir Edward Mark Somerset, Bt. (1882)

Milborne-Swinnerton-Pilkington, Sir Thomas Henry, Bt. (S. 1635)

Milburn, Sir Anthony Rupert, Bt. (1905)

†Miles, Sir Philip John, Bt. (1859)

Millais, Sir Geoffroy Richard Everett, Bt. (1885)

Millar, Prof. Sir Fergus Graham Burtholme, Kt.

Miller, Sir Anthony Thomas, Bt. (1705)

Miller, Sir Donald John, Kt., FRSE, FRENG

Miller, Air Marshal Sir Graham Anthony, KBE

Miller, Sir Jonathan Wolfe, Kt., CBE

Miller, Sir Robin Robert William, Kt.

Miller, Sir Ronald Andrew Baird, Kt., CBE

Miller of Glenlee, Sir Stephen William Macdonald, Bt. (1788)

Mills, Sir Ian, Kt.

Mills, Sir Jonathan Edward Harland (John), Kt., FRSE

Mills, Sir Keith Edward, GBE

Mills, Sir Peter Frederick Leighton, Bt. (1921)

Milman, Sir David Patrick, Bt. (1800)

Milne-Watson, Sir Andrew Michael, Bt. (1937)

Milner, Sir Timothy William Lycett, Bt. (1717)

Mitchell, Rt. Hon. Sir James FitzAllen, KCMG

Mitchell, Very Revd Patrick Reynolds, KCVO

Mitchell, Hon. Sir Stephen George, Kt.

Mitting, Hon. Sir John Edward, Kt.

Moberly, Sir Patrick Hamilton, KCMG

Moir, Sir Christopher Ernest, Bt. (1916)

Molesworth-St Aubyn, Sir William, Bt. (1689)

Molony, Sir John Benjamin, Bt. (1925)

Moncada, Prof. Sir Salvador, Kt.

Montagu, Sir Nicholas Lionel John, KCB

Montagu-Pollock, Sir Guy Maximilian, Bt. (1872)

Montague, Sir Adrian Alastair, Kt., CBE

Montgomery, Sir (Basil Henry) David, Bt. (1801), CVO

Montgomery, Vice-Adm. Sir Charles Percival Ross, KBE, ADC

Montgomery, Prof. Sir James Robert, Kt.

Montgomery-Cuninghame, Sir John Christopher Foggo, Bt. (NS 1672)

Moody-Stuart, Sir Mark, KCMG

Moollan, Sir Abdool Hamid Adam, Kt.

†Moon, Sir Humphrey, Bt. (1887)

Moor, Hon. Sir Philip Drury, Kt.

Moorcroft, Sir William, KBE

Moore, Most Revd Desmond Charles, KBE

Moore, Sir Francis Thomas, Kt.

Moore, Vice Adm. Sir Michael Antony Claës, KBE, LVO

Moore, Sir Peter Alan Cutlack, Bt. (1919)

Moore, Sir Richard William, Bt. (1932)

Moore-Bick, Rt. Hon. Sir Martin James, Kt.

Morauta, Sir Mekere, KCMG, PC

Mordaunt, Sir Richard Nigel Charles, Bt. (1611)

Moree, Hon. Sir Brian, Kt.

Morgan, Vice-Adm. Sir Charles Christopher, KBE

Morgan, Rt. Hon. Sir (Charles) Declan, Kt.

Morgan, Sir Graham, Kt.

Morgan, Hon. Sir Paul Hyacinth, Kt.

Morgan, Sir Terence Keith, Kt., CBE

Morison, Hon. Sir Thomas Richard Atkin, Kt.

Moritz, Sir Michael Jonathan, KBE

Morland, Hon. Sir Michael, Kt.

Morland, Sir Robert Kenelm, Kt.

Morpurgo, Sir Michael Andrew Bridge, Kt., OBE

†Morris, Sir Allan Lindsay, Bt. (1806)

Morris, Sir Andrew Valentine, Kt., OBE

Morris, Air Marshal Sir Arnold Alec, KBE, CB

Morris, Sir Derek James, Kt.

Morris, Sir Keith Elliot Hedley, KBE, CMG

Morris, Prof. Sir Peter John, Kt.

Morris, Hon. Sir Stephen Nathan, Kt.

Morris, Sir Trefor Alfred, Kt., CBE, QPM

Morrison, Sir (Alexander) Fraser, Kt., CBE

Morrison, Sir George Ivan, Kt., OBE

Morrison, Sir Howard Andrew Clive, KCMG, CBE

Morrison-Bell, Sir William Hollin Dayrell, Bt. (1905)

Morrison-Low, Sir Richard Walter, Bt. (1908)

Morritt, Rt. Hon. Sir (Robert) Andrew, Kt., CVO

Morse, Sir Amyas Charles Edward, KCB

Moses, Rt. Hon. Sir Alan George, Kt.

Moses, Very Revd Dr John Henry, KCVO

Moss, Sir David Joseph, KCVO, CMG

Moss, Sir Stephen Alan, Kt.

Moss, Sir Stirling Craufurd, Kt., OBE

Mostyn, Hon. Sir Nicholas Anthony Joseph Ghislain, Kt.

Mostyn, Sir William Basil John, Bt. (1670)

Motion, Sir Andrew, Kt.

Mott, Sir David Hugh, Bt. (1930)

Mottley, Sir Elliott Deighton, KCMG, QC

Mottram, Sir Richard Clive, GCB

†Mount, Sir (William Robert) Ferdinand, Bt. (1921)

Mountain, Sir Edward Brian Stanford, Bt. (1922)

Mowbray, Sir John Robert, Bt. (1880)

Moylan, Rt. Hon. Sir Andrew John Gregory, Kt.

Moynihan, Dr Sir Daniel, Kt.

†Muir, Sir Richard James Kay, Bt. (1892)

Muir-Mackenzie, Sir Alexander Alwyne Henry Charles Brinton, Bt. (1805)

Mulcahy, Sir Geoffrey John, Kt.

Mummery, Rt. Hon. Sir John Frank, Kt.

Munby, Rt. Hon. Sir James Lawrence, Kt.

Munro, Sir Alan Gordon, KCMG

†Munro, Sir Ian Kenneth, Bt. (S. 1634)

Munro, Sir Keith Gordon, Bt. (1825)

Muria, Hon. Sir Gilbert John Baptist, Kt.

Murphy, Sir Jonathan Michael, Kt., QPM

Murray, Sir Andrew, Kt., OBE

Murray, Sir David Edward, Kt.

Murray, Hon. Sir Edward Henry, Kt

Murray, Sir Nigel Andrew Digby, Bt. (S. 1628)

Murray, Sir Patrick Ian Keith, Bt. (S. 1673)

Murray, Sir Robert Sydney, Kt., CBE

Murray, Sir Robin MacGregor, Kt.

†Murray, Sir Rowland William, Bt. (S. 1630)

Muscatelli, Prof. Sir Vito Antonio, Kt., FRSE

Musgrave, Sir Christopher John Shane, Bt. (I. 1782)

Musgrave, Sir Christopher Patrick Charles, Bt. (1611)

Myers, Sir Derek John, Kt.

Myers, Prof. Sir Rupert Horace, KBE

Mynors, Sir Richard Baskerville, Bt. (1964)

Nairn, Sir Michael, Bt. (1904)

Nalau, Sir Jerry Kasip, KBE

Nall, Sir Edward William Joseph, Bt. (1954)

Namaliu, Rt. Hon. Sir Rabbie Langanai, KCMG

Napier, Sir Charles Joseph, Bt. (1867)

Napier, Sir John Archibald Lennox, Bt. (S. 1627)

Narey, Sir Martin James, Kt.

Natzler, Sir David Lionel, KCB

Naylor, Sir Robert, Kt.

Naylor-Leyland, Sir Philip Vyvian, Bt. (1895)

Neal, Sir Eric James, Kt., CVO

Neave, Sir Paul Arundell, Bt. (1795)

†Nelson, Sir Jamie Charles Vernon Hope, Bt. (1912)

Nelson, *Hon.* Sir Robert Franklyn, Kt.

New, *Maj.-Gen.* Sir Laurence Anthony Wallis, Kt., CB, CBE

Newbigging, Sir David Kennedy, Kt., OBE

Newby, *Prof.* Sir Howard Joseph, Kt., CBE

Newey, *Rt. Hon.* Sir Guy Richard, Kt.

Newman, Sir Francis Hugh Cecil, Bt. (1912)

Newman, Sir Geoffrey Robert, Bt. (1836)

Newman, *Vice-Adm.* Sir Roy Thomas, KCB

Newman Taylor, *Prof.* Sir Anthony John, Kt., CBE

Newsam, Sir Peter Anthony, Kt.

Newson-Smith, Sir Peter Frank Graham, Bt. (1944)

Newton, *Revd* George Peter Howgill, Bt. (1900)

Newton, Sir John Garnar, Bt. (1924)

Newton, *Lt.-Gen.* Sir Paul Raymond, KBE

Newton, *Hon.* Sir Roderick Brian, Kt.

Nice, Sir Geoffrey, Kt., QC

Nichol, Sir Duncan Kirkbride, Kt., CBE

Nicholas, Sir David, Kt., CBE

Nicholson, Sir Bryan Hubert, GBE, Kt.

Nicholson, Sir Charles Christian, Bt. (1912)

Nicholson, Sir David, KCB, CBE

Nicholson, *Rt. Hon.* Sir Michael, Kt.

Nicholson, Sir Paul Douglas, KCVO, Kt.

Nicholson, Sir Robin Buchanan, Kt., PHD, FRS, FRENG

Nickell, *Prof.* Sir Stephen John, Kt., CBE, FBA

Nicklin, *Hon.* Sir Matthew James, Kt.

Nicol, *Hon.* Sir Andrew George Lindsay, Kt.

Nightingale, Sir Charles Manners Gamaliel, Bt. (1628)

†Nixon, Sir Simon Michael Christopher, Bt. (1906)

Noble, Sir David Brunel, Bt. (1902)

Noble, Sir Timothy Peter, Bt. (1923)

Nombri, Sir Joseph Karl, Kt., ISO, BEM

Norgrove, Sir David Ronald, Kt.

Norman, Sir Nigel James, Bt. (1915)

Norman, Sir Ronald, Kt., OBE

Norman, Sir Torquil Patrick Alexander, Kt., CBE

Normington, Sir David John, GCB

Norrington, Sir Roger Arthur Carver, Kt., CBE

Norris, *Hon.* Sir Alastair Hubert, Kt.

Norriss, *Air Marshal* Sir Peter Coulson, KBE, CB, AFC

North, *Air Marshal* Sir Barry Mark, KCB, OBE

North, Sir Jeremy William Francis, Bt. (1920)

North, Sir Peter Machin, Kt., CBE, QC, DCL, FBA

Norton, Sir Barry, Kt.

Norton, *Maj.-Gen.* Sir George Pemberton Ross, KCVO, CBE

Norton-Griffiths, Sir Michael, Bt. (1922)

Nossal, Sir Gustav Joseph Victor, Kt., CBE

Nott, *Rt. Hon.* Sir John William Frederic, KCB

Novoselov, *Prof.* Sir Konstantin, Kt.

Nugee, *Hon.* Sir Christopher George, Kt.

Nugent, Sir Christopher George Ridley, Bt. (1806)

†Nugent, Sir Nicholas Myles John, Bt. (I. 1795)

Nugent, Sir (Walter) Richard Middleton, Bt. (1831)

Nunn, Sir Trevor Robert, Kt., CBE

Nunneley, Sir Charles Kenneth Roylance, Kt.

Nursaw, Sir James, KCB, QC

Nurse, Sir Paul Maxime, Kt.

Nuttall, Sir Harry, Bt. (1922)

Nutting, Sir John Grenfell, Bt. (1903), QC

Oakeley, Sir Robert John Atholl, Bt. (1790)

Oakes, Sir Christopher, Bt. (1939)

Oakshott, Sir Thomas Hendrie, Bt. (1959)

O'Brien, Sir Robert Stephen, Kt., CBE

O'Brien, *Rt. Hon.* Sir Stephen Rothwell, KBE

†O'Brien, Sir Timothy John, Bt. (1849)

O'Brien, Sir William, Kt.

O'Connell, Sir Bernard, Kt.

O'Connell, Sir Maurice James Donagh MacCarthy, Bt. (1869)

O'Connor, Sir Denis Francis, Kt., CBE, QPM

Odell, Sir Stanley John, Kt.

Odgers, Sir Graeme David William, Kt.

O'Donnell, Sir Christopher John, Kt.

O'Donoghue, *Lt.-Gen.* Sir Kevin, KCB, CBE

O'Dowd, Sir David Joseph, Kt., CBE, QPM

Ogden, *Dr* Sir Peter James, Kt.

Ogden, Sir Robert, Kt., CBE

Ogilvy, Sir Francis Gilbert Arthur, Bt. (S. 1626)

Ogilvy-Wedderburn, Sir Andrew John Alexander, Bt. (1803)

Ognall, *Hon.* Sir Harry Henry, Kt.

O'Hara, *Hon.* Sir John Ailbe

Ohlson, Sir Peter Michael, Bt. (1920)

Oldham, *Dr* Sir John, Kt., OBE

Olisa, Sir Kenneth Aphunezi, Kt., OBE

Oliver, Sir Craig Stewart, Kt.

Oliver, Sir James Michael Yorrick, Kt.

Oliver, Sir Stephen John Lindsay, Kt., QC

†O'Loghlen, Sir Michael, Bt. (1838)

O'Lone, Sir Marcus James, KCVO

Olver, Sir Richard Lake, Kt.

Omand, Sir David Bruce, GCB

Ondaatje, Sir Christopher, Kt., CBE

O'Nions, *Prof.* Sir Robert Keith, Kt., FRS, PHD

Onslow, Sir Richard Paul Atherton, Bt. (1797)

Openshaw, *Hon.* Sir Charles Peter Lawford, Kt.

O'Rahilly, *Prof.* Sir Stephen Patrick, Kt., FRS

Ord, Sir David Charles, Kt.

Orde, Sir Hugh Stephen Roden, Kt., OBE, QPM

O'Regan, *Dr* Sir Stephen Gerard (Tipene), Kt.

O'Reilly, Sir Anthony John Francis, Kt.

O'Reilly, *Prof.* Sir John James, Kt.

Orr-Ewing, *Hon.* Sir (Alistair) Simon, Bt. (1963)

Orr-Ewing, Sir Archibald Donald, Bt. (1886)

Osborn, Sir Richard Henry Danvers, Bt. (1662)

Osborne, Sir Peter George, Bt. (I. 1629)

O'Shea, *Prof.* Sir Timothy Michael Martin, Kt.

Osmotherly, Sir Edward Benjamin Crofton, Kt., CB

Oswald, Sir (William Richard) Michael, KCVO

Ottaway, *Rt. Hon.* Sir Richard Geoffrey James, Kt.

Otton, Sir Geoffrey John, KCB

Otton, *Rt. Hon.* Sir Philip Howard, Kt.

Ouseley, *Hon.* Sir Duncan Brian Walter, Kt.

Outram, Sir Alan James, Bt. (1858)

Owen, Sir Geoffrey, Kt.

Owen, *Prof.* Sir Michael John, Kt.

Owen, *Hon.* Sir Robert Michael, Kt.

Owen-Jones, Sir Lindsay Harwood, KBE

P-S

Packer, Sir Richard John, KCB

Paget, Sir Henry James, Bt. (1871)

Paget, Sir Richard Herbert, Bt. (1886)

Paice, *Rt. Hon.* Sir James Edward Thornton, Kt.

Paine, Sir Christopher Hammon, Kt., FRCP, FRCR

Pakenham, *Hon.* Sir Michael Aiden, KBE, CMG

Palin, Sir Michael Edward, KCMG, CBE

Palin, *Air Chief Marshal* Sir Roger Hewlett, KCB, OBE

Palmer, Sir Albert Rocky, Kt.

Palmer, Sir (Charles) Mark, Bt. (1886)

Palmer, Sir Geoffrey Christopher John, Bt. (1660)

Palmer, *Rt. Hon.* Sir Geoffrey Winston Russell, KCMG

Palmer, *Prof.* Sir Godfrey Henry Oliver, Kt, OBE
†Palmer, Sir Robert John Hudson, Bt. (1791)
Panter, Sir Howard Hugh, Kt.
Pappano, Sir Antonio, Kt.
Parbo, Sir Arvi Hillar, Kt.
Park, *Hon.* Sir Andrew Edward Wilson, Kt.
Parker, Sir Alan, Kt.
Parker, Sir Alan William, Kt., CBE
Parker, Sir Andrew David, KCB
Parker, *Rt. Hon.* Sir Jonathan Frederic, Kt.
Parker, *Hon.* Sir Kenneth Blades, Kt.
Parker, *Maj.* Sir Michael John, KCVO, CBE
Parker, *Gen.* Sir Nicholas Ralph, KCB, CBE
Parker, Sir Richard (William) Hyde, Bt. (1681)
Parker, Sir (Thomas) John, GBE
Parker, Sir William Peter Brian, Bt. (1844)
Parkes, Sir Edward Walter, Kt., FRENG
Parkinson, Sir Michael, Kt., CBE
Parmley, *Dr* Sir Andrew Charles, Kt.
Parry, *Prof.* Sir Eldryd Hugh Owen, KCMG, OBE
Parry, Sir Emyr Jones, GCMG
Parry-Evans, *Air Chief Marshal* Sir David, GCB, CBE
Parsons, Sir John Christopher, KCVO
Partridge, Sir Michael John Anthony, KCB
Partridge, Sir Nicholas Wyndham, Kt., OBE
Pascoe, *Gen.* Sir Robert Alan, KCB, MBE
Pasley, Sir Robert Killigrew Sabine, Bt. (1794)
Paston-Bedingfeld, Sir Henry Edgar, Bt. (1661)
Patey, Sir William Charters, KCMG
Patten, *Rt. Hon.* Sir Nicholas John, Kt.
Pattie, *Rt. Hon.* Sir Geoffrey Edwin, Kt.
Pattison, *Prof.* Sir John Ridley, Kt., DM, FRCPATH
Pattullo, Sir (David) Bruce, Kt., CBE
Pauncefort-Duncombe, Sir David Philip Henry, Bt. (1859)
Payne, *Prof.* Sir David Neil, Kt., CBE, FRS
Peace, Sir John Wilfrid, Kt.
Peach, *Air Chief Marshal* Sir Stuart William, GBE, KCB, ADC
Pearce, Sir (Daniel Norton) Idris, Kt., CBE, TD
Pears, Sir Trevor Stephen, Kt., CMG
Pearse, Sir Brian Gerald, Kt.
Pearson, Sir David Lee, Kt., CBE
Pearson, Sir Francis Nicholas Fraser, Bt. (1964)
Pearson, Sir Keith, Kt.
Pearson, *Gen.* Sir Thomas Cecil Hook, KCB, CBE, DSO
Pease, Sir Joseph Gurney, Bt. (1882)
Pease, Sir Richard Thorn, Bt. (1920)

Peat, Sir Gerrard Charles, KCVO
Peat, Sir Michael Charles Gerrard, GCVO
Peckham, *Prof.* Sir Michael John, Kt.,
Peek, Sir Richard Grenville, Bt. (1874)
Pelgen, Sir Harry Friedrich, Kt., MBE
Pelham, *Dr* Sir Hugh Reginald Brentnall, Kt., FRS
Pelly, Sir Richard John, Bt. (1840)
Pendry, *Prof.* Sir John Brian, Kt., FRS
Penning, *Rt. Hon.* Sir Michael Allan, Kt.
Penny, *Dr* Nicholas Beaver, Kt., FBA
Penrose, *Prof.* Sir Roger, Kt., OM, FRS
Pepper, *Dr* Sir David Edwin, KCMG
Pepper, *Prof.* Sir Michael, Kt.
Pepperall, *Hon.* Sir Edward Brian, Kt
Pepys, *Prof.* Sir Mark Brian, Kt.
Perowne, *Vice-Adm.* Sir James Francis, KBE
†Perring, Sir John Simon Pelham, Bt. (1963)
Perris, Sir David (Arthur), Kt., MBE
Perry, Sir David Howard, KCB
Perry, Sir Michael Sydney, GBE
Pervez, Sir Mohammed Anwar, Kt., OBE
Petchey, Sir Jack, Kt., CBE
Peters, *Prof.* Sir (David) Keith, GBE, FRCP
Pethica, *Prof.* Sir John Bernard, Kt., FRS
Petit, Sir Dinshaw Manockjee, Bt. (1890)
Peto, Sir Francis Michael Morton, Bt. (1855)
Peto, Sir Henry Christopher Morton Bampfylde, Bt. (1927)
Peto, *Prof.* Sir Richard, Kt., FRS
Petrie, Sir Peter Charles, Bt. (1918), CMG
†Philipson-Stow, Sir (Robert) Matthew, Bt. (1907)
Phillips, Sir (Gerald) Hayden, GCB
Phillips, Sir John David, Kt., QPM
Phillips, Sir Jonathan, KCB
Phillips, Sir Peter John, Kt., OBE
Phillips, Sir Robin Francis, Bt. (1912)
Phillips, *Hon.* Sir Stephen Edmund, Kt.
Phillips, Sir Tom Richard Vaughan, KCMG
Pickard, Sir (John) Michael, Kt.
Picken, *Hon.* Sir Simon Derek, Kt.
Pickthorn, Sir James Francis Mann, Bt. (1959)
†Piers, Sir James Desmond, Bt. (I. 1661)
Pigot, Sir George Hugh, Bt. (1764)
Pigott, *Lt.-Gen.* Sir Anthony David, KCB, CBE
†Pigott, Sir David John Berkeley, Bt. (1808)
Pike, *Lt.-Gen.* Sir Hew William Royston, KCB, DSO, MBE
Pike, Sir Michael Edmund, KCVO, CMG
Pilditch, Sir John Richard, Bt. (1929)
Pile, Sir Anthony John Devereux, Bt. (1900), MBE

Pill, *Rt. Hon.* Sir Malcolm Thomas, Kt.
Pilling, Sir Joseph Grant, KCB
Pinsent, Sir Matthew Clive, Kt., CBE
Pinsent, Sir Thomas Benjamin Roy, Bt. (1938)
Pirmohamed, *Prof.* Sir Hussein Munir, Kt.
Pissarides, *Prof.* Sir Christopher Antoniou, Kt., FBA
Pitcher, Sir Desmond Henry, Kt.
Pitchers, *Hon.* Sir Christopher (John), Kt.
Pitoi, Sir Sere, Kt., CBE
Pitt, Sir Michael Edward, Kt.
Platt, Sir Martin Philip, Bt. (1959)
Pledger, *Air Chief Marshal* Sir Malcolm David, KCB, OBE, AFC
Plender, *Hon.* Sir Richard Owen, Kt.
Plumbly, Sir Derek John, KCMG
Pocock, *Dr* Sir Andrew John, KCMG
Poffley, *Lt.-Gen.* Sir Mark William, KCB, OBE
Poh, Sir Sang Chung, Kt., MBE
Pohai, Sir Timothy, Kt., MBE
Pole, Sir John Chandos, Bt. (1791)
Pole, Sir (John) Richard (Walter Reginald) Carew, Bt. (1628), OBE
Poliakoff, *Prof.* Sir Martyn, Kt., CBE
Polkinghorne, *Revd Canon* John Charlton, KBE
Pollard, Sir Charles, Kt.
†Pollen, Sir Richard John Hungerford, Bt. (1795)
Pollock, Sir David Frederick, Bt. (1866)
Pomeroy, Sir Brian Walter, Kt., CBE
Ponder, *Prof.* Sir Bruce Anthony John, Kt.
Ponsonby, Sir Charles Ashley, Bt. (1956)
Poon, Sir Dickson, Kt., CBE
†Poore, Sir Roger Ricardo, Bt. (1795)
Pope, *Lt.-Gen.* Sir Nicholas Arthur William, KCB, CBE
Popplewell, *Hon.* Sir Andrew John, Kt.
Popplewell, *Hon.* Sir Oliver Bury, Kt.
Porritt, *Hon.* Sir Jonathon Espie, Bt. (1963), CBE
Portal, Sir Jonathan Francis, Bt. (1901)
Porter, *Prof.* Sir Keith Macdonald, Kt.
Potter, *Rt. Hon.* Sir Mark Howard, Kt.
Pound, Sir John David, Bt. (1905)
Pountney, Sir David Willoughby, Kt., CBE
Povey, Sir Keith, Kt., QPM
Powell, Sir Ian Clifford, Kt.
†Powell, Sir James Richard Douglas, Bt. (1897)
Powell, Sir John Christopher, Kt.
Power, Sir Alastair John Cecil, Bt. (1924)
Pownall, Sir Michael Graham, KCB
Poya, Sir Nathaniel, Kt.
Prance, *Prof.* Sir Ghillean Tolmie, Kt., FRS
Prendergast, Sir (Walter) Kieran, KCVO, CMG
Prescott, Sir Mark, Bt. (1938)
Preston, *Prof.* Sir Paul, Kt., CBE

Preston, Sir Philip Charles Henry Hulton, Bt. (1815)

Prevost, Sir Christopher Gerald, Bt. (1805)

Price, Sir Francis Caradoc Rose, Bt. (1815)

Price, Sir Frank Leslie, Kt.

†Prichard-Jones, Sir David John Walter, Bt. (1910)

†Primrose, Sir John Ure, Bt. (1903)

Pringle, *Hon.* Sir John Kenneth, Kt.

Pringle, Sir Norman Murray Archibald Macgregor, Bt. (S. 1683)

Proby, Sir William Henry, Bt. (1952), CBE

Proctor-Beauchamp, Sir Christopher Radstock, Bt. (1745)

Prosser, Sir David John, Kt.

Prosser, Sir Ian Maurice Gray, Kt.

Pryke, Sir Christopher Dudley, Bt. (1926)

Puapua, *Rt. Hon.* Sir Tomasi, GCMG, KBE

Pulford, *Air Chief Marshal* Sir Andrew Douglas, GCB, CBE, ADC

Pullman, Sir Philip Nicholas Outram, Kt., CBE

Purves, Sir William, Kt., CBE, DSO

Purvis, *Vice-Adm.* Sir Neville, KCB

Quan, Sir Henry (Francis), KBE

Quilter, Sir Guy Raymond Cuthbert, Bt. (1897)

Radcliffe, Sir Sebastian Everard, Bt. (1813)

Radda, *Prof.* Sir George Karoly, Kt., CBE, FRS

Rae, Sir William, Kt., QPM

Raeburn, Sir Michael Edward Norman, Bt. (1923)

Rake, Sir Michael Derek Vaughan, Kt.

Ralli, Sir David Charles, Bt. (1912)

Ramakrishnan, *Dr* Sir Venkatraman, Kt.

Ramdanee, Sir Mookteswar Baboolall Kailash, Kt.

Ramphal, Sir Shridath Surendranath, GCMG

Ramphul, Sir Baalkhristna, Kt.

Ramphul, Sir Indurduth, Kt.

Ramsay, Sir Alexander William Burnett, Bt. (1806)

Ramsay, Sir Allan John (Hepple), KBE, CMG

†Ramsay-Fairfax-Lucy, Sir Patrick Samuel Thomas Fulke, Bt. (1836)

Ramsden, Sir David Edward John, Kt., CBE

Ramsden, Sir John Charles Josslyn, Bt. (1689)

Ramsey, *Dr* Sir Frank Cuthbert, KCMG

Ramsey, *Hon.* Sir Vivian Arthur, Kt.

Rankin, Sir Ian Niall, Bt. (1898)

Rasch, Sir Simon Anthony Carne, Bt. (1903)

Rashleigh, Sir Richard Harry, Bt. (1831)

Ratcliffe, Sir James Arthur, Kt.

Ratcliffe, *Prof.* Sir Peter John, Kt., FRS

Ratford, Sir David John Edward, KCMG, CVO

Rattee, *Hon.* Sir Donald Keith, Kt.

Rattle, Sir Simon Dennis, Kt., OM, CBE

Rawlins, *Hon.* Sir Hugh Anthony, Kt.

Rawlins, *Prof.* Sir Michael David, GBE, FRCP, FRCPED

Rawlinson, Sir Anthony Henry John, Bt. (1891)

Rea, *Prof.* Sir Desmond, Kt., OBE

Read, *Prof.* Sir David John, Kt.

Reardon-Smith, Sir (William) Antony (John), Bt. (1920)

Reddaway, Sir David Norman, KCMG, MBE

Redgrave, Sir Steven Geoffrey, Kt., CBE

Redmayne, Sir Giles Martin, Bt. (1964)

Redmond, Sir Anthony Gerard, Kt.

Redwood, *Rt. Hon.* Sir John Alan, Kt.

Redwood, Sir Peter Boverton, Bt. (1911)

Reed, *Prof.* Sir Alec Edward, Kt., CBE

Reedie, Sir Craig Collins, GBE

Rees, Sir David Allan, Kt., PHD, DSC, FRS

Rees, Sir Richard Ellis Meuric, Kt., CBE

Reffell, *Adm.* Sir Derek Roy, KCB

Reich, Sir Erich Arieh, Kt.

Reid, Sir Charles Edward James, Bt. (1897)

Reid, Sir David Edward, Kt.

Reid, *Rt. Hon.* Sir George, Kt.

Reid, Sir (Philip) Alan, GCVO

Reid, Sir Robert Paul, Kt.

Reid, Sir William Kennedy, KCB

Reiher, Sir Frederick Bernard Carl, KCMG, KBE

Renals, Sir Stanley Michael, Bt. (1895)

Renouf, Sir Clement William Bailey, Kt.

Renshaw, Sir John David Bine, Bt. (1903)

Renwick, Sir Richard Eustace, Bt. (1921)

Reynolds, Sir James Francis, Bt. (1923)

Reynolds, Sir Peter William John, Kt., CBE

Rhodes, Sir John Christopher Douglas, Bt. (1919)

Ribat, *Most Revd* John, KBE

Rice, *Prof.* Sir Charles Duncan, Kt.

Rice, *Maj.-Gen.* Sir Desmond Hind Garrett, KCVO, CBE

Rice, Sir Timothy Miles Bindon, Kt.

Richard, Sir Cliff, Kt., OBE

Richards, Sir Brian Mansel, Kt., CBE, PHD

Richards, *Rt. Hon.* Sir David Anthony Stewart, Kt.

Richards, Sir David Gerald, Kt.

Richards, Sir Francis Neville, KCMG, CVO

Richards, *Prof.* Sir Michael Adrian, Kt., CBE

Richards, *Rt. Hon.* Sir Stephen Price, Kt.

Richardson, Sir Anthony Lewis, Bt. (1924)

Richardson, Sir Thomas Legh, KCMG

Richardson-Bunbury, Sir Thomas William, Bt. (I. 1787)

Richmond, Sir David Frank, KBE, CMG

Richmond, *Prof.* Sir Mark Henry, Kt., FRS

Ricketts, Sir Stephen Tristram, Bt. (1828)

Ricks, *Prof.* Sir Christopher Bruce, Kt.

Riddell, Sir Walter John Buchanan, Bt. (S. 1628)

Ridgway, *Lt.-Gen.* Sir Andrew Peter, KBE, CB

Ridley, Sir Adam (Nicholas), Kt.

Ridley, Sir Michael Kershaw, KCVO

Rifkind, *Rt. Hon.* Sir Malcolm Leslie, KCMG

Rigby, Sir Anthony John, Bt. (1929)

Rigby, Sir Peter, Kt.

Rimer, *Rt. Hon.* Sir Colin Percy Farquharson, Kt.

Ripley, Sir William Hugh, Bt. (1880)

Ritako, Sir Thomas Baha, Kt., MBE

Ritblat, Sir John Henry, Kt.

Ritchie, *Prof.* Sir Lewis Duthie, Kt., OBE

Rivett-Carnac, Sir Jonathan James, Bt. (1836)

Rix, *Rt. Hon.* Sir Bernard Anthony, Kt.

Robb, Sir John Weddell, Kt.

Robbins, Sir Oliver, KCMG, CB

Roberts, Sir Derek Harry, Kt., CBE, FRS, FRENG

Roberts, *Prof.* Sir Edward Adam, KCMG

Roberts, Sir Gilbert Howland Rookehurst, Bt. (1809)

Roberts, Sir Hugh Ashley, GCVO

Roberts, Sir Ivor Anthony, KCMG

†Roberts, Sir James Elton Denby Buchanan, Bt. (1909)

Roberts, *Dr* Sir Richard John, Kt.

Roberts, Sir Samuel, Bt. (1919)

Roberts, *Maj.-Gen.* Sir Sebastian John Lechmere, KCVO, OBE

Robertson, *Rt. Hon.* Sir Hugh Michael, KCMG

Robertson, Sir Simon Manwaring, Kt.

Robey, Sir Simon Christopher Townsend, Kt.

Robins, Sir Ralph Harry, Kt., FRENG

Robinson, Sir Anthony, Kt.

Robinson, Sir Bruce, KCB

†Robinson, Sir Christopher Philipse, Bt. (1854)

Robinson, Sir Gerrard Jude, Kt.

Robinson, Sir Ian, Kt.

Robinson, Sir John James Michael Laud, Bt. (1660)

Robinson, *Dr* Sir Kenneth, Kt.

Robinson, Sir Peter Frank, Bt. (1908)

Robson, Sir Stephen Arthur, Kt., CB

Roch, *Rt. Hon.* Sir John Ormond, Kt.

Roche, Sir David O'Grady, Bt. (1838)

Roche, Sir Henry John, Kt.

Rodgers, Sir (Andrew) Piers (Wingate Aikin-Sneath), Bt. (1964)

Rogers, *Air Chief Marshal* Sir John Robson, KCB, CBE

Rogers, Sir Mark Ivan, KCMG

Rogers, Sir Peter, Kt.

Rollo, *Lt.-Gen.* Sir William Raoul, KCB, CBE

†Ropner, Sir Henry John William, Bt. (1952)

Ropner, Sir Robert Clinton, Bt. (1904)

Rose, Sir Arthur James, Kt., CBE

Rose, *Rt. Hon.* Sir Christopher Dudley Roger, Kt.

†Rose, Sir David Lancaster, Bt. (1874)

†Rose, *Gen.* Sir (Hugh) Michael, KCB, CBE, DSO, QGM

Rose, Sir John Edward Victor, Kt.

Rose, Sir Julian Day, Bt. (1872 and 1909)

Rosenthal, Sir Norman Leon, Kt.

Ross, *Maj.* Sir Andrew Charles Paterson, Bt. (1960)

Ross, *Lt.-Gen.* Sir Robert Jeremy, KCB, OBE

Ross, *Lt.-Col.* Sir Walter Hugh Malcolm, GCVO, OBE

Ross, Sir Walter Robert Alexander, KCVO

Rossi, Sir Hugh Alexis Louis, Kt.

Roth, *Hon.* Sir Peter Marcel, Kt.

Rothschild, Sir Evelyn Robert Adrian de, Kt.

Rowe, *Rear-Adm.* Sir Patrick Barton, KCVO, CBE

Rowe-Ham, Sir David Kenneth, GBE

Rowland, Sir Geoffrey Robert, Kt.

Rowley, Sir Mark Peter, Kt., QPM

Rowley, Sir Richard Charles, Bt. (1786 and 1836)

Rowling, Sir John Reginald, Kt.

Royce, *Hon.* Sir Roger John, Kt.

Royden, Sir John Michael Joseph, Bt. (1905)

Rubin, *Prof.* Sir Peter Charles, Kt.

Rudd, Sir (Anthony) Nigel (Russell), Kt.

Ruddock, Sir Paul, Kt.

Rudge, Sir Alan Walter, Kt., CBE, FRS

†Rugge-Price, Sir James Keith Peter, Bt. (1804)

Ruggles-Brise, Sir Timothy Edward, Bt. (1935)

Rumbold, Sir Henry John Sebastian, Bt. (1779)

Rushdie, Sir (Ahmed) Salman, Kt.

Russell, Sir Charles Dominic, Bt. (1916)

Russell, Sir George, Kt., CBE

Russell, Sir Muir, KCB

Russell, Sir Robert, Kt.

†Russell, Sir Stephen (Steve) Charles, Bt. (1812)

Russell Beale, Sir Simon, Kt., CBE

Rutnam, Sir Philip McDougall, KCB

Rutter, *Prof.* Sir Michael Llewellyn, Kt., CBE, MD, FRS

Ryan, Sir Derek Gerald, Bt. (1919)

Rycroft, Sir Richard John, Bt. (1784)

Ryder, *Rt. Hon.* Sir Ernest Nigel, Kt., TD

Sacranie, Sir Iqbal Abdul Karim Mussa, Kt., OBE

Saini, *Hon.* Sir Pushpinder Singh, Kt.

Sainsbury, *Rt. Hon.* Sir Timothy Alan Davan, Kt.

St Clair-Ford, Sir William Sam, Bt. (1793)

St George, Sir John Avenel Bligh, Bt. (I. 1766)

St John, Sir Walter, KCMG, OBE

St John-Mildmay, Sir Walter John Hugh, Bt. (1772)

St Paul, Sir Lyle Kevin, KCMG

Sainty, Sir John Christopher, KCB

Sakora, *Hon.* Sir Bernard Berekia, KBE

Sales, *Rt. Hon.* Sir Philip James, Kt.

Salika, Sir Gibuna Gibbs, KBE

Salisbury, Sir Robert William, Kt.

Salt, Sir Patrick MacDonnell, Bt. (1869)

Salt, Sir (Thomas) Michael John, Bt. (1899)

Salusbury-Trelawny, Sir John William Richard, Bt. (1628)

Salz, Sir Anthony Michael Vaughan, Kt.

Samani, *Prof.* Sir Nilesh Jayantilal, Kt.

Sampson, Sir Colin, Kt., CBE, QPM

Samuel, Sir John Michael Glen, Bt. (1898)

Samuelson, Sir James Francis, Bt. (1884)

Samuelson, Sir Sydney Wylie, Kt., CBE

Samworth, Sir David Chetwode, Kt., CBE

Sanders, Sir Ronald Michael, KCMG

Sanderson, Sir Frank Linton, Bt. (1920), OBE

Sands, Sir Roger Blakemore, KCB

Sants, Sir Hector William Hepburn, Kt.

Sargent, Sir William Desmond, Kt., CBE

Satchwell, Sir Kevin Joseph, Kt.

Saumarez Smith, *Dr* Sir Charles, Kt., CBE, FBA

Saunders, Sir Bruce Joshua, KBE

Saunders, *Hon.* Sir John Henry Boulton, Kt.

Savill, *Prof.* Sir John Stewart, Kt.

Savory, Sir Michael Berry, Kt.

Sawers, Sir Robert John, GCMG

Saxby, *Prof.* Sir Robin Keith, Kt.

Scarlett, Sir John McLeod, KCMG, OBE

Schama, *Prof.* Sir Simon, Kt., CBE, FBA

Schiemann, *Rt. Hon.* Sir Konrad Hermann Theodor, Kt.

Schiff, Sir András, Kt.

Scholar, Sir Michael Charles, KCB

Scholar, Sir Thomas Whinfield, KCB

Scholey, Sir David Gerald, Kt., CBE

Scipio, Sir Hudson Rupert, Kt.

Scott, Sir Christopher James Anderson, Bt. (1909)

Scott, Sir David Richard Alexander, Kt., CBE

Scott, *Prof.* Sir George Peter, Kt.

Scott, Sir Henry Douglas Edward, Bt. (1913)

Scott, Sir James Jervoise, Bt. (1962)

Scott, Sir John Hamilton, KCVO

Scott, Sir Ridley, Kt.

Scott, Sir Robert David Hillyer, Kt.

Scott, Sir Walter John, Bt. (1907)

Scott-Lee, Sir Paul Joseph, Kt., QPM

Scruton, *Prof.* Sir Roger Vernon, Kt.

Seale, Sir Clarence David, Kt.

Seale, Sir John Robert Charters, Bt. (1838)

Sealy, Sir Austin Llewellyn, Kt.

Seaton, HE Sir Samuel Weymouth Tapley, GCMG, CVO

†Sebright, Sir Rufus Hugo Giles, Bt. (1626)

Sedley, *Rt. Hon.* Sir Stephen John, Kt.

Sedwill, Sir Mark, KCMG

†Seely, Sir William Victor Conway, Bt. (1896)

Seeto, Sir Ling James, Kt., MBE

Seeyave, Sir Rene Sow Choung, Kt., CBE

Seldon, *Dr* Sir Anthony Francis, Kt.

Semple, Sir John Laughlin, KCB

Sergeant, Sir Patrick, Kt.

Serota, *Hon.* Sir Nicholas Andrew, Kt., CH

Setchell, Sir Marcus Edward, KCVO

†Seton, Sir Charles Wallace, Bt. (S. 1683)

Seton, Sir Iain Bruce, Bt. (S. 1663)

Seymour, Sir Julian Roger, Kt., CBE

Shadbolt, *Prof.* Sir Nigel Richard, Kt.

Shakerley, Sir Nicholas Simon Adam, Bt. (1838)

Shakespeare, Sir Thomas William, Bt. (1942)

Sharp, Sir Adrian, Bt. (1922)

Sharp, Sir Fabian Alexander Sebastian, Bt. (1920)

Sharp, Sir Leslie, Kt., QPM

Sharples, Sir James, Kt., QPM

Shaw, Sir Charles De Vere, Bt. (1821)

Shaw, *Prof.* Sir John Calman, Kt., CBE

Shaw, Sir Neil McGowan, Kt.

Shaw-Stewart, Sir Ludovic Houston, Bt. (S. 1667)

Shebbeare, Sir Thomas Andrew, KCVO

Sheffield, Sir Reginald Adrian Berkeley, Bt. (1755)

Sheil, *Rt. Hon.* Sir John, Kt.

Sheinwald, Sir Nigel Elton, GCMG

Sheleg, Sir Ehud, Kt.

Shelley, Sir John Richard, Bt. (1611)

Shepherd, Sir Colin Ryley, Kt.

Shepherd, Sir John Alan, KCVO, CMG

Shepherd, Sir Richard Charles Scrimgeour, Kt.

Sher, Sir Antony, KBE

Sherlock, Sir Nigel, KCVO, OBE

Sherston-Baker, Sir Robert George Humphrey, Bt. (1796)

†Shiffner, Sir Michael Goerge Edward, Bt. (1818)

Shinwell, Sir (Maurice) Adrian, Kt.

Shirreff, *Gen.* Sir Alexander Richard David, KCB, CBE

Shortridge, Sir Jon Deacon, KCB

Shuckburgh, Sir James Rupert Charles, Bt. (1660)

Siedentop, *Dr* Sir Larry Alan, Kt., CBE

Silber, *Rt. Hon.* Sir Stephen Robert, Kt.

Silk, Sir Evan Paul, KCB

Silverman, *Prof.* Sir Bernard Walter, Kt.

†Simeon, Sir Stephen George Barrington, Bt. (1815)

Simmonds, *Rt. Hon. Dr* Sir Kennedy Alphonse, KCMG

Simmons, *Air Marshal* Sir Michael George, KCB, AFC

Simms, Sir Neville Ian, Kt., FRENG

Simon, *Rt. Hon.* Sir Peregrine Charles Hugh, Kt.

Simonet, Sir Louis Marcel Pierre, Kt., CBE

Simpson, Sir Peter Austin, Kt., OBE

Simpson, *Dr* Sir Peter Jeffery, Kt.

Sims, Sir Roger Edward, Kt.

Sinclair, Sir Clive Marles, Kt.

Sinclair, Sir Robert John, Kt.

Sinclair, Sir William Robert Francis, Bt. (S. 1704)

Sinclair-Lockhart, Sir Simon John Edward Francis, Bt. (S. 1636)

Singh, Sir Pritpal, Kt.

Singh, *Rt. Hon.* Sir Rabinder, Kt.

Singleton, Sir Roger, Kt., CBE

Sitwell, Sir George Reresby Sacheverell, Bt. (1808)

Skeggs, Sir Clifford George, Kt.

Skehel, Sir John James, Kt., FRS

Skinner, Sir (Thomas) Keith (Hewitt), Bt. (1912)

Skipwith, Sir Alexander Sebastian Grey d'Estoteville, Bt. (1622)

Slade, *Rt. Hon.* Sir Christopher John, Kt.

Slade, Sir Julian Benjamin Alfred, Bt. (1831)

Slater, *Adm.* Sir John (Jock) Cunningham Kirkwood, GCB, LVO

Sleight, Sir Richard, Bt. (1920)

Sloman, Sir David Morgan, Kt.

Smiley, *Lt.-Col.* Sir John Philip, Bt. (1903)

Smith, *Prof.* Sir Adrian Frederick Melhuish, Kt., FRS

Smith, *Hon.* Sir Andrew Charles, Kt.

Smith, Sir Andrew Thomas, Bt. (1897)

Smith, Sir Cornelius Alvin, GCMG

Smith, Sir David Iser, KCVO

Smith, *Prof.* Sir Eric Brian, Kt., PHD

Smith, *Prof.* Sir James Cuthbert, Kt., FRS

Smith, Sir John Alfred, Kt., QPM

Smith, Sir Joseph William Grenville, Kt.

Smith, Sir Kevin, Kt., CBE

Smith, *Hon.* Sir Marcus Alexander, Kt.

Smith, Sir Martin Gregory, Kt.

Smith, Sir Michael John Llewellyn, KCVO, CMG

Smith, Sir (Norman) Brian, Kt., CBE, PHD

Smith, Sir Paul Brierley, Kt., CBE

Smith, *Hon.* Sir Peter Winston, Kt.

Smith, Sir Robert Courtney, Kt., CBE

Smith, Sir Robert Hill, Bt. (1945)

Smith, *Gen.* Sir Rupert Anthony, KCB, DSO, OBE, QGM

Smith, Sir Steven Murray, Kt.

Smith-Dodsworth, Sir David John, Bt. (1784)

Smith-Gordon, Sir (Lionel) Eldred (Peter), Bt. (1838)

Smith-Marriott, Sir Peter Francis, Bt. (1774)

Smurfit, *Dr* Sir Michael William Joseph, KBE

Smyth, Sir Timothy John, Bt. (1956)

Smyth-Osbourne, *Lt.-Gen.* Sir Edward Alexander, KCVO, CBE

Snowden, *Prof.* Sir Christopher Maxwell, Kt.

Snowden, *Hon.* Sir Richard Andrew, Kt.

Snyder, Sir Michael John, Kt.

Soames, *Rt. Hon.* Sir (Arthur) Nicholas Winston, Kt.

Soar, *Adm.* Sir Trevor Alan, KCB, OBE

Sobers, Sir Garfield St Auburn, Kt.

Solomon, Sir Harry, Kt.

Somare, *Rt. Hon.* Sir Michael Thomas, GCMG, CH

Songo, Sir Bernard Paul, Kt., CMG, OBE

Soole, *Hon.* Sir Michael Alexander, Kt.

Sorabji, *Prof.* Sir Richard Rustom Kharsedji, Kt., CBE

Sorrell, Sir John William, Kt., CBE

Sorrell, Sir Martin Stuart, Kt.

Sosa, Sir Manuel, Kt.

Soulsby, Sir Peter Alfred, Kt.

Souter, Sir Brian, Kt.

Southby, Sir John Richard Bilbe, Bt. (1937)

Southern, *Prof.* Sir Edwin Mellor, Kt.

Southgate, Sir Colin Grieve, Kt.

Southgate, Sir William David, Kt.

Southward, *Dr* Sir Nigel Ralph, KCVO

Sparks, *Prof.* Sir Robert Stephen John, Kt., CBE

Sparrow, Sir John, Kt.

Spearman, Sir Alexander Young Richard Mainwaring, Bt. (1840)

Spencer, Sir Derek Harold, Kt., QC

Spencer, *Hon.* Sir Martin Benedict, Kt.

Spencer, *Vice-Adm.* Sir Peter, KCB

Spencer, *Hon.* Sir Robin Godfrey, Kt.

Spencer-Nairn, Sir Robert Arnold, Bt. (1933)

Spicer, Sir Nicholas Adrian Albert, Bt. (1906)

Spiegelhalter, *Prof.* Sir David John, Kt., OBE, FRS

Spiers, Sir Donald Maurice, Kt., CB, TD

Spring, Sir Dryden Thomas, Kt.

Spurling, Sir John Damian, KCVO, OBE

Stacey, *Air Marshal* Sir Graham Edward, KBE, CB

Stadlen, *Hon.* Sir Nicholas Felix, Kt.

Stagg, Sir Charles Richard Vernon, KCMG

Staite, Sir Richard John, Kt., OBE

Stamer, Sir Peter Tomlinson, Bt. (1809)

Stanhope, *Adm.* Sir Mark, GCB, OBE, ADC

Stanier, Sir Beville Douglas, Bt. (1917)

Stanley, *Rt. Hon.* Sir John Paul, Kt.

Starkey, Sir John Philip, Bt. (1935)

Starkey, Sir Richard, Kt., MBE

Starmer, *Rt. Hon.* Sir Keir, KCB, QC

Stear, *Air Chief Marshal* Sir Michael James Douglas, KCB, CBE

Steel, *Vice-Adm.* Sir David George, KBE

Steel, *Hon.* Sir David William, Kt.

Steer, Sir Alan William, Kt.

Stephens, Sir (Edwin) Barrie, Kt.

Stephens, Sir Jonathan Andrew de Sievrac, KCB

Stephens, *Rt. Hon.* Sir (William) Benjamin Synge, Kt.

†Stephenson, Sir Henry Upton, Bt. (1936)

Stephenson, Sir Paul Robert, Kt., QPM

Stephenson, *Prof.* Sir Terence John, Kt.

Sterling, Sir Michael John Howard, Kt.

Stevens, Sir Michael John, KCVO

Stevenson, Sir Hugh Alexander, Kt.

Stewart, Sir Alan d'Arcy, Bt. (I. 1623)

Stewart, Sir Alastair Robin, Bt. (1960)

Stewart, Sir Brian John, Kt., CBE

Stewart, Sir David James Henderson, Bt. (1957)

Stewart, Sir David John Christopher, Bt. (1803)

Stewart, Sir James Moray, KCB

Stewart, Sir (John) Simon (Watson), Bt. (1920)

Stewart, Sir John Young, Kt., OBE

Stewart, Sir Patrick, Kt., OBE

Stewart, *Lt.-Col.* Sir Robert Christie, KCVO, CBE, TD

Stewart, Sir Roderick David, Kt., CBE

Stewart, *Hon.* Sir Stephen Paul, Kt.

Stewart, *Prof.* Sir William Duncan Paterson, Kt., FRS, FRSE

Stewart-Clark, Sir John, Bt. (1918)

Stewart-Richardson, Sir Simon Alaisdair Ian Neile, Bt. (S. 1630)

Stheeman, Sir Robert Alexander Talma, Kt., CB

Stilgoe, Sir Richard Henry Simpson, Kt., OBE

Stirling, Sir Angus Duncan Aeneas, Kt.

Stirling of Garden, *Col.* Sir James, KCVO, CBE, TD

Stirling-Hamilton, Sir Malcolm William Bruce, Bt. (S. 1673)

Stockdale, Sir Thomas Minshull, Bt. (1960)

Stoddart, *Prof.* Sir James Fraser, Kt.

Stoller, Sir Norman Kelvin, Kt., CBE

Stone, Sir Christopher, Kt.
Stone, Sir Roy Alexander, Kt., CBE
Stonhouse, *Revd* Michael Philip, Bt.
(1628 and 1670)
Stonor, *Air Marshal* Sir Thomas Henry,
KCB
Stoppard, Sir Thomas, Kt., OM, CBE
Storey, *Hon.* Sir Richard, Bt., CBE
(1960)
Storr, Sir Peter, KCB
Stothard, Sir Peter Michael, Kt.
Stott, Sir Adrian George Ellingham,
Bt. (1920)
Stoute, Sir Michael Ronald, Kt.
Stoutzker, Sir Ian Isaac, Kt., CBE
Stracey, Sir John Simon, Bt. (1818)
Strachan, Sir Curtis Victor, Kt., CVO
Strachan, Sir Hew Francis Anthony,
Kt.
†Strachey, Sir Henry Leofric
Benvenuto, Bt. (1801)
Straker, Sir Louis Hilton, KCMG
Strang, *Prof.* Sir John Stanley, Kt.
Strang Steel, Sir (Fiennes) Michael, Bt.
(1938), CBE
Stratton, *Prof.* Sir Michael Rudolf, Kt.,
FRS
Strauss, Sir Andrew John, Kt., OBE
Streeter, Sir Gary Nicholas, Kt.
Strickland-Constable, Sir Frederic, Bt.
(1641)
Stringer, Sir Donald Edgar, Kt., CBE
Stringer, Sir Howard, Kt.
Strong, Sir Roy Colin, Kt., CH, PHD,
FSA
†Stronge, Sir James Anselan Maxwell,
Bt. (1803)
†Stuart, Sir Geoffrey Phillip, Bt.
(1660)
Stuart, Sir James Keith, Kt.
†Stuart-Forbes, Sir William Daniel, Bt.
(S. 1626)
Stuart-Menteth, Sir Charles Greaves,
Bt. (1838)
Stuart-Paul, *Air Marshal* Sir Ronald
Ian, KBE
Stuart-Smith, *Hon.* Sir Jeremy Hugh,
Kt
Stuart-Smith, *Rt. Hon.* Sir Murray,
KCMG
Stubbs, Sir William Hamilton, Kt.,
PHD
Stucley, *Lt.* Sir Hugh George
Coplestone Bampfylde, Bt. (1859)
Studd, Sir Edward Fairfax, Bt. (1929)
Studholme, Sir Henry William, Bt.
(1956)
Sturridge, Sir Nicholas Anthony,
KCVO
Stuttard, Sir John Boothman, Kt.
†Style, Sir William Frederick, Bt.
(1627)
Sullivan, *Rt. Hon.* Sir Jeremy Mirth, Kt.
Sullivan, Sir Richard Arthur, Bt.
(1804)
Sunderland, Sir John Michael, Kt.
Supperstone, *Hon.* Sir Michael Alan,
Kt.

Sutherland, Sir John Brewer, Bt.
(1921)
Sutherland, Sir William George
MacKenzie, Kt.
Sutton, Sir Richard Lexington, Bt.
(1772)
Swan, Sir John William David, KBE
Swann, Sir Michael Christopher, Bt.
(1906), TD
Swayne, *Rt. Hon.* Sir Desmond, Kt.,
TD
Sweeney, Sir George, Kt.
Sweeney, *Hon.* Sir Nigel Hamilton, Kt.
Sweeting, *Prof.* Sir Martin Nicholas,
Kt., OBE, FRS
Swift, *Hon.* Sir Jonathan Mark, Kt
Swire, *Rt. Hon.* Sir Hugo George
William, KCMG
Sykes, Sir David Michael, Bt. (1921)
†Sykes, Sir Francis Charles, Bt. (1781)
Sykes, Sir Hugh Ridley, Kt.
Sykes, *Prof.* Sir (Malcolm) Keith, Kt.
Sykes, Sir Richard, Kt.
Sykes, Sir Tatton Christopher Mark,
Bt. (1783)
Symons, *Vice-Adm.* Sir Patrick Jeremy,
KBE
Syms, *Rt. Hon.* Sir Robert Andrew
Raymond, Kt.
†Synge, Sir Allen James Edward, Bt.
(1801)

T-Z

Tanner, Sir David Whitlock, Kt., CBE
Tantum, Sir Geoffrey Alan, Kt., CMG,
OBE
†Tapps-Gervis-Meyrick, Sir George
William Owen, Bt. (1791)
Tate, Sir Edward Nicolas, Bt. (1898)
Taureka, *Dr* Sir Reubeh, KBE
Tauvasa, Sir Joseph James, KBE
Taylor, Sir Hugh Henderson, KCB
Taylor, *Dr* Sir John Michael, Kt., OBE
Taylor, Sir Jonathan McLeod Grigor,
KCMG
Taylor, *Prof.* Sir Martin John, Kt., FRS
Taylor, Sir Nicholas Richard Stuart,
Bt. (1917)
Taylor, *Prof.* Sir William, Kt., CBE
Taylor, Sir William George, Kt.
Teagle, *Vice-Adm.* Sir Somerford
Francis, KBE
Teare, *Hon.* Sir Nigel John Martin, Kt.
Teasdale, *Prof.* Sir Graham Michael,
Kt.
Tebbit, Sir Kevin Reginald, KCB,
CMG
Temple, *Prof.* Sir John Graham, Kt.
Temple, Sir Richard Carnac Chartier,
Bt. (1876)
Temu, *Hon. Dr* Sir Puka, KBE, CMG
Tennyson-D'Eyncourt, Sir Mark
Gervais, Bt. (1930)
Terry, *Air Marshal* Sir Colin George,
KBE, CB
Thatcher, *Hon.* Sir Mark, Bt. (1990)
Thomas, Sir David John Godfrey, Bt.
(1694)

Thomas, Sir Derek Morison David,
KCMG
Thomas, *Prof.* Sir Eric Jackson, Kt.
Thomas, Sir Gilbert Stanley, Kt., OBE
Thomas, Sir Jeremy Cashel, KCMG
Thomas, *Prof.* Sir John Meurig, Kt.,
FRS
Thomas, Sir Keith Vivian, Kt.
Thomas, *Dr* Sir Leton Felix, KCMG,
CBE
Thomas, Sir Philip Lloyd, KCVO,
CMG
Thomas, Sir Quentin Jeremy, Kt., CB
Thomas, Sir William Michael, Bt.
(1919)
Thompson, Sir Christopher Peile, Bt.
(1890)
Thompson, Sir Clive Malcolm, Kt.
Thompson, Sir David Albert, KCMG
Thompson, Sir Jonathan Michael, KCB
Thompson, *Prof.* Sir Michael Warwick,
Kt., DSc
Thompson, Sir Nicholas Annesley, Bt.
(1963)
Thompson, Sir Nigel Cooper, KCMG,
CBE
Thompson, Sir Paul Anthony, Bt.
(1963)
Thompson, Sir Peter Anthony, Kt.
Thompson, *Dr* Sir Richard Paul
Hepworth, KCVO
Thompson, Sir Thomas d'Eyncourt
John, Bt. (1806)
Thomson, Sir Adam McClure, KCMG
Thomson, Sir (Frederick Douglas)
David, Bt. (1929)
Thomson, Sir Mark Wilfrid Home, Bt.
(1925)
Thorne, Sir Neil Gordon, Kt., OBE,
TD
Thornicroft, *Prof.* Sir Graham John, Kt.
Thornton, *Air Marshal* Sir Barry
Michael, KCB
Thornton, Sir (George) Malcolm, Kt.
Thornton, Sir Peter Ribblesdale, Kt.
†Thorold, Sir (Anthony) Oliver, Bt.
(1642)
Thorpe, *Rt. Hon.* Sir Mathew
Alexander, Kt.
Thrift, *Prof.* Sir Nigel John, Kt.
Thurecht, Sir Ramon Richard, Kt.,
OBE
Thwaites, Sir Bryan, Kt., PHD
Tickell, Sir Crispin Charles Cervantes,
GCMG, KCVO
Tidmarsh, Sir James Napier, KCVO,
MBE
Tilt, Sir Robin Richard, Kt.
Tiltman, Sir John Hessell, KCVO
Timmins, *Col.* Sir John Bradford,
KCVO, OBE, TD
Timpson, Sir William John Anthony,
Kt., CBE
Tims, Sir Michael David, KCVO
Tindle, Sir Ray Stanley, Kt., CBE
Tirvengadum, Sir Harry Krishnan, Kt.
Tod, *Vice-Adm.* Sir Jonathan James
Richard, KCB, CBE
Togolo, Sir Melchior Pesa, Kt.

Toka, Sir Mahuru Dadi, Kt., MBE
†Tollemache, Sir Richard John, Bt. (1793)
Tomkys, Sir (William) Roger, KCMG
Tomlinson, Sir John Rowland, Kt., CBE
Tomlinson, Sir Michael John, Kt., CBE
Tomlinson, *Rt. Hon.* Sir Stephen Miles, Kt.
Tooke, *Prof.* Sir John Edward, Kt.
Tooley, Sir John, Kt.
ToRobert, Sir Henry Thomas, KBE
Torpy, *Air Chief Marshal* Sir Glenn Lester, GCB, CBE, DSO
Torrance, *Very Revd Prof.* Iain Richard, KCVO, TD
Torry, Sir Peter James, GCVO, KCMG
†Touche, Sir Eric MacLellan, Bt. (1962)
Touche, Sir William George, Bt. (1920)
Tovadek, Sir Martin, Kt. CMG
Tovua, Sir Paul Joshua, KCMG
ToVue, Sir Ronald, Kt., OBE
Towneley, Sir Simon Peter Edmund Cosmo William, KCVO
Townsley, Sir John Arthur, Kt.
Traill, Sir Alan Towers, GBE
Trainor, *Prof.* Sir Richard Hughes, KBE
Trawen, Sir Andrew Sean, Kt., CMG, MBE
Treacy, *Rt. Hon.* Sir Colman Maurice, Kt.
Treacy, *Hon.* Sir (James Mary) Seamus, Kt.
Treisman, Sir Richard Henry, Kt., FRS
Trescowthick, Sir Donald Henry, KBE
†Trevelyan, Sir Peter John, Bt. (1662 and 1874)
Trezise, Sir Kenneth Bruce, Kt., OBE
Trippier, Sir David Austin, Kt., RD
Tritton, Sir Jeremy Ernest, Bt. (1905)
Trollope, Sir Anthony Simon, Bt. (1642)
Trotter, Sir Neville Guthrie, Kt.
Troubridge, Sir Thomas Richard, Bt. (1799)
Troup, Sir Edward Astley (John), Kt.
Trousdell, *Lt.-Gen.* Sir Philip Charles Cornwallis, KBE, CB
†Truscott, Sir Ralph Eric Nicholson, Bt. (1909)
Tsang, Sir Donald Yam-keun, KBE
Tuck, Sir Christopher John, Bt. (1910)
Tucker, Sir Paul, Kt.
Tucker, *Hon.* Sir Richard Howard, Kt.
Tuckett, *Prof.* Sir Alan John, Kt., OBE
Tuckey, *Rt. Hon.* Sir Simon Lane, Kt.
Tugendhat, *Hon.* Sir Michael George, Kt.
Tuite, Sir Christopher Hugh, Bt. (I. 1622), PHD
Tully, Sir William Mark, KBE
Tunnock, Sir Archibald Boyd, Kt., CBE
Tunstall, Sir Craig, Kt.
†Tupper, Sir Charles Hibbert, Bt. (1888)

Turing, Sir John Dermot, Bt. (S. 1638)
Turnbull, *Prof.* Sir Douglass Matthew, Kt.
Turner, *Hon.* Sir Mark George, Kt.
Turnquest, Sir Orville Alton, GCMG, QC
Tusa, Sir John, Kt.
Tweedie, *Prof.* Sir David Philip, Kt.
Tyrwhitt, Sir Reginald Thomas Newman, Bt. (1919)
Udny-Lister, Sir Edward Julian, Kt.
Ullmann, Sir Anthony James, Kt.
Underhill, *Rt. Hon.* Sir Nicholas Edward, Kt.
Underwood, *Prof.* Sir James Cressee Elphinstone, Kt.
Unwin, Sir (James) Brian, KCB
Ure, Sir John Burns, KCMG, LVO
Urquhart, Sir Brian Edward, KCMG, MBE
Urquhart, *Rt. Revd* David Andrew, KCMG
Usher, Sir Andrew John, Bt. (1899)
Utting, Sir William Benjamin, Kt., CB
Vallance, *Dr* Sir Patrick John Thompson, Kt.
Vardy, Sir Peter, Kt.
Varney, Sir David Robert, Kt.
Vassar-Smith, Sir John Rathbone, Bt. (1917)
Vavasour, Sir Eric Michael Joseph Marmaduke, Bt. (1828)
Veness, Sir David, Kt., CBE, QPM
Vereker, Sir John Michael Medlicott, KCB
Verey, Sir David John, Kt., CBE
Verity, Sir Gary Keith, Kt.
Verney, Sir Edmund Ralph, Bt. (1818)
†Verney, Sir John Sebastian, Bt. (1946)
Vernon, Sir James William, Bt. (1914)
Vestey, Sir Paul Edmund, Bt. (1921)
Vickers, *Prof.* Sir Brian William, Kt.
Vickers, Sir John Stuart, Kt.
Vickers, *Lt.-Gen.* Sir Richard Maurice Hilton, KCB, CVO, OBE
Vickers, Sir Roger Henry, KCVO
Viggers, *Lt.-Gen.* Sir Frederick Richard, KCB, CMG, MBE
Viggers, Sir Peter John, Kt.
Vincent, Sir William Percy Maxwell, Bt. (1936)
Vineall, Sir Anthony John Patrick, Kt.
Virdee, *Prof.* Sir Tejinder Singh, Kt.
von Friesendorff, Sir Rickard Fredrik Knut, Bt. (1661)
Vos, *Rt. Hon.* Sir Geoffrey Charles, Kt.
Vuatha, Sir Tipo, Kt., LVO, MBE
Vunagi, Rt. Revd David, GCMG
†Vyvyan, Sir Ralph Ferrers Alexander, Bt. (1645)
Waena, Sir Nathaniel Rahumaea, GCMG
Waine, *Rt. Revd* John, KCVO
Wainwright, Sir Robert Mark, KCMG
Waite, *Rt. Hon.* Sir John Douglas, Kt.
Waka, Sir Lucas Joseph, Kt., OBE
Wake, Sir Hereward Charles, Bt. (1621)

Wakefield, Sir (Edward) Humphry (Tyrrell), Bt. (1962)
Wakefield, Sir Norman Edward, Kt.
Wakeford, Sir Geoffrey Michael Montgomery, Kt., OBE
Wakeham, *Prof.* Sir William Arnot, Kt.
†Wakeley, Sir Nicholas Jeremy, Bt. (1952)
Waksman, *Hon.* Sir David Michael, Kt.
Wald, *Prof.* Sir Nicholas John, Kt.
Wales, Sir Robert Andrew, Kt.
Waley-Cohen, Sir Stephen Harry, Bt. (1961)
Walker, *Gen.* Sir Antony Kenneth Frederick, KCB
Walker, Sir Charles Ashley Rupert, KBE
Walker, Sir Christopher Robert Baldwin, Bt. (1856)
Walker, Sir David Alan, Kt.
Walker, *Air Vice-Marshal* Sir David Allan, KCVO, OBE
Walker, Sir Harold Berners, KCMG
Walker, Sir John Ernest, Kt., DPHIL, FRS
Walker, *Air Marshal* Sir John Robert, KCB, CBE, AFC
Walker, Sir Malcolm Conrad, Kt., CBE
Walker, Sir Miles Rawstron, Kt., CBE
Walker, Sir Patrick Jeremy, KCB
Walker, *Hon.* Sir Paul James, Kt.
Walker, Sir Rodney Myerscough, Kt.
Walker, Sir Roy Edward, Bt. (1906)
Walker, *Hon.* Sir Timothy Edward, Kt.
Walker, Sir Victor Stewart Heron, Bt. (1868)
Walker-Okeover, Sir Andrew Peter Monro, Bt. (1886)
Walker-Smith, *Hon.* Sir John Jonah, Bt. (1960)
Wall, Sir (John) Stephen, GCMG, LVO
Wall, *Gen.* Sir Peter Anthony, GCB, CBE, ADC
Wallace, *Prof.* Sir David James, Kt., CBE, FRS
Waller, *Rt. Hon.* Sir (George) Mark, Kt.
Waller, Sir John Michael, Bt. (I. 1780)
Waller, *Revd Dr* Sir Ralph, KBE
Wallis, Sir Peter Gordon, KCVO
Wallis, Sir Timothy William, Kt.
Walmsley, *Vice-Adm.* Sir Robert, KCB
Walport, *Dr* Sir Mark Jeremy, Kt.
†Walsham, Sir Gerald Percy Robert, Bt. (1831)
Walters, Sir Dennis Murray, Kt., MBE
Walters, Sir Frederick Donald, Kt.
Walters, Sir Peter Ingram, Kt.
Wamiri, Sir Akapite, KBE
Warby, *Hon.* Sir Mark David John, Kt.
Ward, *Rt. Hon.* Sir Alan Hylton, Kt.
Ward, Sir Austin, Kt., QC
Ward, *Hon.* Sir (Frederik) Gordon (Roy), Kt., OBE
Ward, *Prof.* Sir John MacQueen, Kt., CBE
Ward, Sir Joseph James Laffey, Bt. (1911)
Ward, Sir Timothy James, Kt.

†Wardlaw, Sir Henry Justin, Bt. (NS. 1631)

Waring, Sir (Alfred) Holburt, Bt. (1935)

Warmington, Sir Rupert Marshall, Bt. (1908)

Warner, Sir Gerald Chierici, KCMG

Warner, Sir Philip Courtenay Thomas, Bt. (1910)

Warren, Sir David Alexander, KCMG

Warren, Sir (Frederick) Miles, KBE

Warren, *Hon.* Sir Nicholas Roger, Kt.

Waterlow, Sir Christopher Rupert, Bt. (1873)

Waterlow, Sir (Thomas) James, Bt. (1930)

Waters, *Gen.* Sir (Charles) John, GCB, CBE

Waters, Sir David Mark Rylance (Mark Rylance), Kt.

Waterstone, Sir Timothy, Kt.

Wates, Sir Christopher Stephen, Kt.

Wates, Sir James Garwood Michael, Kt., CBE

Watson, Sir Graham Robert, Kt.

Watson, Sir (James) Andrew, Bt. (1866)

Watson, *Prof.* Sir Robert Tony, Kt., CMG

Watson, Sir Ronald Matthew, Kt., CBE

Watt, *Gen.* Sir Charles Redmond, KCB, KCVO, CBE, ADC

Watts, Sir Philip Beverley, KCMG

Weatherup, *Hon.* Sir Ronald Eccles, Kt.

Webb, *Prof.* Sir Adrian Leonard, Kt.

Webb, *Rt. Hon.* Sir Steven John, Kt.

Webb-Carter, *Maj.-Gen.* Sir Evelyn John, KCVO, OBE

Webster, *Vice-Adm.* Sir John Morrison, KCB

Wedgwood, Sir Ralph Nicholas, Bt. (1942)

Weekes, Sir Everton DeCourcey, KCMG, OBE

Weinberg, Sir Mark Aubrey, Kt.

Weir, *Hon.* Sir Reginald George, Kt.

Weir, Sir Roderick Bignell, Kt.

Welby, Sir (Richard) Bruno Gregory, Bt. (1801)

Welch, Sir John Reader, Bt. (1957)

Weldon, Sir Anthony William, Bt. (I. 1723)

Wellend, *Prof.* Sir Mark Edward, Kt.

Weller, *Prof.* Sir Ian Vincent Derrick, Kt.

Weller, Sir Nicholas John, Kt.

†Wells, Sir Christopher Charles, Bt. (1944)

Wells, *Prof.* Sir Stanley William, Kt., CBE

Wells, Sir William Henry Weston, Kt., FRICS

Wenge, Rt. Revd Girege, KBE

Wessely, *Prof.* Sir Simon Charles, Kt.

Westmacott, Sir Peter John, GCMG, LVO

Weston, Sir Michael Charles Swift, KCMG, CVO

Weston, Sir (Philip) John, KCMG

Whalen, Sir Geoffrey Henry, Kt., CBE

Wheeler, *Rt. Hon.* Sir John Daniel, Kt.

Wheeler, Sir John Frederick, Bt. (1920)

Wheeler, *Gen.* Sir Roger Neil, GCB, CBE

Wheler, Sir Trevor Woodford, Bt. (1660)

Whitaker, Sir John James Ingham (Jack), Bt. (1936)

Whitbread, Sir Samuel Charles, KCVO

Whitchurch, Sir Graeme Ian, Kt., OBE

White, Sir Adrian Edwin, Kt., CBE

White, *Prof.* Sir Christopher John, Kt., CVO

White, Sir David (David Jason), Kt., OBE

White, Sir David Harry, Kt.

White, Sir George Stanley James, Bt. (1904)

White, Sir John Woolmer, Bt. (1922)

White, *Maj.-Gen.* Sir Martin, KCVO, CB, CBE

White, *Prof.* Sir Nicholas John, KCMG, OBE

White, Sir Nicholas Peter Archibald, Bt. (1802)

White, Sir Willard Wentworth, Kt., CBE

White-Spunner, *Lt.-Gen.* Sir Barnabas William Benjamin, KCB, CBE

Whitehead, Sir Philip Henry Rathbone, Bt. (1889)

Whitmore, Sir Clive Anthony, GCB, CVO

Whitmore, Sir Jason Kevin, Bt. (1954)

Whitson, Sir Keith Roderick, Kt.

Whittam Smith, Sir Andreas, Kt., CBE

Wickerson, Sir John Michael, Kt.

Wicks, Sir Nigel Leonard, GCB, CVO, CBE

Wigan, Sir Michael Iain, Bt. (1898)

Wiggin, Sir Richard Edward John, Bt. (1892)

Wiggins, Sir Bradley Marc, Kt., CBE

Wigram, Sir John Woolmore, Bt. (1805)

Wilbraham, Sir Richard Baker, Bt. (1776)

Wild, Sir John Ralston, Kt., CBE

Wiles, *Prof.* Sir Andrew John, KBE

Wilkie, *Hon.* Sir Alan Fraser, Kt.

Wilkins, Sir Michael, Kt.

Wilkinson, Sir (David) Graham (Brook), Bt. (1941)

Willcocks, *Lt.-Gen.* Sir Michael Alan, KCB, CVO

Williams, Sir Anthony Geraint, Bt. (1953)

Williams, Sir (Arthur) Gareth Ludovic Emrys Rhys, Bt. (1918)

Williams, Sir Charles Othniel, Kt.

Williams, Sir Daniel Charles, GCMG, QC

Williams, *Hon.* Sir David Basil, Kt.

Williams, Sir David Reeve, Kt., CBE

Williams, Sir Donald Mark, Bt. (1866)

Williams, *Prof.* Sir (Edward) Dillwyn, Kt., FRCP

Williams, Sir Francis Owen Garbett, Kt., CBE

Williams, *Hon.* Sir (John) Griffith, Kt.

Williams, Sir Nicholas Stephen, Kt.

Williams, *Prof.* Sir Norman Stanley, Kt.

Williams, Sir Paul Michael, Kt., OBE

Williams, Sir Peter Michael, Kt.

Williams, *Prof.* Sir Robert Hughes, Kt.

Williams, Sir (Robert) Philip Nathaniel, Bt. (1915)

Williams, *HE Dr* Sir Rodney Errey Lawrence, GCMG

Williams, *Prof.* Sir Roger, Kt.

Williams, Sir (William) Maxwell (Harries), Kt.

Williams, *Hon.* Sir Wyn Lewis, Kt.

Williams-Bulkeley, Sir Richard Thomas, Bt. (1661)

Williams-Wynn, Sir David Watkin, Bt. (1688)

Williamson, Sir George Malcolm, Kt.

Williamson, Sir Robert Brian, Kt., CBE

Willink, Sir Edward Daniel, Bt. (1957)

Wills, Sir David James Vernon, Bt. (1923)

Wills, Sir David Seton, Bt. (1904)

Wilmot, Sir Henry Robert, Bt. (1759)

Wilmut, *Prof.* Sir Ian, Kt., OBE

Wilsey, *Gen.* Sir John Finlay Willasey, GCB, CBE

Wilshaw, Sir Michael, Kt.

Wilson, *Prof.* Sir Alan Geoffrey, Kt.

Wilson, Sir David Mackenzie, Kt.

Wilson, Sir Franklyn Roosevelt, KCMG

Wilson, Sir James William Douglas, Bt. (1906)

Wilson, *Brig.* Sir Mathew John Anthony, Bt. (1874), OBE, MC

Wilson, *Rt. Hon.* Sir Nicholas Allan Roy, Kt. (Lord Wilson of Culworth)

Wilson, *Prof.* Sir Robert James Timothy, Kt.

Wilson, Sir Robert Peter, KCMG

Wilson, *Air Chief Marshal* Sir (Ronald) Andrew (Fellowes), KCB, AFC

Wilson, Sir Thomas David, Bt. (1920)

Winkley, Sir David Ross, Kt.

Winnington, Sir Anthony Edward, Bt. (1755)

Winship, Sir Peter James Joseph, Kt., CBE

Winsor, Sir Thomas Philip, Kt.

Winter, *Dr* Sir Gregory Winter, Kt., CBE

Winterton, Sir Nicholas Raymond, Kt.

Wiseman, Sir John William, Bt. (1628)

Witty, Sir Andrew, Kt.

Wolfendale, *Prof.* Sir Arnold Whittaker, Kt., FRS

†Wolseley, Sir James Douglas, Bt. (I. 1745)

Wolseley, Sir Stephen Garnet Hugo Charles, Bt. (1628)

†Wombwell, Sir George Philip Frederick, Bt. (1778)

Womersley, Sir Peter John Walter, Bt. (1945)
Woo, Sir Leo Joseph, Kt., MBE
Woo, Sir Po-Shing, Kt.
Wood, Sir Alan Thorpe Richard, Kt., CBE
Wood, Sir Andrew Marley, GCMG
Wood, Sir Anthony John Page, Bt. (1837)
Wood, Sir Ian Clark, KT, GBE
Wood, Sir James Sebastian Lamin, KCMG
Wood, Sir Martin Francis, Kt., OBE
Wood, Sir Michael Charles, KCMG
Wood, Sir Peter John, Kt., CBE
Wood, *Hon.* Sir Roderic Lionel James, Kt.
Woodard, *Rear Adm.* Sir Robert Nathaniel, KCVO
Woodcock, *Vice-Adm.* Sir (Simon) Jonathan, KCB, OBE
Woodhead, *Vice-Adm.* Sir (Anthony) Peter, KCB
Woods, *Prof.* Sir Kent Linton, Kt.
Woods, Sir Robert Kynnersley, Kt., CBE
Woodward, Sir Clive Ronald, Kt., OBE
Woodward, Sir Thomas Jones (Tom Jones), Kt., OBE
Wootton, Sir David Hugh, Kt.
Wormald, Sir Christopher Stephen, KCB

Worsley, Sir William Ralph, Bt. (1838)
Worsthorne, Sir Peregrine Gerard, Kt.
Worthington, Sir Mark, Kt., OBE
Wratten, *Air Chief Marshal* Sir William John, GBE, CB, AFC
Wraxall, Sir Charles Frederick Lascelles, Bt. (1813)
Wrey, Sir George Richard Bourchier, Bt. (1628)
Wright, Sir Allan Frederick, KBE
Wright, Sir David John, GCMG, LVO
Wright, *Hon.* Sir (John) Michael, Kt.
Wright, *Prof.* Sir Nicholas Alcwyn, Kt.
Wright, Sir Peter Robert, Kt., CBE
Wright, *Air Marshal* Sir Robert Alfred, KBE, AFC
Wright, Sir Stephen John Leadbetter, KCMG
Wright, *Dr* Sir William Thompson, Kt., CBE
Wrightson, Sir Charles Mark Garmondsway, Bt. (1900)
Wrigley, *Prof.* Sir Edward Anthony (Sir Tony), Kt., PHD, PBA
Wrixon-Becher, Sir John William Michael, Bt. (1831)
Wroughton, Sir Philip Lavallin, KCVO
Wu, Sir Gordon Ying Sheung, KCMG
Wynne, Sir Graham Robert, Kt., CBE
Yacoub, *Prof.* Sir Magdi Habib, Kt., OM, FRCS
Yaki, Sir Roy, KBE
Yang, *Hon.* Sir Ti Liang, Kt.

Yarrow, Sir Alan Colin Drake, Kt.
Yarrow, Sir Ross William Grant, Bt. (1916)
Yassaie, *Dr* Sir Hossein, Kt.
Yoo Foo, Sir (François) Henri, Kt.
Young, Sir Colville Norbert, GCMG, MBE
Young, Sir Dennis Charles, KCMG
Young, Sir John Kenyon Roe, Bt. (1821)
Young, Sir John Robertson, GCMG
Young, Sir Nicholas Charles, Kt.
Young, Sir Robin Urquhart, KCB
Young, Sir Stephen Stewart Templeton, Bt. (1945), QC
Young, Sir William Neil, Bt. (1769)
Younger, Sir Alexander, KCMG
Younger, *Capt.* Sir John David Bingham, KCVO
Younger Thieriot, Sir Andrew William, Bt. (1911)
Yuwi, Sir Matiabe, KBE
Zacaroli, *Hon.* Sir Antony James, Kt.
Zacca, *Rt. Hon.* Sir Edward, KCMG
Zahedi, *Prof.* Sir Mir Saeed, Kt., OBE
Zambellas, *Adm.* Sir George Michael, GCB, DSC, ADC
Zissman, Sir Bernard Philip, Kt.
Zumla, *Prof.* Sir Alimuddin, Kt.
Zurenuoc, Sir Manasupe Zure, Kt., OBE
Zurenuoc, Sir Zibang, KBE

THE ORDER OF ST JOHN

THE MOST VENERABLE ORDER OF THE HOSPITAL OF ST JOHN OF JERUSALEM (1888)

GCStJ	Bailiff/Dame Grand Cross
KStJ	Knight of Justice/Grace
DStJ	Dame of Justice/Grace
CStJ	Commander
OStJ	Officer
MStJ	Member

Motto, Pro Fide, Pro Utilitate Hominum
(For the faith and in the service of humanity)

The Order of St John, founded in the early 12th century in Jerusalem, was a religious order with a particular duty to care for the sick. In Britain the order was dissolved by Henry VIII in 1540 but the British branch was revived in the early 19th century. The branch was not accepted by the Grand Magistracy of the Order in Rome but its search for a role in the tradition of the hospitallers led to the founding of the St John Ambulance Association in 1877 and later the St John Ambulance Brigade; in 1882 the St John Ophthalmic Hospital was founded in Jerusalem. A royal charter was granted in 1888 establishing the Order of St John as a British Order of Chivalry with the sovereign as its head.

Since October 1999 the whole order worldwide has been governed by a Grand Council which includes a representative from each of the 11 priories (England, Scotland, Wales, Hong Kong, Kenya, Singapore, South Africa, New Zealand, Canada, Australia and the USA). In addition there are also five commanderies in Northern Ireland, Jersey, Guernsey, the Isle of Man and Western Australia. There are also branches in about 30 other Commonwealth countries. Apart from St John Ambulance, the Order is also responsible for the Eye Hospital in Jerusalem. Admission to the order is usually conferred in recognition of service to either one of these institutions. Membership does not confer any rank, style, title or precedence on a recipient.

SOVEREIGN HEAD OF THE ORDER
HM The Queen

GRAND PRIOR
HRH The Duke of Gloucester, KG, GCVO

Lord Prior, Prof. Mark Compton
Prelate, Rt. Revd Timothy Stevens, CBE
Chancellor, Patrick Burgess, OBE
Sub-Prior, John Mah, QC
Secretary-General, Vice-Adm. Sir Paul Lambert, KCB

International Office, 3 Charterhouse Mews, London EC1M 6BB
T 020-7251 3292 **W** www.stjohninternational.org

DAMES

Style, 'Dame' before forename and surname, followed by appropriate post-nominal initials. Where such an award is made to a lady already in possession of a higher title, the appropriate initials follow her name
Envelope, Dame F_ S_, followed by appropriate post-nominal letters. *Letter (formal),* Dear Madam; *(social),* Dear Dame F_. *Spoken,* Dame F_
Husband, Untitled

Dame Grand Cross and Dame Commander are the higher classes for women of the Order of the Bath, the Order of St Michael and St George, the Royal Victorian Order, and the Order of the British Empire. Dames Grand Cross rank after the wives of Baronets and before the wives of Knights Grand Cross. Dames Commanders rank after the wives of Knights Grand Cross and before the wives of Knights Commanders.

Honorary damehoods may be conferred on women who are citizens of countries of which the Queen is not head of state.

LIST OF DAMES *as at 31 December 2020*
Women peers in their own right and life peers are not included in this list. Female members of the royal family are not included in this list; details of the orders they hold can be found within the Royal Family section.

If a dame has a double barrelled or hyphenated surname, she is listed under the first element of the name.

Abaijah, Dame Josephine, DBE
Abramsky, Dame Jennifer Gita, DBE
Acland Hood Gass, Lady (Elizabeth Periam), DCVO
Airlie, The Countess of, DCVO
Allen, *Hon.* Dame Anita Mildred, DBE
Allen, *Prof.* Dame Ingrid Victoria, DBE
Andrews, *Hon.* Dame Geraldine Mary, DBE
Andrews, Dame Julie, DBE
Angiolini, *Rt. Hon.* Dame Elish, DBE, QC
Anionwu, *Prof.* Dame Elizabeth Nneka, DBE
Anson, Lady (Elizabeth Audrey), DBE
Archer, *Dr* Dame Mary Doreen, DBE
Arden, *Rt. Hon.* Dame Mary Howarth (Mrs Mance), DBE
   (Lady Arden of Heswall)
Ashcroft, *Prof.* Dame Frances Mary, DBE, FRS
Asplin, *Rt. Hon.* Dame Sarah Jane (Mrs Sherwin), DBE
Atkins, Dame Eileen, DBE
Atkins, *Prof.* Dame Madeleine Julia, DBE
August, Dame Kathryn, DBE
Bacon, Dame Patricia Anne, DBE
Bailey, Dame Glenda Adrianne, DBE
Bailey, *Prof.* Dame Susan Mary, DBE
Baird, Dame Vera, DBE
Baker, Dame Janet Abbott (Mrs Shelley), CH, DBE
Barbour, Dame Margaret (Mrs Ash), DBE
Barker, Dame Katharine Mary, DBE
Barker-Welch, *Hon.* Dame Maizie Irene, DBE
Barrow, Dame Jocelyn Anita (Mrs Downer), DBE
Barstow, Dame Josephine Clare (Mrs Anderson), DBE
Bassey, Dame Shirley, DBE
Beale, Dame Inga Kristine, DBE
Beard, *Prof.* Dame (Winifred) Mary, DBE
Beasley, *Prof.* Dame Christine Joan, DBE
Beaurepaire, Dame Beryl Edith, DBE
Beckett, *Rt. Hon.* Dame Margaret Mary, DBE
Beer, *Prof.* Dame Gillian Patricia Kempster, DBE, FBA
Beer, *Prof.* Dame Janet Patricia, DBE
Begg, Dame Anne, DBE
Beral, *Prof.* Dame Valerie, DBE
Bertschinger, *Dr* Dame Claire, DBE
Bevan, Dame Yasmin, DBE

Bibby, Dame Enid, DBE
Black, *Prof.* Dame Carol Mary, DBE
Black, *Rt. Hon.* Dame Jill Margaret, DBE (Lady Black of Derwent)
Black, *Prof.* Dame Susan Margaret, DBE, FRSE
Blackadder, Dame Elizabeth Violet, DBE
Blaize, Dame Venetia Ursula, DBE
Blaxland, Dame Helen Frances, DBE
Blume, Dame Hilary Sharon Braverman, DBE
Booth, *Hon.* Dame Margaret Myfanwy Wood, DBE
Bostwick, *Hon.* Dame Janet Gwennett, DBE
Boulding, Dame Hilary, DBE
Bourne, Dame Susan Mary (Mrs Bourne), DBE
Bowe, *Dr* Dame (Mary) Colette, DBE
Bowtell, Dame Ann Elizabeth, DCB
Braddock, *Dr* Dame Christine, DBE
Brain, Dame Margaret Anne (Mrs Wheeler), DBE
Breakwell, *Prof.* Dame Glynis Marie, DBE
Brennan, Dame Maureen, DBE
Brennan, Dame Ursula, DCB
Brewer, *Dr* Dame Nicola Mary, DCMG
Bridges, Dame Mary Patricia, DBE
Brindley, Dame Lynne Janie, DBE
Brittan, Dame Diana (Lady Brittan of Spennithorne), DBE
Brooke, *Rt. Hon.* Dame Annette (Lesley), DBE
Bruce, Dame Susan Margaret, DBE
Bruce, *Prof.* Dame Victoria Geraldine, DBE, FBA, FRSE
Buckland, Dame Yvonne Helen Elaine, DBE
Burnell, *Prof.* Dame Susan Jocelyn Bell, DBE
Burslem, Dame Alexandra Vivien, DBE
Bussell, Dame Darcey Andrea, DBE
Butler, Dame Rosemary Janet Mair, DBE
Byatt, Dame Antonia Susan, DBE, FRSL
Cairncross, Dame Frances Anne, DBE, FRSE
Caldicott, Dame Fiona, DBE, FRCP, FRCPSYCH
Callil, Dame Carmen Thérèse, DBE
Cameron, *Prof.* Dame Averil Millicent, DBE
Campbell-Preston, Dame Frances Olivia, DCVO
Carew Pole, Lady (Mary), DCVO
Carnall, Dame Ruth, DBE
Carnwath, Dame Alison Jane, DBE
Carr, *Rt. Hon.* Dame Sue Lascelles (Mrs Birch), DBE
Cartwright, Dame Silvia Rose, DBE
Chapman, *Prof.* Dame Hilary Anne, DBE
Cheema-Grubb, *Hon.* Dame Bobbie, DBE
Clancy, Dame Claire Elizabeth, DCB
Clark, *Prof.* Dame Jill MacLeod, DBE
Clark, *Prof.* Dame (Margaret) June, DBE, PHD
Cleverdon, Dame Julia Charity, DCVO, CBE
Coates, Dame Sally, DBE
Cockerill, *Hon.* Dame Sara Elizabeth, DBE
Coia, *Dr* Dame Denise Assunta, DBE
Collarbone, Dame Patricia, DBE
Collins, Dame Joan Henrietta, DBE
Connolly, Dame Sarah Patricia, DBE
Contreras, *Prof.* Dame Marcela, DBE
Corley, Dame Elizabeth Pauline Lucy, DBE
Corner, *Prof.* Dame Jessica Lois, DBE
Corsar, *Hon.* Dame Mary Drummond, DBE
Courtice, Dame Veronica Anne (Polly), DBE, LVO
Coward, Dame Pamela Sarah, DBE
Cowley, *Prof.* Dame Sarah Ann, DBE
Cox, *Hon.* Dame Laura Mary, DBE
Cramp, *Prof.* Dame Rosemary Jean, DBE
Cullum, *Prof.* Dame Nicola Anne, DBE
Cunliffe-Lister *Hon.* Dame (Elizabeth) Susan, DCVO
Cutts, *Hon.* Dame Johannah, DBE

Dacon, Dame Monica Jessie, DBE, CMG
Dacre, *Prof.* Dame Jane Elizabeth, DBE
Daniel, Dame Jacqueline Lesley, DBE
Davies, *Prof.* Dame Kay Elizabeth, DBE
Davies, Dame Laura Jane, DBE
Davies, *Rt. Hon.* Dame Nicola Velfor, DBE
Davies, *Prof.* Dame Sally Claire, DBE
Davies, Dame Wendy Patricia, DBE
Davis, Dame Karlene Cecile, DBE
Dawson, *Prof.* Dame Sandra Jane Noble, DBE
de Havilland, Dame Olivia Mary, DBE
De Souza, Dame Rachel Mary, DBE
Dean, *Prof.* Dame Caroline, DBE, FRS
Dell, Dame Miriam Patricia, DBE
Dench, Dame Judith Olivia (Mrs Williams), CH, DBE
Descartes, Dame Marie Selipha Sesenne, DBE, BEM
Dethridge, Dame Kate, DBE
Dick, Dame Cressida Rose, DBE, QPM
Digby, The Lady, DBE
Dobbs, *Hon.* Dame Linda Penelope, DBE
Docherty, Dame Jacqueline, DBE
Dominiczak, *Prof.* Dame Anna Felicja, DBE, FRSE
Donald, *Prof.* Dame Athene Margaret, DBE, FRS
Dowling, *Prof.* Dame Ann Patricia, OM, DBE
Duffield, Dame Vivien Louise, DBE
Duffy, Dame Carol Ann, DBE
Dumont, Dame Ivy Leona, DCMG
Dunnell, Dame Karen, DCB
Dyche, Dame Rachael Mary, DBE
Eady, *Hon.* Dame Jennifer, DBE
Elcoat, Dame Catherine Elizabeth, DBE
Ellison, Dame Jill, DBE
Ellman, Dame Louise Joyce, DBE
Elton, Dame Susan Richenda (Lady Elton), DCVO
Ennis-Hill, Dame Jessica, DBE
Esteve-Coll, Dame Elizabeth Anne Loosemore, DBE
Evans, Dame Anne Elizabeth Jane, DBE
Evans, Dame Madeline Glynne Dervel, DBE, CMG
Evans, Dame Oremi, DBE
Fagan, Dame (Florence) Mary, LG, DCVO
Fairbairn, Dame Carolyn Julie, DBE
Falk, *Hon.* Dame Sarah, DBE
Fallowfield, *Prof.* Dame Lesley Jean, DBE
Farbey, *Hon.* Dame Judith Sarah, DBE
Farnham, Dame Marion (Lady Farnham), DCVO
Fawcett, Dame Amelia Chilcott, DBE
Fielding, Dame Pauline, DBE
Finch, *Prof.* Dame Janet Valerie, DBE
Fisher, *Prof.* Dame Amanda Gray, DBE
Fisher, Dame Jacqueline, DBE
Forgan, Dame Elizabeth Anne Lucy, DBE
Foster, *Hon.* Dame Alison Lee Caroline, DBE
Foster, Dame Jacqueline, DBE
Fradd, Dame Elizabeth, DBE
Francis, *Prof.* Dame Jane Elizabeth, DCMG
Fraser, Lady Antonia, CH, DBE
Fraser, Dame Helen Jean Sutherland, DBE
Frost, Dame Barbara May, DBE
Fry, Dame Margaret Louise, DBE
Furse, Dame Clara Hedwig Frances, DBE
Gadhia, Dame Jayne-Anne, DBE
Gai, *Prof.* Dame Pratibha Laxman (Mrs Gai-Boyes), DBE
Gaymer, Dame Janet Marion, DBE, QC
Ghosh, Dame Helen Frances, DCB
Gibb, Dame Moira Margaret, DBE
Gillan, *Rt. Hon.* Dame Cheryl Elise Kendall, DBE
Glenn, *Prof.* Dame Hazel Gillian, DBE
Glennie, *Dr* Dame Evelyn Elizabeth Ann, CH, DBE
Gloag, Dame Ann Heron, DBE
Gloster, *Rt. Hon.* Dame Elizabeth (Lady Popplewell), DBE
Glover, Dame Audrey Frances, DBE, CMG
Glover, *Prof.* Dame Lesley Anne, DBE, FRSE

Goad, Dame Sarah Jane Frances, DCVO
Goodall, *Dr* Dame (Valerie) Jane, DBE
Goodfellow, *Prof.* Dame Julia Mary, DBE
Gordon, Dame Minita Elmira, GCMG, GCVO
Gordon, *Hon.* Dame Pamela Felicity, DBE
Gow, Dame Jane Elizabeth (Mrs Whiteley), DBE
Grafton, Ann, The Duchess of, GCVO
Grainger, *Dr* Dame Katherine Jane, DBE
Grant, Dame Mavis, DBE
Green, Dame Moya Marguerite, DBE
Green, Dame Pauline, DBE
Gretton, Jennifer, Lady, DCVO
Grey, Dame Beryl Elizabeth (Mrs Svenson), CH, DBE
Griffiths, Dame Marianne, DBE
Grimthorpe, Elizabeth, The Lady, DCVO
Guilfoyle, Dame Margaret Georgina Constance, DBE
Guthardt, *Revd Dr* Dame Phyllis Myra, DBE
Hackitt, Dame Judith Elizabeth, DBE
Hakin, *Dr* Dame Barbara Ann, DBE
Hall, *Prof.* Dame Wendy, DBE
Hallett, Dame Nancy Karen, DBE
Hamilton, *Prof.* Dame Carolyn Paula, DBE
Harbison, Dame Joan Irene, DBE
Harper, Dame Elizabeth Margaret Way, DBE
Harris, Dame Pauline (Lady Harris of Peckham), DBE
Harris, Dame Philippa Jill Olivier, DBE
Hassan, Dame Anna Patricia Lucy, DBE
Hay, Dame Barbara Logan, DCMG, MBE
Henderson, Dame Fiona Douglas, DCVO
Hercus, *Hon.* Dame (Margaret) Ann, DCMG
Higgins, *Prof.* Dame Joan Margaret, DBE
Higgins, *Prof.* Dame Julia Stretton, DBE, FRS
Higgins, *Prof.* Dame Rosalyn, GBE, QC
Hill, *Prof.* Dame Judith Eileen, DBE
Hill, *Prof.* Dame Susan Lesley, DBE
Hine, Dame Deirdre Joan, DBE, FRCP
Hodge, *Rt. Hon.* Dame Margaret (Eve), DBE
Hodgson, Dame Patricia Anne, DBE
Hogg, *Hon.* Dame Mary Claire (Mrs Koops), DBE
Hollows, Dame Sharon, DBE
Holmes, Dame Kelly, DBE
Holroyd, Lady (Margaret Drabble), DBE
Holt, Dame Denise Mary, DCMG
Homer, Dame Linda Margaret, DCB
Hoodless, Dame Elisabeth Anne, DBE
Hoyles, *Prof.* Dame Celia Mary, DBE
Hudson, Dame Alice, DBE
Hufton, *Prof.* Dame Olwen, DBE
Humphrey, *Prof.* Dame Caroline (Lady Rees of Ludlow), DBE
Hunt, Dame Vivian, DBE
Husband, *Prof.* Dame Janet Elizabeth Siarey, DBE
Hussey, Dame Susan Katharine (Lady Hussey of North Bradley), GCVO
Hutton, Dame Deirdre Mary, DBE
Hyde, Dame Helen, DBE
Imison, Dame Tamsyn, DBE
Ion, *Dr* Dame Susan Elizabeth, DBE
Isaacs, Dame Albertha Madeline, DBE
James, Dame Naomi Christine (Mrs Haythorne), DBE
Jefford, *Hon.* Dame Nerys Angharad, DBE
Jiang, *Prof.* Dame Xiangqian (Jane), DBE
John, Dame Susan, DBE
Johnson, *Prof.* Dame Anne Mandall, DBE
Johnston, Dame Rotha Geraldine Diane, DBE
Jones, Dame Gwyneth (Mrs Haberfeld-Jones), DBE
Jordan, *Prof.* Dame Carole, DBE
Joseph, Dame Monica Theresa, DBE
Jowett, Dame Susan, DBE
Judd, *Hon.* Dame Frances, DBE
Julius, *Dr* Dame DeAnne Shirley, DCMG, CBE
Karika, Dame Pauline Margaret Rakera George (Mrs Taripo), DBE

Keeble, *Dr* Dame Reena, DBE
Keegan, Dame Elizabeth Mary, DBE
Keegan, Dame Geraldine Mary Marcella, DBE
Keegan, *Hon.* Dame Siobhan Roisin, DBE
Keith, Dame Penelope Anne Constance (Mrs Timson), DBE
Kekedo, Dame Rosalina Violet, DBE
Kelly, Dame Barbara Mary, DBE
Kelly, Dame Lorna May Boreland, DBE
Kendrick, Dame Fiona Marie, DBE
Kenny, Dame Julie Ann, DBE
Kershaw, Dame Janet Elizabeth Murray (Dame Betty), DBE
Kharas, Dame Zarine, DBE
Khemka, Dame Asha, DBE
Kidu, Lady, DBE
King, *Rt. Hon.* Dame Eleanor Warwick, DBE
Kinnair, Dame Donna, DBE
Kirby, Dame Georgina Kamiria, DBE
Kirkby, Dame (Carolyn) Emma, DBE
Kirwan, *Prof.* Dame Frances Clare, DBE, FRS
Knowles, *Hon.* Dame Gwynneth Frances Dietinde, DBE
Kumar, *Prof.* Dame Parveen June (Mrs Leaver), DBE
La Grenade, *HE* Dame Cécile Ellen Fleurette, GCMG, OBE
Laine, Dame Cleo (Clementine) Dinah (Lady Dankworth), DBE
Laing, *Rt. Hon.* Dame Eleanor Fulton, DBE
Laing, *Hon.* Dame Elisabeth Mary Caroline, DBE
Lake-Tack, *HE* Dame Louise Agnetha, GCMG
Lamb, Dame Dawn Ruth, DBE
Lambert, *Hon.* Dame Christina Caroline, DBE
Lang, *Hon.* Dame Beverley Ann Mcnaughton, DBE
Lannon, *Dr* Dame Frances, DBE
Lansbury Shaw, Dame Angela Brigid, DBE
Lavender, *Prof.* Dame Tina, DBE
Lawson, Dame Lesley (Twiggy), DBE
Leather, Dame Susan Catherine, DBE
Lee, *Prof.* Dame Hermione, DBE
Lee, Dame Laura Elizabeth, DBE
Legge-Bourke, *Hon.* Dame Elizabeth Shân Josephine, DCVO
Lenehan, Dame Christine, DBE
Leslie, Dame Alison Mariot, DCMG
Leslie, Dame Ann Elizabeth Mary, DBE
Lewis, Dame Edna Leofrida (Lady Lewis), DBE
Leyser Day, *Prof.* Dame Henrietta Miriam Ottoline, DBE
Lieven, *Hon.* Dame Nathalie Maria Daniella, DBE
Lively, Dame Penelope Margaret, DBE
Lott, Dame Felicity Ann Emwhyla (Mrs Woolf), DBE
Louisy, Dame (Calliopa) Pearlette, GCMG
Lynn, Dame Vera (Mrs Lewis), CH, DBE
MacArthur, Dame Ellen Patricia, DBE
McBride, *Hon.* Dame Denise Anne, DBE
McCall, Dame Carolyn Julia, DBE
McLean, *Prof.* Dame Angela Ruth, DBE
Macdonald, Dame Mary Beaton, DBE
McDonald, Dame Mavis, DCB
Mace, *Prof.* Dame Georgina, DBE
McGowan, *Hon.* Dame Maura Patricia, DBE
Macgregor, Dame Judith Anne, DCMG, LVO
McGuire, *Rt. Hon.* Dame Anne Catherine, DBE
MacIntyre, *Prof.* Dame Sarah Jane, DBE
Macur, *Rt. Hon.* Dame Julia Wendy, DBE
McVittie, Dame Joan Christine, DBE
Major, Dame Malvina Lorraine (Mrs Fleming), DBE
Major, Dame Norma Christina Elizabeth, DBE
Makin, *Dr* Dame Pamela Louise, DBE
Mantel, *Dr* Dame Hilary Mary, DBE
Manzie, Dame Stella Gordon, DBE
Marsden, *Dr* Dame Rosalind Mary, DCMG
Marsh, Dame Mary Elizabeth, DBE
Marteau, *Prof.* Dame Theresa Mary, DBE
Martin, Dame Louise Livingstone, DBE
Marx, Dame Clare Lucy, DBE
Mason, Dame Monica Margaret, DBE

Mason, *HE* Dame Sandra Prunella, DCMG
Massenet, Dame Natalie Sara, DBE
Matheson, Dame Jilian Norma, DCB
May, *Hon.* Dame Juliet Mary May, DBE
Mayhew Jonas, Dame Judith, DBE
Mellor, Dame Julie Thérèse, DBE
Metge, *Dr* Dame (Alice) Joan, DBE
Middleton, Dame Elaine Madoline, DCMG, MBE
Milburn, Dame Martina Jane, DCVO, CBE
Mills, *Prof.* Dame Anne Jane, DCMG, CBE
Mirren, Dame Helen, DBE
Mitcham, Dame Constance Viola, DBE
Monroe, *Prof.* Dame Barbara, DBE
Moore, Dame Henrietta Louise, DBE, FBA
Moore, Dame Julie, DBE
Moores, Dame Yvonne, DBE
Morgan, *Dr* Dame Gillian Margaret, DBE
Morgan, Dame Shan Elizabeth, DCMG
Morris, Dame Sylvia Ann, DBE
Morrison, *Hon.* Dame Mary Anne, GCVO
Moulder, *Hon.* Dame Jane Clare, DBE
Muirhead, Dame Lorna Elizabeth Fox, DCVO, DBE
Mullaly, *Rt. Revd and Rt. Hon.* Dame Sarah Elisabeth, DBE
Murray, Dame Jennifer Susan, DBE
Nelson, *Prof.* Dame Janet Laughland, DBE
Nelson-Taylor, Dame Nicola Jane, DBE
Neville, Dame Elizabeth, DBE, QPM
Newell, Dame Priscilla Jane, DBE
Ney, Dame Mary Thérèse, DBE
Nimmo, Dame Alison, DBE
O'Brien, Dame Una, DCB
O'Farrell, *Hon.* Dame Finola Mary, DBE
Ogilvie, Dame Bridget Margaret, DBE, PHD, DSc
Oliver, Dame Gillian Frances, DBE
Owen, Dame Susan Jane, DCB
Owers, Dame Anne Elizabeth (Mrs Cook), DBE
Oxenbury, Dame Shirley Ann, DBE
Palmer, Dame Felicity Joan, DBE
Paraskeva, *Rt. Hon.* Dame Janet, DBE
Park, Dame Merle Florence (Mrs Bloch), DBE
Parker, *Hon.* Dame Judith Mary Frances, DBE
Partridge, *Prof.* Dame Linda, DBE
Patel, Dame Indira, DBE
Paterson, Dame Vicki, DBE
Pauffley, *Hon.* Dame Anna Evelyn Hamilton, DBE
Peacock, Dame Alison Margaret, DBE
Pearce, *Prof.* Dame Shirley, DBE
Pedder, Dame Angela Mary, DBE
Penhaligon, Dame Annette (Mrs Egerton), DBE
Pereira, *Hon.* Dame Janice Mesadis, DBE
Perkins, Dame Mary Lesley, DBE
Peters, Dame Mary Elizabeth, LG, CH, DBE
Peyton-Jones, Dame Julia, DBE
Phillips, Dame Jane Elizabeth Ailwen (Sian), DBE
Pienaar, Dame Erica, DBE
Pierce, Dame Karen Elizabeth, DCMG
Pindling, Lady (Marguerite Matilda), GCMG
Platt, Dame Denise, DBE
Plotnikoff, Dame Joyce Evelyn, DBE
Plowright, Dame Joan Ann, DBE
Plunket Greene, Dame Barbara Mary, DBE
Poole, Dame Avril Anne Barker, DBE
Porter, Dame Shirley (Lady Porter), DBE
Powell, Dame Sally Ann Vickers, DBE
Pringle, Dame Anne Fyfe, DCMG
Proudman, *Hon.* Dame Sonia Rosemary Susan, DBE
Pugh, *Dr* Dame Gillian Mary, DBE
Rabbatts, Dame Heather Victoria, DBE
Rafferty, *Rt. Hon.* Dame Anne Judith, DBE
Rantzen, Dame Esther Louise (Mrs Wilcox), DBE
Rawson, *Prof.* Dame Jessica Mary, DBE
Rees, *Prof.* Dame Judith Anne, DBE

Rees, *Prof.* Dame Lesley Howard, DBE
Rees, *Prof.* Dame Teresa Lesley, DBE
Reeves, Dame Helen May, DBE
Refson, Dame Benita, DBE
Rego, Dame Paula Figueiroa, DBE
Reid, Dame Seona Elizabeth, DBE
Reynolds, Dame Fiona Claire, DBE
Rhodes, Dame Zandra Lindsey, DBE
Rice, Lady Susan Ilene, DBE
Richard, Dame Alison (Fettes), DBE
Richardson, Dame Mary, DBE
Rigg, Dame Diana, DBE
Rimington, Dame Stella, DCB
Ritterman, Dame Janet, DBE
Roberts, Dame Jane Elisabeth, DBE
Roberts, *Hon.* Dame Jennifer Mary, DBE
Roberts, *Hon.* Dame Priscilla Jane Stephanie (Lady Roberts), DCVO
Robins, Dame Ruth Laura, DBE
Robinson, *Prof.* Dame Ann Louise
Robinson, *Prof.* Dame Carol Vivien, DBE
Robottom, Dame Marlene, DBE
Roe, Dame Marion Audrey, DBE
Roe, Dame Raigh Edith, DBE
Ronson, Dame Gail, DBE
Roscoe, *Dr* Dame Ingrid Mary, DCVO
Rose, *Rt. Hon.* Dame Vivien Judith, DBE
Ross-Wawrzynski, Dame Dana (Mrs Ross-Wawrzynski), DBE
Rothwell, *Prof.* Dame Nancy Jane, DBE
Routledge, Dame Katherine Patricia, DBE
Ruddock, *Rt. Hon.* Dame Joan Mary, DBE
Runciman of Doxford, The Viscountess, DBE
Russell, *Hon.* Dame Alison Hunter, DBE
Russell, *Dr* Dame Philippa Margaret, DBE
Ryan, Dame Christine, DBE
Sackler, Dame Theresa, DBE
Salmond, *Prof.* Dame Mary Anne, DBE
Saunders, *Dr* Dame Frances Carolyn, DBE, CB
Savill, Dame Rosalind Joy, DBE
Sawyer, *Rt. Hon.* Dame Joan Augusta, DBE
Scardino, Dame Marjorie, DBE
Scott, Dame Catherine Margaret (Mrs Denton), DBE
Scott Thomas, Dame Kristin, DBE
Seward, Dame Margaret Helen Elizabeth, DBE
Sharp, *Rt. Hon.* Dame Victoria Madeleine, DBE
Shaw, *Prof.* Dame Pamela Jean, DBE
Shirley, Dame Stephanie, CH, DBE
Shovelton, Dame Helena, DBE
Sibley, Dame Antoinette (Mrs Corbett), DBE
Sills, *Prof.* Dame Eileen, DBE
Silver, *Dr* Dame Ruth Muldoon, DBE
Simler, *Rt. Hon.* Dame Ingrid Ann (Mrs Bernstein), DBE
Slade, *Hon.* Dame Elizabeth Ann, DBE
Slingo, *Prof.* Dame Julia Mary, DBE
Smith, Dame Dela, DBE
Smith, *Rt. Hon.* Dame Janet Hilary (Mrs Mathieson), DBE
Smith, *Hon.* Dame Jennifer Meredith, DBE
Smith, Dame Margaret Natalie (Maggie) (Mrs Cross), CH, DBE
Snowball, Dame Priscilla (Cilla) Deborah, DBE
Southgate, *Prof.* Dame Lesley Jill, DBE
Spelman, *Rt. Hon.* Dame Caroline Alice, DBE
Spencer, Dame Rosemary Jane, DCMG
Squire, Dame Rosemary Anne, DBE
Stacey, Dame Glenys Jean (Mrs Kyle), DBE
Steel, *Hon.* Dame (Anne) Heather (Mrs Beattie), DBE
Stephens, *Prof.* Dame Elan Cross, DBE
Stocking, Dame Barbara Mary, DBE
Storey, Dame Sarah Joanne, DBE

Strachan, Dame Valerie Patricia Marie, DCB
Strank, *Dr* Dame Angela Rosemary Emily, DBE
Strathern, *Prof.* Dame Anne Marilyn, DBE
Street, Dame Susan Ruth, DCB
Stringer, *Prof.* Dame Joan Kathleen, DBE
Sutherland, Dame Veronica Evelyn, DBE, CMG
Suzman, Dame Janet, DBE
Swift, *Hon.* Dame Caroline Jane (Mrs Openshaw), DBE
Symmonds, Dame Olga Olivia, DBE
Tanner, *Dr* Dame Mary Elizabeth, DBE
Taylor, Dame Meg, DBE
Te Kanawa, Dame Kiri Janette, CH, DBE
Theis, *Hon.* Dame Lucy Morgan, DBE
Thirlwall, *Rt. Hon.* Dame Kathryn Mary, DBE
Thomas, *Prof.* Dame Jean Olwen, DBE
Thomas, Dame Kathrin Elizabeth, DCVO
Thomas, Dame Maureen Elizabeth (Lady Thomas), DBE
Thompson, Dame Emma, DBE
Thompson, Dame Ila Dianne, DBE
Thornton, *Prof.* Dame Janet Maureen, DBE
Thornton, *Hon.* Dame Justine, DBE
Thornton, Dame Sara Joanne, DBE, QPM
Tickell, Dame Clare Oriana, DBE
Tinson, Dame Sue, DBE
Tizard, Dame Catherine Anne, GCMG, GCVO, DBE
Tokiel, Dame Rosa, DBE
Trotter, Dame Janet Olive, DBE
Twelftree, Dame Marcia, DBE
Uchida, Dame Mitsuko, DBE
Uprichard, Dame Mary Elizabeth, DBE
Vitmayer, Dame Janet Mary, DBE
Wagner, Dame Gillian Mary Millicent (Lady Wagner), DBE
Wallace, *Prof.* Dame Helen Sarah, DBE, CMG
Wallis, Dame Sheila Ann, DBE
Walter, Dame Harriet Mary, DBE
Walters, Dame Julie Mary, DBE
Warburton, Dame Arabella, DBE
Warner, *Prof.* Dame Marina Sarah, DBE, FBA
Warwick, Dame Catherine Lilian, DBE
Waterhouse, *Dr* Dame Rachel Elizabeth, DBE
Waterman, *Dr* Dame Fanny, DBE
Watkins, *Prof.* Dame Caroline Leigh, DBE
Watkinson, Dame Angela Eileen, DBE
Webb, *Prof.* Dame Patricia, DBE
Weir, Dame Gillian Constance (Mrs Phelps), DBE
Weller, Dame Rita, DBE
Wells, Dame Rachel Anne, DCVO
Weston, Dame Margaret Kate, DBE
Westwood, Dame Vivienne Isabel, DBE
Whipple, *Hon.* Dame Philippa Jane Edwards, DBE
Whitehead, *Hon.* Dame Annabel Alice Hoyer, DCVO
Whitehead, *Prof.* Dame Margaret McRae, DBE
Whiteread, Dame Rachel, DBE
Wigley, Dame Susan Louise, DCVO
Williams, Dame Josephine, DBE
Willmot, Dame Glenis, DBE
Wilson, Dame Jacqueline, DBE
Wilson-Barnett, *Prof.* Dame Jenifer, DBE
Wilton, Dame Penelope Alice, DBE
Windsor, Dame Barbara, DBE
Winterton, *Rt. Hon.* Dame Rosalie, DBE
Wintour, Dame Anna, DBE
Wolfson de Botton, Dame Janet (Mrs Wolfson de Botton), DBE
Wong Yick-ming, Dame Rosanna, DBE
Woodward, Dame Barbara Janet, DCMG, OBE
Woolf, Dame Catherine Fiona, DBE
Wykes, *Prof.* Dame Til Hilary Margaret, DBE
Yip, *Hon.* Dame Amanda Louise, DBE
Zaffar, Dame Naila, DBE

DECORATIONS AND MEDALS

PRINCIPAL DECORATIONS AND MEDALS IN ORDER OF WEAR

VICTORIA CROSS (VC), 1856 (*see* below)
GEORGE CROSS (GC), 1940 (*see* below)

BRITISH ORDERS OF KNIGHTHOOD
(*see also* Orders of Chivalry)

Order of the Garter
Order of the Thistle
Order of St Patrick
Order of the Bath
Order of Merit
Order of the Star of India
Order of St Michael and George
Order of the Indian Empire
Order of the Crown of India
Royal Victorian Order (Classes I, II and III)
Order of the British Empire (Classes I, II and III)
Order of the Companions of Honour
Distinguished Service Order
Royal Victorian Order (Class IV)
Order of the British Empire (Class IV)
Imperial Service Order
Royal Victorian Order (Class V)
Order of the British Empire (Class V)

BARONET'S BADGE

KNIGHT BACHELOR'S BADGE

INDIAN ORDER OF MERIT (MILITARY)

DECORATIONS, MEDALS FOR GALLANTRY AND DISTINGUISHED CONDUCT

Conspicuous Gallantry Cross (CGC), 1995
Distinguished Conduct Medal (DCM), 1854
Conspicuous Gallantry Medal (CGM), 1874
Conspicuous Gallantry Medal (Flying)
George Medal (GM), 1940
Royal West African Field Force Distinguished Conduct Medal (DCM)
Queen's Police Medal for Gallantry
Queen's Fire Service Medal for Gallantry
Royal Red Cross Class I (RRC), 1883
Distinguished Service Cross (DSC), 1914
Military Cross (MC), December 1914
Distinguished Flying Cross (DFC), 1918
Air Force Cross (AFC), 1918
Royal Red Cross Class II (ARRC)
Order of British India (OBI)
Kaisar-i-Hind Medal
Order of St John
Union of South Africa Queen's Medal for Bravery (Gold)
King's African Rifles Distinguished Conduct Medal
Indian Distinguished Service Medal (IDSM)
Union of South Africa Queen's Medal for Bravery (Silver)
Distinguished Service Medal (DSM), 1914
Military Medal (MM)
Distinguished Flying Medal (DFM)
Air Force Medal (AFM)
Constabulary Medal (Ireland)
Medal for Saving Life at Sea (Sea Gallantry Medal)

Indian Order of Merit (Civil)
Indian Police Medal for Gallantry
Ceylon Police Medal for Gallantry
Sierra Leone Police Medal for Gallantry
Sierra Leone Fire Brigades Medal for Gallantry
Colonial Police Medal for Gallantry
Overseas Territories Police Medal for Gallantry
Queen's Gallantry Medal (QGM), 1974
Royal Victorian Medal (RVM) (Gold, Silver and Bronze)
British Empire Medal (BEM)
Canada Medal
Queen's Police Medal for Distinguished Service (QPM)
Queen's Fire Service Medal for Distinguished Service (QFSM)
Queen's Ambulance Service Medal
Queen's Volunteer Reserves Medal
Queen's Medal for Chiefs

BADGE OF HONOUR

CAMPAIGN MEDALS AND STARS
Including any authorised UN, European Community/Union and NATO medals (in order of date of campaign for which awarded).
   World War medals are worn in the following order:
   First World War, 1914 Star; 1914–15 Star; British War Medal; Mercantile Marine War Medal; Victory Medal; Territorial Force War Medal
   Second World War, 1939–45 Star; Atlantic Star; Arctic Star; Air Crew Europe Star; Africa Star; Pacific Star; Burma Star; Italy Star; France & Germany Star; Defence Medal; Canadian/Newfoundland Volunteer Service Medal; War Medal; Africa Service Medal; India Service Medal; New Zealand War Service Medal; Southern Rhodesia Service Medal; Australian Service Medal

POLAR MEDALS *in order of date*

IMPERIAL SERVICE MEDAL

POLICE MEDALS FOR VALUABLE SERVICE
Indian Police Medal for Meritorious Service
Ceylon Police Medal for Merit
Sierra Leone Police Medal for Meritorious Service
Sierra Leone Fire Brigades Medal for Meritorious Service
Colonial Police Medal for Meritorious Service
Overseas Territories Police Medal for Meritorious Service

JUBILEE, CORONATION AND DURBAR MEDALS
Queen Victoria, King Edward VII, King George V, King George VI, Queen Elizabeth II, Visit Commemoration and Long and Faithful Service Medals

EFFICIENCY AND LONG SERVICE DECORATIONS AND MEDALS
Meritorious Service Medal
Accumulated Campaign Service Medal
Accumulated Campaign Service Medal (2011)
Army Long Service and Good Conduct Medal
Naval Long Service and Good Conduct Medal
Medal for Meritorious Service (Royal Navy 1918–28)
Indian Long Service and Good Conduct Medal
Indian Meritorious Service Medal
Royal Marines Meritorious Service Medal (1849–1947)
Royal Air Force Meritorious Service Medal (1918–1928)

Royal Air Force Long Service and Good Conduct Medal
Medal for Long Service and Good Conduct (Ulster Defence
　Regiment)
Indian Long Service and Good Conduct Medal
Royal West African Frontier Force Long Service and Good Conduct
　Medal
Royal Sierra Leone Military Forces Long Service and Good Conduct
　Medal
King's African Rifles Long Service and Good Conduct Medal
Indian Meritorious Service Medal
Police Long Service and Good Conduct Medal
Fire Brigade Long Service and Good Conduct Medal
African Police Medal for Meritorious Service
Royal Canadian Mounted Police Long Service Medal
Ceylon Police Long Service Medal
Ceylon Fire Services Long Service Medal
Sierra Leone Police Long Service Medal
Colonial Police Long Service Medal
Overseas Territories Police Long Service Medal
Sierra Leone Fire Brigades Long Service Medal
Mauritius Police Long Service and Good Conduct Medal
Mauritius Fire Services Long Service and Good Conduct Medal
Mauritius Prisons Service Long Service and Good Conduct Medal
Colonial Fire Brigades Long Service Medal
Overseas Territories Fire Brigades Long Service Medal
Colonial Prison Service Medal
Overseas Territories Prison Service Medal
Hong Kong Disciplined Services Medal
Army Emergency Reserve Decoration (ERD)
Volunteer Officers' Decoration (VD)
Volunteer Long Service Medal
Volunteer Officers' Decoration (for India and the Colonies)
Volunteer Long Service Medal (for India and the Colonies)
Colonial Auxiliary Forces Officers' Decoration
Colonial Auxiliary Forces Long Service Medal
Medal for Good Shooting (Naval)
Militia Long Service Medal
Imperial Yeomanry Long Service Medal
Territorial Decoration (TD), 1908
Ceylon Armed Services Long Service Medal
Efficiency Decoration (ED)
Territorial Efficiency Medal
Efficiency Medal
Special Reserve Long Service and Good Conduct Medal
Decoration for Officers of the Royal Navy Reserve
Decoration for Officers of the Royal Naval Volunteer Reserve
Royal Naval Reserve Long Service Medal
Royal Naval Volunteer Reserve Long Service Medal
Royal Naval Auxiliary Sick Berth Reserve Long Service and Good
　Conduct Medal
Royal Fleet Reserve Long Service and Good Conduct Medal
Royal Naval Wireless Auxiliary Reserve Long Service and Good
　Conduct Medal
Royal Naval Auxiliary Service Medal
Air Efficiency Award (AE), 1942
Volunteer Reserves Service Medal
Ulster Defence Regiment Medal
Northern Ireland Home Service Medal
Queen's Medal (for Champion Shots of the RN and RM)
Queen's Medal (for Champion Shots of the New Zealand
　Naval Forces)
Queen's Medal (for Champion Shots in the Military Forces)
Queen's Medal (for Champion Shots of the Air Forces)
Cadet Forces Medal, 1950
Coastguard Auxiliary Service Long Service Medal
Special Constabulary Long Service Medal
Canadian Forces Decoration
Royal Observer Corps Medal
Civil Defence Long Service Medal

Ambulance Service (Emergency Duties) Long Service and Good
　Conduct Medal
Royal Fleet Auxiliary Service Medal
Prison Services (Operational Duties) Long Service and Good
　Conduct Medal
Jersey Honorary Police Long Service and Good Conduct Medal
Merchant Navy Medal for Meritorious Service
Ebola Medal for Service in West Africa
National Crime Agency Long Service and Good Conduct Medal
Rhodesia Medal (1980)
Royal Ulster Constabulary Service Medal
Northern Ireland Prison Service Medal
Union of South Africa Commemoration Medal
Indian Independence Medal
Pakistan Medal
Ceylon Armed Services Inauguration Medal
Ceylon Police Independence Medal (1948)
Sierra Leone Independence Medal
Jamaica Independence Medal
Uganda Independence Medal
Malawi Independence Medal
Fiji Independence Medal
Papua New Guinea Independence Medal
Solomon Islands Independence Medal
Service Medal of the Order of St John
Badge of the Order of the League of Mercy
Voluntary Medical Service Medal
Women's Royal Voluntary Service Medal
South African Medal for War Services
Overseas Territories Special Constabulary Medal
Colonial Special Constabulary Medal

COMMONWEALTH REALM'S ORDERS, DECORATIONS
AND MEDALS in order of date

OTHER COMMONWEALTH MEMBER'S ORDERS,
DECORATIONS AND MEDALS in order of date

FOREIGN ORDERS, FOREIGN DECORATIONS AND
FOREIGN MEDALS in order of date

THE VICTORIA CROSS (1856)

FOR CONSPICUOUS BRAVERY

VC

Ribbon, Crimson, for all Services (until 1918 it was blue for
　the Royal Navy)

Instituted on 29 January 1856, the Victoria Cross was awarded
retrospectively to 1854, the first being held by Lt. C. D. Lucas,
RN, for bravery in the Baltic Sea on 21 June 1854 (gazetted
24 February 1857). The first 62 crosses were presented by
Queen Victoria in Hyde Park, London, on 26 June 1857.
　The Victoria Cross is worn before all other decorations, on
the left breast, and consists of a cross-pattée of bronze, 3.8cm
in diameter, with the royal crown surmounted by a lion in the
centre, and beneath there is the inscription For Valour. In July
2015 the tax-free annuity given to holders of the VC,
irrespective of need or other conditions, was increased to
£10,000. At the same time, further annual increases to the
annuity were linked to the CPI rate of inflation. In 1911, the
right to receive the cross was extended to Indian soldiers, and
in 1920 to matrons, sisters and nurses, the staff of the nursing

services and other services pertaining to hospitals and nursing, and to civilians of either sex regularly or temporarily under the orders, direction or supervision of the naval, military, or air forces of the crown.

SURVIVING RECIPIENTS OF THE VICTORIA CROSS
as at 31 December 2020

Apiata, *Cpl.* B. H., VC (New Zealand Special Air Service)
    2004 *Afghanistan*
Beharry, *LSgt* J. G., VC (Princess of Wales's Royal Regiment)
    2005 *Iraq*
Cruickshank, *Flt Lt.* J. A., VC (RAFVR)
    1944 *World War*
Donaldson, *Cpl.* M. G. S., VC (Australian Special Air Service)
    2008 *Afghanistan*
Keighran, *Cpl.* D. A., VC (Royal Australian Regiment)
    2012 *Afghanistan*
Leakey, *Lance Cpl.* J. M., VC (Parachute Regiment)
    2015 *Afghanistan*
Payne, *WO* K., VC, DSC (USA) (Australian Army Training Team)
    1969 *Vietnam*
Rambahadur Limbu, *Capt.,* VC, MVO (10th Princess Mary's Gurkha Rifles)
    1965 *Sarawak*
Roberts-Smith, *Cpl.* B., VC (Australian Special Air Service)
    2010 *Afghanistan*
Sheean, Ord. Seaman E., (Royal Australian Navy)
    2020 World War

THE GEORGE CROSS (1940)
FOR GALLANTRY

GC

Ribbon, Dark blue, threaded through a bar adorned with laurel leaves
Instituted 24 September 1940 (with amendments, 3 November 1942)

The George Cross is worn before all other decorations (except the VC) on the left breast (when worn by a woman it may be worn on the left shoulder from a ribbon of the same width and colour fashioned into a bow). It consists of a plain silver cross with four equal limbs, the cross having in the centre a circular medallion bearing a design showing St George and the Dragon. The inscription *For Gallantry* appears round the medallion and in the angle of each limb of the cross is the royal cypher 'G VI' forming a circle concentric with the medallion. The reverse is plain and bears the name of the recipient and the date of the award. The cross is suspended by a ring from a bar adorned with laurel leaves on dark blue ribbon 3.8cm wide.

The cross is intended primarily for civilians; awards to the fighting services are confined to actions for which purely military honours are not normally granted. It is awarded only for acts of the greatest heroism or of the most conspicuous courage in circumstances of extreme danger. In July 2015 the

tax-free annuity given to holders of the GC, irrespective of need or other conditions, was increased to £10,000. At the same time, further annual increases to the annuity were linked to the CPI rate of inflation. The cross has twice been awarded collectively rather than to an individual: to the island of Malta (1942) and the Royal Ulster Constabulary (1999).

In October 1971 all surviving holders of the Albert Medal and the Edward Medal had their awards translated to the George Cross.

SURVIVING RECIPIENTS OF THE GEORGE CROSS
as at 31 December 2020

If the recipient originally received the Albert Medal (AM) or the Edward Medal (EM), this is indicated by the initials in parentheses.

Bamford, J., GC, 1952
Beaton, J., GC, CVO, 1974
Croucher, *Lance Cpl.* M., GC, 2008
Finney, C., GC, 2003
Gledhill, A. J., GC, 1967
Haberfield, *CSgt.* K. H., GC, 2005
Hughes, *WO2* K. S., GC, 2010
Johnson, *WO1 (SSM)* B., GC, 1990
Lowe, A. R., GC (AM), 1949
Norton, *Maj.* P. A., GC, 2006
Pratt, M. K., GC, 1978
Purves, Mrs M., GC (AM), 1949
Shephard, S. J., GC, 2014
Troulan, D., GC, QGM, 2017
Walker, C., GC, 1972

THE ELIZABETH CROSS (2009)

EC

Instituted 1 July 2009

The Elizabeth Cross consists of a silver cross with a laurel wreath passing between the arms, which bear the floral symbols of England (rose), Scotland (thistle), Ireland (shamrock) and Wales (daffodil). The centre of the cross bears the royal cypher and the reverse is inscribed with the name of the person for whom it is in honour. The cross is accompanied by a memorial scroll and a miniature.

The cross was created to commemorate UK armed forces personnel who have died on operations or as a result of an act of terrorism. It may be granted to and worn by the next of kin of any eligible personnel who died from 1 January 1948 to date. It offers the wearer no precedence. Those that are eligible include the next of kin of personnel who died while serving on a medal earning operation, as a result of an act of terrorism, or on a non-medal earning operation where death was caused by the inherent high risk of the task.

The Elizabeth Cross is not intended as a posthumous medal for the fallen but as an emblem of national recognition of the loss and sacrifice made by the personnel and their families.

CHIEFS OF CLANS IN SCOTLAND

Only chiefs of whole Names or Clans are included, except certain special instances (marked *) who, though not chiefs of a whole Name, were or are for some reason (eg the Macdonald forfeiture) independent. Under decision (*Campbell-Gray,* 1950) that a bearer of a 'double or triple-barrelled' surname cannot be held chief of a part of such, several others cannot be included in the list at present.

THE ROYAL HOUSE: HM The Queen

AGNEW: Sir Crispin Agnew of Lochnaw, Bt., QC
ANSTRUTHER: Tobias Anstruther of Anstruther and Balcaskie
ARBUTHNOTT: Viscount of Arbuthnott
BANNERMAN: Sir David Bannerman of Elsick, Bt.
BARCLAY: Peter C. Barclay of Towie Barclay and of that Ilk
BORTHWICK: Lord Borthwick
BOYLE: Earl of Glasgow
BRODIE: Alexander Brodie of Brodie
BROUN OF COLSTOUN: Sir Wayne Broun of Colstoun, Bt.
BRUCE: Earl of Elgin and Kincardine, KT
BUCHAN: Charles Buchan of Auchmacoy
BURNETT: James C. A. Burnett of Leys
CAMERON: Donald Cameron of Lochiel, CVO
CAMPBELL: Duke of Argyll
CARMICHAEL: Richard Carmichael of Carmichael
CARNEGIE: Duke of Fife
CATHCART: Earl Cathcart
CHARTERIS: Earl of Wemyss and March
CLAN CHATTAN: K. Mackintosh of Clan Chattan
CHISHOLM: Hamish Chisholm of Chisholm (*The Chisholm*)
COCHRANE: Earl of Dundonald
COLQUHOUN: Sir Malcolm Rory Colquhoun of Luss, Bt.
CRANSTOUN: David Cranstoun of that Ilk
CUMMING: Sir Alastair Cumming of Altyre, Bt.
DARROCH: Duncan Darroch of Gourock
DAVIDSON OF DAVIDSTON: Grant Davidson of Davidston
DEWAR: Michael Dewar of that Ilk and Vogrie
DRUMMOND: Earl of Perth
DUNBAR: Sir James Dunbar of Mochrum, Bt.
DUNDAS: David Dundas of Dundas
DURIE: Andrew Durie of Durie, CBE
ELIOTT: Mrs Margaret Eliott of Redheugh
ERSKINE: Earl of Mar and Kellie
FARQUHARSON: Capt. Alwyne Farquharson of Invercauld, MC
FERGUSSON: Sir Charles Fergusson of Kilkerran, Bt.
FORBES: Lord Forbes
FORSYTH: Alistair Forsyth of that Ilk
FRASER: Lady Saltoun
*FRASER (OF LOVAT): Lord Lovat
GAYRE: Reinold Gayre of Gayre and Nigg
GORDON: Marquess of Huntly
GRAHAM: Duke of Montrose
GRANT: Lord Strathspey
GUNN: Iain Gunn of Gunn
GUTHRIE: Alexander Guthrie of Guthrie
HAIG: Earl Haig
HALDANE: Martin Haldane of Gleneagles
HANNAY: David Hannay of Kirkdale and of that Ilk
HAY: Earl of Erroll

HENDERSON: Alistair Henderson of Fordell
HUNTER: Pauline Hunter of Hunterston
IRVINE OF DRUM: Alexander H. R. Irvine of Drum
JARDINE: Sir William Jardine of Applegirth, Bt.
JOHNSTONE: Earl of Annandale and Hartfell
KEITH: Earl of Kintore
KENNEDY: Marquess of Ailsa
KERR: Marquess of Lothian, PC
KINCAID: Madam Arabella Kincaid of Kincaid
LAMONT: Revd Peter Lamont of that Ilk
LEASK: Jonathan Leask of that Ilk
LENNOX: Edward Lennox of that Ilk
LESLIE: Earl of Rothes
LINDSAY: Earl of Crawford and Balcarres, KT, GCVO, PC
LIVINGSTONE (or MACLEA): Niall Livingstone of the Bachuil
LOCKHART: Ranald Lockhart of the Lee
LUMSDEN: Gillem Lumsden of that Ilk and Blanerne
MACALESTER: William St J. McAlester of Loup and Kennox
MACARTHUR: John MacArthur of that Ilk
MCBAIN: James H. McBain of McBain
MACDONALD: Lord Macdonald (*The Macdonald of Macdonald*)
*MACDONALD OF CLANRANALD: Ranald Macdonald of Clanranald
*MACDONALD OF KEPPOCH: Ranald MacDonald of Keppoch
*MACDONALD OF SLEAT (CLAN HUSTEAIN): Sir Ian Macdonald of Sleat, Bt.
*MACDONELL OF GLENGARRY: Ranald MacDonell of Glengarry
MACDOUGALL: Morag MacDougall of MacDougall
MACDOWALL: Fergus Macdowall of Garthland
MACGREGOR: Sir Malcolm MacGregor of MacGregor, Bt.
MACINTYRE: Donald MacIntyre of Glenoe
MACKAY: Lord Reay
MACKENZIE: Earl of Cromartie
MACKINNON: Anne Mackinnon of Mackinnon
MACKINTOSH: John Mackintosh of Mackintosh (*The Mackintosh of Mackintosh*)
MACLACHLAN: Euan MacLachlan of MacLachlan
MACLAINE: Lorne Maclaine of Lochbuie
MACLAREN: Donald MacLaren of MacLaren and Achleskine
MACLEAN: Hon. Sir Lachlan Maclean of Duart, Bt., CVO
MACLENNAN: Ruaraidh MacLennan of MacLennan
MACLEOD: Hugh MacLeod of MacLeod
MACMILLAN: George MacMillan of MacMillan
MACNAB: James W. A. Macnab of Macnab (*The Macnab*)
MACNAGHTEN: Sir Malcolm Macnaghten of Macnaghten and Dundarave, Bt.
MACNEACAIL: John Macneacail of Macneacail and Scorrybreac
MACNEIL OF BARRA: Rory Macneil of Barra (*The Macneil of Barra*)
MACPHERSON: Hon. Sir William Macpherson of Cluny, TD
MACTAVISH: Steven MacTavish of Dunardry
MACTHOMAS: Andrew MacThomas of Finegand
MAITLAND: Earl of Lauderdale
MAKGILL: Viscount of Oxfuird
MALCOLM (MACCALLUM): Robin N. L. Malcolm of Poltalloch

MAR: Countess of Mar

MARJORIBANKS: Andrew Marjoribanks of that Ilk

MATHESON: Sir Alexander Matheson of Matheson, Bt.

MENZIES: David Menzies of Menzies

MOFFAT: Madam Moffat of that Ilk

MONCREIFFE: Hon. Peregrine Moncreiffe of that Ilk

MONTGOMERIE: Earl of Eglinton and Winton

MORRISON: Dr John Ruairidh Morrison of Ruchdi

MUNRO: Hector Munro of Foulis

MURRAY: Duke of Atholl

NESBITT (or NISBET): Mark Nesbitt of that Ilk

OGILVY: Earl of Airlie, KT, GCVO, PC

OLIPHANT: Richard Oliphant of that Ilk

RAMSAY: Earl of Dalhousie

RIDDELL: Sir Walter Riddell of Riddell, Bt.

ROBERTSON: Alexander Robertson of Struan *(Struan-Robertson)*

ROLLO: Lord Rollo

ROSS: David Ross of that Ilk and Balnagowan

RUTHVEN: Earl of Gowrie, PC

SCOTT: Duke of Buccleuch and Queensberry, KT, KBE

SCRYMGEOUR: Earl of Dundee

SEMPILL: Lord Sempill

SHAW: Iain Shaw of Tordarroch

SINCLAIR: Earl of Caithness, PC

SKENE: Dugald Skene of Skene

STIRLING: Fraser Stirling of Cader

STRANGE: Maj. Timothy Strange of Balcaskie

SUTHERLAND: Earl of Sutherland

SWINTON: John Swinton of that Ilk

TROTTER: Alexander Trotter of Mortonhall, CVO

URQUHART: Wilkins F. Urquhart of Urquhart

WALLACE: Andrew Wallace of that Ilk

WEDDERBURN: The Master of Dundee

WEMYSS: Michael Wemyss of that Ilk

THE PRIVY COUNCIL

The sovereign in council, or Privy Council, was the chief source of executive power until the system of cabinet government developed in the 18th century. Now the Privy Council's main functions are to advise the sovereign and to exercise its own statutory responsibilities independent of the sovereign in council.

Membership of the Privy Council is automatic upon appointment to certain government and judicial positions in the UK, eg cabinet ministers must be Privy Counsellors and are sworn in on first assuming office. Membership is also accorded by the Queen to eminent people in the UK and independent countries of the Commonwealth of which she is Queen, on the recommendation of the prime minister. Membership of the council is retained for life, except for very occasional removals.

The administrative functions of the Privy Council are carried out by the Privy Council Office under the direction of the president of the council, who is always a member of the cabinet. (*see also* Parliament)

President of the Council, Rt. Hon. Jacob Rees-Mogg, MP

Clerk of the Council, Richard Tilbrook

Style The Right (or Rt.) Hon._
Envelope, The Right (or Rt.) Hon. F_ S_. Letter, Dear Mr/Miss/Mrs S_. *Spoken,* Mr/Miss/Mrs S_

It is incorrect to use the letters PC after the name in conjunction with the prefix The Right Hon., unless the Privy Counsellor is a peer below the rank of Marquess and so is styled The Right Hon. because of his/her rank.

MEMBERS *as at 31 December 2020*

HRH The Duke of Edinburgh, 1951
HRH The Prince of Wales, 1977
HRH The Duke of Cambridge, 2016
HRH The Duchess of Cornwall, 2016

Abbott, Diane, 2017
Abernethy, *Hon.* Lord (Alastair Cameron), 2005
Adonis, Lord, 2009
Aikens, Sir Richard, 2008
Ainsworth, Robert, 2005
Airlie, Earl of, 1984
Alebua, Ezekiel, 1988
Alexander, Sir Danny, 2010
Alexander, Douglas, 2005
Amos, Baroness, 2003
Anderson of Swansea, Lord, 2000
Andrews, Dame Geraldine, 2020
Anelay of St Johns, Baroness, 2009
Angiolini, Dame Elish, 2006
Anthony, Douglas, 1971
Arbuthnot of Edrom, Lord, 1998
Arden of Heswall, Lady, 2000
Armstrong of Hill Top, Baroness, 1999
Arnold, Sir Richard, 2019
Arthur, *Hon.* Owen, 1995
Ashcroft, Lord, 2012
Ashton of Hyde, Lord, 2019
Ashton of Upholland, Baroness, 2006
Asplin, Dame Sarah, 2017
Astor of Hever, Lord, 2015
Atkins, Sir Robert, 1995
Auld, Sir Robin, 1995
Baker, Sir Jonathan, 2018
Baker, Norman, 2014
Baker, Sir Thomas, 2002
Baker of Dorking, Lord, 1984
Baldry, Sir Tony, 2013
Balls, Ed, 2007
Barclay, Stephen, 2018
Barker of Battle, Lord, 2012
Barron, Sir Kevin, 2001
Barrow, Dean, 2016
Barwell, Lord, 2017
Bassam of Brighton, Lord, 2009

Bates, Lord, 2015
Battle, John, 2002
Bean, Sir David, 2014
Beatson, Sir Jack, 2013
Beckett, Dame Margaret, 1993
Beith, Lord, 1992
Beldam, Sir Roy, 1989
Benn, Hilary, 2003
Benyon, Richard, 2017
Bercow, John, 2009
Berry, Jake, 2019
Birch, Sir William, 1992
Black of Derwent, Lady, 2010
Blackford, Ian, 2017
Blackstone, Baroness, 2001
Blair, Anthony, 1994
Blanchard, Peter, 1998
Blears, Hazel, 2005
Blencathra, Lord, 1995
Blunkett, Lord, 1997
Boateng, Lord, 1999
Bolger, James, 1991
Bonomy, *Hon.* Lord (Iain Bonomy), 2010
Boothroyd, Baroness, 1992
Bottomley of Nettlestone, Baroness, 1992
Boyd of Duncansby, Lord, 2000
Brabazon of Tara, Lord, 2013
Bracadale, *Hon.* Lord (Alistair Campbell), 2013
Bradley, Karen, 2016
Bradley, Lord, 2001
Bradshaw, Ben, 2009
Brake, Thomas, 2011
Braverman, Suella, 2020
Briggs of Westbourne, Lord, 2013
Brodie, *Hon.* Lord (Philip Brodie), 2013
Brokenshire, James, 2015
Brooke, Dame Annette, 2014
Brooke of Sutton Mandeville, Lord, 1988
Brown, Gordon, 1996
Brown, Nicholas, 1997

Brown, Sir Stephen, 1983
Brown of Eaton-under-Heywood, Lord, 1992
Browne of Ladyton, Lord, 2005
Bruce of Bennachie, Lord, 2006
Buckland, Robert, 2019
Burnett of Maldon, Lord, 2014
Burnham, Andy, 2007
Burns, Conor, 2019
Burns, Sir Simon, 2011
Burnton, Sir Stanley, 2008
Burrows, Lord, 2020
Burstow, Paul, 2012
Burt, Alistair, 2013
Butler of Brockwell, Lord, 2004
Butler-Sloss, Baroness, 1988
Buxton, Sir Richard, 1997
Byers, Stephen, 1998
Byrne, Liam, 2008
Byron, Sir Dennis, 2004
Cable, Sir Vincent, 2010
Caborn, Richard, 1999
Cairns, Alun, 2016
Caithness, Earl of, 1990
Cameron, David, 2005
Cameron of Lochbroom, Lord, 1984
Camoys, Lord, 1997
Campbell, Sir Alan, 2014
Campbell, Sir William, 1999
Campbell of Pittenweem, Lord, 1999
Canterbury, Archbishop of, 2013
Carey of Clifton, Lord, 1991
Carloway, *Hon.* Lord (Colin Sutherland), 2008
Carmichael, Alistair, 2010
Carnwath of Notting Hill, Lord, 2002
Carr, Dame Sue, 2020
Carswell, Lord, 1993
Chadwick, Sir John, 1997
Chakrabarti, Baroness, 2018
Chalfont, Lord, 1964
Chalker of Wallasey, Baroness, 1987
Chan, Sir Julius, 1981
Chartres, Rt. Revd Lord, 1995
Chilcot, Sir John, 2004

Christie, Perry, 2004
Clark, Greg, 2010
Clark, Helen, 1990
Clark of Calton, Baroness, 2013
Clark of Windermere, Lord, 1997
Clarke, Charles, 2001
Clarke, Sir Christopher, 2013
Clarke of Nottingham, Lord, 1984
Clarke, Hon. Lord (Matthew Clarke), 2008
Clarke, Thomas, 1997
Clarke of Stone-cum-Ebony, Lord, 1998
Clegg, Sir Nicholas, 2008
Cleverly, James, 2019
Clinton-Davis, Lord, 1998
Clwyd, Ann, 2004
Coffey, Thérèse, 2019
Coghlin, Sir Patrick, 2009
Collins of Mapesbury, Lord, 2007
Cooper, Yvette, 2007
Cope of Berkeley, Lord, 1988
Corbyn, Jeremy, 2015
Corston, Baroness, 2003
Cosgrove, Hon. Lady (Hazel Cosgrove), 2003
Coulson, Sir Peter, 2018
Cox, Geoffrey, 2018
Crabb, Stephen, 2014
Crawford and Balcarres, Earl of, 1972
Creech, Hon. Wyatt, 1999
Cullen of Whitekirk, Lord, 1997
Cunningham of Felling, Lord, 1993
Curry, David, 1996
Darling of Roulanish, Lord, 1997
Darzi of Denham, Lord, 2009
Davey, Sir Edward, 2012
Davidson, Ruth, 2016
Davies, Dame Nicola, 2018
Davies, Ronald, 1997
Davies of Oldham, Lord, 2006
Davis, David, 1997
Davis, Sir Nigel, 2011
Davis, Terence, 1999
de la Bastide, Michael, 2004
Deben, Lord, 1985
Deeny, Sir Donnell, 2017
Denham, John, 2000
Denham, Lord, 1981
Dholakia, Lord, 2010
Dingemans, Sir James, 2019
Dodds of Duncairn, Lord*, 2010
Donaldson, Sir Jeffrey, 2007
Dorrell, Stephen, 1994
Dorrian, Hon. Lady (Leona Dorrian), 2013
Douglas, Dr Denzil, 2011
Dowden, Oliver, 2019
Drakeford, Mark, 2019
Drayson, Lord, 2008
Drummond Young, Hon. Lord (James Drummond Young), 2013
D'Souza, Baroness, 2009
Duncan, Sir Alan, 2010
Duncan Smith, Iain, 2001
Dunne, Philip, 2019
Dyson, Lord, 2001
Eassie, Hon. Lord (Ronald Mackay), 2006
East, Paul, 1998
Edward, Sir David, 2005
Eggar, Timothy, 1995

Elias, Sir Patrick, 2009
Elias, Hon. Dame Sian, 1999
Elis-Thomas, Lord, 2004
Ellis, Michael, 2019
Ellwood, Tobias, 2017
Emslie, Hon. Lord (George Emslie), 2011
Esquivel, Manuel, 1986
Etherton, Sir Terence, 2008
Eustice, George, 2020
Evans, Sir Anthony, 1992
Evans of Bowes Park, Baroness, 2016
Evennett, Sir David, 2015
Falconer of Thoroton, Lord, 2003
Fallon, Sir Michael, 2012
Featherstone, Baroness, 2014
Feldman of Elstree, Lord, 2015
Fellowes, Lord, 1990
Field of Birkenhead, Lord, 1997
Field, Mark, 2015
Flaux, Sir Julian, 2017
Flint, Caroline, 2008
Floyd, Sir Christopher, 2013
Forsyth of Drumlean, Lord, 1995
Foster, Arlene, 2016
Foster of Bath, Lord, 2010
Foulkes of Cumnock, Lord, 2002
Fowler, Lord, 1979
Fox, Liam, 2010
Francois, Mark, 2010
Freedman, Sir Lawrence, 2009
Freeman, Lord, 1993
Freud, Lord, 2015
Fulford, Sir Adrian, 2013
Gage, Sir William, 2004
Gale, Sir Roger, 2019
Garden of Frognal, Baroness, 2015
Garnier, Lord, 2015
Gauke, David, 2016
Geidt, Lord, 2007
Gibb, Nicolas, 2016
Gibson, Sir Peter, 1993
Gill, Hon. Lord (Brian Gill), 2002
Gillan, Dame Cheryl, 2010
Gillen, Sir John, 2014
Girvan, Sir (Frederick) Paul, 2007
Glennie, Hon. Lord (Angus Glennie), 2016
Gloster, Dame Elizabeth, 2013
Goldring, Sir John, 2008
Goldsmith, Lord, 2002
Goldsmith of Richmond Park, Lord, 2019
Goodlad, Lord, 1992
Goodwill, Robert, 2018
Gove, Michael, 2010
Gowrie, Earl of, 1984
Graham, Sir Douglas, 1998
Grayling, Chris, 2010
Green, Damian, 2012
Green, Sir Nicholas, 2018
Greening, Justine, 2011
Grieve, Dominic, 2010
Grocott, Lord, 2002
Gross, Sir Peter, 2010
Gummer, Ben, 2016
Haddon-Cave, Sir Charles, 2018
Hague of Richmond, Lord, 1995
Hailsham, Viscount, 1992
Hain, Lord, 2001
Hale of Richmond, Baroness, 1999
Halfon, Robert, 2015

Hamilton, Hon. Lord (Arthur Hamilton), 2002
Hamilton of Epsom, Lord, 1991
Hammond of Runnymede, Lord, 2010
Hancock, Matthew, 2014
Hands, Gregory, 2014
Hanley, Sir Jeremy, 1994
Hanson, Sir David, 2007
Hardie, Lord, 1997
Hardie Boys, Sir Michael, 1989
Harman, Harriet, 1997
Harper, Mark, 2015
Hart, Simon, 2019
Haselhurst, Lord, 1999
Hattersley, Lord, 1975
Hayes, Sir John, 2013
Hayman, Baroness, 2000
Heald, Sir Oliver, 2016
Healey, John, 2008
Heath, David, 2015
Heathcoat-Amory, David, 1996
Henderson, Sir Launcelot, 2016
Hendry, Charles, 2015
Henley, Lord, 2013
Henry, John, 1996
Herbertof South Downs Lord, 2010
Heseltine, Lord, 1979
Heseltine, Sir William, 1986
Hesketh, Lord, 1991
Hewitt, Patricia, 2001
Hickinbottom, Sir Gary, 2017
Higgins, Lord, 1979
Higgins, Sir Malachy, 2007
Hill, Keith, 2003
Hill of Oareford, Lord, 2013
Hinds, Damian, 2018
Hodge, Dame Margaret, 2003
Hodge, Lord, 2013
Hoffmann, Lord, 1992
Holroyde, Sir Timothy, 2017
Hoon, Geoffrey, 1999
Hooper, Sir Anthony, 2004
Hope of Craighead, Lord, 1989
Hope of Thornes, Lord, 1991
Hordern, Sir Peter, 1993
Howard of Lympne, Lord, 1990
Howarth, Sir George, 2005
Howarth of Newport, Lord, 2000
Howe, Earl, 2013
Howell of Guildford, Lord, 1979
Howells, Kim, 2009
Hoyle, Sir Lindsay, 2013
Hughes, Sir Simon, 2010
Hughes of Ombersley, Lord, 2006
Hughes of Stretford, Baroness, 2004
Hunt, Jeremy, 2010
Hunt, Jonathon, 1989
Hunt of Kings Heath, Lord, 2009
Hunt of Wirral, Lord, 1990
Hurd, Nicholas, 2017
Hurd of Westwell, Lord, 1982
Hutchison, Sir Michael, 1995
Hutton of Furness, Lord, 2001
Inge, Lord, 2004
Ingraham, Hubert, 1993
Ingram, Adam, 1999
Irvine of Lairg, Lord, 1997
Irwin, Sir Stephen, 2016
Jack, Alister, 2019
Jack, Michael, 1997
Jackson, Sir Peter, 2017
Jackson, Sir Rupert, 2008

Jacob, Sir Robert, 2004
Jacobs, Francis, 2005
Janvrin, Lord, 1998
Javid, Sajid, 2014
Jay of Paddington, Baroness, 1998
Jenrick, Robert, 2019
Johnson, Alan, 2003
Johnson, Boris, 2016
Johnson of Marylebone, 2019
Jones, Carwyn, 2010
Jones, David, 2012
Jones, Kevan, 2018
Jones, Lord, 1999
Jopling, Lord, 1979
Judge, Lord, 1996
Jugnauth, Sir Anerood, 1987
Kakkar, Lord, 2014
Kay, Sir Maurice, 2004
Keen of Elie, Lord, 2017
Keene, Sir David, 2000
Keith, Sir Kenneth, 1998
Kelly, Ruth, 2004
Kennedy, Jane, 2003
Kennedy, Sir Paul, 1992
Kerr of Tonaghmore, Lord, 2004
Khan, Sadiq, 2009
Kilmorey, Earl of, 1994
King, Dame Eleanor, 2014
King of Bridgwater, Lord, 1979
Kingarth, *Hon.* Lord (Derek Emslie), 2006
Kinnock, Lord, 1983
Kitchin, Lord, 2011
Knight, Sir Gregory, 1995
Knight of Weymouth, Lord, 2008
Kramer, Baroness, 2014
Kwarteng, Kwasi, 2019
Laing, Dame Eleanor, 2017
Lamb, Sir Norman, 2014
Laming, Lord, 2014
Lammy, David, 2008
Lamont of Lerwick, Lord, 1986
Lancaster of Kimbolton, Lord, 2017
Lang of Monkton, Lord, 1990
Lansley, Lord, 2010
Latasi, Sir Kamuta, 1996
Latham, Sir David, 2000
Laws, David, 2010
Lawson of Blaby, Lord, 1981
Leadsom, Andrea, 2016
Leggatt, Lord George, 2018
Leigh, Sir Edward, 2019
Letwin, Sir Oliver, 2002
Leveson, Sir Brian, 2006
Lewis, Brandon, 2016
Lewis, Dr Clive, 2020
Lewis, Dr Julian, 2015
Lewison, Sir Kim, 2011
Liddell of Coatdyke, Baroness, 1998
Lidington, Sir David, 2010
Lilley, Lord, 1990
Lindblom, Sir Keith, 2015
Llewellyn of Steep, Lord, 2015
Lloyd, Sir Peter, 1994
Lloyd, Sir Timothy, 2005
Lloyd of Berwick, Lord, 1984
Lloyd-Jones, Lord, 2012
Llwyd, Elfyn, 2011
Longmore, Sir Andrew, 2001
Lothian, Marquess of, 1996
Luce, Lord, 1986
Lyne, Sir Roderic, 2009

McAvoy, Lord, 2003
McCartney, Sir Ian, 1999
McCloskey, Sir Bernard, 2019
McCollum, Sir Liam, 1997
McCombe, Sir Richard, 2012
McConnell of Glenscorrodale, Lord, 2001
MacDermott, Sir John, 1987
Macdonald of Tradeston, Lord, 1999
McDonnell, John, 2016
McFadden, Patrick, 2008
McFall of Alcluith, Lord, 2004
McFarlane, Sir Andrew, 2011
MacGregor of Pulham Market, Lord, 1985
McGuire, Dame Anne, 2008
Macintosh, Kenneth, 2016
Mackay, Andrew, 1998
Mackay of Clashfern, Lord, 1979
McKinnon, Sir Donald, 1992
Maclean, *Hon.* Lord (Ranald MacLean), 2001
McLeish, Henry, 2000
McLoughlin, Lord, 2005
McNally, Lord, 2005
McNulty, Anthony, 2007
Mactaggart, Fiona, 2015
Macur, Dame Julia, 2013
McVey, Esther, 2014
Major, Sir John, 1987
Malcolm, *Hon.* Lord (Colin Campbell), 2015
Males, Sir Stephen, 2019
Malloch-Brown, Lord, 2007
Mance, Lord, 1999
Mandelson, Lord, 1998
Marnoch, *Hon.* Lord (Michael Marnoch), 2001
Marwick, Tricia, 2012
Mates, Michael, 2004
Maude of Horsham, Lord, 1992
May, Sir Anthony, 1998
May, Theresa, 2003
Mellor, David, 1990
Menzies, *Hon.* Lord (Duncan Menzies), 2012
Michael, Alun, 1998
Milburn, Alan, 1998
Miliband, David, 2005
Miliband, Ed, 2007
Miller, Maria, 2012
Millett, Lord, 1994
Milling, Amanda, 2020
Milton, Anne, 2015
Mitchell, Andrew, 2010
Mitchell, Sir James, 1985
Mitchell, Dr Keith, 2004
Moore, Michael, 2010
Moore-Bick, Sir Martin, 2005
Morauta, Sir Mekere, 2001
Mordaunt, Penny, 2017
Morgan, Sir Declan, 2009
Morgan of Cotes, Baroness Nicola, 2014
Morris of Aberavon, Lord, 1970
Morris of Yardley, Baroness, 1999
Morritt, Sir Robert, 1994
Moses, Sir Alan, 2005
Moylan, Sir Andrew, 2017
Mulholland, Frank, 2011
Mullally, Rt. Revd Dame Sarah, 2018
Mummery, Sir John, 1996

Munby, Sir James, 2009
Mundell, David, 2010
Murphy, James, 2008
Murphy of Torfaen, Lord, 1999
Murrison, Dr Andrew, 2019
Musa, Wilbert, 2005
Namaliu, Sir Rabbie, 1989
Naseby, Lord, 1994
Neuberger of Abbotsbury, Lord, 2004
Neville-Jones, Baroness, 2010
Newby, Lord, 2014
Newey, Sir Guy, 2017
Nicholson, Sir Michael, 1995
Nimmo Smith, *Hon.* Lord (William Nimmo Smith), 2005
Nokes, Caroline, 2018
Norman, Jesse, 2019
Northover, Baroness, 2015
Nott, Sir John, 1979
Nugee, Sir Christopher, 2020
O'Brien, Mike, 2009
O'Brien, Sir Stephen, 2013
Oppenheim-Barnes, Baroness, 1979
Osborne, George, 2010
Osborne, *Hon.* Lord (Kenneth Osborne), 2001
Ottaway, Sir Richard, 2013
Otton, Sir Philip, 1995
Owen, Lord, 1976
Paeniu, Bikenibeu, 1991
Paice, Sir James, 2010
Palmer, Sir Geoffrey, 1986
Paraskeva, Dame Janet, 2010
Parker, Sir Jonathan, 2000
Patel, Priti, 2015
Paterson, Owen, 2010
Paton, *Hon.* Lady (Ann Paton), 2007
Patten, Lord, 1990
Patten, Sir Nicholas, 2009
Patten of Barnes, Lord, 1989
Patterson, Percival, 1993
Pattie, Sir Geoffrey, 1987
Paul, Lord, 2009
Peel, Earl, 2006
Pendry, Lord, 2000
Penning, Sir Mike, 2014
Penrose, *Hon.* Lord (George Penrose), 2000
Pentland, *Hon.* Lord (Paul Cullen), 2020
Perry, Claire, 2018
Peters, Winston, 1998
Philip, *Hon.* Lord (Alexander Philip), 2005
Phillips, Sir Stephen, 2020
Phillips of Worth Matravers, Lord, 1995
Pickles, Lord, 2010
Pill, Sir Malcolm, 1995
Pincher, Christopher, 2018
Popplewell, Sir Andrew, 2019
Portillo, Michael, 1992
Potter, Sir Mark, 1996
Prashar, Baroness, 2009
Primarolo, Baroness, 2002
Puapua, Sir Tomasi, 1982
Purnell, James, 2007
Quin, Baroness, 1998
Raab, Dominic, 2018
Radice, Lord, 1999
Rafferty, Dame Anne, 2011
Randall of Uxbridge, Lord, 2010

Raynsford, Nick, 2001
Redwood, Sir John, 1993
Rees-Mogg, Jacob, 2019
Reid, Sir George, 2004
Reid of Cardowan, Lord, 1998
Richards, Sir David, 2016
Richards, Sir Stephen, 2005
Riddell, Peter, 2010
Rifkind, Sir Malcolm, 1986
Rimer, Sir Colin, 2007
Rix, Sir Bernard, 2000
Robathan, Lord, 2010
Robertson, Angus, 2015
Robertson, Sir Hugh, 2012
Robertson of Port Ellen, Lord, 1997
Robinson, Peter, 2007
Roch, Sir John, 1993
Rodgers of Quarry Bank, Lord, 1975
Rooker, Lord, 1999
Rose, Sir Christopher, 1992
Rose, Dame Vivien, 2019
Ross, *Hon.* Lord (Donald MacArthur), 1985
Royall of Blaisdon, Baroness, 2008
Rudd, Amber, 2015
Ruddock, Dame Joan, 2010
Ryan, Joan, 2007
Ryder, Sir Ernest, 2013
Ryder of Wensum, Lord, 1990
Sainsbury, Sir Timothy, 1992
Salisbury, Marquess of, 1994
Salmond, Alex, 2007
Sandiford, Lloyd Erskine, 1989
Saville of Newdigate, Lord, 1994
Saville Roberts, Elizabeth, 2019
Sawyer, Dame Joan, 2004
Schiemann, Sir Konrad, 1995
Scotland of Asthal, Baroness, 2001
Scott of Foscote, Lord, 1991
Sedley, Sir Stephen, 1999
Selkirk of Douglas, Lord, 1996
Sentamu, Rt. revd John, 2005
Shapps, Grant, 2010
Sharma, Alok, 2019
Sharp, Dame Victoria, 2013
Sheil, Sir John, 2005
Shelbrooke, Alec, 2019
Shephard of Northwold, Baroness, 1992
Shipley, Jennifer, 1998
Short, Clare, 1997
Shutt of Greetland, Lord, 2009
Simler, Dame Ingrid, 2019
Simmonds, Sir Kennedy, 1984
Simmonds, Mark, 2014
Simon, Sir Peregrine, 2015
Simpson, Keith, 2015
Sinclair, Ian, 1977

Singh, Sir Rabinder, 2017
Skidmore, Chris, 2019
Slade, Sir Christopher, 1982
Smith, Andrew, 1997
Smith, *Hon.* Lady (Anne Smith), 2013
Smith, Jacqueline, 2003
Smith, Dame Janet, 2002
Smith, Julian, 2017
Smith of Basildon, Baroness, 2009
Smith of Finsbury, Lord, 1997
Soames, Sir Nicholas, 2011
Somare, Sir Michael, 1977
Sopoaga, Enele, 2018
Soubry, Anna, 2015
Spellar, John, 2001
Spelman, Dame Caroline, 2010
Spencer, Mark, 2019
Stanley, Sir John, 1984
Starmer, Sir Keir, 2017
Steel of Aikwood, Lord, 1977
Stephens of Creevyloughgare, Lord, 2017
Stewart, Rory, 2019
Stowell of Beeston, Baroness, 2014
Strang, Gavin, 1997
Strathclyde, Lord, 1995
Straw, Jack, 1997
Stride, Melvyn, 2017
Stuart, Freundel, 2013
Stuart of Edgbaston, Baroness, 2015
Stuart-Smith, Sir Jeremy, 2020
Stuart-Smith, Sir Murray, 1988
Stunell, Lord, 2012
Sturgeon, Nicola, 2014
Sullivan, Sir Jeremy, 2009
Sumption, Lord, 2011
Sunak, Rishi, 2019
Sutherland, *Hon.* Lord (Ranald Sutherland), 2000
Swayne, Sir Desmond, 2011
Swire, Sir Hugo, 2010
Symons of Vernham Dean, Baroness, 2001
Tami, Mark, 2018
Taylor of Bolton, Baroness, 1997
Taylor of Holbeach, Lord, 2014
Tebbit, Lord, 1981
Thirlwall, Dame Kathryn, 2017
Thomas, Edmund, 1996
Thomas of Cwmgiedd, Lord, 2003
Thornberry, Emily, 2017
Thorpe, Sir Matthew, 1995
Thurso, Viscount, 2014
Timms, Stephen, 2006
Tipping, Andrew, 1998
Tomlinson, Sir Stephen, 2010
Touhig, Lord, 2006
Treacy, Sir Colman, 2012

Trefgarne, Lord, 1989
Trevelyan, Anne-Marie, 2020
Trimble, Lord, 1997
Truss, Elizabeth, 2014
Tuckey, Sir Simon, 1998
Turnbull, Lord, 2016
Tyler, Lord, 2014
Tyrie, Lord, 2015
Ullswater, Viscount, 1994
Underhill, Sir Nicholas, 2013
Upton, Simon, 1999
Vadera, Baroness, 2009
Vaizey of Didcot, Lord, 2016
Vaz, Keith, 2006
Vaz, Valerie, 2019
Villiers, Theresa, 2010
Vos, Sir Geoffrey, 2013
Waite, Sir John, 1993
Wakeham, Lord, 1983
Waldegrave of North Hill, Lord, 1990
Walker of Gestingthorpe, Lord, 1997
Wallace, Ben, 2017
Wallace of Saltaire, Lord, 2012
Wallace of Tankerness, Lord, 2000
Waller, Sir Mark, 1996
Ward, Sir Alan, 1995
Warner, Lord, 2006
Warsi, Baroness, 2010
Weatherup, Sir Ronald, 2016
Webb, Sir Steven, 2014
Weir, Sir Reginald, 2016
West of Spithead, Lord, 2010
Wheatley, *Hon.* Lord (John Wheatley), 2007
Wheeler, Sir John, 1993
Whittingdale, John, 2015
Whitty, Lord, 2005
Widdecombe, Ann, 1997
Wigley, Lord, 1997
Willetts, Lord, 2010
Williams of Crosby, Baroness, 1974
Williams of Oystermouth, Lord, 2002
Williamson, Gavin, 2015
Willott, Jennifer, 2014
Wills, Lord, 2008
Wilson, Brian, 2003
Wilson, Sammy, 2017
Wilson of Culworth, Lord, 2005
Wingti, Paias, 1987
Winterton, Dame Rosie, 2006
Wolffe, James, 2016
Woodward, Shaun, 2007
Woolf, Lord, 1986
Woolman, *Hon.* Lord (Stephen Woolman), 2020
Wright, Jeremy, 2014
York, Archbishop of, 2020
Young, Edward, 2017
Young of Cookham, Lord, 1993
Young of Graffham, Lord, 1984

PRIVY COUNCIL OF NORTHERN IRELAND

The Privy Council of Northern Ireland had responsibilities in Northern Ireland similar to those of the Privy Council in Great Britain until the Northern Ireland Act 1974. Membership of the Privy Council of Northern Ireland is retained for life. Since the Northern Ireland Constitution Act 1973 no further appointments have been made. The post-nominal initials PC (NI) are used to differentiate its members from those of the Privy Council.

MEMBERS *as at 10 September 2019*
Bailie, Robin, 1971
Dobson, John, 1969
Kilclooney, Lord, 1970

PARLIAMENT

PARLIAMENT IN 2019–20

By Patrick Robathan

Following his larger than expected election victory on 12 December 2019 (majority of 80), Prime Minister Boris Johnson promised that 2020 would be the year the UK finally 'got Brexit done' and that he would instigate his 'levelling up agenda.' What he could not have foreseen was COVID-19. Although he did secure a deal on the UK's exit from the EU at almost the last moment, Parliamentary business was disrupted and dominated by the pandemic. Parliament sat an exceptionally long time in 2020, for 40 weeks, which was the highest since 2010.

The Queen's Speech on 19 December set out plans to 'take us out of the EU, overhaul our immigration system, enshrine in law record investment for the NHS… it will take our country forward with an ambitious One Nation programme to unite and spread opportunity to every corner of our United Kingdom.' It included plans for some 36 Bills. Labour leader Jeremy Corbyn complained 'this Speech shows that what the Government are actually proposing is woefully inadequate for the scale of the problems.' Boris Johnson felt 'as we engage full tilt now in this mission of change, I am filled with invincible confidence in the ability of this nation, our United Kingdom, to renew itself in this generation as we have done so many times in the past. After the dither, after the delay, after the deadlock and after the paralysis and the platitudes, the time has come for change and it is action that the British people will get.' Unusually instead of immediately debating the Queen's Speech on 20 December the House approved the second reading of European Union (Withdrawal Agreement) Bill by 358 votes to 234 and spent the first three days after the Christmas Recess (7/8/9 January) completing consideration of the Bill. On 7 January Defence Secretary Ben Wallace made a statement on the security situation in the Middle East. On 9 January Sports Minister Nigel Adams responded to an urgent question (UQ) from Labour's Carolyn Harris on the deal between the Football Association and Bet365 to screen live football matches. Foreign Office Minister Heather Wheeler made a statement on the Australian Bushfires.

On 13 January MPs returned to the debate on the Queen's Speech and after four days it was passed by 334 votes to 247 on 20 January. On 13 January Foreign Secretary Dominic Raab responded to UQ from Conservative Tobias Ellwood on Iran. On 14 January Transport Minister Paul Maynard replied to UQ from Conservative Caroline Nokes on support available to help Flybe, followed by a statement on the Iran nuclear agreement (Joint Comprehensive Plan of Action) by Dominic Raab. On 16 January Northern Ireland Secretary Julian Smith made a statement on formation of Northern Ireland Executive, followed by Housing, Communities and Local Government Secretary Robert Jenrick on a package of reforms to building safety. On 22 January Minister for Security Brandon Lewis responded to UQ from Shadow Home Secretary Diane Abbott on the Prevent programme. On 23 January Health and Social Care Secretary Matt Hancock made the first statement on the outbreak of a new coronavirus in Wuhan, China.

On 27 January DCMS Minister Matt Warman replied to UQ from Conservative Tom Tugendhat on Huawei's involvement in the UK's 5G network, followed by Minister Policing Kit Malthouse responded to UQ from Lib Dem Sarah Olney on Automated Facial Recognition Surveillance. On 28 January Culture Secretary Lady Morgan of Coates made a statement in the Lords on the security of the telecoms supply chain, 'we will do three things simultaneously: seek to attract established vendors to our country who are not present in the UK; support the emergence of new, disruptive entrants to the supply chain; and promote the adoption of open, interoperable standards that will reduce barriers to entry.' On 30 January Foreign Office Minister Andrew Murrison replied to UQ from Shadow Foreign Secretary Emily Thornberry on President Trump's proposed Middle East peace plan.

On 3 February Dominic Raab made a statement on global Britain, 'now is the time to put our differences aside and come together, so together let us embrace a new chapter for our country, let us move forward united and unleash the enormous potential of the British people, and let us show the world that our finest achievements and our greatest contributions lie ahead.' This was followed by Matt Hancock with an update on the ongoing situation with the Wuhan coronavirus, 'close contacts will be given health advice about symptoms and emergency contact details to use, should they become unwell in the next 14 days. These tried and tested methods of infection control will ensure that we minimise the risk to the public.' Justice Secretary Robert Buckland made a statement about the terror attack in Streatham the previous day. On 4 February for Work and Pensions Minister Will Quince replied to UQ from SNP's Neil Gray on the delay to the full roll-out of Universal Credit, followed by Cabinet Office Minister Chloe Smith responding to UQ from Labour DCMS spokesperson Tracy Brabin on barring of certain journalists from official civil servant media briefings at the direction of special advisers and the arrangements for future lobby and media briefings, followed by a statement from Health Minister Nadine Dorries on the publication of the independent inquiry into disgraced surgeon, Ian Paterson. On 6 February Nigel Adams replied to UQ from Tracy Brabin on plans for BBC Licence Fee.

On 10 February Home Office Minister Kevin Foster responded to UQ from Labour's David Lammy on deportation flights to Jamaica, followed by a statement from Environment Secretary Theresa Villiers on flood response following Storm Ciara. On 11 February Boris Johnson made a statement on transport Infrastructure, 'a new anatomy of British transport— a revolution in the nation's public transport provision. It will be a sign to the world that, in the 21st century, this UK still has the vision to dream big dreams and the courage to bring those dreams about', followed by Matt Hancock updating the House on the Wuhan coronavirus. On 13 February Matt Warman replied to UQ from Conservative Julian Knight on plans for online harms legislation, followed by Nadine Dorries replying to UQ from Conservative Sir Roger Gale on provision and safety of maternity services in East Kent.

After the half-term recess on 24 February Foreign Office Minister James Cleverly replied to UQ from Tobias Ellwood on Syria, followed by a statement from Home Secretary Priti Patel on new points-based immigration system, followed by new Environment Secretary George Eustice on flooding caused by Storm Dennis. On 26 February former Home Secretary, Said Javid, made a personal statement following his resignation from the Government, followed by Matt Hancock with an update on COVID-19. On 27 February Chancellor of the Duchy of Lancaster Michael Gove made a statement on the future relationship with the EU, 'we got Brexit done, and we will use our recovered sovereignty to be a force for good in the world and a fairer nation at home. We want and we will always seek the best possible relationship with our friends and allies in Europe, but we will always put the welfare of the British people first. That means ensuring the British people exercise the democratic control over our destiny for which they voted so decisively.' This was followed by statements from Robert Jenrick on rough sleeping and Home Office Minister Victoria Atkins on child protection.

On 2 March Michael Gove replied to UQ from Jeremy Corbyn on apparent breaches of Ministerial Code following the resignation of Sir Philip Rutnam as Permanent Secretary at Home Office. This was followed by Transport Minister Kelly Tolhurst responding UQ from Labour Transport spokesperson Andy McDonald on airport expansion and then newly appointed Foreign Office Minister Nigel Adams to UQ from Labour's Tulip Siddiq on British citizens imprisoned abroad in countries where coronavirus was spreading rapidly. International Trade Secretary Liz Truss made a statement on UK-US Trade Deal. On 3 March Nigel Adams replied to UQ from Labour's Khalid Mahmood on violence in India and Matt Hancock made a statement about the Government's coronavirus action plan. On 4 March former Leader of the House Andrea Leadsom made a personal statement following her resignation from the Government. On 5 March Kelly Tolhurst made a statement on the collapse of Flybe.

On 9 March Matt Hancock responded to UQ from his Labour Shadow Jonathan Ashworth updating the House on the coronavirus, 'in the UK, as of this morning, there were 319 confirmed cases. Very sadly, this now includes four confirmed deaths. I entirely understand why people are worried and concerned.' On 10 March Nigel Adams replied to UQ from SNP spokesperson Joanna Cherry on refugees at Turkey-Greece border. On 11 March Chancellor of the Exchequer Rishi Sunak delivered his first Budget statement, 'from our national infrastructure strategy to social care and further devolution, this is the Budget of a Government that get things done—creating jobs, cutting taxes, keeping the cost of living low, investing in our NHS, investing in our public services, investing in ideas, backing business, protecting our environment, building roads, building railways, building colleges, building houses and building our Union.' He announced a £30bn package to boost the economy and get the country through the coronavirus outbreak; a suspension of business rates for many firms, extending sick pay and boosting NHS funding, with £12bn specifically targeted at coronavirus measures, including at least £5bn for the NHS and £7bn for business and workers across the UK.

Jeremy Corbyn did not agree. 'The reality is that this Budget is an admission of failure: an admission that austerity has been a failed experiment. It did not solve our economic problems but made them worse. It held back our own recovery and failed even in its own terms.' After four days of debate the Budget was approved on 18 March, The Finance Bill had its second reading on 24 March with third reading completed on 2 July and it gained Royal Assent on 22 July. Also on 11 March Matt Hancock updated the House on the day that the World Health Organisation declared coronavirus a global pandemic, 'we have resolved that we will keep Parliament open. Of course, in some ways this House may have to function differently, but the ability to hold the Government to account and to legislate are as vital in a time of emergency as in normal times.' On 12 March Robert Jenrick published Planning for the Future expanding on the housing measures set out in the Budget. Veterans Minister Johnny Mercer made a statement on veterans' mental health

On 16 March Matt Hancock was allowed to interrupt business to make a statement, 'having agreed a very significant step in the actions that we are taking from within that plan to control the spread of the disease… The measures that I have outlined are unprecedented in peacetime. We are in a war against an invisible killer and we have to do everything we can

to stop it.' Speaker Sir Lindsey Hoyle made a statement on how Parliament would function under the new rules. On 17 March Dominic Raab made a statement advising British nationals against non-essential travel globally, for an initial period of 30 days. On 18 March Education Secretary Gavin Williamson made a statement on changes to the operations of educational settings as a result of the pandemic. On 19 March Economic Secretary to the Treasury John Glen replied to UQ from Conservative Greg Clark on support for wages of employees. Priti Patel made a statement on the Windrush lessons learned review, 'the publication of this review is a small but vital step towards ensuring that the Home Office is trusted by all the people it serves. I encourage anyone who thinks that they have been affected by the Windrush scandal or who requires support or assistance to come forward.' It was agreed that there should be no sittings in Westminster Hall with effect from Friday 20 March until the House otherwise ordered.

On 23 March the Speaker updated MPs on plans for Parliament in lockdown. The Government introduced the Coronavirus Bill which received an unopposed Second Reading and completed all its Common's stages in one day. It was taken in the Lords on 24/25 March and received Royal Assent on 26 March. On 24 March Chief Secretary to the Treasury Steve Barclay responded to UQ from Lib Dem interim leader Sir Edward Davey on financial support for the self-employed in the light of the pandemic. Dominc Raab responded to UQ from Caroline Nokes on measures to assist British citizens abroad to return home. Matt Hancock gave an update, 'our instruction is simple: stay at home. People should only leave their home for one of four reasons: first, to shop for basic necessities, such as food, as infrequently as possible; secondly, to exercise once a day, for example a run, walk or cycle, alone or with members of the same household; thirdly, for any medical need, or to provide care or help to a vulnerable person; and fourthly, to travel to and from work, but only where it cannot be done from home, and employers should be taking every possible step to ensure that staff can work remotely.' On 25 March the Speaker allowed a longer than usual PMQs, 'to serve as an effective replacement for separate statements on the situation of coronavirus.' Friday sittings in the Commons were postponed by at least a month.

On 27 March Rishi Sunak updated the House on the economic response to coronavirus, 'right now, the most important thing for the health of our economy is the health of our people. Our strategy is to protect people and businesses through this crisis, by backing our public services and NHS with increased funding, strengthening our safety net to support those most in need, and supporting people to stay in work and keep their businesses going. Our response is comprehensive, coherent and co-ordinated.' The Finance Bill received an unopposed Second Reading. On 28 April the House observed one-minute's silence to reflect on the sacrifices being made by so many, Michael Gove made a statement on support for public services through the pandemic. On 29 April Nigel Adams made a statement on repatriation of UK Nationals in response to the pandemic.

Returning from the Easter Recess on 21 April MPs passed a motion to allow virtual participation in the House's proceedings and agreed to meet only on Mondays, Tuesdays and Wednesdays. On 22 April newly elected Labour leader Sir Keir Starmer had his first outing at PMQs but faced Dominic Raab as Boris Johnson was in hospital with COVID-19. Matt Hancock gave an update on coronavirus.

On 4 May Work and Pensions Secretary Thérèse Coffey made a statement on the work her Department were doing to provide help to those in need during the pandemic. On 5 May Matt Hancock updated Jonathan Ashworth on the Government's response, 'we have flattened the curve of this epidemic, ensured that the NHS is not overwhelmed and expanded testing capacity to over 100,000 tests a day… we have now built a national testing infrastructure of scale and will be delivering up to 30,000 tests a day to residents and staff in elderly care homes… and we are working to build the resilience of the NHS.' On 6 May the Speaker announced that remote voting would be introduced. Boris Johnson and Sir Keir Starmer had their first face to face PMQs. BEIS Minister Paul Scully responded to UQ from Andy McDonald on guidelines for workplace safety after the lifting of lockdown. International Development Secretary Anne-Marie Trevelyan updated the House on the UK's support for the global effort to tackle the pandemic.

On 11 May Boris Johnson made a statement about the next steps in the battle against coronavirus 'and how we can, with the utmost caution, gradually begin to rebuild our economy and reopen our society.' Conservative Greg Hands made a personal statement apologizing for his misuse of parliamentary stationery. MPs agreed to suspend Conservative Conor Burns from the House for a period of seven days following the recommendations of the Standards Committee into his conduct. On 12 May Rishi Sunak replied to an urgent question from Shadow Chancellor Anneliese Dodds on the Government's economic package in response to the outbreak, 'one of the most comprehensive anywhere in the world. We have provided billions of pounds of cash grants, tax cuts and loans for over 1 million businesses, tens of billions of pounds of deferred taxes, income protection for millions of the self-employed, and a strengthened safety net to protect millions of our most vulnerable people.' Business Secretary Alok Sharma updated the House on the Government's new COVID-19-secure workplace guidance. Transport Secretary Grant Shapps made a statement about the new transport guidance for passengers and operators. On 13 May Gavin Williamson replied to UQ from Lib Dem Education spokesperson Layla Moran on plans to reopen schools as part of the Government's recovery strategy. Robert Jenrick made a statement on COVID-19 and the housing market. The Speaker made a statement on the likely duration of hybrid proceedings and ensuring that those on the estate were safe while business is facilitated.

On 18 May Matt Hancock updated MPs, 'the number of people in hospital with coronavirus is half what it was at the peak…the number of patients in critical care is down by two thirds. Mercifully, the number of deaths across all settings is falling.' On 19 May the Speaker told the Government that it was unacceptable that answering written questions in a timely manner had not continued, 'the Government simply must do better.' Matt Hancock replied to UQ from Labour' Liz Kendall on coronavirus and care homes. Michael Gove responded to UQ from his Shadow Rachel Reeves on the third round of the negotiations on the UK's future relationship with the EU. On 20 May Leader of the House Jacob Rees-Mogg replied to UQ from Lib Dem Chief Whip Alistair Carmichael on conduct of business in the Commons after the Whitsun recess and the necessary motions to continue the online participation of Members. Michael Gove made a statement on the Government's approach to implementing the Northern Ireland protocol as part of the withdrawal agreement with the EU.

Returning from the Whitsun Recess on 2 June Dominic Raab updated the House on UK response to Hong Kong national security legislation. Matt Hancock updated MPs on coronavirus. MPs approved the rules for proceedings during the pandemic. On 3 June Kelly Tolhurst responded to UQ from Conservative Huw Merriman on COVID-19 and the economic impact on aviation. Priti Patel made a statement about the introduction of public health measures at the border in response to coronavirus. On 4 June Minister for Equalities Kemi Badenoch replied to UQ from Labour's Gill Furniss on Public Health England's review of disparities in risks and

outcomes related to the COVID-19. Northern Ireland Minister Robin Walker replied to UQ from DUP Westminster leader Sir Jeffrey Donaldson on abortion regulations for Northern Ireland and then to an urgent question from Labour Northern Ireland spokesperson Louise Haigh on the implementation of the payment scheme for victims of the troubles.

On 8 June Matt Hancock replied to UQ from Jonathan Ashworth on the R value and lockdown, 'thanks to the immense national effort on social distancing, as a country we have made real progress in reducing the number of new infections.' Priti Patel made a statement on public order following demonstrations in the UK after the death of George Floyd in the USA, 'I know that it is the sense of injustice that has driven people to take to the UK streets to protest.' Alistair Carmichael was granted an emergency debate on the conduct of House business during the pandemic. On 9 June Paymaster General Penny Mordaunt replied to UQ from Rachel Reeves on the fourth round of the negotiations on the UK's future relationship with the EU. Gavin Williamson made a statement regarding the wider opening of nurseries, schools and colleges in response to the pandemic. On 10 June Paul Scully replied to UQ from Labour spokesperson Chi Onwurah on support for sub-postmasters wrongly convicted in the Post Office Horizon scandal, 'we are committed to establishing an independent review to consider whether the Post Office has learned the necessary lessons from the Horizon dispute and court case, and to provide an independent and external assessment of its work to rebuild its relationship with its postmasters.' MPs then approved an extension to proxy voting. On 11 June Minister for Housing Christopher Pincher responded to UQ from his Labour Shadow Steve Reed on maintaining public confidence in the probity of the planning process. Robert Buckland made a statement on the Government's plans for the future of probation services in England and Wales.

On 15 June Minister for Health Edward Argar replied to UQ from Greg Clark on reviewing the 2 metre social distancing rule. Priti Patel made a statement on public order following demonstrations in London on a so-called mission to protect the statue of Sir Winston Churchill. On 16 June the Speaker set out the new Division procedure and proxy voting. Financial Secretary to the Treasury Jesse Norman replied to UQ from Anneliese Dodds on the economic outlook and the strategy to protect jobs and the economy in light of upcoming changes to the furlough scheme. Boris Johnson made a statement about the ambitions of a global Britain and the lessons of the pandemic, in particular the merging of the Foreign Office and the Department for International Development. Michael Gove updated MPs on the Government's negotiations on future relationship with the EU. On 17 June Matt Hancock responded to UQ from Jonathan Ashworth on the scientific effort on vaccines. Liz Truss made a statement on UK accession to Comprehensive and Progressive Agreement for Trans-Pacific Partnership. On 18 June Dominic Raab replied to UQ from Lib Dem Wendy Chamberlain on the merger of the Department for International Development with the Foreign and Commonwealth Office.

On 22 June Priti Patel made a statement on the terror attack in Reading at the weekend. Conservative Marcus Fysh made a personal statement on his failure to register unremunerated directorships. On 23 June Boris Johnson made a statement on next steps in the plan to rebuild the economy and reopen society, while waging the struggle against COVID-19. Priti Patel made a statement on the Windrush compensation scheme, 'nothing can ever undo the suffering experienced by members of the Windrush generation. No one should have suffered the uncertainty, complication and hardships brought on by the mistakes of successive Governments. Now is the time for more action to repay that debt of gratitude and to eliminate the challenges that still exist. Only then can we build a stronger, fairer and more successful country for the next generation.' On 25 June Work and Pensions Minister Will Quince responded to UQ from Labour spokesperson Stephen Timms on the Court of Appeal decision on wronged Universal Credit claimants.

On 29 June Home Office Minister Chris Philp replied to UQ from SNP's Alison Thewliss on support and accommodation for asylum seekers during the pandemic following an incident in Glasgow at the weekend. Nigel Adams replied to UQ from Conservative Sir Iain Duncan Smith on the mistreatment by the Chinese Government of Uyghurs in Xinjiang. Later on Matt Hancock made a statement on local action to tackle coronavirus, with the number of recorded deaths at 25, so the Government had been able, carefully, to ease the national restrictions. On 30 June Michael Gove replied to UQ from Shadow Home Secretary Nick Thomas-Symonds on the appointment of the National Security Adviser. Justice Minister Alex Chalk answered UQ from David Lammy on the Government's implementation of the Lammy review, 'enormous progress has been made but… of course there is more to do.' On 1 July Dominic Raab made a statement on developments in Hong Kong, 'we want a positive relationship with China, but we will not look the other way when it comes to Hong Kong and we will not duck our historic responsibilities. We will continue to stand up for the people of Hong Kong, to call out the violations of their freedoms, and to hold China to its international obligations, freely assumed under international law.' On 2 July Gavin Williamson made a statement regarding the full opening of our schools and colleges to all pupils in September.

On 6 July Dominic Raab made a statement on global human rights sanctions regulations, with measures enacted to hold to account the perpetrators of the worst human rights abuses. On 7 July Matt Hancock responded to UQ from Jonathan Ashworth, 'we protected the NHS. We built the new Nightingale hospitals in 10 days. At all times, treatment was available for all. Our medical research has discovered the only drug known to work. We have built, almost from scratch, one of the biggest testing capabilities in the world. We are getting coronavirus cornered, but this is no time to lose our resolve. The virus exists only to spread, so we must all stay alert and enjoy summer safely.' DCMS Minister Caroline Dinenage replied to UQ from Labour Culture spokesperson Jo Stevens on support for arts, culture and heritage industries. On 8 July Rishi Sunak gave an economic update, 'it is a plan to turn our national recovery into millions of stories of personal renewal. It is our plan for jobs.' On 9 July Foreign Office Minister James Cleverly responded to UQ from Father of the House Sir Peter Bottomley on using the Government's relationship with Bahrain to raise the cases of two prisoners who had been sentenced to death. Nadine Dorries made a statement about the independent medicines and medical devices review.

On 13 July Minister for Trade Policy Greg Hands replied to UQ from Labour spokesperson Emily Thornberry on the resumption of the sale of arms to the Saudi-led coalition for use in the war in Yemen. Michael Gove made a statement on preparations for the end of the transition period. On 14 July Culture Secretary Oliver Dowden made a statement on UK telecommunications following the telecoms supply chain review to look at the long-term security of 5G and full-fibre networks. Matt Hancock then updated MPs, 'this deadly virus continues to diminish… for the third consecutive week, total deaths are lower than normal for this time of year.' On 16 July Johnny Mercer replied to UQ from Labour defence spokesperson John Healey on the Overseas Operations Bill's impact on the rights of British troops serving overseas to bring civil liability claims against the MOD and its implications for the Armed Forces Covenant. Alok Sharma published UK

Internal Market White Paper. Late on Matt Hancock made a statement on action against coronavirus and the decisions taken through the day to determine the future of the action needed in Leicester.

On 20 July Dominic Raab made a statement on the latest developments with respect to China and Hong Kong, 'we will stand up for our values, and we will hold China to its international obligations.' Matt Hancock made a further statement on action against coronavirus, which had allowed the Prime Minister to set out a conditional timetable for the further easings of the restrictions. On 21 July Culture Minister John Whittingdale replied to UQ from Lib Dem Daisy Cooper on changes to the licence fee exemptions, programming and job losses at the BBC, 'while the BBC remains operationally and editorially independent from the Government, we will continue to push it on these issues so that we can ensure that the BBC remains closer to the communities that it serves.' Priti Patel made a statement on the progress on the Windrush lessons learned review, 'we are determined to get this right… Home Office is working hard to be more diverse, more compassionate and worthy of the trust of the communities it serves.' On 22 July the Speaker announced an extension to virtual participation in Select Committee meetings. Minister for Security James Brokenshire responded to UQ from Nick Thomas-Symonds on the Intelligence and Security Committee's report into Russia. Christopher Pincher replied to UQ from Labour spokesperson Thangam Debbonaire on implications of the end of the evictions ban for people renting their home. Ben Wallace gave the regular counter-Daesh update.

Returning from the summer recess on 1 September the Speaker informed the House that a Member had been arrested in connection with an investigation into an allegation of a very serious criminal offence (no charges were subsequently made). Matt Hancock updated the House on developments over the summer, 'we will soon be launching a new campaign reminding people of how they can help to stop the spread of coronavirus: Hands, face, space and get a test if you have symptoms. As we learn more and more about this unprecedented virus, so we constantly seek to improve our response to protect the health of the nation and the things we hold dear.' Gavin Williamson made a statement about full opening of schools and colleges and updated the House on the current position regarding exam results for the year's GCSE and A-level students. On 2 September Chris Philp responded to UQ from Nick Thomas-Symonds on those crossing the English Channel in small boats, 'the majority of these crossings are facilitated by ruthless criminal gangs that make money from exploiting migrants who are desperate to come here.' Dominic Raab replied to UQ from his Labour shadow Lisa Nandy on the creation of the Foreign, Commonwealth and Development Office. On 3 September Thérèse Coffey answered UQ from Labour's Jonathan Reynolds on the implementation of the kickstart scheme.

On 7 September Grant Shapps made a statement about international travel corridors allowing people to return to the UK from low-risk countries without quarantine. Kit Malthouse made a statement on the Extinction Rebellion protests and on the incident in Birmingham over the weekend, a fatal stabbing in Lewisham and a serious shooting incident in Suffolk. On 8 September Northern Ireland Secretary Brandon Lewis responded to UQ from Louise Haigh on the UK's commitment to its legal obligations under the Northern Ireland protocol. Matt Hancock updated MPs, 'the threat posed by the virus has not gone away. Now, with winter on the horizon, we must all redouble our efforts and get this virus on the back foot.' On 10 September Matt Hancock made a further statement with a number of new measures that would help get the virus under control and to make the rules clearer, simpler and more enforceable.

On 14 September Liz Truss announced that the UK had reached agreement in principle on a free trade deal with Japan. The United Kingdom Internal Market Bill which Labour spokesperson Ed Milband felt contained 'provisions breaking international law and did not respect the devolution settlements.' received its Second Reading by 340 votes to 263. It was considered in Committee of the Whole House on 15/16/21/22 September and received a third reading on 29 September by 340 votes to 256. It was taken with second reading in the Lords 20 October, was amended in Committee between 26 October and 9 November and was given its Third reading on 2 December. The Bill 'ping-ponged' between the Houses between 8 and 16 December, before the Commons had their way and it received Royal Assent on 17 December. On 15 September Matt Hancock replied to UQ from Jonathan Ashworth, 'the challenges are serious. We must work to overcome them, optimistic in the face even of these huge challenges, and to keep this deadly virus under control.' On 16 September Robert Buckland published Sentencing White Paper. On 17 September Matt Hancock made a statement on plans to put the UK in the strongest possible position for this winter, 'we will soon be facing winter in this fight and, whether on our NHS emergency care wards or in our care homes, we will strain every sinew to give them what they need, so they are well equipped for this pandemic and, indeed, for the years ahead.'

On 21 September Matt Hancock made a further statement, 'the number of new cases in Europe is now higher than during the peak in March. The virus is spreading. We are at a tipping point. I set out today the measures the Government are taking so far. We are working right now on what further measures may be necessary.' On 22 September Boris Johnson made a statement on the response to the rising number of coronavirus cases, 'the Government will introduce new restrictions in England, carefully judged to achieve the maximum reduction in the R number with the minimum damage to lives and livelihoods.' On 23 September Christopher Pincher replied to UQ from Lib Dem Tim Farron on the end of the eviction moratorium. Michael Gove updated MPs on preparations for the end of the transition period that was just 100 days away. The House agreed to extend proxy voting. On 24 September Liz Truss (as Minister for Women and Equalities) replied to an urgent question from Conservative Crispin Blunt on the response to the consultation on the Gender Recognition Act 2004. Rishi Sunak set out the next phase of the planned economic response, 'plans that seek to strike a finely judged balance between managing the virus and protecting the jobs and livelihoods of millions.' Dominic Raab made a statement on the situation in Belarus following presidential elections in August. Conservative David Morris made a personal statement apologising for inadvertently breaching the paid advocacy rule.

On 29 September Gavin Williamson made a statement regarding the return of students to universities. On 30 September Sports Minister Nigel Huddleston replied to UQ from Conservative Tracey Crouch on support for professional and amateur sport. MPs passed Coronavirus Act 2020 (Review of Temporary Provisions) by 330 votes to 24. On 1 October Matt Hancock delivered an update and outlined a hospitality curfew, 'the second peak is highly localised, and in some parts of the country the virus is spreading fast. Our strategy is to suppress the virus, protecting the economy, education and the NHS, until a vaccine can make us safe.' Gavin Williamson made a statement regarding lifetime skills guarantee and post-16 education.

On 5 October Paul Scully responded to UQ from Labour's Kevan Jones on 44 Post Office prosecutions overturned by Criminal Cases Review Commission. Matt Hancock updated the House, 'now more than ever, with winter ahead, we must all remain vigilant and get the virus under control.' On 6 October Steve Barclay replied to UQ from Anneliese Dodds on economic support available in areas of the country subject to additional public health restrictions.

On 12 October Boris Johnson made a statement on how the Government intended to fulfil the simultaneous objectives of saving lives and protecting the NHS while keeping children in school and the economy running, 'the stark reality of the second wave of the virus is that the number of cases has quadrupled in the last three weeks…This is not how we want to live our lives, but this is the narrow path we have to tread between the social and economic trauma of a full lockdown and the massive human and, indeed, economic cost of an uncontained epidemic.' On 13 October Steve Barclay replied to UQ from Anneliese Dodds on economic support available in areas of the country subject to additional public health restrictions. The latest Coronavirus Regulations were passed by 299 votes to 82. On 15 October Matt Hancock made a further statement, 'the threat remains grave and serious. In Europe, positive cases are up 40 per cent from one week ago, and in Italy, Belgium and the Netherlands, they have doubled in the last fortnight. Here, we sadly saw the highest figure for daily deaths since early June… I know that those measures are not easy, but I also know that they are vital.'

On 19 October Michael Gove updated the House on the Government's negotiations with the EU on future trading relationships and the work of the UK/EU Joint Committee. Matt Hancock made a further statement, 'as winter draws in, the virus is on the offensive: 40 million coronavirus cases have now been recorded worldwide. Weekly deaths in Europe have increased by 33 per cent and here in the UK, deaths have tragically doubled in the last 12 days. The situation remains perilous.' On 20 October Matt Hancock made a late statement, 'it is the penetration of coronavirus into older age groups that gives the NHS the greatest cause for concern.' On 21 October Edward Argar made a statement on restrictions in South Yorkshire. On 22 October Rishi Sunak delivered an economic update, 'we have an economic plan that will protect the jobs and livelihoods of the British people, wherever they live and whatever their situation… we will listen and respond to people's concerns as the situation demands.' Kemi Badenoch made a statement on the disparate impact of COVID-19.

Returning from a short recess on 2 November Boris Johnson was told off by the Speaker for letting the main elements of his statement be announced over the weekend, welcoming the announcement of a leak inquiry. Boris Johnson made his statement on measures the UK must take to contain the autumn surge, protect the NHS and save lives, 'the R is still above one in every part of England—as it is across much of Europe—and the virus is spreading even faster than the reasonable worst-case scenario.' On 3 November Steve Barclay responded to UQ from Anneliese Dodds on economic support available during and after the recently announced lockdown. James Cleverly replied to UQ from Tulip Siddiq on Nazanin Zaghari-Ratcliffe. Labour's Dr Rosena Allin-Khan made a personal statement apologising for the inappropriate use of House stationery for a third time. On 5 November Matt Hancock replied to an urgent question from Conservative Andrew Mitchell on the impact of new coronavirus regulations on terminally ill adults travelling abroad for an assisted death. Rishi Sunak gave an economic update, 'we are providing significant extra support to protect jobs and livelihoods in every region and nation of UK: an extension to the coronavirus job retention scheme; more generous support to the self-employed and paying that support more quickly; cash grants of up to £3,000 per month for businesses that are closed, worth over a billion pounds every month; £1.6 billion for English councils to support their local economy and local healthcare response; longer to apply for our loan schemes and the future fund; the chance to top up bounce back loans; and an extension to mortgage payment holidays. That is all on top of more than £200 billion of fiscal support since March.' James Brokenshire made a statement regarding the terrorism threat level, following recent events in France and Vienna.

On 9 November Foreign Office Minister Wendy Morton responded to UQ from Caroline Nokes on steps taken to secure the return of Jonathan Taylor to the UK in order to complete inquiries into corruption by SBM Offshore. Rishi Sunak updated the House on plans for financial services, 'they will be essential to our economic recovery from coronavirus, creating jobs and growth right across our country. As we leave the EU and start a new chapter in the history of financial services in this country, we want to renew the UK's position as the world's pre-eminent financial centre.' Thérèse Coffey made a statement on supporting disadvantaged families. On 10 November Defence Minister Jeremy Quin replied to UQ from John Healey on deployment of the armed forces to assist civilian authorities in dealing with the continuing pandemic. Matt Hancock updated the House, 'this is a disease that strikes at what it is to be human, at the social bonds that unite us. We must come together as one to defeat this latest threat to humanity. There are many hard days ahead, many hurdles to overcome, but our plan is working. I am more sure than ever that we will prevail together.' On 11 November now Housing Minister Kelly Tolhurst replied to UQ from Thangam Debbonaire on preventing homelessness and protecting rough sleepers during the second national lockdown. On 12 November Nigel Adams replied to UQ from Layla Moran on disqualification of pro-democracy lawmakers in Hong Kong, 'yesterday was another sad day for the people of Hong Kong.' Oliver Dowden outlined the Government's plans to mark HM the Queen's platinum jubilee in 2022.

On 16 November Jacob Rees-Mogg responded to UQ from Conservative John Baron on participation in debates, 'the clinically extremely vulnerable should not go into work, we should work with the House authorities to find a solution.' On 17 November Trade Minister Greg Hands replied to UQ from Emily Thornberry on parliamentary scrutiny of future Continuity Trade Agreements. On 18 November Robin Walker responded to UQ from Louise Haigh on preparations for implementation of the Northern Ireland Protocol. Robert Jenrick replied to UQ from Justin Madders on the towns fund. On 19 November Edward Argar replied to UQ from Conservative Sir Christopher Chope on his Department's poor performance in answering written questions. Boris Johnson updated the House on the Government's integrated review of foreign, defence, security and development policy, which would conclude 'early next year.' Nigel Huddleston made a statement on financial support for the sports sector.

On 23 November Boris Johnson made a statement on the winter plan, 'for the first time since this wretched virus took hold, we can see a route out of the pandemic.' On 24 November Christopher Pincher responded to UQ from Labour's Clive Betts on whether leaseholders were expected to pay for the removal of dangerous cladding from their homes. On 25 October Rishi Sunak outlined the Spending Review 2020. On 26 November Matt Hancock made a further statement, 'sadly, there is no quick fix… hope is on the horizon, but we still have further to go, so we must all dig deep. The end is in sight. We must not give up now. We must follow these new rules and make sure that our actions today will save lives in future and help get our country through this.' Dominic Raab made a statement on official development assistance, 'we have concluded after extensive consideration and with regret that we cannot for the moment meet our target of spending 0.7 per cent of gross national income on ODA, and we will move to a target of 0.5 per cent next year.'

On 30 November Chris Philp responded to UQ from Labour's Bell Ribeiro-Addy on the scheduled mass deportation by charter plane to Jamaica, 'they are all foreign national offenders who between them have served 228 years plus a life sentence in prison.' George Eustice made a statement on the agricultural transition plan. Brandon Lewis made a statement on the Supreme Court judgment in the case of Patrick Finucane. On 2 December Paul Scully replied to UQ from Edward Miliband on support for business and the retention of jobs on the high street in light of the announcement of Arcadia entering administration and Debenhams going into liquidation. Matt Hancock made a statement about vaccines, 'today marks a new chapter in our fight against this virus… I am delighted to inform the House that the MHRA has issued the clinical authorisation of the Pfizer/BioNTech vaccine.' On 3 December Gavin Williamson made a statement regarding testing and examinations in schools and colleges next year, 'we will not let covid damage the life chances of an entire year of students by cancelling next year's exams. We support Ofqual's decision that, in awarding next year's GCSEs, AS and A-levels, grading will be as generous and will maintain a similar profile as those grades awarded this year.' Robert Buckland made a statement on the recovery of courts and tribunals.

On 7 December Paymaster General Penny Mordaunt replied to UQ from Rachel Reeves on progress of the negotiations on the UK's future relationship with the EU and the end of the transition period. Nigel Adams responded to UQ from SNP's Alan Smyth on sentencing of three Hong Kong pro-democracy activists. On 8 December Matt Hancock replied to UQ from Jonathan Ashworth announcing the first person in the world to receive a clinically authorised vaccine, 'this marks the start of the NHS's Herculean task to deploy vaccine right across the UK… this simple act of vaccination is a tribute to scientific endeavour, human ingenuity and the hard work of so many people. Today marks the start of the fight back against our common enemy, coronavirus.' After a rebuke from the Speaker on the way the announcement had been handled Nigel Huddleston announced a review of the Gambling Act. On 9 December Michael Gove updated the House on the implementation of the Northern Ireland protocol as part of the withdrawal agreement with the EU. Defence Minister James Heappey made a statement on support for the UN stabilisation mission in Mali. The Taxation (Post-transition Period) Bill received its Second reading and Committee stage. On 10 December Penny Mordaunt replied to UQ from Rachel Reeves on the progress of negotiations on the UK's future relationship with the EU. Nadine Dorries made a statement on publication of the initial report from the Ockenden review into events at Shrewsbury and Telford Hospital NHS Trust.

On 14 December Matt Hancock announced that the NHS had begun vaccinations through GPs in England and in care homes in Scotland, 'day by day, we are giving hope to more people and making this country safer… it will take time for its benefits to be felt far and wide, so we must persevere because the virus remains as dangerous as it has always been.' Alok Sharma published the energy White Paper setting out immediate steps to achieve UK climate ambitions. On 15 December Labour's Chris Bryant made a personal statement apologising for his heckling during Prime Minister's questions and when he challenged the authority of the Chair. Oliver Dowden published the Government's response to the online harms consultation, 'we are proposing groundbreaking regulations that will make tech companies legally responsible for the online safety of their users… this will rebuild public trust and restore public confidence in the tech that has not only powered us through the pandemic, but will power us into the recovery.' On 16 December Chris Philp replied to UQ from

Caroline Nokes on whether changes to the immigration rules would reduce the numbers of asylum seekers in supported accommodation. Nigel Adams replied to UQ from Sir Iain Duncan Smith on the overwhelming evidence of the Chinese Government's use of Uyghur slave labour in Xinjiang. The Trade (Disclosure of Information) Bill completed all its Commons stages in one day. On 17 December Matt Hancock gave an update confirming tougher restrictions, 'where they are necessary, we must put them in place to prevent the NHS from being overwhelmed and to protect life.' Robert Jenrick announced the provisional Local Government Finance Settlement. MPs then rose for the Christmas Recess.

On 23 December Parliament was recalled to approve the European Union (Future Relationship) Bill enacting the EU/UK agreement on leaving the EU. Boris Johnson introduced the Bill by saying, 'having taken back control of our money, our borders, our laws and our waters by leaving the European Union on 31 January, we now seize this moment to forge a fantastic new relationship with our European neighbours based on free trade and friendly co-operation,' Sir Keir Starmer felt,

'a thin deal is better than no deal... I do hope that this will be a moment when our country can come together and look to a better future... The leave/remain argument is over—whichever side we were on, the divisions are over. We now have an opportunity to forge a new future: one outside the EU, but working closely with our great partners, friends and allies... We will always have shared values, experiences and history, and we can now also have a shared future.' Second reading was passed by 521 votes to 73. Whilst unhappy - especially Labour peer Lord Adonis, '"we have sustained a total and unmitigated defeat" - those were Winston Churchill's words on the Munich agreement 82 years ago. Alas, they apply word for word to the Brexit agreement we are being asked to rubber-stamp today', the Lords also passed the Bill unamended by 466 votes to 101. The Bill received Royal Assent at 12.30 am on 31 December, the last possible day. While the Lords debated the Bill, Matt Hancock made his final statement of the year, announcing approval had been granted for use of the Oxford University/AstraZeneca vaccine.

CONSTITUTION OF THE UK

The UK constitution is not contained in any single document but has evolved over time, formed by statute, common law and convention. A constitutional monarchy, the UK is governed by ministers of the crown in the name of the sovereign, who is head both of the state and of the government.

The organs of government are the legislature (parliament), the executive and the judiciary. The executive comprises HM government (the cabinet and other ministers), government departments and local authorities (*see* the Government, Public Bodies and Local Government). The judiciary (*see* Law Courts and Offices) pronounces on the law, both written and unwritten, interprets statutes and is responsible for the enforcement of the law; the judiciary is independent of both the legislature and the executive.

THE MONARCHY

The sovereign personifies the state and is, in law, an integral part of the legislature, head of the executive, head of the judiciary, commander-in-chief of all armed forces of the crown and supreme governor of the Church of England. In the Channel Islands and the Isle of Man, which are crown dependencies, the sovereign is represented by a lieutenant-governor. In the member states of the Commonwealth of which the sovereign is head of state, her representative is a governor-general; in UK overseas territories the sovereign is usually represented by a governor, who is responsible to the British government.

Although in practice the powers of the monarchy are now very limited, and restricted mainly to the advisory and ceremonial, there are important acts of government which require the participation of the sovereign. These include summoning, proroguing and dissolving parliament, giving royal assent to bills passed by parliament, appointing important office-holders like government ministers, judges, bishops and governors, conferring peerages, knighthoods and other honours, and granting pardon to a person wrongly convicted of a crime. The sovereign appoints the prime minister; by convention this office is held by the leader of the political party which enjoys, or can secure, a majority of votes in the House of Commons. In international affairs the sovereign, as head of state, has the power to declare war and make peace, to recognise foreign states and governments, to conclude treaties and to annex or cede territory. However, as the sovereign entrusts executive power to ministers of the crown and acts on the advice of her ministers, which she cannot ignore, royal prerogative powers are in practice exercised by ministers, who are responsible to parliament.

Ministerial responsibility does not diminish the sovereign's importance to the smooth working of government. She holds meetings of the Privy Council (*see* below), gives audiences to her ministers and other officials at home and overseas, receives accounts of cabinet decisions, reads dispatches and signs state papers; she must be informed and consulted on every aspect of national life, and she must show complete impartiality.

COUNSELLORS OF STATE
If the sovereign travels abroad for more than a few days or suffers from a temporary illness, it is necessary to appoint members of the royal family, known as counsellors of state, under letters patent to carry out the chief functions of the monarch, including the holding of Privy Councils and giving royal assent to acts passed by parliament. The normal procedure is to appoint two or more members of the royal family remaining in the UK from among the sovereign's spouse and the four adults next in succession, provided they have reached the age of 21. There are currently four members of the

royal family from which the counsellors of state are appointed: the Prince of Wales, the Duke of Cambridge, Prince Harry and the Duke of York.

In the event of the sovereign on accession being under the age of 18 years, or by infirmity of mind or body, rendered incapable of performing the royal functions, provision is made for a regency.

THE PRIVY COUNCIL

The sovereign in council, or Privy Council, was the chief source of executive power until the system of cabinet government developed. Its main function today is to advise the sovereign on the approval of various statutory functions and acts of the royal prerogative. These powers are exercised through orders in council and royal proclamations, approved by the Queen at meetings of the Privy Council. The council is also able to exercise a number of statutory duties without approval from the sovereign, including powers of supervision over the registering bodies for the medical and allied professions. These duties are exercised through orders of council.

Although appointment as a privy counsellor is for life, only those who are currently government ministers are involved in the day-to-day business of the council. A full council is summoned only on the death of the sovereign or when the sovereign announces his or her intention to marry. (For a full list of privy counsellors, *see* the Privy Council section.)

There are a number of advisory Privy Council committees whose meetings the sovereign does not attend. Some are prerogative committees, such as those dealing with legislative matters submitted by the legislatures of the Channel Islands and the Isle of Man or with applications for charters of incorporation; and some are provided for by statute, for example those for the universities of Oxford and Cambridge and some Scottish universities.

Administrative work is carried out by the Privy Council Office under the direction of the Lord President of the Council, a cabinet minister.

JUDICIAL COMMITTEE OF THE PRIVY COUNCIL
Supreme Court Building, Parliament Square, London SW1P 3BD
T 020-7960 1500 **W** www.jcpc.uk

The Judicial Committee of the Privy Council is the court of final appeal from courts of the UK dependencies, courts of independent Commonwealth countries which have retained the right of appeal and courts of the Channel Islands and the Isle of Man. It also hears very occasional appeals from a number of ancient and ecclesiastical courts.

The committee is composed of privy counsellors who hold, or have held, high judicial office. Only three or five judges hear each case, and these are usually justices of the supreme court.

Chief Executive, Vicky Fox

PARLIAMENT

Parliament is the supreme law-making authority and can legislate for the UK as a whole or for any parts of it separately (the Channel Islands and the Isle of Man are crown dependencies and not part of the UK). The main functions of parliament are to pass laws, to enable the government to raise taxes and to scrutinise government policy and administration, particularly proposals for expenditure. International treaties and agreements are customarily presented to parliament before ratification.

Parliament can trace its roots to two characteristics of Anglo-Saxon rule: the *witan* (a meeting of the king, nobles and advisors) and the *moot* (county meetings where local matters were discussed). However, it was the parliament that Simon de

Montfort called in 1265 that is accepted as the forerunner to modern parliament, as it included non-noble representatives from counties, cities and towns alongside the nobility. The nucleus of early parliaments at the beginning of the 14th century were the officers of the king's household and the king's judges, joined by such ecclesiastical and lay magnates as the king might summon to form a prototype 'House of Lords', and occasionally by the knights of the shires, burgesses and proctors of the lower clergy. By the end of Edward III's reign a 'House of Commons' was beginning to appear; the first known Speaker was elected in 1377.

Parliamentary procedure is based on custom and precedent, partly formulated in the standing orders of both houses of parliament. Each house has the right to control its own internal proceedings and to commit for contempt. The system of debate in the two houses is similar; when a motion has been moved, the Speaker proposes the question as the subject of a debate. Members speak from wherever they have been sitting. Questions are decided by a vote on a simple majority. Draft legislation is introduced, in either house, as a bill. Bills can be introduced by a government minister or a private member, but in practice the majority of bills which become law are introduced by the government. To become law, a bill must be passed by each house (for parliamentary stages, *see* Parliamentary Information) and then sent to the sovereign for the royal assent, after which it becomes an act of parliament.

Proceedings of both houses are public, except on extremely rare occasions. The minutes (called *Votes and Proceedings,* in the Commons and *House of Lords Minutes of Proceedings* in the Lords) and the speeches *(The Official Report of Parliamentary Debates,* Hansard) are published daily. Proceedings are also recorded for transmission on radio and television and stored in the Parliamentary Recording Unit before transfer to the British Library Sound Archive. Television cameras have been allowed into the House of Lords since 1985 and into the House of Commons since 1989; committee meetings may also be televised.

The Fixed Term Parliament Act 2011 fixed the duration of a parliament at five years in normal circumstances, the term being reckoned from the date given on the writs for the new parliament. The term of a parliament has been prolonged by legislation in such rare circumstances as the two World Wars (31 January 1911 to 25 November 1918; 26 November 1935 to 15 June 1945). The life of a parliament is divided into sessions, usually of one year in length, beginning and ending most often in May.

DEVOLUTION
The Scottish parliament and the National Assembly for Wales have legislative power over all devolved matters, for example matters not reserved to Westminster or otherwise outside its powers. The Northern Ireland Assembly has legislative authority in the fields previously administered by the Northern Ireland departments. The assembly was suspended in October 2002 and dissolved in April 2003, before being reinstated on 8 May 2007. The assembly was suspended between January 2017 and January 2020 because of policy disagreements between power-sharing parties. For further information, *see* Devolved Government

THE HOUSE OF LORDS
London SW1A 0PW
T 020-7219 3107
E hlinfo@parliament.uk W www.parliament.uk

The House of Lords is the second chamber, or 'Upper House', of the UK's bicameral parliament. Until the beginning of the 20th century, the House of Lords had considerable power, being able to veto any bill submitted to it by the House of Commons. Since the introduction of the Parliament Acts 1911 and 1949, however, it has no powers over money bills and its power of veto over public legislation has been reduced over time to the power to delay bills for up to one session of parliament (usually one year). Today the main functions of the House of Lords are to contribute to the legislative process, to act as a check on the government, and to provide a forum of expertise. Its judicial role as final court of appeal ended in 2009 with the establishment of a new UK Supreme Court (*see* Law Courts and Offices section).

The House of Lords has a number of select committees. Some relate to the internal affairs of the house – such as its House of Lords Commission – while others carry out important investigative work on matters of public interest. The main committees are: the Communications Committee; the Constitution Committee; the Economic Affairs Committee; the European Union Committee; and the Science and Technology Committee. House of Lords' investigative committees look at broad issues and do not mirror government departments as the select committees in the House of Commons do.

The Constitutional Reform Act 2005 significantly altered the judicial function of the House of Lords and the role of the Lord Chancellor as a judge and its presiding officer. The Lord Chancellor is no longer the presiding officer of the House of Lords nor head of the judiciary in England and Wales, but remains a cabinet minister (the Lord Chancellor and Secretary of State for Justice), and is currently a member of the House of Commons. The function of the presiding officer of the House of Lords was devolved to the newly created post of the Speaker of the House of Lords, commonly known as Lord Speaker. The first Lord Speaker elected by the House was the Rt. Hon. Baroness Hayman on 4 July 2006.

Membership of the House of Lords comprises mainly of life peers created under the Life Peerages Act 1958, along with 92 hereditary peers and a small number of Lords of Appeal in Ordinary, for example law lords, who were created under the Appellate Jurisdiction Act 1876*. The Archbishops of Canterbury and York, the Bishops of London, Durham and Winchester, and the 21 senior diocesan bishops of the Church of England are also members.

The House of Lords Act 1999 provides for 92 hereditary peers to remain in the House of Lords until further reform of the House has been carried out. Of these, 75 (42 Conservative, 28 crossbench, three Liberal Democrat and two Labour) were elected by hereditary peers in their political party or crossbench grouping. In addition, 15 office holders were elected by the whole house. Two hereditary peers with royal duties, the Earl Marshal and the Lord Great Chamberlain, have also remained members. Since November 2002, by-elections have been held to replace elected hereditary peers who have died, and since 2014 to replace those who retire permanently from the House. By-elections are held under the Alternative Vote System, and must take place within three months of a vacancy occurring. (*see also* The Peerage).

Peers are disqualified from sitting in the house if they are:
- absent for an entire parliamentary session which is longer than six months (under the House of Lords Reform Act 2014), unless they are on leave of absence (*see* below)
- not a British citizen, a Commonwealth citizen (under the British Nationality Act 1981) or a citizen of the Republic of Ireland
- under the age of 21
- undischarged bankrupts or, in Scotland, those whose estate is sequestered
- holders of a disqualifying judicial office
- members of the European parliament
- convicted of treason

Bishops cease to be members of the house when they retire.

Members who do not wish to attend sittings of the House of Lords may apply for leave of absence for the duration of a parliament. Since the passage of the House of Lords Reform Act 2014, members of the House may also retire permanently by giving notice in writing to the Clerk of the Parliaments.

Members of the House of Lords, who are not paid a salary, may claim a daily allowance of £305 (or may elect to claim a reduced daily allowance of £153) per sitting day – but only if they attend a sitting of the House and/or committee proceedings.
* Although the office of Lord of Appeal in Ordinary no longer exists, law lords created under the Appellate Jurisdiction Act 1876 remain members of the House. Those in office at the time of the establishment of the Supreme Court became justices of the UK Supreme Court and are not permitted to sit or vote in the House of Lords until they retire.

COMPOSITION *as at 19 November 2020*

Archbishops and bishops	26
Life peers under the Appellate Jurisdiction Act 1876 and the Life Peerages Act 1958*	687
Hereditary peers under the House of Lords Act 1999†	86
Total	799

* Excluding 19 peers on leave of absence
† Excluding two peers on leave of absence

STATE OF THE PARTIES* *as at 19 November 2020*

Conservative	259
Crossbench	182
Labour	178
Liberal Democrats	88
Non-affiliated	50
Archbishops and bishops	26
Other parties	15
Lord Speaker	1
Total	799

* Excluding peers on leave of absence

HOUSE OF LORDS PAY FOR SENIOR STAFF 2018–19*

Senior staff are placed in the following pay bands according to their level of responsibility and taking account of other factors such as experience and marketability.

Judicial group 4	£185,197
Senior band 3	£111,500–£158,805
Senior band 2	£90,500–£119,850
Senior band 1A	£75,956–£105,560
Senior band 1	£69,000–£93,380

* Latest available data

OFFICERS AND OFFICIALS

The house is presided over by the Lord Speaker, whose powers differ from those of the Speaker of the House of Commons. The Lord Speaker has no power to rule on matters of order because the House of Lords is self-regulating. The maintenance of the rules of debate is the responsibility of all the members who are present.

A panel of deputy speakers is appointed by Royal Commission. The first deputy speaker is the Chair of Committees, a salaried officer of the house appointed at the beginning of each session. He or she chairs a number of 'domestic' committees relating to the internal affairs of the house. The first deputy speaker is assisted by a panel of deputy chairs, headed by the salaried Principal Deputy Chair of

Committees, who is also chair of the European Union Committee of the house.

The Clerk of the Parliaments is the accounting officer and the chief permanent official responsible for the administration of the house. The Lady Usher of the Black Rod is responsible for security and other services and also has royal duties as secretary to the Lord Great Chamberlain.

Lord Speaker, Rt. Hon. Lord Fowler
Senior Deputy Speaker of the House of Lords, Rt. Hon. Lord McFall of Alcluith
Principal Deputy Chair of Committees, Earl of Kinnoull
Clerk of the Parliaments, Edward Ollard
Clerk Assistant, Sarah Davies
Reading Clerk and Clerk of the Overseas Office, Jake Vaughan
Lady Usher of the Black Rod, Sarah Clarke, OBE
Yeoman Usher of the Black Rod, Brig. Neil Baverstock
Commissioner for Lords' Standards, Lucy Scott-Moncrieff, CBE
Counsel to the Chair of Committees, J. Cooper
Registrar of Lords' Interests, Tom Wilson
Clerk of Committees, Tom Goldsmith
Legal Adviser to the Human Rights Committee, Eleanor Hourigan
Director of Library Services, Penny Young
Director of Facilities, Carl Woodall
Finance Director, Fehintola Akinlose
Director of Parliamentary Digital Service, Rob Greig
Director of Human Resources, Nigel Sully
Clerk of Legislation, Liam Smyth
Principal Clerk of Select Committees, Tom Healey
Director of Parliamentary Archives, Adrian Brown

LORD GREAT CHAMBERLAIN'S OFFICE
Lord Great Chamberlain, 7th Marquess of Cholmondeley, KCVO

SELECT COMMITTEES
The main House of Lords select committees, as at November 2020, are as follows:

Committee of Selection – Chair, Rt. Hon. Lord McFall of Alcluith
Common Frameworks Scrutiny – Chair, Baroness Andrews, OBE
Communications and Digital – Chair, Lord Gilbert of Panteg
Conduct – Chair, Rt. Hon. Lord Mance
Constitution – Chair, Rt. Hon. Baroness Taylor of Bolton
COVID-19 – Chair, Baroness Lane-Fox of Soho, CBE
Delegated Powers and Regulatory Reform – Chair, Rt. Hon. Lord Blencathra
Democracy and Digital Technologies – Chair, Lord Puttnam, CBE
Economic Affairs – Chair, Rt. Hon. Lord Forsyth of Drumlean
Electoral Registration Act 2013 – Chair, Rt. Hon. Lord Shutt of Greetland, OBE
European Union – Chair, Earl of Kinnoull
European Union – Sub-committees:
  Environment – Chair, Lord Teverson
  Goods – Chair, Baroness Verma
  International Agreements – Chair, Rt. Hon. Lord Goldsmith, QC
  Security and Justice – Chair, Lord Ricketts, GCMG, GCVO
  Services – Chair, Baroness Donaghy, CBE, FRSA
Finance – Chair, Baroness Doocey, OBE
Food, Poverty, Health and Environment – Chair, Lord Krebs
Gambling Industry – Chair, Lord Grade of Yarmouth, CBE
High Speed Rail – Chair, Rt. Hon. Lord Hope of Craighead, KT
House – Chair, Rt. Hon. Lord Fowler
Hybrid Instruments – Chair, Rt. Hon. Lord McFall of Alcluith
International Relations and Defence – Chair, Rt. Hon. Baroness Anelay of St Johns, DBE

Liaison – Chair, Rt. Hon. Lord McFall of Alcluith
National Plan for Sport and Recreation – Chair, Lord Willis of
   Knaresborough
Procedure and Privileges – Chair, Rt. Hon. Lord McFall of
   Alcluith
Public Services – Chair, Rt. Hon. Baroness Armstrong of Hill
   Top
Risk Assessment and Risk Planning – Chair, Rt. Hon. Lord
   Arbuthnot of Erdrom
Science and Technology – Chair, Lord Patel, KT
Secondary Legislation Scrutiny – Chair, Lord Hodgson of Astley
   Abbotts, CBE
Services – Chair, Rt. Hon. Lord Laming, CBE, DL
Standing Orders (Private Bills) – Chair, Rt. Hon. Lord McFall of
   Alcluith

THE HOUSE OF COMMONS
London SW1A 0AA
T 020-7219 3000 **W** www.parliament.uk

HOUSE OF COMMONS ENQUIRY SERVICE
14 Tothill Street, London SW1H 9NB
T 020-7219 4272 **E** hcinfo@parliament.uk

The members of the House of Commons are elected by universal adult suffrage. For electoral purposes, the UK is divided into constituencies, each of which returns one member to the House of Commons, the member being the candidate who obtains the largest number of votes cast in the constituency. To ensure equitable representation, the four Boundary Commissions keep constituency boundaries under review and recommend any redistribution of seats which may seem necessary because of population movements etc. At the 2010 general election the number of seats increased from 646 to 650. Of the present 650 seats, there are 533 for England, 40 for Wales, 59 for Scotland and 18 for Northern Ireland.

NUMBER OF SEATS IN THE HOUSE OF COMMONS BY COUNTRY

	2005	2020
England	529	533
Wales	40	40
Scotland	59	59
Northern Ireland	18	18
Total	646	650

ELECTIONS
Elections are by secret ballot, each elector casting one vote; voting is not compulsory. (For entitlement to vote in parliamentary elections, *see* Legal Notes.) When a seat becomes vacant between general elections, a by-election is held.

British subjects and citizens of the Irish Republic can stand for election as MPs provided they are 18 or over and not subject to disqualification. Those disqualified from sitting in the house include:
- undischarged bankrupts
- people sentenced to more than one year's imprisonment

- members of the House of Lords (but hereditary peers not sitting in the Lords are eligible)
- holders of certain offices listed in the House of Commons Disqualification Act 1975, for example members of the judiciary, civil service, regular armed forces, police forces, some local government officers and some members of public corporations and government commissions

A candidate does not require any party backing but his or her nomination for election must be supported by the signatures of ten people registered in the constituency. A candidate must also deposit £500 with the returning officer, which is forfeit if the candidate does not receive more than 5 per cent of the votes cast. All election expenses at a general election, except the candidate's personal expenses, are subject to a statutory limit of £8,700, plus six pence for each elector in a borough constituency or nine pence for each elector in a county constituency.

See also members of parliament for a current alphabetical list.

STATE OF THE PARTIES *as at 20 November 2020*

Party	Seats
Conservative	364
Labour	200
Scottish National Party	47
Liberal Democrats	11
Democratic Unionist Party	8
Sinn Fein (have not taken their seats)	7
Independent*	5
Plaid Cymru	3
Social Democratic and Labour Party	2
Green	1
Alliance	1
The Speaker	1
Total	650

* MPs either suspended or who have had the whip withdrawn: two Labour, one Conservative, one Scottish National Party, one Plaid Cymru.

BUSINESS
The week's business of the house is outlined each Thursday by the leader of the house, after consultation between the chief government whip and the chief opposition whip. A quarter to a third of the time will be taken up by the government's legislative programme and the rest by other business. As a rule, bills likely to raise political controversy are introduced in the Commons before going on to the Lords, and the Commons claims exclusive control in respect of national taxation and expenditure. Bills such as the finance bill, which imposes taxation, and the consolidated fund bills, which authorise expenditure, must begin in the Commons. A bill of which the financial provisions are subsidiary may begin in the Lords, and the Commons may waive its rights in regard to Lords' amendments affecting finance.

The Commons has a public register of MPs' financial and certain other interests; this is published annually as a House of Commons paper. Members must also disclose any relevant financial interest or benefit in a matter before the house when taking part in a debate, in certain other proceedings of the house, or in consultations with other MPs, with ministers or with civil servants.

MEMBERS' PAY AND ALLOWANCES

Since 1911 members of the House of Commons have received salary payments; facilities for free travel were introduced in 1924. Salary rates for the last 30 years are as follows:

1989 Jan – £24,107	2004 Apr – £57,485
1990 Jan – £26,701	2005 Apr – £59,095
1991 Jan – £29,970	2006 Apr – £59,686
1992 Jan – £30,854	2007 Apr – £61,181
1993 Jan – £30,854	2008 Apr – £63,291
1994 Jan – £31,687	2009 Apr – £64,766
1995 Jan – £33,189	2010 Apr – £65,738
1995 Jan – £33,189	2011 Apr – £65,738
1996 Jan – £34,085	2012 Apr – £65,738
1996 Jul – £43,000	2013 Apr – £66,396
1997 Apr – £43,860	2014 Apr – £67,060
1998 Apr – £45,066	2015 May – £74,000
1999 Apr – £47,008	2016 Apr – £74,962
2000 Apr – £48,371	2017 Apr – £76,011
2001 Apr – £49,822	2018 Apr – £77,379
2002 Apr – £55,118	2019 Apr – £79,468
2003 Apr – £56, 358	2020 Apr – £81,932

The Independent Parliamentary Standards Authority (IPSA) was established under the Parliamentary Standards Act 2009 and is responsible for the independent regulation and administration of the MPs' Scheme of Business Costs and Expenses, as well as for paying the salaries of MPs and their staff members. Since May 2011, the IPSA has also been responsible for determining MPs' pay and setting the level of any increase to their salary.

For 2019–20, the office costs expenditure budget is £28,800 for London area MPs and £25,910 for non-London area MPs. The maximum annual staff budget for London area MPs is £188,860 and £177,550 for non-London area MPs.

Since 1972 MPs have been able to claim reimbursement for the additional cost of staying overnight away from their main residence while on parliamentary business. This is not payable to London area MPs and those MPs who reside in 'grace and favour' accommodation. Accommodation expenses for MPs claiming rental payments in the London area is capped at £23,010 a year; outside of the London area each constituency is banded according to rental values in the area and capped at £16,120. For MPs who own their own homes, mortgage interest and associated expenses up to £5,410 are payable.

For ministerial salaries *see* Government Departments.

MEMBERS' PENSIONS

Pension arrangements for MPs were first introduced in 1964. Under the Parliamentary Contributory Pension Fund CARE (career-averaged revalued earnings) scheme, MPs receive a pension on retirement based upon their salary in their final year, and upon accumulating proportions of pensionable earnings over each year of membership. MPs contributions are payable at a rate of 11.09 per cent of pay. Exchequer contributions are paid at a rate recommended by the Government Actuary and meet the balance of the cost of providing MP's retirement benefits. Pensions are normally payable upon retirement at age 65 to those who are no longer MPs. Abated pensions may be payable to members aged 55 or over. Pensions are also payable to spouses and other qualifying partners of deceased scheme members at the rate of three-eighths of the deceased member's pension. In the case of members who die in service, an enhanced spouse's or partner's pension and a lump sum equal to two times pensionable salary is payable. There are also provisions in place for dependants and MPs of any age who retire due to ill health. All pensions are CPI index-linked.

The House of Commons Members' Fund provides for annual or lump sum grants to ex-MPs, their widows or widowers, and children of those who either ceased to serve as an MP prior to the PCPF being established or who are experiencing hardship. Historically, income to the Fund has been derived from individual contributions from MPs (£24 per annum), an Exchequer contribution (a maximum of £215,000 per annum) and the return on investments. Under the provision of the House of Commons Members Fund Act 2016 the trustees can suspend or increase MP contributions up to a maximum of 0.2 per cent of an member's ordinary salary. The 2016 Act also removed the Exchequer contribution.

HOUSE OF COMMONS PAY BANDS FOR SENIOR STAFF

Senior Staff are placed in the following Senior Civil Service pay bands. These pay bands are for 2019–20 and apply to the most senior staff in departments and agencies.

Pay Band 1	£71,000–£117,800
Pay Band 1A*	£71,000–£128,900
Pay Band 2	£93,000–£162,500
Pay Band 3	£120,000–£208,100
Permanent Secretaries	£150,000–£200,000

* Pay Band 1A is now effectively a closed grade, although existing staff will remain on this grade

OFFICERS AND OFFICIALS

The House of Commons is presided over by the Speaker, who has considerable powers to maintain order. A deputy speaker, called the Chairman of Ways and Means, and two deputy chairs may preside over sittings of the House of Commons; they are elected by the house, and, like the Speaker, neither speak nor vote other than in their official capacity.

The staff of the house are employed by a commission chaired by the Speaker. The heads of the six House of Commons departments are permanent officers of the house, not MPs. The Clerk of the House is the principal adviser to the Speaker on the privileges and procedures of the house, the conduct of the business of the house, and committees. The Serjeant-at-Arms is responsible for security and ceremonial functions of the house.

Speaker, Rt. Hon. Sir Lindsay Hoyle, MP

Chairman of Ways and Means, Rt. Hon. Dame Eleanor Laing, DBE, MP

First Deputy Chairman of Ways and Means, Rt. Hon. Dame Rosie Winterton, DBE, MP

Second Deputy Chairman of Ways and Means, Nigel Evans, MP

House of Commons Commission, Rt. Hon. Sir Lindsay Hoyle, MP *(chair);* Ian Ailles *(Director-General of the House of Commons);* Dr John Benger *(Clerk of the House);* Sir Paul Beresford, MP; Jane McCall *(external member);* Dr Rima Makarem *(external member);* Rt. Hon. Jacob Rees-Mogg, MP *(Leader of the House);* Rt. Hon. Valerie Vaz, MP *(Shadow Leader of the House);* Sir Charles Walter, MP; Rt. Hon. Dame Rosie Winterton, DBE, MP; Pete Wishart, MP

Secretary of the Commission, Marianne Cwynarski

Assistant Secretary, Robert Cope

OFFICE OF THE SPEAKER

Speaker's Secretary, Helen Wood

Trainbearer, Jim Davey

Speaker's Counsel, Saira Salimi

Chaplain to the Speaker, Revd Canon Patricia Hillas

OFFICE OF THE CLERK OF THE HOUSE

Clerk of the House, Dr John Benger

PARLIAMENTARY COMMISSIONER FOR STANDARDS

Parliamentary Commissioner for Standards, Kathryn Stone, OBE

PARLIAMENTARY SECURITY DIRECTOR
Parliamentary Security Director, Eric Hepburn, CBE

GOVERNANCE OFFICE
Head of Office, Marianne Cwynarski

DEPARTMENT OF CHAMBER AND COMMITTEE
SERVICES
Clerk Assistant and Managing Director, Sarah Davies

COMMITTEE OFFICE
Clerk of Committees, Paul Evans

DEPARTMENTAL SELECT COMMITTEES *as at
September 2019*
Administration – Chair, Sir Charles Walker, KBE, MP
Arms Export Controls – Chair, Mark Garnier, MP
Backbench Business – Chair, Ian Mearns, MP
Business, Energy and Industrial Strategy – Chair, Darren Jones,
  MP
Defence – Chair, Rt. Hon. Tobias Ellwood, MP
Digital, Culture, Media and Sport – Chair, Julian Knight, MP
Education – Chair, Rt. Hon. Robert Halfon, MP
Environment, Food and Rural Affairs – Chair, Neil Parish, MP
Environmental Audit – Chair, Rt. Hon. Philip Dunne, MP
European Scrutiny – Chair, Sir William Cash, MP
European Statutory Instruments – Chair, Andrew Jones, MP
Finance – Chair, Lillian Greenwood, MP
Foreign Affairs – Chair, Tom Tugendhat, MP
Future Relationship with the EU – Chair, Rt. Hon. Hilary Benn,
  MP
Health and Social Care – Chair, Rt. Hon. Jeremy Hunt, MP
Home Affairs – Chair, Rt. Hon. Yvette Cooper, MP
Housing, Communities and Local Government, Chair, Clive Betts,
  MP
International Development – Chair, Sarah Champion, MP
International Trade – Chair, Angus Brendan MacNeil, MP
Justice – Chair, Sir Robert Neill, MP
Liaison – Chair, Sir Bernard Jenkin, MP
Northern Ireland Affairs – Chair, Simon Hoare, MP
Petitions – Chair, Catherine McKinnerll, MP
Privileges – Chair, Chris Bryant, MP
Procedure – Chair, Rt. Hon. Karen Bradley, MP
Public Accounts – Chair, Meg Hillier, MP
Public Administration and Constitutional Affairs – Chair, William
  Wragg, MP
Regulatory Reform – Chair, Stephen McPartland, MP
Science and Technology – Chair, Rt. Hon. Greg Clark, MP
Scottish Affairs – Chair, Pete Wishart, MP
Selection – Chair, Bill Wiggin, MP
Standards – Chair, Chris Bryant, MP
Statutory Instruments – Chair, Jessica Morden, MP
Transport – Chair, Huw Merringham, MP
Treasury – Chair, Rt. Hon. Mel Stride, MP
Welsh Affairs – Chair, Rt. Hon. Stephen Crabb, MP
Women and Equalities – Chair, Rt. Hon. Caroline Nokes, MP
Work and Pensions – Chair, Rt. Hon. Stephen Timms, MP

SCRUTINY UNIT
Head of Unit, David Lloyd
Head of Financial Scrutiny, Larry Honeysett

VOTE OFFICE
Deliverer of the Vote, Tom McVeagh

CHAMBER BUSINESS DIRECTORATE
Clerk of Legislation, Liam Laurence Smyth

OFFICIAL REPORT DIRECTORATE (HANSARD)
Editor, Alex Newton

SERJEANT-AT-ARMS DIRECTORATE
Serjeant-at-Arms, Ugbana Oyet

DEPARTMENT OF FINANCE
Head of Finance, Ebenezer Oduwole

DEPARTMENT OF HUMAN RESOURCES AND
CHANGE
Director-General, Andrew Walker

DEPARTMENT OF INFORMATION SERVICES
Director-General and Librarian, Penny Young
Curator of Works of Art, Melissa Hamnett
Keeper of Historic Collections, Mary-Jane Tsang
Collections Care Manager, Caroline Babington
Collections Information Manager, Natasha Wood

PARLIAMENTARY DIGITAL SERVICE (PDS)
Director of Parliamentary Digital Service, Tracey Jessup

OTHER PRINCIPAL OFFICERS
Clerk of the Crown in Chancery, Ceri King
Parliamentary and Health Service Ombudsman, Robert Behrens,
  CBE

NATIONAL AUDIT OFFICE
157–197 Buckingham Palace Road, London SW1W 9SP
T 020-7798 7000
E enquiries@nao.gsi.gov.uk **W** www.nao.org.uk

The National Audit Office came into existence under the
National Audit Act 1983 to replace and continue the work of
the former Exchequer and Audit Department. The act
reinforced the office's total financial and operational
independence from the government and brought its head, the
Comptroller and Auditor-General, into a closer relationship
with parliament as an officer of the House of Commons.

The National Audit Office (NAO) scrutinises public
spending on behalf of parliament, helping it to hold
government departments to account and helping public
service managers improve performance and service delivery.
The NAO audits the financial statements of all government
departments and a wide range of other public bodies. It
regularly publishes 'value for money' reports on the efficiency
and effectiveness of how public resources are used.

Chair, Lord Bichard, KCB
Comptroller and Auditor-General, Gareth Davies
Executive Directors, Abdool Kara; Daniel Lambauer; Elaine
  Lewis; Kate Mathers; Rebecca Sheeran; Max Tse

PARLIAMENTARY INFORMATION

The following is a short glossary of aspects of the work of
parliament. Unless otherwise stated, references are to House of
Commons procedures.

BILL – Proposed legislation is termed a bill. The stages of a
public bill (for private bills, *see* below) in the House of
Commons are as follows:

First reading: This stage introduces the legislation to the
house and, for government bills, merely constitutes an order
to have the bill printed.

Second reading: The debate on the principles of the bill.

Committee stage: The detailed examination of a bill, clause by
clause. In most cases this takes place in a public bill committee,
or the whole house may act as a committee. Public bill
committees may take evidence before embarking on detailed
scrutiny of the bill. Very rarely, a bill may be examined by a
select committee.

Report stage: Detailed review of a bill as amended in
committee, on the floor of the house, and an opportunity to
make further changes.

Third reading: Final debate on the full bill in the Commons.

Public bills go through the same stages in the House of Lords, but with important differences: the committee stage is taken in committee of the whole house or in a grand committee, in which any peer may participate. There are no time limits, all amendments are debated, and further amendments can be made at third reading.

A bill may start in either house, and has to pass through both houses to become law. Both houses have to agree the final text of a bill, so that amendments made by the second house are then considered in the originating house, and if not agreed, sent back or themselves amended, until agreement is reached.

CHILTERN HUNDREDS – A nominal office of profit under the crown, the acceptance of which requires an MP to vacate his/her seat. The Manor of Northstead is similar. These are the only means by which an MP may resign.

CONSOLIDATED FUND BILL – A bill to authorise the issue of money to maintain government services. The bill is dealt with without debate.

EARLY DAY MOTION – A motion put on the notice paper by an MP without, in general, the real prospect of its being debated. Such motions are expressions of back-bench opinion.

FATHER OF THE HOUSE – The MP whose continuous service in the House of Commons is the longest. The present Father of the House is the Sir Peter Bottomley, MP.

GRAND COMMITTEES – There are three grand committees in the House of Commons, one each for Northern Ireland, Scotland and Wales; they consider matters relating specifically to that country. In the House of Lords, bills may be sent to a grand committee instead of a committee of the whole house (*see also* Bill).

HOURS OF MEETING – The House of Commons normally meets on Mondays at 2.30pm, Tuesdays and Wednesdays at 11.30am, Thursdays at 9.30am and some Fridays at 9.30am. (*See also* Westminster Hall Sittings, below.) The House of Lords normally meets at 2.30pm Mondays and Tuesdays, 3pm on Wednesdays and at 11am on Thursdays. The House of Lords occasionally sits on Fridays at 10am.

LEADER OF THE OPPOSITION – In 1937 the office of leader of the opposition was recognised and a salary was assigned to the post. In 2020–21 this is £147,103 (including a parliamentary salary of £81,932). The present leader of the opposition is the Rt. Hon. Sir Keir Starmer, KBC, QC, MP.

THE LORD CHANCELLOR – The office of Lord High Chancellor of Great Britain was significantly altered by the Constitutional Reform Act 2005. Previously, the Lord Chancellor was (*ex officio*) the Speaker of the House of Lords, and took part in debates and voted in divisions in the House of Lords. The Department for Constitutional Affairs was created in 2003, and became the Ministry of Justice in 2007, incorporating most of the responsibilities of the Lord Chancellor's department. The role of Speaker has been transferred to the post of Lord Speaker. The Constitutional Reform Act 2005 also brought to an end the Lord Chancellor's role as head of the judiciary. A Judicial Appointments Commission was created in April 2006, and a supreme court (separate from the House of Lords) was established in 2009.

THE LORD GREAT CHAMBERLAIN – The Lord Great Chamberlain is a Great Officer of State, the office being hereditary since the grant of Henry I to the family of De Vere, Earls of Oxford. It is now a joint hereditary office rotating on the death of the sovereign between the Cholmondeley, Carington and Ancaster families.

The Lord Great Chamberlain, currently the 7th Marquess of Cholmondeley, is responsible for the royal apartments in the Palace of Westminster, the Royal Gallery, the administration of the Chapel of St Mary Undercroft and, in conjunction with the Lord Speaker and the Speaker of the House of Commons, Westminster Hall. The Lord Great Chamberlain has the right to perform specific services at a coronation and has particular responsibility for the internal administrative arrangements within the House of Lords for state openings of parliament.

THE LORD SPEAKER – The first Lord Speaker of the House of Lords, the Rt. Hon. Baroness Hayman, took up office on 4 July 2006. The Lord Speaker is independent of the government and elected by members of the House of Lords rather than appointed by the prime minister. Although the Lord Speaker's primary role is to preside over proceedings in the House of Lords, she does not have the same powers as the Speaker of the House of Commons. For example, the Lord Speaker is not responsible for maintaining order during debates, as this is the responsibility of the house as a whole. The Lord Speaker sits in the Lords on one of the woolsacks, which are couches covered in red cloth and stuffed with wool.

MOTHER OF THE HOUSE – Introduced by Theresa May in 2017, the Mother of the House is the female MP whose continuous service is the longest. The inaugural and present Mother of the House is Rt. Hon. Harriet Harman, QC, MP.

OPPOSITION DAY – A day on which the topic for debate is chosen by the opposition. There are 20 such days in a normal session. On 17 days, subjects are chosen by the leader of the opposition; on the remaining three days by the leader of the next largest opposition party.

PARLIAMENT ACTS 1911 AND 1949 – Under these acts, bills may become law without the consent of the Lords, though the House of Lords has the power to delay a public bill for a parliamentary session.

PRIME MINISTER'S QUESTIONS – The prime minister answers questions from 12 to 12.30pm on Wednesdays.

PRIVATE BILL – A bill promoted by a body or an individual to give powers additional to, or in conflict with, the general law, and to which a special procedure applies to enable people affected to object.

PRIVATE MEMBER'S BILL – A public bill promoted by an MP or peer who is not a member of the government.

PRIVATE NOTICE QUESTION – A question adjudged of urgent importance on submission to the Speaker (in the Lords, the Lord Speaker), answered at the end of oral questions.

PRIVILEGE – The House of Commons has rights and immunities to protect it from obstruction in carrying out its duties. These are known as parliamentary privilege and enable Members of Parliament to debate freely. The most important privilege is that of freedom of speech. MPs cannot be prosecuted for sedition or sued for libel or slander over anything said during proceedings in the house. This enables them to raise in the house questions affecting the public good which might be difficult to raise outside owing to the possibility of legal action against them. The House of Lords has similar privileges.

QUESTION TIME – Oral questions are answered by ministers in the Commons from 2.30 to 3.30pm on Mondays, 11.30am to 12.30pm on Tuesdays and Wednesdays, and 9.30 to 10.30am on Thursdays. Questions are also taken for half an hour at the start of the Lords sittings.

ROYAL ASSENT – The royal assent is signified by letters patent to such bills and measures as have passed both Houses of Parliament (or bills which have been passed under the Parliament Acts 1911 and 1949). The sovereign has not given royal assent in person since 1854. On occasion, for instance in the prorogation of parliament, royal assent may be pronounced to the two houses by Lords Commissioners. More usually royal assent is notified to each house sitting separately in accordance with the Royal Assent Act 1967. The old French formulae for royal assent are then endorsed on the acts by the Clerk of the Parliaments.

The power to withhold assent resides with the sovereign but has not been exercised in the UK since 1707.

SELECT COMMITTEES – Consisting usually of 10 to 15 members of all parties, select committees are a means used by both houses in order to investigate certain matters.

Most select committees in the House of Commons are tied to departments: each committee investigates subjects within a government department's remit. There are other select committees dealing with matters such as public accounts (ie the spending by the government of money voted by parliament) and European legislation, and also committees advising on procedures and domestic administration of the house. Major select committees usually take evidence in public; their evidence and reports are published on the parliament website and in hard copy by The Stationery Office (TSO). House of Commons select committees are reconstituted after a general election.

In the House of Lords, select committees do not mirror government departments but cover broader issues. There is a select committee on the European Union (EU), which has six sub-committees dealing with specific areas of EU policy, a select committee on science and technology, a select committee on economic affairs and also one on the constitution. There is also a select committee on delegated powers and regulatory reform and one on privileges and conduct. In addition, *ad hoc* select committees have been set up from time to time to investigate specific subjects. There are also joint committees of the two houses, eg the committees on statutory instruments and on human rights.

THE SPEAKER – The Speaker of the House of Commons is the spokesperson and chair of the Chamber. He or she is elected by the house at the beginning of each parliament or when the previous Speaker retires or dies. The Speaker neither speaks in debates nor votes in divisions except when the voting is equal.

VACANT SEATS – When a vacancy occurs in the House of Commons during a session of parliament, the writ for the by-election is moved by a whip of the party to which the member whose seat has been vacated belonged. If the house is in recess, the Speaker can issue a warrant for a writ, should two members certify to him that a seat is vacant.

WESTMINSTER HALL SITTINGS – Following a report by the Modernisation of the House of Commons Select Committee, the Commons decided in May 1999 to set up a second debating forum. It is known as 'Westminster Hall' and sittings are in the Grand Committee Room on some Mondays from 4.30pm to 7.30pm, Tuesdays and Wednesdays from 9.30am to 11.30am and from 2.30pm to 5.30pm, and Thursdays from 1.30pm to 4.30pm. Sittings are open to the public at the times indicated.

WHIPS – In order to secure the attendance of members of a particular party in parliament, particularly on the occasion of an important vote, whips (originally known as 'whippers-in') are appointed. The written appeal or circular letter issued by them is also known as a 'whip', its urgency being denoted by the number of times it is underlined. Failure to respond to a three-line whip is tantamount in the Commons to secession (at any rate temporarily) from the party. Whips are provided with office accommodation in both houses, and government and some opposition whips receive salaries from public funds.

PARLIAMENTARY ARCHIVES
Houses of Parliament, London SW1A 0PW
T 020-7219 3074 E archives@parliament.uk
W www.parliament.uk/archives

Since 1497, the records of parliament have been kept within the Palace of Westminster. They are in the custody of the Clerk of Parliaments. In 1946 the House of Lords Record Office, which became the Parliamentary Archives in 2006, was established to supervise their preservation and their availability to the public. Some 3 million documents are preserved, including acts of parliament from 1497, journals of the House of Lords from 1510, minutes and committee proceedings from 1610, and papers laid before parliament from 1531. Among the records are the Petition of Right, the death warrant of Charles I, the Declaration of Breda, and the Bill of Rights. Records are made available through a public search room.

Director of the Parliamentary Archives, Adrian Brown

GOVERNMENT OFFICE

The government is the body of ministers responsible for the administration of national affairs, determining policy and introducing into parliament any legislation necessary to give effect to government policy. The majority of ministers are members of the House of Commons but members of the House of Lords, or of neither house, may also hold ministerial responsibility. The prime minister is, by current convention, always a member of the House of Commons.

THE PRIME MINISTER

The office of prime minister, which had been in existence for nearly 200 years, was officially recognised in 1905 and its holder was granted a place in the table of precedence. The prime minister, by tradition also First Lord of the Treasury and Minister for the Civil Service, is appointed by the sovereign and is usually the leader of the party which enjoys, or can secure, a majority in the House of Commons. Other ministers are appointed by the sovereign on the recommendation of the prime minister, who also allocates functions among ministers and has the power to dismiss ministers from their posts.

The prime minister informs the sovereign on state and political matters, advises on the dissolution of parliament, and makes recommendations for important crown appointments, ie the award of honours, etc.

As the chair of cabinet meetings and leader of a political party, the prime minister is responsible for translating party policy into government activity. As leader of the government, the prime minister is responsible to parliament and to the electorate for the policies and their implementation.

The prime minister also represents the nation in international affairs, for example summit conferences.

THE CABINET

The cabinet developed during the 18th century as an inner committee of the Privy Council, which was the chief source of executive power until that time. The cabinet is composed of about 20 ministers chosen by the prime minister, usually the heads of government departments (generally known as secretaries of state unless they have a special title, for example Chancellor of the Exchequer), the leaders of the two houses of parliament, and the holders of various traditional offices.

The cabinet's functions are the final determination of policy, control of government and coordination of government departments. The exercise of its functions is dependent upon the incumbent party's (or parties') majority support in the House of Commons. Cabinet meetings are held in private, taking place once or twice a week during parliamentary sittings and less often during a recess. Proceedings are confidential, the members being bound by their oath as privy counsellors not to disclose information about the proceedings.

The convention of collective responsibility means that the cabinet acts unanimously even when cabinet ministers do not all agree on a subject. The policies of departmental ministers must be consistent with the policies of the government as a whole, and once the government's policy has been decided, each minister is expected to support it or resign.

The convention of ministerial responsibility holds a minister, as the political head of his or her department, accountable to parliament for the department's work. Departmental ministers usually decide all matters within their responsibility, although on matters of political importance they normally consult their colleagues collectively. A decision by a departmental minister is binding on the government as a whole.

POLITICAL PARTIES

Before the reign of William and Mary, the principal officers of state were chosen by and were responsible to the sovereign alone, and not to parliament or the nation at large. Such officers acted sometimes in concert with one another but more often independently, and the fall of one did not, of necessity, involve that of others, although all were liable to be dismissed at any moment.

In 1693 the Earl of Sunderland recommended to William III the advisability of selecting a ministry from the political party which enjoyed a majority in the House of Commons, and the first united ministry was drawn in 1696 from the Whigs, to which party the king owed his throne. This group became known as the 'junto' and was regarded with suspicion as a novelty in the political life of the nation, being a small section meeting in secret apart from the main body of ministers. It may be regarded as the forerunner of the cabinet and in the course of time it led to the establishment of the principle of joint responsibility of ministers, so that internal disagreement caused a change of personnel or resignation of the whole body of ministers.

The accession of George I, who was unfamiliar with the English language, led to a disinclination on the part of the sovereign to preside at meetings of his ministers and caused the emergence of a prime minister, a position first acquired by Robert Walpole in 1721 and retained by him without interruption for 20 years and 326 days. The office of prime minister was formally recognised in 1905 when it was established by royal warrant.

DEVELOPMENT OF PARTIES

In 1828 the Whigs became known as Liberals, a name originally given by opponents to imply laxity of principles, but gradually accepted by the party to indicate its claim to be pioneers and champions of political reform and progressive legislation. In 1861 a Liberal Registration Association was founded and Liberal Associations became widespread. In 1877 a National Liberal Federation was formed, with its headquarters in London. The Liberal Party was in power for long periods during the second half of the 19th century and for several years during the first quarter of the 20th century, but after a split in the party in 1931, the numbers elected remained small. In 1988 a majority of the Liberals agreed on a merger with the Social Democratic Party under the title Social and Liberal Democrats; since 1989 they have been known as the Liberal Democrats. A minority continue separately as the Liberal Party.

Soon after the change from Whig to Liberal, the Tory Party became known as Conservative, a name believed to have been invented by John Wilson Croker in 1830 and to have been generally adopted around the time of the passing of the Reform Act of 1832 – to indicate that the preservation of national institutions was the leading principle of the party. After the Home Rule crisis of 1886 the dissentient Liberals entered into a compact with the Conservatives, under which the latter undertook not to contest their seats, but a separate Liberal Unionist organisation was maintained until 1912, when it was united with the Conservatives.

Labour candidates for parliament made their first appearance at the general election of 1892, when there were 27 standing as Labour or Liberal-Labour. In 1900 the Labour Representation Committee (LRC) was set up in order to establish a distinct Labour group in parliament, with its own whips, its own policy, and a readiness to cooperate with any party which might be engaged in promoting legislation in the direct interests of labour. In 1906 the LRC became known as the Labour Party.

The Scottish National Party (SNP) was founded in 1934 to campaign for independence for Scotland and a referendum on the subject was held in September 2014 which culminated in a 'no' to independence result.

The Democratic Unionist Party (DUP) was founded in 1971 to resist moves by the Ulster Unionist Party which were considered a threat to the Union. Its aim is to maintain Northern Ireland as an integral part of the UK.

Sinn Fein first emerged in the 1900s as a federation of nationalist clubs. It is a left-wing republican party who rejects British Sovereignty following a policy of abstentionism at Westminster and strives for a united Ireland.

Plaid Cymru was founded in 1926 to provide an independent political voice for Wales and to campaign for self-government in Wales.

The Social Democratic and Labour Party is an Irish nationalist party founded in 1970, which during the Troubles (1960s–1998) distinguished itself from Sinn Fein by rejecting violence.

The Alliance Party of Northern Ireland is a non-sectarian centrist party that advocates co-operation between nationalists and unionists; it was founded in 1970.

The Green Party was founded in 1973 and campaigns for social and environmental justice. The party began as 'People', was renamed the Ecology Party, and became the Green Party in 1985.

GOVERNMENT AND OPPOSITION

The government is formed by the party which wins the largest number of seats in the House of Commons at a general election, or which has the support of a majority of members in the House of Commons. By tradition, the leader of the majority party is asked by the sovereign to form a government, while the largest minority party becomes the official opposition with its own leader and a shadow cabinet. Leaders of the government and opposition sit on the front benches of the Commons with their supporters (the backbenchers) sitting behind them.

FINANCIAL SUPPORT

Financial support for opposition parties in the House of Commons was introduced in 1975 and is commonly known as Short Money, after Edward Short, the leader of the house at that time, who introduced the scheme. Short Money is only payable to those parties that secured at least two seats, or one seat and more than 150,000 votes, at the previous general election and is only intended to provide assistance for parliamentary duties. Opposition parties share £201,007 in travel expenses and receive £18,297.43 for every seat won at the most recent general election plus £36.54 for every 200 votes gained by the party (the figures are uprated annually in line with CPI). Short Money allocations for 2019–20 were:

DUP	£195,702.81
Green	£180,826.51
Labour	£6,563,156.52
Liberal Democrats	£898,384.12
Plaid Cymru	£103,693.35
SDPL	£90,980.65
SNP	£1,110,894.19

The sum paid to Sinn Fein and any other party that may choose not to take their seats in the House of Commons is calculated on the same basis as Short Money, but is known as Representative Money. Sinn Fein's allocation in 2019–20 was £165,304.55.

For the financial year which commenced on 1 April 2018, the leader of the opposition's office was allocated £852,491.98 for running costs.

Financial support for opposition parties in the House of Lords was introduced in 1996 and is commonly known as Cranborne Money, after former leader of the house, Viscount Cranborne.

The following list of political parties are those with at least one MP or sitting member of the House of Lords in the present parliament.

CONSERVATIVE PARTY
Conservative Campaign Headquarters, 4 Matthew Parker Street, London SW1H 9HQ
T 020-7222 9000 **W** www.conservatives.com

Parliamentary Party Leader, Rt. Hon. Boris Johnson, MP
Leader in the Lords, Rt. Hon. Baroness Evans of Bowes Park
Leader in the Commons and Lord President of the Council, Rt. Hon. Jacob Rees-Mogg, MP
Co-Chairs, Ben Elliot; Rt. Hon. Amanda Milling, MP
Deputy Chairman, Lord Sharpe of Epsom, OBE
Party Treasurer, Sir Ehud Sheleg

GREEN PARTY
The Biscuit Factory, Unit 201 A Block, 100 Clements Road, London SE16 4DG
T 020-3691 9400 **E** office@greenparty.org.uk
W www.greenparty.org.uk

Party Leaders, Sian Berry, AM; Jonathan Bartley
Deputy Leader, Amelia Womack
Chair, Liz Reason
Finance Coordinator, Jon Nott

LABOUR PARTY
Labour Central, Kings Manor, Newcastle upon Tyne NE1 6PA
T 0845-092 2299 **W** www.labour.org.uk

General Secretary, David Evans
General Secretary, Welsh Labour, Louise Magee
General Secretary, Michael Sharpe

SHADOW CABINET
Leader of the Opposition, Rt. Hon. Sir Keir Starmer, KCB, QC, MP
Deputy Leader, Angela Rayner, MP
Chancellor of the Exchequer, Anneliese Dodds, PHD, MP
Foreign Secretary, Lisa Nandy, MP
Home Secretary, Nick Thomas-Symonds, MP
Cabinet Office, Rachel Reeves, MP
Lord Chancellor and Secretary of State for Justice, Rt. Hon. David Lammy, MP

Secretary of State for Business, Energy and Industrial Strategy, Rt. Hon. Ed Miliband, MP
Secretary of State for Communities and Local Government, Steve Reed, OBE, MP
Secretary of State for Defence, Rt. Hon. John Healey, MP
Secretary of State for Digital, Culture, Media and Sport, Jo Stevens, MP
Secretary of State for Education, Kate Green, OBE, MP
Secretary of State for Employment Rights, Andy McDonald, MP

Secretary of State for Environment, Food and Rural Affairs, Luke Pollard, MP
Secretary of State for Health and Social Care, Jonathan Ashworth, MP
Secretary of State for Housing, Thangam Debbonaire, MP
Secretary of State for International Development, Preet Kaur Gill, MP
Secretary of State for International Trade, Rt. Hon. Emily Thornberry, MP
Secretary of State for Scotland, Ian Murray, MP
Secretary of State for Transport, Jim McMahon, MP
Chief Secretary to the Treasury, Bridget Phillipson, MP
Secretary of State for Wales, Nia Griffith, MP
Secretary of State for Northern Ireland, Louise Haigh, MP
Secretary of State for Work and Pensions, Jonathan Reynolds, MP
Minister for Mental Health, Dr Rosena Allin-Khan, MP
Minister for Voter Engagement and Youth Affairs, Cat Smith, MP
Minister for Women and Equalities, Marsha De Cordova, MP
Leader of the House of Commons, Rt. Hon. Valerie Vaz, MP
Leader of the House of Lords, Rt. Hon. Baroness Smith of Basildon
Attorney General, Lord Falconer of Thoroton, QC

LABOUR WHIPS
Chief Whip (Commons), Rt. Hon. Nick Brown, MP
Chief Whip (Lords), Rt. Hon. Lord McAvoy

LIBERAL DEMOCRATS
8–10 Great George Street, London SW1P 3AE
T 020-7022 0988 **E** info@libdems.org.uk **W** www.libdems.org.uk

Parliamentary Party Leader, Rt. Hon. Sir Ed Davey, MP
Deputy Party Leader, Daisy Cooper, MP
Leader in the Lords, Rt. Hon. Lord Newby, OBE
President, Mark Pack

NORTHERN IRELAND DEMOCRATIC UNIONIST PARTY
91 Dundela Avenue, Belfast BT4 3BU
T 028-9047 1155
E info@mydup.com **W** www.mydup.com

Parliamentary Party Leader, Rt. Hon. Arlene Foster, MLA
Deputy Leader & House of Commons Group Leader, Rt. Hon. Nigel Dodds, OBE, MP
Chair, Lord Morrow, MLA

PLAID CYMRU – THE PARTY OF WALES
Ty Gwynfor, Anson Court, Atlantic Wharf, Caerdydd CF10 4AL
T 029-2047 2272 **E** post@plaidcymru.org **W** www.partyof.wales

Party Leader, Adam Price, AM
Hon. Party President, Rt. Hon. Lord Wigley
Parliamentary Group Leader, Rt. Hon. Liz Saville Roberts, MP
Chair, Alun Ffred Jones
Chief Executive, Gareth Clubb

SCOTTISH NATIONAL PARTY
Gordon Lamb House, 3 Jackson's Entry, Edinburgh EH8 8PJ
T 0800-633 5432 **E** info@snp.org **W** www.snp.org

Westminster Parliamentary Party Leader, Rt. Hon. Ian Blackford, MP
Westminster Parliamentary Party Chief Whip, Patrick Grady, MP
First Minister of Scotland and Leader of the SNP, Rt. Hon. Nicola Sturgeon, MSP
Deputy Leader, Keith Brown, MSP
Party President, Ian Hudghton
National Treasurer, Colin Beattie, MSP
Chief Executive, Peter Murrell

SINN FEIN
53 Falls Road, Belfast BT12 4PD
T 028-9034 7350 **E** admin@sinnfein.ie **W** www.sinnfein.ie

Party President, Mary Lou McDonald, TD
Vice-President, Michelle O'Neill, MLA
Chair, Declan Kearney, MLA

PUBLIC ACTS OF PARLIAMENT 2019–20

Public acts included in this list are those which received royal assent between 31 July 2019 and 31 December 2020. The date stated after each act is the date on which it came into operation. For further information see **W** www.legislation.gov.uk

Kew Gardens (Leases) Act 2019 ch. 25 (9 September 2019) provides that the Secretary of State's powers in relation to the management of the Royal Botanic Gardens, Kew, include the power to grant a lease in respect of land for a period of up to 150 years.

European Union (Withdrawal) (No. 2) Act 2019 (repealed) ch. 26 (23 January 2020) Act repealed (23.1.2020) by European Union (Withdrawal Agreement) Act 2020

Parliamentary Buildings (Restoration and Renewal) Act 2019 ch. 27 (8 October 2019) makes provision in connection with works for or in connection with the restoration of the Palace of Westminster and other works relating to the Parliamentary Estate; and for connected purposes.

Census (Return Particulars and Removal of Penalties) Act 2019 ch. 28 (8 October 2019) amends the *Census Act 1920* and the *Census Act (Northern Ireland) 1969* in relation to the provision of particulars about sexual orientation and gender identity.

Early Parliamentary General Election Act 2019 ch. 29 (31 October 2019) makes provision for a parliamentary general election to be held on 12 December 2019.

Northern Ireland Budget Act 2019 ch. 30 (31 October) authorises the issue out of the Consolidated Fund of Northern Ireland of certain sums for the service of the year ending 31 March 2020; to appropriate those sums for specified purposes; to authorise the Department of Finance in Northern Ireland to borrow on the credit of the appropriated sums; and to authorise the use for the public service of certain resources (including accruing resources) for that year.

Historical Institutional Abuse (Northern Ireland) Act 2019 ch. 31 (5 November 2019) establishes the Historical Institutional Abuse Redress Board and to confer an entitlement to compensation in connection with children who were resident in certain institutions in Northern Ireland; and to establish the Commissioner for Survivors of Institutional Childhood Abuse.

European Union (Withdrawal Agreement) Act 2020 ch. 1 (23 January 2020) implements, and makes other provisions in connection with, the agreement between the United Kingdom and the EU under Article 50(2) of the Treaty on European Union which sets out the arrangements for the United Kingdom's withdrawal from the EU.

Direct Payments to Farmers (Legislative Continuity) Act 2020 ch. 2 (30 January 2020) makes provision for the incorporation of the Direct Payments Regulation into domestic law; for enabling an increase in the total maximum amount of direct payments under that Regulation; and for connected purposes.

Terrorist Offenders (Restriction of Early Release) Act 2020 ch. 3 (26 February 2020) make provision about the release on licence of offenders convicted of terrorist offences or offences with a terrorist connection; and for connected purposes.

Supply and Appropriation (Anticipation and Adjustments) Act 2020 ch. 4 (16 March 2020) authorises the use of resources for the years ending with 31 March 2020 and 31 March 2021; to authorise the issue of sums out of the Consolidated Fund for those years; and to appropriate the supply authorised by this Act for the year ending with 31 March 2020.

NHS Funding Act 2020 ch. 5 (16 March 2020) makes provision regarding the funding of the health service in England in respect of each financial year until the financial year that ends with 31 March 2024.

Contingencies Fund Act 2020 ch. 6 (25 March 2020) makes provision increasing the maximum capital of the Contingencies Fund for a temporary period.

Coronavirus Act 2020 ch. 7 (25 March 2020) makes provision in connection with coronavirus; and for connected purposes

Windrush Compensation Scheme (Expenditure) Act 2020 ch. 8 (8 June 2020) provides for the payment out of money provided by Parliament of expenditure incurred by the Secretary of State or a government department under, or in connection with, the Windrush Compensation Scheme.

Sentencing (Pre-consolidation Amendments) Act 2020 ch. 9 (8 June 2020) gives effect to Law Commission recommendations relating to commencement of enactments relating to sentencing law and to make provision for pre-consolidation amendments of sentencing law.

Birmingham Commonwealth Games Act 2020 ch. 10 (25 June 2020) makes provision about the Commonwealth Games that are to be held principally in Birmingham in 2022; and for connected purposes.

Divorce, Dissolution and Separation Act 2020 ch. 11 (25 June 2020) makes in relation to marriage and civil partnership in England and Wales provision about divorce, dissolution and separation; and for connected purposes.

Corporate Insolvency and Governance Act 2020 ch. 12 (25 June 2020) makes provision about companies and other entities in financial difficulty; and to make temporary changes to the law relating to the governance and regulation of companies and other entities.

Supply and Appropriation (Main Estimates) Act 2020 ch. 13 (22 July 2020) authorises the use of resources for the year ending with 31 March 2021; to authorise both the issue of sums out of the Consolidated Fund and the application of income for that year; and to appropriate the supply authorised for that year by this Act and by the Supply and Appropriation (Anticipation and Adjustments) Act 2020.

Finance Act 2020 ch. 14 (22 July 2020) grants certain duties, to alter other duties, and to amend the law relating to the national debt and the public revenue, and to make further provision in connection with finance.

Stamp Duty Land Tax (Temporary Relief) Act 2020 ch. 15 (22 July 2020) makes provision to reduce for a temporary period the amount of stamp duty land tax chargeable on the acquisition of residential property.

Business and Planning Act 2020 ch. 16 (22 July 2020) makes provision relating to the promotion of economic recovery and growth.

Sentencing Act 2020 ch. 17 (22 October 2020) consolidates certain enactments relating to sentencing.

Extradition (Provisional Arrest) Act 2020 ch. 18 (22 October 2020) creates a power of arrest, without warrant, for the purpose of extraditing people for serious offences.

Prisoners (Disclosure of Information About Victims) Act 2020 ch. 19 (4 November 2020) requires the Parole Board to take into account any failure by a prisoner serving a sentence for unlawful killing or for taking or making an indecent image of a child to disclose information about the victim.

Immigration and Social Security Co-ordination (EU Withdrawal) Act 2020 ch. 20 (11 November 2020) makes provision to end rights to free movement of persons under retained EU law and to repeal other retained EU law relating to immigration; to confer power to modify retained direct EU legislation relating to social security co-ordination; and for connected purposes.

Agriculture Act 2020 ch. 21 (11 November 2020) authorises expenditure for certain agricultural and other purposes; to makes provision about direct payments following the United Kingdom's departure from the European Union and about payments in response to exceptional market conditions affecting agricultural markets; confers power to modify retained direct EU legislation relating to agricultural and rural development payments and public market intervention and private storage aid; makes provision about reports on food security; makes provision about the acquisition and use of information connected with food supply chains; confers powers to make regulations about the imposition of obligations on business purchasers of agricultural products, marketing standards, organic products and the classification of carcasses; makes provision for reports relating to free trade agreements; makes provision for the recognition of associations of agricultural producers which may benefit from certain exemptions from competition law; makes provision about fertilisers; makes provision about the identification and traceability of animals; makes provision about red meat levy in Great Britain; makes provision about agricultural tenancies; confers power to make regulations about securing compliance with the WTO Agreement on Agriculture; and for connected purposes.

Fisheries Act 2020 ch. 22 (23 November 2020) makes provision in relation to fisheries, fishing, aquaculture and marine conservation; to make provision about the functions of the Marine Management Organisation; and for connected purposes.

Social Security (Up-rating of Benefits) Act 2020 ch. 23 (23 November 2020) makes provision relating to the up-rating of certain social security benefits.

Private International Law (Implementation of Agreements) Act 2020 ch. 24 (14 December 2020) implements the Hague Conventions of 1996, 2005 and 2007 and to provide for the implementation of other international agreements on private international law.

Parliamentary Constituencies Act 2020 ch. 25 (14 December 2020) makes provision about reports of the Boundary Commissions under the Parliamentary Constituencies Act 1986; to make provision about the number of parliamentary constituencies and other rules for the distribution of seats; and for connected purposes.

Taxation (Post-transition Period) Act 2020 ch. 26 (17 December 2020) makes provision (including the imposition and regulation of new duties of customs) in connection with goods in Northern Ireland and their movement into or out of Northern Ireland; to make provision amending certain enactments relating to value added tax, excise duty or insurance premium tax; to make provision in connection with the recovery of unlawful state aid in relation to controlled foreign companies; and for connected purposes.

United Kingdom Internal Market Act 2020 ch. 27 (17 December 2020) makes provision in connection with the internal market for goods and services in the United Kingdom (including provision about the recognition of professional and other qualifications); makes provision in connection with provisions of the Northern Ireland Protocol relating to trade and state aid; authorises the provision of financial assistance by Ministers of the Crown in connection with economic development, infrastructure, culture, sport and educational or training activities and exchanges; makes regulation of the provision of distortive or harmful subsidies a reserved or excepted matter; and for connected purposes.

Trade (Disclosure of Information) Act 2020 ch. 28 (17 December 2020) makes provision about the disclosure of information relating to trade.

European Union (Future Relationship) Act 2020 ch. 29 (31 December 2020) makes provision to implement, and make other provision in connection with, the Trade and Cooperation Agreement; to make further provision in connection with the United Kingdom's future relationship with the EU and its member States; makes related provision about passenger name record data, customs and privileges and immunities; and for connected purposes.

MEMBERS OF PARLIAMENT *as at 20 November 2020*

KEY

* Previously an MP for this seat in the 2017–19 parliament

† Previously an MP for this seat in any parliament prior to the 2017–19 parliament

‡ Previously an MP for a different seat in any previous parliament

§ Currently suspended from the parliamentary Conservative Party

℃ Currently suspended from the parliamentary Labour Party

* **Abbott**, Rt. Hon. Diane (*b.* 1953) *Lab., Hackney North & Stoke Newington,* Maj. 33,188

* **Abrahams**, Debbie (*b.* 1960) *Lab., Oldham East & Saddleworth,* Maj. 1,499

* **Adams**, Nigel (*b.* 1966) *C., Selby & Ainsty,* Maj. 20,137

* **Afolami**, Bim (*b.* 1986) *C., Hitchin & Harpenden,* Maj. 6,895

* **Afriyie**, Adam (*b.* 1965) *C., Windsor,* Maj. 20,079

Khan, Imran Ahman (*b.* 1973) *C., Wakefield,* Maj. 3, 358

Aiken, Nickie (*b.* 1969) *C. Cities of London and Westminster,* Maj. 3,953

* **Aldous**, Peter (*b.* 1961) *C., Waveney,* Maj. 18,002

* **Ali**, Rushanara (*b.* 1975) *Lab., Bethnal Green & Bow,* Maj. 37,524

Ali, Tahir (*b.*) 1971) *Lab., Birminham Hall Green,* Maj. 28,508

* **Allan**, Lucy (*b.* 1964) *C., Telford,* Maj. 10,941

* **Allen**, Heidi (*b.* 1975) *Ind., Cambridgeshire South,* Maj. 15,952

* **Allin-Khan**, Dr Rosena (*b.* 1977) *Lab., Tooting,* Maj. 14,307

Amesbury, Mike (*b.* 1969) *Lab., Weaver Vale,* Maj. 562

*‡ **Amess**, Sir David (*b.* 1952) *C., Southend West,* Maj. 14,459

Anderson, Fleur (*b.* 1971) *L. Putney,* Maj. 4,774

Anderson, Lee (*b.* 1967) *C. Ashfield,* Maj. 5,733

Anderson, Stuart (*b.* 1976) *C. Wolverhampton South West,* Maj. 1,661

* **Andrew**, Stuart (*b.* 1971) *C., Pudsey,* Maj. 3,517

† **Ansell**, Caroline (*b.* 1971) *C., Eastbourne* Maj. 4,331

* **Antoniazzi**, Tonia (*b.* 1971) *Lab., Gower,* Maj. 1,837

* **Argar**, Edward (*b.* 1977) *C., Charnwood,* Maj. 22,397

* **Ashworth**, Jonathan (*b.* 1978) *Lab. Co-op, Leicester South,* Maj. 22,675

Atherton, Sarah (*b.* 1967) *C., Wrexham,* Maj. 2,131

* **Atkins**, Victoria (*b.* 1976) *C., Louth & Horncastle,* Maj. 28,868

Bacon, Gareth (*b.* 1972) *C., Orpington* Maj. 22,378

* **Bacon**, Richard (*b.* 1962) *C., Norfolk South,* Maj. 21,275

* **Badenoch**, Kemi (*b.* 1980) *C., Saffron Walden,* Maj. 29,594

Bailey, Shaun (*b.* 1992) *C. West Bromwich West,* Maj. 3,799

Baillie, Siobhan, (*b.* 1981) *C. Stroud,* Maj. 3,840

Baker, Duncan (*b.* 1979) *C., North Norfolk,* Maj. 14,395

* **Baker**, Steve (*b.* 1971) *C., Wycombe,* Maj. 4,214

* **Baldwin**, Harriett (*b.* 1960) *C., Worcestershire West,* Maj. 24,449

* **Barclay**, Rt. Hon. Stephen (*b.* 1972) *C., North East Cambridgeshire,* Maj. 29,993

* **Bardell**, Hannah (*b.* 1984) *SNP, Livingston,* Maj. 13,435

Barker, Paula (*b.* 1972) *Lab., Liverpool Wavertree* Maj. 27,085

* **Baron**, John (*b.* 1959) *C., Basildon & Billericay,* Maj. 20,412

Baynes, Simon (*b.* 1960) *C. Clwyd South,* Maj. 1,239

*‡ **Beckett**, Rt. Hon. Dame Margaret, DBE (*b.* 1943) *Lab., Derby South,* Maj. 6,019

* **Begley**, Órfhlaith (*b.* 1991) *SF, Tyrone West,* Maj. 7,478

Begum, Apsana (*b.* 1990) *L. Poplar and Limehouse* Maj. 28,904

* **Bell**, Aaron (*b.* 1980) *C., Newcastle-under-Lyme,* Maj. 7,446

* **Benn**, Rt. Hon. Hilary (*b.* 1953) *Lab., Leeds Central,* Maj. 19,270

* **Benton**, Scott (*b.* 1960) *C., Blackpool South,* Maj. 3,690

* **Beresford**, Sir Paul (*b.* 1946) *C., Mole Valley,* Maj. 12,041

* **Berry**, Rt. Hon. Jake (*b.* 1978) *C., Rossendale & Darwen,* Maj. 9,522

* **Betts**, Clive (*b.* 1950) *Lab., Sheffield South East,* Maj. 4,289

Bhatti, Saqib, MBE (*b.* 1985) *C. Meriden* Maj. 22,836

* **Black**, Mhairi (*b.* 1994) *SNP, Paisley & Renfrewshire South,* Maj. 10,679

* **Blackman**, Bob (*b.* 1956) *C., Harrow East,* Maj. 8,170

* **Blackman**, Kirsty (*b.* 1986) *SNP, Aberdeen North,* Maj. 12,670

Blake, Olivia (*b.* 1990) *L., Sheffield Hallam,* Maj. 712

* **Blomfield**, Paul (*b.* 1953) *Lab., Sheffield Central,* Maj. 27,273

* **Blunt**, Crispin (*b.* 1960) *C., Reigate,* Maj. 18,310

* **Bone**, Peter (*b.* 1952) *C., Wellingborough,* Maj. 18,540

Bonnar, Steven (*b.* 1982) *SNP, Coatbridge, Chryston and Bellshill,* Maj. 5,624

*‡ **Bottomley**, Sir Peter (*b.* 1944) *C., Worthing West,* Maj. 14,823

* **Bowie**, Andrew (*b.* 1988) *C., Aberdeenshire West & Kincardine,* Maj. 843

* **Brabin**, Tracy (*b.* 1961) *Lab. Co-op, Batley & Spen,* Maj. 3,525

* **Bradley**, Ben (*b.* 1989) *C., Mansfield,* Maj. 16,306

* **Bradley**, Rt. Hon. Karen (*b.* 1970) *C., Staffordshire Moorlands,* Maj. 16,428

* **Bradshaw**, Rt. Hon. Ben (*b.* 1960) *Lab., Exeter,* Maj. 10,403

* **Brady**, Sir Graham (*b.* 1967) *C., Altrincham & Sale West,* Maj. 6,139

* **Brady**, Mickey (*b.* 1950) *SF, Newry & Armagh,* Maj. 9,287

* **Braverman**, Rt. Hon. Suella (*b.* 1980) *C., Fareham,* Maj. 26,086

* **Brennan**, Kevin (*b.* 1959) *Lab., Cardiff West,* Maj. 10,986

* **Brereton**, Jack (*b.* 1991) *C., Stoke-on-Trent South,* Maj. 11,271

* **Bridgen**, Andrew (*b.* 1964) *C., Leicestershire North West,* Maj. 20,400

* **Brine**, Steve (*b.* 1974) *C., Winchester,* Maj. 985

Bristow, Paul (*b.* 1979) *C. Peterborough,* Maj. 2,580

Britcliffe, Sara (*b.* 1995) *C. Hyndburn,* Maj. 2,951

* **Brock**, Deidre (*b.* 1961) *SNP, Edinburgh North & Leith,* Maj. 12,808

*‡ **Brokenshire**, Rt. Hon. James (*b.* 1968) *C., Old Bexley & Sidcup,* Maj. 18,952

* **Brown**, Alan (*b.* 1970) *SNP, Kilmarnock & Loudoun,* Maj. 12,659

* **Brown**, Lyn (*b.* 1960) *Lab., West Ham,* Maj. 32,388

* **Brown**, Rt. Hon. Nick (*b.* 1950) *Lab., Newcastle upon Tyne East,* Maj. 15,463

Browne, Anthony (*b.* 1967) *C., South Cambridgeshire,* Maj. 2,904

* **Bruce**, Fiona (*b.* 1957) *C., Congleton,* Maj. 18,561

* **Bryant**, Chris (*b.* 1962) *Lab., Rhondda,* Maj. 11,115

Buchan, Felicity, *C. Kensington,* Maj. 150

* **Buck**, Karen (*b.* 1958) *Lab., Westminster North,* Maj. 10,759

* **Buckland**, Rt. Hon. Robert (*b.* 1968) *C., Swindon South,* Maj. 6,625

* **Burden**, Richard (*b.* 1954) *Lab., Birmingham Northfield,* Maj. 4,667

* **Burghart**, Alex (*b.* 1977) *C., Brentwood & Ongar,* Maj. 29,065

* **Burgon**, Richard (*b.* 1980) *Lab., Leeds East,* Maj. 5,531

* **Burns**, Rt. Hon. Conor (*b.* 1972) *C., Bournemouth West,* Maj. 10,150

*‡ **Butler**, Dawn (*b.* 1969) *Lab., Brent Central,* Maj. 20,870

Butler, Rob (*b.* 1967) *C., Aylesbury,* Maj. 17,373

Byrne, Ian (*b.* 1972) *Lab., Liverpool West Derby,* Maj. 29,984

* **Byrne**, Rt. Hon. Liam (*b.* 1970) *Lab., Birmingham Hodge Hill*, Maj. 28,655
* **Cadbury**, Ruth (*b.* 1959) *Lab., Brentford & Isleworth*, Maj. 10,514
* **Cairns**, Rt. Hon. Alun (*b.* 1970) *C., Vale of Glamorgan*, Maj. 3,562
Callaghan Amy (*b.* 1992) *SNP, Dunbartonshire East*, Maj. 149
* **Cameron**, Dr Lisa (*b.* 1972) *SNP, East Kilbride, Strathaven & Lesmahagow*, Maj. 13,322
* **Campbell**, Rt. Hon. Sir Alan (*b.* 1957) *Lab., Tynemouth*, Maj. 4,857
* **Campbell**, Gregory (*b.* 1953) *DUP, Londonderry East*, Maj. 9,607
* **Carden**, Dan (*b.* 1987) *Lab., Liverpool Walton*, Maj. 30,520
* **Carmichael**, Rt. Hon. Alistair (*b.* 1965) *LD, Orkney & Shetland*, Maj. 2,507
Carter, Andy (*b.* 1974) *C., Warrington South* Maj. 2,010
* **Cartlidge**, James (*b.* 1974) *C., Suffolk South*, Maj. 22,903
* **Cash**, Sir William (*b.* 1940) *C., Stone*, Maj. 19,945
Cates, Miriam (*b.* 1982) *C. Penistone & Stocksbridge*, Maj. 7,210
* **Caulfield**, Maria (*b.* 1974) *C., Lewes*, Maj. 2,457
* **Chalk**, Alex (*b.* 1977) *C., Cheltenham*, Maj. 981
Chamberlain, Wendy (*b.* 1976) *LD, North East Fife*, Maj. 1,316
* **Champion**, Sarah (*b.* 1969) *Lab., Rotherham*, Maj. 3,121
* **Chapman**, Douglas (*b.* 1955) *SNP, Dunfermline & Fife West*, Maj. 10,699
Charalambous, Bambos (*b.* 1967) *Lab., Enfield Southgate*, Maj. 4,450
* **Cherry**, Joanna (*b.* 1966) *SNP, Edinburgh South West*, Maj. 11,982
* **Chishti**, Rehman (*b.* 1978) *C., Gillingham & Rainham*, Maj. 15,119
*‡ **Chope**, Sir Christopher, OBE (*b.* 1947) *C., Christchurch*, Maj. 24,617
* **Churchill**, Jo (*b.* 1964) *C., Bury St Edmunds*, Maj. 24,988
Clark, Feryal (*b.* 1979) *Lab, Enfield North*, Maj. 6,492
* **Clark**, Rt. Hon. Greg, PHD (*b.* 1967) *C., Tunbridge Wells*, Maj. 14,645
Clarke, Simon (*b.* 1984) *C., Middlesbrough South & Cleveland East*, Maj. 11,626
Clarke, Theo (*b.* 1985) *C. Stafford*, Maj. 14,377
Clarke-Smith, Brendan (*b.* 1980) *C. Bassetlaw*, Maj. 14,013
Clarkson, Chris (*b.* 1982) *C., Heywood & Middleton*, Maj. 663
* **Cleverly**, Rt. Hon. James (*b.* 1969) *C., Braintree*, Maj. 24,673
* **Clifton-Brown**, Sir Geoffrey (*b.* 1953) *C., Cotswolds, The*, Maj. 20,214
* **Coffey**, Rt. Hon. Thérèse, PHD (*b.* 1971) *C., Suffolk Coastal*, Maj. 20,553
Colburn, Elliot (*b.* 1992) *C. Carshalton and Wallington*, Maj. 629
* **Collins**, Damian (*b.* 1974) *C., Folkestone & Hythe*, Maj. 21,337
* **Cooper**, Rosie (*b.* 1950) *Lab., Lancashire West*, Maj. 8,336
* **Cooper**, Rt. Hon. Yvette (*b.* 1969) *Lab., Normanton, Pontefract & Castleford*, Maj. 18,297
* **Corbyn**, Rt. Hon. Jeremy (*b.* 1949) *Ind., Islington North*, Maj. 26,188
* **Costa**, Alberto (*b.* 1971) *C., Leicestershire South*, Maj. 24,004
* **Courts**, Robert (*b.* 1978) *C., Witney*, Maj. 15,177
Coutinho, Claire (*b.* 1985) *C. East Surrey*, Maj. 24,040
* **Cowan**, Ronnie (*b.* 1959) *SNP, Inverclyde*, Maj. 7,512
* **Cox**, Rt. Hon. Geoffrey (*b.* 1960) *C., Devon West & Torridge*, Maj. 24,992
* **Coyle**, Neil (*b.* 1978) *Lab., Bermondsey & Old Southwark*, Maj. 16,126
* **Crabb**, Rt. Hon. Stephen (*b.* 1973) *C., Preseli Pembrokeshire*, Maj. 5,062

* **Crawley**, Angela (*b.* 1987) *SNP, Lanark & Hamilton East*, Maj. 5,187
* **Creasy**, Stella, PHD (*b.* 1977) *Lab. Co-op, Walthamstow*, Maj. 30,862
Crosbie, Virginia (*b.* 1969) *C., Ynys Mon*, Maj. 1,968
* **Crouch**, Tracey (*b.* 1975) *C., Chatham & Aylesford*, Maj. 18,540
* **Cruddas**, Jon (*b.* 1962) *Lab., Dagenham & Rainham*, Maj. 293
*‡ **Cryer**, John (*b.* 1964) *Lab., Leyton & Wanstead*, Maj. 20,808
* **Cummins**, Judith (*b.* 1967) *Lab., Bradford South*, Maj. 2,346
* **Cunningham**, Alex (*b.* 1955) *Lab., Stockton North*, Maj. 1,027
* **Daby**, Janet (*b.* 1972) *Lab., Lewisham East*, Maj. 17,008
Daly, James (*b.* 1976) *C., Bury North*, Maj. 105
*† **Davey**, Rt. Hon. Sir Edward (*b.* 1965) *LD, Kingston & Surbiton*, Maj. 10,489
* **David**, Wayne (*b.* 1957) *Lab., Caerphilly*, Maj. 6,833
* **Davies**, David (*b.* 1970) *C., Monmouth*, Maj. 9,982
Davies, Gareth (*b.* 1984), *C., Grantham and Stamford*, Maj. 26,003
*‡ **Davies**, Geraint (*b.* 1960) *Lab. Co-op, Swansea West*, Maj. 8,116
† **Davies**, Dr James (*b.* 1980) *C., Vale of Clwyd*, Maj. 1,827
‡ **Davies**, Mims (*b.* 1975) *C., Mid Sussex*, Maj. 18,197
* **Davies**, Philip (*b.* 1972) *C., Shipley*, Maj. 6,242
Davies-Jones, Alex (*b.* 1988) *Lab., Pontypridd*, Maj. 5,887
* **Davis**, Rt. Hon. David (*b.* 1948) *C., Haltemprice & Howden*, Maj. 20,329
Davison, Dehenna (*b.* 1993) *C., Bishop Aukland*, Maj. 7,962
*‡ **Day**, Martyn (*b.* 1971) *SNP, Linlithgrow & Falkirk East*, Maj. 11,266
* **De Cordova**, Marsha (*b.* 1976) *Lab., Battersea*, Maj. 5,668
* **Debbonaire**, Thangam (*b.* 1966) *Lab., Bristol West*, Maj. 28,219
* **Dhesi**, Tanmanjeet Singh (*b.* 1978) *Lab., Slough*, Maj. 13,640
* **Dinenage**, Caroline (*b.* 1971) *C., Gosport*, Maj. 23,278
Dines, Sarah, *C., Derbyshire Dales*, Maj. 17,381
* **Djanogly**, Jonathan (*b.* 1965) *C., Huntingdon*, Maj. 19,383
* **Docherty**, Leo (*b.* 1976) *C., Aldershot*, Maj. 16,698
* **Docherty-Hughes**, Martin (*b.* 1971) *SNP, Dunbartonshire West*, Maj. 9,553
* **Dodds**, Anneliese, PHD (*b.* 1978) *Lab. Co-op, Oxford East*, Maj. 17,832
* **Donaldson**, Rt. Hon. Sir Jeffrey (*b.* 1962) *DUP, Lagan Valley*, Maj. 6,499
* **Donelan**, Michelle (*b.* 1984) *C., Chippenham*, Maj. 11,288
Doogan, Dave (*b.* 1973) *SNP, Angus*, Maj. 3,795
Dorans, Allan (*b.* 1955) *SNP, Ayr, Carrick & Cumnock*, Maj. 2,329
* **Dorries**, Nadine (*b.* 1957) *C., Bedfordshire Mid*, Maj. 24,664
* **Double**, Steve (*b.* 1966) *C., St Austell & Newquay*, Maj. 16,526
* **Doughty**, Stephen (*b.* 1980) *Lab. Co-op, Cardiff South & Penarth*, Maj. 12,737
* **Dowd**, Peter (*b.* 1957) *Lab., Bootle*, Maj. 34,556
* **Dowden**, Rt. Hon. Oliver, CBE (*b.* 1978) *C., Hertsmere*, Maj. 21,313
* **Doyle-Price**, Jackie (*b.* 1969) *C., Thurrock*, Maj. 11,482
* **Drax**, Richard (*b.* 1958) *C., Dorset South*, Maj. 17,153
* **Dromey**, Jack (*b.* 1948) *Lab., Birmingham Erdington*, Maj. 3,601
‡ **Drummond**, Flick (*b.* 1962) *C., Meon Valley*, Maj. 23,555
* **Duddridge**, James (*b.* 1971) *C., Rochford & Southend East*, Maj. 12,286
* **Duffield**, Rosie (*b.* 1971) *Lab., Canterbury*, Maj. 1,836
* **Duguid**, David (*b.* 1970) *C., Banff & Buchan*, Maj. 4,118
* **Duncan Smith**, Rt. Hon. Sir Iain (*b.* 1954) *C., Chingford & Woodford Green*, Maj. 1,262
* **Dunne**, Rt. Hon. Philip (*b.* 1958) *C., Ludlow*, Maj. 23,648
* **Eagle**, Angela (*b.* 1961) *Lab., Wallasey*, Maj. 18,322

* **Eagle**, Maria (*b.* 1961) *Lab., Garston & Halewood,* Maj. 31,624

Eastwood, Colum (*b.* 1983) *SDLP, Foyle,* 17,110

Eastwood, Mark (*b.* 1971) *C., Dewsbury,* 1,561

* **Edwards**, Jonathan (*b.* 1976) *Ind., Carmarthen East & Dinefwr,* Maj. 1,809

Edwards, Ruth, *C., Rushcliffe,* Maj. 7,643

* **Efford**, Clive (*b.* 1958) *Lab., Eltham,* Maj. 3,197

* **Elliott**, Julie (*b.* 1963) *Lab., Sunderland Central,* Maj. 2,964

* **Ellis**, Rt. Hon. Michael (*b.* 1967) *C., Northampton North,* Maj. 5,507

* **Ellwood**, Rt. Hon. Tobias (*b.* 1966) *C., Bournemouth East,* Maj. 8,806

* **Elmore**, Chris (*b.* 1983) *Lab., Ogmore,* Maj. 7,805

Elphicke, Natalie, OBE (*b.* 1970) *C., Dover,* Maj. 12,278

Eshalmoi, Florence (*b.* 1980) *Lab Co-op, Vauxhall,* Maj. 19,612

* **Esterson**, Bill (*b.* 1966) *Lab., Sefton Central,* Maj. 15,122

* **Eustice**, Rt. Hon. George (*b.* 1971) *C., Camborne & Redruth,* Maj. 8,700

* **Evans**, Chris (*b.* 1976) *Lab. Co-op, Islwyn,* Maj. 15,356

Evans, Dr Luke (*b.* 1983) *C. Bosworth,* Maj. 26,278

* **Evans**, Nigel (*b.* 1957) *C., Ribble Valley,* Maj. 18,439

* **Evennett**, Rt. Hon. Sir David (*b.* 1949) *C., Bexleyheath & Crayford,* Maj. 13,103

* **Fabricant**, Michael (*b.* 1950) *C., Lichfield,* Maj. 23,638

Farris, Laura (*b.* 1978) *C., Newbury,* Maj. 16,047

* **Farron**, Tim (*b.* 1970) *LD, Westmorland & Lonsdale,* Maj. 1,934

Farry, Stephen (*b.* 1971) *Alliance, North Down,* Maj. 2,968

Fell, Simon (*b.* 1980) *C. Barrow and Furness,* Maj. 5,789

* **Fellows**, Marion (*b.* 1949) *SNP, Motherwell & Wishaw,* Maj. 6,268

Ferrier, Margaret (*b.* 1960) *SNP, Rutherglen & Hamilton West,* 5,230

Finucane, John (*b.* 1980) *SF, Belfast North,* 23,078

* **Fletcher**, Colleen (*b.* 1954) *Lab., Coventry North East,* Maj. 7,692

Fletcher, Katherine (*b.* 1976) *C., South Ribble,* Maj. 11,199

Fletcher, Mark (*b.* 1985) *C., Bolsover,* Maj. 5,299

Fletcher, Nick (*b.* 1972) *C., Don Valley,* Maj. 3,630

Flynn, Stephen (*b.* 1988) *SNP, Aberdeen South,* Maj. 3,982

Ford, Vicky (*b.* 1967) *C., Chelmsford,* Maj. 17,621

* **Foster**, Kevin (*b.* 1978) *C., Torbay,* Maj. 17,749

* **Fovargue**, Yvonne (*b.* 1956) *Lab., Makerfield,* Maj. 4,740

* **Fox**, Rt. Hon. Dr Liam (*b.* 1961) *C., Somerset North,* Maj. 17,536

* **Foxcroft**, Vicky (*b.* 1977) *Lab., Lewisham Deptford,* Maj. 32,913

Foy, Mary (*b.* 1968) *Lab., City of Durham,* Maj. 5,025

* **Francois**, Rt. Hon. Mark (*b.* 1965) *C., Rayleigh & Wickford,* Maj. 31,000

* **Frazer**, Lucy (*b.* 1972) *C., Cambridgeshire South East,* Maj. 11,490

* **Freeman**, George (*b.* 1967) *C., Norfolk Mid,* Maj. 22,594

* **Freer**, Mike (*b.* 1960) *C., Finchley & Golders Green,* Maj. 6,562

‡ **Fuller**, Richard (*b.* 1962) *C., North East Bedfordshire,* Maj. 24,283

* **Furniss**, Gill (*b.* 1957) *Lab., Sheffield Brightside & Hillsborough,* Maj. 12,274

* **Fysh**, Marcus (*b.* 1970) *C., Yeovil,* Maj. 16,181

* **Gale**, Rt. Hon. Sir Roger (*b.* 1943) *C., Thanet North,* Maj. 17,189

* **Gardiner**, Barry (*b.* 1957) *Lab., Brent North,* Maj. 8,079

* **Garnier**, Mark (*b.* 1963) *C., Wyre Forest,* Maj. 21,413

* **Ghani**, Nusrat (*b.* 1972) *C., Wealden,* Maj. 25,655

* **Gibb**, Rt. Hon. Nick (*b.* 1960) *C., Bognor Regis & Littlehampton,* Maj. 22,503

* **Gibson**, Patricia (*b.* 1968) *SNP, Ayrshire North & Arran,* Maj. 8,521

Gibson, Peter (*b.* 1975) *C., Darlington,* Maj. 3,294

Gideon, Jo (*b.* 1952) *C., Stoke-on-Trent Central,* Maj. 670

*† **Gildernew**, Michelle (*b.* 1970) *SF, Fermanagh & South Tyrone,* Maj. 57

Gill, Preet (*b.* 1972) *Lab. Co-op, Birmingham Edgbaston,* Maj. 5,614

* **Gillan**, Rt. Hon. Dame Cheryl, DBE (*b.* 1952) *C., Chesham & Amersham,* Maj. 16,223

* **Girvan**, Paul (*b.* 1963) *DUP, Antrim South,* Maj. 2,689

* **Glen**, John (*b.* 1974) *C., Salisbury,* Maj. 19,736

* **Glindon**, Mary (*b.* 1957) *Lab., Tyneside North,* Maj. 9,561

* **Goodwill**, Rt. Hon. Robert (*b.* 1956) *C., Scarborough & Whitby,* Maj. 10,270

* **Gove**, Rt. Hon. Michael (*b.* 1967) *C., Surrey Heath,* Maj. 18,349

* **Grady**, Patrick (*b.* 1980) *SNP, Glasgow North,* Maj. 5,601

* **Graham**, Richard (*b.* 1958) *C., Gloucester,* Maj. 10,277

* **Grant**, Helen (*b.* 1961) *C., Maidstone & The Weald,* Maj. 21,772

* **Grant**, Peter (*b.* 1961) *SNP, Glenrothes,* Maj. 11,757

* **Gray**, James (*b.* 1954) *C., Wiltshire North,* Maj. 17,626

* **Gray**, Neil (*b.* 1986) *SNP, Airdrie & Shotts,* Maj. 5,201

* **Grayling**, Rt. Hon. Chris (*b.* 1962) *C., Epsom & Ewell,* Maj. 17,873

* **Green**, Chris (*b.* 1973) *C., Bolton West,* Maj. 8,855

* **Green**, Rt. Hon. Damian (*b.* 1956) *C., Ashford,* Maj. 24,029

* **Green**, Kate (*b.* 1960) *Lab., Stretford & Urmston,* Maj. 16,417

* **Greenwood**, Lilian (*b.* 1966) *Lab., Nottingham South,* Maj. 12,568

* **Greenwood**, Margaret (*b.* 1959) *Lab., Wirral West,* Maj. 3,003

Griffith, Andrew (*b.* 1971) *C., Arundel & South Downs,* Maj. 22,521

* **Griffith**, Nia (*b.* 1956) *Lab., Llanelli,* Maj. 4,670

Griffiths, Kate (*b.* 1971) *C., Burton,* Maj. 14,496

‡ **Grogan**, John (*b.* 1961) *Lab., Keighley,* Maj. 249

Grundy, James (*b.* 1980) *C., Leigh,* Maj. 1,965

Gullis, Jonathan (*b.* 1990) *C., Stoke-on-Trent North,* Maj. 6,286

* **Gwynne**, Andrew (*b.* 1974) *Lab., Denton & Reddish,* Maj. 6,175

* **Haigh**, Louise (*b.* 1987) *Lab., Sheffield Heeley,* Maj. 8,520

* **Halfon**, Rt. Hon. Robert (*b.* 1969) *C., Harlow,* Maj. 14,063

* **Hall**, Luke (*b.* 1986) *C., Thornbury & Yate,* Maj. 12,369

* **Hamilton**, Fabian (*b.* 1955) *Lab., Leeds North East,* Maj. 17,089

* **Hammond**, Stephen (*b.* 1962) *C., Wimbledon,* Maj. 628

* **Hancock**, Rt. Hon. Matt (*b.* 1978) *C., Suffolk West,* Maj. 23,194

* **Hands**, Rt. Hon. Greg (*b.* 1965) *C., Chelsea & Fulham,* Maj. 11,241

Hanna, Claire (*b.* 1980) *SDLP, Belfast South,* Maj. 15,401

Hanvey, Neale (*b.* 1964) *SNP, Kirkcaldy and Cowdenbeath,* 1,243

* **Hardy**, Emma (*b.* 1980) *Lab., Hull West & Hessle,* Maj. 2,856

* **Harman**, Rt. Hon. Harriet (*b.* 1950) *Lab., Camberwell & Peckham,* Maj. 33,780

* **Harper**, Rt. Hon. Mark (*b.* 1970) *C., Forest of Dean,* Maj. 15,869

* **Harris**, Carolyn (*b.* 1960) *Lab., Swansea East,* Maj. 7,970

* **Harris**, Rebecca (*b.* 1967) *C., Castle Point,* Maj. 26,634

* **Harrison**, Trudy (*b.* 1976) *C., Copeland,* Maj. 5,842

Hart, Sally-Ann (*b.* 1968) *C., Hastings and Rye,* Maj. 4,043

* **Hart**, Simon (*b.* 1963) *C., Carmarthen West & Pembrokeshire South,* Maj. 7,745

* **Hayes**, Helen (*b.* 1974) *Lab., Dulwich & West Norwood,* Maj. 27,310

* **Hayes**, Rt. Hon. Sir John, CBE (b. 1958) C., *South Holland & The Deepings*, Maj. 30,838

* **Hazzard**, Chris (b. 1984) SF, *Down South*, Maj. 1,620

* **Heald**, Sir Oliver (b. 1954) C., *Hertfordshire North East*, Maj. 18,189

* **Healey**, Rt. Hon. John (b. 1960) *Lab., Wentworth & Dearne*, Maj. 2,165

* **Heappey**, James (b. 1981) C., *Wells*, Maj. 9,991

* **Heaton-Harris**, Chris (b. 1967) C., *Daventry*, Maj. 26,080

* **Henderson**, Gordon (b. 1948) C., *Sittingbourne & Sheppey*, Maj. 24,479

* **Hendrick**, Sir Mark (b. 1958) *Lab. Co-op, Preston*, Maj. 12,146

* **Hendry**, Drew (b. 1964) SNP, *Inverness, Nairn, Badenoch & Strathspey*, Maj. 10,440

Henry, Darren (b. 1968) C., *Broxtowe*, Maj. 5,331

Higginbotham, Antony (b. 1989) C., *Burnley*, Maj. 1,352

* **Hill**, Mike (b. 1963) *Lab., Hartlepool*, Maj. 3, 595

* **Hillier**, Meg (b. 1969) *Lab. Co-op, Hackney South & Shoreditch*, Maj. 33,985

* **Hinds**, Rt. Hon. Damian (b. 1969) C., *Hampshire East*, Maj. 19,696

* **Hoare**, Simon (b. 1969) C., *Dorset North*, Maj. 24,301

* **Hobhouse**, Wera (b. 1960) LD, *Bath*, Maj. 12,322

* **Hodge**, Rt. Hon. Dame Margaret, DBE (b. 1944) *Lab., Barking*, Maj. 15,427

* **Hodgson**, Sharon (b. 1966) *Lab., Washington & Sunderland West*, Maj. 3,723

Holden, Richard (b. 1985) C., *North West Durham*, Maj. 1,144

* **Hollern**, Kate (b. 1955) *Lab., Blackburn*, Maj. 18,3042

* **Hollinrake**, Kevin (b. 1963) C., *Thirsk & Malton*, Maj. 25,154

* **Hollobone**, Philip (b. 1964) C., *Kettering*, Maj. 16,765

* **Holloway**, Adam (b. 1965) C., *Gravesham*, Maj. 15,581

Holmes, Paul (b. 1988) C., *Eastleigh*, Maj. 15,607

Hopkins, Rachel (b. 1972) *Lab., Luton South*, Maj. 8,756

* **Hosie**, Stewart (b. 1963) SNP, *Dundee East*, Maj. 13,375

* **Howarth**, Rt. Hon. Sir George (b. 1949) *Lab., Knowsley*, Maj. 39,942

* **Howell**, John (b. 1955) C., *Henley*, Maj. 14,053

* **Hoyle**, Rt. Hon. Sir Lindsay (b. 1957) *Speaker, Chorley*, Maj. 17,392

* **Huddleston**, Nigel (b. 1970) C., *Worcestershire Mid*, Maj. 28,018

Hudson, Neil, PHD (b. 1971) C., *Penrith & The Border*, Maj. 18,519

* **Hughes**, Eddie (b. 1968) C., *Walsall North*, Maj. 11,965

Hunt, Jane (b. 1966) C. *Loughborough*, Maj. 7,169

* **Hunt**, Rt. Hon. Jeremy (b. 1966) C., *Surrey South West*, Maj. 8,817

Hunt, Tom (b. 1988) C., *Ipswich*, Maj. 5,479

* **Huq**, Rupa, PHD (b. 1972) *Lab., Ealing Central & Acton*, Maj. 13,300

* **Hussain**, Imran (b. 1978) *Lab., Bradford East*, Maj. 18,144

* **Jack**, Rt. Hon. Alister (b. 1964) C., *Dumfries & Galloway*, Maj. 1,805

* **Jardine**, Christine (b. 1960) LD, *Edinburgh West*, Maj. 3,769

* **Jarvis**, Dan (b. 1972) *Lab., Barnsley Central*, Maj. 3,571

* **Javid**, Rt. Hon. Sajid (b. 1969) C., *Bromsgrove*, Maj. 23,106

* **Jayawardena**, Ranil (b. 1986) C., *Hampshire North East*, Maj. 35,280

* **Jenkin**, Sir Bernard (b. 1959) C., *Harwich & Essex North*, Maj. 20,182

Jenkinson, Mark (b. 1982) C., *Workington*, Maj. 4,176

* **Jenkyns**, Andrea (b. 1974) C., *Morley & Outwood*, Maj. 11,267

* **Jenrick**, Rt. Hon. Robert (b. 1982) C., *Newark*, Maj. 21,836

*‡ **Johnson**, Rt. Hon. Boris (b. 1964) C., *Uxbridge & Ruislip South*, Maj. 7,210

* **Johnson**, Dr Caroline (b. 1977) C., *Sleaford & North Hykeham*, Maj. 32,565

* **Johnson**, Dame Diana, DBE (b. 1966) *Lab., Hull North*, Maj. 7,593

* **Johnson**, Gareth (b. 1969) C., *Dartford*, Maj. 19,160

Johnson, Kim (b. 1960) *Lab., Liverpool Riverside*, Maj. 41,170

Johnston, David, OBE (b. 1981) C., *Wantage*, Maj. 12,653

* **Jones**, Andrew (b. 1963) C., *Harrogate & Knaresborough*, Maj. 9,675

* **Jones**, Darren (b. 1986) *Lab., Bristol North West*, Maj. 5,692

* **Jones**, Rt. Hon. David (b. 1952) C., *Clwyd West*, Maj. 14,402

Jones, Fay (1985) C., *Brecon and Radnorshire*, Maj. 7,131

* **Jones**, Gerald (b. 1970) *Lab., Merthyr Tydfil & Rhymney*, Maj. 10,606

* **Jones**, Rt. Hon. Kevan (b. 1964) *Lab., Durham North*, Maj. 4,742

* **Jones**, Marcus (b. 1974) C., *Nuneaton*, Maj. 13,144

* **Jones**, Ruth, (b. 1962) *Lab., Newport West* Maj. 902

* **Jones**, Sarah (b. 1972) *Lab., Croydon Central*, Maj. 5,949

* **Jupp**, Simon (b. 1985) C., *Devon East*, Maj. 6,708

* **Kane**, Mike (b. 1969) *Lab., Wythenshawe & Sale East*, Maj. 10,396

* **Kawczynski**, Daniel (b. 1972) C., *Shrewsbury & Atcham*, Maj. 11,217

Kearns, Alicia (b. 1988) C., *Rutland and Melton*, Maj. 26,924

* **Keegan**, Gillian (b. 1968) C., *Chichester*, Maj. 21,490

* **Keeley**, Barbara (b. 1952) *Lab., Worsley & Eccles South*, Maj. 3,219

* **Kendall**, Liz (b. 1971) *Lab., Leicester West*, Maj. 4,212

* **Khan**, Afzal, CBE (b. 1958) *Lab., Manchester Gorton*, Maj. 30,339

* **Kinnock**, Stephen (b. 1970) *Lab., Aberavon*, Maj. 10,490

*‡ **Knight**, Rt. Hon. Sir Greg (b. 1949) C., *Yorkshire East*, Maj. 22,787

* **Knight**, Julian (b. 1972) C., *Solihull*, Maj. 21,273

Kruger, Danny, MBE (b. 1974) C., *Devizes*, Maj. 23,993

* **Kwarteng**, Rt. Hon. Kwasi, PHD (b. 1975) C., *Spelthorne*, Maj. 18,393

* **Kyle**, Peter, DPHIL (b. 1970) *Lab., Hove*, Maj. 17,044

* **Laing**, Rt. Hon. Dame Eleanor, DBE (b. 1958) C., *Epping Forest*, Maj. 22,173

* **Lake**, Ben (b. 1993) PC, *Ceredigion*, Maj. 6,329

* **Lammy**, Rt. Hon. David (b. 1972) *Lab., Tottenham*, Maj. 30,175

* **Lamont**, John (b. 1976) C., *Berwickshire, Roxburgh & Selkirk*, Maj. 5,148

Largan, Robert (b. 1987) C., *High Peak*, Maj. 590

* **Latham**, Pauline, OBE (b. 1948) C., *Derbyshire Mid*, Maj. 15,385

* **Lavery**, Ian (b. 1963) *Lab., Wansbeck*, Maj. 814

* **Law**, Chris (b. 1969) SNP, *Dundee West*, Maj. 12,259

* **Leadsom**, Rt. Hon. Andrea, CBE (b. 1963) C., *Northamptonshire South*, Maj. 27,761

* **Leigh**, Rt. Hon. Sir Edward (b. 1950) C., *Gainsborough*, Maj. 22,967

Levy, Ian (b. 1966) C., *Blyth Valley*, Maj. 712

* **Lewell-Buck**, Emma (b. 1978) *Lab., South Shields*, Maj. 9,585

* **Lewer**, Andrew, MBE (b. 1971) C., *Northampton South*, Maj. 4,697

* **Lewis**, Rt. Hon. Brandon, CBE (b. 1971) C., *Great Yarmouth*, Maj. 17,663

* **Lewis**, Clive (b. 1971) *Lab., Norwich South*, Maj. 12,760

* **Lewis**, Rt. Hon. Julian, DPHIL (b. 1951) *Ind., New Forest East*, Maj. 25,251

* **Liddell-Grainger**, Ian (b. 1959) C., *Bridgwater & Somerset West*, Maj. 24,439

* **Linden**, David (b. 1990) SNP, *Glasgow East*, Maj. 5,566

*‡ **Lloyd**, Tony (b. 1950) *Lab., Rochdale*, Maj. 9,668

Lockhart, Carla (b. 1985) DUP, *Upper Bann*, Maj. 20,501

* **O'Hara**, Brendan (b. 1963) SNP, Argyll & Bute, Maj. 4,110
† **Olney**, Sarah (b. 1977) LD, Richmond Park, Maj. 7,766
* **Onwurah**, Chi (b. 1965) Lab., Newcastle upon Tyne Central, Maj. 12,278
* **Opperman**, Guy (b. 1965) C., Hexham, Maj. 10,549
Oppong-Asare, Abena (b. 1982) Lab., Erith and Thamesmead, Maj. 3,758
* **Osamor**, Kate (b. 1968) Lab. Co-op, Edmonton, Maj. 16,015
Osborne, Kate, Lab., Jarrow, Maj. 7,120
† **Oswald**, Kirsten (b. 1972) SNP, East Renfrewshire, Maj. 5,426
Owatemi, Taiwo (b. 1992) Lab., Coventry North West, Maj. 208
Owen, Sarah (b. 1983) Lab., Luton North, Maj. 9,247
* **Paisley**, Hon. Ian (b. 1960) DUP, Antrim North, Maj. 12,721
* **Parish**, Neil (b. 1956) C., Tiverton & Honiton, Maj. 24,239
* **Patel**, Rt. Hon. Priti (b. 1972) C., Witham, Maj. 24,082
* **Paterson**, Rt. Hon. Owen (b. 1956) C., Shropshire North, Maj. 22,949
* **Pawsey**, Mark (b. 1957) C., Rugby, Maj. 13,447
* **Peacock**, Stephanie (b. 1986) Lab., Barnsley East, Maj. 3,217
* **Penning**, Rt. Hon. Sir Mike (b. 1957) C., Hemel Hempstead, Maj. 14,563
* **Pennycook**, Matthew (b. 1982) Lab., Greenwich & Woolwich, Maj. 18,464
* **Penrose**, John (b. 1964) C., Weston-Super-Mare, Maj. 17,121
* **Percy**, Andrew (b. 1977) C., Brigg & Goole, Maj. 21,941
* **Perkins**, Toby (b. 1970) Lab., Chesterfield, Maj. 1,451
* **Phillips**, Jess (b. 1981) Lab., Birmingham Yardley, Maj. 10,659
* **Phillipson**, Bridget (b. 1983) Lab., Houghton & Sunderland South, Maj. 3,115
* **Philp**, Chris (b. 1976) C., Croydon South, Maj. 12,339
* **Pincher**, Rt. Hon. Christopher (b. 1969) C., Tamworth, Maj. 19,634
* **Pollard**, Luke (b. 1980) Lab. Co-op, Plymouth Sutton & Devonport, Maj. 4,757
* **Poulter**, Dr Dan (b. 1978) C., Suffolk Central & Ipswich North, Maj. 23,391
* **Pow**, Rebecca (b. 1960) C., Taunton Deane, Maj. 11,700
* **Powell**, Lucy (b. 1974) Lab. Co-op, Manchester Central, Maj. 29,089
* **Prentis**, Hon. Victoria (b. 1971) C., Banbury, Maj. 16,813
* **Pritchard**, Mark (b. 1966) C., Wrekin, The, Maj. 18,726
* **Pursglove**, Tom (b. 1988) C., Corby, Maj. 10,268
* **Quin**, Jeremy (b. 1968) C., Horsham, Maj. 21,127
* **Quince**, Will (b. 1982) C., Colchester, Maj. 9,423
* **Qureshi**, Yasmin (b. 1963) Lab., Bolton South East, Maj. 7,598
* **Raab**, Rt. Hon. Dominic (b. 1974) C., Esher & Walton, Maj. 2,743
Randall Tom, C., Gedling, Maj. 679
* **Rayner**, Angela (b. 1980) Lab., Ashton Under Lyne, Maj. 4,263
* **Redwood**, Rt. Hon. Sir John, DPHIL (b. 1951) C., Wokingham, Maj. 7,383
* **Reed**, Steve (b. 1963) Lab. Co-op, Croydon North, Maj. 24,673
* **Rees**, Christina (b. 1954) Lab. Co-op, Neath, Maj. 5,637
* **Rees-Mogg**, Rt. Hon. Jacob (b. 1969) C., Somerset North East, Maj. 14,729
* **Reeves**, Ellie (b. 1980) Lab., Lewisham West & Penge, Maj. 21,543
* **Reeves**, Rachel (b. 1979) Lab., Leeds West, Maj. 10,564
* **Reynolds**, Jonathan (b. 1980) Lab. Co-op, Stalybridge & Hyde, Maj. 2,946
Ribeiro-Addy, Bell (b. 1985) Lab, Streatham, 17,690
Richards, Nicola (b. 1994) C., West Bromwich East, Maj. 1,593
Richardson, Angela, C., Guildford, Maj. 3,337
* **Rimmer**, Marie (b. 1947) Lab., St Helens South & Whiston, Maj. 19,122
Roberts, Rob, C., Delyn, Maj. 865
* **Robertson**, Laurence (b. 1958) C., Tewkesbury, Maj. 22,410
* **Robinson**, Gavin (b. 1984) DUP, Belfast East, Maj. 1,819
* **Robinson**, Mary (b. 1955) C., Cheadle, Maj. 2,336

* **Rodda**, Matt (b. 1966) Lab., Reading East, Maj. 5,924
* **Rosindell**, Andrew (b. 1966) C., Romford, Maj. 17,893
* **Ross**, Douglas (b. 1983) C., Moray, Maj. 513
* **Rowley**, Lee (b. 1980) C., Derbyshire North East, Maj. 12,876
Russell, Dean (b. 1976) C., Watford, 4,433
* **Russell-Moyle**, Lloyd (b. 1986) Lab. Co-op, Brighton Kemptown, Maj. 8,061
* **Rutley**, David (b. 1961) C., Macclesfield, Maj. 10,711
Sambrook, Gary (b. 1989) C., Birmingham Northfield, Maj. 1,640
* **Saville Roberts**, Rt. Hon. Liz (b. 1964) PC, Dwyfor Meirionnydd, Maj. 4,740
Saxby, Selaine (b. 1970) C., North Devon, Maj. 14,813
* **Scully**, Paul (b. 1968) C., Sutton & Cheam, Maj. 8,351
* **Seely**, Bob (b. 1966) C., Isle of Wight, Maj. 23,737
* **Selous**, Andrew (b. 1962) C., Bedfordshire South West, Maj. 18,583
* **Shah**, Naz (b. 1973) Lab., Bradford West, Maj. 27,019
* **Shannon**, Jim (b. 1955) DUP, Strangford, Maj. 7,071
* **Shapps**, Rt. Hon. Grant (b. 1968) C., Welwyn Hatfield, Maj. 10,955
* **Sharma**, Rt. Hon. Alok (b. 1967) C., Reading West, Maj. 4,117
* **Sharma**, Virendra (b. 1947) Lab., Ealing Southall, Maj. 16,084
* **Sheerman**, Barry (b. 1940) Lab. Co-op, Huddersfield, Maj. 20,509
* **Shelbrooke**, Rt. Hon. Alec (b. 1976) C., Elmet & Rothwell, Maj. 17,353
* **Sheppard**, Tommy (b. 1959) SNP, Edinburgh East, Maj. 10,417
* **Siddiq**, Tulip (b. 1982) Lab., Hampstead & Kilburn, Maj. 14,188
Simmonds, David, CBE (b. 1976) C., Ruislip, Northwood & Pinner, Maj. 16,394
* **Skidmore**, Rt. Hon. Chris (b. 1981) C., Kingswood, Maj. 11,220
* **Slaughter**, Andy (b. 1960) Lab., Hammersmith, Maj. 17,847
Smith, Alyn (b. 1973) SNP, Stirling, Maj. 9,254
* **Smith**, Cat (b. 1985) Lab., Lancaster & Fleetwood, Maj. 2,380
* **Smith**, Chloe (b. 1982) C., Norwich North, Maj. 4,738
Smith, Greg (b. 1979) C., Buckingham, Maj. 20,411
* **Smith**, Henry (b. 1969) C., Crawley, Maj. 8,360
* **Smith**, Jeff (b. 1963) Lab., Manchester Withington, Maj. 27,905
* **Smith**, Rt. Hon. Julian, CBE (b. 1971) C., Skipton & Ripon, Maj. 23,694
* **Smith**, Nick (b. 1960) Lab., Blaenau Gwent, Maj. 8,647
* **Smith**, Royston (b. 1964) C., Southampton Itchen, Maj. 4,498
* **Smyth**, Karin (b. 1964) Lab., Bristol South, Maj. 9,859
* **Sobel**, Alex (b. 1975) Lab. Co-op, Leeds North West, Maj. 10,749
† **Solloway**, Amanda (b. 1961) C., Derby North, Maj. 2,540
*‡ **Spellar**, Rt. Hon. John (b. 1947) Lab., Warley, Maj. 11,511
* **Spelman**, Rt. Hon. Dame Caroline, DBE (b. 1958) C., Meriden, Maj. 19,198
Spencer, Dr Ben (b. 1981) C., Runnymede and Weybridge, Maj. 18,270
* **Spencer**, Rt. Hon. Mark (b. 1970) C., Sherwood, Maj. 16,186
Stafford, Alexander (b. 1987) C., Rother Valley, Maj. 14,377
* **Starmer**, Rt. Hon. Sir Keir, KCB (b. 1962) Lab., Holborn & St Pancras, Maj. 27,763
* **Stephens**, Chris (b. 1973) SNP, Glasgow South West, Maj. 4,900
* **Stephenson**, Andrew (b. 1981) C., Pendle, Maj. 6,186
* **Stevens**, Jo (b. 1966) Lab., Cardiff Central, Maj. 17,196
Stevenson, Jane (b. 1971) C., Wolverhampton North East, 4,080
* **Stevenson**, John (b. 1963) C., Carlisle, Maj. 8,319
* **Stewart**, Bob, DSO (b. 1949) C., Beckenham, Maj. 14,258
* **Stewart**, Iain (b. 1972) C., Milton Keynes South, Maj. 6,944

GENERAL ELECTION 2019 RESULTS

UK Turnout

Electorate (E.) 47,587,254 Turnout (T.) 32,026,222 (67.3%)

The results of voting in each of the 650 parliamentary constituencies at the general election on 12 December 2019 are given below.

KEY

swing N/A indicates a constituency for which the swing data cannot be calculated because one of the top two parties in the 2017 General Election did not field a candidate in the seat in 2019.

ABBREVIATIONS OF POLITICAL PARTIES

Active Dem.	Movement for Active Democracy
AD	Apolitical Democrats
Alliance	Alliance Party of Northern Ireland
AP	All People's Party
APNI	APNI Party
AWAP	Abolish the Welsh Assembly Party
AWP	Animal Welfare Party
BA	Brexit Alliance
Blue	Blue Revolution
BNP	British National Party
Bournemouth	Bournemouth Independent Alliance
BPE	Bus-Pass Elvis Party
Bradford	Better for Bradford
Brexit	The Brexit Party
Bristol	Independents for Bristol
C.	Conservative
Change	Alter Change
ChangeUK	The Independent Group for Change
Ch. P.	The Christian Party
CISTA	Cannabis is Safer than Alcohol
Citizens	Citizens Independent Social Thought Alliance
Co. Gd	Common Good
Comm.	Communist Party of Britain
Comm. Lge	Communist League
Community	Communities United Party
Compass	Compass Party
Concordia	Concordia
CPA	Christian Peoples Alliance
Croydon	Putting Croydon First
CSP	Common Sense Party
DDI	Demos Direct Initiative
Digital	Digital Democracy
DUP	Democratic Unionist Party
DVP	Democrats and Veterans Party
Eccentric	The Eccentric Party of Great Britain
Elmo	Give Me Back Elmo
Elvis	Church of the Militant Elvis
Eng. Dem.	English Democrats
Eng. Ind.	English Independence

For Britain	The For Britain Movement
Friends	Friends Party
GM Homeless	Greater Manchester Homeless Voice
Good	The Common Good
Green	Green Party
Green Soc.	Alliance for Green Socialism
Guildford	Guildford Greenbelt Group
Humanity	Humanity
Ind.	Independent
IPP	Immigrants Political Party
JACP	Justice & Anti-Corruption Party
Just	The Just Political Party
Lab.	Labour
Lab. Alt	Labour Alternative
Lab. Co-op	Labour and Co-operative
LD	Liberal Democrat
Lib.	The Liberal Party
Lib. GB	Liberty Great Britain
Libertarian	Libertarian Party
Lincs Ind.	Lincolnshire Independents
Loony	Monster Raving Loony Party
Love	One Love Party
MC	The Magna Carta Party
Money	Money Free Party
ND	No description
NE	The North East Party
NF	National Front
NHAP	National Health Action Party
North	Putting North of England People First
Northern	Northern Party
Open	Open Borders Party
Patria	Patria
PBP	People Before Profit Alliance
PC	Plaid Cymru
Peace	Peace Party
PF	People First
Pilgrim	The Pilgrim Party
Pirate	Pirate Party UK
Poole	The Party for Poole People Ltd
Populist	Populist Party
PUP	Progressive Unionist Party
Radical	The Radical Party

Realist	The Realists' Party
Rebooting	Rebooting Democracy
Referendum	Scotland's Independence Referendum Party
Renew	Renew Party
Respect	The Respect Party
Rochdale	Rochdale First Party
Roman	The Roman Party
S. New	Something New
SCP	Scottish Christian Party
SDLP	Social Democratic and Labour Party
SF	Sinn Fein
SNP	Scottish National Party
Soc.	Socialist Party
Soc. Dem.	Social Democratic Party
Soc. Lab.	Socialist Labour Party
Southampton	Southampton Independents
Southend	Southend Independent Association
Southport	The Southport Party
Sovereign	Independent Sovereign Democratic Britain
Space	Space Navies Party
Speaker	The Speaker
SPGB	The Socialist Party of Great Britain
SSP	Scottish Socialist Party
Thanet	Party for a United Thanet
TUSC	Trade Unionist and Socialist Coalition
TUV	Traditional Unionist Voice
UKEUP	UK European Union Party
UKIP	UK Independence Party
UUP	Ulster Unionist Party
Wessex Reg.	Wessex Regionalists
Wigan	Wigan Independents
Women	Women's Equality Party
Worth	The New Society of Worth
WP	Workers' Party
WRP	Workers' Revolutionary Party
WVPTFP	War Veteran's Pro-Traditional Family Party
Yorks	Yorkshire First
Yorkshire	The Yorkshire Party
Young	Young People's Party UK

ENGLAND

ALDERSHOT
E. 72,617 T. 47,932 (66.01%)   C. hold
Leo Docherty, C.   27,980
Howard Kaye, Lab.   11,282
Alan Hilliar, LD   6,920
Donna Wallace, Green   1,750
C. majority 16,698 (34.84%)
5.70% swing Lab. to C.

ALDRIDGE-BROWNHILLS
E. 60,138 T. 39,342 (65.42%)   C. hold
Wendy Morton, C.   27,850
David Morgan, Lab.   8,014
Ian Garrett, LD   2,371
Bill McComish, Green   771
Mark Beech, Loony   336
C. majority 19,836 (50.42%)
7.43% swing Lab. to C.

ALTRINCHAM & SALE WEST
E. 73,096 T. 54,763 (74.92%)   C. hold
Graham Brady, C.   26,311
Andrew Western, Lab.   20,172
Angela Smith, LD   6,036
Geraldine Coggins, Green   1,566
Neil Taylor, Lib   454
Iram Kiani, Ind.   224
C. majority 6,139 (11.21%)
0.48% swing C. to Lab.

AMBER VALLEY
E. 69,976 T. 45,567 (65.12%)   C. hold
Nigel Mills, C.   29,096
Adam Thompson, Lab.   12,210
Kate Smith, LD   2,873
Lian Pizzey, Green   1,388
C. majority 16,886 (37.06%)
9.47% swing Lab. to C.

ARUNDEL & SOUTH DOWNS
E. 81,726 T. 61,408 (75.14%)   C. hold
Andrew Griffith, C.   35,566
Alison Bennett, LD   13,045
Bella Sankey, Lab.   9,722
Isabel Thurston, Green   2,519
Robert Wheal, Ind.   556
C. majority 22,521 (36.67%)
8.87% swing C. to LD

ASHFIELD
E. 78,204 T. 48,980 (62.63%)   C. gain
Lee Anderson, C.   19,231
Jason Zadrozny, Ashfield   13,498
Natalie Fleet, Lab.   11,971
Martin Daubney, Brexit   2,501
Rebecca Wain, LD   1,105
Rose Woods, Green   674
C. majority 5,733 (11.70%)
7.85% swing Lab. to C.

ASHFORD
E. 89,550 T. 60,059 (67.07%)   C. hold
Damian Green, C.   37,270
Dara Farrell, Lab.   13,241
Adrian Gee-Turner, LD   6,048
Mandy Rossi, Green   2,638
Susannah De Sanvil, Ind.   862
C. majority 24,029 (40.01%)
5.41% swing Lab. to C.

ASHTON-UNDER-LYNE
E. 68,497 T. 38,559 (56.29%)   Lab. hold
Angela Rayner, Lab.   18,544
Dan Costello, C.   14,281
Derek Brocklehurst, Brexit   3,131
George Rice, LD   1,395
Lee Huntbach, Green   1,208
Lab. majority 4,263 (11.06%)
8.67% swing Lab. to C.

AYLESBURY
E. 86,665 T. 60,576 (69.90%)   C. hold
Rob Butler, C.   32,737
Liz Hind, Lab.   15,364
Steven Lambert, LD   10,081
Coral Simpson, Green   2,394
C. majority 17,373 (28.68%)
1.83% swing Lab. to C.

BANBURY
E. 90,113 T. 62,921 (69.82%)   C. hold
Victoria Prentis, C.   34,148
Suzette Watson, Lab.   17,335
Tim Bearder, LD   8,831
Ian Middleton, Green   2,607
C. majority 16,813 (26.72%)
3.29% swing Lab. to C.

BARKING
E. 77,946 T. 44,499 (57.09%)   Lab. hold
Margaret Hodge, Lab.   27,219
Tamkeen Shaikh, C.   11,792
Karen Batley, Brexit   3,186
Ann Haigh, LD   1,482
Shannon Butterfield, Green   820
Lab. majority 15,427 (34.67%)
5.33% swing Lab. to C.

BARNSLEY CENTRAL
E. 65,277 T. 36,903 (56.53%)   Lab. hold
Dan Jarvis, Lab.   14,804
Victoria Felton, Brexit   11,233
Iftikhar Ahmed, C.   7,892
Will Sapwell, LD   1,176
Tom Heyes, Green   900
Ryan Williams, Yorkshire   710
Donald Wood, Ind.   188
Lab. majority 3,571 (9.68%)
swing N/A

BARNSLEY EAST
E. 69,504 T. 38,070 (54.77%)   Lab. hold
Stephanie Peacock, Lab.   14,329
Jim Ferguson, Brexit   11,112
Adam Gregg, C.   10,377
Sophie Thornton, LD   1,330
Richard Trotman, Green   922
Lab. majority 3,217 (8.45%)
swing N/A

BARROW & FURNESS
E. 70,158 T. 46,046 (65.63%)   C. gain
Simon Fell, C.   23,876
Chris Altree, Lab.   18,087
Loraine Birchall, LD   2,025
Ged McGrath, Brexit   1,355
Chris Loynes, Green   703
C. majority 5,789 (12.57%)
6.51% swing Lab. to C.

BASILDON & BILLERICAY
E. 69,906 T. 44,128 (63.12%)   C. hold
John Baron, C.   29,590
Andrew Gordon, Lab.   9,178
Edward Sainsbury, LD   3,741
Stewart Goshawk, Green   1,395
Simon Breedon, Soc Dem   224
C. majority 20,412 (46.26%)
8.21% swing Lab. to C.

BASILDON SOUTH & THURROCK EAST
E. 74,441 T. 45,297 (60.85%)   C. hold
Stephen Metcalfe, C.   29,973
Jack Ferguson, Lab.   10,051
Kerry Smith, Ind.   3,316
Michael Bukola, LD   1,957
C. majority 19,922 (43.98%)
9.80% swing Lab. to C.

BASINGSTOKE
E. 82,926 T. 54,713 (65.98%)   C. hold
Maria Miller, C.   29,593
Kerena Marchant, Lab.   15,395
Sashi Mylvaganam, LD   6,841
Jonathan Jenkin, Green   2,138
Alan Stone, ND   746
C. majority 14,198 (25.95%)
4.52% swing Lab. to C.

BASSETLAW
E. 80,035 T. 50,841 (63.52%)   C. gain
Brendan Clarke-Smith, C.   28,078
Keir Morrison, Lab.   14,065
Debbie Soloman, Brexit   5,366
Helen Tamblyn-Saville, LD   3,332
C. majority 14,013 (27.56%)
18.42% swing Lab. to C.

BATH
E. 67,725 T. 52,138 (76.98%)   LD hold
Wera Hobhouse, LD   28,419
Annabel Tall, C.   16,097
Mike Davies, Lab.   6,639
Jimi Ogunnusi, Brexit   642
Bill Blockhead, Ind.   341
LD majority 12,322 (23.63%)
6.07% swing C. to LD

BATLEY & SPEN
E. 79,558 T. 52,927 (66.53%)
                          Lab. Co-op hold
Tracy Brabin, Lab. Co-op   22,594
Mark Brooks, C.   19,069
Paul Halloran, Woollen   6,432
John Lawson, LD   2,462
Clive Minihan, Brexit   1,678
Ty Akram, Green   692
Lab. Co-op majority 3,525 (6.66%)
5.00% swing Lab. to C.

BATTERSEA
E. 79,309 T. 59,977 (75.62%)   Lab. hold
Marsha De Cordova, Lab.   27,290
Kim Caddy, C.   21,622
Mark Gitsham, LD   9,150
Lois Davis, Green   1,529
Jake Thomas, Brexit   386
Lab. majority 5,668 (9.45%)
2.53% swing C. to Lab.

BEACONSFIELD
E. 77,720 T. 57,868 (74.46%)   C. gain
Joy Morrissey, C.   32,477
Dominic Grieve, Ind.   16,765
Alexa Collins, Lab.   5,756
Zoe Hatch, Green   2,033
Adam Cleary, Ind.   837
C. majority 15,712 (27.15%)
swing N/A

BECKENHAM
E. 68,671 T. 50,555 (73.62%)   C. hold
Bob Stewart, C.   27,282
Marina Ahmad, Lab.   13,024
Chloe-Jane Ross, LD   8,194
Ruth Fabricant, Green   2,055
C. majority 14,258 (28.20%)
0.51% swing C. to Lab.

BEDFORD
E. 71,579 T. 47,301 (66.08%)   Lab. hold
Mohammad Yasin, Lab.   20,491
Ryan Henson, C.   20,346
Henry Vann, LD   4,608
Adrian Spurrell, Green   960
Charles Bunker, Brexit   896
Lab. majority 145 (0.31%)
0.66% swing Lab. to C.

BEDFORDSHIRE MID
E. 87,795 T. 64,717 (73.71%)   C. hold
Nadine Dorries, C.   38,692
Rhiannon Meades, Lab.   14,028
Rachel McGann, LD   8,171
Gareth Ellis, Green   2,478
Alan Victor, Ind.   812
Ann Kelly, Loony   536
C. majority 24,664 (38.11%)
2.44% swing Lab. to C.

BEDFORDSHIRE NORTH EAST
E. 90,679 T. 65,018 (71.70%)   C. hold
Richard Fuller, C.   38,443
Julian Vaughan, Lab.   14,160
Daniel Norton, LD   7,999
Adam Zerny, Ind.   2,525
Philippa Fleming, Green   1,891
C. majority 24,283 (37.35%)
2.43% swing Lab. to C.

BEDFORDSHIRE SOUTH WEST
E. 79,926 T. 53,307 (66.70%)   C. hold
Andrew Selous, C.   32,212
Callum Anderson, Lab.   13,629
Emma Matanle, LD   5,435
Andrew Waters, Green   2,031
C. majority 18,583 (34.86%)
4.70% swing Lab. to C.

**BERMONDSEY & OLD
SOUTHWARK**
E. 93,313 T. 58,615 (62.82%)   Lab. hold
Neil Coyle, Lab.   31,723
Humaira Ali, LD   15,597
Andrew Baker, C.   9,678
Alex Matthews, Brexit   1,617
Lab. majority 16,126 (27.51%)
2.67% swing LD to Lab.

BERWICK-UPON-TWEED
E. 59,939 T. 42,109 (70.25%)   C. hold
Anne-Marie Trevelyan, C.   23,947
Trish Williams, Lab.   9,112
Tom Hancock, LD   7,656
Thomas Stewart, Green   1,394
C. majority 14,835 (35.23%)
3.66% swing Lab. to C.

BETHNAL GREEN & BOW
E. 88,169 T. 60,562 (68.69%)   Lab. hold
Rushanara Ali, Lab.   44,052
Nicholas Stovold, C.   6,528
Josh Babarinde, LD   5,892
Shahrar Ali, Green   2,570
David Axe, Brexit   1,081
Vanessa Hudson, AWP   439
Lab. majority 37,524 (61.96%)
1.40% swing C. to Lab.

BEVERLEY & HOLDERNESS
E. 79,683 T. 53,542 (67.19%)   C. hold
Graham Stuart, C.   33,250
Chloe Hopkins, Lab.   12,802
Denis Healy, LD   4,671
Andy Shead, Yorkshire   1,441
Isabel Pires, Green   1,378
C. majority 20,448 (38.19%)
6.49% swing Lab. to C.

BEXHILL & BATTLE
E. 81,968 T. 59,093 (72.09%)   C. hold
Huw Merriman, C.   37,590
Christine Bayliss, Lab.   11,531
Martin Saunders, LD   7,280
Jonathan Kent, Green   2,692
C. majority 26,059 (44.10%)
3.41% swing Lab. to C.

BEXLEYHEATH & CRAYFORD
E. 65,466 T. 43,246 (66.06%)   C. hold
David Evennett, C.   25,856
Anna Day, Lab.   12,753
David McBride, LD   2,819
Tony Ball, Green   1,298
Graham Moore, Eng Dem   520
C. majority 13,103 (30.30%)
5.11% swing Lab. to C.

BIRKENHEAD
E. 63,762 T. 42,329 (66.39%)   Lab. gain
Mick Whitley, Lab.   24,990
Frank Field, BSJP   7,285
Claire Rowles, C.   5,540
Stuart Kelly, LD   1,620
Darren Lythgoe, Brexit   1,489
Pat Cleary, Green   1,405
Lab. majority 17,705 (41.83%)
swing N/A

BIRMINGHAM EDGBASTON
E. 68,828 T. 42,328 (61.50%)
                                   Lab. Co-op hold
Preet Gill, Lab. Co-op   21,217
Alex Yip, C.   15,603
Colin Green, LD   3,349
Phil Simpson, Green   1,112
David Wilks, Brexit   1,047
Lab. Co-op majority 5,614 (13.26%)
1.30% swing Lab. to C.

BIRMINGHAM ERDINGTON
E. 66,148 T. 35,229 (53.26%)   Lab. hold
Jack Dromey, Lab.   17,720
Robert Alden, C.   14,119
Wendy Garcarz, Brexit   1,441
Ann Holtom, LD   1,301
Rob Grant, Green   648
Lab. majority 3,601 (10.22%)
4.68% swing Lab. to C.

BIRMINGHAM HALL GREEN
E. 80,283 T. 52,911 (65.91%)   Lab. hold
Tahir Ali, Lab.   35,889
Penny-Anne O'Donnell, C.   7,381
Roger Godsiff, Ind.   4,273
Izzy Knowles, LD   3,673
Rosie Cuckston, Brexit   877
Patrick Cox, Green   818
Lab. majority 28,508 (53.88%)
4.31% swing Lab. to C.

BIRMINGHAM HODGE HILL
E. 78,295 T. 45,003 (57.48%)   Lab. hold
Liam Byrne, Lab.   35,397
Akaal Sidhu, C.   6,742
Jill Dagnan, Brexit   1,519
Waheed Rafiq, LD   760
Jane McKears, Green   328
Hilda Johani, CPA   257
Lab. majority 28,655 (63.67%)
1.60% swing Lab. to C.

BIRMINGHAM LADYWOOD
E. 74,912 T. 42,118 (56.22%)   Lab. hold
Shabana Mahmood, Lab.   33,355
Mary Noone, C.   4,773
Lee Dargue, LD   2,228
Alex Nettle, Green   931
Andrew Garcarz, Brexit   831
Lab. majority 28,582 (67.86%)
0.83% swing Lab. to C.

BIRMINGHAM NORTHFIELD
E. 73,694 T. 43,098 (58.48%)   C. gain
Gary Sambrook, C.   19,957
Richard Burden, Lab.   18,317
Jamie Scott, LD   1,961
Keith Rowe, Brexit   1,655
Eleanor Masters, Green   954
Kenneth Lowry, UKIP   254
C. majority 1,640 (3.81%)
7.16% swing Lab. to C.

BIRMINGHAM PERRY BARR
E. 72,006 T. 42,147 (58.53%)   Lab. hold
Khalid Mahmood, Lab.   26,594
Raaj Shamji, C.   11,277
Gerry Jerome, LD   1,901
Annette Willcox, Brexit   1,382
Kefentse Dennis, Green   845
Thomas Braich, Yeshua   148
Lab. majority 15,317 (36.34%)
2.63% swing Lab. to C.

BIRMINGHAM SELLY OAK
E. 82,665 T. 49,467 (59.84%) Lab. hold
Steve McCabe, Lab.   27,714
Hannah Campbell, C.   15,300
Dave Radcliffe, LD   3,169
Joe Peacock, Green   1,848
Joseph Tawonezvi, Brexit   1,436
Lab. majority 12,414 (25.10%)
2.97% swing Lab. to C.

BIRMINGHAM YARDLEY
E. 74,704 T. 42,678 (57.13%) Lab. hold
Jess Phillips, Lab.   23,379
Vincent Garrington, C.   12,720
Roger Harmer, LD   3,754
Mary McKenna, Brexit   2,246
Christopher Garghan, Green   579
Lab. majority 10,659 (24.98%)
6.13% swing Lab. to C.

BISHOP AUCKLAND
E. 68,170 T. 44,805 (65.73%) C. gain
Dehenna Davison, C.   24,067
Helen Goodman, Lab.   16,105
Nicholas Brown, Brexit   2,500
Ray Georgeson, LD   2,133
C. majority 7,962 (17.77%)
9.47% swing Lab. to C.

BLACKBURN
E. 71,229 T. 44,736 (62.81%) Lab. hold
Kate Hollern, Lab.   29,040
Claire Gill, C.   10,736
Rick Moore, Brexit   2,770
Beth Waller-Slack, LD   1,130
Reza Hossain, Green   741
Rizwan Shah, Ind.   319
Lab. majority 18,304 (40.92%)
0.98% swing Lab. to C.

BLACKLEY & BROUGHTON
E. 73,372 T. 38,618 (52.63%) Lab. hold
Graham Stringer, Lab.   23,887
Alexander Elias, C.   9,485
James Buckley, Brexit   2,736
Iain Donaldson, LD   1,590
David Jones, Green   920
Lab. majority 14,402 (37.29%)
5.79% swing Lab. to C.

BLACKPOOL NORTH &
CLEVELEYS
E. 63,691 T. 38,804 (60.93%) C. hold
Paul Maynard, C.   22,364
Chris Webb, Lab.   13,768
Sue Close, LD   1,494
Duncan Royle, Green   735
Neil Holden, Ind.   443
C. majority 8,596 (22.15%)
8.61% swing Lab. to C.

BLACKPOOL SOUTH
E. 57,688 T. 32,752 (56.77%) C. gain
Scott Benton, C.   16,247
Gordon Marsden, Lab.   12,557
David Brown, Brexit   2,009
Bill Greene, LD   1,008
Becky Daniels, Green   563
Gary Coleman, Ind.   368
C. majority 3,690 (11.27%)
9.24% swing Lab. to C.

BLAYDON
E. 67,853 T. 45,681 (67.32%) Lab. hold
Liz Twist, Lab.   19,794
Adrian Pepper, C.   14,263
Michael Robinson, Brexit   5,833
Vicky Anderson, LD   3,703
Diane Cadman, Green   1,279
Kathy King, Lib   615
Lisabela Marschild, Space   118
Lee Garrett, ND   76
Lab. majority 5,531 (12.11%)
7.96% swing Lab. to C.

BLYTH VALLEY
E. 64,429 T. 40,859 (63.42%) C. gain
Ian Levy, C.   17,440
Susan Dungworth, Lab. Co-   16,728
op
Mark Peart, Brexit   3,394
Thom Chapman, LD   2,151
Dawn Furness, Green   1,146
C. majority 712 (1.74%)
10.19% swing Lab. to C.

BOGNOR REGIS &
LITTLEHAMPTON
E. 77,488 T. 51,223 (66.10%) C. hold
Nick Gibb, C.   32,521
Alan Butcher, Lab.   10,018
Francis Oppler, LD   5,645
Carol Birch, Green   1,826
David Kurten, UKIP   846
Andrew Elston, Ind.   367
C. majority 22,503 (43.93%)
4.93% swing Lab. to C.

BOLSOVER
E. 75,157 T. 45,938 (61.12%) C. gain
Mark Fletcher, C.   21,791
Dennis Skinner, Lab.   16,492
Kevin Harper, Brexit   4,151
David Hancock, LD   1,759
David Kesteven, Green   758
Ross Walker, Ind.   517
Natalie Hoy, Ind.   470
C. majority 5,299 (11.54%)
11.45% swing Lab. to C.

BOLTON NORTH EAST
E. 67,564 T. 43,556 (64.47%) C. gain
Mark Logan, C.   19,759
David Crausby, Lab.   19,381
Trevor Jones, Brexit   1,880
Warren Fox, LD   1,847
Liz Spencer, Green   689
C. majority 378 (0.87%)
4.64% swing Lab. to C.

BOLTON SOUTH EAST
E. 69,163 T. 40,604 (58.71%) Lab. hold
Yasmin Qureshi, Lab.   21,516
Johno Lee, C.   13,918
Mark Cunningham, Brexit   2,968
Kev Walsh, LD   1,411
David Figgins, Green   791
Lab. majority 7,598 (18.71%)
6.15% swing Lab. to C.

BOLTON WEST
E. 73,191 T. 49,298 (67.36%) C. hold
Chris Green, C.   27,255
Julie Hilling, Lab.   18,400
Rebecca Forrest, LD   2,704
Paris Hayes, Green   939
C. majority 8,855 (17.96%)
8.06% swing Lab. to C.

BOOTLE
E. 74,832 T. 49,174 (65.71%) Lab. hold
Peter Dowd, Lab.   39,066
Tarsilo Onuluk, C.   4,510
Kim Knight, Brexit   2,610
Rebecca Hanson, LD   1,822
Mike Carter, Green   1,166
Lab. majority 34,556 (70.27%)
0.86% swing Lab. to C.

BOSTON & SKEGNESS
E. 68,895 T. 41,696 (60.52%) C. hold
Matt Warman, C.   31,963
Ben Cook, Lab.   6,342
Hilary Jones, LD   1,963
Peter Watson, Ind.   1,428
C. majority 25,621 (61.45%)
11.40% swing Lab. to C.

BOSWORTH
E. 81,537 T. 56,432 (69.21%) C. hold
Luke Evans, C.   36,056
Rick Middleton, Lab.   9,778
Michael Mullaney, LD   9,096
Mick Gregg, Green   1,502
C. majority 26,278 (46.57%)
6.95% swing Lab. to C.

BOURNEMOUTH EAST
E. 74,127 T. 49,274 (66.47%) C. hold
Tobias Ellwood, C.   24,926
Corrie Drew, Lab.   16,120
Philip Dunn, LD   5,418
Alasdair Keddie, Green   2,049
Ben Aston, ND   447
Emma Johnson, Ind.   314
C. majority 8,806 (17.87%)
0.77% swing Lab. to C.

BOURNEMOUTH WEST
E. 74,211 T. 45,977 (61.95%) C. hold
Conor Burns, C.   24,550
David Stokes, Lab.   14,400
Jon Nicholas, LD   4,931
Simon Bull, Green   2,096
C. majority 10,150 (22.08%)
2.38% swing Lab. to C.

BRACKNELL
E. 79,206 T. 54,350 (68.62%) C. gain
James Sunderland, C.   31,894
Paul Bidwell, Lab.   12,065
Kaweh Beheshtizadeh, LD   7,749
Derek Florey, Green   2,089
Olivio Barreto, Ind.   553
C. majority 19,829 (36.48%)
3.91% swing Lab. to C.

BRADFORD EAST
E. 73,206 T. 44,184 (60.36%) Lab. hold
Imran Hussain, Lab.	27,825
Linden Kemkaran, C.	9,681
Jeanette Sunderland, LD	3,316
Jonathan Barras, Brexit	2,700
Andy Stanford, Green	662

Lab. majority 18,144 (41.06%)
1.98% swing Lab. to C.

BRADFORD SOUTH
E. 69,046 T. 39,741 (57.56%) Lab. hold
Judith Cummins, Lab.	18,390
Narinder Sekhon, C.	16,044
Kulvinder Manik, Brexit	2,819
Alun Griffiths, LD	1,505
Matthew Edwards, Green	983

Lab. majority 2,346 (5.90%)
5.21% swing Lab. to C.

BRADFORD WEST
E. 70,694 T. 44,261 (62.61%) Lab. hold
Naz Shah, Lab.	33,736
Mohammed Afzal, C.	6,717
Derrick Hodgson, Brexit	1,556
Mark Christie, LD	1,349
Darren Parkinson, Green	813
Azfar Bukhari, ND	90

Lab. majority 27,019 (61.04%)
6.47% swing C. to Lab.

BRAINTREE
E. 75,208 T. 50,499 (67.15%) C. hold
James Cleverly, C.	34,112
Joshua Garfield, Lab.	9,439
Dominic Graham, LD	4,779
Jo Beavis, Ind.	1,488
David Mansell, Ind.	420
Alan Dorkins, Ind.	261

C. majority 24,673 (48.86%)
6.83% swing Lab. to C.

BRENT CENTRAL
E. 84,204 T. 49,132 (58.35%) Lab. hold
Dawn Butler, Lab.	31,779
David Brescia, C.	10,909
Deborah Unger, LD	4,844
William Relton, Green	1,600

Lab. majority 20,870 (42.48%)
5.53% swing Lab. to C.

BRENT NORTH
E. 83,772 T. 51,879 (61.93%) Lab. hold
Barry Gardiner, Lab.	26,911
Anjana Patel, C.	18,832
Paul Lorber, LD	4,065
Suzie O'Brien, Brexit	951
Simon Rebbitt, Green	850
Noel Coonan, Ind.	169
Elcena Jeffers, Ind.	101

Lab. majority 8,079 (15.57%)
7.33% swing Lab. to C.

BRENTFORD & ISLEWORTH
E. 85,770 T. 58,326 (68.00%) Lab. hold
Ruth Cadbury, Lab.	29,266
Seena Shah, C.	18,752
Helen Cross, LD	7,314
Daniel Goldsmith, Green	1,829
Lucy O'Sullivan, Brexit	1,165

Lab. majority 10,514 (18.03%)
0.87% swing Lab. to C.

BRENTWOOD & ONGAR
E. 75,253 T. 52,941 (70.35%) C. hold
Alex Burghart, C.	36,308
Oliver Durose, Lab.	7,243
David Kendall, LD	7,187
Paul Jeater, Green	1,671
Robin Tilbrook, Eng Dem	532

C. majority 29,065 (54.90%)
4.77% swing Lab. to C.

BRIDGWATER & SOMERSET WEST
E. 85,327 T. 57,652 (67.57%) C. hold
Ian Liddell-Grainger, C.	35,827
Oliver Thornton, Lab.	11,388
Bill Revans, LD	7,805
Mickie Ritchie, Green	1,877
Fares Moussa, Lib	755

C. majority 24,439 (42.39%)
7.94% swing Lab. to C.

BRIGG & GOOLE
E. 65,939 T. 43,402 (65.82%) C. hold
Andrew Percy, C.	30,941
Majid Khan, Lab.	9,000
David Dobbie, LD	2,180
Jo Baker, Green	1,281

C. majority 21,941 (50.55%)
11.56% swing Lab. to C.

BRIGHTON KEMPTOWN
E. 69,833 T. 48,533 (69.50%)
Lab. Co-op hold
Lloyd Russell-Moyle, Lab.	25,033
Co-op	
Joe Miller, C.	16,972
Ben Thomas, LD	2,964
Alexandra Phillips, Green	2,237
Graham Cushway, Brexit	1,327

Lab. Co-op majority 8,061 (16.61%)
1.72% swing Lab. to C.

BRIGHTON PAVILION
E. 79,057 T. 57,998 (73.36%)
Green hold
Caroline Lucas, Green	33,151
Adam Imanpour, Lab.	13,211
Emma Hogan, C.	10,176
Richard Milton, Brexit	770
Citizen Skwith, Loony	301
Bob Dobbs, Ind.	212
Nigel Furness, UKIP	177

Green majority 19,940 (34.38%)
4.46% swing Lab. to Green

BRISTOL EAST
E. 73,867 T. 52,154 (70.61%) Lab. hold
Kerry McCarthy, Lab.	27,717
Sarah Codling, C.	16,923
Nicholas Coombes, LD	3,527
Conan Connolly, Green	2,106
Tim Page, Brexit	1,881

Lab. majority 10,794 (20.70%)
2.84% swing Lab. to C.

BRISTOL NORTH WEST
E. 76,273 T. 55,885 (73.27%) Lab. hold
Darren Jones, Lab.	27,330
Mark Weston, C.	21,638
Chris Coleman, LD	4,940
Heather Mack, Green	1,977

Lab. majority 5,692 (10.19%)
0.69% swing C. to Lab.

BRISTOL SOUTH
E. 84,079 T. 55,196 (65.65%) Lab. hold
Karin Smyth, Lab.	27,895
Richard Morgan, C.	18,036
Andrew Brown, LD	4,227
Tony Dyer, Green	2,713
Robert de Vito Boutin,	2,325
Brexit	

Lab. majority 9,859 (17.86%)
5.77% swing Lab. to C.

BRISTOL WEST
E. 99,253 T. 75,528 (76.10%) Lab. hold
Thangam Debbonaire, Lab.	47,028
Jess Barnard, Green	18,809
Suria Aujla, C.	8,822
Neil Hipkiss, Brexit	869

Lab. majority 28,219 (37.36%)
7.85% swing Lab. to Green

BROADLAND
E. 78,151 T. 56,977 (72.91%) C. hold
Jerome Mayhew, C.	33,934
Ben Barnard, Lab.	12,073
Ben Goodwin, LD	9,195
Andrew Boswell, Green	1,412
Simon Rous, Universal	363

C. majority 21,861 (38.37%)
5.06% swing Lab. to C.

BROMLEY & CHISLEHURST
E. 66,711 T. 45,566 (68.30%) C. hold
Bob Neill, C.	23,958
Angela Wilkins, Lab.	13,067
Julie Ireland, LD	6,621
Mary Ion, Green	1,546
Zion Amodu, CPA	255
Jyoti Dialani, Renew	119

C. majority 10,891 (23.90%)
1.67% swing Lab. to C.

BROMSGROVE
E. 75,079 T. 54,272 (72.29%) C. hold
Sajid Javid, C.	34,408
Rory Shannon, Lab.	11,302
David Nicholl, LD	6,779
Kevin White, Green	1,783

C. majority 23,106 (42.57%)
5.95% swing Lab. to C.

BROXBOURNE
E. 73,182 T. 46,706 (63.82%) C. hold
Charles Walker, C.	30,631
Sean Waters, Lab.	10,824
Julia Bird, LD	3,970
Nicholas Cox, Green	1,281

C. majority 19,807 (42.41%)
4.58% swing Lab. to C.

BROXTOWE
E. 73,895 T. 55,272 (74.80%) C. gain
Darren Henry, C.	26,602
Greg Marshall, Lab.	21,271
Anna Soubry, Change	4,668
Kat Boettge, Green	1,806
Amy Dalla Mura, Eng Dem	432
Teck Khong, Ind.	321
David Bishop, Elvis	172

C. majority 5,331 (9.65%)
4.05% swing Lab. to C.

BUCKINGHAM

E. 83,146   T. 63,458 (76.32%)   C. hold
Greg Smith, C.   37,035
Stephen Dorrell, LD   16,624
David Morgan, Lab.   7,638
Andrew Bell, Brexit   1,286
Ned Thompson, Ind.   681
Antonio Vitiello, Eng Dem   194
C. majority 20,411 (32.16%)
swing N/A

BURNLEY

E. 64,343   T. 38,984 (60.59%)   C. gain
Antony Higginbotham, C.   15,720
Julie Cooper, Lab.   14,368
Gordon Birtwistle, LD   3,501
Stewart Scott, Brexit   3,362
Charlie Briggs, Burnley   1,162
Laura Fisk, Green   739
Karen Helsby Entwistle, Ind.   132
C. majority 1,352 (3.47%)
9.62% swing Lab. to C.

BURTON

E. 75,030   T. 48,738 (64.96%)   C. hold
Kate Griffiths, C.   29,560
Louise Walker, Lab.   15,064
Adam Wain, LD   2,681
Kate Copeland, Green   1,433
C. majority 14,496 (29.74%)
4.81% swing Lab. to C.

BURY NORTH

E. 68,802   T. 46,841 (68.08%)   C. gain
James Daly, C.   21,660
James Frith, Lab.   21,555
Gareth Lloyd-Johnson, LD   1,584
Alan McCarthy, Brexit   1,240
Charlie Allen, Green   802
C. majority 105 (0.22%)
4.68% swing Lab. to C.

BURY SOUTH

E. 75,152   T. 50,274 (66.90%)   C. gain
Christian Wakeford, C.   22,034
Lucy Burke, Lab.   21,632
Richard Kilpatrick, LD   2,315
Andrea Livesey, Brexit   1,672
Ivan Lewis, Ind.   1,366
Glyn Heath, Green   848
Michael Boyle, Ind.   277
Gemma Evans, Women   130
C. majority 402 (0.80%)
6.25% swing Lab. to C.

BURY ST EDMUNDS

E. 89,644   T. 61,957 (69.11%)   C. hold
Jo Churchill, C.   37,770
Cliff Waterman, Lab.   12,782
Helen Geake, Green   9,711
Paul Hopfensperger, Ind.   1,694
C. majority 24,988 (40.33%)
5.33% swing Lab. to C.

CALDER VALLEY

E. 79,287   T. 57,793 (72.89%)   C. hold
Craig Whittaker, C.   29,981
Josh Fenton-Glynn, Lab.   24,207
Javed Bashir, LD   2,884
Richard Phillips, Lib   721
C. majority 5,774 (9.99%)
4.47% swing Lab. to C.

CAMBERWELL & PECKHAM

E. 89,042   T. 56,492 (63.44%)   Lab. hold
Harriet Harman, Lab.   40,258
Peter Quentin, C.   6,478
Julia Ogiehor, LD   5,087
Claire Sheppard, Green   3,501
Cass Cass-Horne, Brexit   1,041
Joshua Ogunleye, WRP   127
Lab. majority 33,780 (59.80%)
2.60% swing Lab. to C.

CAMBORNE & REDRUTH

E. 70,250   T. 50,367 (71.70%)   C. hold
George Eustice, C.   26,764
Paul Farmer, Lab.   18,064
Florence MacDonald, LD   3,504
Karen La Borde, Green   1,359
Paul Holmes, Lib   676
C. majority 8,700 (17.27%)
7.01% swing Lab. to C.

CAMBRIDGE

E. 79,951   T. 53,729 (67.20%)   Lab. hold
Daniel Zeichner, Lab.   25,776
Rod Cantrill, LD   16,137
Russell Perrin, C.   8,342
Jeremy Caddick, Green   2,164
Peter Dawe, Brexit   1,041
Miles Hurley, Ind.   111
Jane Robins, Soc Dem   91
Keith Garrett, Rebooting   67
Lab. majority 9,639 (17.94%)
2.35% swing Lab. to LD

CAMBRIDGESHIRE NORTH EAST

E. 83,699   T. 52,964 (63.28%)   C. hold
Steve Barclay, C.   38,423
Diane Boyd, Lab.   8,430
Rupert Moss-Eccardt, LD   4,298
Ruth Johnson, Green   1,813
C. majority 29,993 (56.63%)
8.36% swing Lab. to C.

CAMBRIDGESHIRE NORTH WEST

E. 94,909   T. 64,533 (67.99%)   C. hold
Shailesh Vara, C.   40,307
Cathy Cordiner-Achenbach,   14,324
Lab.
Bridget Smith, LD   6,881
Nicola Day, Green   3,021
C. majority 25,983 (40.26%)
6.06% swing Lab. to C.

CAMBRIDGESHIRE SOUTH

E. 87,288   T. 66,929 (76.68%)   C. gain
Anthony Browne, C.   31,015
Ian Sollom, LD   28,111
Dan Greef, Lab.   7,803
C. majority 2,904 (4.34%)
14.41% swing C. to LD

CAMBRIDGESHIRE SOUTH EAST

E. 86,769   T. 64,385 (74.20%)   C. hold
Lucy Frazer, C.   32,187
Pippa Heylings, LD   20,697
James Bull, Lab.   10,492
Edmund Fordham, Ind.   1,009
C. majority 11,490 (17.85%)
8.25% swing C. to LD

CANNOCK CHASE

E. 74,813   T. 46,313 (61.91%)   C. hold
Amanda Milling, C.   31,636
Anne Hobbs, Lab.   11,757
Paul Woodhead, Green   2,920
C. majority 19,879 (42.92%)
12.70% swing Lab. to C.

CANTERBURY

E. 80,203   T. 60,113 (74.95%)   Lab. hold
Rosie Duffield, Lab.   29,018
Anna Firth, C.   27,182
Claire Malcomson, LD   3,408
Michael Gould, Ind.   505
Lab. majority 1,836 (3.05%)
1.36% swing C. to Lab.

CARLISLE

E. 65,105   T. 42,873 (65.85%)   C. hold
John Stevenson, C.   23,659
Ruth Alcroft, Lab.   15,340
Julia Aglionby, LD   2,829
Fiona Mills, UKIP   1,045
C. majority 8,319 (19.40%)
6.68% swing Lab. to C.

CARSHALTON & WALLINGTON

E. 72,926   T. 49,098 (67.33%)   C. gain
Elliot Colburn, C.   20,822
Tom Brake, LD   20,193
Ahmad Wattoo, Lab.   6,081
James Woudhuysen, Brexit   1,043
Tracey Hague, Green   759
Ashley Dickenson, CPA   200
C. majority 629 (1.28%)
1.99% swing LD to C.

CASTLE POINT

E. 69,643   T. 44,277 (63.58%)   C. hold
Rebecca Harris, C.   33,971
Katie Curtis, Lab.   7,337
John Howson, LD   2,969
C. majority 26,634 (60.15%)
8.97% swing Lab. to C.

CHARNWOOD

E. 79,556   T. 55,365 (69.59%)   C. hold
Edward Argar, C.   35,121
Gary Godden, Lab.   12,724
Kate Tipton, LD   4,856
Laurie Needham, Green   2,664
C. majority 22,397 (40.45%)
5.42% swing Lab. to C.

CHATHAM & AYLESFORD

E. 71,642   T. 43,340 (60.50%)   C. hold
Tracey Crouch, C.   28,856
Vince Maple, Lab.   10,316
David Naghi, LD   2,866
Geoff Wilkinson, Green   1,090
John Gibson, CPA   212
C. majority 18,540 (42.78%)
9.74% swing Lab. to C.

CHEADLE

E. 74,639   T. 55,903 (74.90%)   C. hold
Mary Robinson, C.   25,694
Tom Morrison, LD   23,358
Zahid Chauhan, Lab.   6,851
C. majority 2,336 (4.18%)
2.04% swing C. to LD

CHELMSFORD
E. 80,481 T. 57,122 (70.98%)   C. hold
Vicky Ford, C.   31,934
Marie Goldman, LD   14,313
Penny Richards, Lab.   10,295
Mark Lawrence, Loony   580
C. majority 17,621 (30.85%)
5.34% swing C. to LD

CHELSEA & FULHAM
E. 67,110 T. 46,821 (69.77%)   C. hold
Greg Hands, C.   23,345
Nicola Horlick, LD   12,104
Matt Uberoi, Lab.   10,872
Samuel Morland, AWP   500
C. majority 11,241 (24.01%)
8.83% swing C. to LD

CHELTENHAM
E. 81,043 T. 59,357 (73.24%)   C. hold
Alex Chalk, C.   28,486
Max Wilkinson, LD   27,505
George Penny, Lab.   2,921
George Ridgeon, Loony   445
C. majority 981 (1.65%)
1.43% swing C. to LD

CHESHAM & AMERSHAM
E. 72,542 T. 55,685 (76.76%)   C. hold
Cheryl Gillan, C.   30,850
Dan Gallagher, LD   14,627
Matt Turmaine, Lab.   7,166
Alan Booth, Green   3,042
C. majority 16,223 (29.13%)
9.26% swing C. to LD

CHESTER, CITY OF
E. 76,057 T. 54,560 (71.74%)   Lab. hold
Chris Matheson, Lab.   27,082
Samantha George, C.   20,918
Bob Thompson, LD   3,734
Nicholas Brown, Green   1,438
Andy Argyle, Brexit   1,388
Lab. majority 6,164 (11.30%)
2.48% swing Lab. to C.

CHESTERFIELD
E. 71,030 T. 45,186 (63.62%)   Lab. hold
Toby Perkins, Lab.   18,171
Leigh Higgins, C.   16,720
John Scotting, Brexit   4,771
Emily Coy, LD   3,985
Neil Jackson, Green   1,148
John Daramy, Ind.   391
Lab. majority 1,451 (3.21%)
8.41% swing Lab. to C.

CHICHESTER
E. 85,499 T. 61,243 (71.63%)   C. hold
Gillian Keegan, C.   35,402
Kate O'Kelly, LD   13,912
Jay Morton, Lab.   9,069
Heather Barrie, Green   2,527
Adam Brown, Libertarian   224
Andrew Emerson, Patria   109
C. majority 21,490 (35.09%)
6.89% swing C. to LD

CHINGFORD & WOODFORD GREEN
E. 65,393 T. 48,444 (74.08%)   C. hold
Iain Duncan Smith, C.   23,481
Faiza Shaheen, Lab.   22,219
Geoff Seeff, LD   2,744
C. majority 1,262 (2.61%)
1.29% swing C. to Lab.

CHIPPENHAM
E. 77,225 T. 57,099 (73.94%)   C. hold
Michelle Donelan, C.   30,994
Helen Belcher, LD   19,706
Martha Anachury, Lab.   6,399
C. majority 11,288 (19.77%)
4.67% swing C. to LD

CHIPPING BARNET
E. 79,960 T. 57,569 (72.00%)   C. hold
Theresa Villiers, C.   25,745
Emma Whysall, Lab.   24,533
Isabelle Parasram, LD   5,932
Gabrielle Bailey, Green   1,288
John Sheffield, Advance   71
C. majority 1,212 (2.11%)
0.73% swing Lab. to C.

CHORLEY
E. 78,177 T. 39,870 (51.00%)
                                    Speaker hold
Lindsay Hoyle, Speaker   26,831
Mark Brexit-Smith, Ind.   9,439
James Melling, Green   3,600
Speaker majority 17,392 (43.62%)
swing N/A

CHRISTCHURCH
E. 71,521 T. 51,951 (72.64%)   C. hold
Christopher Chope, C.   33,894
Mike Cox, LD   9,277
Andrew Dunne, Lab.   6,568
Chris Rigby, Green   2,212
C. majority 24,617 (47.39%)
7.13% swing C. to LD

CITIES OF LONDON & WESTMINSTER
E. 63,700 T. 42,723 (67.07%)   C. hold
Nickie Aiken, C.   17,049
Chuka Umunna, LD   13,096
Gordon Nardell, Lab.   11,624
Zack Polanski, Green   728
Jill McLachlan, CPA   125
Dirk van Heck, Lib   101
C. majority 3,953 (9.25%)
13.14% swing C. to LD

CLACTON
E. 70,930 T. 43,506 (61.34%)   C. hold
Giles Watling, C.   31,438
Kevin Bonavia, Lab.   6,736
Callum Robertson, LD   2,541
Chris Southall, Green   1,225
Andy Morgan, ND   1,099
Colin Bennett, Ind.   243
Just-John Sexton, Loony   224
C. majority 24,702 (56.78%)
10.46% swing Lab. to C.

CLEETHORPES
E. 73,689 T. 46,339 (62.88%)   C. hold
Martin Vickers, C.   31,969
Ros James, Lab.   10,551
Roy Horobin, LD   2,535
Jodi Shanahan, Green   1,284
C. majority 21,418 (46.22%)
12.24% swing Lab. to C.

COLCHESTER
E. 82,625 T. 53,373 (64.60%)   C. hold
Will Quince, C.   26,917
Tina McKay, Lab.   17,494
Martin Goss, LD   7,432
Mark Goacher, Green   1,530
C. majority 9,423 (17.65%)
3.53% swing Lab. to C.

COLNE VALLEY
E. 84,174 T. 60,910 (72.36%)   C. gain
Jason McCartney, C.   29,482
Thelma Walker, Lab.   24,379
Cahal Burke, LD   3,815
Sue Harrison, Brexit   1,286
Darryl Gould, Green   1,068
Owen Aspinall, Yorkshire   548
Melanie Roberts, UKIP   230
Colin Peel, Ind.   102
C. majority 5,103 (8.38%)
4.95% swing Lab. to C.

CONGLETON
E. 80,930 T. 57,233 (70.72%)   C. hold
Fiona Bruce, C.   33,747
Jo Dale, Lab.   15,186
Paul Duffy, LD   6,026
Richard McCarthy, Green   1,616
Jane Smith, AWP   658
C. majority 18,561 (32.43%)
4.99% swing Lab. to C.

COPELAND
E. 61,693 T. 42,523 (68.93%)   C. hold
Trudy Harrison, C.   22,856
Tony Lywood, Lab.   17,014
John Studholme, LD   1,888
Jack Lenox, Green   765
C. majority 5,842 (13.74%)
4.89% swing Lab. to C.

CORBY
E. 86,151 T. 60,484 (70.21%)   C. hold
Tom Pursglove, C.   33,410
Beth Miller, Lab.   23,142
Chris Stanbra, LD   3,932
C. majority 10,268 (16.98%)
6.25% swing Lab. to C.

CORNWALL NORTH
E. 69,935 T. 51,678 (73.89%)   C. hold
Scott Mann, C.   30,671
Danny Chambers, LD   15,919
Joy Bassett, Lab.   4,516
Elmars Liepins, Lib   572
C. majority 14,752 (28.55%)
7.21% swing LD to C.

CORNWALL SOUTH EAST

E. 71,825   T. 53,655 (74.70%)   C. hold
Sheryll Murray, C.   31,807
Gareth Derrick, Lab.   10,836
Colin Martin, LD   8,650
Martha Green, Green   1,493
Jay Latham, Lib   869
C. majority 20,971 (39.08%)
3.15% swing Lab. to C.

COTSWOLDS, THE

E. 81,939   T. 61,176 (74.66%)   C. hold
Geoffrey Clifton-Brown, C.   35,484
Liz Webster, LD   15,270
Alan MacKenzie, Lab.   7,110
Sabrina Poole, Green   3,312
C. majority 20,214 (33.04%)
5.63% swing C. to LD

COVENTRY NORTH EAST

E. 76,002   T. 44,444 (58.48%)   Lab. hold
Colleen Fletcher, Lab.   23,412
Sophie Richards, C.   15,720
Iddrisu Sufyan, Brexit   2,110
Nukey Proctor, LD   2,061
Matthew Handley, Green   1,141
Lab. majority 7,692 (17.31%)
8.10% swing Lab. to C.

COVENTRY NORTH WEST

E. 75,240   T. 47,744 (63.46%)   Lab. hold
Taiwo Owatemi, Lab.   20,918
Clare Golby, C.   20,710
Greg Judge, LD   2,717
Joshua Richardson, Brexit   1,956
Stephen Gray, Green   1,443
Lab. majority 208 (0.44%)
8.39% swing Lab. to C.

COVENTRY SOUTH

E. 70,970   T. 45,044 (63.47%)   Lab. hold
Zarah Sultana, Lab.   19,544
Mattie Heaven, C.   19,143
Stephen Richmond, LD   3,398
James Crocker, Brexit   1,432
Becky Finlayson, Green   1,092
Ed Manning, Ind.   435
Lab. majority 401 (0.89%)
8.01% swing Lab. to C.

CRAWLEY

E. 74,207   T. 49,899 (67.24%)   C. hold
Henry Smith, C.   27,040
Peter Lamb, Lab.   18,680
Khalil Yousuf, LD   2,728
Iain Dickson, Green   1,451
C. majority 8,360 (16.75%)
5.93% swing Lab. to C.

CREWE & NANTWICH

E. 80,321   T. 54,032 (67.27%)   C. gain
Kieran Mullan, C.   28,704
Laura Smith, Lab.   20,196
Matthew Theobald, LD   2,618
Matt Wood, Brexit   1,390
Te Ata Browne, Green   975
Andrew Kinsman,   149
Libertarian
C. majority 8,508 (15.75%)
7.92% swing Lab. to C.

CROYDON CENTRAL

E. 81,410   T. 54,045 (66.39%)   Lab. hold
Sarah Jones, Lab.   27,124
Mario Creatura, C.   21,175
Simon Sprague, LD   3,532
Esther Sutton, Green   1,215
Peter Sonnex, Brexit   999
Lab. majority 5,949 (11.01%)
0.55% swing C. to Lab.

CROYDON NORTH

E. 88,466   T. 55,609 (62.86%)
                              Lab. Co-op hold
Steve Reed, Lab. Co-op   36,495
Donald Ekekhomen, C.   11,822
Claire Bonham, LD   4,476
Rachel Chance, Green   1,629
Chidi Ngwaba, Brexit   839
Candace Mitchell, CPA   348
Lab. Co-op majority 24,673 (44.37%)
4.96% swing Lab. to C.

CROYDON SOUTH

E. 83,977   T. 59,358 (70.68%)   C. hold
Chris Philp, C.   30,985
Olga Fitzroy, Lab.   18,646
Anna Jones, LD   7,503
Peter Underwood, Green   1,782
Kathleen Garner, UKIP   442
C. majority 12,339 (20.79%)
1.08% swing Lab. to C.

DAGENHAM & RAINHAM

E. 71,043   T. 43,735 (61.56%)   Lab. hold
Jon Cruddas, Lab.   19,468
Damian White, C.   19,175
Tom Bewick, Brexit   2,887
Sam Fisk, LD   1,182
Azzees Minott, Green   602
Ron Emin, Ind.   212
Terry London, Ind.   209
Lab. majority 293 (0.67%)
4.74% swing Lab. to C.

DARLINGTON

E. 66,395   T. 43,498 (65.51%)   C. gain
Peter Gibson, C.   20,901
Jenny Chapman, Lab.   17,607
Anne-Marie Curry, LD   2,097
Dave Mawson, Brexit   1,544
Matthew Snedker, Green   1,057
Monty Brack, Ind.   292
C. majority 3,294 (7.57%)
7.45% swing Lab. to C.

DARTFORD

E. 82,209   T. 54,022 (65.71%)   C. hold
Gareth Johnson, C.   34,006
Sacha Gosine, Lab.   14,846
Kyle Marsh, LD   3,735
Mark Lindop, Green   1,435
C. majority 19,160 (35.47%)
5.57% swing Lab. to C.

DAVENTRY

E. 77,493   T. 57,403 (74.08%)   C. hold
Chris Heaton-Harris, C.   37,055
Paul Joyce, Lab.   10,975
Andrew Simpson, LD   7,032
Clare Slater, Green   2,341
C. majority 26,080 (45.43%)
3.19% swing Lab. to C.

DENTON & REDDISH

E. 66,579   T. 38,588 (57.96%)   Lab. hold
Andrew Gwynne, Lab.   19,317
Iain Bott, C.   13,142
Martin Power, Brexit   3,039
Dominic Hardwick, LD   1,642
Gary Lawson, Green   1,124
Farmin Lord F'Tang F'Tang   324
Dave, Loony
Lab. majority 6,175 (16.00%)
9.77% swing Lab. to C.

DERBY NORTH

E. 73,212   T. 47,017 (64.22%)   C. gain
Amanda Solloway, C.   21,259
Tony Tinley, Lab.   18,719
Gregory Webb, LD   *   3,450
Alan Graves, Brexit   1,908
Helen Hitchcock, Green   1,046
Chris Williamson, Ind.   635
C. majority 2,540 (5.40%)
4.77% swing Lab. to C.

DERBY SOUTH

E. 73,079   T. 42,462 (58.10%)   Lab. hold
Margaret Beckett, Lab.   21,690
Ed Barker, C.   15,671
Joe Naitta, LD   2,621
Timothy Prosser, Brexit   2,480
Lab. majority 6,019 (14.18%)
5.33% swing Lab. to C.

DERBYSHIRE DALES

E. 65,060   T. 50,016 (76.88%)   C. hold
Sarah Dines, C.   29,356
Claire Raw, Lab.   11,975
Robert Court, LD   6,627
Matt Buckler, Green   2,058
C. majority 17,381 (34.75%)
2.92% swing Lab. to C.

DERBYSHIRE MID

E. 67,437   T. 49,356 (73.19%)   C. hold
Pauline Latham, C.   29,027
Emma Monkman, Lab.   13,642
Felix Dodds, LD   4,756
Sue MacFarlane, Green   1,931
C. majority 15,385 (31.17%)
4.06% swing Lab. to C.

DERBYSHIRE NORTH EAST

E. 72,360   T. 49,217 (68.02%)   C. hold
Lee Rowley, C.   28,897
Chris Peace, Lab.   16,021
Ross Shipman, LD   3,021
Frank Adlington-Stringer,   1,278
Green
C. majority 12,876 (26.16%)
10.24% swing Lab. to C.

DERBYSHIRE SOUTH

E. 79,365   T. 53,381 (67.26%)   C. hold
Heather Wheeler, C.   33,502
Robert Pearson, Lab.   14,167
Lorraine Johnson, LD   3,924
Amanda Baker, Green   1,788
C. majority 19,335 (36.22%)
6.74% swing Lab. to C.

DEVIZES
E. 73,379 T. 50,954 (69.44%)   C. hold
Danny Kruger, C.   32,150
Jo Waltham, LD   8,157
Rachael Schneider, Lab.   7,838
Emma Dawnay, Green   2,809
C. majority 23,993 (47.09%)
3.18% swing C. to LD

DEVON CENTRAL
E. 74,926 T. 58,072 (77.51%)   C. hold
Mel Stride, C.   32,095
Lisa Robillard Webb, Lab.   14,374
Alison Eden, LD   8,770
Andy Williamson, Green   2,833
C. majority 17,721 (30.52%)
1.70% swing Lab. to C.

DEVON EAST
E. 86,841 T. 64,073 (73.78%)   C. hold
Simon Jupp, C.   32,577
Claire Wright, Ind.   25,869
Dan Wilson, Lab.   2,870
Eleanor Rylance, LD   1,771
Henry Gent, Green   711
Peter Faithfull, Ind.   275
C. majority 6,708 (10.47%)
1.42% swing C. to Ind.

DEVON NORTH
E. 75,853 T. 55,581 (73.27%)   C. hold
Selaine Saxby, C.   31,479
Alex White, LD   16,666
Finola ONeill, Lab.   5,097
Robbie Mack, Green   1,759
Steve Cotten, Ind.   580
C. majority 14,813 (26.65%)
9.44% swing LD to C.

DEVON SOUTH WEST
E. 72,535 T. 53,367 (73.57%)   C. hold
Gary Streeter, C.   33,286
Alex Beverley, Lab.   11,856
Sima Davarian, LD   6,207
Ian Poyser, Green   2,018
C. majority 21,430 (40.16%)
5.12% swing Lab. to C.

DEVON WEST & TORRIDGE
E. 79,831 T. 59,730 (74.82%)   C. hold
Geoffrey Cox, C.   35,904
David Chalmers, LD   10,912
Siobhan Strode, Lab.   10,290
Chris Jordan, Green   2,077
Bob Wootton, Ind.   547
C. majority 24,992 (41.84%)
1.51% swing LD to C.

DEWSBURY
E. 81,253 T. 56,389 (69.40%)   C. gain
Mark Eastwood, C.   26,179
Paula Sherriff, Lab.   24,618
John Rossington, LD   2,406
Philip James, Brexit   1,874
Simon Cope, Green   1,060
Sir Archibald Earl Eaton   252
Stanton, Loony
C. majority 1,561 (2.77%)
4.32% swing Lab. to C.

DON VALLEY
E. 75,356 T. 45,437 (60.30%)   C. gain
Nick Fletcher, C.   19,609
Caroline Flint, Lab.   15,979
Paul Whitehurst, Brexit   6,247
Mark Alcock, LD   1,907
Kate Needham, Green   872
Chris Holmes, Yorkshire   823
C. majority 3,630 (7.99%)
9.61% swing Lab. to C.

DONCASTER CENTRAL
E. 71,389 T. 41,581 (58.25%)   Lab. hold
Rosie Winterton, Lab.   16,638
Roberto Weeden-Sanz, C.   14,360
Surjit Duhre, Brexit   6,842
Paul Horton, LD   1,748
Leon French, Yorkshire   1,012
Frank Sheridan, Green   981
Lab. majority 2,278 (5.48%)
9.03% swing Lab. to C.

DONCASTER NORTH
E. 72,362 T. 40,698 (56.24%)   Lab. hold
Ed Miliband, Lab.   15,740
Katrina Sale, C.   13,370
Andy Stewart, Brexit   8,294
Joe Otten, LD   1,476
Stevie Manion, Yorkshire   959
Frank Calladine, Eng Dem   309
Eddie Todd, ND   220
Wendy Bailey, Ind.   188
Neil Wood, Ind.   142
Lab. majority 2,370 (5.82%)
13.66% swing Lab. to C.

DORSET MID & POOLE NORTH
E. 65,426 T. 48,930 (74.79%)   C. hold
Michael Tomlinson, C.   29,548
Vikki Slade, LD   14,650
Joanne Oldale, Lab.   3,402
Natalie Carswell, Green   1,330
C. majority 14,898 (30.45%)
0.67% swing C. to LD

DORSET NORTH
E. 75,956 T. 56,107 (73.87%)   C. hold
Simon Hoare, C.   35,705
David Chadwick, LD   11,404
Pat Osborne, Lab.   6,737
Ken Huggins, Green   2,261
C. majority 24,301 (43.31%)
4.02% swing C. to LD

DORSET SOUTH
E. 72,924 T. 51,058 (70.02%)   C. hold
Richard Drax, C.   30,024
Carralyn Parkes, Lab.   12,871
Nick Ireland, LD   5,432
Jon Orrell, Green   2,246
Joseph Green, Ind.   485
C. majority 17,153 (33.60%)
5.53% swing Lab. to C.

DORSET WEST
E. 80,963 T. 60,925 (75.25%)   C. gain
Chris Loder, C.   33,589
Edward Morello, LD   19,483
Claudia Sorin, Lab.   5,729
Kelvin Clayton, Green   2,124
C. majority 14,106 (23.15%)
4.44% swing C. to LD

DOVER
E. 76,355 T. 50,701 (66.40%)   C. gain
Natalie Elphicke, C.   28,830
Charlotte Cornell, Lab.   16,552
Simon Dodd, LD   2,895
Beccy Sawbridge, Green   1,371
Nathan Sutton, Ind.   916
Eljai Morais, Women   137
C. majority 12,278 (24.22%)
5.91% swing Lab. to C.

DUDLEY NORTH
E. 61,936 T. 36,684 (59.23%)   C. gain
Marco Longhi, C.   23,134
Melanie Dudley, Lab.   11,601
Ian Flynn, LD   1,210
Mike Harrison, Green   739
C. majority 11,533 (31.44%)
15.75% swing Lab. to C.

DUDLEY SOUTH
E. 60,731 T. 36,576 (60.23%)   C. hold
Mike Wood, C.   24,835
Lucy Caldicott, Lab.   9,270
Jonathan Bramall, LD   1,608
Cate Mohr, Green   863
C. majority 15,565 (42.56%)
11.17% swing Lab. to C.

DULWICH & WEST NORWOOD
E. 84,663 T. 55,778 (65.88%)   Lab. hold
Helen Hayes, Lab.   36,521
Jonathan Bartley, Green   9,211
Jane Lyons, C.   9,160
Julia Stephenson, Brexit   571
Anthony Hodgson, CPA   242
John Plume, UKIP   73
Lab. majority 27,310 (48.96%)
9.08% swing Lab. to Green

DURHAM, CITY OF
E. 71,271 T. 48,859 (68.55%)   Lab. hold
Mary Foy, Lab.   20,531
William Morgan, C.   15,506
Amanda Hopgood, LD   7,935
Lesley Wright, Brexit   3,252
Jonathan Elmer, Green   1,635
Lab. majority 5,025 (10.28%)
7.65% swing Lab. to C.

DURHAM NORTH
E. 66,796 T. 42,195 (63.17%)   Lab. hold
Kevan Jones, Lab.   18,639
Ed Parson, C.   13,897
Peter Telford, Brexit   4,693
Craig Martin, LD   2,879
Derek Morse, Green   1,126
Ken Rollings, Ind.   961
Lab. majority 4,742 (11.24%)
9.33% swing Lab. to C.

DURHAM NORTH WEST
E. 72,166 T. 47,663 (66.05%)   C. gain
Richard Holden, C.   19,990
Laura Pidcock, Lab.   18,846
John Wolstenholme, Brexit   3,193
Michael Peacock, LD   2,831
Watts Stelling, Ind.   1,216
David Sewell, Green   1,173
David Lindsay, Ind.   414
C. majority 1,144 (2.40%)
10.38% swing Lab. to C.

EALING CENTRAL & ACTON
E. 75,510 T. 54,807 (72.58%) Lab. hold
Rupa Huq, Lab.	28,132
Julian Gallant, C.	14,832
Sonul Badiani, LD	9,444
Kate Crossland, Green	1,735
Samir Alsoodani, Brexit	664

Lab. majority 13,300 (24.27%)
0.34% swing Lab. to C.

EALING NORTH
E. 74,473 T. 49,631 (66.64%)
Lab. Co-op hold
James Murray, Lab. Co-op	28,036
Anthony Pickles, C.	15,767
Henrietta Bewley, LD	4,370
Jeremy Parker, Green	1,458

Lab. Co-op majority 12,269 (24.72%)
6.39% swing Lab. to C.

EALING SOUTHALL
E. 64,580 T. 42,217 (65.37%) Lab. hold
Virendra Sharma, Lab.	25,678
Tom Bennett, C.	9,594
Tariq Mahmood, LD	3,933
Darren Moore, Green	1,688
Rosamund Beattie, Brexit	867
Suzanne Fernandes, CPA	287
Hassan Zulkifal, WRP	170

Lab. majority 16,084 (38.10%)
5.42% swing Lab. to C.

EASINGTON
E. 61,182 T. 34,583 (56.52%) Lab. hold
Grahame Morris, Lab.	15,723
Clare Ambrosino, C.	9,142
Julie Maughan, Brexit	6,744
Dominic Haney, LD	1,526
Susan McDonnell, NE Party	1,448

Lab. majority 6,581 (19.03%)
10.96% swing Lab. to C.

EAST HAM
E. 97,942 T. 54,628 (55.78%) Lab. hold
Stephen Timms, Lab.	41,703
Scott Pattenden, C.	8,527
Michael Fox, LD	2,158
Alka Sehgal Cuthbert, Brexit	1,107
Mike Spracklin, Green	883
Kamran Malik, Communities	250

Lab. majority 33,176 (60.73%)
4.85% swing Lab. to C.

EASTBOURNE
E. 79,307 T. 55,134 (69.52%) C. gain
Caroline Ansell, C.	26,951
Stephen Lloyd, LD	22,620
Jake Lambert, Lab.	3,848
Stephen Gander, Brexit	1,530
Ken Pollock, Ind.	185

C. majority 4,331 (7.86%)
5.33% swing LD to C.

EASTLEIGH
E. 83,880 T. 58,971 (70.30%) C. hold
Paul Holmes, C.	32,690
Lynda Murphy, LD	17,083
Sam Jordon, Lab.	7,559
Ron Meldrum, Green	1,639

C. majority 15,607 (26.47%)
0.86% swing LD to C.

EDDISBURY
E. 73,700 T. 52,971 (71.87%) C. gain
Edward Timpson, C.	30,095
Terry Savage, Lab.	11,652
Antoinette Sandbach, LD	9,582
Louise Jewkes, Green	1,191
Andrea Allen, UKIP	451

C. majority 18,443 (34.82%)
5.77% swing Lab. to C.

EDMONTON
E. 65,568 T. 40,341 (61.53%)
Lab. Co-op hold
Kate Osamor, Lab. Co-op	26,217
James Hockney, C.	10,202
David Schmitz, LD	2,145
Benjamin Maydon, Green	862
Sachin Sehgal, Brexit	840
Sabriye Warsame, Ind.	75

Lab. Co-op majority 16,015 (39.70%)
4.32% swing Lab. to C.

ELLESMERE PORT & NESTON
E. 70,327 T. 48,746 (69.31%) Lab. hold
Justin Madders, Lab.	26,001
Alison Rodwell, C.	17,237
Ed Gough, LD	2,406
Christopher Stevens, Brexit	2,138
Chris Copeman, Green	964

Lab. majority 8,764 (17.98%)
2.19% swing Lab. to C.

ELMET & ROTHWELL
E. 80,957 T. 58,225 (71.92%) C. hold
Alec Shelbrooke, C.	33,726
David Nagle, Lab.	16,373
Stewart Golton, LD	5,155
Penny Stables, Green	1,775
Matthew Clover, Yorkshire	1,196

C. majority 17,353 (29.80%)
6.67% swing Lab. to C.

ELTHAM
E. 64,084 T. 43,689 (68.17%) Lab. hold
Clive Efford, Lab.	20,550
Louie French, C.	17,353
Charley Hasted, LD	2,941
Steve Kelleher, Brexit	1,523
Matt Stratford, Green	1,322

Lab. majority 3,197 (7.32%)
3.16% swing Lab. to C.

ENFIELD NORTH
E. 68,066 T. 45,050 (66.19%) Lab. gain
Feryal Clark, Lab.	23,340
Joanne Lab.an, C.	16,848
Guy Russo, LD	2,950
Isobel Whittaker, Green	1,115
Ike Ijeh, Brexit	797

Lab. majority 6,492 (14.41%)
3.34% swing Lab. to C.

ENFIELD SOUTHGATE
E. 65,055 T. 47,276 (72.67%) Lab. hold
Bambos Charalambous, Lab.	22,923
David Burrowes, C.	18,473
Rob Wilson, LD	4,344
Luke Balnave, Green	1,042
Parag Shah, Brexit	494

Lab. majority 4,450 (9.41%)
0.20% swing C. to Lab.

EPPING FOREST
E. 74,305 T. 50,268 (67.65%) C. hold
Eleanor Laing, C.	32,364
Vicky Ashworth Te Velde, Lab.	10,191
Jon Whitehouse, LD	5,387
Steven Neville, Green	1,975
Thomas Hall, Young	181
Jon Newham, Soc Dem	170

C. majority 22,173 (44.11%)
4.09% swing Lab. to C.

EPSOM & EWELL
E. 81,138 T. 59,451 (73.27%) C. hold
Chris Grayling, C.	31,819
Steve Gee, LD	13,946
Ed Mayne, Lab.	10,226
Janice Baker, Green	2,047
Clive Woodbridge, Ind.	1,413

C. majority 17,873 (30.06%)
8.52% swing C. to LD

EREWASH
E. 72,519 T. 48,814 (67.31%) C. hold
Maggie Throup, C.	27,560
Catherine Atkinson, Lab.	16,954
James Archer, LD	2,487
Brent Poland, Green	1,115
Des Ball, Ind.	388
Richard Shaw, Ind.	188
Roy Dunn, Ind.	122

C. majority 10,606 (21.73%)
6.31% swing Lab. to C.

ERITH & THAMESMEAD
E. 65,399 T. 41,384 (63.28%) Lab. hold
Abena Oppong-Asare, Lab.	19,882
Joe Robertson, C.	16,124
Tom Bright, Brexit	2,246
Sam Webber, LD	1,984
Claudine Letsae, Green	876
Richard Mitchell, CPA	272

Lab. majority 3,758 (9.08%)
6.72% swing Lab. to C.

ESHER & WALTON
E. 81,184 T. 63,084 (77.70%) C. hold
Dominic Raab, C.	31,132
Monica Harding, LD	28,389
Peter Ashurst, Lab.	2,838
Kylie Keens, Ind.	347
Baron Badger, Loony	326
Kyle Taylor, Advance	52

C. majority 2,743 (4.35%)
18.46% swing C. to LD

EXETER
E. 82,043 T. 56,192 (68.49%) Lab. hold
Ben Bradshaw, Lab.	29,882
John Gray, C.	19,479
Joe Levy, Green	4,838
Leslie Willis, Brexit	1,428
Daniel Page, Ind.	306
Duncan Odgers, UKIP	259

Lab. majority 10,403 (18.51%)
5.28% swing Lab. to C.

FAREHAM
E. 78,337   T. 57,250 (73.08%)   C. hold
Suella Braverman, C.   36,459
Matthew Randall, Lab.   10,373
Matthew Winnington, LD   8,006
Nick Lyle, Green   2,412
C. majority 26,086 (45.57%)
3.88% swing Lab. to C.

FAVERSHAM & KENT MID
E. 73,404   T. 50,394 (68.65%)   C. hold
Helen Whately, C.   31,864
Jenny Reeves, Lab.   9,888
Hannah Perkin, LD   6,170
Hannah Temple, Green   2,103
Gary Butler, Ind.   369
C. majority 21,976 (43.61%)
4.30% swing Lab. to C.

FELTHAM & HESTON
E. 80,932   T. 47,811 (59.08%)
                          Lab. Co-op hold
Seema Malhotra, Lab. Co-op   24,876
Jane Keep, C.   17,017
Hina Malik, LD   3,127
Martyn Nelson, Brexit   1,658
Tony Firkins, Green   1,133
Lab. Co-op majority 7,859 (16.44%)
6.49% swing Lab. to C.

FILTON & BRADLEY STOKE
E. 74,016   T. 53,752 (72.62%)   C. hold
Jack Lopresti, C.   26,293
Mhairi Threlfall, Lab.   20,647
Louise Harris, LD   4,992
Jenny Vernon, Green   1,563
Elaine Hardwick, Citizens   257
C. majority 5,646 (10.50%)
1.13% swing Lab. to C.

FINCHLEY & GOLDERS GREEN
E. 77,573   T. 55,109 (71.04%)   C. hold
Mike Freer, C.   24,162
Luciana Berger, LD   17,600
Ross Houston, Lab.   13,347
C. majority 6,562 (11.91%)
14.22% swing C. to LD

FOLKESTONE & HYTHE
E. 88,273   T. 59,005 (66.84%)   C. hold
Damian Collins, C.   35,483
Laura Davison, Lab.   14,146
Simon Bishop, LD   5,755
Georgina Treloar, Green   2,706
Henry Bolton, Ind.   576
Colin Menniss, Soc Dem   190
Rohen Kapur, Young   80
Andy Thomas, SPGB   69
C. majority 21,337 (36.16%)
4.99% swing Lab. to C.

FOREST OF DEAN
E. 71,438   T. 51,475 (72.06%)   C. hold
Mark Harper, C.   30,680
Di Martin, Lab. Co-op   14,811
Chris McFarling, Green   4,681
Julian Burrett, Ind.   1,303
C. majority 15,869 (30.83%)
6.24% swing Lab. to C.

FYLDE
E. 66,847   T. 46,659 (69.80%)   C. hold
Mark Menzies, C.   28,432
Martin Mitchell, Lab.   11,821
Mark Jewell, LD   3,748
Gina Dowding, Green   1,731
Andy Higgins, Ind.   927
C. majority 16,611 (35.60%)
5.10% swing Lab. to C.

GAINSBOROUGH
E. 76,343   T. 51,046 (66.86%)   C. hold
Edward Leigh, C.   33,893
Perry Smith, Lab.   10,926
Lesley Rollings, LD   5,157
Mary Cavill, Ind.   1,070
C. majority 22,967 (44.99%)
5.95% swing Lab. to C.

GARSTON & HALEWOOD
E. 76,116   T. 53,326 (70.06%)   Lab. hold
Maria Eagle, Lab.   38,578
Neva Novaky, C.   6,954
Kris Brown, LD   3,324
Jake Fraser, Brexit   2,943
Jean-Paul Roberts, Green   1,183
Hazel Williams, Lib   344
Lab. majority 31,624 (59.30%)
0.38% swing Lab. to C.

GATESHEAD
E. 64,449   T. 38,145 (59.19%)   Lab. hold
Ian Mearns, Lab.   20,450
Jane MacBean, C.   13,250
Peter Maughan, LD   2,792
Rachel Cabral, Green   1,653
Lab. majority 7,200 (18.88%)
11.17% swing Lab. to C.

GEDLING
E. 71,438   T. 49,953 (69.92%)   C. gain
Tom Randall, C.   22,718
Vernon Coaker, Lab.   22,039
Anita Prabhakar, LD   2,279
Graham Hunt, Brexit   1,820
Jim Norris, Green   1,097
C. majority 679 (1.36%)
5.22% swing Lab. to C.

GILLINGHAM & RAINHAM
E. 73,549   T. 45,958 (62.49%)   C. hold
Rehman Chishti, C.   28,173
Andy Stamp, Lab.   13,054
Alan Bullion, LD   2,503
George Salomon, Green   1,043
Rob McCulloch Martin,   837
UKIP
Peter Cook, Ind.   229
Roger Peacock, CPA   119
C. majority 15,119 (32.90%)
6.80% swing Lab. to C.

GLOUCESTER
E. 81,332   T. 53,764 (66.10%)   C. hold
Richard Graham, C.   29,159
Fran Boait, Lab. Co-op   18,882
Rebecca Trimnell, LD   4,338
Michael Byfield, Green   1,385
C. majority 10,277 (19.12%)
4.45% swing Lab. to C.

GOSPORT
E. 73,482   T. 48,453 (65.94%)   C. hold
Caroline Dinenage, C.   32,226
Tom Chatwin, Lab.   8,948
Martin Pepper, LD   5,473
Zoe Aspinall, Green   1,806
C. majority 23,278 (48.04%)
6.63% swing Lab. to C.

GRANTHAM & STAMFORD
E. 81,502   T. 56,003 (68.71%)   C. gain
Gareth Davies, C.   36,794
Kathryn Salt, Lab.   10,791
Harrish Bisnauthsing, LD   6,153
Anne Gayfer, Green   2,265
C. majority 26,003 (46.43%)
5.46% swing Lab. to C.

GRAVESHAM
E. 73,234   T. 47,560 (64.94%)   C. hold
Adam Holloway, C.   29,580
Lauren Sullivan, Lab.   13,999
Ukonu Obasi, LD   2,584
Marna Gilligan, Green   1,397
C. majority 15,581 (32.76%)
6.84% swing Lab. to C.

GREAT GRIMSBY
E. 61,409   T. 33,087 (53.88%)   C. gain
Lia Nici, C.   18,150
Melanie Onn, Lab.   10,819
Christopher Barker, Brexit   2,378
Ian Barfield, LD   1,070
Loyd Emmerson, Green   514
Nigel Winn, Ind.   156
C. majority 7,331 (22.16%)
14.69% swing Lab. to C.

GREAT YARMOUTH
E. 71,957   T. 43,462 (60.40%)   C. hold
Brandon Lewis, C.   28,593
Mike Smith-Clare, Lab. Co-   10,930
op
James Joyce, LD   1,661
Anne Killett, Green   1,064
Dave Harding, VPP   631
Adrian Myers, Ind.   429
Margaret McMahon-Morris,   154
Ind.
C. majority 17,663 (40.64%)
11.29% swing Lab. to C.

GREENWICH & WOOLWICH
E. 79,997   T. 53,120 (66.40%)   Lab. hold
Matthew Pennycook, Lab.   30,185
Thomas Turrell, C.   11,721
Rhian O'Connor, LD   7,253
Victoria Rance, Green   2,363
Kailash Trivedi, Brexit   1,228
Eunice Odesanmi, CPA   245
Sushil Gaikwad, Ind.   125
Lab. majority 18,464 (34.76%)
2.12% swing Lab. to C.

GUILDFORD

E. 77,729 T. 58,651 (75.46%) C. gain

Angela Richardson, C.	26,317
Zoe Franklin, LD	22,980
Anne Rouse, Lab.	4,515
Anne Milton, Ind.	4,356
John Morris, Peace	483

C. majority 3,337 (5.69%)
12.50% swing C. to LD

HACKNEY NORTH & STOKE NEWINGTON

E. 92,451 T. 56,864 (61.51%) Lab. hold

Diane Abbott, Lab.	39,972
Benjamin Obese-Jecty, C.	6,784
Alex Armitage, Green	4,989
Ben Mathis, LD	4,283
Richard Ings, Brexit	609
Haseeb Ur-Rehman, Renew	151
Lore Lixenberg, ND	76

Lab. majority 33,188 (58.36%)
2.03% swing Lab. to C.

HACKNEY SOUTH & SHOREDITCH

E. 89,380 T. 54,439 (60.91%)

Lab. Co-op hold

Meg Hillier, Lab. Co-op	39,884
Mark Beckett, C.	5,899
Dave Raval, LD	4,853
Tyrone Scott, Green	2,948
Robert Lloyd, Brexit	744
Jonty Leff, WRP	111

Lab. Co-op majority 33,985 (62.43%)
3.05% swing Lab. to C.

HALESOWEN & ROWLEY REGIS

E. 68,300 T. 42,345 (62.00%) C. hold

James Morris, C.	25,607
Ian Cooper, Lab.	13,533
Ryan Priest, LD	1,738
James Windridge, Green	934
Jon Cross, Ind.	232
Ian Fleming, Ind.	190
Tim Weller, Ind.	111

C. majority 12,074 (28.51%)
8.34% swing Lab. to C.

HALIFAX

E. 71,904 T. 46,458 (64.61%) Lab. hold

Holly Lynch, Lab.	21,496
Kashif Ali, C.	18,927
Sarah Wood, Brexit	2,813
James Baker, LD	2,276
Bella Jessop, Green	946

Lab. majority 2,569 (5.53%)
2.80% swing Lab. to C.

HALTEMPRICE & HOWDEN

E. 71,062 T. 49,779 (70.05%) C. hold

David Davis, C.	31,045
George Ayre, Lab.	10,716
Linda Johnson, LD	5,215
Angela Stone, Green	1,764
Richard Honnoraty, Yorkshire	1,039

C. majority 20,329 (40.84%)
5.45% swing Lab. to C.

HALTON

E. 71,930 T. 46,203 (64.23%) Lab. hold

Derek Twigg, Lab.	29,333
Charles Rowley, C.	10,358
Janet Balfe, Brexit	3,730
Stephen Gribbon, LD	1,800
David O'Keefe, Green	982

Lab. majority 18,975 (41.07%)
5.12% swing Lab. to C.

HAMMERSMITH

E. 74,759 T. 51,966 (69.51%) Lab. hold

Andy Slaughter, Lab.	30,074
Xingang Wang, C.	12,227
Jessie Venegas, LD	6,947
Alex Horn, Green	1,744
James Keyse, Brexit	974

Lab. majority 17,847 (34.34%)
0.68% swing Lab. to C.

HAMPSHIRE EAST

E. 76,478 T. 56,895 (74.39%) C. hold

Damian Hinds, C.	33,446
David Buxton, LD	13,750
Gaynor Austin, Lab.	6,287
Zoe Parker, Green	2,600
Jim Makin, UKIP	616
Eddie Trotter, JACP	196

C. majority 19,696 (34.62%)
6.93% swing C. to LD

HAMPSHIRE NORTH EAST

E. 78,954 T. 59,270 (75.07%) C. hold

Ranil Jayawardena, C.	35,280
Graham Cockarill, LD	15,069
Barry Jones, Lab.	5,760
Culann Walsh, Green	1,754
Tony Durrant, Ind.	831
"Howling Laud" Hope, Loony	576

C. majority 20,211 (34.10%)
9.65% swing C. to LD

HAMPSHIRE NORTH WEST

E. 83,083 T. 58,918 (70.91%) C. hold

Kit Malthouse, C.	36,591
Luigi Gregori, LD	10,283
Liz Bell, Lab.	9,327
Lance Mitchell, Green	2,717

C. majority 26,308 (44.65%)
3.85% swing C. to LD

HAMPSTEAD & KILBURN

E. 82,432 T. 57,385 (69.61%) Lab. hold

Tulip Siddiq, Lab.	28,080
Johnny Luk, C.	13,892
Matt Sanders, LD	13,121
David Stansell, Green	1,608
James Pointon, Brexit	684

Lab. majority 14,188 (24.72%)
0.96% swing Lab. to C.

HARBOROUGH

E. 79,366 T. 57,319 (72.22%) C. hold

Neil O'Brien, C.	31,698
Celia Hibbert, Lab.	14,420
Zuffar Haq, LD	9,103
Darren Woodiwiss, Green	1,709
Robin Lambert, Ind.	389

C. majority 17,278 (30.14%)
4.28% swing Lab. to C.

HARLOW

E. 68,078 T. 43,354 (63.68%) C. hold

Robert Halfon, C.	27,510
Laura McAlpine, Lab.	13,447
Charlotte Cane, LD	2,397

C. majority 14,063 (32.44%)
8.38% swing Lab. to C.

HARROGATE & KNARESBOROUGH

E. 77,914 T. 56,937 (73.08%) C. hold

Andrew Jones, C.	29,962
Judith Rogerson, LD	20,287
Mark Sewards, Lab.	5,480
Kieron George, Yorkshire	1,208

C. majority 9,675 (16.99%)
7.51% swing C. to LD

HARROW EAST

E. 72,120 T. 49,491 (68.62%) C. hold

Bob Blackman, C.	26,935
Pamela Fitzpatrick, Lab.	18,765
Adam Bernard, LD	3,791

C. majority 8,170 (16.51%)
6.53% swing Lab. to C.

HARROW WEST

E. 72,477 T. 47,922 (66.12%)

Lab. Co-op hold

Gareth Thomas, Lab. Co-op	25,132
Anwara Ali, C.	16,440
Lisa-Maria Bornemann, LD	4,310
Rowan Langley, Green	1,109
Richard Jones, Brexit	931

Lab. Co-op majority 8,692 (18.14%)
4.15% swing Lab. to C.

HARTLEPOOL

E. 70,855 T. 41,037 (57.92%) Lab. hold

Mike Hill, Lab.	15,464
Stefan Houghton, C.	11,869
Richard Tice, Brexit	10,603
Andy Hagon, LD	1,696
Joe Bousfield, Ind.	911
Kevin Cranney, Soc Lab.	494

Lab. majority 3,595 (8.76%)
4.76% swing Lab. to C.

HARWICH & ESSEX NORTH

E. 74,153 T. 51,963 (70.08%) C. hold

Bernard Jenkin, C.	31,830
Stephen Rice, Lab.	11,648
Mike Beckett, LD	5,866
Peter Banks, Green	1,945
Richard Browning-Smith, Ind.	411
Tony Francis, Ind.	263

C. majority 20,182 (38.84%)
5.38% swing Lab. to C.

HASTINGS & RYE

E. 80,524 T. 54,274 (67.40%) C. gain

Sally-Ann Hart, C.	26,896
Peter Chowney, Lab.	22,853
Nick Perry, LD	3,960
Paul Crosland, Ind.	565

C. majority 4,043 (7.45%)
3.41% swing Lab. to C.

HAVANT
E. 72,130   T. 45,959 (63.72%)   C. hold
Alan Mak, C.   30,051
Rosamund Knight, Lab.   8,259
Paul Gray, LD   5,708
John Colman, Green   1,597
Alan Black, Soc Dem   344
C. majority 21,792 (47.42%)
6.48% swing Lab. to C.

HAYES & HARLINGTON
E. 72,356   T. 43,994 (60.80%)   Lab. hold
John McDonnell, Lab.   24,545
Wayne Bridges, C.   15,284
Alexander Cunliffe, LD   1,947
Harry Boparai, Brexit   1,292
Christine West, Green   739
Chika Amadi, CPA   187
Lab. majority 9,261 (21.05%)
8.42% swing Lab. to C.

HAZEL GROVE
E. 65,457   T. 44,269 (67.63%)   C. hold
William Wragg, C.   21,592
Lisa Smart, LD   17,169
Tony Wilson, Lab.   5,508
C. majority 4,423 (9.99%)
1.25% swing C. to LD

HEMEL HEMPSTEAD
E. 74,033   T. 51,271 (69.25%)   C. hold
Mike Penning, C.   28,968
Nabila Ahmed, Lab.   14,405
Sammy Barry, LD   6,317
Sherief Hassan, Green   1,581
C. majority 14,563 (28.40%)
5.17% swing Lab. to C.

HEMSWORTH
E. 73,726   T. 43,907 (59.55%)   Lab. hold
Jon Trickett, Lab.   16,460
Louise Calland, C.   15,280
Waj Ali, Brexit   5,930
Ian Womersley, Ind.   2,458
James Monaghan, LD   1,734
Martin Roberts, Yorkshire   964
Lyn Morton, Green   916
Pete Wilks, Ind.   165
Lab. majority 1,180 (2.69%)
9.73% swing Lab. to C.

HENDON
E. 82,661   T. 55,075 (66.63%)   C. hold
Matthew Offord, C.   26,878
David Pinto-Duschinsky,   22,648
Lab.
Clareine Enderby, LD   4,628
Portia Vincent-Kirby, Green   921
C. majority 4,230 (7.68%)
2.81% swing Lab. to C.

HENLEY
E. 76,660   T. 58,759 (76.65%)   C. hold
John Howell, C.   32,189
Laura Coyle, LD   18,136
Zaid Marham, Lab.   5,698
Jo Robb, Green   2,736
C. majority 14,053 (23.92%)
10.16% swing C. to LD

HEREFORD & HEREFORDSHIRE SOUTH
E. 72,085   T. 49,646 (68.87%)   C. hold
Jesse Norman, C.   30,390
Anna-Maria Coda, Lab.   10,704
Lucy Hurds, LD   6,181
Diana Toynbee, Green   2,371
C. majority 19,686 (39.65%)
4.96% swing Lab. to C.

HEREFORDSHIRE NORTH
E. 70,252   T. 51,033 (72.64%)   C. hold
Bill Wiggin, C.   32,158
Phillip Howells, LD   7,302
Joe Wood, Lab.   6,804
Ellie Chowns, Green   4,769
C. majority 24,856 (48.71%)
0.78% swing C. to LD

HERTFORD & STORTFORD
E. 82,407   T. 60,094 (72.92%)   C. hold
Julie Marson, C.   33,712
Chris Vince, Lab.   14,092
Chris Lucas, LD   8,596
Lucy Downes, Green   2,705
Alistair Lindsay, UKIP   681
Brian Percival, Ind.   308
C. majority 19,620 (32.65%)
0.46% swing Lab. to C.

HERTFORDSHIRE NORTH EAST
E. 76,123   T. 55,327 (72.68%)   C. hold
Oliver Heald, C.   31,293
Kelley Green, Lab.   13,104
Amy Finch, LD   8,563
Tim Lee, Green   2,367
C. majority 18,189 (32.88%)
1.29% swing Lab. to C.

HERTFORDSHIRE SOUTH WEST
E. 80,449   T. 61,191 (76.06%)   C. gain
Gagan Mohindra, C.   30,327
David Gauke, Ind.   15,919
Ali Aklakul, Lab.   7,228
Sally Symington, LD   6,251
Tom Pashby, Green   1,466
C. majority 14,408 (23.55%)
swing N/A

HERTSMERE
E. 73,971   T. 52,203 (70.57%)   C. hold
Oliver Dowden, C.   32,651
Holly Kal-Weiss, Lab.   11,338
Stephen Barrett, LD   6,561
John Humphries, Green   1,653
C. majority 21,313 (40.83%)
4.19% swing Lab. to C.

HEXHAM
E. 61,324   T. 46,150 (75.26%)   C. hold
Guy Opperman, C.   25,152
Penny Grennan, Lab.   14,603
Stephen Howse, LD   4,672
Nick Morphet, Green   1,723
C. majority 10,549 (22.86%)
1.44% swing Lab. to C.

HEYWOOD & MIDDLETON
E. 80,162   T. 47,488 (59.24%)   C. gain
Chris Clarkson, C.   20,453
Liz McInnes, Lab.   19,790
Colin Lambert, Brexit   3,952
Anthony Smith, LD   2,073
Nigel Ainsworth-Barnes,   1,220
Green
C. majority 663 (1.40%)
8.34% swing Lab. to C.

HIGH PEAK
E. 74,343   T. 54,173 (72.87%)   C. gain
Robert Largan, C.   24,844
Ruth George, Lab.   24,254
David Lomax, LD   2,750
Alan Graves, Brexit   1,177
Robert Hodgetts-Haley,   1,148
Green
C. majority 590 (1.09%)
2.70% swing Lab. to C.

HITCHIN & HARPENDEN
E. 76,321   T. 58,871 (77.14%)   C. hold
Bim Afolami, C.   27,719
Sam Collins, LD   20,824
Kay Tart, Lab.   9,959
Sid Cordle, CPA   268
Peter Marshall, Advance   101
C. majority 6,895 (11.71%)
15.37% swing C. to LD

HOLBORN & ST PANCRAS
E. 87,236   T. 56,786 (65.09%)   Lab. hold
Keir Starmer, Lab.   36,641
Alexandra Hayward, C.   8,878
Matthew Kirk, LD   7,314
Kirsten De Keyser, Green   2,746
Hector Birchwood, Brexit   1,032
Mohammad Bhatti, UKIP   138
Thomas Scripps, Soc Eq   37
Lab. majority 27,763 (48.89%)
1.41% swing Lab. to C.

HORNCHURCH & UPMINSTER
E. 80,765   T. 53,974 (66.83%)   C. hold
Julia Lopez, C.   35,495
Tele Lawal, Lab.   12,187
Thomas Clarke, LD   3,862
Peter Caton, Green   1,920
David Furness, BNP   510
C. majority 23,308 (43.18%)
5.80% swing Lab. to C.

HORNSEY & WOOD GREEN
E. 81,814   T. 61,105 (74.69%)   Lab. hold
Catherine West, Lab.   35,126
Dawn Barnes, LD   15,884
Ed McGuinness, C.   6,829
Jarelle Francis, Green   2,192
Daniel Corrigan, Brexit   763
Helen Spiby-Vann, CPA   211
Salah Wakie, Ind.   100
Lab. majority 19,242 (31.49%)
8.93% swing Lab. to LD

HORSHAM

E. 86,730   T. 63,242 (72.92%)   C. hold

Jeremy Quin, C.	35,900
Louise Potter, LD	14,773
Michael Jones, Lab.	9,424
Catherine Ross, Green	2,668
Jim Duggan, Peace	477

C. majority 21,127 (33.41%)
6.90% swing C. to LD

HOUGHTON & SUNDERLAND SOUTH

E. 68,835   T. 39,811 (57.84%)   Lab. hold

Bridget Phillipson, Lab.	16,210
Christopher Howarth, C.	13,095
Kevin Yuill, Brexit	6,165
Paul Edgeworth, LD	2,319
Richard Bradley, Green	1,125
Richard Elvin, UKIP	897

Lab. majority 3,115 (7.82%)
10.96% swing Lab. to C.

HOVE

E. 74,313   T. 56,391 (75.88%)   Lab. hold

Peter Kyle, Lab.	32,876
Robert Nemeth, C.	15,832
Beatrice Bass, LD	3,731
Ollie Sykes, Green	2,496
Angela Hancock, Brexit	1,111
Dame Dixon, Loony	195
Charlotte Sabel, Ind.	150

Lab. majority 17,044 (30.22%)
1.17% swing Lab. to C.

HUDDERSFIELD

E. 65,525   T. 41,882 (63.92%)
Lab. Co-op hold

Barry Sheerman, Lab. Co-op	20,509
Ken Davy, C.	15,572
James Wilkinson, LD	2,367
Andrew Cooper, Green	1,768
Stuart Hale, Brexit	1,666

Lab. Co-op majority 4,937 (11.79%)
7.80% swing Lab. to C.

HULL EAST

E. 65,745   T. 32,442 (49.35%)   Lab. hold

Karl Turner, Lab.	12,713
Rachel Storer, C.	11,474
Marten Hall, Brexit	5,764
Bob Morgan, LD	1,707
Julia Brown, Green	784

Lab. majority 1,239 (3.82%)
12.28% swing Lab. to C.

HULL NORTH

E. 65,515   T. 34,203 (52.21%)   Lab. hold

Diana Johnson, Lab.	17,033
Holly Whitbread, C.	9,440
Derek Abram, Brexit	4,771
Mike Ross, LD	2,084
Richard Howarth, Green	875

Lab. majority 7,593 (22.20%)
8.12% swing Lab. to C.

HULL WEST & HESSLE

E. 60,409   T. 31,356 (51.91%)   Lab. hold

Emma Hardy, Lab.	13,384
Scott Bell, C.	10,528
Michelle Dewberry, Brexit	5,638
David Nolan, LD	1,756
Mike Lammiman, Green	50

Lab. majority 2,856 (9.11%)
7.05% swing Lab. to C.

HUNTINGDON

E. 84,657   T. 59,147 (69.87%)   C. hold

Jonathan Djanogly, C.	32,386
Samuel Sweek, Lab.	13,003
Mark Argent, LD	9,432
Daniel Laycock, Green	2,233
Paul Bullen, Ind.	1,789
Tom Varghese, Ind.	304

C. majority 19,383 (32.77%)
4.27% swing Lab. to C.

HYNDBURN

E. 70,910   T. 42,406 (59.80%)   C. gain

Sara Britcliffe, C.	20,565
Graham Jones, Lab.	17,614
Gregory Butt, Brexit	2,156
Adam Waller-Slack, LD	1,226
Katrina Brockbank, Green	845

C. majority 2,951 (6.96%)
9.91% swing Lab. to C.

ILFORD NORTH

E. 72,963   T. 50,123 (68.70%)   Lab. hold

Wes Streeting, Lab.	25,323
Howard Berlin, C.	20,105
Mark Johnson, LD	2,680
Neil Anderson, Brexit	960
David Reynolds, Green	845
Donald Akhigbe, CPA	210

Lab. majority 5,218 (10.41%)
3.90% swing Lab. to C.

ILFORD SOUTH

E. 84,957   T. 53,477 (62.95%)   Lab. gain

Sam Tarry, Lab.	35,085
Ali Azeem, C.	10,984
Mike Gapes, Change	3,891
Ashburn Holder, LD	1,795
Munish Sharma, Brexit	1,008
Rosemary Warrington, Green	714

Lab. majority 24,101 (45.07%)
4.91% swing Lab. to C.

IPSWICH

E. 75,525   T. 49,579 (65.65%)   C. gain

Tom Hunt, C.	24,952
Sandy Martin, Lab.	19,473
Adrian Hyyrylainen-Trett, LD	2,439
Nicola Thomas, Brexit	1,432
Barry Broom, Green	1,283

C. majority 5,479 (11.05%)
6.34% swing Lab. to C.

ISLE OF WIGHT

E. 113,021 T. 74,442 (65.87%)   C. hold

Bob Seely, C.	41,815
Richard Quigley, Lab.	18,078
Vix Lowthion, Green	11,338
Carl Feeney, Network	1,542
Karl Love, Ind.	874
Daryll Pitcher, Ind.	795

C. majority 23,737 (31.89%)
1.80% swing Lab. to C.

ISLINGTON NORTH

E. 75,162   T. 53,805 (71.59%)   Lab. hold

Jeremy Corbyn, Lab.	34,603
Nick Wakeling, LD	8,415
James Clark, C.	5,483
Caroline Russell, Green	4,326
Yosef David, Brexit	742
Nick Brick, Loony	236

Lab. majority 26,188 (48.67%)
7.65% swing Lab. to LD

ISLINGTON SOUTH & FINSBURY

E. 70,489   T. 47,816 (67.83%)   Lab. hold

Emily Thornberry, Lab.	26,897
Kate Pothalingam, LD	9,569
Jason Charalambous, C.	8,045
Talia Hussain, Green	1,987
Paddy Hannam, Brexit	1,136
Lord Sandys Of Bunhill, Loony	182

Lab. majority 17,328 (36.24%)
7.25% swing Lab. to LD

JARROW

E. 65,103   T. 40,736 (62.57%)   Lab. gain

Kate Osborne, Lab.	18,363
Nick Oliver, C.	11,243
Richard Monaghan, Brexit	4,122
John Robertson, Ind.	2,991
David Wilkinson, LD	2,360
James Milne, Green	831
Shaun Sadler, Ind.	614
Mark Conway, Soc Dem	212

Lab. majority 7,120 (17.48%)
11.32% swing Lab. to C.

KEIGHLEY

E. 72,778   T. 52,600 (72.27%)

Robbie Moore, C.	25,298
John Grogan, Lab.	23,080
Tom Franks, LD	2,573
Waqas Khan, Brexit	850
Mark Barton, Yorkshire	667
Matthew Rose, Soc Dem	132

C. majority 2,218 (4.22%)
2.35% swing Lab. to C.

KENILWORTH & SOUTHAM

E. 68,156   T. 52,597 (77.17%)   C. hold

Jeremy Wright, C.	30,351
Richard Dickson, LD	9,998
Antony Tucker, Lab.	9,440
Alison Firth, Green	2,351
Nicholas Green, Loony	457

C. majority 20,353 (38.70%)
6.27% swing C. to LD

KENSINGTON

E. 64,609 T. 43,762 (67.73%) C. gain

Felicity Buchan, C.	16,768
Emma Dent Coad, Lab.	16,618
Sam Gyimah, LD	9,312
Vivien Lichtenstein, Green	535
Jay Aston Colquhoun, Brexit	384
Roger Phillips, CPA	70
Harriet Gore, Touch	47
Scott Dore, WRP	28

C. majority 150 (0.34%)
0.20% swing Lab. to C.

KETTERING

E. 73,187 T. 49,361 (67.45%) C. hold

Philip Hollobone, C.	29,787
Clare Pavitt, Lab.	13,022
Chris Nelson, LD	3,367
Jim Hakewill, Ind.	1,642
Jamie Wildman, Green	1,543

C. majority 16,765 (33.96%)
6.29% swing Lab. to C.

KINGSTON & SURBITON

E. 81,975 T. 60,846 (74.23%) LD hold

Ed Davey, LD	31,103
Aphra Brandreth, C.	20,614
Leanne Werner, Lab.	6,528
Sharron Sumner, Green	1,038
Scott Holman, Brexit	788
James Giles, Ind.	458
Chinners Chinnery, Loony	193
Roger Glencross, UKIP	124

LD majority 10,489 (17.24%)
5.30% swing C. to LD

KINGSWOOD

E. 68,972 T. 49,314 (71.50%) C. hold

Chris Skidmore, C.	27,712
Nicola Bowden-Jones, Lab.	16,492
Dine Romero, LD	3,421
Joseph Evans, Green	1,200
Angelika Cowell, AWP	489

C. majority 11,220 (22.75%)
3.68% swing Lab. to C.

KNOWSLEY

E. 84,060 T. 54,938 (65.36%) Lab. hold

George Howarth, Lab.	44,374
Rushi Millns, C.	4,432
Tim McCullough, Brexit	3,348
Paul Woodruff, Green	1,262
Joe Slupsky, LD	1,117
Ray Catesby, Lib	405

Lab. majority 39,942 (72.70%)
1.69% swing Lab. to C.

LANCASHIRE WEST

E. 73,346 T. 52,663 (71.80%) Lab. hold

Rosie Cooper, Lab.	27,458
Jack Gilmore, C.	19,122
Simon Thomson, LD	2,560
Marc Stanton, Brexit	2,275
John Puddifer, Green	1,248

Lab. majority 8,336 (15.83%)
2.83% swing Lab. to C.

LANCASTER & FLEETWOOD

E. 70,059 T. 45,219 (64.54%) Lab. hold

Cat Smith, Lab.	21,184
Louise Thistlethwaite, C.	18,804
Peter Jackson, LD	2,018
Leanne Murray, Brexit	1,817
Caroline Jackson, Green	1,396

Lab. majority 2,380 (5.26%)
4.61% swing Lab. to C.

LEEDS CENTRAL

E. 90,971 T. 49,284 (54.18%) Lab. hold

Hilary Benn, Lab.	30,413
Peter Fortune, C.	11,143
Paul Thomas, Brexit	2,999
Jack Holland, LD	2,343
Ed Carlisle, Green	2,105
William Clouston, Soc Dem	281

Lab. majority 19,270 (39.10%)
5.30% swing Lab. to C.

LEEDS EAST

E. 67,286 T. 39,052 (58.04%) Lab. hold

Richard Burgon, Lab.	19,464
Jill Mortimer, C.	13,933
Sarah Wass, Brexit	2,981
David Dresser, LD	1,796
Shahab Adris, Green	878

Lab. majority 5,531 (14.16%)
8.30% swing Lab. to C.

LEEDS NORTH EAST

E. 70,580 T. 50,500 (71.55%) Lab. hold

Fabian Hamilton, Lab.	29,024
Amjad Bashir, C.	11,935
Jon Hannah, LD	5,665
Rachel Hartshorne, Green	1,931
Inaya Iman, Brexit	1,769
Celia Foote, Green Soc	176

Lab. majority 17,089 (33.84%)
0.89% swing C. to Lab.

LEEDS NORTH WEST

E. 67,741 T. 49,283 (72.75%)

Lab. Co-op hold

Alex Sobel, Lab. Co-op	23,971
Stewart Harper, C.	13,222
Kamran Hussain, LD	9,397
Martin Hemingway, Green	1,389
Graeme Webber, Brexit	1,304

Lab. Co-op majority 10,749 (21.81%)
1.32% swing Lab. to C.

LEEDS WEST

E. 67,727 T. 40,281 (59.48%) Lab. hold

Rachel Reeves, Lab.	22,186
Mark Dormer, C.	11,622
Phillip Mars, Brexit	2,685
Dan Walker, LD	1,787
Victoria Smith, Green	1,274
Ian Cowling, Yorkshire	650
Daniel Whetstone, Soc Dem	46
Mike Davies, Green Soc	31

Lab. majority 10,564 (26.23%)
5.79% swing Lab. to C.

LEICESTER EAST

E. 78,432 T. 49,421 (63.01%) Lab. hold

Claudia Webbe, Lab.	25,090
Bhupen Dave, C.	19,071
Nitesh Dave, LD	2,800
Tara Baldwin, Brexit	1,243
Melanie Wakley, Green	888
Sanjay Gogia, Ind.	329

Lab. majority 6,019 (12.18%)
15.30% swing Lab. to C.

LEICESTER SOUTH

E. 77,665 T. 50,147 (64.57%)

Lab. Co-op hold

Jonathan Ashworth, Lab. Co-op	33,606
Natalie Neale, C.	10,931
Chris Coghlan, LD	2,754
Mags Lewis, Green	1,669
James Potter, Brexit	1,187

Lab. Co-op majority 22,675 (45.22%)
3.38% swing Lab. to C.

LEICESTER WEST

E. 64,918 T. 34,775 (53.57%) Lab. hold

Liz Kendall, Lab.	17,291
Amanda Wright, C.	13,079
Ian Bradwell, LD	1,808
Jack Collier, Brexit	1,620
Ani Goddard, Green	977

Lab. majority 4,212 (12.11%)
8.69% swing Lab. to C.

LEICESTERSHIRE NORTH WEST

E. 78,935 T. 53,821 (68.18%) C. hold

Andrew Bridgen, C.	33,811
Terri Eynon, Lab.	13,411
Grahame Hudson, LD	3,614
Carl Benfield, Green	2,478
Edward Nudd, Ind.	367
Dan Liddicott, Libertarian	140

C. majority 20,400 (37.90%)
6.54% swing Lab. to C.

LEICESTERSHIRE SOUTH

E. 80,520 T. 57,469 (71.37%) C. hold

Alberto Costa, C.	36,791
Tristan Koriya, Lab.	12,787
Phil Knowles, LD	5,452
Nick Cox, Green	2,439

C. majority 24,004 (41.77%)
4.45% swing Lab. to C.

LEIGH

E. 77,417 T. 46,979 (60.68%) C. gain

James Grundy, C.	21,266
Joanne Platt, Lab. Co-op	19,301
James Melly, Brexit	3,161
Mark Clayton, LD	2,252
Ann O'Bern, Ind.	551
Leon Peters, UKIP	448

C. majority 1,965 (4.18%)
12.28% swing Lab. to C.

LEWES
E. 71,503 T. 54,851 (76.71%)   C. hold
Maria Caulfield, C.   26,268
Oli Henman, LD   23,811
Kate Chappell, Lab.   3,206
Johnny Denis, Green   1,453
Paul Cragg, ND   113
C. majority 2,457 (4.48%)
2.84% swing C. to LD

LEWISHAM DEPTFORD
E. 80,617 T. 55,368 (68.68%)   Lab. hold
Vicky Foxcroft, Lab.   39,216
Gavin Haran, C.   6,303
Bobby Dean, LD   5,774
Andrea Carey Fuller, Green   3,085
Moses Etienne, Brexit   789
Tan Bui, Ind.   130
John Lloyd, Green Soc   71
Lab. majority 32,913 (59.44%)
1.94% swing Lab. to C.

LEWISHAM EAST
E. 67,857 T. 44,815 (66.04%)   Lab. hold
Janet Daby, Lab.   26,661
Sam Thurgood, C.   9,653
Ade Fatukasi, LD   5,039
Rosamund Adoo-Kissi-   1,706
Debrah, Green
Wesley Pollard, Brexit   1,234
Maureen Martin, CPA   277
Mark Barber, Ind.   152
Richard Galloway, Young   50
Elder Roger Mighton, Ind.   43
Lab. majority 17,008 (37.95%)
3.50% swing Lab. to C.

LEWISHAM WEST & PENGE
E. 74,615 T. 52,100 (69.83%)   Lab. hold
Ellie Reeves, Lab.   31,860
Aisha Cuthbert, C.   10,317
Alex Feakes, LD   6,260
James Braun, Green   2,390
Teixeira Hambro, Brexit   1,060
Katherine Hortense, CPA   213
Lab. majority 21,543 (41.35%)
1.10% swing Lab. to C.

LEYTON & WANSTEAD
E. 64,852 T. 44,547 (68.69%)   Lab. hold
John Cryer, Lab.   28,836
Noshaba Khiljee, C.   8,028
Ben Sims, LD   4,666
Ashley Gunstock, Green   1,805
Zulf Jannaty, Brexit   785
Henry Scott, Ind.   427
Lab. majority 20,808 (46.71%)
1.13% swing Lab. to C.

LICHFIELD
E. 76,751 T. 53,993 (70.35%)   C. hold
Michael Fabricant, C.   34,844
Dave Robertson, Lab.   11,206
Paul Ray, LD   5,632
Andrea Muckley, Green   1,743
John Madden, Ind.   568
C. majority 23,638 (43.78%)
4.53% swing Lab. to C.

LINCOLN
E. 74,778 T. 50,629 (67.71%)   C. gain
Karl McCartney, C.   24,267
Karen Lee, Lab.   20,753
Caroline Kenyon, LD   2,422
Sally Horscroft, Green   1,195
Reece Wilkes, Brexit   1,079
Rob Bradley, Ind.   609
Charles Shaw, Lib   304
C. majority 3,514 (6.94%)
5.05% swing Lab. to C.

LIVERPOOL RIVERSIDE
E. 80,310 T. 52,789 (65.73%)   Lab. gain
Kim Johnson, Lab.   41,170
Sean Malkeson, C.   4,127
Tom Crone, Green   3,017
Rob McAllister-Bell, LD   2,696
David Leach, Brexit   1,779
Lab. majority 37,043 (70.17%)
2.34% swing Lab. to C.

LIVERPOOL WALTON
E. 62,628 T. 40,786 (65.12%)   Lab. hold
Dan Carden, Lab.   34,538
Alex Phillips, C.   4,018
Ted Grant, Green   814
David Newman, LD   756
Billy Lake, Lib   660
Lab. majority 30,520 (74.83%)
1.16% swing Lab. to C.

LIVERPOOL WAVERTREE
E. 63,458 T. 43,377 (68.36%)   Lab. gain
Paula Barker, Lab.   31,310
Catherine Mulhern, C.   4,225
Richard Kemp, LD   4,055
Adam Heatherington, Brexit   1,921
Kay Inckle, Green   1,365
Mick Coyne, Lib   501
Lab. majority 27,085 (62.44%)
2.54% swing Lab. to C.

LIVERPOOL WEST DERBY
E. 65,640 T. 43,989 (67.02%)   Lab. hold
Ian Byrne, Lab.   34,117
Tom Bradley, C.   4,133
Ray Pearson, Brexit   2,012
Steve Radford, Lib   1,826
Paul Parr, LD   1,296
William Ward, Green   605
Lab. majority 29,984 (68.16%)
2.35% swing Lab. to C.

LOUGHBOROUGH
E. 79,776 T. 54,631 (68.48%)   C. hold
Jane Hunt, C.   27,954
Stuart Brady, Lab.   20,785
Ian Sharpe, LD   4,153
Wes Walton, Green   1,504
Queenie Tea, Ind.   235
C. majority 7,169 (13.12%)
2.62% swing Lab. to C.

LOUTH & HORNCASTLE
E. 79,648 T. 52,332 (65.70%)   C. hold
Victoria Atkins, C.   38,021
Ellie Green, Lab.   9,153
Ross Pepper, LD   4,114
The Iconic Arty-Pole, Loony   1,044
C. majority 28,868 (55.16%)
8.97% swing Lab. to C.

LUDLOW
E. 69,442 T. 50,225 (72.33%)   C. hold
Philip Dunne, C.   32,185
Heather Kidd, LD   8,537
Kuldip Sahota, Lab.   7,591
Hilary Wendt, Green   1,912
C. majority 23,648 (47.08%)
2.57% swing C. to LD

LUTON NORTH
E. 68,185 T. 42,589 (62.46%)   Lab. gain
Sarah Owen, Lab.   23,496
Jeet Bains, C.   14,249
Linda Jack, LD   2,063
Sudhir Sharma, Brexit   1,215
Simon Hall, Green   771
Muhammad Rehman, Ind.   646
Serena Laidley, Women   149
Lab. majority 9,247 (21.71%)
4.55% swing Lab. to C.

LUTON SOUTH
E. 69,338 T. 42,064 (60.67%)   Lab. gain
Rachel Hopkins, Lab.   21,787
Parvez Akhtar, C.   13,031
Gavin Shuker, ND   3,893
Garry Warren, Brexit   1,601
Ben Foley, Green   995
Mohammed Ashraf, Ind.   489
John French, Luton   268
Lab. majority 8,756 (20.82%)
4.68% swing Lab. to C.

MACCLESFIELD
E. 76,216 T. 53,867 (70.68%)   C. hold
David Rutley, C.   28,292
Neil Puttick, Lab.   17,581
Neil Christian, LD   5,684
James Booth, Green   2,310
C. majority 10,711 (19.88%)
2.02% swing Lab. to C.

MAIDENHEAD
E. 76,668 T. 56,492 (73.68%)   C. hold
Theresa May, C.   32,620
Joshua Reynolds, LD   13,774
Patrick McDonald, Lab.   7,882
Emily Tomalin, Green   2,216
C. majority 18,846 (33.36%)
10.09% swing C. to LD

MAIDSTONE & THE WEALD
E. 76,110 T. 51,680 (67.90%)   C. hold
Helen Grant, C.   31,220
Dan Wilkinson, Lab.   9,448
James Willis, LD   8,482
Stuart Jeffery, Green   2,172
Yolande Kenward, Ind.   358
C. majority 21,772 (42.13%)
3.94% swing Lab. to C.

MAKERFIELD
E. 74,190 T. 44,259 (59.66%)   Lab. hold
Yvonne Fovargue, Lab.   19,954
Nick King, C.   15,214
Ross Wright, Brexit   5,817
John Skipworth, LD   2,108
Sheila Shaw, Green   1,166
Lab. majority 4,740 (10.71%)
9.07% swing Lab. to C.

MALDON
E. 72,641   T. 50,408 (69.39%)   C. hold
John Whittingdale, C. — 36,304
Stephen Capper, Lab. — 6,263
Colin Baldy, LD — 5,990
Janet Band, Green — 1,851
C. majority 30,041 (59.60%)
6.46% swing Lab. to C.

MANCHESTER CENTRAL
E. 94,247   T. 52,289 (55.48%)
Lab. Co-op hold
Lucy Powell, Lab. Co-op — 36,823
Shaden Jaradat, C. — 7,734
John Bridges, LD — 3,420
Sarah Chadwick, Brexit — 2,335
Melanie Horrocks, Green — 1,870
Dennis Leech, Soc Eq — 107
Lab. Co-op majority 29,089 (55.63%)
3.81% swing Lab. to C.

MANCHESTER GORTON
E. 76,419   T. 44,545 (58.29%)   Lab. hold
Afzal Khan, Lab. — 34,583
Sebastian Lowe, C. — 4,244
Jackie Pearcey, LD — 2,448
Eliza Tyrrell, Green — 1,697
Lesley Kaya, Brexit — 1,573
Lab. majority 30,339 (68.11%)
0.47% swing Lab. to C.

MANCHESTER WITHINGTON
E. 76,530   T. 52,995 (69.25%)   Lab. hold
Jeff Smith, Lab. — 35,902
John Leech, LD — 7,997
Shengke Zhi, C. — 5,820
Lucy Bannister, Green — 1,968
Stephen Ward, Brexit — 1,308
Lab. majority 27,905 (52.66%)
1.54% swing Lab. to LD

MANSFIELD
E. 77,131   T. 49,273 (63.88%)   C. hold
Ben Bradley, C. — 31,484
Sonya Ward, Lab. — 15,178
Sarah Brown, LD — 1,626
Sid Pepper, Ind. — 527
Stephen Harvey, ND — 458
C. majority 16,306 (33.09%)
15.49% swing Lab. to C.

MEON VALLEY
E. 75,737   T. 54,829 (72.39%)   C. hold
Flick Drummond, C. — 35,271
Lewis North, LD — 11,716
Matthew Bunday, Lab. — 5,644
Malcolm Wallace, Green — 2,198
C. majority 23,555 (42.96%)
5.94% swing C. to LD

MERIDEN
E. 85,368   T. 54,161 (63.44%)   C. hold
Saqib Bhatti, C. — 34,358
Teresa Beddis, Lab. — 11,522
Laura McCarthy, LD — 5,614
Steve Caudwell, Green — 2,667
C. majority 22,836 (42.16%)
3.51% swing Lab. to C.

MIDDLESBROUGH
E. 60,759   T. 32,140 (52.90%)   Lab. hold
Andy McDonald, Lab. — 17,202
Ruth Betson, C. — 8,812
Antony High, Ind. — 4,548
Faye Clements, Brexit — 2,168
Thomas Crawford, LD — 816
Hugh Alberti, Green — 546
Lab. majority 8,390 (26.10%)
6.41% swing Lab. to C.

MIDDLESBROUGH SOUTH & CLEVELAND EAST
E. 72,339   T. 47,817 (66.10%)   C. hold
Simon Clarke, C. — 28,135
Lauren Dingsdale, Lab. — 16,509
Jemma Joy, LD — 1,953
Sophie Brown, Green — 1,220
C. majority 11,626 (24.31%)
11.09% swing Lab. to C.

MILTON KEYNES NORTH
E. 91,535   T. 62,543 (68.33%)   C. hold
Ben Everitt, C. — 30,938
Charlynne Pullen, Lab. — 24,683
Aisha Mir, LD — 4,991
Catherine Rose, Green — 1,931
C. majority 6,255 (10.00%)
3.50% swing Lab. to C.

MILTON KEYNES SOUTH
E. 96,343   T. 64,007 (66.44%)   C. hold
Iain Stewart, C. — 32,011
Hannah O'Neill, Lab. — 25,067
Saleyha Ahsan, LD — 4,688
Alan Francis, Green — 1,495
Stephen Fulton, Ind. — 539
Amarachi Ogba, CPA — 207
C. majority 6,944 (10.85%)
4.09% swing Lab. to C.

MITCHAM & MORDEN
E. 70,014   T. 45,741 (65.33%)   Lab. hold
Siobhain McDonagh, Lab. — 27,964
Toby Williams, C. — 11,482
Luke Taylor, LD — 3,717
Jeremy Maddocks, Brexit — 1,202
Pippa Maslin, Green — 1,160
Des Coke, CPA — 216
Lab. majority 16,482 (36.03%)
4.19% swing Lab. to C.

MOLE VALLEY
E. 74,665   T. 57,110 (76.49%)   C. hold
Paul Beresford, C. — 31,656
Paul Kennedy, LD — 19,615
Brian Bostock, Lab. — 2,965
Lisa Scott-Conte, Green — 1,874
Robin Horsley, Ind. — 536
Geoffrey Cox, UKIP — 464
C. majority 12,041 (21.08%)
10.73% swing C. to LD

MORECAMBE & LUNESDALE
E. 67,397   T. 45,310 (67.23%)   C. hold
David Morris, C. — 23,925
Lizzi Collinge, Lab. — 17,571
Owen Lambert, LD — 2,328
Chloe Buckley, Green — 938
Darren Clifford, Ind. — 548
C. majority 6,354 (14.02%)
5.48% swing Lab. to C.

MORLEY & OUTWOOD
E. 78,803   T. 51,930 (65.90%)   C. hold
Andrea Jenkyns, C. — 29,424
Deanne Ferguson, Lab. — 18,157
Craig Dobson, LD — 2,285
Chris Bell, Green — 1,107
Dan Woodlock, Yorkshire — 957
C. majority 11,267 (21.70%)
8.84% swing Lab. to C.

NEW FOREST EAST
E. 73,552   T. 50,786 (69.05%)   C. hold
Julian Lewis, C. — 32,769
Julie Hope, Lab. — 7,518
Bob Johnston, LD — 7,390
Nicola Jolly, Green — 2,434
Andrew Knight, AWP — 675
C. majority 25,251 (49.72%)
3.45% swing Lab. to C.

NEW FOREST WEST
E. 70,867   T. 50,306 (70.99%)   C. hold
Desmond Swayne, C. — 32,113
Jack Davies, LD — 7,710
Jo Graham, Lab. — 6,595
Nick Bubb, Green — 3,888
C. majority 24,403 (48.51%)
4.35% swing C. to LD

NEWARK
E. 75,855   T. 54,722 (72.14%)   C. hold
Robert Jenrick, C. — 34,650
James Baggaley, Lab. — 12,814
David Watts, LD — 5,308
Jay Henderson, Green — 1,950
C. majority 21,836 (39.90%)
3.47% swing Lab. to C.

NEWBURY
E. 83,414   T. 59,998 (71.93%)   C. hold
Laura Farris, C. — 34,431
Lee Dillon, LD — 18,384
James Wilder, Lab. — 4,404
Stephen Masters, Green — 2,454
Ben Holden-Crowther, Ind. — 325
C. majority 16,047 (26.75%)
6.66% swing C. to LD

NEWCASTLE UPON TYNE CENTRAL
E. 57,845   T. 37,474 (64.78%)   Lab. hold
Chi Onwurah, Lab. — 21,568
Emily Payne, C. — 9,290
Ali Avaei, LD — 2,709
Mark Griffin, Brexit — 2,542
Tay Pitman, Green — 1,365
Lab. majority 12,278 (32.76%)
3.75% swing Lab. to C.

NEWCASTLE UPON TYNE EAST
E. 63,796   T. 43,365 (67.97%)   Lab. hold
Nick Brown, Lab. — 26,049
Robin Gwynn, C. — 10,586
Wendy Taylor, LD — 4,535
Nick Hartley, Green — 2,195
Lab. majority 15,463 (35.66%)
5.30% swing Lab. to C.

NEWCASTLE UPON TYNE NORTH
E. 68,486   T. 46,999 (68.63%)   Lab. hold
Catherine McKinnell, Lab.   21,354
Mark Lehain, C.   15,589
Nicholas Cott, LD   4,357
Richard Ogden, Brexit   4,331
Alistair Ford, Green   1,368
Lab. majority 5,765 (12.27%)
4.58% swing Lab. to C.

NEWCASTLE-UNDER-LYME
E. 68,211   T. 44,739 (65.59%)   C. gain
Aaron Bell, C.   23,485
Carl Greatbatch, Lab.   16,039
Nigel Jones, LD   2,361
Jason Cooper, Brexit   1,921
Carl Johnson, Green   933
C. majority 7,446 (16.64%)
8.36% swing Lab. to C.

NEWTON ABBOT
E. 72,533   T. 52,556 (72.46%)   C. hold
Anne Marie Morris, C.   29,190
Martin Wrigley, LD   11,689
James Osben, Lab.   9,329
Megan Debenham, Green   1,508
David Halpin, Ind.   840
C. majority 17,501 (33.30%)
0.81% swing C. to LD

NORFOLK MID
E. 81,975   T. 56,186 (68.54%)   C. hold
George Freeman, C.   35,051
Adrian Heald, Lab.   12,457
Steffan Aquarone, LD   7,739
P J O'Gorman, Ind.   939
C. majority 22,594 (40.21%)
5.66% swing Lab. to C.

NORFOLK NORTH
E. 70,729   T. 50,823 (71.86%)   C. gain
Duncan Baker, C.   29,792
Karen Ward, LD   15,397
Emma Corlett, Lab.   3,895
Harry Gwynne, Brexit   1,739
C. majority 14,395 (28.32%)
17.53% swing LD to C.

NORFOLK NORTH WEST
E. 72,080   T. 46,602 (64.65%)   C. hold
James Wild, C.   30,627
Jo Rust, Lab.   10,705
Rob Colwell, LD   3,625
Andrew De Whalley, Green   1,645
C. majority 19,922 (42.75%)
7.25% swing Lab. to C.

NORFOLK SOUTH
E. 86,214   T. 62,484 (72.48%)   C. hold
Richard Bacon, C.   36,258
Beth Jones, Lab.   14,983
Christopher Brown, LD   8,744
Ben Price, Green   2,499
C. majority 21,275 (34.05%)
3.38% swing Lab. to C.

NORFOLK SOUTH WEST
E. 78,455   T. 51,466 (65.60%)   C. hold
Liz Truss, C.   35,507
Emily Blake, Lab.   9,312
Josie Ratcliffe, LD   4,166
Pallavi Devulapalli, Green   1,645
Earl Elvis Of Outwell,   836
Loony
C. majority 26,195 (50.90%)
7.98% swing Lab. to C.

NORMANTON, PONTEFRACT & CASTLEFORD
E. 84,527   T. 48,259 (57.09%)   Lab. hold
Yvette Cooper, Lab.   18,297
Andrew Lee, C.   17,021
Deneice Florence-Jukes,   8,032
Brexit
Tom Gordon, LD   3,147
Laura Walker, Yorkshire   1,762
Lab. majority 1,276 (2.64%)
13.42% swing Lab. to C.

NORTHAMPTON NORTH
E. 59,265   T. 39,539 (66.72%)   C. hold
Michael Ellis, C.   21,031
Sally Keeble, Lab.   15,524
Martin Sawyer, LD   2,031
Katherine Pate, Green   953
C. majority 5,507 (13.93%)
5.96% swing Lab. to C.

NORTHAMPTON SOUTH
E. 62,712   T. 40,835 (65.12%)   C. hold
Andrew Lewer, C.   20,914
Gareth Eales, Lab.   16,217
Jill Hope, LD   2,482
Scott Mabbutt, Green   1,222
C. majority 4,697 (11.50%)
4.34% swing Lab. to C.

NORTHAMPTONSHIRE SOUTH
E. 90,840   T. 66,908 (73.65%)   C. hold
Andrea Leadsom, C.   41,755
Gen Kitchen, Lab.   13,994
Chris Lofts, LD   7,891
Denise Donaldson, Green   2,634
Josh Phillips, Ind.   463
Stuart McCutcheon, ND   171
C. majority 27,761 (41.49%)
3.18% swing Lab. to C.

NORWICH NORTH
E. 67,172   T. 46,285 (68.91%)   C. hold
Chloe Smith, C.   23,397
Karen Davis, Lab.   18,659
Dave Thomas, LD   2,663
Adrian Holmes, Green   1,078
David Moreland, UKIP   488
C. majority 4,738 (10.24%)
4.57% swing Lab. to C.

NORWICH SOUTH
E. 77,845   T. 51,673 (66.38%)   Lab. hold
Clive Lewis, Lab.   27,766
Mike Spencer, C.   15,006
James Wright, LD   4,776
Catherine Rowett, Green   2,469
Sandy Gilchrist, Brexit   1,656
Lab. majority 12,760 (24.69%)
2.84% swing Lab. to C.

NOTTINGHAM EAST
E. 66,262   T. 40,004 (60.37%)   Lab. gain
Nadia Whittome, Lab.   25,735
Victoria Stapleton, C.   8,342
Robert Swift, LD   1,954
Chris Leslie, Change   1,447
Damian Smith, Brexit   1,343
Michelle Vacciana, Green   1,183
Lab. majority 17,393 (43.48%)
3.17% swing Lab. to C.

NOTTINGHAM NORTH
E. 66,495   T. 35,320 (53.12%)
Lab. Co-op hold
Alex Norris, Lab. Co-op   17,337
Stuart Bestwick, C.   12,847
Julian Carter, Brexit   2,686
Christina Morgan-Danvers,   1,582
LD
Andrew Jones, Green   868
Lab. Co-op majority 4,490 (12.71%)
8.21% swing Lab. to C.

NOTTINGHAM SOUTH
E. 79,485   T. 48,134 (60.56%)   Lab. hold
Lilian Greenwood, Lab.   26,586
Marc Nykolyszyn, C.   14,018
Barry Holliday, LD   3,935
John Lawson, Brexit   2,012
Cath Sutherland, Green   1,583
Lab. majority 12,568 (26.11%)
2.70% swing Lab. to C.

NUNEATON
E. 70,226   T. 45,190 (64.35%)   C. hold
Marcus Jones, C.   27,390
Zoe Mayou, Lab.   14,246
Richard Brighton-Knight,   1,862
LD
Keith Kondakor, Green   1,692
C. majority 13,144 (29.09%)
9.40% swing Lab. to C.

OLD BEXLEY & SIDCUP
E. 66,104   T. 46,145 (69.81%)   C. hold
James Brokenshire, C.   29,786
David Tingle, Lab.   10,834
Simone Reynolds, LD   3,822
Matt Browne, Green   1,477
Carol Valinejad, CPA   226
C. majority 18,952 (41.07%)
4.44% swing Lab. to C.

OLDHAM EAST & SADDLEWORTH
E. 72,173   T. 46,164 (63.96%)   Lab. hold
Debbie Abrahams, Lab.   20,088
Tom Lord, C.   18,589
Paul Brierley, Brexit   2,980
Sam Al-Hamdani, LD   2,423
Paul Errock, Oldham   1,073
Wendy Olsen, Green   778
Amoy Lindo, Ind.   233
Lab. majority 1,499 (3.25%)
7.07% swing Lab. to C.

OLDHAM WEST & ROYTON

E. 73,063   T. 44,434 (60.82%)

		Lab. Co-op hold
Jim McMahon, Lab. Co-op	24,579	
Kirsty Finlayson, C.	13,452	
Helen Formby, Brexit	3,316	
Garth Harkness, LD	1,484	
Dan Jerrome, Green	681	
Debbie Cole, Oldham	533	
Anthony Prince, UKIP	389	

Lab. Co-op majority 11,127 (25.04%)
6.26% swing Lab. to C.

ORPINGTON

E. 68,884   T. 48,721 (70.73%)   C. hold

Gareth Bacon, C.	30,882
Simon Jeal, Lab.	8,504
Allan Tweddle, LD	7,552
Karen Wheller, Green	1,783

C. majority 22,378 (45.93%)
3.68% swing Lab. to C.

OXFORD EAST

E. 77,947   T. 49,359 (63.32%)

	Lab. Co-op hold
Anneliese Dodds, Lab. Co-op	28,135
Louise Staite, C.	10,303
Alistair Fernie, LD	6,884
David Williams, Green	2,392
Roger Carter, Brexit	1,146
David Henwood, Ind.	238
Chaka Artwell, Ind.	143
Phil Taylor, Ind.	118

Lab. Co-op majority 17,832 (36.13%)
3.54% swing Lab. to C.

OXFORD WEST & ABINGDON

E. 76,953   T. 58,824 (76.44%)   LD hold

Layla Moran, LD	31,340
James Fredrickson, C.	22,397
Rosie Sourbut, Lab.	4,258
Allison Wild, Brexit	829

LD majority 8,943 (15.20%)
6.92% swing C. to LD

PENDLE

E. 65,289   T. 44,460 (68.10%)   C. hold

Andrew Stephenson, C.	24,076
Azhar Ali, Lab.	17,890
Gordon Lishman, LD	1,548
Clare Hales, Green	678
John Richardson, Ind.	268

C. majority 6,186 (13.91%)
5.53% swing Lab. to C.

PENISTONE & STOCKSBRIDGE

E. 70,925   T. 49,520 (69.82%)   C. gain

Miriam Cates, C.	23,688
Francyne Johnson, Lab.	16,478
Hannah Kitching, LD	5,054
John Booker, Brexit	4,300

C. majority 7,210 (14.56%)
8.61% swing Lab. to C.

PENRITH & THE BORDER

E. 67,555   T. 47,824 (70.79%)   C. gain

Neil Hudson, C.	28,875
Sarah Williams, Lab. Co-op	10,356
Matt Severn, LD	5,364
Ali Ross, Green	2,159
Jonathan Davies, Cumbria	1,070

C. majority 18,519 (38.72%)
2.24% swing Lab. to C.

PETERBOROUGH

E. 72,560   T. 47,801 (65.88%)   C. gain

Paul Bristow, C.	22,334
Lisa Forbes, Lab.	19,754
Beki Sellick, LD	2,334
Mike Greene, Brexit	2,127
Joseph Wells, Green	728
Luke Ferguson, Ind.	260
Tom Rogers, CPA	151
The Very Raving Mr P, Loony	113

C. majority 2,580 (5.40%)
3.33% swing Lab. to C.

PLYMOUTH MOOR VIEW

E. 69,430   T. 44,239 (63.72%)   C. hold

Johnny Mercer, C.	26,831
Charlotte Holloway, Lab. Co-op	13,934
Sarah Martin, LD	2,301
Ewan Melling Flavell, Green	1,173

C. majority 12,897 (29.15%)
9.05% swing Lab. to C.

PLYMOUTH SUTTON & DEVONPORT

E. 77,852   T. 53,176 (68.30%)

	Lab. Co-op hold
Luke Pollard, Lab. Co-op	25,461
Rebecca Smith, C.	20,704
Ann Widdecombe, Brexit	2,909
Graham Reed, LD	2,545
James Ellwood, Green	1,557

Lab. Co-op majority 4,757 (8.95%)
2.17% swing Lab. to C.

POOLE

E. 73,992   T. 50,451 (68.18%)   C. hold

Robert Syms, C.	29,599
Sue Aitkenhead, Lab. Co-op	10,483
Victoria Collins, LD	7,819
Barry Harding-Rathbone, Green	1,702
David Young, Ind.	848

C. majority 19,116 (37.89%)
4.69% swing Lab. to C.

POPLAR & LIMEHOUSE

E. 91,760   T. 61,276 (66.78%)   Lab. hold

Apsana Begum, Lab.	38,660
Sheun Oke, C.	9,756
Andrew Cregan, LD	8,832
Neil Jameson, Green	2,159
Catherine Cui, Brexit	1,493
Andy Erlam, Ind.	376

Lab. majority 28,904 (47.17%)
0.03% swing C. to Lab.

PORTSMOUTH NORTH

E. 71,299   T. 45,910 (64.39%)   C. hold

Penny Mordaunt, C.	28,172
Amanda Martin, Lab.	12,392
Antonia Harrison, LD	3,419
Lloyd Day, Green	1,304
George Madgwick, ND	623

C. majority 15,780 (34.37%)
6.63% swing Lab. to C.

PORTSMOUTH SOUTH

E. 74,186   T. 47,425 (63.93%)   Lab. hold

Stephen Morgan, Lab.	23,068
Donna Jones, C.	17,705
Gerald Vernon-Jackson, LD	5,418
John Kennedy, Brexit	994
Steven George, JACP	240

Lab. majority 5,363 (11.31%)
3.91% swing C. to Lab.

PRESTON

E. 59,672   T. 33,790 (56.63%)

	Lab. Co-op hold
Mark Hendrick, Lab. Co-op	20,870
Michele Scott, C.	8,724
Rob Sherratt, Brexit	1,799
Neil Darby, LD	1,737
Michael Welton, Green	660

Lab. Co-op majority 12,146 (35.95%)
4.11% swing Lab. to C.

PUDSEY

E. 73,212   T. 54,215 (74.05%)   C. hold

Stuart Andrew, C.	26,453
Jane Aitchison, Lab.	22,936
Ian Dowling, LD	3,088
Quinn Daley, Green	894
Bob Buxton, Yorkshire	844

C. majority 3,517 (6.49%)
2.94% swing Lab. to C.

PUTNEY

E. 65,542   T. 50,467 (77.00%)   Lab. gain

Fleur Anderson, Lab.	22,780
Will Sweet, C.	18,006
Sue Wixley, LD	8,548
Fergal McEntee, Green	1,133

Lab. majority 4,774 (9.46%)
6.39% swing C. to Lab.

RAYLEIGH & WICKFORD

E. 78,959   T. 54,901 (69.53%)   C. hold

Mark Francois, C.	39,864
David Flack, Lab.	8,864
Ron Tindall, LD	4,171
Paul Thorogood, Green	2,002

C. majority 31,000 (56.47%)
7.04% swing Lab. to C.

READING EAST

E. 77,465   T. 55,918 (72.18%)   Lab. hold

Matt Rodda, Lab.	27,102
Craig Morley, C.	21,178
Imogen Shepherd-DuBey, LD	5,035
David McElroy, Green	1,549
Mitchell Feierstein, Brexit	852
Yemi Awolola, CPA	202

Lab. majority 5,924 (10.59%)
1.90% swing C. to Lab.

READING WEST
E. 74,623   T. 50,392 (67.53%)   C. hold
Alok Sharma, C.   24,393
Rachel Eden, Lab. Co-op   20,276
Meri O'Connell, LD   4,460
Jamie Whitham, Green   1,263
C. majority 4,117 (8.17%)
1.31% swing Lab. to C.

REDCAR
E. 65,855   T. 40,842 (62.02%)   C. gain
Jacob Young, C.   18,811
Anna Turley, Lab. Co-op   15,284
Jacqui Cummins, Brexit   2,915
Karen King, LD   2,018
Frankie Wales, Ind.   1,323
Rowan McLaughlin, Green   491
C. majority 3,527 (8.64%)
15.46% swing Lab. to C.

REDDITCH
E. 65,391   T. 44,067 (67.39%)   C. hold
Rachel Maclean, C.   27,907
Rebecca Jenkins, Lab.   11,871
Bruce Horton, LD   2,905
Claire Davies, Green   1,384
C. majority 16,036 (36.39%)
10.05% swing Lab. to C.

REIGATE
E. 74,842   T. 53,156 (71.02%)   C. hold
Crispin Blunt, C.   28,665
Susan Gregory, Lab.   10,355
John Vincent, LD   10,320
Jonathan Essex, Green   3,169
Julia Searle, UKIP   647
C. majority 18,310 (34.45%)
0.86% swing Lab. to C.

RIBBLE VALLEY
E. 79,247   T. 55,284 (69.76%)   C. hold
Nigel Evans, C.   33,346
Giles Bridge, Lab.   14,907
Chantelle Seddon, LD   4,776
Paul Yates, Green   1,704
Tony Johnson, Ind.   551
C. majority 18,439 (33.35%)
4.72% swing Lab. to C.

RICHMOND PARK
E. 82,696   T. 65,067 (78.68%)   LD gain
Sarah Olney, LD   34,559
Zac Goldsmith, C.   26,793
Sandra Keen, Lab.   3,407
Caroline Shah, Ind.   247
John Usher, Ind.   61
LD majority 7,766 (11.94%)
6.00% swing C. to LD

RICHMOND (YORKS)
E. 82,601   T. 57,703 (69.86%)   C. hold
Rishi Sunak, C.   36,693
Thom Kirkwood, Lab.   9,483
Philip Knowles, LD   6,989
John Yorke, Green   2,500
Laurence Waterhouse,   1,077
Yorkshire
Nick Jardine, Ind.   961
C. majority 27,210 (47.16%)
3.31% swing Lab. to C.

ROCHDALE
E. 78,909   T. 47,447 (60.13%)   Lab. hold
Tony Lloyd, Lab.   24,475
Atifa Shah, C.   14,807
Chris Green, Brexit   3,867
Andy Kelly, LD   3,312
Sarah Croke, Green   986
Lab. majority 9,668 (20.38%)
4.62% swing Lab. to C.

ROCHESTER & STROOD
E. 82,056   T. 51,926 (63.28%)   C. hold
Kelly Tolhurst, C.   31,151
Teresa Murray, Lab.   14,079
Graham Colley, LD   3,717
Sonia Hyner, Green   1,312
Roy Freshwater, UKIP   1,080
Chris Spalding, Ind.   587
C. majority 17,072 (32.88%)
7.28% swing Lab. to C.

ROCHFORD & SOUTHEND EAST
E. 75,624   T. 46,136 (61.01%)   C. hold
James Duddridge, C.   27,063
Ashley Dalton, Lab.   14,777
Keith Miller, LD   2,822
Navin Kumar, Ind.   1,107
Jason Pilley, PFP   367
C. majority 12,286 (26.63%)
7.44% swing Lab. to C.

ROMFORD
E. 72,350   T. 47,231 (65.28%)   C. hold
Andrew Rosindell, C.   30,494
Angelina Leatherbarrow,   12,601
Lab.
Ian Sanderson, LD   2,708
David Hughes, Green   1,428
C. majority 17,893 (37.88%)
5.15% swing Lab. to C.

ROMSEY & SOUTHAMPTON NORTH
E. 68,228   T. 51,390 (75.32%)   C. hold
Caroline Nokes, C.   27,862
Craig Fletcher, LD   16,990
Claire Ransom, Lab.   5,898
Geoff Bentley, UKIP   640
C. majority 10,872 (21.16%)
7.37% swing C. to LD

ROSSENDALE & DARWEN
E. 72,771   T. 48,822 (67.09%)   C. hold
Jake Berry, C.   27,570
Alyson Barnes, Lab.   18,048
Paul Valentine, LD   2,011
Sarah Hall, Green   1,193
C. majority 9,522 (19.50%)
6.55% swing Lab. to C.

ROTHER VALLEY
E. 74,802   T. 48,698 (65.10%)   C. gain
Alexander Stafford, C.   21,970
Sophie Wilson, Lab.   15,652
Allen Cowles, Brexit   6,264
Colin Taylor, LD   2,553
Emily West, Green   1,219
Nigel Short, Ind.   1,040
C. majority 6,318 (12.97%)
10.41% swing Lab. to C.

ROTHERHAM
E. 61,688   T. 35,651 (57.79%)   Lab. hold
Sarah Champion, Lab.   14,736
Gerri Hickton, C.   11,615
Paul Hague, Brexit   6,125
Adam Carter, LD   2,090
Dennis Bannan, Yorkshire   1,085
Lab. majority 3,121 (8.75%)
10.64% swing Lab. to C.

RUGBY
E. 72,340   T. 50,814 (70.24%)   C. hold
Mark Pawsey, C.   29,255
Debbie Bannigan, Lab.   15,808
Rana Das-Gupta, LD   4,207
Becca Stevenson, Green   1,544
C. majority 13,447 (26.46%)
5.23% swing Lab. to C.

RUISLIP, NORTHWOOD & PINNER
E. 73,191   T. 52,904 (72.28%)   C. hold
David Simmonds, C.   29,391
Peymana Assad, Lab.   12,997
Jonathan Banks, LD   7,986
Sarah Green, Green   1,646
Femy Amin, AWP   325
Tracy Blackwell, Ind.   295
Julian Wilson, Ind.   264
C. majority 16,394 (30.99%)
2.40% swing Lab. to C.

RUNNYMEDE & WEYBRIDGE
E. 77,196   T. 53,289 (69.03%)   C. gain
Ben Spencer, C.   29,262
Robert King, Lab.   10,992
Rob O'Carroll, LD   9,236
Benjamin Smith, Green   1,876
Stewart Mackay, Ind.   777
Lorna Rowland, Ind.   670
Nicholas Wood, UKIP   476
C. majority 18,270 (34.28%)
0.34% swing C. to Lab.

RUSHCLIFFE
E. 77,055   T. 60,505 (78.52%)   C. gain
Ruth Edwards, C.   28,765
Cheryl Pidgeon, Lab.   21,122
Jason Billin, LD   9,600
Matthew Faithfull, UKIP   591
John Kirby, Ind.   427
C. majority 7,643 (12.63%)
0.55% swing C. to Lab.

RUTLAND & MELTON
E. 82,711   T. 58,310 (70.50%)   C. hold
Alicia Kearns, C.   36,507
Andy Thomas, Lab.   9,583
Carol Weaver, LD   7,970
Alastair McQuillan, Green   2,875
Marietta King, UKIP   917
Anthony Watchorn, Ind.   458
C. majority 26,924 (46.17%)
3.02% swing Lab. to C.

SAFFRON WALDEN
E. 87,017   T. 63,086 (72.50%)   C. hold
Kemi Badenoch, C.   39,714
Mike Hibbs, LD   12,120
Thomas Van De Bilt, Lab.   8,305
Coby Wing, Green   2,947
C. majority 27,594 (43.74%)
2.02% swing C. to LD

SALFORD & ECCLES

E. 82,202　T. 50,632 (61.59%)　Lab. hold
Rebecca Long-Bailey, Lab.　28,755
Attika Choudhary, C.　12,428
Matt Mickler, Brexit　4,290
Jake Overend, LD　3,099
Bryan Blears, Green　2,060
Lab. majority 16,327 (32.25%)
3.97% swing Lab. to C.

SALISBURY

E. 74,560　T. 53,730 (72.06%)　C. hold
John Glen, C.　30,280
Victoria Charleston, LD　10,544
Tom Corbin, Lab.　9,675
Rick Page, Green　2,486
King Arthur Pendragon, Ind.　745
C. majority 19,736 (36.73%)
5.05% swing C. to LD

SCARBOROUGH & WHITBY

E. 74,393　T. 49,724 (66.84%)　C. hold
Robert Goodwill, C.　27,593
Hugo Fearnley, Lab.　17,323
Robert Lockwood, LD　3,038
Lee Derrick, Yorkshire　1,770
C. majority 10,270 (20.65%)
6.92% swing Lab. to C.

SCUNTHORPE

E. 61,955　T. 37,750 (60.93%)　C. gain
Holly Mumby-Croft, C.　20,306
Nic Dakin, Lab.　13,855
Jerry Gorman, Brexit　2,044
Ryk Downes, LD　875
Peter Dennington, Green　670
C. majority 6,451 (17.09%)
12.81% swing Lab. to C.

SEDGEFIELD

E. 64,325　T. 41,566 (64.62%)　C. gain
Paul Howell, C.　19,609
Phil Wilson, Lab.　15,096
David Bull, Brexit　3,518
Dawn Welsh, LD　1,955
John Furness, Green　994
Michael Joyce, Ind.　394
C. majority 4,513 (10.86%)
12.71% swing Lab. to C.

SEFTON CENTRAL

E. 69,760　T. 50,880 (72.94%)　Lab. hold
Bill Esterson, Lab.　29,254
Wazz Mughal, C.　14,132
Keith Cawdron, LD　3,386
Paul Lomas, Brexit　2,425
Alison Gibbon, Green　1,261
Angela Preston, Lib　285
Carla Burns, Renew　137
Lab. majority 15,122 (29.72%)
0.13% swing Lab. to C.

SELBY & AINSTY

E. 78,715　T. 56,418 (71.67%)　C. hold
Nigel Adams, C.　33,995
Malik Rofidi, Lab.　13,858
Katharine Macy, LD　4,842
Mike Jordan, Yorkshire　1,900
Arnold Warneken, Green　1,823
C. majority 20,137 (35.69%)
5.57% swing Lab. to C.

SEVENOAKS

E. 71,777　T. 50,956 (70.99%)　C. hold
Laura Trott, C.　30,932
Gareth Willis, LD　10,114
Seamus McCauley, Lab.　6,946
Paul Wharton, Green　1,974
Paulette Furse, Ind.　695
Sean Finch, Libertarian　295
C. majority 20,818 (40.85%)
7.26% swing C. to LD

SHEFFIELD BRIGHTSIDE & HILLSBOROUGH

E. 69,333　T. 39,600 (57.12%)　Lab. hold
Gill Furniss, Lab.　22,369
Hannah Westropp, C.　10,095
Johnny Johnson, Brexit　3,855
Stephen Porter, LD　1,517
Christine Gilligan Kubo, Green　1,179
Shane Harper, UKIP　585
Lab. majority 12,274 (30.99%)
7.36% swing Lab. to C.

SHEFFIELD CENTRAL

E. 89,849　T. 50,913 (56.67%)　Lab. hold
Paul Blomfield, Lab.　33,968
Janice Silvester-Hall, C.　6,695
Alison Teal, Green　4,570
Colin Ross, LD　3,237
Paul Ward, Brexit　1,969
Jack Carrington, Yorkshire　416
Barry James, Ind.　30
Chris Marsden, Soc Eq　28
Lab. majority 27,273 (53.57%)
2.19% swing Lab. to C.

SHEFFIELD HALLAM

E. 72,763　T. 56,885 (78.18%)　Lab. gain
Olivia Blake, Lab.　19,709
Laura Gordon, LD　18,997
Ian Walker, C.　14,696
Natalie Thomas, Green　1,630
Terence McHale, Brexit　1,562
Michael Virgo, UKIP　168
Elizabeth Aspden, Ind.　123
Lab. majority 712 (1.25%)
1.24% swing Lab. to LD

SHEFFIELD HEELEY

E. 66,940　T. 42,695 (63.78%)　Lab. hold
Louise Haigh, Lab.　21,475
Gordon Gregory, C.　12,955
Tracy Knowles, Brexit　3,538
Simon Clement-Jones, LD　2,916
Paul Turpin, Green　1,811
Lab. majority 8,520 (19.96%)
5.66% swing Lab. to C.

SHEFFIELD SOUTH EAST

E. 67,832　T. 41,998 (61.91%)　Lab. hold
Clive Betts, Lab.　19,359
Marc Bayliss, C.　15,070
Kirk Kus, Brexit　4,478
Rajin Chowdhury, LD　2,125
Alex Martin, Yorkshire　966
Lab. majority 4,289 (10.21%)
8.42% swing Lab. to C.

SHERWOOD

E. 77,948　T. 52,709 (67.62%)　C. hold
Mark Spencer, C.　32,049
Jerry Hague, Lab.　15,863
Timothy Ball, LD　2,883
Esther Cropper, Green　1,214
Simon Rood, Ind.　700
C. majority 16,186 (30.71%)
10.48% swing Lab. to C.

SHIPLEY

E. 74,029　T. 54,004 (72.95%)　C. hold
Philip Davies, C.　27,437
Jo Pike, Lab.　21,195
Caroline Jones, LD　3,188
Celia Hickson, Green　1,301
Darren Longhorn, Yorkshire　883
C. majority 6,242 (11.56%)
1.40% swing Lab. to C.

SHREWSBURY & ATCHAM

E. 82,237　T. 59,065 (71.82%)　C. hold
Daniel Kawczynski, C.　31,021
Julia Buckley, Lab.　19,804
Nat Green, LD　5,906
Julian Dean, Green　1,762
Hannah Locke, Ind.　572
C. majority 11,217 (18.99%)
3.80% swing Lab. to C.

SHROPSHIRE NORTH

E. 83,257　T. 56,513 (67.88%)　C. hold
Owen Paterson, C.　35,444
Graeme Currie, Lab.　12,495
Helen Morgan, LD　5,643
John Adams, Green　1,790
Robert Jones, Salop　1,141
C. majority 22,949 (40.61%)
5.60% swing Lab. to C.

SITTINGBOURNE & SHEPPEY

E. 83,917　T. 51,394 (61.24%)　C. hold
Gordon Henderson, C.　34,742
Clive Johnson, Lab.　10,263
Ben Martin, LD　3,213
Monique Bonney, Ind.　1,257
Sam Collins, Green　1,188
Mad Mike Young, Loony　404
Lee McCall, Ind.　327
C. majority 24,479 (47.63%)
9.02% swing Lab. to C.

SKIPTON & RIPON

E. 78,673　T. 58,724 (74.64%)　C. hold
Julian Smith, C.　34,919
Brian McDaid, Lab.　11,225
Andrew Murday, LD　8,701
Andy Brown, Green　2,748
Jack Render, Yorkshire　1,131
C. majority 23,694 (40.35%)
2.99% swing Lab. to C.

SLEAFORD & NORTH HYKEHAM

E. 94,761　T. 66,554 (70.23%)　C. hold
Caroline Johnson, C.　44,683
Linda Edwards-Shea, Lab.　12,118
Oliver Craven, LD　5,355
Marianne Overton, Lincs　1,999
Simon Tooke, Green　1,742
Caroline Coram, Ind.　657
C. majority 32,565 (48.93%)
5.29% swing Lab. to C.

SLOUGH
E. 87,632　T. 51,038 (58.24%)　Lab. hold
Tan Dhesi, Lab.　29,421
Kanwal Toor Gill, C.　15,781
Aaron Chahal, LD　3,357
Delphine Gray-Fisk, Brexit　1,432
Julian Edmonds, Green　1,047
Lab. majority 13,640 (26.73%)
2.29% swing Lab. to C.

SOLIHULL
E. 78,760　T. 55,344 (70.27%)　C. hold
Julian Knight, C.　32,309
Nick Stephens, Lab. Co-op　11,036
Ade Adeyemo, LD　9,977
Rosemary Sexton, Green　2,022
C. majority 21,273 (38.44%)
1.09% swing Lab. to C.

SOMERSET NORTH
E. 80,194　T. 62,055 (77.38%)　C. hold
Liam Fox, C.　32,801
Hannah Young, Lab.　15,265
Ashley Cartman, LD　11,051
Phil Neve, Green　2,938
C. majority 17,536 (28.26%)
0.34% swing Lab. to C.

SOMERSET NORTH EAST
E. 73,665　T. 56,308 (76.44%)　C. hold
Jacob Rees-Mogg, C.　28,360
Mark Huband, Lab.　13,631
Nick Coates, LD　12,422
Fay Whitfield, Green　1,423
Shaun Hughes, Ind.　472
C. majority 14,729 (26.16%)
3.61% swing Lab. to C.

SOMERTON & FROME
E. 85,866　T. 64,896 (75.58%)　C. hold
David Warburton, C.　36,230
Adam Boyden, LD　17,017
Sean Dromgoole, Lab.　8,354
Andrea Dexter, Green　3,295
C. majority 19,213 (29.61%)
3.21% swing C. to LD

SOUTH HOLLAND & THE DEEPINGS
E. 75,990　T. 49,179 (64.72%)　C. hold
John Hayes, C.　37,338
Mark Popple, Lab.　6,500
Davina Kirby, LD　3,225
Martin Blake, Green　1,613
Rick Stringer, Ind.　503
C. majority 30,838 (62.71%)
6.61% swing Lab. to C.

SOUTH RIBBLE
E. 75,344　T. 53,784 (71.38%)　C. hold
Katherine Fletcher, C.　30,028
Kim Snape, Lab.　18,829
Jo Barton, LD　3,720
Andy Fewings, Green　1,207
C. majority 11,199 (20.82%)
3.64% swing Lab. to C.

SOUTH SHIELDS
E. 62,793　T. 37,882 (60.33%)　Lab. hold
Emma Lewell-Buck, Lab.　17,273
Oni Oviri, C.　7,688
Glenn Thompson, Brexit　6,446
Geoff Thompson, Ind.　3,658
William Shepherd, LD　1,514
Sarah McKeown, Green　1,303
Lab. majority 9,585 (25.30%)
5.14% swing Lab. to C.

SOUTHAMPTON ITCHEN
E. 72,293　T. 47,421 (65.60%)　C. hold
Royston Smith, C.　23,952
Simon Letts, Lab.　19,454
Liz Jarvis, LD　2,503
Osman Sen-Chadun, Green　1,040
Kim Rose, UKIP　472
C. majority 4,498 (9.49%)
4.71% swing Lab. to C.

SOUTHAMPTON TEST
E. 70,113　T. 44,994 (64.17%)　Lab. hold
Alan Whitehead, Lab.　22,256
Steven Galton, C.　16,043
Joe Richards, LD　3,449
Philip Crook, Brexit　1,591
Katherine Barbour, Green　1,433
Kev Barry, ND　222
Lab. majority 6,213 (13.81%)
5.36% swing Lab. to C.

SOUTHEND WEST
E. 69,043　T. 46,537 (67.40%)　C. hold
David Amess, C.　27,555
Aston Line, Lab.　13,096
Nina Stimson, LD　5,312
Seventy-seven Joseph, Ind.　574
C. majority 14,459 (31.07%)
4.94% swing Lab. to C.

SOUTHPORT
E. 70,837　T. 48,180 (68.02%)　C. hold
Damien Moore, C.　22,914
Liz Savage, Lab.　18,767
John Wright, LD　6,499
C. majority 4,147 (8.61%)
1.27% swing Lab. to C.

SPELTHORNE
E. 70,929　T. 49,510 (69.80%)　C. hold
Kwasi Kwarteng, C.　29,141
Pavitar Mann, Lab.　10,748
David Campanale, LD　7,499
Paul Jacobs, Green　2,122
C. majority 18,393 (37.15%)
5.18% swing Lab. to C.

ST ALBANS
E. 73,721　T. 57,599 (78.13%)　LD gain
Daisy Cooper, LD　28,867
Anne Main, C.　22,574
Rebecca Lury, Lab.　5,000
Simon Grover, Green　1,004
Jules Sherrington, ND　154
LD majority 6,293 (10.93%)
10.82% swing C. to LD

ST AUSTELL & NEWQUAY
E. 79,930　T. 55,776 (69.78%)　C. hold
Steve Double, C.　31,273
Felicity Owen, Lab.　14,747
Tim Styles, LD　5,861
Dick Cole, Kernow　1,660
Collin Harker, Green　1,609
Richard Byrne, Lib　626
C. majority 16,526 (29.63%)
4.54% swing Lab. to C.

ST HELENS NORTH
E. 75,593　T. 47,561 (62.92%)　Lab. hold
Conor McGinn, Lab.　24,870
Joel Charles, C.　12,661
Malcolm Webster, Brexit　5,396
Pat Moloney, LD　2,668
David Van Der Burg, Green　1,966
Lab. majority 12,209 (25.67%)
5.49% swing Lab. to C.

ST HELENS SOUTH & WHISTON
E. 79,058　T. 50,313 (63.64%)　Lab. hold
Marie Rimmer, Lab.　29,457
Richard Short, C.　10,335
Daniel Oxley, Brexit　5,353
Brian Spencer, LD　2,886
Kai Taylor, Green　2,282
Lab. majority 19,122 (38.01%)
4.01% swing Lab. to C.

ST IVES
E. 68,795　T. 51,399 (74.71%)　C. hold
Derek Thomas, C.　25,365
Andrew George, LD　21,081
Alana Bates, Lab.　3,553
Ian Flindall, Green　954
Robert Smith, Lib　314
John Harris, People　132
C. majority 4,284 (8.33%)
3.86% swing LD to C.

STAFFORD
E. 72,572　T. 51,149 (70.48%)　C. hold
Theo Clarke, C.　29,992
Joyce Still, Lab.　15,615
Alex Wagner, LD　3,175
Emma Carter, Green　2,367
C. majority 14,377 (28.11%)
6.61% swing Lab. to C.

STAFFORDSHIRE MOORLANDS
E. 65,485　T. 43,656 (66.67%)　C. hold
Karen Bradley, C.　28,192
Darren Price, Lab.　11,764
Andrew Gant, LD　2,469
Douglas Rouxel, Green　1,231
C. majority 16,428 (37.63%)
6.69% swing Lab. to C.

STAFFORDSHIRE SOUTH
E. 73,692　T. 50,005 (67.86%)　C. hold
Gavin Williamson, C.　36,520
Adam Freeman, Lab.　8,270
Chris Fewtrell, LD　3,280
Claire McIlvenna, Green　1,935
C. majority 28,250 (56.49%)
6.01% swing Lab. to C.

STALYBRIDGE & HYDE

E. 73,873   T. 42,368 (57.35%)

Lab. Co-op hold

Jonathan Reynolds, Lab. Co-op	19,025
Tayub Amjad, C.	16,079
Julian Newton, Brexit	3,591
Jamie Dwan, LD	1,827
Julie Wood, Green	1,411
John Edge, Lib	435

Lab. Co-op majority 2,946 (6.95%)

6.04% swing Lab. to C.

STEVENAGE

E. 71,562   T. 47,683 (66.63%)   C. hold

Stephen McPartland, C.	25,328
Jill Borcherds, Lab.	16,766
Lisa Nash, LD	4,132
Victoria Snelling, Green	1,457

C. majority 8,562 (17.96%)

5.55% swing Lab. to C.

STOCKPORT

E. 65,457   T. 41,715 (63.73%)   Lab. gain

Navendu Mishra, Lab.	21,695
Isy Imarni, C.	11,656
Wendy Meikle, LD	5,043
Lee Montague-Trenchard, Brexit	1,918
Helena Mellish, Green	1,403

Lab. majority 10,039 (24.07%)

5.39% swing Lab. to C.

STOCKTON NORTH

E. 66,676   T. 41,156 (61.73%)   Lab. hold

Alex Cunningham, Lab.	17,728
Steven Jackson, C.	16,701
Martin Walker, Brexit	3,907
Aidan King, LD	1,631
Mark Burdon, NE Party	1,189

Lab. majority 1,027 (2.50%)

8.95% swing Lab. to C.

STOCKTON SOUTH

E. 76,895   T. 54,802 (71.27%)   C. gain

Matt Vickers, C.	27,764
Paul Williams, Lab.	22,504
Brendan Devlin, LD	2,338
John Prescott, Brexit	2,196

C. majority 5,260 (9.60%)

5.62% swing Lab. to C.

STOKE-ON-TRENT CENTRAL

E. 55,424   T. 32,070 (57.86%)   C. gain

Jo Gideon, C.	14,557
Gareth Snell, Lab. Co-op	13,887
Tariq Mahmood, Brexit	1,691
Steven Pritchard, LD	1,116
Adam Colclough, Green	819

C. majority 670 (2.09%)

6.92% swing Lab. to C.

STOKE-ON-TRENT NORTH

E. 84,357   T. 40,134 (47.58%)   C. gain

Jonathan Gullis, C.	20,974
Ruth Smeeth, Lab.	14,688
Richard Watkin, Brexit	2,374
Peter Andras, LD	1,268
Alan Borgars, Green	508
Matt Dilworth, Ind.	322

C. majority 6,286 (15.66%)

10.65% swing Lab. to C.

STOKE-ON-TRENT SOUTH

E. 64,499   T. 39,604 (61.40%)   C. hold

Jack Brereton, C.	24,632
Mark McDonald, Lab.	13,361
Rosalyn Gordon, LD	1,611

C. majority 11,271 (28.46%)

13.43% swing Lab. to C.

STONE

E. 69,378   T. 49,843 (71.84%)   C. hold

Bill Cash, C.	31,687
Mike Stubbs, Lab.	11,742
Alec Sandiford, LD	4,412
Tom Adamson, Green	2,002

C. majority 19,945 (40.02%)

2.52% swing Lab. to C.

STOURBRIDGE

E. 69,891   T. 45,689 (65.37%)   C. hold

Suzanne Webb, C.	27,534
Pete Lowe, Lab.	13,963
Chris Bramall, LD	2,523
Andi Mohr, Green	1,048
Aaron Hudson, Ind.	621

C. majority 13,571 (29.70%)

6.73% swing Lab. to C.

STRATFORD-ON-AVON

E. 74,038   T. 55,048 (74.35%)   C. hold

Nadhim Zahawi, C.	33,343
Dominic Skinner, LD	13,371
Felix Ling, Lab.	6,222
Dave Passingham, Green	2,112

C. majority 19,972 (36.28%)

6.89% swing C. to LD

STREATHAM

E. 84,788   T. 56,513 (66.65%)   Lab. gain

Bell Ribeiro-Addy, Lab.	30,976
Helen Thompson, LD	13,286
Rory O'Broin, C.	9,060
Scott Ainslie, Green	2,567
Penelope Becker, Brexit	624

Lab. majority 17,690 (31.30%)

15.36% swing Lab. to LD

STRETFORD & URMSTON

E. 72,356   T. 50,067 (69.20%)   Lab. hold

Kate Green, Lab.	30,195
Mussadak Mirza, C.	13,778
Anna Fryer, LD	2,969
Gary Powell, Brexit	1,768
Jane Leicester, Green	1,357

Lab. majority 16,417 (32.79%)

3.23% swing Lab. to C.

STROUD

E. 84,534   T. 65,930 (77.99%)   C. gain

Siobhan Baillie, C.	31,582
David Drew, Lab. Co-op	27,742
Molly Scott Cato, Green	4,954
Desi Latimer, Brexit	1,085
Glenville Gogerly, Libertarian	567

C. majority 3,840 (5.82%)

3.45% swing Lab. to C.

SUFFOLK CENTRAL & IPSWICH NORTH

E. 76,201   T. 56,250 (73.82%)   C. hold

Dan Poulter, C.	35,253
Emma Bonner-Morgan, Lab.	11,862
James Sandbach, LD	6,485
Daniel Pratt, Green	2,650

C. majority 23,391 (41.58%)

5.59% swing Lab. to C.

SUFFOLK COASTAL

E. 81,910   T. 58,308 (71.19%)   C. hold

Therese Coffey, C.	32,958
Cameron Matthews, Lab.	12,425
Jules Ewart, LD	8,719
Rachel Smith-Lyte, Green	2,713
Tony Love, Ind.	1,493

C. majority 20,533 (35.21%)

3.82% swing Lab. to C.

SUFFOLK SOUTH

E. 76,201   T. 53,495 (70.20%)   C. hold

James Cartlidge, C.	33,276
Elizabeth Hughes, Lab.	10,373
David Beavan, LD	6,702
Robert Lindsay, Green	3,144

C. majority 22,903 (42.81%)

5.04% swing Lab. to C.

SUFFOLK WEST

E. 80,192   T. 51,437 (64.14%)   C. hold

Matt Hancock, C.	33,842
Claire Unwin, Lab.	10,648
Elfreda Tealby-Watson, LD	4,685
Donald Allwright, Green	2,262

C. majority 23,194 (45.09%)

6.06% swing Lab. to C.

SUNDERLAND CENTRAL

E. 72,677   T. 43,476 (59.82%)   Lab. hold

Julie Elliott, Lab.	18,336
Tom D'Silva, C.	15,372
Viral Parikh, Brexit	5,047
Niall Hodson, LD	3,025
Rachel Featherstone, Green	1,212
Dale Mckenzie, Ind.	484

Lab. majority 2,964 (6.82%)

7.67% swing Lab. to C.

SURREY EAST

E. 83,148   T. 59,690 (71.79%)   C. gain

Claire Coutinho, C.	35,624
Alex Ehmann, LD	11,584
Frances Rehal, Lab.	8,247
Joseph Booton, Green	2,340
Helena Windsor, Ind.	1,374
Martin Hogbin, Loony	521

C. majority 24,040 (40.27%)

4.45% swing C. to LD

SURREY HEATH

E. 81,349   T. 58,654 (72.10%)   C. hold

Michael Gove, C.	34,358
Alasdair Pinkerton, LD	16,009
Brahma Mohanty, Lab.	5,407
Sharon Galliford, Green	2,252
David Roe, UKIP	628

C. majority 18,349 (31.28%)

11.03% swing C. to LD

SURREY SOUTH WEST

E. 79,129 T. 60,340 (76.26%)   C. hold

Jeremy Hunt, C.	32,191
Paul Follows, LD	23,374
Tim Corry, Lab.	4,775

C. majority 8,817 (14.61%)
15.63% swing C. to LD

SUSSEX MID

E. 85,141 T. 62,762 (73.72%)   C. hold

Mims Davies, C.	33,455
Robert Eggleston, LD	15,258
Gemma Bolton, Lab.	11,218
Deanna Nicholson, Green	2,234
Baron von Thunderclap, Loony	550
Brett Mortensen, Advance	47

C. majority 18,197 (28.99%)
7.59% swing C. to LD

SUTTON & CHEAM

E. 71,760 T. 50,487 (70.36%)   C. hold

Paul Scully, C.	25,235
Hina Bokhari, LD	16,884
Bonnie Craven, Lab.	7,200
Claire Jackson-Prior, Green	1,168

C. majority 8,351 (16.54%)
3.95% swing C. to LD

SUTTON COLDFIELD

E. 75,638 T. 52,325 (69.18%)   C. hold

Andrew Mitchell, C.	31,604
David Knowles, Lab.	12,332
Jenny Wilkinson, LD	6,358
Ben Auton, Green	2,031

C. majority 19,272 (36.83%)
3.91% swing Lab. to C.

SWINDON NORTH

E. 82,441 T. 55,115 (66.85%)   C. hold

Justin Tomlinson, C.	32,584
Kate Linnegar, Lab.	16,413
Katie Critchlow, LD	4,408
Andy Bentley, Green	1,710

C. majority 16,171 (29.34%)
7.08% swing Lab. to C.

SWINDON SOUTH

E. 73,118 T. 50,746 (69.40%)   C. hold

Robert Buckland, C.	26,536
Sarah Church, Lab. Co-op	19,911
Stan Pajak, LD	4,299

C. majority 6,625 (13.06%)
4.12% swing Lab. to C.

TAMWORTH

E. 71,580 T. 46,056 (64.34%)   C. hold

Christopher Pincher, C.	30,542
Christopher Bain, Lab. Co-op	10,908
Rob Wheway, LD	2,426
Andrew Tilley, Green	935
Robert Bilcliff, UKIP	814
John Wright, Ind.	431

C. majority 19,634 (42.63%)
8.21% swing Lab. to C.

TATTON

E. 69,018 T. 48,967 (70.95%)   C. hold

Esther McVey, C.	28,277
James Weinberg, Lab.	10,890
Jonathan Smith, LD	7,712
Nigel Hennerley, Green	2,088

C. majority 17,387 (35.51%)
2.70% swing Lab. to C.

TAUNTON DEANE

E. 88,675 T. 63,733 (71.87%)   C. hold

Rebecca Pow, C.	34,164
Gideon Amos, LD	22,464
Liam Canham, Lab.	4,715
John Hunt, Ind.	2,390

C. majority 11,700 (18.36%)
3.42% swing C. to LD

TELFORD

E. 68,921 T. 42,825 (62.14%)   C. hold

Lucy Allan, C.	25,546
Katrina Gilman, Lab.	14,605
Shana Roberts, LD	2,674

C. majority 10,941 (25.55%)
11.97% swing Lab. to C.

TEWKESBURY

E. 83,958 T. 61,140 (72.82%)   C. hold

Laurence Robertson, C.	35,728
Alex Hegenbarth, LD	13,318
Lara Chaplin, Lab.	9,310
Cate Cody, Green	2,784

C. majority 22,410 (36.65%)
4.92% swing C. to LD

THANET NORTH

E. 72,811 T. 48,178 (66.17%)   C. hold

Roger Gale, C.	30,066
Coral Jones, Lab.	12,877
Angie Curwen, LD	3,439
Rob Edwards, Green	1,796

C. majority 17,189 (35.68%)
6.73% swing Lab. to C.

THANET SOUTH

E. 73,302 T. 48,257 (65.83%)   C. hold

Craig Mackinlay, C.	27,084
Rebecca Gordon-Nesbitt, Lab.	16,497
Martyn Pennington, LD	2,727
Becky Wing, Green	1,949

C. majority 10,587 (21.94%)
4.55% swing Lab. to C.

THIRSK & MALTON

E. 80,979 T. 56,588 (69.88%)   C. hold

Kevin Hollinrake, C.	35,634
David Yellen, Lab.	10,480
Dinah Keal, LD	6,774
Martin Brampton, Green	2,263
John Hall, Yorkshire	881
Steve Mullins, Ind.	245
Gordon Johnson, ND	184
Michael Taylor, Soc Dem	127

C. majority 25,154 (44.45%)
5.24% swing Lab. to C.

THORNBURY & YATE

E. 69,492 T. 52,243 (75.18%)   C. hold

Luke Hall, C.	30,202
Claire Young, LD	17,833
Rob Logan, Lab.	4,208

C. majority 12,369 (23.68%)
0.07% swing C. to LD

THURROCK

E. 79,655 T. 47,467 (59.59%)   C. hold

Jackie Doyle-Price, C.	27,795
John Kent, Lab.	16,313
Stewart Stone, LD	1,510
James Woollard, Ind.	1,042
Ben Harvey, Green	807

C. majority 11,482 (24.19%)
11.75% swing Lab. to C.

TIVERTON & HONITON

E. 82,953 T. 59,613 (71.86%)   C. hold

Neil Parish, C.	35,893
Liz Pole, Lab.	11,654
John Timperley, LD	8,807
Colin Reed, Green	2,291
Margaret Dennis, UKIP	968

C. majority 24,239 (40.66%)
3.21% swing Lab. to C.

TONBRIDGE & MALLING

E. 77,380 T. 57,003 (73.67%)   C. hold

Tom Tugendhat, C.	35,784
Richard Morris, LD	8,843
Dylan Jones, Lab.	8,286
April Clark, Green	4,090

C. majority 26,941 (47.26%)
4.86% swing C. to LD

TOOTING

E. 76,933 T. 58,473 (76.01%)   Lab. hold

Rosena Allin-Khan, Lab.	30,811
Kerry Briscoe, C.	16,504
Olly Glover, LD	8,305
Glyn Goodwin, Green	2,314
Adam Shakir, Brexit	462
Roz Hubley, Soc Dem	77

Lab. majority 14,307 (24.47%)
1.05% swing Lab. to C.

TORBAY

E. 75,054 T. 50,426 (67.19%)   C. hold

Kevin Foster, C.	29,863
Lee Howgate, LD	12,114
Michele Middleditch, Lab.	6,562
Sam Moss, Green	1,239
James Channer, Ind.	648

C. majority 17,749 (35.20%)
3.64% swing LD to C.

TOTNES

E. 69,863 T. 52,182 (74.69%)   C. gain

Anthony Mangnall, C.	27,751
Sarah Wollaston, LD	15,027
Louise Webberley, Lab.	8,860
John Kitson, ND	544

C. majority 12,724 (24.38%)
8.20% swing C. to LD

TOTTENHAM

E. 75,740   T. 46,856 (61.86%)   Lab. hold

David Lammy, Lab.	35,621
James Newhall, C.	5,446
Tammy Palmer, LD	3,168
Emma Chan, Green	1,873
Abdul Turay, Brexit	527
Andrew Bence, Soc Dem	91
Frank Sweeney, WRP	88
Jonathan Silberman, Comm Lge	42

Lab. majority 30,175 (64.40%)
2.85% swing Lab. to C.

TRURO & FALMOUTH

E. 76,719   T. 59,190 (77.15%)   C. hold

Cherilyn Mackrory, C.	27,237
Jennifer Forbes, Lab.	22,676
Ruth Gripper, LD	7,150
Tom Scott, Green	1,714
Paul Nicholson, Lib	413

C. majority 4,561 (7.71%)
0.51% swing Lab. to C.

TUNBRIDGE WELLS

E. 74,816   T. 54,650 (73.05%)   C. hold

Greg Clark, C.	30,119
Ben Chapelard, LD	15,474
Antonio Weiss, Lab.	8,098
Christopher Camp, Ind.	488
Nigel Peacock, Ind.	471

C. majority 14,645 (26.80%)
10.12% swing C. to LD

TWICKENHAM

E. 84,901   T. 64,503 (75.97%)   LD hold

Munira Wilson, LD	36,166
Isobel Grant, C.	22,045
Ranjeev Walia, Lab.	5,476
Stuart Wells, Brexit	816

LD majority 14,121 (21.89%)
3.58% swing C. to LD

TYNEMOUTH

E. 77,261   T. 56,034 (72.53%)   Lab. hold

Alan Campbell, Lab.	26,928
Lewis Bartoli, C.	22,071
John Appleby, LD	3,791
Ed Punchard, Brexit	1,963
Julia Erskine, Green	1,281

Lab. majority 4,857 (8.67%)
5.92% swing Lab. to C.

TYNESIDE NORTH

E. 78,902   T. 50,429 (63.91%)   Lab. hold

Mary Glindon, Lab.	25,051
Dean Carroll, C.	15,490
Andrew Husband, Brexit	5,254
Chris Boyle, LD	3,241
John Buttery, Green	1,393

Lab. majority 9,561 (18.96%)
9.10% swing Lab. to C.

UXBRIDGE & RUISLIP SOUTH

E. 70,369   T. 48,187 (68.48%)   C. hold

Boris Johnson, C.	25,351
Ali Milani, Lab.	18,141
Joanne Humphreys, LD	3,026
Mark Keir, Green	1,090
Geoffrey Courtenay, UKIP	283
Lord Buckethead, Loony	125
Count Binface, Ind.	69
Alfie Utting, Ind.	44
Yace Yogenstein, ND	23
Norma Burke, Ind.	22
Bobby Smith, ND	8
William Tobin, ND	5

C. majority 7,210 (14.96%)
2.09% swing Lab. to C.

VAUXHALL

E. 88,647   T. 56,333 (63.55%)   Lab. Co-op hold

Florence Eshalomi, Lab. Co-op	31,615
Sarah Lewis, LD	12,003
Sarah Bool, C.	9,422
Jacqueline Bond, Green	2,516
Andrew McGuinness, Brexit	641
Salah Faissal, Ind.	136

Lab. Co-op majority 19,612 (34.81%)
0.99% swing Lab. to LD

WAKEFIELD

E. 70,192   T. 45,027 (64.15%)   C. gain

Imran Ahmad-Khan, C.	21,283
Mary Creagh, Lab.	17,925
Peter Wiltshire, Brexit	2,725
Jamie Needle, LD	1,772
Ryan Kett, Yorkshire	868
Stephen Whyte, Ind.	454

C. majority 3,358 (7.46%)
6.08% swing Lab. to C.

WALLASEY

E. 66,310   T. 46,492 (70.11%)   Lab. hold

Angela Eagle, Lab.	29,901
James Baker, C.	11,579
Martin York, Brexit	2,037
Vicky Downie, LD	1,843
Lily Clough, Green	1,132

Lab. majority 18,322 (39.41%)
4.41% swing Lab. to C.

WALSALL NORTH

E. 67,177   T. 36,556 (54.42%)   C. hold

Eddie Hughes, C.	23,334
Gill Ogilvie, Lab.	11,369
Jennifer Gray, LD	1,236
Mark Wilson, Green	617

C. majority 11,965 (32.73%)
12.95% swing Lab. to C.

WALSALL SOUTH

E. 68,024   T. 42,472 (62.44%)   Lab. hold

Valerie Vaz, Lab.	20,872
Gurjit Bains, C.	17,416
Gary Hughes, Brexit	1,660
Paul Harris, LD	1,602
John Macefield, Green	634
Akheil Mehboob, Ind.	288

Lab. majority 3,456 (8.14%)
6.02% swing Lab. to C.

WALTHAMSTOW

E. 70,268   T. 48,335 (68.79%)   Lab. Co-op hold

Stella Creasy, Lab. Co-op	36,784
Shade Adoh, C.	5,922
Meera Chadha, LD	2,874
Andrew Johns, Green	1,733
Paul Campbell, Brexit	768
Deborah Longe, CPA	254

Lab. Co-op majority 30,862 (63.85%)
1.33% swing Lab. to C.

WANSBECK

E. 63,339   T. 40,509 (63.96%)   Lab. hold

Ian Lavery, Lab.	17,124
Jack Gebhard, C.	16,310
Eden Webley, Brexit	3,141
Stephen Psallidas, LD	2,539
Steve Leyland, Green	1,217
Michael Flynn, CPA	178

Lab. majority 814 (2.01%)
11.29% swing Lab. to C.

WANTAGE

E. 90,875   T. 67,173 (73.92%)   C. hold

David Johnston, C.	34,085
Richard Benwell, LD	21,432
Jonny Roberts, Lab.	10,181
Mark Gray, Ind.	1,475

C. majority 12,653 (18.84%)
10.41% swing C. to LD

WARLEY

E. 62,421   T. 37,239 (59.66%)   Lab. hold

John Spellar, Lab.	21,901
Chandra Kanneganti, C.	10,390
Michael Cooper, Brexit	2,469
Bryan Manley-Green, LD	1,588
Kathryn Downs, Green	891

Lab. majority 11,511 (30.91%)
5.04% swing Lab. to C.

WARRINGTON NORTH

E. 72,235   T. 46,667 (64.60%)   Lab. hold

Charlotte Nichols, Lab.	20,611
Wendy Maisey, C.	19,102
David Crowther, LD	3,071
Elizabeth Babade, Brexit	2,626
Lyndsay McAteer, Green	1,257

Lab. majority 1,509 (3.23%)
8.26% swing Lab. to C.

WARRINGTON SOUTH

E. 86,015   T. 61,899 (71.96%)   C. gain

Andy Carter, C.	28,187
Faisal Rashid, Lab.	26,177
Ryan Bate, LD	5,732
Clare Aspinall, Brexit	1,635
Kevin Hickson, Soc Dem	168

C. majority 2,010 (3.25%)
3.68% swing Lab. to C.

WARWICK & LEAMINGTON
E. 76,373 T. 54,205 (70.97%) Lab. hold

Matt Western, Lab.	23,718
Jack Rankin, C.	22,929
Louis Adam, LD	4,995
Jonathan Chilvers, Green	1,536
Tim Griffiths, Brexit	807
Bob Dhillon, Ind.	153
Xander Bennett, Soc Dem	67

Lab. majority 789 (1.46%)
0.39% swing Lab. to C.

WARWICKSHIRE NORTH
E. 70,271 T. 45,914 (65.34%) C. hold

Craig Tracey, C.	30,249
Claire Breeze, Lab. Co-op	12,293
Richard Whelan, LD	2,069
James Platt, Green	1,303

C. majority 17,956 (39.11%)
10.53% swing Lab. to C.

WASHINGTON & SUNDERLAND WEST
E. 66,278 T. 37,513 (56.60%) Lab. hold

Sharon Hodgson, Lab.	15,941
Valerie Allen, C.	12,218
Howard Brown, Brexit	5,439
Carlton West, LD	2,071
Michal Chantkowski, Green	1,005
Keith Jenkins, UKIP	839

Lab. majority 3,723 (9.92%)
10.98% swing Lab. to C.

WATFORD
E. 83,359 T. 58,065 (69.66%) C. hold

Dean Russell, C.	26,421
Chris Ostrowski, Lab.	21,988
Ian Stotesbury, LD	9,323
Michael McGetrick, Soc Dem	333

C. majority 4,433 (7.63%)
2.03% swing Lab. to C.

WAVENEY
E. 82,791 T. 51,129 (61.76%) C. hold

Peter Aldous, C.	31,778
Sonia Barker, Lab.	13,776
Elfrede Brambley-Crawshaw, Green	2,727
Helen Korfanty, LD	2,603
Dave Brennan, CPA	245

C. majority 18,002 (35.21%)
8.86% swing Lab. to C.

WEALDEN
E. 83,038 T. 60,907 (73.35%) C. hold

Nus Ghani, C.	37,043
Chris Bowers, LD	11,388
Angie Smith, Lab.	9,377
Georgia Taylor, Green	3,099

C. majority 25,655 (42.12%)
4.36% swing C. to LD

WEAVER VALE
E. 70,551 T. 50,713 (71.88%) Lab. hold

Mike Amesbury, Lab.	22,772
Adam Wordsworth, C.	22,210
Daniela Parker, LD	3,300
Nicholas Goulding, Brexit	1,380
Paul Bowers, Green	1,051

Lab. majority 562 (1.11%)
3.33% swing Lab. to C.

WELLINGBOROUGH
E. 80,764 T. 51,913 (64.28%) C. hold

Peter Bone, C.	32,277
Andrea Watts, Lab.	13,737
Suzanna Austin, LD	4,078
Marion Turner-Hawes, Green	1,821

C. majority 18,540 (35.71%)
6.16% swing Lab. to C.

WELLS
E. 84,124 T. 61,295 (72.86%) C. hold

James Heappey, C.	33,336
Tessa Munt, LD	23,345
Kama McKenzie, Lab.	4,034
Dave Dobbs, Ind.	373
Susie Quatermass, Motherworld	207

C. majority 9,991 (16.30%)
1.92% swing LD to C.

WELWYN HATFIELD
E. 74,892 T. 52,053 (69.50%) C. hold

Grant Shapps, C.	27,394
Rosie Newbigging, Lab.	16,439
Paul Zukowskyj, LD	6,602
Oliver Sayers, Green	1,618

C. majority 10,955 (21.05%)
3.39% swing Lab. to C.

WENTWORTH & DEARNE
E. 74,536 T. 41,557 (55.75%) Lab. hold

John Healey, Lab.	16,742
Emily Barley, C.	14,577
Stephen Cavell, Brexit	7,019
Janice Middleton, LD	1,705
Lucy Brown, Yorkshire	1,201
David Bettney, Soc Dem	313

Lab. majority 2,165 (5.21%)
14.24% swing Lab. to C.

WEST BROMWICH EAST
E. 62,111 T. 35,975 (57.92%) C. gain

Nicola Richards, C.	16,804
Ibrahim Dogus, Lab.	15,211
Christian Lucas, Brexit	1,475
Andy Graham, LD	1,313
Mark Redding, Green	627
George Galloway, Ind.	489
Colin Rankine, Yeshua	56

C. majority 1,593 (4.43%)
12.08% swing Lab. to C.

WEST BROMWICH WEST
E. 64,576 T. 34,459 (53.36%) C. gain

Shaun Bailey, C.	17,419
James Cunningham, Lab.	13,620
Franco D'Aulerio, Brexit	1,841
Flo Clucas, LD	915
Keir Williams, Green	664

C. majority 3,799 (11.02%)
11.69% swing Lab. to C.

WEST HAM
E. 97,942 T. 60,200 (61.46%) Lab. hold

Lyn Brown, Lab.	42,181
Sara Kumar, C.	9,793
Eimear O'Casey, LD	4,161
Danny Keeling, Green	1,780
Emma Stockdale, Brexit	1,679
Paul Jobson, CPA	463
Humera Kamran, Communities	143

Lab. majority 32,388 (53.80%)
3.37% swing Lab. to C.

WESTMINSTER NORTH
E. 65,519 T. 42,911 (65.49%) Lab. hold

Karen Buck, Lab.	23,240
Jamie Macfarlane, C.	12,481
George Lee, LD	5,593
Holly Robinson, Green	1,064
Cyrus Parvin, Brexit	418
Gabriela Fajardo Palacios, CPA	115

Lab. majority 10,759 (25.07%)
0.76% swing Lab. to C.

WESTMORLAND & LONSDALE
E. 67,789 T. 52,712 (77.76%) LD hold

Tim Farron, LD	25,795
James Airey, C.	23,861
Phillip Black, Lab.	2,293
Steven Bolton, Brexit	763

LD majority 1,934 (3.67%)
1.08% swing C. to LD

WESTON-SUPER-MARE
E. 82,526 T. 55,614 (67.39%) C. hold

John Penrose, C.	31,983
Tim Taylor, Lab.	14,862
Patrick Keating, LD	6,935
Suneil Basu, Green	1,834

C. majority 17,121 (30.79%)
5.16% swing Lab. to C.

WIGAN
E. 75,680 T. 45,042 (59.52%) Lab. hold

Lisa Nandy, Lab.	21,042
Ashley Williams, C.	14,314
William Malloy, Brexit	5,959
Stuart Thomas, LD	2,428
Peter Jacobs, Green	1,299

Lab. majority 6,728 (14.94%)
9.39% swing Lab. to C.

WILTSHIRE NORTH
E. 73,283 T. 54,758 (74.72%) C. hold

James Gray, C.	32,373
Brian Mathew, LD	14,747
Jon Fisher, Lab.	5,699
Bonnie Jackson, Green	1,939

C. majority 17,626 (32.19%)
5.20% swing C. to LD

WILTSHIRE SOUTH WEST
E. 77,970 T. 54,895 (70.41%) C. hold

Andrew Murrison, C.	33,038
Emily Pomroy-Smith, Lab.	11,408
Ellen Nicholson, LD	8,015
Julie Phillips, Green	2,434

C. majority 21,630 (39.40%)
2.97% swing Lab. to C.

WIMBLEDON
E. 68,232 T. 53,027 (77.72%) C. hold
Stephen Hammond, C.	20,373
Paul Kohler, LD	19,745
Jackie Schneider, Lab.	12,543
Graham Hadley, Ind.	366

C. majority 628 (1.18%)
15.39% swing C. to LD

WINCHESTER
E. 75,582 T. 58,890 (77.92%) C. hold
Steve Brine, C.	28,430
Paula Ferguson, LD	27,445
George Baker, Lab.	2,723
Teresa Skelton, JACP	292

C. majority 985 (1.67%)
7.91% swing C. to LD

WINDSOR
E. 75,038 T. 53,750 (71.63%) C. hold
Adam Afriyie, C.	31,501
Julian Tisi, LD	11,422
Peter Shearman, Lab.	8,147
Fintan McKeown, Green	1,796
David Buckley, Ind.	508
Wisdom Da Costa, Ind.	376

C. majority 20,079 (37.36%)
8.48% swing C. to LD

WIRRAL SOUTH
E. 57,280 T. 43,547 (76.02%) Lab. hold
Alison McGovern, Lab.	22,284
Stewart Gardiner, C.	16,179
Christopher Carubia, LD	2,917
Martin Waring, Brexit	1,219
Harry Gorman, Green	948

Lab. majority 6,105 (14.02%)
2.20% swing Lab. to C.

WIRRAL WEST
E. 55,550 T. 42,918 (77.26%) Lab. hold
Margaret Greenwood, Lab.	20,695
Laura Evans, C.	17,692
Andy Corkhill, LD	2,706
John Coyne, Green	965
John Kelly, Brexit	860

Lab. majority 3,003 (7.00%)
2.60% swing Lab. to C.

WITHAM
E. 70,402 T. 49,344 (70.09%) C. hold
Priti Patel, C.	32,876
Martin Edobor, Lab.	8,794
Sam North, LD	4,584
James Abbott, Green	3,090

C. majority 24,082 (48.80%)
5.47% swing Lab. to C.

WITNEY
E. 83,845 T. 61,305 (73.12%) C. hold
Robert Courts, C.	33,856
Charlotte Hoagland, LD	18,679
Rosa Bolger, Lab. Co-op	8,770

C. majority 15,177 (24.76%)
5.17% swing C. to LD

WOKING
E. 75,455 T. 53,937 (71.48%) C. hold
Jonathan Lord, C.	26,396
Will Forster, LD	16,629
Gerry Mitchell, Lab.	8,827
Ella Walding, Green	1,485
Troy De Leon, UKIP	600

C. majority 9,767 (18.11%)
9.22% swing C. to LD

WOKINGHAM
E. 83,957 T. 61,997 (73.84%) C. hold
John Redwood, C.	30,734
Phillip Lee, LD	23,351
Annette Medhurst, Lab.	6,450
Kizzi Johannessen, Green	1,382
Annabel Mullin, Advance	80

C. majority 7,383 (11.91%)
14.40% swing C. to LD

WOLVERHAMPTON NORTH EAST
E. 61,829 T. 34,281 (55.44%) C. gain
Jane Stevenson, C.	17,722
Emma Reynolds, Lab.	13,642
Vishal Khatri, Brexit	1,354
Richard Maxwell, LD	960
Andrea Cantrill, Green	603

C. majority 4,080 (11.90%)
12.23% swing Lab. to C.

WOLVERHAMPTON SOUTH EAST
E. 63,006 T. 33,443 (53.08%) Lab. hold
Pat McFadden, Lab.	15,522
Ahmed Ejaz, C.	14,287
Raj Chaggar, Brexit	2,094
Ruth Coleman-Taylor, LD	1,019
Kathryn Gilbert, Green	521

Lab. majority 1,235 (3.69%)
9.88% swing Lab. to C.

WOLVERHAMPTON SOUTH WEST
E. 60,895 T. 41,136 (67.55%) C. gain
Stuart Anderson, C.	19,864
Eleanor Smith, Lab.	18,203
Bart Ricketts, LD	2,041
Leo Grandison, Brexit	1,028

C. majority 1,661 (4.04%)
4.60% swing Lab. to C.

WORCESTER
E. 73,475 T. 50,898 (69.27%) C. hold
Robin Walker, C.	25,856
Lynn Denham, Lab.	19,098
Stephen Kearney, LD	3,666
Louis Stephen, Green	1,694
Martin Potter, Ind.	584

C. majority 6,758 (13.28%)
4.20% swing Lab. to C.

WORCESTERSHIRE MID
E. 78,221 T. 56,123 (71.75%) C. hold
Nigel Huddleston, C.	37,426
Helen Russell, Lab.	9,408
Margaret Rowley, LD	6,474
Sue Howarth, Green	2,177
Barmy Lord Brockman, Loony	638

C. majority 28,018 (49.92%)
3.79% swing Lab. to C.

WORCESTERSHIRE WEST
E. 76,267 T. 57,530 (75.43%) C. hold
Harriett Baldwin, C.	34,909
Beverley Nielsen, LD	10,410
Samantha Charles, Lab.	9,496
Martin Allen, Green	2,715

C. majority 24,499 (42.58%)
4.74% swing C. to LD

WORKINGTON
E. 61,370 T. 41,599 (67.78%) C. gain
Mark Jenkinson, C.	20,488
Sue Hayman, Lab.	16,312
David Walker, Brexit	1,749
Neil Hughes, LD	1,525
Nicky Cockburn, Ind.	842
Jill Perry, Green	596
Roy Ivinson, ND	87

C. majority 4,176 (10.04%)
9.73% swing Lab. to C.

WORSLEY & ECCLES SOUTH
E. 75,219 T. 44,825 (59.59%) Lab. hold
Barbara Keeley, Lab.	20,446
Arnie Saunders, C.	17,227
Seamus Martin, Brexit	3,224
Joe Johnson-Tod, LD	2,510
Daniel Towers, Green	1,300

Lab. majority 3,101 (6.92%)
5.72% swing Lab. to C.

WORTHING EAST & SHOREHAM
E. 75,195 T. 53,155 (70.69%) C. hold
Tim Loughton, C.	27,104
Lavinia O'Connor, Lab.	19,663
Ashley Ridley, LD	4,127
Leslie Groves Williams, Green	2,006
Sophie Cook, ND	255

C. majority 7,441 (14.00%)
2.19% swing Lab. to C.

WORTHING WEST
E. 78,587 T. 54,648 (69.54%) C. hold
Peter Bottomley, C.	30,475
Beccy Cooper, Lab.	15,652
Jamie Bennett, LD	6,024
Jo Paul, Green	2,008
David Aherne, Ind.	489

C. majority 14,823 (27.12%)
2.47% swing Lab. to C.

WREKIN, THE
E. 70,693 T. 48,890 (69.16%) C. hold
Mark Pritchard, C.	31,029
Dylan Harrison, Lab.	12,303
Thomas Janke, LD	4,067
Tim Dawes, Green	1,491

C. majority 18,726 (38.30%)
9.50% swing Lab. to C.

WYCOMBE
E. 78,094 T. 54,756 (70.12%) C. hold
Steve Baker, C.	24,766
Khalil Ahmed, Lab.	20,552
Toni Brodelle, LD	6,543
Peter Sims, Green	1,454
Julia Wassell, Wycombe	926
Vijay Srao, UKIP	324
Edmund Gemmell, Ind.	191

C. majority 4,214 (7.70%)
2.30% swing C. to Lab.

WYRE & PRESTON NORTH
E. 75,168 T. 52,924 (70.41%) C. hold
Ben Wallace, C.   31,589
Joanne Ainscough, Lab.   14,808
John Potter, LD   4,463
Ruth Norbury, Green   1,729
David Ragozzino, Ind.   335
C. majority 16,781 (31.71%)
4.22% swing Lab. to C.

WYRE FOREST
E. 78,079 T. 50,561 (64.76%) C. hold
Mark Garnier, C.   32,960
Robin Lunn, Lab.   11,547
Shazu Miah, LD   4,081
John Davis, Green   1,973
C. majority 21,413 (42.35%)
8.14% swing Lab. to C.

WYTHENSHAWE & SALE EAST
E. 76,313 T. 44,759 (58.65%) Lab. hold
Mike Kane, Lab.   23,855
Peter Harrop, C.   13,459
Simon Lepori, LD   3,111
Julie Fousert, Brexit   2,717
Rob Nunney, Green   1,559
Caroline Bellamy, Comm   58
Lge
Lab. majority 10,396 (23.23%)
4.68% swing Lab. to C.

YEOVIL
E. 82,468 T. 59,260 (71.86%) C. hold
Marcus Fysh, C.   34,588
Mick Clark, LD   18,407
Terry Ledlie, Lab.   3,761
Diane Wood, Green   1,629
Tony Capozzoli, Ind.   689
Tom Fox, Constitution   186
C. majority 16,181 (27.31%)
1.26% swing LD to C.

YORK CENTRAL
E. 74,899 T. 49,505 (66.10%)
                         Lab. Co-op hold
Rachael Maskell, Lab. Co-op   27,312
Fabia Tate, C.   13,767
James Blanchard, LD   4,149
Tom Franklin, Green   2,107
Nicholas Szkiler, Brexit   1,479
Andrew Snedden, Yorkshire   557
Andrew Dunn, Soc Dem   134
Lab. Co-op majority 13,545 (27.36%)
3.81% swing Lab. to C.

YORK OUTER
E. 74,673 T. 55,347 (74.12%) C. hold
Julian Sturdy, C.   27,324
Anna Perrett, Lab.   17,339
Keith Aspden, LD   9,992
Scott Marmion, Ind.   692
C. majority 9,985 (18.04%)
1.80% swing Lab. to C.

YORKSHIRE EAST
E. 80,871 T. 52,769 (65.25%) C. hold
Greg Knight, C.   33,988
Catherine Minnis, Lab.   11,201
Dale Needham, LD   4,219
Tim Norman, Yorkshire   1,686
Mike Jackson, Green   1,675
C. majority 22,787 (43.18%)
7.69% swing Lab. to C.

WALES

ABERAVON
E. 50,747 T. 31,598 (62.27%) Lab. hold
Stephen Kinnock, Lab.   17,008
Charlotte Lang, C.   6,518
Glenda Davies, Brexit   3,108
Nigel Hunt, PC   2,711
Sheila Kingston-Jones, LD   1,072
Captain Beany, Ind.   731
Giorgia Finney, Green   450
Lab. majority 10,490 (33.20%)
8.59% swing Lab. to C.

ABERCONWY
E. 44,699 T. 31,865 (71.29%) C. gain
Robin Millar, C.   14,687
Emily Owen, Lab.   12,653
Lisa Goodier, PC   2,704
Jason Edwards, LD   1,821
C. majority 2,034 (6.38%)
2.20% swing Lab. to C.

ALYN & DEESIDE
E. 62,783 T. 43,008 (68.50%) Lab. hold
Mark Tami, Lab.   18,271
Sanjoy Sen, C.   18,058
Simon Wall, Brexit   2,678
Donna Lalek, LD   2,548
Susan Hills, PC   1,453
Lab. majority 213 (0.50%)
5.60% swing Lab. to C.

ARFON
E. 42,215 T. 29,074 (68.87%) PC hold
Hywel Williams, PC   13,134
Steffie Williams Roberts,   10,353
Lab.
Gonul Daniels, C.   4,428
Gary Gribben, Brexit   1,159
PC majority 2,781 (9.57%)
4.62% swing Lab. to PC

BLAENAU GWENT
E. 50,736 T. 30,219 (59.56%) Lab. hold
Nick Smith, Lab.   14,862
Richard Taylor, Brexit   6,215
Laura Jones, C.   5,749
Peredur Owen Griffiths, PC   1,722
Chelsea-Marie Annett, LD   1,285
Stephen Priestnall, Green   386
Lab. majority 8,647 (28.61%)
swing N/A

BRECON & RADNORSHIRE
E. 55,490 T. 41,319 (74.46%) C. gain
Fay Jones, C.   21,958
Jane Dodds, LD   14,827
Tomos Davies, Lab.   3,944
Lady Lily The Pink, Loony   345
Jeff Green, Christian   245
C. majority 7,131 (17.26%)
1.09% swing C. to LD

BRIDGEND
E. 63,303 T. 42,236 (66.72%) C. gain
Jamie Wallis, C.   18,193
Madeleine Moon, Lab.   17,036
Jonathan Pratt, LD   2,368
Leanne Lewis, PC   2,013
Robert Morgan, Brexit   1,811
Alex Harris, Green   815
C. majority 1,157 (2.74%)
6.80% swing Lab. to C.

CAERPHILLY
E. 63,166 T. 40,117 (63.51%) Lab. hold
Wayne David, Lab.   18,018
Jane Pratt, C.   11,185
Lindsay Whittle, PC   6,424
Nathan Gill, Brexit   4,490
Lab. majority 6,833 (17.03%)
6.11% swing Lab. to C.

CARDIFF CENTRAL
E. 64,037 T. 41,822 (65.31%) Lab. hold
Jo Stevens, Lab.   25,605
Meirion Jenkins, C.   8,426
Bablin Molik, LD   6,298
Gareth Pearce, Brexit   1,006
Sian Caiach, Gwlad   280
Akil Kata, Ind.   119
Brian Johnson, SPGB   88
Lab. majority 17,179 (41.08%)
0.76% swing Lab. to C.

CARDIFF NORTH
E. 68,438 T. 52,666 (76.95%) Lab. hold
Anna McMorrin, Lab.   26,064
Mo Ali, C.   19,082
Rhys Taylor, LD   3,580
Steffan Webb, PC   1,606
Chris Butler, Brexit   1,311
Michael Cope, Green   820
Richard Jones, Ind.   203
Lab. majority 6,982 (13.26%)
2.62% swing C. to Lab.

CARDIFF SOUTH & PENARTH
E. 78,837   T. 50,579 (64.16%)

Lab. Co-op hold

Stephen Doughty, Lab. Co-op	27,382
Philippa Broom, C.	14,645
Dan Schmeising, LD	2,985
Nasir Adam, PC	2,386
Tim Price, Brexit	1,999
Ken Barker, Green	1,182

Lab. Co-op majority 12,737 (25.18%)
2.06% swing Lab. to C.

CARDIFF WEST
E. 68,508   T. 46,177 (67.40%)   Lab. hold

Kevin Brennan, Lab.	23,908
Carolyn Webster, C.	12,922
Boyd Clack, PC	3,864
Callum Littlemore, LD	2,731
Nick Mullins, Brexit	1,619
David Griffin, Green	1,133

Lab. majority 10,986 (23.79%)
1.56% swing Lab. to C.

CARMARTHEN EAST & DINEFWR
E. 57,407   T. 41,002 (71.42%)   PC hold

Jonathan Edwards, PC	15,939
Havard Hughes, C.	14,130
Maria Carroll, Lab.	8,622
Peter Prosser, Brexit	2,311

PC majority 1,809 (4.41%)
4.31% swing PC to C.

CARMARTHEN WEST & PEMBROKESHIRE SOUTH
E. 58,629   T. 42,114 (71.83%)   C. hold

Simon Hart, C.	22,183
Marc Tierney, Lab.	14,438
Rhys Thomas, PC	3,633
Alistair Cameron, LD	1,860

C. majority 7,745 (18.39%)
5.51% swing Lab. to C.

CEREDIGION
E. 56,250   T. 40,105 (71.30%)   PC hold

Ben Lake, PC	15,208
Amanda Jenner, C.	8,879
Mark Williams, LD	6,975
Dinah Mulholland, Lab.	6,317
Gethin James, Brexit	2,063
Chris Simpson, Green	663

PC majority 6,329 (15.78%)
2.46% swing C. to PC

CLWYD SOUTH
E. 53,919   T. 36,306 (67.33%)   C. gain

Simon Baynes, C.	16,222
Susan Elan Jones, Lab.	14,983
Chris Allen, PC	2,137
Calum Davies, LD	1,496
Jamie Adams, Brexit	1,468

C. majority 1,239 (3.41%)
7.52% swing Lab. to C.

CLWYD WEST
E. 57,714   T. 40,203 (69.66%)   C. hold

David Jones, C.	20,403
Jo Thomas, Lab.	13,656
Elfed Williams, PC	3,907
David Wilkins, LD	2,237

C. majority 6,747 (16.78%)
4.16% swing Lab. to C.

CYNON VALLEY
E. 51,134   T. 30,236 (59.13%)   Lab. hold

Beth Winter, Lab.	15,533
Pauline Church, C.	6,711
Rebecca Rees-Evans, Brexit	3,045
Geraint Benney, PC	2,562
Andrew Chainey, Cynon	1,322
Steve Bray, LD	949
Ian Mclean, Soc Dem	114

Lab. majority 8,822 (29.18%)
6.22% swing Lab. to C.

DELYN
E. 54,552   T. 38,370 (70.34%)   C. gain

Rob Roberts, C.	16,756
David Hanson, Lab.	15,891
Andrew Parkhurst, LD	2,346
Nigel Williams, Brexit	1,971
Paul Rowlinson, PC	1,406

C. majority 865 (2.25%)
6.51% swing Lab. to C.

DWYFOR MEIRIONNYDD
E. 44,362   T. 29,928 (67.46%)   PC hold

Liz Saville Roberts, PC	14,447
Tomos Davies, C.	9,707
Graham Hogg, Lab.	3,998
Louise Hughes, Brexit	1,776

PC majority 4,740 (15.84%)
0.07% swing PC to C.

GOWER
E. 61,762   T. 44,482 (72.02%)   Lab. hold

Tonia Antoniazzi, Lab.	20,208
Francesca O'Brien, C.	18,371
John Davies, PC	2,288
Sam Bennett, LD	2,236
Rob Ross, Brexit	1,379

Lab. majority 1,837 (4.13%)
1.52% swing Lab. to C.

ISLWYN
E. 55,423   T. 34,350 (61.98%)

Lab. Co-op hold

Chris Evans, Lab. Co-op	15,356
Gavin Chambers, C.	9,892
James Wells, Brexit	4,834
Zoe Hammond, PC	2,286
Jo Watkins, LD	1,313
Catherine Linstrum, Green	669

Lab. Co-op majority 5,464 (15.91%)
7.86% swing Lab. to C.

LLANELLI
E. 60,513   T. 38,233 (63.18%)   Lab. hold

Nia Griffith, Lab.	16,125
Tamara Reay, C.	11,455
Mari Arthur, PC	7,048
Susan Boucher, Brexit	3,605

Lab. majority 4,670 (12.21%)
8.80% swing Lab. to C.

MERTHYR TYDFIL & RHYMNEY
E. 56,322   T. 32,246 (57.25%)   Lab. hold

Gerald Jones, Lab.	16,913
Sara Jones, C.	6,307
Colin Jones, Brexit	3,604
Mark Evans, PC	2,446
David Hughes, Ind.	1,860
Brendan D'Cruz, LD	1,116

Lab. majority 10,606 (32.89%)
7.90% swing Lab. to C.

MONMOUTH
E. 67,094   T. 50,217 (74.85%)   C. hold

David Davies, C.	26,160
Yvonne Murphy, Lab.	16,178
Alison Willott, LD	4,909
Ian Chandler, Green	1,353
Hugh Kocan, PC	1,182
Martyn Ford, Ind.	435

C. majority 9,982 (19.88%)
1.69% swing Lab. to C.

MONTGOMERYSHIRE
E. 48,997   T. 34,214 (69.83%)   C. hold

Craig Williams, C.	20,020
Kishan Devani, LD	7,882
Kait Duerden, Lab.	5,585
Gwyn Wigley Evans, Gwlad	727

C. majority 12,138 (35.48%)
4.43% swing LD to C.

NEATH
E. 56,416   T. 36,756 (65.15%)

Lab. Co-op hold

Christina Rees, Lab. Co-op	15,920
Jon Burns, C.	10,283
Daniel Williams, PC	4,495
Simon Briscoe, Brexit	3,184
Adrian Kingston-Jones, LD	1,485
Megan Lloyd, Green	728
Philip Rogers, Ind.	594
Carl Williams, Soc Dem	67

Lab. Co-op majority 5,637 (15.34%)
8.83% swing Lab. to C.

NEWPORT EAST
E. 58,554   T. 36,282 (61.96%)   Lab. hold

Jessica Morden, Lab.	16,125
Mark Brown, C.	14,133
Julie Price, Brexit	2,454
Mike Hamilton, LD	2,121
Cameron Wixcey, PC	872
Peter Varley, Green	577

Lab. majority 1,992 (5.49%)
8.12% swing Lab. to C.

NEWPORT WEST
E. 66,657   T. 43,433 (65.16%)   Lab. hold

Ruth Jones, Lab.	18,977
Matthew Evans, C.	18,075
Ryan Jones, LD	2,565
Cameron Edwards, Brexit	1,727
Jonathan Clark, PC	1,187
Amelia Womack, Green	902

Lab. majority 902 (2.08%)
5.47% swing Lab. to C.

OGMORE
E. 57,581   T. 35,390 (61.46%)   Lab. hold

Chris Elmore, Lab.	17,602
Sadie Vidal, C.	9,797
Christine Roach, Brexit	2,991
Luke Fletcher, PC	2,919
Anita Davies, LD	1,460
Tom Muller, Green	621

Lab. majority 7,805 (22.05%)
7.61% swing Lab. to C.

PONTYPRIDD
E. 60,327   T. 39,060 (64.75%)   Lab. hold
Alex Davies-Jones, Lab.	17,381
Sam Trask, C.	11,494
Fflur Elin, PC	4,990
Steve Bayliss, Brexit	2,917
Mike Powell, Ind.	1,792
Sue Prior, Ind.	337
Jonathan Bishop, ND	149

Lab. majority 5,887 (15.07%)
6.81% swing Lab. to C.

PRESELI PEMBROKESHIRE
E. 59,586   T. 42,419 (71.19%)   C. hold
Stephen Crabb, C.	21,381
Philippa Thompson, Lab.	16,319
Cris Tomos, PC	2,776
Tom Hughes, LD	1,943

C. majority 5,062 (11.93%)
5.59% swing Lab. to C.

RHONDDA
E. 50,262   T. 29,642 (58.97%)   Lab. hold
Chris Bryant, Lab.	16,115
Hannah Jarvis, C.	4,675
Branwen Cennard, PC	4,069
John Watkins, Brexit	3,733
Simon Berman, LD	612
Shaun Thomas, Green	438

Lab. majority 11,440 (38.59%)
7.67% swing Lab. to C.

SWANSEA EAST
E. 58,450   T. 33,579 (57.45%)   Lab. hold
Carolyn Harris, Lab.	17,405
Denise Howard, C.	9,435
Tony Willicombe, Brexit	2,842
Geraint Havard, PC	1,905
Chloe Hutchinson, LD	1,409
Chris Evans, Green	583

Lab. majority 7,970 (23.74%)
6.86% swing Lab. to C.

SWANSEA WEST
E. 57,078   T. 35,830 (62.77%)
Lab. Co-op hold
Geraint Davies, Lab. Co-op	18,493
James Price, C.	10,377
Michael O'Carroll, LD	2,993
Gwyn Williams, PC	1,984
Peter Hopkins, Brexit	1,983

Lab. Co-op majority 8,116 (22.65%)
2.89% swing Lab. to C.

TORFAEN
E. 61,743   T. 37,176 (60.21%)   Lab. hold
Nick Thomas-Symonds, Lab.	15,546
Graham Smith, C.	11,804
David Thomas, Brexit	5,742
John Miller, LD	1,831
Morgan Bowler-Brown, PC	1,441
Andrew Heygate-Browne, Green	812

Lab. majority 3,742 (10.07%)
8.29% swing Lab. to C.

VALE OF CLWYD
E. 56,649   T. 37,213 (65.69%)   C. gain
James Davies, C.	17,270
Chris Ruane, Lab.	15,443
Glenn Swingler, PC	1,552
Peter Dain, Brexit	1,477
Gavin Scott, LD	1,471

C. majority 1,827 (4.91%)
5.53% swing Lab. to C.

VALE OF GLAMORGAN
E. 76,508   T. 54,807 (71.64%)   C. hold
Alun Cairns, C.	27,305
Belinda Loveluck-Edwards, Lab.	23,743
Anthony Slaughter, Green	3,251
Laurence Williams, Gwlad	508

C. majority 3,562 (6.50%)
1.21% swing Lab. to C.

WREXHAM
E. 49,734   T. 33,532 (67.42%)   C. gain
Sarah Atherton, C.	15,199
Mary Wimbury, Lab. Co-op	13,068
Carrie Harper, PC	2,151
Tim Sly, LD	1,447
Ian Berkeley-Hurst, Brexit	1,222
Duncan Rees, Green	445

C. majority 2,131 (6.36%)
5.79% swing Lab. to C.

YNYS MON
E. 51,925   T. 36,552 (70.39%)   C. gain
Virginia Crosbie, C.	12,959
Mary Roberts, Lab.	10,991
Aled Ap Dafydd, PC	10,418
Helen Jenner, Brexit	2,184

C. majority 1,968 (5.38%)
9.73% swing Lab. to C.

SCOTLAND

ABERDEEN NORTH
E. 62,489   T. 37,413 (59.87%)
	SNP hold
Kirsty Blackman, SNP	20,205
Ryan Houghton, C.	7,535
Nurul Ali, Lab.	4,939
Isobel Davidson, LD	2,846
Seb Leslie, Brexit	1,008
Guy Ingerson, Green	880

SNP majority 12,670 (33.87%)
7.64% swing C. to SNP

ABERDEEN SOUTH
E. 65,719   T. 45,630 (69.43%)   SNP gain
Stephen Flynn, SNP	20,380
Douglas Lumsden, C.	16,398
Ian Yuill, LD	5,018
Shona Simpson, Lab.	3,834

SNP majority 3,982 (8.73%)
9.70% swing C. to SNP

ABERDEENSHIRE WEST & KINCARDINE
E. 72,640   T. 53,345 (73.44%)   C. hold
Andrew Bowie, C.	22,752
Fergus Mutch, SNP	21,909
John Waddell, LD	6,253
Paddy Coffield, Lab.	2,431

C. majority 843 (1.58%)
6.91% swing C. to SNP

AIRDRIE & SHOTTS
E. 64,008   T. 39,772 (62.14%)
	SNP hold
Neil Gray, SNP	17,929
Helen McFarlane, Lab.	12,728
Lorraine Nolan, C.	7,011
William Crossman, LD	1,419
Rosemary McGowan, Green	685

SNP majority 5,201 (13.08%)
6.28% swing Lab. to SNP

ANGUS
E. 63,952   T. 43,170 (67.50%)   SNP gain
Dave Doogan, SNP	21,216
Kirstene Hair, C.	17,421
Ben Lawrie, LD	2,482
Monique Miller, Lab.	2,051

SNP majority 3,795 (8.79%)
7.69% swing C. to SNP

ARGYLL & BUTE
E. 66,525   T. 48,050 (72.23%)
	SNP hold
Brendan O'Hara, SNP	21,040
Gary Mulvaney, C.	16,930
Alan Reid, LD	6,832
Rhea Barnes, Lab.	3,248

SNP majority 4,110 (8.55%)
2.90% swing C. to SNP

AYR, CARRICK & CUMNOCK
E. 71,970   T. 46,592 (64.74%)   SNP gain
Allan Dorans, SNP	20,272
Martin Dowey, C.	17,943
Duncan Townson, Lab.	6,219
Helena Bongard, LD	2,158

SNP majority 2,329 (5.00%)
5.50% swing C. to SNP

AYRSHIRE CENTRAL
E. 69,742   T. 46,534 (66.72%)
	SNP hold
Philippa Whitford, SNP	21,486
Derek Stillie, C.	16,182
Louise McPhater, Lab.	6,583
Emma Farthing, LD	2,283

SNP majority 5,304 (11.40%)
4.29% swing C. to SNP

AYRSHIRE NORTH & ARRAN
E. 73,534   T. 48,154 (65.49%)

		SNP hold
Patricia Gibson, SNP		23,376
David Rocks, C.		14,855
Cameron Gilmore, Lab.		6,702
Louise Young, LD		2,107
David Nairn, Green		1,114

SNP majority 8,521 (17.70%)
5.02% swing C. to SNP

BANFF & BUCHAN
E. 66,655   T. 42,260 (63.40%)   C. hold

David Duguid, C.	21,182
Paul Robertson, SNP	17,064
Alison Smith, LD	2,280
Brian Balcombe, Lab.	1,734

C. majority 4,118 (9.74%)
0.44% swing SNP to C.

BERWICKSHIRE, ROXBURGH & SELKIRK
E. 74,518   T. 53,146 (71.32%)   C. hold

John Lamont, C.	25,747
Calum Kerr, SNP	20,599
Jenny Marr, LD	4,287
Ian Davidson, Lab.	2,513

C. majority 5,148 (9.69%)
5.72% swing C. to SNP

CAITHNESS, SUTHERLAND & EASTER ROSS
E. 46,930   T. 31,457 (67.03%)   LD hold

Jamie Stone, LD	11,705
Karl Rosie, SNP	11,501
Andrew Sinclair, C.	5,176
Cheryl McDonald, Lab.	1,936
Sandra Skinner, Brexit	1,139

LD majority 204 (0.65%)
2.98% swing LD to SNP

COATBRIDGE, CHRYSTON & BELLSHILL
E. 72,943   T. 48,221 (66.11%)   SNP gain

Steven Bonnar, SNP	22,680
Hugh Gaffney, Lab.	17,056
Nathan Wilson, C.	6,113
David Stevens, LD	1,564
Patrick McAleer, Green	808

SNP majority 5,624 (11.66%)
7.59% swing Lab. to SNP

CUMBERNAULD, KILSYTH & KIRKINTILLOCH EAST
E. 66,079   T. 45,686 (69.14%)

	SNP hold
Stuart McDonald, SNP	24,158
James McPhilemy, Lab.	11,182
Roz McCall, C.	7,380
Susan Murray, LD	2,966

SNP majority 12,976 (28.40%)
9.34% swing Lab. to SNP

DUMFRIES & GALLOWAY
E. 74,580   T. 51,429 (68.96%)   C. hold

Alister Jack, C.	22,678
Richard Arkless, SNP	20,873
Ted Thompson, Lab.	4,745
McNabb Laurie, LD	3,133

C. majority 1,805 (3.51%)
3.71% swing C. to SNP

DUMFRIESSHIRE, CLYDESDALE & TWEEDDALE
E. 68,330   T. 49,153 (71.93%)   C. hold

David Mundell, C.	22,611
Amanda Burgauer, SNP	18,830
Nick Chisholm, Lab.	4,172
John Ferry, LD	3,540

C. majority 3,781 (7.69%)
5.79% swing C. to SNP

DUNBARTONSHIRE EAST
E. 66,075   T. 53,031 (80.26%)   SNP gain

Amy Callaghan, SNP	19,672
Jo Swinson, LD	19,523
Pam Gosal, C.	7,455
Callum McNally, Lab.	4,839
Carolynn Scrimgeour, Green	916
Rosie Dickson, Ind.	221
Donald MacKay, UKIP	208
Liam McKechnie, Scot Family	197

SNP majority 149 (0.28%)
5.29% swing LD to SNP

DUNBARTONSHIRE WEST
E. 66,517   T. 45,140 (67.86%)

	SNP hold
Martin Docherty, SNP	22,396
Jean Mitchell, Lab.	12,843
Alix Mathieson, C.	6,436
Jennifer Lang, LD	1,890
Peter Connolly, Green	867
Andrew Muir, Ind.	708

SNP majority 9,553 (21.16%)
7.99% swing Lab. to SNP

DUNDEE EAST
E. 66,210   T. 45,277 (68.38%)

	SNP hold
Stewart Hosie, SNP	24,361
Philip Scott, C.	10,986
Rosalind Garton, Lab.	6,045
Michael Crichton, LD	3,573
George Morton, Ind.	312

SNP majority 13,375 (29.54%)
7.03% swing C. to SNP

DUNDEE WEST
E. 64,431   T. 41,579 (64.53%)

	SNP hold
Chris Law, SNP	22,355
Jim Malone, Lab.	10,096
Tess White, C.	5,149
Daniel Coleman, LD	2,468
Stuart Waiton, Brexit	1,271
Quinta Arrey, CPA	240

SNP majority 12,259 (29.48%)
7.94% swing Lab. to SNP

DUNFERMLINE & FIFE WEST
E. 76,652   T. 53,482 (69.77%)

	SNP hold
Douglas Chapman, SNP	23,727
Cara Hilton, Lab. Co-op	13,028
Moira Benny, C.	11,207
Rebecca Bell, LD	4,262
Mags Hall, Green	1,258

SNP majority 10,699 (20.00%)
9.18% swing Lab. to SNP

EAST KILBRIDE, STRATHAVEN & LESMAHAGOW
E. 81,224   T. 56,337 (69.36%)

	SNP hold
Lisa Cameron, SNP	26,113
Monique McAdams, Lab.	12,791
Gail MacGregor, C.	11,961
Ewan McRobert, LD	3,760
Erica Bradley-Young, Green	1,153
David Mackay, UKIP	559

SNP majority 13,322 (23.65%)
8.25% swing Lab. to SNP

EAST LOTHIAN
E. 81,600   T. 58,513 (71.71%)   SNP gain

Kenny MacAskill, SNP	21,156
Martin Whitfield, Lab.	17,270
Craig Hoy, C.	15,523
Robert O'Riordan, LD	4,071
David Sisson, UKIP	493

SNP majority 3,886 (6.64%)
6.08% swing Lab. to SNP

EDINBURGH EAST
E. 69,424   T. 47,815 (68.87%)

	SNP hold
Tommy Sheppard, SNP	23,165
Sheila Gilmore, Lab.	12,748
Eleanor Price, C.	6,549
Jill Reilly, LD	3,289
Claire Miller, Green	2,064

SNP majority 10,417 (21.79%)
6.96% swing Lab. to SNP

EDINBURGH NORTH & LEITH
E. 81,336   T. 59,344 (72.96%)

	SNP hold
Deidre Brock, SNP	25,925
Gordon Munro, Lab. Co-op	13,117
Iain McGill, C.	11,000
Bruce Wilson, LD	6,635
Steve Burgess, Green	1,971
Robert Speirs, Brexit	558
Heather Astbury, Renew	138

SNP majority 12,808 (21.58%)
9.35% swing Lab. to SNP

EDINBURGH SOUTH
E. 66,188   T. 49,732 (75.14%)   Lab. hold

Ian Murray, Lab.	23,745
Catriona MacDonald, SNP	12,650
Nick Cook, C.	8,161
Alan Beal, LD	3,819
Kate Nevens, Green	1,357

Lab. majority 11,095 (22.31%)
5.06% swing Lab. to SNP

EDINBURGH SOUTH WEST
E. 73,501   T. 52,131 (70.93%)

	SNP hold
Joanna Cherry, SNP	24,830
Callum Laidlaw, C.	12,848
Sophie Cooke, Lab.	7,478
Tom Inglis, LD	4,971
Ben Parker, Green	1,265
David Ballantine, Brexit	625
Mev Brown, Soc Dem	114

SNP majority 11,982 (22.98%)
10.38% swing C. to SNP

EDINBURGH WEST
E. 72,507   T. 54,533 (75.21%)   LD hold
Christine Jardine, LD   21,766
Sarah Masson, SNP   17,997
Graham Hutchison, C.   9,283
Craig Bolton, Lab.   4,460
Elaine Gunn, Green   1,027
LD majority 3,769 (6.91%)
0.63% swing SNP to LD

FALKIRK
E. 84,472   T. 55,872 (66.14%)
                                        SNP hold
Johnny McNally, SNP   29,351
Lynn Munro, C.   14,403
Safia Ali, Lab.   6,243
Austin Reid, LD   3,990
Tom McLaughlin, Green   1,885
SNP majority 14,948 (26.75%)
7.00% swing C. to SNP

FIFE NORTH EAST
E. 60,905   T. 45,878 (75.33%)   LD gain
Wendy Chamberlain, LD   19,763
Stephen Gethins, SNP   18,447
Tony Miklinski, C.   5,961
Wendy Haynes, Lab.   1,707
LD majority 1,316 (2.87%)
1.44% swing SNP to LD

GLASGOW CENTRAL
E. 69,230   T. 40,105 (57.93%)
                                        SNP hold
Alison Thewliss, SNP   19,750
Faten Hameed, Lab.   13,276
Flora Scarabello, C.   3,698
Ewan Hoyle, LD   1,952
Elaine Gallagher, Green   1,429
SNP majority 6,474 (16.14%)
4.92% swing Lab. to SNP

GLASGOW EAST
E. 67,381   T. 38,483 (57.11%)
                                        SNP hold
David Linden, SNP   18,357
Kate Watson, Lab.   12,791
Thomas Kerr, C.   5,709
James Harrison, LD   1,626
SNP majority 5,566 (14.46%)
7.13% swing Lab. to SNP

GLASGOW NORTH
E. 57,130   T. 36,191 (63.35%)
                                        SNP hold
Patrick Grady, SNP   16,982
Pam Duncan-Glancy, Lab.   11,381
Tony Curtis, C.   3,806
Andrew Chamberlain, LD   2,394
Cass Macgregor, Green   1,308
Dionne Cocozza, Brexit   320
SNP majority 5,601 (15.48%)
6.15% swing Lab. to SNP

GLASGOW NORTH EAST
E. 61,075   T. 33,925 (55.55%)   SNP gain
Anne McLaughlin, SNP   15,911
Paul Sweeney, Lab. Co-op   13,363
Lauren Bennie, C.   3,558
Nicholas Moohan, LD   1,093
SNP majority 2,548 (7.51%)
4.14% swing Lab. to SNP

GLASGOW NORTH WEST
E. 63,402   T. 39,735 (62.67%)
                                        SNP hold
Carol Monaghan, SNP   19,678
Patricia Ferguson, Lab.   11,319
Ade Aibinu, C.   6,022
James Speirs, LD   2,716
SNP majority 8,359 (21.04%)
7.22% swing Lab. to SNP

GLASGOW SOUTH
E. 70,891   T. 47,443 (66.92%)
                                        SNP hold
Stewart McDonald, SNP   22,829
Johann Lamont, Lab. Co-op   13,824
Kyle Thornton, C.   6,237
Carole Ford, LD   2,786
Dan Hutchison, Green   1,251
Danyaal Raja, Brexit   516
SNP majority 9,005 (18.98%)
7.22% swing Lab. to SNP

GLASGOW SOUTH WEST
E. 64,575   T. 36,847 (57.06%)
                                        SNP hold
Chris Stephens, SNP   17,643
Matt Kerr, Lab. Co-op   12,743
Thomas Haddow, C.   4,224
Ben Denton-Cardew, LD   1,435
Peter Brown, Brexit   802
SNP majority 4,900 (13.30%)
6.56% swing Lab. to SNP

GLENROTHES
E. 65,762   T. 41,546 (63.18%)
                                        SNP hold
Peter Grant, SNP   21,234
Pat Egan, Lab.   9,477
Amy Thomson, C.   6,920
Jane Ann Liston, LD   2,639
Victor Farrell, Brexit   1,276
SNP majority 11,757 (28.30%)
10.11% swing Lab. to SNP

GORDON
E. 79,629   T. 55,916 (70.22%)   SNP gain
Richard Thomson, SNP   23,885
Colin Clark, C.   23,066
James Oates, LD   5,913
Heather Herbert, Lab.   3,052
SNP majority 819 (1.46%)
3.16% swing C. to SNP

INVERCLYDE
E. 60,622   T. 39,903 (65.82%)
                                        SNP hold
Ronnie Cowan, SNP   19,295
Martin McCluskey, Lab.   11,783
Haroun Malik, C.   6,265
Jacci Stoyle, LD   2,560
SNP majority 7,512 (18.83%)
8.92% swing Lab. to SNP

INVERNESS, NAIRN, BADENOCH &
STRATHSPEY
E. 78,057   T. 54,810 (70.22%)
                                        SNP hold
Drew Hendry, SNP   26,247
Fiona Fawcett, C.   15,807
Robert Rixson, LD   5,846
Lewis Whyte, Lab.   4,123
Ariane Burgess, Green   1,709
Les Durance, Brexit   1,078
SNP majority 10,440 (19.05%)
4.86% swing C. to SNP

KILMARNOCK & LOUDOUN
E. 74,517   T. 47,631 (63.92%)
                                        SNP hold
Alan Brown, SNP   24,216
Caroline Hollins, C.   11,557
Kevin McGregor, Lab.   9,009
Edward Thornley, LD   2,444
Stef Johnstone, Libertarian   405
SNP majority 12,659 (26.58%)
5.46% swing C. to SNP

KIRKCALDY & COWDENBEATH
E. 72,853   T. 47,005 (64.52%)   SNP gain
Neale Hanvey, SNP   16,568
Lesley Laird, Lab.   15,325
Kathleen Leslie, C.   9,449
Gill Cole-Hamilton, LD   2,903
Scott Rutherford, Green   1,628
Mitch William, Brexit   1,132
SNP majority 1,243 (2.64%)
1.60% swing Lab. to SNP

LANARK & HAMILTON EAST
E. 77,659   T. 53,072 (68.34%)
                                        SNP hold
Angela Crawley, SNP   22,243
Shona Haslam, C.   17,056
Andrew Hilland, Lab.   10,736
Jane Pickard, LD   3,037
SNP majority 5,187 (9.77%)
4.62% swing C. to SNP

LINLITHGOW & FALKIRK EAST
E. 87,044   T. 57,775 (66.37%)
                                        SNP hold
Martyn Day, SNP   25,551
Charles Kennedy, C.   14,285
Wendy Milne, Lab.   10,517
Sally Pattle, LD   4,393
Marc Bozza, Brexit   1,257
Gillian Mackay, Green   1,184
Mark Tunnicliff, VPP   588
SNP majority 11,266 (19.50%)
6.12% swing C. to SNP

LIVINGSTON
E. 82,285   T. 54,592 (66.35%)
                                        SNP hold
Hannah Bardell, SNP   25,617
Damian Timson, C.   12,182
Caitlin Kane, Lab.   11,915
Charles Dundas, LD   3,457
Cameron Glasgow, Green   1,421
SNP majority 13,435 (24.61%)
4.46% swing C. to SNP

MIDLOTHIAN

E. 70,544   T. 48,221 (68.36%)   SNP gain

Owen Thompson, SNP	20,033
Danielle Rowley, Lab.	14,328
Rebecca Fraser, C.	10,467
Steve Arrundale, LD	3,393

SNP majority 5,705 (11.83%)
6.89% swing Lab. to SNP

MORAY

E. 71,035   T. 48,825 (68.73%)   C. hold

Douglas Ross, C.	22,112
Laura Mitchell, SNP	21,599
Jo Kirby, Lab.	2,432
Fiona Campbell Trevor, LD	2,269
Rob Scorer, UKIP	413

C. majority 513 (1.05%)
3.84% swing C. to SNP

MOTHERWELL & WISHAW

E. 68,856   T. 44,420 (64.51%)

SNP hold

Marion Fellows, SNP	20,622
Angela Feeney, Lab.	14,354
Meghan Gallacher, C.	7,150
Christopher Wilson, LD	1,675
Neil Wilson, UKIP	619

SNP majority 6,268 (14.11%)
6.68% swing Lab. to SNP

NA H-EILEANAN AN IAR

E. 21,106   T. 14,477 (68.59%)

SNP hold

Angus MacNeil, SNP	6,531
Alison MacCorquodale, Lab.	4,093
Jennifer Ross, C.	3,216
Neil Mitchison, LD	637

SNP majority 2,438 (16.84%)
5.02% swing Lab. to SNP

OCHIL & PERTHSHIRE SOUTH

E. 78,776   T. 57,813 (73.39%)   SNP gain

John Nicolson, SNP	26,882
Luke Graham, C.	22,384
Lorna Robertson, Lab.	4,961
Iliyan Stefanov, LD	3,204
Stuart Martin, UKIP	382

SNP majority 4,498 (7.78%)
6.99% swing C. to SNP

ORKNEY & SHETLAND

E. 34,211   T. 23,160 (67.70%)   LD hold

Alistair Carmichael, LD	10,381
Robert Leslie, SNP	7,874
Jennifer Fairbairn, C.	2,287
Coilla Drake, Lab.	1,550
Robert Smith, Brexit	900
David Barnard, Ind.	168

LD majority 2,507 (10.82%)
4.39% swing LD to SNP

PAISLEY & RENFREWSHIRE NORTH

E. 72,007   T. 49,682 (69.00%)

SNP hold

Gavin Newlands, SNP	23,353
Alison Taylor, Lab.	11,451
Julie Pirone, C.	11,217
Ross Stalker, LD	3,661

SNP majority 11,902 (23.96%)
9.18% swing Lab. to SNP

PAISLEY & RENFREWSHIRE SOUTH

E. 64,385   T. 43,084 (66.92%)

SNP hold

Mhairi Black, SNP	21,637
Moira Ramage, Lab.	10,958
Mark Dougan, C.	7,571
Jack Clark, LD	2,918

SNP majority 10,679 (24.79%)
9.35% swing Lab. to SNP

PERTH & PERTHSHIRE NORTH

E. 72,600   T. 54,076 (74.48%)

SNP hold

Pete Wishart, SNP	27,362
Angus Forbes, C.	19,812
Peter Barrett, LD	3,780
Angela Bretherton, Lab.	2,471
Stuart Powell, Brexit	651

SNP majority 7,550 (13.96%)
6.96% swing C. to SNP

RENFREWSHIRE EAST

E. 72,232   T. 55,357 (76.64%)   SNP gain

Kirsten Oswald, SNP	24,877
Paul Masterton, C.	19,451
Carolann Davidson, Lab.	6,855
Andrew McGlynn, LD	4,174

SNP majority 5,426 (9.80%)
9.29% swing C. to SNP

ROSS, SKYE & LOCHABER

E. 54,229   T. 39,869 (73.52%)

SNP hold

Ian Blackford, SNP	19,263
Craig Harrow, LD	9,820
Gavin Berkenheger, C.	6,900
John Erskine, Lab.	2,448
Kate Brownlie, Brexit	710
Donald Boyd, SCP	460
Richard Lucas, Scot Family	268

SNP majority 9,443 (23.69%)
2.17% swing LD to SNP

RUTHERGLEN & HAMILTON WEST

E. 80,918   T. 53,794 (66.48%)   SNP gain

Margaret Ferrier, SNP	23,775
Ged Killen, Lab. Co-op	18,545
Lynne Nailon, C.	8,054
Mark McGeever, LD	2,791
Janice Mackay, UKIP	629

SNP majority 5,230 (9.72%)
5.12% swing Lab. to SNP

STIRLING

E. 68,473   T. 52,620 (76.85%)   SNP gain

Alyn Smith, SNP	26,895
Stephen Kerr, C.	17,641
Mary Ross, Lab.	4,275
Fayzan Rehman, LD	2,867
Bryan Quinn, Green	942

SNP majority 9,254 (17.59%)
8.94% swing C. to SNP

NORTHERN IRELAND

ANTRIM EAST

E. 64,830   T. 37,261 (57.47%)

DUP hold

Sammy Wilson, DUP	16,871
Danny Donnelly, Alliance	10,165
Steve Aiken, UUP	5,475
Oliver McMullan, SF	2,120
Aaron Rankin, C.	1,043
Angela Mulholland, SDLP	902
Philip Randle, Green	685

DUP majority 6,706 (18.00%)
11.87% swing DUP to Alliance

ANTRIM NORTH

E. 77,134   T. 44,051 (57.11%)

DUP hold

Ian Paisley, DUP	20,860
Robin Swann, UUP	8,139
Patricia O'Lynn, Alliance	6,231
Cara McShane, SF	5,632
Margaret McKillop, SDLP	2,943
Stephen Palmer, Ind.	246

DUP majority 12,721 (28.88%)
11.40% swing DUP to UUP

ANTRIM SOUTH

E. 71,711   T. 42,974 (59.93%)

DUP hold

Paul Girvan, DUP	15,149
Danny Kinahan, UUP	12,460
John Blair, Alliance	8,190
Declan Kearney, SF	4,887
Roisin Lynch, SDLP	2,288

DUP majority 2,689 (6.26%)
0.59% swing DUP to UUP

BELFAST EAST

E. 66,245   T. 42,445 (64.07%)

DUP hold

Gavin Robinson, DUP	20,874
Naomi Long, Alliance	19,055
Carl McClean, UUP	2,516

DUP majority 1,819 (4.29%)
7.74% swing DUP to Alliance

BELFAST NORTH
E. 72,225   T. 49,037 (67.89%)

		SF gain
John Finucane, SF	23,078	
Nigel Dodds, DUP	21,135	
Nuala McAllister, Alliance	4,824	

SF majority 1,943 (3.96%)
4.25% swing DUP to SF

BELFAST SOUTH
E. 69,984   T. 47,352 (67.66%)

		SDLP gain
Claire Hanna, SDLP	27,079	
Emma Little Pengelly, DUP	11,678	
Paula Bradshaw, Alliance	6,786	
Michael Henderson, UUP	1,259	
Chris McHugh, Aontu	550	

SDLP majority 15,401 (32.52%)
18.55% swing DUP to SDLP

BELFAST WEST
E. 65,644   T. 38,782 (59.08%)

		SF hold
Paul Maskey, SF	20,866	
Gerry Carroll, PBP	6,194	
Frank McCoubrey, DUP	5,220	
Paul Doherty, SDLP	2,985	
Donnamarie Higgins, Alliance	1,882	
Monica Digney, Aontu	1,635	

SF majority 14,672 (37.83%)
9.36% swing SF to PBP

DOWN NORTH
E. 67,099   T. 40,643 (60.57%)

		Alliance gain
Stephen Farry, Alliance	18,358	
Alex Easton, DUP	15,390	
Alan Chambers, UUP	4,936	
Matthew Robinson, C.	1,959	

Alliance majority 2,968 (7.30%)
18.07% swing DUP to Alliance

DOWN SOUTH
E. 79,175   T. 49,762 (62.85%)

		SF hold
Chris Hazzard, SF	16,137	
Michael Savage, SDLP	14,517	
Glyn Hanna, DUP	7,619	
Patrick Brown, Alliance	6,916	
Jill Macauley, UUP	3,307	
Paul Brady, Aontu	1,266	

SF majority 1,620 (3.26%)
0.78% swing SF to SDLP

FERMANAGH & SOUTH TYRONE
E. 72,848   T. 50,762 (69.68%)

		SF hold
Michelle Gildernew, SF	21,986	
Tom Elliott, UUP	21,929	
Adam Gannon, SDLP	3,446	
Matthew Beaumont, Alliance	2,650	
Caroline Wheeler, Ind.	751	

SF majority 57 (0.11%)
0.76% swing SF to UUP

FOYLE
E. 74,346   T. 47,144 (63.41%)

		SDLP gain
Colum Eastwood, SDLP	26,881	
Elisha McCallion, SF	9,771	
Gary Middleton, DUP	4,773	
Anne McCloskey, Aontu	2,032	
Shaun Harkin, PBP	1,332	
Rachael Ferguson, Alliance	1,267	
Darren Guy, UUP	1,088	

SDLP majority 17,110 (36.29%)
18.33% swing SF to SDLP

LAGAN VALLEY
E. 75,735   T. 45,405 (59.95%)

		DUP hold
Jeffrey Donaldson, DUP	19,586	
Sorcha Eastwood, Alliance	13,087	
Robbie Butler, UUP	8,606	
Ally Haydock, SDLP	1,758	
Gary McCleave, SF	1,098	
Gary Hynds, C.	955	
Alan Love, UKIP	315	

DUP majority 6,499 (14.31%)
17.07% swing DUP to Alliance

LONDONDERRY EAST
E. 69,246   T. 39,302 (56.76%)

		DUP hold
Gregory Campbell, DUP	15,765	
Cara Hunter, SDLP	6,158	
Dermot Nicholl, SF	6,128	
Chris McCaw, Alliance	5,921	
Richard Holmes, UUP	3,599	
Sean McNicholl, Aontu	1,731	

DUP majority 9,607 (24.44%)
6.42% swing DUP to SDLP

NEWRY & ARMAGH
E. 81,226   T. 50,779 (62.52%)

		SF hold
Mickey Brady, SF	20,287	
William Irwin, DUP	11,000	
Pete Byrne, SDLP	9,449	
Jackie Coade, Alliance	4,211	
Sam Nicholson, UUP	4,204	
Martin Kelly, Aontu	1,628	

SF majority 9,287 (18.29%)
2.51% swing SF to DUP

STRANGFORD
E. 66,928   T. 37,485 (56.01%)

		DUP hold
Jim Shannon, DUP	17,705	
Kellie Armstrong, Alliance	10,634	
Philip Smith, UUP	4,023	
Joe Boyle, SDLP	1,994	
Grant Abraham, C.	1,476	
Maurice Macartney, Green	790	
Ryan Carlin, SF	555	
Robert Stephenson, UKIP	308	

DUP majority 7,071 (18.86%)
14.24% swing DUP to Alliance

TYRONE WEST
E. 66,259   T. 41,186 (62.16%)

		SF hold
Orfhlaith Begley, SF	16,544	
Thomas Buchanan, DUP	9,066	
Daniel McCrossan, SDLP	7,330	
Stephen Donnelly, Alliance	3,979	
Andy McKane, UUP	2,774	
James Hope, Aontu	972	
Susan Glass, Green	521	

SF majority 7,478 (18.16%)
2.81% swing SF to DUP

ULSTER MID
E. 70,449   T. 44,620 (63.34%)

		SF hold
Francie Molloy, SF	20,473	
Keith Buchanan, DUP	10,936	
Denise Johnston, SDLP	6,384	
Mel Boyle, Alliance	3,526	
Neil Richardson, UUP	2,611	
Conor Rafferty, Ind.	690	

SF majority 9,537 (21.37%)
3.12% swing SF to DUP

UPPER BANN
E. 82,887   T. 50,045 (60.38%)

		DUP hold
Carla Lockhart, DUP	20,501	
John O'Dowd, SF	12,291	
Eoin Tennyson, Alliance	6,433	
Doug Beattie, UUP	6,197	
Dolores Kelly, SDLP	4,623	

DUP majority 8,210 (16.41%)
0.41% swing SF to DUP

THE GOVERNMENT

As at 25 November 2020

THE CABINET

Prime Minister, First Lord of the Treasury, Minister for the Union and Minister for the Civil Service
Rt. Hon. Boris Johnson, MP
Chancellor of the Exchequer
Rt. Hon. Rishi Sunak, MP
Secretary of State for Foreign, Commonwealth and Development Affairs and First Secretary of State
Rt. Hon. Dominic Raab, MP
Secretary of State for the Home Department
Rt. Hon. Priti Patel, MP
Chancellor of the Duchy of Lancaster and Minister for the Cabinet Office
Rt. Hon. Michael Gove, MP
Lord Chancellor and Secretary of State for Justice
Rt. Hon. Robert Buckland, QC, MP
Secretary of State for Defence
Rt. Hon. Ben Wallace, MP
Secretary of State for Health and Social Care
Rt. Hon. Matt Hancock, MP
Secretary of State for Business, Energy and Industrial Strategy
Rt. Hon. Alok Sharma, MP
Secretary of State for International Trade and President of the Board of Trade and Minister for Women and Equalities
Rt. Hon. Elizabeth Truss, MP
Secretary of State for Work and Pensions
Rt. Hon. Thérèse Coffey, MP
Secretary of State for Education
Rt. Hon. Gavin Williamson, CBE, MP
Secretary of State for Environment, Food and Rural Affairs
Rt. Hon. George Eustice, MP
Secretary of State for Housing, Communities and Local Government
Rt. Hon. Robert Jenrick, MP
Secretary of State for Transport
Rt. Hon. Grant Shapps, MP
Secretary of State for Northern Ireland
Rt. Hon. Julian Lewis, MP
Secretary of State for Scotland
Rt. Hon. Alister Jack, MP
Secretary of State for Wales
Rt. Hon. Simon Hart, MP
Leader of the House of Lords and Lord Privy Seal
Rt. Hon. Baroness Evans of Bowes Park
Secretary of State for Digital, Culture, Media and Sport
Rt. Hon. Oliver Dowden, CBE, MP
Minister without Portfolio
Rt. Hon. Amanda Milling, MP

ALSO ATTENDING CABINET MEETINGS
Chief Secretary to the Treasury
Rt. Hon. Steve Barclay, MP
Lord President of the Council and Leader of the House of Commons
Rt. Hon. Jacob Rees-Mogg, MP
Parliamentary Secretary to the Treasury and Chief Whip
Rt. Hon. Mark Spencer, MP
Attorney-General
Rt. Hon. Suella Braverman, QC, MP
Minister for Business, Energy and Clean Growth
Rt. Hon. Kwasi Kwarteng, MP
Minister of State for Housing
Rt. Hon. Christopher Pincher, MP

Minister of State for Media and Data
Rt. Hon. John Whittingdale, OBE, MP
Minister of State for the Middle East and North Africa
Rt. Hon. James Cleverly, MP
Minister of State for Pacific and Environment
Rt. Hon. Lord Zac Goldsmith
Minister of State for School Standards
Rt. Hon. Nick Gibb, MP
Minister of State for Security
Rt. Hon. James Brokenshire, MP
Minister of State for Trade Policy
Rt. Hon. Greg Hands, MP
Deputy Leader of the House of Lords
Rt. Hon. Earl Howe
Finance Secretary to the Treasury
Rt. Hon. Jesse Norman, MP
Paymaster-General
Rt. Hon. Penny Mordaunt, MP
Solicitor General
Rt. Hon. Michael Ellis, QC, MP

LAW OFFICERS

Attorney-General
Rt. Hon. Suella Braverman, QC, MP
Solicitor-General
Rt. Hon. Michael Ellis, QC, MP
Advocate-General for Scotland
Keith Stewart, QC

MINISTERS OF STATE

Business, Energy and Industrial Strategy
Rt. Hon. Kwasi Kwarteng, MP
Cabinet Office
Lord Agnew§
Chloe Smith, MP
Lord True, CBE
Defence
Baroness Goldie, DL
Jeremy Quin
Digital, Culture, Media and Sport
Caroline Dinenage, MP
Rt Hon. John Whittingdale, OBE, MP
Education
Michelle Donelan, MP
Rt. Hon. Nick Gibb, MP
Environment, Food and Rural Affairs
Lord Zac Goldsmith†
Foreign, Commonwealth and Development Office
Lord Ahmad of Wimbledon
Nigel Adams, MP
Rt. Hon. James Cleverly, MP
Health and Social Care
Edward Argar, MP
Nadine Dorries, MP
Helen Whately, MP
Home Office
Rt. Hon. James Brokenshire, MP
Kit Malthouse, MP*

Housing, Communities and Local Government
Lord Stephen Greenhalgh‡
Luke Hall, MP
Rt. Hon. Christopher Pincher, MP
International Trade
Rt. Hon. Greg Hands, MP
Justice
Lucy Frazer, QC, MP
Northern Ireland Office
Robin Walker, MP
Transport
Chris Heaton-Harris, MP
Andrew Stephenson, MP
Work and Pensions
Justin Tomlinson, MP

* Jointly held with the Ministry of Justice
† Jointly held with FCO
‡ Jointly held with the Home Office
§ Jointly held with the Treasury

UNDER-SECRETARIES OF STATE

Business, Energy and Industrial Strategy
Lord Callahan
Paul Scully, MP
Amanda Solloway, MP
Nadhim Zahawi, MP
Cabinet Office
Johnny Mercer, MP*
Defence
James Heappey, MP
Digital, Culture, Media and Sport
Baroness Barran, MBE
Nigel Huddleston, MP††
Matt Warman, MP
Education
Baroness Berridge of The Vale of Catmose†
Vicky Ford, MP
Gillian Keegan, MP
Environment, Food and Rural Affairs
Lord Gardiner of Kimble
Rebecca Pow, MP
Victoria Prentis, MP
Foreign, Commonwealth and Development Office
James Duddridge, MP
Wendy Morton, MO
Health and Social Care
Jo Churchill, MP
Lord Bethell of Romford
Home Office
Victoria Atkins, MP
Kevin Foster, MP
Chris Philp, MP§
Housing, Communities and Local Government
Kelly Tolhurst, MP
International Trade
Kemi Badenoch, MP₵
Baroness Berridge of The Vale of Catmose‡
Ranil Jayawardena, MP
Graham Stuart, MP
Justice
Alex Chalk, MP††
Office of the Secretary of State for Scotland
David Duguid, MP‡‡
Iain Stewart, MP
Transport
Robert Courts, MP
Rachel Maclean, MP
Baroness Vere of Norbiton

Office of the Secretary of State for Wales
David Davies, MP††
Work and Pensions
Mims Davies, MP
Guy Opperman, MP
Will Quince, MP
Baroness Deborah Stedman-Scott, OBE, DL

* Jointly held with the MOD
† Alongside role at DfT
‡ Alongside role at the DfE
§ Jointly held with the MoJ
₵ Alongside role as Exchequer Secretary to the Treasury
** Jointly held with UK Export Finance
†† Alongside role as Assistant Whip
‡‡ Alongside role as government Whip

OTHER MINISTERS

Business, Energy and Industrial Strategy
Lord Grimstone of Boscobel Kt* *(Minister for Investment)*
Cabinet Office
Julia Lopez, MP *(Parliamentary Secretary)*
Home Office
Baroness Williams of Trafford *(Lords Minister)*
Treasury
Kemi Badenoch, MP *(Exchequer Secretary)*
John Glen, MP *(Economic Secretary)*

* Jointly held with DfT

GOVERNMENT WHIPS

HOUSE OF LORDS

Lords Chief Whip and Captain of the Honourable Corps of Gentlemen-at-Arms
Rt. Hon. Lord Ashton of Hyde
Deputy Chief Whip and Captain of the Queen's Bodyguard of the Yeomen of the Guard
Earl of Courtown
Lords-in-Waiting
Lord Parkinson of Whitley Bay
Viscount Younger of Leckie
Baronesses-in-Waiting
Baroness Bloomfield of Hinton Waldrist
Baroness Penn
Baroness Scott of Bybrook, OBE

HOUSE OF COMMONS

Chief Whip and Parliamentary Secretary to the Treasury
Rt. Hon. Mark Spencer, MP
Deputy Chief Whip and Treasurer of HM Household
Stuart Andrew, MP
Government Whip and Comptroller of HM Household
Mike Feer, MP
Government Whip and Vice-Chamberlain of HM Household
Marcus Jones, MP
Lords Commissioners of HM Treasury (Whips)
David Duguid, MP*; Rebecca Harris, MP; James Morris, MP; David Rutley, MP; Maggie Throup, MP; Michael Tomlinson, MP
Assistant Whips
Maria Caulfield, MP; Alex Chalk, MP; David Davies, MP†; Leo Docherty, MP; Nigel Huddleston, MP; Eddie Hughes, MP; Tom Pursglove, MP;

*Alongside role as Under-Secretary of State at the Scottish Office
† Alongside role as Under-Secretary of State at the Welsh Office
‡ Alongside role as Under-Secretary of State at the Ministry of Justice
§ Alongside role as Under-Secretary of State at DCMS

GOVERNMENT DEPARTMENTS

THE CIVIL SERVICE

The civil service helps the government develop and deliver its policies as effectively as possible. It works in three types of organisations – departments, executive agencies, and non-departmental government bodies (NDPBs). Under the Next Steps programme, launched in 1988, many semi-autonomous executive agencies were established to carry out much of the work of the civil service. Executive agencies operate within a framework set by the responsible minister which specifies policies, objectives and available resources. All executive agencies are set annual performance targets by their minister. Each agency has a chief executive, who is responsible for the day-to-day operations of the agency and who is accountable to the minister for the use of resources and for meeting the agency's targets. The minister accounts to parliament for the work of the agency.

There are currently 423,770 civil servants on a full-time equivalent (FTE) basis and 456,410 on a headcount basis. FTE is a measure that counts staff according to the proportion of full-time hours that they work. Almost three-quarters of all civil servants work outside London and the south-east. All government departments and executive agencies are responsible for their own pay and grading systems for civil servants outside the senior civil service.

SALARIES 2020–21

MINISTERIAL SALARIES
Ministers who are members of the House of Commons receive a parliamentary salary of £81,932 in addition to the ministerial salary.

Prime minister	£79,936
Cabinet minister (Commons)	£71,673
Cabinet minister (Lords)	£105,216
Minister of state (Commons)	£34,367
Minister of state (Lords)	£82,153
Parliamentary under-secretary (Commons)	£24,678
Parliamentary under-secretary (Lords)	£71,551

SPECIAL ADVISERS' SALARIES
Special advisers to government ministers are paid out of public funds; their salaries are negotiated individually, but are usually in the range of £57,000 to £145,000.

CIVIL SERVICE SALARIES	
Senior Civil Servants	
Permanent secretary	£150,000–£200,000
Band 3	£120,000–£208,100
Band 2	£93,000–£162,500
Band 1	£71,000–£117,800

Staff are placed in pay bands according to their level of responsibility and taking account of other factors such as experience and marketability. Movement within and between bands is based on performance.

GOVERNMENT DEPARTMENTS

For more information on government departments, *see* **W** www.gov.uk/government/organisations

ATTORNEY-GENERAL'S OFFICE
Attorney-General's Office, 120 Petty France, London SW1H 9EA
T 020-7271 2492 **E** correspondence@attorneygeneral.gov.uk
W www.gov.uk/government/organisations/attorney-generals-office

The law officers of the crown for England and Wales are the Attorney-General and the Solicitor-General. The Attorney-General, assisted by the Solicitor-General, is the chief legal adviser to the government and is also ultimately responsible for all crown litigation. They have overall responsibility for the work of the Law Officers' Departments (the Treasury Solicitor's Department, the Crown Prosecution Service – incorporating the Revenue and Customs Prosecutions Office – and the Serious Fraud Office, and HM Crown Prosecution Service Inspectorate). The Attorney-General also oversees the armed forces' prosecuting authority and the government legal service. They have a specific statutory duty to superintend the discharge of their duties by the Director of Public Prosecutions (who heads the Crown Prosecution Service) and the Director of the Serious Fraud Office. The Attorney-General has specific responsibilities for the enforcement of the criminal law and also performs certain public interest functions, for example protecting charities and appealing unduly lenient sentences. They also deal with questions of law arising in bills and with issues of legal policy.

Following the devolution of power to the Northern Ireland Assembly on 12 April 2010, the assembly now appoints the Attorney-General for Northern Ireland. The Attorney-General for England and Wales holds the office of Advocate-General for Northern Ireland, with significantly reduced responsibilities in Northern Ireland. The Attorney-General's Office is supported by four executive agencies and public bodies.

Attorney-General, Rt. Hon. Suella Braverman, QC, MP
Parliamentary Private Secretary, vacant
Principal Private Secretary, Josh Dodd
Deputy Principal Private Secretary, Samuel Chivers
Solicitor-General, Rt. Hon. Michael Ellis, QC, MP

MANAGEMENT BOARD
Director-General (Interim), Shehzad Charania, MBE
Deputy Legal Secretary and Head of Operations, Michelle Crotty

DEPARTMENT FOR BUSINESS, ENERGY AND INDUSTRIAL STRATEGY
1 Victoria Street, London SW1H 0ET
T 020-7215 5000 **E** enquiries@beis.gov.uk **W** www.gov.uk/government/organisations/department-for-business-energy-and-industrial-strategy

The Department for Business, Energy and Industrial Strategy (BEIS) was established in July 2016 following the appointment of Theresa May as prime minister. It merged the Department of Business, Innovation and Skills and the Department of Energy and Climate Change. BEIS brings together responsibilities for business, industrial strategy, science, innovation, energy and climate change, and is supported by 45 executive agencies and public bodies. It is responsible for: developing and delivering a comprehensive industrial strategy and leading the government's relationship with business; ensuring that the UK has secure, reliable, affordable and clean energy supplies; ensuring the UK remains at the forefront of science, research and innovation; and tackling climate change.

Secretary of State for Business, Energy and Industrial Strategy, Rt. Hon. Alok Sharma, MP
Parliamentary Private Secretary, Jo Gideon, MP
Special Advisers, Samantha Magnus; Marc Pooler
Minister of State, Rt. Hon. Kwasi Kwarteng, MP
Parliamentary Private Secretary, Mark Fletcher, MP
Parliamentary Under-Secretary of State, Lord Callanan (Climate Change and Corporate Responsibility)
Parliamentary Under-Secretary of State, Paul Scully, MP (Small Business, Consumers and Labour Markets)
Parliamentary Under-Secretary of State, Amanda Solloway, MP (Science, Research and Innovation)
Parliamentary Under-Secretary of State, Nadim Zahawi, MP (Business and Industry)
Minister for Investment, Lord Grimstone of Boscobel Kt*

* Jointly held with DfIT

MANAGEMENT BOARD
Permanent Secretary, Sarah Munby
Members, Julian Critchlow (Energy Transformation and Clean Growth); Ashley Ibbett (Trade, Europe and Analysis); Prof. Paul Monks (BEIS Chief Scientific Adviser); Jee Samant (Market Frameworks); Jo Shanmugalingam (Industrial Strategy, Science and Innovation); Doug Watkins (Corporate Services); Joanna Whittington (Energy and Security)
Non-Executive Members, Archie Norman (Lead); Nigel Boardman; Stephen Carter; Dame Carolyn McCall, DBE; Leena Nair; Kathryn Parsons; Stuart Quickenden
Special Representatives, Rt. Hon. Anne-Marie Trevelyan, MP (Adaptation and Resilience for COP26 Presidency)

BETTER REGULATION EXECUTIVE
1 Victoria Street, London SW1 0ET
T 020-7215 5000 E enquiries@beis.gov.uk
W www.gov.uk/government/policy-teams/better-regulation-executive

The Better Regulation Executive (BRE) is a joint BEIS/Cabinet Office unit which leads on delivering the government's manifesto commitment to reduce the overall burden on business, in order to increase growth and create jobs. Each government department is, however, responsible for delivering its part of the deregulation agenda within the framework put in place by the BRE.

Non-Executive Chair, Lord Curry of Kirkharle, CBE
Chief Executive, Graham Turnock

CABINET OFFICE
70 Whitehall, London SW1A 2AS
T 020-7276 1234
W www.gov.uk/government/organisations/cabinet-office

The Cabinet Office, alongside the Treasury, sits at the centre of the government, with an overarching purpose of making government work better. It supports the prime minister and the cabinet, helping to ensure effective development, coordination and implementation of policy and operations across all government departments. The Cabinet Office also leads work to ensure that the Civil Service provides the most effective and efficient support to the government to meet its objectives. The department is headed by the Minister for the Cabinet Office. The Cabinet Office is responsible for: supporting collective government; supporting the National Security Council and the Joint Intelligence Organisation, coordinating the government's response to crises and managing the UK's cyber security; promoting efficiency and reform across government through innovation, better procurement and project management, and by transforming the delivery of services; promoting the release of government data, and making the way government works more transparent; improving the capability and effectiveness of the Civil Service; and political constitution and reform.

The priorities of the Cabinet Office include: supporting the prime minister and cabinet to deliver the government's programme; driving efficiencies and reforms to improve the government's performance; creating a more united democracy; and strengthening and securing the UK at home and abroad. The Cabinet Office employs around 8,800 staff and is supported by 23 executive agencies and public bodies.

Prime Minister, First Lord of the Treasury, Minister for the Union and Minister for the Civil Service, Rt. Hon. Boris Johnson, MP
Parliamentary Private Secretaries, Alex Burghart, MP; Trudy Harrison, MP
Principal Private Secretary, Martin Reynolds, CMG
Chief of Staff, Baron Ed Udny-Lister
Special Advisers (Senior), Nikki Da Costa (Legislative Affairs); David Frost, CMG (Europe); Andrew Griffith, MP (Business); Oliver Lewis; Munira Mirza (Policy)
Chancellor of the Duchy of Lancaster and Minister for the Cabinet Office, Rt. Hon. Michael Gove, MP
Parliamentary Private Secretary, Kevin Hollinrake, MP
Special Advisers, Josh Grimstone; Henry Newman; Charlie Rowley
Lord President of the Council, Rt. Hon. Jacob Rees-Mogg, MP
Parliamentary Private Secretary, Lucy Allan, MP
Special Advisers, Fred de Frossard; Beatrice Timpson
Lord Privy Seal and Leader of the House of Lords, Rt. Hon Baroness Evans of Bowed Park
Parliamentary Private Secretary, Christ Green, MP
Special Advisers, Annabelle Eyre; James Price; Hannah Ellis; Yasmin Kalhori
Minister without Portfolio, Rt. Hon. Amanda Milling, MP
Paymaster-General, Rt. Hon. Penny Mordaunt, MP
Minister of State, Chloe Smith, MP (Constitution and Devolution)
Minister of State, Lord Agnew (Efficiency and Transformation)*
Minister of State, Lord True, CBE
Parliamentary Under-Secretary of State, Johnny Mercer, MP (Minister for Defence, People and Veterans)†
Parliamentary Secretary, Julia Lopez, MP

*Jointly held with the Treasury
† Jointly held with the MoD

MANAGEMENT BOARD
Cabinet Secretary and Head of the Civil Service, Simon Case, CVO
Permanent Secretary and Chief Operating Officer for the Civil Service, Alex Chisholm
First Parliamentary Counsel, Elizabeth Gardiner, CB, QC
Chair of the Joint Intelligence Committee, Sir Simon Gass, KCMG, CVO
Chief People Officer, Rupert McNeil
Government Chief Commercial Officer, Gareth Rhys Williams
Executive Director, Government Communications, Alex Aiken
Prime Minister's International Affairs Adviser, Deputy National Security Adviser, David Quarrey, CMG
Director-General, UK Governance, Lucy Smith
Director-General, Government Property, Mike Parsons
Chief Security Officer, Dominic Fortescue
Director-General, Government Digital Service (Interim), Fiona Deans
Chief Executive, Infrastructure and Projects Authority, Nick Smallwood

Director-General, Government Service, Kevin Cunnington
Deputy National Security Adviser, Alex Ellis
Deputy Cabinet Secretary, Helen MacNamara
Lead Non-Executive Board Member, Rt. Hon. Gisela Stuart
Non-Executive Board Members, Anand Aithal; Mike Ashley; Karen Blackett, OBE; Henry De Zoete; Baroness Finn; Lord Hogan-Howe

SPECIAL REPRESENTATIVE
Kevin Cunnington *(Digital Envoy for the UK)**

*Alongside role as Director-General, International Government Service

HONOURS AND APPOINTMENTS BOARD
Room G-39, Horse Guards Road, London SW1A 2HQ
T 020-7276 2777
Chair, Simon Case, CVO

OFFICE OF THE LEADER OF THE HOUSE OF COMMONS
70 Whitehall, London SW1A 2AS
T 020-7276 1005 E commonsleader@cabinetoffice.gov.uk
W www.gov.uk/government/organisations/
the-office-of-the-leader-of-the-house-of-commons

The Office of the Leader of the House of Commons is responsible for the arrangement of government business in the House of Commons and for planning and supervising the government's legislative programme. The Leader of the House of Commons upholds the rights and privileges of the house and acts as a spokesperson for the government as a whole.

The leader reports regularly to the cabinet on parliamentary business and the legislative programme. In their capacity as leader of the house, they are a member of the House of Commons Commission. They also chair the cabinet committee on the legislative programme. As Lord President of the Council, they are a member of the cabinet and in charge of the Office of the Privy Council.

The Deputy Leader of the House of Commons supports the leader in handling the government's business in the house. They are responsible for monitoring MPs' and peers' correspondence.

Lord President of the Privy Council and Leader of the House of Commons, Rt. Hon. Jacob Rees-Mogg, MP
Parliamentary Private Secretary, Lucy Allan, MP
Special Advisers, Fred de Frossard; Beatrice Timpson

OFFICE OF THE LEADER OF THE HOUSE OF LORDS
Room 20, Principal Floor, West Front, House of Lords, London SW1A 0PW
T 020-7219 3200 E psleaderofthelords@cabinetoffice.gov.uk
W www.gov.uk/government/organisations/
office-of-the-leader-of-the-house-of-lords

The Office of the Leader of the House of Lords provides support to the leader in their parliamentary and ministerial duties, which include leading the government benches in the House of Lords; the delivery of the government's business in the Lords; taking part in formal ceremonies such as the state opening of parliament; and giving guidance to the House of Lords on matters of procedure and order.

Lord Privy Seal and Leader of the House of Lords, Rt. Hon. Baroness Evans of Bowes Park
Parliamentary Private Secretary, Chris Green, MP
Special Advisers, Annabelle Eyre *(Senior)*; Hannah Ellis; Yasmin Kalhori; James Price
Deputy Leader of the House of Lords, Rt. Hon. Earl Howe

PRIME MINISTER'S OFFICE
10 Downing Street, London SW1A 2AA
W www.gov.uk/government/organisations/
prime-ministers-office-10-downing-street

Prime Minister, Rt. Hon. Boris Johnson, MP
Parliamentary Private Secretaries, Alex Burghart, MP; Trudy Harrison, MP
Principal Private Secretary, Martin Reynolds, CMG
Chief of Staff, Baron Ed Udny-Lister
Special Advisers (Senior), Nikki Da Costa *(Legislative Affairs)*; David Frost, CMG *(Europe)*; Andrew Griffith, MP *(Business)*; Oliver Lewis; Munira Mirza *(Policy)*
Special Advisers, Rosie Bate-Williams; Hugh Bennett; Henry Cook; Jack Doyle; Lucia Hodgson; Ben Gascoigne; Sophie Lis; Damon Poole; Chloe Sarfaty; Sophia True; Cleo Watson; Chloe Westley
Director of Communications, vacant
Prime Minister's Official Spokesman, James Slack, CBE
Prime Minister's Official Speech Writer, Alex Marklew
Press Secretary, Allegra Stratton
Head of Operations, Shelley Williams-Walker
Head of Implementation Unit, Jonathan Nancekivell-Smith
Research and Briefing, Declan Lyons; Marcus Natale; Sheridan Westlake

PRIVATE OFFICES GROUP
Director-General, Propriety and Ethics and Head of Private Offices Group, vacant

UK GOVERNANCE GROUP
Head of UK Governance, Lucy Smith

CABINET OFFICE CORPORATE SERVICES
Executive Director, Government Communications, Alex Aiken
Chief Financial Officer, Richard Hornby
Human Resources Director, Jo Rodrigues

NATIONAL SECURITY
Comprises the National Security Secretariat and the Joint Intelligence Organisation. The National Security Secretariat is responsible for providing policy advice to the National Security Council, where ministers discuss national security issues at a strategic level; coordinating and developing foreign and defence policy across government; coordinating policy, ethical and legal issues across the intelligence community, managing its funding and priorities, and dealing with the Intelligence and Security Committee which calls it to account; developing effective protective security policies and capabilities for government; improving the UK's resilience to respond to and recover from emergencies, and maintaining facilities for the effective coordination of government response to crises; and providing strategic leadership for cyber security in the UK, in line with the National Cyber Security Strategy.

NATIONAL SECURITY SECRETARIAT
Chief Security Officer, Dominic Fortescue
Deputy National Security Advisers, Alex Ellis; David Quarrey, CMG

JOINT INTELLIGENCE ORGANISATION
Chair of the Joint Intelligence Committee, Sir Simon Gass, KCMG, CVO

INDEPENDENT OFFICES

CIVIL SERVICE COMMISSION
1 Horse Guards Road, London SW1A 2HQ
T 020-7271 0831
W www.civilservicecommission.independent.gov.uk

The Civil Service Commission regulates the requirement that selection for appointment to the Civil Service must be on merit on the basis of fair and open competition; the commission publishes its recruitment principles and audit departments and agencies' performance against these. Commissioners personally chair competitions for the most senior jobs in the civil service. In addition, the commission hears complaints from civil servants under the Civil Service Code.

The commission was established as a statutory body in November 2010 under the provisions of the Constitutional Reform and Governance Act 2010.

Commissioners, Jane Burgess; Jan Cameron; Natalie Campbell; Isabel Doverty; Margaret Edwards; Rosie Glazebrook; Sarah Laessig; June Milligan; Joe Montgomery; Ian Watmore; Kevin Woods

THE COMMISSIONER FOR PUBLIC APPOINTMENTS
G/8, 1 Horse Guards Road, London SW1A 2HQ
T 020-7271 6729 E publicappointments@csc.gov.uk
W http://publicappointmentscommissioner.independent.gov.uk

The Commissioner for Public Appointments is responsible for monitoring, regulating and reporting on ministerial appointments (including those made by Welsh government ministers) to public bodies. The commissioner can investigate complaints about the way in which appointments were made.

Commissioner for Public Appointments, Peter Riddell
Chief Executive Commission Secretariat, Peter Lawrence, OBE

OFFICE OF THE PARLIAMENTARY COUNSEL
1 Horse Guards Road, London SW1A 2HQ
T 02-7276 6586 E opc@cabinetoffice.gov.uk W www.gov.uk/government/organisations/office-of-the-parliamentary-counsel

The Office of the Parliamentary Counsel is a group of government lawyers who specialise in drafting government bills; advising departments on the rules and procedures of Parliament; reviewing orders and regulations which amend Acts of Parliament; and assisting the government on a range of legal and constitutional issues.

Parliamentary Counsel, Elizabeth Gardiner

GOVERNMENT EQUALITIES OFFICE
Sanctuary Buildings, 16–20 Great Smith Street, London SW1P 3BT
T 0808-800 0082 W www.gov.uk/government/organisations/government-equalities-office

The Government Equalities Office (GEO) is responsible for the government's overall strategy on equality. Its work includes leading the development of a more integrated approach on equality across government with the aim of improving equality and reducing discrimination and disadvantage for all. The office is also responsible for leading policy on gender equality, sexual orientation and transgender equality matters.

Minister for Women and Equalities, Rt. Hon. Elizabeth Truss, MP*
Parliamentary Under-Secretary of State, Kemi Badenoch *(Equalities)†*
Parliamentary Under-Secretary of State, Baroness Berridge of the Vale of Catmose *(Women)†*
Director (Interim), Elysia McCaffrey

* Alongside role as Secretary of State for International Trade and President of the Board of Trade
† Alongside role as Under-Secretary of State for the School System in the DfE

MINISTRY OF DEFENCE
Main Building, Whitehall, London SW1A 2HB
T 020-7218 9000 W www.gov.uk/government/organisations/ministry-of-defence

For further information on the responsibilities and remit of the MoD *see* the Defence Chapter.

Secretary of State for Defence, Rt. Hon. Ben Wallace, MP
Parliamentary Private Secretary, Jack Brereton, MP
Special Adviser, Peter Quentin
Minister of State, Baroness Goldie *(Lords)*
Minister of State, Jeremy Quin, MP *(Defence Procurement)*
Parliamentary Under-Secretary of State and Minister for Armed Forces, James Heappey, MP
Parliamentary Under-Secretary of State and Minister for Defence People and Veterans, Johnny Mercer, MP*

*Jointly held with the Cabinet Office

SENIOR MILITARY OFFICIALS
Chief of the Defence Staff, Gen. Sir Nick Carter, GCB, CBE, DSO, ADC Gen
Vice-Chief of the Defence Staff, Adm. Sir Tim Fraser, KCB, ADC
Chief of Naval Staff and First Sea Lord, Adm. Tony Radakin, CB, ADC
Chief of the General Staff, Gen. Sir Mark Carleton-Smith, KCB, CBE, ADC Gen
Chief of the Air Staff, Air Chief Marshal Mike Wigston, CBE, ADC
Commander of Joint Forces Command, Gen. Sir Patrick Sanders, KCB, CBE, DSO, ADC Gen
Deputy Commander of Strategic Command, Lt.-Gen. Rob Magowan, CB, CBE

MANAGEMENT BOARD
Permanent Secretary, Sir Stephen Lovegrove, KCB
Members, Mike Baker, CBE *(Chief Operating Officer);* Lt.-Gen. Doug Chalmers *(Deputy Chief of Defence Staff (Military Strategy and Operations));* Charlie Forte *(Chief Information Officer);* Prof. Robin Grimes, FRS, FRENG *(Chief Scientific Adviser (Nuclear));* Air Marshal Richard Knighton *(Deputy Chief of the Defence Staff (Financial and Military Capability));* Angus Lapsley *(Strategy and International);* Prof. Dame Angela McLean, DBE *(Chief Scientific Adviser);* Vanessa Nicholls *(Nuclear);* Charlie Pate *(Finance);* Maj.-Gen. James Swift *(Chief of Defence People);* Dominic Wilson *(Security Policy)*
Non-Executive Members, Brian McBride *(Lead);* Danuta Gray; Simon Henry; Robin Marshall

DEPARTMENT FOR DIGITAL, CULTURE, MEDIA AND SPORT
100 Parliament Street, London SW1A 2BQ
E enquiries@culture.gov.uk W www.gov.uk/government/organisations/department-for-digital-culture-media-sport

The Department for Digital, Culture, Media and Sport (DCMS) was established in July 1997 (as the Department for Culture, Media and Sport) and aims to improve the quality of life for all those in the UK through cultural and sporting activities while championing the tourism, creative and leisure industries. It is responsible for government policy relating to the arts, sport, the National Lottery, tourism, libraries, museums and galleries, broadcasting, creative industries – including film and the music industry – press freedom and regulation, licensing, gambling, the historic environment, telecommunications and online and media ownership and mergers. In July 2017, the department was rebranded to reflect its growing commitment and responsibility regarding digital infrastructure, communication and cyber security.

The department is also responsible for 45 agencies and public bodies that help deliver the department's strategic aims and objectives, the listing of historic buildings and scheduling of ancient monuments, the export licensing of cultural goods, and the management of the Government Art Collection and the Royal Historic Palaces. It has the responsibility for humanitarian assistance in the event of a disaster, as well as for the organisation of the annual Remembrance Day ceremony at the Cenotaph.

Secretary of State for Digital, Culture, Media and Sport, Rt. Hon. Oliver Dowden, CBE, MP

Special Advisers, Jamie Njoku-Goodwin; Lucy Noakes; Mike Crowhurst

Minister of State, Caroline Dinenage, MP *(Digital and Culture)*

Minister of State, Rt. Hon. John Whittingdale, OBE, MP *(Media and Data)*

Parliamentary Under-Secretary of State, Baroness Barran, MBE *(Civil Society)*

Parliamentary Under-Secretary of State, Nigel Huddlestone, MP *(Sport, Tourism and Heritage)**

Parliamentary Under-Secretary of State, Matt Warman, MP *(Digital Infrastructure)*

*Alongside role as Assistant Whip

MANAGEMENT BOARD

Permanent Secretary, Sarah Healey

Members, Clare Dove, CBE *(Voluntary, Community and Social Enterprise Representative);* Jacinda Humphry *(Finance and Commercial Director)* Helen Judge *(Culture, Sport and Civil Society);* Sam Lister *(Strategy and Operations);* Neil Mendoza *(Cultural Recovery and Renewal);* Prof. Tom Rodden *(Chief Scientific Adviser);* Susannah Storey *(Digital and Media);*

Non-Executive Members, Charles Alexander *(Lead);* Sherry Coutu, CBE; Hermant Patel; Baroness Laura Wyld

DEPARTMENT FOR EDUCATION

Piccadilly Gate, Store Street, Manchester M1 2WD
T 0370-000 2288 **W** www.gov.uk/government/organisations/department-for-education

The Department for Education (DfE) was established in May 2010 in place of the Department for Children, Schools and Families (DCSF), in order to refocus the department on its core purpose of supporting teaching and learning. The department is responsible for education and children's services, while the Department for Business, Energy and Industrial Strategy is responsible for higher education. The DfE is supported by 18 executive agencies and public bodies.

The department's objectives include keeping pace with academic standards as measured internationally, and improving technical education in line with international systems.

Secretary of State for Education, Rt. Hon. Gavin Williamson, CBE, MP

Parliamentary Private Secretary, Scott Mann, MP

Special Advisers, Iain Mansfield; Innes Taylor; Angus Walker

Minister of State, Rt. Hon. Nick Gibb, MP *(School Standards)*

Minister of State, Michelle Donelan, MP *(Universities)*

Parliamentary Under-Secretary of State, Baroness Berridge of The Vale of Catmose *(School System)*

Parliamentary Under-Secretary of State, Vicky Ford, MP *(Children and Families)*

Parliamentary Under-Secretary of State, Gillian Keegan, MP *(Apprenticeships and Skills)*

* Jointly held with the DfIT

MANAGEMENT BOARD

Permanent Secretary, Susan Acland-Hood

Members, Mike Green *(Chief Operating Officer, Operations Group);* Paul Kett *(Higher and Further Education Group);*

Andrew McCully, CB, CBE *(Early Years and Schools);* Elaine Milner *(ex officio);* Indra Morris *(Social Care, Mobility and Disadvantage);* Lucy Smith *(COVID-19 Response and Schools Recovery)*

Non-Executive Members, Richard Pennycook *(Lead);* Ian Ferguson, CBE; Irene Lucas; Baroness Ruby McGregor-Smith, CBE; Toby Peyton-Jones; Nick Timothy, CBE

DEPARTMENT FOR ENVIRONMENT, FOOD AND RURAL AFFAIRS

Seacole Building, 2 Marsham Street, London SW1P 4DF
T 03459-335577 **E** defra.helpline@defra.gov.uk
W www.gov.uk/government/organisations/department-for-environment-food-rural-affairs

The Department for Environment, Food and Rural Affairs (DEFRA) is responsible for government policy on the environment, rural matters and farming and food production. In association with the agriculture departments of the Scottish government, the National Assembly for Wales and the Northern Ireland Office, the department is responsible for helping negotiating the grounds for Britain's exit from the EU. Its remit includes international agricultural and food trade policy.

The department's strategic priorities are a smooth exit from the EU; climate change adaptation; the protection of natural resources and the countryside; and sustainable rural communities. DEFRA, which is supported by 33 executive agencies and public bodies, is also the lead government department for responding to emergencies in animal and plant diseases, flooding, food and water supply, dealing with the consequences of a chemical, biological, radiological or nuclear incident, and other threats to the environment.

Secretary of State for Environment, Food and Rural Affairs, Rt. Hon. George Eustice, MP

Parliamentary Private Secretary, Caroline Ansell, MP

Special Adviser, Emma Pryor

Minister of State, Rt. Hon. Zac Goldsmith, MP *(Pacific and the Environment)**

Parliamentary Under-Secretary of State, Lord Gardiner of Kimble *(Rural Affairs and Biosecurity)*

Parliamentary Under-Secretary of State, Rebecca Pow, MP

Parliamentary Under-Secretary of State, Victoria Prentis, MP

* Jointly held with the FCDO

MANAGEMENT BOARD

Permanent Secretary, Tamara Finkelstein

Members, Prof. Gideon Henderson *(Chief Scientific Adviser);* David Hill *(Environment, Rural and Marine);* Sarah Homer *(Chief Operating Officer);* Emma Howard Boyd *(ex officio);* Tony Juniper, CBE *(ex officio);* David Kennedy *(Food, Farming and Biosecurity);* James Quinault *(Europe, International and Constitution Group)*

Non-Executive Members, Henry Dimbleby *(Lead);* Elizabeth Buchanan; Colin Day; Ben Goldsmith; Lizzie Noel

FOREIGN, COMMONWEALTH AND DEVELOPMENT OFFICE

King Charles Street, London SW1A 2AH
T 020-7008 5000 **E** fcdo.correspondence@fcdo.gov.uk
W www.gov.uk/government/organisations/foreign-commonwealth-development-office

The Foreign, Commonwealth and Development Office (FCDO) was formed in September 2020 from a merger between the Foreign and Commonwealth Office and the Department for International Development ahead of the UK's presidency of the G7 and COP26 in 2021. It provides the means of communication between the British government and other governments – and international governmental organisations – on all matters falling within the field of international relations and development. The FCDO employs over 17,300 people in 280 places across the world through a network of embassies, consulates, and development programmes that help to protect and promote national interests. FCO diplomats are skilled in understanding and influencing what is happening abroad, supporting British citizens who are travelling and living overseas, helping to manage migration into Britain, promoting British trade and other interests abroad and encouraging foreign investment in the UK.

The FCDO is responsible for promoting sustainable development and reducing poverty, and honouring the UK's international commitments including the United Nations' Sustainable Development Goals. It aims to make British overseas aid more effective by improving transparency and value for money; focusing British international development policy on economic growth and wealth creation; improving the coherence and performance of British development policy in fragile and conflict-affected countries; improving the lives of girls and women through better education, greater choice on family planning and preventing violence; and acting on climate change and encouraging adaptation and low-carbon growth in developing countries. It provides regional and national programmes throughout the world, including in dependent UK Overseas Territories, and gives UK Aid through multi-country global programmes and multilateral institutions like the World Bank and United Nations. The FCDO is supported by 12 executive agencies and public bodies.

Secretary of State for Foreign, Commonwealth and Development Affairs, First Secretary of State, Rt. Hon. Dominic Raab, MP
Parliamentary Private Secretary, Gareth Johnson, MP
Special Advisers, Beth Armstrong; Simon Finkelstien
Minister of State, Nigel Adams, MP *(Asia)*
Minister of State, Lord Ahmad of Wimbledon *(South Asia and the Commonwealth)*
Minister of State, Rt. Hon. James Cleverly, MP *(Middle East and North Africa)*
Minister of State, Rt. Hon. Lord Zac Goldsmith *(Pacific and the Environment)**
Parliamentary Under-Secretary of State, James Duddridge, MP *(Africa)*
Parliamentary Under-Secretary of State, Wendy Morton, MP *(European Neighbourhood and the Americas)*

* Jointly held with DEFRA

SPECIAL REPRESENTATIVES
Lord Ahmad of Wimbledon *(Prime Minister's Special Representative on Preventing Sexual Violence in Conflict);* Gareth Bayley *(Afghanistan and Pakistan);* Nick Bridge *(Climate Change);* Nick Dyer *(Special Envoy for Famine Prevention and Humanitarian Affairs);* Robert Fairweather, OBE *(Sudan and South Sudan);* Philip Parham *(Commonwealth);* Rt. Hon. Lord Pickles *(UK Special Envoy for Post-Holocaust Issues);* Jennifer Townson *(Migration and Modern Slavery Envoy);* Rt. Hon. Marie-Trevelyan, MP *(Adaptation and Resilience for COP26 Presidency)*

MANAGEMENT BOARD
Permanent Under-Secretary, Sir Philip Barton, KCMG, OBE
Political Director, Sir Tim Barrow, GCMG, LVO, MBE
Members, Jenny Bates *(Indo-Pacific);* Juliet Chua *(Finance and Corporate);* Thomas Drew, CMG *(Middle East, North Africa, Afghanistan and Pakistan);* Dr Rachel Glennerster *(Chief Economist);* Nic Hailey, CMG *(Transformation);* Kumar Iyer *(Delivery);* Sir Iain Macleod, KCMG *(Legal);* Moazzam Malik *(Africa);* Vijay Rangarajan *(Americas and Overseas Territories)*
Non-Executive Members, Baroness Helena Morrissey *(Lead);* John Coffey; Ann Cormack, MBE; Beverley Tew

CDC GROUP
123 Victoria Street, London SW1E 6DE
T 020-7963 4700 E enquiries@cdcgroup.com
W www.cdcgroup.com

Founded in 1948, CDC is the UK's Development Finance Institution wholly owned by the UK government. It invests to create jobs and build businesses in developing countries in Africa and South Asia. In 2019 CDC's new investment commitments totalled £1.66bn to 690 businesses in Africa and 377 businesses in South Asia, helping to create new jobs across these regions. CDC is a public limited company with a portfolio worth £4.7bn.

Chair, Sir Graham Wrigley
Chief Executive, Nick O'Donohoe

DEPARTMENT OF HEALTH AND SOCIAL CARE
39 Victoria Street, London SW1H 0EU
T 020-7210 4850 W www.gov.uk/government/organisations/department-of-health-and-social-care

The Department of Health and Social Care (DHSC) leads, shapes and funds health and social care in England, making sure people have the support, care and treatment they need and that this is delivered in a compassionate, respectful and dignified manner.

The DHSC leads across health and care by creating national policies and legislation to meet current and future challenges. It provides funding, assures the delivery and continuity of services and accounts to parliament in a way that represents the best interests of patients, the public and the taxpayer. The DHSC is supported by 29 executive agencies and public bodies.

Secretary of State for Health and Social Care, Rt. Hon. Matthew Hancock, MP
Parliamentary Private Secretary, Steve Double, MP
Special Advisers, Emma Dean; Allan Nixon; Ed Taylor
Minister of State, Edward Argar, MP *(Health)*
Minister of State, Nadine Dorries, MP *(Patient Safety, Suicide Prevention and Mental Health)*
Minister of State, Helen Whately, MP *(Care)*
Parliamentary Under-Secretary of State, Lord Bethell of Romford *(Innovation)*
Parliamentary Under-Secretary of State, Jo Churchill, MP *(Prevention, Public Health and Primary Care)*

DEPARTMENTAL BOARD
Permanent Secretary, Sir Chris Wormald, KCB
Members, Matthew Gould *(CEO of NHSX);* Jonathan Marron *(Community and Social Care);* Lee McDonough *(Acute Care and Workforce);* Clara Swinson *(Global and Public Health);* Prof. Chris Whitty *(Chief Scientific Adviser, Chief Medical Officer);* David Williams *(Second Permanent Secretary, Finance and Group Operations)*

SPECIAL REPRESENTATIVES
Prof. Dame Sally Davies, DBE *(UK Special Envoy on Antimicrobial Resistance)*

HOME OFFICE
2 Marsham Street, London SW1P 4DF
T 020-7035 4848 **E** public.enquiries@homeoffice.gov.uk
W www.gov.uk/government/organisations/home-office

The Home Office deals with those internal affairs in England and Wales which have not been assigned to other government departments. The Secretary of State for the Home Department is the link between the Queen and the public, and exercises certain powers on her behalf, including that of the royal pardon.

The Home Office aims to build a safe, just and tolerant society and to maintain and enhance public security and protection; to support and mobilise communities so that they are able to shape policy and improvement for their locality, overcome nuisance and anti-social behaviour, maintain and enhance social cohesion and enjoy their homes and public spaces peacefully; to deliver departmental policies and responsibilities fairly, effectively and efficiently; and to make the best use of resources. These objectives reflect the priorities of the government and the home secretary in areas of crime, citizenship and communities, namely to work on the problems caused by illegal drug use; shape the alcohol strategy, policy and licensing conditions; keep the UK safe from the threat of terrorism; reduce and prevent crime, and ensure people feel safe in their homes and communities; secure the UK border and control immigration; consider applications to enter and stay in the UK; issue passports and visas; to support visible, responsible and accountable policing by empowering the public and freeing up the police to fight crime; and oversee the fire and rescue services.

The Home Office delivers these aims through the immigration services, its 30 executive agencies and non-departmental public bodies, and by working with partners in private, public and voluntary sectors, individuals and communities. The home secretary is also the link between the UK government and the governments of the Channel Islands and the Isle of Man.

Secretary of State for the Home Department, Rt. Hon. Priti Patel, MP
Parliamentary Private Secretary, Mike Wood, MP
Special Advisers, Hannah Guerin; Harry Methley; Charlotte Miller; Michael Young
Minister of State, Rt. Hon. James Brokenshire, CBE, MP *(Security)*
Minister of State, Lord Stephen Greenhalgh *(Building Safety and Communities)**
Minister of State, Kit Malthouse, MP *(Crime and Policing)*†
Minister of State, Baroness Williams of Trafford *(Lords)*
Parliamentary Under-Secretary of State, Victoria Atkins, MP *(Safeguarding)*
Parliamentary Under-Secretary of State, Kevin Foster, MP *(Future Borders and Immigration)*
Parliamentary Under-Secretary of State, Chris Philp, MP *(Immigration Compliance and the Courts)*†

* Jointly held with the MHCLG
† Jointly held with the MoJ

MANAGEMENT BOARD
Permanent Secretary, Sir Matthew Rycroft, CBE
Second Permanent Secretary, Shona Dunn
Members, Simon Baugh *(Communications);* Joanna Davinson *(Chief Digital, Data and Technology Officer);* Charu Gorasia *(Capabilities and Resources);* Jill Hatcher *(Chief People Officer);* Tricia Hayes *(Crime, Policing and Fire);* Tyson Hepple *(Immigration Enforcement);* Tom Hurd *(Security and Counter-Terrorism);* Julia Kinniburgh *(Serious and Organised Crime Group);* Paul Lincoln *(Border Force);* Marc Owen, OBE *(Visas and Citizenship);* Abi Tierney *(UK Visas and Immigration, Her Majesty's Passport Office);* Glyn Williams, CB *(Borders, Immigration and Citizenship)*
Non-Executive Members, Sue Langley, OBE *(Lead);* James Cooper; Michael Fuller, QPM; Suzy Levy; John Paton; Tim Robinson; Phil Swallow

MINISTRY OF HOUSING, COMMUNITIES AND LOCAL GOVERNMENT
2 Marsham Street, London SW1P 4DF
T 0303-444 0000 **W** www.gov.uk/government/organisations/ministry-of-housing-communities-and-local-government

The Ministry of Housing, Communities and Local Government was formed in January 2018 uniting housing, communities and civil renewal functions with responsibility for regeneration, neighbourhood renewal and local government. The ministry is tasked with increasing the national housing supply and home ownership; supporting public services; and devolving power and budgets to boost local growth in England. The ministry is supported by 12 executive agencies and public bodies.

Secretary of State for Housing, Communities and Local Government, Rt. Hon. Robert Jenrick, MP
Parliamentary Private Secretary, Andrea Jenkyns, MP
Special Advisers, Olivia Oates; Tom Kennedy
Minister of State, Luke Hall, MP *(Regional Growth and Local Government)*
Minister of State, Rt. Hon. Christopher Pincher, MP *(Housing)*
Parliamentary Under-Secretary of State, Lord Stephen Greenhalgh *(Building Safety and Communities)**
Parliamentary Under-Secretary of State, Kelly Tolhurst, MP *(Rough Sleeping and Housing)*

* Jointly held with the Home Office

MANAGEMENT BOARD
Permanent Secretary, Jeremy Pocklington
Members, Ruth Bailey *(People Capability and Change);* Lise-Anne Boissiere *(Strategy, Communications and Private Office);* Catherine Frances *(Local Government and Public Services);* Emran Mian *(Decentralisation and Growth);* Prof. Alan Penn *(Chief Scientific Adviser);* Matt Thurstan *(Chief Financial Officer);* Chris Townsend *(Shielding Programme);* Tracey Waltho *(Housing and Planning)*
Non-Executive Members, Michael Jary *(Lead);* Pam Chesters, CBE; Dame Mary Ney, DBE

SPECIAL REPRESENTATIVES
UK Special Envoy for Post-Holocaust Issues, Rt. Hon. Lord Pickles

DEPARTMENT FOR INTERNATIONAL TRADE
King Charles Street, Whitehall, London SW1A 2AH
T 020-7215 5000 **W** www.gov.uk/government/organisations/department-for-international-trade

The Department for International Trade was formed in July 2016 following the UK referendum to leave the European Union. The department is responsible for promoting British trade and investment around the world, striking and extending trade agreements between the UK and non-EU states.

Secretary of State for International Trade and President of the Board of Trade, Rt. Hon. Elizabeth Truss, MP
Parliamentary Private Secretary, Saqib Bhatti, MP
Special Advisers, Sophie Jarvis; Adam Jones
Minister of State, Rt. Hon. Greg Hands, MP *(Trade Policy)*
Minister for Investment, Lord Grimstone of Boscobel Kt*
Parliamentary Under-Secretary of State, Kemi Badenoch, MP *(Equalities)*†

Parliamentary Under-Secretary of State, Baroness Berridge of the Vale of Catmose *(Women)*‡

Parliamentary Under-Secretary of State, Ranil Jayawardena, MP *(International Trade)*

Parliamentary Under-Secretary of State, Graham Stuart, MP *(Exports)*§

* Jointly held with the DBEIS
† Alongside role as Exchequer Secretary to the Treasury
‡ Alongside role as Under-Secretary of State for the School System in DfE
§ Jointly held with UK Export Finance

MANAGEMENT BOARD

Permanent Secretary, Antonia Romeo
Second Permanent Secretary and Chief Trade Negotiation Adviser, Crawford Falconer
Members, John Alty *(Trade Policy);* John Mahon *(Exports);* Mark Slaughter *(Investment);* Louis Taylor *(UK Export Finance);* Catherine Vaughan *(Chief Operating Officer)*
Non-Executive Members, Julie Currie, Noel Harwerth, Sir Stephen O'Brien

MINISTRY OF JUSTICE

102 Petty France, London SW1H 9AJ
T 020-3334 3555
W www.gov.uk/government/organisations/ministry-of-justice

The Ministry of Justice (MoJ) was established in May 2007. MoJ is headed by the Lord Chancellor and Secretary of State for Justice who is responsible for improvements to the justice system so that it better serves the public. They are also responsible for some areas of constitutional policy.

The MoJ's key priorities are to reduce reoffending by using the skills of the public, private and voluntary sectors; build a prison and probation service that delivers maximum value for money; to promote the rule of law globally; and to modernise the courts and justice system. The MoJ has a budget of around £10bn and is supported by 34 executive agencies and public bodies to achieve its targets.

The Lord Chancellor and Secretary of State for Justice is the government minister responsible to parliament for the judiciary, the court system and prisons and probation. The Lord Chief Justice has been the head of the judiciary since 2006.

MoJ incorporates HM Prison and Probation Service; HM Courts and Tribunals Service; the Legal Aid Agency; and the Youth Justice Board.

Lord Chancellor and Secretary of State for Justice, Rt. Hon. Robert Buckland, QC, MP
Parliamentary Private Secretary, Neil O'Brien, MP
Special Advisers, Ben Jafari; Rajiv Shah; Alex Wild
Minister of State, Kit Malthouse, QC, MP *(Crime and Policing)**
Parliamentary Under-Secretary of State, Alex Chalk, MP†
Parliamentary Under-Secretary of State, Chris Philp, MP *(Immigration Compliance and the Courts)**
HM Advocate-General for Scotland, Keith Stewart, QC

* Jointly held with the Home Office
† Alongside role as Assistant Whip

MANAGEMENT BOARD

Permanent Secretary (Interim), Mike Driver
Members, Susan Acland-Hood *(Chief Executive and Board member, HM Courts and Tribunals Service);* Phil Copple *(Prisons);* Jo Farrar *(Chief Executive Officer, HM Prison and Probation Service);* Naomi Mallick *(Legal);* James McEwen *(Interim Chief Financial Officer, Director General of CFO Group);* Amy Rees *(Probation and Wales);* Dr Neil Wooding *(Chief People Officer)*
Non-Executive Members, Mark Rawlinson *(Lead);* Nick Campsie; Shirley Cooper; Paul Smith

NORTHERN IRELAND OFFICE

1 Horse Guards Road, London SW1A 2HQ
Stormont House, Stormont Estate, Belfast BT4 3SH
T 028-9052 0700 **E** comms@nio.gov.uk
W www.gov.uk/government/organisations/northern-ireland-office

The Northern Ireland Office was established in 1972, when the Northern Ireland (Temporary Provisions) Act transferred the legislative and executive powers of the Northern Ireland parliament and government to the UK parliament and a secretary of state. Under the terms of the 1998 Good Friday Agreement, power was devolved to the Northern Ireland Assembly in 1999. The assembly took on responsibility for the relevant areas of work previously undertaken by the departments of the Northern Ireland Office, covering agriculture and rural development, the environment, regional development, social development, education, higher education, training and employment, enterprise, trade and investment, culture, arts and leisure, health, social services, public safety and finance and personnel. In October 2002 the Northern Ireland Assembly was suspended and Northern Ireland returned to direct rule, but despite repeated setbacks, devolution was restored in May 2007. In January 2017 Martin McGuinness resigned as Deputy First Minister of Northern Ireland. Under the joint protocols that govern the power-sharing agreement, which requires the government to be comprised of both unionists and nationalists, if either the first minister or the deputy resigns and a replacement is not nominated by the relevant party within seven days then a snap election must be called. The assembly was formerly dissolved on 25 January 2017 and devolved government was not restored until 10 January 2020, when a new deal was brokered. For further details, *see* Devolved Government.

The Northern Ireland Office is supported by three executive agencies and public bodies and is responsible for the smooth working of the devolution settlement; representing Northern Ireland interests within the UK government and similarly representing the UK government in Northern Ireland; working in partnership with the Northern Ireland Executive for a stable, prosperous Northern Ireland; and supporting and implementing political agreements to increase stability.

Secretary of State for Northern Ireland, Rt. Hon. Brandon Lewis, CBE, MP
Parliamentary Private Secretary, Sarah Dines, MP
Special Advisers, Isabel Bruce; Oliver Legard; Dr David Sheils
Minister of State, Robin Walker, MP

OFFICE OF THE ADVOCATE-GENERAL FOR SCOTLAND

Queen Elizabeth House, Edinburgh, EH8 8FT
T 0131-244 0359 **E** enquiries@advocategeneral.gov.uk
Dover House, Whitehall, London SW1A 2AU
T 020-7270 6720
W www.gov.uk/government/organisations/office-of-the-advocate-general-for-scotland

The Advocate-General for Scotland is one of the three law officers of the crown, alongside the Attorney-General and the Solicitor-General for England and Wales. It acts as the legal adviser to the UK government on Scottish law and supports the Advocate-General. The office is divided into the Legal Secretariat, based mainly in London, and the Office of the Solicitor to the Advocate-General, based in Edinburgh.

The post was created as a consequence of the constitutional changes set out in the Scotland Act 1998, which created a devolved Scottish parliament. The Lord Advocate and the Solicitor-General for Scotland then became part of the Scottish government and the Advocate-General took over their previous role as legal adviser to the UK government on Scots law. *See also* Devolved Government *and* Ministry of Justice.

HM Advocate-General for Scotland and MoJ Spokesperson for the Lords, Keith Stewart, QC
Private Secretary, Nathan Lappin

MANAGEMENT BOARD
Director and Solicitor to the Advocate-General, Neil Taylor
Head of Advisory and Legislation Division, Victoria MacDonald
Members, Shona Bathgate *(Head of HMRC Division);* Fiona Robertson *(Head of Litigation Division);* Chris Stephen *(Legal Secretary to the Advocate General)*

OFFICE OF THE SECRETARY OF STATE FOR SCOTLAND
Dover House, Whitehall, London SW1A 2AU
Queen Elizabeth House, Edinburgh EH8 8FT
T 0131-244 9010 **E** enquiries@scotlandoffice.gsi.gov.uk
W www.gov.uk/government/organisations/
office-of-the-secretary-of-state-for-scotland

The Office of the Secretary of State for Scotland represents Scottish interests within the UK government in matters reserved to the UK parliament. The Secretary of State for Scotland maintains the stability of the devolution settlement for Scotland; delivers secondary legislation under the Scotland Act 1998; is responsible for the conduct and funding of the Scottish parliament elections; manages the Scottish vote provision and authorises the monthly payment of funds from the UK consolidated fund to the Scottish consolidated fund; and publishes regular information on the state of the Scottish economy.

Matters reserved to the UK parliament include the constitution, foreign affairs, defence, international development, the civil service, financial and economic matters, national security, immigration and nationality, misuse of drugs, trade and industry, various aspects of energy regulation (for example coal, electricity, oil, gas and nuclear energy), various aspects of transport, social security, employment, abortion, genetics, surrogacy, medicines, broadcasting and equal opportunities. Devolved matters include health and social work, education and training, local government and housing, justice and police, agriculture, forestry, fisheries, the environment, tourism, sports, heritage, economic development and internal transport. It is supported by one public body. *See also* Devolved Government *and* Ministry of Justice.

Secretary of State for Scotland, Rt. Hon. Alister Jack, MP
Parliamentary Private Secretary, Ruth Edwards, MP
Special Advisers, Magnus Gardham
Principal Private Secretary, Victoria Jones
Parliamentary Under-Secretary of State, David Duguid, MP*
Parliamentary Under-Secretary of State, Iain Stewart, MP

* Alongside role as Whip, Lord Commissioner of HM Treasury

MANAGEMENT BOARD
Director, Gillian McGregor, CBE
Members, Alison Evans *(Constitutional Policy);* Rebecca Hackett *(Policy Delivery and Relationship Management);* Rachel Irvine *(Constitutional Policy);* Nick Leake *(Policy Delivery and Relationship Management);* Anna Macmillan *(Communications)*

DEPARTMENT FOR TRANSPORT
Great Minster House, 33 Horseferry Road, London SW1P 4DR
T 0300-330 3000 **W** www.gov.uk/government/organisations/
department-for-transport

The Department for Transport (DfT) works with its agencies, partners and local authorities to support the transport network that helps the UK's businesses and gets people and goods travelling around the country. It oversees transport investment and strategic direction in England and Wales, while seeking to

promote low-carbon travel and reduce pollution. The DfT sets standards for safety and security in transport and is supported by 24 executive agencies and public bodies.

Secretary of State for Transport, Rt. Hon. Grant Shapps, MP
Parliamentary Private Secretary, Laura Trott, MP
Special Advisers, Rupert Reid; Neil Tweedie
Minister of State, Chris Heaton-Harris, MP
Minister of State, Andrew Stephenson, MP
Parliamentary Under-Secretary of State, Andrew Courts, MP
Parliamentary Under-Secretary of State, Rachel Maclean, MP
Parliamentary Under-Secretary of State, Baroness Vere of Norbiton

MANAGEMENT BOARD
Permanent Secretary, Bernadette Kelly, CB
Members, Prof. Phil Blythe *(Chief Scientific Adviser);* Gareth Davies, *(Aviation, Maritime, International and Security);* Ruth Hannant *(Rail Group);* Nick Joyce *(Resources and Strategy Group);* Clive Maxwell *(High Speed Rail and Major Projects);* Polly Payne *(Rail Group);* Emma Ward *(Roads, laces and Environment Group);* Brett Welch *(Legal Director)*
Non-Executive Members, Ian King *(Lead);* Richard Aitken-Davies; Richard Keys; Tony Poulter; Tracy Westall

HM TREASURY
1 Horse Guards Road, London SW1A 2HQ
T 020-7270 5000 **E** public.enquiries@hmtreasury.gov.uk
W www.gov.uk/government/organisations/hm-treasury

HM Treasury is the country's economics and finance ministry, and is responsible for formulating and implementing the government's financial and economic policy. It aims to raise the rate of sustainable growth, boost prosperity, and provide the conditions necessary for universal economic and employment opportunities. The Lord High Commissioners of HM Treasury are the First Lord of the Treasury (who is also the prime minister), the Chancellor of the Exchequer and six junior lords. This board of commissioners is assisted at present by the chief secretary, the parliamentary secretary (who is also the government chief whip in the House of Commons), the financial secretary, the economic secretary, the exchequer secretary and efficiency and transformation minister. The prime minister as first lord is not primarily concerned with the day-to-day aspects of Treasury business; neither are the parliamentary secretary and the junior lords as government whips. Treasury business is managed by the Chancellor of the Exchequer and the other Treasury ministers, assisted by the permanent secretary.

The chief secretary is responsible for public expenditure, including spending reviews and strategic planning; in-year control; public-sector pay and pensions; Annually Managed Expenditure and welfare reform; efficiency in public services; procurement and capital investment. He also has responsibility for the Treasury's interest in devolution.

The financial secretary has responsibility for financial services policy including banking and financial services reform and regulation; financial stability; city competitiveness; wholesale and retail markets in the UK, Europe and internationally; and the Financial Services Authority. His other responsibilities include banking support; bank lending; UK Financial Investments; Equitable Life; and personal savings and pensions policy. He also provides support to the chancellor on EU and wider international finance issues.

The exchequer secretary is a title only used occasionally, normally when the post of paymaster-general is allocated to a minister outside of the Treasury. The exchequer secretary's responsibilities include strategic oversight of the UK tax system; corporate and small business taxation, with input from the commercial secretary; departmental minister for HM

Revenue and Customs and the Valuation Office Agency; and lead minister on European and international tax issues.

The economic secretary's responsibilities include environmental issues such as taxation of transport, international climate change and energy; North Sea oil taxation; tax credits and child poverty; assisting the chief secretary on welfare reform; charities and the voluntary sector; excise duties and gambling; stamp duty land tax; EU Budget; the Royal Mint; and departmental minister for HM Treasury Group.

The Minister for Efficiency and Transformation is responsible for supporting the Chancellor of the Duchy of Lancaster and the chief secretary to implement cross-government efficiency and public-sector transformation by improved planning and procurement.

HM Treasury is supported by 14 executive agencies and public bodies.

Prime Minister and First Lord of the Treasury, Rt. Hon. Boris Johnson, MP
Parliamentary Private Secretaries, Alex Burghart, MP; James Heappey, MP
Chancellor of the Exchequer, Rt. Hon. Rishi Sunak, MP
Parliamentary Private Secretary, James Cartlidge, MP
Special Advisers, Liam Booth-Smith; Nerissa Chesterfield; Cass Horowitz; Douglas McNeill; Michael Webb; Rupert Yorke
Chief Secretary to the Treasury, Rt. Hon. Steve Barclay, MP
Special Adviser, Aled Maclean-Jones
Financial Secretary to the Treasury, Rt. Hon. Jesse Norman, MP
Economic Secretary to the Treasury, John Glen, MP
Exchequer Secretary to the Treasury, Kemi Badenoch, MP*
Minister of State for Efficiency and Transformation, Lord Agnew†
Parliamentary Secretary to the Treasury (Chief Whip), Rt. Hon. Mark Spencer, MP
Special Advisers, Sophie Bolsover; Simon Burton; David Sforza
Lords Commissioners of HM Treasury (Whips), David Duguid, MP‡; Rebecca Harris, MP§; James Morris; MP; David Rutley, MP; Maggie Throup, MP; Michael Tomlinson, MP℃
Assistant Whips, Maria Caulfield, MP; Alex Chalk, MP**; David Davies, MP††; Leo Docherty, MP; Nigel Huddleston, MP‡‡; Eddie Hughes, MP; Tom Pursglove, MP

* Alongside role at the DfT
† Jointly held with the Cabinet Office
‡ Alongside role at the Scotland Office
§ Alongside role at the DfT
℃ Alongside role at the DWP
** Alongside role at the MoJ
†† Alongside role at the Wales Office
‡‡ Alongside role at DCMS

MANAGEMENT BOARD
Permanent Secretary, Sir Tom Scholar, KCB
Second Permanent Secretary, Charles Roxburgh
Executive Members, Mark Bowman *(International and EU);* Katharine Braddick *(Financial Services);* Philip Duffy *(Growth and Productivity);* Cat Little *(Public Spending);* Clare Lombardelli *(Chief Economic Adviser);* Beth Russell *(Tax and Welfare)*
Non-Executive Member, Rt. Hon. Lord Hill, CBE *(Lead);* Gay Huey Evans, OBE; Richard Meddings; Tim Score

UK GOVERNMENT INVESTMENTS
1 Victoria Street, London SW1H 0ET
T 020-7215 4720 E enquiries@UKGI.org.uk
W www.ukgi.org.uk/

UK Government Investments (UKGI) is the government's centre of expertise in corporate finance and corporate governance. UKGI Limited began operating on 1 April 2016 as a government company, wholly owned by HM Treasury, which brought together the functions of the Shareholder Executive (formerly part of the Department for Business, Energy and Industrial Strategy) and UK Financial Investments. UKGI's principle investments are to: prepare and execute all significant corporate asset sales by the UK government; advise on all major UK government financial interventions into corporate structures; act as shareholder for those arm's length bodies of the UK government that are structured to allow a meaningful shareholder function and for other UK government assets facing complex transformations; and to advise on major UK government negotiations with corporates.

Chief Executive, Mark Russell, CBE

Chair, Charles Donald
Board, Andrew Duff; Lord Jitesh Gadhia; Jane Guyett; Clare Hollingsworth; Robin Lawther; Hon. Sir James Leigh-Pemberton *(Deputy Chair);* Sarah Munby; Charles Roxburgh; Caroline Thompson

OFFICE OF TAX SIMPLIFICATION
HM Treasury, 1 Horse Guards Road, London SW1A 2HQ
E ots@ots.gov.uk
W www.gov.uk/government/organisations/office-of-tax-simplification

The chancellor and exchequer secretary to HM Treasury launched the Office of Tax Simplification (OTS) on 20 July 2010 to provide the government with independent advice on simplifying the UK tax system. The OTS is part of HM Treasury and provides the government with independent advice on simplifying the UK tax system. It carries out projects investigating complex areas of the tax system and makes recommendations to the chancellor in reports which are published on its website.

Chair, Kathryn Cearns, OBE
Tax Director, Bill Dodwell

ROYAL MINT LTD
PO Box 500, Llantrisant, Pontyclun CF72 8YT
W www.royalmint.com

From 1975 the Royal Mint operated as a trading fund and was established as an executive agency in 1990. Since 2010 it has operated as Royal Mint Ltd, a company 100 per cent owned by HM Treasury, with an exclusive contract to supply all coinage for the UK.

The Royal Mint actively competes in world markets for a share of the available circulating coin business and about half of the coins and blanks it produces annually are exported. It is the leading export mint, accounting for around 15 per cent of the world market. The Royal Mint also manufactures special proof and uncirculated quality coins in gold, silver and other metals; military and civil decorations and medals; commemorative and prize medals; and royal and official seals.

Master of the Mint, Chancellor of the Exchequer *(ex officio)*
Chair, Graham Love
Chief Executive, Anne Jessopp

UK EXPORT FINANCE
1 Horse Guards Road, London SW1A 2HQ
T 020-7271 8010 E customer.service@ukexportfinance.gov.uk
W www.gov.uk/government/organisations/uk-export-finance

UK Export Finance is the UK's export credit agency. It helps UK exporters by providing insurance to them and guarantees to banks to share the risks of providing export finance. Additionally, it can make loans to overseas buyers of goods and services from the UK. UK Export Finance is the operating name of the Export Credits Guarantee Department.

The priorities of UK Export Finance are to fulfil its statutory remit to support exports; operate within the policy and financial objectives established by the government, which includes international obligations; and to recover the maximum amount of debt in respect of claims paid, taking account of the government's policy on debt forgiveness. It is a ministerial department supported by one public body, the Export Guarantees Advisory Council.

Secretary of State for International Trade and President of the Board of Trade, Rt. Hon. Elizabeth Truss, MP
Special Advisers, Sophie Jarvis; Adam Jones
Parliamentary Under Secretary of State, Graham Stuart, MP *(Minister for Exports)**
* Jointly held with the DfIT

MANAGEMENT BOARD
Chief Executive, Louis Taylor
Chair, Noel Harwerth
Members, Cameron Fox *(Chief Finance and Operating Officer)*; Shane Lynch *(Resources)*; Davinder Mann *(Legal and Compliance)*; Madelaine McTernan *(UK Government Investments)*; Samir Parkash *(Chief Risk Officer)*; Richard Simon-Lewis *(Business Development, Marketing and Communications)*; Gordon Welsh *(Head of the Business Group)*
Non-Executive Members, Alistair Clark; Shalini Khemka; Andrew Mitchell, CMG; Oliver Peterken; Lawrence Weiss; Kimberly Wiehl

OFFICE OF THE SECRETARY OF STATE FOR WALES
Gwydyr House, Whitehall, London SW1A 2NP
T 020-7270 0534 E correspondence@walesoffice.gov.uk
1 Caspian Point, Caspian Way, Cardiff CF10 4BQ
W www.gov.uk/government/organisations/
office-of-the-secretary-of-state-for-wales

The Office of the Secretary of State for Wales, informally known as the Wales Office, was established in 1999 when most of the powers of the Welsh Office were handed over to the National Assembly for Wales. It is the department of the Secretary of State for Wales, who is the key government figure liaising with the devolved government in Wales and who represents Welsh interests in the cabinet and parliament. The secretary of state has the right to attend and speak at sessions of the National Assembly (and must consult the assembly on the government's legislative programme). *See also* Devolved Government *and* Ministry of Justice.

Secretary of State for Wales, Rt. Hon. Simon Hart, MP
Parliamentary Private Secretary, Sarah Atherton, MP
Special Adviser, Jack Sellers
Principal Private Secretary, Sarah Jennings
Parliamentary Under-Secretary of State, David Davies, MP
* Alongside role as assistant Whip

MANAGEMENT BOARD
Director, Glynne Jones
Members, Ashok Ahir *(Communications)*; Louise Parry *(Policy)*; Kate Starkey *(Policy)*; Geth Williams *(Constitution and Policy)*
Non-Executive Members, Alison White

DEPARTMENT FOR WORK AND PENSIONS
Caxton House, Tothill Street, London SW1H 9NA
W www.gov.uk/government/organisations/
department-for-work-pensions

The Department for Work and Pensions was formed in June 2001 from parts of the former Department of Social Security, the Department for Education and Employment and the Employment Service. The department helps unemployed people of working age into work, helps employers to fill their vacancies and provides financial support to people unable to help themselves, through back-to-work programmes. The department also administers the child support system, social security benefits and the social fund. In addition, the department has reciprocal social security arrangements with other countries. It is the largest department in the government, employing 80,790 people in 2020, and is supported by 15 executive agencies and public bodies.

Secretary of State for Work and Pensions, Rt. Hon. Thérèse Coffey, MP
Parliamentary Private Secretary, Bim Afolami, MP
Special Advisers, Alex Hitchcock; Rhiannon Padley
Minister of State, Justin Tomlinson, MP *(Disabled People, Health and Work)*
Parliamentary Under-Secretary of State, Mims Davies, MP *(Employment)*
Parliamentary Under-Secretary of State, Guy Opperman, MP *(Pensions and Financial Inclusion)*
Parliamentary Under-Secretary of State, Will Quince, MP *(Welfare Delivery)*
Parliamentary Under-Secretary of State, Baroness Stedman-Scott, OBE *(Lords)*

MANAGEMENT BOARD
Permanent Secretary, Peter Schofield
Members, Debbie Alder, CB *(People and Capability)*; Neil Couling, CBE *(Change and Universal Credit)*; Emma Haddad *(Service Excellence)*; Nick Joicey *(Finance)*; John-Paul Marks *(Work and Health Services)*; Jonathan Mills *(Policy Group)*; Simon McKinnon *(Digital and Information Officer)*

EXECUTIVE AGENCIES

Executive agencies are well-defined business units that carry out services with a clear focus on delivering specific outputs within a framework of accountability to ministers. They can be set up or disbanded without legislation, and they are organisationally independent from the department they are answerable to. In the following list the agencies are shown in the accounts of their sponsor departments. Legally they act on behalf of the relevant secretary of state. Their chief executives also perform the role of accounting officers, which means they are responsible for the money spent by their organisations. Staff employed by agencies are civil servants.

DEPARTMENT FOR BUSINESS, ENERGY AND INDUSTRIAL STRATEGY

COMPANIES HOUSE
Crown Way, Cardiff CF14 3UZ
T 0303-123 4500 E enquiries@companieshouse.gov.uk
W www.gov.uk/government/organisations/companies-house

Companies House incorporates and dissolves limited companies, examines and stores company information delivered under the Companies Act and related legislation; and makes this information available to the public.

Chief Executive, Louise Smyth

THE INSOLVENCY SERVICE
4 Abbey Orchard Street, London SW1P 2HT
T 020-7637 1110
W www.gov.uk/government/organisations/insolvency-service

The role of the service includes administration and investigation of the affairs of bankruptcies, individuals subject to debt relief orders, partnerships and companies in compulsory liquidation; dealing with the disqualification of directors in all corporate failures; authorising and regulating the insolvency profession; providing banking and investment services for bankruptcy and liquidation estate funds; assessing and paying statutory entitlement to redundancy payments when an employer cannot, or will not, pay its employees; and advising ministers and the public on insolvency, redundancy and related issues. The service has around 1,700 staff, operating from 22 locations across Great Britain.

Inspector-General and Chief Executive, Dean Beale

INTELLECTUAL PROPERTY OFFICE
Concept House, Cardiff Road, Newport NP10 8QQ
T 0300-300 2000 E information@ipo.gov.uk
W www.gov.uk/government/organisations/
intellectual-property-office

The Intellectual Property Office (an operating name of the Patent Office) was set up in 1852 to act as the UK's sole office for the granting of patents. It was established as an executive agency in 1990 and became a trading fund in 1991. The office is responsible for the granting of intellectual property (IP) rights, which include patents, trade marks, designs and copyright.

Comptroller-General and Chief Executive, Tim Moss

MET OFFICE
FitzRoy Road, Exeter, Devon EX1 3PB
T 0370-900 0100 E enquiries@metoffice.gov.uk
W www.metoffice.gov.uk

The Met Office is the UK's National Weather Service, operating as an executive agency of BEIS after having transferred from the MoD in July 2011. Founded in 1854, it is a world leader in providing weather and climate services and processes up to 215 billion weather observations a day from across the world.

Chief Executive, Prof. Penelope Endersby
Chief Scientist, Prof. Stephen Belcher

UK SPACE AGENCY
Polaris House, North Star Avenue, Swindon, Wiltshire SN2 1SZ
T 020-7215 5000 E info@ukspaceagency.gov.uk
W www.gov.uk/government/organisations/uk-space-agency

The UK Space Agency was established on 23 March 2010 and became an executive agency on 1 April 2011. It was created to provide a single voice for UK space ambitions, and is responsible for all strategic decisions on the UK civil space programme. Responsibilities of the UK Space Agency include coordinating UK civil space activity; supporting academic research; nurturing the UK space industry; raising the profile of UK space activities at home and abroad; working to increase understanding of space science and its practical benefits; inspiring the next generation of UK scientists and engineers; licencing the launch and operation of UK spacecraft; and promoting co-operation with the European Space programme. It aims to capture 10 per cent of the global market for space by 2030.

Chief Executive, Dr Graham Turnock

CABINET OFFICE

CROWN COMMERCIAL SERVICE
Floor 9, The Capital Building, Old Hall Street, Liverpool L3 9PP
T 0345-410 2222 E info@crowncommercial.gov.uk
W www.gov.uk/government/organisations/
crown-commercial-service

The Crown Commercial Service (CCS) is an executive agency of the Cabinet Office, bringing together policy, advice and direct buying; providing commercial services to the public sector; and saving money for the taxpayer. The CCS works with over 17,000 customer organisations in the public sector.

Chief Executive, Simon Tse

GOVERNMENT PROPERTY AGENCY
E enquiries@gpa.gov.uk
W www.gov.uk/government/organisations/
government-property-agency

Formed in April 2018, the Government Property Agency delivers property and workplace solutions across the government, and aims to improve the efficiency and effectiveness of the Government Estate. It owns and operates the central government general purpose estate and aims to improve working environments for civil servants while making efficiency savings.

Chair, Pat Ritchie
Chief Executive, Steven Boyd

MINISTRY OF HOUSING, COMMUNITIES AND LOCAL GOVERNMENT

PLANNING INSPECTORATE
Temple Quay House, 2 The Square, Temple Quay, Bristol BS1 6PN
T 0303-444 5000 E enquiries@planninginspectorate.gov.uk
W www.gov.uk/government/organisations/planning-inspectorate

The main work of the inspectorate consists of processing planning and enforcement appeals, national infrastructure planning applications, and holding examinations into local development plans. It also deals with listed building consent appeals; advertisement appeals; rights of way cases; cases arising from the Environmental Protection and Water acts, the Transport and Works Act 1992 and other highways legislation; and reporting on planning applications called in for decision by the Ministry of Housing, Communities and Local Government and the Welsh government. It seeks to foster economic growth through sustainable development, particularly in energy and transport.

Chief Executive, Sarah Richards

THE QUEEN ELIZABETH II CONFERENCE CENTRE
Broad Sanctuary, London SW1P 3EE
T 020-7798 4000 W www.qeiicentre.london

The centre provides secure conference facilities for national and international government and private sector use, with a capacity of up to 2,500 delegates.

Chief Executive, Mark Taylor

MINISTRY OF DEFENCE
See also Defence Chapter.

DEFENCE ELECTRONICS AND COMPONENTS AGENCY
Welsh Road, Deeside, Flintshire CH5 2LS T 01244-847694
E decainfo@deca.mod.uk
W www.gov.uk/government/organisations/
defence-electronics-and-components-agency

The Defence Electronics and Components Agency (DECA) provides maintenance, repair, overhaul, upgrade and procurement in avionics, electronics and components fields to support the MoD. As a 'trading' executive agency DECA is run along commercial lines, with funding for DECA's activities being generated entirely by payments for delivery of services provided to the MoD and other private sector customers. DECA currently has an annual turnover of around £25m and employs over 400 staff across its head office and main operating centre in North Wales, a site in Stafford and various deployed locations across the UK.

Chief Executive, Geraint Spearing

DEFENCE EQUIPMENT AND SUPPORT

Ministry of Defence, Maple0a,#2043, MoD Abbey Wood, Bristol BS34 8JH **T** 0117-9130893
W www.gov.uk/government/organisations/
defence-electronics-and-components-agency

Defence Equipment and Support is a trading entity that oversees the purchase of equipment and services for the armed forces and MoD, including the procurement of ships, submarines, aircraft, vehicles, weapons, medical supplies, clothing and food. It employs around 12,000 civil servants and military personnel.

Chief Executive, Sir Simon Bollom

DEFENCE SCIENCE AND TECHNOLOGY LABORATORY

Porton Down, Salisbury, Wiltshire SP4 0JQ
T 01980-950000 **E** centralenquiries@dstl.gov.uk
W www.gov.uk/defence-science-and-technology-laboratory

The Defence Science and Technology Laboratory (DSTL) supplies specialist science and technology services to the MoD and wider government.

Chair, Adrian Belton
Chief Executive, Gary Aitkenhead

UK HYDROGRAPHIC OFFICE

Admiralty Way, Taunton, Somerset TA1 2DN
T 01823-484444 **E** customerservices@ukho.gov.uk
W www.gov.uk/uk-hydrographic-office

The UK Hydrographic Office (UKHO) collects and supplies hydrographic and geospatial data for the Royal Navy and merchant shipping to protect lives at sea. Working with other national hydrographic offices, UKHO sets and raises global standards of hydrography, cartography and navigation.

Chief Executive (Acting), Rear-Adm. Peter Sparkes

DEPARTMENT FOR EDUCATION

THE EDUCATION AND SKILLS FUNDING AGENCY

Department for Education, Piccadilly Gate, Shore Street, Manchester M1 2WD
W www.gov.uk/government/organisations/
education-and-skills-funding-agency

Formed in April 2017 after a merger of the Education Funding Agency (EFA) and the Skills Funding Agency (SFA), the Education and Skills Funding Agency (ESFA) is the DfE's delivery agency for funding and compliance. It manages £58bn of funding each year to support all state-provided education and training for children and young people aged 3 to 19, and intervenes where there is evidence of mismanagement of funds or risk of failure. The ESFA also supports the delivery of building and maintenance programmes for schools, academies, free schools and sixth-form colleges. It also administers the National Careers Service, the National Apprenticeship Service and the Learning Records Service.

Chief Executive, Eileen Milner

STANDARDS AND TESTING AGENCY

Ground Floor, South Building, Cheylesmore House, 5 Quinton Road, Coventry CV1 2WT
T 0300-303 3013 **E** assessments@education.gov.uk
W www.gov.uk/government/organisations/
standards-and-testing-agency

The Standards and Testing Agency (STA) opened in October 2011 and is responsible for the development and delivery of all statutory assessments from early years to the end of Key Stage 2.

Chief Executive, Una Bennett

TEACHING REGULATION AGENCY

Ground Floor, South Building, Cheylesmore House, 5 Quinton Road, Coventry CV1 2WT
T 0207-593 5394 **E** qts.enquiries@education.gov.uk
W www.gov.uk/government/organisations/
teaching-regulation-agency

Established in April 2018, the Teaching Regulation Agency is responsible for regulating the teaching profession, maintaining a database of qualified teachers in England and is the awarding body for Qualified Teacher Status (QTS).

Chief Executive, Alan Meyrick

DEPARTMENT FOR ENVIRONMENT, FOOD AND RURAL AFFAIRS

ANIMAL AND PLANT HEALTH AGENCY

Woodham Lane, New Haw, Addlestone, Surrey KT15 3NB
E enquiries@apha.gov.uk
W www.gov.uk/government/organisations/
animal-and-plant-health-agency

The Animal and Plant Health Agency (APHA) was launched in October 2014. It merged the former Animal Health and Veterinary Laboratories Agency with parts of the Food and Environment Research Agency responsible for plant and bee health to create a single agency responsible for animal, plant and bee health.

APHA is responsible for identifying and controlling endemic and exotic diseases and pests in animals, plants and bees, and surveillance of new and emerging pests and diseases; scientific research in areas such as bacterial, viral, prion and parasitic diseases, vaccines and food safety and act as an international reference laboratory for many farm animal diseases; facilitating international trade in animals, products of animal origin, and plants; protecting endangered wildlife through licensing and registration; managing a programme of apiary inspections, diagnostics, research and development, training and advice; and regulating the safe disposal of animal by-products to reduce the risk of potentially dangerous substances entering the food chain.

The agency provides all or some of these services to DEFRA and the Scottish and Welsh governments.

Chief Executive, Chris Hadkiss

CENTRE FOR ENVIRONMENT, FISHERIES AND AQUACULTURE SCIENCE (CEFAS)

Pakefield Road, Lowestoft, Suffolk NR33 0HT
T 01502-562244 **W** www.gov.uk/government/organisations/
centre-for-environment-fisheries-and-aquaculture-science

Established in April 1997, the agency provides research and consultancy services in fisheries science and management, aquaculture, fish health and hygiene, environmental impact assessment, and environmental quality assessment.

Chief Executive (Interim), Tim Green

RURAL PAYMENTS AGENCY

PO Box 69, Reading RG1 3YD
T 0300-0200 301 **E** ruralpayments@defra.gov.uk
W www.gov.uk/government/organisations/rural-payments-agency

The RPA was established in 2001. It pays out over £2bn each year to support the farming and food sector and is responsible for Common Agricultural Policy (CAP) schemes in England. In addition it manages over 40 other rural economy and community schemes. It is also responsible for improving agricultural productivity; boosting rural economies through development schemes; operating cattle tracing services; conducting inspections of farms, processing plants and fresh produce markets in England; providing import and export licences for the agri-food sector; and regulating the dairy and farm produce markets.

Chief Executive, Paul Caldwell

VETERINARY MEDICINES DIRECTORATE

Woodham Lane, New Haw, Addlestone, Surrey KT15 3LS
T 01932-336911 **E** postmaster@vmd.gov.uk
W www.gov.uk/government/organisations/
veterinary-medicines-directorate

The Veterinary Medicines Directorate is responsible for all aspects of the authorisation and control of veterinary medicines, including post-authorisation surveillance of residues in animals and animal products. It is also responsible for the development and enforcement of legislation concerning veterinary medicines and the provision of policy advice to ministers.

Chief Executive, Prof. Peter Borriello

FOREIGN, COMMONWEALTH AND DEVELOPMENT OFFICE

WILTON PARK

Wiston House, Steyning, West Sussex BN44 3DZ
T 01903-815020 **W** www.wiltonpark.org.uk

Wilton Park organises international affairs conferences and is hired out to government departments and commercial users. It organises over 50 events a year, helping to develop international policy and advance practical solutions to global issues.

Chief Executive (Interim), Colin Smith

DEPARTMENT OF HEALTH AND SOCIAL CARE

MEDICINES AND HEALTHCARE PRODUCTS REGULATORY AGENCY (MHRA)

10 South Colonnade, London E14 4PU
T 020-3080 6000 **E** info@mhra.gov.uk **W** www.gov.uk/
government/organisations/
medicines-and-healthcare-products-regulatory-agency

The MHRA, which also includes the National Institute for Biological Standards and Control (NIBSC) and the Clinical Practice Research Datalink (CPRD), is responsible for regulating all medicines, medical devices and blood components for transfusion in the UK by ensuring they work and are acceptably safe.

Chair, Stephen Lightfoot
Chief Executive, Dr June Raine, CBE

PUBLIC HEALTH ENGLAND

Wellington House, 133–155 Waterloo Road, London SE1 8UG
T 020-7654 8000 **E** enquiries@phe.gov.uk
W www.gov.uk/government/organisations/public-health-england

Public Health England (PHE) began operating in April 2013 and is responsible for protecting and improving the health and wellbeing of the nation; reducing health inequalities; protecting the nation from public health hazards; preparing for and responding to public health emergencies; and researching, collecting and analysing data to improve understanding of and solutions to public health problems. PHE employs 5,500 staff who are mostly scientists, researchers and public health professionals. It has eight local centres and four regions in England and works closely with public health professionals in Wales, Scotland, Northern Ireland and internationally.

Chief Executive (Interim), Michael Brodie

MINISTRY OF JUSTICE

CRIMINAL INJURIES COMPENSATION AUTHORITY (CICA)

Alexander Bain House, Atlantic Quay, 15 York Street, Glasgow G2 8JQ **T** 0300-003 3601
W www.gov.uk/government/organisations/
criminal-injuries-compensation-authority

CICA is the executive agency responsible for administering the Criminal Injuries Compensation Scheme in England, Scotland and Wales (separate arrangements apply in Northern Ireland). CICA handles over 30,000 applications for compensation each year, paying more than £130m to victims of violent crime. Appeals against decisions made by CICA can be put to the First-tier Tribunal (Criminal Injuries Compensation) *see* Tribunals.

Chief Executive, Linda Brown

HM COURTS AND TRIBUNALS SERVICE

102 Petty France, London SW1H 9AJ
W www.gov.uk/government/organisations/
hm-courts-and-tribunals-service

HM Courts Service and the Tribunals Service merged in April 2011 to form HM Courts and Tribunals Service, an integrated agency providing support for the administration of justice in courts and tribunals. As an agency within the MoJ it operates as a partnership between the Lord Chancellor, the Lord Chief Justice and the Senior President of Tribunals. It is responsible for the administration of the criminal, civil and family courts and tribunals in England and Wales and non-devolved tribunals in Scotland and Northern Ireland. The agency's work is overseen by a board headed by an independent chair working with non-executive, executive and judicial members.

Chief Executive, Susan Acland-Hood

HM PRISON AND PROBATION SERVICE

102 Petty France, London SW1H 9EX
T 01633-630941 **E** public.enquiries@noms.gsi.gov.uk
W www.gov.uk/government/organisations/
her-majestys-prison-and-probation-service

HM Prison and Probation Service (HMPPS) was established in April 2017, and is responsible for the roll out of government policies concerning the welfare of offenders and communities, and for reducing levels of reoffending by the rehabilitation of offenders through education and training schemes. HM Prison Service operates as an executive agency of HMPPS and is responsible for keeping those sentenced to prison in custody, and helping them lead law-abiding and useful lives both in prison and after they have been released. The agency runs 109 of the 123 prisons in England and Wales, and is also responsible for managing probation services and supporting effective offender management.

Chief Executive, Jo Farrar

LEGAL AID AGENCY

Unit B8, Berkley Way, Viking Business Park, Jarrow NE31 1SF
T 0300-200 2020 **E** contactcivil@justice.gov.uk
W www.gov.uk/government/organisations/legal-aid-agency

The Legal Aid Agency provides civil and criminal legal aid and advice in England and Wales. Formed in April 2013 as part of the Legal Aid, Sentencing and Punishment of Offenders Act 2012, the agency replaced the Legal Services Commission, a non-departmental public body of the MoJ.
Chief Executive (Interim), Jane Harbottle

OFFICE OF THE PUBLIC GUARDIAN

PO Box 16185, Birmingham B2 2WH
T 0300-456 0300 **E** customerservices@publicguardian.gov.uk
W www.gov.uk/government/organisations/
office-of-the-public-guardian

The Office of the Public Guardian (OPG) works within the Mental Capacity Act 2005 and Guardianship (Missing Persons) Act 2017 to support and protect those who lack the mental capacity to make decisions for themselves. It supports the Public Guardian in the registration of Enduring Powers of Attorney (EPA) and Lasting Powers of Attorney (LPA), and the supervision of deputies appointed by the Court of Protection. The OPG also has responsibility for investigating and acting on allegations of abuse by attorneys and deputies. The OPG's responsibility extends across England and Wales.

Chief Executive and Public Guardian, Nick Goodwin

DEPARTMENT FOR TRANSPORT

DRIVER AND VEHICLE LICENSING AGENCY (DVLA)
Longview Road, Swansea SA6 7JL
W www.gov.uk/government/organisations/
driver-and-vehicle-licensing-agency

The DVLA, established as an executive agency in 1990, maintains registers of drivers and vehicles in Great Britain. The information collated by the DVLA helps to improve road safety, reduce vehicle related crime, support environmental initiatives and limit vehicle tax evasion. The DVLA maintains over 49 million driver records and over 40 million vehicle records and collects over £6bn a year in vehicle tax.

Chief Executive, Julie Lennard

DRIVER AND VEHICLE STANDARDS AGENCY
Fourth Floor, The Axis Building, 112 Upper Parliament Street, Nottingham NG1 6LP
W www.gov.uk/government/organisations/
driver-and-vehicle-standards-agency

Formed by the merger of the Driving Standards Agency and the Vehicle and Operator Services Agency in 2014, the Driver and Vehicle Standards Agency (DVSA) is responsible for improving road safety in the UK by setting standards for driving and motorcycling, and ensuring drivers, vehicle operators and MOT garages understand and comply with roadworthiness standards. It additionally provides a range of licensing, testing, education and enforcement services.

Chief Executive, Gareth Llewellyn

MARITIME AND COASTGUARD AGENCY
Spring Place, 105 Commercial Road, Southampton SO15 1EG
T 020-3817 2000 E infoline@mcga.gov.uk W www.gov.uk/
government/organisations/maritime-and-coastguard-agency

The agency's aims are to prevent loss of life, continuously improve maritime safety and protect the marine environment. It produces legislation and guidance on maritime matters, and oversees certification to seafarers.

Chief Executive, Brian Johnson

VEHICLE CERTIFICATION AGENCY
1 Eastgate Office Centre, Eastgate Road, Bristol BS5 6XX
T 0300-330 5797 E W www.vehicle-certification-agency.gov.uk

The agency is the UK authority responsible for ensuring that new road vehicles, agricultural tractors, off-road vehicles and vehicle parts have been designed and constructed to meet internationally agreed standards of safety and environmental protection.

Chief Executive, Pia Wilkes

HM TREASURY

GOVERNMENT INTERNAL AUDIT AGENCY
10 Victoria Street, London SW1H 0NB
E Correspondence@giaa.gov.uk W www.gov.uk/government/
organisations/government-internal-audit-agency

Launched in April 2015, the Government Internal Audit Agency (GIAA) helps ensure government and the wider public sector provide services effectively. GIAA offers quality assurance on organisation's systems and processes, based on an objective assessment of the governance, risk management and control arrangements in place.

Chief Executive, Elizabeth Honer

NATIONAL INFRASTRUCTURE COMMISSION
1 Horse Guards Road, London SW1A 2HQ
E Correspondence@giaa.gov.uk W www.gov.uk/government/
organisations/government-internal-audit-agency

The National Infrastructure Commission was permanently established in January 2017 to provide the government with expert, impartial advice on significant long-term infrastructure challenges. During each parliament it is tasked with undertaking a national infrastructure assessment and monitoring the government's progress.

Chair, Sir John Armitt, CBE

UK DEBT MANAGEMENT OFFICE
Eastcheap Court, 11 Philpot Lane, London EC3M 8UD
T 020-7862 6500 W www.dmo.gov.uk

The UK Debt Management Office (DMO) was launched as an executive agency of HM Treasury in April 1998. The Chancellor of the Exchequer determines the policy and financial framework within which the DMO operates, but delegates operational decisions on debt and cash management and the day-to-day running of the office to the chief executive. The DMO's remit is to carry out the government's debt management policy of minimising financing costs over the long term, and to minimise the cost of offsetting the government's net cash flows over time, while operating at a level of risk approved by ministers in both cases. The DMO is also responsible for providing loans to local authorities through the Public Works Loan Board, and for managing the assets of certain public-sector bodies through the Commissioners for the Reduction of the National Debt.

Chief Executive, Sir Robert Stheeman, CB

NON-MINISTERIAL GOVERNMENT DEPARTMENTS

Non-ministerial government departments are part of central government but are not headed by a minister and are not funded by a sponsor department. They are created to implement specific legislation, but do not have the ability to change it. Departments may have links to a minister, but the minister is not responsible for the department's overall performance. Staff employed by non-ministerial departments are civil servants.

CHARITY COMMISSION
T 0300-066 9197 W www.gov.uk/government/organisations/
charity-commission

The Charity Commission is established by law as the independent regulator and registrar of charities in England and Wales. Its aim is to provide the best possible regulation of these charities in order to ensure their legal compliance and increase their efficiency, accountability and effectiveness, as well as to encourage public trust and confidence in them. The commission maintains a register of over 166,000 charities. It is accountable to both parliament and the First-tier Tribunal (Charity), and the chamber of the Upper Tribunal or high court for decisions made in exercising the commission's legal powers. The Charity Commission has offices in London, Liverpool, Taunton and Newport.

Chair, Rt. Hon. Baroness Stowell of Beeston, MBE
Chief Executive, Helen Stephenson, CBE

COMPETITION AND MARKETS AUTHORITY

The Cabot, 25 Cabot Square, London E14 4QZ
T 020-3738 6000 **E** general.enquiries@cma.gov.uk
W www.gov.uk/government/organisations/
competition-and-markets-authority

The Competition and Markets Authority (CMA) is the UK's primary competition and consumer authority. It is an independent non-ministerial government department with responsibility for carrying out investigations into mergers, markets and the regulated industries and enforcing competition and consumer law. In April 2014 it took over the functions of the Competition Commission and the competition and certain consumer functions of the Office of Fair Trading under the Enterprise Act 2002, as amended by the Enterprise and Regulatory Reform Act 2013.

Chair, Jonathan Scott
Chief Executive, Dr Andrea Coscelli, CBE

CROWN PROSECUTION SERVICE

102 Petty France, London SW1H 9EA
T 020-3357 0899 **E** enquiries@cps.gov.uk **W** www.cps.gov.uk

The Crown Prosecution Service (CPS) is the independent body responsible for prosecuting people in England and Wales. The CPS was established as a result of the Prosecution of Offences Act 1985. It works closely with the police to advise on lines of inquiry and to decide on appropriate charges and other disposals in all but minor cases. *See also* Law Courts and Offices.

Director of Public Prosecutions, Max Hill, QC
Chief Executive, Rebecca Lawrence

FOOD STANDARDS AGENCY

Floor 6 & 7, Clive House, 70 Petty France, London SW1H 9EX
T 0330-332 7149 **E** helpline@food.gov.uk
W www.food.gov.uk

Established in April 2000, the FSA is a non-ministerial government body responsible for food safety and hygiene in England, Wales and Northern Ireland. The agency has the general function of developing policy in these areas and provides information and advice to the government, other public bodies and consumers. The FSA also works with local authorities to enforce food safety regulations and has staff working in UK meat plants to check that the requirements of the regulations are being met.

Chair, Heather Hancock
Chief Executive, Emily Miles

FOOD STANDARDS AGENCY NORTHERN IRELAND,
  10C Clarendon Road, Belfast BT1 3BG **E** infosani@food.gov.uk
FOOD STANDARDS AGENCY WALES, 11th Floor, South
  Gate House, Wood Street, Cardiff CF10 1EW
  E walesadminteam@food.gov.uk

FORESTRY COMMISSION

620 Bristol Business Park, Coldharbour Lane, Bristol BS16 1EJ
T 0300-067 4000 **E** nationalenquiries@forestrycommission.gov.uk
W www.gov.uk/government/organisations/forestry-commission

The Forestry Commission is the non-ministerial government department responsible for forestry policy in England. It is supported by two executive agencies: Forest Research, which carries out scientific research and technical development relevant to forestry, and Forestry England, responsible for managing around 1,500 woods and forests.

In April 2013 the functions of its Welsh division, Forestry Commission Wales, were subsumed into Natural Resources Wales, a new body established by the Welsh government to regulate and manage natural resources in Wales.

In April 2019 responsibility for forestry in Scotland was devolved to two new Scottish government agencies: Forestry and Land Scotland and Scottish Forestry, who are accountable to the Scottish ministers.

The commission's principal objectives are to protect and expand England's forests and woodlands; enhance the economic value of forest resources; conserve and improve the biodiversity, landscape and cultural heritage of forests and woodlands; develop opportunities for woodland recreation; and increase public understanding of, and community participation in, forestry. It does this by managing public forests in its care to implement these objectives; by supporting other woodland owners with grants, regulation, advice and tree felling licences; and, through its Forest Research agency, by carrying out scientific research and technical development in support of these objectives.

Chair, Sir William Worsley
Chief Executive, Forest Research, Prof. James Pendlebury
Chief Executive, Forestry England, Mike Seddon

GOVERNMENT ACTUARY'S DEPARTMENT

Finlaison House, 15–17 Furnival Street, London EC4A 1AB
T 020-7211 2601 **E** enquiries@gad.gov.uk
Queen Elizabeth House, 1 Sibbald Walk, Edinburgh EH8 8FT
T 0131-467 0324 **E** scottish-enquiries@gad.gov.uk
W www.gov.uk/government/organisations/
government-actuarys-department

The Government Actuary's Department (GAD) was established in 1919 and provides actuarial advice to the public sector in the UK and overseas, and also to the private sector, where consistent with government policy. The GAD provides advice on occupational pension schemes, social security and National Insurance, investment and strategic risk management, insurance analysis and advice, financial risk management, and healthcare financing.

Government Actuary, Martin Clarke
Deputy Government Actuary, Colin Wilson

GOVERNMENT LEGAL DEPARTMENT

102 Petty France, Westminster, London SW1H 9GL
T 020-7210 3000 **E** thetreasurysolicitor@governmentlegal.gov.uk
W www.gov.uk/government/organisations/
government-legal-department

The Treasury Solicitor's Department became the Government Legal Department (GLD) in April 2015. The department provides legal advice to government on the development, design and implementation of government policies and decisions, and represents the government in court. It is superintended by the Attorney-General. The permanent secretary of the GLD, the Treasury Solicitor, is also the Queen's Proctor, and is responsible for collecting ownerless goods *(bona vacantia)* on behalf of the crown.

HM Procurator-General and Treasury Solicitor (Interim), Peter
  Fish, CB
Directors-General, Stephen Braviner-Roman; Susanna
  McGibbon
Head of Bona Vacantia, Caroline Harold

HM LAND REGISTRY

Trafalgar House, 1 Bedford Park, Croydon CR0 2AQ
T 0300-006 0411
W www.gov.uk/government/organisations/land-registry

A government department and trading fund of BEIS, HM Land Registry maintains the Land Register – the definitive source of information for more than 25 million property titles in England and Wales. The Land Register has been open to public inspection since 1990.

Chief Land Registrar and Chief Executive, Simon Hayes

HM REVENUE AND CUSTOMS (HMRC)
100 Parliament Street, London SW1A 2BQ
Income Tax Enquiries 0300-200 3300
National Insurance Enquiries 0300-200 3500
VAT Enquiries 0300-200 3700
W www.gov.uk/government/organisations/hm-revenue-customs

HMRC was formed following the integration of the Inland Revenue and HM Customs and Excise, which was made formal by parliament in April 2005. It collects and administers direct taxes (capital gains tax, corporation tax, income tax, inheritance tax and national insurance contributions), indirect taxes (excise duties, insurance premium tax, petroleum revenue tax, stamp duty, stamp duty land tax, stamp duty reserve tax and value-added tax) and environmental taxes (climate change levy, landfill tax, aggregates levy, emissions trading and energy efficiency scheme). HMRC also pays and administers child benefit and tax credits, in addition to being responsible for national minimum wage enforcement and recovery of student loans. HMRC also administers the Government Banking Service.

Chief Executive and First Permanent Secretary, Jim Hara
Deputy Chief Executive and Second Permanent Secretary, Angela
    MacDonald

VALUATION OFFICE AGENCY
Wingate House, 93–107 Shaftesbury Avenue, London W1D 5BU
T 0300-050 1501 (England); 0300-505505 **T** 0300-505505 (Wales)
W www.gov.uk/government/organisations/valuation-office-agency

Established in 1991, the Valuation Office is an executive agency of HM Revenue and Customs. It is responsible for compiling and maintaining the business rating and council tax valuation lists for England and Wales; valuing property throughout Great Britain for the purposes of taxes administered by HMRC; providing statutory and non-statutory property valuation services in England, Wales and Scotland; and giving policy advice to ministers on property valuation matters. In April 2009 the VOA assumed responsibility for the functions of The Rent Service, which provided a rental valuation service to local authorities in England, and fair rent determinations for landlords and tenants.

Chief Executive (Interim), Jonathan Russell, CB

NATIONAL ARCHIVES
Kew, Richmond, Surrey TW9 4DU
T 020-8876 3444 **W** www.nationalarchives.gov.uk

The National Archives is a non-ministerial government department which incorporates the Public Record Office, Historical Manuscripts Commission, Office of Public Sector Information and Her Majesty's Stationery Office. As the official archive of the UK government, it preserves, protects and makes accessible the historical collection of official records.

The National Archives also manages digital information including the UK government web archive which contains over 1.7 billion digital documents, and devises solutions for keeping government records readable now and in the future.

The organisation administers the UK's public records system under the Public Records Acts of 1958 and 1967. The records it holds span 1,000 years – from the Domesday Book to the latest government papers to be released – and fill more than 104 miles of shelving.

Chief Executive and Keeper, Jeff James

NATIONAL CRIME AGENCY
Units 1–6 Citadel Place, Tinworth Street, London SE11 5EF
T 0370-496 7622 **E** communication@nca.gov.uk
W www.nationalcrimeagency.gov.uk

The National Crime Agency (NCA) is an operational crime fighting agency introduced under the Crime and Courts Act 2013, which became fully operational in October 2013. The NCA's remit is to fight serious and organised crime, strengthen UK borders, tackle fraud, modern slavery, human trafficking and cyber crime, and protect children and young people. The agency provides leadership through its organised crime, border policing, economic crime and Child Exploitation and Online Protection Centre commands, the National Cyber Crime Unit and specialist capability teams.

Director-General, Lynne Owens, CBE, QPM

NATIONAL SAVINGS AND INVESTMENTS
Glasgow G58 1SB
T 08085-007007 **W** www.nsandi.com

NS&I (National Savings and Investments) came into being in 1861 when the Palmerston government set up the Post Office Savings Bank, a savings scheme which aimed to encourage working-class wage earners 'to provide for themselves against adversity and ill health'. NS&I was established as a government department in 1969. It is responsible for the design, marketing and administration of savings and investment products for personal savers and investors, including premium bonds. It has over 25 million customers and around £179bn invested. *See also* Banking and Finance, National Savings.

Chief Executive, Ian Ackerley

OFFICE OF GAS AND ELECTRICITY MARKETS (OFGEM)
10 South Colonnade, Canary Wharf, London E14 4PU
T 020-7901 7000 **W** www.ofgem.gov.uk

OFGEM is the regulator for Britain's gas and electricity industries. Its role is to protect and advance the interests of consumers by promoting competition where possible, and through regulation only where necessary. OFGEM operates under the direction and governance of the Gas and Electricity Markets Authority, which makes all major decisions and sets policy priorities for OFGEM. OFGEM's powers are provided for under the Gas Act 1986 and the Electricity Act 1989, as amended by the Utilities Act 2000. It also has enforcement powers under the Competition Act 1998 and the Enterprise Act 2002.

Chair, Martin Cave
Chief Executive, Jonathan Brearley

OFFICE OF RAIL AND ROAD
25 Cabot square, London E14 4QZ
T 020-7282 2000 **E** contact.cct@orr.gov.uk **W** www.orr.gov.uk

The Office of the Rail and Road (ORR) was established in July 2004 under the Railways and Transport Safety Act 2003. It replaced the Office of the Rail Regulator.

In April 2006, ORR assumed new responsibilities as a combined safety and economic regulator under the Railways Act 2005. It also has concurrent jurisdiction with the Competition and Market Authority under the Competition Act 1998 as the competition authority for the railways.

As the railway industry's independent health and safety and economic regulator, its principal functions are to: ensure that Network Rail and HS1 manage the national network efficiently and in a way that meets the needs of its users;

encourage continuous health and safety performance; secure compliance with relevant health and safety law, including taking enforcement action as necessary; develop policy and enhance relevant railway health and safety legislation; and license operators of railway assets, setting the terms for access by operators to the network and other railway facilities, and enforce competition and consumer law in the rail sector.

In April 2015, under the Infrastructure Act 2015, ORR assumed responsibility for monitoring Highways England's management and development of the strategic road network – the motorways and main 'A' roads in England. In this role ORR ensures that the network is managed efficiently, safely and sustainably, for the benefit of road users and the public.

On 16 March 2015, ORR signed an agreement with the French rail regulator ARAF to establish a collaborative regulatory approach for consistent independent regulation across the Channel tunnel network.

ORR is led by a board appointed by the Secretary of State for Transport.

Chair, Declan Collier
Chief Executive (Interim), John Larkinson

OFFICE OF QUALIFICATIONS AND EXAMINATIONS REGULATION (OFQUAL)

Earlsdon Park, 53–55 Butts Road, Coventry CV1 3BH
T 0300-303 3344 **E** public.enquiries@ofqual.gov.uk
W www.gov.uk/government/organisations/ofqual

OFQUAL became the independent regulator of qualifications, examinations and assessments on 1 April 2010. It is responsible for maintaining standards, improving confidence and distributing information about qualifications and examinations, as well as regulating general and vocational qualifications in England.

Chief Regulator, Dame Glenys Stacey
Chair, Roger Taylor

OFFICE FOR STANDARDS IN EDUCATION, CHILDREN'S SERVICES AND SKILLS (OFSTED)

Aviation House, 125 Kingsway, London WC2B 6SE
T 0300-123 1231 **E** enquiries@ofsted.gov.uk
W www.gov.uk/government/organisations/ofsted

Ofsted was established under the Education (Schools Act) 1992 and was relaunched on 1 April 2007 with a wider remit, bringing together four formerly separate inspectorates. It works to raise standards in services through the inspection and regulation of care for children and young people, and inspects education and training for children of all ages. *See also* Education.

HM Chief Inspector, Amanda Spielman
Chair, Dame Christine Ryan

SERIOUS FRAUD OFFICE

2–4 Cockspur Street, London SW1Y 5BS
T 020-7239 7272 **E** public.enquiries@sfo.gov.uk
W www.sfo.gov.uk

The Serious Fraud Office is an independent government department that investigates and, where appropriate, prosecutes serious or complex fraud, bribery and corruption. It is part of the UK criminal justice system with jurisdiction over England, Wales and Northern Ireland but not Scotland, the Isle of Man or the Channel Islands. The office is headed by a director who is superintended by the Attorney-General.

Director, Lisa Osofsky

SUPREME COURT OF THE UNITED KINGDOM

Parliament Square, London SW1P 3BD
T 020-7960 1900 **E** enquiries@supremecourt.uk
W www.supremecourt.uk

The Supreme Court of the United Kingdom is the highest domestic judicial authority; it replaced the appellate committee of the House of Lords (the house functioning in its judicial capacity) in October 2009. It is the final court of appeal for cases heard in Great Britain and Northern Ireland (except for criminal cases from Scotland). Cases concerning the interpretation and application of European Union law, including preliminary rulings requested by British courts and tribunals, are decided by the Court of Justice of the European Union (CJEU), and the supreme court can make a reference to the CJEU in appropriate cases. Additionally, in giving effect to rights contained in the European Convention on Human Rights, the supreme court must take account of any decision of the European Court of Human Rights.

The supreme court also assumed jurisdiction in relation to devolution matters under the Scotland Act 1998 (now partly superseded by the Scotland Act 2012), the Northern Ireland Act 1988 and the Government of Wales Act 2006; these powers were transferred from the Judicial Committee of the Privy Council. Ten of the 12 Lords of Appeal in Ordinary (Law Lords) from the House of Lords transferred to the 12-member supreme court when it came into operation (at the same time one law lord retired and another was appointed Master of the Rolls). All new justices of the supreme court are now appointed by an independent selection commission, and, although styled Rt. Hon. Lord, are not members of the House of Lords. Peers who are members of the judiciary are disqualified from sitting or voting in the House of Lords until they retire from their judicial office.

Chief Executive, Vicky Fox

UK STATISTICS AUTHORITY

1 Drummond Gate, London SW1V 2QQ
E authority.enquiries@statistics.gov.uk
W www.statisticsauthority.gov.uk

The UK Statistics Authority was established in April 2008 by the Statistics and Registration Service Act 2007 as an independent body operating at arm's length from government, reporting to the UK parliament and the devolved legislatures. Its overall objective is to promote and safeguard the production and publication of official statistics and ensure their quality and comprehensiveness. The authority's main functions are the oversight of the Office for National Statistics (ONS); monitoring and reporting on all UK official statistics, which includes around 30 central government departments and the devolved administrations; and the production of a code of practice for statistics and the assessment of official statistics against the code.

BOARD
Chair, Sir David Norgrove
Board Members, Sam Beckett *(Second Permanent Secretary);* Prof. Sir Ian Diamond, FBA, FRSE, FACSS *(National Statistician);* Ed Humpherson *(Director General of Regulation)*
Non-Executive Members, Helen Boaden; Richard Dobbs; Prof. David Hand, OBE; Prof. Jonathan Haskel, OBE; Sian Jones *(Deputy Chair);* Nora Nanayakkara; Prof. David Spiegelhalter; Prof. Anne Trefethen

OFFICE FOR NATIONAL STATISTICS (ONS)

Cardiff Road, Newport NP10 8XG
T 0845-601 3034 **E** info@ons.gov.uk **W** www.ons.gov.uk

The ONS was created in 1996 by the merger of the Central Statistical Office and the Office of Population Censuses and Surveys. In April 2008 it became the executive office of the UK Statistics Authority. As part of these changes, the office's responsibility for the General Register Office transferred to HM Passport Office of the Home Office.

The ONS is responsible for preparing, interpreting and publishing key statistics on the government, economy and society of the UK. Its key responsibilities include designing, managing and running the Census and providing statistics on health and other demographic matters in England and Wales; the production of the UK National Accounts and other economic indicators; the organisation of population censuses in England and Wales and surveys for government departments and public bodies.

National Statistician and Permanent Secretary, John Pullinger

Second Permanent Secretary, Sam Beckett
Director-Generals, Jonathan Athow; Iain Bell; Alison Pritchard

WATER SERVICES REGULATION AUTHORITY (OFWAT)
Centre City Tower, 7 Hill Street, Birmingham B5 4UA
W www.ofwat.gov.uk

OFWAT is the independent economic regulator of the water and sewerage companies in England and Wales. It is responsible for ensuring that the water industry in England and Wales provides household and business customers with a good quality service and value for money. This is done by ensuring that the companies provide customers with a good quality, efficient service at a fair price; limiting the prices companies can charge; monitoring the companies' performance and taking action, including enforcement, to protect customers' interests; setting the companies efficiency targets; making sure the companies deliver the best for consumers and the environment in the long term; and encouraging competition where it benefits consumers.

Chair, Jonson Cox
Chief Executive, Rachel Fletcher

PUBLIC BODIES

The following section is a listing of public bodies and other civil service organisations: it is not a complete list of these organisations, which total over 400.

Whereas executive agencies are either part of a government department or are one in their own right (*see* Government Departments), public bodies carry out their functions to a greater or lesser extent at arm's length from central government. Ministers are ultimately responsible to parliament for the activities of the public bodies sponsored by their department and in almost all cases (except where there is separate statutory provision) ministers make the appointments to their boards. Departments are responsible for funding and ensuring good governance of their public bodies.

The term 'public body' is a general one which includes public corporations, such as the BBC; NHS bodies; and non-departmental public bodies (NDPBs).

ADJUDICATOR'S OFFICE
PO Box 10280, Nottingham NG2 9PF
T 0300-057 1111 **W** www.gov.uk/government/organisations/the-ajudicator-s-office

The Adjudicator's Office investigates complaints from individuals and businesses about the way that HM Revenue and Customs and the Valuation Office Agency have handled a person's affairs. The Adjudicator's Office will only consider a complaint after the respective organisation's internal complaints procedure has been exhausted. It also reviews Home Office decisions on entitlement to compensation under the Windrush Compensation Scheme.

The Adjudicator, Helen Megarry

ADVISORY, CONCILIATION AND ARBITRATION SERVICE (ACAS)
22nd Floor, Euston Tower, 286 Euston Road, London NW1 3JJ
T 0300-123 1100 **W** www.acas.org.uk

The Advisory, Conciliation and Arbitration Service was set up under the Employment Protection Act 1975 (the provisions now being found in the Trade Union and Labour Relations (Consolidation) Act 1992).

ACAS is largely funded by the Department for Business, Energy and Industrial Strategy. A council sets its strategic direction, policies and priorities, and ensures that the agreed strategic objectives and targets are met. It consists of a chair and 11 employer, trade union and independent members, appointed by the Secretary of State for Business, Energy and Industrial Strategy.

ACAS aims to improve organisations and working life through better employment relations, to provide up-to-date information, independent advice and high-quality training, and to work with employers and employees to solve problems and improve performance.

ACAS has regional offices in Birmingham, Bristol, Cardiff, Fleet, Glasgow, Leeds, Manchester, Mildenhall, Newcastle upon Tyne and Nottingham. The head office is in London.

Chair, Sir Brendan Barber
Chief Executive, Susan Clews

ADVISORY COUNCIL ON NATIONAL RECORDS AND ARCHIVES
The National Archives, Kew, Surrey TW9 4DU
T 020-8392 5248
E advisorycouncilsecretary@nationalarchives.gov.uk
W http://www.nationalarchives.gov.uk/about/our-role/advisory-council

The Advisory Council on National Records and Archives advises the Secretary of State for Digital, Culture, Media and Sport on issues relating to public records that are over 20 years old including public access to them. The council meets four times a year, and its main task is to consider requests for the extended closure of public records; it also reaches decisions regarding government departments that want to keep records. It is chaired by the Master of the Rolls.

The Forum on Historical Manuscripts and Academic Research, a sub-committee of the Advisory Council, provides advice to the Chief Executive of The National Archives and Keeper of Public Records on matters relating to historical manuscripts, records and archives, other than public records.

Chair, Rt. Hon. Sir Terence Etherton *(Master of the Rolls)*

AGRICULTURE AND HORTICULTURE DEVELOPMENT BOARD
Stoneleigh Park, Kenilworth, Warwickshire CV8 2TL
T 024-7669 2051 **E** info@ahdb.org.uk **W** www.ahdb.org.uk

The Agriculture and Horticulture Development Board (AHDB) is funded by the agriculture and horticulture industries through statutory levies, with the duty to improve efficiency and competitiveness within six sectors: beef and lamb in England; cereals and oilseeds in the UK; commercial horticulture in Great Britain; milk in Great Britain; pigs in England; and potatoes in Great Britain. The AHDB represents around 70 per cent of total UK agricultural output. Levies raised from the six sectors are ring-fenced to ensure that they can only be used to the benefit of the sectors from which they were raised.

Chair, Nicholas Saphir
Independent members, George Lyon; Sarah Pumfrett; Janet Swadling
Sector members, Hayley Campbell-Gibbons *(Horticulture);* Alison Levett *(Potatoes);* Adam Quinney *(Beef and Lamb);* Mike Sheldon *(Pork);* Richard Soffe *(Dairy);* Paul Temple *(Cereals and Oilseeds)*
Chief Executive, Jane King

ARCHITECTURE AND DESIGN SCOTLAND
9 Bakehouse Close, 146 Canongate, Edinburgh EH8 8DD
T 0131-556 6699 **E** info@ads.org.uk **W** www.ads.org.uk

Architecture and Design Scotland (A&DS) was established in 2005 by the Scottish government as the national champion for good architecture, urban design and planning in the built environment; it works with a wide range of organisations at national, regional and local levels.

Chair, Ann Allen
Chief Executive, Jim MacDonald

ARMED FORCES' PAY REVIEW BODY
8th Floor, Fleetbank House, 2–6 Salisbury Square, London EC4Y 8JX
T 020-7211 8175 **W** www.gov.uk/government/organisations/
armed-forces-pay-review-body

The Armed Forces' Pay Review Body was appointed in 1971. It advises the prime minister and the Secretary of State for Defence on the pay and allowances of members of naval, military and air forces of the Crown.

Chair, Peter Maddison, QPM
Members, Brendan Connor, JP; Jenni Douglas-Todd; Willie Entwisle, OBE, MVO; Kerry Holden; Prof. Ken Mayhew; Julian Miller

ARTS COUNCIL ENGLAND
21 Bloomsbury Street, London WC1B 3HF
E enqiries@artscouncil.org.uk **W** www.artscouncil.org.uk

Arts Council England is the national development agency for the arts in England. Using public money from government and the National Lottery, it supports a range of artistic activities, including theatre, music, literature, dance, photography, digital art, carnival and crafts. Between 2018 and 2022, Arts Council England planned to invest £408m a year in 829 arts organisations, museums and libraries within its national portfolio. However, the economic impact of the coronavirus pandemic in 2020 resulted in significant losses for the entire sector and emergency state funding was announced in July. Administered by Arts Council England, the Cultural Relief Fund allocated £1.57bn of grants, repayable finance and capital investment to institutions and individuals.

The governing body, the national council, comprises 14 members, who are appointed by the Secretary of State for Digital, Culture, Media and Sport usually for a term of four years. There are also five councils, responsible for the agreement of area strategies, plans and priorities for action within the national framework.

Chair, Sir Nicholas Serota, CH
National Council Members, Helen Birchenough; Prof. Roni Brown; Michael Eakin; Ciara Eastell, OBE; Sukhy Johal, MBE; David Joseph; Ruth Mackenzie, CBE; Catherine Mallyon; Andrew Miller; George Mpanga; Elisabeth Murdoch; Paul Roberts, OBE; Tessa Ross; Kate Willard
Chief Executive, Darren Henley, OBE

ARTS COUNCIL OF NORTHERN IRELAND
Linen Hill House, 23 Linenhall Street, Lisburn BT28 1FJ
T 028-9262 3555 **E** info@artscouncil-ni.org
W www.artscouncil-ni.org

The Arts Council of Northern Ireland is the prime distributor of government funds in support of the arts in Northern Ireland. It is funded by the Department for Communities and from National Lottery funds.

Chair, John Edmund
Members, Dr Katy Radford, MBE *(Vice-Chair);* Julie Andrews; Lynne Best; Liam Hannaway; Sean Kelly; Una McRory; Mairtin O Muilleoir; Cian Smyth
Chief Executive, Roisin McDonough

ARTS COUNCIL OF WALES
Bute Place, Cardiff CF10 5AL
T 0330-123 2733 **W** www.arts.wales

The Arts Council of Wales was established in 1994 by royal charter and is the development body for the arts in Wales. It funds arts organisations with funding from the Welsh government and is the distributor of National Lottery funds to the arts in Wales. It is known by its Welsh name, Cyngor Celfyddydau Cymru.

Chair, Phil George
Members, Iwan Bala; Lhosa Daly; Devinda De Silva; Andy Eagle; Kate Eden; Michael Griffiths, OBE; Tadur Hallam; Alison Mears Esswood; Andrew Miller; Victoria Pravis; Dafydd Rhys; Marian Wyn Jones; Sarah Younan
Chief Executive, Nick Capaldi

AUDIT SCOTLAND
102 West Port, Edinburgh EH3 9DN
T 0131-625 1500 **E** info@audit-scotland.gov.uk
W www.audit-scotland.gov.uk

Audit Scotland was set up in 2000 to provide services to the Accounts Commission and the Auditor-General for Scotland. Together they help to ensure that public-sector bodies in Scotland are held accountable for the proper, efficient and effective use of public funds.

Audit Scotland's is responsible for auditing 222 public bodies, including: 72 Scottish government bodies (including the police, fire and Scottish Water) and the Scottish parliament; 23 NHS bodies; 32 councils; 73 joint boards and committees (including 30 health integration boards); 21 further education colleges; and one European Agricultural Fund.

Audit Scotland carries out financial and regularity audits to ensure that public-sector bodies adhere to the highest standards of financial management and governance. It also carries out performance audits to ensure that these bodies achieve the best value for money. All of Audit Scotland's work in connection with local authorities is carried out for the Accounts Commission; its other work is undertaken for the Auditor-General.

Chair, Prof. Alan Alexander, OBE
Auditor-General, Stephen Boyle
Chair of the Accounts Commission (Interim), Elma Murray, OBE

BANK OF ENGLAND
Threadneedle Street, London EC2R 8AH
T 020-3461 4444 **E** enquiries@bankofengland.co.uk
W www.bankofengland.co.uk

The Bank of England was incorporated in 1694 under royal charter. It was nationalised in 1946 under the Bank of England Act of that year which gave HM Treasury statutory powers over the bank. It is the banker of the government and it manages the issue of banknotes. Since 1998 it has been operationally independent and its Monetary Policy Committee has been responsible for setting short-term interest rates to meet the government's inflation target. Its responsibility for banking supervision was transferred to the Financial Services Authority in the same year. As the central reserve bank of the country, the Bank of England keeps the accounts of British banks, and of most overseas central banks; the larger banks and building societies are required to maintain with it a proportion of their cash resources. The bank's core purposes are monetary stability and financial stability. The Banking Act 2009 increased the responsibilities of the bank, including giving it a new financial stability objective and creating a special resolution regime for dealing with failing banks.

In 2012, through the Prudential Regulation Authority (PRA), the bank became responsible for the prudential regulation and supervision of banks, building societies, credit unions, insurers and major investment firms.

COURT OF DIRECTORS
Governor, Andrew Bailey
Deputy Governors, Dr Ben Broadbent *(Monetary Policy);* Sir Jon Cunliffe, CB *(Financial Stability);* Sir Dave Ramsden *(Markets and Banking);* Sam Woods *(Prudential Regulation)*

Non-Executive Members, Bradley Fried *(Chair, Court of Directors);* Anne Glover, CBE; Baroness Harding of Winscombe; Ron Kalifa, OBE; Diana Noble, CBE; Frances O'Grady; Dorothy Thompson

FINANCIAL POLICY COMMITTEE
Members, Andrew Bailey; Dr Colette Bowe, DBE; Alex Brazier; Dr Ben Broadbent; Sir Jon Cunliffe, CB; Jonathan Hall; Anil Kashyap; Donald Kohn; Sir Dave Ramsden; Nikhil Rathi; Charles Roxburgh; Elisabeth Stheeman; Sam Woods

MONETARY POLICY COMMITTEE
Members, Dr Ben Broadbent; Mark Carney; Sir Jon Cunliffe, CB; Andy Haldane; Jonathan Haskel; Sir Dave Ramsden; Michael Saunders; Silvana Tenreyro; Dr Gertian Vlieghe

PRUDENTIAL REGULATION COMMITTEE
Members, Andrew Bailey; David Belsham; Julia Black, CBE, FBA; Dr Ben Broadbent; Norval Bryson; Sir Jon Cunliffe, CB; Jill May; Nikhil Rathi; Sir Dave Ramsden; Sam Woods; Mark Yallop

Chief Operating Officer, Joanna Place
General Counsel, Sonya Branch
Chief Cashier and Director of Notes, Sarah John

BOUNDARY COMMISSIONS

The commissions, established in 1944, are constituted under the Parliamentary Constituencies Act 1986 (as amended). The Speaker of the House of Commons is the *ex officio* chair of all four commissions in the UK.

The last reviews of UK parliament constituencies were undertaken using the electoral register from 1 December 2015; these reviews were submitted by the commissions in September 2018.

ENGLAND
Room 3.26, 1 Horse Guards Road, London SW1A 2HQ
T 020-7276 1102
E information@boundarycommissionengland.gov.uk
W http://boundarycommissionforengland.independent.gov.uk

Deputy Chair, Hon. Mr Justice Nicol

WALES
Hastings House, Fitzalan Court, Cardiff CF24 0BL
T 029-2046 4819 **E** enquiries@boundaries.wales
W www.bcomm-wales.gov.uk

Deputy Chair, Hon. Ms Justice Jefford, DBE, QC

SCOTLAND
Thistle House, 91 Haymarket Terrace, Edinburgh EH12 5HD
T 0131-244 2001 **E** bcs@scottishboundaries.gov.uk
W www.bcomm-scotland.independent.gov.uk

Deputy Chair, Hon. Lord Matthews

NORTHERN IRELAND
The Bungalow, Stormont House, Stormont Estate, Belfast BT4 3SH
T 028-9052 7821 **E** contact@boundarycommission.org.uk
W www.boundarycommission.org.uk

Deputy Chair, Hon. Ms Justice McBride, DBE

BRITISH BROADCASTING CORPORATION (BBC)

BBC Broadcasting House, Portland Place, London W1A 1AA
W www.bbc.co.uk

The BBC was incorporated under royal charter in 1926 as successor to the British Broadcasting Company Ltd. The BBC's current charter, which came into force on 1 January 2017 and extends to 31 December 2027, recognises the BBC's editorial

independence and sets out its public purposes. The BBC Board was formed under the new charter and is responsible for ensuring that the Corporation fulfils its mission and public purposes by setting the strategic direction of the BBC, establishing its creative remit, setting the budget and determining the framework for assessing performance. As part of the new charter, The Office of Communications (OFCOM) was awarded sole regulatory responsibility for the BBC. The BBC is financed by television licence revenue to ensure it remains independent from political control.

BBC BOARD
Chair, Sir David Clementi
Director-General, Tim Davie, CBE
National Members, Steve Morrison *(Scotland);* Dr Ashley Steel *(England);* Dame Elan Closs Stephens, DBE *(Wales)*
Members, Tim Davie *(CEO BBC Studios);* Ken MacQuarrie *(Nations and Regions);* Charlotte Moore *(Chief Content Officer);* Nicholas Serota, CH *(Senior Independent Director);* Francesca Unsworth *(News and Current Affairs)*
Non-Executive Members, Shirley Garrood; Baroness Grey-Thompson, DBE; Ian Hargreaves, CBE; Tom Ilube

EXECUTIVE COMMITTEE
Director-General, Tim Davie, CBE
Directors, Kerris Bright *(Chief Customer Officer);* Tom Fussell *(Interim CEO, BBC Studios);* Glyn Isherwood *(Chief Financial Officer);* Ken MacQuarrie *(Nations and Regions);* Charlotte Moore *(Chief Content Officer);* Gautam Rangarajan *(Strategy and Performance);* June Sarpong *(Creative Diversity);* Bob Shennan *(Managing Director);* Francesca Unsworth *(News and Current Affairs)*

CHANNEL AND PLATFORM HEADS
Chief Content Officer, Charlotte Moore
Controller BBC Two, Patrick Holland
Controller BBC Three, Fiona Campbell
Editor BBC Four, Cassian Harrison
Controller of Programming and iPlayer, Dan McGolpin
Director of Sport, Barbara Slater
Head of Content BBC Children's, Cheryl Taylor

GENRE CONTROLLERS
Entertainment, Kate Phillips
Factual, Alison Kirkham
Drama, Piers Wenger
Comedy, Shane Allen

Production, BBC Radio and Music, Bob Shennan

BRITISH COUNCIL

Bridgewater House, 58 Whitworth Street, Manchester M1 6BB
T 0161-957 7755
W www.britishcouncil.org

The British Council was established in 1934, incorporated by royal charter in 1940 and granted a supplemental charter in 1993. It is an independent, non-political organisation which promotes Britain abroad and is the UK's international organisation for educational and cultural relations. The British Council is represented in over 100 countries.

Chair, Stevie Spring, CBE
Chief Executive, Sir Ciarán Devane

BRITISH FILM INSTITUTE

21 Stephen Street, London W1T 1LN
W www.bfi.org.uk

The BFI, established in 1933, offers opportunities for people throughout the UK to experience, learn and discover more about the world of film and moving image culture. It incorporates the BFI National Archive, the BFI Reuben

Library, BFI Southbank, BFI Distribution, the annual BFI London Film Festival as well as the BFI FLARE: London LGBT Film Festival, and the BFI IMAX cinema. It also publishes the monthly *Sight and Sound* magazine and provides advice and support for regional cinemas and film festivals across the UK.

Following the closure of the UK Film Council in April 2011, the BFI became the lead body for film in the UK, in charge of allocating lottery money for the development and production of new British films.

Chair (Interim), Pat Butler
Chief Executive, Ben Roberts

BRITISH LIBRARY
96 Euston Road, London NW1 2DB
Boston Spa, Wetherby, W. Yorks LS23 7BQ
T 0330-333 1144 **E** customer-services@bl.uk **W** www.bl.uk

The British Library was established in 1973. It is the UK's national library and one of the world's greatest research libraries. It aims to serve scholarship, research, industry, commerce and all other major users of information. The Library's collection has developed over 250 years and exceeds 170 million items, including books, journals, manuscripts, maps, stamps, music, patents, newspapers and sound recordings in all written and spoken languages. The library is now based at two sites: London St Pancras and Boston Spa, W. Yorks. The library's sponsoring department is the Department for Digital, Culture, Media and Sport. Up to 3 million digitised items are added to the collection each year.

BRITISH LIBRARY BOARD
Chair, Dame Carol Black, DBE, FRCP
*Members,*Jana Bennett, OBE; Delroy Beverley; Dr Robert Black, CBE, FRSE; Tracy Chevalier, FRSL; Lord Janvrin, GCB, GCVO, QSO, PC; Roly Keating; Patrick Plant; Dr Venki Ramakrishnan; Dr Jeremy Silver; Laela Tabrizi; Dr Simon Thurley, CBE; Dr Wei Yang

EXECUTIVE
Chief Executive, Roly Keating
Chief Librarian, Liz Jolly
Chief Operating Officer, Phil Spence

BRITISH MUSEUM
Great Russell Street, London WC1B 3DG
T 020-7323 8000
W www.britishmuseum.org

The British Museum houses the national collection of antiquities, ethnography, coins and paper money, medals, prints and drawings. The British Museum dates from 7 June 1753, when parliament approved the holding of a public lottery to raise funds for the purchase of the collections of Sir Hans Sloane and the Harleian manuscripts, and for their proper housing and maintenance. The building (Montagu House) was opened in 1759. The existing buildings were erected between 1823 and the present day, and the original collection has increased to its current dimensions by gifts and purchases. Total government grant-in-aid for 2018–19 was £52.5m.

Chair, Sir Richard Lambert
Trustees, Prof. Dame Mary Beard DBE, FSA, FBA; Hon. Nigel Boardman; Cheryl Carolus; Elizabeth Corley, CBE; Patricia Cumper, MBE; Clarissa Farr; Prof. Chris Gosden, FBA; Muriel Gray; Philipp Hildebrand; Dame Vivian Hunt, DBE; Sir Deryck Maughan; Sir Charles Mayfield; Mark Pears, CBE; Grayson Perry, CBE, RA; Sir Paul Ruddock, FSA; Lord Sassoon; Baroness (Minouche) Shafik, DBE *(Deputy Chair)*; George Weston; Prof. Dame Sarah Worthington, DBE, QC (Hon), FBA

OFFICERS
Director, Dr Hartwig Fischer
Deputy Directors, Joanna Mackle; Jonathan Williams; Christopher Yates

KEEPERS
Keeper of Africa, Oceania and the Americas, Lissant Bolton
Keeper of Ancient Egypt and Sudan, Neal Spencer
Keeper of Asia, Jane Portal
Deputy Keeper of Britain, Europe and Prehistory, Jill Cook
Keeper of Coins and Medals, Philip Attwood
Keeper of Greece and Rome, J. Lesley Fitton
Keeper of the Middle East, Jonathan N. Tubb
Keeper of Portable Antiquities and Treasure, Roger Bland
Keeper of Prints and Drawings, Hugo Chapman

BRITISH PHARMACOPOEIA COMMISSION
151 Buckingham Palace Road, London SW1W 9SZ
T 020-3080 6561 **E** bpcom@mhra.gov.uk
W www.pharmacopoeia.com

The British Pharmacopoeia Commission sets standards for medicinal products used in human and veterinary medicines and is responsible for publication of *British Pharmacopoeia* (a publicly available statement of the standard that a medicinal substance or product must meet throughout its shelf-life), *British Pharmacopoeia (Veterinary)* and *British Approved Names.* It has 17 members, including two lay members, who are appointed on behalf of the Secretary of State for Health and Social Care by the Department of Health and Social Care.

Chair, Prof. Kevin Taylor
Vice-Chair, Prof. Alastair Davidson

CARE QUALITY COMMISSION
Citygate, Gallowgate, Newcastle upon Tyne NE1 4PA
T 0300-061 6161 **E** enquiries@cqc.org.uk **W** www.cqc.org.uk

The Care Quality Commission (CQC) is the independent regulator of health and adult social care services in England, ensuring health and social care services provide people with safe, effective, compassionate, high-quality care and encouraging them to improve. CQC monitors, inspects and regulates services to make sure they meet fundamental standards of quality and safety and publishes performance ratings to help people choose care.

Chair, Peter Wyman, CBE
Board Members, Prof. Ted Baker; Rosie Benneyworth; Sir Robert Francis, QC; Jora Gill; Paul Rew; Mark Saxton; Liz Sayce, OBE; Kate Terroni; Kirsty Shaw
Chief Executive, Ian Trenholm

CENTRAL ARBITRATION COMMITTEE
Fleetbank House, 2-6 Salisbury Square, London EC4Y 8JX
T 0330-109 3610 **E** enquiries@cac.gov.uk
W www.gov.uk/government/organisations/central-arbitration-committee

The Central Arbitration Committee (CAC) is a permanent independent body with statutory powers whose main function is to adjudicate on applications relating to the statutory recognition and de-recognition of trade unions for collective bargaining purposes, where such recognition or de-recognition cannot be agreed voluntarily. In addition, the CAC has a statutory role in determining disputes between trade unions and employers over the disclosure of information for collective bargaining purposes, and in resolving applications and complaints under the information and consultation regulations, and performs a similar role in relation to the legislation on the European Works Council, European companies, European cooperative societies and cross-border mergers. The CAC and its predecessors have also provided voluntary arbitration in collective disputes.

Chair, Stephen Redmond

CERTIFICATION OFFICE FOR TRADE UNIONS AND EMPLOYERS' ASSOCIATIONS

Lower Ground Floor, Fleetbank House, 2-6 Salisbury Square, London EC4Y 8JX
T 0330-109 3602 **E** info@certoffice.org
W www.gov.uk/government/organisations/certification-officer

The Certification Office is an independent statutory authority. The Certification Officer is appointed by the Secretary of State for Business, Energy and Industrial Strategy and is responsible for maintaining a list of trade unions and employers' associations; ensuring compliance with statutory requirements and keeping available for public inspection annual returns from trade unions and employers' associations; determining complaints concerning trade union elections, certain ballots and certain breaches of trade union rules; ensuring observance of statutory requirements governing mergers between trade unions and between employers' associations; overseeing the political funds and finances of trade unions and employers' associations; and for certifying the independence of trade unions.

Certification Officer, Sarah Bedwell

CHURCH COMMISSIONERS

Church House, Great Smith Street, London SW1P 3AZ
T 020-7898 1000 **E** commissioners.enquiry@churchofengland.org
W www.churchofengland.org/about/leadership-and-governance/church-commissioners

The Church Commissioners were established in 1948 by the amalgamation of Queen Anne's Bounty (established 1704) and the Ecclesiastical Commissioners (established 1836). They are responsible for the management of some of the Church of England's assets, the income from which is predominantly used to help pay for the stipend and pension of the clergy and to support the church's work throughout the country. The commissioners own UK and global company shares, over 120,000 acres of forestry estate, a residential estate in central London, and commercial property across Great Britain, plus an interest in overseas property via managed funds. They also carry out administrative duties in connection with pastoral reorganisation and closed churches.

The 33 commissioners are: the Archbishops of Canterbury and of York; eleven people elected by the General Synod, comprising four bishops, three clergy and four lay persons; three Church Estates Commissioners; two cathedral deans; nine people appointed by the crown and the archbishops; six holders of state office, comprising the Prime Minister, the Lord Chancellor, the Lord President of the Council, the Secretary of State for Digital, Culture, Media and Sport, the Speaker of the House of Commons and the Lord Speaker.

CHURCH ESTATES COMMISSIONERS
First, Loretta Minghella, OBE
Second, Andrew Selous, MP
Third, Dr Eve Poole

OFFICERS
Chief Executive and Secretary, Gareth Mostyn
Official Solicitor, Revd Alexander McGregor

COAL AUTHORITY

200 Lichfield Lane, Mansfield, Notts NG18 4RG
T 0345-762 6848 **E** thecoalauthority@coal.gov.uk
W www.gov.uk/government/organisations/the-coal-authority

The Coal Authority was established under the Coal Industry Act 1994 to manage certain functions previously undertaken by British Coal, including ownership of unworked coal. It is responsible for licensing coal mining operations and for providing information on coal reserves and past and future coal mining. It settles subsidence damage claims which are not the responsibility of licensed coal mining operators. It deals with the management and disposal of property, and with surface hazards such as abandoned coal mine entries and mine water discharges. The Coal Authority's powers were extended alongside the Energy Act 2011 to enable it to deal with metal mine subsidence issues and deliver a metal mine water treatment programme.

Chair, Stephen Dingle
Chief Executive, Lisa Pinney, MBE

COMMITTEE ON STANDARDS IN PUBLIC LIFE

1 Horse Guards Road, London SW1A 2HQ
T 020-7271 2685 **E** public@public-standards.gov.uk
W www.gov.uk/government/organisations/the-committee-on-standards-in-public-life

The Committee on Standards in Public Life (CSPL) was set up in October 1994. It is formed of 8 people appointed by the prime minister, comprising the chair, three political members nominated by the leaders of the three main political parties and four independent members. The CSPL advises the prime minister on ethical standards across the whole of public life in the UK. It monitors and reports on issues relating to the standards of conduct of all public office holders. It is responsible for promoting the seven principles of public life, being: selflessness; integrity; objectivity; accountability; openness; honesty; and leadership.

Chair, Lord Jonathan Evans of Weardale, KCB, DL
Members, Rt. Hon. Dame Margaret Beckett, DBE, PC, MP; Dr Jane Martin, CBE; Dame Shirley Pearce, DBE; Monisha Shah; Rt. Hon. Lord Andrew Stunell, OBE; Rt. Hon. Jeremy Wright, QC, MP

COMMONWEALTH WAR GRAVES COMMISSION

2 Marlow Road, Maidenhead, Berks SL6 7DX
T 01628-634221 **E** enquiries@cwgc.org **W** www.cwgc.org

The Commonwealth War Graves Commission (CWGC) was founded by royal charter in 1917. It is responsible for the commemoration of around 1.7 million members of the forces of the Commonwealth who lost their lives in the two world wars. More than one million graves are maintained in over 23,000 burial grounds across 154 countries. Over three-quarters of a million men and women who have no known grave or who were cremated are commemorated by name on memorials built by the commission.

The funds of the commission are derived from the six participating governments: the UK, Canada, Australia, New Zealand, South Africa and India.

President, HRH the Duke of Kent, KG, GCMG, GCVO, ADC
Chair, Secretary of State for Defence
Vice-Chair, Lt.-Gen. Sir William Rollo, KCB, CBE
Members, High Commissioners in London for Australia, Canada, India, New Zealand and South Africa; Rt. Hon. Philip Dunne, MP; Sir Tim Hitchens, KCVO, CMG; Vice-Adm. Peter Hudson, CB, CBE; Diana Johnson, MP, DBE;

Dame Judith Mayhew Jonas, DBE; Vasuki Shastry; Air Marshal David Walker, CB, CBE, AFC
Director-General (Acting), Barry Murphy

COMPETITION SERVICE
Victoria House, Bloomsbury Place, London WC1A 2EB
T 020-7979 7979 **W** www.catribunal.org.uk

The Competition Service is the financial corporate body by which the Competition Appeal Tribunal is administered and through which it receives funding for the performance of its judicial functions.

Registrar, Charles Dhanowa, OBE, QC

CONSUMER COUNCIL FOR WATER
Victoria Square House, Victoria Square, Birmingham, B2 4AJ
T 0300-034 2222 **E** enquiries@ccwater.org.uk
W www.ccwater.org.uk

The Consumer Council for Water was established in 2005 under the Water Act 2003 to represent consumers' interests in respect of price, service and value for money from their water and sewerage services, and to investigate complaints from customers about their water company. There are four regional committees in England and one in Wales.

Chair, Robert Light
Chief Executive, Emma Clancy

CORPORATION OF TRINITY HOUSE
Trinity House, Tower Hill, London EC3N 4DH
T 020-7481 6900 **E** enquiries@trinityhouse.co.uk
W www.trinityhouse.co.uk

The Corporation of Trinity House of Deptford Strond is the UK's largest-endowed maritime charity, established formally by royal charter by Henry VIII in 1514, with statutory duties as the General Lighthouse Authority (GLA) for England, Wales, the Channel Islands and Gibraltar. Its remit is to assist the safe passage of a variety of vessels through some of the busiest sea-lanes in the world; it does this by inspecting and auditing almost 11,000 local aids to navigation, ranging from lighthouses to a satellite navigation service. The corporation also has certain statutory jurisdiction over aids to navigation maintained by local harbour authorities and is responsible for marking or dispersing wrecks dangerous to navigation, except those occurring within port limits or wrecks of HM ships.

The statutory duties of Trinity House are funded by the General Lighthouse Fund, which is provided from light dues levied on commercial vessels calling at ports in the British Isles, based on the net registered tonnage of the vessel. Light Dues are paid into the General Lighthouse Fund under the stewardship of the Department for Transport. The fund finances the work of Trinity House and the Northern Lighthouse Board (Scotland and the Isle of Man). The corporation is a deep-sea pilotage authority, authorised by the Secretary of State for Transport to license deep-sea pilots. In addition, Trinity House is a charitable organisation that maintains a number of retirement homes for mariners and their dependants, funds a four-year training scheme for those seeking a career in the merchant navy, and also dispenses grants to a wide range of maritime charities. Trinity House's maritime and corporate charities are entirely self-funded by incomes derived from endowed funds.

The corporation is controlled by a court of 31 elected Elder Brethren, who oversee the corporate and lighthouse boards. The Elder Brethren also act as nautical assessors in marine cases in the Admiralty Division of the High Court.

ELDER BRETHREN
Master, HRH the Princess Royal, KG, KT, GCVO
Deputy Master, Capt. Ian McNaught, CVO
Wardens, Capt. Nigel Palmer, OBE *(Rental)*; Rear-Adm. David Snelson, CB *(Nether)*; Rear-Adm. David Snelson, CB
Elder Brethren, HRH the Duke of Edinburgh, KG, KT, OM, GBE; HRH the Prince of Wales, KG, KT, GCB; HRH the Duke of York, KG, GCVO, ADC; Capt. Roger Barker; Adm. Lord Boyce, KG, GCB, OBE; Capt. Lord Browne of Madingley, FRS, FRENG; Capt. John Burton-Hall, RD, RNR; Viscount Cobham; Cdre Robert Dorey, RFA; Capt. Sir Malcolm Edge, KCVO; Capt. Ian Gibb, MBE; Malcolm Glaister; Capt. Duncan Glass, OBE; Capt. Stephen Gobbi; Lord Greenway, Bt.; Rear-Adm. Sir Jeremy de Halpert, KCVO, CB; Capt. Nigel Hope, RD, RNR; Lord Mackay of Clashfern, KT, PC; Sir John Major, KG, CH, PC; Capt. Peter Mason, CBE; Cdre Peter Melson, CVO, CBE, RN; Capt. David Orr; Sir John Parker, GBE; Douglas Potter; Capt. Nigel Pryke; Richard Sadler; Lord Robertson of Port Ellen, KT, GCMG, PC; Rear-Adm. Sir Patrick Rowe, KCVO, CBE; Cdre James Scorer, RN; Simon Sherrard; Adm. Sir Jock Slater, GCB, LVO; Cdre David Squire, CBE, RFA; Vice-Adm. Lord Sterling of Plaistow, GCVO, CBE, RNR; Capt. Colin Stewart, LVO; Capt. Thomas Woodfield, OBE; Capt. Richard Woodman, LVO; Cdre William Walworth, CBE; Adm. Sir George Zambellas, CB

OFFICERS
Secretary, Thomas Arculus
Director of Business Services, Ton Damen, RA
Director of Navigational Requirements, Capt. Roger Barker
Director of Operations, Cdre Rob Dorey

CREATIVE SCOTLAND
Waverley Gate, 2–4 Waterloo Place, Edinburgh EH1 3EG
T 0330-333 2000 **E** enquiries@creativescotland.com
W www.creativescotland.com

Creative Scotland is the organisation tasked with leading the development of the arts, creative and screen industries across Scotland. It was created in 2010 as an amalgamation of the Scottish Arts Council and Scottish Screen, and it encourages and sustains the arts through investment in the form of grants, bursaries, loans and equity. It aims to invest in talent; artistic production; audiences, access and participation; and the cultural economy. Total Scottish government grant-in-aid funding for 2019–20 is £62m.

Chair, Robert Wilson
Board, Ewan Angus; David Brew; Duncan Cockburn; Stephanie Fraser; Philip Long; Sarah Munro; Elizabeth Partyka; David Strachan
Chief Executive, Iain Munro

CRIMINAL CASES REVIEW COMMISSION
5 St Philip's Place, Birmingham B3 2PW
T 0121-233 1473 **E** info@ccrc.gov.uk **W** www.ccrc.gov.uk

The Criminal Cases Review Commission is the independent body set up under the Criminal Appeal Act 1995. It is a non-departmental public body reporting to parliament via the Lord Chancellor and Secretary of State for Justice. It is responsible for investigating possible miscarriages of justice in England, Wales and Northern Ireland, and deciding whether or not to refer cases back to an appeal court. Members of the commission are appointed in accordance with the Office of the Commissioner for Public Appointments' code of practice.

Chair, Helen Pitcher, OBE
Members, David Brown, QFSM; Cindy Butts; Ian Comfort;
Rachel Ellis; Jill Gramann; Johanna Higgins; Linda Lee;
Christine Smith, QC; Robert Ward, CBE, QC (Hon)
Chief Executive, Karen Kneller

CROFTING COMMISSION
Great Glen House, Leachkin Road, Inverness IV3 8NW
T 01463-663439 E info@crofting.gov.scot
W www.crofting.scotland.gov.uk

The Crofting Commission was established on 1 April 2012,
taking over the regulation of crofting from the Crofters
Commission. The aim of the Crofting Commission is to
regulate crofting, to promote the occupancy of crofts, active
land use, and shared management of the land by crofters, as a
means of sustaining and enhancing rural communities in
Scotland.

Chief Executive, Bill Barron

CROWN ESTATE
1 St James's Market, London SW1Y 4AH
T 020-7851 5000 E enquiries@thecrownestate.co.uk
W www.thecrownestate.co.uk

The Crown Estate is part of the hereditary possessions of the
sovereign 'in right of the crown', managed under the
provisions of the Crown Estate Act 1961. It had a capital value
of £13.4bn in 2020, which included substantial blocks of
urban property, primarily in London, sizeable portions of
coastal and rural land, and offshore windfarms. The Crown
Estate has a duty to maintain and enhance the capital value of
estate and the income obtained from it. Under the terms of the
act, the estate pays its revenue surplus to the Treasury every
year.

Chair and First Commissioner, Robin Budenberg, CBE
Chief Executive and Second Commissioner, Daniel Labbad

DISCLOSURE AND BARRING SERVICE
PO Box 3961, Royal Wootton Bassett SN4 4HF
T 0300-020 0190 E customerservices@dbs.gov.uk
W www.gov.uk/government/organisations/
disclosure-and-barring-service

The Disclosure and Barring Service (DBS) is an executive non-
departmental public body of the Home Office. It helps
employers make safer recruitment decisions and prevent
unsuitable people from working with vulnerable groups,
including children. It was formed in December 2012 and
replaced the Criminal Records Bureau (CRB) and Independent
Safeguarding Authority (ISA). The DBS is responsible for the
children's barred list and adults' barred list for England, Wales
and Northern Ireland.

Chair, Dr Gillian Fairfield
Chief Executive, Eric Robinson

ENVIRONMENT AGENCY
PO Box 544, Rotherham S60 1BY
T 0370-850 6506 E enquiries@environment-agency.gov.uk
Incident Hotline 0800-807060
W www.gov.uk/government/organisations/environment-agency

Established in 1996 under the Environment Act 1995, the
Environment Agency is a non-departmental public body
sponsored by the Department for Environment, Food and
Rural Affairs. In April 2013, Natural Resources Wales took
over the Environment Agency's responsibilities in Wales.
Around 68 per cent of the agency's funding is from the
government, with the rest raised from various charging
schemes. The agency is responsible for pollution prevention

and control in England and for the management and use of
water resources, including flood defences, fisheries and
navigation. Its remit also includes: scrutinising potentially
hazardous business operations; helping businesses to use
resources more efficiently; taking action against those who do
not take environmental responsibilities seriously; looking after
wildlife; working with farmers; helping people get the most
out of their environment; and improving the quality of inner
city areas and parks by restoring rivers and lakes.

The Environment Agency has head offices in Bristol and
London, as well as offices across England, divided into 14
regions. Its total grant-in-aid for 2018–19 was £850m.

Chair, Emma Howard Boyd
Board Members, Harvey Bradshaw; John Curtin; John Leyland;
Toby Wilson
Chief Executive, Sir James Bevan

EQUALITY AND HUMAN RIGHTS COMMISSION
Arndale House, The Arndale Centre, Manchester M4 3AQ
T 0161-829 8327 E correspondence@equalityhumanrights.com
W www.equalityhumanrights.com

The Equality and Human Rights Commission (EHRC) is a
statutory body, established under the Equality Act 2006 and
launched in October 2007. It inherited the responsibilities of
the Commission for Racial Equality, the Disability Rights
Commission and the Equal Opportunities Commission. The
EHRC's purpose is to reduce inequality, eliminate
discrimination, strengthen relations between people, and
promote and protect human rights. It enforces equality
legislation on age, disability, gender reassignment, marriage
and civil partnership, pregnancy and maternity, race, religion
or belief, sex and sexual orientation, and encourages
compliance with the Human Rights Act 1998 throughout
England, Wales and Scotland.

Chair, Baroness Kishwer Falkner of Margravine
Deputy Chair, Caroline Waters, OBE
Commissioners, Suzanne Baxter; Jessica Butcher, MBE; Pavita
Cooper; David Goodhart; Alasdair Henderson; Susan
Johnston, OBE; Mark McLane; Helen Mahy, CBE; Baron
Bernard Ribeiro of Achimota and Ovington, CBE; Dr
Lesley Sawers, OBE *(Scotland Commissioner);* Sue-Mei
Thompson
Chief Executive, Rebecca Hilsenrath

EQUALITY COMMISSION FOR NORTHERN IRELAND
Equality House, 7–9 Shaftesbury Square, Belfast BT2 7DP
T 028-9050 0600 E information@equalityni.org
W www.equalityni.org

The Equality Commission was set up in 1999 under the
Northern Ireland Act 1998 and is responsible for promoting
equality, keeping the relevant legislation under review,
eliminating discrimination on the grounds of age, race,
disability, sex and sexual orientation, gender (including marital
and civil partner status, gender reassignment, pregnancy and
maternity), religion and political opinion, and for overseeing
the statutory duties on public authorities to promote equality
of opportunity and good relations.

Chief Commissioner, Geraldine McGahey
Deputy Chief Commissioner, Neil Anderson
Chief Executive, Dr Evelyn Collins, CBE

GAMBLING COMMISSION

Victoria Square House, Victoria Square, Birmingham B2 4BP
T 0121-230 6666 **E W** www.gamblingcommission.gov.uk

The Gambling Commission was established under the Gambling Act 2005, and took over the role previously occupied by the Gaming Board for Great Britain in regulating and licensing all commercial gambling – apart from spread betting and the National Lottery – for example casinos, bingo, betting, remote gambling (online and by phone), gaming machines and lotteries. It also advises local and central government on related issues, and is responsible for the protection of children and the vulnerable from being harmed by gambling. In October 2013, the Gambling Commission took over all the responsibilities of the National Lottery Commission in regulating the National Lottery. The commission is sponsored by the Department for Digital, Culture, Media and Sport, with its work funded by licence fees paid by the gambling industry.

Chair, Dr Bill Moyes
Commissioners, Terry Babbs; John Baillie; Brian Bannister; Carol Brady; Stephen Cohen; Jo Hill; Trevor Pearce, CBE, QPM; Catherine Seddon;
Chief Executive, Neil McArthur, MBE

HEALTH AND SAFETY EXECUTIVE

Redgrave Court, Merton Road, Bootle, Merseyside L20 7HS
T 0300-790 6787 **W** www.hse.gov.uk

The Health and Safety Commission (HSC) and the Health and Safety Executive (HSE) merged in April 2008 to form a single national regulatory body – the HSE – responsible for promoting the cause of better health and safety at work. The HSE is sponsored by the Department for Work and Pensions.

HSE regulates all industrial and commercial sectors except operations in the air and at sea. This includes agriculture, construction, manufacturing, services, transport, mines, offshore oil and gas, quarries and major hazard sites in chemicals and petrochemicals.

HSE is responsible for developing and enforcing health and safety law; providing guidance and advice; commissioning research; conducting inspections and accident and ill-health investigations; developing standards; and licensing or approving some work activities such as asbestos removal.

Chair, Sarah Newton, FRSA
Board Members, Janice Crawford; Martin Esom; Susan Johnson, OBE; John McDermid; Prof. Ged Nichols, OBE; Ken Robertson; Kevin Rowan; Claire Sullivan
Chief Executive, Sarah Albon

HER MAJESTY'S OFFICERS OF ARMS

COLLEGE OF ARMS (HERALDS' COLLEGE)

130 Queen Victoria Street, London EC4V 4BT
T 020-7248 2762 **W** www.college-of-arms.gov.uk

The Sovereign's Officers of Arms (King's, Heralds and Pursuivants of Arms) were first incorporated by Richard III in 1484. The powers vested by the crown in the Earl Marshal (the Duke of Norfolk) with regard to state ceremonial are largely exercised through the college. The college is also the official repository of the arms and pedigrees of English, Welsh, Northern Irish and Commonwealth (except Canadian) families and their descendants, and its records include official copies of the records of the Ulster King of Arms, the originals of which remain in Dublin. The 13 officers of the college specialise in genealogical and heraldic work for their respective clients.

Arms have long been, and still are, granted by letters patent from the Kings of Arms. A right to arms can only be established by the registration in the official records of the College of Arms of a pedigree showing direct male line descent from an ancestor already appearing therein as being entitled to arms, or by making application through the College of Arms for a grant of arms. Grants are made to corporations as well as to individuals.

Earl Marshal, the Duke of Norfolk

KINGS OF ARMS
Garter, Thomas Woodcock, CVO, FSA
Clarenceux, Patric Dickinson, LVO
Norroy and Ulster, Timothy Duke, FSA

HERALDS
Lancaster, Robert Noel
Somerset, David White
Richmond, Clive Cheesman, FSA
York, Peter O'Donoghue, FSA
Chester, Hon. Christopher Fletcher-Vane
Windsor, John Allen-Petrie

PURSUIVANTS
Rouge Dragon, Adam Tuck
Bluemantle, Mark Scott
Portcullis, vacant
Rouge Croix, vacant

COURT OF THE LORD LYON

HM New Register House, Edinburgh EH1 3YT
T 0131-556 7255 **E** lyonoffice@gov.scot
W www.courtofthelordlyon.scot

Her Majesty's Officers of Arms in Scotland perform ceremonial duties and, in addition, may be consulted by members of the public on heraldic and genealogical matters in a professional capacity.

KING OF ARMS
Lord Lyon King of Arms, Dr Joseph Morrow, CBE, QC

HERALDS
Rothesay, Sir Crispin Agnew of Lochnaw, Bt., QC
Snawdoun, Elizabeth Roads, LVO, FSA, FSA SCOT
Marchmont, Hon. Adam Bruce, WS

PURSUIVANTS
Dingwall, Yvonne Holton
Unicorn, Liam Devlin
Carrick, George Way of Plean

EXTRAORDINARY OFFICERS
Orkney Herald Extraordinary, vacant
Angus Herald Extraordinary, vacant
Ross Herald Extraordinary, vacant
Islay Herald Extraordinary, vacant
Linlithgow Pursuivant Extraordinary, John Stirling, WS
Falkland Pursuivant Extraordinary, Roderick Macpherson

HIGHLANDS AND ISLANDS ENTERPRISE

An Lòchran, 10 Inverness Campus, Inverness IV2 5NA
T 01463-245245 **E** enquiries@hient.co.uk **W** www.hie.co.uk

Highlands and Islands Enterprise (HIE) was set up under the Enterprise and New Towns (Scotland) Act 1991. Its role is to deliver community and economic development in line with the Scottish government economic strategy. It focuses on four priorities: supporting businesses and social enterprises; strengthening communities and fragile areas; developing growth sectors; and creating the conditions for a competitive and low carbon region. HIE's budget for 2020–21 was £58.2m.

Chair, Alistair Dodds, CBE
Chief Executive, Charlotte Wright

HISTORIC ENGLAND

Cannon Bridge House, 25 Dowgate Hill, London EC4R 2YA
T 0370-333 0607 **E** customers@historicengland.org.uk
W www.historicengland.org.uk

Established under the National Heritage Act 1983, Historic England, officially the Historic Buildings and Monuments Commission for England, has three statutory purposes: to secure the preservation of ancient monuments and historic buildings; to promote the preservation and enhancement of the character and appearance of conservation areas; and to promote the public's enjoyment of, and advance their knowledge of, ancient monuments and historic buildings. In 2018–19 Historic England received £91.6m grant-in-aid from the Department for Digital, Culture, Media and Sport.

Chair, Sir Laurie Magnus
Commissioners, Alex Balfour; Nicholas Boys Smith; Prof. Martin Daunton; Sandie Dawe, CBE; Ben Derbyshire; Sandra Dinneen; Paul Farmer; Prof. Helena Hamerow; Victoria Harley; Rosemarie MacQueen, MBE; Michael Morrison; Patrick Newberry; Charles O'Brien; Susie Thornberry; Richard Upton; Sue Wilkinson
Chief Executive, Duncan Wilson, OBE

HISTORIC ENVIRONMENT SCOTLAND

Longmore House, Salisbury Place, Edinburgh EH9 1SH
T 0131-668 8600 **W** www.historicenvironment.scot

Historic Environment Scotland is the lead public body established to investigate, care for and promote Scotland's historic environment. It is the result of the bringing together of two of Scotland's leading heritage bodies, Historic Scotland and the Royal Commission on Ancient and Historical Monuments Scotland, and has been formed to help deliver the Our Place in Time strategy. It is responsible for more than 300 properties of national importance, including Edinburgh Castle, Skara Brae and Fort George, and for collections that include more than 5 million drawings, photographs, negatives and manuscripts, along with Scotland's National Collection of Aerial Photography, containing more than 26 million aerial images. The Historic Environment Scotland's draft budget from the Scottish government for 2020–21 was £42.8m.

Chair, Jane Ryder, OBE
Trustees, Ian Brennan; Dr Janet Brennan; Trudi Craggs; Andrew Davies; Emma Hard; Terry Levinthal; Dr Coinneach Maclean; Dr Fiona McLean; Ian Robertson; Dr Paul Stollard; Dr Ken Thomson; Jane Williamson
Chief Executive, Alex Paterson

HISTORIC ROYAL PALACES

Apartment 39A, Hampton Court Palace, Surrey KT8 9AU
T 0333-320 6000 **E** info@hrp.org.uk **W** www.hrp.org.uk

Historic Royal Palaces was established in 1998 as a royal charter body with charitable status and is contracted by the Secretary of State for Digital, Culture, Media and Sport to manage unoccupied palaces on his behalf. The palaces – the Tower of London, Hampton Court Palace, the Banqueting House, Kensington Palace and Kew Palace – are owned by the Queen on behalf of the nation. In April 2014, Historic Royal Palaces was also appointed responsible for the management of Hillsborough Castle in Northern Ireland under contract with the Secretary of State for Northern Ireland.

The organisation is governed by a board comprising a chair and 11 non-executive trustees. The chief executive is accountable to the board of trustees and ultimately to parliament. Historic Royal Palaces receives no funding from the government or the Crown.

TRUSTEES
Chair, Rupert Gavin
Appointed by the Queen, Zeinab Badawi; Tim Knox *(ex officio, Director of the Royal Collection Trust);* Sir Michael Stevens, CVO *(ex officio, the Keeper of the Privy Purse)*
Appointed by the Secretary of State, Gen. Lord Houghton of Richmond, GCB, CBE, DL *(ex officio, the Constable of the Tower of London);* Jane Kennedy; Sarah Jenkins; Carole Souter, CBE; Robert Swannell, CBE; Sue Wilkinson, MBE; Dr Jo Twist, OBE; Prof. Michael Wood

OFFICER
Chief Executive, John Barnes

HOMES ENGLAND

50 Victoria Street, Westminster, London SW1H 0TL
T 0300-123 4500 **E** enquiries@homesengland.gov.uk
W www.gov.uk/government/organisations/homes-england

Homes England is an executive non-departmental public body, sponsored by the Ministry of Housing, Communities and Local Government to facilitate delivery of sufficient new homes by bringing together land, money, expertise, planning and compulsory purchase powers. It replaced the Homes and Communities Agency in January 2018, adopting the new trading name Homes England. Along with it, its regulation directorate, which undertakes the functions of the Regulation Committee, refers to itself as the Regulator of Social Housing. Homes England invests mostly in building new homes, but also in creating employment floorspace nationwide, as well as bringing forward public land for development and increasing the speed with which it is made available.

Chief Executive, Nick Walkley
Chief of Staff, Amy Casterton

HUMAN TISSUE AUTHORITY (HTA)

151 Buckingham Palace Road, London SW1W 9SZ
T 020-7269 1900 **E W** www.hta.gov.uk

The Human Tissue Authority (HTA) was established in April 2005 under the Human Tissue Act 2004, and is sponsored and part-funded by the Department of Health and Social Care. It regulates organisations that remove, store and use tissue for research, medical treatment, post-mortem examination, teaching and display in public. The HTA also gives approval for organ and bone marrow donations from living people. Under the EU tissues and cells directives, the HTA is one of the two designated competent authorities for the UK responsible for regulating tissues and cells. The HTA is also the sole competent authority for the UK under the EU organ donation directive.

Chair, Lynne Berry, CBE
Chief Executive, Allan Marriott-Smith

IMPERIAL WAR MUSEUMS (IWM)

Lambeth Road, London SE1 6HZ
T 020-7416 5000 **E W** www.iwm.org.uk

IWM is the world's leading authority on conflict and its impact, focusing on Britain, its former empire and the Commonwealth from the First World War to the present. IWM aims to enrich people's understanding of the causes, course and consequences of war and conflict.

IWM comprises the organisation's flagship, IWM London; IWM North in Trafford, Manchester; IWM Duxford in Cambridgeshire; the Churchill War Rooms in Whitehall; and HMS *Belfast* in the Pool of London.

The total grant-in-aid for 2019–20 is £19.74m.

President, HRH the Duke of Kent, KG, GCMG, GCVO, ADC
Chair, Matthew Westerman
Trustees, Desmond Bowen, CB, CMG; HE Hon. George
   Brandis, QC; Hugh Bullock; HE Janice Charette;
   Elizabeth Cleaver; HE Bede Cory; Lt.-Gen. Andrew
   Figgures, CB, CBE; HE Ruchi Ghanashyam; HE Manisha
   Gunasekera; Angus Lapsley; Margaret Macmillan, CH;
   Tim Marlow, OBE; HE Mohammad Nafees Zakaria;
   Suzanna Raine; HE Nomatemba Tambo; Tamsin Todd;
   Mark Urban; Guy Weston
Director-General, Diane Lees, CBE
Directors, John Brown *(Commercial Services and Operations)*; Jon
   Card *(Collections and Governance)*; Graeme Etheridge
   (Change); Gill Webber *(Content and Public Programmes)*

INFORMATION COMMISSIONER'S OFFICE
Wycliffe House, Water Lane, Wilmslow, Cheshire SK9 5AF
T 0303-123 1113 **W** www.ico.org.uk

The Information Commissioner's Office (ICO) oversees and
enforces the freedom of information acts of 2000 and 2004,
the Data Protection Act 2018, and the Network and
Information Systems Regulations 2018. Its objective it to
promote public access to official information and protecting
personal information.

The Data Protection Act 2018, which replaced legislation
passed in 1998, sets out rules for the processing of personal
information and applies to records held on computers and some
paper files. The freedom of information acts are designed to
help end the culture of unnecessary secrecy and open up the
inner workings of the public sector to citizens and businesses.

The ICO also enforces and oversees the privacy and electronic
communications regulations 2003 and the environmental
regulations 2004. It also has limited responsibilities under the
INSPIRE regulations 2009 and DRR regulations 2014.

The Information Commissioner reports annually to
parliament on the performance of his/her functions under the
acts and has obligations to assess breaches of the acts. Since
April 2010 the ICO has been able to fine organisations up to
€20m, or 4 per cent of their total annual worldwide turnover,
for serious breaches of the Data Protection Act.

Information Commissioner, Elizabeth Denham, CBE

INDUSTRIAL INJURIES ADVISORY COUNCIL
First Floor, Caxton House, Tothill Street, London SW1H 9NA
T 020-7449 5618 **E** iiac@dwp.gov.uk
W www.gov.uk/government/organisations/
industrial-injuries-advisory-council

The Industrial Injuries Advisory Council was established under
the National Insurance (Industrial Injuries) Act 1946, which
came into effect on 5 July 1948. Statutory provisions
governing its work are set out in the Social Security
Administration Act 1992 and corresponding Northern Ireland
legislation. The council usually consists of 17 members,
including a chair, appointed by the Secretary of State for Work
and Pensions, and has three tasks: to advise on the prescription
of diseases; to consider and advise on draft regulations and
proposals concerning the industrial injuries disablement
benefit scheme referred to the council by the Secretary of State
for Work and Pensions or the Department for Communities in
Northern Ireland; and to advise on any other matter concerning
the scheme or its administration.

Chair, Dr Leslie Rushton, OBE

JOINT NATURE CONSERVATION COMMITTEE
Monkstone House, City Road, Peterborough PE1 1JY
T 01733-562626 **W** www.jncc.gov.uk

The committee was established under the Environmental
Protection Act 1990, reconstituted by the Natural
Environment and Rural Communities Act 2006, and extended
by the Offshore Marine Conservation (Natural Habitats)
Regulations 2007 and the Marine and Coastal Access Act
2009. It advises the government and devolved administrations
on UK and international nature conservation issues. Its work
contributes to maintaining and enriching biological diversity,
conserving geological features and sustaining natural systems.

Chair, Prof. Chris Gilligan, CBE
Chief Executive, Marcus Yeo

LAW COMMISSION
1st Floor, Tower, 52 Queen Anne's Gate, London SW1H 9AG
T 020-3334 0200 **E** enquiries@lawcommission.gov.uk
W www.lawcom.gov.uk

The Law Commission was set up under the Law Commissions
Act 1965 to make proposals to the government for the
examination of the law in England and Wales and for its
revision to ensure it is fair, modern, simple and cost effective.
It recommends to the lord chancellor programmes for the
examination of different branches of the law and suggests
whether the examination should be carried out by the
commission itself or by some other body. The commission is
also responsible for the preparation of Consolidation and
Statute Law (Repeals) Bills.

Chair, Sir Nicholas Green
Commissioners, Prof. Sarah Green; Prof. Nicholas Hopkins;
   Prof. Penney Lewis; Nicholas Paines, QC
Chief Executive, Phil Golding

NATIONAL ARMY MUSEUM
Royal Hospital Road, Chelsea, London SW3 4HT
T 020-7730 0717 **E** info@nam.ac.uk **W** www.nam.ac.uk

The National Army Museum shares the stories of the British
Army and its soldiers. It was established by royal charter in
1960 and moved to its current site in Chelsea in 1971. The
museum re-opened in spring 2017 following a major
redevelopment project. The new museum features five state-of-
the-art galleries, housing a wide array of artefacts, paintings,
photographs, uniforms and equipment; a café; a shop; and
learning and research facilities.

Chair, Gen. Sir Richard Shirreff, KCB, CBE
Council Members, Patrick Aylmer; Dr Jonathan Boff; Judith
   Donovan, CBE; John Duncan, OBE; Lt.-Gen. Sir Simon
   Mayall, KBE, CB; Guy Perricone; Paul Schreier; Jessica
   Spungin; Sabine Vandenbroucke; William Wells
Director, Justin Maciejewski, DSO, MBE

NATIONAL GALLERIES OF SCOTLAND
73 Belford Road, Edinburgh EH4 3DS
T 0131-624 6200 **E** enquiries@nationalgalleries.org
W www.nationalgalleries.org

The National Galleries of Scotland comprise three galleries in
Edinburgh: the National Gallery of Scotland, the Scottish
National Portrait Gallery and the Scottish National Gallery of
Modern Art. There are also partner galleries at Paxton House,
Berwickshire, and Duff House, Banffshire. It also owns the
Granton Centre for Art, a purpose built storage facility.

TRUSTEES

Chair, Benny Higgins

Trustees, Audrey Carlin; Alistair Dodds; Edward Green; Tari Lang; Prof. Nicholas Pearce; Lynn Richmond; Dr Hannah Rudman; Chris Sibbald; Rucelle Soutar; Willie Watt; Andrew Wilson

OFFICERS

Director-General, Sir John Leighton
Directors, Dr Line Clausen Pedersen *(Collection and Research);* Jo Coomber *(Public Engagement);* Jacqueline Ridge *(Conservation and Collection Management);* Bryan Robertson *(Chief Operating Officer)*

NATIONAL GALLERY

Trafalgar Square, London WC2N 5DN
T 020-7747 2885 **E** information@ng-london.org.uk
W www.nationalgallery.org.uk

The National Gallery, which houses a collection of paintings in the western European tradition from the 13th to the 20th century, was founded in 1824, following a parliamentary grant of £57,000 for the purchase of the Angerstein collection of pictures. The present site was first occupied in 1838; an extension to the north of the building with a public entrance in Orange Street was opened in 1975; the Sainsbury Wing was opened in 1991; and the Getty Entrance opened off Trafalgar Square at the east end of the main building in 2004. Total government grant-in-aid for 2019–20 was £24.7m.

BOARD OF TRUSTEES

Chair, Lord Hall of Birkenhead, CBE

Trustees, Dame Moya Greene, DBE; Catherine Goodman, LVO; Doug Gurr; Katrin Henkel; Sir John Kingman; Rosemary Leith; David Marks; Tonya Nelson; Charles Sebag-Montefiore; Stuart Roden; John Singer; Molly Stevens

OFFICERS

Director of the National Gallery, Dr Gabriele Finaldi
Deputy Director, Dr Susan Foister *(Public Programmes and Partnerships)*
Directors, Dr Caroline Campbell *(Collections and Research);* Andy Hibbert *(Finance and Operations);* Dr Chris Michaels *(Digital)*

NATIONAL HERITAGE MEMORIAL FUND

International House, 1 Katherine's Way, London E1W 1UN
T 020-7591 6044 **E** NHMF_Enquiries@nhmf.org.uk
W www.nhmf.org.uk

The National Heritage Memorial Fund was set up under the National Heritage Act 1980 in memory of people who have given their lives for the United Kingdom. The fund provides grants to organisations based in the UK, mainly so that they can buy items of outstanding interest and of importance to the national heritage. These must either be at risk or have a memorial character. The fund is administered by a chair and trustees who are appointed by the prime minister.

The National Heritage Memorial Fund receives an annual grant from the Department for Digital, Culture, Media and Sport. Under the National Lottery etc. Act 1993, the trustees of the fund became responsible for the distribution of funds for both the National Heritage Memorial Fund and the Heritage Lottery Fund. Total annual government grant-in-aid is £5m.

Chair (Interim), René Olivieri
Trustees, Maria Adebowale-Schwarte; Baroness Andrews, OBE, FSA; Jim Dixon; Dr Claire Feehily; Sarah Flannigan; Perdita Hunt, OBE, DL; Ray Macfarlane; David Stocker
Chief Executive, Ros Kerslake, OBE

NATIONAL LIBRARY OF SCOTLAND

George IV Bridge, Edinburgh EH1 1EW
T 0131-623 3700 **E W** www.nls.uk

The library, which was formally opened as the Advocates' Library in 1689, became the National Library of Scotland in 1925. It contains over 26 million printed items in multiple formats including: books, manuscripts, archives, websites, newspapers, maps, music, moving images and sound, along with the John Murray Archive. One of only six legal deposit libraries, it receives more than 4,000 new items a week. It has an unrivalled Scottish collection as well as online catalogues and digital resources which can be accessed through the Library's website. Material can be consulted in the library branches in Edinburgh and Glasgow, which are open to anyone with a valid library card.

The National Library of Scotland Act 2012 modernised the composition and responsibilities of the board. Board members are appointed by the Scottish ministers.

Chair (Interim), Simon Learoyd
Board members, Noreen Adams; Elizabeth Carmichal, CBE; Ruth Crawford, QC; Helen Durndell; Dianne Haley; Alan Horn; Iain Marley; Lesley McPherson; Prof. Adrienne Scullion; Amina Shah; Prof. Melissa Terras; Robert Wallen
National Librarian and Chief Executive, Dr John Scally
Heads of Department, John Coll *(Access);* Jackie Cromarty *(External Relations);* Anthony Gillespie *(Business Support);* Stuart Lewis *(Digital);* Joesph Marshall *(Collections Management);* Robin Smith *(Collections and Research)*

NATIONAL LIBRARY OF WALES/ LLYFRGELL GENEDLAETHOL CYMRU

Aberystwyth, Ceredigion, Wales SY23 3BU
T 01970-632800 **E** gofyn@llgc.org.uk **W** www.library.wales

The National Library of Wales was founded by royal charter in 1907, and is funded by the Welsh government. It contains about 6 million books and newspapers, 40,000 manuscripts, four million deeds and documents, 1.5 million maps, prints and drawings, and a sound and moving image collection. It specialises in manuscripts and books relating to Wales and the Celtic peoples. It is the repository for pre-1858 Welsh probate records, manorial records and tithe documents, and certain legal records. Admission to the reading rooms is by reader's ticket, but entry to the exhibition programme is free.

Funding from the Welsh government totalled £11.8m in 2019–20.

President, Meri Huws

Trustees, Lord Aberdare; Michael Cavanagh; Gwilym Dyfri Jones; Quentin Howard; Dr Anwen Jones; Dr Gwenllian Lansdown Davies; Dr Elin Royles; Dr Elizabeth Siberry; Hugh Thomas; Eleri Twynog Humphries; Carl Williams; Steve Williams; Lee Yale-Helms *(Treasurer)*
Chief Executive and Librarian, Pedr ap Llwyd

NATIONAL MUSEUM OF THE ROYAL NAVY

HM Naval Base (PP66), Portsmouth PO1 3NH
T 023-9289 1370 **W** www.nmrn.org.uk

The National Museum of the Royal Navy comprises ten museums: HMS *Victory,* HMS *Caroline,* HMS *M.33,* HMS *Warrior,* the National Museum of the Royal Navy Portsmouth, the National Museum of the Royal Navy Hartlepool, the Fleet Air Arm Museum, the Royal Navy Submarine Museum, the New Royal Marines Museum, and the Explosion Museum of Naval Firepower. The Fleet Air Museum is located at RNAS Yeovilton, Somerset, and HMS Caroline is located at

Alexandra Dock, Belfast, while the other eight are situated in Portsmouth and Gosport.

Chair, Adm. Sir Philip Jones, GCB, DL
Trustees, Mark Anderson; Michael Bedingfield; Katherine Biggs; Philip Dolling; Helen Jackson; Cllr Donna Jones; Mike Gambazzi; Helen Jackson; Vice-Adm. Sir Adrian Johns, KCB, CBE, ADC; Maj.-Gen. Jeffrey Mason, MBE; Rear-Adm. Jonathan Pentreath, CB, OBE; Hon. Mary Montagu-Scott; Tim Schadla-Hall; John Scott; Alison Start; Gavin Whitter
Director-General, Prof. Dominic Tweddle

NATIONAL LOTTERY COMMUNITY FUND
1 Plough Place, London EC4A 1DE
T 0289-568 0143
E general.enquiries@tnlcommunityfund.org.uk
W www.tnlcommunityfund.org.uk

The National Lottery Community Fund, formerly the Big Lottery Fund, awarded over £588m of National Lottery funds in 2019–20; 83.3 per cent in grants under £10,000. The Fund supports health, education, environmental and charitable projects.

Chair (Interim), Tony Burton, CBE
Regional Chairs, Kate Beggs *(Northern Ireland);* Neil Ritch *(Scotland);* Elly de Baker *(England);* John Rose *(Wales)*
Chief Executive, Dawn Austwick, OBE

NATIONAL MUSEUM WALES/ AMGUEDDFA CYMRU
Cathays Park, Cardiff CF10 3NP
T 0300-111 2333 **W** https://museum.wales

National Museum Wales *(Amgueddfa Cymru)* is the body that runs Wales' seven national museums. It comprises National Museum Cardiff; St Fagans: National Waterfront Museum, Swansea; Big Pit: National Coal Museum, Blaenafon; National Roman Legion Museum, Caerleon; National Slate Museum, Llanberis; National Wool Museum, Dre-fach Felindre; and National Collections Centre, Nantgarw.

President, Roger Lewis
Vice-President, Dr Carol Bell
Trustees, Hywel John *(Treasurer);* Baroness Andrews, OBE; Dr Catherine Duigan; Dr Madeleine Havard; Gwyneth Hayward; Carys Howell; Rachel Hughes; Rob Humphries, CBE; Dr Hywel Jones, CMG; Michael Prior
Director-General, David Anderson, OBE

NATIONAL MUSEUMS LIVERPOOL
127 Dale Street, Liverpool L2 2JH
W www.liverpoolmuseums.org.uk

Regulated by the Department of Digital, Culture, Media and Sport, National Museums Liverpool is a group of museums and collections, comprising eight venues: International Slavery Museum, Lady Lever Art Gallery, Merseyside Maritime Museum, Museum of Liverpool, Seized! (UK Border Force National Museum), Sudley House, Walker Art Gallery and World Museum.

Chair, Sir David Henshaw
Trustees, Heather Blyth; James Chapman; Michelle Charters; Sarah Dean; Paul Eccleson; David Fleming; Heather Lauder; Rita McLean; Andrew McCluskey; Philip Price; Ian Rosenblatt, OBE; Max Steinberg, CBE; Virginia Tandy
Director National Museums Liverpool, Laura Pye
Directors, Mark Davies *(People);* Stephanie Donaldson *(Business Resources);* Janet Dugdale *(Museums and Participation);*

Stacey Hammond *(Business Development);* Mairi Johnson *(Estates);* Melanie Lewis *(Commercial and Business Development);* Karen O'Connor *(Commercial Enterprises);* Sandra Penketh *(Galleries and Collections Management);* Fiona Philpott *(Exhibitions);* Carol Rogers *(House of Memories);* David Spilsbury *(Finance);* David Watson *(Audiences and Media)*

NATIONAL MUSEUMS NORTHERN IRELAND
Cultra, Holywood, Northern Ireland BT18 0EU
T 0280-042 8428 **E** info@nmni.com **W** www.nmni.com

Across three unique sites National Museums Northern Ireland cares for and presents inspirational collections reflecting the creativity, innovation, history, culture and people of Northern Ireland and beyond.

Together the Ulster Museum, Ulster Folk and Transport Museum and Ulster American Folk Park contain 1.4 billion objects and offer a unique opportunity to experience the heritage and way of life of Northern Ireland.

Chair, Miceal McCoy
Vice-Chair, Prof. Garth Earls
Trustees, Dr Riann Coulter; Deirdre Devlin; William Duddy; Dr Leon Litvack; Prof. Karen Fleming; Hazel Francey; Daphne Harshaw; Charlotte Jess; Dr Rosemary Kelly, OBE; Alan McFarland; Dr George McIlroy; Catherine Molloy; Dr Robert Whan
Chief Executive, Kathryn Thomson

NATIONAL MUSEUMS SCOTLAND
Chambers Street, Edinburgh EH1 1JF
T 0300-123 6789 **E** info@nms.ac.uk **W** www.nms.ac.uk

National Museums Scotland provides advice, expertise and support to the museums community across Scotland, and undertakes fieldwork that often involves collaboration at local, national and international levels. National Museums Scotland comprises the National Museum of Scotland, the National War Museum, the National Museum of Rural Life, the National Museum of Flight and the National Museums Collection Centre. Its collections represent more than two centuries of collecting and include Scottish and classical archaeology, decorative and applied arts, world cultures and social history and science, technology and the natural world.

Up to 15 trustees can be appointed by the Minister for Culture, Tourism and External Affairs for a term of four years, and may serve a second term.

Chair, Ian Russell, CBE
Trustees, Ann Allen, MBE; Prof. Mary Bownes, OBE, FRSE; Adam Bruce; Gordon Drummond; Chris Fletcher; Dr Brian Lang, CBE, FRSE; Lynda Logan; Dr Catriona Macdonald; Janet Stevenson; Eilidh Wiseman; Dr Laura Young, MBE
Director, Dr Chris Breward

NATIONAL PORTRAIT GALLERY
St Martin's Place, London WC2H 0HE
T 020-7306 0055 **W** www.npg.org.uk

The National Portrait Gallery was established in 1856. Today the Gallery collects portraits of those who have made, or are making, a significant contribution to British history and culture. The Collection is free to visit, and includes works across all media, from painting and sculpture to photography and digital portraits. To complement the Collection, the Gallery stages exhibitions, displays, talks and events throughout the year which explore the nature of portraiture. The Gallery loans exhibitions, displays and individual portraits to organisations across the UK and internationally as part of its ongoing commitment to sharing the Collection as widely as possible.

Chair of the Board of Trustees, David Ross
Director, Dr Nicholas Cullinan

NATURAL ENGLAND
County Hall, Spetchley Road, Worcester WR5 2NP
T 0300-060 3900 **E** enquiries@naturalengland.org.uk
W www.gov.uk/government/organisations/natural-england

Natural England is the government's adviser on the natural environment, providing practical scientific advice on how to look after England's landscapes and wildlife.

The organisation's remit is to ensure sustainable stewardship of the land and sea so that people and nature can thrive.

Natural England works with farmers and land managers; business and industry; planners and developers; national and local government; charities and conservationists; interest groups and local communities to help them improve their local environment.

Chair, Tony Juniper, CBE
Chief Executive, Marian Spain

NATURAL HISTORY MUSEUM
Cromwell Road, London SW7 5BD
T 020-7942 5000 **W** www.nhm.ac.uk

The Natural History Museum, which houses 80 million natural history specimens, originates from the natural history departments of the British Museum, which grew extensively during the 19th century; in 1860 it was agreed that the natural history collections should be separated from the British Museum's collections of books, manuscripts and antiquities. Part of the site of the 1862 International Exhibition in South Kensington was acquired for the new museum, and the museum opened to the public in 1881. In 1963 the Natural History Museum became completely independent, although eight members of the board are still selected by the prime minister, once by the Department for Digital, Culture, Media and Sport, and three by the board itself. The Natural History Museum at Tring, bequeathed by the second Lord Rothschild, has formed part of the museum since 1937. The Geological Museum merged with the Natural History Museum in 1986. In September 2009 the Natural History Museum opened the Darwin Centre, which contains public galleries, a high-tech interactive area known as the Attenborough Studio and scientific research facilities.

Chair, Lord Green of Hurstpierpoint
Trustees, Prof. Sir John Beddington, CMG, FRS; Harris Bokhari, OBE; Dame Frances Cairncross, DBE, FRSE; Prof. Yadvinder Malhi, FRS; Anand Mahindra; Hilary Newiss; Robert Noel; Simon Patterson; Prof. Stephen Sparks, CMG, FRS, CBE; Dr Sarah Thomas; Prof. Dame Janet Thornton, DBE, FRS, FMEDSCI; Dr Kim Winser, OBE
Museum Director, Doug Gurr
Directors, Neil Greenwood *(Finance and Corporate Services);* Dt Tim Littlewood *(Science);* Fiona McWilliams *(Development);* Clare Matterson, CBE *(Engagement)*

NATURAL RESOURCES WALES
Ty Cambria, 29 Newport Road, Cardiff CF24 0TP
T 0300-065 3000 **E** enquiries@naturalresourceswales.gov.uk
W www.naturalresources.wales

Natural Resources Wales *(Cyfoeth Naturiol Cymru)* is the principal adviser to the Welsh government on the environment. It became operational in April 2013 following a merger of the Countryside Council for Wales, Environment Agency Wales and the Forestry Commission Wales. It is responsible for ensuring that the natural resources of Wales are sustainably maintained, enhanced and used; now and in the future.

Chair, Sir David Henshaw
Board Members, Karen Balmer; Chris Blake; Catherine Brown; Julia Cherret; Geraint Davies; Howard Davies; Dr Elizabeth Haywood; Zoë Henderson; Prof. Steve Ormerod, FCIEEM; Dr Rosie Plummer; Prof. Peter Rigby, FRS, FMEDSCI
Chief Executive, Clare Pillman

NHS PAY REVIEW BODY
8th Floor, Fleetbank House, 2-6 Salisbury Square, London EC4Y 8JX
T 020-7211 8295 **W** www.gov.uk/government/organisations/nhs-pay-review-body

The NHS Pay Review Body (NHSPRB) advises the prime minister, Secretary of State for Health and ministers in Scotland, Wales and Northern Ireland on the remuneration of all paid staff under agenda for change and employed in the NHS. The review body was established in 1983 for nurses and allied health professionals. Its remit has since expanded to cover just under 1.5 million staff, ie almost all staff in the NHS, with the exception of dentists, doctors and very senior managers.

Chair, Philippa Hird
Members, Richard Cooper; Patricia Gordon; Neville Hounsome; Stephanie Marston; Karen Mumford; Anne Phillimore; Prof. David Ulph, CBE

NORTHERN IRELAND HUMAN RIGHTS COMMISSION
Fourth Floor, Alfred House, 19-21 Alfred Street, Belfast BT2 8ED
T 028-9024 3987 **E** info@nihrc.org **W** www.nihrc.org

The Northern Ireland Human Rights Commission is a non-departmental public body, established by the Northern Ireland Act 1998 and set up in March 1999. Its purpose is to protect and promote human rights in Northern Ireland. Its main functions include reviewing the law and practice relating to human rights, advising government and the Northern Ireland Assembly, and promoting an awareness of human rights. It can also investigate human rights violations and take cases to court. The members of the commission are appointed by the Secretary of State for Northern Ireland.

Chief Commissioner, Les Allamby
Commissioners, Helen Henderson; Jonathan Kearney; David Lavery, CB; Maura Muldoon; Eddie Rooney; Stephen White, OBE
Chief Executive, Dr David Russell

NORTHERN LIGHTHOUSE BOARD
84 George Street, Edinburgh EH2 3DA
T 0131-473 3100 **E** enquiries@nlb.org.uk **W** www.nlb.org.uk

The Northern Lighthouse Board is the general lighthouse authority for Scotland and the Isle of Man and owes its origin to an act of parliament passed in 1786. At present there are 19 commissioners who operate under the Merchant Shipping Act 1995.

The commissioners control 206 lighthouses, 170 lighted and unlighted buoys, 26 beacons, 35 AIS (automatic identification system) stations, 29 radar beacons, four DGPS (differential global positioning system) stations and an ELORAN (long-range navigation) system. *See also* Transport.

Chair, Capt. Michael Brew
Vice-Chair, Capt. Alastair Beveridge

Commissioners, Lord Advocate; Solicitor-General for Scotland; Lord Provosts of Edinburgh, Glasgow, and Aberdeen; Convener of Highland Council; Provost of Argyll and Bute Council; Sheriffs-Principal of South Strathclyde, Dumfries and Galloway, Tayside, Central and Fife, North Strathclyde, Grampian, Highlands and Islands, Lothian and Borders, and Glasgow and Strathkelvin; Brian Archibald; Hugh Shaw, OBE; Elaine Wilkinson; Rob Woodward
Chief Executive, Mike Bullock, MBE

NUCLEAR DECOMMISSIONING AUTHORITY

Herdus House, Westlakes Science and Technology Park, Moor Row, Cumbria CA24 3HU
T 01925-802001 **E** enquiries@nda.gov.uk
W www.gov.uk/government/organisations/nuclear-decommissioning-authority

The Nuclear Decommissioning Authority (NDA) was created under the Energy Act 2004. It is a strategic authority that owns 17 sites plus associated civil nuclear liabilities and assets of the public sector, previously under the control of the UK Energy Authority and British Nuclear Fuels. The NDA's responsibilities include decommissioning and cleaning up civil nuclear facilities; ensuring the safe management of waste products, both radioactive and non-radioactive; implementing government policy on the long-term management of nuclear waste; developing UK-wide low-level waste strategy plans; and scrutinising the decommissioning plans of EDF Energy.

Total planned expenditure for 2019–20 was £3.112bn, with total grant-in-aid standing at £2.210bn. The remaining £0.902bn will come from commercial operations.

Chair, Dr Ros Rivaz
Chief Executive, David Peattie

OFFICE FOR BUDGET RESPONSIBILITY

14T, 102 Petty France, London SW1H 9AJ
T 020-3334 6117 **E** OBR.Enquiries@obr.uk **W** www.obr.uk

The Office for Budget Responsibility (OBR) was created in 2010 to provide independent and authoritative analysis of the UK's public finances. It has five main roles: producing forecasts for the economy and public finances; judging progress towards the government's fiscal targets; evaluating fiscal risks; assessing the long-term sustainability of the public finances; and scrutinising HM Treasury's costing of tax and welfare spending measures.

Chair, Richard Hughes
Committee Members, Prof. Sir Charles Bean; Andy King

OFFICE OF COMMUNICATIONS (OFCOM)

Riverside House, 2A Southwark Bridge Road, London SE1 9HA
T 0300-123 3000 **W** www.ofcom.org.uk

OFCOM was established in 2003 under the Office of Communications Act 2002 as the independent regulator and competition authority for the UK communications industries with responsibility, for television, video-on-demand, radio, telecommunications and wireless communications services.

Following the passing of the Postal Services Act 2011, OFCOM also assumed regulatory responsibility for postal services.

Chair, Lord Burns
Deputy Chair, Maggie Carver
Board Members, Kevin Bakhurst; Angela Dean *(Audit and Risk);* Bob Downes *(Scotland);* David Jones *(Wales);* Graham Mather; Tim Suter; Ben Verwaayen
Chief Executive, Melanie Dawes

OFFICE OF MANPOWER ECONOMICS (OME)

8th Floor, Fleetbank House, 2–6 Salisbury Square, London EC4Y 8JX
T 020-7211 8165 **E** omeenquiries@beis.gov.uk **W** www.gov.uk/government/organisations/office-of-manpower-economics

The Office of Manpower Economics (OME) was established in 1971. It is an independent non-statutory organisation responsible for providing an independent secretariat to eight independent review bodies: the Armed Forces' Pay Review Body (AFPRB); the Review Body on Doctors' and Dentists' Remuneration (DDRB); the NHS Pay Review Body (NHSPRB); the Prison Service Pay Review Body (PSPRB); the School Teachers' Review Body (STRB); the Senior Salaries Review Body (SSRB); the Police Remuneration Review Body (PRRB); and the National Crime Agency Remuneration Review Body (NCARRB). In total these pay bodies make recommendations impacting 2.5 million workers – around 45 per cent of public sector staff – and with a total pay bill of £100bn.

Director, David Fry

ORDNANCE SURVEY

Adanac Drive, Southampton SO16 0AS
T 0345-605 0505 **E** customerservices@os.uk **W** www.ordnancesurvey.co.uk

Ordnance Survey is the national mapping agency for Great Britain, which can trace its roots back to 1745. It is a public corporation of the Department for Business, Energy and Industrial Strategy.

Chief Executive, Steve Blair

PARADES COMMISSION

2nd Floor, Andras House, 60 Great Victoria Street, Belfast BT2 7BB
T 028-9089 5900 **E** info@paradescommissionni.org **W** www.paradescommission.org

The Parades Commission is an independent, quasi-judicial body set up under the Public Processions (Northern Ireland) Act 1998. Its function is to encourage and facilitate local accommodation of contentious parades; where this is not possible, the commission is empowered to make legal determinations about such parades, which may include imposing conditions on aspects of the notified parade (such as restrictions on routes/areas and exclusion of certain groups with a record of bad behaviour).

The chair and members are appointed by the Secretary of State for Northern Ireland; the membership must, as far as is practicable, be representative of the community in Northern Ireland.

Chair, Anne Henderson
Members, Joelle Black; Sarah Havlin; Paul Hutchinson; Colin Kennedy; Anne Marshall; Geraldine McGahey

PAROLE BOARD FOR ENGLAND AND WALES

3rd Floor, 10 South Colonnade, Canary Wharf, London E14 4PU
T 020-3880 0885 **E** info@paroleboard.gov.uk **W** www.gov.uk/government/organisations/parole-board

The Parole Board was established in 1968 under the Criminal Justice Act 1967 and became an independent executive non-departmental public body on 1 July 1996 under the Criminal Justice and Public Order Act 1994. It is the body that protects the public by making risk assessments about prisoners to decide who may safely be released into the community and who must remain in, or be returned to, custody. Board decisions are taken at two main types of panels of up to three members: 'paper panels' for the majority of cases, or oral hearings for decisions concerning prisoners serving life or indeterminate sentences for public protection. The Parole Board held 5,380 oral hearings in 2018–19; 49 per cent were released.

Chair, Caroline Corby
Chief Executive, Martin Jones

PAROLE BOARD FOR SCOTLAND
Saughton House, Broomhouse Drive, Edinburgh EH11 3XD
T 0131-244 8373 **E** enquiries@paroleboard.scot
W www.scottishparoleboard.scot

The board is an independent judicial body directs and advises the Scottish ministers on the release of prisoners on licence, and related matters.

Chair, John Watt

PENSION PROTECTION FUND (PPF)
Renaissance, 12 Dingwall Road, Croydon CR0 2NA
T 0345-600 2541 **E** information@ppf.co.uk
W www.pensionprotectionfund.org.uk

The PPF became operational in 2005. It was established to pay compensation to members of eligible defined-benefit pension schemes, when a qualifying insolvency event in relation to the employer occurs and where there is a lack of sufficient assets in the pension scheme. The PPF also administers the Financial Assistance Scheme, which helps members whose schemes wound-up before 2005. It is also responsible for the Fraud Compensation Fund (which provides compensation to occupational pension schemes that suffer a loss that can be attributed to dishonesty). The chair and board of the PPF are appointed by, and accountable to, the Secretary of State for Work and Pensions, and are responsible for paying compensation, calculating annual levies (which help fund the PPF), and setting and overseeing investment strategy.

Chair, Arnold Wagner, OBE
Chief Executive, Oliver Morley, CBE

PENSIONS REGULATOR
Napier House, Trafalgar Place, Brighton BN1 4DW
T 0345-600 0707 **E** customersupport@tpr.gov.uk
W www.thepensionsregulator.gov.uk

The Pensions Regulator was established in 2005 as the regulator of workplace pension schemes in the UK, replacing the Occupational Pensions Regulatory Authority (OPRA). It aims to make sure employers put their staff into a pension scheme and pay money into it (automatic enrolment) and to protect the benefits of occupational and personal pension scheme members by working with trustees, employers, pension providers and advisers. The regulator's work focuses on encouraging better management and administration of schemes, ensuring that final salary schemes have a sensible funding plan, and encouraging money purchase schemes to provide members with the information that they need to make informed choices about their pension fund. The Pensions Act 2004 and the Pensions Act 2008 gave the regulator a range of powers which can be used to protect scheme members, but a strong emphasis is placed on educating and enabling those responsible for managing pension schemes, and powers are used only where necessary. The regulator offers free online resources to help trustees, employers, professionals and advisers understand their role, duties and obligations.

Chair, Mark Boyle
Chief Executive, Charles Counsell

POLICE ADVISORY BOARD FOR ENGLAND AND WALES
Home Office, 6th Floor Fry, 2 Marsham Street, London SW1P 4DF
E pabewsecretariat@homeoffice.gov.uk
W www.gov.uk/government/organisations/police-advisory-board-for-england-and-wales

The Police Advisory Board for England and Wales was established in 1965 by section 46 of the Police Act 1964 and provides advice to the home secretary on general questions affecting the police in England and Wales. It also considers draft regulations under the Police Act 1996 about matters such as recruitment, diversity and collaboration between forces.

Independent Chair, Elizabeth France

PRISON SERVICE PAY REVIEW BODY
8th Floor, Fleetbank House, 2-6 Salisbury Square, London EC4Y 8JX
T 020-7211 8259 **E** PSPRB@beis.gov.uk
W www.gov.uk/government/organisations/prison-services-pay-review-body

The Prison Service Pay Review Body was set up in 2001. It makes independent recommendations on the pay of prison governors, operational managers, prison officers and related grades for the Prison Service in England and Wales, and for the Northern Ireland Prison Service.

Chair, Tim Flesher, CB
Members, Mary Carter; Luke Corkill; Prof. Andy Dickerson; Judith Gillespie, CBE; Leslie Manasseh, MBE; Paul West, QPM

PRIVY COUNCIL OFFICE
Room G/04, 1 Horse Guards Road, London SW1A 2HQ
E enquiries@pco.gov.uk
W https://privycouncil.independent.gov.uk

The primary function of the office is to act as the secretariat to the Privy Council. It is responsible for the arrangements leading to the making of all royal proclamations and orders in council; for certain formalities connected with ministerial changes; for considering applications for the granting (or amendment) of royal charters; for the scrutiny and approval of by-laws and statutes of chartered institutions and of the governing instruments of universities and colleges; and for the appointment of high sheriffs and Privy Council appointments to governing bodies. Under the relevant acts, the office is responsible for the approval of certain regulations and rules made by the regulatory bodies of the medical and certain allied professions.

The Lord President of the Council is the ministerial head of the office and presides at meetings of the Privy Council. The Clerk of the Council is the administrative head of the Privy Council office.

Lord President of the Council and Leader of the House of Commons, Rt. Hon. Jacob Rees-Mogg
Clerk of the Council, Richard Tilbrook
Head of Secretariat and Deputy Clerk, Ceri King
Deputy Clerk, Christopher Berry

REVIEW BODY ON DOCTORS' AND DENTISTS' REMUNERATION
8th Floor, Fleetbank House, 2-6 Salisbury Square, London EC4Y 8JX
T 020-7211 8184 **W** www.gov.uk/government/organisations/review-body-on-doctors-and-dentists-remuneration

The Review Body on Doctors' and Dentists' Remuneration was set up in 1971. It advises the prime minister, the secretary of state for health and social care, first ministers in Scotland, Wales and Northern Ireland, and the ministers for Health and

Social Care, in England, Scotland, Wales and Northern Ireland on the remuneration of doctors and dentists taking any part in the National Health Service.

Chair, Christopher Pilgrim
Members, David Bingham; Helen Jackson; Prof. Peter Kopelman, MD, FRCP, FFPH; James Malcomson; John Matheson, CBE; Nora Nanayakkara

ROYAL AIR FORCE MUSEUM
Grahame Park Way, London NW9 5LL
T 020-8205 2266 E london@rafmuseum.org
W www.rafmuseum.org.uk

The museum has two sites, one at the former airfield at Colindale, in North London, and the second at Cosford, in the West Midlands, both of which illustrate the development of aviation from before the Wright brothers to the present-day RAF. The museum's collection across both sites consists of over 170 aircraft, as well as artefacts, aviation memorabilia, fine art and photographs.

Chair, Air Chief Marshal Sir Andrew Pulford, GCB, CBE, DL
Trustees, Peter Bateson; Laurie Benson; Dr Carol Cole; Dr Rodney Eastwood, MBE; Richard Holman; Catriona Lougher; Julie McGarvey; Andrew Reid; Nick Sanders; Mike Schindler
Chief Executive, Maggie Appleton, MBE

ROYAL BOTANIC GARDEN EDINBURGH
Arboretum Place, Edinburgh EH3 5NZ
T 0172-760254 W www.rbge.org.uk

The Royal Botanic Garden Edinburgh (RBGE) originated as the Physic Garden, established in 1670 beside the Palace of Holyroodhouse. The garden moved to its present site at Inverleith, Edinburgh, in 1820. There are also three regional gardens: Benmore Botanic Garden, near Dunoon, Argyll; Logan Botanic Garden, near Stranraer, Wigtownshire; and Dawyck Botanic Garden, near Stobo, Peeblesshire. Since 1986 RBGE has been administered by a board of trustees established under the National Heritage (Scotland) Act 1985. It receives an annual grant from the Scottish government's Environment and Forestry Directorate.

The RBGE is an international centre for scientific research on plant diversity and for horticulture education and conservation. It has an extensive library, a herbarium with almost three million preserved plant specimens, and over 13,500 species in the living collections.

Chair, Dominic Fry
Trustees, Raoul Curtis-Machin; Prof. Beverley Glover; Dr David Hamilton; Dr Ian Jardine; Prof. Thomas Meagher; Diana Murray; Prof. Ian Wall, FRSE
Regius Keeper, Simon Milne, MBE

ROYAL BOTANIC GARDENS, KEW
Kew Gardens, Richmond, London TW9 3AB
T 020-8332 5655 E info@kew.org
Wakehurst, Ardingly, W. Sussex RH17 6TN
T 01444-894066 E wakehurst@kew.org
W www.kew.org

Kew Gardens was originally laid out as a private garden for the now demolished White House for George III's mother, Princess Augusta, in 1759. The gardens were much enlarged in the 19th century, notably by the inclusion of the grounds of the former Richmond Lodge. In 1965 Kew acquired the gardens at Wakehurst on a long lease from the National Trust. Under the National Heritage Act 1983 a board of trustees was set up to administer the gardens, which in 1984 became an independent body supported by grant-in-aid from the

Department for Environment, Food and Rural Affairs. In 2016, restoration work was completed on Temperate House and the Giant pagoda.

The functions of RBG, Kew are to carry out research into plant sciences, to disseminate knowledge about plants and to provide the public with the opportunity to gain knowledge and enjoyment from the gardens' collections. There are extensive national reference collections of living and preserved plants and a comprehensive library and archive. The main emphasis is on plant conservation and biodiversity; Wakehurst houses the Millennium Seed Bank Partnership, which is the largest *ex situ* conservation project in the world – it is home to 2.4 billion seeds from 97 countries.

Chair, Dame Amelia Fawcett, DBE, CVO
Trustees, Nick Baird, CMG, CVO; Prof. Liam Dolan; Catherine Dugmore; Sarah Flannigan; Valerie Gooding, CBE; Krishnan Guru-Murthy; Prof. Sue Hartley, OBE; Ian Karet; Jantiene Klein Roseboom van der Veer; Michael Lear; Sir Derek Myers
Director, Richard Deverell

ROYAL COMMISSION ON THE ANCIENT AND HISTORICAL MONUMENTS OF WALES
Ffordd Penglais, Aberystwyth SY23 3BU
T 01970-621200 E nmr.wales@rcahmw.gov.uk
W www.rcahmw.gov.uk

The Royal Commission on the Ancient and Historical Monuments of Wales, established in 1908, is the investigation body and national archive for the historic environment of Wales. It has the lead role in ensuring that Wales's archaeological, built and maritime heritage is authoritatively recorded, and seeks to promote the understanding and appreciation of this heritage nationally and internationally. The commission is funded by the Welsh government.

Chair, Prof. Nancy Edwards, FSA
Commissioners, Neil Beagrie, FRSA; Chris Brayne; Caroline Crewe-Read, FRSA; Dr Louise Emanuel; Catherine Hardman, FSA; Thomas Lloyd, OBE, FSA; Dr Hayley Roberts; Jonathan Vining
Secretary, Christopher Catling

ROYAL MUSEUMS GREENWICH
National Maritime Museum, Greenwich, London SE10 9NF
T 020-8858 4422 E RMGenquiries@rmg.co.uk
W www.rmg.co.uk

Royal Museums Greenwich comprises the National Maritime Museum, the Queen's House and the Royal Observatory Greenwich, and also works in collaboration with the Cutty Sark Trust. The National Maritime Museum provides information on the maritime history of Great Britain and is the largest institution of its kind in the world, with over 2.5 million items related to seafaring, navigation and astronomy. Originally the home of Charles I's Queen, Henrietta Maria, the Queen's House was built between 1616–18, although it was structurally altered between 1629–35. It now contains a fine-art collection. The Royal Observatory, Greenwich is the home of Greenwich Mean Time and the prime meridian of the world. It also contains London's only planetarium, Harrison's timekeepers and the UK's largest refracting telescope.

Chair, Sir Charles Dunstone, CVO
Trustees, Joyce Bridges, CBE; Dr Fiona Butcher; Dr Helen Czerski; Prof. Julian Dowdeswell; Dr Aminul Hoque, MBE; Alastair Marsh; Jeremy Penn; Eric Reynolds; Adm. Sir Mark Stanhope, GCB, OBE
Director, Paddy Rodgers

SCHOOL TEACHERS' REVIEW BODY

8th Floor, Fleetbank House, 2-6 Salisbury Square, London EC4Y 8JX
T 020-7211 8463 W www.gov.uk/government/organisations/
school-teachers-review-body

The School Teachers' Review Body was set up under the School Teachers' Pay and Conditions Act 1991. It is required to examine and make recommendations on such matters relating to the statutory conditions of employment of school teachers in England and Wales. It reports to the education secretary and the prime minister.

Chair, Dr Patricia Rice
Members, Sir Robert Burgess; Ken Clark; Harriet Kemp; John Lakin; Lynne Lawrence; Martin Post; Dr Andrew Walker

SCIENCE MUSEUM GROUP

W www.sciencemuseumgroup.org.uk

SCIENCE MUSEUM
Exhibition Road, London SW7 2DD
T 0800-047 8124 E info@sciencemuseum.ac.uk
W www.sciencemuseum.org.uk

SCIENCE AND INDUSTRY MUSEUM
Liverpool Road, Castlefield, Manchester M3 4FP
T 0161-832 2244 E contact@scienceandindustrymuseum.org.uk
W www.scienceandindustrymuseum.org.uk

NATIONAL RAILWAY MUSEUM AND LOCOMOTION
NRM York, Leeman Road, York YO26 4XJ
T 0333-016 1010 E info@railwaymuseum.org.uk
W www.railwaymuseum.org.uk
Locomotion, Shildon, Co. Durham DL4 2RE
T 01904-685780 E info@locomotion.org.uk
W www.locomotion.org.uk

NATIONAL SCIENCE AND MEDIA MUSEUM
Pictureville, Bradford BD1 1NQ
T 0844-856 3797 E talk.nsmm@scienceandmediamuseum.org.uk
W www.scienceandmediamuseum.org.uk

The Science Museum Group (SMG) consists of the Science Museum; the Science and Industry Museum, Manchester; the National Railway Museum, York; the National Science and Media Museum, Bradford; and Locomotion at Shildon. The Science Museum houses the national collections of science, technology, industry and medicine and attracts around 3.2 million visits annually. The museum began as the science collection of the South Kensington Museum and first opened in 1857. In 1883 it acquired the collections of the Patent Museum and in 1909 the science collections were transferred to the new Science Museum, leaving the art collections with the Victoria and Albert Museum. The Wellcome Wing was opened in July 2000.

The Trustees of the Science Museum Group have statutory duties under the National Heritage Act 1983 for the general management and control of SMG.

Total government grant in aid for 2019–20 was £67.7m.

Chair, Dame Mary Archer, DBE
Trustees, Prof. Brian Cantor; Judith Donovan, CBE; Dr Sarah Dry; Sharon Flood; Prof. Russell Foster, CBE, FRS, FMEDSCI; Dr Hannah Fry; Prof. Ludmilla Jordanova, FRHS, FRSM; Prof. Ajit Lalvani; Iain McIntosh; Lopa Patel; Prof. David Phoenix, OBE; Sarah Staniforth; Steven Underwood; Anton Valk, CBE; Dame Fiona Woolf, CBE
Director of Science Museum, Sir Ian Blatchford
Director of Science & Industry Museum, Sally MacDonald
Director of National Science and Media Museum, Jo Quinton-Tulloch
Director of National Railway Museum, Judith McNicol

SCOTTISH CRIMINAL CASES REVIEW COMMISSION

Portland House, 17 Renfield Street, Glasgow G2 5AH
T 0141-270 7030 E info@sccrc.org.uk W www.sccrc.org.uk

The commission is a non-departmental public body, funded by the Scottish Government Justice Directorate, and established under the Criminal Procedure (Scotland) Act 1995 in April 1999. It assumed the role previously performed by the Secretary of State for Scotland to consider alleged miscarriages of justice in Scotland and refer cases meeting the relevant criteria to the high court for determination. Members are appointed by the Queen on the recommendation of the first minister; senior executive staff are appointed by the commission.

Chair, Bill Matthews
Members, Prof. Jim Fraser; Raymond McMenamin; Elaine Noad; Dr Alex Quinn; Laura Reilly; Carol Gammie
Chief Executive and Principal Solicitor, Gerard Sinclair

SCOTTISH ENTERPRISE

Atrium Court, 50 Waterloo Street, Glasgow G2 6HQ
T 0300-013 3385
W www.scottish-enterprise.com

Scottish Enterprise was established in 1991 and its purpose is to stimulate the sustainable growth of Scotland's economy. It is mainly funded by the Scottish government and is responsible to the Scottish ministers. Working in partnership with the private and public sectors, Scottish Enterprise invests £300–350m annually to further the development of Scotland's economy by helping ambitious and innovative businesses grow and become more successful. Scottish Enterprise is particularly interested in supporting companies that provide renewable energy, encourage trade overseas, increase innovation, and those that will help Scotland become a low-carbon economy. Total anticipated Scottish government funding for 2019–20 was £295.4m.

Chair, Lord Smith of Kelvin, KT, CH
Chief Executive (Interim), Linda Hannah

SCOTTISH ENVIRONMENT PROTECTION AGENCY (SEPA)

Erskine Court, Castle Business Park, Stirling FK9 4TZ
T 0300-099 6699 W www.sepa.org.uk

SEPA was established in 1996 and is the public body responsible for environmental protection in Scotland. It regulates potential pollution to land, air and water; the storage, transport and disposal of controlled waste; and the safekeeping and disposal of radioactive materials. It does this within a complex legislative framework of acts of parliament, EU directives and regulations, granting licences to operations of industrial processes and waste disposal. SEPA also operates Floodline (T 0345-988 1188), a public service providing information on the possible risk of flooding 24 hours a day, 365 days a year.

Chair, Bob Downes
Members, Franceska van Dijk; Michelle Francis; Nicola Gordon; Martin Hill; Craig Hume; Julie Hutchinson; Harpreet Kohli; Nick Martin; Philip Matthews
Chief Executive, Terry A'Hearn

SCOTTISH LAW COMMISSION

140 Causewayside, Edinburgh EH9 1PR
T 0131-668 2131 E info@scotlawcom.gov.uk
W www.scotlawcom.gov.uk

The Scottish Law Commission, established in 1965, keeps the law in Scotland under review and makes proposals for its development and reform. It is responsible to the Scottish ministers through the Scottish government constitution, law and courts directorate.

Chair, Rt. Hon. Lady Paton
Commissioners, David Bartos; Prof. Gillian Black; Kate Dowdalls, QC; Prof. Frankie McCarthy
Chief Executive, Malcolm McMillan

SCOTTISH LEGAL AID BOARD

Thistle House, 91 Haymarket Terrace, Edinburgh EH12 5HE
T 0131-226 7061 **E** general@slab.org.uk **W** www.slab.org.uk

The Scottish Legal Aid Board was set up under the Legal Aid (Scotland) Act 1986 to manage legal aid in Scotland. It is designed to help individuals on low or modest incomes gain access to the legal system. It reports to the Scottish government. Board members are appointed by Scottish ministers.

Chair, Ray MacFarlane
Members, Brian Baverstock; Rani Dhir, MBE; Marieke Dwarshuis; Stephen Humphreys; Tim McKay; Raymond McMenamin; Sheriff John Morris, QC; Sarah O'Neill; Paul Reid; David Sheldon, QC; Lesley Ward
Chief Executive, Colin Lancaster

SCOTTISH NATURAL HERITAGE (SNH)

Great Glen House, Leachkin Road, Inverness IV3 8NW
T 01463-725000 **E** enquiries@nature.scot **W** www.nature.scot

SNH was established in 1992 under the Natural Heritage (Scotland) Act 1991. It is the government's adviser on all aspects of nature and landscape across Scotland and its role is to help the public understand, value and enjoy Scotland's nature, as well as to support those people and organisations that manage it.

Chair, Dr Mike Cantlay, OBE
Chief Executive and Accountable Officer, Francesca Osowska
Directors, Robbie Kernahan *(Sustainable Growth);* Jane Macdonald *(Business Services and Transformation);* Eileen Stuart *(Nature and Climate Change)*

SEAFISH

18 Logie Mill, Logie Green Road, Edinburgh EH7 4HS
T 0131-558 3331 **E** seafish@seafish.co.uk **W** www.seafish.org

Established under the Fisheries Act 1981, Seafish works with all sectors of the UK seafood industry to satisfy consumers, raise standards, improve efficiency and secure a sustainable and profitable future. Services range from research and development, economic consulting, market research and training and accreditation through to legislative advice for the seafood industry. It is sponsored by the four UK fisheries departments, which appoint the board, and receives 80 per cent of its funding through a levy on seafood.

Chair, Brian Young
Chief Executive, Marcus Coleman

SECURITY AND INTELLIGENCE SERVICES

GOVERNMENT COMMUNICATIONS HEADQUARTERS (GCHQ)

Hubble Road, Cheltenham GL51 0EX
T 01242-221491 **W** www.gchq.gov.uk

GCHQ produces signals intelligence in support of national security and the UK's economic wellbeing, and in the prevention or detection of serious crime. It is the national authority for cyber security and provides advice and assistance to government departments, the armed forces and other national infrastructure bodies on the security of their communications and information systems. GCHQ was placed on a statutory footing by the Intelligence Services Act 1994 and is headed by a director who is directly accountable to the foreign secretary.

Director, Jeremy Fleming

SECRET INTELLIGENCE SERVICE (MI6)

PO Box 1300, London SE1 1BD
Anti-Terrorist Hotline 0800-789 321 **W** www.sis.gov.uk

Established in 1909 as the Foreign Section of the Secret Service Bureau, the Secret Intelligence Service produces secret intelligence in support of the government's security, defence, foreign and economic policies. It was placed on a statutory footing by the Intelligence Services Act 1994 and is headed by a chief, known as 'C', who is directly accountable to the foreign secretary.

Chief, Richard Moore, CMG

SECURITY SERVICE (MI5)

PO Box 3255, London SW1P 1AE
T 0800-111 4645 **Anti-Terrorist Hotline** 0800-789 321
W www.mi5.gov.uk

The Security Service is responsible for security intelligence work against covertly organised threats to the UK. It is organised into ten branches, each with dedicated areas of responsibility, which include countering terrorism, espionage and the proliferation of weapons of mass destruction. The Security Service also provides security advice to a wide range of organisations to help reduce vulnerability to threats from individuals, groups or countries hostile to UK interests. The home secretary has parliamentary accountability for the Security Service. There is a network of regional offices around the UK, plus a Northern Ireland headquarters.

Director-General, Ken McCallum

SENIOR SALARIES REVIEW BODY

8th Floor, Fleetbank House, 2-6 Salisbury Square, London EC4Y 8JX
T 020-7211 8315 **E** SSRB@BEIS.gov.uk **W** www.gov.uk/government/organisations/review-body-on-senior-salaries

The Senior Salaries Review Body (formerly the Top Salaries Review Body) was set up in 1971 and advises the prime minister, the Lord Chancellor, the defence secretary, the health secretary and the home secretary on the remuneration of the judiciary, senior civil servants, senior officers of the armed forces, certain senior managers in the NHS, police and crime commissioners and chief police officers. In 1993 its remit was extended to cover the pay, pensions and allowances of MPs, ministers and others whose pay is determined by the Ministerial and Other Salaries Act 1975, and also the allowances of peers. If asked, it advises on the pay of officers and members of the devolved parliament and assemblies.

Chair, Dr Martin Read, CBE
Members, Pippa Greenslade; Sir Adrian Johns, KCB, CBE, DL; Pippa Lambert; Peter Maddison, QPM; David Sissling; Sharon Witherspoon, MBE

STUDENT LOANS COMPANY LTD

100 Bothwell Street, Glasgow G2 7JD
T 0300-100 0607 (England); 0300-200 4050 (Wales); 0300-555 0505 (Scotland); 0300-100 0077 (Northern Ireland)
W www.gove.uk/government/organisations/student-loans-company

The Student Loans Company (SLC) is owned by the Department for Education. It processes and administers financial assistance, in the form of grants and loans, for undergraduates who have secured a place at university or college. The SLC also provides loans for tuition fees, which are paid directly to the university or college. In 2016 the SLC introduced the provision of loans to postgraduates in accordance with government policy. The SLC supports over 1 million students per year and has a loan book worth £156.5bn.

Chair, Peter Lauener
Chief Executive, Paula Sussex

TATE
W www.tate.org.uk

TATE BRITAIN
Millbank, London SW1P 4RG
T 020-7887 8888 **E** information@tate.org.uk

TATE MODERN
Bankside, London SE1 9TG
T 020-7887 8888 **E** information@tate.org.uk

TATE LIVERPOOL
Royal Albert Dock, Liverpool L3 4BB
T 015-1702 7400 **E** visiting.liverpool@tate.org.uk

TATE ST IVES
Porthmeor Beach, St Ives, Cornwall TR26 1TG
T 01736-796226 **E** visiting.stives@tate.org.uk

Tate comprises four art galleries: Tate Britain and Tate Modern in London, Tate Liverpool and Tate St Ives.

Tate Britain, which opened in 1897, displays the national collection of British art from 1500 to the present day – with special attention and dedicated space given to Blake, Turner and Constable.

Opened in May 2000, Tate Modern displays the Tate collection of international modern art dating from 1900 to the present day. It includes works by Dalí, Picasso, and Matisse, as well as many contemporary works. It is housed in the former Bankside Power Station in London, which was redesigned by the Swiss architects Herzog and de Meuron, and in the neighbouring and purpose-built Switch House, which was designed by Herzog and de Meuron and opened in 2016.

Tate Liverpool opened in 1988 and houses mainly 20th-century art, and Tate St Ives, which features work by artists from and working in St Ives and includes the Barbara Hepworth Museum and Sculpture Garden, opened in 1993.

BOARD OF TRUSTEES
Chair, Lionel Barber
Trustees, John Booth; Farooq Chaudhry, OBE; Tim Davie, CBE; Dame Jayne-Anne Gadhia, DBE; Dame Moya Greene, DBE; Katrin Henkel; Anna Loew; Michael Lynton; Dame Seona Reid, DBE; Roland Rudd; James Timpson, OBE; Jane Wilson

OFFICERS
Director, Tate, Maria Balshaw, CBE
Executive Group (Directors), Anne Barlow *(Tate St Ives);* Vicky Cheetham *(COO);* Anna Cutler *(Learning and Research);* Alex Farquharson *(Tate Britain);* Helen Legg *(Tate Liverpool);* Rosemary Lynch *(Collection Care);* Frances Morris *(Tate Modern);* Stephen Wingfield *(Finance and Estates)*

TOURISM BODIES
Visit Britain, Visit Scotland, Visit Wales and the Northern Ireland Tourist Board are responsible for developing and marketing the tourist industry in their respective regions. Visit Wales is not listed here as it is part of the Welsh government, within the Department for Heritage, and not a public body.

VISITBRITAIN
151 Buckingham Palace Road, London SW1W 9SZ
T 020-7578 1000 **W** www.visitbritain.org
Chair, Rt. Hon. Lord McLoughlin, CH
Chief Executive, Sally Balcombe

VISITSCOTLAND
Ocean Point One, 94 Ocean Drive Edinburgh EH6 6JH
T 0131-472 2222 **E** info@visitscotland.com
W www.visitscotland.com
Chair, Lord Thurso
Chief Executive, Malcolm Roughead, OBE

NORTHERN IRELAND TOURIST BOARD
Floors 10–12, Linum Chambers, Bedford Square, Bedford Street, Belfast BT2 7ES **T** 028-9023 1221
E info@tourismni.com **W** www.tourismni.com
Chair, Terence Brannigan
Chief Executive, John McGrillen

TRANSPORT FOR LONDON (TFL)
4th Floor, 14 Pier Walk, London SE10 0ES
T 0343-222 1234 **W** www.tfl.gov.uk

TfL was created in July 2000 and is the integrated body responsible for the capital's transport system. Its role is to implement the Mayor of London's transport strategy and manage the transport services across London, for which the mayor has responsibility. These services include TfL Rail, London's buses, London Underground, London Overground, the Docklands Light Railway (DLR), London Trams, London River Services and Victoria Coach Station. TfL also runs the Emirates Air Line and the London Transport Museum. In a joint venture with the Department for Transport, TfL is responsible for the construction of Crossrail – a new railway linking Reading and Heathrow in the west, to Shenfield and Abbey Wood in the east. The 73-mile section through London, which was due to open in December 2018, is expected to be operational in 2022. In 2017 TfL announced plans for Crossrail 2, a railway running between Surrey and Hertfordshire.

TfL is responsible for managing the Congestion Charging scheme and the Transport for London road network, London's 'red routes', which make up 5 per cent of the city's roads, but carry around 30 per cent of the traffic. It manages, maintains and operates over 6,000 traffic lights and regulates the city's taxis and private hire vehicles. TfL runs the Santander Cycle Hire scheme, allowing customers to hire a bicycle from £2, and the Dial-a-ride scheme, a door-to-door service for disabled people unable to use buses, trams or the London Underground.

Chair, Rt. Hon. Sadiq Khan
Members, Heidi Alexander *(Deputy Chair);* Julian Bell; Kay Carberry, CBE; Prof. Greg Clark, CBE; Bronwen Handyside; Ron Kalifam OBE; Anne McMeel; Dr Alice Maynard, CBE; Dr Mee Ling Ng, OBE; Dr Nelson Ogunshakin, OBE; Mark Phillips; Dr Nina Skorupska, CBE; Dr Lynn Sloman; Ben Story
Commissioner, Mike Brown, MVO

UK ATOMIC ENERGY AUTHORITY
Culham Science Centre, Abingdon, Oxfordshire OX14 3DB
T 01235-528822 **W** www.gov.uk/government/organisations/uk-atomic-energy-authority

The UK Atomic Energy Authority (UKAEA) was established by the Atomic Energy Authority Act 1954 and took over responsibility for the research and development of the sustainable civil nuclear power programme. The UKAEA reports to the Department for Business, Energy and Industrial Strategy and is responsible for managing UK fusion research, including operating the Joint European Torus (JET) on behalf of the UKAEA's European partners at its site in Culham, Oxfordshire. Culham also houses the facilities for Materials Research, Remote Access in Challenging Environments and Oxford Advanced Skills. In October 2009, as part of the government's Operation Efficiency Programme, the authority sold its commercial arm, UKAEA Limited; as a result, the UKAEA no longer provides nuclear decommissioning services.

Chair, Prof. David Gann, CBE
Chief Executive, Prof. Ian Chapman

UK SPORT
21 Bloomsbury Street, London WC1B 3HF
T 020-7211 5100 **E** info@uksport.gov.uk **W** www.uksport.gov.uk

UK Sport was established by royal charter in 1997 and is accountable to parliament through the Department for Digital, Culture, Media and Sport. Its mission is to lead sport in the UK to world-class success. This means working with partner organisations to deliver medals at the Olympic and Paralympic Games and organising, bidding for and staging major sporting events in the UK; increasing the UK's sporting activity and influence overseas; and promoting sporting conduct, ethics and diversity in society. UK Sport is funded by a mix of grant-in-aid and National Lottery income, and invests around £100m a year in high-performance sport.

Chair, Dame Katherine Grainger, DBE
Chief Executive, Sally Monday

VICTORIA AND ALBERT MUSEUM
Cromwell Road, London SW7 2RL
T 020-7942 2000 **E** hello@vam.ac.uk **W** www.vam.ac.uk

The Victoria and Albert Museum (V&A) is the national museum of art, design and performance. It descends directly from the Museum of Manufactures, which opened in Marlborough House in 1852 after the Great Exhibition of 1851. The museum was moved in 1857 to become part of the South Kensington Museum. It was renamed the Victoria and Albert Museum in 1899. It also houses the National Art Library, which holds over 950,000 books dedicated to the study of fine and decorative arts from around the world. V&A Dundee was opened in September 2018 and contains the restored Charles Rennie Macintosh Oak Room; the building was designed by Kengo Kuma and cost £80.1m.

The museum's collections span over 5,000 years of human creativity, including paintings, sculpture, architecture, ceramics, furniture, fashion and textiles, theatre and performance, photography, glass, jewellery, book arts, Asian art and design and metalwork. Materials relating to childhood are displayed at the V&A Museum of Childhood at Bethnal Green, which opened in 1872 and is the most important surviving example of the type of glass and iron construction used by Joseph Paxton for the Great Exhibition.

Chair, Nicholas Coleridge, CBE
Trustees, Jonathan Anderson; Martin Bartle; Allegra Berman; David Bomford; Dr Genevieve Davies; Ben Elliot; Nick Hoffman; Amanda Levete, CBE; Steven Murphy; Prof. Lynda Nead; Kavita Puri; Marc St John; Caroline Silver; Amanda Spielman; Dr Paul Thompson; Nigel Webb
Director, Dr Tristram Hunt

WALLACE COLLECTION
Hertford House, Manchester Square, London W1U 3BN
T 020-7563 9500 **E** collection@wallacecollection.org
W www.wallacecollection.org

The Wallace Collection was bequeathed to the nation by the widow of Sir Richard Wallace, in 1897, and Hertford House was subsequently acquired by the government. The collection contains works by Titian and Rembrandt, and includes porcelain, furniture and an array of arms and armour.

Chair, António Horta-Osório
Trustees, Marilyn Berk; Jennifer Eady, QC; Eric Ellul; Dounia Nadar; Jessica Pulay; Jemima Rellie; Kate de Rothschild-Agius; Dr Ashok Roy; Timothy Schroder
Director, Dr Xavier Bray

DEVOLVED GOVERNMENT

WALES

NATIONAL ASSEMBLY FOR WALES
Cardiff Bay, Cardiff CF99 1NA
T 0300-200 6565 W www.assemblywales.org

The National Assembly for Wales has been in existence since 1999, following a 'yes' vote in the 1997 referendum. However, the way the assembly is structured and its powers have changed over time.

The UK Act that created the assembly was the Government of Wales Act 1998. This stated that the Assembly was a 'corporate body' which meant that the Welsh government and the assembly were a single organisation. Also, it could not pass its own acts. It could, however make orders and regulations, known as secondary legislation.

The Government of Wales Act 2006 created a formal legal separation between:
- the legislative branch: the National Assembly for Wales, made up of 60 assembly members, and
- the executive branch: the Welsh government, made up of the First Minister, Welsh cabinet secretaries and the Counsel General

The act allowed the assembly to seek the power to make laws from the UK parliament. The laws were known as 'measures' of the National Assembly for Wales ('assembly measures'). The power to make laws ('legislative competence') was granted through clauses in Westminster bills or through legislative competence orders. These had to be approved by parliament and by the assembly. This is how the third assembly operated between 2007 and 2011.

The Government of Wales Act 2006 also contained provision for the assembly to make its own lawns without the permission of the UK parliament. These provisions could only be triggered by:
- two-thirds of all assembly members voting in favour of a referendum
- the approval of the UK government and parliament to hold a referendum
- a 'yes' vote in a referendum of the Welsh public

A referendum held on 3 March 2011 resulted in a 'yes' vote in favour of bringing into force part four of the Government of Wales Act 2006. This has meant that since the 2011 National Assembly of Wales election the assembly has been able to pass laws on all subjects in the devolved areas without first needing the agreement of the UK parliament.

During an assembly election, the people of Wales have two votes. One vote is for their constituency assembly member who represents local areas. Wales is divided into 40 constituencies and each is represented by one assembly member (AM).

The other vote is for a party or independent candidate to represent the voter's region. Wales is divided into five regions – North Wales, Mid and West Wales, South Wales West, South Wales East and South Wales Central.

This system means that the overall number of seats held by each political party more closely reflects the share of the vote that the party receives.

The 60 assembly members who are elected make decisions regarding many things that affect life in Wales – health, education, housing and transport. Their job is to make sure that the Welsh government's decisions are in the best interests of Wales and its people.

The National Assembly for Wales does this by:

- scrutinising the policies the Welsh government sets and the decisions it makes
- scrutinising suggestions for laws, proposing changes and voting on whether they should be passed
- asking questions to Welsh government and making suggestions about policies
- voting on how the Welsh government spends its budget every year

The assembly also makes laws for Wales. A law can be put forward by the Welsh government, an individual assembly member, or an assembly committee or the Assembly Commission. The majority of laws are put forward by the Welsh government.

The assembly operates in both Welsh and English and all its legislation is made bilingually.

In July 2018 the National Assembly of Wales Commission announced plans to lower the minimum voting age for assembly elections to 16 years. They also announced plans to change the name of the assembly to Welsh Parliament/Senedd Cymru. The assembly intends to legislate both changes prior to the next assembly elections in 2021.

ASSEMBLY COMMISSION
The Assembly Commission was created under the Government of Wales Act 2006 to ensure that the assembly is provided with the property, staff and services required for it to carry out its functions. The commission also sets the National Assembly's strategic aims, objectives, standards and values. The Assembly Commission consists of the presiding officer, plus four other assembly members, one nominated by each of the four party groups. The five commissioners are accountable to the National Assembly.

Presiding Officer, Elin Jones, AM
Deputy Presiding Officer, Ann Jones, AM
Commissioners, Suzy Davies, AM; Siân Gwenllian, AM, David Rowlands, AM, Joyce Watson, AM
Chief Executive and Clerk of the Assembly, Manon Antoniazzi

ASSEMBLY COMMITTEES
The Business Committee, chaired by the Presiding Officer and established on 24 May 2016, is responsible for facilitating the effective organisation of assembly proceedings. The rest of the assembly committees *as at* August 2019 are:

Children, Young People and Education
  Chair, Lynne Neagle, AM
Climate Change, Environment and Rural Affairs
  Chair, Mike Hedges, AM
Constitutional and Legislative Affairs
  Chair, Mick Antoniw, AM
Culture, Welsh Language and Communications
  Chair, Bethan Sayed, AM
Economy, Infrastructure and Skills
  Chair, Russell George, AM
Equality, Local Government and Communities
  Chair, John Griffiths, AM
External Affairs and Additional Legislation
  Chair, David Rees, AM
Finance
  Chair, Llyr Gruffydd, AM
Health, Social Care and Sport
  Chair, Dai Lloyd, AM
Petitions
  Chair, Janet Finch-Saunders, AM

Public Accounts
  Chair, Nick Ramsay, AM
Scrutiny of the First Minister
  Chair, Ann Jones, AM
Standards of Conduct
  Chair, Jayne Bryant, AM

SALARIES* 2019–20

First Minister	£147,983
Presiding Officer	£110,987
Cabinet Secretary	£105,701
Minister/Deputy Presiding Officer	£89,846
Assembly Commissioners	£81,390
Assembly Member (AM)	£67,649

* All salaries include the AM salary

MEMBERS OF THE NATIONAL ASSEMBLY FOR WALES as at 31 August 2019

KEY
* Elected via a by-election since the 2016 National Assembly election
† Replacement from the party list since the 2016 National Assembly election
‡ Previously AM for PC
§ Previously AM for UKIP
℃ Previously an Ind. AM
** Previously an AM for C.

Antoniw, Mick, *Lab., Pontypridd*, Maj. 5,327
ap Iorwerth, Rhun, *PC, Ynys Môn*, Maj. 9,510
Asghar, Mohammad, *C., South Wales East region*
Bennett, Gareth, *UKIP, South Wales Central region*
Blythyn, Hannah, *Lab., Delyn*, Maj. 3,582
Bowden, Dawn, *Lab., Merthyr Tydfil and Rhymney*, Maj. 5,486
§ **Brown**, Michelle, *Ind., North Wales region*
Bryant, Jayne, *Lab., Newport West*, Maj. 4,115
Burns, Angela, *C., Carmarthen West and South Pembrokeshire*, Maj. 3,373
David, Hefin, *Lab., Caerphilly*, Maj. 1,575
Davies, Alun, *Lab., Blaenau Gwent*, Maj. 650
Davies, Andrew R. T., *C., South Wales Central region*
Davies, Paul, *C., Preseli Pembrokeshire*, Maj. 3,930
Davies, Suzy, *C., South Wales West region*
Drakeford, Rt. Hon. Mark, *Lab., Cardiff West*, Maj. 1,176
‡ **Elis-Thomas**, Rt. Hon. Lord, *Ind., Dwyfor Meirionnydd*, Maj. 6,406
Evans, Rebecca, *Lab., Gower*, Maj. 1,829
Finch-Saunders, Janet, *C., Aberconwy*, Maj. 754
George, Russell, *C., Montgomeryshire*, Maj. 3,339
Gething, Vaughan, *Lab., Cardiff South and Penarth*, Maj. 6,921
Griffiths, John, *Lab., Newport East*, Maj. 4,896
Griffiths, Lesley, *Lab., Wrexham*, Maj. 1,325
Gruffydd, Llyr, *PC, North Wales region*
Gwenllian, Siân, *PC, Arfon*, Maj. 4,162
Hamilton, Neil, *UKIP, Mid and West Wales region*
Hedges, Mike, *Lab., Swansea East*, Maj. 7,452
Howells, Vikki, *Lab., Cynon Valley*, Maj. 5, 994
Hutt, Jane, *Lab., Vale of Glamorgan*, Maj. 777
Irranca-Davies, Huw, *Lab., Ogmore*, Maj. 9,468
Isherwood, Mark, *C., North Wales region*
James, Julie, *Lab., Swansea West*, Maj. 5,080
† **Jewell**, Delyth, *PC, South Wales East region*
Jones, Ann, *Lab., Vale of Clwyd*, Maj. 768
§ **Jones**, Caroline, *Brexit, South Wales West region*
Jones, Rt. Hon. Carwyn, *Lab., Bridgend*, Maj. 5,623
Jones, Elin, *PC, Ceredigion*, Maj. 2,408

Jones, Helen Mary, *PC, Mid and West Wales region*
℃ **Jones**, Mandy, *Brexit, North Wales region*
Lloyd, Dai, *PC, South Wales West region*
‡ **McEvoy**, Neil, *Ind., South Wales Central region*
Melding, David, *C. South Wales Central region*
Miles, Jeremy, *Lab. Neath*, Maj. 2,923
Millar, Darren, *C., Clwyd West*, Maj. 5,063
Morgan, Eluned *Lab., Mid and West Wales region*
Morgan, Julie, *Lab., Cardiff North*, Maj. 3,667
Neagle, Lynne, *Lab., Torfaen*, Maj. 4,498
Passmore, Rhianon, *Lab., Islwyn*, Maj. 5,106
Price, Adam, *PC, Carmarthen East and Dinefwr*, Maj. 8,700
Ramsay, Nick, *C., Monmouth*, Maj. 5,147
Rathbone, Jenny, *Lab., Cardiff Central*, Maj. 817
§ ** **Reckless**, Mark, *Brexit, South Wales East*
Rees, David, *Lab, Aberavon*, Maj. 6,402
§ **Rowlands**, David J., *Brexit, South Wales East region*
* **Sargeant**, Jack, *Lab., Alyn and Deeside* Maj. 6,545
Sayed, Bethan, *PC, South Wales West region*
Skates, Ken, *Lab., Clwyd South*, Maj. 3,016
Waters, Lee, *Lab., Llanelli*, Maj. 382
Watson, Joyce, *Lab., Mid and West Wales region*
Williams, Kirsty, *LD, Brecon and Radnorshire*, Maj. 8,170
Wood, Leanne, *PC, Rhondda*, Maj. 3,359

STATE OF THE PARTIES *as at 31 August 2019*

	Constituency AMs	Regional AMs	AM total
Labour (Lab.)	*27	2	29
Conservative (C.)	6	5	11
Plaid Cymru (PC)	†5	5	10
Brexit Party (Brexit)	0	4	4
UKIP	0	2	2
Independent (Ind.)	1	2	3
Liberal Democrats (LD)	1	0	1
Total	40	20	60

* Includes the Deputy Presiding Officer
† Includes the Presiding Officer

WELSH GOVERNMENT
Cathays Park, Cardiff CF10 3NQ
T 0300-060 4400 W www.gov.wales

The Welsh government is the devolved government of Wales. It is accountable to the National Assembly for Wales, the Welsh legislature which represents the interests of the people of Wales, and makes laws for Wales. The Welsh government and the National Assembly for Wales were established as separate institutions under the Government of Wales Act 2006.

The Welsh government comprises the first minister, who is usually the leader of the largest party in the National Assembly for Wales; up to 14 cabinet secretaries and ministers and deputy ministers; and a counsel-general (the chief legal adviser).

Following the referendum on 3 March 2011 on granting further law-making powers to the National Assembly, the Welsh government's functions now include the ability to propose bills to the National Assembly on subjects within 20 set areas of policy. Subject to limitations prescribed by the Government of Wales Act 2006, acts of the National Assembly may make any provision that could be made by act of parliament. The 20 areas of responsibility devolved to the National Assembly for Wales (and within which Welsh ministers exercise executive functions) are: agriculture, fisheries, forestry and rural development; ancient monuments and historic buildings; culture; economic development; education and training; environment; fire and rescue services and promotion of fire safety; food; health and health services; highways and transport; housing; local government; the National Assembly for Wales; public administration; social welfare; sport and recreation; tourism; town and county planning; water and flood defence; and the Welsh language.

CABINET

Ministers
First Minister of Wales, Rt. Hon. Mark Drakeford, AM
Economy and Transport, Ken Skates, AM
Education, Kirsty Williams, AM
Environment, Energy and Rural Affairs, Lesley Griffiths, AM
Finance and Trefnydd (Leader of the House), Rebecca Evans, AM
Health and Social Services, Vaughan Gething, AM
Housing and Local Government, Julie James, AM
International Relations and the Welsh Language, Eluned Morgan, AM
Counsel-General and Brexit Minister, Jeremy Miles, AM

Deputy Ministers
Culture, Sport and Tourism, Rt. Hon. Lord Elis-Thomas, AM
Economy and Transport, Lee Waters, AM
Health and Social Services, Julie Morgan, AM
Housing and Local Government, Hannah Blythyn, AM
Chief Whip, Jane Hutt, AM

MANAGEMENT BOARD

Permanent Secretary, Dame Shan Morgan, DCMG
Director-Generals, Tracey Burke *(Education and Public Services);* Desmond Clifford *(Office of the First Minister and Brexit);* Dr Andrew Goodall, CBE *(Health and Social Services);* Andrew Slade *(Economy, Skills and Natural Resources)*
Directors, Jeff Godfrey *(Legal Services);* Peter Kennedy *(HR);* David Richards *(Governance and Ethics)*
Head of Organisational Development and Engagement, Natalie Pearson
Board Equality and Diversity Champion, Gillian Baranski
Finance Director, Gawain Evans
Non-Executive Directors, Ellen Donovan; Jeff Farrar; Ann Keane; Gareth Lynn

DEPARTMENTS

Permanent Secretary's Group – Welsh Treasury, Finance, Governance and HR

DIRECTORATES

Office of the First Minister and Brexit
Education and Public Services
Health and Social Services
Economy, Skills and Natural Resources

NATIONAL ASSEMBLY ELECTION RESULTS *as at 5 May 2016*

Electorate (E.) 2,248,050 Turnout (T.) 45.3%
See General Election Results for a list of party abbreviations

ABERAVON (S. WALES WEST)
E. 49,074 T. 20,852 (42.49%)

David Rees, Lab.	10,578
Bethan Jenkins, PC	4,176
Glenda Davies, UKIP	3,119
David Jenkins, C.	1,342
Helen Ceri Clarke, LD	1,248
Jonathan Tier, Green	389

Lab. majority 6,402 (30.70%)
9.31% swing Lab. to PC

ABERCONWY (WALES N.)
E. 44,960 T. 22,038 (49.02%)

Janet Finch-Saunders, C.	7,646
Trystan Lewis, PC	6,892
Mike Priestley, Lab.	6,039
Sarah Lesiter-Burgess, LD	781
Petra Haig, Green	680

C. majority 754 (3.42%)
2.15% swing C. to PC

ALYN AND DEESIDE (WALES N.)
E. 62,697 T. 21,696 (34.60%)

Carl Sargeant, Lab.	9,922
Mike Gibbs, C.	4,558
Michelle Brown, UKIP	3,765
Jacqui Hurst, PC	1,944
Pete Williams, LD	980
Martin Bennewith, Green	527

Lab. majority 5,364 (24.72%)
0.11% swing C. to Lab.

ARFON (WALES N.)
E. 39,269 T. 19,994 (50.92%)

Sian Gwenllian, PC	10,962
Sion Jones, Lab.	6,800
Martin Peet, C.	1,655
Sara Lloyd Williams, LD	577

PC majority 4,162 (20.82%)
4.86% swing PC to Lab.

BLAENAU GWENT (S. WALES EAST)
E. 50,574 T. 21,291 (42.10%)

Alun Davies, Lab.	8,442
Nigel Copner, PC	7,792
Kevin Boucher, UKIP	3,423
Tracey West, C.	1,334
Brendan D'Cruz, LD	300

Lab. majority 650 (3.05%)
27.73% swing Lab. to PC

BRECON AND RADNORSHIRE (WALES MID AND W.)
E. 53,793 T. 30,367 (56.45%)

Kirsty Williams, LD	15,898
Gary Price, C.	7,728
Alex Thomas, Lab.	2,703
Thomas Turton, UKIP	2,161
Freddy Greaves, PC	1,180
Grenville Ham, Green	697

LD majority 8,170 (26.90%)
8.59% swing C. to LD

BRIDGEND (S. WALES WEST)
E. 60,195 T. 26,851 (44.61%)

Carwyn Jones, Lab.	12,166
George Jabbour, C.	6,543
Caroline Jones, UKIP	3,919
James Radcliffe, PC	2,569
Jonathan Pratt, LD	1,087
Charlie Barlow, Green	567

Lab. majority 5,623 (20.94%)
3.62% swing Lab. to C.

CAERPHILLY (S. WALES EAST)
E. 62,449 T. 27,115 (43.42%)

Hefin David, Lab.	9,584
Lindsay Whittle, PC	8,009
Sam Gould, UKIP	5,954
Jane Pratt, C.	2,412
Andrew Creak, Green	770
Aladdin Ayesh, LD	386

Lab. majority 1,575 (5.81%)
6.72% swing Lab. to PC

CARDIFF CENTRAL (S. WALES CENTRAL)
E. 57,177 T. 26,068 (45.59%)

Jenny Rathbone, Lab.	10,016
Eluned Parrott, LD	9,199
Joel Williams, C.	2,317
Glyn Wise, PC	1,951
Mohammed Islam, UKIP	1,223
Amelia Womack, Green	1,150
Jane Croad, Ind.	212

Lab. majority 817 (3.13%)
1.49% swing LD to Lab.

CARDIFF NORTH (S. WALES CENTRAL)
E. 65,927 T. 37,452 (56.81%)

Julie Morgan, Lab.	16,766
Jayne Cowan, C.	13,099
Haydn Rushworth, UKIP	2,509
Elin Walker Jones, PC	2,278
John Dixon, LD	1,130
Fiona Burt, Ind.	846
Chris von Ruhland, Green	824

Lab. majority 3,667 (9.79%)
2.31% swing C. to Lab.

CARDIFF SOUTH AND PENARTH (S. WALES CENTRAL)
E. 76,110 T. 30,276 (39.78%)

Vaughan Gething, Lab.	13,274
Ben Gray, C.	6,353
Dafydd Davies, PC	4,320
Hugh Moelwyn Hughes, UKIP	3,716
Nigel Howells, LD	1,345
Anthony Slaughter, Green	1,268

Lab. majority 6,921 (22.86%)
0.04% swing C. to Lab.

CARDIFF WEST (S. WALES CENTRAL)
E. 66,040 T. 31,960 (48.39%)

Mark Drakeford, Lab.	11,381
Neil McEvoy, PC	10,205
Sean Driscoll, C.	5,617
Gareth Bennett, UKIP	2,629
Hannah Pudner, Green	1,032
Cadan ap Tomos, LD	868
Eliot Freedman, Ind.	132
Lee Woolls, FTC	96

Lab. majority 1,176 (3.68%)
11.71% swing Lab. to PC

CARMARTHEN EAST AND DINEFWR (WALES MID AND W.)
E. 55,395 T. 29,751 (53.71%)

Adam Price, PC	14,427
Stephen Jeacock, Lab.	5,727
Matthew Paul, C.	4,489
Neil Hamilton, UKIP	3,474
William Powell, LD	837
Freya Amsbury, Green	797

PC majority 8,700 (29.24%)
7.17% swing Lab. to PC

CARMARTHEN WEST AND SOUTH PEMBROKESHIRE (WALES MID AND W.)
E. 56,886 T. 29,237 (51.40%)

Angela Burns, C.	10,355
Marc Tierney, Lab.	6,982
Simon Thomas, PC	5,459
Allan Brookes, UKIP	3,300
Chris Overton, Ind.	1,638
Val Bradley, Green	804
Alistair Cameron, LD	699

C. majority 3,373 (11.54%)
3.10% swing Lab. to C.

CEREDIGION (WALES MID AND W.)
E. 51,230 T. 29,485 (57.55%)

Elin T Jones, PC	12,014
Elizabeth Evans, LD	9,606
Gethin James, UKIP	2,665
Felix Aubel, C.	2,075
Iwan Wyn Jones, Lab.	1,902
Brian Williams, Green	1,223

PC majority 2,408 (8.17%)
1.03% swing LD to PC

CLWYD SOUTH (WALES N.)
E. 54,185 T. 22,159 (40.90%)

Ken Skates, Lab.	7,862
Simon Baynes, C.	4,846
Mabon ap Gwynfor, PC	3,861
Mandy Jones, UKIP	2,827
Aled Roberts, LD	2,289
Duncan Rees, Green	474

Lab. majority 3,016 (13.61%)
0.17% swing C. to Lab.

CLWYD WEST (WALES N.)
E. 57,657 T. 26,226 (45.49%)

Darren Millar, C.	10,831
Llyr Gruffydd, PC	5,768
Jo Thomas, Lab.	5,246
David Edwards, UKIP	2,985
Victor Babu, LD	831
Julian Mahy, Green	565

C. majority 5,063 (19.31%)
0.52% swing C. to PC

CYNON VALLEY (S. WALES CENTRAL)
E. 50,292 T. 19,236 (38.25%)

Vikki Howells, Lab.	9,830
Cerith Griffiths, PC	3,836
Liz Wilks, UKIP	3,460
Lyn Hudson, C.	1,177
John Matthews, Green	598
Michael Wallace, LD	335

Lab. majority 5,994 (31.16%)
1.78% swing Lab. to PC

DELYN (WALES N.)
E. 53,490 T. 23,159 (43.30%)

Hannah Blythyn, Lab.	9,480
Huw Williams, C.	5,898
Nigel Williams, UKIP	3,794
Paul Rowlinson, PC	2,269
Tom Rippeth, LD	1,718

Lab. majority 3,582 (15.47%)
1.52% swing C. to Lab.

DWYFOR MEIRIONNYDD (WALES MID AND W.)
E. 43,304 T. 20,236 (46.73%)

Dafydd Elis-Thomas, PC	9,566
Neil Fairlamb, C.	3,160
Ian MacIntyre, Lab.	2,443
Frank Wykes, UKIP	2,149
Louise Hughes, Ind.	1,259
Steve Churchman, LD	916
Alice Hooker-Stroud, Green	743

PC majority 6,406 (31.66%)
2.77% swing C. to PC

GOWER (S. WALES WEST)
E. 60,631 T. 30,187 (49.79%)

Rebecca Evans, Lab.	11,982
Lyndon Jones, C.	10,153
Colin Beckett, UKIP	3,300
Harri Roberts, PC	2,982
Sheila Kingston-Jones, LD	1,033
Abi Cherry-Hamer, Green	737

Lab. majority 1,829 (6.06%)
6.05% swing Lab. to C.

ISLWYN (S. WALES EAST)
E. 54,465 T. 22,309 (40.96%)

Rhianon Passmore, Lab.	10,050
Joe Smyth, UKIP	4,944
Lyn Ackerman, PC	4,349
Paul Williams, C.	1,775
Matthew Kidner, LD	597
Katy Beddoe, Green	594

Lab. majority 5,106 (22.89%)

LLANELLI (WALES MID AND W.)
E. 59,651 T. 28,116 (47.13%)

Lee Waters, Lab.	10,267
Helen Mary Jones, PC	9,885
Ken Rees, UKIP	4,132
Stefan Ryszewski, C.	1,937
Sian Caiach, PF	1,113
Guy Smith, Green	427
Gemma Bowker, LD	355

Lab. majority 382 (1.36%)
0.53% swing PC to Lab.

MERTHYR TYDFIL AND RHYMNEY (S. WALES EAST)
E. 53,754 T. 20,683 (38.48%)

Dawn Bowden, Lab.	9,763
David Rowlands, UKIP	4,277
Brian Thomas, PC	3,721
Elizabeth Simon, C.	1,331
Bob Griffin, LD	1,122
Julie Colbran, Green	469

Lab. majority 5,486 (26.52%)

MONMOUTH (S. WALES EAST)
E. 64,197 T. 31,401 (48.91%)

Nick Ramsay, C.	13,585
Catherine Fookes, Lab.	8,438
Tim Price, UKIP	3,092
Debby Blakebrough, Ind.	1,932
Jonathan Clark, PC	1,824
Veronica German, LD	1,474
Chris Were, Green	910
Stephen Morris, Eng Dem	146

C. majority 5,147 (16.39%)
2.00% swing C. to Lab.

MONTGOMERYSHIRE (WALES MID AND W.)
E. 48,682 T. 23,600 (48.48%)

Russell George, C.	9,875
Jane Dodds, LD	6,536
Des Parkinson, UKIP	2,458
Aled Morgan Hughes, PC	2,410
Martyn Singleton, Lab.	1,389
Richard Chaloner, Green	932

C. majority 3,339 (14.15%)
2.01% swing LD to C.

NEATH (S. WALES WEST)
E. 55,395 T. 25,363 (45.79%)

Jeremy Miles, Lab.	9,468
Alun Llewelyn, PC	6,545
Richard Pritchard, UKIP	3,780
Peter Crocker-Jaques, C.	2,179
Steve Hunt, Ind.	2,056
Frank Little, LD	746
Lisa Rapado, Green	589

Lab. majority 2,923 (11.52%)
7.63% swing Lab. to PC

NEWPORT EAST (S. WALES EAST)
E. 55,499 T. 20,688 (37.28%)
John Griffiths, Lab.	9,229
James Peterson, UKIP	4,333
Munawar Mughal, C.	3,768
Paul Halliday, LD	1,481
Tony Salkeld, PC	1,386
Peter Varley, Green	491

Lab. majority 4,896 (23.67%)

NEWPORT WEST (S. WALES EAST)
E. 62,169 T. 27,751 (44.64%)
Jayne Bryant, Lab.	12,157
Matthew Evans, C.	8,042
Michael Ford, UKIP	3,842
Simon Coopey, PC	1,645
Liz Newton, LD	880
Pippa Bartolotti, Green	814
Bill Fearnley-Whittingstall, Ind.	333
Gruff Meredith, WSov	38

Lab. majority 4,115 (14.83%)
1.75% swing Lab. to C.

OGMORE (S. WALES WEST)
E. 54,502 T. 23,356 (42.85%)
Huw Irranca-Davies, Lab.	12,895
Tim Thomas, PC	3,427
Elizabeth Kendall, UKIP	3,233
Jamie Wallis, C.	2,587
Anita Davies, LD	698
Laurie Brophy, Green	516

Lab. majority 9,468 (40.54%)
3.36% swing Lab. to PC

PONTYPRIDD (S. WALES CENTRAL)
E. 58,277 T. 25,338 (43.48%)
Mick Antoniw, Lab.	9,986
Chad Rickard, PC	4,659
Joel James, C.	3,884
Edwin Allen, UKIP	3,322
Mike Powell, LD	2,979
Ken Barker, Green	508

Lab. majority 5,327 (21.02%)
8.18% swing Lab. to PC

PRESELI PEMBROKESHIRE (WALES MID AND W.)
E. 56,414 T. 28,397 (50.34%)
Paul Davies, C.	11,123
Dan Lodge, Lab.	7,193
John Osmond, PC	3,957
Howard Lillyman, UKIP	3,286
Bob Kilmister, LD	1,677
Frances Bryant, Green	1,161

C. majority 3,930 (13.84%)
2.92% swing Lab. to C.

RHONDDA (S. WALES CENTRAL)
E. 49,758 T. 23,486 (47.20%)
Leanne Wood, PC	11,891
Leighton Andrews, Lab.	8,432
Stephen Clee, UKIP	2,203
Maria Hill, C.	528
Pat Matthews, Green	259
Rhys Taylor, LD	173

PC majority 3,459 (14.73%)
24.19% swing Lab. to PC

SWANSEA EAST (S. WALES WEST)
E. 57,589 T. 20,576 (35.73%)
Mike Hedges, Lab.	10,726
Clifford Johnson, UKIP	3,274
Dic Jones, PC	2,744
Sadie Vidal, C.	1,729
Charlene Webster, LD	1,574
Tony Young, Green	529

Lab. majority 7,452 (36.22%)

SWANSEA WEST (S. WALES WEST)
E. 54,593 T. 22,202 (40.67%)
Julie James, Lab.	9,014
Craig Lawton, C.	3,934
Dai Lloyd, PC	3,225
Rosie Irwin, UKIP	3,058
Chris Holley, LD	2,012
Gareth Tucker, Green	883
Brian Johnson, SPGB	76

Lab. majority 5,080 (22.88%)
0.77% swing C. to Lab.

TORFAEN (S. WALES EAST)
E. 60,246 T. 22,978 (38.14%)
Lynne Neagle, Lab.	9,688
Susan Boucher, UKIP	5,190
Graham Smith, C.	3,931
Matthew Woolfall-Jones, PC	2,860
Steve Jenkins, Green	681
Alison Willott, LD	628

Lab. majority 4,498 (19.58%)

VALE OF CLWYD (WALES N.)
E. 56,322 T. 24,183 (42.94%)
Ann Jones, Lab.	9,560
Sam Rowlands, C.	8,792
Paul Davies-Cooke, UKIP	2,975
Mair Rowlands, PC	2,098
Gwyn Williams, LD	758

Lab. majority 768 (3.18%)
7.11% swing Lab. to C.

VALE OF GLAMORGAN (S. WALES CENTRAL)
E. 71,177 T. 37,798 (53.10%)
Jane Hutt, Lab.	14,655
Ross England, C.	13,878
Ian Johnson, PC	3,871
Lawrence Andrews, UKIP	3,662
Denis Campbell, LD	938
Alison Haden, Green	794

Lab. majority 777 (2.06%)
4.65% swing Lab. to C.

WREXHAM (WALES N.)
E. 51,567 T. 20,354 (39.47%)
Lesley Griffiths, Lab.	7,552
Andrew Atkinson, C.	6,227
Carrie Harper, PC	2,631
Jeanette Bassford-Barton, UKIP	2,393
Beryl Blackmore, LD	1,140
Alan Butterworth, Green	411

Lab. majority 1,325 (6.51%)
5.67% swing Lab. to C.

YNYS MON (WALES N.)
E. 50,345 T. 25,167 (49.99%)
Rhun ap Iorwerth, PC	13,788
Julia Dobson, Lab.	4,278
Simon Wall, UKIP	3,212
Clay Theakston, C.	2,904
Gerry Wolff, Green	389
Thomas Crofts, LD	334
Daniel ap Eifion Jones, Ind.	262

PC majority 9,510 (37.79%)
11.29% swing Lab. to PC

REGIONS *as at 5 May 2016*
E. 2,248,050 T. 45.3%

MID AND WEST WALES
E. 425,355 T. 215,840 (50.74%)

PC	56,754	(26.29%)
C.	44,461	(20.60%)
Lab.	41,975	(19.45%)
UKIP	25,042	(11.60%)
LD	23,554	(10.91%)
Abolish	10,707	(4.96%)
Green	8,222	(3.81%)
PF	1,496	(0.69%)
Ch. P.	1,103	(0.51%)
Loony	1,071	(0.50%)
Loc. Ind.	1,032	(0.48%)
Welsh Comm	423	(0.20%)

PC majority 12,293 (5.70%)
2.02% swing C. to PC (2011 PC majority 3,479)

ADDITIONAL MEMBERS
Joyce Watson, *Lab.*
Eluned Morgan, *Lab.*
Simon Thomas, *PC*
Neil Hamilton, *UKIP*

NORTH WALES
E. 470,492 T. 204,490 (43.46%)

Lab.	57,528	(28.13%)
PC	47,701	(23.33%)
C	45,468	(22.23%)
UKIP	25,518	(12.48%)
Abolish	9,409	(4.60%)
LD	9,345	(4.57%)
Green	4,789	(2.34%)
Loc Ind.	1,865	(0.91%)
Loony	1,355	(0.66%)
Ind.	926	(0.45%)
Welsh Comm	586	(0.29%)

Lab. majority 9,827 (4.81%)
2.98% swing Lab. to PC (2011 Lab. majority 10,476)

ADDITIONAL MEMBERS
Mark Isherwood, *C.*
Llyr Gruffydd, *PC*
Nathan Gill, *UKIP*
Michelle Brown, *UKIP*

SOUTH WALES CENTRAL
E. 494,758 T. 231,133 (46.72%)

Lab.	78,366	(33.91%)
PC	48,357	(20.92%)
C.	42,185	(18.25%)
UKIP	23,958	(10.37%)
LD	14,875	(6.44%)
Abolish	9,163	(3.96%)
Green	7,949	(3.44%)
Women	2,807	(1.21%)
Loony	1,096	(0.47%)
TUSC	736	(0.32%)
Ind.	651	(0.28%)
Comm	520	(0.22%)
FTC	470	(0.20%)

Lab. majority 30,009 (12.98%)
7.24% swing Lab. to PC (2011 Lab. majority 39,694)

ADDITIONAL MEMBERS
Andrew Davies, *C.*
David Melding, *C.*
Neil McEvoy, *PC*
Gareth Bennett, *UKIP*

SOUTH WALES EAST
E. 463,353 T. 194,091 (41.89%)

Lab.	74,424	(38.34%)
UKIP	34,524	(17.79%)
C.	33,318	(17.17%)
PC	29,686	(15.29%)
Abolish	7,870	(4.05%)
LD	6,784	(3.50%)
Green	4,831	(2.49%)
Loony	1,115	(0.57%)
TUSC	618	(0.32%)
Welsh Comm	492	(0.25%)
NF	429	(0.22%)

Lab. majority 39,900 (20.56%)
9.93% swing Lab. to UKIP (2011 Lab. majority 47,240)

ADDITIONAL MEMBERS
Oscar Asghar, *C.*
Steffan Lewis, *PC*
Mark Reckless, *UKIP*
David Rowlands, *UKIP*

SOUTH WALES WEST
E. 391,979 T. 169,189 (43.16%)

Lab.	66,903	(39.54%)
PC	29,050	(17.17%)
C.	25,414	(15.02%)
UKIP	23,096	(13.65%)
LD	10,946	(6.47%)
Abolish	7,137	(4.22%)
Green	4,420	(2.61%)
Loony	1,106	(0.65%)
TUSC	686	(0.41%)
Welsh Comm	431	(0.25%)

Lab. majority 37,853 (22.37%)
5.17% swing Lab. to PC (2011 Lab. majority 44,309)

ADDITIONAL MEMBERS
Suzy Davies, *C.*
Bethan Jenkins, *PC*
Dai Lloyd, *PC*
Caroline Jones, *UKIP*

SCOTLAND

SCOTTISH PARLIAMENT
Edinburgh EH99 1SP
T 0131-348 5000/ 0800-092 7500
E info@parliament.scot
W www.parliament.scot

In July 1997 the government announced plans to establish a Scottish parliament. In a referendum on 11 September 1997 about 60 per cent of the electorate voted. Of those who voted, 74.3 per cent voted in favour of the parliament and 63.5 per cent voted in support of granting the parliament having tax-raising powers. Elections are normally held every four years, but the current session is scheduled to last for five years. The first elections were held on 6 May 1999, when around 59 per cent of the electorate voted. The first meeting was held on 12 May 1999 and the Scottish parliament was officially opened on 1 July 1999 at the Assembly Hall, Edinburgh. A new building to house the parliament was opened, in the presence of the Queen, at Holyrood on 9 October 2004. On 5 May 2016 the fifth elections to the Scottish parliament took place.

The Scottish parliament has 129 members (including the presiding officer), comprising 73 constituency members and 56 additional regional members, drawn from the party lists. It can introduce primary legislation and has the power to set rates and bands for income tax on non-savings and non-dividend income for Scottish taxpayers.

Members of the Scottish parliament are elected using the additional member system, the same system used to elect London Assembly and Welsh Assembly members. Under the additional member system the electorate has two votes; the first to elect their constituency member via the 'first past the post' method of voting and the second to elect their regional members. The 56 regional seats are filled proportionally from the parties' lists according to their share of the vote on the second ballot paper. By-elections are held for constituency seat vacancies but not for regional seat vacancies which are filled by the next candidate on the list from the same political party in which the vacancy arose.

The areas for which the Scottish parliament is responsible include: civil and criminal justice; education; health; environment; economic development; local government; housing; police; fire services; planning; financial assistance to industry; tourism; heritage and the arts; agriculture; social work; sports; public registers and records; forestry; food standards; some aspects of transport; and some areas of welfare.

SALARIES* as at 1 April 2019

First Minister	£155,680
Cabinet Secretary/ Presiding Officer	£111,359
Minister/ Deputy Presiding Officer	£93,510
MSP†	£63,579
Lord Advocate	£126,000
Solicitor-General for Scotland	£108,718

* All salaries include the MSP salary
† Reduced by two-thirds if the member is also an MP or MEP

The Presiding Officer, Ken Macintosh, MSP
Deputy Presiding Officers, Linda Fabiani, MSP; Christine Grahame, MSP

MEMBERS OF THE SCOTTISH PARLIAMENT as at September 2019

KEY
* Elected via a by-election since the 2016 Scottish parliament election
† Replacement from the party list since the 2016 Scottish parliament election under the additional member system
‡ The Presiding Officer was elected as a regional member for Labour but has no party affiliation while in post

Adam, George, SNP, Paisley, Maj. 5,199
Adamson, Clare, SNP, Motherwell and Wishaw, Maj. 6,223
Allan, Alasdair, SNP, Na h-Eileanan an Iar, Maj. 3,496
Arthur, Tom, SNP, Renfrewshire South, Maj. 4,408
Baillie, Jackie, Lab., Dumbarton, Maj. 109
Baker, Claire, Lab., Mid Scotland and Fife region
Balfour, Jeremy, C., Lothian region
† Ballantyne, Michelle, C., South Scotland region
Beamish, Claudia, Lab., South Scotland region
Beattie, Colin, SNP, Midlothian North and Musselburgh, Maj. 7,035
Bibby, Neil, Lab., West Scotland region
† Bowman, Bill, C., North East Scotland region
† Boyack, Sarah, Lab., Lothian region
Briggs, Miles, C. Lothian region
Brown, Keith, SNP, Clackmannanshire and Dunblane, Maj. 6,721
Burnett, Alexander, C., Aberdeenshire West, Maj. 900
Cameron, Donald, C., Highlands and Islands region
Campbell, Aileen, SNP, Clydesdale, Maj. 5,979
Carlaw, Jackson, CB, C., Eastwood, Maj. 1.610
Carson, Finlay, C., Galloway and West Dumfries, Maj. 1,514
Chapman, Peter, C., North East Scotland region
Coffey, Willie, SNP, Kilmarnock and Irvine Valley, Maj. 11,194
Cole-Hamilton, Alex, LD, Edinburgh Western, Maj. 2,960
Constance, Angela, SNP, Almond Valley, Maj. 8,393
Corry, Maurice, C., West Scotland region
Crawford, Bruce, SNP, Stirling, Maj. 6,718
Cunningham, Roseanna, SNP, Perthshire South and Kinross-shire, Maj. 1,422
Davidson, Ruth, C., Edinburgh Central, Maj. 610
Denham, Ash, SNP, Edinburgh Eastern, Maj. 5,087
Dey, Graeme, SNP, Angus South, Maj. 4,304
Doris, Bob, SNP, Glasgow Maryhill and Springburn, Maj. 5,602
Dornan, James, SNP, Glasgow Cathcart, Maj. 9,390
Ewing, Annabelle, SNP, Cowdenbeath, Maj. 3,041
Ewing, Fergus, SNP, Inverness and Nairn, Maj. 10,857
Fabiani, Linda, SNP, East Kilbride, Maj. 10,979
Fee, Mary, Lab., West Scotland region
Findlay, Neil, Lab., Lothian region
Finnie, John, Green, Highlands and Islands region
FitzPatrick, Joe, SNP, Dundee City West, Maj. 8,828
Forbes, Kate, SNP, Skye, Lochaber and Badenoch, Maj. 9,043
Fraser, Murdo, C., Mid Scotland and Fife region
Freeman, Jeane, SNP, Carrick, Cumnock and Doon Valley, Maj. 6,006
Gibson, Kenneth, SNP, Cunninghame North, Maj. 8,724
Gilruth, Jenny, SNP, Mid Fife and Glenrothes, Maj. 8,276
Golden, Maurice, C., West Scotland region
Gougeon, Mairi, SNP, Angus North and Mearns, Maj. 2,472
Grahame, Christine, SNP, Midlothian South, Tweeddale and Lauderdale, Maj. 5,868
Grant, Rhoda, Lab., Highlands and Islands region
Gray, Iain, Lab., East Lothian, Maj. 1,127
Greene, Jamie, C., West Scotland region

Greer, Ross, *Green, West Scotland region*
Griffin, Mark, *Lab., Central Scotland region*
† Halcro Johnston, Jamie, *C., Highlands and Islands region*
* Hamilton, Rachael, *C., Ettrick, Roxburgh and Berwickshire*, Maj. 9,338
Harper, Emma, *SNP, South Scotland region*
Harris, Alison, *C., Central Scotland region*
Harvie, Patrick, *Green, Glasgow region*
Haughey, Clare, *SNP, Rutherglen*, Maj. 3,743
Hepburn, Jamie, *SNP, Cumbernauld and Kilsyth*, Maj. 9,478
Hyslop, Fiona, *SNP, Linlithgow*, Maj. 9,335
Johnson, Daniel, *Lab., Edinburgh Southern*, Maj. 1,123
Johnstone, Alison, *Green, Lothian region*
Kelly, James, *Lab., Glasgow region*
Kerr, Liam, *C., North East Scotland region*
Kidd, Bill, *SNP, Glasgow Anniesland*, Maj. 6,153
Lamont, Johann, *Lab., Glasgow region*
Lennon, Monica, *Lab., Central Scotland region*
Leonard, Richard, *Lab., Central Scotland region*
Lindhurst, Gordon, *C., Lothian region*
Lochhead, Richard, *SNP, Moray*, Maj. 2,875
Lockhart, Dean, *C., Mid Scotland and Fife region*
Lyle, Richard, *SNP, Uddingston and Bellshill*, Maj. 4,809
McAlpine, Joan, *SNP, South Scotland region*
McArthur, Liam, *LD, Orkney Islands*, Maj. 4,534
MacDonald, Angus, *SNP, Falkirk East*, Maj. 8,312
MacDonald, Gordon, *SNP, Edinburgh Pentlands*, Maj. 2,456
Macdonald, Lewis, *Lab., North East Scotland region*
McDonald, Mark, *Ind., Aberdeen Donside*, Maj. 11,630
MacGregor, Fulton, *SNP, Coatbridge and Chryston*, Maj. 3,779
‡ Macintosh, Ken, *no party affiliation, West Scotland region*
Mackay, Derek, *SNP, Renfrewshire North and West*, Maj. 7,373
Mackay, Rona, *SNP, Strathkelvin and Bearsden*, Maj. 8,100
McKee, Ivan, *SNP, Glasgow Provan*, Maj. 4,783
McKelvie, Christina, *SNP, Hamilton, Larkhall and Stonehouse*, Maj. 5,437
McMillan, Stuart, *SNP, Greenock and Inverclyde*, Maj. 8,230
McNeill, Pauline, *Lab., Glasgow region*
Macpherson, Ben, *SNP, Edinburgh Northern and Leith*, Maj. 6,746
Maguire, Ruth, *SNP, Cunninghame South*, Maj. 5,693
Marra, Jenny, *Lab., North East Scotland region*
Martin, Gillian, *SNP, Aberdeenshire East*, Maj. 5,837
Mason, John, *SNP, Glasgow Shettleston*, Maj. 7,323
† Mason, Tom, *C., North East Scotland region*
Matheson, Michael, *SNP, Falkirk West*, Maj. 11,280
Mitchell, Margaret, *C., Central Scotland region*
Mountain, Edward, *C., Highlands and Islands region*
Mundell, Oliver, *C., Dumfriesshire*, Maj. 1,230
Neil, Alex, *SNP, Airdrie and Shotts*, Maj. 6,192
Paterson, Gil, *SNP, Clydebank and Milngavie*, Maj. 8,432
Rennie, Willie, *LD, North East Fife*, Maj. 3,465
Robison, Shona, *SNP, Dundee City East*, Maj. 10,898
Ross, Gail, *SNP, Caithness, Sutherland and Ross*, Maj. 3,913
Rowley, Alex, *Lab., Mid Scotland and Fife region*
Rumbles, Mike, *LD, North East Scotland region*
Ruskell, Mark, *Green, Mid Scotland and Fife region*
Russell, Michael, *SNP, Argyll and Bute*, Maj. 5,978
Sarwar, Anas, *Lab., Glasgow region*
Scott, John, *C., Ayr*, Maj. 750
Simpson, Graham, *C., Central Scotland region*
Smith, Elaine, *Lab., Central Scotland region*
Smith, Liz, *C., Mid Scotland and Fife region*
Smyth, Colin, *Lab., South Scotland region*
Somerville, Shirley-Anne, *SNP, Dunfermline*, Maj. 4,558
Stevenson, Stewart, *SNP, Banffshire and Buchan Coast*, Maj. 6,583

Stewart, Alexander, *C., Mid Scotland and Fife region*
Stewart, David, *Lab., Highlands and Islands region*
Stewart, Kevin, *SNP, Aberdeen Central*, Maj. 4,349
Sturgeon, Nicola, *SNP, Glasgow Southside*, Maj. 9,593
Swinney, John, *SNP, Perthshire North*, Maj. 3,336
Todd, Maree, *SNP, Highlands and Islands region*
Tomkins, Adam, *C., Glasgow region*
Torrance, David, *SNP, Kirkcaldy*, Maj. 7,395
Watt, Maureen, *SNP, Aberdeen South and North Kincardine*, Maj. 2,755
Wells, Annie, *C., Glasgow region*
Wheelhouse, Paul, *SNP, South Scotland region*
White, Sandra, *SNP, Glasgow Kelvin*, Maj. 4,048
Whittle, Brian, *C., South Scotland region*
Wightman, Andy, *Green, Lothian region*
* Wishart, Beatrice, *LD, Shetland Islands* Maj. 1,837
Yousaf, Humza, *SNP, Glasgow Pollok*, Maj. 6,482

STATE OF THE PARTIES *as at August 2019*

	Constituency MSPs	Regional MSPs	Total
Scottish National Party (SNP)	58	4	62
Scottish Conservative and Unionist Party (C.)	7	24	31
Scottish Labour Party (Lab.)	3	20	23
Scottish Green Party (Green)	0	6	6
Scottish Liberal Democrats (LD)	3	1	4
Independent (Ind.)	1	–	1
*Presiding Officer	–	1	1
vacancy	1	0	1
Total	73	56	129

SCOTTISH GOVERNMENT
St Andrew's House, Regent Road, Edinburgh EH1 3DG
T 0300-244 4000
E ceu@gov.scot W www.gov.scot

The devolved government for Scotland is responsible for most of the issues of day-to-day concern to the people of Scotland, including health, education, justice, rural affairs and transport.

The Scottish government was known as the Scottish executive when it was established in 1999, following the first elections to the Scottish parliament. There has been a majority Scottish National Party administration since the elections in May 2011.

The government is led by a first minister who is nominated by the parliament and in turn appoints the other Scottish ministers who make up the cabinet.

Civil servants in Scotland are accountable to Scottish ministers, who are themselves accountable to the Scottish parliament.

CABINET
First Minister, Rt. Hon. Nicola Sturgeon, MSP
Deputy First Minister and Cabinet Secretary for Education and Skills, John Swinney, MSP

Cabinet Secretaries
Communities and Local Government, Aileen Campbell, MSP
Culture, Tourism and External Affairs, Fiona Hyslop, MSP
Environment, Climate Change and Land Reform, Roseanna Cunningham, MSP
Finance, Economy and Fair Work, Derek Mackay, MSP
Government Business and Constitutional Relations, Michael Russell, MSP
Health and Sport, Jeane Freeman, MSP
Justice, Humza Yousaf, MSP
Rural Economy, Fergus Ewing, MSP
Social Security and Older People, Shirley-Anne Somerville, MSP
Transport, Infrastructure and Connectivity, Michael Matheson, MSP

Ministers
Business, Fair Work and Skills, Jamie Hepburn, MSP
Childcare and Early Years, Maree Todd, MSP
Community Safety, Ash Denham, MSP
Energy, Connectivity and the Islands, Paul Wheelhouse, MSP
Europe, Migration and International Development, Ben
    Macpherson, MSP
Further Education, Higher Education and Science, Richard
    Lochhead, MSP
Local Government, Housing and Planning, Kevin Stewart, MSP
Mental Health, Clare Haughey, MSP
Older People and Equalities, Christina McKelvie, MSP
Parliamentary Business and Veterans, Graeme Dey, MSP
Public Finance and Digital Economy, Kate Forbes
Public Health, Sport and Wellbeing, Joe FitzPatrick, MSP
Rural Affairs and the Natural Environment, Mairi Gougeon, MSP
Trade, Investment and Innovation, Ivan McKee, MSP

LAW OFFICERS
Lord Advocate, James Wolffe, QC
Solicitor-General for Scotland, Alison di Rollo

STRATEGIC BOARD
Permanent Secretary, Leslie Evans
Director-General Constitution and External Affairs, Ken Thomson
Director-General, Economy, Liz Ditchburn
Director-General, Education, Communities and Justice, Paul
    Johnston
Director-General, Scottish Exchequer, Alyson Stafford
Director-General, Health and Social Care, Malcolm Wright
Director-General, Organisational Development and Operations,
    Lesley Fraser

GOVERNMENT DEPARTMENTS

CONSTITUTION AND EXTERNAL AFFAIRS
St Andrew's House, Regent Road, Edinburgh EH1 3DG
Director-General, Ken Thomson
Directorates: Constitution and Cabinet; EU Directorate; EU
    Exit and Transition; External Affairs; Legal Services
    (Solicitor to the Scottish Government); Parliamentary
    Counsel

ECONOMY
St Andrew's House, Regent Road, Edinburgh EH1 3DG
Director-General, Liz Ditchburn
Directorates: Agriculture and Rural Economy; Chief
    Economist; Culture, Tourism and Major Events; Economic
    Development; Economic Policy and Capability; Energy
    and Climate Change; Environment and Forestry; Fair
    Work, Employability and Skills; International Trade and
    Investment; Marine Scotland; Scottish Development
    International; Scottish National Investment Bank
Executive Agencies: Accountant in Bankruptcy; Drinking Water
    Quality Regulator; Forestry and Land Scotland; James
    Hutton Institute; Moredun Research Institute; National
    Records of Scotland; Scottish Agricultural College;
    Scottish Forestry; Transport Scotland; Waterwatch
    Scotland

EDUCATION, COMMUNITIES AND JUSTICE
St Andrew's House, Regent Road, Edinburgh EH1 3DG
Director-General Paul Johnston
Directorates: Advance Learning and Science; Children and
    Families; Early Learning and Childcare Programme;
    Education Analytical Services; Housing and Social Justice;
    Justice; Learning; Local Government and Communities;
    Safer Communities

Executive Agencies: Disclosure Scotland; Education Scotland;
    HM Chief Inspector of Prosecution in Scotland; HM
    Inspectorate of Constabulary; HM Inspectorate of Prisons;
    Inspectorate of Prosecution in Scotland; Justice of the
    Peace Advisory Committee; Scottish Prison Service;
    Student Awards Agency for Scotland; Visiting Committees
    for Scottish Penal Establishments

SCOTTISH EXCHEQUER
Victoria Quay, Edinburgh, EH6 6QQ
Director-General, Alyson Stafford
Directorates: Budget and Sustainability; Internal Audit and
    Assurance; Performance and Outcomes; Taxation
Executive Agency: Audit Scotland

HEALTH AND SOCIAL CARE
St Andrew's House, Regent Road, Edinburgh EH1 3DG
*Director-General Health and Social Care and Chief Executive NHS
    Scotland,* Malcolm Wright
Directorates: Chief Medical Officer; Chief Nursing Officer;
    Community Health and Social Care; Corporate
    Governance and Value; Health Finance; Health
    Performance and Delivery; Health Workforce, Leadership
    and Service Reform; Healthcare Quality and
    Improvement; Mental Health; Office of the Chief
    Executive NHS Scotland; Performance and Delivery;
    Population Health
Executive Agency: Scottish Children's Reporters
    Administration

ORGANISATIONAL DEVELOPMENT AND OPERATIONS
St Andrew's House, Regent Road, Edinburgh EH1 3DG
Directorates: Communications, Ministerial Support and
    Facilities; Digital; Financial Management; People; Social
    Security; Scottish Procurement and Commercial
Executive Agencies: Scottish Public Pensions Agency; Social
    Security Scotland

NON-MINISTERIAL DEPARTMENTS

FOOD STANDARDS SCOTLAND
Pilgrim House, Old Ford Road, Aberdeen AB11 5RL **T** 01224-285100
W www.foodstandards.gov.scot
Chief Executive, Geoff Ogle
NATIONAL RECORDS OF SCOTLAND
General Register House, 2 Princes Street, Edinburgh EH1 3YY
T 0131-334 0380 **W** www.nrscotland.gov.uk
Registrar General and Keeper of the Records of Scotland, Paul
    Lowe
OFFICE OF THE SCOTTISH CHARITY REGULATOR
2nd Floor, Quadrant House, 9 Riverside Drive, Dundee DD1 4NY
T 01382-220446 **W** www.oscr.org.uk
Chief Executive, Maureen Mallon *(interim)*
REGISTERS OF SCOTLAND
Meadowbank House, 153 London Road, Edinburgh, Midlothian EH8
7AU **T** 0800-169 9391 **W** www.ros.gov.uk
Keeper, Jennifer Henderson
REVENUE SCOTLAND
PO Box 24068, Victoria Quay, Edinburgh EH6 9BR **T** 0300-020 0310
W www.revenue.scot
Chief Executive, Dr Keith Nicholson
SCOTTISH COURTS AND TRIBUNALS SERVICE
Saughton House, Broomhouse Drive, Edinburgh EH11 3XD
T 0131-444 3300 **W** www.scotcourts.gov.uk
Chief Executive, Eric McQueen
SCOTTISH HOUSING REGULATOR
Buchanan House, 58 Port Dundas Road, Glasgow G4 0HF
T 0141-242 5642 **W** www.scottishhousingregulator.gov.uk
Chief Executive, George Walker

SCOTTISH PARLIAMENT ELECTION RESULTS *as at 5 May 2016*

Electorate (E.) 4,099,407 Turnout (T.) 55.6%
See General Election Results for a list of party abbreviations

ABERDEEN CENTRAL
(Scotland North East Region)
E. 57,195 T. 26,704 (46.69%)

Kevin Stewart, SNP	11,648
Lewis Macdonald, Lab.	7,299
Tom Mason, C.	6,022
Ken McLeod, LD	1,735

SNP majority 4,349 (16.29%)
6.92% swing Lab. to SNP

ABERDEEN DONSIDE
(Scotland North East Region)
E. 61,200 T. 30,981 (50.62%)

Mark McDonald, SNP	17,339
Liam Kerr, C.	5,709
Greg Williams, Lab.	5,672
Isobel Davidson, LD	2,261

SNP majority 11,630 (37.54%)
4.82% swing SNP to C.

ABERDEEN SOUTH & KINCARDINE NORTH
(Scotland North East Region)
E. 59,710 T. 32,340 (54.16%)

Maureen Watt, SNP	13,604
Ross Thomson, C.	10,849
Alison Evison, Lab.	5,603
John Waddell, LD	2,284

SNP majority 2,755 (8.52%)
9.49% swing SNP to C.

ABERDEENSHIRE EAST
(Scotland North East Region)
E. 62,844 T. 34,753 (55.30%)

Gillian Martin, SNP	15,912
Colin Clark, C.	10,075
Christine Jardine, LD	6,611
Sarah Flavell, Lab.	2,155

SNP majority 5,837 (16.80%)
16.90% swing SNP to C.

ABERDEENSHIRE WEST
(Scotland North East Region)
E. 59,576 T. 35,198 (59.08%)

Alexander Burnett, C.	13,400
Dennis Robertson, SNP	12,500
Mike Rumbles, LD	7,262
Sarah Christina Duncan, Lab.	2,036

C. majority 900 (2.56%)
12.03% swing SNP to C.

AIRDRIE & SHOTTS
(Scotland Central Region)
E. 53,899 T. 26,573 (49.30%)

Alex Neil, SNP	13,954
Richard Leonard, Lab.	7,762
Eric Holford, C.	4,164
Louise Young, LD	693

SNP majority 6,192 (23.30%)
7.46% swing Lab. to SNP

ALMOND VALLEY
(Lothian Region)
E. 64,901 T. 34,872 (53.73%)

Angela Constance, SNP	18,475
Neil Findlay, Lab.	10,082
Stephanie Smith, C.	5,308
Charles Dundas, LD	1,007

SNP majority 8,393 (24.07%)
3.02% swing Lab. to SNP

ANGUS NORTH & MEARNS
(Scotland North East Region)
E. 54,268 T. 29,379 (54.14%)

Mairi Evans, SNP	13,417
Alex Johnstone, C.	10,945
John Ruddy, Lab.	2,752
Euan Davidson, LD	2,265

SNP majority 2,472 (8.41%)
10.41% swing SNP to C.

ANGUS SOUTH
(Scotland North East Region)
E. 56,278 T. 31,929 (56.73%)

Graeme Dey, SNP	15,622
Kirstene Hair, C.	11,318
Joanne McFadden, Lab.	3,773
Clive Sneddon, LD	1,216

SNP majority 4,304 (13.48%)
12.40% swing SNP to C.

ARGYLL & BUTE
(Highlands and Islands Region)
E. 48,804 T. 29,476 (60.40%)

Michael Russell, SNP	13,561
Alan Reid, LD	7,583
Donald Cameron, C.	5,840
Mick Rice, Lab.	2,492

SNP majority 5,978 (20.28%)
9.07% swing SNP to LD

AYR
(Scotland South Region)
E. 61,558 T. 37,615 (61.10%)

John Scott, C.	16,183
Jennifer Dunn, SNP	15,433
Brian McGinley, Lab.	5,283
Robbie Simpson, LD	716

C. majority 750 (1.99%)
0.67% swing C. to SNP

BANFFSHIRE & BUCHAN COAST
(Scotland North East Region)
E. 59,155 T. 28,683 (48.49%)

Stewart Stevenson, SNP	15,802
Peter Chapman, C.	9,219
Nathan Morrison, Lab.	2,372
David Evans, LD	1,290

SNP majority 6,583 (22.95%)
12.96% swing SNP to C.

CAITHNESS, SUTHERLAND & ROSS
(Highlands and Islands Region)
E. 55,176 T. 32,207 (58.37%)

Gail Ross, SNP	13,937
Jamie Stone, LD	10,024
Struan Mackie, C.	4,912
Leah Franchetti, Lab.	3,334

SNP majority 3,913 (12.15%)
6.96% swing SNP to LD

CARRICK, CUMNOCK & DOON VALLEY
(Scotland South Region)
E. 58,548 T. 31,680 (54.11%)

Jeane Freeman, SNP	14,690
Carol Mochan, Lab.	8,684
Lee Lyons, C.	7,666
Dawud Islam, LD	640

SNP majority 6,006 (18.96%)
4.98% swing Lab. to SNP

CLACKMANNANSHIRE & DUNBLANE
(Mid Scotland and Fife Region)
E. 50,557 T. 29,746 (58.84%)

Keith Brown, SNP	14,147
Craig Miller, Lab.	7,426
Alexander Stewart, C.	6,915
Christopher McKinlay, LD	1,258

SNP majority 6,721 (22.59%)
4.72% swing Lab. to SNP

CLYDEBANK & MILNGAVIE
(Scotland West Region)
E. 54,761 T. 32,838 (59.97%)

Gil Paterson, SNP	16,158
Gail Casey, Lab.	7,726
Maurice Golden, C.	6,029
Frank Bowles, LD	2,925

SNP majority 8,432 (25.68%)
11.58% swing Lab. to SNP

CLYDESDALE
(Scotland South Region)
E. 58,471 T. 33,619 (57.50%)

Aileen Campbell, SNP	14,821
Alex Allison, C.	8,842
Claudia Beamish, Lab.	6,895
Danny Meikle, Ind.	1,332
Bev Gauld, CSSInd.	909
Jennifer Jamieson Ball, LD	820

SNP majority 5,979 (17.78%)
8.88% swing SNP to C.

COATBRIDGE & CHRYSTON
(Scotland Central Region)
E. 54,169 T. 28,334 (52.31%)

Fulton MacGregor, SNP	13,605
Elaine Smith, Lab.	9,826
Robyn Halbert, C.	2,868
John Wilson, Green	1,612
Jenni Lang, LD	423

SNP majority 3,779 (13.34%)
12.56% swing Lab. to SNP

COWDENBEATH
(Mid Scotland and Fife Region)
E. 54,596 T. 29,734 (54.46%)

Annabelle Ewing, SNP	13,715
Alex Rowley, Lab.	10,674
Dave Dempsey, C.	4,251
Bryn Jones, LD	1,094

SNP majority 3,041 (10.23%)
7.54% swing Lab. to SNP

CUMBERNAULD & KILSYTH
(Scotland Central Region)
E. 49,964 T. 28,308 (56.66%)

Jamie Hepburn, SNP	17,015
Mark Griffin, Lab.	7,537
Anthony Newman, C.	3,068
Irene Lang, LD	688

SNP majority 9,478 (33.48%)
9.89% swing Lab. to SNP

CUNNINGHAME NORTH
(Scotland West Region)
E. 55,647 T. 31,965 (57.44%)

Kenneth Gibson, SNP	16,587
Jamie Greene, C.	7,863
Johanna Baxter, Lab.	6,735
Charity Pierce, LD	780

SNP majority 8,724 (27.29%)
5.83% swing SNP to C.

CUNNINGHAME SOUTH
(Scotland South Region)
E. 50,215 T. 25,695 (51.17%)

Ruth Maguire, SNP	13,416
Joe Cullinane, Lab.	7,723
Billy McClure, C.	3,940
Ruby Kirkwood, LD	616

SNP majority 5,693 (22.16%)
5.76% swing Lab. to SNP

DUMBARTON
(Scotland West Region)
E. 55,098 T. 33,598 (60.98%)

Jackie Baillie, Lab.	13,522
Gail Robertson, SNP	13,413
Maurice Corry, C.	4,891
Aileen Morton, LD	1,131
Andrew Muir, Ind.	641

Lab. majority 109 (0.32%)
2.71% swing Lab. to SNP

DUMFRIESSHIRE
(Scotland South Region)
E. 60,698 T. 36,260 (59.74%)

Oliver Mundell, C.	13,536
Joan McAlpine, SNP	12,306
Elaine Murray, Lab.	9,151
Richard Brodie, LD	1,267

C. majority 1,230 (3.39%)
10.99% swing Lab. to C.

DUNDEE EAST
(Scotland North East Region)
E. 55,261 T. 28,437 (51.46%)

Shona Robison, SNP	16,509
Richard McCready, Lab.	5,611
Bill Bowman, C.	4,969
Craig Duncan, LD	911
Leah Ganley, TUSC	437

SNP majority 10,898 (38.32%)
1.57% swing SNP to Lab.

DUNDEE WEST
(Scotland North East Region)
E. 53,830 T. 27,788 (51.62%)

Joe FitzPatrick, SNP	16,070
Jenny Marra, Lab.	7,242
Nicola Ross, C.	2,826
Daniel Coleman, LD	1,008
Jim McFarlane, TUSC	642

SNP majority 8,828 (31.77%)
2.79% swing Lab. to SNP

DUNFERMLINE
(Scotland Mid and Fife Region)
E. 57,740 T. 32,909 (57.00%)

Shirley-Anne Somerville, SNP	14,257
Cara Hilton, Lab.	9,699
James Reekie, C.	5,797
James Calder, LD	3,156

SNP majority 4,558 (13.85%)
5.92% swing Lab. to SNP

EAST KILBRIDE
(Scotland Central Region)
E. 61,134 T. 34,629 (56.64%)

Linda Fabiani, SNP	19,371
LizAnne Handibode, Lab.	8,392
Graham Simpson, C.	5,857
Paul McGarry, LD	1,009

SNP majority 10,979 (31.70%)
12.59% swing Lab. to SNP

EAST LOTHIAN
(Scotland South Region)
E. 60,848 T. 37,913 (62.31%)

Iain Gray, Lab.	14,329
DJ Johnston-Smith, SNP	13,202
Rachael Hamilton, C.	9,045
Ettie Spencer, LD	1,337

Lab. majority 1,127 (2.97%)
1.25% swing SNP to Lab.

EASTWOOD
(Scotland West Region)
E. 53,085 T. 36,255 (68.30%)

Jackson Carlaw, C.	12,932
Stewart Maxwell, SNP	11,321
Ken Macintosh, Lab.	11,081
John Duncan, LD	921

C. majority 1,611 (4.44%)
5.70% swing Lab. to C.

EDINBURGH CENTRAL
(Lothian Region)
E. 59,581 T. 34,169 (57.35%)

Ruth Davidson, C.	10,399
Alison Dickie, SNP	9,789
Sarah Boyack, Lab.	7,546
Alison Johnstone, Green	4,644
Hannah Bettsworth, LD	1,672
Tom Laird, SLP	119

C. majority 610 (1.79%)
9.73% swing SNP to C.

EDINBURGH EASTERN
(Lothian Region)
E. 62,817 T. 35,397 (56.35%)

Ash Denham, SNP	16,760
Kezia Dugdale, Lab.	11,673
Nick Cook, C.	5,700
Cospatric D'Inverno, LD	1,264

SNP majority 5,087 (14.37%)
3.55% swing Lab. to SNP

EDINBURGH NORTHERN & LEITH
(Lothian Region)
E. 67,273 T. 37,102 (55.15%)

Ben Macpherson, SNP	17,322
Lesley Hinds, Lab.	10,576
Iain McGill, C.	6,081
Martin Veart, LD	1,779
Jack Caldwell, Ind.	1,344

SNP majority 6,746 (18.18%)
10.05% swing Lab. to SNP

EDINBURGH PENTLANDS
(Lothian Region)
E. 55,241 T. 33,353 (60.38%)

Gordon MacDonald, SNP	13,181
Gordon Lindhurst, C.	10,725
Blair Heary, Lab.	7,811
Emma Farthing-Sykes, LD	1,636

SNP majority 2,456 (7.36%)
0.76% swing C. to SNP

EDINBURGH SOUTHERN
(Lothian Region)
E. 59,587 T. 38,259 (64.21%)

Daniel Johnson, Lab.	13,597
Jim Eadie, SNP	12,474
Miles Briggs, C.	9,972
Pramod Subbaraman, LD	2,216

Lab. majority 1,123 (2.94%)
2.49% swing SNP to Lab.

EDINBURGH WESTERN
(Lothian Region)
E. 61,666 T. 39,766 (64.49%)

Alex Cole-Hamilton, LD	16,645
Toni Giugliano, SNP	13,685
Sandy Batho, C.	5,686
Cat Headley, Lab.	3,750

LD majority 2,960 (7.44%)
7.74% swing SNP to LD

ETTRICK, ROXBURGH &
BERWICKSHIRE
(Scotland South Region)
E. 54,506 T. 33,095 (60.72%)
John Lamont, C.   18,257
Paul Wheelhouse, SNP   10,521
Jim Hume, LD   2,551
Barrie Cunning, Lab.   1,766

C. majority 7,736 (23.38%)
2.43% swing SNP to C.

FALKIRK EAST
(Scotland Central Region)
E. 60,271 T. 32,524 (53.96%)
Angus MacDonald, SNP   16,720
Craig Martin, Lab.   8,408
Callum Laidlaw, C.   6,342
James Munro, LD   1,054

SNP majority 8,312 (25.56%)
6.50% swing Lab. to SNP

FALKIRK WEST
(Scotland Central Region)
E. 59,812 T. 32,083 (53.64%)
Michael Matheson, SNP   18,260
Mandy Telford, Lab.   6,980
Alison Harris, C.   5,877
Gillian Cole-Hamilton, LD   966

SNP majority 11,280 (35.16%)
7.39% swing Lab. to SNP

FIFE MID & GLENROTHES
(Scotland Mid and Fife Region)
E. 53,241 T. 28,547 (53.62%)
Jenny Gilruth, SNP   15,555
Kay Morrison, Lab.   7,279
Alex Stewart-Clark, C.   4,427
Jane-Ann Liston, LD   1,286

SNP majority 8,276 (28.99%)
6.54% swing Lab. to SNP

FIFE NORTH EAST
(Scotland Mid and Fife Region)
E. 54,052 T. 34,063 (63.02%)
Willie Rennie, LD   14,928
Roderick Campbell, SNP   11,463
Huw Bell, C.   5,646
Rosalind Garton, Lab.   2,026

LD majority 3,465 (10.17%)
9.45% swing SNP to LD

GALLOWAY & WEST DUMFRIES
(Scotland South Region)
E. 56,321 T. 33,363 (59.24%)
Finlay Carson, C.   14,527
Aileen McLeod, SNP   13,013
Fiona O'Donnell, Lab.   4,876
Andrew Metcalf, LD   947

C. majority 1,514 (4.54%)
0.83% swing SNP to C.

GLASGOW ANNIESLAND
(Glasgow Region)
E. 57,884 T. 29,016 (50.13%)
Bill Kidd, SNP   15,007
Bill Butler, Lab.   8,854
Adam Tomkins, C.   4,057
James Speirs, LD   1,098

SNP majority 6,153 (21.21%)
10.59% swing Lab. to SNP

GLASGOW CATHCART
(Glasgow Region)
E. 60,871 T. 30,637 (50.33%)
James Dornan, SNP   16,200
Soryia Siddique, Lab.   6,810
Kyle Thornton, C.   4,514
Margot Clark, LD   1,703
Brian Smith, TUSC   909
Chris Creighton, Ind.   501

SNP majority 9,390 (30.65%)
12.29% swing Lab. to SNP

GLASGOW KELVIN
(Glasgow Region)
E. 62,203 T. 28,442 (45.72%)
Sandra White, SNP   10,964
Patrick Harvie, Green   6,916
Michael Shanks, Lab.   5,968
Sheila Mechan, C.   3,346
Carole Ford, LD   1,050
Tom Muirhead, Ind.   198

SNP majority 4,048 (14.23%)

GLASGOW MARYHILL &
SPRINGBURN
(Glasgow Region)
E. 53,647 T. 23,612 (44.01%)
Bob Doris, SNP   13,109
Patricia Ferguson, Lab.   7,507
John Anderson, C.   2,305
James Harrison, LD   691

SNP majority 5,602 (23.73%)
15.01% swing Lab. to SNP

GLASGOW POLLOK
(Glasgow Region)
E. 61,350 T. 27,943 (45.55%)
Humza Yousaf, SNP   15,316
Johann Lamont, Lab.   8,834
Thomas Haddow, C.   2,653
Isabel Nelson, LD   585
Ian Leech, TUSC   555

SNP majority 6,482 (23.20%)
12.96% swing Lab. to SNP

GLASGOW PROVAN
(Glasgow Region)
E. 56,169 T. 24,077 (42.87%)
Ivan McKee, SNP   13,140
Paul Martin, Lab.   8,357
Annie Wells, C.   2,062
Tom Coleman, LD   518

SNP majority 4,783 (19.87%)
15.35% swing Lab. to SNP

GLASGOW SHETTLESTON
(Glasgow Region)
E. 58,021 T. 25,375 (43.73%)
John Mason, SNP   14,198
Thomas Rannachan, Lab.   6,875
Thomas Kerr, C.   3,151
Jamie Cocozza, TUSC   583
Giovanni Caccavello, LD   568

SNP majority 7,323 (28.86%)
13.05% swing Lab. to SNP

GLASGOW SOUTHSIDE
(Glasgow Region)
E. 52,141 T. 24,903 (47.76%)
Nicola Sturgeon, SNP   15,287
Fariha Thomas, Lab.   5,694
Graham Hutchison, C.   3,100
Kevin Lewsey, LD   822

SNP majority 9,593 (38.52%)
9.64% swing Lab. to SNP

GREENOCK & INVERCLYDE
(Scotland West Region)
E. 55,171 T. 31,725 (57.50%)
Stuart McMillan, SNP   17,032
Siobhan McCready, Lab.   8,802
Graeme Brooks, C.   4,487
John Watson, LD   1,404

SNP majority 8,230 (25.94%)
13.88% swing Lab. to SNP

HAMILTON, LARKHALL &
STONEHOUSE
(Scotland Central Region)
E. 57,656 T. 28,885 (50.10%)
Christina McKelvie, SNP   13,945
Margaret McCulloch, Lab.   8,508
Margaret Mitchell, C.   5,596
Eileen Baxendale, LD   836

SNP majority 5,437 (18.82%)
5.05% swing Lab. to SNP

INVERNESS & NAIRN
(Highlands and Islands Region)
E. 66,619 T. 38,317 (57.52%)
Fergus Ewing, SNP   18,505
Edward Mountain, C.   7,648
David Stewart, Lab.   6,719
Carolyn Caddick, LD   5,445

SNP majority 10,857 (28.33%)
5.80% swing SNP to C.

KILMARNOCK & IRVINE VALLEY
(Scotland South Region)
E. 62,620 T. 34,385 (54.91%)
Willie Coffey, SNP   19,047
Dave Meechan, Lab.   7,853
Brian Whittle, C.   6,597
Rebecca Plenderleith, LD   888

SNP majority 11,194 (32.55%)
6.87% swing Lab. to SNP

KIRKCALDY
(Scotland Mid and Fife Region)
E. 59,533 T. 31,108 (52.25%)
David Torrance, SNP   16,358
Claire Baker, Lab.   8,963
Martin Laidlaw, C.   4,568
Lauren Jones, LD   1,219

SNP majority 7,395 (23.77%)
11.56% swing Lab. to SNP

LINLITHGOW
(Lothian Region)
E. 71,434 T. 38,407 (53.77%)
Fiona Hyslop, SNP   19,362
Angela Moohan, Lab.   10,027
Charles Kennedy, C.   7,699
Dan Farthing-Sykes, LD   1,319

SNP majority 9,335 (24.31%)
6.17% swing Lab. to SNP

MIDLOTHIAN NORTH &
MUSSELBURGH
(Lothian Region)
E. 63,360 T. 34,685 (54.74%)

Colin Beattie, SNP	16,948
Bernard Harkins, Lab.	9,913
Jeremy Balfour, C.	6,267
Jacquie Bell, LD	1,557

SNP majority 7,035 (20.28%)
5.12% swing Lab. to SNP

MIDLOTHIAN SOUTH,
TWEEDDALE & LAUDERDALE
(Scotland South Region)
E. 60,204 T. 35,581 (59.10%)

Christine Grahame, SNP	16,031
Michelle Ballantyne, C.	10,163
Fiona Dugdale, Lab.	5,701
Kris Chapman, LD	3,686

SNP majority 5,868 (16.49%)
7.63% swing SNP to C.

MORAY
(Highlands and Islands Region)
E. 61,969 T. 33,421 (53.93%)

Richard Lochhead, SNP	15,742
Douglas Ross, C.	12,867
Sean Morton, Lab.	3,547
Jamie Paterson, LD	1,265

SNP majority 2,875 (8.60%)
14.83% swing SNP to C.

MOTHERWELL & WISHAW
(Scotland Central Region)
E. 57,045 T. 29,111 (51.03%)

Clare Adamson, SNP	15,291
John Pentland, Lab.	9,068
Meghan Gallacher, C.	3,991
Yvonne Finlayson, LD	761

SNP majority 6,223 (21.38%)
11.89% swing Lab. to SNP

NA H-EILEANAN AN IAR
(Highlands and Islands Region)
E. 21,695 T. 13,206 (60.87%)

Alasdair Allan, SNP	6,874
Rhoda Grant, Lab.	3,378
Ranald Fraser, C.	1,499
John Cormack, SCP	1,162
Ken MacLeod, LD	293

SNP majority 3,496 (26.47%)
5.10% swing SNP to Lab.

ORKNEY
(Highlands and Islands Region)
E. 16,997 T. 10,534 (61.98%)

Liam McArthur, LD	7,096
Donna Heddle, SNP	2,562
Jamie Halcro Johnston, C.	435
Gerry McGarvey, Lab.	304
Paul Dawson, Ind.	137

LD majority 4,534 (43.04%)
16.20% swing SNP to LD

PAISLEY
(Scotland West Region)
E. 51,673 T. 29,464 (57.02%)

George Adam, SNP	14,682
Neil Bibby, Lab.	9,483
Paul Masterton, C.	3,533
Eileen McCartin, LD	1,766

SNP majority 5,199 (17.65%)
8.34% swing Lab. to SNP

PERTHSHIRE NORTH
(Scotland and Mid Fife Region)
E. 54,255 T. 34,025 (62.71%)

John Swinney, SNP	16,526
Murdo Fraser, C.	13,190
Anna McEwan, Lab.	2,604
Peter Barrett, LD	1,705

SNP majority 3,336 (9.80%)
12.38% swing SNP to C.

PERTHSHIRE SOUTH & KINROSS-
SHIRE
(Scotland and Mid Fife Region)
E. 59,397 T. 36,149 (60.86%)

Roseanna Cunningham, SNP	15,315
Liz Smith, C.	13,893
Scott Nicholson, Lab.	3,389
Willie Robertson, LD	3,008
Craig Finlay, Community	544

SNP majority 1,422 (3.93%)
9.51% swing SNP to C.

RENFREWSHIRE NORTH & WEST
(Scotland West Region)
E. 50,555 T. 30,807 (60.94%)

Derek Mackay, SNP	14,718
David Wilson, C.	7,345
Mary Fee, Lab.	7,244
Rod Ackland, LD	888
Jim Halfpenny, TUSC	414
Peter Morton, Ind.	198

SNP majority 7,373 (23.93%)
1.02% swing C. to SNP

RENFREWSHIRE SOUTH
(Scotland West Region)
E. 49,422 T. 29,681 (60.06%)

Thomas Arthur, SNP	14,272
Paul O'Kane, Lab.	9,864
Ann Le Blond, C.	4,752
Tristan Gray, LD	793

SNP majority 4,408 (14.85%)
12.21% swing Lab. to SNP

RUTHERGLEN
(Glasgow Region)
E. 60,702 T. 32,952 (54.28%)

Clare Haughey, SNP	15,222
James Kelly, Lab.	11,479
Taylor Muir, C.	3,718
Robert Brown, LD	2,533

SNP majority 3,743 (11.36%)
8.96% swing Lab. to SNP

SHETLAND ISLANDS
(Highlands and Islands Region)
E. 17,784 T. 11,041 (62.08%)

Tavish Scott, LD	7,440
Danus Skene, SNP	2,545
Robina Barton, Lab.	651
Cameron Smith, C.	405

LD majority 4,895 (44.33%)
4.45% swing SNP to LD

SKYE, LOCHABER & BADENOCH
(Highlands and Islands Region)
E. 59,537 T. 36,505 (61.31%)

Kate Forbes, SNP	17,362
Angela MacLean, LD	8,319
Robbie Munro, C.	5,887
Linda Stewart, Lab.	3,821
Ronnie Campbell, Ind.	1,116

SNP majority 9,043 (24.77%)
4.56% swing LD to SNP

STIRLING
(Scotland and Mid Fife Region)
E. 55,785 T. 34,189 (61.29%)

Bruce Crawford, SNP	16,303
Dean Lockhart, C.	9,585
Rebecca Bell, Lab.	6,885
Elisabeth Wilson, LD	1,416

SNP majority 6,718 (19.65%)
7.03% swing SNP to C.

STRATHKELVIN & BEARSDEN
(Scotland West Region)
E. 62,598 T. 39,188 (62.60%)

Rona Mackay, SNP	17,060
Andrew Polson, C.	8,960
Margaret McCarthy, Lab.	8,288
Katy Gordon, LD	4,880

SNP majority 8,100 (20.67%)
4.21% swing SNP to C.

UDDINGSTON & BELLSHILL
(Central Scotland Region)
E. 57,556 T. 29,543 (51.33%)

Richard Lyle, SNP	14,424
Michael McMahon, Lab.	9,615
Andrew Morrison, C.	4,693
Kaitey Blair, LD	811

SNP majority 4,809 (16.28%)
9.57% swing Lab. to SNP

REGIONS *as at 5 May 2016*
E. 4,099,407 T. 55.6%

GLASGOW
E. 522,988 T. 248,109 (47.44%)

SNP	111,101	(44.78%)
Lab.	59,151	(23.84%)
C.	29,533	(11.90%)
Green	23,398	(9.43%)
LD	5,850	(2.36%)
UKIP	4,889	(1.97%)
Solidarity	3,593	(1.45%)
RISE	2,454	(0.99%)
UP	2,453	(0.99%)
Women	2,091	(0.84%)
Animal	1,819	(0.73%)
SCP	1,506	(0.61%)
Ind.	271	(0.11%)

SNP majority 51,950 (20.94%)
8.05% swing Lab. to SNP (2011 SNP majority 10,078)
ADDITIONAL MEMBERS

Adam Tomkins, *C.*	James Kelly, *Lab.*
Annie Wells, *C.*	Pauline McNeill, *Lab.*
Anas Sarwar, *Lab.*	Patrick Harvie, *Green*
Johann Lamont, *Lab.*	

HIGHLANDS AND ISLANDS
E. 348,581 T. 205,313 (58.90%)

SNP	81,600	(39.74%)
C.	44,693	(21.77%)
LD	27,223	(13.26%)
Lab.	22,894	(11.15%)
Green	14,781	(7.20%)
UKIP	5,344	(2.60%)
Ind.	3,689	(1.80%)
SCP	3,407	(1.66%)
RISE	889	(0.43%)
Solidarity	793	(0.39%)

SNP majority 36,907 (17.98%)
8.95% swing SNP to C. (2011 SNP majority 59,198)
ADDITIONAL MEMBERS

Douglas Ross, *C.*	David Steward, *Lab.*
Edward Mountain, *C.*	Maree Todd, *SNP*
Donald Cameron, *C.*	John Finnie, *Green*
Rhoda Grant, *Lab.*	

LOTHIAN
E. 565,860 T. 327,178 (57.82%)

SNP	118,546	(36.23%)
C.	74,972	(22.91%)
Lab.	67,991	(20.78%)
Green	34,551	(10.56%)
LD	18,479	(5.65%)
UKIP	5,802	(1.77%)
Women	3,877	(1.18%)
RISE	1,641	(0.50%)
Solidarity	1,319	(0.40%)

SNP majority 43,574 (13.32%)
7.10% swing SNP to C. (2011 SNP majority 40,409)
ADDITIONAL MEMBERS

Miles Briggs, *C.*	Neil Findlay, *Lab.*
Gordon Lindhurst, *C.*	Alison Johnstone, *Green*
Jeremy Balfour, *C.*	Andy Wightman, *Green*
Kezia Dugdale, *Lab.*	

SCOTLAND CENTRAL
E. 511,506 T. 270,706 (52.92%)

SNP	129,082	(47.68%)
Lab.	67,103	(24.79%)
C.	43,602	(16.11%)
Green	12,722	(4.70%)
UKIP	6,088	(2.25%)
LD	5,015	(1.85%)
Solidarity	2,684	(0.99%)
SCP	2,314	(0.85%)
RISE	1,636	(0.60%)
Ind.	460	(0.17%)

SNP majority 61,979 (22.90%)
5.92% swing Lab. to SNP (2011 SNP majority 25,802)
ADDITIONAL MEMBERS

Margaret Mitchell, *C.*	Monica Lennon, *Lab.*
Graham Simpson, *C.*	Mark Griffin, *Lab.*
Alison Harris, *C.*	Elaine Smith, *Lab.*
Richard Leonard, *Lab.*	

SCOTLAND MID AND FIFE
E. 499,156 T. 291,172 (58.33%)

SNP	120,128	(41.26%)
C.	73,293	(25.17%)
Lab.	51,373	(17.64%)
LD	20,401	(7.01%)
Green	17,860	(6.13%)
UKIP	5,345	(1.84%)
RISE	1,073	(0.37%)
Solidarity	1,049	(0.36%)
SLP	650	(0.22%)

SNP majority 46,835 (16.08%)
7.50% swing SNP to C. (2011 SNP majority 52,068)
ADDITIONAL MEMBERS

Murdo Fraser, *C.*	Alex Rowley, *Lab.*
Liz Smith, *C.*	Claire Baker, *Lab.*
Dean Lockhart, *C.*	Mark Ruskell, *Green*
Alexander Stewart, *C.*	

SCOTLAND NORTH EAST
E. 579,317 T. 307,006 (52.99%)

SNP	137,086	(44.65%)
C.	85,848	(27.96%)
Lab.	38,791	(12.64%)
LD	18,444	(6.01%)
Green	15,123	(4.93%)
UKIP	6,376	(2.08%)
SCP	2,068	(0.67%)
Solidarity	992	(0.32%)
Nat Front	617	(0.20%)
RISE	599	(0.20%)
SLP	552	(0.18%)
Comm Brit	510	(0.17%)

SNP majority 51,238 (16.69%)
10.95% swing SNP to C. (2011 SNP majority 96,856)
ADDITIONAL MEMBERS

Alex Johnstone, *C.*	Jenny Marra, *Lab.*
Ross Thomson, *C.*	Lewis Macdonald, *Lab.*
Peter Chapman, *C.*	Mike Rumbles, *LD*
Liam Kerr, *C.*	

SCOTLAND SOUTH
E. 533,774 T. 314,192 (58.86%)

SNP	120,217	(38.26%)
C.	100,753	(32.07%)
Lab.	56,072	(17.85%)
Green	14,773	(4.70%)
LD	11,775	(3.75%)
UKIP	6,726	(2.14%)
CSSInd.	1,485	(0.47%)
Solidarity	1,294	(0.41%)
RISE	1,097	(0.35%)

SNP majority 19,464 (6.19%)
7.65% swing SNP to C. (2011 SNP majority 43,675)
ADDITIONAL MEMBERS

Rachel Hamilton, C.	Joan McAlpine, SNP
Brian Whittle, C.	Emma Harper, SNP
Claudia Beamish, Lab.	Paul Wheelhouse, SNP
Colin Smyth, Lab.	

SCOTLAND WEST
E. 538,225 T. 322,076 (59.84%)

SNP	135,827	(42.17%)
Lab.	72,544	(22.52%)
C.	71,528	(22.21%)
Green	17,218	(5.35%)
LD	12,097	(3.76%)
UKIP	5,856	(1.82%)
Solidarity	2,609	(0.81%)
SCP	2,391	(0.74%)
RISE	1,522	(0.47%)
SLP	484	(0.15%)

SNP majority 63,283 (19.65%)
5.44% swing Lab. to SNP (2011 SNP majority 24,776)
ADDITIONAL MEMBERS

Jamie Green, C.	Mary Fee, Lab.
Maurice Golden, C.	Ken Macintosh, Lab.
Maurice Corry, C.	Ross Greer, Green
Neil Bibby, Lab.	

NORTHERN IRELAND

NORTHERN IRELAND ASSEMBLY
Parliament Buildings, Stormont, Belfast BT4 3XX
T 028-9052 1137 **E** info@niassembly.gov.uk
W www.niassembly.gov.uk

The Northern Ireland Assembly was established as a result of the Belfast Agreement (also known as the Good Friday Agreement) in April 1998. The agreement was endorsed through a referendum held in May 1998 and subsequently given legal force through the Northern Ireland Act 1998.

The Northern Ireland Assembly has full legislative and executive authority for all matters that are the responsibility of the government's Northern Ireland departments – known as transferred matters. Excepted and reserved matters are defined in schedules 2 and 3 of the Northern Ireland Act 1998 and remain the responsibility of UK parliament.

The first assembly election occurred on 25 June 1998 and the 108 members elected met for the first time on 1 July 1998.

On 29 November 1999 the assembly appointed ten ministers as well as the chairs and deputy chairs for the ten statutory departmental committees. Devolution of powers to the Northern Ireland Assembly occurred on 2 December 1999, following several delays concerned with Sinn Fein's inclusion in the executive while Irish Republican Army (IRA) weapons were yet to be decommissioned.

Since the devolution of powers, the assembly has been suspended by the Secretary of State for Northern Ireland on four occasions. The first was between 11 February and 30 May 2000, with two 24-hour suspensions on 10 August and 22 September 2001 – all owing to a lack of progress in decommissioning. The final suspension took place on 14 October 2002 after unionists walked out of the executive following a police raid on Sinn Fein's office investigating alleged intelligence gathering.

The assembly was formally dissolved in April 2003 in anticipation of an election, which eventually took place on 26 November 2003. The results of the election changed the balance of power between the political parties, with an increase in the number of seats held by the Democratic Unionist Party (DUP) and Sinn Fein (SF), so that they became the largest parties. The assembly was restored to a state of suspension following the November election while political parties engaged in a review of the Belfast Agreement aimed at fully restoring the devolved institutions.

In July 2005 the leadership of the IRA formally ordered an end to its armed campaign; it authorised a representative to engage with the Independent International Commission on Decommissioning in order to verifiably put the arms beyond use. On 26 September 2005 General John de Chastelain, the chair of the commission, along with two independent church witnesses confirmed that the IRA's entire arsenal of weapons had been decommissioned.

Following the passing of the Northern Ireland Act 2006 the secretary of state created a non-legislative fixed-term assembly, whose membership consisted of the 108 members elected in the 2003 election. It first met on 15 May 2006 with the remit of making preparations for the restoration of devolved government; its discussions informed the next round of talks called by the British and Irish governments held at St Andrews. The St Andrews agreement of 13 October 2006 led to the establishment of the transitional assembly.

The Northern Ireland (St Andrews Agreement) Act 2006 set out a timetable to restore devolution, and also set the date for the third election to the assembly as 7 March 2007. The DUP and SF again had the largest number of Members of the Legislative Assembly (MLAs) elected, and although the initial restoration deadline of 26 March was missed, the leaders of the DUP and SF (Revd Dr Ian Paisley and Gerry Adams respectively) took part in a historic meeting and made a joint commitment to establish an executive committee in the assembly to which devolved powers were restored on 8 May 2007.

RECENT DEVELOPMENTS
Assembly elections took place on 5 May 2016 to elect the 108 members of the legislative assembly for a fifth term. The fifth assembly collapsed on 9 January 2017 when Martin McGuinness resigned as Deputy First Minister. Under the joint protocols that govern the power-sharing agreement, if either the first minister or the deputy resigns and a replacement is not nominated by the relevant party within seven days, then a snap election must be called. The assembly was formerly dissolved at midnight on 25 January 2017 and the most recent assembly elections were held on 2 March 2017 to elect the 90 members of the legislative assembly. Under the Assembly Members (Reduction of Numbers) Act Northern Ireland 2016, the number of assembly members was reduced from 108 to 90 – five members to be elected by each constituency, rather than six.

Following the March 2017 election, negotiations to form an executive missed both the normal three week deadline and an extended deadline of 29 June 2017 set by the Secretary of State for Northern Ireland. The sixth assembly remains suspended until an executive is formed.

THE SINGLE TRANSFERABLE VOTE SYSTEM
Members of the Northern Ireland Assembly are elected by the single transferable vote system from 18 constituencies – five per constituency. Under the single transferable vote system every voter has a single vote that can be transferred from one candidate to another. Voters number their candidates in order of preference. Where candidates reach their quota of votes and are elected, surplus votes are transferred to other candidates according to the next preference on each voter's ballot slip. The candidate in each round with the fewest votes is eliminated and their surplus votes are redistributed according to the voter's next preference. The process is repeated until the required number of members are elected.

SALARIES*

	From 1 January 2019
Speaker	£55,848
Deputy Speaker	£37,388
Commission member	£40,688
MLA	£35,888

* MLA salaries were reduced on 1 November 2018 and further reduced on 1 January 2019 for the present period while there is no executive

NORTHERN IRELAND ASSEMBLY
MEMBERS *as at August 2019*
KEY
* Replacement from the party list since the 2 March 2017 Northern Ireland Assembly election

Agnew, Steven, *Green, Down North*
Aiken, Dr Steve, OBE, *UUP, Antrim South*
Allen, Andy, *UUP, Belfast East*
Allister, Jim, *TUV, Antrim North*
Archibald, Caoimhe, *SF, Londonderry East*
Armstrong, Kellie, *Alliance, Strangford*
Bailey, Clare, *Green, Belfast South*
Barton, Rosemary, *UUP, Fermanagh and South Tyrone*
Beattie, Doug, MC, *UUP, Upper Bann*
Beggs, Roy, *UUP, Antrim East*
* **Blair**, John, *Alliance, Antrim South*

Boylan, Cathal, *SF, Newry and Armagh*
Bradley, Maurice, *DUP, Londonderry East*
Bradley, Paula, *DUP, Belfast North*
Bradley, Sinéad, *SDLP, Down South*
Bradshaw, Paula, *Alliance, Belfast South*
Buchanan, Keith, *DUP, Ulster Mid*
Buchanan, Thomas, *DUP, Tyrone West*
Buckley, Jonathan, *DUP, Upper Bann*
Bunting, Joanne, *DUP, Belfast East*
Butler, Robbie, *UUP, Lagan Valley*
Cameron, Pam, *DUP, Antrim South*
Carroll, Gerry, *PBP, Belfast West*
Catney, Pat, *SDLP, Lagan Valley*
Chambers, Alan, *UUP, Down North*
* Clarke, Trevor, *DUP, Antrim South*
Dallat, John, *SDLP, Londonderry East*
Dickson, Stewart, *Alliance, Antrim East*
Dillon, Linda, *SF, Ulster Mid*
Dolan, Jemma, *SF, Fermanagh and South Tyrone*
Dunne, Gordon, *DUP, Down North*
Durkan, Mark, *SDLP, Foyle*
Easton, Alex, *DUP, Down North*
Eastwood, Colum, *SDLP, Foyle*
Ennis, Sinéad, *SF, Down South*
Farry, Dr Stephen, *Alliance, Down North*
Fearon, Megan, *SF, Newry and Armagh*
Flynn, Órlaithí, *SF, Belfast West*
Foster, Arlene, *DUP, Fermanagh and South Tyrone*
Frew, Paul, *DUP, Antrim North*
* Gildernew, Colm, *SF, Fermanagh and South Tyrone*
Givan, Paul, *DUP, Lagan Valley*
Hamilton, Simon, *DUP, Strangford*
Hanna, Claire, *SDLP, Belfast South*
* Hendron, Máire, *Alliance, Belfast East*
Hilditch, David, *DUP, Antrim East*
Humphrey, William, *DUP, Belfast North*
Irwin, William, *DUP, Newry and Armagh*
Kearney, Declan, *SF, Antrim South*
* Kelly, Catherine, *SF, Tyrone West*
Kelly, Dolores, *SDLP, Upper Bann*
Kelly, Gerry, *SF, Belfast North*
Lockhart, Carla, *DUP, Upper Bann*
Long, Naomi, *Alliance, Belfast East*
Lunn, Trevor, *Alliance, Lagan Valley*
Lynch, Seán, *SF, Fermanagh and South Tyrone*
Lyons, Gordon, *DUP, Antrim East*
Lyttle, Chris, *Alliance, Belfast East*
McAleer, Declan, *SF, Tyrone West*
McCann, Fra, *SF, Belfast West*
McCartney, Raymond, *SF, Foyle*
McCrossan, Daniel, *SDLP, Tyrone West*
McGlone, Patsy, *SDLP, Ulster Mid*
McGrath, Colin, *SDLP, Down South*
McGuigan, Philip, *SF, Antrim North*
* McHugh, Maoliosa, *SF, Tyrone West*
McIlveen, Michelle, *DUP, Strangford*
McNulty, Justin, *SDLP, Newry and Armagh*
Mallon, Nichola, *SDLP, Belfast North*
Maskey, Alex, *SF, Belfast West*
Middleton, Gary, *DUP, Foyle*
* Mullan, Karen, *SF, Foyle*
Murphy, Conor, *SF, Newry and Armagh*
Nesbitt, Mike, *UUP, Strangford*
Newton, Robin, *DUP, Belfast East*
Ní Chuilín, Carál, *SF, Belfast North*
O'Dowd, John, *SF, Upper Bann*
O'Neill, Michelle, *SF, Ulster Mid*
Ó Muilleoir, Máirtín, *SF, Belfast South*
Poots, Edwin, *DUP, Lagan Valley*

Robinson, George, *DUP, Londonderry East*
* Rogan, Emma, *SF, Down South*
Sheehan, Pat, *SF, Belfast West*
* Sheerin, Emma, *SF, Ulster Mid*
Stalford, Christopher, *DUP, Belfast South*
Stewart, John, *UUP, Antrim East*
Storey, Mervyn, *DUP, Antrim North*
Sugden, Claire, *Ind., Londonderry East*
Swann, Robin, *UUP, Antrim North*
Weir, Peter, *DUP, Down North*
Wells, Jim, *DUP, Down South*

STATE OF THE PARTIES *as at 2 March 2017 election*

Party	Seats
Democratic Unionist Party (DUP)	28
Sinn Fein (SF)	27
Social Democratic and Labour Party (SDLP)	12
Ulster Unionist Party (UUP)	10
Alliance Party of Northern Ireland (Alliance)	8
Green Party (Green)	2
People Before Profit Alliance (PBP)	1
Traditional Unionist Voice (TUV)	1
Independents (Ind.)	1
Total	90

NORTHERN IRELAND EXECUTIVE
Stormont Castle, Stormont, Belfast BT4 3TT
T 028-9052 8400
W www.northernireland.gov.uk

The Northern Ireland Executive comprises the first minister, deputy first minister, two junior ministers and eight departmental ministers.

The executive exercises authority on behalf of the Northern Ireland Assembly, and takes decisions on significant issues and matters which cut across the responsibility of two or more ministers.

The executive also agrees proposals put forward by ministers for new legislation in the form of 'executive bills' for consideration by the assembly. It is also responsible for drawing up a programme for government and an agreed budget for approval by the assembly. Ministers of the executive are nominated by the political parties in the Northern Ireland Assembly. The number of ministers which a party can nominate is determined by its share of seats in the assembly. The first minister and deputy first minister are nominated by the largest and second largest parties respectively and act as chairs of the executive. Each executive minister has responsibility for a specific Northern Ireland government department.

EXECUTIVE COMMITTEE OF MINISTERS
There are currently no executive ministers in post since the most recent assembly elections which took place on 2 March 2017. Negotiations to appoint the executive committee of ministers in charge of the nine government departments failed to meet both the three-week deadline following the election and an extended deadline of 29 June 2017 set by the Secretary of State for Northern Ireland. The assembly remains suspended until an executive is formed.

NORTHERN IRELAND EXECUTIVE DEPARTMENTS
THE EXECUTIVE OFFICE, Stormont Castle, Stormont, Belfast BT4 3TT **T** 028-9052 8400 **W** www.executiveoffice-ni.gov.uk
DEPARTMENT OF AGRICULTURE, ENVIRONMENT AND RURAL AFFAIRS, Dundonald House, Upper Newtownards Road, Belfast BT4 3SB **T** 0300-200 7850 **W** www.daera-ni.gov.uk

DEPARTMENT FOR COMMUNITIES, Causeway Exchange, 1–7 Bedford Street, Belfast BT2 7EG **T** 028-9082 9000 **W** www.communities-ni.gov.uk

DEPARTMENT FOR THE ECONOMY, Netherleigh, Massey Avenue, Belfast BT4 2JP **T** 028-9052 9900 **W** www.economy-ni.gov.uk

DEPARTMENT OF EDUCATION, Rathgael House, Balloo Road, Bangor, Co. Down BT19 7PR **T** 028-9127 9279 **W** www.education-ni.gov.uk

DEPARTMENT OF FINANCE, Clare House, 303 Airport Road, Belfast BT3 9ED **T** 028-9185 8111 **W** www.finance-ni.gov.uk

DEPARTMENT OF HEALTH, Castle Buildings, Stormont, Belfast BT4 3SQ **T** 028-9052 0500 **W** www.health-ni.gov.uk

DEPARTMENT FOR INFRASTRUCTURE, Clarence Court, 10–18 Adelaide Street, Belfast BT2 8GB **T** 028-9054 0540 **W** www.infrastructure-ni.gov.uk

DEPARTMENT OF JUSTICE, Block B, Castle Buildings, Stormont Estate, Belfast BT4 3SG **T** 028-9076 3000 **W** www.justice-ni.gov.uk

NORTHERN IRELAND AUDIT OFFICE
106 University Street, Belfast BT7 1EU
T 028-9025 1000 **E** info@niauditoffice.gov.uk
W www.niauditoffice.gov.uk

The Northern Ireland Audit Office supports the Comptroller and Auditor-General in fulfilling his responsibilities. He is responsible for authorising the issue of money from central government funds to Northern Ireland departments and for both financial and value for money audits of central government bodies in Northern Ireland, including, Northern Ireland departments, executive agencies, executive non-departmental public bodies and health and social care bodies.

Comptroller and Auditor-General, Kieran Donnelly, CB

OFFICE OF THE ATTORNEY-GENERAL FOR NORTHERN IRELAND
PO Box 1272, Belfast BT1 9LU
T 028-9072 5333 **E** contact@attorneygeneralni.gov.uk
W www.attorneygeneralni.gov.uk

With the devolution of justice responsibilities on 12 April 2010, the Justice (Northern Ireland) Act 2002 was enacted which established a new post of Attorney-General for Northern Ireland. The Attorney-General acts as the chief legal adviser to the Northern Ireland executive for both civil and criminal matters that fall within the devolved powers of the assembly. He is the executive's most senior representative in the courts and responsible for protecting the public interest in matters of law; overseeing the legal work of the in-house advisers to the executive and its departments; and for the appointment of the director and deputy director of the Public Prosecution Service for Northern Ireland. The Attorney-General participates in the assembly proceedings to the extent permitted by its standing orders, but does not vote in the assembly.

The post of Attorney-General is statutorily independent of the first minister, deputy first minister, the executive and the executive departments.

Attorney-General for Northern Ireland, John Larkin, QC

NORTHERN IRELAND ASSEMBLY ELECTION RESULTS *as at 2 March 2017*

Electorate (E.) 1,254,709 Turnout (T.) 64.8%
First = number of first-preference votes
See General Election Results for a list of party abbreviations

ANTRIM EAST
E. 62,933 T. 37,836 (60.12%)

	First	Round Elected
David Hilditch, DUP	6,000	3
Roy Beggs, UUP	5,121	6
Stewart Dickson, Alliance, DUP	4,179	6
Gordon Lyons, DUP	3,851	8
Oliver McMullan, SF	3,701	
John Stewart, UUP	3,377	9
Stephen Ross, DUP	3,313	
Danny Donnelly, Alliance	1,817	
Noel Jordan, UKIP	1,579	
Ruth Wilson, TUV	1,534	
Margaret McKillop, SDLP	1,524	
Dawn Patterson, Green	777	
Conor Sheridan, Lab. Alt	393	
Alan Dunlop, Lab. C	152	
Ricky Best, Ind.	106	

ANTRIM NORTH
E. 76,739 T. 48,518 (63.22%)

	First	Round Elected
Philip McGuigan, SF	7,600	6
Paul Frew, DUP	6,975	7
Mervyn Storey, DUP	6,857	7
Jim Allister, TUV	6,214	7
Robin Swann, UUP	6,022	6
Phillip Logan, DUP	5,708	
Connor Duncan, SDLP	3,519	
Patricia O'Lynn, Alliance	2,616	
Timothy Gaston, TUV	1,505	
Mark Bailey, Green	530	
Monica Digney, Ind.	435	
Adam McBride, Ind.	113	

ANTRIM SOUTH
E. 68,475 T. 42,726 (62.40%)

	First	Round Elected
Declan Kearney, SF	6,891	4
Steve Aiken, UUP	6,287	5
David Ford, Alliance	5,278	7
Paul Girvan, DUP	5,152	8
Pam Cameron, DUP	4,604	8
Trevor Clarke, DUP	4,522	
Roisin Lynch, SDLP	4,024	
Adrian Cochrane-Watson, UUP	2,505	
Richard Cairns, TUV	1,353	
Ivanka Antova, PBP	530	
David McMaster, Ind.	503	
Eleanor Bailey, Green	501	
Mark Logan, C.	194	

BELFAST EAST
E. 64,788 T. 40,828 (63.02%)

	First	Round Elected
Naomi Long, Alliance	7,610	1
Joanne Bunting, DUP	6,007	9
Andy Allen, UUP	5,275	9
Chris Lyttle, Alliance	5,059	8
Robin Newton, DUP	4,729	11
David Douglas, DUP	4,431	
John Kyle, PUP	2,658	
Georgina Milne, Green	1,447	
Mairead O'Donnell, SF	1,173	
Andrew Girvin, TUV	917	
Courtney Robinson, CCLA	442	
Sheila Bodel, C.	275	
Séamas de Faoite, SDLP	250	
Jordy McKeag, Ind.	84	

BELFAST NORTH
E. 68,187 T. 42,119 (61.77%)

	First	Round Elected
Gerry Kelly, SF	6,275	7
Caral Ni Chuilin, SF	5,929	7
Nichola Mallon, SDLP	5,431	7
Paula Bradley, DUP	4,835	6
William Humphrey, DUP	4,418	6
Nelson McCausland, DUP	4,056	
Nuala McAllister, Alliance	3,487	
Robert Foster, UUP	2,418	
Julie-Anne Corr-Johnston, PUP	2,053	
Fiona Ferguson, PBP	1,559	
Malachai O'Hara, Green	711	
Gemma Weir, WP	248	
Adam Millar, Ind.	66	

BELFAST SOUTH
E. 61,309 T. 43,465 (70.89%)

	First	Round Elected
Máirtín Ó Muilleoir, SF	7,610	1
Claire Hanna, SDLP	6,559	6
Paula Bradshaw, Alliance	5,595	6
Christopher Stalford, DUP	4,529	9
Emma Little-Pengelly, DUP	4,446	
Clare Bailey, Green	4,247	9
Michael Henderson, UUP	3,863	
Emmet McDonough-Brown, Alliance	2,053	
Naomh Gallagher, SDLP	1,794	
Padraigin Mervyn, PBP	760	
John Hiddleston, TUV	703	
Sean Burns, Lab. Alt	531	
George Jabbour, C.	200	
Lily Kerr, WP	163	

BELFAST WEST
E. 61,309 T. 40,930 (66.76%)

	First	Round Elected
Orlaithi Flynn, SF	6,918	1
Alex Maskey, SF	6,346	3
Fra McCann, SF	6,201	4
Pat Sheehan, SF	5,466	4
Gerry Carroll, PBP	4,903	3
Frank McCoubrey, DUP	4,063	
Alex Attwood, SDLP	3,452	
Michael Collins, PBP	1,096	
Sorcha Eastwood, Alliance	747	
Fred Rodgers, UUP	486	
Connor Campbell, WP	415	
Ellen Murray, Green	251	

DOWN NORTH
E. 64,461 T. 38,174 (59.22%)

	First	Round Elected
Alex Easton, DUP	8,034	1
Alan Chambers, UUP	7,151	1
Stephen Farry, Alliance	7,014	1
Gordon Dunne, DUP	6,118	2
Steven Agnew, Green	5,178	7
Melanie Kennedy, Ind.	1,246	
William Cudworth, UUP	964	
Caoimhe McNeill, SDLP	679	
Frank Shivers, C.	641	
Kieran Maxwell, SF	591	
Chris Carter, Ind.	92	
Gavan Reynolds, Ind.	31	

DOWN SOUTH
E. 75,415 T. 49,934 (66.21%)

	First	Round Elected
Sinéad Ennis, SF	10,256	1
Chris Hazzard, SF	8,827	1
Jim Wells, DUP	7,786	5
Sinéad Bradley, SDLP	7,323	3
Colin McGrath, SDLP	5,110	7
Patrick Brown, Alliance	4,535	
Harold McKee, UUP	4,172	
Lyle Rea, TUV	630	
Hannah George, Green	483	
Patrick Clarke, Ind.	192	
Gary Hynds, C.	85	

FERMANAGH AND SOUTH TYRONE
E. 73,100 T. 53,075 (72.61%)

	First	Round Elected
Arlene Foster, DUP	8,479	2
Michelle Gildernew, SF	7,987	3
Jemma Dolan, SF	7,767	3
Maurice Morrow, DUP	7,102	
Sean Lynch, SF	6,254	4
Rosemary Barton, UUP	6,060	4
Richie McPhillips, SDLP	5,134	
Noreen Campbell, Alliance	1,437	
Alex Elliott, TUV	780	
Donal O'Cofaigh, Lab. Alt	643	
Tanya Jones, Green	550	
Richard Dunn, C.	70	

FOYLE
E. 69,718 T. 45,317 (65.00%)

	First	Round Elected
Elisha McCallion, SF	9,205	1
Colum Eastwood, SDLP	7,240	3
Raymond McCartney, SF	7,145	2
Mark H. Durkan, SDLP	6,948	5
Gary Middleton, DUP	5,975	6
Eamon McCann, PBP	4,760	
Julia Kee, UUP	1,660	
Colm Cavanagh, Alliance	1,124	
Shannon Downey, Green	242	
John Lindsay, CISTA	196	
Stuart Canning, C.	77	
Arthur McGuinness, Ind.	44	

LAGAN VALLEY
E. 72,621 T. 45,440 (62.50%)

	First	Round Elected
Paul Givan, DUP	8,035	1
Robbie Butler, UUP	6,846	7
Trevor Lunn, Alliance	6,105	7
Edwin Poots, DUP	6,013	8
Brenda Hale, DUP	4,566	
Jenny Palmer, UUP	4,492	
Pat Catney, SDLP	3,795	8
Peter Doran, SF	1,801	
Samuel Morrison, TUV	1,389	
Dan Barrios-O'Neill, Green	912	
Jonny Orr, Ind.	856	
Matthew Robinson, C.	183	
Keith John Gray, Ind.	76	

LONDONDERRY EAST
E. 67,392 T. 42,248 (62.69%)

	First	Round Elected
Caoimhe Archibald, SF	5,851	12
Maurice Bradley, DUP	5,444	9
Cathal ohOisin, SF	4,953	
Claire Sugden, Ind.	4,918	8
George Robinson, DUP	4,715	9
Adrian McQuillan, DUP	3,881	
John Dallat, SDLP	3,319	12
William McCandless, UUP	2,814	
Chris McCaw, Alliance	1,841	
Gerry Mullan, Ind.	1,204	
Jordan Armstrong, TUV	1,038	
Russell Watton, PUP	879	
Gavin Campbell, PBP	492	
Anthony Flynn, Green	305	
David Harding, C.	219	

NEWRY AND ARMAGH
E. 80,140 T. 55,625 (69.41%)

	First	Round Elected
William Irwin, DUP	9,760	1
Cathal Boylan, SF	9,197	1
Justin McNulty, SDLP	8,983	2
Megan Fearon, SF	8,881	2
Conor Murphy, SF	8,454	3
Danny Kennedy, UUP	7,256	
Jackie Coade, Alliance	1,418	
Emmet Crossan, CISTA	704	
Rowan Tunnicliffe, Green	265	

STRANGFORD
E. 64,393 T. 39,239 (60.94%)

	First	Round Elected
Simon Hamilton, DUP	6,221	5
Kellie Armstrong, Alliance	5,813	4
Michelle McIlveen, DUP	5,728	9
Mike Nesbitt, UUP	5,323	9
Peter Weir, DUP	3,543	11
Joe Boyle, SDLP	3,045	
Philip Smith, UUP	2,453	
Jimmy Menagh, Ind.	1,627	
Jonathan Bell, Ind.	1,479	
Stephen Cooper, TUV	1,330	
Dermot Kennedy, SF	1,110	
Ricky Bamford, Green	918	
Scott Benton, C.	195	

TYRONE WEST
E. 64,258 T. 44,907 (69.89%)

	First	Round Elected
Thomas Buchanan, DUP	9,064	1
Michaela Boyle, SF	7,714	1
Barry McElduff, SF	7,573	1
Daniel McCrossan, SDLP	6,283	5
Declan McAleer, SF	6,034	5
Alicia Clarke, UUP	3,654	
Stephen Donnelly, Alliance	1,252	
Sorcha McAnespy, Ind.	864	
Charlie Chittick, TUV	851	
Ciaran McClean, Green	412	
Barry Brown, CISTA	373	
Corey French, Ind.	98	
Roisin McMackin, Ind.	85	
Susan-Anne White, Ind.	41	
Roger Lomas, C.	27	

ULSTER MID
E. 69,396 T. 50,228 (72.38%)

	First	Round Elected
Michelle, O'Neill, SF	10,258	1
Keith Buchanan, DUP	9,568	1
Ian Milne, SF	8,143	2
Linda Dillon, SF	7,806	2
Patsy McGlone, SDLP	6,419	5
Sandra Overend, UUP	4,516	
Hannah Loughrin, TUV	1,244	
Fay Watson, Alliance	1,017	
Hugh McCloy, Ind.	247	
Stefan Taylor, Green	243	
Hugh Scullion, WP	217	

UPPER BANN
E. 83,431 T. 52,174 (62.54%)

	First	Round Elected
Carla Lockhart, DUP	9,140	1
John O'Dowd, SF	8,220	5
Jonathan Buckley, DUP	7,745	4
Nuala Toman, SF	6,108	
Doug Beattie, UUP	5,467	5
Jo-Anne Dobson, UUP	5,132	
Dolores Kelly, SDLP	5,127	6
Tara Doyle, Alliance	2,720	
Roy Ferguson, TUV	1,035	
Simon Lee, Green	555	
Colin Craig, WP	218	
Ian Nickels, C.	81	

REGIONAL GOVERNMENT

LONDON

GREATER LONDON AUTHORITY (GLA)

City Hall, The Queen's Walk, London SE1 2AA
T 020-7983 4000 **E** mayor@london.gov.uk **W** www.london.gov.uk

On 7 May 1998 London voted in favour of the formation of the Greater London Authority (GLA). The first elections to the GLA took place on 4 May 2000 and the new authority took over its responsibilities on 3 July 2000. In July 2002 the GLA moved to one of London's most spectacular buildings, newly built on a brownfield site on the south bank of the Thames, adjacent to Tower Bridge. The fifth and most recent election to the GLA took place on 5 May 2016; the May 2020 mayoral and assembly elections were delayed until May 2021 due to the coronavirus pandemic.

The structure and objectives of the GLA stem from its main areas of responsibility: transport, policing, fire and emergency planning, economic development, planning, culture and health. There are five functional bodies which form part of the wider GLA group and report to the GLA: the Mayor's Office for Policing and Crime (MOPAC), Transport for London (TfL), the London Fire Commissioner, the London Legacy Development Corporation, and the Old Oak and Park Royal Development Corporation.

The GLA consists of a directly elected mayor, the Mayor of London, and a separately elected assembly, the London Assembly. The mayor has the key role in decision making, with the assembly responsible for regulating and scrutinising these decisions, and investigating issues of importance to Londoners. In addition, the GLA has around 950 permanent staff to support the activities of the mayor and the assembly, which are overseen by a head of paid service. The mayor may appoint two political advisers and not more than ten other members of staff, though he does not necessarily exercise this power, but he does not appoint the chief executive, the monitoring officer or the chief finance officer. These must be appointed jointly by the assembly and the mayor.

Every aspect of the assembly and its activities must be open to public scrutiny and therefore accountable. The assembly holds the mayor to account through scrutiny of his strategies, decisions and actions. Mayor's Question Time, conducted on ten occasions a year at City Hall, is carried out by direct questioning at assembly meetings and by conducting detailed investigations in committee.

People's Question Time, held twice a year, and Talk London (**W** www.london.gov.uk/talk-london) give Londoners the chance to question and express their opinions to the mayor and the assembly about plans, priorities and policies for London.

The role of the mayor can be broken down into a number of key areas:
- to represent and promote London at home and abroad and speak up for Londoners
- to devise strategies and plans to tackle London-wide issues, such as crime, transport, housing, planning, economic development and regeneration, environment, public services, society and culture, sport and health; and to set budgets for TfL, MOPAC, London Fire Commissioner and the London Legacy Development Corporation
- the mayor is chair of TfL, and is responsible for the Metropolitan Police's priorities and performance

The role of the assembly can be broken down into a number of key areas:
- to hold the mayor to account by examining his decisions and actions
- to have the power to amend the mayor's budget by a majority of two-thirds
- to have the power to summon the mayor, senior staff of the GLA and functional bodies
- to investigate issues of London-wide significance and make proposals to appropriate stakeholders
- to examine the work of MOPAC and to review the police and crime plan for London through the Police and Crime Committee

MAYORAL TEAM
Mayor, Sadiq Khan
Deputy Mayors, Rajesh Agrawal *(Business);* Heidi Alexander *(Transport);* Tom Copley *(Housing and Residential Development);* Sophie Linden *(Policing and Crime);* Joanne McCartney, AM *(Education and Childcare);* Jules Pipe, CBE *(Planning, Regeneration and Skills);* Shirley Rodrigues *(Environment and Energy);* Justine Simons, OBE *(Culture and the Creative Industries);* Dr Fiona Twycross, AM *(Fire and Resilience);* Debbie Weekes-Bernard *(Social Integration, Social Mobility and Community Engagement)*
Chief of Staff, David Bellamy
Directors, Dr Nick Bowes *(Policy);* Patrick Hennessy *(Communications);* Leah Kreitzman *(External and International Affairs);* Jack Stenner *(Political and Public Affairs)*
Special Appointments, Theo Blackwell, MBE *(Chief Digital Officer);* Dr Tom Coffey, OBE *(Health Adviser);* Amy Lamé *(Night Czar);* Dr Will Norman *(Walking and Cycling Commissioner);* Lib Peck *(Director of the Violence Reduction Unit);* Claire Waxman *(Victims Commissioner)*

ELECTIONS AND VOTING SYSTEMS
The assembly is elected every four years at the same time as the mayor, and consists of 25 members. There is one member from each of the 14 GLA constituencies topped up with 11 London-wide members who are either representatives of political parties or individuals standing as independent candidates.

Two distinct voting systems are used to appoint the existing mayor and the assembly. The mayor is elected using the supplementary vote system (SVS). With SVS, electors have two votes: one to give a first choice for mayor and one to give a second choice; they cannot vote twice for the same candidate. If one candidate gets more than half of all the first-choice votes, they become mayor. If no candidate gets more than half of the first-choice votes, the two candidates with the most first-choice votes remain in the election and all the other candidates drop out. The second-choice votes on the ballot papers are then counted. Where these second-choice votes are for the two remaining candidates, they are added to the first-choice votes these candidates already have. The candidate with the most first- and second-choice votes combined becomes the Mayor of London.

The assembly is appointed using the additional member system (AMS). Under AMS, electors have two votes. The first vote is for a constituency candidate. The second vote is for a party list or individual candidate contesting the London-wide assembly seats. The 14 constituency members are elected under the first-past-the-post system, the same system used in general and local elections. Electors vote for one candidate and the candidate with the most votes wins. The additional members are drawn from party lists or are independent candidates; they are chosen using a form of proportional representation.

The Greater London Returning Officer (GLRO) is the independent official responsible for running the election in London. He is supported in this by returning officers in each of the 14 London constituencies.

GLRO for 2016 Election, Jeff Jacobs

TRANSPORT FOR LONDON (TFL)

TfL is the integrated body responsible for London's transport system. Its role is to implement the mayor's transport strategy for London and manage transport services across the capital for which the mayor has responsibility. TfL is directed by a management board whose members are chosen for their understanding of transport matters and are appointed by the mayor, who chairs the board. TfL's role is:

• to manage the London Underground, buses, Croydon Tramlink, London Overground and the Docklands Light Railway (DLR)
• to manage a 580km network of main roads and all 6,000 of London's traffic lights
• to regulate taxis and minicabs
• to run the London River Services, Victoria Coach Station and London Transport Museum
• to help to coordinate the Dial-a-Ride, Capital Call and Taxicard schemes for door-to-door services for transport users with mobility problems

The London Borough Councils maintain the role of highway and traffic authorities for 95 per cent of London's roads. A congestion charge for motorists driving into central London between the hours of 7am and 6.30pm, Monday to Friday (excluding public holidays) was introduced in February 2003. In February 2007, the charge zone roughly doubled in size after a westward expansion and the charging hours were shortened, to finish at 6pm. In January 2011, the westward expansion was removed from the charging zone and an automated payment system was introduced. As at December 2020 the daily congestion charge is £15.00. (**W** www.tfl.gov.uk/modes/driving/congestion-charge).

TfL introduced a low emission zone (LEZ) for London in February 2008; the LEZ covers most of Greater London and is in constant operation for larger vans, minibuses, lorries, buses and other heavy vehicles that do not meet the LEZ emissions standards (cars and motorcycles are exempt). The daily charge is £100 for larger vans, minibuses and other specialist vehicles and £200 for lorries, buses and coaches, although emissions standards are set to become tougher from 1 March 2021. (**W** www.tfl.gov.uk/modes/driving/low-emission-zone).

Since April 2019 a new ultra low emission zone (ULEZ) has operated constantly in central London and covers the same area of central London as the congestion charge. Most vehicles, including cars and vans, need to meet the ULEZ emissions standards or their drivers must pay a daily charge, in addition to the congestion charge and, if applicable, the LEZ, to drive within the zone. As at December 2020 the charge is £12.50 for most vehicle types, including cars, motorcycles and vans (up to and including 3.5 tonnes) and £100 for heavier vehicles, including lorries (over 3.5 tonnes) and buses/coaches (over 5 tonnes). From 25 October 2021 ULEZ is set to expand to create a single larger zone bounded by the north and south circular roads. (**W** www.tfl.gov.uk/modes/driving/ultra-low-emission-zone).

Since January 2009, Londoners over pensionable age (or over 60 if born before 1950) and those with eligible disabilities are entitled to free travel on the capital's transport network at any time. War veterans who are receiving ongoing payments under the war pensions scheme, or those receiving guaranteed income payments under the armed forces compensation scheme can travel free at any time on bus, underground, DLR, tram and London Overground services and at certain times on National Rail services.

In the summer of 2010, the London cycle hire scheme launched with 6,000 new bicycles for hire from 400 docking stations across eight boroughs, the City and the Royal parks. The scheme has been expanded and there are now around 11,500 bicycles available and over 750 docking stations.

Commissioner of TfL, Andy Byford

MAYOR'S OFFICE FOR POLICING AND CRIME (MOPAC)

The Mayor's Office for Policing and Crime (MOPAC) was set up in response to the Police Reform and Social Responsibility Act 2011, replacing the Metropolitan Police Authority. MOPAC is headed by the mayor, or the appointed statutory deputy mayor for policing and crime. Operational responsibility for policing in London belongs to the Metropolitan Police Commissioner. The major areas of focus of MOPAC are:

• operational policing and crime reduction including counter terrorism
• ensuring the Metropolitan Police effectively reduce gang crime and violence in London and coordinating support for communities and local organisations to prevent gang activities
• criminal justice, including preventing reoffending, reducing crime and decreasing demand within the criminal justice system in addition to reducing alcohol and drug abuse.

The Police and Crime Committee consisting of nine elected members of the London Assembly scrutinises the work of MOPAC and meets regularly to hold to account the Deputy Mayor for Policing and Crime.

Deputy Mayor for Policing and Crime, Sophie Linden

LONDON FIRE COMMISSIONER

Under the Policing and Crime Act 2017, the London Fire Commissioner replaced the London Fire and Emergency Planning Authority (LFEPA) and was tasked with overseeing the London Fire Brigade, the fire and rescue authority for London. It consists of three main structural bodies: operational staff and firefighters, control staff and emergency responders, and a non-uniformed support team. Operational staff provide the only full-time fire service in the UK.

The Mayor of London sets its budget, approves its London Safety Plan, and can direct it to act. The London Fire Commissioner is further scrutinised by the Fire, Resilience and Emergency Planning (FREP) Committee of the London Assembly.

Commissioner, Andy Roe

LONDON LEGACY DEVELOPMENT CORPORATION

Following the London 2012 Olympic Games, the London Legacy Development Corporation was made responsible for the long-term planning, development, management and maintenance of the Queen Elizabeth Olympic Park (formerly the Olympic Park) and its facilities. The organisation is tasked with transforming the area into a thriving neighbourhood.

Chair, Sir Peter Hendy, CBE

SALARIES *as at December 2020*

Mayor	£152,734
Chief of Staff	£137,243
Deputy Mayors	
Housing and Residential Development	£132,664
Business	£132,664
Culture and the Creative Industries	£132,664
Transport	£132,664
Environment and Energy	£132,664
Policing and Crime	£127,513
Planning, Regeneration and Skills	£132,664
Social Integration, Social Mobility and Engagement	£132,664
Fire and Resilience	£132,664
Stautory Deputy Mayor (Education and Childcare)	£105,269
Chair of the Assembly	£70,225
Assembly Member	£58,543

STATE OF THE PARTIES *as at December 2020*

Party	Seats
Labour (Lab.)	12
Conservative (C.)	8
Green	2
Brexit Alliance (BA)	2
Liberal Democrats (LD)	1

LONDON ASSEMBLY COMMITTEES

Chair, Audit Panel, Susan Hall, AM
Chair, Budget and Performance Committee, Susan Hall, AM
Chair, Budget Monitoring Sub-Committee, Susan Hall, AM
Chair, Confirmation Hearings Committee, Andrew Boff, AM
Chair, Economy Committee, Leonie Cooper, AM
Chair, Environment Committee, Caroline Russell, AM
Chair, Fire, Resilience and Emergency Planning Committee, Andrew Dismore, AM
Chair, GLA Oversight Committee, Len Duvall, OBE, AM
Chair, Health Committee, Dr Onkar Sahota, AM
Chair, Housing Committee, Murad Queshi, AM
Chair, Planning and Regeneration Committee, Andrew Boff, AM
Chair, Police and Crime Committee, Unmesh Desai, AM
Chair, Transport Committee, Dr Alison Moore

LONDON ASSEMBLY MEMBERS

as at December 2020

Arbour, Tony, *C., South West,* Maj. 21,444
Arnold, Jennette, OBE, *Lab., North East,* Maj. 101,742
Bacon, Gareth, MP, *C., Bexley and Bromley,* Maj. 41,669
Bailey, Shaun, *C., London-wide*
Berry, Siân, *Green, London-wide*
Boff, Andrew, *C., London-wide*
Cooper, Leonie, *Lab., Merton and Wandsworth,* Maj. 4,301
Desai, Unmesh, *Lab., City and East,* Maj. 89,629
Devenish, Tony, *C., West Central,* Maj. 14,564
Dismore, Andrew, *Lab., Barnet and Camden,* Maj. 16,240
Duvall, Len, OBE, *Lab., Greenwich and Lewisham,* Maj. 54,895
Eshalomi, Florence, MP, *Lab., Lambeth and Southwark,* Maj. 62,243
Gavron, Nicky, *Lab., London-wide*
Hall, Susan, *C., London-wide*
Kurten, David, *BA, London-wide*
McCartney, Joanne, *Lab., Enfield and Haringey,* Maj. 51,152
Moore, Dr Alison, *Lab., London-wide*
O'Connell, Steve, *C., Croydon and Sutton,* Maj. 11,614
Pidgeon, Caroline, MBE, *LD, London-wide*
Prince, Keith, *C. Havering and Redbridge,* Maj. 1,438
Murad, Qureshi, *Lab. and Co-op, London-wide*
Russell, Caroline, *Green, London-wide*
Sahota, Dr Onkar, *Lab., Ealing and Hillingdon,* Maj. 15,933
Shah, Navin, *Lab., Brent and Harrow,* Maj. 20,755
Whittle, Peter, *BA, London-wide*

Chair of the London Assembly, Navin Shah

MAYORAL ELECTION RESULTS

as at 5 May 2016

Electorate 5,739,011 Turnout 45.6%

First	Party	Votes	%
Sadiq Khan	Lab.	1,148,716	44.2
Zac Goldsmith	C.	909,755	35.0
Siân Berry	Green	150,673	5.8
Caroline Pidgeon	LD	120,005	4.6
Peter Whittle	UKIP	94,373	3.6
Sophie Walker	Women	53,055	2.0
George Galloway	Respect	37,007	1.4
Paul Golding	Brit. First	31,372	1.2
Lee Harris	CISTA	20,537	0.8
David Furness	BNP	13,325	0.5
Prince Zylinski	Ind.	13,202	0.5
Ankit Love	One Love	4,941	0.2

Second	Party	Votes	%
Sadiq Khan	Lab.	161,427	65.5
Zac Goldsmith	C.	84,859	34.5

LONDON ASSEMBLY ELECTION RESULTS *as at 5 May 2016*

E. Electorate T. Turnout

See General Election Results for a list of party abbreviations

CONSTITUENCIES
E. 5,739,011 T 45.6%

BARNET AND CAMDEN
E. 387,844 T. 47.44%

Andrew Dismore, Lab.	81,482
Daniel Thomas, C.	65,242
Stephen Taylor, Green	16,996
Zack Polanski, LD	11,204
Joseph Langton, UKIP	9,057

Lab. majority 16,240

BEXLEY AND BROMLEY
E. 404,342 T. 46.94%

Gareth Bacon, C.	87,460
Sam Russell, Lab.	45,791
Frank Gould, UKIP	30,485
Roisin Robertson, Green	12,685
Julie Ireland, LD	12,145
Veronica Obadara, APP	1,243

C. majority 41,669

BRENT AND HARROW
E. 381,778 T. 45.76%

Navin Shah, Lab.	79,902
Joel Davidson, C.	59,147
Anton Georgiou, LD	11,534
Jafar Hassan, Green	9,874
Rathy Alagaratnam, UKIP	9,074
Akib Mahmood, Respect GG	5,170

Lab. majority 20,755

CITY AND EAST
E. 503,301 T. 42.01%

Unmesh Desai, Lab.	122,175
Chris Chapman, C.	32,546
Rachel Collinson, Green	18,766
Peter Harris, UKIP	18,071
Elaine Bagshaw, LD	10,714
Rayne Mickail, Respect GG	6,772
Amina Gichinga, TBTC	1,368
Aaron D'Souza, APP	1,009

Lab. majority 89,629

CROYDON AND SUTTON
E. 401,660 T. 45.29%

Steve O'Connell, C.	70,156
Marina Ahmad, Lab.	58,542
Amna Ahmad, LD	18,859
Peter Staveley, UKIP	18,338
Tracey Hague, Green	13,513
Madonna Lewis, APP	1,386
Richard Edmonds, NF	1,106

C. majority 11,614

EALING AND HILLINGDON
E. 444,168 T. 45.25%

Onkar Sahota, Lab.	86,088
Dominic Gilham, C.	70,155
Alex Nieora, UKIP	15,832
Meena Hans, Green	15,758
Francesco Fruzza, LD	13,154

Lab. majority 15,933

ENFIELD AND HARINGEY
E. 377,060 T. 44.73%

Joanne McCartney, Lab.	91,075
Linda Kelly, C.	39,923
Ronald Stewart, Green	15,409
Nicholas da Costa, LD	12,038
Neville Watson, UKIP	9,042
Godson Azu, APP	1,172

Lab. majority 51,152

GREENWICH AND LEWISHAM
E. 362,376 T. 45.08%

Len Duvall, Lab.	85,735
Adam Thomas, C.	30,840
Imogen Solly, Green	20,520
Paul Oakley, UKIP	13,686
Julia Fletcher, LD	11,303
Ajaratu Bangura, APP	1,275

Lab. majority 54,895

HAVERING AND REDBRIDGE
E. 383,234 T. 44.63%

Keith Prince, C.	64,483
Ivana Bartoletti, Lab.	63,045
Lawrence Webb, UKIP	26,788
Lee Burkwood, Green	9,617
Ian Sanderson, LD	7,105

C. majority 1,438

LAMBETH AND SOUTHWARK
E. 426,966 T. 43.98%

Florence Eshalomi, Lab.	96,946
Robert Flint, C.	34,703
Rashid Nix, Green	25,793
Michael Bukola, LD	21,489
Idham Ramadi, UKIP	6,591
Kevin Parkin, SPGB	1,333
Amadu Kanumansa, APP	906

Lab. majority 62,243

MERTON AND WANDSWORTH
E. 374,126 T. 49.56%

Leonie Cooper, Lab.	77,340
David Dean, C.	73,039
Esther Obiri-Darko, Green	14,682
Adrian Hyyrylainen-Trett, LD	10,732
Elizabeth Jones, UKIP	8,478
Thamilini Kulendran, Ind.	1,142

Lab. majority 4,301

NORTH EAST
E. 500,432 T. 45.72%

Jennette Arnold, Lab.	134,307
Sam Malik, C.	32,565
Samir Jeraj, Green	29,401
Terry Stacy, LD	14,312
Freddy Vachha, UKIP	11,315
Tim Allen, Respect GG	5,068
Bill Martin, SPGB	1,293
Jonathan Silberman, Comm L	536

Lab. majority 101,742

SOUTH WEST
E. 435,877 T. 49.04%

Tony Arbour, C.	84,381
Martin Whelton, Lab.	62,937
Rosina Robson, LD	30,654
Andree Frieze, Green	19,745
Alexander Craig, UKIP	14,983
Adam Buick, SPGB	1,065

C. majority 21,444

WEST CENTRAL
E. 348,740 T. 43.96%

Tony Devenish, C.	67,775
Mandy Richards, Lab.	53,211
Jennifer Nadel, Green	14,050
Annabel Mullin, LD	10,577
Clive Egan, UKIP	7,708

C. majority 14,564

LONDON-WIDE MEMBERS

Conservative Party	*Labour Party*
Kemi Badenoch	Fiona Twycross
Andrew Boff	Tom Copley
Shaun Bailey	Nicky Gavron

Green Party	*UKIP*
Sian Berry	Peter Whittle
Caroline Russell	David Kurten

Liberal Democrats
Caroline Pidgeon

LOCAL GOVERNMENT

Major changes in local government were introduced in England and Wales in 1974 and in Scotland in 1975 by the Local Government Act 1972 and the Local Government (Scotland) Act 1973. Additional alterations were made in England by the Local Government Acts of 1985, 1992 and 2000.

The structure in England was based on two tiers of local authorities (county councils and district councils) in the non-metropolitan areas; and a single tier of metropolitan councils in the six metropolitan areas of England and London borough councils in London.

Following reviews of the structure of local government in England by the Local Government Commission (now the Boundary Commission for England), 46 unitary (all-purpose) authorities were created between April 1995 and April 1998 to cover certain areas in the non-metropolitan counties. The remaining county areas continue to have two tiers of local authorities. The county and district councils in the Isle of Wight were replaced by a single unitary authority in April 1995; the former counties of Avon, Cleveland, Humberside and Berkshire were replaced by unitary authorities; and Hereford & Worcester was replaced by a new county council for Worcestershire (with district councils) and a unitary authority for Herefordshire. In April 2009 the county areas of Cornwall, Durham, Northumberland, Shropshire and Wiltshire were given unitary status and two new unitary authorities were created for Bedfordshire (Bedford and Central Bedfordshire) and Cheshire (Cheshire East and Cheshire West & Chester) replacing the two-tier county/district system in these areas.

In April 2019 Dorset's nine councils merged into two unitary authorities. Bournemouth and Poole unitary authorities merged with Christchurch district council to become Bournemouth, Christchurch and Poole (BCP) unitary authority, while Dorset unitary authority was formed from Dorset County Council together with East Dorset, North Dorset, Purbeck, Weymouth & Portland and West Dorset district councils. Also in April 2019, in what is expected to be a continuing trend in order to share resources and make financial savings, a total of six district councils merged into three new district authorities. The three councils, East Suffolk, West Suffolk and Somerset West and Taunton, continue to operate at district level. Similarly, in April 2020 four non-metropolitan districts in Buckinghamshire merged with Buckinghamshire County Council to form a new unitary authority, Buckinghamshire Council.

The Local Government (Wales) Act 1994 and the Local Government etc (Scotland) Act 1994 abolished the two-tier structure in Wales and Scotland with effect from April 1996, replacing it with a single tier of unitary authorities.

In Northern Ireland a reform programme to reduce the number of local authorities from 26 to 11 began in 2012 when legislation finalising the boundaries of the new 11 local government district authorities was approved by the Northern Ireland Assembly. The Local Government Act (Northern Ireland) 2014 received royal assent on 12 May 2014, providing the legislative framework for the 11 new councils. On 1 April 2015 additional functions, previously the responsibility of the Northern Ireland executive, fully transferred to the new district authorities.

ELECTIONS

Local elections are normally held on the first Thursday in May. Generally, all citizens of the UK, the Republic of Ireland, Commonwealth and other European Union citizens who are 18 years or over and resident on the qualifying date in the area for which the election is being held, are entitled to vote at local government elections. A register of electors is prepared and published annually by local electoral registration officers.

A returning officer has the overall responsibility for an election. Voting takes place at polling stations, arranged by the local authority and under the supervision of a presiding officer specially appointed for the purpose. Candidates, who are subject to various statutory qualifications and disqualifications designed to ensure that they are suitable to hold office, must be nominated by electors for the electoral area concerned.

In England, the Local Government Boundary Commission for England is responsible for carrying out periodic reviews of electoral arrangements, to consider whether the boundaries of wards or divisions within a local authority need to be altered to take account of changes in electorate; structural reviews, to consider whether a single, unitary authority should be established in an area instead of an existing two-tier system; and administrative boundary reviews of district or county authorities.

The Local Democracy and Boundary Commission for Wales, the Local Government Boundary Commission for Scotland and the local government boundary commissioner for Northern Ireland (appointed when required by the Boundary Commission for Northern Ireland) are responsible for reviewing the electoral arrangements and boundaries of local authorities within their respective regions.

The Local Government Act 2000 provided for the secretary of state to change the frequency and phasing of elections in England and Wales.

LOCAL GOVERNMENT BOUNDARY COMMISSION FOR ENGLAND, SW1H 0TL1st Floor, Windsor House, 50 Victoria Street, London SW1H 0TL **T** 0330-500 1525
E reviews@lgbce.org.uk **W** www.lgbce.org.uk

LOCAL DEMOCRACY AND BOUNDARY COMMISSION FOR WALES, Ground Floor, Hastings House, Fitzalan Court, Cardiff CF24 0BL **T** 029-2046 4819
E enquiries@boundaries.wales **W** www.ldbc.gov.wales

LOCAL GOVERNMENT BOUNDARY COMMISSION FOR SCOTLAND, Thistle House, 91 Haymarket Terrace, Edinburgh EH12 5HD **T** 0131-244 2001
E lgbcs@scottishboundaries.gov.uk
W www.lgbc-scotland.gov.uk

BOUNDARY COMMISSION FOR NORTHERN IRELAND, The Bungalow, Stormont House, Stormont Estate, Belfast BT4 3SH **T** 028-9052 7821
E contact@boundarycommission.org.uk
W www.boundarycommission.org.uk

LOCAL GOVERNMENT DEVOLUTION

Local government is a devolved matter in Scotland, Wales and Northern Ireland.

In England, under the Cities and Local Government Devolution Act 2016, multiple local authorities can combine and take on more functions, over and above those they were allowed to take on under previous legislation. In order for a combined or 'regional' authority to be given these extra powers a mayor must be elected for the region by the electorate in the combined-authority area. The first six combined authority mayoral elections took place in May 2017. The exact functions the combined authority and mayor manage varies depending on the devolution agreement reached with central government, but the directly elected 'metro' mayor does have powers and responsibilities to make strategic decisions across whole city regions. This is in contrast to existing city mayors (which are also directly elected) or local council leaders that only make decisions for, and on behalf of, their local authority (*see* Internal Organisation). To date, ten combined authorities have been established, eight of which have a mayor and a devolution agreement with national government (*see* Combined Authorities for a complete list).

INTERNAL ORGANISATION

The council as a whole is the final decision-making body within any authority. Councils are free to a great extent to make their own internal organisational arrangements. The Local Government Act, given royal assent on 28 July 2000, allows councils to adopt one of three broad categories of constitution which include a separate executive:

- A directly elected mayor with a cabinet selected by that mayor
- A cabinet, either elected by the council or appointed by its leader
- A directly elected mayor and council manager

Normally, questions of policy are settled by the full council, while the administration of the various services is the responsibility of committees of councillors. Day-to-day decisions are delegated to the council's officers, who act within the policies laid down by the councillors.

FINANCE

Local government in England, Wales and Scotland is financed from four sources: council tax, non-domestic rates, government grants and income from fees and charges for services.

COUNCIL TAX

Council tax is a local tax levied by each local council. Liability for the council tax bill usually falls on the owner-occupier or tenant of a dwelling which is their sole or main residence. Council tax bills may be reduced because of the personal circumstances of people resident in a property and there are discounts in the case of dwellings occupied by fewer than two adults.

In England, unitary and metropolitan authorities are responsible for collecting their own council tax. In areas where there are two tiers of local authority, each county and district authority sets its own council tax rate; the district authorities collect the combined council tax and the county councils claim their share from the district councils' collection funds. In Wales and Scotland each unitary authority sets its own council tax rate and is responsible for collection.

The tax relates to the value of the dwelling. In England and Scotland each dwelling is placed in one of eight valuation bands, ranging from A to H, based on the property's estimated market value as at 1 April 1991. In Wales there are nine bands, ranging from A to I, based on the estimated market value of property as at 1 April 2003.

The valuation bands and ranges of values in England, Wales and Scotland are:

England

A	Up to £40,000	E	£88,001–£120,000
B	£40,001–£52,000	F	£120,001–£160,000
C	£52,001–£68,000	G	£160,001–£320,000
D	£68,001–£88,000	H	Over £320,001

Wales

A	Up to £44,000	F	£162,001–£223,000
B	£44,001–£65,000	G	£223,001–£324,000
C	£65,001–£91,000	H	£324,001–£424,000
D	£91,001–£123,000	I	Over £424,000
E	£123,001–£162,000		

Scotland

A	Up to £27,000	E	£58,001–£80,000
B	£27,001–£35,000	F	£80,001–£106,000
C	£35,001–£45,000	G	£106,001–£212,000
D	£45,001–£58,000	H	Over £212,000

The council tax within a local area varies between the different bands according to proportions laid down by law. The charge attributable to each band as a proportion of the Band D charge set by the council is:

A	67%	F	144%
B	78%	G	167%
C	89%	H	200%
D	100%	I*	233%
E	122%		

* Wales only

The Band D council tax bill for 2019–20, inclusive of adult social care and parish precepts, for each authority area is given in the complete lists of local authorities for England, London, Wales and Scotland which follow. There may be variations from the given figure within each district council area because of different parish or community precepts being levied, the personal circumstances of the residents in a property or in the case of dwellings occupied by fewer than two adults.

Domestic property in Northern Ireland is subjected to a rateable system based on the capital value of a property as at 1 January 2005 *see* Northern Ireland, Finance for further information.

NON-DOMESTIC RATES

Non-domestic (business) rates are collected by billing authorities; these are the district councils in those areas of England with two tiers of local government and unitary authorities in other parts of England, in Wales and in Scotland. In respect of England and Wales, the Local Government Finance Act 1988 provides for liability for rates to be assessed on the basis of a poundage (multiplier) tax on the rateable value of property (hereditaments). Separate multipliers are set by the Ministry of Housing, Communities and Local Government (MHCLG) in England, the Welsh government and the Scottish government. Rates are collected by the billing authority for the area where a property is located. Rate income collected by billing authorities is paid into a national non-domestic rating (NNDR) pool and redistributed to individual authorities on the basis of the adult population figure as prescribed by MHCLG, the Welsh government or the Scottish government. The rates pools are maintained separately in England, Wales and Scotland. Actual payment of rates in certain cases is subject to transitional arrangements, to phase in the larger increases and reductions in rates resulting from the effects of the latest revaluation.

The most recent rating lists for England, Wales and Scotland came into effect on 1 April 2017. The rateable values on these lists are derived from the rental value of property as at 1 April 2015 and determined on certain statutory assumptions by the Valuation Office Agency in England and Wales, and by local area assessors in Scotland. New property which is added to the list, and significant changes to existing property, necessitate amendments to the rateable value on the same basis. Rating lists (valuation rolls in Scotland) remain in force until the next general revaluation, which usually takes place every five years to reflect changes in the property market.

A revaluation of non-domestic properties in Northern Ireland was completed at the start of 2015, enforced after 1 April 2015, and a revised rate introduced on 1 April 2020 based on the rental value of the property as at 1 April 2018.

Certain types of property are exempt from rates, for example agricultural land and buildings, buildings used for the training or welfare of disabled people and buildings registered for public religious worship. Charities and other non-profit-making organisations may receive full or partial relief and relief schemes for small businesses are available in England, Wales, Scotland and Northern Ireland. Empty commercial property in England and Wales is exempt from business rates for the first three months that the property is vacant, empty industrial property for six months and listed buildings are exempt until re-occupied; after which full business rates are normally payable. In Scotland empty commercial property is entitled to a 50 per cent discount on business rates for the first three months and a 10 per cent discount thereafter, empty industrial buildings are entitled to full relief for six months and a 10 per cent discount thereafter and empty listed buildings and properties with a rateable value of less than £1,700 are entirely exempt. In Northern Ireland all vacant non-domestic property, which has been previously occupied for at least six weeks, is entirely exempt from rates for three months, after this period, rates are billed at 50 per cent of the normal occupied amount.

COMPLAINTS

In England the Local Government and Social Care Ombudsman investigates complaints of injustice arising from maladministration by local authorities about most council services, including planning, some housing issues, social care, some education and schools issues, children's services, housing benefit, council tax, transport and highways, environment and waste, neighbour nuisance and antisocial behaviour and service failure by local authorities, schools and all registered social care providers, including all adult social care complaints. The Local Government Ombudsman will not usually consider a complaint unless the local authority concerned has had an opportunity to investigate and reply to a complainant.

The functions of the Local Government Ombudsman for Wales were subsumed into the office of Public Services Ombudsman for Wales on 1 April 2006 and the Scottish Public Services Ombudsman is responsible for complaints regarding the maladministration of local government in Scotland.

The Office of Northern Ireland Public Services Ombudsman (NIPSO) was established in April 2016, replacing and expanding the functions of the Northern Ireland Assembly Ombudsman and Commissioner for Complaints. NIPSO provides an independent review of complaints of members of the public, where they believe they have sustained an injustice or hardship as a result or inaction of a public service provider. NIPSO additionally ensures that public services improve as a result of the complaints brought to them by the public. The professional, independent and impartial service is provided free of charge to the citizens of Northern Ireland.

LOCAL GOVERNMENT AND SOCIAL CARE
OMBUDSMAN, PO Box 4771, Coventry CV4 0EH
T 0300-061 0614 W www.lgo.org.uk
Ombudsman, Michael King
PUBLIC SERVICES OMBUDSMAN FOR WALES, 1 Ffordd
yr Hen Gae, Pencoed CF35 5LJ T 0300-790 0203
E ask@ombudsman.wales W www.ombudsman-wales.org.uk
Ombudsman, Nick Bennett

SCOTTISH PUBLIC SERVICES OMBUDSMAN, Bridgeside
House, 99 McDonald Road, Edinburgh EH7 4NS
T 0800-377 7330 E ask@spso.org.scot W www.spso.org.uk
Ombudsman, Rosemary Agnew
NORTHERN IRELAND PUBLIC SERVICES
OMBUDSMAN, Progressive House, 33 Wellington Place,
Belfast BT1 6HN T 028-9023 3821 E nipso@nipso.org.uk
W www.nipso.org.uk
Ombudsman, Margaret Kelly

THE QUEEN'S REPRESENTATIVES

The lord-lieutenant of a county is the permanent local representative of the Crown in that county. The appointment of lord-lieutenants is now regulated by the Lieutenancies Act 1997. They are appointed by the sovereign on the recommendation of the prime minister. The retirement age is 75. The office of lord-lieutenant dates from 1551, and its holder was originally responsible for maintaining order and for local defence in the county. The duties of the post include attending on royalty during official visits to the county, performing certain duties in connection with the armed forces (and in particular the reserve forces), and making presentations of honours and awards on behalf of the Crown. In England, Wales and Northern Ireland, the lord-lieutenant usually also holds the office of *Custos Rotulorum.* As such, he or she acts as head of the county's commission of the peace (which recommends the appointment of magistrates).

The office of sheriff (from the Old English *shire-reeve*) of a county was created in the tenth century. The sheriff was the special nominee of the sovereign, and the office reached the peak of its influence under the Norman kings. The Provisions of Oxford (1258) laid down a yearly tenure of office. Since the mid-16th century the office has been purely civil, with military duties taken over by the lord-lieutenant of the county. The sheriff (commonly known as 'high sheriff') attends on royalty during official visits to the county, acts as the returning officer during parliamentary elections in county constituencies, attends the opening ceremony when a high court judge goes on circuit, executes high court writs, and appoints under-sheriffs to act as deputies. The appointments and duties of the sheriffs in England and Wales are laid down by the Sheriffs Act 1887.

The serving high sheriff submits a list of names of possible future sheriffs to a tribunal, which chooses three names to put to the sovereign. The tribunal nominates the high sheriff annually on 12 November and the sovereign picks the name of the sheriff to succeed in the following year. The term of office runs from 25 March to the following 24 March (the civil and legal year before 1752). No person may be chosen twice in three years if there is any other suitable person in the county.

CIVIC DIGNITIES

District councils in England and local councils in Wales may petition for a royal charter granting borough or 'city' status to the council.

In England and Wales the chair of a borough or county borough council may be called a mayor, and the chair of a city council may be called a lord mayor (if lord mayoralty has been conferred on that city). Parish councils in England and community councils in Wales may call themselves 'town councils', in which case their chair is the town mayor.

In Scotland the chair of a local council may be known as a convenor; a provost is the mayoral equivalent. The chair of the councils for the cities of Aberdeen, Dundee, Edinburgh and Glasgow are lord provosts.

ENGLAND

The country of England lies between 55° 46′ and 49° 57′ 30″ N. latitude (from a few miles north of the mouth of the Tweed to the Lizard), and between 1° 46′ E. and 5° 43′ W. longitude (from Lowestoft to Land's End). England is bounded on the north by the Cheviot Hills; on the south by the English Channel; on the east by the Straits of Dover (Pas de Calais) and the North Sea; and on the west by the Atlantic Ocean, Wales and the Irish Sea. It has a total area of 130,309 sq. km (50,313 sq. miles).

There are currently 339 local authorities, divided into 25 county councils, 188 district councils, 56 unitary authorities (including the Isles of Scilly), and 126 single-tier authorities including 36 metropolitan boroughs and 33 London Boroughs (including the Corporation of London). *See* Local Government, London for information on London Borough councils and the Corporation of London.

POPULATION
The population at the mid-2019 estimate was 56,286,961 (27,827,831 males; 28,459,130 females), a 0.55 per cent increase on mid-2018. The average density of the population at the mid-2019 estimate was 432 persons per sq. km (1,113 per sq. mile).

The populations of most of the unitary authorities are in the range of 100,000 to 500,000. The district councils have populations broadly in the range of 60,000 to 200,000; some, however, have larger populations, because of the need to avoid dividing large towns, or because they were formed from the merger of multiple district councils, and some in mainly rural areas have smaller populations.

The main conurbations outside Greater London – Tyne and Wear, West Midlands, Merseyside, Greater Manchester, West Yorkshire and South Yorkshire – are divided into 36 metropolitan boroughs, most of which have a population of over 200,000.

ELECTIONS
For districts, counties and for around 9,000 towns and parishes, there are elected councils, consisting of directly elected councillors. The councillors elect one of their number as chair annually.

In general, councils can have whole council elections, elections by thirds or elections by halves. However all metropolitan authorities must hold elections by thirds. The electoral cycle of any new unitary authority is specified in the appropriate statutory order under which it is established.

COMBINED AUTHORITIES
Under the Cities and Local Government Devolution Act 2016, multiple local authorities can combine and take on more functions, over and above those they were allowed to take on under previous legislation. In order for a combined or 'regional' authority to be given these extra powers a mayor must be elected for the region by the electorate in the combined-authority area. The first six combined authority mayoral elections took place in May 2017.

The exact functions the combined authority and mayor manage varies depending on the devolution agreement reached with central government, but the directly elected 'metro' mayor does have powers and responsibilities to make strategic decisions across whole city regions. This is in contrast to existing city mayors (which are also directly elected) or local council leaders that only make decisions for, and on behalf of, their local authority.

On 2 November 2018, the North East combined authority was divided into two. The boundaries of the re-constituted North East combined authority now cover the local authorities of Durham, Gateshead, South Tyneside and Sunderland, while the boundaries of the newly created North of Tyne combined authority cover the local authorities of Newcastle, North Tyneside and Northumberland. As at July 2019, ten combined authorities had been established, eight of which have a mayor and a devolution agreement with national government. The combined authorities comprise constituent and non-constituent councils and other local authorities. Constituent councils have full voting rights and cannot be a member of another combined authority. Non-constituent councils usually have restricted voting rights, although this decision rests with the combined authority. In addition, non-constituent councils can be a member of more than one combined authority, as long as this is also on a non-constituent basis. *See* the list of Combined Authorities for details of the devolved regions, their mayors and constituent councils.

COUNCIL FUNCTIONS
In areas with a two-tier system of local governance, functions are divided between the district and county authorities, with those functions affecting the larger area or population generally being the responsibility of the county council. A few functions continue to be exercised over the larger area by joint bodies, made up of councillors from each authority within the area.

Generally the allocation of functions is as follows:

County councils: education; strategic planning; traffic, transport and highways; fire service; consumer protection; refuse disposal; smallholdings; social care; libraries

District councils: local planning; housing; highways (maintenance of certain urban roads and off-street car parks); building regulations; environmental health; refuse collection; cemeteries and crematoria; collection of council tax and non-domestic rates

Unitary and metropolitan councils: their functions are all those listed above, except that the fire service is exercised by a joint body

Concurrently by county and district councils: recreation (parks, playing fields, swimming pools); museums; encouragement of the arts, tourism and industry

PARISH COUNCILS
Parish or town councils are the most local tier of government in England. There are currently 10,219 parishes in England, of which 8,859 have councils. Since February 2008 local councils have been able to create new parish councils without seeking approval from the government. Around 80 per cent of parish councils represent populations of less than 2,500; parishes with no parish council can be grouped with neighbouring parishes under a common parish council. A parish council comprises at least five members, the number being fixed by the district council. Elections are held every four years, at the time of the election of the district councillor for the ward including the parish. Full parish councils must be formed for those parishes with more than 999 electors – below this number, parish meetings comprising the electors of the parish must be held at least twice a year.

Parish council functions include: allotments; encouragement of arts and crafts; community halls, recreational facilities (for example open spaces, swimming pools), cemeteries and crematoria; and many minor functions. They must also be given an opportunity to comment on planning applications. They may, like county and district councils, spend limited sums for the general benefit of the parish. They levy a precept on the district councils for their funds. Parish precepts for 2020–21 total £580m, an increase of 2.9 per cent on 2019–20.

FINANCE

Total revenue expenditure by all local authorities in England for 2020-21 was £102.4bn; of this £33.1bn was estimated to be raised through council tax, £16.5bn from the business rate retention scheme and £51.5bn from government grants. The remainder will be derived from additional COVID-19 government grants, and also drawn from local authority reserves.

Since April 2013 local authorities retain a share of business rates and keep the growth on that share (the 'rate retention scheme'). Revenue support grant is paid to local authorities to enable all authorities in the same class to broadly set the same council tax; in 2020–21 revenue support grant totals £1.6bn. In addition central government pays specific grants in support of revenue expenditure on particular services. Police grant totals £7.9bn in 2020–21. In 2020–21, local authorities' allocated adult social care expenditure increased by £568m on 2019–20, to £17.7bn, and children's social care rose by £529m to £9.8bn.

In response to COVID-19 the government introduced several additional grants in 2020–21, including £3.2bn of emergency funding and £5bn of cashflow support, a £500m hardship fund, and grants to small businesses worth £12.3bn.

In England, the average council tax per dwelling for 2020–21 is £1,385, an increase of 4.4 per cent from 2019–20. The average council tax bill for a Band D dwelling (occupied by two adults, including adult social care and parish precepts) for 2020–21 is £1,818, an increase of 3.9 per cent from 2019–20. The average Band D council tax is £1,895 in shire districts, £1,809 in metropolitan areas, £1,886 in unitary authority areas and £1,534 in London.

The non-domestic rating multiplier for England for 2020–21 is 51.2p (49.9p for small businesses). The City of London is able to set a different multiplier from the rest of England; for 2019–20 this is 52p (50.7p for small businesses).

Under the Local Government and Housing Act 1989, local authorities have four main ways of paying for capital expenditure: borrowing and other forms of extended credit; capital grants from central government towards some types of capital expenditure; 'usable' capital receipts from the sale of land, houses and other assets; and revenue.

The amount of capital expenditure which a local authority can finance by borrowing (or other forms of credit) is effectively limited by the credit approvals issued to it by central government. Most credit approvals can be used for any kind of local authority capital expenditure; these are known as basic credit approvals. Others (supplementary credit approvals) can be used only for the kind of expenditure specified in the approval, and so are often given to fund particular projects or services.

Local authorities can use all capital receipts from the sale of property or assets for capital spending, except in the case of sales of council houses. Generally, the 'usable' part of a local authority's capital receipts consists of 25 per cent of receipts from the sale of council houses and 50 per cent of other housing assets such as shops or vacant land. The balance has to be set aside as provision for repaying debt and meeting other credit liabilities.

EXPENDITURE

Budgeted revenue expenditure for 2020–21 is:

Service	£ million
Education	34,349
Highways and transport	3,915
Children's social care	9,814
Adult social care	17,686
Public health	3,313
Housing (excluding HRA)	1,864
Cultural	2,189
Environmental	5,414
Planning & development	1,378
Police	12,986
Fire and rescue	2,284
Central	3,066
Other	525
Total Service Expenditure	98,782
*Housing benefits	15,899
Parish precepts	580
†Levies & trading account and other adjustments	(522)
Total Net Current Expenditure	114,735
Non-current Expenditure and External Receipts	
Capital expenditure charged to revenue account	1,665
Housing benefits subsidies	(15,857)
Community infrastructure levy	(120)
Capital financing and debt servicing	4,894
REVENUE EXPENDITURE	102,389

HRA = Housing Revenue Account
* Includes all mandatory and non-mandatory housing benefits
† Includes Integrated Transport Authority levy, Waste Disposal Authority levy, London Pensions Fund Authority levy and other levies

RELIEF

There is a marked division between the upland and lowland areas of England. In the extreme north the Cheviot Hills (highest point, the Cheviot, 815m/2,674ft) form a natural boundary with Scotland. Running south from the Cheviots, though divided from them by the Tyne Gap, is the Pennine range (highest point, Cross Fell, 893m/2,930ft), the main orological feature of the country. The Pennines culminate in the Peak District of Derbyshire (Kinder Scout, 636m/2,088ft). West of the Pennines are the Cumbrian mountains, which include Scafell Pike (978m/3,210ft), the highest peak in England, and to the east are the Yorkshire Moors, their highest point being Urra Moor (454m/1,490ft).

In the west, the foothills of the Welsh mountains extend into the bordering English counties of Shropshire (the Wrekin, 407m/1,334ft; Long Mynd, 516m/1,694ft) and Hereford and Worcester (the Malvern Hills – Worcestershire Beacon, 425m/1,394ft). Extensive areas of highland and moorland are also to be found in the south-western peninsula formed by Somerset, Devon and Cornwall, principally Exmoor (Dunkery Beacon, 519m/1,704ft), Dartmoor (High Willhays, 621m/2,038ft) and Bodmin Moor (Brown Willy, 420m/1,377ft). Ranges of low, undulating hills run across the south of the country, including the Cotswolds in the Midlands and south-west, the Chilterns to the north of London, and the North (Kent) and South (Sussex) Downs of the south-east coastal areas.

The lowlands of England lie in the Vale of York, East Anglia and the area around the Wash. The lowest-lying are the Cambridgeshire Fens in the valleys of the Great Ouse and the river Nene, which are below sea-level in places. Since the 17th century extensive drainage has brought much of the Fens under cultivation. The North Sea coast between the Thames and the Humber, low-lying and formed of sand and shingle for the most part, is subject to erosion and defences against further incursion have been built along many stretches.

HYDROGRAPHY

The Severn is the longest river in Great Britain, rising on the north-eastern slopes of Plynlimon (Wales) and entering England in Shropshire, with a total length of 354km (220 miles) from its source to its outflow into the Bristol Channel, where it receives the Bristol Avon on the east and the Wye on the west; its other tributaries are the Vyrnwy, Tern, Stour, Teme and Upper (or Warwickshire) Avon. The Severn is tidal below Gloucester, and a high bore or tidal wave sometimes reverses the flow as high as Tewkesbury (21.75km/13.5 miles above Gloucester). The Severn Tunnel was begun in 1873 and completed in 1886 at a cost of £2m and after many difficulties caused by flooding. It is 7km (4 miles 628 yards) in length (of which 3.67km/2.25 miles are under the river). The Severn road bridge between Haysgate, Gwent, and Almondsbury, Glos, with a centre span of 988m (3,240ft), was opened in 1966.

The longest river wholly in England is the Thames, with a total length of 346km (215 miles) from its source in the Cotswold hills to the Nore. The Thames is tidal to Teddington (111km/69 miles from its mouth) and forms county boundaries almost throughout its course; on its banks are situated London, Windsor Castle, Eton College and Oxford University. Of the remaining English rivers, those flowing into the North Sea are the Tyne, Wear, Tees, Ouse and Trent from the Pennine Range, the Great Ouse (257km/160 miles), which rises in Northamptonshire, and the Orwell and Stour from the hills of East Anglia. Flowing into the English Channel are the Sussex Ouse from the Weald, the Itchen from the Hampshire hills, and the Axe, Teign, Dart, Tamar and Exe from the Devonian hills. Flowing into the Irish Sea are the Mersey, Ribble and Eden from the western slopes of the Pennines and the Derwent from the Cumbrian mountains.

The English Lakes, notable for their picturesque scenery and poetic associations, lie in Cumbria's Lake District, designated a UNESCO World Heritage Site in 2017 for its cultural significance. The largest lakes are Windermere (14.7 sq. km/5.7 sq. miles), Ullswater (8.8 sq. km/3.4 sq. miles) and Derwent Water (5.3 sq. km/2.0 sq. miles).

FLAG

The flag of England is the cross of St George, a red cross on a white field (cross gules in a field argent). The cross of St George, the patron saint of England, has been used since the 13th century.

ISLANDS

The Isle of Wight is separated from Hampshire by the Solent. The capital, Newport, stands at the head of the estuary of the Medina, and Cowes (at the mouth) is the chief port. Other centres are Ryde, Sandown, Shanklin, Ventnor, Freshwater, Yarmouth, Totland Bay, Seaview and Bembridge.

Lundy (the name is derived from the Old Norse for 'puffin island'), 18km (11 miles) north-west of Hartland Point, Devon, is around 5km (3 miles) long and almost 1km (half a mile) wide on average, with a total area of around 452 hectares (1,116 acres), and a population of 28. It became the property of the National Trust in 1969 and is financed, administered and maintained by the Landmark Trust. Lundy is principally a bird sanctuary; the waters around the island were formerly designated as a marine conservation zone in 2013.

The Isles of Scilly comprise around 140 islands and skerries (total area, 10 sq. km/6 sq. miles) situated 45 km (28 miles) south-west of Land's End in Cornwall. Only five are inhabited: St Mary's, St Agnes, Bryher, Tresco and St Martin's. The 2019 mid-year population estimate was 2,242. The entire group has been designated an Area of Outstanding Natural Beauty because of its unique flora and fauna. Tourism and the winter/spring flower trade for the home market form the basis of the economy of the islands.

EARLY HISTORY

Archaeological evidence suggests that England has been inhabited since at least the Palaeolithic period, though the extent of the various Palaeolithic cultures was dependent upon the degree of glaciation. The succeeding Neolithic and Bronze Age cultures have left abundant remains throughout the country; the best-known of these are the henges and stone circles of Stonehenge (ten miles north of Salisbury, Wilts) and Avebury (Wilts). In the latter part of the Bronze Age the Goidels, a people of the Celtic race, invaded the country and brought with them Celtic civilisation and dialects; as a result place names in England bear witness to the spread of the invasion across the whole region.

THE ROMAN CONQUEST

The Roman conquest of Gaul (57–50 BC) brought Britain into close contact with Roman civilisation, but although Julius Caesar raided the south of Britain in 55 and 54 BC, conquest was not undertaken until nearly 100 years later. In AD 43 the Emperor Claudius dispatched Aulus Plautius, with a well-equipped force of 40,000, and himself followed with reinforcements in the same year. Success was delayed by the resistance of Caratacus (Caractacus), the British leader from AD 48–51, who was finally captured and sent to Rome, and by a great revolt in AD 61 led by Boudicca (Boadicea), Queen of the Iceni, but the south of Britain was secured by AD 70, and Wales and the area north to the Tyne by about AD 80.

In AD 122, the Emperor Hadrian visited Britain and built a continuous rampart, since known as Hadrian's Wall, from Wallsend to Bowness (Tyne to Solway). The work was entrusted by the Emperor Hadrian to Aulus Platorius Nepos, legate of Britain from AD 122 to 126, and it was intended to form the northern frontier of the Roman Empire.

The Romans administered Britain as a province under a governor, with a well-defined system of local government, each Roman municipality ruling itself and its surrounding territory, while London was the centre of the road system and the seat of the financial officials of the Province of Britain. Colchester, Lincoln, York, Gloucester and St Albans stand on the sites of five Roman municipalities, and Wroxeter, Caerleon, Chester, Lincoln and York were at various times the sites of legionary fortresses. Well-preserved Roman towns have been uncovered at or near Silchester (Calleva Atrebatum), ten miles south of Reading, Wroxeter (Viroconium Cornoviorum), near Shrewsbury and St Albans (Verulamium) in Hertfordshire.

Four main groups of roads radiated from London, and a fifth (the Fosse) ran obliquely from Lincoln through Leicester, Cirencester and Bath to Exeter. Of the four groups radiating from London, one ran south-east to Canterbury and the coast of Kent, a second to Silchester and thence to parts of western Britain and south Wales, a third (later known as Watling Street) ran through St Albans to Chester, with various branches, and the fourth reached Colchester, Lincoln, York and the eastern counties.

In the fourth century Britain was subjected to raids along the east coast by Saxon pirates, which led to the establishment of a system of coastal defences from the Wash to Southampton Water, with forts at Brancaster, Burgh Castle (Yarmouth), Walton (Felixstowe), Bradwell, Reculver, Richborough, Dover, Lympne, Pevensey and Porchester (Portsmouth). The Irish (Scoti) and Picts in the north were also becoming more aggressive and from around AD 350 incursions became more frequent and more formidable. As the Roman Empire came increasingly under attack towards the end of the fourth century, many troops were removed from Britain for service in other parts of the empire. The island was eventually cut off from Rome by the Teutonic conquest of Gaul, and with the withdrawal of the last Roman garrison early in the fifth century, the Romano-British were left to themselves.

SAXON SETTLEMENT
According to legend, the British King Vortigern called in the Saxons to defend his lands against the Picts. The Saxon chieftains Hengist and Horsa landed at Ebbsfleet, Kent, and established themselves in the Isle of Thanet, but the events during the one-and-a-half centuries between the final break with Rome and the re-establishment of Christianity are unclear. However, it would appear that over the course of this period the raids turned into large-scale settlement by invaders traditionally known as Angles (England north of the Wash and East Anglia), Saxons (Essex and southern England) and Jutes (Kent and the Weald), which pushed the Romano-British into the mountainous areas of the north and west. Celtic culture outside Wales and Cornwall survives only in topographical names. Various kingdoms established at this time attempted to claim overlordship of the whole country, hegemony finally being achieved by Wessex (with the capital at Winchester) in the ninth century. This century also saw the beginning of raids by the Vikings (Danes), which were resisted by Alfred the Great (871–899), who fixed a limit on the advance of Danish settlement by the Treaty of Wedmore (878), giving them the area north and east of Watling Street on the condition that they adopt Christianity.

In the tenth century the kings of Wessex recovered the whole of England from the Danes, but subsequent rulers were unable to resist a second wave of invaders. England paid tribute *(Danegeld)* for many years, and was invaded in 1013 by the Danes and ruled by Danish kings (including Cnut) from 1016 until 1042, when Edward the Confessor was recalled from exile in Normandy. On Edward's death in 1066 Harold Godwinson (brother-in-law of Edward and son of Earl Godwin of Wessex) was chosen to be King of England. After defeating (at Stamford Bridge, Yorkshire, 25 September 1066) an invading army under Harald Hadraada, King of Norway (aided by the outlawed Earl Tostig of Northumbria, Harold's brother), Harold was himself defeated at the Battle of Hastings on 14 October 1066, and the Norman conquest secured the throne of England for Duke William of Normandy, a cousin of Edward the Confessor.

CHRISTIANITY
Christianity reached the Roman province of Britain from Gaul in the third century (or possibly earlier). Alban, traditionally Britain's first martyr, was put to death as a Christian during the persecution of Diocletian (22 June 303) at his native town *Verulamium,* and the bishops of *Londinium, Eboracum* (York), and *Lindum* (Lincoln) attended the Council of Arles in 314. However, the Anglo-Saxon invasions submerged the Christian religion in England until the sixth century: conversion was undertaken in the north from 563 by Celtic missionaries from Ireland led by St Columba, and in the south by a mission sent from Rome in 597 which was led by St Augustine, who became the first archbishop of Canterbury. England appears to have been converted again by the end of the seventh century and followed, after the Council of Whitby in 663, the practices of the Roman Church, which brought the kingdom into the mainstream of European thought and culture.

PRINCIPAL CITIES

There are 51 cities in England and space constraints prevent us from including profiles of them all. Below is a selection of England's principal cities with the date on which city status was conferred in parentheses. Other cities are Bradford (pre-1900), Chelmsford (2012), Chichester (pre-1900), Coventry (pre-1900), Derby (1977), Ely (pre-1900), Exeter (pre-1900), Gloucester (pre-1900), Hereford (pre-1900), Kingston-upon-Hull (pre-1900), Lancaster (1937), Lichfield (pre-1900), London (pre-1900), Peterborough (pre-1900), Plymouth (1928), Portsmouth (1926), Preston (2002), Ripon (pre-1900), Salford (1926), Stoke-on-Trent (1925), Sunderland (1992), Truro (pre-1900), Wakefield (pre-1900), Wells (pre-1900), Westminster (pre-1900), Wolverhampton (2000) and Worcester (pre-1900).

Certain cities have also been granted a lord mayoralty – this grant confers no additional powers or functions and is purely honorific. Cities with lord mayors are Birmingham, Bradford, Bristol, Canterbury, Chester, Coventry, Exeter, Kingston-upon-Hull, Leeds, Leicester, Liverpool, London, Manchester, Newcastle-upon-Tyne, Norwich, Nottingham, Oxford, Plymouth, Portsmouth, Sheffield, Stoke-on-Trent, Westminster and York.

BATH (PRE-1900)
Bath stands on the river Avon between the Cotswold Hills to the north and the Mendips to the south, and was originally a small roman town *(Aquae Sulis)* with a baths and temple complex built around naturally occurring hot springs. In the early 18th century Bath became England's premier spa town where the rich and celebrated members of fashionable society gathered to 'take the waters' and enjoy the town's theatres and concert rooms. During this period the architect John Wood laid the foundations of a new Georgian city built using the honey-coloured stone for which Bath is famous today. Since 1987 the city has been listed as a UNESCO World Heritage Site.

Contemporary Bath is a thriving tourist destination and remains a leading cultural, religious and historical centre with many art galleries and historic sites including the Pump Room (1790); the Royal Crescent (1767); the Circus (1754); the 18th-century Assembly Rooms (housing the Museum of Costume); Pulteney Bridge (1771); the Guildhall and the Abbey, now over 500 years old, which is built on the site of a Saxon monastery. In 2006 the Bath Thermae Spa was completed and the hot springs reopened to the public for the first time since 1978.

BIRMINGHAM (PRE-1900)
Birmingham is Britain's second largest city, with a population of over one million. The generally accepted derivation of 'Birmingham' is the *ham* (dwelling-place) of the *ing* (family) of *Beorma,* presumed to have been Saxon. During the Industrial Revolution the town grew into a major manufacturing centre, known as the 'city of a thousand trades', and in 1889 was granted city status. By the 18th century, Birmingham was the main European producer of items such as buckles, medals and coins. Today, around 40 per cent of all the UK's handmade jewellery is produced in Birmingham's Jewellery Quarter. Another product of the Industrial Revolution are the city's 34 miles (56km) of canals.

Recent developments include Millennium Point, which houses Thinktank, the Birmingham science museum, and Brindleyplace, a development of shops, offices and leisure facilities on a former industrial site clustered around canals. In 2003 the Bullring shopping centre was officially opened as part of the city's urban regeneration programme.

The principal buildings are the Town Hall (1834–50), the Council House (1879), Victoria Law Courts (1891), the University of Birmingham (1906–9), the 13th-century church of St Martin in the Bull Ring (rebuilt 1873), the cathedral (formerly St Philip's Church) (1711), the Roman Catholic cathedral of St Chad (1839–41), the Assay Office (1773), the Rotunda (1964) and the National Exhibition Centre (1976).

BRIGHTON AND HOVE (2000)

Brighton and Hove is situated on the south coast of England, around 96km (60 miles) south of London. Originally a fishing village called Brighthelmstone, it was transformed into a fashionable seaside resort in the 18th century when Dr Richard Russell popularised the benefits of his 'sea-water cure'; as one of the closest beaches to London, Brighton began to attract wealthy visitors. One of these was the Prince Regent (the future King George IV), who first visited in 1783 and became so fond of the city that in 1807 he bought the former farmhouse he had been renting, and gradually turned it into Brighton's most recognisable building, the Royal Pavilion. The Pavilion is renowned for its Indo-Saracenic exterior, featuring minarets and an enormous central dome designed by John Nash, combined with the lavish chinoiserie of Frederick Crace's and Robert Jones' interiors. Queen Victoria sold the Pavilion to Brighton's municipal authority in 1850.

Brighton and Hove's Regency heritage can also be seen in the numerous elegant squares and crescents designed by Amon Wilds and Augustin Busby that dominate the seafront.

BRISTOL (PRE-1900)

Bristol was a royal borough before the Norman conquest. The earliest form of the name is *Bricgstow*. Due to the city's position close to the mouth of the River Avon, it was an important location for marine trade for centuries and prospered greatly from the transatlantic slave trade during the 18th century.

The principal buildings include the 12th-century cathedral with Norman chapter house and gateway; the 14th-century church of St Mary Redcliffe; Wesley's Chapel, Broadmead; the Merchant Venturers' Almshouses; the Council House (1956); the Guildhall; the Exchange (erected from the designs of John Wood in 1743); Cabot Tower; the university and Clifton College.

The Clifton Suspension Bridge, with a span of 214m (702ft) over the Avon, was projected by Isambard Kingdom Brunel in 1836 but was not completed until 1864. Brunel's SS *Great Britain*, the first ocean-going propeller-driven ship, now forms a museum at the western dockyard, from where she was originally launched in 1843. The docks themselves have been extensively restored and redeveloped; the 19th-century two-storey former tea warehouse is now the Arnolfini Centre for Contemporary Arts, and an 18th-century sail-loft houses the Architecture Centre. On Princes Wharf, 1950s transit sheds have been renovated and converted into the museum of Bristol, M Shed, which opened in 2011.

CAMBRIDGE (1951)

Cambridge, a settlement far older than its ancient university, lies on the River Cam (or Granta). Its industries include technology research and development, and biotechnology. Among its open spaces are Jesus Green, Sheep's Green, Coe Fen, Parker's Piece, Christ's Pieces, the University Botanic Garden, and the 'Backs' – lawns and gardens through which the Cam winds behind the principal line of college buildings. Historical sites east of the Cam include King's Parade, Great St Mary's Church, Gibbs' Senate House and King's College Chapel.

University and college buildings provide the outstanding features of Cambridge's architecture but several churches (especially St Bene't's, the oldest building in the city, and Holy Sepulchre or the Round Church) are also notable. The Guildhall (1937) stands on a site of which at least part has held municipal buildings since 1224. In 2009 the University of Cambridge celebrated its 800th anniversary.

CANTERBURY (PRE-1900)

Canterbury, seat of the Archbishop of Canterbury, the primate of the Church of England, dates back to prehistoric times. It was the Roman *Durovernum Cantiacorum* and the Saxon *Cant-wara-byrig* (stronghold of the men of Kent). It was here in 597 that St Augustine began the conversion of the English to Christianity, when Ethelbert, King of Kent, was baptised.

Of the Benedictine St Augustine's Abbey, burial place of the Jutish kings of Kent, only ruins remain. According to Bede, St Martin's Church, on the eastern outskirts of the city, was the place of worship of Queen Bertha, the Christian wife of King Ethelbert, before the advent of St Augustine. In 1170 the rivalry of Church and State culminated in the murder of Archbishop Thomas Becket in Canterbury Cathedral, by Henry II's knights. His shrine became a great centre of pilgrimage, as described in Chaucer's *Canterbury Tales*. After the Reformation pilgrimages ceased, the prosperity of the city was strengthened by an influx of Huguenot refugees, who introduced weaving. The poet and playwright Christopher Marlowe was born and raised in Canterbury and the city is home to the 1,200-seat Marlowe Theatre, which reopened to the public in 2011, following an extensive £25m rebuild.

The cathedral, with its architecture ranging from the 11th to the 15th centuries, is famous worldwide. Visitors are attracted particularly to the Martyrdom, the Black Prince's Tomb and the Warriors' Chapel.

The medieval city walls are built on Roman foundations and the 14th-century West Gate is one of the finest buildings of its kind in the country.

CHESTER (PRE-1900)

Chester is situated on the River Dee. Its recorded history dates from the first century when the Romans founded the fortress of *Deva*. The city's name is derived from the latin *Castra* (a camp or encampment). During the middle ages, Chester was the principal port of north-west England but declined with the silting of the Dee estuary and competition from Liverpool. The city was also an important military centre, notably during Edward I's Welsh campaigns and the Elizabethan Irish campaigns. During the Civil War, Chester supported the king and was besieged from 1643 to 1646. Chester's first charter was granted c.1175 and the city was incorporated in 1506. The office of sheriff is the earliest created in the country (1120s), and in 1992 the mayor, who also enjoys the title 'Admiral of the Dee', was made a lord mayor.

The city's architectural features include the city walls (an almost complete two-mile circuit), the unique 13th-century Rows (covered galleries above the street-level shops), the Victorian Gothic town hall (1869), the castle (rebuilt 1788 and 1822) and numerous half-timbered buildings. The cathedral was a Benedictine abbey until the dissolution of the monasteries. Chester racecourse is the oldest racecourse in Britain, believed to have origins in the 13th century. The first recorded horserace was in 1539 during the reign of Henry VIII. Chester also houses the ruins of a Roman amphitheatre, built in the late first century AD.

DURHAM (PRE-1900)

The city of Durham's prominent Norman cathedral and castle are set high on a wooded peninsula overlooking the River Wear. The cathedral was founded as a shrine for the body of St Cuthbert in 995. The present building dates from 1093 and among its many treasures is the tomb of the Venerable Bede (673–735). Durham's prince bishops had unique powers up to 1836, being lay rulers as well as religious leaders. As a palatinate, Durham could have its own army, nobility, coinage and courts. The castle was the main seat of the prince bishops for nearly 800 years; it is now used as a college by the University of Durham. The university, founded in the early 19th century on the initiative of Bishop William Van Mildert, is England's third oldest.

Annual events include Durham's regatta in June (claimed to be the oldest rowing event in Britain) and the annual Durham

Miners' Gala in July. Durham County Cricket Club was established in 1882.

LEEDS (PRE-1900)

Leeds, situated in the lower Aire valley, was first incorporated by Charles I in 1626. The earliest forms of the name are *Loidis* or *Ledes,* the origins of which are obscure.

The principal buildings are the Civic Hall (1933), the Town Hall (1858), the Municipal Buildings and Art Gallery (1884) with the Henry Moore Gallery (1982), the Corn Exchange (1863) and the university. The parish church of St Peter was rebuilt in 1841 and granted minister status in 2012. The 17th-century St John's Church has a fine interior with a famous English Renaissance screen; the last remaining 18th-century church in the city is Holy Trinity in Boar Lane (1727). Kirkstall Abbey (about three miles from the centre of the city), founded by Henry de Lacy in 1152, is one of the most complete examples of a Cistercian house now remaining. The Royal Armouries Museum forms part of a group of museums that house the national collection of antique arms and armour. The Grand Theatre and Opera House is home to Northern Ballet and Opera North.

LEICESTER (1919)

Leicester is situated in central England. The city was an important Roman settlement and also one of the five 'burghs' or boroughs of the Danelaw. In 1485 Richard III was buried in Leicester following his death at the nearby Battle of Bosworth; his remains were subsequently lost during the sixteenth century but rediscovered underneath a car park in 2012, and reburied at Leicester Cathedral in 2015. In 1589 Queen Elizabeth I granted a charter to the city and the ancient title was confirmed by letters patent in 1919.

The textile industry was responsible for Leicester's early expansion and the city still maintains a strong manufacturing base. Cotton mills and factories are now undergoing extensive regeneration and are being converted into offices, apartments, bars and restaurants. The principal buildings include the two universities (the University of Leicester and De Montfort University), as well as the Town Hall, the 13th-century Guildhall, De Montfort Hall, Leicester Cathedral, the Jewry Wall (the UK's highest standing Roman wall), St Nicholas Church and St Mary de Castro church. The motte and Great Hall of Leicester can be seen from the castle gardens, situated next to the River Soar.

LINCOLN (PRE-1900)

Situated 64km (40 miles) inland on the river Witham, Lincoln derives its name from a contraction of *Lindum Colonia,* the settlement founded in AD 48 by the Romans to command the crossing of Ermine Street and Fosse Way. Sections of the third-century Roman city wall can be seen, including an extant gateway (Newport Arch). The Romans also drained the surrounding fenland and created a canal system, laying the foundations of Lincoln's agricultural prosperity and also the city's importance in the medieval wool trade as a port and staple town.

As one of the five 'burghs' or boroughs of the Danelaw, Lincoln was an important trading centre in the ninth and tenth centuries and prosperity from the wool trade lasted until the 14th century. This wealth enabled local merchants to build parish churches, of which three survive, and there are also remains of a 12th-century Jewish community. However, the removal of the staple to Boston in 1369 heralded a decline, from which the city only recovered fully in the 19th century, when improved fen drainage made Lincoln agriculturally important. Improved canal and rail links led to industrial development, mainly in the manufacture of machinery and engineering products.

The castle was built shortly after the Norman Conquest and is unusual in having two mounds; on one motte stands a keep (Lucy's Tower) added in the 12th century. It currently houses one of the four surviving copies of the Magna Carta. The cathedral was begun *c.*1073 but was mostly destroyed by fire and earthquake in the 12th century. Rebuilding was begun by St Hugh and completed over a century later. It is believed the cathedral was the tallest building in the world between 1311 and 1548, when the central tower spire collapsed and was never rebuilt. Other notable architectural features are the 12th-century High Bridge, the oldest in Britain still to carry buildings, and the Guildhall, situated above the 15th-century Stonebow gateway.

LIVERPOOL (PRE-1900)

Liverpool, on the north bank of the river Mersey, 5km (3 miles) from the Irish Sea, is the UK's foremost port for Atlantic trade.

There are 2,100 acres of dockland on both sides of the river and the Gladstone and Royal Seaforth Docks can accommodate tanker-sized vessels. Liverpool Free Port was opened in 1984.

Liverpool was created a free borough in 1207 and was given city status in 1880. From the early 18th century it expanded rapidly with the growth of industrialisation and the transatlantic slave trade. Surviving buildings from this period include the Bluecoat Chambers (1717, formerly the Bluecoat School), and the Town Hall (1754, rebuilt to the original design 1795). Notable from the 19th and 20th centuries are the Anglican cathedral (built from the designs of Sir Giles Gilbert Scott, it took 74 years to construct), and the Catholic Metropolitan Cathedral (designed by Sir Frederick Gibberd, consecrated 1967). Both of these cathedrals are situated on Hope Street, named after the merchant William Hope, which is the only street in the UK with a cathedral at either end. The refurbished Albert Dock (designed by Jesse Hartley) contains the Merseyside Maritime Museum, the International Slavery Museum, the Beatles Story and the Tate Liverpool art gallery. The Museum of Liverpool opened in 2011.

MANCHESTER (PRE-1900)

Manchester (the *Mamucium* of the Romans, who occupied it in AD 79) is a commercial and industrial centre connected with the sea by the Manchester Ship Canal, 57km (35.5 miles) long, opened in 1894 and accommodating ships up to 15,000 tons. During the Industrial Revolution the city had a thriving cotton industry and by 1853 there were over 100 cotton mills, which dominated the city's landscape.

The principal buildings are the Town Hall, erected in 1877 from the designs of Alfred Waterhouse, with a large extension of 1938; the Royal Exchange (1869, enlarged 1921); the Central Library (1934); Heaton Hall; the 17th-century Chetham Library; the Rylands Library (1900), which includes the Althorp collection; the university precinct; the 15th-century cathedral (formerly the parish church); the Manchester Central conference and exhibition centre and the Bridgewater Hall (1996) concert venue. Manchester is the home of the Hallé Orchestra, the Royal Northern College of Music, the Royal Exchange Theatre and numerous public art galleries.

The town received its first charter of incorporation in 1838 and was created a city in 1853.

NEWCASTLE UPON TYNE (PRE-1900)

Newcastle upon Tyne, on the north bank of the River Tyne, is 13km (8 miles) from the North Sea. A cathedral and university city, it is the administrative, commercial and cultural centre for north-east England and the principal port.

The principal buildings include the Castle Keep (12th century), Black Gate (13th century), Blackfriars (13th century), West Walls (13th century), St Nicholas Cathedral (15th century, fine lantern tower), St Andrew's Church (12th–14th century), St John's (14th–15th century), All Saints (1786 by Stephenson), St Mary's Roman Catholic Cathedral (1844), Trinity House (17th century), Sandhill (16th-century houses), Guildhall (Georgian), Grey Street (1834–9), Central Station (1846–50) and the Central Library (1969). Open spaces include the Town Moor (927 acres).

Numerous bridges span the Tyne at Newcastle, including the Tyne Bridge (1928) and the Tilting Millennium Bridge (2001) which links the city with Gateshead to the south.

The city's name is derived from the 'new castle' (1080) erected as a defence against the Scots. In 1265 defensive walls over two miles in length were built around the city as further protection; parts of these walls remain today and can be found to the west of the city centre.

NORWICH (PRE-1900)

Norwich grew from an early Anglo-Saxon settlement near the confluence of the rivers Yare and Wensum, and now serves as the provincial capital for the predominantly agricultural region of East Anglia. The name is thought to relate to the most northerly of a group of Anglo-Saxon villages or *wics*. The city's first known charter was granted in 1158 by Henry II.

Norwich serves its surrounding area as a market town and commercial centre. From the 14th century until the Industrial Revolution, Norwich was the regional centre of the woollen industry. Now the biggest single industry is financial services and principal trades are engineering, printing and shoemaking. The University of East Anglia is on the city's western boundary and admitted its first students in 1963. Norwich is accessible to seagoing vessels by means of the river Yare, entered at Great Yarmouth, 32km (20 miles) to the east.

Among many historic buildings are the cathedral (completed in the 12th century and surmounted by a 15th-century spire 96m (315ft) in height); the keep of the Norman castle (now a museum and art gallery); the 15th-century flint-walled Guildhall; some 30 medieval parish churches; St Andrew's and Blackfriars' Halls; the Tudor houses preserved in Elm Hill and the Georgian Assembly House.

NOTTINGHAM (PRE-1900)

Nottingham stands on the river Trent. *Snotingaham* or *Notingeham,* the 'homestead of the people of Snot', is the Anglo-Saxon name for the Celtic settlement of *Tigguocobauc,* or the house of caves. In 878, Nottingham became one of the five 'burghs' or boroughs of the Danelaw. William the Conqueror ordered the construction of Nottingham Castle, while the town itself developed rapidly under Norman rule. Its laws and rights were formally recognised by Henry II's charter in 1155. The castle became a favoured residence of King John. In 1642 Charles I raised his personal standard at Nottingham Castle at the start of the Civil War.

Architecturally, Nottingham has a wealth of notable buildings, particularly those designed in the Victorian era by T. C. Hine and Watson Fothergill. The city council owns the castle (of Norman origin but restored in 1878), Wollaton Hall (1580–8), Newstead Abbey (once the home of Lord Byron), the Guildhall (1888) and the Council House (1929). St Mary's, St Peter's and St Nicholas' churches are of interest, as is the Roman Catholic cathedral (Pugin, 1842–4). Nottingham was granted city status in 1897.

OXFORD (PRE-1900)

Oxford is a university city, an important industrial centre and a market town.

Oxford is known for its architecture, its oldest specimens being the reputedly Saxon tower of St Michael's Church, the remains of the Norman castle and city walls, and the Norman church at Iffley. It also has many Gothic buildings, such as the

Divinity Schools, the Old Library at Merton College, William of Wykeham's New College, Magdalen and Christ Church colleges and many other college buildings. Later centuries are represented by the Laudian Quadrangle at St John's College, the Renaissance Sheldonian Theatre by Sir Christopher Wren, Trinity College Chapel, All Saints Church, Hawksmoor's mock-Gothic at All Souls College, and the 18th-century Queen's College. In addition to individual buildings, High Street and Radcliffe Square both form interesting architectural compositions. Most of the colleges have gardens, those of Magdalen, New College, St John's and Worcester being the largest.

The Oxford University Museum of Natural History, renowned for its spectacular neo-Gothic architecture, houses the university's scientific collections of zoological, entomological and geological specimens and is attached to the neighbouring Pitt Rivers Museum, which houses ethnographic and archaeological objects from around the world. The Ashmolean is the city's museum of art and archaeology and Modern Art Oxford hosts a programme of contemporary art exhibitions.

ST ALBANS (PRE-1900)

The origins of St Albans, situated on the river Ver, stem from the Roman town of *Verulamium.* Named after the first Christian martyr in Britain, who was executed there, St Albans has developed around the Norman abbey and the cathedral church (consecrated 1115), which was built partly of materials from the old Roman city. The museums house Iron Age and Roman artefacts and the Roman theatre, unique in Britain, has a stage as opposed to an amphitheatre. Archaeological excavations in the city centre have revealed evidence of pre-Roman, Saxon and medieval occupation.

The town's significance grew to the extent that it was a signatory and venue for the drafting of the Magna Carta. It was also the scene of riots during the Peasants' Revolt, the French King John was imprisoned there after the Battle of Poitiers, and heavy fighting took place there during the Wars of the Roses.

Previously controlled by the Abbot, the town achieved a charter in 1553 and city status in 1877. The street market, first established in 1553, is still an important feature of the city, as are many hotels and inns, surviving from the days when St Albans was an important coach stop. St Albans is also noted for its clock tower, built between 1403 and 1412, the only remaining medieval town belfry in England.

SALISBURY (PRE-1900)

The history of Salisbury centres around the cathedral and cathedral close. The city evolved from an Iron Age camp a mile to the north of its current position which was strengthened by the Romans and called *Serviodunum.* The Normans built a castle and cathedral on the site and renamed it Sarum. In 1220 Bishop Richard Poore and the architect Elias de Derham decided to build a new Gothic-style cathedral. The cathedral was completed 38 years later and a community known as New Sarum, now called Salisbury, grew around it. Originally the cathedral had a squat tower; the 123m (404ft) spire that makes the cathedral the tallest medieval structure in the world was added c.1315. A walled close with houses for the clergy was built around the cathedral; the Medieval Hall still stands today, alongside buildings dating from the 13th to the 20th century, including some designed by Sir Christopher Wren.

A prosperous wool and cloth trade allowed Salisbury to flourish until the 17th century. When the wool trade declined new crafts were established, including cutlery, leather and basket work, saddlery, lacemaking, joinery and malting. By 1750 it had become an important road junction and coaching centre and in the Victorian era the railways enabled a new age of expansion and prosperity.

SHEFFIELD (PRE-1900)

Sheffield is situated at the confluence of the rivers Sheaf, Porter, Rivelin and Loxley with the river Don and was created a city in 1893.

The parish church of St Peter and St Paul, founded in the 12th century, became the cathedral church of the diocese of Sheffield in 1914. The Roman Catholic Cathedral Church of St Marie (founded 1847) was made a cathedral for the new diocese of Hallam in 1980; parts of the present building date from c.1435. The principal buildings are the Town Hall (1897), the Cutlers' Hall (1832), City Hall (1932), Graves Art Gallery (1934), and the Millennium Gallery (2001). The Grade II listed Park Hill housing estate was built between 1957 and 1961, and renovation work is set to be completed in 2022. The City Museum and Mappin Art Gallery (1874) reopened to the public as the Weston Park Museum in 2006 after undergoing a major £19m redevelopment, housing Sheffield's archaeology, natural history, art and social history collections, it underwent further refurbishment in 2016.

The restored Lyceum Theatre, which dates from 1897, reopened in 1990 and The Crucible Theatre (1971), famous for hosting the World Snooker Championship, was refurbished between 2007 and 2009 and officially reopened in 2010. Three major sporting and entertainment venues were opened between 1990 and 1991: Sheffield Arena, now FlyDSA Arena, and Ponds Forge, which houses an Olympic sized swimming pool and the UK's deepest diving pool, home to the GB Diving Squad. The Don Valley Stadium, completed in 1990, was demolished in 2013 and the site redeveloped as the Olympic Legacy Park, which includes a research centre, sport centre and educational facilities for local universities, opened in 2018. The Leadmill, Sheffield's longest-running independent live music venue, opened in 1980.

SOUTHAMPTON (1964)

Southampton is a major seaport on the south coast of England, situated between the mouths of the Test and Itchen rivers. Southampton's natural deep-water harbour has made the area an important settlement since the Romans built the first port (known as *Clausentum*) in the first century, and Southampton's port has witnessed several important departures, including those of Henry V in 1415 for the Battle of Agincourt, the *Mayflower* in 1620, and the RMS *Titanic* in 1912.

The city's strategic importance, not only as a seaport but also as a centre for aircraft production, meant that it was heavily bombed during the Second World War. However, many historically significant structures remain, including the Wool House, dating from 1417 and now used as the Maritime Museum; parts of the Norman city walls, which are among the most complete in the UK; the Bargate, which was originally the main gateway into the city; God's House Tower, now the Museum of Archaeology; St Michael's, the city's oldest church; and the Tudor Merchants Hall.

WINCHESTER (PRE-1900)

Winchester, the ancient capital of England, is situated on the river Itchen. The city is rich in architecture of all types, and especially notable is the cathedral. Built in 1079–93 the cathedral exhibits examples of Norman, early English and Perpendicular styles and is the burial place of author Jane Austen. Winchester College, founded in 1382, is one of the country's most famous public schools, and the original building (1393) remains largely unaltered. St Cross Hospital, another great medieval foundation, lies one mile south of the city. The almshouses were founded in 1136 by Bishop Henry de Blois, and Cardinal Henry Beaufort added a new almshouse of 'Noble Poverty' in 1446. The chapel and dwellings are of great architectural interest, and visitors may still receive the 'Wayfarer's Dole' of bread and ale, a tradition now 900 years old.

Excavations have done much to clarify the origins and development of Winchester. Part of the forum and several of the streets from the Roman town have been discovered. Excavations in the cathedral close have uncovered the entire site of the Anglo-Saxon cathedral (known as the Old Minster) and parts of the New Minster which was built by Alfred the Great's son, Edward the Elder, and is the burial place of the Alfredian dynasty. The original burial place of St Swithun, before his remains were translated to a site in the present cathedral, was also uncovered.

Excavations in other parts of the city have cast much light on Norman Winchester, notably on the site of the Royal Castle (adjacent to which the new Law Courts have been built) and in the grounds of Wolvesey Castle, where the great house built by bishops Giffard and Henry de Blois in the 12th century has been uncovered. The Great Hall, built by Henry III between 1222 and 1236, survives and houses the Arthurian Round Table.

YORK (PRE-1900)

The city of York is an archiepiscopal seat. Its recorded history dates from AD 71, when the Roman Ninth Legion established a base under Petilius Cerealis that would later become the fortress of *Eburacum*, or *Eboracum*. In Anglo-Saxon times the city was the royal and ecclesiastical centre of Northumbria, and after capture by a Viking army in AD 866 it became the capital of the Viking kingdom of Jorvik. By the 14th century the city had become a great mercantile centre, mainly because of its control of the wool trade, and was used as the chief base against the Scots. Under the Tudors its fortunes declined, although Henry VIII made it the headquarters of the Council of the North. Excavations on many sites, including Coppergate, have greatly expanded knowledge of Roman, Viking and medieval urban life. The JORVIK Viking Centre (reopened in 2017) takes visitors on a journey through a reconstructed 10th century Viking-age York.

The city is rich in examples of architecture of all periods. The earliest church was built in AD 627 and, from the 12th to 15th centuries, the present Minster was built in a succession of styles.

LORD-LIEUTENANTS AND HIGH SHERIFFS

Area	Lord-Lieutenant	High Sheriff (2020–21)
Bedfordshire	Helen Nellis	Susana Lousada
Berkshire	James Puxley	Mary Riall
Bristol	Peaches Golding, OBE	Dr John Manley
Buckinghamshire	Sir Henry Aubrey-Fletcher, Bt., KCVO	Andrew Farncombe
Cambridgeshire	Julie Spence, OBE, QPM	Brig. Tim Seal, TD
Cheshire	David Briggs, MBE	Nick Hopkinson, MBE
Cornwall	Col. Edward Bolitho, OBE	Kate Holborow
Cumbria	Claire Hensman	Julie Barton
Derbyshire	Elizabeth Fothergill, CBE	Tony Walker, CBE
Devon	David Fursdon	Gerald Hine-Haycock
Dorset	Angus Campbell	George Streatfeild
Durham	Susan Snowden	David Gray
East Riding of Yorkshire	James Dick, OBE	Andrew Horncastle, MBE
East Sussex	Peter Field	Andrew Blackman
Essex	Jennifer Tolhurst	Julie Fosh
Gloucestershire	Edward Gillespie, OBE	Helen Lovatt
Greater London	Sir Kenneth Olisa, OBE	John Garbutt
Greater Manchester	Sir Warren Smith, KVCO	Dr Eamonn O'Neal
Hampshire	Nigel Atkinson	Revd Sue Colman
Herefordshire	Edward Harley, OBE	Patricia Thomas
Hertfordshire	Robert Voss, CBE	The Hon. Henry Holland-Hibbert
Isle of Wight	Susan Sheldon	Caroline Peel
Kent	Lady Annabel Colgrain of Ide Hill	Remony Milwater
Lancashire	Lord Shuttleworth, KG, KCVO	Catherine Penny
Leicestershire	Michael Kapur, OBE	Alison Smith, MBE
Lincolnshire	Toby Dennis	Michael Scott
Merseyside	Mark Blundell	His Hon John Roberts
Norfolk	Lady Dannatt, MBE	Lady Roberts
North Yorkshire	Johanna Ropner	David Kerfoot, MBE
Northamptonshire	James Saunders Watson	Paul Parsons
Northumberland	Duchess of Northumberland	Tom Fairfax
Nottinghamshire	Sir John Peace	Dame Elizabeth Fradd, DBE
Oxfordshire	Tim Stevenson, OBE	Amanda Ponsonby, MBE
Rutland	Dr Sarah Furness	Richard Cole
Shropshire	Anna Turner	Dean Harris
Somerset	Anne Maw	Mary-Clare Rodwell
South Yorkshire	Andrew Coombe	Carole O'Neill
Staffordshire	Ian Dudson, CBE	Commander Charles Bagot-Jewitt
Suffolk	Clare, Countess of Euston	Bridget McIntyre, MBE
Surrey	Michael More-Molyneux	Shahid Azeem
Tyne and Wear	Susan Winfield, OBE	Sarah Stewart, OBE
Warwickshire	Timothy Cox	Joe Greenwall, CBE
West Midlands	John Crabtree, OBE	Wade Lyn, CBE
West Sussex	Susan Pyper	Dr Timothy Fooks
West Yorkshire	Edmund Anderson	Jonathan Thornton
Wiltshire	Sarah Troughton	Maj.-Gen. Ashley Truluck, CB, CBE
Worcestershire	Lt.-Col. Patrick Holcroft, LVO, OBE	Lt.-Col. Mike Jackson, OBE

COMBINED AUTHORITIES

Authority	Constituent Councils*	Pop. †	Mayor, Political Party
Cambridgeshire & Peterborough	Cambridge, Cambridgeshire, E. Cambridgeshire, Fenland, Huntingdonshire, Peterborough, S. Cambridgeshire	855,796	James Palmer, C.
Greater Manchester	Bolton, Bury, Manchester, Oldham, Rochdale, Salford, Stockport, Tameside, Trafford, Wigan	2,835,686	Andy Burnham, Lab.
Liverpool City Region	Halton, Knowsley, Liverpool, St Helens, Sefton, Wirral	1,559,320	Steve Rotheram, Lab.
North East	Durham, Gateshead, S. Tyneside, Sunderland	1,160,830	None
North of Tyne	Newcastle Upon Tyne, N. Tyneside, Northumberland	833,167	Jamie Driscoll, Lab.
Sheffield City Region	Barnsley, Doncaster, Rotherham, Sheffield	1,409,020	Dan Jarvis, Lab.
Tees Valley	Darlington, Hartlepool, Middlesbrough, Redcar & Cleveland, Stockton-On-Tees	675,944	Ben Houchen, C.
West of England	Bath & N. E. Somerset, Bristol, S. Gloucestershire	941,752	Tim Bowles, C.
West Midlands	Birmingham, Coventry, Dudley, Sandwell, Solihull, Walsall, Wolverhampton	2,916,458	Andy Street, C.
West Yorkshire	Bradford, Calderdale, Kirklees, Leeds, Wakefield	2,332,469	None

COUNTY COUNCILS

Council & Administrative HQ	Telephone	Population†	Council Tax‡	Chief Executive§
Cambridgeshire, Cambridge	0345-045 5200	653,537	£1,359	Gillian Beasley
Cumbria, Carlisle	01228-606060	500,012	£1,441	Katherine Fairclough
Derbyshire, Matlock	01629-580000	802,694	£1,349	E. Alexander; H. Jones; J. Parfrement
Devon, Exeter	0345-155 1015	802,375	£1,439	Dr Phil Norrey
East Sussex, Lewes	0345-608 0190	557,229	£1,492	Becky Shaw
Essex, Chelmsford	0845-7430 430	1,489,189	£1,321	Gavin Jones
Gloucestershire, Gloucester	01452-425000	637,070	£1,345	Peter Bungard
Hampshire, Winchester	0300-555 1375	1,382,542	£1,286	John Coughlan, CBE
Hertfordshire, Hertford	0300-123 4040	1,189,519	£1,414	Owen Mapley
Kent, Maidstone	0300-041 4141	1,581,555	£1,351	David Cockburn
Lancashire, Preston	0300-123 6701	1,219,799	£1,400	Angie Ridgwell
Leicestershire, Leicester	0116-232 3232	706,155	£1,344	John Sinnott
Lincolnshire, Lincoln	01522-552222	761,224	£1,338	Debbie Barnes, OBE
Norfolk, Norwich	0344-800 8020	907,760	£1,417	Tom McCabe
North Yorkshire, Northallerton	01609-780780	618,054	£1,363	Richard Flinton
Northamptonshire, Northampton	0300-126 1000	753,278	£1,285	Theresa Grant
Nottinghamshire, Nottingham	0115-982 3823	828,224	£1,535	Anthony May
Oxfordshire, Oxford	01865-792422	691,667	£1,527	Yvonne Rees
Somerset, Taunton	0300-123 2224	562,225	£1,289	vacant
Staffordshire, Stafford	0300-111 8000	879,560	£1,296	John Henderson, CB
Suffolk, Ipswich	03456-606 6067	761,350	£1,344	Nicola Beach
Surrey, Kingston upon Thames	0345-600 9009	1,196,236	£1,511	Joanna Killian
Warwickshire, Warwick	01926-410410	577,933	£1,489	Monica Fogarty
West Sussex, Chichester	01243-777100	863,980	£1,439	Becky Shaw
Worcestershire, Worcester	01905-763763	595,786	£1,311	Paul Robinson

*See the following pages for information on individual constituent councils

† Source: Office for National Statistics – Mid-2019 Population Estimates (Crown copyright)

‡ Average 2020–21 Band D council tax in the county area inclusive of the adult social care precept, but exclusive of precepts for fire authorities and Police and Crime Commissioners. County councils claim their share of the combined council tax from the collection funds of the district authorities within their area. Band D council tax bills for the billing authority are given on the following pages

§ Or equivalent postholder

DISTRICT COUNCILS

District Council	Telephone	Pop.*	Council Tax†	Chief Executive‡
Adur	01273-263000	64,301	£1,963	Alex Bailey
Allerdale	01900-702702	97,761	£1,960	Andrew Seekings
Amber Valley	01773-570222	128,147	£1,883	Sylvia Delahay & Julian Townsend
Arun	01903-737500	160,758	£1,903	Nigel Lynn
Ashfield	01623-450000	127,918	£2,045	Carol Cooper-Smith *(interim)*
Ashford	01233-331111	130,032	£1,848	Tracey Kerly
Babergh	01473-822801	92,036	£1,820	Arthur Charvonia
Barrow-in-Furness	01229-876543	67,049	£1,954	Sam Plum
Basildon	01268-533333	187,199	£1,880	Scott Logan
Basingstoke and Deane	01256-844844	176,582	£1,880	Ian Doll *(interim)*
Bassetlaw	01909-533533	117,459	£2,059	Neil Taylor
Blaby	0116-275 0555	101,526	£1,920	Jane Toman
Bolsover	01246-242424	80,562	£1,981	Karen Hanson & Lee Hickin
Boston	01205-314200	70,173	£1,842	Rob Barlow
Braintree	01376-552525	152,604	£1,824	Andy Wright
Breckland	01362-656870	139,968	£1,872	Nathan Elvery
Brentwood	01277-312500	77,021	£1,805	Jonathan Stephenson
Broadland	01603-431133	130,783	£1,891	Trevor Holden
Bromsgrove	01527-881288	99,881	£1,876	Kevin Dicks
Broxbourne	01992-785555	97,279	£1,750	Jeff Stack
Broxtowe	0115-917 7777	114,033	£2,039	Ruth Hyde, OBE
Burnley	01282-425011	88,920	£1,996	Mick Cartledge
CAMBRIDGE	01223-457000	124,798	£1,866	Andrew Grant *(interim)*
Cannock Chase	01543-462621	100,762	£1,845	Tony McGovern
CANTERBURY	01227-862000	165,394	£1,866	Colin Carmichael
CARLISLE	01228-817000	108,678	£1,943	Dr Jason Gooding
Castle Point	01268-882200	90,376	£1,865	David Marchant
Charnwood	01509-263151	185,851	£1,860	Rob Mitchell
CHELMSFORD	01245-606606	178,388	£1,831	Nick Eveleigh
Cheltenham	01242-262626	116,306	£1,823	Gareth Edmundson
Cherwell	01295-227001	150,503	£1,974	Yvonne Rees
Chesterfield	01246-345345	104,900	£1,839	Huw Bowen
Chichester	01243-785166	121,129	£1,868	Diane Shepherd
Chorley	01257-515151	118,216	£1,893	Gary Hall
Colchester	01206-282222	194,706	£1,822	Adrian Pritchard
Copeland	01946-598300	68,183	£1,970	Pat Graham
Corby	01536-464000	72,218	£1,801	Jonathan Waterworth & Paul Goult
Cotswold	01285-623000	89,862	£1,817	Robert Weaver
Craven	01756-700600	57,142	£1,943	Paul Shevlin
Crawley	01293-438000	112,409	£1,848	Natalie Brahma-Pearl
Dacorum	01442-228000	154,763	£1,835	Claire Hamilton
Dartford	01322-343434	112,606	£1,847	Sheri Green & Sarah Martin
Daventry	01327-871100	85,950	£1,858	Ian Vincent
Derbyshire Dales	01629-761100	72,325	£1,926	Paul Wilson
Dover	01304-821199	118,131	£1,894	Nadeem Aziz
East Cambridgeshire	01353-665555	89,840	£1,888	John Hill
East Devon	01395-516551	146,284	£1,967	Mark Williams
East Hampshire	01730-266551	122,308	£1,784	Gill Kneller
East Hertfordshire	01279-655261	149,748	£1,864	Richard Cassidy
East Lindsey	01507-601111	141,727	£1,801	Rob Barlow
East Northamptonshire	01832-742000	94,527	£1,876	David Oliver
East Staffordshire	01283-508000	119,754	£1,875	Andy O'Brien
East Suffolk	03330-162000	249,461	£1,810	Stephen Baker
Eastbourne	01323-410000	103,745	£2,039	Robert Cottrill
Eastleigh	023-8068 8000	133,584	£1,768	Nick Tustian
Eden	01768-817817	53,253	£1,958	vacant
Elmbridge	01372-474474	136,795	£2,009	Robert Moran
Epping Forest	01992-564000	131,689	£1,816	Georgina Blakemore
Epsom and Ewell	01372-732000	80,627	£1,985	Kathryn Beldon
Erewash	0115-907 2244	115,371	£1,857	Jeremy Jaroszek
EXETER	01392-277888	131,405	£1,909	Karime Hassan
Fareham	01329-236100	116,233	£1,732	Peter Grimwood
Fenland	01354-654321	101,850	£1,973	Paul Medd
Folkestone and Hythe	01303-853000	112,996	£1,967	Dr Susan Priest
Forest of Dean	01594-810000	86,791	£1,870	Jan Britton
Fylde	01253-658658	80,780	£1,928	Allan Oldfield

Gedling	0115-901 3901	117,896	£2,033	Mike Hill
GLOUCESTER	01452-396396	129,28	£1,816	Jon McGinty
Gosport	023-9258 4242	84,838	£1,798	David Williams
Gravesham	01474-564422	106,939	£1,853	Stuart Bobby
Great Yarmouth	01493-856100	99,336	£1,863	Sheila Oxtoby
Guildford	01483-505050	148,998	£1,991	James Whiteman
Hambleton	01619-779977	91,594	£1,858	Dr Justin Ives
Harborough	01858-828282	93,807	£1,865	Norman Proudfoot
Harlow	01279-446655	87,067	£1,877	Brian Keane
Harrogate	01423-500600	160,831	£1,966	Wallace Sampson
Hart	01252-622122	97,073	£1,826	Patricia Hughes & Daryl Phillips
Hastings	01424-451066	92,661	£2,058	Jane Hartnell
Havant	023-9244 6019	126,220	£1,776	Gill Kneller
Hertsmere	020-8207 2277	104,919	£1,825	Sajida Bijle
High Peak	0345-129 7777	92,666	£1,869	Andrew Stokes
Hinckley and Bosworth	01455-238141	113,136	£1,836	Bill Cullen
Horsham	01403-215100	143,791	£1,857	Glen Chip
Huntingdonshire	01480-388388	177,963	£1,925	Jo Lancaster
Hyndburn	01254-388111	81,043	£1,934	David Welsby
Ipswich	01473-432000	136,913	£1,936	Russell Williams
Kettering	01536-410333	101,766	£1,824	Graham Soulsby
King's Lynn and West Norfolk	01553-616200	151,383	£1,876	Lorraine Gore
LANCASTER	01524-582000	146,038	£1,931	Kieran Keane
Lewes	01273-471600	103,268	£2,111	Robert Cottrill
Lichfield	01543-308000	104,756	£1,830	Diane Tilley
LINCOLN	01522-881188	99,299	£1,869	Angela Andrews
Maidstone	01622-602000	171,826	£1,933	Alison Broom
Maldon	01621-854477	64,926	£1,858	P. Dodson; R. Holmes; C. Leslie
Malvern Hills	01684-862151	78,698	£1,857	Vic Allison
Mansfield	01623-463463	109,313	£2,039	Hayley Barsby
Melton	01664-502502	51,209	£1,888	Edd de Coverly
Mendip	0300-3038588	115,587	£1,882	Stuart Brown
Mid Devon	01884-255255	82,311	£2,021	Stephen Walford
Mid Suffolk	01449-720711	103,895	£1,812	Arthur Charvonia
Mid Sussex	01444-458166	151,022	£1,883	Kathryn Hall
Mole Valley	01306-885001	87,245	£1,974	Karen Brimacombe
New Forest	023-8028 5000	180,086	£1,836	Bob Jackson
Newark and Sherwood	01636-650000	122,421	£2,100	John Robinson
Newcastle-under-Lyme	01782-717717	129,441	£1,815	Martin Hamilton
North Devon	01271-327711	97,145	£2,006	Ken Miles
North East Derbyshire	01246-231111	101,462	£1,949	Karen Hanson & Lee Hickin
North Hertfordshire	01462-474000	133,570	£1,871	Anthony Roche
North Kesteven	01529-414155	116,915	£1,853	Ian Fytche
North Norfolk	01263-513811	104,837	£1,895	Steve Blatch
North Warwickshire	01827-715341	65,264	£1,990	Steve Maxey
North West Leicestershire	01530-454545	103,611	£1,883	Beverley Smith
Northampton	0300-330 7000	224,610	£1,851	George Candler
NORWICH	0344-980 3333	140,573	£1,949	Stephen Evans
Nuneaton and Bedworth	024-7637 6376	129,883	£1,966	Brent Davis & Simone Hines
Oadby and Wigston	0116-288 8961	57,015	£1,874	Anne Court
OXFORD	01865-249811	152,457	£2,064	Gordon Mitchell
Pendle	01282-661661	92,112	£2,050	Dean Langton & Philip Mousdale
PRESTON	01772-906900	143,135	£2,012	Adrian Phillips
Redditch	01527-64252	85,261	£1,867	Kevin Dicks
Reigate and Banstead	01737-276000	148,748	£2,022	vacant
Ribble Valley	01200-425111	60,888	£1,860	Marshal Scott
Richmondshire	01748-829100	53,730	£1,955	Tony Clark
Rochford	01702-318111	87,368	£1,881	Angela Hutchings *(acting)*
Rossendale	01706-217777	71,482	£1,962	Neil Shaw
Rother	01424-787000	96,080	£2,036	Malcolm Johnston
Rugby	01788-533533	108,935	£1,944	Mannie Ketley
Runnymede	01932-838383	89,424	£1,952	Paul Turrell
Rushcliffe	0115-981 9911	119,184	£2,056	Kath Marriott
Rushmoor	01252-398398	94,599	£1,776	Paul Shackley
Ryedale	01653-600666	55,380	£1,955	Stacey Burlet
ST ALBANS	01727-866100	148,482	£1,840	Amanda Foley
Scarborough	01723-232323	108,757	£1,966	Michael Greene
Sedgemoor	0845-408 2540	123,178	£1,836	Allison Griffin
Selby	01757-705101	90,620	£1,945	Janet Waggott
Sevenoaks	01732-227000	120,750	£1,944	Dr Pav Ramewal

Somerset West and Taunton	0300-304 8000	155,115	£1,814	James Hassett
South Cambridgeshire	0345-045 0500	159,086	£1,907	Liz Watts
South Derbyshire	01283-595795	107,261	£1,844	Frank McArdle
South Hams	01803-861234	87,004	£1,991	Andy Bates
South Holland	01775-761161	95,019	£1,808	Nathan Elvery
South Kesteven	01476-406080	142,424	£1,791	Karen Bradford
South Lakeland	01539-733333	105,088	£1,945	Lawrence Conway
South Norfolk	01508-533633	140,880	£1,917	Trevor Holden
South Northamptonshire	01327-322322	94,490	£1,889	Richard Ellis
South Oxfordshire	01235-520202	142,057	£1,965	Mark Stone
South Ribble	01772-421491	110,788	£1,918	vacant
South Somerset	01935-462462	168,345	£1,874	Alex Parmley
South Staffordshire	01902-696000	112,436	£1,779	Dave Heywood
Spelthorne	01784-451499	99,844	£1,987	Daniel Mouawad
Stafford	01785-619000	137,280	£1,782	Tim Clegg
Staffordshire Moorlands	0345-605 3010	98,435	£1,805	Andrew Stokes
Stevenage	01438-242242	87,845	£1,828	Matt Partridge
Stratford-on-Avon	01789-267575	130,089	£1,933	Dave Buckland
Stroud	01453-766321	119,964	£1,909	Kathy O'Leary
Surrey Heath	01276-707100	89,305	£2,026	Damian Roberts
Swale	01795-417850	150,082	£1,846	Larissa Reed
Tamworth	01827-709709	76,696	£1,780	Anthony Goodwin
Tandridge	01883-722000	88,129	£2,208	Jackie King *(acting)*
Teignbridge	01626-361101	134,163	£2,001	Phil Shears
Tendring	01255-686868	146,561	£1,809	Ian Davidson
Test Valley	01264-368000	126,160	£1,755	Andy Ferrier
Tewkesbury	01684-295010	92,019	£1,788	Mike Dawson
Thanet	01843-577000	141,922	£1,921	Madeline Homer
Three Rivers	01923-776611	93,323	£1,844	Joanne Wagstaffe
Tonbridge and Malling	01732-844522	132,153	£1,909	Julie Beilby
Torridge	01237-428700	68,267	£1,984	Steve Hearse
Tunbridge Wells	01892-526121	118,724	£1,876	William Benson
Uttlesford	01799-510510	91,284	£1,779	Dawn French
Vale of White Horse	01235-520202	136,007	£1,961	Mark Stone
Warwick	01926-410410	143,753	£1,930	Chris Elliott
Watford	01923-226400	96,577	£1,886	Donna Nolan
Waverley	01483-523333	126,328	£2,031	Tom Horwood
Wealden	01323-443322	161,475	£2,091	Trevor Scott
Wellingborough	01933-229777	79,707	£1,786	Liz Elliott
Welwyn & Hatfield	01707-357000	123,043	£1,867	Ka Ng *(interim)*
West Devon	01822-813600	55,796	£2,067	Andy Bates
West Lancashire	01695-577177	114,306	£1,908	Jacqui Sinnott-Lacey
West Lindsey	01427-676676	95,667	£1,878	Ian Knowles
West Oxfordshire	01993-861000	110,643	£1,937	Giles Hughes
West Suffolk	01284-763233	179,045	£1,821	Ian Gallin
WINCHESTER	01962-840222	124,859	£1,798	Laura Taylor
Woking	01483-755855	100,793	£2,027	Ray Morgan, OBE
WORCESTER	01905-722233	101,222	£1,818	David Blake
Worthing	01903-239999	110,570	£1,881	Alex Bailey
Wychavon	01386-565000	129,433	£1,793	Vic Allison
Wyre	01253-891000	112,091	£1,908	Garry Payne
Wyre Forest	01562-732928	101,291	£1,880	Ian Miller

* *Source:* Office for National Statistics – *Mid-2019 Population Estimates* (Crown copyright)
† Band D council tax bill for 2020–21 inclusive of adult social care and parish precepts
‡ Or equivalent postholder
Councils in CAPITAL LETTERS have city status

METROPOLITAN BOROUGH COUNCILS

Metropolitan Borough Council	Telephone	Pop.*	Council Tax†	Chief Executive‡
Barnsley	01226-770770	246,866	£1,820	Sarah Norman
BIRMINGHAM	0121-303 1111	1,141,814	£1,668	Chris Naylor *(interim)*
Bolton	01204-333333	287,550	£1,821	Tony Oakman
BRADFORD	01274-432001	539,776	£1,708	Kersten England
Bury	0161-253 5000	190,990	£1,911	Geoff Little, OBE
Calderdale	01422-288001	211,455	£1,823	Robin Tuddenham
COVENTRY	0500-834 333	371,521	£1,909	Dr Martin Reeves
Doncaster	01302-736000	311,890	£1,707	Damian Allen
Dudley	0300-555 2345	321,596	£1,606	Kevin O'Keefe
Gateshead	0191-433 3000	202,055	£2,045	Sheena Ramsey
Kirklees	01484-221000	439,787	£1,839	Jacqui Gedman
Knowsley	0151-489 6000	150,862	£1,892	Mike Harden
LEEDS	0113-222 4444	793,139	£1,720	Tom Riordan
LIVERPOOL	0151-233 3000	498,042	£2,027	Tony Reeves
MANCHESTER	0161-234 5000	552,858	£1,725	Joanne Roney, OBE
NEWCASTLE UPON TYNE	0191-278 7878	302,820	£1,930	Pat Ritchie
North Tyneside	0191-643 5991	207,913	£1,852	Paul Hanson
Oldham	0161-770 3000	237,110	£1,977	Dr Carolyn Wilkins, OBE
Rochdale	01706-647474	222,412	£1,945	Steve Rumbelow
Rotherham	01709-382121	265,411	£1,885	Sharon Kemp
St Helens	01744-676789	180,585	£1,821	Kath O'Dwyer
SALFORD	0161-794 4711	258,834	£1,940	Tom Stannard
Sandwell	0121-569 2200	328,450	£1,682	David Stevens
Sefton	0345 140 0845	276,410	£1,958	Dwayne Johnson
SHEFFIELD	0114-273 4567	584,853	£1,899	Kate Josephs
Solihull	0121-704 8001	216,374	£1,655	Nick Page
South Tyneside	0191-427 7000	150,976	£1,850	vacant
Stockport	0161-480 4949	293,423	£1,990	Pam Smith
SUNDERLAND	0191-520 5555	277,705	£1,692	Patrick Melia
Tameside	0161-342 8355	226,493	£1,828	Steven Pleasant. MBE
Trafford	0161-912 2000	237,354	£1,644	Sara Todd
WAKEFIELD	0845-850 6506	348,312	£1,735	Merran McRae
Walsall	01922-650000	285,478	£2,007	Dr Helen Paterson
Wigan	01942-244991	328,662	£1,616	Alison McKenzie-Folan
Wirral	0151-606 2000	324,011	£1,896	Paul Satoor
WOLVERHAMPTON	01902-551155	263,357	£1,906	Tim Johnson

* *Source:* Office for National Statistics – *Mid-2019 Population Estimates* (Crown copyright)
† Band D council tax bill for 2020–21 inclusive of adult social care and parish precepts
‡ Or equivalent postholder
Councils in CAPITAL LETTERS have city status

UNITARY COUNCILS

Unitary Council	Telephone	Pop.*	Council Tax†	Chief Executive‡
Bath and North East Somerset	01225-477000	193,282	£1,803	Will Godfrey
Bedford	01234-267422	173,292	£1,908	Philip Simpkins
Blackburn with Darwen	01254-585585	149,696	£1,857	Denise Park
Blackpool	01253-477477	139,446	£1,901	Neil Jack
Bournemouth, Christchurch and Poole (BCP)	01202-451451	395,331	£1,842	Graham Farrant
Bracknell Forest	01344-352000	122,529	£1,716	Timothy Wheadon
BRIGHTON AND HOVE	01273-290000	290,885	£1,955	Geoff Raw
BRISTOL	0117-922 2000	463,377	£2,061	Mike Jackson
Buckinghamshire	0300-131 6000	543,973	£1,903	Rachel Shimmin, OBE
Central Bedfordshire	0300-300 8000	288,648	£1,996	Marcel Coiffait
Cheshire East	0300-123 5500	384,152	£1,851	Lorraine O'Donnell
Cheshire West and Chester	0300-123 8123	343,071	£1,902	Andrew Lewis
Cornwall	0300-123 4100	569,578	£1,943	Kate Kennally
Darlington	01325-380651	106,803	£1,892	Paul Wildsmith
DERBY	01332-293111	257,302	£1,778	Paul Simpson
Dorset	01305-221000	378,508	£2,119	Matt Prosser
DURHAM	0300-026000	530,094	£2,071	John Hewitt (interim)
East Riding of Yorkshire	01482-393939	341,173	£1,875	Caroline Lacey
Halton	0303-333 4300	129,410	£1,789	David Parr, OBE
Hartlepool	01429-266522	93,663	£2,092	Denise McGuckin
Herefordshire	01432-260000	192,801	£1,954	Alistair Neill
Isle of Wight	01983-821000	141,771	£1,965	John Metcalfe
Isles of Scilly§	01720-424000	2,224	£1,550	Paul Masters
KINGSTON-UPON-HULL	01482-609100	259,778	£1,741	Matt Jukes
LEICESTER	0116-254 1000	354,224	£1,915	vacant
Luton	01582-546000	213,052	£1,850	Robin Porter
Medway	01634-333333	278,556	£1,760	Neil Davies
Middlesbrough	01642-245432	140,980	£2,050	Tony Parkinson
Milton Keynes	01908-691691	269,457	£1,747	Michael Bracey
North East Lincolnshire	01472-313131	159,563	£1,923	Rob Walsh
North Lincolnshire	01724-296296	172,292	£1,875	Denise Hyde
North Somerset	01934-888888	215,052	£1,813	Jo Walker
Northumberland	0345-600 6400	322,900	£1,985	Daljit Lally, OBE
NOTTINGHAM	0115-915 5555	332,900	£2,119	Mel Barrett
PETERBOROUGH	01733-747474	201,041	£1,715	Gillian Beasley
PLYMOUTH	01752-668000	262,100	£1,885	Tracey Lee
PORTSMOUTH	023-9282 2251	214,905	£1,733	David Williams
Reading	0118-937 3787	161,780	£1,976	Peter Sloman
Redcar and Cleveland	0164-277 4774	137,150	£1,995	John Sampson
Rutland	01572-722577	39,927	£2,125	Mark Andrews (interim)
Shropshire	0345-678 9000	323,136	£1,850	Andy Begley
Slough	01753-475111	149,539	£1,708	Josie Wragg
South Gloucestershire	01454-868009	285,093	£1,929	Dave Perry
SOUTHAMPTON	023-8083 3000	252,520	£1,847	Sandy Hopkins
Southend-on-Sea	01702-215000	183,125	£1,718	Alison Griffin
Stockton-on-Tees	01642-393939	197,348	£2,006	Julie Danks
STOKE-ON-TRENT	01782-234567	256,375	£1,660	Jon Rouse
Swindon	01793-463000	222,193	£1,828	Susie Kemp
Telford and Wrekin	01952-380000	179,854	£1,733	David Sidaway
Thurrock	01375-652652	174,341	£1,605	Lyn Carpenter
Torbay	01803-201201	136,262	£1,809	Anne-Marie Bond (interim)
Warrington	01925-443322	210,014	£1,881	Prof. Steven Broomhead
West Berkshire	01635-42400	158,450	£1,917	Nick Carter
Wiltshire	0300-456 0100	500,024	£1,935	Terence Herbert
Windsor and Maidenhead	01628-683800	151,422	£1,384	Duncan Sharkey
Wokingham	0118-974 6000	171,119	£1,893	Susan Parsonage
YORK	01904-551550	210,618	£1,734	Ian Floyd

* *Source:* Office for National Statistics – *Mid-2019 Population Estimates* (Crown copyright)
† Band D council tax bill for 2020–21 inclusive of adult social care and parish precepts
‡ Or equivalent postholder
§ Under the Isles of Scilly Clause the council has additional functions to other unitary authorities
Councils in CAPITAL LETTERS have city status

SINGLE-TIER & COUNTY COUNCIL AREAS IN ENGLAND

1 Stockton-on-Tees
2 Middlesbrough
3 Blackpool
4 Blackburn
  with Darwen
5 Bolton
6 Bury
7 Rochdale
8 Salford
9 Oldham
10 Liverpool
11 Knowsley
12 St Helens
13 Halton
14 Warrington
15 Trafford
16 Manchester
17 Tameside
18 Stockport
19 Nottingham
20 Telford and
   Wrekin
21 Wolverhampton

22 Walsall
23 Sandwell
24 Dudley
25 Birmingham
26 Solihull
27 Coventry
28 Peterborough
29 South Glos
30 Bristol
31 Bath and
   NE Somerset
32 Windsor and
   Maidenhead
33 Slough
34 Reading
35 Wokingham
36 Bracknell Forest
37 Thurrock
38 Southend
39 Medway
40 Plymouth
41 Torbay

LONDON

1 Hillingdon
2 Harrow
3 Barnet
4 Enfield
5 Waltham Forest
6 Redbridge
7 Barking and Dagenham
8 Havering
9 Ealing
10 Brent
11 Camden
12 Haringey
13 Islington
14 Hackney
15 Newham
16 Hounslow
17 Hammersmith and Fulham

18 Kensington and Chelsea
19 City of Westminster
20 City of London
21 Tower Hamlets
22 Richmond upon Thames
23 Wandsworth
24 Lambeth
25 Southwark
26 Lewisham
27 Greenwich
28 Bexley
29 Kingston upon Thames
30 Merton
31 Sutton
32 Croydon
33 Bromley

LONDON

The Greater London Council was abolished in 1986 and London was divided into 32 borough councils, which have a status similar to the metropolitan borough councils in the rest of England, and the City of London Corporation.

In March 1998 the government announced proposals for a Greater London Authority (GLA) covering the area of the 32 London boroughs and the City of London, which would comprise a directly elected mayor and a 25-member assembly. A referendum was held in London on 7 May 1998 and 72 per cent of voters balloted in favour of the GLA. A London mayor was elected on 4 May 2000 and the authority assumed its responsibilities on 3 July 2000 (see also Regional Government).

LONDON BOROUGH COUNCILS

The London boroughs have whole council elections every four years, in the year immediately following the county council election year. The most recent elections took place on 3 May 2018.

The borough councils have responsibility for the following functions: building regulations, cemeteries and crematoria, consumer protection, education, youth employment, environmental health, electoral registration, food, drugs, housing, leisure services, libraries, local planning, local roads, museums, parking, recreation (parks, playing fields, swimming pools), refuse collection and street cleaning, social services, town planning and traffic management.

LONDON BOROUGH COUNCILS

Council	Telephone	Pop.*	Council Tax†	Chief Executive‡
Barking and Dagenham	020-8592 4500	212,906	£1,617	Claire Symonds
Barnet	020-8359 2000	395,869	£1,606	John Hooton
Bexley	020-8303 7777	248,287	£1,735	Jackie Belton
Brent	020-8937 1234	329,771	£1,645	Carolyn Downs
Bromley	020-8464 3333	332,336	£1,597	Ade Adetosoye, OBE
Camden	020-7974 4444	270,029	£1,624	Jenny Rowlands
CITY OF LONDON CORPORATION	020-7606 3030	9,721	£1,007	John Barradell, OBE
Croydon	020-8726 6000	386,710	£1,784	Katherine Kerswell
Ealing	020-8825 5000	341,806	£1,571	Paul Najsarek
Enfield	020-8379 1000	333,794	£1,696	Ian Davis
Greenwich	020-8854 8888	287,942	£1,548	Debbie Warren
Hackney	020-8356 5000	281,120	£1,512	Tim Shields
Hammersmith and Fulham	020-8748 3020	185,143	£1,124	Kim Smith
Haringey	020-8489 0000	268,647	£1,705	Zina Etheridge
Harrow	020-8863 5611	251,160	£1,855	Sean Harriss
Havering	01708-434343	259,552	£1,796	Andrew Blake-Herbert
Hillingdon	01895-250111	306,870	£1,515	Fran Beasley
Hounslow	020-8583 2000	271,523	£1,607	Niall Bolger
Islington	020-7527 2000	242,467	£1,598	Linzi Roberts-Egan
Kensington and Chelsea	020-7361 3000	156,129	£1,254	Barry Quirk, CBE
Kingston upon Thames	020-8547 5000	177,507	£1,945	Ian Thomas, CBE
Lambeth	020-7926 1000	326,034	£1,502	Andrew Travers
Lewisham	020-8314 6000	305,842	£1,646	Kim Wright
Merton	020-8274 4901	206,548	£1,614	Ged Curran
Newham	020-8430 2000	353,134	£1,383	Althea Loderick
Redbridge	020-8554 5000	305,222	£1,690	Andy Donald
Richmond upon Thames	020-8891 1411	198,019	£1,872	Paul Martin
Southwark	020-7525 5000	318,830	£1,441	Eleanor Kelly
Sutton	020-8770 5000	206,349	£1,761	Helen Bailey
Tower Hamlets	020-7364 5000	324,745	£1,392	Will Tuckley
Waltham Forest	020-8496 3000	276,983	£1,760	Martin Esom
Wandsworth	020-8871 6000	329,677	£800	Paul Martin
WESTMINSTER	020-7641 6000	261,317	£782	Stuart Love

* Source: Office for National Statistics – Mid-2019 Population Estimates (Crown copyright)
† Band D council tax bill for 2020–21 inclusive of adult social care and parish precepts
‡ Or equivalent postholder
Councils in CAPITAL LETTERS have city status

CITY OF LONDON CORPORATION

The City of London Corporation is the local authority for the City of London. Its legal definition is the 'Mayor and Commonalty and Citizens of the City of London'. It is governed by the Court of Common Council, which consists of the lord mayor, 24 other aldermen and 100 common councillors. The lord mayor and two sheriffs are nominated annually by the City guilds (the livery companies) and elected by the Court of Aldermen. Aldermen and councillors are elected from the 25 wards into which the City is divided; councilmen must stand for re-election every four years. The council is a legislative assembly, and there are no political parties.

The corporation has the same functions as the London borough councils. In addition, it runs the City of London Police; is the health authority for the Port of London; has health control of animal imports throughout Greater London, including at Heathrow airport; owns and manages public open spaces throughout Greater London; runs the central criminal court; and runs Billingsgate, New Spitalfields and Smithfield markets.

The City of London is the historic centre at the heart of London known as 'the square mile', around which the vast metropolis has grown over the centuries. The City's residential population was 9,721 at the mid-2019 estimate and in addition, around 522,000 people work in the City. The City is an international financial and business centre, generating about £30bn a year for the British economy. It includes the head offices of the principal banks, insurance companies and mercantile houses, in addition to buildings ranging from the historic Roman Wall and the 15th-century Guildhall, to the massive splendour of St Paul's Cathedral and the architectural beauty of Christopher Wren's spires.

The City of London was described by Tacitus in AD 62 as 'a busy emporium for trade and traders'. Under the Romans it became an important administration centre and hub of the road system. Little is known of London in Saxon times, when it formed part of the kingdom of the East Saxons. In 886 Alfred recovered London from the Danes and reconstituted it a burgh under his son-in-law. In 1066 the citizens submitted to William the Conqueror who in 1067 granted them a charter, which is still preserved, establishing them in the rights and privileges they had hitherto enjoyed.

THE MAYORALTY

The mayoralty was probably established about 1189, the first mayor being Henry Fitz Ailwyn who filled the office for 23 years and was succeeded by Fitz Alan (1212–14). A new charter was granted by King John in 1215, directing the mayor to be chosen annually, which has been done ever since, though in early times the same individual often held the office more than once. A familiar instance is that of 'Whittington, thrice Lord Mayor of London' (in reality four times: 1397, 1398, 1406 and 1419); and many modern cases have occurred. The earliest instance of the phrase 'lord mayor' in English is in 1414. It was used more generally in the latter part of the 15th century and became invariable from 1535 onwards. At Michaelmas the liverymen in Common Hall choose two aldermen who have served the office of sheriff for presentation to the Court of Aldermen, and one is chosen to be lord mayor for the following mayoral year.

LORD MAYOR'S DAY

The Lord Mayor of the City of London was previously elected on the feast of St Simon and St Jude (28 October), and from the time of Edward I, at least, was presented to the King or to the Barons of the Exchequer on the following day, unless that day was a Sunday. The day of election was altered to 16 October in 1346, and after some further changes was fixed for Michaelmas Day in 1546, but the ceremonies of admittance and swearing-in of the lord mayor continued to take place on 28 and 29 October respectively until 1751. In 1752, at the reform of the calendar, the lord mayor was continued in office until 8 November, the 'new style' equivalent of 28 October. The lord mayor is now presented to the Lord Chief Justice at the Royal Courts of Justice on the second Saturday in November to make the final declaration of office, having been sworn in at Guildhall on the preceding day. The procession to the Royal Courts of Justice is popularly known as the Lord Mayor's Show.

REPRESENTATIVES

Aldermen are mentioned in the 11th century and their office is of Saxon origin. They were elected annually between 1377 and 1394, when an act of parliament of Richard II directed them to be chosen for life. Aldermen now serve a six-year term of office before submitting themselves for re-election.

The Common Council was, at an early date, substituted for a popular assembly called the *Folkmote*. At first only two representatives were sent from each ward, but now each of the City's 25 wards is represented by an alderman and at least two common councillors (the number depending on the size of the ward). Common councillors are elected every four years at all-out ward elections.

OFFICERS

Sheriffs were Saxon officers; their predecessors were the *wic-reeves* and *portreeves* of London and Middlesex. At first they were officers of the Crown, and were named by the Barons of the Exchequer; but Henry I (in 1132) gave the citizens permission to choose their own sheriffs, and the annual election of sheriffs became fully operative under King John's charter of 1199. The citizens lost this privilege, as far as the election of the sheriff of Middlesex was concerned, by the Local Government Act 1888; but the liverymen continue to choose two sheriffs of the City of London, who are appointed on Midsummer Day and take office at Michaelmas.

The office of chamberlain is an ancient one, the first contemporary record of which is 1237. The Town Clerk (or common clerk) is first mentioned in 1274.

ACTIVITIES

The work of the City of London Corporation is assigned to a number of committees which make decisions on behalf of the Court of Common Council or which make recommendations for decisions by the court. The committees are extensive given the diverse services delivered by the City Corporation and include: Audit and Risk Management; Barbican Centre; Barbican Residential; Board of Governors of the City of London Freeman's School, City of London School, City of London School for Girls and the Guildhall School of Music and Drama; The City Bridge Trust; Community and Children's Services; Culture, Heritage and Libraries; Education; Epping Forest and Commons; Establishment; Finance; Freedom Applications; Gresham (City Side); Hampstead Heath, Highgate Wood and Queen's Park; Health and Wellbeing; Investment; Licensing; Markets; Open Spaces and City Gardens; Pensions Board; Planning and Transportation; Police; Policy and Resources; Port Health and Environmental Services; Standards; and West Ham Park. There are numerous other sub-committees which report to the City of London Corporation's committees.

The City's estate, in the possession of which the City of London Corporation differs from other municipalities, is largely managed by the property investment board.

The Honourable the Irish Society, which manages the City Corporation's estates in Ulster, consists of a governor, two other aldermen and 12 common councilmen.

THE LORD MAYOR 2019–21*

The Rt. Hon. the Lord Mayor, William Russell
Executive Director of Mansion House and the Central Criminal Court, Vic Annells

* Serving a two-year term due to the coronavirus pandemic

THE SHERIFFS 2019–21*

Alderman Michael Mainelli (Broad Street); Christopher Hayward

* Serving a two-year term due to the coronavirus pandemic

OFFICERS, ETC

Town Clerk, John Barradell
Chamberlain, Peter Kane
Chief Commoner (2020), Brian Mooney
Clerk, The Honourable the Irish Society, H. E. J. Montgomery, MBE

THE ALDERMEN

with office held and date of appointment to that office

Name and Ward	Common Councilman	Alderman	Sheriff	Lord Mayor
Ian Luder, *Castle Baynard*	1998	2005	2007	2008
Nicholas Anstee, *Aldersgate*	1987	1996	2003	2009
Sir David Wootton, *Langbourn*	2002	2005	2009	2011
Sir Roger Gifford, *Cordwainer*	–	2004	2008	2012
Sir Alan Yarrow, *Bridge & Bridge Wt.*	–	2007	2011	2014
Dr Sir Andrew Parmley, *Vintry*	1992	2001	2014	2016
Sir Charles Bowman, *Lime Street*	–	2013	2015	2017
Peter Estlin, *Coleman Street*	–	2013	2016	2018
William Russell, *Bread Street*	–	2013	2016	2019

All the above have passed the Civic Chair

	Common Councilman	Alderman	Sheriff
Alison Gowman, *Dowgate*	1991	2002	–
David Graves, *Cripplegate*	–	2008	–
John Garbutt, *Walbrook*	–	2009	–
Timothy Hailes, *Bassishaw*	–	2013	2017
Prof. Michael Mainelli, *Broad Street*	–	2013	2019
Vincent Keaveny, *Farringdon Wn.*	–	2013	2018
Baroness Scotland of Asthal, QC, *Bishopsgate*	–	2015	–
Robert Howard, *Cornhill*	2011	2015	–
Alistair King, *Queenhithe*	–	2016	–
Gregory Jones, QC, *Farringdon Wt.*	2013	2017	–
Prem Goyal, *Portsoken*	2017	2017	–
Nicholas Lyons, *Tower*	2017	2017	–
Emma Edhem, *Candlewick*	2018	2018	–
Robert Hughes-Penney, *Cheap*	2004–12	2018	–
Susan Langley, *Aldgate*	–	2018	–
Bronek Masojada, *Billingsgate*	–	2019	–

THE COMMON COUNCIL

Deputy: each common councillor so described serves as deputy to the alderman of her/his ward.

Abrahams, G. C. (2000)	*Farringdon Wt.*
Absalom, *Deputy* J. D. (1994)	*Farringdon Wt.*
Addy, C. K. (2017)	*Farringdon Wt.*
Ali, M. (2017)	*Portsoken*
Ameer, R. B. (2017)	*Vintry*
Anderson, R. K. (2013)	*Aldersgate*
Barr, A. R. M. (2017)	*Cordwainer*
Barrow, *Deputy* D. G. F. (2007)	*Aldgate*
Bastow, A. M. (2017)	*Aldersgate*
Bell, M. (2017)	*Farringdon Wn.*
Bennett, *Deputy* J. A. (2005)	*Broad Street*
Bennett, P. G. (2016)	*Walbrook*
Bensted-Smith, N. M. (2014)	*Cheap*
Boden, C. P. (2013)	*Castle Baynard*
Bostock, R. M. (2017)	*Cripplegate*
Bottomley, *Deputy* K. D. F. (2015)	*Bridge & Bridge Wt.*
Bradshaw, *Deputy* D. J. (1991)	*Cripplegate Wn.*
Broeke, T. (2017)	*Cheap*
Cassidy, *Deputy* M. J., CBE (1980)	*Coleman Street*
Chadwick, *Deputy* R. A. H., OBE (1994)	*Tower*
Chapman, *Deputy* J. D. (2006)	*Langbourn*
Christian, D. G. (2016)	*Lime Street*
Clementi, T. C. (2017)	*Lime Street*
Colthurst, H. N. A. (2013)	*Lime Street*
Crossan, R. P. (2017)	*Aldersgate*
Dostalova, K. H. (2013)	*Farringdon Wn.*
Duckworth, S. D., OBE (2000)	*Bishopsgate Wn.*
Dunphy, P. G. (2009)	*Cornhill*
Durcan, J. M. (2017)	*Cripplegate*
Edwards, J. E. (2019)	*Farringdon Wn.*
Everett, *Deputy* K. M. (1984)	*Candlewick*
Fairweather, A. H. (2016)	*Tower*
Fernandes, S. A. (2009)	*Coleman Street*
Fletcher, J. W. (2011)	*Portsoken*
Fredericks, M. B. (2008)	*Tower*
Graham, T. (2019)	*Cordwainer*
Haines, C. W. (2017)	*Queenhithe*
Haines, *Deputy* Revd S. D. (2005)	*Cornhill*
Harrower, G. G. (2015)	*Bassishaw*
Hayward, C. M. (2013)	*Broad Street*
Hill, C. (2017)	*Farringdon Wn.*
Hoffman, *Deputy* T. D. D. (2002)	*Vintry*
Holmes, A. (2013)	*Farringdon Wn.*
Hudson, M. (2007)	*Castle Baynard*
Hyde, *Deputy* W. (2011)	*Bishopsgate Wt.*
Ingham Clark, *Deputy* J. (2013)	*Billingsgate*
James, *Deputy* C. (2008)	*Farringdon Wn.*
Jones, *Deputy* H. L. M. (2004)	*Portsoken*
Joshi, S. J. (2018)	*Bishopsgate*
Knowles-Cutler, A. (2017)	*Castle Baynard*
Lawrence, G. A. (2002)	*Farringdon Wt.*
Levene, T. C. (2017)	*Bridge and Bridge Wt.*
Littlechild, V. (2009)	*Cripplegate Wn.*
Lloyd-Owen, N. M. C. (2018)	*Castle Baynard*
Lodge, O. A. W., TD (2009)	*Bread Street*
Lord, *Deputy* C. E., OBE (2001)	*Farringdon Wt.*
Martinelli, P. N. (2013)	*Farringdon Wt.*
Mayer, A. P. (2017)	*Bishopsgate*
Mayhew, J. P. (1996)	*Aldersgate*
McGuinness, *Deputy* C. S. (1997)	*Castle Baynard*
McMurtie, A. S. (2013)	*Coleman Street*
Mead, W., OBE (1997)	*Farringdon Wt.*
Merrett, *Deputy* R. A. (2009)	*Bassishaw*
Meyers, *Deputy* A. G. D. (2017)	*Aldgate*
Mooney, (Chief Commoner) *Deputy* B. D. F. (1998)	*Queenhithe*
Morris, H. F. (2008)	*Aldgate*
Moss, *Deputy* A. M. (2013)	*Cheap*
Moys, S. D. (2001)	*Aldgate*
Murphy, B. D. (2017)	*Bishopsgate*
Nash, *Deputy* J. C., OBE (1983)	*Aldersgate*
Newman, B. P., CBE (1989)	*Aldersgate*
Packham, G. D. (2013)	*Castle Baynard*
Patel, D. (2013)	*Aldgate*
Pearson, S. J. (2017)	*Cripplegate*
Petrie, J. (2018)	*Billingsgate*
Pimlott, W. (2017)	*Cripplegate*

Pleasance, J. L. (2013) — *Langbourn*
Pollard, *Deputy* J. H. G. (2002) — *Dowgate*
Priest, H. J. S. (2009) — *Castle Baynard*
Pritchard, J. P. (2017) — *Portsoken*
Quilter, S. D. (1998) — *Cripplegate Wt.*
Regan, *Deputy* R. D., OBE (1998) — *Farringdon Wn.*
Rogula, *Deputy* E. (2008) — *Lime Street*
de Sausmarez, H. J. (2015) — *Candlewick*
Sayed, R. (2017) — *Farringdon Wt.*
Scott, J. G. S. (1999) — *Broad Street*
Seaton, I. C. N. (2009) — *Cornhill*
Sells, O. M., QC (2017) — *Farringdon Wt.*
Shilson, *Deputy*, G. R. E. (2009) — *Bread Street*
Simons, J. L. (2004) — *Castle Baynard*
Sleigh, *Deputy* T. C. C. (2013) — *Bishopsgate Wt.*
Smith, G. M. (2013) — *Farringdon Wn.*
Snyder, *Deputy* Sir Michael (1986) — *Cordwainer*
Thompson, D. J. (2004) — *Aldgate*
Tomlinson, *Deputy* J. (2004) — *Cripplegate Wt.*
Tumbridge, J. R. (2009) — *Tower*
Upton, J. W. D. (2017) — *Farringdon Wt.*
Wheatley, M. R. P. H. D. (2013) — *Dowgate*
Woodhouse, *Deputy* P. J. (2013) — *Langbourn*
Wright, D. L. (2019) — *Coleman Street*

THE CITY GUILDS (LIVERY COMPANIES)

The livery companies of the City of London grew out of early medieval religious fraternities and began to emerge as trade and craft guilds, retaining their religious aspect, in the 12th century. From the early 14th century, only members of the trade and craft guilds could call themselves citizens of the City of London. The guilds began to be called livery companies, because of the distinctive livery worn by the most prosperous guild members on ceremonial occasions, in the late 15th century.

By the early 19th century the power of the companies within their trades had begun to wane, but those wearing the livery of a company continued to play an important role in the government of the City of London. Liverymen still have the right to nominate the Lord Mayor and sheriffs, and most members of the Court of Common Council are liverymen.

The constitution of the livery companies has been unchanged for centuries. There are three ranks of membership: freemen, liverymen and assistants. A person can become a freeman by patrimony (through a parent having been a freeman); by servitude (through having served an apprenticeship to a freeman); or by redemption (by purchase).

Election to the livery is the prerogative of the company, who can elect any of its freemen as liverymen. Assistants are usually elected from the livery and form a court of assistants which is the governing body of the company. The master (in some companies called the prime warden) is elected annually from the assistants.

The register for 2020 lists 25,949 liverymen of the guilds entitled to vote at elections at common hall.

The order of precedence, omitting extinct companies, is given in parentheses after the name of each company in the list below. In certain companies the election of master or prime warden for the year does not take place until the autumn. In such cases the master or prime warden for 2019–20, rather than 2020–21, is given.

The Twelve Great Companies are given in order of civic precedence and appear first in the list below; the remaining guilds are listed in alphabetical order. Parish clerks and watermen and lightermen have requested to remain with no livery and are marked with a '*'.

MERCERS (1). *Hall*, Mercers' Hall, 6 Frederick's Place, London EC2R 8AB *Livery*, 250.
Clerk, Rob Abernethy
Master, Mark Aspinall

GROCERS (2). *Hall*, Grocers' Hall, Princes Street, London EC2R 8AD *Livery*, 360.
Clerk, Brig. Greville Bibby, CBE
Master, Rupert Uloth

DRAPERS (3). *Hall*, Drapers' Hall, Throgmorton Avenue, London EC2N 2DQ *Livery*, 290.
Clerk, Col. Richard Winstanley, OBE
Master, Timothy Orchard

FISHMONGERS (4). *Hall*, Fishmongers' Hall, London Bridge, London EC4R 9EL *Livery*, 330.
Clerk, Cdre Toby Williamson, MVO
Prime Warden, David Jones

GOLDSMITHS (5). *Hall*, Goldsmiths' Hall, Foster Lane, London EC2V 6BN *Livery*, 280.
Clerk, Sir David Reddaway, KCMG, MBE
Prime Warden, Richard Fox

MERCHANT TAYLORS (6/7). *Hall*, Merchant Taylors' Hall, 30 Threadneedle Street, London EC2R 8JB *Livery*, 360.
Clerk, Rear-Adm. John Clink, CBE
Master, Jane Hall

SKINNERS (6/7). *Hall*, Skinners' Hall, 8 Dowgate Hill, London EC4R 2SP *Livery*, 390.
Clerk, Maj.-Gen. Andrew Kennett, CB, CBE
Master, John Emms

HABERDASHERS (8). *Hall*, Haberdashers' Hall, 18 West Smithfield, London EC1A 9HQ *Livery*, 325.
Clerk, Cdre Philip Thicknesse, RN
Master, Daniel Hochberg

SALTERS (9). *Hall*, Salters' Hall, 4 London Wall Place, London EC2Y 5DE *Livery*, 180.
Clerk, vacant
Master, Dr Elizabeth Nodder

IRONMONGERS (10). *Hall*, Ironmongers' Hall, Shaftesbury Place, London EC2Y 8AA *Livery*, 115.
Clerk, Col. Charlie Knaggs, OBE
Master, John Biles

VINTNERS (11). *Hall*, Vintners' Hall, Upper Thames Street, London EC4V 3BG *Livery*, 390.
Clerk, Brig. Jonathan Bourne-May
Master, Christopher Davey

CLOTHWORKERS (12). *Hall*, Clothworkers' Hall, Dunster Court, London EC3R 7AH *Livery*, 210.
Clerk, Joss Stuart-Grumbar
Master, Alex Nelson

ACTUARIES (91). 2nd Floor, 2 London Wall Place, London EC2Y 5AU *Livery*, 260.
Clerk, Lyndon Jones
Master, Julie Griffiths

AIR PILOTS AND AIR NAVIGATORS (81). Air Pilots House, 52A Borough High Street, London SE1 1XN *Livery*, 550.
Clerk, Paul Tacon
Master, John Towell

APOTHECARIES (58). *Hall*, Apothecaries' Hall, 14 Black Friars Lane, London EC4V 6EJ *Livery*, 1,200.
Clerk, Nick Royle
Master, Prof. Michael Farthing

ARBITRATORS (93). 28 The Meadway, Cuffley EN6 4ES *Livery*, 145.
Clerk, Biagio Fraulo
Master, Margaret Bickford-Smith, QC

ARMOURERS AND BRASIERS (22). *Hall*, Armourers' Hall, 81 Coleman Street, London EC2R 5BJ *Livery*, 130.
Clerk, Peter Bateman
Master, Mike Goulette

ARTS SCHOLARS (110). 5 Queen Anne's Gate, White House Walk, Farnham GU9 9AN *Livery*, 150.
Clerk, Lt.-Col. Chris Booth
Master, John Spanner, TD

BAKERS (19). *Hall*, Bakers' Hall, 9 Harp Lane, London EC3R 6DP *Livery*, 235.
Clerk, Lance Whitehouse
Master, Christopher Freeman

BARBERS (17). *Hall*, Barber-Surgeons' Hall, Monkwell Square, London EC2Y 5BL *Livery*, 250.
Clerk, Malachy Doran
Master, Nicolas Goddard

BASKETMAKERS (52). 11 South Way, Seaford BN25 4JG *Livery*, 200.
Clerk, Sarah Sinclair
Prime Warden, Lewis Block, FCSI

BLACKSMITHS (40). Painters' Hall, 9 Little Trinity Lane, London EC4V 2AD *Livery*, 260.
Clerk, Jill Moffatt
Prime Warden, Alderman Alastair King

BOWYERS (38). Fosters Lodge, Duck Street, Warminster BA12 7AL *Livery*, 100.
Clerk, Lt.-Col. Tony Marinos
Master, David Laxton

BREWERS (14). *Hall*, Brewers' Hall, Aldermanbury Square, London EC2V 7HR *Livery*, 200.
Clerk, Col. Michael O'Dwyer, OBE
Master, Richard Fuller

BRODERERS (48). Orchard House, Vicarage Lane, Steeple Ashton BA14 6HH *Livery*, 120.
Clerk, Brig. Bill Aldridge, CBE
Master, Toby Gunter

BUILDERS MERCHANTS (88). 4 College Hill, London EC4R 2RB *Livery*, 210.
Clerk, Virginia Rounding
Master, Stewart Price

BUTCHERS (24). Butchers' Hall, 87 Bartholomew Close, London EC1A 7EB *Livery*, 650.
Clerk, Maj.-Gen. Jeff Mason, MBE, RM
Master, Andrew Parker

CARMEN (77). Plaisterers' Hall, 1 London Wall, London EC2Y 5JU *Livery*, 500.
Clerk, Julian Litchfield
Master, Col. Simon Bennett, TD

CARPENTERS (26). *Hall*, Carpenters' Hall, 1 Throgmorton Avenue, London EC2N 2JJ *Livery*, 150.
Clerk, Brig. Tim Gregson, MBE
Master, Michael Morrison

CHARTERED ACCOUNTANTS (86). 35 Ascot Way, Bicester OX26 1AG *Livery*, 290.
Clerk, Jonathan Grosvenor
Master, Graeme Gordon

CHARTERED ARCHITECTS (98). 53 Lychgate Drive, Horndean PO8 9QE *Livery*, 160.
Clerk, Phil Gibbs
Master, John Assael

CHARTERED SECRETARIES AND ADMINISTRATORS (87). 3rd Floor, Saddlers' Hall, 40 Gutter Lane, London EC2V 6BR *Livery*, 210.
Clerk, Keith Povey
Master, Edward Nicholl

CHARTERED SURVEYORS (85). 75 Meadway Drive, Horsell, Woking GU21 4TF *Livery*, 330.
Clerk, Colin Peacock
Master, Ken Morgan

CLOCKMAKERS (61). 1 Throgmorton Avenue, London EC2N 2BY *Livery*, 285.
Clerk, Camilla Szymanowska
Master, Joanna Migdal

COACHMAKERS AND COACH-HARNESS MAKERS (72). The Old Barn, Church Lane, Glentham LN8 2EL *Livery*, 430.
Clerk, Cdr Mark Leaning
Master, Sarah Adams-Diffey

CONSTRUCTORS (99). 5 Delft Close, Southampton SO31 7TQ *Livery*, 135.
Clerk, Kim Tyrrell
Master, Arthur Seymour

COOKS (35). 18 Solent Drive, Warsash SO31 9HB *Livery*, 70.
Clerk, Vice-Adm. Peter Wilkinson, CB, CVO
Master, Cdre David Smith, CBE

COOPERS (36). *Hall*, Coopers' Hall, 13 Devonshire Square, London EC2M 4TH *Livery*, 250.
Clerk, Cdr Stephen White
Master, Bill Scott

CORDWAINERS (27). Clothworkers' Hall, Dunster Court, London EC3R 7AH *Livery*, 170.
Clerk, Penny Graham
Master, Peter Lamble

CURRIERS (29). Oak Lodge, 4 Greenhill Lane, Wimborne BH21 2RN *Livery*, 110.
Clerk, Adrian Rafferty
Master, Mary McNeill

CUTLERS (18). *Hall*, Cutlers' Hall, Warwick Lane, London EC4M 7BR *Livery*, 90.
Clerk, Rupert Meacher
Master, Dr Caroline Herbert, MBE

DISTILLERS (69). 1 The Sanctuary, London SW1P 3JT *Livery*, 320.
Clerk, Edward Macey-Dare
Master, Jonathan Driver

DYERS (13). *Hall*, Dyers' Hall, 10 Dowgate Hill, London EC4R 2ST *Livery*, 140.
Clerk, Russell Vaizey
Prime Warden, James Rothwell

EDUCATORS (109). 8 Little Trinity Lane, London EC4V 2AN *Livery*, 200.
Clerk, Christian Jensen
Master, Richard Evans

ENGINEERS (94). Saddlers' House, 44 Gutter Lane, London EC2V 6BR *Livery*, 310.
Clerk, Col. David Swann, CBE
Master, Prof. Gordon Masterton

ENVIRONMENTAL CLEANERS (97). Woodfield Cottage, The Street, Mortimer RG7 3DW *Livery*, 160.
Clerk, Philip Morrish
Master, John Shonfeld

FAN MAKERS (76). Skinners' Hall, 8 Dowgate Hill, London EC4R 2SP *Livery*, 190.
Clerk, Martin Davies
Master, Colin Bramall

FARMERS (80). *Hall*, The Farmers' and Fletchers' Hall, 3 Cloth Street, London EC1A 7LD *Livery*, 355.
Clerk, Graham Bamford
Master, Richard Whitlock

FARRIERS (55). 19 Queen Street, Chipperfield, Kings Langley WD4 9BT *Livery*, 330.
Clerk, Charlotte Clifford
Master, John Wilsher

FELTMAKERS (63). Post Cottage, Hook RG29 1DA *Livery*, 200.
Clerk, Maj. Jollyon Coombs
Master, Lady Gilly Yarrow

FIREFIGHTERS (103). 3rd Floor, Wax Chandlers' Hall, 6 Gresham Street, London EC2V 7AD *Livery*, 140.
Clerk, Steven Tamcken
Master, Frances Blois

FLETCHERS (39). *Hall*, 37 Wallingford Avenue, London W10 6PZ *Livery*, 150.
Clerk, Kate Pink
Master, Stuart Robbens

FOUNDERS (33). *Hall*, Founders' Hall, 1 Cloth Fair, London EC1A 7JQ *Livery*, 165.
Clerk, Andrew Bell
Master, Anthony Whiteoak Robinson

FRAMEWORK KNITTERS (64). The Grange, Walton Road, Lutterworth LE17 5RU *Livery*, 185.
Clerk, Shaun Mackaness
Master, Ian Grundy

FRUITERERS (45). The Old Bakery, Bull Lane, Ketton PE9 3TB *Livery*, 260.
Clerk, John Grant
Master, David Simmons

FUELLERS (95). Skinners' Hall, 8 Dowgate Hill, London
EC4R 2SP *Livery*, 160.
Clerk, Crde. Bill Walworth, CBE
Master, HRH Prince Edward, Earl of Wessex, KG, GCVO

FURNITURE MAKERS (83). *Hall*, Furniture Makers' Hall, 12
Austin Friars, London EC2N 2HE *Livery*, 220.
Clerk, Jonny Westbrooke
Master, David Woodward

GARDENERS (66). Ingrams, Ingram's Green, Midhurst
GU29 0LJ *Livery*, 295.
Clerk, Maj. Jeremy Herrtage
Master, Dr Heather Barrett-Modd, OBE

GIRDLERS (23). *Hall*, Girdlers' Hall, Basinghall Avenue, London
EC2V 5DD *Livery*, 80.
Clerk, Brig. Murray Whiteside, OBE
Master, Maj.-Gen. Sir Sebastian Roberts, KCVO, OBE

GLASS SELLERS (71). 238 Nelson Road, Whitton *Livery*, 132.
Clerk, Paul Wenham
Master, Richard Katz

GLAZIERS AND PAINTERS OF GLASS (53). *Hall*, Glaziers'
Hall, 9 Montague Close, London SE1 9DD *Livery*, 180.
Clerk, Liz Wicksteed
Master, Michael Dalton

GLOVERS (62). Seniors Farmhouse, Semley, Shaftesbury
SP7 9AX *Livery*, 250.
Clerk, Lt.-Col. Mark Butler
Master, Richard Morris

GOLD AND SILVER WYRE DRAWERS (74). Lye Green
Forge, Lye Green, Crowborough TN6 1UU *Livery*, 280.
Clerk, Cdr Mark Dickens
Master, Michael Gunston

GUNMAKERS (73). The Proof House, 48–50 Commercial Road,
London E1 1LP *Livery*, 360.
Clerk, Adrian Mundin, MVO
Master, Roderick Richmond-Watson

HACKNEY CARRIAGE DRIVERS (104). 17 Barton Court
Avenue, New Milton BH25 7EP *Livery*, 105.
Clerk, position abolished
Master, Rick Alford

HORNERS (54). 12 Coltsfoot Close, Ixworth
IP31 2NJ *Livery*, 200.
Clerk, Jonathan Mead, FRSA
Master, Martin Muirhead

INFORMATION TECHNOLOGISTS (100). *Hall*, Information
Technologists' Hall, 39A Bartholomew Close, London
EC1A 7JN *Livery*, 380.
Clerk, Susan Hoefling
Master, Mark Holford

INNHOLDERS (32). *Hall*, Innholders' Hall, 30 College Street,
London EC4R 2RH *Livery*, 100.
Clerk, Charles Henty
Master, Keith Harrison

INSURERS (92). PO Box 55873, London N18 9DJ *Livery*, 365.
Clerk, Victoria King
Master, David Sales

INTERNATIONAL BANKERS (106). 12 Austin Friars, London
EC2N 2HE *Livery*, 190.
Clerk, Nicholas Westgarth
Master, Robert Merrett

JOINERS AND CEILERS (41). 3 Dury Road, Barnet
EN5 5PU *Livery*, 130.
Clerk, Alistair MacQueen
Master, James de Sausmarez

LAUNDERERS (89). Glaziers' Hall, 9 Montague Close, London
SE1 9DD *Livery*, 175.
Clerk, Margaret Campbell
Master, Maj. Jack Strachan, MBE

LEATHERSELLERS (15). 7 St Helen's Place, London
EC3A 6AB *Livery*, 150.
Clerk, David Santa-Olalla, DSO, MC
Master, Jonathan Muirhead, OBE, DL

LIGHTMONGERS (96). Tallow Chandlers' Hall, 4 Dowgate Hill,
London EC4R 2SH *Livery*, 150.
Clerk, Victoria McKay
Master, Father Peter Harris

LORINERS (57). 30 Elm Park, Royal Wootton Bassett
SN4 7TA *Livery*, 350.
Clerk, Honor Page
Master, Susan Douthwaite

MAKERS OF PLAYING CARDS (75). 35 Ascot Way, Bicester
E14 3WE *Livery*, 150.
Clerk, Annie Prowse
Master, Giles Stockton

MANAGEMENT CONSULTANTS (105). Skinners' Hall, 8
Dowgate Hill, London EC4R 2SP *Livery*, 130.
Clerk, Julie Fox
Master, Denise Fellows

MARKETORS (90). Plaisterers' Hall, One London Wall, London
EC2Y 5JU *Livery*, 250.
Clerk, John Hammond
Master, Lesley Wilson

MASONS (30). 8 Little Trinity Lane, London
EC4V 2AN *Livery*, 190.
Clerk, Maj. Giles Clapp
Master, Dr Christine Rigden

MASTER MARINERS (78). *Hall*, HQS Wellington, Temple
Stairs, London WC2R 2PN *Livery*, 188.
Clerk, Scott Hanlon
Master, Capt. Derek Chadburn

MUSICIANS (50). 1 Speed Highwalk, Barbican
EC2Y BDX *Livery*, 420.
Clerk, Hugh Lloyd
Master, John Nichols

NEEDLEMAKERS (65). PO Box 73635, London
SW14 9BY *Livery*, 195.
Clerk, Fiona Sedgwick
Master, Andrew Whitton

PAINTER-STAINERS (28). *Hall*, Painters' Hall, 9 Little Trinity
Lane, London EC4V 2AD *Livery*, 270.
Clerk, Christopher Twyman
Master, Peter Huddleston

PATTENMAKERS (70). 3 The High Street, Sutton Valence
ME17 3AG *Livery*, 210.
Clerk, Col. Robert Murfin, TD
Master, Dr David Best

PAVIORS (56). Paviors' House, Charterhouse, London
EC1M 6AN *Livery*, 310.
Clerk, John Freestone
Master, Hugh MacDougald

PEWTERERS (16). *Hall*, Pewterers' Hall, Oat Lane, London
EC2V 7DE *Livery*, 140.
Clerk, Cdre. Mike Walliker, CBE
Master, Chris Hudson, MBE

PLAISTERERS (46). *Hall*, Plaisterers' Hall, 1 London Wall,
London EC2Y 5JU *Livery*, 230.
Clerk, Col. Garth Manger, OBE
Master, Margaret Coates

PLUMBERS (31). Carpenters' Hall, 1 Throgmorton Avenue,
London EC2N 2JJ *Livery*, 340.
Clerk, Adrian Mumford
Master, Dr Peter Rumley

POULTERS (34). 20 Waltham Road, Woodford Green
IG8 8DN *Livery*, 220.
Clerk, Julie Pearce
Master, Reginald Beer

SADDLERS (25). *Hall*, Saddlers' Hall, 40 Gutter Lane, London
EC2V 6BR *Livery*, 90.
Clerk, Brig. Philip Napier, OBE
Prime Warden, Nicholas Mason

SCIENTIFIC INSTRUMENT MAKERS (84). Glaziers' Hall, 9
Montague Close, London SE1 9DD *Livery*, 180.
Clerk, Dr Misha Hebel
Master, Martyn Weatley

SCRIVENERS (44). HQS Wellington, Temple Stairs, Victoria
Embankment, London WC2R 2PN *Livery*, 200.
Clerk, Capt. Arnold Lustman
Master, Barry Theobald-Hicks

SECURITY PROFESSIONALS (108). 4 Holmere Farm
Cottages, Goose Green, Ashill IP25 7AS *Livery*, 180.
Clerk, Patricia Boswell
Master, Yasmeen Stratton

SHIPWRIGHTS (59). Ironmonger's Hall, Shaftesbury Place,
London EC2Y 8AA *Livery*, 420.
Clerk, Lt.-Col. Richard Cole-Mackintosh
Prime Warden, John Denholm

SOLICITORS (79). 4 College Hill, London
EC4R 2RB *Livery*, 410.
Clerk, Linzi James
Master, Robert Bell

SPECTACLE MAKERS (60). Apothecaries' Hall, Black Friars
Lane, London EC4V 6EL *Livery*, 380.
Clerk, Helen Perkins
Master, Huntly Taylor

STATIONERS AND NEWSPAPER MAKERS (47). *Hall*,
Stationers' Hall, Ave Maria Lane, London
EC4M 7DD *Livery*, 530.
Clerk, William Alden, MBE
Master, The Rt. Revd Dr Stephen Platten

TALLOW CHANDLERS (21). *Hall*, Tallow Chandlers' Hall, 4
Dowgate Hill, London EC4R 2SH *Livery*, 180.
Clerk, Brig. David Homer, MBE
Master, Oliver Kirby-Johnson

TAX ADVISERS (107). 10 Deena Close, Queen's Drive
W3 0HR *Livery*, 160.
Clerk, Stephen Henderson
Master, Sue Christensen

TIN PLATE WORKERS (ALIAS WIRE WORKERS) (67).
PO Box 71002, London W4 9FH *Livery*, 180.
Clerk, Dr Piers Baker
Master, Laurence Mutkin

TOBACCO PIPE MAKERS AND TOBACCO BLENDERS
(82). 14 Montpelier Road, Sutton SM1 4QE *Livery*, 135.
Clerk, Sandra Stocker
Master, Adam Bennett

TURNERS (51). Skinner's Hall, 8 Dowgate Hill, London
EC4R 2SP *Livery*, 190.
Clerk, Alex Robertson
Master, Melissa Scott

TYLERS AND BRICKLAYERS (37). 15 Heathway, Chaldon
Cateram CR3 5DN *Livery*, 160.
Clerk, John Brooks
Master, Dr Michel Saminaden

UPHOLDERS (49). Pembroke Lodge, 162 Tonbridge Road,
Hildenborough TN11 9HP *Livery*, 160.
Clerk, Susan Nevard
Master, Wendy Shorter-Blake, MBE

WATER CONSERVATORS (102). The Lark, 2 Bell Lane, Bury
St Edmunds IP28 8SE *Livery*, 175.
Clerk, Ralph Riley
Master, Rob Casey

WAX CHANDLERS (20). *Hall*, Wax Chandlers' Hall, 6 Gresham
Street, London EC2V 7AD *Livery*, 120.
Clerk, Richard Moule
Master, Susan Green

WEAVERS (42). Saddlers' House, Gutter Lane, London
EC2V 6BR *Livery*, 130.
Clerk, James Gaselee
Upper Bailiff, William Makower

WHEELWRIGHTS (68). 90 Fernside Road, London
SW12 8LJ *Livery*, 210.
Clerk, Susie Morris
Master, His Excellency Air Chief Marshal Sir Stephen Dalton

WOOLMEN (43). 153 Leathwaite Road,
SW11 6RW *Livery*, 160.
Clerk, Duncan Crole
Master, Alderman Sir David Wootton

WORLD TRADERS (101). 13 Hall Gardens, St Albans
AL4 0QF *Livery*, 220.
Clerk, Gaye Duffy
Master, Peter Alvey

PARISH CLERKS (90). Acreholt, 33 Medstead Road, Beech,
Alton GU34 4AD *Members*, 90.
Clerk, Alana Coombes
Master, Nigel Thompson

WATERMEN AND LIGHTERMEN (No Livery*). *Hall*,
Watermen's Hall, 16–18 St Mary at Hill, London
EC3R 8EF *Craft Owning Freemen*, 380.
Clerk, Colin Middlemiss
Master, Tony Maynard

WALES

Cymru

The principality of Wales (Cymru) occupies the extreme west of the central southern portion of the island of Great Britain, with a total area of 20,736 sq. km (8,006 sq. miles). It is bordered in the north by the Irish Sea, in the south by the Bristol Channel, in the east by the English counties of Cheshire West and Chester, Shropshire, Herefordshire and Gloucestershire, and in the west by St George's Channel.

Across the Menai Straits is Ynys Mon (Isle of Anglesey) (715 sq. km/276 sq. miles), communication with which is facilitated by the Menai Suspension Bridge (305m/1,000ft long) built by Thomas Telford in 1826, and by the Britannia Bridge (351m/1,151ft), a two-tier road and rail truss arch design, rebuilt in 1972 after a fire destroyed the original tubular railway bridge built by Robert Stephenson in 1850. Holyhead harbour, on Holy Isle (north-west of Anglesey), provides ferry services to Dublin (113km/70 miles).

The Local Government (Wales) Act 1994 abolished the two-tier structure of eight county and 37 district councils which had existed since 1974, and replaced it, from 1 April 1996, with 22 unitary authorities. The new authorities were elected in May 1995. Each unitary authority inherited all the functions of the previous county and district councils, except fire services (which are provided by three combined fire authorities, composed of representatives from the unitary authorities) and national parks (which are the responsibility of three independent national park authorities).

POPULATION

The population at the mid-2019 estimate was 3,138,631 (1,554,678 males; 1,598,201 females). The average density of the population at the mid-2019 estimate was 152 persons per sq. km (392 per sq. mile).

COMMUNITY COUNCILS

In Wales communities are the equivalent of parishes in England. Unlike England, where many areas are not in any parish, communities have been established for the whole of Wales, 870 communities in all. Community meetings may be convened as and when desired.

Community or town councils exist in over 730 of the communities and further councils may be established at the request of a community meeting. Community councils have broadly the same range of powers as English parish councils. Community councillors are elected for a term of four years.

ELECTIONS

Elections usually take place every four years; the last elections took place on 4 May 2017.

FINANCE

Total budgeted revenue expenditure by all local authorities for 2020–21 was £8.7bn, an increase of 4.1 per cent on 2019–20. Total budget requirement, which excludes expenditure financed by specific and special government grants and any use of reserves, was £6.9bn. This comprises revenue support grant of £3.5bn, support from the national non-domestic rate pool of £1.1bn, police grant of £241m and £2.1bn to be raised through council tax. The non-domestic rating multiplier for Wales for 2020–21 is 53.5p. The average Band D council tax levied in Wales for 2020–21 is £1,667, comprising county councils £1,354, police and crime commissioners £275 and community councils £38.

EXPENDITURE

Local authority budgeted revenue expenditure for 2020–21 is:

Service	£ million
Education	2,7893.2
Social services	2,053.8
Housing*	1,022.0
Local environmental services	394.6
Roads and transport	282.3
Libraries, culture, heritage, sport & recreation	193.5
Planning, economic & community development	80.4
Council tax collection	32.1
Debt financing	301.6
Central administrative & other revenue expenditure	398.3
Police	816.6
Fire	166.8
National parks	19.2
Gross revenue expenditure	8,654.7
Less specific & special government grants	(1,897.3)
Net revenue expenditure	6,757.4
Less appropriations from reserves	(118.0)
Council tax reduction scheme	278.2
BUDGET REQUIREMENT	6,917.6

* Includes housing benefit and provision for the homeless, not council owned housing

RELIEF

Wales is a country of extensive tracts of high plateau and shorter stretches of mountain ranges deeply dissected by river valleys. Lower-lying ground is largely confined to the coastal belt and the lower parts of the valleys. The highest mountains are those of Snowdonia in the north-west (Snowdon, 1,085m/3,559ft and Aran Fawddwy, 906m/2,971ft). Snowdonia is also home to Cader Idris (Pen y Gadair, 892m/2,928ft). Other high peaks are to be found in the Cambrian range (Plynlimon, 752m/2,467ft), and the Black Mountains, Brecon Beacons and Black Forest ranges in the south-east (Pen y Fan, 886m/2,906ft; Waun Fâch, 811m/2,660ft; Carmarthen Van, 802m/2,630ft).

HYDROGRAPHY

The principal river in Wales is the Severn, which flows from the slopes of Plynlimon to the English border. The Wye (209km/130 miles) also rises on the slopes of Plynlimon. The Usk (90km/56 miles) flows into the Bristol Channel through Gwent. The Dee (113km/70 miles) rises in Bala Lake and flows through the Vale of Llangollen, where an aqueduct (built by Thomas Telford in 1805) carries the Pontcysyllte branch of the Shropshire Union Canal across the valley. The estuary of the Dee is the navigable portion; it is 23km (14 miles) in length and about 8km (5 miles) in breadth. The Towy (109km/68 miles), Teifi (80km/50 miles), Taff (64km/40 miles), Dovey (48km/30 miles), Taf (40km/25 miles) and Conway (39km/24 miles) are wholly Welsh rivers.

The largest natural lake is Bala (Llyn Tegid) in Gwynedd, nearly 7km (4 miles) long and 1.6km (1 mile) wide. Lake Vyrnwy is an artificial reservoir, about the size of Bala, and forms the water supply of Liverpool; Birmingham's water is supplied from reservoirs in the Elan and Claerwen valleys.

FLAG

The flag of Wales, the Red Dragon (*Y Ddraig Goch*), is a red dragon on a field divided by white over green (*per fess argent and vert a dragon passant gules).* The flag was augmented in 1953 by a royal badge on a shield encircled with a riband bearing the words *Ddraig Goch Ddyry Cychwyn* and imperially crowned, but this augmented flag is rarely used.

WELSH LANGUAGE

At the 2011 census the percentage of people, aged three years and over, recorded as able to speak Welsh was:

Blaenau Gwent	7.8	Neath Port Talbot	15.3
Bridgend	9.7	Newport	9.3
Caerphilly	11.2	Pembrokeshire	19.2
Cardiff	11.1	Powys	18.6
Carmarthenshire	43.9	Rhondda Cynon Taf	12.3
Ceredigion	47.3	Swansea	11.4
Conwy	27.4	Torfaen	9.8
Denbighshire	24.6	Vale of Glamorgan	10.8
Flintshire	13.2	Wrexham	12.9
Gwynedd	65.4	Ynys Mon	
Merthyr Tydfil	8.9	(Isle of Anglesey)	57.2
Monmouthshire	9.9	*Total in Wales*	19.0

EARLY HISTORY

The earliest inhabitants of whom there is any record appear to have been subdued or exterminated by the Goidels (a people of Celtic race) in the Bronze Age. A further invasion of Celtic Brythons and Belgae followed in the ensuing Iron Age. The Roman conquest of southern Britain and Wales was for some time successfully opposed by Caratacus (Caractacus or Caradog), chieftain of the Catuvellauni and son of Cunobelinus (Cymbeline). South-east Wales was subjugated and the legionary fortress at Caerleon-on-Usk established by around AD 75–7; the conquest of Wales was completed by Agricola around AD 78. Communications were opened up by the construction of military roads from Chester to Caerleon-on-Usk and Caerwent, and from Chester to Conwy (and thence to Carmarthen and Neath). Christianity was introduced in the fourth century, during the Roman occupation.

ANGLO-SAXON ATTACKS

The Anglo-Saxon invaders of southern Britain drove the Celts into the mountain stronghold of Wales, and into Strathclyde (Cumberland and south-west Scotland) and Cornwall, giving them the name of *Waelisc* (Welsh), meaning 'foreign'. The West Saxons' victory of Deorham (AD 577) isolated Wales from Cornwall and the battle of Chester (AD 613) cut off communication with Strathclyde and northern Britain. In the eighth century the boundaries of the Welsh were further restricted by the annexations of Offa, King of Mercia, and counter-attacks were largely prevented by the construction of an artificial boundary from the Dee to the Wye (Offa's Dyke).

In the ninth century Rhodri Mawr (844–878) united the country and successfully resisted further incursions of the Saxons by land and raids of Norse and Danish pirates by sea, but at his death his three provinces of Gwynedd (north), Powys (central) and Deheubarth (south) were divided among his three sons, Anarawd, Mervyn and Cadell. Cadell's son Hywel Dda ruled a large part of Wales and codified its laws but the provinces were not united again until the rule of Llewelyn ap Seisyllt (husband of the heiress of Gwynedd) from 1018 to 1023.

THE NORMAN CONQUEST

After the Norman conquest of England, William I created palatine counties along the Welsh frontier, and the Norman barons began to make encroachments into Welsh territory. The Welsh princes recovered many of their losses during the civil wars of Stephen's reign (1135–54), and in the early 13th century Owen Gruffydd, prince of Gwynedd, was the dominant figure in Wales. Under Llywelyn ap Iorwerth (1194–1240) the Welsh united in powerful resistance to English incursions and Llywelyn's privileges and *de facto* independence were recognised in the Magna Carta. His grandson, Llywelyn ap Gruffydd, was the last native prince; he was killed in 1282 during hostilities between the Welsh and English, allowing Edward I of England to establish his authority over the country. On 7 February 1301, Edward of Caernarvon, son of Edward I, was created Prince of Wales, a title subsequently borne by the eldest son of the sovereign.

Strong Welsh national feeling continued, expressed in the early 15th century in the rising led by Owain Glyndwr, but the situation was altered by the accession to the English throne in 1485 of Henry VII of the Welsh House of Tudor. Wales was politically annexed by England under the Act of Union of 1535, which extended English laws to the principality and gave it parliamentary representation for the first time.

EISTEDDFOD

The Welsh are a distinct nation, with a language and literature of their own; the national bardic festival (Eisteddfod), instituted by Prince Rhys ap Griffith in 1176, is still held annually.

PRINCIPAL CITIES

There are six cities in Wales (with date city status conferred): Bangor (pre-1900), Cardiff (1905), Newport (2002), St Asaph (2012), St David's (1994) and Swansea (1969).

Cardiff and Swansea have also been granted lord mayoralties.

CARDIFF

Cardiff *(Caerdydd)*, at the mouth of the rivers Taff, Rhymney and Ely, is the capital city of Wales. The city has changed dramatically in recent years following the regeneration of Cardiff Bay and construction of a barrage, which has created a permanent freshwater lake and waterfront for the city. As the capital city, Cardiff is home to the National Assembly for Wales and is a major administrative, retail, business and cultural centre.

The city is home to many fine buildings, including the City Hall, Cardiff Castle, Llandaff Cathedral, the National Museum of Wales, university buildings, law courts and the Temple of Peace and Health. The Millennium Stadium opened in 1999 and has hosted high-profile events since 2001.

SWANSEA

Swansea *(Abertawe)* is a seaport with a population of 239,023 at the 2011 census. The Gower peninsula was brought within the city boundary under local government reform in 1974.

The principal buildings are the Norman castle (rebuilt *c.*1330), the Royal Institution of South Wales, founded in 1835 (including library), the University of Swansea at Singleton and the Guildhall, containing Frank Brangwyn's British Empire panels. The Dylan Thomas Centre, formerly the old Guildhall, was restored in 1995. More recent buildings include the County Hall, the Maritime Quarter Marina, the Wales National Pool and the National Waterfront Museum.

Swansea was chartered by the Earl of Warwick (1158–84), and further charters were granted by King John, Henry III, Edward II, Edward III and James II, Oliver Cromwell and the Marcher Lord William de Breos. It was formally invested with city status in 1969.

LORD-LIEUTENANTS AND HIGH SHERIFFS

Area	Lord-Lieutenant	High Sheriff (2020–21)
Clwyd	Henry Fetherstonhaugh, OBE	David Wynne-Finch
Dyfed	Sara Edwards	Sharron Lusher
Gwent	Brig. Robert Aiken, CBE	Timothy Russen
Gwynedd	Edmund Bailey	David Williams
Mid Glamorgan	Prof. Peter Vaughan, QPM	Jason Edwards
Powys	Tia Jones	Rhian Duggan
S. Glamorgan	Morfudd Meredith	Andrew Howell
W. Glamorgan	Roberta Fleet	Debra Evans-Williams

LOCAL COUNCILS

Council	Administrative HQ	Telephone	Pop.*	Council Tax†	Chief Executive
Blaenau Gwent	Ebbw Vale	01495-311556	69,862	£2,009	Michelle Morris
Bridgend	Bridgend	01656-643643	147,049	£1,862	Mark Shephard
Caerphilly	Hengoed	01443-815588	181,075	£1,471	Christina Harrhy (interim)
CARDIFF	Cardiff	029-2087 2087	366,903	£1,541	Dr Paul Orders
Carmarthenshire	Carmarthen	01267-234567	188,771	£1,667	Wendy Walters
Ceredigion	Aberaeron	01545-570881	72,695	£1,661	Eifion Evans
Conwy	Conwy	01492-574000	117,203	£1,682	Iwan Davies
Denbighshire	Ruthin	01824-706101	95,696	£1,729	Judith Greenhalgh
Flintshire	Mold	01352-752121	156,100	£1,679	Colin Everett
Gwynedd	Caernarfon	01766-771000	124,560	£1,769	Dilwyn Williams
Merthyr Tydfil	Merthyr Tydfil	01685-725000	60,326	£1,944	Ellis Cooper
Monmouthshire	Cwmbran	01633-644644	94,590	£1,717	Paul Matthews
Neath Port Talbot	Port Talbot	01639-686868	143,315	£1,935	Stephen Phillips
NEWPORT	Newport	01633-656656	154,676	£1,478	Bev Owen (interim)
Pembrokeshire	Haverfordwest	01437-764551	125,818	£1,445	Ian Westley
Powys	Llandrindod Wells	01597-827460	132,435	£1,692	Dr Caroline Turner
Rhondda Cynon Taff	Tonypandy	01443-425005	241,264	£1,799	Chris Bradshaw
SWANSEA	Swansea	01792-636000	246,993	£1,696	Phil Roberts
Torfaen	Pontypool	01495-762200	93,961	£1,690	Alison Ward, CBE
Vale of Glamorgan	Barry	01446-700111	133,587	£1,629	Rob Thomas
Wrexham	Wrexham	01978-292000	135,957	£1,575	Ian Barncroft
Ynys Mon (Isle of Anglesey)	Ynys Mon	01248-750057	70,043	£1,642	Annwen Morgan

* Source: Office for National Statistics – Mid-2019 Population Estimates (Crown copyright)
† Band D council tax bill for 2020–21.
Councils in CAPITAL LETTERS have city status

Key	Council	Key	Council
1	Anglesey (Ynys Mon)	12	Merthyr Tydfil
2	Blaenau Gwent	13	Monmouthshire
3	Bridgend	14	Neath Port Talbot
4	Caerphilly	15	NEWPORT
5	CARDIFF	16	Pembrokeshire
6	Carmarthenshire	17	Powys
7	Ceredigion	18	Rhondda Cynon Taff
8	Conwy	19	SWANSEA
9	Denbighshire	20	Torfaen
10	Flintshire	21	Vale of Glamorgan
11	Gwynedd	22	Wrexham

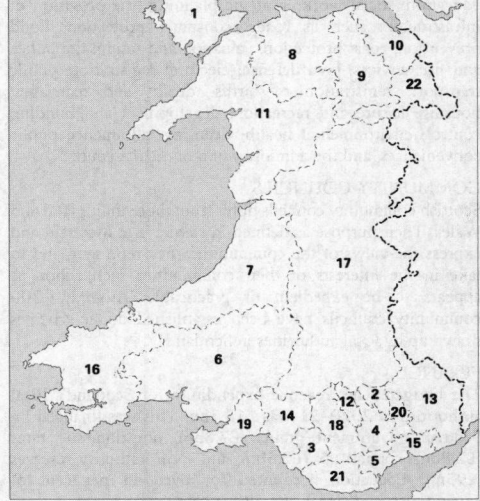

SCOTLAND

Scotland occupies the northern portion of the main island of Great Britain and includes the Inner and Outer Hebrides, Orkney, Shetland and many other islands. It lies between 60° 51′ 30″ and 54° 38′ N. latitude and between 1° 45′ 32″ and 6° 14′ W. longitude, with England to the south-east, the North Channel and the Irish Sea to the south-west, the Atlantic Ocean on the north and west, and the North Sea on the east.

The greatest length of the mainland (Cape Wrath to the Mull of Galloway) is 441km (274 miles), and the greatest breadth (Buchan Ness to Applecross) is 248km (154 miles). The customary measurement of the island of Great Britain is from the site of John o' Groats house, near Duncansby Head, Caithness, to Land's End, Cornwall, a total distance of 970km (603 miles) in a straight line and approximately 1,448km (900 miles) by road.

The Local Government etc (Scotland) Act 1994 abolished the two-tier structure of nine regional and 53 district councils which had existed since 1975 and replaced it, from April 1996, with 29 unitary authorities on the mainland; the three islands councils remained. The new authorities were elected in April 1995.

In July 1999 the Scottish parliament assumed responsibility for legislation on local government.

The total area of Scotland is 77,911 sq. km (30,081 sq. miles).

POPULATION
The population at the mid-2019 estimate was 5,463,300 (2,663,003 males; 2,800,297 females). The average density of the population at the mid-2019 estimate was 70 persons per sq. km (181 per sq. mile).

ELECTIONS
The unitary authorities consist of directly elected councillors. The Scottish Local Government (Elections) Act 2002 moved elections from a three-year to a four-year cycle. The last local authority elections took place in May 2017.

FUNCTIONS
The functions of the councils and islands councils are: education; social work; strategic planning; the provision of infrastructure such as roads; consumer protection; flood prevention; coast protection; valuation and rating; the police and fire services; civil defence; electoral registration; public transport; registration of births, deaths and marriages; housing; leisure and recreation; development and building control; environmental health; licensing; allotments; public conveniences; and the administration of district courts.

COMMUNITY COUNCILS
Scottish community councils differ from those in England and Wales. Their purpose as defined in statute is to ascertain and express the views of the communities they represent, and to take in the interests of their communities such action as appears to be expedient or practicable. Around 1,200 community councils have been established under schemes drawn up by local authorities in Scotland.

FINANCE
The budgeted net revenue expenditure for Scotland's local authorities in 2020–21 was £13.3bn. This was financed by Scottish government grants (£7.8bn), non-domestic rates (£2.8bn), council tax (£2.6bn), and local authority reserves (£95m). Education accounted for over 45 per cent of expenditure, and social care 27 per cent.

The non-domestic tax rate for 2020–21 is 49.8p. Intermediate businesses (rateable value in excess of £51,000) pay 51.1p and higher businesses (rateable value in excess of £95,000) pay 52.4p, which contributes towards the cost of the small business bonus scheme. Non-domestic properties with a rateable value of £15,000 or less do not have to pay business rates. The average Band D council tax for 2020–21 is £1,300.

EXPENDITURE
Local authority budgeted net revenue expenditure for 2020–21 is:

Service	£ million
Education	6,070
Social work	3,572
Environmental services	691
Culture & related service	556
Roads & transport	377
Planning & development	211
All other services	685
Non-service expenditure	1,164
TOTAL	13,327

RELIEF
There are three natural orographic divisions of Scotland. The southern uplands have their highest points in Merrick (843m/ 2,766ft), Rhinns of Kells (814m/2,669ft) and Cairnsmuir of Carsphairn (797m/2,614ft), in the west; and the Tweedsmuir Hills in the east (Broad Law 840m/2,756ft; Dollar Law 817m/2,682ft; Hartfell 808m/2,651ft).

The central lowlands, formed by the valleys of the Clyde, Forth and Tay, divide the southern uplands from the Highlands, which extend from close to the extreme north of the mainland to the central lowlands, and are divided into a northern and a southern system by the Great Glen.

The Grampian Mountains, the southern Highland system, include in the west Ben Nevis (1,345m/4,412ft), the highest point in the British Isles, and in the east the Cairngorm Mountains (Ben Macdui 1,309m/4,296ft; Braeriach 1,295m/4,248ft; Cairn Gorm 1,245m/4,084ft). The north-west Highlands contain the mountains of Wester and Easter Ross (Carn Eige 1,183m/3,880ft; Sgurr na Lapaich 1,151m/ 3,775ft).

Created, like the central lowlands, by a major geological fault, the Great Glen (97km/60 miles long) runs between Inverness and Fort William, and contains Loch Ness, Loch Oich and Loch Lochy. These are linked to each other and to the north-east and south-west coasts of Scotland by the Caledonian Canal, providing a navigable passage between the Moray Firth and the Inner Hebrides.

HYDROGRAPHY
The western coast is fragmented by peninsulas and islands, and indented by fjords (sea-lochs), the longest of which is Loch Fyne (68km/42 miles long) in Argyll. Although the east coast tends to be less fractured and lower, there are several great drowned inlets (firths), including the Firth of Forth, Firth of Tay and the Moray Firth, as well as the Firth of Clyde in the west.

The lochs are the principal hydrographic feature. The largest in Scotland and in Britain is Loch Lomond (70 sq. km/27 sq. miles), in the Grampian valleys, and the longest and deepest is Loch Ness (39km/24 miles long and 244m/800ft deep), in the Great Glen.

The longest river is the Tay (188km/117 miles), noted for its salmon. It flows into the North Sea, with Dundee on the estuary, which is spanned by the Tay Bridge (3,136m/10,289ft) opened in 1887 and the Tay Road Bridge (2,245m/7,365ft) opened in 1966. Other noted salmon rivers are the Dee (145km/90 miles) which flows into the North Sea at Aberdeen, and the Spey (177km/110 miles), the swiftest flowing river in the British Isles, which flows into the Moray Firth. The Tweed, which gave its name to the woollen cloth produced along its banks, marks in the lower stretches of its 154km (96 mile) course the border between Scotland and England.

The most important river commercially is the Clyde (171km/106 miles), formed by the junction of the Daer and Portrail water, which flows through the city of Glasgow to the Firth of Clyde. During its course it passes over the picturesque Falls of Clyde, Bonnington Linn (9m/30ft), Corra Linn (26m/84ft), Dundaff Linn (3m/10ft) and Stonebyres Linn (24m/80ft), above and below Lanark. The Forth (106km/66 miles), upon which stands Edinburgh, the capital, is spanned by the Forth Railway Bridge (1890), which is 1,625m (5,330ft) long, and the Forth Road Bridge (1964), which has a total length of 1,876m (6,156ft) (over water) and a single span of 914m (3,000ft).

The highest waterfall in Scotland, and the British Isles, is Eas a'Chùal Aluinn with a total height of 201m (658ft), which falls from Glas Bheinn in Sutherland. The Falls of Glomach, on a head-stream of the Elchaig in Wester Ross, have a drop of 113m (370ft).

GAELIC LANGUAGE
According to the 2011 census, 1.1 per cent (58,000 people) of the population of Scotland aged three and over were able to speak the Scottish form of Gaelic. This was a slight decrease from the 1.2 per cent recorded at the 2001 census.

LOWLAND SCOTTISH LANGUAGE
Several regional lowland Scottish dialects, known variously as Scots, Lallans or Doric, are widely spoken. According to the 2011 census, 43 per cent of the population of Scotland aged three and over stated they could do one or a combination of read, write, speak or understand Scots. A question on Scots was not included in the 2001 census.

FLAG
The flag of Scotland is known as the Saltire. It is a white diagonal cross on a blue field (saltire argent in a field azure) and represents St Andrew, the patron saint of Scotland.

THE SCOTTISH ISLANDS

ORKNEY
The Orkney Islands (total area 972 sq. km/376 sq. miles) lie about 10km (six miles) north of the mainland, separated from it by the Pentland Firth. Of the 90 islands and islets (holms and skerries) in the group, about one-third are inhabited.

The total population at the 2011 census was 21,349; the 2011 populations of the islands shown here include those of smaller islands forming part of the same council district.

Mainland, 17,162	Inner Holm, 1
Auskerry, 5	Norh Ronaldsay, 72
Burray, 409	Papa Westray, 90
Eday, 160	Rousay, 216
Egilsay, 26	Sanday, 494
Flotta, 8	Shapinsay, 307
Gairsay, 3	South Ronaldsay, 909
Graemsay, 28	Stronsay, 349
Holm of Grimbister, 3	Westray, 588
Hoy, 419	Wyre, 29

The islands are rich in prehistoric and Scandinavian remains, the most notable being the Stone Age village of Skara Brae, the burial chamber of Maes Howe, the many brochs (towers) and the 12th-century St Magnus Cathedral. Scapa Flow, between the Mainland and Hoy, was the war station of the British Grand Fleet from 1914 to 1919 and the scene of the scuttling of the surrendered German High Seas Fleet (21 June 1919).

Most of the islands are low-lying and fertile, and farming (principally beef cattle) is the main industry. Flotta, to the south of Scapa Flow, is the site of the oil terminal for the Piper, Claymore and Tartan fields in the North Sea.

The capital is Kirkwall (population 7,045) situated on Mainland.

SHETLAND
The Shetland Islands have a total area of 1,427 sq. km (551 sq. miles) and had a population at the 2011 census of 23,167. They lie about 80km (50 miles) north of the Orkneys, with Fair Isle about half way between the two groups. Out Stack, off Muckle Flugga, 1.6km (one mile) north of Unst, is the most northerly part of the British Isles (60° 51' 30" N. lat.).

There are over 100 islands, of which 16 are inhabited. Populations at the 2011 census were:

Mainland, 18,765	Muckle Roe, 130
Bressay, 368	Papa Stour, 15
Bruray, 24	Trondra, 135
East Burra, 76	Unst, 632
Fair Isle, 68	Vaila, 2
Fetlar, 61	West Burra, 776
Foula, 38	Whalsay, 1,061
Housay, 50	Yell, 966

Shetland's many archaeological sites include Jarlshof, Mousa and Clickhimin, and its long connection with Scandinavia has resulted in a strong Norse influence on its place names and dialect.

Industries include fishing, knitwear and farming. In addition to the fishing fleet there are fish processing factories, and the traditional handknitting of Fair Isle and Unst is now supplemented with machine-knitted garments. Farming is mainly crofting, with sheep being raised on the moorland and hills of the islands. Since 1970s the islands have been at the centre of the North Sea oil industry, with pipelines from the Brent and Ninian fields running to the terminal at Sullom Voe, one of the largest in Europe. Although much quieter than at the height of oil production in the late 1990s, the terminal marked a milestone 40-year anniversary since first oil in November 2018.

The capital is Lerwick (population 6,958) situated on Mainland. Lerwick is the main centre for supply services for offshore oil exploration and development.

THE HEBRIDES
Until the late 13th century the Hebrides included other Scottish islands in the Firth of Clyde, the peninsula of Kintyre (Argyll), the Isle of Man and the (Irish) Isle of Rathlin. The origin of the name is probably the Greek *Eboudai,* latinised as *Hebudes* by Pliny, and corrupted to its present form. The Norwegian name *Sudreyjar* (Southern Islands) was latinised as *Sodorenses,* a name that survives in the Anglican bishopric of Sodor and Man.

There are over 500 islands and islets, of which about 100 are inhabited, though mountainous terrain and extensive peat bogs mean that only a fraction of the total area is under cultivation. Stone, Bronze and Iron Age settlement has left many remains, including those at Callanish on Lewis, and Norse colonisation influenced language, customs and place names. Occupations include farming (mostly crofting and stock-raising), fishing and the manufacture of tweeds and other woollens. Tourism is an important part of the economy.

The Inner Hebrides lie off the west coast of Scotland and are relatively close to the mainland. The largest and best-known is Skye (area 1,665 sq. km/643 sq. miles; pop. 10,008; chief town, Portree), which contains the Cuillin Hills (Sgurr Alasdair, 993m/3,257ft), Bla Bheinn (928m/3,046ft), the Storr (719m/2,358ft) and the Red Hills (Beinn na Caillich, 732m/2,403ft). Other islands in the Highland council area include Raasay (pop. 161), Eigg (pop. 83), Muck (pop. 27) and Rhum (pop. 22).

Further south the Inner Hebridean islands include Arran (pop. 4,629), containing Goat Fell (874m/2,868ft); Coll (pop. 195) and Tiree (pop. 653); Colonsay (pop. 124) and Oronsay (pop. 8); Easdale (pop. 59); Gigha (pop. 163); Islay (area 608 sq. km/235 sq. miles; pop. 3,228); Jura (area 414 sq. km/160 sq. miles; pop. 196), with a range of hills culminating in the Paps of Jura (Beinn-an-Oir, 785m/2,576ft, and Beinn Chaolais, 755m/2,477ft); Lismore (pop. 192); Luing (pop. 195); and Mull (area 950 sq. km/367 sq. miles; pop. 2,800; chief town Tobermory), containing Ben More (1,174m/3,852 ft).

The Outer Hebrides, separated from the mainland by the Minch, now form the Eilean Siar (Western Isles) council (area 2,897 sq. km/1,119 sq. miles; pop. 27,684). The main islands are Lewis with Harris (area 1,994 sq. km/770 sq. miles, pop. 21,031), whose chief town, Stornoway, is the administrative seat; North Uist (pop. 1,254); South Uist (pop. 1,754); Benbecula (pop. 1,303) and Barra (pop. 1,174). Other inhabited islands include Great Bernera (252), Berneray (138), Eriskay (143), Grimsay (169), Scalpay (291) and Vatersay (90).

EARLY HISTORY

There is evidence of human settlement in Scotland dating from the third millennium BC, the earliest settlers being Mesolithic hunters and fishermen. Early in the second millennium BC, Neolithic farmers began to cultivate crops and rear livestock; their settlements were on the west coast and in the north, and included Skara Brae and Maeshowe (Orkney). Settlement by the early Bronze Age 'Beaker Folk', so-called from the shape of their drinking vessels, in eastern Scotland dates from about 1800 BC. Further settlement is believed to have occurred from 700 BC onwards, as tribes were displaced from further south by new incursions from the Continent and the Roman invasions from AD 43.

Julius Agricola, the Roman governor of Britain AD 77–84, extended the Roman conquests in Britain by advancing into Caledonia, culminating with a victory at Mons Graupius, probably in AD 84; he was recalled to Rome shortly after and his forward policy was not pursued. Hadrian's Wall, mostly completed by AD 30, marked the northern frontier of the Roman empire except for the period between about AD 144 and 190 when the frontier moved north to the Forth-Clyde isthmus and a turf wall, the Antonine Wall, was manned.

After the Roman withdrawal from Britain, there were centuries of warfare between the Picts, Scots, Britons, Angles and Vikings. The Picts, generally accepted to be descended from the indigenous Iron Age people of northern Scotland, occupied the area north of the Forth. The Scots, a Gaelic-speaking people of northern Ireland, colonised the area of Argyll and Bute (the kingdom of Dalriada) in the fifth century AD and then expanded eastwards and northwards. The Britons, speaking a Brythonic Celtic language, colonised Scotland from the south from the first century BC; they lost control of south-eastern Scotland (incorporated into the kingdom of Northumbria) to the Angles in the early seventh century but retained Strathclyde (south-western Scotland and Cumbria). Viking raids from the late eighth century were followed by Norse settlement in the western and northern isles, Argyll, Caithness and Sutherland from the mid-ninth century onwards.

UNIFICATION

The union of the areas which now comprise Scotland began in AD 843 when Kenneth MacAlpin, king of the Scots from c.834, also became king of the Picts, joining the two lands to form the kingdom of Alba (comprising Scotland north of a line between the Forth and Clyde rivers). Lothian, the eastern part of the area between the Forth and the Tweed, seems to have been leased to Kenneth II of Alba (reigned 971–995) by Edgar of England c.973, and Scottish possession was confirmed by Malcolm II's victory over a Northumbrian army at Carham c.1016. At about this time Malcolm II (reigned 1005–34) placed his grandson Duncan on the throne of the British kingdom of Strathclyde, bringing under Scots rule virtually all of what is now Scotland.

The Norse possessions were incorporated into the kingdom of Scotland from the 12th century onwards. An uprising in the mid-12th century drove the Norse from most of mainland Argyll. The Hebrides were ceded to Scotland by the Treaty of Perth in 1266 after a Norwegian expedition in 1263 failed to maintain Norse authority over the islands. Orkney and Shetland fell to Scotland in 1468–9 as a pledge for the unpaid dowry of Margaret of Denmark, wife of James III, although Danish claims of suzerainty were relinquished only with the marriage of Anne of Denmark to James VI in 1590.

From the 11th century, there were frequent wars between Scotland and England over territory and the extent of England's political influence. The failure of the Scottish royal line with the death of Margaret of Norway in 1290 led to disputes over the throne which were resolved by the adjudication of Edward I of England. He awarded the throne to John Balliol in 1292 but Balliol's refusal to be a puppet king led to war. Balliol surrendered to Edward I in 1296 and Edward attempted to rule Scotland himself. Resistance to Scotland's loss of independence was led by William Wallace, who defeated the English at Stirling Bridge (1297), and Robert Bruce, crowned in 1306, who held most of Scotland by 1311 and routed Edward II's army at Bannockburn (1314). England recognised the independence of Scotland in the Treaty of Northampton in 1328. Subsequent clashes include the disastrous battle of Flodden (1513) in which James IV and many of his nobles fell.

THE UNION

In 1603 James VI of Scotland succeeded Elizabeth I on the throne of England (his mother, Mary Queen of Scots, was the great-granddaughter of Henry VII), his successors reigning as sovereigns of Great Britain. Political union of the two countries did not occur until 1707.

THE JACOBITE REVOLTS

After the abdication (by flight) in 1688 of James VII and II, the crown devolved upon William III (grandson of Charles I) and Mary II (elder daughter of James VII and II). In 1689 Graham of Claverhouse roused the Highlands on behalf of James VII and II, but died after a military success at Killiecrankie. After the death of Anne (younger daughter of James VII and II), the throne devolved upon George I (great-grandson of James VI and I). In 1715, armed risings on behalf of James Stuart (the Old Pretender, son of James VII and II) led to the indecisive battle of Sheriffmuir, and the Jacobite movement died down until 1745, when Charles Stuart (the Young Pretender) defeated the Royalist troops at Prestonpans and advanced to Derby (1746). From Derby, Charles Stuart's forces fell back on the defensive and were finally crushed at Culloden (16 April 1746) by an army led by the Duke of Cumberland, son of George II.

PRINCIPAL CITIES

ABERDEEN

Aberdeen, 209km (130 miles) north-east of Edinburgh, received its charter as a Royal Burgh in 1124. Scotland's third largest city, Aberdeen lies between two rivers, the Dee and the Don, facing the North Sea; the city has a strong maritime history and is today a major centre for offshore oil exploration and production. It is also an ancient university town and distinguished research centre.

Places of interest include King's College, St Machar's Cathedral, Brig o' Balgownie, Duthie Park and Winter Gardens, Hazlehead Park, Kirk of St Nicholas, Mercat Cross, Marischal College and Marischal Museum, Provost Skene's House, Gordon Highlanders Museum, Aberdeen Science Centre (formerly Satrosphere), and Aberdeen Maritime Museum. Closed in 2015 for a major £35m redevelopment, Aberdeen Art Gallery, which first opened in 1885 and comprises the Cowdray Hall concert venue and the city's Remembrance Hall, reopened in November 2019.

DUNDEE

The Royal Burgh of Dundee is situated on the north bank of the Tay estuary. The city's port and dock installations are important to the offshore oil industry and the airport also provides servicing facilities.

The unique City Churches – three churches under one roof, together with the 15th-century St Mary's Tower – are the most prominent architectural feature. Dundee is home to two historic ships: the Dundee-built RRS *Discovery* which took Capt. Scott to the Antarctic lies alongside Discovery Quay, and the frigate *Unicorn,* the only British-built wooden warship still afloat, is moored in Victoria Dock. Places of interest include Mills Observatory, the Tay road and rail bridges, Dundee Contemporary Arts centre, The McManus (Dundee's art gallery and museum), Claypotts Castle, Broughty Castle, Verdant Works (textile heritage centre) and the Dundee Science Centre (formerly Sensation).V&A Dundee was opened in September 2018 at a cost of £80.1m.

EDINBURGH

Edinburgh is the capital city and seat of government in Scotland. The new Scottish parliament building designed by Enric Miralles was completed in 2004 and is open to visitors. The city is built on a group of hills and both the Old and New Towns are inscribed on the UNESCO World Cultural and Natural Heritage List for their cultural significance.

Other places of interest include the castle, which houses the Stone of Scone and also includes St Margaret's Chapel, the oldest building in Edinburgh, and near it, the Scottish National War Memorial; the Palace of Holyroodhouse, the Queen's official residence in Scotland; Parliament House, the present seat of the judicature; Princes Street; three universities (Edinburgh, Heriot-Watt, Napier); St Giles' Cathedral; St Mary's (Scottish Episcopal) Cathedral (Sir George Gilbert Scott); General Register House (Robert Adam); the National Library of Scotland, the Signet Library; the Royal Scottish Academy and National Galleries Scotland – comprising the Scottish National Gallery, the Scottish National Portrait Gallery and the Scottish National Gallery of Modern Art.

GLASGOW

Glasgow, a Royal Burgh, is Scotland's largest city and its principal commercial and industrial centre. The city occupies the north and south banks of the Clyde, formerly one of the chief commercial estuaries in the world.

The chief buildings are the 13th-century Gothic cathedral, the university (Sir George Gilbert Scott), the City Chambers, the Royal Concert Hall, St Mungo Museum of Religious Life and Art, Pollok House, Kelvingrove Art Gallery and Museum, the Gallery of Modern Art, the Riverside Museum: Scotland's Museum of Transport and Travel (Zaha Hadid), Mitchell Library and the Burrell Collection museum, which is currently undergoing a major refurbishment and is due to re-open in Spring 2021. The iconic School of Art designed by Charles Rennie Mackintosh (fully completed in 1909) is being rebuilt after it was devastated by two fires; the first in 2014 and the second in 2018. The city is home to the Royal Scottish National Orchestra, Scottish Opera, Scottish Ballet, BBC Scotland and Scottish Television (STV).

Inverness was granted city status in 2000, Stirling in 2002 and Perth in 2012. Aberdeen, Dundee, Edinburgh and Glasgow have also been granted lord mayoralty/lord provostship.

LORD-LIEUTENANTS

Title	Name
Aberdeen City*	Lord Provost Barney Crockett
Aberdeenshire	Alexander Mason
Angus	Patricia Sawers
Argyll and Bute	Jane MacLeod
Ayrshire & Arran	Iona McDonald
Banffshire	Christopher Simpson
Berwickshire	Jeannna Swan
Caithness	Rt. Hon. Viscount Thurso, PC
Clackmannanshire	Lt.-Col. Johnny Stewart, LVO
Dumfries	Lady Fiona MacGregor of MacGregor (Fiona Armstrong)
Dunbartonshire	Jill Young, MBE
Dundee City*	Lord Provost Ian Borthwick
East Lothian	Maj. Michael Williams, MBE
Edinburgh City*	Rt. Hon. Lord Provost Frank Ross
Eilean Siar (Western Isles)	Donald Martin
Fife	Robert Balfour
Glasgow City*	Rt. Hon. Lord Provost Philip Braat
Inverness	Donald Cameron of Lochiel, CVO
Kincardineshire	Alistair Macphie
Lanarkshire	Lady Susan Haughey, CBE
Midlothian	Lt.-Col. Richard Callander, LVO, OBE, TD
Moray	Maj.-Gen. the Hon. Seymour Monro, CBE, LVO
Nairnshire	George Asher
Orkney	Elaine Grieve
Perth & Kinross	Gordon Leckie
Renfrewshire	Col. Peter McCarthy
Ross & Cromarty	Joanie Whiteford
Roxburgh, Ettrick & Lauderdale	Duke of Buccleuch and Queensberry, KT, KBE
Shetland	Robert Hunter
Stirling & Falkirk	Alan Simpson, OBE
Sutherland	Dr Monica Main, CVO
The Stewartry of Kirkcudbright	Elizabeth Gilroy
Tweeddale	Prof. Sir Hew Strachan
West Lothian	Moira Niven, MBE
Wigtown	Aileen Brewis

* The Lord Provosts of the four cities of Aberdeen, Dundee, Edinburgh and Glasgow are Lord-Lieutenants *ex officio* for those districts

LOCAL COUNCILS

Council	Administrative Headquarters	Telephone	Pop.*	Council Tax†	Chief Executive
ABERDEEN	Aberdeen	0300-020 0291	228,670	£1,377	Angela Scott
Aberdeenshire	Aberdeen	0845-608 1207	261,210	£1,301	Jim Savege
Angus	Forfar	0345-277 7778	116,200	£1,207	Margo Williamson
Argyll and Bute	Lochgilphead	01546-602127	85,870	£1,368	Pippa Milne
Clackmannanshire	Alloa	01259-450000	51,540	£1,305	Nikki Bridle
Dumfries and Galloway	Dumfries	030-3333 3000	148,860	£1,223	Gavin Stevenson
DUNDEE	Dundee	01382-434000	149,320	£1,379	David Martin
East Ayrshire	Kilmarnock	01563-576000	122,010	£1,375	Eddie Fraser
East Dunbartonshire	Kirkintilloch	0300-123 4510	108,640	£1,309	Gerry Cornes
East Lothian	Haddington	01620-827827	107,090	£1,303	Monica Patterson
East Renfrewshire	Giffnock	0141-577 3000	95,530	£1,290	Lorraine McMillan
EDINBURGH	Edinburgh	0131-200 2000	524,930	£1,339	Andrew Kerr
Eilean Siar (Western Isles)	Stornoway	01851-703773	26,720	£1,193	Malcolm Burr
Falkirk	Falkirk	01324-506070	160,890	£1,226	Kenneth Lawrie
Fife	Glenrothes	0345-155 0000	373,550	£1,281	Steve Grimmond
GLASGOW	Glasgow	0141-287 2000	633,120	£1,386	Annemarie O'Donnell
Highland	Inverness	01349-886606	235,830	£1,332	Donna Manson
Inverclyde	Greenock	01475-717171	77,800	£1,332	Aubrey Fawcett
Midlothian	Dalkeith	0131-270 7500	92,460	£1,409	Dr Grace Vickers
Moray	Elgin	01343-543451	95,820	£1,323	Roderick Burns
North Ayrshire	Irvine	01294-310000	134,740	£1,343	Craig Hatton
North Lanarkshire	Motherwell	01698-403200	341,370	£1,221	Des Murray
Orkney	Kirkwall	01856-873535	22,270	£1,208	John Mundell (interim)
Perth and Kinross	Perth	01738-475000	151,950	£1,318	Karen Reid
Renfrewshire	Paisley	0300-300 0300	179,100	£1,315	Sandra Black
Scottish Borders	Melrose	01835-824000	115,510	£1,254	Rob Dickson & David Robertson
Shetland	Lerwick	01595-693535	22,920	£1,206	Maggie Sandison
South Ayrshire	Ayr	0300-123 0900	112,610	£1,345	Eileen Howat
South Lanarkshire	Hamilton	0303-123 1015	320,530	£1,203	Cleland Sneddon
STIRLING	Stirling	0845-277 7000	94,210	£1,344	Carol Beattie
West Dunbartonshire	Dumbarton	01389-737000	88,930	£1,294	Joyce White, OBE
West Lothian	Livingston	01506-280000	183,100	£1,276	Graham Hope

* *Source*: Office for National Statistics – *Mid-2019 Population Estimates* (Crown copyright)
† Average Band D council tax bill 2020–21.
Councils in CAPITAL LETTERS have city status

Key	Council	Key	Council
1	Aberdeen City	17	Inverclyde
2	Aberdeenshire	18	Midlothian
3	Angus	19	Moray
4	Argyll and Bute	20	North Ayrshire
5	City of Edinburgh	21	North Lanarkshire
6	Clackmannanshire	22	Orkney
7	Dumfries and Galloway	23	Perth and Kinross
8	Dundee City	24	Renfrewshire
9	East Ayrshire	25	Scottish Borders
10	East Dunbartonshire	26	Shetland
11	East Lothian	27	South Ayrshire
12	East Renfrewshire	28	South Lanarkshire
13	Falkirk	29	Stirling
14	Fife	30	West Dunbartonshire
15	Glasgow City	31	Western Isles (Eilean Siar)
16	Highland	32	West Lothian

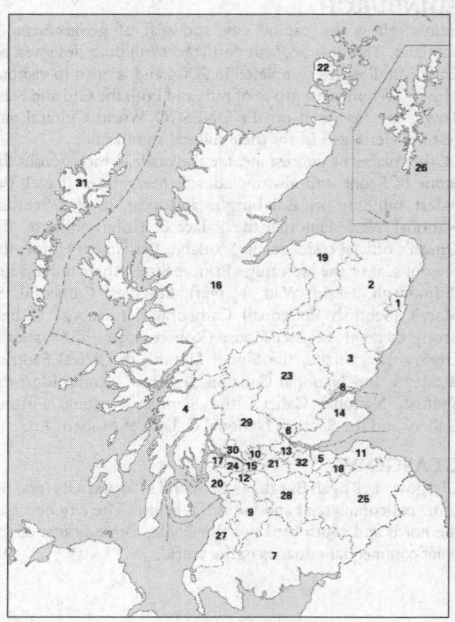

NORTHERN IRELAND

Northern Ireland has a total area of 13,793 sq. km (5,326 sq. miles).

In 2012 a reform programme began to reduce the number of district councils from 26 to 11. The Local Government Act (Northern Ireland) received royal assent on 12 May 2014 providing new governance arrangements for local councils and made transitional provisions for the transfer of staff, assets and liabilities etc to the new 11 councils. On 1 April 2015 additional functions, that were previously the responsibility of the Northern Ireland executive, fully transferred to the new district authorities.

POPULATION
The population of Northern Ireland at the mid-2019 estimate was 1,893,667 (932,717 males; 960,950 females). The estimated average density of population at mid-2019 was 137 persons per sq. km (353 per sq. mile).

ELECTIONS
Elections to the 11 councils took place on 2 May 2019.

FUNCTIONS
The councils are responsible for approving business and financial plans, setting domestic and non-domestic rates. Since April 2016 councils have also been responsible for urban regeneration and community development.

The district councils are responsible for:

Direct Service Provision of a wide range of local services, including: building control-inspection and the regulation of new buildings; byelaw enforcement; cemeteries; community centres; cultural facilities; dog control; environmental health; food safety; health and safety; local economic development; local planning; off-street parking (except park and ride schemes); parks, open spaces and playgrounds; public conveniences; recycling and waste management; registration of births, deaths and marriages; sport, leisure and recreational facilities; and street cleaning. District councils also have a role in community development and safety; sports development; summer schemes; and tourism.

Representation: nominating representatives to sit as members of the various statutory bodies responsible for the administration of regional services such as education, health and social services, libraries and road safety committees

FINANCE
Government in Northern Ireland is part-funded by a system of rates, which supplement the Northern Ireland budget from the UK government. The ratepayer receives a combined tax bill consisting of the regional rate, set by the Northern Ireland executive, and the district rate, which is set by each district council. The regional and district rates are both collected by Land and Property Services (part of the Department of Finance). The product of the district rates is paid over to each council while the product of the regional rate supports expenditure by the departments of the executive and assembly.

Since April 2007 domestic rates bills have been based on the capital value of a property, rather than the rental value. The capital value is defined as the price the property might reasonably be expected to realise had it been sold on the open market on 1 January 2005. Non-domestic rates bills are based on the rental value of the property as at 1 April 2013.

Rate bills are calculated by multiplying the property's net annual rental value (in the case of non-domestic property), or capital value (in the case of domestic property), by the regional and district rate poundages respectively.

For 2020–21 the overall average domestic poundage is 0.8427p compared to 0.8302p in 2012–20. The overall average non-domestic rate poundage in 2020–21 is 53.02p compared to 59.53p in 2019–20.

FLAG
The official national flag of Northern Ireland is the Union Flag.

PRINCIPAL CITIES
In addition to Belfast and Londonderry, three other places in Northern Ireland have been granted city status: Armagh (1994), Lisburn (2002) and Newry (2002).

BELFAST
Belfast, the administrative centre of Northern Ireland, is situated at the mouth of the River Lagan at its entrance to Belfast Lough. The city grew to be a great industrial centre, owing to its easy access by sea to Scottish coal and iron.

The principal buildings are of a relatively young age and include the parliament buildings at Stormont, the City Hall, Waterfront Hall, the Law Courts, the Public Library and the Ulster Museum, situated in the botanic gardens. The Metropolitan Arts Centre (MAC), an award-winning arts venue designed by Belfast-based architectural practice Hall McKnight, was completed in February 2019 and is situated opposite St Anne's Cathedral. In March 2012, Titanic Belfast opened on the banks of the Lagan River on the site of the shipyard where RMS *Titanic* was built and launched. The museum forms the centrepiece of a new mixed-use maritime quarter.

Belfast received its first charter of incorporation in 1613 and was created a city in 1888; the title of lord mayor was conferred in 1892.

LONDONDERRY
Londonderry (originally Derry) is situated on the River Foyle, and has important associations with the City of London. The Irish Society was created by the City of London in 1610, and under its royal charter of 1613 it fortified the city and was for a long time closely associated with its administration. Because of this connection the city was incorporated in 1613 under the new name of Londonderry.

The city is famous for the great siege of 1688–9, when for 105 days the town held out against the forces of James II. The city walls are still intact and form a circuit of 1.6 km (one mile) around the old city.

Interesting buildings are the Protestant cathedral of St Columb's (1633) and the Guildhall, reconstructed in 1912 and containing a number of beautiful stained glass windows, many of which were presented by the livery companies of London.

CONSTITUTIONAL HISTORY
Northern Ireland is subject to the same fundamental constitutional provisions which apply to the rest of the UK. It had its own parliament and government from 1921 to 1972, but after increasing civil unrest the Northern Ireland (Temporary Provisions) Act 1972 transferred the legislative and executive powers of the Northern Ireland parliament and government to the UK parliament and a secretary of state. The

Northern Ireland Constitution Act 1973 provided for devolution in Northern Ireland through an assembly and executive, but a power-sharing executive formed by the Northern Ireland political parties in January 1974 collapsed in May 1974 and Northern Ireland returned to direct rule governance under the provisions of the Northern Ireland Act 1974, placing the Northern Ireland department under the direction and control of the Northern Ireland secretary.

In December 1993 the British and Irish governments published the Joint Declaration, complementing their political talks and making clear that any settlement would need to be founded on principles of democracy and consent.

On 12 January 1998 the British and Irish governments issued a joint document, *Propositions on Heads of Agreement,* proposing the establishment of various new cross-border bodies; further proposals were presented on 27 January. A draft peace settlement was issued by the talks' chair, US Senator George Mitchell, on 6 April 1998 but was rejected by the Unionists the following day. On 10 April agreement was reached between the British and Irish governments and the eight Northern Ireland political parties still involved in the talks (the Good Friday Agreement). The agreement provided for an elected Northern Ireland Assembly, a North/South Ministerial Council, and a British-Irish Council comprising representatives of the British, Irish, Channel Islands and Isle of Man governments and members of the new assemblies for Scotland, Wales and Northern Ireland. Further points included the abandonment of the Republic of Ireland's constitutional claim to Northern Ireland, the decommissioning of weapons, the release of paramilitary prisoners and changes in policing.

The agreement was ratified in referendums held in Northern Ireland and the Republic of Ireland on 22 May 1998. In the UK, the Northern Ireland Act received royal assent in November 1998.

On 28 April 2003 the secretary of state again assumed responsibility for the direction of the Northern Ireland departments on the dissolution of the Northern Ireland Assembly, following its initial suspension from midnight on 14 October 2002. In 2006, following the passing of the Northern Ireland Act, the secretary of state created a non-legislative fixed-term assembly which would cease to operate either when the political parties agreed to restore devolution, or on 24 November 2006 (whichever occurred first). In October 2006 a timetable to restore devolution was drawn up (St Andrews Agreement) and a transitional Northern Ireland Assembly was formed on 24 November. The transitional assembly was dissolved in January 2007 in preparation for elections to be held on 7 March; following the elections a power-sharing executive was formed and the new 108-member Northern Ireland Assembly became operational on 8 May 2007.

A breakdown of trust between the parties following the Renewable Heat Incentive scandal resulted in the dissolution of the 5th assembly and executive on 26 January 2017 and a new election took place in March 2017. Following this election negotiations to form an executive missed both the normal three week deadline and an extended deadline of 29 June 2017 and the sixth assembly was suspended until 11 January 2020. For further information *see* Devolved Government.

LORD-LIEUTENANTS AND HIGH SHERIFFS

County	Lord-Lieutenant	High Sheriff (2020)
Antrim	David McCorkell	Rupert Cramsie
Armagh	Earl of Caledon, KCVO	Michael Dickson
Belfast City	Fionnuala Jay-O'Boyle, CBE	Nicola Verner
Down	David Lindsay	Austin Baird
Fermanagh	Viscount Brookeborough, KG	Breda McGrenaghan, BEM
Londonderry	Alison Millar	Ross Wilson, BEM
Londonderry City	Dr Angela Garvey	James Doherty
Tyrone	Robert Scott, OBE	Gordon Aiken, BEM

LOCAL COUNCILS

Council	Telephone	Population*	Chief Executive
Antrim & Newtownabbey	028-9448 1311	143,504	Jacqui Dixon
Ards & North Down	0300-013 3333	161,725	Stephen Reid
Armagh City, Banbridge & Craigavon	0300-030 0900	216,205	Roger Wilson
Belfast City	028-9027 0549	343,542	Suzanne Wylie
Causeway Coast & Glens	028-7034 7034	144,838	David Jackson, MBE
Derry City & Strabane	028-7138 2204	151,284	John Kelpie
Fermanagh & Omagh	0300-303 1777	117,397	Brendan Hegarty
Lisburn & Castlereagh	028-9250 9250	146,002	David Burns
Mid & East Antrim	028-9335 8000	139,274	Anne Donaghy
Mid Ulster	0300-013 2132	148,528	Adrian McCreesh
Newry, Mourne & Down	028-3031 3037	181,368	Marie Ward

* *Source:* Office for National Statistics – *Mid-2019 Population Estimates* (Crown copyright)

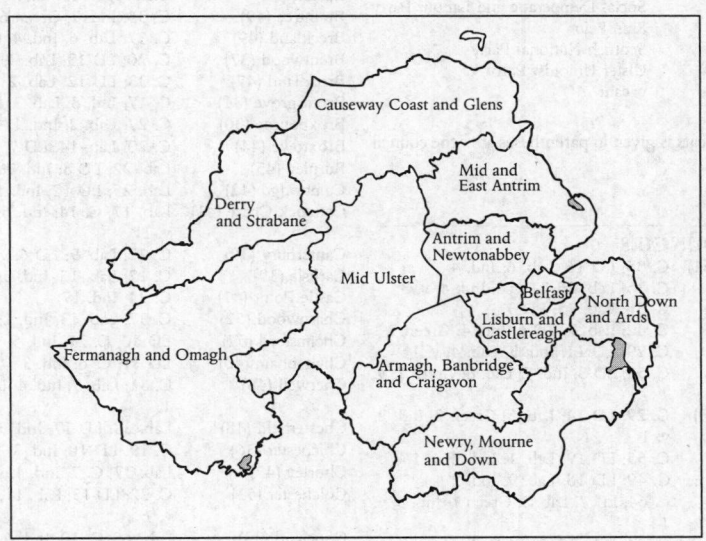

POLITICAL COMPOSITION OF COUNCILS

Most local elections were cancelled in 2020 because of the coronavirus pandemic. Listed are the the the composition of councils as at December 2020

Abbreviations

All.	Alliance
C.	Conservative
DUP	Democratic Unionist Party
Green	Green
Ind.	Independent or other party
Lab.	Labour
LD	Liberal Democrat
PC	Plaid Cymru
SDLP	Social Democratic and Labour Party
SF	Sinn Fein
SNP	Scottish National Party
UUP	Ulster Unionist Party
v.	vacant

Total number of seats is given in parentheses after the council name.

ENGLAND

COUNTY COUNCILS

Cambridgeshire (61)	C. 35; LD 16; Lab. 6; Ind. 4
Cumbria (84)	C. 35; Lab. 26; LD 16; Ind. 4; v. 3
Derbyshire (64)	C. 36; Lab. 25; LD 3
Devon (60)	C. 42; Lab. 7; LD 6; Ind. 4; Green 1
East Sussex (50)	C. 29; LD 11; Ind. 5; Lab. 4; v. 1
Essex (75)	C. 52; LD 8; Ind. 7; Lab. 6; Green 1; v. 1
Gloucestershire (53)	C. 29; LD 14; Lab. 5; Green 2; Ind. 2; v. 1
Hampshire (78)	C. 55; LD 19; Lab. 1; Ind. 2; v. 1
Hertfordshire (78)	C. 49; LD 18; Lab. 9; Ind. 2
Kent (81)	C. 64; LD 7; Lab. 5; Green 1; Ind. 3; v. 1
Lancashire (84)	C. 44; Lab. 30; LD 4; Ind. 4; Green 1; v. 1
Leicestershire (55)	C. 36; LD 13; Lab. 6
Lincolnshire (70)	C. 54; Lab. 5; Ind. 9; LD 1; v. 1
Norfolk (84)	C. 54; Lab. 16; LD 9; Ind. 4; v. 1
North Yorkshire (72)	C. 52; Ind. 12; Lab. 4; LD 4
Northamptonshire (57)	C. 40; Lab. 11; Ind. 3; LD 2; v. 1
Nottinghamshire (66)	C. 32; Lab. 22; Ind. 11; LD 1
Oxfordshire (63)	C. 30; Lab. 14; LD 13; Ind. 5
Somerset (55)	C. 33; LD 14; Ind. 3; Lab. 3; Green 2
Staffordshire (62)	C. 51; Lab. 10; Ind. 1
Suffolk (75)	C. 49; Lab. 11; LD 5; Ind. 6; Green 3; v. 1
Surrey (81)	C. 57; Ind. 13; LD 9; Lab. 1; Green 1
Warwickshire (57)	C. 34; Lab. 8; LD 8; Ind. 2; Green 2; v. 3
West Sussex (70)	C. 51; LD 8; Lab. 4; Ind. 6; v. 1
Worcestershire (57)	C. 41; Lab. 8; LD 2; Green 2; Ind. 3; v. 3

DISTRICT COUNCILS

Adur (29)	C. 15; Lab. 7; Ind. 5; v. 2
Allerdale (49)	Ind. 17; C. 15; Lab. 12; v. 5
Amber Valley (45)	Lab. 23; C. 16; Green 1; Ind. 2; v. 3
Arun (54)	C. 21; LD 18; Ind. 11; Green 2; Lab. 1; v. 1
Ashfield (35)	Ind. 29; C. 3; Lab. 2; v. 1
Ashford (47)	C. 25; Ind. 13; Lab. 6; Green 2; v. 1
Babergh (32)	C. 13; Ind. 10; Green 4; LD 3; Lab. 2
Barrow-in-Furness (36)	Lab. 23; C. 11; v. 2
Basildon (42)	C. 19; Lab. 15; Ind. 7; v. 1
Basingstoke and Deane (60)	C. 28; Lab. 13; Ind. 11; LD 7; v. 1
Bassetlaw (48)	Lab. 37; C. 5; Ind. 5; LD 1
Blaby (39)	C. 24; Lab. 6; LD 6; Green 1; Ind. 1; v. 1
Bolsover (37)	Lab. 17; Ind. 15; C. 3; v. 2
Boston (30)	Ind. 15; C. 13; Lab. 2
Braintree (49)	C. 33; Ind. 7; Green 6; Lab. 2; v. 1
Breckland (49)	C. 37; Lab. 6; Ind. 4; Green 2
Brentwood (37)	C. 20; LD 13; Lab. 3; Ind. 1
Broadland (47)	C. 33; LD 12; Lab. 2
Bromsgrove (31)	C. 17; Ind. 8; Lab. 3; LD 3
Broxbourne (30)	C. 27; Lab. 2; Ind. 1
Broxtowe (44)	C. 20; Lab. 14; LD 7; Ind. 3
Burnley (45)	Lab. 22; LD 8; Ind. 7; C. 6; Green 2
Cambridge (42)	Lab. 25; LD 12; Ind. 1; v. 4
Cannock Chase (41)	Lab. 17; C. 14; Ind. 6; LD 2; Green 1; v. 1
Canterbury (39)	C. 22; Lab. 9; LD 6; v. 2
Carlisle (39)	C. 17; Lab. 15; Ind. 5; LD 1; Green 1
Castle Point (41)	C. 24; Ind. 17
Charnwood (52)	C. 37; Lab. 13; Ind. 1; Green 1
Chelmsford (57)	LD 30; C. 21; Ind. 5; v. 1
Cheltenham (40)	LD 31; C. 6; Ind. 3
Cherwell (48)	C. 31; Lab. 9; Ind. 4; LD 2; Green 1; v. 1
Chesterfield (48)	Lab. 28; LD 17; Ind. 3
Chichester (36)	C. 19; LD 10; Ind. 3; Lab. 2; Green 2
Chorley (47)	Lab. 37; C. 7; Ind. 1; v. 2
Colchester (51)	C. 22; LD 13; Lab. 11; Ind. 3; Green 1; v. 1
Copeland (33)	Lab. 16; C. 10; Ind. 6; v. 1
Corby (29)	Lab. 22; C. 4; Ind. 1; v. 2
Cotswolds (34)	LD 18; C. 14; Green 1; Ind. 1
Craven (30)	C. 15; Ind. 8; Lab. 3; Green 2; LD 1; v. 1
Crawley (36)	C. 17; Lab. 17; Ind. 2; v. 1
Dacorum (51)	C. 31; LD 18; Ind. 1; v. 1
Dartford (42)	C. 29; Lab. 9; Ind. 4
Daventry (36)	C. 29; Lab. 4; LD 2; Ind. 1
Derbyshire Dales (39)	C. 20; LD 8; Lab. 6; Ind. 3; Green 2
Dover (32)	C. 19; Lab. 12; Ind. 1
East Cambridgeshire (28)	C. 15; LD 11; Ind. 2
East Devon (60)	Ind. 31; C. 19; LD 8; Green 2
East Hampshire (43)	C. 32; LD 8; Lab. 2; Ind. 1
East Hertfordshire (50)	C. 40; LD 6; Lab. 2; Green 2
East Lindsey (55)	C. 30; Ind. 18; Lab. 6; LD 1
East Northamptonshire (40)	C. 36; Ind. 3; Lab. 1
East Staffordshire (39)	C. 25; Lab. 9; Ind. 2; LD 1; v. 2
East Suffolk (55)	C. 39; Lab. 7; Green 4; LD 3; Ind. 1; v. 1
Eastbourne (27)	LD 17; C. 9; v. 1
Eastleigh (39)	LD 33; Ind. 2; Ind. 3; C. 2; v. 1

Eden (38)   C. 13; LD 11; Ind. 9; Lab. 2; Green 2; v. 1

Elmbridge (48)   Ind. 21; C. 18; LD 7; v. 2

Epping Forest (58)   C. 35; Ind. 15; Green 3; LD 3; v. 2

Epsom and Ewell (38)   Ind. 32; Lab. 3; LD 2; C. 1

Erewash (47)   C. 27; Lab. 18; LD 1; Ind. 1

Exeter (39)   Lab. 28; C. 6; LD 2; Ind. 1; Green 1; v. 1

Fareham (31)   C. 21; Ind. 5; LD 4; v. 1

Fenland (39)   C. 25; Ind. 10; LD 2; Green 1

Folkestone and Hythe (30)   C. 13; Green 6; Lab. 5; LD 2; Ind. 4

Forest of Dean (38)   Ind. 15; C. 9; Green 6; Lab. 5; LD 2; v. 1

Fylde (51)   C. 31; Ind. 19; LD 1

Gedling (41)   Lab. 29; C. 8; Ind. 2; LD 2

Gloucester (39)   C. 19; Lab. 8; LD 9; Ind. 1; v. 2

Gosport (34)   C. 18; LD 14; Lab. 2

Gravesham (44)   Lab. 22; C. 19; Ind. 2; v. 1

Great Yarmouth (39)   C. 20; Lab. 15; Ind. 4

Guildford (48)   Ind. 24; LD 17; C. 4; Lab. 2; v. 1

Hambleton (28)   C. 24; Ind. 2; LD 1; Lab. 1

Harborough (34)   C. 22; LD 11; Lab. 1

Harlow (33)   Lab. 19; C. 12; v. 2

Harrogate (40)   C. 31; LD 7; Ind. 2

Hart (33)   Ind. 11; C. 11; LD 10; v. 1

Hastings (32)   Lab. 23; C. 8; Ind. 1

Havant (38)   C. 33; Lab. 2; Ind. 2; LD 1

Hertsmere (39)   C. 29; Lab. 6; LD 3; v. 1

High Peak (43)   Lab. 22; C. 16; LD 3; Green 2

Hinckley and Bosworth (34)   LD 21; C. 11; Lab. 2

Horsham (48)   C. 32; LD 12; Green 2; Ind. 1; v. 1

Huntingdonshire (52)   C. 30; Ind. 11; LD 7; Lab. 4

Hyndburn (35)   Lab. 25; C. 6; Ind. 2; v. 2

Ipswich (48)   Lab. 36; C. 8; LD 3; v. 1

Kettering (36)   C. 22; Lab. 7; Ind. 4; LD 1; v. 2

King's Lynn and West Norfolk (55)   C. 29; Ind. 15; Lab. 9; LD 1; Green 1

Lancaster (60)   Ind. 21; Lab. 14; C. 12; Green 10; LD 2; v. 1

Lewes (41)   C. 17; LD 9; Green 8; Lab. 3; Ind. 2; v. 2

Lichfield (47)   C. 34; Lab. 10; Ind. 1; LD 1; v. 1

Lincoln City (33)   Lab. 24; C. 9

Maidstone (55)   C. 24; LD 20; Ind. 6; Lab. 4; v. 1

Maldon (31)   Ind. 21; C. 8; v. 2

Malvern Hills (38)   C. 13; Ind. 10; LD 9; Green 5; Lab. 1

Mansfield (36)   Ind. 20; Lab. 14; C. 2

Melton (28)   C. 20; Ind. 7; Green 1

Mendip (47)   LD 24; C. 11; Green 10; Ind. 2

Mid Devon (42)   C. 17; LD 11; Ind. 9; Green 2

Mid Suffolk (34)   C. 16; Green 12; LD 5; Ind. 1

Mid Sussex (54)   C. 34; LD 13; Ind. 3; Green 3; v. 1

Mole Valley (41)   LD 22; C. 11; Ind. 8

New Forest (60)   C. 46; LD 13; Ind. 1

Newark and Sherwood (39)   C. 27; Lab. 7; Ind. 3; LD 2

Newcastle-under-Lyme (44)   Lab. 19; C. 19; Ind. 4; LD 2

North Devon (42)   LD 21; C. 12; Ind. 7; Green 2

North East Derbyshire (53)   C. 30; Lab. 18; LD 3; Ind. 2

North Hertfordshire (49)   C. 21; Lab. 15; LD 11; v. 2

North Kesteven (43)   Ind. 21; C. 21; v. 1

North Norfolk (40)   LD 28; C. 8; Ind. 4

North Warwickshire (35)   C. 20; Lab. 14; Ind. 1

North West Leicestershire (38)   C. 20; Lab. 9; LD 4; Ind. 3; Green 1; v. 1

Northampton (45)   C. 24; Lab. 16; LD 3; Ind. 1; v. 1

Norwich (39)   Lab. 27; Green 8; LD 3; v. 1

Nuneaton and Bedworth (34)   Lab. 17; C. 14; Ind. 2; Green 1

Oadby and Wigston (26)   LD 24; C. 2

Oxford (48)   Lab. 32; LD 8; Green 2; Ind. 3; v. 3

Pendle (49)   C. 20; Lab. 15; LD 10; Ind. 1; v. 3

Preston (48)   Lab. 30; LD 9; C. 8; v. 1

Redditch (29)   C. 18; Lab. 10; v. 1

Reigate and Banstead (45)   C. 29; Ind. 7; Green 5; LD 3; v. 1

Ribble Valley (40)   C. 27; LD 10; Ind. 2; v. 1

Richmondshire (24)   Ind. 11; C. 9; LD 3; Green 1

Rochford (39)   C. 26; Ind. 6; LD 3; Green 2; v. 2

Rossendale (36)   Lab. 19; C. 13; Ind. 4

Rother (38)   C. 14; Ind. 13; LD 7; Lab. 3; Green 1

Rugby (42)   C. 24; LD 9; Lab. 9

Runnymede (41)   C. 25; Ind. 10; LD 3; Lab. 2; Green 1

Rushcliffe (44)   C. 29; Lab. 7; Ind. 3; LD 3; Green 2

Rushmoor (39)   C. 26; Lab. 10; LD 1; v. 2

Ryedale (30)   Ind. 17; C. 11; LD 2

St Albans (58)   LD 24; C. 24; Lab. 5; Ind. 4; Green 1

Scarborough (46)   Ind. 17; C. 14; Lab. 13; Green 2

Sedgemoor (48)   C. 29; Lab. 11; LD 7; Ind. 1

Selby (31)   C. 16; Lab. 8; Ind. 7

Sevenoaks (54)   C. 46; Ind. 4; LD 3; Lab. 1

Somerset West and Taunton (59)   LD 32; Ind. 13; C. 9; Lab. 3; Green 2

South Cambridgeshire (45)   LD 28; C. 11; Ind. 2; Lab. 2; v. 2

South Derbyshire (36)   C. 22; Lab. 14; Ind. 7; v. 3

South Hams (31)   C. 15; LD 10; Green 3; Ind. 2; v. 1

South Holland (37)   C. 24; Ind. 13

South Kesteven (56)   C. 38; Ind. 12; Lab. 3; LD 2; v. 1

South Lakeland (51)   LD 30; C. 13; Lab. 3; Green 1; v. 4

South Norfolk (46)   C. 35; LD 10; Lab. 1

South Northamptonshire (42)   C. 32; LD 6; Ind. 3; v. 1

South Oxfordshire (36)   LD 12; C. 9; Ind. 6; Green 5; Lab. 3; v. 1

South Ribble (50)   C. 23; Lab. 21; LD 5; v. 1

South Somerset (60)   LD 40; C. 14; Green 1; Ind. 5

South Staffordshire (49)   C. 37; Ind. 8; Green 3; Lab. 1

Spelthorne (39)   C. 16; Ind. 12; LD 7; Lab. 2; Green 2

Stafford (40)   C. 22; Lab. 10; Ind. 7; Green 1

Staffordshire Moorlands (56)   C. 25; Ind. 16; Lab. 13; LD 1; v. 1

Stevenage (39)   Lab. 27; C. 7; LD 5

Stratford-on-Avon (36)   C. 19; LD 12; Ind. 4; Green 1

Stroud (51)   C. 21; Lab. 16; Green 9; LD 2; Ind. 2; v. 1

Surrey Heath (35)   C. 16; LD 9; Ind. 6; Green 2; Lab. 1; v. 1

Swale (47)   C. 16; Ind. 13; Lab. 11; LD 5; Green 2

Tamworth (30)   C. 21; Lab. 5; Ind. 4

Tandridge (42)   C. 15; Ind. 15; LD 9; v. 3

Teignbridge (47)   LD 24; C. 12; Ind. 11

Tendring (48)   Ind. 19; C. 19; Lab. 6; LD. 2; v. 2

Test Valley (43)   C. 22; LD 12; Ind. 6; v. 3

Tewkesbury (38)   C. 23; LD 8; Ind. 6; Green 1

Thanet (56)   C. 25; Lab. 19; Ind. 8; Green 3; v. 1

Three Rivers (39)   LD 22; C. 11; Lab. 3; Ind. 3

Tonbridge and Malling (54)   C. 39; LD 9; Ind. 3; Green 2; Lab. 1

Torridge (36) Ind. 18; C. 11; Lab. 3; LD 2; Green 2
Tunbridge Wells (48) C. 28; LD 10; Ind. 5; Lab. 4; v. 1
Uttlesford (39) Ind. 26; LD 5; C. 4; Ind. 2; v. 2
Vale of White Horse (38) LD 30; C. 6; Green 1; v. 1
Warwick (44) C. 19; LD 9; Green 8; Lab. 5; Ind. 3
Watford (36) LD 26; Lab. 10
Waverley (57) C. 23; Ind. 16; LD 14; Green 2; Lab. 2
Wealden (45) C. 30; Ind. 6; LD 4; Green 2; v. 3
Wellingborough (36) C. 25; Lab. 9; Ind. 1; v. 1
Welwyn Hatfield (48) C. 23; Lab. 13; LD 12
West Devon (31) C. 15; Ind. 12; LD 2; Green 2
West Lancashire (54) Lab. 29; C. 19; Ind. 6
West Lindsey (36) C. 16; LD 12; Ind. 7; v. 1
West Oxfordshire (49) C. 29; LD 9; Lab. 9; Ind. 2
West Suffolk (64) C. 37; Ind. 19; Lab. 5; Green 1
Winchester (45) LD 26; C. 15; Ind. 3; v. 1
Woking (30) C. 14; LD 10; Ind. 3; Lab. 3
Worcester (35) C. 16; Lab. 15; Green 3; LD 1
Worthing (37) C. 23; Lab. 10; LD 3; Ind. 1
Wychavon (45) C. 34; LD 6; Green 2; Ind. 2; v. 1
Wyre (50) C. 37; Lab. 8; Ind. 5
Wyre Forest (33) Ind. 15; C. 12; LD 3; Lab. 2; Green 1

LONDON BOROUGH COUNCILS

Barking and Dagenham (51) Lab. 51
Barnet (63) C. 36; Lab. 24; LD 2; v. 1
Bexley (45) C. 34; Lab. 10; Ind. 1
Brent (63) Lab. 59; C. 3; LD 1
Bromley (60) C. 50; Lab. 8; Ind. 2
Camden (54) Lab. 43; C. 7; LD 3; Green 1
Croydon (70) Lab. 41; C. 29
Ealing (69) Lab. 56; C. 6; LD 4; v. 3
Enfield (63) Lab. 40; C. 16; Ind. 5; v. 2
Greenwich (51) Lab. 40; C. 9; v. 2
Hackney (57) Lab. 49; C. 4; v. 4
Hammersmith and Fulham (46) Lab. 35; C. 11
Haringey (57) Lab. 41; LD 15; Ind. 1
Harrow (63) Lab. 35; C. 27; Ind. 1
Havering (54) C. 25; Ind. 24; Lab. 5
Hillingdon (65) C. 43; Lab. 21; v. 1
Hounslow (60) Lab. 49; C. 10; v. 1
Islington (48) Lab. 45; C. 1; LD 1; Green 1
Kensington and Chelsea (50) C. 35; Lab. 13; LD 1; Ind. 1
Kingston upon Thames (48) LD 37; C. 9; Ind. 1; v. 1
Lambeth (63) Lab. 57; Green 5; C. 1
Lewisham (54) Lab. 51; Ind. 1; v. 2
Merton (60) Lab. 34; C. 17; LD 6; Ind. 3
Newham (60) Lab. 59; v. 1
Redbridge (63) Lab. 49; C. 12; v. 2
Richmond upon Thames (54) LD 39; C. 11; Green 3; v. 1
Southwark (63) Lab. 48; LD 14; Ind. 1
Sutton (54) LD 33; C. 18; Ind. 3
Tower Hamlets (45) Lab. 41; C. 1; LD 1; Ind. 2
Waltham Forest (60) Lab. 46; C. 13; v. 1
Wandsworth (60) C. 33; Lab. 26; Ind. 1
Westminster (60) C. 41; Lab. 19

METROPOLITAN BOROUGHS

Barnsley (63) Lab. 48; Ind. 7; LD 4; C. 3; v. 1
Birmingham (101) Lab. 64; C. 25; LD 8; Green 1; v. 3
Bolton (60) Con. 18; Lab. 18; Ind. 15; LD 7; v. 2
Bradford (90) Lab. 52; C. 20; LD 7; Ind. 7; Green 2; v. 2
Bury (51) Lab. 28; C. 16; LD 4; Ind. 3

Calderdale (51) Lab. 28; C. 12; LD 7; Ind. 4
Coventry (54) Lab. 39; C. 13; Ind. 1; v. 1
Doncaster (55) Lab. 41; C. 8; Ind. 6
Dudley (72) Lab. 35; C. 34; Ind. 2; v. 1
Gateshead (66) Lab. 51; LD 12; Ind. 2; v. 1
Kirklees (69) Lab. 32; C. 16; LD 10; Ind. 7; Green 3; v. 1
Knowsley (45) Lab. 36; LD 3; Green 3; Ind. 1; v. 2
Leeds (99) Lab. 56; C. 23; LD 7; Ind. 9; Green 3; v. 1
Liverpool (90) Lab. 71; LD 10; Green 4; Ind. 4; v. 1
Manchester (96) Lab. 92; LD 2; v. 2
Newcastle-upon-Tyne (78) Lab. 50; LD 20; Ind. 4; v. 4
North Tyneside (60) Lab. 49; C. 7; Ind. 1; LD 1; v. 2
Oldham (60) Lab. 46; LD 8; C. 4; Ind. 2
Rochdale (60) Lab. 44; C. 10; LD 3; Ind. 3
Rotherham (63) Lab. 42; Ind. 17; LD 1; v. 3
St Helens (48) Lab. 35; LD 4; C. 3; Green 2; Ind. 2; v. 2
Salford (60) Lab. 50; C. 8; Ind. 1; v. 1
Sandwell (72) Lab. 62; Ind. 5; v. 5
Sefton (66) Lab. 41; LD 12; C. 6; Ind. 5; v. 2
Sheffield (84) Lab. 45; LD 26; Green 8; Ind. 1; v. 4
Solihull (51) C. 26; Green 14; LD 5; Lab. 3; Ind. 2; v. 1
South Tyneside (54) Lab. 44; Ind. 6; Green 1; v. 3
Stockport (63) Lab. 26; LD 26; C. 8; Ind. 3
Sunderland (75) Lab. 50; C. 12; LD 8; Ind. 3; Green 1; v. 1
Tameside (57) Lab. 51; C. 5; Green 1
Trafford (63) Lab. 34; C. 19; LD 3; Green 3; Ind. 1; v. 3
Wakefield (63) Lab. 47; C. 11; Ind. 1; LD 1; v. 3
Walsall (62) C. 31; Lab. 26; LD 2; Ind. 1
Wigan (75) Lab. 57; Ind. 10; C. 7; v. 1
Wirral (66) Lab. 31; C. 19; LD 6; Green 2; Ind. 4; v. 4
Wolverhampton (60) Lab. 47; C. 10; v. 3

UNITARY COUNCILS

Bath and North East Somerset (59) LD 37; C. 11; Ind. 6; Lab. 5
Bedford (40) LD 15; Lab. 11; C. 11; Green 2; Ind. 1
Blackburn with Darwen (51) Lab. 33; C. 12; LD 2; Ind. 2; v. 2
Blackpool (42) Lab. 22; C. 14; Ind. 4; v. 2
Bournemouth, Christchurch & Poole (BCP) (76) C. 36; Ind. 19; LD 14; Lab. 3; Green 2; v. 2
Bracknell Forest (42) C. 38; Lab. 3; LD 1
Brighton and Hove (54) Green 19; Lab. 17; C. 13; Ind. 5
Bristol (70) Lab. 34; C. 14; Green 11; LD 9; v. 2
Buckinghamshire (194) C. 151; LD 17; Ind. 16; Lab. 9; Green 1
Central Bedfordshire (59) C. 42; Ind. 13; LD 3; Lab. 1
Cheshire East (82) C. 32; Lab. 24; Ind. 21; LD 4; v. 1
Cheshire West and Chester (70) Lab. 34; C. 29; Ind. 3; LD 2; Green 1; v. 1
Cornwall (123) C. 44; Ind. 40; LD 34; Lab. 4; v. 1
Darlington (50) C. 22; Lab. 19; Ind. 4; LD 3; Green 2
Derby (51) C. 19; Lab. 15; Ind. 9; LD 8
Dorset (82) C. 43; LD 29; Ind. 5; Green 4; Lab. 1
Durham (126) Lab. 70; Ind. 31; LD 15; C. 10
East Riding of Yorkshire (67) C. 47; Ind. 10; LD 9; v. 1
Halton (56) Lab. 50; LD 3; C. 2; v. 2
Hartlepool (33) Ind. 20; Lab. 6; C. 4; v. 3
Herefordshire (53) Ind. 26; C. 13; Green 7; LD 6; v. 1

Isle of Wight (40)   C. 25; Ind. 13; LD 2
*Isles of Scilly (16)   Ind. 16
Kingston-upon-Hull (57)   Lab. 30; LD 24; C. 2; v. 1
Leicester (54)   Lab. 51; LD 1; Ind. 1; v. 1
Luton (48)   Lab. 33; LD 12; C. 3
Medway (55)   C. 32; Lab. 20; Ind. 3
Middlesbrough (46)   Ind. 25; Lab. 18; C. 3
Milton Keynes (57)   Lab. 22; C. 17; LD 15; Ind. 2; v. 1
North East Lincolnshire (42)   C. 23; Lab. 14; LD 4; Ind. 1
North Lincolnshire (43)   C. 24; Lab. 14; Ind. 1; v. 1
North Somerset (50)   Ind. 16; C. 13; LD 11; Lab. 6; Green 3; v. 1
Northumberland (67)   C. 32; Lab. 23; Ind. 8; LD. 3; v. 1
Nottingham (55)   Lab. 50; Ind. 3; C. 2
Peterborough (60)   C. 26; Lab. 17; LD 9; Ind. 4; Green 2; v. 2
Plymouth (57)   Lab. 30; C. 17; Ind. 10
Portsmouth (42)   LD 17; C. 14; Lab. 6; Ind. 5
Reading (46)   Lab. 30; C. 10; Green 4; LD 2
Redcar and Cleveland (59)   Ind. 21; Lab. 15; LD 13; C. 8; v. 2
Rutland (27)   C. 17; Ind. 6; LD 3; Green 1
Shropshire (74)   C. 47; LD 12; Lab. 7; Ind. 7; Green 1
Slough (42)   Lab. 35; C. 4; Ind. 2; v. 1
South Gloucestershire (61)   C. 32; LD 17; Lab. 11; v. 1
Southampton (48)   Lab. 30; C. 18
Southend-on-Sea (51)   C. 20; Lab. 13; Ind. 11; LD 5; v. 2
Stockton-on-Tees (56)   Lab. 24; Ind. 15; C. 13; LD 1; v. 3
Stoke-on-Trent (44)   C. 19; Lab. 14; Ind. 10; v. 1
Swindon (57)   C. 30; Lab. 22; LD 2; Ind. 2; v. 1
Telford and Wrekin (54)   Lab. 35; C. 13; LD 4; Ind. 1; v. 1
Thurrock (49)   C. 28; Lab. 16; Ind. 5
Torbay (36)   C. 16; LD 11; Ind. 8; v. 1
Warrington (58)   Lab. 42; LD 12; Ind. 2; C. 1; v. 1
West Berkshire (43)   C. 24; LD 16; Green 3
Wiltshire (98)   C. 63; LD 21; Ind. 10; Lab. 3; v. 1
Windsor and Maidenhead (41)   C. 22; LD 10; Ind. 9
Wokingham (54)   C. 31; LD 15; Lab. 4; Ind. 3; v. 1
York (47)   LD 21; Lab. 17; Green 3; Ind. 4; C. 2

* Twelve councillors are elected by the residents of the isle of St Mary's and one councillor each are elected by the residents of the four other islands (Bryher, St Agnes, St Martin's and Tresco)

WALES

Blaenau Gwent (41)   Ind. 28; Lab. 13; PC 1
Bridgend (54)   Lab. 26; Ind. 16; C. 8; PC 2; LD 1; v. 1
Caerphilly (73)   Lab. 49; PC 18; Ind. 6
Cardiff (75)   Lab. 38; C. 21; LD 11; Ind. 5
Carmarthenshire (74)   PC 38; Ind. 19; Lab. 17
Ceredigion (42)   PC 20; Ind. 14; LD 8
Conwy (59)   Ind. 25; C. 14; PC 9; Lab. 6; LD 4; v. 1
Denbighshire (47)   C. 15; Lab. 11; Ind. 11; PC 9; v. 1
Flintshire (70)   Lab. 34; Ind. 24; C. 6; LD 5; v. 1
Gwynedd (75)   PC 39; Ind. 33; Lab. 1; LD 1; v. 1
Merthyr Tydfil (33)   Ind. 18; Lab. 15
Monmouthshire (43)   C. 25; Lab. 10; Ind. 5; LD 3

Neath Port Talbot (64)   Lab. 38; PC 15; Ind. 9; LD 1' v. 1
Newport (50)   Lab. 30; C. 12; Ind. 5; LD 2
Pembrokeshire (60)   Ind. 35; C. 11; Lab. 7; PC 6; LD 1
Powys (73)   Ind. 31; C. 17; LD 14; Lab. 8; PC 2; Green 1
Rhondda Cynon Taff (75)   Lab. 47; PC 17; Ind. 8; C. 3
Swansea (72)   Lab. 47; C. 9; Ind. 8; LD 7; v. 1
Torfaen (44)   Lab. 27; Ind. 12; C. 4; v. 1
Vale of Glamorgan (47)   C. 25; Lab. 14; Ind. 14; PC 4
Wrexham (52)   Ind. 25; Lab. 11; C. 9; PC 4; LD 2; v. 1
Ynys Mon (Isle of Anglesey) (30)   PC 13; Ind. 12; Lab. 2; LD 1; v. 2

SCOTLAND

Aberdeen (45)   SNP 19; C. 10; Lab. 9; LD 3; Ind. 4
Aberdeenshire (70)   SNP 19; C. 18; Ind. 17; LD 14; Green 1; Lab. 1
Angus (28)   Ind. 9; SNP 9; C. 8; LD 2
Argyll and Bute (36)   SNP 11; Ind. 9; C. 9; LD 5; v. 2
Clackmannanshire (18)   SNP 8; Lab. 5; C. 4; Ind. 1
Dumfries and Galloway (43)   C. 16; SNP 10; Lab. 9; Ind. 7; LD 1
Dundee (29)   SNP 14; Lab. 8; C. 3; LD 2; Ind. 2
East Ayrshire (32)   SNP 14; Lab. 9; C. 6; Ind. 3
East Dunbartonshire (22)   SNP 7; C. 6; LD 6; Lab. 2; Ind. 1
East Lothian (22)   Lab. 9; C. 7; SNP 6
East Renfrewshire (18)   C. 5; SNP 5; Lab. 4; LD 1; Ind. 3
Edinburgh (63)   C. 17; SNP 16; Lab. 11; Green 8; LD 6; Ind. 5
Eilean Siar (Western Isles) (31)   Ind. 22; SNP 7; C. 2
Falkirk (30)   SNP 12; Lab. 8; C. 6; Ind. 4
Fife (75)   SNP 30; Lab. 23; C. 14; LD 7; Ind. 1
Glasgow (85)   SNP 36; Lab. 30; C. 7; Green 7; Ind. 4; v. 1
Highland (74)   Ind. 32; SNP 18; C. 10; LD 9; Lab. 3; Green 1; v. 1
Inverclyde (22)   Lab. 8; SNP 7; Ind. 4; C. 2; LD 1
Midlothian (18)   Lab. 6; SNP 7; C. 5
Moray (26)   C. 9; SNP 8; Ind. 8; Lab. 1
North Ayrshire (33)   Lab. 11; SNP 11; C. 7; Ind. 4
North Lanarkshire (77)   Lab. 30; SNP 29; C. 8; Ind. 8; v. 2
Orkney Islands (21)   Ind. 20; Green 1
Perth and Kinross (40)   C. 17; SNP 13; LD 5; Ind. 3; Lab. 1; v. 1
Renfrewshire (43)   SNP 19; Lab. 13; C. 8; Ind. 1; LD 1; v. 1
Scottish Borders (34)   C. 14; SNP 8; Ind. 9; LD 2; v. 1
Shetland Islands (22)   Ind. 21; SNP 1
South Ayrshire (28)   C. 12; SNP 9; Lab. 5; Ind. 2
South Lanarkshire (64)   SNP 25; Lab. 17; C. 13; LD 3; Ind. 6
Stirling (23)   C. 8; SNP 8; Lab. 4; Green 1; Ind. 1
West Dunbartonshire (22)   SNP 10; Lab. 8; Ind. 2; C. 2
West Lothian (33)   SNP 12; Lab. 12; C. 7; Ind. 1; v. 1

NORTHERN IRELAND

Antrim & Newtownabbey (40)	DUP 14; UUP 8; All. 7; SF 5; SDLP 4; Ind. 2
Ards & North Down (40)	DUP 13; All. 10; UUP 8; Ind. 7; SDLP 2
Armagh City, Banbridge & Craigavon (41)	DUP 11; UUP 10; SF 10; SDLP 4; All. 3; Ind. 1; v. 2
Belfast City (60)	SF 18; DUP 14; All. 10; Ind. 10; SDLP 6; UUP 2
Causeway Coast & Glens (40)	DUP 14; SF 9; UUP 6; SDLP 4; All. 2; Ind. 5
Derry City & Strabane (40)	SF 11; SDLP 11; DUP 7; Ind. 6; All. 2; UUP 2; v. 1
Fermanagh & Omagh (40)	SF 14; UUP 10; SDLP 5; DUP 5; Ind. 5; All. 1
Lisburn & Castlereagh (40)	DUP 15; UUP 11; All. 9; SDLP 2; SF 2; Ind. 1
Mid & East Antrim (40)	DUP 16; Ind. 8; All. 7; UUP 6; SF 2; SDLP 1
Mid Ulster (40)	SF 17; DUP 9; UUP 6; SDLP 5; Ind. 3
Newry, Mourne & Down (41)	SF 16; SDLP 11; Ind. 5; UUP 3; DUP 4; All. 2

THE ISLE OF MAN

Ellan Vannin

The Isle of Man is an island situated in the Irish Sea, at latitude 54° 3′–54° 25′ N. and longitude 4° 18′–4° 47′ W., nearly equidistant from England, Scotland and Ireland. Although the early inhabitants were of Celtic origin, the Isle of Man was part of the Norwegian Kingdom of the Hebrides until 1266, when this was ceded to Scotland. Subsequently granted to the Stanleys (Earls of Derby) in the 15th century and later to the Dukes of Atholl, it was brought under the administration of the Crown in 1765. The island forms the bishopric of Sodor and Man.

The total land area is 572 sq. km (221 sq. miles). The 2016 census showed a resident population of 83,314 (men, 41,269; women, 42,045). The main language in use is English. Around 1,660 people are able to speak the Manx Gaelic language.

CAPITAL – ΨDouglas; population, 26,997 (2016). ΨCastletown (3,216) is the ancient capital; the other towns are ΨPeel (5,374) and ΨRamsey (7,845)

FLAG – A red flag charged with three conjoined armoured legs in white and gold

NATIONAL DAY – 5 July (Tynwald Day)

GOVERNMENT

The Isle of Man is a self-governing Crown dependency, with its own parliamentary, legal and administrative system. The British government is responsible for international relations and defence. Prior to Britain's withdrawal from the European Union, the island's special relationship with the EU was limited to trade alone and did not extend to financial aid; it neither contributed money to nor received funds from the EU budget. The Lieutenant-Governor is the Queen's personal representative on the island.

The legislature, Tynwald, is the oldest parliament in the world in continuous existence. It has two branches: the Legislative Council and the House of Keys. The council consists of the President of Tynwald, the Bishop of Sodor and Man, the Attorney-General (who does not have a vote) and eight members elected by the House of Keys. The House of Keys has 24 members, elected by universal adult suffrage. The branches sit separately to consider legislation and sit together, as Tynwald Court, for most other parliamentary purposes.

The presiding officer of Tynwald Court is the President of Tynwald, elected by the members, who also presides over sittings of the Legislative Council. The presiding officer of the House of Keys is the Speaker, who is elected by members of the house.

The principal members of the Manx government are the chief minister and eight departmental ministers, who comprise the Council of Ministers.

Lieutenant-Governor, HE Sir Richard Gozney, KCMG, CVO
President of Tynwald, Hon. Steve Rodan, OBE
Speaker, House of Keys, Hon. Juan Paul Watterson, SHK
Deputy Speaker, House of Keys, Chris Robertshaw, MHK
The First Deemster and Clerk of the Rolls, His Hon. Andrew Corlett
Clerk of Tynwald, Secretary to the House of Keys and Counsel to the Speaker, Roger Phillips
Clerk of the Legislative Council and Deputy Clerk of Tynwald, Jonathan King
HM Attorney-General, John Quinn, QC
Chief Minister, Hon. Howard Quayle, MHK
Chief Secretary, Will Greenhow

ECONOMY

Much of the income generated in the island is earned in the services sector with financial and professional services accounting for 45.1 per cent of the national income. Two other significant sectors are e-gaming and ICT, contributing 17.6 per cent and 6.9 per cent respectively, to the national income. The island has tariff-free access to EU markets for its engineering, farming and fishing products prior to the end of Britain's withdrawal period from the EU, set to end on 1 January 2021.

In November 2020 the island's unemployment rate was 1.8 per cent and the CPI rate of inflation was 0.2 per cent.

FINANCE

The budget for 2020–21 provides for gross revenue expenditure of £1,066m. The principal sources of government revenue are direct and indirect taxes. Income tax is payable at a rate of 10 per cent on the first £6,500 of taxable income for single resident individuals and 20 per cent on the balance, after personal allowances of £14,250. These bands are doubled for married couples. The rate of income tax for trading companies is zero per cent except for income from banking and major retail operations which is taxed at 10 per cent, and land and property which is taxed at 20 per cent. By agreement with the British government, the island keeps most of its rates of indirect taxation (VAT and duties) the same as those in the UK. However, VAT on tourist accommodation, domestic property, repairs and renovations is charged at 5 per cent. Taxes are also charged on property (rates), but these are comparatively low.

The major government expenditure items are social security payments, health and education. The island makes an annual contribution to the UK for defence and other external services.

Ψ = sea port

THE CHANNEL ISLANDS

The Channel Islands, situated off the north-west coast of France (at a distance of 16km (10 miles) at their closest point), are the only portions of the Dukedom of Normandy still belonging to the Crown, to which they have been attached since the Norman Conquest of 1066. They were the only British territory to come under German occupation during the Second World War, following invasion on 30 June and 1 July 1940. Guernsey and Jersey were relieved by British forces on 9 May 1945, Sark on 10 May 1945 and Alderney on 16 May 1945; 9 May (Liberation Day) is now observed as a bank and public holiday in Guernsey and Jersey.

The islands consist of Jersey (11,630ha/28,717 acres), Guernsey (6,340ha/15,654 acres), and the dependencies of Guernsey: Alderney (795ha/1,962 acres), Brecqhou (30ha/74 acres), Great Sark (419ha/1,035 acres), Little Sark (97ha/239 acres), Herm (130ha/320 acres), Jethou (18ha/44 acres) and Lihou (15ha/38 acres) – a total of 19,474ha/48,083 acres, or 195 sq. km/75 sq. miles.

Official figures estimated the population of Jersey as 106,800 at the end of 2018. Guernsey uses a rolling electronic census system and the most recent figures showed the population of Guernsey to be 63,021 (December 2019) and Alderney 2,019 (March 2018). Sark's population is estimated to be around 600. The official language is English but French is often used for ceremonial purposes. A Norman-French *patois* is also spoken by a few in Jersey, Guernsey and Sark.

GOVERNMENT

The islands are Crown dependencies with their own legislative assemblies (the States of Jersey, the States of Alderney, the States of Deliberation in Guernsey and the Chief Pleas in Sark), systems of local administration and law, and their own courts. *Projets de Loi* (Acts) passed by the States require the sanction of the Queen-in-council. The UK government is responsible for defence and international relations, although the islands are increasingly entering into agreements with other countries in their own right. The Channel Islands are not members of the European Union but had trading rights with the free movement of goods within the EU prior to Britain's withdrawal; as of November 2020 their future arrangement remained unclear. A common customs tariff, levies and agricultural and import measures apply to trade between the islands and non-member countries.

In both Jersey and Guernsey bailiwicks the Lieutenant-Governor and Commander-in-Chief, who is appointed by the Crown, is the personal representative of the Queen and the official channel of communication between the Crown (via the Privy Council) and the islands' governments.

The head of government in both Jersey and Guernsey is the Chief Minister. Jersey has a ministerial system of government; the executive comprises the Council of Ministers and consists of a chief minister and eleven other ministers. The ministers are assisted by up to nine assistant ministers. Members of the States who are not in the executive are able to sit on a number of scrutiny panels and the Public Accounts Committee to examine the policy of the executive and hold ministers to account. Guernsey is administered by a number of committees. The Policy and Resources committee is the senior committee responsible for leadership and coordination of the work of the States and is presided over by the Chief Minister, in addition there are six principal committees with mandated responsibilities. The States of Deliberation is the island's parliamentary assembly. Alderney has a legislature comprising a President and ten members elected by universal suffrage. Sark has a directly elected legislature of 28 members *(conseillers)* who serve on a number of committees.

Justice is administered by the royal courts of Jersey and Guernsey, each consisting of the bailiff and 12 elected jurats. The bailiffs of Jersey and Guernsey, appointed by the Crown, are presidents of the royal courts of their respective islands. Each bailiff is the *ex-officio* presiding officer in their respective parliaments and, by convention, the civic head.

The Church of England in each bailiwick is under the jurisdiction of the Dean of Jersey and the Dean of Guernsey respectively. The Bishop of Dover (Diocese of Canterbury) has episcopal oversight of the Channel Islands.

ECONOMY

A mild climate and good soil have led to the development of intensive systems of agriculture and horticulture. Earnings from tourism are important but the main source of income is banking and finance: the low rates of income and corporation tax and the absence of death duties make the islands an important offshore financial centre. The financial services sector contributes over 50 per cent of GDP in Jersey and 40 per cent of GVA in Guernsey. In addition, there is no VAT or equivalent tax in Guernsey and only small goods and services tax in Jersey (5 per cent since 1 June 2011). The international stock exchange is located in Guernsey, which also has a thriving e-gaming sector.

Principal exports are agricultural produce and flowers; imports are chiefly machinery, manufactured goods, food, fuel and chemicals. Trade with the UK is regarded as internal.

British currency is legal tender in the Channel Islands but each bailiwick issues its own coins and notes (*see* Currency section). They also issue their own postage stamps; UK stamps are not valid.

JERSEY

Lieutenant-Governor and Commander-in-Chief of Jersey, HE Air
   Chief Marshal Sir Stephen Dalton, GCB, *from* 2017
Chief of Staff, Maj. Justin Oldridge
Bailiff of Jersey, Timothy J. Le Cocq, QC
Deputy Bailiff, Robert J. MacRae, QC
Attorney-General, Mark Temple, QC
Receiver-General, David Pett
Solicitor-General, Matthew Jowitt, QC
Greffier of the States, Mark Egan
States Treasurer, Richard Bell
Chief Minister, Senator John Le Fondré

FINANCE

	2018	2019
Revenue income	£799,205,000	£845,370,000
Revenue expenditure	£759,303,000	£782,413,000
Capital expenditure	£18,077,000*	£68,946,000

* Much reduced due to a major new hospital project being postponed.

CHIEF TOWN – ѰSt Helier, on the south coast
FLAG – A white field charged with a red saltire cross, and
   the arms of Jersey in the upper centre

GUERNSEY AND DEPENDENCIES

Lieutenant-Governor and Commander-in-Chief of the Bailiwick of Guernsey and its Dependencies, Vice-Adm. Sir Ian Corder, KBE, CB

Presiding Officer of the Royal Court and of the States of Deliberation, Bailiff Richard McMahon, QC

Deputy Presiding Officer of the Royal Court and States of Deliberation, Deputy Bailiff Jessica Roland

HM Procureur and Receiver-General (Attorney-General), Megan Pullum, QC

HM Comptroller (Solicitor-General), Robert Titterington, QC

GUERNSEY

President of the Policy and Resources Committee, Deputy Peter Ferbrache

Chief Executive, Paul Whitfield

FINANCE

	2018	2019
Revenue income	£455,601,000	£476,876,000
Other income	£38,838,000	£152,778,000
Revenue expenditure	£452,182,000	£479,529,000
Capital expenditure	£37,057,000	£32,487,000
Other expenditure	£21,419,000	£12,082,000

CHIEF TOWNS – ΨSt Peter Port, on the east coast of Guernsey; St Anne on Alderney

FLAG – White, bearing a red cross of St George, with a gold cross of Normandy overall in the centre

ALDERNEY

President of the States, William Tate
Chief Executive, vacant
Greffier, Jonathan Anderson

SARK

Sark was the last European territory to abolish feudal parliamentary representation. Elections for a democratic legislative assembly took place in December 2008, with the *conseillers* taking their seats in the newly constituted Chief Pleas in January 2009.

Seigneur of Sark, Maj. Christopher Beaumont
Seneschal, Jeremy la Trobe-Bateman
Speaker, Lt.-Col. Reginald Guille, MBE
Greffier, Trevor Hamon

OTHER DEPENDENCIES

Herm and Lihou are owned by the States of Guernsey; Herm is leased, Lihou is uninhabited. Jethou is leased by the Crown to the States of Guernsey and is sub-let by the States. Brecqhou is within the legislative and judicial territory of Sark.

Ψ = seaport

LAW COURTS AND OFFICES

SUPREME COURT OF THE UNITED KINGDOM

The Supreme Court of the United Kingdom is the highest domestic judicial authority; it replaced the appellate committee of the House of Lords (the house functioning in its judicial capacity) on 1 October 2009. It is the final court of appeal for cases heard in Great Britain and Northern Ireland (except for criminal cases from Scotland). Cases concerning the interpretation and application of European Union law, including preliminary rulings requested by British courts and tribunals, which are decided by the Court of Justice of the European Union (CJEU) (*see* European Union), and the supreme court can make a reference to the CJEU in appropriate cases. Additionally, in giving effect to rights contained in the European Convention on Human Rights, the supreme court must take account of any decision of the European Court of Human Rights.

The supreme court also assumed jurisdiction in relation to devolution matters under the Scotland Act 1998 (now partly superseded by the Scotland Act 2012), the Northern Ireland Act 1988 and the Government of Wales Act 2006; these powers were transferred from the Judicial Committee of the Privy Council. Ten of the 12 Lords of Appeal in Ordinary (Law Lords) from the House of Lords transferred to the 12-member supreme court when it came into operation (at the same time one law lord retired and another was appointed Master of the Rolls). All new justices of the supreme court are now appointed by an independent selection commission, and, although styled *Rt. Hon. Lord,* are not members of the House of Lords. Peers who are members of the judiciary are disqualified from sitting or voting in the House of Lords until they retire from their judicial office. *See* Life Peers for a list of such peers (§).

President of the Supreme Court (£234,184), Rt. Hon. Lord Reed
  born 1956, *apptd* 2019 (from January 2020)
Deputy President of the Supreme Court (£226,193), vacant

JUSTICES OF THE SUPREME COURT *as at November 2019* (each £226,193)
Style, The Rt. Hon. Lord/Lady–

Rt. Hon. Lord Kerr of Tonaghmore, *born* 1948, *apptd* 2009
Rt. Hon. Lord Wilson of Culworth, *born* 1945, *apptd* 2011
Rt. Hon. Lord Carnwath of Notting Hill, CVO, *born* 1945, *apptd* 2012
Rt. Hon. Lord Hodge, *born* 1953, *apptd* 2013
Rt. Hon. Lady Black of Derwent, DBE, *born* 1954, *apptd* 2017
Rt. Hon. Lord Lloyd-Jones, *born* 1952, *apptd* 2017
Rt. Hon. Lord Briggs of Westbourne, *born* 1954, *apptd* 2017
Rt. Hon. Lady Arden of Heswall, DBE, *born* 1947, *apptd* 2018
Rt. Hon. Lord Kitchin, *born* 1955, *apptd* 2018
Rt. Hon. Lord Sales, *born* 1962, *apptd* 2019

UNITED KINGDOM SUPREME COURT
Parliament Square, London SW1P 3BD **T** 020-7960 1900
Chief Executive, Mark Ormerod, CB

JUDICATURE OF ENGLAND AND WALES

The legal system in England and Wales is divided into criminal law and civil law. Criminal law is concerned with acts harmful to the community and the rules laid down by the state for the benefit of citizens, whereas civil law governs the relationships and transactions between individuals. Administrative law is a kind of civil law usually concerning the interaction of individuals and the state, and most cases are heard in tribunals specific to the subject (*see* Tribunals section). Scotland and Northern Ireland possess legal systems that differ from the system in England and Wales in law, judicial procedure and court structure, but retain the distinction between criminal and civil law.

Under the provisions of the Criminal Appeal Act 1995, a commission was set up to direct and supervise investigations into possible miscarriages of justice and to refer cases to the appeal courts on the grounds of conviction and sentence; these functions were formerly the responsibility of the home secretary.

HIERARCHY OF ENGLISH AND WELSH COURTS

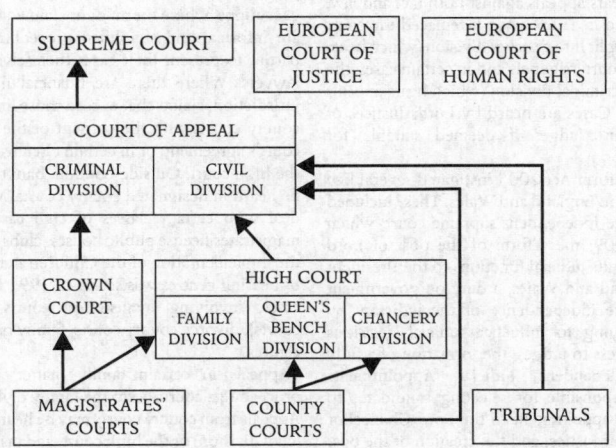

SENIOR COURTS OF ENGLAND AND WALES

The senior courts of England and Wales (until September 2009 known as the supreme court of judicature of England and Wales) comprise the high court, the crown court and the court of appeal. The President of the Courts of England and Wales, a new title given to the Lord Chief Justice under the Constitutional Reform Act 2005, is the head of the judiciary.

The high court was created in 1875 and combined many previously separate courts. Sittings are held at the royal courts of justice in London or at around 120 district registries outside the capital. It is the superior civil court and is split into three divisions – the chancery division, the Queen's bench division and the family division – each of which is further divided. The chancery division is headed by the Chancellor of the High Court and is concerned mainly with equity, trusts, tax and bankruptcy, while also including two specialist courts, the patents court and the companies court. The Queen's bench division (QBD) is the largest of the three divisions, and is headed by its own president. It deals with common law (ie tort, contract, debt and personal injuries), some tax law, eg VAT tribunal appeals, and encompasses the admiralty court and the commercial court. The QBD also administers the technology and construction court. The family division was created in 1970 and is headed by its own president, who is also Head of Family Justice, and hears cases concerning divorce, access to and custody of children, and other family matters. The divisional court of the high court sits in the family and chancery divisions, and hears appeals from the magistrates' courts and county courts.

The crown court was set up in 1972 and sits at 77 centres throughout England and Wales. It deals with more serious (indictable) criminal offences, which are triable before a judge and jury, including treason, murder, rape, kidnapping, armed robbery and Official Secrets Act offences. It also handles cases transferred from the magistrates' courts where the magistrate decides his or her own power of sentence is inadequate, or where someone appeals against a magistrate's decision, or in a case that is triable 'either way' where the accused has chosen a jury trial. The crown court centres are divided into three tiers: high court judges, circuit judges and sometimes recorders (part-time circuit judges), sit in first-tier centres, hearing the most serious criminal offences (eg murder, treason, rape, manslaughter) and some civil high court cases. The second-tier centres are presided over by high court judges, circuit judges or recorders and also deal with the most serious criminal cases. Third-tier courts deal with the remaining criminal offences, with circuit judges or recorders presiding.

The court of appeal hears appeals against both fact and law, and was last restructured in 1966 when it replaced the court of criminal appeal. It is split into the civil division (which hears appeals from the high court, tribunals and in certain cases, the county courts) and the criminal division (which hears appeals from the crown court). Cases are heard by Lords Justices of Appeal and high court judges if deemed suitable for reconsideration.

The Constitutional Reform Act 2005 instigated several key changes to the judiciary in England and Wales. These included the establishment of the independent supreme court, which opened in October 2009; the reform of the post of Lord Chancellor, transferring its judicial functions to the President of the Courts of England and Wales; a duty on government ministers to uphold the independence of the judiciary by barring them from trying to influence judicial decisions through any special access to judges; the formation of a fully transparent and independent Judicial Appointments Commission that is responsible for selecting candidates to recommend for judicial appointment to the Lord Chancellor and Secretary of State for Justice; and the creation of the post of Judicial Appointments and Conduct Ombudsman.

CRIMINAL CASES

In criminal matters the decision to prosecute (in the majority of cases) rests with the Crown Prosecution Service (CPS), which is the independent prosecuting body in England and Wales. The CPS is headed by the director of public prosecutions, who works under the superintendence of the Attorney-General. Certain categories of offence continue to require the Attorney-General's consent for prosecution.

Most minor criminal cases (summary offences) are dealt with in magistrates' courts, usually by a bench of three unpaid lay magistrates (justices of the peace) sitting without a jury and assisted on points of law and procedure by a legally trained clerk. There are approximately 23,000 justices of the peace. In some courts a full-time, salaried and legally qualified district judge (magistrates' court) – formerly known as a stipendiary judge – presides alone. There are 140 district judges and 170 deputy district judges operating in around 330 magistrates' courts in England and Wales. Magistrates' courts deal with 95 per cent of all criminal cases. Magistrates' courts also house some family proceedings courts (which deal with relationship breakdown and childcare cases) and youth courts. Cases of medium seriousness (known as 'offences triable either way') where the defendant pleads not guilty can be heard in the crown court for a trial by jury, if the defendant so chooses. Preliminary proceedings in a serious case to decide whether there is evidence to justify committal for trial in the crown court are dealt with in the magistrates' courts.

The 77 centres that the crown court sits in are divided into seven regions. There are over 600 circuit judges and 1,000 recorders (part-time circuit judges); expected to sit for 30 days a year. A jury is present in all trials that are contested.

Appeals from magistrates' courts against sentence or conviction are made to the crown court, and appeals upon a point of law are made to the high court, which may ultimately be appealed to the supreme court. Appeals from the crown court, either against sentence or conviction, are made to the court of appeal (criminal division). Again, these appeals may be brought to the supreme court if a point of law is contested, and if the house considers it is of sufficient importance.

CIVIL CASES

Most minor civil cases – including contract, tort (especially personal injuries), property, divorce and other family matters, bankruptcy etc – are dealt with by the county courts, of which there are around 200 (see **W** www.justice.gov.uk for further details). Cases are heard by circuit judges, recorders or district judges. For cases involving small claims (with certain exceptions, where the amount claimed is £5,000 or less) there are informal and simplified procedures designed to enable parties to present their cases themselves without recourse to lawyers. Where there are financial limits on county court jurisdiction, claims that exceed those limits may be tried in the county courts with the consent of the parties, subject to the court's agreement, or in certain circumstances on transfer from the high court. Outside London, bankruptcy proceedings can be heard in designated county courts. Magistrates' courts also deal with certain classes of civil case, and committees of magistrates license public houses, clubs and betting shops. For the implementation of the Children Act 1989, a new structure of hearing centres was set up in 1991 for family proceedings cases, involving magistrates' courts (family proceedings courts), divorce county courts, family hearing centres and care centres.

Appeals in certain family matters heard in the family proceedings courts go to the family division of the high court. Appeals from county courts may be heard in the court of appeal (civil division) or the high court, and may go on to the supreme court.

CORONERS' COURTS

Unlike the unified courts system, administered by HM Courts and Tribunals Service, there are 92 separate coroners' jurisdictions in England and Wales. Each jurisdiction is locally funded and resourced by local authorities. Coroners are barristers, solicitors or medical practitioners of not less than five years standing, who continue in their legal or medical practices when not sitting as coroners. Some 32 coroners are 'full-time' coroners and are paid an annual salary regardless of their caseload. The remainder are paid according to the number of cases referred to them. The coroner's jurisdiction is territorial – it is the location of the dead body which dictates which coroner has jurisdiction in any particular case.

The coroners' courts investigate violent and unnatural deaths or sudden deaths where the cause is unknown. Doctors, the police, various public authorities or members of the public may bring cases before a coroner. Where a death is sudden and the cause is unknown, the coroner may order a post-mortem examination to determine the cause of death rather than hold an inquest in court. An inquest must be held, however, if a person died in a violent or unnatural way, or died in prison or other unusual circumstances. If the coroner suspects murder, manslaughter or infanticide, then they must summon a jury.

Coroners are required to appoint a deputy or assistant deputy to act in their stead if they are out of the district or otherwise unable to act. Deputies and assistant deputies have the same professional qualifications as the coroner. In exceptionally high-profile or complex cases, a serving judge may be appointed as a deputy coroner.

SENIOR JUDICIARY OF ENGLAND AND WALES

Lord Chief Justice of England and Wales and Head of Criminal Justice (£262,264), Rt. Hon. Lord Burnett of Maldon, *born* 1958, *apptd* 2017

Master of the Rolls and Head of Civil Justice (£234,184), Rt. Hon. Sir Terence Etherton, *born* 1951, *apptd* 2016

President of the Queen's Bench Division (£226,193), Rt. Hon. Dame Victoria Sharp, DBE, *born* 1956, *apptd* 2019

President of the Family Division and Head of Family Justice (£226,193), Rt. Hon. Sir Andrew McFarlane, *born* 1954, *apptd* 2018

Chancellor of the High Court (£226,193), Rt. Hon. Sir Geoffrey Vos, *born* 1955, *apptd* 2016

SENIOR COURTS OF ENGLAND AND WALES

COURT OF APPEAL

Presiding Judge, Criminal Division, Lord Chief Justice of England and Wales

Presiding Judge, Civil Division, Master of the Rolls

Vice-President, Civil Division (£215,094), Rt. Hon. Sir Nicholas Underhill *born* 1952, *apptd* 2018

Vice-President, Criminal Division (£215,094), Rt. Hon. Lady Heather Hallett, DBE, *born* 1949, *apptd* 2013

LORD JUSTICES OF APPEAL *as at September 2019* (each £215,094)
Style, The Rt. Hon. Lord/Lady Justice [surname]

Rt. Hon. Sir Andrew Longmore, *born* 1944, *apptd* 2001
Rt. Hon. Lady Heather Hallett, DBE, *born* 1949, *apptd* 2005
Rt. Hon. Sir Nicholas Patten, *born* 1950, *apptd* 2009
Rt. Hon. Sir Peter Gross, *born* 1952, *apptd* 2010
Rt. Hon. Dame Anne Rafferty, DBE, *born* 1950, *apptd* 2011
Rt. Hon. Sir Nigel Davis, *born* 1951, *apptd* 2011
Rt. Hon. Sir Kim Lewison, *born* 1952, *apptd* 2011
Rt. Hon. Sir Colman Treacy, *born* 1949, *apptd* 2012
Rt. Hon. Sir Richard McCombe, *born* 1952, *apptd* 2012

Rt. Hon. Sir Ernest Ryder, TD, *born* 1957, *apptd* 2013
Rt. Hon. Sir Nicholas Underhill, *born* 1952, *apptd* 2013
Rt. Hon. Sir Christopher Floyd, *born* 1951, *apptd* 2013
Rt. Hon. Sir Adrian Fulford, *born* 1953, *apptd* 2013
Rt. Hon. Dame Julia Macur, DBE, *born* 1957, *apptd* 2013
Rt. Hon. Sir David Bean, *born* 1954, *apptd* 2014
Rt. Hon. Dame Eleanor King, DBE, *born* 1957, *apptd* 2014
Rt. Hon. Sir Peregrine Simon, *born* 1950, *apptd* 2015
Rt. Hon. Sir Keith Lindblom, *born* 1956, *apptd* 2015
Rt. Hon. Sir David Richards, *born* 1951, *apptd* 2015
Rt. Hon. Sir Nicholas Hamblen, *born* 1957, *apptd* 2016
Rt. Hon. Sir Stephen Irwin, *born* 1953, *apptd* 2016
Rt. Hon. Sir Launcelot Henderson, *born* 1951, *apptd* 2016
Rt. Hon. Sir Julian Flaux, *born* 1955, *apptd* 2016
Rt. Hon. Dame Kathryn Thirlwall, DBE, *born* 1957, *apptd* 2017
Rt. Hon. Sir Gary Hickinbottom, *born* 1955, *apptd* 2017
Rt. Hon. Sir Andrew Moylan, *born* 1953, *apptd* 2017
Rt. Hon. Sir Timothy Holroyde, *born* 1955, *apptd* 2017
Rt. Hon. Sir Peter Jackson, *born* 1955, *apptd* 2017
Rt. Hon Sir Guy Newey, *born* 1959, *apptd* 2017
Rt. Hon Sir Rabinder Singh, *born* 1964, *apptd* 2017
Rt. Hon. Dame Sarah Asplin, DBE, *born* 1959, *apptd* 2017
Rt. Hon. Sir George Leggatt, *born* 1957, *apptd* 2018
Rt. Hon. Sir Peter Coulson, *born* 1958, *apptd* 2018
Rt. Hon. Sir Jonathan Baker, *born* 1955, *apptd* 2018
Rt. Hon. Sir Charles Haddon-Cave, *born* 1956, *apptd* 2018
Rt. Hon. Sir Nicholas Green, *born* 1958, *apptd* 2018
Rt. Hon. Dame Nicola Davies, DBE, *born* 1953, *apptd* 2018
Rt. Hon. Sir Stephen Males, *born* 1955, *apptd* 2019
Rt. Hon. Dame Vivien Rose, DBE, *born* 1960, *apptd* 2019
Rt. Hon. Dame Ingrid Simler, DBE, *born* 1963, *apptd* 2019

Ex Officio Judges, Lord Chief Justice of England and Wales; Master of the Rolls; President of the Queen's Bench Division; President of the Family Division; Chancellor of the High Court

COURTS-MARTIAL APPEAL COURT

Judges, Lord Chief Justice of England and Wales; Master of the Rolls; Lord Justices of Appeal; Judges of the High Court of Justice

HIGH COURT

CHANCERY DIVISION

Chancellor of the High Court (£226,193), Rt. Hon. Sir Geoffrey Vos, *born* 1955, *apptd* 2016
Clerk, Natalie Ford
Legal Secretary, Vannina Ettori

JUDGES *as at September 2019* (each £188,901)
Style, The Hon. Mr/Mrs/Ms Justice [surname]

Hon. Sir George Mann, *born* 1951, *apptd* 2004
Hon. Sir Paul Morgan, *born* 1952, *apptd* 2007
Hon. Sir Alastair Norris, *born* 1950, *apptd* 2007
Hon. Sir Gerald Barling, *born* 1949, *apptd* 2007
Hon. Sir Richard Arnold, *born* 1961, *apptd* 2008
Hon. Sir Peter Roth, *born* 1952, *apptd* 2009
Hon. Sir Robert Hildyard, *born* 1952, *apptd* 2011
Hon. Sir Colin Birss, *born* 1964, *apptd* 2013
Hon. Sir Christopher Nugee, *born* 1959, *apptd* 2013
Hon. Sir Richard Snowden, *born* 1962, *apptd* 2015
Hon. Sir Marcus Smith, *born* 1967, *apptd* 2017
Hon. Sir Antony Zacaroli, *born* 1963, *apptd* 2017
Hon. Sir Timothy Fancourt, *born* 1964, *apptd* 2018
Hon. Dame Sarah Falk, DBE, *born* 1962, *apptd* 2018

The Chancery Division also includes three specialist courts: the Companies Court, the Patents Court and the Bankruptcy Court.

QUEEN'S BENCH DIVISION
President (£226,193), Rt. Hon. Dame Victoria Sharp, DBE, *born* 1956, *apptd* 2019
Vice-President (£215,094), vacant

JUDGES *as at September 2019* (each £188,901)
Style, The Hon. Mr/Mrs/Ms Justice [surname]

Hon. Sir Paul Walker, *born* 1954, *apptd* 2004
Hon. Sir Nigel Teare, *born* 1952, *apptd* 2006
Hon. Sir Nigel Sweeney, *born* 1954, *apptd* 2008
Hon. Sir Andrew Nicol, *born* 1951, *apptd* 2009
Hon. Sir Michael Supperstone, *born* 1950, *apptd* 2010
Hon. Sir Robin Spencer, *born* 1955, *apptd* 2010
Hon. Sir Andrew Popplewell, *born* 1959, *apptd* 2011
Hon. Dame Beverley Lang, DBE, *born* 1955, *apptd* 2011
Hon. Sir Jeremy Stuart-Smith, *born* 1955, *apptd* 2012
Hon. Sir Mark Turner, *born* 1959, *apptd* 2013
Hon. Sir Jeremy Baker, *born* 1958, *apptd* 2013
Hon. Sir Stephen Stewart, *born* 1953, *apptd* 2013
Hon. Sir Robert Jay, *born* 1959, *apptd* 2013
Hon. Sir James Dingemans, *born* 1964, *apptd* 2013
Hon. Sir Clive Lewis, *born* 1960, *apptd* 2013
Hon. Dame Sue Carr, DBE, *born* 1964, *apptd* 2013
Hon. Sir Stephen Phillips, *born* 1961, *apptd* 2013
Hon. Dame Geraldine Andrews, DBE, *born* 1959, *apptd* 2013
Hon. Dame Elisabeth Laing, DBE, *born* 1956, *apptd* 2014
Hon. Sir William Davis, *born* 1954, *apptd* 2014
Hon. Sir Mark Warby, *born* 1958, *apptd* 2014
Hon. Sir Andrew Edis, *born* 1957, *apptd* 2014
Hon. Sir James Goss, *born* 1953, *apptd* 2014
Hon. Dame Maura McGowan, DBE, *born* 1957, *apptd* 2014
Hon. Sir Robin Knowles, *born* 1960, *apptd* 2014
Hon. Sir Ian Dove, *born* 1963, *apptd* 2014
Hon. Sir David Holgate, *born* 1956, *apptd* 2014
Hon. Sir Timothy Kerr, *born* 1958, *apptd* 2015
Hon. Sir Simon Picken, *born* 1966, *apptd* 2015
Hon. Dame Philippa Whipple, DBE, *born* 1966, *apptd* 2015
Hon. Sir Peter Fraser, *born* 1963, *apptd* 2015
Hon. Sir Neil Garnham, *born* 1959, *apptd* 2015
Hon. Dame Bobbie Cheema-Grubb, DBE *born* 1966, *apptd* 2015
Hon. Sir Michael Soole, *born* 1954, *apptd* 2015
Hon. Dame Juliet May, DBE, *born* 1961, *apptd* 2015
Hon. Sir Stephen Morris, *born* 1957, *apptd* 2016
Hon. Dame Nerys Jefford, DBE, *born* 1962, *apptd* 2016
Hon. Sir Nicholas Lavender, *born* 1964, *apptd* 2016
Hon. Dame Finola O'Farrell, DBE, *born* 1960, *apptd* 2016
Hon. Sir Andrew Baker, *born* 1965, *apptd* 2016
Hon. Sir Julian Goose, *born* 1961, *apptd* 2017
Hon. Sir Peter Lane, *born* 1953, *apptd* 2017
Hon. Sir Simon Bryan, *born* 1965, *apptd* 2017
Hon. Dame Jane Moulder, DBE, *born* 1960, *apptd* 2017
Hon. Sir Martin Spencer, *born* 1956, *apptd* 2017
Hon. Sir Julian Knowles, *born* 1969, *apptd* 2017
Hon. Dame Amanda Yip, DBE, *born* 1969, *apptd* 2017
Hon. Sir Matthew Nicklin, *born* 1970, *apptd* 2017
Hon. Sir Akhlaq Choudhury, *born* 1967, *apptd* 2017
Hon. Dame Sara Cockerill, DBE, *born* 1968, *apptd* 2017
Hon. Dame Christina Lambert, DBE, *born* 1963, *apptd* 2018
Hon. Sir Christopher Butcher, *born* 1962, *apptd* 2018
Hon. Sir Richard Jacobs, *born* 1956, *apptd* 2018
Hon. Sir David Waksman, *born* 1957, *apptd* 2018
Hon. Dame Johannah Cutts, DBE, *born* 1964, *apptd* 2018
Hon. Sir Jonathan Swift, *born* 1964, *apptd* 2018
Hon. Sir Edward Pepperall, *born* 1966, *apptd* 2018
Hon. Sir Edward Murray, *born* 1958, *apptd* 2018
Hon. Dame Judith Farbey, DBE, *born* 1965, *apptd* 2018
Hon. Clive Freedman, *born* 1955, *apptd* 2018
Hon. Dame Justine Thornton, *born* 1970, *apptd* 2019
Hon. Dame Jennifer Eady, DBE, *born* 1965, *apptd* 2019
Hon. Sir John Cavanagh, *born* 1960, *apptd* 2019
Hon. Dame Alison Foster, *born* 1957, *apptd* 2019
Hon. Sir Pushpinder Saini, *born* 1968, *apptd* 2019
Hon. Sir Jeremy Johnson, *born* 1971, *apptd* 2019
Hon. Sir Martin Chamberlain, *born* 1974, *apptd* 2019

The Queen's Bench Division also includes the Divisional Court, the Admiralty Court, Commercial Court and Technology and Construction Court.

FAMILY DIVISION
President (£226,193), Rt. Hon. Sir Andrew McFarlane, *born* 1954, *apptd* 2018

JUDGES *as at September 2019* (each £188,901)
Style, The Hon. Mr/Mrs/Ms Justice [surname]

Hon. Sir Edward Holman, *born* 1947, *apptd* 1995
Hon. Sir Nicholas Mostyn, *born* 1957, *apptd* 2010
Hon. Dame Lucy Theis, DBE, *born* 1960, *apptd* 2010
Hon. Sir Philip Moor, *born* 1959, *apptd* 2011
Hon. Sir Stephen Cobb, *born* 1962, *apptd* 2013
Hon. Sir Michael Keehan, *born* 1960, *apptd* 2013
Hon. Sir Anthony Hayden, *born* 1961, *apptd* 2013
Hon. Dame Alison Russell, DBE, *born* 1958, *apptd* 2014
Hon. Sir Roderick Newton, *born* 1958, *apptd* 2014
Hon. Dame Jennifer Roberts, DBE, *born* 1953, *apptd* 2014
Hon. Sir Alistair MacDonald, *born* 1970, *apptd* 2015
Hon. Sir Peter Francis, *born* 1958, *apptd* 2016
Hon. Dame Gwynneth Knowles, DBE *born* 1962, *apptd* 2017
Hon. Sir Jonathan Cohen, *born* 1951, *apptd* 2017
Hon. Sir David Williams, *born* 1961, *apptd* 2017
Hon. Dame Nathalie Lieven, DBE, *born* 1964, *apptd* 2019
Hon. Dame Frances Judd, DBE, *born* 1961, *apptd* 2019

COURTS, DIVISIONS AND OFFICES OF THE HIGH COURT OF ENGLAND AND WALES

ADMINISTRATIVE COURT
Royal Courts of Justice, London WC2A 2LL
T 020-7947 6655
Judge in charge of the Administrative Court (£188,901), Hon. Mr Justice Supperstone
Registrar of Criminal Appeals, Master of the Crown Office and Queen's Coroner and Attorney (£140,289), Master Beldam

ADMIRALTY COURT
Ground Floor, 7 Rolls Building, Fetter Lane, London EC4A 1NL
T 020-7947 6112
Admiralty Judge (£188,901), Hon. Mr Justice Teare
Clerk, Paul Doerr
Registrar (£112,542), vacant

CIRCUIT COMMERCIAL COURT (formerly Mercantile Court)
Ground Floor, 7 Rolls Building, Fetter Lane, London EC4A 1NL
T 020-7947 6112

CHANCERY DIVISION
7 Rolls Building, Fetter Lane, London EC4A 1NL **T** 020-7947 7391
Chief Chancery Master (£140,289), Chief Master Marsh *apptd* 2014
Masters of Chancery (£112,542), Master Clark *apptd* 2015; Master Kaye *apptd* 2019; Master Matthews *apptd* 2015; Master Shuman *apptd* 2017; Master Teverson *apptd* 2005

COMMERCIAL COURT
Ground Floor, 7 Rolls Building, Fetter Lane, London EC4A 1NL
T 020-7947 7501
Judge in charge of the Commercial Court (£188,901), Hon. Mr
Justice Teare
Clerk, Paul Doerr

COURT OF APPEAL CIVIL DIVISION
Royal Courts of Justice, London WC2A 2LL **T** 020-7947 6916

COURT OF APPEAL CRIMINAL DIVISION
Royal Courts of Justice, London WC2A 2LL **T** 020-7947 6011

COURT OF PROTECTION
First Avenue House, 42–49 High Holborn, London WC1V 6NP
T 0300-456 4600
Senior Judge and Master of the Court of Protection (£140,289),
Her Hon. Judge Hilder, *apptd* 2017

FAMILY DIVISION
Royal Courts of Justice, London WC2A 2LL **T** 020-7947 6000

INSOLVENCY AND COMPANIES LIST
7 Rolls Building, Fetter Lane, London EC4A 1NL
T 020-7947 6294
Chief Registrar (140,289), Nicholas Briggs *apptd* 2017
Insolvency and Companies Court Judges (£112,542), Judge
Barber *apptd* 2009; Judge Burton *apptd* 2018; Judge Jones
apptd 2012; Judge Mullen *apptd* 2018; Judge Prentis *apptd*
2018

INTELLECTUAL PROPERTY ENTERPRISE COURT
7 Rolls Building, Fetter Lane, London EC4A 1NL
T 020-7947 7783 **E** ipec@hmcts.gsi.gov.uk
Judge in Charge, His Hon. Judge Hacon
Clerk, Irram Khan

PATENTS COURT
7 Rolls Building, Fetter Lane, London EC4A 1NL
T 020-7073 1789
Judge in Charge, Hon. Mr Justice Arnold
Clerk, Pauline Drewett

PLANNING COURT
Royal Courts of Justice, London WC2A 2LL
T 020-7947 6655

QUEEN'S BENCH DIVISION
Judge in Charge of the Queen's Bench Civil List, Hon. Mr Justice
Stewart
Senior Master and Queen's Remembrancer (£140,289), Senior
Master Fontaine *apptd* 2014
Masters of the Queen's Bench Division (£112,542), Master Cook
apptd 2011; Master Davison *apptd* 2016; Master Eastman
apptd 2009; Master Gidden *apptd* 2012; Master McCloud
apptd 2010; Master Thornett *apptd* 2016; Master Yoxall
apptd 2002

SENIOR COURT COSTS OFFICE
Thomas More Building, Royal Courts of Justice, London WC2A 2LL
T 020-7947 6000
Senior Costs Judge (Chief Taxing Master) (£140,289), Chief
Master Gordon-Saker *apptd* 2014
Cost Judges (Taxing Masters) (£112,542), Master Brown *apptd*
2016; Master Haworth *apptd* 2006; Master James *apptd*
2015; Master Leonard *apptd* 2010; Master Nagalingam
apptd 2017; Master Rowley *apptd* 2013; Master Whalan
apptd 2015

TECHNOLOGY AND CONSTRUCTION COURT (TCC)
Ground Floor, 7 Rolls Building, Fetter Lane, London EC4A 1NL
T 020-7947 7156
Judge in charge of the TCC (£188,901), Hon. Mr Justice Fraser

COURT FUNDS OFFICE

Sunderland SR43 3AB **T** 0300-020 0199 **E** enquiries@cfo.gsi.gov.uk

The Court Funds Office (CFO), established in 1726, provides
a banking and administration service for the civil courts
throughout England and Wales, including the High Court.

ELECTION PETITIONS OFFICE

Room E113, Royal Courts of Justice, Strand, London WC2A 2LL
T 020-7947 6877

The office accepts petitions and deals with all matters relating
to the questioning of parliamentary, European parliament,
local government and parish elections, and with applications
for relief under the 'representation of the people' legislation.

Prescribed Officer, The Senior Master and Senior Remembrancer
(£140,289), B. Fontaine

EXAMINERS OF THE COURT

A panel of 18 advocates and solicitor advocates, of at least three
years standing, is empowered to take examination of witnesses
in all divisions of the High Court.

Examiners, Tony Baumgartner; Naomi Candlin; Angharad
Davies; Judy Dawson; Alison Green; Nicholas Hill; Mathias
Kelly; John Leslie; Simon Lewis; Josh Lewison; Susan Lindsey;
Andrew McLoughlin; Christopher McNall; Michael Salter;
Ashley Serr; Frederico Singarajah; Lara Spencer; John
Hamilton

OFFICIAL SOLICITOR AND PUBLIC TRUSTEE

Victory House, 30–34 Kingsway, London WC2B 6EX
E enquiries@ospt.gov.uk

The Official Solicitor and the Public Trustee are independent
statutory office holders. Their office (OSPT) is an arms-length
body of the Ministry of Justice that exists to support their work.
The Official Solicitor provides access to the justice system to
those who are vulnerable by virtue of minority or lack of mental
capacity. The Public Trustee acts as executor or administrator
of estates and as the appointed trustee of settlements, providing
an effective executor and trustee service of last resort.

Official Solicitor to the Senior Courts and the Public Trustee, Sarah
Castle
Deputy Public Trustee, Janet Peel
Deputy Official Solicitors, Brid Breathnach; Elaine Brown; Janet
Ilett

PROBATE REGISTRIES

London Probate Department, 7th Floor, First Avenue House, 42–49
High Holborn, London WC1V 6NP **T** 020-7421 8509

Probate registries issue grants of probate and grants of letters
of administration. The principal probate registry is situated in
central London and there are 11 district probate registries in
Birmingham, Brighton, Bristol, Cardiff, Ipswich, Leeds,
Liverpool, Manchester, Newcastle, Oxford and Winchester,
and a further 18 probate sub-registries. Probate registries are
administered by HM Courts and Tribunals Service.

JUDGE ADVOCATES GENERAL

The Judge Advocate General is the judicial head of the Service justice system, and the leader of the judges who preside over trials in the court martial and other Service courts. The defendants are service personnel from the Royal Navy, the army and the Royal Air Force, and civilians accompanying them overseas.

JUDGE ADVOCATE GENERAL OF THE FORCES
9th Floor, Thomas More Building, Royal Courts of Justice, Strand, London WC2A 2LL **T** 020-7218 8095

Judge Advocate General (£151,497), His Hon. Judge Blackett
Vice-Judge Advocate General (£132,075), Judge Hunter
Assistant Judge Advocates General (£112,542), J. P. Camp; R. D. Hill; A. M. Large; A. J. B. McGrigor
Style, Judge [surname]

CROWN COURT CENTRES

The crown court sits in 77 court centres across England and Wales. It deals with serious criminal cases which include:
- cases sent for trial by magistrates' courts because the offences are 'indictable only' (ie those which can only be heard by the crown court)
- 'either way' offences (which can be heard in a magistrates' court, but can also be sent to the crown court if the defendant chooses a jury trial)
- defendants convicted in magistrates' courts, but sent to the Crown Court for sentencing due to the seriousness of the offence
- appeals against decisions of magistrates' courts

First-tier centres deal with both civil and criminal cases and are served by high court and circuit judges. Second-tier centres deal with criminal cases only and are served by high court and circuit judges. Third-tier centres deal with criminal cases only and are served only by circuit judges.

In London, the high court acts as the first-tier centre, sitting at the Royal Courts of Justice, and the second-tier is the Central Criminal Court.

CIRCUIT JUDGES

Circuit judges are barristers of at least seven years' standing or recorders of at least five years' standing. Circuit judges serve in the county courts and the crown court.

Style, His/Her Hon. Judge [surname]
Senior Presiding Judge, Rt. Hon. Lady Justice Macur, DBE
Deputy Senior Presiding Judge, Rt. Hon Lady Justice Thirlwall, DBE
Senior Circuit Judges, each £151,497
Circuit Judges at the Central Criminal Court, London (Old Bailey Judges), each £151,497
Circuit Judges, each £140,289

MIDLAND CIRCUIT
Presiding Judges, Hon. Mrs Justice Carr; Hon. Mr Justice Jeremy Baker
NORTH-EASTERN CIRCUIT
Presiding Judges, Hon. Mr Justice Goss; Hon. Mr Justice Lavender
NORTHERN CIRCUIT
Presiding Judges, Hon. Mr Justice William Davis; Hon. Mr Justice Dove
SOUTH-EASTERN CIRCUIT
Presiding Judges, Hon. Mrs Justice McGowan; Hon. Mr Justice Edis; Hon. Mrs Justice Whipple; Hon. Mrs Justice Cheema-Grubb
WALES CIRCUIT
Presiding Judges, Hon. Mr Justice Lewis; Hon. Mr Justice Picken

WESTERN CIRCUIT
Presiding Judges, Hon. Mrs Justice May; Hon. Mr Justice Garnham

DISTRICT JUDGES

District judges, formerly known as registrars of the court, are solicitors of at least seven years' standing and serve in county courts.
District Judges, each £112,542

DISTRICT JUDGES (MAGISTRATES' COURTS)

District judges (magistrates' courts), formerly known as stipendiary magistrates, serve in magistrates courts where they hear criminal cases, youth cases and some civil proceedings. Many also hear family cases in the single family court. Some may be authorised to handle extradition proceedings and terrorist cases. District judges (magistrates' courts) are appointed following competition conducted by the Judicial Appointments Commission.
District Judges (Magistrates' Courts), each £112,542

OFFICE OF THE CHIEF MAGISTRATE
181 Marylebone Road, London NW1 5BR
T 020-3126 3100

The Chief Magistrate (senior district judge) is responsible for hearing many of the sensitive or complex cases – extradition and special jurisdiction cases in particular – in the magistrates' courts. The Chief Magistrate also supports and guides district judges (magistrates' courts), and liaises with the senior judiciary and presiding judges on matters pertaining to magistrates' courts.

The Office of the Chief Magistrate provides administration support to both the Chief Magistrate and to all the district judges sitting at magistrates' courts in England and Wales.

Chief Magistrate, Emma Arbuthnot
Deputy Chief Magistrate, Tanweer Ikram

CROWN PROSECUTION SERVICE

102 Petty France, London SW1H 9EA
T 020-3357 0899 **E** enquiries@cps.gov.uk **W** www.cps.gov.uk

The Crown Prosecution Service (CPS) is responsible for prosecuting cases investigated by the police in England and Wales, with the exception of cases conducted by the Serious Fraud Office and certain minor offences.

The CPS is headed by the director of public prosecutions (DPP), who works under the superintendence of the attorney-general. The service is divided into 14 regional teams across England and Wales, with each area led by a chief crown prosecutor.

Director of Public Prosecutions, Max Hill, QC
Chief Executive, Rebecca Lawrence
Directors, Jean Ashton, OBE *(Business Services);* Sue Hemming *(Legal Services);* Gregor McGill *(Legal Services)*

CPS AREAS
EAST MIDLANDS, 2 King Edward Court, King Edward Street, Nottingham NG1 1EL **T** 0115-852 3300
  Chief Crown Prosecutor, Janine Smith
EAST OF ENGLAND, County House, 100 New London Road, Chelmsford, Essex CM2 0RG **T** 01245-455800
  Chief Crown Prosecutor, Chris Long
LONDON, 1st Floor, Zone A, 102 Petty France, London SW1H 9EA **T** 020-3357 7000
  Chief Crown Prosecutor London North, Ed Beltrami, CBE
  Chief Crown Prosecutor London South, Claire Lindley

MERSEY–CHESHIRE, 2nd Floor, Walker House, Exchange Flags, Liverpool L2 3YL **T** 0151-239 6400
Chief Crown Prosecutor, Siobhan Blake

NORTH EAST, St Ann's Quay, 112 Quayside, Newcastle Upon Tyne, NE1 3BD **T** 0191-260 4200
Chief Crown Prosecutor, Andrew Penhale

NORTH WEST, 1st Floor, Stocklund House, Castle Street, Carlisle CA3 8SY **T** 01228-882900
Chief Crown Prosecutor, Martin Goldman

SOUTH EAST, Riding Gate House, 37 Old Dover Road, Canterbury, Kent CT1 3JG **T** 01227-866000
Chief Crown Prosecutor, Frank Ferguson

SOUTH WEST, 5th Floor, Kite Wing, Temple Quay House, 2 The Square, Bristol BS1 6PN **T** 0117-930 2800
Chief Crown Prosecutor, Victoria Cook

THAMES AND CHILTERN, Eaton Court, 112 Oxford Road, Reading, Berks RG1 7LL **T** 01727-798700
Chief Crown Prosecutor, Jaswant Kaur Narwal

WALES, 20th Floor, Capital Tower, Greyfriars Road, Cardiff CF10 3PL **T** 029-2080 3800
Chief Crown Prosecutor, Barry Hughes

WESSEX, 3rd Floor, Black Horse House, 8–10 Leigh Road, Eastleigh, Hants SO50 9FH **T** 0238-067 3800
Chief Crown Prosecutor, Joanne Jakymec

WEST MIDLANDS, Colmore Gate, 2 Colmore Row, Birmingham B3 2QA **T** 0121-262 1300
Chief Crown Prosecutor, Grace Ononiwu, OBE

YORKSHIRE AND HUMBERSIDE, 27 Park Place, Leeds LS1 2SZ **T** 0113-290 2700
Chief Crown Prosecutor, Gerry Wareham

HER MAJESTY'S COURTS AND TRIBUNALS SERVICE

1st Floor, 102 Petty France, London SW1H 9AJ
W www.gov.uk/government/organisations/hm-courts-and-tribunals-service

Her Majesty's Courts Service and the Tribunals Service merged on 1 April 2011 to form HM Courts and Tribunals Service. It is an agency of the Ministry of Justice, operating as a partnership between the Lord Chancellor, the Lord Chief Justice and the Senior President of Tribunals. It is responsible for administering the criminal, civil and family courts and tribunals in England and Wales and non-devolved tribunals in Scotland and Northern Ireland.

Chief Executive, Susan Acland-Hood

JUDICIAL APPOINTMENTS COMMISSION

5th Floor, Clive House, 70 Petty France, London SW1H 9EX
T 020-3334 0123 **E** jaas@judicialappointments.gov.uk
W www.judicialappointments.gov.uk

The Judicial Appointments Commission was established as an independent non-departmental public body in April 2006 by the Constitutional Reform Act 2005. Its role is to select judicial office holders independently of government (a responsibility previously held by the Lord Chancellor) for courts and tribunals in England and Wales, and for some tribunals whose jurisdiction extends to Scotland or Northern Ireland. It has a statutory duty to encourage diversity in the range of persons available for selection and is sponsored by the Ministry of Justice and accountable to parliament through the Lord Chancellor. It is made up of a total of 15 commissioners: seven judicial (including one non-legal), two professional, five lay and the chair.

Chair, Rt. Hon. Prof. Lord Kakkar
Vice-Chair, Rt. Hon. Dame Anne Rafferty, DBE
Commissioners, Judge Mathu Asokan; Her Hon. Judge Anuja Dhir; Emir Khan Feisal; Jane Furness, CBE; Sue Hoyle;

Andrew Kennon; Sarah Lee; Judge Fiona Monk; Brie Stevens-Hoare, QC; His Hon. Judge Phillip Sycamore; Sir Simon Wessely; Dame Philippa Whipple, DBE
Chief Executive, Richard Jarvis

JUDICIAL OFFICE

The Judicial Office was established in April 2006 to support the judiciary in discharging its responsibilities under the Constitutional Reform Act 2005. It is led by a chief executive, who reports to the Lord Chief Justice and Senior President of Tribunals rather than to ministers, and its work is directed by the judiciary rather than by the administration of the day. The Judicial Office incorporates the Judicial College, sponsorship of the Family and Civil Justice Councils, the Office for Judicial Complaints and Office of the Chief Coroner.

Chief Executive, Andrew Key

JUDICIAL COMMITTEE OF THE PRIVY COUNCIL

The Judicial Committee of the Privy Council is the final court of appeal for the United Kingdom overseas territories (*see* UK Overseas Territories section), crown dependencies and those independent Commonwealth countries which have retained this avenue of appeal and the sovereign base areas of Akrotiri and Dhekelia in Cyprus. The committee also hears appeals against pastoral schemes under the Pastoral Measure 1983, and deals with appeals from veterinary disciplinary bodies.

Until October 2009, the Judicial Committee of the Privy Council was the final arbiter in disputes as to the legal competence of matters done or proposed by the devolved legislative and executive authorities in Scotland, Wales and Northern Ireland. This is now the responsibility of the UK Supreme Court.

The members of the Judicial Committee are the justices of the supreme court, and Privy Counsellors who hold or have held high judicial office in the United Kingdom or in certain designated courts of Commonwealth countries from which appeals are taken to committee.

JUDICIAL COMMITTEE OF THE PRIVY COUNCIL
Parliament Square, London SW1P 3BD **T** 020-7960 1500
W www.jcpc.uk
Chief Executive, Mark Ormerod
Registrar of the Privy Council, Louise di Mambro

SCOTTISH JUDICATURE

Scotland has a legal system separate from, and differing greatly from, the English legal system in enacted law, judicial procedure and the structure of courts.

In Scotland the system of public prosecution is headed by the Lord Advocate and is independent of the police, who have no say in the decision to prosecute. The Lord Advocate, discharging his functions through the Crown Office in Edinburgh, is responsible for prosecutions in the high court, sheriff courts and justice of the peace courts. Prosecutions in the high court are prepared by the Crown Office and conducted in court by one of the law officers, by an advocate-depute, or by a solicitor advocate. In the inferior courts the decision to prosecute is made and prosecution is preferred by procurators fiscal, who are lawyers and full-time civil servants subject to the directions of the Crown Office. A permanent legally qualified civil servant, known as the crown agent, is responsible for the running of the Crown Office and the organisation of the Procurator Fiscal Service, of which he or she is the head.

Scotland is divided into six sheriffdoms, each with a full-time sheriff principal. The sheriffdoms are further divided into sheriff court districts, each of which has a legally qualified resident sheriff or sheriffs, who are the judges of the court.

In criminal cases sheriffs principal and sheriffs have the same powers; sitting with a jury of 15 members, they may try more serious cases on indictment, or, sitting alone, may try lesser cases under summary procedure. Minor summary offences are dealt with in justice of the peace courts, which replaced district courts formerly operated by local authorities, and presided over by lay justices of the peace (of whom some 500 regularly sit in court) and, in Glasgow only, by stipendiary magistrates. Juvenile offenders (children under 16) may be brought before an informal children's hearing comprising three local lay people. The superior criminal court is the high court of justiciary which is both a trial and an appeal court. Cases on indictment are tried by a high court judge, sitting with a jury of 15, in Edinburgh and on circuit in other towns. Appeals from the lower courts against conviction or sentence are also heard by the high court, which sits as an appeal court only in Edinburgh. There is no further appeal to the UK supreme court in criminal cases.

In civil cases the jurisdiction of the sheriff court extends to most kinds of action. Appeals against decisions of the sheriff may be made to the sheriff principal and thence to the court of session, or direct to the court of session, which sits only in Edinburgh. The court of session is divided into the inner and the outer house. The outer house is a court of first instance in which cases are heard by judges sitting singly, sometimes with a jury of 12. The inner house, itself subdivided into two divisions of equal status, is mainly an appeal court. Appeals may be made to the inner house from the outer house as well as from the sheriff court. An appeal may be made from the inner house to the UK supreme court.

The judges of the court of session are the same as those of the high court of justiciary, with the Lord President of the court of session also holding the office of Lord Justice General in the high court. Senators of the College of Justice are Lords Commissioners of Justiciary as well as judges of the court of session. On appointment, a senator takes a judicial title, which is retained for life. Although styled The Hon./Rt. Hon. Lord, the senator is not a peer, although some judges are peers in their own right.

The office of coroner does not exist in Scotland. The local procurator fiscal inquires privately into sudden or suspicious deaths and may report findings to the crown agent. In some cases a fatal accident inquiry may be held before the sheriff.

COURT OF SESSION AND HIGH COURT OF JUSTICIARY

The Lord President and Lord Justice General (£234,184), Rt. Hon. Lord Carloway, *born* 1954, *apptd* 2015
Private Secretary, Paul Gilmour

INNER HOUSE
Lords of Session (each £215,094)

FIRST DIVISION
The Lord President

Rt. Hon. Lord Menzies (Duncan Menzies), *born* 1953, *apptd* 2012
Rt. Hon. Lady Smith (Anne Smith), *born* 1955, *apptd* 2012
Rt. Hon. Lord Brodie (Philip Brodie), *born* 1950, *apptd* 2012
Rt. Hon. Lady Clark of Calton (Lynda Clark), *born* 1949, *apptd* 2013
Rt. Hon. Lord Glennie (Angus Glennie), *born* 1950, *apptd* 2016

SECOND DIVISION
Lord Justice Clerk (£226,193), Rt. Hon. Lady Dorrian (Leeona Dorrian), *born* 1957, *apptd* 2016

Rt. Hon. Lady Paton (Ann Paton), *born* 1952, *apptd* 2007
Rt. Hon. Lord Drummond Young (James Drummond Young), *born* 1950, *apptd* 2013
Rt. Hon. Lord Malcolm (Colin M. Campbell), *born* 1953, *apptd* 2015
Hon. Lord Turnbull (Alan Turnbull), *born* 1958, *apptd* 2016

OUTER HOUSE
Lords of Session (each £188,901)

Hon. Lord Kinclaven (Alexander F. Wylie, OBE), *born* 1951, *apptd* 2005
Hon. Lord Brailsford (S. Neil Brailsford), *born* 1954, *apptd* 2006
Hon. Lord Uist (Roderick Macdonald), *born* 1951, *apptd* 2006
Hon. Lord Matthews (Hugh Matthews), *born* 1953, *apptd* 2007
Hon. Lord Woolman (Stephen Woolman), *born* 1953, *apptd* 2008
Hon. Lord Pentland (Paul Cullen), *born* 1957, *apptd* 2008
Hon. Lord Bannatyne (Iain Peebles, QC), *born* 1954, *apptd* 2008
Hon. Lady Stacey (Valerie E. Stacey), *born* 1954, *apptd* 2009
Hon. Lord Tyre (Colin Tyre, CBE), *born* 1956, *apptd* 2010
Hon. Lord Doherty (J. Raymond Doherty), *born* 1958, *apptd* 2010
Rt. Hon. Lord Boyd of Duncansby (Colin Boyd), *born* 1953, *apptd* 2012
Hon. Lord Burns (David Burns), *born* 1952, *apptd* 2012
Hon. Lady Scott (Margaret Scott), *born* 1960, *apptd* 2012
Hon. Lady Wise (Morag Wise), *born* 1963, *apptd* 2013
Hon. Lord Armstrong (Iain Armstrong), *born* 1956, *apptd* 2013
Hon. Lady Rae (Rita Rae), *born* 1950, *apptd* 2014
Hon. Lady Wolffe (Sarah Wolffe, QC), *apptd* 2014
Hon. Lord Beckett (John Beckett, QC), *apptd* 2016
Hon. Lord Clark (Alistair Clark, QC), *born* 1955, *apptd* 2016
Hon. Lord Ericht (Andrew Stewart, QC), *born* 1963, *apptd* 2016
Hon. Lady Carmichael (Ailsa Carmichael, QC), *born* 1969, *apptd* 2016
Rt. Hon. Lord Mulholland (Frank Mulholland, QC), *born* 1959, *apptd* 2016
Hon. Lord Summers (Alan Summers, QC), *born* 1964, *apptd* 2017
Hon. Lord Arthurson (Paul Arthurson, QC), *born* 1964, *apptd* 2017

COURT OF SESSION AND HIGH COURT OF JUSTICIARY
Parliament House, Parliament Square, Edinburgh EH1 1RQ
T 0131-225 2595

Director and Principal Clerk of Session and Justiciary, Gillian Prentice
Deputy Principal Clerk of Session, Diane Machin
Deputy Principal Clerk of Justiciary, Joe Moyes
Depute in Charge of the Court of Session Office, Christina Bardsley
Officer in Charge of the Justiciary Office, Ross Martin
Keeper of the Rolls, Trish Fiddes
Assistant Keeper of the Rolls, Grahame Simpson
Appeals Manager, Alex McKay
Clerking Services Manager, Chris Fyffe
Court Manager, Zac Conway

JUDICIAL APPOINTMENTS BOARD FOR SCOTLAND
Thistle House, 91 Haymarket Terrace, Edinburgh EH12 5HE
T 0131-528 5101 W www.judicialappointments.scot

The board's remit is to provide the first minister with the names of candidates recommended for appointment to the court posts of senator of the college of justice, chair of the Scottish Land Court, sheriff principal, sheriff and part-time sheriff. It is also responsible for recommending individuals to the office of vice-president of the Upper Tribunal; chamber and deputy chamber presidents of the First-tier Tribunal; and members of the Upper Tribunal and First-tier Tribunal.

Chair, Nicola Gordon
Chief Executive, John Craig

JUDICIAL OFFICE FOR SCOTLAND
Parliament House, Edinburgh EH1 1RQ
T 0131-240 6677 **W** www.scotland-judiciary.org.uk

The Judicial Office for Scotland came into being on 1 April 2010 as part of the changes introduced by the Judiciary and Courts (Scotland) Act 2008. It provides support for the Lord President in his role as head of the Scottish judiciary with responsibility for the training, welfare, deployment and conduct of judges and the efficient disposal of business in the courts.

Executive Director, Tim Barraclough

SCOTTISH COURTS AND TRIBUNALS SERVICE
Saughton House, Broomhouse Drive, Edinburgh EH11 3XD
T 0131-444 3300 **W** www.scotcourts.gov.uk

The Scottish Courts and Tribunals Service (SCTS) is an independent body which was established on 1 April 2010 under the Judiciary and Courts (Scotland) Act 2008. Its function is to provide administrative support to Scottish courts and tribunals and to the judiciary of courts, including the High Court of Justiciary, Court of Session, sheriff courts and justice of the peace courts, and to the Office of the Public Guardian and Accountant of Court.

Chief Executive, Eric McQueen

SCOTTISH GOVERNMENT JUSTICE DIRECTORATE
St Andrew's House, Edinburgh EH1 3DG
T 0131-244 4000

The Justice Directorate is responsible for the appointment of judges and sheriffs to meet the needs of the business of the supreme and sheriffs court in Scotland. It is also responsible for providing resources for the efficient administration of certain specialist courts and tribunals.

Director (Justice), Neil Rennick

SCOTTISH LAND COURT
126 George Street, Edinburgh EH2 4HH
T 0131-271 4360 **W** www.scottish-land-court.org.uk

The court deals with disputes relating to agricultural and crofting land in Scotland.

Chair (£151,497), Hon. Lord Miningish (Roderick John MacLeod, QC)
Deputy Chair, Iain Maclean
Members, Tom Campbell; John Smith
Principal Clerk, Barbara Brown

SHERIFF COURTS
The majority of cases in Scotland are handled by one of the 39 sheriff courts. Criminal cases are heard by a sheriff and a jury (solemn procedure) but can be heard by a sheriff alone (summary procedure). Civil cases are heard by a single sheriff.
Scotland is split into six sheriffdoms, each headed by a sheriff principal.

SALARIES
Sheriff Principal, £151,497
Sheriff, £140,289

SHERIFFDOMS
GLASGOW AND STRATHKELVIN
Sheriff Principal, Craig Turnbull
GRAMPIAN, HIGHLAND AND ISLANDS
Sheriff Principal, Derek Pyle
LOTHIAN AND BORDERS
Sheriff Principal, Mhairi Stephen, QC
NORTH STRATHCLYDE
Sheriff Principal, Duncan Murray
SOUTH STRATHCLYDE, DUMFRIES AND GALLOWAY
Sheriff Principal, Ian Abercrombie, QC
TAYSIDE, CENTRAL AND FIFE
Sheriff Principal, Marysia Lewis

JUSTICE OF THE PEACE COURTS
Justice of the peace courts replaced district courts and are a unique feature of Scotland's judicial system. Justices of the peace are lay magistrates who either sit alone, or in a bench of three, and deal with summary crimes such as speeding and careless driving. In court, justices have access to solicitors, who fulfil the role of legal advisers or clerks of court.

A justice of the peace court can be presided over by a stipendiary magistrate – a legally qualified solicitor or advocate who sits alone. They deal with more serious summary business similar to sheriffs, such as drink driving and assault. All sheriffs principal have powers to appoint stipendiary magistrates, but at present there are no justice of the peace courts in the sheriff court districts of Lerwick, Kirkwall, Wick, Stornoway, Lochmaddy and Portree.

CROWN OFFICE AND PROCURATOR FISCAL SERVICE
25 Chambers Street, Edinburgh EH1 1LA
T 0300-020 3000 **W** www.copfs.gov.uk

The Crown Office and Procurator Fiscal Service (COPFS) is Scotland's prosecution service. COPFS receive reports about crimes from the police and other reporting agencies and then decide what action to take, including whether to prosecute someone. It is also responsible for looking into deaths that need further explanation and investigating allegations of criminal conduct against police officers.

Lord Advocate, Rt. Hon. James Wolffe, QC
Solicitor-General, Alison Di Rollo, QC
Crown Agent, David Harvie

COURT OF THE LORD LYON
HM New Register House, Edinburgh EH1 3YT
T 0131-556 7255 **W** www.courtofthelordlyon.scot

The Court of the Lord Lyon is the Scottish Court of Chivalry (including the genealogical jurisdiction of the *Ri-Sennachie* of Scotland's Celtic kings). The Lord Lyon King of Arms has jurisdiction, subject to appeal to the Court of Session and the House of Lords, in questions of heraldry and the right to bear arms. The court also administers the Public Register of All Arms and Bearings and the Public Register of All Genealogies in Scotland. Pedigrees are established by decrees of Lyon Court and by letters patent. As Royal Commissioner in Armory, the Lord Lyon grants patents of arms to virtuous and well-deserving Scots and to petitioners (personal or corporate) in the Queen's overseas realms of Scottish connection, and also issues birthbrieves. For information on Her Majesty's Officers of Arms in Scotland, *see* the Court of the Lord Lyon in the Public Bodies section.

Lord Lyon King of Arms, Dr Joseph Morrow, CBE, QC
Lyon Clerk and Keeper of the Records, Russell Hunter
Procurator Fiscal, Alexander Green

NORTHERN IRELAND JUDICATURE

In Northern Ireland the legal system and the structure of courts closely resemble those of England and Wales; there are, however, often differences in enacted law.

The court of judicature of Northern Ireland comprises the court of appeal, the high court of justice and the crown court. The practice and procedure of these courts is similar to that in England. The superior civil court is the high court of justice, from which an appeal lies to the Northern Ireland court of appeal; the UK supreme court is the final civil appeal court.

The crown court, served by high court and county court judges, deals with criminal trials on indictment. Cases are heard before a judge and, except those certified by the Director of Public Prosecutions under the Justice and Security Act 2007, a jury. Appeals from the crown court against conviction or sentence are heard by the Northern Ireland court of appeal; the UK supreme court is the final court of appeal.

The decision to prosecute in criminal cases in Northern Ireland rests with the Director of Public Prosecutions.

Minor criminal offences are dealt with in magistrates' courts by a legally qualified district judge (magistrates' courts) and, where an offender is under the age of 18, by youth courts each consisting of a district judge (magistrates' courts) and two lay magistrates (at least one of whom must be a woman). There are approximately 200 lay magistrates in Northern Ireland. Appeals from magistrates' courts are heard by the county court, or by the court of appeal on a point of law or an issue as to jurisdiction.

Magistrates' courts in Northern Ireland can deal with certain classes of civil case but most minor civil cases are dealt with in county courts. Judgments of all civil courts are enforceable through a centralised procedure administered by the Enforcement of Judgments Office.

COURT OF JUDICATURE
The Royal Courts of Justice, Chichester Street, Belfast BT1 3JF
T 0300-200 7812 **W** www.courtsni.gov.uk

Lord Chief Justice of Northern Ireland (£234,184), Rt. Hon. Sir Declan Morgan, *born* 1952, *apptd* 2009

LORDS JUSTICES OF APPEAL (£215,094)
Style, The Rt. Hon. Lord/Lady Justice [surname]

Rt. Hon. Sir Benjamin Stephens, *born* 1954, *apptd* 2017
Hon. Sir Seamus Treacy, *born* 1956, *apptd* 2017

Hon. Sir Bernard McCloskey, *born* 1956, *apptd* 2019

HIGH COURT JUDGES (£188,901)
Style, The Hon. Mr/Mrs/Ms Justice [surname]

Hon. Sir Paul Maguire, *born* 1952, *apptd* 2012
Hon. Sir Mark Horner, *born* 1956, *apptd* 2012
Hon. Sir John O'Hara, *born* 1956, *apptd* 2013
Hon. Sir Adrian Colton, *born* 1959, *apptd* 2015
Hon. Dame Denise McBride, DBE, *apptd* 2015
Hon. Dame Siobhan Keegan, DBE, *apptd* 2015
Hon. Sir Gerry McAlinden, *apptd* 2018
Hon. Sir Ian Huddleston, *apptd* 2019

MASTERS OF THE HIGH COURT (£112,542)
Presiding Master, Master McCorry, *apptd* 2001
Masters, Master Bell *apptd* 2006; Master Hardstaff, *apptd* 2014; Master Kelly, *apptd* 2005; Master McGivern *apptd* 2015; Master Sweeney, *apptd* 2015; Master Wells, *apptd* 2005

COUNTY COURTS

JUDGES (£151,498†)
Style, His/Her Hon. Judge [surname]

Judge Babington *apptd* 2004; Judge Crawford *apptd* 2015; Judge Devlin *apptd* 2011; Judge Fowler, QC *apptd* 2011; Judge Gilpin *apptd* 2019; Judge Kerr, QC *apptd* 2012; Judge Kinney *apptd* 2012; Judge Lynch, QC *apptd* 2004; Judge McCaffrey *apptd* 2016; Judge McColgan, QC *apptd* 2013; Judge McCormick *apptd* 2018; Judge McFarland *apptd* 1998; Judge McReynolds *apptd* 2004; Judge Miller, QC *apptd* 2009; Judge Rafferty, QC *apptd* 2016; Judge Ramsay, QC *apptd* 2014; Judge Sherrard *apptd* 2012; Judge Smyth *apptd* 2010

† County court judges are paid £151,498 so long as they are required to carry out significantly different work from their counterparts elsewhere in the UK

RECORDERS
Belfast (£163,617), Judge McFarland
Londonderry (£151,497), Judge Babington

DISTRICT JUDGES (£112,542)
Only barristers and solicitors with ten years' standing are eligible to become district judges. There are usually four district judges in Northern Ireland:

Presiding District Judge Brownlie *apptd* 1997; District Judge Collins *apptd* 2000; District Judge Duncan *apptd* 2014

MAGISTRATES' COURTS

DISTRICT JUDGES (MAGISTRATES' COURTS) (£112,542)
There are usually 21 district judges (magistrates' courts) in Northern Ireland:

Presiding District Judge Bagnall *apptd* 2003; District Judge Brady *apptd* 2016; District Judge Broderick *apptd* 2013; District Judge Conner *apptd* 1999; District Judge Copeland *apptd* 1993; District Judge Hamill *apptd* 1999; District Judge Henderson *apptd* 2005; District Judge Kelly *apptd* 1997; District Judge Keown *apptd* 2018; District Judge E. King *apptd* 2005; District Judge P. King *apptd* 2013; District Judge McElholm *apptd* 1998; District Judge McGarrity *apptd* 2019; District Judge McNally *apptd* 2003; District Judge P. Magill *apptd* 2018; District Judge Meehan *apptd* 2002; District Judge Mullan *apptd* 2016; District Judge Prytherch *apptd* 2005; District Judge Ranaghan *apptd* 2017; District Judge Watters *apptd* 1998

NORTHERN IRELAND COURTS AND TRIBUNALS SERVICE
23–27 Oxford Street, Belfast BT1 3LA
T 0300-200 7812 **W** www.justice-ni.gov.uk/topics/courts-and-tribunals
Chief Executive (acting), Peter Luney

CROWN SOLICITOR'S OFFICE
Royal Courts of Justice, Chichester Street, Belfast BT1 3JE
T 028-9054 2555
Crown Solicitor, Fiona Chamberlain

PUBLIC PROSECUTION SERVICE
Belfast Chambers, 93 Chichester Street, Belfast BT1 3JR
T 028-9089 7100 **W** www.ppsni.gov.uk
Director of Public Prosecutions, Stephen Herron

TRIBUNALS

Information on all the tribunals listed here, with the exception of the independent tribunals and the tribunals based in Scotland, Wales and Northern Ireland, can be found online (W www.gov.uk/government/organisations/hm-courts-and-tribunals-service).

HM COURTS AND TRIBUNALS SERVICE

102 Petty France, London SW1H 9AJ
W www.gov.uk/government/organisations/hm-courts-and-tribunals-service
W www.gov.uk/find-court-tribunal

HM Courts Service and the Tribunals Service merged on 1 April 2011 to form HM Courts and Tribunals Service, an integrated agency providing support for the administration of justice in courts and tribunals. It is an agency within the Ministry of Justice, operating as a partnership between the Lord Chancellor, the Lord Chief Justice and the Senior President of Tribunals. It is responsible for the administration of the criminal, civil and family courts and tribunals in England and Wales and non-devolved tribunals in Scotland

and Northern Ireland. The agency's work is overseen by a board headed by an independent chair working with non-executive, executive and judicial members.

A two-tier tribunal system, comprising the First-tier Tribunal and Upper Tribunal, was established on 3 November 2008 as a result of radical reform under the Tribunals, Courts and Enforcement Act 2007. Both of these tiers are split into a number of separate chambers. These chambers group together individual tribunals (also known as 'jurisdictions') which deal with similar work or require similar skills. Cases start in the First-tier Tribunal and there is a right of appeal to the Upper Tribunal. Some tribunals transferred to the new two-tier system immediately, with more transferring between 2009 and 2011. The exception is employment tribunals, which remain outside this structure. The Act also allowed legally qualified tribunal chairs and adjudicators to swear the judicial oath and become judges.

Senior President, Rt. Hon. Sir Ernest Ryder, TD
Vice-President of the Unified Tribunals, Hon. Sir Keith Lindblom
Chief Executive, Susan Acland-Hood

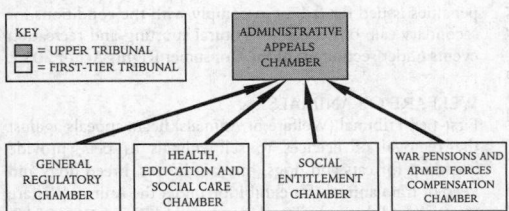

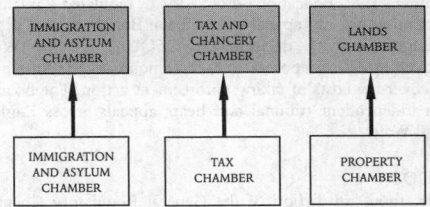

FIRST-TIER TRIBUNAL

The main function of the First-tier Tribunal is to hear appeals by citizens against decisions of the government. In most cases appeals are heard by a panel made up of one judge and two specialists in their relevant field, known as 'members'. Both judges and members are appointed through the Independent Judicial Appointments Commission. Most of the tribunals administered by central government are part of the First-tier Tribunal, which is split into seven separate chambers.

GENERAL REGULATORY CHAMBER

For all jurisdictions: General Regulatory Chamber, HMCTS, PO Box 9300, Leicester LE1 8DJ T 0300-123 4504
E grc@justice.gov.uk
Chamber President, Judge McKenna

CHARITY
Under the Charities Act 2011 (only applicable to England and Wales), First-tier Tribunal (Charity) hears appeals against the decisions of the Charity Commission, applications for the review of decisions made by the Charity Commission and considers references from the Attorney-General or the Charity Commission on points of law.

COMMUNITY RIGHT TO BID
The Community Right to Bid jurisdiction of the General Regulatory Chamber was established in January 2013 and hears appeals against review decisions made by local authorities to list your property as a community asset and

give local communities the right to bid for it if you decide to sell. Individuals have the right to appeal against a listing decision under the Localism Act 2011 and the assets of community value (England) regulations 2012.

CONSULTANT LOBBYISTS
First-tier Tribunal (Consultant Lobbyists) hears appeals against penalties imposed for an offence under section 12 of the Transparency of Lobbying, Non-Party Campaigning and Trade Union Administration Act 2014 by the Office of the Registrar of Consultant Lobbyists.

CONVEYANCING
The professional regulation jurisdiction hears appeals against decisions made by the Council for Licensed Conveyancers under the Legal Services Act 2007.

COPYRIGHT LICENSING
Under the copyright (regulation of relevant licensing bodies) regulations 2014 a copyright licensing body may appeal to a First-tier Tribunal (Copyright Licensing) against a government decision to fine or impose a code of conduct on their organisation.

DRIVING INSTRUCTORS
First-tier Tribunal (Driving Instructors) hears appeals against decisions made by the Registrar of Approved Driving Instructors under the Road Traffic Act 1988, Transport Act 2000 and the Motor Cars (Driving Instruction) Regulations 2005. Its jurisdiction covers England, Scotland and Wales.

ELECTRONIC COMMUNICATIONS AND POSTAL SERVICES

Hears appeals against decisions made by the Interception of Communications Commissioner under the Regulation of Investigatory Powers (Monetary Penalty Notices and Consents for Interceptions) Regulations 2011.

ENVIRONMENT

First-tier Tribunal (Environment) was created to decide appeals regarding civil sanctions made by environmental regulators. Established in April 2010, the jurisdiction of the tribunal extends to England and Wales.

ESTATE AGENTS

First-tier Tribunal (Estate Agents) hears appeals, under the Estate Agents Act 1979, against decisions made by the Office of Fair Trading pertaining to orders prohibiting a person from being employed as an estate agent when that person has been, for example, convicted of fraud or another offence involving dishonesty. The tribunal also hears appeals relating to decisions refusing to revoke or vary a prohibition order or warning order, as well as appeals regarding the issuing of a warning order when a person has not fulfilled their obligations under the Act.

EXAM BOARDS

Under the Education Act 1997 regulated awarding organisations can appeal to the Exam Board tribunal if they disagree with a decision by OFQUAL or the Welsh government to impose a fine, the amount of the fine, or to recover the costs of taking enforcement action. The board is an independent tribunal and hears appeals across England and Wales.

FOOD

The food jurisdiction of the General Regulatory Chamber was established in January 2013 and hears appeals against some of the decisions taken by the Food Standards Agency, Department for Environment, Food and Rural Affairs and local authority trading standards departments. It also deals with appeals against decisions under the Fish Labelling (England) Regulations.

GAMBLING

First-tier Tribunal (Gambling) hears and decides appeals against decisions made by the Gambling Commission under the Gambling Act 2005.

IMMIGRATION SERVICES

First-tier Tribunal (Welfare of Animals) hears appeals against the removal of licences to sell animals as pets, provide boarding for cats and dogs, hire out horses, breed dogs and keep or train animals for exhibition under the Animal Welfare (Licensing of Activities Involving Animals) Regulations 2018.

INFORMATION RIGHTS

First-tier Tribunal (Information Rights) determines appeals against notices issued by the Information Commissioner under the Freedom of Information Act 2000 and other regulations.

When a minister of the crown issues a certificate on the grounds of national security, the appeal must be transferred to the Administrative Appeals Chamber of the Upper Tribunal on receipt.

LETTING AND MANAGING AGENTS

First-tier Tribunal (Letting and Managing Agents) hears appeals against a decision by a local authority or the Trading Standards Office to impose a fine on an agent for not being a member of an approved complaints scheme or for not clearly publicising fees under The Redress Schemes for Lettings Agency Work and Property Management Work (Requirements to Belong to a Scheme etc) (England) Order 2014 and schedule 9 of the Consumer Rights Act 2015.

MICROCHIPPING DOGS

Established under the Microchipping of Dogs (England) Regulations 2015, appeals can be made to First-Tier Tribunal (Microchipping Dogs) against a decision by the Department for the Environment and Rural Affairs to ban or stop an individual from microchipping dogs or from running a database on microchipped dogs. Dog owners can also appeal against a notice to microchip their dog served by the police or local authority.

PENSIONS REGULATION

First-tier Tribunal (Pensions) hears appeals against decisions made by the Pensions Regulator under section 44 of the Pensions Act 2008. Appeals under section 102 of the Act are heard by the Tax and Chancery Chamber of the Upper Tribunal.

SECONDARY TICKETING

First-tier Tribunal (Secondary Ticketing) hears appeals against penalties issued for failing to comply with the conditions for secondary sale of tickets for cultural sporting and recreation events under section 90 of the Consumer Rights Act of 2015.

WELFARE OF ANIMALS

First-tier Tribunal (Welfare of Animals) hears appeals against the removal of licences to sell animals as pets, provide boarding for cats and dogs, hire out horses, breed dogs and keep or train animals for exhibition under the Animal Welfare (Licensing of Activities Involving Animals) Regulations 2018.

HEALTH, EDUCATION AND SOCIAL CARE CHAMBER

Chamber President, His Hon. Judge Sycamore

CARE STANDARDS

First-tier Tribunal (Care Standards), 1st Floor Darlington Magistrates' Court, Parkgate DL1 1RU
T 01325-289350 E cst@justice.gov.uk

First-tier Tribunal (Care Standards) was established under the Protection of Children Act 1999 and considers appeals in relation to decisions made by the Secretary of State for Education, the Secretary of State for Health, the Care Quality Commission, Ofsted or the Care Council for Wales about the inclusion of individuals' names on the list of those considered unsuitable to work with children or vulnerable adults, restrictions from teaching and employment in schools/further education institutions, and the registration of independent schools. It also deals with general registration decisions made about care homes, children's homes, childcare providers, nurses' agencies, social workers, residential family centres, independent hospitals and fostering agencies.

MENTAL HEALTH

PO Box 8793, 5th Floor, Leicester LE1 8BN
T 0300-123 2201 E MHRTEnquiries@justice.gov.uk

The First-tier Tribunal (Mental Health) hears applications and references for people detained under the Mental Health Act 1983 (as amended by the Mental Health Act 2007). There are separate mental health tribunals for Wales and Scotland.

PRIMARY HEALTH LISTS

First-tier Tribunal (Primary Health Lists), 1st Floor Darlington
Magistrates' Court, Parkgate DL1 1RU **T** 01325-289350

First-tier Tribunal (Primary Health Lists) hears appeals against
decisions made by the NHS Commissioning Board to not
include, to remove or to change the conditions of inclusion
for medical practitioners and providers on the NHS medical,
dental, ophthalmic or pharmaceutical lists.

SPECIAL EDUCATIONAL NEEDS AND DISABILITY

First-tier Tribunal (SEND), 1st Floor Darlington Magistrates' Court,
Parkgate DL1 1RU
T 01325-289350 **E** send@justice.gov.uk

First-tier Tribunal (Special Educational Needs and Disability)
considers parents' appeals against the decisions of local
authorities about children's special educational needs if
parents cannot reach agreement with the local authority. It
also considers claims of disability discrimination in schools.

IMMIGRATION AND ASYLUM CHAMBER

Chamber President, Judge Clements
PO Box 6987, Leicester LE1 6ZX
T 0300-123 1711 **E** customer.service@justice.gov.uk

The Immigration and Asylum Chamber is an independent
tribunal dealing with appeals against decisions made by the
Home Office concerning immigration, asylum and nationality
matters.

PROPERTY CHAMBER

Chamber President, Judge McGrath
10 Alfred Place, London WC1E 7LR
T 020-7291 7250 **E** alr@justice.gov.uk

The First-tier Tribunal (Property Chamber) handles
applications, appeals and references relating to disputes over
property and land. It serves the private-rented and leasehold
property market in England regarding rent increases,
leasehold disputes, improvement notices under the Housing
Act 2004, land registration matters and agricultural land and
drainage matters.

SOCIAL ENTITLEMENT CHAMBER

Chamber President, His Hon. Judge Aitken

ASYLUM SUPPORT

2nd Floor, Anchorage House, 2 Clove Crescent, London E14 2BE
T 0800-681 6509

First-tier Tribunal (Asylum Support) deals with appeals
against decisions made by the Home Office. The Home Office
decides whether asylum seekers, failed asylum seekers and/or
their dependants are entitled to support and accommodation
on the grounds of destitution, as provided by the Immigration
and Asylum Act 1999. The tribunal can only consider appeals
against a refusal or termination of support. It can, if
appropriate, require the Secretary of State for the Home
Department to reconsider the original decision, substitute the
original decision with the tribunal's own decision or dismiss
the appeal.

CRIMINAL INJURIES COMPENSATION

20 York Street, Glasgow G2 8GT **T** 0300-790 6234
E cic.enquiries@justice.gov.uk

First-tier Tribunal (Criminal Injuries Compensation)
determines appeals against review decisions made by the
Criminal Injuries Compensation Authority on applications for
compensation made by victims of violent crime.

SOCIAL SECURITY AND CHILD SUPPORT

England and Wales **T** 0300-123 1142
Scotland **T** 0300-790 6234

First-tier Tribunal (Social Security and Child Support)
arranges and hears appeals against decisions made by the
Department for Work and Pensions and HM Revenue and
Customs regarding social security benefits. Appeals considered
include those concerned with: attendance, bereavement and
carer's allowances; child benefit; child support; the
compensation recovery scheme (including NHS recovery
claims); diffuse mesotheliomia and the industrial injuries
disablement benefit payment schemes; income support;
jobseeker's allowance; tax credits; universal credit; and vaccine
damage payment.

TAX CHAMBER

Chamber President, Judge Sinfield
PO Box 16972, Birmingham B16 6TZ
T 0300-123 1024 **E** taxappeals@justice.gov.uk

First-tier Tribunal Tax Chamber hears most appeals against
decisions made by HM Revenue and Customs in relation to
income tax, corporation tax, capital gains tax, inheritance tax,
stamp duty land tax, statutory sick and maternity pay, national
insurance contributions and VAT or duties. The tribunal also
hears some appeals relating to goods seized by HM Revenue
and Customs or Border Force and against some decisions
made by the National Crime Agency. Appeals can be made
by individuals or organisations, single taxpayers or large
multinational companies. First-tier Tribunal (Tax) also hears
appeals against certain decisions made by a compliance
officer, an independent office holder appointed by the
Independent Parliamentary Standards Authority, the
organisation responsible for determining and paying MP
expenses. Appeals can be made by current or former MPs
under the Parliamentary Standards Act 2009. The jurisdiction
is UK-wide.

WAR PENSIONS AND ARMED FORCES
COMPENSATION CHAMBER

Acting Chamber President, Judge Sehba Storey
5th Floor, Fox Court, 14 Gray's Inn Road, London WC1X 8HN
T 020-3206 0701 **E** armedforces.chamber@justice.gov.uk

The War Pensions and Armed Forces Compensation Chamber
of the First-tier Tribunal hears appeals brought by ex-
servicemen and women against decisions by Veterans UK
regarding pensions, compensation and other amounts under
the war pensions legislation for injuries sustained before 5
April 2005, and under the armed forces compensation scheme
for injuries after that date.

UPPER TRIBUNAL

Comprising four separate chambers, the Upper Tribunal deals
mostly with appeals from, and enforcement of, decisions
taken by the First-tier Tribunal, but it also handles some cases
that do not go through the First-tier Tribunal. Additionally,
it has assumed some of the supervisory powers of the courts
to deal with the actions of tribunals, government departments
and some other public authorities. All the decision-makers of
the Upper Tribunal are judges or expert members sitting in a
panel chaired by a judge, and are specialists in the areas of
law they handle. Over time their decisions are expected to
build comprehensive case law for each area covered by the
tribunals.

ADMINISTRATIVE APPEALS CHAMBER

Chamber President, Hon. Dame Judith Farbey, DBE

England and Wales, 5th Floor, 7 Rolls Building, Fetter Lane, London EC4A 1NL **T** 020-7071 5662
E adminappeals@justice.gov.uk

Scotland, George House, 126 George Street, Edinburgh EH2 4HH
T 0131-271 4310 **E** UTAACmailbox@gov.scot

Northern Ireland, Tribunal Hearing Centre, 2nd Floor, Royal Courts of Justice, Chichester Street, Belfast BT1 3JF
T 028-9072 4883 **E** tribunalsunit@courtsni.gov.uk

The Administrative Appeals Chamber appeals against decisions made by certain lower tribunals and organisations including: social security and child support, war pensions and armed forces compensation, mental health, special education needs or disabilities, disputes heard by the General Regulatory Chamber, decisions made by the Disclosure and Barring Service, decisions made by the Traffic Commissioner (or the Transport Regulation Unit in Northern Ireland), Special Education Needs Tribunal for Wales, Mental Health Review Tribunal for Wales and the Pensions Appeal Tribunal in Northern Ireland (only for assessment appeals under the War Pensions Scheme). It also handles applications for judicial review of decisions made by: First-tier Tribunal (Criminal Injuries Compensation) and other first-tier tribunals where there is no right of appeal.

IMMIGRATION AND ASYLUM CHAMBER

Chamber President, Hon. Sir Peter Lane

1A Field House, 15–25 Bream's Buildings, London EC4A 1DZ
T 0300-123 1711 **E** FieldHouseCorrespondence@justice.gov.uk

The Immigration and Asylum Chamber hears appeals against decisions made by the First-tier Tribunal (Immigration and Asylum) relating to visa and asylum applications and the right to enter or stay in the UK. The chamber also deals with applications for judicial review of certain decisions made by the Home Office relating to immigration, asylum and human rights claims.

LANDS CHAMBER

Chamber President, Hon. Sir David Holgate

5th Floor, 7 Rolls Buildings, London EC4A 1NL
T 020-7612 9710 **E** lands@justice.gov.uk

The Lands Chamber is responsible for handling appeals against decisions made by the First-tier Tribunal (Property Chamber) (except decisions about land registration), the Residential Property Tribunal in Wales and the Leasehold Valuation Tribunal in Wales, It is also responsible for handling applications for cases regarding decisions about rates made by the Valuation Tribunal in England or Wales, compensation for the compulsory purchase of land, discharge or modification of land affected by a 'restrictive covenant', compensation for the effect on land affected by public works, a tree preservation order, compensation for damage to land damaged by subsidence from mining, the valuation of land or buildings for Capital Gains Tax or Inheritance Tax purposes and compensation for blighted land.

TAX AND CHANCERY CHAMBER

Chamber President, Hon. Sir Antony Zacaroli

5th Floor, 7 Rolls Buildings, London EC4A 1NL
T 020-7612 9730 **E** uttc@justice.gov.uk

The Tax and Chancery Chamber hears appeals against decisions made by the First-tier Tribunal (Tax), the land registration division of the First-tier Tribunal (Property Chamber) and the General Regulatory Chamber in cases relating to charities. The chamber also hears appeals against decisions issued by the Financial Conduct Authority, the Prudential Regulation Authority, the Pensions Regulator, the Bank of England, HM Treasury and OFGEM.

SPECIAL IMMIGRATION APPEALS COMMISSION

15–25 Bream's Buildings, London EC4A 1DZ
T 0300-123 1711

The commission was set up under the Special Immigration Appeals Commission Act 1997. It remains separate from the First-tier and Upper Tribunal structure but is part of HM Courts and Tribunals Service. Its main function is to consider appeals against orders for deportation or exclusion, or orders withdrawing or refusing British nationality, in cases which involve considerations of national security.

Chair, Hon. Dame Elisabeth Laing, DBE

EMPLOYMENT TRIBUNALS

Employment Tribunal Central Office England and Wales, PO Box 10218, Leicester LE1 8EG **T** 0300-123 1024

Employment Tribunal Central Office Scotland, PO Box 27105, Glasgow G2 9JR **T** 0300-790 6234

Employment tribunals hear claims regarding matters of employment law, redundancy, dismissal, contract disputes, sexual, racial and disability discrimination and related areas of dispute which may arise in the workplace.

President (England and Wales), Judge Doyle
President (Scotland), Judge Simon

EMPLOYMENT APPEAL TRIBUNAL

Employment Appeal Tribunal England and Wales, 5th Floor, 7 Rolls Buildings, Fetter Lane, London EC4A 1NL **T** 020-7273 1041
E londoneat@justice.gov.uk

Employment Appeal Tribunal Scotland, George House, 126 George Street, Edinburgh, EH2 4HH **T** 0131-225 3963
E edinburgheat@justice.gov.uk

The Employment Appeal Tribunal hears appeals (on points of law only) arising from decisions made by employment tribunals.

President, Hon. Mr Justice Choudhury

SCOTTISH COURTS AND TRIBUNALS SERVICE

Saughton House, Broomhouse Drive, Edinburgh EH11 3XD
T 0131-444 3300

W www.scotcourts.gov.uk **E** enquiries@scotcourts.gov.uk

The Tribunals (Scotland) Act 2014 created a new, simplified statutory framework for tribunals in Scotland, bringing existing jurisdictions together and providing a structure for new ones. The Act created two new tribunals, the First-tier Tribunal for Scotland and the Upper Tribunal for Scotland.

The Lord President is the head of the Scottish Courts and Tribunals Service and has delegated various functions to the President of Scottish Tribunals.

President of Scottish Tribunals, Rt. Hon. Lady Smith (Anne Smith)

UPPER TRIBUNAL FOR SCOTLAND

The Glasgow Tribunals Centre, 20 York Street, Glasgow G2 8GT
T 0141-302 5880
E uppertribunalforscotland@scotcourtstribunals.gov.uk

The Upper Tribunal hears appeals on decisions of the chambers of the First-tier Tribunal.

FIRST-TIER TRIBUNAL

The First-tier Tribunal is organised into five chambers.

GENERAL REGULATORY CHAMBER
George House, 126 George Street, Edinburgh EH2 4HH
T 0131-271 4340 **E** Charityappeals@scotcourtstribunals.gov.uk

HEALTH AND EDUCATION CHAMBER
20 York Street, Glasgow G2 8GT
T 0141-302 5860

HOUSING AND PROPERTY CHAMBER
20 York Street, Glasgow G2 8GT
T 0141-302 5900

SOCIAL SECURITY CHAMBER
20 York Street, Glasgow G2 8GT
T 0141-302 5858

TAX CHAMBER
George House, 126 George Street, Edinburgh EH2 4HH
T 0131-271 4385 **E** taxchamber@scotcourtstribunals.gov.uk

The Scottish Courts and Tribunals Service currently provides administrative support for the following Scottish tribunals:

COUNCIL TAX REDUCTION REVIEW PANEL, 20 York
Street, Glasgow G2 8GT **T** 0141-302 5840
E ctrrpadmin@scotcourtstribunals.gov.uk
W www.counciltaxreductionreview.scotland.gov.uk

THE LANDS TRIBUNAL FOR SCOTLAND, George House,
126 George Street, Edinburgh EH2 4HH **T** 0131-271 4350
E LTS_mailbox@scotcourtstribunals.gov.uk
W www.lands-tribunal-scotland.org.uk
President, Hon. Lord Minginish (Roderick MacLeod)

THE MENTAL HEALTH TRIBUNAL FOR SCOTLAND,
Bothwell House, First Floor, Hamilton Business Park, Caird Park,
Hamilton ML3 0QA **T** 0800-345 7060
E mhtsTeam1@scotcourtstribunals.gov.uk
W www.mhtscotland.gov.uk
President, Dr Joe Morrow, CBE

THE PENSIONS APPEAL TRIBUNAL SCOTLAND,
126 George Street, Edinburgh EH2 4HH **T** 0131-271 4340
E PAT_Info_Mailbox@scotcourtstribunals.gov.uk
W www.patscotland.org.uk
President, Marion Caldwell, QC

NORTHERN IRELAND COURTS AND TRIBUNALS SERVICE

Department of Justice, Block B, Castle Buildings, Stormont Estate,
Belfast BT4 3SG
T 028-9076 3000 **W** www.justice-ni.gov.uk/topics/
courts-and-tribunals
Lord Chief Justice of Northern Ireland, Rt. Hon. Sir Declan
Morgan

The Northern Ireland Courts and Tribunals Service currently provides administrative support for the following Northern Ireland tribunals. All the tribunals below, unless otherwise specified, can be contacted at: 2nd Floor, Royal Courts of Justice, Chichester Street, Belfast BT1 3JF **T** 0300-200 7812
E tribunalsunit@courtsni.gov.uk

THE APPEALS SERVICE, 6th Floor, Oyster House, 12
Wellington Place, Belfast BT1 6GE **T** 028-9054 4000
E appeals.service.belfast@dsdni.gov.uk
THE CARE TRIBUNAL
Chairs, Diane Drennan, Stephen Quinn
THE CHARITY TRIBUNAL
CRIMINAL INJURIES COMPENSATION APPEALS
PANEL NORTHERN IRELAND,
E cicapnicustomer@courtsni.gov.uk
Chair, Patricia McKaigue
LANDS TRIBUNAL
MENTAL HEALTH REVIEW TRIBUNAL
NORTHERN IRELAND HEALTH AND SAFETY
TRIBUNAL
NORTHERN IRELAND TRAFFIC PENALTY TRIBUNAL
NORTHERN IRELAND VALUATION TRIBUNAL
OFFICE OF SOCIAL SECURITY COMMISSIONERS AND
CHILD SUPPORT COMMISSIONERS
Chief Commissioner, Kenneth Mullan
PAROLE COMMISSIONERS FOR NORTHERN
IRELAND, Laganside Court, Mezzanine 1st Floor,
Oxford Street, Belfast BT1 3LL **T** 028-9041 2969
E info@parolecomni.org.uk
Chief Commissioner, Christine Glenn
PENSIONS APPEAL COMMISSIONERS
PENSIONS APPEAL TRIBUNALS
RENT ASSESSMENT PANEL, Cleaver House, 3 Donegall
Square North, Belfast BT1 5GA **T** 028-9051 8518
E appeals.service.belfast@dsdni.gov.uk
SPECIAL EDUCATIONAL NEEDS AND DISABILITY
TRIBUNAL

INDEPENDENT TRIBUNALS

The following represents a selection of tribunals not administered by HM Courts and Tribunals Service.

CIVIL AVIATION AUTHORITY
Aviation House, Beehive Ringroad, Crawley, W. Sussex RH6 0YR
T 0330-022 1500 **W** www.caa.co.uk

The Civil Aviation Authority (CAA) does not have a separate tribunal department as such, but for certain purposes the CAA must conform to tribunal requirements, for example, to deal with appeals against the refusal or revocation of aviation licences and certificates issued by the CAA, and the allocation of routes outside of the EU to airlines.

The chair and non-executive members who may sit on panels for tribunal purposes are appointed by the Secretary of State for Transport.

Chair, Dame Deirdre Hutton, DBE

COMPETITION APPEAL TRIBUNAL
Victoria House, Bloomsbury Place, London WC1A 2EB
T 020-7979 7979 **W** www.catribunal.org.uk

The Competition Appeal Tribunal (CAT) is a specialist tribunal established to hear certain cases in the sphere of UK competition and economic regulatory law. It hears appeals against decisions of the Competition and Markets Authority (CMA) and the sectoral regulators in respect of infringements of competition law and with respect to mergers and markets. The CAT also has jurisdiction to award damages in respect of infringements of EU or UK competition law and to hear appeals against decisions of the Office of Communications (OFCOM) in telecommunications matters.

President, Hon. Sir Peter Roth

COPYRIGHT TRIBUNAL
4 Abbey Orchard Street, London SW1P 2HT
T 020-7034 2836 **E** copyright.tribunal@ipo.gov.uk
W www.gov.uk/government/organisations/copyright-tribunal

The Copyright Tribunal resolves disputes over the terms and conditions of licences offered by, or licensing schemes operated by, collective management organisations in the copyright and related rights area. Its decisions are appealable to the high court on points of law only.

Chair, His Hon. Judge Hacon

INDUSTRIAL TRIBUNALS AND THE FAIR EMPLOYMENT TRIBUNAL (NORTHERN IRELAND)
Killymeal House, 2 Cromac Quay, Ormeau Road, Belfast BT7 2JD
T 028-9032 7666 **E** mail@employmenttribunalsni.org
W www.employmenttribunalsni.org

The industrial tribunal system in Northern Ireland was set up in 1965 and has a similar remit to the employment tribunals in the rest of the UK. There is also a Fair Employment Tribunal, which hears and determines individual cases of alleged religious or political discrimination in employment. Employers can appeal to the Fair Employment Tribunal if they consider the directions of the Equality Commission to be unreasonable, inappropriate or unnecessary, and the Equality Commission can make application to the tribunal for the enforcement of undertakings or directions with which an employer has not complied.

President, Eileen McBride, CBE

INVESTIGATORY POWERS TRIBUNAL
PO Box 33220, London SW1H 9ZQ
T 020-7035 3711 **E** info@ipt-uk.com **W** www.ipt-uk.com

The Investigatory Powers Tribunal replaced the Interception of Communications Tribunal, the Intelligence Services Tribunal, the Security Services Tribunal and the complaints function of the commissioner appointed under the Police Act 1997.

The Regulation of Investigatory Powers Act 2000 (RIPA) provides for a tribunal made up of senior members of the legal profession, independent of the government and appointed by the Queen, to consider all complaints against the intelligence services and those against public authorities in respect of powers covered by RIPA; and to consider proceedings brought under section 7 of the Human Rights Act 1998 against the intelligence services and law enforcement agencies in respect of these powers.

President, Rt. Hon, Sir Rabinder Singh

SOLICITORS' DISCIPLINARY TRIBUNAL
3rd Floor, Gate House, 1 Farringdon Street, London EC4M 7LG
T 020-7329 4808 **E** enquiries@solicitorsdt.com
W www.solicitorstribunal.org.uk

The Solicitors' Disciplinary Tribunal is an independent statutory body whose members are appointed by the Master of the Rolls. The tribunal adjudicates upon alleged breaches of the rules and regulations applicable to solicitors and their firms, including the Solicitors' Code of Conduct 2007. It also decides applications by former solicitors for restoration to the Roll.

Chair, Edward Nally

SCOTTISH SOLICITORS' DISCIPLINE TRIBUNAL
Unit 3.5, The Granary Business Centre, Coal Road, Cupar, Fife KY15 5YQ
T 01334-659099 **E** enquiries@ssdt.org.uk **W** www.ssdt.org.uk

The Scottish Solicitors' Discipline Tribunal is an independent statutory body with a panel of 24 members, 12 of whom are solicitors appointed by the Lord President of the Court of Session. Its principal function is to consider complaints of misconduct against solicitors in Scotland.

Chair, Nicholas Whyte

TRAFFIC PENALTY TRIBUNAL
Springfield House, Water Lane, Wilmslow, Cheshire SK9 5BG
T 0800-160 1999 **E** help@trafficpenaltytribunal.gov.uk
W www.trafficpenaltytribunal.gov.uk

The Traffic Penalty Tribunal adjudicators consider appeals in relation to penalty charge notices issued by local authorities in England (outside London) and Wales for parking and bus lane contraventions and, additionally in Wales, moving traffic contraventions. The tribunal also considers appeals in relation to penalties issued by the Secretary of State for Transport for failing to pay a charge at the Dartford river crossing, the Durham peninsular congestion charging zone and the Mersey Gateway bridge crossings.

Chief Adjudicator, Caroline Sheppard, OBE

VALUATION TRIBUNAL FOR ENGLAND
2nd Floor, 120 Leman Street, London E1 8EU
T 020-7246 3900 **W** www.valuationtribunal.gov.uk

The Valuation Tribunal for England (VTE) came into being on 1 October 2009, replacing 56 valuation tribunals in England. Provision for the VTE was made in the Local Government and Public Involvement in Health Act 2007. The VTE hears appeals concerning council tax and non-domestic (business) rates, as well as a small number of appeals against drainage boards' assessments of drainage rates. A separate panel is constituted for each hearing, and consists of a chair and usually one or two other members.

The Valuation Tribunal Service (VTS) was created as a corporate body by the Local Government Act 2003, and is responsible for providing or arranging the services required for the operation of the Valuation Tribunal for England. The VTS board consists of a chair and members appointed by the secretary of state. The VTS is sponsored by the Ministry of Housing, Communities and Local Government.

President (VTE), Gary Garland
Chair (VTS), Robin Evans

VALUATION TRIBUNAL FOR WALES
W www.valuationtribunal.wales

The Valuation Tribunal for Wales (VTW) was established by the Valuation Tribunal for Wales Regulations 2010, and hears and determines appeals concerning council tax, non-domestic rating and drainage rates in Wales. The governing council, comprising the president, four regional representatives and one member who is appointed by the Welsh government, performs the management functions on behalf of the tribunal. There are a number of VTW offices across Wales and contact details for these can be found on the website listed above.

President, Carol Cobert

OMBUDSMAN SERVICES

The following section is a listing of selected ombudsman services. Ombudsmen are a free, independent and impartial means of resolving certain disputes outside of the courts. These disputes are, in the majority of cases, concerned with whether something has been badly or unfairly handled (for example owing to delay, neglect, inefficiency or failure to follow proper procedures). Most ombudsman schemes are established by statute; they cover various public and private bodies and generally examine matters only after the relevant body has been given a reasonable opportunity to deal with the complaint.

After conducting an investigation an ombudsman will usually issue a written report, which normally suggests a resolution to the dispute and often includes recommendations concerning the improvement of procedures.

OMBUDSMAN ASSOCIATION

PO Box 343, Carshalton, Surrey SM5 9BX
E secretary@ombudsmanassociation.org
W www.ombudsmanassociation.org

The Ombudsman Association was established in 1994 and exists to provide information to the government, public bodies and the public about ombudsmen and other complaint-handling services in the UK and Ireland. An ombudsman scheme must meet four criteria in order to attain full Ombudsman Association membership: independence from the organisations the ombudsman has the power to investigate, fairness, effectiveness and public accountability. Complaint Handler membership is open to complaint-handling bodies that do not meet these criteria in full. Ombudsmen schemes from the UK, Ireland, British crown dependencies and overseas territories may apply to the Ombudsman Association for membership. The Ombudsman Association publishes a quarterly magazine containing news about ombudsmen and complaint-handling services in the UK, Ireland and overseas, along with topical articles of interest to members of the Association.

Chair, Nick Bennett

The following is a selection of organisations that are members of the Ombudsman Association.

FINANCIAL OMBUDSMAN SERVICE

Exchange Tower, London E14 9SR
T 020-7964 1000 E complaint.info@financial-ombudsman.org.uk
W www.financial-ombudsman.org.uk

The Financial Ombudsman Service settles individual disputes between businesses providing financial services and their customers. The service examines complaints about most financial matters, including banking, insurance, mortgages, pensions, savings, loans and credit cards. *See also* Banking and Finance.

Chief Ombudsman and Chief Executive, Caroline Wayman

HOUSING OMBUDSMAN SERVICE

Exchange Tower, London E14 9GE
T 0300-111 3000 E info@housing-ombudsman.org.uk
W www.housing-ombudsman.org.uk

The Housing Ombudsman Service was established in 1997 to deal with complaints and disputes involving tenants and housing associations and social landlords, certain private-sector landlords and managing agents. The ombudsman has a statutory jurisdiction over all registered social landlords in England. Private and other landlords can join the service on a voluntary basis. On 1 April 2013 a new Housing Ombudsman Service was launched with an extended jurisdiction covering all housing associations and local authorities.

Ombudsman, Andrea Keenoy *(interim)*

INDEPENDENT OFFICE FOR POLICE CONDUCT

90 High Holborn, London WC1V 6BH
T 0300-020 0096 E enquiries@policeconduct.gov.uk
W www.policeconduct.gov.uk

Established under the Policing and Crime Act 2017, the Independent Office for Police Conduct (IOPC) succeeded the Independent Police Complaints Commission (IPCC) in January 2018. The IOPC is responsible for carrying out independent investigations into serious incidents or allegations of misconduct by those serving with the police forces in England and Wales, as well as Police and Crime Commissioners in England and Wales and the London Mayor's Office for Policing and Crime (MOPAC). The IOPC's director-general and its regional directors must not have worked for the police in any capacity prior to their appointment. It has the power to initiate, undertake and oversee investigations and is also responsible for the way in which complaints are handled by local police forces. The IOPC is also responsible for serious complaints and conduct matters relating to staff at the National Crime Agency (NCA), Her Majesty's Revenue and Customs (HMRC), and the Gangmasters and Labour Abuse Authority.

Director-General, Michael Lockwood

LEGAL OMBUDSMAN

PO Box 6806, Wolverhampton WV1 9WJ
T 0300-555 0333 E enquiries@legalombudsman.org.uk
W www.legalombudsman.org.uk

The Legal Ombudsman was set up by the Office for Legal Complaints under the Legal Services Act 2007 and is the single body for all consumer legal complaints in England and Wales. It replaced the Office of the Legal Services Ombudsman in 2010. The Legal Ombudsman aims to resolve disputes between individuals and authorised legal practitioners, including barristers, law cost draftsmen, legal executives, licensed conveyancers, notaries, patent attorneys, probate practitioners, registered European lawyers, solicitors and trade mark attorneys. The Legal Ombudsman is an independent and impartial organisation and deals with various types of complaints against legal services, such as wills, family issues, personal injury and buying or selling a house.

Chief Ombudsman, Rebecca Marsh

LOCAL GOVERNMENT AND SOCIAL CARE OMBUDSMAN

PO Box 4771, Coventry CV4 0EH
T 0300-061 0614 W www.lgo.org.uk

The Local Government and Social Care Ombudsman deals with complaints about most council services, including planning, some housing issues, social care, some education and schools issues, children's services, housing benefit, council tax, transport and highways, environment and waste, neighbour nuisance and antisocial behaviour and service failure by local authorities, schools and all registered social care providers, including all adult social care complaints. The Ombudsman's powers to investigate include complaints about publicly and privately funded social care.

If a complaint is about both health and social care services, a joint investigation with the Health Service Ombudsman can be carried out with the Social Care Ombudsman as the single point of contact.

Local Government and Social Care Ombudsman, Michael King

NORTHERN IRELAND PUBLIC SERVICES OMBUDSMAN

33 Wellington Place, Belfast BT1 6HN
T 028-9023 3821 **E** nipso@nipso.org.uk
W www.nipso.org.uk

The Office of Northern Ireland Public Services Ombudsman (NIPSO) was established in April 2016, replacing and expanding the functions of the Northern Ireland Assembly Ombudsman and Commissioner for Complaints. NIPSO provides an independent review of complaints of members of the public, where they believe they have sustained an injustice or hardship as a result or inaction of a public service provider. NIPSO additionally ensures that public services improve as a result of the complaints brought to them by the public. The professional, independent and impartial service is provided free of charge to the citizens of Northern Ireland.

Ombudsman, Marie Anderson

OFFICE OF THE PENSIONS OMBUDSMAN

10 South Colonnade, Canary Wharf, London E14 4PU
T 0800-917 4487 **E** enquiries@pensions-ombudsman.org.uk
W www.pensions-ombudsman.org.uk

The Pensions Ombudsman can investigate and decide complaints and disputes regarding the way occupational and personal pension schemes are administered and managed. Unless there are special circumstances, this only usually includes issues and disputes that have arisen within the past three years. The Pensions Ombudsman is also the Ombudsman for the Pension Protection Fund (PPF) and the Financial Assistance Scheme (which offers help to those who were a member of an under-funded defined benefit pension scheme that started to wind-up in specific financial circumstances between 1 January 1997 and 5 April 2005).

Pensions Ombudsman, Anthony Arter
Deputy Pensions Ombudsman, Karen Johnston

OMBUDSMAN SERVICES

3300 Daresbury Park, Warrington WA4 4HS
W www.ombudsman-services.org

Ombudsman Services was founded in 2002 and provides independent dispute resolution for the communications, copyright licensing and energy sectors. Ombudsman Services ceased dealing with complaints concerning the property sector in 2018.

Ombudsman Services: Communications investigates complaints from consumers about companies which provide communication services to the public.

Ombudsman Services: Copyright Licensing helps to resolve complaints about bodies that either own or administer, on behalf of third parties, the licensing of copyright materials.

Ombudsman Services: Energy helps to resolve complaints from consumers about energy (gas and electricity companies). This service is also responsible for handling investigations concerning the government's Green Deal policy, which launched in 2013, and offers long-term loans towards energy-saving home improvements.

Chair, Lord Tim Clement-Jones, CBE
Chief Ombudsman, Matthew Vickers

OMBUDSMAN SERVICES: COMMUNICATIONS
PO Box 730, Warrington WA4 6WU
T 0330-440 1614

OMBUDSMAN SERVICES: COPYRIGHT LICENSING
PO Box 1124, Warrington WA4 9GH
T 0330-440 1601

OMBUDSMAN SERVICES: ENERGY
PO Box 966, Warrington WA4 9DF
T 0330-440 1624

PARLIAMENTARY AND HEALTH SERVICE OMBUDSMAN

Millbank Tower, Millbank, London SW1P 4QP
T 0345-015 4033
W www.ombudsman.org.uk

The Parliamentary Commissioner for Administration (commonly known as the Parliamentary Ombudsman) is independent of government and is an officer of parliament. He is responsible for investigating complaints referred to him by MPs from members of the public who claim to have sustained injustice in consequence of maladministration by or on behalf of government departments and certain non-departmental public bodies in the UK. Certain types of action by government departments or bodies are excluded from investigation.

The Health Service Ombudsman is responsible for investigating complaints about services funded by the National Health Service in England that have not been dealt with by the service providers to the satisfaction of the complainant. This includes complaints about doctors, dentists, pharmacists and opticians. Complaints can be referred directly by the member of the public who claims to have sustained injustice or hardship in consequence of the failure in a service provided by a relevant organisation.

The two offices of the Parliamentary and Health Service Ombudsman are traditionally held by the same person.

Parliamentary Ombudsman and Health Service Ombudsman, Robert Behrens, CBE

PRISONS AND PROBATION OMBUDSMAN

Third Floor, 10 South Colonnade, London E14 4PU
T 020-7633 4100 **E** mail@ppo.gov.uk
W www.ppo.gov.uk

The Prisons and Probation Ombudsman investigates complaints from prisoners, people on probation and immigration detainees, deaths of prisoners, residents of probation-service approved premises and those held in immigration removal centres. The ombudsman is appointed by the Secretary of State for Justice and works closely with the Ministry of Justice. All deaths that occur in prison are investigated and an anonymised fatal incident report is written after each investigation.

Ombudsman, Sue McAllister, CB

PROPERTY OMBUDSMAN

Milford House, 43–55 Milford Street, Salisbury SP1 2BP
T 01722-333306
W www.tpos.co.uk

The Property Ombudsman (TPO) scheme was established in 1998 and provides a free, impartial and independent service for dealing with unresolved disputes between property agents and buyers, sellers, tenants and landlords of property in the UK.

The ombudsman's role is to consider complaints against the agents' obligation to act in accordance with the TPO codes of practice and to propose a full and final resolution to the dispute. Consumers are not bound by the Ombudsman's decision, but registered agents are.

TPO is the primary dispute-resolution service for the property industry.

Ombudsman, Katrine Sporle, CBE

PUBLIC SERVICES OMBUDSMAN FOR WALES

1 Ffordd yr Hen Gae, Pencoed CF35 5LJ
T 0300-790 0203 **E** ask@ombudsman-wales.org.uk
W www.ombudsman.wales

The office of Public Services Ombudsman for Wales was established, with effect from 1 April 2006, by the Public Services Ombudsman (Wales) Act 2005. The ombudsman, who is appointed by the Queen, investigates complaints of injustice caused by maladministration or service failure by public services such as the Assembly Commission (and public bodies sponsored by the assembly); Welsh government; National Health Service bodies, including GPs, family health service providers and hospitals; registered social landlords; local authorities, including community councils; fire and rescue authorities; police authorities; the Arts Council of Wales; national park authorities; and countryside and environmental organisations.

Ombudsman, Nick Bennett

REMOVALS INDUSTRY OMBUDSMAN SCHEME

PO Box 1535, High Wycombe HP12 9EE
T 020-8144 3790 **E** ombudsman@removalsombudsman.co.uk
W www.removalsombudsman.co.uk

The Removals Industry Ombudsman Scheme was established to resolve disputes between removal companies that are members of the scheme and their clients, both domestic and commercial. It comprises a board of four members, only one of whom has any connection with the removals industry. The ombudsman investigates complaints such as breaches of contract, unprofessional conduct, delays, excessive charges or breaches in the code of practice. The National Guild of Removers and Storers is currently the principal member.

Ombudsman, Tony Kaye

SCOTTISH PUBLIC SERVICES OMBUDSMAN

Bridgeside House, 99 McDonald Road, Edinburgh EH7 4NS
T 0800-377 7330
W www.spso.org.uk

The Scottish Public Services Ombudsman (SPSO) was established in 2002. The SPSO is the final stage for complaints about public services in Scotland. Its service is free and independent. SPSO investigates complaints about the Scottish government, its agencies and departments; the Scottish Parliamentary Corporate Body; colleges and universities; councils; housing associations; NHS Scotland; prisons; some water and sewerage service providers; and most other Scottish public bodies. The ombudsman looks at complaints regarding poor service or administrative failure and can usually only look at those that have been through the formal complaints process of the organisation concerned. It also has a statutory function in improving complaints handling in public services, which it carries out through its Complaints Standards Authority.

Scottish Public Services Ombudsman, Rosemary Agnew

WATERWAYS OMBUDSMAN

PO Box 854, Altrincham WA15 5JS
T 0161-980 4858 **E** enquiries@waterways-ombudsman.org
W www.waterways-ombudsman.org

Since July 2012, the Waterways Ombudsman has investigated complaints about the Canal and River Trust and its subsidiaries (such as British Waterways Marinas Limited). The ombudsman does not consider complaints about canals in Scotland, which are the responsibility of the Scottish Public Services Ombudsman.

Ombudsman, Sarah Daniel

THE POLICE SERVICE

There are 45 police forces in the United Kingdom: 43 in England and Wales, including the Metropolitan Police and the City of London Police, Police Scotland and the Police Service of Northern Ireland. The Isle of Man, Jersey and Guernsey have their own forces responsible for policing in their respective islands and bailiwicks. The National Crime Agency, which became operational in October 2013, is responsible for preventing organised crime and strengthening UK borders.

Since 1964, police authorities – separate independent bodies for each police force – were responsible for the supervision of local policing in England and Wales. Following the government's white paper *Policing in the 21st Century* it was concluded that, in order to make the police more accountable, police authorities should be replaced with a directly elected commissioner for each force, supported by a police and crime panel made up of representatives from each local authority in a police force area. In November 2012, following the enactment of the Police Reform and Social Responsibility Act 2011, the first elections to install police and crime commissioners (PCCs) were held in November 2012 across England and Wales; the most recent elections took place in May 2016. The PCCs are responsible for appointing the chief constable of their force, establishing local priorities and setting budgets. The PCCs are not in place to run their local force but rather to hold them to account. The Mayor of London, through the Deputy Mayor for Policing and Crime and supported by the Mayor's Office for Policing and Crime (MOPAC), acts as the PCC for the Metropolitan Police. Since 2017 the Mayor of Greater Manchester fulfils the PCC responsibilities for this area's force. The City of London Corporation acts as the police authority for the City of London Police.

Under the Police and Fire Reform (Scotland) Act 2012, Police Scotland was established on 1 April 2013, merging the eight separate territorial police forces, the Scottish Crime and Drug Enforcement Agency and the Association of Chief Police Officers in Scotland. Responsible for policing the whole of Scotland, Police Scotland is the second largest force in the UK after the Metropolitan Police. The service is led by a chief constable who is supported by a team of four deputy constables, assistant chief constables and three directors. The Scottish Police Authority, established in October 2012, is responsible for maintaining policing, promoting policing principles, the continuous improvement of policing and holds the Chief Constable to account. In Northern Ireland, the Northern Ireland Policing Board, an independent public body consisting of 19 political and independent members, fulfils a similar role.

Police forces in England, Scotland and Wales are financed by central and local government grants and a precept on the council tax. The Police Service of Northern Ireland is wholly funded by central government.

The home secretary, the Scottish government and the Northern Ireland Minister of Justice are responsible for the organisation, administration and operation of the police service. They regulate police ranks, discipline, hours of duty and pay and allowances. All police forces are subject to inspection by HM Inspectorate of Constabulary, which reports to the home secretary and the Northern Ireland Minister of Justice. Police forces in Scotland are inspected by HM Inspectorate of Constabulary for Scotland which operates independently of the Scottish government.

COMPLAINTS

Established under the Policing and Crime Act 2017, the Independent Office for Police Conduct (IOPC) succeeded the Independent Police Complaints Commission (IPCC) in January 2018. The IOPC is responsible for carrying out independent investigations into serious incidents or allegations of misconduct by those serving with the police forces in England and Wales, as well as Police and Crime Commissioners in England and Wales and the London Mayor's Office for Policing and Crime (MOPAC). The IOPC's director-general and its regional directors must not have worked for the police in any capacity prior to their appointment. It has the power to initiate, undertake and oversee investigations and is also responsible for the way in which complaints are handled by local police forces. The IOPC is also responsible for serious complaints and conduct matters relating to staff at the National Crime Agency (NCA).

Complaints about the police must first be recorded with the relevant police force and the local force will attempt to resolve the matter internally. Certain serious complaints are automatically referred to the IOPC. The IOPC or police force may refer the case to the Crown Prosecution Service, which will decide whether to bring criminal charges against the officer/s involved.

On 1 April 2013, under the Police and Fire Reform (Scotland) Act 2012 which brought together Scotland's eight police services into the single Police Service of Scotland, the remit of the Police Complaints Commissioner for Scotland (PCCS) was expanded to include investigations into the most serious incidents concerning the police. To reflect this change, the PCCS was renamed the Police Investigations and Review Commissioner (PIRC).

The Police Ombudsman for Northern Ireland provides an independent police complaints system for Northern Ireland, dealing with all stages of the complaints procedure. Complaints that cannot be resolved informally are investigated and the ombudsman recommends a suitable course of action to the Chief Constable of the Police Service of Northern Ireland or the Northern Ireland Policing Board based on the investigation's findings. The ombudsman may recommend that a police officer be prosecuted, but the decision to prosecute a police officer rests with the Director of Public Prosecutions.

INDEPENDENT OFFICE FOR POLICE CONDUCT, PO Box 473, Sale M33 0BW **T** 0300-020 0096
E enquiries@policeconduct.gov.uk
W www.policeconduct.gov.uk
Director-General, Michael Lockwood

POLICE INVESTIGATIONS AND REVIEW COMMISSIONER, Hamilton House, Hamilton Business Park, Caird Park, Hamilton ML3 0QA **T** 01698-542900
E enquiries@pirc.gov.scot **W** www.pirc.scotland.gov.uk
Police Investigations and Review Commissioner, Kate Frame

POLICE OMBUDSMAN FOR NORTHERN IRELAND, New Cathedral Buildings, Writers' Square, 11 Church Street, Belfast BT1 1PG **T** 028-9082 8600 **E** info@policeombudsman.org
W www.policeombudsman.org
Police Ombudsman, Dr Michael Maguire

POLICE SERVICES

COLLEGE OF POLICING

Leamington Road, Ryton-on-Dunsmore, Coventry CV8 3EN
T 0800-496 3322 E contactus@college.pnn.police.uk
W www.college.police.uk

The College of Policing was established in December 2012 as the first professional body set up for policing. It works on behalf of the public to raise professional standards in policing and to assist forces to reduce crime and protect the public. It engages with the public through the Police and Crime Commissioners to ensure that it is responsive to the issues of greatest concern.

The government has designated the college as a centre for reviewing and testing practices and interventions to identify which are effective in reducing crime. It makes this information accessible for all in policing, particularly frontline practitioners. The college also supports continuous professional development and sets national standards for promotion and progression.

Chief Executive, Mike Cunningham, QPM
Chair, Millie Banerjee, CBE

NATIONAL CRIME AGENCY

Units 1–6 Citadel Place, Tinworth Street, London SE11 5EF
T 0370-496 7622
E communication@nca.gov.uk
W www.nationalcrimeagency.gov.uk

Established under the Crime and Courts Act 2013 the National Crime Agency (NCA) became fully operational in October 2013. The NCA is a non-ministerial government department.

The NCA's remit is to fight organised crime, including child sexual exploitation, modern slavery and human trafficking, illegal firearms, cyber crime and money laundering.

The director-general has independent operational direction and control over the NCA's activities and, through the home secretary, is accountable to parliament.

Director-General, Lynne Owens, CBE, QPM

UK MISSING PERSONS UNIT

PO Box 58358, London NW1W 9LA T 0800-234 6034
E ukmpu@nca.gov.uk
W www.missingpersons.police.uk

The UK Missing Persons Unit, part of the National Crime Agency, acts as the centre for the exchange of information connected with the search for missing persons nationally and internationally alongside the police and other related organisations. The unit focuses on cross-matching missing persons with unidentified persons or bodies by maintaining records, including a dental index of ante-mortem chartings of long-term missing persons and post-mortem chartings from unidentified bodies.

Information is supplied and collected for all persons who have been missing in the UK for over 72 hours (or fewer where police deem appropriate), foreign nationals reported missing in the UK, UK nationals reported missing abroad and all unidentified bodies and persons found within the UK.

SPECIALIST FORCES

BRITISH TRANSPORT POLICE

25 Camden Road, London NW1 9LN T 0800-405040
E first_contact@btp.pnn.police.uk
W www.btp.police.uk
Strength (August 2019), 3,069

British Transport Police is the national police force for the railways in England, Wales and Scotland, including the London Underground system, Docklands Light Railway, Glasgow Subway, Midland Metro tram system, Sunderland Metro, London Tramlink and the Emirates Air Line cable car.

The chief constable reports to the British Transport Police Authority. The members of the authority are appointed by the transport secretary and include representatives from the rail industry as well as independent members. Officers are paid the same salary as those in other police forces.

Chief Constable, Paul Crowther, OBE

CIVIL NUCLEAR CONSTABULARY

Building F6, Culham Science Centre, Abingdon,
Oxfordshire OX14 3DB T 0300-313 5400
W www.gov.uk/government/organisations/
civil-nuclear-constabulary
*Strength, c.*1,500

The Civil Nuclear Constabulary (CNC) is overseen by the Civil Nuclear Police Authority, an executive non-departmental public body sponsored by the Department for Business, Energy and Industrial Strategy. The CNC is a specialised armed force that protects civil nuclear sites and nuclear materials. The constabulary is responsible for policing UK civil nuclear industry facilities and for escorting nuclear material between establishments within the UK and worldwide.

Chief Constable, Simon Chesterman, QPM
Deputy Chief Constable, Chris Armitt, QPM

MINISTRY OF DEFENCE POLICE

Ministry of Defence Police HQ, Wethersfield, Braintree, Essex
CM7 4AZ T 01371-854000
W www.mod.police.uk
Strength (July 2018), 2,733

Part of the Ministry of Defence Police and Guarding Agency, the Ministry of Defence Police is a statutory civil police force with particular responsibility for the security and policing of the MoD environment. It contributes to the physical protection of property and personnel within its jurisdiction and provides a comprehensive police service to the MoD as a whole.

Chief Constable, Andy Adams
Deputy Chief Constable, Gareth Wilson

THE SPECIAL CONSTABULARY

Strength (March 2019), 10,640

The Special Constabulary is a force of trained volunteers who support and work with their local police force, usually for a minimum of 16 hours a month. Special constables are thoroughly grounded in the basic aspects of police work, such as self-defence, powers of arrest, common crimes and preparing evidence for court, before they can begin to carry out any police duties. Once they have completed their training, they have the same powers as a regular officer and wear a similar uniform. The Metropolitan Police Service have further information on their website.

POLICE FORCES

The telephone number for each local police force in England, Wales, Scotland and Northern Ireland is **T** 101

Force	Strength†	Chief Constable	Police and Crime Commissioner
ENGLAND			
Avon and Somerset	2,676	Andy Marsh, QPM	Sue Mountstevens
Bedfordshire	1,164	Jon Boutcher, QPM	Kathryn Holloway
Cambridgeshire	1,447	Nick Dean	Jason Ablewhite
Cheshire	2,006	Darren Martland	David Keane
Cleveland	1,198	Richard Lewis	Barry Coppinger
Cumbria	1,160	Michelle Skeer, QPM	Peter McCall
Derbyshire	1,767	Peter Goodman	Hardyal Dhindsa
Devon and Cornwall	3,000	Shaun Sawyer, QPM	Alison Hernandez
Dorset	1,223	James Vaughan, QPM	Martyn Underhill
Durham	1,118	Jo Farrell	Ron Hogg
Essex	3,071	Ben-Julian Harrington	Roger Hirst
Gloucestershire	1,073	Rod Hansen	Martin Surl
Greater Manchester	6,444	Ian Hopkins, QPM	Mayor of Greater Manchester
Hampshire	2,697	Olivia Pinkney	Michael Lane
Hertfordshire	2,009	Charlie Hall, QPM	David Lloyd
Humberside	1,889	Lee Freeman	Keith Hunter
Kent	3,553	Alan Pughsley, QPM	Matthew Scott
Lancashire	2,895	Andy Rhodes	Clive Grunshaw
Leicestershire	1,829	Simon Cole, QPM	Lord Bach
Lincolnshire	1,096	Bill Skelly	Marc Jones
Merseyside	3,396	Andy Cooke, QPM	Jane Kennedy
Norfolk	1,609	Simon Bailey, QPM	Lorne Green
North Yorkshire	1,377	Lisa Winward	Julia Mulligan
Northamptonshire	1,187	Nick Adderley	Stephen Mold
Northumbria	3,081	Winton Keenen	Kim McGuiness
Nottinghamshire	1,936	Craig Guilford	Paddy Tipping
South Yorkshire	2,370	Stephen Watson, QPM	Dr Alan Billings
Staffordshire	1,567	Gareth Morgan	Matthew Ellis
Suffolk	1,172	Steve Jupp	Tim Passmore
Surrey	1,882	Nick Ephgrave	David Munro
Sussex	2,629	Giles York, QPM	Katy Bourne
Thames Valley	4,149	Francis Habgood, QPM	Anthony Stansfeld
Warwickshire	817	Martin Jelley, QPM	Philip Seccombe
West Mercia	1,989	Anthony Bangham	John-Paul Campion
West Midlands	6,495	Dave Thompson, QPM	David Jamieson
West Yorkshire	5,137	John Robins, QPM	Mark Burns-Williamson, OBE
Wiltshire	992	Kier Pritchard	Angus Macpherson
WALES			
Dyfed-Powys	1,145	Mark Collins	Dafydd Llywelyn
Gwent	1,308	Pam Kelly *(acting)*	Jeff Cuthbert
North Wales	1,458	Carl Foulkes	Arfon Jones
South Wales	2,986	Matt Jukes	Rt. Hon. Alun Michael
POLICE SCOTLAND	17,251	Iain Livingstone, QPM	–
POLICE SERVICE OF NORTHERN IRELAND	6,716	Simon Byrne	–

ISLANDS	Strength†	Chief Constable	Telephone
Isle of Man	236	Gary Roberts	01624-631212
States of Jersey	189	Rob Bastable	01534-612612
Guernsey	146	Rauri Hardy	01481-725111

† Size of force (full-time equivalent; excluding long-term absentees) as at 31 March 2019

LONDON FORCES

CITY OF LONDON POLICE

182 Bishopsgate, London EC2M 4NP **T** 020-7601 2222
W www.cityoflondon.police.uk
Strength (June 2019), 756

The City of London has one of the most important financial centres in the world and the force has particular expertise in fraud investigation. The force concentrates on: economic crime, counter terrorism and community policing. It has a wholly elected police authority, the police committee of the City of London Corporation, which appoints the commissioner.

Commissioner, Ian Dyson, QPM
Assistant Commissioner, Alistair Sutherland, QPM
Commander, Karen Baxter *(Economic Crime)*

METROPOLITAN POLICE SERVICE

New Scotland Yard, Broadway, London SW1H 0BG
T 020-7230 1212 **W** www.met.police.uk
Strength (June 2019), 30,059

Commissioner, Cressida Dick, CBE, QPM
Deputy Commissioner, Sir Stephen House, QPM

The Metropolitan Police Service (MPS) is divided into four main areas for operational purposes:

FRONTLINE POLICING
Most of the day-to-day policing of London is carried out by 32 borough operational command units operating within the same boundaries as the London borough councils.

Assistant Commissioner, Mark Simmons

SPECIALIST OPERATIONS
Counter Terrorism Command is responsible for the prevention and disruption of terrorist activity, domestic extremism and related offences within London and nationally. It provides an explosives disposal and chemical, biological, radiological and nuclear capability in London, assists the security services in fulfilling their roles and provides a point of contact for international partners.

Protection Command is responsible for the protection and security of high-profile persons, such as the royal family, prime minister and visiting heads of state.

Security Command works with authorities at the Houses of Parliament to provide security for peers, MPs, employees and visitors to the Palace of Westminster.

Assistant Commissioner & National Coordinator for Counter Terrorism Policing, Neil Basu

MET OPERATIONS
Met Operations provides two main services: reducing the harm caused by serious crime and criminal networks and providing specialist policing services across London.

Assistant Commissioner, Nick Ephgrave

PROFESSIONALISM
The Directorate of Professionalism's key aims are to uphold and improve professional standards across the MPS. It works with the IOPC to establish good practice, reduce bureaucracy and review decision making. It also works with the CPS to ensure timely investigations of complaints and conduct matters.

Assistant Commissioner, Helen Ball

STAFF ASSOCIATIONS

Police officers are not permitted to join a trade union or to take strike action. All ranks have their own staff associations.

NATIONAL POLICE CHIEFS' COUNCIL (NPCC), 10 Victoria Street, London SW1H 0NN **T** 020-3276 3795
W www.npcc.police.uk
Chair, Barbara Scott

ENGLAND AND WALES

POLICE FEDERATION OF ENGLAND AND WALES, Federation House, Highbury Drive, Leatherhead, Surrey KT22 7UY **T** 01372-352050 **W** www.polfed.org
National Secretary, Alex Duncan
POLICE SUPERINTENDENTS' ASSOCIATION OF ENGLAND AND WALES, 67A Reading Road, Pangbourne, Reading RG8 7JD **T** 0118-984 4005 **W** www.policesupers.com
National Secretary, Chief Supt. Dan Murphy

SCOTLAND

ASSOCIATION OF SCOTTISH POLICE SUPERINTENDENTS, Scottish Police College, Kincardine, Fife FK10 4BE **T** 01259-732122
W www.scottishpolicesupers.org.uk
General Secretary, Craig Suttie
SCOTTISH POLICE FEDERATION, 5 Woodside Place, Glasgow G3 7QF **T** 0300-303 0027 **W** www.spf.org.uk
General Secretary, Calum Steele

NORTHERN IRELAND

POLICE FEDERATION FOR NORTHERN IRELAND, 77–79 Garnerville Road, Belfast BT4 2NX **T** 028-9076 4200
W www.policefed-ni.org.uk
Chair, Mark Lindsay
SUPERINTENDENTS' ASSOCIATION OF NORTHERN IRELAND, **T** 028-9092 2201
E SuptAssociation@psni.pnn.police.uk

RATES OF PAY *as at 1 September 2019*

Chief Constable of Greater Manchester or W. Midlands*	£199,386
Chief Constable	£142,896–£186,099
Deputy Chief Constable	£119,637–£152,871
Assistant Chief Constable/ Commander	£103,023–£116,313
Chief Superintendent	£84,849–£89,511
Superintendent	
in rank on or after 1 April 2014	£68,460–£80,859
in rank before 1 April 2014	£68,460–£79,758
Chief Inspector†	£56,910 (£59,175)–£60,219 (£62,469)
Inspector†	£51,414 (£53,664)–£55,767 (£58,038)
Sergeant	£41,499–£45,099
Constable	
apptd on or after 1 April 2013	£20,880–£40,128
apptd before 1 April 2013	£25,560–£40,128
Metropolitan Police	
Commissioner	£285,792
Deputy Commissioner	£235,944
City of London Police	
Commissioner	£176,802
Assistant Commissioner	£145,830
Police Scotland	
Chief Constable	£214,404
Deputy Chief Constable	£174,741
Assistant Chief Constable	£118,485
Police Service of Northern Ireland	
Chief Constable	£207,489
Deputy Chief Constable	£168,582

* Also applicable to the four Assistant Commissioners of the MPS
† London salary in parentheses. All other officers (not MPS or City of London Commissioners) working in London receive an additional payment of £2,505 per annum

THE PRISON SERVICE

The prison services in the UK are the responsibility of the Secretary of State for Justice, the Scottish Secretary for Justice and the Minister of Justice in Northern Ireland. The chief executive (director-general in Northern Ireland), officers of HM Prison and Probation Service (HMPPS), the Scottish Prison Service (SPS) and the Northern Ireland Prison Service are responsible for the day-to-day running of the system.

There are 122 prison establishments in England and Wales, 15 in Scotland and three in Northern Ireland. Convicted prisoners are classified according to their assessed security risk and are housed in establishments appropriate to that level of security. There are no open prisons in Northern Ireland. Female prisoners are housed in women's establishments or in separate wings of mixed prisons. Remand prisoners are, where possible, housed separately from convicted prisoners. Offenders under the age of 21 are usually detained in a Young Offender Institution, which may be a separate establishment or part of a prison. Appellant and failed asylum seekers are held in Immigration Removal Centres, or in separate units of other prisons.

Fifteen prisons are now run by the private sector in England and Wales, and in England, Wales and Scotland all escort services have been contracted out to private companies. In Scotland, two prisons (Kilmarnock and Addiewell) were built and financed by the private sector and are being operated by private contractors.

There are independent prison inspectorates in England, Wales and Scotland which report annually on conditions and the treatment of prisoners. The Chief Inspector of Criminal Justice in Northern Ireland and HM Inspectorate of Prisons for England and Wales perform an inspectorate role for prisons in Northern Ireland. Every prison establishment also has an independent monitoring board made up of local volunteers.

Any prisoner whose complaint is not satisfied by the internal complaints procedures may complain to the prisons and probation ombudsman for England and Wales, the Scottish public services ombudsman or the prisoner ombudsman for Northern Ireland. The prisons and probation inspectors, the prisons ombudsman and the independent monitoring boards report to the home secretary and to the Minister of Justice in Northern Ireland.

PRISON STATISTICS

The current projections forecast that the prison population in England and Wales will grow to 85,800 by June 2022.

PRISON POPULATION 2019 (UK)

	Remand	Sentenced	Other
ENGLAND AND WALES	8,957	72,860	817
Male	8,437	69,576	739
Female	520	3,284	28
SCOTLAND	1,808	6,416	–
Male	1,697	6,125	–
Female	111	291	–
N. IRELAND*	436	987	–
Male	414	944	–
Female	22	43	–
UK TOTAL	11,201	80,263	1,584

* Figures from September 2018
Sources: MoJ; Scottish Prison Service; NI Prison Service

PRISON CAPACITY (ENGLAND AND WALES)
as at July 2019

Male prisoners	79,211
Female prisoners	3,831
Total	83,042
Useable operational capacity	85,131
Under home detention curfew supervision	2,884

Source: MoJ – Prisons and Probation Statistics

SENTENCED PRISON POPULATION BY SEX AND OFFENCE (ENGLAND AND WALES) as at 31 March 2019

	Male	Female
Violence against the person	18,342	948
Sexual offences	13,234	125
Robbery	6,840	324
Theft offences	8,494	590
Criminal damage and arson	1,052	95
Drugs offences	10,579	436
Possession of weapons	2,854	113
Public order offences	1,148	41
Miscellaneous crimes against society	2,820	177
Fraud offences	1,079	169
Summary non-motoring	2,502	224
Summary motoring	350	10
Offence not recorded	233	26
Total	69,527	3,278

Source: MoJ – Prisons and Probation Statistics

SENTENCED POPULATION BY LENGTH OF SENTENCE (ENGLAND AND WALES)
as at 31 March 2019

	British	Other Nationalities or Not Recorded
Less than 12 months	4,432	522
12 months to less than 4 years	14,140	1,628
4 years to less than life	31,285	3,441
Indeterminate	8,561	875
Total*	58,418	6,466

* Figures do not include civil (non-criminal) prisoners or fine defaulters
Source: MoJ – Prisons and Probation Statistics

AVERAGE DAILY POPULATION BY TYPE OF CUSTODY 2019 (SCOTLAND)

Remand	1,489
Convicted awaiting sentence	319
Sentenced	6,416
Total	8,224

Source: SPS

SUICIDES IN PRISON (ENGLAND AND WALES)
Dec. 2017–Dec. 2018

Total	92

Source: MoJ

THE PRISON SERVICES

HM PRISON AND PROBATION SERVICE

102 Petty France, London SW1H 9AJ
T 0163-363 0941 **E** public.enquiries@noms.gsi.gov.uk
W www.gov.uk/government/organisations/
her-majestys-prison-and-probation-service

HM Prison and Probation Service (HMPPS) was formed on 1 April 2017, incorporating the National Offender Management Service (NOMS) and HM Prisons. HMPPS is responsible for implementing government policy concerning the welfare of prison populations and local communities, working closely with HM Prison Service to oversee the management of public sector prisons in England and Wales.

SALARIES (ENGLAND AND WALES)
from 1 April 2019

All salary ranges given are for the average across England and Wales (includes inner and outer London salaries) and are based on a 37-hour-week inclusive of the required hours allowance (Governors, Deputy Governors and Heads of Function) or the additional 17 per cent unsocial hours payment for all other grades.

Governor	£68,604–£97,859
Deputy Governor	£48,656–£79,520
Head of Function	£43,545–£54,810
Custodial Manager	£31,615–£40,319
Supervising/Specialist Officer	£28,101–£35,988
Prison Officer	£22,293–£29,518
Operational Support Grade	£20,095–£24,829

HM PRISON AND PROBATION SERVICE BOARD
Chief Executive, Jo Farrar
Executive Directors, Ian Blakeman *(Performance);* Phil Copple *(Prisons);* Amy Rees *(HMPPS Wales and Strategy);* Adrian Scott *(Electronic Monitoring Programme and Procurement);* Helga Swindenbank *(Youth Custody Service)*

OPERATING COSTS OF HM PRISON AND PROBATION SERVICE 2018–19

Operating income	(£245,575,000)
Total operating expenditure	£5,072,722,000
Staff costs	£2,146,359,000
Net operating expenditure	£4,827,147,000

Source: HM Prison and Probation Service – *Annual Report and Accounts 2018–19*

SCOTTISH PRISON SERVICE (SPS)

Calton House, 5 Redheughs Rigg, Edinburgh EH12 9HW
T 0131-330 3500 **E** gaolinfo@sps.pnn.gov.uk
W www.sps.gov.uk

SALARIES
from 1 April 2018

Governor in Charge	£64,771–£73,365
Deputy Governor	£52,361–£60,790
Head of Operations	£42,301–£50,547
Unit Manager	£34,440–£42,941
First Line Manager	£28,071–£36,175
Residential Officer	£23,564–£30,356
Operations Officer	£18,871–£23,372

SPS BOARD
Chief Executive, Colin McConnell
Directors, Caroline Johnston *(Strategy and Stakeholder Engagement, interim);* James Kerr *(Operations);* Ruth Sutherland *(Corporate Services, interim)*
Non-Executive Directors, K. Hampton; R. Molan; H. Monro; G. Scott; G. Stillie

OPERATING COSTS OF SPS 2017–18

Staff costs	£170,437,000
Total income	(£7,389,000)
Total operating expenditure	£331,518,000
Net operating expenditure	£324,129,000

Source: SPS – *Annual Report and Accounts 2017–18*

NORTHERN IRELAND PRISON SERVICE

Dundonald House, Upper Newtownards Road, Belfast BT4 3SU
T 028-9052 2922 **E** niprisonservice@nics.gov.uk
W www.justice-ni.gov.uk/topics/prisons

SALARIES
from 1 April 2018

Governor in Charge (Maghaberry)	£75,875–£82,375
Governor in Charge	£68,535–£75,035
Head of Function	£54,350–£58,775
Head of Unit	£48,750–£52,600
Senior Prison Officer	£37,680–£42,276
Main Grade Prison Officer	£34,121–£38,688
Custody Prison Officer	£23,950–£29,470
Operational Support Grade	£23,950
Prisoner Custody Officer (PCO)*	£20,026–£21,798

* 35-hour/week

MANAGEMENT BOARD
Director-General (Chair), Ronnie Armour
Permanent Secretary, Peter May
Directors, Louise Blair *(Finance);* Paul Doran *(Rehabilitation);* Brendan Giffen *(Strategy and Governance);* Austin Treacy, OBE *(Prisons);* Jacqui Wallace *(HR)*
Non-Executive Directors, Dale Ashford; Claire Keatinge

OPERATING COSTS OF NORTHERN IRELAND PRISON SERVICE 2016–17

Staff costs	£61,606,000
Operating income	£2,732,000
Total operating expenditure	£106,602,000
Net operating expenditure	£103,870,000

Source: NI Prison Service – *Annual Report and Accounts 2017–18*

PRISON ESTABLISHMENTS

ENGLAND AND WALES *as at June 2019*

Prison	Address	Capacity	Prisoners	Governor/Director
†‡ ALTCOURSE	Liverpool L9 7LH	1,164	1,147	Steve Williams
ASHFIELD	Bristol BS16 9QJ	400	398	Martin Booth
*‡ ASKHAM GRANGE	York YO23 3FT	128	112	Natalie McKee
‡ AYLESBURY	Bucks HP20 1EH	209	200	Laura Sapwell
BEDFORD	Bedford MK40 1HG	411	347	Patrick Butler
BELMARSH	London SE28 0EB	906	806	Rob Davis, OBE
BERWYN	Wrexham, LL13 9QE	1,400	1,361	Nick Leader
BIRMINGHAM	Birmingham B18 4AS	977	925	Paul Newton
BLANTYRE HOUSE	Kent TN17 2NH	–	–	James Bourke
†‡ BRINSFORD	Wolverhampton WV10 7PY	577	554	Heather Whithead
†‡ BRISTOL	Bristol BS7 8PS	520	463	Steve Cross
BRIXTON	London SW2 5XF	798	737	Dave Bamford
* BRONZEFIELD	Middlesex TW15 3JZ	567	530	Ian Whiteside
BUCKLEY HALL	Lancs OL12 9DP	459	'449	Rob Knight
BULLINGDON	Oxon OX25 1PZ	1,114	1,055	Ian Blakeman
BURE	Norfolk NR10 5GB	656	653	Simon Rhoden
† CARDIFF	Cardiff CF24 0UG	779	722	Helen Ryder
CHANNINGS WOOD	Devon TQ12 6DW	724	690	Richard Luscombe
‡ CHELMSFORD	Essex CM2 6LQ	700	665	Penny Bartlett
COLDINGLEY	Surrey GU24 9EX	426	421	Jo Sims
‡ COOKHAM WOOD	Kent ME1 3LU	188	164	Paul Durham
DARTMOOR	Devon PL20 6RR	640	628	Bridie Oakes-Richards
‡ DEERBOLT	Co. Durham DL12 9BG	387	354	Gavin O'Malley
DONCASTER (private prison)	Doncaster DN5 8UX	1,145	1,081	Jerry Spencer
† DOVEGATE (private prison)	Staffs ST14 8XR	1,160	1,150	John Hewitson
* DOWNVIEW	Surrey SM2 5PD	293	273	Natasha Wilson
* DRAKE HALL	Staffs ST21 6LQ	340	333	Carl Hardwick
† DURHAM	Durham DH1 3HU	996	918	Phil Husband (*acting*)
* EAST SUTTON PARK	Kent ME17 3DF	101	96	Robin Eldridge
* EASTWOOD PARK	Glos GL12 8DB	432	396	Suzy Dymond-White
† ELMLEY	Kent ME12 4DZ	1,212	1,159	Paul Woods
ERLESTOKE	Wilts SN10 5TU	524	507	Tim Knight
†‡ EXETER	Devon EX4 4EX	545	488	Dave Atkinson
FEATHERSTONE	Wolverhampton WV10 7PU	637	611	Babafemi Dada
†‡ FELTHAM	Middx TW13 4ND	568	470	Emily Martin
FORD	W. Sussex BN18 0BX	544	538	Stephen Fradley
‡ FOREST BANK	Salford M27 8FB	1,460	1,430	Matt Spencer
* FOSTON HALL	Derby DE65 5DN	336	286	Andrea Black
FRANKLAND	Durham DH1 5YD	852	838	Gavin O'Malley
FULL SUTTON	York YO41 1PS	574	521	Gareth Sands
GARTH	Preston PR26 8NE	845	817	Steve Pearson
GARTREE	Leics LE16 7RP	'708	678	Ali Barker
GRENDON	Bucks HP18 0TL	568	538	Jamie Bennett
GUYS MARSH	Dorset SP7 0AH	396	387	Jamie Lucas
HATFIELD (AND MOORLAND)	S. Yorks DN7 6EL	1,384	1,328	Julie Spence
HAVERIGG	Cumbria LA18 4NA	269	264	Tony Corcoran
HEWELL	Worcs B97 6QS	1,115	1,094	Clare Pearson
HIGH DOWN	Surrey SM2 5PJ	1,203	1,107	Sally Hill
HIGHPOINT	Suffolk CB8 9YG	1,325	1,279	Nigel Smith
‡ HINDLEY	Lancs WN2 5TH	578	547	Mark Livingston
‡ HOLLESLEY BAY	Suffolk IP12 3JW	485	481	Gary Newnes
HOLME HOUSE	Stockton-on-Tees TS18 2QU	1,210	1,199	Chris Dyer
HULL	Hull HU9 5LS	1,036	989	Anthony Oliver
HUMBER	E. Yorks HU15 2JZ	1,062	937	Marcella Goligher
§ HUNTERCOMBE	Oxon RG9 5SB	480	464	David Redhouse
‡ ISIS	Thamesmead SE28 0NZ	628	622	Emily Thomas
ISLE OF WIGHT	Isle of Wight PO30 5RS	1,053	1,016	Doug Graham
KIRKHAM	Lancs PR4 2RN	657	644	Dan Cooper
KIRKLEVINGTON GRANGE	Cleveland TS15 9PA	283	279	Angie Petit
†‡ LANCASTER FARMS	Lancaster LA1 3QZ	560	551	Peter Francis
LEEDS	Leeds LS12 2TJ	1,212	1,066	Steven Robson
LEICESTER	Leicester LE2 7AJ	411	302	Jim Donaldson
‡ LEWES	E. Sussex BN7 1EA	606	514	Stephen Fradley
LEYHILL	Glos GL12 8BT	515	511	Neil Lavis
† LINCOLN	Lincoln LN2 4BD	629	514	Paul Yates
LINDHOLME	Doncaster DN7 6EE	945	938	Simon Walters
LITTLEHEY	Cambs PE28 0SR	1,220	1,205	Stephen Ruddy
LIVERPOOL	Liverpool L9 3DF	700	670	Pia Sinha
LONG LARTIN	Worcs WR11 8TZ	602	584	Jamie Bennett
* LOW NEWTON	Durham DH1 5YA	352	314	Gabrielle Lee
LOWDHAM GRANGE (private prison)	Notts NG14 7DA	888	878	Mark Hanson

Prison	Address	Average Daily	Max. Number	Governor/Director
§ MAIDSTONE	Kent ME14 1UZ	600	585	Dave Atkinson
† MANCHESTER	Manchester M60 9AH	1,072	918	Rob Young
§ MORTON HALL	Lincoln LN6 9PT	392	254	Karen Head
The MOUNT	Herts HP3 0NZ	1,028	990	Kevin Leggett
*‡ NEW HALL	W. Yorks WF4 4XX	425	358	Natalie McKee
NORTH SEA CAMP	Lincs PE22 0QX	420	411	Michelle Quirke
NORTHUMBERLAND	Northumberland NE65 9XG	1,348	1,342	Nick Leader
† NORWICH	Norfolk NR1 4LU	773	719	Declan Moore
NOTTINGHAM	Notts NG5 3AG	800	787	Phil Novis
OAKWOOD	W. Midlands WV10 7QD	2,106	2,080	John McLaughlin
ONLEY	Warks CV23 8AP	734	730	Matthew Tilt
‡ PARC	Bridgend CF35 6AP	1,699	1,631	Janet Wallsgrove
PENTONVILLE	London N7 8TT	1,098	1,065	Darren Hughes
* PETERBOROUGH	Peterborough PE3 7PD	1,240	1,149	Damian Evans
‡ PORTLAND	Dorset DT5 1DL	530	518	Steve Hodson
PRESTON	Lancs PR1 5AB	811	697	Steve Lawrence
RANBY	Notts DN22 8EU	1,038	1,014	Nigel Hirst
RISLEY	Cheshire WA3 6BP	1,014	1,066	Nicki Smith
‡ ROCHESTER	Kent ME1 3QS	695	680	Dean Gardiner
RYE HILL	Warks CV23 8SZ	664	660	Pete Small
* SEND	Surrey GU23 7LJ	282	268	Carlene Dixon
STAFFORD	Stafford ST16 3AW	751	750	Ralph Lubkowski
STANDFORD HILL	Kent ME12 4AA	464	459	Dawn Mauldon
STOCKEN	Rutland LE15 7RD	913	864	Neil Thomas
† STOKE HEATH	Shropshire TF9 2JL	782	755	John Huntington
* STYAL	Cheshire SK9 4HR	486	461	Kate Robinson
‡ SUDBURY	Derbys DE6 5HW	581	579	Adrian Turner
SWALESIDE	Kent ME12 4AX	1,112	1,064	Mark Icke
SWANSEA	Swansea SA1 3SR	497	419	Graham Barrett
‡ SWINFEN HALL	Staffs WS14 9QS	594	574	Ian West
THAMESIDE	London SE28 0FJ	1,232	1,200	Craig Thomson
THORN CROSS	Cheshire WA4 4RL	385	384	Mick Povall
USK/PRESCOED	Monmouthshire NP15 1XP	526	519	Giles Mason
VERNE	Dorset DT5 1EQ	580	480	David Bourne
WAKEFIELD	W. Yorks WF2 9AG	750	723	Tom Wheatley
WANDSWORTH	London SW18 3HU	1,540	1,496	Jeanne Bryant
WARREN HILL	Suffolk IP12 3BF	258	240	Dave Nickolson
WAYLAND	Norfolk IP25 6RL	940	931	Sonia Walsh
WEALSTUN	W. Yorks LS23 7AZ	832	804	Diane Lewis
‡ WERRINGTON	Stoke-on-Trent ST9 0DX	118	116	Ian Darlington
‡ WETHERBY	W. Yorks LS22 5ED	336	223	Andrew Dickinson
WHATTON	Nottingham NG13 9FQ	841	836	Lynn Saunders, OBE
WHITEMOOR	Cambs PE15 0PR	458	451	Will Styles
WINCHESTER	Winchester SO22 5DF	500	474	James Bourke
WOODHILL	Bucks MK4 4DA	622	571	Nicola Marfleet
WORMWOOD SCRUBS	London W12 0AE	1,096	1,039	Sarah Pennington
WYMOTT	Preston PR26 8LW	1,169	1,149	Graham Beck

SCOTLAND *as at June 2019*

Prison	Address	Average Daily	Max. Number	Governor/Director
ADDIEWELL	West Lothian EH55 8QA	696	702	Ian Whitehead
†‡ BARLINNIE	Glasgow G33 2QX	1,127	1,195	Michael Stoney
CASTLE HUNTLY (Open Estate)	Dundee DD2 5HL	189	X	Gerry Michie
*†‡ CORNTON VALE	Stirling FK9 5NU	86	96	Jacqueline Clinton
† DUMFRIES	Dumfries DG2 9AX	172	180	Linda Dorward
*† EDINBURGH	Edinburgh EH11 3LN	872	913	David Abernethy
GLENOCHIL	Tullibody FK10 3AD	641	667	Andrew Hodge
*‡ GRAMPIAN	Peterhead AB42 2YY	449	474	Mike Hebden (*acting*)
*† GREENOCK	Greenock PA16 9AJ	248	257	Karen Smith
† INVERNESS	Inverness IV2 3HH	110	137	Stephen Coyle
† KILMARNOCK (private prison)	Kilmarnock KA1 5AA	499	509	Michael Guy
LOW MOSS	Glasgow G64 2PZ	757	778	James Farish
† PERTH	Perth PH2 8AT	617	654	Fraser Munro
*†‡ POLMONT	Falkirk FK2 0AB	470	522	Brenda Stewart
SHOTTS	Lanarkshire ML7 4LE	531	540	Allister Purdie

NORTHERN IRELAND *as at June 2019*

Prison	Address	Prisoners	Governor/Director
* HYDEBANK WOOD	Belfast BT8 8NA	152	Richard Taylor
†§ MAGHABERRY	Co. Antrim BT28 2NF	857	David Kennedy
MAGILLIGAN	Co. Londonderry BT49 0LR	430	Richard Taylor

* Women's establishment or establishment with units for women
† Remand Centre or establishment with units for remand prisoners
‡ Young Offender Institution or establishment with units for young offenders
§ Immigration Removal Centre or establishment with units for immigration detainees

DEFENCE

The armed forces of the UK comprise the Royal Navy, the Army and the Royal Air Force (RAF). The Queen is Commander-in-Chief of all the armed forces. The Secretary of State for Defence is responsible for the formulation and content of defence policy and for providing the means by which it is conducted. The formal legal basis for the conduct of defence in the UK rests on a range of powers vested by statute and letters patent in the Defence Council, chaired by the Secretary of State for Defence. Beneath the ministers lies the top management of the Ministry of Defence (MoD), headed jointly by the Permanent Secretary and the Chief of the Defence Staff. The Permanent Secretary is the government's principal civilian adviser on defence and has the primary responsibility for policy, finance, management and administration. The Permanent Secretary is also personally accountable to parliament for the expenditure of all public money allocated to defence purposes. The Chief of the Defence Staff is the professional head of the armed forces in the UK and the principal military adviser to the secretary of state and the government.

The Defence Board is the executive of the Defence Council. Chaired by the Permanent Secretary, it acts as the main executive board of the Ministry of Defence, providing senior level leadership and strategic management of defence.

The Central Staff, headed by the Vice-Chief of the Defence Staff and the Second Permanent Under-Secretary of State, is the policy core of the department. Defence Equipment and Support, headed by the Chief of Defence Materiel, is responsible for purchasing defence equipment and providing logistical support to the armed forces.

A permanent Joint Headquarters for the conduct of joint operations was set up at Northwood in 1996. The Joint Headquarters connects the policy and strategic functions of the MoD head office with the conduct of operations and is intended to strengthen the policy/executive division.

The UK pursues its defence and security policies through its membership of NATO (to which most of its armed forces are committed), the Organisation for Security and Cooperation in Europe and the UN (*see* International Organisations section).

STRENGTH OF THE REGULAR ARMED FORCES

	Royal Navy	Army	RAF	All Services
1975 strength	76,200	167,100	95,000	338,300
2000 strength	42,850	110,050	54,720	207,620
2005 strength	39,940	109,290	51,870	201,100
2010 strength	38,730	108,920	44,050	191,700
2011 strength	37,660	106,240	42,460	186,360
2012 strength	35,540	104,250	40,000	179,800
2013 strength	33,960	99,730	37,030	170,710
2014 strength	33,330	91,070	35,230	159,630
2015 strength	32,740	87,060	33,930	153,720
2016 strength	32,502	85,038	33,456	150,966
2017 strength	32,544	83,561	33,261	149,366
2018 strength	32,483	81,116	32,957	146,556
2019 strength	32,537	79,029	32,862	144,428
2020 strength	33,050	78,876	32,820	144,746

Source: MoD – Defence Statistics (Tri-Service)

UK REGULAR ARMED FORCES BY RANK 2020

Officers	27,752
Other Ranks	117,565

Source: MoD – Defence Statistics (Tri-Service)

UK regular forces include trained and untrained personnel and nursing services, but exclude Gurkhas, full-time reserve service personnel, mobilised reservists and naval activated reservists. As at 1 July 2020 these groups numbered:

All Gurkhas	3,752
Full-time reserve service	5,345
Mobilised reservists	2,854
Army	2,200
RAF	434
Royal Navy	220

Source: MoD – Defence Statistics (Tri-Service)

CIVILIAN PERSONNEL

2000 level	121,300
2005 level	107,680
2006 level	102,970
2007 level	95,790
2008 level	89,499
2009 level	86,621
2010 level	85,850
2011 level	83,063
2012 level	71,008
2013 level	65,400
2014 level	62,501
2015 level	58,161
2016 level	56,243
2017 level	56,675
2018 level	56,865
2019 level	57,760
2020 level	58,256

Source: MoD – Defence Statistics (Tri-Service)

UK REGULAR FORCES: DEATHS

In 2018 there were a total of 61 deaths among the UK regular armed forces, of which 12 were serving in the Royal Navy and Royal Marines, 38 in the Army and 11 in the RAF. The largest single cause of death was cancers, which accounted for 10 deaths (16 per cent of the total) in 2018. Land transport accidents accounted for 10 deaths (16 per cent) and other accidents provisionally accounted for a further 22 deaths (36 per cent). There was one death as a result of hostile action. Suicides and open verdicts accounted for five deaths.

NUMBER OF DEATHS AND MORTALITY RATES

	2015	2016	2017	2018	2019
Total number	60	72	73	61	66
Royal Navy	11	17	12	12	9
Army	39	41	40	38	40
RAF	10	14	11	11	17
Mortality rates per thousand					
Tri-service rate	0.39	0.47	0.42	0.41	0.45
Navy	0.32	0.52	0.36	0.34	0.27
Army	0.45	0.47	0.49	0.46	0.54
RAF	0.28	0.36	0.27	0.29	0.43

Source: MoD National Statistics

NUCLEAR FORCES

The Vanguard Class SSBN (ship submersible ballistic nuclear) provides the UK's strategic nuclear deterrent. Each Vanguard Class submarine is capable of carrying 16 Trident II D5 missiles equipped with nuclear warheads.

There is a ballistic missile early warning system station at RAF Fylingdales in North Yorkshire.

ARMS CONTROL

The 1990 Conventional Armed Forces in Europe (CFE) Treaty, which commits all NATO and former Warsaw Pact members to limiting their holdings of five major classes of conventional weapons, has been adapted to reflect the changed geo-strategic environment and negotiations continue for its implementation. The Open Skies Treaty, which the UK signed in 1992 and entered into force in 2002, allows for the overflight of states parties by other states parties using unarmed observation aircraft.

The UN Convention on Certain Conventional Weapons (as amended 2001), which bans or restricts the use of specific types of weapons that are considered to cause unnecessary or unjustifiable suffering to combatants, or to affect civilians indiscriminately, was ratified by the UK in 1995. In 1968 the UK signed and ratified the Nuclear Non-Proliferation Treaty, which came into force in 1970 and was indefinitely and unconditionally extended in 1995. In 1996 the UK signed the Comprehensive Nuclear Test Ban Treaty and ratified it in 1998. The UK is a party to the 1972 Biological and Toxin Weapons Convention, which provides for a worldwide ban on biological weapons, and the 1993 Chemical Weapons Convention, which came into force in 1997 and provides for a verifiable worldwide ban on chemical weapons.

DEFENCE BUDGET

DEPARTMENTAL EXPENDITURE LIMITS

£ billion

	2020–21
Resource DEL	30.8
Capital DEL	10.6
Total	41.4

Source: HM Treasury – *The Budget 2020* (Crown copyright)

MINISTRY OF DEFENCE

Main Building, Whitehall, London SW1A 2HB
T 020-7218 9000
W www.gov.uk/government/organisations/ministry-of-defence

Secretary of State for Defence, Rt. Hon. Ben Wallace, MP
Parliamentary Private Secretary, Jack Brereton, MP
Special Advisers, Peter Quentin
Minister of State, Jeremy Quin, MP *(Armed Forces)*
Minister of State, Baroness Goldie *(Lords)*
Parliamentary Under-Secretary of State and Minister for the Armed Forces, James Heappey, MP
Parliamentary Under-Secretary of State and Minister for Defence People and Veterans, Johnny Mercer, MP

CHIEFS OF STAFF

Chief of the Defence Staff, Gen. Sir Nick Carter, GCB, CBE, DSO, ADC
Vice-Chief of the Defence Staff, Adm. Sir Tim Fraser, KCB, ADC
Chief of Naval Staff and First Sea Lord, Adm. Tony Radakin, CB, ADC
Second Sea Lord and Deputy Chief of Naval Staff, Vice-Adm. Nicholas Hine, CB
Chief of the General Staff, Gen. Sir Mark Carleton-Smith, KCB, CBE, ADC
Deputy Chief of the General Staff, Lt.-Gen. Christopher Tickell, CBE

Chief of the Air Staff, Air Chief Marshal Mike Wigston, CBE, ADC
Assistant Chief of the Air Staff, Air Vice-Marshal Ian Gale, MBE
Commander of Strategic Command, Gen. Patrick Sanders, KCB, CBE, DSO, ADC
Deputy Commander of Strategic Command, Lt.-Gen. Rob Magowan, CB, CBE

SENIOR OFFICIALS

Permanent Secretary, Sir Stephen Lovegrove, KCB
Chief Scientific Adviser, Prof. Dame Angela McLean, DBE
Chief Scientific Adviser (Nuclear), Prof. Robin Grimes, FRS, FRENG
Director-General Finance, Charlie Pate

THE DEFENCE COUNCIL

The Defence Council is chaired by the Secretary of State, and comprises the other ministers, the Permanent Under-Secretary, the Chief of Defence Staff and senior service officers and officials who head the armed services and the department's major corporate functions. It provides the formal legal basis for the conduct of UK defence through a range of powers vested in it by statute and letters patent.

THE DEFENCE BOARD

The Defence Board is the main corporate board of the MoD, providing senior level leadership and strategic management of defence. The Defence Board is the highest committee in the MoD, responsible for the full range of defence business, other than the conduct of operations.

MANAGEMENT BOARD

Permanent Secretary, Sir Stephen Lovegrove, KCB
Members, Mike Baker, CBE *(Chief Operating Officer);* Lt.-Gen. Doug Chalmers *(Deputy Chief of Defence Staff (Military Strategy and Operations));* Charlie Forte *(Chief Information Officer);* Prof. Robin Grimes, FRS, FRENG *(Chief Scientific Adviser (Nuclear));* Air Marshal Richard Knighton *(Deputy Chief of the Defence Staff (Financial and Military Capability));* Angus Lapsley *(Strategy and International);* Prof. Dame Angela McLean, DBE *(Chief Scientific Adviser);* Vanessa Nicholls *(Nuclear);* Charlie Pate *(Finance);* Lt.-Gen. James Swift, OBE *(Chief of Defence People);* Dominic Wilson *(Security Policy)*
Non-Executive Members, Brian McBride *(Lead);* Simon Henry; Danuta Gray; Robin Marshall

CENTRAL STAFF

Vice-Chief of the Defence Staff, Adm. Sir Tim Fraser, KCB, ADC

STRATEGIC COMMAND

Commander of Strategic Command, Gen. Patrick Sanders, CBE, DSO, ADC
Deputy Commander of Strategic Command, Lt.-Gen. Rob Magowan, CB, CBE
Commander of Joint Operations, Vice-Adm. Benjamin Key, CBE
Chief of Defence Intelligence, Lt.-Gen. Jim Hockenhull, OBE
Chief Defence Logistics Support, Lt.-Gen. Richard Wardlaw, OBE

FLEET COMMAND

First Sea Lord, Adm. Tony Radakin, CB, ADC
Fleet Commander and Chief Naval Warfare Officer, Vice-Adm. Jeremy Kyd, CBE

NAVAL HOME COMMAND

Second Sea Lord, Vice-Adm. Nicholas Hine, CB

LAND FORCES

Commander Field Army, Lt.-Gen. Ivan Jones, CB
Deputy Commander Field Army, Maj.-Gen. Celia Harvey, OBE, QVRM, TD

AIR COMMAND

Deputy Commander Operations and Air Member for Operations, Air Marshal Gerry Mayhew, CBE

Deputy Commander Capability and Air Member for Personnel and Capability, Air Marshal Andrew Turner, CB, CBE

DEFENCE EQUIPMENT AND SUPPORT

Chief Executive, Sir Simon Bollom

Deputy Chief Executive, Adrian Baguley

Director General (Ships), Vice-Adm. Chris Gardner, CBE

Director General (Land), Chris Bushell

Chief of Materiel (Air), Air Marshal Sir Julian Young, CB, KBE

EXECUTIVE AGENCIES

For a full list, *see* Executive Agencies: Ministry of Defence.

DEFENCE ELECTRONICS AND COMPONENTS AGENCY

Welsh Road, Deeside, Flintshire CH5 2LS **T** 01244-847694
E decainfo@deca.mod.uk
W www.gov.uk/defence-electronics-and-components-agency

The Defence Electronics and Components Agency (DECA) provides maintenance, repair, overhaul, upgrade and procurement in avionics, electronics and components fields to support the MoD. As a 'trading' executive agency DECA is run along commercial lines with funding for DECA's activities being generated entirely by payments for delivery of services provided to the MoD and other private sector customers. DECA currently has an annual turnover of around £25m and employs over 400 staff across its head office and main operating centre in North Wales, a site in Stafford and various deployed locations across the UK.

Chief Executive, Geraint Spearing

DEFENCE SCIENCE AND TECHNOLOGY LABORATORY

Porton Down, Salisbury, Wiltshire SP4 0JQ **T** 01980-950000
E centralenquiries@dstl.gov.uk
W www.gov.uk/defence-science-and-technology-laboratory

The Defence Science and Technology Laboratory (DSTL) supplies specialist science and technology services to the MoD and wider government.

Chief Executive, Adrian Belton

UK HYDROGRAPHIC OFFICE

Admiralty Way, Taunton, Somerset TA1 2DN
T 01823-484444
E customerservices@ukho.gov.uk
W www.gov.uk/uk-hydrographic-office

The UK Hydrographic Office (UKHO) collects and supplies hydrographic and geospatial data for the Royal Navy and merchant shipping, to protect lives at sea. Working with other national hydrographic offices, UKHO sets and raises global standards of hydrography, cartography and navigation.

Chief Executive (Acting), Rear-Adm. Peter Sparkes

ARMED FORCES TRAINING AND RECRUITMENT

From Naval Bases at Portsmouth, Plymouth, the Clyde in Scotland and a small team at Northwood in Middlesex, Flag Officer Sea Training (FOST) provides Fleet Operational Sea Training for all surface ships, submarines, Royal Fleet Auxiliaries and Strike Groups of the Royal Navy. All aspects of naval training are offered by FOST including new entry, officer, Royal Marine, submarine, surface and aviation training. FOST also offers specialist training in a number of areas including hydrography, meteorology, oceanography, marine engineering and diving.

The Army Recruiting and Training Division (ARTD) is responsible for the four key areas of army training: soldier initial training, at the School of Infantry or at one of the army's four other facilities; officer initial training at the Royal Military Academy Sandhurst; trade training at one of the army's specialist facilities; and resettlement training for those about to leave the army. Trade training facilities include: the Armour Centre; the Infantry Battle School; the Infantry Training Centre, Catterick; the Royal School of Military Engineering and the Army Aviation Centre.

The Royal Air Force No. 22 (Training) Group is responsible for the recruitment, selection, initial and professional training of RAF personnel as well as providing trained specialist personnel to the armed forces as a whole, such as providing the army air corps with trained helicopter pilots. The group is split into five areas: RAF College Cranwell; the Air Cadet Organisation (ACO); the Directorate of Flying Training (DFT); the Directorate of Ground Training; and the Defence College of Technical Training.

The Defence College of Technical Training provides technical training to all three services and includes the Defence School of Communications Information Systems (DSCIS); the Defence School of Electronic and Mechanical Engineering (DSEME); and the Defence School of Marine Engineering (DSMarE).

USEFUL WEBSITES

W www.royalnavy.mod.uk
W www.army.mod.uk
W www.raf.mod.uk

THE ROYAL NAVY

In Order of Seniority as at 1 January 2021

LORD HIGH ADMIRAL OF THE UNITED KINGDOM
HRH The Prince Philip, Duke of Edinburgh, KG, KT, OM,
GCVO, GBE, GBE, ONZ, QSO, AK, PC, GCL, CMM
apptd 2011

ADMIRALS OF THE FLEET
HRH The Prince Philip, Duke of Edinburgh, KG, KT, OM,
GCVO, GBE, GBE, ONZ, QSO, AK, PC, GCL, CMM,
apptd 1953
Sir Benjamin Bathurst, GCB, *apptd* 1995
HRH The Prince of Wales, KG, KT, GCB, OM, AK, QSO,
CC, ADC, *apptd* 2012
Lord Boyce, KG, GCB, OBE, *apptd* 2014

ADMIRALS
(Former Chiefs or Vice Chiefs of Defence Staff and First Sea
Lords who remain on the active list)
Slater, Sir Jock, GCB, LVO, *apptd* 1991
Essenhigh, Sir Nigel, GCB, *apptd* 1998
West of Spithead, Lord, GCB, DSC, PC, *apptd* 2000
Band, Sir Jonathon, GCB, *apptd* 2002
Stanhope, Sir Mark, GCB, OBE, *apptd* 2004
Zambellas, Sir George, GCB, DSC, *apptd* 2012
Jones, Sir Philip, KCB, ADC, *apptd* 2016
Messenger, Sir Gordon, KBC, DSO *apptd* 2016

ADMIRALS
HRH The Princess Royal, KG, KT, GCVO, QSO *(Adm. Chief
Commandant for Women in the Royal Navy; Cdre-in-Chief
Portsmouth)*
Radakin, Antony, CB, ADC *(First Sea Lord and Chief of Naval
Staff)*
Fraser, Tim, KBC, ADC *(Vice-Chief of the Defence Staff)*

VICE-ADMIRALS
HRH The Duke of York, KG, GCVO, ADC *(Cdre-in-Chief
Fleet Air Arm)*
Key, Benjamin, KCB, CBE *(Chief of Joint Operations)*
Bennett, Paul, CB, OBE *(Chief of Staff, Supreme Allied Cdr
(Transformation))*
Kyd, Jeremy, CBE *(Fleet Cdr and Chief Naval Warfare Officer)*
Gardner, Chris, CBE *(Director General (Ships))*
Hine, Nicholas, CB *(Second Sea Lord and Deputy Chief of Naval
Staff)*
Blount, Keith, CB, OBE *(Cdr Maritime Command)*
Thompson, Richard, CBE *(Director General (Air))*

LIEUTENANT-GENERALS
Magowan, Robert, CB, CBE *(Deputy Cdr UK Strategic
Command)*

REAR-ADMIRALS
Beckett, Keith, CBE *(Chief Strategic Systems Executive)*
Hodgson, Timothy, CB, MBE *(Director Submarine Capability)*
Halton, Paul, OBE *(Director Submarine Readiness)*
Robinson, Guy, OBE *(Deputy Cdr Naval Striking and Support
Forces NATO)*
Briers, Matthew *(Director Carrier Strike)*
Morley, James *(Director Capability UK Strategic Command)*
Toy, Malcolm *(Director (Technical) Military Aviation Authority)*
Kyte, Andrew, CB *(Assistant Chief of the Defence Staff (Logistics
Operations))*

Beard, Hugh *(Assistant Chief of Naval Staff (Capability and Force
Design))*
Connell, Martin, CBE *(Director Force Generation)*
Burns, Andrew, OBE *(Director Develop)*
Marshall, Paul, CBE *(Director Naval Acquisition)*
Macleod, James, CB *(Assistant Chief of Defence Staff (Personnel
Capability) and Defence Services Secretary)*
Hally, Philip, MBE *(Director People and Training; Naval
Secretary)*
Betton, Andrew, OBE *(Deputy Cdr Joint Force Command
Norfolk)*
Asquith, Simon, OBE *(Commander Operations)*
Sparkes, Peter *(National Hydrographer; Chief Executive UK
Hydrographic Office (acting))*
Utley, Michael, CB, OBE *(Commander UK Strike Force)*
Hatcher, Rhett *(Director Data Acquisition)*
Lower, Iain *(Assistant Chief of the Naval Staff)*

ROYAL MARINES

CAPTAIN-GENERAL
Position in abeyance

GENERAL
Messenger, Sir Gordon, KCB, DSO*, OBE, ADC

MAJOR-GENERALS
Bevis, Timothy, CBE *(Director Operations and Plans,
International Military Staff)*
Magowan, Robert, CB, CBE *(Assistant Chief of the Defence Staff
(Capability and Force Design))*
Holmes, Matthew, CBE, DSO *(Cdr UK Amphibious Forces and
Commandant-General Royal Marines)*
Jenkins, Gwyn, OBE *(Assistant Chief of Naval Staff (Policy))*
Stickland, Charles, CB, OBE *(Assistant Chief of the Defence Staff
(Commitments))*
Morris, Jim, DSO *(Director of Joint Warfare)*

The Royal Marines, formed in 1664, are the Royal Navy's
elite, amphibious commando force. Capable of operating in
the littoral, land and maritime environment their principal
operational formation is an all-arms force, 3 Commando
Brigade RM, comprising of:

- 40 and 45 Commando RM, based in Taunton and
  Arbroath, are the force's very high readiness response and
  forward presence units
- 42 Commando RM, based in Plymouth, is the maritime
  operations commando unit. They are optimised for
  boarding operations and maritime interdiction as well as
  partnering and assistance operations alongside key
  international allies
- 47 Commando Raiding Group RM, the commando force's
  surface manoeuvre specialists, provide littoral manoeuvre
  support to the whole force and enable all its activity. They
  are based in Devonport Naval Base, Plymouth
- 43 Commando Fleet Protection Group RM provide
  specialist military support for the protection of the nation's
  strategic nuclear deterrent. They are based in Faslane Naval
  Base, Scotland
- 30 Commando Information Exploitation Group RM are the
  force's information, surveillance and reconnaissance
  specialists. They are based in Plymouth
- Commando Logistics Regiment RM provide intimate
  logistical and medical support to every unit in the force.
  They are located in Chivenor, North Devon

- 24 Commando Royal Engineers and 29 Commando Royal Artillery, based in Chivenor and Plymouth, provide the force with specialist engineering and fires capability

The Royal Marines also provide detachments for warships and land-based naval parties as required.

ROYAL MARINES RESERVES (RMR)

The Royal Marines Reserve is a commando-trained volunteer force with the principal role of supporting the Royal Marines. This can be through mobilisation or other full-time or part-time service. The RMR consists of approximately 670 trained ranks who are distributed between the four RMR Units in the UK. Approximately 10 per cent of the RMR are working with the regular corps on long-term attachments within all of the Royal Marines regular units.

OTHER PARTS OF THE NAVAL SERVICE

FLEET AIR ARM

The Fleet Air Arm (FAA) provides the Royal Navy with a multi-role aviation combat capability able to operate autonomously at short notice worldwide in all environments, over the sea and land. The FAA numbers some 4,500 regulars and 430 reserves. It operates some 200 combat aircraft and more than 50 support/training aircraft.

ROYAL FLEET AUXILIARY (RFA)

The Royal Fleet Auxiliary is a 1,852-strong civilian-manned flotilla of 13 ships owned by the MoD. Its primary role is to supply the Royal Navy and host nations while at sea with fuel, ammunition, food and spares, enabling them to maintain operations away from their home ports. It also provides amphibious support and secure sea transport for military units and their equipment. The ships routinely support and embark Royal Naval Air Squadrons.

ROYAL NAVAL RESERVE (RNR)

The Royal Naval Reserve is an integral part of the Royal Navy. It is an auxiliary and contingent force of around 3,000 trained personnel who provide support to maritime operations and wider defence tasks in peacetime or conflict.

The Royal Naval Reserve has 15 units throughout the UK, one of which, HMS Ferret, provides specialist intelligence capability. Basic training is provided at HMS Raleigh, Torpoint in Cornwall for ratings and at the Britannia Royal Naval College, Dartmouth in Devon for officers.

Reservists usually serve part-time unless mobilised for an operational tour of duty and are expected to fulfil a commitment of 24 days a year, comprising 12 days continuous training and 12 days non-continuous training.

QUEEN ALEXANDRA'S ROYAL NAVAL NURSING SERVICE

The first nursing sisters were appointed to naval hospitals in 1884 and the Queen Alexandra's Royal Naval Nursing Service (QARNNS) gained its current title in 1902. Today QARNNS is a branch of the Royal Naval Medical Service that is committed to supporting the medical component of Royal Naval operational capability. QARNNS trains and employs nurses in a wide variety of specialities including emergency nursing, intensive care, burns and plastics, trauma and orthopaedics, surgical, medical and ophthalmology.

QARNNS is ready to deploy anywhere in the world to support global naval operations; recent deployments have included fighting the Ebola outbreak in Sierra Leone and helping to save lives in the Mediterranean.

Patron, HRH Princess Alexandra, the Hon. Lady Ogilvy, KG, GCVO

Head of the Naval Nursing Service, Capt. Lisa Taylor

HM FLEET
as at December 2020

Submarines	
Vanguard Class	Vanguard, Vengeance, Victorious, Vigilant
Trafalgar Class	Talent, Trenchant, Triumph
Astute Class	Artful, Astute, Ambush, Audacious
Aircraft Carrier	Queen Elizabeth, Prince of Wales
Landing Platform Dock (Albion Class)	Albion, Bulwark
Destroyers	
Daring Class (Type 45)	Daring, Dauntless, Defender, Diamond, Dragon, Duncan
Frigates	
Duke Class (Type 23)	Argyll, Iron Duke, Kent, Lancaster, Monmouth, Montrose, Northumberland, Portland, Richmond, St Albans, Somerset, Sutherland, Westminster
Mine Warfare Vessels	
Hunt Class	Brocklesby, Cattistock, Chiddingfold, Hurworth, Ledbury, Middleton
Sandown Class	Bangor, Blyth, Grimsby, Pembroke, Penzance, Ramsey, Shoreham
Patrol Vessels	
Archer Class P2000 Training Boats	Archer, Biter, Blazer, Charger, Example, Exploit, Explorer, Express, Puncher, Raider, Ranger, Sabre, Scrimatar, Smiter, Tracker, Trumpeter
Pursuer and Dasher Vessels	
Fast Patrol Boats	Sabre, Scimitar
River Class	Forth, Medway, Mersey, Severn, Tamar, Trent, Tyne, Spey
Survey Vessels	
Ice Patrol Ship	Protector
Ocean Survey Vessel	Scott
Coastal Survey Vessel	Magpie
Multi-Role Survey Vessels	Echo, Enterprise

ROYAL FLEET AUXILIARY

Landing Ship Dock (Auxiliary)	RFA Cardigan Bay, RFA Mounts Bay, RFA Lyme Bay
Tide Class	RFS Tideforce, RFA Tiderace, RFA Tidespring, RFA Tidesurge
Wave Class	RFA Wave Knight, RFA Wave Ruler
Fort Class	RFA Fort Austin, RFA Fort Rosalie, RFA Fort Victoria
Casualty Receiving Ship/ Aviation Training Facilities	RFA Argus

THE ARMY

In Order of Seniority as at 1 December 2020

THE QUEEN

FIELD MARSHALS
HRH The Prince Philip, Duke of Edinburgh, KG, KT, OM, GCVO, GBE, GBE, ONZ, QSO, AK, PC, GCL, CMM, *apptd* 1953
Sir John Chapple, GCB, CBE, *apptd* 1992
HRH The Duke of Kent, KG, GCMG, GCVO, ADC, *apptd* 1993
Lord Inge, KG, GCB, PC, *apptd* 1994
HRH The Prince of Wales, KG, KT, GCB, OM, AK, QSO, CC, ADC, *apptd* 2012
Lord Guthrie of Craigiebank, GCB, GCVO, OBE, *apptd* 2012
Lord Walker of Aldringham, GCB, CMG, CBE, *apptd* 2014

FORMER CHIEFS OF STAFF
Gen. Sir Roger Wheeler, GCB, CBE, *apptd* 1997
Gen. Sir Mike Jackson, GCB, CBE, DSO, *apptd* 2003
Gen. Sir Timothy Granville-Chapman, GBE, KCB, *apptd* 2005
Gen. Lord Dannatt, GCB, CBE, MC, *apptd* 2006
Gen. Lord Richards of Herstmonceux, GCB, CBE, DSO, *apptd* 2009
Gen. Lord Houghton of Richmond, GCB, CBE, *apptd* 2009
Gen. Sir Peter Wall, GCB, CBE, *apptd* 2010
Gen. Sir Richard Barrons, KCB, CBE, *apptd* 2013
Gen. Sir Christopher Deverell, KCB, MBE, *apptd* 2016

GENERALS
Carter, Sir Nicholas, KCB, CBE, DSO, ADC *(Chief of the Defence Staff)*
Carleton-Smith, Sir Mark, KCB, CBE, ADC *(Chief of the General Staff)*
Sanders, Sir Patrick, KCB, CBE, DSO, ADC *(Cdr Joint Forces Command)*
Radford, T., CB, DSO, OBE *(Deputy Supreme Allied Cdr Europe)*

LIEUTENANT-GENERALS
Lorimer, Sir John, KCB, DSO, MBE *(Defence Senior Adviser to the Middle East)*
Nugee, R., CB, CVO, CBE *(Climate Change and Sustainability Strategy Lead)*
Cripwell, R., CB, CBE *(Deputy Cdr NATO Land Command Izmir)*
Urch T., CBE *(Cdr Home Command)*
Chalmers, D., DSO, OBE *(Deputy Chief of the Defence Staff (Military Strategy and Operations))*
Hockenhull, J., OBE *(Chief of Defence Intelligence)*
Skeates, S., CBE *(Deputy Cdr Joint Force Command Brunssum)*
Jones, I., CB *(Cdr Field Army)*
Smyth-Osbourne, Sir Edward, KCVO, CBE *(Cdr Allied Rapid Reaction Corps)*
Tickell, C., CBE *(Deputy Chief of the General Staff)*
Wardlaw, R., OBE *(Chief of Defence Logistics and Support)*
Hill, G., CBE *(Deputy Cdr Resolute Support)*
Swift, J., OBE *(Chief of Defence People)*
Bathurst, Sir Ben, KCVO, CBE *(UK Military Representative, HQ NATO)*

MAJOR-GENERALS
Stanford, R., MBE *(Senior British Loan Service Officer – Oman)*
Bramble, W., CBE *(Deputy Cdr NATO Rapid Deployable Corps – Italy)*
Cave, I., CBE *(pending assignment; Cdr Home Command designate (from June 2021))*
Brooks-Ward, S., CVO, OBE, TD, VR *(Assistant Chief of the Defence Staff (Reserves and Cadets))*
Jones, R., CBE *(Standing Joint Force Cdr, Standing Joint Force HQ)*
Hyams, T., OBE *(Military Secretary and General Officer Scotland)*
Borton, N., DSO, MBE *(Chief of Staff (Operations), Permanent Joint HQ; Cdr Allied Rapid Reaction Corps designate (from December 2021))*
Illingworth, J., OBE *(Director Land Warfare)*
Gedney, F., OBE *(pending assignment; Senior British Loan Service Officer (Oman) designate (from January 2021))*
Wooddisse, R., CBE, MC *(Assistant Chief of the General Staff; Crd Field Army designate (from April 2021))*
Capps, D., CBE *(Commandant Royal Military Academy Sandhurst)*
Ford, K., CBE *(Director Policy and Capabilities Division, International Military Staff, HQ NATO)*
Copinger-Symes, T., CBE *(Director Military Digitisation)*
Walker, C., DSO *(MoD; Deputy Chief of Defence Staff (Military Strategy and Operations) designate (from June 2021))*
Cole, J., OBE *(Director Information)*
Deakin, G., CBE *(Deputy Chief of Staff Plans, Joint Force Command Naples)*
Cain, P., QHP *(Director Defence Healthcare)*
Ghika, C., CBE *(GOC London District and Maj.-Gen. The Household Division)*
Sexton, N. *(Director Engagement and Communications)*
Weir, C., DSO, MBE *(Chief of Staff Field Army)*
Bennett, J., CBE *(Director Capability)*
Langston, C., CB, QHC, CF *(Chaplain-General)*
Nesmith, S. *(Director Personnel)*
Hamilton, S., CBE *(Director Support)*
Roe, A. *(Chief Executive Defence Academy and Commandant Joint Service Command and Staff College)*
Strickland, G., DSO, MBE *(Deputy Commanding General, HQ III (USA) Corps)*
Harrison, A., DSO, MBE *(Senior British Military Advisor, US Central Command)*
McMahon, S., CBE *(pending assignment)*
Bruce of Crionaich, A., OBE, VR *(Governor of Edinburgh Castle)*
Taylor A. *(Director Army Legal Services)*
Bowder, J., OBE *(GOC 6th Division)*
Mead, J., OBE *(Chief of Staff, Headquarters Allied Rapid Reaction Corps)*
Spencer, R. *(Director Delivery, Intelligence and Expeditionary Services, Defence Digital Service Delivery and Operations)*
Southall, D., CBE *(Director Army Basing and Infrastructure)*
Thomson, R., CBE, DSO, *(Cdr British Forces Cyprus and Administrator of the Sovereign Base Areas)*
Crook, D., *(Director Land Equipment, Defence Equipment and Support)*
Elviss, M., MBE *(GOC 3rd Division)*
Eastman, D., MBE *(GOC Regional Command)*
Hutchings, OBE *(Director Joint Support, UK Strategic Command)*
Harvey, C., OBE, QVRM, TD, VR *(Deputy Cdr Field Army)*
Bell, C., CBE *(GOC ARITC)*
Humphrey, S., CBE *(pending retirement)*

Walton-Knight, R., CBE *(Director Strategy and Planning, Defence Infrastructure Organisation)*

Amison, D., CBE *(Director Development, Concepts and Doctrine Centre)*

Copsey, K., OBE *(Deputy Cdr Combined Joint Task Force, Operation Inherent Resolve)*

Anderton-Brown, R., *(Director Multi-Domain Integration Change Programme, UK Strategic Command)*

Collins, C., DSO, OBE *(GOC 1st Division)*

Graham, S., VR *(Director Reserves)*

CONSTITUTION OF THE ARMY

The army consists of the Regular Army, the Regular Reserve and the Army Reserve. It is commanded by the Chief of the General Staff, who is the professional Head of Service and Chair of the Executive Committee of the Army Board, which provides overall strategic policy and direction to the Commander Land Forces (formerly Commander-in-Chief, Land Forces). There are four subordinate commands that report to the Commander Land Forces: the Field Army; Support Command, headed by the Adjutant General; Force Development and Capability Command and the Joint Helicopter Command. The army is divided into functional arms and services, subdivided into regiments and corps (listed below in order of precedence).

During 2008, as part of the Future Army Structure (FAS) reform programme, the infantry was re-structured into large multi-battalion regiments, which involved amalgamations and changes in title for some regiments. The main changes at divisional, brigade and unit level occurred largely between mid-2014 and mid-2015. As at April 2020 there were 32 Regular Army battalions in the infantry, 16 Army Reserves battalions and 15 Royal Armoured Corps regiments. The 2010 Strategic Defence and Security Review laid out the commitments expected of the UK Armed Forces and, as a result, Army 2020 was created to replace FAS.

All enquiries with regard to records of serving personnel (Regular and Reserve) should be directed to: The Army Personnel Centre Help Desk, Kentigern House, 65 Brown Street, Glasgow G2 8EX T 0345-600 9663. Enquirers should note that the Army is governed in the release of personal information by various acts of parliament.

ORDER OF PRECEDENCE OF CORPS AND REGIMENTS OF THE BRITISH ARMY

ARMS

HOUSEHOLD CAVALRY
    The Life Guards
    The Blues and Royals (Royal Horse Guards and 1st Dragoons)

ROYAL HORSE ARTILLERY
(when on parade, the Royal Horse Artillery take precedence over the Household Cavalry)

ROYAL ARMOURED CORPS
    1st the Queen's Dragoon Guards
    The Royal Scots Dragoon Guards (Carabiniers and Greys)
    The Royal Dragoon Guards
    The Queen's Royal Hussars (The Queen's Own and Royal Irish)
    The Royal Lancers
    The King's Royal Hussars
    The Light Dragoons
    Royal Tank Regiment

ROYAL REGIMENT OF ARTILLERY
(with the exception of the Royal Horse Artillery (*see* above))

CORPS OF ROYAL ENGINEERS

ROYAL CORPS OF SIGNALS

REGIMENTS OF FOOT GUARDS
    Grenadier Guards
    Coldstream Guards
    Scots Guards
    Irish Guards
    Welsh Guards

REGIMENTS OF INFANTRY
    The Royal Regiment of Scotland
    The Princess of Wales's Royal Regiment (Queen and Royal Hampshire's)
    The Duke of Lancaster's Regiment (King's, Lancashire and Border)
    The Royal Regiment of Fusiliers
    The Royal Anglian Regiment
    The Rifles
    The Yorkshire Regiment
    The Mercian Regiment
    The Royal Welsh
    The Royal Irish Regiment
    The Parachute Regiment
    The Royal Gurkha Rifles

SPECIAL AIR SERVICE

ARMY AIR CORPS

SERVICES

ROYAL ARMY CHAPLAINS' DEPARTMENT

THE ROYAL LOGISTIC CORPS

ROYAL ARMY MEDICAL CORPS

CORPS OF ROYAL ELECTRICAL AND MECHANICAL ENGINEERS

ADJUTANT-GENERAL'S CORPS

ROYAL ARMY VETERINARY CORPS

SMALL ARMS SCHOOL CORPS

ROYAL ARMY DENTAL CORPS

INTELLIGENCE CORPS

ROYAL ARMY PHYSICAL TRAINING CORPS

QUEEN ALEXANDRA'S ROYAL ARMY NURSING CORPS

CORPS OF ARMY MUSIC

THE ROYAL MONMOUTHSHIRE ROYAL ENGINEERS (MILITIA) (THE ARMY RESERVE)

THE HONOURABLE ARTILLERY COMPANY (THE ARMY RESERVE)

REST OF THE ARMY RESERVE

EQUIPMENT

VEHICLES

Combat Vehicles	Bulldog, Challenger 2, Stormer, Warrior
Reconnaissance Vehicles	Coyote, FUCHS, Jackal 2, Samaritan, Sampson, Scimitar, Spartan, Sultan
Protected Patrol Vehicles	Foxhound, Husky, Mastiff, Panther, Ridgback, RWMIK Land Rover, Wolfhound
Engineering Equipment	BR90 Bridge, Challenger Armoured Repair & Recovery Vehicle, Explosive Ordnance Disposal, M3 Amphibious Bridging Vehicle, Terrier, Titan Armoured Bridge Launcher, Trojan Armoured Vehicle
Artillery and Air Defence	AS90, Desert Hawk, L118 Light Gun, M270B1 Multiple Launch Rocket System, Rapier, Starstreak High Verlocity Missile
Aircraft	AH-64E Apache Attack Helicopter, Airbus 135 Juno, Bell 212, Gazelle, Watchkeeper, Wildcat Mk1

THE ARMY RESERVE

The Army Reserve (formerly the Territorial Army (TA)) is part of the UK's reserve land forces and provides support to the regular army at home and overseas. The Army Reserve is divided into three types of unit: national, regional, and sponsored. Army Reserve soldiers serving in regional units complete a minimum of 27 days training a year, comprising some evenings, weekends and an annual two-week camp. National units normally specialise in a specific role or trade, such as logistics, IT, communications or medical services. Members of national units have a lower level of training commitment and complete 19 days training a year. Sponsored reserves are individuals who will serve, as members of the workforce of a company contracted to the MoD, in a military capacity and have agreed to accept a reserve liability to be called up for active service in a crisis. In 2012 the Secretary of State for Defence issued a consultation paper *Future Reserves 2020: Delivering the Nation's Security Together,* which outlined plans to invest an additional £1.8bn in the Reserve Forces over a ten-year period, for the Reserve Forces to be more integrated with the regular forces and to have a more significant role within the armed forces as a whole.

QUEEN ALEXANDRA'S ROYAL ARMY NURSING CORPS

The Queen Alexandra's Royal Army Nursing Corps (QARANC) was founded in 1902 as Queen Alexandra's Imperial Military Nursing Service and gained its present title in 1949. The QARANC has trained nurses for the register since 1950 and also trains and employs healthcare assistants. Nursing officers, Nursing soldiers, healthcare assistants and student nurses of the QARANC deliver a high quality, adaptable and dedicated nursing care wherever the Army needs it and can find themselves working in a variety of settings. These can vary from NHS hospitals with military units, to ground based environments such as medical regiments and field hospitals. QARANC personnel deal with a wide range of medical situations, with civilian and military patients in the UK, to military casualties of war and conflict. Work locations vary between clinical roles and instructional positions at training bases. Currently, Army nurses are based and deployed in the UK, Germany, Cyprus, Canada, Poland, Brunei, Nepal, Kenya and Sierra Leone.

Colonel-in-Chief, HRH The Countess of Wessex, GCVO
Colonels Commandant, Col. Jane Davis, OBE, QVRM, TD; Col. Carol Kefford

THE ROYAL AIR FORCE

As at 31 December 2020

THE QUEEN

MARSHALS OF THE ROYAL AIR FORCE
HRH The Prince Philip, Duke of Edinburgh, KG, KT, OM, GCVO, GBE, GBE, ONZ, QSO, AK, PC, GCL, CMM, *apptd* 1953
HRH The Prince of Wales,KG, KT, GCB, OM, AK, QSO, CC, ADC, *apptd* 2012

FORMER CHIEFS OF THE AIR STAFF

MARSHALS OF THE ROYAL AIR FORCE
Lord Craig of Radley, GCB, OBE, *apptd* 1988
Lord Stirrup, KG, GCB, AFC, *apptd* 2014

AIR CHIEF MARSHALS
Sir Michael Graydon, GCB, CBE, *apptd* 1991
Sir Richard Johns, GCB, KCVO, OBE, *apptd* 1994
Sir Glenn Torpy, GCB, CBE, DSO, *apptd* 2006
Sir Stephen Dalton, GCB, *apptd* 2009
Sir Andrew Pulford, GCB, CBE, *apptd* 2013
Sir Stephen Hillier, KCB, CBE, DFC *apptd* 2016

AIR RANK LIST

AIR CHIEF MARSHALS
Peach, Sir Stuart, GBE, KCB *(Chair of the Military Committee, NATO)*
Wigston, Sir Michael, KCB, CBE, ADC *(Chief of the Air Staff)*

AIR MARSHALS
Young, J., CB, OBE *(pending retirement)*
Stringer, E., CB, CBE *(Director-General Joint Force Development)*
Knighton, R., CB *(Deputy Chief of the Defence Staff, Military Capability)*
Gray, S., CB, OBE *(Director-General Defence Safety Authority)*
Turner, A., CB, CBE *(Deputy Cdr Capability and Air Member for Personnel and Capability)*
Mayhew, G., CBE *(Deputy Cdr Operations and Air Member for Operations)*

AIR VICE-MARSHALS
Bethell, K., CBE *(Director Combat Air; pending retirement)*
Byford, M. *(Chief of Staff (Personnel) and Air Secretary)*
Colman, N., OBE *(Commander Joint Helicopter Command)*
Duguid, I., CB, CBE *(Air Officer Commanding No. 11 Group)*
Ellis, J., *(Chaplain-in-Chief and Director-General Chaplaincy Service (RAF))*
Ellard, S. *(Air Officer Commanding No. 38 Group)*
Gale, I., MBE *(Assistant Chief of the Air Staff (Strategy))*
Gillespie, A., CBE *(Air Officer Commanding No. 2 Group)*
Hart, M., CBE *(Head of Joint Terrorism Analysis Centre)*
Hill, R., CBE *(Director Defence Support Transformation)*
James, W., CBE *(pending retirement)*
Jennings, T., OBE *(Director Legal Services (RAF))*
Maddison, R., OBE *(Air Officer Commanding No. 22 Group)*

Marshall, A., OBE *(Air Officer Commanding No. 1 Group)*
Moore, C., CBE *(Defence Digital Director Service Operations)*
Reid, A., CB, QHP *(Surgeon General)*
Russell, G., CB *(Director Helicopters)*
Sampson, M., CBE, DSO *(Director Ministry of Defence Saudi Armed Forces Projects)*
Shell, S., CB, CBE *(Director Military Aviation Authority)*
Smeath, M., CBE *(Defence Attaché, British Defence Staff, Washington D.C.)*
Smith, A., *(Assistant Chief of Defence Staff (Global Engagement and Military Strategy))*
Smyth, H., OBE *(Director Space)*
Stringer, J., CBE *(Director Strategy, Uk Strategic Command)*
Taylor, L., OBE *(Chief of Staff Capability)*
Tunnicliffe, G., CVO *(Deputy Commandant, Royal College of Defence Studies)*
Vallely, I., OBE *(Cdr Cyber, Intelligence, Surveillance and Reconnaissance)*
Walton, C., QHP *(Director Defence Medical Personnel and Training)*

CONSTITUTION OF THE RAF

The RAF consists of a single command, Air Command, based at RAF High Wycombe. RAF Air Command was formed on 1 April 2007 from the amalgamation of Strike Command and Personnel and Training Command.

Air Command consists of four groups, each organised around specific operational duties. No. 1 Group is the coordinating organisation for the tactical fast-jet forces responsible for attack, offensive support and air defence operations. No. 2 Group provides air combat support including air transport and air-to-air refuelling; intelligence surveillance; targeting and reconnaissance; and force protection. No. 11 Group, formed in 2018, is a multi-domain operations group tasked with co-ordinating and integrating data from air, space and cyber activities into the planning and execution of operations. No. 22 Group recruits personnel and provides trained specialist personnel to the RAF, as well as to the Royal Navy and the Army (*see also* Armed Forces Training and Recruitment).

RAF EQUIPMENT

AIRCRAFT

Combat	F35B Lightning II, Typhoon FGR4
Training	Embraer Phenom 100, Hawk T1, Hawk T2, 120TP Prefect, Texan T1, Tutor T1, Viking T1
Surveillance	P-8A Poseidon, MQ-9 Reaper, RC-135W Rivet Joint, Sentinel R1, E-3D Sentry AEW1, Shadow R1
Transport	Atlas, BAe146, C17 Globemaster III, C-130J Hercules, Voyager

HELICOPTERS

Helicopters	Chinook, Griffin HAR2, Puma HC2
Training	Airbus H135 Juno, Airbus H145 Jupiter
Transport	Leonardo GrandNew

ROYAL AUXILIARY AIR FORCE

The Auxiliary Air Force was formed in 1924 to train an elite corps of civilians to serve their country in flying squadrons in their spare time. In 1947 the force was awarded the prefix 'royal' in recognition of its distinguished war service and the Sovereign's Colour for the RAuxAF was presented in 1989. The RAuxAF continues to recruit civilians who undertake military training in their spare time, with a standard minimum commitment of 27 days a year. With the amendments to the reserve service made under the Defence Reform Act 2014, reservists can now be employed to support the RAF across the full spectrum of military tasks. There are currently 27 squadrons with the RAuxAF, with a total establishment of just under 3,200 posts, with reservist posts being available in the majority of trades.

Air Commodore-in-Chief, HM The Queen
Commandant General, Air Vice-Marshal Ranald Munro, CBE, TD, VR, DL
Inspector, Capt. J. White

PRINCESS MARY'S ROYAL AIR FORCE NURSING SERVICE

The Princess Mary's Royal Air Force Nursing Service (PMRAFNS) was formed on 1 June 1918 as the Royal Air Force Nursing Service. In June 1923, His Majesty King George V gave his royal assent for the Royal Air Force Nursing Service to be known as the Princess Mary's Royal Air Force Nursing Service. The Princess Mary's Royal Air Force Nursing Service (PMRAFNS) is committed to providing a skilled, knowledgeable and able nursing workforce to deliver high quality care, whilst being responsive to the dynamic nature of RAF Nursing in peacetime and on operations.

Patron and Air Chief Commandant, HRH Princess Alexandra, The Hon. Lady Ogilvy, KG, GCVO
Matron-in-Chief, Gp Capt. Fionnuala Bradley

SERVICE SALARIES

Pay16 was introduced on 1 April 2016, replacing the previous Pay 2000 scheme for all regular and reserve personnel on the main pay spines up to and including the rank of Commodore/Brigadier/ Air Commodore (*see* following page for table of relative rank). Compared with Pay 2000 the total number of increments has been reduced and personnel, with the exception of Lieutenants, remain on the same salary for the first two years in rank.

The following rates of pay apply from 1 April 2020 and are rounded to the nearest pound.

The pay rates shown are for army personnel. The rates also apply to personnel of equivalent rank and pay band in the other services.

Rank	Annual Salary
Second Lieutenant	£27,818
LIEUTENANT	
On appointment	£33,436
After 1 year in rank	£34,610
After 2 years in rank	£35,784
After 3 years in rank	£36,958
CAPTAIN	
On appointment	£42,850
After 2 years in rank	£44,201
After 3 years in rank	£45,552
After 4 years in rank	£46,904
After 5 years in rank	£48,255
After 6 years in rank	£49,606
After 7 years in rank	£50,957
MAJOR	
On appointment	£53,975
After 2 years in rank	£55,753
After 3 years in rank	£57,531
After 4 years in rank	£59,309
After 5 years in rank	£61,087
After 10 years in rank	£68,599
After 12 years in rank	£71,370
LIEUTENANT-COLONEL	
On appointment	£75,754
After 2 years in rank	£77,753
After 3 years in rank	£79,741
After 4 years in rank	£81,735
After 5 years in rank	£83,729
After 6 years in rank	£85,723
After 7 years in rank	£87,716
COLONEL	
On appointment	£91,776
After 2 years in rank	£93,295
After 3 years in rank	£94,814
After 4 years in rank	£96,332
After 5 years in rank	£97,851
After 6 years in rank	£99,369
After 7 years in rank	£100,888
BRIGADIER	
On appointment	£109,368
After 2 years in rank	£110,475
After 3 years in rank	£111,581
After 4 years in rank	£112,688
After 5 years in rank	£113,794

PAY SYSTEM FOR SENIOR MILITARY OFFICERS

Pay rates effective as at 1 April 2020 for all military officers of 2* rank and above (excluding medical and dental officers). All pay rates are rounded to the nearest pound.

Rank	Annual Salary
MAJOR-GENERAL (2*)	
Scale 1	£120,800
Scale 2	£123,160
Scale 3	£125,568
Scale 4	£128,024
Scale 5	£130,529
Scale 6	£133,083
LIEUTENANT-GENERAL (3*)	
Scale 1	£140,549
Scale 2	£147,438
Scale 3	£154,671
Scale 4	£160,746
Scale 5	£165,485
Scale 6	£170,367
GENERAL (4*)	
Scale 1	£184,348
Scale 2	£188,956
Scale 3	£193,681
Scale 4	£198,523
Scale 5	£202,493
Scale 6	£206,543

Field Marshal – appointments to this rank will not usually be made in peacetime. The salary for holders of the rank is equivalent to the salary of a 5-star General, a salary created only in times of war. In peacetime, the equivalent rank to Field Marshal is the Chief of the Defence Staff. As at 1 April 2020, the annual salary range for the Chief of the Defence Staff is £265,588–£281,844.

OFFICERS COMMISSIONED FROM THE SENIOR RANKS

Rank	Annual salary
Level 15	£57,274
Level 14	£56,900
Level 13	£56,506
Level 12	£55,743
Level 11	£54,984
Level 10	£54,216
Level 9	£53,452
Level 8	£52,688
Level 7*	£51,735
Level 6	£51,147
Level 5	£50,550
Level 4†	£49,370
Level 3	£48,782
Level 2	£48,181
Level 1‡	£47,005

* Officers commissioned from the ranks with more than 15 years' service enter on level 7

† Officers commissioned from the ranks with between 12 and 15 years' service enter on level 4

‡ Officers commissioned from the ranks with less than 12 years' service enter on level 1

SOLDIERS' SALARIES

Pay16 was introduced on 1 April 2016, replacing the previous Pay 2000 scheme for all regular and reserve personnel on the main pay spines up to and including the rank of Commodore/ Brigadier/ Air Commodore (*see* below for table of relative rank). Rank remains the key determinant of pay, but the 'high' and 'low' bands under the Pay 2000 scheme were removed and replaced with 4 supplements (*Supp.*) under which trades are allocated. All ranks in a particular trade are treated the same for pay supplement purposes. Compared with Pay 2000 the total number of increments has been reduced and personnel remain on increment Level 1 for the first two years in rank, with the exception of Privates who remain on increment Level 2 for two years.

Rates of pay effective from 1 April 2020 (rounded to the nearest pound) are:

Rank	Supp. 1	Supp. 2	Supp. 3	Supp 4
PRIVATE				
Level 1	20,400	–	–	–
Level 2	21,230	–	–	–
Level 3	22,641	22,908	23,185	23,185
Level 4	23,825	24,902	24,451	24,785
Level 5	24,981	25,340	25,790	26,124
Level 6	26,137	26,656	27,202	27,549
LANCE CORPORAL				
(levels 7 to 9 also applicable to Privates)				
Level 7	27,327	27,961	28,507	29,004
Level 8	28,592	29,342	29,916	30,445
Level 9	29,921	30,748	31,397	32,009

CORPORAL				
Level 1	31,870	32,797	33,699	34,536
Level 2	32,721	33,668	34,597	35,432
Level 3	33,206	34,338	35,375	36,263
Level 4	33,660	34,807	36,120	37,135
Level 5	34,139	35,285	36,775	37,875
SERGEANT				
Level 1	35,854	37,061	38,628	39,896
Level 2	36,747	38,043	39,615	41,079
Level 3	37,672	39,071	40,588	42,132
Level 4	38,609	40,200	41,601	43,227
Level 5	39,556	41,221	42,666	44,365
STAFF SERGEANT				
Level 1	40,358	42,056	43,581	45,340
Level 2	40,994	42,789	44,361	46,078
Level 3	41,652	43,449	45,142	46,857
Level 4	42,288	44,085	45,943	47,407
Level 5	42,953	44,749	46,866	48,407
WARRANT OFFICER CLASS II				
(also applicable to Staff Sergeants)				
Level 1	43,896	45,930	48,191	49,762
Level 2	44,836	46,870	48,880	50,289
Level 3	45,725	47,520	49,231	50,664
Level 4	46,500	48,166	49,545	50,979
Level 5	47,293	48,798	49,841	51,275
WARRANT OFFICER CLASS I				
Level 1	50,839	–	–	52,314
Level 2	51,133	–	–	52,761
Level 3	51,717	–	–	53,267
Level 4	52,301	–	–	53,779
Level 5	52,837	–	–	54,262

RELATIVE RANK – ARMED FORCES

Royal Navy
1 Admiral of the Fleet
2 Admiral (Adm.)
3 Vice-Admiral (Vice-Adm.)
4 Rear-Admiral (Rear-Adm.)
5 Commodore (Cdre)
6 Captain (Capt.)
7 Commander (Cdr)
8 Lieutenant-Commander (Lt.-Cdr)
9 Lieutenant (Lt.)
10 Sub-Lieutenant (Sub-Lt.)
11 Midshipman

Army
1 Field Marshal
2 General (Gen.)
3 Lieutenant-General (Lt.-Gen.)
4 Major-General (Maj.-Gen.)
5 Brigadier (Brig.)
6 Colonel (Col.)
7 Lieutenant-Colonel (Lt.-Col.)
8 Major (Maj.)
9 Captain (Capt.)
10 Lieutenant (Lt.)
11 Second Lieutenant (2nd Lt.)

Royal Air Force
1 Marshal of the RAF
2 Air Chief Marshal
3 Air Marshal
4 Air Vice-Marshal
5 Air Commodore (Air Cdre)
6 Group Captain (Gp Capt.)
7 Wing Commander (Wg Cdr)
8 Squadron Leader (Sqn Ldr)
9 Flight Lieutenant (Flt Lt)
10 Flying Officer (FO)
11 Pilot Officer (PO)

EDUCATION

THE UK EDUCATION SYSTEM

The structure of the education system in the UK is a devolved matter with each of the countries of the UK having separate systems under separate governments. There are differences between the school systems in terms of the curriculum, examinations and final qualifications and, at university level, in terms of the nature of some degrees and in the matter of tuition fees. The systems in England, Wales and Northern Ireland are similar and have more in common with one another than the Scottish system, which differs significantly.

Education in England is overseen by the Department for Education (DfE), with university research covered by the Department for Business, Energy and Industrial Strategy (DfBEIS).

Responsibility for education in Wales lies with the Department for Education and Skills (DfES) within the Welsh government. Ministers in the Scottish government are responsible for education in Scotland, led by the directorates of Learning and Lifelong Learning, while in Northern Ireland responsibility lies with the Department of Education and the Department for the Economy within the Northern Ireland government.

DEPARTMENT FOR EDUCATION **T** 0370-000 2288
 W www.gov.uk/government/organisations/
 department-for-education
DEPARTMENT FOR EDUCATION AND SKILLS (DFES)
 T 0300-060 4400 **W** www.gov.wales/topics/educationandskills
SCOTTISH GOVERNMENT – EDUCATION
 T 0300-244 4000 **W** www.gov.scot/education
DEPARTMENT OF EDUCATION (NI) **T** 028-9127 9279
 W www.education-ni.gov.uk
DEPARTMENT FOR THE ECONOMY **T** 028-9052 9900
 W www.economy-ni.gov.uk

RECENT DEVELOPMENTS

All four nations grappled with the fallout from the coronavirus pandemic, with huge financial and learning implications for all. Exams were cancelled in 2020 in all nations, with grades based on teacher assessments. Only Scotland opted to cancel exams in 2021, while England, Wales and Northern Ireland will proceed having made changes to content and assessment. T levels began in earnest in England alongside a focus on further education with changes announced and a white paper planned. Wales continued with moves to reform its education system, with Northern Ireland starting to consider similarly wide ranging reforms.

ENGLAND

- In June 2020 , £1bn was announced to mitigate lost teaching time, including £650m for state schools to lift educational outcomes and a £350m tutoring scheme specifically for the most disadvantaged during 2020–21, while £96m was allocated for small group tutoring to help disadvantaged 16 to 19-year-old students whose studies were disrupted
- GCSE, AS and A-levels were cancelled and grades given based on teachers' judgements in 2020 as a result of COVID-19 disruption to education. In 2021, exams will go ahead with changes to 15 A-level subjects and 25 GCSEs
- From September all new primary school pupils will take the new reception baseline assessment (RBA) that will replace SATs in year 2. The one-to-one exercise done in 20 minutes with a teacher in an informal setting will be taken by all children in their first six weeks of primary school
- 'Early adopter' schools began using the revised Early Years Foundation Stage (EYFS) framework in September, before statutory national roll out in September 2021. The reforms focus on improving outcomes in language, literacy and maths and cut paperwork for teachers so they can spend more time teaching and interacting with pupils
- Pupil funding rose in 2021 to a minimum of £5,150 per secondary pupil and a minimum of £4,000 per primary pupil as part of a £14.4bn three-year settlement
- Up to 3,000 new school places are to be created for children with special educational needs and disabilities (SEND), providing tailored support and specialist equipment. Staffed by specially trained teachers, the 35 new special free schools are expected from September 2022
- Schools in England will get £320m towards sport and physical education in 2020–21
- The government agreed a 3.1 per cent overall pay rise for teachers, including increasing the starting salary for new teachers by 5.5 per cent and the upper and lower boundaries of the pay ranges for all other teachers by 2.75 per cent. There is a commitment to increase teachers' starting salaries to £30,000 by 2022–23. It sought advice on new national professional qualifications to help teachers progress their careers, as part of a teacher recruitment and retention strategy
- The government will help employers and FE providers deliver the high-quality industry placements required of new T Level qualifications by providing new guidance for employers and students, extending the Employer Support Fund pilot and procuring an organisation with the appropriate expertise to support 2020, 2021 and 2022 providers. Over 180 education providers will be able to deliver a range of high-quality T Level courses from 2022, across subject areas such as Law, Engineering and Manufacturing, Digital, Construction, Health, Science and Education. Investment of £95 through the T Level Capital Fund and £15m for the T Level Professional Development (TLPD)
- In August 2019, £400m was announced for school sixth forms and colleges in 2020–21, including: £65m to cover the cost of delivering courses in six expensive subject areas: building and construction, hospitality and catering, engineering, transportation operations and maintenance, manufacturing technologies and science; and £55m for high value courses such as STEM subjects; and £35m for students on level 3 courses (A-level equivalent) who have not yet achieved a GCSE pass in maths and English
- A 10-year schools and colleges rebuilding programme will start in 2020–21 with the first 50 projects, supported by over £1bn in funding. Investment will be targeted at school buildings in the worst condition across England, including substantial investment in the North and the Midlands
- More than 180 colleges will receive a share of £200m to repair and refurbish buildings and campuses, as part of a £1.5bn investment to transform colleges over the next five years
- 20 colleges will divide £5.4m to share good practice, knowledge and experience to drive up the standard of education and training on offer to their local communities, including support to develop high quality digital content to provide improved remote and blended learning

- An overhaul of technical and vocational education in Britain will see lesser known qualifications that sit between A-level and degrees, such as CertHE, DipHE and foundation degrees, rebranded as 'Higher Technical Qualifications' and quality approved to attract more people to study them. Employers will define the skills and requirements needed, then newly approved digital qualifications are due to start in 2022, with health, sciences and construction qualifications to follow in 2023. The Institute for Apprenticeships and Technical Education will work with Ofsted and the Office for Students to make sure the quality of courses is consistently high across HE and FE institutions
- Other measures to transform technical education included £120m to establish up to eight more Institutes of Technology, collaborations between FE colleges, universities and employers offering higher technical education and training mainly at Levels 4 and 5 (above A-levels and T levels but below degree level) in key sectors such as digital, construction, advanced manufacturing and engineering
- Efforts to stabilise university research after COVID-19 were made in May, June and September 2020, including a funding scheme to cover up to 80 per cent of a university's income losses from a decline in international students, £200m to support researchers' salaries across the UK, and £80m redistributed from existing UK Research and Innovation funds. Bureaucracy in universities and research will also be reduced to help focus on high-quality teaching and research
- £100m of public funding was brought forward to 2020–21 to help protect vital university research activities, and around £2.6bn of tuition fee payments to help universities manage financial risks
- A temporary limit was set on the number of full-time undergraduate UK and EU students English higher education providers could recruit for 2020–21, based on their forecasts for the next academic year, plus an additional 5 per cent. The government also allowed for a discretionary 10,000 extra places, with 5,000 ring-fenced for nursing, midwifery or allied health courses to support the country's vital public services
- Students studying to become paramedics, radiographers and physiotherapists will be among those receiving £5,000 maintenance grants from September 2020. Extra payments worth up to £3,000 per academic year will be available for eligible students
- £24m was pledged to 18 universities and partners to deliver 2,500 places on artificial intelligence and data science conversion courses in 28 universities and colleges in England, with 1,000 scholarships offered to students from underrepresented backgrounds
- England's first Space Engineering Technician apprenticeship will be available to students from January 2021. A degree equivalent (level 6) space engineering diploma is expected to be available to students from September 2021
- Students in England could receive university offers only once they have obtained their final grades under proposals to change the current admissions system. The government plans to consult on proposals for post-qualification university admissions that would remove the unfairness of inaccurate predicated grades. This will not affect university applications for 2021 and different options will be assessed after the consultation ends

WALES

- A level, AS, GCSE, Skills Challenge Certificate and Welsh Baccalaureate grades in Wales were awarded on the basis of centre assessment grades. In summer 2021, current AS learners will choose whether to only sit the A2 units, with the A level grade based on their performance in the A2 units, or sit both the AS and A2 units and be awarded the best grade from either route. Those due to sit GCSE will sit only the units they plan to take in summer 2021, with their GCSE grade based on that performance only, or sit the Year 10 units in summer 2021, along with the Year 11 units. They will be awarded the best grade from either route
- A new Early Childhood Education and Care (ECEC) approach launched in 2019 that will reform the provision of early years care to ensure children get the best possible start in life
- Revised guidance on Curriculum for Wales was published and an additional £15m given to support teachers preparing for its implementation
- A new Additional Learning Needs code and regulations are expected to be brought to the assembly in February 2021 to start in September 2021
- The government agreed an overall pay rise of 3.1 per cent – 3.75 per cent for teachers on the main pay scale – while starting salaries for new teachers increased by 8.48 per cent, performance-related pay progression ended and national pay scales were reintroduced. College staff received a pay rise of 2.75 per cent to bring their pay level to that of schoolteachers
- A new all-Wales 'National Masters in Education' programme will be available for teaching from September 2021. The Welsh government will support up to 500 early career education professionals to take the qualification. The aim is to strengthen recruitment and retention, professional learning and the relationship between the HE sector and Wales' education reform programme
- The £10m Skills Development Fund designed for colleges to address gaps in job-specific skills in their areas, as identified by local employers, will continue. £5m will again be available for colleges to invest in staff professional development, including developing digital and Welsh-language skills
- Funding for 2020–21 included £5m to cover the costs of safely bringing back FE learners to take qualifications; £15m for catch up costs of 16–19 learners, £460,000 to support additional costs of allowing Independent Living Skills learners to return to college in September, and nearly £18m to cover the costs of bringing vocational learners safely back for practical face-to-face learning
- A COVID-19 resilience plan stopped performance measures for further education, work-based learning and adult learning outcomes from being produced for 2019–20 and suspended Estyn inspections
- A vision for post compulsory education and training sector (PCET) was unveiled in November 2020 to combat Brexit, COVID-19 and climate change. A new Commission for Tertiary Education and Research (CTER), as proposed in the draft Tertiary Education and Research (Wales) Bill – the introduction of which was delayed to 2021 after COVID-19 – would have extensive funding, planning and regulatory powers, enabling it to improve quality, efficiency and efficacy across the higher education sector. It would bring together further education, including sixth forms, adult community learning, work-based learning and universities

SCOTLAND

- In its work programme for 2020–21, the Scottish government set out measures to help mitigate the impact of COVID-19. These included: a 'Youth Guarantee' to keep 19 to 24-year-olds in training, work or education; £2m to help residential outdoor education; £50m to recruit new teachers and support staff; £1.5m for school staff, and £5m to tackle digital exclusion. An Education Recovery Group was set up to help schools and universities return after lockdown

- In 2020, exams were cancelled and qualifications were awarded based on teacher estimates. Higher and Advanced Higher exams will not go ahead in 2021 either, replaced again with awards based on teacher judgement of pupils' attainment
- Children and young people with additional support needs will be now be directly involved in the decisions that affect them following an independent review. A progress report is due in October 2021
- The government invested a further £182m in the Attainment Scotland Fund and confirmed more than £250m of Pupil Equity Funding will be made available to 97 per cent of schools in 2020–21 and 2021–22
- A new £15m Apprenticeship Employer Grant will help increase the number of employers able to take on an apprentice or help employees obtain new skills. Pathway Apprenticeships will help school leavers up to age 18 train and get qualifications through 1,200 work experience, volunteering and work-based learning opportunities
- A range of measures to support colleges and universities included a one-off £75m to universities to protect world-leading research, £10m for estates development, and early access to £11.4m of Higher Education Hardship Funds. The Scottish Funding Council estimated the country's universities would lose around £72m in academic year 2019–20 as a result of COVID-19 and predicted an operating deficit of between £384m and £651m in 2020–21 as the number of international students decline
- It was confirmed that EU students will have to pay tuition fees from 2021–22 unless Scotland rejoins the EU

NORTHERN IRELAND
- GCSE, AS and A-level exams will go ahead in 2021, with more generous grading across all qualifications, significant reductions in content to be assessed, support materials for GCSE maths and a reserve examination series in early July for A2 candidates who miss exams through illness or self-isolating. Year 14 pupils will not have to take AS examinations and, in the majority of GCSE qualifications a specified module will be omitted from assessment. All assessments in GCSE Maths will be retained but the speaking and listening component for GCSE English Language will be omitted. The timetable for the summer exam series will be delayed by one week with exams starting no earlier than 12 May 2021, but concluding by 30 June. Results will issue at the end of August
- A *New Decade New Approach* set out the priorities of the newly restored Northern Ireland Assembly in January 2020. A wide-ranging review of education will consider the education journey and outcomes of children and young people, support for schools and settings, and system level design. It will begin later in 2021 once an independent panel is appointed. It is expected to last 18 months
- A consultation on how to improve provision of education for children and young people with special educational needs launched, along with £7.5m for a new SEN framework to provide additional resources for schools. Proposed changes include a defined period in which assessments must be carried out and decisions implemented. Children and parents will also have new rights that will ensure services meet their needs. The Education Authority will be required to publish an annual plan of SEN provision arrangements and each child with SEN will be required to have a Personal Learning Plan. Each school will have to have a Learning Support Coordinator
- This followed the Children and Young People's Strategy 2019–29 unveiled in December 2019 that set out a strategic

framework for improving the well-being of children and young people in Northern Ireland. One goal, that children and young people 'learn and achieve', will include a Department of Education led programme to transform the education system
- Almost £64m to help schools manage Education Authority pressures, COVID-19 pressures and for free school meals was announced in October 2020. It included £49.4m to cover additional costs and £12.8m for special educational needs. A further £1.4m went towards providing free school meals over the extended half-term break
- Up to £4m will be invested in new and existing nurture groups across Northern Ireland in 2020–21, including establishing 15 new and funding 31 existing nurture groups in primary schools, and a Nurture Advisory Service in the Education Authority
- A pay rise for teachers was agreed in April 2020, ending all industrial action. All teachers in Northern Ireland were awarded a pay rise of 2.25 per cent payable from September 2017 and an additional 2 per cent payable from September 2018
- Some 12 primary schools, five post-primary schools and one special school will benefit from an estimated capital investment of £45m under the Schools Enhancement Programme
- In FE, the Northern Regional College will get a £40m boost to develop its campus, and £4.6m for 3,000 free online digital skills training places for people whose employment was disrupted by the pandemic
- In HE, £5.6m was set aside to alleviate student hardship in 2020–21

STATE SCHOOL SYSTEM

PRE-SCHOOL
Pre-school education is not compulsory.

In England, a free place is available for every 3- and 4-year-old whose parents want one, although parents may use as little or as much of their entitlement as they choose. All 3- and 4-year-olds, and disadvantaged 2-year-olds, are entitled to 15 hours a week of free early education over 38 weeks of the year until they reach compulsory school age (the term following their fifth birthday). Working parents of 3- and 4-year-old children may be eligible for up to 30 hours free childcare. Free places are funded by local authorities and are delivered by a range of approved providers in the maintained and non-maintained sectors: nursery schools, nursery classes in primary schools, private schools, private day nurseries, voluntary playgroups, pre-schools and registered childminders. In order to receive funding, providers must be working towards the early learning goals and the Early Years Foundation Stage curriculum, must be inspected on a regular basis by Ofsted and must meet any conditions set by the local authority.

In Wales, every child is entitled to receive free Foundation Phase education for a minimum of two hours a day from the term following their third birthday. The Flying Start scheme allows disadvantaged 2- to 3-year-olds 2.5 hours childcare a week for 39 weeks. Up to 30 hours a week of free childcare is available to working parents of 3- to 4-year-olds from 2020, made up of a minimum of 10 hours early education and a maximum of 20 hours of childcare.

In Scotland, councils have a duty to provide a pre-school education for all 3- and 4-year-olds, and some disadvantaged 2- to 3-year-olds, whose parents request one. From August 2020, education authorities were obliged to offer 1,140 hours of free pre-school education a year, but this was revoked in March 2020 to allow local authorities to focus on the pandemic response (*see also* Recent Developments).

In Northern Ireland, pre-school education is available to all children in the year before they are due to start primary one. Most settings offer 2.5 hours a day, five days a week for at least 38 weeks a year, but some offer full-time places of 4.5 hours a day.

PRIMARY AND SECONDARY SCHOOLS

By law, full-time education starts at the age of five for children in England, Scotland and Wales and at the age of four in Northern Ireland (where the child's age after 1 July determines when they start). In practice, most children in the UK start school before their fifth birthday: in England all children are entitled to a primary school place from the September after their fourth birthday.

Children in England are required to stay in education or training until the end of the academic year in which they turn 18. In all other parts of the UK, compulsory schooling ends at age 16, but children born between certain dates may leave school before their 16th birthday; most young people stay in some form of education until 17 or 18.

Primary education consists mainly of infant schools for children aged 5 to 7, junior schools for those aged 7 to 11, and combined infant and junior schools for both age groups. Scotland has only primary schools with no infant/junior division.

In a few parts of England there are schools catering for ages 5 to 10 as the first stage of a three-tier system of first (lower), middle and secondary (upper) schools.

Children usually leave primary school and move on to secondary school at the age of 11 (or 12 in Scotland). In the few areas of England that have a three-tier system, middle schools cater for children for three to four years between the ages of 8 and 14, depending on the local authority.

Secondary schools cater for children aged 11 to 16 and, if they have a sixth form, for those who choose to stay on to the age of 18. From the age of 16, students may move instead to further education colleges or work-based training.

Most UK secondary schools are co-educational. The largest secondary schools have more than 1,500 pupils and around 60 per cent of secondary pupils in the UK are in schools that take more than 1,000 pupils.

Most state-maintained secondary schools in England, Wales and Scotland are comprehensive schools, which admit pupils without reference to ability. In England there remain some areas with grammar schools, catering for pupils aged 11 to 18, which select pupils on the basis of high academic ability. Nearly two-thirds of state secondary schools in England (2,700) are now academies: academies are funded directly by the state rather than being maintained by local authorities. Northern Ireland still has 66 grammar schools; the 11-plus has been officially discontinued but schools, or consortia of schools, use their own unregulated entry tests.

More than 90 per cent of pupils in the UK attend publicly funded schools and receive free education. The rest (6.5 per cent) attend privately funded 'independent' schools which charge fees, or are educated at home.

The bulk of the UK government's expenditure on school education is through local authorities (Education and Library Boards (ELBs) in Northern Ireland), which pass on state funding to schools and other educational institutions.

SPECIAL EDUCATION

Schools and local authorities in England and Wales, Education and Library Boards (ELBs) in Northern Ireland and education authorities in Scotland are required to identify and secure provision for children with special educational needs and to involve parents in decisions (see also Recent Developments.) The majority of children with special educational needs are educated in ordinary mainstream schools, sometimes with supplementary help from outside specialists. Parents of children with special educational needs (referred to as additional support needs in Scotland and additional learning needs in Wales) have a right of appeal to independent tribunals if their wishes are not met.

Special educational needs provision may be made in maintained special schools, special units attached to mainstream schools or in mainstream classes themselves, all funded by local authorities. There are also non-maintained special schools run by voluntary bodies, mainly charities, who may receive grants from central government for capital expenditure and equipment but whose other costs are met primarily from the fees charged to local authorities for pupils placed in the schools. Some independent schools also provide education wholly or mainly for children with special educational needs.

ADDITIONAL SUPPORT NEEDS TRIBUNALS FOR
    SCOTLAND **T** 0141-302 5860
    W www.healthandeducationchamber.scot
FIRST-TIER TRIBUNAL (SPECIAL EDUCATIONAL
    NEEDS AND DISABILITY) **T** 01325-289350
    W www.gov.uk/special-educational-needs-disability-tribunal
INFORMATION ADVICE AND SUPPORT SERVICES
    NETWORK FOR SEND **E** iassn@ncb.org.uk
    W https://councilfordisabledchildren.org.uk/
    information-advice-and-support-services-network
SPECIAL EDUCATIONAL NEEDS TRIBUNAL FOR
    WALES **T** 01597-829800 **W** www.sentw.gov.uk

HOME EDUCATION

In England and Wales parents have the right to educate their children at home and do not have to be qualified teachers to do so. Home-educated children do not have to follow the National Curriculum or take national tests. Nor do they need a fixed timetable, formal lessons or to observe school hours, days or terms. However, by law parents must ensure that the home education provided is full-time and suitable for the child's age, ability and aptitude and, if appropriate, for any special educational needs. Parents have no legal obligation to notify the local authority that a child is being educated at home, but if they take a child out of school, they must notify the school in writing and the school must report this to the local authority. Local authorities can make informal enquiries of parents to establish that a suitable education is being provided. For children in special schools, parents must seek the consent of the local authority before taking steps to educate them at home.

In Northern Ireland, ELBs monitor the quality of home provision and provide general guidance on appropriate materials and exam types through regular home visits.

The home schooling law in Scotland is similar to that of England. One difference, however, is that if parents wish to take a child out of school they must have permission from the local education authority.

HOME EDUCATION ADVISORY SERVICE
    T 01707-371854 **W** www.heas.org.uk
HOME EDUCATION IN NORTHERN IRELAND
    W www.hedni.org
SCHOOLHOUSE HOME EDUCATION ASSOCIATION
    (SCOTLAND) **T** 01307-463120
    E contact@schoolhouse.org.uk **W** www.schoolhouse.org.uk
EDUCATION OTHERWISE **T** 0845-4786345
    W www.educationotherwise.org

FURTHER EDUCATION

In the UK, further education (FE) is generally understood as post-secondary education, ie any education undertaken after an individual leaves school that is below higher education level. FE therefore embraces a wide range of general and vocational study, full-time or part-time, undertaken by people of all ages from 16 upwards who may be self-funded, employer-funded or state-funded.

There are three types of technical and applied qualifications for 16- to 19-year-olds: level 3 tech levels which equip people to specialise in specific technical jobs; level 2 technical certificates to help them get employment or progress to another tech level; and applied general qualifications which prepare them to continue general education at advanced level through applied learning.

FE in the UK is often undertaken at further education colleges, although some takes place on employers' premises. Many of these colleges offer some courses at higher education level; some FE colleges teach certain subjects to 14- to 16-year-olds under collaborative arrangements with schools. Colleges' income comes from public funding, student fees and work for and with employers.

HIGHER EDUCATION

Higher education (HE) in the UK describes courses of study, provided in universities, specialist colleges of higher education and in some FE colleges, where the level of instruction is above that of A-level or equivalent exams.

All UK universities and colleges that provide HE are autonomous bodies with their own internal systems of governance. They are not owned by the state. However, most receive a portion of their income from state funds distributed by the Office for Students in England, the Higher Education Funding Council for Wales, the Scottish Funding Council or the Department for the Economy in Northern Ireland. The rest of their income comes from a number of sources including fees from home and overseas students, government funding for research, endowments and work with or for business.

EXPENDITURE

PUBLIC SECTOR EXPENDITURE ON EDUCATION
(Real terms adjusted to 2019–20 price levels) £bn

2014–15	93.0
2015–16	92.1
2016–17	89.6
2017–18	89.8
2018–19	92.4

Source: HM Treasury – *Public Expenditure Statistical Analyses (PESA)* July 2020

SCHOOLS

UK SCHOOLS BY CATEGORY

	England	Wales
Maintained nursery schools	389	9
*Maintained primary schools	16,784	1,247
Maintained secondary schools	3,456	183
Pupil Referral Units	349	–
Maintained Special schools	993	41
†Non-maintained Special schools	58	–
†Academies	9,041	–
‡Independent schools	2,331	75
Total	24,360	1,555

* Includes 107 middle schools in England and 22 in Wales

† Includes City Technology Colleges, University Technology Colleges, studio schools and free schools; excludes voluntary and private pre-school education centres and academies and free schools alternative provision
‡ Data as at 2019 as not collected in 2020 owing to the coronavirus pandemic
Source: DfE & Welsh government, January 2020

SCOTLAND

Publicly funded schools	5,052
Nursery	2,576
Primary	2,004
Secondary	358
Special	114
Independent schools	92
Total	5,144

Source: Scottish government, December 2020

NORTHERN IRELAND

Maintained nursery schools	95
Maintained primary schools	794
Maintained secondary schools	127
Grammar schools	66
*Special schools	40
Independent schools	14
Total	1,136

* Includes one hospital school
Source: DENI, February 2020

ENGLAND AND WALES

In England and Wales, publicly funded schools are referred to as 'state schools'. Local authorities have a duty to ensure there is a suitable place for every school-age child resident in their area.

The most common types of state funded school are:
* *community schools*, which are sometimes called local authority maintained schools. They are not influenced by business or religious groups and follow the national curriculum
* *foundation schools* and *voluntary schools*, which are funded by the local authority but have more freedom to change the way they do things. Sometimes they are supported by representatives from religious groups
* *academies* and *free schools*, which are run by not-for-profit academy trusts, independent from the local authority. They have more freedom to change how they run things and can follow a different curriculum
* *grammar schools*, which can be run by the local authority, a foundation body or an academy trust; they select pupils based on academic ability

Special schools with pupils aged 11 and older can specialise in one of the four areas of special educational needs: communication and interaction; cognition and learning; social, emotional and mental health; sensory and physical needs.

Faith schools have to follow the national curriculum, but they can choose what they teach in religious studies. They may have different admissions criteria and staffing policies to state schools, although anyone can apply for a place. *Faith academies* do not have to teach the national curriculum and have their own admissions processes.

Free schools are funded by the government but are not run by the local authority so have more control over how they do things and do not have to follow the national curriculum. They are "all-ability" schools so cannot use academic selection processes. They are run on a not-for-profit basis and can be set up by groups like: charities; universities; independent schools; community and faith groups; teachers; parents and businesses.

University technical colleges specialising in subjects like engineering and construction are a type of free school where pupils study academic and practical subjects leading to technical qualifications. *Studio schools* are small free schools teaching mainstream qualifications through project-based learning.

Academies are run by an academy trust with more control over how they do things than community schools. They are inspected by Ofsted and have to follow the same rules on admissions, special educational needs and exclusion as other state schools and students sit the same exams. Academies have greater freedoms over how they use their budgets, set staff pay and conditions and deliver the curriculum. They do not have to follow the national curriculum and can set their own term times.

England now has increasing numbers of Academies. Those set up before the Academies Act 2010 were sponsored by business, faith or voluntary groups who contributed to funding their land and buildings, while the government covered the running costs at a level comparable to other local schools. The Academies Act 2010 streamlined the process of becoming an academy, enabled high-performing schools to convert without a sponsor and allowed primary and special schools to become academies. All academies now receive funding from central government at the level they would have received if still maintained by their local authority, with extra funding only to cover those services the local authority no longer provides. As at October 2020 there were 9,323 open academies, 85.8 per cent of all state-funded schools.

All but three *City technology colleges* – independent schools in urban areas that are free to go to – have now converted into academies.

State boarding schools provide free education but charge fees for boarding. Most are academies, some are free schools and some are run by local authorities.

Private or 'independent' schools charge fees to attend instead of being funded by the government. Pupils do not have to follow the national curriculum. They must be registered with the government and are inspected regularly.

In Wales, Welsh-medium primary and secondary schools were first established in the 1950s and 1960s, originally in response to the wishes of Welsh-speaking parents who wanted their children to be educated through the medium of the Welsh language. Now, many children who are not from Welsh-speaking homes also attend Welsh-medium and bilingual schools throughout Wales. There are 420 Welsh-medium primary schools where instruction is mainly or solely in the Welsh language, six Welsh-medium middle schools and 49 Welsh-medium secondary schools, where more than half of foundation subjects (other than English and Welsh) and religious education are taught wholly or partly in Welsh.

SCOTLAND

Most schools in Scotland, known as 'publicly funded' schools, are state-funded and charge no fees. Funding is met from resources raised by the Scottish local authorities and from an annual grant from the Scottish government. Scotland does not have school governing bodies like the rest of the UK: local authorities retain greater responsibility for the management and performance of publicly funded schools. Headteachers manage at least 80 per cent of a school's budget, covering staffing, furnishings, repairs, supplies, services and energy costs. Spending on new buildings, modernisation projects and equipment is financed by the local authority within the limits set by the Scottish government.

Scotland has 370 state-funded *faith schools*, the majority of which are Catholic. It has no grammar schools.

Integrated community schools form part of the Scottish government's strategy to promote social inclusion and to raise educational standards. They encourage closer and better joint working among education, health and social work agencies and professionals, greater pupil and parental involvement in schools, and improved support and service provision for vulnerable children and young people.

Scotland has eight *grant-aided schools* that are independent of local authorities but supported financially by the Scottish government. These schools are managed by boards and most of them provide education for children and young people with special educational needs.

NORTHERN IRELAND

Most schools in Northern Ireland are maintained by the state and generally charge no fees, though fees may be charged in preparatory departments of some grammar schools. There are different types of state-funded schools, each under the control of management committees, which also employ the teachers.

Controlled schools (nursery, primary, special, secondary and grammar schools) are managed by Northern Ireland's five ELBs through boards of governors consisting of teachers, parents, members of the ELB and transferor representatives (mainly from the Protestant churches).

Catholic maintained schools (nursery, primary, special and secondary) are under the management of boards of governors consisting of teachers, parents and members nominated by the employing authority, the Council for Catholic Maintained Schools (CCMS).

Other maintained schools (primary, special and secondary) are, in the main, Irish-medium schools that provide education in an Irish-speaking environment. The Department of Education has a duty to encourage and facilitate the development of Irish-medium education. Northern Ireland has 29 standalone Irish-medium schools, most of them primary schools, and 11 Irish-medium units attached to English-medium host schools.

Voluntary schools are mainly grammar schools (66 in 2020), which select most pupils according to academic ability. They are managed by boards of governors consisting of teachers, parents and, in most cases, representatives from the Department of Education and the ELB.

Integrated schools (primary and secondary) educate pupils from both the Protestant and Catholic communities as well as those of other faiths and no faith; each school is managed by a board of governors. There are at present 65 integrated schools maintained by the state, 27 of which are controlled schools.

Since 2013 all pupils are guaranteed access to a wide range of courses, with a minimum of 24 courses at Key Stage 4, and 27 at post-16. At least one-third of the courses on offer will be academic and another third will be vocational. Schools work with other schools, FE colleges and other providers to widen the range of courses on offer.

INDEPENDENT SCHOOLS

Around 6.5 per cent of UK schoolchildren are educated by privately funded 'independent' schools that charge fees and set their own admissions policies. Independent schools are required to meet certain minimum standards but need not teach the National Curriculum. *See also* Independent Schools.

INSPECTION

ENGLAND

The Office for Standards in Education, Children's Services and Skills (Ofsted) is the main body responsible for inspecting education in English schools. As well as inspecting all publicly funded and some independent schools, Ofsted inspects a range of other services in England, including childcare, children's homes, pupil referral units, local authority children's services, further education, initial teacher training and publicly funded adult skills training. Inspection reports, recommendations and statistical information are published on Ofsted's website.

Ofsted is an independent, non-ministerial government department that reports directly to parliament, headed by Her Majesty's Chief Inspector (HMCI). Ofsted is required to promote improvement in the public services that it inspects; ensure that these services focus on the interests of their users – children, parents, learners and employers; and see that these services are efficient, effective and promote value for money. A new 'common inspection regime' came into effect in September 2015 to make inspections of different settings with similar age groups more coherent.

Since September 2019, Ofsted adopted a revised inspection framework focused less on exam and test results, more on the quality, breadth and depth of the education provided and on supporting underperforming schools. Inspectors' view of an education provider's overall effectiveness will be based on four other judgements: quality of education; students' behaviour and attitudes; their personal development; and leadership and management. Judgements will still be expressed using continue to be awarded under the current four-point grading scale: outstanding; good; requires improvement; and inadequate.

OFFICE FOR STANDARDS IN EDUCATION,
   CHILDREN'S SERVICES AND SKILLS T 0300-123 1231
   W www.gov.uk/government/organisations/ofsted

WALES
Estyn is the education and training inspectorate for Wales. It is independent of, but funded by, the Welsh government and is led by Her Majesty's Chief Inspector of Education and Training in Wales.

Estyn's role is to inspect quality and standards in education and training in Wales, including in primary, secondary, special and independent schools, pupil referral units, publicly funded nursery schools and settings, further education, adult community-based and work-based learning, local authorities and teacher education and training.

Estyn also provides advice on quality and standards in education and training to the Welsh government and others and its remit includes making public good practice based on inspection evidence. Estyn publishes on its website the findings of its inspection reports, its recommendations and statistical information.

The inspection regime will be suspended from September 2020 to August 2021 to enable Estyn to make changes to the system in line with the education reforms in Wales.

HER MAJESTY'S INSPECTORATE FOR EDUCATION
   AND TRAINING IN WALES T 029-2044 6446
   W www.estyn.gov.uk

SCOTLAND
Education Scotland is in charge of inspection and review, supporting quality and improvement in Scottish education. The executive agency of the Scottish government operates independently and impartially while being directly accountable to Scottish ministers for the standards of its work. The agency is responsible for delivering measurable year-on-year improvements, with maximum efficiency, by promoting excellence, building on strengths, and identifying and addressing underperformance. Since August 2015, inspections take account of national expectations of progress in implementing Curriculum for Excellence.

Inspection reports and reviews, recommendations, examples of good practice and statistical information are published on Education Scotland's website.

EDUCATION SCOTLAND T 0131-244 4330 W https://education.gov.scot

NORTHERN IRELAND
The Education and Training Inspectorate (ETINI) provides inspection services for the Department of Education and the Department for the Economy in Northern Ireland.

ETINI carries out inspections of all schools, pre-school services, special education, further education colleges, initial teacher training, training organisations, and curriculum advisory and support services. ETINI carries out a Sustaining Improvement Inspection (SII) for 'high capacity' special, primary and post-primary schools and Monitoring Inspection (MIn) is more proportionate to risk and aims to focus resources where they will have most impact on learners. Schools are notified 48 hours before either inspection, or two weeks before a full inspection.Since September 2013 regional colleges of further education have received four weeks' notice of inspection, while all other organisations have received two weeks' notice. All inspections were paused on 18 March 2020 until further notice to support schools during the challenge of COVID-19.

The inspectorate's role is to improve services and provide ministers with evidence-based advice to assist in policy formulation. It publishes the findings of its inspection reports, its recommendations and statistical information on its website.

EDUCATION AND TRAINING INSPECTORATE
   T 028-9127 9726 W www.etini.gov.uk

THE NATIONAL CURRICULUM

ENGLAND
The National Curriculum, first introduced in 1988, is mandatory in all local authority maintained state schools for children from age five onwards.

Until age five, or the end of Reception Year in primary school, children are in the Early Years Foundation Stage (EYFS), which has its own learning and development requirements for children in nursery and primary schools. Changes to the EYFS came into effect in 2012, 2014 and 2017. These included simplifying the statutory assessment of children's development at age five; reducing the number of early learning goals from 69 to 17; focusing on seven areas of learning and development (communication and language; physical development; personal, social and emotional development; literacy; mathematics; understanding the world; and expressive arts and design) and, for parents, a new progress check on their child's development between the ages of two and three. More reforms in part to help reception age children gain a better grasp of language, literacy and maths are due in September 2021 (see also Recent Developments).

After the Foundation Stage the National Curriculum is organised into 'Key Stages', and sets out the core subjects that must be taught and the standards or attainment targets for each subject at each Key Stage.

- Key Stage 1 covers Years 1 and 2 of primary school, for children aged 5–7
- Key Stage 2 covers Years 3 to 6 of primary school, for children aged 7–11
- Key Stage 3 covers Years 7 to 9 of secondary school, for children aged 11–14
- Key Stage 4 covers Years 10 and 11 of secondary school, for children aged 14–16

Within the framework of the National Curriculum, schools may plan and organise teaching and learning in the way that best meets the needs of their pupils, but maintained schools are expected to follow the programmes of study associated with particular subjects. The programmes of study describe the subject knowledge, skills and understanding that pupils are expected to have developed by the end of each Key Stage.

The government brought in a new National Curriculum for England for maintained primary and secondary schools from September 2014. From September 2017 schools have taught the new programmes of study to all pupils in all Key Stages.

COMPULSORY SUBJECTS IN KEY STAGES 1 AND 2	
English	Design and technology
Mathematics	Geography
Science	History
Art and design	Music
Computing	Physical education (incl. swimming)

Foreign languages are compulsory in Key Stage 2, but not Key Stage 1: schools can choose from French, German, Italian, Mandarin, Spanish, Latin and Ancient Greek.

At Key Stage 3, compulsory subjects include those compulsory for Key Stage 2 (though the language taught should be a modern foreign language) plus citizenship.

Pupils in Key Stage 4 study a mix of compulsory and optional subjects in preparation for national examinations such as GCSEs. The compulsory subjects are English, mathematics, science, citizenship, computing and physical education. Key Stage 4 pupils also have to undertake careers education and work-related learning. In addition, schools must offer at least one subject from each of four 'entitlement' areas: arts (art and design, music, dance, drama and media arts); design and technology; humanities (history and geography); and modern foreign languages. To meet the entitlement requirements, schools must ensure that courses in these areas lead to approved qualifications, and must allow pupils to take courses in all four areas if they wish to do so.

Schools must teach religious education (RE) at all key stages, although parents have the right to withdraw children from all or part of the subject. From September 2020, primary schools must teach relationships and health education, while secondary schools must provide sex, relationships and health education.

ASSESSMENT

Statutory assessment must be undertaken for all pupils in publicly funded schools in the relevant years. It first takes place towards the end of reception when teachers assess children's development in 17 early learning goals across seven learning areas to form an early years foundation stage profile (EYFSP). Pupils receive a phonics screening check at the end of the first year in Key Stage 1, repeated the following year if necessary. Teacher assessments in English, mathematics and science take place at the end of Key Stage 1 (Year 2) and Key Stage 2 (Year 6); at the end of Key Stage 3 (Year 9) teachers assess progress in all subjects being studied. National tests in English and mathematics take place in Year 6. At Key Stage 4, national examinations are the main form of assessment.

The assessment process for English at the end of Key Stage 2 now involves three elements: English reading; English grammar, punctuation and spelling.

Key stage 2 results no longer use the previous system of levels. Instead, test results are converted into 'scaled scores', with a score of 100 being the expected standard. Any score below 100 means the pupil is working 'towards the expected standard'; any score above 100 means the pupil is working 'above the expected standard'. Previously the expected standard was a level 4.

From September 2020, children will take a new reception baseline assessment (RBA) within the first six weeks of starting school. This would focus on maths, and literacy, communication and development with the results used to assess how much progress schools are making with their pupils. Results for individual children or schools will not be published (see also Recent Developments). This paves the way for removing national curriculum assessments or SATs at the end of Key Stage 1 from 2022–23. An online multiplication tables check also now takes place in Year 4.

Each year the Department for Education publishes on its website performance tables covering every school, college and local authority. The primary school tables are based mainly on the results of the tests taken by children at the end of Key Stage 2 when they are usually aged 11; since 2010 teacher assessment results are also included.

Headline indicators in the secondary school tables are: pupils' average progress and attainment across eight specified subjects; percentages of pupils achieving passes and strong passes (grades 5 and above) in English and maths; percentages of pupils entering and achieving strong passes in the English Baccalaureate (the EBacc is made up of English, maths, two sciences, a language and history or geography); and the percentage of pupils staying in education or employment for at least two terms after Key Stage 4.

DEPARTMENT FOR EDUCATION T 0370-000 2288
   W www.gov.uk/government/organisations/
   department-for-education

WALES

Guidance on the new curriculum for 3- to 16-year-olds in Wales was published in January 2020 ahead of implementation in 2022 for learners up to and including Year 7. Secondary schools will then be expected to roll out their curricular on a year-by-year basis with Year 8 in September 2023 through to Year 11 in September 2026.

The purposes of the curriculum in Wales are to develop children and young people as to:

• Ambitious, capable learners, ready to learn throughout their lives
• Enterprising, creative contributors, ready to play a full part in life and work
• Ethical, informed citizens of Wales and the world
• Healthy, confident individuals, ready to lead fulfilling lives as valued members of society

This will be underpinned by integral skills: creativity and innovation; critical thinking and problem-solving; personal effectiveness; and planning and organising, as well as literacy, numeracy and digital skills. Assessment will be focused on identifying students' progress and preparing them for life after school.

Schools are expected to write their own curriculum, it must include:

• Six areas of learning and experience from age 3 to 16 years
• Three cross-curriculum responsibilities: literacy, numeracy and digital competence
• Progression reference points at ages 5, 8, 11, 14 and 16
• Achievement outcomes which describe expected achievements at each progression reference point

The six Areas of Learning and Experience will be:

• Expressive arts
• Health and well-being
• Humanities (including RE which should remain compulsory to age 16)
• Languages, literacy and communication (including Welsh, which should remain compulsory to age 16, and modern foreign languages)
• Mathematics and numeracy
• Science and technology (including computer science)

Schools must also teach relationships and sexuality education.

Welsh is compulsory for pupils at all key stages, either as a first or as a second language. In 2010, 16.5 per cent of pupils were taught Welsh as a first language. In April 2012, the Minister for Education and Skills approved an action plan to raise standards and attainment in Welsh second language education.

ASSESSMENT

Statutory testing at the end of Key Stage 2 was removed for pupils in Wales from 2004–5, leaving only statutory teacher assessment which takes place at the end of Key Stage 1 (the Foundation Phase) and Key Stage 3, and is being strengthened by moderation and accreditation arrangements.

A National Literacy and Numeracy Framework (LNF), outlining the skills 5- to 15-year-olds are expected to acquire, became statutory from September 2013. For literacy, this means children should become accomplished in reading for information, writing for information and expressing themselves fluently and grammatically in speech. In numeracy, children are expected to develop numerical reasoning and use number skills, measuring skills and data skills.

National reading and numeracy tests – 'personalised assessments' – for pupils in Years 2 to 9 started in Wales in May 2013 and will be entirely online from 2021–22. The tests are designed to give teachers a clearer insight into a learner's development and progress, to allow them to intervene at an earlier stage if learners are falling behind.

The reading test includes a statutory 'core' test, and a set of optional test materials to help teachers to investigate learners' strengths and development needs in more depth.

The numeracy test is split into two papers: numerical procedures and numerical reasoning. The procedural paper consists of a set of questions designed to assess the basic, essential numeracy skills such as addition, multiplication and division. The numerical reasoning test assesses learners' ability to find the most effective ways to solve everyday numeracy problems.

Learners in Welsh-medium schools take a reading test in Welsh only in Years 2 and 3, but in both English and Welsh from Year 4 onwards. Schools have the option to use both tests in Year 3. Learners take the numeracy test in either English or Welsh.

THE WELSH GOVERNMENT – EDUCATION AND SKILLS **W** https://hwb.gov.wales/curriculum-for-wales

SCOTLAND

The curriculum in Scotland is not prescribed by statute but is the responsibility of education authorities and individual schools. However, schools and authorities are expected to follow the Scottish government's guidance on management and delivery of the curriculum, which is primarily through Education Scotland.

Scotland is now implementing *Curriculum for Excellence,* which aims to provide more autonomy for teachers, greater choice and opportunity for pupils and a single coherent curriculum for all children and young people aged 3 to 18.

The purpose of Curriculum for Excellence is encapsulated in 'the four capacities': to enable each child or young person to be a successful learner, a confident individual, a responsible citizen and an effective contributor. It focuses on providing a broad curriculum that develops skills for learning, skills for life and skills for work, with a sustained focus on literacy and numeracy. The period of education from pre-school through to the end of secondary stage 3, when pupils reach 14, aims to provide every young person in Scotland with this broad general education.

Curriculum for Excellence sets out 'experiences and outcomes', which describe broad areas of learning and what is to be achieved within them. They are:

- Expressive arts (including art and design, dance, drama, music)
- Health and well-being (including physical education, food and health, relationships and sexual health and mental, physical and social well-being)
- Languages
- Mathematics
- Religious and moral education
- Sciences
- Social studies (including history, geography, society and economy)
- Technologies (including business, computing, food and textiles, craft, design, engineering and graphics)

The experiences and outcomes are written at five levels with progression to examinations and qualifications during the senior phase, which covers secondary stages 4 to 6 when students are generally aged 14 to 17. The framework is designed to be flexible so that pupils can progress at their own pace.

Level	Stage
Early	The pre-school years and primary 1 (ages 3–5), or later for some
First	To the end of primary 4 (age 8), but earlier or later for some
Second	To the end of primary 7 (age 11), but earlier or later for some
Third and Fourth	Secondary 1 to secondary 3 (ages 12–14), but earlier for some. The fourth level experiences and outcomes are intended to allow choice, and young people's programmes will not include all of the fourth level outcomes
Senior phase	Secondary 4 to secondary 6 (ages 15–18), and college or other studies

Under the new curriculum, assessment of students' progress and achievements from ages 3 to 15 is carried out by teachers who base their assessment judgments on a range of evidence rather than single assessment instruments such as tests. Teachers have access to an online National Assessment Resource, which provides a range of assessment material and national exemplars across the curriculum areas.

In the senior phase, young people aged 16 to 18, including those studying outside school, build up a portfolio of national qualifications, awarded by the Scottish Qualifications Authority (SQA).

Provision is made for teaching in Gaelic in many parts of Scotland and the number of pupils in Gaelic-medium education, from nursery to secondary, is growing.

EDUCATION SCOTLAND **T** 0113-1244 4330 **W** https:// education.gov.scot
SCOTTISH QUALIFICATIONS AUTHORITY
T 0345-279 1000 **W** www.sqa.org.uk

NORTHERN IRELAND

Children aged four to 16 in all grant-aided schools in Northern Ireland must be taught the curriculum put in place in September 2009. The statutory curriculum for Years 1 to 12 places greater emphasis on developing skills and preparing young people for life and work.

This curriculum includes a Foundation Stage to cover Years 1 and 2 of primary school, to allow a more appropriate learning style for the youngest pupils and to ease the transition from pre-school. Key Stage 1 covers primary Years 3 and 4, until children are 8, and Key Stage 2 covers primary Years 5, 6 and 7, until children are 11. Post-primary, Key Stage 3 covers Years 8, 9 and 10 and Key Stage 4 covers Years 11 and 12.

The primary curriculum is made up of the following areas of learning:

- Language and literacy
- Mathematics and numeracy
- The arts
- The world around us
- Personal development and mutual understanding
- Physical education
- Religious education

The post-primary curriculum includes a new area of learning for life and work, made up of employability, personal development, local and global citizenship and home economics (at Key Stage 3). It is also made up of RE and the following areas of learning:

- Language and literacy
- Mathematics and numeracy
- Modern languages
- The arts
- Environment and society
- Physical education
- Science and technology

At Key Stage 4, there are nine areas of learning, but statutory requirements are reduced to learning for life and work, physical education and RE. The aim is to provide greater choice and flexibility for pupils and allow them access to a wider range of academic and vocational courses provided under the revised curriculum's 'Entitlement Framework' (EF).

Since September 2013, schools have been required to provide pupils with access to at least 18 courses at Key Stage 4 and 21 courses at post-16. This increased to 24 and 27 courses respectively in September 2015. At least one third of the courses must be 'general' with one third 'applied'. The remaining third is at the discretion of each school. Individual pupils decide on the number and mix of courses they wish to follow.

RE is a compulsory part of the Northern Ireland curriculum, although parents have the right to withdraw their children from part or all of RE or collective worship. Schools have to provide RE in accordance with a core syllabus drawn up by the province's four main churches (Church of Ireland, Presbyterian, Methodist and Roman Catholic) and specified by the Department of Education.

Revised assessment and reporting arrangements were introduced when the curriculum was revised. The focus from Foundation to Key Stage 3 is on 'Assessment for Learning'. This programme includes classroom-based teacher assessment, computer-based assessment of literacy and numeracy and pupils deciding on their strengths and weaknesses and how they might progress to achieve their potential. Assessment information is given to parents in an annual report. Pupils at Key Stage 4 and beyond continue to be assessed through public examinations.

The Council for the Curriculum, Examinations and Assessment (CCEA), a non-departmental public body reporting to the Department of Education in Northern Ireland, is unique in the UK in combining the functions of a curriculum advisory body, an awarding body and a qualifications regulatory body. It advises the government on what should be taught in Northern Ireland's schools and colleges, ensures that the qualifications and examinations offered by awarding bodies in Northern Ireland are of an appropriate quality and standard and, as the leading awarding body itself, offers a range of qualifications including GCSEs, A-levels and AS-levels.

The CCEA hosts a dedicated curriculum website covering all aspects of the revised curriculum, assessment and reporting.

COUNCIL FOR THE CURRICULUM, EXAMINATIONS AND ASSESSMENT **T** 028-9026 1200 **W** www.ccea.org.uk

QUALIFICATIONS

ENGLAND, WALES AND NORTHERN IRELAND

There is a very wide range of public examinations and qualifications available, accredited by the Office of Qualifications and Examinations Regulation (OFQUAL) in England, Qualifications Wales in Wales and the Council for the Curriculum, Examinations and Assessment (CCEA) in Northern Ireland. Up-to-date information on all accredited qualifications and awarding bodies is available online at the Register of Regulated Qualifications website.

The qualifications frameworks group all accredited qualifications into levels. All the qualifications within a level place similar demands on individuals as learners. Entry level, for example, covers basic knowledge and skills in English, maths and ICT not geared towards specific occupations, level 3 includes qualifications such as A-levels which are appropriate for those wishing to go on to higher education, level 7 covers Master's degrees and vocational qualifications appropriate for senior professionals and managers and level 8 is equivalent to a doctorate.

Young people aged 14 to 19 in schools or (post-16) colleges or apprenticeships may gain academic qualifications such as GCSEs, AS-levels and A-levels; qualifications linked to particular career fields, like diplomas; vocational qualifications such as BTECs and NVQs; and functional key or basic skills qualifications.

In October 2015, both the National Qualifications Framework (NQF) formerly used in England, Wales and Northern Ireland and its successor the Qualifications and Credit Framework (QCF) for England and Northern Ireland were replaced by the Regulated Qualifications Framework (RQF) for England and the Credit and Qualifications Framework for Wales (CQFW). In Northern Ireland the Council for the Curriculum, Examinations and Assessment (CCEA) regulates qualifications. There is also a Framework for Higher Education Qualifications (FHEQ) for England, Wales and Northern Ireland.

In England, Wales and Northern Ireland there are nine qualification levels:

Entry level – each entry-level qualification is available at three sub-levels: 1, 2 and 3, with level 3 the most difficult. Entry-level qualifications are: entry-level award; entry-level certificate (ELC); entry-level diploma; entry-level English for speakers of other languages (ESOL); entry-level essential skills; entry-level functional skills; Skills for Life.

Level 1 qualifications are: first certificate; GCSE – grade D, E, F or G (3, 2 or 1 in the new grading structure); level 1 award; level 1 certificate; level 1 diploma; level 1 ESOL; level 1 essential skills; level 1 functional skills; level 1 national vocational qualification (NVQ); music grades 1, 2 and 3.

Level 2 qualifications are: CSE – grade 1; GCSE – grade A*, A, B or C (4 or above in the new grading structure); intermediate apprenticeship; level 2 award; level 2 certificate; level 2 diploma; level 2 ESOL; level 2 essential skills; level 2 functional skills; level 2 national certificate; level 2 national diploma; level 2 NVQ; music grades 4 and 5; O level – grade A, B or C.

Level 3 qualifications are: A level – grade A*, A, B, C, D or E; access to higher education; diploma; advanced apprenticeship; applied general; AS level; international Baccalaureate diploma; level 3 award; level 3 certificate; level 3 diploma; level 3 ESOL; level 3 national certificate; level 3 national diploma; level 3 NVQ; music grades 6, 7 and 8; tech level.

Level 4 qualifications are: certificate of higher education (CertHE); higher apprenticeship; higher national certificate (HNC); level 4 award; level 4 certificate; level 4 diploma; level 4 NVQ.

Level 5 qualifications are: diploma of higher education (DipHE); foundation degree; higher national diploma (HND); level 5 award; level 5 certificate; level 5 diploma; level 5 NVQ.

Level 6 qualifications are: degree apprenticeship; degree with honours – for example bachelor of arts (BA) with honours, bachelor of science (BSc) with honours; graduate certificate; graduate diploma; level 6 award; level 6 certificate; level 6 diploma; level 6 NVQ; ordinary degree without honours.

Level 7 qualifications are: integrated master's degree, for example master of engineering (MEng); level 7 award; level 7 certificate; level 7 diploma; level 7 NVQ; master's degree, for example master of arts (MA), master of science (MSc); postgraduate certificate; postgraduate certificate in education (PGCE); postgraduate diploma.

Level 8 qualifications are: doctorate, for example doctor of philosophy (PHD or DPHIL); level 8 award; level 8 certificate; level 8 diploma.

FRAMEWORK FOR HIGHER EDUCATION QUALIFICATIONS (FHEQ)

This framework applies to degrees, diplomas, certificates and other academic awards (other than honorary degrees and higher doctorates) granted by a higher education provider in the exercise of its degree awarding powers. It starts at RQF level 4 and goes up to level 8 and includes the following qualifications: Certificate of Higher Education; Diploma of Higher Education; Bachelor's degrees; Master's degrees; and Doctoral degrees.

COUNCIL FOR THE CURRICULUM, EXAMINATIONS AND ASSESSMENT (NORTHERN IRELAND)
T 028-9026 1200 **W** www.ccea.org.uk

QUALIFICATIONS WALES **T** 01633-373222
W www.qualificationswales.org

REGISTER OF REGULATED QUALIFICATIONS
W http://register.ofqual.gov.uk

OFFICE OF QUALIFICATIONS AND EXAMINATIONS REGULATION (OFQUAL) **T** 0300-303 3344
W www.ofqual.gov.uk

GCSE

The vast majority of pupils in their last year of compulsory schooling in England, Wales and Northern Ireland take at least one General Certificate of Secondary Education (GCSE) exam, though GCSEs may be taken at any age. GCSEs assess the performance of pupils on a subject-specific basis and are mostly taken after a two-year course. They are available in more than 50 subjects, most of them academic subjects, though some, known as vocational or applied GCSEs, involve the study of a particular area of employment and the development of work-related skills. Some subjects are also offered as short-course qualifications, equivalent to half a standard GCSE, or as double awards, equivalent to two GCSEs.

For many years GCSEs were assessed on coursework completed by students during the course as well as exams at the end, and GCSE certificates were awarded on an eight-point scale from A* to G. In most subjects two different papers, higher tier and foundation tier, were provided for different ranges of ability, with grades A*–D available to students taking the higher paper and grades C–G available from the foundation paper.

In England, all traditional GCSEs have been replaced by new GCSEs or, in some subjects, withdrawn. The new GCSEs no longer involve modules and coursework, just exam assessment at the end of the two-year course; a very few subjects (such as music technology) may include an element of non-exam assessment. Only maths, science and foreign language GCSEs will be tiered. New GCSEs are graded 9 to 1, rather than A* to G.

The changeover to new GCSEs was phased in. In September 2015 schools began teaching revised GCSEs in English language, English literature and mathematics, for exams in 2017. Teaching of revised GCSEs in ancient and modern foreign languages, art and design, biology, chemistry, citizenship, computer science, double science, dance, drama, food preparation and nutrition, geography, history, music, physics, physical education and religious studies started in September 2016 for exams in 2018. Teaching in 14 other subjects started in September 2017 for exams in 2019.

In 2017 English language, English literature and maths were the first subjects to be graded from 9 to 1. Another 20 subjects were graded 9 to 1 in 2018, with most others following in 2019. During this transition, students received a mixture of letter and number grades. It will take until summer 2020 for all reformed GCSEs to be graded on the new scale.

In Northern Ireland, new CCEA GCSEs were introduced for first teaching in 2017, with first awards in 2019. They are graded on a 9 grade system from A*-G with a new C* grade.

All GCSE specifications, assessments and grading procedures are monitored by OFQUAL, QW and the CCEA.

Since September 2010 state schools have been allowed to offer pupils International GCSE (iGCSE) qualifications in key subjects including English, mathematics, science and ICT. Though iGCSEs were considered more rigorous than traditional GCSEs, the government regards the new GCSEs in these subjects as superior, and iGCSE results no longer count in school performance tables from 2017, or later, depending on the subject.

GCE A-LEVEL AND AS-LEVEL

GCE (General Certificate of Education) Advanced levels (A-levels) are the qualifications used by most young people in England, Wales and Northern Ireland to gain entry to university.

A-levels are subject-based qualifications. They are mostly taken by UK students aged 16 to 19 over a two-year course in school sixth forms or at college, but can be taken at any age. They are available in more than 45, mostly academic, subjects, though there are some A-levels in vocational areas, often termed 'applied A-levels'.

Traditionally, A-level qualifications consisted of two parts: advanced subsidiary (AS) and A2 units. The AS was a qualification assessed at the standard expected of a learner half way through an A-level course, normally consisting of two units that together contributed 50 per cent towards the full A-level. The A2 was the second half of a full A-level qualification. It was assessed at the standard expected of a learner at the end of a full A-level course, and normally consisted of two units that together made up the remaining 50 per cent of the full A-level qualification. Each unit was graded A–E, with an A* grade available to exceptional candidates since 2010.

An extended project was introduced in September 2008 as a separate qualification. It is a single piece of work on a topic of the student's own choosing that requires a high degree of planning, preparation, research and autonomous working. Awards are graded A–E and the extended project is accredited as half an A-level.

Since September 2013, students in England in their first or second year of A-level studies have not been allowed to sit A-level exams in January. A-levels are still examined unit by unit, but all exams are taken in the summer.

Revised AS and A-levels were introduced in phases from 2015 to 2017. All assessment of the new A-levels now takes place at the end of the two-year course and the AS has become a standalone qualification rather than contributing to a full A-level qualification.

Since September 2015, students have been taught the new-style AS-levels and A-levels in art and design, biology, business, chemistry, computer science, economics, English language, English language and literature, English literature, history, physics, psychology and sociology. New AS and A-levels in ancient languages, dance, drama and theatre, geography, modern foreign languages (French, German and Spanish), music, physical education and religious studies started to be taught in September 2016.

From September 2017, new-style A-levels were introduced in: accounting, ancient history, archaeology, classical civilisation, design and technology, electronics, film studies, geology, government and politics, history of art, law, maths and further maths, media studies, music technology, philosophy and statistics.

As a result of COVID-19 disruption to education, in 2021 exams will go ahead in England, Wales and Northern Ireland with changes to 15 A-level subjects and 25 GCSEs. Changes include: changes to how content is assessed in GCSE geography, history and ancient history; a choice of topics on which students are required to answer questions in their English literature exams; a reduction in geography, geology and environmental science fieldwork at GCSE and A-level; modern foreign languages GCSE students will be given a grade of pass, merit or distinction (or 'not classified') for their spoken language skills by teachers, alongside their 9 to 1 grade; a range of modifications to the non-exam assessment arrangements in a number of subjects to accommodate potential public health requirements, for example, GCSE food preparation and nutrition, GCSE, AS and A level music and GCSE physical education. *See also* Recent Developments.

INTERNATIONAL BACCALAUREATE

The International Baccalaureate (IB) offers four educational programmes for students aged 3 to 19: IB primary years programme, IB middle years programme, IB diploma programme, IB career-related certificate.

Some 155 'IB World Schools' in the UK offer at least one IB programme.

The IB diploma programme for students aged 16 to 19 is based around detailed academic study of a wide range of subjects, including languages, the arts, science, maths, history and geography, leading to a single qualification recognised by UK universities.

The IB diploma is made up of a compulsory 'core' plus six separate subjects where individuals have some choice over what they study. The compulsory core contains three elements: theory of knowledge; creativity, action and service; and a 4,000-word extended essay.

The IB diploma normally takes two years to complete and most of the assessment is done through externally marked examinations. Candidates are awarded points for each part of the programme, up to a maximum of 45. A candidate must score 24 points or more to achieve a full diploma.

Successfully completing the diploma earns points on the 'UCAS tariff', the UK system for allocating points to qualifications used for entry to higher education. An IB diploma total of 24 points is worth 260 UCAS points – the same as a B and two C grades at A-level. The maximum of 45 points earns 720 UCAS points – equivalent to six A-levels at grade A.

WELSH BACCALAUREATE

The Welsh Baccalaureate Qualification (WBQ), available for 14- to 19-year-olds in Wales, combines a compulsory core, which incorporates personal development skills, with options from existing academic and vocational qualifications, such as A-levels, GCSEs and NVQs, to make one broader award. The WBQ can be studied in English or Welsh, or a combination of the two. Candidates who meet the requirements of the compulsory core and options relevant to each level of the qualification are awarded the Welsh Baccalaureate Foundation, Intermediate or Advanced Diploma as appropriate.

WJEC (Welsh Joint Education Committee), which administers the WBQ, has also developed two new WBQs at level 1 and level 2 suitable for delivery over one year and with a particular focus on employability.

A revised and more rigorous Welsh Baccalaureate has been taught since September 2015. It is based on a graded Skills Challenge Certificate and supporting qualifications. The aim is to enable learners to develop and demonstrate an understanding of, and proficiency in, essential and employability skills: communication, numeracy, digital literacy, planning and organisation, creativity and innovation, critical thinking and problem solving, and personal effectiveness. The emphasis is on applied and purposeful learning and opportunities for assessment in a range of real life contexts through three 'challenge briefs' and an individual project.

APPLIED GENERAL, TECH LEVEL AND T LEVEL QUALIFICATIONS

As part of changes to the 16-19 performance tables, existing vocational qualifications were designated 'Tech levels' if they met specific criteria. Students achieving a Tech level qualification, a level 3 maths qualification and an extended project could be counted as achieving a 'TechBacc' (Technical Baccalaureate) performance measure in the post-16 school and college performance tables from 2016.

From 2017, post-16 performance tables have also recognised Applied General Qualifications, which take the same time to complete as AS-levels and focus on broader study of a technical area. These are advanced (level 3) qualifications that allow 16- to 19-year-old students to develop transferable knowledge and skills. They allow entry to a range of higher education courses, either by meeting the entry requirements in their own right or by adding value to other qualifications such as A-levels.

From September 2020, new 'T Level' qualifications started for students aged 16-19 wanting to specialise in a technical occupation. The two-year courses follow GCSEs and are equivalent to three A-levels and have been developed in collaboration with employers and businesses so that the content meets the needs of industry and prepares students for work, further training or study. T Levels offer students a mixture of classroom learning and 'on-the-job' experience during an industry placement of at least 315 hours (approximately 45 days).

T Levels take as long to complete as A-levels and, like A-levels, are at level 3. They are based on the same standards as apprenticeships, designed by employers, and will offer around 1,800 hours of study over two years, including a 315 hour (45-day) work placement.

T Levels include compulsory elements:
- A technical qualification which includes core skills, theory, and concepts for the industry area
- Specialist occupational skills and knowledge of the career
- An industry placement with an employer
- A minimum standard in maths and English, if students have not already achieved this

Students who complete a T Level will receive an overall grade of pass, merit, distinction or distinction*; a separate grade for the core component using A* to E, and a separate grade for each occupational specialism, shown as pass, merit or distinction. Students will be awarded a nationally recognised certificate showing a breakdown of what they have achieved. It will also confirm that a student has met the minimum requirements for maths and English qualifications.

T-levels in digital production, design and development; design, surveying and planning, and education started in September 2020. From Autumn 2021, T-levels will be available in: building services engineering; digital business services; digital support and services; health; healthcare science; onsite construction; and science. More T-levels are expected from Autumn 2022.

Students who want to go on to higher education must achieve at least an overall pass grade to receive UCAS Tariff points, as Detailed below:

T Level Overall Grade	UCAS Tariffs	A Level
Distinction* (A* on the core and distinction in the occupational specialism)	168	AAA*
Distinction	144	AAA
Merit	120	BBB
Pass (C or above on the core)	96	CCC
Pass (D or E on the core)	72	DDD

BTECS, OCR NATIONALS AND OTHER VOCATIONAL QUALIFICATIONS

Vocational qualifications can range from general qualifications where a person learns skills relevant to a variety of jobs, to specialist qualifications designed for a particular sector. They are available from several awarding bodies, such as City & Guilds, Edexcel and OCR, and can be taken at many different levels. All vocational and work-related qualifications fit into the Regulated Qualifications Framework (RQF).

BTEC qualifications and OCR Nationals are particular types of work-related qualifications, available in a wide range of subjects, including: art and design, business, health and social care, information technology, media, public services, science and sport. The qualifications offer a mix of theory and practice, can include work experience and can be part of an Apprenticeship. They can be studied full-time at college or school, or part-time at college.

Learners complete a range of assignments, case studies and practical activities, as well as a portfolio of evidence that shows what work has been completed.

Since 2016, the quality and assessment of all vocational courses offered by schools and colleges to 14- to 19-year-olds has been strengthened. The standards of reformed BTECs, along with Cambridge OCR National Certificates and Vocational Certificates (V-Certs), equal those of GCSE A*–C grades. All vocational qualifications are graded (previously many were simply pass/fail) and all have a 25 per cent externally examined component. New Substantial Vocational Qualifications at level 2 provide 16- to 19-year-old students seeking entry at a more basic level to a skilled trade or occupation with qualifications that are valued by employers.

NVQs

A National Vocational Qualification (NVQ) is a 'competence-based' qualification that is recognised by employers. Individuals learn practical, work-related tasks designed to help them develop the skills and knowledge to do a particular job effectively. NVQs can be taken in school, at college or by people already in work. There are more than 1,300 different NVQs available from the vast majority of business sectors. NVQs exist at levels 1 to 5 on the RQF. An NVQ qualification at level 2 or 3 can also be taken as part of an Apprenticeship.

Functional Skills

Functional skills qualifications were launched during 2010, for all learners aged 14 and above. They test practical skills that allow people to work confidently, effectively and independently in life, and are available only in England. Wales and Northern Ireland have literacy and numeracy qualifications known as 'Essential Skills'.

In England, the government is reforming functional skills qualifications in English and mathematics, with reformed qualifications first taught from September 2019.

Apprenticeships

Apprenticeships combine on-the-job training with nationally recognised qualifications, allowing individuals to gain skills and qualifications while working and earning a wage. More than 200 different types of apprenticeships are available, offering over 1,500 job roles; they take between one and five years to complete. There are four levels available:

- Intermediate Apprenticeships – at level 2 on the Regulated Qualifications Framework (RQF), they are equivalent to five good GCSE passes (9–4)
- Advanced Apprenticeships – at level 3 on the RQF, they are equivalent to two A-level passes/Level 3 Diploma/ International Baccalaureate
- Higher Apprenticeships – levels 4, 5, 6 and 7 equivalent to Foundation degree and above
- Degree Apprenticeships – added in 2015 (RQF level 6 and 7) equivalent to a bachelor's or master's degree

In England, the National Apprenticeship Service (NAS), launched in 2009, is responsible for the delivery of apprenticeships and provides an online vacancy matching system. The way in which the government funds the training and assessment costs of apprenticeships was revised in May 2017, when the apprenticeship levy was introduced and the Institute for Apprenticeships and Technical Education was created. Sponsored by the Department for Education, the institute is focused on supporting employers in developing apprenticeships. In 2018–19, 742,000 people participated in an apprenticeship in England, with 393,400 apprenticeship starts and 185,100 achievements. Degree apprenticeships are growing in number with numerous universities grouping together to offer full bachelor's or master's degree programmes. Currently the scheme is only available in England and Wales, though applications can be made from all parts of the UK. The Welsh government and the Department for the Economy are responsible for the apprenticeship programmes in Wales and Northern Ireland respectively.

INSTITUTE FOR APPRENTICESHIPS AND TECHNICAL EDUCATION W www.instituteforapprenticeships.org

NATIONAL APPRENTICESHIP SERVICE (NAS) T 0800-015 0400 W www.gov.uk/apply-apprenticeship

REGISTER OF APPRENTICESHIP TRAINING PROVIDERS W www.gov.uk/guidance/ register-of-apprenticeship-training-providers

SCOTLAND

Scotland has its own system of public examinations and qualifications. The Scottish Qualifications Authority (SQA) is Scotland's national body for qualifications, responsible for developing, accrediting, assessing and certificating all Scottish qualifications apart from university degrees and some professional body qualifications.

There are qualifications at all levels of attainment. Almost all school candidates gain SQA qualifications in the fourth year of secondary school and most obtain further qualifications in the fifth or sixth year or in further education colleges. Increasingly, people also take qualifications in the workplace.

SQA, with partners such as Universities Scotland, has introduced the Scottish Credit and Qualifications Framework (SCQF) as a way of comparing and understanding Scottish qualifications. It includes qualifications across academic and vocational sectors and compares them by giving a level and credit points. There are 12 levels in the SCQF, level 1 being the least difficult and level 12 the most difficult. The number of SCQF credit points shows how much learning has to be done to achieve the qualification. For instance, one SCQF credit point equals about 10 hours of learning including assessment.

Since reforms introduced in 2013, qualifications in Scotland are divided into academic National Qualifications and more practical-based Qualifications for Work.

National Qualifications
- National 1 units are assessed as a pass or fail by a teacher or lecturer. They could lead to National 2 courses or awards at SCQF level 1 or 2
- National 2 courses are made up of units assessed as pass or fail by a teacher or lecturer. Learners need to pass all units to achieve the qualification. They could lead to National 3 courses or awards at SCQF level 2 or 3
- National 3 courses comprise three National Units assessed as pass or fail by a teacher or lecturer. They could lead to related courses at National 4, awards at SQCF level 3 or 4, National Certificates or National Progression Awards or employment opportunities
- National 4 courses are made up of units, including an added value unit, which assesses learners' performance across the course. They could lead to National 5 courses, units or awards at SCQF level 4 or 5, National Certificate or National Progression Awards, or Modern Apprenticeships or other employment opportunities
- National 5 courses are assessed through exams, coursework or both, most of which is marked by the Scottish Qualifications Authority. Courses are graded A to D or 'no award'. They could lead to Higher courses, units or awards at SCQF level 5 or 6, National Certificate or National Progression Awards, Foundation Apprenticeships or a Modern Apprenticeship at SCQF level 6
- Higher courses are made up of exams or coursework (units will be removed from 2018–19) or both, marked by the SQA, or teachers or lecturers in some cases. They could lead to Advanced Higher courses, units or awards at SCQF level 6 or 7, National Certificate or National Progression Awards, Higher National Certificate or Higher National Diplomas, or Modern Apprenticeships at SCQF level 7
- Advanced Higher courses are made up of exams or coursework (units will be removed from 2019–20) or both, marked by the SQA, or teachers or lecturers in some cases. They could lead to a Higher National Diploma, undergraduate degree or a Technical Apprenticeship at SCQF level 8
- Skills for Work courses encourage learners to become familiar with the world of work. They are available in a variety of areas such as construction, hairdressing and hospitality (**W** www.sqa.org.uk/skillsforwork)
- Scottish Baccalaureates are qualifications at SCQF level 7, and are available for learners in S5 and S6. They exist in Expressive Arts, Languages, Science, and Social Sciences and are awarded as a pass or distinction. Learners undertake an interdisciplinary project, which allows them to develop and show evidence of initiative, responsibility, and independent working – skills of value in the world of higher education (**W** www.sqa.org.uk/baccalaureates)

Qualifications For Work
- Introduction to Work Place Skills qualification is designed to help 'can do' learners to develop core and employability skills. It comprises an employer-assessed work experience placement of a minimum of 150 hours. Successful completion allows learners to go to Certificate of Work Readiness, further training, education or employment (**W** www.sqa.org.uk/introtowork)
- Certificate of Work Readiness award includes an employer-assessed work experience placement and is available through colleges and training providers working in partnership with employers (**W** www.sqa.org.uk/workready).
- Foundation Apprenticeships are new, work-based learning qualifications for secondary school pupils and allow pupils in S4 to S6 to complete elements of a Modern Apprenticeship while still at school. Depending on their subject, pupils study towards Foundation Apprenticeships alongside their other subjects and spend part of their school week at college or with a local employer. By December 2017, some 18,700 young people had started apprenticeships. (**W** www.apprenticeships.scot/foundation-apprenticeships).
- Modern Apprenticeships offer anyone aged over 16 paid employment combined with the opportunity to train for jobs at craft, technician and management level. They are developed by the industry or sector in which they will be implemented. (**W** www.sqa.org.uk/modernapprenticeships or **W** www.apprenticeships.scot)
- SQA Awards are flexible and nationally recognised. They provide learners with opportunities to acquire skills, recognise achievement and promote confidence
- Wider Achievement qualifications provide young people with the opportunity to have learning and skills formally recognised, whether developed in or outside the classroom. Available at a number of levels in subjects including Employability, Leadership and Enterprise, these qualifications help schools deliver skills for learning, life and work
- Scottish Vocational Qualifications are based on national standards drawn up by people from industry, commerce and education covering a wide range of occupations
- Professional Development Awards develop the skills of those already in professional employment and can be embedded within another qualification such as a Higher National Certificate or Diploma
- National Certificates prepare people for employment, development or progression to advanced study. They are aimed at 16-18 year olds and are at SCQF levels 2 to 6
- National Progression Awards assess a defined set of skills and knowledge in specialist vocational areas, linking to National Occupational Standards, which are the basis of SVQs
- Higher National qualifications are offered by colleges, universities and other training centres. Higher National Certificates, Higher National Diplomas and Professional Development Awards are designed to meet employers' needs and can give candidates access to second or third year entry at university

As part of the Curriculum for Excellence programme SQA developed revised National qualifications that became available in schools from August 2013, replacing Standard Grade, Intermediate and Access qualifications at all levels. New Higher qualifications became available from August 2014 and Advanced Higher qualifications from August 2015:

SCQF level	National qualifications
1 & 2	National 1 & 2
3	National 3
4	National 4
5	National 5
6	Higher
7	Advanced Higher

Revised qualifications were available alongside existing qualifications until 2015–16. Final results for existing Access, Intermediate, Higher and Advanced Higher qualifications were issued in August 2015.

Since 2017–18 mandatory unit assessments have been removed from the National 5 qualification to reduce teacher and pupil workload. Course assessments for National 5 – a combination of exam and coursework – were strengthened to maintain their integrity, breadth and standards.

Mandatory unit assessment was removed for Higher courses from 2018–19 and FOR Advanced Higher courses from 2019–20.

THE SCOTTISH QUALIFICATIONS AUTHORITY (SQA)
    T 0345-279 1000 W www.sqa.org.uk
SCOTTISH CREDIT AND QUALIFICATIONS
    FRAMEWORK (SCQF) T 0845-270 7371
    W www.scqf.org.uk
SKILLS DEVELOPMENT SCOTLAND (SDS)
    T 0800-917 8000 W www.skillsdevelopmentscotland.co.uk

FURTHER EDUCATION AND LIFELONG LEARNING

ENGLAND

The further education (FE) system in England provides a wide range of education and training opportunities for young people and adults. From the age of 16, young people who wish to remain in education, but not in a school setting, can undertake further education (including skills training) in an FE college. There are two main types of college in the FE sector: sixth form colleges and general further education (GFE) colleges. Some FE colleges focus on a particular area, such as art and design or agriculture and horticulture. Each institution decides its own range of subjects and courses. Students at FE colleges can study for a wide and growing range of academic and/or work-related qualifications, from entry level to higher education level.

The Department for Business, Innovation and Skills was responsible for the FE sector and for funding adult FE until July 2016, when these responsibilities passed to the Department for Education, which already funded all education and training for 16- to 18-year-olds.

The proportion of 16- to 18-year-olds in education or training has risen steadily over recent years, driven by increases in state-funded schools and in higher education. The 'September Guarantee', introduced in 2007, offers a place in post-16 education or training to all 16- and 17-year-olds who want one. The latest statistics, for 2019, show 81.6 per cent of young people in full-time education and apprenticeships, with 6.6 per cent not in education, employment or training.

The Education and Skills Funding Agency (ESFA) replaced the Skills Funding Agency and the Education Funding Agency in April 2017. The ESFA is accountable for £59bn of funding for the education and training sector, regulating academies, FE colleges, employers and training providers, intervening where there is risk of failure or where there is evidence of mismanagement of public funds, and delivering major projects in the education and skills sector, such as school capital programmes, the National Careers Service, the digital Apprenticeship Service and National Apprenticeship Service.

In November 2010, the government announced a new strategy for FE, including more adult apprenticeships; fully-funded training for 19- to 24-year-olds undertaking their first full level 2 (GCSE equivalent) or first level 3 qualification; and fully-funded basic skills training for people who left school without basic skills in reading, writing and mathematics. 'Train to Gain', the programme that funded trainees sponsored by employers, was replaced in July 2011 by a programme focused on helping small employers to train low-skilled staff. In April 2012 the National Careers Service was created.

In April 2013, the government announced plans to make the skills system more responsive and to create new traineeships.

There are currently nine centres of training excellence called National Skills Academies, led, funded and designed by employers, in various stages of development. Each academy offers specialist training in a key sector of the economy, working in partnership with colleges, schools and independent training providers.

Among the many voluntary bodies providing adult education, the Workers' Educational Association (WEA) is the UK's largest, operating throughout England and Scotland. It provides part-time courses to adults in response to local need in community centres, village halls, schools, pubs or workplaces. Similar but separate WEA organisations operate in Wales and Northern Ireland.

Since 2016, the Learning and Work Institute promotes lifelong learning opportunities for adults in England and Wales.

LEARNING AND WORK INSTITUTE T 0116-204 4200
    W www.learningandwork.org.uk
THE EDUCATION AND SKILLS FUNDING AGENCY
    W www.gov.uk/government/organisations/
    education-and-skills-funding-agency
WORKERS' EDUCATIONAL ASSOCIATION (WEA)
    T 0300-303346 W www.wea.org.uk
EDUCATION AND TRAINING FOUNDATION
    T 020-3740 8280 W www.et-foundation.co.uk
FEDERATION FOR INDUSTRY SECTOR SKILLS &
    STANDARDS
    W www.fisss.org/sector-skills-council-body/directory-of-sscs/

WALES

In Wales, the aims and makeup of the FE system are similar to those outlined for England. The Welsh government funds a wide range of learning programmes for young people through its 15 FE colleges, local authorities and private organisations. The Welsh government has set out plans to improve learning opportunities for all post-16 learners in the shortest possible time, to increase the engagement of disadvantaged young people in the learning process, and to transform the learning network to increase learner choice, reduce duplication of provision and encourage higher-quality learning and teaching in all post-16 provision.

Responsibility for adult and continuing education lies with the Department for Education and Skills (DfES) within the Welsh government. Wales operates a range of programmes to support skills development, including subsidised work-based training courses for employees and the Workforce Development Programme, where employers can use the free services of experienced skills advisers to develop staff training plans.

COLLEGES WALES **T** 029-2052 2500
  W www.collegeswales.ac.uk

ADULT LEARNING WALES **T** 029-2023 5277
  W www.adultlearning.wales

LEARNING AND WORK INSTITUTE **T** 029-2037 0900
  W www.learningandwork.wales

WEA SOUTH WALES **T** 029-2023 5277
  W www.swales.wea.org.uk

SCOTLAND

Following a series of mergers, Scotland has 26 FE colleges (known simply as colleges), which are at the forefront of lifelong learning, education, training and skills in Scotland. Colleges cater for the needs of learners both in and out of employment and at all stages in their lives. Colleges' courses span much of the range of learning needs, from specialised vocational education and training through to general educational programmes. The level of provision ranges from essential life skills and provision for students with learning difficulties to HNCs and HNDs. Some colleges, notably those in the Highlands and Islands, also deliver degrees and postgraduate qualifications.

A shift in study patterns is taking place within the college sector as colleges concentrate on full-time courses aimed at helping people gain employment and no longer fund short courses lasting less than ten hours. Overall figures are stable, but this change has led to a decline in part-time study and an increase in full-time study.

The Scottish Funding Council (SFC) is the statutory body responsible for funding teaching and learning provision, research and other activities in Scotland's colleges. Overall strategic direction for the sector is provided by the Lifelong Learning Directorate of the Scottish government, which provides annual guidance to the SFC and liaises closely with bodies such as Colleges Scotland, the Scottish Qualifications Authority and the FE colleges themselves to ensure that policies remain relevant and practical.

The Scottish government takes responsibility for community learning and development in Scotland while Skills Development Scotland, a non-departmental public body, is charged with improving Scotland's skills performance by linking skills supply and demand and helping people and organisations to learn, develop and make use of these skills to greater effect.

ILA SCOTLAND **T** 0800-917 8000
  W www.myworldofwork.co.uk/learn-and-train/funding

COLLEGES SCOTLAND **T** 01786-892100
  W www.collegesscotland.ac.uk

SCOTTISH FUNDING COUNCIL **T** 0131-313 6500
  W www.sfc.ac.uk

SKILLS DEVELOPMENT SCOTLAND **T** 0800-917 8000
  W www.skillsdevelopmentscotland.co.uk

NORTHERN IRELAND

FE in Northern Ireland is provided through six regional multi-campus colleges and the College of Agriculture, Food and Rural Affairs. Most secondary schools also have a sixth form which students may attend for two additional years to complete their AS-levels and A-levels.

Colleges Northern Ireland acts as the representative body for the six FE colleges which, like their counterparts in the rest of the UK, are independent corporate bodies each managed by their own governing body. The range of courses that they offer spans essential skills, a wide choice of vocational and academic programmes and higher education programmes. Most full-time students in the six colleges are aged 16 to 19, while most part-time students are over 19.

The Department for the Economy is responsible for the policy, strategic development and financing of the statutory FE sector and for lifelong learning, and also provides support to a small number of non-statutory FE providers. The Educational Guidance Service for Adults, an independent, not-for-profit organisation, has a network of local offices based across Northern Ireland that provide services to adult learners, learning advisers, providers, employers and others interested in improving access to learning for adults.

THE EDUCATIONAL GUIDANCE SERVICE FOR
  ADULTS **E** info@egsa.org.uk **W** www.egsa.org.uk

NI DIRECT FE COLLEGES
  W www.nidirect.gov.uk/contacts/further-education-fe-colleges

FINANCIAL SUPPORT

England has a bursary scheme of up to £1,200 a year for full-time 16- to 19-year-old students facing financial hardship. Two types of bursary exist: vulnerable student bursary and discretionary bursary. Help with transport costs is also possible for some students. This scheme replaced the Education Maintenance Allowance (EMA), which gave 16- to 19-year-olds from low-income families a weekly allowance to continue in education.

There are EMA schemes in Scotland, Wales and Northern Ireland, but with slightly different eligibility conditions. Students must apply to the EMA scheme for the part of the UK where they intend to study. In Northern Ireland 16- to 19-year-old students who meet the relevant criteria and live in a household that has an annual income of £20,500 or less a year (£22,500 if more than one young person in the household qualifies for child benefit) automatically get £30 a week in 2020–21. There is a possibility of two £200 bonus payments too.

Colleges and learning providers award learner support funds directly to new students aged 19 and over.

Care to Learn is available in England to help young parents under the age of 20, who are caring for their own child or children while they are in some form of publicly funded learning (below higher education level), with the costs of childcare and travel. The scheme is not income-assessed and pays up to £160 a week (£175 in London) to cover costs.

Dance and Drama Awards (DaDA) are state-funded scholarships for students aged 16 to 23 enrolled at one of 19 private dance and drama schools in England, who are taking specified courses at National Certificate or National Diploma level. Awards, based on household income, cover some of students' tuition fees and from £1,350 to £5,185 of maintenance in 2020–21.

Young people studying away from home because their chosen course is not available locally may qualify for the *Residential Support Scheme* (up to £3,458 outside London and £4,079 in London for household incomes of less than £21,000).

Information and advice on funding support and applications are available from the Learner Support helpline (**T** 0800-121 8989) or on the GOV.UK website (*see* below).

Discretionary Support Funds (DSF) are available in colleges and school sixth forms to help students who have trouble meeting the costs of participating in further education.

In Wales, students aged 19 or over on FE courses may be eligible for the *Welsh Government Learning Grant FE* (previously the Assembly Learning Grant for Further Education). This is a means-tested payment of up to £1,500 for full-time students and up to £750 for those studying part-time. *Discretionary Assistance Funds* are also available to all students in Wales suffering hardship.

In Scotland, FE students can apply to their college for discretionary support in the form of *Further Education Bursaries,* which can include allowances for maintenance, travel, study, childcare and additional support needs. *Individual Training*

Accounts, which replaced *Individual Learning Accounts* from October 2017, allow eligible students up to £200 towards a single course or training episode per year.

In Northern Ireland, FE students with annual household incomes below £21,330 may be eligible for *Further Education Awards* of up to £2,092, non-refundable assistance, administered on behalf of the five Education and Library Boards by the Western Education and Library Board.

EDUCATION AUTHORITY **W** www.eani.org.uk

GOV.UK **W** www.gov.uk/further-education-courses/financial-help

MY WORLD OF WORK **W** www.myworldofwork.co.uk

STUDENT FINANCE WALES **T** 0300-200 4050
   W www.studentfinancewales.co.uk

HIGHER EDUCATION

Publicly funded higher education (HE) in the UK is provided in universities, higher education colleges and other specialist HE institutions, and in a significant number of FE colleges offering higher education courses.

Since the closure of the Higher Education Funding Council for England (HEFCE) in March 2018, universities and university colleges are funded through UK Research and Innovation (UKRI); *see also* Recent Developments).

The Higher Education Funding Council for Wales (HEFCW) distributes funding for HE in Wales through Wales' eight HEIs, the Open University in Wales and some FE colleges.

The Scottish Funding Council (SFC) – which is also responsible for FE in Scotland – is the national strategic body responsible for funding HE teaching and research in Scotland's 19 HEIs and 26 colleges.

In Northern Ireland, HE is provided by two universities, two university colleges, six regional institutes of further and higher education and the Open University (OU), which operates UK-wide. Northern Ireland has no higher education funding body; the Department for the Economy fulfils that role.

All UK universities and a number of HE colleges award their own degrees and other HE qualifications. HE providers who do not have their own degree-awarding powers offer degrees under 'validation arrangements' with other institutions that do have those powers. The OU, for example, runs a validation service which enables a number of other institutions to award OU degrees, after the OU has assured itself that the academic standards of their courses are as high as the OU's own standards.

Each HE institution is responsible for the standards of the awards it makes and the quality of the education it provides to its students, and each has its own internal quality assurance procedures. External quality assurance for HE institutions throughout the UK is provided by the Quality Assurance Agency for Higher Education (QAA).

The QAA is independent of government, funded by subscriptions from all publicly funded UK universities and colleges of HE. Its main role is to safeguard the standards of HE qualifications. It does this by defining standards for HE through a framework known as the academic infrastructure. QAA carries out reviews of the quality of UK HE institutions via a system known as 'institutional audits', advises on a range of HE quality issues and publishes reports on its website.

DEPARTMENT FOR THE ECONOMY (NI)
   T 028-9052 9900 **W** www.economy-ni.gov.uk

HIGHER EDUCATION FUNDING COUNCIL FOR
   WALES **T** 029-2085 9698 **W** www.hefcw.ac.uk

RESEARCH ENGLAND **T** 0117-905 7600 **W** https://re.ukri.org

SCOTTISH FUNDING COUNCIL **T** 0131-313 6500
   W www.sfc.ac.uk

THE QUALITY ASSURANCE AGENCY FOR HIGHER
   EDUCATION **T** 01452-557000 **W** www.qaa.ac.uk

STUDENTS APPLYING TO UNIVERSITY			
	2019	2020	*Difference*
Total applicants by 30 Jan*	638,030	652,790	2%

* Deadline for 2020 cycle
Source: UCAS

STUDENTS IN HIGHER EDUCATION 2018–19*		
	Full-time	*Part-time*
HE students	1,883,155	500,810
Postgraduate students	356,650	229,080
Undergraduate students	1,526,505	271,730

* Includes UK, EU and non-EU students
Source: Higher Education Statistics Authority (HESA) 2020

UK HIGHER EDUCATION QUALIFICATIONS AWARDED 2018–19		
	Full-time	*Part-time*
First degrees	397,540	27,005
Other undergraduate qualifications	46,620	24,950
Postgraduate Certificate in Education	20,545	930
Other postgraduate research and taught qualifications	203,975	79,570
Total qualifications awarded	668,685	132,450

Source: HESA 2020

COURSES

HE institutions in the UK mainly offer courses leading to the following qualifications. These qualifications go from levels 4 to 8 on England's Regulated Qualifications Framework, levels 7 to 12 on Scotland's Credit and Qualifications Framework. Individual HEIs may not offer all of these.

Certificates of Higher Education (CertHE) are awarded after one year's full-time study (or equivalent). If available to students on longer courses, they certify that students have reached a minimum standard in their first year.

Diplomas of Higher Education (DipHE) and other *Higher Diplomas* are awarded after two to three years' full-time study (or equivalent). They certify that a student has achieved a minimum standard in first- and second-year courses and, in the case of nursing, third-year courses. They can often be used for entry to the third year of a related degree course.

Foundation degrees are awarded after two years of full-time study (or equivalent). These degrees combine academic study with work-based learning, and have been designed jointly by universities, colleges and employers with a particular area of work in mind. They are usually accepted as a basis for entry to the third year of a related degree course. These courses are due to be streamlined and renamed 'Higher Technical Qualifications' under plans to revamp further education in England (see also Recent Developments).

Bachelor's degrees, also referred to as *first degrees,* have different titles, Bachelor of Arts (BA) and Bachelor of Science (BSc) being the most common. In England, Wales and Northern Ireland most Bachelor's degree courses are 'with Honours' and awarded after three years of full-time study, although in some subjects the courses last longer. In Scotland, where young people may leave school and go to university a year younger, HE institutions typically offer Ordinary Bachelor's degrees after three years' study and Bachelor's degrees with Honours after four years. Honours degrees are graded as first, upper second (2:1), lower second (2:2), or third. HEIs in England, Wales and Northern Ireland may allow students who fail the first year of an Honours degree by a small margin to transfer to an Ordinary degree course, if they have one. Ordinary degrees may also be awarded to Honours degree students who do not finish an Honours degree course but complete enough of it to earn a pass.

Postgraduate or *Higher degrees.* Graduates may go on to take *Master's degrees,* which involve one or two years' work and can be taught or research-based. They may also take one-year postgraduate diplomas and certificates, often linked to a specific profession, such as the *Postgraduate Certificate in Education* (PGCE) required to become a state school teacher. A *doctorate,* leading to a qualification such as Doctor of Philosophy – a PHD or DPHIL – usually involves at least three years of full-time research.

The framework for HE qualifications in England, Wales and Northern Ireland (FHEQ) and the framework for qualifications of HE institutions in Scotland can both be found on the QAA website, which describes the achievement represented by HE qualifications.

ADMISSIONS
When preparing to apply to a university or other HE college, individuals can compare facts and figures on institutions and courses using the government's Unistats website. This includes details of students' views from the annual National Student Survey. They can also consult the results of the Teaching Excellence Framework, which is an official survey of teaching quality in universities listed on the Office for Students' website.

For the vast majority of full-time undergraduate courses, individuals need to apply online through UCAS, the organisation responsible for managing applications to HE courses in the UK. More than half a million people wanting to study at a university or college each year use this UCAS service, which has useful online tools to help students find the right course.

UCAS also provides two specialist applications services used by more than 50,000 people each year: the Conservatoires UK Admissions Service (CUKAS), for those applying to UK music conservatoires, and the Graduate Teacher Training Registry (GTTR), for postgraduate applications for initial teacher training courses in England and Wales and some in Scotland. Details of initial teacher training courses in Scotland can also be obtained from Universities Scotland and from Teach in Scotland, the website created by the Scottish government to promote teaching.

Each university or college sets its own entry requirements. These can be in terms of particular exam grades or total points on the 'UCAS tariff' (UCAS's system for allocating points to different qualifications on a common basis), or be non-academic, like having a health check. HE institutions will make 'firm offers' to candidates who have already gained the qualifications they present for entry, and 'conditional offers' to those who have yet to take their exams or obtain their results. Conditional offers often require a minimum level of achievement in a specified subject, for example '300 points to include grade A at A-level Chemistry'. If candidates' achievements are lower than specified in their conditional offers, the university or college may not accept them; then, if they still wish to go into HE, they need to find another institution through the UCAS 'clearing' process.

The government is looking into whether to change to a post-qualification admissions system (*see also* Recent Developments.)

The Open University conducts its own admissions. It is the UK's only university dedicated to distance learning and the UK's largest for part-time HE. Because it is designed to be 'open' to all, no qualifications are needed for entry to the majority of its courses.

Individuals can search thousands of UK postgraduate courses and research opportunities on UK graduate careers website Prospects. The application process for postgraduate

places can vary between institutions. Most universities and colleges accept direct applications and many accept applications through UKPASS, a free, centralised online service run by UCAS that allows individuals to submit up to ten different applications, track their progress and attach supporting material, such as references.

UNISTATS **W** http://unistats.direct.gov.uk
TEACHING EXCELLENCE FRAMEWORK
  W www.officeforstudents.org.uk/advice-and-guidance/teaching
UCAS **T** 0371-468 0468 **W** www.ucas.com
UNIVERSITIES SCOTLAND **T** 0131-226 1111
  W www.universities-scotland.ac.uk
TEACH IN SCOTLAND **T** 0845-345 4745
  W https://teachinscotland.scot
PROSPECTS **T** 0161-277 5200 **W** www.prospects.ac.uk
UKPASS **T** 0371-334 4447 **W** http://ukpass.ac.uk

TUITION FEES AND STUDENT SUPPORT

TUITION FEES
Higher Education institutions (HEIs) in England, Wales and Northern Ireland charge tuition fees for full-time HE courses. Although students from outside the EU can be charged the full cost of their courses, the tuition fees that universities may charge undergraduate degree students from the UK and other EU countries is capped at £9,250 for 2020–21, while for all other international students the fees are variable. In Scotland, tuition fees for 2020–21 are £1,820 for full-time Scottish-domiciled or EU students and capped at £9,250 for full-time students from the rest of the UK (England, Wales and Northern Ireland). In Wales, maximum tuition fees are £, while in Northern Ireland they are £4,275 for resident and EU students, otherwise £9,250.

Full-time students do not have to pay their fees themselves before or during their course, as tuition fee loans are available to cover the full cost; these do not have to be repaid until the student is working and earning more than a specified amount (*see* Student Loans, Grants and Bursaries).

EU students starting courses in 2020–21 will pay home student level fees for the duration of their course. For courses starting in academic year 2021–22, however, EU, other EEA and Swiss nationals will no longer be eligible for home fee status undergraduate, postgraduate, and advanced learner financial support from Student Finance England. This change will also apply to further education funding for those aged 19 or over, and funding for apprenticeships.

STUDENT LOANS, GRANTS AND BURSARIES

England
Students starting their first full-time HE course in 2020–21 can apply through Student Finance England for financial support. Two student loans are available from the government: a tuition fee loan of up to £9,250 for 2020–21, or up to £6,165 for a private university or college, or £11,100 for an accelerated degree course; and a maintenance loan (for students aged under 60) to help with living expenses of up to £9,203 for those living away from home (£12,010 if studying away from home in London), or up to £7,747 for those living with their parents during term time, or up to £10,539 if living and studying abroad for a year.

The tuition fee loan is not affected by household income and is paid directly to the relevant HE institution. A proportion (currently 65 per cent) of the maximum maintenance loan is available irrespective of household income while the rest depends on an income assessment. Student Finance England usually pays the money into the student's own bank account in three instalments, one at the start of each term.

Repayment of both loans does not start until the April after the student has left university or college, or before they are earning £19,390 a year, £1,615 a month or £372 a week in the UK (£21,000 for postgraduate loans).

At this point the individual's employer will deduct 9 per cent of any salary above the starting limit through the Pay As You Earn (PAYE) system (6 per cent for postgraduate loans). The self-employed make repayments through their tax returns. Student loans accrue interest from the date they are paid out, until they are repaid in full. Generally, the interest rate for student loans is set in September each year. The latest rate can be found online (W www.studentloanrepayment.co.uk).

Maintenance loans replaced grants for all new full-time students from 2016. Students can apply in 2020–21 for maintenance loans of up to £9,203 a year (£12,010 in London) – the maximum amount applying only to students with a household income of less than £25,000 a year. Special support grants will also be replaced by maintenance loans.

Students needing extra help may also be entitled to receive disabled students' allowance, adult dependants' grant, childcare grant or parents' learning allowance.

Part-time Higher Education Students are entitled to tuition fee loans (which replaced grants) of up to £5,981 in 2020–21.

Details are available on the Student Finance England website (W www.gov.uk/student-finance/loans-and-grants). There is a student finance calculator on the website to work out what financial support is available.

Universities and other higher education providers offer their own grants and bursaries, with differing criteria. Bursaries do not have to be repaid. Students should always check with the institution they are planning to attend to find out what extra financial support may be available.

If the student's chosen HE institution runs the additional fee support scheme, it could provide extra financial help if the student is on a low income and in certain other circumstances. For students in financial difficulty help may also be available through the institution's access to learning fund.

Wales

Welsh students starting a full-time HE course in 2020–21 can apply through Student Finance Wales for the forms of financial support described below.

The system of tuition fee and maintenance loans and grants in Wales is similar to England's, particularly for new students, but continuing Welsh students can also receive a substantial tuition fee grant. Maximum maintenance loans are: up to £8,100 for students living away from home (£10,124 if studying away from home in London) and up to £6,885 for those living with their parents during term time.

Welsh-domiciled students may apply for a Welsh government learning grant of up to £10,124 to help meet general living costs. This is paid in three instalments, one at the start of each term, like the student maintenance loan. The amount that a student gets depends on household income. The maximum grant is available to those with a household income of £18,370 or under. Those with an income of £59,200 or over will receive £1,000.

There is also a special support grant for single parents, student parents or those with disabilities, which is worth up to £5,161 a year in 2020–21. It is paid directly to students and is not offset against student loan borrowing.

Students can use the student finance calculator on the Student Finance Wales website to work out what financial support they may be entitled to.

Welsh HE institutions also hold financial contingency funds to provide discretionary assistance to students experiencing financial difficulties.

For 2020–21 part-time undergraduate higher education students and continuing students studying at least 25 per cent of an equivalent full-time course are entitled to receive a fee loan of £2,625 (£6,935 for a course at a publicly funded university or college elsewhere in the UK, or £4,625 at a private university or college). The maximum amount of grants and loans available is £5,433.75 depending on household income and course intensity.

Childcare Grants, Parents' Learning Allowance, Adult Dependants' Grant, and Disabled Students' Allowances are also available.

STUDENT FINANCE WALES **T** 0300-200 4050
 W www.studentfinancewales.co.uk

Scotland

Students starting a full-time HE course in 2020–21 can apply through the Student Awards Agency for Scotland for financial support. Full-time Scottish-domiciled or EU students enrolling on a course in 2020 will be eligible to have their tuition fees (£1,285 for a HND/HNC; £1,820 for a degree or equivalent) paid for the duration of their studies through the Student Awards Agency for Scotland (applications for tuition fee payment should be made annually). Tuition fees for full-time students from the rest of the UK (England, Wales and Northern Ireland) are capped at £9,250 for 2020–21, for which loans are available from the relevant body (Student Finance England, Student Finance Wales or Student Finance Northern Ireland). Living cost support is mainly provided through a student loan, the majority of which is income-assessed. The maximum loan for 2020–21 is £7,750.

The young students' bursary (YSB) is available to young students from low-income backgrounds and is non-repayable. Eligible students receive this bursary instead of part of the student loan, thus reducing their level of repayable debt. In 2020–21 the maximum annual support provided through YSB is £2,000 if household income is £20,999 or less a year.

The independent students' bursary (ISB) similarly replaces part of the loan and reduces repayable debt for low-income students independent of parental support. The maximum paid is £1,000 a year to those whose household income is £20,999 or less a year.

In 2020–21, students who have come from a care setting will be eligible to apply for a non-means-tested bursary of £8,100.

Travel expenses are included within the student loan. There are supplementary grants available to certain categories of students such as lone parents (£1,305). Extra help is also available to those who have a disability, learning difficulty or mental health problem.

STUDENT AWARDS AGENCY FOR SCOTLAND
 T 0300-555 0505 **W** www.saas.gov.uk

Northern Ireland

Students starting a full-time HE course in 2020–21 can apply through Student Finance Northern Ireland for financial support. The arrangements for both full-time and part-time students are similar to those for England. The main difference is that the income-assessed maintenance grant (or special support grant for students on certain income-assessed benefits) for new full-time students studying at UK universities and colleges is worth up to £3,475 (for household incomes of £19,203 or less).

Universities and colleges in Northern Ireland can charge up to £4,275 for tuition fees in academic year 2020–21, and students can get a loan for up to this amount. There are tuition fee loans of up to £9,250 for students studying in England, Scotland and Wales.

Loans are available for living costs: £3,750 for study in Northern Ireland, £4,840 for study elsewhere in the UK (£6,780 in London).

STUDENT FINANCE NORTHERN IRELAND
T 0300-100 0077 W www.studentfinanceni.co.uk

Disabled Students' Allowances

Disabled Students' Allowances (DSAs) are grants available throughout the UK to help meet the extra course costs that full-time, part-time and postgraduate (taught or research) students can face as a direct result of a disability, ongoing health condition, mental health condition or specific learning difficulty. They help disabled people to study in HE on an equal basis with other students. They are paid on top of the standard student finance package and do not have to be repaid. The amount that an individual gets depends on the type of extra help needed, not on household income.

In all parts of the UK, the following three allowances are available: a specialist equipment or large items allowance for the entire course (2020–21 maximum rates vary from £5,849 in Northern Ireland to £5,266 in England); an annual non-medical helper allowance (2020–21 maximum rates for full-time students vary from £23,258 in England to £20,938 in Northern Ireland); and an annual general or basic allowance (2020–21 maximum rates for full-time students vary from £1,954 in England to £1,759 in Northern Ireland). Reasonable spending on extra disability-related travel costs can also be reimbursed. Eligible individuals should apply as early as possible to the relevant UK awarding authority.

POSTGRADUATE AWARDS
In England in 2020–21, postgraduate loans for a masters course of £11,222 and doctoral loans of up to £26,445 are available to cover tuition and living costs for the duration of study, dependent on course, age and nationality or residency as well as other factors. Some courses such as a Postgraduate Certificate in Education (PGCE) allow students to qualify for the finance package usually available only to undergraduates. There are also bursaries available for social work and some medical students.

In Wales, masters loans of up to £17,489 and doctoral loans of up to £26,445 are available, while in Northern Ireland up to £5,500 is available to cover course fees only. In Scotland, eligible full-time and part-time postgraduate students can get tuition fee loans of up to £5,500, while only full-time students can apply for living cost loans of up to £4,500.

There is heavy competition for other postgraduate funding. Individuals can search for postgraduate awards and scholarships on two websites: Hot Courses and Prospects. They can also search for grants available from educational trusts, often reserved for students from poorer backgrounds or for those who have achieved academic excellence, on W www.gov.uk/grant-bursary-adult-learners or the Family Action website.

DEPARTMENT FOR THE ECONOMY (DE),
   NORTHERN IRELAND T 028-9052 9900
   W www.nidirect.gov.uk/articles/postgraduate-awards
FAMILY ACTION T 020-7254 6251
   W www.family-action.org.uk
HOT COURSES W www.hotcourses.com
POSTGRADUATE SEARCH W www.postgraduatesearch.com
PROSPECTS W www.prospects.ac.uk
STUDENT AWARDS AGENCY FOR SCOTLAND (SAAS)
   T 0300-555 0505 W www.saas.gov.uk

TEACHER TRAINING
See Professional Education/Teaching.

EMPLOYEES AND SALARIES

QUALIFIED TEACHERS IN MAINTAINED SCHOOLS
Full-time equivalent, thousands (2019–20)

	England	Wales	Scotland	NI	UK
Nursery and primary schools	*221.2	*14.1	25.8	8.2	269.5
Secondary schools	204.7	10.7	23.5	9.3	248.2
Special schools	24.3	0.8	1.9	0.9	27.9
Total	453.8	25.8	†52.1	18.4	550.1

* Includes middle schools in England and Wales
† Includes all centrally employed teachers
Source: gov.uk; wales.gov; scot.gov and education-ni.gov.uk, 2020

SUPPORT STAFF IN MAINTAINED SCHOOLS, ENGLAND AND WALES (2019–20)
Full-time equivalent, thousands

	England	Wales
Teaching assistants	265.2	15.6
Other support staff	226.8	11.3
Total	492.0	26.8

Source: gov.uk and wales.gov, 2020

ACADEMIC STAFF IN UK HIGHER EDUCATION INSTITUTIONS (2018–19)

	Full-time	Part-time	Total
Professors	16,840	4,680	21,520
Non-professors	126,670	68,875	195,545
Teaching only	19,925	46,430	66,335
Teaching and research	80,880	17,720	98,600
Research only	41,775	9,085	50,860
Neither teaching nor research	930	320	1,250

Source: HESA 2020

SALARIES

State school teachers in England and Wales are employed by local authorities or the governing bodies of their schools. All teachers are eligible for membership of the Teachers' Pension Scheme.

There are teaching and learning responsibility payments for specific posts, special needs work and recruitment and retention factors which may be awarded at the discretion of the school governing body or the local authority. There are separate pay ranges for Headteachers and other school leaders. Academies are free to set their own salaries.

In 2013 every school was required to revise its pay and appraisal policies, setting out how pay progression would, in future, be linked to a teacher's performance. From September 2014, school governing bodies were given more flexibility, within the national pay ranges, to determine the pay of headteachers and other school leaders. In July 2020 the Secretary of State for Education announced a pay award from September 2020 of between 5.5 and 2.75 per cent for teachers on the main scale and of 2.75 per cent for those on upper pay scales. From September 2020 the pay of school leaders ranges from £42,195 to £117,197 a year outside London and from £50,167 to £125,098 a year in Inner London.

After completing initial teacher training and achieving qualified teacher status (QTS), newly qualified teachers (NQTs) in maintained schools can expect to start on a salary of £25,714 a year in England and Wales (or £32,517 in Inner London).

In January 2020, the English government proposed an uplift to £26,000 for starting salaries in England and Wales potentially rising to £30,000 by 2022. In July, the government agreed a 3.1 per cent overall pay rise for teachers (*see also* Recent Developments).

The pay ranges for teachers in England and Wales from September 2020 are:

Main pay range (including NQTs)	
London fringe	£26,948–£38,174
Outer London	£29,915–£41,136
Inner London	£32,157–£42,624
Rest of England and Wales	£25,714–£36,961
Upper pay range	
London fringe	£39,864–£42,780
Outer London	£42,559–£45,766
Inner London	£46,971–£50,935
Rest of England and Wales	£38,690–£41,604

The Scottish Negotiating Committee for Teachers determines teachers' pay in Scotland on a seven-point scale where the entry point is for newly qualified teachers undertaking their probationary year. Experienced, ambitious teachers who reach the top of the main pay scale are eligible to become chartered teachers and earn more on a separate pay spine. However, to do so they must study for further professional qualifications. Headteachers and deputies have a separate pay spine as do 'principals' or heads of department. Additional allowances are payable to teachers in circumstances such as working in distant islands and remote schools. Teaching salaries in Scotland were increased by 1 per cent in April 2017 and by a further 1 per cent in January 2018.

Salary scales for teachers in Scotland from 1 April 2020:

Headteacher/deputy headteacher	£51,207–£98,808
Principal teacher	£45,150–£58,269
Chartered teacher	£42,696–£50,772
Main grade	£27,498–£41,412

Teachers in Northern Ireland have broadly similar pay scales to teachers in England and Wales. Classroom teachers who take on teaching and learning responsibilities outside their normal classroom duties may be awarded one of five teaching allowances. In April 2020, the Department for Education published agreed revised pay scales with a backdated uplift of 2.25 per cent from September 2017 and 2 per cent payable from September 2018 in Northern Ireland. From 1 September 2018, details as follows:

Principal (headteacher)	£45,540–£112,934
School leaders	£40,256–£44,427
Classroom teacher (upper pay scale)	£36,731–£39,498
Classroom teacher (main pay scale)	£23,199–£33,906
Unqualified teacher	£14,760
Teaching allowances	£1,985–£12,800

Since 2007, most academic staff in HE across the UK are paid on a single national pay scale as a result of a national framework agreement negotiated by the HE unions and HE institutions. Staff are paid according to rates on a 51-point national pay spine and academic and academic-related staff are graded according to a national grading structure. As HE institutions are autonomous employers, precise job grades and salaries may vary but the following table outlines salaries that typically tally with certain job roles in HE. As a result of the economic impact of the COVID-19 pandemic, employers opted for a zero per cent uplift in the pay award for 2020–21, so pay remains at previous levels:

Principal lecturer	£50,132–£58,089
Senior lecturer	£39,609–£48,677
Lecturer	£33,199–£38,460
Junior researcher	£26,243–£32,236

UNIVERSITIES

The following is a list of universities, which are those institutions that have been granted degree-awarding powers by either a royal charter or an act of parliament, or have been permitted to use the word 'university' (or 'university college') by the Privy Council. There are other recognised bodies in the UK with degree-awarding powers, as well as institutions offering courses leading to a degree from a recognised body. Further information is available at W www.gov.uk/recognised-uk-degrees

Student figures represent the number of undergraduate (UG) and postgraduate (PG) students based on information available at July 2019.

Higher Education institutions in England, Wales and Northern Ireland charge tuition fees for full-time HE courses. Although students from outside the EU can be charged the full cost of their courses, the tuition fees that universities may charge undergraduate degree students from the UK and other EU countries is capped at £9,250 for 2020–21. In Scotland, tuition fees for 2020–21 are £1,820 for full-time Scottish-domiciled or EU students and capped at £9,250 for full-time students from the rest of the UK (England, Wales and Northern Ireland). In Wales, maximum tuition fees are £9,000, while in Northern Ireland they are £4,395 for resident and EU students, otherwise £9,250. For detailed information on tuition fees and student loans, including for the devolved administrations, *see* Education, Higher Education, Tuition Fees and Student Support.

RESEARCH EXCELLENCE FRAMEWORK
The research excellence framework (REF) is the system for assessing the quality of research in UK higher education institutions. The next REF assessment will be published in 2021, further information on this and the existing 2014 REF assessment can be found at W www.ref.ac.uk.

TEACHING EXCELLENCE FRAMEWORK
The teaching excellence framework (TEF) rates teaching in universities and colleges and provides information about teaching provision and student outcomes. Participation for institutions is voluntary and open to universities and colleges in England, Wales, Scotland and Northern Ireland. A list of participating institutions and their current ratings (gold, silver, bronze or provisional) can be found on the Office for Students website (W www.officeforstudents.org.uk/advice-and-guidance/teaching/tef-outcomes).

UNIVERSITY OF ABERDEEN (1495)
King's College, Aberdeen AB24 3FX T 01224-272000
W www.abdn.ac.uk
Students: 10,255 UG; 4,115 PG
Chancellor, HRH the Duchess of Rothesay, GCVO, PC
Vice-Chancellor, Prof. George Boyne
University Secretary, Caroline Inglis

UNIVERSITY OF ABERTAY DUNDEE (1994)
Bell Street, Dundee DD1 1HG T 01382-308000
W www.abertay.ac.uk
Students: 3,605 UG; 450 PG
Chancellor, Lord Cullen of Whitekirk, KT, PC, FRSE
Vice-Chancellor, Prof. Nigel Seaton, FRENG
University Secretary, Sheena Stewart

ABERYSTWYTH UNIVERSITY (1872)
Penglais, Aberystwyth SY23 3FL T 01970-62311 1
W www.aber.ac.uk
Students: 7,035 UG; 1,150 PG
Chancellor, Lord Thomas of Cwmgiedd, PC, QC
Vice-Chancellor, Prof. Elizabeth Treasure
University Secretary, Geraint Pugh

ANGLIA RUSKIN UNIVERSITY (1992)
Chelmsford Campus, Bishop Hall Lane, Chelmsford CM1 1SQ
T 01245-493131 E answers@anglia.ac.uk W www.aru.ac.uk
Students: 19,010 UG; 4,490 PG
Chancellor, Lord Ashcroft, KCMG, PC
Vice-Chancellor, Prof. Roderick Watkins
Secretary and Clerk, Paul Bogle

ARTS UNIVERSITY BOURNEMOUTH (2012)
Wallisdown BH12 5HH T 01202-533011 W www.aub.ac.uk
Students: 3,365 UG; 125 PG
Chancellor, Prof. Sir Christopher Frayling
Vice-Chancellor, Prof. Paul Gough, CBE
University Secretary, Jon Reynard

UNIVERSITY OF THE ARTS LONDON (2003 (Formerly The London Institute (1986), renamed 2004))
272 High Holborn, London WC1V 7EY T 020-7514 6000
W www.arts.ac.uk
Students: 15,120 UG; 3,850 PG
Chancellor, Grayson Perry, CBE, RA
Vice-Chancellor, Sir Nigel Carrington
Secretary and Registrar, Stephen Marshall

COLLEGES
CAMBERWELL COLLEGE OF ARTS (1898)
45–65 Peckham Road, London SE5 8UF
T 020-7514 6301
W www.arts.ac.uk/camberwell
Head of College, Prof. David Crow
CENTRAL SAINT MARTINS COLLEGE OF ART AND DESIGN (1854)
Granary Building, 1 Granary Square, London N1C 4AA
T 020-7514 7444
W www.arts.ac.uk/csm
Head of College, Prof. Jeremy Till
CHELSEA COLLEGE OF ARTS (1895)
16 John Islip Street, London SW1P 4JU
T 020-7514 7751
W www.arts.ac.uk/chelsea
Head of College, Prof. David Crow
LONDON COLLEGE OF COMMUNICATION (1894)
Elephant and Castle, London SE1 6SB
T 020-7514 6500
W www.arts.ac.uk/cc
Head of College, Natalie Brett
LONDON COLLEGE OF FASHION (1963)
20 John Prince's Street, London W1G 0BJ
T 020-7514 7400
W www.arts.ac.uk/fashion
Head of College, Prof. Frances Corner, OBE
WIMBLEDON COLLEGE OF ART (1930)
Merton Hall Road, London SW19 3QA
T 020-7514 9641
W www.arts.ac.uk/wimbledon
Head of College, Prof. David Crow

ASTON UNIVERSITY (1966)
Aston Triangle, Birmingham B4 7ET T 0121-204 3000
W www2.aston.ac.uk
Students: 11,850 UG; 2,765 PG
Chancellor, Sir John Sunderland
Vice-Chancellor, Prof. Alec Cameron
Chief Operating Officer, Neil Scott

BANGOR UNIVERSITY (1884)
Gwynedd LL57 2DG T 01248-3511 51 W www.bangor.ac.uk
Students: 8,455 UG; 2,700 PG
Chancellor, George Meyrick
Vice-Chancellor, Prof. Graham Upton (interim)
University Secretary, Dr Kevin Mundy

UNIVERSITY OF BATH (1966)
Bath BA2 7AY T 01225-388388 W www.bath.ac.uk
Students: 13,275 UG; 4,275 PG
Chancellor, HRH the Earl of Wessex, KG, GCVO
Vice-Chancellor, Prof. Ian White, FRENG
University Secretary, Mark Humphriss

BATH SPA UNIVERSITY (2005)
Newton Park, Bath BA2 9BN T 01225-875875
E enquiries@bathspa.ac.uk W www.bathspa.ac.uk
Students: 6,320 UG; 1,670 PG
Chancellor, Jeremy Irons
Vice-Chancellor, Prof. Sue Rigby
Registrar, Christopher Ellicott

UNIVERSITY OF BEDFORDSHIRE (1993)
University Square, Luton LU1 3JU T 01234-400400
W www.beds.ac.uk
Students: 10,475 UG; 2,325 PG
Chancellor, Rt. Hon. John Bercow, MP
Vice-Chancellor, Bill Rammell
Registrar, Jenny Jenkin

UNIVERSITY OF BIRMINGHAM (1900)
Edgbaston, Birmingham B15 2TT T 0121-414 3344
W www.birmingham.ac.uk
Students: 22,710 UG; 12,205 PG
Chancellor, Lord Bilimoria, CBE
Vice-Chancellor and Principal, Prof. Sir David Eastwood
Registrar and Secretary, Lee Sanders

BIRMINGHAM CITY UNIVERSITY (1992)
University House, 15 Bartholemew Row, Birmingham B5 5JU
T 0121-331 5000 W www.bcu.ac.uk
Students: 19,790 UG; 4,785 PG
Chancellor, Sir Lenny Henry, CBE
Vice-Chancellor, Prof. Philip Plowden
University Secretary, Karen Stephenson

UNIVERSITY COLLEGE BIRMINGHAM (2012)
Summer Rowe, Birmingham B3 1JB T 0121-604 1000
E admissions@ucb.ac.uk W www.ucb.ac.uk
Students: 4,425 UG; 520 PG
Vice-Chancellor and Principal, Prof. Ray Linforth, OBE

BISHOP GROSSETESTE UNIVERSITY (2013)
Longdales Road, Lincoln LN1 3DY T 01522-527347
E enquiries@bishopg.ac.uk W www.bishopg.ac.uk
Students: 1,705 UG; 550 PG
Chancellor, Dame Judith Mayhew-Jonas, DBE
Vice-Chancellor, Revd. Canon Prof. Peter Neil
Registrar and University Secretary, Dr Anne Craven

UNIVERSITY OF BOLTON (2005)
Deane Road, Bolton BL3 5AB T 01204-900600
E enquiries@bolton.ac.uk W www.bolton.ac.uk
Students: 5,340 UG; 1,205 PG
Chancellor, Earl of St Andrews
Vice-Chancellor, Prof. George E. Holmes
Registrar and Secretary, Sue Duncan, LLD

BOURNEMOUTH UNIVERSITY (1992)
Fern Barrow, Poole BH12 5BB T 01202-961916
E enquiries@bournemouth.ac.uk W www.bournemouth.ac.uk
Students: 15,420 UG; 3,265 PG
Chancellor, Kate Adie, CBE
Vice-Chancellor, Prof. John Vinney
Chief Operating Officer, Jim Andrews

UNIVERSITY OF BRADFORD (1966)
Richmond Road, Bradford BD7 1DP T 01274-232323
W www.bradford.ac.uk
Students: 7,695 UG; 2,420 PG
Chancellor, Kate Swann
Vice-Chancellor and Principal, Prof. Brian Cantor, CBE
University Secretary, Riley Power

UNIVERSITY OF BRIGHTON (1992)
Mithras House, Lewes Road, Brighton BN2 4AT T 01273-600900
W www.brighton.ac.uk
Students: 17,700 UG; 3,855 PG
Vice-Chancellor, Prof. Debra Humphris, FRCP
Secretary and Registrar, Stephen Dudderidge

UNIVERSITY OF BRISTOL (1909)
Beacon House, Queens Road, Bristol BS8 1QU T 0117-928 9000
W www.bristol.ac.uk
Students: 18,270 UG; 6,585 PG
Chancellor, Sir Paul Nurse, FRS, FMEDSCI
Vice-Chancellor, Prof. Hugh Brady
Registrar, Lucinda Parr

BRUNEL UNIVERSITY LONDON (1966)
Kingston Lane, Uxbridge UB8 3PH T 01895-274000
E admissions@brunel.ac.uk W www.brunel.ac.uk
Students: 10,545 UG; 3,365 PG
Chancellor, Sir Richard Sykes
Vice-Chancellor, Prof. Julia Buckingham, CBE, PHD, DSc, FRSA
Chief Operating Officer, Paul Thomas, CBE

UNIVERSITY OF BUCKINGHAM (1983)
Buckingham MK18 1EG T 01280-814080
E info@buckingham.ac.uk W www.buckingham.ac.uk
Students: 1,465 UG; 1,395 PG
Chancellor, The Hon. Lady Keswick
Vice-Chancellor, Sir Anthony Seldon, PHD, FRSA
University Secretary, Emma Potts

BUCKS NEW UNIVERSITY (2007)
High Wycombe Campus, Queen Alexandra Road, High Wycombe
HP11 2JZ T 01494-522141 E advice@bucks.ac.uk
W www.bucks.ac.uk
Students: 8,030 UG; 1,060 PG
Vice-Chancellor, Prof. Nick Braisby
Academic Registrar and Secretary, Ellie Smith

UNIVERSITY OF CAMBRIDGE (1209)
The Old Schools, Trinity Lane, Cambridge CB2 1TN
T 01223-337733 W www.cam.ac.uk
Students: 12,540 UG; 7,970 PG
Chancellor, Lord Sainsbury of Turville, FRS (King's)
Vice-Chancellor, Prof. Stephen J. Toope (Clare Hall)
High Steward, Lord Watson of Richmond, CBE (Jesus)
Deputy High Steward, Mrs A. Lonsdale, CBE (Murray Edwards)
Commissary, Lord Judge, PC (Magdalene)
Pro-Vice-Chancellors, Prof. G. Virgo, QC (Downing); Prof. E. Ferran, FBA (St Catharine's); Prof. C. Abell, FRS, FMEDSCI (Christ's); Prof. A. Neely (Sidney Sussex); Prof. D. Cardwell, FRENG (Fitzwilliam)
Proctors (2019–20), Dr Timothy Dickens (Peterhouse); Francis Knights (Fitzwilliam)
Deputy Proctors (2019–20), Dr Gemma Burgess (Newnham); Gordon Chesterman (St Edmund's)
Orator, Dr R. Thompson (Selwyn)
Registrary, E. Rampton (Sidney Sussex)
Librarian, Dr J. Gardner (Selwyn)
Director of the Fitzwilliam Museum, L. Syson
Interim Academic Secretary, Dr. R. Coupe
Director of Finance, J. Hughes (Wolfson)
Executive Director of Development, Ms A. Traub
Esquire Bedells, Mrs N. Hardy (Jesus); Ms S. Scarlett (Lucy Cavendish)
University Advocate, Dr R. Thornton (Emmanuel)
Deputy University Advocate, Dr J. Seymour (Sidney Sussex)

COLLEGES AND HALLS
(with dates of foundation)
CHRIST'S (1505)
Master, Prof. J. Stapleton, FBA
CHURCHILL (1960)
Master, Prof. Dame Athene Donald, DBE, FRS
CLARE (1326)
Master, Lord Grabiner, QC
CLARE HALL (1966)
President, Prof. D. Ibbetson, FBA
CORPUS CHRISTI (1352)
Master, Prof. C. Kelly
DARWIN (1964)
Master, Prof. C. Fowler, FRAS, FGS
DOWNING (1800)
Master, A. Bookbinder
EMMANUEL (1584)
Master, Dame Fiona Reynolds, DBE
FITZWILLIAM (1966)
Master, Baroness Morgan of Huyton
GIRTON (1869)
Mistress, Prof. S. Smith, FRSE FBA
GONVILLE AND CAIUS (1348)
Master, Dr. P. Rogerson
HOMERTON (1976)
Principal, Prof. G. Ward, FRSA
HUGHES HALL (1885)
President, Dr A. Freeling
JESUS (1496)
Master, Sonita Alleyne, OBE, FRA, FRSA
KING'S (1441)
Provost, Prof. M. Proctor, FRS
LUCY CAVENDISH (1965)
President, Dame Madeleine Atkins, DBE, FACSS
MAGDALENE (1542)
Master, Rt. Revd Lord Williams of Oystermouth, PC, FBA
MURRAY EDWARDS (1954)
President, Dame Barbara Stocking, DBE

NEWNHAM (1871)
Principal, Ms A. Rose
PEMBROKE (1347)
Master, Lord Smith of Finsbury, PC
PETERHOUSE (1284)
Master, Bridget Kendall, MBE
QUEENS' (1448)
President, Prof. Lord Eatwell
ROBINSON (1977)
Warden, Prof. A. D. Yates
ST CATHARINE'S (1473)
Master, Prof. Sir Mark Welland, FRS, FRENG
ST EDMUND'S (1896)
Master, Ms C. Arnold, OBE
ST JOHN'S (1511)
Master, Prof. Sir Christopher Dobson, FRS, FMEDSCI
SELWYN (1882)
Master, R. Mosey
SIDNEY SUSSEX (1596)
Master, Prof. R. Penty, FRENG
TRINITY (1546)
Master, Dame Sally Davies, DBE, FRS
TRINITY HALL (1350)
Master, Revd Canon Dr J. Morris, FRHISTS
WOLFSON (1965)
President, Prof. J. Clarke, FRS, FMEDSCI

CANTERBURY CHRIST CHURCH UNIVERSITY (2005)
North Holmes Road, Canterbury CT1 1QU T 01227-767700
E admissions@canterbury.co.uk W www.canterbury.ac.uk
Students: 11,765 UG; 2,690 PG
Chancellor, Most Revd and Rt. Hon. Archbishop of Canterbury
Vice-Chancellor, Prof. Rama Thirunamachandran
Director of Academic Administration, Cathy Lambert

CARDIFF UNIVERSITY (1883)
Cardiff CF10 3AT T 029-2087 4000 W www.cardiff.ac.uk
Students: 23,480 UG; 8,455 PG
Chancellor, Baroness Randerson
Vice-Chancellor, Prof. Colin Riordan
Chief Operating Officer, Deborah Collins

CARDIFF METROPOLITAN UNIVERSITY (1865)
Western Avenue, Cardiff CF5 2YB T 029-2041 6070
W www.cardiffmet.ac.uk
Students: 8,330 UG; 2,100 PG
President and Vice-Chancellor, Prof. Cara Carmichael Aitchison, FACSS, FRGS, FHEA
Chief Operating Officer, John Cappock

UNIVERSITY OF CENTRAL LANCASHIRE (1992)
Preston PR1 2HE T 01772-201201 E cenquiries@uclan.ac.uk
W www.uclan.ac.uk
Students: 18,020 UG; 4,980 PG
Chancellor, Ranvir Singh
Vice-Chancellor, Lynne Livesey (interim)
University Secretary, Ian Fisher

UNIVERSITY OF CHESTER (Founded in 1839 as Chester Diocesan Training College; gained University status in 2005)
Parkgate Road, Chester CH1 4BJ T 01244-511000
E enquiries@chester.ac.uk W www.chester.ac.uk
Students: 10,945 UG; 4,465 PG
Chancellor, Gyles Brandreth
Vice-Chancellor, Canon Prof. Tim Wheeler
University Secretary, Adrian Lee

UNIVERSITY OF CHICHESTER (2005)
College Lane, Chichester PO19 6PE **T** 01243-816000
E help@chi.ac.uk **W** www.chi.ac.uk
Students: 4,465 UG; 1,055 PG
Vice-Chancellor, Prof. Jane Longmore
University Secretary, Sophie Egleton

COVENTRY UNIVERSITY (1992)
Priory Street, Coventry CV1 5FB **T** 024-7688 7688
W www.coventry.ac.uk
Students: 27,895 UG; 6,230 PG
Chancellor, Margaret Casely-Hayford
Vice-Chancellor, Prof. John Latham
Academic Registrar, Kate Quantrell

CRANFIELD UNIVERSITY (1969)
Cranfield MK43 0AL **T** 01234-750111 **E** info@cranfield.ac.uk
W www.cranfield.ac.uk
Students: 4,355 PG (postgraduate only)
Chancellor, Baroness Young of Old Scone
Vice-Chancellor, Prof. Sir Peter Gregson
University Secretary, Gregor Douglas

UNIVERSITY FOR THE CREATIVE ARTS (2008)
Falkner Road, Farnham GU9 7DS **T** 01252-722441
W www.uca.ac.uk
Students: 6,260 UG; 360 PG
Chancellor, Prof. Magdalene Odundo, OBE
Vice-Chancellor, Prof. Bashir Makhoul
University Secretary, Marion Wilks

UNIVERSITY OF CUMBRIA (2007)
Fusehill Street, Carlisle CA1 2HH **T** 01228-616234
W www.cumbria.ac.uk
Students: 5,860 UG; 1,720 PG
Chancellor, Most Revd and Rt. Hon. Archbishop of York
Vice-Chancellor, Prof. Julie Mennell
Registrar and Secretary, Jean Brown

DE MONTFORT UNIVERSITY (1992)
The Gateway, Leicester LE1 9BH **T** 0116-255 1551
E enquiry@dmu.ac.uk **W** www.dmu.ac.uk
Students: 20,855 UG; 4,845 PG
Chancellor, Baroness Lawrence of Clarendon, OBE
Vice-Chancellor, Prof. Andy Callop (interim)

UNIVERSITY OF DERBY (1992)
Kedleston Road, Derby DE22 1GB **T** 01332-590500
E askadmissions@derby.ac.uk **W** www.derby.ac.uk
Students: 14,595 UG; 3,895 PG
Chancellor, Earl of Burlington
Vice-Chancellor and Principal, Prof. Kathryn Mitchell
Registrar, June Hughes

UNIVERSITY OF DUNDEE (1967)
Nethergate, Dundee DD1 4HN **T** 01382-383000
W www.dundee.ac.uk
Students: 10,715 UG; 4,390 PG
Chancellor, Dame Jocelyn Bell Burnell, DBE, FRS, FRSE, FRAS
Vice-Chancellor and Principal, Prof. Andrew Atherton
University Secretary, Dr James McGeorge

DURHAM UNIVERSITY (1832)
The Palatine Centre, Stockton Road, Durham DH1 3LE
T 0191-334 2000 **W** www.dur.ac.uk
Students: 13,835 UG; 4,495 PG
Chancellor, Sir Thomas Allen, CBE
Vice-Chancellor, Prof. Stuart Corbridge
University Secretary, Jennifer Sewel

COLLEGES
COLLINGWOOD (1972)
Principal, Prof. J. Elliott
GREY (1959)
Master, Prof. T. Allen
HATFIELD (1846)
Master, Prof. A. M. MacLarnon
JOHN SNOW (2001)
Principal, Prof. C. Summerbell
JOSEPHINE BUTLER (2006)
Principal, A. Simpson
ST AIDAN'S (1947)
Principal, S. F. Frenk
ST CHAD'S (1904)
Principal, M. Masson
ST CUTHBERT'S SOCIETY (1888)
Principal, Prof. E. Archibald
ST HILD AND ST BEDE (1839)
Principal, Prof. S. Forrest
ST JOHN'S (1909)
Principal, Revd Dr D. Wilkinson
ST MARY'S (1899)
Principal, Prof. M. Dawn
SOUTH (2020)
Principal, Prof. T. Luckhurst
STEPHENSON (2001)
Principal, Prof. R. Lynes
TREVELYAN (1966)
Principal, Prof. A. Adeyeye
UNIVERSITY (1832)
Master, Dr R. Lawrie (acting)
USTINOV (2003)
Principal, S. Prescott (acting)
VAN MILDERT (1965)
Principal, Prof. D. Harper

UNIVERSITY OF EAST ANGLIA (1963)
Norwich Research Park, Norwich NR4 7TJ **T** 01603-456161
E admissions@uea.ac.uk **W** www.uea.ac.uk
Students: 12,985 UG; 4,970 PG
Chancellor, Karen Jones, CBE
Vice-Chancellor, Prof. David Richardson

UNIVERSITY OF EAST LONDON (1898)
University Way, London E16 2RD **T** 020-8223 3000
E study@uel.ac.uk **W** www.uel.ac.uk
Students: 9,695 UG; 3,390 PG
Chancellor, Shabir Randeree, CBE
Vice-Chancellor, Prof. Amanda Broderick
University Secretary, Tristan Foote (acting)

EDGE HILL UNIVERSITY (2006)
St Helens Road, Ormskirk L39 4QP **T** 01695-575171
W www.edgehill.ac.uk
Students: 11,050 UG; 3,205 PG
Chancellor, Prof. Tanya Byron
Vice-Chancellor, Dr John Cater, CBE
University Secretary, Lynda Brady

UNIVERSITY OF EDINBURGH (1583)
Old College, South Bridge, Edinburgh EH8 9YL **T** 0131-650 1000
E communications.office@ed.ac.uk **W** www.ed.ac.uk
Students: 22,095 UG; 10,795 PG
Chancellor, HRH the Princess Royal, KG, KT, GCVO
Vice-Chancellor and Principal, Prof. Peter Mathieson, FRCP,
  FRCPE
University Secretary, Sarah Smith

EDINBURGH NAPIER UNIVERSITY (1992)
Sighthill Campus, Edinburgh EH11 4BN **T** 0333-900 6040
W www.napier.ac.uk
Students: 10,280 UG; 2,830 PG
Chancellor, David Eustace
Vice-Chancellor, Prof. Andrea Nolan, OBE
Secretary, David Cloy

UNIVERSITY OF ESSEX (1965)
Wivenhoe Park, Colchester CO4 3SQ **T** 01206-873333
E admit@essex.ac.uk **W** www.essex.ac.uk
Students: 11,370 UG; 3,390 PG
Chancellor, Rt. Hon. John Bercow, MP
Vice-Chancellor, Prof. Anthony Forster, DPHIL
Registrar, Bryn Morris

UNIVERSITY OF EXETER (1955)
Stocker Road, Exeter EX4 4PY **T** 01392-661000
W www.exeter.ac.uk
Students: 18,480 UG; 5,565 PG
Chancellor, Lord Myners, CBE
Vice-Chancellor, Prof. Sir Steve Smith, FACSS
Registrar and Secretary, Mike Shore-Nye

FALMOUTH UNIVERSITY (2012)
Falmouth Campus, Woodlane, Falmouth TR11 4RH
T 01326-211077 **W** www.falmouth.ac.uk
Students: 5,605 UG; 400 PG
Chancellor, Dawn French
Vice-Chancellor, Prof. Anne Carlisle, OBE

UNIVERSITY OF GLASGOW (1451)
University Avenue, Glasgow G12 8QQ **T** 0141-330 2000
E student.recruitment@glasgow.ac.uk **W** www.gla.ac.uk
Students: 20,805 UG; 8,920 PG
Chancellor, Prof. Sir Kenneth Calman, KCB, FRCS, FRSE
Vice-Chancellor, Prof. Sir Anton Muscatelli, FRSE, FACSS
Registrar, David Bennion

GLASGOW CALEDONIAN UNIVERSITY (1993)
City Campus, Cowcaddens Road, Glasgow G4 0BA
T 0141-331 3000 **E** ukroenquiries@gcu.ac.uk **W** www.gcu.ac.uk
Students: 13,575 UG; 2,875 PG
Chancellor, Annie Lennox, OBE
Vice-Chancellor, Prof. Pamela Gillies, CBE, FRSE
University Secretary, Jan Hulme

UNIVERSITY OF GLOUCESTERSHIRE (2001)
The Park, Cheltenham GL50 2RH **T** 03330-141414
E admissions@glos.ac.uk **W** www.glos.ac.uk
Students: 7,080 UG; 1,415 PG
Chancellor, Baroness Fritchie, DBE
Vice-Chancellor, Stephen Marston
Secretary and Registrar, Dr Matthew Andrews

UNIVERSITY OF GREENWICH (1992)
Old Royal Naval College, Park Row, London SE10 9LS
T 020-8331 8000 **E** courseinfo@gre.ac.uk **W** www.gre.ac.uk
Students: 14,740 UG; 4,065 PG
Chancellor, Lord Boateng, PC, QC
Vice-Chancellor, Prof. David Maguire
Secretary, Peter Garrod

HARPER ADAMS UNIVERSITY (2012)
Newport TF10 8NB **T** 01952-820280
E admissions@harper-adams.ac.uk **W** www.harper-adams.ac.uk
Students: 4,805 UG; 505 PG
Chancellor, HRH the Princess Royal, KG, KT, GCVO
Vice-Chancellor, David Llewellyn
University Secretary, Dr Catherine Baxter

HARTPURY UNIVERSITY AND COLLEGE (2017)
Hartpury House, Gloucester GL19 3BE
E admissions@hartpury.ac.uk **W** www.hartpury.ac.uk
Students: 1,800
Vice-Chancellor and Chief Executive, Russell Marchant
Vice-Principal and Deputy Chief Executive, Lynn Forrester-Walker

HERIOT-WATT UNIVERSITY (1966)
Edinburgh EH14 4AS **T** 0131-449 5111 **E** enquiries@hw.ac.uk
W www.hw.ac.uk
Students: 7660 UG; 3,250 PG
Chancellor, Dr Robert Buchan
Vice-Chancellor, Prof. Richard A. Williams, OBE, FRSE, FRENG
University Secretary, Ann Marie Dalton-Pillay

UNIVERSITY OF HERTFORDSHIRE (1992)
Hatfield AL10 9AB **T** 01707-284000 **W** www.herts.ac.uk
Students: 18,840 UG; 5,565 PG
Chancellor, Marquess of Salisbury, KG, KCVO, PC
Vice-Chancellor, Prof. Quintin McKellar, CBE
Secretary and Registrar, Sue Grant

**UNIVERSITY OF THE HIGHLANDS AND ISLANDS
(2011)**
Ness Walk, Inverness IV3 5SQ **T** 01463-279190 **W** www.uhi.ac.uk
Students: 8,470 UG; 850 PG
Chancellor, HRH the Princess Royal, KG, KT, GCVO
Vice-Chancellor, Prof. Crichton Lang (interim)
Chief Operating Officer, Fiona Larg

UNIVERSITY OF HUDDERSFIELD (1992)
Queensgate, Huddersfield HD1 3DH **T** 01484-422288
W www.hud.ac.uk
Students: 14,165 UG; 4,080 PG
Chancellor, HRH the Duke of York, KG, GCVO, ADC(P)
Vice-Chancellor, Prof. Bob Cryan, CBE, DL, FRENG
University Secretary, Michaela Boryslawskyj

UNIVERSITY OF HULL (1927)
Cottingham Road, Hull HU6 7RX **T** 01482-346311
W www.hull.ac.uk
Students: 13,390 UG; 2,200 PG
Chancellor, Baroness Bottomley of Nettlestone, PC
Vice-Chancellor, Prof. Susan Lea, PHD
Registrar, Jeanette Strachan

IMPERIAL COLLEGE LONDON (1907)
South Kensington SW7 2AZ **T** 020-7589 5111
W www.imperial.ac.uk
Students: 9,730 UG; 8,645 PG
President, Prof. Alice Gast
Provost, Prof. Ian Walmsley, FRS
Secretary and Registrar, David Ashton

KEELE UNIVERSITY (1962)
Keele ST5 5BG **T** 01782-732000 **E** admissions@keele.ac.uk
W www.keele.ac.uk
Students: 8,510 UG; 2,360 PG
Chancellor, Sir Jonathon Porritt, CBE
Vice-Chancellor, Prof. Trevor McMillan
Academic Registrar, Dr Helen Galbraith

UNIVERSITY OF KENT (1965)
Canterbury CT2 7NZ **T** 01227-764000 **E** information@kent.ac.uk
W www.kent.ac.uk
Students: 15,905 UG; 3,920 PG
Chancellor, Gavin Esler
Vice-Chancellor & Principal, Prof. Karen Cox
Provost, David Nightingale

KINGSTON UNIVERSITY (1992)
River House, 53–57 High Street, Kingston upon Thames KT1 1LQ
T 020-8417 9000 E admissionsops@kingston.ac.uk
W www.kingston.ac.uk
Students: 13,625 UG; 4,010 PG
Chancellor, Bonnie Greer, OBE
Vice-Chancellor, Prof. Stephen Spier
University Secretary, Keith Brennan

UNIVERSITY OF LANCASTER (1964)
Bailrigg, Lancaster LA1 4YW T 01524-65201
W www.lancaster.ac.uk
Students: 10,220 UG; 3,990 PG
Chancellor, Rt. Hon. Alan Milburn
Vice-Chancellor, Prof. Mark E. Smith, PHD
University Secretary, Nicola Owen

UNIVERSITY OF LEEDS (1904)
Leeds LS2 9JT T 0113-243 1751 W www.leeds.ac.uk
Students: 25,430 UG; 8,990 PG
Chancellor, Prof. Dame Jane Francis, DCMG
Vice-Chancellor, Sir Alan Langlands
University Secretary, Roger Gair

LEEDS ARTS UNIVERSITY (2017)
Blenheim Walk, Leeds LS2 9AQ T 0113-202 8000
W www.leeds-art.ac.uk
Students: 1,570 UG; 35 PG
Vice-Chancellor, Prof. Simone Wonnacott

LEEDS BECKETT UNIVERSITY (1992)
City Campus, Leeds LS1 3HE T 0113-812 0000
W www.leedsbeckett.ac.uk
Students: 18,615 UG; 4,955 PG
Chancellor, Sir Bob Murray, CBE
Vice-Chancellor, Prof. Peter Slee
Secretary and Registrar, Jenny Share

LEEDS TRINITY UNIVERSITY (2012)
Brownberrie Lane, Leeds LS18 5HD T 0113-283 7100
E hello@leedstrinity.ac.uk W www.leedstrinity.ac.uk
Students: 2,725 UG; 640 PG
Chancellor, Deborah McAndrew
Vice-Chancellor, Prof. Margaret House, OBE
Chief Operating Officer, Phill Dixon

UNIVERSITY OF LEICESTER (1957)
University Road, Leicester LE1 7RH T 0116-252 2522
W www.le.ac.uk
Students: 12,555 UG; 4,855 PG
Chancellor, Lord Willets, PC
Vice-Chancellor, Prof. E Burke (acting)
Registrar, David Hall

UNIVERSITY OF LINCOLN (1992)
Brayford Pool, Lincoln LN6 7TS T 01522-882000
E enquiries@lincoln.ac.uk W www.lincoln.ac.uk
Students: 12,645 UG; 2,325 PG
Chancellor, Lord Adebowale, CBE
Vice-Chancellor, Prof. Mary Stuart, CBE
Registrar, Chris Spendlove

UNIVERSITY OF LIVERPOOL (1903)
Brownlow Hill, Liverpool L69 7ZX T 0151-794 2000
W www.liverpool.ac.uk
Students: 22,070 UG; 6,725 PG
Chancellor, Colm Tóibín
Vice-Chancellor, Prof. Dame Janet Beer, DBE

LIVERPOOL HOPE UNIVERSITY (2005)
Hope Park, Liverpool L16 9JD T 0151-291 3000
E enquiry@hope.ac.uk W www.hope.ac.uk
Students: 3,910 UG; 1,290 PG
Chancellor, Lord Guthrie of Craigiebank, GCB, LVO, OBE
Vice-Chancellor and Rector, Prof. Gerald Pillay
University Secretary, Graham Donelan

LIVERPOOL JOHN MOORES UNIVERSITY (1992)
Kingsway House, 2nd Floor, Hatton Garden, Liverpool L3 2QP
T 0151-231 2121 E courses@ljmu.ac.uk W www.ljmu.ac.uk
Students: 18,875 UG; 4,350 PG
Chancellor, Rt. Hon. Sir Brian Leveson
Vice-Chancellor, Mark Power
Registrar, Liz McGough

UNIVERSITY OF LONDON (1836)
Senate House, Malet Street, London WC1E 7HU T 020-7862 8000
W www.london.ac.uk

Chancellor, HRH the Princess Royal, KG, KT, GCVO
Vice-Chancellor, Prof. Wendy Thomson, CBE
University Secretary, Chris Cobb

COLLEGES
BIRKBECK
Malet Street, London WC1E 7HX
Students: 7,155 UG; 4,785 PG
President, Baroness Bakewell, DBE
Master, Prof. David Latchman, CBE
CITY
Northampton Square, London EC1V 0HB
Students: 10,640 UG; 9,140 PG
President, Prof. Sir Paul Curran
COURTAULD INSTITUTE OF ART
Somerset House, Strand, London WC2R 0RN
Students: 205 UG; 300 PG
Director, Prof. Deborah Swallow
GOLDSMITHS
New Cross, London SE14 6NW
Students: 6,545 UG; 3,455 PG
Warden, Patrick Loughrey
INSTITUTE OF CANCER RESEARCH
15 Cotswold Road, Sutton, Surrey SM2 5NG
Students: 290 PG (postgraduate only)
Chief Executive, Prof. Paul Workman
KING'S COLLEGE LONDON
(includes Guy's, King's and St Thomas's Schools of
Medicine, Dentistry and Biomedical Sciences)
Strand, London WC2R 2LS
Students: 18,925 UG; 13,345 PG
Principal, Prof. Edward Byrne
LONDON BUSINESS SCHOOL
Regent's Park, London NW1 4SA
Students: 1,915 PG (postgraduate only)
Dean, François Ortalo-Magné
**LONDON SCHOOL OF ECONOMICS AND POLITICAL
SCIENCE**
Houghton Street, London WC2A 2AE
Students: 4,835 UG; 6,790 PG
Director, Dame Minouche Shafik, DBE
**LONDON SCHOOL OF HYGIENE AND TROPICAL
MEDICINE**
Keppel Street, London WC1E 7HT
Students: 1,085 PG (postgraduate only)
Director, Prof. Baron Peter Piot, KCMG, MD, PHD

QUEEN MARY'S
(incorporating St Bartholomew's and the London School of Medicine and Dentistry)
Mile End Road, London E1 4NS
Students: 13,935 UG; 6,135 PG
Principal, Prof. Colin Bailey
ROYAL ACADEMY OF MUSIC
Marylebone Road, London NW1 5HT
Students: 415 UG; 430 PG
Principal, Prof. Jonathan Freeman-Attwood, CBE
ROYAL CENTRAL SCHOOL OF SPEECH AND DRAMA
Eton Avenue, London NW3 3HY
Students: 685 UG; 405 PG
Principal, Prof. Gavin Henderson, CBE
ROYAL HOLLOWAY
Egham Hill, Egham, Surrey TW20 0EX
Students: 7,725 UG; 2,835 PG
Principal, Prof. Paul Layzell
ROYAL VETERINARY COLLEGE
Royal College Street, London NW1 0TU
Students: 1,995 UG; 545 PG
Principal, Prof. Stuart Reid
SOAS
Thornhaugh Street, Russell Square, London WC1H 0XG
Students: 3,155 UG; 3,115 PG
Director, Baroness Amos, CH, PC
ST GEORGE'S
Cranmer Terrace, London SW17 0RE
Students: 3,935 UG; 1,035 PG
Principal, Prof. Jenny Higham
UCL
(including the Institute of Neurology, Eastman Dental Institute, School of Pharmacy and Institute of Education)
Gower Street, London WC1E 6BT
Students: 19,705 UG; 20,310 PG
Provost and President, Prof. Michael Arthur, FRCP, FMEDSCI
UNIVERSITY OF LONDON INSTITUTE IN PARIS
9–11 rue de Constantine, 75340 Paris Cedex 07, France
Chief Executive, Dr Tim Gore, OBE

INSTITUTES
SCHOOL OF ADVANCED STUDY
Senate House, Malet Street, London WC1H 0XG
Dean and Chief Executive, Prof. Rick Rylance
The school consists of nine institutes:
INSTITUTE OF ADVANCED LEGAL STUDIES
Charles Clore House, 17 Russell Square, London WC1B 5DR
Director, Prof. Carl Stychin
INSTITUTE OF CLASSICAL STUDIES
Senate House, Malet Street, London WC1E 7HU
Director, Prof. Greg Woolf, FSA
INSTITUTE OF COMMONWEALTH STUDIES
Senate House, Malet Street, London WC1E 7HU
Director, Prof. Philip Murphy
INSTITUTE OF ENGLISH STUDIES
Senate House, Malet Street, London WC1E 7HU
Director, Prof. Clare A. Lees
INSTITUTE OF HISTORICAL RESEARCH
Senate House, Malet Street, London WC1E 7HU
Director, Prof. Jo Fox
INSTITUTE OF LATIN AMERICAN STUDIES
Senate House, Malet Street, London WC1E 7HU
Director, Prof. Linda Newson, OBE
INSTITUTE OF MODERN LANGUAGES RESEARCH
Senate House, Malet Street, London WC1E 7HU
Director, Prof. Catherine Davies
INSTITUTE OF PHILOSOPHY
Senate House, Malet Street, London WC1E 7HU
Director, Prof. Barry Smith

THE WARBURG INSTITUTE
Woburn Square, London WC1H 0AB
Director, Prof. Bill Sherman

LONDON METROPOLITAN UNIVERSITY (2002)
166–220 Holloway Road, London N7 8DB T 020-7423 0000
W www.londonmet.ac.uk
Students: 7,920 UG; 2,375 PG
Patron, HRH the Duke of York, KG, GCVO, ADC(P)
Vice-Chancellor, Prof. Lynn Dobbs
University Secretary, Chris Ince

LONDON SOUTH BANK UNIVERSITY (1992)
103 Borough Road, London SE1 0AA T 020-7815 7815
E course.enquiry@lsbu.ac.uk W www.lsbu.ac.uk
Students: 12,320 UG; 4,810 PG
Chancellor, Sir Simon Hughes, PC
Vice-Chancellor, Prof. David Phoenix
University Secretary, James Stevenson

LOUGHBOROUGH UNIVERSITY (1966)
Epinal Way, Loughborough LE11 3TU T 01509-222222
W www.lboro.ac.uk
Students: 13,110 UG; 4,205 PG
Chancellor, Lord Coe, CH, OBE
Vice-Chancellor, Prof. Robert Allison
Chief Operating Officer, Richard Taylor

UNIVERSITY OF MANCHESTER (2004. Formed by the amalgamation of Victoria University of Manchester (1851; reorganised 1880 and 1903) and the University of Manchester Institute of Science and Technology (1824))
Oxford Road, Manchester M13 9PL T 0161-306 6000
W www.manchester.ac.uk
Students: 27,505 UG; 12,640 PG
Chancellor, Lemn Sissay, MBE
Vice-Chancellor, Prof. Dame Nancy Rothwell, DBE, FRS
Secretary and Registrar, Patrick Hackett

MANCHESTER METROPOLITAN UNIVERSITY (1992)
All Saints, Manchester M15 6BH T 0161-247 2000
W www2.mmu.ac.uk
Students: 26,605 UG; 6,475 PG
Chancellor, Lord Mandelson, PC
Vice-Chancellor, Prof. Malcolm Press
Chief Operating Officer, Prof. Karen Moore

MIDDLESEX UNIVERSITY (1992)
Hendon Campus, London NW4 4BT T 020-8411 5555
W www.mdx.ac.uk
Students: 14,920 UG; 4,770 PG
Chancellor, Dame Janet Ritterman, DBE
Vice-Chancellor, Prof. Tim Blackman
Chief Operating Officer, Sophie Bowen, PHD

NEWCASTLE UNIVERSITY (1963)
Newcastle upon Tyne NE1 7RU T 0191-208 6000
W www.ncl.ac.uk
Students: 19,860 UG; 6,615 PG
Chancellor, Prof. Sir Liam Donaldson
Vice-Chancellor, Prof. Chris Day, FRS, DPHIL
Registrar, Dr. John Hogan

NEWMAN UNIVERSITY, BIRMINGHAM (2013)
Genners Lane, Birmingham B32 3NT T 0121-476 1181
E admissions@newman.ac.uk W www.newman.ac.uk
Students: 2,220 UG; 540 PG
Vice-Chancellor, Prof. Scott Davidson
Secretary and Registrar, Andrea Bolshaw

UNIVERSITY OF NORTHAMPTON (2005)

Waterside Campus, University Drive, Northampton NN1 5PH
T 01604-735500 E bc.applicationservices@northumbria.ac.uk
W www.northampton.ac.uk
Students: 9,655 UG; 2,310 PG
Chancellor, Revd Richard Coles
Vice-Chancellor, Prof. Nick Petford, PHD, DSc
Chief Operating Officer, Terry Neville, OBE

NORTHUMBRIA UNIVERSITY AT NEWCASTLE (1992)

Ellison Building, Ellison Place, Newcastle upon Tyne NE1 8ST
T 0191-232 6002 E course.enquiries@northumbria.ac.uk
W www.northumbria.ac.uk
Students: 21,150 UG; 5,495 PG
Chancellor, Baroness Grey-Thompson, DBE
Vice-Chancellor, Prof. Andrew Wathey, CBE, DPHIL

NORWICH UNIVERSITY OF THE ARTS (2012)

Francis House, 3–7 Redwell Street, Norwich NR2 4SN
T 01603-610561 E info@nua.ac.uk W www.nua.ac.uk
Students: 2,115 UG; 105 PG
Vice-Chancellor, Prof. John Last, OBE, FRSA
Academic Registrar, Angela Tubb

UNIVERSITY OF NOTTINGHAM (1948)

University Park, Nottingham NG7 2RD T 0115-951 5151
W www.nottingham.ac.uk
Students: 24,605 UG; 8,495 PG
Chancellor, Sir Andrew Witty
Vice-Chancellor, Prof. Shearer West
Registrar, Dr Paul Greatrix

NOTTINGHAM TRENT UNIVERSITY (1992)

50 Shakespeare Street, Nottingham NG1 4FQ T 0115-941 8418
W www.ntu.ac.uk
Students: 24,520 UG; 6,370 PG
Chancellor, Sir John Peace
Vice-Chancellor, Prof. Edward Peck
Chief Operating Officer, Steve Denton

OPEN UNIVERSITY (1969)

Walton Hall, Milton Keynes MK7 6AA T 0300-303 5303
W www.open.ac.uk
Students: 108,990 UG; 8,945 PG
Chancellor, Baroness Lane-Fox of Soho, CBE
Acting Vice-Chancellor, Prof. Mary Kellett
University Secretary, Dr Jonathan Nicholls

UNIVERSITY OF OXFORD (c.12th century)

University Offices, Wellington Square, Oxford OX1 2JD
T 01865-270000 E information.office@admin.ox.ac.uk
W www.ox.ac.uk
Students: 14,640 UG; 10,275 PG
Chancellor, Lord Patten of Barnes, CH, PC (Balliol, St Antony's)
Vice-Chancellor, Prof. Louise Richardson, FRSE
Pro-Vice-Chancellors, Dr D. Prout, CB (Queen's); Prof. M.
   Williams (New College); Dr R. Easton (New College);
   Prof. A. Trefethen (St Cross); Prof. Chas Bountra
   (Merton); Prof. P.S. Grant (St Catherine's)
Registrar, G. Aitken
Academic Registrar, Dr S. Shaikh
Public Orator, Dr J. Katz (All Souls)
Director of University Library Services and Bodley's Librarian, R.
   Ovenden (Balliol)
Director of the Ashmolean Museum, Dr A. Sturgis (Worcester)
Director of the Museum of the History of Science, Dr S.
   Ackermann (Linacre)
Director of the Pitt Rivers Museum, Dr L. Van Broekhoven
   (Linacre)
Director of the University Museum of Natural History, Prof. P.
   Smith (Kellogg)
Chief Executive of Oxford University Press, N. Portwood (Exeter)
Keeper of Archives, S. Bailey (Linacre)
Director of Estates, P. Goffin (Jesus)
Director of Finance, L. Pearson (New College)

COLLEGES AND HALLS *(with dates of foundation)*

ALL SOULS (1438)
Warden, Prof. Sir John Vickers, FBA
BALLIOL (1263)
Master, Dame Helen Ghosh, DCB
BLACKFRIARS HALL (1221)
Regent, Very Revd Dr Simon Gaine, OP
BRASENOSE (1509)
Principal, John Bowers, QC
CAMPION HALL (1896)
Master, Revd James Hanvey
CHRIST CHURCH (1546)
Dean, Very Revd Prof. Martyn Percy
CORPUS CHRISTI (1517)
President, Dr Helen Moore
EXETER (1314)
Rector, Prof. Sir Rick Trainor, KBE
GREEN TEMPLETON (2008)
Principal, Prof. Denise Lievesley, CBE
HARRIS MANCHESTER (1889)
Principal, Very Revd Prof. Jane Shaw
HERTFORD (1740)
Principal, Will Hutton
JESUS (1571)
Principal, Prof. Sir Nigel Shadbolt, FRS, FREng
KEBLE (1870)
Warden, Sir Jonathan Phillips, KCB
KELLOGG (1990)
President, Prof. Jonathan M. Michie
LADY MARGARET HALL (1878)
Principal, Alan Rusbridger
LINACRE (1962)
Principal, Dr Nick Brown
LINCOLN (1427)
Rector, Prof. Henry Woudhuysen, FBA
MAGDALEN (1458)
President, Prof. Sir David Clary, FRS
MANSFIELD (1886)
Principal, Helen Mountfield, QC
MERTON (1264)
Warden, Prof. Irene Tracey, FMedSci
NEW COLLEGE (1379)
Warden, Miles Young
NUFFIELD (1958)
Warden, Sir Andrew Dilnot, CBE
ORIEL (1326)
Provost, Neil Mendoza
PEMBROKE (1624)
Master, Dame Lynne Brindley, DBE, FRSA
QUEEN'S (1341)
Provost, Prof. Paul Madden, FRS, FRSE
REGENT'S PARK COLLEGE (1810)
Principal, Revd Dr Robert Ellis
ST ANNE'S (1878)
Principal, Helen King, QPM
ST ANTONY'S (1953)
Warden, Prof. Roger Goodman
ST BENET'S HALL (1897)
Master, Prof. Richard Cooper
ST CATHERINE'S (1963)
Master, Prof. Peter Battle
ST CROSS (1965)
Master, Carole Souter, CBE
ST EDMUND HALL (C. 1278)
Principal, Prof. Katherine Willis, CBE
ST HILDA'S (1893)
Principal, Prof. Sir Gordon Duff, FRCP, FRSE, FMedSci

ST HUGH'S (1886)
Principal, Dame Elish Angiolini, PC, DBE, QC
ST JOHN'S (1555)
President, Prof. Margaret J. Snowling, FBA, CBE
ST PETER'S (1929)
Principal, Mark Damazer, CBE
ST STEPHEN'S HOUSE (1876)
Principal, Revd Canon Dr Robin Ward
SOMERVILLE (1879)
Principal, Baroness Royall of Blaisdon, PC
TRINITY (1554)
President, Dame Hilary Boulding, DBE
UNIVERSITY (1249)
Master, Sir Ivor Crewe
WADHAM (1610)
Warden, Lord Macdonald of River Glaven, QC
WOLFSON (1981)
President, Sir Tim Hitchens, KCVO, CMG
WORCESTER (1714)
Provost, Prof. Sir Jonathan Bate, CBE, FBA, FRSL
WYCLIFFE HALL (1877)
Principal, Revd Michael Lloyd

OXFORD BROOKES UNIVERSITY (1992)
Gipsy Lane, Oxford OX3 0BP T 01865-741111
E query@brookes.ac.uk W www.brookes.ac.uk
Students: 13,120 UG; 4,055 PG
Chancellor, Dame Dr Katherine Grainger, DBE
Vice-Chancellor, Prof. Alistair Fitt
Registrar, Brendan Casey

UNIVERSITY OF PLYMOUTH (1992)
Drake Circus, Plymouth PL4 8AA T 01752-600600
E admissions@plymouth.ac.uk W www.plymouth.ac.uk
Students: 17,740 UG; 3,030 PG
Chancellor, Lord Kestenbaum
Vice-Chancellor, Prof. Judith Petts, CBE
University Secretary, Gordon Stewart

PLYMOUTH MARJON UNIVERSITY (2012)
Derriford Road, Plymouth PL6 8BH T 01752-636700
E admissions@marjon.ac.uk W www.marjon.ac.uk
Students: 2,140 UG; 495 PG
Vice-Chancellor, Prof. Rob Warner
Registrar, Stephen Plant

UNIVERSITY OF PORTSMOUTH (1992)
University House, Winston Churchill Avenue, Portsmouth PO1 2UP
T 023-9284 8484 E info@port.ac.uk W www.port.ac.uk
Students: 20,305 UG; 4,090 PG
Chancellor, Karen Blackett, OBE
Vice-Chancellor, Prof. Graham Galbraith, PHD
Chief Operating Officer, Bernie Topham

QUEEN MARGARET UNIVERSITY (2007)
Edinburgh EH21 6UU T 0131-474 0000 W www.qmu.ac.uk
Students: 3,430 UG; 1,745 PG
Chancellor, Prue Leith, CBE
Vice-Chancellor, Sir Paul Grice, FRSE
Secretary, Prof. Irene Hynd

QUEEN'S UNIVERSITY BELFAST (1908)
University Road, Belfast BT7 1NN T 028-9024 5133
E comms.office@qub.ac.uk W www.qub.ac.uk
Students: 18,630 UG; 5,855 PG
Chancellor, vacant
Vice-Chancellor, Prof. Ian Greer, FRCP,
Registrar, Joanne Clague

RAVENSBOURNE UNIVERSITY LONDON (2018)
Greenwich Peninsula, 6 Penrose Way, London SE10 0EW
T 020-3040 3500 W www.ravensbourne.ac.uk
Students: 2,475 UG; 55 PG
Interim Director and Chief Operating Officer, Andy Cook

UNIVERSITY OF READING (1926)
Whiteknights, PO Box 217, Reading RG6 6AH T 0118-987 5123
W www.reading.ac.uk
Students: 12,380 UG; 4,620 PG
Chancellor, Lord Waldegrave of North Hill, PC
Vice-Chancellor, Prof. Robert Van de Noort
University Secretary, Dr Richard Messer

RICHMOND, AMERICAN INTERNATIONAL
UNIVERSITY (1972 (obtained UK degree awarding powers
2018))
Queens Road, Richmond-upon-Thames TW10 6JP
T 0208 322 8200 W www.richmond.ac.uk
Students: 1,600
Principal and Vice-Chancellor, Prof. Lawrence S. Abeln
Provost, Phil Davies

ROBERT GORDON UNIVERSITY (1992)
Garthdee House, Garthdee Road, Aberdeen AB10 7QB
T 01224-262000 E admissions@rgu.ac.uk W www.rgu.ac.uk
Students: 9,175 UG; 3,355 PG
Chancellor, Sir Ian Wood, KT, GBE
Vice-Chancellor, Prof. John Harper
Academic Registrar, Hilary Douglas

ROEHAMPTON UNIVERSITY (2004)
Erasmus House, Roehampton Lane, London SW15 5PU
T 020-8392 3000 E Info@roehampton.ac.uk
W www.roehampton.ac.uk
Students: 10,155 UG; 1,750 PG
Chancellor, Dame Jacqueline Wilson, DBE, FRSL
Vice-Chancellor, Prof. Jean-Noël Ezingeard
University Secretary, Mark Ellul

ROYAL AGRICULTURAL UNIVERSITY (2013)
Stroud Road, Cirencester GL7 6JS T 01285-652531
E admissions@rau.ac.uk W www.rau.ac.uk
Students: 1,045 UG; 145 PG
Vice-Chancellor, Prof. Joanna Price
Chief Operating Officer, Susan O'Neill

ROYAL COLLEGE OF ART (1967)
Kensington Gore, London SW7 2EU T 020-7590 4444
E info@rca.ac.uk W www.rca.ac.uk
Students: 2,105 PG (postgraduate only)
Chancellor, Sir Jonathan Ive, KBE
Vice-Chancellor, Dr Paul Thompson
Chief Operating Officer (interim), Jocelyn Prudence

UNIVERSITY OF ST ANDREWS (1413)
St Andrews KY16 9AJ T 01334-476161 W www.st-andrews.ac.uk
Students: 8,625 UG; 2,110 PG
Chancellor, Lord Campbell of Pittenweem, CH, CBE, PC, QC
Vice-Chancellor, Prof. Sally Mapstone, FRSE
Academic Registrar, Marie-Noël Earley

ST MARY'S UNIVERSITY (2014)
Waldegrave Road, Strawberry Hill, Twickenham TW1 4SX
T 020-8240 4000 W www.stmarys.ac.uk
Students: 3,860 UG; 1,450 PG
Chancellor, Cardinal Vincent Nichols
Vice-Chancellor, Prof. Francis Campbell
University Secretary, Andrew Bogg

UNIVERSITY OF SALFORD (1967)
The Crescent, Salford M5 4WT **T** 0161-295 5000
W www.salford.ac.uk
Students: 15,985 UG; 4,305 PG
Chancellor, Jackie Kay, MBE
Vice-Chancellor, Prof. Helen Marshall
University Secretary, Alison Blackburn

UNIVERSITY OF SHEFFIELD (1905)
Western Bank, Sheffield S10 2TN **T** 0114-222 2000
E study@sheffield.ac.uk **W** www.sheffield.ac.uk
Students: 19,760 UG; 9,915 PG
Chancellor, Lady Justice Rafferty, DBE, PC
President and Vice-Chancellor, Prof. Koen Lamberts

SHEFFIELD HALLAM UNIVERSITY (1992)
City Campus, Howard Street, Sheffield S1 1WB **T** 011 4-225 5555
E enquiries@shu.ac.uk **W** www.shu.ac.uk
Students: 24,320 UG; 6,410 PG
Chancellor, Baroness Kennedy of The Shaws, FRSA, QC
Vice-Chancellor, Prof. Sir Chris Husbands
Chief Operating Officer, Richard Calvert

UNIVERSITY OF SOUTHAMPTON (1952)
University Road, Southampton SO17 1BJ **T** 023-8059 5000
W www.southampton.ac.uk
Students: 17,000 UG; 7,620 PG
Chancellor, Ruby Wax, OBE
Vice-Chancellor (interim), Prof. Mark Spearing
Chief Operating Officer, Ian Dunn

SOUTHAMPTON SOLENT UNIVERSITY (2005)
East Park Terrace, Southampton SO14 0YN **T** 023-8201 3000
E ask@solent.ac.uk **W** www.solent.ac.uk
Students: 10,015 UG; 560 PG
Chancellor, Theo Paphitis
Vice-Chancellor, Prof. Graham Baldwin
University Secretary, Caroline Carpenter

UNIVERSITY OF SOUTH WALES (1992)
Pontypridd CF37 1DL **T** 0345-576 0101 **W** www.southwales.ac.uk
Students: 18,360 UG; 4,500 PG
Chancellor, Rt. Revd Lord Williams of Oystermouth, PC, DPHIL
Vice-Chancellor, Prof. Julie Lydon, OBE
Academic Registrar, Sara Moggridge

STAFFORDSHIRE UNIVERSITY (1992)
College Road, Stoke-on-Trent ST4 2DE **T** 01782-294000
W www.staffs.ac.uk
Students: 12,305 UG; 2,045 PG
Chancellor, Lord Stafford
Vice-Chancellor, Prof. Liz Barnes
Chief Operating Officer, Ian Blachford

UNIVERSITY OF STIRLING (1967)
Stirling FK9 4LA **T** 01786-473171 **W** www.stir.ac.uk
Students: 8,745 UG; 3,835 PG
Chancellor, Lord McConnell of Glenscorrodale, PC
Vice-Chancellor, Prof. Gerry McCormac, FRSE
University Secretary, Eileen Schofield

UNIVERSITY OF STRATHCLYDE (1964)
16 Richmond Street, Glasgow G1 1XQ **T** 0141-552 4400
E corporatecomms@strath.ac.uk **W** www.strath.ac.uk
Students: 14,860 UG; 7,435 PG
Chancellor, Lord Smith of Kelvin, KT, CH
Vice-Chancellor, Prof. Sir Jim McDonald, FRSE, FRENG
Academic Registrar, Dr Veena O'Halloran

UNIVERSITY OF SUFFOLK (2016)
Waterfront Building, Neptune Quay, Ipswich IP4 1QJ
T 01473-338000 **W** www.uos.ac.uk
Students: 4,910 UG; 465 PG
Chancellor, Dr Helen Pankhurst
Vice-Chancellor, Prof. Helen Langton
Secretary and Registrar, Tim Greenacre

UNIVERSITY OF SUNDERLAND (1992)
Edinburgh Building, Chester Road, Sunderland SR1 3SD
T 0191-515 2000 **E** student.helpline@sunderland.ac.uk
W www.sunderland.ac.uk
Students: 11,320 UG; 2,750 PG
Chancellor, Emeli Sandé, MBE
Vice-Chancellor, Sir David Bell, KCB
Chief Operating Officer, Steve Knight

UNIVERSITY OF SURREY (1966)
Guildford GU2 7XH **T** 01483-300800 **E** admissions@surrey.ac.uk
W www.surrey.ac.uk
Students: 13,225 UG; 3,720 PG
Chancellor, HRH the Duke of Kent, KG, GCMG, GCVO
Vice-Chancellor, Prof. G. Q. Max Lu
Registrar, Sarah Litchfield

UNIVERSITY OF SUSSEX (1961)
Sussex House, Brighton BN1 9RH **T** 01273-606755
E information@sussex.ac.uk **W** www.sussex.ac.uk
Students: 13,000 UG; 4,800 PG
Chancellor, Sanjeev Bhaskar, OBE
Vice-Chancellor, Prof. Adam Tickell
Chief Operating Officer, Dr Tim Westlake

SWANSEA UNIVERSITY (1920)
Singleton Park, Swansea SA2 8PP **T** 01792-205678
W www.swansea.ac.uk
Students: 16,850 UG; 3,565 PG
Chancellor, Prof. Dame Jean Thomas, DBE, FMEDSCI, FLSW,
    FRS
Vice-Chancellor, Prof. Paul Boyle
Registrar, Andrew Rhodes

TEESIDE UNIVERSITY (1992)
Middlesbrough TS1 3BX **T** 01642-218121 **E** enquiries@tees.ac.uk
W www.tees.ac.uk
Students: 15,830 UG; 2,545 PG
Chancellor, Paul Drechsler, CBE
Vice-Chancellor, Prof. Paul Croney, CBE
Chief Operating Officer, Malcolm Page

UNIVERSITY OF ULSTER (1984)
Cromore Road, Coleraine BT52 1SA **T** 028-7012 3456
W www.ulster.ac.uk
Students: 18,365 UG; 5,350 PG
Chancellor, James Nesbitt, OBE
Vice-Chancellor, Prof. Paddy Nixon
University Secretary, Eamon Mullan

**UNIVERSITY OF WALES, TRINITY SAINT DAVID
(1828)**
Carmarthen Campus, SA31 3EP **T** 01267-676767
W www.uwtsd.ac.uk
Students: 8,495 UG; 1,785 PG
Vice-Chancellor, Prof. Medwin Hughes, FRSA

UNIVERSITY OF WARWICK (1965)
Coventry CV4 7AL **T** 024-7652 3523 **W** www.warwick.ac.uk
Students: 16,520 UG; 9,185 PG
Chancellor, Baroness Ashton of Upholland, GCMG, PC
Vice-Chancellor, Prof. Stuart Croft
Registrar, Rachel Sandby Thomas, CB

UNIVERSITY OF WEST LONDON (1992)
St Mary's Road, London W5 5RF **T** 0800-036 8888
W www.uwl.ac.uk
Students: 8,985 UG; 1,785 PG
Chancellor, Laurence S. Geller, CBE
Vice-Chancellor, Prof. Peter John
University Secretary, Marion Lowe

UNIVERSITY OF WESTMINSTER (1992)
309 Regent Street, London W1B 2HW **T** 020-7911 5000
E course-enquiries@westminster.ac.uk **W** www.westminster.ac.uk
Students: 14,890 UG; 4,350 PG
Chancellor, Lady Sorrell, OBE
Vice-Chancellor and Rector, Dr Peter Bonfield
University Secretary, John Cappock

UNIVERSITY OF THE WEST OF ENGLAND (1992)
Frenchay Campus, Coldharbour Lane, Bristol BS16 1QY
T 0117-965 6261 **E** infopoint@uwe.ac.uk **W** www.uwe.ac.uk
Students: 21,520 UG; 7,270 PG
Chancellor, Sir Ian Carruthers, OBE
Vice-Chancellor, Prof. Steve West, CBE
Registrar, Rachel Cowie

UNIVERSITY OF THE WEST OF SCOTLAND (2007)
Paisley PA1 2BE **T** 0141-848 3000 **E** ask@uws.ac.uk
W www.uws.ac.uk
Students: 13,465 UG; 2,970 PG
Chancellor, Rt. Hon. Dame Elish Angiolini, DBE, QC
Vice-Chancellor and Principal, Prof. Craig Mahoney
Chief Operating Officer, Susan Mitchell

UNIVERSITY OF WINCHESTER (2005)
Winchester SO22 4NR **T** 01962-841515
E enquiries@winchester.ac.uk **W** www.winchester.ac.uk
Students: 6,290 UG; 1,290 PG
Chancellor, Alan Titchmarsh, MBE
Vice-Chancellor, Prof. Joy Carter, CBE
Registrar, Dee Povey

UNIVERSITY OF WOLVERHAMPTON (1992)
Wulfruna Street, Wolverhampton WV1 1LY **T** 01902-321000
E enquiries@wlv.ac.uk **W** www.wlv.ac.uk
Students:·16,055 UG; 3,575 PG
Chancellor, Lord Paul, PC
Vice-Chancellor, Prof. Geoff Layer, OBE
Academic Registrar, Dr Jo Wright

UNIVERSITY OF WORCESTER (1946)
Henwick Grove, Worcester WR2 6AJ **T** 01905-855000
E study@worc.ac.uk **W** www.worcester.ac.uk
Students: 8,945 UG; 1,855 PG
Chancellor, HRH the Duke of Gloucester, KG, GCVO
Vice Chancellor, Prof. David Green, CBE
Registrar, Kevin Pickess

WREXHAM GLYNDWR UNIVERSITY (2008)
Mold Road, Wrexham LL11 2AW **T** 01978-290666
E enquiries@glyndwr.ac.uk **W** www.glyndwr.ac.uk
Students: 5,130 UG; 610 PG
Chancellor, Colin Jackson, CBE
Vice-Chancellor, Maria Hinfelaar

WRITTLE UNIVERSITY COLLEGE (2015)
Lordship Road, Chelmsford CM1 3RR **T** 01245-424200
E info@writtle.ac.uk **W** www.writtle.ac.uk
Students: 720 UG; 90 PG
Chancellor, Baroness Jenkin of Kennington
Vice-Chancellor, Prof. Tim Middleton
University Secretary, Andrew Williamson

UNIVERSITY OF YORK (1963)
York YO10 5DD **T** 01904-320000 **W** www.york.ac.uk
Students: 13,810 UG; 5,010 PG
Chancellor, Prof. Sir Malcolm Grant, CBE
Vice-Chancellor (acting), Prof. Saul Tendler, PHD
Registrar and Secretary, Jo Horsburgh, PHD

YORK ST JOHN UNIVERSITY (2006)
Lord Mayor's Walk, York YO31 7EX **T** 01904-624624
E admissions@yorksj.ac.uk **W** www.yorksj.ac.uk
Students: 5,460 UG; 785 PG
Chancellor, Most Revd and Rt. Hon. Archbishop of York
Vice-Chancellor, Prof. Karen Stanton
University Secretary, Dr Amanda Wilcox

PROFESSIONAL EDUCATION

The organisations selected below provide specialist training, conduct examinations or are responsible for maintaining a register of those with professional qualifications in their sector, thereby controlling entry into a profession.

EU RECOGNITION

It is possible for those with professional qualifications obtained in the UK to have these recognised in other European countries. Further information can be obtained from:

UK NARIC, Suffolk House, 68–70 Suffolk Road, Cheltenham GL50 2ED **T** 0871-330 7033 **W** www.naric.org.uk/naric

ACCOUNTANCY

Salary range for chartered accountants: Certified £25,000 (starting), rising to £26,000–£45,000+ (qualified); £40,000–£100,000+ at senior levels
Management £28,000 (starting); £32,000 (CIMA student); £62,000 (average); £46,000–£129,000+ at senior levels
Public finance £12,000–£35,000 (starting); £35,000–£50,000 (qualified); £50,000–£70,000 (5 years post-qualification experience); £80,000+ at senior levels

Chartered Accountancy trainees can be school-leavers or graduates. They usually undertake a three-year training contract with an approved employer culminating in professional exams provided by ICAEW, ICAS or CAI. Success in the exams and membership of one of the professional bodies, which offers continuous professional development and regulation, allows the use of the designation 'chartered accountant' and the letters ACA, FCA or CA.

The Association of Chartered Certified Accountants (ACCA) is the global body for professional accountants. The ACCA aims to offer business-relevant qualifications to students in a range of business sectors and countries seeking a career in accountancy, finance and management. The ACCA Qualification consists of up to 13 examinations, practical experiences and a professional ethics module. Chartered certified accountants can use the designatory letters ACCA.

Chartered global management accountants focus on accounting for businesses, and most do not work in accountancy practices but in industry, commerce, not-for-profit and public-sector organisations. Graduates who have not studied a business or accounting degree must complete the Chartered Institute of Management Accountants (CIMA) Certificate in Business Accounting before progressing to the CIMA Professional Qualification, which requires three years of practical experience and 12 examinations. In May 2011, CIMA and the American Institute of Certified Public Accountants (AICPA) agreed on the creation of a new professional designation, the Chartered Global Management Accountant (CGMA), which represents a worldwide standard in management accounting.

The Chartered Institute of Public Finance and Accountancy (CIPFA) is the professional body for people working in public finance. Chartered public finance accountants usually work for public bodies, but they can also work in the private sector. To gain chartered public finance accountant status (CPFA), trainees must complete a professional qualification in public sector accountancy. CIPFA also offers a postgraduate diploma for those already working in leadership positions.

ASSOCIATION OF CHARTERED CERTIFIED ACCOUNTANTS (ACCA), The Adelphi, 1–11 John Adam Street, London WC2N 6AU **T** 0141-582 2000
E info@accaglobal.com **W** www.accaglobal.com
Chief Executive, Helen Brand, OBE

CHARTERED ACCOUNTANTS IRELAND (CAI), 47–49 Pearse Street, Dublin 2 **T** 0353-1637 7200
W www.charteredaccountants.ie
Chief Executive, Barry Dempsey

CHARTERED INSTITUTE OF MANAGEMENT ACCOUNTANTS (CIMA), The Helicon, One South Place, London EC2M 2RB **T** 020-8849 2251
E cima.contact@aicpa-cima.com **W** www.cimaglobal.com
Chief Executive, Andrew Harding

CHARTERED INSTITUTE OF PUBLIC FINANCE AND ACCOUNTANCY (CIPFA), 77 Mansell Street, London E1 8AN **T** 020-7543 5600 **E** customerservices@cipfa.org
W www.cipfa.org
Chief Executive, Rob Whiteman

INSTITUTE OF CHARTERED ACCOUNTANTS IN ENGLAND AND WALES (ICAEW), Chartered Accountants' Hall, Moorgate Place, London EC2R 6EA
T 020-7920 8100 **E** general.enquiries@icaew.com
W www.icaew.com
Chief Executive, Michael Izza

INSTITUTE OF CHARTERED ACCOUNTANTS OF SCOTLAND (ICAS), CA House, 21 Haymarket Yards, Edinburgh EH12 5BH **T** 0131-347 0100 **E** enquiries@icas.com
W www.icas.com
Chief Executive, Bruce Cartwight

ACTUARIAL SCIENCE

Salary range: £25,000–£35,000 for graduate trainees; £40,000–£55,000 after qualification; £60,000+ for senior roles; £200,000+ for senior directors

Actuaries apply financial and statistical theories to solve business problems. These problems usually involve analysing future financial events in order to assess investment risks. To qualify, graduate trainees must complete 15 exams and three years worth of actuarial work-based training; most graduate trainees take between three and six years to qualify. Students can become Associate members of the Institute and Faculty of Actuaries (IFoA) and gain the right to describe themselves as an actuary and to use the letters AIA or AFA. Members of the profession who wish to continue their studies to an advanced level, or who specialise in a particular actuarial field, may take further specialist exams to qualify as a Fellow and bear the designations FIA or FFA.

The IFoA is the UK's chartered professional body dedicated to educating, developing and regulating actuaries based both in the UK and internationally. As at June 2019, the IFoA represent and regulate 32,938 members and oversee their education at all stages of qualification and development throughout their careers.

The Financial Reporting Council (FRC) is the unified independent regulator for corporate reporting, auditing, actuarial practice, corporate governance and the professionalism of accountants and actuaries. In 2012, the FRC assumed responsibility for setting and maintaining technical actuarial standards independently of the profession, as well as overseeing the regulation of the accountancy and actuarial professions by their respective professional bodies.

FINANCIAL REPORTING COUNCIL (FRC), 8th Floor, 125
London Wall, London EC2Y 5AS T 020-7492 2300
E enquiries@frc.org.uk W www.frc.org.uk
Chief Executive, Stephen Haddrill

INSTITUTE AND FACULTY OF ACTUARIES (IFoA), 7th
Floor, Holborn Gate, 326–330 High Holborn, London WC1V 7PP
T 020-7632 2100 E careers@actuaries.org.uk
W www.actuaries.org.uk
Chief Executive, Derek Cribb

ARCHITECTURE

Salary range: architectural assistant (part I) £18,000–£22,000;
(part II) £22,000–£35,000; fully qualified £32,000–£45,000;
senior associate, partner or director £45,000–£70,000

It takes a minimum of seven years to become an architect,
involving three stages: a three-year first degree, a two-year
second degree or diploma and two years of professional
experience followed by the successful completion of a
professional practice examination.

The Architects Registration Board (ARB) is the independent
regulator for the profession. It was set up by an act of
parliament in 1997 and is responsible for maintaining the
register of UK architects, prescribing qualifications that lead to
registration as an architect, investigating complaints about the
conduct and competence of architects and ensuring that only
those who are registered offer their services as an architect.
Following registration with ARB an architect can apply for
chartered membership of the Royal Institute of British
Architects (RIBA). RIBA, the UK body for architecture and the
architectural profession, received its royal charter in 1837 and
validates courses at over 50 schools of architecture in the UK;
it also validates overseas courses. RIBA provides support and
guidance for its members in the form of training, technical
services and events and sets standards for the education of
architects.

The Chartered Institute of Architectural Technologists is the
international qualifying body for Chartered Architectural
Technologists and Architectural Technicians.

ARCHITECTS REGISTRATION BOARD (ARB) 8
Weymouth Street, London W1W 5BU T 020-7580 5861
E info@arb.org.uk W www.arb.org.uk
Registrar and Chief Executive, Karen Holmes

CHARTERED INSTITUTE OF ARCHITECTURAL
TECHNOLOGISTS 397 City Road, London EC1V 1NH
T 020-7278 2206 E info@ciat.org.uk W www.ciat.org.uk
Chief Executive, Francesca Berriman, MBE

ROYAL INCORPORATION OF ARCHITECTS IN
SCOTLAND 15 Rutland Square, Edinburgh EH1 2BE
T 0131-229 7545 E info@rias.org.uk W www.rias.org.uk
President, Prof. Robin Webster, OBE

ROYAL INSTITUTE OF BRITISH ARCHITECTS (RIBA)
66 Portland Place, London W1B 1AD T 020-7580 5533
E info@riba.org W www.architecture.com
Chief Executive, Alan Vallance

ENGINEERING

Salary range:
Civil/structural £22,000–£30,000 (graduate); £50,000
(members of the Institution of Civil Engineers (ICE)); £81,447
(fellows of ICE)
Chemical £28,600 average (graduate); £78,500+ (chartered)
Electrical £26,000 (graduate); £35,000–£60,000 with
experience; £60,000+ (chartered)

The Engineering Council holds the national registers of
Engineering Technicians (EngTech), Incorporated Engineers
(IEng), Chartered Engineers (CEng) and Information and
Communication Technology Technicians (ICTTech). It also
sets and maintains the internationally recognised standards of
competence and ethics that govern the award and retention of
these titles.

To apply for the EngTech, IEng, CEng or ICTTech titles, an
individual must be a member of one of the 36 engineering
institutions and societies (listed below) currently licensed by
the Engineering Council to assess candidates. Applicants must
demonstrate that they possess a range of technical and personal
competences and are committed to keeping these up-to-date.

ENGINEERING COUNCIL, 5th Floor, Woolgate Exchange, 25
Basinghall Street, London EC2V 5HA T 020-3206 0500
W www.engc.org.uk
Chief Executive, Alasdair Coates

LICENSED MEMBERS

BCS – The Chartered Institute for IT W www.bcs.org
British Institute of Non-Destructive Testing W www.bindt.org
Chartered Institute of Plumbing and Heating Engineering
W www.ciphe.org.uk
Chartered Institution of Building Services Engineers
W www.cibse.org
Chartered Institution of Highways and Transportation
W www.ciht.org.uk
Chartered Institution of Water and Environmental Management
W www.ciwem.org
Energy Institute W www.energyinst.org
Institute of Acoustics W www.ioa.org.uk
Institute of Cast Metals Engineers W www.icme.org.uk
Institute of Healthcare Engineering and Estate Management
W www.iheem.org.uk
Institute of Highway Engineers W www.theihe.org
Institute of Marine Engineering, Science and Technology
W www.imarest.org
Institute of Materials, Minerals and Mining
W www.iom3.org
Institute of Measurement and Control
W www.instmc.org
Institute of Physics W www.iop.org
Institute of Physics and Engineering in Medicine
W www.ipem.ac.uk
Institute of Water W www.instituteofwater.org.uk
Institution of Agricultural Engineers
W www.iagre.org
Institution of Chemical Engineers W www.icheme.org
Institution of Civil Engineers W www.ice.org.uk
Institution of Engineering Designers
W www.institution-engineering-designers.org.uk
Institution of Engineering and Technology
W www.theiet.org
Institution of Fire Engineers W www.ife.org.uk
Institution of Gas Engineers and Managers
W www.igem.org.uk
Institution of Lighting Professionals W www.theilp.org.uk
Institution of Mechanical Engineers W www.imeche.org
Institution of Railway Signal Engineers W www.irse.org
Institution of Royal Engineers W www.instre.org
Institution of Structural Engineers W www.istructe.org
Nuclear Institute W www.nuclearinst.com
Permanent Way Institution W www.thepwi.org
Royal Aeronautical Society W www.aerosociety.com
Royal Institution of Naval Architects W www.rina.org.uk
Society of Environmental Engineers W www.environmental.org.uk
Society of Operations Engineers W www.soe.org.uk
The Welding Institute W www.theweldinginstitute.com

HEALTHCARE

CHIROPRACTIC

Salary range: £30,000–£50,000 starting salary; with own practice £50,000–£100,000 (depending on experience and size of practice)

Chiropractors diagnose and treat conditions caused by problems with joints, ligaments, tendons and nerves of the body. The General Chiropractic Council (GCC) is the independent statutory regulatory body for chiropractors and its role and remit is defined in the Chiropractors Act 1994. The GCC sets the criteria for the recognition of chiropractic degrees and for standards of proficiency and conduct. Details of the institutions offering degree programmes are available on the GCC website (*see* below). It is illegal for anyone in the UK to use the title 'chiropractor' unless registered with the GCC.

The British Chiropractic Association, Scottish Chiropractic Association, McTimoney Chiropractic Association and United Chiropractic Association are the representative bodies for the profession and are sources of further information.

BRITISH CHIROPRACTIC ASSOCIATION, 59 Castle
Street, Reading RG1 7SN **T** 0150-663 9607
E enquiries@chiropractic-uk.co.uk **W** www.chiropractic-uk.co.uk
Executive Director, Tom Mullarkey, MBE

GENERAL CHIROPRACTIC COUNCIL (GCC), Park
House, 186 Kennington Park Road, London SE11 4BT
T 020-7713 5155 **E** enquiries@gcc-uk.org **W** www.gcc-uk.org
Chief Executive and Registrar, Nick Jones

SCOTTISH CHIROPRACTIC ASSOCIATION, The Old
Barn, Houston Road, Houston, Renfrewshire PA6 7BH
T 0141-404 0260 **E** admin@sca-chiropractic.org
W www.sca-chiropractic.org
Administrator, Morag Cairns

DENTISTRY

Salary range: see Health: Employees and Salaries

The General Dental Council (GDC) is the organisation that regulates dental professionals in the UK. All dentists, dental hygienists, dental therapists, dental technicians, clinical dental technicians, dental nurses and orthodontic therapists must be registered with the GDC to work in the UK.

There are various different routes to qualify for registration as a dentist, including holding a degree from a UK university, completing the GDC's qualifying examination or holding a relevant European Economic Area or overseas diploma. The GDC's purpose is to protect the public through the regulation of UK dental professionals. It keeps up-to-date registers of dental professionals and works to set standards of dental practice, behaviour and education.

Founded in 1880, the British Dental Association (BDA) is the professional association and trade union for dentists in the UK. It represents dentists working in general practice, in community and hospital settings, in academia, research and the armed forces, and includes dental students.

BRITISH DENTAL ASSOCIATION (BDA), 64 Wimpole
Street, London W1G 8YS **T** 020-7935 0875 **E** enquiries@bda.org
W www.bda.org
Chief Executive, Martin Woodrow *(acting)*

GENERAL DENTAL COUNCIL (GDC), 37 Wimpole Street,
London W1G 8DQ **T** 020-7167 6000 **E** information@gdc-uk.org
W www.gdc-uk.org
Chief Executive, Ian Brack

MEDICINE

Salary range: see Health: Employees and Salaries

The General Medical Council (GMC) regulates medical education and training in the UK. This covers undergraduate study (usually five years), the two-year foundation programme taken by doctors directly after graduation and all subsequent postgraduate study, including speciality and GP training.

All doctors must be registered with the GMC, which is responsible for protecting the public. It does this by promoting high standards of medical education and training, fostering good medical practice, keeping a register of qualified doctors and taking action where a doctor's fitness to practise is in doubt. Doctors are eligible for full registration upon successful completion of the first year of training after graduation.

Following the foundation programme, many doctors undertake specialist training (provided by the colleges and faculties listed below) to become either a consultant or a GP. Once specialist training has been completed, doctors are awarded the Certificate of Completion of Training (CCT) and are eligible to be placed on either the GMC's specialist register or its GP register.

The British Medical Association (BMA) is a trade union and professional body for doctors in the UK, providing individual and collective representation, as well as information and professional guidance and support.

BRITISH MEDICAL ASSOCIATION (BMA), BMA House,
Tavistock Square, London WC1H 9JP **T** 020-7387 4499
E info.public@bma.org.uk **W** www.bma.org.uk
President, Prof. Dinesh Bhugra, CBE

GENERAL MEDICAL COUNCIL (GMC), Regent's Place, 350
Euston Road, London NW1 3JN **T** 0161-923 6602
E gmc@gmc-uk.org **W** www.gmc-uk.org
Chief Executive, Charlie Massey

WORSHIPFUL SOCIETY OF APOTHECARIES OF
LONDON, Black Friars Lane, London EC4V 6EJ
T 020-7236 1189 **E** clerksec@apothecaries.org
W www.apothecaries.org
Master, Prof. Martin Rossor

SPECIALIST TRAINING COLLEGES AND FACULTIES

Faculty of Occupational Medicine **W** www.facoccmed.ac.uk
Faculty of Public Health **W** www.fph.org.uk
Joint Committee on Surgical Training **W** www.jcst.org
Joint Royal Colleges of Physicians Training Board
W www.jrcptb.org.uk
Royal College of Anaesthetists **W** www.rcoa.ac.uk
Royal College of Emergency Medicine www.rcem.ac.uk
Royal College of General Practitioners **W** www.rcgp.org.uk
Royal College of Obstetricians and Gynaecologists
W www.rcog.org.uk
Royal College of Ophthalmologists **W** www.rcophth.ac.uk
Royal College of Paediatrics and Child Health
W www.rcpch.ac.uk
Royal College of Pathologists **W** www.rcpath.org
Royal College of Physicians, London **W** www.rcplondon.ac.uk
Royal College of Psychiatrists **W** www.rcpsych.ac.uk
Royal College of Radiologists **W** www.rcr.ac.uk

MEDICINE, SUPPLEMENTARY PROFESSIONS

The standard of professional education for arts therapists, biomedical scientists, chiropodists and podiatrists, clinical scientists, dietitians, hearing aid dispensers, occupational therapists, operating department practitioners, orthoptists, paramedics, physiotherapists, practitioner psychologists, prosthetists and orthotists, radiographers, social workers in England and speech and language therapists are regulated by the Health and Care Professions Council (HCPC), which only registers those practitioners who meet certain standards of training, professional skills, behaviour and health. The HCPC can take action against professionals who do not meet these standards or falsely declare they are registered. Each profession regulated by the HCPC has at least one professional title that is protected by law.

HEALTH AND CARE PROFESSIONS COUNCIL (HCPC), Park House, 184–186 Kennington Park Road, London SE11 4BU **T** 0300-500 6184 **E** registration@hcpc-uk.org **W** www.hcpc-uk.org *Chief Executive and Registrar,* Marc Seale

ART, DRAMA AND MUSIC THERAPIES
Salary range: £26,000–£37,000 (starting); £31,000–£43,000 with experience; £40,000–£50,000 (senior and principal therapists)

An art, drama or music therapist encourages people to express their feelings and emotions through art, such as painting and drawing, drama or music. A postgraduate qualification in the relevant therapy is required. Details of accredited training programmes in the UK can be obtained from the following organisations:

BRITISH ASSOCIATION FOR MUSIC THERAPY, 24–27 White Lion Street, London N1 9PD **T** 020-7837 6100 **E** info@bamt.org **W** www.bamt.org *Chair,* Ben Saul

BRITISH ASSOCIATION OF ART THERAPISTS, 24–27 White Lion Street, London N1 9PD **T** 020-7686 4216 **E** info@baat.org **W** www.baat.org *Chief Executive,* Dr Val Huet

BRITISH ASSOCIATION OF DRAMATHERAPISTS, PO Box 1257, Cheltenham, Gloucestershire GL50 9YX **T** 01242-235515 **E** info@badth.org.uk **W** www.badth.org.uk *Chair,* Madeline Anderson-Warren *(acting)*

BIOMEDICAL SCIENCES
Salary range: £22,128–£28,746 (starting); £26,565–£35,577 with experience; £31,696–£48,514 for senior roles

The Institute of Biomedical Science (IBMS) is the professional body for biomedical scientists in the UK. Biomedical scientists carry out investigations on tissue and body fluid samples to diagnose disease and monitor the progress of a patient's treatment. The IBMS sets quality standards for the profession through training, education, assessments, examinations and continuous professional development.

INSTITUTE OF BIOMEDICAL SCIENCE (IBMS), 12 Coldbath Square, London EC1R 5HL **T** 020-7713 0214 **E** mail@ibms.org **W** www.ibms.org *Chief Executive,* Jill Rodney

CHIROPODY AND PODIATRY
Salary range: £23,000–£4; £42,000–£85,000 (consultant podiatrist or specialist registrar in practice)

Chiropodists and podiatrists assess, diagnose and treat problems of the lower leg and foot. The College of Podiatry (formerly Society of Chiropodists and Podiatrists) is the professional body and trade union for the profession. Qualifications granted and degrees recognised by the society are approved by the HCPC. HCPC registration is required in order to use the titles chiropodist and podiatrist.

COLLEGE OF PODIATRY, Quartz House, 207 Providence Square, Mill Street, London SE1 2EW **T** 020-7234 8620 **E** reception@scpod.org **W** www.cop.org.uk *Chief Executive,* Steve Jamieson

CLINICAL SCIENCE
Salary range: £25,000–£99,000

Clinical scientists conduct tests in laboratories in order to diagnose and manage disease. The Association of Clinical

Scientists is responsible for setting the criteria for competence of applicants to the HCPC's register and for presenting a Certificate of Attainment to candidates following a successful assessment. This certificate will allow direct registration with the HCPC.

ASSOCIATION OF CLINICAL SCIENTISTS, 130–132 Tooley Street, London SE1 2TU **T** 020-7940 8960 **E** info@assclinsci.org **W** www.assclinsci.org *Chair,* Prof. Richard Lerski

DIETETICS
Salary range: £23,000–£43,000

Dietitians advise patients on how to improve their health and counter specific health problems through diet. The British Dietetic Association, established in 1936, is the professional association for dietitians. Full membership is open to UK-registered dietitians, who must also be registered with the HCPC.

BRITISH DIETETIC ASSOCIATION, 5th Floor, Charles House, 148–149 Great Charles Street Queensway, Birmingham B3 3HT **T** 0121-200 8080 **E** info@bda.uk.com **W** www.bda.uk.com *Chief Executive,* Andy Burman

MENTAL HEALTH
Salary range: Clinical psychologist £26,000, rising to £31,000+ after qualification; £48,000–£83,000 at senior levels
Counselling psychologist £26,000–£35,000 (starting), rising to £31,500–£41,500 (qualified) and up to £82,000 at senior levels
Educational psychologist £22,000, rising to £48,211 (fully qualified) and up to £66,000 at senior levels
Psychotherapist £26,250–£35,250 (starting), rising to £55,000 with experience

Psychologists and counsellors are mental health professionals who can work in a range of settings including prisons, schools and hospitals. The British Psychological Society (BPS) is the representative body for psychology and psychologists in the UK. The BPS is responsible for the development, promotion and application of psychology for the public good. The Association of Educational Psychologists (AEP) represents the interests of educational psychologists. The British Association for Counselling and Psychotherapy (BACP) sets educational standards and provides professional support to counsellors, psychotherapists and others working in counselling, psychotherapy or counselling-related roles. The BPS website provides more information on the different specialisations that may be pursued by psychologists.

ASSOCIATION OF EDUCATIONAL PSYCHOLOGISTS (AEP), 4 The Riverside Centre, Frankland Lane, Durham DH1 5TA **T** 0191-384 9512 **E** enquiries@aep.org.uk **W** www.aep.org.uk *President,* Lisa O'Connor

BRITISH ASSOCIATION FOR COUNSELLING AND PSYCHOTHERAPY (BACP), BACP House, 15 St John's Business Park, Lutterworth, Leicestershire LE17 4HB **T** 01455-883300 **E** bacp@bacp.co.uk **W** www.bacp.co.uk *President,* David Weaver

BRITISH PSYCHOLOGICAL SOCIETY (BPS), St Andrews House, 48 Princess Road East, Leicester LE1 7DR **T** 0116-254 9568 **E** info@bps.org.uk **W** www.bps.org.uk *President,* Kate Bullen

OCCUPATIONAL THERAPY
Salary range: £22,000–£41,500; £40,000–£58,000 for consultancy roles

Occupational therapists work with people who have physical, mental and/or social problems, either from birth or as a result of accident, illness or ageing, and aim to make them as independent as possible. The professional qualification and eligibility for registration may be obtained upon successful completion of a validated course in any of the educational institutions approved by the College of Occupational Therapists, which is the professional body for occupational therapy in the UK. The courses are normally degree-level and based in higher education institutions.

COLLEGE OF OCCUPATIONAL THERAPISTS, 106–114 Borough High Street, London SE1 1LB T 020-7357 6480 E hello@rcot.co.uk W www.rcot.co.uk
Chief Executive, Julia Scott

ORTHOPTICS
Salary range: £24,200 (graduate), rising to £30,000–£86,600 in senior posts

Orthoptists undertake the diagnosis and treatment of all types of squint and other anomalies of binocular vision, working in close collaboration with ophthalmologists. The all-graduate workforce comes from three universities: the University of Liverpool, the University of Sheffield and Glasgow Caledonian University.

BRITISH AND IRISH ORTHOPTIC SOCIETY, 5th Floor, Charles House, 148–9 Great Street Queensway, Birmingham B3 3HT T 0344-209 0754 E bios@orthoptics.org.uk
W www.orthoptics.org.uk
Chair, Rowena McNamara

PARAMEDICAL SERVICES
Salary range: £23,000–£36,600; £59,000–£71,000 for consultancy roles

Paramedics deal with accidents and emergencies, assessing patients and carrying out any specialist treatment and care needed in the first instance. The body that represents ambulance professionals is the College of Paramedics.

COLLEGE OF PARAMEDICS, The Exchange, Express Park, Bristol Road, Bridgwater TA6 4RR T 01278-420014 E membership@collegeofparamedics.co.uk
W www.collegeofparamedics.co.uk
Chief Executive, Gerry Egan

PHYSIOTHERAPY
Salary range: £23,000–£49,000; £60,000 (management roles)

Physiotherapists are concerned with movement and function and deal with problems arising from injury, illness and ageing. Full-time three- or four-year degree courses are available at around 40 higher education institutions in the UK. Information about courses leading to state registration is available from the Chartered Society of Physiotherapy.

CHARTERED SOCIETY OF PHYSIOTHERAPY, 14 Bedford Row, London WC1R 4ED T 020-7306 6666
W www.csp.org.uk
Chief Executive, Karen Middleton, CBE

PROSTHETICS AND ORTHOTICS
Salary range: £21,000 on qualification, up to £67,000 as a consultant

Prosthetists provide artificial limbs, while orthotists provide devices to support or control a part of the body. It is necessary to obtain an honours degree to become a prosthetist or orthotist. Training is centred at the University of Salford and the University of Strathclyde.

BRITISH ASSOCIATION OF PROSTHETISTS AND ORTHOTISTS, Unit 3010, Mile End Mill, Abbey Mill Business Centre, Paisley PA1 1JS T 0141-561 7217 E enquiries@bapo.com
W www.bapo.com
Chair, Lynne Rowley

RADIOGRAPHY
Salary range: £22,000–£43,000, rising to £69,100 in consultancy posts

In order to practise both diagnostic and therapeutic radiography in the UK, it is necessary to have successfully completed a course of education and training recognised by the HCPC. Such courses are offered by around 24 universities throughout the UK and lead to the award of a degree in radiography. Further information is available from the Society of Radiographers, the trade union and professional body which represents the whole of the radiographic workforce in the UK.

SOCIETY OF RADIOGRAPHERS, 207 Providence Square, Mill Street, London SE1 2EW T 020-7740 7200 W www.sor.org
Chief Executive, Richard Evans, OBE

SPEECH AND LANGUAGE THERAPY
Salary range: £23,000–£43,000

Speech and language therapists (SLTs) work with people with communication, swallowing, eating and drinking problems. The Royal College of Speech and Language Therapists is the professional body for speech and language therapists and support workers. Alongside the HCPC, it accredits education and training courses leading to qualification.

ROYAL COLLEGE OF SPEECH AND LANGUAGE THERAPISTS, 2 White Hart Yard, London SE1 1NX T 020-7378 1200 W www.rcslt.org
Chief Executive, Kamini Gadhok, MBE

NURSING
Salary range: see Health: Employees and Salaries

In order to practise in the UK, all nurses and midwives must be registered with the Nursing and Midwifery Council (NMC). The NMC is a statutory regulatory body that establishes and maintains standards of education, training, conduct and performance for nursing and midwifery. Courses leading to registration are currently at a minimum of degree level. All take a minimum of three years if undertaken full-time. The NMC approves programmes run jointly by higher education institutions with their healthcare service partners who offer clinical placements. The nursing part of the register has four fields of practice: adult, children's (paediatric), learning disability and mental health nursing. In most cases students must select one specific field to study before applying to an institution. Some universities run courses which offer the simultaneous study of two nursing fields. In addition, those studying to become adult nurses gain experience of nursing in relation to medicine, surgery, maternity care and nursing in the home. The NMC also sets standards for programmes leading to registration as a midwife and a range of post-registration courses including specialist practice programmes, nurse prescribing and those for teachers of nursing and midwifery. The NMC has a part of the register for specialist community public health nurses and approves programmes for health visitors, occupational health nurses and school nurses.

The Royal College of Nursing is the largest professional union for nursing in the UK, representing qualified nurses, midwives, healthcare assistants and nursing students in the NHS and the independent sector.

NURSING AND MIDWIFERY COUNCIL (NMC), 23
Portland Place, London W1B 1PZ **T** 020-7637 7181
E ukenquiries@nmc-uk.org **W** www.nmc.org.uk
Chief Executive and Registrar, Andrea Sutcliffe, CBE

ROYAL COLLEGE OF NURSING, 20 Cavendish Square,
London W1G 0RN **T** 020-7409 3333 **W** www.rcn.org.uk
Chief Executive and General Secretary, Dame Donna Kinnair,
DBE

OPTOMETRY AND DISPENSING OPTICS

Salary range: Optometrist £20,000–£85,000 (NHS); £14,000–
£65,000+ (private)
Dispensing Optician £14,000–£45,000+

There are various routes to qualification as a dispensing
optician. Qualification takes three years in total, and can be
completed by combining a distance learning course or day
release while working as a trainee under the supervision of a
qualified and registered optician. Alternatively, students can do
a two-year full-time course followed by one year of supervised
practice with a qualified and registered optician. Training must
be done at a training establishment approved by the regulatory
body – the General Optical Council (GOC). There are six
training establishments which are approved by the GOC:
ABDO (Association of British Dispensing Opticians) College,
Anglia Ruskin University, Bradford College, City and
Islington College, City University and Glasgow Caledonian
University. After the completion of training to fit contact lenses
and attaining the ABDO Level 6 certificate in contact lens
practice qualification, a Contact Lens Optician may apply to be
included in the GOC Speciality Register. Students are also able
to complete a Foundation or Undergraduate degree in
Ophthalmic Dispensing, offered by ABDO in conjunction
with Canterbury Christ Church University. All routes are
concluded by professional qualifying examinations, successful
completion of which leads to the awarding of the Level 6
Fellowship Diploma of the Association of British Dispensing
Opticians (FBDO) by ABDO. FBDO holders are able to
register with the GOC following the awarding of their
diploma, with registration being compulsory for all practising
dispensing opticians.

Continuing Education and Training (CET) is a statutory
requirement for all registered dispensing opticians and contact
lens opticians to retain GOC registration.

ASSOCIATION OF BRITISH DISPENSING OPTICIANS
(ABDO), Godmersham Park, Godmersham, Canterbury, Kent
CT4 7DT **T** 01227-733905 **E** general@abdo.org.uk
W www.abdo.org.uk
General Secretary, Sir Anthony Garrett, CBE

COLLEGE OF OPTOMETRISTS, 42 Craven Street, London
WC2N 5NG **T** 020-7839 6000 **W** www.college-optometrists.org
Chief Executive, Ian Humphreys

GENERAL OPTICAL COUNCIL (GOC), 10 Old Bailey,
London EC4M 7NG **T** 020-7580 3898 **E** goc@optical.org
W www.optical.org
Chief Executive and Registrar, Lesley Longstone, CB

OSTEOPATHY

Salary Range: £20,000–£100,000+

Osteopathy is a system of diagnosis and treatment for a wide
range of conditions. It works with the structure and function
of the body, and is based on the principle that the well-being
of an individual depends on the skeleton, muscles, ligaments
and connective tissues functioning smoothly together. The
General Osteopathic Council (GOsC) regulates the practice of
osteopathy in the UK and maintains a register of those entitled
to practise. It is a criminal offence for anyone to describe
themselves as an osteopath unless they are registered with the
GOsC.

To gain entry to the register, applicants must hold a
recognised qualification from an osteopathic education
institute accredited by the GOsC; this involves a four- to five-
year honours degree programme combined with clinical
training.

GENERAL OSTEOPATHIC COUNCIL (GOsC), Osteopathy
House, 176 Tower Bridge Road, London SE1 3LU
T 020-7357 6655 **E** info@osteopathy.org.uk
W www.osteopathy.org.uk
Chief Executive and Registrar, Leonie Milliner

PHARMACY

Salary range: £30,000–£70,000 (community); £26,500–
£100,000 (hospital)

Pharmacists are involved in the preparation and use of
medicines, from the discovery of their active ingredients to
their use by patients. Pharmacists also monitor the effects of
medicines, both for patient care and for research purposes.

The General Pharmaceutical Council (GPhC) is the
independent regulatory body for pharmacists in England,
Scotland and Wales, having taken over the regulating function
of the Royal Pharmaceutical Society in 2010. The GPhC
maintains the register of pharmacists, pharmacy technicians
and pharmacy premises; it also sets national standards for
training, ethics, proficiency and continuing professional
development. The Pharmaceutical Society of Northern Ireland
(PSNI) performs the same role in Northern Ireland. In order to
register, students must complete a four-year degree in
pharmacy that is accredited by either the GPhC or the PSNI,
followed by one year of pre-registration training at an
approved pharmacy; they must then pass an entrance
examination.

GENERAL PHARMACEUTICAL COUNCIL (GPhC), 25
Canada Square, London, E14 5LQ **T** 020-3713 8000
E info@pharmacyregulation.org
W www.pharmacyregulation.org
Chief Executive and Registrar, Duncan Rudkin

PHARMACEUTICAL SOCIETY OF NORTHERN
IRELAND (PSNI), 73 University Street, Belfast BT7 1HL
T 028-9032 6927 **E** info@psni.org.uk **W** www.psni.org.uk
Chief Executive, Trevor Patterson

ROYAL PHARMACEUTICAL SOCIETY, 66 East Smithfield,
London, E1W 1AW **T** 020-7572 2737 **E** support@rpharms.com
W www.rpharms.com
Chief Executive, Paul Bennett

INFORMATION MANAGEMENT

Salary range: Archivist £22,443 (newly qualified); £25,000–
£45,000 (with experience); £55,000 in senior posts
Information Officer £18,000–£31,000 (starting); £21,000–
£28,000 (newly qualified); £26,000–£50,000+ in senior and
chartered posts
Librarian £16,000–£20,000 (trainee); £22,500–£29,500
(assistant librarian); £30,000–£40,000 (experienced);
£43,000–£70,000 (chief/head librarian)

The Chartered Institute of Library and Information
Professionals (CILIP) is the leading professional body for
librarians, information specialists and knowledge managers.
The Archives and Records Association is the professional body
for archivists and record managers.

ARCHIVES AND RECORDS ASSOCIATION, Prioryfield
House, 20 Canon Street, Taunton, Somerset TA1 1SW
T 01823-327077 **E** ara@archives.org.uk **W** www.archives.org.uk
Chief Executive, John Chambers

CHARTERED INSTITUTE OF LIBRARY AND
INFORMATION PROFESSIONALS (CILIP), 7 Ridgmount
Street, London WC1E 7AE **T** 020-7255 0500 **E** info@cilip.org.uk
W www.cilip.org.uk
Chief Executive, Nick Poole

JOURNALISM

Salary range: £12,000–£18,000 (trainee); £25,000 for
established journalists, rising to £35,000–£65,000+ for those
with over a decade's experience in print media, as high as
£80,000+ for top/high-profile broadcast journalists.

The National Council for the Training of Journalists (NCTJ)
accredits courses for journalists run by a number of different
education providers throughout the United Kingdom; it also
provides professional support to journalists.

The Broadcast Journalism Training Council (BJTC) is an
association of the UK's main broadcast journalism employers
and accredits courses in broadcast journalism.

BROADCAST JOURNALISM TRAINING COUNCIL
(BJTC), Sterling House, 20 Station Road, Gerard's Cross,
Buckinghamshire, SL9 8EL **T** 0845-600 8789 **E** sec@bjtc.org.uk
W www.bjtc.org.uk
Chief Executive, Jon Godel

NATIONAL COUNCIL FOR THE TRAINING OF
JOURNALISTS (NCTJ), The New Granary, Station Road,
Newport, Saffron Walden, Essex CB11 3PL **T** 01799-544014
E info@nctj.com **W** www.nctj.com
Chief Executive, Joanne Butcher

LAW

There are three types of practising lawyers: barristers, notaries
and solicitors. Solicitors tend to work as a group in firms, and
can be approached directly by individuals. They advise on a
variety of legal issues and must decide the most appropriate
course of action, if any. Notaries have all the powers of a
solicitor other than the conduct of litigation. Most of them
are primarily concerned with the preparation and
authentication of documents for use abroad. Barristers are
usually self-employed. If a solicitor believes that a barrister is
required, he or she will instruct one on behalf of the client;
the client will not have contact with the barrister without the
solicitor being present.

When specialist expertise is needed, barristers give opinions
on complex matters of law, and when clients require
representation in the higher courts (crown courts, the high
court, the court of appeal and the supreme court), barristers
provide a specialist advocacy service. However, solicitors –
who represent their clients in the lower courts such as
magistrates' courts and county courts – can also apply for
advocacy rights in the higher courts instead of briefing a
barrister.

THE BAR

Salary range: £12,000–£50,000 (pupillage); £50,000–
£200,000 (qualified); £65,000–£1,000,000+ with ten years
experience

The governing body of the Bar of England and Wales is the
General Council of the Bar, also known as the Bar Council.
Since January 2006, the regulatory functions of the Bar
Council (including regulating the education and training
requirements for those wishing to enter the profession) have
been undertaken by the Bar Standards Board.

In the first (or 'academic') stage of training, aspiring
barristers must obtain a law degree of a good standard (at
least second class). Alternatively, those with a non-law degree
(at least second class) may complete a one-year full-time or

two-year part-time Common Professional Examination (CPE)
or Graduate Diploma in Law (GDL).

The second (vocational) stage is the completion of the Bar
Professional Training Course (BPTC), which is available at a
number of validated institutions in the UK and must be
applied for one year in advance. All barristers must join one
of the four Inns of Court prior to commencing the BPTC.

Students are 'called to the Bar' by their Inn after completion
of the vocational stage, but cannot practise as a barrister until
completion of the third stage, which is called 'pupillage'.
Being called to the Bar does not entitle a person to practise as
a barrister – successful completion of pupillage is now a
prerequisite. Pupillage lasts for two six-month periods: the
'first six' and the 'second six'. The former consists of
shadowing an experienced barrister, while the latter involves
appearing in court as a barrister. Chambers can then offer a
long term 'tenancy' to students. Students who are not given
'tenancy' may take a 'third six'.

In Northern Ireland admission to the Bar is controlled by
the Bar of Northern Ireland; admission as an Advocate to the
Scottish Bar is through the Faculty of Advocates.

BAR STANDARDS BOARD 289-293 High Holborn, London,
WC1V 7HZ **T** 020-7611 1444
E contactus@barstandardsboard.org.uk
W www.barstandardsboard.org.uk
Chair of the Bar Council, Rt. Hon. Baroness Blackstone

FACULTY OF ADVOCATES, Parliament Square, Edinburgh
EH1 1RF **T** 0131-226 5071 **E** info@advocates.org.uk
W www.advocates.org.uk
Dean, Gordon Jackson, QC

GENERAL COUNCIL OF THE BAR (THE BAR
COUNCIL), 289–293 High Holborn, London WC1V 7HZ
T 020-7242 0082 **E** contactus@barcouncil.org.uk
W www.barcouncil.org.uk
Chief Executive, Malcolm Cree, CBE

THE BAR OF NORTHERN IRELAND, 91 Chichester Street,
Belfast BT1 3JQ **T** 028-9024 1523 **W** www.barofni.com
Chief Executive, David Mulholland

THE INNS OF COURT

HONOURABLE SOCIETY OF GRAY'S INN, 8 South
Square, London WC1R 5ET **T** 020-7458 7900
W www.graysinn.org.uk
Under-Treasurer, Brig. Anthony Harking, OBE

HONOURABLE SOCIETY OF LINCOLN'S INN, Treasury
Office, Lincoln's Inn, London WC2A 3TL **T** 020-7405 1393
E mail@lincolnsinn.org.uk **W** www.lincolnsinn.org.uk
Treasurer, Rt. Hon. Lord Justice McCombe

HONOURABLE SOCIETY OF THE INNER TEMPLE,
Treasury Office, Inner Temple, 1 Mitre Court, London EC4Y 7BS
T 020-7797 8250 **E** enquiries@innertemple.org.uk
W www.innertemple.org.uk
Treasurer, Rt. Hon. Lord Hughes of Ombersley

HONOURABLE SOCIETY OF THE MIDDLE TEMPLE,
Treasury Office, Ashley Building, Middle Temple Lane, London
EC4Y 9BT **T** 020-7427 4800 **E** education@middletemple.org.uk
W www.middletemple.org.uk
Chief Executive, Guy Perricone

NOTARIES PUBLIC

Notaries are qualified lawyers with a postgraduate diploma in
notarial practice. Once a potential notary has passed the
postgraduate diploma, they can petition the Court of Faculties
for a 'faculty'. After the faculty is granted, the notary is able
to practise; however, for the first two years this must be under
the supervision of an experienced notary. The admission and

regulation of notaries in England and Wales is a statutory function of the Faculty Office. This jurisdiction was confirmed by the Courts and Legal Services Act 1990. The Notaries Society of England and Wales is the representative body for practising notaries.

THE FACULTY OFFICE, 1 The Sanctuary, Westminster, London SW1P 3JT **T** 020-7222 5381
  E faculty.office@1thesanctuary.com
  W www.facultyoffice.org.uk
  Registrar, Howard Dellar
THE NOTARIES SOCIETY OF ENGLAND AND WALES, PO Box 1023, Ipswich IP1 9XB
  E admin@thenotariessociety.org.uk
  W www.thenotariessociety.org.uk
  Secretary, Christopher Vaughan

SOLICITORS

Salary range: Trainee solicitors paid at least the national minimum wage; £25,000–£65,000 after qualification; £100,000+ (associate or partner)

Graduates from any discipline can train to be a solicitor; however, if the undergraduate degree is not in law, a one-year conversion course – either the Common Professional Examination (CPE) or the Graduate Diploma in Law (GDL) – must be completed. The next stage, and the beginning of the vocational phase, is the Legal Practice Course (LPC), which takes one year and is obligatory for both law and non-law graduates. The LPC provides professional instruction for prospective solicitors and can be completed on a full-time and part-time basis. Trainee solicitors then enter the final stage, which is a paid period of supervised work that lasts two years for full-time contracts. The employer that provides the training contract must be authorised by the Solicitors Regulation Authority (SRA) (the regulatory body of the Law Society of England and Wales), the Law Society of Scotland or the Law Society of Northern Ireland. The SRA also monitors the training contract to ensure that it provides the trainee with the expertise to qualify as a solicitor.

Conveyancers are specialist property lawyers, dealing with the legal processes involved in transferring buildings, land and associated finances from one owner to another. This was the sole responsibility of solicitors until 1987 but under current legislation it is now possible for others to train as conveyancers.

COUNCIL FOR LICENSED CONVEYANCERS (CLC), WeWork, 131 Finsbury Pavement, London EC2A 1NT
  T 020-3859 0904 **E** clc@clc-uk.org **W** www.clc-uk.org
  Chief Executive, Sheila Kumar
THE LAW SOCIETY OF ENGLAND AND WALES, The Law Society's Hall, 113 Chancery Lane, London WC2A 1PL
  T 020-7242 1222 **W** www.lawsociety.org.uk
  Chief Executive, Paul Tennant, OBE
LAW SOCIETY OF NORTHERN IRELAND, 96 Victoria Street, Belfast BT1 3GN **T** 028-9023 1614**W** www.lawsoc-ni.org
  Chief Executive, Alan Hunter
LAW SOCIETY OF SCOTLAND, Atria One, 144 Morrison Street, Edinburgh EH3 8EX **T** 0131-226 7411
  E lawscot@lawscot.org.uk **W** www.lawscot.org.uk
  Chief Executive, Lorna Jack
SOLICITORS REGULATION AUTHORITY (SRA), The Cube, 199 Wharfside Street, Birmingham B1 1RN
  T 0370-606 2555 **W** www.sra.org.uk
  Chief Executive, Paul Philip

SOCIAL WORK

Salary range: £22,000 (newly qualified); £40,000 (with experience); £26,565–£35,577 (NHS)

Social workers tend to specialise in either adult or children's services. Social Work England obtains regulatory responsibility from the Health and Care Professions Council (HCPC) on 2 December 2019, taking on responsibility for setting standards of conduct and practice for social care workers and their employers, regulating the workforce and social work education and training. A degree or postgraduate qualification is needed in order to become a social worker.

SOCIAL WORK ENGLAND, 1 North Bank, Blonk Street, Sheffield S3 8JY **W** www.socialworkengland.org.uk
  Chief Executive, Colum Conway

SURVEYING

Salary range: £20,000–£25,000 (starting); £50,000 (senior); up to £100,000+ (partners and directors)

The Royal Institution of Chartered Surveyors (RICS) is the professional body that represents and regulates property professionals including land surveyors, valuers, auctioneers, quantity surveyors and project managers. Entry to the institution, following completion of a RICS-accredited degree, is through completion of the Assessment of Professional Competence (APC), which involves a period of practical training concluded by a final assessment of competence. Entry as a technical surveyor requires completion of the Assessment of Technical Competence (ATC), which mirrors the format of the APC. The different levels of RICS membership are MRICS (member) or FRICS (fellow) for chartered surveyors, and AssocRICS for associate members.

Relevant courses can also be accredited by the Chartered Institute of Building (CIOB), which represents managers working in a range of construction disciplines. The CIOB offers four levels of membership to those who satisfy its requirements: FCIOB (fellow), MCIOB (member), ICIOB (incorporated) and ACIOB (associate).

CHARTERED INSTITUTE OF BUILDING (CIOB), 1 Arlington Square, Downshire Way, Bracknell RG12 1WA **T** 01344-630700 **E** reception@ciob.org.uk **W** www.ciob.org
  Chief Executive, Caroline Gumble
ROYAL INSTITUTION OF CHARTERED SURVEYORS (RICS), Parliament Square, London SW1P 3AD **T** 024-7686 8555 **E** contactrics@rics.org **W** www.rics.org
  Chief Executive, Sean Tompkins

TEACHING

Salary range: school teachers £24,373–£49,571; school leaders £41,065–£121,749 (for more detailed information *see* Education: Employees and Salaries)

Since 1 April 2018, the Teaching Regulation Agency, an executive agency sponsored by the Department for Education, is responsible for maintaining the register of qualified teachers in England and is the awarding body for Qualified Teacher Status (QTS). The Education Workforce Council in Wales and the General Teaching Council for Scotland fulfil this responsibility in their respective administrations. In Northern Ireland teacher registration is the responsibility of the General Teaching Council for Northern Ireland. Registration is a legal requirement in order to teach in local authority maintained schools. UCAS Teacher Training is the body through which to apply for postgraduate teacher training in the UK. To become a qualified teacher in a state school, all entrants must have a degree and gain QTS, which includes a minimum of 24 weeks in at least two different schools and academic study of teaching. QTS is not required to teach in independent schools, academies or free schools, but it is a definite advantage. Another route is through School-centred Initial Teacher Training (SCITT), where practical, hands-on teacher training is delivered by experienced, practising teachers in their own government-approved school.

Many courses also award an academic qualification known as the Postgraduate Certificate in Education (PGCE) in England and Wales and the Professional Graduate Diploma in Education (PGDE) in Scotland. Once training is completed, applicants spend a year in school as a newly qualified teacher (NQT).

Teachers in Further Education (FE) need not have QTS, though new entrants to FE may be required to work towards a specified FE qualification by employers. A range of courses are offered and usually require one year of study in addition to 100 hours of teaching experience. Similarly, academic staff in Higher Education require no formal teaching qualification, but are expected to obtain a qualification that meets standards set by the Higher Education Academy.

Details of routes to gaining QTS in England are available from the Department for Education, the Teaching Regulation Agency and UCAS. In the devolved administrations information is available from the Welsh government, Teach in Scotland and from the Department of Education in Northern Ireland.

In July 2017, the College of Teaching became the Chartered College of Teaching. Under the terms of its royal charter, it provides professional qualifications and membership to teachers and those involved in education in the UK and overseas.

ADVANCE HE Innovation Way, York Science Park, Heslington, York YO10 5BR **T** 0330–041 6201
E enquiries@advance-he.ac.uk **W** www.advance-he.ac.uk
Chief Executive, Alison Johns

CHARTERED COLLEGE OF TEACHING, 9–11 Endsleigh Gardens, London WC1H 0EH **T** 020-7911 5589
E hello@chartered.college **W** www.chartered.college
Chief Executive, Prof. Dame Alison Peacock, DBE

DEPARTMENT OF EDUCATION NORTHERN IRELAND, Rathgael House, Balloo Road, Rathgill, Bangor BT19 7PR **T** 028-9127 9279 **E** DE.DEWebMail@education-ni.gov.uk
W www.education-ni.gov.uk

EDUCATION WORKFORCE COUNCIL, 9th Floor, Eastgate House, 35–43 Newport Road, Cardiff CF24 0AB
T 029-2046 0099 **E** information@ewc.wales **W** www.ewc.wales
Chief Executive, Hayden Llewellyn

GENERAL TEACHING COUNCIL FOR NORTHERN IRELAND, 3rd Floor, Albany House, 73–75 Great Victoria Street, Belfast BT2 7AF **T** 028-9033 3390 **E** info@gtcni.org.uk
W www.gtcni.org.uk
Chair, David Canning, OBE

GENERAL TEACHING COUNCIL FOR SCOTLAND, Clerwood House, 96 Clermiston Road, Edinburgh EH12 6UT
T 0131-314 6000 **E** gtcs@gtcs.org.uk **W** www.gtcs.org.uk
Chief Executive, Ken Muir

TEACHING REGULATION AGENCY, Ground Floor South, Cheylesmore House, 5 Quinton Road, Coventry CV1 2WT
T 0207 593 5394 **E** qts.enquiries@education.gov.uk
W www.gov.uk/government/organisations/teaching-regulation-agency
Chief Executive, Alan Meyrick

UCAS TEACHER TRAINING, Rosehill, New Barn Lane, Cheltenham GL52 3LZ **T** 0371-468 0469
W www.ucas.com/teaching-in-the-uk
Chief Executive, Clare Marchant

VETERINARY MEDICINE

Salary range: £30,000 (newly qualified); £43,200–£64,870 (with experience); £72,360 (20+ years experience)

The regulatory body for veterinary surgeons in the UK is the Royal College of Veterinary Surgeons (RCVS); which keeps the register of those entitled to practise veterinary medicine, the register of veterinary nurses and veterinary practice premises (on behalf of the Veterinary Medicines Directorate). Holders of recognised degrees from any of the seven UK university veterinary schools that have been approved by the RCVS or from certain EU or overseas universities are entitled to be registered, and holders of certain other degrees may take a statutory membership examination. The UK's RCVS-approved veterinary schools are located at the University of Bristol, the University of Cambridge, the University of Edinburgh, the University of Glasgow, the University of Liverpool, University of Nottingham and the Royal Veterinary College in London; all veterinary degrees last for five years except that offered at Cambridge, which lasts for six.

The British Veterinary Association is the national representative body for the UK veterinary profession. The British Veterinary Nursing Association is the professional body representing veterinary nurses.

BRITISH VETERINARY ASSOCIATION, 7 Mansfield Street, London W1G 9NQ **T** 020-7636 6541 **E** bvahq@bva.co.uk
W www.bva.co.uk
Chief Executive, David Calpin

BRITISH VETERINARY NURSING ASSOCIATION, 79 Greenway Business Centre, Harlow Business Park, Harlow, Essex CM19 5QE **T** 01279-408644 **E** bvna@bvna.co.uk
W www.bvna.org.uk
Honorary Treasurer, Erika Feilberg

ROYAL COLLEGE OF VETERINARY SURGEONS (RCVS), Belgravia House, 62–64 Horseferry Road, London SW1P 2AF **T** 020-7222 2001 **E** info@rcvs.org.uk
W www.rcvs.org.uk
Chief Executive, Lizzie Lockett

INDEPENDENT SCHOOLS

Independent schools (non-maintained mainstream schools) charge fees and are owned privately or managed under special trusts, with profits being used for the benefit of the schools concerned. As at January 2019 there were 2,486 non-maintained mainstream schools in the UK, educating 580,955 pupils; 6.6 per cent of the total school-age population.

The Independent Schools Council (ISC), formed in 1974, acts on behalf of the seven independent schools' associations which constitute it. These associations are:

Association of Governing Bodies of Independent Schools (AGBIS)
Girls' Schools Association (GSA)
Headmasters' & Headmistresses' Conference (HMC)
Independent Association of Prep Schools (IAPS)
Independent Schools Association (ISA)
Independent Schools' Bursars Association (ISBA)
The Society of Heads

In January 2019 there were 536,109 pupils being educated in 1,364 schools in membership of associations within the Independent Schools Council (ISC). Most schools not in membership of an ISC association are likely to be privately owned. The Independent Schools Inspectorate (ISI) was demerged from ISC with effect from 1 January 2008 and is legally and operationally independent of ISC. ISI works as an accredited inspectorate of schools in membership of the ISC associations under a framework agreed with the Department for Education (DfE). A school must pass an ISI accreditation inspection to qualify for membership of an association within ISC.

In 2019 at GCSE 23.1 per cent of all exams taken by candidates in ISC associations' member schools were awarded a grade 9 (compared to the national average of 4.5 per cent), and at A-level 17.2 per cent of entries were awarded an A* grade (national average, 8 per cent). In 2019 a total of 176,633 pupils (34 per cent) at schools in ISC associations were receiving help with their fees, mainly in the form of bursaries and scholarships from the schools. ISC schools provided £864m of assistance with fees.

INDEPENDENT SCHOOLS COUNCIL, First Floor, 27 Queen Anne's Gate, London SW1H 9BU T 020-7766 7070
W www.isc.co.uk

The list of schools below was compiled from the *Independent Schools Yearbook 2018–19* (ed. Judy Mott, published by Bloomsbury Publishing) which includes schools whose heads are members of one of the ISC's five Heads' Associations. Further details are available online (W www.isyb.co.uk).

The fees shown below represent the upper limit payable for the year 2018–19.

School	Web Address	Termly Fees Day	Board	Head
ENGLAND				
Abbey Gate College, Cheshire	www.abbeygatecollege.co.uk	£4,280	–	Mrs T. Pollard
Abbot's Hill School, Herts	www.abbotshill.herts.sch.uk	£6,172	–	Mrs E. Thomas
Abbotsholme School, Derbys, Staffs	www.abbotsholme.co.uk	£7,495	£10,995	R. Barnes
Abingdon School, Oxon	www.abingdon.org.uk	£6,650	£11,070	M. Windsor
Adcote School, Shrops	www.adcoteschool.org.uk	£4,946	£9,032	Mrs D. Browne
AKS Lytham, Lancs	www.akslytham.com	£3,929	–	M. Walton
Aldenham School, Herts	www.aldenham.com	£7,538	£11,078	J. Fowler
Alderley Edge School for Girls, Cheshire	www.aesg.co.uk	£4,150	–	Mrs H. Jeys
Alleyn's School, London, SE22	www.alleyns.org.uk	£6,617	–	Dr G. Savage
Ampleforth College, N. Yorks	www.ampleforth.org.uk/college	£8,212	£11,808	Miss D. Rowe
Ardingly College, W. Sussex	www.ardingly.com	£7,870	£11,470	B. Figgis
Ashford School, Kent	www.ashfordschool.co.uk	£5,600	£12,000	M. Hall
Austin Friars, Cumbria	www.austinfriars.co.uk	£4,880	–	M. Harris
Bablake School, W. Midlands	www.bablake.com	£3,898	–	A. Wright
Badminton School, Bristol	www.badmintonschool.co.uk	£5,475	£12,525	Mrs R. Tear
Bancroft's School, Essex	www.bancrofts.org	£6,041	–	S. Marshall
Barnard Castle School, Durham	www.barnardcastleschool.org.uk	£4,650	£8,400	A. Jackson
Bedales School, Hants	www.bedales.org.uk	£9,505	£12,095	M. Bashaarat
Bede's Senior School, E. Sussex	www.bedes.org	£7,370	£11,720	P. Goodyer
Bedford Girls' School, Beds	www.bedfordgirlsschool.co.uk	£4,468	–	Miss J. MacKenzie
Bedford Modern School, Beds	www.bedmod.co.uk	£4,468	–	A. Tate
Bedford School, Beds	www.bedfordschool.org.uk	£6,344	£10,730	J. Hodgson
Bedstone College, Shrops	www.bedstone.org	£4,885	£8,840	D. Gajadharsingh
Beechwood Sacred Heart School, Kent	www.beechwood.org.uk	£5,375	£9,950	Mrs H. Rowe
Benenden School, Kent	www.benenden.kent.sch.uk	–	£12,650	Mrs S. Price
Berkhamsted, Herts	www.berkhamsted.com	£6,880	£11,530	R. Backhouse
Bethany School, Kent	www.bethanyschool.org.uk	£6,155	£10,500	F. Healy
Birkdale School, S. Yorks	www.birkdaleschool.org.uk	£4,330	–	P. Harris
Birkenhead School, Merseyside	www.birkenheadschool.co.uk	£3,998	–	P. Vicars
Bishop's Stortford College, Herts	www.bishopsstortfordcollege.org	£6,613	£10,237	J. Gladwin
Blackheath High School, London, SE3	www.blackheathhighschool.gdst.net	£5,498	–	Mrs C. Chandler-Thompson
Blundell's School, Devon	www.blundells.org	£7,470	£11,735	B. Wielenga
Bolton School Boys' Division, Lancs	www.boltonschool.org/seniorboys	£3,992	–	P. Britton
Bolton School Girls' Division, Lancs	www.boltonschool.org/seniorgirls	£3,992	–	Miss S. Hincks

School	Website	Day	Boarding	Head
Bootham School, N. Yorks	www.boothamschool.com	£5,995	£10,155	C. Jeffrey
Bournemouth Collegiate School, Dorset	www.bournemouthcollegiateschool.co.uk	£4,810	£9,890	R. Slatford
Box Hill School, Surrey	www.boxhillschool.com	£6,570	£13,310	C. Lowde
Bradfield College, Berks	www.bradfieldcollege.org.uk	£9,975	£12,468	Dr C. Stevens
Bradford Grammar School, W. Yorks	www.bradfordgrammar.com	£4,223	–	Dr S. Hinchliffe
Bredon School, Glos	www.bredonschool.org	£7,315	£11,715	K. Claeys
Brentwood School, Essex	www.brentwoodschool.co.uk	£6,315	£12,376	D. Davies
Brighton & Hove High School, E. Sussex	www.bhhs.gdst.net	£4,807	–	Ms J. Smith
Brighton College, E. Sussex	www.brightoncollege.org.uk	–	£13,190	R. Cairns
Bristol Grammar School, Bristol	www.bristolgrammarschool.co.uk	£4,870	–	J. Barot
Bromley High School, Kent	www.bromleyhigh.gdst.net	£5,697	–	Mrs A. Drew
Bromsgrove School, Worcs	www.bromsgrove-school.co.uk	£5,555	£12,430	P. Clague
Bruton School for Girls, Somerset	www.brutonschool.co.uk	£5,935	£10,110	Mrs N. Botterill
Bryanston School, Dorset	www.bryanston.co.uk	£10,438	£12,728	Ms S. Thomas
Burgess Hill Girls, W. Sussex	www.burgesshillgirls.com	£6,400	£11,400	Mrs L. Laybourn
Bury Grammar School Boys, Lancs	www.burygrammar.com	£3,585	–	Mrs J. Anderson
Bury Grammar School Girls, Lancs	www.burygrammar.com	£3,585	–	Mrs J. Anderson
Caterham School, Surrey	www.caterhamschool.co.uk	£6,300	£12,190	C. Jones
Channing School, London, N6	www.channing.co.uk	£6,470	–	Mrs B. Elliott
Charterhouse, Surrey	www.charterhouse.org.uk	–	£13,055	Dr A. Peterken
Cheltenham College, Glos	www.cheltenhamcollege.org	£9,195	£12,260	Mrs N. Huggett
Cheltenham Ladies' College, Glos	www.cheltladiescollege.org	£8,270	£12,315	Ms E. Jardine-Young
Chetham's School of Music, Greater Manchester	www.chethams.com	–	–	A. Jones
Chigwell School, Essex	www.chigwell-school.org	£5,995	£10,011	M. Punt
Christ's Hospital, W. Sussex	www.christs-hospital.org.uk	£5,930	£11,480	S. Reid
Churcher's College, Hants	www.churcherscollege.com	£5,140	–	S. Williams
City of London Freemen's School, Surrey	www.freemens.org	£6,081	£10,260	R. Martin
City of London School, London, EC4	www.cityoflondonschool.org.uk	£5,967	–	A. Bird
City of London School for Girls, London, EC2	www.clsg.org.uk	£6,128	–	Mrs E. Harrop
Claremont Fan Court School, Surrey	www.claremontfancourt.co.uk	£5,890	–	W. Brierly
Clayesmore School, Dorset	www.clayesmore.com	£8,740	£11,910	Mrs J. Thomson
Clifton College, Bristol	www.cliftoncollege.com	£8,230	£12,390	Dr T. Greene
Clifton High School, Bristol	www.cliftonhigh.co.uk	£4,985	–	Dr A. Neill
Cobham Hall, Kent	www.cobhamhall.com	£7,401	£11,517	Ms M. Roberts
Cokethorpe School, Oxon	www.cokethorpe.org.uk	£6,400	–	D. Ettinger
Colfe's School, London, SE12	www.colfes.com	£5,643	–	R. Russell
Colston's, Bristol	www.colstons.org	£4,650	–	J. McCullough
Concord College, Shrops	www.concordcollegeuk.com	£4,903	£13,967	N. Hawkins
Cranford House, Oxon	www.cranfordhouse.net	£5,680	–	Dr J. Raymond
Cranleigh School, Surrey	www.cranleigh.org	£10,390	£12,635	M. Reader
Croydon High School, Surrey	www.croydonhigh.gdst.net	£5,552	–	Mrs E. Pattison
Culford School, Suffolk	www.culford.co.uk	£6,500	£10,580	J. Johnson-Munday
Dauntsey's School, Wilts	www.dauntseys.org	£6,330	£10,480	M. Lascelles
Dean Close School, Glos	www.deanclose.org.uk	£8,200	£11,939	Mrs E. Taylor
Denstone College, Staffs	www.denstonecollege.org	£5,293	£8,407	M. Norris
Derby Grammar School, Derbys	www.derbygrammar.org	£4,483	–	Dr R. Norris
Derby High School, Derbys	www.derbyhigh.derby.sch.uk	£4,290	–	Mrs A. Chapman
Dover College, Kent	www.dovercollege.org.uk	£5,350	£10,500	G. Doodes
d'Overbroeck's, Oxon	www.doverbroecks.com	£7,950	£12,900	J. Cuff
Downe House, Berks	www.downehouse.net	£9,165	£12,510	Mrs E. McKendrick
Downside School, Somerset	www.downside.co.uk	£6,417	£11,287	A. Hobbs
Dulwich College, London, SE21	www.dulwich.org.uk	£6,816	£14,227	Dr J. Spence
Dunottar School, Surrey	www.dunottarschool.com	£5,345	–	M. Tottman
Durham High School for Girls, Durham	www.dhsfg.org.uk	£4,375	–	Mrs S. Niblock
Eastbourne College, E. Sussex	www.eastbourne-college.co.uk	£7,710	£11,750	T. Lawson
Edgbaston High School, W. Midlands	www.edgbastonhigh.co.uk	£4,258	–	Dr R. Weeks
Ellesmere College, Shrops	www.ellesmere.com	£6,123	£10,977	B. Wignall
Eltham College, London, SE9	www.elthamcollege.london	£5,925	–	G. Sanderson
Emanuel School, London, SW11	www.emanuel.org.uk	£6,194	–	R. Milne
Epsom College, Surrey	www.epsomcollege.org.uk	£8,422	£12,421	J. Piggot
Eton College, Berks	www.etoncollege.com	–	£13,556	S. Henderson
Ewell Castle School, Surrey	www.ewellcastle.co.uk	£5,564	–	S. Edmonds
Exeter School, Devon	www.exeterschool.org.uk	£4,410	–	B. Griffin
Farnborough Hill, Hants	www.farnborough-hill.org.uk	£4,932	–	Mrs A. Neil
Farringtons School, Kent	www.farringtons.org.uk	£4,870	£10,560	Mrs D. Nancekievill
Felsted School, Essex	www.felsted.org	£7,850	£11,995	C. Townsend

School	Website			Head
Forest School, London, E17	www.forest.org.uk	£6,227	–	M. Hodges
Framlingham College, Suffolk	www.framcollege.co.uk	£6,642	£10,328	P. Taylor
Francis Holland School, London, NW1	www.fhs-nw1.org.uk	£6,680	–	C. Fillingham
Francis Holland School, London, SW1	www.fhs-sw1.org.uk	£6,970	–	Mrs L. Elphinstone
Frensham Heights, Surrey	www.frensham.org	£6,410	£9,890	R. Clarke
Fulneck School, W. Yorks	www.fulneckschool.co.uk	£4,375	£8,485	P. Taylor
Gateways School, W. Yorks	www.gatewaysschool.co.uk	£4,538	–	Dr T. Johnson
Giggleswick School, N. Yorks	www.giggleswick.org.uk	£6,475	£10,715	M. Turnbull
The Godolphin and Latymer School, London, W6	www.godolphinandlatymer.com	£7,205	–	Dr F. Ramsey
Godolphin School, Wilts	www.godolphin.org	£7,030	£10,675	Mrs E. Hattersley
The Grange School, Cheshire	www.grange.org.uk	£3,835	–	Mrs D. Leonard
Gresham's School, Norfolk	www.greshams.com	£8,140	£11,660	D. Robb
Guildford High School – Senior School, Surrey	www.guildfordhigh.co.uk	£5,664	–	Mrs F. Boulton
The Haberdashers' Aske's Boys' School, Herts	www.habsboys.org.uk	£6,782	–	G. Lock
Haberdashers' Aske's School for Girls, Herts	www.habsgirls.org.uk	£6,131	–	Miss B. O'Connor
Halliford School, Middx	www.hallifordschool.co.uk	£5,320	–	J. Davies
Hampshire Collegiate School, Hants	www.hampshirecs.org.uk	£5,253	£8,925	C. Canning
Hampton School, Middx	hamptonschool.org.uk	£6,685	–	K. Knibbs
Harrogate Ladies' College, N. Yorks	www.hlc.org.uk	£5,345	£12,170	Mrs S. Brett
Harrow School, Middx	www.harrowschool.org.uk	–	£13,350	A. Land
Headington School, Oxon	www.headington.org	£6,417	£12,762	Mrs C. Jordan
Heathfield School, Berks	www.heathfieldschool.net	£7,600	£12,210	Mrs M. Legge
Hereford Cathedral School, Herefords	www.herefordcs.com	£4,627	–	P. Smith
Hethersett Old Hall School, Norfolk	www.hohs.co.uk	£5,210	£8,020	S. Crump
Highclare School, W. Midlands	www.highclareschool.co.uk	£4,215	–	Dr R. Luker
Highgate School, London, N6	www.highgateschool.org.uk	£6,990	–	A. Pettitt
Hill House School, S. Yorks	www.hillhouse.doncaster.sch.uk	£4,400	–	D. Holland
Hurstpierpoint College, W. Sussex	www.hppc.co.uk	£7,950	£9,985	T. Manly
Hymers College, E. Yorks	www.hymerscollege.co.uk	£3,786	–	D. Elstone
Ibstock Place School, London, SW15	www.ibstockplaceschool.co.uk	£6,960	–	Mrs A. Sylvester-Johnson
Immanuel College, Herts	www.immanuelcollege.co.uk	£5,890	–	G. Griffin
Ipswich High School, Suffolk	www.ipswichhighschool.co.uk	£4,708	–	Ms O. Carlin
Ipswich School, Suffolk	www.ipswich.school	£5,193	£10,057	N. Weaver
James Allen's Girls' School (JAGS), London, SE22	www.jags.org.uk	£5,997	–	Mrs S. Huang
The John Lyon School, Middx	www.johnlyon.org	£6,194	–	Miss K. Haynes
Kent College, Kent	www.kentcollege.com	£6,105	£11,497	Dr D. Lamper
Kimbolton School, Cambs	www.kimbolton.cambs.sch.uk	£5,265	£8,760	J. Belbin
King Edward VI High School for Girls, W. Midlands	www.kehs.org.uk	£4,296	–	Mrs A. Clark
King Edward VI School, Hants	www.kes.hants.sch.uk	£5,350	–	J. Thould
King Edward's School, Somerset	www.kesbath.com	£4,825	–	M. Boden
King Edward's School, W. Midlands	www.kes.org.uk	£4,410	–	K. Phillips
King Edward's Witley, Surrey	www.kesw.org	£6,820	£10,665	J. Attwater
King Henry VIII School, W. Midlands	www.khviii.com	£3,898	–	J. Slack
King William's College, Isle of Man	www.kwc.im	£6,520	£9,882	J. Buchanan
King's College School, London, SW19	www.kcs.org.uk	£7,200	–	A. Halls
King's College, Taunton, Somerset	www.kings-taunton.co.uk	£7,460	£11,055	R. Biggs
King's Ely, Cambs	www.kingsely.org	£7,153	£10,355	Mrs S. Freestone
King's High School, Warwicks	www.kingshighwarwick.co.uk	£4,325	–	R. Nicholson
The King's School, Kent	www.kings-school.co.uk	£9,165	£12,485	P. Roberts
The King's School, Cheshire	www.kingschester.co.uk	£4,505	–	G. Hartley
The King's School, Cheshire	www.kingsmac.co.uk	£4,330	–	Dr S. Hyde
King's Rochester, Kent	www.kings-rochester.co.uk	£6,440	£10,530	B. Charles
The King's School, Worcs	www.ksw.org.uk	£4,663	–	M. Armstrong
The Kingsley School, Warwicks	www.thekingsleyschool.com	£4,418	–	Ms H. Owens
Kingsley School, Devon	www.kingsleyschoolbideford.co.uk	£4,460	£8,945	P. Last
Kingston Grammar School, Surrey	www.kgs.org.uk	£6,410	–	S. Lehec
Kingswood School, Somerset	www.kingswood.bath.sch.uk	£5,061	£10,909	S. Morris
Kirkham Grammar School, Lancs	www.kirkhamgrammar.co.uk	£3,875	£7,355	D. Berry
Lady Eleanor Holles, Middx	www.lehs.org.uk	£5,576	–	Mrs H. Hanbury
Lancing College, W. Sussex	www.lancingcollege.co.uk	£8,190	£11,995	D. Oliver
Latymer Upper School, London, W6	www.latymer-upper.org	£6,710	–	D. Goodhew
The Grammar School at Leeds, W. Yorks	www.gsal.org.uk	£4,596	–	Mrs S. Woodroofe
Leicester Grammar School, Leics	www.lgs-senior.org.uk	£4,343	–	J. Watson
Leicester High School for Girls, Leics	www.leicesterhigh.co.uk	£4,065	–	A. Whelpdale
Leighton Park School, Berks	www.leightonpark.com	£7,326	£11,915	M. Judd

Leweston School, Dorset	www.leweston.co.uk	£5,140	£10,185	Mrs K. Reynolds
The Leys, Cambs	www.theleys.net	£7,345	£10,975	M. Priestley
Lichfield Cathedral School, Staffs	www.lichfieldcathedralschool.com	£4,605	–	Mrs S. Hannam
Lincoln Minster School, Lincolns	www.lincolnminsterschool.co.uk	£4,608	£9,022	M. Wallace
Lingfield College, Surrey	www.lingfieldcollege.co.uk	£5,104	–	R. Bool
Longridge Towers School, Northumberland	www.lts.org.uk	£4,550	£9,250	J. Lee
Lord Wandsworth College, Hants	www.lordwandsworth.org	£10,600	£11,100	A. Williams
Loughborough Grammar School, Leics	www.lsf.org/grammar	£4,183	£9,584	D. Byrne
Loughborough High School, Leics	www.lsf.org/high	£4,183	–	Dr F. Miles
Luckley House School, Berks	www.luckleyhouseschool.org	£5,540	£9,694	Mrs J. Tudor
LVS Ascot, Berks	www.lvs.ascot.sch.uk	£5,657	£10,077	Mrs C. Cunniffe
Magdalen College School, Oxon	www.mcsoxford.org	£6,159	–	Miss H. Pike
Malvern College, Worcs	www.malverncollege.org.uk	£8,485	£13,153	K. Metcalfe
The Manchester Grammar School, Greater Manchester	www.mgs.org	£4,190	–	Dr M. Boulton
Manchester High School for Girls, Greater Manchester	www.manchesterhigh.co.uk	£3,958	–	Mrs C. Hewitt
Manor House School, Bookham, Surrey	www.manorhouseschool.org	£5,801	–	Ms T. Fantham
The Marist School – Senior Phase, Berks	www.themarist.com	£4,870	–	K. McCloskey
Marlborough College, Wilts	www.marlboroughcollege.org	–	£12,605	Mrs L. Moelwyn-Hughes
Marymount International School, Surrey	www.marymountlondon.com	£7,925	£13,475	Mrs M. Frazier
Mayfield School, E. Sussex	www.mayfieldgirls.org	£7,000	£11,300	Miss A. Beary
The Maynard School, Devon	www.maynard.co.uk	£4,416	–	Miss S. Dunn
Merchant Taylors' Boys' School, Merseyside	www.merchanttaylors.com	£3,798	–	D. Wickes
Merchant Taylors' Girls' School, Merseyside	www.merchanttaylors.com	£3,798	–	Mrs C. Tao
Merchant Taylors' School, Middx	www.mtsn.org.uk	£6,899	–	S. Everson
Mill Hill School, London, NW7	millhill.org.uk	£7,047	£11,239	Mrs J. Sanchez
Millfield, Somerset	millfieldschool.com	£8,535	£12,870	G. Horgan
Milton Abbey School, Dorset	www.miltonabbey.co.uk	£6,750	£12,850	Mrs J. Fremont-Barnes
Monkton Combe School, Somerset	www.monktoncombeschool.com	£6,970	£11,115	C. Wheeler
More House School, London, SW1	www.morehouse.org.uk	£6,650	–	Mrs A. Leach
Moreton Hall, Shrops	www.moretonhall.org	£9,575	£11,625	J. Forster
Mount House School, Herts	www.mounthouse.org.uk	£5,010	–	T. Mullins
Mount Kelly, Devon	www.mountkelly.com	£5,840	£10,190	G. Ayling
Mount St Mary's College, Derbys	www.msmcollege.com	£4,695	£9,995	Dr N. Cuddihy
New Hall School, Essex	www.newhallschool.co.uk	£6,626	£10,002	Mrs K. Jeffrey
Newcastle High School for Girls, Tyne and Wear	www.newcastlehigh.gdst.net	£4,341	–	M. Tippett
Newcastle School for Boys, Tyne and Wear	www.newcastleschool.co.uk	£4,161	–	D. Tickner
Newcastle-under-Lyme School, Staffs	www.nuls.org.uk	£3,993	–	M. Getty
North London Collegiate School, Middx	www.nlcs.org.uk	£6,676	–	Mrs S. Clark
Norwich High School, Norfolk	www.norwichhigh.gdst.net	£4,854	–	Mrs K. Malaisé
Norwich School, Norfolk	www.norwich-school.org.uk	£5,404	–	S. Griffiths
Notre Dame School, Surrey	www.notredame.co.uk	£5,590	–	Mrs A. King
Notting Hill and Ealing High School, London, W13	www.nhehs.gdst.net	£6,187	–	M. Shoults
Nottingham Girls' High School, Notts	www.nottinghamgirlshigh.gdst.net	£4,527	–	Miss J. Keller
Nottingham High School, Notts	www.nottinghamhigh.co.uk	£4,955	–	K. Fear
Oakham School, Rutland	www.oakham.rutland.sch.uk	£6,845	£11,220	N. Lashbrook
Ockbrook School, Derbys	www.ockbrooksch.co.uk	£4,390	–	T. Brooksby
Oldham Hulme Grammar School, Lancs	www.ohgs.co.uk	£3,745	–	C. Mairs
The Oratory School, Oxon	www.oratory.co.uk	£8,322	£11,433	J. Smith
Oundle School, Northants	www.oundleschool.org.uk	£7,935	£12,230	Mrs S. Kerr-Dineen
Our Lady's Abingdon Senior School, Oxon	www.olab.org.uk	£5,350	–	S. Oliver
Oxford High School, Oxon	www.oxfordhigh.gdst.net	£5,182	–	Dr P. Hills
Palmers Green High School, London, N21	www.pghs.co.uk	£5,310	–	Mrs W. Kempster
Pangbourne College, Berks	www.pangbourne.com	£8,295	£11,730	T. Garnier
The Perse Upper School, Cambs	www.perse.co.uk	£5,774	–	E. Elliott
The Peterborough School, Cambs	www.thepeterboroughschool.co.uk	£4,956	–	A. Meadows
Pipers Corner School, Bucks	www.piperscorner.co.uk	£6,130	–	Mrs H. Ness-Gifford
Pitsford School, Northants	www.pitsfordschool.com	£4,902	–	Dr C. Walker
Plymouth College, Devon	www.plymouthcollege.com	£5,225	£9,995	J. Cohen
Pocklington School, E. Yorks	www.pocklingtonschool.com	£4,873	£9,497	T. Seth
Portland Place School, London, W1B	www.portland-place.co.uk	£7,040	–	D. Bradbury
The Portsmouth Grammar School, Hants	www.pgs.org.uk	£5,317	–	Dr A. Cotton
Portsmouth High School, Hants	www.portsmouthhigh.co.uk	£4,662	–	Mrs J. Prescott
Princess Helena College, Herts	www.princesshelenacollege.co.uk	£6,741	£9,800	Mrs S. Davis

Princethorpe College, Warwicks	www.princethorpe.co.uk	£4,231	–	E. Hester
Prior Park College, Somerset	www.priorparkschools.com	£5,585	£10,315	J. Murphy-O'Connor
The Purcell School, Herts	www.purcell-school.org	£8,656	£11,025	P. Bambrough
Putney High School, London, SW15	www.putneyhigh.gdst.net	£6,300	–	Mrs S. Longstaff
Queen Anne's School, Berks	www.qas.org.uk	£8,045	£11,860	Mrs J. Harrington
Queen Elizabeth's Hospital (QEH), Bristol	www.qehbristol.co.uk	£4,802	–	S. Holliday
Queen Mary's School, N. Yorks	www.queenmarys.org	£6,325	£8,630	Mrs C. Cameron
Queen's College, London, London, W1G	www.qcl.org.uk	£6,375	–	R. Tillett
Queen's College, Somerset	www.queenscollege.org.uk	£6,150	£10,660	Dr L. Earps
Queen's Gate School, London, SW7	www.queensgate.org.uk	£6,850	–	Mrs R. Kamaryc
Queenswood School, Herts	www.queenswood.org	£8,125	£10,900	Mrs J. Cameron
Radley College, Oxon	www.radley.org.uk	–	£12,775	J. Moule
Ratcliffe College, Leics	www.ratcliffecollege.com	£5,429	£8,653	J. Reddin
The Read School, N. Yorks	www.readschool.co.uk	£4,132	£9,482	Mrs R. Ainley
Reading Blue Coat School, Berks	www.rbcs.org.uk	£5,565	–	J. Elzinga
Reddam House Berkshire, Berks	www.reddamhouse.org.uk	£5,760	£10,935	Mrs T. Howard
Redmaids' High School, Bristol	www.redmaidshigh.co.uk	£5,025	–	Mrs I. Tobias
Reed's School, Surrey	www.reeds.surrey.sch.uk	£8,225	£10,600	M. Hoskins
Reigate Grammar School, Surrey	www.reigategrammar.org	£6,240	–	S. Fenton
Rendcomb College, Glos	www.rendcombcollege.org.uk	£7,775	£10,500	R. Jones
Repton School, Derbys	www.repton.org.uk	£8,831	£11,904	M. Semmence
RGS Worcester, Worcs	www.rgsw.org.uk	£4,360	–	J. Pitt
Rishworth School, W. Yorks	www.rishworth-school.co.uk	£4,220	£9,995	Dr P. Silverwood
Roedean Moira House Girls School, E. Sussex	www.roedeanmoirahouse.co.uk	£6,020	£11,140	A. Wood
Roedean School, E. Sussex	www.roedean.co.uk	£7,165	£12,855	O. Blond
Rossall School, Lancs	www.rossall.org.uk	£4,360	£12,450	J. Quartermain
Royal Grammar School, Surrey	www.rgsg.co.uk	£6,095	–	Dr J. Cox
Royal Grammar School, Tyne and Wear	www.rgs.newcastle.sch.uk	£4,388	–	J. Fern
Royal Hospital School, Suffolk	www.royalhospitalschool.org	£5,830	£10,865	S. Lockyer
The Royal Masonic School for Girls, Herts	www.rmsforgirls.org.uk	£5,825	£9,945	K. Carson
Royal Russell School, Surrey	www.royalrussell.co.uk	£6,160	£12,175	C. Hutchinson
Rugby School, Warwicks	www.rugbyschool.co.uk	£7,479	£11,920	P. Green
Ryde School with Upper Chine, Isle of Wight	www.rydeschool.org.uk	£4,410	–	M. Waldron
Rye St Antony, Oxon	www.ryestantony.co.uk	£5,110	£8,645	Mrs S. Ryan
St Albans High School for Girls, Herts	www.stahs.org.uk	£6,265	–	Mrs J. Brown
St Albans School, Herts	www.st-albans.herts.sch.uk	£6,200	–	J. Gillespie
St Augustine's Priory School, London, W5	www.sapriory.com	£5,231	–	Mrs S. Raffray
St Bede's College, Greater Manchester	www.sbcm.co.uk	£3,775	–	L. d'Arcy
St Benedict's School, London, W5	www.stbenedicts.org.uk	£5,615	–	A. Johnson
St Catherine's School, Surrey	www.stcatherines.info	£6,125	£10,095	Mrs A. Phillips
St Catherine's School, Middx	www.stcatherineschool.co.uk	£4,970	–	Mrs J. McPherson
St Christopher School, Herts	www.stchris.co.uk	£6,025	£10,550	R. Palmer
St Columba's College, Herts	www.stcolumbascollege.org	£5,233	–	D. Buxton
St Dominic's Grammar School, Staffs	www.stdominicsgrammarschool.co.uk	£4,404	–	P. McNabb
St Dunstan's College, London, SE6	www.stdunstans.org.uk	£5,732	–	N. Hewlett
St Edmund's College, Herts	www.stedmundscollege.org	£5,935	£10,305	P. Durán
St Edmund's School Canterbury, Kent	www.stedmunds.org.uk	£6,822	£11,656	E. O'Connor
St Edward's, Oxford, Oxon	www.stedwardsoxford.org	£10,095	£12,615	S. Jones
St Edward's School, Glos	www.stedwards.co.uk	£5,920	–	Mrs P. Clayfield
St Gabriel's, Berks	www.stgabriels.co.uk	£5,806	–	R. Smith
St George's College, Weybridge, Surrey	www.stgeorgesweybridge.com	£6,395	–	Mrs R. Owens
St George's, Ascot, Berks	www.stgeorges-ascot.org.uk	£7,600	£11,820	Mrs E. Hewer
St Helen & St Katharine, Oxon	www.shsk.org.uk	£5,490	–	Mrs R. Dougall
St Helen's School, Middx	www.sthelens.london	£5,816	–	Dr M. Short
St James Senior Boys' School, Surrey	www.stjamesboys.co.uk	£6,310	–	D. Brazier
St James Senior Girls' School, London, W14	www.stjamesgirls.co.uk	£6,700	–	Mrs S. Labram
St John's College, Hants	www.stjohnscollege.co.uk	£4,030	£8,695	Mrs M. Maguire
St Joseph's College, Suffolk	www.stjos.co.uk	£5,050	£11,590	Mrs D. Clarke
St Lawrence College, Kent	www.slcuk.com	£5,333	£11,945	A. Spencer
St Mary's School Ascot, Berks	www.st-marys-ascot.co.uk	£9,210	£12,930	Mrs M. Breen
St Mary's Calne, Wilts	www.stmaryscalne.org	£9,675	£12,975	Dr F. Kirk
St Mary's School, Essex	www.stmaryscolchester.org.uk	£4,995	–	Mrs H. Vipond
St Mary's College, Merseyside	www.stmarys.ac	£3,720	–	M. Kennedy
St Mary's School, Bucks	www.stmarysschool.co.uk	£5,660	–	Mrs P. Adams
St Mary's School, Dorset	www.stmarys.eu	£6,950	£10,490	Mrs M. Young
St Nicholas' School, Hants	www.st-nicholas.hants.sch.uk	£4,786	–	Dr O. Wright
St Paul's Girls' School, London, W6	www.spgs.org	£8,297	–	Mrs S. Fletcher
St Paul's School, London, SW13	www.stpaulsschool.org.uk	£8,344	£12,537	Professor Mark Bailey

St Peter's School, York, N. Yorks	www.stpetersyork.org.uk	£6,025	£10,010	J. Walker
St Swithun's School, Hants	www.stswithuns.com	£6,855	£11,200	Ms J. Gandee
Scarborough College, N. Yorks	www.scarboroughcollege.co.uk	£4,898	£8,267	G. Emmett
Seaford College, W. Sussex	www.seaford.org	£7,130	£11,030	J. Green
Sevenoaks School, Kent	www.sevenoaksschool.org	£7,785	£12,432	Dr K. Ricks
Shebbear College, Devon	www.shebbearcollege.co.uk	£4,325	£8,775	S. Weale
Sheffield High School for Girls, S. Yorks	www.sheffieldhighschool.org.uk	£4,325	–	Mrs N. Gunson
Sherborne Girls, Dorset	www.sherborne.com	£7,095	£11,960	Dr R. Sullivan
Sherborne School, Dorset	www.sherborne.org	£10,125	£12,500	D. Luckett
Shiplake College, Oxon	www.shiplake.org.uk	£7,410	£11,025	A. Davies
Shrewsbury School, Shrops	www.shrewsbury.org.uk	£8,745	£13,040	L. Winkley
Sibford School, Oxon	www.sibfordschool.co.uk	£4,913	£9,548	T. Spence
Solihull School, W. Midlands	www.solsch.org.uk	£4,331	–	D. Lloyd
South Hampstead High School, London, NW3	shhs.gdst.net	£6,218	–	Mrs V. Bingham
Stafford Grammar School, Staffs	www.staffordgrammar.co.uk	£4,260	–	M. Darley
Stamford High School, Lincolns	www.ses.lincs.sch.uk	£5,106	£9,482	W. Phelan
Stamford School, Lincolns	www.ses.lincs.sch.uk	£5,106	£9,482	W. Phelan
The Stephen Perse Foundation, Cambs	www.stephenperse.com	£5,850	–	Miss P. Kelleher
Stockport Grammar School, Cheshire	www.stockportgrammar.co.uk	£3,900	–	Dr P. Owen
Stonar, Wilts	www.stonarschool.com	£5,500	£10,135	Dr S. Divall
Stonyhurst College, Lancs	www.stonyhurst.ac.uk	£6,650	£12,100	J. Browne
Stover School, Devon	www.stover.co.uk	£8,730	£4,260	R. Notman
Stowe School, Bucks	www.stowe.co.uk	£6,330	£12,220	Dr A. Wallersteiner
Streatham & Clapham High School, London, SW16	www.schs.gdst.net	£5,874	–	Dr M. Sachania
Sutton Valence School, Kent	www.svs.org.uk	£7,135	£11,115	B. Grindlay
Sydenham High School, London, SE26	www.sydenhamhighschool.gdst.net	£5,579	–	Mrs K. Woodcock
Talbot Heath, Dorset	www.talbotheath.org	£4,801	£8,364	Mrs A. Holloway
Tettenhall College, W. Midlands	www.tettenhallcollege.co.uk	£4,627	£10,533	D. Williams
Thetford Grammar School, Norfolk	www.thetfordgrammar.co.uk	£4,555	–	M. Brewer
Tonbridge School, Kent	www.tonbridge-school.co.uk	£10,114	£13,482	J. Priory
Tormead School, Surrey	www.tormeadschool.org.uk	£5,150	–	Mrs C. Foord
Tring Park School for the Performing Arts, Herts	www.tringpark.com	£7,125	£11,135	S. Anderson
Trinity School, Surrey	www.trinity-school.org	£5,816	–	A. Kennedy
Trinity School, Devon	www.trinityschool.co.uk	£4,100	£9,259	L. Coen
Truro School, Cornwall	www.truroschool.com	£4,690	£9,355	A. Gordon-Brown
Tudor Hall, Oxon	www.tudorhallschool.com	£7,365	£11,870	Miss W. Griffiths
University College School, London, NW3	www.ucs.org.uk	£6,776	–	M. Beard
Uppingham School, Rutland	www.uppingham.co.uk	£8,771	£12,530	Dr R. Maloney
Walthamstow Hall, Kent	www.walthamstow-hall.co.uk	£6,690	–	Miss S. Ferro
Warminster School, Wilts	www.warminsterschool.org.uk	£5,110	£10,880	M. Mortimer
Warwick School, Warwicks	www.warwickschool.org	£4,398	£9,586	Dr D. Smith
Welbeck – The Defence Sixth Form College, Leics	www.dsfc.ac.uk	£6,666	–	J. Middleton
Wellingborough School, Northants	www.wellingboroughschool.org	£5,330	–	A. Holman
Wellington College, Berks	www.wellingtoncollege.org.uk	£9,680	£13,250	J. Thomas
Wellington School, Somerset	www.wellingtonschool.org.uk	£5,075	£10,270	H. Price
Wells Cathedral School, Somerset	www.wells-cathedral-school.com	£6,124	£10,255	A. Tighe
West Buckland School, Devon	www.westbuckland.com	£5,020	£10,240	P. Stapleton
Westfield School, Tyne and Wear	www.westfield.newcastle.sch.uk	£4,530	–	N. Walker
Westholme School, Lancs	www.westholmeschool.com	£3,760	–	Mrs L. Horner
Westminster School, London, SW1	www.westminster.org.uk	£9,058	£13,084	P. Derham
Westonbirt School, Glos	www.westonbirt.org	£4,995	£9,750	Mrs N. Dangerfield
Wimbledon High School, London, SW19	www.wimbledonhigh.gdst.net	£6,270	–	Mrs J. Lunnon
Winchester College, Hants	www.winchestercollege.org	–	£13,304	Dr T. Hands
Windermere School, Cumbria	www.windermereschool.co.uk	£5,820	£9,950	I. Lavender
Wisbech Grammar School, Cambs	www.wisbechgrammar.com	£4,449	–	C. Staley
Withington Girls' School, Greater Manchester	www.wgs.org	£4,084	–	Mrs S. Haslam
Woldingham School, Surrey	www.woldinghamschool.co.uk	£7,480	£12,180	Mrs A. Hutchinson
Wolverhampton Grammar School, W. Midlands	www.wgs.org.uk	£4,554	–	Mrs K. Crewe-Read
Woodbridge School, Suffolk	www.woodbridgeschool.org.uk	£5,500	£10,295	Dr R. Robson
Woodhouse Grove School, W. Yorks	www.woodhousegrove.co.uk	£4,525	£9,340	J. Lockwood
Worth School, W. Sussex	www.worthschool.org.uk	£7,910	£11,230	S. McPherson
Wrekin College, Shrops	www.wrekincollege.com	£5,975	£8,440	T. Firth
Wychwood School, Oxon	www.wychwoodschool.org	£5,300	£9,300	Mrs A. Johnson
Wycliffe College, Glos	www.wycliffe.co.uk	£6,995	£11,740	N. Gregory
Wycombe Abbey, Bucks	www.wycombeabbey.com	–	£12,980	Mrs R. Wilkinson
The Yehudi Menuhin School, Surrey	www.menuhinschool.co.uk	–	–	Mrs K. Clanchy

WALES

The Cathedral School Llandaff, Cardiff	www.cathedral-school.co.uk	£4,238	–	Mrs C. Sherwood
Christ College, Brecon	www.christcollegebrecon.com	£5,892	£9,217	G. Pearson
Howell's School Llandaff, Cardiff	www.howells-cardiff.gdst.net	£4,461	–	Mrs S. Davis
Monmouth School for Boys, Monmouth	www.habsmonmouth.org	£5,272	£10,687	Dr A. Daniel
Monmouth School for Girls, Monmouth	www.habsmonmouth.org	£4,926	£10,687	Mrs J. Miles
Myddelton College, Denbigh	www.myddeltoncollege.com	£4,000	£9,366	M. Roberts
Rougemont School, Newport	www.rougemontschool.co.uk	£4,512	–	R. Carnevale
Ruthin School, Ruthin	www.ruthinschool.co.uk	£4,666	£11,500	T. Belfield

SCOTLAND

The High School of Dundee, Dundee	www.highschoolofdundee.org.uk	£4,333	–	Dr J. Halliday
The Edinburgh Academy, Edinburgh	www.edinburghacademy.org.uk	£3,792	–	B. Welsh
Fettes College, Edinburgh	www.fettes.com	£9,400	£11,600	G. Stanford
George Heriot's School, Edinburgh	www.george-heriots.com	£4,174	–	Mrs L. Franklin
The Glasgow Academy, Glasgow	www.theglasgowacademy.org.uk	£4,128	–	P. Brodie
The High School of Glasgow, Glasgow	www.highschoolofglasgow.co.uk	£4,256	–	J. O'Neill
Glenalmond College, Perth	www.glenalmondcollege.co.uk	£8,617	£11,502	H. Ouston
Gordonstoun, Elgin	www.gordonstoun.org.uk	£9,445	£12,765	Mrs L. Kerr
Kelvinside Academy, Glasgow	www.kelvinsideacademy.org.uk	£4,220	–	I. Munro
Kilgraston School, Bridge of Earn	www.kilgraston.com	£5,880	£10,045	Mrs D. MacGinty
Lomond School, Helensburgh	www.lomondschool.com	£3,990	£9,250	Mrs J. Urquhart
Loretto School, Musselburgh	www.loretto.com	£7,775	£11,420	G. Hawley
Merchiston Castle School, Edinburgh	www.merchiston.co.uk	£8,070	£10,970	J. Anderson
Morrison's Academy, Crieff	www.morrisonsacademy.org	£4,332	–	G. Warren
Robert Gordon's College, Aberdeen	www.rgc.aberdeen.sch.uk	£4,377	–	S. Mills
St Aloysius' College, Glasgow	www.staloysius.org	£4,275	–	M. Bartlett
St Columba's School, Kilmacolm	www.st-columbas.org	£4,032	–	Mrs A. Angus
St Leonards School, St Andrews	www.stleonards-fife.org	£4,736	£11,551	Dr M. Carslaw
St Margaret's School for Girls, Aberdeen	www.st-margaret.aberdeen.sch.uk	£5,292	–	Miss A. Tomlinson
Strathallan School, Perth	www.strathallan.co.uk	£7,470	£11,000	M. Lauder

NORTHERN IRELAND

Campbell College, Belfast	www.campbellcollege.co.uk	£930	£4,915	R. Robinson
The Royal School Dungannon, Dungannon	www.royaldungannon.com	£50	£3,550	D. Burnett

CHANNEL ISLANDS

Elizabeth College, Guernsey	www.elizabethcollege.gg	£3,995	–	Mrs J. Palmer
Victoria College, Jersey	www.victoriacollege.je	£1,916	–	A. Watkins

NATIONAL ACADEMIES OF SCHOLARSHIP

The national academies are self-governing bodies whose members are elected as a result of achievement and distinction in the academy's field. Within their discipline, the academies provide advice, support education and exceptional scholars, stimulate debate, promote UK research worldwide and collaborate with international counterparts.

The UK's four national academies – the Royal Society, the British Academy, the Royal Academy of Engineering and the Academy of Medical Sciences – receive funding from the Department for Business, Energy and Industrial Strategy (BEIS) for key programmes that help deliver government priorities. The total amount of resource funding allocated by BEIS to the four national academies for 2019–20 is £195m. The Royal Society of Edinburgh is aided by funds provided by the Scottish government. In addition to government funding, the national academies generate additional income from donations, membership contributions, trading and investments.

ACADEMY OF MEDICAL SCIENCES (1998)

41 Portland Place, London W1B 1QH
T 020-3141 3200 W www.acmedsci.ac.uk

Founded in 1998, the Academy of Medical Sciences is the independent body in the UK representing the diversity of medical science. The Academy seeks to improve health through research, as well as to promote medical science and its translation into benefits for society.

The academy is self-governing and receives funding from a variety of sources, including the fellowship, charitable donations, government and industry.

Fellows are elected from a broad range of medical sciences: biomedical, clinical and population based. The academy includes in its remit veterinary medicine, dentistry, nursing, medical law, economics, sociology and ethics. Elections are from nominations put forward by existing fellows.

There are around 1,200 fellows and 42 honorary fellows.

President, Prof. Sir Robert Lechler, PMEDSCI
Executive Director, Dr Rachel Quinn *(interim)*

BRITISH ACADEMY (1902)

10–11 Carlton House Terrace, London SW1Y 5AH
T 020-7969 5200 W www.thebritishacademy.ac.uk

The British Academy is an independent, self-governing learned society for the promotion of the humanities and social sciences. It was founded in 1901 and granted a royal charter in 1902. The British Academy supports advanced academic research and is a channel for the government's support of research in those disciplines.

The fellows are scholars who have attained distinction in one of the branches of study that the academy exists to promote. Candidates must be nominated by existing fellows. There are just over 1,000 fellows, around 30 honorary fellows and 300 corresponding fellows overseas.

President, Prof. Sir David Cannadine
Chief Executive, Dr Robin Jackson *(interim)*

ROYAL ACADEMY OF ENGINEERING (1976)

3 Carlton House Terrace, London SW1Y 5DG
T 020-7766 0600 W www.raeng.org.uk

The Royal Academy of Engineering was established as the Fellowship of Engineering in 1976. It was granted a royal charter in 1983 and its present title in 1992. It is an independent, self-governing body whose object is the pursuit, encouragement and maintenance of excellence in the whole field of engineering, in order to promote the advancement of the science, art and practice of engineering for the benefit of the public.

Election to the fellowship is by invitation only, from nominations supported by the body of fellows. There are around 1,500 fellows, 40 honorary fellows and 100 international fellows. The Duke of Edinburgh is the senior fellow and the Princess Royal and the Duke of Kent are both royal fellows.

President, Prof. Dame Ann Dowling, OM, DBE, FRENG, FRS
Chief Executive, Dr Hayaatun Sillem

ROYAL SOCIETY (1660)

6–9 Carlton House Terrace, London SW1Y 5AG
T 020-7451 2500 W www.royalsociety.org

The Royal Society is an independent academy promoting the natural and applied sciences. Founded in 1660 and granted a royal charter in 1662, the society has three roles: as the UK academy of science, as a learned society and as a funding agency. It is an independent, self-governing body under a royal charter, promoting and advancing all fields of physical and biological sciences, of mathematics and engineering, medical and agricultural sciences and their application.

Fellows are elected for their contributions to science, both in fundamental research resulting in greater understanding, and also in leading and directing scientific and technological progress in industry and research establishments. Each year up to 52 new fellows, who must be citizens or residents of the Commonwealth or Ireland, and up to ten foreign members may be elected. In addition one honorary fellow may also be elected annually from those not eligible for election as fellows or foreign members. There are around 1,700 fellows and foreign members and eight honorary members covering all scientific disciplines. The Queen is the patron of the Royal Society, and there are also five royal fellows.

President, Sir Venki Ramakrishnan, PRS
Executive Director, Dr Julie Maxton, CBE

ROYAL SOCIETY OF EDINBURGH (1783)

22–26 George Street, Edinburgh EH2 2PQ
T 0131-240 5000 W www.rse.org.uk

The Royal Society of Edinburgh (RSE) is an educational charity and Scotland's national academy. An independent body with charitable status, its multidisciplinary membership represents a knowledge resource for the people of Scotland. Granted its royal charter in 1783 for the 'advancement of learning and useful knowledge', the society organises conferences, debates and lectures; conducts independent inquiries; facilitates international collaboration and showcases the country's research and development capabilities; provides educational activities for primary and secondary school students; and awards prizes and medals. The society also awards over £2m annually to Scotland's top researchers and entrepreneurs working in Scotland.

There are over 1,750 fellows, including honorary fellows and corresponding fellows overseas.

President, Prof. Dame Anne Glover
Chief Executive, Dr Rebekah Widdowfield

PRIVATELY FUNDED ARTS ACADEMIES

The Royal Academy and the Royal Scottish Academy support the visual arts community in the UK, hold educational events and promote interest in the arts. They are entirely privately funded through contributions by 'friends' (regular donors who receive benefits such as free entry, previews and magazines), bequests, corporate donations and exhibitions.

ROYAL ACADEMY OF ARTS (1768)

Burlington House, Piccadilly, London W1J 0BD
T 020-7300 8000 **W** www.royalacademy.org.uk

Founded by George III in 1768, the Royal Academy of Arts is an independent, self-governing society devoted to the encouragement and promotion of the fine arts.

Membership of the academy is limited to 100 academicians, all of whom are either painters, engravers, printmakers, draughtsmen, sculptors or architects. There must always be at least 14 sculptors, 12 architects and eight printmakers among the academicians. Candidates must be professionally active in the UK and are nominated and elected by the existing academicians. The members are known as royal academicians (RAs) and are responsible for both the governance and direction of the academy. When RAs reach the age of 75, they become senior academicians and can no longer serve as officers or on the committees.

The title of honorary academician is awarded to a small number of distinguished artists who are not resident in the UK; as at July 2019, there were 34 honorary academicians. Unlike the RAs, they do not take part in the governance of the academy and are unable to vote.

President, Christopher Le Brun, PRA
Secretary and Chief Executive, Axel Rüger

ROYAL SCOTTISH ACADEMY (1838)

The Mound, Edinburgh EH2 2EL
T 0131-225 6671 **W** www.royalscottishacademy.org

Founded in 1826 and led by a body of academicians comprising eminent artists and architects, the Royal Scottish Academy (RSA) is an independent voice for cultural advocacy and one of the largest supporters of artists in Scotland. The Academy administers a number of scholarships, awards and residencies and has a historic collection of Scottish artworks, recognised by the Scottish government as being of national significance. The Academy is independent from local or national government funding, relying instead on bequests, legacies, sponsorship and earned income.

Academicians have to be Scots by birth or domicile, and are elected from the disciplines of art and architecture following nominations put forward by the existing membership. There are also a small number of honorary academicians – distinguished artists and architects, writers, historians and musicians – who do not have to be Scottish. As at July 2019 there were 135 academicians and 41 honorary academicians.

President, Joyce W. Cairns, PRSA
Secretary, Robbie Bushe, RSA
Treasurer, Robin Webster, RSA

RESEARCH COUNCILS

The government funds research through nine research councils, supported by the Department for Business, Energy and Industrial Strategy (BEIS) through UK Research and Innovation (for further information *see* **W** www.ukri.org). The councils support research and training in universities and other higher education and research facilities.

Under the Higher Education and Research Act 2017, the existing seven research councils, Innovate UK and the research and knowledge exchange functions of the former Higher Education Funding Council for England (HEFCE) were subsumed into a new single funding body, UK Research and Innovation (UKRI), which became operational in April 2018. Research England is a new council within UKRI, taking forward the England-only responsibilities of HEFCE in relation to research and knowledge exchange. Innovate UK is a non-departmental public body which works with companies and partner organisations to facilitate scientific and technological development for the UK economy.

Quality-related research funding is administered through UKRI. Additional funds may also be provided by other government departments, devolved administrations and other international bodies. The councils also receive income for research specifically commissioned by government departments and the private sector, and income from charitable sources.

ARTS AND HUMANITIES RESEARCH COUNCIL

Polaris House, North Star Avenue, Swindon SN2 1FL
T 01793-416000 **W** www.ahrc.ukri.org

The AHRC is the successor organisation to the Arts and Humanities Research Board and was incorporated by royal charter and established in 2005. It provides funding for postgraduate training and research in the arts and humanities; in any one year, the AHRC makes approximately 700 research awards and around 2,000 postgraduate scholarships. Awards are made after a rigorous peer review system, which ensures the quality of applications.

Executive Chair, Prof. Andrew Thompson, DPHIL

BIOTECHNOLOGY AND BIOLOGICAL SCIENCES RESEARCH COUNCIL

Polaris House, North Star Avenue, Swindon SN2 1UH
T 01793-413200 **W** www.bbsrc.ukri.org

Established by royal charter in 1994, the BBSRC is the UK funding agency for research in the non-clinical life sciences. It funds research into how all living organisms function and behave, benefiting the agriculture, food, health, pharmaceutical and chemical sectors. To deliver its mission, the BBSRC supports research and training in universities and research centres throughout the UK, including providing strategic research grants to the eight institutes listed below. In June 2015, the institutes founded the National Institutes of Bioscience (NIB) partnership in order to increase the impact of bioscience research and to strengthen the UK's reputation in the field.

Chair, Prof. Melanie Welham

INSTITUTES

BABRAHAM INSTITUTE, Babraham Hall, Cambridge CB22 3AT **T** 01223-496000
Director, Prof. Michael Wakelam

INSTITUTE FOR BIOLOGICAL, ENVIRONMENTAL AND RURAL SCIENCES (ABERYSTWYTH UNIVERSITY), Penglais, Aberystwyth SY23 3DA
T 01970-621986
Director, Prof. Mike Gooding
EARLHAM INSTITUTE, Norwich Research Park, Colney, Norwich NR4 7UZ **T** 01603-450001
Director, Prof. Neil Hall
JOHN INNES CENTRE, Norwich Research Park, Colney, Norwich NR4 7UH **T** 01603-450000
Director, Prof. Dale Sanders
PIRBRIGHT INSTITUTE, Ash Road, Woking, Surrey GU24 0NF
T 01483-232441
Director, Dr Bryan Charleston
QUADRAM INSTITUTE, Norwich Research Park, Norwich, Norfolk NR4 7UA **T** 01603-255000
Director, Prof. Ian Charles
ROSLIN INSTITUTE (UNIVERSITY OF EDINBURGH), Easter Bush, Midlothian EH25 9RG **T** 0131-651 9100
Director, Prof. Eleanor Riley
ROTHAMSTED RESEARCH, Harpenden, Herts AL5 2JQ
T 01582-763133
Director, Prof. Achim Dobermann

ECONOMIC AND SOCIAL RESEARCH COUNCIL

Polaris House, North Star Avenue, Swindon SN2 1UJ
T 01793-413000 **W** www.esrc.ukri.org

The ESRC was established by royal charter in 1965 as an organisation for funding and promoting research and postgraduate training in the social sciences. It supports independent research which has an impact on business, the public sector and civil society and also provides advice, disseminates knowledge and promotes public understanding in these areas.

The ESRC has a total budget of around £202m and provides funding to over 4,000 researchers and postgraduate students in academic institutions and independent research institutes.

Executive Chair, Prof. Jennifer Rubin

ENGINEERING AND PHYSICAL SCIENCES RESEARCH COUNCIL

Polaris House, North Star Avenue, Swindon SN2 1ET
T 01793-444000 **W** www.epsrc.ukri.org

Formed in 1994 by royal charter, the EPSRC is the UK government's main agency for funding research and training in engineering and the physical sciences in universities and other organisations throughout the UK. The EPSRC invests around £800m a year in a broad range of subjects – from mathematics to materials science, and from information technology to structural engineering. It also provides advice, disseminates knowledge and promotes public understanding in these areas.

Executive Chair, Prof. Lynn Gladden, CBE

MEDICAL RESEARCH COUNCIL

Polaris House, North Star Avenue, Swindon SN2 1FL
T 01793-416200 **W** www.mrc.ukri.org

The MRC is a publicly funded organisation dedicated to improving human health. The MRC supports research across the entire spectrum of medical sciences, in universities, hospitals, centres and institutes.

Chair, Prof. Fiona Watt
Chair, Infections and Immunity Board, Prof. Paul Kaye
Chair, Molecular and Cellular Medicine Board, Prof. Anne Ferguson-Smith
Chair, Neurosciences and Mental Health Board, Prof. Patrick Chinnery
Chair, Population and Systems Medicine Board, Prof. Paul Elliott
Chair, Regenerative Medicine Research Board, Prof. Martin Wilkins

NATURAL ENVIRONMENT RESEARCH COUNCIL

Polaris House, North Star Avenue, Swindon SN2 1EU
T 01793-411500 **W** www.nerc.ukri.org

NERC is the leading funder of independent research, training and innovation in environmental science in the UK. Its work covers the full range of atmospheric, earth, biological, terrestrial and aquatic sciences. NERC invests around £330m a year in research exploring how we can sustainably benefit from our natural resources, predict and respond to natural hazards and understand environmental change. NERC works closely with policymakers and industry to support sustainable economic growth in the UK and around the world.
Executive Chair, Prof. Duncan Wingham

RESEARCH CENTRES

BRITISH ANTARCTIC SURVEY, High Cross, Madingley Road, Cambridge CB3 OET **T** 01223-221400
Director, Prof. Dame Jane Francis, DCMG
BRITISH GEOLOGICAL SURVEY, Kingsley Dunham Centre, Keyworth, Nottingham NG12 5GG **T** 0115-936 3100
Executive Director, Prof. John Ludden
CENTRE FOR ECOLOGY AND HYDROLOGY, Maclean Building, Benson Lane, Crowmarsh Gifford, Wallingford OX10 8BB **T** 01491-838800
Director, Prof. Mark Bailey
NATIONAL CENTRE FOR ATMOSPHERIC SCIENCE, NCAS Headquarters, School of Earth and Environment, University of Leeds, Leeds LS2 9JT **T** 0113-343 6408
Director, Prof. Stephen Mobbs

NATIONAL CENTRE FOR EARTH OBSERVATION, Michael Atiyah Building, University of Leicester, University Road, Leicester LE1 7RH **T** 0116-252 2016
Director, Prof. John Remedios
NATIONAL OCEANOGRAPHY CENTRE, University of Southampton Waterfront Campus, European Way, Southampton SO14 3ZH **T** 0238-059 6666
Director, Prof. Ed Hill, OBE

SCIENCE AND TECHNOLOGY FACILITIES COUNCIL

Polaris House, North Star Avenue, Swindon SN2 1SZ
T 01793-442000 **W** www.stfc.ukri.org

Formed by royal charter in 2007, through the merger of the Council for the Central Laboratory of the Research Councils and the Particle Physics and Astronomy Research Council, the STFC is a non-departmental public body reporting to BEIS.

The STFC invests in large national and international research facilities, while delivering science and technology expertise for the UK. The council is involved in research projects such as the Diamond Light Source Synchrotron and the Large Hadron Collider, and develops new areas of science and technology. The EPSRC has transferred its responsibility for nuclear physics to the STFC.

Executive Chair, Prof. Mark Thompson

RESEARCH CENTRES

BOULBY UNDERGROUND SCIENCE FACILITY, Boulby Mine, Loftus, Saltburn-by-the-Sea, Cleveland TS13 4UZ **T** 01287-646300
CHILBOLTON OBSERVATORY, Chilbolton, Stockbridge, Hampshire SO20 6BJ **T** 01264-860391
DARESBURY LABORATORY, SciTech Daresbury, Keckwick Lane, Warrington WA4 4AD **T** 01925-603000
RUTHERFORD APPLETON LABORATORY, Harwell Campus, Didcot OX11 0QX **T** 01235-445000
UK ASTRONOMY TECHNOLOGY CENTRE, Royal Observatory Edinburgh, Blackford Hill, Edinburgh EH9 3HJ **T** 0131-668 8100

HEALTH

COVID-19 IN 2019–20

By Jenni Reid

While a global pandemic has long been a concern of academics, governments and international organisations, few predicted that 2020 would be the year one emerged, or quite the extent of the socioeconomic impact one would have. Virtually no nation has escaped the effects of the novel coronavirus COVID-19 entirely, but the specific impacts – whether to public health, tourism, business or everyday life – have varied widely around the world.

THE SPREAD OF COVID-19
At the end of December 2019, the Wuhan Municipal Health Commission in China reported a cluster of pneumonia cases with an unknown cause. The World Health Organization (WHO) quickly began advising countries on detecting and managing a new coronavirus, based on its experiences with SARS and MERS. On 13 January, the first infection was reported outside of China, in Thailand. By the end of January, low numbers of cases had been detected in countries across Asia and Oceania, as well as in the Middle East, North America and Europe.

In February, the effects of the outbreak were largely being felt in Asia. Chinese cities restricted citizens' movements, countries began banning flights from China, and others introduced mandatory quarantine periods for people arriving from certain countries. Several cruise ships were prevented from docking by countries which feared passengers bringing the virus with them. By the end of the month, small numbers of deaths linked to the virus, now known as COVID-19 or severe acute respiratory syndrome coronavirus 2, were being reported around the world. On 25 February, the WHO announced there were more cases outside of China than within it: the virus had gone global. Italy appeared to be the European hotspot, with seven deaths reported by the end of February, and cases in nearby countries were traced back to it.

In March, it became clear that COVID-19 would cause disruption to many nations on a scale unprecedented in recent memory. On 11 March, the WHO assessed that due to the virus's 'alarming' levels of spread and severity, the situation could be characterised as a pandemic. The same day, the US barred entry to foreign nationals travelling from China, Iran and most European countries. Mass gatherings were banned, to varying degrees, around the world. States of emergency were declared. Schools, workplaces and hospitality venues closed. Flights were cancelled, and some countries closed their borders almost entirely. Countries or cities implemented what quickly became known as 'lockdowns', with citizens told to stay at home unless necessary. In some places this was backed up by fines or other punitive measures, in others it remained a recommendation. Events that were cancelled or postponed in 2020 ranged from the Tokyo Olympic and Paralympic games and the COP21 Climate Summit, to thousands of sporting events, music festivals, concerts, theatre productions and conferences.

While intergovernmental agencies like the WHO provided advice throughout the year, the world's response to its newest pandemic was marked by a fragmented approach. Even blocs like the European Union had little coordination in their responses, with different stances taken at different times on issues such as border restrictions, mask wearing, lockdowns and testing. The arrival of vaccines developed by several companies, which began to be rolled out in some countries in December, provided some much-needed hope for an end to the pandemic. Yet it also saw UN Secretary General Antonio Guterres urge rich nations to make greater contributions to ensure it will be available around the world, and to warn against 'vaccine nationalism.'

On 31 December, one year after the first cases of what would later be identified as COVID-19 were reported, there had been over 83.9 million confirmed cases and over 1.8 million deaths linked to the virus worldwide. Europe and the Americas accounted for the lion's share of those cases, with Asia and Africa making up much smaller portions and Oceania barely any. The trend of cumulative cases and deaths worldwide was still moving up, and those figures pre-dated an expected rise in cases in many Western countries due to household mixing over Christmas and New Year's Eve. This data is imperfect, as countries carried out different levels of testing and disagreed on exactly how to measure deaths that followed infections. Still, it was apparent at the end of the year that several major economies in the Americas and Europe had taken the biggest hit both to their economies and their citizens' health, including the US and the UK.

COVID-19 IN THE UK
The first two cases of COVID-19 in the UK were reported on 30 January in York, England. The UK's official case tally did not begin to rise significantly until March, though it is likely the virus was spreading more rapidly than realised at the time. COVID-19 had its first major impact on UK public life on 16 March, when Prime Minister Boris Johnson held a press conference in which he urged people to work from home and avoid pubs, restaurants and other public spaces. The stated aim was to avoid overwhelming the National Health Service, due to an expected rise in hospitalisations.

On 18 March, schools in England, Wales and Scotland were shut down until further notice. On 20 March, a day after China reported zero local infections for the first time, the UK government ordered all pubs, restaurants, gyms and social venues to close. On 23 March, Johnson told all Britons they should only go outside to shop for essentials, to exercise for one hour each day, or to work if doing so at home was not possible. Those who did not comply were liable to pay a fine, and emergency legislation was passed to enable police enforcement. Several government figures were infected with the coronavirus during the succeeding weeks, including Johnson. The prime minister entered intensive care on 6 April due to the severity of his case. He recovered and was discharged on 14 April, and returned to work on 27 April.

The two months from 23 March were widely referred to as the UK's first 'lockdown'. The rules announced on that date largely remained in force until 15 June, when non-essential shops and places of worship were allowed to reopen. On 22 June, the public was given permission to meet outdoors in groups of up to six people, and to form a 'support bubble' with one other household to meet indoors. Pubs, restaurants and hotels began to reopen from 4 July. From 10 July, Britons were allowed to holiday without quarantining on their return in a list of countries from a 'travel corridor' list, where cases were judged sufficiently low, with the list updated weekly. Wedding receptions with limited numbers were allowed from 15 August.

The first lockdown largely succeeded in what government scientific advisors referred to as 'flattening the curve', by slowing the rate of new daily cases and eventually causing the number of cases to plateau. The NHS did not become overwhelmed (meaning COVID-19 patients being denied life-saving treatment due to a lack of resources), and a network of emergency hospitals that was established in venues such as conference centres and sports stadiums went largely unused. Cases went from over 4,000 per day throughout April to just over 1,400 per day at the end of May, to just over 600 per day at the end of June. However, the total death toll during this period was significant, rising from 1,172 at the start of lockdown on 27 March to 37,531 by the end of June.

Meanwhile, the daily case rate began to rise again as soon as society 'opened up' in July, hitting 800 cases by the end of the month and nearly 2,000 by the end of August. The summertime loosening of restrictions was tightened again in early September, when a UK-wide ban on gatherings of more than six people came into force. But at the same time, most children returned to school, many students arrived in university halls, leisure travel remained permitted and hospitality venues stayed open. New daily cases soared over the next two months, hitting a peak of 31,060 on 9 November (the number was substantially higher than at the peak of the first lockdown due to the wider availability of testing).

From September onwards, the UK nations began to take different approaches to tackling the pandemic, with decisions on covid-prevention measures taken by the devolved governments. Regional rules were also introduced: for example, areas of Leicestershire were placed back into lockdown on 29 June due to a surge in local infections, followed by parts of the north of England. On 12 October, England was placed into a 'three tier' system, with regions in the country placed under different restrictions based on their COVID-19 figures. On 14 October, Northern Ireland closed all pubs and restaurants. On 19 October, Wales entered a two-week 'firebreak' lockdown with only essential activities permitted. On 21 October, Scotland launched its own five-tier system.

Up to the year's end, the nations continued to move their regions into different levels of restrictions. The government was criticised for announcing that some household mixing would be allowed for a five-day period over Christmas in England, only to reverse this decision on 19 December. Following a dip in new daily cases due to lockdown measures through November, cases rose massively from 1 December to the end of the year, with 52,796 new cases on 31 December alone. By the end of the year, 73,512 Britons had died within 28 days of a positive coronavirus test.

THE ECONOMY
The pandemic had a dramatic impact on the UK economy in 2020. This was for a variety of reasons, most notably lockdown measures which included the instruction to stay at home unless necessary, and the resulting effect on businesses. The UK's GDP shrank by 19.8 per cent between April and June, the biggest slump since quarterly records began in 1955. In August, the ONS announced a cumulative 22.1 per cent fall in GDP in the first six months of 2020. This was among the highest drops in Europe, second only to the 22.7 per cent seen in Spain, and more than double the 10.6 per cent fall in the United States. A strong rebound was seen in the third quarter of the year, with a record 16 per cent expansion reported from July to September. But this news was tempered by the detail of a September slowdown, with experts predicting a weak fourth quarter. The Office for Budget Responsibility predicted the UK economy would shrink by 11.3 per cent overall in 2020.

The government rolled out numerous policies to attempt to counter the economic fallout. This began with the March 2020 budget, which brought with it the flagship Coronavirus Job Retention Scheme (CJRS), commonly referred to as the furlough scheme. The government initially covered 80 per cent of the wages of employees who were unable to work as a result of the pandemic, subject to a cap of £2,500 per month. These employees could not work for the company that had furloughed them, though they could volunteer or take on additional work that did not breach their contract. In May, when use of the scheme was at its highest, 30 per cent of the nation's workforce was furloughed. Gradual changes were made to the scheme from 1 July, when employers were able to bring back furloughed workers part-time. From 1 August, employers were asked to pay National Insurance and pension contributions for the hours employees were furloughed. From 1 September, the government's salary contribution was lowered to 70 per cent, and it dipped again to 60 per cent in October. Following several extensions, the CJRS was set to last until the end of April 2021, with further extension possible.

Financial support was also given to self-employed workers, who were able to claim through the Self-Employment Income Support Scheme (SEISS). This was open to people with annual profits of less than £50,000 who usually received at least half their income from self-employment, and whose work was adversely affected by the pandemic. Two grants were made available in 2020, in July and October, the first representing 80 per cent of average monthly trading profits, the second 70 per cent. Two more were set to be paid out in 2021.

By late 2020 it was difficult to say exactly how many jobs and livelihoods were preserved by the CJRS and SEISS, though it was likely in the thousands. However, the government was criticised for announcing one extension to the CJRS, from November to the end of March 2021, at very short notice, by which point some staff had already been laid off. Some also argued that jobs could have been saved had employers known the scheme would last for more than a year. Meanwhile, around 3 million people were estimated to have been ineligible for either scheme, including sole company directors, people who had been self-employed for less than a year, and people who normally moved between employment and self-employment.

While the CJRS and SEISS ran beyond the end of the year, the effects of the pandemic were already showing in employment figures. The UK unemployment rate rose to 4.9 per cent from July through September, 1.2 per cent higher than a year earlier and 0.7 per cent higher than in the previous quarter. Overall there were 819,000 fewer workers on UK company payrolls in November than in February. The biggest reductions over this period were in hospitality (297,000), retail and wholesale (160,000), manufacturing (115,000), culture and recreation (89,000) and admin and support services (58,000). In November, there were 2.7 million people claiming Jobseeker's Allowance or Universal Credit, 1.4 million more than in February. The OECD predicted UK unemployment would rise to an average of 7.4 per cent in 2021, up from 4 per cent pre-pandemic. The Bank of England expected unemployment to reach a high of 7.7 per cent in April to June 2021, though stated it could rise as high as 10 per cent, and further government support could alleviate this.

Many businesses were hit hard by the volatility of 2020, and policy measures to help them included Statutory Sick Pay refunds for coronavirus-related absences, a Coronavirus Business Interruption Loan Scheme for SMEs, Local Restrictions Support grants, and selected VAT cuts. Another was 'Eat Out To Help Out', a UK-wide scheme which saw the government subsidise a 50 per cent discount on food and soft drinks purchased in restaurants, cafes and pubs from Monday to Wednesday throughout August, in a bid to boost trade. By some measures the scheme was a success, with more than 49,000 businesses making a claim under the scheme and many calling for its continuation into the autumn. However, it was also criticised for its impact on the spread of the virus, with one study by the University of Warwick linking it to a sixth of new coronavirus case clusters over the summer.

The impact of COVID-19 on business could not be staved off entirely, and entire industries were pushed to crisis point, particularly hospitality, leisure, travel and tourism. Tens of thousands of pubs, restaurants, bars and hotels were put at risk of closure; pub groups including Marston's and Greene King cut jobs; and the airline Flybe and travel group Thomas Cook were pushed from precarious financial situations into collapse. The embattled British high street took a further blow, with big names including the Arcadia Group, Debenhams, Edinburgh Woollen Mill, Laura Ashley and Cath Kidston all entering administration. Nonetheless, the UK's company liquidation rate actually fell year-on-year in the 12 months ending in the third quarter of 2020, which the government attributed to financial support for businesses and the temporary prohibition of the use of statutory demands and certain winding-up petitions from 27 April to the end of the year.

Some businesses did well from the pandemic, including the major supermarket chains and web-only supermarket Ocado; Reckitt Benckiser, the producer of Dettol; and online gambling companies. The housing market was essentially suspended in late March, with the government telling people to delay home moves and preventing new viewings. But when it resumed in mid-May, with the government announcing a cut in stamp duty in England and Northern Ireland until 31 March and similar measures in place in Wales and Scotland, the market boomed. UK house prices increased by an average 7.6 per cent in the year to November, according to mortgage lender Halifax, and the end of June to the end of November saw the fastest five-month rise since 2004. Trends noted by housing websites included increased desires for gardens, as well as 'detached', 'rural' and 'secluded' homes, as lockdowns and the work-from-home lifestyle fuelled a desire for more space and fresh air.

The 2020 Autumn Budget was deferred to March 2021, when a full 'recovery plan' for the UK economy was set to be announced. As the year ended, cases of COVID-19 in the UK were soaring and most areas were under strict restrictions, raising the prospect of a grim remainder of the winter. In December, the Organisation for Economic Co-operation and Development (OECD) predicted that among major economies, the UK's would face the biggest hit from the pandemic second only to Argentina, and that it would be 6 per cent smaller than before the pandemic at the end of 2021. At this point it expects the overall global economy to be back to pre-pandemic levels. Also in December, the Office for Budget Responsibility (OBR) predicted the UK government would need to borrow £394bn to fund a tax shortfall and £280bn in public spending to tackle the pandemic, a cost that was over 80 per cent higher than the average among other G7 economies. It also estimated the UK was on course for a 90 per cent deeper decline in economic output in 2020, and almost 60 per cent more deaths. This was on top of the uncertainty posed by the UK's exit from the European Union, which was finally completed in 2020. While a trade deal was reached in December, it included additional barriers to trade, and the OBR forecasted a long-term loss of output of around 4 per cent compared with if the UK had remained in the EU.

SOCIETY

The pandemic had numerous effects on society and social issues, many of them negative. ONS figures published in August found that depression among British adults had doubled during the pandemic. Studies also showed an increase in rates of loneliness during lockdown periods. Women's Aid reported a significant rise in domestic violence linked to the pandemic. Meanwhile, hospitals were placed in the difficult position of having to restrict visitations, leading to thousands of people giving birth, undergoing serious treatments, or even dying with limited or no in-person contact with family or friends.

There were huge repercussions for non-covid-related healthcare during the pandemic. The NHS shut down or significantly reduced many areas of non-covid care during April, May and June. During this period, the British Medical Association estimated there were up to 286,000 fewer urgent cancer referrals, 25,900 fewer patients starting first cancer treatments following a decision to treat, and between 1.32 and 1.50 million fewer elective admissions than would usually be expected. NHS waiting times also reached a record high in England over the summer, according to a study published in the *British Medical Journal*.

The Social Care Institute for Excellence (SCIE) reported in September that the pandemic took a 'grim toll on social care in England'. Sector workers said many care homes had insufficient space to isolate people who had caught the virus. Others reported a lack of personal protective equipment, leaving staff as well as residents at risk. The same SCIE report stated that the pandemic exposed 'the deep levels of inequalities which exist in society, with evidence telling us that Black, Asian and minority ethnic (BAME) communities, adults with learning disabilities, and those on the lowest incomes, have been disproportionately affected.' A study by the University of Manchester in November estimated that 29,400 more care home residents died during the first 23 weeks of the pandemic than would be expected from historical trends, through causes directly and indirectly attributable to COVID-19.

Almost 700,000 people, including 120,000 children, fell into poverty as a result of the pandemic, according to analysis by thinktank The Legatum Institute. This took the number of people living in poverty in the UK to more than 15 million, or 23 per cent of the population. The Legatum Institute also found that an additional 700,000 people were prevented from falling into poverty by the temporary £20-a-week boost to universal credit which was introduced in April.

Homelessness was also impacted by COVID-19. Thousands of people were placed in temporary housing during the first lockdown, through what in England was called the 'Everyone In' scheme. Similar initiatives took place in Wales, Scotland and Northern Ireland. This saw local authorities find accommodation for all homeless people on their radar, regardless of factors such as perceived need, responsibility or immigration status. Chiefly using newly empty student accommodation and hotels, more than 29,000 people were housed in England alone, which medical journal *The Lancet* estimated avoided 1,164 covid-related hospital admissions and 266 deaths. Still, hundreds of people slipped through the cracks and continued to sleep rough throughout the year. This was especially due to the number of newly homeless people, exacerbated by the economic downturn and people in precarious housing situations being pushed into homelessness due to social distancing, restrictions on travel and other factors.

Significant disruption was caused to children's and higher education in 2020. Almost all schools in the UK closed on or around 20 March, except to the children of essential workers, and did not reopen until the new school year began in September. The Nuffield Trust described the result as an 'unprecedented disruption to the education of children and young people.' Teachers gave online lessons, and schools were tasked with both providing remote support for pupils and making sure they had a basic level of equipment. This included laptops, tablets and internet connectivity provided by the government, though some schools still reported an insufficient supply.

When children did return to school in September, the environment was still highly disrupted. Schools followed their own approaches for dividing children into 'bubbles': if one child in the bubble became ill, even with a cold, it sometimes led to dozens of children being sent home to isolate for two weeks. Teachers were leading lessons from behind masks and face shields. There was fierce debate between politicians, education authorities, teachers and others about whether to close schools early as cases soared in late autumn and winter. While the risk to children from COVID-19 appeared to be very low, schools were described as 'vectors for transmission', putting parents and teachers at greater risk. This came up against the strain put on parents from keeping children home, as well as the mental health and short- to long-term educational impact on children themselves.

All school leavers' exams, including A Levels, GCSEs, National Highers and Advanced Highers, were cancelled in 2020. Instead, exam boards calculated grades for students based on a combination of teacher assessments, class rankings and the past performance of their schools. The system was widely criticised as unfair, particularly for penalising students from disadvantaged backgrounds or who attended traditionally weaker-performing schools. Following a public outcry and student protests, by 17 August the administrations in England, Wales, Northern Ireland and Scotland all decided to allow students to receive teacher-assessed grades if they were higher than their standardised grades.

Students starting or returning to university in 2020 had a first term like no other. Those entering university accommodation were largely banned from socialising with people beyond their new flatmates, while the vast majority of teaching was done online. Where COVID-19 cases were discovered, some accommodation blocks were placed entirely into lockdown,

with university administrators dropping off food and drink for students outside doors. The situation caused widespread anger and frustration among students, leading to the biggest wave of student rent strikes in 40 years.

TAKING STOCK

Describing the events of 2020 as 'unprecedented' became so commonplace that it turned into a running joke on social media. Yet the word is undoubtedly a fitting one for the wrenching societal and economic changes that took place, from a Conservative government embracing massive public sector borrowing and placing stringent limitations on public life, to the months-long closure of schools, offices, restaurants, pubs, hotels, theatres, cinemas and more. So many words shot to prominence that the *Oxford English Dictionary* team was unable to choose just one as its Word of the Year, instead highlighting several, including COVID-19, WFH (work from home), lockdown, circuit-breaker, support bubble, keyworker and furlough.

The pandemic's long-term effects are still to be revealed. Some believe it will lead many businesses to shift to a home-working model to save on costly city centre office space, for example, or turbocharge the dominance of online services like door-to-door delivery platforms. Mask-wearing on public transport, or when someone is sick, might become a common sight; or it might fade into memory. What is certain is that individuals will feel the impact in the years and decades to come: whether that's the adults to be hit by the predicted rise in unemployment; the children whose education has been unsettled; or the tens of thousands who have lost loved ones to COVID-19.

NATIONAL HEALTH SERVICE

The National Health Service (NHS) came into being on 5 July 1948 under the National Health Service Act 1946, covering England and Wales and, under separate legislation, Scotland and Northern Ireland. The NHS is now administered by the Secretary of State for Health (in England), the Welsh government, the Scottish government and the Northern Ireland Executive.

The function of the NHS is to provide a comprehensive health service designed to secure improvement in the physical and mental health of the people and to prevent, diagnose and treat illness. It was founded on the principle that treatment should be provided according to clinical need rather than ability to pay, and should be free at the point of delivery.

Hospital, mental, dental, nursing, ophthalmic and ambulance services and facilities for the care of expectant and nursing mothers and young children are provided by the NHS to meet all reasonable requirements. Rehabilitation services such as occupational therapy, physiotherapy, speech therapy and surgical and medical appliances are supplied where appropriate. Specialists and consultants who work in NHS hospitals can also engage in private practice, including the treatment of their private patients in NHS hospitals.

STRUCTURE

The structure of the NHS remained relatively stable for the first 30 years of its existence. In 1974, a three-tier management structure comprising regional health authorities, area health authorities and district management teams was introduced in England, and the NHS became responsible for community health services. In 1979, area health authorities were abolished and district management teams were replaced by district health authorities.

The National Health Service and Community Care Act 1990 provided for more streamlined regional health authorities and district health authorities, and for the establishment of family health services authorities (FHSAs) and NHS trusts. The concept of the 'internal market' was introduced into health care, whereby care was provided through NHS contracts where health authorities or boards and GP fundholders (the purchasers) were responsible for buying health care from hospitals, non-fundholding GPs, community services and ambulance services (the providers). The Act also paved the way for the community care reforms, which were introduced in April 1993, and changed the way care is administered for older people, the mentally ill, the physically disabled and people with learning disabilities.

ENGLAND

Under the Health and Social Care Act 2012, which gained royal assent in March 2012, The NHS in England underwent a complete operational and budgetary restructure at a cost of approximately £1.4bn.

Hospitals were extensively affected by the overhaul, with the cap on income from private hospital patients increased from 1.5 per cent to 49 per cent. All hospitals will become foundation trusts, competing for treatment contracts from clinical commissioning groups (CCGs).

On 1 April 2013 the new commissioning board, NHS England, took on full statutory responsibilities; at the same time, strategic health authorities (SHAs) and primary care trusts (PCTs) which, alongside the Department of Health, had been responsible for NHS planning and delivery, were abolished. NHS England is an executive non-departmental public body of the Department of Health and Social Care (DHSC) with a remit to:

- provide national leadership to improve the quality of care
- oversee the operation of clinical commissioning groups
- allocate resources to clinical commissioning groups
- commission primary care and specialist services

The secretary of state has ultimate responsibility for the provision of a comprehensive health service in England and for ensuring the system works to its optimum capacity to meet the needs of its patients. The DHSC is responsible for strategic leadership of the health and social care systems, but is not the headquarters of the NHS, nor does it directly manage any NHS organisations.

In October 2014, NHS England published *Five Year Forward View* which committed the organisation to further change, including additional decentralisation and a greater emphasis on out-of-hospital care and preventative medicine. In January 2019 the *NHS Long Term Plan* was published outlining NHS England's healthcare plans for the next ten years; subsequently, around 1,250 primary care networks were formed after July 2019 from almost all existing general practices to better work at scale, covering populations of 30,000–50,000 people.

NHS ENGLAND, PO Box 16738, Redditch B97 9PT
T 0300-311 2233 E england.contactus@nhs.net
W www.england.nhs.uk
Chief Executive, Simon Stevens

CLINICAL COMMISSIONING GROUPS (CCGS)

On 1 April 2013, PCTs, which controlled 80 per cent of the NHS budget and commissioned most NHS services, were abolished. They were replaced with CCGs which took on many of the functions of the PCTs in addition to some functions previously assumed by the Department of Health. All GP practices now belong to a CCG which also includes other health professionals, such as nurses. CCGs commission most services, including:

- mental health and learning disability services
- planned hospital care
- rehabilitative care
- urgent and emergency care (including out-of-hours)
- most community health services

CCGs can commission any service provider that meets NHS standards and costs. These can be NHS hospitals, social enterprises, charities, or private-sector providers. There are around 135 CCGs in England, which together are responsible for around two-thirds of the NHS budget, around £80bn in 2020–21.

HEALTH AND WELLBEING BOARDS

Every upper-tier local authority has established a health and wellbeing board to act as a forum for local commissioners across the NHS, social care, public health and other services. There are more than 150 health and wellbeing boards in England, which are intended to:

- encourage integrated commissioning of health and social care services
- increase democratic input into strategic decisions about health and wellbeing services
- strengthen working relationships between health and social care

PUBLIC HEALTH ENGLAND (PHE)

Established on 1 April 2013, PHE provides national leadership and expert services to support public health and also works with local government and the NHS to respond to emergencies. PHE's responsibilities are to:

- make the public healthier and reduce differences between the health of different groups by advising the government; supporting action by the NHS, local government and the public; and promoting healthier lifestyles
- protect the public from health hazards
- prepare for and respond to public health emergencies
- share information and expertise, and prepare for future public health challenges

- support the NHS and local authorities to prepare for and provide social care, and develop the public health system and its specialist workforce

REGULATION

Since the restructuring of the NHS in England began in April 2013, some elements of the regulation system have changed. Responsibility for the regulation of particular aspects of care is shared across a number of different bodies, including the Care Quality Commission (CQC), and individual professional regulatory bodies, such as the General Medical Council, Nursing and Midwifery Council, General Dental Council and the Health and Care Professions Council. Regulation of the market is performed by the Department of Health and NHS Improvement.

CARE QUALITY COMMISSION (CQC)

The CQC regulates all health and social care services in England, including those provided by the NHS, local authorities, private companies or voluntary organisations. In addition it protects the interests of people detained under the Mental Health Act. The CQC ensures that all essential standards of quality and safety are met where care is provided, from hospitals to private care homes. By law all NHS providers (such as hospitals and ambulance services) must register with the CQC to show they are protecting people from the risk of infection. The CQC possesses a range of legal powers and duties and will take action if providers do not meet essential standards of quality or safety.

NHS IMPROVEMENT

NHS Improvement is responsible for overseeing NHS foundation trusts, NHS trusts and independent providers, helping them give patients consistently high quality, safe and compassionate care within local health systems that are financially sustainable. In April 2019 NHS Improvement fully integrated into NHS England to act as a single organisation as part of the *NHS Long Term Plan*, but it retains a separate board.

HEALTHWATCH

Healthwatch England was established in October 2012 following the restructuring of the NHS. The organisation functions at a national and local level as an independent consumer body, gathering and representing the views of the public about health and social care services in England.

CARE QUALITY COMMISSION, 151 Buckingham Palace Road, London SW1W 9SZ **T** 03000-616161 **W** www.cqc.org.uk
Chief Executive, Ian Trenholm

NHS IMPROVEMENT, Skipton House, 80 London Road, London SE1 6LH **T** 0113-825 0000
E enquiries@improvement.nhs.uk
Chief Operating Officer, Amanda Pritchard

HEALTHWATCH, 151 Buckingham Palace Road, London SW1W 9SZ **T** 0300-068 3000 **W** www.healthwatch.co.uk
National Director, Imelda Redmond, CBE

AUTHORITIES AND TRUSTS

REGIONS

In April 2019, as outlined in the *NHS Long Term Plan*, all NHS trusts were re-organised into seven integrated regional teams to ensure the commissioning of high quality primary care and specialised services at a local level across England.

ACUTE TRUSTS

Hospitals in England are managed by acute trusts. There were around 135 acute non-specialist trusts, of which 84 have foundation trust status and 17 acute specialist trusts, of which 16 have foundation trust status. Acute trusts ensure hospitals provide high-quality healthcare and spend money efficiently.

They employ a large sector of the NHS workforce, including doctors, nurses, pharmacists, midwives and health visitors. Acute trusts also employ those in supplementary medical professions, such as physiotherapists, radiographers and podiatrists, in addition to many other non-medical staff.

AMBULANCE TRUSTS

There are 10 ambulance services (five foundation trusts) in England, providing emergency services to healthcare.

CLINICAL SENATES AND STRATEGIC CLINICAL NETWORKS

Clinical senates are advisory groups of experts from across health and social care. There are 12 senates covering England comprising clinical leaders from across the healthcare system, in addition to members from social care and public health.

There are 12 strategic clinical networks across England, comprising groups of clinical experts covering a particular disease, patient or professional group. They offer advice to CCGs and NHS England.

Neither organisation is a statutory body, and although they comment on CCG plans to NHS England, they are unable to veto them.

FOUNDATION TRUSTS

NHS foundation trusts are independent legal entities with unique governance arrangements. Each NHS foundation trust has a duty to consult and involve a board of governors in the strategic planning of its organisation. They have financial freedoms and can raise capital from both the public and private sectors within borrowing limits determined by projected cash flows and based on affordability.

MENTAL HEALTH TRUSTS

There are 69 mental health trusts in England, 42 of which have foundation trust status.

WALES

The NHS Wales was reorganised according to Welsh Assembly commitments laid out in the *One Wales* strategy which came into effect in October 2009. There are now seven local health boards (LHBs) that are responsible for delivering all health care services within a geographical area, rather than the trust and local health board system that existed previously. Community health councils (CHCs) are statutory lay bodies that represent the public for the health service in their region. There are currently eight CHCs.

NHS TRUSTS

There are three NHS trusts in Wales. The Welsh Ambulance Services NHS Trust is for emergency services; the Velindre NHS Trust offers specialist services in cancer care; while Public Health Wales serves as a unified public health organisation for Wales.

LOCAL HEALTH BOARDS

The websites of the seven LHBs, and contact details for community health councils and NHS trusts, are available in the *NHS Wales Directory* (**W** www.wales.nhs.uk).

ANEURIN BEVAN, Headquarters, Lodge Road, Caerleon, Newport NP18 3XQ **T** 01873-732732
Chief Executive, Judith Paget, CBE

BETSI CADWALADR, Ysbyty Gwynedd, Penrhosgarnedd, Bangor, Gwynedd LL57 2PW **T** 01248-384384
Chief Executive, Gill Harris *(acting)*

CARDIFF AND VALE, Cardigan House, University Hospital of Wales, Heath Park, Cardiff CF14 4XW **T** 029-2074 7747
Chief Executive, Len Richards

CWM TAF MORGANNWG, Ynysmeurig House, Navigation Park, Abercynon CF45 4SN **T** 01443-744800
Chief Executive, Paul Mears

HYWEL DDA, Corporate Offices, Ystwyth Building, Hafan Derwen, Jobswell Road, Carmarthen SA31 3BB **T** 01267-235151
Chief Executive, Steve Moore

POWYS, Glasbury House, Bronllys Hospital, Bronllys, Brecon, Powys LD3 0LS **T** 01874-771661
Chief Executive, Carol Shillabeer

SWANSEA BAY, One Talbot Gateway, Baglan Energy Park, Baglan, Port Talbot SA12 7BR **T** 01656-683344
Chief Executive, Tracy Myhill

SCOTLAND

The Scottish government Health and Social Care directorates are responsible both for NHS Scotland and for the development and implementation of health and community care policy. The chief executive of NHS Scotland leads the central management of the NHS, is accountable to ministers for the efficiency and performance of the service and heads the Health Department which oversees the work of the 14 regional health boards. These boards provide strategic management for the entire local NHS system and are responsible for ensuring that services are delivered effectively and efficiently.

In addition to the 14 regional health boards there are a further seven special boards and one public health body, which provide national services, such as the Scottish ambulance service and NHS Health Scotland. Healthcare Improvement Scotland, was formed on 1 April 2011 by the Public Services Reform Act 2010 to improve the quality of Scottish healthcare.

REGIONAL HEALTH BOARDS

AYRSHIRE AND ARRAN, Eglinton House, Ailsa Hospital, Dalmellington Road, Ayr KA6 6AB **T** 0800-169 1441
W www.nhsaaa.net
Chief Executive, John Burns

BORDERS, Borders General Hospital, Melrose, Roxburghshire TD6 9BS **T** 01896-826000 **W** www.nhsborders.scot.nhs.uk
Chief Executive, Ralph Roberts

DUMFRIES AND GALLOWAY, Mountainhall Treatment Centre, Dumfries DG1 4AP **T** 01387-246246
W www.nhsdg.co.uk
Chief Executive, Jeff Ace

EILEAN SIAR (WESTERN ISLES), 37 South Beach Street, Stornoway, Isle of Lewis HS1 2BB **T** 01851-702997
W www.wihb.scot.nhs.uk
Chief Executive, Gordon Jamieson

FIFE, Hayfield House, Hayfield Road, Kirkcaldy, Fife KY2 5AH **T** 01592-643355 **W** www.nhsfife.org
Chief Executive, Carol Potter

FORTH VALLEY, Carseview House, Castle Business Park, Stirling FK9 4SW **T** 01786-463031 **W** www.nhsforthvalley.com
Chief Executive, Cathie Cowan

GRAMPIAN, Summerfield House, 2 Eday Road, Aberdeen AB15 6RE **T** 0345-456 6000 **W** www.nhsgrampian.org
Chief Executive, Prof. Caroline Hiscox

GREATER GLASGOW AND CLYDE, J. B. Russell House, Gartnavel Royal Hospital Campus, 1055 Great Western Road, Glasgow G12 0XH **T** 0141-201 4444 **W** www.nhsggc.org.uk
Chief Executive, Jane Grant

HIGHLAND, Assynt House, Beechwood Park, Inverness IV2 3BW **T** 01463-704000 **W** www.nhshighland.scot.nhs.uk
Chief Executive, Pam Dudek

LANARKSHIRE, Kirklands, Fallside Road, Bothwell G71 8BB **T** 0300-303 0243 **W** www.nhslanarkshire.org.uk

Chief Executive, Heather Knox *(interim)*

LOTHIAN, Waverley Gate, 2–4 Waterloo Place, Edinburgh EH1 3EG **T** 0131-536 9000 **W** www.nhslothian.scot.nhs.uk
Chief Executive, Calum Campbell

ORKNEY, The Balfour, Foreland Road, Kirkwall, Orkney KW15 1NZ **T** 01856-888100 **W** www.ohb.scot.nhs.uk
Chief Executive, Michael Dickson *(interim)*

SHETLAND, Upper Floor Montfield, Burgh Road, Lerwick ZE1 0LA **T** 01595-743060 **W** www.shb.scot.nhs.uk
Chief Executive, Michael Dickson

TAYSIDE, Ninewells Hospital & Medical School, Dundee DD1 9SY **T** 01382-660111 **W** www.nhstayside.scot.nhs.uk
Chief Executive, Grant Archibald

NORTHERN IRELAND

On 1 April 2009 the four health and social services boards in Northern Ireland were replaced by a single health and social care board for the whole of Northern Ireland. The board, together with its five local commissioning groups are responsible for improving the health and social wellbeing of people in the area for which they are responsible, planning and commissioning services, and coordinating the delivery of services in a cost-effective manner. In March 2016, the health minister announced plans to abolish the health and social care board, with all commissioning powers to be transferred to the Department of Health and a new group being established to hold the five Northern Ireland trusts to account. As at December 2020, no further decision regarding the future of the board had been taken and the board remains operational.

HEALTH AND SOCIAL CARE BOARD, 12–22 Linenhall Street, Belfast BT2 8BS **T** 030-0555 0115
W www.hscboard.hscni.net
Chief Executive, Sharon Gallagher

FINANCE

The NHS is still funded mainly through general taxation, although in recent years more reliance has been placed on the NHS element of national insurance contributions, patient charges and other sources of income.

NHS England's total budget for 2020–21, including the Long Term Plan funding settlement but excluding emergency coronavirus funding, was set at £305bn in March 2020. Expenditure for the NHS in Wales, Scotland and Northern Ireland is set by the devolved governments.

EMPLOYEES AND SALARIES

NHS ENGLAND STAFF 2020
Full-time equivalent

Total	1,161,858
Doctors	121,726
Ambulance staff	17,201
Midwives	21,892
Nurses and health visitors	302,033
Scientific, therapeutic and technical staff	149,144
Clinical support staff	363,448
Infrastructure support staff	184,548
Other staff	1,864
Source: NHS Digital. Excludes dental staff	

SALARIES
Many general practitioners (GPs) are self-employed and hold contracts, either on their own or as part of a Clinical Commissioning Group (CCG). The profit of GPs varies

according to the services they provide for their patients and the way they choose to provide these services. Salaried GPs who are part of a CCG earn between £60,8455 and £91,228. Most NHS dentists are self-employed contractors. A contract for dentists was introduced on 1 April 2006 which provides dentists with an annual income in return for carrying out an agreed amount, or units, of work. A salaried dentist employed by the NHS, who works mainly with community dental services earns between £41,766 and £89,333.

BASIC SALARIES FOR HOSPITAL MEDICAL AND DENTAL STAFF 2020–21

Consultant (2003 contract)	£82,096–£110,683
Associate specialist	£57,705–£94,988
Speciality doctor	£41,158–£76,751
Core/higher training year 3+	£49,036
Core training year 1 & 2	£38,694
Foundation doctor year 2	£32,691
Foundation doctor year 1	£28,243

NURSES

From 1 December 2004 the *Agenda for Change* pay system was introduced throughout the UK for all NHS staff with the exception of medical and dental staff, doctors in public health medicine and the community health service. Nurses' salaries are incorporated in the *Agenda for Change* nine band pay structure, which provides additional payments for flexible working such as providing out-of-hours services, working weekends and nights and being on-call. There is also additional payments for those staff who work in high-cost areas such as London.

SALARIES FOR NURSES AND MIDWIVES 2020–21

Nurse/Midwife consultant	£53,168–£87,754
Modern matron	£45,753–£51,668
Nurse advanced/team manager	£38,890–£44,503
Midwife higher level	£38,890–£44,503
Nurse specialist/team leader	£31,365–£37,890
Hospital/community midwife	£31,365–£37,890
Registered nurse/entry level midwife*	£24,907–£30,615

*The starting salary in Wales and Northern Ireland is currently the same as in England. The starting salary is £25,100 in Scotland.

HEALTH SERVICES

PRIMARY CARE

Primary care comprises the services provided by general practitioners, community health centres, pharmacies, dental practices and opticians. Primary nursing care includes the work carried out by practice nurses, community nurses, community midwives and health visitors.

PRIMARY MEDICAL SERVICES

In England, primary medical services (PMS) are provided by 35,416 full-time equivalent GPs, working in around 6,800 GP practices, with 60.6 million registered patients.

In Wales, responsibility for primary medical services rests with local health boards (LHBs), in Scotland with the 14 regional health boards and in Northern Ireland with the Health and Social Care Board.

Any vocationally trained doctor may provide general or personal medical services. GPs may also have private fee-paying patients, but not if that patient is already an NHS patient on that doctor's patient list.

A person who is ordinarily resident in the UK is eligible to register with a GP (or PMS provider) for free primary care treatment. Should a patient have difficulty in registering with

a doctor, he or she should contact the local CCG for help. When a person is away from home he/she can still access primary care treatment from a GP if they ask to be treated as a temporary resident. In an emergency any doctor in the service will give treatment and advice.

GPs or CCGs are responsible for the care of their patients 24 hours a day, seven days a week, but can fulfil the terms of their contract by delegating or transferring responsibility for out-of-hours care to an accredited provider.

In addition, NHS walk-in centres (WICs) throughout England are usually open seven days a week, from early in the morning until late in the evening. They are nurse-led and provide treatment for minor illnesses and injuries, health information and self-help advice. Some WICs are not able to treat young children.

HEALTH COSTS

Some people are exempt from, or entitled to help with, health costs such as prescription charges, ophthalmic and dental costs, and in some cases help towards travel costs to and from hospital.

The following list is intended as a general guide to those who may be entitled to help, or who are exempt from some of the charges relating to the above:

- children under 16 and young people in full-time education who are under 19
- people aged 60 or over
- pregnant women and women who have had a baby in the last 12 months and have a valid maternity exemption certificate (MatEx)
- people, or their partners, who are in receipt of income support, income-based jobseeker's allowance and/or income-based employment and support allowance
- people in receipt of the pension credit
- diagnosed glaucoma patients, people who have been advised by an ophthalmologist that they are at risk of glaucoma and people aged 40 or over who have an immediate family member who is a diagnosed glaucoma patient
- NHS in-patients
- NHS out-patients for all prescribed contraceptives, medication given at a hospital, NHS walk-in centre, personally administered by a GP or supplied at a hospital or primary care trust clinic for the treatment of tuberculosis or a sexually transmissible infection
- out-patients of the NHS Hospital Dental Service
- people registered blind or partially sighted
- people who need complex lenses
- war pensioners whose treatment/prescription is for their accepted disablement and who have a valid exemption certificate
- people who are entitled to, or named on, a valid NHS tax credit exemption or HC2 certificate
- people who have a medical exemption (MedEx) certificate, including those with cancer or diabetes

People in other circumstances may also be eligible for help; *see* www.nhs.uk/using-the-nhs/help-with-health-costs for further information.

WALES

On 1 April 2007 all prescription charges (including those for medical supports and appliances and wigs) for people living in Wales were abolished. The above guide still applies for NHS dental and optical charges although all people aged under 25 living in Wales are also entitled to free dental examinations.

SCOTLAND

On 1 April 2011 all prescription charges in Scotland were abolished. Those entitled to free prescriptions in Scotland include patients registered with a Scottish GP and receiving a prescription from a Scottish pharmacy, and Scottish patients who have an English GP and an entitlement card.

NORTHERN IRELAND
On 1 April 2010 all prescription charges in Northern Ireland were abolished. All prescriptions dispensed in Northern Ireland are free, even for patients visiting from England, Wales or Scotland.

PHARMACEUTICAL SERVICES
Patients may obtain medicines and appliances under the NHS from any pharmacy whose owner has entered into arrangements with the CCG to provide this service. There are also some suppliers who only provide special appliances. In rural areas, where access to a pharmacy may be difficult, patients may be able to obtain medicines, etc, from a dispensing doctor.

In England, a charge of £9.15 is payable for each item supplied (except for contraceptives for which there is no charge), unless the patient is exempt and the declaration on the back of the prescription form is completed. Prescription prepayment certificates (£29.65 valid for three months, £105.90 valid for a year) may be purchased by those patients not entitled to exemption who require frequent prescriptions.

DENTAL SERVICES
Dentists, like doctors, may take part in the NHS and also have private patients. Dentists are responsible to the local health provider in whose areas they provide services. Patients may go to any dentist who is taking part in the NHS and is willing to accept them. There is a three-tier payment system based on the individual course of treatment required.

NHS DENTAL CHARGES *from 1 April 2020*

	England/Wales
Band 1* – Examination, diagnosis, preventive care (eg x-rays, scale and polish)	£23.80/£14.70
Band 2 – Band 1 + basic additional treatment (eg fillings and extractions)	£65.20/£47.00
Band 3 – Bands 1 and 2 + all other treatment (eg crowns, dentures and bridges)	£282.80/£203.00

* Urgent and out-of-hours treatment is also charged at this tier

The cost of individual treatment plans should be known prior to treatment and some dental practices may require payment in advance. There is no charge for writing a prescription or removing stitches and only one charge is payable for each course of treatment even if more than one visit to the dentist is required. If additional treatment is required within two months of visiting the dentist and this is covered by the course of treatment most recently paid for (for example, payment was made for the second tier of treatment but an additional filling is required) then this will be provided free of charge.

SCOTLAND AND NORTHERN IRELAND
Scotland and Northern Ireland have yet to simplify their charging systems. NHS dental patients pay 80 per cent of the cost of the individual items of treatment provided up to a maximum of £384. An NHS dental examination in Scotland is free of charge for everyone.

GENERAL OPHTHALMIC SERVICES
General ophthalmic services are administered by local health providers. Testing of sight may be carried out by any ophthalmic medical practitioner or ophthalmic optician (optometrist). The optician must give the prescription to the patient, who can take this to any supplier of glasses to have them dispensed. Only registered opticians can supply glasses to children and to people registered as blind or partially sighted.

Free eyesight tests and help towards the cost are available to people in certain circumstances. Help is also available for the purchase of glasses or contact lenses. In Scotland eye examinations, which include a sight test, are free to all UK residents. Help is also available for the purchase of glasses or contact lenses to those entitled to help with health costs in the same way it is available to those in England and Wales.

CHILD HEALTH SERVICES
Pre-school services at GP surgeries or child health clinics provide regular monitoring of children's physical, mental and emotional health and development and advise parents on their children's health and welfare.

NHS 111 AND NHS 24
NHS 111 is a website and 24-hour nurse-led advice telephone service for England, Wales and Northern Ireland, dealing with non-urgent health issues. It provides medical advice as well as directing people to the appropriate part of the NHS for treatment if necessary. (T 111 W www.111.nhs.uk & www.111.wales.nhs.uk).

NHS 24 provides an equivalent service for Scotland (T 111 W www.nhs24.scot).

SECONDARY CARE AND OTHER SERVICES

HOSPITALS
NHS hospitals provide acute and specialist care services, treating conditions which normally cannot be dealt with by primary care specialists, and provide for medical emergencies. The figures below are representative of the period 1 April 2019–31 March 2020. As such, they exclude the significant increase in bed capacity that was introduced by the government in early April 2020 in response to the coronavirus pandemic.

HOSPITAL CHARGES
Acute or foundation trusts can provide hospital accommodation in single rooms or small wards, if not required for patients who need privacy for medical reasons. The patient is still an NHS patient, but there may be a charge for these additional facilities. Acute or foundation trusts can charge for certain patient services that are considered to be additional treatments over and above the normal hospital service provision. There is no blanket policy to cover this and each case is considered in the light of the patient's clinical need. However, if an item or service is considered to be an integral part of a patient's treatment by their clinician, then a charge should not be made.

In some NHS hospitals, accommodation and services are available for the treatment of private patients where it does not interfere with care for NHS patients. Income generated by treating private patients is then put back into local NHS services. Private patients undertake to pay the full costs of medical treatment, accommodation, medication and other related services. Charges for private patients are set locally.

NUMBER OF BEDS 2019–20

	Average daily	
	available beds	occupation of beds
England	142,745	126,758
Wales*	10,564	9,170
Scotland	13,156	11,406
Northern Ireland	5,780	4,831

* Figures are for 2018–19

Sources: NHS England, Welsh government, ISD Scotland, Northern Ireland Executive

WAITING LISTS

During 2020, the COVID-19 pandemic adversely affected the NHS, and consequently the figures listed below are significantly lower than in previous years.

England
During June 2020, 94,354 referral to treatment (RTT) patients started admitted treatment and 662,634 started non-admitted treatment. Of the admitted patients, 92 per cent were waiting up to 37.4 weeks, and for patients waiting to start treatment 52 per cent were treated within 18 weeks of referral. The median waiting time was 17.6 weeks.
Wales
During September 2020, 72.2 per cent of 232,127 patients were treated within 26 weeks and 84.8 per cent were treated within 36 weeks of the date the referral letter was received by the hospital.
Scotland
In the quarter ending September 2020, 66.9 per cent of patients with fully measurable journeys were seen within the 18 week referral to treatment (RTT) standard. In the same quarter, 72.1 per cent of patients waiting for a new outpatient appointment were seen within 12 weeks.
Northern Ireland
By September 2020 the aim was for at least 50 per cent of patients to wait no longer than 9 weeks for a first out-patient appointment, with no patient waiting longer than 52 weeks. The total number of people waiting for a first outpatient appointment at the end of September 2020 was 160,663, of these 65.4 per cent had been waiting over 9 weeks and 44.8 per cent had been waiting over 26 weeks.

AMBULANCE SERVICE

The NHS provides emergency ambulance services free of charge via the 999 emergency telephone service. Air ambulances, provided through local charities and partially funded by the NHS, are used throughout the UK. They assist with cases where access may be difficult or heavy traffic could hinder road progress. Non-emergency ambulance services are provided free to patients who are deemed to require them on medical grounds.

Since 1 April 2001 all services have had a system of call prioritisation. Since 2017, ambulances have been expected to reach Red 1 – calls requiring a defibrillator – and Red 2 emergency calls within seven minutes, at least 75 per cent of the time. Non-emergency calls are categorised as Green 1, 2, 3 or 4, with category Green 4 calls being the least serious. Green calls are generally responded to between 20 minutes and one hour.

In 2016 it was agreed that all ambulance staff were to be re-banded from a band 5 to a band 6 under the *Agenda for Change* pay scale. In 2020, the NHS employed 18,299 qualified ambulance staff in England earning between £19,737 (emergency care assistant) and £37,890 (senior paramedic).

BLOOD AND TRANSPLANT SERVICES

There are four national bodies which coordinate the blood donor programme and transplant and related services in the UK. Donors give blood at local centres on a voluntary basis.

NHS BLOOD AND TRANSPLANT, 500, North Bristol Park, Filton, Bristol, BR34 7QH **T** 0300-123 2323 **W** www.nhsbt.nhs.uk

WELSH BLOOD SERVICE, Ely Valley Road, Talbot Green, Pontyclun CF72 9WB **T** 0800-252 2266 **W** www.welsh-blood.org.uk

SCOTTISH NATIONAL BLOOD TRANSFUSION SERVICE, The Jack Copland Centre, 52 Research Avenue North, Herriot-Watt Research Park, Edinburgh EH14 4BE **T** 0131-314 5510 **W** www.scotblood.co.uk

NORTHERN IRELAND BLOOD TRANSFUSION SERVICE, Lisburn Road, Belfast BT9 7TS **T** 028-9032 1414 **W** www.nibts.hscni.net

HOSPICES

Hospice or palliative care may be available for patients with life-threatening illnesses. It may be provided at the patient's home, in a voluntary or NHS hospice or at hospital, and is intended to ensure the best possible quality of life for the patient, and to provide help and support to both the patient and the patient's family. Hospice UK coordinates NHS and voluntary services in England, Wales and Northern Ireland; the Scottish Partnership for Palliative Care performs the same function in Scotland.

HOSPICE UK, Hospice House, 34–44 Britannia Street, London WC1X 9JG **T** 020-7520 8200 **W** www.hospiceuk.org

SCOTTISH PARTNERSHIP FOR PALLIATIVE CARE, CBC House, 24 Canning Street, Edinburgh EH3 8EG **T** 0131-272 2735 **W** www.palliativecarescotland.org.uk

COMPLAINTS

Patient advice and liaison services (PALS) have been established for every NHS and PCT in England. PALS can give advice on local complaints procedure, or resolve concerns informally. If the case is not resolved locally or the complainant is not satisfied with the way a local NHS body or practice has dealt with their complaint, they may approach the Parliamentary and Health Service Ombudsman in England, the Scottish Public Services Ombudsman, Public Services Ombudsman for Wales or the Northern Ireland Public Services Ombudsman. *See* Ombudsman Services.

HEALTH ADVICE AND MEDICAL TREATMENT ABROAD

IMMUNISATION

Country-by-country guidance is set out on the website **W** www.fitfortravel.nhs.uk

RECIPROCAL ARRANGEMENTS

Prior to 1 Jan 2021, the European Health Insurance Card (EHIC) had allowed UK residents access to state-provided healthcare while temporarily travelling in all European Economic Area (EEA) countries and Switzerland, either free or at a reduced cost. From 1 January 2021, the EHIC was no longer valid for most travellers except pensioners living in the EU, EU nationals living in the UK before the end of 2020, students studying in the EEA, 'frontier workers' living and working in different states, and dependents of these groups. A card is free, valid for up to five years and should be obtained before travelling. Full eligibility criteria can be found online (**W** www.ehic.org.uk), where applications can also be made.

Visitors from countries with which the UK has bilateral health care agreements are currently able to receive emergency health care on the NHS on the same terms as is available to UK residents. After 1 January 2021, when the Brexit transition period ends, European Economic Area nationals may lose this entitlement or it will be dependent on arrangements made with individual countries. The UK also has bilateral agreements with several other countries, including Australia and New Zealand, for the free provision of urgent medical treatment.

SOCIAL WELFARE

SOCIAL SERVICES

The Secretary of State for Health (in England), the Welsh government, the Scottish government and the Secretary of State for Northern Ireland are responsible, under the Local Authority Social Services Act 1970, for the provision of social services for older people, disabled people, families and children, and those with mental disorders. Personal social services are administered by local authorities according to policies, with standards set by central and devolved government. Each authority has a director and a committee responsible for the social services functions placed upon them. Local authorities provide, enable and commission care after assessing the needs of their population. The private and voluntary sectors also play an important role in the delivery of social services, and an estimated 7 million people in the UK provide substantial regular care for a member of their family.

The Care Quality Commission (CQC) was established in April 2009, bringing together the independent regulation of health, mental health and adult social care. Prior to 1 April 2009 this work was carried out by three separate organisations: the Healthcare Commission, the Mental Health Act Commission and the Commission for Social Care Inspection. The CQC is responsible for the registration of health and social care providers, the monitoring and inspection of all health and adult social care, issuing fines, public warnings or closures if standards are not met and for undertaking regular performance reviews. Since April 2007 the Office for Standards in Education, Children's Services and Skills (Ofsted) has been responsible for inspecting and regulating all care services for children and young people in England. Both Ofsted and CQC collate information on local care services and make this information available to the public.

The Care Inspectorate Wales, an operationally independent part of the Welsh government, is responsible for the regulation and inspection of all social care services in Wales.

In Scotland, the Care Inspectorate, is the independent care services regulator for Scotland.

The Department of Health is responsible for social care in Northern Ireland.

CARE QUALITY COMMISSION (CQC), Citygate, Gallowgate, Newcastle upon Tyne NE1 4PA **T** 0300-061 6161 **W** www.cqc.org.uk

OFFICE FOR STANDARDS IN EDUCATION, CHILDREN'S SERVICES AND SKILLS (Ofsted), Piccadilly Gate, Store Street, Manchester M1 2WD **T** 0300-123 1231 **E** enquiries@ofsted.gov.uk **W** www.gov.uk/government/organisations/ofsted

CARE INSPECTORATE WALES (CIW), Welsh Government Office, Sarn Mynach, Llandudno Junction LL31 9RZ **T** 0300-790 0126 **E** ciw@gov.wales **W** www.careinspectorate.wales

CARE INSPECTORATE, Compass House, 11 Riverside Drive, Dundee DD1 4NY **T** 0345 600 9527 **E** enquiries@careinspectorate.com **W** www.careinspectorate.com

DEPARTMENT OF HEALTH, Castle Buildings, Stormont, Belfast BT4 3SQ **T** 028-9052 0500 **E** webmaster@health-ni.gov.uk **W** www.health-ni.gov.uk

ADULT SOCIAL CARE WORKFORCE ESTIMATES (ENGLAND)

Total: all job roles	1,600,000
Managerial	119,000
Regulated professional	83,000
Direct care	1,220,000
Other	180,000

Source: Skills for Care, 2018

OLDER PEOPLE

Services for older people are designed to enable them to remain living in their own homes for as long as possible. Local authority services include advice, domestic help, meals in the home, alterations to the home to aid mobility, emergency alarm systems, day and/or night attendants, laundry services and the provision of day centres and recreational facilities. Charges may be made for these services. Respite care may also be provided in order to allow carers temporary relief from their responsibilities.

Local authorities and the private sector also provide 'sheltered housing' for older people, sometimes with resident wardens.

If an older person is admitted to a residential home, charges are made according to a means test; if the person cannot afford to pay, the costs are met by the local authority.

DISABLED PEOPLE

Services for disabled people are designed to enable them to remain living in their own homes wherever possible. Local authority services include advice, adaptations to the home, meals in the home, help with personal care, occupational therapy, educational facilities and recreational facilities. Respite care may also be provided in order to allow carers temporary relief from their responsibilities.

Special housing may be available for disabled people who can live independently, and residential accommodation for those who cannot.

FAMILIES AND CHILDREN

Local authorities are required to provide services aimed at safeguarding the welfare of children in need and, wherever possible, allowing them to be brought up by their families. Services include advice, counselling, help in the home and the provision of family centres. Many authorities also provide short-term refuge accommodation for women and children.

DAY CARE

In allocating day care places to children, local authorities give priority to children with special needs, whether in terms of their health, learning abilities or social needs. Since September 2001, Ofsted has been responsible for the regulation and registration of all early years childcare and education provision in England (previously the responsibility of the local authorities). All day care and childminding services that care for children under eight years of age for more than two hours a day must register with Ofsted and are inspected at least every two years. In 2018 there were an estimated 81,500 childcare providers in England.

CHILD PROTECTION

Children considered to be at risk of physical injury, neglect or sexual abuse are placed on the local authority's child protection register. Local authority social services staff, schools, health visitors and other agencies work together to prevent and detect cases of abuse. As at 31 March 2018, there was a total of 61,500 children on child protection registers or subject to a child protection plan in the UK. In England, there were 53,790 children on child protection registers, of these, 25,820 were at risk of neglect, 4,120 of physical abuse, 2,180 of sexual abuse and 18,860 of emotional abuse. At 31 March (July in Scotland) 2018 there were 2,960 children on child protection registers in Wales, 2,668 in Scotland and 2,082 in Northern Ireland.

LOCAL AUTHORITY CARE

Local authorities are required to provide accommodation for children who have no parents or guardians or whose parents or guardians are unable or unwilling to care for them. A family proceedings court may also issue a care order where a child is being neglected or abused, or is not attending school; the court must be satisfied that this would positively contribute to the well-being of the child.

The welfare of children in local authority care must be properly safeguarded. Children may be placed with foster families, who receive payments to cover the expenses of caring for the child or children, or in residential care.

Children's homes may be run by the local authority or by the private or voluntary sectors; all homes are subject to inspection procedures. As at 31 March 2018, 75,420 children in England were in the care of local authorities, of these, 55,200 were in foster placements and 8,530 were in children's homes, hostels or secure units.

ADOPTION

Local authorities are required to provide an adoption service, either directly or via approved voluntary societies. In the year to 31 March 2018, 2,230 children in local authority care in England were placed for adoption.

PEOPLE WITH LEARNING DISABILITIES

Services for people with learning disabilities are designed to enable them to remain living in the community wherever possible. Local authority services include short-term care, support in the home, the provision of day care centres, and help with other activities outside the home. Residential care is provided for the severely or profoundly disabled.

MENTALLY ILL PEOPLE

Under the care programme approach, mentally ill people should be assessed by specialist services and receive a care plan. A key worker should be appointed for each patient and regular reviews of the person's progress should be conducted. Local authorities provide help and advice to mentally ill people and their families, and places in day centres and social centres. Social workers can apply for a mentally disturbed person to be compulsorily detained in hospital. Where appropriate, mentally ill people are provided with accommodation in special hospitals, local authority accommodation, or at homes run by private or voluntary organisations. Patients who have been discharged from hospitals may be placed on a supervision register.

NATIONAL INSURANCE

The National Insurance (NI) scheme operates under the Social Security Contributions and Benefits Act 1992 and the Social Security Administration Act 1992, and orders and regulations made thereunder. The scheme is financed by contributions payable by earners, employers and others (see below). Money collected under the scheme is used to finance the National Insurance Fund (from which contributory benefits are paid) and to contribute to the cost of the National Health Service.

NATIONAL INSURANCE FUND

Estimated receipts, payments and statement of balances of the National Insurance Fund for 2019–20:

Receipts	£ million
Net national insurance contributions	108,706
Compensation from the Consolidated Fund for statutory payments recoveries	2,760
Income from investments	305
State scheme premiums	0
Other receipts	0
TOTAL RECEIPTS	111,771

Payments	£ million
Benefits	
At present rates	102,008
Increase due to proposed rate changes	2,515
Administration costs	743
Redundancy fund payments	295
Transfer to Northern Ireland	737
Other payments	188
TOTAL PAYMENTS	106,486

Balances	£ million
Balance at the beginning of the year	27,337
Excess of receipts over payments	5,285
BALANCE AT END OF YEAR	32,622

CONTRIBUTIONS

There are six classes of National Insurance contributions (NICs):

Class 1	paid by employees and their employers
Class 1A	paid by employers who provide employees with certain benefits in kind for private use, such as company cars
Class 1B	paid by employers who enter into a pay as you earn (PAYE) settlement agreement (PSA) with HM Revenue and Customs
Class 2	paid by self-employed people
Class 3	voluntary contributions paid to protect entitlement to the state pension for those who do not pay enough NI contributions in another class
Class 4	paid by the self-employed on their taxable profits over a set limit. These are normally paid by self-employed people in addition to class 2 contributions. Class 4 contributions do not count towards benefits.

The lower and upper earnings limits and the percentage rates referred to below apply from April 2019 to April 2020.

CLASS 1

Class 1 primary (employee) contributions are paid where a person:

- is an employed earner (employee), office holder (eg company director) or employed under a contract of service in Great Britain or Northern Ireland
- is 16 or over and under state pension age
- earns at or above the earnings threshold of £166.00 per week (including overtime pay, bonus, commission, etc, without deduction of superannuation contributions)

Class 1 contributions are made up of primary and secondary contributions. Primary contributions are those paid by the employee and these are deducted from earnings by the employer. Since 6 April 2001 the employee's and employer's earnings thresholds have been the same. Primary contributions are not paid on earnings below the earnings threshold of £166.00 per week. However, between the lower earnings limit of £118.00 per week and the earnings threshold of £166.00 per week, NI contributions are treated as having been paid to protect the benefit entitlement position of lower earners. Contributions are payable at the rate of 12 per cent on earnings between the earnings threshold and the upper earnings limit of £962.00 per week. Above the upper earnings limit 2 per cent is payable.

Some married women or widows pay a reduced rate of 5.85 per cent on earnings between the earnings threshold and upper earnings limits and 2 per cent above this. It is no longer possible to elect to pay the reduced rate but those who had reduced liability before 12 May 1977 may retain it for as long as certain conditions are met.

Secondary contributions are paid by employers of employed earners at the rate of 13.8 per cent on all earnings above the earnings threshold of £166.00 per week. There is a zero rate between the earnings threshold and the upper threshold of £962 per week for employers of relevant apprentices and employed earners under the age of 21.

CLASS 2
Class 2 contributions are paid where a person is self-employed and is 16 or over and under state pension age. Contributions are paid at a flat rate of £3.00 per week regardless of the amount earned. However, those with profits of less than £6,365 a year can apply for small profits exception. Those granted exemption from class 2 contributions may pay class 2 or class 3* contributions voluntarily. Self-employed earners (whether or not they pay class 2 contributions) may also be liable to pay class 4 contributions based on profits. There are special rules for those who are concurrently employed and self-employed.

Married women and widows can no longer choose not to pay class 2 contributions but those who elected not to pay class 2 contributions before 12 May 1977 may retain the right for as long as certain conditions are met.

Class 2 contributions are assessed and collected annually by HM Revenue and Customs (HMRC) as part of the self-assessment tax bill. For self-employed people that do not pay tax through self-assessment, a bill is issued by HMRC by the end of October.

CLASS 3
Class 3 contributions are voluntary flat-rate contributions of £15.00 per week payable by persons over the age of 16 who would otherwise be unable to qualify for retirement pension and certain other benefits because they have an insufficient record of class 1 or class 2 contributions. This may include those who are not working, those not liable for class 1 or class 2 contributions, or those excepted from class 2 contributions. Married women and widows who on or before 11 May 1977 elected not to pay class 1 (full rate) or class 2 contributions cannot pay class 3 contributions while they retain this right. Class 3 contributions are collected by HMRC by quarterly bills or monthly direct debit. One-off payments can also be made.

CLASS 4
Self-employed people whose profits and gains are over £8,632 a year pay class 4 contributions in addition to class 2 contributions. This applies to self-employed earners over 16 and under the state pension age. Class 4 contributions are calculated at 9 per cent of annual profits or gains between £8,632 and £50,000 and 2 per cent above. Class 4 contributions are assessed and collected annually by HMRC as part of the self-assessment tax bill. It is possible, in some circumstances, to apply for exceptions from liability to pay class 4 contributions or to have the amount of contribution reduced.

PENSIONS

Many people will qualify for a state pension; however, there are further pension choices available, such as workplace, personal and stakeholder pensions. There are also other non-pension savings and investment options.

STATE PENSION

From 6 April 2016, the system of basic and additional state pension was replaced with a new scheme for people reaching state pension age after that date (ie men born on or after 6 April 1951, and women born on or after 6 April 1953).

Those that reached state pension age before this date continue to receive their state pension in line with the old rules.

The earliest state pension can be claimed is at state pension age, people can delay claiming it to earn weekly state pension or a lump sum payment.

NEW STATE PENSION
The full rate of the new state pension, for people reaching state pension age on or after 6 April 2016, is £168.60 per week for a single person in 2019–20. The amount received is based on the individual's national insurance record.

An individual's 'starting amount', part of the new state pension, is based on NI contributions and credits made before 6 April 2016 and will be the higher of either:
- the amount received under the old state pension rules (including basic state pension and additional state pension)
- the amount received if the new state pension had been in place from the start of their working life

A deduction may be made to these amounts for periods an individual was contracted out of the additional state pension because they were in a certain type of workplace, personal or stakeholder pension.

If the individual's starting amount is less than the full new state pension (£168.60 per week) more qualifying years can be added to their national insurance record after 5 April 2016 until the individual reaches the full rate of new state pension or reaches state pension age – whichever is first. If the individual's starting amount is more than the full new state pension of £168.60 per week, then the amount above the full new state pension (the 'protected payment') is paid on top of the full new state pension.

If an individual did not make NI contributions or get NI credits prior to 6 April 2016 than their state pension will be calculated entirely under the new state pension rules.

Further information about the new state pension can be found online (www.gov.uk/new-state-pension).

CATEGORY A OR B STATE PENSION
The category A or B state pension scheme is paid to individuals who reached state pension age before 6 April 2016 and is based on their own contributions or those made by a deceased spouse or civil partner. The full weekly rate in 2019–20 is £129.20.

For further information see Benefits, State Pension: Categories A and B.

WORKING LIFE
The working life is from the start of the tax year (6 April) in which a person reaches 16 to the end of the tax year (5 April) before the one in which they reach state pension age (see State Pension Age).

QUALIFYING YEARS
A 'qualifying year' is a tax year in which a person has sufficient earnings upon which they have paid, are treated as having paid, or have been credited with national insurance (NI) contributions (see National Insurance Credits).

For people reaching state pension age on or after 6 April 2016 a full new state pension (£168.60 per week in 2019–20) is payable to those individuals who have 35 qualifying years on their national insurance record. Individuals usually need at least ten qualifying years and will receive a proportion of the new state pension if they have between ten and 35 qualifying years.

For people who reached state pension age between 6 April 2010 and 5 April 2016 a full category A or B pension (£129.20 per week in 2019–20) is payable to those individuals who have 30 qualifying years on their national insurance record. Someone with less than 30 qualifying years will be entitled to a proportion of the full category A or B pension based on the number of qualifying years they have. Just one qualifying year, achieved through paid or credited contributions, will give entitlement to the basic state pension worth one-thirtieth of the full basic state pension.

For people who reached state pension age before 6 April 2010, women normally needed 39 qualifying years for a full basic state pension (£129.20 per week in 2019–20) and men normally needed 44 qualifying years. A reduced-rate basic state pension was payable if the number of qualifying years was less than 90 per cent of the individual's working life, but to receive any state pension at all, a person must have had enough qualifying years, normally ten or 11, to receive a basic state pension of at least 25 per cent of the full rate.

The state pension of transgender people may be affected for those that changed their gender or started claiming state pension before 4 April 2005; claims for those who legally changed their gender and started claiming state pension on or after 4 April 2005 are based on the individual's legal gender.

NATIONAL INSURANCE CREDITS
Those in receipt of carer's allowance, working tax credit (with a disability premium), jobseeker's allowance, employment and support allowance, unemployability supplement, statutory sick pay, maternity allowance, statutory maternity, paternity or statutory adoption pay may have class 1 NI contributions credited to them each week. People may also get credits if they are unemployed and looking for work or too sick to work, even if they are not in receipt of any benefit, although the credits must be applied for in these circumstances. Since April 2010, spouses and civil partners of members of HM forces may get credits if they are on an accompanied assignment outside the UK. Those who reach state pension age on or after 6 April 2016 can apply for NI credits for periods before April 2010 during which they were married to, or in a civil partnership with, a member of HM forces and accompanied them on a posting outside the UK. Persons undertaking certain training courses or jury service or who have been wrongly imprisoned for a conviction which is quashed on appeal may also get class 1 NI credits for each week they fulfil certain conditions. Class 1 credits may also be available to men approaching state pension age, born before 6 October 1953 who live in the UK for at least 183 days a year and who don't work, earn enough to make a qualifying year or are self-employed with profits of less than £6,365. Class 1 NI credits count toward all future contributory benefits.

A class 3 NI credit for basic state pension and bereavement benefit purposes is awarded, where required, for each week universal credit, working tax credit (without a disability premium) or child benefit, for a child under 12, has been received. Class 3 credits may also be awarded, on application, to approved foster carers and people caring for others for at least 20 hours a week. Since 6 April 2011, class 3 credits have been available to adults under state pension age who care for a family member under 12. Further information regarding eligibility for NI credits is available online (www.gov.uk/national-insurance-credits/eligibility)

STATE PENSION AGE
From 6 November 2018 state pension age is 65 for both men and women and this will increase to age 66 for both men and women by October 2020. The Pensions Act 2014 makes provision for a regular review of state pension age. Reviews will take place at least once every six years and will take into account up-to-date life expectancy data and the findings of an independently led review, which will consider wider factors such as variation in life expectancy and employment opportunities for older workers. Further information can be obtained from the online state pension calculator (W www.gov.uk/state-pension-age).

USING THE NI CONTRIBUTION RECORD OF ANOTHER TO CLAIM A STATE PENSION
Married people or civil partners who reached state pension age before 6 April 2016 whose own NI record is incomplete may get a lower-rate basic state pension calculated using their partner's NI contribution record. This can be up to £77.45 a week in 2019–20.

People who reached state pension age before 6 April 2016 will continue to be able to use these provisions, even if their spouse or civil partner reaches state pension age on or after that date. However, contributions their spouse or civil partner pays, or is credited with, following implementation of the new system will only count towards their own state pension. This means that only the NI record of the spouse or civil partner up to and including 2015–16 will be used to calculate any derived entitlement.

People who reached state pension age on or after 6 April 2016 will not be able to claim state pension on their spouse's or civil partner's NI record. There will be special arrangements for women who had opted to pay the married women's and widows reduced rate contributions before May 1977.

NON-CONTRIBUTORY STATE PENSIONS
A non-contributory state pension may be payable to those aged 80 or over who live in England, Scotland or Wales, and have done so for a total of ten years or more for any continuous period in the 20 years after their 60th birthday, if they are not entitled to another category of state pension, or are entitled to one below the rate of £77.45 a week in 2019–20 (*see also* Benefits, State Pension for people aged 80 and over).

GRADUATED RETIREMENT BENEFIT
Graduated Retirement Benefit (GRB) is based on the amount of graduated NI contributions paid into the GRB scheme between April 1961 and April 1975 (*see also* Benefits, Graduated Retirement Benefit). It is normally paid as an increase to a main state pension. For those reaching state pension age under the new state pension rules, it will be included in the calculation of their basic amount.

HOME RESPONSIBILITIES PROTECTION
From 6 April 1978 until 5 April 2010, it was possible for people who had low income or were unable to work because they cared for children or a sick or disabled person at home to reduce the number of qualifying years required for basic state pension. This was called home responsibilities protection (HRP); the number of years for which HRP was given was deducted from the number of qualifying years needed. HRP could, in some cases, also qualify the recipient for additional state pension. From April 2003 to April 2010 HRP was also available to approved foster carers.

From 6 April 2010, HRP was replaced by weekly credits for parents and carers. A class 3 national insurance credit is also given, where eligible, towards state pension and bereavement benefits for spouses and civil partners. An earnings factor credit towards additional state pension was also awarded. Any years of HRP accrued before 6 April 2010 were converted into qualifying years of credits for people reaching state pension age after that date, up to a maximum of 22 years for state pension purposes.

ADDITIONAL STATE PENSION

The additional state pension is an extra sum paid on top of a basic state pension to men born before 6 April 1951 or women born before 1953. Individuals born after these dates will get the new state pension instead and won't qualify for the additional state pension, although they might still be able to inherit additional state pension from their partner. Additional state pension is paid automatically if an individual is eligible for it, unless they contracted out of it. There is no fixed amount for the additional state pension, the amount paid depends on the amount of earnings a person has, or is treated as having, between the lower and upper earnings limits for each complete tax year between 6 April 1978 and the tax year before they reach state pension age. The additional state pension is paid with the basic state pension.

From 1978 to 2002, additional state pension was called the State Earnings-Related Pension Scheme (SERPS). SERPS covered all earnings by employees from 6 April 1978 to 5 April 1997 on which standard rate class 1 NI contributions had been paid, and earnings between 6 April 1997 and 5 April 2002 if the standard rate class 1 NI contributions had been contracted-in.

In 2002, SERPS was reformed through the state second pension, by improving the pension available to low and moderate earners and extending access to certain carers and people with long-term illness or disability. If earnings on which class 1 NI contributions have been paid or can be treated as paid are above the annual NI lower earnings limit (£6,136 for 2019–2020) but below the primary threshold (£8,632 for 2019–2020), the state second pension regards this as earnings of £8,632 and it is treated as equivalent. Certain carers and people with long-term illness and disability will be considered as having earned at the primary threshold for each complete tax year since 2002–3 even if they do not work at all, or earn less than the annual NI lower earnings limit.

The amount of additional state pension paid also depends on when a person reaches state pension age; changes phased in from 6 April 1999 mean that pensions are calculated differently from that date.

ADDITIONAL STATE PENSION INHERITANCE

Men or women widowed before 6 October 2002 may inherit all of their late spouse's SERPS pension. Since 6 October 2002, the maximum percentage of SERPS pension that a person can inherit from a late spouse or civil partner depends on their late spouse's or civil partner's date of birth:

Maximum SERPS entitlement	d.o.b. (men)	d.o.b. (women)
100%	5/10/37 or earlier	5/10/42 or earlier
90%	6/10/37 to 5/10/39	6/10/42 to 5/10/44
80%	6/10/39 to 5/10/41	6/10/44 to 5/10/46
70%	6/10/41 to 5/10/43	6/10/46 to 5/10/48
60%	6/10/43 to 5/10/45	6/10/48 to 5/7/50
50%	6/10/45 or later	6/7/50 or later

The maximum state second pension a person can inherit from a spouse or civil partner is 50 per cent. If a person is bereaved before they have reached their state pension age, inherited SERPS or state second pension can be paid as part of widowed parent's allowance (in the case of a person who has dependent children) or otherwise only from state pension age. If they remarry or form a new civil partnership before state pension age they lose the right to inherit any state pension.

NEW STATE PENSION INHERITANCE

A person who reached state pension age before 6 April 2016 will still be able to inherit additional state pension under the existing rules. However, if their late spouse or civil partner reaches state pension age on or after that date, the amount they can inherit will be based on the deceased's contributions up to 5 April 2016 only.

A person reaching state pension age on or after 6 April 2016 whose deceased spouse or civil partner reached state pension age or died before that date will be able to inherit additional state pension under the current rules. If the deceased spouse or civil partner is also in the new state pension the survivor may inherit half of any 'protected payment'. A person will have a protected payment if their state pension calculated under current rules is more than the full rate of new state pension at April 2016. The protected payment is the amount of the excess.

In order for a person reaching state pension age on or after 6 April 2016 to qualify for an inherited amount the marriage or civil partnership must have begun before that date; and, in the case of a person widowed under state pension age, they must not remarry or form a new civil partnership before state pension age.

STATE PENSION STATEMENTS

The Department for Work and Pensions provide state pension statements. These statements give an estimate of the state pension an individual may get based on their current NI contribution record.

There is also an online state pension calculator (W www.gov.uk/check-state-pension).

PRIVATE PENSIONS

CONTRACTED-OUT PENSIONS

From 6 April 2012, employees have not been able to contract-out of the state second pension through a money purchase (defined contribution) occupational pension scheme or a personal or stakeholder pension. Anyone contracted-out via these schemes, from that date, was automatically contracted back into the additional state pension. Although those rights built up before the abolition date can be used to provide pension benefits. These changes did not affect contracting-out via a salary-related occupational pension scheme (also known as contracted-out defined benefit (DB) or final salary schemes), which provide a pension related to earnings and the length of pensionable service. However, the introduction of the single-tier pension scheme in April 2016 closed the additional state pension for those reaching state pension age after this date, and contracting out on a DB basis ended.

STAKEHOLDER PENSION SCHEMES

Introduced in 2001, stakeholder pensions are available to everyone but are principally for moderate earners who do not have access to a good value company pension scheme. Stakeholder pensions must meet minimum standards to make sure they are flexible, portable and annual management charges are capped. The minimum contribution is £20.

AUTOMATIC ENROLMENT INTO WORKPLACE PENSIONS

Under the Pensions Act 2008 automatic enrolment into workplace pensions was phased in between October 2012 and February 2018, from when all employers must automatically enrol their workers who meet the age and earnings criteria into a workplace pension. This applies to people who are not already in a qualifying workplace pension scheme and who:

- earn at least £10,000 per annum
- are aged 22 or over
- are under state pension age
- ordinarily work in the UK

Employees who meet the above requirements are entitled to opt out of the scheme at any time if they wish to do so; if they opt out within one calendar month of enrolment they will get back any money already paid in, otherwise payments will usually stay in the pension until retirement. Employees can opt back in at any time by writing to their employer, although they do not have to accept the employer back into their workplace scheme if they they have opted in and opted out within the past 12 months. Employers will automatically re-enrol those that have opted out every three years (from the date they were first enrolled) and will write to the employee when they do this. Employees can leave the scheme again, but only once they have been re-enrolled.

Additionally certain employees can also choose to opt in to the scheme. Currently, employees can opt in if they are:
• aged 16 to 21, or state pension age to 74
• earning above £6,032 up to and including £10,000 per annum
If they remain in the scheme, they, together with their employer, will pay into it every month. The government will also contribute through tax relief. Further information is available at **W** www.gov.uk/workplace-pensions

COMPLAINTS
The Pensions Advisory Service provides information and guidance to members of the public, on state, company, personal and stakeholder schemes. They also help any member of the public who has a problem, complaint or dispute with their occupational or personal pensions.

There are two bodies for pension complaints. The Financial Ombudsman Service deals with complaints which predominantly concern the sale and/or marketing of occupational, stakeholder and personal pensions. The Pensions Ombudsman deals with complaints regarding the management (after sale or marketing) of occupational, stakeholder and personal pensions.

The Pensions Regulator is the UK regulator for work-based pension schemes; it concentrates its resources on schemes where there is the greatest risk to the security of members' benefits, promotes good administration practice for all work-based schemes and works with trustees, employers and professional advisers to put things right when necessary.

WAR PENSIONS AND THE ARMED FORCES COMPENSATION SCHEME
Veterans UK is part of the Ministry of Defence. It was formed on 1 April 2007 to provide services to both serving personnel and veterans.

Veterans UK is responsible for the administration of the war pensions scheme and the armed forces compensation scheme (AFCS) to members of the armed forces in respect of disablement or death due to service. They are also responsible for the administration of the armed forces pension scheme (AFPS), which provides occupational pensions for ex-service personnel.

THE WAR PENSIONS SCHEME
War disablement pension is awarded for the disabling effects of any injury, wound or disease which was the result of, or was aggravated by, service in the armed forces prior to 6 April 2005. Claims are only considered once the person has left the armed forces. The amount of pension paid depends on the severity of disablement, which is assessed by comparing the health of the claimant with that of a healthy person of the same age and sex. The person's earning capacity or occupation are not taken into account in this assessment. A pension is awarded if the person has a disablement of 20 per cent or more and a lump sum is usually payable to those with a disablement of less than 20 per cent. No award is made for noise-induced sensorineural hearing loss where the assessment of disablement is less than 20 per cent. Where an assessment of disablement is at 40 per cent or more, an age addition is automatically given when the pensioner reaches 65.

A pension is payable to war widows, widowers and surviving civil partners where the spouse's or civil partner's death was due to, or hastened by, service in the armed forces prior to 6 April 2005 or where the spouse or civil partner was in receipt of a war disablement pension constant attendance allowance (or would have been if not in hospital) at the time of death. A pension is also payable to widows, widowers or surviving civil partners if the spouse or civil partner was receiving the war disablement pension at the 80 per cent rate or higher in conjunction with unemployability supplement at the time of death. War widows, widowers and surviving civil partners receive a standard rank-related rate, but a lower weekly rate is payable to war widows, widowers and surviving civil partners of personnel of the rank of Major or below who are under the age of 40, without children and capable of maintaining themselves. This is increased to the standard rate at age 40. Allowances are paid for children and adult dependants. An age allowance is automatically given when the widow, widower or surviving civil partner reaches 65 and increased at ages 70 and 80.

Pensioners living overseas receive the same pension rates as those living in the UK. All war disablement pensions and allowances and pensions for war widows, widowers and surviving civil partners are tax-free in the UK; this does not always apply in overseas countries due to different tax laws.

SUPPLEMENTARY ALLOWANCES
A number of supplementary allowances may be awarded to a war pensioner and are intended to meet various needs. The principal supplementary allowances are unemployability supplement, allowance for lowered standard of occupation, constant attendance allowance and war pensions mobility supplement. Others include exceptionally severe disablement allowance, severe disablement occupational allowance, treatment allowance, comforts allowance, clothing allowance, age allowance and widow/widower/surviving civil partner's age allowance. Rent and children's allowances are also available with pensions for war widows, widowers and surviving civil partners.

ARMED FORCES COMPENSATION SCHEME
The armed forces compensation scheme (AFCS) became effective on 6 April 2005 and covers all regular (including Gurkhas) and reserve personnel whose injury, ill health or death is caused predominantly by service on or after 6 April 2005. There are time limits under this scheme and generally claims must be made within seven years of the injury occurring or from first seeking medical advice about an illness. There are some exceptions to this time limit, the main one being for a late-onset illness. Claims for a late-onset illness can be made, after discharge, at any time after the event to which it relates, providing the claim is made within three years of medical advice being sought.

The AFCS provides compensation where service in the armed forces is the only or predominant cause of injury, illness or death. Any other personal accident cover held by the individual is not taken into account when determining an AFCS award. Under the terms of the scheme a tax-free lump sum is payable to service or ex-service personnel based on a 15-level tariff, graduated according to the seriousness of the injury. If multiple injuries are sustained in the same incident compensation for each injury, up to the scheme maximum, is awarded. For those with the most serious injuries and illness a tax-free, index-linked monthly payment – a guaranteed income payment or GIP – is paid for life from the point of discharge. A taxable survivor's GIP (SGIP) will also be paid to surviving spouses, civil partners and unmarried partners who meet certain criteria. GIP and SGIP are calculated by multiplying the pensionable pay of the service person by a factor that depends on the age at the person's last birthday. The younger the person, the higher the factor, because there are more years to normal retirement age.

ARMED FORCES INDEPENDENCE PAYMENT

Armed forces independence payment (AFIP) is designed to provide financial support for service personnel and veterans who have been seriously injured to cover the extra costs they may incur as a result of their injury. It is administered by Veterans UK as part of AFCS although payments are made by the Department for Work and Pensions (DWP). It is non-taxable and non-means-tested.

Service personnel and veterans awarded a GIP of 50 per cent or higher under the AFCS are eligible. Those eligible for AFIP are not required to undergo an assessment and will keep the payment for as long as they are entitled to receive a GIP of 50 per cent or higher.

DEPARTMENT FOR WORK AND PENSIONS BENEFITS

Payments under the AFCS and the war pensions scheme may affect income related benefits from the DWP. In particular any supplementary allowances in payment with war pensions. Any state pension for which a war widow, widower or surviving civil partner qualifies for on their own NI contribution record can be paid in addition to monies received under the war pensions scheme.

CLAIMS AND QUESTIONS

Further information on the war pensions scheme, the AFCS and contact details for Veterans Welfare Service centres can be obtained from Veterans UK (T 0808-191 4218, if calling from the UK or, if living overseas, T (+44) (1253) 866-043).

VETERANS UK, Norcross Lane, Thornton-Cleveleys FY5 3WP
E veterans-uk@mod.gov.uk W www.gov.uk/government/organisations/veterans-uk

TAX CREDITS

Tax credits are administered by HM Revenue and Customs (HMRC). They are based on an individual's or couple's household income and current circumstances. Adjustments can be made during the year to reflect changes in income and/or circumstances. Tax credits are being replaced by universal credit. Further information regarding the qualifying conditions for tax credits, how to claim and the rates payable is available online at (W www.gov.uk/browse/benefits/tax-credits).

WORKING TAX CREDIT

Working tax credit is a payment from the government to support people on low incomes. New claims may only be made by those who are in receipt of a severe disability premium. Those who do not meet this criteria may be eligible for universal credit if they are of working age, or pension credits if they are of qualifying age.

For those in receipt of working tax credit (where this has not been replaced by universal credit) the amount received depends on individual circumstances and income. The basic amount is up to £1,960 per annum and extra 'elements' are paid on top of this:

Element	Amount per annum
Couple applying together	up to £2,010
Single parent	up to £2,010
An individual working at least 30 hours a week	up to £810
An individual with a disability	up to £3,165
An individual with a severe disability	up to £1,365*

* Usually in addition to the disability payment

Childcare Element

Those already in receipt of tax credits, may still be able to claim for the childcare element. In families with children where a lone parent works at least 16 hours a week, or couples who work at least 24 hours a week between them with one partner working at least 16 hours a week, or where one partner works at least 16 hours a week and the other is disabled, an in-patient in hospital, or in prison, the family is entitled to the childcare element of working tax credit. Depending on circumstances this payment can contribute up to £122.50 a week towards childcare costs for one child and up to £210.00 a week for two or more children. Families can only claim if they use an approved childcare provider.

CHILD TAX CREDIT

Child tax credit has been replaced by universal credit for most people. The credit is made up of a main 'family' element of up to £545 a year with an additional 'child' payment of up to £2,780 a year for each child in a household born before 6 April 2017. For children born after this date, only the 'child' element of child tax credit will apply for the first two children in a household with no 'family element', however there are exceptions to this two-child rule. An additional payment is paid for children with a disability, plus a further payment for children who are severely disabled. New child tax credit claims are still possible for individuals who are eligible for a severe disability premium and have legal responsibility and care for any child who is 16 years and younger.

BENEFITS

The following is intended as a general guide to the benefits system. Conditions of entitlement and benefit rates change annually and all prospective claimants should check exact entitlements and rates of benefit directly with their local Jobcentre Plus office, pension centre or online (W www.gov.uk/browse/benefits). Leaflets relating to the various benefits and contribution conditions for different benefits are available from local Jobcentre Plus offices.

UNIVERSAL CREDIT

Universal credit (UC) is a single benefit which combines benefits for in and out of work support, housing and childcare costs, with additional payments for people who have disabilities or caring responsibilities. UC is gradually being rolled out to all new and existing claimants in all local authority areas in the country, replacing six means-tested benefits with a single monthly payment. The six benefits being replaced by UC are:

- Income-based jobseeker's allowance (JSA)
- Income-related employment and support allowance (ESA)
- Income support
- Child tax credit
- Working tax credit
- Housing benefit

The UC full service completed its roll-out for all new claimants in December 2018 and is available in all parts of the UK. It is expected that existing claimants of the above six benefits will be moved to UC between November 2020 and December 2023. This will follow a pilot involving up to 10,000 people moved between July 2019 and July 2020.

The amount of UC awarded is determined by the circumstances of the claimant, this includes income and number of dependants in the household. It consists of a basic 'standard allowance' and additional payments as applicable to the claimant's circumstances. UC can be claimed while working, but the monthly payment will reduce gradually as the claimant earns more.

Standard monthly allowance from April 2019

Single, under 25	£251.77
Single, over 25	£317.82
Couple, both under 25	£395.20
Couple, one or both over 25	£498.89

Additional monthly payments from April 2019

Disability or health condition	£336.20
Carer allowance	£160.20
First child born before 6 April 2017	£277.08
First child born after 6 April 2017	£231.67
Second child	£231.67
Childcare for one child (max.)	£646.35
Childcare for two or more children (max.)	£1,108.04
Child with a disability	
Lower rate addition	£126.11
Higher rate addition	£392.08

For more information and to check eligibility visit **W** www.gov.uk/universal-credit

CONTRIBUTORY BENEFITS

Entitlement to contributory benefits depends on national insurance contribution conditions being satisfied either by the claimant or by someone on the claimant's behalf (depending on the kind of benefit). The class or classes of national insurance contribution relevant to each benefit are:

Jobseeker's allowance (contribution-based)	Class 1
Employment and Support Allowance (contributory)	Class 1 or 2
Widow's benefit and bereavement benefit	Class 1, 2 or 3
State pensions, categories A and B	Class 1, 2 or 3

The system of contribution conditions relates to yearly levels of earnings on which national insurance (NI) contributions have been paid.

JOBSEEKER'S ALLOWANCE

Jobseeker's allowance (JSA) replaced unemployment benefit and income support for unemployed people under state pension age from 7 October 1996. There are three different types of JSA: 'new style' JSA, contribution-based JSA and income-based JSA. Following the roll out of universal credit (UC) new claimants can only claim contribution-based JSA if they are entitled to the severe disability premium, existing claimants will transfer to 'new style' JSA in line with UC roll-out in their area. JSA is paid at a personal rate (ie additional benefit for dependants is not paid) to those who have made sufficient Class 1 NI contributions in the previous two or three tax years. Savings and partner's earnings are not taken into account and payment can be made for up to six months. Rates of JSA correspond to income support rates.

Claims are made through Jobcentre Plus. A person wishing to claim JSA must generally be unemployed or working on average less than 16 hours a week, capable of work and available for any work which he or she can reasonably be expected to do, usually for at least 40 hours a week. The claimant must agree and sign a 'jobseeker's agreement', which will set out his or her plans to find work, and must actively seek work. If the claimant refuses work or training the benefit may be sanctioned for between one and 26 weeks. On successfully claiming the 'new style' JSA, UC payments will be reduced.

A person will be sanctioned from JSA for up to 26 weeks if he or she has left a job voluntarily without just cause or through misconduct. In these circumstances, it may be possible to receive hardship payments, particularly where the claimant or the claimant's family is vulnerable, eg if sick or pregnant, or with children or caring responsibilities.

Weekly Rates from April 2019

Person aged under 25	£57.90
Person aged 25 or over	£73.10

EMPLOYMENT AND SUPPORT ALLOWANCE

From 27 October 2008, employment and support allowance (ESA) replaced incapacity benefit and income support paid on the grounds of incapacity or disability. There are three different types of ESA: 'new style' ESA, contribution-based ESA and income-related ESA. Those eligible for UC may be able to get UC at the same time or instead of 'new style' ESA. Contributory ESA is available to those who have limited capability for work but cannot get statutory sick pay from their employer; new claimants must be in receipt of the severe disability premium otherwise they can only apply for 'new style' ESA. Those over pensionable age are not entitled to ESA. Apart from those who qualify under the special provisions for people incapacitated in youth, entitlement to contributory ESA is based on a person's NI contribution record. The amount of contributory ESA payable may be reduced where the person receives more than a specified amount of occupational or personal pension. Contributory ESA is paid only in respect of the person claiming the benefit – there are no additional amounts for dependants.

Those with the most severe health conditions or disabilities will receive the support component, which is more than the work-related activity component. Claimants in receipt of the support component are not required to engage in work-related activities, although they can volunteer to do so or undertake permitted work if their condition allows.

Weekly Rates from April 2019

ESA plus work-related activity component	up to £102.15
ESA plus support component	up to £111.65

BEREAVEMENT SUPPORT PAYMENT

Bereavement support payment replaced bereavement payment, widowed parent's allowance and bereavement allowance for those whose spouse or civil partner died on or after 6 April 2017. It may be paid to those under state pension age at the time of their spouse or civil partner's death and whose spouse or civil partner had paid National Insurance contributions for at least 25 weeks or died because of an accident at work or a disease caused by work.

It consists of an initial one-off payment followed by up to 18 monthly payments. There are two rates: those in receipt of, or entitled to, child benefit or those who were pregnant when their spouse or civil partner died receive the higher rate. In order to receive the full amount claims must be made within three months of the death of the spouse or civil partner. After three months, claims can still be made up to 21 months after the spouse or civil partner's death but the payments will be less.

Rates from April 2019

Standard rate	
lump sum	£2,500.00
monthly payment	£100.00
Higher rate	
lump sum	£3,500.00
monthly payment	£350.00

NEW STATE PENSION

The new state pension is payable to men and women who reach state pension age on or after 6 April 2016 (ie men born on or after 6 April 1951 or women born on or after 6 April

1953). Those that reached state pension age before this date continue to receive state pension under the old rules.

The full new state pension of £168.60 a week in 2019–20 is payable to those individuals who have 35 qualifying years on their national insurance record. Individuals usually need at least ten qualifying years and will receive a proportion of the new state pension if they have between ten and 35 qualifying years. The starting amount is the higher of the amount receivable under the old state pension rules (category A and B) and the amount the individual would receive had the new state pension been in place at the start of their working life. The amount received includes a deduction for those who were contracted out of the additional state pension.

Each qualifying year on an individual's national insurance record after 5 April 2016 adds £4.82 a week to the new state pension. The exact amount can be calculated by dividing £168.60 by 35 and then multiplying by the number of qualifying years after 5 April 2016. Additional qualifying years can be added to a person's national insurance record until the person reaches the full new state pension amount or the state pension age – whichever is first.

Those individuals who have accrued an amount, before 5 April 2016, which is above the new full state pension – a 'protected payment' – have this paid on top of the full new state pension.

The new state pension increases each year by whichever is the highest:
- earnings – the average percentage growth in wages (in Great Britain)
- prices – the percentage growth in prices in the UK as measured by the Consumer Prices Index (CPI)
- 3 per cent

Any protected payment increases each year in line with CPI.

The new state pension can be deferred beyond state pension age and will increase by 1 per cent for every nine weeks it is deferred, as long as it is deferred for at least nine weeks. This equates to just under 5.8 per cent for every full year a new state pension is deferred. The new state pension can only be deferred once and for a period of at least nine weeks (there is no upper limit).

Weekly Rate from April 2019	
Full new state pension	£168.60

STATE PENSION: CATEGORIES A AND B
Category A pension is payable for life to men and women who reach state pension age, who satisfy the contributions conditions and who claim for it. Category B pension may be payable to married women, married men and civil partners who are not entitled to a basic state pension on their own NI contributions or whose own basic state pension entitlement is less than £77.45 a week in 2019–20. It is based on their spouse or civil partner's NI contributions and is payable when both members of the couple have reached state pension age. Married men and civil partners may only be able to qualify for a category B pension if their wife or civil partner was born on or after 6 April 1950. Category B pension is also payable to widows, widowers and surviving civil partners who are bereaved before state pension age if they were previously entitled to widowed parent's allowance or bereavement allowance based on their late spouse's or civil partner's NI contributions. If they were receiving widowed parent's allowance on reaching state pension age, they could qualify for a category B pension payable at the same rate as their widowed parent's allowance comprising a basic pension, plus, if applicable, the appropriate share of their late spouse's or late civil partner's additional state pension. If their widowed

parent's allowance had stopped before they reached state pension age, or they had been getting bereavement allowance at any time before state pension age, their category B pension will consist of inheritable additional state pension only. No basic state pension is included, although they may qualify for a basic state pension or have their own basic state pension improved by substituting their late spouse's or late civil partner's NI records for their own.

Widows who are bereaved when over state pension age can qualify for a category B pension regardless of the age of their husband when he died. This is payable at the same rate as the basic state pension the widow's late husband was entitled to (or would have been entitled to) at the time of his death. It can also be paid to widowers and civil partners who are bereaved when over state pension age if their wife or civil partner had reached state pension age when they died. Widowers and surviving civil partners who reached state pension age on or after 6 April 2010 and bereaved when over state pension age can qualify for a category B pension regardless of the age of their wife or civil partner when they died.

Where a person is entitled to both a category A and category B pension then they can be combined to give a composite pension, but this cannot be more than the full rate pension. Where a person is entitled to more than one category A or category B pension then only one can be paid. In such cases the person can choose which to get; if no choice is made, the most favourable one is paid.

A person may defer claiming their pension beyond state pension age. In doing so they may earn increments which will increase the weekly amount paid by 1 per cent per five weeks of deferral (equivalent to 10.4 per cent/year) when they claim their state pension. If a person delays claiming for at least 12 months they are given the option of a one-off taxable lump sum, instead of a pension increase, based on the weekly pension deferred, plus interest of at least 2 per cent above the Bank of England base rate. Since 6 April 2010, a category B pension has been treated independently of the spouse's or partner's pension. It is possible to take a category B pension even if the spouse or partner has deferred theirs.

It is no longer possible to claim an increase on a state pension for another adult (known as adult dependency increase). Those who received the increase before April 2010 can keep receiving it until the conditions are no longer met or until 5 April 2020, whichever is first.

Provision for children is made through universal credit. An age addition of 25p a week is payable with a state pension if a pensioner is aged 80 or over.

Since 1989 pensioners have been allowed to have unlimited earnings without affecting their state pension. *See also* Pensions.

Weekly Rates from April 2019	
Category A or B pension for a single person	£129.20
Category B pension based on spouse or civil partner's NI contributions	£77.45

GRADUATED RETIREMENT BENEFIT
Graduated retirement benefit (GRB) is based on the amount of graduated NI contributions paid into the GRB scheme between April 1961 and April 1975; however, it is still paid in addition to any state pension to those who made the relevant contributions. A person will receive graduated retirement benefit based on their own contributions, even if not entitled to a basic state pension. Widows, widowers and surviving civil partners may inherit half of their deceased spouse's or civil partner's entitlement, but none that the deceased spouse or civil partner may have been eligible for from a former spouse or civil partner. If a person defers

making a claim beyond state pension age, they may earn an increase or a one-off lump sum payment in respect of their deferred graduated retirement benefit; calculated in the same way as for a category A or B state pension.

NON-CONTRIBUTORY BENEFITS
These benefits are paid from general taxation and are not dependent on NI contributions.

JOBSEEKER'S ALLOWANCE (INCOME-BASED)
Those who do not qualify for contribution-based jobseeker's allowance (JSA) and those who have exhausted their entitlement to contribution-based JSA may qualify for income-based JSA. Universal credit and 'new style' Jobseeker's Allowance (JSA) has replaced income-based JSA for most people, only those in receipt of, or eligible for, a benefit with a severe disability premium and those who recently stopped getting a benefit with a severe disability premium and still meet the eligibility requirements can make a new claim for income-based JSA.

The amount paid depends on age, whether they are single or a couple and amount of income and savings. To get income-based JSA the claimant must usually be aged 18 or over but below state pension age, although there are some exceptions for 16- or 17-year-olds. The rules of entitlement are the same as for contribution-based JSA.

Weekly Rates from April 2019	
Person aged under 25	£57.90
Person aged 25 or over	£73.10
Couple, both aged 18 or over	£114.85

MATERNITY ALLOWANCE
Maternity allowance (MA) is a benefit available for pregnant women who cannot get statutory maternity pay (SMP) from their employer or have been employed/self-employed during or close to their pregnancy. In order to qualify for payment, a woman must have been employed and/or self-employed for at least 26 weeks in the 66-week period up to and including the week before the baby is due (test period). These weeks do not have to be in a row and any part weeks worked will count towards the 26 weeks. She must also have an average weekly earning of at least £30 (maternity allowance threshold) over any 13 weeks of the woman's choice within the test period.

Self-employed women who pay class 2 NI contributions or who hold a small earnings exception certificate are deemed to have enough earnings to qualify for MA.

A woman can choose to start receiving MA from the 11th week before the week in which the baby is due (if she stops work before then) up to the day following the day of birth. The exact date MA starts will depend on when the woman stops work to have her baby or if the baby is born before she stops work. However, where the woman is absent from work wholly or partly due to her pregnancy in the four weeks before the week the baby is due to be born, MA will start the day following the first day of absence from work. MA is paid for a maximum of 39 weeks.

Women who are not eligible for statutory maternity pay or the higher amount of MA may be eligible for a reduced rate of MA for either a 39-week or a 14-week period. For example, women who have not made enough Class 2 NI contributions or who take part in the business of their self-employed spouse or civil partner, for at least 26 weeks in the 66 weeks before their baby is due, and the work they do is unpaid.

Weekly Rates from April 2019	
Standard rate	£148.68 or 90 per cent of the woman's average weekly earnings if less than £148.68
39-week reduced rate	£27.00
14-week reduced rate	£27.00

CHILD BENEFIT
A person responsible for one or more children under 16 (or under 20 if they stay in approved education or training) is entitled to claim child benefit. There's no limit to the number of children that can be claimed for, but only one person can receive child benefit for a child. Child benefit is taxable if the claimant or their partner's individual income is over £50,000. An individual can choose not to receive child benefit payments, but they should still fill in the claim form in order to get National Insurance credits and to ensure the child is registered to get a National Insurance number when they become 16-years-old

Weekly Rates from April 2019	
Eldest/only child	£20.70
Each subsequent child	£13.70

GUARDIAN'S ALLOWANCE
Guardian's allowance is payable to a person who is bringing up a child or young person because the child's parents have died, or in some circumstances, where only one parent has died. To receive the allowance the person must be in receipt of child benefit for the child or young person, although they do not have to be the child's legal guardian.

Weekly Rate (in addition to child benefit) from April 2019	
Each child	£17.60

CARER'S ALLOWANCE
Carer's allowance (CA) is a benefit payable to people who spend at least 35 hours a week caring for a severely disabled person. To qualify for CA a person must be caring for someone in receipt of one of the following benefits:
- attendance allowance
- disability living allowance (middle or highest care rate)
- personal independence payment (daily living component)
- constant attendance allowance, paid at not less than the normal maximum rate with an industrial injuries disablement benefit or at the basic (full-day) rate with a war disablement pension
- armed forces independence payment

Weekly Rate from April 2019	
Carer's allowance	£66.15

ATTENDANCE ALLOWANCE
This may be payable to people aged 65 or over who need help with personal care because they are physically or mentally disabled, and who have needed help for a period of at least six months. Attendance allowance has two rates: the lower rate is for day or night care, and the higher rate is for day and night care. People not expected to live for more than six months because of a progressive disease can receive the highest rate of attendance allowance straight away.

Weekly Rates from April 2019	
Higher rate	£87.65
Lower rate	£58.70

PERSONAL INDEPENDENCE PAYMENT (PIP)

Personal independence payment (PIP) replaced disability living allowance (DLA) for people aged 16 to 64 on 8 April 2013. PIP has two components: the daily living component and the mobility component, with each offering two different benefit rates: standard and enhanced. Whether one or both components are claimed depends on the requirements of the individual. Claimants are assessed on their ability to carry out everyday activities, with the majority of claims evaluated via an interview. Claimants with a terminal illness automatically receive the enhanced daily living component.

Weekly Rates from April 2019	
Daily living component	
Standard	£58.70
Enhanced	£87.65
Mobility component	
Standard	£23.20
Enhanced	£61.20

STATE PENSION FOR PEOPLE AGED 80 AND OVER

A state pension, referred to as category D pension, is provided for people aged 80 and over if they are not entitled to another category of state pension or are entitled to a state pension that is less than £77.45 a week. The person must live in Great Britain and have done so for a period of ten years or more in any continuous 20-year period since their 60th birthday.

Weekly Rate from April 2019	
Single person	£77.45
Age addition	£0.25

INCOME SUPPORT

Broadly speaking income support is a benefit for those aged between 16 and pension credit qualifying age, whose income is below a certain level, work on average less than 16 hours a week and are:

- bringing up children alone
- registered sick or disabled
- a student who is also a lone parent or disabled
- caring for someone who is sick or elderly

Income support is being replaced by universal credit, new claims for income support can only be made by those entitled to the severe disability premium or those in receipt of it in the last month and who are still eligible.

Income support is not payable if the claimant, or claimant and partner, have capital or savings in excess of £16,000 – and deductions are made for capital and savings in excess of £6,000. For people permanently in residential care and nursing homes, deductions apply for capital over £10,000. A permanent address is not needed to claim income support.

Sums payable depend on fixed allowances laid down by law for people in different circumstances. If both partners are eligible for income support, either may claim it for the couple. People receiving income support may be able to receive housing benefit and help with healthcare. They may also be eligible for help with exceptional expenses from the Social Fund. Special rates may apply to some people living in residential care or nursing homes.

INCOME SUPPORT PREMIUMS

Income support premiums are extra weekly payments for those with additional needs. People qualifying for more than one premium will normally only receive the highest single premium for which they qualify. However, family premium, disabled child premium, severe disability premium and carer premium are payable in addition to other premiums.

Child tax credit replaced premiums for people with children for all new income support claims from 6 April 2004. People with children who were already in receipt of income support in April 2004 and have not claimed child tax credit may qualify for:

- the family premium if they have at least one child
- the disabled child premium if they have a child who receives disability living allowance or is registered blind
- the enhanced disability child premium if they have a child in receipt of the higher rate disability living allowance care component

Carers may qualify for the carer premium if they or their partner are in receipt of carer's allowance and Long-term sick or disabled people may qualify for the disability premium, the severe disability premium or the enhanced disability premium. People with a partner at state pension age may qualify for the pensioner premium.

WEEKLY RATES OF INCOME SUPPORT
from April 2019

Single person	
Aged under 18	£57.90
aged 25+	£73.10
Aged under 18 and a single parent	£57.90
Aged 18+ and a single parent	£73.10

Couples	
Both under 18	£57.90
Both under 18, in certain circumstances	£87.50
One under 18, one under 25	£57.90
One under 18, one aged 25+	£73.10
Both aged 18+	£114.85

Premiums	
Carer premium	£36.85
Severe disability premium	£65.85
Enhanced disability premium	
Single person	£16.80
Couples	£24.10
Pensioner premium (couple)	£140.40

PENSION CREDIT

To qualify for pension credit you must have reached state pension age. Since 15 May 2019 only couples where both parties have reached state pension age, or one party is in receipt of housing benefit for people aged over state pension age, are eligible for pension credit. Couples not in receipt of pension credit could backdate their claim until 13 August 2019. Those already in receipt of pension credit under the old rules on 15 May 2019 will continue to receive it while they remain eligible. If their entitlement stops for any reason they can not start getting it again until they are eligible under the new rules. Those not entitled to pension credit can apply for universal credit instead.

Income from state pension, private pensions, earnings and most benefits are taken into account when calculating the pension credit. For savings and capital in excess of £10,000, £1 for every £500 or part of £500 held is taken into account as income when working out entitlement to pension credit.

There are two elements to pension credit:

THE GUARANTEE CREDIT

The guarantee credit guarantees a minimum income of £167.25 for single people and £255.25 for couples, with additional elements for people who have severe disabilities and caring responsibilities.

Weekly Rates from April 2019	
Additional amount for severe disability	
Single person	£65.85
Couple (one qualifies)	£65.85
Couple (both qualify)	£131.70
Additional amount for carers	£36.85

THE SAVINGS CREDIT
Savings Credit is only available to individuals and couples that reached state pension age before 6 April 2016. Those that have been in receipt of savings credit since before 6 April 2016, will continue to receive it as long as there are no breaks in their entitlement. If eligibility ceases the individual or couple will not be able to claim it again.

The savings credit is calculated by taking into account any qualifying income above the savings credit threshold. For 2019–20 the threshold is £144.38 for single people and £229.67 for couples. The maximum savings credit is £13.73 a week (£15.35 a week for couples).

HOUSING BENEFIT
Housing benefit is designed to help people with rent (including rent for accommodation in guesthouses, lodgings or hostels), but does not cover mortgage payments. This benefit is being replaced by universal credit (UC). Since May 2019, only new claimants in receipt of a severe disability premium, who have reached state pension age or who live in temporary accommodation or sheltered housing are eligible to make a claim for housing benefit. Couples are only eligible if both have reached state pension age or one party has reached state pension age and started claiming housing benefit or pension credit (as a couple) before 15 May 2019.

The amount of benefit paid depends on:
• the income of the claimant, and partner if there is one, including earned income, unearned income (any other income including some other benefits) and savings
• number of dependants
• certain extra needs of the claimant, partner or any dependants
• number and gross income of people sharing the home who are not dependent on the claimant
• how much rent is paid

Housing benefit is not payable if the claimant, or claimant and partner, have savings in excess of £16,000. The amount of benefit is affected if savings held exceed £6,000 (£10,000 for people living in residential care and nursing homes). Housing benefit is not paid for meals, fuel or certain service charges that may be included in the rent. Deductions are also made for most non-dependants who live in the same accommodation as the claimant (and their partner). If the claimant is living with a partner or civil partner there can only be one claim.

The maximum amount of benefit (which is not necessarily the same as the amount of rent paid) may be paid where the claimant is in receipt of income support, income-based jobseeker's allowance, the guarantee element of pension credit or where the claimant's income is less than the amount allowed for their needs. Any income over that allowed for their needs will mean that their benefit is reduced.

LOCAL HOUSING ALLOWANCE
Local Housing Allowance (LHA) is the name given to housing benefit for private renters. LHA rates are calculated for every local area based on local rents. The maximum amount of support a household can claim will depend on where they live, the minimum number of bedrooms they need and their income.

COUNCIL TAX REDUCTION
From April 2013, council tax benefit was replaced by council tax reduction. Nearly all the rules that apply to housing benefit apply to council tax reduction, which helps people on low incomes to pay council tax bills. The amount payable depends on how much council tax is paid and who lives with the claimant. The benefit may be available to those receiving income support, income-based jobseeker's allowance, the guarantee element of pension credit or to those whose income is less than that allowed for their needs. Any income over that allowed for their needs will mean that they will receive less help with their council tax reduction. Deductions are made for non-dependants.

A full council tax bill is based on at least two adults living in a home. Residents may receive a 25 per cent reduction on their bill if they count as an adult for council tax and live on their own. If the property is the resident's main home and there is no-one who counts as an adult, the reduction is 50 per cent.

THE SOCIAL FUND
REGULATED PAYMENTS
Sure Start Maternity Grant
Sure start maternity grant (SSMG) is a one-off payment of £500 (or £1,000 for multiple births of three or more) to help people in England, Wales and Northern Ireland on low incomes pay for essential items for new babies that are expected, born, adopted, the subject of a parental order (following a surrogate birth) or, in certain circumstances, the subject of a residency order. SSMG can be claimed any time within 11 weeks of the expected birth and up to six months after the birth, adoption or date of parental or residency order. Those eligible are people in receipt of universal credit, income support, income-based jobseeker's allowance, pension credit, child tax credit at a rate higher than the family element or working tax credit where a disability or severe disability element is in payment. SSMG is only available if there are no other children under 16 in the family, unless the claimant is expecting a multiple birth. There are also exceptions for those who have taken on responsibility for another's child (eg through adoption, legal guardianship or a parental order). Expectant parents in Scotland may be eligible for a pregnancy and baby payment as part of the 'best start' grant. *See* www.mygov.scot/best-start-grant for further information.

Funeral Expenses Payment
Payable to help cover the necessary cost of burial or cremation, a new burial plot, moving the body, the purchase of official documents and certificates and certain other expenses plus an additional payment of up to £700 for any other funeral expenses, such as the funeral director's fees, the coffin or flowers. Those eligible are people receiving universal credit, income support, income-based jobseeker's allowance, pension credit, child tax credit at a higher rate than the family element, working tax credit where a disability or severe disability element is in payment, council tax benefit or housing benefit who have good reason for taking responsibility for the funeral expenses, such as partner, child or parent of the deceased. These payments are recoverable from any estate of the deceased.

Cold Weather Payments
A payment of £25 per seven-day period between 1 November and 31 March when the average temperature is recorded at or forecast to be 0°C or below over seven consecutive days in the qualifying person's area. Payments are made to people on universal credit, pension credit or child tax credit with a disability element, those on income support whose benefit includes a pensioner or disability premium, and those on

income-based jobseeker's allowance or employment and support allowance who have a child who is disabled or under the age of five. Payments are made automatically and do not have to be repaid.

Winter Fuel Payments
For 2019–20 the winter fuel payment is £200 for households with someone born on or before 5 April 1954 and £300 for households with someone aged 80 or over. The rate paid is based on the person's age and circumstances in the 'qualifying week' between 16 and 22 September 2019. The majority of eligible people are paid automatically between November and December, although a few need to claim. Payments do not have to be repaid.

Christmas Bonus
The Christmas bonus is a one-off tax-free £10 payment made before Christmas to those people in receipt of a qualifying benefit in the qualifying week (usually the first full week of December).

DISCRETIONARY PAYMENTS

Finance Support – Northern Ireland
The Northern Ireland (Welfare Reform) Act 2016 introduced Finance Support to replace Crisis Loans and Community Care Grants on 31 October 2016. Since 31 October 2016, people suffering a financial crisis are able to apply for a discretionary support loan or short term benefit advance from the Finance Support Service (**W** www.nidirect.gov.uk/contacts/contacts-az/ finance-support-service-times-crisis-and-need). To receive discretionary support, the applicant must have a crisis which places themselves or their family's health, safety or wellbeing at significant risk. Applicants must be a resident of Northern Ireland and be over 18-years-old (16-years-old if they do not have any parental support) and be earning less than the national living wage. If eligible, the applicant may be offered a discretionary support loan or grant; usually no more than three loans and one grant can be awarded within a 12-month period.

Short-term benefit advances are available to those that have an urgent financial need that may impact the applicant or their family's health, safety or wellbeing. The applicant must be able to afford to repay the advance within 12 weeks.

If an applicant's combined discretionary support and short-term benefit advance debt is £1,000 or more they will not be able to get further support until their debt falls below this limit.

Budgeting Loans
These are interest-free loans to people who have been receiving universal credit, income support, income-based jobseeker's allowance or income-related employment and support allowance or pension credit for the past six months, for intermittent expenses that may be difficult to budget for. Those claiming universal credit can apply for a budgeting advance instead. The smallest borrowable amount is £100.

SAVINGS
Savings of £1,000 (£2,000 if the applicant or their partner is aged 63 or over) are taken into account for budgeting loans. Savings are not taken into account for sure start maternity grant, funeral payments, cold weather payments, winter fuel payments or the Christmas bonus.

INDUSTRIAL INJURIES AND DISABLEMENT BENEFITS
The Industrial Injuries Scheme, administered under the Social Security Contributions and Benefits Act 1992, provides a range of benefits designed to compensate for disablement resulting from an industrial accident (ie an accident arising out of and in the course of an earner's employment) or from a prescribed disease due to the nature of a person's employment. Those who are self-employed are not covered by this scheme.

INDUSTRIAL INJURIES DISABLEMENT BENEFIT
A person may be able to claim industrial injuries disablement benefit if they are ill or disabled due to an accident or incident that happened at work or in connection with work in England, Scotland or Wales. The amount of benefit awarded depends on the person's age and the degree of disability as assessed by a doctor.

The benefit is payable whether the person works or not and those who are incapable of work are entitled to draw other benefits, such as statutory sick pay or incapacity benefit, in addition to industrial injuries disablement benefit. It may also be possible to claim the following allowances:
* reduced earnings allowance for those who are unable to return to their regular work or work of the same standard and who had their accident (or whose disease started) before 1 October 1990. At state pension age this is converted to retirement allowance
* constant attendance allowance for those with a disablement of 100 per cent who need constant care. There are four rates of allowance depending on how much care the person needs
* exceptionally severe disablement allowance can be claimed in addition to constant care attendance allowance at one of the higher rates for those who need constant care permanently

Weekly Rates from April 2019

Degree of disablement	Aged 18+ or with dependants
100 per cent	£179.00
90	£161.10
80	£143.20
70	£125.30
60	£107.40
50	£89.50
40	£71.60
30	£53.70
20	£35.80
Unemployability supplement	£110.65
Reduced earnings allowance (max)	£71.60
Retirement allowance (max)	£17.90
Constant attendance allowance (normal max rate)	£71.60
Exceptionally severe disablement allowance	£71.60

OTHER BENEFITS
People who are disabled because of an accident or disease that was the result of work that they did before 5 July 1948 are not entitled to industrial injuries disablement benefit. They may, however, be entitled under the Workmen's Compensation Scheme or the Pneumoconiosis, Byssinosis and Miscellaneous Diseases Benefit Scheme. People who suffer from certain industrial diseases caused by dust can make a claim for an additional payment under the Pneumoconiosis Act 1979 if they are unable to get damages from the employer responsible.

Diffuse Mesothelioma Payments (2008 Scheme)
Since 1 October 2008 any person suffering from the asbestos-related disease, diffuse mesothelioma, who is unable to make a claim under the Pneumoconiosis Act 1979, have not received payment in respect of the disease from an employer, via a civil claim or elsewhere, and are not entitled to compensation from a MoD scheme, can claim a one-off lump sum payment. The scheme covers people whose exposure to asbestos occurred in the UK and was not as a result of their work (ie they lived near a factory using asbestos). The amount paid depends on the age of the person when the disease was diagnosed, or the date of the claim if the diagnosis date is not

known. The current rate is £92,259 for those who were diagnosed aged 37 and under to £14,334 for persons aged 77 and over at the time of diagnosis. Since 1 October 2009 claims must be received within 12 months of the date of diagnosis. If the sufferer has died, their dependants may be able to claim, but must do so within 12 months of the date of death.

CLAIMS AND QUESTIONS

Entitlement to benefit and regulated Social Fund payments is determined by a decision maker on behalf of the Secretary of State for the Department for Work and Pensions. A claimant who is dissatisfied with that decision can ask for an explanation. He or she can dispute the decision by applying to have it revised or, in particular circumstances, superseded. The claimant can appeal to the First-tier Tribunal (Social Security and Child Support). There is a further right of appeal to the Administrative Appeals Chamber of the Upper Tribunal (see Tribunals).

Decisions on claims and applications for housing benefit and council tax benefit are made by local authorities. The explanation, dispute and appeals process is the same as for other benefits.

All decisions on applications to the discretionary Social Fund are made by Jobcentre Plus Social Fund decision makers. Applicants can ask for a review of the decision within 28 days of the date on the decision letter. As above, the claimant has a right of appeal to the First-tier Tribunal (Social Security and Child Support).

EMPLOYER PAYMENTS

STATUTORY MATERNITY PAY

Employers pay statutory maternity pay (SMP) to pregnant women who have been employed by them, full or part-time, continuously for at least 26 weeks into the 15th week before the week the baby is due, and whose earnings on average at least equal the lower earnings limit applied to NI contributions (£118 a week if the end of the qualifying week is in the 2019–20 tax year). SMP can be paid for a period of up to 39 weeks. If the qualifying conditions are met women will receive a payment of 90 per cent of their average earnings for the first six weeks, followed by 33 weeks at £148.68 or 90 per cent of the woman's average weekly earnings if this is less than £148.68. SMP can be paid, at the earliest, 11 weeks before the week in which the baby is due, up to the day following the birth. Women can decide when they wish their maternity leave and pay to start and can work until the baby is born. However, where the woman is absent from work wholly or partly due to her pregnancy in the four weeks before the week the baby is due to be born, SMP will start the day following the first day of absence from work.

Employers are reimbursed for 92 per cent of the SMP they pay. Small employers with annual gross NI payments of £45,000 or less recover 103 per cent of the SMP paid out.

STATUTORY PATERNITY PAY

Employers pay statutory paternity pay (SPP) to employees who are taking leave when a child is born or placed for adoption. To qualify the employee must:
- be the father or the intended parent (ie in a surrogacy arrangement)
- be the husband or partner of the mother (or adopter) – this includes same-sex partners
- be the child's adopter
- have been employed continuously by the same employer for at least 26 weeks ending with the 15th week before the baby is due (or the week in which the adopter is notified of having been matched with a child)

- continue working for the employer up to the child's birth (or placement for adoption) and give the correct notice
- be earning an average of at least £118 a week (before tax)

Employees who meet these conditions receive payment of £148.68 or 90 per cent of the employee's average weekly earnings if this is less than £148.68. The employee can choose to be paid for one or two consecutive weeks. The SPP period can not start before the birth of the child or date of placement for adoption and must be completed within eight weeks of that date. SPP is not payable for any week in which the employee works. Employers are reimbursed in the same way as for statutory maternity pay.

STATUTORY ADOPTION PAY

Employers pay statutory adoption pay (SAP) to employees taking adoption leave from their employers. To qualify for SAP the employee must:
- have been continuously employed by the same employer for at least 26 weeks ending up to any day in the week in which they were matched with a child
- be earning an average of at least £118 a week (before tax) during the 'relevant' eight week period
- have given the correct notice and provided proof of the adoption or surrogacy
- have permission from a UK authority, in cases where the child is being adopted from abroad

Employees who meet these conditions receive payment of £148.68 or 90 per cent of their average weekly earnings if this is less than £148.68 for up to 39 weeks. The earliest SAP can be paid from is two weeks before the expected date of placement (UK adoptions), on the date the employee is matched with a child (UK adoptions), on arrival of the child in the UK or within 28 days of this date (overseas adoptions) or the day or day after the child's birth in surrogacy arrangements. Where a couple adopt a child, only one of them may receive SAP, the other may be able to receive statutory paternity pay if they meet the eligibility criteria. Employers are reimbursed in the same way as for statutory maternity pay.

STATUTORY SHARED PARENTAL PAY

The Children and Families Act 2014 provided parents greater flexibility to maternity and paternity provisions. Shared parental leave (SPL) provides up to 50 weeks of leave and 37 weeks of pay for couples having a baby or adopting a child. The leave and pay is shared between the couple in the first year after the birth or, in the case of adoption, placement of the child. SPL is flexible and can be used in blocks separated by periods of work, or taken all in one go. Couples can also choose to be off work together or to stagger the leave and pay. There are different eligibility criteria for birth and adoptive parents. For further information see W www.gov.uk/shared-parental-leave-and-pay

The current rate of statutory shared parental pay is £148.68 a week or 90 per cent of the employee's average weekly earnings if this is less than £148.68. The earnings threshold is the same as for SMP and SPP (£118 a week (before tax)).

STATUTORY SICK PAY

Employers pay statutory sick pay (SSP) for up to 28 weeks, to any employee incapable of work for four or more consecutive days (including non-working days). Employees must have done some work under their contract of service, have average weekly earnings of at least £118 a week (before tax) and inform their employer they are sick before their employer's deadline, or within seven days if their employer does not have a deadline. SSP is a daily payment and is usually paid for the days that an employee would normally work. SSP is paid at £94.25 a week and is subject to PAYE and NI contributions.

THE WATER INDUSTRY

In the UK, the water industry provides clean and safe drinking water to over 60 million homes and has an estimated annual economic impact of over £15bn. It supplies around 17 billion litres of water a day to domestic and commercial customers and collects and treats more than 16 billion litres of wastewater a day. It also manages assets that include around 1,400 water treatment and 9,350 wastewater treatment works, 550 impounding reservoirs, over 6,500 service reservoirs/water towers and 800,000km of water mains and sewers.

Water services in England and Wales are provided by private companies. In Scotland and Northern Ireland there are single authorities, Scottish Water and Northern Ireland Water, that are publicly owned companies answerable to their respective governments. In drinking water quality tests carried out in 2018 by the Drinking Water Inspectorate, the water industry in England and Wales achieved 99.95 per cent compliance with the standards required by the EU Drinking Water Directive; Scotland achieved 99.91 per cent and Northern Ireland 99.88 per cent.

In 2016, the Drinking Water Inspectorate (DWI) introduced the Compliance Risk Index (CRI) to illustrate the risk arising from failing to meet water safety standards and the proportion of consumers potentially at risk. In 2019, the CRI for England and Wales was 2.80, an improvement on 3.87 in 2018.

Water UK is the industry association that represents all UK water and wastewater service suppliers at national and European level and is funded directly by its members, the service suppliers for England, Scotland, Wales and Northern Ireland, of which each has a seat on the Water UK Council.

WATER UK, 3rd Floor, 36 Broadway, London SW1H 0BH
T 020-7344 1844 W www.water.org.uk
Chief Executive, Christine McGourty

ENGLAND AND WALES

In England and Wales, the Secretary of State for Environment, Food and Rural Affairs and the Welsh government have overall responsibility for water policy and oversee environmental standards for the water industry.

The statutory consumer representative body for water services is the Consumer Council for Water.

CONSUMER COUNCIL FOR WATER, 1st Floor, Victoria Square House, Victoria Square, Birmingham B2 4AJ
T 0300-034 2222 (England) & 0300-034 3333 (Wales)
W www.ccwater.org.uk

REGULATORY BODIES
The Water Services Regulation Authority (OFWAT) was established in 1989 when the water and sewerage industry in England and Wales was privatised. Its statutory role and duties are laid out under the Water Industry Act 1991 and it is the independent economic regulator of the water and sewerage companies in England and Wales. OFWAT's main duties are to ensure that the companies can finance and carry out their statutory functions and to protect the interests of water customers. OFWAT is a non-ministerial government department headed by a board following a change in legislation introduced by the Water Act 2003.

Under the Competition Act 1998, from 1 March 2000 the Competition Appeal Tribunal has heard appeals against the regulator's decisions regarding anti-competitive agreements and abuse of a dominant position in the marketplace. The Water Act 2003 placed a new duty on OFWAT to contribute to the achievement of sustainable development.

The Environment Agency has statutory duties and powers in relation to water resources, pollution control, flood defence, fisheries, recreation, conservation and navigation in England and Wales. It is also responsible for issuing permits, licences, consents and registrations such as industrial licences to extract water and fishing licences.

The Drinking Water Inspectorate (DWI) is the drinking water quality regulator for England and Wales, responsible for assessing the quality of drinking water supplied by the water companies and investigating any incidents affecting drinking water quality, initiating prosecution where necessary. The DWI science and policy group provides scientific advice on drinking water policy to DEFRA and the Welsh government.

OFWAT, Centre City Tower, 7 Hill Street, Birmingham B5 4UA
W www.ofwat.gov.uk
Chair, Jonson Cox
Chief Executive, Rachel Fletcher

METHODS OF CHARGING
In England and Wales, most domestic customers still pay for domestic water supply and sewerage services through charges based on the rateable value of their property. Currently around half of household customers in England and Wales have a metered supply. Nearly all non-household customers are charged according to consumption.

Under the Water Industry Act 1999, water companies can continue basing their charges on the old rateable value of the property. Domestic customers can continue paying on an unmeasured basis unless they choose to pay according to consumption. After having a meter installed (which is free of charge), a customer can revert to unmeasured charging within 12 months. However, water companies may charge by meter for new homes, or homes where there is a high discretionary use of water. Domestic, school and hospital customers cannot be disconnected for non-payment.

In December 2019, OFWAT finalised its 2019 price review decisions for household water bills for the five-year period to 2025. This means that average bills for water and wastewater customers in England and Wales will decreased by around 12 per cent, before adjustments for inflation, between 2020 and 2025; an average household bill decrease of around £50 compared with the previous period.

AVERAGE HOUSEHOLD BILLS 2018–21 *(£)*
WATER AND SEWERAGE COMPANIES

	2018–19	2019–20	2020–21
	(£)	(£)	(£)
Anglian	429	438	412
Dwr Cymru	445	445	451
Hafren Dyfrdwy	289	296	300
Northumbrian	403	411	326
Severn Trent	347	356	358
South West	499	487	470
Southern	396	440	391
Thames	385	396	394
United Utilities	435	443	420
Wessex	489	487	447
Yorkshire	387	392	406
Average	404	413	397

WATER ONLY COMPANIES

	2018–19	2019–20	2020–21
	(£)	(£)	(£)
Affinity*	191	188	175
Bournemouth	147	150	136
Bristol	184	187	177
Cambridge	141	139	139
Essex and Suffolk	258	257	223
Portsmouth	105	106	102
South East	210	211	210
South Staffs	147	146	149
SES	195	199	187
Average	191	192	186

* Average figures from central, east and south-east regions
Source: Water UK

SCOTLAND

In 2002 the three existing water authorities in Scotland (East of Scotland Water, North of Scotland Water and West of Scotland Water) merged to form Scottish Water. Scottish Water, which serves more than 2.5 million households and provides 1.4 billion litres of water per day while removing almost one billion litres of waste water, is a public sector company, structured and managed like a private company, but remains answerable to the Scottish parliament. Scottish Water is regulated by the Water Industry Commission for Scotland (established under the Water Services (Scotland) Act 2005), the Scottish Environment Protection Agency (SEPA) and the Drinking Water Quality Regulator for Scotland. The Water Industry Commissioner is responsible for regulating all aspects of economic and customer service performance, including water and sewerage charges. SEPA, created under the Environment Act 1995, is responsible for environmental issues, including controlling pollution and promoting the cleanliness of Scotland's rivers, lochs and coastal waters. The Public Services Reform (Scotland) Act 2010 transferred the complaints handling function of Waterwatch Scotland regarding Scottish Water, to the Scottish Public Services Ombudsman. Consumer Futures represented the views and interests of Scottish Water customers but became part of Citizens Advice Scotland in 2014.

METHODS OF CHARGING
Scottish Water sets charges for domestic and non-domestic water and sewerage provision through charges schemes which are regulated by the Water Industry Commission for Scotland. In February 2004 the harmonisation of all household charges across the country was completed following the merger of the separate authorities under Scottish Water. In October 2010 the Water Industry Commission for Scotland published *The Strategic Review of Charges 2021–2027*, stating that annual price rises would not increase at more than £2 a month above inflation for any Scottish household. For the year 2020–21, the combined service charge, covering the water supply and waste water collection, increased by 0.9 per cent on the previous year; resulting in an annual average household bill of £372.

CITIZENS ADVICE SCOTLAND, **W** www.cas.org.uk
DRINKING WATER QUALITY REGULATOR FOR SCOTLAND, Area 3-J South, Victoria Quay, Edinburgh EH6 6QQ **T** 0131-244 0190 **W** www.dwqr.scot
SCOTTISH ENVIRONMENT PROTECTION AGENCY, Third Floor, Silvan House, 231 Corstorphine Road, Edinburgh EH12 7AT **T** 0131-449 7296 **W** www.sepa.org.uk
SCOTTISH PUBLIC SERVICES OMBUDSMAN, Bridgewater House, 99 McDonald Rd, Edinburgh EH7 4NS **T** 0800-377 7330 **W** www.spso.org.uk

SCOTTISH WATER, Castle House, 6 Castle Drive, Dunfermline KY11 8GG **T** 0800-077 8778 **W** www.scottishwater.co.uk
Chief Executive, Douglas Millican
WATER INDUSTRY COMMISSION FOR SCOTLAND, First Floor, Moray House, Forthside Way, Stirling FK8 1QZ **T** 01786-430200 **W** www.watercommission.co.uk

NORTHERN IRELAND

Formerly an executive agency of the Department for Regional Development, Northern Ireland Water is a government-owned company but with substantial independence from government. Northern Ireland Water was set up as a result of government reform of water and sewerage services in April 2007. It is responsible for policy and coordination with regard to the supply, distribution and cleanliness of water, and the provision and maintenance of sewerage services. It supplies 560 million litres of clean water a day to around 840,000 households and treats 330 million litres of waste water each day. The Northern Ireland Authority for Utility Regulation (known as the Utility Regulator) is responsible for regulating the water services provided by Northern Ireland Water. The Drinking Water Inspectorate, a unit in the Northern Ireland Environment Agency (NIEA), regulates drinking water quality. Another NIEA unit, the Water Management Unit, has responsibility for the protection of the aquatic environment. The Consumer Council for Northern Ireland is the consumer representative body for water services.

METHODS OF CHARGING
The water and sewerage used by metered domestic customers in Northern Ireland is currently paid for by the Department for Infrastructure (un-metered domestic customers pay 50 per cent of the full charge), however the future of the subsidy system is uncertain. Non-domestic customers in Northern Ireland became subject to water and sewerage charges and trade effluent charges where applicable in April 2008.

CONSUMER COUNCIL FOR NORTHERN IRELAND, Seatem House, 28–32 Alfred Street, Belfast BT2 8EN **T** 028-9025 1600 **W** www.consumercouncil.org.uk
NORTHERN IRELAND AUTHORITY FOR UTILITY REGULATION, Queens House, 14 Queen Street, Belfast BT1 6ED **T** 028-9031 1575 **W** www.uregni.gov.uk
NORTHERN IRELAND WATER, Westland House, 40 Old Westland Road, Belfast BT14 6TE **T** 0345-744 0088 **W** www.niwater.com
Chief Executive, Sara Venning

WATER SERVICE COMPANIES

WATER UK MEMBERS
AFFINITY WATER, Tamblin Way, Hatfield, Herts AL10 9EZ **T** 0345-357 2407 **W** www.affinitywater.co.uk
ALBION WATER, Harpenden Hall, Southdown Road, Harpenden, Herts AL5 1TE **T** 03300-342020 **W** www.albionwater.co.uk
ANGLIAN WATER SERVICES LTD, Lancaster House, Lancaster Way, Huntingdon PE29 6YJ **T** 01480-32300 **W** www.anglianwater.co.uk
BRISTOL WATER PLC, Bridgwater Road, Bristol BS13 7AX **T** 0345-702 3797 **W** www.bristolwater.co.uk
CAMBRIDGE WATER COMPANY, 90 Fulborn Road, Cambridge CB1 9JN **T** 01223-706050 **W** www.cambridge-water.co.uk
DWR CYMRU (WELSH WATER), Pentwyn Road, Nelson, Treharris, Mid Glamorgan CF46 6LY **T** 0800-052 0145 **W** www.dwrcymru.co.uk

ESSEX & SUFFOLK WATER PLC (subsidiary of Northumbrian Water Ltd), Sandon Valley House, Cannon Barnes Road, Chelmsford CM3 8BD **T** 0345-782 0111
W www.eswater.co.uk

HAFREN DYFRDWY WATER Packsaddle/ Wrexham Road, Rhostyllen, Wrexham, Clwyd LL14 4EH **T** 0330-678 0679
W www.hdcymru.co.uk

ICOSA WATER LTD, Sophia House, 28 Cathedral Road, Cardiff CF11 9LI **T** 0330-111 0780 **W** www.icosawater.co.uk

INDEPENDENT WATER NETWORKS, Driscoll 2, Ellen Street, Cardiff CF10 4BP **T** 029-2002 8711 **W** www.iwnl.co.uk

LEEP UTILITIES, The Greenhouse, MediaCityUK, Salford M50 2EQ **T** 0345-122 6786 **W** www.leeputilities.co.uk

NORTHERN IRELAND WATER, Westland House, Old Westland Road, Belfast BT14 6TE **T** 0345-733 0088
W www.niwater.com

NORTHUMBRIAN WATER LTD, Northumbria House, Abbey Road, Pity Me, Durham DH1 5FJ **T** 0345-717 1100
W www.nwl.co.uk

PORTSMOUTH WATER PLC, PO Box 99, West Street, Havant, Hants PO9 1LG **T** 023-9249 9888
W www.portsmouthwater.co.uk

SCOTTISH WATER, Castle House, 6 Castle Drive, Carnegie Campus, Dunfermline KY11 8GG **T** 0800-077 8778
W www.scottishwater.co.uk

SEVERN TRENT WATER PLC, PO Box 407, Darlington DL1 9WD **T** 0345-570 0500 **W** www.stwater.co.uk

SOUTH EAST WATER LTD, Rocfort Road, Snodland, Kent ME6 5AH **T** 0333-000 0001 **W** www.southeastwater.co.uk

SOUTH STAFFS WATER PLC, Green Lane, Walsall WS2 7PD **T** 0845-607 0456 **W** www.south-staffs-water.co.uk

SOUTH WEST WATER LTD, Peninsula House, Rydon Lane, Exeter EX2 7HR **T** 0344-346 1010
W www.southwestwater.co.uk

SOUTHERN WATER SERVICES LTD, Southern House, Yeoman Road, Worthing BN13 3NX **T** 0330-303 0277
W www.southernwater.co.uk

SES WATER PLC, London Road, Redhill, Surrey RH1 1LJ **T** 01737-772000 **W** www.seswater.co.uk

THAMES WATER UTILITIES LTD, Clearwater Court, Vastern Road, Reading RG1 8DB **T** 0800-980 8800
W www.thameswater.co.uk

UNITED UTILITIES WATER PLC, Haweswater House, Lingley Mere Business Park, Great Sankey, Warrington WA5 3LP **T** 0345-672 2888 **W** www.unitedutilities.com

VEOLIA WATER PROJECTS, 210 Pentonville Road, London N1 9JY**T** 020-7812 5000 **W** www.veolia.co.uk

WESSEX WATER SERVICES LTD, Claverton Down, Bath BA2 7WW **T** 0345-6004 600 **W** www.wessexwater.co.uk

YORKSHIRE WATER SERVICES LTD, Western House, Western Way, Bradford BD6 2LZ **T** 0345-124 2424
W www.yorkshirewater.com

ASSOCIATE MEMBERS
(not members of Water UK)

GUERNSEY WATER, PO Box 30, Brickfield House, St Andrew, Guernsey GY1 3AS **T** 01481-239500 **W** www.water.gg

IRISH WATER (UISCE EIREANN), Colvill House, 24–26 Talbot Street, Dublin 1 **T** (+353) (1) 707 2828 **W** www.water.ie

JERSEY WATER, Mulcaster House, Westmount Road, St Helier, Jersey JE1 1DG **T** 01534-707300 **W** www.jerseywater.je

TIDEWAY (BAZALGETTE TUNNEL LTD), Cottons Centre, Cottons Land, London SE1 2QG **T** 0800-308 080
W www.tideway.london

ENERGY

The main primary sources of energy in Britain are coal, oil, natural gas, renewables and nuclear power. The main secondary sources are electricity, coke and smokeless fuels and petroleum products. The UK was a net importer of fuels in the 1970s, however as a result of growth in oil and gas production from the North Sea, the UK became a net exporter of energy for most of the 1980s. Output decreased in the late 1980s following the Piper Alpha disaster until the mid-1990s, after which the UK again became a net exporter. Since 2004, the UK has reverted back to become a net importer of energy. However, in 2019 the UK net import gap decreased for the sixth consecutive year – from the 2013 peak of 104 million tonnes of oil equivalent – to 70 million tonnes of oil equivalent, accounting for 35.2 per cent of the total energy used in the UK.

The Department for Business, Energy and Industrial Strategy (DBEIS) is responsible for promoting energy efficiency.

INDIGENOUS PRODUCTION OF PRIMARY FUELS
Million tonnes of oil equivalent

	2018	2019
Primary oils	55.7	56.8
Natural gas	38.9	37.8
Primary electricity	20.5	20.4
Coal	1.8	1.5
Bioenergy and waste	13.5	13.8
Total	130.4	130.2

Source: DBEIS

INLAND ENERGY CONSUMPTION BY PRIMARY FUEL
Million tonnes of oil equivalent

	2018	2019
Natural gas	75.3	74.3
Petroleum	68.8	68.0
Coal	8.6	6.1
Nuclear electricity	14.1	13.3
Bioenergy and waste	17.5	18.9
Wind and hydro electricity	6.5	7.2
Net Imports	1.6	1.8
Total	192.4	189.5

Source: DBEIS

TRADE IN FUELS AND RELATED MATERIALS (2019)

	Quantity, million tonnes of oil equivalent	Value £m
Imports		
Crude oil	57.1	19,480
Petroleum products	36.3	16,375
Natural gas	44.5	6,965
Coal and other solid fuel	10.5	1,600
Electricity	2.1	1,015
Total	150.6	45,435
Exports		
Crude oil	49.1	18,290
Petroleum products	22.7	11,245
Natural gas	7.5	1,125
Coal and other solid fuel	0.9	90
Electricity	0.3	140
Total	80.5	30,890

Source: DBEIS, ONS

OIL

Until the 1960s Britain imported almost all its oil supplies. In 1969 oil was discovered in the Arbroath field in the North Sea. The first oilfield to be brought into production was Argyll in 1975, and since the mid-1970s Britain has been a major producer of crude oil.

To date, the UK has produced around 3.9 billion tonnes of oil. It is estimated that there are around 481 million tonnes remaining to be produced. Licences for exploration and production are granted to companies by the Oil and Gas Authority. As at July 2019, there were 285 offshore oil and gas fields in production. Total UK oil production peaked in 1999 but is now on a long-term trajectory of gradual decline. Production stood at 52.2 million tonnes in 2019, just over a third of the 1999 level. Profits from oil production are subject to a special tax regime with different taxes applying depending on the date of approval of each field.

INDIGENOUS PRODUCTION AND REFINERY RECEIPTS
Thousand tonnes

	2018	2019
Indigenous production	51,234	52,186
Crude oil	47,550	48,743
*NGLs	3,320	3,074
Refinery receipts	58,397	59,158

* Natural Gas Liquids: condensates and petroleum gases derived at onshore treatment plants
Source: DBEIS

DELIVERIES OF PETROLEUM PRODUCTS FOR INLAND CONSUMPTION BY ENERGY USE
Thousand tonnes

	2018	2019
Transport	49,999	49,470
Industry	2,397	2,153
Domestic	2,290	2,267
Other	3,351	3,381
Total	58,388	57,271

Source: DBEIS

COAL

Mines were in private ownership until 1947 when they were nationalised and came under the management of the National Coal Board, later the British Coal Corporation. The corporation held a near monopoly on coal production until 1994 when the industry was restructured. Under the Coal Industry Act 1994, the Coal Authority was established to take over ownership of coal reserves and to issue licences to private mining companies. The Coal Authority is also responsible for the physical legacy of mining, eg subsidence damage claims that are not the responsibility of licensees, and for holding and making available all existing records. It also publishes current data on the coal industry on its website (**W** www.gov.uk/government/organisations/the-coal-authority).

The mines owned by the British Coal Corporation were sold as five separate businesses in 1994 and coal production is now undertaken entirely in the private sector. Coal output was around 50 million tonnes a year in 1994 but has since declined. In 2019, coal output stood at a record low of 2.2 million tonnes, a decrease of 16 per cent on 2018 and about 7 per cent of the value recorded at the start of the century. The decrease was mainly due to a decrease in demand for coal fired electricity. Deep mine production of coal virtually ceased and accounted for only 5 per cent of production, while surface mined production decreased by 19 per cent. As at 31 December 2019, there were eight deep mines and nine surface mines in production in the UK, additionally one deep mine and one surface mine are in 'care and maintenance'.

The main consumer of coal in the UK is the electricity supply industry. Coal supplies 3 per cent of the UK's electricity needs, but as indigenous production has declined imports have continued to make up the shortfall and now represent 82 per cent of UK coal supply, 37 per cent of which is currently supplied from Russia.

UK government policy is to meet the long-term challenges posed by climate change while continuing to ensure secure, clean and affordable energy. Coal's carbon emissions are high compared to other fuels so the UK government is committed to ending unabated coal generation by 2024. In the future generating mix carbon emissions will need to be managed through the introduction of abatement technologies including carbon capture and storage (CCS).

CCS attempts to mitigate the effects of global warming by capturing the carbon dioxide emissions from power stations that burn fossil fuels, preventing the gas from being released into the atmosphere, and storing it in underground geological formations. CCS is still in its infancy and only through its successful demonstration and development will it be possible for coal to remain a part of a low-carbon UK energy mix. As part of a wider package of reforms to the electricity market, the government will also be introducing an Emissions Performance Standard, which will limit the emissions from new fossil fuel power stations.

INLAND COAL USE
Thousand tonnes

	2018	2019
Fuel producers		
Electricity generators	6,655	2,906
Coke manufacture	1,766	1,809
Blast furnaces	1,156	1,135
Heat generation	6	6
Patent fuel manufacture	194	144
Final consumption		
Industry	1,581	1,426
Transport	15	15
Domestic	518	492
Public administration	26	19
Commercial	5	5
Agriculture	0	0
Miscellaneous	7	7

Source: DBEIS

COAL PRODUCTION AND FOREIGN TRADE
Thousand tonnes

	2018	2019
Surface mining	2,556	2,067
Deep-mined	24	99
Imports	10,144	6,529
Exports	(634)	(740)
*Total supply	11,922	7,971
Total demand	11,929	7,963

* Includes stock change
Source: DBEIS

GAS

From the late 18th century gas in Britain was produced from coal. In the 1960s town gas began to be produced from oil-based feedstocks using imported oil. In 1965 gas was discovered in the North Sea in the West Sole field, which became the first gasfield in production in 1967, and from the late 1960s natural gas began to replace town gas. From October 1998 Britain was connected to the continental European gas system via a pipeline from Bacton, Norfolk to Zeebrugge, Belgium. Gas is transported through 278,000km of mains pipeline including 7,600km of high-pressure gas pipelines owned and operated in the UK by National Grid Gas plc.

The gas industry in Britain was nationalised in 1949 and operated as the Gas Council. The Gas Council was replaced by the British Gas Corporation in 1972 and the industry became more centralised. The British Gas Corporation was privatised in 1986 as British Gas plc. In 1993 the Monopolies and Mergers Commission found that British Gas's integrated business in Great Britain as a gas trader and the owner of the gas transportation system could operate against the public interest. In February 1997, British Gas demerged its trading arm to become two separate companies, BG plc and Centrica plc. In February 2016, Royal Dutch Shell announced that it had acquired BG Group, whose principal business was finding and developing gas reserves and building gas markets. Its core operations are located in the UK, South America, Egypt, Trinidad and Tobago, Kazakhstan and India. Centrica runs the trading and services operations under the British Gas brand name in Great Britain. In October 2000 BG demerged its pipeline business, Transco, which became part of Lattice Group, finally merging with the National Grid Group in 2002 to become National Grid Transco plc.

In July 2005 National Grid Transco plc changed its name to National Grid plc and Transco plc became National Grid Gas plc. In the same year National Grid Gas also completed the sale of four of its eight gas distribution networks. The distribution networks transport gas at lower pressures, which eventually supply the consumers such as domestic customers. The Scotland and south-east of England networks were sold to Scotia Gas Networks. The Wales and south-west network was sold to Wales & West Utilities and the network in the north-east to Northern Gas Networks. This was the biggest change in the corporate structure of gas infrastructure since privatisation in 1986.

Competition was gradually introduced into the industrial gas market from 1986. Supply of gas to the domestic market was opened to companies other than British Gas, starting in April 1996 with a pilot project in the West Country and Wales, with the rest of the UK following soon after.

Declines in UK indigenous gas production and increasing demand led to the UK becoming a net importer of gas once more in 2004. With the depletion of the UK Continental Shelf reserves, UK annual gas production has experienced decline since the turn of the century, where annual production is 65 per cent below the peak recorded in 2000. As part of the Energy Act 2008, the government planned to strengthen regulation of the offshore gas supply infrastructure, to allow private sector investment to help maintain UK energy supplies.

In 2012, it was estimated that there could be over 200 trillion cubic feet of untapped gas underneath Lincolnshire. Trapped inside rock formations, the gas is known as shale gas and the process to release the gas is called hydraulic fracturing or fracking, whereby water, chemicals and sand are pumped into a drilled well at high pressure. A further investigation by the British Geological Survey in 2012 claimed that there could in fact be up to 1,300 trillion cubic feet of gas but opponents to the process raised concerns that fracking results in more greenhouse gas emissions than conventional gas, damages the environment significantly and that it may cause seismic tremors.

CENTRICA PLC, Millstream, Maidenhead Road, Windsor, Berkshire SL4 5GD **T** 01753-494000 **W** www.centrica.com
Chair, Scott Wheway
Chief Executive, Chris O'Shea

NATIONAL GRID PLC, 1–3 Strand, London WC2N 5EH
T 0207-0043 000 **W** www.nationalgrid.com
Chair, Sir Peter Gershon, CBE
Chief Executive, John Pettigrew

UK GAS CONSUMPTION BY INDUSTRY
GWh

	2018	2019
Domestic	312,770	309,934
Industry	102,966	101,766
Public administration	37,697	36,961
Commercial	47,541	47,871
Agriculture	995	1,078
Non-energy use	4,807	4,663
Miscellaneous	10,105	9,837
Total gas consumption	516,880	512,110
Source: DBEIS		

ELECTRICITY

The first power station in Britain generating electricity for public supply began operating in 1882. In the 1930s a national transmission grid was developed, and it was reconstructed and extended in the 1950s and 1960s. Power stations were operated by the Central Electricity Generating Board.

Under the Electricity Act 1989, 12 regional electricity companies, responsible for the distribution of electricity from the national grid to consumers, were formed from the former area electricity boards in England and Wales. Four companies were formed from the Central Electricity Generating Board: three generating companies (National Power plc, Nuclear Electric plc and Powergen plc) and the National Grid Company plc, which owned and operated the transmission system in England and Wales. National Power and Powergen were floated on the stock market in 1991.

National Power was demerged in October 2000 to form two separate companies: International Power plc and Innogy plc, which manages the bulk of National Power's UK assets. Nuclear Electric was split into two parts in 1996.

The National Grid Company was floated on the stock market in 1995 and formed a new holding company, National Grid Group. National Grid Group completed a merger with Lattice in 2002 to form National Grid Transco, a public limited company (*see* Gas).

Following privatisation, generators and suppliers in England and Wales traded via the Electricity Pool. A competitive wholesale trading market known as NETA (New Electricity Trading Arrangements) replaced the Electricity Pool in March 2001, and was extended to include Scotland via the British Electricity Transmissions and Trading Arrangements (BETTA) in 2005. As part of BETTA, National Grid became the system operator for all transmission. The introduction of competition into the domestic electricity market was completed in May 1999.

In Scotland, three new companies were formed under the Electricity Act 1989: Scottish Power plc and Scottish Hydro-Electric plc, which were responsible for generation, transmission, distribution and supply; and Scottish Nuclear Ltd. Scottish Power and Scottish Hydro-Electric were floated on the stock market in 1991. Scottish Hydro-Electric merged with Southern Electric in 1998 to become Scottish and Southern Energy plc. Scottish Nuclear was incorporated into British Energy in 1996. In 2009, British Energy was acquired by French multinational EDF and rebranded EDF Energy.

In Northern Ireland, Northern Ireland Electricity plc (NIE) was set up in 1993 under a 1991 Order in Council. In 1993 it was floated on the stock market and in 1998 it became part of the Viridian Group (now Energia Group) and was responsible for distribution and supply until NIE was sold to the Electricity Supply Board of Ireland in December 2010. In June 2010, Airtricity became the first new electricity supplier since the Northern Ireland electricity market was opened to competition in 2007.

On 14 December 2020 the government published 'Powering our Net Zero Future', a White Paper with net zero and efforts to fight climate change at its core. This built on a 2011 White Paper 'Planning Our Electric Future: a White Paper for Secure, Affordable and Low-carbon Electricity' which recognised that extensive investment was needed to update the grid and build new power stations. Currently, 17.3 per cent of the UK electricity generation comes from nuclear reactors, a process by which uranium atoms are split to produce heat through a chemical process known as fission. While nuclear power stations will close gradually over the next decade, with only one expected to produce power beyond 2030, there are plans in place for a new generation of reactors to be built, the first of which is expected to be running by 2025. A significant proportion of the UK's electricity still comes from burning fossil fuels and, in 2019, natural gas provided 40.6 per cent of electricity generation, coal provided 2.1 per cent – a record low – and 0.3 per cent was provided from oil. However, the picture is changing; renewables generated a record of 37.1 per cent of the UK's electricity in 2019, up from 33.1 per cent in 2018.

Interconnecting cables import and export electricity to Europe. These link the UK to the grids of France, the Netherlands and Ireland. A new 'interconnector' was launched in January 2019, connecting the UK to the Belgian grid. In 2019, the UK was a net importer of electricity via these cables, totalling 21.1TWh (terawatt hours), or 6.1 per cent of electricity supplied to the UK grid. The UK's only net exporting system was the Ireland-Wales interconnector.

On 30 September 2003 the Electricity Association, the industry's main trade association, was replaced with three separate trade bodies: the Association of Electricity Producers; the Energy Networks Association; and the Energy Retail Association. In April 2012, following a merger between the Association of Electricity Producers, the Energy Retail Association and the UK Business Council for Sustainable Energy, Energy UK – the new trade association for the gas and electricity sector – was established.

ENERGY NETWORKS ASSOCIATION, 4 More London Riverside, London SE1 2AU **T** 020-7706 5100
W www.energynetworks.org
Chief Executive, David Smith

ENERGY UK, 1st Floor, 26 Finsbury Square, London EC2A 1DS
T 020-7930 9390 **W** www.energy-uk.org.uk
Chief Executive, Emma Pinchbeck

ELECTRICITY PRODUCTION, SUPPLY AND
CONSUMPTION
GWh

	2018	2019
Electricity produced		
Nuclear	65,064	56,184
Hydro	5,444	5,935
Wind, wave and solar photovoltaics	69,651	77,267
Coal	16,831	6,891
Oil	1,063	1,119
Gas	131,490	131,931
Other renewables	34,954	37,314
Other	5,780	6,363
Total	330,277	323,005
Electricity supplied		
Production	330,277	323,005
*Other sources	2,498	1,756
Imports	21,332	24,556
Exports	(2,225)	(3,385)
Total	351,883	345,931
Electricity consumed		
Industry	93,871	91,617
Transport	4,984	5,456
Other	201,589	198,187
Domestic	105,065	103,825
Public administration	18,248	17,744
Commercial	73,961	72,413
Agriculture	4,316	4,205
Total	300,444	295,259

* Pumped storage production
Source: DBEIS

GAS AND ELECTRICITY SUPPLIERS

With the gas and electricity markets open, most suppliers offer their customers both services. The majority of gas/electricity companies have become part of larger multi-utility companies, often operating internationally.

As part of measures to reduce the UK's carbon output, the government has outlined plans to introduce 'smart meters' to all UK homes. Smart meters perform the traditional meter function of measuring energy consumption, in addition to more advanced functions such as allowing energy suppliers to communicate directly with their customers and removing the need for meter readings and bill estimates. The meters also allow domestic customers to have direct access to energy consumption information.

The following list comprises a selection of major suppliers offering gas and electricity. After E.ON absorbed Npower, one of its major competitors, in April 2019, the 'Big Six' energy suppliers in the UK became the 'Big Five'. In 2020, SSE Energy Services was sold to OVO Energy, a new challenger and now a major supplier. Nonetheless, in recent years the dominance of these companies has been declining. The 'Big Five', including OVO Energy, claimed a combined market share 72.8 per cent in 2020, down from 90.2 per cent in 2015. Organisations in italics are subsidiaries of the companies listed in capital letters directly above.

ENGLAND, SCOTLAND AND WALES

CENTRICA PLC, Millstream, Maidenhead Road, Windsor, Berkshire SL4 5GD **T** 01753-494000 **W** www.centrica.com
British Gas, PO Box 227, Rotherham S98 1PD **T** 0800-072 8625 **W** www.britishgas.co.uk
EDF ENERGY, 90 Whitfield Street, London W1T 4EZ **T** 0333-200 5100 **W** www.edfenergy.com
E.ON UK, Westward Way Business Park, Coventry, CV4 8LG **T** 0345-052 0000 **W** www.eonenergy.com
Npower, Windmill Business Park, Whitehall Way, Swindon SN5 6PB **T** 0800-073 3000 **W** www.npower.com

OVO ENERGY, 1 Rivergate Temple Quay, Bristol, BS1 6ED **T** 0330-303 5063 **W** www.ovoenergy.com
SCOTTISH POWER, 320 St Vincent Street, Glasgow G2 5AD **T** 0800-027 0072 **W** www.scottishpower.co.uk

NORTHERN IRELAND

AIRTRICITY (a member of SSE plc), Millennium House, 25 Great Victoria Street, Belfast BT2 7AQ **T** 0345-600 9093 **W** www.sseairtricity.com/uk
ELECTRIC IRELAND, 1 Cromac Quay, The Gasworks, Belfast BT7 2JD **T** 0345-600 5335 **W** www.electricireland.com
POWERNI (a member of Energia Group), 120 Malone Road, Belfast BT9 5HT **T** 0345-745 5455 **W** www.powerni.co.uk

REGULATION OF THE GAS AND ELECTRICITY INDUSTRIES

The Office of Gas and Electricity Markets (OFGEM) regulates the gas and electricity industries in Great Britain. It was formed in 1999 by the merger of the Office of Gas Supply and the Office of Electricity Regulation. OFGEM's overriding aim is to protect and promote the interests of all gas and electricity customers by promoting competition and regulating monopolies. It is governed by an authority and its powers are provided for under the Gas Act 1986, the Electricity Act 1989, the Competition Act 1998, the Utilities Act 2000, the Enterprise Act 2002 and the Consumer Rights Ace 2015.

THE OFFICE OF GAS AND ELECTRICITY MARKETS (OFGEM), 10 South Colonnade, Canary Wharf, London E14 4PU **T** 020-7901 7000 **W** www.ofgem.gov.uk

NUCLEAR POWER

Nuclear reactors began to supply electricity to the national grid in 1956. There are presently 15 reactors at eight sites which generated 17.3 per cent of the UK's electricity in 2019. Approximately half of this capacity is due to be retired by 2025. In December 2015, the final Magnox reactor, and last remaining nuclear plant in Wales (Wylfa 1) began decommissioning after 44 years of operation. This left 14 active advanced gas-cooled reactors (AGR) and one pressurised water reactor (PWR), Sizewell B in Suffolk. The AGRs and PWR are owned by a private company, EDF Energy. Apart from Sizewell B, which first produced power in 1995, the seven other sites are expected to close by 2035. The UK's ageing nuclear power stations have seen the decline of nuclear generation over the past decade, as a result of prolonged outages which have reduced operational nuclear capacity, with the 2019 share of generation the lowest since 2010.

In June 2011, eight new sites across the UK were selected for locations of new nuclear power stations, and EDF Energy was contracted to construct four new European Pressurised Reactors (EPRs), two of which were scheduled to be established at Hinkley Point, with the other two at Sizewell. However, the future many of these projects looks uncertain due to delays, lower energy demand, cheaper renewable energy and developers pulling out. The fate of the two EPRs at Sizewell C has yet to be determined.

Hinkley Point C, which was the first new nuclear power plant to begin construction in the UK in 20 years, is due to commission in the mid-2020s. The French firm EDF Energy, which is set to finance two-thirds of the site, had approved the funding but critics warned of environmental damage, increasing costs and concern over the implications of nuclear sites being built in the UK by foreign investors. However, in September 2016, the prime minister gave the go ahead for the nuclear power station after the government imposed significant new safeguards for future projects. The initial estimated cost of £18bn has since increased to £21.5–22.5bn. The combined 3.2GW capacity of its two EPRs is expected to deliver around 7 per cent of the country's current electricity needs, which is enough to power the equivalent of six million homes. Nuclear power continues to be a reliable source of low carbon electricity, with analysis suggesting that additional nuclear beyond Hinkley Point C will be required as the UK seeks to achieve net-zero carbon emissions by 2050.

The UK Energy White Paper, published in December 2020, outlines plans for advanced nuclear innovation, including a £385 million fund for the development of Small Modular Reactors (SMRs) and Advanced Modular Reactors (AMRs). The estimated worth of the global market for SMRs and AMRs is expected to be between £250bn and £400bn by 2035. With the controversially high costs associated with large-scale nuclear power plants, SMRs have the potential to provide cost-competitive nuclear power by the early-2030s and may be suitable for a wide range of sites across the country.

In April 2005 the responsibility for the decommissioning of civil nuclear reactors and other nuclear facilities used in research and development was handed to the Nuclear Decommissioning Authority (NDA). The NDA is a non-departmental public body, funded mainly by the DBEIS. The total planned expenditure for the NDA in 2020–21 was £3.5bn. Until April 2007, UK Nirex was responsible for the disposal of intermediate and some low-level nuclear waste. After this date Nirex was integrated into the NDA and renamed the Radioactive Waste Management directorate.

There are currently 17 nuclear sites owned by the NDA that are in various stages of decommissioning, including the world's first commercial power station at Calder Hall on the Sellafield site in Cumbria and Windscale, which produced plutonium in the 1950s to be used for military purposes. The responsibilities of the NDA include: decommissioning and cleaning up nuclear facilities; ensuring that all waste, including radioactive and non-radioactive products, are safely managed; developing nationwide strategies and plans for Low Level Waste; implementing a long-term plan for the management of nuclear waste; and scrutinising EDF Energy's decommissioning plans, which includes the fleet of AGR nuclear stations.

In 2019, electricity supplied from nuclear sources accounted for 56TWh, equating to 17.3 per cent of total electricity generation or 7.3 per cent of total energy supplied.

Nuclear power has its advantages: reactors emit virtually no carbon dioxide and uranium prices remain relatively steady. However, the advantages of low emissions are countered by the high costs of construction and difficulties in disposing of nuclear waste. Currently, the only method is to store it securely until it has slowly decayed to safe levels. Public distrust persists despite the advances in safety technology. Following the tsunami which struck Japan in March 2011 and the level 7 meltdowns of three reactors in the Fukushima Daiichi Nuclear Plant, the safety of nuclear reactors was brought further into public interest and became a government priority.

SAFETY AND REGULATION
The Office for Nuclear Regulation (ONR) is responsible for regulation of nuclear safety and security across the UK. The Civil Nuclear Constabulary, a specialised armed force created in April 2005, is responsible for policing the industry.

RENEWABLE SOURCES

Progress was made towards the UK's target of consuming 15 per cent of energy from renewable sources by 2020, introduced in the 2009 EU Renewable Directive, as 12.3 per cent of energy consumption came from renewable sources in 2019, up from 11.2 per cent in 2018. Renewable sources provided 37.1 per cent of the electricity generated in the UK in 2019, up from 33.1 per cent in 2018, with record annual generations for wind, solar and bioenergy. This rise is attributed to a 6.5 per cent increase in capacity and a decrease in total electricity generation. Yearly weather conditions were

unfavourable (for wind) but sunlight hours (solar) and average rainfall (hydro) were up slightly on 2018.

In 2019 onshore wind was the leading technology in terms of capacity for a second year in a row, at 29.9 per cent, closely followed by solar photovoltaics (28.3 per cent), which had been the leading technology from 2015 and 2017. Onshore wind capacity increased by 4.2 per cent from 2018, and average wind speeds were up so that onshore wind generation increased by 6.5 per cent. The largest increase in capacity was for offshore wind which increased by 21 per cent from 2018, generation from offshore wind also increased by 20 per cent in 2019. Despite no new capacity in 2019, hydro generation increased by 9.0 per cent as a result of more rainfall. Solar photovoltaic generation grew by just 1.4 per cent as average sunlight hours were down and capacity increased by just 2.1 per cent. Meanwhile, heat generation from renewable sources increased by 2.4 per cent, primarily due to increases in generation from wood fuel.

The government's principal mechanism for developing renewable energy sources is the Contracts for Difference (CfD) scheme. The CfD scheme recently replaced the Renewables Obligation (RO) which had been in place since 2002. It aims to increase the contribution of electricity from renewables in the UK by offering long-term contracts to new low carbon electricity generators. These guarantee a certain price for their generated electricity, which helps to tackle the risks and uncertainties associated with investing in renewables. The RO closed to new capacity in March 2017, but will continue to provide support to existing generators for 20 years.

The Feed-in Tariff (FIT) scheme has run alongside CfDs and the RO, providing incentives to encourage the uptake of small-scale low carbon electricity generation technologies, principally renewables such as solar photovoltaics, wind and hydro-electricity. The scheme was hugely successful in attracting investment; however, the scheme closed to new registrations in April 2019. Following this, the government laid legislation in June 2019 to introduce a new supplier-led smart export guarantee (SEG) in Great Britain from 1 January 2020. Under the SEG, licensed electricity suppliers (with 150,000 domestic customers or more) are required to offer small-scale low-carbon generators a price per kWh for electricity exported to the grid.

In addition to these schemes, the Renewable Heat Incentive (RHI) aims to promote the use of renewable heating systems. The RHI was originally introduced in November 2011 to provide a long-term financial incentive to support the uptake of renewable heat in the non-domestic sector. In April 2014, the RHI was extended to cover the domestic sector replacing the renewable heat premium payment scheme which closed in March 2013. Participants of the scheme receive tariff payments for the heat generated from an eligible renewable heating system which is heating a single dwelling.

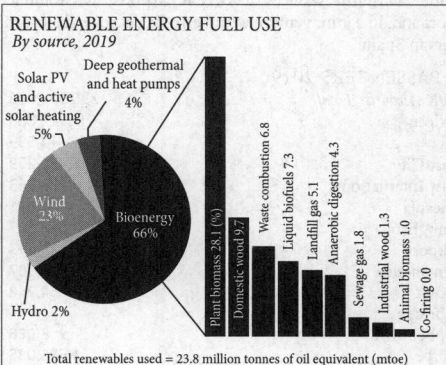

RENEWABLE ENERGY FUEL USE
By source, 2019

Solar PV and active solar heating 5%

Deep geothermal and heat pumps 4%

Wind 23%

Bioenergy 66%

Hydro 2%

Plant biomass 28.1 (%)
Domestic wood 9.7
Waste combustion 6.8
Liquid biofuels 7.3
Landfill gas 5.1
Anaerobic digestion 4.3
Sewage gas 1.8
Industrial wood 1.3
Animal biomass 1.0
Co-firing 0.0

Total renewables used = 23.8 million tonnes of oil equivalent (mtoe)

Source: Department for Business, Energy and Industrial Strategy, 2019

TRANSPORT

CIVIL AVIATION

Since the privatisation of British Airways in 1987, UK airlines have been operated entirely by the private sector. In 2019, total capacity of British airlines amounted to 58 billion tonne-km. UK airlines carried around 153 million passengers; 142 million on scheduled services and 11 million on charter flights. Passenger traffic through UK airports increased by 2 per cent in 2019. Traffic at the six main London area airports (Gatwick, Heathrow, London City, Luton, Southend and Stansted) increased by 2 per cent over 2018 and other UK regional airports saw an increase of 1 per cent.

Leading British airlines include British Airways, EasyJet, Tui Airways and Virgin Atlantic. Irish airline Ryanair also operates frequent flights from the UK.

There are around 126 licensed civil aerodromes in Britain, with Heathrow and Gatwick handling the highest volume of passengers.

The Civil Aviation Authority (CAA), an independent statutory body, is responsible for the regulation of UK airlines. This includes economic and airspace regulation, air safety, consumer protection and environmental research and consultancy. All commercial airline companies must be granted an air operator's certificate, which is issued by the CAA to operators meeting the required safety standards. The CAA issues airport safety licences, which must be obtained by any airport used for public transport and training flights. All British-registered aircraft must be granted an airworthiness certificate, and the CAA issues professional licences to pilots, flight crew, ground engineers and air traffic controllers. The CAA also manages the Air Travel Organiser's Licence (ATOL), the UK's principal travel protection scheme. The CAA's costs are met entirely from charges on those whom it regulates; there is no direct government funding of the CAA's work.

The Transport Act 2000 separated the CAA from its subsidiary, National Air Traffic Services (NATS), which provides air traffic control services to aircraft flying in UK airspace and over the eastern part of the North Atlantic. NATS is a public private partnership (PPP) between the Airline Group (a consortium of UK airlines), which holds 42 per cent of the shares; NATS staff, who hold 5 per cent; UK airport operator LHR Airports Limited, which holds 4 per cent, and the government, which holds 49 per cent and a golden share. NATS handled 2.6m flights in 2019, from its centres at Swanwick, Hampshire and Prestwick, Ayrshire. NATS also provides air traffic services at 14 UK airports; at Gibraltar Airport and, in a joint venture with Ferrovial, at several airport towers in Spain.

AIR PASSENGERS 2019

All UK Airports: Total	296,924,188
Aberdeen	2,912,883
Barra	14,599
Belfast City	2,455,259
Belfast International	6,278,563
Benbecula	34,691
Birmingham	12,650,607
Blackpool	15,213
Bournemouth	803,307
Bristol	8,964,242
Cambridge	–
Campbeltown	8,086
Cardiff	1,656,085
City of Derry (Eglinton)	203,777
Doncaster Sheffield	1,407,862
Dundee	20,917
Durham Tees Valley	142,080
East Midlands	4,675,411
Edinburgh	14,737,497
Exeter	1,021,784
Gatwick	46,086,089
Glasgow	8,847,100
Gloucestershire	–
Heathrow	80,890,031
Humberside	204,463
Inverness	938,232
Islay	34,992
Isle of Man	854,676
Isles of Scilly (St Mary's)	93,927
Kirkwall	172,625
Lands End (St Just)	64,056
Leeds Bradford	3,992,862
Lerwick (Tingwall)	3,309
Liverpool	5,045,991
London City	5,122,271
Luton	18,216,207
Lydd	39
Manchester	29,397,357
Newcastle	5,203,624
Newquay	461,478
Norwich	530,238
Oxford (Kidlington)	–
Prestwick	640,055
Scatsta	109,480
Shoreham	–
Southampton	1,781,457
Southend	2,035,535
Stansted	28,124,292
Stornoway	131,441
Sumburgh	267,456
Teeside	150,735
Tiree	12,178
Wick	13,149
Channel Islands Airports	2,698,478
Alderney	53,155
Guernsey	882,374
Jersey	1,762,949

Source: Civil Aviation Authority

CAA, Aviation House, Beehive Ringroad, Crawley, West Sussex RH6 0YR **T** 0330-022 1500 **W** www.caa.co.uk

Heathrow Airport	**T** 0844-335 1801
Gatwick Airport	**T** 0344-892 0322
Manchester Airport	**T** 0808-169 7030
Stansted Airport	**T** 0844-335 1803

BRITISH AIRLINES

BRITISH AIRWAYS, PO Box 365, Waterside, Harmondsworth UB7 0GB **T** 0844-493 0787 **W** www.britishairways.com

EASYJET, Hangar 89, London Luton Airport LU2 9PF **T** 0330-365 5000 **W** www.easyjet.com

TUI AIRWAYS, Wigmore House, Wigmore Place, Wigmore Lane, Luton, Beds LU2 9TN **T** 0203-451 2688 **W** www.tui.co.uk

VIRGIN ATLANTIC, Fleming Way, Crawley, W. Sussex RH10 9DF **T** 0344-874 7747 **W** www.virginatlantic.com

RAILWAYS

The railway network in Britain was developed by private companies in the 19th century. In 1948 the main railway companies were nationalised and were run by a public authority, the British Transport Commission. The commission was replaced by the British Railways Board in 1963, operating as British Rail. On 1 April 1994, responsibility for managing the track and railway infrastructure passed to a newly formed company, Railtrack plc. In October 2001 Railtrack was put into administration under the Railways Act 1993. In October 2002 Railtrack was taken out of administration and replaced by the not-for-profit company Network Rail. The British Railways Board continued as operator of all train services until 1996–7, when they were sold or franchised to the private sector.

The Strategic Rail Authority (SRA) was created to provide strategic leadership to the rail industry and formally came into being on 1 February 2001 following the passing of the Transport Act 2000. In January 2002 it published its first strategic plan, setting out the strategic priorities for Britain's railways over the next ten years. In addition to its coordinating role, the SRA was responsible for allocating government funding to the railways and awarding and monitoring the franchises for operating rail services.

On 15 July 2004 the transport secretary announced a new structure for the rail industry in the white paper *The Future of Rail*. These proposals were implemented under the Railways Act 2005, which abolished the SRA, passing most of its functions to the Department for Transport; established the Rail Passengers Council as a single national body, dissolving the regional committees; and gave devolved transport to Scotland and Wales more say in decisions at a local level. In addition, responsibility for railway safety regulation was transferred to the Office of Rail Regulation from the Health and Safety Executive.

OFFICE OF RAIL AND ROAD

The Office of Rail and Road (ORR), previously known as the Office of Rail Regulation, was established on 5 July 2004 by the Railways and Transport Safety Act 2003, replacing the Office of the Rail Regulator. In April 2015 it acquired responsibility for monitoring Highways England in addition to its existing role as the railway industry's economic and safety regulator and changed its name to better reflect its functions. The ORR regulates Network Rail's stewardship of the national network, licenses operators, approves network access agreements, and enforces domestic competition law. The ORR is a non-ministerial government department led by a board appointed by the Secretary of State for Transport and chaired by Declan Collier.

SERVICES

For privatisation, under the Railways Act 1993, domestic passenger services were divided into 25 train operating units, which were franchised to private sector operators via a competitive tendering process. The train operators formed the Association of Train Operating Companies (ATOC) to act as the official voice of the passenger rail industry and provide its members with a range of services enabling them to comply with conditions imposed on them through their franchise agreements and operating licences.

As at December 2020 there were 31 passenger train operating companies: Avanti West Coast, c2c, Caledonian Sleeper, Chiltern Railways, CrossCountry, East Midlands Railway, Eurostar, Gatwick Express, Grand Central, Great Northern, Great Western Railway, Greater Anglia, Heathrow Express, Hull Trains, Island Line, London North Eastern Railway, London Northwestern Railway, London Overground, London Underground, Merseyrail, Northern, ScotRail, South Western Railway, Southeastern, Southern, Stansted Express, TfL Rail, Thameslink, TransPennine Express, Transport for Wales, West Midlands Railway.

Network Rail publishes a national timetable which contains details of rail services operated over the UK network and sea ferry services which provide connections with Ireland, the Isle of Man, the Isle of Wight, the Channel Islands and some European destinations.

The national rail enquiries service offers information about train times and fares for any part of the country, Transport for London (TfL) provides London-specific travel information for all modes of travel and Eurostar provides information for international channel tunnel rail services:

NATIONAL RAIL ENQUIRIES
  T 0345-748 4950 **W** www.nationalrail.co.uk

TRANSPORT FOR LONDON
  T 0343-222 1234 **W** www.tfl.gov.uk

EUROSTAR
  T 0343-186186 **W** www.eurostar.com

CONSUMER WATCHDOGS

Previously known as Passenger Focus, Transport Focus is the national consumer watchdog for bus, tram, coach and rail passengers in England. Under The Infrastructure Act 2015 Transport Focus's role was expanded to also represent users of the strategic road network. The entity is funded by the Department for Transport and is an executive non-departmental public body.

Established in July 2000, London TravelWatch is the operating name of the official watchdog organisation representing the interests of transport users in and around the capital. Officially known as the London Transport Users' Committee, it is sponsored and funded by the London Assembly and is independent of the transport operators. London TravelWatch represents users of buses, the Underground, river and rail services in and around London, including Eurostar and Heathrow Express, Croydon Tramlink and the Docklands Light Railway. The interests of pedestrians, cyclists and motorists are also represented, as are those of taxi users.

FREIGHT

On privatisation in 1996, British Rail's bulk freight operations were sold to North and South Railways – subsequently called English, Welsh and Scottish Railways (EWS). In 2007, EWS was bought by Deutsche Bahn and is now DB Cargo UK. The other major companies in the rail freight sector are: Colas Rail, Direct Rail Services, Freightliner and GB Railfreight (GBRf). In 2019–20 total volume of freight moved by rail amounted to 16.6 billion net tonne-kilometres, the lowest total since 1996–7 due to the coronavirus pandemic and a sharp fall in coal transportation.

NETWORK RAIL

Network Rail is responsible for the tracks, bridges, tunnels, level crossings, viaducts and main stations that form Britain's rail network. In addition to providing the timetables for the passenger and freight operators, Network Rail is also responsible for all the signalling and electrical control equipment needed to operate the rail network and for monitoring and reporting performance across the industry.

In September 2014, Network Rail was reclassified as a public body after being privately run since 2002 as a commercial business which was directly accountable to its members. The members had similar rights to those of shareholders in a public company except they did not receive dividends or share capital and thereby had no financial interest in Network Rail. On 1 July 2015, the 46 public members were dismissed and the company is now accountable directly to parliament through the Secretary of State for Transport. Network Rail is regulated by the ORR and all of its profits are reinvested into maintaining and upgrading the rail infrastructure. In 2019–20 a total of 1.7 billion passenger journeys were made on the rail network, a reduction of 0.8 per cent on 2018–19.

LONDON TRAVELWATCH, Europoint 5–11, Lavington Street, London SE1 0NZ T 020-3176 2999
  W www.londontravelwatch.org.uk

NETWORK RAIL, 1 Eversholt Street, London NW1 2DN
  T 0345-711 4141 W www.networkrail.co.uk

OFFICE OF RAIL AND ROAD, 25 Cabot Square, London E14 4QZ T 020-7282 2000 W www.orr.gov.uk

TRANSPORT FOCUS, Fleetbank House, 2–6 Salisbury Square, London EC4Y 8AE T 0300-123 2350
  W www.transportfocus.org.uk

RAIL SAFETY
On 1 April 2006 responsibility for health and safety policy and enforcement on the railways transferred from the Health and Safety Executive to the Office of Rail Regulation (ORR).

ACCIDENTS ON RAILWAYS

	2018–19	2019–20
Rail incident fatalities		
Passengers	17	12
Railway employees	2	4

SUICIDES AND ATTEMPTED SUICIDES 2019–20
Fatalities   283

Source: RSSB – *Annual Safety Performance Report 2019–20*

OTHER RAIL SYSTEMS
Responsibility for the London Underground passed from the government to the Mayor and Transport for London on 15 July 2003, with a public-private partnership already in place. Plans for a public-private partnership for London Underground were pushed through by the government in February 2002 despite opposition from the Mayor of London and a range of transport organisations. Under the PPP, long-term contracts with private companies were estimated to enable around £16bn to be invested in renewing and upgrading the London Underground's infrastructure over 15 years. In July 2007, Metronet, which was responsible for two of three PPP contracts, went into administration; TfL took over both contracts. Responsibility for stations, trains, operations, signalling and safety remains in the public sector. In 2019–20, there were 2.1 billion passenger journeys.

In addition to Glasgow Subway (12.7 million passenger journeys in 2019–20) and Edinburgh Trams (7.45 million passenger journeys in 2019), Britain has eight other light rail and tram systems: Blackpool Tramway, Docklands Light Railway (DLR), London Tramlink, Manchester Metrolink, Midland Metro, Nottingham Express Transit (NET), Sheffield Supertram and Tyne and Wear Metro. These eight accounted for 263.4 million passenger journeys in 2019–20; a decrease of 4.2 per cent on 2018–19 figures.

THE CHANNEL TUNNEL
The earliest recorded scheme for a submarine transport connection between Britain and France was in 1802. Tunnelling began simultaneously on both sides of the Channel three times: in 1881, in the early 1970s, and on 1 December 1987, when construction workers bored the first of the three tunnels which form the Channel Tunnel. Engineers 'holed through' the first tunnel (the service tunnel) on 1 December 1990 and tunnelling was completed in June 1991. The tunnel was officially inaugurated by the Queen and President Mitterrand of France on 6 May 1994.

The submarine link comprises two rail tunnels, each carrying trains in one direction, which measure 7.6m (24.93ft) in diameter. Between them lies a smaller service tunnel, measuring 4.8m (15.75ft) in diameter. The service tunnel is linked to the rail tunnels by 130 cross-passages for maintenance and safety purposes. The tunnels are 50km (31 miles) long, 38km (24 miles) of which is under the seabed at an average depth of 40m (132ft). The rail terminals are situated at Folkestone and Calais, and the tunnels go underground at Shakespeare Cliff, Dover and Sangatte, west of Calais.

HIGH SPEED 1
The Channel Tunnel rail link, High Speed 1, runs from Folkestone to St Pancras station, London, with intermediate stations at Ashford and Ebbsfleet in Kent.

Construction of the rail link was financed by the private sector with a substantial government contribution. A private sector consortium, London and Continental Railways Ltd (LCR), comprising Union Railways and the UK operator of Eurostar, owns the rail link and was responsible for its design and construction. The rail link was constructed in two phases: phase one, from the Channel Tunnel to Fawkham Junction, Kent, began in October 1998 and opened to fare-paying passengers on 28 September 2003; phase two, from Southfleet Junction to St Pancras, was completed in November 2007.

Eurostar provides direct services from the UK (London) to Avignon (5 hours 49 minutes), Calais (55 minutes), Disneyland Paris (2 hours 49 minutes), Lille (1 hour 22 minutes), Lyon (4 hours 41 minutes), Marseille (6 hours 26 minutes) and Paris (2 hours 16 minutes) in France; Brussels (1 hour 53 minutes) in Belgium; and Amsterdam (3 hours 52 minutes) and Rotterdam (3 hours 13 minutes) in the Netherlands.

HIGH SPEED 2
A second high speed rail link connecting London and Birmingham, with branches to Manchester and Leeds, was first proposed in 2009 and the legislative process started in 2012. Following significant opposition, particularly from environmental groups, an independent review was conducted in 2019 and Prime Minister Boris Johnson confirmed the project would proceed in February 2020. Construction started in September on phase one, between London and Birmingham, and is set to be completed in 2031. The second phase is expected to open in 2040, at a total cost of £106bn. It is Europe's largest infrastructure project.

ROADS

HIGHWAY AUTHORITIES
The powers and responsibilities of highway authorities in England and Wales are set out in the Highways Act 1980; for Scotland there is separate legislation.

Responsibility for motorways and other trunk roads in Great Britain rests in England with the Secretary of State for Transport, in Scotland with the Scottish government, and in Wales with the Welsh government. The highway authority for non-trunk roads in England, Wales and Scotland is, in general, the local authority in whose area the roads lie. With the establishment of the Greater London Authority in July 2000, Transport for London became the highway authority for roads in London.

In Northern Ireland the Department for Infrastructure is responsible for public roads and their maintenance and construction.

FINANCE

In England all aspects of trunk road and motorway funding are provided directly by the government to Highways England, which operates, maintains and improves a network of motorways and trunk roads around 6,920km (4,300 miles) long, on behalf of the secretary of state. Since 2001 the length of the network that the Highways England is responsible for has been decreasing owing to a policy of de-trunking, which transfers responsibility for non-core roads to local authorities. The government's second road investment strategy, published in 2020, outlines Highways England's five-year objectives which include 12 major new road projects and 52 other schemes. The budget for 2020–25 is £27.4bn, and this includes maintenance, major schemes, traffic management, technology improvements, other programmes and administration costs.

Government support for local authority capital expenditure on roads and other transport infrastructure is provided through grant and credit approvals as part of the Local Transport Plan (LTP). Local authorities bid for resources on the basis of a five-year programme built around delivering integrated transport strategies. As well as covering the structural maintenance of local roads and the construction of major new road schemes, LTP funding also includes smaller-scale safety and traffic management measures with associated improvements for public transport, cyclists and pedestrians.

In Northern Ireland all roads, some 26,000km (16,160 miles) are managed by the Department for Infrastructure (DfI) for Northern Ireland as the sole road authority. The road network is made up of some 300km (185 miles) of motorway, 1,300km (810 miles) of trunk roads and 25,000km (15,534miles) of other roads. The department is also responsible for maintaining some 10,000km (6,210 miles) of footpaths and 5,800 bridges.

For the financial year 2020–21 the DfI open resourcing budget was £418m, and planned expenditure on all infrastructure was £544m. This included maintenance, capital schemes, traffic management and technology improvements.

The Transport Act 2000 gave English and Welsh local authorities (outside London) powers to introduce road-user charging or workplace parking levy schemes. The act requires that the net revenue raised is used to improve local transport services and facilities for at least ten years. The aim is to reduce congestion and encourage greater use of alternative modes of transport. Schemes developed by local authorities require government approval. The UK's first toll road, the M6 Toll, opened in December 2003 and runs for 43.5km (27 miles) around Birmingham from junction 3a to junction 11a on the M6.

Charging schemes in London are allowed under the 1999 Greater London Authority Act. The Central London Congestion Charge Scheme began on 17 February 2003 *(see also Regional Government London).*

ROAD LENGTHS 2019
Miles

	England	Wales	Scotland	Great Britain
Major Roads	22,355	2,720	6,734	31,809
Motorways	1,941	88	296	2,325
Minor Roads	166,793	18,306	30,146	215,246
Total	189,148	21,026	36,880	247,055

Source: Department for Transport

BUSES

The majority of bus services outside London are provided on a commercial basis by private operators. Local authorities have powers to subsidise services where needs are not being met by a commercial service.

Since April 2008 men and women who have attained the state pension age and disabled people who qualify under the categories listed in the Transport Act 2000 have been able to travel for free on any local bus across England between 9.30am and 11pm Monday to Friday and all day on weekends and bank holidays. Local authorities recompense operators for the reduced fare revenue. The age of eligibility for concessionary travel is the female state pension age, regardless of your gender. A similar scheme from age 60 operates in Wales and within London, although there is no time restriction. In Scotland, people aged 60 and over and disabled people have been able to travel for free on any local or long-distance bus since April 2006.

In London, Transport for London (TfL) has overall responsibility for setting routes, service standards and fares for the bus network. Almost all routes are competitively tendered to commercial operators.

In Northern Ireland, passenger transport services are provided by Ulsterbus, Metro (formerly Citybus) and Glider, a new service added in 2018, three wholly owned subsidiaries of the Northern Ireland Transport Holding Company. Along with Northern Ireland Railways, Ulsterbus, Metro and Glider operate under the brand name of Translink and are publicly owned. Ulsterbus is responsible for virtually all bus services in Northern Ireland except Belfast city services, which are operated by Metro and Glider, which connects East Belfast, West Belfast and the Titanic Quarter through the city centre. People living in Northern Ireland aged 60 and over can travel on buses and trains for free once they have obtained a SmartPass from Translink.

LOCAL BUS PASSENGER JOURNEYS 2019–20
No. of journeys (millions)

England	4,069
London	2,091
Scotland	366
Wales	89
Total	4,524

Source: Department for Transport

TAXIS AND PRIVATE HIRE VEHICLES

A taxi is a public transport vehicle with fewer than nine passenger seats, which is licensed to 'ply for hire'. This distinguishes taxis from private hire vehicles (PHVs) which must be booked in advance through an operator. In London, taxis and private hire vehicles are licensed by the Public Carriage Office (PCO), part of TfL. At the end of March 2020 there were 19,000 taxis and 96,000 PHVs licensed in London. Outside London, local authorities are responsible for the licensing of taxis and private hire vehicles operational in their respective administrative areas. At the end of March 2020 there were 67,900 licensed taxis and 230,900 licensed PHVs in England.

ROAD TRAFFIC BY VEHICLE TYPE (UK) 2019

	Billion vehicle miles
All motor vehicles	356.5
Cars & taxis	278.2
Light goods vehicles	55.5
Heavy goods vehicles	17.4
Motorcycles	3
Buses & coaches	2.4

Source: Department for Transport

ROAD SAFETY

The key findings from the Department for Transport's 2019 annual road casualty report found that the total number of reported casualties of all severities in Great Britain in 2019 was 153,158; a 5 per cent decrease from 2018. Of these a total of 1,752 people were killed in 2019; a decrease of almost 2 per cent from 2018. Serious injuries accounted for 25,945 of the casualties and slight injuries for 125,461. Total reported child casualties (0–15 years) decreased by 5 per cent to 13,574 in 2019.

ROAD ACCIDENT CASUALTIES

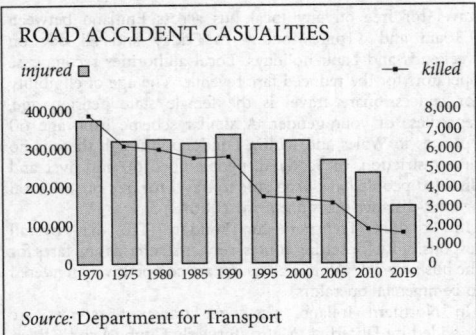

injured □   ● *killed*

Source: Department for Transport

DRIVING LICENCES

It is necessary to hold a valid full licence in order to drive unaccompanied on public roads in the UK. Learner drivers must obtain a provisional driving licence before starting to learn to drive and must then pass theory and practical tests to obtain a full driving licence.

There are separate tests for driving motorcycles, cars, passenger-carrying vehicles (PCVs) and large goods vehicles (LGVs). Drivers must hold full car entitlement before they can apply for PCV or LGV entitlements.

The Driver and Vehicle Licensing Agency (DVLA) ceased the issue of paper licences in March 2000, but those currently in circulation will remain valid until they expire or the details on them change. The photocard driving licence was introduced to comply with the second EC directive on driving licences. This requires a photograph of the driver to be included on all UK licences issued from July 2001. The photocard licence must be renewed every ten years, with fines of up to £1,000 for failure to do so.

To apply for a first photocard driving licence, individuals are required to either apply online or complete the form *Application for a Driving Licence* (D1) and submit by post.

The minimum age for driving motor cars, light goods vehicles up to 3.5 tonnes and motorcycles is 17 (moped, 16). Drivers who collect 12 or more penalty points within three years of qualifying lose their licence and are required to take another test. Forms and leaflets are available from post offices and online (**W** www.gov.uk/dvlaforms or **W** www.gov.uk/government/organisations/driver-and-vehicle-licensing-agency).

The DVLA is responsible for issuing driving licences, registering and licensing vehicles, and collecting excise duty in Great Britain. The Driver and Vehicle Agency (DVA), has similar responsibilities in Northern Ireland.

DRIVING LICENCE FEES *as at December 2020*

	online*/postal
Provisional licence	
Car, motorcycle or moped	£34/£43
Bus or lorry	Free
Changing a provisional licence to a full licence	Free
Renewal	
Renewing an expired licence (must be renewed every 10 years)	£14/£17
At age 70 and over	Free
For medical reasons	Free
Bus or lorry driver entitlement	Free
After disqualification	£65
After disqualification for some drink driving offences†	£90
After revocation (under the New Drivers Act)	£50
Replacing a lost, stolen, defaced or destroyed licence	£20/£20
Adding an entitlement to a full licence	Free
Exchanging	
a paper licence for a photocard licence‡	£20/£20
a full Northern Ireland licence for a full GB licence	Free

a full GB licence for a full EU/EEA or other designated foreign licence	Free
a full EU/EEA or other designated foreign licence for a full GB licence	£43
Changing	
name or address	Free
photo	£14/£17

* Not all services are available online; in these instances just the postal fee is shown. Licence fees differ in Northern Ireland (**W** www.nidirect.gov.uk/the-cost-of-a-driving-licence).

† For an alcohol-related offence where the DVLA need to arrange medical enquiries

‡ If a paper licence is exchanged for a photocard at the same time as name or address details are changed there is no charge

DRIVING TESTS

The Driver and Vehicle Standards Agency (DVSA) is responsible for improving road safety in Great Britain by setting standards for driving and motorcycling and making sure drivers, vehicle operators and MOT garages understand and follow roadworthiness standards. The agency also provides a range of licensing, testing, education and enforcement services.

DRIVING TESTS TAKEN AND PASSED
2019–2020

	Number Taken	Percentage Passed
Practical Test		
Car	1,599,504	45.9
Motorcycle Module 1	51,921	72.1
Motorcycle Module 2	50,993	71.0
PCV	7,345	60.0
LGV	70,288	58.9
Theory Test		
Car	1,865,740	47.1
Motorcycle	64,924	70.7
PCV		
Multiple choice	8,210	62.9
Hazard perception	6,874	79.8
Driver CPC*	5,334	52.7
LGV		
Multiple choice	55,110	60.7
Hazard perception	43,882	81.2
Driver CPC*	33,510	68.8

LGV = Large goods vehicle; PCV = Passenger-carrying vehicle
* Driver Certificate of Professional Competence – legal requirement for all professional bus, coach and lorry drivers
Source: DVSA

The theory and practical driving tests can be booked online (**W** www.gov.uk/book-driving-test) or by phone (**T** 0300-2001122).

DRIVING TEST FEES *as at December 2020*

	Weekday/evening, weekend & bank holidays
Theory tests	
Car and motorcycle	£23.00/£23.00
Bus and lorry	
Multiple choice	£26.00/£26.00
Hazard perception	£11.00/£11.00
Driver CPC†	£23.00/£23.00
Practical tests	
Car	£62.00/£75.00
Tractor and other specialist vehicles	£62.00/£75.00
Motorcycle	
Module 1 (off-road)	£15.50/£15.50
Module 2 (on-road)	£75.00/£88.50
Lorry and bus	£115.00/£141.00
Driver CPC†	£55.00/£63.00
Car and trailer	£115.00/£141.00
Extended tests for disqualified drivers	
Car	£124.00/£150.00
Motorcycle Module 1 (on-road)	£150.00/£177.00

* After 4.30pm
† Driver Certificate of Professional Competence – legal requirement for all professional bus, coach and lorry drivers

VEHICLE LICENCES

Registration and first licensing of vehicles is through local offices of the DVLA in Swansea. Local facilities for relicensing are available at any post office which deals with vehicle licensing. Applicants will need to take their vehicle registration document (V55/5) or, if this is not available, the applicant must complete form V62. Forms are available at post offices and online (**W** www.gov.uk/dvlaforms)

MOTOR VEHICLES LICENSED (UK)
As at 30 September 2020

	Thousands
All cars	32,869.9
Light goods vehicles	4,342.5
Motorcycles	1,384.3
Heavy goods vehicles	507.9
Buses and coaches	144.4
Other vehicles*	806.3
Total	40,055.4

* Includes rear diggers, lift trucks, rollers, ambulances, Hackney Carriages, three-wheelers and agricultural vehicles
Source: Department for Transport

VEHICLE EXCISE DUTY

Details of the present duties chargeable on motor vehicles are available at post offices and online (**W** www.gov.uk/government/publications/rates-of-vehicle-tax-v149). The Vehicle Excise and Registration Act 1994 provides *inter alia* that any vehicle kept on a public road but not used on roads is chargeable to excise duty as if it were in use. All non-commercial vehicles constructed before 1 January 1973 are exempt from vehicle excise duty. Any vehicle licensed on or after 31 January 1998, not in use and not kept on public roads must be registered as SORN (Statutory Off Road Notification) to be exempted from vehicle excise duty. From 1 January 2004 the registered keeper of a vehicle remains responsible for taxing a vehicle or making a SORN declaration until that liability is formally transferred to a new keeper.

All rates of duty can also be paid by direct debit – the 6-month direct debit rate is slightly cheaper than the non-direct debit rate listed below. There is also the option to pay vehicle duty by direct debit monthly instalments.

RATES OF DUTY *from 1 April 2020*

	6 months	12 months
Cars registered on or after 1 April 2017*†		
petrol/diesel car	£82.50	£150.00
alternative fuel car	£77.00	£140.00
Cars registered on or after 1 March 2001		
Under 1,549cc	£90.75	£165.00
Over 1,549cc	£148.50	£270.00
Light goods vehicles registered on or after 1 March 2001		
	£77.00	£140.00
Euro 4 light goods vehicles registered between 1 March 2003 and 31 December 2006		
	£77.00	£140.00
Euro 5 light goods vehicles registered between 1 January 2009 and 31 December 2010		
	£77.00	£140.00
Motorcycles (with or without sidecar)		
Not over 150cc	–	£20.00
151–400cc	–	£44.00
401–600cc	£36.85	£67.00
600cc+	£51.15	£93.00
Tricycles		
Not over 150cc	–	£20.00
All others	£51.15	£93.00

* Different first year licence rates based on CO_2 emissions are payable at first registration
† Cars with a list price of over £40,000 at first registration pay an additional £325 on the standard 12-month rate above for five years from the start of the second tax payment

RATES OF DUTY FOR CARS REGISTERED BETWEEN 1 MARCH 2001 AND 1 APRIL 2017
from 1 April 2020

	CO_2 Emissions	Petrol and Diesel Car		Alternative Fuel Car	
	(g/km)	6 months	12 months	6 months	12 months
A	Up to 100	–	£0.00	–	£0.00
B	101–110	–	£20.00	–	£10.00
C	111–120	–	£30.00	–	£20.00
D	121–130	£68,75	£125.00	£63.25	£115.00
E	131–140	£82.50	£150.00	£77.00	£140.00
F	141–150	£90.75	£165.00	£85.25	£155.00
G	151–165	£112.75	£205.00	£107.25	£195.00
H	166–175	£132.00	£240.00	£126.50	£230.00
I	176–185	£145.75	£265.00	£140.25	£255.00
J	186–200	£167.75	£305.00	£162.25	£295.00
K*	201–255	£181.50	£330.00	£176.00	£320.00
L	226–255	£310.75	£565.00	£305.25	£555.00
M	255+	£319.00	£580.00	£313.50	£570.00

* Includes cars that have a CO_2 emission figure over 225g/km but were registered before 23 March 2006

MOT TESTING

Cars, motorcycles, motor caravans, light goods and dual-purpose vehicles more than three years old must be covered by a current MOT test certificate. However, some vehicles (ie minibuses, ambulances and taxis) may require a certificate at one year old. All certificates must be renewed annually. Only MOT testing stations showing a blue sign with three triangles and an official 'MOT: Test: Fees and Appeals' poster may carry out an approved MOT. The MOT testing scheme is administered by the Driver and Vehicle Standards Agency (DVSA) on behalf of the Secretary of State for Transport.

A fee is payable to MOT testing stations. The current maximum fees are:

For cars, private hire and public service vehicles, motor caravans, dual purpose vehicles, ambulances and taxis (all up to eight passenger seats)	£54.85
For motorcycles	£29.65
For motorcycles with sidecar	£37.80
For three-wheeled vehicles (up to 450kg unladen weight)	£37.80

*Private passenger vehicles and ambulances with:

9–12 passenger seats	£57.30 (£64.00)
13–16 passenger seats	£59.55 (£80.50)
16+ passenger seats	£80.65 (£124.50)
Goods vehicles (3,000–3,500kg)	£58.60

* Figures in parentheses include seatbelt installation check

SHIPPING AND PORTS

Sea trade has always played a central role in Britain's economy. By the 17th century Britain had built up a substantial merchant fleet and by the early 20th century it dominated the world shipping industry. In 2019 the UK registered trading fleet decreased by 34 per cent in gross tonnage (GT) compared to 2018, to 10.5 million GT, the 24th largest trading fleet in the world. At the end of 2019, the number of UK registered trading vessels was 1,177, an annual decrease of 10 per cent. This sharp decline, after several years of stability, was likely due to uncertainty over the UK's exit from the EU. The UK registered share of the world fleet fell to 0.5 per cent on a deadweight tonnage basis and 0.7 per cent when measured using GT, compared with 0.8 per cent and 1.1 per cent respectively in 2018.

Freight is carried by liner and bulk services, almost all scheduled liner services being containerised. About 95 per cent by weight of Britain's overseas trade is carried by sea. Passengers and vehicles are carried by roll-on, roll-off ferries, hovercraft, cruise ships and high-speed catamarans. In 2019 the number of international short-sea route passengers to and from the UK decreased by 6 per cent to 18.4 million.

Lloyd's of London provides the most comprehensive shipping intelligence service in the world. *Lloyd's List* (www.lloydslistintelligence.com) lists over 126,000 ocean-going vessels and gives the latest known report of each.

PORTS

There are 51 major ports in the UK. Total freight tonnage handled by UK ports in 2019 was 486.1 million tonnes, broadly level with 2018 (483.3 million tonnes). The largest ports in terms of freight tonnage in 2018 were Grimsby and Immingham (54.1 million tonnes), London (54 million tonnes), Milford Haven (35 million tonnes), Liverpool (34.3 million tonnes) and Southampton (33.2 million tonnes). Belfast (18.5 million tonnes) is the principal freight port in Northern Ireland.

Broadly speaking, ports are owned and operated by private companies, local authorities or self-owning bodies, known as trust ports. The largest operator is Associated British Ports which owns 21 ports.

MARINE SAFETY

The Maritime and Coastguard Agency (MCA) is an executive agency of the Department for Transport responsible for implementing the government's maritime safety policy in the UK and works to prevent the loss of life on the coast and at sea.

HM Coastguard maintains a 24-hour search and rescue response and coordination capability for the whole of the UK coast and the internationally agreed search and rescue region. HM Coastguard is responsible for mobilising and organising resources in response to people in distress at sea, or at risk of injury or death on the UK's cliffs or shoreline.

The MCA also inspects and surveys ships to ensure that they are meeting UK and international safety rules, provides certification to seafarers, registers vessels and responds to pollution from shipping and offshore installations.

Locations hazardous to shipping in coastal waters are marked by lighthouses and other lights and buoys. The lighthouse authorities are the Corporation of Trinity House (for England, Wales and the Channel Islands), the Northern Lighthouse Board (for Scotland and the Isle of Man), and the Commissioners of Irish Lights (for Northern Ireland and the Republic of Ireland). Trinity House maintains 66 lighthouses, nine light vessels/floats, 508 buoys, 18 beacons, 52 radar beacons, seven DGPS (differential global positioning system) stations* and three AIS (automatic identification system) stations. The Northern Lighthouse Board maintains 206 lighthouses, 204 buoys, 25 beacons, 29 radar beacons, 46 AIS stations and four DGPS stations; and Irish Lights looks after 67 lighthouses, 183 buoys, 20 beacons, and three DGPS stations, with AIS in operation on 48 lighthouses.

Harbour authorities are responsible for pilotage within their harbour areas; and the Ports Act 1991 provides for the transfer of lights and buoys to harbour authorities where these are used mainly for local navigation.

* DGPS is a satellite-based navigation system

UK-OWNED TRADING VESSELS
500 gross tons and over, as at end 2019

Type of vessel	No.	Gross tonnage
Tankers	98	2,945,000
Fully cellular container	73	3,172,000
Dry bulk carriers	68	2,660,000
Ro-Ro (passenger & cargo)	77	901,000
Passenger (incl cruise)	33	2,044,000
Other general cargo	110	355,000
Specialised carriers	12	413,000
All vessels	471	12,485,000

Source: Department for Transport

UK SEA PASSENGER* MOVEMENTS 2019

Type of journey	No. of passenger movements
Short-sea routes	18,404,000
Cruises beginning or ending at a UK port*	2,171,000
Long sea journeys	75,000
Total	20,651,000

* Passengers are included at both departure and arrival if their journeys begin and end at a UK seaport

Source: Department for Transport

UK SHIPPING FORECAST AREAS

Weather bulletins for shipping are broadcast daily on BBC Radio 4 at 00h 48m, 05h 20m, 12h 01m and 17h 54m. All transmissions are broadcast on long wave at 198kHz and the 00h 48m and 05h 20m transmissions are also broadcast on FM 92–95. The bulletins consist of a gale warning summary, general synopsis, sea-area forecasts and coastal station reports. In addition, gale warnings are broadcast at the first available programme break after receipt. If this does not coincide with a news bulletin, the warning is repeated after the next news bulletin. Shipping forecasts and gale warnings are also available on the Met Office and BBC Weather websites.

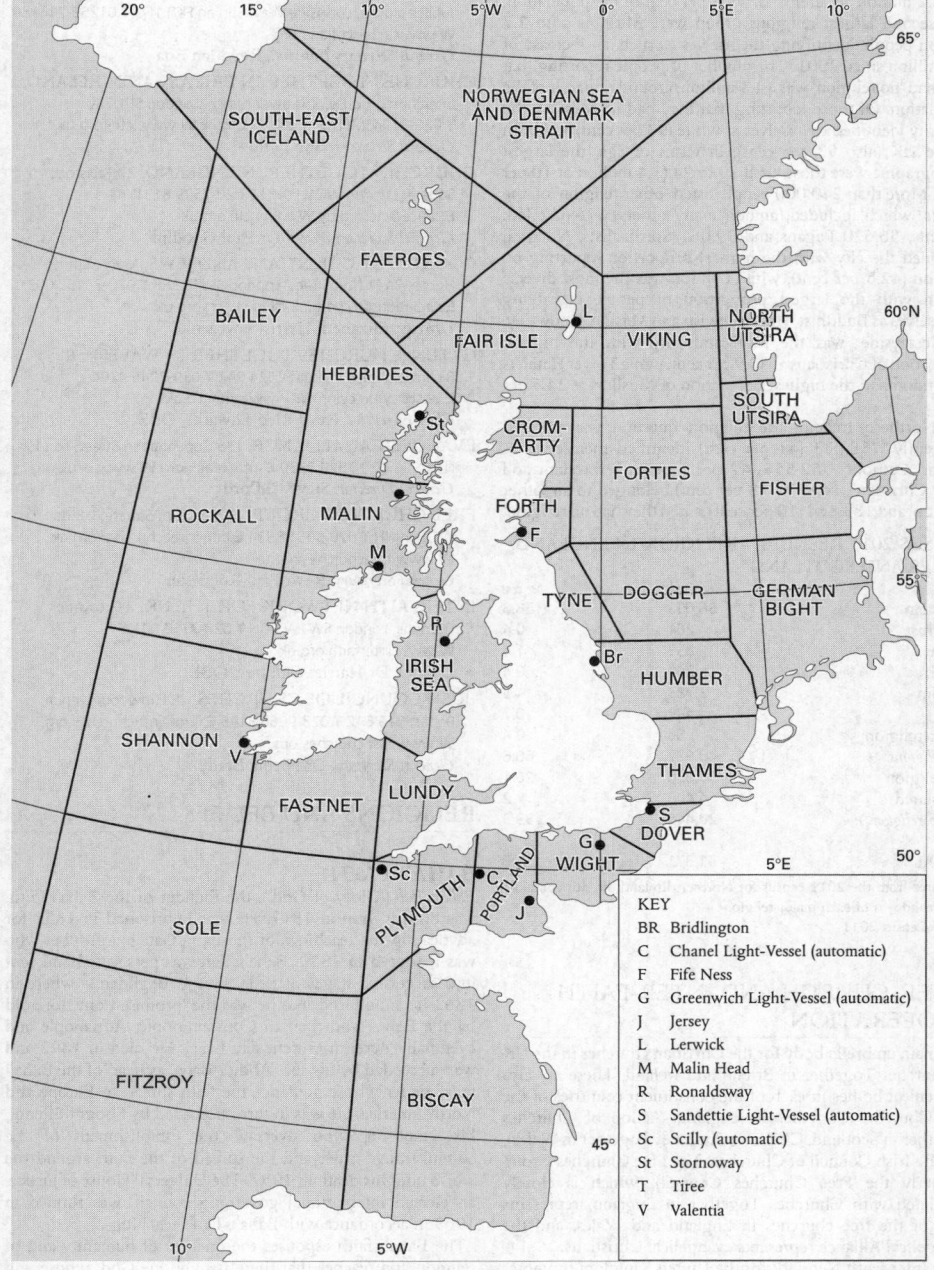

KEY

BR	Bridlington
C	Chanel Light-Vessel (automatic)
F	Fife Ness
G	Greenwich Light-Vessel (automatic)
J	Jersey
L	Lerwick
M	Malin Head
R	Ronaldsway
S	Sandettie Light-Vessel (automatic)
Sc	Scilly (automatic)
St	Stornoway
T	Tiree
V	Valentia

RELIGION IN THE UK

The 2011 census in England and Wales included a voluntary question on religion; 92.8 per cent of the population chose to answer the question. Christianity remained the largest religion, despite a decrease of 4 million people from the 2001 census, to 33.2 million adherents, or 59.3 per cent of the population. The second largest religious group were Muslims with 2.7 million people identifying themselves as such, an increase of 1.2 million since 2001. The number of people reporting that they had 'no religion' was 14.1 million, around a quarter of the population. Of those reporting that they had no religion, the majority identified themselves as white (93 per cent) and born in the UK (also 93 per cent); in terms of age, the largest demographic were those aged 20 to 24 (1.4 million or 10 per cent). More than 240,000 people listed 'other religion' on the census, which included, among many others, 176,632 Jedi Knights, 56,620 Pagans and 39,061 Spiritualists. Norwich remained the city with the highest proportion reporting no religion (42.5 per cent), while London was the most diverse region with the largest proportion of people classifying themselves as Buddhist, Hindu, Jewish and Muslim. Knowsley, in Merseyside, was the local authority with the highest proportion of Christians at 80.9 per cent, while Tower Hamlets in London had the highest population of Muslims at 34.5 per cent.

In Northern Ireland, the religion question was phrased differently; 738,033 (41 per cent) identified themselves as Roman Catholic, 752,555 (42 per cent) as 'Protestant and other Christian', 14,859 (0.8 per cent) belonged to an 'other religion' and 183,164 (10 per cent) stated they had no religion.

CENSUS 2011 RESULTS – RELIGION IN ENGLAND, WALES AND SCOTLAND*

	thousands	per cent
Christian	36,093	58.8
Buddhist	261	0.4
Hindu	833	1.4
Jewish	269	0.4
Muslim	2,783	4.5
Sikh	432	0.7
Other religion	256	0.4
All religions	40,927	66.6
No religion	16,038	26.1
Not stated	4,406	7.2
All no religion/not stated	20,444	33.3
TOTAL	61,371	100

* Figures from the 2011 census for Northern Ireland did not contain a full breakdown of each major religion
Source: Census 2011

INTER-CHURCH AND INTER-FAITH COOPERATION

The main umbrella body for the Christian churches in the UK is Churches Together in Britain and Ireland. There are also ecumenical bodies in each of the constituent countries of the UK: Churches Together in England, Action of Churches Together in Scotland, CYTUN (Churches Together in Wales), and the Irish Council of Churches. The Free Churches Group (formerly the Free Churches Council), which is closely associated with Churches Together in England, represents most of the free churches in England and Wales, and the Evangelical Alliance represents evangelical Christians.

The Inter Faith Network for the United Kingdom promotes cooperation between faiths, and the Council of Christians and

Jews works to improve relations between the two religions. Churches Together in Britain and Ireland also has a commission on inter-faith relations.

ACTION OF CHURCHES TOGETHER IN SCOTLAND, Jubilee House, Forthside Way, Stirling FK8 1QZ **T** 01259-216980 **W** www.acts-scotland.org
General Secretary (interim), Revd Ian Boa

CHURCHES TOGETHER IN BRITAIN AND IRELAND, Interchurch House, 35 Lower Marsh, London SE1 7RL **T** 020-3794 2288 **E** info@ctbi.org.uk **W** www.ctbi.org.uk
General Secretary, Bob Fyffe

CHURCHES TOGETHER IN ENGLAND, 27 Tavistock Square, London WC1H 9HH **T** 020-7529 8131 **E** office@cte.org.uk **W** www.cte.org.uk
General Secretary, Revd Dr Paul Goodliff

COUNCIL OF CHRISTIANS AND JEWS, Mary Sumner House, 24 Tufton Street, London SW1P 3RB **T** 020-3515 3003 **E** cjrelations@ccj.org.uk **W** www.ccj.org.uk
Director, Elizabeth Harris-Sawczenko

CYTUN (CHURCHES TOGETHER IN WALES), 58 Richmond Road, Cardiff CF24 3AT **T** 029-2046 4204 **E** post@cytun.cymru **W** www.cytun.co.uk
Chief Executive, Revd Aled Edwards, OBE

EVANGELICAL ALLIANCE, 176 Copenhagen Street, London N1 0ST **T** 020-7520 3830 **E** info@eauk.org **W** www.eauk.org
General Director, Steve Clifford

FREE CHURCHES GROUP, 27 Tavistock Square, London WC1H 9HH **T** 020-3651 8334 **E** info@freechurches.org.uk **W** www.freechurches.org.uk
General Secretary, Revd Paul Rochester

INTERFAITH NETWORK FOR THE UK, 2 Grosvenor Gardens, London SW1W 0DH **T** 020-7730 0410 **W** www.interfaith.org.uk
Director, Dr Harriet Crabtree, OBE

IRISH COUNCIL OF CHURCHES, 48 Elmwood Avenue, Belfast BT9 6AZ **T** 028-9066 3145 **E** info@irishchurches.org **W** www.irishchurches.org
General Secretary, Dr Nicola Brady

RELIGIONS AND BELIEFS

BAHA'I FAITH

Baha'u'llah ('Glory of God'), the founder of the Baha'i faith, was born in Iran in 1817. He was imprisoned in 1852 for advocating the teachings of the Bab ('Gate'), a prophet who was martyred in 1850. Baha'u'llah was persecuted and sent into successive stages of exile, first to Baghdad – where in 1863 he announced that he was the 'promised one' foretold by the Bab – and then to Constantinople, Adrianople and eventually Acre, in present day Israel. He died in 1892 and was succeeded by his son, Abdu'l-Baha, as head of the Baha'i faith, under whose guidance the faith spread to Europe and North America. He was in turn succeeded by Shoghi Effendi, his grandson, who oversaw the establishment of the administrative order and the spread of the faith around the world until his death in 1957. The Universal House of Justice, an elected international governing council, was formed in 1963 in accordance with Baha'u'llah's teachings.

The Baha'i faith espouses the oneness of humanity and of religion and teaches that there is only one God, whose will has been revealed to mankind by a series of messengers, such as Zoroaster, Abraham, Moses, Buddha, Krishna, Christ, Muhammad, the Bab and Baha'u'llah, who were seen as the founders of separate religions, but whose common purpose was to bring God's message to mankind. The Baha'i faith attributes the differences in teachings between religions to humanity's changing needs. Baha'i teachings include that all races and both sexes are equal and deserving of equal opportunities and treatment, that education is a fundamental right and that extremes of wealth and poverty should be eliminated. In addition, the faith exhorts mankind to establish a world federal system to promote peace and unity.

In an effort to translate these principles into action, Baha'is have initiated an educational process across the world that seeks to raise the capacity of people of all ages and from all backgrounds to contribute towards the betterment of society. There is no clergy; each local community elects a local spiritual assembly to tend to its administrative needs. A national spiritual assembly is elected annually by locally elected delegates, and every five years the national spiritual assemblies meet together to elect the Universal House of Justice, the supreme international governing body of the Baha'i Faith. Worldwide there are over 13,000 local spiritual assemblies and nearly 7 million followers, with around 7,000 in the UK.

BAHA'I COMMUNITY OF THE UK, 27 Rutland Gate, London SW7 1PD T 020-7584 2566 E opa@bahai.org.uk
W www.bahai.org.uk
Director, Office of Public Affairs, Padideh Sabeti

BUDDHISM
Buddhism originated in what is now the Bihar area of northern India in the teachings of Siddhartha Gautama, who became the *Buddha* ('Enlightened One'). In the Thai or Suriyakati calendar the beginning of the Buddhist era is dated from the death of Buddha; the year 2020 is therefore 2563 by the Thai Buddhist reckoning.

Fundamental to Buddhism is the concept of rebirth, whereby each life carries with it the consequences of the conduct of earlier lives (known as the law of *karma*) and this cycle of death and rebirth is broken only when the state of *nirvana* has been reached. Buddhism steers a middle path between belief in personal continuity and the belief that death results in total extinction.

While doctrine does not have a pivotal position in Buddhism, a statement of four 'Noble Truths' is common to all its schools and varieties. These are: suffering is inescapable in even the most fortunate of existences; craving is the root cause of suffering; abandonment of the selfish mindset is the way to end suffering; and bodily and mental discipline, accompanied by the cultivation of wisdom and compassion, provides the spiritual path ('Noble Eightfold Path') to accomplish this. Buddhists deny the idea of a creator and prefer to emphasise the practical aspects of moral and spiritual development.

The schools of Buddhism can be broadly divided into three: *Theravada,* the generally monastic-led tradition practised in Sri Lanka and South East Asia; *Mahayana,* the philosophical and popular traditions of the Far East; and *Esoteric,* the Tantric-derived traditions found in Tibet and Mongolia and, to a lesser extent, China and Japan. The extensive Theravada scriptures are contained in the *Pali Canon,* which dates in its written form from the first century BC. Mahayana and Esoteric schools have Sanskrit-derived translations of these plus many more additional scriptures as well as exegetical material.

In the East the new and full moons and the lunar quarter days were (and to a certain extent, still are) significant in determining the religious calendar. Most private homes contain a shrine where offerings, worship and other spiritual practices (such as meditation, chanting or mantra recitation)

take place on a daily basis. Buddhist festivals vary according to local traditions within the different schools and there is little uniformity – even in commemorating the birth, enlightenment and death of the Buddha.

There is no governing authority for Buddhism in the UK. Communities representing all schools of Buddhism operate independently. The Buddhist Society was established in 1924; it runs courses, lectures and meditation groups, and publishes books about Buddhism. The Network of Buddhist Organisations was founded in 1993 to promote fellowship and dialogue between Buddhist organisations and to facilitate cooperation in matters of common interest.

There are estimated to be at least 490 million Buddhists worldwide. Of the 248,000 Buddhists in England and Wales (according to the 2011 census), 72,000 are white British (the majority are converts), 49,000 Chinese, 93,000 'other Asian' and 36,000 are 'other ethnic'.

THE BUDDHIST SOCIETY, 58 Eccleston Square, London SW1V 1PH T 020-7834 5858 E info@thebuddhistsociety.org
W www.thebuddhistsociety.org
President, Dr Desmond Biddulph, CBE
LONDON BUDDHIST CENTRE, 51 Roman Road, London E2 0HU T 020-8981 1225 E contact@lbc.org.uk
W www.lbc.org.uk
Chair, Dharmachari Subhuti
THE NETWORK OF BUDDHIST ORGANISATIONS, PO Box 4147, Maidenhead SL60 1DN T 0845-345 8978
E nboadmin@nbo.org.uk W www.nbo.org.uk
Chair, Juliet Hackney
SOKA GAKKAI UK, Taplow Court Grand Cultural Centre, Cliveden Road, Taplow, Berkshire SL6 0ER T 01628-773163
W www.sgi-uk.org
General Director, Robert Harrap
TIBET HOUSE TRUST, Tibet House, 1 Culworth Street, London NW8 7AF T 020-7722 5378
E secretary@tibet-house-trust.co.uk
W www.tibet-house-trust.co.uk
Chair, Sonam Tsering Frasi

CHRISTIANITY
Christianity is a monotheistic faith based on the person and teachings of Jesus Christ, and all Christian denominations claim his authority. Central to its teaching is the concept of God and his son Jesus Christ, who was crucified and resurrected in order to enable mankind to attain salvation.

The Jewish scriptures predicted the coming of a *Messiah,* an 'anointed one', who would bring salvation. To Christians, Jesus of Nazareth, a Jewish rabbi (teacher) who was born in Palestine, was the promised Messiah. Jesus' birth, teachings, crucifixion and subsequent resurrection are recorded in the *Gospels,* which, together with other scriptures that summarise Christian belief, form the *New Testament.* This, together with the Hebrew scriptures – entitled the *Old Testament* by Christians – makes up the Bible, the sacred texts of Christianity.

Christians believe that sin distanced mankind from God, and that Jesus was the son of God, sent to redeem mankind from sin by his death. In addition, many believe that Jesus will return again at some future date, triumph over evil and establish a kingdom on earth, thus inaugurating a new age. The Gospel assures Christians that those who believe in Jesus and obey his teachings will be forgiven their sins and will be resurrected from the dead.

The Apostles were Jesus' first converts and are recognised by Christians as the founders of the Christian community. Early Christianity spread rapidly throughout the eastern provinces of the Roman Empire but was subjected to great persecution until AD 313, when Emperor Constantine's Edict of Toleration confirmed its right to exist. Christianity was established as the religion of the Roman Empire in AD 381.

Between AD 325 and 787 there were seven Oecumenical Councils at which bishops from the entire Christian world assembled to resolve various doctrinal disputes. The estrangement between East and West began after Constantine moved the centre of the Roman Empire from Rome to Constantinople, and it grew after the division of the Roman Empire into eastern and western halves. Linguistic and cultural differences between Greek East and Latin West served to encourage separate ecclesiastical developments which became pronounced in the tenth and early 11th centuries. Administration of the church was divided between five ancient patriarchates: Rome and all the West, Constantinople (the imperial city – the 'New Rome'), Jerusalem and all of Palestine, Antioch and all the East, and Alexandria and all of Africa. Of these, only Rome was in the Latin West and after the schism in 1054, Rome developed a structure of authority centralised on the Papacy, while the Orthodox East maintained the style of localised administration. Papal authority over the doctrine and jurisdiction of the church in Western Europe was unrivalled after the split with the Eastern Orthodox Church until the Protestant Reformation in the 16th century.

Christian practices vary widely between different Christian churches, but prayer, charity and giving (for the maintenance of the church buildings, for the work of the church, and to those in need) are common to all. In addition, certain days of observance, ie the *Sabbath, Easter* and *Christmas,* are celebrated by most Christians. The Orthodox, Roman Catholic and Anglican churches celebrate many more days of observance, based on saints and significant events in the life of Jesus. The belief in sacraments, physical signs believed to have been ordained by Jesus Christ to symbolise and convey spiritual gifts, varies greatly between Christian denominations; *baptism* and the *Eucharist* are practised by most Christians. Baptism, symbolising repentance and faith in Jesus, is an act marking entry into the Christian community; the Eucharist, the ritual re-enactment of the Last Supper, Jesus' final meal with his disciples, is also practised by most denominations. Other sacraments, such as anointing the sick, the laying on of hands to symbolise the passing on of the office of priesthood or to heal the sick, and speaking in tongues, where it is believed that the person is possessed by the Holy Spirit, are less common. In denominations where infant baptism is practised, confirmation (where the person confirms the commitments made on their behalf in infancy) is common. Matrimony and the ordination of priests are also widely believed to be sacraments. Many Protestants regard only baptism and the Eucharist to be sacraments; the Quakers and the Salvation Army reject the use of sacraments.

See Churches for contact details of the Church of England, the Roman Catholic Church and other Christian churches in the UK.

HINDUISM

Hinduism has no historical founder but had become highly developed in India by *c.*2500 BC. Its adherents originally called themselves Aryans; Muslim invaders first called the Aryans 'Hindus' (derived from 'Sindhu', the name of the river Indus) in the eighth century.

Most Hindus hold that *satya* (truthfulness), honesty, sincerity and devotion to God are essential for good living. They believe in one supreme spirit *(Brahman),* and in the transmigration of *atman* (the soul). Most Hindus accept the doctrine of *karma* (consequences of actions), the concept of *samsara* (successive lives) and the possibility of all atmans achieving *moksha* (liberation from samsara) through *jnana* (knowledge), *yoga* (meditation), *karma* (work or action) and *bhakti* (devotion).

Most Hindus offer worship to *murtis* (images of deities) representing different incarnations or aspects of Brahman, and follow their *dharma* (religious and social duty) according to the traditions of their *varna* (social class), *ashrama* (stage in life), *jaiti* (caste) and *kula* (family).

Hinduism's sacred texts are divided into *shruti* ('that which is heard'), including the *Vedas,* and *smriti* ('that which is remembered'), including the *Ramayana,* the *Mahabharata,* the *Puranas* (ancient myths), and the sacred law books. Most Hindus recognise the authority of the *Vedas,* the oldest holy books, and accept the philosophical teachings of the *Upanishads,* the *Vedanta Sutras* and the *Bhagavad-Gita.*

Hindus believe Brahman to be omniscient, omnipotent, limitless and all-pervading. Brahman is usually worshipped in its deity form. Brahma, Vishnu and Shiva are the most important deities or aspects of Brahman worshipped by Hindus; their respective consorts are Saraswati, Lakshmi and Durga or Parvati, also known as Shakti. There are believed to have been ten *avatars* (incarnations) of Vishnu, of whom the most important are Rama and Krishna. Other popular gods are Ganesha, Hanuman and Subrahmanyam. All Hindu gods are seen as aspects of the supreme spirit (Brahman), not as competing deities.

Orthodox Hindus revere all gods and goddesses equally, but there are many denominations, including the Hare-Krishna movement (ISKCon), the Arya Samaj and the Swaminarayan Hindu mission, in which worship is concentrated on one deity. The *guru* (spiritual teacher) is seen as the source of spiritual guidance.

Hinduism does not have a centrally trained and ordained priesthood. The pronouncements of the *shankaracharyas* (heads of monasteries) of Shringeri, Puri, Dwarka and Badrinath are heeded by the orthodox but may be ignored by the various sects.

The commonest form of worship is *puja,* in which water, flowers, food, fruit, incense and light are offered to the deity. Puja may be done either in a home shrine or a *mandir* (temple). Many British Hindus celebrate *samskars* (purification rites), to name a baby, for the sacred thread (an initiation ceremony), marriage and cremation.

The largest communities of Hindus in Britain are in Leicester, London, Birmingham and Bradford, and developed as a result of immigration from India, eastern Africa and Sri Lanka.

There are an estimated 800 million Hindus worldwide; there are around 817,000 adherents, according to the 2011 census in England and Wales, and around 135 temples in the UK.

ARYA SAMAJ LONDON, 69 Argyle Road, London W13 0LY
  T 020-8991 1732 **E** aryasamajlondon@yahoo.co.uk
  W www.aryasamajlondon.org.uk
  General Secretary, Amrit Lal Bhardwaj

BHARATIYA VIDYA BHAVAN, 4A Castletown Road, London W14 9HE **T** 020-7381 3086 **E** info@bhavan.net
  W www.bhavan.net
  Executive Director, Dr N. M Nandakumara

BHAKTIVEDANTA MANOR: INTERNATIONAL SOCIETY FOR KRISHNA CONSCIOUSNESS (ISKCON), Bhaktivedanta Manor, Dharam Marg, Hilfield Lane, Aldenham, Watford, Herts WD25 8EZ **T** 01923-851000
  E info@krishnatemple.com **W** www.bhaktivedantamanor.co.uk
  Temple President, Gauri Das

NATIONAL COUNCIL OF HINDU TEMPLES (UK), c/o Shree Sanatan Mandir, 84 Weymouth Street, Leicester LE4 6FQ
  T 0771-781 4357 **E** info@nchtuk.org **W** www.nchtuk.org
  General Secretary, Satish K. Sharma

SWAMINARAYAN HINDU MISSION (SHRI
SWAMINARAYAN MANDIR), 105–119 Brentfield Road,
London NW10 8
LD **T** 020-8965 2651 **E** info@londonmandir.baps.org
W www.londonmandir.baps.org

HUMANISM

Humanism traces its roots back to ancient times, with Chinese,
Greek, Indian and Roman philosophers expressing Humanist
ideas some 2,500 years ago. Confucius, the Chinese
philosopher who lived *c.*500 BC, believed that religious
observances should be replaced with moral values as the basis
of social and political order and that 'the true way' is based
on reason and humanity. He also stressed the importance of
benevolence and respect for others, and believed that the
individual situation should be considered rather than the
global application of traditional rules.

Humanists believe that there is no God or other supernatural
being, that humans have only one life (Humanists do not
believe in an afterlife or reincarnation) and that humans can
live ethical and fulfilling lives without religious beliefs
through a moral code derived from a shared history, personal
experience and thought. There are no sacred Humanist texts.
Particular emphasis is placed on science as the only reliable
source of knowledge of the universe. Many Humanists
recognise a need for ceremonies to mark important occasions
in life and the British Humanist Association has a network of
celebrants who are trained and accredited to conduct baby
namings, weddings and funerals. The British Humanist
Association's campaigns for a secular state (a state based on
freedom of religious or non-religious belief with no privileges
for any particular set of beliefs) are based on equality and
human rights. The association also campaigns for inclusive
schools that meet the needs of all parents and pupils,
regardless of their religious or non-religious beliefs. According
to figures from the 2011 census, there are just over 15,000
Humanists in England and Wales.

BRITISH HUMANIST ASSOCIATION, 39 Moreland Street,
London EC1V 8BB **T** 020-7324 3060 **E** info@humanism.org.uk
W www.humanism.org.uk
Chief Executive, Andrew Copson

ISLAM

Islam (which means 'peace arising from submission to the will
of Allah' in Arabic) is a monotheistic religion which was
taught in Arabia by the Prophet Muhammad, who was born
in Mecca (Al-Makkah) in 570 AD. Islam spread to Egypt,
north Africa, Spain and the borders of China in the century
following the Prophet's death, and is now the predominant
religion in Indonesia, the near and Middle East, northern and
parts of western Africa, Pakistan, Bangladesh, Malaysia and
some of the former Soviet republics. There are also large
Muslim communities in other countries.

For Muslims (adherents of Islam), there is one God *(Allah)*,
who holds absolute power. Muslims believe that Allah's
commands were revealed to mankind through the prophets,
who include Abraham, Moses and Jesus, but that Allah's
message was gradually corrupted until revealed finally and in
perfect form to Muhammad through the angel *Jibril* (Gabriel)
over a period of 23 years. This last, incorruptible message is
said to have been recorded in the *Qur'an* (Koran), which
contains 114 divisions called *surahs,* each made up of *ayahs* of
various lengths, and is held to be the essence of all previous
scriptures. The *Ahadith* are the records of the Prophet
Muhammad's deeds and sayings (the *Sunnah*) as practised and
recounted by his immediate followers. A culture and a system
of law and theology gradually developed to form a distinctive
Islamic civilisation. Islam makes no distinction between sacred
and worldly affairs and provides rules for every aspect of

human life. The *Shariah* is the sacred law of Islam based
primarily upon prescriptions derived from the *Qur'an* and the
Sunnah of the Prophet.

The 'five pillars of Islam' are *shahadah* (a declaration of faith
in the oneness and supremacy of Allah and the messengership
of Muhammad); *salat* (formal prayer, to be performed five
times a day facing the *Ka'bah* (the most sacred shrine in the
holy city of Mecca)); *zakat* (welfare due, paid annually on all
savings at the rate of 2.5 per cent); *sawm* (fasting during the
month of Ramadan from dawn until sunset); and *hajj*
(pilgrimage to Mecca made once in a lifetime if the believer is
financially and physically able). Some Muslims would add
jihad as the sixth pillar (striving for the cause of good and
resistance to evil).

Two main groups developed among Muslims. *Sunni* Muslims
accept the legitimacy of Muhammad's first four *caliphs*
(successors as head of the Muslim community) and of the
authority of the Muslim community as a whole. About 90 per
cent of Muslims are Sunni Muslims.

Shi'ites recognise only Muhammad's son-in-law Ali as his
rightful successor and the *Imams* (descendants of Ali, not to be
confused with *imams,* who are prayer leaders or religious
teachers) as the principal legitimate religious authority. The
largest group within Shi'ism is *Twelver Shi'ism,* which has
been the official school of law and theology in Iran since the
16th century; other subsects include the *Ismailis,* the *Druze*
and the *Alawis,* the latter two differing considerably from the
main body of Muslims. The *Ibadis* of Oman are neither Sunni
nor Shia, deriving from the strictly observant *Khariji*
(Seceders). There is no organised priesthood, but learned men
such as imams, *ulama,* and *ayatollahs* are accorded great respect.
The *Sufis* are the mystics of Islam. Mosques are centres for
worship and teaching and also for social and welfare activities.

Islam was first recorded in western Europe in the eighth
century AD when 800 years of Muslim rule began in Spain.
Later, Islam spread to eastern Europe. More recently, Muslims
came to Europe from Africa, the Middle East and Asia in the
late 19th century. Both the Sunni and Shia traditions are
represented in Britain, but the majority of Muslims in Britain
adhere to Sunni Islam. Efforts to establish a representative
national body for Muslims in Britain resulted in the founding,
in 1997, of the Muslim Council of Britain. In addition, there
are many other Muslim organisations in the UK. There are
around 1.6 billion Muslims worldwide, with around 2.8
million adherents in England, Wales and Scotland and about
1,500 mosques in the UK.

ISLAMIC CULTURAL CENTRE – THE LONDON
CENTRAL MOSQUE, 146 Park Road, London NW8 7RG
T 020-7724 3363 **E** info@iccuk.org **W** www.iccuk.org
Director-General, Dr Ahmad Al-Dubayan

MUSLIM COUNCIL OF BRITAIN, PO Box 57330, London
E1 2WJ **T** 0845-262 6786 **E** admin@mcb.org.uk
W www.mcb.org.uk
Secretary-General, Harun Rashid Khan

MUSLIM LAW (SHARIAH) COUNCIL UK, 20–22 Creffield
Road, London W5 3RP **T** 0208-992 6636
E info@shariahcouncil.org **W** www.shariahcouncil.org
Chair, Dr Mohamed Benotman

MUSLIM WORLD LEAGUE LONDON, 46 Goodge Street,
London W1T 4LU **T** 020-7636 7568 **E** info@mwllo.org.uk
W www.mwllo.org.uk
Director, Dr Ahmed Makhdoom

JAINISM

Jainism traces its history to Vardhamana Jnatriputra, known
as *Tirthankara Mahavira* ('the Great Hero') whose traditional
dates were 599–527 BC. Jains believe he was the last of the
current era in a series of 24 *Jinas* (those who overcome all
passions and desires) or *Tirthankaras* (those who show a way
across the ocean of life) stretching back to remote antiquity.

Born to a noble family in north-eastern India (presently the state of Bihar), he renounced the world for the life of a wandering ascetic and after 12 years of austerity and meditation he attained enlightenment. He then preached his message until, at the age of 72, he left the mortal world and achieved total liberation *(moksha)* from the cycle of death and rebirth.

Jains declare that the Hindu rituals of transferring merit are not acceptable as each living being is responsible for its own actions. They recognise some of the minor deities of the Hindu pantheon, but the supreme objects of worship are the Tirthankaras. The pious Jain does not ask favours from the Tirthankaras, but seeks to emulate their example in his or her own life.

Jains believe that the universe is eternal and self-subsisting, that there is no omnipotent creator God ruling it and the destiny of the individual is in his or her own hands. *Karma,* the fruit of past actions, is believed to determine the place of every living being and rebirth may be in the heavens, on earth as a human, an animal or other lower being, or in the hells. The ultimate goal of existence for Jains is *moksha,* a state of perfect knowledge and tranquillity for each individual soul, which can be achieved only by gaining enlightenment.

The Jainist path to liberation is defined by the three jewels: *Samyak Darshan* (right perception), *Samyak Jnana* (right knowledge) and *Samyak Charitra* (right conduct). Of the five fundamental precepts of the Jains, *Ahimsa* (non-injury to any form of being, in any mode: thought, speech or action) is the first and foremost, and was popularised by Gandhi as *Ahimsa paramo dharma* (non-violence is the supreme religion).

The largest population of Jains can be found in India but there are approximately 30,000 Jains in Britain, with sizeable communities in North America, East Africa, Australia and smaller groups in many other countries.

INSTITUTE OF JAINOLOGY, Unit 18, Silicon Business Centre, 28 Wadsworth Road, Perivale, Greenford, Middx UB6 7JZ
T 020-8997 2300 E info@jainology.org W www.jainology.org
Chair, Nemu Chandaria, OBE

JUDAISM

Judaism is the oldest monotheistic faith. The primary text of Judaism is the Hebrew bible or *Tanakh,* which records how the descendants of Abraham were led by Moses out of their slavery in Egypt to Mount Sinai where God's law *(Torah)* was revealed to them as the chosen people. The *Talmud,* which consists of commentaries on the *Mishnah* (the first text of rabbinical Judaism), is also held to be authoritative, and may be divided into two main categories: the *halakeh* (dealing with legal and ritual matters) and the *aggadah* (dealing with theological and ethical matters not directly concerned with the regulation of conduct). The *midrash* comprises rabbinic writings containing biblical interpretations in the spirit of the aggadah. The halakah has become a source of division: orthodox Jews regard Jewish law as derived from God and therefore unalterable; progressive Jews seek to interpret it in the light of contemporary considerations; and conservative Jews aim to maintain most of the traditional rituals but to allow changes in accordance with tradition. Reconstructionist Judaism, a 20th-century movement, regards Judaism as a culture rather than a theological system and accepts all forms of Jewish practice.

The family is the basic unit of Jewish ritual, with the synagogue playing an important role as the centre for public worship and religious study. A synagogue is led by a group of laymen who are elected to office. The Rabbi is primarily a teacher and spiritual guide. The *Sabbath* is the central religious observance. Most British Jews are descendants of either the *Ashkenazim* of central and eastern Europe or the *Sephardim* of Spain, Portugal and the Middle East.

The Chief Rabbi of the United Hebrew Congregations of the Commonwealth is appointed by a Chief Rabbinate Conference, and is the rabbinical authority of the mainstream Orthodox sector of the Ashkenazi Jewish community, the largest body of which is the United Synagogue. His formal ecclesiastical authority is not recognised by the Reform Synagogues of Great Britain (the largest progressive group), the Union of Liberal and Progressive Synagogues, the Spanish and Portuguese Jews' Congregation or the Assembly of Masorti Synagogues. He is, however, generally recognised both outside the Jewish community and within it as the public religious representative of the totality of British Jewry. The Chief Rabbi is President of the London *Beth Din* (Court of Judgment), a rabbinic court. The *Dayanim* (Judges) adjudicate in disputes or on matters of Jewish law and tradition; they also oversee dietary law administration, marriage, divorce and issues of personal status.

The Board of Deputies of British Jews, established in 1760, is the representative body of British Jewry. The basis of representation is through the election of deputies by synagogues and communal organisations. It protects and promotes the interests of British Jewry, acts as the central voice of the community and seeks to counter anti-Jewish discrimination and anti-Semitic activities.

There are approximately 13.9 million Jews worldwide; in the UK there are an estimated 290,000 adherents and over 400 synagogues.

OFFICE OF THE CHIEF RABBI, 305 Ballards Lane, London N12 8GB T 020-8343 6301 E info@chiefrabbi.org
W www.chiefrabbi.org
Chief Rabbi, Ephraim Mirvis

BETH DIN (THE UNITED SYNAGOGUE), 305 Ballards Lane, London N12 8GB T 020-8343 6270 E info@bethdin.org.uk
W www.theus.org.uk
President, Michael Goldstein
Dayanim, Menachem Gelley *(Rosh Beth Din);* Ivan Binstock; Shmuel Simons

MASORTI JUDAISM, Alexander House, 3 Shakespeare Road, London N3 1XE T 020-8349 6650 E enquiries@masorti.org.uk
W www.masorti.org.uk
Executive Director, Matt Plen

BOARD OF DEPUTIES OF BRITISH JEWS, 1 Torriano Mews, London NW5 2RZ T 020-7543 5400 E info@bod.org.uk
W www.bod.org.uk
Chief Executive, Gillian Merron

FEDERATION OF SYNAGOGUES, 65 Watford Way, London NW4 3AQ T 020-8202 2263
E info@federationofsynagogues.com
W www.federationofsynagogues.com
Chief Executive, Rabbi Ari Lazarus

LIBERAL JUDAISM, The Montagu Centre, 21 Maple Street, London W1T 4BE T 020-7580 1663
E montagu@liberaljudaism.org W www.liberaljudaism.org
Chief Executive, Rabbi Danny Rich

THE MOVEMENT FOR REFORM JUDAISM, The Sternberg Centre for Judaism, 80 East End Road, London N3 2SY
T 020-8349 5640 E admin@reformjudaism.org.uk
W www.reformjudaism.org.uk
Senior Rabbi, Laura Janner-Klausner

THE SEPHARDI COMMUNITY, 119–121 Brent Street, London NW4 2DX T 020-7289 2573 E admin@spsyn.org.uk
W www.sephardi.org.uk
Executive Director, David Arden

UNITED SYNAGOGUE HEAD OFFICE, Adler House, 735 High Road, London N12 0US T 020-8343 8989
W www.theus.org.uk
Chief Executive, Dr Stephen Wilson

PAGANISM

Paganism draws on the ideas of the Celtic people of pre-Roman Europe and is closely linked to Druidism. The first historical record of Druidry comes from classical Greek and Roman writers of the third century BC, who noted the existence of Druids among a people called the Keltoi who inhabited central and southern Europe. The word druid may derive from the Indo-European 'dreo-vid', meaning 'one who knows the truth'. In practice it was probably understood to mean something like 'wise-one' or 'philosopher-priest'.

Paganism is a pantheistic nature-worshipping religion which incorporates beliefs and ritual practices from ancient times. Pagans place much emphasis on the natural world and the ongoing cycle of life and death is central to their beliefs. Most Pagans believe that they are part of nature and not separate from, or superior to it, and seek to live in a way that minimises harm to the natural environment (the word Pagan derives from the Latin *Paganus*, meaning 'rural'). Paganism strongly emphasises the equality of the sexes, with women playing a prominent role in the modern Pagan movement and goddess worship featuring in most ceremonies. Paganism cannot be defined by any principal beliefs because it is shaped by each individual's experiences.

The Pagan Federation was founded in 1971 to provide information on Paganism, campaigns on issues which affect Paganism and provides support to members of the Pagan community. Within the UK the Pagan Federation is divided into 12 districts each with a district manager and a regional coordinator. Local meetings are called 'moots' and take place in private homes, pubs or coffee bars. The Pagan Federation publishes a quarterly journal, *Pagan Dawn*, formerly *The Wiccan* (founded in 1968). The federation also publishes other material, arranges members-only and public events and maintains personal contact by letter with individual members and the wider Pagan community. Regional gatherings and conferences are held throughout the year.

THE PAGAN FEDERATION, Suite 1, The Werks, 45 Church Road, Hove BN3 2BE E info@paganfederation.co.uk
W www.paganfed.org
President, Robin Taylor

SIKHISM

The Sikh religion dates from the birth of Guru Nanak in the Punjab in 1469. 'Guru' means teacher but in Sikh tradition has come to represent the divine presence of God giving inner spiritual guidance. Nanak's role as the human vessel of the divine guru was passed on to nine successors, the last of whom (Guru Gobind Singh) died in 1708. The immortal guru is now held to reside in the sacred scripture, *Guru Granth Sahib*, and so to be present in all Sikh gatherings.

Guru Nanak taught that there is one God and that different religions are like different roads leading to the same destination. He condemned religious conflict, ritualism and caste prejudices. The fifth Guru, Guru Arjan Dev, largely compiled the Sikh Holy scripture, a collection of hymns (*gurbani*) known as the *Adi Granth*. It includes the writings of the first five gurus and the ninth guru, and selected writings of Hindu and Muslim saints whose views are in accord with the gurus' teachings. Guru Arjan Dev also built the Golden Temple at Amritsar, the centre of Sikhism. The tenth guru, Guru Gobind Singh, passed on the guruship to the sacred scripture, Guru Granth Sahib, and founded the *Khalsa*, an order intended to fight against tyranny and injustice. Male initiates to the order added 'Singh' to their given names and women added 'Kaur'. Guru Gobind Singh also made the wearing of five symbols obligatory: *kaccha* (a special undergarment), *kara* (a steel bangle), *kirpan* (a small sword), *kesh* (long unshorn hair, and consequently the wearing of a turban) and *kangha* (a comb). These practices are still compulsory for those Sikhs who are initiated into the Khalsa (the *Amritdharis*). Those who do not seek initiation are known as *Sehajdharis*.

There are no professional priests in Sikhism; anyone with a reasonable proficiency in the Punjabi language can conduct a service. Worship can be offered individually or communally, and in a private house or a *gurdwara* (temple). Sikhs are forbidden to eat meat prepared by ritual slaughter; they are also asked to abstain from smoking, alcohol and other intoxicants. Such abstention is compulsory for the Amritdharis.

There are about 24 million Sikhs worldwide and, according to the 2011 census, there are 432,000 adherents in England, Wales and Scotland. Every gurdwara manages its own affairs; there is no central body in the UK. The Sikh Missionary Society provides an information service.

SIKH MISSIONARY SOCIETY UK, 10 Featherstone Road, Southall, Middx UB2 5AA T 020-8574 1902
E info@sikhmissionarysociety.org
W www.sikhmissionarysociety.org

ZOROASTRIANISM

Zoroastrians are followers of the Iranian prophet Spitaman Zarathushtra (or Zoroaster in its hellenised form) who lived *c.*1200–1500 BC. Zoroastrians were persecuted in Iran following the Arab invasion of Persia in the seventh century AD and a group (who are known as Parsis) migrated to India in the ninth century AD to avoid harassment and persecution. Zarathushtra's words are recorded in 17 hymns called the *Gathas*, which, together with other scriptures, form the *Avesta*.

Zoroastrianism teaches that there is one God, *Ahura Mazda* ('Wise Lord'), and that all creation stems ultimately from God; the Gathas teach that human beings have free will, are responsible for their own actions and can choose between good and evil. It is believed that choosing *Asha* (truth or righteousness), with the aid of *Vohu Manah* (good mind), leads to happiness for the individual and society, whereas choosing evil leads to unhappiness and conflict. The *Gathas* also encourage hard work, good deeds and charitable acts. Zoroastrians believe that after death the immortal soul is judged by God, and is then sent to paradise or hell, where it will stay until the end of time to be resurrected for the final judgment.

In Zoroastrian places of worship, an urn containing fire is the central feature; the fire symbolises purity, light and truth and is a visible symbol of the *Fravashi* or *Farohar* (spirit), the presence of Ahura Mazda in every human being. Zoroastrians respect nature and much importance is attached to cultivating land and protecting air, earth and water.

The Zoroastrian Trust Funds of Europe is the main body for Zoroastrians in the UK. Founded in 1861 as the Religious Funds of the Zoroastrians of Europe, it disseminates information on the Zoroastrian faith, provides a place of worship and maintains separate burial grounds for Zoroastrians. It also holds religious and social functions and provides assistance to Zoroastrians as considered necessary, including the provision of loans and grants to students of Zoroastrianism, and participates in inter-faith educational activities.

There are approximately 150,000 Zoroastrians worldwide, of which around 4,000 reside in England and Wales, mainly in London and the South East.

ZOROASTRIAN TRUST FUNDS OF EUROPE, Zoroastrian Centre, 440 Alexandra Avenue, Harrow, Middx HA2 9TL
T 020-8866 0765 E secretary@ztfe.com W www.ztfe.com
President, Malcolm Deboo

CHURCHES

There are two established (ie state) churches in the UK: the Church of England and the Church of Scotland. There are no established churches in Wales or Northern Ireland, though the Church in Wales, the Scottish Episcopal Church and the Church of Ireland are members of the Anglican Communion.

THE CHURCH OF ENGLAND

The Church of England is divided into the two provinces of Canterbury and York, each under an archbishop. The two provinces are subdivided into 42 dioceses, the newest of which came into existence on 20 April 2014. The new Diocese of Leeds was formed from the amalgamation of the former dioceses of Bradford, Ripon and Leeds and Wakefield.

Legislative provision for the Church of England is made by the General Synod, established in 1970. It also discusses and expresses opinion on any other matter of religious or public interest. The General Synod has 483 members in total, divided between three houses: the House of Bishops, the House of Clergy and the House of Laity. It is presided over jointly by the Archbishops of Canterbury and York and normally meets twice a year. The synod has the power, delegated by parliament, to frame statute law (known as a 'measure') on any matter concerning the Church of England. A measure must be laid before both houses of parliament, who may accept or reject it but cannot amend it. Once accepted the measure is submitted for royal assent and then has the full force of law. In addition to the General Synod, there are synods at diocesan level. The entire General Synod is re-elected once every five years. The tenth General Synod was inaugurated by the Queen on 23 November 2015.

THE ARCHBISHOPS' COUNCIL

The Archbishops' Council was established in January 1999. Its creation was the result of changes to the Church of England's national structure proposed in 1995 and subsequently approved by the synod and parliament. The council's purpose, set out in the National Institutions Measure 1998, is 'to coordinate, promote and further the work and mission of the Church of England'. It reports to the General Synod. The Archbishops' Council comprises the Archbishops of Canterbury and York, ex officio, the prolocutors elected by the convocations of Canterbury and York, the chair and vice-chair of the House of Laity, two bishops, two clergy and two lay persons elected by their respective houses of the General Synod, the Church Estates Commissioner, and up to six persons appointed jointly by the two archbishops.

There are also a number of national boards, councils and other bodies working on matters such as social responsibility, mission, Christian unity and education, which report to the General Synod through the Archbishops' Council.

GENERAL SYNOD OF THE CHURCH OF ENGLAND/ ARCHBISHOPS' COUNCIL, Church House, Great Smith Street, London SW1P 3AZ T 020-7898 1000
Secretary-General, William Nye, LVO

THE ORDINATION AND CONSECRATION OF WOMEN

The canon making it possible for women to be ordained to the priesthood was promulgated in the General Synod in February 1994 and the first 32 women priests were ordained on 12 March 1994.

On 14 July 2014 the General Synod approved the Bishops and Priests (Consecration and Ordination of Women) Measure which made provision for the consecration of women as bishops and for the continuation of provision for the ordination of women. The Revd Elizabeth Lane was consecrated as the first female bishop on 26 January 2015 when she became Bishop Suffragan of Stockport in the diocese of Chester. The first female diocesan bishop, Rachel Treweek, was consecrated as the 41st Bishop of Gloucester on 22 July 2015.

PORVOO DECLARATION

The Porvoo Declaration was approved by the General Synod of the Church of England in July 1995. Churches that approve the declaration regard baptised members of each other's churches as members of their own, and allow free interchange of episcopally ordained ministers within the rules of each church.

MEMBERSHIP AND MINISTRY

	Full-time Diocesan Clergy 2017		Electoral Roll Membership 2017
	Male	Female	
Bath and Wells	132	52	29,800
Birmingham	108	42	15,800
Blackburn	132	24	28,200
Bristol	70	29	14,700
Canterbury	97	27	20,700
Carlisle	72	16	17,600
Chelmsford	222	85	40,800
Chester	138	53	38,900
Chichester	217	31	47,000
Coventry	79	29	15,300
Derby	94	38	15,000
Durham	95	43	18,900
Ely	75	41	17,500
Europe	63	5	11,600
Exeter	154	33	26,000
Gloucester	77	40	21,400
Guildford	119	48	26,300
Hereford	58	25	14,700
Leeds	218	89	38,900
Leicester	79	37	15,900
Lichfield	179	56	38,200
Lincoln	102	53	21,300
Liverpool	119	60	23,800
London	427	86	76,100
Manchester	135	63	28,000
Newcastle	86	32	13,800
Norwich	125	45	17,800
Oxford	264	96	51,800
Peterborough	94	47	17,900
Portsmouth	64	27	14,300
Rochester	145	40	25,900
St Albans	163	70	31,800
St Edmundsbury and Ipswich	79	36	19,000
Salisbury	132	60	35,200
Sheffield	94	32	15,500
Sodor and Man	15	3	2,000
Southwark	231	87	43,600
Southwell and Nottingham	76	31	17,500
Truro	48	34	13,200
Winchester	119	33	28,200
Worcester	74	34	14,500
York	139	54	28,600
Channel Islands	26	4	–
Total	5,235	1,870	1,053,000

In 2017, 102,250 people were baptised, 38,420 people were married in parish churches, the Church of England had an electoral roll membership of 1.05 million, and each week an average 895,300 people (all ages) attended services. There were 15,583 churches; 377 senior clergy (including bishops, archdeacons and cathedral clergy); 7,270 parochial stipendiary clergy; 100 non-parochial stipendiary clergy; 3,060 self-supporting ministers; 1,070 ordained chaplains; 5,180 readers or licensed lay ministers in active ministry; and 3,310 readers or licensed lay ministers with permission to officiate (active emeriti).

STIPENDS

The stipends below are for those appointed on or after 1 April 2004; transitional arrangements are in place for those appointed prior to this date. The national minimum stipend from 1 April 2019 is £24,770; under common tenure all full-time office-holders must receive stipend, or stipend together with other income related to their office, of at least this amount.

	2019–20
Archbishop of Canterbury	£83,400
Archbishop of York	£71,470
Bishop of London	£65,510
Diocesan bishops	£45,270
Suffragan bishops	£36,930
Deans	£36,930
Archdeacons	£35,400
Residentiary canons	*£28,580
Incumbents and clergy of similar status	*£26,470

* National stipend benchmark: adjusted regionally to reflect variations in the cost of living

CANTERBURY

105TH ARCHBISHOP AND PRIMATE OF ALL ENGLAND

Most Revd and Rt. Hon. Justin Welby, *cons.* 2011, *apptd* 2013; Lambeth Palace, London SE1 7JU
Signs Justin Cantuar:

BISHOPS SUFFRAGAN

Dover, vacant

Ebbsfleet, Rt. Revd Jonathan Goodall, *cons.* 2013, *apptd* 2013; Hill House, Treetops, The Mount, Caversham, Reading RG4 7RE
Richborough, Rt. Revd Norman Banks, *cons.* 2011, *apptd* 2011; Parkside House, Abbey Mill Lane, St Albans AL3 4HE
Maidstone, Rt. Revd Roderick Thomas, *cons.* 2015, *apptd* 2015; The Bishop's Lodge, Church Road, Worth, Crawley RH10 7RT

DEAN

Very Revd Robert Willis, *apptd* 2001

Dean of Jersey (A Peculiar), Very Revd Mike Keirle, *apptd* 2017
Dean of Guernsey (A Peculiar), Very Revd Tim Barker, *apptd* 2015

Organist (Canterbury Cathedral), David Flood, FRCO, *apptd* 1988

ARCHDEACONS

Ashford, Ven. Darren Miller, *apptd* 2018
Canterbury, Ven. Jo Kelly Moore *apptd* 2017
Maidstone, Ven. Stephen Taylor, *apptd* 2011

Vicar-General of Province and Diocese, Chancellor Sheila Cameron, QC
Commissary-General, Morag Ellis, QC
Joint Registrars of the Province, Canon John Rees; Stephen Slack
Diocesan Registrar and Legal Adviser, Owen Carew Jones

Diocesan Secretary, Julian Hills, Diocesan House, Lady Wootton's Green, Canterbury CT1 1NQ T 01227-459401

YORK

97TH ARCHBISHOP AND PRIMATE OF ENGLAND

Most Revd and Rt. Hon. Dr John Sentamu, *cons.* 1996, *trans.* 2005; Bishopthorpe, York YO23 2GE
Signs Sentamu Ebor:

BISHOPS SUFFRAGAN

Hull, Rt. Revd Alison White, *cons.* 2015, *apptd* 2015; Hullen House, Woodfield Lane, Hessle, Hull HU13 0ES
Selby, Rt. Revd John Thomson, *cons.* 2014, *apptd* 2014; 6 Pinfold Garth, Malton YO17 7XQ
Whitby, Rt. Revd Paul Fergson, *cons.* 2014, *apptd* 2014; 21 Thornton Road, Stainton TS8 9DS

PRINCIPAL EPISCOPAL VISITOR

Beverley, Rt. Revd Glyn Webster, *cons.* 2013, *apptd* 2013; Holy Trinity Rectory, Micklegate, York YO1 6LE

DEAN

Very Revd Jonathan Frost, *apptd* 2019

Director of Music, Robert Sharpe, *apptd* 2008

ARCHDEACONS

Cleveland, Ven. Samantha Rushton, *apptd* 2015
East Riding, Ven. Andy Broom, *apptd* 2014
York, vacant

Chancellor of the Diocese, His Hon. Judge Collier, QC, *apptd* 2006
Acting Registrar and Legal Secretary, Louise Connacher
Diocesan Secretary, Canon Peter Warry, Diocesan House, Amy Johnson Way, York YO30 4XT T 01904-699500

LONDON (CANTERBURY)

133RD BISHOP

Rt. Revd Dame Sarah Mullally, DBE, *cons.* 2015, *apptd* 2017; Bishop of London's Office, St Michael Paternoster Royal, College Hill, London EC4R 2RL
Signs Sarah Londin:

AREA BISHOPS

Edmonton, Rt. Revd Robert Wickham, *cons.* 2015, *apptd* 2015; 27 Thurlow Road, London NW3 5PP
Kensington, Rt. Revd Graham Tomlin, *cons.* 2015, *apptd* 2015; Dial House, Riverside, Twickenham TW1 3DT
Stepney, Rt. Revd Joanne Grenfell, *cons.* 2019, *apptd* 2019; 63 Coburn Road, London E3 2DB
Willesden, Rt. Revd Peter Broadbent, *cons.* 2001, *apptd* 2001; 173 Willesden Lane, London NW6 7YN

BISHOP SUFFRAGAN

Islington, Rt. Revd Ric Thorpe, *cons.* 2015, *apptd* 2015; St Edmund the King, Lombard Street, London, EC3V 9EA
Fulham, Rt. Revd Jonathan Baker, *cons.* 2011, *apptd* 2013; The Vicarage, 5 St Andrew Street, London EC4A 3AF

DEAN OF ST PAUL'S

Very Revd Dr David Ison, PHD, *apptd* 2012

Director of Music, Andrew Carwood, *apptd* 2007

ARCHDEACONS

Hackney, Ven. Liz Adekunle, *apptd* 2016
Hampstead, Ven. John Hawkins, *apptd* 2015
London, Ven. Luke Miller, *apptd* 2016
Middlesex, Ven. Stephan Welch, *apptd* 2006
Northolt, Ven. Duncan Green, *apptd* 2013
Two Cities, vacant

Chancellor, Nigel Seed, QC, *apptd* 2002
Registrar and Legal Secretary, Paul Morris

Diocesan Secretary, Richard Gough, London Diocesan House, 36 Causton Street, London SW1P 4AU **T** 020-7932 1100

DURHAM (YORK)

74TH BISHOP

Rt. Revd Paul Butler, *cons.* 2004, *trans.* 2013; Auckland Castle, Bishop Auckland DL14 7NR
Signs Paul Dunelm:

BISHOP SUFFRAGAN

Jarrow, Rt. Revd Sarah Clark, *cons.* 2019, *apptd* 2019; Bishop's House, 25 Ivy Lane, Low Fell, Gateshead NE9 6QD

DEAN

Very Revd Andrew Tremlett, *apptd* 2015

Organist, Daniel Cook, *apptd* 2017

ARCHDEACONS

Auckland, Ven. Rick Simpson, *apptd* 2017
Durham, Ven. Ian Jagger, *apptd* 2006
Sunderland, Ven. Bob Cooper, *apptd* 2018

Chancellor, Adrian Iles, *apptd* 2017
Registrar and Legal Secretary, Philip Wills, *apptd* 2018

Diocesan Secretary, Andrew Thurston, Diocesan Office, Cuthbert House, Stonebridge, Durham DH1 3RY **T** 01388-660010

WINCHESTER (CANTERBURY)

97TH BISHOP

Rt. Revd Tim Dakin, cons. 2012, *apptd* 2011; Bishop's Office, Wolvesey, Winchester SO23 9ND
Signs Tim Winton:

BISHOPS SUFFRAGAN

Basingstoke, Rt. Revd David Williams, *cons.* 2014, *apptd* 2014; Diocesan Office, Old Alresford Place, Alresford, Hants SO24 9DH
Southampton, Rt. Revd Deborah Sellin, *cons.* 2019, *apptd* 2019; Diocesan Office, Old Alresford Place, Alresford, Hants SO24 9DH

DEAN

Very Revd Catherine Ogle, *apptd* 2017

Director of Music, Andrew Lumsden, *apptd* 2002

ARCHDEACONS

Bournemouth, Ven. Dr Peter Rouch, *apptd* 2011
Winchester, Ven. Richard Brand, *apptd* 2016
For Mission Development, Ven. Paul Moore, *apptd* 2014

Chancellor, Cain Ormondroyd, *apptd* 2017
Registrar and Legal Secretary, Sue de Candole

Chief Executive, Andrew Robinson, Old Alresford Place, Alresford, Hants SO24 9DH **T** 01962-737300

BATH AND WELLS (CANTERBURY)

79TH BISHOP

Rt. Revd Peter Hancock, *cons.* 2010, *apptd* 2014; The Bishop's Palace, Wells, Somerset BA5 2PD
Signs Peter Bath & Wells:

BISHOP SUFFRAGAN

Taunton, Rt. Revd Ruth Worsley, *cons.* 2015, *apptd* 2015; The Bishop's Palace, Market Place, Wells BA5 2PD

DEAN

Very Revd John Davies, *apptd* 2016

Organist, Matthew Owens, *apptd* 2005

ARCHDEACONS

Bath, Ven. Dr Adrian Youings, *apptd* 2017
Taunton, Ven. Simon Hill, *apptd* 2016
Wells, Ven. Anne Gell, *apptd* 2017

Chancellor, Timothy Briden, *apptd* 1993
Registrar and Legal Secretary, Roland Callaby

Diocesan Secretary, Nick May, The Old Deanery, St Andrew's Street, Wells, Somerset BA5 2UG **T** 01749-670777

BIRMINGHAM (CANTERBURY)

9TH BISHOP

Rt. Revd David Urquhart, KCMG *cons.* 2000, *apptd* 2006; Bishop's Croft, Old Church Road, Harborne, Birmingham B17 0BG
Signs David Birmingham:

BISHOP SUFFRAGAN

Aston, Anne Hollinghurst, *cons.* 2015, *apptd* 2015, Bishop's Lodge, 16 Coleshill Street, Sutton Coldfield B72 1SH

DEAN

Very Revd Matt Thompson, *apptd* 2017

Director of Music, David Hardie, *apptd* 2018

ARCHDEACONS

Aston, Ven. Simon Heathfield, *apptd* 2014
Birmingham, Ven. Jenny Tomlinson, *apptd* 2019

Chancellor, Mark Powell, QC, *apptd* 2012
Registrar and Legal Secretary, Vicki Simpson

Diocesan Secretary, Andrew Halstead, 1 Colmore Row, Birmingham B3 2BJ **T** 0121-426 0400

BLACKBURN (YORK)

9TH BISHOP

Rt. Revd Julian Henderson, *cons.* 2013, *apptd* 2013; Bishop's House, Ribchester Road, Blackburn BB1 9EF
Signs Julian Blackburn

BISHOPS SUFFRAGAN

Burnley, Rt. Revd Philip North, *cons.* 2015, *apptd* 2015; Dean House, 449 Padiham Road, Burnley BB12 6TE
Lancaster, Rt. Revd Dr Jill Duff, *cons.* 2018, *apptd* 2018; Shireshead Vicarage, Whinney Brow, Forton, Preston PR3 0AE

DEAN

Very Revd Peter Howell-Jones, *apptd* 2016

Organist and Director of Music, John Robinson, *apptd* 2019

ARCHDEACON

Blackburn, Ven. Mark Ireland, *apptd* 2015
Lancaster, vacant

Chancellor, His Hon. Judge Bullimore, *apptd* 1990
Registrar and Legal Secretary, Revd Paul Benfield

Diocesan Secretary, Graeme Pollard, Diocesan Office, Clayton House, Walker Office Park, Blackburn BB1 2QE **T** 01254-503070

BRISTOL (CANTERBURY)

56TH BISHOP

Rt. Revd Vivienne Faull, *cons.* 2018, *apptd* 2018; 58A High Street, Winterbourne, Bristol BS36 1JQ
Signs Vivienne Bristol

BISHOP SUFFRAGAN

Swindon, Rt. Revd Dr Lee Rayfield, *cons.* 2005, *apptd* 2005; Mark House, Field Rise, Swindon, Wiltshire SN1 4HP

DEAN
Very Revd David Hoyle, *apptd* 2010

Organist and Director of Music, Mark Lee, *apptd* 1998

ARCHDEACONS
Bristol, Ven. Neil Warwick, *apptd* 2019
Malmesbury, Ven. Christopher Bryan, *apptd* 2019

Chancellor, Revd Justin Gau
Registrar and Legal Secretary, Roland Callaby

Diocesan Secretary, Oliver Home, First Floor, Hillside House, 1500
Parkway North, Stoke Gifford, Bristol BS34 8YU **T** 0117-9060100

CARLISLE (YORK)

67TH BISHOP
Rt. Revd James Newcome, *cons.* 2002, *apptd* 2009; Bishop's
House, Ambleside Road, Keswick CA12 4DD
Signs James Carliol

BISHOP SUFFRAGAN
Penrith, Revd Dr Emma Ineson, *cons.* 2019, *apptd* 2018; Holm
Croft, 13 Castle Road, Kendal, Cumbria LA9 7AU

DEAN
Very Revd Mark Boyling, *apptd* 2004

Director of Music, Mark Duthie, *apptd* 2017

ARCHDEACONS
Carlisle, Ven. Lee Townend, *apptd* 2017
West Cumberland, Ven. Dr Richard Pratt, *apptd* 2009
Westmorland and Furness, Ven. Vernon Ross, *apptd* 2017

Chancellor, Geoffrey Tattersall, QC, *apptd* 2003
Registrar and Legal Secretary, Jane Lowdon

Diocesan Secretary, Derek Hurton, Church House, 19–24
Friargate, Penrith, Cumbria CA11 7XR **T** 01768-807777

CHELMSFORD (CANTERBURY)

10TH BISHOP
Rt. Revd Stephen Cottrell, *cons.* 2004, *apptd* 2010;
Bishopscourt, Main Road, Margaretting, Ingatestone, Essex CM4
0HD
Signs Stephen Chelmsford

BISHOPS SUFFRAGAN
Barking, Rt. Revd Peter Hill, *cons.* 2014, *apptd* 2014; Barking
Lodge, Verulam Avenue, London E17 8ES
Bradwell, Rt. Revd Dr John Perumbalath, *cons.* 2018, *apptd*
2018; Bishop's House. Orsett Road, Horndon-on-the-Hill, Essex
SS17 8NS
Colchester, Rt. Revd Roger Morris, *cons.* 2014, *apptd* 2014; 1
Fitzwater Road, Colchester, Essex CO3 3SS

DEAN
Very Revd Nicholas Henshall, *apptd* 2013

Director of Music, James Davy, *apptd* 2012

ARCHDEACONS
Barking, Ven. Christopher Burke, *apptd* 2019
Chelmsford, Ven. Elizabeth Snowden, *apptd* 2016
Colchester, Ven. Ruth Patten, *apptd* 2019
Harlow, Ven. Vanessa Herrick, *apptd* 2017
Southend, Ven. Mike Lodge, *apptd* 2017
Stansted, Ven. Robin King, *apptd* 2013
West Ham, Ven. Elwin Cockett, *apptd* 2007

Chancellor, George Pulman, QC, *apptd* 2001
Registrar and Legal Secretary, Aiden Hargreaves-Smith

Chief Executive, Joel Gowen, 53 New Street, Chelmsford, Essex
CM1 1AT **T** 01245-294400

CHESTER (YORK)

41ST BISHOP
vacant

BISHOPS SUFFRAGAN
Birkenhead, Rt. Revd Keith Sinclair, *cons.* 2007, *apptd* 2007;
Bishop's Lodge, 67 Bidston Road, Prenton CH43 6TR
Stockport, vacant; Bishop's Lodge, Back Lane, Dunham, Altrincham
WA14 4SG

DEAN
Very Revd Dr Timothy Stratford, *apptd* 2018

Organist and Director of Music, Philip Rushforth, FRCO,
apptd 2008

ARCHDEACONS
Chester, Ven. Dr Michael Gilbertson, *apptd* 2010
Macclesfield, Ven. Ian Bishop, *apptd* 2011

Chancellor, His Hon. Judge Turner, QC, *apptd* 1998
Registrar and Legal Secretary, Lisa Moncur

Diocesan Secretary, George Colville, Church House, 5500
Daresbury Park, Daresbury, Warrington WA4 4GE
T 01928-718834

CHICHESTER (CANTERBURY)

103RD BISHOP
Rt. Revd Dr Martin Warner, *cons.* 2010, *apptd* 2012; The
Palace, Chichester PO19 1PY
Signs Martin Cicestr:

BISHOPS SUFFRAGAN
Horsham, vacant

Lewes, Rt. Revd Richard Jackson, *cons.* 2014, *apptd* 2014;
Ebenezer House, Kingston Ridge, Kingston, Lewes BN7 3JU

DEAN
Very Revd Stephen Waine, *apptd* 2015

Organist, Charles Harrison, *apptd* 2014

ARCHDEACONS
Brighton and Lewes, Ven. Martin Lloyd Williams, *apptd* 2015
Chichester, Ven. Luke Irvine-Capel, *apptd* 2019
Horsham, Ven. Fiona Windsor, *apptd* 2014
Hastings, Ven. Edward Dowler, *apptd* 2016

Chancellor, Prof. Mark Hill, QC
Deputy Registrar and Legal Secretary, Darren Oliver

Diocesan Secretary, Gabrielle Higgins, Diocesan Church House,
211 New Church Road, Hove, E. Sussex BN3 4ED
T 01273-421021

COVENTRY (CANTERBURY)

9TH BISHOP
Rt. Revd Dr Christopher Cocksworth, *cons.* 2008, *apptd*
2008; The Bishop's House, 23 Davenport Road, Coventry
CV5 6PW
Signs Christopher Coventry

BISHOP SUFFRAGAN
Warwick, Rt. Revd John Stroyan, *cons.* 2005, *apptd* 2005;
Warwick House, School Hill, Offchurch, Leamington Spa CV33 9AL

DEAN
Very Revd John Witcombe, *apptd* 2013

Director of Music, Mr Kerry Beaumont, *apptd* 2006

ARCHDEACONS

Archdeacon Missioner, Ven. Barry Dugmore, *apptd* 2019
Archdeacon Pastor, Ven. Sue Field *apptd* 2017

Chancellor, His Hon. Judge Eyre, *apptd* 2009
Registrar and Legal Secretary, Mary Allanson
Diocesan Secretary, Ruth Marlow, Cathedral & Diocesan Offices, 1 Hilltop, Coventry CV1 5AB **T** 024-7652 1200

DERBY (CANTERBURY)

8TH BISHOP

Rt. Revd. Elizabeth Lane, *cons.* 2015, *apptd* 2019; The Bishop's Office, 6 King Street, Duffield DE56 4EU
Signs Elizabeth Derby

BISHOP SUFFRAGAN

Repton, Rt. Revd Jan McFarlane, *cons.* 2016, *apptd* 2016; Repton House, 39 Hickton Road, Swanwick, Alfreton DE55 1AF

DEAN

Very Revd Dr Stephen Hance, *apptd* 2017

Director of Music, Alexander Binns, *apptd* 2019

ARCHDEACONS

Chesterfield, Ven. Carol Coslett, *apptd* 2018
Derby, Ven. Dr Christopher Cunliffe, *apptd* 2006

Chancellor, His Hon. Judge Bullimore, *apptd* 1981
Registrar and Legal Secretary, Nadine Waldron
Diocesan Secretary, Rachel Morris, Derby Church House, Full Street, Derby DE1 3DR **T** 01332-388650

ELY (CANTERBURY)

69TH BISHOP

Rt. Revd Stephen Conway, *cons.* 2006, *apptd* 2011; The Bishop's House, Ely CB7 4DW
Signs Stephen Ely

BISHOP SUFFRAGAN

Huntingdon, Rt. Revd Dr Dagmar Winter, *cons.* 2019, *apptd* 2019; 14 Lynn Road, Ely, Cambs CB6 1DA

DEAN

Very Revd Mark Bonney, *apptd* 2012

Director of Music, Edmund Aldhouse, *apptd* 2018

ARCHDEACONS

Cambridge, Ven. Dr Alex Hughes, *apptd* 2014
Huntingdon and Wisbech, Ven. Hugh McCurdy, *apptd* 2005

Chancellor, His Hon. Judge Leonard, QC
Registrar, Howard Dellar
Diocesan Secretary, Paul Evans, Bishop Woodford House, Barton Road, Ely, Cambs CB7 4DX **T** 01353-652701

EXETER (CANTERBURY)

71ST BISHOP

Rt. Revd Robert Atwell, *cons.* 2008, *apptd* 2014; The Palace, Exeter EX1 1HY
Signs Robert Exon:

BISHOPS SUFFRAGAN

Crediton, Rt. Revd Jackie Searle, *cons.* 2018, *apptd* 2018; 32 The Avenue, Tiverton EX16 4HW
Plymouth, Rt. Revd Nick McKinnel, *cons.* 2012, *trans.* 2015; 108 Molesworth Road, Stoke, Plymouth PL3 4AQ

DEAN

Very Revd Jonathan Greener, *apptd* 2017

Director of Music, Timothy Noon, *apptd* 2016

ARCHDEACONS

Barnstaple, Ven. Mark Butchers, *apptd* 2015
Exeter, Ven. Andrew Beane, *apptd* 2019
Plymouth, Ven. Nick Shutt, *apptd* 2019
Totnes, Ven. Douglas Dettmer, *apptd* 2015

Chancellor, Hon. Sir Andrew McFarlane
Registrar and Legal Secretary, Alison Stock
Diocesan Secretary, Stephen Hancock, The Old Deanery, The Cloisters, Exeter EX1 1HS **T** 01392-272686

GIBRALTAR IN EUROPE (CANTERBURY)

4TH BISHOP

Rt. Revd Robert Innes, PHD, *cons.* 2014, *apptd* 2014; Office of the Bishop in Europe, 47, rue Capitaine Crespel – boite 49, 1050 Brussels, Belgium

BISHOP SUFFRAGAN

In Europe, Rt. Revd David Hamid, *cons.* 2002, *apptd* 2002; 14 Tufton Street, London SW1P 3QZ

Dean, Cathedral Church of the Holy Trinity, Gibraltar, vacant

Chancellor, Pro-Cathedral of St Paul, Valletta, Malta, Canon Simon Godfrey
Chancellor, Pro-Cathedral of the Holy Trinity, Brussels, Belgium, Ven. Dr Paul Vrolijk

ARCHDEACONS

Eastern, Canon Adèle Kelham *(acting)*
France, Ven. Meurig Williams
Germany and Northern Europe, Canon John Newsome *(acting)*
Gibraltar, Ven. Geoffrey Johnston *(interim)*
Italy and Malta, Ven. Geoffrey Johnston *(acting)*
North-West Europe, Ven. Dr Paul Vrolijk
Switzerland, Canon Adèle Kelham

Chancellor, Prof. Mark Hill, QC
Registrar and Legal Secretary, Aiden Hargreaves-Smith
Diocesan Secretary, Andrew Caspari 14 Tufton Street, London SW1P 3QZ **T** 020-7898 1155

GLOUCESTER (CANTERBURY)

41ST BISHOP

Rt. Revd Rachel Treweek, *cons.* 2015, *apptd* 2015; 2 College Green, Gloucester GL1 2LR
Signs Rachel Gloucestr

BISHOP SUFFRAGAN

Tewkesbury, Rt. Revd Robert Springett, *cons.* 2016, *apptd* 2016; 2 College Green, Gloucester GL1 2LR

DEAN

Very Revd Stephen Lake, *apptd* 2011

Director of Music, Adrian Partington, *apptd* 2007

ARCHDEACONS

Cheltenham, Ven. Phil Andrew, *apptd* 2017
Gloucester, Ven. Hilary Dawson, *apptd* 2019

Chancellor and Vicar-General, June Rodgers, *apptd* 1990
Registrar and Legal Secretary, Jos Moule
Diocesan Secretary, Ben Preece Smith, Church House, College Green, Gloucester GL1 2LY **T** 01452-410022

GUILDFORD (CANTERBURY)

10TH BISHOP

Rt. Revd Andrew Watson, *cons.* 2008, *apptd* 2014; Willow Grange, Woking Road, Guildford, Surrey GU4 7QS
Signs Andrew Guildford

BISHOP SUFFRAGAN

Dorking, Rt Revd Jo Wells, *cons.* 2016, *apptd* 2016; Dayspring, 13 Pilgrim's Way, Guildford, Surrey GU4 8AD

DEAN

Very Revd Dianna Gwilliams, *apptd* 2013

Organist, Katherine Dienes-Williams, *apptd* 2007

ARCHDEACONS
Dorking, vacant
Surrey, Ven. Paul Davies, *apptd* 2017

Chancellor, Andrew Jordan
Registrar and Legal Secretary, Howard Dellar
Diocesan Secretary, Peter Coles, Church House, 20 Alan Turing Road, Guildford GU2 7YF **T** 01483-790300

HEREFORD (CANTERBURY)

105TH BISHOP

Rt. Revd Richard Frith, cons. 1998, apptd 2014; Bishop's House, The Palace, Hereford HR4 9BN
Signs Richard Hereford

BISHOP SUFFRAGAN

Ludlow, Rt. Revd Alistair Magowan, *cons.* 2009, *apptd* 2009; Bishop's House, Corvedale Road, Craven Arms, Shropshire SY7 9BT

DEAN

Very Revd Michael Tavinor, *apptd* 2002

Organist and Director of Music, Geraint Bowen, FRCO, *apptd* 2001

ARCHDEACONS
Hereford, Ven. Derek Chedzey, *apptd* 2018
Ludlow, Rt. Revd Alistair Magowan, *apptd* 2009

Chancellor, His Hon. Judge Kaye, QC
Registrar and Legal Secretary, Howard Dellar
Diocesan Secretary, Sam Pratley, The Palace, Hereford HR4 9BL **T** 01432-373300

LEEDS (YORK)

1ST BISHOP OF LEEDS

Rt. Revd Nicholas Baines, *cons.* 2003, *apptd* 2014; Hollin House, Weetwood Avenue, Leeds LS16 5NG
Signs Nicholas Leeds

AREA BISHOPS

Bradford, Rt. Revd Dr Toby Howarth, *cons.* 2014, *apptd* 2014; 47 Kirkgate, Shipley BD18 3EH
Huddersfield, Rt. Revd Jonathan Gibbs, *cons.* 2014, *apptd* 2014; University of Huddersfield, Ground Floor, Sir John Ramsden Court, Huddersfield HD1 3AQ
Ripon, Rt. Revd Dr Helen-Ann Hartley, *cons.* 2014, *apptd* 2018; The Bishop's Office, Redwood, New Road, Sharow, Ripon HG4 5BS
Wakefield, Rt. Revd Anthony Robinson, *cons.* 2002, *apptd* 2014; Pontefract House 181A Manygates Lane, Sandal, Wakefield WF2 7DR

SUFFRAGAN BISHOP

Richmond, Rt. Revd Paul Slater, *cons.* 2015, apptd 2015; Church House, 17–19 York Place, Leeds LS1 2EX

DEANS
Bradford, Very Revd Jerry Lepine, *apptd* 2013
Ripon, Very Revd John Dobson, *apptd* 2014
Wakefield, Very Revd Simon Cowling, *apptd* 2018

Directors of Music, Alexander Berry (Bradford), *apptd* 2017; Andrew Bryden (Ripon), *apptd* 2003; Thomas Moore (Wakefield), *apptd* 2010

ARCHDEACONS
Bradford, Ven. Andrew Jolley, *apptd* 2016
Halifax, Ven. Dr Anne Dawtry, *apptd* 2011
Leeds, Ven. Paul Ayers, *apptd* 2017
Richmond and Craven, Ven. Jonathan Gough, *apptd* 2019
Pontefract, Ven. Peter Townley, *apptd* 2008

Chancellor, Prof. Mark Hill, QC
Registrar and Legal Secretary, Peter Foskett
Diocesan Secretary, Debbie Child; Church House, 17–19 York Place, Leeds LS1 2EX **T** 0113-200 0540

LEICESTER (CANTERBURY)

7TH BISHOP

Rt Revd Martyn Snow, *cons.* 2013, *apptd* 2016; Bishop's Lodge, 10 Springfield Road, Leicester LE2 3BD
Signs Martyn Leicester

SUFFRAGAN BISHOP

Loughborough, Rt. Revd Guli Francis-Dehqani, *cons.* 2017, *apptd* 2017; c/o Bishop's Lodge, 10 Springfield Road, Leicester LE2 3BD

DEAN

Very Revd David Monteith, *apptd* 2013

Director of Music, Dr Christopher Ouvry-Johns

ARCHDEACONS
Leicester, Ven. Richard Worsfold, *apptd* 2018
Loughborough, Ven. Claire Wood, *apptd* 2017

Chancellor, Mark Blackett-Ord
Registrar and Legal Secretary, Lee Coley
Diocesan Secretary, Jonathan Kerry, St Martin's House, 7 Peacock Lane, Leicester LE1 5PZ **T** 0116-261 5200

LICHFIELD (CANTERBURY)

99TH BISHOP

Rt. Revd Dr Michael Ipgrave, OBE, *cons.* 2012, *apptd* 2016; 22 The Close, Lichfield, WS13 7LG
Signs Michael Lich:

AREA BISHOPS

Shrewsbury, Rt. Revd Sarah Bullock, *cons.* 2019, *apptd* 2019; Athlone House, 68 London Road, Shrewsbury SY2 6PG
Stafford, Rt. Revd Geoffrey Annas, *cons.* 2010, *apptd* 2010; Ash Garth, Broughton Crescent, Barlaston, Stoke-on-Trent ST12 9DD
Wolverhampton, Rt. Revd Clive Gregory, *cons.* 2007, *apptd* 2007; 61 Richmond Road, Wolverhampton WV3 9JH

DEAN

Very Revd Adrian Dorber, *apptd* 2005

Director of Music, Ben Lamb, *apptd* 2010
Organist, Martyn Rawles, *apptd* 2010

ARCHDEACONS
Lichfield, vacant
Salop, Ven. Paul Thomas, *apptd* 2011
Stoke-on-Trent, Ven. Matthew Parker, *apptd* 2013
Walsall, Ven. Julian Francis, *apptd* 2019

Chancellor, His Hon. Judge Eyre, *apptd* 2012
Joint Registrars and Legal Secretaries, Niall Blackie; Andrew Wynne

Diocesan Secretary, Julie Jones, St Mary's House, The Close, Lichfield, Staffs WS13 7LD **T** 01543-306030

LINCOLN (CANTERBURY)

72ND BISHOP
Rt. Revd Christopher Lowson, *cons.* 2011, *apptd* 2011; Bishop's Office, The Old Palace, Minster Yard, Lincoln LN2 1PU
Signs Christopher Lincoln

BISHOPS SUFFRAGAN
Grantham, Rt. Revd Dr Nicholas Chamberlain, *cons.* 2015, *apptd* 2015; The Old Palace, Minster Yard, Lincoln LN2 1PU
Grimsby, Rt. Revd Dr David Court (acting diocesan bishop), *cons.* 2014, *apptd* 2014; The Old Palace, Minster Yard, Lincoln LN2 1PU

DEAN
Very Revd Christine Wilson, *apptd* 2016 (currently on leave of absence)

Director of Music, Aric Prentice, *apptd* 2003

ARCHDEACONS
Boston, Ven. Dr Justine Allain Chapman, *apptd* 2013
Lincoln, Ven. Gavin Kirk, *apptd* 2016
Stow and Lindsey, Ven. Mark Steadman, *apptd* 2015

Chancellor, His Hon. Judge Bishop
Registrar and Legal Secretary, Ian Blaney

Diocesan Secretary, Revd David Dadswell, Edward King House, Minster Yard, Lincoln LN2 1PU **T** 01522-504050

LIVERPOOL (YORK)

8TH BISHOP
Rt. Revd Paul Bayes, *cons.* 2010, *apptd* 2014; Bishop's Lodge, Woolton Park, Liverpool L25 6DT
Signs Paul Liverpool

BISHOP SUFFRAGAN
Warrington, Rt. Revd Bev Mason, *cons.* 2018, *apptd* 2018; 34 Central Avenue, Eccleston Park, Prescot L34 2QP

DEAN
Very Revd Susan Jones, PHD, *apptd* 2018

Director of Music, Lee Ward, *apptd* 2017

ARCHDEACONS
Liverpool, Ven. Mike McGurk, *apptd* 2017
Knowlsey & Sefton, Ven. Pete Spiers *apptd* 2015
St Helens & Warrington, Ven. Peter Preece, *apptd* 2015
Wigan & West Lancashire, Ven. Jennifer McKenzie, *apptd* 2015

Chancellor, His Hon. Judge Wood, QC
Registrar and Legal Secretary, Howard Dellar

Diocesan Secretary, Mike Eastwood, St James House, 20 St James Street, Liverpool L1 7BY **T** 0151-709 9722

MANCHESTER (YORK)

12TH BISHOP
Rt. Revd Dr David Walker, *cons.* 2000, *apptd* 2013; Bishopscourt, Bury New Road, Salford M7 4LE
Signs David Manchester

BISHOPS SUFFRAGAN
Bolton, Rt. Revd Mark Ashcroft, *cons.* 2016, *apptd* 2016; Bishop's Lodge, Walkenden Road, Walkenden M28 2WH
Middleton, Rt. Revd Mark Davies, *cons.* 2008, *apptd* 2008; The Hollies, Manchester Road, Rochdale OL11 3QY

DEAN
Very Revd Rogers Govender, *apptd* 2006

Organist, Christopher Stokes, *apptd* 1992

ARCHDEACONS
Bolton, Ven. Jean Burgess, *apptd* 2018
Manchester, Ven. Karen Lund, *apptd* 2017
Rochdale, Ven. Cherry Vann, *apptd* 2008
Salford, Ven. David Sharples, *apptd* 2009

Chancellor, Canon Geoffrey Tattersall, QC
Registrar and Legal Secretary, Jane Monks

Diocesan Secretary, Helen Platts, Diocesan Church House, 90 Deansgate, Manchester M3 2GH **T** 0161-828 1400

NEWCASTLE (YORK)

12TH BISHOP
Rt. Revd Christine Elizabeth Hardman, *cons.* 2015, apptd 2015; Bishop's House, 29 Moor Road South, Gosforth, Newcastle upon Tyne NE3 1PA
Signs Christine Newcastle

SUFFRAGAN BISHOP
Berwick Rt. Revd Mark Tanner, *cons.* 2016, *apptd* 2016; Berwick House, Longhirst Road, Pegswood, Morpeth NE61 6XF

DEAN
Very Revd Geoff Miller, *apptd* 2018

Director of Music, Ian Roberts, *apptd* 2016

ARCHDEACONS
Lindisfarne, Ven. Dr Peter Robinson, *apptd* 2008
Northumberland, Ven. Mark Wroe, *apptd* 2019

Chancellor, Euan Duff, *apptd* 2013
Registrar and Legal Secretary, Jane Lowdon

Diocesan Secretary, Canon Shane Waddle, Church House, St John's Terrace, North Shields NE29 6HS **T** 0191-270 4100

NORWICH (CANTERBURY)

72ND BISHOP
Rt. Revd Graham Usher, *cons.* 2014, *apptd* 2019; Bishop's House, Norwich NR3 1SB
Signs Graham Norvic:

BISHOPS SUFFRAGAN
Lynn, Rt. Revd Jonathan Meyrick, *cons.* 2011, *apptd* 2011; The Old Vicarage, Castle Acre, King's Lynn PE32 2AA
Thetford, Rt. Revd Alan Winton, PHD, *cons.* 2009, *apptd* 2009; The Red House, 53 Norwich Road, Stoke Holy Cross, Norwich NR14 8AB

DEAN
Very Revd Jane Hedges, *apptd* 2014

Master of Music, Ashley Grote, *apptd* 2012

ARCHDEACONS
Lynn, Ven. Ian Bentley, *apptd* 2018
Norfolk, Ven. Steven Betts, *apptd* 2012
Norwich, Ven. Karen Hutchinson, *apptd* 2016

Chancellor, Ruth Arlow, *apptd* 2012
Registrar and Legal Secretary, Stuart Jones
Diocesan Secretary, Richard Butler, Diocesan House, 109 Dereham Road, Easton, Norwich, Norfolk NR9 5ES T 01603-880853

OXFORD (CANTERBURY)

44TH BISHOP
Rt. Revd Steven Croft, *cons.* 2009, *apptd* 2016; Church House Oxford, Langford Locks, Kidlington, Oxford OX5 1GF
Signs Steven Oxon:

AREA BISHOPS
Buckingham, Rt. Revd Dr Alan Wilson, *cons.* 2003, *apptd* 2003; Sheridan, Grimms Hill, Great Missenden, Bucks HP16 9BD
Dorchester, Rt. Revd Colin Fletcher, *cons.* 2000, *apptd* 2000; Arran House, Sandy Lane, Yarnton, Oxon OX5 1PB
Reading, vacant; Bishop's House, Tidmarsh Lane, Tidmarsh, Reading RG8 8HA

DEAN OF CHRIST CHURCH
Very Revd Martyn Percy, PHD, *apptd* 2014

Organist, Steven Grahl, *apptd* 2018

ARCHDEACONS
Berkshire, Ven. Olivia Graham, *apptd* 2013
Buckingham, Ven. Guy Elsmore, *apptd* 2016
Dorchester, Ven. Judy French, *apptd* 2014
Oxford, Ven. Martin Gorick, *apptd* 2013

Chancellor, His Hon. Judge Hodge, QC, *apptd* 2019
Joint Registrars and Legal Secretaries, Darren Oliver; Revd Canon John Rees
Diocesan Secretary, Mark Humphriss, Church House Oxford, Langford Locks, Kidlington, Oxford OX5 1GF T 01865-208200

PETERBOROUGH (CANTERBURY)

38TH BISHOP
Rt. Revd Donald Allister, *cons.* 2010, *apptd* 2009; Bishop's Lodging, The Palace, Peterborough PE1 1YA
Signs Donald Petriburg:

BISHOP SUFFRAGAN
Brixworth, Rt. Revd John Holbrook, *cons.* 2011, *apptd* 2011; Orchard Acre, 11 North Street, Mears Ashby, Northants NN6 0DW

DEAN
Very Revd Christopher Dalliston, *apptd* 2018

Director of Music, Tansy Castledine, *apptd* 2018

ARCHDEACONS
Northampton, Ven. Richard Ormston, *apptd* 2014
Oakham, Ven. Gordon Steele, *apptd* 2012

Chancellor, David Pittaway, QC, *apptd* 2005
Registrar and Legal Secretary, Anna Spriggs
Diocesan Secretary, Andrew Roberts, Diocesan Office, The Palace, Peterborough PE1 1YB T 01733-887000

PORTSMOUTH (CANTERBURY)

9TH BISHOP
Rt. Revd Christopher Foster, *cons.* 2010, *apptd* 2010; Bishopsgrove, 26 Osborn Road, Fareham, Hants PO16 7DQ
Signs Christopher Portsmouth

DEAN
Very Revd Anthony Cane, *apptd* 2019

Organist, David Price, *apptd* 1996

ARCHDEACONS
Isle of Wight, Ven. Peter Leonard, *apptd* 2019
Portsdown, vacant
The Meon, Ven. Gavin Collins, *apptd* 2011

Chancellor, His Hon. Judge Waller, CBE
Registrar and Legal Secretary, Hilary Tyler
Diocesan Secretary, Victoria James, Diocesan Offices, 1st Floor, Peninsular House, Wharf Road, Portsmouth PO2 8HB T 023-9289 9664

ROCHESTER (CANTERBURY)

107TH BISHOP
Rt. Revd James Langstaff, *cons.* 2004, *apptd* 2010; Bishopscourt, 24 St Margaret's Street, Rochester ME1 1TS
Signs, James Roffen:

BISHOP SUFFRAGAN
Tonbridge, Rt. Revd Simon Burton-Jones, *cons.* 2018, *apptd* 2018; 25 Shoesmith Lane, Kings Hill, Kent ME19 4FF

DEAN
Very Revd Dr Philip Hesketh, *apptd* 2016

Interim Director of Music, Adrian Bawtree, *apptd* 2018

ARCHDEACONS
Bromley & Bexley, Ven. Dr Paul Wright, *apptd* 2003
*Rochester,*Ven. Andrew Wooding Jones, *apptd* 2018
Tonbridge, Ven. Julie Conalty *apptd* 2017

Chancellor, The Worshipful John Gallagher
Registrar and Legal Secretary, Owen Carew-Jones
Diocesan Secretary, vacant, St Nicholas Church, Boley Hill, Rochester ME1 1SL T 01634-560000

ST ALBANS (CANTERBURY)

10TH BISHOP
Rt. Revd Dr Alan Smith, *cons.* 2001, *apptd* 2009, *trans.* 2009; Abbey Gate House, St Albans AL3 4HD
Signs Alan St Albans

BISHOPS SUFFRAGAN
Bedford, Rt. Revd Richard Atkinson, OBE, *cons.* 2012, *apptd* 2012; Bishop's Lodge, Bedford Road, Cardington, Bedford MK44 3SS
Hertford, Rt. Revd Dr Michael Beasley, *cons.* 2015, *apptd* 2015; Bishopswood, 3 Stobarts Close, Knebworth SG3 6ND

DEAN
Very Revd Dr Jeffrey John, *apptd* 2004

Organist, Andrew Lucas, *apptd* 1998

ARCHDEACONS
Bedford, Ven. Dave Middlebrook, *apptd* 2019
Hertford, Ven. Janet Mackenzie, *apptd* 2016
St Albans, Ven. Jonathan Smith, *apptd* 2008

Chancellor, Lyndsey de Mestre, QC
Deputy Registrars, Jonathan Baldwin; Owen Carew-Jones
Diocesan Secretary, Susan Pope, Holywell Lodge, 41 Holywell Hill, St Albans AL1 1HE T 01727-854532

ST EDMUNDSBURY AND IPSWICH (CANTERBURY)

11TH BISHOP

Rt. Revd Martin Seeley, *cons.* 2015, *apptd* 2015; The Bishop's House, 4 Park Road, Ipswich IP1 3ST
Signs Martin St Edmundsbury and Ipswich

BISHOP SUFFRAGAN

Dunwich, Rt. Revd Michael Harrison, PHD, *cons.* 2016, *apptd* 2015; Robin Hall, Chapel Lane, Mendlesham, Stowmarket IP14 5SQ

DEAN

Very Revd Joe Hawes, *apptd* 2018

Director of Music, James Thomas, *apptd* 1997

ARCHDEACONS

Ipswich, Ven. Rhiannon King, *apptd* 2019
Sudbury, Ven. Dr David Jenkins, *apptd* 2010
Suffolk, Ven. Ian Morgan, *apptd* 2012
Rural Mission, Ven. Sally Gaze, *apptd* 2019

Chancellor, David Etherington, QC
Registrar and Legal Secretary, James Hall

Diocesan Secretary, Anna Hughes, Diocesan Office, St Nicholas Centre, 4 Cutler Street, Ipswich IP1 1UQ **T** 01473-298500

SALISBURY (CANTERBURY)

78TH BISHOP

Rt. Revd Nicholas Holtam, *cons.* 2011, *apptd* 2011; South Canonry, 71 The Close, Salisbury SP1 2ER
Signs Nicholas Sarum

BISHOPS SUFFRAGAN

Ramsbury, Rt. Revd Dr Andrew Rumsey, *cons.* 2019, *apptd* 2018; Church House, Crane Street, Salisbury SP1 2QB
Sherborne, Rt. Revd Karen Gorham, *cons.* 2016, *apptd* 2015; The Sherborne Office, St Nicholas' Church Centre, 30 Wareham Road, Corfe Mullen BH21 3LE

DEAN

Very Revd Nicholas Papadopulos *apptd* 2018

Director of Music, David Halls, *apptd* 2005

ARCHDEACONS

Dorset, Ven. Antony MacRow-Wood, *apptd* 2015
Sarum, Ven. Alan Jeans, *apptd* 2003
Sherborne, Ven. Penny Sayer, *apptd* 2018
Wilts, Ven. Sue Groom, *apptd* 2016

Chancellor, Canon Ruth Arlow, *apptd* 2016
Registrar and Legal Secretary, Sue de Candole

Diocesan Secretary, David Pain, Church House, Crane Street, Salisbury SP1 2QB **T** 01722-411922

SHEFFIELD (YORK)

8TH BISHOP

Rt. Revd Dr Peter Wilcox, *cons.* 2017, *apptd* 2017; Bishopscroft, Snaithing Lane, Sheffield S10 3LG
Signs Peter Sheffield

BISHOP SUFFRAGAN

Doncaster, vacant

DEAN

Very Revd Peter Bradley, *apptd* 2003

Director of Music, Thomas Corns, *apptd* 2017

ARCHDEACONS

Doncaster, Ven. Steve Wilcockson, *apptd* 2012
Sheffield and Rotherham, Ven. Malcolm Chamberlain, *apptd* 2013

Chancellor, Her Hon. Judge Sarah Singleton, QC, *apptd* 2014
Registrar and Legal Secretary, Andrew Vidler

Diocesan Secretary, Heidi Adcock, Church House, 95–99 Effingham Street, Rotherham S65 1BL **T** 01709-309100

SODOR AND MAN (YORK)

82ND BISHOP

Rt. Revd Peter Eagles, *cons.* 2017, *apptd* 2017; Thie yn Aspick, 4 The Falls, Douglas, Isle of Man IM4 4PZ
Signs Peter Sodor as Mannin

ARCHDEACON OF MAN

Ven. Andrew Brown, *apptd* 2011

Vicar-General and Chancellor, Howard Connell
Registrar, Louise Connacher

Diocesan Secretary, Andrew Swithinbank, c/o Thie yn Aspick, 4 The Falls, Douglas, Isle of Man IM4 4PZ **T** 07624-314590

SOUTHWARK (CANTERBURY)

10TH BISHOP

Rt. Revd Christopher Chessun, *cons.* 2005, *apptd* 2011; Trinity House, 4 Chapel Court, Borough High Street, London SE1 1HW
Signs Christopher Southwark

AREA BISHOPS

Croydon, Rt. Revd Jonathan Clark, *cons.* 2012, *apptd* 2012; St Matthew's House, 100 George Street, London CR0 1PE
Kingston upon Thames, Rt. Revd Dr Richard Cheetham, *cons.* 2002, *apptd* 2002; 620 Kingston Road, Raynes Park, London SW20 8DN
Woolwich, Rt. Revd Dr Karowei Dorgu, *cons.* 2017, *apptd* 2017; Trinity House, 4 Chapel Court, Borough High Street, London SE1 1HW

DEAN

Very Revd Andrew Nunn, *apptd* 2011

Director of Music, Ian Keatley, *apptd* 2019

ARCHDEACONS

Croydon, Ven. Christopher Skilton, *apptd* 2013
Lambeth, Ven. Simon Gates, *apptd* 2013
Lewisham & Greenwich, Ven. Alastair Cutting, *apptd* 2013
Reigate, Ven. Moira Astin, *apptd* 2016
Southwark, Ven. Dr Jane Steen, *apptd* 2013
Wandsworth, Ven. John Kiddle, *apptd* 2015

Chancellor, Philip Petchey
Registrar and Legal Secretary, Paul Morris

Diocesan Secretary, Ruth Martin, Trinity House, 4 Chapel Court, Borough High Street, London SE1 1HW **T** 020-7939 9400

SOUTHWELL AND NOTTINGHAM (YORK)

12TH BISHOP

Rt. Revd Paul Williams, *cons.* 2009, *trans.* 2015; Jubilee House, Westgate, Southwell NG25 0JH
Signs Paul Southwell and Nottingham

BISHOP SUFFRAGAN

Sherwood, Rt. Revd Anthony Porter, *cons.* 2006, *apptd* 2006; Jubilee House, Westgate, Southwell NG25 0JH

DEAN
Very Revd Nicola Sullivan, *apptd* 2016

Rector Chori, Paul Provost, *apptd* 2017

ARCHDEACONS
Newark, Ven. David Picken, *apptd* 2012
Nottingham, Ven. Phil Williams, *apptd* 2019

Chancellor, His Hon. Judge Ockelton
Registrar and Legal Secretary, Amanda Redgate
Chief Executive, Nigel Spraggins, Jubilee House, Westgate, Southwell, Notts NG25 0JH **T** 01636-814331

TRURO (CANTERBURY)

16TH BISHOP
Rt. Revd Philip Mounstephen, *cons.* 2018, *apptd* 2018; Lis Escop, Feock, Truro TR3 6QQ
Signs Philip Truro

BISHOP SUFFRAGAN
St Germans, Rt. Revd Christopher Goldsmith, DPHIL, *cons.* 2013, *apptd* 2013; Lis Escop, Feock, Truro TR3 6QQ

DEAN
Very Revd Roger Bush, *apptd* 2012

Organist and Director of Music, Chris Gray, *apptd* 2008

ARCHDEACONS
Bodmin, Ven. Audrey Elkington, *apptd* 2011
Cornwall, Ven. Paul Bryer, *apptd* 2019

Chancellor, Timothy Briden, *apptd* 1998
Registrar and Legal Secretary, Jos Moule

Diocesan Secretary, Esther Pollard, Church House, Woodlands Court, Truro Business Park, Threemilestone, Truro TR4 9NH **T** 01872-274351

WORCESTER (CANTERBURY)

113TH BISHOP
Rt. Revd Dr John Inge, *cons.* 2003, *apptd* 2007; The Bishop's Office, The Old Palace, Deansway, Worcester WR1 2JE
Signs John Wigorn

SUFFRAGAN BISHOP
Dudley, vacant; Bishop's House, 60 Bishop's Walk, Cradley Heath, West Midlands B64 7RH

DEAN
Very Revd Dr Peter Atkinson, *apptd* 2006

Director of Music, Samuel Hudson, *apptd* 2018

ARCHDEACONS
Dudley, Ven. Nikki Groarke, *apptd* 2014
Worcester, Ven. Robert Jones, *apptd* 2014

Chancellor, Charles Mynors, *apptd* 1999
Registrar and Legal Secretary, Stuart Ness

Diocesan Secretary, John Preston, The Old Palace, Deansway, Worcester WR1 2JE **T** 01905-20537

ROYAL PECULIARS

WESTMINSTER
The Collegiate Church of St Peter

Dean, vacant
Canon Steward, Revd Anthony Ball

Chapter Clerk, Receiver-General and Registrar, Paul Baumann, CBE; Chapter Office, 20 Dean's Yard, London SW1P 3PA
Organist, James O'Donnell, *apptd* 2000
Legal Secretary, Christopher Vyse, *apptd* 2000

WINDSOR
The Queen's Free Chapel of St George within Her Castle of Windsor

Dean, Rt. Revd David Conner, KCVO, *apptd* 1998
Chapter Clerk, Charlotte Manley, CVO, OBE, *apptd* 2003; Chapter Office, The Cloisters, Windsor Castle, Windsor, Berks SL4 1NJ
Director of Music, James Vivian, *apptd* 2013

OTHER ANGLICAN CHURCHES

THE CHURCH IN WALES

The Anglican Church was the established church in Wales from the 16th century until 1920, when the estrangement of the majority of Welsh people from Anglicanism resulted in disestablishment. Since then the Church in Wales has been an autonomous province consisting of six sees. The bishops are elected by an electoral college comprising elected lay and clerical members, who also elect one of the diocesan bishops as Archbishop of Wales.

The legislative body of the Church in Wales is the Governing Body, which has 138 members divided between the three orders of bishops, clergy and laity. Its president is the Archbishop of Wales and it meets twice annually. Its decisions are binding upon all members of the church. The church's property and finances are the responsibility of the Representative Body. There are 44,875 members of the Church in Wales, with 410 stipendiary clergy and 563 parishes.

THE REPRESENTATIVE BODY OF THE CHURCH IN WALES, 2 Callaghan Square, Cardiff CF10 5BT
T 029-2034 8200 *Secretary,* Simon Lloyd
13TH ARCHBISHOP OF WALES, Most Revd John Davies (Bishop of Swansea and Brecon), *elected* 2017
Signs John Cambrensis

BISHOPS
Bangor (81st), Rt. Revd Andrew John, *b.* 1964, *cons.* 2008, *elected* 2008; Ty'r Esgob, Bangor, Gwynedd LL57 2SS
Signs Andrew Bangor. *Stipendiary clergy,* 45
Llandaff (103rd), Rt. Revd June Osborne, *b.* 1953, *cons.* 2017, *elected* 2017; Llys Esgob, The Cathedral Green, Llandaff, Cardiff CF5 2YE
Signs June Landav. *Stipendiary clergy,* 107
Monmouth (11th), vacant; Bishopstow, Stow Hill, Newport NP20 4EA
Stipendiary clergy, 45
St Asaph (76th), Rt. Revd Gregory Cameron, *b.* 1959, *cons.* 2009, *elected* 2009; Esgobty, Upper Denbigh Road, St Asaph, Denbighshire LL17 0TW
Signs Gregory Llanelwy. *Stipendiary clergy,* 76
St David's (129th), Rt. Revd Joanna Penberthy, *b.* 1960, *cons.* 2017, *elected* 2016; Llys Esgob, Abergwili, Carmarthen SA31 2JG
Signs Joanna Tyddewi. *Stipendiary clergy,* 82
Swansea and Brecon (9th), Most Revd John Davies (also Archbishop of Wales), *b.* 1953, *cons.* 2008, *trans.* 2017; Ely Tower, Castle Square, Brecon, Powys LD3 9DJ
Signs John Cambrensis. *Stipendiary clergy,* 55

The stipend for a diocesan bishop of the Church in Wales is £45,956 a year for 2019–20.

SCOTTISH EPISCOPAL CHURCH

The Scottish Episcopal Church was founded after the Act of Settlement (1690) established the presbyterian nature of the Church of Scotland. The Scottish Episcopal Church is a member of the worldwide Anglican Communion. The governing authority is the General Synod, which consists of the Church's seven bishops, the conveners of the provincial Standing Committee, the conveners of the boards, the Church's representatives on the Anglican Consultative Council and 124 elected members (62 from the clergy and 62 from the laity). The General Synod meets once a year. The bishop who convenes and presides at meetings of the General Synod is called the 'primus' and is elected by his fellow bishops.

As at December 2018 there were 28,647 members of the Scottish Episcopal Church, seven bishops, around 500 serving clergy and 300 churches and places of worship.

THE GENERAL SYNOD OF THE SCOTTISH
  EPISCOPAL CHURCH, 21 Grosvenor Crescent, Edinburgh
  EH12 5EE **T** 0131-225 6357 **W** www.scotland.anglican.org
  Secretary-General, John Stuart

PRIMUS OF THE SCOTTISH EPISCOPAL CHURCH,
  Most Revd Mark Strange (Bishop of Moray, Ross and
  Caithness), *elected* 2017

BISHOPS
Aberdeen and Orkney, Rt. Revd Anne Dyer, *b.* 1957, *cons.*
  2018, *elected* 2017. *Clergy,* 50
Argyll and the Isles, Rt. Revd Kevin Pearson, *b.* 1954, *cons.*
  2011, *elected* 2010. *Clergy,* 25
Brechin, Rt. Revd Andrew Swift, *b.* 1968, *cons.* 2018, *elected*
  2018. *Clergy,* 30
Edinburgh, Rt. Revd Dr John Armes, *b.* 1955, *cons.* 2012,
  elected 2012. *Clergy,* 160
Glasgow and Galloway, vacant. *Clergy,* 110
Moray, Ross and Caithness, Most Revd Mark Strange, *b.* 1961,
  cons. 2007, *elected* 2007. *Clergy,* 60
St Andrews, Dunkeld and Dunblane, Rt. Revd Ian Paton, *elected*
  2018. *Clergy,* 75
The minimum stipend of a diocesan bishop of the Scottish
Episcopal Church for 2019 is £39,705 (ie 1.5 times the
standard clergy stipend of £26,470).

CHURCH OF IRELAND

The Anglican Church was the established church in Ireland from the 16th century but never secured the allegiance of the majority and was disestablished in 1871. The Church of Ireland is divided into the provinces of Armagh and Dublin, each under an archbishop. The provinces are subdivided into 12 dioceses.

The legislative body is the General Synod, which has 660 members in total, divided between the House of Bishops (12 members) and the House of Representatives (216 clergy and 432 laity). The Archbishop of Armagh is elected by the House of Bishops; other episcopal elections are made by an electoral college.

There are around 375,000 members of the Church of Ireland, 249,000 in Northern Ireland and 126,000 in the Republic of Ireland. There are two archbishops, ten bishops and 441 stipendiary clergy.

CENTRAL OFFICE, Church of Ireland House, Church Avenue,
  Rathmines, Dublin D06 CF67 **T** (+353) (1) 497 8422
  *Chief Officer and Secretary-General of the Representative Church
  Body,* David Ritchie

PROVINCE OF ARMAGH
Archbishop of Armagh, Primate of all Ireland and Metropolitan,
  Most Revd Richard Clarke, PHD, *b.* 1949, *cons.* 1996,
  trans. 2012. *Clergy,* 42

BISHOPS
Clogher, Rt. Revd John McDowell, *b.* 1956, *cons.* 2011, *elected*
  2011. *Clergy,* 23
Connor, Rt. Revd Alan Abernethy, *b.* 1957, *cons.* 2007, *elected*
  2007. *Clergy,* 70

Derry and Raphoe, vacant. *Clergy,* 46
Down and Dromore, Rt. Revd Harold Miller, *b.* 1950, *cons.*
  1997, *elected* 1997. *Clergy,* 79
Kilmore, Elphin and Ardagh, Rt. Revd Ferran Glenfield, PHD
  b. 1954, *cons.* 2013, *elected* 2013. *Clergy,* 22
Tuam, Killala and Achonry, Rt. Revd Patrick Rooke, *b.* 1955,
  cons. 2011, *elected* 2011. *Clergy,* 10

PROVINCE OF DUBLIN
*Archbishop of Dublin, Bishop of Glendalough, Primate of Ireland
  and Metropolitan,* Most Revd Michael Jackson, PHD,
  DPHIL, *b.* 1956, *cons.* 2002, *trans.* 2011. *Clergy,* 61

BISHOPS
Cashel, Ferns and Ossory, Rt. Revd Michael Burrows, *b.* 1961,
  cons. 2006, *elected* 2006. *Clergy,* 32
Cork, Cloyne and Ross, Rt. Revd Paul Colton, PHD, *b.* 1960,
  cons. 1999, *elected* 1999. *Clergy,* 25
Limerick, Killaloe and Ardfert, Rt. Revd Kenneth Kearon, *b.*
  1953, *cons.* 2015, *elected* 2014. *Clergy,* 16
Meath and Kildare, Most Revd Patricia Storey, *b.* 1960, *cons.*
  2013, *elected* 2013. *Clergy,* 15

OVERSEAS

PRIMATES
Primates and Archbishops of Aotearoa, New Zealand and Polynesia,
  Most Revd Philip Richardson; Most Revd Don Tamihere
Primate of Australia, Most Revd Phillip Freier
Primate of Brazil, Most Revd Naudal Alves Gomes
Archbishop of the Province of Burundi, Most Revd Martin
  Nyaboho
Primate of Canada, Most Revd Linda Nicholls
Archbishop of the Province of Central Africa, Most Revd Albert
  Chama
Primate of the Central Region of America, Rt. Revd Julio
  Thompson
Primate of Chile, Most Revd Héctor Zavala Muñoz
Archbishop of the Province of Congo, Most Revd Zacharie
  Masimango Katanda
Archbishop of Hong Kong Sheng Kung Hui, Most Revd Paul
  Kwong
Archbishop of the Province of the Indian Ocean, Most Revd James
  Wong Yin Song
Primate of Japan (Nippon Sei Ko Kai), Most Revd Nathaniel
  Makoto Uematsu
Archbishop of Jerusalem and the Middle East, Most Revd Suheil
  Dawani
Primate and Archbishop of All Kenya, Most Revd Jackson Ole
  Sapit
Primate of Korea, Most Revd Moses Nagjun Yoo
Archbishop of Melanesia, Most Revd George Takeli
Presiding Bishop of Mexico, Most Revd Francisco Moreno
Archbishop of the Province of Myanmar (Burma), Most Revd
  Stephen Oo
Metropolitan and Primate of All Nigeria, Most Revd Nicholas
  Okoh
Archbishop of Papua New Guinea, Rt. Revd Allan Migi
Prime Bishop of the Philippines, Most Revd Joel Atiwag Pachao
Archbishop of the Province of Rwanda, Most Revd Laurent
  Mbanda
Archbishop of the Province of South East Asia, Most Revd Ng
  Moon Hing
Primate of Southern Africa, Most Revd Dr Thabo Makgoba
Presiding Bishop of South America, Most Revd Gregory
  Venables
Primate of the Province of South Sudan, Most Revd Justin Badi
  Arama
Archbishop of the Province of Sudan, Most Revd Ezekiel Kumir
  Kondo

Archbishop of Tanzania, Most Revd Maimbo Mndolwa
Archbishop of the Province of Uganda, Most Revd Stanley
  Ntagali
Presiding Bishop of the USA, Most Revd Michael Curry
Primate and Metropolitan of the Province of West Africa, Most
  Revd Dr Daniel Sarfo
Archbishop of the Province of the West Indies, Most Revd
  Howard Gregory

OTHER CHURCHES AND EXTRA-PROVINCIAL DIOCESES

Anglican Church of Bermuda, extra-provincial to Canterbury
  Bishop, Rt. Revd Nicholas Dill
Church of Ceylon, extra-provincial to Canterbury
  Bishop of Colombo, Rt. Revd Dhiloraj Canagasabey
  Bishop of Kurunegala, Rt. Revd Keerthisiri Fernando
Episcopal Church of Cuba, Rt. Revd Griselda Del Carpio
Falkland Islands, extra-provincial to Canterbury
  Bishop, Rt. Revd Timothy Thornton (Bishop to the Forces)
Lusitanian Church (Portuguese Episcopal Church), extra-provincial
  to Canterbury
  Bishop, Rt. Revd Jose Cabral
Reformed Episcopal Church of Spain, extra-provincial to Canterbury
  Bishop, Rt. Revd Carlos López-Lozano

MODERATION OF CHURCHES IN FULL COMMUNION WITH THE ANGLICAN COMMUNION

Church of Bangladesh, Most Revd Samuel Mankhin
Church of North India, Most Revd Dr Prem Chand Singh
Church of South India, Most Revd Thomas Oommen
Church of Pakistan, Most Revd Humphrey Peters

CHURCH OF SCOTLAND

The Church of Scotland is the national church of Scotland. The church is reformed in doctrine, and presbyterian in constitution; ie based on a hierarchy of courts of ministers and elders and, since 1990, of members of a diaconate. At local level the Kirk Session consists of the parish minister and ruling elders. At district level the presbyteries, of which there are 44 in Britain, consist of all the ministers in the district, one ruling elder from each congregation, and those members of the diaconate who qualify for membership. The General Assembly is the supreme authority, and is presided over by a Moderator chosen annually by the Assembly. The sovereign, if not present in person, is represented by a Lord High Commissioner who is appointed each year by the Crown. In May 2019 the General Assembly voted in favour of replacing the Council of Assembly with a new 12-person body, the Assembly Trustees, from June 2019. The Assembly Trustees appoint a chief officer, who has oversight of budgets and staff, and other office bearers.

The Church of Scotland has around 360,000 members, 780 parish ministers and 30,000 elders. The majority of parishes are in Scotland, but there are also churches in England, Europe and overseas.

Lord High Commissioner (2019–20), Duke of Buccleuch and
  Queensberry, KT, KBE
Moderator of the General Assembly (2019–20), Rt. Revd Colin
  Sinclair
Principal Clerk, Revd Dr George Whyte
Procurator, James McNeill, QC
Law Agent and Solicitor of the Church, Mary Macleod
Parliamentary Officer, Chloe Clemmons
General Treasurer, Anne Macintosh
Convener to the Assembly Trustees, Very Revd D John Chalmers
CHURCH OFFICE, 121 George Street, Edinburgh EH2 4YN
T 0131-225 5722

PRESBYTERIES AND CLERKS

Aberdeen, Revd Dr John Ferguson
Abernethy, Revd James MacEwan
Angus, Revd Dr Ian McLean
Annandale and Eskdale, Revd Adam Dillon
Ardrossan, Jean Hunter
Argyll, Dr Christopher Brett
Ayr, Revd Kenneth Elliott
Buchan, Revd Sheila Kirk
Caithness, Revd Ronald Johnstone
Dumbarton, David Sinclair
Dumfries and Kirkcudbright, Revd Donald Campbell
Dundee, Revd James Wilson
Dunfermline, Revd Iain Greenshields
Dunkeld and Meigle, Revd John Russell
Duns, David Philp
Edinburgh, Revd Marjory McPherson
England, Revd Alistair Cumming
Falkirk, Revd Andrew Sarle
Glasgow, Revd George Cowie
Gordon, Revd Euan Glen
Greenock and Paisley, Revd Dr Peter McEnhill
Hamilton, Revd Dr Gordon McCracken
International, Revd Jim Sharp
Inverness, Revd Trevor Hunt
Irvine and Kilmarnock, Steuart Dey
Jedburgh, Revd Lisa-Jane Rankin
Jerusalem, Revd Joanna Oakley-Levstein
Kincardine and Deeside, Revd Hugh Conkey
Kirkcaldy, Revd Alan Kimmitt
Lanark, Revd Bryan Kerr
Lewis, John Cunningham
Lochaber, Revd Donald McCorkindale
Lochcarron-Skye, Revd John Murray
Lothian, John McCulloch
Melrose and Peebles, Revd Victoria Linford
Moray, Dr Alastair Gray
Orkney, Dr Mike Partridge
Perth, Revd Colin Caskie
Ross, Cath Chambers
St Andrews, Revd Nigel Robb
Shetland, Revd Deborah Dobby
Stirling, Revd Alan Miller
Sutherland, Revd Ian McCree
Uist, Revd Gavin Elliott
West Lothian, Revd Duncan Shaw
Wigtown and Stranraer, Sam Scobie
The stipends for ministers in the Church of Scotland in 2019 range from £27,585–£33,899, depending on length of service.

ROMAN CATHOLIC CHURCH

The Roman Catholic Church is a worldwide Christian church acknowledging as its head the Bishop of Rome, known as the Pope (father). Despite its widespread usage, 'Pope' is actually an unofficial term. The Annuario Pontificio, (Pontifical Yearbook) lists eight official titles: Bishop of Rome, Vicar of Jesus Christ, Successor of the Prince of the Apostles, Supreme Pontiff of the Universal Church, Primate of Italy, Archbishop and Metropolitan of the Roman Province, Sovereign of the State of the Vatican City and Servant of the Servants of God.

The Pope leads a communion of followers of Christ, who believe they continue His presence in the world as servants of faith, hope and love to all society. The Pope is held to be the successor of St Peter and thus invested with the power which was entrusted to St Peter by Jesus Christ. A direct line of succession is therefore claimed from the earliest Christian communities. With the fall of the Roman Empire the Pope also became an important political leader. His territory is now limited to the 0.44 sq. km (0.17 sq. miles) of the Vatican City State, created to provide some independence to the Pope from Italy and other nations. The episcopal jurisdiction of the Roman Catholic Church is called the Holy See.

The Pope exercises spiritual authority over the church with the advice and assistance of the Sacred College of Cardinals, the supreme council of the church. The number of cardinals was fixed at 70 by Pope Sixtus V in 1586 but has increased steadily since the pontificate of John XXIII. On 28 February 2013, the date of Pope Benedict XVI's resignation, there were 207 cardinals.

Following the death or resignation of the Pope, the members of the College of Cardinals under the age of 80 are called to the Vatican to elect a successor. They are known as cardinal electors and form an assembly called the conclave. The conclave, which comprised 115 cardinal electors when it convened in March 2013, conducts a secret ballot in complete seclusion to elect the next Pope. A two-thirds majority is necessary before the vote can be accepted as final. When a cardinal receives the necessary number of votes, the Dean of the Sacred College formally asks him if he will accept election and the name by which he wishes to be known. On his acceptance of the office of Supreme Pontiff, the conclave is dissolved and the first Cardinal Deacon announces the election to the assembled crowd in St Peter's Square.

The Pope has full legislative, judicial and administrative power over the whole Roman Catholic Church. He is aided in his administration by the curia, which is made up of a number of departments. The Secretariat of State is the central office for carrying out the Pope's instructions and is presided over by the Cardinal Secretary of State. It maintains relations with the departments of the curia, with the episcopate, with the representatives of the Holy See in various countries, governments and private persons. The congregations and pontifical councils are the Pope's ministries and include departments such as the Congregation for the Doctrine of Faith, whose field of competence concerns faith and morals; the Congregation for the Clergy and the Congregation for the Evangelisation of Peoples, the Pontifical Council for the Family and the Pontifical Council for the Promotion of Christian Unity.

The Holy See, composed of the Pope and those who help him in his mission for the church, is recognised by the Conventions of Vienna as an international moral body. Apostolic nuncios are the Pope's diplomatic representatives; in countries where no formal diplomatic relations exist between the Holy See and that country, the papal representative is known as an apostolic delegate.

According to the 2019 Pontifical Yearbook the number of baptised Roman Catholics worldwide was 1,313 million in 2017 and there were 414,582 priests.

SUPREME PONTIFF
His Holiness Pope Francis (Jorge Mario Bergoglio), *born* Buenos Aires, Argentina, 17 December 1936; *ordained priest* 13 December 1969; *appointed Archbishop* (of Buenos Aires), 28 February 1998; *created Cardinal* 21 February 2001; *assumed pontificate* 13 March 2013

PONTIFF EMERITUS
His Holiness Pope Benedict XVI (Joseph Ratzinger), *born* Bavaria, Germany, 16 April 1927; *ordained priest* 29 June 1951; *appointed Archbishop* (of Munich), 24 March 1977; *created Cardinal* 27 June 1977; *assumed pontificate* 19 April 2005; *resigned pontificate* 28 February 2013

SECRETARIAT OF STATE
Secretary of State, His Eminence Cardinal Pietro Parolin
First Section (General Affairs), Most Revd Edgar Peña Parra (Titular Archbishop of Thélepte)
Second Section (Relations with Other States), Most Revd Paul Gallagher (Titular Archbishop of Hodelm)

BISHOPS' CONFERENCE
The Catholic Bishops' Conference of England and Wales is the permanent assembly of Catholic Bishops and Ordinaries in the two member countries. The membership of the Conference comprises the Archbishops, Bishops and Auxiliary Bishops of the 22 Dioceses within England and Wales, the Bishop of the Forces (Military Ordinariate), the Apostolic Eparchs of the Ukrainian Church and Syro-Malabar Catholics in Great Britain, the Ordinary of the Personal Ordinariate of Our Lady of Walsingham, and the Apostolic Prefect of the Falkland Islands. The Conference is headed by a president and vice-president. There are six departments, each with an episcopal chair: Christian Life and Worship, Dialogue and Unity, Education and Formation, Evangelisation and Catechesis, International Affairs, and Social Justice.

The Bishops' Conference Standing Committee is made up of two directly elected bishops in addition to the Metropolitan Archbishops and chairs from each of the above departments. The committee has general responsibility for continuity of policy between the plenary sessions of the conference, preparing the conference agenda and implementing its decisions.

The administration of the Bishops' Conference is funded by a levy on each diocese, according to income. A general secretariat in London coordinates and supervises the Bishops' Conference administration activities. There are also other agencies and consultative bodies affiliated to the conference.

The Bishops' Conference of Scotland is the permanently constituted assembly of the eight bishops of Scotland. The conference is headed by the president (Rt. Revd. Hugh Gilbert, Bishop of Aberdeen). The conference establishes various agencies which perform advisory functions in relation to the conference. The more important of these agencies are called commissions; each one is headed by a bishop president who, with the other members of the commissions, are appointed by the conference.

The Irish Catholic Bishops' Conference (also known as the Irish Episcopal Conference) has as its president the Most Revd Eamon Martin (Archbishop of Armagh and Primate of All Ireland). Its membership comprises all the archbishops and bishops of Ireland. It appoints various commissions and agencies to assist with the work of the Catholic Church in Ireland.

The Catholic Church in the UK has over 900,000 mass attendees, 5,500 priests and 4,550 churches.

Bishops' Conferences secretariats:

ENGLAND AND WALES, 39 Eccleston Square, London SW1V 1BX **T** 020-7630 8220 **W** www.cbcew.org.uk
  General Secretary, Revd Christopher Thomas
SCOTLAND, 64 Aitken Street, Airdrie ML6 6LT **T** 01236-764061
  W www.bcos.org.uk
  General Secretary, Fr James Grant
IRELAND, Columba Centre, Maynooth, County Kildare W23 P6D3 **T** (+353) (1) 505 3000 **E** info@catholicbishops.ie
  W www.catholicbishops.ie
  Episcopal Secretary, Most Revd Kieran O'Reilly (Archbishop of Cashel and Emly)
  Executive Secretary, Mgr Gearóid Dullea

GREAT BRITAIN

APOSTOLIC NUNCIO TO GREAT BRITAIN

HE Most Revd Edward Joseph Adams (Titular Archbishop of Scala), *apptd* 2017. *Apostolic Nunciature*, 54 Parkside, London SW19 5NE **T** 020-8944 7189

ENGLAND AND WALES

THE MOST REVD ARCHBISHOPS

Westminster, HE Cardinal Vincent Nichols, *cons.* 1992, *apptd* 2009 *Auxiliaries*, John Sherrington, *cons.* 2011; Nicholas Hudson, *cons.* 2014; Paul McAleenan, *cons.* 2016; John Sherrington, *cons.* 2011. *Clergy*, 318. *Archbishop's House*, Ambrosden Avenue, London SW1P 1QJ **T** 020-7798 9033

Birmingham, Bernard Longley, *cons.* 2003, *apptd* 2009 *Auxiliaries*, William Kenney, *cons.* 1987; David McGough, *cons.* 2005; Robert Byrne, *cons.* 2014. *Clergy*, 430. *Archbishop's House*, 8 Shadwell Street, Birmingham B4 6EY **T** 0121-236 9090

Cardiff, George Stack, *cons.* 2001, *apptd* 2011. *Clergy*, 47. *Archbishop's House*, 41–43 Cathedral Road, Cardiff CF11 9HD **T** 029-2022 0411

Liverpool, Malcolm McMahon, *cons.* 2000, *apptd* 2014 *Auxiliary*, Tom Williams, *cons.* 2003. *Clergy*, 402. *Archbishop's House*, 19 Salisbury Road, Cressington Park, Liverpool L19 0PH **T** 0151-494 0686

Southwark, John Wilson, *cons.* 2016, *apptd* 2019 *Auxiliaries*, Patrick Lynch, *cons.* 2006; Paul Hendricks, *cons.* 2006. *Clergy*, 366. *Archbishop's House*, 150 St George's Road, London SE1 6HX **T** 020-7928 2495

THE RT. REVD BISHOPS

Arundel and Brighton, Richard Moth, *cons.* 2009, *apptd* 2015. *Clergy*, 95. *Bishop's House*, High Oaks, Old Brighton Road North, Pease Pottage RH11 9AJ **T** 01293-526428

Brentwood, Alan Williams, *cons.* 2014, *apptd* 2014. *Clergy*, 170. *Bishop's Office*, Cathedral House, Ingrave Road, Brentwood, Essex CM15 8AT **T** 01277-232266

Clifton, Declan Lang, *cons.* 2001, *apptd* 2001. *Clergy*, 153. *Bishop's House*, St Ambrose, North Road, Leigh Woods, Bristol BS8 3PW **T** 0117-973 3072

East Anglia, Alan Hopes, *cons.* 2003, *apptd* 2013. *Clergy*, 129. *Diocesan Curia*, The White House, 21 Upgate, Poringland, Norwich NR14 7SH **T** 01508-492202

Hallam, Ralph Heskett, *cons.* 2010, *apptd* 2014. *Clergy*, 71. *Bishop's House*, 75 Norfolk Road, Sheffield S2 2SZ **T** 0114-278 7988

Hexham and Newcastle, Robert Byrne, *cons.* 2014, *apptd* 2019. *Clergy*, 164. *Bishop's House*, 800 West Road, Newcastle upon Tyne NE5 2BJ **T** 0191-228 0003

Lancaster, Paul Swarbrick, *cons.* 2018, *apptd* 2018. *Clergy*, 97. *Bishop's Office*, The Pastoral Centre, Balmoral Road, Lancaster LA1 3BT **T** 01524-596050

Leeds, Marcus Stock, *cons.* 2014, *apptd* 2014. *Clergy*, 193. *Diocesan Curia*, Hinsley Hall, 62 Headingley Lane, Leeds LS6 2BX **T** 0113-230 4533

Menevia (Wales), vacant. *Clergy*, 60. *Diocesan Office*, 27 Convent Street, Swansea SA1 2BX **T** 01792-644017

Middlesbrough, Terence Drainey, *cons.* 2008, *apptd* 2007. *Clergy*, 50. *Diocesan Curia*, 16 Cambridge Road, Middlesbrough TS5 5NN **T** 01642-850505

Northampton, Peter Doyle, *cons.* 2005, *apptd* 2005. *Clergy*, 116. *Bishop's House*, Marriott Street, Northampton NN2 6AW **T** 01604-715635

Nottingham, Patrick McKinney, *cons.* 2015, *apptd* 2015. *Clergy*, 166. *Bishop's House*, 27 Cavendish Road East, The Park, Nottingham NG7 1BB **T** 0115-947 4786

Plymouth, Mark O'Toole, *cons.* 2014, *apptd* 2013. *Clergy*, 50. *Bishop's House*, 45 Cecil Street, Plymouth PL1 5HW **T** 01752-224414

Portsmouth, Philip Egan, *cons.* 2012, *apptd* 2012. *Clergy*, 214. *Bishop's House*, Bishop Crispian Way, Portsmouth, Hants PO1 3HG **T** 023-9282 0894

Salford, John Arnold, *cons.* 2006, *apptd* 2014. *Clergy*, 218. *Diocesan Curia*, Wardley Hall, Worsley, Manchester M28 2ND **T** 0161-794 2825

Shrewsbury, Mark Davies, *cons.* 2010, *apptd* 2010. *Clergy* 112. *Diocesan Curia*, 2 Park Road South, Prenton, Wirral CH43 4UX **T** 0151-652 9855

Wrexham (Wales), Peter Brignall, *cons.* 2012, *apptd* 2012. *Clergy*, 16. *Bishop's House*, Sontley Road, Wrexham LL13 7EW **T** 01978-262726

SCOTLAND

THE MOST REVD ARCHBISHOPS

St Andrews and Edinburgh, Leo Cushley, *cons.* 2013, *apptd* 2013. *Clergy*, 50. *Archdiocesan Offices*, 100 Strathearn Road, Edinburgh EH9 1BB **T** 0131-623 8900

Glasgow, Philip Tartaglia, *cons.* 2005, *apptd* 2012. *Clergy*, 198. *Diocesan Curia*, 196 Clyde Street, Glasgow G1 4JY **T** 0141-226 5898

THE RT. REVD BISHOPS

Aberdeen, Hugh Gilbert, *cons.* 2011, *apptd* 2011. *Clergy*, 47. *Bishop's House*, 3 Queen's Cross, Aberdeen AB15 4XU **T** 01224-319154

Argyll and the Isles, Brian McGee, *cons.* 2016, *apptd* 2015. *Clergy*, 32. *Diocesan Office* Bishop's House, Esplanade, Oban, Argyll PA34 5AB **T** 01631-567436

Dunkeld, Stephen Robson, *cons.* 2012, *apptd* 2013. *Clergy*, 43. *Diocesan Curia*, 24–28 Lawside Road, Dundee DD3 6XY **T** 01382-225453

Galloway, William Nolan, *cons.* 2015, *apptd* 2014. *Clergy*, 19. *Diocesan Office*, 8 Corsehill Road, Ayr KA7 2ST **T** 01292-266750

Motherwell, Joseph Toal, *cons.* 2008, *trans.* 2014. *Clergy*, 123. *Diocesan Curia*, Coursington Road, Motherwell ML1 1PP **T** 01698-269114

Paisley, John Keenan, *cons.* 2014, *apptd* 2014. *Clergy*, 75. *Diocesan Curia*, Cathedral Precincts, Incle Street, Paisley PA1 1HR **T** 0141-847 6131

BISHOPRIC OF THE FORCES

Rt. Revd Paul Mason, *cons.* 2016, *apptd* 2018. *Administration*, RC Bishopric of the Forces, Wellington House, St Omer Barracks, Thornhill Road, Aldershot, Hants GU11 2BG **T** 01252-348234

IRELAND

There is one hierarchy for the whole of Ireland. Several of the dioceses have territory partly in the Republic of Ireland and partly in Northern Ireland.

APOSTOLIC NUNCIO TO IRELAND

Most Revd Jude Thaddeus Okolo (Titular Archbishop of Novica), *apptd* 2017. *Apostolic Nunciature*, 183 Navan Road, Dublin 7 **T** (+353) (1) 838 0577

THE MOST REVD ARCHBISHOPS

Armagh, Eamon Martin (*also* Primate of All Ireland), *cons.* 2013, *apptd* 2014. *Archbishop Emeritus*, HE Cardinal Seán Brady *cons.* 1995, *elevated* 2007. *Auxiliary*, Michael Router, *cons.* 2019. *Clergy*, 135. *Bishop's Residence*, Ara Coeli, Cathedral Road, Armagh BT61 7QY **T** 028-3752 2045

Cashel and Emly, Kieran O'Reilly, *cons.* 2010, *apptd* 2015. *Clergy*, 83. *Archbishop's House*, Thurles, Co. Tipperary **T** (+353) (504) 21512

Dublin, Diarmuid Martin (*also* Primate of Ireland), *cons.* 1999, *apptd* Coadjutor Archbishop 2003, *succeeded as Archbishop* 2004. *Auxiliary*, Éamonn Walsh, *cons.* 1990. *Clergy*, 389. *Archbishop's House*, Drumcondra, Dublin 9 **T** (+353) (1) 837 3732

Tuam, Dr Michael Neary, *cons.* 1992, *apptd* 1995. *Clergy*, 110. *Archbishop's House*, Tuam, Co. Galway **T** (+353) (93) 24166

THE MOST REVD BISHOPS

Achonry, vacant. *Clergy*, 50. *Bishop's House*, Edmondstown, Ballaghaderreen, Co. Roscommon **T** (+353) (94) 986 0034

Ardagh and Clonmacnois, Francis Duffy, *cons.* 2013, *apptd* 2013. *Clergy*, 60. *Diocesan Office*, St Mel's, Longford **T** (+353) (43) 334 6432

Clogher, Lawrence Duffy, *cons.* 2019, *apptd* 2019. *Clergy*, 74. *Bishop's House*, Monaghan **T** (+353) (47) 81019

Clonfert, John Kirby, *cons.* 1988, *apptd* 1988. *Clergy*, 37. *Bishop's House*, Coorheen, Loughrea, Co. Galway **T** (+353) (91) 841560

Cloyne, William Crean, *cons.* 2013, *apptd* 2013. *Clergy*, 126. *Diocesan Office*, Cobh, Co. Cork **T** (+353) (21) 481 1430

Cork and Ross, Fintan Gavin, *cons.* 2019, *apptd* 2019. *Clergy*, 133. *Diocesan Office*, Cork and Ross Offices, Redemption Road, Cork **T** (+353) (21) 430 1717

Derry, Dónal McKeown, *cons.* 2001, *apptd* 2014. *Clergy*, 108. *Bishop's House*, PO Box 227, Derry BT48 9YG **T** 028-7126 2302

Down and Connor, Noël Treanor, *cons.* 2008, *apptd* 2008. *Clergy*, 199. *Bishop's Residence*, Lisbreen, 73 Somerton Road, Belfast, Co. Antrim BT15 4DE **T** 028-9077 6185

Dromore, vacant. *Clergy*, 33. *Bishop's House*, 44 Armagh Road, Newry, Co. Down BT35 6PN **T** 028-3026 2444

Elphin, Kevin Doran, *cons.* 2014, *apptd* 2014. *Clergy*, 66. *Bishop's House*, Temple St, St Mary's, Sligo **T** (+353) (71) 915 0106

Ferns, Denis Brennan, *cons.* 2006, *apptd* 2006. *Clergy*, 88. *Bishop's House*, Summerhill, Wexford **T** (+353) (53) 912 2177

Galway, Kilmacduagh and Kilfenora, Brendan Kelly, *cons.* 2008, *apptd* 2018. *Clergy*, 57. *Diocesan Office*, The Cathedral, Galway **T** (+353) (91) 563566

Kerry, Ray Browne, *cons.* 2013, *apptd* 2013. *Clergy*, 88. *Bishop's House*, Killarney, Co. Kerry **T** (+353) (64) 663 1168

Kildare and Leighlin, Denis Nulty, *cons.* 2013, *apptd* 2013. *Clergy*, 72. *Bishop's House*, Old Dublin Road, Carlow Town **T** (+353) (59) 917 6725

Killala, John Fleming, *cons.* 2002, *apptd* 2002. *Clergy*, 40. *Bishop's House*, Ballina, Co. Mayo **T** (+353) (96) 21518

Killaloe, Fintan Monahan, *cons.* 2016, *apptd* 2016. *Clergy*, 95. *Diocesan Office*, Westbourne, Ennis, Co. Clare **T** (+353) (65) 682 8638

Kilmore, vacant. *Clergy*, 67. *Bishop's House*, Cullies, Cavan, Co. Cavan **T** (+353) (49) 433 1496

Limerick, Brendan Leahy, *cons.* 2013, *apptd* 2013. *Clergy*, 109. *Diocesan Office*, Social Service Centre, Henry Street, Limerick **T** (+353) (61) 315856

Meath, Thomas Deenihan, *cons.* 2018, *apptd* 2018. *Clergy*, 120. *Bishop's House*, Dublin Road, Mullingar, Co. Westmeath **T** (+353) (44) 934 8841

Ossory, Dermot Farrell, *cons.* 2018, *apptd* 2018. *Clergy*, 81. *Diocesan Office*, James's Street, Kilkenny **T** (+353) (56) 776 2448

Raphoe, Alan McGuckian, *cons.* 2017, *apptd* 2017. *Clergy*, 80. *Bishop's House*, Ard Adhamhnáin, Letterkenny, Co. Donegal **T** (+353) (74) 912 1208

Waterford and Lismore, Alphonsus Cullinan, *cons.* 2015, *apptd* 2015. *Clergy*, 114. *Bishop's House*, John's Hill, Waterford **T** (+353) (51) 874463

OTHER CHURCHES IN THE UK

ASSOCIATED PRESBYTERIAN CHURCHES OF SCOTLAND

The Associated Presbyterian Churches came into being in 1989 as a result of a division within the Free Presbyterian Church of Scotland. The Associated Presbyterian Churches is reformed and evangelistic in nature and emphasises the importance of doctrine based primarily on the Bible and secondly on the Westminster Confession of Faith. There are an estimated 500 members, 8 ministers and 18 congregations in Scotland. There are also congregations in Canada.

ASSOCIATED PRESBYTERIAN CHURCHES OF SCOTLAND, Bruach Taibh, 2 Borve, Arnisort, Isle of Skye IV51 9PS **T** 01470-582264 **W** www.apchurches.org
Presbytery Clerk, Revd J.R. Ross Macaskill

BAPTIST CHURCH

Baptists trace their origins to John Smyth, who in 1609 in Amsterdam reinstituted the baptism of conscious believers as the basis of the fellowship of a gathered church. Members of Smyth's church established the first Baptist church in England in 1612. They came to be known as 'General' Baptists and their theology was Arminian, whereas a later group of Calvinists who adopted the baptism of believers came to be known as 'Particular' Baptists. The two sections of the Baptists were united into one body in 1891: the Baptist Union of Great Britain and Ireland (renamed the Baptist Union of Great Britain in 1988).

Baptists emphasise the complete autonomy of the local church, although individual churches are linked in various kinds of associations. There are international bodies (such as the Baptist World Alliance) and national bodies, but some Baptist churches belong to neither. However, in Great Britain the majority of churches and associations belong to the Baptist Union of Great Britain. There are also Baptist unions in Wales, Scotland and Ireland and there is some overlap of membership.

There are currently around 135,000 members, 2,500 ministers and 2,080 churches associated with the Baptist Union of Great Britain. The Baptist Union of Great Britain is one of the founder members of the European Baptist Federation (1948) and the Baptist World Alliance (1905); the latter represents 42 million members worldwide.

In the Baptist Union of Wales (Undeb Bedyddwyr Cymru) there are 11,355 members, 88 pastors and 386 churches, including those in England.

In the Baptist Union of Scotland there are 11,500 members and 161 churches.

BAPTIST UNION OF GREAT BRITAIN, Baptist House, PO Box 44, 129 Broadway, Didcot, Oxon OX11 8RT **T** 01235-517700 **W** www.baptist.org.uk
President (2019–20), Revd Ken Benjamin
General Secretary, Lynn Green

BAPTIST UNION OF WALES, Y Llwyfan, College Road, Carmarthen SA31 3EQ **T** 01267-245660 **E** mennajones@ubc.cymru **W** www.buw.org.uk
President of the Welsh Assembly (2019–20), David Peregrine
President of the English Assembly (2019–20), Janet Matthews
General Secretary of the Baptist Union of Wales, Revd Judith Morris

BAPTIST UNION OF SCOTLAND, 48 Speirs Wharf, Glasgow G4 9TH **T** 0141-423 6169 **E** admin@scottishbaptist.org.uk **W** www.scottishbaptist.com
General Director, Revd Martin Hodson

THE BRETHREN

The Brethren was founded in Dublin in 1827–8, basing itself on the structures and practices of the early church and rejecting denominationalism and clericalism. Many groups sprang up; the group at Plymouth became the best known, resulting in its designation by others as the 'Plymouth Brethren'. Early worship had a prescribed form but quickly assumed an unstructured, non-liturgical format.

There are services devoted to worship, usually involving the breaking of bread, and separate preaching meetings. There is no salaried ministry.

A theological dispute led in 1848 to schism between the Open Brethren and the Closed or Exclusive Brethren, each branch later suffering further divisions.

Open Brethren churches are run by appointed elders and are completely independent, but freely cooperate with each other. Exclusive Brethren churches believe in a universal fellowship between congregations. They do not have appointed elders, but use respected members of their congregation to perform certain administrative functions.

There are a number of publishing houses that publish Brethren-related literature. Chapter Two is the main supplier of such literature in the UK; it also has a Brethren history archive which is available for use by appointment.

CHAPTER TWO, 3 Conduit Mews, London SE18 7AP
   T 020-8316 5389 E info@chaptertwobooks.org.uk
   W www.chaptertwobooks.org.uk

CONGREGATIONAL FEDERATION
The Congregational Federation was founded by members of Congregational churches in England and Wales who did not join the United Reformed Church in 1972. There are also churches in Scotland and France affiliated to the federation. The federation exists to encourage congregations of believers to worship in free assembly, but it has no authority over them and emphasises their right to independence and self-governance.

The federation has around 7,000 members, 187 accredited ministers and 265 churches in England, Wales and Scotland.

CONGREGATIONAL FEDERATION, 8 Castle Gate,
   Nottingham NG1 7AS T 0115-911 1460
   E admin@congregational.org.uk W www.congregational.org.uk
   President of the Federation (2019–20), Revd Dr Janet Wootton
   General Secretary, Yvonne Campbell

FELLOWSHIP OF INDEPENDENT EVANGELICAL CHURCHES
The Fellowship of Independent Evangelical Churches (FIEC) was founded by Revd E. J. Poole-Connor (1872–1962) in 1922. In 1923 the fellowship published its first register of non-denominational pastors, evangelists and congregations who had accepted the doctrinal basis for the fellowship.

Members of the fellowship have two primary convictions: firstly to defend the evangelical faith, and secondly that evangelicalism is the bond that unites the fellowship, rather than forms of worship or church government.

The FIEC exists to promote the welfare of non-denominational Bible churches and to give expression to the fundamental doctrines of evangelical Christianity. It supports individual churches by providing resources and advising churches on current theological, moral, social and practical issues.

There are currently around 600 churches affiliated to the fellowship.

FELLOWSHIP OF INDEPENDENT EVANGELICAL
   CHURCHES, 39 The Point, Market Harborough, Leics LE16
   7QU T 01858-434540 E admin@fiec.org.uk W www.fiec.org.uk
   National Director, John Stevens

FREE CHURCH OF ENGLAND
The Free Church of England, otherwise called the Reformed Episcopal Church, is an independent episcopal church, constituted according to the historic faith, tradition and practice of the Church of England. Its roots lie in the 18th century, but it started to grow significantly from the 1840s onwards, as clergy and congregations joined it from the established church in protest against the Oxford Movement. The historic episcopate was conferred on the English church in 1876 through bishops of the Reformed Episcopal Church (which had broken away from the Protestant Episcopal Church in the USA in 1873). A branch of the Reformed Episcopal Church was founded in the UK and this merged with the Free Church of England in 1927 to create the present church. The Orders of the Free Church of England are recognised by the Church of England.

Worship is according to the *Book of Common Prayer* and some modern liturgy is permissible. Only men are ordained to the orders of deacon, presbyter and bishop.

The Free Church of England has two dioceses, 19 congregations and around 900 members in England. There is one congregation in St Petersburg, Russia and three congregations and six missions in Brazil.

THE FREE CHURCH OF ENGLAND, 329 Wolverhampton
   Road West, Willenhall, W. Midlands WV13 2RL T 01902-607335
   W www.fcofe.org.uk
   Bishop Primus, Rt. Revd Dr John Fenwick (Bishop of the Northern Diocese)
   General Secretary, Rt. Revd Paul Hunt (Bishop of the Southern Diocese)

FREE CHURCH OF SCOTLAND
The Free Church of Scotland was formed in 1843 when over 400 ministers withdrew from the Church of Scotland as a result of interference in the internal affairs of the church by the civil authorities. In 1900, all but 26 ministers joined with others to form the United Free Church (most of which rejoined the Church of Scotland in 1929). In 1904 the remaining 26 ministers were recognised by the House of Lords as continuing the Free Church of Scotland.

The church maintains strict adherence to the Westminster Confession of Faith (1648) and accepts the Bible as the sole rule of faith and conduct. Its general assembly meets annually. It also has links with reformed churches overseas. The Free Church of Scotland has about 13,000 members, 90 ministers and 100 congregations.

FREE CHURCH OF SCOTLAND, 15 North Bank Street,
   The Mound, Edinburgh EH1 2LS T 0131-226 5286
   E offices@freechurchofscotland.org.uk W www.freechurch.org
   Chief Executive, Scott Matheson

FREE PRESBYTERIAN CHURCH OF SCOTLAND
The Free Presbyterian Church of Scotland was formed in 1893 by two ministers of the Free Church of Scotland who refused to accept a Declaratory Act passed by the Free Church General Assembly in 1892. The Free Presbyterian Church of Scotland is Calvinistic in doctrine and emphasises observance of the Sabbath. It adheres strictly to the Westminster Confession of Faith (1648).

The church has about 700 members in Scotland. It has 17 ministers and 40 churches in the UK.

FREE PRESBYTERIAN CHURCH OF SCOTLAND,
   133 Woodlands Road, Glasgow G3 6LE
   E outreach@fpchurch.org.uk W www.fpchurch.org.uk
   Moderator (2019–20), Revd Roderick McLeod
   Clerk of the Synod, Revd Keith Watkins

HOLY APOSTOLIC CATHOLIC ASSYRIAN CHURCH OF THE EAST

The Holy Apostolic Catholic Assyrian Church of the East traces its beginnings to the middle of the first century. It spread from Upper Mesopotamia throughout the territories of the Persian Empire. The Assyrian Church of the East became theologically separated from the rest of the Christian community following the Council of Ephesus in 431. The church is headed by the Catholicos Patriarch and is episcopal in government. The liturgical language is Syriac (Aramaic). The Assyrian Church of the East and the Roman Catholic Church agreed a common Christological declaration in 1994, and a process of dialogue between the Assyrian Church of the East and the Chaldean Catholic Church, which is in communion with Rome but shares the Syriac liturgy, was instituted in 1996.

The church has around 325,000 members in the Middle East, India, Russia, Europe, North America and Australasia. In Great Britain there is one parish, which is situated in London. The church in Great Britain forms part of the Diocese of Europe under HG Mar Odisho Oraham.

HOLY APOSTOLIC CATHOLIC ASSYRIAN CHURCH OF THE EAST, St Mary's Church Hall, 62 Greenford Avenue, Hanwell, London W7 3QP T 0786-873 7112

INDEPENDENT METHODIST CHURCHES

The Independent Methodist Churches were formed in 1805 and remained independent when the Methodist Church in Great Britain was formed in 1932. They are mainly concentrated in the industrial areas of the north of England.

The churches are Methodist in doctrine but their organisation is congregational. All the churches are members of the Independent Methodist Connexion of Churches. The controlling body of the Connexion is the Annual Meeting, to which churches send delegates. The Connexional President is elected every two years. Between annual meetings the affairs of the Connexion are handled by the Connexional Committee and departmental committees. Ministers are appointed by the churches and trained through the Connexion. The ministry is open to both men and women.

There are 1,600 members, 70 ministers and 74 churches in Great Britain.

INDEPENDENT METHODIST RESOURCE CENTRE, The Resource Centre, Fleet Street, Wigan WN5 0DS T 01942-223526 E resourcecentre@imchurches.org.uk W www.imchurches.org.uk
General Secretary, Brian Rowney

LUTHERAN CHURCH

Lutheranism is based on the teachings of Martin Luther, the German leader of the Protestant Reformation. The authority of the scriptures is held to be supreme over church tradition. The teachings of Lutheranism are explained in detail in 16th-century confessional writings, particularly the Augsburg Confession. Lutheranism is one of the largest Protestant denominations and it is particularly strong in northern Europe and the USA. Some Lutheran churches are episcopal, while others have a synodal form of organisation; unity is based on doctrine rather than structure. Most Lutheran churches are members of the Lutheran World Federation, based in Geneva.

Lutheran services in Great Britain are held in 15 languages to serve members of different nationalities. Services usually follow ancient liturgies. English-language congregations are members either of the Lutheran Church in Great Britain or of the Evangelical Lutheran Church of England. The Lutheran Church in Great Britain and other Lutheran churches in Britain are members of the Lutheran Council of Great Britain, which represents them and coordinates their common work.

There are around 70 million Lutherans worldwide, with around 180,000 members in Great Britain.

THE LUTHERAN COUNCIL OF GREAT BRITAIN, 30 Thanet Street, London WC1H 9QH T 020-7554 9753 E enquiries@lutheran.org.uk W www.lutheran.org.uk
Chair, Revd Torbjorn Holt
General Secretary, Malcolm Bruce

METHODIST CHURCH

The Methodist movement started in England in 1729 when the Revd John Wesley, an Anglican priest, and his brother Charles met with others in Oxford and resolved to conduct their lives by 'rule and method'. In 1739 the Wesleys began evangelistic preaching and the first Methodist chapel was founded in Bristol in the same year. In 1744 the first annual conference was held, at which the Articles of Religion were drawn up. Doctrinal emphases included repentance, faith, the assurance of salvation, social concern and the priesthood of all believers. After John Wesley's death in 1791 the Methodists withdrew from the established church to form the Methodist Church. Methodists gradually drifted into many groups, but in 1932 the Wesleyan Methodist Church, the United Methodist Church and the Primitive Methodist Church united to form the Methodist Church in Britain.

The governing body is the Conference. The Conference meets annually and consists of two parts: the ministerial and representative sessions. The Methodist Church is structured as a 'Connexion' of churches, circuits and districts. The local churches in a defined area form a circuit, and a number of these 368 circuits make up each of the 31 districts. The latest 2019 Statistics for Mission show that as at October 2018 the Methodist Church in Britain had 173,000 members, 1,600 active ministers and 4,271 local churches.

THE METHODIST CHURCH IN BRITAIN, Methodist Church House, 25 Marylebone Road, London NW1 5JR T 020-7486 5502 E enquiries@methodistchurch.org.uk W www.methodist.org.uk
Conference President (2019–20), Revd Barbara Glasson
Conference Vice-President (2019–20), Clive Marsh
Conference Secretary, Doug Swanney

THE METHODIST CHURCH IN IRELAND
The Methodist Church in Ireland is autonomous but has close links with British Methodism. As at December 2014 it had 45,828 members, 121 active ministers and 270 lay preachers.

METHODIST CHURCH IN IRELAND, 1 Fountainville Avenue, Belfast BT9 6AN T 028-9032 4554 E secretary@irishmethodist.org W www.irishmethodist.org
President of the Conference (2019–20), Revd Sam McGuffin
Lay Leader of the Conference (2019–20), Lynda Neilands
Secretary, Revd Tom McKnight

ORTHODOX CHURCHES

EASTERN ORTHODOX CHURCH
The Eastern (or Byzantine) Orthodox Church is a communion of self-governing Christian churches that recognises the honorary primacy of the Ecumenical Patriarch of Constantinople.

The position of Orthodox Christians is that the faith was fully defined during the period of the Oecumenical Councils. In doctrine it is strongly trinitarian, and stresses the mystery and importance of the sacraments. It is episcopal in government. The structure of the Orthodox Christian year differs from that of western churches.

Orthodox Christians throughout the world are estimated to number about 300 million; there are around 300,000 in the UK.

GREEK ORTHODOX CHURCH (PATRIARCHATE OF ANTIOCH)

The church is led by John X, Patriarch of Antioch, who was enthroned in February 2013. The Archdiocese of the British Isles and Ireland has 18 parishes, including St George's Cathedral in London, and 27 clergy.

ANTIOCHIAN ORTHODOX ARCHDIOCESE OF THE BRITISH ISLES AND IRELAND, St George's Cathedral, 1a Redhill Street, London NW1 4BG **T** 020-7383 0403
E fr.s.gholam@antiochianorth.co.uk
W www.antiochian-orthodox.co.uk
Archbishop, Metropolitan Silouan Oner

GREEK ORTHODOX CHURCH (PATRIARCHATE OF CONSTANTINOPLE)

The presence of Greek Orthodox Christians in Britain dates back at least to 1677 when Archbishop Joseph Geogirenes of Samos fled from Turkish persecution and came to London. The present Greek cathedral in Moscow Road, Bayswater, was opened for public worship in 1879, and the Diocese of Thyateira and Great Britain was established in 1922. There are now around 100 parishes and one monastery in the UK, served by one archbishop, three bishops and around 120 clergy.

THE PATRIARCHATE OF CONSTANTINOPLE IN GREAT BRITAIN, Archdiocese of Thyateira and Great Britain, Thyateira House, 5 Craven Hill, London W2 3EN
T 020-7723 4787 **E** mail@thyateira.org.uk
W www.thyateira.org.uk
Archbishop, Nikitas of Thyateira and Great Britain

THE RUSSIAN ORTHODOX CHURCH (PATRIARCHATE OF MOSCOW)

The records of Russian Orthodox Church activities in Britain date from the visit to England of Tsar Peter I in the early 18th century. Clergy were sent from Russia to serve the chapel established to minister to the staff of the Imperial Russian Embassy in London.

In 2007, after an 80-year division, the Russian Orthodox Church Outside Russia agreed to become an autonomous part of the Russian Orthodox Church, Patriarchate of Moscow. The reunification agreement was signed by Patriarch Alexy II, 15th Patriarch of Moscow and All Russia and Metropolitan Laurus, leader of the Russian Orthodox Church Outside Russia on 17 May at a ceremony at Christ the Saviour Cathedral in Moscow. Patriarch Alexy II died on 5 December 2008. Metropolitan Kirill of Smolensk and Kaliningrad was enthroned as the 16th Patriarch of Moscow and All Russia on 1 February 2009, having been elected by a secret ballot of clergy on 27 January 2009.

The diocese of Sourozh is the diocese of the Russian Orthodox Church in Great Britain and Ireland and is led by Bishop Matthew of Sourozh.

DIOCESE OF SOUROZH, Diocesan Office, Cathedral of the Dormition of the Mother of God and All Saints, 67 Ennismore Gardens, London SW7 1NH **T** 020-7584 0096
W www.sourozh.org
Diocesan Hierarch, Bishop Matthew of Sourozh

SERBIAN ORTHODOX CHURCH (PATRIARCHATE OF SERBIA)

There are seven parishes in Great Britain and around 4,000 members. Great Britain is part of the Diocese of Great Britain and Scandinavia, which is led by Bishop Dositey. The church can be contacted via the church of St Sava in London.

SERBIAN ORTHODOX CHURCH IN GREAT BRITAIN, Church of Saint Sava, 89 Lancaster Road, London W11 1QQ
T 020-7727 8367 **E** crkva@spclondon.org.uk
W www.spclondon.org.uk
Archpriest, Very Revd Goran Spaic

OTHER NATIONALITIES

The Patriarchates of Romania and Bulgaria (Diocese of Western Europe) have memberships estimated at 20,000 and 2,000 respectively, while the Georgian Orthodox Church has around 500 members. The Belarusian (membership estimated at 2,400) and Latvian (membership of around 100).

ORIENTAL ORTHODOX CHURCHES

The term 'Oriental Orthodox Churches' is now generally used to describe a group of six ancient eastern churches (Armenian, Coptic, Eritrean, Ethiopian, Indian (Malankara) and Syrian) which rejected the Christological definition of the Council of Chalcedon (AD 451). There are around 50 million members worldwide of the Oriental Orthodox Churches and over 20,000 in the UK.

ARMENIAN ORTHODOX CHURCH (CATHOLICOSATE OF ETCHMIADZIN)

The Armenian Orthodox Church is led by HH Karekin II, Catholicos of All Armenians. HG Bishop Hovakim Manukyan was appointed Primate of the Armenian Church in the UK and Ireland in 2015.

ARMENIAN CHURCH IN THE UK AND IRELAND, The Armenian Vicarage, 27 Haven Green, London W5 2NZ
T 020-8998 9210 **W** www.armeniandiocese.org.uk
Primate, HG Bishop Hovakim Manukyan

COPTIC ORTHODOX CHURCH

The Coptic Orthodox Church is headed by Pope Tawadros II, who was appointed in November 2012. There are three dioceses in the UK: the Midlands, led by HG Bishop Missael; Ireland, Scotland and north-east England, led by HG Bishop Antony; and the Papal Diocese which is led by HG Bishop Angaelos and covers all the remaining parishes in the UK.

CATHEDRAL OF ST GEORGE AT THE COPTIC ORTHODOX CHURCH CENTRE, Shephalbury Manor, Broadhall Way, Stevenage, Herts SG2 8NP **T** 020-7993 9001
W www.copticcentre.com
Bishop, HG Bishop Angaelos

BRITISH ORTHODOX CHURCH

The British Orthodox Church is a small autonomous Orthodox jurisdiction, originally deriving from the Syrian Orthodox Church. It was canonically part of the Coptic Orthodox Patriarchate of Alexandria from 1994–2015. As it ministers to British people, all of its services are in English.

THE BRITISH ORTHODOX CHURCH, 10 Heathwood Gardens, Charlton, London SE7 8EP **T** 020-8854 3090
E info@britishorthodox.org **W** www.britishorthodox.org
Metropolitan, Abba Seraphim

ERITREAN ORTHODOX TEWAHEDO CHURCH

The Eritrean Orthodox Church was granted independence in 1994 by Pope Shenouda III, following the declaration of Eritrea's independence from Ethiopia in 1993. In 2006, the Eritrean government removed the third patriarch, Abune Antonios, from office and imprisoned him; the government replaced him with Abune Dioskoros in 2007, although the Oriental Orthodox Churches continue to recognise Antonios as the rightful patriarch. The diocesan bishop for North America, Europe and the Middle East is HG Abune Makarios.

ETHIOPIAN ORTHODOX TAWAHEDO CHURCH

The Ethiopian Orthodox Church was administratively part of the Coptic Orthodox Church of Alexandria until 1959, when it was granted its own patriarch by the Coptic Orthodox Pope of Alexandria and Patriarch of All Africa, Cyril VI. The current patriarch is HH Abune Mathias. The church in London was established in 1976.

ETHIOPIAN ORTHODOX TAWAHEDO CHURCH, St Mary of Zion, PO Box 56856, London N13 5US **T** 020-8807 5885 **E** pc@tserhasion.org.uk **W** www.stmaryofzion.co.uk
Priest-in-Charge, Melake Sion Habte Mariam

INDIAN ORTHODOX CHURCH

The Indian Orthodox Church, also known as the Malankara Orthodox Church, traces its origins to the first century. The head of the Malankara Orthodox Church is HH Baselios Marthoma Paulose II. The mother church of all the parishes in the UK and the Republic of Ireland is St Gregorios Church in London. The London parish has around 280 families as practising members.

INDIAN ORTHODOX CHURCH, St Gregorios Indian Orthodox Church, Cranfield Road, Brockley, London SE4 1UF **T** 020-8691 9456 **E** ioclondon@gmail.com **W** www.ioclondon.co.uk
Diocesan Metropolitan, HG Dr Mathews Mar Thimothios
Vicar, Revd Fr Aby P Varghese

SYRIAN ORTHODOX CHURCH

The Syrian (Syriac) Orthodox Church of Antioch is an Oriental Orthodox Church based in the Eastern Mediterranean headed by HH Moran Mor Ignatius Aphrem II. The Patriarchate Vicariate in the UK is represented by HE Archbishop Mor Athanasius Toma Dawod.

SYRIAN ORTHODOX CHURCH IN THE UK, St Thomas Cathedral, 7–11 Armstrong Road, London W3 7JL **T** 020-8749 5834 **E** enquiry-uk@syrianorthodoxchurch.net **W** www.syrianorthodoxchurch.net
Archbishop, HE Mor Athanasius Toma Dawod

PENTECOSTAL CHURCHES

Pentecostalism is inspired by the descent of the Holy Spirit upon the apostles at Pentecost. The movement began in Los Angeles, USA, in 1906 and is characterised by baptism with the Holy Spirit, divine healing, speaking in tongues (glossolalia) and a literal interpretation of the scriptures.

The Pentecostal movement in Britain dates from 1907. Initially, groups of Pentecostalists were led by laymen and did not organise formally. However, in 1915 the Elim Foursquare Gospel Alliance (more commonly called the Elim Pentecostal Church) was founded in Ireland by George Jeffreys and currently has about 550 churches, 68,500 adherents and 650 accredited ministers. In 1924 about 70 independent assemblies formed a fellowship called Assemblies of God in Great Britain and Ireland, which now incorporates around 600 churches, around 75,000 adherents and 1,000 ministers.

The Apostolic Church grew out of the 1904–5 Christian revivals in South Wales and was established in 1916. The Apostolic Church has around 90 churches, 7,000 adherents and 100 ministers in the UK. The New Testament Church of God was established in England in 1953 and has over 130 congregations, 11,000 members and over 300 ministers across England and Wales.

There are about 105 million Pentecostalists worldwide, with over 350,000 adherents in the UK.

THE APOSTOLIC CHURCH, Suite 105, Crystal House, New Bedford Road, Luton LU1 1HS **T** 020-7587 1802 **E** admin@apostolic-church.org **W** www.apostolic-church.org
National Leader, Tim Jack

ASSEMBLIES OF GOD, National Ministry Centre, Mattersey, Doncaster DN10 5HD **T** 017-7781 7663 **E** info@aog.org.uk **W** www.aog.org.uk

THE ELIM PENTECOSTAL CHURCH, Elim International Centre, De Walden Road, Malvern WR14 4DF **T** 0345-302 6750 **W** www.elim.org.uk
General Superintendent, Chris Cartwright

THE NEW TESTAMENT CHURCH OF GOD, 3 Cheyne Walk, Northampton NN1 5PT **T** 01604-824222 **E** mmcc@ntcg.org.uk **W** www.ntcg.org.uk
Administrative Bishop, Donald Bolt

PRESBYTERIAN CHURCH IN IRELAND

Irish Presbyterianism traces its origins back to the Plantation of Ulster in 1606, when English and Scottish Protestants began to settle on the land confiscated from the Irish chieftains. The first presbytery was established in Ulster in 1642 by chaplains of a Scottish army that had been sent to crush a Catholic rebellion in 1641.

The Presbyterian Church in Ireland is reformed in doctrine and belongs to the World Alliance of Reformed Churches. Structurally, the 536 congregations are grouped in 19 presbyteries under the General Assembly. This body meets annually and is presided over by a moderator who is elected for one year. The ongoing work of the church is undertaken by boards under which there are specialist committees.

There are over 225,000 members and 326 active ministers of Irish presbyterian churches in Ireland and Northern Ireland.

THE PRESBYTERIAN CHURCH IN IRELAND, Assembly Buildings, 2–10 Fisherwick Place, Belfast BT1 6DW **T** 028-9032 2284 **E** info@presbyterianireland.org **W** www.presbyterianireland.org
Moderator (2019–20), Rt. Revd Dr William Henry
Clerk of Assembly and General Secretary, Revd Trevor Gribben

PRESBYTERIAN CHURCH OF WALES

The Presbyterian Church of Wales or Calvinistic Methodist Church of Wales is Calvinistic in doctrine and presbyterian in constitution. It was formed in 1811 when Welsh Calvinists severed the relationship with the established church by ordaining their own ministers. It secured its own confession of faith in 1823 and a Constitutional Deed in 1826, and since 1864 the General Assembly has met annually, presided over by a moderator elected for a year. The doctrine and constitutional structure of the Presbyterian Church of Wales was confirmed by act of parliament in 1931–2.

The Church has 20,000 members, 55 ministers and 600 congregations.

THE PRESBYTERIAN CHURCH OF WALES, Tabernacle Chapel, 81 Merthyr Road, Whitchurch, Cardiff CF14 1DD **T** 029-2062 7465 **E** swyddfa.office@ebcpcw.org.uk **W** www.ebcpcw.cymru
Moderator (2019–20), Revd Brian Matthews
General Secretary, Revd Meirion Morris

RELIGIOUS SOCIETY OF FRIENDS (QUAKERS)

Quakerism is a religious denomination which was founded in the 17th century by George Fox and others in an attempt to revive what they saw as the original 'primitive Christianity'. The movement, at first called Friends of the Truth, started in the Midlands, Yorkshire and north-west England, but there are now Quakers all over the UK and in 36 countries around the world. The colony of Pennsylvania, founded by William Penn, was originally a Quaker settlement.

Quakers place an emphasis on the experience of God in daily life rather than on sacraments or religious occasions. There is no church calendar. Worship is largely silent and there are no appointed ministers; the responsibility for conducting a meeting is shared equally among those present. Religious tolerance and social reform have always been important to Quakers, together with a commitment to peace and non-violence in resolving disputes.

There are more than 23,000 'friends' or Quakers in Great Britain. There are around 475 places where Quaker meetings are held, many of them Quaker-owned Friends Meeting

Houses. The Britain Yearly Meeting is the name given to the central organisation of Quakers in Britain.

THE RELIGIOUS SOCIETY OF FRIENDS (QUAKERS) IN BRITAIN, Friends House, 173–177 Euston Road, London NW1 2BJ **T** 020-7663 1000 **E** enquiries@quaker.org.uk **W** www.quaker.org.uk
General Secretary, Oliver Robertson

SALVATION ARMY
The Salvation Army is an international Christian organisation working in 126 countries worldwide. As a church and registered charity, The Salvation Army is funded through donations from its members, the general public and, where appropriate, government grants.

The Salvation Army was founded by Methodists William and Catherine Booth in the East End of London in 1865 and marked its 150th anniversary on 2 July 2015. It now has around 40,000 members and 1,067 Salvation Army Officers (full-time ministers) in the UK. There are over 700 local church and community centres, 62 residential support centres for homeless people, 16 care homes for older people and six substance-misuse centres. It also runs a clothing recycling programme, charity shops, foodbanks, a prison-visiting service and a family-tracing service. In 1878 it adopted a quasi-military command structure intended to inspire and regulate its endeavours and to reflect its view that the church was engaged in spiritual warfare.

UK TERRITORIAL HEADQUARTERS, 101 Newington Causeway, London SE1 6BN **T** 020-7367 4500 **E** info@salvationarmy.org.uk **W** www.salvationarmy.org.uk
UK Territorial Leaders, Commissioners Anthony and Gillian Cotterill

SEVENTH-DAY ADVENTIST CHURCH
The Seventh-day Adventist Church is a worldwide Christian church marked by its observance of Saturday as the Sabbath and by its emphasis on the imminent second coming of Jesus Christ. Adventists summarise their faith in '28 fundamental beliefs'.

The church grew out of the Millerite movement in the USA during the mid-19th century and was formally established in 1863. The church has a worldwide membership of over 17 million. In the UK and Ireland there are 37,917 members worshipping in around 300 churches and companies.

SEVENTH-DAY ADVENTIST CHURCH HQ, Stanborough Park, Watford WD25 9JZ **T** 01923-672251 **E** info@adventist.org.uk **W** www.adventist.org.uk
President, Pastor Ian Sweeney
Executive Secretary, John Sturridge

THE (SWEDENBORGIAN) NEW CHURCH
The New Church is based on the teachings of the 18th-century Swedish scientist and theologian Emanuel Swedenborg (1688–1772), who believed that Jesus Christ appeared to him and instructed him to reveal the spiritual meaning of the Bible. He claimed to have visions of the spiritual world, including heaven and hell, and conversations with angels and spirits. He published several theological works, including descriptions of the spiritual world and a Bible commentary.

Swedenborgians believe that the second coming of Jesus Christ is taking place, being not an actual physical reappearance of Christ, but rather his return in spirit. It is also believed that concurrent with our life on earth is life in a parallel spiritual world, of which we are usually unconscious until death. There are around 30,000 Swedenborgians worldwide, with around 600 members, 18 churches and five ministers in the UK.

THE GENERAL CONFERENCE OF THE NEW CHURCH, Purley Chase Centre, Purley Chase Lane, Mancetter, Atherstone CV9 2RQ **T** 01827-712370 **W** www.generalconference.org.uk

UNDEB YR ANNIBYNWYR CYMRAEG
Undeb Yr Annibynwyr Cymraeg (the Union of Welsh Independents) was formed in 1872 and is a voluntary association of Welsh Congregational churches and personal members. It is mainly Welsh-speaking. Congregationalism in Wales dates back to 1639 when the first Welsh Congregational church was opened in Gwent.

Member churches are traditionally congregationalist in organisation and Calvinistic in doctrine, although a wide range of interpretations are permitted. Each church has complete independence in the governance and administration of its affairs.

The Union has around 24,000 members, 80 ministers and 400 member churches.

UNDEB YR ANNIBYNWYR CYMRAEG, 5 Axis Court, Riverside Business Park, Swansea Vale, Swansea SA7 0AJ **T** 01792-795888 **E** undeb@annibynwyr.org **W** www.annibynwyr.org
President, Revd Jill-Hailey Harries
President Elect, Revd Beti-Wyn James
General Secretary, Revd Dyfrig Rees

UNITED REFORMED CHURCH
The United Reformed Church (URC) was first formed by the union of most of the Congregational churches in England and Wales with the Presbyterian Church of England in 1972. It is Calvinistic in doctrine, and its followers form independent self-governing congregations bound under God by covenant, a principle laid down in the writings of Robert Browne (1550–1633). From the late 16th century the movement was driven underground by persecution, but the cause was defended at the Westminster Assembly in 1643 and the Savoy Declaration of 1658 laid down its principles. Congregational churches formed county associations and in 1832 these associations merged to form the Congregational Union of England and Wales.

In the 1960s there was close cooperation locally and nationally between congregational and presbyterian churches. This led to union negotiations and a Scheme of Union, supported by an act of parliament in 1972. In 1981 a further unification took place, with the Reformed Association of Churches of Christ becoming part of the URC. In 2000 a third union took place, with the Congregational Union of Scotland. At its basis the URC reflects local church initiative and responsibility with a conciliar pattern of oversight.

The URC is divided into 13 synods, each with a synod moderator. There are 1,406 churches which serve 49,517 members. There are 401 stipendiary ministers.

The General Assembly is the central body, and comprises around 400 representatives, mainly appointed by the synods, of which half are lay persons and half are ministers. Since 2010 the General Assembly has met biennially to elect two moderators (one lay and one ordained), who then become the public representatives of the URC.

UNITED REFORMED CHURCH, 86 Tavistock Place, London WC1H 9RT **T** 020-7916 2020 **E** urc@urc.org.uk **W** www.urc.org.uk
Moderators of the General Assembly 2018–20, Revd Nigel Uden; Derek Estill
General Secretary, Revd John Proctor

WESLEYAN REFORM UNION

The Wesleyan Reform Union was founded by Methodists who left or were expelled from Wesleyan Methodism in 1849 following a period of internal conflict. Its doctrine is conservative evangelical and its organisation is congregational, each church having complete independence in the government and administration of its affairs. The union has around 1,250 members, 20 ministers and 96 churches.

THE WESLEYAN REFORM UNION, Church Street, Jump,
   Barnsley S74 0HZ **T** 01226-891608 **E** admin@thewru.co.uk
   W www.thewru.com
   President, Revd Colin Braithwaite

NON-TRINITARIAN CHURCHES

CHRISTADELPHIAN

Christadelphians believe that the Bible is the word of God and that it reveals both God's dealings with mankind in the past and his plans for the future. These plans centre on the work of Jesus Christ, who it is believed will return to Earth to establish God's kingdom. The Christadelphian group was founded in the USA in the 1850s by Englishman Dr John Thomas.

THE CHRISTADELPHIAN MAGAZINE AND
   PUBLISHING ASSOCIATION, 404 Shaftmoor Lane, Hall
   Green, Birmingham B28 8SZ **T** 0121-777 6328
   W www.thechristadelphian.com

CHURCH OF CHRIST, SCIENTIST

The Church of Christ, Scientist was founded by Mary Baker Eddy in the USA in 1879 to 'reinstate primitive Christianity and its lost element of healing'. Christian Science teaches the need for spiritual regeneration and salvation from sin, but it is best known for its reliance on prayer alone in the healing of sickness. Adherents believe that such healing is the result of divine laws, or divine science, and is in direct line with that practised by Jesus Christ (revered, not as God, but as the son of God) and by the early Christian church.

The denomination consists of The First Church of Christ, Scientist, in Boston, Massachusetts, USA ('The Mother Church') and its branch churches in almost 80 countries worldwide. The Bible and Mary Baker Eddy's book, *Science and Health with Key to the Scriptures,* are used for daily spiritual guidance and healing by all members and are read at services. There are no clergy; those engaged in full-time healing are called Christian Science practitioners, of whom there are around 1,500 worldwide.

No membership figures are available, since Mary Baker Eddy felt that numbers are no measure of spiritual vitality and ruled that such statistics should not be published. There are almost 2,000 branch churches worldwide, including 100 in the UK.

CHRISTIAN SCIENCE COMMITTEE ON PUBLICATION
   UK AND IRELAND, Golden Cross House, 8 Duncannon
   Street, London WC2N 4JF **T** 020-8150 0245
   E londoncs@csps.com **W** http://ukchristianscience.com
   District Manager for the UK and Ireland, Robin Harragin Hussey

CHURCH OF JESUS CHRIST OF LATTER-DAY SAINTS

The Church of Jesus Christ of Latter-day Saints ('Mormons') was founded in New York State, USA, in 1830, and came to Britain in 1837.

Mormons are Christians who claim to belong to the 'restored church' of Jesus Christ. They believe that true Christianity died when the last original apostle died, but that it was given back to the world by God and Jesus Christ through Joseph Smith, the church's founder and first president. They accept and use the Bible as scripture, but believe in continuing revelation from God; Mormons also use additional scriptures, including *The Book of Mormon: Another Testament of Jesus Christ.* The importance of the family is central to the church's beliefs and practices. Polygamy was formally discontinued in 1890.

The church has no paid ministry: local congregations are headed by a leader chosen from among their number. The world governing body, based in Utah, USA, is led by a president, believed to be the chosen prophet, and his two counsellors. There are over 15 million members worldwide, with 185,848 members and 333 congregations in the UK.

THE CHURCH OF JESUS CHRIST OF LATTER-DAY
   SAINTS, London Temple Visitors' Centre, West Park Road,
   Newchapel, Surrey RH7 6HW **T** 01342-831400
   W www.lds.org.uk

JEHOVAH'S WITNESSES

The movement now known as Jehovah's Witnesses grew from a Bible study group formed by Charles Taze Russell in 1872 in Pennsylvania, USA. In 1896 it adopted the name of the Watch Tower Bible and Tract Society, and in 1931 its members became known as Jehovah's Witnesses.

Jehovah's Witnesses believe in the Bible as the word of God, and consider it to be inspired and historically accurate. They take the scriptures literally, except where there are obvious indications that they are figurative or symbolic, and reject the doctrine of the Trinity. Witnesses also believe that all those approved of by Jehovah will have eternal life on a cleansed and beautified earth; only 144,000 will go to heaven to rule with Jesus Christ. They believe that the second coming of Christ began in 1914, that his thousand-year reign over the earth is imminent, and that armageddon (a final battle in which evil will be defeated) will precede Christ's rule of peace. Jehovah's Witnesses refuse to take part in military service and do not accept blood transfusions.

The world governing body is based in New York, USA. There is no paid ministry, but each congregation has elders assigned to look after various duties and every Witness takes part in the public ministry in their neighbourhood. There are 8.3 million Jehovah's Witnesses worldwide, with around 136,000 Witnesses in Great Britain organised into around 1,500 congregations.

BRITISH HEADQUARTERS, The Ridgeway, London NW7 1RN
   T 020-8906 2211 **W** www.jw.org/en

UNITARIAN AND FREE CHRISTIAN CHURCHES

Unitarianism has its historical roots in the Judaeo-Christian tradition but rejects the deity of Christ and the doctrine of the Trinity. There is no fixed creed and it allows the individual to take insights from all of the world's faiths and philosophies. It is accepted that beliefs may evolve in the light of personal experience.

Unitarian communities first became established in Poland and Transylvania in the 16th century. The first avowedly Unitarian place of worship in Britain opened in London in 1774. The General Assembly of Unitarian and Free Christian Churches came into existence in 1928 as the result of the amalgamation of two earlier organisations.

There are around 3,400 Unitarians in Great Britain in 170 self-governing congregations and fellowship groups.

GENERAL ASSEMBLY OF UNITARIAN AND FREE
   CHRISTIAN CHURCHES, Essex Hall, 1–6 Essex Street,
   London WC2R 3HY **T** 020-7240 2384 **E** info@unitarian.org.uk
   W www.unitarian.org.uk
   President (2019–20), Revd Celia Cartwright
   Chief Officer, Liz Slade

COMMUNICATIONS

POSTAL SERVICES

On 15 October 2013, under the Postal Services Act 2011, Royal Mail was privatised when it was listed on the London Stock Exchange. The government initially retained a 30 per cent stake in Royal Mail, however it sold its remaining shares in 2015. Royal Mail Group ltd operates Royal Mail, Parcelforce Worldwide and General Logistics Systems (GLS). Under the same 2011 Act, the Post Office became independent of Royal Mail Group on 1 April 2012. The government, through the Department for Business, Energy and Industrial Strategy (BEIS), holds a special share in Post Office ltd. The Post Office has a strategic agreement in place to continue to supply Royal Mail products and services through its network and also has the same group holding company (Royal Mail Holdings plc), which holds shares in both Post Office ltd and Royal Mail Group ltd. Neither Royal Mail Holdings plc, nor BEIS, have any involvement in the day-to-day operations of the Post Office.

Royal Mail is the sole provider of the 'universal service': postal products and associated minimum service standards that must be available to all addresses in the UK.

Following the passing of the Postal Services Act 2011, the Office of Communications (OFCOM) assumed regulatory responsibility for postal services. OFCOM's primary responsibility is to secure the provision of a universal postal service with regard to its financial sustainability.

ROYAL MAIL GROUP LTD, 100 Victoria Embankment, London EC4Y 0HQ **T** 0345-774 0740
  W www.royalmailgroup.com
OFCOM, Riverside House, 2A Southwark Bridge Road, London SE1 9HA **T** 0207-981 3000
  W www.ofcom.org.uk

PRICING IN PROPORTION

Since 2006 Royal Mail has priced mail according to its size as well as its weight. The system is intended to reflect the fact that larger, bulkier items cost more to handle than smaller, lighter ones. There are five basic categories of correspondence:

LETTER: *Length* up to 240mm, *width* up to 165mm, *thickness* up to 5mm, *weight* up to 100g; eg most cards and postcards
LARGE LETTER: *Length* up to 353mm, *width* up to 250mm, *thickness* up to 25mm, *weight* up to 750g; eg most A4 documents and magazines
SMALL PARCEL: *Length* up to 450mm, *width* up to 350mm, *depth* up to 160mm, *weight* up to 2kg; eg books, clothes and gifts
MEDIUM PARCEL: *Length* up to 610mm, *width* up to 460mm, *depth* up to 460mm, *weight* up to 20kg; eg gifts, shoes, heavy or bulky items
ROLLED OR CYLINDER SHAPED PARCEL: The length of the item plus twice the diameter must not exceed 104cm, with the greatest dimension being no more than 90cm; eg posters and prints

Items larger than those listed above can only be sent via Parcelforce:

STANDARD PARCELFORCE: *Length* up to 150cm, with a combined length and girth of less than 300cm, *weight* up to 30kg
LARGE PARCELFORCE*: *Length* up to 250cm, with a combined length and girth of less than 500cm, *weight* up to 30kg

* Only available at selected Post Office branches

INLAND POSTAL SERVICES

Following are the details of a number of popular postal services along with prices correct as at December 2020. For a full list of prices *see* **W** www.royalmail.com

FIRST AND SECOND CLASS

Format	Maximum weight	First class	Second class
Letter/postcard	100g	£0.85	£0.66
Large letter	100g	£1.29	£0.96
	250g	£1.83	£1.53
	500g	£2.39	£1.99
	750g	£3.30	£2.70
Small parcel	1,000g	£3.85	£3.20
	2,000g	£5.57	£3.20
Medium parcel	1,000g	£6.00	£5.30
	2,000g	£9.02	£5.30
	5,000g	£15.85	£8.99
	10,000g	£21.90	£20.25
	20,000g	£33.40	£28.55

First class post is normally delivered on the following working day and second class within three working days. Prices are exempt from VAT.

STANDARD PARCELFORCE

Maximum weight	Lowest tariff*
2kg	£12.12
5kg	£13.14
10kg	£16.62
15kg	£23.40
20kg	£28.80
25kg	£40.08
30kg	£44.22

* The rate listed includes VAT, compensation up to £100 and is for delivery within 48 hours

OVERSEAS POSTAL SERVICES

For charging purposes Royal Mail divides the world into four zones: UK, Europe, World Zone 1 (including the Americas, Africa, the Middle East, the Far East and S. E. Asia) and World Zone 2 (including Australia, British Indian Ocean Territory, Fiji, New Zealand, Papua New Guinea, Singapore and Samoa). There is a complete listing on the Royal Mail website (**W** www.royalmail.com/international-zones)

INTERNATIONAL ECONOMY MAIL RATES*

Maximum weight		Standard tariff
Letters up to 100g†		
10g		£1.45
20g		£1.45
100g		£1.45

	Large letters	Small parcels/ printed papers
100g	£3.00	£4.85
250g	£4.00	£5.20
500g	£4.90	£7.45
750g	£5.90	£8.70
1,000g	–	£9.50
2,000g	–	£12.95

* Formerly Surface Mail
† Can only be sent by International Economy to destinations outside of Europe

Printed papers only add £1.35 for each additional 250g, or part thereof, up to 5,000g

INTERNATIONAL STANDARD MAIL RATES*

Weight up to and including	Europe	World Zone 1	World Zone 2
Letters			
10g	£1.70	£1.70	£1.70
20g	£1.70	£1.70	£1.70
100g	£1.70	£2.55	£2.55
Large letters			
100g	£3.25	£4.20	£4.20
250g	£4.25	£5.70	£6.80
500g	£5.25	£8.00	£9.85
750g	£6.25	£10.65	£13.55
Small parcels and printed papers			
100g	£5.80	£7.15	£8.35
250g	£5.95	£8.30	£9.90
500g	£7.80	£12.10	£14.50
750g	£9.05	£14.85	£17.60
1,000g	£10.20	£17.65	£20.85
2,000g	£13.00	£23.30	£28.55

Printed papers only add £1.40 for Europe, £1.90 for World Zone 1 or £2.35 for World Zone 2 for each additional 250g, or part thereof, up to 5,000g

* Formerly Airmail

SPECIAL DELIVERY SERVICES

INTERNATIONAL TRACKED AND SIGNED FOR SERVICES
There are various services available: *International Tracked & Signed* provides full end-to-end tracking, signature on delivery and online delivery confirmation to over 60 destinations; *International Tracked* provides the same, but without a signature on delivery, to over 50 destinations; and *International Signed* is tracked within the UK, a signature is taken on delivery and is available to over 155 destinations. All Tracked and Signed For services deliver to Europe within 3–5 working days, and worldwide within 5–7 working days. Proof of posting and compensation up to £50 is provided as standard. Additional compensation up to £250 can be provided for an extra fee.

SAME DAY
A courier service which provides same day delivery of urgent items in most places in the UK. With collection within the hour of booking, satellite tracking, delivery confirmation and automatic compensation up to £2,500, and for an additional fee, up to £10,000, the service is charged on a loaded mile basis **T** 0330-088 5522

SIGNED FOR
A service which offers proof of delivery including a signature from the receiver and compensation cover up to £50. The first class service is delivered the next working day and prices vary from £2.25 to £34.40 depending on the size and weight of the item. The second class service allows two to three working days for delivery with charges of £2.06 to £29.55.

SPECIAL DELIVERY GUARANTEED
A guaranteed next working day delivery service by 9am or 1pm with a refund option guaranteed for late delivery. With many options available, Royal Mail offers a full list of prices online **W** www.royalmail.com/personal/uk-delivery/special-delivery

OTHER SERVICES

KEEPSAFE
Mail is held for up to 100 days while the addressee is away, and is delivered when the addressee returns. Prices start at £16.00 for 10 days up to £82.00 for 100 days.

PASSPORT CHECK & SEND
For a fee, paper and child passport applications are checked to ensure they meet the requirements set by HM Passport Office and are dispatched to HM Passport Office by secure post.

In November 2018 a digital check and send passport service, available at over 700 branches, was launched for the renewal of adult passports. For a fee of £16.00, and on submission of the old passport, counter staff will take photographs, submit an electronic application and dispatch the old passport to HM Passport Office by special delivery. The new passport will be received from HM Passport Office within three weeks. **W** www.postoffice.co.uk/passport-check-send.

POST OFFICE BOX
A Post Office (PO) Box provides a short and memorable alternative address. Mail is held at a local delivery office until the addressee is ready to collect it, or delivered to a street address for an extra fee. Prices start at £35.10 for one month or £168.00 for six months or £283.50 for a year.

POSTCODE FINDER
Customers can search an online database to find UK postcodes and addresses. For more information *see* Royal Mail's postcode finder **W** www.royalmail.com/postcode-finder

REDELIVERY
Customers can request a redelivery of an item for up to 18 days if it was unable to be delivered and the person is unable to collect from the address on the delivery notification card. A 48-hour notice period is required for redelivery. Redelivery can be arranged to the customer's house, an alternative local address or, for a fee of £0.70 payable on collection, to a local post office branch.

REDIRECTION
Customers may arrange the redirection of their mail via post, at the Post Office or online, subject to verification of their identity. The service is available for three months, six months or 12 months. Prices start at £33.99 for redirection to a UK destination for a single applicant; a full price list is available at **W** www.royalmail.com/personal/receiving-mail/redirection

TRACK AND TRACE
An online service for customers to track the progress of items sent using any special delivery tracked and signed for service. It is accessible from **W** www.royalmail.com/track-your-item

CONTACTS
PARCELFORCE **T** 0344-800 4466 **W** www.parcelforce.com
POST OFFICE **T** 0345-722 3355 **W** www.postoffice.co.uk

TELECOMMUNICATIONS

4G AND 5G

Mobile network technology has improved dramatically since the launch in 1985 of the first-generation global system for mobile communications (GSM), which offered little or no data capability. In 1992 Vodafone launched a new GSM network, usually referred to as 2G or second generation, which used digital encoding and allowed voice and low-speed data communications. This technology was extended, via the enhanced data transfer rate of 2.5G, to 3G – a family of mobile standards that provide high bandwidth support to applications such as voice- and video-calling, data transfer, television streaming and full internet access.

EE was the first operator to launch 4G in late 2012 and by April 2013 the service was available in ten cities where the broadband speed was doubled to more than 20 megabits per second (Mbps). O2 and Vodafone subsequently launched their 4G networks in late August 2013 while 3 began their service in December 2013.

By the end of 2017, there were 58.4 million 4G subscribers, an increase of 6 million (11.5 per cent) from the previous year. The number of 4G subscribers at the end of 2017 comprised 63.5 per cent of the total number of all active mobile subscribers in the UK. 4G coverage improved in 2017, with 58 per cent of all indoor premises covered by all four networks, up from 40 per cent in 2016. Geographic areas covered by all four networks increased from 21 per cent in 2016 to 43 per cent in 2017 and geographic areas with no coverage from any network decreased from 37 per cent in 2016 to 22 per cent in 2017. The ability to connect to a good 4G service continues to vary according to location; in urban areas, good 4G data services of at least 2Mbps is available at 83 per cent of premises, in contrast, only 41 per cent of premises can access good quality data services in rural areas.

In February 2015, OFCOM stated that 5G data connections could be available in the UK by 2020 and in December 2017, the organisation that governs cellular standards, The 3rd Generation Partnership Project (3GPP), signed off on a universal standard, called 5G NR. EE officially switched on its 5G services in Belfast, Birmingham, Cardiff, Edinburgh, London and Manchester on 30 May 2019, becoming the first company to launch 5G in the UK. EE planned to extend 5G to a further ten cities in the UK by the end of 2019 and launched a 5G home broadband service in June 2019. O2 launched 5G in the UK's four capital cities in 2019 and Vodafone launched in 19 cities in 2019, starting with seven cities in July. 3 launched its 5G services in the second half of 2019. All four mobile network providers have 5G-capable devices on the market.

The headline benefit of 5G is speed. 5G is expected to reach speeds in excess of 1,000Mbps or 1Gbps (1 gigabit per second). In comparison maximum download speeds are 384Kbps (kilobits per second) for 3G, 100Mbps for 4G and 300Mbps for 4G+. However, actual download speeds depend on a variety of factors, such as distance from a base station and how many other people are using the network at the same time. As at April 2019 EE provided the fastest 4G connection with an average download speed of 29.6 Mbps; Vodafone, 3 and O2 offered average download speeds of 21.0Mbps, 18.0Mbps and 14.1Mbps respectively. So, although 5G is targeting a download speed of over 1Gbps, average mobile download speeds are expected to be in the region of 80 to 100 Mbps.

FIXED-LINE SERVICES

The total number of fixed-line services in the UK declined for the first time in 2017; from a total of 33.6 million connections in 2016 to 33.1 million in 2017. The decrease in landlines was as a result of businesses switching to mobile and voice over internet protocol (VoIP) services, such as Skype. Fixed voice call minutes continued to decline, from 54 billion in 2017, to 9.5 billion in 2019; part of a steady decline from the 103 billion minutes recorded in 2012.

The decrease in business lines was partly offset by a 1 per cent increase in the number of residential landlines, attributed to growing fixed broadband take-up – most households in the UK need a landline to be able to access fixed broadband services. Fixed broadband connections totalled 26.8 million in 2019, compared to 26.0 million in 2017.

MOBILE PHONE USAGE

At the end of 2019 the total number of mobile subscriptions in the UK had increased by 0.9 million to 84.9 million since the previous year. The volume of SMS and MMS messages sent continued to decline, decreasing to 2.7 billion; a further decline from 90 billion in 2016. The decline in text messaging is likely to be a result of the increasing number of smartphones being used for communication, with social media platforms and instant messaging services such as Whatsapp and iMessenger providing alternatives to SMS. Total outgoing mobile calls decreased to 39.6 billion minutes in 2019, compared with an increase from 143 to 151 billion minutes from 2015 to 2016. Average monthly data use per mobile connection further increased from 1.3 gigabytes in 2016 to 1.9 gigabytes in 2017 and from just 0.9 gigabytes in 2015.

UK adults spent most of their time online on the smartphone in March 2018. Of the total minutes spent online by the entire UK digital population in March 2018, 62 per cent was via the smartphone, followed by the desktop/ laptop (25 per cent) and tablet (13 per cent). In 2018, nearly half (48 per cent) of UK internet users stated that smartphones were their most important device for accessing the internet. This was higher for younger adults, with 72 per cent regarding their smartphones as their most important device for accessing the internet. In contrast, only 17 per cent of those aged over 54 perceived the smartphone as the most important device.

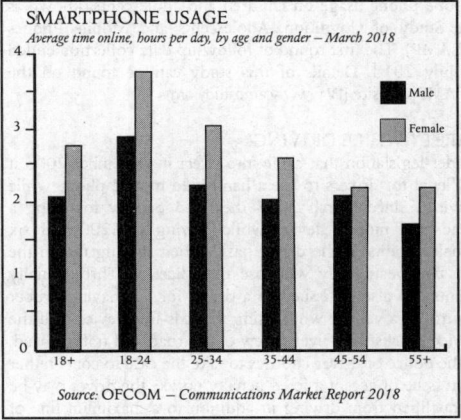

SMARTPHONE USAGE

Average time online, hours per day, by age and gender – March 2018

■ Male
■ Female

18+ 18-24 25-34 35-44 45-54 55+

Source: OFCOM – Communications Market Report 2018

HEALTH

In 1999 the Independent Expert Group on Mobile Phones (IEGMP) was established to examine the possible effects on health of mobile phones, base stations and transmitters. The main findings of the IEGMP's report *Mobile Phones and Health,* published in May 2000, were:

- exposure to radio frequency radiation below guideline levels did not cause adverse health effects to the general population
- the use of mobile phones by drivers of any vehicle can increase the chance of accidents
- the widespread use of mobile phones by children for non-essential calls should be discouraged as if there are unrecognised adverse health effects children may be more vulnerable
- there is no general risk to the health of people living near to base stations on the basis that exposures are expected to be much lower than guidelines set by the International Commission on Non-Ionising Radiation Protection

The government set up the Mobile Telecommunications Health and Research (MTHR) programme in 2001 to undertake independent research into the possible health risks from mobile telephone technology. The MTHR programme published its report in September 2007 concluding that, in the short term, neither mobile phones nor base stations have been found to be associated with any biological or adverse health effects. An international cohort study into the possible long-term health effects of mobile phone use was launched by the MTHR in April 2010. The study is known as COSMOS and aims to follow the health of 250,000 mobile phone users from five countries over 20 to 30 years. Details of the study can be found on the COSMOS website (**W** www.thecosmosproject.org).

A national measurement programme to ensure that emissions from mobile phone base stations do not exceed the ICNIRP guideline levels is overseen by OFCOM and annual audits of these levels can be found on the sitefinder part of its website. Public Health England is responsible for providing information and advice on the health effects of electromagnetic fields, including those emitted from mobile phones and base stations. In April 2012, the HPA's independent Advisory Group on Non-ionising Radiation published a report concluding that there was no convincing evidence that mobile phone technologies cause adverse effects on human health.

In 2014, the Department of Health and Social Care commissioned the world's biggest study into the effects of mobile phone usage on children and adolescents, known as the Study of Cognition, Adolescents and Mobile Phones (SCAMP). The first round of follow-up data collection ended in July 2018. Details of this study can be found on the SCAMP website (**W** www.scampstudy.org).

SAFETY WHILE DRIVING

Under legislation that came into effect in December 2003 it is illegal for drivers to use a hand-held mobile phone while driving. Since March 2017 the fixed penalty for using a hand-held mobile device while driving is £200 and six penalty points. If the driver passed their driving test in the last two years, they will lose their licence. Three penalty points can also be issued to a driver for not having proper control of a vehicle while using a hands-free device or if the device blocks the driver's view of the road and traffic ahead. If the police or driver chooses to take the case to court rather than issue or accept a fixed penalty notice, the driver may be disqualified from driving in addition to a maximum fine of £1,000 for car drivers and £2,500 for drivers of buses, coaches or heavy goods vehicles. The only exceptions for using a mobile phone while driving are to call the emergency services, when it is unsafe or impractical to stop, or when the driver is safely parked.

REGULATION

Under the Communications Act 2003, OFCOM is the independent regulator and competition authority for the UK communications industries, with responsibilities across television, radio, telecommunications and wireless communications services. Competition in the communications market is also regulated by the Competition and Markets Authority, although OFCOM takes the lead in competition investigations in the UK market. The Competition Appeal Tribunal hears appeals against OFCOM's decisions.

CONTACTS

OFCOM, Riverside House, 2A Southwark Bridge Road, London SE1 9HA **T** 020-7981 3000
   W www.ofcom.org.uk

INTERNET

The UK ranks 31st in the world for broadband speed with an average speed of 16.51Mbps. At May 2017, OFCOM reported 100 per cent coverage in the UK at a download speed of 44Mbps, up from 37Mbps in 2016. Superfast broadband is now available in 91 per cent of the UK at a speed of 77Mbps and OFCOM are continually working to boost superfast and ultrafast connections. There were 26 million fixed broadband connections in the UK at the end of 2017, 49 per cent of which were superfast connections.

In 2018 87 per cent of UK adults (aged 16+) had broadband internet access at home. The most frequently cited reason for not having internet access was that they did not need it (45 per cent). Of adults without home internet access, 14 per cent said they were likely to get it in the next year. Home internet access varies significantly according to age group. At the beginning of 2019, 95 per cent of those aged 16 to 24 reported they had home internet access, as opposed to only 75 per cent of those aged over 55+.

In 2018 the most popular internet activity was general browsing, with 69 per cent of adults having browsed the internet in the past week. Sending emails was the second most common activity, with 66 per cent of adults reporting to have done this in the last week. Just under half of adults (44 per cent) reported they had shopped online in the last week, a reduction from 76 per cent in 2017, and around half of UK adults had used online banking and social media in the last week. In 2016, 42 per cent of internet users claimed to use the same password for most, if not all websites and in 2018, a quarter of internet users said they did not carry out appropriate checks before entering their personal or financial information online.

In the UK 77 per cent of internet users had a profile or account on a social media or messaging site or app in 2018, unchanged since 2016. Facebook remained the most-visited social platform, reaching 41 million internet users aged 13+ in 2018 (90 per cent of the total UK internet audience). However Facebook began to see a downward trend in the number of people aged under 35 accessing the platform; with the number of people aged 18 to 24 decreasing by 4 per cent in the year to March 2018, in contrast, visitors among those aged over 54 increased to 24 per cent (2.2 million people) in the same period. Snapchat and Facebook-owned Instagram saw an increase in online audiences, with 22.7 million adults visiting Snapchat in March 2018, fractionally less than Instagram with 23.1 million. However, Snapchat had much larger year-on-year growth than Instagram (122 per cent, compared with 22 per cent). Much of the growth was driven by an increased number of adults aged 25+ visiting the platform.

In March 2018 the organisation with the largest online audience in the UK was Google (41.9 million unique visitors aged 18+), closely followed by Facebook and BBC (40.2 million and 39.5 million respectively) and Amazon (37.7 million), pushing Microsoft down to fifth place with 37 million unique visitors. Within the Google portfolio, YouTube was the most popular platform (40 million), followed by Google Search (37 million), Google Maps (25 million) and Gmail (23 million).

GLOSSARY OF TERMS

The following is a list of selected internet terms. It is by no means exhaustive but is intended to cover those that the average computer user might encounter.

BANNER AD: An advertisement on a web page that links to a corresponding website when clicked.

BLOG: Short for 'web log' – an online personal journal that is frequently updated and intended to be read by the public. Blogs are kept by 'bloggers' and are commonly available as RSS feeds.

BOOKMARKS: A method of storing links or automatic pathways within web browsers which allow a user to quickly return to a webpage. Referred to as 'Favourites' in Internet Explorer.

BROWSER: Typically refers to a 'web browser' program that allows a computer user to view web page content on their computer, eg Firefox, Internet Explorer or Safari.

CLICK-THROUGH: The number of times a web user 'clicks through' a paid advertisement link to the corresponding website.

CLOUD COMPUTING: The use of IT resources as an on-demand service across a network; through cloud computing, software, advanced computation and archived information can be accessed remotely, without the user needing local dedicated hardware.

COOKIE: A piece of information placed on a user's hard disk by a web server. Cookies contain data about the user's activity on a website, and are returned to the server whenever a browser makes further requests. They are important for remembering information such as login and registration details, 'shopping cart' data, user preferences etc, and are often set to expire after a fixed period.

DOMAIN: A set of words or letters, separated by dots, used to identify an internet server, eg www.whitakersalmanack.com, where 'www' denotes a web (http) server, 'whitakersalmanack' denotes the organisation name and 'com' denotes that the organisation is a company.

ENCRYPTION: The conversion of information or data into a code in order to prevent unauthorised access.

FIREWALL: A protection system designed to prevent unauthorised access to or from a private network.

FTP: File Transfer Protocol – a set of network rules enabling a user to exchange files with a remote server.

HACKER: A person who attempts to break or 'hack' into websites. Motives typically involve the desire to procure personal information such as addresses, passwords or credit card details. Hackers may also delete code or incorporate traces of malicious code to damage the functionality of a website.

HIT: A single request from a web browser for a single item from a web server. In order for a web browser to display a page that contains three graphics, four 'hits' would occur at the server: one for the HTML page and one for each of the three graphics. Therefore the number of hits on a website is not synonymous with the number of visitors.

HTML: HyperText Mark-up Language – a programming language used to denote or mark up how an internet page should be presented to a user from an HTTP server via a web browser.

HTTP: HyperText Transfer Protocol – an internet protocol whereby a web server sends web pages, images and files to a web browser.

HYPERLINK: A piece of specially coded text that users can click on to navigate to the web page, or element of a web page, associated with that link's code. Links are typically distinguished through the use of bold, underlined or differently coloured text.

JAVA: A programming language used widely on the internet.

MALWARE: A combination of the words 'malicious' and 'software'. Malware is software designed with the intention of infiltrating a computer and damaging its system.

OPEN-SOURCE: Describes a computer program that has its source code (the instructions that make up a program) freely available for viewing and modification.

PAGERANK: A link analysis algorithm used by search engines that assigns a numerical value based on a website's relevance and reputation. In general, a site with a higher pagerank has more traffic than a site with a lower one.

PHISHING: The fraudulent practice of sending emails to acquire personal information by masquerading as a legitimate company.

PODCAST: A form of audio and video broadcasting using the internet. Although the word is a portmanteau of 'iPod' and broadcasting, podcasting does not require the use of an iPod. A podcaster creates a list of files and makes it available in the RSS 2.0 format. The list can then be obtained using podcast 'retriever' software which makes the files available to digital devices (including iPods); users may then listen or watch at their convenience.

RSS FEED: Rich Site Summary or RDF Site Summary or Real Simple Syndication – a commonly used protocol for syndication and sharing of content, originally developed to facilitate the syndication of news articles, now widely used to share the content of blogs.

SEO: Search Engine Optimisation – the process of optimising the content of a web page to ensure that it is indexed by search engines.

SERVER: A node on a network that provides service to the terminals on the network. These computers have higher hardware specifications, ie more resources and greater speed, in order to handle large amounts of data.

SOCIAL NETWORKING: The practice of using a web-hosted service such as Facebook or Twitter to upload and share content and build friendship networks.

SPAM: A term used for unsolicited, generally junk, email.

TRAFFIC: The number of visitors to a website.

TWITTER: An online microblogging service that allows users to stay connected through the exchange of 140-character posts, known as 'tweets'.

URL: Uniform Resource Locator – address of a file accessible on the internet, eg http://www.whitakersalmanack.com

USER-GENERATED CONTENT (UGC): Refers to various media content produced or primarily influenced by end-users, as opposed to traditional media producers such as licensed broadcasters and production companies. These forms of media include digital video, blogging, podcasting, mobile phone photography and wikis.

WIKI: A website or database developed collaboratively by a community of users, allowing any user to add or edit content.

CONSERVATION AND HERITAGE

NATURAL ENVIRONMENTS IN 2019–20

By Peter Marren

NATURE UNDER LOCKDOWN

Travel restrictions meant that far fewer people travelled abroad in 2020. One outcome of the spring lockdown was that we grew to know our home patch perhaps better than ever before. In the absence of heavy traffic and overhead planes we could hear birdsong and the hum of bees and felt closer to nature than usual. 'There is no salve quite like nature for an anxious mind', noted the Director of Kew Gardens (though his gardens were unfortunately closed). There was also a big increase in the use of natural history webcams. Beaches and places such as the Lake District and the New Forest received even more visitors than usual. The downside was an increase in litter, especially when those normally employed to clean up our messes were furloughed. There were also heathland fires caused by portable barbecues, including a bad one at Wareham Forest in Dorset, and outbreaks of vandalism.

The quiet and weeks of sunshine brought unusual sightings such as the wild goats leaving their clifftop home to wander the streets of Llandudno. There were reports of birds nesting in empty car parks, and of the first cuckoo heard in west London for twenty years. People gathered at harbours to watch dolphins and porpoises undisturbed by boat traffic. It was, however, a difficult year for conservation charities whose income from visitors was curtailed after most properties were closed. Their incomes were already under strain after the withdrawal of European funds, and further stretched by emergencies such as the flooding of autumn 2019 and ash dieback. The National Trust had to dispense with its education officers as it sought to seal a £200m hole in its finances. Plantlife laid off nearly a quarter of its staff. Collectively the Wildlife Trusts lost £10m every month. Conservation projects were placed in abeyance after employees were furloughed. The knock-on effects on wildlife will be significant.

HIGH SPEED TWO

In February 2020, the government approved the HS2 high-speed railway, both for the immediate London-Birmingham phase and its later stages to Manchester and Leeds. After a delay forced by protestors on environmental grounds, construction began in September. Tunnelling through the Chilterns will commence early in 2021. The costs of the project, which in 2010 were estimated at £30–36bn, have already spiralled to £80–88bn and may eventually top £100bn. Even if the project runs on time, the Manchester stage will not be complete until 2040.

HS2 is to be a low-carbon enterprise, using electric trains powered by renewables. The developers are also committed to a policy of 'no net loss' in biodiversity. All the same, construction will damage or destroy a great many wildlife habitats along the route. The Wildlife Trusts claim that the line and its associated works will pass through, or close to, five sites of international importance, 31 Sites of Special Scientific Interest (SSSIs), 693 'local wildlife sites' and 108 ancient woods, not to mention 18 Wildlife Trust nature reserves. It will also require the removal of many old hedges and disrupt roosts and hunting territories of bats and owls. There are concerns that the tunnelling and other works will affect the groundwater and chalk aquifers. HS2 ltd disputes all these figures.

In mitigation, HS2 ltd plans to plant millions of trees and create new habitats such as ponds within what it refers to as a 'green corridor'. It will also salvage soil from wildlife habitats in its path. The line will be crossed by 16 'green bridges' and numerous underpasses. The broad idea is that natural habitats lost during construction will be replaced by planting and landscaping. HS2's full ecological report runs to 55,000 pages. Even so, the Wildlife Trusts are unimpressed and believe that the no-net-loss policy is in fact unachievable. As *The Guardian* journalist Patrick Barkham expressed it, this is a project where 'natural destruction is smoothed over with plenty of tree-planting, newt ponds and nice green talk.'

EVER MORE AMBITIOUS TREE PLANTING TARGETS

In the General Election of 2019, all the main political parties made extravagant pledges to expand Britain's forests. The Conservatives promised to plant thirty million trees each year. The Liberal Democrats and Scottish Nationalist Party proposed to double that. The Green Party wishes to plant 700 million trees over the next ten years. Right out in front was the Labour Party which proposed to plant two *billion* trees by 2040. Their enthusiasm is shared by many environmentalists. Friends of the Earth would like to double Britain's tree cover by planting up 3 million hectares – an area one-and-a-half times the size of Wales. The Woodland Trust heads a consortium aiming to plant 50 million trees over the next 25 years to create a 'Northern Forest', stretching across the Pennines from Liverpool to Hull. The National Trust pledged to plant 20 million trees on its own properties in England and Wales at a cost of about £5 per tree.

The aim of all this planting is not to satisfy Britain's timber needs so much as amenity and carbon storage. The National Trust, for example, hopes to achieve net-zero carbon emissions in this way. Like all green plants, trees reduce the impact of climate change by removing carbon dioxide – the main greenhouse gas – from the atmosphere and storing it as wood: trunks, roots, branches. At present the world's forests store roughly 45 per cent of all land carbon. Trees also filter out pollutants, prevent flooding, and of course they make people happy.

But there are nonetheless environmental drawbacks to a free-for-all planting policy. Firstly it seems to deny a tree's natural ability to regenerate by itself. Next, some of the trees will be planted on natural grassland and heathland, or boggy moors – habitats which are in much shorter supply than woodland. The wildlife benefits of dense plantations of young trees are strictly limited, and there are fears that planting will take the lion's share of government grants such as the £40m pledged for 'green spaces'.

Perhaps most significantly, young trees are not, in fact, very effective at storing carbon. They will become more so as they grow and mature, but whether many of these planted saplings will survive to become mature trees is open to doubt. Several recent academic studies have cast further doubt on whether mass planting is in fact a cost-effective, or even a sensible, policy. This debate is bound to run and run, since so many bodies are now committed to tree planting, strategically and financially.

THE STATE OF OUR BIRDS

Birds are considered to be a good indication of the broad state of wildlife in Britain. They are the only species for which good data is available and the determinants well understood. Regular health checks on breeding birds have revealed significant long-term changes, while short-term change tends to bounce up and down from year to year. Roughly speaking the winners and losers balance one another, and for about 40 per cent of our birds there has been little overall change. No one would be surprised to learn that jackdaws and wood pigeons have more than doubled their numbers since the 1970s, or that the turtle dove, tree sparrow and nightingale are no longer common everyday species.

Milder winters are boosting the numbers of wrens and blackcaps, while species like the nuthatch are extending their range northwards, probably in repose to climate change. Goldfinches have increased thanks to nut feeders but the greenfinch, which also enjoys feeders, has declined through disease and eating mouldy peanuts! Some of our migrant birds are suffering because of what is happening in other countries, including drought, habitat loss and shooting. Birdwatchers from the 1970s would be amazed by the numbers of avocets and black-tailed godwits along our muddy shores, but shocked by the scarcity of breeding curlews and lapwings in the lowlands, and wonder what has happened to the yellow wagtails that used to scuttle about under the feet of cattle. They would observe the growing number of little egrets with wonder, but be appalled to learn that the kittiwake is now an endangered species through its steep rate of decline. It seems to be a victim of the impact of climate change on the sea, which has diminished its food supply and hence its ability to feed its chicks.

Most raptors have increased their numbers. The red kite, introduced to England and Scotland in the 1990s, is now too numerous to count regularly, but there are certainly far more than the 'official' figure of 1,800 breeding pairs. The reintroduced white-tailed sea eagle is slowly expanding its range in Scotland, and has been introduced to the Isle of Wight. Peregrines are now nesting in many towns and cities. Even the hen harrier, which is persecuted illegally, managed 15 successfully breeding pairs in England, the highest total since 2006. Only the kestrel has bucked the trend and is in 'moderate decline'.

The RSPB believes there is room for optimism. Some of our rarer birds, such as corncrakes in the western isles and cirl buntings in Devon, have been saved by management for their needs, with the cooperation of farmers and crofters. Although many farm birds, migrant songbirds and seabirds have declined, government agri-environment schemes are having a positive effect, and current plans to replace EU farm subsidies for 'public goods', including wildlife, bode well.

THE STATE OF OUR INSECTS

A paper published in the journal *Biological Conservation* in February 2019 produced alarming evidence of insect decline across the world. In a review of the best 73 studies on the subject, the paper concluded that 40 per cent of the world's insects are declining and that one third are endangered. The rate of extinction appears to be eight times that of birds or mammals. Worse, the total mass of insects has fallen by 2.5 per cent per year for the last 25–30 years, a rate that would ensure the extinction of the world's insects within the coming half century, with catastrophic consequences to agriculture and ecosystems. The paper concluded gloomily that 'unless we change our ways of producing food, insects as a whole will go down the path of extinction'.

There is some confirmation of this in Germany, which found an alarming decrease in flying insects even on nature reserves, and in Britain where butterflies and moths are monitored by volunteers. One gauge of this is the much smaller number of insects that we find in our houses even on warm humid days in mid-summer. Another is the much lower number of moths coming to traps, and the near disappearance of some species,

including the once well-known garden tiger moth. The rate of decline in Britain is higher than the European average. The causes of the crash are likely numerous, but systematic use of pesticides has been fingered as a likely contributor, as have chemical fertilisers that drift into nearby fields and freshwater.

One group that has suffered disproportionately is dung beetles. They provide a vital role as nature's dustmen, clearing up corpses and animal dung, and one of them, the scarab, was adopted by the ancient Egyptians as a symbol of resurrection and transformation. Unfortunately much of farmland dung is effectively toxic to beetles because the animals have been treated with insecticides to kill intestinal worms. Yet dung beetles are themselves useful to farmers by reducing the rate of nematode worm infections and reducing pest flies by rapidly breaking down the dung. By recycling nutrients into the soil they also aid the growth of grass. The loss of dung beetles has knock-on effects on the animals that feed on them, such as bats. Broadly speaking, our dependence on chemicals is having alarming effects on wildlife and natural food-chains.

BEAVERS EXPANDING THEIR RANGE

The Eurasian beaver (a different species from the better-known Canadian beaver) is a native animal which was hunted to extinction in Britain about 600 years ago. After long debate, a trial to see whether beavers could adapt to the modern British landscape began in 2009 in Knapdale, a remote forested area in western Scotland. That trial was deemed a success. At the same time, beavers escaping from captivity have established themselves on the River Tay catchment in Scotland and also the River Otter in Devon. In both places they are increasing their range naturally, and the Tay now has the largest number of wild-living beavers in Britain, estimated in 2018 at 114 active territories and upwards of 320 individual animals. Since then they have spread further into the Trossachs and the River Forth, and have even been spotted in the Glasgow area.

In November 2016 the Scottish government announced that the beaver could remain as a protected species. In 2019 it also agreed to allow the beavers to expand their range naturally without any need for further releases. Yet the success of the Scottish beavers has not been without friction. There is a mitigation scheme in place for removing the animals where they are causing trouble, but some 87 animals were shot by farmers in 2019.

On the River Otter the government has also accepted that the beavers can remain and expand their range, finding new areas to settle 'as they need'. Formal legal protection came into force in May 2019. On nearby Exmoor the National Trust's release of beavers on its Holnicote estate has already resulted in a dam and 'instant wetland'. Releases within fenced enclosures are much more numerous. Natural England has issued 13 such licenses since 2017, from Cumbria to Cornwall, and more are in the pipeline, including the 'wildland' at Knepp in Sussex, and the Exmoor estate owned by the Prime Minister's father. A breeding stock of beavers is to be Stanley Johnson's 80th birthday present. Some of these captive beavers will undoubtedly escape to form free-range wild colonies.

In time to come the beaver will probably be a familiar wild animal in Britain, with places where they can be watched without disturbing them. The beaver is regarded by ecologists as a keystone species that creates its own habitat of wet channels, deep pools and well-gnawed woodland, while improving water quality in the process. Other animals such as kingfishers and trout benefit from their activities. From being an endangered species not long ago, the Eurasian beaver has been nursed back to ecological health in most European countries, and Britain looks like being no exception.

CLIMATE CHANGE BENEFITS DRAGONFLIES – BUT NOT BUTTERFLIES

Books about dragonflies published before the present century will need to be rewritten. Previously Britain and Ireland had

38 resident species of dragonflies (including the smaller damselflies). Today we have at least 47 species, with more likely to cross the sea soon and join them. Moreover some of our hitherto rare species, such as the Norfolk Hawker and the Scarce Chaser, are increasing their range. Dragonflies, it seems, are very mobile species and able to take advantage of the warming climate. We can watch it happening in detail, year on year, because dragonfly-watching has become very popular. They are 'honorary birds', taken up by birders as an extra group to enjoy watching with binoculars.

The past two summers have been notable ones for dragonflies. Numbers of migratory Southern Migrant Hawkers, Vagrant Hawkers and Lesser Emperors have reached an all-time high, and newcomers such as Southern Emerald, Willow Damselfly and Small Red-eyed Damselfly are rapidly expanding their range northwards. The latest coloniser is the Dainty Damselfly, *Coenagrion scitulum*. Three-quarters of a century ago, this species briefly colonised the coast of Essex but disappeared after the floods of 1953. It has now returned and is breeding happily in a newly dug pond in Kent. The downside to our growing list of dragonflies is that some of the northern species may suffer, especially if hotter, drier summers become the norm.

Our butterflies, on the other hand, have remained much the same. The extinct Large Blue has been introduced successfully from Swedish stock, and the Chequered Skipper, extinct in England (but not Scotland) since 1976, was introduced into Rockingham Forest from Belgian stock in 2018. The one clear beneficiary of climate change is the Long-tailed Blue, formerly a very rare migrant with only a handful of British records. It is now a regular visitor to the south coast, and has established temporary breeding colonies here and there. Moreover in 2020 a former resident, the Large Tortoiseshell, bred successfully for the first time in half a century. European species, such as the Southern Small White and the Short-tailed Blue are moving northwards in response to climate change and have now reached the English Channel. They may be the next colonisers.

WORST YEAR YET FOR ASH

Ash die-back is a fungal disease which blocks the passages of the living tree and results in its death. Once a tree is infected, nothing other than the tree's natural defences can prevent the advance of the disease. It has already killed the majority of ash trees across northern Europe. The disease was first detected in Britain in 2012 on saplings in a tree nursery, and quickly spread into nearby woodland. It is now well-established throughout the UK and will have to take its course. Ash is the third commonest native tree with an estimated 126 million mature trees in woodland and 60 million more in hedgerows and open countryside. The death of the ash will have even greater impacts on the landscape than did Dutch elm disease in the 1970s.

Die-back has been making steady inroads into Britain's ash trees since its discovery, but 2020 has been the worst year yet. Disease may have been aided by the stresses caused by late winter flooding, late frosts and an abnormally hot, dry spring. The National Trust, which had been felling around 5,000 trees a year, had to fell at least 20,000 in 2020, especially in the Cotswolds and south-west England. Among the landscapes affected by the loss of this tree are those made famous by the paintings of John Constable, and the ashwoods of the Lake District that inspired Beatrix Potter. Some estates are now felling healthy trees too since felling the dead ones is more hazardous and expensive. Around 955 species of invertebrates, mosses and lichens are associated with ash, and some of them depend on it. Ash die-back is estimated to cost the economy at least £15bn, including not only the removal costs but also the contribution the trees make to carbon storage and to air and water purification.

There are a few reasons for hope. It may well be that some trees are resistant to the disease, given that ash is genetically highly variable in Britain. There are also signs that the disease is slower in mature trees than younger ones, and that many isolated trees are escaping infection so far. The tree may also be more resistant in mixed woods than those dominated by ash. Given the rate at which ash saplings appear from seed, there is a possibility that the tree may self-select varieties that can resist the disease.

NO-GO ZONES FOR PHEASANTS

An estimated 60 million pheasants and red-legged partridges are released in England each year for shooting. This represents a considerable scaling-up from the 4 million or so birds released in the early 1970s, and in biomass terms it makes the pheasant the most abundant bird in England. However the pheasant is not a native species – their wild range is further east, in Asia and south-east Europe. Legally they are classed not as wild birds but as livestock. Most pheasants are raised in pens in woodland and released in late summer, ready for the winter shooting season. The impact of so many large omnivorous birds on native wildlife has not been investigated (perhaps no one is eager to sponsor research that may harm their interests). There is however anecdotal evidence that pheasants prey on young lizards, snakes and slow-worms. They also impact on woodland plants and invertebrates, while unwanted pheasant carcasses are routinely dumped in pits where they attract foxes and crows. This in turn increases predation on ground-nesting birds, many of which are in decline.

The campaign group Wild Justice argued successfully that the lack of regulation on pheasant releases contravenes EU wildlife protection rules. From February 2021 shooting interests will now require a license to release pheasants or red-legged partridges within 500 metres of a protected site, technically defined as either a SAC (Special Area of Conservation), or a SPA (Special Protection Area for birds). The RSPB (Royal Society for the Protection of Birds) welcomed the decision. Such licensing may reduce the current pheasant population by 7 million or so. The Environment Minister, George Eustice, noted judiciously that the move 'highlighted the need for a better understanding of how any localised impacts might be mitigated and existing arrangements strengthened'.

Shooting interests argue that the licensing is disproportionate, and that more evidence is needed to justify it. Moreover, they argue, pheasant shooting has preserved many small woods and encouraged management that benefits wildlife, such as the maintenance of broad open rides. Wild Justice, on the other hand, sees the 500-metre buffer area as a compromise, and will continue to campaign for a wider 1,000-metre zone around protected sites and a ban on the use of lead ammunition.

NATURAL HISTORY ON THE SCHOOL SYLLABUS

Natural history is to be taught in schools from 2022 as an optional GCSE subject. The growing 'disconnect' between young people and nature is widely recognised, and was demonstrated recently when only half the children asked could recognise a stinging nettle and only a fifth could recognise a bumblebee. Children spend more time indoors than earlier generations, and few of them are allowed to roam as in the past. Yet an awareness of nature is widely recognised as being good for us, benefitting mental health and tackling such social issues as depression and obesity. Of course it would also help the natural environment if more young people had some knowledge of it.

The campaign to teach natural history in schools was led by Mary Colwell, who four years ago launched a petition for a GCSE in the subject. Backed by the Green MP Caroline Lucas, and with encouragement from the then environment minister

Michael Gove, the idea was taken forward by senior educationalists. Its advocates needed to convince civil servants and teachers that natural history is not the same thing as biology, and is a genuine educational gap. It is envisaged as a much broader subject embracing not only science but history, geography and the arts, as well as developing field skills. In May 2020 the proposal was formally approved and moved onto the consultation stage. It is expected that teachers will be assisted by nature experts, field centres and museums, particularly the Natural History Museum. Mary Colwell hopes that the GCSE will 'make nature part of British society again'.

NATURAL CAPITAL

The new buzzword in conservation is 'natural capital'. It is envisaged as the total stock of natural resources in any given area: rocks, soil, water, air and all living things. Fertile soil and clean water underwrite economies and make human life possible. Other natural assets provide what are termed ecosystem services, that is, goods and services based on the natural systems of the earth. Essentially, natural capital is an economist's way of viewing nature. It appeals to politicians and planners.

At the government's bidding, Natural England has spent much of the year producing Natural Capital 'atlases' for every English county and city region. These are now available online. They are seen as a framework 'to inform our understanding of the state of our natural assets'. To some this is a helpful way to value the natural world, including wildlife. To others it is a distortion of science by the cold arithmetic of money. The environmental critic George Monbiot, for instance, summed up Natural Capital as 'gibberish'.

BUILT HERITAGE IN 2019–20

By Matthew Saunders

COVID-19

Like everything in the United Kingdom in 2020, life in the world of historic buildings was dominated and diverted by the COVID-19 pandemic. For all those sites dependent on the visitor, the financial effect was potentially disastrous whilst fundraising campaigns were drastically limited by the ban on public gatherings. Westminster Abbey alone forecast a shortfall in 2020 of £12m. The Historic Houses Association, which brings together private country house owners, found, in a survey of members, that many had paused capital works, despite the fact that before COVID-19, there had already been an accumulated backlog of repairs of £1.4bn. Government came dramatically to the rescue, both indirectly through its furlough scheme for staff unable to work and directly through unprecedented cash injections, beginning with £1.57m in a Culture Recovery Fund, (including the Heritage Stimulus Fund) launched in the summer and disbursed in the autumn. This embraced £270m on loans, £880m in grants, £100m to national cultural institutions and £120m to the English Heritage Trust (the latter to keep it on course for the government's aim of financial self-sufficiency by 2023). Beneficiaries (given in full on **W** www.gov.uk/government/news) included national organisations such as Historic Royal Palaces, The Landmark Trust, English Heritage, The Churches Conservation Trust and The Friends of Friendless Churches, individual sites like the vast mansion at Wentworth Woodhouse in Yorkshire, Waltham Abbey Gunpowder Mills and a goodly number of churches and cathedrals, and local bodies like The Great Yarmouth Preservation Trust, The Modernist Society in Manchester and conservation practitioners such as The Skillington Workshop. The National Lottery Heritage Fund, Historic England, Cadw (in Wales) and

Historic Scotland were all channels for the distribution of much of this injection of funds but were also recast into fire-fighting mode when it came to disbursing their own grant monies. No new NLHF grants were offered in 2020–21 and the reopening to fresh applications from 2021–22 remains limited, as most funds were directed to the rescue and stabilization of existing projects and past customers.

As the physical retail unit, many of which are housed in historic town centres, became one of the most threatened of all building types, as Lockdowns hit hard, the pre-existing allocation by the Chancellor of some £95m to the Heritage Action Zones, nearly all of them in urban centres, became considerably more relevant. The grants, distributed by Historic England, were announced in early October. Amounts of £2m or thereabouts went to Tottenham, Hastings, Wednesbury, Plymouth, Gloucester, Kirkham, Sowerby Bridge and Huddersfield, with other appreciable beneficiaries at Bacup, Hexham, Tewkesbury, Bedford, Dunstable, Lincoln, Buxton, Gosport, Chatham and Kettering.

The principal proposal for constitutional change in the course of the year, indeed the most significant overhaul of the planning system for decades, was that laid out in *Planning for the Future*, published at the beginning of August. The system of heritage protection emerged with a clean bill of health, with no changes proposed in the listed building consent system. However, unintended indirect consequences are highly likely in the future, due to decision-making made less by discretionary judgment in individual cases and more by following a set rulebook. No decision has yet been made on a proposal in Wales, first recommended late in 2018, that the separate listed building consent regime in Wales be abolished and merged with planning permission.

Britain has more listed buildings, at 550,000 (400,000 in England) than any other country apart from Italy. The most effective form is statutory listing, in one of three grades, which requires a dedicated permission, known as listed building consent for works of demolition, alteration or extension. This is administered by Historic England through the Secretary of State for Digital, Culture, Media and Sport. Parallel to that is the system of Local Listing, operated by 45 per cent of local planning authorities. This is 'non-statutory' in that demolishing entries on such a list does not need express permission but becomes a material consideration when an associated planning application is lodged. Both regimes came under close attention in 2020 with the publication in November of the Saunders Report on The Future of the National Heritage List for England, commissioned by Historic England, and the announcement earlier in the year by the Ministry responsible for local listing, DCLG, that a budget of £700,000 was being set aside to stimulate the creation of further such Lists. Additions to the statutory lists in 2020 included the picturesque villa known as Eller How at Lindale in the Lake District, created by the renowned local practice known as 'Websters of Kendal', the former studio and workshop of Barbara Hepworth at St Ives and the BBC Recording Studio at Maida Vale with 24 additions from among post-war designed landscapes to the (non-statutory) Register of Parks and Gardens.

NEW ATTRACTIONS

2020 was a highly inauspicious year for the new venture but some did come on stream. A new rehearsal studio for the Halle Orchestra, in Manchester, based in the listed former church of St Peter in Ancoats (1859) was opened in November 2019 as was The Fratry (new reception area for visitors) at Carlisle Cathedral, in July 2020, on the back of a £2m National Lottery grant. The most triumphant was undoubtedly the completion in the summer of the new Spa Hotel as the centrepiece of the Grade 1 listed 'The Crescent' at Buxton in Derbyshire. The

Crescent has been at risk for forty years and it was only the determination of the developer, Trevor Osborne and the huge grants, totalling £24m from the National Lottery Heritage Fund (NLHF) that finally saw the project through. The new archives of the Church of England in the grounds of Lambeth Palace, paid for, without grant aid, by the Church Commissioners and containing some of the country's greatest treasures, is to admit the public (as it has done within the Palace itself since 1610) early in 2021. Openings projected for 2021 include the new visitor centre at Lincoln Cathedral, the new galleries at Northampton Museum and the Corinium Museum, Cirencester, a brand new museum for Petersfield in Hampshire and the new centre for Suffolk archives on Ipswich Waterfront to be termed 'The Hold'. 'Round Two' NLHF grants confirmed in 2020 promised vital kickstarts for major schemes to conserve and convert one of the greatest High Victorian buildings of the North, the Grade 1 listed Town Hall at Rochdale (NLHF grant £8.3m), that to repair and open up the 'Pitman's Parliament' at Redhill, Co.Durham (£400,000), the placing of the 'Coventry Tapestry' in, and associated repairs to, the Grade 1 listed St Mary's Guildhall in that city (£1,762,700), Exeter Cathedral (£4,290,500), Evesham Abbey Trust (£788,300) and St Peter's church Sudbury, Suffolk (£1.67m) to open this redundant church for wider community use. Further areas of Jewish history were opened up with the new museum in the cemetery of 1873 at Willesden in North West London whilst the future of one of the most memorable recent gardens, that known as The Laskett, at Much Birch in Herefordshire, created by Sir Roy Strong and his late wife, Julia Trevelyan Oman around a villa of 1830, is assured by its passing for preservation in perpetuity to the horticultural charity known as 'Perennial'. And in a similar act of philanthropy, Sir James and Lady Deirdre Dyson have announced plans for a brand new art gallery, open to the public, in the grounds of their Grade 1 listed house by James Wyatt, Dodington Park, Gloucestershire. But in such a traumatic year as 2020, there have steps back as well as forward. Kneller Hall, at Twickenham, the imposing listed home to Royal Military School of Music of 1848 is set to close in 2021, the plans to create a centre for mental health in the former church of St Mary at Quay in Ipswich, owned by the Churches Conservation Trust have collapsed and the seventy-year-old Stamford-based organization known as 'Men of the Stones', set up to protect the masonry skills of the limestone belt has been closed down and its funds transferred. One of the most architecturally splendid of all Benedictine monasteries, Downside Abbey in Somerset, has announced that it is to shut (although the school is to survive) and the charming Museum of Mechanical Music based in a former church at Portfield near Chichester is no more. The Annual Report 2018–19 of the Methodist Church Conservation Section, published in 2020, highlighted the closure of four historic chapels – High House Church at Ireshopburn, Durham, Darlington Street Chapel, Wolverhampton and the major chapels at Redruth, Cornwall and Williton, Somerset.

ADVANCES IN KNOWLEDGE

Publications have suffered less than buildings. The year saw important additions in the Pevsner *Buildings of England* volumes with the revision of *Nottinghamshire* with that for *County Durham* promised for March 2021. There were significant new accounts of *Arts & Crafts Churches* by Alec Hamilton, porches on East Anglian medieval churches (by Helen Lunnon), additions (covering Derbyshire and Staffordshire) within the ongoing *Corpus of Anglo-Saxon Sculpture,* issued by the British Academy, the architecture of the Cooperative Movement (by Lynn Pearson) and Historic England's account of the development of Ramsgate. There were biographies of Sir Edward Maufe, architect, inter alia, of Guildford Cathedral (by Juliet Dunmur), of J.F.Bentley, the designer of Wesminster (RC) Cathedral (by Peter Howell) and of Edward L'Anson, and his son and grandson (by Peter Jefferson). *Somerset Architects and Surveyors: A Biographical Dictionary of Building Professionals, Artists and Craftsmen 1720-1939* by Russell Lillford, was published in 2020 on the website of the Somerset Building Preservation Trust. *Excellent Essex* by Gillian Darley, an episodic overview of the history, buildings and radicals of that county was a particular critical success.

Plans were announced to celebrate the tercentenary of the death of Sir Christopher Wren in 1723 (WREN300) and towards the end of the year a society to celebrate one of the country's greatest wood (and stone) carvers, Grinling Gibbons, received charitable status. It will launch formally in 2021 and events planned to celebrate his tercentenary include a major exhibition on the man and his work.

NATIONAL PARKS

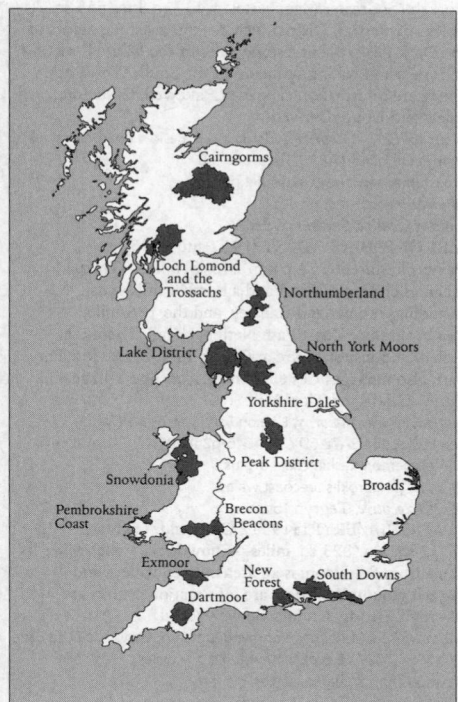

ENGLAND AND WALES

There are ten national parks in England, and three in Wales. In addition, the Norfolk and Suffolk Broads are considered to have equivalent status to a national park. Under the National Parks and Access to the Countryside Act 1949, as clarified by the Natural Environment and Rural Communities Act 2006, the two purposes of the national parks are to conserve and enhance the parks' natural beauty, wildlife and cultural heritage, and to promote opportunities for the understanding and enjoyment of the special qualities of national parks by the public. If there is a conflict between the two purposes, then conservation takes precedence.

Natural England is the statutory body that has the power to designate national parks in England, and Natural Resources Wales (formerly Countryside Council for Wales) is responsible for national parks in Wales. Designations in England are confirmed by the Secretary of State for Environment, Food and Rural Affairs and those in Wales by the Welsh government. The designation of a national park does not affect the ownership of the land or remove the rights of the local community. The majority of the land in the national parks is owned by private landowners (around 75 per cent) or by bodies such as the National Trust and the Forestry Commission. The national park authorities own only a small percentage of the land themselves.

The Environment Act 1995 replaced the existing national park boards and committees with free-standing national park authorities (NPAs). NPAs are the sole local planning authorities for their areas and as such influence land use and development, and deal with planning applications. NPAs are responsible for carrying out the statutory purposes of national parks stated above.

In pursuing these purposes they have a statutory duty to seek to foster the economic and social well-being of the communities within national parks. The NPAs publish management plans setting out overarching policies for their area and appoint their own officers and staff.

The Broads Authority was established under the Norfolk and Suffolk Broads Act 1988 and meets the requirement for the authority to have a navigation function in addition to a regard for the needs of agriculture, forestry and the economic and social interests of those who live or work in the Broads.

MEMBERSHIP

Membership of English NPAs comprises local authority appointees, members directly appointed by the Secretary of State for Environment, Food and Rural Affairs and members appointed by the secretary after consultation with local parishes. Under the Natural Environment and Rural Communities Act 2006 every district, county or unitary authority with land in a national park is entitled to appoint at least one member unless it chooses to opt out. The total number of local authority and parish members must exceed the number of national members.

Brecon Beacons, Northumberland, Pembrokeshire Coast and Snowdonia NPAs have 18 members; Dartmoor has 19; the Lake District and North York Moors have 20; the Broads has 21; Exmoor, the New Forest 22; Yorkshire Dales 25; South Downs 27; and the Peak District 30.

In Wales, two-thirds of NPA members are appointed by the constituent local authorities and one-third by the Welsh government, advised by Natural Resources Wales.

FUNDING

Core funding for the English NPAs and the Broads Authority is provided by central government through the Department for Environment, Food and Rural Affairs (DEFRA) National Park Grant.

In Wales, the three national parks are funded by the Welsh government; for 2020–21 budgeted gross revenue expenditure totals £19.2m and capital expenditure £5.4m.

All NPAs and the Broads Authority can take advantage of grants from other bodies including lottery and European grants.

The national parks (with date that designation was confirmed) are:

BRECON BEACONS (1957), Powys (66 per cent)/ Carmarthenshire/Rhondda, Cynon and Taff/Merthyr Tydfil/Blaenau Gwent/Monmouthshire, 1,344 sq. km/ 519 sq. miles – The park is centred on the Brecon Beacons mountain range, which includes the three highest mountains in southern Britain (Pen y Fan, Corn Du and Cribyn), but also includes the valleys of the rivers Usk and Wye, the Black Mountains to the east and the Black Mountain to the west. There is a visitor centre at Libanus, a tourist information centre at Abergavenny and community run information centres in Llandovery and Brecon.
National Park Authority, Plas y Ffynnon, Cambrian Way, Brecon, Powys LD3 7HP **T** 01874-624437 **W** www.beacons-npa.gov.uk
Chief Executive, Vacant

BROADS (1989), Norfolk/Suffolk, 303 sq. km/117 sq. miles – The Broads is located between Norwich and Great Yarmouth on the flood plains of the six rivers flowing through the area to the sea. The area is one of fens, winding waterways, woodland and marsh. The 60 or so broads are man-made, and many are connected to the rivers by dykes, providing over 200km (125 miles) of navigable waterways. There are information centres at Hoveton, Whitlingham Country Park and How Hill National Nature Reserve. There are yacht stations at Norwich, Reedham and Great Yarmouth.

Broads Authority, Yare House, 62–64 Thorpe Road, Norwich NR1 1RY **T** 01603-610734 **W** www.broads-authority.gov.uk
Chief Executive, Dr John Packman

DARTMOOR (1951), Devon, 953 sq. km / 368 sq. miles – The park consists of moorland and rocky granite tors, and is rich in prehistoric remains. There are visitor centres at Haytor, Princetown (main visitor centre) and Postbridge.
National Park Authority, Parke, Bovey Tracey, Devon TQ13 9JQ
T 01626-832093 **E** hq@dartmoor.gov.uk
W www.dartmoor.gov.uk
Chief Executive, Kevin Bishop

EXMOOR (1954), Somerset (71 per cent) / Devon (29 per cent), 694 sq. km / 268 sq. miles – Exmoor is a moorland plateau, with steep wooded slopes that extend along the coastline and is inhabited by wild Exmoor ponies and red deer. There are many ancient remains and burial mounds. There are national park centres at Dunster, Dulverton and Lynmouth.
National Park Authority, Exmoor House, Dulverton, Somerset TA22 9HL **T** 01398-323665 **E** info@exmoor-nationalpark.gov.uk
W www.exmoor-nationalpark.gov.uk
Chief Executive, Sarah Bryan

LAKE DISTRICT (1951), Cumbria, 2,362 sq. km / 912 sq. miles – The Lake District includes England's highest mountains (Scafell Pike, Helvellyn and Skiddaw) but it is most famous for its glaciated lakes. In 2017 the Lake District was inscribed as a UNESCO World Heritage Site for its cultural significance *see also* World Heritage Sites. There are national park information centres at Bowness-on-Windermere, Keswick, Ullswater and a visitor centre at Brockhole, Windermere.
National Park Authority, Murley Moss, Oxenholme Road, Kendal, Cumbria LA9 7RL **T** 01539-724555
E hq@lakedistrict.gov.uk **W** www.lakedistrict.gov.uk
Chief Executive, Richard Leafe

NEW FOREST (2005), Hampshire, 570 sq. km / 220 sq. miles – The forest has been protected since 1079 when it was declared a royal hunting forest. The area consists of forest, ancient woodland, heathland, farmland, coastal saltmarsh and mudflats. Managed by the ancient system of commoning, the landscape is shaped by grazing animals and contains a range of rare plants and animals.
National Park Authority, Town Hall, Avenue Road, Lymington, Hants SO41 9ZG **T** 01590-646600
E enquiries@newforestnpa.gov.uk **W** www.newforestnpa.gov.uk
Chief Executive, Alison Barnes

NORTH YORK MOORS (1952), North Yorkshire (96 per cent) / Redcar and Cleveland, 1,434 sq. km / 554 sq. miles – The park consists of dales woodland, moorland and coast, and includes the Hambleton Hills and the Cleveland Way national trail. There are national park centres at Danby and Sutton Bank.
National Park Authority, The Old Vicarage, Bondgate, Helmsley, York YO62 5BP **T** 01439-772700
E general@northyorkmoors.org.uk
W www.northyorkmoors.org.uk
Chief Executive, Tom Hind

NORTHUMBERLAND (1956), Northumberland, 1,049 sq. km / 405 sq. miles – The park is an area of hill country, comprising open moorland, blanket bogs and very small patches of ancient woodland, stretching from Hadrian's Wall to the Scottish border. Visitor information is available from the Sill National Landscape Discovery Centre on Hadrian's Wall.
National Park Authority, Eastburn, South Park, Hexham, Northumberland NE46 1BS **T** 01434-605555
E enquiries@nnpa.org.uk
W www.northumberlandnationalpark.org.uk
Chief Executive, Tony Gates

PEAK DISTRICT (1951), Derbyshire (64 per cent) / Staffordshire / South Yorkshire / Cheshire / West Yorkshire / Greater Manchester, 1,437 sq. km / 555 sq. miles – The Peak District includes the gritstone moors of the Dark Peak, the limestone dales of the White Peak and the crags and rolling farmland of the South West Peak. There are information centres at Bakewell, Castleton, Edale and Upper Derwent.
National Park Authority, Aldern House, Baslow Road, Bakewell, Derbyshire DE45 1AE **T** 01629-816200
E customer.service@peakdistrict.gov.uk
W www.peakdistrict.gov.uk
Chief Executive, Sarah Fowler

PEMBROKESHIRE COAST (1952 and 1995), Pembrokeshire, 615 sq. km / 240 sq. miles – The park includes cliffs, moorland and a number of islands, including Skomer and Ramsey, and the 186-mile Pembrokeshire Coast Path National Trail. There is a gallery and visitor centre at Oriel y Parc, St Davids. The park also manages Castell Henllys Iron Age Village and Carew Castle and Tidal Mill.
National Park Authority, Llanion Park, Pembroke Dock, Pembrokeshire SA72 6DY **T** 01646-624800
E info@pembrokeshirecoast.org.uk
W www.pembrokeshirecoast.wales
Chief Executive, Tegryn Jones

SNOWDONIA / ERYRI (1951), Gwynedd / Conwy, 2,132 sq. km / 823 sq. miles – Snowdonia, which takes its name from Snowdon, is an area of deep valleys and rugged mountains. There are information centres at Aberdyfi, Beddgelert and Betws y Coed.
National Park Authority, Penrhyndeudraeth, Gwynedd LL48 6LF
T 01766-770274 **E** park@snowdonia.gov.wales
W www.snowdonia.gov.wales
Chief Executive, Emyr Williams

THE SOUTH DOWNS (2010), West Sussex / Hampshire, 1,624 sq. km / 627 sq. miles – The South Downs contains a diversity of natural habitats, including flower-studded chalk grassland, ancient woodland, flood meadow, lowland heath and rare chalk heathland. There are visitor centres at Beachy Head, Queen Elizabeth Country Park in Hampshire and Seven Sisters Country Park in East Sussex.
National Park Authority, North Street, Midhurst, W. Sussex GU29 9DH **T** 01730-814810 **W** www.southdowns.gov.uk
Chief Executive, Trevor Beattie

YORKSHIRE DALES (1954), North Yorkshire (71 per cent) / Cumbria (28 per cent) / Lancashire (1 per cent), 2,179 sq. km / 841 sq. miles – The Yorkshire Dales is composed primarily of limestone overlaid in places by millstone grit. The three peaks of Ingleborough, Whernside and Pen-y-ghent are within the park. There are information centres at Grassington, Hawes, Aysgarth Falls, Malham and Reeth.
National Park Authority, Yoredale, Bainbridge, Leyburn, N. Yorks DL8 3EL **T** 0300-456 0030 **E** info@yorkshiredales.org.uk
W www.yorkshiredales.org.uk
Chief Executive, David Butterworth

SCOTLAND

On 9 August 2000 the national parks (Scotland) bill received royal assent, giving parliament the ability to create national parks in Scotland. The Act gives Scottish parks wider powers than in England and Wales, including statutory responsibilities for the local economy and rural communities. The board of the Cairngorms NPA comprises 19 members; seven appointed by the Scottish ministers, a further seven nominated to the board by the five local authorities in the park area and five locally elected members. The board of Loch Lomond and the Trossachs NPA comprises 17 members; five elected by the community and 12 appointed by Scottish Ministers, six of whom are nominated by local authorities. In Scotland, the national parks are central government bodies and are wholly funded by the Scottish government. Due to the financial hardships caused by COVID-19, the budget for 2020–21 will run a deficit of £398,000.

CAIRNGORMS (2003), North-East Scotland, 4,528 sq. km/1,748 sq. miles – The Cairngorms national park is the largest in the UK, covering around 6 per cent of Scotland. It displays a vast collection of landforms, including five of the six highest mountains in the UK and contains 25 per cent of Britain's threatened species. The near natural woodlands contain remnants of the original ancient Caledonian pine forest. There are 13 visitor centres within the park.
National Park Authority, 14 The Square, Grantown-on-Spey, Morayshire PH26 3HG **T** 01479-873535
E enquiries@cairngorms.co.uk **W** www.cairngorms.co.uk
Chief Executive, Grant Moir

LOCH LOMOND AND THE TROSSACHS (2002), Argyll and Bute/Perth and Kinross/Stirling/West Dunbartonshire, 1,865 sq. km/720 sq. miles – The park boundaries encompass lochs, rivers, forests, 21 mountains above 914m (3,000ft) including Ben More, the highest at 1,174m (3,852ft) and a further 20 mountains between 762m (2,500ft) and 914m (3,000ft). There is a national park centre in Balmaha and several other visitor centres across the park which are administered by VisitScotland.
National Park Authority, Carrochan, Carrochan Road, Balloch G83 8EG **T** 01389-722600 **E** info@lochlomond-trossachs.org
W www.lochlomond-trossachs.org
Chief Executive, Gordon Watson

NORTHERN IRELAND
There is a power to designate national parks in Northern Ireland under the Nature Conservation and Amenity Lands Order (Northern Ireland) 1985, but there are currently no national parks in Northern Ireland.

AREAS OF OUTSTANDING NATURAL BEAUTY

ENGLAND AND WALES
Under the National Parks and Access to the Countryside Act 1949, provision was made for the designation of areas of outstanding natural beauty (AONBs). Natural England is responsible for designating AONBs in England and Natural Resources Wales for the Welsh AONBs. Designations in England are confirmed by the Secretary of State for Environment, Food and Rural Affairs and those in Wales by the Welsh government. The Countryside and Rights of Way (CROW) Act 2000 placed greater responsibility on local authorities to protect AONBs and made it a statutory duty for relevant authorities to produce a management plan for their AONB area. The CROW Act also provided for the creation of conservation boards for larger and more complex AONBs.

The primary objective of the AONB designation is to conserve and enhance the natural beauty of the area. Where an AONB has a conservation board, it has the additional purpose of increasing public understanding and enjoyment of the special qualities of the area; the board has greater weight should there be a conflict of interests between the two. In addition, the board is also required to foster the economic and social well-being of the local communities but without incurring significant expenditure in doing so. Overall responsibility for AONBs lies with the relevant local authorities or conservation board. To coordinate planning and management responsibilities between local authorities in whose area they fall, AONBs are overseen by a joint advisory committee (or similar body) which includes representatives from the local authorities, landowners, farmers, residents and conservation and recreation groups. Core funding for AONBs is provided by central government through DEFRA, local authorities and Natural Resources Wales.

The 46 AONBs (with date designation confirmed) are:

ARNSIDE AND SILVERDALE (1972), Cumbria/Lancashire, 75 sq. km/29 sq. miles

BLACKDOWN HILLS (1991), Devon/Somerset, 370 sq. km/143 sq. miles

CANNOCK CHASE (1958), Staffordshire, 68 sq. km/26 sq. miles

CHICHESTER HARBOUR (1964), Hampshire/West Sussex, 74 sq. km/29 sq. miles

CHILTERNS (1965; extended 1990), Bedfordshire/Buckinghamshire/Hertfordshire/Oxfordshire, 839 sq. km/324 sq. miles

CLWYDIAN RANGE AND DEE VALLEY (1985; extended 2011), Denbighshire/Flintshire, 389 sq. km/150 sq. miles

CORNWALL (1959; Camel Estuary 1983), 958 sq. km/370 sq. miles

COTSWOLDS (1966; extended 1990), Gloucestershire/Oxfordshire/Warwickshire/Wiltshire/Worcestershire, 2,046 sq. km/790 sq. miles

CRANBORNE CHASE AND WEST WILTSHIRE DOWNS (1983), Dorset/Hampshire/Somerset/Wiltshire, 983 sq. km/380 sq. miles

DEDHAM VALE (1970; extended 1978, 1991), Essex/Suffolk, 90 sq. km/35 sq. miles

DORSET (1959), Dorset/Somerset, 1,129 sq. km/436 sq. miles

EAST DEVON (1963), 268 sq. km/103 sq. miles

FOREST OF BOWLAND (1964), Lancashire/North Yorkshire, 803 sq. km/310 sq. miles

GOWER (1956), Swansea, 188 sq. km/73 sq. miles

HIGH WEALD (1983), East Sussex/Kent/Surrey/West Sussex, 1,461 sq. km/564 sq. miles

HOWARDIAN HILLS (1987), North Yorkshire, 204 sq. km/79 sq. miles

ISLE OF WIGHT (1963), 189 sq. km/73 sq. miles

ISLES OF SCILLY (1976), 16 sq. km/6 sq. miles

KENT DOWNS (1968), 878 sq. km/339 sq. miles

LINCOLNSHIRE WOLDS (1973), 558 sq. km/215 sq. miles

LLYN (1957), Gwynedd, 155 sq. km/60 sq. miles

MALVERN HILLS (1959), Gloucestershire/Worcestershire, 105 sq. km/41 sq. miles

MENDIP HILLS (1972; extended 1989), Somerset, 198 sq. km/76 sq. miles

NIDDERDALE (1994), North Yorkshire, 603 sq. km/233 sq. miles

NORFOLK COAST (1968), 451 sq. km/174 sq. miles

NORTH DEVON (1960), 171 sq. km/66 sq. miles

NORTH PENNINES (1988), Cumbria/Durham/North Yorkshire/Northumberland, 1,983 sq. km/766 sq. miles

NORTH WESSEX DOWNS (1972), Hampshire/Oxfordshire/Wiltshire, 1,730 sq. km/668 sq. miles

NORTHUMBERLAND COAST (1958), 138 sq. km/64 sq. miles

QUANTOCK HILLS (1957), Somerset, 99 sq. km/38 sq. miles

SHROPSHIRE HILLS (1959), 804 sq. km/310 sq. miles

SOLWAY COAST (1964), Cumbria, 115 sq. km/44 sq. miles

SOUTH DEVON (1960), 337 sq. km/130 sq. miles

SUFFOLK COAST AND HEATHS (1970), 403 sq. km/156 sq. miles

SURREY HILLS (1958), 419 sq. km/162 sq. miles

TAMAR VALLEY (1995), Cornwall/Devon, 190 sq. km/73 sq. miles

WYE VALLEY (1971), Gloucestershire/Herefordshire/ Monmouthshire, 326 sq. km/126 sq. miles

YNYS MON (ISLE OF ANGLESEY) (1967), 221 sq. km/85 sq. miles

NORTHERN IRELAND

The Department of Agriculture, Environment and Rural Affairs (Northern Ireland), with advice from the Council for Nature Conservation and the Countryside, designates AONBs in Northern Ireland. Dates given are those of designation.

ANTRIM COAST AND GLENS (1988), Co. Antrim, 725 sq. km/280 sq. miles

BINEVENAGH (2006), Co. Londonderry, 166 sq. km/64 sq. miles

CAUSEWAY COAST (1989), Co. Antrim, 42 sq. km/ 16 sq. miles

LAGAN VALLEY (1965), Co. Down, 39 sq. km/15 sq. miles

MOURNE (1986), Co. Down, 580 sq. km/224 sq. miles

RING OF GULLION (1991), Co. Armagh, 153 sq. km/59 sq. miles

SPERRIN (1968; extended 2008), Co. Tyrone/Co. Londonderry, 1,182 sq. km/456 sq. miles

STRANGFORD LOUGH (2010), Co. Down, 528 sq. km/ 204 sq. miles

NATIONAL SCENIC AREAS

In Scotland, national scenic areas have a broadly equivalent status to AONBs. Scottish Natural Heritage recognises areas of national scenic significance. As at October 2020, there were 40, covering a land area of 1,020,495 hectares (2,521,694 acres) and a marine area of 357,864 hectares (884,299 acres).

Development within national scenic areas is dealt with by local authorities, who are required to consult Scottish Natural Heritage concerning certain categories of development. Disagreements between Scottish Natural Heritage and local authorities are referred to the Scottish government. Land management uses can also be modified in the interest of scenic conservation.

ASSYNT-COIGACH, Highland, 129,824ha/222,884 acres

BEN NEVIS AND GLEN COE, Highland, 92,278ha/ 228,024 acres

CAIRNGORM MOUNTAINS, Highland/Aberdeenshire/ Moray, 65,541ha/161,955 acres

CUILLIN HILLS, Highland, 27,320ha/67,509 acres

DEESIDE AND LOCHNAGAR, Aberdeenshire, 39,787ha/ 98,316 acres

DORNOCH FIRTH, Highland, 15,782ha/38,998 acres

EAST STEWARTRY COAST, Dumfries and Galloway, 9,620ha/23,772 acres

EILDON AND LEADERFOOT, Borders, 3,877ha/9,580 acres

FLEET VALLEY, Dumfries and Galloway, 5,854ha/14,466 acres

GLEN AFFRIC, Highland, 18,837ha/46,547 acres

GLEN STRATHFARRAR, Highland, 4,027ha/9,951 acres

HOY AND WEST MAINLAND, Orkney Islands, 24,407ha/60,311 acres

JURA, Argyll and Bute, 30,317ha/74,915 acres

KINTAIL, Highland, 17,149/42,376 acres

KNAPDALE, Argyll and Bute, 32,832ha/81,130 acres

KNOYDART, Highland, 50,696ha/125,272 acres

KYLE OF TONGUE, Highland, 24,488ha/60,511 acres

KYLES OF BUTE, Argyll and Bute, 5,739ha/14,181 acres

LOCH LOMOND, Argyll and Bute, 28,077ha/69,380 acres

LOCH NA KEAL, Mull, Argyll and Bute, 44,250ha/ 109,344 acres

LOCH RANNOCH AND GLEN LYON, Perthshire and Kinross, 48,625ha/120,155 acres

LOCH SHIEL, Highland, 13,045ha/32,235 acres

LOCH TUMMEL, Perthshire and Kinross, 9,013ha/22,272 acres

LYNN OF LORN, Argyll and Bute, 15,726ha/38,860 acres

MORAR, MOIDART AND ARDNAMURCHAN, Highland, 36,956ha/91,320 acres

NITH ESTUARY, Dumfries and Galloway, 14,337ha/ 35,427 acres

NORTH ARRAN, North Ayrshire, 27,304ha/67,470 acres

NORTH-WEST SUTHERLAND, Highland, 26,565ha/ 65,643 acres

RIVER EARN, Perthshire and Kinross, 3,108ha/7,680 acres

RIVER TAY, Perthshire and Kinross, 5,708ha/14,105 acres

ST KILDA, Eilean Siar (Western Isles), 6,966ha/17,213 acres

SCARBA, LUNGA AND THE GARVELLACHS, Argyll and Bute, 6,542ha/16,166 acres

SHETLAND, Shetland Isles, 41,833ha/130,371 acres

SMALL ISLANDS, Highland, 47,235ha/116,720 acres

SOUTH LEWIS, HARRIS AND NORTH UIST, Eilean Siar (Western Isles), 202,388ha/500,111 acres

SOUTH UIST MACHAIR, Eilean Siar (Western Isles), 13,314ha/32,900 acres

THE TROSSACHS, Stirling, 4,850ha/11,985 acres

TROTTERNISH, Highland, 7,916ha/19,561 acres

UPPER TWEEDDALE, Borders, 12,770ha/31,555 acres

WESTER ROSS, Highland, 163,456ha/403,908 acres

THE NATIONAL FOREST

The National Forest is one of the UK's biggest environmental projects, creating a forest across 518.5 sq. km (200.2 sq. miles) of Derbyshire, Leicestershire and Staffordshire. Since the early 1990s, more than 8.9 million trees have been planted to create over 7,000ha of new woodland landscapes. Forest cover has increased from 6 per cent to 20 per cent, with the aim of eventually covering approximately one-third of the designated area.

Since its establishment in 1995, the National Forest Company leads the project and is responsible for delivery of the government-approved National Forest Strategy, sponsored by DEFRA. Priorities include continued forest creation and management, economic development of the area for recreation and tourism, and engaging local communities in the forest to improve quality of life.

NATIONAL FOREST COMPANY, Enterprise Glade, Bath Yard, Moira, Swadlincote, Derbyshire DE12 6BA

T 01283-551211 W www.nationalforest.org

Chief Executive, John Everitt

SITES OF SPECIAL SCIENTIFIC INTEREST

A site of special scientific interest (SSSI) is a legal notification applied to land in England, Scotland or Wales which Natural England (NE), Scottish Natural Heritage (SNH) or Natural Resources Wales (NRW) identifies as being of special interest because of its flora, fauna, geological or physiographical features. In some cases, SSSIs are managed as nature reserves.

NE, SNH and NRW must notify the designation of an SSSI to the local planning authority, every owner/occupier of the land, and the environment secretary, the Scottish ministers or the Welsh government. The Environment Agency (in England), water companies and internal drainage authorities and a number of other interested parties are also formally notified.

Objections to the notification of an SSSI can be made and ultimately considered at a full meeting of the board of NE or, in Wales, a subgroup committee of the NRW board. In Scotland an objection will be dealt with by the main board of SNH or an appropriate subgroup.

The protection of these sites depends on the cooperation of individual landowners and occupiers. Owner/occupiers must consult NE, SNH or NRW and gain written consent before they can undertake certain listed activities on the site. Funds are available through management agreements and grants to assist owners and occupiers in conserving sites' interests. Sites can also be protected by management schemes, management notices and other enforcement mechanisms. As a last resort a site can be purchased.

SSSIs in Britain as at June 2019:

	Number	Hectares	Acres
England	4,125	1,096,608	2,709,777
Scotland	1,423	1,022,883	2,527,599
Wales	1,077	262,233	647,993

Sources: Natural England; © Natural Resources Wales and database right (all rights reserved); Scottish Natural Heritage

NORTHERN IRELAND

In Northern Ireland areas of special scientific interest (ASSIs) are designated by the Department of Agriculture, Environment and Rural Affairs (Northern Ireland).

NATIONAL NATURE RESERVES

National Nature Reserves are defined in the National Parks and Access to the Countryside Act 1949 as modified by the Natural Environment and Rural Communities Act 2006. National Nature Reserves may be managed solely for the purpose of conservation, or for both the purposes of conservation and recreation, providing this does not compromise the conservation purpose.

NE, SNH or NRW can declare as a national nature reserve land which is held and managed as a nature reserve under an agreement; land held and managed by NE, SNH or NRW; or land held and managed as a nature reserve by an approved body. NE, SNH or NRW can make by-laws to protect reserves from undesirable activities; these are subject to confirmation by the Secretary of State for Environment, Food and Rural Affairs, the Welsh government or the Scottish ministers.

National nature reserves in Britain as at June 2019:

	Number	Hectares	Acres
England	224	93,912	232,062
Scotland	43	154,262	381,190
Wales	76	26,362	65,143

Sources: Natural England; © Natural Resources Wales and database right (all rights reserved); Scottish Natural Heritage

NORTHERN IRELAND

Nature reserves are established and managed by the Department of Agriculture, Environment and Rural Affairs (Northern Ireland), with advice from the Council for Nature Conservation and the Countryside. Nature reserves are declared under the Nature Conservation and Amenity Lands (Northern Ireland) Order 1985.

LOCAL NATURE RESERVES

Local Nature Reserves are defined in the National Parks and Access to the Countryside Act 1949 (as amended by the Natural Environment and Rural Communities Act 2006) as land designated for the study and preservation of flora and fauna, or of geological or physiographical features. Local Nature Reserves also have a statutory obligation to provide opportunities for the enjoyment of nature or open air recreation, providing this does not compromise the conservation purpose of the reserve. Local authorities in England, Scotland and Wales have the power to acquire, declare and manage reserves in consultation with NE, SNH and NRW. There is similar legislation in Northern Ireland, where the consulting organisation is the Environment Agency.

Any organisation, such as water companies, educational trusts, local amenity groups and charitable nature conservation bodies, such as wildlife trusts, may manage local nature reserves, provided that a local authority has a legal interest in the land. This means that the local authority must either own it, lease it or have a management agreement with the landowner.

Designated local nature reserves in Britain as at June 2019:

	Number	Hectares	Acres
England	1,622	41,954	103,671
Scotland	75	10,780	26,638
Wales	95	6,187	15,289

Sources: Natural England; © Natural Resources Wales and database right (all rights reserved); Scottish Natural Heritage

There are also local nature reserves in Northern Ireland.

FOREST RESERVES

The Forestry Commission is the government department responsible for forestry policy throughout Great Britain. Forestry is a devolved matter, with the separate Forestry Commissions for England, Scotland and Wales reporting directly to their appropriate minister. The equivalent body in Northern Ireland is the Forest Service, an agency of the Department of Agriculture and Rural Development for Northern Ireland. The Forestry Commission in each country is led by a director who is also a member of the GB Board of Commissioners. As at October 2020, UK woodland certified by the Forestry Commission (including Forestry Commission-managed woodland) amounted to around 1,394,000ha (3,444,644 acres): 323,000ha (798,149 acres) in England, 145,000ha (360,773 acres) in Wales, 859,000ha (2,122,632 acres) in Scotland and 66,000ha (163,089 acres) in Northern Ireland.

There are forest nature reserves in Northern Ireland, designated and administered by the Forest Service.

MARINE NATURE RESERVES

Marine protected areas provide protection for marine flora and fauna, and geological and physiographical features on land covered by tidal waters or parts of the sea in or adjacent to the UK. These areas also provide opportunities for study and research.

ENGLAND AND WALES

The Marine and Coastal Access Act 2009 created a new kind of statutory protection for marine protected areas in England and Wales, marine conservation zones (MCZs), which are designed to increase the protection of species and habitats deemed to be of national importance. The Secretary of State for Environment, Food and Rural Affairs and the Welsh ministers have the power to designate MCZs. Individual

MCZs can have varying levels of protection: some include specific activities that are appropriately managed, while others prohibit all damaging and disturbing activities. The act converted the waters around Lundy Island, a former marine protected area, to MCZ status in 2010 and this was formerly designated as such in 2013. Similarly, the marine nature reserve in the waters around Skomer was reclassified and designated an MCZ in 2014; forming the only MCZ solely in Welsh waters.

In 2009, Natural England and the Joint Nature Conservation Committee (JNCC) gave sea-users and stakeholders the ability to recommend potential MCZs to the UK government by establishing four regional projects. On 21 November 2013, the government announced the creation of 27 MCZs, covering an area of around 9,700 sq. km, to protect wildlife including seahorses, coral reefs and oyster beds from dredging and bottom-trawling. In January 2016, 23 additional MCZs were designated and in May 2019, a further 41 sites were added to the list, bringing the total to 91. The new MCZ designations means that around 30 per cent of English waters are considered protected. Information on all 91 MCZs (with date designation confirmed) can be found online
W　　　　　www.gov.uk/government/collections/marine-conservation-zone-designations-in-england

SCOTLAND

In July 2014, under the Marine (Scotland) Act 2010, the Scottish government designated 17 marine protected areas (MPAs) in Scottish inshore territorial waters (Clyde Sea Sill; East Caithness Cliffs; Fetlar to Haroldswick; Loch Creran; Loch Sunart; Loch Sunart to the Sound of Jura; Loch Sween; Lochs Duich, Long and Alsh; Monarch Isles; Mousa to Boddam; Noss Head; Papa Westray; Small Isles; South Arran; Upper Loch Fyne and Loch Goil; Wester Ross; and Wyre and Rousay Sounds). In 2017 Loch Carron was designated an inshore MPA.

A further 13, also in July 2014, were designated in offshore waters under the UK Marine and Coastal Access Act 2009. These are: Central Fladen; East of Gannet and Montrose Fields; Faroe–Shetland Sponge Belt; Firth of Forth Banks Complex; Geikie Slide and Hebridean Slope; Hatton–Rockall Basin; North-east Faroe Shetland Channel; North-west Orkney; Norwegian Boundary Sediment Plain; Rosemary Bank Seamount; The Barra Fan and Hebrides Terrace Seamount; Turbot Bank; and West Shetland Shelf.

NORTHERN IRELAND

The Marine Act (Northern Ireland) 2013 includes provisions for establishing Marine Conservation Zones (MCZs), as well as a system of marine planning, fisheries management and marine licensing. MCZs may be designated for various purposes including the conservation of marine species and habitats, taking fully into account any economic, cultural or social consequences of doing so. The Act also allows the NI Department of Agriculture, Environment and Rural Affairs to make byelaws to protect MCZs from damage caused by unregulated activities such as anchoring, kite surfing or jet skiing. It is an offence to intentionally or recklessly destroy or damage a protected feature of an MCZ.

As at October 2020 there were five MCZs in Northern Ireland. Strangford Lough was Northern Ireland's only marine nature reserve, established in 1995 under the Nature Conservation and Amenity Lands Order (Northern Ireland) 1985, but it was redesignated as Northern Ireland's first MCZ on the introduction of the Marine Act (Northern Ireland) 2013. After a consultation period, the NI Department of Agriculture, Environment and Rural Affairs announced four new MCZ's in December 2016; Carlingford Lough, Outer Belfast Lough, Rathlin and Waterfoot.

INTERNATIONAL CONVENTIONS

The UK is party to a number of international conventions.

BERN CONVENTION

The 1979 Bern Convention on the Conservation of European Wildlife and Natural Habitats came into force in the UK in June 1982. There are 51 contracting parties and a number of other states attend meetings as observers.

The aims are to conserve wild flora and fauna and their habitats, especially where this requires the cooperation of several countries, and to promote such cooperation. The convention imposes legal obligations on contracting parties, protecting over 500 wild plant species and more than 1,000 wild animal species.

All parties to the convention must promote national conservation policies and take account of the conservation of wild flora and fauna when setting planning and development policies. The contracting parties are invited to submit reports to the standing committee every four years.

SECRETARIAT OF THE BERN CONVENTION STANDING COMMITTEE, Council of Europe, Avenue de l'Europe, F-67075 Strasbourg Cedex, France
W www.coe.int/bernconvention

BIOLOGICAL DIVERSITY

The UK ratified the Convention on Biological Diversity (CBD) in June 1994. As at October 2020 there were 196 parties to the convention.

There are seven programmes addressing agricultural biodiversity, marine and coastal biodiversity and the biodiversity of inland waters, dry and sub-humid lands, islands, mountains and forests. On 29 January 2000 the Conference of the Parties adopted a supplementary agreement to the convention known as the Cartagena Protocol on Biosafety. The protocol seeks to protect biological diversity from potential risks that may be posed by introducing modified living organisms, resulting from biotechnology, into the environment. As at October 2020, 173 countries were party to the protocol; the UK joined on 17 February 2004. The Nagoya Protocol on Access and Benefit-sharing was adopted in October 2010 and entered into force on 12 October 2014. It provides international rules and procedure on liability and redress for damage to biodiversity resulting from living modified organisms. As at October 2020, 128 countries were party to the protocol; the UK became party on 22 May 2016. The Nagoya-Kuala Lumpur Supplementary Protocol on Liability and Redress was adopted as a supplementary agreement to the Cartagena Protocol on Biosafety. It aims to contribute to the conservation and sustainable use of biodiversity by providing international rules and procedures in the field of liability and redress relating to living modified organisms; requiring that response measures are taken in the event of damage resulting from living modified organisms, or where there is sufficient likelihood that damage will result if timely response measures are not taken. The Nagoya-Kuala Lumpur Supplementary Protocol entered into force on 5 March 2018; as at October 2020 44 countries, including the UK, were party to the protocol.

The UK Biodiversity Action Plan (UKBAP), published in 1994, was the UK government's response to the CBD at the 1992 Rio Earth Summit. The UK Post-2010 Biodiversity Framework replaced UKBAP when it was published in 2012 by DEFRA and the devolved administrations. The framework covers the period 2011–20 and forms the UK government's response to the strategic plan of the CBD. It includes five internationally agreed strategic goals to be achieved by 2020:

to address the underlying causes of biodiversity loss by making biodiversity a mainstream issue across government and society; to reduce the direct pressures on biodiversity and promote sustainable use; to safeguard ecosystems, species and genetic diversity; to enhance the benefits to all from biodiversity and ecosystem services; and to enhance implementation through participatory planning, knowledge management and capacity building. The list of priority species and habitats under the biodiversity framework covers 1,150 species and 65 habitats and is administered by the Joint Nature Conservation Committee (JNCC).

SECRETARIAT OF THE CONVENTION ON BIOLOGICAL DIVERSITY, 413, Saint Jacques Street, suite 800, Montreal, QC H2Y 1N9 Canada
T +1514-288 2220 E secretariat@cbd.int W www.cbd.int
JNCC, Monkstone House, City Road, Peterborough PE1 1JY
T 01733-562626 W www.jncc.defra.gov.uk

BONN CONVENTION

The 1979 Convention on Conservation of Migratory Species of Wild Animals (also known as the CMS or Bonn Convention) came into force in the UK in October 1985. As at October 2020, 131 countries were party to the convention.

It requires the protection of listed endangered migratory species and encourages international agreements covering these and other threatened species.

Seven agreements have been concluded to date under the convention. They aim to conserve African-Eurasian migratory waterbirds; albatrosses and petrels; European bats; cetaceans of the Black Sea, Mediterranean and contiguous Atlantic area; small cetaceans in the Baltic, north-east Atlantic, Irish and North Seas; gorillas and their habitats; and seals in the Wadden Sea. A further 19 memorandums of understanding have been agreed for West-African populations of the African elephant, aquatic warbler, bukhara deer, cetaceans of the Pacific Islands, dugongs (large marine mammals), middle-European population of the great bustard, high Andean flamingos, huemuls (Andean deer), manatee and small cetaceans of Western Africa and Macaronesia, marine turtles of the Atlantic coast of Africa, Indian Ocean and South East Asia, migratory birds of prey in Africa and Eurasia, migratory grassland birds of southern South America, migratory sharks, eastern-Atlantic populations of the Mediterranean monk seal, ruddy-headed goose, saiga antelope, Siberian crane and the slender-billed curlew. In addition, there are four special species initiatives for: African carnivores, central Asian mammals, Sahelo–Saharan megafauna and the central Asian flyway.

UNEP/CMS SECRETARIAT, Platz der Vereinten Nationen 1, 53113 Bonn, Germany T (+49) (228) 815 2401
E cms.secretariat@cms.int W www.cms.int

CITES

The 1973 Convention on International Trade in Endangered Species of Wild Fauna and Flora (CITES), which entered into force in 1975, is an agreement between governments to ensure that international trade in specimens of wild animals and plants does not threaten their survival. The convention came into force in the UK in October 1976 and there are currently 183 member countries. Countries party to the convention ban commercial international trade in an agreed list of endangered species and regulate and monitor trade in other species that might become endangered. The convention accords varying degrees of protection to approximately 30,000 species of plants and 5,800 species of animals, whether they are traded as live specimens or as products derived from them.

The Conference of the Parties to CITES meets every two to three years to review the convention's implementation. The Animal and Plant Health Agency at the Department for Environment, Food and Rural Affairs carries out the government's responsibilities under CITES.

CITES is implemented in the EU through a series of EC regulations known as the Wildlife Trade Regulations.

CITES SECRETARIAT, Palais des Nations, Avenue de la Paix 8-14, 1211 Genève 10, Switzerland T (+41) (22) 917 8139/40
E info@cites.org W www.cites.org

INTERNATIONAL CONVENTION FOR THE REGULATION OF WHALING

The International Convention for the Regulation of Whaling was signed in Washington DC in 1946 and currently has 89 member countries.

The measures in the convention provide for the complete protection of certain species; designate specified areas as whale sanctuaries; set limits on the numbers and size of whales which may be taken; prescribe open and closed seasons and areas for whaling; and prohibit the capture of suckling calves and female whales accompanied by calves. The International Whaling Commission meets biennially to review and revise these measures.

INTERNATIONAL WHALING COMMISSION, The Red House, 135 Station Road, Impington, Cambridge CB24 9NP
T 01223-233971 E secretariat@iwc.int W www.iwc.int

OSPAR

The Convention for the Protection of the Marine Environment of the North-East Atlantic (the OSPAR Convention) was adopted in Paris, France in September 1992 and entered into force in March 1998. The OSPAR Convention replaced both the Oslo Convention (1972) and the Paris Convention (1974), with the intention of providing a comprehensive approach to addressing all sources of pollution which may affect the maritime area, and matters relating to the protection of the maritime environment. An annex on biodiversity and ecosystems was adopted in 1998 to cover non-polluting human activities that can adversely affect the sea.

Fifteen countries plus the European Union are party to the convention; the UK ratified OSPAR in 1998. The OSPAR Commission makes decisions and recommendations and sets out actions to be taken by the contracting parties. The OSPAR Secretariat administers the work under the convention, coordinates the work of the contracting parties and runs the formal meeting schedule of OSPAR.

OSPAR COMMISSION, The Aspect, 12 Finsbury Square, London EC2A 1AS T 020-7430 5200 E secretariat@ospar.org
W www.ospar.org

RAMSAR CONVENTION

The 1971 Convention on Wetlands of National Importance, called the Ramsar Convention, is an inter-governmental treaty that provides for the conservation and sustainable use of wetlands and their resources. The Convention entered into force in the UK in 1976.

Governments that are contracting parties to the convention must designate wetlands for inclusion in the List of Wetlands of International Importance (the 'Ramsar List') and include wetland conservation considerations in their land-use planning. As at October 2020, the Convention's 171 contracting parties had designated 2,414 wetland sites, covering 252,537,889 hectares. The UK currently has 175 designated sites covering 1,283,040 hectares.

The contracting parties meet every three years to assess progress. The 13th Meeting of the Conference of the

Contracting Parties to the Ramsar Convention on Wetlands took place in Dubai, UAE in October 2018.

RAMSAR CONVENTION SECRETARIAT, Rue Mauverney 28, CH-1196 Gland, Switzerland **T** (+41) (22) 999 0170 **E** ramsar@ramsar.org **W** https://www.ramsar.org

UK LEGISLATION

The Wildlife and Countryside Act 1981 gives legal protection to a wide range of wild animals and plants. Every five years the statutory nature conservation agencies (Natural England, Natural Resources Wales and Scottish Natural Heritage), working jointly through the Joint Nature Conservation Committee, are required to review schedules 5 (animals, other than birds) and 8 (plants) of the Wildlife and Countryside Act 1981. They make recommendations to the Secretary of State for Environment, Food and Rural Affairs, the Welsh ministers and the Scottish government for changes to these schedules. The most recent variations of schedules 5 and 8 for England came into effect on 1 October 2011, following the fifth quinquennial review. The sixth review was submitted to DEFRA, the Welsh government and the Scottish government in April 2014; once these governments have considered the review, they will respond formally and publish amendments to the Wildlife and Countryside Act (1981).

Under section 9 of the act it is an offence to kill, injure, take, possess or sell (whether alive or dead) any wild animal included in schedule 5 of the act and to disturb its place of shelter and protection or to destroy that place. However certain species listed on schedule 5 are protected against some, but not all, of these activities.

Under section 13 of the act it is illegal without a licence to pick, uproot, sell or destroy plants listed in schedule 8. Since January 2001, under the Countryside and Rights of Way Act 2000, persons found guilty of an offence under part 1 of the Wildlife and Countryside Act 1981 face a maximum penalty of up to £5,000 and/or up to a six-month custodial sentence per specimen.

BIRDS

The act lays down a close season for birds (listed on Schedule 2, part 1) from 1 February to 31 August inclusive, each year. Variations to these dates are made for:

Black grouse – 10 December to 20 August (10 December – 1 September for Somerset, Devon and New Forest)
Capercaillie – 1 February to 30 September (England and Wales only)
Grey partridge – 1 February to 1 September
Pheasant – 1 February to 1 October
Ptarmigan and Red grouse – 10 December to 12 August
Red-legged partridge – 1 February to 1 September
Snipe – 1 February to 11 August
Woodcock – 1 February to 30 September (England and Wales); 1 February to 31 August (Scotland)
Birds listed on schedule 2, part 1 (below high water mark) (*see* below) – 21 February to 31 August
Wild duck and wild geese, in or over any area below the high-water mark of ordinary spring tides – 21 February to 31 August
Sundays and Christmas Day in Scotland, and Sundays for any area of England or Wales prescribed by the Secretary of State.

Birds listed on schedule 2, part 1, which may be killed or taken outside the close season are: capercaillie (England and Wales only); coot; certain wild duck (gadwall, goldeneye, mallard, Northern pintail, common pochard, Northern shoveler, teal, tufted duck, Eurasian wigeon); certain wild geese (Canada, greylag, pink-footed, white-fronted (in England and Wales only); golden plover; moorhen; snipe; and woodcock.

Section 16 of the 1981 act allows licences to be issued on either an individual or general basis, to allow the killing, taking and sale of certain birds for specified reasons such as public health and safety. All other wild birds are fully protected by law throughout the year.

ANIMALS PROTECTED BY SCHEDULE 5

Adder *(Vipera berus)*
Anemone, Ivell's Sea *(Edwardsia ivelli)*
Anemone, Starlet Sea *(Nematosella vectensis)*
Apus *(Triops cancriformis)*
Bat, Horseshoe, all species *(Rhinolophidae)*
Bat, Typical, all species *(Vespertilionidae)*
Beetle *(Hypebaeus flavipes)*
Beetle, Bembridge Water *(Paracymus aeneus)*
Beetle, Lesser Silver Water *(Hydrochara caraboides)*
Beetle, Mire Pill *(Curimopsis nigrita)*
Beetle, Moccas *(Hypebaeus flavipes)*
Beetle, Rainbow Leaf *(Chrysolina cerealis)*
Beetle, Spangled Water *(Graphoderus zonatus)*
Beetle, Stag *(Lucanus cervus)*
Beetle, Violet Click *(Limoniscus violaceus)*
Beetle, Water *(Paracymus aeneus)*
Burbot *(Lota lota)*
Butterfly, Adonis Blue *(Lysandra bellargus)*
Butterfly, Black Hairstreak *(Strymonidia pruni)*
Butterfly, Brown Hairstreak *(Thecla betulae)*
Butterfly, Chalkhill Blue *(Lysandra coridon)*
Butterfly, Chequered Skipper *(Carterocephalus palaemon)*
Butterfly, Duke of Burgundy Fritillary *(Hamearis lucina)*
Butterfly, Glanville Fritillary *(Melitaea cinxia)*
Butterfly, Heath Fritillary *(Mellicta athalia* or *Melitaea athalia)*
Butterfly, High Brown Fritillary *(Argynnis adippe)*
Butterfly, Large Blue *(Maculinea arion)*
Butterfly, Large Copper *(Lycaena dispar)*
Butterfly, Large Heath *(Coenonympha tullia)*
Butterfly, Large Tortoiseshell *(Nymphalis polychloros)*
Butterfly, Lulworth Skipper *(Thymelicus acteon)*
Butterfly, Marsh Fritillary *(Eurodryas aurinia)*
Butterfly, Mountain Ringlet *(Erebia epiphron)*
Butterfly, Northern Brown Argus *(Aricia artaxerxes)*
Butterfly, Pearl-bordered Fritillary *(Boloria euphrosyne)*
Butterfly, Purple Emperor *(Apatura iris)*
Butterfly, Silver Spotted Skipper *(Hesperia comma)*
Butterfly, Silver-studded Blue *(Plebejus argus)*
Butterfly, Small Blue *(Cupido minimus)*
Butterfly, Swallowtail *(Papilio machaon)*
Butterfly, White Letter Hairstreak *(Stymonida w-album)*
Butterfly, Wood White *(Leptidea sinapis)*
Cat, Wild *(Felis silvestris)*
Cicada, New Forest *(Cicadetta montana)*
Crayfish, Atlantic Stream *(Austropotamobius pallipes)*
Cricket, Field *(Gryllus campestris)*
Cricket, Mole *(Gryllotalpa gryllotalpa)*
Damselfly, Southern *(Coenagrion mercuriale)*
Dolphin, all species *(Cetacea)*
Dormouse *(Muscardinus avellanarius)*
Dragonfly, Norfolk Aeshna *(Aeshna isosceles)*
Frog, Common *(Rana temporaria)*
Frog, Pool, Northern Clade *(Pelophylax lessonae)*
Goby, Couch's *(Gobius couchii)*
Goby, Giant *(Gobius cobitis)*
Grasshopper, Wart-biter *(Decticus verrucivorus)*
Hatchet Shell, Northern *(Thyasira gouldi)*
Hydroid, Marine *(Clavopsella navis)*
Lagoon Snail, De Folin's *(Caecum armoricum)*
Lagoon Worm, Tentacled *(Alkmaria romijni)*

Leech, Medicinal *(Hirudo medicinalis)*
Lizard, Sand *(Lacerta agilis)*
Lizard, Viviparous *(Lacerta vivipara)*
Marten, Pine *(Martes martes)*
Moth, Barberry Carpet *(Pareulype berberata)*
Moth, Black-veined *(Siona lineata* or *Idaea lineata)*
Moth, Fiery Clearwing *(Bembecia chrysidiformis)*
Moth, Fisher's Estuarine *(Gortyna borelii)*
Moth, New Forest Burnet *(Zygaena viciae)*
Moth, Reddish Buff *(Acosmetia caliginosa)*
Moth, Slender Scotch Burnet *(Zygaena loti)*
Moth, Sussex Emerald *(Thalera fimbrialis)*
Moth, Talisker Burnet *(Zygaena lonicerae)*
Mussel, Fan *(Atrina fragilis)*
Mussel, Freshwater Pearl *(Margaritifera margaritifera)*
Newt, Great Crested (or Warty) *(Triturus cristatus)*
Newt, Palmate *(Triturus helveticus)*
Newt, Smooth *(Triturus vulgaris)*
Otter, Common *(Lutra lutra)*
Porpoise, all species *(Cetacea)*
Sandworm, Lagoon *(Armandia cirrhosa)*
Sea Fan, Pink *(Eunicella verrucosa)*
Sea Slug, Lagoon *(Tenellia adspersa)*
Sea-mat, Trembling *(Victorella pavida)*
Seahorse, Short Snouted (England only)
(Hippocampus hippocampus)
Seahorse, Spiny (England only) *(Hippocampus guttulatus)*
Shad, Allis *(Alosa alosa)*
Shad, Twaite *(Alosa fallax)*
Shark, Angel (England only) *(Squatina squatina)*
Shark, Basking *(Cetorhinus maximus)*
Shrimp, Fairy *(Chirocephalus diaphanus)*
Shrimp, Lagoon Sand *(Gammarus insensibilis)*
Shrimp, Tadpole (Apus) *(Triops cancriformis)*
Skate, White *(Rostroraja alba)*
Slow-worm *(Anguis fragilis)*
Snail, Glutinous *(Myxas glutinosa)*
Snail, Roman (England only) *(Helix pomatia)*
Snail, Sandbowl *(Catinella arenaria)*
Snake, Grass *(Natrix natrix* or *Natrix helvetica)*
Snake, Smooth *(Coronella austriaca)*
Spider, Fen Raft *(Dolomedes plantarius)*
Spider, Ladybird *(Eresus niger)*
Squirrel, Red *(Sciurus vulgaris)*
Sturgeon *(Acipenser sturio)*
Toad, Common *(Bufo bufo)*
Toad, Natterjack *(Bufo calamita)*
Turtle, Flatback *(Cheloniidae/Natator Depressus)*
Turtle, Green Sea *(Chelonia mydas)*
Turtle, Hawksbill *(Eretmochelys imbricate)*
Turtle, Kemp's Ridley Sea *(Lepidochelys kempii)*
Turtle, Leatherback Sea *(Dermo chelys coriacea)*
Turtle, Loggerhead Sea *(Caretta caretta)*
Turtle, Olive Ridley *(Lepidochelys olivacea)*
Vendace *(Coregonus albula)*
Vole, Water *(Arvicola terrestris)*
Walrus *(Odobenus rosmarus)*
Whale, all species *(Cetacea)*
Whitefish *(Coregonus lavaretus)*

PLANTS PROTECTED BY SCHEDULE 8

Adder's Tongue, Least *(Ophioglossum lusitanicum)*
Alison, Small *(Alyssum alyssoides)*
Anomodon, Long-leaved *(Anomodon longifolius)*
Beech-lichen, New Forest *(Enterographa elaborata)*
Blackwort *(Southbya nigrella)*
Bluebell *(Hyacinthoides non-scripta)*
Bolete, Royal *(Boletus regius)*
Broomrape, Bedstraw *(Orobanche caryophyllacea)*

Broomrape, Oxtongue *(Orobanche loricata)*
Broomrape, Thistle *(Orobanche reticulata)*
Cabbage, Lundy *(Rhynchosinapis wrightii)*
Calamint, Wood *(Calamintha sylvatica)*
Caloplaca, Snow *(Caloplaca nivalis)*
Catapyrenium, Tree *(Catapyrenium psoromoides)*
Catchfly, Alpine *(Lychnis alpina)*
Catillaria, Laurer's *(Catellaria laureri)*
Centaury, Slender *(Centaurium tenuiflorum)*
Cinquefoil, Rock *(Potentilla rupestris)*
Cladonia, Convoluted *(Cladonia convoluta)*
Cladonia, Upright Mountain *(Cladonia stricta)*
Clary, Meadow *(Salvia pratensis)*
Club-rush, Triangular *(Scirpus triquetrus)*
Colt's-foot, Purple *(Homogyne alpina)*
Cotoneaster, Wild *(Cotoneaster integerrimus)*
Cottongrass, Slender *(Eriophorum gracile)*
Cow-wheat, Field *(Melampyrum arvense)*
Crocus, Sand *(Romulea columnae)*
Crystalwort, Lizard *(Riccia bifurca)*
Cudweed, Broad-leaved *(Filago pyramidata)*
Cudweed, Jersey *(Gnaphalium luteoalbum)*
Cudweed, Red-tipped *(Filago lutescens)*
Cut-grass *(Leersia oryzoides)*
Diapensia *(Diapensia lapponica)*
Dock, shore *(Rumex rupestris)*
Earwort, Marsh *(Jamesoniella undulifolia)*
Eryngo, Field *(Eryngium campestre)*
Fern, Dickie's Bladder *(Cystopteris dickieana)*
Fern, Killarney *(Trichomanes speciosum)*
Flapwort, Norfolk *(Leiocolea rutheana)*
Fleabane, Alpine *(Erigeron borealis)*
Fleabane, Small *(Pulicaria vulgaris)*
Fleawort, South Stack *(Tephroseris integrifolia ssp maritima)*
Frostwort, Pointed *(Gymnomitrion apiculatum)*
Fungus, Hedgehog *(Hericium erinaceum)*
Galingale, Brown *(Cyperus fuscus)*
Gentian, Alpine *(Gentiana nivalis)*
Gentian, Dune *(Gentianella uliginosa)*
Gentian, Early *(Gentianella anglica)*
Gentian, Fringed *(Gentianella ciliata)*
Gentian, Spring *(Gentiana verna)*
Germander, Cut-leaved *(Teucrium botrys)*
Germander, Water *(Teucrium scordium)*
Gladiolus, Wild *(Gladiolus illyricus)*
Goblin Lights *(Catolechia wahlenbergii)*
Goosefoot, Stinking *(Chenopodium vulvaria)*
Grass-poly *(Lythrum hyssopifolia)*
Grimmia, Blunt-leaved *(Grimmia unicolor)*
Gyalecta, Elm *(Gyalecta ulmi)*
Hare's-ear, Sickle-leaved *(Bupleurum falcatum)*
Hare's-ear, Small *(Bupleurum baldense)*
Hawk's-beard, Stinking *(Crepis foetida)*
Hawkweed, Northroe *(Hieracium northroense)*
Hawkweed, Shetland *(Hieracium zetlandicum)*
Hawkweed, Weak-leaved *(Hieracium attenuatifolium)*
Heath, Blue *(Phyllodoce caerulea)*
Helleborine, Red *(Cephalanthera rubra)*
Helleborine, Young *(Epipactis youngiana)*
Horsetail, Branched *(Equisetum ramosissimum)*
Hound's-tongue, Green *(Cynoglossum germanicum)*
Knawel, Perennial *(Scleranthus perennis)*
Knotgrass, Sea *(Polygonum maritimum)*
Lady's-Slipper *(Cypripedium calceolus)*
Lecanactis, Churchyard *Lecanactis hemisphaerica)*
Lecanora, Tarn *(Lecanora archariana)*
Lecidea, Copper *(Lecidea inops)*
Leek, Round-headed *(Allium sphaerocephalon)*
Lettuce, Least *(Lactuca saligna)*

Lichen, Arctic Kidney *(Nephroma arcticum)*
Lichen, Ciliate Strap *(Heterodermia leucomelos)*
Lichen, Coralloid Rosette *(Heterodermia propagulifera)*
Lichen, Ear-lobed Dog *(Peltigera lepidophora)*
Lichen, Forked Hair *(Bryoria furcellata)*
Lichen, Golden Hair *(Teloschistes flavicans)*
Lichen, Orange-fruited Elm *(Caloplaca luteoalba)*
Lichen, River Jelly *(Collema dichotomum)*
Lichen, Scaly Breck *(Squamarina lentigera)*
Lichen, Starry Breck *(Buellia asterella)*
Lily, Snowdon *(Lloydia serotina)*
Liverwort *(Petallophyllum ralfsi)*
Liverwort, Lindenberg's Leafy *(Adelanthus lindenbergianus)*
Lungwort, Tree *(Lobaria pulmonaria)*
Marsh-mallow, Rough *(Althaea hirsuta)*
Marshwort, Creeping *(Apium repens)*
Milk-parsley, Cambridge *(Selinum carvifolia)*
Moss *(Drepanocladius vernicosus)*
Moss, Alpine Copper *(Mielichoferia mielichoferi)*
Moss, Baltic Bog *(Sphagnum balticum)*
Moss, Blue Dew *(Saelania glaucescens)*
Moss, Blunt-leaved Bristle *(Orthotrichum obtusifolium)*
Moss, Bright Green Cave *(Cyclodictyon laetevirens)*
Moss, Cordate Beard *(Barbula cordata)*
Moss, Cornish Path *(Ditrichum cornubicum)*
Moss, Derbyshire Feather *(Thamnobryum angustifolium)*
Moss, Dune Thread *(Bryum mamillatum)*
Moss, Flamingo *(Desmatodon cernuus)*
Moss, Glaucous Beard *(Barbula glauca)*
Moss, Green Shield *(Buxbaumia viridis)*
Moss, Hair Silk *(Plagiothecium piliferum)*
Moss, Knothole *(Zygodon forsteri)*
Moss, Large Yellow Feather *(Scorpidium turgescens)*
Moss, Millimetre *(Micromitrium tenerum)*
Moss, Multi-fruited River *(Cryphaea lamyana)*
Moss, Nowell's Limestone *(Zygodon gracilis)*
Moss, Polar Feather *(Hygrohypnum polare)*
Moss, Rigid Apple *(Bartramia stricta)*
Moss, Round-leaved Feather *(Rhyncostegium rotundifolium)*
Moss, Schleicher's Thread *(Bryum schleicheri)*
Moss, Triangular Pygmy *(Acaulon triquetrum)*
Moss, Vaucher's Feather *(Hypnum vaucheri)*
Mudwort, Welsh *(Limosella australis)*
Naiad, Holly-leaved *(Najas marina)*
Naiad, Slender *(Najas flexilis)*
Nail, Rock *(Calicium corynellum)*
Orache, Stalked *(Halimione pedunculata)*
Orchid, Early Spider *(Ophrys sphegodes)*
Orchid, Fen *(Liparis loeselii)*
Orchid, Ghost *(Epipogium aphyllum)*
Orchid, Lapland Marsh *(Dactylorhiza lapponica)*
Orchid, Late Spider *(Ophrys fuciflora)*
Orchid, Lizard *(Himantoglossum hircinum)*
Orchid, Military *(Orchis militaris)*
Orchid, Monkey *(Orchis simia)*

Pannaria, Caledonia *(Panneria ignobilis)*
Parmelia, New Forest *(Parmelia minarum)*
Parmentaria, Oil Stain *(Parmentaria chilensis)*
Pear, Plymouth *(Pyrus cordata)*
Penny-cress, Perfoliate *(Thlaspi perfoliatum)*
Pennyroyal *(Mentha pulegium)*
Pertusaria, Alpine Moss *(Pertusaria bryontha)*
Physcia, Southern Grey *(Physcia tribacioides)*
Pigmyweed *(Crassula aquatica)*
Pine, Ground *(Ajuga chamaepitys)*
Pink, Cheddar *(Dianthus gratianopolitanus)*
Pink, Childing *(Petroraghia nanteuilii)*
Pink, Deptford (England and Wales only) *(Dianthus armeria)*
Plantain, Floating Water *(Luronium natans)*
Polypore, Oak *(Buglossoporus pulvinus)*
Pseudocyphellaria, Ragged *(Pseudocyphellaria lacerata)*
Psora, Rusty Alpine *(Psora rubiformis)*
Puffball, Sandy Stilt *(Battarraea phalloides)*
Ragwort, Fen *(Senecio paludosus)*
Ramping-fumitory, Martin's *(Fumaria martinii)*
Rampion, Spiked *(Phyteuma spicatum)*
Restharrow, Small *(Ononis reclinata)*
Rock-cress, Alpine *(Arabis alpina)*
Rock-cress, Bristol *(Arabis stricta)*
Rustwort, Western *(Marsupella profunda)*
Sandwort, Norwegian *(Arenaria norvegica)*
Sandwort, Teesdale *(Minuartia stricta)*
Saxifrage, Drooping *(Saxifraga cernua)*
Saxifrage, Marsh *(Saxifraga hirilus)*
Saxifrage, Tufted *(Saxifraga cespitosa)*
Solenopsora, Serpentine *(Solenopsora liparina)*
Solomon's-seal, Whorled *(Polygonatum verticillatum)*
Sow-thistle, Alpine *(Cicerbita alpina)*
Spearwort, Adder's-tongue *(Ranunculus ophioglossifolius)*
Speedwell, Fingered *(Veronica triphyllos)*
Speedwell, Spiked *(Veronica spicata)*
Spike-rush, Dwarf *(Eleocharis parvula)*
Star-of-Bethlehem, Early *(Gagea bohemica)*
Starfruit *(Damasonium alisma)*
Stonewort, Bearded *(Chara canescens)*
Stonewort, Foxtail *(Lamprothamnium papulosum)*
Strapwort *(Corrigiola litoralis)*
Sulphur-tresses, Alpine *(Alectoria ochroleuca)*
Threadmoss, Long-leaved *(Bryum neodamense)*
Turpswort *(Geocalyx graveolens)*
Violet, Fen *(Viola persicifolia)*
Viper's-grass *(Scorzonera humilis)*
Water-plantain, Ribbon-leaved *(Alisma gramineum)*
Wood-sedge, Starved *(Carex depauperata)*
Woodsia, Alpine *(Woodsia alpina)*
Woodsia, Oblong *(Woodsia ilvenis)*
Wormwood, Field *(Artemisia campestris)*
Woundwort, Downy *(Stachys germanica)*
Woundwort, Limestone *(Stachys alpina)*
Yellow-rattle, Greater *(Rhinanthus serotinus)*

WORLD HERITAGE SITES

The Convention Concerning the Protection of the World Cultural and Natural Heritage was adopted by the United Nations Educational, Scientific and Cultural Organization (UNESCO) in 1972 and ratified by the UK in 1984. As at October 2020, 194 states were party to the convention. The convention provides for the identification, protection and conservation of cultural and natural sites of outstanding universal value.

Cultural sites may be:
- an extraordinary exponent of human creative genius
- sites representing architectural and technological innovation or cultural interchange
- sites of artistic, historic, aesthetic, archaeological, scientific, ethnologic or anthropologic value
- 'cultural landscapes', ie sites whose characteristics are marked by significant interactions between human populations and their natural environment
- exceptional examples of a traditional settlement or land- or sea-use, especially those threatened by irreversible changes.
- unique or exceptional examples of a cultural tradition or a civilisation either still present or extinct

Natural sites may be:
- those displaying critical periods of earth's history
- superlative examples of on-going ecological and biological processes in the evolution of ecosystems
- those exhibiting remarkable natural beauty and aesthetic significance or those where extraordinary natural phenomena are witnessed
- the habitat of threatened species and plants

Governments which are party to the convention nominate sites in their country for inclusion in the World Heritage List. Nominations are considered by the World Heritage Committee, an inter-governmental committee composed of 21 representatives of the parties to the convention. The committee is advised by the International Council on Monuments and Sites (ICOMOS), the International Centre for the Study of the Preservation and Restoration of Cultural Property (ICCROM) and the International Union for the Conservation of Nature (IUCN). ICOMOS evaluates and reports on proposed cultural and mixed sites, ICCROM provides expert advice and training on how to conserve and restore cultural property and IUCN provides technical evaluations of natural heritage sites and reports on the state of conservation of listed sites.

A prerequisite for inclusion in the World Heritage List is the existence of an effective legal protection system in the country in which the site is situated and a detailed management plan to ensure the conservation of the site. Inclusion in the list does not confer any greater degree of protection on the site than that offered by the national protection framework.

If a site is considered to be in serious danger of decay or damage, the committee may add it to the World Heritage in Danger List. Sites on this list may benefit from particular attention or emergency measures to allay threats and allow them to retain their world heritage status, or in extreme cases of damage or neglect they may lose their world heritage status completely. A total of 53 sites are currently inscribed on the World Heritage in Danger List.

Financial support for the conservation of sites on the World Heritage List is provided by the World Heritage Fund, administered by the World Heritage Committee. The fund's income is derived from compulsory and voluntary contributions from the states party to the convention and from private donations.

WORLD HERITAGE CENTRE, UNESCO, 7 Place de Fontenoy, 75352 Paris 07 SP, France **W** https://whc.unesco.org

DESIGNATED SITES

As at 10 July 2019, following the 43rd session of the World Heritage Committee, 1,121 sites across 167 countries were on the World Heritage List. The 44th session of the World Heritage Committee was delayed until 2021, due to COVID-19; no new UNESCO sites were designated in 2020. Of these, 28 are in the UK and four in UK overseas territories; 27 are listed for their cultural significance (†), four for their natural significance (*) and one for both cultural and natural significance. Liverpool's Maritime Mercantile City is the only UK site on the List of World Heritage in Danger. The year in which sites were designated appears in the first set of parentheses. The number in the second set of parentheses denotes the position of each site on the map below.

WORLD HERITAGE SITES IN THE UK

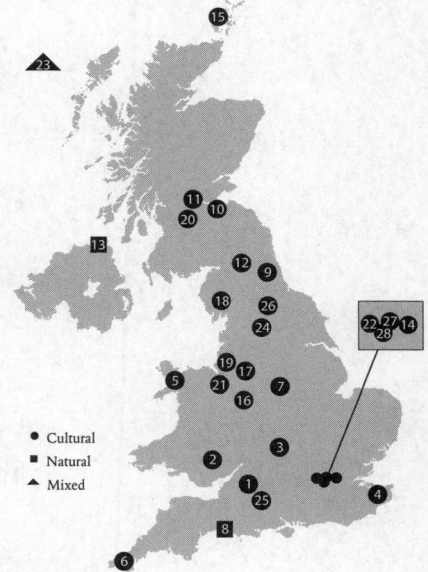

UNITED KINGDOM
†Bath – the city (1987). (1)
†Blaenarvon industrial landscape, Wales (2000). (2)
†Blenheim Palace and Park, Oxfordshire (1987). (3)
†Canterbury Cathedral, St Augustine's Abbey, St Martin's Church, Kent (1988). (4)
†Castle and town walls of King Edward I, north Wales – Beaumaris, Caernarfon Castle, Conwy Castle, Harlech Castle (1986). (5)
†Cornwall and west Devon mining landscape (2006). (6)
†Derwent Valley Mills, Derbyshire (2001). (7)
*Dorset and east Devon coast (2001). (8)
†Durham Cathedral and Castle (1986). (9)
†Edinburgh old and new towns (1995). (10)
†Forth Bridge, Firth of Forth, Scotland (2015). (11)

†Frontiers of the Roman Empire – Hadrian's Wall, northern England; Antonine Wall, central Scotland (1987, 2005, 2008). (12)

*Giant's Causeway and Causeway coast, Co. Antrim (1986). (13)

†Greenwich, London – maritime Greenwich, including the Royal Naval College, Old Royal Observatory, Queen's House, town centre (1997). (14)

†Heart of Neolithic Orkney (1999). (15)

†Ironbridge Gorge, Shropshire – the world's first iron bridge and other early industrial sites (1986). (16)

†Jodrell Bank Observatory, Cheshire (2019). (17)

†Lake District, Cumbria (2017). (18)

†Liverpool – six areas of the maritime mercantile city (2004). (19)

†New Lanark, South Lanarkshire, Scotland (2001). (20)

†Pontcysyllte Aqueduct and Canal, Wrexham, Wales (2009). (21)

†Royal Botanic Gardens, Kew (2003). (22)

†*St Kilda, Eilean Siar (Western Isles) (1986). (23)

†Saltaire, West Yorkshire (2001). (24)

†Stonehenge, Avebury and related megalithic sites, Wiltshire (1986). (25)

†Studley Royal Park, Fountains Abbey, St Mary's Church, N. Yorkshire (1986). (26)

†Tower of London (1988). (27)

†Westminster Abbey, Palace of Westminster, St Margaret's Church, London (1987). (28)

UK OVERSEAS TERRITORIES

*Henderson Island, Pitcairn Islands, South Pacific Ocean (1988)

*Gough Island and Inaccessible Island (part of Tristan da Cunha), South Atlantic Ocean (1995)

†Historic town of St George and related fortifications, Bermuda (2000)

†Gorham's Cave Complex, Gibraltar (2016)

HISTORIC BUILDINGS AND MONUMENTS

ENGLAND

Under the Planning (Listed Buildings and Conservation Areas) Act 1990, the Secretary of State for Digital, Culture, Media and Sport has a statutory duty to approve buildings or groups of buildings in England that are of special architectural or historic interest. Since April 2015 the list of such buildings is maintained by Historic England who are also responsible for making recommendations to the secretary of state for additions, removals and amendments to the list. Under the Ancient Monuments and Archaeological Areas Act 1979 as amended by the National Heritage Act 1983, the secretary of state is also responsible for compiling a schedule of ancient monuments. Decisions are taken on the advice of Historic England. A searchable database of all nationally designated heritage assets, The National Heritage List for England (NHLE), is available online: **W** www.historicengland.org.uk/listing/the-list.

LISTED BUILDINGS

Listed buildings are classified into Grade I, Grade II* and Grade II. As at October 2020, there were approximately 400,000 listed buildings in England, of which approximately 90 per cent are Grade II listed. Almost all pre-1700 buildings are listed, as are most buildings of 1700 to 1850. Historic England surveys particular types of buildings with a view to making recommendations for listing. The main purpose of listing is to ensure that care is taken in deciding the future of a building. No changes which affect the architectural or historic character of a listed building can be made without listed building consent (in addition to planning permission where relevant). Applications for consent are normally dealt with by the local planning authority, although Historic England is always consulted about proposals affecting Grade I and Grade II* properties. It is a criminal offence to demolish a listed building, or alter it in such a way as to affect its character, without consent.

SCHEDULED MONUMENTS

As at October 2020, there were approximately 20,000 scheduled monuments in England. All monuments proposed for scheduling are considered to be of national importance. Where buildings are both scheduled and listed, ancient monuments legislation takes precedence. The main purpose of scheduling a monument is to preserve it for the future and to protect it from damage, destruction or any unnecessary interference. Once a monument has been scheduled, scheduled monument consent is required before any works can be carried out. The scope of the control is more extensive and more detailed than that applied to listed buildings, but certain minor works, as detailed in the Ancient Monuments (Class Consents) Order 1994, may be carried out without consent. It is a criminal offence to carry out unauthorised work to scheduled monuments.

WALES

Under the Planning (Listed Buildings and Conservation Areas) Act 1990 and the Ancient Monuments and Archaeological Areas Act 1979, the National Assembly for Wales is responsible for listing buildings and scheduling monuments in Wales on the advice of Cadw (the Welsh government's historic environment division) and the Royal Commission on the Ancient and Historical Monuments of Wales (RCAHMW). The criteria for evaluating buildings are similar to those in England

and the same listing system is used. As at Octobe 2020, there were approximately 30,000 listed buildings and 4,200 scheduled monuments in Wales. A list of National Historic Assets of Wales is available online: **W** https://cadw.gov.wales/historicenvironment/recordsv1.

SCOTLAND

Under the Planning (Listed Buildings and Conservation Areas) (Scotland) Act 1997 and the Ancient Monuments and Archaeological Areas Act 1979, Scottish ministers are responsible for listing buildings and scheduling monuments in Scotland on the advice of Historic Environment Scotland. The Historic Environment Scotland Act 2014 sets out Historic Environment Scotland's role and legal status. The criteria for evaluating buildings are similar to those in England but an A, B, C categorisation is used. As at October 2020, there were approximately 47,500 listed buildings and 8,300 scheduled monuments in Scotland. A list of historic buildings and monuments in Scotland is available online: **W** https://portal.historicenvironment.scot/search.

NORTHERN IRELAND

Under the Planning (Northern Ireland) Act 2011 and the Historic Monuments and Archaeological Objects (Northern Ireland) Order 1995, the Historic Environment Division (part of the Department for Communities, Northern Ireland) is responsible for listing buildings and scheduling monuments. The Historic Buildings Council for Northern Ireland and the relevant district council must be consulted on listing proposals, and the Historic Monuments Council for Northern Ireland must be consulted on scheduling proposals. The criteria for evaluating buildings are similar to those in England but an A, B+, B1 and B2 categorisation is used. As at As at May 2019 the most up to date figure was recorded as 8,916 listed buildings and 1,994 scheduled monuments in Norther Ireland.

ENGLAND

English Heritage cares for over 400 historic monuments, buildings and places. For more information on English Heritage properties, including those listed below, the official website is **W** www.english-heritage.org.uk

For more information on National Trust properties in England, including those listed below, the official website is **W** www.nationaltrust.org.uk

KEY
(EH) English Heritage property
(NT) National Trust property
* UNESCO World Heritage Site (*see also* World Heritage Sites)

A LA RONDE (NT), Exmouth, Devon EX8 5BD **T** 01395-265514
  Unique 16-sided house completed *c.*1796
ALNWICK CASTLE, Alnwick, Northumberland NE66 1NG
  T 01665-511100 **W** www.alnwickcastle.com
  Seat of the Dukes of Northumberland since 1309; Italian Renaissance-style interior; gardens with spectacular water features
ALTHORP, Northants NN7 4HQ **T** 01604-770006
  W www.spencerofalthorp.com
  Spencer family seat built in 1508; home to the annual Althorp Literary Festival and Althorp Food and Drink Festival

ANGLESEY ABBEY (NT), Quy Road, Lode, Cambridge CB25
9EJ **T** 01223-810080
Jacobean house (c.1600) with gardens and a working
watermill (Lode Mill) on the site of a 12th-century priory;
fine furnishings and a unique clock collection

APSLEY HOUSE (EH), London W1J 7NT **T** 020-7499 5676
Built by Robert Adam 1771–8; home of the Dukes of
Wellington since 1817 and known as 'No. 1 London';
collection of fine and decorative arts

ARUNDEL CASTLE, Arundel, W. Sussex BN18 9AB
T 01903-882173 **W** www.arundelcastle.org
Castle dating from the Norman Conquest; seat of the
Dukes of Norfolk

AUDLEY END HOUSE AND GARDENS (EH), Saffron
Walden, Essex, CB11 4JF **T** 01799-522842 **T** 01799-522842
Jacobean house converted from a Benedictine monastery;
given to Sir Thomas Audley by King Henry VIII.

AVEBURY (EH/NT), Wilts SN8 1RF **T** 01672-539250
Remains of stone circles constructed 4,000 years ago
enclosing part of the later village of Avebury

BANQUETING HOUSE, Whitehall, London SW1A 2ER
T 020-3166 6000 **W** www.hrp.org.uk/banquetinghouse
Designed by Inigo Jones in 1619; ceiling paintings by
Rubens; site of the execution of Charles I

BASILDON PARK (NT), Reading, Berks RG8 9NR
T 01491-672382
Palladian mansion built in 1776–83 by John Carr

BATTLE ABBEY (EH), Battle, E. Sussex TN33 0AD **T** 870 333
1181
Remains of the abbey founded by William the Conqueror
on the site of the Battle of Hastings

BEESTON CASTLE (EH), Cheshire CW6 9TX **T** 01829-260464
Built in the 13th century by Ranulf, sixth Earl of Chester,
on the site of an Iron Age hillfort

BELVOIR CASTLE, Grantham, Lincs NG32 1PE
T 01476-871001 **W** www.belvoircastle.com
Seat of the Dukes of Rutland; 19th-century Gothic-style
castle; notable art collection

BERKELEY CASTLE, Glos GL13 9BQ **T** 01453-810303
W www.berkeley-castle.com
Completed late 12th century; site of the murder of
Edward II (1327)

BIRDOSWALD ROMAN FORT (EH), Brampton, Cumbria
CA8 7DD **T** 01697-747602
Stretch of Hadrian's Wall with Roman wall fort, turret
and milecastle

*BLENHEIM PALACE, Woodstock, Oxon OX20 1UL
T 01993-810530 **W** www.blenheimpalace.com
Seat of the Dukes of Marlborough and Winston
Churchill's birthplace; house designed by Vanbrugh;
landscaped parkland by Capability Brown

BLICKLING ESTATE (NT), Blickling, Norfolk NR11 6NF
T 01263-738030
Jacobean house with state rooms; extensive gardens,
temple and 18th-century orangery

BODIAM CASTLE (NT), Bodiam, E. Sussex TN32 5UA
T 01580-830196
Well-preserved medieval moated castle built in 1385

BOLSOVER CASTLE (EH), Bolsover, Derbys S44 6PR
T 01246-822844
17th-century castle on site of medieval fortress

BOSCOBEL HOUSE (EH), Bishops Wood, Shrops ST19 9AR
T 01902-850244
Timber-framed 17th-century hunting lodge; refuge of
fugitive Charles II from parliamentary troops

BOUGHTON HOUSE, Kettering, Northants NN14 1BJ
T 01536-515731 **W** www.boughtonhouse.org.uk
17th-century house with French-style additions; home of
the Dukes of Buccleuch and Queensbury

BOWOOD HOUSE, Calne, Wilts SN11 0LZ **T** 01249-812102
W www.bowood.org/bowood-house-gardens/house/
18th-century house in Capability Brown park, featuring
Robert Adam orangery and renowned pinetum and
arboretum

BUCKFAST ABBEY, Buckfastleigh, Devon TQ11 0EE
T 01364-645500 **W** www.buckfast.org.uk
Benedictine monastery on medieval foundations

BUCKINGHAM PALACE, London SW1A 1AA
T 030-3123 7300 **W** www.royalcollection.org.uk
Purchased by George III in 1761, and the Sovereign's
official London residence since 1837; 19 state rooms,
including the Throne Room, and Queen's Gallery

BUCKLAND ABBEY (NT), Yelverton, Devon PL20 6EY
T 01822-853607
13th-century Cistercian monastery; home of Sir Francis
Drake

BURGHLEY HOUSE, Stamford, Lincs PE9 3JY **T** 01780-752451
W www.burghley.co.uk
Late Elizabethan house built by William Cecil, first Lord
Burghley

CARISBROOKE CASTLE (EH), Newport, Isle of Wight PO30
1XY **T** 01983-522107
Norman castle; museum; prison of Charles I 1647–8

CARLISLE CASTLE (EH), Carlisle, Cumbria CA3 8UR
T 01228-591922
Medieval castle; prison of Mary, Queen of Scots

CASTLE ACRE PRIORY (EH), King's Lynn, Norfolk PE32 2XD
T 01760-755394
Remains include 12th-century church and prior's lodgings

CASTLE DROGO (NT), Drewsteignton, Devon EX6 6PB
T 01647-433306
Granite castle designed by Lutyens in 1911

CASTLE HOWARD, N. Yorks YO60 7DA **T** 01653-648333
W www.castlehoward.co.uk
Designed by Vanbrugh 1699–1726; mausoleum designed
by Hawksmoor

CASTLE RISING CASTLE (EH), King's Lynn, Norfolk PE31
6AH **T** 01553-631330 **W** www.castlerising.co.uk
12th-century keep with gatehouse and bridge, surrounded
by 20 acres of defensive earthworks

CHARLES DARWIN'S HOME (DOWN HOUSE) (EH),
Downe, Kent BR6 7JT **T** 01689-859119
The family home where Darwin wrote *On the Origin of
Species*

CHARTWELL (NT), Westerham, Kent TN16 1PS
T 01732-868381
Home and studio of Sir Winston Churchill

CHATSWORTH, Bakewell, Derbys DE45 1PP **T** 01246-565300
W www.chatsworth.org
Tudor mansion set in magnificent parkland; seat of the
Dukes of Devonshire

CHESTERS ROMAN FORT (EH), Chollerford,
Northumberland NE46 4EU **T** 870 333 1181
Roman cavalry fort built to guard Hadrian's Wall

CHYSAUSTER ANCIENT VILLAGE (EH), Penzance,
Cornwall TR20 8XA **T** 870 333 1181
Remains of nearly 2,000-year-old Celtic settlement; eight
stone-walled homesteads

CLANDON PARK (NT), Guildford, Surrey GU4 7RQ
T 01483-222482
18th-century Palladian mansion and gardens, with an
original Maori meeting house, brought back from New
Zealand in 1892

CLIFFORD'S TOWER (EH), York YO1 9SA **T** 01904-646940
13th-century keep built on a mound; remains of a castle
built by William the Conqueror

CORBRIDGE ROMAN TOWN (EH), Corbridge,
Northumberland NE45 5NT **T** 870 333 1181
Excavated central area of a Roman garrison town

CORFE CASTLE (NT), Wareham, Dorset BH20 5EZ
T 01929-481294
Former royal castle, dating from the 11th century and
partially ruined during the English Civil War

CROFT CASTLE AND PARKLAND (NT), Yarpole,
Herefordshire HR6 9PW T 01568-780246
17th-century quadrangular manor house with Georgian-
Gothic interior; built close to the ruin of pre-Conquest
border castle

DEAL CASTLE (EH), Deal, Kent CT14 7BA T 870 333 1181
Largest of the coastal defence forts built by Henry VIII;
shaped like a rose with six inner and outer bastions

*DERWENT VALLEY MILLS, Belper, Derbyshire DE56 1YD
T 01629-536831 W www.derwentvalleymills.org
Series of 18th- and 19th-century cotton mills; birthplace
of the modern factory

DOVER CASTLE (EH), Dover, Kent CT16 1HU T 01304-211067
Castle with Roman, Saxon and Norman features; tunnels
used as secret wartime operations rooms

DR JOHNSON'S HOUSE, London EC4A 3DE T 020-7353 3745
W www.drjohnsonshouse.org
300-year-old townhouse of Samuel Johnson 1748–59

DUNSTANBURGH CASTLE (EH/NT), Alnwick,
Northumberland NE66 3TT T 01665-576231
14th-century castle ruins on a headland, with a substantial
twin-towered gatehouse-keep

ELTHAM PALACE (EH), Greenwich, London SE9 5QE
T 020-8294 2548
Art Deco mansion next to remains of medieval palace once
occupied by Henry VIII; moated gardens

FARLEIGH HUNGERFORD CASTLE (EH), Bath, Somerset
BA2 7RS T 01225-754026
Late 14th-century castle with inner and outer courts;
chapel with rare medieval wall paintings

FARNHAM CASTLE KEEP (EH), Farnham, Surrey GU9 0AG
T 01252-721194 W www.farnhamcastle.com
Large 12th-century castle keep with motte and bailey wall

FISHBOURNE ROMAN PALACE,Chichester, W. Sussex PO19
3QR T 01243-785859 W http://sussexpast.co.uk
Excavated Roman palace with largest collection of in situ
mosaics in the UK

*FOUNTAINS ABBEY (NT), Ripon, N. Yorks HG4 3DY
T 01765-608888
Ruined Cistercian monastery and corn mill; site includes
Studley Royal, a Georgian water garden and deer park

FRAMLINGHAM CASTLE (EH), Framlingham, Suffolk IP13
9BP T 870 333 1181
Castle (c.1200) with high curtain walls enclosing an
almshouse (1639); once the refuge of Mary I

FURNESS ABBEY (EH), Barrow-in-Furness, Cumbria LA13 0PJ
T 01229-823420
Remains of an abbey founded in 1124 by Stephen, later
king of England

GLASTONBURY ABBEY, Glastonbury, Somerset BA6 9EL
T 01458-832267 W www.glastonburyabbey.com
12th-century abbey, destroyed by fire in 1184 and later
rebuilt; site of early Christian settlement; ruined in 1539
during dissolution of monasteries

GOODRICH CASTLE (EH), Ross-on-Wye, Herefordshire HR9
6HY T 01600-890538
Remains of 12th- and 13th-century castle; contains a
famous mortar that ruined the castle in 1646

GREENWAY (NT), Brixham, Devon TQ5 0ES T 01803-842382
Large woodland; walled garden; location of Agatha
Christie's holiday home and inspiration for several
settings in her books, including the murder in *Dead Man's
Folly*

*GREENWICH, London SE10 9NF T 020-8305 5235
W www.visitgreenwich.org.uk
Former Royal Observatory (founded 1675) home to the
Meridian Line, *Cutty Sark* and National Maritime Museum;
the Queen's House, designed for Queen Anne, wife of
James I, by Inigo Jones; Painted Hall and neoclassical
Chapel (Old Royal Naval College)

GRIME'S GRAVES (EH), Thetford, Norfolk IP26 5DE
T 01842-810656
Neolithic flint mines, dug over 5,000 years ago; one shaft
has been been excavated

GUILDHALL, London EC2V 7HH T 020-7332 1313
W www.guildhall.cityoflondon.gov.uk
Centre of civic government of the City of London built
c.1441; facade built 1788–9

HADDON HALL, Bakewell, Derbys DE45 1LA T 01629-812855
W www.haddonhall.co.uk
Well-preserved 12th-century manor house

HAILES ABBEY (EH), Cheltenham, Glos GL54 5PB
T 01242-602398
Ruins of a 13th-century Cistercian monastery

HAM HOUSE AND GARDEN (NT), Richmond, Surrey TW10
7RS T 020-8940 1950
Grand Stuart house with lavish interiors and formal
gardens

HAMPTON COURT PALACE, East Molesey, Surrey KT8 9AU
T 020-3166 6000 W www.hrp.org.uk/hampton-court-palace
Palace originally built for Cardinal Wolsey in the early
16th-century, famous as the home of Henry VIII, his
wives and children, with a 17th-century Baroque palace
by Wren commissioned by William III and Mary II in
1689; Royal Tennis Court and world-renowned maze

HARDWICK HALL (NT), Chesterfield, Derbys S44 5QJ
T 01246-850430
Elizabethan house built for Bess of Hardwick

HARDY'S COTTAGE (NT), Higher Bockhampton, Dorset DT2
8QJ T 01305-262366
Birthplace and home of Thomas Hardy

HAREWOOD HOUSE, Leeds, W. Yorks LS17 9LG
T 0113-218 1010 W https://harewood.org
18th-century house designed by John Carr and Robert
Adam; park by Capability Brown

HATFIELD HOUSE, Hatfield, Herts AL9 5NB T 01707-287010
W www.hatfield-house.co.uk
Jacobean house built by Robert Cecil; features surviving
wing of Royal Palace of Hatfield (c.1485), the childhood
home of Elizabeth I

HELMSLEY CASTLE (EH), Helmsley, N. Yorks YO62 5AB
T 01439-770442
12th-century keep and curtain wall with 16th-century
buildings; spectacular earthwork defences

HEVER CASTLE, Edenbridge, Kent TN8 7NG T 01732-865224
W www.hevercastle.co.uk
13th-century double-moated castle; childhood home of
Anne Boleyn

HOLKHAM HALL, Wells-next-the-Sea, Norfolk NR23 1AB
T 01328-710227 W www.holkham.co.uk
Palladian mansion; notable fine art collection

HOUSESTEADS ROMAN FORT (EH), Hexham,
Northumberland NE47 6NN T 870 333 1181
Excavated Roman infantry fort on Hadrian's Wall with
museum

*IRONBRIDGE GORGE, Ironbridge, Shropshire
T 01952-433424W www.ironbridge.org.uk
Important Industrial Revolution site, featuring the world's
first iron bridge

KEDLESTON HALL (NT), Derbys DE22 5JH T 01332-842191
Palladian mansion built 1759–65; complete Robert Adam
interiors; museum of Asian artefacts

KELMSCOTT MANOR, Lechlade, Glos GL7 3HJ
T 01367-252486 W www.sal.org.uk/kelmscott-manor/
Built c.1600; summer home of William Morris, with
products of Morris and Co.

KENILWORTH CASTLE (EH), Kenilworth, Warks CV8 1NG
T 01926-852078
Largest castle ruin in England; Norman keep with 13th-
century outer walls; once home to Robert Dudley

KENSINGTON PALACE, Kensington Gardens, London W8 4PX
T 020-3166 6000 W www.hrp.org.uk/kensington-palace
Built in 1605 and enlarged by Wren; birthplace of Queen
Victoria

KENWOOD HOUSE (EH), Hampstead , London NW3 7JR
T 020-8348 1286
Neoclassical villa on the edge of Hampstead Heath,
housing the Iveagh bequest of paintings and furniture

KEW PALACE, Richmond, Surrey TW9 3AE T 020-3166 6000
W www.hrp.org.uk/kew-palace
Red-brick mansion (c.1631); includes Queen Charlotte's
Cottage, used by King George III and family as a
summerhouse

KINGSTON LACY (NT), Wimborne Minster, Dorset BH21 4EA
T 01202-883402
17th-century mansion with 19th-century alterations;
important art collection

KNEBWORTH HOUSE, Knebworth, Herts SG3 6PY
T 01438-812661 W www.knebworthhouse.com
Tudor manor house concealed by 19th-century Gothic
decoration; Lutyens gardens

KNOLE (NT), Sevenoaks, Kent TN15 0RP T 01732-462100
House built in 1456, set in 1,000-acre deer park; fine art
and furniture collection; birthplace of Vita Sackville-West

LAMBETH PALACE, London SE1 7JU T 020-7898 1200
W www.archbishopofcanterbury.org/about-lambeth-palace
Official residence of the Archbishop of Canterbury since
the 13th century

LANERCOST PRIORY (EH), nr Brampton, Cumbria CA8 2HQ
T 01697-73030 W www.lanercostpriory.org.uk
The nave of the Augustinian priory's church, c.1166, is
still used; remains of other claustral buildings and
beautifully preserved cloisters

LANHYDROCK (NT), Bodmin, Cornwall PL30 5AD
T 01208-265950
House dating from the 17th century; 50 rooms, including
kitchen and nursery

LEEDS CASTLE, Maidstone, Kent ME17 1PL T 01622-765400
W www.leeds-castle.com
Castle dating from the 12th century, situated in 500 acres
of parkland and gardens; used as a royal palace by Henry
VIII

LEVENS HALL, nr Kendal, Cumbria LA8 0PD T 01539-560321
W www.levenshall.co.uk
Elizabethan house with unique topiary garden (1694);
steam engine collection

LINCOLN CASTLE, Lincoln, Lincs LN1 3AA T 01522-554559
W www.lincolncastle.com
Built by William the Conqueror in 1068 on a Roman site;
one of only two double-motted castles in Britain

LINDISFARNE PRIORY (EH), Holy Island, Northumberland
TD15 2RX T 01289-389200
Founded in AD 635; re-established in the 12th century as
a Benedictine priory, now ruined

LITTLE MORETON HALL (NT), Congleton, Cheshire CW12
4SD T 01260-272018
Iconic timber-framed moated Tudor manor house with
knot garden

LONGLEAT HOUSE, Warminster, Wilts BA12 7NW
T 01985-844400 W www.longleat.co.uk
Elizabethan house in Italian Renaissance style; Capability
Brown parkland with lakes; safari park

LULLINGSTONE ROMAN VILLA (EH), Eynsford, Kent DA4
0JA T 870 333 1181
Large villa occupied for much of the Roman period;
collection of Roman artefacts and unique Christian
paintings

MIDDLEHAM CASTLE (EH), Middleham, N. Yorks DL8 4QG
T 01969-623899
12th-century keep within later fortifications; childhood
home of Richard III

MONTACUTE HOUSE (NT), Montacute, Somerset TA15 6XP
T 01935-823289
Elizabethan Renaissance mansion, with collection of
portraits from the period

MOUNT GRACE PRIORY (EH), Northallerton, N. Yorks DL6
3JG T 01609-883494
Well-preserved Carthusian priory with remains of
monastic buildings

OLD SARUM (EH), Salisbury, Wilts SP1 3SD T 01722-335398
Iron Age hill fort enclosing remains of Norman castle and
cathedral

ORFORD CASTLE (EH), Orford, Suffolk IP12 2ND T 870 333
1181
Polygonal tower keep c.1170 and remains of coastal
defence castle built by Henry II

OSBORNE HOUSE (EH), East Cowes, Isle of Wight PO32 6JT
T 01983-200022
Queen Victoria's seaside residence; built by Thomas
Cubitt in Italian Renaissance style; summer house, Swiss
Cottage and museum

OSTERLEY PARK AND HOUSE (NT), Isleworth, Middx TW7
4RB T 020-8232 5050
18th-century neoclassical mansion with Tudor stable
block

PENDENNIS CASTLE (EH), Falmouth, Cornwall TR11 4LP
T 01326-316594
Well-preserved 16th-century coastal defence castle

PENSHURST PLACE, Penshurst, Kent TN11 8DG
T 01892-870307 W www.penshurstplace.com
Medieval house featuring Baron's Hall (1341) and
gardens (1346); toy museum

PETWORTH HOUSE (NT), Petworth, W. Sussex GU28 9LR T
01798-342207
Late 17th-century house set in Capability Brown
landscaped deer park; fine art collection

PEVENSEY CASTLE (EH), Pevensey, E. Sussex BN24 5LE
T 870 333 1181
Walls of a fourth-century Roman fort; remains of an 11th-
century castle

POLESDEN LACEY (NT), nr Dorking, Surrey RH5 6BD
T 01372-452048
Regency villa remodelled in the Edwardian era; fine
paintings and furnishings; walled rose garden

PORTCHESTER CASTLE (EH), Portchester, Hants PO16 9QW
T 02392-378291
Walls of a late Roman fort enclosing a Norman keep and
an Augustinian priory church

POWDERHAM CASTLE, Kenton, Devon EX6 8JQ
T 01626-890243 W www.powderham.co.uk
Medieval castle with 18th- and 19th-century alterations,
including James Wyatt music room

RABY CASTLE, Staindrop, Co. Durham DL2 3AH
T 01833-660202 W www.raby.co.uk
14th-century castle with walled gardens

RAGLEY HALL, Alcester, Warks B49 5NJ T 01789-762090
W www.ragley.co.uk
17th-century Palladian house with gardens and lake

RICHBOROUGH ROMAN FORT (EH), Sandwich, Kent
CT13 9JW T 01304-612013
Remains of a Roman Saxon Shore fortress; landing-site of
the Claudian invasion in AD 43

RICHMOND CASTLE (EH), Richmond, N. Yorks DL10 4QW
T 870 333 1181
12th-century keep with 11th-century curtain wall

RIEVAULX ABBEY (EH), nr Helmsley, N. Yorks YO62 5LB
T 01439-798228
Remains of a Cistercian abbey founded *c.*1132

ROCHESTER CASTLE (EH), Rochester, Kent ME1 1SW
T 01634-335882
11th-century castle partly on the Roman city wall, with a well-preserved square keep of *c.*1127

ROCKINGHAM CASTLE, Market Harborough, Leics LE16 8TH
T 01536-770240 **W** www.rockinghamcastle.com
Built by William the Conqueror; formal gardens and 400-year-old 'elephant' hedge

ROMAN BATHS, Abbey Church Yard, Bath BA1 1LZ
T 01225-477785 **W** www.romanbaths.co.uk
Extensive remains of a Roman temple and bathing complex which still flows with natural thermal water; museum

ROYAL PAVILION, Brighton BN1 1EE **T** 03000-290900
W https://brightonmuseums.org.uk/royalpavilion
Unique palace of George IV, in Indo-gothic style with chinoiserie interiors and Regency gardens

ST AUGUSTINE'S ABBEY (EH), Canterbury, Kent CT1 1PF
T 01227-767345
Remains of Benedictine monastery founded in 598

ST MAWES CASTLE (EH), St Mawes, Cornwall TR2 5DE
T 01326-270526
Coastal defence castle built by Henry VIII

ST MICHAEL'S MOUNT (NT), Marazion, Cornwall TR17 0HS
T 01736-710265 **W** www.stmichaelsmount.co.uk
12th-century church and castle with later additions, situated on an iconic rocky island

*SALTAIRE VILLAGE, nr Shipley, W. Yorks **T** 01274-433678
W www.saltairevillage.info
Victorian industrial village founded by mill owner Titus Salt for his workers; *see also* World Heritage Sites

SANDRINGHAM, Norfolk PE35 6EN **T** 01485-545400
W www.sandringhamestate.co.uk
The Queen's private residence; neo-Jacobean house built in 1870 with gardens and country park

SCARBOROUGH CASTLE (EH), Scarborough, N. Yorks YO11 1HY **T** 01723-372451
Remains of 12th-century keep and curtain walls

SHERBORNE CASTLE, Sherborne, Dorset DT9 5NR
T 01935-813182 **W** www.sherbornecastle.com
16th-century castle built by Sir Walter Raleigh set in Capability Brown landscaped gardens

SHUGBOROUGH ESTATE (NT), Milford, Staffs ST17 0XB
T 01889-880166
Late 17th century house in 18th-century park with monuments, temples and pavilions in the Greek Revival style; seat of the Earls of Lichfield

SISSINGHURST CASTLE GARDEN (NT), Nr Cranbrook, Kent TN17 2AB **T** 01580-710700
Early 14th century site, purchased by Vita Sackville-West in the 1930s where the writer, poet and Bloomsbury Group member created the famous gardens

SKIPTON CASTLE, Skipton, N. Yorks BD23 1AW
T 01756-792442 **W** www.skiptoncastle.co.uk
Well-preserved D-shaped medieval castle with six round towers and inner courtyard

SMALLHYTHE PLACE (NT), Tenterden, Kent TN30 7NG
T 01580-762334
Half-timbered 16th-century house

*STONEHENGE (EH), nr Amesbury, Wilts SP4 7DE
T 0370-333 1181
World-famous prehistoric monument comprising concentric stone circles surrounded by a ditch and bank

STONOR PARK, Henley-on-Thames, Oxon RG9 6HF
T 01491-638587 **W** www.stonor.com
Medieval house with Georgian facade; refuge for Catholic recusants after the Reformation

STOURHEAD (NT), Nr Mere, Wilts BA12 6QD **T** 01747-841152
18th-century Palladian mansion with world-renowned landscape gardens; King Alfred's Tower

STRATFIELD SAYE HOUSE, Hants RG7 2BT **T** 01256-882694
W www.wellingtonestates.co.uk/stratfield-saye-house
House built 1630–40; home of the Dukes of Wellington since 1817

STRATFORD-UPON-AVON, Warks **T** 01789-868191
W www.stratford-upon-avon.co.uk
Shakespeare's Birthplace Trust with Shakespeare Centre; Anne Hathaway's Cottage; Holy Trinity Church, where Shakespeare is buried

STRAWBERRY HILL HOUSE, Twickenham TW1 4ST
T 020-8744 1241 **W** www.strawberryhillhouse.org.uk
Early Gothic Revival villa built between 1749 and 1776 for Horace Walpole (1717–97)

SUDELEY CASTLE, Winchcombe, Glos GL54 5JD
T 01242-604244 **W** www.sudeleycastle.co.uk
Castle built in 1442; once owned by Richard III and former home of Catherine Parr, sixth wife of Henry VIII; restored in the 19th century

SULGRAVE MANOR, nr Banbury, Oxon OX17 2SD
T 01295-760205 **W** www.sulgravemanor.org.uk
Tudor and Georgian house; home of George Washington's family

SUTTON HOUSE (NT), Hackney, London E9 6JQ
T 020-8986 2264
Tudor house, built in 1535 by Sir Ralph Sadleir

SYON HOUSE, Brentford, Middx TW8 8JF **T** 020-8560 0882
W www.syonpark.co.uk
Built on the site of a former monastery; Robert Adam interior; Capability Brown park

TINTAGEL CASTLE (EH), Tintagel, Cornwall PL34 0HE
T 01840-770328
13th-century cliff-top castle and 5th–6th-century Celtic settlement; linked with Arthurian legend

TOWER OF LONDON, London EC3N 4AB **T** 020-3166 6000
W www.hrp.org.uk/tower-of-london
Royal palace and fortress begun by William the Conqueror in 1078; houses the Crown Jewels

TYNEMOUTH PRIORY AND CASTLE (EH), Tyne and Wear NE30 4BZ **T** 01912-571090
Remains of a Benedictine priory, founded *c.*1090, moated castle-towers, a gatehouse and keep on Saxon monastic site

UPPARK (NT), Petersfield, W. Sussex GU31 5QR
T 01730-825415
17th-century house, restored after fire; Fetherstonhaugh art collection; 18th-century dolls' house

WALMER CASTLE (EH), Deal, Kent CT14 7LJ **T** 01304-364288
One of Henry VIII's coastal defence castles, now the residence of the Lord Warden of the Cinque Ports

WARKWORTH CASTLE (EH), Warkworth, Northumberland NE65 0UJ **T** 01665-711423
14th-century keep amid earlier ruins, with hermitage upstream

WHITBY ABBEY (EH), Whitby, N. Yorks YO22 4JT
T 01947-603568
Remains of Norman church on the site of a monastery founded in AD 657

WILTON HOUSE, nr Salisbury, Wilts SP2 0BJ **T** 01722-746700
W www.wiltonhouse.com
17th-century house on the site of a Tudor house and ninth-century nunnery; Palladian bridge

WINDSOR CASTLE, Windsor, Berks SL4 1NJ **T** 030-3123 7304
  W www.rct.org.uk/visit/windsor-castle
  Official residence of the Queen; oldest royal residence still
  in regular use; largest inhabited castle in the world. Also
  St George's Chapel; Queen Mary's Dolls' House
WOBURN ABBEY, Woburn, Beds MK17 9WA **T** 01525-290333
  W www.woburn.co.uk
  Built on the site of a Cistercian abbey; seat of the Dukes
  of Bedford; art collection
WROXETER ROMAN CITY (EH), nr Shrewsbury, Shropshire
  SY5 6PH **T** 01743-761330
  Second-century public baths and part of the forum of the
  Roman town of *Viroconium*

WALES
For more information on Cadw properties, including those
listed below, the official website is **W** www.cadw.wales.gov.uk
For more information on National Trust properties in Wales,
including those listed below, the official website is
W www.nationaltrust.org.uk

KEY
(C) Property of Cadw: Welsh Historic Monuments
(NT) National Trust property
* UNESCO World Heritage Site (*see also* World Heritage Sites)

*BEAUMARIS CASTLE (C), Anglesey LL58 8AP
  T 01248-810361
  Concentrically planned 13th-century castle, still virtually
  intact
*BLAENAVON, Blaenavon NP4 9AS **T** 01495-742333
  W www.visitblaenavon.co.uk
  18th- and 19th-century industrial landscape associated
  with coal and iron production
CAERLEON ROMAN BATHS AND AMPHITHEATRE
  (C), Newport NP18 1AE **T** 01633-422518
  Rare example of a legionary bath-house and late first-
  century arena surrounded by bank for spectators
*CAERNARFON CASTLE (C), Gwynedd LL55 2AY
  T 01286-677617 **W** www.caernarfon-castle.co.uk
  Huge fortress with polygonal towers built between 1283
  and 1330, initially for King Edward I of England; setting
  for the investiture of Prince Charles in 1969
CAERPHILLY CASTLE (C), Caerphilly CF83 1JD
  T 029-2088 3143
  Concentrically planned castle (*c.*1270) notable for its scale
  and use of water defences
CARDIFF CASTLE, Cardiff CF10 3RB **T** 029-2087 8100
  W www.cardiffcastle.com
  Norman keep built on site of Roman fort; 'fairytale'
  gothic-revival mansion added in the 19th century
CASTELL COCH (C), Tongwynlais, Cardiff CF15 7JS
  T 029-2081 0101
  'Fairytale'-style castle, rebuilt 1872–91 on medieval
  foundations
CHEPSTOW CASTLE (C), Monmouthshire NP16 5EY
  T 01291-624065
  Rectangular keep amid extensive fortifications; developed
  throughout the Middle Ages
*CONWY CASTLE (C), Gwynedd LL32 8AY **T** 01492-592358
  Built for Edward I in 1283–9 on narrow rocky outcrop;
  features eight towers and two barbicans
CRICCIETH CASTLE (C), Gwynedd LL52 0DP
  T 01766-522227
  Native Welsh 13th-century castle, taken and altered by
  Edward I and Edward II
DENBIGH CASTLE (C), Denbighshire LL16 3NB
  T 01745-813385
  Remains of the castle (begun 1282), including triple-
  towered gatehouses

DYFFRYN GARDENS (NT), St Nicholas, Cardiff CF5 6SU
  T 029-2059 3328
  Edwardian gardens designed by Thomas Mawson,
  overlooked by a grand Edwardian mansion
*HARLECH CASTLE (C), Gwynedd LL46 2YH **T** 01766-780552
  Well-preserved castle, constructed 1283–95, on an
  outcrop above the former shoreline; withstood seven-year
  siege 1461–8
PEMBROKE CASTLE, Pembrokeshire SA71 4LA
  T 01646-681510 **W** https://pembrokecastle.co.uk
  Castle founded in 1093; Great Tower built in late 12th
  century; birthplace of King Henry VII
PENRHYN CASTLE (NT), Bangor, Gwynedd LL57 4HT
  T 01248-353084
  Neo-Norman castle built in the 19th century; railway and
  dolls' museums; private art collection
*PONTCYSYLLTE AQUEDUCT AND CANAL, Trevor,
  Wrexham LL20 7TY **T** 01978-822912
  W www.pontcysyllte-aqueduct.co.uk
  Longest and highest aqueduct in Great Britain; designed
  by Thomas Telford and finished in 1805
POWIS CASTLE (NT), Welshpool, Powys SY21 8RF
  T 01938-551944
  Medieval castle with interior in variety of styles; 17th-
  century gardens; Clive of India museum
RAGLAN CASTLE (C), Monmouthshire NP15 2BT
  T 01291-690228
  Remains of 15th-century castle with moated hexagonal
  keep
ST DAVIDS BISHOP'S PALACE (C), Pembrokeshire SA62 6PE
  T 01437-720517
  Remains of residence of Bishops of St Davids built 1328–
  47
TINTERN ABBEY (C), Tintern, Monmouthshire NP16 6SE
  T 01291-689251
  Remains of 13th-century church and conventual buildings
  of a 12th-century Cistercian monastery
TRETOWER COURT AND CASTLE (C), Nr Crickhowell,
  Powys NP8 1RD **T** 01874-730279
  Medieval manor house rebuilt in the 15th century, with
  remains of 12th-century castle nearby

SCOTLAND
For more information on Historic Environment Scotland
properties, including those listed below, the official website is
W www.historicenvironment.scot
For more information on National Trust for Scotland
properties, including those listed below, the official website is
W www.nts.org.uk

KEY
(HES) Historic Environment Scotland property
(NTS) National Trust for Scotland property
* Part of the Heart of Neolithic Orkney UNESCO World
Heritage Site

ABBOTSFORD HOUSE, Melrose, Roxburghshire TD6 9BQ
  T 01896-752043 **W** www.scottsabbotsford.co.uk
  Home of Sir Walter Scott; features historic Scottish relics
  and formal gardens
BALMORAL CASTLE, Ballater, Aberdeenshire AB35 5TB
  T 01339-742534 **W** www.balmoralcastle.com
  Baronial-style castle built for Victoria and Albert; the
  Queen's private residence
BLACKHOUSE, ARNOL (HES), Lewis, Western Isles HS2 9DB
  T 01851-710395
  Traditional Lewis thatched house

BLAIR CASTLE, Blair Atholl, Perthshire PH18 5TL
 T 01796-481207 **W** www.blair-castle.co.uk
 Mid-18th-century mansion with 13th-century tower; seat
 of the Dukes and Earls of Atholl
BOWHILL, Selkirk, Scottish Borders TD7 5ET **T** 01750-22204
 W www.bowhillhouse.co.uk
 Present house dates mainly from 1812; Seat of the Dukes
 of Buccleuch and Queensberry; fine collection of paintings
BROUGH OF BIRSAY (HES), Orkney KW17 2LX
 T 01856-841815
 Remains of Norse and Pictish village on the tidal island of
 Birsay
CAERLAVEROCK CASTLE (HES), Glencaple, Dumfries and
 Galloway DG1 4RU **T** 01387-770244
 Unique triangular 13th-century moated castle with
 classical Renaissance additions
CAIRNPAPPLE HILL (HES), Torphichen, West Lothian
 T 01506-634622
 Neolithic ceremonial site and Bronze Age burial chambers
CALANAIS STANDING STONES (HES), Lewis, Western Isles
 HS2 9DY **T** 01851-621422
 Standing stones in a cross-shaped setting, dating from
 between 2900 and 2600 BC
CATERTHUNS (BROWN AND WHITE) (HES), Menmuir,
 nr Brechin, Angus
 Two large Iron Age hill forts
CAWDOR CASTLE, Nairn, Moray IV12 5RD **T** 01667-404401
 W www.cawdorcastle.com
 14th-century keep with 15th- and 17th-century additions
CLAVA CAIRNS (HES), nr Inverness, Inverness-shire IV2 5EU
 T 0131-668 8600
 Bronze Age cemetery complex of cairns and standing
 stones
CRATHES CASTLE (NTS), nr Banchory, Aberdeenshire AB31
 5QJ **T** 01330-844525
 16th-century baronial castle in woodland, fields and
 gardens
CULZEAN CASTLE (NTS), Maybole, Ayrshire KA19 8LE
 T 01655-884455
 18th-century Robert Adam castle with oval staircase and
 circular saloon
DRYBURGH ABBEY (HES), nr Melrose, Roxburghshire TD6
 0RQ **T** 01835-822381
 12th-century abbey containing the tomb of Sir Walter
 Scott
DUNVEGAN CASTLE, Skye IV55 8WF **T** 01470-521206
 W www.dunvegancastle.com
 13th-century castle with later additions; home of the
 chiefs of the Clan MacLeod
EDINBURGH CASTLE (HES), Edinburgh EH1 2NG
 T 0131-225 9846 **W** www.edinburghcastle.scot
 Fortress perched on extinct volcano; houses the Scottish
 Crown Jewels, Scottish National War Memorial, Scottish
 United Services Museum
EDZELL CASTLE (HES), nr Brechin, Angus DD9 7UE
 T 01356-648631
 Ruined 16th-century tower house on medieval
 foundations; early 17th-century walled garden
EILEAN DONAN CASTLE, Dornie, Ross and Cromarty IV40
 8DX **T** 01599-555202 **W** www.eileandonancastle.com
 13th-century castle situated at the meeting point of three
 sea lochs; Jacobite relics
ELGIN CATHEDRAL (HES), Moray IV30 1HU **T** 01343-547171
 13th-century cathedral and octagonal chapterhouse
FLOORS CASTLE, Kelso, Roxburghshire TD5 7SF
 T 01573-223333 **W** www.floorscastle.com
 Largest inhabited castle in Scotland; seat of the Dukes of
 Roxburghe; built in the 1720s by William Adam

FORT GEORGE (HES), Ardersier, Inverness-shire IV2 7TD
 T 01667-460232
 18th-century fort; still a working army barracks
GLAMIS CASTLE, Forfar, Angus DD8 1RJ **T** 01307-840393
 W www.glamis-castle.co.uk
 Seat of the Lyon family (later Earls of Strathmore and
 Kinghorne) since 1372; the setting for Shakespeare's
 Macbeth
GLASGOW CATHEDRAL (HES), Lanarkshire G4 0QZ
 T 0141-552 8198 **W** www.glasgowcathedral.org.uk
 Late 12th-century cathedral with vaulted crypt
GLENELG BROCHS (HES), Glenelg, Ross and Cromarty
 T 0131-668 8600
 Two 2,000-year-old broch towers (Dun Telve and Dun
 Troddan) with well-preserved structural features
HOPETOUN HOUSE, South Queensferry, West Lothian EH30
 9RW **T** 0131-331 2451 **W** www.hopetoun.co.uk
 Designed by Sir William Bruce in 1699 and enlarged by
 William Adam 1721–48
HUNTLY CASTLE (HES), Aberdeenshire AB54 4SH
 T 01466-793191
 Ruin of a 16th- and 17th-century baronial residence
INVERARAY CASTLE, Argyll PA32 8XE **T** 01499-302203
 W www.inveraray-castle.com
 Gothic-style 18th-century castle designed by William
 Adam and Roger Morris; seat of the Dukes of Argyll
IONA ABBEY (HES), Iona, Argyll PA76 6SQ **T** 01681-700512
 Monastery founded by St Columba in AD 563; remains a
 popular Christian pilgrimage site
JARLSHOF (HES), Sumburgh Head, Shetland ZE3 9JN
 T 01950-460112
 Prehistoric settlement with later ninth-century Norse
 additions
JEDBURGH ABBEY (HES), Roxburghshire TD8 6JQ
 T 01835-863925
 Ruined Augustinian abbey founded *c*.1138; display of
 early Christian artefacts
KISIMUL CASTLE (HES), Castlebay, Barra, Western Isles HS9
 5UZ **T** 01871-810313
 Medieval island home of the Clan MacNeil
LINLITHGOW PALACE (HES), Kirkgate, Linlithgow, West
 Lothian EH49 7AL **T** 01506-842896
 Ruined royal palace, founded in 1424, set in park;
 birthplace of James V and Mary, Queen of Scots
*MAESHOWE (HES), Stenness, Orkney KW16 3LB
 Neolithic chambered tomb with Viking runes
MEIGLE SCULPTURED STONES (HES), Meigle, Perthshire
 PH12 8SB **T** 01828-640612
 Twenty-six carved Pictish stones dating from the late
 eighth to the late tenth centuries
MELROSE ABBEY (HES), Roxburghshire TD6 9LG
 T 01896-822562
 Ruin of Cistercian abbey founded *c*.1136 by David I;
 museum of medieval objects
MOUSA BROCH (HES), Island of Mousa, Shetland ZE2 9HP
 Finest surviving Iron Age broch tower *c*.100 BC
NEW ABBEY CORN MILL (HES), Dumfriesshire DG2 8BX
 T 01387-850260
 Working water-powered mill built in the late 18th
 century
*NEW LANARK, South Lanarkshire ML11 9DB **T** 01555-661345
 W www.newlanark.org
 18th-century village built around a cotton mill
PALACE OF HOLYROODHOUSE, Edinburgh EH8 8DX
 T 0303-123 7306 **W** www.royalcollection.org.uk
 The Queen's official Scottish residence; home to Mary,
 Queen of Scots; main part of the palace built 1671–9
 close to ruined 12th-century Augustinian abbey

*RING OF BRODGAR (HES), Stenness, Orkney
T 01856-841815
Neolithic circle of upright stones surrounded by circular ditch

ROSSLYN CHAPEL, Roslin, Midlothian EH25 9PU
T 0131-440 2159 W www.rosslynchapel.com
Historic church built between 1446 and 1484 with unique stone carvings

ST ANDREWS CASTLE AND CATHEDRAL (HES), Fife
KY16 9AR (castle); 9QL (cathedral) T 01334-477196 (castle); 01334-472563 (cathedral)
Ruins of 13th-century castle, the former residence of bishops of St Andrews, and remains of the largest cathedral in Scotland; museum

SCONE PALACE, Perth, Perthshire PH2 6BD T 01738-552300
W www.scone-palace.co.uk
Georgian-Gothic house built 1802–12; originally the site of a 12th-century church

*SKARA BRAE (HES), Sandwick, Orkney KW16 3LR
T 01856-841815
Neolithic village with adjacent replica house

SMAILHOLM TOWER (HES), nr Kelso, Roxburghshire TD5 7PG T 01573-460365
Well-preserved 15th-century tower-house

STIRLING CASTLE (HES), Stirlingshire FK8 1EJ
T 01786-450000 W www.stirlingcastle.scot
Great Hall and gatehouse built for James IV c.1500; palace built for James V in 1538; site of coronations including Mary, Queen of Scots

*STONES OF STENNESS (HES), Stenness, Orkney KW16 3JZ
T 0131-668 8600
Four surviving Neolithic standing stones and the uprights of a three-stone dolmen

TANTALLON CASTLE (HES), North Berwick, East Lothian EH39 5PN T 01620-892727
Ruined 14th-century curtain wall with towers

THREAVE CASTLE (HES), Dumfries, Kirkcudbrightshire DG7 1TJ T 07711-223101
Ruined late 14th-century tower on an island; accessible only by boat

URQUHART CASTLE (HES), Drumnadrochit, Inverness-shire IV63 6XJ T 01456-450551
13th-century castle remains on the banks of Loch Ness

NORTHERN IRELAND

For the Northern Ireland Department for Communities, the official website is W www.discovernorthernireland.com
For more information on National Trust properties in Northern Ireland, including those listed below, the official website is W www.nationaltrust.org.uk

KEY
(NIDC) Property in the care of the Northern Ireland Department for Communities
(NT) National Trust property

CARRICKFERGUS CASTLE (NIDC), Carrickfergus, Co. Antrim BT38 7BG T 028-9335 1273
Castle built in 1177 and taken by King John in 1210; garrisoned until 1928. From March 2019 the Inner Ward and Great Tower are closed to the public for renovation

CASTLE COOLE (NT), Enniskillen, Co. Fermanagh BT74 6JY
T 028-6632 2690
18th-century neoclassical mansion in parkland; designed by James Wyatt

CASTLE WARD (NT), Strangford, Co. Down BT30 7BA
T 028-4488 1204
18th-century house with Classical and Gothic facades

DEVENISH MONASTIC SITE (NIDC), nr Enniskillen, Co. Fermanagh T 028-9082 3207
Island monastery founded in the sixth century by St Molaise; church dating from 13th century

DOWNHILL DEMESNE AND HEZLETT HOUSE (NT), Castlerock, Co. Londonderry BT51 4RP T 028-7084 8728
Ruins of 18th-century mansion and a 17th-century cottage in landscaped estate including Mussenden Temple

DUNLUCE CASTLE (NIDC), Bushmills, Co. Antrim BT57 8UY
T 028-2073 1938
Ruins of 16th-century stronghold of the McDonnells

FLORENCE COURT (NT), Enniskillen, Co. Fermanagh BT92 1DB T 028-6634 8249
Mid-18th-century house with Rococo decoration

GREY ABBEY (NIDC), Greyabbey, Co. Down BT22 2NQ
T 028-9082 3207
Substantial remains of a Cistercian abbey founded in 1193 set in landscaped parkland

MOUNT STEWART (NT), Newtownards, Co. Down BT22 2AD
T 028-4278 8387
19th-century neoclassical house; octagonal Temple of the Winds

NENDRUM MONASTIC SITE (NIDC), Mahee Island, Co. Down T 028-9082 3207
Pre-Norman island monastery founded in the fifth century by St Machaoi; has links to St. Patrick

PATTERSON'S SPADE MILL (NT), Templepatrick, Co. Antrim BT39 0AP T 028-9443 3619
Last working water-driven spade mill in the UK

TULLY CASTLE (NIDC), Derrygonnelly, Co. Fermanagh
T 028-9082 3207
Remains of a fortified house and bawn built c.1619

MUSEUMS AND GALLERIES

There are approximately 2,500 museums and galleries in the UK. As at October 2020, 1,572 of these were fully accredited by Arts Council England and a further 170 museums held provisional accreditation. Accreditation indicates that the museum or gallery has an appropriate constitution, is soundly financed, has adequate collection management standards and public services and has access to professional curatorial advice. These applications are assessed by either Arts Council England; the Museums, Archives and Libraries division of the Welsh government; Museums Galleries Scotland or the Northern Ireland Museums Council.

The following is a selection of museums and art galleries in the UK. Opening hours and admission charges vary. Further information about museums and galleries in the UK is available from the Museums Association (**T** 020-7566 7800 **W** www.museumsassociation.org).

W www.weareculture24.org.uk includes a database of all the museums and galleries in the UK.

ENGLAND
* England's national museums and galleries, which receive funding from a government department, such as the DCMS or MoD. These institutions are deemed to have collections of national importance, and the government is able to call upon their staff for expert advice.

ALTON
Jane Austen's House Museum, Chawton, Hants GU34 1SD
T 01420-83262 **W** www.janeaustens.house
17th-century house which tells the author's story
BARNARD CASTLE
The Bowes Museum, Co. Durham DL12 8NP **T** 01833-690606
W www.thebowesmuseum.org.uk
Public gallery in a French châteaux style featuring archaeology, fashion and ceramics. Houses one of the largest collections of Spanish art in the country
BATH
American Museum, Claverton Manor BA2 7BD **T** 01225-460503
W www.americanmuseum.org
American decorative arts from the 17th to 20th centuries
Fashion Museum, Bennett Street BA1 2QH **T** 01225-477789
W www.fashionmuseum.co.uk
Fashion from the 17th century to the present day
Victoria Art Gallery, Bridge Street BA2 4AT **T** 01225-477233
W www.victoriagal.org.uk
European Old Masters and British art since the 15th century
BEAMISH
Beamish Museum, Co. Durham DH9 0RG **T** 0191-370 4000
W www.beamish.org.uk
Living working museum of a northern industrial town during Georgian, Victorian and Edwardian times
BEAULIEU
National Motor Museum, Hants SO42 7ZN **T** 01590-612345
W www.beaulieu.co.uk
Former royal estate within the New Forest national park home to Beaulieu Abbey, Palace House and the National Motor Museum
BIRMINGHAM
Aston Hall, Trinity Road B6 6JD **T** 0121-348 8100
W www.birminghammuseums.org.uk/aston
Jacobean House containing paintings, furniture and tapestries from the 17th to 19th centuries

Barber Institute of Fine Arts, University of Birmingham, Edgbaston B15 2TS **T** 0121-414 7333 **W** www.barber.org.uk
Extensive coin collection; fine arts, including Old Masters
Birmingham Museum and Art Gallery, Chamberlain Square B3 3DH
T 0121-348 8000 **W** www.birminghammuseums.org.uk/bmag
Includes notable collection of Pre-Raphaelite art
Museum of the Jewellery Quarter, Vyse Street, B18 6HA
T 0121-348 8140
W www.birminghammuseums.org.uk/jewellery
Preserved jewellery workshop
Sarehole Mill, Cole Bank Road, B13 0BD **T** 0121-348 8160
W www.birminghammuseums.org.uk/sarehole
A 250-year-old watermill renowned for its association with author J. R. R. Tolkien
Thinktank, Curzon Street B4 7XG **T** 0121-348 8000
W www.birminghammuseums.org.uk/thinktank
Science museum featuring over 200 hands-on displays and a Planetarium
BOURNEMOUTH
Russell-Cotes Art Gallery and Museum, East Cliff Promenade BH1 3AA **T** 01202-451858 **W** www.russellcotes.com
Seaside villa housing 19th- and 20th-century art and sculptures from around the world
BOVINGTON
Tank Museum, Dorset BH20 6JG **T** 01929-405096
W www.tankmuseum.org
Collection of 300 tanks from their invention in 1915 to the modern conflict in Afghanistan
BRADFORD
Bradford Industrial Museum, Moorside Mills, Moorside Road, Eccleshill BD2 3HP **T** 01274-435900
W www.bradfordmuseums.org
Steam power, machinery and motor vehicle exhibits
Cartwright Hall Art Gallery, Lister Park BD9 4NS **T** 01274-431212
W www.bradfordmuseums.org
British 19th- and 20th-century fine art, contemporary prints and south Asian art
National Science and Media Museum,* BD1 1NQ **T 0800-047 8124
W www.scienceandmediamuseum.org.uk
The science and culture of image and sound technologies, film and television with interactive exhibits and experiments; features an IMAX cinema and the only permanent Cinerama screen in Europe
BRIGHTON
Booth Museum of Natural History, Dyke Road BN1 5AA
T 03000-290900 **W** www.brightonmuseums.org.uk/booth
Zoology, botany and geology collections; British birds in recreated habitats
Brighton Museum and Art Gallery, Royal Pavilion Gardens BN1 1EE
T 03000-290900 **W** www.brightonmuseums.org.uk/brighton
Includes fine art and design, fashion, world art; Sussex history
Royal Pavilion, 4/5 Pavilion Buildings BN1 1EE **T** 0300-0290900
W https://brightonmuseums.org.uk/royalpavilion
Regency seaside pleasure palace for George IV built in the visual style of India and China; includes the Prince Regent and Indian Military Hospital galleries
BRISTOL
Arnolfini, Narrow Quay BS1 4QA **T** 0117-917 2300
W www.arnolfini.org.uk
Experimental contemporary visual arts, dance, performance, music; talks and workshops

Blaise Castle House Museum, Henbury Road BS10 7QS
T 0117-903 9818
W www.bristolmuseums.org.uk/blaise-castle-house-museum
18th-century mansion; social history collections
Bristol Museum and Art Gallery, Queen's Road BS8 1RL
T 0117-922 3571
W www.bristolmuseums.org.uk/bristol-museum-and-art-gallery
Includes Victorian, Edwardian and French fine art;
archaeology, local history and natural sciences
M Shed, Prince's Wharf BS1 4RN **T** 0117-352 6600
W www.bristolmuseums.org.uk/m-shed
The story of Bristol's heritage of engineering, transport,
music and industry
Red Lodge Museum, Park Row BS1 5LJ **T** 0117-921 1360
W www.bristolmuseums.org.uk/red-lodge-museum
House museum showcasing original historical interiors
from the Tudor to Victorian periods
CAMBRIDGE
Fitzwilliam Museum, Trumpington Street CB2 1RB
T 01223-332900 **W** www.fitzmuseum.cam.ac.uk
Antiquities, fine and applied arts, clocks, ceramics,
manuscripts, furniture, sculpture, coins and medals
*Imperial War Museum Duxford, Duxford CB22 4QR
T 01223-835000 **W** www.iwm.org.uk/visits/iwm-duxford
Displays of military and civil aircraft, tanks and naval
exhibits
Museum of Archaeology and Anthropology, Downing Street CB2
3DZ **T** 01223-333516 **W** www.maa.cam.ac.uk
Global archaeological and anthropological collections;
photography and modern art collections
Museum of Zoology, Downing Street CB2 3EJ **T** 01223-336650
W www.museum.zoo.cam.ac.uk
Extensive assortment of zoological specimens; includes the
collections of Charles Darwin and Alfred Russel Wallace
Sedgwick Museum of Earth Sciences, Downing Street CB2 3EQ
T 01223-333456 **W** www.sedgwickmuseum.org
Extensive geological collection
Whipple Museum of the History of Science, Free School Lane CB2
3RH **T** 01223-330906 **W** www.hps.cam.ac.uk/whipple
Scientific instruments from the 14th century to the present
CARLISLE
Tullie House Museum and Art Gallery, Castle Street CA3 8TP
T 01228-618718 **W** www.tulliehouse.co.uk
Jacobean house with fine art, local social history,
prehistoric archaeology and natural sciences including
Hadrian's Wall exhibit
CHATHAM
The Historic Dockyard, ME4 4TE **T** 01634-823800
W www.thedockyard.co.uk
Maritime attractions including HMS *Cavalier,* the UK's last
Second World War destroyer
Royal Engineers Museum, Prince Arthur Road, Gillingham ME7 1UR
T 01634-822312 **W** www.re-museum.co.uk
Regimental history, ethnography, decorative art and
photography
CHELTENHAM
The Wilson Art Gallery and Museum, Clarence Street GL50 3JT
T 01242-387488 **W** www.cheltenhammuseum.org.uk
Arts and crafts, local heroes, fine art and natural history
CHESTER
Grosvenor Museum, Grosvenor Street CH1 2DD **T** 01244-972197
W www.grosvenormuseum.westcheshiremuseums.co.uk
Roman collections, natural history, art, Chester silver,
local history and costume
CHICHESTER
Weald and Downland Open Air Museum, Singleton PO18 0EU
T 01243-811363 **W** www.wealddown.co.uk
Rebuilt vernacular buildings from south-east England;
includes medieval houses and a working watermill; craft
demonstrations, Tudor kitchen and cooking

COLCHESTER
Colchester Castle Museum, Castle Park CO1 1TJ **T** 01206-282939
W www.colchestercastlepark.co.uk/colchester-castle
Largest Norman keep in Europe standing on foundations
of the Roman Temple of Claudius
COVENTRY
Coventry Transport Museum, Hales Street CV1 1JD
T 024-7623 4270 **W** www.transport-museum.com
Extensive collection of motor vehicles and bicycles; land
speed record-holding car
Herbert Art Gallery and Museum, Jordan Well CV1 5QP
T 024-7623 7521 **W** www.theherbert.org
Local history, archaeology, industry and visual arts
DERBY
Derby Museum and Art Gallery, The Strand DE1 1BS
T 01332-641901 **W** www.derbymuseums.org/museumartgallery
Includes paintings by Joseph Wright of Derby, origins of
Derby and military history
Pickford's House Museum, Friar Gate DE1 1DA **T** 01332-715181
W www.derbymuseums.org/pickfords-house
Georgian town house designed by architect Joseph
Pickford; museum of Georgian life and costume
DEVIZES
Wiltshire Museum, Library and Gallery, Long Street SN10 1NS
T 01380-727369 **W** www.wiltshiremuseum.org.uk
Natural and local history; art gallery; archaeological finds
from prehistoric, Roman and Saxon sites
DOVER
Dover Museum, Market Square CT16 1PH **T** 01304-201066
W www.dovermuseum.co.uk
Contains the Dover Bronze Age Boat Gallery and
archaeological finds from Bronze Age, Roman and Saxon
sites
EXETER
Royal Albert Memorial Museum and Art Gallery, Queen Street EX4
3RX **T** 01392-265858 **W** www.rammuseum.org.uk
Natural history; archaeology; worldwide fine and
decorative art including Exeter silver
GATESHEAD
BALTIC Centre for Contemporary Art, NE8 3BA **T** 0191-478 1810
W www.baltic.art
Contemporary art exhibitions and events
Shipley Art Gallery, Prince Consort Road NE8 4JB **T** 0191-477 1495
W www.shipleyartgallery.org.uk
Contemporary crafts
GAYDON
British Motor Museum, Banbury Road, Warks CV35 0BJ
T 01926-641188 **W** www.britishmotormuseum.co.uk
The world's largest collection of British cars with nearly
300 vehicles spanning the classic, vintage and veteran eras
GLOUCESTER
Gloucester Waterways Museum, Gloucester Docks GL1 2EH
T 01452-318200 **W** www.gloucesterwaterwaysmuseum.org.uk
200-year history of Britain's canals and inland waterways
GOSPORT
Royal Navy Submarine Museum, Haslar Jetty Road, Hants PO12 2AS
T 023-9251 0354 **W** www.nmrn.org.uk/submarine-museum
Underwater warfare exhibition, including submarines
HMS *Alliance* and HMS *Holland 1* – the Royal Navy's first
submarine
GRASMERE
Dove Cottage and the *Wordsworth Museum,* Cumbria LA22 9SH
T 015394-35544 **W** www.wordsworth.org.uk
William Wordsworth's manuscripts, home and garden
HOVE
Hove Museum and Art Gallery, New Church Road BN3 4AB
T 03000-290900 **W** www.brightonmuseums.org.uk/hove
Toys, cinema, local history and fine art collections
HULL

Ferens Art Gallery, Queen Victoria Square HU1 3RA
T 01482-300300 W www.hcandl.co.uk/ferens-art-gallery
European Old Masters, Victorian, Edwardian and
contemporary British art

Hull and East Riding Museum of Archaeology, High Street, HU1
1NQ T 01482-300300
W www.hcandl.co.uk/hull-and-east-riding-museum
Local history from the pre-historic to the present day

Hull Maritime Museum, Queen Victoria Square HU1 3DX
T 01482-300300 W www.hcandl.co.uk/maritime-museum
Hull's maritime heritage including whaling, fishing,
navigation and merchant trade

Wilberforce House, 23–25 High Street HU1 1NQ T 01482-300300
W www.hcandl.co.uk/wilberforce-house
Birthplace of abolitionist William Wilberforce; history of
the transatlantic slave trade

HUNTINGDON

The Cromwell Museum, Grammar School Walk PE29 3LF
T 01480-708008 W www.cromwellmuseum.org
Portraits and memorabilia relating to Oliver Cromwell

IPSWICH

Christchurch Mansion and *Wolsey Art Gallery*, Christchurch Park
IP4 2BE T 01473-433554 W www.cimuseums.org.uk
Tudor house with paintings by Gainsborough, Constable
and other Suffolk artists; furniture and 18th-century
ceramics; temporary exhibitions

KEIGHLEY

The Brontë Parsonage Museum, Haworth, W. Yorks BD22 8DR
T 01535-642323 W www.bronte.org.uk
The former home of the literary Brontë family

KESWICK

Derwent Pencil Museum, Southey Works CA12 5NG
T 01900-609590 W www.derwentart.com
500-year history of the pencil; demonstration events and
workshops throughout the year

LEEDS

Armley Mills, Leeds Industrial Museum, Canal Road, Armley
LS12 2QF T 0113-378 3173
W museumsandgalleries.leeds.gov.uk/armleymills
Once the world's largest woollen mill, now a museum for
textiles and Leeds' industrial heritage

Leeds Art Gallery, The Headrow LS1 3AA T 0113-378 5350
W museumsandgalleries.leeds.gov.uk/artgallery
Includes English watercolours, sculpture, contemporary
art and prints from the region's artists

Royal Armouries Museum, Armouries Drive LS10 1LT
T 0113-220 1961 W www.royalarmouries.org
National collection of over 8,500 items of arms and
armour from BC to present over five galleries: War,
Tournament, Oriental, Self Defence and Hunting

LEICESTER

New Walk Museum and Art Gallery, 53 New Walk LE1 7EA
T 0116-255 4900
W www.leicester.gov.uk/leisure-and-culture/
museums-and-galleries
Natural and cultural history; ancient Egypt gallery;
European art including works by the German
expressionists and ceramics by Picasso

LINCOLN

The Collection, Danes Terrace LN2 1LP T 01522-782040
W www.thecollectionmuseum.com
Artefacts from the Stone Age to the Roman, Viking and
Medieval eras; adjacent art gallery; collections of
contemporary art and craft, sculpture, porcelain, clocks
and watches

Museum of Lincolnshire Life, Burton Road LN1 3LY
T 01522-782040
W www.lincolnshire.gov.uk/museumoflincolnshirelife
Social history; agricultural, industrial, military and
commercial exhibits

LIVERPOOL

**International Slavery Museum*, Royal Albert Dock L3 4AQ
T 0151-478 4499 W www.liverpoolmuseums.org.uk/ism
Explores historical and contemporary aspects of slavery

**Lady Lever Art Gallery*, Wirral CH62 5EQ T 0151-478 4136
W www.liverpoolmuseums.org.uk/ladylever
Paintings, furniture and porcelain

**Merseyside Maritime Museum*, Royal Albert Dock L3 4AQ
T 0151-478 4499 W www.liverpoolmuseums.org.uk/maritime
Floating exhibits, working displays and craft
demonstrations; incorporates the *UK Border Agency
National Museum*

**Museum of Liverpool*, Pier Head L3 1DG T 0151-478 4545
W www.liverpoolmuseums.org.uk/mol
Explores the significance of the city's geography, history
and culture

* *Sudley House*, Mossley Hill Road L18 8BX T 0151-478 4016
W www.liverpoolmuseums.org.uk/sudley
Late 18th- and 19th-century paintings in former
shipowner's home

*Tate Liverpool, Albert Dock L3 4BB T 0151-1702 7400
W www.tate.org.uk/liverpool
20th-century paintings and sculpture

**Walker Art Gallery*, William Brown Street L3 8EL
T 0151-478 4199 W www.liverpoolmuseums.org.uk/walker
Paintings and decorative arts from the 13th century to the
present day

**World Museum Liverpool*, William Brown Street L3 8EN
T 0151-478 4393 W www.liverpoolmuseums.org.uk/wml
Includes Egyptian mummies, weapons and classical
sculpture; planetarium, aquarium, vivarium and natural
history centre

LONDON: GALLERIES

Barbican Art Gallery, Barbican Centre, Silk Street EC2Y 8DS
T 020-7638 4141 W www.barbican.org.uk
Art, music, theatre, dance and film exhibitions

Courtauld Institute of Art Gallery, Somerset House, Strand
WC2R 0RN T 020-3947 7777 W www.courtauld.ac.uk
Fine art from the early renaissance to the 20th century,
including impressionist and post-impressionist paintings

Dennis Severs' House, 18 Folgate Street E1 6BX T 020-7247 4013
W www.dennissevershouse.co.uk
Candlelit recreation of a Huguenot silk weaver's home

Dulwich Picture Gallery, Gallery Road SE21 7AD T 020-8693 5254
W www.dulwichpicturegallery.org.uk
England's first public art gallery; designed by Sir John
Soane to house 17th- and 18th-century paintings

Estorick Collection of Modern Italian Art, Canonbury Square
N1 2AN T 020-7704 9522 W www.estorickcollection.com
Early 20th-century Italian drawings, paintings, sculptures
and etchings, with an emphasis on Futurism

Hayward Gallery, Belvedere Road SE1 8XX T 020-7960 4200
W www.southbankcentre.co.uk
Temporary exhibitions

*National Gallery, Trafalgar Square WC2N 5DN T 020-7747 2885
W www.nationalgallery.org.uk
Western painting from the 13th to 19th centuries; early
Renaissance collection in the Sainsbury Wing

**National Portrait Gallery*, St Martin's Place WC2H 0HE
T 020-7306 0055 W www.npg.org.uk
Portraits of eminent people in British history

Photographers' Gallery, Ramillies Street W1F 7LW T 020-7087 9300
W www.thephotographersgallery.org.uk
Temporary exhibitions; permanent camera obscura

The Queen's Gallery, Buckingham Palace SW1A 1AA
T 020-7766 7300 W www.rct.uk
Art from the Royal Collection

Royal Academy of Arts, Burlington House, Piccadilly W1J 0BD
   T 020-7300 8090 **W** www.royalacademy.org.uk
   British art since 1768 and temporary exhibitions; annual
   Summer Exhibition
Saatchi Gallery, Duke of York's HQ, King's Road SW3 4RY
   T 020-7811 3070 **W** www.saatchigallery.com
   Contemporary art including paintings, photographs,
   sculpture and installations
Serpentine Gallery, Kensington Gardens W2 3XA **T** 020-7402 6075
   W www.serpentinegallery.org
   Temporary exhibitions of British and international
   contemporary art
*Tate Britain, Millbank SW1P 4RG **T** 020-7887 8888
   W www.tate.org.uk/britain
   British art from the 16th century to the present;
   international modern art
*Tate Modern, Bankside SE1 9TG **T** 020-7887 8888
   W www.tate.org.uk/modern
   International modern art from 1900 to the present
*Wallace Collection, Manchester Square W1U 3BN
   T 020-7563 9500 **W** www.wallacecollection.org
   Old Masters; French 18th-century paintings, furniture,
   armour, porcelain, clocks and sculpture
Whitechapel Art Gallery, Whitechapel High Street E1 7QX
   T 020-7522 7888 **W** www.whitechapelgallery.org
   Temporary exhibitions of modern art
LONDON: MUSEUMS
Bank of England Museum, Bartholomew Lane EC2R 8AH
   T 020-3461 4444 **W** www.bankofengland.co.uk/museum
   History of the Bank of England since 1694
*British Museum, Great Russell Street WC1B 3DG **T** 020-7323 8000
   W www.britishmuseum.org
   Collection of art and antiquities spanning 2 million years
   of human history; temporary exhibitions; houses the Elgin
   Marbles from the Parthenon
Brunel Museum, Rotherhithe SE16 4LF **T** 020-7231 3840
   W www.brunel-museum.org.uk
   Explores the engineering achievements of Isambard
   Kingdom Brunel and his father, Marc Brunel
Charles Dickens Museum, Doughty Street WC1N 2LX
   T 020-7405 2127 **W** www.dickensmuseum.com
   Dickens's home from 1837–9; manuscripts, personal
   items and paintings
*Churchill War Rooms, King Charles Street SW1A 2AQ
   T 020-7416 5000 **W** www.iwm.org.uk/visits/churchill-war-rooms
   Underground rooms used by Churchill and the
   government during the Second World War
Cutty Sark, King William Walk SE10 9HT **T** 020-8858 4422
   W www.rmg.co.uk/cuttysark
   The world's last remaining tea clipper; re-opened in April
   2012 following extensive restoration
Design Museum, Kensington High Street W8 6AG **T** 020-3862 5900
   W www.designmuseum.org
   The development of design and the mass-production of
   consumer objects
Garden Museum, Lambeth Palace Road SE1 7LB **T** 020-7401 8865
   W www.gardenmuseum.org.uk
   History and development of gardens and gardening;
   temporary exhibitions, symposia and events
*HMS Belfast, The Queen's Walk SE1 2JH **T** 020-7940 6300
   W www.iwm.org.uk/hms-belfast
   Life and work on board a Second World War cruiser
*Horniman Museum and Gardens, London Road SE23 3PQ
   T 020-8699 1872 **W** www.horniman.ac.uk
   Museum of anthropology, musical instruments and natural
   history; aquarium; reference library; gardens

*Imperial War Museum, Lambeth Road SE1 6HZ **T** 020-7416 5000
   W www.iwm.org.uk
   All aspects of the two World Wars and other military
   operations involving Britain and the Commonwealth since
   1914
Jewish Museum, Albert Street NW1 7NB **T** 020-7284 7384
   W www.jewishmuseum.org.uk
   Jewish life, history, art and religion
London Metropolitan Archives, Northampton Road EC1R 0HB
   T 020-7332 3820 **W** www.cityoflondon.gov.uk/lma
   Material on the history of London and its people dating
   from 1067 to the present day
London Museum of Water and Steam, Green Dragon Lane TW8 0EN
   T 020-8568 4757 **W** www.waterandsteam.org.uk
   Large collection of steam engines; reopened in 2014 after
   refurbishment
London Transport Museum, Covent Garden Piazza WC2E 7BB
   T 034-3222 5000 **W** www.ltmuseum.co.uk
   Vehicles, photographs and graphic art relating to the
   history of transport in London
MCC Museum, Lord's Cricket Ground, St John's Wood NW8 8QN
   T 020-7616 8500 **W** www.lords.org/tours-and-museum
   Cricket exhibits including the Ashes Urn, kits, paintings
   and W. G. Grace exhibit
Migration Museum, Lambeth High Street SE1 7AG
   E info@migrationmuseum.org **W** www.migrationmuseum.org
   Opened in 2017, tells the story of migration through the
   ages and how it has affected and transformed Britain
*Museum of Childhood (V&A), Cambridge Heath Road E2 9PA
   T 020-7942 2000 **W** www.vam.ac.uk/moc
   Toys, games and exhibits relating to the social history of
   childhood from the 17th century to the present
*Museum of London, London Wall EC2Y 5HN **T** 020-7001 9844
   W www.museumoflondon.org.uk
   History of London from prehistoric times to the present
   day; Galleries of Modern London
Museum of London Docklands, West India Quay, Canary Wharf
   E14 4AL **T** 020-7001 9844
   W www.museumoflondon.org.uk/docklands
   Explores the story of London's river, port and people over
   2,000 years; includes the London Sugar Slavery Gallery
National Archives Museum, Kew TW9 4DU **T** 020-8876 3444
   W www.nationalarchives.gov.uk/museum
   Displays treasures from the archives, including the
   Domesday Book and Magna Carta
*National Army Museum, Royal Hospital Road SW3 4HT
   T 020-7730 0717 **W** www.nam.ac.uk
   Five-hundred-year history of the British soldier; exhibits
   include model of the Battle of Waterloo and recreated
   First World War trench
*National Maritime Museum, Romney Road SE10 9NF
   T 020-8858 4422
   W www.rmg.co.uk/national-maritime-museum
   Maritime history of Britain; collections include globes,
   clocks, telescopes and paintings; comprises the main
   building, the Royal Observatory and the Queen's House
*Natural History Museum, Cromwell Road SW7 5BD
   T 020-7942 5000 **W** www.nhm.ac.uk
   Natural history collections and interactive Darwin Centre
Petrie Museum of Egyptian Archaeology, University College London,
   Malet Place WC1E 6BT **T** 020-3108 9000
   W www.ucl.ac.uk/museums/petrie
   Egyptian and Sudanese archaeology featuring around
   80,000 objects
Postal Museum, 15–20 Phoenix Place, WC1X 0DL **T** 0300-030 0700
   W www.postalmuseum.org
   British postal service and communications from Tudor
   times to the present; interactive galleries, archives and
   subterranean mail train ride

*Royal Air Force Museum, Grahame Park Way NW9 5LL
T 020-8205 2266 W www.rafmuseum.org.uk
Aviation from before the Wright brothers to the present

Royal Mews, Buckingham Palace SW1W 0QH T 020-7766 7302
W www.rct.uk/visit/royalmews
State vehicles, including the Queen's gold state coach;
home to the Queen's horses; guided tours

*Science Museum, Exhibition Road SW7 2DD T 0800-047 8124
W www.sciencemuseum.org.uk
Science, technology, industry and medicine exhibitions;
children's interactive gallery; IMAX cinema

Shakespeare's Globe Exhibition, New Globe Walk, Bankside SE1 9DT
T 020-7902 1400 W www.shakespearesglobe.com
Recreation of Elizabethan theatre using 16th-century
techniques; includes a tour of the theatre

*Sir John Soane's Museum, Lincoln's Inn Fields WC2A 3BP
T 020-7405 2107 W www.soane.org
Art and antiquities collected by Soane throughout his
lifetime; authentic Georgian and Victorian interior

Tower Bridge Exhibition, SE1 2UP T 020-7403 3761
W www.towerbridge.org.uk
History of the bridge and display of Victorian steam
machinery; panoramic views from walkways

*Victoria and Albert Museum, Cromwell Road SW7 2RL
T 020-7942 2000 W www.vam.ac.uk
Includes the National Art Library and the Gilbert
Collection; fine and applied art and design; furniture,
glass, textiles, theatre and dress collections; temporary
exhibitions

Wellcome Collection, Euston Road NW1 2BE T 020-7611 2222
W www.wellcomecollection.org
Contemporary and historic exhibitions and collections
including the Wellcome Library

Wimbledon Lawn Tennis Museum, Church Road SW19 5AE
T 020-8944 1066 W www.wimbledon.com/museum
Tennis trophies, fashion and memorabilia; view of Centre
Court

MALTON

Eden Camp, N. Yorks YO17 6RT T 01653-697777
W www.edencamp.co.uk
Restored POW camp and Second World War
memorabilia

MANCHESTER

Gallery of Costume, Platt Hall, Rusholme M14 5LL T 0161-245 7245
W www.manchesterartgallery.org
Exhibits from the 17th century to the present day

*Imperial War Museum North, Trafford Wharf Road M17 1TZ
T 0207-416 5000 W www.iwm.org.uk/north
History of war from the 20th century to the present

Manchester Art Gallery, Mosley Street M2 3JL T 0161-235 8888
W www.manchesterartgallery.org
European fine and decorative art from the 17th to 20th
centuries

Manchester Museum, Oxford Road M13 9PL T 0161-275 2648
W www.museum.manchester.ac.uk
Collections include decorative arts, natural history and
zoology; three Ancient Worlds galleries

*Museum of Science and Industry, Liverpool Road M3 4FP
T 0800-047 8124 W www.scienceandindustrymuseum.org.uk
On site of world's oldest passenger railway station;
galleries relating to space, energy, power, transport,
aviation, textiles and social history

National Football Museum, Cathedral Gardens M4 3BG
T 0161-605 8200 W www.nationalfootballmuseum.com
Home to the FIFA, FA and Football League collections
including the 1966 World Cup final ball

People's History Museum, Left Bank, Spinningfields M3 3ER
T 0161-838 9190 W www.phm.org.uk
History of British political and working life

The Whitworth, Oxford Road M15 6ER T 0161-275 7450
W www.whitworth.manchester.ac.uk
Fine and modern art, wallpapers, prints, textiles and
sculptures

MILTON KEYNES

Bletchley Park National Codes Centre, Bucks MK3 6EB
T 01908-640404 W www.bletchleypark.org.uk
Home of British codebreaking during the Second World
War; Enigma machine; computer museum and Alan
Turing gallery

The National Museum of Computing Block H, Bletchley Park, MK3
6EB T 01908-374708 W www.tnmoc.org
Charts the development of computing from the 1940s
onwards and houses the world's largest collection of
functional historical computers, including the Colossus
and the WITCH

NEWCASTLE UPON TYNE

Discovery Museum, Blandford Square NE1 4JA T 0191-232 6789
W www.discoverymuseum.org.uk
Science and industry, local history, fashion; Tyneside's
maritime history; digital jukebox of 2,000 film and TV
titles from the BFI National Archive

Great North Museum: Hancock, Barras Bridge NE2 4PT
T 0191-222 6765 W www.greatnorthmuseum.org.uk
Natural and ancient history; planetarium; Living Planet
display incorporates live animal tanks and aquaria

Laing Art Gallery, New Bridge Street NE1 8AG T 0191-278 1611
W www.laingartgallery.org.uk
19th and 20th century art including local painters;
ceramics, glass, Japanese decorative arts and prints

NEWMARKET

Palace House: National Heritage Centre for Horseracing and
Sporting Art, Palace Street CB8 8EP T 01638-667314
W www.palacehousenewmarket.co.uk
Collection of horseracing memorabilia, British Sporting
Art from around the UK and home of the retraining of
racehorses

NORTH SHIELDS

Stephenson Railway Museum, Middle Engine Lane NE29 8DX
T 0191-277 7135 W www.stephensonrailwaymuseum.org.uk
Locomotive engines and rolling stock; open April through
November and school holidays outside this period

NOTTINGHAM

Natural History Museum, Wollaton Hall, Wollaton NG8 2AE
T 0115-876 3100 W www.wallatonhall.org.uk
Geology, botany and zoology specimens housed in an
Elizabethan mansion

OXFORD

Ashmolean Museum, Beaumont Street OX1 2PH T 01865-278000
W www.ashmolean.org
Art and archaeology including Egyptian, Minoan, Anglo-
Saxon and Chinese exhibits; largest collection of Raphael
drawings in the world

Modern Art Oxford, Pembroke Street OX1 1BP T 01865-722733
W www.modernartoxford.org.uk
Temporary exhibitions

Museum of the History of Science, Broad Street OX1 3AZ
T 01865-277293 W www.hsm.ox.ac.uk
Displays include early scientific instruments, chemical
apparatus, clocks and watches

Oxford University Museum of Natural History, Parks Road
OX1 3PW T 01865-272950 W www.oumnh.ox.ac.uk
Entomology, geology, mineralogy and petrology, and
zoology

Pitt Rivers Museum, South Parks Road OX1 3PP T 01865-613000
W www.prm.ox.ac.uk
Anthropological and archaeological artefacts

PLYMOUTH

The Box Plymouth, Tavistock Place PL4 8AX
  W www.theboxplymouth.com
  Local archives and study; fine and decorative arts; world cultures; temporary exhibitions

PORTSMOUTH

Charles Dickens Birthplace, Old Commercial Road PO1 4QL
  T 023-9282 1879 **W** www.charlesdickensbirthplace.co.uk
  Reproduction Regency house; Dickens memorabilia

The D-Day Story, Clarence Esplanade, Southsea PO5 3NT
  T 023-9288 2555 **W** www.theddaystory.com
  The evacuation of Dunkirk, the D-Day landings and the Battle of Normandy exhibitions with over 10,000 objects and artefacts including the Overlord embroidery

Portsmouth Historic Dockyard, HM Naval Base PO1 3LJ
  T 023-9283 9766 **W** www.historicdockyard.co.uk
  Incorporates the *National Museum of the Royal Navy** (PO1 3NH **T** 023-9289 1370 **W** www.nmrn.org.uk), HMS *Victory* (PO1 3NH **T** 023-9283 9766 **W** www.hms-victory.com), HMS *Warrior* (PO1 3QX **T** 023-9283 9766 **W** www.hmswarrior.org), *Mary Rose* (PO1 3LX **T** 077-166 3973 **W** www.maryrose.org) and *Action Stations* (PO1 3LJ **T** 023-9283 9766 **W** www.actionstations.org)
  History of the Royal Navy and of the dockyard; warships and technology spanning 500 years

PRESTON

Harris Museum and Art Gallery, Market Square PR1 2PP
  T 01772-258248 **W** www.theharris.org.uk
  British art since the 18th century; ceramics, glass, costume and local history; contemporary exhibitions

ST ALBANS

Verulamium Museum, St Michael's Street AL3 4SW
  T 01727-751810 **W** www.stalbansmuseums.org.uk
  Remains of Iron Age settlement and the third-largest city in Roman Britain

ST IVES

**Tate St Ives*, Porthmeor Beach, Cornwall TR26 1TG
  T 01736-796226 **W** www.tate.org.uk/stives
  Modern art, much by artists associated with St Ives; includes the Barbara Hepworth Museum and Sculpture Garden; open after 2014 part closure

SALISBURY

Salisbury & South Wiltshire Museum, The Close SP1 2EN
  T 01722-332151 **W** www.salisburymuseum.org.uk
  Local history and archaeology; Stonehenge exhibits

SHEFFIELD

Graves Gallery, Surrey Street S1 1XZ **T** 0114-278 2600
  W www.museums-sheffield.org.uk
  Twentieth-century British art; European art spanning four centuries

Millennium Galleries, Arundel Gate S1 2PP **T** 0114-278 2600
  W www.museums-sheffield.org.uk
  Incorporates four different galleries: the Special Exhibition Gallery, the Craft and Design Gallery, the Metalwork Gallery and the Ruskin Gallery, which houses John Ruskin's collection of paintings, drawings, books and medieval manuscripts

Weston Park Museum, Western Bank S10 2TP **T** 0114-278 2600
  W www.museums-sheffield.org.uk
  World and local history; art and temporary exhibitions

SOUTHAMPTON

City Art Gallery, Commercial Road SO14 7LP **T** 023-8083 3007
  W www.southamptoncityartgallery.com
  Western art from the Renaissance to the present

SeaCity Museum, Havelock Road SO14 7FY **T** 023-8083 3007
  W www.seacitymuseum.co.uk
  Opened in 2012, the museum tells the story of the city's maritime past and present

SOUTH SHIELDS

Arbeia Roman Fort, Baring Street NE33 2BB **T** 0191-277 2170
  W www.arbeiaromanfort.org.uk
  Excavated ruins; reconstructions of original buildings

South Shields Museum and Art Gallery, Ocean Road NE33 2JA
  T 0191-211 5599 **W** www.southshieldsmuseum.org.uk
  South Tyneside history; interactive art gallery

STOKE-ON-TRENT

Etruria Industrial Museum, Lower Bedford Street ST4 7AF
  T 07900-267711 **W** www.etruriamuseum.org.uk
  Britain's sole surviving steam-powered potter's mill

Gladstone Pottery Museum, Uttoxeter Road, Longton ST3 1PQ
  T 01782-237777 **W** www.stokemuseums.org.uk/gpm
  The last complete Victorian pottery factory in Britain

Potteries Museum and Art Gallery, Bethesda Street ST1 3DW
  T 01782-232323 **W** www.stokemuseums.org.uk/pmag
  Pottery, china and porcelain collections and a Mark XVI Spitfire

The Wedgwood Museum, Barlaston ST12 9ER **T** 01782-371900
  W www.wedgwoodmuseum.org.uk
  The story of Josiah Wedgwood and the company he founded

SUNDERLAND

Sunderland Museum and Winter Gardens, Burdon Road SR1 1PP
  T 0191-553 2323 **W** www.sunderlandculture.org.uk
  Fine and decorative art, local history and gardens

TELFORD

Ironbridge Gorge Museums, TF8 7DQ **T** 01952-433424
  W www.ironbridge.org.uk
  Ten museums including The Museum of the Gorge; The Iron Bridge and Tollhouse; Blists Hill (late Victorian working town); Brosely Pipeworks; Coalbrookdale Museum of Iron; Coalport China Museum; Jackfield Tile Museum; Tar Tunnel; Darby Houses

WAKEFIELD

Hepworth Wakefield, Gallery Walk WF1 5AW **T** 01924-247360
  W www.hepworthwakefield.org
  Historic and modern art; temporary exhibitions of contemporary art

National Coal Mining Museum for England, New Road, Overton WF4 4RH **T** 01924-848806 **W** www.ncm.org.uk
  Includes underground tours of one of Britain's oldest working mines

Yorkshire Sculpture Park, West Bretton WF4 4LG **T** 01924-832631
  W www.ysp.co.uk
  Open-air sculpture gallery including works by Henry Moore, Barbara Hepworth and others in 500 acres of parkland

WEYBRIDGE

Brooklands Museum, Brooklands Road KT13 0QN **T** 01932-857381
  W www.brooklandsmuseum.com
  Birthplace of British motorsport; world's first purpose-built motor racing circuit

WILMSLOW

Quarry Bank Mill and Styal Estate, Wilmslow SK9 4LA
  T 01625-527468 **W** www.nationaltrust.org.uk/quarry-bank
  Europe's most powerful working waterwheel owned by the National Trust illustrating history of cotton industry; costumed guides at restored Apprentice House

WINCHESTER

Winchester Science Centre and Planetarium, Telegraph Way, Hants SO21 1HZ **T** 01962-863791
  W www.winchestersciencecentre.org
  Interactive science centre and planetarium

WORCESTER

City Art Gallery and Museum, Foregate Street WR1 1DT
  T 01905-25371
  W www.museumsworcestershire.org.uk/museums/worcester-city-art-gallery-museum
  Includes the Regimental museum, 19th-century chemist shop and changing art exhibitions

Museum of Royal Worcester, Severn Street WR1 2ND
 T 01905-21247 **W** www.museumofroyalworcester.org
  Worcester porcelain from 1751 to the present day
YEOVIL
Fleet Air Arm Museum, RNAS Yeovilton, Somerset BA22 8HT
 T 01935-840565 **W** www.fleetairarm.com
  History of naval aviation; historic aircraft, including
  Concorde 002
YORK
Beningbrough Hall, Beningbrough YO30 1DD **T** 01904-472027
 W www.nationaltrust.org.uk/beningbrough-hall
  18th-century house with portraits from the National
  Portrait Gallery; parklands and gardens
JORVIK Viking Centre, Coppergate YO1 9WT **T** 01904-615505
 W www.jorvikvikingcentre.co.uk
  Reconstruction of Viking York based on archaeological
  evidence
*National Railway Museum, Leeman Road YO26 4XJ
 T 0800-047 8124 **W** www.railwaymuseum.org.uk
  Includes locomotives, rolling stock and carriages
York Art Gallery, Exhibition Square, YO1 7EW **T** 01904 687687
 W www.yorkartgallery.org.uk
  600 years of British and European painting; ceramics and
  sculpture
York Castle Museum, Eye of York YO1 9RY **T** 01904-687687
 W www.yorkcastlemuseum.org.uk
  Includes Kirkgate, a reconstructed Victorian street;
  costume and military collections
Yorkshire Museum, Museum Gardens YO1 7FR **T** 01904-687687
 W www.yorkshiremuseum.org.uk
  Yorkshire life from Roman to medieval times; geology
  and biology; York observatory

WALES
* Members of National Museum Wales, a public body that
receives its core funding from the Welsh government

ABERYSTWYTH
Ceredigion Museum, Terrace Road SY23 2AQ **T** 01970-633088
 W www.ceredigionmuseum.wales
  Local history, housed in a restored Edwardian theatre
Silver Mountain Experience, Ponterwyd SY23 3AB **T** 01970-890620
 W www.silvermountainexperience.co.uk
  Tours of an 18th-century silver mine, with interactive
  challenges and games for children
BLAENAFON
*Big Pit National Coal Museum, Torfaen NP4 9XP
 T 030-0111 2333 **W** www.museum.wales/bigpit
  Colliery with an underground tour and exhibitions of
  modern mining equipment
BODELWYDDAN
Bodelwyddan Castle, Denbighshire LL18 5YA **T** 01745-584060
 W www.bodelwyddan-castle.co.uk
  Art gallery within an historic house; features temporary art
  exhibits
CAERLEON
*National Roman Legion Museum, NP18 1AE **T** 030-0111 2333
 W www.museum.wales/roman
  Features the oldest recorded piece of writing in Wales;
  pottery, Roman era gemstones
CARDIFF
*National Museum Cardiff, Cathays Park CF10 3NP
 T 030-0111 2333 **W** www.museum.wales/cardiff
  Houses Wales's national art, archaeology and natural
  history collections
*St Fagans: National History Museum, St Fagans CF5 6XB
 T 030-0111 2333 **W** www.museum.wales/stfagans
  Open-air museum with re-erected buildings, agricultural
  equipment and costume

TECHNIQUEST, Stuart Street CF10 5BW **T** 029-2047 5475
 W www.techniquest.org
  Interactive science exhibits, planetarium and science
  theatre
CRICCIETH
Lloyd George Museum, Llanystumdwy LL52 0SH **T** 01766-522071
 W www.gwynedd.llyw.cymru
  Childhood home of David Lloyd George
DRE-FACH FELINDRE
*National Wool Museum, Llandysul SA44 5UP **T** 030-0111 2333
 W www.museum.wales/wool
  Exhibitions, a working woollen mill and craft workshops
LLANBERIS
*National Slate Museum, Gwynedd LL55 4TY **T** 030-0111 2333
 W www.museum.wales/slate
  Former slate quarry with original machinery and plant;
  slate crafts demonstrations; working waterwheel
LLANDRINDOD WELLS
National Cycle Collection, Automobile Palace, Temple Street
 LD1 5DL **T** 01597-825531 **W** www.cyclemuseum.org.uk
  Approximately 250 bicycles on display, from 1819 to the
  present
PRESTEIGNE
Judge's Lodging Museum, Broad Street LD8 2AD **T** 01544-260650
 W www.judgeslodging.org.uk
  Restored apartments, courtroom, cells and servants'
  quarters
SWANSEA
Glynn Vivian Art Gallery, Alexandra Road SA1 5DZ
 T 01792-516900 **W** www.swansea.gov.uk/glynnvivian
  Fine art and ceramics from 1700 to the present
*National Waterfront Museum, Oystermouth Road SA1 3RD
 T 030-0111 2333 **W** www.museum.wales/swansea
  Wales during the Industrial Revolution
Swansea Museum, Victoria Road SA1 1SN **T** 01792-653763
 W www.swanseamuseum.co.uk
  Paintings, Egyptian artifacts, transport and nautical
  collections; war time Swansea
TENBY
Tenby Museum and Art Gallery, Castle Hill SA70 7BP **T** 01834-
 842809 **W** www.tenbymuseum.org.uk
  Local archaeology, history, geology and art

SCOTLAND
* Members of National Museums Scotland or National
Galleries of Scotland, which are non-departmental public
bodies funded by, and accountable to, the Scottish government

ABERDEEN
Aberdeen Art Gallery, Schoolhill AB10 1FQ **T** 0300-020 0293
 W www.aagm.co.uk
  Paintings, sculptures and graphics; temporary exhibitions
Aberdeen Maritime Museum, Shiprow AB11 5BY **T** 0300-020 0293
 W www.aagm.co.uk
  Maritime history, including shipbuilding and North Sea
  oil
AYR
Robert Burns Birthplace Museum, Murdoch's Lone, Alloway
 KA7 4PQ **T** 0129-244 3700 **W** www.burnsmuseum.org.uk
  Comprises Burns Cottage, birthplace of the poet, gardens
  and a museum
EDINBURGH
Britannia, Leith EH6 6JJ **T** 0131-555 5566
 W www.royalyachtbritannia.co.uk
  Former royal yacht with royal barge and royal family
  picture gallery

City Art Centre, Market Street EH1 1DE **T** 0131-529 3993
W www.edinburghmuseums.org.uk
Rolling programme of exhibitions including historic and modern photography; contemporary art, design and architecture

Museum of Childhood, High Street EH1 1TG **T** 0131-529 4142
W www.edinburghmuseums.org.uk
Toys, games, clothes and exhibits relating to the social history of childhood

Museum of Edinburgh, Canongate, Royal Mile EH8 8DD
T 0131-529 4143 **W** www.edinburghmuseums.org.uk
Local history, silver, glass and Scottish pottery

National Museum of Flight, East Fortune Airfield, East Lothian
EH39 5LF **T** 0300-123 6789 **W** www.nms.ac.uk/flight
Aviation from the early 20th century to the present

National Museum of Scotland, Chambers Street EH1 1JF
T 0300-123 6789 **W** www.nms.ac.uk/scotland
Scottish history; world cultures; natural world; art and design; science and technology

National War Museum of Scotland, Edinburgh Castle EH1 2NG
T 0300-123 6789 **W** www.nms.ac.uk/war
Scotland's military history housed within Edinburgh Castle

Scottish National Gallery, The Mound EH2 2EL **T** 0131-624 6200
W www.nationalgalleries.org
Fine art from the early Renaissance to the end of the 19th century

Scottish National Gallery of Modern Art, Belford Road EH4 3DR
T 0131-624 6200 **W** www.nationalgalleries.org
Contemporary art featuring British, French and Russian collections; outdoor sculpture park

Scottish National Portrait Gallery, Queen Street EH2 1JD
T 0131-624 6200 **W** www.nationalgalleries.org/portraitgallery
Portraits of eminent people in Scottish history; Photography Gallery; Victorian Library

The Writers' Museum, Lady Stair's Close EH1 2PA
T 0131-529 4901 **W** www.edinburghmuseums.org.uk
Exhibitions relating to Robert Burns, Sir Walter Scott and Robert Louis Stevenson

FORT WILLIAM
West Highland Museum, Cameron Square PH33 6AJ
T 01397-702169 **W** www.westhighlandmuseum.org.uk
Highland life; Military, Victorian and Jacobite collections

GLASGOW
Burrell Collection, Pollokshaws Road G43 1AT **T** 0141-287 2550
W www.glasgowlife.org.uk/museums
Paintings by major artists; medieval art, Chinese and Islamic art

Gallery of Modern Art, Royal Exchange Square G1 3AH
T 0141-287 3050 **W** www.glasgowlife.org.uk/museums
Collection of contemporary Scottish and world art

Hunterian, University of Glasgow G12 8QQ **T** 0141-330 4221
W www.gla.ac.uk/hunterian
Rennie Mackintosh and Whistler collections; coins; Scottish paintings; Pacific ethnographic collection; archaeology; medicine

Kelvingrove Art Gallery & Museum, Argyle Street G3 8AG
T 0141-357 3929 **W** www.glasgowlife.org.uk/museums
Includes Old Masters; natural history; arms and armour

Museum of Piping, McPhater Street G4 0HW **T** 0141-353 0220
W www.thepipingcentre.co.uk
The history and origins of bagpiping

Museum of Rural Life, Philipshill Road, East Kilbride G76 9HR
T 0300-123 6789 **W** www.nms.ac.uk/rural
History of rural life and work

People's Palace and Winter Gardens, Glasgow Green G40 1AT
T 0141-276 0788 **W** www.glasgowlife.org.uk/museums
Social history of Glasgow since 1750

Riverside Museum, 100 Pointhouse Place G3 8RS **T** 0141-287 2720
W www.glasgowlife.org.uk/museums
Scotland's museum of transport and travel; the Tall Ship *Glenlee*, a Clyde-built sailing ship, is berthed alongside

St Mungo Museum of Religious Art and Life, Castle Street G4 0RH
T 0141-276 1625 **W** www.glasgowlife.org.uk/museums
Exhibits detailing the world's major religions; oldest Zen garden in Britain

NORTHERN IRELAND
* Members of National Museums Northern Ireland, a public body sponsored by the Department for Communities, Northern Ireland executive.

ARMAGH
Armagh County Museum, The Mall East BT61 9BE
T 028-3752 3070 **W** www.nimc.co.uk
Local history; fine art; archaeology; crafts

BANGOR
North Down Museum, Town Hall BT20 4BT **T** 028-9127 1200
W www.andculture.org.uk
Local history from the Bronze age to the present

BELFAST
Titanic Belfast, Queen's Road, Titanic Quarter BT3 9EP
T 028-9076 6386 **W** www.titanicbelfast.com
The story of RMS *Titanic* from her conception to demise; Shipyard ride and ocean exploration centre

Ulster Museum, Botanic Gardens BT9 5AB **T** 0289-044 0000
W www.nmni.com/um
Irish antiquities; natural and local history; fine and applied arts

W5, Queen's Quay BT3 9QQ **T** 028-9046 7700
W www.w5online.co.uk
Interactive science and technology centre

HOLYWOOD
Ulster Folk and Transport Museum, Cultra BT18 0EU
T 028-9042 8428 **W** www.nmni.com/uftm
Open-air museum with original buildings from Ulster town and rural life *c*.1900; indoor galleries including Irish rail and road transport

LONDONDERRY
The Tower Museum, Union Hall Place BT48 6LU **T** 028-7137 2411
W www.derrystrabane.com/towermuseum
Tells the story of Ireland through the history of Londonderry

NEWTOWNARDS
The Somme Heritage Centre, Bangor Road BT23 7PH
T 028-9182 3202 **W** www.sommeassociation.com
Commemorates the part played by Irish forces in the First World War

OMAGH
Ulster American Folk Park, Castletown, Co. Tyrone BT78 5QU
T 028-8224 3292 **W** www.nmni.com/uafp
Open-air museum telling the story of Ulster's emigrants to America; restored or recreated dwellings and workshops; ship and dockside gallery

SIGHTS OF LONDON

For historic buildings, museums and galleries in London, *see* the Historic Buildings and Monuments, and Museums and Galleries sections.

BRIDGES

The bridges over the Thames in London, from east to west, are:

Tower Bridge (268m/880ft by 18m/60ft), architect: Horace Jones, engineer: John Wolfe Barry, opened 1894

London Bridge (262m/860ft by 32m/105ft), original 13th-century stone bridge rebuilt and opened 1831 (engineer: John Rennie), reconstructed in Arizona when current London Bridge opened 1973 (architect: Lord Holford, engineer: Mott, Hay and Anderson)

Cannon Street Railway Bridge (261m/855ft), engineers: John Hawkshaw and John Wolfe Barry, originally named Alexandra Bridge, opened 1866; renovated 1979–82

Southwark Bridge (244m/800ft by 17m/56ft), engineer: John Rennie, originally named Queen Street Bridge, opened 1819; rebuilt 1912–21 (architect: Ernest George, engineer: Mott, Hay and Anderson)

Millennium Bridge (325m/1,066ft by 4m/13ft), architect: Foster and Partners, engineer: Ove Arup and Partners, opened 2000; reopened after modification 2002

Blackfriars Railway Bridge (284m/933ft), engineers: John Wolfe Barry and Henri Marc Brunel, originally named St Paul's Railway Bridge, opened 1886

Blackfriars Bridge (294m/963ft by 32m/105ft), engineer: Robert Mylne, opened 1769; rebuilt 1869 (engineer: Joseph Cubitt); widened 1909

Waterloo Bridge (366m/1,200ft by 24m/80ft), engineer: John Rennie, opened 1817; rebuilt 1945 (architect: Sir Giles Gilbert Scott, engineer: Rendel, Palmer and Triton)

Golden Jubilee Bridges (325m/1,066ft by 4.7m/15ft), architect: Lifschutz Davidson, engineer: WSP Group, opened 2002; commonly known as the Hungerford Footbridges

Hungerford Railway Bridge (366m/1,200ft), engineer: Isambard Kingdom Brunel, suspension bridge opened 1845; present railway bridge opened 1864 (engineer: John Hawkshaw); widened in 1886

Westminster Bridge (228m/748ft by 26m/85ft), engineer: Charles Labelye, opened 1750; rebuilt 1862 (architect: Charles Barry, engineer: Thomas Page)

Lambeth Bridge (237m/776ft by 18m/60ft), engineer: Peter W. Barlow, original suspension bridge opened 1862; current structure opened 1932 (architect: Reginald Blomfield, engineer: George W. Humphreys)

Vauxhall Bridge (231m/759ft by 24m/80ft), engineer: James Walker, opened 1816; redesigned and opened 1906 (architect: William Edward Riley, engineers: Alexander Binnie and Maurice Fitzmaurice)

Grosvenor Railway Bridge (213m/699ft), engineer: John Fowler, opened 1860; rebuilt 1965; also known as the Victoria Railway Bridge

Chelsea Bridge (213m/699ft by 25m/83ft), original suspension bridge opened 1858 (engineer: Thomas Page); rebuilt 1937 (architects: George Topham Forrest and E. P. Wheeler, engineer: Rendel, Palmer and Triton)

Albert Bridge (216m/710ft by 12m/40ft), engineer: Rowland M. Ordish, opened 1873; restructured 1884 (engineer: Joseph Bazalgette); strengthened 1971–3

Battersea Bridge (204m/670ft by 17m/56ft), engineer: Henry Holland, opened 1771; rebuilt 1890 (engineer: Joseph Bazalgette)

Battersea Railway Bridge (204m/670ft), engineer: William Baker, opened 1863; also known as Cremorne Bridge

Wandsworth Bridge (189m/619ft by 18m/60ft), engineer: Julian Tolmé, opened 1873; rebuilt 1940 (architect: E. P. Wheeler, engineer: T. Pierson Frank)

Putney Railway Bridge (229m/750ft), engineers: W. H. Thomas and William Jacomb, opened 1889; also known as the Fulham Railway Bridge or the Iron Bridge – it has no official name

Putney Bridge (213m/699ft by 23m/74ft), architect: Jacob Ackworth, original wooden bridge opened 1729; current granite structure completed in 1886 (engineer: Joseph Bazalgette). The starting point of the Boat Race

Hammersmith Bridge (210m/688ft by 10m/33ft), engineer: William Tierney Clarke; the first suspension bridge in London, originally built 1827; rebuilt 1887 (engineer: Joseph Bazalgette)

Barnes Railway Bridge (also footbridge, 110m/360ft), engineer: Joseph Locke, opened 1849; rebuilt 1895 (engineers: London and South Western Railway); the original structure stands unused

Chiswick Bridge (137m/450ft by 21m/70ft), architect: Herbert Baker, engineer: Alfred Dryland, opened 1933. The bridge marks the end point of the Boat Race

Kew Railway Bridge (175m/575ft), engineer: W. R. Galbraith, opened 1869

Kew Bridge (110m/360ft by 17m/56ft), engineer: Robert Tunstall, original timber bridge built 1759; replaced by a Portland stone structure in 1789 (engineer: James Paine); current granite bridge renamed King Edward VII Bridge in 1903, but still known as Kew Bridge (engineers: John Wolfe Barry and Cuthbert Brereton)

Richmond Lock (91m/300ft by 11m/36ft), engineer: F. G. M. Stoney, lock and footbridge opened 1894

Twickenham Bridge (85m/280ft by 21m/70ft), architect: Maxwell Ayrton, engineer: Alfred Dryland, opened 1933

Richmond Railway Bridge (91m/300ft), engineer: Joseph Locke, opened 1848; rebuilt 1906–8 (engineer: J. W. Jacomb-Hood)

Richmond Bridge (85m/280ft by 10m/33ft), architect: James Paine, engineer: Kenton Couse, built 1777; widened 1939

Teddington Lock (198m/650ft), engineer: G. Pooley, two footbridges opened 1889; marks the end of the tidal reach of the Thames

Kingston Railway Bridge architects: J. E. Errington and W. R. Galbraith, engineer: Thomas Brassey, opened 1863

Kingston Bridge (116m/382ft), engineer: Edward Lapidge, built 1825–8; widened 1911–14 (engineers: Basil Mott and David Hay) and 1999–2001

Hampton Court Bridge, engineers: Samuel Stevens and Benjamin Ludgator, built 1753; replaced by iron bridge 1865; present bridge opened 1933 (architect: Edwin Lutyens, engineer: W. P. Robinson)

CEMETERIES

In 1832, in response to the overcrowding of burial grounds in London, the government authorised the establishment of seven non-denominational cemeteries that would encircle the city. These large cemeteries, known as the 'magnificent seven', were seen by many Victorian families as places in which to demonstrate their wealth and stature, and as a result there are some highly ornate graves and tombs.

THE MAGNIFICENT SEVEN

Abney Park, Stoke Newington, N16 (13ha/32 acres), established 1840; tomb of William and Catherine Booth, founders of the Salvation Army, and memorials to many nonconformists and dissenters

Brompton, Old Brompton Road, SW10 (16.5ha/40 acres), established 1840; graves of Sir Henry Cole, Emmeline Pankhurst, John Wisden

Highgate, Swains Lane, N6 (15ha/38 acres), established 1839; graves of Douglas Adams, George Eliot, Eric Hobsbawm, Michael Faraday, Karl Marx, Ralph Miliband and Christina Rossetti

Kensal Green, Harrow Road, W10 (29ha/72 acres), established 1833; tombs of Charles Babbage, Isambard Kingdom Brunel, Wilkie Collins, George Cruikshank, Tom Hood, Leigh Hunt, Harold Pinter, William Makepeace Thackeray, Anthony Trollope

Nunhead, Linden Grove, SE15 (21ha/52 acres), established 1840; closed in 1969, restored and opened for burials

Tower Hamlets, Southern Grove, E3 (11ha/27 acres), established 1841, 350,000 interments; bombed heavily during the Second World War and closed to burials in 1966; now a nature reserve

West Norwood Cemetery and Crematorium, Norwood High Street, SE27 (17ha/42 acres), established 1837; tombs of C. W. Alcock, Mrs Beeton, Sir Henry Tate and Joseph Whitaker (*Whitaker's Almanack*)

OTHER CEMETERIES

Bunhill Fields, City Road, EC1 (1.6ha/4 acres), 17th-century nonconformist burial ground containing the graves of William Blake, John Bunyan and Daniel Defoe

City of London Cemetery and Crematorium, Aldersbrook Road, E12 (81ha/200 acres), established 1856; grave of Bobby Moore

Golders Green Crematorium, Hoop Lane, NW11 (5ha/12 acres), established 1902; retains the ashes of Kingsley Amis, Lionel Bart, Enid Blyton, Marc Bolan, Sigmund Freud, Keith Moon, Ivor Novello, Bram Stoker and H. G. Wells

Hampstead, Fortune Green Road, NW6 (10.5ha/26 acres), established 1876; graves of Alan Coren, Kate Greenaway, Joseph Lister and Marie Lloyd

MARKETS

Billingsgate, Trafalgar Way, E14 (fish), a market site for over 1,000 years, with the Lower Thames Street site dating from 1876; moved to the Isle of Dogs in 1982; owned and run by the City of London Corporation

Borough, Southwark Street, SE1 (vegetables, fruit, meat, dairy, bread), established on present site in 1756; privately owned and run

Brick Lane, E1 (jewellery, vintage clothes, bric-a-brac, food), open Saturday and Sunday

Brixton, SW9 (African-Caribbean food, music, clothing), open Monday to Saturday

Broadway, E8 (food, fashion, crafts), re-established in 2004, open Saturday

Camden Lock, NW1 (second-hand clothing, jewellery, alternative fashion, crafts), established in 1973

Columbia Road, E2 (flowers), dates from 19th century; became dedicated flower market in the 20th century

Covent Garden, WC2 (antiques, handicrafts, jewellery, clothing, food), originally a fruit and vegetable market (*see* New Covent Garden market); it has been trading in its current form since 1980

Grays, Davies Street, W1K (antiques), indoor market in listed building, established 1977

Greenwich, SE10 (crafts, fashion, food), market revived in the 1980s

Leadenhall, Gracechurch Street, EC3V (meat, poultry, cheese, clothing), site of market since 14th century; present hall built 1881; owned and run by the City of London Corporation

New Covent Garden, SW8 (wholesale vegetables, fruit, flowers), established in 1670 under a charter of Charles II; relocated from central London in 1974

New Spitalfields, E10 (vegetables, fruit), established 1682, modernised 1928, moved out of the City to Leyton in 1991, open Monday to Saturday

Old Spitalfields, E1 (arts, crafts, books, clothes, organic food, antiques), continues to trade on the original Spitalfields site on Commercial Street

Petticoat Lane, Middlesex Street, E1, a market has existed on the site for over 500 years, now a Sunday morning market selling almost anything

Portobello Road, W11, originally for herbs and horse-trading from 1870; became famous for antiques after the closure of the Caledonian Market in 1948

Smithfield, EC1 (meat, poultry), built 1866–8, refurbished 1993–4; the site of St Bartholomew's Fair from 12th to 19th century; owned and run by the City of London Corporation, open Monday to Friday

MONUMENTS

CENOTAPH

Whitehall, SW1. The Cenotaph (from the Greek meaning 'empty tomb') was built to commemorate 'The Glorious Dead' and is a memorial to all ranks of the sea, land and air forces who gave their lives in the service of the Empire during the First World War. Designed by Sir Edwin Lutyens and constructed in plaster as a temporary memorial in 1919, it was replaced by a permanent structure of Portland stone and unveiled by George V on 11 November 1920, Armistice Day. An additional inscription was made in 1946 to commemorate those who gave their lives in the Second World War

FOURTH PLINTH

Trafalgar Square, WC2. The fourth plinth (1841) was designed for an equestrian statue that was never built due to lack of funds. From 1999 temporary works have been displayed on the plinth including *Ecce Homo* (Mark Wallinger), *Monument* (Rachel Whiteread), *Alison Lapper Pregnant* (Marc Quinn) and *One & Other* (Antony Gormley). Since March 2018 *The Invisible Enemy Should Not Exist* (Michael Rakowitz) a recreation of the Lamassu, a winged bull and protective deity that stood at the entrance to the Nergal Gate of Nineveh from *c.*700 BC until it was destroyed by Islamic State in 2015, has occupied the plinth. The Lamassu is made from 10,500 empty Iraqi date syrup cans, representing a once-renowned industry now decimated by war. In 2020 it will be replaced by *The End* (Heather Phillipson); a sculpture portraying a giant dollop of cream upon which sits a fly, a cherry and a drone that will film Trafalgar Square from above

LONDON MONUMENT

(Commonly called the Monument), Monument Street, EC3. Built to designs by Sir Christopher Wren and Robert Hooke between 1671 and 1677, the Monument commemorates the Great Fire of London, which broke out in Pudding Lane on 2 September 1666. The fluted Doric column is 36.6m

(120ft) high, the moulded cylinder above the balcony supporting a flaming vase of gilt bronze is an additional 12.8m (42ft), and the column is based on a square plinth 12.2m (40ft) high (with fine carvings on the west face), making a total height of 61.6m (202ft) – the tallest isolated stone column in the world, with views of London from a gallery at the top (311 steps)

OTHER MONUMENTS
(sculptor's name in parentheses):

7 July Memorial (Carmody Groarke), Hyde Park

Afghanistan and Iraq War Memorial (Day), Victoria Embankment

African and Caribbean War Memorial, Windrush Square, Brixton

Viscount Alanbrooke (Roberts-Jones), Whitehall

Albert Memorial (Scott), Kensington Gore

Battle of Britain (Day), Victoria Embankment

Beatty (Wheeler), Trafalgar Square

Belgian Gratitude (setting by Blomfield, statue by Rousseau), Victoria Embankment

Boadicea (or Boudicca), *Queen of the Iceni* (Thornycroft), Westminster Bridge

Brunel (Marochetti), Victoria Embankment

Burghers of Calais (Rodin), Victoria Tower Gardens, Westminster

Burns (Steell), Embankment Gardens

Canada Memorial (Granche), Green Park

Carlyle (Boehm), Chelsea Embankment

Cavalry (Jones), Hyde Park

Edith Cavell (Frampton), St Martin's Place

Charles I (Le Sueur), Trafalgar Square

Charles II (Gibbons), Royal Hospital, Chelsea

Churchill (Roberts-Jones), Parliament Square

Cleopatra's Needle (20.9m/68.5ft high, *c.*1500 BC, erected in London in 1878; the sphinxes are Victorian), Thames Embankment

Clive (Tweed), King Charles Street

Captain Cook (Brock), The Mall

Oliver Cromwell (Thornycroft), outside Westminster Hall

Cunningham (Belsky), Trafalgar Square

Gen. Charles de Gaulle (Conner), Carlton Gardens

Diana, Princess of Wales Memorial Fountain (Gustafson Porter), Hyde Park

Disraeli, Earl of Beaconsfield (Raggi), Parliament Square

Duke of Cambridge (Jones), Whitehall

Duke of York (37.8m/124ft column, with statue by Westmacott), Carlton House Terrace

Edward VII (Mackennal), Waterloo Place

Elizabeth I (Kerwin, 1586, oldest outdoor statue in London; from Ludgate), Fleet Street

Eros (Shaftesbury Memorial) (Gilbert), Piccadilly Circus

Lord Dowding (Winter), Strand

Millicent Fawcett (Wearing), Parliament Square

Marechal/Marshall Foch (Mallisard, copy of one in Cassel, France), Grosvenor Gardens

Charles James Fox (Westmacott), Bloomsbury Square

Yuri Gagarin (Novikov, copy of Russian statue), The Mall

Mahatma Gandhi (Jackson), Parliament Square

George III (Cotes Wyatt), Cockspur Street

George IV (Chantrey), Trafalgar Square

George V (Reid Dick and Scott), Old Palace Yard

George VI (McMillan), Carlton Gardens

Gladstone (Thornycroft), Strand

Guards' (Crimea; Bell), Waterloo Place

Guards Division (Ledward, figures, Bradshaw, cenotaph), Horse Guards' Parade

Haig (Hardiman), Whitehall

Sir Arthur (Bomber) Harris (Winter), Strand

Gen. Henry Havelock (Behnes), Trafalgar Square

International Brigades Memorial (Spanish Civil War) (Ian Walters), Jubilee Gardens, South Bank

Irving (Brock), north side of National Portrait Gallery

Isis (Gudgeon), Hyde Park

James II (Gibbons), Trafalgar Square

Jellicoe (McMillan), Trafalgar Square

Samuel Johnson (Fitzgerald), opposite St Clement Danes

Kitchener (Tweed), Horse Guards' Parade

Abraham Lincoln (Saint-Gaudens, copy of one in Chicago), Parliament Square

Mandela (Walters), Parliament Square

Milton (Montford), St Giles, Cripplegate

Mountbatten (Belsky), Foreign Office Green

Gen. Charles James Napier (Adams), Trafalgar Square

Nelson (Railton), Trafalgar Square, with Landseer's lions (cast from guns recovered from the wreck of the *Royal George*)

Florence Nightingale (Walker), Waterloo Place

Palmerston (Woolner), Parliament Square

Sir Keith Park (Johnson), Waterloo Place

Peel (Noble), Parliament Square

Pitt (Chantrey), Hanover Square

Portal (Nemon), Embankment Gardens

Prince Albert (Bacon), Holborn Circus

Queen Elizabeth Gate (Lund and Wynne), Hyde Park Corner

Queen Mother (Jackson), Carlton Gardens

Raleigh (McMillan), Greenwich

Richard I (Coeur de Lion) (Marochetti), Old Palace Yard

Roberts (Bates), Horse Guards' Parade

Franklin D. Roosevelt (Reid Dick), Grosvenor Square

Royal Air Force (Blomfield), Victoria Embankment

Royal Air Force Bomber Command Memorial (O'Connor), Green Park

Royal Artillery (Great War) (Jagger and Pearson), Hyde Park Corner

Royal Artillery (South Africa) (Colton), The Mall

Captain Scott (Lady Scott), Waterloo Place

Shackleton (Jagger), Kensington Gore

Shakespeare (Fontana, copy of one by Scheemakers in Westminster Abbey), Leicester Square

Smuts (Epstein), Parliament Square

Sullivan (Goscombe John), Victoria Embankment

Trenchard (McMillan), Victoria Embankment

Victoria Memorial (Webb and Brock), in front of Buckingham Palace

Raoul Wallenberg (Jackson), Great Cumberland Place

George Washington (Houdon copy), Trafalgar Square

Wellington (Boehm), Hyde Park Corner

Wellington (Chantrey), outside Royal Exchange

John Wesley (Adams Acton), City Road

Westminster School (Crimea) (Scott), Broad Sanctuary

William III (Bacon), St James's Square

Wolseley (Goscombe John), Horse Guards' Parade

PARKS, GARDENS AND OPEN SPACES

CITY OF LONDON CORPORATION OPEN SPACES
W www.cityoflondon.gov.uk

Ashtead Common (202ha/500 acres), Surrey

Burnham Beeches and *Fleet Wood* (220ha/540 acres), Bucks. Acquired by the City of London for the benefit of the public in 1880, Fleet Wood (26ha/65 acres) being presented in 1921

Coulsdon Common (51ha/127 acres), Surrey

Epping Forest (2,476ha/6,118 acres), Essex. Acquired by the City of London in 1878 and opened to the public in 1882. The Queen Elizabeth Hunting Lodge, built for Henry VIII in 1543, lies at the edge of the forest. The present forest is 19.3km (12 miles) long by around 3km (2 miles) wide, approximately one-tenth of its original area

*Epping Forest Buffer Land (735ha/1,816 acres), Waltham Abbey/Epping

Farthing Downs and New Hill (95ha/235 acres), Surrey

Hampstead Heath (275ha/680 acres), NW3. Including Golders Hill (15ha/36 acres) and Parliament Hill (110ha/271 acres)

Highgate Wood (28ha/70 acres), N6/N10

Kenley Common (56ha/139 acres), Surrey

Queen's Park (12ha/30 acres), NW6

Riddlesdown (43ha/104 acres), Surrey

Spring Park (20ha/50 acres), Kent

Stoke Common (80ha/198 acres), Bucks. Ownership was transferred to the City of London in 2007

West Ham Park (31ha/77 acres), E15

West Wickham Common (10ha/26 acres), Kent

Also over 150 smaller open spaces within the City of London, including *Finsbury Circus* and *St Dunstan-in-the-East*

* Includes Copped Hall Park, Woodredon Estate and Warlies Park

OTHER PARKS AND GARDENS

CHELSEA PHYSIC GARDEN, 66 Royal Hospital Road SW3 4HS **T** 020-7352 5646 **W** www.chelseaphysicgarden.co.uk
A garden of general botanical research and education, maintaining a wide range of rare and unusual plants; established in 1673 by the Society of Apothecaries

HAMPTON COURT PARK AND GARDENS (328ha/810 acres), Surrey KT8 9AU **T** 0844-482 7777 **W** www.hrp.org.uk
Also known as Home Park, the park lies beyond the palace's formal gardens. It contains a herd of deer and a 750-year-old oak tree from the original park

HOLLAND PARK (22.5ha/54 acres), Ilchester Place W8 **T** 020-7361 3000 **W** www.rbkc.gov.uk
The largest park in the Royal Borough of Kensington and Chelsea, includes the Kyoto Garden

KEW, ROYAL BOTANIC GARDENS (120ha/300 acres), Richmond, Surrey TW9 3AB **T** 020-8332 5655 **W** www.kew.org
Founded in 1759 and declared a UNESCO World Heritage Site in 2003

THAMES BARRIER PARK (9ha/22acres), North Woolwich Road E16 2HP **T** 020-7476 3741 Opened in 2000, landscaped gardens with spectacular views of the Thames Barrier

ROYAL PARKS

W www.royalparks.org.uk

Bushy Park (450ha/1,099 acres), Middx. Adjoins Hampton Court; contains an avenue of horse-chestnuts enclosed in a fourfold avenue of limes planted by William III

Green Park (19ha/47 acres), W1. Between Piccadilly and St James's Park, with Constitution Hill leading to Hyde Park Corner

Greenwich Park (74ha/183 acres), SE10. Enclosed by Humphrey, Duke of Gloucester, and laid out by Charles II from the designs of Le Nôtre. On a hill in Greenwich Park is the Royal Observatory (founded 1675). Its buildings are now managed by the National Maritime Museum (**T** 020-8858 4422 **W** www.rmg.co.uk
) and the earliest building is named Flamsteed House, after John Flamsteed (1646–1719), the first astronomer royal

Hyde Park (142ha/350 acres), W1/W2. From Park Lane to Kensington Gardens and incorporating the Serpentine lake, Apsley House, the Achilles Statue, Rotten Row and the Ladies' Mile; fine gateway at Hyde Park Corner. To the north-east is Marble Arch, originally erected by George IV at the entrance to Buckingham Palace and re-erected in the present position in 1851. At Hyde Park Corner stands Wellington Arch, built in 1825–7, it opened to the public in 2012 following major renovation

Kensington Gardens (107ha/265 acres), W2/W8. From the western boundary of Hyde Park to Kensington Palace; contains the Albert Memorial, Serpentine Gallery, Diana, Princess of Wales' Memorial Playground and the Peter Pan statue

The Regent's Park and *Primrose Hill* (197ha/487 acres), NW1. From Marylebone Road to Primrose Hill surrounded by the Outer Circle; divided by the Broad Walk leading to the Zoological Gardens

Richmond Park (1,000ha/2,500 acres), Surrey. Designated a National Nature Reserve, a Site of Special Scientific Interest and a Special Area of Conservation

St James's Park (23ha/57 acres), SW1. From Whitehall to Buckingham Palace; ornamental lake of 4.9ha (12 acres); the Mall leads from Admiralty Arch to Buckingham Palace

PLACES OF HISTORICAL AND CULTURAL INTEREST

1 Canada Square

Canary Wharf E14 5AB **T** 020-7418 2000
W www.canarywharf.com
Also known as 'Canary Wharf', the steel and glass skyscraper is designed to sway 35cm in the strongest winds

20 Fenchurch Street

W https:/skygarden.london
Designed by architect Rafael Viñoly the skyscraper was completed in March 2014. The top three storeys are home to the Sky Garden, London's highest public garden with viewing platforms, bars, restaurants and an open air terrace. Access to the Sky Garden is free, but tickets must be booked in advance

30 St Mary Axe

EC3A 8BF **W** www.30stmaryaxe.com
Completed in 2004 and commonly known as the 'Gherkin', each of the floors rotates five degrees from the one below

122 Leadenhall Street

EC3V 4AB **T** 020-7220 8950 **W** www.theleadenhallbuilding.com
The distinctive 225m (737ft) asymmetrical Leadenhall Building, designed by architects Rogers Stirk Harbour & Partners, was completed in 2014

Alexandra Palace

Alexandra Palace Way N22 7AY **T** 020-8365 2121
W www.alexandrapalace.com
The Victorian palace was severely damaged by fire in 1980 but was restored, and reopened in 1988. Alexandra Palace now provides modern facilities for exhibitions, conferences, banquets and leisure activities. There is a winter ice rink, a boating lake and a conservation area. Restoration of the east wing and Victorian theatre was completed in 2018

Barbican Centre

Silk Street EC2Y 8DS **T** 020-7638 4141 **W** www.barbican.org.uk
Owned, funded and managed by the City of London Corporation, the Barbican Centre opened in 1982 and houses the Barbican Theatre, a studio theatre called The Pit and the Barbican Hall; it is also home to the London Symphony Orchestra. There are three cinemas, six conference rooms, two art galleries, a sculpture court, a lending library, trade and banqueting facilities and a conservatory

British Library

St Pancras, 96 Euston Road NW1 2DB **T** 0330-333 1144
W www.bl.uk
The largest building constructed in the UK in the 20th century with basements extending 24.5m underground. Holdings include the *Magna Carta*, the Gutenburg Bible, Shakespeare's First Folio, Beatles manuscripts and the first edition of *The Times* from 1788. Holds temporary exhibitions on a range of topics

Central Criminal Court

Old Bailey EC4M 7EH **T** 020-7192 2739
W www.cityoflondon.gov.uk

The highest criminal court in the UK, the 'Old Bailey' is located on the site of the old Newgate Prison. Trials held here have included those of Oscar Wilde, Dr Crippen and the Yorkshire Ripper. The courthouse has been rebuilt several times since 1674; Edward VII officially opened the current neo-baroque building in 1907

Charterhouse

Charterhouse Square EC1M 6AN **T** 020-7253 9503
W www.thecharterhouse.org

A Carthusian monastery from 1371 to 1538, purchased in 1611 by Thomas Sutton, who endowed it as a residence for aged men 'of gentle birth' and a school for poor scholars (removed to Godalming in 1872)

Downing Street

SW1A 2AA **W** www.number10.gov.uk

Number 10 Downing Street is the official town residence of the prime minister and number 11 of the Chancellor of the Exchequer. The street was named after Sir George Downing, Bt., soldier and diplomat, who was MP for Morpeth 1660–84

George Inn

The George Inn Yard SE1 1NH **T** 020-7407 2056
W www.nationaltrust.org.uk/george-inn

The last galleried inn in London, built in 1677. Now owned by the National Trust and run as an ordinary public house

Horse Guards

Whitehall SW1

Archway and offices built about 1753. The changing of the guard takes place daily at 11am (10am on Sundays) and the inspection at 4pm. Only those with the Queen's permission may drive through the gates and archway into *Horse Guards Parade*, where the colour is 'trooped' on the Queen's official birthday

HOUSES OF PARLIAMENT

T 020-7219 3000 **W** www.parliament.uk
House of Commons, Westminster SW1A 0AA
House of Lords, Westminster SW1A 0PW

The royal palace of Westminster, originally built by Edward the Confessor, was the normal meeting place of Parliament from about 1340. St Stephen's Chapel was used from about 1550 for the meetings of the House of Commons, which had previously been held in the Chapter House or Refectory of Westminster Abbey. The House of Lords met in an apartment of the royal palace. The fire of 1834 destroyed much of the palace, and the present Houses of Parliament were erected on the site from the designs of Sir Charles Barry and Augustus Welby Pugin between 1840 and 1867. The chamber of the House of Commons was destroyed by bombing in 1941, and a new chamber designed by Sir Giles Gilbert Scott was used for the first time in 1950. *Westminster Hall and the Crypt Chapel* was the only part of the old palace of Westminster to survive the fire of 1834. It was built by William II from 1097 to 1099 and altered by Richard II between 1394 and 1399. The hammerbeam roof of carved oak dates from 1396–8. The Hall was the scene of the trial of Charles I. *The Victoria Tower* of the House of Lords is 98.5m (323ft) high and *The Elizabeth Tower* of the House of Commons is 96.3m (316ft) high and contains 'Big Ben', the great bell said to be named after Sir Benjamin Hall, First Commissioner of Works when the original bell was cast in 1856. This bell, which weighed 16 tons 11 cwt, was found to be cracked in 1857. The present bell (13.5 tons) is a recasting of the original and was first brought into use in 1859. The dials of the clock

are 7m (23ft) in diameter, the hands being 2.7m (9ft) and 4.3m (14ft) long (including balance piece).

During session, tours of the Houses of Parliament are only available to UK residents who have made advance arrangements through an MP or peer. Overseas visitors are no longer provided with permits to tour the Houses of Parliament during session, although they can tour on Saturdays and during the summer opening and attend debates for both houses in the Strangers' Galleries. During the summer recess, tickets for tours of the Houses of Parliament can be booked online, by telephone (**T** 020-7219 4114) or bought on site at the ticket office located at the front of Portcullis House SW1A 2LW. The Strangers' Gallery of the House of Commons is open to the public when the house is sitting. To acquire tickets in advance, UK residents should write to their local MP and overseas visitors should apply to their embassy or high commission in the UK for a permit. If none of these arrangements has been made, visitors should join the public queue outside St Stephen's Entrance, where there is also a queue for entry to the House of Lords Gallery

INNS OF COURT

The Inns of Court are ancient unincorporated bodies of lawyers which for more than five centuries have had the power to call to the Bar those of their members who have qualified for the rank or degree of Barrister-at-Law. There are four Inns of Court as well as many lesser inns:

Lincoln's Inn, WC2A 3TL **T** 020-7405 1393
W www.lincolnsinn.org.uk

The most ancient of the inns with records dating back to 1422. The hall and library buildings are from 1845, although the library is first mentioned in 1474; the old hall (late 15th century) and the chapel were rebuilt c.1619–23

Inner Temple, King's Bench Walk EC4Y 7HL **T** 020-7797 8250
W www.innertemple.org.uk
Middle Temple, Middle Temple Lane EC4Y 9BT
T 020-7427 4800 **W** www.middletemple.org.uk

Records for the Inner and Middle Temple date back to the beginning of the 16th century. The site was originally occupied by the Order of Knights Templar c.1160–1312. The two inns have separate halls thought to have been formed c.1350. The division between the two societies was formalised in 1732 with Temple Church and the Masters House remaining in common. The Inner Temple Garden is normally open to the public on weekdays between 12.30pm and 3pm

Temple Church, EC4Y 7BB **T** 020-7353 8559
W www.templechurch.com

The nave forms one of five remaining round churches in England

Gray's Inn, South Square WC1R 5ET **T** 020-7458 7800
W www.graysinn.info

Founded early 14th century; hall 1556–8

No other 'Inns' are active, but there are remains of *Staple Inn,* a gabled front on Holborn (opposite Gray's Inn Road). *Clement's Inn* (near St Clement Danes Church), *Clifford's Inn,* Fleet Street, and *Thavies Inn,* Holborn Circus, are all rebuilt. *Serjeants' Inn,* Fleet Street, and another (demolished 1910) of the same name in Chancery Lane, were composed of Serjeants-at-Law, the last of whom died in 1922

Institute of Contemporary Arts

The Mall SW1Y 5AH **T** 020-7930 3647 **W** www.ica.art

Exhibitions of modern art in the fields of film, theatre, new media and the visual arts

Lloyd's

Lime Street EC3M 7HA **T** 020-7327 1000 **W** www.lloyds.com

International insurance market which evolved during the 17th century from Lloyd's Coffee House. The present building was opened for business in May 1986, and houses the Lutine Bell. Underwriting is on three floors with a total area of 10,591 sq. m (114,000 sq. ft). The Lloyd's building is not open to the general public

London Central Mosque and the Islamic Cultural Centre
Park Road NW8 7RG **T** 020-7725 2152 **W** www.iccuk.org
The focus for London's Muslims; established in 1944 but not completed until 1977, the mosque can accommodate about 5,000 worshippers; guided tours are available

London Eye
South Bank SE1 7PB **W** www.londoneye.com
Opened in March 2000 as London's millennium landmark, this 137m (450ft) observation wheel is the tallest cantilevered observation wheel in the world. The wheel provides a 30-minute ride offering panoramic views of the capital

London Zoo
Regent's Park NW1 4RY **T** 0344-225 1826 **W** www.zsl.org
Opened in 1828 by the Zoological Society of London (ZSL) to house an array of exotic and endangered animals with an emphasis on scientific research and conservation

Madame Tussauds
Marylebone Road NW1 5LR **T** 0871-894 3000
W www.madametussauds.com
Waxwork exhibition

Mansion House
Cannon Street EC4N 8BH **T** 020-7626 2500
W www.cityoflondon.gov.uk
The official residence of the Lord Mayor. Built in the 18th century in the Palladian style. Open to groups by appointment only

Marlborough House
Pall Mall SW1Y 5HX **T** 020-7747 6500
W www.thecommonwealth.org
Built by Wren for the first Duke of Marlborough and completed in 1711, the house reverted to the Crown in 1835. In 1863 it became the London house of the Prince of Wales and was the London home of Queen Mary until her death in 1953. In 1959 Marlborough House was given by the Queen as the headquarters for the Commonwealth Secretariat and it was opened as such in 1965. The Queen's Chapel, Marlborough Gate, was begun in 1623 from the designs of Inigo Jones for the Infanta Maria of Spain, and completed for Queen Henrietta Maria. Marlborough House is not open to the public

Neasden Temple
BAPS Shri Swaminarayan Mandir, Brentfield Road, Neasden NW10 8LD **T** 020-8965 2651 **W** http://londonmandir.baps.org
When built, it was the first and largest traditional Hindu Mandir outside of India; opened in 1995

Port of London
Port of London Authority, Royal Pier Road, Kent DA12 2BG
T 01474-562200 **W** www.pla.co.uk
The Port of London covers the tidal section of the river Thames from Teddington to the seaward limit (the outer Tongue buoy and the Sunk light vessel), a distance of 153km (95 miles). The governing body is the Port of London Authority (PLA). Cargo is handled at privately operated riverside terminals between Fulham and Canvey Island, including the enclosed dock at Tilbury, 40km (25 miles) below London Bridge. Passenger vessels and cruise liners can be handled at moorings at Greenwich, Tower Bridge and Tilbury

Queen Elizabeth Olympic Park
Stratford E20 **T** 0800-072 2110
W www.queenelizabetholympicpark.co.uk
Built for the London 2012 Olympic and Paralympic Games, the park, which included the Olympic Stadium,

Velodrome and Aquatics Centre has been redeveloped to provide 227ha (560 acres) of parkland with play areas, outside arts and theatre spaces, waterways and wetlands. The north of the park, which includes the Copper Box Arena sport venue, re-opened to the public in 2013. The south of the park, which re-opened in April 2014, incorporates three venues for arts and sports events and the *ArcelorMittal Orbit,* designed by Sir Anish Kapoor and Cecil Balmond; it is the UK's tallest sculpture (114.5m/ 376ft) and has two accessible observation floors

Roman Remains
The city wall of Roman *Londinium* was largely rebuilt during the medieval period but sections may be seen near the White Tower in the Tower of London; at Tower Hill; at Coopers' Row; at All Hallows, London Wall, its vestry being built on the remains of a semi-circular Roman bastion; at St Alphage, London Wall, showing a succession of building repairs from the Roman until the late medieval period; and at St Giles, Cripplegate. Sections of the great forum and basilica, more than 165 sq. m (1,776 sq. ft), have been encountered during excavations in the area of Leadenhall, Gracechurch Street and Lombard Street. Traces of Roman activity along the river include a massive riverside wall built in the late Roman period, and a succession of Roman timber quays along Lower and Upper Thames Street. Finds from these sites can be seen at the Museum of London.
Other major buildings are the amphitheatre at Guildhall, remains of bath-buildings in Upper and Lower Thames Street, and the temple of Mithras in Walbrook

Royal Albert Hall
Kensington Gore SW7 2AP **T** 020-7589 3203
W www.royalalberthall.com
The elliptical hall, one of the largest in the world, was completed in 1871; since 1941 it has been the venue each summer for the Promenade Concerts founded in 1895 by Sir Henry Wood. Other events include pop and classical music concerts, dance, opera, sporting events, conferences and banquets

Royal Courts of Justice
Strand WC2A 2LL **T** 020-7947 6000 **W** www.justice.gov.uk
Victorian Gothic building that is home to the high court. Visitors are free to watch proceedings

Royal Hospital, Chelsea
Royal Hospital Road SW3 4SR **T** 020-7881 5200
W www.chelsea-pensioners.co.uk
Founded by Charles II in 1682, and built by Wren; opened in 1692 for old and disabled soldiers. The extensive grounds include the former Ranelagh Gardens and are the venue for the Chelsea Flower Show each May

Royal Naval College
Greenwich SE10 9NN **T** 020-8269 4747 **W** www.ornc.org
The building was the Greenwich Hospital until 1869. It was built by Charles II, largely from designs by John Webb, and by Queen Mary II and William III, from designs by Wren. It stands on the site of an ancient abbey, a royal house and Greenwich Palace, which was constructed by Henry VII. Henry VIII, Mary I and Elizabeth I were born in the royal palace and Edward VI died there. The Painted Hall, designed by Wren, reopened in March 2019 after a major two-year conservation project to restore its vividly painted interior by Sir James Thornhill

Royal Opera House
Covent Garden WC2E 9DD **T** 020-7240 1200 **W** www.roh.org.uk
Home of The Royal Ballet (1931) and The Royal Opera (1946). The Royal Opera House is the third theatre to be built on the site, opening 1858; the first was opened in 1732

St James's Palace

Pall Mall SW1A 1BQ **W** www.royal.uk

Built by Henry VIII, only the Gatehouse and Presence Chamber remain; later alterations were made by Wren and Kent. Representatives of foreign powers are still accredited 'to the Court of St James's'. *Clarence House* (1825), the official London residence of the Prince of Wales, stands within the St James's Palace estate

St Paul's Cathedral

St Paul's Churchyard EC4M 8AD **T** 020-7246 8350

W www.stpauls.co.uk

Built 1675–1710. The cross on the dome is 111m (365ft) above ground level, the inner cupola 66.4m (218ft) above the floor. 'Great Paul' in the south-west tower weighs nearly 17 tons. The organ by Father Smith (enlarged by Willis and rebuilt by Mander) is in a case carved by Grinling Gibbons, who also carved the choir stalls

Shakespeare's Globe

New Globe Walk SE1 9DT **T** 020-7902 1500

W www.shakespearesglobe.com

Reconstructed in 1997, the open-air playhouse is a unique resource for the works of William Shakespeare through performance and education; a new indoor replica Jacobean theatre staged its first public performance in January 2014

Shard

London Bridge SE1 **T** 0344 449-7222 **W** www.the-shard.com

Completed in May 2012, the skyscraper stands at 310m (1,016ft) and possesses a unique facade of 11,000 glass panels and a 360-degree viewing gallery

Somerset House

Strand WC2R 1LA **T** 020-7845 4600

W www.somersethouse.org.uk

The river facade (183m/600ft long) was built in 1776–1801 from the designs of Sir William Chambers; the eastern extension, which houses part of King's College, was built by Smirke in 1829–35. Somerset House was the property of Lord Protector Somerset, at whose attainder in 1552 the palace passed to the Crown, and it was a royal residence until 1692. Somerset House has recently undergone extensive renovation and is home to the Embankment Galleries and the Courtauld Gallery. Open-air concerts and ice-skating (Nov–Jan) are held in the courtyard

SOUTH BANK, SE1

Arts complex on the south bank of the river Thames which consists of:

BFI Southbank **T** 020-7928 3232 **W** www.bfi.org.uk

Opened in 1952 and administered by the British Film Institute, has four auditoria of varying capacities. Venue for the annual London Film Festival

The *Royal Festival Hall* **T** 020-7960 4200

W www.southbankcentre.co.uk

Opened in 1951 for the Festival of Britain, adjacent are the *Queen Elizabeth Hall,* the *Purcell Room* and the *Hayward Gallery*

The *Royal National Theatre,* **T** 020-7452 3000

W www.nationaltheatre.org.uk

Opened in 1976; comprises the Olivier, the Lyttelton and Dorfman theatres. The Cottesloe Theatre closed in February 2013 and, following refurbishment reopened in 2014 as the Dorfman Theatre

Southwark Cathedral

London Bridge SE1 9DA **T** 020-7367 6700

W www.cathedral.southwark.anglican.org

Mainly 13th century, but the nave is largely rebuilt. The tomb of John Gower (1330–1408) is between the Bunyan and Chaucer memorial windows in the north aisle; Shakespeare's effigy, backed by a view of Southwark and the Globe Theatre, is in the south aisle; the tomb of Bishop Andrewes (d. 1626) is near the screen. The Lady Chapel was the scene of the consistory courts of the reign of Mary (Gardiner and Bonner) and is still used as a consistory court. John Harvard, after whom Harvard University is named, was baptised here in 1607, and the chapel by the north choir aisle is his memorial chapel

Thames Embankments

Sir Joseph Bazalgette (1819–91) constructed the *Victoria Embankment,* on the north side from Westminster to Blackfriars for the Metropolitan Board of Works, 1864–70 (the seats, of which the supports of some are a kneeling camel, laden with spicery, and of others a winged sphinx, were presented by the Grocers' Company and by W. H. Smith, MP, in 1874); the *Albert Embankment,* on the south side from Westminster Bridge to Vauxhall, 1866–9, and the Chelsea Embankment, 1871–4. The total cost exceeded £2m. Bazalgette also inaugurated the London main drainage system, 1858–65. A medallion *(Flumini vincula posuit)* has been placed on a pier of the *Victoria Embankment* to commemorate the engineer

Thames Flood Barrier

W www.environment-agency.gov.uk

Officially opened in May 1984, though first used in February 1983, the barrier consists of ten rising sector gates which span approximately 520m from bank to bank of the Thames at Woolwich Reach. When not in use the gates lie horizontally, allowing shipping to navigate the river normally; when the barrier is closed, the gates turn through 90 degrees to stand vertically more than 50 feet above the river bed. The barrier took eight years to complete and can be raised within about 90 minutes

Trafalgar Tavern

Park Row, Greenwich SE10 9NW **T** 020-3887 9886

W www.trafalgartavern.co.uk

Regency-period riverside public house built in 1837. Charles Dickens and William Gladstone were patrons

Wembley Stadium

Wembley HA9 0WS **W** www.wembleystadium.com

The second largest stadium in Europe; hosts major sporting events and music concerts

Westminster Abbey

SW1P 3PA **T** 020-7222 5152 **W** www.westminster-abbey.org

Founded as a Benedictine monastery over 1,000 years ago, the church was rebuilt by Edward the Confessor in 1065 and again by Henry III in the 13th century. The abbey is the resting place for monarchs including Edward I, Henry III, Henry V, Henry VII, Elizabeth I, Mary I and Mary, Queen of Scots, and has been the setting of coronations since that of William the Conqueror in 1066. In Poets' Corner there are memorials to many literary figures, and many scientists and musicians are also remembered here. The grave of the Unknown Warrior is to be found in the nave

Westminster Cathedral

Francis Street SW1P 1QW **T** 020-7798 9055

W www.westminstercathedral.org.uk

Roman Catholic cathedral built 1895–1903 from the designs of John Francis Bentley. The campanile is 83m (273ft) high

Wimbledon All England Lawn Tennis Club

Church Road SW19 5AE **T** 020-8944 1066

W www.wimbledon.com

Venue for the Wimbledon Championships. Includes the Wimbledon Lawn Tennis Museum

HALLMARKS

Hallmarks are the symbols stamped on gold, silver, palladium or platinum articles to indicate that they have been tested at an official Assay Office and that they conform to one of the legal standards. The marking of gold and silver articles to identify the maker was instituted in England in 1363 under a statute of Edward III. In 1478 the Assay Office in Goldsmiths' Hall was established and all gold and silversmiths were required to bring their wares to be date-marked by the Hall, hence the term 'hallmarked'.

With certain exceptions, all gold, silver, palladium or platinum articles are required by law to be hallmarked before they are offered for sale. Current hallmarking requirements come under the UK Hallmarking Act 1973 and subsequent amendments. The act is built around the principle of description, where it is an offence for any person to apply to an unhallmarked article a description indicating that it is wholly or partly made of gold, silver, palladium or platinum. There is an exemption by weight: compulsory hallmarks are not needed on gold and palladium under 1g, silver under 7.78g and platinum under 0.5g. Also, some descriptions, such as rolled gold and gold plate, are permissible. The British Hallmarking Council is a statutory body created as a result of the Hallmarking Act. It ensures adequate provision for assaying and hallmarking, supervises the assay offices and ensures the enforcement of hallmarking legislation. The four assay offices at London, Birmingham, Sheffield and Edinburgh operate under the act.

BRITISH HALLMARKING COUNCIL Secretariat, c/o
Shakespeare Martineau, 60 Gracechurch Street, London EC3V OHR **W** www.gov.uk/government/organisations/british-hallmarking-council

COMPULSORY MARKS

Since January 1999 UK hallmarks have consisted of three compulsory symbols – the sponsor's mark, the millesimal fineness (purity) mark and the assay office mark. The distinction between UK and foreign articles has been removed, and more finenesses are now legal, reflecting the more common finenesses elsewhere in Europe.

SPONSOR'S MARK

Formerly known as the maker's mark, the sponsor's mark was instituted in England in 1363. Originally a device such as a bird or fleur-de-lis, now it consists of a combination of at least two initials (usually a shortened form of the manufacturer's name) and a shield design. The London Assay Office offers 45 standard shield designs but other designs are possible by arrangement.

MILLESIMAL FINENESS MARK

The millesimal fineness (purity) mark indicates the number of parts per thousand of pure metal in the alloy. The current finenesses allowed in the UK are:

Gold   999; 990; 916 (22 carat); 750 (18 carat); 585 (14 carat); 375 (9 carat)
Silver   999; 958 (Britannia); 925 (sterling); 800
Palladium   999; 950; 500
Platinum   999; 950; 900; 850

ASSAY OFFICE MARK

This mark identifies the particular assay office at which the article was tested and marked. The British assay offices are:

 LONDON, Goldsmiths' Hall, Gutter Lane, London EC2V 8AQ **T** 020-7606 8971 **W** www.assayofficelondon.co.uk

 BIRMINGHAM, 1 Moreton Street, Birmingham B1 3AX **T** 0121-236 6951 **W** www.theassayoffice.co.uk

 SHEFFIELD, Guardians' Hall, Beulah Road, Hillsborough, Sheffield S6 2AN **T** 0114-231 2121 **W** www.assayoffice.co.uk

 EDINBURGH, Goldsmiths' Hall, 24 Broughton Street, Edinburgh EH1 3RH **T** 0131-556 1144 **W** www.edinburghassayoffice.co.uk

Assay offices formerly existed in other towns, eg Chester, Exeter, Glasgow, Newcastle, Norwich and York, each having its own distinguishing mark.

OPTIONAL MARKS

Since 1999 traditional pictorial marks such as a crown for gold, the Britannia for 958 silver, the lion passant for 925 Sterling silver (lion rampant in Scotland) and the orb for 950 platinum may be added voluntarily to the millesimal mark. In 2010 a pictorial mark of the Greek goddess Pallas Athene was introduced for 950 palladium.

 Gold – a crown

 Sterling silver (Scotland)

 Britannia silver

 Platinum – an orb

 Sterling silver (England)

 Palladium – the Greek goddess Pallas Athene

DATE LETTER

The date letter shows the year in which an article was assayed and hallmarked. Each alphabetical cycle has a distinctive style of lettering or shape of shield. The date letters were different at the various assay offices and the particular office must be established from the assay office mark before reference is made to tables of date letters. Date letter marks became voluntary from 1 January 1999.

The table which follows shows one specimen shield and letter used by the London Assay Office on silver articles for each alphabetical cycle from 1498. The same letters are found on gold articles but the surrounding shield may differ. Until 1 January 1975, each hallmark covered two calendar years as the letter changed annually in May on St Dunstan's Day (the patron saint of silversmiths). Since 1 January 1975, each date letter has indicated a calendar year from January to December and each office has used the same style of date letter and shield for all articles.

LONDON (GOLDSMITHS' HALL) DATE LETTERS

	from	*to*		*from*	*to*
	1498–9	1517–18		1756–7	1775–6
	1518–19	1537–8		1776–7	1795–6
	1538–9	1557–8		1796–7	1815–16
	1558–9	1577–8		1816–17	1835–6
	1578–9	1597–8		1836–7	1855–6
	1598–9	1617–18		1856–7	1875–6
	1618–19	1637–8		1876–7 (A to M square shield, N to Z as shown)	1895–6
	1638–9	1657–8		1896–7	1915–16
	1658–9	1677–8		1916–17	1935–6
	1678–9	1696–7		1936–7	1955–6
	1697 (from March, 1697 only)	1715–16		1956–7	1974
	1716–17	1735–6		1975	1999
	1736–7	1738–9		2000	
	1739–40	1755–6			

OTHER MARKS

FOREIGN GOODS

Foreign goods imported into the UK are required to be hallmarked before sale, unless they already bear a convention mark or a hallmark struck by an independent assay office in the European Economic Area which is deemed to be equivalent to a UK hallmark.

The following are the assay office marks used for gold imported articles until the end of 1998. For silver and platinum the symbols remain the same but the shields differ in shape.

 London   *Sheffield*

 Birmingham   *Edinburgh*

CONVENTION HALLMARKS

The UK has been a signatory to the International Convention on Hallmarks since 1972. A convention hallmark struck by the UK assay offices is recognised by all member countries in the convention and, similarly, convention marks from member countries are legally recognised in the UK. There are currently 20 members of the hallmarking convention: Austria, Croatia, Cyprus, Czech Republic, Denmark, Finland, Hungary, Ireland, Israel, Latvia, Lithuania, the Netherlands, Norway, Poland, Portugal, Slovakia, Slovenia, Sweden, Switzerland, and the UK.

A convention hallmark comprises four marks: a sponsor's mark, a common control mark, a fineness mark, and an assay office mark.

Examples of common control marks (figures differ according to fineness, but the style of each mark remains the same for each article):

GOLD	SILVER	PALLADIUM	PLATINUM
375	800	950	850

COMMEMORATIVE MARKS

There are other marks to commemorate special events: the silver jubilee of King George V and Queen Mary in 1935, the coronation of Queen Elizabeth II in 1953, her silver jubilee in 1977, and her golden jubilee in 2002. During 1999 and 2000 there was a voluntary additional Millennium Mark. A mark to commemorate the Queen's diamond jubilee in 2012 was available from July 2011 to October 2012:

BANKING AND FINANCE

BUSINESS AND FINANCE IN 2019–20

By Lisa Carden

It's almost impossible to know where – and how – to begin. 2020 was a brutal year for the UK. Tens of thousands of people have fallen victim to the COVID-19 pandemic, despite the best efforts of a committed and courageous NHS, and what most of us regarded as 'normal' life has been put on hold. Many of the restrictions instituted by the government in order to suppress the spread of the coronavirus will have affected us both as employees, employers, and consumers. So, what are the main talking points?

BREXIT: THE NEVER-ENDING STORY
Almost implausibly, a trade deal had still not been done as of early December 2020. More than four years after the UK's first vote to leave the EU – and subsequently reinforced by two general elections – discussions went down to the very wire. Fishing rights – in terms of both access and quotas – remained a principal sticking point, as did the concept of a 'level playing field' in business competition, and dispute resolution. At last, an early Christmas miracle occurred when an agreement was finally reached on 24 December, but it will be months before the real-life consequences of the deal are apparent to all.

What *is* already clear, however, is the sheer amount of paperwork involved in the UK's final break with the EU is enormous: Jim Harra, chief executive of HM Revenue and Customs, said in December 2020 that the 'administrative burden' of filling in customs forms once the transition is over would be £7.5bn per year (this figure was first mooted in 2018 and, according to Mr Harra, still stands). The whole issue of customs was an extremely fraught one as 2020 wound to a close: freight was getting stuck in UK ports as a result of delays linked to the impact of the coronavirus and pre-Brexit stock movement, so much so that Honda had to pause production at its Swindon plant due to a parts shortage. Builders were also reporting problems in accessing timber, roof tiles, power tools, and even screws, and they weren't alone in experiencing supply-chain issues. (It should be noted that the UK was just one of numerous countries suffering freight woes, and ports were congested around the world: for example, at one point in late November, the *LA Times* reported that twelve cargo ships were anchored south of Los Angeles waiting for a berth, while the ports of Los Angeles and Long Beach were already full to capacity.)

While it had always been suspected that negotiations between the UK and EU would come down the last possible minute, what transpired was *so* last minute that British retailers, exporters, and suppliers were left desperately trying to prepare – at the government's request – for a future about which they had been given no details. Key questions about vital issues such as tariffs, fees, stock movements, pre-existing contracts, and future work prospects were left unanswered. The official slogan of 'Check, Change, Go' belied the enormity of the situation. In the face of this, the news that the multinational INEOS, owned by Brexit supporter Jim Radcliffe, announced that it would be building a manufacturing plant for its Grenadier off-road vehicle on the French/German border rather than in Bridgend, as had been suggested, was particularly poorly timed.

LOCKDOWN BLUES
On the evening of 23 March 2020, the prime minister addressed the UK. He explained that (and as had widely been expected) in order to stop the spread of the coronavirus, the nation should work from home wherever possible, reduce social contact with others and shop only for essentials. To that end, supermarkets would remain open (with social distancing procedures in place), along with pharmacists and a handful of other outlets, but pretty much everything was closed. The hospitality and travel industries shut their doors and the country fell quiet.

Many white-collar office-based businesses and organisations would continue to function (after a fashion) thanks to a range of 'virtual' meetings solutions (see below), but what of those that relied on people crossing the threshold? The very backbone of British high streets – from pubs to bookshops, cafes to hairdressers – was gone in the blink of an eye. How could these businesses keep going? The government stepped in, offering a Coronavirus Job Retention Scheme (more commonly referred to as 'furlough') that would, in effect, pay a large proportion (80 per cent) of employees' wages for a specified time period (furlough has now been extended several times and at the time of writing will be in place until April 2021). Grants and loans were also made available throughout the year (some during the first, national lockdown and others later in the year during the local restrictions). Assistance for the self-employed came in the form of the Self-Employed Income Support Scheme, which offered a grant to those businesses that had seen a dramatic fall in demand due to the impact of the pandemic or had been forced to close temporarily because of it). In all, the government claimed it had offered an 'unprecedented' financial aid package of over £200m, saving 9 million jobs in the process. And it is certainly true that the support was welcome.

There were, however, some gaps in the coverage, and the self-employed were at a particular disadvantage if: a) their business was relatively new, and thus had no 'track record' to be judged on; b) they had been in effect, too successful, having an average trading profit of over £50,000 for the three tax years immediately prior to the pandemic; or c) owners (perfectly legally) paid themselves a salary and dividends through their company. In such situations, they did not qualify for government assistance. According to the Institute of Fiscal Studies, almost a fifth (18 per cent) of those for whom self-employment accounts for the bulk of their income were left out in the cold.

Despite the government's efforts, and although many businesses took advantage of an online presence to keep trading during both the initial lockdown and the subsequent local restrictions, a good number of the UK's most famous and best-loved trading names did not survived COVID-19. In the space of 24 hours during early December, 25,000 jobs were put at risk when Sir Philip Green's Arcadia Group – which includes brands such as Topshop, Dorothy Perkins and Burton – went into administration, and Debenhams, which first opened in 1813, went into liquidation (it had been in trouble for some time). Even John Lewis was not immune: in August 2020, it announced plans to close eight stores, some of which were relatively small but one – in Birmingham – was opened only in 2015 as part of an enormously expensive regeneration project near to the city's New Street Station. And these were just a handful of the famous retail names that fell by the wayside over the twelve months. Worryingly, the immediate future does not look brighter: in November 2020, the chief executive of Fortnum & Mason, Ewan Venters, said in an interview with Radio 4's *Today* programme that he expected a third of leading retail brands to have vanished by the end of March 2021.

For hospitality and personal care businesses, the on/off nature of the restrictions was particularly problematic. Even though many were able to trade throughout July, August, and even September (once appropriately covid-secure), the regional lockdowns that were rolled out during the late autumn meant that it simply wasn't worth opening up again until 2021. This is certainly the case in Wales, which had a 'firebreak' lockdown from 23 October to 9 November, swiftly followed by further restrictions less than a month later, as part of which pubs were not allowed to serve alcohol. The country's largest Welsh-owned brewery, Brains, said it would shut 100 of its pubs until the New Year and estimated that the firebreak had cost the company over £1.5m. Both England and Scotland implemented (slightly different) tier systems, under which pubs could open in the less severely-hit areas, while the situation in Northern Ireland remained unpredictable: a 'circuit-breaker' lockdown that was due to end in late November was extended at very short notice for a further two weeks, leaving both retail and hospitality in the region in disarray.

The overall effects of the pandemic on jobs and the UK's longer-term economic future are staggering. In his Spending Review in late November 2020, Rishi Sunak, Chancellor of the Exchequer, warned that the UK's economic emergency had 'only just begun'. Government borrowing was expected to exceed £390bn in 2020 alone, while expenditure on tackling COVID-19 would be in the region of £280bn. Unemployment figures had risen by 300,000 on 2019, up to 1.62 million. Winter was coming, in every sense.

PARADIGM SHIFTS

There were, however, some pockets of good news. For obvious reasons, the demand for online food shopping soared during 2020, and although access to those services was problematic during the spring lockdown, things evened out in time for the subsequent autumn restrictions (which varied in duration and detail across the UK). While nearly all of the UK's supermarkets had an online operation too, Ocado was the only one that was digital-only. It had been popular for some time but – famously – had only made a profit in three of the twenty years it has been operational. The game certainly changed during 2020, despite a challenging start when an extensive warehouse fire in February cost the business over £200m. In July, however, its chief executive and co-founder, Tim Steiner, announced that half-year sales had reached £1bn, a rise of over 25 per cent in retail revenues. By early November 2020, share price rises meant that Ocado was worth £18bn – almost on a par with Tesco. Groceries aside – these are now, in fact, part of a jointly owned business with Marks & Spencer, whose products Ocado has stocked since September 2020 following the end of its previous deal with Waitrose – Ocado's tech solutions may prove to be a longer-term source of revenue. As a *Guardian* article reported in November 2020, Ocado had licensed its software and picking robots to supermarkets around the world and in so doing hoped to make further inroads into a market estimated to be worth over £7.5 *trillion*.

One of the unexpected trends of the pandemic has perhaps been an acceleration of change. During the spring restrictions, many workplaces closed. All over the country, people speedily carved out 'offices' in their homes and got used to 'Zooming' – that is, holding meetings over the eponymous online video-conferencing service. Formed in California in 2011, Zoom allowed people to (just about) go about their day jobs by seeing and speaking to colleagues, clients, suppliers and so on. A host of other options were available, of course, many of which (such as Microsoft Teams and Google Classroom) were adopted by UK schools as they attempted to maintain their pupils' education and motivation, but Zoom became emblematic of the nation's attempts to remain engaged and productive. The company's worth leapt as a result: in August 2020, the BBC reported that revenues had rocketed by more than 300 per cent for the three months to end of July, reaching over $660m (£450m), while profits jumped to $186m. Although growth will probably be less marked in the years ahead, demand is likely to remain high for the first quarter of 2021, with many offices not expected to open up fully before late spring.

Other industries – traditional and otherwise – also saw some positive effects from a hugely challenging time. Publishing is just one of the creative industries of which the UK can be rightly proud, and books continued to be a source of solace for many during 2020. Audiobooks have been increasingly popular over recent years – a report published by Deloitte Insights in December 2019 estimated that the global audiobook market would be worth $3.5bn during 2020, a jump of 25 per cent – but the pandemic was an extra catalyst to an established trend. Ebooks also benefited: after their heyday about a decade ago – when it was suggested that they were the future of books full stop – digital versions of books had remained relatively popular (arguably thanks to Amazon's Kindle device) but were no longer setting the world on fire. Given that only 'essential shops' were open for most of the spring, though, and that Amazon de-prioritised book deliveries for a time, their speed of delivery and ease of use meant that ebooks became popular again. According to a *Guardian* story in November 2020, sales were up 17 per cent on the previous year, and ebooks were on track to have their best year since 2015. (The government's removal of VAT on them was also a boon.) Even though print books were harder to come by than normal during the spring, some publishers had a good year overall. Bloomsbury, for example, had its highest first half results since 2008, and was able to repay roughly £700,000 to members of staff who took a pay cut to see the firm through the early phase of the pandemic. The end of the autumn restrictions in England did bring good news for booksellers, though: *The Bookseller* magazine reported a 'pre-Christmas bonanza' as more shops re-opened and shoppers emerged.

The other creative industries, however, took a battering. Cinemas and theatres alike had to shut in the spring and while some cinemas were able to reopen briefly over the summer, the autumn COVID-19 restrictions were an unfortunate end to a bad year. It is likely some will not open again, although there was some good news in December 2020 for those towns and cities with Cineworld venues: it was announced that these would reopen in the UK in March 2021, earlier than anticipated when in October 2020 it was announced that they would all close temporarily.

One of the biggest unknowns going forward will be the impact of home screening options, which allow us to watch films at home via the TV or on computer. Prior to the pandemic, services such as Netflix, Amazon Prime, and Sky Box Office had (broadly speaking) co-existed with standard cinema offerings, although the more traditional film establishment had been rather lukewarm towards Netflix-originated films when it came to awards season (see the reaction to Alfonso Cuarón's 2019 film, *Roma*), often because such productions aired on the TV at the same time as they were released into cinemas, thereby reducing revenue. Again, restrictions imposed due to the pandemic sped up the pace of change. Although some box office blockbusters were been held back so that they could appear on (literal) big screens first – most notably *No Time to Die*, Daniel Craig's final outing as James Bond, which is now expected to appear in October 2021 (and the postponement of which forced Cineworld's hand in the same month of 2020) – many were just being streamed first (as was the case with Disney's reboot of *Mulan*). More worryingly for cinema chains, in early December 2020, HBO Max in the US announced that it would stream many of Warner Bros'. 2021 titles at no extra cost to existing subscribers for one month: given that these films include a raft of productions that could well be the highlight of any other year by themselves – such as *Wonder Woman 1984*, *Matrix 4* and *Dune* – cinema chains have every right to be worried. At the time of writing, it is probable that these films will be streamed in the UK at the same time.

Exercising at home was another area of growth in 2020, given the complex patchwork of closures and reopenings of gyms and recreational facilities across the UK since March, not to mention concerns about social distancing and hygiene precautions. Classes of all types switched to Zoom, free sessions were available on YouTube and sales of equipment soared. As a BBC article explained, road bikes and exercise bikes enjoyed a healthy uplift in sales during the spring. Perhaps one of the highest-profile home exercise regimes was Peloton, which offered a range of live-streamed or on-demand classes, some using a branded stationary bike or treadmill. Peloton is, to put it bluntly, not cheap: at the time of writing, the 'original' bike costs £1,750 alone, and then users need to factor in £39 per month for classes (cheaper alternatives, not including the bike, are also available). The cost didn't seem to put people off, however: in September 2020, the company announced that it had doubled its membership numbers at the end of June, and now had over 3 million – twice as many as the same time in 2019. The increase in subscribers meant that revenue was now in excess of $600m (over £400m), and the company was on track to make a profit for the first time. Supply-chain issues meant there was a backlog in getting some hardware to new customers, but as a long winter beckoned, exercising at home is an attractive option for many at the moment.

The popularity of meal kits also soared during 2020, as people's shopping and eating habits changed. Hello Fresh was a key player in this market: customers could buy ingredients and a set of cooking instructions for meals of varying sizes and types (to suit their household), all of which was delivered to their home. As *The Financial Times* reported in November 2020, Hello Fresh doubled its revenues between July and September 2020: demand was up 120 per cent on the same time last year, and the German-owned company's sales reached €970m.

Competitors of all sizes were eager to take a bite of this particular cherry, however: the giant conglomerate Nestlé sank $950m into its acquisition of the US pre-prepared food chain, Freshly, while in the UK, the start-up Gousto went from strength to strength. In the first six months of 2020 it more than matched its 2019 total revenues of £83m, it announced plans to double its workforce to 2,000 by 2022 and secured another £25m of investment from some of its existing backers, bringing the total investment in the business to £155m.

Perhaps the most surprising trend of the spring restrictions across the UK was that alcohol sales *fell*: according to a report released by Nielsen Datatrack in September 2020, volume fell from 2 billion litres in 2019 for the seventeen weeks up to 11 July to 1.3 billion in 2020. Clearly much of this can be ascribed to licensed premises having to close their doors during that time. People were very much at liberty to drink at home, though, and supermarket alcohol sales during this period were in excess of £7.5bn. Beer, cider, wine and spirits all rose in popularity during the first lockdown but it will probably come as no surprise that Champagne sales were lacking in fizz, tumbling by £9m on last year.

In the spirit of necessity being the mother of invention, some of the UK's independent brewers and distillers diversified when lockdown hit. Aberdeen-based Brewdog, for example, started making hand sanitiser when national stocks ran low during the first wave of the pandemic; not to be outdone, a number of gin distilleries rallied to the cause and – from the Isle of Harris to West London – put their production facilities to a different use.

STRAPPED FOR CASH?

Paying by card became the norm in 2020. The news in early December that the Bank of England was rather hazy about the whereabouts of £50bn worth of banknotes, however, seemed to be taking this new approach to its very limits. (A vivid example in a *Guardian* article on this issue explained that the money was equivalent to an 800-mile-high stack of £5 notes.) The Public Accounts Committee at the House of Commons took a dim view, with its chair, Meg Hillier (MP for Hackney South and Shoreditch) saying that the Bank of England: '[needs] to be more concerned about where the missing £50bn is. Depending where it is and what it's being used for, that amount of money could have material implications for public policy and the public purse. The Bank needs to get a better handle on the national currency it controls.' The Bank replied that it was not the public's responsibility to explain where they stored or used their notes – at home, abroad or (probably the key issue) for illicit purposes – and thus the notes were not 'lost' at all.

Perhaps the wider issue here was access to cash. Even with a shift to digital payments, elderly people or those in more rural locations and on low incomes do still need to be able to withdraw money – many small businesses still trade in cash too – but the number of free cashpoints is falling. According to Which?, both NatWest and Barclays have each closed 500 branches since 2015, and TSB is expected to shut over 150 in 2021. By contrast, the number of cashpoints charging a fee rose by over 4,000, according to the Public Accounts Committee. The Treasury has published a report on expanding cash access and has committed to introduce legislation on this issue.

A WINTER'S TALE

As 2020 stumbled to a close, there was at last some good news in the form of three potential vaccines for coronavirus. Work began on them in the spring, and partly thanks to the fact crucial testing phases ran in parallel rather than sequentially it meant they were able to get to market in ten months rather than ten years. The first out of the blocks was created by Pfizer and the German company BioNTech: the UK was the first country in the world to approve its use, and vaccinations began on 8 December 2020: rather splendidly, the second person to receive the vaccine – following 91-year-old Margaret Keenan, at University Hospital, Coventry – shared a name with that icon of the Midlands, William Shakespeare. Also, under consideration by the Medicines and Healthcare products Regulatory Agency (MHRA) was a vaccine produced by the US firm Moderna, and one produced in a joint effort between Oxford University and AstraZeneca. While BioNTech was first, the Oxford option has attracted a good deal of attention in the UK, quite understandably, although there has been some confusion about its efficacy and correct dosing requirements. From a business perspective, AstraZeneca won plaudits for saying it would not make a profit on the vaccine while the pandemic lasted, although it is not yet known how that would be quantified.

AstraZeneca is a British/Swedish multinational company, its UK roots stretching back to the world's first chemical company, ICI. It is a key player in an important industry both nationally and globally: while recent UK figures are hard to come by – even the facts and figures featured on the website Association of the British Pharmaceutical Industry only go up to 2016/17 – the global statistics are staggering. Projected global spending on medicines by 2024 was $1.6 trillion, while the projected 2019 revenue for just one drug – Opdivo, manufactured by Bristol–Myers Squibb – was $3.6bn.

Given these numbers, 'Big Pharma' is a commonly used pejorative group name for these huge businesses, and there have certainly been instances in the past where outcomes have been very far from ideal. However, the way in which the industry – and its collaborators in academia – have pulled together in the face of threat to life as we know it, has been nothing short of jaw-dropping. If the biggest lesson we can take from 2020 is that knowledge, expertise and collaboration can make a genuine difference, then perhaps the year won't have been in vain after all.

BANKING AND PERSONAL FINANCE

There are two main types of deposit-taking institutions: banks and building societies, although National Savings and Investments also provides savings products. Banks and building societies are regulated by the Prudential Regulation Authority, part of the Bank of England (*see* Financial Services Regulation), and National Savings and Investments is accountable to HM Treasury.

The main institutions within the British banking system are the Bank of England (the central bank), retail banks, investment banks and overseas banks. In its role as the central bank, the Bank of England acts as banker to the government and as a note-issuing authority; it also oversees the efficient functioning of payment and settlement systems.

Since May 1997, the Bank of England has had operational responsibility for monetary policy. At monthly meetings of its monetary policy committee the Bank sets the interest rate at which it will lend to the money markets.

OFFICIAL INTEREST RATES 2006–19	
3 August 2006	4.75%
9 November 2006	5.00%
11 January 2007	5.25%
10 May 2007	5.50%
5 July 2007	5.75%
6 December 2007	5.50%
7 February 2008	5.25%
10 April 2008	5.00%
8 October 2008	4.50%
6 November 2008	3.00%
4 December 2008	2.00%
8 January 2009	1.50%
5 February 2009	1.00%
5 March 2009	0.50%
4 August 2016	0.25%
2 November 2017	0.50%
2 August 2018	0.75%

RETAIL BANKING

Retail banks offer a wide variety of financial services to individuals and companies, including current and deposit accounts, loan and overdraft facilities, credit and debit cards, investment services, pensions, insurance and mortgages. All banks offer internet and telephone banking facilities and the majority also offer traditional branch services.

The Financial Ombudsman Service provides independent and impartial arbitration in disputes between banks and their customers (*see* Financial Services Regulation).

PAYMENT CLEARINGS

The Payment Systems Regulator (PSR), a subsidiary of the Financial Conduct Authority (*see* Financial Services Regulation), is the economic regulator for the £81 trillion payment systems industry in the UK. Funded by an annual levy on the firms it regulates, it was established on 1 April 2015. The PSR's statutory objectives are:

- to ensure that payment systems are operated and developed in a way that considers and promotes the interests of all the businesses and consumers that use them
- to promote effective competition in the markets for payment systems and services – between operators, payment service providers and infrastructure providers
- to promote development and innovation in payment systems, in particular the infrastructure used to operate these systems

DESIGNATED PAYMENT SYSTEMS

The PSR can only use its regulatory powers in relation to payment systems designated by HM Treasury, which regularly reviews this list. The current designated payment systems are: BACS, C&C (Cheque & Credit), CHAPS, Faster Payments Scheme (FPS), LINK, Northern Ireland Cheque Clearing (NICC), MasterCard, Visa Europe (Visa).

PSR, 12 Endeavour Square, Stratford, London E20 1JN
T 020-7066 1000 **E** contactus@psr.org.uk **W** www.psr.org.uk
Chair, Charles Randell, CBE

MAJOR RETAIL BANKS' FINANCIAL RESULTS 2018

Bank group	Profit/(loss) before taxation £ million	Profit/(loss) after taxation £ million	Total assets £ million
Barclays Bank	3,494	2,372	1,133,283
Cooperative Bank	(141)	(69)	23,103
HSBC UK Bank	1,064	763	238,939
Lloyds Banking Group	5,960	4,400	797,598
RBS Group	3,359	2,084	694,235
Santander UK	1,545	1,104	283,372
TSB Banking Group	(105)	(63)	41,124
Virgin Money Group	119	81	45,116

GLOSSARY OF FINANCIAL TERMS

The following provides a glossary of a selection of financial terms currently in general use and does not constitute any sort of financial advice which should always be sort from a regulated provider *see also* Financial Services Regulation.

ACCIDENT, SICKNESS AND UNEMPLOYMENT (ASU) INSURANCE – Is a short-term income protection policy that replaces an individual's income for a pre-defined amount of time, should they become unable to work due to accident, sickness or involuntary redundancy. Unemployment protection insurance can also be brought as a standalone product, as can accident and sickness protection. *See also* PPI.

AER (ANNUAL EQUIVALENT RATE) – A notional rate quoted on savings and investment products which demonstrates the return on interest, when compounded and paid annually.

APR (ANNUAL PERCENTAGE RATE) – Calculates the total amount of interest payable over the whole term of a product (such as an investment or loan), allowing consumers to compare rival products on a like-for-like basis. Companies offering loans, credit cards, mortgages or overdrafts are required by law to provide the APR rate. Where typical APR is shown, it refers to the company's typical borrower and so is given as a best example; rate and costs may vary depending on individual circumstances.

ANNUITY – A type of insurance policy that provides regular income in exchange for a lump sum. The annuity can be bought from a company other than the existing pension provider.

ATM (AUTOMATED TELLER MACHINES) – Commonly referred to as cash machines. Users can access their bank accounts using a card for simple transactions such as withdrawing money and viewing an account balance. Some banks and independent ATM deployers charge for transactions.

BANKER'S DRAFT – A cheque drawn on a bank against a cash deposit. Considered to be a secure way of receiving money in instances where a cheque could 'bounce' or where it is not desirable to receive cash.

BASE RATE – The interest rate set by the Bank of England at which it will lend to financial institutions. This acts as a benchmark for all other interest rates.

BASIS POINT – Unit of measure (usually one-hundredth of a percentage point) used to express movements in interest rates, foreign rates or bond yields.

BUY-TO-LET – The purchase of a residential property for the sole purpose of letting to a tenant. Not all lenders provide mortgage finance for this purpose. Buy-to-let lenders assess projected rental income (typical expectations are between 125 and 130 per cent of the monthly interest payment) in addition to, or instead of, the borrower's income. Buy-to-let mortgages are available as either interest only or repayment.

CAPITAL GAIN/LOSS – Increase/decrease in the value of a capital asset when it is sold or transferred compared to its initial worth.

CAPPED RATE MORTGAGE – The interest rate applied to a loan is guaranteed not to rise above a certain rate for a set period of time; the rate can therefore fall but will not rise above the capped rate. The level at which the cap is fixed is usually higher than for a fixed rate mortgage for a comparable period of time. The lender normally imposes early redemption penalties within the first few years.

CASH CARD – Issued by banks and building societies for withdrawing cash from ATMs.

CHARGE CARD – Charge cards, eg American Express and Diners Club, can be used in a similar way to credit cards but the debt must be settled in full each month.

CHIP AND PIN CARD – A credit/debit card which incorporates an embedded chip containing unique owner details. When used with a PIN, such cards offer greater security as they are less prone to fraud.

CONTACTLESS PAYMENT – A system that uses radio-frequency identification (RFID) or near-field communication (NFC) for making secure payments via a credit, debit or smart card or another device, such as a smartphone, with an embedded chip and antenna which need to be in close proximity to a reader at the point of sale. Occasional PIN verification is required to authenticate the user and purchases are typically limited to small value sales.

CREDIT CARD – Normally issued with a credit limit, credit cards can be used for purchases until the limit is reached. There is normally an interest-free period on the outstanding balance of up to 56 days. Charges can be avoided if the balance is paid off in full within the interest-free period. Alternatively part of the balance can be paid and in most cases there is a minimum amount set by the issuer (normally a percentage of the outstanding balance) which must be paid on a monthly basis. Some card issuers charge an annual fee and most issuers belong to at least one major credit card network, eg Mastercard or Visa.

CREDIT RATING – Overall credit worthiness of a borrower based on information from a credit reference agency, such as Experian or Equifax, which holds details of credit agreements, payment records, county court judgments etc for all adults in the UK. This information is supplied to lenders who use it in their credit scoring or underwriting systems to calculate the risk of granting a loan to an individual and the probability that it will be repaid. Each lender sets their own criteria for credit worthiness and may accept or reject a credit application based on an individual's credit rating.

CRITICAL ILLNESS COVER – Insurance that covers borrowers against critical illnesses such as stroke, heart attack or cancer and is designed to protect mortgage or other loan payments.

DEBIT CARD – Debit cards were introduced on a large scale in the UK in the mid-1980s, replacing cash and cheques to purchase goods and services. Funds are automatically withdrawn from an individual's bank account after making a purchase and no interest is charged. They can also be used to withdraw cash from ATMs in the UK and abroad.

DIRECT DEBIT – An instruction from a customer to their bank, which authorises the payee to charge costs to the customer's bank account.

DISCOUNTED MORTGAGE – Discounted mortgages guarantee an interest rate set at a margin below the standard variable rate for a period of time. The discounted rate will move up or down with the standard variable rate, but the payment rate will retain the agreed differential below the standard variable rate. The lender normally imposes early redemption penalties within the first few years.

EARLY REDEMPTION PENALTY – *see* Redemption Penalty

ENDOWMENT MORTGAGE – Refers to a mortgage loan arranged on an interest-only basis where the capital is intended to be repaid by one or more endowment policies. The borrower has two distinct arrangements: one with the lender for the mortgage and one with the insurer for the endowment policy. The borrower can change either arrangement if they wish.

EQUITY – When applied to real estate, equity is the difference between the value of a property and the amount outstanding on any loan secured against it. Negative

BANK FAMILY TREE

Includes the major retail banks operating in the UK as at April 2019. For financial results for these banks *see* Banking and Personal Finance. Building societies are only included in instances where they demutualised to become a bank.

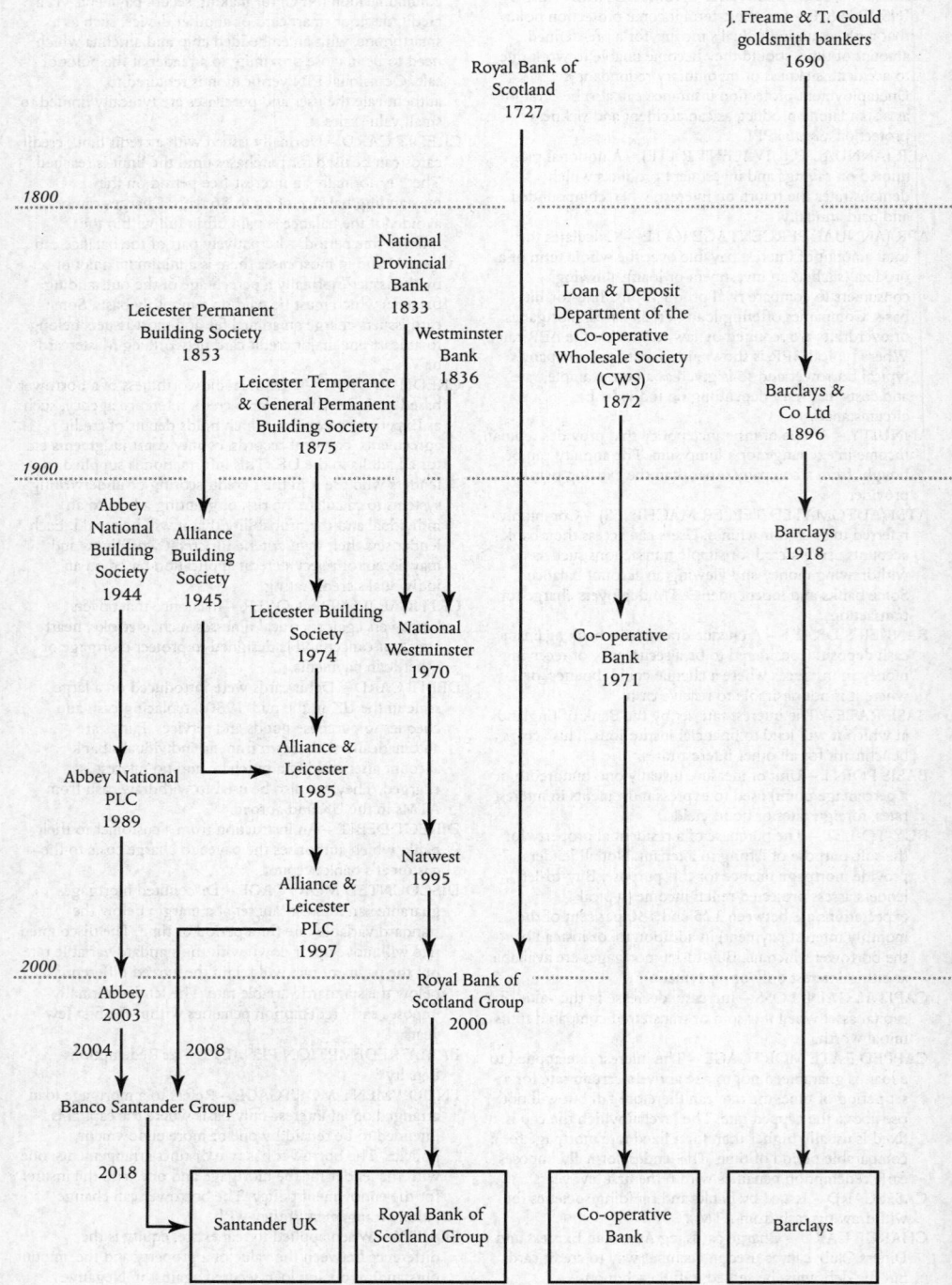

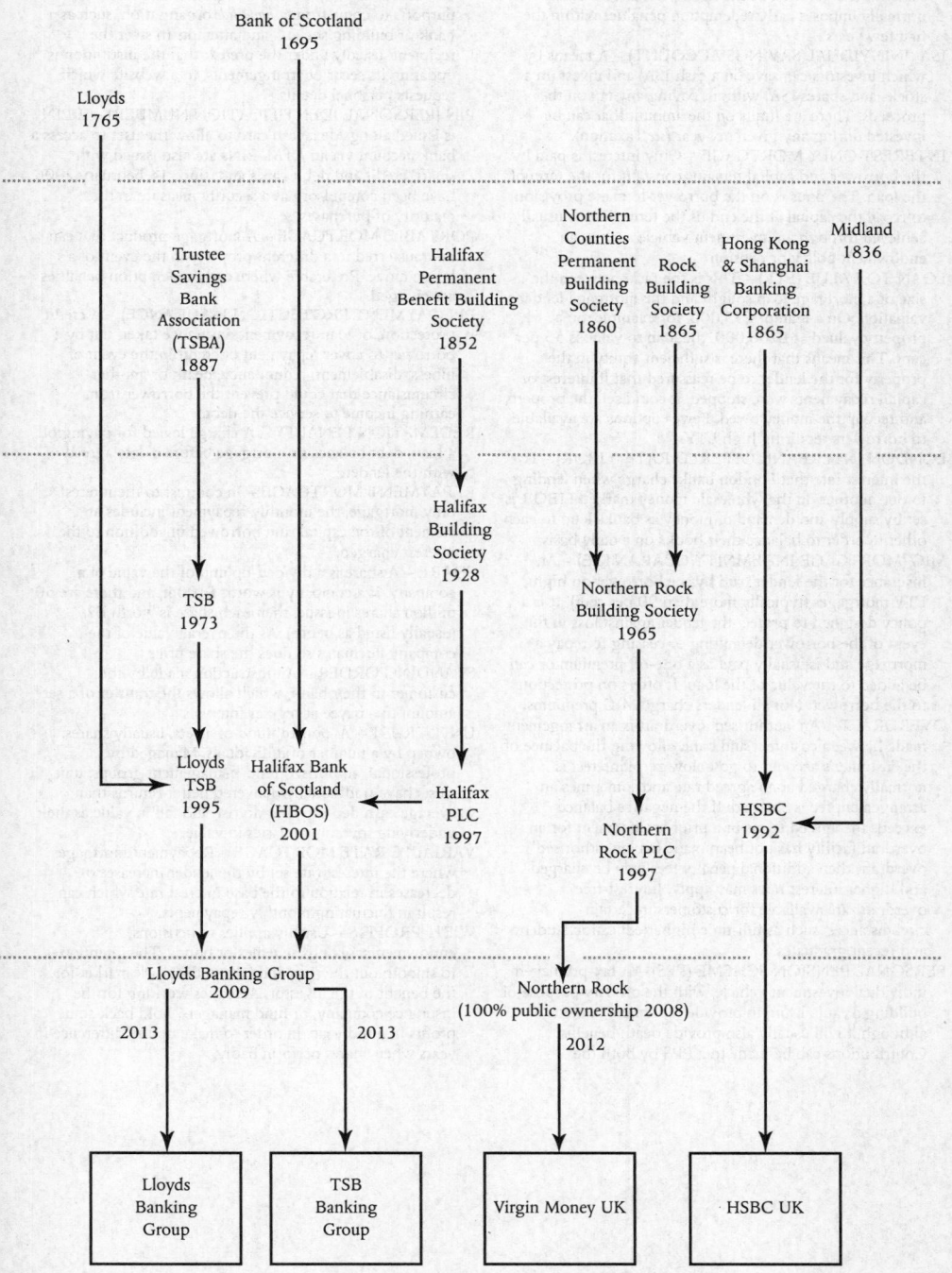

equity occurs when the loan is greater than the market value of the property.

FIXED RATE MORTGAGE – A repayment mortgage where the interest rate on the loan is fixed for a set amount of time, normally a period of between one and ten years. The interest rate does not vary with changes to the base rate resulting in the monthly mortgage payment remaining the same for the duration of the fixed period. The lender normally imposes early redemption penalties within the first few years.

ISA (INDIVIDUAL SAVINGS ACCOUNT) – A means by which investors can save (in a cash ISA) and invest (in a stocks and shares ISA) without paying any tax on the proceeds. There are limits on the amount that can be invested during any given tax year (see Taxation).

INTEREST ONLY MORTGAGE – Only interest is paid by the borrower and capital remains constant for the term of the loan. The onus is on the borrower to make provision to repay the capital at the end of the term. This is usually achieved through an investment vehicle such as an endowment policy or pension.

LOAN TO VALUE (LTV) – This is the ratio between the size of a mortgage loan sought and the mortgage lender's valuation. On a loan of £55,000, for example, on a property valued at £100,000, the loan to value is 55 per cent. This means that there is sufficient equity in the property for the lender to be reassured that if interest or capital repayments were stopped, it could sell the property and recoup the money owed. Fewer options are available to borrowers requiring high LTV.

LONDON INTERBANK OFFERED RATE (LIBOR) – Is the interest rate that London banks charge when lending to one another on the wholesale money market. LIBOR is set by supply and demand of money as banks lend to each other in order to balance their books on a daily basis.

MIG (MORTGAGE INDEMNITY GUARANTEE) – An insurance for the lender paid by the borrower on high LTV mortgages (typically more than 90 per cent). It is a policy designed to protect the lender against loss in the event of the borrower defaulting or ceasing to repay a mortgage and is usually paid as a one-off premium or can be added to the value of the loan. It offers no protection to the borrower. Not all lenders charge MIG premiums.

OVERDRAFT – An 'authorised' overdraft is an arrangement made between customer and bank allowing the balance of the customer's account to go below zero; interest is normally charged at an agreed rate and sometimes an arrangement fee is charged. If the negative balance exceeds the agreed terms or a prior arrangement for an overdraft facility has not been made (an 'unauthorised' overdraft) then additional penalty fees may be charged and higher interest rates may apply. Interest-free overdrafts are available for customers in certain circumstances, such as full-time higher education students and recent graduates.

PERSONAL PENSION SCHEME (PPS) – A tax-privileged individual investment vehicle, with the primary purpose of building a capital sum to provide retirement benefits, although it will usually also provide death benefits. Contributions can be made to a PPS by both the

individual and, if they are not self-employed, their employer. Contributions are exempt from tax and the retirement age may be selected at any time, usually from age 55. Up to 25 per cent of the pension fund may be taken as a tax-free cash sum on retirement. See also Social Welfare, Pensions.

PHISHING – A fraudulent attempt to obtain bank account details and security codes through an email. The email purports to come from a bona fide organisation, such as a bank or building society, and attempts to steer the recipient, usually under the pretext that the institution is updating its security arrangements, to a website which requests personal details.

PIN (PERSONAL IDENTIFICATION NUMBER) – A PIN is issued alongside a cash card to allow the user to access a bank account via an ATM. PINs are also issued with smart, credit and debit cards and, since 14 February 2006, have been compulsory as a security measure in the majority of purchases.

PORTABLE MORTGAGE – A mortgage product that can be transferred to a different property in the event of a house move. Preferable where early redemption penalties are charged.

PPI (PAYMENT PROTECTION INSURANCE) – A credit protection, or loan repayment, insurance taken out by a borrower to cover repayment of credit in the event of illness, disablement, redundancy, death or another circumstance that could prevent the borrower from earning income to service the debt.

REDEMPTION PENALTY – A charge levied for paying off a loan, debt balance or mortgage before a date agreed with the lender.

REPAYMENT MORTGAGE – In contrast to the interest only mortgage, the monthly repayment includes an element of the capital sum borrowed in addition to the interest charged.

SHARE – A share is a divided-up unit of the value of a company. If a company is worth £100m, and there are 50 million shares in issue, then each share is worth £2 (usually listed as pence). As the overall value of the company fluctuates so does the share price.

STANDING ORDER – An instruction made by the customer to their bank, which allows the transfer of a set amount to a payee at regular intervals.

UNIT TRUST – A 'pooled' fund of assets, usually shares, owned by a number of individuals. Managed by professional, authorised fund-management groups, unit trusts have traditionally delivered better returns than average cash deposits, but do rise and fall in value as their underlying investment varies in value.

VARIABLE RATE MORTGAGE – Repayment mortgages where the interest rate set by the lender increases or decreases in relation to the base interest rate which can result in fluctuating monthly repayments.

WITH-PROFITS – Usually applies to pensions, endowments, savings schemes or bonds. The intention is to smooth out the rises and falls in the stock market for the benefit of the investor. Actuaries working for the insurance company, or fund managers, hold back some profits in good years in order to make up the difference in years when shares perform badly.

BRITISH CURRENCY

The unit of currency is the pound sterling (£) of 100 pence. The decimal system was introduced on 15 February 1971.

COIN

Gold Coins	Nickel-Brass Coins
One hundred pounds £100*	Two pounds £2 (pre-1997)◖
Fifty pounds £50*	One pound £1
Twenty-five pounds £25*	
Ten pounds £10*	*Cupro-Nickel Coins*
Five pounds £5	Crown £5 (since 1990)◖
Two pounds £2	50 pence 50p
Sovereign £1	Crown 25p (pre-1990)◖
Half-sovereign 50p	20 pence 20p
Silver Coins	*Nickel-plated Steel Coins***
(Britannia coins)*	10 pence 10p
Two pounds £2	5 pence 5p
One pound £1	
50 pence 50p	*Bronze Coins*
Twenty pence 20p	2 pence 2p
	1 penny 1p
Maundy Money†	
Fourpence 4p	*Copper-plated Steel Coins††*
Threepence 3p	2 pence 2p
Twopence 2p	1 penny 1p
Penny 1p	
Bi-colour Coins‡	
Two pounds £2	
One pound £1§	

* Britannia coins: gold bullion introduced 1987; silver, 1997
† Ceremonial money given annually by the sovereign on Maundy Thursday to as many elderly men and women as there are years in the sovereign's age
‡ Cupro-nickel centre and nickel-brass outer ring
§ The 12-sided £1 entered circulation on 28 March 2017
◖ Commemorative coins; not intended for general circulation
** Since September 1992; in 1998 the 2p was additionally struck in bronze
†† Pre-2012 the 10p and 5p coins were struck in cupro-nickel

GOLD COIN

Gold ceased to circulate during the First World War. Since then controls on buying, selling and holding gold coin have been imposed at various times but have subsequently been revoked. Under the Exchange Control (Gold Coins Exemption) Order 1979, gold coins may now be imported and exported without restriction, except gold coins which are more than 50 years old and valued at a sum in excess of £8,000.

Value Added Taxation on the sale of gold coins was revoked in 2000.

SILVER COIN

Prior to 1920 silver coins were struck from sterling silver, an alloy of which 925 parts in 1,000 were silver. In 1920 the proportion of silver was reduced to 500 parts. Since 1947 all 'silver' coins, except Maundy money, have been struck from cupro-nickel, an alloy of 75 parts copper and 25 parts nickel, except for the 20p, composed of 84 parts copper, 16 parts nickel. Maundy coins continue to be struck from sterling silver.

BRONZE COIN

Bronze, introduced in 1860 to replace copper, is an alloy consisting mainly of copper with small amounts of zinc and tin. Bronze was replaced by copper-plated steel in September 1992 with the exception of 1998 when the 2p was made in both copper-plated steel and bronze.

LEGAL TENDER *as at May 2019*

	Legal up to
Gold*	any amount
£2	any amount
£1	any amount
50p	£10
20p	£10
10p	£5
5p	£5
2p	20p
1p	20p

* Dated 1838 onwards, if not below least current weight

£5 (Crown since 1990) and 25p (Crown pre-1990) up to £10 are also legal tender under the Coinage Act 1971 but, as for all commemorative coins, are not designed for general circulation and are unlikely to be accepted by banks and shops.

The following coins have ceased to be legal tender:

Farthing	31 Dec 1960
Halfpenny (½d)	31 Jul 1969
Half-crown	31 Dec 1969
Threepence	31 Aug 1971
Penny (1d)	31 Aug 1971
Sixpence	30 Jun 1980
Halfpenny (½p)	31 Dec 1984
Old 5 pence	31 Dec 1990
Old 10 pence	30 Jun 1993
Old 50 pence	28 Feb 1998
Old £1 (nickel-brass/round)	15 Oct 2017

The Channel Islands and the Isle of Man issue their own coinage, which is legal tender only in the island of issue.

COIN STANDARDS

	Metal	Standard weight (g)	Standard diameter (mm)
1p	bronze	3.56	20.30
1p	copper-plated steel	3.56	20.30
2p	bronze	7.12	25.90
2p	copper-plated steel	7.12	25.90
5p	cupro-nickel	3.25	18.00
5p	nickel-plated steel	3.25	18.00
10p	nickel-plated steel	6.50	24.50
20p	cupro-nickel	5.00	21.40
25p Crown	cupro-nickel	28.28	38.61
50p	cupro-nickel	8.00	27.30
£1	nickel-brass, nickel-plated brass alloy	8.75	23.43
£2	nickel-brass	15.98	28.40
£2	nickel-brass, cupro-nickel	12.00	28.40
£5 Crown	cupro-nickel	28.28	38.61

The 'remedy' is the amount of variation from standard permitted in weight and fineness of coins when first issued from the Royal Mint.

THE TRIAL OF THE PYX

The Trial of the Pyx is the examination by a jury to ascertain that coins made by the Royal Mint, which have been set aside in the pyx (or box), are of the proper weight, diameter and composition required by law. The trial is held annually, presided over by the Queen's Remembrancer, with a jury of freemen of the Company of Goldsmiths.

BANKNOTES

Bank of England notes are issued in denominations of £5, £10, £20 and £50 for the amount of the fiduciary note issue, and are legal tender in England and Wales.

LEGAL TENDER

A new-style £20 note, the first in series F, was introduced in March 2007. A £50 note, the second in the F series, and the first banknote issued by the Bank of England to feature two portraits on the reverse, was issued in November 2011. The first polymer G series banknote, a £5 note featuring Sir Winston Churchill, was issued in September 2016, a £10 polymer note featuring Jane Austen followed in September 2017 and a £20 polymer note featuring the artist J. M. W. Turner will be issued in 2020.

The historical figures portrayed in the F and G series are:

£5	Sep 2016–date	Sir Winston Churchill
£10	Sep 2017–date	Jane Austen
£20	Mar 2007–date	Adam Smith
£50	Nov 2011–date	Matthew Boulton and James Watt

NOTE CIRCULATION

Note circulation is highest at the two peak spending periods of the year: around Christmas and during the summer holiday period.

The Bank of England measures the value of notes in circulation on the last day of February each year. The value of notes in circulation (£ million) at the end of February 2018 and 2019 was:

	2018	2019
£5	1,910	1,979
£10	7,789	10,524
£20	42,692	40,129
£50	16,508	17,210
Other notes*	4,351	4,330
Total	73,250	74,171

* Includes higher value notes used as backing for the note issues of authorised banks in Scotland and Northern Ireland

WITHDRAWN BANKNOTES

Banknotes which are no longer legal tender are payable when presented at the head office of the Bank of England in London.

The white notes for £10, £20, £50, £100, £500 and £1,000, which were issued until April 1943, ceased to be legal tender in May 1945, and the white £5 note in March 1946.

The white £5 note issued between October 1945 and September 1956, the £5 notes issued between 1957 and 1963 (bearing a portrait of Britannia) and the first series to bear a portrait of the Queen, issued between 1963 and 1971, ceased to be legal tender in March 1961, June 1967 and September 1973 respectively.

The series of £1 notes issued during the years 1928 to 1960 and the 10 shilling notes issued from 1928 to 1961 (those without the royal portrait) ceased to be legal tender in May and October 1962 respectively. The £1 note first issued in March 1960 (bearing on the back a representation of Britannia) and the £10 note first issued in February 1964 (bearing a lion on the back), both bearing a portrait of the Queen on the front, ceased to be legal tender in June 1979. The £1 note first issued in 1978 ceased to be legal tender on 11 March 1988. The 10 shilling note was replaced by the 50p coin in October 1969, and ceased to be legal tender on 21 November 1970.

The D series of banknotes was introduced from 1970 and ceased to be legal tender from the dates shown below. The predominant identifying feature of each note was the portrayal on the back of a prominent figure from British history:

£1	Feb 1978–Mar 1988	Sir Isaac Newton
£5	Nov 1971–Nov 1991	Duke of Wellington
£10	Feb 1975–May 1994	Florence Nightingale
£20	Jul 1970–Mar 1993	William Shakespeare
£50	Mar 1981–Sep 1996	Sir Christopher Wren

The £1 coin was introduced on 21 April 1983 to replace the £1 note. No £1 notes have been issued since 1984 and in March 1998 the outstanding notes were written off in accordance with the provision of the Currency Act 1983.

The E series of notes was introduced from June 1990, replacing the D series. E series notes were withdrawn from circulation on the dates shown below:

£5	Jun 1990–Nov 2003	George Stephenson
£5	May 2002–May 2017	Elizabeth Fry
£10	Apr 1992–Jul 2003	Charles Dickens
£10	Nov 2000–Mar 2018	Charles Darwin
£20	Jun 1991–Feb 2001	Michael Faraday
£20	Jun 1999–Jun 2010	Sir Edward Elgar
£50	Apr 1994–Apr 2014	Sir John Houblon

Scotland – Banknotes are issued by three Scottish banks. The Royal Bank of Scotland issues notes for £1, £5, £10, £20, £50 and £100. Bank of Scotland and the Clydesdale Bank issue notes for £5, £10, £20, £50 and £100. All three banks have replaced paper £5 and £10 with polymer notes. Scottish notes are not legal tender in the UK but they are an authorised currency.

Northern Ireland – Banknotes are issued by four banks in Northern Ireland. The Bank of Ireland and the Ulster Bank issue notes for £5 (polymer), £10 (polymer), £20, £50 and £100. The First Trust Bank retains the right to issue notes for £10, £20, £50 and £100 until midnight on 30 June 2020, when it will cease to do so. Danske Bank (formerly Northern Bank) issue notes for £10 (polymer) and £20. Northern Ireland notes are not legal tender in the UK but they are an authorised currency.

Channel Islands – The States of Guernsey issues its own currency notes and coinage. The notes are for £1, £5, £10, £20 and £50, and the coins are for 1p, 2p, 5p, 10p, 20p, 50p and £2. The Guernsey round £1 coin was withdrawn from circulation in October 2017 with the introduction of the UK 12-sided coin, which is used alongside the £1 note.

The States of Jersey issues its own currency notes and coinage. The notes are for £1, £5, £10, £20, £50 and £100, and the coins are for 1p, 2p, 5p, 10p, 20p, 50p and £2. The Jersey round £1 coin was withdrawn from circulation in October 2017 with the introduction of the UK 12-sided coin, which is used alongside the £1 note.

The Isle of Man – The Isle of Man government issues notes for £1, £5, £10, £20 and £50. Although these notes are only legal tender in the Isle of Man, they may be exchanged at face value at certain UK banks at their discretion. The Isle of Man issues coins for 1p, 2p, 5p, 10p, 20p, 50p, £1, £2 and £5.

COST OF LIVING AND INFLATION RATES

The first cost of living index to be calculated took July 1914 as 100 and was based on the pattern of expenditure of working-class families in 1914. The cost of living index was superseded in 1947 by the general index of retail prices (RPI), although the older term is still popularly applied.

The Harmonised Index of Consumer Prices (HICP) was introduced in 1997 to enable comparisons within the European Union using an agreed methodology. In 2003 the National Statistician renamed the HICP the Consumer Prices Index (CPI) to reflect its role as the main target measure of inflation for macroeconomic purposes. In March 2013 CPIH, an additional index which includes owner-occupiers' housing costs, was introduced.

The RPI and indices based on it continue to be published alongside the CPI. Private-sector pensions and index-linked gilts continue to be calculated with reference to RPI or its derivatives.

CPI AND RPI

The CPI and RPI measure the changes month by month in the average level of prices of goods and services purchased by households in the UK. The indices are compiled using a selection of around 700 goods and services, and the prices charged for these items are collected at regular intervals at about 140 locations throughout the country, from the internet and over the phone. The Office for National Statistics (ONS) reviews the components of the indices once a year to reflect changes in consumer preferences and the establishment of new products. The table below shows changes made by the ONS to the CPI 'shopping basket' in 2019.

The CPI excludes a number of items that are included in the RPI, mainly related to housing, such as council tax, and a range of owner-occupier housing costs, such as mortgage payments. The CPI covers all private households, whereas the RPI excludes the top 4 per cent by income and pensioner households which derive at least three-quarters of their income from state benefits. The two indices use different methodologies to combine the prices of goods and services, which means that since 1996 the CPI inflation measure is less than the RPI inflation measure.

CHANGES TO THE 'SHOPPING BASKET' OF GOODS AND SERVICES IN 2019

The table below shows changes to the CPI* basket of goods and services made by the ONS in 2019 in order to reflect changes in consumer preferences and the establishment of new products.

Goods and services group	Removed items	New items
Food	–	popcorn; peanut butter
Non-alcoholic beverages	cola flavoured drink	flavoured tea (eg herbal/ fruit); regular cola drink (bottle); diet/ sugar-free cola drink (bottle)
Clothing	–	adult hat/ cap
Furniture, furnishings & carpets	three-piece non-leather suite	non-leather settee
Glassware, tableware & household utensils	crockery set	bakeware (baking tray or roasting tin); dinner plate
Non-durable household goods	washing powder	washing liquid/ gel
Operation of personal transport equipment	brake fitting in fast-fit auto centre	wheel alignment
Audio-visual equipment & related products	hi-fi	portable speaker (eg Bluetooth speaker); smart speaker
Recreational items, gardens & pets	complete dry dog food	dog treats
Books, newspapers & stationery	envelopes	child's fiction book, 6–12-years-old
Catering services	staff restaurant soft drink	–
Personal care	–	electric toothbrush
Financial services	unit trust initial charge	–

* RPI goods and services are grouped together under different classifications

INFLATION RATE

The 12-monthly percentage change in the 'all items' index of the RPI or CPI is referred to as the rate of inflation. As the most familiar measure of inflation, the RPI is often referred to as the 'headline rate of inflation'. The CPI is the main measure of inflation for macroeconomic purposes and forms the basis of the government's inflation target, which is currently 2 per cent. The percentage change in prices between any two months/years can be obtained using this formula:

$$\frac{\text{Later date RPI/CPI} - \text{Earlier date RPI/CPI}}{\text{Earlier date RPI/CPI}} \times 100$$

For example, to find the CPI rate of inflation for 2006, using the annual averages for 2005 and 2006:

$$\frac{79.9 - 78.1}{78.1} \times 100$$

On 16 February 2016 the reference year for all CPI indices was re-based to 2015=100, replacing the 2005=100 series. The change of reference period does not apply to the RPI, which remains unchanged. The CPI rate of inflation figure given in the Annual Indices table may differ by plus or minus 0.1 percentage points from the figure calculated by the above equation.

The RPI and CPI figures are published around the the middle of each month in an indices bulletin on the ONS website (**W** www.ons.gov.uk/economy/inflationandpriceindices).

PURCHASING POWER OF THE POUND

Changes in the internal purchasing power of the pound may be defined as the 'inverse' of changes in the level of prices: when prices go up, the amount which can be purchased with a given sum of money goes down. To find the purchasing power of the pound in one month or year, given that it was 100p in a previous month or year, the calculation would be:

$$100p \times \frac{\text{Earlier month/year RPI}}{\text{Later month/year RPI}}$$

Thus, if the purchasing power of the pound is taken to be 100p in 1975, the comparable purchasing power in 2000 would be:

$$100p \times \frac{34.2}{170.3} = 20.1p$$

For longer term comparisons, it has been the practice to use an index which has been constructed by linking together the RPI for the period 1962 to date; an index derived from the consumers' expenditure deflator for the period from 1938 to 1962; and the pre-war 'cost of living' index for the period 1914 to 1938. This long-term index enables the internal purchasing power of the pound to be calculated for any year from 1914 onwards. It should be noted that these figures can only be approximate.

ANNUAL INDICES

	Annual average RPI (1987 = 100)	Purchasing power of £ (1998 = 1.00)	Annual average CPI (2015 = 100)*	Annual average CPIH† (2015=100)*	Rate of inflation (RPI/ CPI/ CPIH)†
1914	2.8	58.18			
1915	3.5	46.54			
1920	7.0	23.27			
1925	5.0	32.58			
1930	4.5	36.20			
1935	4.0	40.72			
1938	4.4	37.02			
There are no official figures for 1939–45					
1946	7.4	22.01			
1950	9.0	18.10			
1955	11.2	14.54			
1960	12.6	12.93			
1965	14.8	11.00			
1970	18.5	8.80			
1975	34.2	4.76			
1980	66.8	2.44			
1985	94.6	1.72			
1990	126.1	1.29			9.5/ 7.0
1995	149.1	1.09			3.5/ 2.6
1998	162.9	1.00	71.2		3.4/ 1.6
2000	170.3	0.96	72.7		3.0/ 0.8
2005	192.0	0.85	78.1	79.4	2.8/ 2.1
2006	198.1	0.82	79.9	81.4	3.2/ 2.3/ 2.5
2007	206.6	0.79	81.8	83.3	4.3/ 2.3/ 2.4
2008	214.8	0.76	84.7	86.2	4.0/ 3.6/ 3.5
2009	213.7	0.76	86.6	87.9	−0.5/ 2.2/ 2.0
2010	223.6	0.73	89.4	90.1	4.6/ 3.3/ 2.5
2011	235.2	0.69	93.4	93.6	5.2/ 4.5/ 3.8
2012	242.7	0.67	96.1	96.0	3.2/ 2.8/ 2.6
2013	250.1	0.65	98.5	98.2	3.0/ 2.6/ 2.3
2014	256.0	0.64	100.0	99.6	2.4/ 1.5/ 1.5
2015	258.5	0.63	100.0	100.0	1.0/ 0.0/ 0.4
2016	263.1	0.62	100.7	101.0	1.8/ 0.7/ 1.0
2017	272.5	0.60	103.4	103.6	3.6/ 2.7/ 2.6
2018	281.6	0.58	105.9	106.0	3.3/ 2.5/ 2.3

ECONOMIC STATISTICS

TRADE

TRADE IN GOODS
£ million

	Exports	Imports	Balance
2014	293,116	415,187	(122,071)
2015	286,752	404,562	(117,810)
2016	299,073	431,725	(132,652)
2017	338,739	475,774	(137,035)
2018	350,651	488,744	(138,093)

Source: ONS (Crown copyright)

BALANCE OF PAYMENTS, 2018

Current Account	£ million
Trade in goods and services	
Trade in goods	(138,093)
Trade in services	107,124
Total trade in goods and services	(30,969)
Income	
Compensation of employees	(171)
Investment income	(25,376)
Other	(1,103)
Total income	(26,650)
Total secondary income	(24,025)
TOTAL (CURRENT BALANCE)	(81,644)

Source: ONS (Crown copyright)

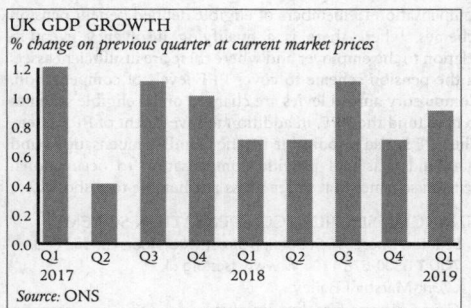

UK GDP GROWTH
% change on previous quarter at current market prices

Q1 Q2 Q3 Q4 / Q1 Q2 Q3 Q4 / Q1
2017   2018   2019
Source: ONS

UK EMPLOYMENT

DISTRIBUTION OF THE WORKFORCE

	Mar 2018	Mar 2019
Workforce jobs	34,949,000	35,537,000
HM forces	154,000	152,000
Self-employment jobs	4,496,000	4,657,000
Employees jobs	30,271,000	30,701,000
Government-supported trainees	28,000	27,000

Source: ONS – Labour Market Statistics 2019 (Crown copyright)

EMPLOYED AND UNEMPLOYED
thousands, all aged 16+

	Apr–Jun 2018		Apr–Jun 2019	
	Number	Rate (%)	Number	Rate (%)
Employed	32,386	61.1	32,811	61.6
Unemployed	1,362	4.0	1,329	3.9

Source: ONS – Labour Market Statistics 2019 (Crown copyright)

DURATION OF UNEMPLOYMENT, APR–JUN 2019

All unemployed	1,329,000
Less than 6 months	793,000
6 months–1 year	194,000
1 year +	342,000
2 years +	169,000

Source: ONS – Labour Market Statistics 2019 (Crown copyright)

MEDIAN EARNINGS, 2018
full-time, £

	All	Male	Female
Gross annual	24,006.00	29,425.00	18,735.00
Gross weekly	460.00	555.00	369.90
Hourly	12.78	14.10	11.50

Source: ONS (Crown copyright)

LABOUR STOPPAGES BY DURATION, 2018

1 day	12
2–3 days	22
4 days	6
5–10 days	23
11+ days	18
All stoppages	81

Source: ONS (Crown copyright)

LABOUR DISPUTES BY INDUSTRY, 2018

Industry Group	Working Days Lost
Mining, quarrying, electricity, gas, air con.	100
Manufacturing	3,000
Sewage, waste management, water supply	4,600
Construction	5,800
Wholesale & retail, motor vehicles, accommodation, food	900
Transport & storage	42,600
Information & Communication	10,600
Financial, professional, scientific, administration	4,000
Public administration & defence	15,900
Education	179,400
Human health and social work	4,900
Other	800
All industries & services	272,600

Source: ONS (Crown copyright)

TRADE UNIONS

Year	No. of unions	Total membership
2013–14	166	7,086,116
2014–15	160	7,010,527
2015–16	160	6,948,725
2016–17	151	6,865,056
2017–18	146	6,875,231

Source: Annual Report of the Certification Officer 2017–18

FINANCIAL SERVICES REGULATION

Under the Financial Services and Markets Act 2000, as amended by the Financial Services Act (2012), the Financial Conduct Authority and the Prudential Regulation Authority are responsible for financial regulation in the UK.

FINANCIAL CONDUCT AUTHORITY

The Financial Conduct Authority (FCA) is responsible for supervising the conduct of over 58,000 financial services firms and financial markets in the UK and for regulating the prudential standards of those firms – over 18,000 – not regulated by the Prudential Regulation authority. The FCA has three statutory objectives:
• to secure an appropriate degree of protection for consumers
• to protect and enhance the integrity of the UK financial system
• to promote effective market competition in the interests of consumers

The FCA is accountable to HM Treasury and therefore to parliament, but is operationally independent of the government and is funded entirely by the firms which it regulates. The FCA is governed by a board appointed by HM Treasury, but day-to-day decisions and staff management are the responsibility of the executive committee.

The FCA's annual budget for ongoing regulatory activity (ORA) in 2019–20 is £537.7m, a 2 per cent increase from 2018–19. The 2019–20 annual funding requirement totals £558.5m, an increase of 2.7 per cent due to the increase in the ORA budget and an additional £5m allocated for the costs associated with withdrawing from the European Union.

THE FINANCIAL SERVICES REGISTER
The Financial Services Register lists financial services firms and individuals in the UK who are authorised by the FCA and PRA (see Prudential Regulation Authority) to do business and specifies which activity each firm or individual is regulated to undertake and what products or services each is approved to provide.

FINANCIAL CONDUCT AUTHORITY, 12 Endeavour Square, London E20 1JN T 020-7066 1000 W www.fca.org.uk
Chair, Charles Randell, CBE
Chief Executive, Andrew Bailey

PRUDENTIAL REGULATION AUTHORITY

The Prudential Regulation Authority (PRA), part of the Bank of England, works alongside the FCA and is responsible for the prudential regulation and supervision of around 1,500 banks, building societies, credit unions, insurers and major investment firms. The PRA has three statutory objectives:
• to promote the safety and soundness of the firms it regulates
• to contribute to securing an appropriate degree of protection for those who are, or may become, insurance policyholders
• to facilitate effective competition

The members of the PRA's committee are: the Governor of the Bank of England (chair); the three Deputy Governors for Financial Stability, Markets and Banking, and Prudential Regulation; the chief executive of the FCA; a member appointed by the Governor with the approval of the chancellor; and six other external members appointed by the chancellor.

The PRA's budget for 2019–20 is £273m.

PRUDENTIAL REGULATION AUTHORITY, 20 Moorgate, London EC2R 6DA T 020-3461 4444
E enquiries@bankofengland.co.uk
W www.bankofengland.co.uk/prudential-regulation
Chief Executive, Sam Woods

COMPENSATION

Created under the Financial Services and Markets Act (2000), the Financial Services Compensation Scheme (FSCS) is the UK's statutory fund of last resort for customers of authorised financial services firms. It provides compensation if a firm authorised by the FCA or PRA is unable, or likely to be unable, to pay claims against it. In general this is when a firm has stopped trading and has insufficient assets to meet claims, or is in insolvency. This includes, banks, building societies and credit unions; firms providing debt management, mortgage and endowment advice; insurance firms; insurance brokers; investment firms; payment protection insurance firms and pension companies. The FSCS is independent of the UK regulators (FCA and PRA), with separate staff and premises. However, the FCA and PRA appoint the directors. The chair's appointment (and removal) is subject to HM Treasury approval. The FSCS is funded by an annual levy on every firm authorised by the UK regulators.

The Pension Protection Fund (PPF) is a statutory fund established under the Pensions Act 2004 and became operational on 6 April 2005. The fund was set up to pay compensation to members of eligible defined benefit pension schemes, where there is a qualifying insolvency event in relation to the employer and where there are insufficient assets in the pension scheme to cover PPF levels of compensation. Compulsory annual levies are charged on all eligible schemes to help fund the PPF, in addition to investment of PPF assets. The PPF is also responsible for the Fraud Compensation Fund – a fund that will provide compensation to occupational pension schemes that suffer a loss attributable to dishonesty.

FINANCIAL SERVICES COMPENSATION SCHEME, Beaufort House, 15 St Botolph Street, 10th Floor, London EC3A 7QU T 0800-678 1100 W www.fscs.org.uk
Chair, Marshall Bailey
Chief Executive, Caroline Rainbird
PENSION PROTECTION FUND, Renaissance, 12 Dingwall Road, Croydon CR0 2NA T 0345-600 2541
E information@ppf.co.uk W www.ppf.co.uk
Chair, Arnold Wagner, OBE
Chief Executive, Oliver Morley, CBE

DESIGNATED PROFESSIONAL BODIES

Professional firms are exempt from requiring direct regulation by the FCA if they carry out only certain restricted activities that arise out of, or are complementary to, the provision of professional services, such as arranging the sale of shares on the instructions of executors or trustees, or providing services to small, private companies. These firms are, however, supervised by designated professional bodies (DPBs). There are a number of safeguards to protect consumers dealing with firms that do not require direct regulation. These arrangements include:
• the FCA's power to ban a specific firm from taking advantage of the exemption and to restrict the regulated activities permitted to the firms

- rules which require professional firms to ensure that their clients are aware that they are not authorised persons
- a requirement for the DPBs to supervise and regulate the firms and inform the FCA on how the professional firms carry on their regulated activities

See Professional Education section for contact details of the following DPBs:

Association of Chartered Certified Accountants
Council for Licensed Conveyancers
Institute of Actuaries
Institute of Chartered Accountants in England and Wales
Institute of Chartered Accountants in Ireland
Institute of Chartered Accountants of Scotland
Law Society of England and Wales
Law Society of Northern Ireland
Law Society of Scotland
Royal Institution of Chartered Surveyors

RECOGNISED INVESTMENT EXCHANGES

The FCA currently supervises seven recognised investment exchanges (RIEs) in the UK; recognition confers an exemption from the need to be authorised to carry out regulated activities in the UK. The RIEs are organised markets on which member firms can trade investments such as equities and derivatives. The RIEs are listed with their year of recognition in parentheses:

CBOE EUROPE (2013), 5th Floor, The Monument Building, 11 Monument Street, London EC3R 8AF **T** 020-7012 8900 **W** https://markets.cboe.com

EURONEXT LONDON (2014), 10th Floor, 110 Cannon Street, London EC4N 6EU **T** 020-7076 0900 **W** www.euronext.com/en

ICE FUTURES EUROPE (2001), 5th Floor Milton Gate, 60 Chiswell Street, London EC1Y 4SA **T** 020-7065 7700 **W** www.theice.com

INTERNATIONAL PROPERTY SECURITIES EXCHANGE (IPSX) UK (2019), 8–10 Hill Street, London W1J 5NG **T** 020-3931 8800 **W** www.ipsx.com

LONDON METAL EXCHANGE (2001), 10 Finsbury Square, London EC2A 1AJ **T** 020-7113 8888 **W** www.lme.com

LONDON STOCK EXCHANGE (2001), 10 Paternoster Square, London EC4M 7LS **T** 020-7797 1000 **W** www.londonstockexchange.com

NEX EXCHANGE (2007), London Fruit and Wool Exchange, 1 Duval Square, London E1 6PW **T** 020-7818 9774 **W** www.nexexchange.com

RECOGNISED CLEARING HOUSES AND CENTRAL COUNTERPARTIES

The Bank of England is responsible for recognising and supervising central counterparties (CCPs) and clearing houses (RCHs). CCPs and RCHs provide clearing and settlement services for transactions in foreign exchange, securities, options and derivatives on recognised investment exchanges. There are currently three UK CCPs authorised under the European Market Infrastructure regulation (EMIR) and one recognised RCH (dates of authorisation and recognition are given in parentheses):

EUROCLEAR UK AND IRELAND (RCH, 2001), 33 Cannon Street, London EC4M 5SB **T** 020-7849 0000 **W** www.euroclear.com

ICE CLEAR EUROPE (CCP, 2016), 5th Floor, Milton Gate, 60 Chiswell Street, London EC1Y 4SA **T** 020-7065 7600 **W** www.theice.com/clear-europe

LCH (LONDON CLEARING HOUSE) (CCP, 2014), Aldgate House, 33 Aldgate High Street, London EC3N 1EA **T** 020-7426 7000 **W** www.lch.com

LME (LONDON METAL EXCHANGE) CLEAR (CCP, 2014), 10 Finsbury Square, London EC2A 1AJ **T** 020-7113 8888 **W** www.lme.com/LME-Clear

OMBUDSMAN SCHEMES

The Financial Ombudsman Service was set up by the Financial Services and Markets Act 2000 to provide consumers with a free, independent service for resolving disputes with authorised financial firms. It can consider complaints about most financial matters including: banking; credit cards and store cards; financial advice; hire purchase and pawnbroking; insurance; loans and credit; money transfer; mortgages; payday lending and debt collecting; payment protection insurance; pensions; savings and investments; stocks, shares, unit trusts and bonds.

Complainants must first complain to the firm involved. They do not have to accept the ombudsman's decision and are free to go to court if they wish, but if a decision is accepted, it is binding for both the complainant and the firm.

The Pensions Ombudsman can investigate and decide complaints and disputes regarding the way occupational and personal pension schemes are administered and managed. Unless there are special circumstances, this only usually includes issues and disputes that have arisen within the past three years. The Pensions Ombudsman is also the Ombudsman for the Pension Protection Fund (PPF) and the Financial Assistance Scheme (which offers help to those who were a member of an under-funded defined benefit pension scheme that started to wind-up in specific financial circumstances between 1 January 1997 and 5 April 2005).

FINANCIAL OMBUDSMAN SERVICE, Exchange Tower, Harbour Exchange, London E14 9SR **Helpline** 0800-023 4567 **T** 020-7964 1000 **W** www.financial-ombudsman.org.uk *Chief Ombudsman,* Caroline Wayman

PENSIONS OMBUDSMAN, 10 South Colonnade, Canary Wharf, London E14 4PU **T** 0800-917 4487 **E** enquiries@pensions-ombudsman.org.uk **W** www.pensions-ombudsman.org.uk *Pensions Ombudsman,* Anthony Arter *Deputy Pensions Ombudsman,* Karen Johnston

THE TAKEOVER PANEL

The Panel on Takeovers and Mergers is an independent body, established in 1968, whose main functions are to issue and administer the City code and to ensure equality of treatment and opportunity for all shareholders in takeover bids and mergers. The panel's statutory functions are set out in the Companies Act 2006.

The panel comprises up to 36 members representing a spread of expertise in takeovers, securities markets, industry and commerce. The chair, at least one deputy chair and up to 20 other members are nominated by the panel's own nomination committee. The remaining 12 members are nominated by professional bodies representing the accountancy, financial advice, insurance, investment and pension industries; the Association for Financial Markets in Europe; the Confederation of British Industry; the Quoted Companies Alliance; and UK Finance.

THE TAKEOVER PANEL, One Angel Court, London EC2R 7HJ **T** 020-7382 9026 **E** supportgroup@thetakeoverpanel.org.uk **W** www.thetakeoverpanel.org.uk *Chair,* Michael Crane, QC

INSURANCE

AUTHORISATION AND REGULATION OF INSURANCE COMPANIES

Since 1 April 2013, under the Financial Services Act 2012, the prudential supervision of over 60,000 banks, insurers and other financial services firms is the responsibility of the Prudential Regulation Authority (PRA), an operationally independent subsidiary of the Bank of England. The Financial Conduct Authority (FCA) is responsible for consumer protection, promoting competition and markets oversight. All life insurers, general insurers, reinsurers, insurance and reinsurance brokers, financial advisers and composite firms are statutorily regulated. *See also* Financial Services Regulation.

Firms wishing to effect or carry out contracts of insurance must be granted authorisation to do so. The PRA assesses applicant insurers from a prudential perspective, using the same framework that is employed for supervision of existing insurers. The FCA then assesses applicants from a conduct perspective. Although the PRA manages the authorisation process, an insurer will be granted authorisation only where both the FCA and the PRA are satisfied that they meet their relevant requirements.

There are around over 1,200 insurance organisations and friendly societies with authorisation to transact one or more class of insurance business in the UK. Although the UK left the EU on 31 January 2020, it continued to be treated for most purposes as if it was still an EU member state during the transition period and most EU law continued to apply. *See also* Brexit.

COMPLAINTS

Disputes between consumers and financial businesses can be referred to the Financial Ombudsman Service (FOS). Consumers with a complaint about any form of money matter, including bank accounts, insurance, mortgages, savings, credit and claims management companies must first take the matter to the highest level within the provider. The provider has to provide a 'final response' within eight weeks. If the complaint remains unresolved consumers can refer the complaint, free of charge, to the FOS. Since 1 April 2020 the FOS compensation limits are £355,000 for acts or omissions by firms on or after 1 April 2019 and £160,000 for acts or omissions by firms before 1 April 2019, even if the complaint is referred to the FOS after this date. Award limits are automatically adjusted each year in line with inflation as measured by the Consumer Prices Index (CPI).

Businesses falling under the EU definition of a micro enterprise (businesses with a turnover of up to €2m and fewer than ten employees) may also refer a matter to the FOS. In 2018–19, 39 per cent of new complaints about financial services companies related to payment protection insurance (down 45 per cent). Other types of insurance, such as motor, buildings and life insurance, accounted for 10 per cent (down from 11 per cent) of the total number of 1.6 million complaints received. *See also* Financial Services Regulation.

ASSOCIATION OF BRITISH INSURERS

Over 90 per cent of the domestic business of UK insurance companies is transacted by the 200 members of the Association of British Insurers (ABI). The ABI is a trade association which protects and promotes the interests of all its insurance company members. Only insurers authorised in the EU are eligible for membership. Brokers, intermediaries, financial advisers and claims handlers may not join the ABI, but may have their own trade associations. Legal firms, consultants, price comparison websites and other firms which help insurers deliver their services may join the ABI as associate members.

ASSOCIATION OF BRITISH INSURERS (ABI), One America Square, 17 Crosswall, London EC3N 2LB
T 020-7600 3333 W www.abi.org.uk
Chair, Amanda Blanc (Group Chief Executive Officer, AVIVA plc)
Director-General, Huw Evans

BALANCE OF PAYMENTS

In 2018, financial and insurance services contributed £132bn to the UK economy, 6.9 per cent of the total. The UK trade surplus for insurance and pensions was around £63bn.

WORLDWIDE MARKET

In 2019 the UK insurance industry was the largest in Europe and the fourth largest in the world behind the USA, China and Japan. China continued to be the biggest growth area, increasing its premium income by 7.4 per cent in 12 months.

Market	Premium income ($bn)
USA	2,460
China	617
Japan	459
UK	366

TAKEOVERS AND MERGERS

In an industry as competitive as insurance, where products can be very similar, price can often be the most important factor for consumers when choosing a product. This makes increasing a company's market share through increased sales extremely difficult. An alternative strategy can be through takeovers and mergers.

Allianz continued to be among the most active in 2019–20 with the announcement in May 2019 of their purchase of LV General Insurance from Liverpool Victoria Friendly Society for £1.08bn and the general insurance division of Legal and General for £242m. Both deals were completed in January 2020 and moved Allianz to the UK's second largest general insurer.

In January 2019, Markerstudy Group announced the purchase of Co-op Insurance Services for £185m. Progress on this acquisition was slow due to the COVID-19 pandemic, opposition from the trade union UNITE and the complicated structure of the deal. The sale was finally completed in December 2020.

Over the last few years RSA has been linked with a number of companies as a takeover or merger target. These have included Aviva, Zurich and Allianz but nothing had been agreed until November 2020 when it was confirmed that Canadian insurer Intact Financial Corp. and Danish insurer Tryg A/S had agreed to purchase RSA Insurance Group Plc for a total of £7.2bn, the biggest acquisition of a UK-listed company in 2020. Under the deal, RSA will be broken up with Tryg taking the Swedish and Norwegian operations for £4.2bn and Intact taking the Canadian, UK and international business for £3bn. Both companies will jointly own RSA's Danish company.

In August 2020 motor Insurer Hastings Direct was purchased by Finnish Insurer SAMPO and South African consortium RMI for £1.66bn, and in October 2020 Ageas insurance sold their 50 per cent stake in Tesco underwriting to Tesco Bank, giving the latter full ownership of the company.

BREXIT

Although COVID-19 has grabbed much of the world's attention, the issue of Brexit and its impact on the UK Insurance Industry has not gone away.

The Insurance and financial services sector are very important to the UK and its economy. The UK is the fourth largest insurance and long-term savings industry in the world and the largest in the EU. Certainly, the insurance industry made no secret of being firmly in the 'remain' camp in the Brexit debate, with the ABI, British Insurance Brokers' Association (BIBA) and Lloyd's all stressing the volatility and uncertainty they believed a 'leave' vote would create. But the result in June 2016 proved that their lobbying had not persuaded enough voters.

While leaving the EU may present opportunities to expand global markets and the demand for insurance products will certainly not reduce, the referendum result left the industry with a number of concerns, not least the need for the UK government to negotiate a very complicated trade agreement, or at least interim measures, in a short space of time.

The UK formally left the EU on 31 January 2020, entering into an 11-month transition period. At the time of writing it is still not clear whether or not a trade deal can be agreed and whether insurance and financial services will be included in any deal and on what terms.

In the absence of a specific agreement, the main effect on insurance consumers will be that from 1 January 2021 anyone travelling to Europe will need to have health insurance cover to replace the provisions of the European Health Insurance Card (EHIC). This card had guaranteed to provide a UK traveller with the same state-provided healthcare that was available to a resident of the EU country they are visiting. This provision will cease on 1 January.

In the same way, if there is no agreement on the UK's participation in the Green Card Free Circulation Zone, which is separate from the main negotiations, anyone taking their vehicle to the EU will be required to carry with them a Green Card. This is a document that has to be issued by insurers to confirm correct insurance cover is in place to satisfy the law in the countries to be visited. Having a Green Card every time a vehicle crosses into or out of an EU country could add additional delay and inconvenience to every private and commercial driver, particularly those who regularly drive between Northern Ireland and the Republic.

For insurance companies, after 1 January 2020, if there is no specific agreement, UK insurers and brokers will not have 'passporting rights' to EU countries. This currently allows firms registered in the EEA to do business in all other EEA states without additional authorisation from each country. Many insurers have already opened EU-based subsidiaries to avoid the complication of the loss of passporting rights will present.

As has been the case since the referendum, the insurance industry will wait for definite news on the outcome of trade negotiations.

COVID-19 AND THE INSURANCE INDUSTRY

Like all others, the insurance industry has been hit by restrictions and lockdowns imposed to reduce the spread of COVID-19. As a result, insurance staff joined the 49 per cent of UK workers who were working from home. Where this

was not possible, the industry adapted its working practices and IT systems, as appropriate.

There were, however, specific areas of cover that were impacted directly or were altered as a result of the pandemic.

LIFE INSURANCE

With a very small number of exceptions, life insurance policies all pay out on death by any cause. As a result, between 1 March and 31 May 2020 the life insurance industry paid out over £90m in COVID-19 related death claims.

Some insurers were also prepared to offer payment holidays for some types of life insurance.

BUSINESS INSURANCE

Early in the pandemic there was criticism by some business leaders and politicians because business interruption insurers refused claims for lost profits caused by business closures, due to lockdown. In May 2020, in an open letter to the Association of British Insurers, almost 700 business owners accused the industry of an 'abrogation of responsibility.' A week later a beer and pub industry coalition sent a similar open letter. The industry responded by pointing out that it was not possible to buy a policy covering business interruption caused by a COVID-19 pandemic anywhere in the world. A very small number of firms had covered themselves for closure caused by notifiable diseases but these diseases were usually specifically listed in the policy and did not include COVID-19, as it was a very new virus.

TRAVEL INSURANCE

Initially, the main focus of travel insurers was dealing with claims for curtailment of trips and repatriation of people caught in areas closed or locked-down following COVID-19 outbreaks. The majority of travel insurance policies also covered medical expenses for people needing treatment for COVID-19 related conditions contracted while abroad and cancellation of trips where the Foreign, Commonwealth and Development Office (FCDO) had advised against travel. These claims had cost around £275m by December 2020.

Going forward, travel insurance will not cover anyone travelling against FCDO advice but will be automatically extended for travellers unable to return home due to quarantine or lockdowns.

HOME INSURANCE

In March 2020, as the COVID-19 restrictions and the first lockdown were announced, household insurers confirmed that any office-based worker who needed to work from home during the pandemic could do so without affecting their home contents insurance cover or needing to tell their insurers.

MOTOR INSURANCE

A number of additional support measures were announced for private car policyholders:

- If a person could not work from home and needed to drive to their workplace, insurers agreed to include this 'commuting cover' without notification and free of charge
- Anyone using their vehicle to help with community activity like delivering medicines or groceries or voluntary responders carrying patients or equipment were also covered automatically
- Key workers who needed to drive to a different place of work because of re-deployment or who had to work on multiple sites were automatically given cover for these activities

CHARITABLE

Possibly as a result of the bad publicity over business interruption insurance, in May 2020 the insurance and long-term savings industry launched a COVID-19 Support Fund to provide immediate relief to charities affected by COVID-19, as well as a longer-term programme of support for people, communities, and issues where there is the greatest need. It was supported by members of the ABI (Association of British Insurers), The British Insurance Brokers' Association (BIBA), Lloyd's, and The London Market Group (LMG). Its aim was to raise £100m which was achieved by September 2020.

UK insurance companies (ie excluding Lloyd's and London Market insurers) estimated that the cost of claims arising from the COVID-19 pandemic will be over £1.2bn.

GENERAL INSURANCE

In October 2018, the Financial Conduct Authority announced a market study into how insurers charge their customers for the most common types of general insurance, home and motor cover. The study was prompted by suggestions in the media and from consumer organisations that customers who remained with the same insurer over a period of years were paying more for exactly the same product than new customers. An interim report was published in October 2019 and the final report was released in September 2020. The FCA concluded that the pricing of these products was unclear and that some loyal customers could find themselves worse off than new ones. The FCA produced a number of proposals including:

• An automatic remedy for customers who find they are not being given the same deal as new customers
• Requirements on insurers to submit pricing data to FCA so they can check the new rules are being followed
• Moves towards the prohibition of automatic renewal of policies

The FCA believes the proposed remedies will improve competition, lower costs for supplying insurance, and, on average, reduce the prices paid by consumers. The FCA estimates that its proposals will save consumers £3.7bn over 10 years.

Flood and storm damage claims continued to be a headache for property insurers. Storms and flooding in the North of England and the Midlands in October and November 2019 costing £110m were swiftly followed by Storms Ciara and Dennis in February 2020, which produced 82,000 further claims costing around £363m. Following these flooding events the government asked Amanda Blanc, CEO of AVIVA Insurance, to conduct a review of the extent of insurance coverage in Doncaster, one of the worst hit areas. The report found that although a substantial number of homes and businesses had insurance cover some policies excluded flood cover despite it being available with other insurers. Private landlords were also criticised for not being transparent with tenants about the cover they had.

Finally, motor insurance policyholders had some good news in 2020 as the cost of an average comprehensive motor policy remained at a four-year low. The average price in 2020 was £460, £8 lower than in 2019.

TOP FIVE GENERAL INSURANCE COMPANIES IN THE UK 2018

Insurance Company	Gross written premium (£bn)
1. AVIVA	11.2
2. AIG	5.3
3. AXA	4.5
4. RSA	4.1
5. Zurich	3.6

LONDON INSURANCE MARKET

In recent years it has become increasingly difficult to define the London Insurance Market business. Many businesses operate in London as branch offices of parent companies located elsewhere in the world and may no longer separately identify as London Market premiums. What is acknowledged is that, despite the growth of other international centres, London remains the world's leading market for internationally traded insurance and reinsurance, its business comprising mainly overseas non-life large and high-exposure risks. The market is centred on the square mile of the City of London, which provides the required financial, banking, legal and other support services. Around 56 per cent of London market business is transacted at Lloyd's of London, the remainder through insurance companies and protection and indemnity clubs. In 2018 the market had a written gross premium income of £63.96bn. Around 200 Lloyd's brokers service the market.

The trade association for the international insurers and reinsurers writing primarily non-marine insurance and all classes of reinsurance business in the London market is the International Underwriting Association (IUA).

INTERNATIONAL UNDERWRITING ASSOCIATION,
  1 Minster Court, Mincing Lane, London EC3R 7AA
  T 020-7617 4444 **W** www.iua.co.uk
  Chair, Malcolm Newman
  Chief Executive, Dave Matcham

LLOYD'S OF LONDON

Lloyd's of London is an international market for almost all types of general insurance. Lloyd's currently has the capacity to accept insurance premiums of around £33bn. Much of this business comes from outside the UK and makes a valuable contribution to the balance of payments.

A policy is underwritten at Lloyd's by a mixture of private and corporate members. Specialist underwriters accept insurance risks at Lloyd's on behalf of members (referred to as 'names') grouped in syndicates. There are currently 93 syndicates of varying sizes, each managed by one of the 53 underwriting agents approved by the Council of Lloyd's.

Members divide into three categories: corporate organisations, individuals who have no limit to their liability for losses, and those who have an agreed limit (known as NameCos). Currently there are around 2,000 members of which around 200 are individuals.

Lloyd's is incorporated by an act of parliament (Lloyd's Acts 1871 onwards) and was governed by an 18-person council, and an 11-person Lloyd's Franchise Board. In November 2019 it was announced that as from 1 June 2020 these two boards would be merged into a single 15-member body – the Lloyd's Council.

Lloyd's corporation is a non-profit making body chiefly financed by its members' subscriptions. It provides the premises, administrative staff and services for Lloyd's underwriting syndicates. It does not, however, assume corporate liability for the risks accepted by its members. Individual members are responsible to the full extent of their personal means for their underwriting affairs unless they have converted to limited liability companies.

Lloyd's syndicates have no direct contact with the public. All business is transacted through insurance brokers accredited by the Corporation of Lloyd's. In addition, non-Lloyd's brokers in the UK, when guaranteed by Lloyd's brokers, are able to deal directly with Lloyd's motor syndicates, a facility that has made the Lloyd's market more accessible to the insuring public.

Under the Financial Services and Markets Act 2000, Lloyd's is regulated by the FCA and the PRA. However, in situations where Lloyd's internal regulatory and compensation arrangements are more far-reaching – as for example with the Lloyd's Central Fund which safeguards claim payments to policyholders – the regulatory role is delegated to the Council of Lloyd's.

DEVELOPMENTS IN 2019–20

Like all businesses, the Lloyd's market found the spring of 2020 extremely difficult as COVID-19 spread rapidly around the world causing devastation for individuals, communities and the world economy.

The market was able to continue to function through a programme of remote working (even Lloyd's famous underwriting room was forced to close), the use of a digital platform for arranging cover known as PPL and the use of the previously designed Lloyd's emergency trading protocol. The significant volatility of global financial markets had its effect on the value of the market's assets but these have been closely monitored and a plan put in place to mitigate the risks as far as possible. The extent of the market's liability for claims arising from COVID-19 is not yet clear but, as with any potential large loss event, market reports are already being collected and assessed.

2019 saw Lloyd's net resources increase by 9 per cent to £30.6bn.

It also proved to be a better year for the market with an overall profit of £2.5bn compared to losses of £2.0bn in 2017 and £1.0bn in 2018. Most underwriting results were better as a result of improved pricing. Pre-covid investment returns also showed signs of improvement at £3,537m (2018: £504m), a return of 4.8 per cent (2018: 0.7 per cent).

The greatest turnaround in underwriting results saw property underwriting move to a small £12m profit from a loss of £700m in 2018. The motor insurance underwriting result remained stable with a small profit of £12m (£11m in 2018).

Major claims (catastrophes) for the market cost £1.81bn, down from £2.91bn in 2018 net of reinsurance. After a quiet first half of 2019, Japan was hit, firstly by Typhoon Faxai then Typhoon Hagibis causing extensive flood and wind damage. Hurricane Dorian caused substantial damage in the Bahamas. There were also wildfires in the US and Australia and rioting in Chile.

2019 was also the first full year of trading for Lloyd's Europe (previously called Lloyd's Brussels) which will enable the market to continue to underwrite European business irrespective of the outcome of Brexit trade talks.

LLOYD'S OF LONDON, One Lime Street, London EC3M 7HA
T 020-7327 1000 W www.lloyds.com
Chair, Bruce Carnegie-Brown
Chief Executive, John Neal

LLOYD'S SEGMENTAL RESULTS 2019 *(£m)*

	Gross written premiums	Net earned premiums	Underwriting result
Reinsurance	11,418	7,841	(434)
Casualty	9,459	6,793	(390)
Property	9,856	6,815	(12)
Marine Aviation and Transit	2,802	2,343	(199)
Motor	1,053	955	11
Energy	1,500	1,008	27
Life	87	66	1
Total from syndicate operations	35,905	25,821	(972)

HEALTH AND PRIVATE MEDICAL INSURANCE

Over the four-year period between 2015 and 2019, the number of people covered by personal health insurance dropped to 1.2 million – a fall of nearly 10 per cent. Over the same period corporate health insurance saw a 5 per cent drop to 3.5 million. The industry laid the blame for these falls firmly at the door of the government, pointing out that over the same period Insurance Premium Tax had doubled from 6 per cent to 12 per cent, one of the highest rates in Europe. Other contributing factors included price rises of 15 per cent for personal cover and 8 per cent for corporate insurance. These were blamed on increases in medical costs driven by the use of more sophisticated technologies and treatments.

BRITISH INSURANCE COMPANIES

The following insurance company figures refer to members and certain non-members of the ABI.

DOMESTIC PROPERTY CLAIMS STATISTICS 2018

Type	Payment (£m)
Theft	422
Fire	520
Weather	585
Escape of water	877
Domestic subsidence	195
Accidental damage	325
other domestic claims	325
Total	3,249

WORLDWIDE GENERAL BUSINESS TRADING RESULTS *(£m)*

	2017	2018
Net written premiums	45,959	48,214
Underwriting results	1,679	1,935
Investment income	2,136	1,969
Overall trading profit	3,815	3,904
Profit as percentage of premium income	8%	8%

LIFE AND LONG-TERM INSURANCE AND PENSIONS

Although regulatory and product development activity was severely restricted by the pandemic, there were developments in a number of on-going issues, particularly in the pensions area.

In 2015 the government introduced a series of reforms that removed the requirement that pension pots had to be invested in a guaranteed income for life. Instead, savers who had reached 55 were able to access their pension savings and have total freedom over whether its left alone, invested for their retirement or spent.

To mark five years since those reforms, the ABI published a report in February 2020 calling for further measures to address a number of issues:

• The risk that savers may face a retirement in poverty because they have used their pension savings for holidays or consumer goods (this has become more pertinent as there is now evidence that the financial hardships caused by the COVID-19 pandemic may force more people to withdraw funds)

• The lack of suitable financial advice to enable savers to make informed decisions

• That the true impact of the reforms may not be apparent for decades

The Government and regulators have yet to respond.

Work continued throughout 2019 and 2020 on the establishment of a pensions dashboard. This is the online system that will allow individuals to see, in one place, all the private and company pensions they have contributed to in their working life. A system of this kind requires complex setting up and data standards as well as stringent security and privacy measures. The next steps, in 2021, will be the building integration and testing of the digital architecture.

Since 2013 the payment of commission by life insurance and pension companies to financial advisers who sell their investment products has been banned. It was replaced by a fee-based system involving an initial charge for becoming a client and an ongoing annual percentage charge. The intention was to create a fairer system that avoids mis-selling but a survey by the Association of British Insurers (ABI) found that 72 per cent of people were not prepared to pay for financial advice. The most popular alternative options were Government websites (29 per cent), family members (23 per cent) and online information (22 per cent). The FCA will now consider the report and decide if reform is needed.

PROTECTION INSURANCE CLAIMS 2019

Type of product	No. of claims paid*	% of new claims paid	Total value paid (£ thousand)	Average claim paid (£)
Critical illness	17,995	91.60	1,215,957	67,573.28
Term Life	39,638	97.40	3,073,382	77,535.28
Total permanent disability	474	71.70	32,345	68,174.00
Whole of life	229,197	99.99	794,106	3,464.73
Income protection	16,591	87.20	669,397	17,728.80
All protection products	303,896	98.30	5,785,187	19,037.00

* Figures are for new claims, as well as all income protection claims in payment

UK LONG-TERM INSURANCE NET PREMIUM INCOME

Year	Life & annuities	Individual pensions	Occupational pensions	Income protection & other business	Total
2008	36,300	30,523	62,820	1,541	131,183
2009	20,336	27,725	68,988	1,473	118,521
2010	19,241	28,218	64,033	1,482	112,975
2011	16,008	27,401	71,680	1,456	116,545
2012	14,893	33,219	71,148	1,862	121,122
2013	9,944	25,119	80,192	1,457	116,712
2014	9,985	23,721	70,826	1,290	105,822
2015	10,461	35,194	76,188	1,290	123,133
2016	12,679	29,684	75,634	1,553	119,551
2017	11,685	59,817	91,039	2,511	165,052
2018	10,275	49,462	110,582	2,489	172,807

THE NATIONAL DEBT

HISTORY

The early 1700s saw the meteoric rise of the banking and financial markets in Great Britain, with the emerging stock market revolving around government funds. The ability to raise money by means of creating debt through the issue of bills and bonds heralded the beginning of the national debt.

The war years of 1914–18 saw an increase in the national debt from £650m at the start of the war to £7,500m by 1919. The Treasury developed new expertise in foreign exchange, currency, credit and price control in order to manage the post-war economy. The slump of the 1930s necessitated the restructuring of the UK economy following the Second World War (the national debt stood at £21bn by its end) and the emphasis was placed on economic planning and financial relations.

The relatively high period of inflation in the 1970s and 1980s led to the rise of the national debt in nominal terms from £36bn in 1972 to £197bn in 1987 and then to £419bn in March 1998. Although in nominal terms the national debt has risen sharply in recent years, as a percentage of GDP it has decreased dramatically since the end of the Second World War, when it stood at 250 per cent of GDP (for current figures, see table below).

THE UK DEBT MANAGEMENT OFFICE

The decision in 1997 to transfer monetary policy to the Bank of England, while the Treasury retained control of fiscal policy, led to the creation of the UK Debt Management Office (DMO) as an executive agency of HM Treasury in April 1998. Initially the DMO was responsible only for the management of government marketable debt and for issuing gilts. In April 2000 responsibility for exchequer cash management and for issuing Treasury bills (short-dated securities with maturities of less than one year) was transferred from the Bank of England to the DMO. The national debt also includes the (non-marketable) liabilities of National Savings and Investments and other public sector and foreign currency debt.

In 2002 the operations of the long-standing statutory functions of the Public Works Loan Board, which lends capital to local authorities, and the Commissioners for the Reduction of the National Debt, which manages the investment portfolios of certain public funds, were integrated within the DMO.

UK PUBLIC SECTOR NET DEBT

	£ billion	per cent of GDP
2017–18 (outturn)	1,779	85.0
2018–19 (forecast)	1,810	83.7
2019–20 (forecast)	1,851	82.8

Source: HM Treasury – The Budget 2018 (Crown copyright)

NATIONAL SAVINGS AND INVESTMENTS

NS&I (National Savings and Investments) is both a non-ministerial government department and an executive agency of the Chancellor of the Exchequer. It is one of the UK's largest savings organisations, with 25 million customers and around £157bn invested. When people invest in NS&I they are lending money to the government which pays them interest or prizes in return. All deposits are 100 per cent financially secure because they are guaranteed by HM Treasury.

TAX-FREE PRODUCTS

PREMIUM BONDS
Introduced in 1956, premium bonds enable savers to enter a regular draw for tax-free prizes, while retaining the right to get their money back. A sum equivalent to interest on each bond is put into a prize fund and distributed by monthly prize draws. The prizes are drawn by ERNIE (electronic random number indicator equipment) and are free of all UK income tax and capital gains tax. Two £1m jackpots are drawn each month in addition to other tax-free prizes ranging in value from £25 to £100,000.

Bonds are in units of £1, with a minimum purchase of £25, up to a maximum holding limit of £50,000 per person. Bonds become eligible for prizes once they have been held for one clear calendar month following the month of purchase. Each £1 unit can win only one prize per draw, but it will be awarded the highest for which it is drawn. Bonds remain eligible for prizes until they are repaid.

The scheme offers a facility to reinvest prize wins automatically. Upon completion of an automatic prize reinvestment mandate, holders receive new bonds which are immediately eligible for future prize draws. Bonds can only be held in the name of an individual and not by organisations.

INDIVIDUAL SAVINGS ACCOUNTS
Since April 1999 NS&I has offered cash individual savings accounts (ISAs). Its Direct ISA, launched in April 2006, can be opened and managed online and by telephone with a minimum investment of £1 and a maximum investment of £20,000 in the 2019–20 tax year. Interest for the Direct ISA is calculated daily, added to the account annually on 6 April and is free of tax.

Its Junior ISA, launched in August 2017 as a successor to children's bonds, can be opened for children under 18 by those with parental responsibility or, by a young person aged 16 or 17 for themselves. There is a minimum investment of £1 and a maximum investment of £4,368 in the 2019–20 tax year. It can only be opened and managed online and there are no withdrawals allowed until the young person reaches 18. Interest is accrued daily, added to the account annually on 6 April and is free of tax.

OTHER PRODUCTS

INCOME BONDS
NS&I income bonds were introduced in 1982. They are suitable for those who want to receive regular monthly payments of interest while preserving the full cash value of their capital. The minimum holding for each investment is £500 and the maximum £1m per person. A variable rate of interest is calculated on a day-to-day basis and paid monthly. Interest is taxable but is paid gross without deduction of tax at source.

GUARANTEED GROWTH AND GUARANTEED INCOME BONDS
Guaranteed growth and guaranteed income bonds, re-launched in December 2017, offer a lump sum investment that earns a fixed rate of interest over either a one-year term or a three-year term. The minimum holding is £500 to a maximum of £10,000 per person or trust per issue. For the guaranteed growth bond interest is calculated daily and added to the bond on each anniversary of the investment. The guaranteed income bond has interest paid monthly. Interest on both bonds is taxable but is paid gross without deduction of tax at source.

SAVINGS AND INVESTMENT ACCOUNTS
The direct saver account was launched in March 2010. Accounts can be opened by an individual aged at least 16, or jointly. Customers are able to invest between £1 and £2m per person. The account can be managed online or by telephone and funds can be withdrawn at any time. Interest is paid gross without deduction of tax at source.

The investment account can be opened with a minimum balance of £20 and has a maximum limit of £1m. The interest is paid gross without deduction of tax at source.

FURTHER INFORMATION
Further information regarding products and their current availability can be obtained online (W www.nsandi.com), by telephone (T 0808-500 7007) or by writing to: NS&I, Glasgow G58 1SB.

THE LONDON STOCK EXCHANGE

The London Stock Exchange Group (LSEG) serves the needs of companies by providing facilities for raising capital. It also operates marketplaces for members to trade financial instruments. including equities, bonds and derivatives, on behalf of investors and institutions such as pension funds and insurers.

LSEG's key subsidiary companies are the London Stock Exchange, Borsa Italiana, MTS (a trading platform for European government and corporate bonds), Turquoise (a trading platform for European equities) and FTSE (a global index provider).

Headquartered in London, with significant operations in Italy, France, North America and Sri Lanka, the group employs around 4,500 people.

HISTORY

The London Stock Exchange is one of the world's oldest stock exchanges, dating back more than 300 years to its origins in the coffee houses of 17th-century London. It was formally established as a membership organisation in 1801.

MAJOR DEVELOPMENTS

'BIG BANG'
In 1986 a package of reforms which are now known as 'Big Bang' transformed the London Stock Exchange and the City of London, liberalising the way in which banks and stock-broking firms operated and facilitating greater foreign investment. The London Stock Exchange ceased granting voting rights to individual members and became a private company. The 'Big Bang' also saw the start of a move towards fully electronic trading and the closure of the trading floor.

INTRODUCTION OF SETS
In October 1997, the Exchange introduced SETS, its electronic order book. The system enhanced the efficiency and transparency of trading on the Exchange, allowing trades to be executed automatically and anonymously rather than negotiated by telephone.

DEMUTUALISATION AND LISTING
The London Stock Exchange demutualised in 2000 and listed on its own main market in 2001.

MERGER WITH BORSA ITALIANA
In October 2007 the London Stock Exchange merged with the Italian stock exchange, Borsa Italiana, creating London Stock Exchange Group (LSEG).

DIVERSIFICATION
Since 2009 LSEG has diversified its business beyond the listing and trading of UK and Italian equities:
• In 2009 LSEG purchased Sri Lankan technology company MillenniumIT which provides technology to stock

exchanges, brokerages and regulators around the world. It also supplies the trading technology to LSEG's own markets
• In 2010 LSEG acquired a majority stake in Turquoise, a platform facilitating the trading of stocks listed in 19 European countries and the USA
• In 2011 LSEG became the owner of FTSE, the international business which creates and manages financial indices
• In 2013 LSEG purchased a majority stake in LCH (London Clearing House) (*see also* Financial Services Regulation, Recognised Clearing Houses and Central Counterparties)

UK EQUITY MARKETS

LSEG offers a range of listing options for companies, according to their size, history and requirements:
• The Main Market has the highest standards of regulation and disclosure obligations and is overseen by the UK Listing Authority (UKLA), a division of the Financial Conduct Authority (FCA). A Main Market listing enables established companies to raise capital, widen their investor base and have their shares traded alongside global peers. They are also eligible for inclusion in key indices, such as the FTSE 100 and the FTSE 250
• The Alternative Investment Market (AIM), established in June 1995, is specially designed to meet the needs of small and growing companies. It enables them to raise capital and broaden their investor base in a more flexible regulatory environment, while still being traded on an internationally recognised market. AIM companies retain an experienced Nominated Adviser (or 'Nomad') firm, which is responsible for ensuring the company's suitability for the market
• The Professional Securities Market (PSM), established in July 2005, allows companies to target professional investors only, on a market that offers greater flexibility in accounting standards
• The Specialist Fund Segment (SFS), established as the Specialist Fund Market (SFM) in November 2007, is a part of the London Stock Exchange's regulated Main Market designed for highly specialised investment entities, such as hedge funds or private equity funds, that wish to target institutional, professional, professionally advised and knowledgeable investors

As at 30 April 2019 there were 5,739 companies listed on LSEG's primary markets, with a combined market value of £2,052,073m: 1,770 on the Main Market (1,431 on the UK main market and 398 on the international main market), 3,852 on the AIM, 16 on the PSM and 35 entities on the SFS.

LONDON STOCK EXCHANGE, 10 Paternoster Square, London EC4M 7LS T 020-7797 1000
W www.londonstockexchange.com
Chair, Don Robert
Chief Executive, David Schwimmer

TAXATION

The government raises money to pay for public services such as education, health and the social welfare system through tax. Each year the Chancellor of the Exchequer's Budget sets out how much it will cost to provide these services and how much tax is therefore needed to pay for them. The tax is collected by HM Revenue and Customs (HMRC). There are several different types of tax:

- income tax payable on earnings, pensions, state benefits, savings and investments
- capital gains tax (CGT) payable on the disposal of certain assets
- inheritance tax (IHT) payable on estates upon death and certain lifetime gifts
- stamp duty payable when purchasing property and shares
- value added tax (VAT) payable on goods and services
- certain other duties such as fuel duty on petrol and excise duty on alcohol and tobacco

Corporation tax raises funds from companies and small businesses.

New taxation measures and changes to the administration of the taxation system are normally announced by the incumbent Chancellor of the Exchequer in the government's annual Budget in the autumn, with a spring statement on government spending forecasts.

The government has a stated policy of investing resources into reducing tax evasion and avoidance by both individuals and companies. Information and updates on the latest measures can be found on the government's website: www.gov.uk/government/policies/tax-evasion-and-avoidance).

The government also has an ongoing drive to simplify the UK tax system via the Office of Tax Simplification (OTS). Details of the OTS and its work can also be found on the government's website (**W** www.gov.uk/government/organisations/office-of-tax-simplification). The OTS welcomes views from individuals and can be contacted via email (**E** ots@ots.gov.uk).

HELP AND INFORMATION ON TAXATION

For information and help on any aspect of personal taxation, call the HMRC helpline (**T** 0300-200 3300). The lines are open 8am to 8pm from Monday to Friday, 8am to 4pm on Saturday, and 9am to 5pm on Sunday. For general queries (not specific cases) you can also use Twitter, starting your query with @HMRCcustomers.

HMRC no longer has a network of enquiry centres, because visitor numbers had dropped dramatically.

The HMRC website (**W** www.gov.uk/government/organisations/hm-revenue-customs) provides wide-ranging information.

INCOME TAX

Income tax is assessed on different sorts of income. Not all types of income are taxable and individuals are entitled to certain reliefs and allowances which reduce or, in some cases, cancel out their income tax bill.

An individual's taxable income is assessed each tax year, starting on 6 April and ending on 5 April the following year. The information below relates specifically to the year of assessment 2019–20, ending on 5 April 2020, and has only limited application to earlier years. Changes due to come into operation at a later date are briefly mentioned where information is available. Types of income that are taxable include:

- earnings from employment or profits from self-employment
- most pensions income, including state, company and personal pensions

- interest over the savings allowance
- income (dividends) from shares
- income from property
- income received from a trust
- certain state benefits
- an individual's share of any joint income

There are certain sorts of income on which individuals never pay tax. These are ignored altogether when working out how much income tax an individual may need to pay. Types of income that are not taxable include:

- certain state benefits and tax credits, such as child benefit, working tax credit, child tax credit, pension credit, attendance allowance, personal independence payment, housing benefit and maternity allowance
- winter fuel payments
- income from National Savings and Investments savings certificates
- interest, dividends and other income from various tax-free investments, notably individual savings accounts (ISAs)
- premium bond and national lottery prizes

PERSONAL ALLOWANCE

Every individual resident in the UK has a 'personal allowance' for tax purposes. This is the amount of taxable income that an individual can earn or receive each year tax-free. This tax year (2019–20) the basic personal allowance or tax-free amount is £12,500, an increase of £650 from the 2018–19 figure of £11,850. The personal allowance is for all taxpayers regardless of age.

Income tax is only due on an individual's taxable income that is above his or her tax-free allowance. Spouses and civil partners are taxed separately, with each entitled to his or her personal allowance. Each spouse or civil partner may obtain other allowances and reliefs where the required conditions are satisfied.

The personal allowance is available for all individuals with income up to £100,000. Those individuals with an 'adjusted net income' above the £100,000 limit have their personal allowance reduced by half the excess (£1 for every £2) they have over that limit until their personal allowance is reduced to nil.

An individual's 'adjusted net income' is calculated in a series of steps. The starting point is 'net income', which is the total of the individual's income subject to income tax less specified deductions such as payments made gross to pension schemes or trading losses. This net income is then reduced by the grossed-up amount of the individual's Gift Aid contributions to charities and the grossed-up amount of the individual's pension contributions that have received tax relief at source. The final step is to add back any relief for payments to trade unions or police organisations deducted in arriving at the individual's net income. The result is the individual's adjusted net income.

MARRIAGE ALLOWANCE

Some married couples and civil partners, made up of one non-taxpayer and one basic rate taxpayer, are eligible for a marriage allowance, which lets them share some of the non-taxpayer's unused annual income tax allowance. In the 2019–20 tax year, the allowance allows a spouse or civil partner with an income less than £12,500 to transfer up to £1,250 of their unused personal allowance to their higher-income partner. So long as the person receiving the transfer is a basic rate taxpayer, which, in most cases, means having an income of between £12,500 and £50,000 (£43,430 in Scotland), this transferable tax allowance is worth up to £250 in 2019–20.

BLIND PERSON'S ALLOWANCE
If an individual is registered blind or is unable to perform any work for which eyesight is essential, he or she can claim blind person's allowance, an extra amount of tax-free income added to the personal allowance. In 2019–20 the blind person's allowance is £2,450, irrespective of age or income. If an individual is married or in a civil partnership and cannot use all of the allowance because of insufficient income, the unused part of the allowance can be passed to the spouse or civil partner.

PROPERTY AND TRADING ALLOWANCES
These allowances benefit 'micro-entrepreneurs' who use one or more of a wide range of money-making activities to supplement their income. Individuals with property or trading income do not need to declare or pay tax on the first £1,000 they earn from each source per year. Should they earn more than that amount they will have to declare it to HMRC, but they can still take advantage of the allowance.

Property income qualifying for relief under the property allowance could be any income that an individual makes from renting out a residence, home, building, property or land – even from renting out a driveway as a parking space, for example, or renting out a room via websites like Airbnb.

Trading income qualifying for the allowance can be income from any sale of goods or services. An individual could do tasks such as cleaning or odd jobs, hiring out their own equipment such as power tools, or selling goods through websites like eBay or Etsy.

INCOME TAX ALLOWANCES

	2018–19	2019–20
Personal allowance	£11,850	£12,500
Income limit for personal allowance	£100,000	£100,000
Marriage allowance	£1,190	£1,250
Blind person's allowance	£2,390	£2,450
Property allowance	£1,000	£1,000
Trading allowance	£1,000	£1,000

CALCULATING INCOME TAX DUE
Individuals' liability to pay income tax is determined by establishing their level of taxable income for the year. For married couples and civil partners, income must be allocated between the couple by reference to the individual who is beneficially entitled to that income. Where income arises from jointly held assets, it is normally apportioned equally between the partners. If, however, the beneficial interests in jointly held assets are not equal, in most cases couples can make a special declaration to have income apportioned by reference to the actual interests in that income.

To work out an individual's liability for tax, his or her taxable income must be allocated between three different types:
- earned income (excluding income from savings and dividends)
- income from savings
- company dividends from shares and other equity-based investments

After the tax-free personal allowance plus any deductible allowances and reliefs have been taken into account, the amount of tax an individual pays is calculated using different tax rates and a series of tax bands. Each tax band applies to a slice of an individual's income after tax allowances and any reliefs have been taken into account.

SCOTLAND
Since the start of the tax year 2017–18, the Scottish government has been able to set the rates and bands for tax on income from earnings, pensions and most other taxable income in Scotland. The tax raised is paid to the Scottish government.

Income from savings and dividends continues to be taxed at the same rate as in the rest of the UK.

UK INCOME TAX BANDS AND RATES 2018–19

England, Wales & NI	Band*	Rate
Basic rate	£0–37,500	20%
Higher rate	£37,501–150,000	40%
Additional rate	£150,000+	45%
Scotland		
Starter rate	£0–2,049	19%
Basic rate	£2,050–12,444	20%
Intermediate rate	£12,445–30,930	21%
Higher rate	£30,931–£150,000	40%
Top rate	£150,000+	46%

The first calculation is applied to earned income, which includes income from employment or self-employment, most pension income and rental income, plus the value of a wide range of employee 'benefits in kind' such as company cars, living accommodation and private medical insurance (for more information on benefits in kind, see later section on Payment of Income Tax). In working out the amount of an individual's net taxable earnings, all expenses incurred 'wholly, exclusively and necessarily' in the performance of his or her employment duties, together with the cost of business travel, may be deducted. Fees and subscriptions to certain professional bodies may also be deducted. Redundancy payments and other sums paid on the termination of an employment are assessable income, but the first £30,000 is normally tax-free provided the payment is not linked with the recipient's retirement or performance.

For UK taxpayers other than Scottish residents, the first £37,500 of taxable income remaining after the tax-free allowance and any deductible allowances and reliefs have been taken into account is taxed at the basic rate of 20 per cent. Taxable income between £37,501 and £150,000 is taxed at the higher rate of 40 per cent. Taxable income above £150,001 is taxed at the additional rate of 45 per cent.

Savings and dividend income is added to an individual's other taxable income and taxed last. This means that tax on such sorts of income is based on an individual's highest income tax band.

SAVINGS INCOME
The second calculation is applied to any income from savings received by an individual. Savings income includes interest paid on bank and building society accounts, interest paid on accounts from providers like credit unions or National Savings and Investments, interest distributions (but not dividend distributions) from authorised unit trusts, open-ended investment companies and investment trusts, interest from peer-to-peer lending, government or company bonds and life annuity payments.

The appropriate rate at which savings income must be taxed is determined by adding income from savings to an individual's other taxable income (excluding dividends). Savings interest may be set against the personal allowance (if that is not used up on income from employment or pension), the starting rate for savings income and the personal savings allowance.

The starting rate of tax for savings income allows an individual to earn up to £5,000 of interest tax-free in 2019–20, but this amount is reduced by £1 for every £1 of their non-savings income above the personal allowance threshold. For example, a person earning £16,000 from their employment:

- their personal allowance of £12,500 is set against their income, leaving £3,500 taxable
- this taxable amount reduces their starting rate for savings, but they can still receive up to £1,500 (£5,000 less £3,500) of tax-free interest on their savings

In addition, the personal savings allowance (PSA) allows a basic rate taxpayer to earn their first £1,000 of savings income tax-free. A higher rate taxpayer may earn their first £500 of savings income tax-free. Additional rate taxpayers do not get a PSA. Interest from ISAs (*see* Tax-Free Savings) do not count towards this limit.

It is an individual's responsibility to inform HMRC if they earn savings income above the PSA on which tax is payable; any tax owed will normally be collected via the individual's tax code.

Tax on interest over the allowance is paid at the individual's usual rate of income tax, that is for a taxpayer not resident in Scotland 20 per cent for basic rate taxpayers, 40 per cent for higher rate taxpayers and 45 per cent for additional rate taxpayers. If savings income falls on both sides of a tax band, the relevant amounts are taxed at the rates for each tax band.

DIVIDEND INCOME

The third and final income tax calculation is on UK dividends, which means income from shares in UK companies and other share-based investments.

All taxpayers now have a £2,000 tax-free dividend allowance. This means that individuals do not have to pay tax on the first £2,000 of their dividend income, no matter what non-dividend income they have. The allowance is available to anyone who has dividend income.

Dividends received that exceed the £2,000 allowance are treated as the top band of income. This means that if an individual's divided income takes them from one income tax band into the next, they will then pay the higher dividend rate on that portion of income.

TAX RATES ON DIVIDENDS OVER £2,000

Band	2019–20
Basic rate	7.5%
Higher rate	32.5%
Additional rate	38.1%

If there is significant change to an individual's savings or other income, whatever his or her current tax bracket, it is the individual's responsibility to contact HMRC immediately, even if he or she does not normally complete a tax return. This enables HMRC to work out whether more tax should be paid, or if a refund is due.

TAX-FREE SAVINGS

There is a small selection of savings and investment products that are tax-free. This means that there is no tax to pay on any income generated in the form of interest or dividends, nor on any increase in the value of the capital invested. Their tax-efficient status has been granted by the government in order to give people an incentive to save more. For this reason there are usually limits and restrictions on the amount of money an individual may invest in such savings and investments.

Individual savings accounts (ISAs) are the best known among tax-efficient savings and investments. There are four types: cash ISAs, stocks and shares ISAs, innovative finance ISAs (earning interest and capital gains free of tax on loans made via peer-to-peer lending platforms) and lifetime ISAs. Money may be invested in one of each type of ISA each tax year, up to an overall annual subscription limit, which is £20,000 in 2019–20. This may be paid into one ISA or split between some or all of the other types, although no more than £4,000 may be paid into a lifetime ISA in one tax year.

To be eligible to invest in ISAs and receive all profits free of tax, individuals must be:

- aged 16 or over to hold a cash ISA
- aged 18 or over for a stocks and shares or innovative finance ISA
- aged 18 or over but under 40 for a lifetime ISA
- resident in the UK or, if not resident in the UK, a Crown servant or their spouse or civil partner

An ISA must be in an individual's name and cannot be held jointly with another person, but spouses and civil partners may inherit their partner's ISA allowance after death.

The lifetime ISA introduced in April 2017 may be opened by UK residents between the ages of 18 and 40, and allows individuals to save up to £4,000 a year between the ages of 18 and 50. Savings put into the account before their 50th birthday will qualify for a government bonus of 25 per cent, up to £1,000 a year. An individual may use their savings and bonus towards the purchase of a first-time home worth up to £450,000. Alternatively, they may choose to keep the account as retirement savings until their 60th birthday, after which date they can withdraw all the money tax-free.

There are also long-term, tax-free savings accounts for children called Junior ISAs. The investment limit for these in 2019–20 is £4,368 per child. Parents or guardians with parental responsibility can open Junior ISAs for children aged under 18 who live in the UK. However, while parents can open and manage Junior ISAs for their children, the invested money belongs to the child, who can take control of their account when they are 16 and withdraw the money when they are 18. Children aged 16 and 17 can open their own Junior ISA as well as an adult cash ISA. Junior ISAs automatically turn into an adult ISA when the child turns 18.

The Help to Buy ISA is one of a number of government measures to help individuals save towards buying their first home. Aspiring first-time buyers aged 16 or over who open a Help to Buy ISA before 30 November 2019 may continue to save up to £200 a month and the government boosts their savings by 25 per cent, up to a maximum of £3,000 per person. If, therefore, an individual saves £12,000, the government bonus boosts their total savings to £15,000. The minimum government bonus is £400, meaning that the individual must save at least £1,600 to qualify for the scheme. There is no monthly minimum investment.

Savings held in a Help to Buy ISA can be accessed at any time, but the government payment is only added if and when the savings are used as a deposit on a first and only home in the UK. The bonus is available on home purchases of up to £450,000 in London and up to £250,000 outside London. Qualifying properties must be purchased with a mortgage and must be lived in by the purchaser and not rented out.

Those who hold an account may continue saving into their account, but must claim their bonus by 1 December 2030.

Further details about ISAs are available via the HMRC's savings helpline (**T** 0300-200 3300).

DEDUCTIBLE ALLOWANCES AND RELIEF

Income taxpayers may be entitled to certain tax-deductible allowances and reliefs as well as their personal allowances. Examples include the married couple's allowance and maintenance payments relief, *see* below. Unlike the tax-free allowances, these are not amounts of income that an individual can receive tax-free but amounts by which their tax bill can be reduced.

MARRIED COUPLE'S ALLOWANCE

A married couple's allowance (MCA) is available to taxpayers who are married or are in a civil partnership where at least one partner was born before 6 April 1935 and they usually live together. Eligible couples can start to claim the MCA from the year of marriage or civil partnership registration.

The MCA is restricted to give relief at a fixed rate of 10 per cent, which means that – unlike the personal allowance – it is not income that can be received without paying tax. Instead, it reduces an individual's tax bill by up to a fixed amount of 10 per cent of the amount of the allowance to which they are entitled.

In 2019–20, the maximum MCA is £8,915 and is therefore worth £891.50 off a couple's tax bill. In 2019–20 this maximum is reduced by £1 for every £2 the highest earner's income exceeds £29,600, to a minimum MCA of £3,450. The minimum always applies, regardless of the level of the highest earner's income.

For marriages before 5 December 2005, the allowance is based on the husband's income; for marriages and civil partnerships after that date, the allowance is based on the income of the highest earner. A couple can decide to have the minimum amount of the allowance split equally between them, or transfer the whole of the minimum MCA from one to the other. If an individual does not have enough income to use all of his or her share of the MCA, the unused part of it can be transferred to his or her spouse or civil partner. A couple can inform HMRC of their decision before the start of the new tax year in which they want the decision to take effect.

MAINTENANCE PAYMENTS RELIEF
An allowance is available to reduce an individual's tax bill for maintenance payments he or she makes to his or her ex-spouse or former civil partner in certain circumstances. To be eligible:
- one or other partner must have been born before 6 April 1935
- the couple must be legally separated or divorced
- the maintenance payments being made must be under a court order
- the payments must be for the maintenance of an ex-spouse or former civil partner (provided he or she is not now remarried or in a new civil partnership) or for children who are under 21.

For the tax year 2019–20, this allowance can reduce an individual's tax bill by:
- 10 per cent of £3,260 (maximum £326) – this applies where an individual makes maintenance payments of £3,260 or more a year
- 10 per cent of the amount the individual has actually paid – this applies where an individual makes maintenance payments of less than £3,260 a year

An individual cannot claim a tax reduction for any voluntary payments he or she makes for a child, ex-spouse or former civil partner. To claim maintenance payments relief, individuals should call the HMRC helpline (**T** 0300-200 3300).

TAX RELIEF FOR LANDLORDS
Up to April 2017 individual landlords were able to deduct all their costs, including mortgage interest, from their profits before they paid tax. Wealthier landlords received tax relief at 40 per cent and 45 per cent.

This calculation has been changing for properties other than furnished holiday lettings. From April 2020, tax relief on financing costs will only be at the basic rate. Property profits (excluding interest costs) and other income will be assessed, and then amount of tax due will be reduced by the amount of the interest multiplied by the basic rate of income tax. This change only applies to landlords who are individuals, including where they operate through a partnership. It does not apply to companies who rent out property. *See* **W** www.gov.uk/government/news/changes-to-tax-relief-for-residential-landlords.

CHARITABLE DONATIONS
A number of charitable donations qualify for tax relief. Individuals can increase the value of regular or one-off charitable gifts of money, however small, by using the Gift Aid scheme that allows charities or community amateur sports clubs (CASCs) to reclaim 20 per cent basic rate tax relief on donations they receive. If a taxpayer gives £10 using Gift Aid, for example, the donation is worth £12.50 to the charity or CASC.

Individuals who pay 40 per cent higher rate income tax can claim back the difference between the 40 per cent and the 20 per cent basic rate of income tax on the total (gross) value of their donations. For example, a 40 per cent tax payer donates £100; the total value of this donation to the charity or CASC is £125, of which the individual can claim back 20 per cent (£25) for themselves. Similarly, those who pay 45 per cent additional rate income tax can claim back the difference between the 45 per cent and the 20 per cent basic rate on the total (gross) value of their donations. On a £100 donation, this means they can claim back £31.25. Scottish taxpayers who pay tax at rates higher than the basic 20 per cent rate can claim extra tax relief.

In order to make a Gift Aid donation, individuals need to make a Gift Aid declaration. The charity or CASC will normally ask an individual to complete a simple form. One form can cover every gift made to the same charity or CASC for whatever period chosen, including both gifts made in the past and in the future. Charities are able to claim a Gift Aid-type tax refund on small donations in various circumstances, *see* **W** www.gov.uk/claim-gift-aid/small-donations-scheme.

Individuals can use Gift Aid provided the amount of income tax and/or capital gains tax they have paid in the tax year in which their donations are made is at least equal to the amount of basic rate tax the charity or CASC is reclaiming on their gifts. It is the responsibility of the individual to make sure this is the case. If an individual makes Gift Aid donations and has not paid sufficient tax, they may have to pay the shortfall to HMRC. The Gift Aid scheme is not available for non-taxpayers.

Individuals who complete a tax return and are due a tax refund can ask HMRC to treat all or part of it as a Gift Aid donation.

For employees or those in receipt of an occupational pension, a tax-efficient way of making regular donations to charities is to use the payroll giving scheme. It allows the donations to be paid from a salary or pension before income tax is deducted. This effectively reduces the cost of giving for donors, which may allow them to give more.

For example, it costs a basic rate taxpayer only £8 in take-home pay to give £10 to charity from their pre-tax pay. Where a donor pays 40 per cent higher rate tax, that same £10 donation costs the taxpayer £6, and for donors who pay the additional 45 per cent rate tax, it costs £5.50.

Anyone who pays tax through the pay as you earn (PAYE) system (*see* Payment of Income Tax) can give to any charity of their choosing in this way, providing their employer or pension provider offers the payroll giving scheme. There is no limit to the amount individuals can donate.

Details of tax-efficient charitable giving methods can be found at **W** www.gov.uk/donating-to-charity.

TAX RELIEF ON PENSION CONTRIBUTIONS
Pensions are long-term investments designed to help ensure that people have enough income in retirement. The government encourages individuals to save towards a pension by offering tax relief on their contributions. Tax relief reduces an individual's tax bill or increases their pension fund.

The way tax relief is given on pension contributions depends on whether an individual pays into a company, public service or personal pension scheme.

For employees who pay into a company or public service pension scheme, most employers take the pension contributions from the employee's pay before deducting tax, which means that the individual – whether they pay income tax at the basic or higher rate – gets full tax relief straight away. Some employers, however, use the same method of paying pension contributions as that used by personal pension scheme payers described below.

Individuals who pay into a personal pension scheme normally make contributions from their net salary; that is, after tax has been deducted. For each pound that individuals contribute to their pension from net salary, the pension provider claims tax back from the government at the basic rate of 20 per cent and reinvests it on behalf of the individual into the scheme. In practice this means that for every £80 an individual pays into their pension, they receive £100 in their pension fund.

Subject to certain income related limits (see below) higher rate taxpayers currently get 40 per cent tax relief on money they put into a pension. On contributions made from net salary, the first 20 per cent is claimed back from HMRC by the pension scheme in the same way as for a lower rate taxpayer. It is then up to individuals to claim back the other 20 per cent from HMRC, either when they fill in their annual tax return. In a similar fashion, individuals subject to the 45 per cent additional rate of income tax can get 45 per cent tax relief on their pension contributions.

Non-taxpayers can still pay into a personal pension scheme and benefit from 20 per cent basic rate relief on the first £2,880 a year they contribute. In practice this means that the government tops up their £2,880 contribution to make it £3,600, which is the current universal pension allowance. Such pension contributions may be made on behalf of a non-taxpayer by another individual. An individual may, for example, contribute to a pension on behalf of a husband, wife, civil partner, child or grandchild. Tax relief will be added to their contribution at the basic rate, again on up to £2,880 a year benefiting the recipient, but their own tax bill will not be affected.

In any one tax year, individuals can get tax relief on pension contributions made into any number and type of registered pension schemes of up to 100 per cent of their annual earnings, irrespective of age, up to a maximum 'annual allowance'. For the tax year 2019–20 the annual allowance for most individuals is £40,000. This £40,000 annual allowance is reduced by £1 for every £2 of income between £150,000 and £210,000, so that those earning £210,000 and over have a £10,000 annual allowance.

Everyone also has a 'lifetime allowance' which defines the total amount a taxpayer can save in their pension fund and still get tax relief at their highest rate of income tax on all their contributions. The lifetime allowance is £1.055m in 2019–20, increased from £1.03m in 2018–19.

For information on pensions and tax relief visit W   www.gov.uk/browse/working/workplace-personal-pensions. Another useful source of information and advice is the Pensions Advisory Service (TPAS), an independent voluntary organisation grant-aided by the government, at W www.pensionsadvisoryservice.org.uk; or the pensions helpline is on T 0300-123 1047.

PAYMENT OF INCOME TAX

Employees have their income tax deducted from their wages throughout the year by their employer, who sends it on to HMRC. Those in receipt of a company pension have their tax deducted in the same way by their pension provider. This system of collecting income tax is known as 'pay as you earn' (PAYE).

BENEFITS IN KIND

The PAYE system is also used to collect tax on certain employee benefits or 'benefits in kind' that employees or directors receive from their employer as part of their remuneration package. These include company cars, living accommodation, private medical insurance paid for by the employer or cheap or free loans from the employer. Some of these benefits are tax-free, including employer-paid contributions into an employee's pension fund, cheap or free canteen meals, works buses, in-house sports facilities, reasonable relocation expenses, provision of a mobile phone and workplace nursery places provided for the children of employees. Tax is paid on the 'taxable value' of any taxable benefit.

Employers submit returns for individual employees to HMRC on form P11D, with details of any benefits they have been given. Employees should get a copy of this form by 6 July following the end of the tax year and must enter the value of the benefits they have received on their tax return for the relevant year, even if tax has already been paid on them under PAYE. Benefits in kind may be taxed under PAYE by being offset against personal tax allowances in an individual's PAYE code. Otherwise tax will be collected after the end of the tax year by the issue of an assessment on the value of the benefits.

SELF ASSESSMENT

Individuals who are not on PAYE, notably the self-employed, need to complete a self assessment tax return each year online (W www.gov.uk/log-in-file-self-assessment-tax-return), and pay any income tax owed in twice-yearly instalments. Some individuals with more complex tax affairs, such as those who earn money from rents or investments above a certain level, may also need to make a self assessment return even if they are on PAYE. HMRC uses the figures supplied on the tax return to work out the individual's tax bill, or they can choose to work it out themselves. It is called self assessment because individuals are responsible for making sure the details they provide are correct.

Some people still prefer to file a paper tax return. The forms can be downloaded from W www.gov.uk/government/publications/self-assessment-tax-return-sa100, but it should be noted that the deadline for returning a paper form is earlier than the online version.

Central to the self assessment system is the requirement for individuals to register online if they should complete a self assessment return. Individuals have six months from when the tax year ends to report any new income. The registration process is online (W www.gov.uk/log-in-file-self-assessment-tax-return), but it is important to allow enough time for the process – HMRC recommend allowing up to 20 working days extra for a first online return.

TAX RETURN FILING AND PAYMENT DEADLINES

There are also key deadlines for filing (sending in) completed tax returns and paying the tax due. Failure to do so can incur penalties, interest charges and surcharges.

KEY FILING DATES FOR SELF ASSESSMENT RETURNS

Date	Why the date is important
31 Oct*	Deadline for filing paper returns* for tax year ending the previous 5 April
30 Dec	Deadline for online filing where the amount owed for tax year ending the previous 5 April is less than £3,000 and the taxpayer wants HMRC to collect any tax due through their PAYE tax code
31 Jan†	Deadline for online filing of returns for tax year ending the previous 5 April

* Or three months from the date the return was requested if this was after 31 July
† Or three months from the date the return was requested if this was after 31 October

KEY SELF ASSESSMENT PAYMENT DATES

Date   *What payment is due?*

31 Jan   Deadline for paying the balance of any tax owed – the 'balancing payment' – for the tax year ending the previous 5 April. It is also the date by which a taxpayer must make any first 'payment on account' (advance payment) for the current tax year. For example, on 31 January 2020 a taxpayer may have to pay both the balancing payment for the year 2018–19 and the first payment on account for 2019–20.

31 Jul   Deadline for making a second payment on account for the current tax year

LATE FILING AND PAYMENT PENALTIES

Late filing of tax returns incurs an automatic £100 penalty, although individuals may appeal against the penalty if they have a reasonable excuse.

- Over three months late – £10 each day, up to a maximum of £900, in addition to the penalty above
- Over six months late – an additional £300 or 5 per cent of the tax due, whichever is the higher, in addition to the penalty above
- Over 12 months late – a further £300 or 5 per cent of the tax due, whichever is the higher. In serious cases HMRC reserve the right to ask for 100 per cent of the tax due instead. In both instances this is in addition to the penalty above

Late payment of tax owing incurs interest at 3.25 per cent.

Interest is due on all outstanding amounts, including any unpaid penalties, until payment is received in full. Individuals may calculate the penalties they owe for late self assessment tax returns and payments online (**W** www.gov.uk/estimate-self-assessment-penalties).

TAX CREDITS

Child tax credit, working tax credit and the new universal credit are paid to qualifying individuals. Although the titles of these credits incorporate the word 'tax', they do not affect the amount of income tax payable or repayable. They are forms of social security benefits. *See* Social Welfare.

CAPITAL GAINS TAX

Capital gains tax (CGT) is a tax on the gain or profit that an individual makes when they sell, give away or otherwise dispose of certain assets, for example shares, land or buildings. An individual potentially has to pay CGT on gains they make from any disposal of taxable assets during a tax year. There is a tax-free allowance and some additional reliefs that may reduce an individual's CGT bill. The following information relates to the tax year 2019–20 ending on 5 April 2020.

CGT is paid by individuals who are either resident or ordinarily resident in the UK for the tax year, executors or administrators – 'personal representatives' – responsible for a deceased person's financial affairs and trustees of a settlement. Non-residents are not usually liable to CGT unless they carry on a business in the UK through a branch or agency. However, from April 2015, the government introduced a CGT charge on gains made by non-residents disposing of UK residential property. Special CGT rules apply to individuals who used to live and work in the UK but have since left the country.

CAPITAL GAINS CHARGEABLE TO CGT

Typically, individuals have made a gain if they sell an asset for more than they paid for it. It is the gain that is taxed, not the amount the individual receives for the asset. For example, a man buys shares for £1,000 and later sells them for £3,000.

He has made a gain of £2,000 (£3,000 less £1,000). If someone gives an asset away, the gain will be based on the difference between what the asset was worth when originally acquired and its worth at the time of disposal. The same is true when an asset is sold for less than its full worth in order to give away part of the value. For example, a woman buys a property for £120,000 and three years later, when the property's market value has risen to £180,000, she gives it to her son. The son may pay nothing for the property, or pay less than its true worth, for example £100,000. Either way, she has made a gain of £60,000 (£180,000 less £120,000).

If an individual disposes of an asset he or she received as a gift, the gain is worked out according to the market value of the asset when it was received. For example, a man gives his sister a painting worth £8,000. She pays nothing for it. Later she sells the painting for £10,000. For CGT purposes, she is treated as making a gain of £2,000 (£10,000 less £8,000). If an individual inherits an asset, the estate of the person who died does not pay CGT at the time. If the inheritor later disposes of the asset, the gain is worked out by looking at the market value at the time of the death (the probate value). For example, a woman acquires some shares for £5,000 and leaves them to her niece when she dies. No CGT is payable at the time of death when the shares are worth £8,000. Later the niece sells the shares for £10,000. She has made a gain of £2,000 (£10,000 less £8,000).

Individuals may also have to pay CGT if they dispose of part of an asset or exchange one asset for another. Similarly, CGT may be payable if an individual receives a capital sum of money from an asset without disposing of it, for example where he or she receives compensation when an asset is damaged.

Assets that may lead to a CGT charge when they are disposed of include:

- shares in a company that are not held in an ISA or PEP
- units in a unit trust
- land and buildings (though not normally an individual's main home – *see* 'Disposal of a home' section for details)
- personal possessions, including jewellery, paintings, antiques and other personal effects, individually worth £6,000 or more
- business assets

EXEMPT GAINS

Certain kinds of assets do not give rise to a chargeable gain when they are disposed of. Assets exempt from CGT include:

- a car
- an individual's main home, if certain conditions are met
- tax-free investments such as assets held in an ISA or PEP
- UK government gilts or 'bonds' (including premium bonds)
- personal belongings, including jewellery, paintings and antiques, individually worth £6,000 or less
- betting, lottery or pools winnings

DISPOSAL OF A HOME: PRIVATE RESIDENCE RELIEF

When an individual sells their own home they automatically qualify for private residence relief, which means they do not have to pay any CGT provided that:

- the property has been their only home or main residence since they bought it, and
- they have used it as their home and for no other purpose

Even if an individual has not lived in the property for all of the time that they owned it, they may still be entitled to the full relief.

Under the relief rules, the final 18 months of ownership are always treated as if the individual lived in the property even if they did not. This means that if an individual moves out of one home and into a new one, they have up to 18 months in which to sell their former home without incurring any CGT on the sale proceeds.

Full relief is granted to individuals when they sell their home if they could not live in it for periods because they were working abroad. Full relief is also granted if an individual is prevented from living in the home for periods totalling a maximum of four years because their job required them to work elsewhere in the UK. In both cases, however, for the property to qualify for full relief, the general rule is that it must have been the individual's only or main home both before and after they worked away.

Individuals can also get full relief when they sell their home if they have lived away from it for reasons other than working away, provided all of the following apply:
- they were not living away from the home for more than three years in total during the time they owned the property
- they were not entitled to private residence relief on any other property during that time
- the property was their only or main home both before and after they lived elsewhere

There are instances when individuals may not get the full amount of private residence relief when they sell their home. These include if:
- the grounds, including all buildings, are larger than 5,000 square metres
- any part of the home has been used exclusively for business purposes
- all or part of the home has been let out (or more than one lodger has been taken in at a time). The owner may, however, be entitled to another form of CGT relief – letting relief – instead
- the main reason the property was bought was to make a profit from a quick sale

If an individual lives in – not just owns – more than one property, they can 'nominate' which should be treated as their main home for private residence relief purposes. Married couples or those in a civil partnership must make such a nomination jointly as they are only entitled to private residence relief on one house between them.

There is a calculator to help individuals work out how much private residence relief they may be entitled to when selling their main residence at **W** www.gov.uk/tax-relief-selling-home.

OTHER TRANSACTIONS NOT CHARGEABLE TO CGT

Certain other kinds of disposal similarly do not give rise to a chargeable gain. For example, individuals who are married or in a civil partnership and live together may sell or give assets to their spouse or civil partner without having to pay CGT. Individuals may not, however, give or sell assets cheaply to their children without having to consider CGT. There is no CGT to pay on assets given to a registered charity.

CALCULATING CGT

CGT is worked out for each tax year and is charged on the total of an individual's taxable gains after taking into account certain costs and reliefs that can reduce or defer chargeable gains, allowable losses made on assets to which CGT normally applies and an annual exempt (tax-free) amount that applies to every individual. If the total of an individual's net gains in a tax year is less than the annual exempt amount (AEA), the individual will not have to pay CGT. For the tax year 2019–20 the AEA is £12,000. If an individual's net gains are more than the AEA, they pay CGT on the excess. Should any part of the exemption remain unused, this cannot be carried forward to a future year.

There are certain reliefs available that may eliminate, reduce or defer CGT. Some reliefs are available to many people while others are available only in special circumstances. Some reliefs are given automatically while others are given only if they are claimed. Some of the costs of buying, selling and improving assets may be deducted from total gains when working out an individual's chargeable gain.

RATES OF TAX

The net gains remaining, if any, calculated after subtracting the AEA, deducting costs and taking into account all CGT reliefs, incur liability to capital gains tax. Individuals pay CGT at a rate of 10 per cent on gains up to the unused amount of the basic rate income tax band (if any) and at 20 per cent on gains above that amount. Rates for individuals for gains on residential property not eligible for private residence relief (*see* above) are charged at a rate of 18 per cent up to any unused amount of the basic rate income tax band and at 28 per cent on gains above that amount. The CGT rate charged to trustees and personal representatives is 28 per cent on residential property and 20 per cent on other chargeable assets.

An individual can report any CGT they need to pay (*see* below):
- straight away using the 'real time' Capital Gains Tax service
  W www.gov.uk/capital-gains-tax/report-and-pay-capital-gains-tax*
- annually in a self assessment tax return

* It should be noted that if the 'real time' service is used but the individual needs to submit a tax return for another reason, then their gains have to be reported again through self assessment

VALUATION OF ASSETS

The disposal proceeds (the amount received as consideration for the disposal of an asset) are the sum used to establish the gain or loss once certain allowable costs have been deducted. In most cases this is straightforward because the disposal proceeds are the amount actually received for disposing of the asset. This may include cash payable now or in the future and the value of any asset received in exchange for the asset disposed of. However, in certain circumstances, the disposal proceeds may not accurately reflect the value of the asset and the individual may be treated as disposing of an asset for an amount other than the actual amount (if any) that they received. This applies, in particular, where an asset is transferred as a gift or sold for a price known to be below market value. Disposal proceeds in such transactions are deemed to be equal to the market value of the asset at the time it was disposed of rather than the actual amount (if any) received for it.

Market value represents the price that an asset might reasonably be expected to fetch upon sale in the open market. In the case of unquoted shares or securities, it is assumed that the hypothetical purchaser in the open market would have available all the information that a prudent prospective purchaser of shares or securities might reasonably require if that person were proposing to purchase them from a willing vendor by private treaty and at arm's length. The market value of unquoted shares or securities will often be established following negotiations with the specialist HMRC Shares and Assets Valuation department. The valuation of land and interests in land in the UK is dealt with by the Valuation Office Agency. Special rules apply to determine the market value of shares quoted on the London Stock Exchange.

ALLOWABLE COSTS

When working out a chargeable gain, once the actual or notional disposal proceeds have been determined, certain allowable costs may be deducted. There is a general rule that no costs that could be taken into account when working out income or losses for income tax purposes may be deducted. Subject to this, allowable costs are:
- acquisition costs – the actual amount spent on acquiring the asset or, in certain circumstances, the equivalent market value

- incidental costs of acquiring the asset, such as fees paid for professional advice, valuation costs, stamp duty and advertising costs to find a seller
- enhancement costs – incurred for the purpose of enhancing the value of the asset (not including normal maintenance and repair costs)
- expenditure on defending or establishing a person's rights over the asset
- incidental costs of disposing of the asset, such as fees paid for professional advice, valuation costs, stamp duty and advertising costs to find a buyer

If an individual disposes of part of his or her interest in an asset, or part of a holding of shares of the same class in the same company, or part of a holding of units in the same unit trust, he or she can deduct the relevant part of the allowable costs of the asset or holding when working out the chargeable gain.

ENTREPRENEURS' RELIEF

Entrepreneurs' relief allows individuals in business and some trustees to claim relief on the first £10m of gains made on the disposal of any of the following:

- all or part of a business
- the assets of a business after it has ceased
- certain shares in a company.

The relief is available to taxpayers as individuals if they are in business, for example as a sole trader or as a partner in a trading business, or if they hold shares in their own personal trading company. This relief is not available for companies.

Depending on the type of disposal, certain qualifying conditions need to be met throughout a qualifying one-year period. For example, if an individual is selling all or part of their business, they must have owned the business during a one-year period that ends on the date of the disposal.

Where all gains qualify for entrepreneurs' relief, CGT is charged at 10 per cent. An individual can make claims for this relief on more than one occasion as long as the lifetime total of all their claims does not exceed £10m of gains qualifying for relief.

BUSINESS ASSET ROLLOVER RELIEF

When certain types of business asset are sold or disposed of and the proceeds are reinvested in new qualifying trading assets, business asset rollover relief makes it possible to 'rollover' or postpone the payment of any CGT that would normally be due. The gain is deducted from the base cost of the new asset and only becomes chargeable to CGT on the eventual disposal of that replacement asset, unless a further rollover situation then develops. Full relief is available if all the proceeds from the original asset are reinvested in the qualifying replacement asset.

For example, a trader sells a freehold office for £75,000 and makes a gain of £30,000. All of the proceeds are reinvested in a new freehold business premises costing £90,000. The trader can postpone the whole of the £30,000 gain made on the sale of the old office, as all of the proceeds have been reinvested. When the trader eventually sells the new business premises and the CGT bill becomes payable, the cost of the new premises will be treated as £60,000 (£90,000 less the £30,000 gain).

If only part of the proceeds from the disposal of an old asset is reinvested in a new one, different rules may apply, but it may still be possible to postpone paying tax on part of the gain until the eventual disposal of the new asset.

Relief is only available if the acquisition of the new asset takes place within a period between 12 months before and 36 months after the disposal of the old asset. However, HMRC may extend this time limit at their discretion where there is a clear intention to acquire a replacement asset. The most common types of business asset that qualify for rollover relief are land, buildings occupied and used for the purposes of trade, and fixed plant and machinery. Assets used for the commercial letting of furnished holiday accommodation qualify if certain conditions are satisfied.

GIFT HOLD-OVER RELIEF

The gift of an asset is treated as a disposal made for a consideration equal to market value, with a corresponding acquisition by the transferee at an identical value. In the case of gifts of business assets made by individuals and a limited range of trustees, a form of hold-over relief may be available. This relief, which must be claimed, in effect enables liability for CGT to be deferred and passed to the person to whom the gift is made. Relief is limited to the transfer of certain assets, including the following:

- gifts of assets used for the purposes of a business carried on by the donor or his or her personal company
- gifts of shares in trading companies that are not listed on a stock exchange
- gifts of shares or securities in the donor's personal trading company
- gifts of agricultural land and buildings that would qualify for inheritance tax agricultural property relief
- gifts that are chargeable transfers for inheritance tax purposes
- certain types of gifts that are specifically exempt from inheritance tax

Hold-over relief is automatically due on certain sorts of gifts, including gifts to charities and community amateur sports clubs, and gifts of works of art where certain undertakings have been given. There are certain rules to prevent gifts hold-over relief being used for tax avoidance purposes. For example, restrictions may apply where an individual gifts assets to trustees administering a trust in which the individual retains an interest, or the assets transferred comprise a dwelling-house. Subject to these exceptions, the effect of a valid claim for hold-over relief is similar to a claim for rollover relief on the disposal of business assets.

OTHER CGT RELIEFS

There are certain other CGT reliefs available on the disposal of property, shares and business assets. For detailed information on all CGT reliefs and for more general guidance on CGT, visit **W** www.gov.uk/personal-tax/capital-gains-tax.

REPORTING AND PAYING CGT

Individuals are responsible for telling HMRC about capital gains on which they have to pay tax, either:

- on their self assessment tax return by filling in the capital gains supplementary pages (the return explains how to obtain these pages if needed), or
- by visiting **W** www.gov.uk/capital-gains-tax/report-and-pay-capital-gains-tax, which explains what information to gather before following the link on that page to the 'real time' capital gains tax service

There is a time limit for claiming capital losses. The deadline is four years from 31 January after the end of the tax year in which the loss was made.

INHERITANCE TAX

Inheritance tax (IHT) is a tax on the value of a person's estate on death and on certain gifts made by an individual during his or her lifetime, usually payable within six months of death. Broadly speaking, a person's estate is everything he or she owned at the time of death, including property, possessions, money and investments, less his or her debts. Not everyone pays IHT. It only applies if the taxable value of an estate is above the current IHT threshold. If an estate, including any assets held in trust and gifts made within seven years of death, is less than the threshold (in the nil-rate band), no IHT will be due.

A claim can be made to transfer any unused IHT nil-rate band on a person's death to the estate of their surviving spouse or civil partner. This applies where the IHT nil-rate band of the first deceased spouse or civil partner was not fully used in calculating the IHT liability of their estate. When the surviving spouse or civil partner dies, the unused amount may be added to their own nil-rate band (*see* below for details).

IHT used to be something only very wealthy individuals needed to consider. This is no longer the case. The fact that the IHT threshold has not kept pace with house price inflation in recent years means that the estates of some 'ordinary' taxpayers are now liable for IHT purely because of the value of their home. However, there are a number of ways that individuals – while still alive – can legally reduce the IHT bill that will apply to their estates on death. Several valuable IHT exemptions are available (explained further below) which allow individuals to pass on assets during their lifetime or in their will without any IHT being due. Detailed information on IHT is available at **W** www.gov.uk/inheritance-tax. Further help is also available from the probate and inheritance tax helpline (**T** 0300-123 1072).

DOMICILE

Liability to IHT depends on an individual's domicile at the time of any gift or on death. Domicile is a complex legal concept and what follows explains some of the main issues. An individual is domiciled in the country where he or she has a permanent home. Domicile is different from nationality or residence, and an individual can only have one domicile at any given time.

A 'domicile of origin' is normally acquired from the individual's father on birth, so this may not be the country in which the individual is born. For example, a child born in Germany to a father who is working there, but whose permanent home is in the UK, will have the UK as his or her domicile of origin. Until a person legally changes his or her domicile, it will be the same as that of the person on whom they are legally dependent.

Individuals can legally acquire a new domicile – a 'domicile of choice' – from the age of 16 by leaving the current country of domicile, settling in another country and providing strong evidence of intention to live there permanently or indefinitely. Women who were married before 1974 acquired their husband's domicile and still retain it until they legally acquire a new domicile.

For IHT purposes, there is a concept of 'deemed domicile'. This means that even if a person is not domiciled in the UK under general law, he or she is treated as domiciled in the UK at the time of a transfer (ie at the time of a lifetime gift or on death) if he or she was:

• domiciled in the UK at any time in the three years immediately before the transfer, or
• 'resident' in the UK in at least 17 of the 20 income tax years of assessment ending with the year in which a transfer is made

Where a person is domiciled, or treated as domiciled, in the UK at the time of a gift or on death, the location of assets is immaterial and full liability to IHT arises. A non-UK domiciled individual is also liable to IHT, but only on chargeable property in the UK.

The assets of spouses and registered civil partners are not merged for IHT purposes, except that the IHT value of assets owned by one spouse or civil partner may be affected if the other also owns similar assets (eg shares in the same company or a share in their jointly owned house). Each spouse or partner is treated as a separate individual entitled to receive the benefit of his or her exemptions, reliefs and rates of tax.

IHT EXEMPTIONS

There are some important exemptions that allow individuals to legally pass assets on to others, both before and after their death – without being subject to IHT.

Exempt Beneficiaries

Assets can be given away to certain people and organisations without any IHT having to be paid. These gifts, which are exempt whether individuals make them during their lifetime or in their will, include gifts to:

• a spouse or civil partner, even if the couple is legally separated (but not if they are divorced or the civil partnership has been dissolved). Note that gifts to an unmarried partner or a partner with whom the donor has not formed a civil partnership are not exempt
• a 'qualifying' charity established in the EU or another specified country
• some national institutions, including national museums, universities and the National Trust
• UK political parties

Annual Exemption

The first £3,000 of gifts made each tax year by each individual is exempt from IHT. If this exemption is not used, or not wholly used in any year, the balance may be carried forward to the following year only. A couple, therefore, may give away a total of £6,000 per tax year between them or £12,000 if they have not used their previous year's annual exemptions.

Wedding Gifts / Civil Partnership Ceremony Gifts

Some gifts are exempt from IHT because of the type of gift or reason for making it. Wedding or civil partnership ceremony gifts made to either of the couple are exempt from IHT up to certain amounts:

• gifts by a parent or step-parent, £5,000
• gifts by a grandparent or great-grandparent, £2,500
• gifts by anyone else, £1,000

The gift must be made on or shortly before the date of the wedding or civil partnership ceremony. If the ceremony is called off but the gift is made, this exemption will not apply.

Small Gifts

An individual can make small gifts, up to the value of £250, to any number of people in any one tax year without them being liable for IHT. However, a larger sum such as £500 cannot be given and exemption claimed for the first £250. Note that this exemption cannot be used with any other exemption when giving to the same person. For example, a parent cannot combine a 'small gifts exemption' with a 'wedding/civil partnership ceremony gift exemption' to give a child £5,250 when he or she gets married or forms a civil partnership. Neither may an individual combine a 'small gifts exemption' with the 'annual exemption' to give someone £3,250. Note that it is possible to use the 'annual exemption' with any other exemption, such as the 'wedding/civil partnership ceremony gift exemption'. For example, if a child marries or forms a civil partnership, the parent who has not made any other taxable transfers in the year can give him or her a total IHT-free gift of £8,000 by combining £5,000 under the wedding/civil partnership gift exemption and £3,000 under the annual exemption.

Normal Expenditure

Any gifts made out of an individual's after-tax income (not capital) are exempt from IHT if they are part of their normal expenditure and do not result in a fall in their standard of living. These can include regular payments to someone, such as an allowance or gifts for Christmas or a birthday, and regular premiums paid on a life insurance policy for someone else.

Maintenance Gifts
An individual can make IHT-free maintenance payments to his or her spouse or registered civil partner, ex-spouse or former civil partner, relatives dependent because of old age or infirmity, and children (including adopted children and step-children) who are under 18 or in full-time education.

POTENTIALLY EXEMPT TRANSFERS
If an individual makes a gift to either another individual or a certain type of trust and it is not covered by one of the above exemptions, it is known as a 'potentially exempt transfer' (PET). A PET is only free of IHT on two strict conditions:
- the gift must be made at least seven years before the donor's death; if the donor does not survive seven years after making the gift, it will be liable for IHT
- the gift must be made as a true gift with no strings attached (technically known as a 'gift with reservation of benefit'). This means that the donor must give up all rights to the gift and stop benefiting from it in any way

If a gift is made and the donor does retain some benefit from it, then it will still count as part of the donor's estate no matter how long he or she lives after making it. For example, a father could make a lifetime gift of his home to his child, on condition that he continue to live in it. HMRC would not accept this as a true gift unless he paid his child a full commercial rent to do so, because he would be considered to still have a material interest in the gifted home. Its value, therefore, would still be liable for IHT.

In some circumstances a gift with strings attached might give rise to an income tax charge on the donor based on the value of the benefit he or she retains. In this case the donor can choose whether to pay the income tax or have the gift treated as a gift with reservation.

CHARGEABLE TRANSFERS
Any remaining lifetime gifts that are not (potentially or otherwise) exempt transfers are chargeable transfers or 'chargeable gifts', meaning that they incur liability to IHT. Chargeable transfers comprise mainly gifts to or from companies and gifts to particular types of trust. There is an immediate charge to IHT on chargeable gifts, and additional tax may be payable if the donor dies within seven years of making a chargeable gift.

DEATH
Immediately before the time of death an individual is deemed to make a transfer of value. This transfer will comprise the value of assets forming part of the deceased's estate after subtracting most liabilities. Any exempt transfers may be excluded, such as transfers for the benefit of a surviving spouse or civil partner and charities. Death may also trigger three additional liabilities:
- on a PET made within the seven years before death, which loses its potential status and becomes chargeable to IHT
- on the value of gifts made with reservation may incur liability if any benefit was enjoyed within the seven years before the death
- additional tax may become payable for chargeable lifetime transfers made within the seven years before the death

The 'personal representative' (the person nominated to handle the affairs of the deceased person) arranges to value the estate and pay any IHT that is due. One or more personal representatives can be nominated in a person's will, in which case they are known as the 'executors'. If a person dies without leaving a will a court can nominate the personal representative, who is then known as the 'administrator'. Valuing the deceased person's estate is one of the first things a personal representative

needs to do. The representative will not normally be able to take over management of the estate (called 'applying for probate') until all or some of any IHT that is due has been paid.

VALUATIONS
When valuing a deceased person's estate, all assets (property, possessions and money) owned at the time of death and certain assets given away during the seven years before death must be included. The valuation must accurately reflect what those assets would reasonably fetch in the open market at the date of death. The value of all of the assets that the deceased owned should include:
- his or her share of any assets owned jointly with someone else, for example a house owned with a partner
- any assets that are held in a trust, from which the deceased had the right to benefit
- any assets given away, but in which he or she kept an interest (gifts with reservation)
- PETs given away within the last seven years

Most estate assets can be valued quite easily, for example money in bank accounts or stocks and shares. In other instances the help of a professional valuer may be needed. Advice on how to value different assets, including joint or trust assets, is available at **W** www.gov.uk/valuing-estate-of-someone-who-died.

When valuing an estate, special relief is made available for certain assets. The two main reliefs are agricultural property relief and business relief, outlined below. Once all assets have been valued, the next step is to deduct from the total assets everything that the deceased person owed, such as unpaid bills, outstanding mortgages, other loans and their funeral expenses.

The value of all of the assets, less the deductible debts, is their estate. IHT is only payable on any value above the threshold for the tax year. It is payable at the current rate of 40 per cent. This rate is reduced to 36 per cent where 10 per cent or more of a net estate (after deducting IHT exemptions, reliefs and the nil-rate band) is left to charity.

RELIEF FOR SELECTED ASSETS

Agricultural Property
If an individual owns agricultural property and it is part of a working farm, it is possible to pass on some of this property free of IHT, either during that individual's lifetime or on their death. Agricultural property generally includes land or pasture used in the growing of crops or intensive rearing of animals for food consumption. It can also include farmhouses and farm cottages. The agricultural property can be owner-occupied or let. Relief is only due if the transferor has owned the property and it has been occupied for agricultural purposes for a minimum period.

The chargeable value transferred, either in a lifetime gift or on death, must be determined. This value may then be reduced by a percentage. Depending on the type of property, it will normally qualify for relief of 100 per cent.

Business Relief
Business relief is available on transfers of certain types of business and of business assets if they qualify as relevant business property and the transferor has owned them for a minimum period. The relief can be claimed for transfers made during the person's lifetime or on their death. Where the chargeable value transferred is attributable to relevant business property, the business relief reduces that value by either 50 or 100 per cent, depending on the type of asset. Business relief may be claimed on relevant business property, including property and buildings or assets such as unlisted shares or machinery.

It is a general requirement that the property must have been retained for a period of two years before the transfer or death, and restrictions may be necessary if the property has not been used wholly for business purposes. The same property cannot obtain both business property relief and the relief available for agricultural property.

CALCULATION OF TAX PAYABLE

The calculation of IHT payable adopts the use of a cumulative or 'running' total. Each chargeable lifetime transfer is added to the total if it was made within seven years of the donor's death. To the running total this produces is added the total value of the estate at death. If the total exceeds the inheritance tax threshold (the 'nil-rate band') IHT becomes payable. The rate of tax that is paid is determined by the element that causes the estate to exceed the threshold; gifts use up all or part of the nil-rate band first.

Lifetime Chargeable Transfers

The value transferred by total chargeable transfers during the deceased's lifetime must be added to the seven-year running total to calculate whether any IHT is due. If the nil-rate band is exceeded, tax will be imposed on the excess at the rate of 20 per cent. However, if the donor dies within a period of seven years from the date of the chargeable lifetime transfer, additional tax may be due. This is calculated by applying tax at the full rate of 40 per cent (rather than 20 per cent). The amount of tax is then reduced by applying taper relief, which is a percentage of the full rate of 40 per cent. This percentage is governed by the number of years from the date of the lifetime gift to the date of death, as follows:

TAPER RELIEF

Years between transfer and death	Taper relief %
More than 3 but not more than 4	20%
More than 4 but not more than 5	40%
More than 5 but not more than 6	60%
More than 6 but not more than 7	80%

Should this exercise produce liability greater than that previously paid at the 20 per cent rate on the lifetime transfer, the difference must be paid in additional tax. Where the calculation shows an amount falling below tax paid on the lifetime transfer, no additional liability can arise nor will the shortfall become repayable.

Taper relief is only available if the calculation discloses a liability to IHT. There is no liability if the lifetime transfer falls within the nil-rate band.

Potentially Exempt Transfers

Where a PET loses immunity from liability to IHT because the donor dies within seven years of making the transfer, the value transferred enters into the running total. Any liability to IHT will be calculated by applying the full rate of 40 per cent, reduced by taper relief if applicable. Again, liability to IHT can only arise if the nil-rate band is exceeded.

Death

On death, IHT is due on the value of the deceased's estate plus the running total of gifts made in the seven years before death if that comes to more than the nil-rate band. IHT is then charged at the full rate of 40 per cent on the amount in excess of the nil-rate band.

Settled Property and Trusts

Trusts are special legal arrangements that can be used by individuals to control how their assets are distributed to their beneficiaries and minimise their IHT liability. Complex rules apply to establish IHT liability on 'settled property' which includes property held in trust, and individuals are advised to take expert legal advice when setting up trusts.

RATES OF TAX

There are four rates:

- nil-rate
- lifetime rate of 20 per cent
- full rate of 40 per cent
- reduced rate of 36 per cent applicable to taxable estates where 10 per cent of the net estate has been left to charity (see above)

The basic nil-rate band threshold is £325,000 for 2019–20. In 2015 the government announced that the nil-rate band would remain at this figure until April 2021. Any excess over this level is taxable at the relevant rate.

ADDITIONAL THRESHOLD (RNRB)

The additional threshold (or residence nil-rate band) was introduced from April 2017, applying where a residence the deceased owns and has lived in passes on their death to direct descendants. The additional threshold is £150,000 in 2019–20 and £175,000 in 2020–21. It will increase in line with the consumer prices index (CPI) from 2021–22 onwards. Any unused nil-rate band may be transferred to the surviving spouse or civil partner.

The RNRB will also be available when an individual downsizes or ceases to own a home and other assets of an equivalent value are passed on death to direct descendants. These changes apply for deaths on or after 6 April 2017 where the deceased downsized or disposed of a property after 7 July 2015.

There is a tapered withdrawal of the RNRB for estates with a net value of more than £2m. This will be at a rate of £1 for every £2 over the additional threshold. Guidance on the additional threshold can be found at **W** www.gov.uk/guidance/inheritance-tax-residence-nil-rate-band.

TRANSFER OF NIL-RATE BAND

Transfers of property between spouses or civil partners are generally exempt from IHT. This means that someone who dies leaving some or all of their property to their spouse or civil partner may not have fully used up their nil-rate band. Any nil-rate band unused on the first death can be used when the surviving spouse or civil partner dies. A transfer of unused nil-rate band from a deceased spouse or civil partner may be made to the estate of their surviving spouse or civil partner.

Where a valid claim to transfer unused nil-rate band is made, the nil-rate band that is available when the surviving spouse or civil partner dies is increased by the proportion of the nil-rate band unused on the first death. For example, if on the first death the chargeable estate is £150,000 and the nil-rate band is £300,000, 50 per cent of the nil-rate band would be unused. If the nil-rate band when the survivor dies is £329,000, then that would be increased by 50 per cent to £493,500. The amount of the nil-rate band that can be transferred does not depend on the value of the first spouse or civil partner's estate. Whatever proportion of the nil-rate band is unused on the first death is available for transfer to the survivor.

The amount of additional nil-rate band that can be accumulated by any one surviving spouse or civil partner is limited to the value of the nil-rate band in force at the time of their death. This may be relevant where a person dies having survived more than one spouse or civil partner.

Where these rules have effect, personal representatives do not have to claim for the unused nil-rate band to be transferred at the time of the first death. Any claims for transfer of unused nil-rate band amounts are made by the personal representatives of the estate of the second spouse or civil partner to die when they make an IHT return.

Guidance on how to transfer the nil-rate band can be found at **W** www.gov.uk/government/publications/claim-the-residence-nil-rate-band-rnrb-iht435.

PAYMENT OF TAX

IHT is normally due six months after the end of the month in which the death occurs or the chargeable transaction takes place. This is referred to as the 'due date'. Tax on some assets, such as business property, certain shares and securities and land and buildings (including the deceased person's home), can be deferred and paid in equal instalments over ten years, though interest will be charged in most cases. If IHT is due on lifetime gifts and transfers, the person who received the gift or assets (the transferee) is normally liable to pay the IHT, though any IHT already paid at the time of a transfer into a trust or company will be taken into account. If tax owed is not paid by the due date, interest is charged on any unpaid IHT, no matter what caused the delay in payment.

HMRC has developed an online service to support the administration of IHT. This does away with the need to complete paper forms and enables individuals to proceed with their application for probate and submit IHT accounts online:

- if you are dealing with the estate of someone who has died, there is some guidance about the basic processes at **W** www.gov.uk/valuing-estate-of-someone-who-died and this page also gives links to make the relevant return
- to get a payment reference number, go to **W** www.gov.uk/paying-inheritance-tax/get-a-reference-number at least three weeks before the payment is due
- forms and worksheets for calculating IHT liabilities are available at **W** www.gov.uk/government/publications/inheritance-tax-inheritance-tax-account-iht100

CORPORATION TAX

Corporation tax is a tax on a company's profits, including all its income and gains. This tax is payable by UK resident companies and by non-resident companies carrying on a trade in the UK through a permanent establishment. The following comments are confined to companies resident in the UK. The word 'company' is also used to include:

- members' clubs, societies and associations
- trade associations
- housing associations
- groups of individuals carrying on a business but not as a partnership (for example, cooperatives)

A company's taxable income is charged by reference to income or gains arising in its 'accounting period', which is normally 12 months long. In some circumstances accounting periods can be shorter than 12 months, but never longer. The accounting period is normally the period for which a company's accounts are drawn up, but the two periods do not have to coincide.

If a company is liable to pay corporation tax on its profits, several things must be done. HMRC must be informed that the company exists and is liable for tax. A self assessment company tax return plus full accounts and calculation of tax liability must be filed by the statutory filing date, normally 12 months after the end of the accounting period. Companies have to work out their own tax liability and have to pay their tax without prior assessment by HMRC. Records of all company expenditure and income must be kept in order to work out the tax liability correctly. Companies are liable to penalties if they fail to carry out these obligations.

There is a radically simpler way for small self-employed businesses, such as sole traders and partnerships, to calculate their tax. Such businesses with receipts of £150,000 or less are able to work out their income on a cash basis and use simplified expenses rules, rather than having to follow the rules for larger businesses. Limited companies and limited liability partnerships can not use the cash basis. If a small business uses cash basis accounting and the business grows during the tax year, it can stay in the scheme up to a total business turnover of £300,000 a year.

Corporation tax information is available at **W** www.gov.uk/browse/business/business-tax and companies may file their company tax returns online (**W** www.gov.uk/file-your-company-accounts-and-tax-return).

RATE OF TAX

The rate of corporation tax is fixed for a financial year starting on 1 April and ending on the following 31 March. If a company's accounting period does not coincide with the financial year, its profits must be apportioned between the financial years and the tax rates for each financial year applied to those profits. The corporation tax liability is the total tax for both financial years.

The rate of corporation tax has been 19 per cent since 1 April 2017, but will decrease to 17 per cent for the financial year commencing 1 April 2020.

ALLOWANCES AND RELIEFS

Businesses can claim capital allowances, on certain purchases or investments. This means that a proportion of these costs can be deducted from a business' taxable profits and reduce its tax bill. Capital allowances are currently available on plant and machinery such as equipment and business vehicles. Reliefs are also available for research and development, profits from patented inventions and certain creative industries. The amount of the allowance or relief depends on what is being claimed for.

Detailed information on allowances and reliefs is available at **W** www.gov.uk/corporation-tax-rates/allowances-and-reliefs.

PAYMENT OF TAX

Corporation tax liabilities are normally due and payable in a single lump sum not later than nine months and one day after the end of the accounting period. For 'large' companies – those with profits over £1.5m – there is a requirement to pay corporation tax in four quarterly instalments. Where a company is a member of a group, the profits of the entire group must be merged to establish whether the company is 'large'.

HMRC runs a Business Payment Support Service (BPSS) which allows businesses facing temporary financial difficulties more time to pay their tax bills. Traders concerned about their ability to meet corporation tax, VAT or other payments owed to HMRC can call the BPSS Line (**T** 0300-200 3835) seven days a week. This helpline is for new enquiries only, not for traders who have already been contacted by HMRC about an overdue payment. For details of the service, visit **W** www.gov.uk/government/organisations/hm-revenue-customs/contact/business-payment-support-service.

CAPITAL GAINS

Chargeable gains arising to a company are calculated in a manner similar to that used for individuals. However, companies are not entitled to the CGT annual exemption. Companies incur liability to corporation tax rather than CGT on chargeable gains. Tax is due on the full chargeable gain of an accounting period after subtracting relief for any losses.

GROUPS OF COMPANIES

Each company within a group is separately charged corporation tax on profits, gains and income. However, where one group member realises a trading loss for which special rules apply, a claim may be made to offset the taxable loss against profits of some other member of the same group. These rules do not apply to capital losses. The transfer of capital assets from one member of a group to a fellow member will usually incur no liability to tax on chargeable gains.

SPORTS CLUBS

Though corporation tax is payable by unincorporated associations (including most sports clubs) on their profits, a substantial exemption from liability to corporation tax is available to qualifying registered community amateur sports clubs (CASCs). Sports clubs that are registered as CASCs are exempt from liability to corporation tax on:

- profits from trading where the turnover of the trade is less than £50,000 in a 12-month period
- income from letting property where the gross rental income is less than £30,000 in a 12-month period
- bank and building society interest received
- chargeable gains
- any Gift Aid donations

All of the exemptions depend upon the club having been a registered CASC for the whole of the relevant accounting period and the income or gains being used only for qualifying purposes. If the club has only been a registered CASC for part of an accounting period the exemption amounts of £50,000 (for trading) and £30,000 (for income from property) are reduced proportionately. Only interest and gains received after the club is registered are exempted. Full details can be found at **W** www.gov.uk/government/publications/community-amateur-sports-clubs-detailed-guidance-notes.

CHARITIES

Charities do not pay corporation tax on profits from their charitable activities. To minimise their liability, they often operate their trading activities through a subsidiary company.

VALUE ADDED TAX

Value added tax (VAT) is a tax on consumption which is collected at each stage in the supply chain. It is included in the sale price of taxable goods and services and paid at the point of purchase. Each EU country has its own rates of VAT. VAT is charged on most business transactions involving the supply of goods and services by VAT registered traders in the UK and Isle of Man. It is also charged on goods and some services imported from places outside the EU and on goods and some services coming into the UK from the other EU countries. VAT is administered by HMRC. A wide range of information on VAT, including VAT forms, is available online (**W** www.gov.uk/topic/business-tax/vat) and HMRC also runs a VAT enquiries helpline (**T** 0300-200 3700).

HMRC have confirmed that the UK will continue to have a VAT system after it leaves the EU. The revenue that VAT provides is vital for funding public services. The VAT rules relating to UK domestic transactions will continue to apply to businesses as they do now.

RATES OF TAX

There are three rates of VAT in the UK:
- the standard rate, payable on most goods and services in the UK, is 20 per cent
- the reduced rate – currently 5 per cent – is payable on certain goods and services, including domestic fuel and power, children's car seats, women's sanitary products, smoking cessation products and the installation of energy-saving materials such as wall insulation and solar panels
- the zero rate applies to certain items, including, children's clothes, books, newspapers, most food and drink, and drugs and aids for disabled people. There are numerous exceptions to the zero-rated categories, including: confectionery, potato crisps, alcoholic drinks, soft drinks and items sold for consumption in a restaurant or café. Takeaway cold items such as sandwiches are zero-rated, but hot foods like fish and chips are not.

REGISTRATION

All traders, including professional persons and companies, must register for VAT if they are making 'taxable supplies' of a value exceeding the registration threshold. All goods and services that are VAT rated are defined as 'taxable supplies'. This includes zero-rated items, which must be included when calculating the total value of a trader's taxable supplies – his or her 'taxable turnover'. The limits that govern mandatory registration are amended periodically.

An unregistered trader must register for VAT if:
- at the end of any month the total value of his or her taxable turnover (not just profit) for the past 12 months or less is more than the current VAT threshold of £85,000

or

- at any time he or she has reasonable grounds to expect that his or her taxable turnover will be more than the current registration threshold of £85,000 in the next 30 days alone

VAT registration must be completed within 30 days. Most businesses register online, but some need to download a form (**W** www.gov.uk/vat-registration/how-to-register). Traders who do not register at the correct time can be fined. Traders must charge VAT on their taxable supplies from the effective date of registration.

Traders who only supply zero-rated goods may not have to register for VAT even if their taxable turnover goes above the registration threshold. However, a trader in this position must inform HMRC first and apply to be 'exempt from registration'.

A trader whose taxable turnover does not reach the mandatory registration limit may choose to register for VAT voluntarily. This step may be thought advisable to recover input tax (*see* below) or to compete with other registered traders.

Registered traders may submit an application for deregistration if their taxable turnover subsequently falls. An application for deregistration can be made if the taxable turnover for the 12 months beginning on the application date is not expected to exceed £83,000.

INPUT TAX

Traders suffer input tax when buying in goods or services for the purposes of their business. It is the VAT that traders pay out to their suppliers on goods and services coming *in* to their business. Relief can usually be obtained for input tax suffered by registered traders, either by setting that tax against output tax due on sales or by repayment. Most items of input tax can be relieved in this manner. Where a registered trader makes both exempt supplies and taxable supplies to his customers or clients, there may be some restriction in the amount of input tax that can be recovered.

OUTPUT TAX

When making a taxable supply of goods or services, registered traders must account for output tax on the value of that supply. Output tax is the term used to describe the VAT on the goods and services that they supply or sell, so the goods or services are going *out* of the business. It is collected from customers on each sale by increasing the price by the VAT. Failure to make the required addition will not remove liability to pay the output tax to HMRC.

The liability to account for output tax, and also relief for input tax, may be affected where a trader is using a special secondhand goods scheme.

EXEMPT SUPPLIES

VAT is not chargeable on certain goods and services because the law deems them 'exempt' from VAT. These include:
- the provision of burial and cremation facilities
- insurance
- loans of money
- certain types of education and training
- most property transactions, unless the owner has opted to tax the property

Exempt supplies do not enter into the calculation of taxable turnover that governs liability to mandatory registration (*see* above). Such supplies made by a registered trader may limit the amount of input tax that can be relieved.

COLLECTION OF TAX

Registered traders submit VAT returns for accounting periods usually of three months in duration, but arrangements can be made to submit returns on a monthly basis. Very large traders – those whose annual VAT liability exceeds £2.3m – must make payments on account on a monthly basis, with the quarterly return used to determine the balancing payment. The return will show the output tax due for supplies made by the trader in the accounting period and the input tax for which relief is claimed. If the output tax exceeds input tax the balance must be remitted at the time of the VAT return. Where input tax suffered exceeds the output tax due, the registered trader may claim the excess from HMRC.

In this way, each trader in the supply chain collects the tax relating to the value added by their business. Where the supply is made to a person who is not a registered trader there can be no recovery of input tax and it is on this person that the final burden of VAT eventually falls.

As part of the Making Tax Digital initiative, most registered traders are required to use the Making Tax Digital service to keep records digitally and use software to submit their VAT returns from 1 April 2019. From 1 October 2019 the following organisations will also need to use the digital service:

- trusts
- not-for-profit organisations that are not set up as a company
- VAT divisions and groups
- public sector entities required to provide additional information on their VAT return (eg government departments and NHS trusts)
- local authorities
- public corporations
- traders based overseas
- those required to make payments on account
- annual accounting scheme users

For further information see **W** www.gov.uk/guidance/making-tax-digital-for-vat.

Exemptions from Making Tax Digital are available to those:
- that can not use computers, software or the internet due to age, disability or where they live
- or whose business are subject to an insolvency procedure
- that object to using computers on religious grounds

Applications for exemptions should be made to: HMRC – VAT Written Enquiries Team, Portcullis House, 21 India Street, Glasgow G2 4PZ or **T** 0300-200 3700. Applicants must state their VAT registration number, business name and address, details of how they currently file their VAT Return, and the reason they think they're exempt from Making Tax Digital.

Where goods are acquired by a UK trader from a supplier within the EU, the trader must also account for the tax due on acquisition. At the time of writing, the future of these arrangements is uncertain.

There are a number of simplified arrangements to make VAT accounting easier for businesses, particularly small businesses, and there is advice on the HMRC website about how to choose the most appropriate scheme for a business:

Cash Accounting Scheme
This scheme allows businesses to only pay VAT on the basis of payments received from their customers rather than on invoice dates or time of supply. This is useful for businesses with cash flow problems. Businesses may use the cash accounting scheme if estimated taxable turnover is £1.35m or less for the next 12 months. There is no need to apply for the scheme – eligible businesses may start using it at the beginning of a new tax period. If a trader opts to use this scheme, he or she can do so until the taxable turnover reaches £1.6m. For further information see **W** www.gov.uk/vat-cash-accounting-scheme.

Annual Accounting Scheme
If estimated taxable turnover is £1.35m or less in the next 12 months, the trader may join the annual accounting scheme which allows them to make nine monthly or three quarterly instalments during the year based on an estimate of their total annual VAT bill. At the end of the year they submit a single return and any balance due. The advantages of this scheme for businesses are easier budgeting and cash flow planning, because fixed payments are spread regularly throughout the year. Once a trader has joined the annual accounting scheme, membership may continue until the annual taxable turnover reaches £1.6m. This scheme is not helpful where businesses receive a refund of VAT, because it delays receipt of the refund. For more information see **W** www.gov.uk/vat-annual-accounting-scheme.

Flat Rate Scheme
This scheme allows small businesses with an annual taxable turnover of £150,000 or less to save on administration by paying VAT as a set flat percentage of their annual turnover instead of accounting internally for VAT on each individual 'in and out'. The percentage rate used is governed by the trade sector into which the business falls. The scheme can no longer be used once annual income exceeds £230,000.

Under this scheme, it is not possible to reclaim the VAT on purchases, except for certain assets over £2,000. For further information see **W** www.gov.uk/vat-flat-rate-scheme.

A business can not use the Flat Rate Scheme and the Cash Accounting Scheme at the same time.

Retail Schemes
There are special schemes that offer retailers an alternative if it is impractical for them to issue invoices for a large number of supplies direct to the public. These schemes include a provision to claim relief from VAT on bad debts where goods or services are supplied to a customer who does not pay for them. For further information see **W** www.gov.uk/vat-retail-schemes.

VAT FACT SUMMARY *from 1 April 2019*

Standard rate	20%
Reduced rate	5%
Registration (last 12 months or next 30 days)	over £85,000
Deregistration (next 12 months)	under £83,000
Cash accounting scheme	up to £1,350,000
Exit limit	£1,600,000
Annual accounting scheme	up to £1,350,000
Exit limit	£1,600,000
Flat rate scheme	up to £150,000
Exit limit	£230,000

STAMP DUTY

Stamp duty is payable by the buyer based on the purchase price of a property, stocks and shares. For the majority of people, contact with stamp duty arises when they buy a property. This section aims to provide a broad overview of stamp duty as it may affect the average person.

STAMP DUTY LAND TAX

Stamp duty land tax (SDLT) covers the purchase of houses, flats and other land, buildings and certain leases in the UK.

Buyers of property are responsible for completing a land transaction return form, SDLT1, which contains all information regarding the purchase that is relevant to HMRC and paying SDLT, though the solicitor or licensed conveyancer acting for them in a land transaction will normally complete the relevant paperwork. Once HMRC has received the completed land transaction return and the payment of any SDLT due, a certificate, SDLT5, will be issued that enables a solicitor or licensed conveyancer to register the property in the new owner's name at the land registry.

The threshold for notification of residential property is currently £40,000. This means that taxpayers entering into a transaction involving residential or non-residential property where the chargeable consideration is less than £40,000 do not need to notify HMRC about the transaction. Further information can be found online: **W** www.gov.uk/government/organisations/hm-revenue-customs/contact/stamp-duty-land-tax.

Since 1 April 2015 stamp duty has no longer applied to land transactions in Scotland. These are now subject to land and buildings transaction tax, details of which can be found online (**W** www.gov.uk/sdlt-scottish-transactions).

RATES OF SDLT

SDLT is charged at different rates and has thresholds for different types of property and different values of transaction. The tax rate and payment threshold can vary according to whether the property is in residential or non-residential use and whether it is freehold or leasehold.

SDLT on purchases of residential property is charged at increasing rates for each portion of the price.

SDLT ON RESIDENTIAL PROPERTY 2018–19

Portion of the transaction value	SDLT is charged at
Up to £125,000	zero
Between £125,001 and £250,000	2 per cent
Between £250,001 and £925,000	5 per cent
Between £925,001 and £1,500,000	10 per cent
Over £1,500,000	12 per cent

For example, on a property bought for £275,000, a total of £3,750 is payable in SDLT. This is made up of: nothing on the first £125,000, £2,500 (2 per cent) on the next £125,000, and £1,250 (5 per cent) on the remaining £25,000.

Higher rates of SDLT apply to purchases of additional residential properties such as second homes and buy-to-let properties. The higher rates are 3 per cent above the standard rates of SDLT. They do not apply to purchases of caravans, mobile homes, houseboats or property under £40,000.

HIGHER RATE SDLT ON ADDITIONAL RESIDENTIAL PROPERTY 2018–19

Portion of the transaction value	SDLT is charged at
Up to £125,000	3 per cent
Between £125,001 and £250,000	5 per cent
Between £250,001 and £925,000	8 per cent
Between £925,001 and £1,500,000	13 per cent
Over £1,500,000	15 per cent

Each of these higher rates again applies to the portion of the consideration that falls within each rate band. For example, on a buy-to-let property bought for £300,000, a total of £14,000 is payable in higher rate SDLT. This is made up of: £3,750 (3 per cent) on the first £125,000, £6,250 (5 per cent) on the next £125,000, and £4,000 (8 per cent) on the remaining £50,000.

The SDLT on purchases of non-residential and mixed-use property is charged at increasing rates for each portion of the price (in the same way that it is charged on purchases of residential property).

SDLT ON NON-RESIDENTIAL AND MIXED USE PROPERTY PURCHASES 2018–19

Portion of the transaction value	SDLT is charged at
Up to £150,000	zero
Between £150,001 and £250,000	2 per cent
Over £250,001	5 per cent

FIRST TIME BUYERS

From November 2017, first time buyers of homes worth between £300,000 and £500,000 will not pay SDLT on the first £300,000. They will pay the normal rates of SDLT on the price above that. This will save £1,660 on the average first-time property. This zero rate does not apply to first time buy-to-let or holiday home purchases, although those that are investing in buy-to-let property as first time buyers, will still get some relief as they will pay the standard residential rates rather than the higher buy-to-let rates. It is estimated that 80 per cent of people buying their first home will pay no SDLT.

This relief does not apply for those buying properties over £500,000.

CALCULATING SDLT

To work out the amount of SDLT payable on residential or non-residential property, a SDLT calculator is available online (**W** www.tax.service.gov.uk/calculate-stamp-duty-land-tax/#/intro).

STAMP DUTY RESERVE TAX

Stamp duty or stamp duty reserve tax (SDRT) is payable at the rate of 0.5 per cent when shares are purchased. Stamp duty is payable when the shares are transferred using a stock transfer form, whereas SDRT is payable on 'paperless' share transactions where the shares are transferred electronically without using a stock transfer form. Most share transactions nowadays are paperless and settled by stockbrokers through CREST (the electronic settlement and registration system). SDRT therefore now accounts for the majority of taxation collected on share transactions effected through the London Stock Exchange.

The flat rate of 0.5 per cent is based on the amount paid for the shares, not what they are worth. If, for example, shares are bought for £2,000, £10 SDRT is payable, whatever the value of the shares themselves. If shares are transferred for free, no SDRT is payable.

A higher rate of 1.5 per cent is payable where shares are transferred into a 'depositary receipt scheme' or a 'clearance service'. These are special arrangements where the shares are held by a third party.

CREST automatically deducts the SDRT and sends it to HMRC. A stockbroker will settle up with CREST for the cost of the shares and the SDRT and then bill the purchaser for these and the broker's fees. If shares are not purchased through CREST, the stamp duty must be paid by the purchaser to HMRC.

UK stamp duty or SDRT is not payable on the purchase of foreign shares, though there may be foreign taxes to pay. SDRT is already accounted for in the price paid for units in unit trusts or shares in open-ended investment companies.

Further information on SDRT is available via the stamp taxes helpline on **T** 0300-200 3510 or the government information website (**W** www.gov.uk/topic/business-tax/stamp-duty-on-shares).

LEGAL NOTES

These notes outline certain aspects of the law as they might affect the average person. They are intended only as a broad guideline and are by no means definitive. The law is constantly changing so expert advice should always be taken. In some cases, sources of further information are given in these notes.

It is always advisable to consult a solicitor without delay. Anyone who does not have a solicitor can contact the following for assistance in finding one: Citizens Advice (W www.citizensadvice.org.uk), the Community Legal Service (W www.gov.uk) or the Law Society of England and Wales. For assistance in Scotland, contact Citizens Advice Scotland (W www.cas.org.uk) or the Law Society of Scotland.

Legal aid schemes exist to make the help of a lawyer available to those who would not otherwise be able to afford one. Entitlement for most types of legal aid depends on an individual's means but a solicitor or Citizens Advice will be able to advise on this.

LAW SOCIETY OF ENGLAND AND WALES, 113 Chancery Lane, London WC2A 1PL **T** 020-7242 1222
W www.lawsociety.org.uk

LAW SOCIETY OF SCOTLAND, Atria One, 144 Morrison Street, Edinburgh EH8 8EX **T** 0131-226 7411
W www.lawscot.org.uk

ABORTION

Abortion is governed by the Abortion Act 1967. Under its provisions, a legally induced abortion must be:
- performed by a registered medical practitioner
- carried out in an NHS hospital or other approved premises
- certified by two registered medical practitioners, acting in good faith, on the basis of one or more of the following grounds:
1. that the pregnancy has not exceeded its 24th week and that the continuance of the pregnancy would involve risk, greater than if the pregnancy were terminated, of injury to the physical or mental health of the pregnant woman or any existing children of her family
2. that the termination is necessary to prevent grave permanent injury to the physical or mental health of the pregnant woman
3. that the continuance of the pregnancy would involve risk to the life of the pregnant woman, greater than if the pregnancy were terminated
4. that there is a substantial risk that if the child were born it would suffer from such physical or mental abnormalities as to be seriously handicapped.

In determining whether the continuance of a pregnancy would involve such risk of injury to health as is mentioned in the first and second grounds, account may be taken of the pregnant woman's actual or reasonably foreseeable environment.

The requirements relating to the opinion of two registered medical practitioners and to the performance of the abortion at an NHS hospital or other approved place cease to apply in circumstances where a registered medical practitioner is of the opinion, formed in good faith, that a termination is immediately necessary to save the life, or to prevent grave permanent injury to the physical or mental health, of the pregnant woman.

The Abortion Act 1967 does not apply to Northern Ireland. Despite a 2015 high court ruling that Northern Ireland's law on abortion is inconsistent with the European Convention on Human Rights, abortion is only permitted where there is a serious long-term risk to the health of the mother.

FAMILY PLANNING ASSOCIATION (UK), 23–28 Penn Street, London N1 5DL **T** 020-7608 5240 **W** www.fpa.org.uk

BRITISH PREGNANCY ADVISORY SERVICE (BPAS), 20 Timothys Bridge Road, Stratford-upon-Avon CV37 9BF
T 0345-730 4030 **W** www.bpas.org

ADOPTION OF CHILDREN

The Adoption and Children Act 2002 reformed the framework for domestic and intercountry adoption in England and Wales and some parts of it extend to Scotland and Northern Ireland. The Children and Adoption Act 2006, recently amended by the Children and Families Act 2014, introduced further provisions for adoptions involving a foreign element.

WHO MAY APPLY FOR AN ADOPTION ORDER

A couple (whether married or two people living as partners in an enduring family relationship) may apply for an adoption order where both of them are over 21 or where one is only 18 but the natural parent and the other is 21. An adoption order may be made for one applicant where that person is 21 and: a) the court is satisfied that person is the partner of a parent of the person to be adopted; or b) they are not married and are not civil partners; or c) married or in a civil partnership but they are separated from their spouse or civil partner and living apart with the separation likely to be permanent; or d) their spouse/civil partner is either unable to be found, or their spouse/civil partner is incapable by reason of ill-health of making an application. There are certain qualifying conditions an applicant must meet, eg residency in the British Isles.

ARRANGING AN ADOPTION

Adoptions may generally only be arranged by an adoption agency or by way of an order from the high court; breach of the restrictions on who may arrange an adoption would constitute a criminal offence. When deciding whether a child should be placed for adoption, the court or adoption agency must consider all the factors set out in the 'welfare checklist' – the paramount consideration being the child's welfare, throughout his or her life. These factors include the child's wishes, needs, age, sex, background and any harm which the child has suffered or is likely to suffer. At all times, the court or adoption agency must bear in mind that delay is likely to prejudice a child's welfare.

ADOPTION ORDER

Once an adoption has been arranged, a court order is necessary to make it legal; this may be obtained from the high court, county court or magistrates' court (including the family proceedings court). An adoption order may not be given unless the court is satisfied that the consent of the child's natural parents (or guardians) has been given correctly. Consent can be dispensed with on two grounds: where the parent or guardian cannot be found or is incapable of giving consent, or where the welfare of the child so demands.

An adoption order extinguishes the parental responsibility that a person other than the adopters (or adopter) has for the child. Where an order is made on the application of the partner of the parent, that parent keeps parental responsibility. Once adopted, the child has the same status as a child born to the adoptive parents, but may lose rights to the estates of those losing their parental responsibility.

REGISTRATION AND CERTIFICATES
All adoption orders made in England and Wales are required to be registered in the Adopted Children Register which also contains particulars of children adopted under registrable foreign adoptions. The General Register Office keeps this register from which certificates may be obtained in a similar way to birth certificates. The General Register Office also has equivalents in Scotland and Northern Ireland.

TRACING NATURAL PARENTS OR CHILDREN WHO HAVE BEEN ADOPTED
An adult adopted person may apply to the Registrar-General to obtain a certified copy of his/her birth certificate. Adoption agencies and adoption support agencies should provide services to adopted persons to assist them in obtaining information about their adoption and facilitate contact with their relatives. There is an Adoption Contact Register which provides a safe and confidential way for birth parents and other relatives to assure an adopted person that contact would be welcome. CoramBAAF (see below) can provide addresses of organisations which offer advice, information and counselling to adopted people, adoptive parents and people who have had their children adopted.

CORAMBAAF ADOPTION AND FOSTERING
ACADEMY, 41 Brunswick Square, London WC1N 1AZ
T 020-7520 0300 W https://corambaaf.org.uk

SCOTLAND
The relevant legislation is the Adoption and Children (Scotland) Act 2007 which came into force on 28 September 2009. In addition, adoptions with a foreign element are governed by the Adoptions with a Foreign Element (Scotland) Regulations 2009. Pre-2009 adoptions are governed by Part IV of the Adoption (Scotland) Act 1978. The provisions of the 2007 act are similar to those described above. In Scotland, petitions for adoption are made to the sheriff court or the court of session.

ADOPTION AND FOSTERING ALLIANCE SCOTLAND,
Foxglove Offices/GF2, 14 Links Place, Edinburgh EH6 7EZ
T 0131-322 8490 W www.afascotland.com

BIRTHS (REGISTRATION)
It is the duty of the parents of a child born in England or Wales to register the birth within 42 days of the date of birth at the register office in the district in which the baby was born. If it is inconvenient to go to the district where the birth took place, the information for the registration may be given to a registrar in another district, who will send your details to the appropriate register office. Failure to register the birth within 42 days without reasonable cause may leave the parents liable to a penalty. If a birth has not been registered within 12 months of its occurrence it is possible for the late registration of the birth to be authorised by the Registrar-General, provided documentary evidence of the precise date and place of birth are satisfactory.

Births that take place in England may only be registered in English, but births that take place in Wales may be registered bilingually in Welsh and English. In order to do this, the details must be given in Welsh and the registrar must be able to understand and write in Welsh.

If the parents of the child were married to each other at the time of the birth (or conception), either the mother or the father may register the birth alone. If the parents were not married to each other at the time of the child's birth (or conception), the father's particulars may be entered in the register only where he attends the register office with the mother and they sign the birth register together or the mother can choose to register the child's birth without the father's details. Where an unmarried parent is unable to attend the register office, either parent may submit to the registrar a statutory declaration of acknowledgement of parentage (this form may be obtained from any registrar in England or Wales or online at W www.gro.gov.uk); alternatively a parental responsibility agreement or appropriate court order may be produced to the registrar.

If the father's details are not included in the birth register, it may be possible to re-register the birth at a later date. If the parents can not register the birth of their child the following people may do so:
- an administrative member of staff of the hospital where the child was born
- a person who was present at the birth
- a person who is responsible for the child

Upon registration of the birth a short (containing only the child's details) or full (containing the child's and parents' details) certificate can be issued at a cost of £11.00 each. It may be possible to register the birth while still at hospital. Hospitals will advise individually whether this is possible.

SAME-SEX COUPLES
Male couples must get a parental order from the court before they can be registered as parents. Female couples can include both of their names on the child's birth certificate when registering the birth; however the rules differ depending on whether or not they are in a civil partnership.

In the case of female civil partners, either woman can register the birth on her own if all of the following are true:
- the mother had the child by donor insemination or fertility treatment
- she was married or in a civil partnership at the time of the treatment

When a mother is not in a civil partnership, her partner can be seen as the child's second parent if both women:
- were treated together in the UK by a licensed clinic
- have made a 'parenthood agreement'

However, for both parents' details to be recorded on the birth certificate, the parents must do one of the following:
- register the birth jointly
- complete a 'statutory declaration of acknowledgement of parentage' form and one parent takes the signed form when she registers the birth
- get a document from the court (eg a court order) giving the second female parent parental responsibility and one parent shows the document when she registers the birth

BIRTHS ABROAD
A child's birth abroad must be registered according to the regulations in the country where the child was born. The local authorities will issue a local birth certificate. The local birth certificate should be accepted in the UK, for example when registering a child with a school or doctor, but the certificate may be required to be translated and certified in English.

Once the child's birth has been registered locally, the birth may be registered with the UK authorities (only if the child was born on or after 1 January 1983). There is no obligation to register a child's birth with the UK authority; however, by registering the birth with the UK authority the birth will be recorded with the General Register Offices and a consular birth registration certificate can be ordered.

SCOTLAND

In Scotland the birth of a child must be registered within 21 days at the registration office of any registration district in Scotland.

If the child is born, either in or out of Scotland, on a ship, aircraft or land vehicle that ends its journey at any place in Scotland, the child, in most cases, will be registered as if born in that place.

CERTIFICATES OF BIRTHS, DEATHS OR MARRIAGES

Certificates of births, marriages and deaths that have taken place in England and Wales since 1837 can be obtained from the General Register Office (GRO).

Marriage or death certificates may also be obtained from the minister of the church in which the marriage or funeral took place. Any register office can advise about the best way to obtain certificates.

The fees for certificates are:

Online application:
- full certificate of birth, marriage, death or adoption, £14.00
- full certificate of birth, marriage, death or adoption with GRO reference supplied, £11.00

By postal/phone/fax application:
- full certificate of birth, marriage, death or adoption, £14.00
- full certificate of birth, marriage, death or adoption with GRO reference supplied, £11.00
- extra copies of the same birth, marriage or death certificate issued at the same time, £11.00

A priority service is available for a fee of £35.00 with GRO reference supplied and £38.00 without.

A complete set of the GRO indexes including births, deaths and marriages, civil partnerships, adoptions and provisional indexes for births and deaths are available at the British Library, City of Westminster Archives Centre, Manchester Central Library, Newcastle City Library, Library of Birmingham, Bridgend Reference and Information Library and Plymouth Central Library. Copies of GRO indexes may also be held at some libraries, family history societies, local records offices and The Church of Jesus Christ of Latter Day Saints family history centres. Some organisations may not hold a complete record of indexes and a small fee may be charged by some of them. GRO indexes are also available online.

The Society of Genealogists has many records of baptisms, marriages and deaths prior to 1837.

SCOTLAND

Certificates of births, deaths or marriages that have taken place in Scotland since 1855 can be obtained from the National Records of Scotland (formerly the General Register Office for Scotland) or from the appropriate local registrar.

Applicable fees – local registrar:
- each extract or abbreviated certificate of birth, death, marriage, civil partnership or adoption within a month of registration, £10.00
- each extract or abbreviated certificate of birth, death, marriage, civil partnership or adoption outwith a month of registration, £15.00

A priority service is available for an additional fee.

The National Records of Scotland also keeps the Register of Divorces (including decrees of declaration of nullity of marriage), and holds parish registers dating from before 1855.

Applicable fees – National Records of Scotland:
- personal application, or postal, telephone or fax order: £15.00

A priority service for a response within 24 hours is available for an additional fee of £15.00. Online fees (excluding postage) are £12.00 or £27.00 for a priority service.

A search of birth, death and marriage records including records of Church of Scotland parishes and other statutory records can be done at the Scotland's People Centre. There are also indexes to some of the old parish registers death and burial records in the library at the centre and indexes and images of census records from 1841–1911 are available. The charges for a full or part-day search pass is £15.00.

Online searching is also available. For more information, visit **W** www.scotlandspeople.gov.uk

THE GENERAL REGISTER OFFICE, General Register Office, Certificate Services Section, PO Box 2, Southport PR8 2JD **T** 0300-123 1837 **W** www.gro.gov.uk/gro/content/certificates

THE NATIONAL RECORDS OF SCOTLAND, HM General Register House, 2 Princes Street, Edinburgh EH1 3YT **T** 0131-334 0380 **W** www.nrscotland.gov.uk

SCOTLAND'S PEOPLE CENTRE, General Register House, 2 Princes Street, Edinburgh EH1 3YY **W** www.scotlandspeople.gov.uk

THE SOCIETY OF GENEALOGISTS, 14 Charterhouse Buildings, Goswell Road, London EC1M 7BA **T** 020-7251 8799 **W** www.sog.org.uk

BRITISH NATIONALITY

There are different types of British nationality status: British citizenship; British overseas citizenship; British national (overseas); British overseas territories citizenship; British protected persons; and British subjects. The most widely held of these is British citizenship. Everyone born in the UK before 1 January 1983 became a British citizen when the British Nationality Act 1981 came into force, with the exception of children born to certain diplomatic staff working in the UK at the time. Individuals born outside the UK before 1 January 1983 but who at that date were citizens of the UK and colonies and had a right of abode in the UK also became British citizens. British citizens have the right to live permanently in the UK and are free to leave and re-enter the UK at any time.

A person born on or after 1 January 1983 in the UK (including, for this purpose, the Channel Islands and the Isle of Man) is entitled to British citizenship if he/she falls into one of the following categories:
- he/she has a parent who is a British citizen
- he/she has a parent who is settled in the UK
- he/she is a newborn infant found abandoned in the UK
- his/her parents subsequently settle in the UK or become British citizens and an application is made before he/she is 18
- he/she lives in the UK for the first ten years of his/her life and is not absent for more than 90 days in each of those years
- he/she is adopted in the UK and one of the adopters is a British citizen
- the home secretary consents to his/her registration while he/she is a minor
- if he/she has always been stateless and lives in the UK for a period of five years before his/her 22nd birthday
- if he/she has been born on or after 13 January 2010 to a parent who is a member of the UK armed forces
- if he/she has been born on or after 13 January 2010 and a parent becomes a member of the UK armed forces, and an application is made before he/she is 18

A person born outside the UK may acquire British citizenship if he/she falls into one of the following categories:
- he/she has a parent who is a British citizen otherwise than by descent, eg a parent who was born in the UK

- he/she has a parent who is a British citizen serving the crown or a European community institution overseas and was recruited to that service in the UK (including qualifying territories for those born on or after 21 May 2002) or in the European Community (for services within an EU institution); or if the applicant himself/herself has at any time been in crown, or similar, service under the government of a British overseas territory
- if he/she has been born on or after 13 January 2010 to a parent who is a member of the UK armed forces serving outside the UK and qualifying territories, is of good character and (if he/she is a minor at the time of application) all parents then alive consent in signed writing
- the home secretary consents to his/her registration while he/she is a minor
- he/she is a British overseas territories citizen, a British overseas citizen, a British subject or a British protected person and has been lawfully resident in the UK for five years
- he/she is a British overseas territories citizen who acquired that citizenship from a connection with Gibraltar
- he/she is adopted or naturalised

Where parents are married, the status of either may confer citizenship on their child. Since July 2006, both parents are able to pass on nationality even if they are not married, provided that there is satisfactory evidence of paternity. For children born before July 2006, it must be shown that there is parental consent and that the child would have an automatic claim to citizenship or entitlement to registration had the parents been married. Where parents are not married, the status of the mother determines the child's citizenship.

Under the 1981 act, Commonwealth citizens and citizens of the Republic of Ireland were entitled to registration as British citizens before 1 January 1983. In 1983, citizens of the Falkland Islands were granted British citizenship.

Renunciation of British citizenship must be registered with the home secretary and will be revoked if no new citizenship or nationality is acquired within six months. If the renunciation was required in order to retain or acquire another citizenship or nationality, the citizenship may be reacquired only once. If the renunciation was for another reason, the home secretary may allow reacquisition more than once, depending on the circumstances. The secretary of state may deprive a person of a citizenship status if he or she is satisfied that the person has done anything seriously prejudicial to the vital interests of the UK, or a British overseas territory, unless making the order would have the effect of rendering such a person stateless. A person may also be deprived of a citizenship status which results from his registration or naturalisation if the secretary of state is satisfied that the registration or naturalisation was obtained by fraud, false representation or concealment of a material fact.

BRITISH DEPENDENT TERRITORIES CITIZENSHIP
Since 26 February 2002, this category of nationality no longer exists and has been replaced by British overseas territory citizenship.

If a person had this class of nationality only by reason of a connection to the territory of Hong Kong, they lost it automatically when Hong Kong was returned to the People's Republic of China. However, if after 30 June 1997, they had no other nationality and would have become stateless, or were born after 30 June 1997 and would have been born stateless (but had a parent who was a British national (overseas) or a British overseas citizen), they became a British overseas citizen.

BRITISH OVERSEAS CITIZENSHIP
Under the 1981 act, as amended by the British Overseas Territories Act 2002, this type of citizenship was conferred on any UK and colonies citizens who did not become either a British citizen or a British overseas territories citizen on 1 January 1983 and as such is now, for most purposes, only acquired by persons who would otherwise be stateless.

BRITISH OVERSEAS TERRITORIES CITIZENSHIP
This category of nationality replaced British dependent territories citizenship. Most commonly, this form of nationality is acquired where, after 31 December 1982, a person was a citizen of the UK and colonies and did not become a British citizen, and that person, and their parents or grandparents, were born, registered or naturalised in the specified British overseas territory. However, on 21 May 2002, people became British citizens if they had British overseas territories citizenship by connection with any British overseas territory, except for the sovereign base areas of Akrotiri and Dhekelia in Cyprus.

RESIDUAL CATEGORIES
British subjects, British protected persons and British nationals (overseas) may be entitled to registration as British citizens on completion of five years' legal residence in the UK.

Citizens of the Republic of Ireland who were also British subjects before 1 January 1949 can retain that status if they fulfil certain conditions.

EUROPEAN UNION CITIZENSHIP
At the time of writing, British citizens (including Gibraltarians who are registered for this purpose) are also EU citizens and are entitled to travel freely to other EU countries to work, study, reside and set up a business. EU citizens have the same rights with respect to the UK. However, on the day the UK leaves the EU, European freedom of movement will end for all EU citizens (including citizens of Switzerland, Norway, Iceland and Liechtenstein) and their family members in the UK, and for all British citizens living in the EU.

The EU and the UK have negotiated the terms of the UK's withdrawal from the EU. Under the withdrawal agreement, EU law, in the main, would continue to apply in the UK from when the UK leaves the EU until 31 December 2020. This means that the freedom of movement would also continue until this date. In the case of no agreement between the UK and the EU, the freedom of movement would end after the withdrawal date.

NATURALISATION
Naturalisation is granted at the discretion of the home secretary. The basic requirements are lawful residence in the UK in the five years immediately preceding application (three years if the applicant is married to, or is the civil partner of a British citizen), good character, adequate knowledge of the English, Welsh or Scottish Gaelic language, passing the UK citizenship test and an intention to reside permanently in the UK.

The good character requirement applies to adults and children over the age of 10 and in assessing this the Home Office will take into account a range of factors, including any convictions, cautions, civil judgements, bankruptcies, financial soundness and any instances of failure to comply with immigration laws. If a person is deemed not to be of good character their naturalisation application will be refused. In January 2019 the Home Office updated its guidance as to how caseworkers should assess whether or not someone meets the good character requirement. The changes to the guidance apply to all applications made after 16 January 2019 and mainly relate to children, certain immigration offences and genuine mistakes made by the applicant.

STATUS OF ALIENS
Aliens, being persons without any of the above forms of British nationality, may not hold public office or vote in

Britain and they may not own a British ship or aircraft. Citizens of the Republic of Ireland and Commonwealth citizens are not deemed to be aliens. Certain provisions of the Immigration and Asylum Act 1999 make provision about immigration and asylum and about procedures in connection with marriage by superintendent registrar's certificate.

CONSUMER LAW

SALE OF GOODS
The law in this area is enacted to protect buyers who deal as 'consumers' (where the seller is selling in the course of a business, the goods are of a type ordinarily bought for private use and the goods are purchased by a buyer who is not a business buyer).

A sale of goods contract is the most common type of contract. These are governed by the Consumer Rights Act 2015 (CRA), which was designed to modernise and simplify the law in this area by codifying consumer legislation, most notably incorporating the Sale of Goods Act 1979.

The CRA provides protection for buyers by implying terms into every business-to-consumer sale of goods contract. These terms include:
- that the goods must be of a standard such that a reasonable person would deem them to be of satisfactory quality, considering, among other relevant factors, any description of the goods given by the seller and their price. The goods should be of satisfactory quality for the purpose for which they are usually intended, as well as in appearance, and they should not pose safety concerns. Should, prior to purchase, any issue affecting the quality of the goods be made clear to the consumer, then the term will not be applied. The same is true if, prior to purchase, the consumer has the opportunity to make a reasonable examination of the goods or a sample of them which would reveal any issue affecting their quality
- that goods must be suitable for the purpose for which the consumer has, expressly or implicitly, stated that they are intended. This term is applicable regardless of whether or not goods of such a nature are usually intended for this purpose, unless the consumer is advised otherwise by the trader and ignores such advice
- that any description of the goods provided by the seller must be accurate. If the seller provides both a description and a sample, the goods must ultimately correspond with the description, irrespective of whether they mostly correspond with the sample. This term is included even when the goods have been exposed for supply prior to purchase and selected by the consumer
- that goods will match any sample or model provided by the seller before purchase. In the case of the provision of a sample or a model, the goods must match the sample or model with the exception of any difference made clear to the consumer prior to purchase. Where a sample is provided, there must be no defect to the goods that a reasonable examination of the sample would not reveal
- that, in the event that the contract includes the installation of the goods, it is the duty of the seller to install or ensure that the goods are installed correctly
- that, in the event that goods include digital content, such digital content must comply with the contract for the provision of such content, or the goods will be considered as breaching the contract; and
- that the seller has the right to sell the goods, and that the goods have and will continue to have no charge or encumbrance that has not been made clear to the consumer prior to purchase. In the case of the hire of goods, the trader must have the right to transfer the goods for such a purpose

Under the CRA, which draws together and slightly amends the pre-existing rules under the Unfair Contract Terms Act 1977 and the Unfair Terms in Consumer Contracts Regulations 1999, these terms can not be excluded from contracts by the seller.

In a sale of secondhand goods by auction (at which individuals have the opportunity of attending the sale in person), a buyer does not deal as a consumer.

HIRE-PURCHASE AGREEMENTS
Terms similar to those implied in contracts of sales of goods are implied into contracts of hire-purchase, under the CRA. The Act limits the exclusion of these implied terms as before.

SUPPLY OF GOODS AND SERVICES
Before the CRA, the Supply of Goods and Services Act 1982 regulated other types of contracts (including for services, contracts under which ownership of goods pass and contracts for hire of goods). This Act has now also been amalgamated into the CRA. Similar terms to those above are implied into such contracts, however there are additional terms including:
- that the supplier will use reasonable care and skill in carrying out the service
- that the supplier will carry out the service in a reasonable time (unless the time has been agreed)
- that the supplier will make a reasonable charge (unless the charge or mechanism for its calculation has already been agreed)

The CRA Act limits the exclusion of these implied terms in a similar manner as before.

DIGITAL CONTENT
The CRA is the first statute to address the sale and supply of digital products, defined as 'data which are produced and supplied in digital form.' The Act applies to any digital content which is purchased or that which comes free alongside purchased services or goods. As above, implied terms for quality, fitness for purpose and adherence to description will be imposed on all consumer contracts. However, there is an extra term for contracts for digital content: that the seller has the right to provide such content.

These terms also apply to any future update or modification of the content. Should such future alterations fail to meet these standards, then the breach will be treated as having occurred at the time of supply rather than the point at which it was adapted.

Where digital content causes damage to other digital content or devices, and this could have been prevented where the seller had exercised reasonable skill and care, then that seller will be required to remedy the breach.

UNFAIR TERMS
The CRA has also consolidated the provisions of the Unfair Terms in Consumer Contracts Regulations 1999 that protected consumers against the imposition of unfair consumer contract terms. Where the terms have not been individually negotiated (ie where the terms were drafted in advance so that the consumer was unable to influence those terms), a term will be deemed unfair if it operates to the detriment of the consumer (ie causes a significant imbalance in the parties' rights and obligations arising under the contract). An unfair term does not bind the consumer but the contract may continue to bind the parties if it is capable of existing without the unfair term. The CRA contains a non-exhaustive list of terms that are regarded as potentially unfair. When a term does not fall into such a category, whether it will be regarded as fair or not will depend on many factors, including the nature of the goods or services, the surrounding circumstances (such as the bargaining strength of both parties) and the other terms in the contract.

CONSUMER PROTECTION

The Consumer Protection from Unfair Trading Regulations 2008 (CPRs) replaced much previous consumer protection regulation, including the majority of the Trade Descriptions Act 1968. The CPRs prohibit 31 specific practices, including pyramid schemes. In addition the CPRs prohibit business sellers from making misleading actions and misleading omissions, which cause, or are likely to cause, the average consumer to take a different transactional decision. There is also a general duty not to trade unfairly. The CPRs were amended by the Consumer Protection (Amendment) Regulations 2014, which entered into force on 1 October 2014 and introduced a new direct civil right of redress for consumers against businesses for misleading and aggressive practices, as well as extending the CPRs to cover misleading and aggressive demands for payment.

Under the Consumer Protection Act 1987, producers of goods are liable for any injury, death or damage to any property exceeding £275 caused by a defect in their product (subject to certain defences).

Consumers are also afforded protection under the Consumer Contracts (Information, Cancellation and Additional Charges) Regulations 2013 (CCRs), which came into force on 13 June 2014 and require certain information to be provided to the consumer.

The Financial Guidance and Claims Act 2018 makes provision to ensure members of the public are able to access free and impartial money guidance, pensions guidance and debt advice, and to ensure that they are able to access high-quality claims handling services by strengthening the regulation of claims management companies.

The CPA, CPRs and CCRs implement EU legislation and will be amended accordingly on the day that the UK exits the EU.

CONSUMER CREDIT

In matters relating to the provision of credit (or the supply of goods on hire or hire-purchase), consumers are also protected by the Consumer Credit Act 1974 (as amended by the Consumer Credit Act 2006). The Act was most recently amended by a number of statutory instruments made under the Financial Services and Markets Act 2000. These came into force on 1 April 2014 and represent a major overhaul of the consumer credit regime which was carried out in order to implement the recent EU Consumer Credit Directive. Under the new regime, responsibility for consumer credit regulation has been transferred from the Office of Fair Trading (OFT), which has ceased to exist, to the Financial Conduct Authority (FCA). Previously, a licence issued by the OFT was required in order to conduct a consumer credit, consumer hire or an ancillary credit business, subject to certain exemptions. The requirement to obtain a licence from the OFT has been replaced by the need to obtain authorisation from the FCA to carry out a consumer credit 'regulated' activity, which is likewise subject to certain exemptions. Provisions of the 1974 Act as amended include:

• in order for a creditor to enforce a regulated agreement, the agreement must comply with certain formalities and must be properly executed. An improperly executed regulated agreement is enforceable only on an order of the court. The debtor must also be given specified information by the creditor or his/her broker or agent during the negotiations which take place before the signing of the agreement. The agreement must also state certain information to ensure that the debtor or hirer is aware of the rights and duties conferred or imposed on him/her and the protection and remedies available to him/her under the Act
• the right to withdraw from or cancel some contracts depending on the circumstances. For example, subject to certain exceptions, a borrower may withdraw from a regulated credit agreement within 14 days without giving any reason. The exceptions include agreements for credit exceeding £60,260 and agreements secured on land. The right to withdraw applies only to the credit agreement itself and not to goods or services purchased with it. The borrower must also repay the credit and any interest
• if the debtor is in breach of the agreement, the creditor must serve a default notice before taking any action such as repossessing the goods
• if the agreement is a hire purchase or conditional sale agreement, the creditor cannot repossess the goods without a court order if the debtor has paid one third of the total price of the goods
• in agreements where the relationship between the creditor and the debtor is unfair to the debtor, the court may alter or set aside some of the terms of the agreement

It is intended that the statutory basis of consumer credit regulation, under the 1974 Act, will be replaced by a rules-based approach under the new regime. The FCA will be reviewing the statutory framework over the next few years and will develop rule-based alternatives where possible.

Consumer credit legislation will be amended on the day the UK exits the EU.

SCOTLAND

The legislation governing the sale and supply of goods applies to Scotland as follows:
• the Consumer Rights Act 2015 (with the exception of chapter three)
• the Sale of Goods Act 1979 applies with some modifications and it has been amended by the Sale and Supply of Goods Act 1994
• the Supply of Goods (Implied Terms) Act 1973 applies
• the Supply of Goods and Services Act 1982 does not extend to Scotland but some of its provisions were introduced by the Sale and Supply of Goods Act 1994
• only Parts II and III of the Unfair Contract Terms Act 1977 apply
• the Trade Descriptions Act 1968 applies with minor modifications
• the Consumer Credit Act 1974 applies
• the Consumer Credit Act 2006 applies
• the Consumer Protection Act 1987 applies
• the General Product Safety Regulations 2005 apply
• the Unfair Terms in Consumer Contracts (Amendment) Regulations 2001 apply
• the Consumer Protection (Distance Selling) Regulations 2000 apply
• the Consumer Protection from Unfair Trading Regulations 2008 apply

PROCEEDINGS AGAINST THE CROWN

Until 1947, proceedings against the Crown were generally possible only by a procedure known as a petition of right, which put the private litigant at a considerable disadvantage. The Crown Proceedings Act 1947 placed the Crown (not the sovereign in his/her private capacity, but as the embodiment of the state) largely in the same position as a private individual and made proceedings in the high court involving the Crown subject to the same rules as any other case. The act did not, however, extinguish or limit the Crown's prerogative or statutory powers, and it continued the immunity of HM ships and aircraft. It also left certain Crown privileges unaffected. The act largely abolished the special procedures which previously applied to civil proceedings by and against the Crown. Civil proceedings may be initiated against the appropriate government department or, if there is doubt regarding which is the appropriate department, against the attorney-general.

In Scotland proceedings against the Crown founded on breach of contract could be taken before the 1947 act and no special procedures applied. The Crown could, however, claim certain special pleas. The 1947 act applies in part to Scotland and brings the practice of the two countries as closely together as the different legal systems permit. As a result of the Scotland Act 1998, actions against government departments should be raised against the Lord Advocate or the advocate-general. Actions should be raised against the Lord Advocate where the department involved administers a devolved matter. Devolved matters include agriculture, education, housing, local government, health and justice. Actions should be raised against the advocate-general where the department is dealing with a reserved matter. Reserved matters include defence, foreign affairs and social security.

DEATHS

WHEN A DEATH OCCURS

If the death (including stillbirth) was expected, the doctor who attended the deceased during their final illness should be contacted. If the death was sudden or unexpected, the family doctor (if known) and police should be contacted. If the cause of death is quite clear, the doctor will provide:
- a medical certificate that shows the cause of death
- a formal notice that states that the doctor has signed the medical certificate and that explains how to get the death registered
- if the death was known to be caused by a natural illness but the doctor wishes to know more about the cause of death, he/she may ask the relatives for permission to carry out a post-mortem examination

In England and Wales a coroner is responsible for investigating deaths occurring:
- when there is no doctor who can issue a medical certificate of cause of death
- no doctor has treated the deceased during his or her last illness or when the doctor attending the patient did not see him or her within 14 days before death, or after death
- the death occurred during an operation or before recovery from the effect of an anaesthetic
- the death was sudden and unexplained or attended by suspicious circumstances
- the death might be due to an industrial injury, disease or poisoning
- the death might be due to accident, violence, neglect or abortion
- the death occurred in prison or in police custody
- the cause of death is unknown

The doctor will write on the formal notice that the death has been referred to the coroner; if the post-mortem shows that death was due to natural causes, the coroner may issue a notification which gives the cause of death so that the death can be registered. If the cause of death was violent or unnatural, is still undetermined after a post-mortem, or took place in prison or police custody, the coroner must hold an inquest. The coroner must hold an inquest in these circumstances even if the death occurred abroad (and the body has been returned to England or Wales).

In Scotland the office of coroner does not exist. The local procurator fiscal inquires into sudden or suspicious deaths. A fatal accident inquiry will be held before the sheriff where the death has resulted from an accident during the course of the employment of the person who has died, or where the person who has died was in legal custody or a child required to be kept or detained in secure accommodation, or where the Lord Advocate deems it in the public interest that an inquiry be held.

REGISTERING A DEATH

In England and Wales the death can be registered at any register office, although if it is registered by the registrar of births and deaths for the district in which it occurred, the necessary documents can be obtained on the same day. A death which occurs in Scotland can be registered in any registration district in Scotland. Information concerning a death can be given before any registrar of births and deaths in England and Wales. The registrar will pass the relevant details to the registrar for the district where the death occurred, who will then register the death.

In England and Wales the death must normally be registered within five days (unless the registrar says this period can be extended); in Scotland within eight days. If the death has been referred to the coroner/local procurator fiscal it cannot be registered until the registrar has received authority from the coroner/local procurator fiscal to do so. Failure to register a death involves a penalty in England and Wales and may lead to a court decree being granted by a sheriff in Scotland. A stillbirth normally needs to be registered within 42 days, and at the latest within three months. In many cases this can be done at the hospital or at the local register office. In Scotland this must be done within 21 days.

If the death occurred at a house or hospital, the death may be registered by:
- any relative of the deceased
- any person present at the death
- any person making the funeral arrangements
- an administrator from the hospital
- in Scotland, the deceased's executor or legal representative

For deaths that took place elsewhere, the death may be registered by:
- any relative of the deceased
- someone present at the death
- someone who found the body
- a person in charge of the body
- any person making the funeral arrangements

The majority of deaths are registered by a relative of the deceased. The registrar would normally allow one of the other listed persons to register the death only if there were no relatives available.

The person registering the death should take the medical certificate of the cause of death (signed by a doctor) with them; it is also useful, though not essential, to take the deceased's birth and marriage/civil partnership certificates, council tax bill, driving licence, passport or NHS medical card. The details given to the registrar must be absolutely correct, otherwise it may be difficult to change them later. The person registering the death should check the entry carefully before it is signed. The registrar will issue a certificate for burial or cremation, and a certificate of registration of death (form BD8, commonly known as a 'death certificate' which is issued for social security purposes if the deceased received a state pension or benefits) – both free of charge. A death certificate is a certified copy of the entry in the death register; copies can be provided on payment of a fee and may be required for the following purposes, in particular by the executor or administrator when sorting out the deceased's affairs:
- the will
- bank and building society accounts
- savings bank certificates and premium bonds
- insurance policies
- pension claims

If the death occurred abroad or on a foreign ship or aircraft, the death should be registered according to the local regulations of the relevant country and a death certificate should be obtained. In many countries the death can also be registered with the British consulate in that country and a record will be kept at the General Register Office. This avoids the expense of bringing the body back.

After 12 months (three months in Scotland) of death or the finding of a dead body, no death can be registered without the written authority of the registrar-general.

BURIAL AND CREMATION

In most circumstances in England and Wales a certificate for burial or cremation must be obtained from the registrar before the burial or cremation can take place. If the death has been referred to the coroner, an order for burial or a certificate for cremation must be obtained. In Scotland a death or still birth must be registered in order that the appropriate certificate can be obtained to allow burial or cremation of the body.

Funeral costs can normally be repaid out of the deceased's estate and should be given priority over any other claims. If the deceased has left a will it may contain directions concerning the funeral; however, these directions need not be followed by the executor.

The deceased's papers should also indicate whether a grave space had already been arranged. This information will be contained in a document known as a 'Deed of Grant'. Most town churchyards and many suburban churchyards are no longer open for burial because they are full. Most cemeteries are non-denominational and may be owned by local authorities or private companies; fees vary.

If the body is to be cremated, an application form, two cremation certificates, one signed by the doctor who issued the medical certificate and the other signed by a different doctor confirming the first certificate (for which there is a charge) or a certificate for cremation if the death was referred to the coroner must be completed in addition to the certificate for burial or cremation (the form is not required if the coroner has issued a certificate for cremation). All the forms are available from the funeral director or crematorium. Most crematoria are run by local authorities, the fees can include the medical referee's fee and the use of the chapel. Ashes may be scattered, buried in a churchyard or cemetery, or kept.

The registrar must be notified of the date, place and means of disposal of the body within 96 hours (England and Wales) or three days (Scotland).

If the death occurred abroad or on a foreign ship or aircraft, a local burial or cremation may be arranged. If the body is to be brought back to England or Wales, a death certificate from the relevant country or an authorisation for the removal of the body from the country of death from the coroner or relevant authority, together with a certificate of embalming, will be required. The British consulate can help to arrange this documentation. To arrange a funeral in England or Wales, a certified translation of a foreign death certificate or a death certificate issued in Scotland or Northern Ireland which must show the cause of death, is needed, together with a certificate of no liability to register from the registrar in England and Wales in whose sub-district it is intended to bury or cremate the body. If burial is intended they will issue a certificate for burial. If it is intended to cremate the body, a cremation order will be required from the Home Office or a certificate for cremation. If the body is to be cremated in Scotland, a certificate permitting this must be obtained from the Death Certification Review Service run by Healthcare Improvement Scotland.

THE GENERAL REGISTER OFFICE, General Register Office, PO Box 2, Southport PR8 2JD **T** 0300-123 1837
W www.gro.gov.uk/gro/content/certificates

THE NATIONAL RECORDS OF SCOTLAND, New Register House, 3 West Register Street, Edinburgh EH1 3YT
T 0131-334 0380 **W** www.nrscotland.gov.uk

DIVORCE, DISSOLUTION AND RELATED MATTERS

Divorce is the legal process which ends a marriage. The process is the same whether the parties are of the opposite or same sex pursuant to the Marriage (Same Sex Couples) Act 2013. Dissolution is a similar process which ends a civil partnership. Divorce and dissolution should be distinguished from judicial separation which does not legally dissolve the marriage/civil partnership but removes the legal requirement for a married couple to live together.

DIVORCE

There are two bars to divorce and dissolution: the 'one-year rule' and jurisdiction.

An application for a matrimonial order for divorce may only be presented to the court after one year of marriage. The spouse who lodges this document is known as the 'applicant petitioner' throughout the divorce proceedings and the other spouse is the 'respondent'.

Whether the English court may or may not have jurisdiction to deal with any divorce will depend on where the parties spent their married life and whether or not one party has retained their residence or domicile in England (and Wales). If there is a dispute as to which of two jurisdictions should host the divorce, where the two jurisdictions likely to be relevant are EU countries then the usual rule is that the divorce takes place in the country where the petition is filed first. The exception to this rule is Denmark, which opted out of the EU regulation which determines forums in this way.

If the two countries are not within the EU, or one of them is Denmark, then the forum of divorce may be determined by which is the more appropriate or convenient *(forum conveniens)*. In these circumstances, an election of a jurisdiction in a pre-nuptial agreement can be very important in resolving that dispute, although it cannot override the 'first in time' rule between EU countries (except Denmark) referred to above (save in the case of maintenance claims).

Some EU countries have signed up to the Convention on the Recognition of Divorces and Legal Separations which would allow a couple to elect a choice of law even in EU countries whereby one country would be required to apply the law of another. For the time being, England has not signed up to that convention and would apply English law only.

The UK's withdrawal from the EU will undoubtedly have an impact on the law in this area, since various European instruments apply (as outlined above) in determining in which country and jurisdiction a couple get divorced. In the case of a no-deal Brexit, the 'first-in-time' rules will no longer apply between the UK and the remaining EU member states and the UK would revert to the pre-EU *forum conveniens* rules.

There is only one ground for divorce, namely that the marriage has broken down irretrievably. This ground must be 'proved' by one of the five following facts:

- the respondent has committed adultery and the petitioner finds it intolerable to live with the respondent (an applicant can not file for divorce based on their own adultery)
- the respondent has behaved in such a way that the petitioner cannot reasonably be expected to live with the respondent
- the respondent has deserted the petitioner for a continuous period of at least two years immediately prior to the petition
- the applicant and respondent have lived apart for a continuous period of two years immediately prior to the petition and the respondent agrees to a divorce
- the applicant and respondent have lived apart for a continuous period of five years immediately prior to the petition

If the court is satisfied that the petitioner has proved one of those facts then it must grant a decree nisi (*see* below) unless it is satisfied that the marriage has not broken down.

Periods of up to six months' cohabitation are permitted for attempts at reconciliation without prejudicing the matrimonial proceedings. If the parties continue to live together for more than six months following discovery of adultery, the applicant will not be able to rely on the fact of adultery to prove the marriage has irretrievably broken down and may also adversely affect the applicant's chances of establishing arguments of unreasonable behaviour.

NO-FAULT DIVORCE

The majority of people are not prepared to wait two or five years to divorce and so are forced by the current legislation to apportion blame (adultery or unreasonable behaviour). Following the supreme court case of *Owens v Owens* in 2018, the government announced plans to introduce no-fault divorce and, in April 2019, it was confirmed the government will introduce new legislation to implement the planned changes. Removing blame from the divorce process has come as a welcome development to family lawyers. Following reform, a couple (or one party) would need to notify the court that their marriage has irretrievably broken down. The 'five facts' will be removed, a minimum six-month period will be required to enable couples to 'reflect' on their decision and the ability to contest a divorce will be abolished. Parallel changes will be made to the law governing the dissolution of civil partnerships. The proposed legislation will not cover other areas of matrimonial law such as financial provision.

DECREE NISI

If the judge is satisfied that the petitioner has proved the marriage has irretrievably broken down, a date will be set for the pronouncement of the decree nisi in open court. The decree nisi confirms the grounds for divorce have been met; the marriage will not be legally dissolved until the decree absolute. Neither party needs to attend and all the proceedings up to this point are usually carried out on paper.

DECREE ABSOLUTE

The final step in the divorce procedure is to obtain a decree absolute which formally ends the marriage. The petitioner can apply for this six weeks and one day after the date of the decree nisi. If the petitioner does not apply the respondent can apply, but only after three months from the earliest date on which the petitioner could have applied.

A decree absolute will not usually be granted until the parties have agreed, or the court has dealt with, the parties' financial situation (*see* below for details of financial provision).

DISSOLUTION OF CIVIL PARTNERSHIPS

The legal process for dissolution of a civil partnership follows a model closely based on divorce. Irretrievable breakdown of the partnership is the sole ground for dissolution. The facts to be proved to establish this are the same as for divorce, with the exception of adultery which, due to its legal definition, can only apply to opposite sex couples. Sexual activity with a third party can, however, be used as an example of unreasonable behaviour.

FINANCIAL RELIEF ANCILLARY TO DIVORCE, NULLITY AND JUDICIAL SEPARATION

Following a petition for divorce, nullity or judicial separation, it is open to either spouse or former spouse to make a claim for financial provision provided they have not remarried. It is common practice for such an application to be made at the same time, or shortly after, a divorce petition has been issued. Although most are agreed or settled by the parties themselves, where the parties are unable to agree, the courts have wide powers to make financial provision where a marriage breaks down. Orders can be made for:

- spousal maintenance (periodical payments) which can be capitalised into a lump sum
- lump sum payments
- adjustment or transfer of interests in property
- adjustment of interests in trusts and settlements
- orders relating to pensions

EXERCISE OF THE COURT'S POWERS TO ORDER FINANCIAL PROVISION

The court must exercise its powers so as to achieve an outcome which is fair between the parties, although it has a wide discretion in determining what is a fair financial outcome. It will consider the worldwide assets of both parties, whether liquid or illiquid. In exercising its discretion, the court has to consider a range of statutory factors including:

- the income, earning capacity, property and other financial resources which either party has or is likely to have in the foreseeable future, including, in the case of earning capacity, any increase in that capacity which it would in the opinion of the court be reasonable to expect a party to the marriage to take steps to acquire
- the financial needs, obligations and responsibilities which each of the parties to the marriage has or is likely to have in the foreseeable future
- the standard of living enjoyed by the family before the breakdown of the marriage
- the age of each party to the marriage and the duration of the marriage
- any physical or mental disability of either of the parties to the marriage
- the contribution which each of the parties has made or is likely to make in the foreseeable future to the welfare of the family, including any contribution by looking after the home or caring for the family
- the conduct of each of the parties, if that conduct is such that it would in the opinion of the court be inequitable to disregard it
- the value to each of the parties to the marriage of any benefit which, by reason of the dissolution of that marriage, that party will lose the chance of acquiring

When considering the above factors, the court must give first consideration to the welfare of any child of the family.

The court has a duty when exercising its powers to consider whether a 'clean break' would be appropriate. A clean break severs the financial ties between the parties and would provide no continuing capital payments or spousal periodical payments.

The court has a wide discretion in considering these factors in order to achieve an outcome it considers to be fair. The court's approach changed dramatically following the House of Lords decision of *White v White* in October 2000 where it was said that, after providing for the parties' reasonable needs, the remaining assets should be shared. In that case, it was established that the contributions made by both breadwinner and homemaker are to be regarded as equal and the court's main objective must be to achieve a fair outcome. More recent case law has gone further in establishing that the starting point should be an equal division of matrimonial assets. In lower net worth cases, any departure from an equal division is usually justified on the basis of need.

In high net worth cases, however, a departure from equality is frequently justified not just on the basis of need but also of compensation and non-matrimonial property. In the House of Lords cases of Miller and McFarlane the court refined the thinking in the White case to say that the court should strive to achieve a fair result by considering three strands:

- the needs of the parties going forward
- compensation for any economic disparity between the parties (such as where one party has sacrificed their career to become a full-time parent)
- sharing

NUPTIAL AGREEMENTS

Nuptial agreements are legal agreements drawn up prior to (pre-nuptial) or during (post-nuptial) marriage or civil partnership to regulate financial arrangements and division of assets in the event of divorce or dissolution. Such agreements are not currently binding in England and Wales. In October 2010, the supreme court gave judgment in *Radmacher v Granatino* which made it clear that a nuptial agreement can carry considerable weight (and will most likely be binding) provided the spouses freely and fully agree to its terms, are aware of its implications and it is fair to hold the parties to it, given the circumstances at the time of the court hearing. However, the court will still be able to decide as to whether the agreement is fair and whether the terms setting out the financial provision on divorce should be enforced in whole or in part. The supreme court gave some guidelines on when a pre-nuptial agreement would be considered 'fair', but ultimately it depends on the facts of the individual case.

FINANCIAL PROVISION ON DISSOLUTION OF A CIVIL PARTNERSHIP

The Civil Partnership Act 2004 makes provisions for financial relief for civil partners generally and extends the same rights and responsibilities invoked by marriage. Again the court must consider a number of factors when exercising its discretion and must take into account all of the circumstances of the case while giving first consideration to the welfare of any child of the family who is under 18. The list of statutory factors the court must consider resemble those for marriage and it is likely that the interpretation of these factors will be based on the court's interpretation of the factors relating to marriage.

COHABITING COUPLES

There is no such thing as a common law spouse. Unmarried couples do not benefit from the same statutory protection afforded to married couples. Instead, the rights of cohabitees are based on property law and trust interests. Therefore, it is advisable to consider entering into a contract, or 'cohabitation agreement', which establishes how money, property and the care of any children should be divided in the event of a relationship breakdown.

The Cohabitation Rights bill 2017–19 seeks to introduce certain protections for cohabitees during their lifetime and on death, it received its first reading in the House of Lords on 5 July 2017 and second reading on 15 March 2019, but has made no further progress. Thus, cohabitation agreements continue to be governed by the same general principles of property, trust, and contract law.

FINANCIAL PROVISION FOR CHILDREN

Under the Child Support Act 1991, all parents are under a legal obligation to support their children financially. A parent who does not have day-to-day care of a child is under a duty to pay child maintenance to the parent who does.

Parents can arrange child maintenance themselves (a so-called 'family based arrangement') or, where the parties are not able to reach an agreement, one party may apply to the Child Maintenance Service (CMS), (formerly the Child Support Agency (CSA)) to carry out an assessment.

Since 31 December 2017, CMS handles all child maintenance arrangements. The CSA no longer takes on new cases but still handles cases opened before 25 November 2013.

There is a £20 application fee for applying to CMS (unless the applicant is under the age of 18, a victim of domestic abuse, or lives in Northern Ireland), which covers the costs for calculating the amount of child maintenance, the provision to both parties of a yearly updated calculation using HMRC data and provision of information about payment services.

There are three different methods of calculating child support under the statutory child maintenance schemes:

- the 'old' scheme (for all applications up until 3 March 2003)
- the net income scheme (for applications from 3 March 2003)
- the gross income scheme (for all new applications since 25 November 2013)

All CMS child maintenance calculations will be dealt with under the gross income scheme. CMS uses the paying parent's gross weekly income (using information obtained from HMRC) as a starting point to work out the rate of child maintenance a non-resident parent should be liable for. Once the gross income information is received, the CMS applies a specific formula to work out the level of child maintenance payable. The child maintenance calculation may only be reassessed annually, unless the income variation is 25 per cent or more or in cases involving long-term illness or redundancy. It is a criminal offence to make a false statement or representation to or withhold information from the CMS and also to fail to notify CMS of a change of address or other change of circumstances.

Under the gross income scheme, it is mandatory for parents to have a conversation with the Child Maintenance Options (CMO) team to discuss their choices and consider alternatives before they proceed with their application. The CMO will discuss the various options available to parents if they cannot agree a 'family-based arrangement' between themselves:

- 'Direct Pay' (previously known as 'Maintenance Direct' under CSA arrangements) which enables parents to keep control of making and receiving payments. The statutory service works out the payment amounts for parents but will not be involved in collection
- 'Collect and Pay' (previously known as the 'full collection service' under CSA arrangements) whereby CMS calculates how much maintenance the paying parent owes. If the Collect and Pay Service is used, parties will be required to pay a fee for use of the service. Paying parents are required to pay a 20 per cent fee on top of their regular child maintenance payment and receiving parents will have 4 per cent of their child maintenance payment deducted from the total they receive

If payments are not made on time there is a spectrum of collection actions and enforcement powers (the range of which was increased in December 2018) available to the CMS to collect arrears, although they can only be used if a case is on the 'Collect and Pay' scheme. CMS will contact the paying parent to seek continuing payments. Where there is persistent non-payment, the CMS is able to take money directly from the paying parent, either from their earnings or bank account, or to take court action. There are CMS fees for pursuing enforcement action, which may affect the eventual amount of child maintenance received by the receiving party. Since December 2018, the government has had the power to write-off arrears that accumulated when a case was administered by the CSA, if no payment towards those arrears has been made for three months, and subject to certain other conditions.

Further changes were introduced in December 2018 including how CMS calculates child maintenance for complex earnings giving CMS the right to make deductions from joint accounts and unlimited partnership accounts and the power to disqualify a payment parents from holding or obtaining a passport if they have consistently avoided paying their child maintenance debt.

Provision is also made under Schedule 1 of the Children Act 1989 for unmarried parents, step-parents and guardians to apply to the court for periodical payments, lump sum and property adjustment orders.

SCOTLAND

Although some provisions are similar to those for England and Wales, there is separate legislation for Scotland covering nullity of marriage, judicial separation, divorce and ancillary matters. The principal legislation in relation to family law in Scotland is the Family Law (Scotland) Act 1985. The Family Law (Scotland) Act 2006 came into force on 4 May 2006, and introduced reforms to various aspects of Scottish family law. The following is confined to major points on which the law in Scotland differs from that of England and Wales.

An action for judicial separation or divorce may be raised in the court of session; it may also be raised in the sheriff court if either party was resident in the sheriffdom for 40 days immediately before the date of the action or for 40 days ending not more than 40 days before the date of the action and has no known residence in Scotland at that date. The fee for starting a divorce petition in the sheriff court is £156.

The grounds for raising an action of divorce in Scotland are set down in The Divorce (Scotland) Act 1976 and have been subject to reform in terms of the 2006 act. The current grounds for divorce are:

- the defender has committed adultery. When adultery is cited as proof that the marriage has broken down irretrievably, it is not necessary in Scotland to prove that it is also intolerable for the pursuer to live with the defender
- the defender's behaviour is such that the pursuer cannot reasonably be expected to cohabit with the defender
- there has been no cohabitation between the parties for one year prior to the raising of the action for divorce, and the defender consents to the granting of decree of divorce
- there has been no cohabitation between the parties for two years prior to the raising of the action for divorce
- the marriage has broken down irretrievably
- an interim gender recognition certificate under the Gender Recognition Act 2004 has, after the date of marriage, been issued to either party to the marriage. However, as a result of changes under the Marriage and Civil Partnership (Scotland) Act 2014, this ground of divorce will sometimes not be available where a full gender recognition certificate has been issued under the 2004 Act

The previously available ground of desertion was abolished by the 2006 Act.

A simplified procedure for 'do-it-yourself divorce' was introduced in 1983 for certain divorces. If the action is based on one or two years' separation and will not be opposed or because a gender recognition certificate has been issued; there are no children under 16; no financial claims; there is no sign that the applicant's spouse is unable to manage his or her affairs through mental illness or handicap; and there are no other court proceedings underway which might result in the end of the marriage, the applicant can access the appropriate forms to enable him or her to proceed on the Scottish Courts and Tribunals' website. From 25 April 2019 the fee is £125, however the applicant may be exempt from paying the fee if they are in receipt of certain benefits; or if legal advice and assistance is being provided by a solicitor in terms of the Legal Aid (Scotland) Act 1986.

Where a divorce action has been raised, it may be put on hold for a variety of reasons. In all actions for divorce an extract decree, which brings the marriage to an end, will be made available 14 days after the divorce has been granted. Unlike in England, there is no decree nisi, only a final decree of divorce. Parties must ensure that all financial issues have been resolved prior to divorce, as it is not possible to seek further financial provision after divorce has been granted.

FINANCIAL PROVISION

In relation to financial provision on divorce, the first, and most important, principle is fair sharing of the matrimonial property. There is a presumption that fair share means an equal share of the matrimonial property, which can be departed from if justified by special circumstances. In terms of Scots law matrimonial property is defined as all property acquired by either spouse from the date of marriage up to the date of separation. Property acquired before the marriage is not deemed to be matrimonial unless it was acquired for use by the parties as a family home or as furniture for that home. Property acquired after the date of separation is not matrimonial property. Any property acquired by either of the parties by way of gift or inheritance during the marriage is excluded and does not form part of the matrimonial property.

When considering whether to make an award of financial provision a court shall also take account of any economic advantage derived by either party to the marriage as a result of contributions, financial or otherwise, by the other, and of any economic disadvantage suffered by either party for the benefit of the other party. The court must also ensure that the economic burden of caring for a child under the age of 16 is shared fairly between the parties.

A court can also consider making an order requiring one party to pay the other party a periodical allowance for a certain period of time following divorce. Such an order may be appropriate in cases where there is insufficient capital to effect a fair sharing of the matrimonial property. Orders for periodical allowance are uncommon, as courts will favour a 'clean break' where possible.

CHILDREN

The court has the power to award a residence order in respect of any children of the marriage or to make an order regulating the child's contact with the non-resident parent. The court will only make such orders if it is deemed better for the child to do so than to make no order at all, and the welfare of the children is of paramount importance. The fact that a spouse has caused the breakdown of the marriage does not in itself preclude him/her from being awarded residence.

NULLITY

An action for 'declaration of nullity' can be brought if someone with a legitimate interest is able to show that the marriage is void or voidable. Although the grounds on which a marriage may be void or voidable are similar to those on which a marriage can be declared invalid in England, there are some differences. Where a spouse is capable of sexual intercourse but refuses to consummate the marriage, this is not a ground for nullity in Scots law, though it could be a ground for divorce. Where a spouse was suffering from venereal disease at the time of marriage and the other spouse did not know, this is not a ground for nullity in Scots law, neither is the fact that a wife was pregnant by another man at the time of marriage without the knowledge of her husband.

COHABITING COUPLES

The law in Scotland now provides certain financial and property rights for cohabiting couples in terms of the Family Law (Scotland) Act 2006, or 'the 2006 Act'. The relevant 2006 Act provisions do not place cohabitants in Scotland on an equal footing with married couples or civil partners, but provide some rights for cohabitants in the event that the relationship is terminated by separation or death. The provisions relate to couples who cease to cohabit after 4 May 2006.

The legislation provides for a presumption that most contents of the home shared by the cohabitants are owned in equal shares. A former cohabitant can also seek financial provision on termination of the relationship in the form of a capital payment if they can successfully demonstrate that they have been financially disadvantaged, and that conversely the other cohabitant has been financially advantaged, as a consequence of contributions made (financial or otherwise). An order can also be made in respect of the economic burden of caring for a child of whom the cohabitants are the parents. Such a claim must be made no later than one year after the day on which the cohabitants cease to cohabit.

The 2006 Act also provides that a cohabitant may make a claim on their partner's estate in the event of that partner's death, providing that there is no will. A claim of this nature must be made no later than six months after the date of the partner's death.

THE CENTRAL FAMILY COURT, First Avenue House, 42–49 High Holborn, London WC1V 6NP **T** 020-7421 8594

THE COURT OF SESSION, Parliament House, Parliament Square, Edinburgh EH1 1RQ **T** 0131-225 2595
W www.scotcourts.gov.uk

THE CHILD MAINTENANCE SERVICE, **T** 0800-171 2033
W www.gov.uk/child-maintenance

EMPLOYMENT LAW

EMPLOYEES
A fundamental distinction in UK employment law is that drawn between an employee and someone who is self-employed. Further, there is an important, intermediate category introduced by legislation: 'workers' covers all employees but also catches others who do not have full employment status. An 'employee' is someone who has entered into or works under a contract of employment, while a 'worker' has entered into or works under a contract whereby he undertakes to do or perform personally any work or services for another party whose status is not that of a client or customer. Whether or not someone is an employee or a worker as opposed to being genuinely self-employed is an important and complex question, for it determines that person's statutory rights and protections. For certain purposes, such as protection against discrimination, protection extends to some genuinely self-employed people as well as workers and employees.

The greater the level of control that the employer has over the work carried out, the greater the depth of integration of the employee in the employer's business, and the closer the obligations to provide and perform work between the parties, the more likely it is that the parties will be employer and employee.

PAY AND CONDITIONS
The Employment Rights Act 1996 consolidated the statutory provisions relating to employees' rights. Employers must give each employee employed for one month or more a written statement containing the following information:
• names of employer and employee
• date when employment began and the date on which the employee's period of *continuous* employment began (taking into account any employment with a previous employer which counts towards that period)
• the scale, rate or other method of calculating remuneration and intervals at which it will be paid
• job title or description of job
• hours and the permitted place(s) of work and, where there are several such places, the address of the employer
• holiday entitlement and holiday pay
• provisions concerning incapacity for work due to sickness and injury, including provisions for sick pay
• details of pension scheme(s)
• length of notice the employee is obliged to give and entitled to receive in order to terminate the contract of employment
• if the employment is not intended to be permanent, the period for which it is expected to continue or, if it is for a fixed term, the end date of the contract
• details of any collective agreement (including the parties to the agreement) which directly affects the terms of employment
• details of disciplinary and grievance procedures (including the individual to whom a complaint should be made and the process of making that complaint) except those which relate to health and safety at work
• if the employee is to work outside the UK for more than one month, the period of such work and the currency in which

payment is made and any additional remuneration or benefits payable to them
• a note stating whether a contracting-out certificate is in force
This must be given to the employee within two months of the start of their employment.

If the employer does not provide the written statement within two months (or a statement of any changes to these particulars within one month of the changes being made) then the employee can complain to an employment tribunal, which can specify the information that the employer should have given. When, in the context of an employee's successful tribunal claim, the employer is also found to have been in breach of the duty to provide the written statement at the time proceedings were commenced, the tribunal must award the employee two weeks' pay, and may award four weeks' pay, subject to the statutory cap, unless it would be unjust or inequitable to do so.

The Working Time Regulations 1998, the National Minimum Wage Act 1998, Employment Relations Act 1999, the Employment Act 2002 and the Employment Act 2008 now supplement the 1996 Act.

The Employment Rights (Employment Particulars and Paid Annual Leave) (Amendment) Regulations 2018 will come into force on 6 April 2020 and provides that a written statement of terms must be given on or before the first day of employment, rather than within two months of employment starting. In addition, they increase the amount of information that must be included in the statement.

The Employment Rights (Miscellaneous Amendments) Regulations 2019 will also extend the right to a written statement of terms to all workers, rather than just employees, for all new joiners on or after 6 April 2020.

FLEXIBLE WORKING
The Flexible Working Regulations 2014 gives all employees, from 30 June 2014, the right to apply for flexible working after continuously working for the same employer for at least 26 weeks. An employer must consider and decide upon a request within three months and must have a sound business reason for rejecting any request. If an application under the act is not dealt with in accordance with a prescribed procedure, or is rejected on other than specific grounds, the employee may complain to an employment tribunal. In Northern Ireland an employer must hold a meeting with an employee within 28 days of a request for flexible working, and give reasons in writing within a further 14 days.

SICK PAY
Employees absent from work through illness or injury are entitled to receive Statutory Sick Pay (SSP) from the employer from the fourth day of absence for a maximum period of 28 weeks. The right to SSP will cease where an employee has had linked periods of sickness that have spanned a period of three years.

MATERNITY AND PARENTAL RIGHTS
Under the Employment Relations Act 1999, the Employment Act 2002, the Maternity and Parental Leave Regulations 1999 (as amended in 2001, 2002, 2006, 2013 and 2014), the Paternity and Adoption Leave Regulations 2002 and 2003, the Additional Paternity Leave Regulations 2010 and the Shared Parental Leave Regulations 2014, both men and women are entitled to take leave when they become a parent (including by adoption). Women are protected from discrimination, detriment or dismissal by reason of their pregnancy or maternity, including discrimination by association and by perception. Men and adoptive parents are protected from suffering a detriment or dismissal for taking paternity, adoption or parental leave.

Any woman who needs to attend an antenatal appointment on the advice of a registered medical professional is entitled to paid leave from work to attend. All pregnant women are entitled to a maximum period of maternity leave of 52 weeks. This comprises 26 weeks' ordinary maternity leave, followed immediately by 26 weeks' additional maternity leave. A woman who takes ordinary maternity leave normally has the right to return to the job in which she was employed before her absence. If she takes additional maternity leave, she is entitled to return to the same job or, if that is not reasonably practicable, to another job that is suitable and appropriate for her to do. There is a two-week period of compulsory maternity leave, immediately following the birth of the child, wherein the employer is not permitted to allow the mother to work.

A woman will qualify for Statutory Maternity Pay (SMP), which is payable for up to 39 weeks, if she has been continuously employed for not less than 26 weeks by the end of the 15th week before the expected week of childbirth. For further information see Social Welfare, Employer Payments.

Employees are entitled to adoption leave and adoption pay (at the same rates as SMP) subject to fulfilment of similar criteria to those in relation to maternity leave and pay. Where a couple is adopting a child, either one (but not both) of the parents may take adoption leave, and the other may take paternity leave.

Certain employees are entitled to paternity leave on the birth or adoption of a child. To be eligible, the employee must be the child's father, or the partner of the mother or adopter, and meet other conditions. These conditions are, firstly, that they must have been continuously employed for not less than 26 weeks prior to the 15th week before the expected week of childbirth (or, in the case of adoptions, 26 weeks ending with the week in which notification of the adoption match is given) and, secondly, that the employee must have or expect to have responsibility for the upbringing of the child. The employee may take either one week's leave, or two consecutive weeks' leave. This leave may be taken at any time between the date of the child's birth (or placement for adoption) and 56 days later. A statutory payment is available during this period.

For births on or after 5 April 2015, eligible parents are entitled to shared parental leave (SPL) whereby they will be able to share a pot of leave of up to 50 weeks and 37 weeks of pay, after the initial two weeks of maternity leave that is compulsory for the mother (or the equivalent two-week period for the adopter in adoption cases). During that 50 week period, parents can decide to be off work at the same time and/or take it in turns to have periods of leave to look after their child. To be eligible, the employee must be the child's mother, father, adopter, or partner of the mother or adopter, and must have worked for the same employer for not less than 26 weeks prior to the end of the 15th week before the expected week of childbirth (or, in case of adoptions, 26 weeks ending with the week in which notification of the adoption match is given). The amount of leave available is calculated using the mother's entitlement to maternity leave. If a mother reduces maternity leave she and/or her partner may opt to take SPL for the remaining weeks. On taking SPL, a woman will be entitled to statutory shared parental pay, which will generally be at the same rate as SMP, except in the first six weeks of maternity leave, during which a cap applies to shared parental pay but not to SMP.

For more information see Social Welfare, Employer Payments. Any employee with one at least year's continuous service who has, or expects to have, responsibility for a child may take parental leave to care for the child. Each parent is entitled to a total of 18 weeks unpaid parental leave for each child or adopted child. This leave must be taken (at the rate of no more than four weeks a year, and in blocks of whole weeks only) before the child's 18th birthday.

The Parental Bereavement (Leave and Pay) Act 2018 is expected to come into force in April 2020 and will provide the right for all employed parents to take two weeks' leave if they lose a child under the age of 18, or suffer a stillbirth from 24 weeks of pregnancy, together with the right to statutory parental bereavement pay if certain eligibility criteria are met. It is likely that any such leave will need to be taken within 56 days of the child's death.

SUNDAY TRADING

The Sunday Trading Act 1994 allows shops to open on Sunday. The Employment Rights Act 1996 gives shop workers and betting workers the right not to be dismissed, selected for redundancy or to suffer any detriment (such as the denial of overtime, promotion or training) if they refuse to work only on Sundays. This does not apply to those who, under their contracts, are employed to work on Sundays.

TERMINATION OF EMPLOYMENT

An employee may be dismissed without notice if guilty of gross misconduct but in other cases a period of notice must be given by the employer. The minimum periods of notice specified in the Employment Rights Act 1996 are:

- one week if the employee has been continuously employed for one month or more but for less than two years
- one week for each complete year of continuous employment, if the employee has been employed for two years or more, up to a maximum of 12 weeks' notice
- longer periods apply if these are specified in the contract of employment

If an employee is dismissed with less notice than he/she is entitled to by statute, or under their contract if longer, he/she will have a wrongful dismissal claim (unless the employer paid the employee in lieu of notice in accordance with a contractual provision entitling it to do so). This claim for wrongful dismissal can be brought by the employee either in the civil courts or the employment tribunal, but if brought in the tribunal the maximum amount that can be awarded is £25,000.

REDUNDANCY

An employee dismissed because of redundancy may be entitled to redundancy pay. This applies if:

- the employment commenced before 6 April 2012 and the employee has at least one year's continuous service or the employment commenced on or after 6 April 2012 and the employee has at least two years' continuous service
- the employee is dismissed by the employer by reason of redundancy (this can include cases of voluntary redundancy)

Redundancy can mean closure of the entire business, closure of a particular site of the business, or a reduction in the need for employees to carry out work of a particular kind.

An employee may not be entitled to a redundancy payment if offered a suitable alternative job by the same (or an associated) employer. The amount of statutory redundancy pay depends on the employee's length of service, age, and their earnings, subject to a weekly maximum of (currently) £525 (£547 in Northern Ireland). The maximum payment that can be awarded is £15,750. The redundancy payment is guaranteed by the government in cases where the employer becomes insolvent.

UNFAIR DISMISSAL

Complaints of unfair dismissal are dealt with by an employment tribunal. Any employee whose employment commenced before 6 April 2012 with at least one year's continuous service or any employee whose employment commenced on or after 6 April 2012 with at least two year's continuous service (subject to exceptions, including in relation to whistleblowers – see below) can make a complaint to the tribunal. At the tribunal, it is for the employee to show that the employer dismissed them either expressly or constructively and it is for the employer to prove that the dismissal was due to one or more potentially fair reasons: a statutory restriction preventing the continuation of the employee's contract; the employee's capability or qualifications for the job he/she was employed to do; the employee's conduct; redundancy; or some other substantial reason.

If the employer succeeds in showing this, the tribunal must then decide whether the employer acted reasonably in dismissing the employee for that reason. If the employee is found to have been unfairly dismissed, the tribunal can order that he/she be reinstated, re-engaged or compensated. Any person believing that they may have been unfairly dismissed should contact their local Citizens Advice bureau or seek legal advice. A claim must be brought within three months of the date of effective termination of employment.

The normal maximum compensatory award for unfair dismissal is £86,444 as at April 2019 (£86,614 in Northern Ireland). If the dismissal occurred after 6 April 2009 and the employer unreasonably failed to follow the ACAS Code of Practice on Disciplinary and Grievance Procedures in carrying out the dismissal, the tribunal may increase the employee's compensation by up to 25 per cent.

Employees in Northern Ireland can make a complaint to the tribunal if they have at least one year's continuous service.

WHISTLEBLOWING

Under the whistleblowing legislation (Public Interest Disclosure Act 1998, which inserted provisions into the Employment Rights Act 1996) dismissal of an employee is automatically unfair if the reason or principal reason for the dismissal is that the employee has made a protected disclosure. The legislation also makes it unlawful to subject workers (a broad category that includes employees and certain other individuals, such as agency workers) who have made a protected disclosure to any detriment on the ground that they have done so.

For a disclosure to qualify for protection, the claimant must show that he or she has disclosed information, which in his or her reasonable belief tends to show one or more of the following six categories of wrongdoing: criminal offences; breach of any legal obligation; miscarriages of justice; danger to the health and safety of any individual; damage to the environment; or the deliberate concealing of information about any of the other categories. The malpractices can be past, present, prospective or merely alleged.

A qualifying disclosure will only be protected if the manner of the disclosure fulfils certain conditions, which varies according to the type of disclosure. With effect from 25 June 2013, there is no requirement for the disclosure to have been made in 'good faith', although where it appears to the tribunal that the protected disclosure was not made in good faith, the tribunal may reduce any compensatory award it makes by up to 25 per cent if it considers that it is just and equitable to do so in all the circumstances.

Any whistleblower claim in the employment tribunal must normally be brought within three months of the date of dismissal or other act leading to a detriment.

An individual does not need to have been working with the employer for any particular period of time to be able to bring such a claim and compensation is uncapped (and can include an amount for injury to feelings).

DISCRIMINATION

Discrimination in employment on the grounds of sex (including gender reassignment), sexual orientation, being pregnant or on maternity leave, race, colour, nationality, ethnic or national origins, religion or belief, marital or civil partnership status, age or disability is unlawful. Discrimination legislation generally covers direct discrimination, indirect discrimination, harassment and victimisation. Only in limited circumstances can such discrimination be justified (rendering it lawful).

An individual does not need to be employed for any particular period of time to be able to claim discrimination (discrimination can be alleged at the recruitment phase), and discrimination compensation is uncapped (and can include an amount for injury to feelings). These features distinguish the discrimination laws from, for example, the unfair dismissal laws.

The Equality Act 2010 was passed on 8 April 2010 and its main provisions came into force on 1 October 2010. It unifies several pieces of discrimination legislation, providing one definition of direct discrimination, indirect discrimination, harassment and victimisation. The Act applies to those employed in Great Britain but not to employees in Northern Ireland; it is only likely to apply to those predominantly working abroad if there is a strong connection between their work and Great Britain.

The Act provides that:

- it is unlawful to discriminate on the grounds of sex, gender reassignment, being pregnant or on maternity leave, or marital/civil partner status (all but the last of these categories include discrimination by association and by perception). This covers all aspects of employment (including advertising for jobs), but there are some limited exceptions, such as where the essential nature of the job requires it to be given to someone of a particular sex, or where decency and privacy requires it. The act entitles men and women to equality of remuneration for equivalent work or work of the same value
- individuals have the right not to be discriminated against on the grounds of race, colour, nationality, or ethnic or national origins and this applies to all aspects of employment. Employers may also take lawful positive action, including in relation to recruitment and promotion
- discrimination against a disabled person in all aspects of employment is unlawful. This includes protecting carers from discrimination by association with the disabled persons that they look after. The act also imposes a duty on employers to make 'reasonable adjustments' to the arrangements and physical features of the workplace if these place disabled people at a substantial disadvantage compared with those who are not disabled. The definition of a 'disabled person' is wide and includes people diagnosed with HIV, cancer and multiple sclerosis
- discrimination against a person on the grounds of religion or belief (or lack of belief) including discrimination by association and by perception, in all aspects of employment, is unlawful
- discrimination against an individual on the grounds of sexual orientation, including discrimination by association and by perception, in all aspects of employment, is unlawful
- age discrimination in the workplace is unlawful. However, it is lawful to discriminate because of age in relation to benefits based on length of service, redundancy pay (provided that any enhanced redundancy payment scheme operated by the employer is sufficiently similar to the statutory redundancy payment scheme), national minimum wage and insurance benefits.

The responsibility for monitoring equality in society rests with the Equality and Human Rights Commission.

In Northern Ireland similar provisions exist to those that were in force in Great Britain prior to the coming into force of the Equality Act but are contained in separate legislation (although the Disability Discrimination Act 1995 does extend to Northern Ireland).

In Northern Ireland there is one combined body working towards equality and eliminating discrimination, the Equality Commission for Northern Ireland.

WORKING TIME

The Working Time Regulations 1998 impose rules that limit working hours and provide for rest breaks and holidays. The regulations apply to workers and so cover not only employees but also other individuals who undertake to perform personally any work or services (eg freelancers). The regulations are complex and subject to various exceptions and qualifications but the basic provisions relating to adult day workers are as follows:

- No worker is permitted to work more than an average of 48 hours per week (unless they have made a genuine voluntary opt-out of this limit – it is not generally thought to be sufficient to make it a term of the contract that the worker opts out), and a worker is entitled to, but is not required to take, the following breaks:
- 11 consecutive hours' uninterrupted rest in every 24-hour period
- an uninterrupted rest period of 24 hours in each 7-day period or 48 hours in each fortnight (in addition to the daily rest period)
- 20 minutes' rest break provided that the working day is longer than 6 hours
- 5.6 weeks' paid annual leave (28 days full-time). This equates to 4 weeks plus public holidays

There are specific provisions relating to night work, young workers (ie those over school leaving age but under 18) and a variety of workers in specialised sectors (such as off-shore oil rig workers).

HUMAN RIGHTS

On 2 October 2000 the Human Rights Act 1998 came into force in the UK. This act incorporates the European Convention on Human Rights into the law of the UK. The main principles of the act are as follows:

- all legislation must be interpreted and given effect by the courts as compatible with the Convention so far as it is possible to do so. Before the second reading of a new bill the minister responsible for the bill must provide a statement regarding its compatibility with the Human Rights Act
- subordinate legislation (eg statutory instruments) which is incompatible with the Convention can be struck down by the courts
- primary legislation (eg an act of parliament) which is incompatible with the Convention cannot be struck down by a court, but the higher courts can make a declaration of incompatibility which is a signal to parliament to change the law
- all public authorities (including courts and tribunals) must not act in a way which is incompatible with the Convention
- individuals whose Convention rights have been infringed by a public authority may bring proceedings against that authority, but the act is not intended to create new rights as between individuals

The main human rights protected by the Convention are the right to life (article 2); protection from torture and inhuman or degrading treatment (article 3); protection from slavery or forced labour (article 4); the right to liberty and security of the person (article 5); the right to a fair trial (article 6); the right not to be subject to retrospective criminal offences (article 7); the right to respect for private and family life (article 8); freedom of thought, conscience and religion (article 9); freedom of expression (article 10); freedom of association and peaceful assembly (article 11); the right to marry and found a family (article 12); protection from discrimination (article 14); the right to protection of property (article 1 of protocol No.1); the right to education (article 2 of protocol No.1); and the right to free elections (article 3 protocol No.1). Most of the Convention rights are subject to limitations which deem the breach of the right acceptable on the basis it is 'necessary in a democratic society'.

Human rights are also enshrined in the common law (of tort). Although this is of historical significance, the common law (for example the duty of confidentiality) remains especially important regarding violations of human rights that occur between private parties, where the Human Rights Act 1998 does not apply.

PARENTAL RESPONSIBILITY

The Children Act 1989 (as amended by the Children and Families Act 2014) gives both the mother and father parental responsibility for the child if the parents are married to each other at the time of the child's birth. If the parents are not married, only the mother has parental responsibility. The father may acquire it in accordance with the provisions of section 4 of the Children Act 1989. He can do this in one of several ways, including: by being registered as the father on the child's birth certificate with the consent of the mother (only for fathers of children born after 1 December 2003, following changes to the Adoption and Children Act 2002); by applying to the court for a parental responsibility order; by entering into a parental responsibility agreement with the mother which must be in the prescribed form; or by marrying the mother of the child.

Following changes to the Children Act 1989 (introduced by the Children and Families Act 2014), if a court makes a child arrangements order in favour of a father, providing that the child lives with that father, the court must make a parental responsibility order in his favour. If the child arrangements order provides that the child spend time or otherwise have contact with the father, the court must consider whether to make a parental responsibility order (residence orders were replaced by child arrangement orders under the Children and Families Act 2014, but if obtained prior to 22 April 2014 are still valid).

Where a child's parent, who has parental responsibility, marries or enters into a civil partnership with a person who is not the child's parent, the child's parent(s) with parental responsibility can agree for the step-parent to have parental responsibility by entering into a parental responsibility agreement, or the step-parent may acquire parental responsibility by order of the court (section 4A(1) Children Act 1989).

If a child is conceived after 6 April 2009 by female civil partners or female same-sex spouses, under the Human Fertilisation and Embryology Act (HFEA) 2008, both individuals will have parental responsibility for that child. A female, who is not in a civil partnership or same-sex marriage with the mother at the date of the child's birth, but is the child's other parent (by virtue of HFEA 2008), can acquire parental responsibility in the same way as set out above in relation to a father. Parental responsibility will also be acquired if the mother and the child's other parent enter into a civil partnership or (from 13 March 2014) a same-sex marriage after the child's date of birth.

Where the court makes a child arrangements order and a person (who is not the parent or guardian of the child) is named in the order as a person with whom the child is to live, that person will have parental responsibility while the order remains in force. Where the person (who is not the parent or guardian of the child) is named in the order as a person with whom the child is to spend time or otherwise have contact (but not with whom the child is to live), the court may provide in the order for that person to have parental responsibility for the child, while the provisions in the order continue.

An adoption order gives parental responsibility for the child to the adopters. It extinguishes parental responsibility that any person had for the child immediately before the making of the order.

In Scotland, the relevant legislation is the Children (Scotland) Act 1995, which gives the mother parental rights and responsibilities for her child whether or not she is married to the child's father. A father who is married to the mother, either at the time of the child's conception or subsequently, will also have automatic parental rights and responsibilities. Section 3 of the 2006 act provides that an unmarried father will obtain automatic parental responsibilities and rights if he is registered as the father on the child's birth certificate. For unmarried fathers who are not named on the birth certificate, or whose children were born before the 2006 act came into force, it is possible to acquire parental responsibilities and rights by applying to the court or by entering into a parental responsibilities and rights agreement with the mother. The father of any child, regardless of parental rights, has a duty to aliment that child until he/she is 18 (or under 25 if the child is still at an educational establishment or training for employment or for a trade, profession or vocation).

LEGITIMATION
Under the Legitimacy Act 1976, an illegitimate person automatically becomes legitimate when his/her parents marry. This applies even where one of the parents was married to a third person at the time of the birth. In such cases it is necessary to re-register the birth of the child. In Scotland, the status of illegitimacy has been abolished by section 21 of the 2006 act. The Family Law Reform Act 1987 reformed the law so as to remove so far as possible the legal disadvantages of illegitimacy.

JURY SERVICE

In England and Wales, the law concerning juries is largely consolidated in the Juries Act 1974 (as amended by the Criminal Justice and Courts Act 2015). In England and Wales, a person charged with a serious criminal offence is entitled to have their trial heard by a jury in a crown court, except in cases where there is a danger of jury tampering or where jury tampering has taken place.

In civil cases, there is a right to a jury in the Queen's Bench Division of the high court in cases where the person applying for a jury has been accused of fraud, as well as in cases of malicious prosecution or false imprisonment. The same applies to the county court. In all other cases in the Queen's Bench Division only the judge has discretion to order trial with a jury, though such an order is seldom made. In the chancery division of the high court a jury is never used. The same is true in the family division of the high court.

No right to a jury trial exists in Scotland, although more serious offences are heard before a jury. In England and Wales criminal cases and civil cases in the high court are generally heard by a jury of 12 members, but in the county court the jury is smaller, normally consisting of eight members. In the event that a juror is excused the trial can proceed so long as there are at least seven remaining jurors in the county court and nine in the case of the high court or crown court. At an inquest, there must be at least seven and no more than 11 members. In Scotland there are 12 members of a jury in a civil case in the court of session and certain sheriff court cases, and 15 in a criminal trial in the high court of justiciary. Jurors are normally asked to serve for ten working days, during which time they could sit on more than one case. Jurors selected for longer cases are expected to sit for the duration of the trial.

In England and Wales, every 'registered' parliamentary or local government elector between the ages of 18 and 75 who has lived in the UK (including, for this purpose, the Channel Islands and the Isle of Man) for any period of at least five years since reaching the age of 13 is qualified to serve on a jury unless he/she is disqualified.

Those disqualified from jury service include:

- those who have at any time been sentenced by a court in the UK (including, for this purpose, the Channel Islands and the Isle of Man) to a term of imprisonment or youth custody of five years or more
- those who have within the previous ten years served any part of a sentence of imprisonment, youth custody or detention, been detained in a young offenders' institution, received a suspended sentence of imprisonment or order for detention, or received a community order
- those who are on bail in criminal proceedings
- those who have been convicted of a jury misconduct offence
- those who are liable to be detained, who are under guardianship or who are under a community treatment order under the Mental Health Act 1983 or who are in resident in a hospital on account of mental disorder
- Those who lack capacity, as defined under the Mental Capacity Act 2005, to serve as a juror

The court has the discretion to excuse a juror from service, or defer the date of service, if the juror can show there is good reason why he/she should be excused from attending or good reason why his/her attendance should be deferred. It is an offence (punishable by a fine) to fail to attend when summoned, to serve knowing that you are disqualified from service, or to make false representations in an attempt to evade service. If a juror fails to turn up for service, or attends but cannot serve due to being under the influence of drink or drugs, this is punishable as contempt of court. Any party can object to any juror if he/she can show cause to the trial judge.

It may be appropriate for a judge to excuse a juror from a particular case if he is personally concerned in the facts of the particular case, or closely connected with a party to the proceedings or with a prospective witness. The judge may also discharge any juror who, from a mental or physical incapacity, temporary or permanent, or alternatively due to linguistic difficulties, cannot pay proper attention to the evidence.

An individual juror (or the entire jury) can be discharged if it is shown that they or any of their number have, among other things, separated from the rest of the jury without the leave of the court; talked to any person out of court who is not a member of the jury; determined the verdict of the trial by drawing lots; come to a compromise on the verdict; been drunk, or otherwise incapacitated, while carrying out their duties as a juror; exerted improper pressure on the other members of the jury (eg harassment or bullying); declined to take part in the jury's functions; displayed actual or apparent bias (eg racism, sexism or other discriminatory or deliberate hostility); or inadvertently possessed knowledge of the bad character of a party to the proceedings which has not been adduced as evidence in the proceedings. The factual situations that arise are many, and include falling asleep during the trial, asking friends on Facebook for help in making a decision, consulting an ouija board in the course of deliberations, making telephone calls after retirement, and lunching with a barrister not connected with the proceedings.

The Criminal Justice and Courts Act 2015 has introduced four new offences of juror misconduct with a penalty of up to two years in prison. A juror commits an offence if he: (a) intentionally seeks information during a trial where he knows, or ought to reasonably know, that the information sought is or may be relevant to the case; (b) passes on to another juror information obtained through such research; (c) engages in conduct from which it may reasonably be concluded that he intends to try the issue otherwise than on the basis of the evidence presented in the proceedings on the issue; and (d) discloses information about the jury's deliberations, subject to specified exceptions. A person who has been convicted of one of the above offences within the last ten years will be disqualified from jury duty. A judge now has a discretionary power to order members of a jury to surrender their electronic communication devices for a period of time, and a court security officer is authorised to search a juror for a device that a judge has ordered be surrendered.

In England and Wales, the jury's verdict need not be unanimous. In criminal proceedings, and civil proceedings in the high court, the agreement of ten jurors will suffice when there are not fewer than 11 people on the jury (or nine in a jury of ten). In civil proceedings in the county court the agreement of seven or eight jurors will suffice. Where a majority verdict is given, the court must be satisfied that the jury had reasonable time to consider its verdict based on the nature and complexity of the case. In criminal proceedings this must be no less than two hours and ten minutes (allowing time for the jury to settle after retiring).

A juror is immune from prosecution or civil claim in respect of anything said or done by him or her in the discharge of their office. It is an offence for a juror to disclose what happened in the jury room even after the trial is over. A juror may claim travelling expenses, a subsistence allowance and an allowance for other financial loss (eg loss of earnings or benefits, fees paid to carers or child-minders) up to a stated limit. For more information on jury service, visit **W** www.gov.uk/jury-service/overview

SCOTLAND

Qualification criteria for jury service in Scotland are similar to those in England and Wales, except that members of the judiciary are ineligible for ten years after ceasing to hold their post, and others concerned with the administration of justice are only eligible for service five years after ceasing to hold office. Certain persons have the right to apply to be excused – full-time members of the medical, dental, nursing, veterinary and pharmaceutical professions, full-time members of the armed forces, ministers of religion, persons who have served on a jury within the previous five years, persons who have attended court to serve on a jury but were not selected by ballot within the previous two years, members of the Scottish parliament, members of the Scottish government, junior Scottish ministers and those aged 71 years or over. Those who are incapable by reason of a mental disorder may also be excused. Such an application will be accepted if the application is made within 7 days of the person being notified that they may have to serve. For civil trials there is an age limit of 65 years. Those convicted of a crime and sentenced to a period of imprisonment of 5 years or more are automatically disqualified. The maximum fine for a person serving on a jury while knowing himself/herself to be ineligible is £1,000. The maximum fine for failing to attend without good cause in criminal trials is also £1,000, however in civil proceedings the maximum fine is £200.

HER MAJESTY'S COURTS AND TRIBUNALS SERVICE,
102 Petty France, London SW1H 9AJ **T** 0845-456 8770

JURY CENTRAL SUMMONING BUREAU, Freepost LON
19669, Pocock Street, London SE1 0YG **T** 0300-456 1024
E jurysummoning@justice.gov.uk

SCOTTISH COURTS AND TRIBUNALS SERVICE,
Saughton House, Broomhouse Drive, Edinburgh EH11 3XD
T 0131-444 3300
W www.scotcourts.gov.uk

LANDLORD AND TENANT

RESIDENTIAL LETTINGS

The provisions outlined here apply only where the tenant lives in a separate dwelling from the landlord and where the dwelling is the tenant's only or main home. It does not apply to licensees such as lodgers, guests or service occupiers.

The 1996 Housing Act radically changed certain aspects of the legislation referred to below; in particular, the grant of assured and assured shorthold tenancies under the Housing Act 1988.

ASSURED SHORTHOLD TENANCIES

If a tenancy was granted on or after 15 January 1989 and before 28 February 1997, the tenant would have an assured tenancy unless the landlord served notice under section 20 in the prescribed form prior to the commencement of the tenancy, stating that the tenancy is to be an assured shorthold tenancy and the tenancy is for a minimum fixed term period of six months (see below). An assured tenancy gives that tenant greater security. The tenant could, for example, stay in possession of the dwelling for as long as the tenant observed the terms of the tenancy. The landlord cannot obtain possession from such a tenant unless the landlord can establish a specific ground for possession (set out in the Housing Act 1988) and obtains a court order. The rent payable is that agreed with the landlord at the start of the tenancy. The landlord has the right to increase the rent annually by serving a notice. If that happens the tenant can apply to the Residential Property Tribunal in England (or a rent assessment committee in Wales) to assess the open market rent for the property. The tenant or the landlord may request that the committee sets the rent in line with open market rents for that type of property.

Under the Housing Act 1996, all new lettings (below an annual rent threshold of £100,000 since October 2010 in England or December 2011 in Wales) entered into on or after 28 February 1997 (for whatever term) will be assured shorthold tenancies unless the landlord serves a notice stating that the tenancy is not to be an assured shorthold tenancy. This means that the landlord is entitled to possession at the end of the tenancy provided he serves a notice under section 21 Housing Act 1988 and commences the proceedings in accordance with the correct procedure. The landlord must obtain a court order, however, to obtain possession if the tenant refuses to vacate at the end of the tenancy. If the tenancy is an assured shorthold tenancy, the court must grant the order.

REGULATED TENANCIES

Before the Housing Act 1988 came into force on 15 January 1989 there were regulated tenancies; some are still in existence and are protected by the Rent Act 1977. Under this act it is possible for the landlord or the tenant to apply to the local rent officer to have a 'fair' rent registered. The fair rent is then the maximum rent payable.

SECURE TENANCIES

Secure tenancies are generally given to tenants of local authorities, housing associations (before 15 January 1989) and certain other bodies. This gives the tenant security of tenure unless the terms of the agreement are broken by the tenant and it is reasonable to make an order for possession. Those with secure tenancies may have the right to buy their property. In practice this right is generally only available to council tenants. However, the Housing and Planning Act 2016 enables housing associations voluntarily to extend the right to buy. A roll out of the extended right to buy regime has now taken place as the Department for Communities and Local Government published its guidance in April 2018.

The Prevention of Social Housing Fraud Act came into force in October 2013. It creates criminal offences for unlawful sub-letting by secure and assured tenants of social housing.

AGRICULTURAL PROPERTY

Tenancies in agricultural properties are governed by the Agricultural Holdings Act 1986, the Agricultural Tenancies

Act 1995 (both amended by the Regulatory Reform (Agricultural Tenancies) (England and Wales) Order 2006), the Tribunals, Courts and Enforcement Act 2007, the Legal Services Act 2007 and the Rent (Agriculture) Act 1976, which give similar protections to those described above, eg security of tenure, right to compensation for disturbance, etc. Similar provisions are applied to Scotland by the Agricultural Holdings (Scotland) Act 2003 for those leases entered into on or after 27 November 2003. The Agricultural Holdings (Scotland) Act 1991 continues to apply to those leases in Scotland entered into prior to this date and in certain other circumstances outlined by the 2003 act. However, one distinction to note between the 1991 act and the 2003 act is that those leases governed by the former have full security of tenure, subject to certain exceptions, whereas leases under the 2003 act are fixed term arrangements of various durations.

EVICTION

The Protection from Eviction Act 1977 (as amended by the Housing Act 1988 and Nationality, Immigration and Asylum Act 2002) sets out the procedure a landlord must follow in order to obtain possession of property. It is unlawful for a landlord to evict a tenant otherwise than in accordance with the law. For common law tenancies and for Rent Act tenants a notice to quit in the prescribed form giving 28 days notice is required. For secure and assured tenancies a notice seeking possession must be served. It is unlawful for the landlord to evict a person by putting their belongings on to the street, by changing the locks and so on. It is also unlawful for a landlord to harass a tenant in any way in order to persuade him/her to give up the tenancy. The tenant may be able to obtain an injunction to restrain the actions of the landlord and get back into the property and be awarded damages.

LANDLORD RESPONSIBILITIES

Under the Landlord and Tenant Act 1985, where the term of the lease is less than seven years, the landlord is responsible for maintaining the structure and exterior of the property, for sanitation, for heating and hot water, and all installations for the supply of water, gas and electricity.

While the responsibility of maintaining the premises remains intact, since July 2012 landlords are no longer permitted to enter the rental premises for the purpose of viewing their state and condition. This power of entry was revoked by the Protection of Freedoms Act 2012.

LEASEHOLDERS

Strictly speaking, leaseholders have bought a long lease rather than a property and in certain limited circumstances the landlord can end the tenancy. Under the Leasehold Reform Act 1967 (as amended by the Housing Acts 1969, 1974, 1980 and 1985), leaseholders of houses, as opposed to flats, may have the right to buy the freehold or to take an extended lease for a term of 50 years. This applies to leases where the term of the lease is more than 21 years and where the leaseholder has occupied the house as his/her only or main residence for the last two years, or for a total of two years over the last ten. It was the case that a low rent and rateable value test applied to the right to buy the freehold, this is generally no longer the case, although they do remain applicable to the right to a lease extension. The tenant must give the landlord written notice of his desire to acquire the freehold or extend the leasehold.

The Leasehold Reform, Housing and Urban Development Act came into force in 1993 and allows the leaseholders of flats in certain circumstances to buy the freehold of the building in which they live. Owners of certain long leases of flats may also have the right to take an extended act of 90 years plus the unexpired residue of their current lease: although technically a grant of a new lease, these are commonly called 'lease extensions'.

Responsibility for maintenance of the structure, exterior and interior of the building should be set out in the lease. Usually the upkeep of the interior of his/her part of the property is the responsibility of the leaseholder, and responsibility for the structure, exterior and common interior areas is shared between the freeholder and the leaseholder(s).

If leaseholders are dissatisfied with charges made in respect of lease extensions, they are entitled to have their situation evaluated by the First-tier Tribunal (Property Chamber).

The Commonhold and Leasehold Reform Act 2002 makes provision for the freehold estate in land to be registered as commonhold land and for the legal interest in the land to be vested in a 'commonhold association', ie a private limited company.

BUSINESS LETTINGS

The Landlord and Tenant Acts 1927 and 1954 (as amended) give security of tenure to the tenants of most business premises. The landlord can only evict the tenant on one of the grounds laid down in the 1954 act, and in some cases where the landlord repossesses the property the tenant may be entitled to compensation. However, it is commonplace for landlords and tenants to agree that these provisions will not apply to their lease, meaning that no security of tenure is granted.

SCOTLAND

In Scotland assured and short assured tenancies exist for residential lettings entered into after 2 January 1989 and before December 2017 are similar to assured shorthold tenancies in England and Wales. The relevant legislation for these is the Housing (Scotland) Act 1988. However, under the provisions of the Private Housing (Tenancies) (Scotland) Act 2016 all new tenancies for private residential lettings from 1 December 2017 take the form of a private rental tenancy. They provide more security for tenants as the 'no fault ground of repossession' (the equivalent of recovering possession under section 21 of the Housing Act 1988 in England) has been abolished. The act also introduced a model tenancy agreement, rent controls and move the adjudication of disputes from the sheriff court to the Housing and Property Chamber of the First-tier Tribunal.

Most tenancies created before 2 January 1989 were regulated tenancies and the Rent (Scotland) Act 1984 still applies where these exist. The act defines, among other things, the circumstances in which a landlord can increase the rent when improvements are made to the property. It does not apply to tenancies where the landlord is the Crown, a local authority or a housing corporation.

The Antisocial Behaviour etc (Scotland) Act 2004 provides that all private landlords letting property in Scotland must register with the local authority in which the let property is situated, unless the landlord is a local authority, or a registered social landlord. Exceptions also apply to holiday lets, owner-occupied accommodation and agricultural holdings. The act applies to partnerships, trusts and companies as well as to individuals.

Tenancy Deposit Schemes (Scotland) Regulations 2011 require that a landlord must pay deposits taken from tenants into an approved scheme and ensure that the money is held by an approved scheme for the duration of the tenancy. Evidence of registration with the relevant local authority in terms of the 2004 Act must be provided when the deposit is paid over.

Landlords who provide a private residential tenancy must provide new tenants with a Tenant Information Pack. The Tenant Information Pack includes information on the Repairing Standard, and its provision satisfies the separate obligation of a landlord to provide a tenant with written information about the landlord's duty to repair and maintain in terms of the Housing (Scotland) Act 2006.

The Housing (Scotland) Acts of 1987 and 2001 relate to local authority and registered social landlord responsibilities for housing, the right to buy, and local authority secured tenancies. The Housing (Scotland) Act 2010 reformed right-to-buy provisions, modernised social housing regulation, introduced the Scottish social housing charter and replaced the regulatory framework established by the 2001 act. Right-to-buy provisions were then abolished by the Housing (Scotland) Act 2014.

In Scotland, business premises are not controlled by statute to the same extent as in England and Wales, although the Tenancy of Shops (Scotland) Act 1949 gives some security to tenants of shops. Tenants of shops can apply to the sheriff, within 21 days of being served a notice to quit, for a renewal of tenancy if threatened with eviction. This application may be dismissed on various grounds, including where the landlord has offered to sell the property to the tenant at an agreed price or, in the absence of agreement as to price, at a price fixed by a single arbiter appointed by the parties or the sheriff. The act extends to properties where the Crown or government departments are the landlords or the tenants.

Under the Leases Act 1449 the landlord's successors (either purchasers or creditors) are bound by the agreement made with any tenants so long as the following conditions are met:
• the lease, if for more than one year, must be in writing
• there must be a rent
• there must be a term of expiry
• the tenant must have entered into possession
• the subjects of the lease must be land
• the landlord, if owner, must be the proprietor with a recorded title, ie the title deeds recorded in the Register of Sasines or registered in the Land Register

On 28 November 2013 certain leases which were granted for more than 175 years and under which the rent does not exceed £100 a year, converted to heritable titles. Therefore the tenants under these leases will become the owners of the property. Conversion of the lease will be automatic, provided certain conditions are met, unless the tenant opts out. It is possible for the landlord to claim compensation for their loss of income.

LEGAL AID

The Access to Justice Act 1999 transformed what used to be known as the Legal Aid system. The Legal Aid Board was replaced by the Legal Services Commission, which was responsible for the development and administration of two legal funding schemes in England and Wales, namely the Criminal Defence Service and the Community Legal Service. The Criminal Defence Service assisted people who were under police investigation or facing criminal charges. The Community Legal Service was designed to increase access to legal information and advice by involving a much wider network of funders and providers in giving publicly funded legal services. In Scotland, provision of legal aid is governed by the Legal Aid (Scotland) Act 1986, the Legal Profession and Legal Aid (Scotland) Act 2007 and the Scottish Civil Justice Council and Criminal Legal Assistance Act 2013, and administered by the Scottish Legal Aid Board.

Under the Legal Aid, Sentencing and Punishment of Offenders Act 2012 (LASPO), which came into force on 1 April 2013, the Legal Services Commission was abolished and replaced by the newly created Legal Aid Agency. The act has also limited the areas of law that fall within the scope of legal aid funding, especially those related to civil legal services. However, the act does include provisions for funding in exceptional cases, such as where failure to provide legal aid would result in a violation of an individual's human rights or where providing legal aid would serve a wider public interest. Further, the act allows for areas of law to be added or omitted from the scope of legal aid independently, without subsequent legislation.

LASPO took whole areas of law out of scope for legal aid; some areas only qualify if they meet certain criteria. Broadly, the following categories of cases are now out of such scope: (a) family cases where there is no proof of domestic violence, forced marriage or child abduction; (b) immigration cases that do not involve asylum or detention; (c) housing and debt matters unless they constitute an immediate risk to the home; (d) welfare benefit cases except appeals to the upper tribunal or high court; (e) almost all clinical negligence cases; and (f) employment cases that do not involve human trafficking or a contravention of the Equality Act 2010. Funding for cases that fall outside of the scope of legal aid may be available under the Exceptional Case Funding scheme.

The Ministry of Justice published a review of LASPO in February 2019 and a Legal Support Action Plan which outlines changes the government intends to make and the future direction for legal aid support.

LEGAL AID AGENCY, **W** www.gov.uk/government/organisations/legal-aid-agency

CIVIL LEGAL AID

From 1 January 2000, only organisations (such as solicitors or Citizens Advice) with a contract with the Legal Services Commission (now Legal Aid Agency) have been able to give initial help in any civil matter. Moreover, from that date decisions about funding were devolved from the Legal Services Commission to contracted organisations in relation to any level of publicly funded service in family and immigration cases. For other types of case, applications for public funding are made through a solicitor (or other contracted legal services providers) in much the same way as the former Legal Aid.

Under the civil funding scheme there are broadly six levels of service available:
• legal help
• help at court
• family help – either family help (lower) or family help (higher)
• legal representation – either investigative help or full representation
• family mediation
• such other services as authorised by specific orders

ELIGIBILITY

Eligibility for funding from the Legal Aid Agency depends broadly on five factors:
• the level of service sought (*see* above)
• whether the applicant qualifies financially
• the merits of the applicant's case
• a costs-benefits analysis (if the costs are likely to outweigh any benefit that might be gained from the proceedings, funding may be refused)
• whether there is any public interest in the case being litigated (ie whether the case has a wider public interest beyond that of the parties involved, eg a human rights case)

The limits on capital and income above which a person is not entitled to public funding vary with the type of service sought. As of Spring 2017, there is a consultation on government proposals seeking to amend the legal financial eligibility system to accommodate the expansion of Universal Credit. Nothing in the consultation will affect the scope of or eligibility threshold for legal aid, but instead when claimants are passported and so would not have to undergo a full assessment of their means. The consultation closed on 11 May 2017 and the outcome is pending.

The 2012 act also amended the merits criteria so that legal aid may be refused where the case is suitable for alternative funding, such as Conditional Fee Agreements. Children, and individuals on certain welfare benefits, may be relieved from means testing and from the liability to make contributions. Financial eligibility requirements may be waived for individuals applying for an order for protection from domestic violence or forced marriage (though a contribution may be required). The government intend to extend the relief of means testing to parents opposing applications for placement orders or adoption orders by summer 2019.

CONTRIBUTIONS

Some of those who qualify for Legal Aid Agency funding will have to contribute towards their legal costs. Contributions must be paid by anyone who has a disposable income or disposable capital exceeding a prescribed amount. The rules relating to applicable contributions are complex and detailed information can be obtained from the Legal Aid Agency. Individuals on certain welfare benefits may not have to contribute.

STATUTORY CHARGE

A statutory charge is made if a person keeps or gains money or property in a case for which they have received legal aid. This means that the amount paid by the Legal Aid Agency fund on their behalf is deducted from the amount that the person receives. This does not apply if the court has ordered that the costs be paid by the other party (unless the amount paid by the other party does not cover all of the costs). In certain circumstances, the Legal Aid Agency may waive or postpone payment.

CONTINGENCY OR CONDITIONAL FEES

This system was introduced by the Courts and Legal Services Act 1990. It can offer legal representation on a 'no win, no fee' basis. It provides an alternative form of assistance, especially for those cases which are ineligible for funding by the Legal Aid Agency. The main area for such work is in the field of personal injuries.

Not all solicitors offer such a scheme and different solicitors may well have different terms. The effect of the agreement is that solicitors may not make any charges, or may waive some of their charges, until the case is concluded successfully. If a case is won then the losing party will usually have to pay towards costs, with the winning party contributing around one third.

SCOTLAND

Civil legal aid is available for cases in the following:
- the sheriff courts
- the Court of Session
- the Supreme Court
- the Lands Valuation Appeal Court
- the Scottish Land Court
- the Sheriff Appeal Court
- the Lands Tribunal for Scotland
- the Employment Appeal Tribunal
- the Proscribed Organisations Appeal Commission
- the Upper Tribunal for Scotland
- certain appeals before the Social Security Commissioners

Civil legal aid is not available for election petitions, some simple procedure actions, simplified divorce procedures or petitions by a debtor for his own sequestration. In defamation actions additional criteria must be met in order for legal aid to be available.

Eligibility for civil legal aid is assessed in a similar way to that in England and Wales, though the financial limits differ in some respects. A person shall be eligible for civil legal aid if their disposable income does not exceed £26,239 a year. A person may be refused civil aid if their disposable capital exceeds £13,017 and it appears to the Legal Aid board that they can afford to pay without legal aid. Additionally:
- if disposable capital is between £7,853 and £13,017, the applicant will be required to pay a contribution which will be equal to the difference between £7,853 and their disposable capital
- if disposable income is between £3,522 and £11,540, a contribution of one third of the difference between £3,522 and the disposable income may be payable
- if disposable income is between £11,541 and £15,743, one third of the difference between £3,522 and £11,540 plus half the difference between £11,541 and the disposable income may be payable
- if disposable income is between £15,744 and £26,239, a contribution of the following: one third of the difference between £3,522 and £11,540, plus half the difference between £11,541 and £15,743, plus all the remaining disposable income between £15,744 and £26,239 – will be payable

CRIMINAL LEGAL AID

The Legal Aid Agency provides defendants facing criminal charges with free legal representation if they pass a merits test and a means test although children and individuals on certain welfare benefits may be relieved from means testing.

Criminal legal aid covers the cost of preparing a case and legal representation in criminal proceedings. It is also available for appeals against verdicts or sentences in magistrates' courts, the crown court or the court of appeal. It is not available for bringing a private prosecution in a criminal court.

If granted criminal legal aid, either the person may choose their own solicitor or the court will assign one. Contributions to the legal costs may be required. The rules relating to applicable contributions are complex and detailed information can be obtained from the Legal Aid Agency.

DUTY SOLICITORS

LASPO also provides for free initial advice and initial assistance to anyone questioned by the police (whether under arrest or helping the police with their enquiries). No means test or contributions are required for this.

SCOTLAND

Legal advice and assistance operates in a similar way in Scotland. A person is eligible:
- if disposable income does not exceed £245 a week. If disposable income is between £105 and £245 a week, contributions are payable
- if disposable capital does not exceed £1,716 (if the person has dependent relatives, the savings allowance is higher)
- if receiving income support or income-related job seeker's allowance they qualify automatically provided their disposable capital is not over the limit

The procedure for application for criminal legal aid depends on the circumstances of each case. In solemn cases (more serious cases, such as murder) heard before a jury, a person is automatically entitled to criminal legal aid until they are given bail or placed in custody. Thereafter, it is for the court to decide whether to grant legal aid. The court will do this if the person accused cannot meet the expenses of the case without undue hardship on him or his dependants. In less serious cases the procedure depends on whether the person is in custody:
- anyone taken into custody has the right to free legal aid from the duty solicitor up to and including the first court appearance

- if the person is not in custody and wishes to plead guilty, they are not entitled to criminal legal aid but may be entitled to legal advice and assistance, including assistance by way of representation

However, regardless of whether the person is in custody if they wish to plead not guilty, they can apply for criminal legal aid. This must be done within 14 days of the first court appearance at which they made the plea.

The criteria used to assess whether or not criminal legal aid should be granted is similar to the criteria for England and Wales. When meeting with your solicitor, take evidence of your financial position such as details of savings, bank statements, pay slips, pension book or benefits book.

Under the relevant provisions of the Scottish Civil Justice Council and Criminal Legal Assistance Act 2013, a person in receipt of criminal legal aid or criminal assistance by way of representation will be required, in most circumstances, to make contributions where their weekly disposable income is £82 or above or if their disposable capital is £750 or more. The Scottish government has delayed the implementation of these provisions and no timetable has yet been proposed.

THE SCOTTISH LEGAL AID BOARD, Thistle House, 91 Haymarket Terrace, Edinburgh EH12 5HE T 0131-226 7061 W www.slab.org.uk

MARRIAGE

Any two persons may marry provided that:
- they are at least 16 years old on the day of the marriage (in England and Wales persons under the age of 18 must generally obtain the consent of their parents or guardian; if consent is refused an appeal may be made to the high court or the family court)
- they are not related to one another in a way which would prevent their marrying
- they are unmarried (a person who has already been married must produce documentary evidence that the previous marriage has been ended by death, divorce or annulment)
- they are capable of understanding the nature, duties and responsibilities of a marriage
- they consent to the marriage

It is now lawful for same sex couples to marry by way of civil or religious ceremony following the passing of the Marriage (Same Sex Couples) Act 2013, which came into force in March 2014. In addition, an existing marriage will now be able to continue where one or both parties change their legal gender and both parties wish to remain married. Civil partnerships are also still available for same sex couples, although The Marriage (Same Sex Couples) Act 2013 provides that couples in civil partnerships may convert their relationship to a marriage if they wish.

The parties should check the marriage will be recognised as valid in their home country if either is not a British citizen.

DEGREES OF RELATIONSHIP

A marriage between persons within the prohibited degrees of consanguinity, affinity or adoption is void.

Neither party may marry his or her parent, child, grandparent, grandchild, sibling, parent's sibling, sibling's child, adoptive parent, former adoptive parent, adoptive child or former adoptive child. All references to siblings include half-brothers/sisters.

Under the Marriage (Prohibited Degrees of Relationship) Act 1986, some exceptions to the law permit a person to marry certain step-relatives or in-laws.

In addition to the above, a person may not marry a child of their former civil partner, a child of a former spouse, the former civil partner of a grandparent, the former civil partner of a parent, the former spouse of a grandparent, the former spouse of a parent, the grandchild of a former civil partner or the grandchild of a former spouse, unless that relationship is the only reason they cannot marry and both persons are over 21 and the younger party has not at any time before attaining the age of 18 been a child of the family in relation to the other party.

ENGLAND AND WALES

TYPES OF MARRIAGE CEREMONY

It is possible to marry by either religious or civil ceremony. A religious ceremony can take place at a church or chapel of the Church of England or the Church in Wales, or at any other place of worship which has been formally registered by the Registrar-General. Same-sex marriages can also take place in a religious building, provided that the premises have been registered for the marriage of same-sex couples. Applications to register are made to the superintendent register of the registration district where the building is located and then forwarded to the General Register Office to be recorded. It is not possible, however, for same-sex marriages to take place in an Anglican church (although the Church of England is currently considering proposals to give same-sex marriage blessings).

A civil ceremony can take place at a register office, a venue approved by the local authority or any religious premises where permission has been given by the relevant religious organisation and is approved by the local authority.

An application for an approved premises licence must be made by the owners or trustees of the building concerned; it cannot be made by the prospective marriage couple. Approved premises must be regularly open to the public for marriages and civil partnerships; be a seemly and dignified venue; and the venue must be deemed to be a permanent and immovable structure. Open-air ceremonies are prohibited.

Non-Anglican marriages may also be solemnised following the issue of a Registrar-General's licence in other premises where one of the parties is seriously ill, is not expected to recover, and cannot be moved to premises where the marriage could normally be solemnised. The marriage must be solemnised in the place stated on the relevant notice of marriage, which may be one of the parties' place of residence. Detained and house-bound persons may also be married at their usual place of residence on the authority of a superintendent registrar's certificates with proper notice and consents.

MARRIAGE IN THE CHURCH OF ENGLAND OR THE CHURCH IN WALES

Marriage by banns

The marriage can take place in a parish in which one of the parties lives, or in a church in another parish if it is the usual place of worship of either or both of the parties. Further to measures introduced in October 2008, marriages can also take place in a parish where one of the parties has a 'qualifying connection', ie in: a parish where one of the parties was baptised (but not if it was part of a combined rite) or confirmed (where the confirmation was entered into the register book of confirmation for a church or chapel in that parish); a parish where one of the parties lived or habitually attended worship for six months or more; a parish where one of the parents of either of the parties lived for six months or more in the child's lifetime; a parish where one of the parents of either of the parties has habitually attended public worship for six months or more in the child's lifetime; or a parish where a parent or grandparent of either of the parties was married. The banns (ie the announcement of the marriage ceremony) must be called in the parish in which the marriage is to take place on three Sundays before the day of the ceremony; if either or both of the parties lives in a different parish the banns must also be called there. After three months the banns are no longer valid. The minister will not perform the marriage unless satisfied that the banns have been properly called.

Marriage by common licence

The couple and the member of the church who is to conduct the marriage will arrange for a common licence to be issued by the local diocese; this dispenses with the necessity for banns. One of the parties must reside in the parish, must usually worship at the parish church or authorised chapel of that parish, or otherwise have a 'qualifying connection' to the parish. The party must swear that they believe there is no lawful impediment to hinder the solemnisation of the marriage in accordance with the licence. If either party is under 18 years old, evidence of consent by their parent or guardian will be required. Any further eligibility requirements vary from diocese to diocese. The licence is valid for three months.

Marriage by special licence

A special licence is granted at the discretion of the Archbishop of Canterbury where a party has a genuine connection to a particular church or chapel but does not satisfy the legal requirements to marry there. They are also used where the building is not authorised for marriages, such as a private chapel. The parties are usually required to demonstrate that they have a genuine worshipping connection to the church or chapel. The special licence will usually be issued to the officiating priest approximately three weeks prior to the date of the wedding and expire three months after the date of issue. An application for the special licence must be made in hard copy to the registrar of the Faculty Office: 1 The Sanctuary, London SW1P 3JT T 020-7222 5381.

Marriage by certificate

The marriage can be conducted on the authority of a superintendent registrar's certificate, provided that the consent of the minister of the church or chapel where the celebration of the marriage is to take place is obtained. Since 2 March 2015, the marriage of non-EU nationals in the Church of England must take place by superintendent registrar's certificate (unless a special marriage licence is required or certain transitional arrangements apply to them), and will be allowed in any situation where the couple would otherwise have qualified for marriage by banns. In the case of British/EU nationals, the certificate procedure will be only be available if one of the parties lives in the parish for at least seven days or usually worships at the church/chapel.

Registration of the Marriage

Immediately following the solemnisation of a marriage according to the rites of the Church of England, the marriage must be registered in duplicate in two marriage register books provided by the Registrar-General for England and Wales. The entry must contain the particulars of the marriage in the prescribed form and must be signed by the clergyman, the parties to the marriage and two witnesses.

MARRIAGE BY OTHER RELIGIOUS CEREMONY

The parties will need to give notice to the register office at least 28 days before the ceremony. One of the parties must normally live in the registration district where the marriage is to take place or usually worship in the building where they wish to be married. If the building where the parties wish to be married has not been registered, the couple can still have a religious ceremony there, but this will have to follow a separate civil marriage ceremony for it to be valid. If the building is registered, in addition to giving notice to the superintendent registrar it may also be necessary to book a registrar, or authorised person to be present at the ceremony.

CIVIL MARRIAGE

A marriage may be solemnised at any register office, registered building or approved premises in England and Wales, without either of the parties being resident in the same district. The superintendent registrar of the district should be contacted and given notice, and, if the marriage is to take place at approved premises, the necessary arrangements at the venue must also be made.

NOTICE OF MARRIAGE

Where a marriage is intended to take place on the authority of a superintendent registrar's certificates, a notice of the marriage must be given in person to the superintendent registrar of the relevant district.

Both parties must have lived in a registration district in England or Wales for at least seven days immediately before giving notice personally at the local register office. If they live in different registration districts, notice must be given in both districts by the respective party in person. The marriage can take place in any register office or other approved premises in England and Wales no sooner than 28 days after notice has been given, when the superintendent registrar issues a certificate. The parties must get married or register the civil partnership within one year of giving notice.

When giving notice of the marriage it is necessary to provide evidence of name and surname, date of birth, place of residence and nationality, for example, with a passport or birth certificate and a recent bank statement. It will also be necessary to produce official proof, if relevant, that any previous marriage has ended in divorce or death by producing the original decree absolute or death certificate (or a certified copy). If the divorce or annulment documents were granted outside the UK, Channel Islands or Isle of Man the registrar may need to get in touch with the General Register Office to confirm their validity, which will incur further costs of between £50 and £75.

If either party is under 18 years old, evidence of consent by their parent or guardian is required. There are special procedures for those wishing to get married in the UK that are subject to immigration control; the register office will be able to advise on these.

SOLEMNISATION OF THE MARRIAGE

On the day of the wedding there must be at least two other people present who are prepared to act as witnesses and sign the marriage register. A registrar of marriages must be present at a marriage in a register office or at approved premises, but an authorised person may act in the capacity of registrar in a registered building.

If the marriage takes place at approved premises, the room must be separate from any other activity on the premises at the time of the ceremony, and no food or drink can be sold or consumed in the room during the ceremony or for one hour beforehand. In addition, proceedings conducted on approved premises cannot be religious in nature (although predominantly non-religious music and/or readings with incidental references to deities may be included).

The marriage must be solemnised with open doors. At some time during the ceremony the parties must make a declaration that they know of no legal impediment to the marriage and they must also say the contracting words; the declaratory and contracting words may vary according to the form of service. It may also be possible to embellish the marriage vows taken by the couple.

CIVIL FEES

Notice and registration of Marriage at a Register Office

By superintendent registrar's certificate, £35 per person for the notice of the marriage (which is not refundable if the marriage does not in fact take place) and £46 for the registration of the marriage.

Marriage at a Register Office / Approved Premises
Fees for marriage at a register office are set by the local authority responsible. An additional fee will also be payable for the registrar's attendance at the marriage on an approved premises. This is also set locally by the local authority responsible. A further charge is likely to be made by the owners of the building for the use of the premises.

For marriages taking place in a registered religious building, an additional fee (determined by the local authority) is payable for the registrar's attendance at the marriage unless an 'authorised person' has agreed to register the marriage. Additional fees may be charged by the trustees and/or proprietors of the building for the wedding and by the person who performs the ceremony.

ECCLESIASTICAL FEES
(Church of England and Church in Wales)

Marriage by banns
For publication of banns, £30*
For certificate of banns issued at time of publication, £14*
For marriage service, £455*
For marriage certificate at time of registration £11 and £11 thereafter
* These fees are revised from 1 January each calendar year. Some may not apply to the Church in Wales

Marriage by common licence
The fee will be specified by each individual diocese
Marriage by special licence £250*
* This fee is revised on 1 April each calendar year

SCOTLAND

REGULAR MARRIAGES
A regular marriage is one which is celebrated by a minister of religion or authorised registrar or other celebrant. Each of the parties must complete a marriage notice form and return it to the district registrar for the area in which they are to be married, irrespective of where they live, within the three month period prior to the date of the marriage and not later than 29 days prior to that date. The district registrar must then enter the date of receipt and certain details in a marriage book kept for this purpose, and must also enter the names of the parties and the proposed date of marriage in a list which is displayed in a conspicuous place at the registration office until the date of the marriage has passed. All persons wishing to enter into a regular marriage in Scotland must follow the same preliminary procedure regardless of whether they intend to have a religious or civil ceremony. Before the marriage ceremony takes place any person may submit an objection in writing to the district registrar.

A marriage schedule, which is prepared by the registrar, will be issued to one or both of the parties in person up to seven days before a religious marriage; for a civil marriage the schedule will be available at the ceremony. The schedule must be handed to the celebrant before the ceremony starts and it must be signed immediately after the wedding. For religious marriages the schedule must be sent within three days by the parties to the district registrar who must register the marriage as soon as possible thereafter. In civil marriages, the district registrar must register the marriage as soon as possible.

The authority to conduct a religious marriage is deemed to be vested in the authorised celebrant rather than the building in which it takes place; open-air religious ceremonies are therefore permissible in Scotland.

From 10 June 2002 it has been possible, under the Marriage (Scotland) Act 2002, for venues or couples to apply to the local council for a licence to allow a civil ceremony to take place at a venue other than a registration office. To obtain further information, a venue or couple should contact the district registrar in the area they wish to marry.

MARRIAGE BY COHABITATION WITH HABIT AND REPUTE
Prior to the enactment of the Family Law (Scotland) Act 2006, if two people had lived together constantly as husband and wife and were generally held to be such by the neighbourhood and among their friends and relations, a presumption could arise from which marriage could be inferred. Before such a marriage could be registered, however, a decree of declarator of marriage had to be obtained from the court of session. Section 3 of the 2006 act provides that it will no longer be possible for a marriage to be constituted by cohabitation with habit and repute, but it will still be possible for couples whose period of cohabitation began before commencement of the 2006 act to seek a declarator under the old rule of law.

SAME-SEX MARRIAGES
On 12 March 2014 the Scottish government passed the Marriage and Civil Partnership (Scotland) Act 2014. This permits same-sex couples to get married, either in a civil ceremony or a 'religious or belief' ceremony where the religious or belief body has opted-in to solemnising same-sex marriage. Also, certain same-sex couples who have entered into a civil partnership have the option under the act to change their civil partnership to a marriage.

It is still possible for same-sex couples to enter into a civil partnership and this may be a 'religious or belief' civil partnership if the religious or belief body has agreed to perform these.

CIVIL FEES
The fee for submitting a notice of marriage to the district registrar is £30.00 per person. Solemnisation of a civil marriage costs £55.00, while the extract of the entry in the register of marriages attracts a fee of £10.00. The costs of religious marriage ceremonies can vary.

THE GENERAL REGISTER OFFICE, PO Box 2, Southport PR8 2JD **T** 0300-123 1837 **W** www.gro.gov.uk/gro/content/certificates

THE NATIONAL RECORDS OF SCOTLAND, New Register House, 3 West Register Street, Edinburgh EH1 3YT **T** 0131-314 0380 **W** www.nrscotland.gov.uk

TOWN AND COUNTRY PLANNING

There are a number of acts governing the development of land and buildings in England and Wales and advice should always be sought from Citizens Advice or the local planning authority before undertaking building works on any land or property. If development takes place which requires planning permission without permission being given, enforcement action may take place and the situation may need to be rectified. Planning law in Scotland is similar but certain Scotland-specific legislation applies so advice should always be sought.

PLANNING PERMISSION
Planning permission may be needed if the work involves:
- making a material change in use, such as dividing off part of a house for commercial use, eg for a workshop
- subdivision of a residential house into two or more separate homes
- going against the terms of the original planning permission, eg there may be a pre-existing restriction on fences in front gardens within an 'open-plan' estate

- building, engineering or mining works, except for the permitted developments below
- new or wider access to a main road
- additions or extensions to flats or maisonettes
- work which might obstruct the view of road users

Planning permission is not needed to carry out internal alterations or work which does not affect the external appearance of the building, and are not works for making good war damage or works begun after 5 December 1968 for the alteration of a building by providing additional space in it underground.

Under regulations which came into effect on 15 April 2015, there are certain types of development for which the Secretary of State for the Environment, Food and Rural Affairs has granted general permissions (permitted development rights). These include house extensions and additions, outbuildings and garages, other ancillary garden buildings such as swimming pools or ponds, and laying patios, paths or driveways for domestic use. However, all such developments will still be subject to a number of conditions.

Before carrying out any of the above permitted developments you should contact your local planning authority to find out whether the general permission has been modified in your area. For more information, visit **W** www.gov.uk/planning-permission-england-wales/when-you-dont-need-it

OTHER RESTRICTIONS

It may be necessary to obtain other types of permissions before carrying out any development. These permissions are separate from planning permission and apply regardless of whether or not planning permission is needed, eg:

- building regulations will probably apply if a new building is to be erected, if an existing one is to be altered or extended, or if the work involves building over a drain or sewer. The building control department of the local authority will advise on this
- listed building consent must be obtained from the local authority in order to make any alterations to a listed building. This applies to the main building, as well as possibly other structures within the curtilage of the building and/ or its grounds
- local authority approval is necessary if a building (or, in some circumstances, gates, walls, fences or railings) in a conservation area is to be demolished; each local authority keeps a register of all local buildings that are in conservation areas
- many trees are protected by tree preservation orders and must not be pruned or taken down without local authority consent
- bats and many other species are protected, and so Natural England or Natural Resources Wales must be notified before any work is carried out that will affect the habitat of protected species, eg timber treatment, renovation or extensions of lofts
- developments in areas with special designations, such as National Parks, Areas of Outstanding Natural Beauty, National Scenic Areas or in the Norfolk or Suffolk Broads, are subject to greater restrictions. The local planning authority will advise or refer enquirers to the relevant authority

There may also be restrictions contained in the title to the property which require you to get someone else's agreement before carrying out certain developments, and which should be considered when works are planned.

VOTERS' QUALIFICATIONS

Those entitled to vote at parliamentary and local government elections are those who, at the date of taking the poll, are:

- on the electoral roll
- aged 18 years or older (although for Scottish parliament and local government elections in Scotland those aged 16 and older can vote)
- British citizens, qualifying Commonwealth citizens or citizens of the Irish Republic who are resident in the UK
- those who suffer from no other legal bar to voting (eg prisoners). It should be noted that there is some uncertainty regarding the future of the legal bar on prisoners' voting following a decision taken by the European Court of Human Rights
- citizens of any EU member state may vote in local elections if they meet the criteria listed above (save for the nationality requirements). There is some uncertainty regarding future voting rights of EU citizens in light of Brexit. However, it should be noted that there will be no change to the voting rights of EU citizens living in the UK while the UK remains in the EU
- registered to vote as a Crown Servant
- registered to vote as a service voter

British citizens resident abroad are entitled to vote, provided they have been registered to vote in the UK within the last 15 years, as overseas electors in domestic parliamentary elections in the constituency in which they were last resident if they are on the electoral roll of the relevant constituency. The government released a policy statement in October 2016 proposing to abolish the current 15 year time limit for British citizens registering as overseas electors although it is unclear when this proposal will be legislated for. Members of the armed forces and their spouses or civil partners, Crown servants and employees of the British Council who are overseas, along with their spouses and civil partners, are entitled to vote regardless of how long they have been abroad. British citizens who had never been registered as an elector in the UK are not eligible to register as an overseas voter unless they left the UK before they were 18, providing they left the country no more than 15 years ago. Overseas electors may opt to vote by proxy or by postal vote. Overseas voters may not vote in local government elections.

The main categories of people who are not entitled to vote at general elections are:

- sitting peers in the House of Lords
- convicted persons detained in pursuance of their sentences (though remand prisoners, unconvicted prisoners and civil prisoners can vote if on the electoral register). This is currently subject to review, as detailed above
- those convicted within the previous five years of corrupt or illegal election practices
- EU citizens (who may only vote in EU and local government elections)

Under the Representation of the People Act 2000, several new groups of people are permitted to vote for the first time. These include: people who live on barges; people in mental health hospitals (other than those with criminal convictions) and homeless people who have made a 'declaration of local connection'.

REGISTERING TO VOTE

Voters must be entered on an electoral register. The Electoral Registration Officer (ERO) for each council area is responsible for preparing and publishing the register for his area by 1 December each year. Names may be added to the register to reflect changes in people's circumstances as they occur and each month during December to August, the ERO publishes a list of alterations to the published register.

On 10 May 2012, the government introduced the electoral registration and administration bill, which received royal assent on 31 January 2013. The act replaced household registration with individual elector registration, meaning each elector must apply individually to be registered to vote. Individuals will also be asked for identifying information such as date of birth and national insurance number. The act also introduced a number of changes relating to electoral administration and the conduct of elections. Anyone failing to supply information to the ERO when requested, or supplying false information, may be fined by up to £1,000. Further, the ERO may impose a civil penalty on those who fail to make an application for registration when required to do so by the ERO. Application forms and more information are available from the Electoral Commission (**W** www.aboutmyvote.co.uk).

VOTING

Voting is not compulsory in the UK. Those who wish to vote do so in person at the allotted polling station. Postal votes are now available to anyone on request and you do not need to give a reason for using a postal vote.

A proxy (whereby the voter nominates someone to vote in person on their behalf) can be appointed to act in a specific election, for a specified period of time or indefinitely. For the appointment of an indefinite or long-term proxy, the voter needs to specify physical employment, study reasons or a disability to explain why they are making an application. With proxy votes where a particular election is specified, the voter needs to provide details of the circumstances by which they cannot reasonably be expected to go to the polling station. Applications for a proxy are normally available up to six working days before an election, but should the voter fall ill on election day, it is possible to appoint a proxy up until polling day.

On 4 April 2019, a new campaign 'Let Us Vote' was launched with the aim of giving everyone living in the UK the right to vote in elections and referendums. The campaign is seeking new legislation which would allow all UK residents, plus British citizens living abroad, to vote in general elections regardless of their citizenship.

WILLS

A will is used to appoint executors (who will administer the estate), give directions as to the disposal of the body, appoint guardians for children and determine how and to whom property is to be passed. A well-drafted will can operate to reduce the level of inheritance tax which the estate pays. It is best to have a will drawn up by a solicitor, but if a solicitor is not employed the following points must be taken into account:

- if possible the will must not be prepared on behalf of another person by someone who is to benefit from it or who is a close relative of a major beneficiary
- the language used must be clear and unambiguous and it is better to avoid the use of legal terms where the same thing can be expressed in plain language
- it is better to rewrite the whole document if a mistake is made. If necessary, alterations can be made by striking through the words with a pen, and the signature or initials of the testator and the witnesses must be put in the margin opposite the alteration. No alteration of any kind should be made after the will has been executed
- if the person later wishes to change the will or part of it, it is better to write a new will revoking the old. The use of codicils (documents written as supplements or containing modifications to the will) should be left to a solicitor

- the will should be typed or printed, or if handwritten be legible and preferably in ink

The form of a will varies to suit different cases, a solicitor will be able to advise as to wording, however, 'DIY' will-writing kits can be purchased from good stationery shops and many banks offer a will-writing service.

LAPSED LEGATEES

If a person who has been left property in a will dies before the person who made the will, the gift fails and will pass to the person entitled to everything not otherwise disposed of (the residuary estate). If the beneficiary of the residuary estate dies before the person who made the will, the gift of the residuary estate also fails and passes to the closest relative(s) of the testator in accordance with the intestacy rules.

It is always better to draw up a new will if a beneficiary predeceases the person who made the will.

EXECUTORS

It is usual to appoint two executors, although one is sufficient. No more than four persons can deal with the estate of the person who has died. The name and address of each executor should be given in full (the addresses are not essential but including them adds clarity to the document). Executors should be 18 years of age or over. An executor may be a beneficiary of the will.

WITNESSES

A person who is a beneficiary of a will, or the spouse or civil partner of a beneficiary at the time the will is signed, must not act as a witness or else he/she will be unable to take his/her gift. There is nothing preventing the spouse or civil partner of the person making the will from acting as a witness, but as it is rare for a spouse or civil partner not to benefit from the will of his/her spouse or civil partner, an independent witness is usually better.

It is also better that a person does not act as an executor and as a witness, as he/she can take no benefit (including remuneration) under a will to which he/she is witness. In relation to deaths on or after 1 February 2001, however, a professional executor who is also a witness can receive payments due to him or her under a term in the will for services provided as executor.

The identity of the witnesses should be made as explicit as possible, such as by stating their names, addresses, and occupations.

EXECUTION OF A WILL

The person making the will should sign his/her name in the presence of the two witnesses. It is advisable to sign at the foot of the document, so as to avoid uncertainty about the testator's intention. The witnesses must then sign their names while the person making the will looks on. If this procedure is not adhered to, the will may be considered invalid. There are certain exceptional circumstances where these rules are relaxed, eg where the person may be too ill to sign.

CAPACITY TO MAKE A WILL

Anyone aged 18 or over can make a will. However, if there is any suspicion that the person making the will is not, through reasons of infirmity or age, fully in command of his/her faculties, it is advisable to arrange for a medical practitioner to examine the person making the will as near to the time that the testator gives instructions for the will and to when the will is executed (to verify his/her mental capacity and to record that medical opinion in writing), and to ask the examining practitioner to act as a witness. If a person is not mentally able to make a will, the court of protection may do this for him/her by virtue of the Mental Capacity Act 2005.

REVOCATION

A will may be revoked or cancelled in a number of ways:
- a later will revokes an earlier one if it says so; otherwise the

earlier will is by implication revoked by the later one to the extent that it contradicts or repeats the earlier one

- a will is revoked if the original physical document on which it is written is destroyed by the person whose will it is. There must be an intention to revoke the will and an act of destruction. It may not be sufficient to obliterate the will with a pen
- a will is revoked by the testator making a written declaration to this effect executed in the same way as a will
- a will is also revoked when the person marries or forms a civil partnership, unless it is clear from the will that the person intended the will to stand after that particular marriage or civil partnership. A will is not revoked, however, by the conversion of a civil partnership to a marriage, or when the testator is treated as having formed a civil partnership on 5 December 2005 because he/she registered a recognised overseas relationship before that date.
- where a marriage or civil partnership ends in divorce or dissolution or is annulled or declared void, gifts to the spouse or civil partner and the appointment of the spouse or civil partner as executor fail unless the will says that this is not to happen. A former spouse or civil partner is treated as having predeceased the testator. A separation does not change the effect of a married person or civil partner's will.

PROBATE AND LETTERS OF ADMINISTRATION
The grant of probate is granted to the executors named in a will and once granted, the executors are obliged to carry out the instructions of the will. Letters of administration are granted where the deceased died intestate or did not leave a valid will. Letters of administration with will annexed are granted when the deceased did not appoint an executor in the will or the appointed executor(s) are not able or willing to act. The letters of administration give a person, often the next of kin, similar powers and duties to those of an executor.

Applications for the grant of probate or for letters of administration can be made to the Principal Registry of the Family Division, to a district probate registry or to a probate sub-registry. Applicants not using a solicitor will need to send the following documents to the main probate registry of choice: the Probate Application Form (PA1A if the deceased did not leave a will or PA1P if the deceased had a will); the original will and codicils (if any) and three copies of the same; an official copy of the death certificate; and the appropriate tax form (an 'IHT 205' if no inheritance tax is owed; otherwise an 'IHT 421' stamped by HMRC confirming payment of inheritance tax), in addition to a cheque for the relevant probate fee. The applicant will then be invited to an interview at the probate registry of choice where they will swear an oath. Where an applicant is using a solicitor, the PA1 is not necessary and the appropriate oath (for executors or administrators) will be included in the documents to be sent to the probate registry; there is no interview. In both cases, where the estate of the deceased is below £5,000, there is no probate fee to pay. Certain property, up to the value of £5,000, may be disposed of without a grant of probate or letters of administration, as can assets that do not pass under the will such as jointly owned assets which pass automatically on the death of one of the joint holders to the survivor, life policies written in trust, or discretionary pension death benefits.

A new probate regime was scheduled to be in force by April 2019, but due to the immediacy of Brexit, the approval process had been delayed, and at the time of writing there had been no indication from the Ministry of Justice as to when it may come into force. Notwithstanding, the new regime will come into force 21 days after the order is made, unless the approval motion is rejected by parliament and the issue has to be debated and voted on. The new regime stipulates that probate fees will maintained at the current level for estates worth below £50,000 and increased to £6,000 for estates worth over £2m, with a sliding scale for estates worth between £50,000 and £2m.

WHERE TO FIND A PROVED WILL
Since 1858 wills which have been proved, that is wills on which probate or letters of administration have been granted, must have been proved at the Principal Registry of the Family Division or at a district probate registry. The Lord Chancellor has power to direct where the original documents are kept but most are filed where they were proved and may be inspected there and a copy obtained. You can search for a probate record online or by post. The Principal Registry also holds copies of all wills proved at district probate registries and these may be inspected at First Avenue House, High Holborn, London. An index of all grants, both of probate and of letters of administration, is compiled by the Principal Registry and may be seen either at the Principal Registry or at a district probate registry.

It is also possible to discover when a grant of probate or letters of administration is issued by requesting a standing search. In response to a request and for a small fee, a district probate registry will supply the names and addresses of executors or administrators and the registry in which the grant was made, of any grant in the estate of a specified person made in the previous six months or following six months.

PRINCIPAL REGISTRY (FAMILY DIVISION), 7th Floor, 42–49 High Holborn, First Avenue House, London WC1V 6NP
T 020-7421 8509

INTESTACY
Intestacy occurs when someone dies without leaving a will or leaves a will which is invalid or which does not take effect for some reason. Intestacy can be partial, for instance, if there is a valid will which disposes of some but not all of the testator's property. In such cases the person's estate (property, possessions, other assets following the payment of debts) passes to certain members of the family. If a will has been written that disposes of only part of a person's property, these rules apply to the part which is undisposed of.

Some types of property do not follow the intestacy rules, for example, property held as joint tenants, insurance policies taken out for specified individuals or assigned into trust during the testator's lifetime and death benefits under a pension scheme.

Following a lengthy review by the Law Commission, the intestacy rules changed on 1 October 2014.

If the person (intestate) leaves a spouse or a civil partner who survives for 28 days and children (legitimate, illegitimate and adopted children and other descendants), the estate is divided as follows:

- if the estate is worth more than £250,000, the spouse or civil partner takes the 'personal chattels' (household articles, including cars, but nothing used for business purposes or held solely as an investment), £250,000 and half of the rest of the estate absolutely
- the rest of the estate goes to the children*

If the intestate leaves a spouse or civil partner who survives for 28 days but no children, the spouse or civil partner will take the estate in its entirety, regardless of its value.

If there is no surviving spouse or civil partner, the estate is distributed among those who survive the intestate as follows (these provisions remained unchanged at 1 October 2014):

- to surviving children*, but if none to
- parents (equally, if both alive), but if none to
- brothers and sisters of the whole blood* (including issue of deceased ones), but if none to
- brothers and sisters of the half blood* (including issue of deceased ones), but if none to
- grandparents (equally, if more than one), but if none to
- aunts and uncles of the whole blood*, but if none to
- aunts and uncles of the half blood*, but if none to

- the Crown, Duchy of Lancaster or the Duke of Cornwall *(bona vacantia)*

* To inherit, a member of these groups must survive the intestate and attain the age of 18, or marry under that age. If they die under the age of 18 (unless married under that age), their share goes to others, if any, in the same group. If any member of these groups predeceases the intestate leaving children, their share is divided equally among their children.

In England and Wales the provisions of the Inheritance (Provision for Family and Dependants) Act 1975 may allow other people to claim provision from the deceased's assets. This act also applies to cases where a will has been made and allows a person to apply to the court if they feel that the will or rules of intestacy (or both) do not make adequate provision for them. The court can order payment from the deceased's assets or the transfer of property from them if the applicant's claim is accepted. The application must be made within six months of the grant of probate or letters of administration and the following people can make an application:

- the spouse or civil partner
- a former spouse or civil partner who has not remarried or formed a subsequent civil partnership
- a child of the deceased
- someone treated as a child of the deceased's family where the deceased stood in the role of a parent to the applicant
- someone maintained wholly or partly by the deceased
- where the deceased died on or after 1 January 1996, someone who has cohabited for two years before the death in the same household as the deceased and was living as the husband or wife or civil partner of the deceased

SCOTLAND

In Scotland any person over 12 and of sound mind can make a will. The person making the will can only freely dispose of the heritage and what is known as the 'dead's part' of the estate because:

- the spouse or civil partner has the right to inherit one-third of the moveable estate if there are children or other descendants, and one-half of it if there are not
- children are entitled to one-third of the moveable estate if there is a surviving spouse or civil partner, and one-half of it if there is not

The remaining portion of the moveable estate is the dead's part, and legacies and bequests are payable from this. Debts are payable out of the whole estate before any division.

From August 1995, wills no longer needed to be 'holographed' and it is now only necessary to have one witness. The person making the will still needs to sign each page. It is better that the will is not witnessed by a beneficiary although the attestation would still be sound and the beneficiary would not have to relinquish the gift.

As a result of the changes brought in by the Succession (Scotland) Act 2016, from 1 November 2016 a divorce, dissolution or annulment (granted by a UK court) will revoke any provision in a will which confers a benefit or power of appointment on the former spouse or civil partner unless the will expressly provides that the benefit or appointment should still apply in the event of a divorce, dissolution or annulment. Subsequent marriage or civil partnership does not revoke a will but the birth of a child who is not provided for may do so. A will may be revoked by a subsequent will, either expressly or by implication, but in so far as the two can be read together both have effect. If a subsequent will is revoked, the earlier will may be revived provided it was not physically destroyed.

Wills may be registered in the sheriff court Books of the Sheriffdom in which the deceased lived or in the Books of Council and Session at the Registers of Scotland.

CONFIRMATION

Confirmation (the Scottish equivalent of probate) is obtained in the sheriff court of the sheriffdom in which the deceased was domiciled at the time of death. Executors are either 'nominate' (named by the deceased in the will) or 'dative' (appointed by the court in cases where no executor is named in a will or in cases of intestacy). Applicants for confirmation must first provide an inventory of the deceased's estate and a schedule of debts, with an affidavit. In estates under £36,000 gross, confirmation can be obtained under a simplified procedure at reduced fees, with no need for a solicitor. The local sheriff clerk's office can provide assistance.

PRINCIPAL REGISTRY (FAMILY DIVISION), First Avenue House, 42–49 High Holborn, London WC1V 6NP
T 020-7947 6000

REGISTERS OF SCOTLAND, Meadowbank House, 153 London Road, Edinburgh EH8 7AU **T** 0800-169 9391
W www.ros.gov.uk

INTESTACY

The rules of distribution are contained in the Succession (Scotland) Act 1964 and are extended to include civil partners by the Civil Partnership Act 2004.

A surviving spouse or civil partner is entitled to 'prior rights'. Prior rights mean that if certain conditions are met the spouse or civil partner has the right to inherit:

- the matrimonial or family home up to a value of £473,000, or one matrimonial or family home if there is more than one, or, in certain circumstances, the value of the home
- the furnishings and contents of that home, up to the value of £29,000
- a cash sum of £50,000 if the deceased left children or other descendants, or £89,000 if not

These figures are increased from time to time by regulations.

Once prior rights have been satisfied legal rights are settled. Legal rights are:

- *Jus relicti(ae) and rights under the section 131 of the Civil Partnership Act 2004* – the right of a surviving spouse or civil partner to one-half of the net moveable estate, after satisfaction of prior rights, if there are no surviving children; if there are surviving children, the spouse or civil partner is entitled to one-third of the net moveable estate
- *Legitim and rights under the section 131 of the Civil Partnership Act 2004* – the right of surviving children to one-half of the net moveable estate if there is no surviving spouse or civil partner; if there is a surviving spouse or civil partner, the children are entitled to one-third of the net moveable estate after the satisfaction of prior rights

Once prior and legal rights have been satisfied, the remaining estate will be distributed in the following order:

- to descendants
- if no descendants, then to collaterals (ie brothers and sisters) and parents with each being entitled to half of the estate, or if only either parents or collaterals survive, the whole of the estate
- surviving spouse or civil partner
- if no collaterals, parents, spouse or civil partner, then to ascendants collaterals (ie aunts and uncles), and so on in an ascending scale
- if all lines of succession fail, the estate passes to the Crown

Relatives of the whole blood are preferred to relatives of the half blood. Also the right of representation, ie the right of the issue of a person who would have succeeded if he/she had survived the intestate, applies.

The Family Law (Scotland) Act 2006 makes provision to allow an unmarried cohabitant to make a financial claim against the estate of a cohabitant who dies intestate. In general a claim must be made within six months of the deceased's death. The court must take into account certain factors when considering such a claim. If the claim is successful the court has the power to order payment of a capital sum and transfer of property.

In February 2019 the Scottish government launched a consultation on changes to the law of intestate succession.

INTELLECTUAL PROPERTY

Intellectual property is a broad term covering a number of legal rights provided by the government to help people protect their creative works and encourage further innovation. By using these legal rights people can own the things they create and control the way in which others use their innovations. Intellectual property owners can take legal action to stop others using their intellectual property, they can license their intellectual property to others or they can sell it on. Different types of intellectual property utilise different forms of protection including copyright, designs, patents and trade marks, which are all covered below in more detail.

CHANGES TO INTELLECTUAL PROPERTY LAW

Reforms to the Copyright, Designs and Patents Act 1988 came into force on 1 June 2014, giving a number of sectors a legal framework suitable for the digital age, removing unnecessary regulations and enabling these sectors to better preserve and use copyright material. Under the reforms, researchers benefit from a text and data mining exception for non-commercial research and schools, colleges and universities can obtain a licence to use copyright material on interactive whiteboards and in presentations without accidentally infringing copyright. An existing preservation exception was expanded to cover all types of copyright work, and now applies to museums and galleries as well as libraries and archives. The reforms also provided exceptions to copyright for the benefit of disabled people, allowing those with any type of disability which affected access to copyright works to make accessible copies of these works (eg music, film, books) when no commercial alternative existed. Under the Marrakesh Treaty, which entered into force on 11 October 2018, the commercial availability restrictions were removed to allow disabled persons to make accessible copies even when the material is commercially available.

The Intellectual Property Act 2014 came into effect on 1 October 2014. The act modernised intellectual property law to help UK businesses better protect their rights. It also implemented reforms to design legislation and introduced a number of changes to patent law, making it cheaper and easier to use and defend patents. Additional patent rule changes came into effect on 1 October 2016 and 6 April 2017. These streamlined the application process, made procedures more flexible and increased the legal certainty of patents that are granted.

The Intellectual Property (Unjustified Threats) Act 2017 came into effect on 1 October 2017. The act serves to protect businesses against unfair threats of legal action, when no infringement of intellectual property has actually taken place, and to help businesses negotiate fairly over intellectual property disputes and avoid costly litigation.

COPYRIGHT

Copyright protects all original literary, dramatic, musical and artistic works, as well as sound and film recordings and broadcasts. Among the works covered by copyright are novels, computer programs, newspaper articles, sculptures, technical drawings, websites, maps and photographs. Under copyright the creators of these works can control the various ways in which their material may be exploited, the rights broadly covering copying, adapting, issuing (including renting and lending) copies to the public, performing in public, and broadcasting the material (including online). The transfer of copyright works to formats accessible to visually impaired persons without infringement of copyright was enacted in 2002.

Copyright protection in the UK is automatic and there is no official registration system. The creator of a work can help to protect it by including the copyright symbol ©, the name of the copyright owner, and the year in which the work was created. In addition, steps can be taken by the work's creator to provide evidence that they had the work at a particular time (eg by depositing a copy with a bank or solicitor). The main legislation is the Copyright, Designs and Patents Act 1988 (as amended). The term of copyright protection for literary, dramatic, musical (including song lyrics and musical compositions) and artistic works lasts for 70 years after the death of the creator. For film, copyright lasts for 70 years after the director, authors of the screenplay and dialogue, or the composer of any music specially created for the film have all died. Sound recordings are protected for 50 years after their publication (or their first performance if they are not published), and broadcasts for 50 years from the end of the year in which the broadcast/transmission was made. The typographical arrangement of published editions remains under copyright protection for 25 years from the end of the year in which the particular edition was published.

The main international treaties protecting copyright are the Berne Convention for the Protection of Literary and Artistic Works (administered by the World Intellectual Property Organization (WIPO)), the Rome Convention for the Protection of Performers, Producers of Phonograms and Broadcasting Organisations (administered by the the International Labour Organisation, UNESCO and WIPO), the Geneva Phonograms Convention (administered by WIPO), and the Universal Copyright Convention (developed by UNESCO); the UK is a signatory to these conventions. Copyright material created by UK nationals or residents is protected in the countries that have signed one of the above-named conventions by the national law of that country. A list of participating countries may be obtained from the UK Intellectual Property Office. The World Trade Organization's Trade-Related Aspects of Intellectual Property Rights (TRIPS) agreement may also provide copyright protection abroad.

In May 2001 the EU passed a new directive (which became law in the UK in 2003) aimed at harmonising copyright law throughout the EU to take account of the internet and other technologies. More information can be found online (**W** www.ipo.gov.uk).

LICENSING

Use of copyright material without seeking permission in each instance may be permitted under 'blanket' licences available from national copyright licensing agencies. The International Federation of Reproduction Rights Organisations facilitates agreements between its member licensing agencies and on behalf of its members with organisations such as WIPO, UNESCO, the EU and the Council of Europe. More information can be found online (**W** www.ifrro.org).

DESIGN PROTECTION

Design protection covers the outward appearance of an article, and in the UK it takes two forms: registered design and design right, which are not mutually exclusive. Registered design protects the aesthetic appearance of an article, including shape, configuration, pattern or ornament; artistic works such as sculptures are excluded, being generally protected by copyright. To achieve design protection the owner of the design must apply to the Intellectual Property Office. In order to qualify for protection, a design must be new and materially different from earlier UK published designs. Initial registration lasts for five years and can be extended in five-year increments to a maximum of 25 years. The current legislation is the Registered Designs Act 1949 (as amended).

UK applicants wishing to protect their designs in the EU can do so by applying for a Registered Community Design with the EU Intellectual Property Office. Outside the EU separate applications must be made in each country in which protection is sought.

Design right is an automatic right which applies to the shape or configuration of articles and does not require registration. Unlike registered design, two-dimensional designs do not qualify for protection but designs of electronic circuits are protected by design right. Designs must be original and non-commonplace. The term of design right is ten years from first marketing of the design, or 15 years after the creation of the design, whichever is earlier. This right is effective only in the UK. After five years anyone is entitled to apply for a licence of right, which allows others to make and sell products copying the design. The current legislation is Part 3 of the Copyright, Designs and Patents Act 1988.

PATENTS

A patent is a document issued by the UK Intellectual Property Office relating to an invention. It gives the proprietor the right for a limited period to stop others from making, using, importing or selling the invention without the inventor's permission. The patentee pays a fee to cover the costs of processing the patent and must publicly disclose details of the invention.

To qualify for a patent, an invention must be new, must be functional or technical, must exhibit an inventive step, and must be capable of industrial application. The patent is valid for a maximum of 20 years, subject to renewal on the fourth anniversary of when the application was first filed and annually thereafter. The UK Intellectual Property Office, established in 1852, is responsible for ensuring that all stages of an application comply with the Patents Act 1977, and that the invention meets the criteria for a patent. An online patent renewal service is available at: www.gov.uk/renew-patent.

WIPO is responsible for administering many of the international conventions on intellectual property. The Patent Cooperation Treaty allows inventors to file a single application for patent rights in some or all of the contracting states. This application is searched by an International Searching Authority to confirm the invention is novel and that the same concept has not already been made publicly available. The application and search report are then published by the International Bureau of WIPO. It may also be the subject of an (optional) international preliminary examination. Applicants must then deal directly with the patent offices in the countries where they are seeking patent rights. The European Patent Convention allows inventors to obtain patent rights in all the contracting states by filing a single application with the European Patent Office. More information can be found at: W www.ipo.gov.uk.

RESEARCH DISCLOSURES

Research disclosures are publicly disclosed details of inventions. Once published, an invention is considered no longer novel and becomes 'prior art'. Publishing a disclosure is significantly cheaper than applying for a patent; however, unlike a patent, it does not entitle the author to exclusive rights to use or license the invention. Instead, research disclosures are primarily published to ensure the inventor the freedom to use the invention. This works because publishing legally prevents other parties from patenting the disclosed innovation and, in the UK, patent law dictates that by disclosing details of an invention, even the inventor relinquishes their right to a patent.

In theory, publishing details of an invention anywhere should be enough to constitute a research disclosure. However, to be effective, a research disclosure needs to be published in a location which patent examiners will include in their prior art searches. To ensure global legal precedent it must be included in a publication with a recognised date stamp and made publicly available throughout the world.

Research Disclosure, established in 1960 and operated by Questel Ireland Ltd, is the primary publisher of research disclosures. It is the only disclosure service recognised by the Patent Cooperation Treaty as a mandatory search resource which must be consulted by the international search authorities. (W www.researchdisclosure.com).

TRADE MARKS

Trade marks are a means of identification, enabling traders to make their goods and services readily distinguishable from those supplied by others. Trade marks can take the form of words, a logo or a combination of both. Registration prevents other traders using the same or similar trade marks for similar products or services.

In the UK trade marks are registered at the UK Intellectual Property Office. In order to qualify for registration, a trade mark must be capable of distinguishing its proprietor's goods or services from those of other undertakings; it should be non-deceptive, should not describe the goods and services or any characteristics of them, should not be contrary to law or morality and should not be similar or identical to any earlier trade marks for the same or similar goods or services. The owner of a registered trade mark may include an ® symbol next to it, and must renew their registration every ten years to keep it in force. The relevant current legislation is the Trade Marks Act 1994 (as amended).

It is possible to obtain an international trade mark registration, effective in up to 120 countries, under the Madrid system for the international registration of marks, to which the UK is party. British companies can obtain international trade mark registration in those countries party to the system through a single application to WIPO.

EU trade mark regulation is administered by the EU Intellectual Property Office, which registers Community trade marks, valid throughout the EU. The registration of trade marks in individual member states continues in parallel with EU trade marks.

DOMAIN NAMES

An internet domain name (eg www.whitakersalmanack.com) has to be registered separately from a trade mark, and this can be done through a number of registrars which charge varying rates and compete for business. For each top-level domain name (eg uk.com), there is a central registry to store the unique internet names and addresses using that suffix. A list of accredited registrars can be found online (W www.icann.org).

CONTACTS

COPYRIGHT LICENSING AGENCY LTD, 5th Floor, Shackleton House, 4 Battle Bridge Lane, London SE1 2HX T 020-7400 3100 W www.cla.co.uk

EUROPEAN PATENT OFFICE, 80298 Munich, Germany T (+49) 89 2399-0 W www.epo.org

INTELLECTUAL PROPERTY OFFICE, Concept House, Cardiff Road, Newport NP10 8QQ T 0300-300 2000 W www.ipo.gov.uk

WORLD INTELLECTUAL PROPERTY ORGANIZATION, 34 chemin des Colombettes, CH-1211 Geneva 20, Switzerland T (+41) 22 338 9111 W www.wipo.int

THE MEDIA

THE MEDIA IN 2019–20

By Steve Clarke

TELEVISION

The COVID-19 pandemic exerted a profound impact on television during the year under review. In the spring lockdown production was halted across TV. Flagship shows including the soaps were hit; for the first time in almost 60 years the *Coronation Street* set went dark; the veteran soap would celebrate its 60th anniversary in December. With people told to stay at home, other than to exercise, receive health care or to shop for food and medicine, TV ratings soared, especially for news programmes.

THE NATION TURNS TO THE BBC

In the short term, the clear winner was the BBC, which has seen support for its funding less secure under recent governments. Suddenly, the corporation went from being the subject of public criticism from the newly elected Boris Johnson-led government to serving as a vital conduit for ministers to communicate their messages to a deeply traumatised nation. A broadcast by the prime minster on 23 March announcing unprecedented peace-time restrictions on Briton's daily lives was watched by more than 27 million people, the majority – some 15.4 million – tuning into BBC One.

Government ministers, particularly health secretary Matt Hancock, were regularly seen – and heard – on BBC news and current affairs programmes. This represented an extraordinary volte-face as high-profile programmes like BBC Radio 4's *Today* had struggled in vain to get ministers to agree to appear. While political tensions were still evident between some government ministers and key parts of the broadcast media, especially the BBC, the effect of the pandemic tempered this public combativeness

With echoes of wartime radio bulletins, in the spring televised daily press conferences featuring the government's chief medical officer, Chris Witty, and chief scientific officer, Patrick Vallance, flanked by a member of Johnson's team, became a regular feature of life in lockdown.

PIERS MORGAN CAPTURES THE PUBLIC MOOD

As the COVID-19 death toll mounted amidst accusations of government incompetence (the shortage of personal protection equipment was highlighted by all parts of the media) ITV's daytime staple, *Good Morning Britain*, in the view of some commentators came into its own. Presenter Piers Morgan, once a supporter of the Conservative Party, became a vociferous and outspoken opponent of the Johnson administration's handling of the health crisis. In May, Morgan took to Twitter to describe Johnson's failure to sack Dominic Cummings for flouting lockdown rules as a 'disgrace.'

The Guardian's political sketch writer, John Crace, hailed Morgan for capturing the public mood. He was: "The everyman who isn't afraid to use what power he has to call out bullshit and incompetence for what it is. A kind of national group therapy for all those of us who feel powerless."

CHANNEL 4 FREEZES OUT BORIS JOHNSON

The acrimony between some broadcasters and certain politicians was evident in December's especially fractious general election campaign. During a Channel 4 news party leaders' debate on climate change that Johnson had declined to appear on, he was replaced by a melting ice sculpture of the planet.

Such was the anger of some Conservative politicians at what they regarded as a cheap journalistic stunt, they said that privatising the broadcaster would be back on the agenda should Johnson be re-elected. In the event, he was returned to power with an impressive 80-seat majority.

Throughout much of 2020 the sight of TV news anchors and other presenters broadcasting from their homes became part of the 'new normal.' As the health crisis worsened Channel 4 quickly commissioned and broadcast several shows designed to cheer up the UK. *Grayson Perry's Art Club* invited audiences to discover their inner Van Gogh. 'Confined to his home studio, the artist surveils creative acts across the nation from a large computer screen, like a benign cultural security guard,' opined Hettie Judah in the *i*. In a similar mood, Jamie Oliver gave tips on how to prepare basic but nutritious meals in *Keep Cooking and Carry On*.

COVID-19 UPENDS TV BUDGETS

Channel 4 was putting on a brave face. In common with ITV, the economic firestorm of COVID-19 was forcing drastic budget cuts as advertising revenue vanished. The predominantly freelance workforce responsible for most TV production was hit particularly hard as overnight employment dried up.

In early lockdown, the BBC won widespread praise for its Bitesize home-schooling initiative. For mums and dads, the service was a game changer when schools and nurseries closed across the UK in late March. Not everyone was happy, however, as the *Daily Mail* reported one anonymous parent complaining: 'My son's school have decided this is what they'll do in terms of teaching... We don't have a TV licence as we have other online subscriptions. Will we be allowed to access the videos?'

With exquisite timing, on 24 March Disney's much anticipated video-on-demand service, Disney+, launched in the UK. Within a month the family-friendly film and TV online direct-to-consumer platform had acquired 4.3 million subscribers, making Disney+ arguably the most successful UK media debut of all time.

Throughout 2019–20 streaming platforms continued to gain ground at the expense of traditional broadcasters. BritBox, the joint BBC-ITV on-demand service, was launched in November 2019, and made a splash when it brought back *Spitting Image* in the autumn of 2020. In the summer it was revealed that YouTube was the UK's third most popular video service after the BBC and ITV. Ofcom reported that it was no longer only younger audiences watching on-demand services; in significant numbers, the over-55s were getting the Netflix habit too. Netflix *et al.* declines to publish regular viewing figures so accurate information regarding individual shows streamed by these companies is not available. But it was generally assumed that for those under 35 around half their viewing time was spent with streaming platforms. Shows like Netflix's *Tiger King, The Crown* and *The Queen's Gambit* were all ideal lockdown TV.

DRAMA CONTINUES TO OCCUPY CENTRE STAGE

Throughout 2019–20 the main networks continued to provide enough high-end drama series – and the occasional one-off – to remain competitive with the subscription video on demand platforms. BBC Three's adaptation of Sally Rooney's best-selling love story *Normal People* was widely admired. Also outstanding were BBC2's *The Windermere Children*, the story of Nazi concentration camp survivors brought to England as refugees, a feminist take on the Profumo scandal, BBC One's *The Trial of Christine Keeler* starring Sophie Cookson in the title role, and the sublime second series of *My Brilliant Friend* on Sky Atlantic. There was praise too for Sky Atlantic's uber-violent *The Gangs of London*.

Two retellings of recent history also stood out – ITV's *Quiz*, written by James Graham and based on the 'Coughing Major' *Who Wants To Be A Millionaire* incident, and BBC One's *The Salisbury Poisonings*, a three-part reconstruction of how the Wiltshire city reacted to the poisoning of Russian double agent, Sergei Skripal. The story was told from the perspective of local people, notably public health officer Tracy Daszkiewicz, played by Anne-Marie Duff. Screened in June, *The Salisbury Poisonings'* contemporary resonance as the coronavirus pandemic raged added to the programme's impact.

Mindful of the challenge presented by the popularity of its online rivals, the BBC put a lot of effort into promoting one of 2020's most original dramas, *I May Destroy You*, written by and starring Michaela Cole. In *The Guardian*, Lucy Mangan wondered if *I May Destroy You* was the year's best TV drama. 'It is an astonishing, beautiful, thrilling series – a sexual-consent drama if you want the one-line pitch, but so, so much more than that,' she wrote.

BLACK LIVES ON THE FRONT LINE
Another outstanding drama was *Small Axe*, a group of five films directed by the Oscar-winning Steve McQueen. It dealt with the experience of London's West Indian community in the 1960s, 1970s and early 1980s. Of the first film, *Mangrove*, *The Telegraph's* Anita Singh commented: 'Mangrove is a chronicle of racism and the black British experience, a gripping courtroom drama and a beautifully directed period piece. Watched in a packed cinema, I can imagine it is exhilarating. But as a television experience, it is pummelling.'

The murder of George Floyd in May in Minneapolis, USA reignited the Black Lives Matter movement and led to much soul searching by decision makers in British TV. Across the board, broadcasters announced new diversity schemes. In August, at the Edinburgh Television Festival, the historian, writer and broadcaster David Olusoga gave a blistering MacTaggart lecture in which he outlined how systemic racism had blighted his TV career and led to unrepresentative programmes that failed to reflect modern Britain.

Tim Davie, who took over as the BBC's new director general in September, appeared to be listening. He told the Royal Television Society that improving diversity among BBC staff, particularly those in senior jobs, was 'mission critical.' Davie pledged to create a '50-20-12 organisation', referring respectively to the proportion of staff from female, BAME and disabled backgrounds.

THE ROYAL SOAP OPERA REIGNITES
Television's relationship with the British royal family is symbiotic. In November 2019, BBC Two's *Newsnight* broadcasted an exclusive interview with Prince Andrew conducted by Emily Maitlis. He was grilled regarding his relationship with the billionaire paedophile Jeffrey Epstein. There was a consensus that the interview was a PR disaster for the prince but apparently the palace voiced few misgivings. Maitlis told *Radio Times*: 'we know that the palace was happy with the interview. We had plenty of engagement with them after it went out. I think their shock was not at the interview itself, but the reaction it caused in the days and weeks afterwards.' One immediate consequence of the programme was that Prince Andrew 'stepped back' from royal duties. He strenuously denied accusations that he had slept with a teenager at the home of Epstein's friend, Ghislaine Maxwell.

Another BBC royal interview caused ripples during 2019–20 –Martin Bashir's revealing interview with Princess Diana broadcast by *Panorama* in 1995 was placed centre stage. It was alleged by Diana's brother, Earl Spencer, that Bashir had used dirty tricks to secure the interview. The BBC announced a new inquiry to be conducted by Lord Dyson, a former Master of the Rolls, to examine the case.

Season four of *The Crown*, which was launched in the autumn, generated much controversy. Most of it concerned the unflattering light the series shone on Prince Charles' treatment of his young wife, Diana, played by Emma Corrin, who most critics agreed was exceptional in the role. Culture Secretary Oliver Dowden said *The Crown* should carry 'a health' warning to make it clear to audiences that the show was fiction. Opinion formers from both ends of the political spectrum criticised Dowden's idea. More tellingly, some columnists saw contemporary echoes in the depiction of the royal family's attitude to Diana. Writing in *The Guardian*, Rhiannon Lucy Cosslett opined: 'these days, many, many more young women identify as feminists, and as with the treatment of Monica Lewinsky, many of them are looking at the Diana story with horror. This is a generation raised in a celebrity culture obsessed with female pain and, now they are seeing the excoriation of the Duchess of Sussex in the press, they are wondering how much has really changed.'

COMFORT TV COMES TO THE FORE
The deep trauma of coronavirus led to record-breaking audiences in 2019–20 for some of British TV's most popular entertainment shows as people sought distraction from the health emergency. In the autumn the final of *The Great British Bake Off*, made in a so-called 'biosphere' to minimize social contact, was watched by a peak of 10.4 million on Channel 4; the first edition of the 20th season of ITV's *I'm A Celebrity…Get Me Out Of Here*, transferred from the Australian rainforest to a Welsh castle, was watched by a peak of 12 million viewers, the biggest overnight audience since *Gavin and Stacey's* Christmas special in 2019.

In December the final of BBC One's *Strictly Come Dancing*, the first to feature a same-sex couple, was seen by more than 13 million viewers. 'Strictly has provided much needed sparkle to our weekends this autumn,' said acting BBC One controller Kate Phillips. These shows had been made under new protocols designed to keep everybody involved in their production safe from the virus. The ingenuity of TV to adapt to the pandemic would be one of the legacies of a year that no one will ever forget.

RADIO
Radio's unique intimacy came into its own during the pandemic. Exactly how successful the medium was in informing and entertaining the UK during 2019–20 remains unknown because the body that measures radio audiences, RAJAR, suspended their work due to the difficulty of conducting face-to-face interviews with listeners. But there was no doubt that people stranded at home, especially those living alone, appreciated more than ever the special magic that is radio.

As Ofcom observed in its annual report on the BBC published in October: 'our research shows that around a third of adults tuned in to radio for up-to-date information about the pandemic at the start of lockdown and also indicates that listeners continued to turn to radio for companionship and music. Around a fifth of adults turned to BBC radio during the start of lockdown and the BBC's *Coronavirus Newscast* was the most popular podcast at that time.'

DOWNING STREET ENDS *TODAY* BOYCOTT
The spring lockdown had an immediate impact on radio listening. Levels of listening in cars and at workplaces, which

typically accounts for around 40 per cent of all listening, fell. Radio was able to respond quickly to the crisis as home studios were set up apparently seamlessly. The BBC's director of audio James Purnell, interviewed by the Royal Television Society in the summer, revealed that the BBC had considered shutting some of its radio stations. 'At one point, we were planning to close down various stations but, because of the flexibility and ingenuity of our technical staff, we suddenly found that a lot could be done from home,' explained Purnell. He indicated that Radio 4 was an immediate winner from the crisis as listeners turned to the service's news and current affairs coverage.

Number 10 had refused to allow ministers to appear on the flagship *Today* programme since the 2019 December general election. The prime minister's advisors were reportedly furious with the BBC for what they claimed were its anti-Brexit prejudices. The *PoliticsHome* website reported one as saying: 'the *Today* programme is irrelevant, it is not a serious programme anymore so we are not going to engage with it – it is far better for us to put people up on BBC *Breakfast* and *Five Live*." But at the end of February, Conservative MP Edward Argar, a health minister, became the first Government minister to appear on *Today* since the election. Subsequently, ministers regularly featured on the programme.

COMMERCIAL RADIO'S SUCCESS CONTINUES

Figures published for the first quarter of 2020 showed commercial stations such as Magic, Heart, Smooth and Kisstory continuing to put pressure on Radio 2, the UK's most popular station, with an audience of 14.4 million but 1 million fewer than the previous year. LBC reached a record 2.8 million listeners across the UK each week. Classic FM registered its highest audience for 13 years – some 5.5 million a week – while the number of listeners tuning into Radio 3 fell slightly to just under 2 million.

However, as the pandemic tightened its grip on the UK Radio 3 gained a new prominence in national life. With so much grim news, the service provided welcome relief. In May a *Guardian* leader opined: 'in this moment of lockdown, it is to BBC Radio 3 in particular that many are flocking, for it offers a very particular kind of shelter in the current storm. The network provides, above all, an escape: an escape from the news bulletins and speculation, an escape from the wranglings and bunglings, an escape from the sadness and anxiety.'

Listeners were discovering other types of music as well; Radio 1Xtra and Radio 6 Music both benefited from lockdown, and as Miranda Sawyer reported in the *Observer*: "No Signal's live soundclash show 10 v 10 has exploded into success, with hundreds of thousands tuning in worldwide to hear Vybz Kartel tracks played in competition against Wizkid's, or Ian Wright clash with Julie Adenuga with 80s v 90s tunes."

TIMES RADIO MAKES ITS DEBUT

The growing confidence in the commercial sector was evident when in June Times Radio, backed by the newspaper group, News UK, launched. A speech-based rival to Radio 4 had been a long time coming. Critics broadly approved of the new service which had successfully poached some former BBC presenters including Mariella Frostrup and John Pienaar. Writing in *The Sunday Times*, the doyenne of radio critics, Gillian Reynolds commented: 'Times Radio is unique. It is commercial, but doesn't carry commercials. It has acquired presenters and personnel from the BBC, but doesn't sound like a BBC network. It is sponsored by *The Times* and *The Sunday Times*, but will reach listeners who may not read either. As radio stations go, its first day was mostly charming but bland.' One of the first people to be heard on the new station was the unmistakable voice of the prime minister, interviewed by Aasmah Mir and Stig Abell on their breakfast show.

Later in the year there was outrage in Fleet Street and on social media when the BBC revealed that the host of Radio 2's breakfast show, Zoe Ball, was the second highest paid star on the corporation's pay roll – despite a dip in popularity for her show. 'Zoe Ball has lost a million listeners from the Radio 2 breakfast show since she took over from Chris Evans. On Tuesday we learnt that she has had a pay increase of a million pounds. A pound for every listener that she lost,' reckoned the *The Telegraph's* Charlotte Runcie, who was furious at Ball's £1.3m fee. 'How much more would they have paid her if she'd actually added listeners?' the columnist wanted to know. In November, *The Telegraph* told Radio 2 to 'up its game' when Graham Norton left the station to join Virgin.

EXIT MR BREXIT

Another radio presenter attracting controversy was the former UKIP leader, Nigel Farage, whose contract to present a five day a week show for LBC was abruptly terminated in June. A few days before his exit Farage had compared Black Lives Matters protestors to the Taliban for demolishing statues of slave traders. LBC's owner, Global Radio, was criticised by some presenters over its response to the protests, following the death of George Floyd. A Global Radio spokesperson told the BBC the company had taken 'several steps in recent days' to improve its inclusivity, 'including the formation of a BAME committee' adding: 'Global is committed to recruiting the highest level of expertise and experience, regardless of gender, race, sexual orientation or disability. Like a lot of businesses, we are honest enough to say that we are still finding our feet and learning fast.'

THE PRESS

The year 2019–20 was, to say the least, a challenging one for the press, both in terms of covering not only a general election but the biggest crisis to affect the UK since the Second World War. As with so many other areas of society, the pandemic accelerated trends that were present prior to coronavirus – in the newspaper sector falling sales and a still greater reliance on digital publication.

The December battle at the polls between Boris Johnson and Jeremy Corbyn once again brought into stark relief the support that most national papers gave to the Conservative Party. On election day *The Sun* carried a picture of Boris Johnson inside a glowing lightbulb and Jeremy Corbyn inside a dud. The front page read: 'if Boris wins today, a bright future begins tomorrow… but if Red Jez gets in, the lights will go out for good.' The *Daily Mail*, which during the period under review overtook *The Sun* to become Britain's biggest selling paper, emblazoned its front page with the word BORIS in huge type. Its readers were told that 'you MUST brave the deluge [a reference to the wintry weather] to back' the Tory leader.

FLEET STREET TURNS ON JOHNSON?

But as the health emergency began to take its toll and the prime minister's chief adviser, Dominic Cummings, was found to have broken lockdown rules, even the pro-Tory press turned on the government. In May, Cummings' failure to resign led to harsh criticism from the *Daily Mail*, which wanted to know apropos Johnson and Cummings, 'what planet are they on?', adding: 'neither man has displayed a scintilla of contrition for this breach of trust. Do they think we are fools?' Earlier in April *The Sunday Times*, another Conservative-supporting paper, had published an investigative piece headlined: 'Coronavirus: 38 days when Britain sleepwalked into disaster.' The article reported that the prime minister had skipped five meetings of the Cobra emergency committee devoted to the virus and suggested that the government's initial slow response to the pandemic may have costs thousands of lives.

As the second wave of COVID-19 began to surge in the autumn and many opinion formers again challenged the government's competence, *The Independent's* Sean O'Grady wrote: that 'the right-wing, traditionally Tory press in Britain, which is to say almost all of it, has turned a bit nasty.' *Mailonline* reported: 'in the week Boris told a battered Britain it was in for another six months of covid winter misery, his partner Carrie Symonds enjoys five-star Italian holiday at a £600-a-night Lake Como hotel.'

THE CHALLENGE OF REPORTING COVID-19
The ability of journalists to adequately cover what was in many ways a science story was raised by some commentors. Dorothy Byrne, editor at large at Channel 4, wondered if the majority of journalists lacked the necessary science backgrounds to understand the pandemic and therefore were equipped to ask tough questions of the ministers and health officials who at the first peak of the crisis gave televised daily press conference. By common consent, one journalist who undoubtably became required reading was Tim Harford, a regular in *The Financial Times*, and Radio 4 broadcaster. His ability to make sense of the data deluge was invaluable.

The crisis sent newspaper circulations plummeting. ABC figures published in the autumn showed that only the *Observer's* sales were stable. With cities, particularly London, empty of commuters, free papers *Metro* and the *Evening Standard* registered huge declines, of 45 per cent and 39 per cent respectively. Sales of *The Financial Times* showed the biggest fall among paid-for titles, down 37 per cent.

Job cuts at newspapers loomed large. In the summer News UK, owners of *The Sun* and *The Sunday Times*, warned of a reduction in staff while *The Guardian* announced economies that could affect up to 180 jobs, with 70 in editorial. In August, it was reported that the *Evening Standard* was making a third of its staff redundant, with a 40 per cent reduction in newsroom staff. Reach, publishers of *The Daily Mirror*, *Daily Express* and *Daily Star* said it was axing 550 jobs, 12 per cent of its workforce. The move was designed to save £35m a year.

THE FT MAKES HISTORY
During the year under review Fleet Street announced the appointment of two new female editors. At the *Evening Standard*, former reporter Emily Sheffield succeeded George Osborne, who became editor-in-chief; Sheffield is the sister of David Cameron's wife, Samantha. More significantly *The Financial Times* appointed its first ever woman editor since the paper began publishing in 1888, Roula Khalaf, the paper's deputy editor. She succeeded Lionel Barber who was leaving following 14 years in charge.

Another female journalist who was the subject of media interest was the maverick *Guardian* columnist, Suzanne Moore. In November, she revealed she was leaving the paper after more than 300 members of staff accused her of writing a column that in their view was 'transphobic.' She tweeted: 'I have left *The Guardian*. I will very much miss SOME of the people there. For now that's all I can say.'

In a column she had written that a person's sex was a biological classification 'not a feeling.' She and her children were subjected to death and rape threats. They had contacted the police after 'being deemed transphobic by an invisible committee on social media,' she said.

MEGHAN MAULS THE *MAIL*
In the year under review Associated Newspapers, owners of the *Daily Mail*, were sued by the Duchess of Sussex, Meghan Markle, claiming it had unlawfully published one of her private letters, sent by Meghan to her father Thomas Markle. A statement published in October 2019 by the Duke of Sussex said he and Meghan were forced to act against 'relentless propaganda.' Prince Harry said: 'I lost my mother and now I watch my wife falling victim to the same powerful forces.'

In a year of unrelenting bad news, newspapers seized on the inspirational story of centenarian Captain Tom Moore, who incredibly raised over £30m for the NHS during the spring lockdown by walking laps of his garden. His heroic efforts won him a knighthood.

One of true giants of British journalism, Harold Evans died in September. He was 92. Evans was editor of *The Sunday Times* when it published its seminal investigation into the effects of thalidomide, which was subsequently banned. Opined the BBC's media editor, Amol Rajan: 'though he later fell out with Rupert Murdoch, and never forgave him, in his 14 years at the helm of *The Sunday Times* he redefined journalism itself.'

THE INTERNET
The one clear winner from the pandemic was 'Big Tech'. Google, Amazon, Apple and Facebook all made a rapid recovery from a brief coronavirus-induced downturn in 2019–20 as staying and working from home, together with online shopping propelled these behemoths to new heights. 'Three months of lockdown has accelerated ecommerce by four years and households will spend more than ever before online, post-lockdown,' noted *Enders Analysis* in September.

JEFF BEZOS KEEPS GETTING RICHER
In October, *The Financial Times* reported that 'combined sales of the four big tech companies leapt 18 per cent year on year in the latest quarter, to $227bn, 4 per cent higher than expected, while their after-tax profits jumped by 31 per cent, to $39bn. The surge comes in a quarter when companies in the S&P 500 are expected to suffer an overall revenue decline of more than 2 per cent, with earnings down 17 per cent.'

The wealth of Amazon boss, Jeff Bezos, grew to an all-time high of $171.6bn. Prompted by the pandemic, some tech titans made considerable donations to charities – Microsoft's Melinda and Bill Gates gave $305m to COVID-19 causes while Twitter founder Jack Dorsey donated $1bn for pandemic relief.

Ofcom's annual report, *Online Nation*, published in June, showed just how much of our lives are lived online; it revealed that at the height of the spring lockdown, on average UK adults spent four hours and two minutes a day online, up from just under three-and-a-half hours in September 2019.

BOOM TIMES FOR ZOOM
As video conferences became a way of life, Zoom, hardly a household name before the virus struck, became ubiquitous. Between January to April UK Zoom users grew from 659,000 to 13 million, a rise of almost 2,000 per cent. Many believe that even when the pandemic ends online meetings are here to stay.

The service was such a vital part of many people's lockdown lives that Zoom was gold dust for comedians as people struggled with their mute buttons and camera connections. The BBC TV satire, *W1A*, posted a special episode online, *Initial Lockdown Meeting*, in which members of the cast discussed life after lockdown on a Zoom call. More seriously, a writer on the New Yorker, Jeffrey Toobin, was sacked after allegedly exposing himself on Zoom.

AMAZON SCORES AS IT TAKES PREMIER LEAGUE ONLINE – BUT *THE NEW YORK TIMES* CRIES FOUL
In 2019–20 the increasing part played by the tech giants in all our lives was evident prior to the pandemic. For the first time 20 Premier League matches were shown exclusively on Amazon Prime Video over the Christmas period, a move that broke Sky and BT's stranglehold on the game. Most reviewers agreed there was something reassuringly old-fashioned about Amazon's coverage, despite some teething problems affecting the quality of the video stream. 'This bold new world suddenly thrust upon us feels just like the old one. And yet – what took it so long?' observed *The Independent's* sportswriter Vithushan Ehantharajah.

At the retail end of the company's activities, it was estimated that Amazon had created 400,000 new jobs owing to the online shopping boom. However, not for the first time, pointed questions were asked of Amazon's working practices. More than 100 former and current Amazon employees were interviewed for a *New York Times* exposé of the company. It described working conditions devoid of empathy and which push employees to their limits in the name of productivity and efficiency. Bezos said the report was erroneous commenting: '[the article] claims that our intentional approach is to create a soulless, dystopian workplace where no fun is had and no laughter heard. I don't recognise this Amazon and I very much hope you don't, either.'

TIKTOK ENTERS THE MAINSTREAM
The Chinese social media service, TikTok, a favourite for children's home-made video clips, was another tech company on the rise during 2019–20. Ofcom estimated it had 12.9 million UK adult visitors in April, a huge increase from 5.4 million in January. As *Enders Analysis* observed: 'TikTok has confounded regulatory woes in India and the US, and renewed competition from US tech, to post dizzying user growth in every major internet region where it is available, casting off its image as a niche youth product and entering the mainstream.'

As the nation was trapped indoors the online world encouraged people to take more care of themselves. In the spring fitness instructor Joe Wicks became a YouTube phenomenon, thanks to his 20-minute exercise routines. It was estimated that more than 70 per cent of the nation joined in his workouts, which raised £580,000 for the NHS. 'He became the person, outside our nuclear family, who was most present in our lives during lockdown,' observed *The Guardian*.

IS SOCIAL MEDIA A THREAT TO OUR HEALTH?
During the year 2019–20 the pandemic and the US election re-enforced the view that the internet can be a place where conspiracy theories take root and fake news spreads noxiously.

A peer-reviewed study published in the journal *Psychological Medicine* in June suggested that unregulated social media platforms like Facebook and YouTube may present a health risk because they spread conspiracy theories on coronavirus. People who obtain their news from social media were more likely to break lockdown rules, argued the study's authors, who concluded: 'one wonders how long this state of affairs can be allowed to persist while social media platforms continue to provide a worldwide distribution mechanism for medical misinformation.'

In the run-up to and during the November US presidential election, Facebook and Twitter doubled down on their efforts to stop fake news spreading on their sites. When President Donald Trump claimed the election was stolen from him, Facebook and Twitter immediately made it clear that his view was factually incorrect. Other, less well-known social media sites such as Parler were happy to feature posts from QAnon, the pro-Trump conspiracy theory that asserted that some top Democrats were satanic paedophiles.

REGULATORS WAIT IN THE WINGS
In December, the government announced more details of its long anticipated Online Harms Bill. Culture secretary Oliver Dowden told parliament the proposals involved 'decisive action' to protect both children and adults online. 'A 13-year-old should no longer be able to access pornographic images on Twitter, YouTube will not be allowed to recommend videos promoting terrorist ideologies and anti-Semitic hate crimes will need to be removed without delay.' He said that secondary legislation would be introduced to effect 'criminal sanctions for senior managers' if the social media companies failed to act. Critics, however, wondered if these plans would genuinely rid social media of damaging content and what impact lobbying by the tech giants was likely to have before the bill eventually became law. With so much money at their fingertips their powers of persuasion were likely to be considerable.

CROSS-MEDIA OWNERSHIP

The rules surrounding cross-media ownership were overhauled as part of the 2003 Communications Act. The act simplified and relaxed existing rules to encourage dispersion of ownership and new market entry while preventing the most influential media in any community being controlled by too narrow a range of interests. However, transfers and mergers are not solely subject to examination on competition grounds by the competition authorities. The Secretary of State for Digital, Culture, Media and Sport has a broad remit to decide if a transaction is permissible and can intervene on public interest grounds (relating both to newspapers and cross-media criteria, if broadcasting interests are also involved). The Office of Communications (OFCOM) has an advisory role in this context. Government and parliamentary assurances were given that any intervention into local newspaper transfers would be rare and exceptional. Following a request from the Secretary of State for Digital, Culture, Media and Sport in June 2010 for a removal of all restrictions from the ownership of local media, OFCOM recommended the liberalisation of local cross-media regulations to enable a single owner to control newspapers, a TV licence and radio stations in one area.

REGULATION

OFCOM is the regulator for the communication industries in the UK and has responsibility for television, radio, telecommunications and wireless communications services. OFCOM is required to report annually to parliament and exists to further the interests of consumers by balancing choice and competition with the duty to foster plurality; protect viewers and listeners and promote cultural diversity in the media; and to ensure full and fair competition between communications providers.

OFFICE OF COMMUNICATIONS (OFCOM), Riverside House, 2A Southwark Bridge Road, London SE1 9HA
T 020-7981 3000 **W** www.ofcom.org.uk
Chair, Lord Burns, GCB

COMPLAINTS

Under the Communications Act 2003 OFCOM's licensees are obliged to adhere to the provisions of its codes (including advertising, programme standards, fairness, privacy and sponsorship). Complainants should contact the broadcaster in the first instance (details can be found on OFCOM's website); however, if the complainant wishes the complaint to be considered by OFCOM, it will do so. Complaints must be submitted within 20 working days of broadcast, as broadcasters are only required to keep recordings for the following periods: radio, 42 days; television, 90 days; and cable and satellite, 60 days. OFCOM can fine a broadcaster, revoke a licence or take programmes off the air. Since November 2004 complaints relating to individual advertisements on TV or radio have been dealt with by the Advertising Standards Authority.

ADVERTISING STANDARDS AUTHORITY Mid City Place, 71 High Holborn, London WC1V 6QT **T** 020-7492 2222
W www.asa.org.uk
Chief Executive, Guy Parker

TELEVISION

There are six major television channel owners who are responsible for the biggest audience share. They are the British Broadcasting Corporation (BBC), Independent Television (ITV), Channel 4, Channel 5, Sky and UKTV. Overall there are around 480 channels available to viewers, through free-to-air, free-to-view and subscription-based services. Following the completion of the switchover to a digital format in October 2012, analogue transmissions ended and digital-only content was broadcast through a range of services, including terrestrial, satellite, cable and IP.

Beginning as a radio station in 1922, the BBC is the oldest broadcaster in the world. The corporation began a London-only television service from Alexandra Palace in 1936 and achieved nationwide coverage 15 years later. A second station, BBC Two, was launched in 1964. The BBC's other free-to-air channels available in the UK comprise BBC Four, BBC News, BBC Parliament, the children's channels, CBeebies and CBBC, and regional channels including BBC Alba, a gaelic-language channel in Scotland. Many of the BBC's channels have a corresponding HD (high definition) service and there are additionally several local channels. BBC's iPlayer service was launched on Christmas Day 2007 and allows users to view and listen to content instantly, stream live television and download programmes on to a computer, tablet or mobile device for up to 30 days. An integrated service for radio was launched in June 2008. In 2009, iPlayer was extended to more than 20 devices, including mobile phones and games consoles, and an HD service was launched. The BBC services are funded by the licence fee. The corporation also has a commercial arm, BBC Worldwide, which was formed in 1994 and exists to maximise the value of the BBC's programme and publishing assets for the benefit of the licence payer. Its businesses include international programming distribution, magazines, other licensed products, live events and media monitoring.

The ITV (Independent Television) network began broadcasting in 1955 on Channel 3 in the London area, under the Television Act 1954 which made provision for commercial television in the UK. The ITV network originally comprised a number of independent licensees, the majority of which have now merged to form ITV plc. The network generates funds through broadcasting television advertisements. The ITV network channels now include ITV2, ITV3, ITV4, ITVBe, ITV Encore and CiTV, while the network also owns UTV Ireland. The majority of ITV channels have corresponding HD services. ITV Player, similar to iPlayer, was launched December 2008 and rebranded as ITV Hub in November 2015. ITV Network Centre is wholly owned by the ITV companies and undertakes commissioning and scheduling of programmes shown across the ITV network and, as with the other terrestrial channels, 25 per cent of programmes must come from independent producers.

Channel 4 and S4C (Sianel Pedwar Cymru – Channel Four Wales) were launched in 1982 to provide programmes with a distinctive character that appeal to interests not catered for by ITV. Channel 4 has a remit to be innovative, experimental and distinctive. Although publicly owned, Channel 4 receives no public funding and is financed predominantly through advertising, but unlike ITV, Channel 4 is not shareholder-owned. It has expanded to create the stations E4, More4, Film4, 4Music and, in July 2012, catchup channel 4seven. All 4 is Channel 4's online service which enables viewers to download and revisit programmes from the last 30 days as well as access an older archive of footage. All 4 replaced Channel 4's first online platform 4oD (launched in 2006) in March 2015 and in March 2019 a subscription service was added, All 4+, which removes ads from the platform. S4C, the Welsh language public service broadcaster, receives annual funding, £15m in 2018–19, from the Department for Digital, Culture, Media and Sport (DCMS). In March 2018, the government decided that S4C would be entirely funded through the TV licence from 2022, which currently fulfils 90 per cent of its budget. S4C will remain independent and be entitled to receive UK government funding and generate its own revenue. The on-demand service is called S4C Clic and some S4C programmes are also available through BBC iPlayer.

Channel 5 began broadcasting in 1997. It was rebranded Five in 2002 but reverted to its original name, Channel 5, after the station was acquired by Northern & Shell in July 2010. Digital stations 5USA and 5Star (formerly Five Life, then Fiver) were launched in October 2006. My5 (formerly Demand 5) is an online service, launched in June 2008, where viewers can watch and download content from the last 30 days on various platforms.

BSkyB was formed after the merger in 1990 of Sky Television and British Sky Broadcasting. Now known as Sky plc, the company operates across five countries: Italy, Germany, Austria, the UK and Ireland and serves 22 million customers. Sky is one of the UK's largest pay-TV broadcasters and Its television service includes Sky Sports, Sky Cinema, Sky Arts and Sky Atlantic. In 2007, Freeview overtook Sky as the UK's most popular digital service.

In February 2011, a new version of OFCOM's Broadcasting Code came into force, permitting product placement for the first time in UK-produced television programmes. A large 'P' logo designed by OFCOM and broadcasters is displayed at the beginning and end of each programme containing product placement. The first instance of product placement occurred on 28 February 2011.

THE TELEVISION LICENCE

HOW THE LICENCE FEE IS SPENT
2018-19

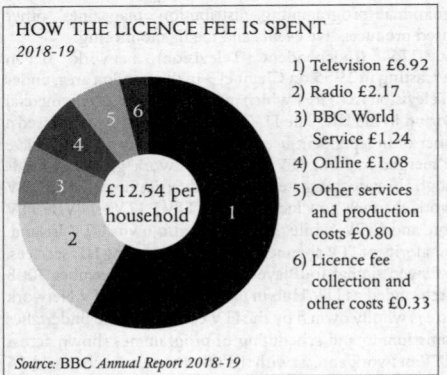

£12.54 per household

1) Television £6.92
2) Radio £2.17
3) BBC World Service £1.24
4) Online £1.08
5) Other services and production costs £0.80
6) Licence fee collection and other costs £0.33

Source: BBC Annual Report 2018-19

In the UK and its dependencies, a television licence is required to receive any publicly broadcast television service, regardless of its source, including commercial, satellite and cable programming. A TV licence registered to a home address allows the viewer to watch television on laptops, tablets and mobile phones outside the place of residence. Since 1 September 2016 a TV licence is required for services such as BBC iPlayer, even if the programme is not being watched live.

The TV licence is classified as a tax, therefore non-payment is a criminal offence. A fine of up to £1,000 can be imposed on those successfully prosecuted. The TV licence is issued on behalf of the BBC as the licensing authority under the Communications Act 2003. In 2018–19 25,927,000 TV licences were purchased, a 37,000 decrease on the number purchased in 2017–18, resulting in a 3.8 per cent decrease in revenue to £3,690m. As at 1 April 2019, an annual colour television licence costs £154.50 and a black and white licence £52.00. Concessions are available for the elderly and people with disabilities. In June 2019, the BBC announced its intention to end free TV licences for those aged 75 and over from June 2020; only households with someone aged 75 and over who is in receipt of pension credit will remain eligible to apply for a free licence. Further details can be found at **W** www.tvlicensing.co.uk/information

DIGITAL TELEVISION

The Broadcasting Act 1996 provided for the licensing of 20 or more digital terrestrial television (DTT) channels (on six frequency channels or 'multiplexes'). The first digital services went on air in autumn 1998.

In June 2002, following the collapse of ITV Digital, the digital terrestrial television licence was awarded to a consortium made up of the BBC, BSkyB and transmitter company Crown Castle by the Independent Television Commission. Freeview was launched on 30 October 2002 with 25 free-to-air channels: it now offers over 70 digital channels, up to 15 HD channels and 30 radio stations and requires the one-off purchase of a set-top box, but is subsequently free of charge with no subscription. In Autumn 2005 ITV and Channel 4 officially became shareholders, each taking a 20 per cent stake. As at 2018, around 20 million homes use Freeview on at least one set, amounting to around 30 per cent of UK households. There is an additional Freeview+ service which works in a similar fashion to Sky+, allowing viewers to record programmes. Over 97 per cent of UK homes have access to digital television.

TELEVISION AUDIENCE SHARE, 2018
per cent

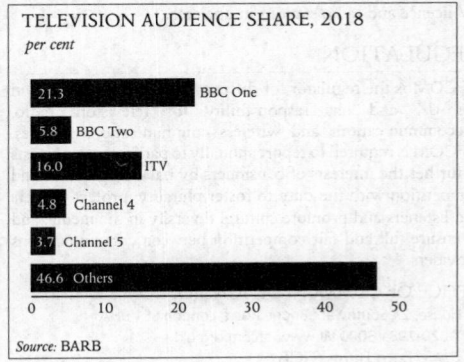

21.3	BBC One
5.8	BBC Two
16.0	ITV
4.8	Channel 4
3.7	Channel 5
46.6	Others

Source: BARB

RECENT DEVELOPMENTS

The internet has now firmly established itself as an alternative to live and programmed TV, particularly for those aged 16 to 34. Since the launch of 4oD in 2006 and BBC iPlayer in 2007, there has been a noticeable shift in the way viewers can watch their favourite programmes. Technological advancements have also contributed to this phenomenon; more than half of the UK population uses a tablet, over 90 per cent of UK homes and businesses have access to superfast broadband and there are millions of public Wi-Fi hotspots across the UK. There is now a much bigger emphasis on catch-up, and subscription video on demand (SVOD) services then ever before, with BBC iPlayer recording 356 million requests in January 2019, an average of 11.5 million requests a day. SVOD services such as Netflix, Now TV and Amazon Prime Video have experienced a surge in popularity, with subscribers able to stream programmes through computers, mobiles, tablets and games consoles on up to four devices at a time. Both Netflix and Amazon Prime Video commission and distribute their own programmes, available exclusively to their subscribers, contributing to their popularity. UK subscriptions to Netflix surpassed those to Sky for the first time in December 2018. and 47 per cent of all UK households currently have an active subscription to at least one SVOD service. The BBC has provided exclusive content and programmes on iPlayer since 2014 and in 2016 moved BBC Three to an online-only service. ITV and Channel 4 both launched their own SVOD services (ITV Hub+, All 4+) in 2018 and 2019 respectively.

Despite the rise in the popularity of tablets, traditional TV sets are still the most popular way to watch television. HD TV provides more vibrant colours, greater detail and increased picture clarity, along with improved sound quality. An HD television screen uses 1,280 by 720 pixels up to 1,920 by 1,080 pixels. HD Ready TVs operate at 720p while full HD TVs tend to operate on 1080p or 1080i; the differences between these three settings are down to the number of lines in the resolution and the type of scanning technology. 'HD Ready' simply means the TV will only operate a higher definition once plugged into a decoder, whereas full HD has this built in. In 2017, the average screen size in the UK was 43.7 inches wide and this is expected to increase to 48.9 inches by 2020, indicating a rapidly increasing trend towards bigger screens. Sales of Smart TVs, which can access apps, browse the internet and stream video, are increasing; around 48 per cent of UK households now own a Smart TV.

In April 2010, Samsung released the first consumer 3D TV; in the same month Sky launched the UK's first dedicated 3D channel. Several sporting events were broadcast in 3D, including the Wimbledon Championships. The BBC began a two-year 3D trial in 2011 but announced in July 2013 it would suspend 3D programming for an indefinite period of time due to a lack of public appetite for the technology and the sale of new 3D TV sets and services has now essentially ceased in the UK. In June 2018, the Facebook owned virtual reality (VR) headset company Oculus launched Oculus TV, intended to create a fully immersive experience.

In September 2012, OFCOM awarded its first local TV licences after announcing plans to broadcast 21 channels in total. In November 2013, Estuary TV, based in Grimsby, was the first to be launched. In March 2013, OFCOM stated plans for a further 30 areas to invite bids for local television services. However in April 2018, OFCOM announced its intention to halt the roll out of new local TV stations due several service providers facing financial difficulties and poor audience figures.

CONTACTS

THE BRITISH BROADCASTING CORPORATION (BBC)

BBC Broadcasting House, Portland Place, London W1A 1AA
   W www.bbc.co.uk
BBC North, Media City UK, Bridge House, Salford Quays, Manchester M50 2BH
   Chair, BBC Board, Sir David Clementi
   Director-General, Lord Hall of Birkenhead, CBE
BBC Worldwide, 1 Television Centre, Wood Lane, London W12 7FA **W** www.bbcworldwide.com

INDEPENDENT TELEVISION (ITV)

London Television Centre, 2 Waterhouse Square, 138-142 Holborn, London EC1N 2AE **W** www.itv.com
   Chair, Sir Peter Bazalgette
   Chief Executive, Dame Carolyn McCall, DBE

INDEPENDENT TELEVISION (ITV) REGIONS

Anglia (eastern England), **W** www.itv.com/anglia
Border (Borders and the Isle of Man), **W** www.itv.com/border
Calendar (Yorkshire), **W** www.itv.com/calendar
Central (east, west and south Midlands), **W** www.itv.com/central
Channel (Channel Islands), **W** www.itv.com/channel
Granada (north-west England), **W** www.itv.com/granada
London, **W** www.itv.com/london
Meridian (south and south-east England), **W** www.itv.com/meridian
STV (Scotland), **W** www.stv.tv
Tyne Tees (north-east England), **W** www.itv.com/tynetees
Ulster (Northern Ireland), **W** www.itv.com/utv

Wales, **W** www.itv.com/wales
West, **W** www.itv.com/west

OTHER TELEVISION COMPANIES

Channel 4 Television, 124 Horseferry Road, London SW1P 2TX
   T 020-7396 4444 **W** www.channel4.com
Channel 5 Broadcasting Ltd, 10 Lower Thames Street, London EC3R 6EN **T** 020-8612 7700 **W** www.channel5.com
Independent Television Network (ITN), 200 Gray's Inn Road, London WC1X 8XZ **T** 020-7833 3000 **W** www.itn.co.uk
Provides news programming and services for ITV, Channel 4 and Channel 5, as well as content for international news providers.
Sianel Pedwar Cymru (S4/C), Canolfan S4/C, Yr Egin, Carmarthen SA31 3EQ **T** 0870-600 4141 **W** www.s4c.cymru
Freeview, DTV Services Ltd, 27 Mortimer Street, London W1T 3JF
   W www.freeview.co.uk

DIRECT BROADCASTING BY SATELLITE TELEVISION

Sky plc, Grant Way, Isleworth, Middlesex TW7 5QD
   T 033-3100 0333 **W** www.sky.com
   Chief Executive, Stephen van Rooyen

RADIO

UK domestic radio services are broadcast across three wavebands: FM, medium wave and long wave (used by BBC Radio 4). In the UK the FM waveband extends in frequency from 87.5MHz to 108MHz and the medium waveband from 531kHz to 1602kHz. A number of radio stations are broadcast in both analogue and digital as well as a growing number in digital alone. As at June 2019, the BBC Radio network controlled around 51.4 per cent of the listening market (*see* BBC Radio section), and the independent sector (*see* Independent Radio section) 45.7 per cent. As at June 2019, a listener tunes into an average of 20.9 hours of radio per week.

ESTIMATED AUDIENCE SHARE

			Percentage
	Apr–Jun 2017	Apr–Jun 2018	Apr–Jun 2019
BBC Radio 1	6.2	5.9	5.7
BBC Radio 2	16.8	17.9	17.4
BBC Radio 3	1.2	1.2	1.2
BBC Radio 4	12.3	11.7	11.9
BBC Radio Five Live	3.4	3.1	3.4
Five Live Sports Extra	0.3	0.3	0.1
BBC 6 Music	1.9	2.4	2.4
BBC Asian Network UK	0.3	0.3	0.2
1Xtra	0.5	0.4	0.4
BBC Local/Regional	7.3	6.7	6.6
BBC World Service	0.9	0.7	0.7
All BBC	52.3	45.0	51.4
All independent	45.0	45.7	45.7
All national independent	16.7	18.1	19.9
All local independent	28.4	27.6	25.9
Other	2.8	2.5	2.8

Source: RAJAR

DIGITAL RADIO

The UK has the world's largest digital radio network, with 103 transmitters, two national Digital Audio Broadcasting (DAB) ensembles and a total of 48 local and regional DAB ensembles, which broadcast around 250 independent and 34 BBC radio stations. The BBC began test transmissions of the DAB Eureka 147 digital radio service in 1990 from the Crystal Palace transmitting station and the service was publicly launched in

1995. As well as DAB, digital televisions, car radios, games consoles, mobile devices and the internet are commonly employed as platforms to listen to radio in the UK. One of the major benefits of DAB is better sound quality than analogue radio, and the availability of a wider choice of stations, in addition to the lack of interference experienced by other broadcast media.

The UK government intends to migrate the majority of AM and FM analogue radio services to digital, based on certain conditions being met such as coverage, listening figures and agreements in relation to funding. In the second quarter of 2018, 50.2 per cent of all radio listening hours in the UK were through digital platforms. From this 50.2 per cent, DAB made up the majority of listenership with 72 per cent. In 2018, over 63 per cent of all UK households were believed to have access to DAB radio.

The BBC's national DAB ensemble has coverage across the UK of around 97 per cent and broadcasts on the frequency 225.648 MHz. Owned and operated by the BBC, the multiplex of broadcasts is transmitted across the UK from a number of sites. Local and regional ensembles, which cover 71.7 per cent of the UK, are transmitted through a number of DAB multiplex operators across the UK, including Digital One and Sound Digital – the two national operators – in addition to local multiplex operators.

There are two criteria that must be met for digital migration to occur:
- at least 50 per cent of radio listening is digital
- national DAB coverage is comparable to FM coverage, and local DAB reaches 90 per cent of the population and all major roads

LICENSING

The Broadcasting Act 1996 provided for the licensing of digital radio services (on multiplexes, where a number of stations share one frequency to transmit their services). To allocate the multiplexes, OFCOM advertises licences for which interested parties can bid. Once the licence has been awarded, the new owner seeks out services to broadcast on the multiplex. The BBC has a separate national multiplex for its services. There are local multiplexes around the country, each broadcasting an average of seven services, plus the local BBC station.

INNOVATIONS

The internet offers a number of advantages compared to other digital platforms such as DAB, including higher sound quality, a greater range of channel availability and flexibility in listening opportunity. Listeners can tune in to the majority of radio stations live on the internet or listen again online generally up to seven days after broadcast. DAB radio does not allow the same interactivity: the data is only able to travel one-way from broadcaster to listener whereas the internet allows a two-way flow of information.

Increases in Wi-Fi hotspots also means listening to radio, podcasts and catch-up programmes is easy to do through tablets and mobile phones; in 2018, over 50 per cent of all reported radio listening was via a digital service. The increase in music streaming services and radio-related apps has had a major effect on music discovery and sharing. In the UK in 2018 the number of streams per week averaged around 550 million. Since 6 July 2014 the UK Official Charts Company has included streaming services in its compilation, with 100 streams the equivalent to one purchase.

Since 2005 most radio stations offer all or part of their programmes as downloadable files, known as podcasts, to listen to on computers, mobiles or tablets. Podcasting technology allows listeners to subscribe in order to automatically receive the latest episodes of regularly transmitted programmes as soon as they become available.

The relationship between radio stations and their audiences is also undergoing change. The quantity and availability of music on the internet has led to the creation of shows dedicated entirely to music sent in by listeners. Another new development in internet-based radio has been personalised radio stations, such as SoundCloud and Spotify. SoundCloud allows users to upload, record, promote and share their music and sounds. Artists who upload their music are given a URL, allowing their music to be embedded anywhere, making it easier to share through social media platforms such as Twitter and Facebook. Users can also create their own playlists and link them to social media platforms. Spotify, available as an app on most smart phones and tablets as well as online, allows listeners access to the track, artist or genre of their choice, or to share and create playlists. It has seen steady growth in popularity since its launch in 2008, with 83 million paying subscribers and 180 million active users globally, as at June 2018. Spotify 'learns as you listen' and makes associated recommendations based on user choices. Radioplayer (**W** www.radioplayer.co.uk), a not-for-profit company backed by the BBC and commercial radio, allows audiences to listen to live and catch-up radio from one place. Over 6 million people per month use the Radioplayer service. There are over 400 stations available and a 'recommended' service which offers station suggestions depending on location, what is trending and the type of music the user likes. Radioplayer launched as a mobile app in 2012 and a tablet app in 2013. Through the tablet app, users sample an average of 4.6 stations a week in comparison with just 2.1 for analogue users. In November 2018, the BBC launched BBC Sounds (**W** www.bbc.co.uk/sounds), a digital platform for all BBC radio and podcast output with the intention of streamlining their audio content on to a single platform, personalised to the individual listener's preferences.

BBC RADIO

BBC Radio broadcasts network services to the UK, Isle of Man and the Channel Islands, with around 34.7 million listeners each week. There is also a tier of national services in Wales, Scotland and Northern Ireland and around 40 local radio stations in England and the Channel Islands. In Wales and Scotland there are also dedicated language services in Welsh and Gaelic respectively. The frequency allocated for digital BBC broadcasts is 225.648MHz.

BBC Radio, Broadcasting House, Portland Place, London W1A 1AA
W www.bbc.co.uk/radio

BBC NETWORK RADIO STATIONS

Radio 1 (contemporary pop music and entertainment news) – 24 hours a day, *Frequencies:* 97–99 FM and digital *Radio 1Xtra* (contemporary urban and hip-hop music, culture and entertainment) – 24 hours a day, digital only

Radio 2 (popular music, entertainment, comedy and the arts) – 24 hours a day, *Frequencies:* 88–91 FM and digital

Radio 3 (classical music, classic drama, documentaries and features) – 24 hours a day, *Frequencies:* 90–93 FM and digital

Radio 4 (news, documentaries, drama, entertainment and cricket on long wave in season) – 5.20am–1am daily, with BBC World Service overnight, *Frequencies:* 92–95 FM/103–105 FM and 198 LW and digital

Radio Five Live (news and sport) – 24 hours a day, *Frequencies:* 909/693 MW and digital *Five Live Sports Extra* (live sport) – schedule varies, digital only

6 Music (contemporary and classic pop and rock music) – 24 hours a day, digital only

Asian Network (news, music and sport) – 5am–1am, with Radio 1Xtra overnight, *Frequencies:* various MW frequencies in Midlands and digital

BBC NATIONAL RADIO STATIONS

Radio Cymru (Welsh-language), *Frequencies:* 92–105 FM and digital

Radio Foyle, Frequencies: 93.1 FM and 792 MW and digital

Radio nan Gaidheal (Gaelic service), *Frequencies:* 103–105 FM and digital

Radio Scotland, Frequencies: 92–95 FM and 810 MW and digital. Local programmes for Orkney, Shetland and Highlands and Islands

Radio Ulster, Frequencies: 1341 MW and 92–95 FM and digital. Local programmes on Radio Foyle

Radio Wales, Frequencies: 657/882 MW and 93–104 FM and digital

BBC WORLD SERVICE

The BBC World Service broadcasts to an estimated weekly audience of 1.5 million people in the UK and 280 million worldwide, in 40 languages including English, and is now available in around 150 capital cities. It no longer broadcasts in Dutch, French for Europe, German, Hebrew, Italian, Japanese or Malay because it was found that most speakers of these languages preferred to listen to the English broadcasts. In 2006 services in ten languages (Bulgarian, Croatian, Czech, Greek, Hungarian, Kazakh, Polish, Slovak, Slovene and Thai) were terminated to provide funding for a new Arabic television channel, which was launched in March 2008. In August 2008 the BBC's Romanian World Service broadcasts were discontinued after 68 years. In January 2011 the BBC announced five more language services would be terminated: Albanian, Caribbean English, Macedonian, Portuguese for Africa and Serbian. The BBC World Service website offers interactive news services in 28 languages including English, Arabic, Chinese, Hindi, Persian, Portuguese for Brazil, Russian, Spanish and Urdu with audiostreaming available.

LANGUAGES

Afaan Oromoo, Amharic, Arabic, Azeri, Bengali, Burmese, Cantonese, English, French, Gujarati, Hausa, Hindi, Igbo, Indonesian, Kinyarwanda, Kirundi, Korean, Kyrgyz, Marathi, Nepali, Nigerian, Nigerian Pidgin, Pashto, Persian, Portuguese, Punjabi, Russian, Sinhala, Somali, Spanish, Swahili, Tamil, Telugu, Tigrinya, Turkish, Ukrainian, Urdu, Uzbek, Yoruba and Vietnamese.

UK frequencies: digital; overnight on BBC Radio 4.

BBC Learning English teaches English worldwide through radio, television and a wide range of published and online courses.

BBC Media Action is a registered charity established in 1999 by BBC World Service, known as the BBC World Service Trust until December 2011. It promotes development through the innovative use of the media in the developing world.

BBC Monitoring tracks the global media for the latest news reports emerging around the world.

BBC WORLD SERVICE, Broadcasting House, Portland Place, London W1A 1AA **W** www.bbc.co.uk/worldservice

INDEPENDENT RADIO

Until 1973, the BBC had a legal monopoly on radio broadcasting in the UK. During this time, the corporation's only competition came from pirate stations located abroad, such as Radio Luxembourg. Christopher Chataway, Minister for Post and Telecommunications, changed this by creating the first licences for commercial radio stations. The Independent Broadcasting Authority (IBA) awarded the first of these licences to the London Broadcasting Company (LBC) to provide London's news and information service. LBC was

followed by Capital Radio, to offer the city's entertainment service, Radio Clyde in Glasgow and BRMB in Birmingham.

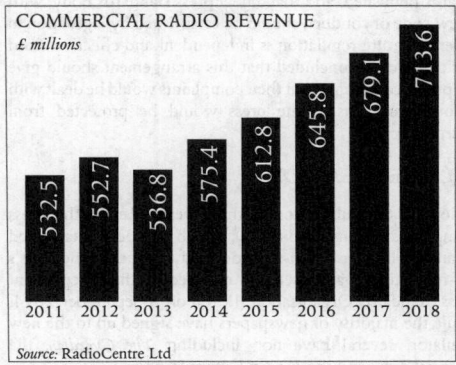

COMMERCIAL RADIO REVENUE
£ millions

2011	2012	2013	2014	2015	2016	2017	2018
532.5	552.7	536.8	575.4	612.8	645.8	679.1	713.6

Source: RadioCentre Ltd

The IBA was dissolved when the Broadcasting Act of 1990 de-regulated broadcasting, to be succeeded by the less rigid Radio Authority (RA). The RA began advertising new licences for the development of independent radio in January 1991. It awarded national and local radio, satellite and cable services licences, and long-term restricted service licences for stations serving non-commercial establishments such as hospitals and universities. The first national commercial digital multiplex licence was awarded in October 1998 and a number of local digital multiplex licences followed. At the end of 2003 the RA was replaced by OFCOM, which now carries out the licensing administration.

RadioCentre was formed in July 2006 as a result of the merger between the Radio Advertising Bureau (RAB) and the Commercial Radio Companies Association (CRCA), the former non-profit trade body for commercial radio companies in the UK, to operate essentially as a union for commercial radio stations.

RadioCentre, 6th Floor, 55 New Oxford Street, London WC1A 1BS
T 020-7010 0600 **W** www.radiocentre.org
Chief Executive, Siobhan Kenny

THE PRESS

The newspaper and periodical press in the UK is large and diverse, catering for a wide variety of views and interests. There is no state control or censorship of the press; however, it is subject to the laws on publication.

The press is not state-subsidised and receives few tax concessions. The income of most newspapers and periodicals is derived largely from sales and from advertising. The Advertising Association reported in July 2018 that national newspaper brands experienced their first increase in advertising spend in seven years in 2017. The UK advertising market in general grew to an estimated £23.5bn in 2018, an increase of 6 per cent.

LEVESON REPORT

The Leveson Inquiry, established under the Inquiries Act 2005, was announced by the prime minister on 13 July 2011 to investigate the role of press and police in the *News of the World* phone-hacking scandal. Lord Justice Leveson was appointed as chair of the inquiry. The hearings began on 14 November 2011 and ended on 24 July 2012 following the testimonies of 650 witnesses.

The Leveson Report was published in late November 2012 and featured several broad and complex recommendations as to how the press should be regulated. The report generally recommended that the press should continue to be self-regulated, with the government allowed no direct power over what is published, and that a new press standards body, with a new code of conduct, should be established by legislation in order to ensure regulation is independent and effective. Lord Justice Leveson concluded that this arrangement should give the public confidence that their complaints would be dealt with seriously and ensure the press would be protected from interference.

SELF-REGULATION

Following the publication of the Leveson Report the Press Complaints Commission (PCC), which had been established in January 1991 as a non-statutory body to operate the press's self-regulation, was closed and replaced by the Independent Press Standards Organisation (IPSO) on 8 September 2014. While the majority of newspapers have signed up to the new regulator, several have not, including *The Guardian*, the *Financial Times* and the *London Evening Standard*.

In 2013 a royal charter on press regulation was granted by the Privy Council to create a watchdog to oversee a new regulator. On 3 November 2014, a fully independent body, the Press Recognition Panel (PRP) was established to consider whether press regulators meet the criteria recommended in the Leveson Report and, if so, to afford these regulators official recognition.

IPSO has not sought recognition from the PRP, but another regulator, IMPRESS, was awarded recognition by the PRP in October 2016.

INDEPENDENT PRESS STANDARDS ORGANISATION,
Gate House, 1 Farringdon Street, London EC4M 7LH
T 0300-123 2220 **E** inquiries@ipso.co.uk **W** www.ipso.co.uk
Chair, Rt. Hon. Sir Alan Moses

PRESS RECOGNITION PANEL, Mappin House, 4 Winsley
Street, London W1W 8HF
E contact@pressrecognitionpanel.org.uk
W www.pressrecognitionpanel.org.uk
Chair, Dr David Wolfe, QC

NEWSPAPERS

Newspapers are mostly financially independent of any political party, though most adopt a political stance in their editorial comments, usually reflecting proprietorial influence. Ownership of the national and regional daily newspapers is concentrated in the hands of large corporations whose interests cover publishing and communications, although *The Guardian* and *The Observer* are owned by the Scott Trust, formed in 1936 to protect the financial and editorial independence of *The Guardian* in perpetuity. The rules on cross-media ownership, as amended by the Broadcasting Act 1996, which limited the extent to which newspaper organisations may become involved in broadcasting, have been relaxed by the Communications Act 2003: newspapers with over a 20 per cent share of national circulation may own national and/or local radio licences.

In October 2010, *The Independent* launched a concise newspaper, *i*, the first new daily newspaper since 1986 but the final editions of *The Independent* and *The Independent on Sunday* were published in March 2016 as the paper moved to digital only. In July 2011, *News of the World* was closed by its parent company, News International, following accusations of phone-hacking. In February 2012 News International printed the first edition of *The Sun on Sunday*, a Sunday format of the daily tabloid paper *The Sun*. In November 2014, the Herald and Times Group launched the Scottish daily *The National,* the first newspaper to actively support Scottish independence. In September 2018, *The Sunday National* was

launched to replace *The Sunday Herald* which ceased publication on 2 September 2018. In February 2016, Trinity Mirror launched a compact daily newspaper, *The New Day* – the first new standalone paper since *The Independent* in 1986 – but it ceased publication in May 2016 after a sharp drop in circulation. There are 11 daily and Sunday national papers and several hundred local papers that are published daily, weekly or twice-weekly. Scotland, Wales and Northern Ireland all have at least one daily and one Sunday national paper.

National Daily Newspapers	June 2018	June 2019	% +/-
The Sun	1,451,584	1,277,947	−12.72
Daily Mail	1,264,810	1,175,653	−7.31
Daily Mirror	562,523	488,829	−14.02
Daily Star	364,448	310,246	−16.07
The Daily Telegraph	370,613	327,345	−12.40
The Times	428,034	399,672	−6.85
Daily Express	338,527	307,662	−9.57
i	248,234	288,801	−8.14
Financial Times	183,319	175,512	−4.35
The Guardian	138,082	132,821	−3.88
Daily Record	145,724	111,543	−26.57
National Sunday Newspapers			
The Sun on Sunday	1,224,119	1,066,147	−13.80
The Mail on Sunday	1,056,916	986,385	−6.90
The Sunday Times	721,808	686,819	−4.97
Sunday Mirror	475,976	403,350	−16.52
The Sunday Telegraph	288,484	258,394	−11.0
Sunday Express	295,294	268,096	−10.12
Daily Star Sunday	220,684	184,914	−17.63
Sunday People	183,784	151,523	−19.24
The Observer	166,317	159,568	−4.14
Sunday Mail	131,716	113,712	−14.67
Sunday Post	115,973	96,422	−18.41

Source: Audit Bureau of Circulations Ltd

Newspapers are usually published in either broadsheet or smaller, tabloid format. The 'quality' daily papers – ie those providing detailed coverage of a wide range of public matters – have traditionally been broadsheets, the more populist newspapers tabloid. In 2004 this correlation between format and content was redefined when two traditionally broadsheet newspapers, *The Times* and *The Independent*, switched to tabloid-sized editions, while *The Guardian* launched a 'Berliner' format in September 2005. In October 2005 *The Independent on Sunday* became the first Sunday broadsheet to be published in the tabloid (or 'compact') size. *The Observer,* like its daily counterpart *The Guardian,* began publishing in the Berliner format in January 2006 and began publishing in tabloid format in January 2018.

NEWSPAPERS ONLINE

The demand to read news instantly and while on the move has increased the popularity of newspaper websites. Most newspapers now operate their own websites in line with their print editions, often including the same material as seen in daily printed editions but can also include video and audio features. Many articles and columns additionally have the option of reader contributions and debate. Certain newspapers charge a subscription fee to access their websites but the majority are free to browse.

NATIONAL PRESS WEBSITE DAILY AVERAGE
BROWSERS

National Press Website	June 2017	June 2018	% +/-
MailOnline	15,406,452	12,622,077	−18.07
metro.co.uk	2,676,403	1,689,148	−36.89
Reach PLC*	10,121,154	8,976,593	−11.31
thesun.co.uk	5,281,981	5,410,691	2.44

* Formerly known as Trinity Mirror Group PLC
Source: Audit Bureau of Circulations Ltd

NATIONAL DAILY NEWSPAPERS

DAILY EXPRESS
Northern & Shell Building, 10 Lower Thames Street, London
EC3R 6EN **T** 020-8612 7000 **W** www.express.co.uk
Editor, Gary Jones

DAILY MAIL
Northcliffe House, 2 Derry Street, London W8 5TT **T** 020-7938 6000
W www.dailymail.co.uk
Editor, Geordie Greig

DAILY MIRROR
1 Canada Square, Canary Wharf, London E14 5AP
T 020-7293 3000 **W** www.mirror.co.uk
Editor, Allison Phillips

DAILY RECORD
1 Central Quay, Glasgow G3 8DA **T** 0141-309 3000
W www.dailyrecord.co.uk
Editor, David Dick

DAILY STAR
Northern & Shell Building, 10 Lower Thames Street, London
EC3R 6EN **T** 020-8612 7000 **W** www.dailystar.co.uk
Editor, Jon Clark

THE DAILY TELEGRAPH
111 Buckingham Palace Road, London SW1W 0DT
T 020-7931 2000 **W** www.telegraph.co.uk
Editor, Chris Evans

FINANCIAL TIMES
Bracken House, 1 Friday Street, London EC4M 9BT
T 020-7873 3000 **W** www.ft.com
Editor, Lionel Barber

THE GUARDIAN
Kings Place, 90 York Way, London N1 9GU **T** 020-3353 2000
W www.theguardian.com
Editor-in-Chief, Katharine Viner

THE HERALD
200 Renfield Street, Glasgow G2 3QB **T** 0141-302 7000
W www.heraldscotland.com
Editor, Graeme Smith

i
2 Derry Street, London W8 5HF **T** 020-7005 2000
W www.inews.co.uk
Editor, Oliver Duff

MORNING STAR
William Rust House, 52 Beachy Road, London E3 2NS
T 020 8510-0815 **W** www.morningstaronline.co.uk
Editor, Ben Chacko

THE NATIONAL
200 Renfield Street, Glasgow, G2 3QB **T** 0141-302 7000
W www.thenational.scot
Editor, Callum Baird

THE SCOTSMAN
Orchard Brae House, 30 Queensferry Road, Edinburgh EH4 2HS
T 0131-311 7311 **W** www.scotsman.com
Editorial Director, Frank O'Donnell

THE SUN
1 London Bridge Street, London SE1 9GF **T** 020-7782 4000
W www.thesun.co.uk
Editor, Tony Gallagher

THE TIMES
1 London Bridge Street, London SE1 9GF **T** 0800-018 5177
W www.thetimes.co.uk
Editor, John Witherow

WEEKLY NEWSPAPERS

DAILY STAR SUNDAY
Northern & Shell Building, 10 Lower Thames Street, London
EC3R 6EN **T** 020-8612 7000 **W** www.dailystar.co.uk/sunday
Editor, Denis Mann

MAIL ON SUNDAY
Northcliffe House, 2 Derry Street, London W8 HFT **T** 020-7938 6000
W www.mailonsunday.co.uk
Editor, Ted Verity

THE OBSERVER
Kings Place, 90 York Way, London N1 9GU **T** 020-3353 2000
W www.theguardian.com/observer
Editor, Paul Webster

THE SUNDAY PEOPLE
1 Canada Square, Canary Wharf, London E14 5AP
T 020-7293 3000 **W** www.people.co.uk
Editor, Peter Willis

SCOTLAND ON SUNDAY
Orchard Brae House, 30 Queensferry Road, Edinburgh EH4 2HS
T 0131-311 7311 **W** www.scotlandonsunday.com
Editorial Director, Frank O'Donnell

THE SUN ON SUNDAY
1 London Bridge Street, London SE1 9GF **T** 020-7782 4000
W www.thesun.co.uk
Editor, Victoria Newton

SUNDAY EXPRESS
Northern & Shell Building, 10 Lower Thames Street, London
EC4R 6EN **T** 020-8612 7000 **W** www.sundayexpress.co.uk
Editor, Gary Jones

SUNDAY MAIL
1 Central Quay, Glasgow G3 8DA **T** 0141-309 3000
W www.sundaymail.com
Editor, Brendan McGinty

SUNDAY MIRROR
1 Canada Square, Canary Wharf, London E14 5AP
T 020-7293 3000 **W** www.sundaymirror.co.uk
Editor, Lloyd Embley

SUNDAY NATIONAL
200 Renfield Street, Glasgow, G2 3QB **T** 0141 302-7000
W www.thenational.scot
Editor, Richard Walker

SUNDAY POST
Skypark, 8 Elliot Place, Glasgow G3 8EP **T** 01382-223131
W www.sundaypost.com
Editor, Richard Prest

SUNDAY TELEGRAPH
111 Buckingham Palace Road, London SW1W 0DT
T 020-7931 2000 **W** www.telegraph.co.uk
Editor, Allister Heath

THE SUNDAY TIMES
1 London Bridge Street, London SE1 9GF **T** 020-7782 5000
W www.thesundaytimes.co.uk
Editor, Martin Ivens

REGIONAL NEWSPAPERS

EAST ANGLIA

CAMBRIDGE NEWS
Cambridge Research Park, Waterbeach CB25 9PD **T** 01223-632200
W www.cambridge-news.co.uk
Editor, David Bartlett

EAST ANGLIAN DAILY TIMES
Portman House, 120 Princes Street, Ipswich IP1 1RS
T 01473-230023 **W** www.eadt.co.uk
Editor, Brad Jones

EASTERN DAILY PRESS
Prospect House, Rouen Road, Norwich NR1 1RE **T** 01603-628311
W www.edp24.co.uk
Editor, David Powles

IPSWICH STAR
Portman House, 120 Princes Street, Ipswich IP1 1RS
T 01473-230023 **W** www.ipswichstar.co.uk
Editor, Brad Jones

NORWICH EVENING NEWS
Prospect House, Rouen Road, Norwich NR1 1RE **T** 01603-628311
W www.eveningnews24.co.uk
Editor, David Powles

EAST MIDLANDS

DERBY TELEGRAPH
2 Siddals Road, Derby DE1 2PB **T** 01332-411888
W www.derbytelegraph.co.uk
Editor, Julie Bayley

THE LEICESTER MERCURY
16 New Walk, Leicester LE1 6TF **T** 0116-251 2512
W www.leicestermercury.co.uk
Editor, George Oliver

LINCOLNSHIRE ECHO
Witham Wharf, Brayford Wharf East, Lincoln LN5 7AY
T 01522-804300 **W** www.lincolnshirelive.co.uk
Editor, Adam Moss

NORTHAMPTON CHRONICLE & ECHO
400 Pavilion Drive, Northants NN4 7PA **T** 01604-467032
W www.northamptonchron.co.uk
Editor, David Summers

NOTTINGHAM POST
City Gate, Tollhouse Hill, Notts NG1 5FS **T** 0115-948 2000
W www.nottinghampost.com
Editor, Mike Sassi

LONDON

EVENING STANDARD
Northcliffe House, 2 Derry Street, London W8 5TT **T** 020-3367 7000
W www.standard.co.uk
Editor, George Osborne

METRO
Northcliffe House, 2 Derry Street, London W8 5TT **T** 020-3615 3480
W www.metro.co.uk
Editor, Ted Young

NORTH EAST

EVENING CHRONICLE
2nd Floor, Eldon Court, Percy Street, Newcastle upon Tyne NE1 7JB
T 0191-201 6446 **W** www.chroniclelive.co.uk
Editor-in-Chief, Neil Hodgkinson

HARTLEPOOL MAIL
North East Business & Innovation Centre, Westfield Enterprise Park
East, Sunderland SR5 2TA **T** 0191-516 6127
W www.hartlepoolmail.co.uk
Editor, Joy Yates

THE JOURNAL
2nd Floor, Eldon Court, Percy Street, Newcastle upon Tyne NE1 7JB
T 0191-201 6446 **W** www.thejournal.co.uk
Editor, Neil Hodgkinson

THE NORTHERN ECHO
PO Box 14, Priestgate, Darlington, Co. Durham DL1 1NF
T 01325-381313 **W** www.thenorthernecho.co.uk
Editor, Hannah Chapman

THE SHIELDS GAZETTE
North East Business & Innovation Centre, Westfield Enterprise Park
East, Sunderland SR5 2TA **T** 0191-516 6127
W www.shieldsgazette.com
Editor, Joy Yates

THE SUNDAY SUN
2nd Floor, Eldon Court, Percy Street, Newcastle upon Tyne NE1 7JB
T 0191-201 6446 **W** www.sundaysun.co.uk
Editor, Neil Hodgkinson

SUNDERLAND ECHO
North East Business & Innovation Centre, Westfield Enterprise Park
East, Sunderland SR5 2TA **T** 0191-501 5800
W www.sunderlandecho.com
Editor, Joy Yates

TEESIDE GAZETTE
1st Floor, Hudson Quay, The Halyard, Middlehaven, Middlesbrough
TS3 6RT **T** 01642-234262 **W** www.gazettelive.co.uk
Editor, Neil Hodgkinson

NORTH WEST

THE BLACKPOOL GAZETTE
Avroe House, Avroe Crescent, Blackpool FY4 2DP **T** 01253-400888
W www.blackpoolgazette.co.uk
Editor, Simon Drury

THE BOLTON NEWS
The Wellsprings, Civic Centre, Bolton BL1 1AR **T** 01204-522345
W www.theboltonnews.co.uk
Editor, Karl Holbrook

CARLISLE NEWS AND STAR
Newspaper House, Dalston Road, Carlisle CA2 5UA
T 01228-612600 **W** www.newsandstar.co.uk
Editor, Chris Story

LANCASHIRE EVENING POST
Stuart House, 89 Caxton Road, Fulwood, Preston PR2 9ZB
T 01772-254841 **W** www.lep.co.uk
Editor, Gillian Parkinson

LANCASHIRE TELEGRAPH
50–54 Church Street, Blackburn, Lancs. BB1 5AL **T** 01254 678678
W www.lancashiretelegraph.co.uk
Editor, Steven Thompson

LIVERPOOL ECHO
5 St Paul's Square, Liverpool L3 9SL **T** 0151-472 2507
W www.liverpoolecho.co.uk
Editor, Alastair Machray

MANCHESTER EVENING NEWS
Mitchell Henry House, Hollinwood Avenue, Chadderton OL9 8EF
T 0161-832 7200 **W** www.manchestereveningnews.co.uk
Editor, Darren Thwaites

NORTH-WEST EVENING MAIL
Abbey Road, Barrow-in-Furness, Cumbria LA14 5QS
T 01229-840100 **W** www.nwemail.co.uk
Editor, Vanessa Sims

SOUTH EAST

THE ARGUS
Dolphin House, 2–5 Manchester Street, Brighton BN2 1TF
T 01273-021400 **W** www.theargus.co.uk
Editor, vacant

ECHO
Newspaper House, Chester Hall Lane, Basildon, Essex SS14 3BL
T 01268-522792 **W** www.echo-news.co.uk
Editor, Chris Hatton

MEDWAY MESSENGER
Medway House, Ginsbury Close, Sir Thomas Longley Road,
Rochester, Kent ME2 4DU **T** 01634-227800
W www.kentonline.co.uk/medway
Editor, Matt Ramsden

THE NEWS, PORTSMOUTH
1000 Lakeside, North Harbour, Portsmouth PO6 3EN
T 023-9266 4488 **W** www.portsmouth.co.uk
Editor, Mark Waldron

OXFORD MAIL
Newsquest Oxfordshire & Wiltshire, Osney Mead, Oxford OX2 0EJ
T 01865-425262 **W** www.oxfordmail.co.uk
Managing Editor, Samantha Harmon

READING CHRONICLE
2–10 Bridge Street, Reading, Berks. RG1 2LU **T** 0118-955 3333
W www.readingchronicle.co.uk
Group Editor, Andrew Colley

THE SOUTHERN DAILY ECHO
Newspaper House, Test Lane, Redbridge, Southampton SO16 9JX
T 023-8042 4777 **W** www.dailyecho.co.uk
Editor, Gordon Sutter

SOUTH WEST

BRISTOL POST
Temple Way, Bristol BS2 0BY **T** 0117-934 3331
W www.bristolpost.co.uk
Editor, Mike Norton

BOURNEMOUTH ECHO
Richmond Hill, Bournemouth BH2 6HH **T** 01202-554601
W www.bournemouthecho.co.uk
Editor, Andy Martin

CORNISH TIMES
The Tindle Suite, Webbs House, Liskeard PL14 6AH
T 01579-342174 **W** www.cornish-times.co.uk
Editor, Andrew Townsend

DORSET ECHO
Fleet House, Hampshire Road, Weymouth, Dorset DT4 9XD
T 01305-830930 **W** www.dorsetecho.co.uk
Editor, Diarmuid MacDonagh

EXETER EXPRESS & ECHO
Queens House, Little Queen Street, Exeter EX4 3LJ **T** 01392-346763
W www.exeterexpressandecho.co.uk
Editor, Rich Booth

GLOUCESTER CITIZEN
Gloucester Quays, St Ann Way, Gloucester GL1 5SH
T 01452-689320 **W** www.gloucestershirelive.co.uk
Editor, Rachael Sugden

GLOUCESTERSHIRE ECHO
Gloucester Quays, St Ann Way, Gloucester GL1
5SH**T** 01452 689320 **W** www.gloucestershirelive.co.uk
Editor, Rachael Sugden

THE HERALD
3rd Floor, Millbay Road, Plymouth PL1 3LF **T** 01752-293000
W www.plymouthherald.co.uk
Editor, Edd Moore

SUNDAY INDEPENDENT
Indy House, Lighterage Hill, Truro TR1 2XR **T** 01579-556970
W www.indyonline.co.uk
Editor, John Collings

SWINDON ADVERTISER
Richmond House, Edison Park, Swindon SN3 3RB **T** 01793-528144
W www.swindonadvertiser.co.uk
Editor, Pete Gavan

TORQUAY HERALD EXPRESS
Queens House, Little Queen Street, Exeter EX4 3LJ **T** 01392-346763
W www.devonlive.com
Editor, Rich Booth

WESTERN DAILY PRESS
Temple Way, Bristol BS99 7HD **T** 0117-934 3000
W www.somersetlive.co.uk
Editor, vacant

THE WESTERN MORNING NEWS
3rd Floor, Millbay Road, Plymouth PL1 3LF **T** 01752-293000
W www.thisiswesternmorningnews.co.uk
Editor, Bill Martin

WEST MIDLANDS

BIRMINGHAM MAIL
Embassy House, 60 Church Street, Birmingham B3 2DJ
T 0121-234 5000 **W** www.birminghammail.co.uk
Editor, Anna Jeys

COVENTRY TELEGRAPH
Corporation Street, Coventry CV1 1FP **T** 024-7663 3633
W www.coventrytelegraph.net
Editor, Keith Perry

EXPRESS & STAR
51–53 Queen Street, Wolverhampton WV1 1ES **T** 01902-313131
W www.expressandstar.com
Editor, Martin Wright

THE SENTINEL
Sentinel House, Bethesda Street, Stoke-on-Trent ST1 3GN
T 01782-864100 **W** www.stokesentinel.co.uk
Editor, Martin Tideswell

SHROPSHIRE STAR
Waterloo Road, Ketley, Telford TF1 5HU **T** 01952-242424
W www.shropshirestar.com
Editor, Martin Wright

WORCESTER NEWS
Berrows House, Hylton Road, Worcester WR2 5JX **T** 01905-748200
W www.worcesternews.co.uk
Editor, Michael Purton

YORKSHIRE AND HUMBERSIDE

GRIMSBY TELEGRAPH
Heritage House, Fisherman's Wharf, Grimsby DN31 1SY
T 01472-808000 **W** www.grimsbytelegraph.co.uk
Editor, Jamie Macaskill

HALIFAX COURIER
The Fire Station, Dean Clough Mills, Halifax HX3 5AX
T 01422-260252 **W** www.halifaxcourier.co.uk
Editor, John Kenealy

THE HUDDERSFIELD DAILY EXAMINER
Pennine Business Park, Longbow Close, Bradley Road, Huddersfield
HD2 1GQ **T** 01484-430000 **W** www.examiner.co.uk
Editor, Wayne Ankers

HULL DAILY MAIL
Blundell's Corner, Beverley Road, Hull HU3 1XS **T** 01482-327111
W www.hulldailymail.co.uk
Editor, Neil Hodgkinson

THE PRESS
PO Box 29, 76–86 Walmgate, York YO1 9YN **T** 01904-567131
W www.yorkpress.co.uk
Editor, Nigel Burton

SCARBOROUGH NEWS
17–23 Aberdeen Walk, Scarborough, N. Yorks YO11 1BB
T 01723-60100 **W** www.thescarboroughnews.co.uk
Editor, Jean MacQuarrie

SHEFFIELD STAR
The Balance, 2 Pinfold Street, Sheffield S1 2GU **T** 0114-276 7676
W www.thestar.co.uk
Editor, Nancy Fielder

TELEGRAPH & ARGUS
Hall Ings, Bradford BD1 1JR **T** 01274-729511
W www.thetelegraphandargus.co.uk
Editor, Nigel Burton

YORKSHIRE EVENING POST
26 Whitehall Road, Leeds LS12 1BE **T** 0113-238 8917
W www.yorkshireeveningpost.co.uk
Editor, Hannah Thaxter

YORKSHIRE POST
26 Whitehall Road, Leeds LS12 1BE **T** 0113-238 8427
W www.yorkshirepost.co.uk
Editor, James Mitchinson

SCOTLAND

THE COURIER
2 Albert Square, Dundee DD1 1DD **T** 01382-575291
W www.thecourier.co.uk
Editor, Richard Neville

DUNDEE EVENING TELEGRAPH
2 Albert Square, Dundee DD1 1DD **T** 01382-575950
W www.eveningtelegraph.co.uk
Editor, Dave Lord

EDINBURGH EVENING NEWS
Orchard Brae House, 30 Queensferry Road, Edinburgh EH4 2HS
T 0131-311 7311 **W** www.edinburghnews.scotsman.com
Editor, Euan McGrory

EVENING EXPRESS
1 Marischal Square, Broad Street, Aberdeen AB10 1BL
T 01224-691212 **W** www.eveningexpress.co.uk
Editor, Craig Walker

GLASGOW EVENING TIMES
200 Renfield Street, Glasgow G2 3QB **T** 0141-302 6600
W www.eveningtimes.co.uk
Editor, Donald Martin

INVERNESS COURIER
New Century House, Stadium Road, Inverness IV1 1FF
T 01463-246575 **W** www.inverness-courier.co.uk
Editor, Andrew Dixon

PAISLEY DAILY EXPRESS
1 Central Quay, Glasgow G3 8DA **T** 0141-887 7911
W www.paisleydailyexpress.co.uk
Editor, Cheryl McEvoy

THE PRESS AND JOURNAL
1 Marischal Square, Broad Street, Aberdeen AB10 1BL
T 01224-690222 **W** www.pressandjournal.co.uk
Editor, Alan McCabe

WALES

THE LEADER
Mold Business Park, Mold, Flintshire CH7 1XY **T** 01352-707707
W www.leaderlive.co.uk
Group Editor, Susan Perry

SOUTH WALES ARGUS
Cardiff Road, Maesglas, Newport NP20 3QN **T** 01633-810000
W www.southwalesargus.co.uk
Editor, Nicole Garnon

SOUTH WALES ECHO
6 Park Street, Cardiff CF10 1XR **T** 029-2024 3602
W www.walesonline.co.uk
Editor, Tryst Williams

SOUTH WALES EVENING POST
Urban Village, High Street, Swansea SA1 1NW **T** 01792-545515
W www.southwales-eveningpost.co.uk
Editor, Jonathan Roberts

WESTERN MAIL
6 Park Street, Cardiff CF10 1XR **T** 029-2024 3635
W www.walesonline.co.uk
Editor, Catrin Pascoe

NORTHERN IRELAND

BELFAST TELEGRAPH
124–144 Royal Avenue, Belfast BT1 1DN **T** 028-9026 4000
W www.belfasttelegraph.co.uk
Editor, Gail Walker

IRISH NEWS
113–117 Donegall Street, Belfast BT1 2GE **T** 028-9032 2226
W www.irishnews.com
Editor, Noel Doran

NEWS LETTER
Arthur House, 41 Arthur Street, Belfast BT1 4GB **T** 028-3839 5577
W www.newsletter.co.uk
Editor, Alistair Bushe

SUNDAY LIFE
124–144 Royal Avenue, Belfast BT1 1EB **T** 028-9026 4000
W www.belfasttelegraph.co.uk/sunday-life
Editor, Martin Breen

CHANNEL ISLANDS

GUERNSEY PRESS
PO Box 57, Braye Road, Vale, Guernsey GY1 3BW **T** 01481-240240
W www.guernseypress.com
Editor, Shaun Green

JERSEY EVENING POST
Guiton House, Five Oaks, St Saviour, Jersey JE4 8XQ
T 01534-611611 **W** www.jerseyeveningpost.com
Editor, Andy Sibcy

PERIODICALS

ART

AESTHETICA
PO Box 371, York YO23 1WL **T** 01904-629137
W www.aestheticamagazine.com
Editor, Cherie Federico

APOLLO
22 Old Queen Street, London SW1H 9HP **T** 020-7961 0150
W www.apollo-magazine.com
Editor, Thomas Marks

ART MONTHLY
12 Carlton House Terrace, London SW1Y 5AH **T** 020-7240 0389
W www.artmonthly.co.uk
Editor, Patricia Bickers

ARTREVIEW
1 Honduras Street, London EC1Y 0TH **T** 020-7490 8138
W www.artreview.com
Editor, Mark Rappolt

TATE ETC.
Tate, Millbank, London SW1P 4RG **T** 020-7887 8724
W www.tate.org.uk/tate-ect
Editor, Simon Grant

BUSINESS AND FINANCE

THE ECONOMIST
20 Cabot Square, London E14 4QW **T** 020-7576 8000
W www.economist.com
Editor, Zanny Minton Beddoes

MANAGEMENT TODAY
Bridge House, 69 London Road, Twickenham TW1 3SP
T 020-8267 5000 **W** www.managementtoday.co.uk
Editor, Adam Gale

MARKETING WEEK
79 Wells Street, London W1T 3QN **T** 020-7292 3711
W www.marketingweek.co.uk
Editor, Russell Parsons

MONEYWEEK
31–32 Alfred Place, London WC1E 7DP **T** 0330-333 9688
W www.moneyweek.com
Editor-in-Chief, Merryn Somerset Webb

PUBLIC FINANCE
78 Chamber Street, London E1 8BL **T** 020-7880 6200
W www.publicfinance.co.uk
Managing Editor, John Watkins

CELEBRITY

CLOSER
Endeavour House, 189 Shaftesbury Avenue, London WC2H 8JG
T 020-7295 5000 **W** www.closeronline.co.uk
Editor, Lisa Burrow

HEAT
Endeavour House, 189 Shaftesbury Avenue, London WC2H 8JG
T 020-7437 9011 **W** www.heatworld.com
Editor, Suzy Cox

HELLO!
Wellington House, 69–71 Upper Ground, London SE1 9PQ
T 020-7667 8901 **W** www.hellomagazine.com
Editor, Rosie Nixon

OK!
10 Lower Thames Street, London EC3R 6EN **T** 020-8612 7000
W www.ok.co.uk
Editor, Kirsty Tyler

CHILDREN'S AND FAMILY

THE BEANO
185 Fleet Street, London EC4A 2HS **W** www.beano.com
Editor, John Anderson

MOTHER & BABY
Bauer Media Group, Media House, Lynchwood, Peterborough
Business Park, Peterborough PE2 6EA **T** 01733- 468000
W www.motherandbaby.co.uk
Editor, Sally Saunders

YOUR CAT
Warners Group Publications, The Maltings, West Street, Bourne,
Lincs PE10 9PH**T** 0177-839 5070 **W** www.yourcat.co.uk
Editor, Emily Wardle

YOUR DOG
Warners Group Publications, The Maltings, West Street, Bourne,
Lincs PE10 9PH **T** 0177-839 5070 **W** www.yourdog.co.uk
Editor, Sarah Wright

CLASSICAL MUSIC AND OPERA

BBC MUSIC
Immediate Media Company Bristol Ltd, Tower House, Colston
Avenue, Bristol BS1 4ST **T** 0117-927 9009
W www.classical-music.com
Editor, Oliver Condy

CLASSICAL MUSIC
Rhinegold House, 20 Rugby Street, London WC1N 3QZ
T 020-7333 1729 **W** www.classicalmusicmagazine.org
Editor, Lucy Thraves

GRAMOPHONE
c/o Mark Allen Group, St Jude's Church, Dulwich Road, London
SE24 0PB **T** 020-7738 5454 **W** www.gramophone.co.uk
Editor, Martin Cullingford

OPERA
36 Black Lion Lane, London W6 9BE **T** 020-8563 8893
W www.opera.co.uk
Editor, John Allison

COMPUTERS AND TECHNOLOGY

PC PRO
31–32 Alfred Place, London WC1E 7DP **T** 020-3890 3890
W www.alphr.com
Editorial Director, Victoria Woollaston

STUFF
Blackfriars Foundary, 154–156 Blackfriars Road, London SE1 8EN
T 020-8267 5036 **W** www.stuff.tv
Editor, James Day

T3
T3 magazine, 5 Pinesway Industrial Estate, Bath BA2 3QS
W www.t3.com
Editor, Matt Bolton

WEB USER
Dennis Publishing, 30 Cleveland Street, London W1T 4JD
T 020-7907 6000 **W** www.webuser.co.uk
Group Editor, Daniel Booth

WIRED
Condé Nast, Vogue House, Hanover Square, London W1S 1JU
T 0844-848 5202 **W** www.wired.co.uk
Editor-in-Chief, Nicholas Thompson

CRAFT

CARDMAKING & PAPERCRAFT
Immediate Media, Vineyard House, 44 Brook Green, London W6
7BT **T** 0117-933 8081 **W** www.cardmakingandpapercraft.com
Editor, Hayley Hawes

SIMPLY KNITTING
Immediate Media, Vineyard House, 44 Brook Green, London W6
7BT **T** 0117-3008 253 **W** www.immediate.co.uk/brands/
simply-knitting
Commissioning Editor, Kirstie McLeod

THE WORLD OF CROSS STITCHING
Immediate Media, Vineyard House, 44 Brook Green, London W6
7BT **T** 0117-314 8351 **W** www.cross-stitching.com
Editor, Hannah Kelly

ENTERTAINMENT

EMPIRE
Endeavour House, 189 Shaftesbury Avenue, London WC2H 8JG
T 020-7437 9011 **W** www.empireonline.com
Editor-in-Chief, Terri White

RADIO TIMES
Vineyard House, 44 Brook Green, London W6 7BT
T 020-7150 5800 **W** www.radiotimes.com
Editorial Director, Mark Frith

SIGHT & SOUND
BFI, 21 Stephen Street, London W1T 1LN **T** 020-7255 1444
W www.bfi.org.uk/sightandsound
Editor, vacant

TIME OUT LONDON
77 Wicklow Street, London WC1X 9JY **T** 020-7813 3000
W www.timeout.com
Editor, Caroline McGinn

TOTAL FILM
Future Publishing Ltd, 1–10 Praed Mews, London W2 1QY
T 020-7042 4831 **W** www.gamesradar.com/totalfilm
Editor, Jane Crowther

FASHION AND BEAUTY

COSMOPOLITAN
House of Hearst, 30 Panton Street, London SW1Y 4AJ
T 020-7439 5000 **W** www.cosmopolitan.co.uk
Editor, Claire Hodgson

ELLE
House of Hearst, 30 Panton Street, London SW1Y 4AJ
T 020-7150 7000 **W** www.elleuk.com
Editor, Farrah Storr

GLAMOUR
Condé Nast, Vogue House, Hanover Square, London W1S 1JU
T 020-7499 9080 **W** www.glamourmagazine.co.uk
Editor-in-Chief, Deborah Joseph

GRAZIA
Endeavour House, 189 Shaftesbury Avenue, London WC2H 8JG
T 0845-601 1356 **W** www.graziadaily.co.uk
Editor, Hattie Brett

HARPER'S BAZAAR
House of Hearst, 30 Panton Street, London SW1Y 4AJ
T 0844-848 5203 **W** www.harpersbazaar.co.uk
Editor-in-Chief, Justine Picardie

MARIE CLAIRE
161 Marsh Wall, London E14 9AP **T** 020-3148 5000
W www.marieclaire.co.uk
Editor-in-Chief, Trish Halpin

VOGUE
Condé Nast, Vogue House, Hanover Square, London W1S 1JU
T 0844-848 5202 **W** www.vogue.co.uk
Editor, Edward Enninful

FOOD AND DRINK

FOOD AND TRAVEL
Suite 51, The Business Centre, Ingate Place, London SW8 3NS
T 020-7501 0511 **W** www.foodandtravel.com
Editor, Michelle Hather

GOOD FOOD
44 Vineyard House, Brook Green, London W6 7BT
T 020-7150 5022 **W** www.bbcgoodfood.com
Editor, Christine Hayes

OLIVE
Vineyard House, 44 Brook Green, London W6 7BT
T 020-7150 5024 **W** www.olivemagazine.com
Editor, Laura Rowe

WHISKY
6 Woolgate Court, St Benedicts Street, Norwich NR2 4AP
T 01603-633 808 **W** www.whiskymag.com
Editor, Rob Allanson

GENERAL INTEREST

BBC HISTORY
Tower House, Fairfax Street, Bristol BS1 3BN **T** 0117-927 9009
W www.historyextra.com
Editor, Rob Attar

BOOKSELLER
Floor 10, Westminster Tower, 3 Albert Embankment, London SE1
7SP **T** 020-3358 0365 **W** www.thebookseller.com
Editor, Philip Jones

HISTORY TODAY
2nd Floor, 9 Staple Inn, London WC1V 7QH **T** 020-3219 7810
W www.historytoday.com
Editor, Paul Lay

LITERARY REVIEW
44 Lexington Street, London W1F OLW **T** 020-7437 9392
W www.literaryreview.co.uk
Editor, Nancy Sladek

NEW STATESMAN
Standard House, 12–13 Essex Street, London WC2R
3AA **T** 020-7936 6400 **W** www.newstatesman.com
Editor, Jason Cowley

PRIVATE EYE
6 Carlisle Street, London W1D 3BN **T** 020-7437 4017
W www.private-eye.co.uk
Editor, Ian Hislop

PROSPECT
5th Floor, 23 Savile Row, London W1S 2ET **T** 020-7255 1281
W www.prospectmagazine.co.uk
Editor, Tom Clark

READER'S DIGEST
The Maltings, West Street, Bourne BH24 9PH **T** 0330-333 2220
W www.readersdigest.co.uk
Editor, Fiona Hicks

SAGA
Saga Publishing Ltd, Enbrook Park, Folkestone, Kent CT20 3SE
T 01303-771111 **W** www.saga.co.uk
Editor, Louise Robinson

THE SPECTATOR
22 Old Queen Street, London SW1H 9HP **T** 020-7961 0200
W www.spectator.co.uk
Editor, Fraser Nelson

TLS (THE TIMES LITERARY SUPPLEMENT)
1 London Bridge Street, London SE1 9GF **T** 020-7782 5000
W www.the-tls.co.uk
Editor, Stig Abell

THE WEEK
31–32 Alfred Place, London WC1E 7DP **T** 020-3890 3890
W www.theweek.co.uk
Editor-in-Chief, Jeremy O'Grady

WHO DO YOU THINK YOU ARE?
Tower House, Fairfax Street, Bristol BS1 3BN **T** 0117-314 7400
W www.whodoyouthinkyouaremagazine.com
Editor, Sarah Williams

HEALTH AND FITNESS

MEN'S FITNESS
31–32 Alfred Place, London WC1E 7DP **T** 020-3890 3890
W www.coachmag.co.uk
Editor, Isaac Williams

RUNNER'S WORLD
33 Broadwick Street, London W1F 9EP **T** 020-7339 4409
W www.runnersworld.co.uk
Editor, Andy Dixon

WW MAGAZINE
The River Group, 1 Neal Street, London WC2H 9QL
T 020-7306 0304 **W** www.weightwatchers.co.uk
Editor, vacant

WOMEN'S HEALTH
House of Hearst, 30 Panton Street, London SW1Y 4AJ
T 0844-322 1773 **W** www.womenshealthmag.com/uk
Editor, Claire Sanderson

HOBBIES AND GAMES

AIRFIX MODEL WORLD
Key Publishing Ltd, PO Box 100, Stamford PE9 1XQ
T 01780-755131 **W** www.airfixmodelworld.com
Editor, Stuart Fone

ANGLING TIMES
Bauer Media Group, Media House, Lynchwood, Peterborough PE2
6EA **T** 01733-395097 **W** www.anglingtimes.co.uk
Editor-in-Chief, Steve Fitzpatrick

BRITISH RAILWAY MODELLING
Warners Group Publications, The Maltings, West Street, Bourne,
Lincs PE10 9PH **T** 01778-391000 **W** www.world-of-railways.co.uk/
brm
Editor, Steve Cole

BRITISH CHESS MAGAZINE
Albany House, 14 Shute End, Wokingham RG40 1BJ
T 01252-514372 **W** www.britishchessmagazine.co.uk
Editors, Milan Dinic; Shaun Taulbut

COIN NEWS
Token Publishing Ltd, 40 Southernhay East, Exeter, Devon EX1 1PE
T 01404-46972 **W** www.tokenpublishing.com
Editor, John Russell

HORNBY
Key Publishing Ltd, PO Box 100, Stamford PE9 1XQ
T 01780-755131 **W** www.hornbymagazine.com
Editor, Mike Wild

HOME AND GARDEN

BBC GARDENERS' WORLD
Immediate Media, 5th Floor, Vineyard House, 44 Brook Green,
London W6 7BT **T** 020-7150 5700 **W** www.gardenersworld.com
Editor, Lucy Hall

GOOD HOUSEKEEPING
House of Hearst, 30 Panton Street, London SW1Y 4AJ
T 020-7439 5000 **W** www.goodhousekeeping.co.uk
Editor-in-chief, Gaby Huddart

HOUSE & GARDEN
Condé Nast Publications, Vogue House, Hanover Square, London
W1S 1JU **T** 020-7499 9080 **W** www.houseandgarden.co.uk
Editor, Hatta Byng

LIVING ETC
TI Media, 161 Marsh Wall, London E14 9SJ **T** 020-3148 5000
W www.housetohome.co.uk/livingetc
Editor, Sarah Spiteri

MEN'S LIFESTYLE

ESQUIRE
House of Hearst, 30 Panton Street, London SW1Y 4AJ
T 020-7439 5000 **W** www.esquire.co.uk
Editor, Alex Bilmes

GAY TIMES
Millivres Prowler Group, Spectrum House, 32-34 Gordon House
Road, London NW5 1LP **T** 020-7424 7400 **W** www.gaytimes.co.uk
Editor, Tag Warner

GQ
Vogue House, 1 Hanover Square, London W1S 1JU
T 020-7499 9080 **W** www.gq-magazine.co.uk
Editor, Dylan Jones

MOTORING

BIKE
Bauer Media, Media House, Lynchwood, Peterborough PE2 6EA
T 01733-468000 **W** www.bikemagazine.co.uk
Editor, Hugo Wilson

CARAVAN
Warners Group Publications, The Maltings, West Street, Bourne, Lincs PE10 9PH **T** 01778-392450 **W** www.outandaboutlive.co.uk
Editor, Daniel Attwood

F1 RACING
Autosport Media, 1 Eton Street, Richmond TW9 1AG
T 020-3405 8100 **W** www.f1racing.co.uk
Editor, Ben Anderson

PRACTICAL CARAVAN
Haymarket Ltd, Bridge House, 69 London Road, Twickenham TW1 3SP **T** 020-8267 5712 **W** www.practicalcaravan.com
Editor, Sarah Wakely

TOP GEAR
Energy Centre, Media Centre, 201 Wood Lane, London W12 7TQ
T 020-7150 5558 **W** www.topgear.com
Editor, Charlie Turner

PHOTOGRAPHY

AMATEUR PHOTOGRAPHER
Pinehurst 2, Pinehurst Road, Farnborough, Hants. GU14 7BF
T 01252-555213 **W** www.amateurphotographer.co.uk
Group Editor, Nigel Atherton

DIGITAL CAMERA
Future Publishing Ltd Quay House, The Ambury, Bath BA1 1UA
W www.digitalcameraworld.com
Editor, James Artaius

DIGITAL PHOTOGRAPHER
Future Publishing Ltd, Quay House, The Ambury, Bath BA1 1UA
T 01202-586200 **W** www.dphotographer.co.uk
Editor-in-Chief, Amy Squibb

POPULAR MUSIC

CLASH
Studio 86, Hackney Downs Studios, 17 Amhurst Terrace, London E8 2BT **T** 020-7628 2312 **W** www.clashmusic.com
Editor-in-Chief, Simon Harper

CLASSIC ROCK
Future Publishing Ltd, Quay House, The Ambury, Bath BA1 1UA
W www.loudersound.com/classic-rock
Editor, Siân Llewellyn

DIY
2nd Floor, Unit 23, Tileyard Studios, Tileyard Road, London N7 9AH
W www.diymag.com
Editor, Sarah Jamieson

GUITARIST
Future Publishing Ltd, Beauford Court, 30 Monmouth Street, Bath BA1 2BW **T** 01225-442244 **W** www.musicradar.com/guitarist
Editor, Jamie Dickson

MOJO
Endeavour House, 189 Shaftesbury Avenue, London WC2H 8JG
T 020-7208 3443 **W** www.mojo4music.com
Editor, John Mulvey

Q
Endeavour House, 189 Shaftesbury Avenue, London WC2H 8JG
T 020-7295 5000 **W** www.qthemusic.com
Editor-in-Chief, John Mulvey

UNCUT
TI Media, 161 Marsh Wall, London E14 9SJ **T** 020-3148 5000
W www.uncut.co.uk
Editor, Michael Bonnier

SCIENCE AND NATURE

BBC WILDLIFE
Immediate Media, Eagle House, Colston Avenue, Bristol BS1 4ST
T 0117-927 9009 **W** www.discoverwildlife.com
Editor, Paul McGuinness

BIRD WATCHING
Bauer Media, Media House, Lynch Wood, Peterborough PE2 6EA
T 01733-468000 **W** www.birdwatching.co.uk
Editor, Matthew Merritt

COUNTRYFILE
9th Floor, Tower House, Fairfax Street, Bristol BS1 3BN
T 0117-927 9009 **W** www.countryfile.com
Editor, Fergus Collins

BBC SCIENCE FOCUS
Immediate Media, Eagle House, Colston Avenue, Bristol BS1 4ST
T 0117-927 9009 **W** www.sciencefocus.com
Editor, Daniel Bennett

HOW IT WORKS
Future Publishing Limited Quay House, The Ambury, Bath BA1 1UA
W www.howitworksdaily.com
Editor-in-Chief, Dave Harfield

NEW SCIENTIST
110 High Holborn, London WC1V 6EU **T** 020-7611 1206
W www.newscientist.com
Editor-in-Chief, Emily Wilson

BBC SKY AT NIGHT
Immediate Media, Eagle House, Colston Avenue, Bristol BS1 4ST **T** 0117-927 9009 **W** www.skyatnightmagazine.com
Editor, Chris Bramley

SPORT

BOXING MONTHLY
Kelsey Media, Cudham Tithe Barn, Berry's Hill, Cudham, Kent TN16 3AG **T** 020-8986 4141 **W** www.boxingmonthly.com
Editor, Graham Houston

THE CRICKETER
Court House, Cleaver Street, London SE11 4DZ **T** 020-3198 1359
W www.thecricketer.com
Editor, Simon Hughes

FOURFOURTWO
Future Publishing Ltd, Quay House, The Ambury, Bath BA1 1UA
T 0844-848 2852 **W** www.fourfourtwo.com
Editor, James Brown

GOLF MONTHLY
TI Media Ltd, Pinehurst 2, Pinehurst Road, Farnborough Business Park, Farnborough, Hants GU14 7BF **T** 01252-555197
W www.golf-monthly.co.uk
Editor, Michael Harris

HORSE & HOUND
TI Media Ltd, 161 Marsh Wall, London E14 9SJ **T** 01252-555029
W www.horseandhound.co.uk
Editor, Pippa Roome

MATCH
Kelsey Media, Cudham Tithe Barn, Berrys Hill, Cudham, Kent, TN16 3AG **T** 01959-541444 **W** www.matchfootball.co.uk
Editor, Stephen Fishlock

RUGBY WORLD
TI Media Ltd, 2nd Floor, Pinehurst 2, Pinehurst Road, Farnborough Business Park, Farnborough, Hants GU14 7BF **T** 01252-555271
W www.rugbyworld.com
Editor, Sarah Mockford

TENNISHEAD
Advantage Publishing (UK) Ltd, Trinity House, Sculpins Lane, Braintree, Essex CM7 4AY **T** 020-8408 7148
W www.tennishead.net
Consultant Editor, Paul Newman

WISDEN CRICKET MONTHLY
PO Box 33, 4th Floor, Kia Oval, Kennington, London, England, SE11 5SS **T** 01293 312094 **W** www.wisden.com
Editor, Phil Walker

WORLD SOCCER
TI Media Ltd, 2nd Floor, Pinehurst 2, Pinehurst Road, Farnborough Business Park, Farnborough, Hants GU14 7BF **T** 020-3148 4817
W www.worldsoccer.com
Editor, Gavin Hamilton

TRAVEL

CONDÉ NAST TRAVELLER
Vogue House, Hanover Square, London W1S 1JU **T** 0844-848 2851
W www.cntraveller.com
Editor, Melinda Stevens

FRANCE
Archant House, 3 Oriel Road, Cheltenham GL50 1BB
T 01242-216050 **W** www.completefrance.com
Editor, Karen Tait

LONELY PLANET
Immediate Media, Eagle House, Colston Avenue, Bristol BS1 4ST
T 0207-150 5000 **W** www.lonelyplanet.com
Editor, Peter Grunert

NATIONAL GEOGRAPHIC TRAVELLER
Unit 310 Highgate Studios, 53–79 Highgate Road, London NW5 1TL
T 020-7253 9906 **W** www.natgeotraveller.co.uk
Editor, Pat Riddell

TRADE AND PROFESSIONAL BODIES

The following is a list of employers' and trade associations and other professional bodies in the UK. It does not represent a comprehensive list. For further professional bodies *see* Professional Education.

ASSOCIATIONS

ABTA – THE TRAVEL ASSOCIATION 30 Park Street, London SE1 9EQ **W** www.abta.com
Chief Executive, Mark Tanzer

ADVERTISING ASSOCIATION Lynton House 7-12, Tavistock Square, London WC1H 9LT **T** 020-7340 1100
E aa@adassoc.org.uk **W** www.adassoc.org.uk
Chief Executive, Stephen Woodford

AEROSPACE DEFENCE SECURITY Salamanca Square, 9 Albert Embankment, London SE1 7SP **T** 020-7091 4500
W www.adsgroup.org.uk
Chief Executive, Paul Everitt

AGRICULTURAL ENGINEERS ASSOCIATION Samuelson House, 62 Forder Way, Peterborough PE7 8JB **T** 0845-644 8748
E info@aea.uk.com **W** www.aea.uk.com
Chief Executive, Ruth Bailey

ASBESTOS REMOVAL CONTRACTORS ASSOCIATION Unit 1, Stretton Business Park 2, Brunel Drive, Stretton DE13 0BY
T 01283-566467 **E** info@arca.org.uk **W** www.arca.org.uk
Chief Executive, Steve Sadley

ASSOCIATION FOR CONSULTANCY AND ENGINEERING Alliance House, 12 Caxton Street, London SW1H 0QL **T** 020-7222 6557 **E** consult@acenet.co.uk
W www.acenet.co.uk
Chief Executive, Hannah Vickers

ASSOCIATION OF ACCOUNTING TECHNICIANS 140 Aldersgate Street, London EC1A 4HY **T** 020-3735 2468
E customersupport@aat.org.uk **W** www.aat.org.uk
Chief Executive, Mark Farrar

ASSOCIATION OF ANAESTHETISTS OF GREAT BRITAIN AND IRELAND 21 Portland Place, London W1B 1PY **T** 020-7631 1650 **E** info@aagbi.org **W** www.aagbi.org
Executive Director, Karin Pappenheim

ASSOCIATION OF BRITISH INSURERS One America Square, London EC3N 2LB **T** 020-7600 3333 **E** info@abi.org.uk
W www.abi.org.uk
Director-General, Huw Evans

ASSOCIATION OF BUSINESS RECOVERY PROFESSIONALS 8th Floor, 120 Aldersgate Street, London EC1A 4JQ **T** 020-7566 4200 **E** association@r3.org.uk
W www.r3.org.uk
Chief Executive, Liz Bingham

ASSOCIATION OF CONVENIENCE STORES LTD Federation House, 17 Farnborough Street, Farnborough GU14 8AG **T** 01252-515001 **E** acs@acs.org.uk
W www.acs.org.uk
Chief Executive, James Lowman

ASSOCIATION OF CORPORATE TREASURERS 69 Leadenhall Street, London EC3A 2BG **T** 020-7847 2540
W www.treasurers.org
Chief Executive, Caroline Stockmann

ASSOCIATION OF DRAINAGE AUTHORITIES Rural Innovation Centre, Avenue H, Stoneleigh Park CV8 2LG
T 024-7699 2889 **E** admin@ada.org.uk **W** www.ada.org.uk
Chief Executive, Innes Thomson, CENG

BOOKSELLERS ASSOCIATION 6 Bell Yard, London WC2A 2JR **T** 020-7421 4640 **E** mail@booksellers.org.uk
W www.booksellers.org.uk
Chief Executive, Meryl Halls

BRITISH ANTIQUE DEALERS' ASSOCIATION 21 John Street, London WC1N 2BF **T** 020-7589 4128 **E** info@bada.org
W www.bada.org
President, Vacant

BRITISH ASSOCIATION OF SOCIAL WORKERS 37 Waterloo Street, Birmingham B2 5PP **T** 0121-622 3911
W www.basw.co.uk
Chief Executive, Dr Roth Allen

BRITISH BEER & PUB ASSOCIATION Ground Floor, 61 Queen Street, London EC4R 1EB **T** 020-7627 9191
E contact@beerandpub.com **W** www.beerandpub.com
Chief Executive, Emma McClarkin

BRITISH CHAMBERS OF COMMERCE 65 Petty France, London SW1H 9EU **T** 020-7654 5800
W www.britishchambers.org.uk
Director-General, Adam Marshall

BRITISH ELECTROTECHNICAL AND ALLIED MANUFACTURERS ASSOCIATION (BEAMA) Rotherwick House, 3 Thomas More Street, London E1W 1YZ
T 020-7793 3000 **E** info@beama.org.uk **W** www.beama.org.uk
Chief Executive, Dr Howard Porter

BRITISH HOROLOGICAL INSTITUTE Upton Hall, Upton, Newark NG23 5TE **T** 01636-813795 **E** info@bhi.co.uk
W www.bhi.co.uk
President, Rt. Hon. Viscount Middleton, FBHI

BRITISH INSTITUTE OF PROFESSIONAL PHOTOGRAPHY The Artistry House, 16 Winckley Square, Preston PR1 3JJ **T** 01772-367968 **E** admin@bipp.com
W www.bipp.com
Chief Executive, Martin Baynes

BRITISH INSURANCE BROKERS' ASSOCIATION 8th Floor, John Stow House, 18 Bevis Marks, London EC3A 7JB
T 0344-770 0266 **E** enquiries@biba.org.uk **W** www.biba.org.uk
Chief Executive, Steve White

BRITISH MARINE FEDERATION Marine House, Thorpe Lea Road, Egham TW20 8BF **T** 01784-473377
E info@britishmarine.co.uk **W** www.britishmarine.co.uk
Chief Executive, Lesley Robinson

BRITISH MEDICAL ASSOCIATION BMA House, Tavistock Square, London WC1H 9JP **T** 020-7387 4499
W www.bma.org.uk
Chief Executive, Tom Grinyer

BRITISH OFFICE SUPPLIES AND SERVICES (BOSS) FEDERATION c/o British Printing Industries Federation, 2 Villiers Court, Copse Drive CV5 9RN **T** 01676-526030
W www.bossfederation.co.uk
Chief Executive, Amy Hutchinson

BPI (BRITISH PHONOGRAPHIC INDUSTRY) Riverside Building, County Hall, Westminster Bridge Road, London SE1 7JA
T 020-7803 1300 **E** general@bpi.co.uk **W** www.bpi.co.uk
Chief Executive, Geoff Taylor

BRITISH PLASTICS FEDERATION 6 Bath Place, London EC2A 3JE **T** 020-7457 5000 **E** reception@bpf.co.uk
W www.bpf.co.uk
Director-General, Philip Law

BRITISH PORTS ASSOCIATION 1st Floor, 30 Park Street, London SE1 9EQ T 020-7260 1780 E info@britishports.org.uk W www.britishports.org.uk
Chief Executive, Richard Ballantyne

BRITISH PRINTING INDUSTRIES FEDERATION Unit 2, Villiers Court, Meriden Business Park CV5 9RN T 01676-526030 W www.britishprint.com
Chief Executive, Charles Jarrold

BRITISH PROPERTY FEDERATION 5th Floor, St Albans House, 57–59 Haymarket, London SW1Y 4QX T 020-7802 0110 E info@bpf.org.uk W www.bpf.org.uk
Chief Executive, Melanie Leech

BRITISH RETAIL CONSORTIUM 100 Avebury Blvd., Milton Keynes MK9 1FH T 020-7854 8900 E info@brc.org.uk W www.brc.org.uk
Director-General, Helen Dickinson, OBE

BRITISH TYRE MANUFACTURERS' ASSOCIATION 5 Berewyk Hall Court, White Colne, Colchester CO6 2QB T 01787-226995 W www.btmauk.com
Chief Executive, Graham Willson

BUILDING SOCIETIES ASSOCIATION 6th Floor, York House, London WC2B 6UJ T 020-7520 5900 W www.bsa.org.uk
Chief Executive, Robin Fieth

CHARTERED ASSOCIATION OF BUILDING ENGINEERS Lutyens House, Billing Brook Road, Northampton NN3 8NW T 01604-404121 W www.cbuilde.com
Chief Executive, Dr Gavin Dunn

CHARTERED INSTITUTE FOR ARCHAEOLOGISTS Power Steele Building, Wessex Hall, Whiteknights Road, Reading RG6 6DE T 0118-966 2841 E admin@archaeologists.net W www.archaeologists.net
Chief Executive, Peter Hinton

CHARTERED INSTITUTE OF ENVIRONMENTAL HEALTH Chadwick Court, 15 Hatfields, London SE1 8DJ T 020-7827 5800 E info@cieh.org W www.cieh.org
Chief Executive, Dawn Welham

CHARTERED INSTITUTE OF JOURNALISTS 2 Dock Offices, Surrey Quays Road, London SE16 2XU T 020-7252 1187 E memberservices@cioj.co.uk W www.cioj.co.uk
General Secretary, Dominic Cooper

CHARTERED INSTITUTE OF PURCHASING AND SUPPLY Easton House, Church Street, Stamford PE9 3NZ T 08458-801188 W www.cips.org
Chief Executive, Malcolm Harrison

CHARTERED INSTITUTE OF TAXATION 30 Monck Street, London SW1P 2AP T 020-7340 0550 W www.tax.org.uk
Chief Executive, Helen Whiteman

CHARTERED INSURANCE INSTITUTE 42–48 High Road, London E18 2JP T 020-8989 8464 E customer.serv@cii.co.uk W www.cii.co.uk
Chief Executive, Sian Fisher

CHARTERED MANAGEMENT INSTITUTE Management House, Cottingham Road, Corby NN17 1TT T 01536-207360 E cmi@managers.org.uk W www.managers.org.uk
Chief Executive, Anne Francke

CHARTERED QUALITY INSTITUTE 2nd Floor North, Chancery Exchange, London EC4A 1AB T 020-7245 6722 E membership@quality.org W www.quality.org
Chief Executive, Vincent Desmond

CHARTERED TRADING STANDARDS INSTITUTE 1 Sylvan Court, Sylvan Way, Basildon SS15 6TH T 01268-582200 E institute@tsi.org.uk W www.tradingstandards.uk
Chief Executive, Leon Livermore

CHEMICAL INDUSTRIES ASSOCIATION Kings Buildings, Smith Square, London SW1P 3JJ T 020-7834 3399 E enquiries@cia.org.uk W www.cia.org.uk
Chief Executive, Steve Elliott

CONFEDERATION OF PAPER INDUSTRIES 1 Rivenhall Road, Swindon SN5 7BD T 01793-889600 E cpi@paper.org.uk W www.paper.org.uk
Director-General, Andrew Large

CONFEDERATION OF PASSENGER TRANSPORT UK Fifth Floor Offices (South), Chancery House, London WC2A 1QS T 020-7240 3131 E admin@cpt-uk.org W www.cpt-uk.org
Chief Executive, Graham Vidler

CONSTRUCTION PRODUCTS ASSOCIATION The Building Centre, 26 Store Street, London WC1E 7BT T 020-7323 3770 W www.constructionproducts.org.uk
Chief Executive, Peter Caplehorn

DAIRY UK 6th Floor, London WC1V 7EP T 020-7405 1484 E info@dairyuk.org W www.dairyuk.org
Chief Executive, Dr Judith Bryans

ENERGY UK 26 Finsbury Square, London EC2A 1DS T 020-7930 9390 W www.energy-uk.org.uk
Chief Executive, Emma Pinchbeck

FEDERATION OF BAKERS 6th Floor, 10 Bloomsbury Way, London WC1A 2SL T 020-7420 7190 E info@fob.uk.com W www.fob.uk.com
Director, Gordon Polson

FEDERATION OF MASTER BUILDERS David Croft House, 25 Ely Place, London EC1N 6TD T 0330-333 7777 W www.fmb.org.uk
Chief Executive, Brian Berry

FSPA (FEDERATION OF SPORTS AND PLAY ASSOCIATIONS) Office 8, Rural Innovation Centre, Unit 169– Avenue H, Kenilworth CV8 2LG T 024-7641 4999 E info@sportsandplay.com W www.sportsandplay.com
Chair, Jack Osborne

FINANCE AND LEASING ASSOCIATION 2nd Floor, Imperial House, 8 Kean Street, London WC2B 4AS T 020-7836 6511 E info@fla.org.uk W www.fla.org.uk
Director-General, Stephen Haddrill

FOOD AND DRINK FEDERATION 6th Floor, London WC1A 2SL T 020-7836 2460 W www.fdf.org.uk
Chief Executive, Ian Wright

FREIGHT TRANSPORT ASSOCIATION LTD Hermes House, St John's Road, Tunbridge Wells TN4 9UZ T 01892-52617 E enquiry@logistics.org.uk W www.logistics.org.uk
President, David Wells

GLASGOW CHAMBER OF COMMERCE 30 George Square, Glasgow G2 1EQ T 0141-204 2121 E chamber@glasgowchamberofcommerce.com W www.glasgowchamberofcommerce.com
Chief Executive, Stuart Patrick

INSTITUTE OF BREWING AND DISTILLING 44A Curlew Street, London SE1 2ND T 020-7499 8144 E customer.support@ibd.org.uk W www.ibd.org.uk
Chief Executive, Dr Jerry Avis

INSTITUTE OF BRITISH ORGAN BUILDING 13 Ryefields, Bury St Edmunds IP31 3TD T 01359-233433 W www.ibo.co.uk
President, Andrew Moyes

INSTITUTE OF CHARTERED FORESTERS 59 George Street, Edinburgh EH2 2JG E icf@charteredforesters.org W www.charteredforesters.org
Executive Director, Shireen Chambers

INSTITUTE OF CHARTERED SECRETARIES AND
ADMINISTRATORS Saffron House, 6–10 Kirby Street,
London EC1N 8TS T 020-7580 4741 E enquiries@icsa.org.uk
W www.icsa.org.uk
Chief Executive, Sara Drake

INSTITUTE OF CHARTERED SHIPBROKERS
30 Park Street, London SE1 9EQ T 020-7357 9722
E enquiries@ics.org.uk W www.ics.org.uk
Interim Director, Robert Hill, FICS

INSTITUTE OF DIRECTORS 116 Pall Mall, London
SW1Y 5ED T 020-3855 4738 E businessinfo@iod.com
W www.iod.com
Director-General, Johnathan Geldart

INSTITUTE OF EXPORT AND INTERNATIONAL
TRADE Export House, Minerva Business Park, Peterborough
PE2 6FT T 01733-404400 W www.export.org.uk
Chair, Terry Scuoler, CBE

INSTITUTE OF FINANCIAL ACCOUNTANTS
CS111, Clerkenwell Workshops, 27–31 Clerkenwell Close,
London EC1R 0AT T 020-3567 5999 E mail@ifa.org.uk
W www.ifa.org.uk
Chief Executive, John Edwards

INSTITUTE OF HEALTHCARE MANAGEMENT
33 Cavendish Square, London W1G 0PW T 020-7182 4066
E contact@ihm.org.uk W www.ihm.org.uk
Chief Executive, Jon Wilks

INSTITUTE OF HOSPITALITY 14 Palmerston Road, Surrey
SM1 4QL T 020-8661 4900 E info@instituteofhospitality.org
W www.instituteofhospitality.org
Chief Executive, Peter Ducker

INSTITUTE OF INTERNAL COMMUNICATION Scorpio
House, Rockingham Drive, MK14 6LY T 01908-232168
E enquiries@ioic.org.uk W www.ioic.org.uk
Chief Executive, Jennifer Sproul

INSTITUTE OF MANAGEMENT SERVICES Lichfield
Business Village, Friary Way, Lichfield WS13 6AA
T 01543-308605 E admin@ims-productivity.com
W www.ims-productivity.com
Chairman, Dr Andrew Muir

INSTITUTE OF QUARRYING McPherson House, 8A Regan
Way, Chilwell NG9 6RZ T 0115-972 9995 E mail@quarrying.org
W www.quarrying.org
Chief Executive, James Thorne

INSTITUTE OF THE MOTOR INDUSTRY Fanshaws,
Hertford SG13 8PQ T 01992-519025 E comms@theimi.org.uk
W www.theimi.org.uk
Chief Executive, Steve Nash

INSTITUTION OF OCCUPATIONAL SAFETY AND
HEALTH The Grange, Highfield Drive, Wigston LE18 1NN
T 0116-257 3100 E reception@iosh.co.uk W www.iosh.co.uk
Chief Executive, James Quinn

IP FEDERATION 60 Gray's Inn Road, London WC1X 8AQ
T 020-7242 3923 E admin@ipfederation.com
W www.ipfederation.com
President, Scott Roberts

LEATHER UK Leather Trade House, Kings Park Road,
Northampton NN3 6JD T 01604-679999 E info@leatheruk.org
W www.leatheruk.org
Director, Dr Kerry Senior

MAGISTRATES' ASSOCIATION 10A Flagstaff House,
St George Wharf, London SW8 2LE T 020-7387 2353
E information@magistrates-association.org.uk
W www.magistrates-association.org.uk
Chief Executive, Jon Collins

MAKE UK, THE MANUFACTURERS' ORGANISATION
Broadway House, Tothill Street, London SW1H 9NQ
T 0808-168 5874 E enquiries@makeuk.org W www.makeuk.org
Chief Executive, Stephen Phipson, CBE

MANAGEMENT CONSULTANCIES ASSOCIATION
5th Floor, 36–38 Cornhill, London EC3V 3NG T 020-7645 7950
E info@mca.org.uk W www.mca.org.uk
Chief Executive, Tamzen Isacsson

MASTER LOCKSMITHS ASSOCIATION 1 Prospect Park,
Rugby CV21 1TF T 01327-262255 E enquiries@locksmiths.co.uk
W www.locksmiths.co.uk
Director, Maria Ging

NATIONAL ASSOCIATION OF BRITISH MARKET
AUTHORITIES The Guildhall, Shropshire SY1 1PZ
T 01691-680713 E nabma@nabma.com W www.nabma.com
Chief Executive, David Preston

NATIONAL ASSOCIATION OF ESTATE AGENTS Arbon
House, 6 Tournament Court, Warwick CV34 6LG
T 01926-496800 W www.naea.co.uk
President, Kirsty Finney

NATIONAL FARMERS' UNION (NFU) Agriculture House,
Stoneleigh Park, Stoneleigh CV8 2LZ T 024-7685 8500
W www.nfuonline.com
Director-General, Terry Jones

NATIONAL FEDERATION OF RETAIL NEWSAGENTS
Bede House, Belmont Business Park, Durham DH1 1TW
T 020-7017 8880 E connect@nrfn.org.uk W www.nfrn.org.uk
Chief Executive, Paul Baxter

NATIONAL LANDLORDS ASSOCIATION 212 Washway
Road, Manchester M33 6RN T 0300-121 6400
W www.nrla.org.uk
Chief Executive, Ben Beadle

NATIONAL MARKET TRADERS FEDERATION Hampton
House, Hawshaw Lane, Barnsley S74 0HA T 01226-749021
E genoffice@nmtf.co.uk W www.nmtf.co.uk
Chief Executive, John Dyson

NATIONAL PHARMACY ASSOCIATION Mallinson House,
38–42 St Peter's Street, Herts AL1 3NP T 01727-858687
E npa@npa.co.uk W www.npa.co.uk
Chief Executive, Mark Lyonette

NEWS MEDIA ASSOCIATION 16-18 New Bridge Road,
London ECV4 6AG T 020-3848 9620 E nma@newsmediauk.org
W www.newsmediauk.org
Chief Executive, David Newell

OIL AND GAS UK *1st Floor*, Paternoster House, 65 St. Paul
Churchyard, London EC4M 8AB T 020-7802 2400
E info@oilandgasuk.co.uk W www.oilandgasuk.co.uk
Chief Executive, Deirdre Michie

PROPERTY CARE ASSOCIATION 11 Ramsay Court,
Kingfisher Way, Huntingdon PE29 6FY T 0148-400 000
E pca@property-care.org W www.property-care.org
Chief Executive, Stephen Hodgson

PUBLISHERS ASSOCIATION 50 Southwark Street, London
SE1 1UN T 020-7378 0504 E mail@publishers.org.uk
W www.publishers.org.uk
Chief Executive, Stephen Lotinga

RADIOCENTRE 6th Floor, 55 New Oxford Street, London
WC1A 1BS T 020-7010 0600 E info@radiocentre.org
W www.radiocentre.org
Chief Executive, Siobhan Kenny

ROAD HAULAGE ASSOCIATION LTD Roadway House,
Bretton Way, Peterborough PE3 8DD T 01733-261131
W www.rha.uk.net
Chief Executive, Richard Burnett

ROYAL ASSOCIATION OF BRITISH DAIRY FARMERS
Dairy House, Unit 31, Abbey Park, Kenilworth CV8 2LY
T 024-7663 9317 E office@rabdf.co.uk W www.rabdf.co.uk
Managing Director, Matthew Knight

ROYAL FACULTY OF PROCURATORS IN GLASGOW
12 Nelson Mandela Place, Glasgow G2 1BT T 0141-332 3593
E library@rfpg.org W www.rfpg.org
Chief Executive, John McKenzie

SHELLFISH ASSOCIATION OF GREAT BRITAIN
Fishmongers' Hall, London Bridge, London EC4R 9EL
T 020-7283 8305 E projects@shellfish.org.uk
W www.shellfish.org.uk
Director, David Jarrad

SOCIETY OF LOCAL AUTHORITY CHIEF EXECUTIVES
AND SENIOR MANAGERS (SOLACE) Off Southgate,
Pontefract, West Yorkshire WF8 1NT T 0207-233 0081
E contact@solace.org.uk W www.solace.org.uk
Directors, Graeme McDonald; Terry McDougall

SOCIETY OF MOTOR MANUFACTURERS AND
TRADERS LTD 71 Great Peter Street, London SW1P 2BN
T 020-7235 7000 W www.smmt.co.uk
Chief Executive, Mike Hawes

TIMBER TRADE FEDERATION The Building Centre, 26
Store Street, London WC1E 7BT T 020-3205 0067 E ttf@ttf.co.uk
W www.ttf.co.uk
Managing Director, David Hopkins

UK CHAMBER OF SHIPPING 30 Park Street, London
SE1 9EQ T 020-7417 2800 E query@ukchamberofshipping.com
W www.ukchamberofshipping.com
Chief Executive, Bob Sanguinetti

UK FASHION AND TEXTILE ASSOCIATION 3 Queen
Square, London WC1N 3AR T 020-7843 9460 E info@ukft.org
W www.ukft.org
Chief Executive, Adam Mansell

UK FINANCE 5th Floor, 1 Angel Court, London EC2R 7HJ
T 020-7706 3333 W www.ukfinance.org.uk
COO, Alastair Gilmartin Smith

UKHOSPITALITY 10 Bloomsbury Way, London WC1A 2SL
T 020-7404 7744 W www.ukhospitality.org.uk
Chairman, Steve Richards

UK PETROLEUM INDUSTRY ASSOCIATION LTD 37–
39 High Holborn, London WC1V 6AA T 020-7269 7600
E info@ukpia.com W www.ukpia.org.uk
Director-General, Stephen Marcos Jones

ULSTER FARMERS' UNION 475 Antrim Road, Belfast
BT15 3DA T 028-9037 0222 E info@ufuhq.com
W www.ufuni.org
Chief Executive, Wesley Aston

THE WINE AND SPIRIT TRADE ASSOCIATION
International Wine and Spirit Centre, 39–45 Bermondsey Street,
London SE1 3XF T 020-7089 3877 E info@wsta.co.uk
W www.wsta.co.uk
Chief Executive, Miles Beale

CBI

Cannon Place, 78 Cannon Street, London EC4N 6HN
T 020-7379 7400 E enquiries@cbi.org.uk W www.cbi.org.uk

The CBI was founded in 1965 and is an independent non-party political body financed by industry and commerce. It works with the UK government, international legislators and policymakers to help UK businesses compete effectively. It is the recognised spokesman for the business viewpoint and is consulted as such by the government.

The CBI speaks for some 190,000 businesses that together employ approximately one-third of the private sector workforce. Member companies, which decide all policy positions, include FTSE 100 index listed companies, small- and medium-size firms, micro businesses, private and family owned businesses, start-ups and trade associations.

The CBI board is chaired by the president and meets four times a year. It is assisted by 14 expert standing committees which advise on the main aspects of policy. There are nine regional councils for England and three national councils for, Wales, Scotland and Northern Ireland. There are also offices in Beijing, Brussels, New Delhi and Washington DC.

President, Lord Karan Bilimoria, CBEDL
Director-General, Tony Danker

WALES, 2 Caspian Point, Caspian Way, Cardiff Bay, Cardiff
CF10 4DQ T 029-2097 7600 E wales.mail@cbi.org.uk
Regional Director, Ian Price

SCOTLAND, 160 West George Street, Glasgow G2 2HQ
T 0141-222 2184 E scotland@cbi.org.uk
Regional Director, Tracy Black

NORTHERN IRELAND, Hamilton House, 3 Joy Street, Belfast
BT2 8LE T 028-9010 1100 E ni.mail@cbi.org.uk
Regional Director, Angela McGowan

TRADE UNIONS

A trade union is an organisation of workers formed for the purpose of collective bargaining over pay and working conditions. Trade unions may also provide legal and financial advice, sickness benefits and education facilities to their members. Legally any employee has the right to join a trade union, but not all employers recognise all or any trade unions. Conversely an employee also has the right not to join a trade union, in particular since the practice of a 'closed shop' system, where all employees have to join the employer's preferred union, is no longer permitted.

THE CENTRAL ARBITRATION COMMITTEE

Fleetbank House, 2–6 Salisbury Square, London EC4Y 8JX
T 0330-109 3610 E enquiries@cac.gov.uk
W www.gov.uk/government/organisations/
central-arbitration-committee

The Central Arbitration Committee's main role is concerned with requests for trade union recognition and de-recognition under the statutory procedures of Schedule A1 of the Employment Rights Act 1999. It also determines disclosure of information complaints under the Trade Union and Labour Relations (Consolidation) Act 1992, considers applications and complaints under the Information and Consultation Regulations 2004, and performs a similar role in relation to European works councils, companies, cooperative societies and cross-border mergers.

Chair, Sir Stephen Redmond
Acting Chief Executive, Maverlie Tavares

TRADES UNION CONGRESS (TUC)

Congress House, 23–28 Great Russell Street, London WC1B 3LS
T 020-7636 4030 E info@tuc.org.uk
W www.tuc.org.uk

The Trades Union Congress (TUC), founded in 1868, is an independent association of trade unions. The TUC promotes the rights and welfare of those in work and helps the unemployed. The TUC brings Britain's unions together to draw up common polices; lobbies the government to implement policies that will benefit people at work; campaigns on economic and social issues; represents working people on public bodies and at the UN employment body – the International Labour Organisation; carries out research on employment-related issues; runs training and education programmes for union representatives; helps unions to develop new services for their members and negotiate with each other; and builds links with other trade union bodies worldwide.

The governing body of the TUC is the annual congress which sets policy. Between congresses, business is conducted by a 56-member general council, which meets every two months to oversee the TUC's work programme and sanction new policy initiatives. Each year, at its first post-congress meeting, the general council appoints an executive committee and the TUC president for that congress year. The executive committee meets monthly to implement and develop policy, manage TUC financial affairs and deal with any urgent business. The president chairs general council and executive meetings and is consulted by the General Secretary on all major issues.

President (2020–21), Gail Cartmail
General Secretary, Frances O'Grady

SCOTTISH TRADES UNION CONGRESS (STUC)

Red Tree Business Unit, 24 Stonelaw Road, Glasgow G73 3TW
T 0141-337 8100
E info@stuc.org.uk W www.stuc.org.uk

The congress was formed in 1897 and acts as a national centre for the trade union movement in Scotland. The STUC promotes the rights to welfare of those in work and helps the unemployed. It helps its member unions to promote membership in new areas and industries, and campaigns for rights at work for all employees, including part-time and temporary workers, whether union members or not. It also makes representations to government and employers. In 2016 the STUC had over 540,000 members from 37 affiliated unions and 20 trade union councils.

The annual congress in April elects a 36-member general council on the basis of six sections.

General Secretary, Roz Foyer

WALES TUC

Wales TUC was established in 1974 to ensure that the role of the TUC was effectively undertaken in Wales. Its structure reflects the four economic regions of Wales and matches the regional committee areas of the National Assembly of Wales. The regional committees oversee the implementation of Wales TUC policy and campaigns in the relevant regions, and liaise with local government, training organisations and regional economic development bodies. The Wales TUC seeks to reduce unemployment, increase the levels of skill and pay, and eliminate discrimination.

The governing body of Wales TUC is the conference, which meets annually in May and elects a general council (usually of around 50 people) that oversees the work of the TUC throughout the year.

There are 49 affiliated unions representing around 400,000 workers.

Acting General Secretary, Shavanah Taj

TUC-AFFILIATED UNIONS
As at December 2020

ACCORD Simmons House, 46 Old Bath Road, Reading
RG10 9QR T 0118-934 1808 E info@accordhq.org
W www.accord-myunion.org
General Secretary, Ged Nichols
Membership: 24,431

ADVANCE 2nd Floor, 16–17 High Street, Tring HP23 5AH
T 01442-891122 E info@advance-union.org
W www.advance-union.org
General Secretary, Linda Rolph
Membership: 6,848

AEGIS THE UNION 1–3 Lochside Crescent, Edinburgh
EH12 9SE T 0131-549 5665 E members@aegistheunion.co.uk
W www.aegistheunion.co.uk
General Secretary, Brian Linn
Membership: 4,570

AEP (ASSOCIATION OF EDUCATIONAL
PSYCHOLOGISTS) 4 The Riverside Centre, Durham DH1 5TA
T 0191-384 9512 E enquiries@aep.org.uk W www.aep.org.uk
General Secretary, Kate Fallon
Membership: 3,396

AFA (ASSOCIATION OF FLIGHT ATTENDANTS) 32 Wingford Road, London SW2 4DS **T** 0208-276 6723 **E** afalhr@unitedafa.org **W** www.afacwa.org
General Secretary, Michael Schwaabe
Membership: 500

ARTISTS' UNION ENGLAND Old Bakery, Carlow Street, London NW1 7LH **E** info@artistsunionengland.org.uk **W** www.artistsunionengland.org.uk
General Secretary, Vacant
Membership: 295

ASLEF (ASSOCIATED SOCIETY OF LOCOMOTIVE ENGINEERS AND FIREMEN) 77 St John Street, London EC1M 4NN **T** 020-7324 2400 **E** info@aslef.org.uk **W** www.aslef.org.uk
General Secretary, Michael Whelan
Membership: 22,078

BALPA (BRITISH AIRLINE PILOTS ASSOCIATION) BALPA House, 5 Heathrow Boulevard, 278 Bath Road, West Drayton UB7 0DQ **T** 020-8476 4000 **E** balpa@balpa.org **W** www.balpa.org
General Secretary, Brian Strutton
Membership: 8,012

BDA (BRITISH DIETETIC ASSOCIATION) 3rd Floor, Interchange Place, 151-165 Edmund Street, Birmingham B3 2TA **T** 0121-200 8021 **W** www.bda.uk.com
General Secretary, Annette Mansell-Green
Membership: 9,073

BFAWU (BAKERS, FOOD AND ALLIED WORKERS' UNION) Stanborough House, Great North Road, Welwyn Garden City AL8 7TA **T** 01707-260150 **E** info@bfawu.org **W** www.bfawu.org
General Secretary, Sarah Woolley
Membership: 17,595

BOS TU (BRITISH ORTHOPTIC SOCIETY TRADE UNION) 5th Floor, Charles House, 148/9 Great Charles Street Queensway, Birmingham B3 3HT **T** 0121-728 5633 **E** bios@orthoptics.org.uk **W** www.orthoptics.org.uk
Chair, Samantha Aitkenhead
Membership: 1,782

COMMUNITY 465C Caledonian Road, London N7 9GX **T** 0800 389 6332 **E** info@community-tu.org **W** www.community-tu.org
General Secretary, Roy Rickhuss
Membership: 31,866

COP (COLLEGE OF PODIATRY) Quartz House, London SE1 2EW **T** 020-7234 8639 **E** reception@scpod.org **W** www.cop.org.uk
General Secretary, Steve Jamieson
Membership: 9,512

CSP (CHARTERED SOCIETY OF PHYSIOTHERAPY) 14 Bedford Row, London WC1R 4ED **T** 020-7306 6666 **E** enquiries@csp.org.uk **W** www.csp.org.uk
Chief Executive, Claire Sullivan
Membership: 40,050

CWU (COMMUNICATION WORKERS UNION) 150 The Broadway, London SW19 1RX **T** 020-8971 7200 **E** info@cwu.org **W** www.cwu.org
General Secretary, Dave Ward
Membership: 191,437

EIS (EDUCATIONAL INSTITUTE OF SCOTLAND) 46 Moray Place, Edinburgh EH3 6BH **T** 0131-225 6244 **E** enquiries@eis.org.uk **W** www.eis.org.uk
General Secretary, Larry Flanagan
Membership: 54,702

EQUITY Guild House, Upper St Martin's Lane, London WC2H 9EG **T** 020-7379 6000 **E** info@equity.org.uk **W** www.equity.org.uk
General Secretary, Paul Flemming
Membership: 43,555

FBU (FIRE BRIGADES UNION) Bradley House, 68 Coombe Road, Kingston upon Thames KT2 7AE **T** 020-8541 1765 **E** office@fbu.org.uk **W** www.fbu.org.uk
General Secretary, Matthew Wrack
Membership: 33,042

FDA Centenary House, 93-95 Borough High Street, London SE1 1NL **T** 020-7401 5555 **E** info@fda.org.uk **W** www.fda.org.uk
General Secretary, Dave Penman
Membership: 16,744

GMB 22 Stephenson Way, London NW1 2HD **T** 020-7391 6700 **E** info@gmb.org.uk **W** www.gmb.org.uk
General Secretary, John Phillips
Membership: 614,494

HCSA (HOSPITAL CONSULTANTS' AND SPECIALISTS' ASSOCIATION) 1 Kingsclere Road, Basingstoke RG25 3JA **T** 01256-771777 **E** conspec@hcsa.com **W** www.hcsa.com
Chief Executive, Dr Paul Donaldson
Membership: 3,229

MU (MUSICIANS' UNION) 60–62 Clapham Road, London SW9 0JJ **T** 020-7582 5566 **E** info@theMU.org **W** www.musiciansunion.org.uk
General Secretary, Horace Trubridge
Membership: 30,421

NAHT (NATIONAL ASSOCIATION OF HEAD TEACHERS) 1 Heath Square, Haywards Heath RH16 1BL **T** 0300-303 0333 **E** info@naht.org.uk **W** www.naht.org.uk
General Secretary, Paul Whiteman
Membership: 28,600

NAPO (TRADE UNION AND PROFESSIONAL ASSOCIATION FOR FAMILY COURT AND PROBATION STAFF) 160 Falcon Road, London SW11 2NY **T** 020-7223 4887 **E** info@napo.org.uk **W** www.napo.org.uk
General Secretary, Ian Lawrence
Membership: 4,996

NARS (NATIONAL ASSOCIATION OF RACING STAFF) The Racing Centre, Fred Archer Way, Newmarket CB8 8NT **T** 01638-663411 **E** admin@naors.co.uk **W** www.naors.co.uk
Chief Executive, George McGrath
Membership: 2,137

NASUWT (NATIONAL ASSOCIATION OF SCHOOLMASTERS/ UNION OF WOMEN TEACHERS) Orion Centre, 5 Upper St Martins Lane, London WC2H 9EA **T** 020-7420 9670 **E** nasuwt@mail.nasuwt.org.uk **W** www.nasuwt.org.uk
General Secretary, Patrick Roach
Membership: 295,565

NATIONAL HOUSE BUILDING COUNCIL STAFF ASSOCIATION NHBC House, Davey Avenue, Milton Keynes MK5 8FP **E** lheritage@nhbc.co.uk **W** www.nhbc.co.uk
Acting Chair, Julia Georgiou
Membership: 686

NAUTILUS INTERNATIONAL 1–2 The Shrubberies, George Lane, London E18 1BD **T** 020-8989 6677 **E** enquiries@nautilusint.org **W** www.nautilusint.org
General Secretary, Mark Dickinson
Membership: 14,590

NEU (NATIONAL EDUCATION UNION) Hamilton House, Mabledon Place, London WC1H 9BD **T** 0345-811 8111 **W** www.neu.org.uk
General Secretaries, Dr Mary Bousted; Kevin Courtney
Membership: 450,150

NGSU (NATIONWIDE GROUP STAFF UNION) Middleton Farmhouse, 37 Main Road, Middleton Cheney OX17 2QT **T** 07793 596244 **E** ngsu@ngsu.org.uk **W** www.ngsu.co.uk
General Secretary, Tim Rose
Membership: 12,666

NSEAD (NATIONAL SOCIETY FOR EDUCATION IN ART AND DESIGN) 3 Mason's Wharf, Potley Lane, Corsham SN13 9FY T 01225-810134 E info@nsead.org W www.nsead.org
General Secretary, Michele Gregson
Membership: 1,240

NUJ (NATIONAL UNION OF JOURNALISTS) 72 Acton Street, London WC1X 9NB T 020-7843 3700 E info@nuj.org.uk
W www.nuj.org.uk
General Secretary, Michelle Stanistreet
Membership: 30,261

NUM (NATIONAL UNION OF MINEWORKERS) Miners' Offices, 2 Huddersfield Road, Barnsley S70 2LS T 01226-215555 E chris.kitchen@num.org.uk W www.num.org.uk
National Secretary, Chris Kitchen
Membership: 319

PCS (PUBLIC AND COMMERCIAL SERVICES UNION) 160 Falcon Road, London SW11 2LN T 020-7924 2727
W www.pcs.org.uk
General Secretary, Mark Serwotka
Membership: 177,750

PFA (PROFESSIONAL FOOTBALLERS' ASSOCIATION) 20 Oxford Court, Manchester M2 3WQ T 0161-236 0575 E info@thepfa.co.uk W www.thepfa.com
Chief Executive, Gordon Taylor
, OBE *Membership*: 2,168

POA (PROFESSIONAL TRADE UNION FOR PRISON, CORRECTIONAL AND SECURE PSYCHIATRIC WORKERS) Cronin House, 245 Church Street, London N9 9HW T 020-8803 0255 E general@poauk.org.uk
W www.poauk.org.uk
General Secretary, Steve Gillan
Membership: 30,011

PROSPECT New Prospect House, 8 Leake Street, London SE1 7NN T 020-7902 6600 E enquiries@prospect.org.uk
W www.prospect.org.uk
General Secretary, Mike Clancy
Membership: 143,770

RCM (ROYAL COLLEGE OF MIDWIVES) 15 Mansfield Street, London W1G 9NH T 030-0303 0444 W www.rcm.org.uk
General Secretary, Gill Walton
Membership: 35,428

RMT (NATIONAL UNION OF RAIL, MARITIME AND TRANSPORT WORKERS) Unity House, 39 Chalton Street, London NW1 1JD T 020-7387 4771 E info@rmt.org.uk
W www.rmt.org.uk
General Secretary, Mick Cash
Membership: 85,474

SOR (SOCIETY OF RADIOGRAPHERS) 207 Providence Square, Mill Street, London SE1 2EW T 020-7740 7200
W www.sor.org
Chief Executive, Richard Evans
Membership: 23,320

TSSA (TRANSPORT SALARIED STAFFS' ASSOCIATION) 2nd Floor, 17 Devonshire Square, London EC2M 4SQ
T 020-7387 2101 E enquiries@tssa.org.uk W www.tssa.org.uk
General Secretary, Manuel Cortes
Membership: 18,494

UCAC (UNDEB CENEDLAETHOL ATHRAWON CYMRU/ NATIONAL UNION OF THE TEACHERS OF WALES) Prif Swyddfa UCAC, Ffordd Penglais, Aberystwyth SY23 3EU T 01970-639950 E ucac@ucac.cymru
W www.ucac.cymru
General Secretary, Dilwyn Roberts-Young
Membership: 4,028

UCU (UNIVERSITY AND COLLEGE UNION) Carlow Street, London NW1 7LH T 020-7756 2500 W www.ucu.org.uk
General Secretary, Jo Grady
Membership: 108,515

UNISON 130 Euston Road, London NW1 2AY T 0800-085 7857
W www.unison.org.uk
General Secretary, Dave Prentis
Membership: 1,193,991

UNITE 128 Theobald's Road, London WC1X 8TN
T 020-7611 2500 W www.unitetheunion.org
General Secretary, Len McCluskey
Membership: 1,233,646

URTU (UNITED ROAD TRANSPORT UNION) Almond House, Oak Green, Cheadle, Hulme SK8 6QL T 0800-526 639 E info@urtu.com W www.urtu.com
General Secretary, Robert Monks
Membership: 9,400

USDAW (UNION OF SHOP, DISTRIBUTIVE AND ALLIED WORKERS) 188 Wilmslow Road, Manchester M14 6LJ T 0161-224 2804 E enquiries@usdaw.org.uk
W www.usdaw.org.uk
General Secretary, Paddy Lillis
Membership: 433,260

WGGB (WRITERS' GUILD OF GREAT BRITAIN) 134 Tooley Street, London SE1 2TU T 020-7833 0777
E admin@writersguild.org.uk W www.writersguild.org.uk
General Secretary, Ellie Peers
Membership: 2,242

NON-AFFILIATED UNIONS
As at December 2020

ASCL (ASSOCIATION OF SCHOOL AND COLLEGE LEADERS) 130 Regent Road, Leicester LE1 7PG
T 0116-299 1122 E info@ascl.org.uk W www.ascl.org.uk
General Secretary, Geoff Barton
Membership: 20,500

BDA (BRITISH DENTAL ASSOCIATION) 64 Wimpole Street, London W1G 8YS T 020-7935 0875 E enquiries@bda.org
W www.bda.org
General Secretary, Eddie Crouch
Membership: 15,000

CIOJ (CHARTERED INSTITUTE OF JOURNALISTS)
T 020-7252 1187 E memberservices@cioj.co.uk
W www.cioj.co.uk
General Secretary, Dominic Cooper
Membership: 1,000 (est.)

SOCIETY OF AUTHORS 24 Bedford Row, London WC1R 4EH
T 020-7373 6642 E info@societyofauthors.org
W www.societyofauthors.org
Chief Executive, Nicola Solomon
Membership: 10,000 (est.)

SSTA (SCOTTISH SECONDARY TEACHERS' ASSOCIATION) West End House, 14 West End Place, Edinburgh EH11 2ED T 0131-313 7300 E info@ssta.org.uk
W www.ssta.org.uk
General Secretary, Seamus Searson
Membership: 6,500 (est.)

SPORTS BODIES

SPORTS COUNCILS

SPORT AND RECREATION ALLIANCE Holborn Tower, 137–145 High Holborn, London WC1V 6PL **T** 020-7976 3900 **E** info@sportandrecreation.org.uk **W** www.sportandrecreation.org.uk
Chief Executive, Lisa Wainwright

SPORT ENGLAND 21 Bloomsbury Street, London WC1B 3HF **T** 0345-850 8508 **E** info@sportengland.org **W** www.sportengland.org
Chief Executive, Tim Hollingsworth

SPORT NORTHERN IRELAND House of Sport, 2A Upper Malone Road, Belfast BT9 5LA **T** 028-9038 1222 **E** info@sportni.net **W** www.sportni.net
Chief Executive, Antoinette McKeown

SPORTSCOTLAND Doges, Templeton on the Green, 62 Templeton Street, Glasgow G40 1DA **T** 0141-534 6500 **E** sportscotland.enquiries@sportscotland.org.uk **W** www.sportscotland.org.uk
Chief Executive, Stewart Harris

SPORT WALES Sophia Gardens, Cardiff CF11 9SW **T** 0300-300 3111 **E** info@sportwales.org.uk **W** www.sport.wales
Chief Executive, Sarah Powell

UK SPORT 21 Bloomsbury Street, London WC1B 3HF **T** 020-7211 5100 **E** info@uksport.gov.uk **W** www.uksport.gov.uk
Chief Executive, Liz Nicholl, CBE

AMERICAN FOOTBALL

BRITISH AMERICAN FOOTBALL ASSOCIATION 1 Franchise Street, Kidderminster DY11 6RE **E** human.resources@britishamericanfootball.org **W** www.britishamericanfootball.org
Chair, Nichole McCulloch

ANGLING

ANGLING TRUST Eastwood House, 6 Rainbow Street, Herefordshire HR6 8DQ **T** 0343-507 7006 **E** admin@anglingtrust.net **W** www.anglingtrust.net
Chief Executive, Mark Lloyd

ARCHERY

ARCHERY GB Lilleshall National Sports Centre, Newport TF10 9AT **T** 0195-267 7888 **E** enquiries@archerygb.org **W** www.archerygb.org
Chief Executive, Neil Armitage

ASSOCIATION FOOTBALL

ENGLISH FOOTBALL LEAGUE EFL House, 10-12 West Cliff, Preston PR1 8HU **T** 01772-325800 **E** enquiries@efl.com **W** www.efl.com
Chief Executive, Shaun Harvey

FOOTBALL ASSOCIATION Wembley Stadium, PO Box 1966, London SW1P 9EQ **T** 0800-169 1863 **E** info@thefa.com **W** www.thefa.com
Chief Executive, Martin Glenn

FOOTBALL ASSOCIATION OF WALES 11–12 Neptune Court, Vanguard Way, Cardiff CF24 5PJ **T** 029-2043 5830 **E** info@faw.co.uk **W** www.faw.cymru
Chief Executive, Jonathan Ford

IRISH FOOTBALL ASSOCIATION Donegal Avenue, Belfast BT12 6LU **T** 028-9066 9458 **E** info@irishfa.com **W** www.irishfa.com
Chief Executive, Patrick Nelson

PREMIER LEAGUE 30 Gloucester Place, London W1U 8PL **T** 020-7864 9000 **E** info@premierleague.com **W** www.premierleague.com
Chief Executive, vacant

SCOTTISH FOOTBALL ASSOCIATION Hampden Park, Glasgow G42 9AY **T** 0141-616 6000 **E** info@scottishfa.co.uk **W** www.scottishfa.co.uk
Chief Executive, Ian Maxwell

SCOTTISH PROFESSIONAL FOOTBALL LEAGUE Hampden Park, Glasgow G42 9DE **T** 0141-620 4140 **E** info@spfl.co.uk **W** www.spfl.co.uk
Chief Executive, Neil Doncaster

ATHLETICS

BRITISH ATHLETICS Athletics House, Alexander Stadium, Birmingham B42 2BE **T** 0121-713 8400 **E** majorevents@britishathletics.org.uk **W** www.britishathletics.org.uk
Chief Executive, Nigel Holl (interim)

ATHLETICS NORTHERN IRELAND Athletics House, Old Coach Road, Belfast BT9 5PR **T** 028-9060 2707 **E** info@athleticsni.org **W** www.athleticsni.org
General Secretary, John Allen

SCOTTISH ATHLETICS Caledonia House, Edinburgh EH12 9DQ **T** 0131-539 7320 **E** admin@scottishathletics.org.uk **W** www.scottishathletics.org.uk
Chief Executive, Mark Munro

WELSH ATHLETICS Cardiff International Sports Stadium, Leckwith Road, Cardiff CF11 8AZ **T** 029-2064 4870 **E** office@welshathletics.org **W** www.welshathletics.org
Chief Executive, Matt Newman

BADMINTON

BADMINTON ENGLAND National Badminton Centre, Bradwell Road, Milton Keynes MK8 9LA **T** 01908-268400 **E** enquiries@badmintonengland.co.uk **W** www.badmintonengland.co.uk
Chief Executive, Adrian Christy

BADMINTON SCOTLAND Sir Craig Reedie Badminton Centre, 40 Bogmoor Place, Glasgow G51 4TQ **T** 0141-445 1218 **E** enquiries@badmintonscotland.org.uk **W** www.badmintonscotland.org.uk
Chief Executive, Keith Russell

BADMINTON WALES Sport Wales National Centre, Sophia Gardens, Cardiff CF11 9SW **T** 029-2033 4938 **E** enquiries@badminton.wales **W** www.badminton.wales
General Manager, Gareth Hall

BASEBALL

BASEBALLSOFTBALL UK Marathon House, 190 Great Dover Street, London SE1 4YB **T** 020-7453 7055 **W** www.baseballsoftballuk.com
Chief Executive, John Boyd

BRITISH BASEBALL FEDERATION Marathon House, 190 Great Dane Street, London SE1 4YB **T** 0207-7453 7055 **W** www.britishbaseballfederation.org
President, Gerry Perez

BASKETBALL

BASKETBALL ENGLAND Etihad Stadium, Rowsley Street, Manchester M11 3FF **T** 0300-600 1170 **E** info@basketballengland.com **W** www.basketballengland.co.uk
Chief Executive, Stewart Kellett

BASKETBALL SCOTLAND Caledonia House, Edinburgh
EH12 9DQ **T** 0131-317 7260
E enquiries@basketball-scotland.com
W www.basketballscotland.co.uk
Chief Executive, Kevin Pringle

BILLIARDS AND SNOOKER

WORLD SNOOKER 75 Whiteladies Road, Bristol BS8 2NT
T 0117-317 8200 **E** info@worldsnooker.com
W www.worldsnooker.com
Chief Executive, Steve Dawson

BOBSLEIGH

BRITISH BOBSLEIGH & SKELETON ASSOCIATION
University of Bath, Claverton Down, Bath BA2 7AY
T 01225-384343 **E** office@thebbsa.co.uk **W** www.thebbsa.co.uk
Chair, Christopher Rodrigues

BOWLS

BOWLS ENGLAND Riverside House, Milverton Hill, Royal
Leamington Spa CV32 5HZ **T** 01926-334609
E enquiries@bowlsengland.com **W** www.bowlsengland.com
Chief Executive, Tony Allcock, MBE
BRITISH ISLES BOWLS COUNCIL
E bibcsecretary@aol.co.uk **W** www.britishislesbowls.com
President, David Graham, OBE
ENGLISH INDOOR BOWLING ASSOCIATION David
Cornwell House, Bowling Green, Melton Mowbray LE13 0FA
T 01664-481900 **E** enquiries@eiba.co.uk **W** www.eiba.co.uk
Chief Executive, Peter Thompson

BOXING

BRITISH BOXING BOARD OF CONTROL 14 North Road,
Cardiff CF10 3DY **T** 029-2036 7000 **E** admin@bbbofc.com
W www.bbbofc.com
General Secretary, Robert Smith
ENGLAND BOXING English Institute of Sport, Coleridge Road,
Sheffield S9 5DA **T** 0114-223 5654
E enquiries@englandboxing.org **W** www.abae.co.uk
Chief Executive, Gethin Jenkins

CANOEING

BRITISH CANOEING National Water Sport Centre, Adbolton
Lane, Nottingham NG12 2LU **T** 0300-011 9500
E info@britishcanoeing.org.uk **W** www.britishcanoeing.org.uk
Chief Executive, David Joy

CHESS

ENGLISH CHESS FEDERATION The Watch Oak, Chain Lane,
Battle TN33 0YD **T** 01424-775222 **E** office@englishchess.org.uk
W www.englishchess.org.uk
Chief Executive, Mike Truran

CRICKET

ENGLAND AND WALES CRICKET BOARD Lord's Cricket
Ground, St John's Wood Road, London NW8 8QZ
T 020-7432 1200 **W** www.ecb.co.uk
Chief Executive, Tom Harrison
MCC Lord's Cricket Ground, London NW8 8QN **T** 020-7616 8500
E reception@mcc.org.uk **W** www.lords.org
Chief Executive and Secretary, Guy Lavender

CROQUET

CROQUET ASSOCIATION Old Bath Road, Cheltenham
GL53 7DF **T** 01242-242318 **E** caoffice@croquet.org.uk
W www.croquet.org.uk
Manager, Mark Suter

CURLING

BRITISH CURLING c/o The Royal Caledonian Curling Club,
Ochil House, Stirling FK7 7XE **E** info@britishcurling.com
W www.britishcurling.org.uk
Chief Executive, Bruce Crawford
SCOTTISH CURLING Ochil House, Stirling FK7 7XE
T 0131-333 3003 **E** office@scottishcurling.org
W www.scottishcurling.org
Chief Executive, Bruce Crawford

CYCLING

BRITISH CYCLING FEDERATION Stuart Street, Manchester
M11 4DQ **T** 0161-274 2000 **E** info@britishcycling.org.uk
W www.britishcycling.org.uk
Chief Executive, Julie Harrington

DARTS

BRITISH DARTS ORGANISATION Unit 4, Glan-y-Llyn
Industrial Estate, Cardiff CF15 7JD **T** 029-2081 1815
E contact@bdodarts.com **W** www.bdodarts.com
Chairman, Derek Jacklin

EQUESTRIANISM

BRITISH EQUESTRIAN FEDERATION Abbey Park,
Kenilworth CV8 2RH **T** 024-7669 8871 **E** info@bef.co.uk
W www.bef.co.uk
Chief Executive, Nick Fellows
BRITISH EVENTING Abbey Park, Kenilworth CV8 2RN
T 024-7669 8856 **E** info@britisheventing.com
W www.britisheventing.com
Chief Executive, David Holmes

ETON FIVES

ETON FIVES ASSOCIATION 45 Sandhills Crescent, Solihull
B91 3UE **T** 07833-600230 **W** www.etonfives.com
Chair, Chris Davies

FENCING

BRITISH FENCING 1 Baron's Gate, 33 Rothschild Road,
London W4 5HT **T** 020-8742 3032
E headoffice@britishfencing.com **W** www.britishfencing.com
Chief Executive, Georgina Usher

GLIDING

BRITISH GLIDING ASSOCIATION 8 Merus Court, Meridian
Business Park, Leicester LE19 1RJ **T** 0116-289 2956
E office@gliding.co.uk **W** www.gliding.co.uk
Chief Executive, Pete Stratten

GOLF

ENGLAND GOLF The National Golf Centre, Woodhall Spa
LN10 6PU **T** 01526-354500 **E** info@englandgolf.org
W www.englandgolf.org
Chief Executive, Nick Pink
THE ROYAL AND ANCIENT GOLF CLUB Golf Place, St
Andrews KY16 9JD **T** 01334-460000
E thesecretary@randagc.org **W** www.randa.org
Chief Executive and Secretary, Martin Slumbers

GYMNASTICS

BRITISH GYMNASTICS Ford Hall, Lilleshall National Sports
Centre, Newport TF10 9NB **T** 0345-129 7129
E information@british-gymnastics.org
W www.british-gymnastics.org
Chief Executive, Jane Allen

HANDBALL

ENGLAND HANDBALL The Halliwell Jones Stadium, Winwick Road, Warrington WA2 7NE T 01925-246482
E office@englandhandball.com W www.englandhandball.com
Chief Executive, David Meli

HOCKEY

ENGLAND HOCKEY Bisham Abbey National Sports Centre, Marlow SL7 1RR T 01628-897500
E enquiries@englandhockey.co.uk W www.englandhockey.co.uk
Chief Executive, Sally Munday
HOCKEY WALES Sport Wales National Centre, Sophia Close, Cardiff CF11 9SW T 0300-300 3126 E info@hockeywales.org.uk
W www.hockeywales.org.uk
Chief Executive, Ria Male (interim)
SCOTTISH HOCKEY UNION Glasgow National Hockey Centre, 8 King's Drive, Glasgow G40 1HB T 0141-550 5999
W www.scottish-hockey.org.uk
Chief Executive, David Sweetman

HORSERACING

BRITISH HORSERACING AUTHORITY 75 High Holborn, London WC1V 6LS T 020-7152 0000
E info@britishhorseracing.com W www.britishhorseracing.com
Chief Executive, Nick Rust
THE JOCKEY CLUB 75 High Holborn, London WC1V 6LS
T 020-7611 1800 E info@thejockeyclub.co.uk
W www.thejockeyclub.co.uk
Chief Executive, Simon Bazalgette

ICE SKATING

NATIONAL ICE SKATING ASSOCIATION English Institute of Sport, Coleridge Road, Sheffield S9 5DA T 0115-988 8060
E info@iceskating.org.uk W www.iceskating.org.uk
Chair, Rob Jones

LACROSSE

ENGLISH LACROSSE ASSOCIATION National Squash Centre and Regional Arena, Gate 13, Manchester M11 3FF
T 0161-974 7757 E info@englandlacrosse.co.uk
W www.englandlacrosse.co.uk
Chief Executive, Mark Coups

LAWN TENNIS

LAWN TENNIS ASSOCIATION National Tennis Centre, 100 Priory Lane, London SW15 5JQ T 020-8487 7000
E info@lta.org.uk W www.lta.org.uk
Chief Executive, Scott Lloyd

MARTIAL ARTS

BRITISH JUDO ASSOCIATION Floor 1, Kudhail House, 238 Birmingham Road, Great Barr B43 7AH T 0121-728 6920
E bja@britishjudo.org.uk W www.britishjudo.org.uk
Chief Executive, Andrew Scoular
BRITISH JU JITSU ASSOCIATION 5 Avenue Parade, Accrington BB5 6PN T 03333-202039 E bjjagb@icloud.com
W www.bjjagb.com
Chairman, Prof. Martin Dixon
BRITISH TAEKWONDO Manchester Regional Arena, Rowsley Street, Manchester M11 3FF T 01623-382020
E admin@britishtaekwondo.org
W www.britishtaekwondo.org.uk
Chair, Jonny Cowan (interim)

MODERN PENTATHLON

PENTATHLON GB Sports Training Village, University of Bath, Bath BA2 7AY T 01225-386808 E admin@pentathlongb.org
W www.pentathlongb.org
Chief Executive, Sara Heath

MOTOR SPORTS

AUTO-CYCLE UNION ACU House, Rugby CV21 2YX
T 01788-566400 E admin@acu.org.uk W www.acu.org.uk
General Secretary, Gary Thompson, MBE
MOTORSPORT UK Motorsport UK House, Riverside Park, Colnbrook SL3 0HG T 01753-765000 W www.motorsportuk.org
Chief Executive, Hugh Chambers
SCOTTISH AUTO CYCLE UNION 28 West Main Street, Uphall EH52 5DW T 01506-858354 E office@sacu.co.uk
W www.sacu.co.uk
Chair, Sandy Mack

MOUNTAINEERING

BRITISH MOUNTAINEERING COUNCIL The Old Church, 177–179 Burton Road, Manchester M20 2BB T 0161-445 6111
E office@thebmc.co.uk W www.thebmc.co.uk
Chief Executive, Dave Turnbull

MULTI-SPORTS BODIES

ACTIVITY ALLIANCE Loughborough University, 3 Oakwood Drive, LE11 3QF T 01509-227750 W www.activityalliance.org.uk
Chief Executive, Barry Horne
BRITISH OLYMPIC ASSOCIATION 60 Charlotte Street, London W1T 2NU T 020-7842 5700 E boa@boa.org.uk
W www.teamgb.com
Chief Executive, Bill Sweeney
BRITISH PARALYMPIC ASSOCIATION 60 Charlotte Street, London W1T 2NU T 020-7842 5789 E info@paralympics.org.uk
W www.paralympics.org.uk
Chief Executive, Mike Sharrock
BRITISH UNIVERSITIES AND COLLEGES SPORT 20–24 Kings Bench Street, London SE1 0QX T 020-7633 5080
E info@bucs.org.uk W www.bucs.org.uk
Chief Executive, Vince Mayne
COMMONWEALTH GAMES ENGLAND 5th floor, Holborn Tower, 137–144 High Holborn, London WC1V 6PL
T 020-7831 3444 E info@teamengland.org
W www.teamengland.org
Chief Executive, Paul Blanchard
COMMONWEALTH GAMES FEDERATION Commonwealth House, 55–58 Pall Mall, London SW1Y 5JH
T 020-7747 6427 E info@thecgf.com W www.thecgf.com
Chief Executive, David Grevemberg, CBE

NETBALL

ENGLAND NETBALL SportPark, 3 Oakwood Drive, Loughborough LE11 3QF T 01509-277850
E info@englandnetball.co.uk W www.englandnetball.co.uk
Chief Executive, Joanna Adams
NETBALL NI Unit F, Curlew Pavilion, Portside Business Park, Belfast BT3 9ED T 028-9073 6320
E bookingsandadmin@netballni.org W www.netballni.org
Chair, Geoff Wilson
NETBALL SCOTLAND Emirates Arena, 1000 London Road, Glasgow G40 3HY T 0141-428 3460
E membership@netballscotland.com
W www.netballscotland.com
Chief Executive, Claire Nelson
WELSH NETBALL ASSOCIATION Sport Wales National Centre, Sophia Gardens, Cardiff CF11 9SW T 029-2033 4950
E welshnetball@welshnetball.com W www.welshnetball.com
Chief Executive, Sarah Jones

ORIENTEERING

BRITISH ORIENTEERING Scholes Mill, Old Coach Road, Matlock DE4 5FY T 01629-583037
E info@britishorienteering.org.uk
W www.britishorienteering.org.uk
Chief Executive, Peter Hart

POLO

THE HURLINGHAM POLO ASSOCIATION Manor Farm, Little Coxwell, Faringdon SN7 7LW T 01367-242828 E enquiries@hpa-polo.co.uk W www.hpa-polo.co.uk
Chief Executive, David Woodd

RACKETS AND REAL TENNIS

TENNIS AND RACKETS ASSOCIATION c/o The Queen's Club, Palliser Road, London W14 9EQ T 020-7835 6937 E office@tennisandrackets.com W www.tennisandrackets.com
Chief Executive, C. S. Davies

ROWING

BRITISH ROWING 6 Lower Mall, London W6 9DJ T 020-8237 6700 E info@britishrowing.org
W www.britishrowing.org
Chief Executive, Andy Parkinson
HENLEY ROYAL REGATTA Regatta Headquarters, Henley-on-Thames RG9 2LY T 01491-572153 W www.hrr.co.uk
Secretary, Daniel Grist

RUGBY LEAGUE

BRITISH AMATEUR RUGBY LEAGUE ASSOCIATION West Yorkshire House, 4 New North Parade, Huddersfield HD1 5JP T 01484-510682 E secretary@barla.org.uk
W www.barla.org.uk
Chair, Sue Taylor
RUGBY FOOTBALL LEAGUE Red Hall, Red Hall Lane, Leeds LS17 8NB T 0330-111 1113 E enquiries@rfl.uk.co.uk
W www.rugby-league.com
Chief Executive, Ralph Rimmer

RUGBY UNION

IRISH RUGBY FOOTBALL UNION 10–12 Lansdowne Road, Dublin 4 T (+353) 1647 3800 E info@irishrugby.ie
W www.irishrugby.ie
Chief Executive, Philip Browne
RUGBY FOOTBALL UNION Rugby House, Twickenham Stadium, 200 Whitton Road, Twickenham TW2 7BA
T 0871-222 2120 E enquiries@therfu.com
W www.englandrugby.com
Chief Executive, Bill Sweeney
RUGBY FOOTBALL UNION FOR WOMEN Rugby House, Twickenham Stadium, 200 Whitton Road, Twickenham TW2 7BA T 0871-222 2120 E enquiries@therfu.com
W www.englandrugby.com
Managing Director, Rosie Williams
SCOTTISH RUGBY UNION BT Murrayfield, Edinburgh EH12 5PJ T 0131-346 5000 E feedback@sru.org.uk
W www.scottishrugby.org
Chief Executive, Mark Dodson
SCOTTISH WOMEN'S RUGBY UNION BT Murrayfield, Edinburgh EH12 5PJ T 0131-346 5000 E feedback@sru.org.uk
W www.scottishrugby.org
Chief Executive, Mark Dodson
WELSH RUGBY UNION Principality Stadium, Westgate Street, Cardiff CF10 1NS T 0844-249 1999 E info@wru.co.uk
W www.wru.wales
Chief Executive, Martyn Phillips

SHOOTING

BRITISH SHOOTING Bisham Abbey National Sports Centre, Marlow Road, Marlow SL7 1RR T 01628-488800
E admin@britishshooting.org.uk W www.britishshooting.org.uk
Chief Executive, Hamish McInnes
CLAY PIGEON SHOOTING ASSOCIATION Edmonton House, National Shooting Centre, Brookwood, Woking GU24 0NP T 01483-485400 E info@cpsa.co.uk
W www.cpsa.co.uk
Chief Executive, Iain Parker

NATIONAL RIFLE ASSOCIATION Bisley Camp, Brookwood GU24 0PB T 01483-797777 E info@nra.org.uk
W www.nra.org.uk
Chief Executive, John Webster
NATIONAL SMALL-BORE RIFLE ASSOCIATION Lord Roberts Centre, Bisley Camp, Woking GU24 0NP
T 01483-485502 W www.nsra.co.uk
Chair, Robert Newman

SKIING AND SNOWBOARDING

GB SNOWSPORT 60 Charlotte Street, London W1T 2NU T 020-7842 5764 E info@gbsnowsport.com
W www.gbsnowsport.com
Chief Executive, Victoria Gosling, OBE

SPEEDWAY

BRITISH SPEEDWAY ACU Headquarters, Wood Street, Rugby CV21 2YX T 01788-560648 E office@speedwaygb.co.uk
W www.speedwaygb.co.uk
Chair, Keith Chapman

SQUASH

ENGLAND SQUASH National Squash Centre, Manchester M11 3FF T 0161-231 4499 W www.englandsquash.com
Chief Executive, Keir Worth
SCOTTISH SQUASH Oriam, Edinburgh EH14 4AS
T 0131-451 8525 E info@scottishsquash.org
W www.scottishsquash.org
Chief Executive, Maggie Still
WALES SQUASH AND RACKETBALL Sport Wales National Centre, Sophia Close, Cardiff CF11 9SW T 0300-300 3121
W www.walessquashandracketball.co.uk
General Manager, Gareth Hall

SUB-AQUA

BRITISH SUB-AQUA CLUB Telford's Quay, South Pier Road, Ellesmere Port CH65 4FL T 0151-350 6200 E info@bsac.com
W www.bsac.com
Chief Executive, Mary Tetley

SWIMMING

SWIM ENGLAND Pavilion 3, Sport Park, Loughborough LE11 3QF T 01509-618700 E customerservices@swimming.org
W www.swimming.org
Chief Executive, Jane Nickerson
SCOTTISH SWIMMING National Swimming Academy, University of Stirling, FK9 4LA T 01786-466520
E info@scottishswimming.com W www.scottishswimming.com
Chief Executive, Forbes Dunlop
SWIM WALES WNPS, Sketty Lane, Swansea SA2 8QG
T 01792-513636 W www.swimwales.org
Chief Executive, Fergus Feeney

TABLE TENNIS

TABLE TENNIS ENGLAND Bradwell Road, Milton Keynes MK8 9LA T 01908-208860 E help@tabletennisengland.co.uk
W www.tabletennisengland.co.uk
Chief Executive, Sara Sutcliffe
TABLE TENNIS SCOTLAND Caledonia House, South Gyle, Edinburgh EH12 9DQ T 0131-317 8077
E info@tabletennisscotland.co.uk
W www.tabletennisscotland.co.uk
Chair, Terry McLernon, MBE
TABLE TENNIS WALES Glanrhyd, Ebbw View, Ebbw Vale NP23 5NU T 01244-571335 W www.tabletennis.wales
Company Secretary, Neil O'Connell

TRIATHLON

BRITISH TRIATHLON PO Box 25, Loughborough LE11 3WX
T 01509-226161 E info@britishtriathlon.org
W www.britishtriathlon.org
Chief Executive, Andy Salmon

VOLLEYBALL

NORTHERN IRELAND VOLLEYBALL ASSOCIATION 7
Greengage Cottages, Ballymoney BT53 6GZ
W www.nivolleyball.com
General Secretary, Paddy Elder

SCOTTISH VOLLEYBALL ASSOCIATION 48 The
Pleasance, Edinburgh EH8 9TJ T 0131-556 4633
E info@scottishvolleyball.org W www.scottishvolleyball.org
Chief Executive, Margaret Ann Fleming

VOLLEYBALL ENGLAND SportPark, Loughborough University,
3 Oakwood Drive, Loughborough LE11 3QF T 01509-227722
E info@volleyballengland.org W www.volleyballengland.org
Chief Executive, Janet Inman

VOLLEYBALL WALES 13 Beckgrove Close, Cardiff CF24 2SE
T 029-2041 6537 E yperkins@cardiffmet.ac.uk
W www.volleyballwales.org
Chair, Yvonne Perkins

WALKING

RACE WALKING ASSOCIATION Hufflers, Heard's Lane,
Brentwood CM15 0SF T 01277-220687
E racewalkingassociation@btinternet.com
W www.racewalkingassociation.com
Hon. General Secretary, Colin Vesty

WATER SKIING

BRITISH WATER SKI AND WAKEBOARD The Forum,
Hanworth Lane, Chertsey KT16 9JX T 01932-560007
E info@bwsf.co.uk W www.bwsw.org.uk
Chief Executive, Patrick Donovan

WEIGHTLIFTING

BRITISH WEIGHT LIFTING St Ann's Mill, Kirkstall Road,
Leeds LS5 3AE T 0113-224 9402
E enquiries@britishweightlifting.org
W www.britishweightlifting.org
Chief Executive, Ashley Metcalfe

WRESTLING

BRITISH WRESTLING ASSOCIATION 41 Great Clowes St,
Salford M7 1RQ T 0161-835 2112 E admin@britishwrestling.org
W www.britishwrestling.org
Chief Executive, Colin Nicholson

YACHTING

ROYAL YACHTING ASSOCIATION RYA House, Ensign
Way, Southampton SO31 4YA T 023-8060 4100
E enquiries@rya.org.uk W www.rya.org.uk
Chief Executive, Sarah Treseder

CHARITIES AND SOCIETIES

The following is a selection of charities, societies and non-profit organisations in the UK and does not represent a comprehensive list. For professional and employment-related organisations, *see* Professional Education and Trade and Professional Bodies.

ABBEYFIELD SOCIETY (1956), St Peter's House, 2 Bricket Road, St Albans AL1 3JW T 01727-857536
E post@abbeyfield.com W www.abbeyfield.com
Chief Executive, David McCullough

ACTIONAID (1972), 33–39 Bowling Green Lane, London EC1R 0BJ T 01460 238000 E supportercontact@actionaid.org
W www.actionaid.org.uk
Chief Executive, Girish Menon

ACTION FOR CHILDREN (1869), 3 The Boulevard, Watford WD18 8AG T 0300 123-2112 E ask.us@actionforchildren.org.uk
W www.actionforchildren.org.uk
Chief Executive, Julie Bentley

ACTION MEDICAL RESEARCH (1952), Vincent House, Horsham RH12 2DP T 01403-210406 E info@action.org.uk
W www.action.org.uk
Chief Executive, Julie Buckler

ACTION ON HEARING LOSS (1911), 1–3 Highbury Station Road, London N1 1SE
T 0808-808 0123, **Textphone** 0808-808 9000
E informationline@hearingloss.org.uk
W www.actiononhearingloss.org.uk
Chief Executive, Mark Atkinson

ACTORS' BENEVOLENT FUND (1882), 6 Adam Street, London WC2N 6AD T 020-7836 6378 E office@abf.org.uk
W www.actorsbenevolentfund.co.uk
General Secretary, Jonathan Ellicott

ACTORS' CHILDREN'S TRUST (1896), 58 Bloomsbury Street, London WC1B 3QT T 020-7636 7868
E robert@actorschildren.org W www.actorschildren.org
Executive Director, Robert Ashby

ADAM SMITH INSTITUTE (1977), 23 Great Smith Street, London SW1P 3DJ T 020-7222 4995 E info@adamsmith.org
W www.adamsmith.org
Director, Dr Eamonn Butler

ADDACTION (1967), Gate House, 1–3 St John's Square, London EC1M 4DH T 020-7251 5860 E info@addaction.org.uk
W www.addaction.org.uk
Chief Executive, Mike Dixon

ADVERTISING STANDARDS AUTHORITY (1962), Mid City Place, 71 High Holborn, London WC1V 6QT
T 020-7492 2222 W www.asa.org.uk
Chief Executive, Guy Parker

AFASIC (1968), 209–211 City Road, London EC1V 1JN
T 020-7490 9410 W www.afasic.org.uk
Chief Executive, Linda Lascelles

AGE CYMRU (2010), Ground Floor, Mariners House, East Moors Road CF24 5TD T 029-2043 1555
E advice@agecymru.org.uk W www.ageuk.org.uk/cymru
Chief Executive, Victoria Lloyd (interim)

AGE SCOTLAND (1943), Causewayside House, 160 Causewayside, Edinburgh EH9 1PR T 0333-323 2400
E info@agescotland.org.uk W www.ageuk.org.uk/scotland
Chief Executive, Brian Sloan

AGE UK (2010), Tavis House, 1–6 Tavistock Square, London WC1H 9NA T 0800-169 8787 E contact@ageuk.org.uk
W www.ageuk.org.uk
Chief Executive, Steph Harland

ALEXANDRA ROSE CHARITY (1912), 5 Mead Lane, Farnham GU9 7DY T 01252-726171 E info@alexandrarose.org
W www.alexandrarose.org.uk
Chief Executive, Jonathan Pauling

ALZHEIMER'S SOCIETY (1979), 43–44 Crutched Friars, London EC3N 2AE T 0330-333 0804
E enquiries@alzheimers.org.uk W www.alzheimers.org.uk
Chief Executive, Jeremy Hughes

AMNESTY INTERNATIONAL UK (1961), The Human Rights Action Centre, 17–25 New Inn Yard, London EC2A 3EA
T 020-7033 1500 E sct@amnesty.org.uk
W www.amnesty.org.uk
UK Director, Kate Allen

AMREF UK (1957), 15–18 White Lion Street, London N1 9PD
T 020-7269 5520 E info@amrefuk.org W www.amrefuk.org
Chief Executive, Frances Longley

ANGLO-BELGIAN SOCIETY (1982), 15 Westmoreland Terrace, London SW1V 4AG
E secretary@anglobelgiansociety.com
W www.anglobelgiansociety.com
Chair, Caroline Colvin, OBE

ANGLO-DANISH SOCIETY (1924), 43 Maresfield Gardens, London NW3 5TF T 07934-236686
E info@anglo-danishsociety.org.uk
W www.anglo-danishsociety.org.uk
Chair, Wayne Harber, OBE

ANGLO-NORSE SOCIETY (1918), 25 Belgrave Square, London SW1X 8QD T 01825 840-043 E info@anglo-norse.org.uk
W www.anglo-norse.org.uk
Chair, Sir Richard Dales, KCVO, CMG

ANIMAL HEALTH TRUST (1942), Lanwades Park, Newmarket CB8 7UU T 01638-751000 E info@aht.org.uk
W www.aht.org.uk
Chief Executive, Dr Mark Vaudin

ANTHONY NOLAN (1974), 2 Heathgate Place, 75–87 Agincourt Road, London NW3 2NU T 0303-303 0303
W www.anthonynolan.org
Chief Executive, Henny Braund

ANTI-SLAVERY INTERNATIONAL (1839), Thomas Clarkson House, The Stableyard, London SW9 9TL
T 020-7501 8920 E info@antislavery.org W www.antislavery.org
CEO, Jasmine O'Connor

ARCHITECTS BENEVOLENT SOCIETY (1850), 43 Portland Place, London W1B 1QH T 020-7580 2823
E help@absnet.org.uk W www.absnet.org.uk
Chief Executive, Robert Ball

ARCHITECTURAL HERITAGE FUND (1976), 3 Spital Yard, London E1 6AQ T 020-7925 0199 E ahf@ahfund.org.uk
W www.ahfund.org.uk
Chief Executive, Matthew McKeague

ARLIS/UK AND IRELAND (1969), National Art Library, Victoria & Albert Museum, London SW7 2RL E info@arlis.net
W www.arlis.net
Chair, Carla Marchesan

ART FUND (1903), 2 Granary Square, King's Cross, London N1C 4BH T 020-7225 4800 E info@artfund.org
W www.artfund.org
Director, Dr Stephen Deuchar

ASSOCIATION FOR LANGUAGE LEARNING (1990), 1A Duffield Road, Derby DE21 5DR T 01332-227779
E info@all-languages.org.uk W www.all-languages.org.uk
Director, Rachel Middleton

ASSOCIATION FOR SCIENCE EDUCATION (1901), College Lane, Hatfield AL10 9AA **T** 01707-283000 **E** info@ase.org.uk **W** www.ase.org.uk
Chief Executive, Shaun Reason

ASSOCIATION FOR THE PROTECTION OF RURAL SCOTLAND (1926), Dolphin House, 4 Hunter Square, Edinburgh EH1 1QW **T** 0131-225 7012 **E** info@aprs.scot **W** www.aprs.scot
Director, John Mayhew

ASSOCIATION OF FINANCIAL MUTUALS (1995), 7 Castle Hill, Caistor LN7 6QL **T** 0844-879 7863 **E** martin@financialmutuals.org **W** www.financialmutuals.org
Chief Executive, Martin Shaw

ASSOCIATION OF GENEALOGISTS AND RESEARCHERS IN ARCHIVES (1968), Box A, 14 Charterhouse Buildings, Goswell Road, London EC1M 7BA **E** info@agra.org.uk **W** www.agra.org.uk
Chair, Sharon Grant

ASSOCIATION OF ROYAL NAVY OFFICERS (1920), 70 Porchester Terrace, London W2 3TP **T** 020-7402 5231 **E** enquiries@arno.org.uk **W** www.arno.org.uk
Director, Cdr Mike Goldthorpe

ASTHMA UK (1927), 18 Mansell Street, London E1 8AA **T** 0300-222 5800 **E** info@asthma.org.uk **W** www.asthma.org.uk
Chief Executive, Kay Boycott

AUDIT BUREAU OF CIRCULATIONS LTD (1931), Saxon House, 211 High Street, Berkhamsted HP4 1AD **T** 01442-870800 **E** enquiries@abc.org.uk **W** www.abc.org.uk
Chair, Derek Morris

AUTISM INITIATIVES (1971), Sefton House, Bridle Road, Merseyside L30 4XR **T** 0151-330 9500 **E** info@autisminitiatives.org **W** www.autisminitiatives.org
Chair, Brian Williams

AUTOMOBILE ASSOCIATION (1905), Fanum House, Basing View, Basingstoke RG21 4EA **T** 0345-607 6727 **E** customersupport@theaa.com **W** www.theaa.com
CEO, Simon Breakwell

BALTIC EXCHANGE (1744), St Mary Axe, London EC3A 8BH **T** 020-7283 9300 **W** www.balticexchange.com
Chief Executive, Mark Jackson

BARNARDO'S (1866), Tanners Lane, Ilford IG6 1QG **T** 020-8550 8822 **W** www.barnardos.org.uk
Chief Executive, Javed Khan

BBC MEDIA ACTION (1999), Ibex House, 42–47 Minories, London EC2N 1DY **T** 020-7481 9797 **E** media.action@bbc.co.uk **W** www.bbc.co.uk/mediaaction
Executive Director, Caroline Nursey, OBE

BCS, THE CHARTERED INSTITUTE FOR IT (1957), 1st Floor, Block D, North Star House, North Star Avenue, Swindon SN2 1FA **T** 01793-417417 **W** www.bcs.org.uk
Chief Executive, Paul Fletcher

BEAT (1989), Unit 1 Chalk Hill House, 19 Rosary Road, Norwich NR1 1SZ
T 0300-123 3355 **Helpline** 0808-801 0677 **Youthline** 0808-801 0711 **E** info@b-eat.co.uk **W** www.beateatingdisorders.org.uk
Chief Executive, Andrew Radford

BIBLE SOCIETY (1804), Stonehill Green, Swindon SN5 7DG **T** 01793-418222 **W** www.biblesociety.org.uk
Chief Executive, Paul Williams

BIBLIOGRAPHICAL SOCIETY (1892), c/o University of London, Institute of English Studies, Senate House, London WC1E 7HU **E** admin@bibsoc.org.uk **W** www.bibsoc.org.uk
Hon. Secretary, Karen Limper-Herz

BIPOLAR UK (1983), 11 Belgrave Road, London SW1V 1RB **T** 0333-323 3880 **E** info@bipolaruk.org.uk **W** www.bipolaruk.org
Chief Executive, Simon Kitchen

BLIND VETERANS UK (1915), 12–14 Harcourt Street, London W1H 4HD **T** 0300 111-2233 **E** info@blindveterans.org.uk **W** www.blindveterans.org.uk
Chief Executive, Maj.-Gen. Nick Caplin, CB

BLISS (1979), Fourth Floor, Maya House, London SE1 1LB **T** 020-7378 1122 **E** ask@bliss.org.uk **W** www.bliss.org.uk
Chief Executive, Caroline Lee-Davey

BLOODWISE (1960), 39–40 Eagle Street, London WC1R 4TH **T** 020-7504 2200 **W** bloodwise.org.uk
Chief Executive, Gemma Peters

BLUE CROSS (1897), Shilton Road, Burford OX18 4PF **T** 0300-777 1897 **W** www.bluecross.org.uk
Chief Executive, Sally de la Bedoyere

BOOK AID INTERNATIONAL (1954), 39–41 Coldharbour Lane, London SE5 9NR **T** 020-7733 3577 **E** info@bookaid.org **W** www.bookaid.org
Chief Executive, Alison Tweed

BOOK TRADE CHARITY (BTBS) (1837), The Foyle Centre, The Retreat, Kings Langley WD4 8LT **T** 01923-263128 **E** info@booktradecharity.org **W** www.btbs.org
Chief Executive, David Hicks

BOOKTRUST (1926), G8 Battersea Studios, 80 Silverthorne Road, London SW8 3HE **T** 020-7801 8800 **E** query@booktrust.org.uk **W** www.booktrust.org.uk
Chief Executive, Diana Gerald

BOTANICAL SOCIETY OF BRITAIN AND IRELAND (1836), 29 West Farm Court, Durham DH7 7RN **T** 07725-862957 **E** enquiries@bsbi.org.uk **W** www.bsbi.org
Chair, Christopher Miles

BOTANICAL SOCIETY OF SCOTLAND (1836), c/o Royal Botanic Garden Edinburgh, 20A Inverleith Row, Edinburgh EH3 5LR **T** 0131-552 7171 **W** www.botanical-society-scotland.org.uk
General Secretaries, Julia Wilson; Liz Lavery

BRISTOL AND GLOUCESTERSHIRE ARCHAEOLOGICAL SOCIETY (1876), 10 Paddock Gardens, Gloucester GL2 0ED **T** 01452-414279 **E** secretary@bgas.org.uk **W** www.bgas.org.uk
Hon. General Secretary, Dr Graham Barton

BRITISH ASSOCIATION FOR EARLY CHILDHOOD EDUCATION (1923), 54 Clarendon Road, Watford WD17 1DU **T** 01923-438995 **E** office@early-education.org.uk **W** www.early-education.org.uk
Chief Executive, Beatrice Merrick

BRITISH ASSOCIATION FOR LOCAL HISTORY (1982), Chester House, 68 Chestergate, Macclesfield SK11 6DY **T** 01625-664524 **E** admin@balh.org.uk **W** www.balh.org.uk
President, Professor Caroline Barron

BRITISH ASTRONOMICAL ASSOCIATION (1890), Burlington House, London W1J 0DU **T** 020-7734 4145 **W** www.britastro.org
President, Callum Potter

BRITISH BOARD OF FILM CLASSIFICATION (1912), 3 Soho Square, London W1D 3HD **T** 020-7440 1570 **E** feedback@bbfc.co.uk **W** www.bbfc.co.uk
President, Patrick Swaffer

BRITISH CATTLE BREEDERS CLUB (1946), Underhill Farm, Glutton Bridge, Buxton SK17 0RN **T** 07966-032079 **E** heidi.bradbury@cattlebreeders.org.uk **W** www.cattlebreeders.org.uk
Chair, Mike Coffey

BRITISH COPYRIGHT COUNCIL (1965), 2 Pancras Square, London N1C 4AG **T** 020-3290 1444 **E** info@britishcopyright.org **W** www.britishcopyright.org
Chairman, Trevor Cook

BRITISH DEAF ASSOCIATION (1890), 3rd Floor, 356 Holloway Road, London N7 6PA **T** 020-7697 4140 **E** bda@bda.org.uk **W** www.bda.org.uk
Executive Director, Damian Barry

BRITISH ECOLOGICAL SOCIETY (1913), Charles Darwin House, 12 Roger Street, London WC1N 2JU **T** 020-7685 2500 **E** hello@britishecologicalsociety.org **W** www.britishecologicalsociety.org *Chief Executive*, Dr Hazel Norman

BRITISH FEDERATION OF WOMEN GRADUATES (1907), 4 Mandeville Courtyard, 142 Battersea Park Road, London SW11 4NB **T** 020-7498 8037 **E** office@bfwg.org.uk **W** www.bfwg.org.uk *President*, Patrice Wellesley-Cole

BRITISH HEART FOUNDATION (1961), Greater London House, 180 Hampstead Road, London NW1 7AW **T** 020-7554 0000 **W** www.bhf.org.uk *Chief Executive*, Simon Gillespie, OBE

BRITISH HEDGEHOG PRESERVATION SOCIETY (1982), Hedgehog House, Dhustone, Ludlow SY8 3PL **T** 01584-890801 **E** info@britishhedgehogs.org.uk **W** www.britishhedgehogs.org.uk *Chief Executive*, Fay Vass

BRITISH HERPETOLOGICAL SOCIETY (1947), 11 Strathmore Place, Montrose DD10 8LQ **E** info@thebhs.org **W** www.thebhs.org *Secretary*, Trevor Rose

BRITISH HORSE SOCIETY (1947), Abbey Park, Stareton, Kenilworth CV8 2XZ **T** 024-7684 0500 **E** enquiry@bhs.org.uk **W** www.bhs.org.uk *Chief Executive*, Sarah Phillips

BRITISH LUNG FOUNDATION (1985), 73–75 Goswell Road, London EC1V 7ER **T** 020-7688 5555, **Helpline** 03000-030 555 **W** www.blf.org.uk *Chief Executive*, Dr Penny Woods

BRITISH MENSA LTD (1946), St John's House, St John's Square, Wolverhampton WV2 4AH **T** 01902-772771 **W** www.mensa.org.uk *Chief Executive*, John Stevenage

BRITISH NATURALISTS' ASSOCIATION (1905), BM 8129, London WC1N 3XX **T** 0844-892-1817 **E** info@bna-naturalists.org **W** www.bna-naturalists.org *Hon. Chair*, Steven Rutherford

BRITISH NUTRITION FOUNDATION (1967), New Derwent House, 69–73 Theobalds Road, London WC1X 8TA **T** 020-7557 7930 **E** postbox@nutrition.org.uk **W** www.nutrition.org.uk *Director-General*, Prof. Judith Buttriss, PHD

BRITISH ORNITHOLOGISTS' UNION (1858), PO Box 417, Peterborough PE7 3FX **T** 01733-844820 **E** bou@bou.org.uk **W** www.bou.org.uk *Chief Operations Officer*, Steve Dudley

BRITISH PHARMACOLOGICAL SOCIETY (1931), The Schild Plot, 16 Angel Gate, London EC1V 2PT **T** 020-7239 0171 **W** www.bps.ac.uk *Chief Executive*, Jonathan Brüün

BRITISH POLIO FELLOWSHIP (1939), CP House, Otterspool Way, Watford WD25 8HR **T** 0800-043 1935 **E** info@britishpolio.org.uk **W** www.britishpolio.org.uk *National Chairman*, David Mitchell

BRITISH RED CROSS (1870), 44 Moorfields, London EC2Y 9AL **T** 0344-871 11 11 , **Textphone** 020-7562 2050 **E** contactus@redcross.org.uk **W** www.redcross.org.uk *Chief Executive*, Mike Adamson

BRITISH SAFETY COUNCIL (1957), 70 Chancellors Road, London W6 9RS **T** 020-3510 8355 **E** customer.service@britsafe.org **W** www.britsafe.org *Chief Executive*, Michael Robinson

BRITISH SCIENCE ASSOCIATION (1831), Wellcome Wolfson Building, London SW7 5HD **E** info@britishscienceassociation.org **W** www.britishscienceassociation.org *Chief Executive*, Katherine Mathieson

BRITISH SUNDIAL SOCIETY (1989), c/o The Royal Astronomical Society, London W1J 0BQ **E** secretary@sundialsoc.org.uk **W** www.sundialsoc.org.uk *Chair*, Dr Frank King

BRITISH TRUST FOR ORNITHOLOGY (1933), The Nunnery, Thetford IP24 2PU **T** 01842-750050 **E** info@bto.org **W** www.bto.org *Director*, Dr Andy Clements

BUCKINGHAMSHIRE ARCHAEOLOGICAL SOCIETY (1847), County Museum, Church Street, Aylesbury HP20 2QP **T** 01296-397200 **E** help@bucksas.org.uk **W** www.bucksas.org.uk *Chair*, Peter Marsden

BUILD AFRICA (1978), 14th Floor, Tower Building, London SE1 7NX **T** 01892-519619 **E** hello@build-africa.org.uk **W** www.build-africa.org *Chief Executive*, Martin Realey

CAFOD (CATHOLIC AGENCY FOR OVERSEAS DEVELOPMENT) (1962), Romero House, 55 Westminster Bridge Road, London SE1 7JB **T** 020-7733 7900 **E** cafod@cafod.org.uk **W** www.cafod.org.uk *Director*, Christine Allen

CALOUSTE GULBENKIAN FOUNDATION (1956), 50 Hoxton Square, London N1 6PB **T** 020-7012 1400 **E** info@gulbenkian.org.uk **W** gulbenkian.pt/uk-branch/ *Director*, Andrew Barnett

CAMBRIAN ARCHAEOLOGICAL ASSOCIATION (1847), Braemar, SA31 2PB **T** 01248-364865 **E** info@cambrians.org.uk **W** www.cambrians.org.uk *General Secretary*, Heather James

CAMERON FUND (1970), BMA House, Tavistock Square, London WC1H 9JP **T** 020-7388 0796 **E** info@cameronfund.org.uk **W** www.cameronfund.org.uk *Chief Executive*, Jill Rowlinson

CAMPAIGN FOR FREEDOM OF INFORMATION (1984), Free Word Centre, 60 Farringdon Road, London EC1R 3GA **T** 020-7324 2519 **E** admin@cfoi.org.uk **W** www.cfoi.org.uk *Director*, Maurice Frankel

CAMPAIGN FOR NUCLEAR DISARMAMENT (1958), Mordechai Vanunu House, 162 Holloway Road, London N7 8DQ **T** 020-7700 2393 **E** enquiries@cnduk.org **W** www.cnduk.org *General Secretary*, Kate Hudson

CAMPAIGN FOR THE PROTECTION OF RURAL WALES (1928), Tŷ Gwyn, 31 High Street, Welshpool SY21 7YD **T** 01938-552525 **E** info@cprwmail.org.uk **W** www.cprw.org.uk *Chair*, Peter Alexander-Fitzgerald

CANCER RESEARCH UK (2002), Angel Building, 407 St John Street, London EC1V 4AD **T** 0300-123 1022 **W** www.cancerresearchuk.org *Chief Executive*, Michelle Mitchell, OBE

CAREERS RESEARCH AND ADVISORY CENTRE (1964), 22 Signet Court, Swanns Road, Cambridge CB5 8LA **T** 01223-460277 **E** enquiries@crac.org.uk **W** www.crac.org.uk *Chief Executive*, Clare Viney

CARERS TRUST (2012), Unit 101, 164-180 Union Street, London SE1 0LH **T** 0300-772 9600 **E** info@carers.org **W** www.carers.org *Chief Executive*, Giles Meyer

CARERS UK (1965), 20 Great Dover Street, London SE1 4LX **T** 020-7378 4999 **E** info@carersuk.org **W** www.carersuk.org *Chief Executive*, Helen Walker

CARNEGIE UNITED KINGDOM TRUST (1913), Andrew Carnegie House, Pittencrieff Street, Dunfermline KY12 8AW **T** 01383-721445 **E** info@carnegieuk.org **W** www.carnegieuktrust.org.uk *President*, William Thomson, CBE

CATHEDRALS FABRIC COMMISSION FOR ENGLAND
(1991), Church House, 27 Great Smith Street, London
SW1P 3AZ **T** 020-7898 1000 **E** enquiries.ccb@c-of-e.org.uk
W www.churchcare.co.uk/cathedrals
Secretary, Thomas Ashley

CATHOLIC TRUTH SOCIETY (1868), 42–46 Harleyford
Road, London SE11 5AY **T** 020-7640 0042 **E** info@ctsbooks.org
W www.ctsbooks.org
General Secretary, Fergal Martin

CATHOLIC UNION OF GREAT BRITAIN (1870),
St Maximillian Kolbe House, 63 Jeddo Road, London W12 9EE
T 020-8749 1321 **W** www.catholicunion.org.uk
President, Rt. Hon. Sir Edward Leigh, MP

CAVELL NURSES' TRUST (1917), Grosvenor House, Prospect
Hill, Redditch B97 4DL **T** 01527-595999
E admin@cavellnursestrust.org **W** www.cavellnursestrust.org
Chief Executive, John Orchard

CENTRAL AND CECIL HOUSING TRUST (1927), Cecil
House, 266 Waterloo Road, London SE1 8RQ **T** 020-7922 5300
E contact-us@ccht.org.uk **W** www.ccht.org.uk
Chief Executive, Julia Ashley

CENTREPOINT (1969), Central House, 25 Camperdown
Street, London E1 8DZ **T** 0800-587 5158
W www.centrepoint.org.uk
Chief Executive, Seyi Obakin, OBE

CEREDIGION HISTORICAL SOCIETY (1909),
78 Maesceinion, Aberystwyth SY23 3QJ
E ymholiadau@cymdeithashanesceredigion.org
W www.ceredigionhistoricalsociety.org
Hon. Secretary, Siân Bowyer

CHANGING FACES (1992), The Squire Centre, 33–37
University Street, London WC1E 6JN **T** 0345-450 0275
E info@changingfaces.org.uk **W** www.changingfaces.org.uk
Chief Executive, Becky Hewitt

CHARITIES AID FOUNDATION (1924), 25 Kings Hill
Avenue, West Malling ME19 4TA **T** 0300-012 3000
W www.cafonline.org
Chief Executive, Sir John Low, CBE

CHARTERED INSTITUTE OF ARBITRATORS (1915),
12 Bloomsbury Square, London WC1A 2LP **T** 020-7421 7444
E info@ciarb.org **W** www.ciarb.org
Director-General, Anthony Abrahams

CHARTERED INSTITUTE OF LINGUISTS (1910),
7th floor, 167 Fleet Street, London EC4A 2EA **T** 020-7940 3100
E info@ciol.org.uk **W** www.ciol.org.uk
Chief Executive, Ann Carlisle

CHARTERED SOCIETY OF FORENSIC SCIENCES
(1959), Office 40, Flexspace, Harrogate HG3 2XA
T 01423-534646 **E** info@csofs.org **W** www.csofs.org
Chief Executive, Dr Anya Hunt

CHATHAM HOUSE (1920), The Royal Institute of International
Affairs, Chatham House, 10 St James's Square, London
SW1Y 4LE **T** 020-7957 5700 **E** contact@chathamhouse.org
W www.chathamhouse.org
Director, Dr Robin Niblett, CMG

CHILD POVERTY ACTION GROUP (1965), 30 Micawber
Street, London N1 7TB **T** 020-7837 7979 **E** info@cpag.org.uk
W www.cpag.org.uk
Chief Executive, Alison Garnham

CHILDREN 1ST (1884), 83 Whitehouse Loan, Edinburgh
EH9 1AT **T** 0131-446 2300 **E** cfs@children1st.org.uk
W www.children1st.org.uk
Chief Executive, Mary Glasgow

CHILDREN'S SOCIETY (1881), Edward Rudolf House,
Margery Street, London WC1X 0JL **T** 0300-303 7000
E supportercare@childrenssociety.org.uk
W www.childrenssociety.org.uk
Chief Executive, Matthew Reed

CHOICE SUPPORT (1987), 1 Hermitage Court, Maidstone
Me16 9NT **T** 01622-722400 **E** enquiries@choicesupport.org.uk
W www.choicesupport.org.uk
Chief Executive, Sarah Maguire

CHRISTIAN AID (1945), 35–41 Lower Marsh, London SE1 7RL
T 020-7620 4444 **E** info@christian-aid.org
W www.christianaid.org.uk
Chief Executive, Amanda Mukwashi

CHRISTIAN AID SCOTLAND (1945), Augustine United
Church, 41 George IV Bridge, Edinburgh EH1 1EL
T 0131-220 1254 **E** edinburgh@christian-aid.org
W www.christianaid.org.uk/scotland
Head of Christian Aid Scotland, Sally Foster-Fulton

CHRISTIAN EDUCATION (2001), 5/6 Imperial Court, 12
Sovereign Road, Birmingham B30 3FH **T** 0121-458 3313
E sales@christianeducation.org.uk
W www.christianeducation.org.uk
Secretary, Zöe Keens

CHURCH BUILDINGS COUNCIL (1921), Church House, 27
Great Smith Street, London SW1P 3NZ **T** 020-7898 1874
E churchcare@churchofengland.org **W** www.churchcare.co.uk
Senior Church Buildings Officer, Dr David Knight

CHURCH LADS' AND CHURCH GIRLS' BRIGADE
(1891), St Martin's House, 2 Barnsley Road, Barnsley S63 6PY
T 01709-876535 **E** contactus@clcgb.org.uk
W www.clcgb.org.uk
Chief Executive, Audrey Simm

CHURCH MISSION SOCIETY (1799), Watlington Road,
Oxford OX4 6BZ **T** 01865-787400
E info@churchmissionsociety.org
W www.churchmissionsociety.org
Chief Executive, Alastair Bateman

CHURCH MONUMENTS SOCIETY (1979), c/o The Society
of Antiquaries, Burlington House, London W1J 0BD
T 0147-658 5012 **E** secretarychurchmonuments@gmail.com
W www.churchmonumentssociety.org
President, Mark Downing

CHURCH UNION (1859), c/o Additional Curates Society, 16
Commercial Street, Birmingham B1 1RS **T** 0121-382 5533
E membership@churchunion.co.uk **W** www.churchunion.co.uk
Chair, Father Darren Smith

CITIZENS ADVICE (1939), 3rd Floor North, 200 Aldersgate,
London EC1A 4HD **T** 03000-231231
W www.citizensadvice.org.uk
Chief Executive, Gillian Guy, CBE

CITY BUSINESS LIBRARY (1970), Aldermanbury, London
EC2V 7HH **T** 020-7332 1812 **E** cbl@cityoflondon.gov.uk
W www.cityoflondon.gov.uk/cbl
Manager, Alexandra Leader

CLASSICAL ASSOCIATION (1903), Cardinal Point, Park
Road, Rickmansworth WD3 1RE **T** 07926-632598
E office@classicalassociation.org **W** www.classicalassociation.org
Hon. Secretary, Dr J. Robson

CLIMATE GROUP (2004), 2nd Floor, Riverside Building,
County Hall, London SE1 7PB **T** 020-7960 2970
E info@theclimategroup.org **W** www.theclimategroup.org
Chief Executive, Helen Clarkson

COMBAT STRESS (1919), Tyrwhitt House, Oaklawn Road,
Leatherhead KT22 0BX **T** 01372-587000
E contactus@combatstress.org.uk **W** www.combatstress.org.uk
Chief Executive, Sue Freeth

COMMUNITY INTEGRATED CARE (1988), Old Market
Court, Miners Way, Widnes WA8 7SP **T** 0151 420 3637
E information@c-i-c.co.uk **W** www.c-i-c.co.uk
Chief Executive, Mark Adams

CONCERN WORLDWIDE (1968), 13–14 Calico House,
Clove Hitch Quay, London SW11 3TN **T** 020-7801 1850
W www.concern.org.uk
Executive Director, Rose Caldwell

THE CONSERVATION VOLUNTEERS (1959), Sedum House, Mallard Way, Doncaster DN4 8DB **T** 01302-388883 **E** information@tcv.org.uk **W** www.tcv.org.uk
Chief Executive, Darren York

CONTEMPORARY APPLIED ARTS (1948), 6 Paddington Street, London W1U 5QG **T** 020-7620 0086 **E** shop@caa.org.uk **W** www.caa.org.uk
Executive Director, Christine Lalumia

CO-OPERATIVES UK (1869), Holyoake House, Hanover Street, Manchester M60 0AS **T** 0161-214 1750 **E** info@uk.coop **W** www.uk.coop
Secretary-General, Ed Mayo

CORAM FAMILY (1739), Coram Campus, 41 Brunswick Square, London WC1N 1AZ **T** 020-7520 0300 **W** www.coram.org.uk
Chief Executive, Dr Carol Homden, CBE

CORONERS' SOCIETY OF ENGLAND AND WALES (1846), HM Coroner's Court, Gerard Majella Courthouse, Liverpool L5 2QD **W** www.coronersociety.org.uk
Chief Coroner, Hon. Judge Mark Lucraft, QC

CORPORATION OF THE CHURCH HOUSE (1888), Church House, Great Smith Street, London SW1P 3AZ **T** 020-7898 1311 **W** www.churchhouse.org.uk
Secretary, Christopher Palmer, CBE

COUNCIL FOR BRITISH ARCHAEOLOGY (1944), Beatrice de Cardi House, 66 Bootham, York YO30 7BZ **T** 01904-671417 **E** info@archaeologyuk.org **W** www.archaeologyuk.org
Director, Dr Mike Heyworth, MBE

COUNCIL FOR WORLD MISSION (1977), 6th Floor, Regus, 50 Broadway, London SW1H 0RG **T** 020-7222 4214 **E** council.uk@cwmission.org **W** www.cwmission.org
General Secretary, Revd Dr Collin Cowan

COUNCIL OF UNIVERSITY CLASSICAL DEPARTMENTS (1972), Institute of Classical Studies, Senate House, Malet Street, London WC1E 7HU **E** director.ics@sas.ac.uk **W** cucd.blogs.sas.ac.uk
Chair, Prof. Helen Lovatt

COUNTRY LAND & BUSINESS ASSOCIATION (1907), 16 Belgrave Square, London SW1X 8PQ **T** 020-7235 0511 **E** mail@cla.org.uk **W** www.cla.org.uk
President, Tim Breitmeyer

COUNTRYSIDE ALLIANCE (1997), 1 Spring Mews, Tinworth Street, London SE11 5AN **T** 020-7840 9220 **W** www.countryside-alliance.org.uk
Chief Executive, Tim Bonner

CPRE (CAMPAIGN TO PROTECT RURAL ENGLAND) (1926), 5–11 Lavington Street, London SE1 0NZ **T** 020-7981 2800 **E** info@cpre.org.uk **W** www.cpre.org.uk
Chief Executive, Crispin Truman

CRAFTS COUNCIL (1971), 44A Pentonville Road, London N1 9BY **T** 020-7806 2500 **E** reception@craftscouncil.org.uk **W** www.craftscouncil.org.uk
Executive Director, Rosy Greenlees, OBE

CRANSTOUN (1969), Thames Mews, Esher KT10 9AD **T** 020-8335 1830 **E** info@cranstoun.org.uk **W** www.cranstoun.org
Chair, Richard Pertwee

CROHN'S AND COLITIS UK (1979), 1 Bishop Square, Hatfield Business Park AL10 9NE **T** 01727-830038 **E** info@crohnsandcolitis.org.uk **W** www.crohnsandcolitis.org.uk
Chief Executive, Sarah Sleet

CRUELTY FREE INTERNATIONAL (1898), 16A Crane Grove, London N7 8NN **T** 020-7700 4888 **E** info@crueltyfreeinternational.org **W** www.crueltyfreeinternational.org
Chief Executive, Michelle Thew

CRUSE BEREAVEMENT CARE (1959), Unit 01, One Victoria Villas, Richmond TW9 2GW **T** 020-8939 9530, **Helpline** 0808-808 1677 **E** info@cruse.org.uk **W** www.cruse.org.uk
Chief Executive, Steven Wibberley

CUMBRIA PAST (1866), Westlands, Westbourne Drive, Lancaster LA1 5EE **T** 01524-67523 **W** www.cumbriapast.com
General Secretary, Marion E. M. McClintock, MBE

CYCLING UK (1878), Parklands, Railton Road, Guildford GU2 9JX **T** 01483-238301 **E** cycling@cyclinguk.org **W** www.cyclinguk.org
Chief Executive, Paul Tuohy

CYSTIC FIBROSIS TRUST (1964), One Aldgate, 2nd Floor, London EC3N 1RE **T** 020-3795 1555 **E** enquiries@cysticfibrosis.org.uk **W** www.cysticfibrosis.org.uk
Chief Executive, David Ramsden

DEMOS (1994), 76 Vincent Square, London SW1P 2PD **T** 020-3878 3955 **E** hello@demos.co.uk **W** www.demos.co.uk
Chief Executive, Polly Mackenzie

DESIGN AND TECHNOLOGY ASSOCIATION (1989), 11 Manor Park, Banbury OX16 3TB **T** 01789-470007 **E** info@data.org.uk **W** www.data.org.uk
Chief Executive, Tony Ryan

DEVON ARCHAEOLOGICAL SOCIETY (1929), Royal Albert Memorial Museum, Queen Street, Exeter EX4 3RX **E** dashonsec@devonarchaeologicalsociety.org.uk **W** www.devonarchaeologicalsociety.org.uk
Hon. Secretary, Debbie Griffiths

DIABETES UK (1934), Wells Lawrence House, 126 Back Church Lane, London E1 1FH **T** 0345-123 2399 **E** helpline@diabetes.org.uk **W** www.diabetes.org.uk
Chief Executive, Chris Askew

DISABILITY RIGHTS UK (1977), Plexal, 14 East Bay Lane, Queen Elizabeth Olympic Park E20 3BS **T** 0330-995 0400 **E** enquiries@disabilityrightsuk.org **W** www.disabilityrightsuk.org
Chief Executive, Kamran Mallick

DITCHLEY FOUNDATION (1958), Ditchley Park, Chipping Norton OX7 4ER **T** 01608-677346 **E** info@ditchley.co.uk **W** www.ditchley.co.uk
Director, James Arroyo, OBE

DOWN'S SYNDROME ASSOCIATION (1970), Langdon Down Centre, 2A Langdon Park, Teddington TW11 9PS **T** 0333-1212300 **E** info@downs-syndrome.org.uk **W** www.downs-syndrome.org.uk
Chief Executive, Carol Boys

EARLY YEARS ALLIANCE (1961), 50 Featherstone Street, London EC1Y 8RT **T** 020-7697 2500 **E** info@eyalliance.org.uk **W** www.eyalliance.org.uk
Chief Executive, Neil Leitch

ECCLESIOLOGICAL SOCIETY (1879), 68 Scholars Road, Balham SW12 0PG **E** admin@ecclsoc.org **W** www.ecclsoc.org
Chairman, Mark Kirby

EDINBURGH CHAMBER OF COMMERCE (1785), Chamber Business Centre, 40 George Street, Edinburgh EH2 2LE **T** 0131-221 2999 **E** info@edinburghchamber.co.uk **W** www.edinburghchamber.co.uk
Chief Executive, Liz McAreavey

EDUCATION SUPPORT PARTNERSHIP (1877), 40A Drayton Park, London N5 1EW **T** 020-7697 2750, **Helpline** 0800-056 2561 **E** enquiries@edsupport.org.uk **W** www.educationsupportpartnership.org.uk
Chief Executive, Sinéad McBrearty

EGYPT EXPLORATION SOCIETY (1882), 3 Doughty Mews, London WC1N 2PG **T** 020-7242 1880 **E** contact@ees.ac.uk **W** www.ees.ac.uk
Director, Dr Carl Graves

ELECTORAL REFORM SOCIETY (1884), 3rd Floor, News Building, 3 London Bridge Street, London SE1 9SG T 020-3743 6066 E ers@electoral-reform.org.uk W www.electoral-reform.org.uk *Chief Executive*, Darren Hughes

ELGAR SOCIETY (1951), 6 Carriage Close, Worcester WR2 6AE T 01905-339371 E vice.chair@elgar.org W elgar.org/elgarsoc/ *Chairman (acting)*, Stuart Freed

EMERGENCY PLANNING SOCIETY (1993), The Hawkhills, Easingwold, York YO61 3EG T 01347-821972 E info@the-eps.org W www.the-eps.org *Chair*, Jacqui Semple

ENABLE SCOTLAND (1954), Inspire House, 3 Renshaw Place, Glasgow ML1 4UF T 01698-737000 E enabledirect@enable.org.uk W www.enable.org.uk *Chief Executive*, Theresa Shearer

ENERGY INSTITUTE (2003), 61 New Cavendish Street, London W1G 7AR T 020-7467 7100 E info@energyinst.org W www.energyinst.org *Chief Executive*, Louise Kingham, OBE

ENGLISH ASSOCIATION (1906), University of Leicester, University Road, Leicester LE1 7RH T 0116-229 7622 E engassoc@le.ac.uk W www.le.ac.uk/engassoc *Chief Executive*, Dr Rebecca Fisher

ENGLISH CHESS FEDERATION (1904), The Watch Oak, Chain Lane, Battle TN33 0YD T 01424-775222 E office@englishchess.org.uk W www.englishchess.org.uk *Chief Executive*, Mike Truran

ENGLISH FOLK DANCE AND SONG SOCIETY (1932), Cecil Sharp House, 2 Regent's Park Road, London NW1 7AY T 020-7485 2206 E info@efdss.org W www.efdss.org *Chief Executive*, Katy Spicer

ENGLISH-SPEAKING UNION OF THE COMMONWEALTH (1918), Dartmouth House, 37 Charles Street, London W1J 5ED T 020-7529 1550 E esu@esu.org W www.esu.org *Director-General*, Jane Easton

EPILEPSY SOCIETY (1892), Chesham Lane, Chalfont St Peter SL9 0RJ T 01494-601300, **Helpline** 01494-601400 W www.epilepsysociety.org.uk *Chief Executive*, Clare Pelham

EQUINOX CARE (1986), 1 Waterloo Gardens, London N1 1TY T 020-3668 9270 E enquiries@equinoxcare.org.uk W www.equinoxcare.org.uk *Chief Executive*, Gill Arukpe

ESPERANTO ASSOCIATION OF BRITAIN (1976), Esperanto House, Station Road, Stoke-on-Trent ST12 9DE T 01782-372 141 E eab@esperanto.org.uk W www.esperanto.org.uk *President*, Ian Carter

FABIAN SOCIETY (1884), 61 Petty France, London SW1H 9EU T 020-7227 4900 E info@fabians.org.uk W www.fabians.org.uk *General Secretary*, Andrew Harrop

FAITH AND THOUGHT (VICTORIA INSTITUTE) (1865), 15 The Drive, Harlow CM20 3QD E admin@faithandthought.org W www.faithandthought.org *President*, Prof. Sir Colin J. Humphreys, CBE

FAMILY ACTION (1869), 24 Angel Gate, City Road, London EC1V 2PT T 020-7254 6251 E info@family-action.org.uk W www.family-action.org.uk *Chief Executive*, David Holmes, CBE

FAUNA & FLORA INTERNATIONAL (1903), The David Attenborough Building, Pembroke Street, Cambridge CB2 3QZ T 01223-571000 E info@fauna-flora.org W www.fauna-flora.org *Chief Executive*, Mark Rose

FEDERATION OF FAMILY HISTORY SOCIETIES (1974), 2 Primrose Avenue, Manchester M41 0TY T 01263-824 951 E info@ffhs.org.uk W www.familyhistoryfederation.com *President*, Dr Nick Barratt

FEDERATION OF SMALL BUSINESSES (1974), Sir Frank Whittle Way, Blackpool FY4 2FE T 0808-2020 888 E customerservices@fsb.org.uk W www.fsb.org.uk *National Chairman*, Mike Cherry, OBE

FIELDS IN TRUST (1925), Unit 2D, Woodstock Studios, 36 Woodstock Grove, London W12 8LE T 020-7427 2110 E info@fieldsintrust.org W www.fieldsintrust.org *Chief Executive*, Helen Griffiths

FIELD STUDIES COUNCIL (1943), Preston Montford, Shrewsbury SY4 1HW T 01743-852100 E enquiries@field-studies-council.org W www.field-studies-council.org *Chief Executive*, Mark Castle, OBE

FIGHT FOR SIGHT (1965), 18 Mansell Street, London E1 8AA T 020-7264 3900 E info@fightforsight.org.uk W www.fightforsight.org.uk *Chief Executive*, Sherine Krause

FIRE FIGHTERS CHARITY (1943), Level 6, Belvedere, Basing View, Basingstoke RG21 4HG T 01256-366566 W www.firefighterscharity.org.uk *Chief Executive*, Jill Tolfrey

FIRE PROTECTION ASSOCIATION (1946), London Road, Moreton-in-Marsh, Glos GL56 0RH T 01608-812500 E fpa@thefpa.co.uk W www.thefpa.co.uk *Managing Director*, Jonathan O'Neill, OBE

FLAG INSTITUTE (1971), HQS Wellington, Victoria Embankment, London WC2R 2PN E info@flaginstitute.org W www.flaginstitute.org *President*, Capt. Malcolm Farrow, OBE, FFI, RN

FOREIGN PRESS ASSOCIATION IN LONDON (1888), 8 St James's Square, London SW1Y 4JU T 020-3727 4319 W www.fpalondon.net *Director*, Deborah Bonetti

FOUNDATION FOR CREDIT COUNSELLING (STEP CHANGE) (1993), Wade House, Merrion Centre, Leeds LS2 8NG T 0800-138 1111 W www.stepchange.org *Chief Executive*, Phil Andrew

FRANCO-BRITISH SOCIETY (1924), 3 Dovedale Studios, 465 Battersea Park Road, London SW11 4LR E francobritsoc@gmail.com W www.franco-british-society.org *Executive Secretary*, Isabelle Gault

FRIENDS OF CATHEDRAL MUSIC (1956), 27 Old Gloucester Street, London WC1N 3XX T 020-3637 2172 E info@fcm.org.uk W www.fcm.org.uk *Chair*, Peter Allwood

FRIENDS OF FRIENDLESS CHURCHES (1957), St Ann's Vestry Hall, 2 Church Entry, London EC4V 5HB T 020-7236 3934 E office@friendsoffriendlesschurches.org.uk W www.friendsoffriendlesschurches.org.uk *Director*, Rachel Morley

FRIENDS OF THE BODLEIAN (1925), Bodleian Library, Broad Street, Oxford OX1 3BG T 01865-277162 E reader.services@bodleian.ox.ac.uk W www.bodleian.ox.ac.uk/bodley/friends *Librarian*, Richard Ovenden

FRIENDS OF THE EARTH SCOTLAND (1978), Thorn House, 5 Rose Street, Edinburgh EH2 2PR T 0131-243 2700 W www.foe.scot *Director*, Dr Richard Dixon

FRIENDS OF THE ELDERLY (1905), 40–42 Ebury Street, London SW1W 0LZ T 020-7730 8263 E enquiries@fote.org.uk W www.fote.org.uk *Chief Executive*, Steve Allen

FRIENDS OF THE NATIONAL LIBRARIES (1931),
PO Box 4291, Reading RG8 9JA
W www.friendsofnationallibraries.org.uk
Chair, Geordie Greig

FUTURES FOR WOMEN (SPTW) (1859), 11 Church Street,
Rugby CV23 9RL E futuresforwomen@btinternet.com
W futuresforwomen.org.uk
Secretary, Ms Jane Hampson

GALLIPOLI ASSOCIATION (1969), 5 Mews House, Roffey
Park, Colegate RH12 4TD T 028-2177 2996
E secretary@gallipoli-association.org
W www.gallipoli-association.org
Hon. Secretary, Sarah Kellam

GAME AND WILDLIFE CONSERVATION TRUST
(1969), Burgate Manor, Fordingbridge SP6 1EF
T 01425-652381 E info@gwct.org.uk W www.gwct.org.uk
Chief Executive, Teresa Dent

GARDENS TRUST (1965), 70 Cowcross Street, London
EC1M 6EJ T 020-7608 2409 E enquiries@thegardenstrust.org
W thegardenstrust.org
Chairman, Dr James Bartos

GEMMOLOGICAL ASSOCIATION OF GREAT BRITAIN
(GEM-A) (1931), 21 Ely Place, London EC1N 6TD
T 020-7404 3334 E information@gem-a.com
W www.gem-a.com
Chief Executive, Alan Hart

GENERAL MEDICAL COUNCIL (1858), 3 Hardman Street,
Manchester M3 3AW T 0161-923 6602 E gmc@gmc-uk.org
W www.gmc-uk.org
Chief Executive, Charlie Massey

GENERAL OPTICAL COUNCIL (1958), 10 Old Bailey,
London EC4M 7NG T 020-7580 3898 E goc@optical.org
W www.optical.org
Chief Executive / Registrar, Vicky McDermott

GEOGRAPHICAL ASSOCIATION (1893), 160 Solly Street,
Sheffield S1 4BF T 0114-296 0088 E info@geography.org.uk
W www.geography.org.uk
Chief Executive, Alan Kinder

GEOLOGICAL SOCIETY OF LONDON (1807),
Burlington House, Piccadilly, London W1J 0BG T 020-7434 9944
E enquiries@geolsoc.org.uk W www.geolsoc.org.uk
President, Prof. Nick Rogers

GEORGIAN GROUP (1937), 6 Fitzroy Square, W1T 5DX
T 020-7529 8920 E office@georgiangroup.org.uk
W www.georgiangroup.org.uk
Secretary, David Adshead

GIRLGUIDING (1910), 17–19 Buckingham Palace Road,
SW1W 0PT T 020-7834 6242 E info@girlguiding.org.uk
W www.girlguiding.org.uk
Chief Guide, Amanda Medler

GIRLS' FRIENDLY SOCIETY IN ENGLAND AND
WALES (1875), Unit 30 Angel Gate, 326 City Road, London
EC1V 2PT T 020-7837 9669 E info@girlsfriendlysociety.org.uk
W girlsfriendlysociety.org.uk
Executive Director, Paul Rompani

GLADSTONE'S LIBRARY (1894), Church Lane, Hawarden
CH5 3DF T 01244-532350 E enquiries@gladlib.org
W www.gladstoneslibrary.org
Warden, Revd Peter Francis

GREENPEACE UK (1979), Canonbury Villas, N1 2PN
T 020-7865 8100 W www.greenpeace.org.uk
Executive Director, John Sauven

GUIDE DOGS (1934), Hillfields, Burghfield Common, Reading
RG7 3YG T 0118-983 5555 E guidedogs@guidedogs.org.uk
W www.guidedogs.org.uk
Chief Executive, Thomas Wright, CBE

GUILD OF FREEMEN OF THE CITY OF LONDON
(1908), Rooms 78/79, 65 London Wall, London EC2M 5TU
T 020-7239 9016 E clerk@guild-freemen-london.co.uk
W www.guild-freemen-london.co.uk
Clerk to the Guild, Christine Cook

GUILD OF GLASS ENGRAVERS (1975), c/o Red House Glass
Cone, High Street, Stourbridge DY8 4AZ T 07834-549925
E enquiries@gge.org.uk W www.gge.org.uk
President, Tracey Sheppard

GUILD OF PASTORAL PSYCHOLOGY (1937), GPP
Administration, Unit 1 Chapleton Lodge, Blackborough End
PE32 1SF T 01553-849849
E administration@guildofpastoralpsychology.org.uk
W www.guildofpastoralpsychology.org.uk
Chair, Jim Keeling

GURKHA WELFARE TRUST (1969), PO Box 2170, 22 Queen
Street, Salisbury SP2 2EX T 01722-323955 E info@gwt.org.uk
W www.gwt.org.uk
Director, Al Howard

GUY'S AND ST THOMAS' CHARITY (1553), Francis House,
9 King's Head Yard, SE1 1NA T 020-7089 4550
E info@gsttcharity.org.uk W www.gsttcharity.org.uk
Chief Executive, Kieron Boyle

HAEMOPHILIA SOCIETY (1950), Willcox House, 140–148
Borough High Street, London SE1 1LB T 020-7939 0780
E info@haemophilia.org.uk W www.haemophilia.org.uk
Chief Executive, Liz Carroll

HAIG HOUSING TRUST (2009), Alban Dobson House, Green
Lane, Morden SM4 5NS T 020-8685 5777
E enquiries@haighousing.org.uk W www.haighousing.org.uk
Chief Executive, James Richardson

HAKLUYT SOCIETY (1846), c/o Map Library, The British
Library, London NW1 2DB T 07568-468066
E office@hakluyt.com W www.hakluyt.com
President, Prof. Jim. Bennett

HANSARD SOCIETY (1944), 5th Floor, 9 King Street,
EC2V 8EA T 020-7710 6070 E contact@hansardsociety.org.uk
W www.hansardsociety.org.uk
Director, Dr Ruth Fox

HARVEIAN SOCIETY OF LONDON (1831), Lettsom
House, 11 Chandos Street, W1G 9EB T 020-7580 1043
E harveiansoclondon@btconnect.com
W www.harveiansocietyoflondon.btck.co.uk
Executive Secretary, Cdr Mike Flynn, FCMI MCPID

HEARING LINK (1947), The Grange, Wycombe Road, Princes
Risborough HP27 9NS T 07526-123255
E enquiries@hearinglink.org W www.hearinglink.org
Chief Operating Officer, Dr Lorraine Gailey

HELP FOR HEROES (2007), Unit 14, Parkers Close, Salisbury
SP5 3RB T 0300-303 9888 W www.helpforheroes.org.uk
Chief Executive, Melanie Waters, OBE

HELP MUSICIANS (MUSICIANS BENEVOLENT FUND)
(1921), 7–11 Britannia Street, London WC1X 9JS
T 020-7239 9100 E info@helpmusicians.org.uk
W www.helpmusicians.org.uk
Chief Executive, James Ainscough

HERALDRY SOCIETY (1947), 53 Hitchin Street, Baldock
SG7 6AQ E info@theheraldrysociety.com
W www.theheraldrysociety.com
Hon. Secretary, John Tunesi of Liongam

HIGH SHERIFFS' ASSOCIATION OF ENGLAND &
WALES (1971), Heritage House, PO Box 21, Baldock SG7 5SH
T 01462-896688 E secretary@highsheriffs.com
W www.highsheriffs.com
Chair, Hon. Hugh Tollemache

HISPANIC AND LUSO BRAZILIAN COUNCIL
(CANNING HOUSE) (1943), Canning House, 126 Wigmore
Street, W1U 3RZ T 020-7811 5600 E events@canninghouse.org
W www.canninghouse.org
Chief Executive, Cristina Cortes

HISTORICAL ASSOCIATION (1906), 59A Kennington Park Road, London SE11 4JH **T** 0300-100 0223
E enquiries@history.org.uk **W** www.history.org.uk
Chief Executive, Rebecca Sullivan

HISTORIC HOUSES ASSOCIATION (1973), 2 Chester Street, London SW1X 7BB **T** 020-7259 5688 **E** info@hha.org.uk
W www.historichouses.org
Director-General, Ben Cowell

HONG KONG ASSOCIATION (1961), Swire House, 59 Buckingham Gate, London SW1E 6AJ **T** 020-7963 9447
E communications@hkas.org.uk **W** www.hkas.org.uk
Executive Director, Lindsay Jones

HONOURABLE SOCIETY OF CYMMRODORION (1751), 157–163, Grays Inn Road, London WC1X 8UE
E secretary@cymmrodorion.org **W** www.cymmrodorion.org
Honorary Secretary, Dr Lynn Williams, FLSW

HOSPITAL SATURDAY FUND (1873), 24 Upper Ground, London SE1 9PD **T** 020-7202 1365 **E** charity@hsf.eu.com
W www.hospitalsaturdayfund.org
Chief Executive, Paul Jackson

HOUSING JUSTICE (2003), 256 Bermondsey Street, London SE1 3UJ **T** 020-3544 8094 **E** info@housingjustice.org.uk
W www.housingjustice.org.uk
Chief Executive, Kathy Mohan

THE HUMANE RESEARCH TRUST (1962), Brook House, 29 Bramhall Lane South, Stockport SK7 2DN **T** 0161-439 8041
E info@humaneresearch.org.uk **W** www.humaneresearch.org.uk
Chair, L. M. Rhoades

I CAN (1888), 31 Angel Gate (Gate 5), Goswell Road, London EC1V 2PT **T** 020-7843 2510 **E** info@ican.org.uk
W www.ican.org.uk
Chief Executive, Bob Reitemeier, CBE

INCORPORATED COUNCIL OF LAW REPORTING FOR ENGLAND AND WALES (1865), Megarry House, 119 Chancery Lane, WC2A 1PP **T** 020-7242 6471
E enquiries@iclr.co.uk **W** www.iclr.co.uk
Chief Executive, Kevin Laws

INCORPORATED SOCIETY OF MUSICIANS (1882), 4–5 Inverness Mews, London W2 3JQ **T** 020-7221 3499
E membership@ism.org **W** www.ism.org
Chief Executive, Deborah Annetts

INDEPENDENT SCHOOLS' BURSARS ASSOCIATION (1932), Bluett House, Unit 11–12, Cliddesden RG25 2JB
T 01256-330369 **E** office@theisba.org.uk
W www.theisba.org.uk
Chief Executive, David Woodgate

INDEPENDENT AGE (1863), 18 Avonmore Road, W14 8RR
T 020-7605 4200 **E** charity@independentage.org
W www.independentage.org
Chief Executive, Shan Nicholas

INDUSTRY AND PARLIAMENT TRUST (1977), Suite 101, 3 Whitehall Court, SW1A 2EL **T** 020-7839 9400
E enquiries@ipt.org.uk **W** www.ipt.org.uk
Chief Executive, Nick Maher

INSTITUTE FOR PUBLIC POLICY RESEARCH (1988), Ground Floor, 14 Buckingham Street, London WC2N 6DF
T 020-7470 6100 **E** info@ippr.org **W** www.ippr.org
Director, Tom Kibasi

INSTITUTE OF CANCER RESEARCH (1909), 123 Old Brompton Road, London SW7 3RP **T** 020-7352 8133
W www.icr.ac.uk
Chief Executive, Prof. Paul Workman

INSTITUTE OF ECONOMIC AFFAIRS (1955), 2 Lord North Street, London SW1P 3LB **T** 020-7799 8900 **E** iea@iea.org.uk
W www.iea.org.uk
Director-General, Mark Littlewood

INSTITUTE OF FOOD SCIENCE AND TECHNOLOGY (1964), 5 Cambridge Court, 210 Shepherd's Bush Road, London W6 7NJ **T** 020-7603 6316 **E** info@ifst.org **W** www.ifst.org
Chief Executive, Jon Poole

INSTITUTE OF HEALTH PROMOTION AND EDUCATION (1962), PO BOX 7409, Lichfield WS14 4LS
E admin@ihpe.org.uk **W** www.ihpe.org.uk
President, Sylvia Cheater

INSTITUTE OF HERALDIC AND GENEALOGICAL STUDIES (1961), 79–82 Northgate, Canterbury CT1 1BA
T 01227-768664 **E** enquiries@ihgs.ac.uk **W** www.ihgs.ac.uk
Principal, Dr Richard Baker

INSTITUTE OF MASTERS OF WINE (1955), 6 Riverlight Quay, London SW11 8EA **T** 020-7383 9130
E info@mastersofwine.org **W** www.mastersofwine.org
Executive Director, Rufus Olins

INSTITUTE OF MATHEMATICS AND ITS APPLICATIONS (1964), Catherine Richards House, 16 Nelson Street, Southend-on-Sea SS1 1EF **T** 01702-354020
E post@ima.org.uk **W** www.ima.org.uk
Executive Director, David Youdan

INSTITUTE OF PHYSICS AND ENGINEERING IN MEDICINE (1997), Fairmount House, 230 Tadcaster Road, York YO24 1ES **T** 01904-610821 **E** office@ipem.ac.uk
W www.ipem.ac.uk
Chief Executive, Rosemary Cook, CBE

INSTITUTION OF ENGINEERING AND TECHNOLOGY (1871), Michael Faraday House, Six Hills Way, Stevenage SG1 2AY **T** 01438-313311 **E** postmaster@theiet.org
W www.theiet.org
Chief Executive & Secretary, Nigel Fine

INTERCONTINENTAL CHURCH SOCIETY (1823), Unit 11, Ensign Business Centre, Westwood Way, Coventry CV4 8JA
T 024-7646 3940 **W** www.ics-uk.org
Mission Director, Revd Richard Bromley

INTERNATIONAL AFRICAN INSTITUTE (1926), School of Oriental and African Studies, Thornhaugh Street, London WC1H 0XG **T** 020-7898 4420 **E** iai@soas.ac.uk
W www.internationalafricaninstitute.org
Honorary Director, Prof. Philip Burnham

INTERNATIONAL CHURCHILL SOCIETY UK (1968), Churchill College, Storey's Way, Cambridge CB3 0DS
T 01223-331646 **E** asmith@winstonchurchill.org
W www.winstonchurchill.org
Executive Director, Andrew Smith

INTERNATIONAL INSTITUTE FOR CONSERVATION OF HISTORIC AND ARTISTIC WORKS (1950), 3 Birdcage Walk, London SW1H 9JJ **T** 020-7799 5500
E iic@iiconservation.org **W** www.iiconservation.org
Secretary-General, Jane Henderson

INTERNATIONAL RESCUE COMMITTEE UK (1997), 100 Wood Street, London EC2V 7AN **T** 020-3983 2727
E contactus@rescue-uk.org **W** www.rescue-uk.org
Executive Director, Sanj Srikanthan

INTERNATIONAL STUDENTS HOUSE (1962), 229 Great Portland Street, London W1W 5PN **T** 020-7631 8300
E accom@ish.org.uk **W** www.ish.org.uk
Chief Executive, Martin Chalker

INTERNATIONAL TREE FOUNDATION (1924), 1 Kings Meadow, Oxford OX2 0DP **T** 01865-922430
E info@internationaltreefoundation.org
W www.internationaltreefoundation.org
Chief Executive, Andy Egan

IRAN SOCIETY (1911), 1a St Martin's House, London NW1 1QB **T** 020-7235 5122 **E** info@iransociety.org
W www.iransociety.org
President, Sir Richard Dalton, KCMG

JAPAN SOCIETY (1891), 13–14 Cornwall Terrace, London NW1 4QP **T** 020-7935 0475 **E** info@japansociety.org.uk
W www.japansociety.org.uk
Chief Executive, Heidi Potter

THE JERUSALEM AND THE MIDDLE EAST CHURCH ASSOCIATION (1929), 1 Hart House, The Hart, Farnham GU9 7HJ **T** 01252-726994 **E** information@jmeca.org.uk **W** www.jmeca.org.uk
Chair, John Clark

JEWISH CARE (1990), Amélie House, Maurice and Vivienne Wohl Campus, London NW11 9DQ **T** 020-8922 2000 **E** info@jcare.org **W** www.jewishcare.org
Chair, Steven Lewis

JOURNALISTS' CHARITY (1864), Dickens House, 35 Wathen Road, Dorking RH4 1JY **T** 01306-887511 **E** enquiries@journalistscharity.org.uk **W** www.journalistscharity.org.uk
Chief Executive, James Brindle

KENT ARCHAEOLOGICAL SOCIETY (1857), Maidstone Museum, St Faith's Street, Maidstone ME14 1LH **E** secretary@kentarchaeology.org.uk **W** www.kentarchaeology.org.uk
Hon. General Secretary, Dr Clive Drew

KING'S FUND (1897), 11–13 Cavendish Square, London W1G 0AN **T** 020-7307 2400 **E** enquiry@kingsfund.org.uk **W** www.kingsfund.org.uk
Chief Executive, Richard Murray

LCIA (LONDON COURT OF INTERNATIONAL ARBITRATION) (1892), 70 Fleet Street, London EC4Y 1EU **T** 020-7936 6200 **E** enquiries@lcia.org **W** www.lcia.org
Director-General, Dr Jacomijn van Haersolte-van Hof

LEAGUE OF THE HELPING HAND (1908), PO Box 342, Burgess Hill RH15 5AQ **T** 01444-236099 **E** secretary@lhh.org.uk **W** www.lhh.org.uk
Chair and Director, Moira Parrott

THE LEPROSY MISSION, ENGLAND, WALES, THE CHANNEL ISLANDS AND THE ISLE OF MAN (1874), Goldhay Way, Peterborough PE2 5GZ **T** 01733-370505 **E** post@tlmew.org.uk **W** www.leprosymission.org.uk
National Director, Peter Waddup

LIBERTY (NATIONAL COUNCIL FOR CIVIL LIBERTIES) (1934), Liberty House, 26–30 Strutton Ground, London SW19 2HR **T** 020-7403 3888 **W** www.libertyhumanrights.org.uk
Director (acting), Corey Stoughton

LINNEAN SOCIETY OF LONDON (1788), Burlington House, London W1J 0BF **T** 020-7434 4479 **E** info@linnean.org **W** www.linnean.org
Executive Secretary, Dr Elizabeth Rollinson

LISTENING BOOKS (1959), 12 Lant Street, London SE1 1QH **T** 020-7407 9417 **E** info@listening-books.org.uk **W** www.listening-books.org.uk
Chief Executive, Bill Dee

LIVABILITY (*c.*1840), 6 Mitre Passage, London SE10 0ER **T** 020-7452 2000 **E** info@livability.org.uk **W** www.livability.org.uk
Chief Executive, Helen England

LOCAL GOVERNMENT ASSOCIATION (1997), 18 Smith Square, London SW1P 3HZ **T** 020-7664 3000 **E** info@local.gov.uk **W** www.local.gov.uk
Chief Executive, Mark Lloyd

LOCAL SOLUTIONS (1974), Mount Vernon Green, Hall Lane, Liverpool L7 8TF **T** 0151-709 0990 **E** info@localsolutions.org.uk **W** www.localsolutions.org.uk
Chief Executive, Steve Hawkins

LONDON AND MIDDLESEX ARCHAEOLOGICAL SOCIETY (1855), c/o Museum of London, London EC2Y 5HN **T** 020-7410 2228 **W** www.lamas.org.uk
Hon. Secretary, Karen Thomas

LONDON CITY MISSION (1835), Nasmith House, 175 Tower Bridge Road, London SE1 2AH **T** 020-7407 7585 **E** enquiries@lcm.org.uk **W** www.lcm.org.uk
Chief Executive, Graham Miller

LONDON COLLEGE OF OSTEOPATHIC MEDICINE (1946), 8–10 Boston Place, London NW1 6QH **T** 020-7262 1128 **W** www.lcom.org.uk
Director, Brian McKenna

LONDON CATALYST (1873), 45 Westminster Bridge Road, London SE1 7JB **T** 020-3828 4204 **E** london.catalyst@peabody.org.uk **W** www.londoncatalyst.org.uk
Director, Victor Willmott

LONDON COUNCILS (2000), 59½ Southwark Street, London SE1 0AL **T** 020-7934 9999 **E** info@londoncouncils.gov.uk **W** www.londoncouncils.gov.uk
Chief Executive, John O'Brien

LONDON INSTITUTE OF FINANCE AND BANKING (1879), 8th Floor, Peninsular House, London EC3R 8LJ **T** 01227-818609 **E** customerservices@libf.ac.uk **W** www.libf.ac.uk
Chief Executive, Alex Fraser

LONDON LIBRARY (1841), 14 St James's Square, London SW1Y 4LG **T** 020-7766 4700 **E** reception@londonlibrary.co.uk **W** www.londonlibrary.co.uk
Director, Philip Marshall

LONDON PLAYING FIELDS FOUNDATION (1890), 58 Bloomsbury Street, London WC1B 3QT **T** 020-7323 0331 **E** enquiries@lpff.org.uk **W** www.lpff.org.uk
Chief Executive, Alex Welsh

LONDON SOCIETY (1912), Mortimer Wheeler House, 46 Eagle Wharf Road, London N1 7ED **E** info@londonsociety.org.uk **W** www.londonsociety.org.uk
Chair, Peter Murray

LOTTERIES COUNCIL (1979), 66 Lincoln's Inn Fields, London WC2A 3LH **T** 07954-723224 **E** tina@lotteriescouncil.org.uk **W** www.lotteriescouncil.org.uk
Chair, Tony Vick

LULLABY TRUST (1971), 11 Belgrave Road, London SW1V 1RB **T** 020-7802 3200 **E** office@lullabytrust.org.uk **W** www.lullabytrust.co.uk
Chief Executive, Jenny Ward (acting)

MACMILLAN CANCER SUPPORT (1911), 89 Albert Embankment, London SE1 7UQ **T** 020-7840 7840 **W** www.macmillan.org.uk
Chief Executive, Lynda Thomas

MAKING MUSIC, THE NATIONAL FEDERATION OF MUSIC SOCIETIES (1935), 8 Holyrood Street, London SE1 2EL **T** 020-7939 6030 **W** www.makingmusic.org.uk
Chief Executive, Barbara Eifler

MARIE CURIE CANCER CARE (1948), 89 Albert Embankment, SE1 7TP **T** 0800-716146 **E** supporter.relations@mariecurie.org.uk **W** www.mariecurie.org.uk
Chief Executive, Matthew Reed

MARINE BIOLOGICAL ASSOCIATION OF THE UK (1884), The Laboratory, Citadel Hill, Plymouth PL1 2BP **T** 01752-426493 **E** info@mba.ac.uk **W** www.mba.ac.uk
President, Prof. Sir John Beddington, CMG FRS

MARINE SOCIETY AND SEA CADETS (1756), 202 Lambeth Road, London SE1 7JW **T** 020-7654 7000 **E** info@ms-sc.org **W** www.ms-sc.org
Chief Executive, Martin Coles

MASONIC CHARITABLE FOUNDATION (1982), 60 Great Queen Street, London WC2B 5AZ **T** 020-3146 3333 **E** info@mcf.org.uk **W** www.mcf.org.uk
Chief Executive, David Innes

MATERNITY ACTION (2008), 52–54 Featherstone Street, London EC1Y 8RT **T** 020-7253 2288 **W** www.maternityaction.org.uk
Director, Rosalind Bragg

MATHEMATICAL ASSOCIATION (1871), 259 London Road, Leicester LE2 3BE T 0116-221 0013 E office@m-a.org.uk W www.m-a.org.uk
President, Prof. Mike Askew

ME ASSOCIATION (1976), 7 Apollo Office Court, Radclive Road, Gawcott MK18 4DF T 01280-818964
W www.meassociation.org.uk
Chair, Neil Riley

MEDIAWATCH-UK (1965), 3 Willow House, Kennington Road, Ashford TN24 0NR T 01233-633936
E info@mediawatchuk.org W www.mediawatchuk.org
Director, Helen Lewington

MEDICAL SOCIETY OF LONDON (1773), Lettsom House, 11 Chandos Street, London W1G 9EB T 020-7580 1043
E info@medsoclondon.org W www.medsoclondon.org
Registrar, Cdr Mike Flynn, FCMI MCPID

MEDICAL WOMEN'S FEDERATION (1917), Tavistock House North, Tavistock Square, London WC1H 9HX
T 020-7387 7765 E admin@medicalwomensfederation.org.uk
W www.medicalwomensfederation.org.uk
President, Dr Henrietta Bowden-Jones

MENCAP (ROYAL MENCAP SOCIETY) (1946), 123 Golden Lane, EC1Y 0RT T 020-7454 0454
E helpline@mencap.org.uk W www.mencap.org.uk
Chief Executive, Jan Tregelles

MENTAL HEALTH FOUNDATION (1972), Colechurch House, 1 London Bridge Walk, London SE1 2SX
T 020-7803 1100 W www.mentalhealth.org.uk
Chief Executive, Mark Rowland

MERCHANT NAVY WELFARE BOARD (1948), 8 Cumberland Place, Southampton SO15 2BH T 023-8033 7799
E enquiries@mnwb.org.uk W www.mnwb.org
Chief Executive, Peter Tomlin, MBE

MHA (1943), Epworth House, 3 Stuart Street, Derby DE1 2EQ
T 01332-296200 E enquiries@mha.org.uk W www.mha.org.uk
Chief Executive, Sam Monaghan

MILITARY HISTORICAL SOCIETY (1948), Lower Brook Farm, Smithy Lane, Rainow SK10 5VP T 0121-711 4712
E flers99@yahoo.com W www.themilitaryhistoricalsociety.co.uk
Chair, Clive Elderton, CBE

MIND (NATIONAL ASSOCIATION FOR MENTAL HEALTH) (1946), 15–19 Broadway, London E15 4BQ
T 020-8519 2122, **Infoline** 0300-123 3393
E supporterrelations@mind.org.uk W www.mind.org.uk
Chief Executive, Paul Farmer, CBE

MINERALOGICAL SOCIETY (1876), 12 Baylis Mews, Twickenham TW1 3HQ T 020-8891 6600 E info@minersoc.org
W www.minersoc.org
Executive Director, Kevin Murphy

MISSING PEOPLE (1993), 284 Upper Richmond Road West, London SW14 7JE T 020-8392 4590
W www.missingpeople.org.uk
Chief Executive, Jo Youle

MISSION TO SEAFARERS (1856), St Michael Paternoster Royal, College Hill, London EC4R 2RL T 020-7248 5202
E info@missiontoseafarers.org W www.missiontoseafarers.org
Secretary General, Revd Andrew Wright

MULTIPLE SCLEROSIS SOCIETY (1953), MS National Centre, 372 Edgware Road, London NW2 6ND T 020-8438 0700
E supportercare@mssociety.org.uk W www.mssociety.org.uk
Chief Executive, Nick Moberly

MUSEUMS ASSOCIATION (1889), 42 Clerkenwell Close, London EC1R 0AZ T 020-7566 7800
E info@museumsassociation.org
W www.museumsassociation.org
Director, Sharon Heal

NABS (1916), 10 Hills Place, London W1F 7SD T 020-7290 7070
W www.nabs.org.uk
Chief Executive, Diana Tickell

NACRO, THE SOCIAL JUSTICE CHARITY (1966), 1st Floor, 46 Loman Street, London SE1 0EH T 0300-123 1889
E helpline@nacro.org.uk W www.nacro.org.uk
Chief Executive, Campbell Robb

NAT (NATIONAL AIDS TRUST) (1987), Aztec House, 397–405 Archway Road, London N6 4EY T 020-7814 6767
E info@nat.org.uk W www.nat.org.uk
Chief Executive, Deborah Gold

NATIONAL BENEVOLENT CHARITY (1812), Peter Hervé House, Eccles Court, Tetbury GL8 8EH T 01666-505500
E office@natben.org.uk W www.natben.org.uk
Chief Executive, Paul Rossi

NATIONAL CAMPAIGN FOR THE ARTS LTD (1985), c/o Cog Design, 11 Greenwich Centre Business Park, London SE10 9QF T 020-8269 1800 E hello@forthearts.org.uk
W forthearts.org.uk
Executive Chair, Michael Smith

NATIONAL CAMPAIGN FOR COURTESY (1986), Walmere, Wrigglebrook Lane, Kingsthorne HR2 8AW
T 020-3633 4650 E courtesy@campaignforcourtesy.org.uk
W www.campaignforcourtesy.org.uk
Chair, John Stokes

NATIONAL CHILDBIRTH TRUST (1956), 30 Euston Square, London NW1 2FB T 0300-330 0770
E enquiries@nct.org.uk W www.nct.org.uk
Chief Executive, Nick Wilkie

NATIONAL COUNCIL OF WOMEN GREAT BRITAIN (1895), 81 Bondgate, Darlington DL3 7JT T 01325-367375
E info@ncwgb.org W www.ncwgb.org
President, Dr Andrena Telford

NATIONAL EXTENSION COLLEGE (1963), Michael Young Centre, School House, Cambridge CB2 8EB T 0800-389 2839
E info@nec.ac.uk W www.nec.ac.uk
Chief Executive, Dr Ros Morpeth

NATIONAL FAMILY MEDIATION (1981), Civic Centre, Paris Street, Exeter EX1 1JN T 0300-400 0636
E general@nfm.org.uk W www.nfm.org.uk
Chief Executive, Jane Robey

NATIONAL FEDERATION OF WOMEN'S INSTITUTES (1915), 104 New Kings Road, London SW6 4LY
T 020-7371 9300 W www.thewi.org.uk
General Secretary, Melissa Green

NATIONAL FOUNDATION FOR EDUCATIONAL RESEARCH IN ENGLAND AND WALES (1946), The Mere, Upton Park, Slough SL1 2DQ T 01753-574123
E enquiries@nfer.ac.uk W www.nfer.ac.uk
Chief Executive, Carole Willis

NATIONAL GARDENS SCHEME CHARITABLE TRUST (1927), East Wing, Hatchlands Park, Guildford GU4 7RT
T 01483-211535 E hello@ngs.org.uk W www.ngs.org.uk
Chair, Martin McMillan, OBE

NATIONAL OPERATIC AND DRAMATIC ASSOCIATION (NODA) (1899), 15 The Metro Centre, Peterborough PE2 7UH T 01733-374790 E info@noda.org.uk
W www.noda.org.uk
Chief Operating Officer, Dale Freeman

NATIONAL SECULAR SOCIETY (1866), 25 Red Lion Square, London WC1R 4RL T 020-7404 3126
E enquiries@secularism.org.uk W www.secularism.org.uk
President, K. P. Wood

NATIONAL TRUST (1895), Heelis, Kemble Drive, Swindon SN2 2NA T 0344-800 1895 E enquiries@thenationaltrust.org.uk
W www.nationaltrust.org.uk
Director-General, Hilary McGrady

NATIONAL TRUST FOR SCOTLAND (1931), Hermiston Quay, Edinburgh EH11 4DF T 0131-458 0200
E information@nts.org.uk W www.nts.org.uk
Chief Executive, Simon Skinner

NATIONAL UNION OF STUDENTS (NUS) (1922), Ian
King House, Snape Road, Macclesfield SK10 2NZ
T 0300-303 8602 W www.nus.org.uk
President, Zamzam Ibrahim

NATIONAL WOMEN'S REGISTER (1966), Unit 23, Vulcan
House, Norwich NR6 6AQ T 01603-406767 E office@nwr.org.uk
W www.nwr.org.uk
Chair of Trustees, Josephine Burt

NEWCOMEN SOCIETY (1920), The Science Museum,
London SW7 2DD T 020-7371 4445 E office@newcomen.com
W www.newcomen.com
President, Robert Taylor

NHS CONFEDERATION (1997), Floor 15, Portland House,
London SW1E 5BH T 020-7799 6666 E enquiries@nhsconfed.org
W www.nhsconfed.org
Chief Executive, Niall Dickson, CBE

NOISE ABATEMENT SOCIETY (1959), 44 Grand Parade,
Brighton BN2 9QA T 01273-823850
E info@noise-abatement.org
W www.noiseabatementsociety.com
Chief Executive, Gloria Elliott

NORFOLK AND NORWICH ARCHAEOLOGICAL
SOCIETY (1846), 64 The Close, Norwich NR1 4DH
E secretary@nnas.info W www.nnas.info
Hon. Secretary, Edmund Perry

NORTH OF ENGLAND ZOOLOGICAL SOCIETY (1934),
Chester Zoo, Chester CH2 1LH T 01244-380280
E reception@chesterzoo.co.uk W www.chesterzoo.org
Chief Executive Officer, Dr Mark Pilgrim

NSPCC (1884), Weston House, 42 Curtain Road, London
EC2A 3NH T 0808-800 5000 E help@nspcc.org.uk
W www.nspcc.org.uk
Chief Executive, Peter Wanless

NUCLEAR INSTITUTE (1962), Phoenix House, 18 King
William Street, London EC4N 7BP T 020-7816 2600
E admin@nuclearinst.com W www.nuclearinst.com
President, John Clarke

NUFFIELD FOUNDATION (1943), 28 Bedford Square,
London WC1B 3JS T 020-7631 0566
E info@nuffieldfoundation.org W www.nuffieldfoundation.org
Director, Timothy Gardam

NUFFIELD TRUST (1940), 59 New Cavendish Street, London
W1G 7LP T 020-7631 8450 E info@nuffieldtrust.org.uk
W www.nuffieldtrust.org.uk
Chief Executive, Nigel Edwards

NUTRITION SOCIETY (1941), 10 Cambridge Court, 210
Shepherds Bush Road, London W6 7NJ T 020-7602 0228
E office@nutritionsociety.org W www.nutritionsociety.org
Chief Executive, Mark Hollingsworth

OFFICERS' ASSOCIATION (1919), First Floor, Mountbarrow
House, London SW1W 9RB T 020-7808 4160
E info@officersassociation.org.uk
W www.officersassociation.org.uk
Chief Executive, Lee Holloway

OPEN-AIR MISSION (1853), 4 Harrier Court, Woodside Road,
Luton LU1 4DQ T 01582-841141 E email@oamission.com
W www.oamission.com
General Secretary, Andy Banton

OPEN SPACES SOCIETY (1865), 25A Bell Street, Henley-on-
Thames RG9 2BA T 01491-573535 E hq@oss.org.uk
W www.oss.org.uk
General Secretary, Kate Ashbrook

OVERSEAS DEVELOPMENT INSTITUTE (1960),
203 Blackfriars Road, London SE1 8NJ T 020-7922 0300
E odi@odi.org W www.odi.org
Executive Director, Simon Gill (acting)

OXFAM GREAT BRITAIN (1942), Oxfam House, John Smith
Drive, Oxford OX4 2JY T 0300-200 1300
E enquiries@oxfam.org.uk W www.oxfam.org.uk
Chief Executive, Dr Dhananjayan Sriskandarajah

OXFORD PRESERVATION TRUST (1927), 10 Turn Again
Lane, Oxford OX1 1QL T 01865-242918
E info@oxfordpreservation.org.uk
W www.oxfordpreservation.org.uk
Director, Debbie Dance OBE

OXFORDSHIRE ARCHITECTURAL AND HISTORICAL
SOCIETY (1839), 99 Wellington Street, Thame OX9 3BW
E secretary@oahs.org.uk W www.oahs.org.uk
President, Geoffrey Tyack

OXFORD UNIVERSITY SOCIETY (1932), University Alumni
Office, Wellington Square, Oxford OX1 2JD T 01865-611610
E enquiries@alumni.ox.ac.uk W www.alumni.ox.ac.uk
Chair, Nicholas Segal

THE PALAEONTOLOGICAL ASSOCIATION (1957),
Alport House, 35 Old Elvet, Durham DH1 3HN T 0191-386 1482
W www.palass.org
Executive Officer, Dr Jo Hellawell

PARLIAMENTARY AND SCIENTIFIC COMMITTEE
(1939), 3 Birdcage Walk, London SW1H 9JJ T 020-7222 7085
E office@scienceinparliament.org.uk
W www.scienceinparliament.org.uk
Chair, Stephen Metcalfe, MP

PATIENTS ASSOCIATION (1963), PO Box 935, Harrow
HA1 3YJ T 020-8423 9111, **Helpline** 020-8423 8999
E helpline@patients-association.com
W www.patients-association.org.uk
Chair, Lucy Watson

PEABODY (1862), 45 Westminster Bridge Road, London
SE1 7JB T 020-7021 4444 E customercareline@peabody.org.uk
W www.peabody.org.uk
Chief Executive, Brendan Sarsfield

PEN INTERNATIONAL (1921), Unit A Koops Mill Mews,
162–164 Abbey Street, London SE1 2AN T 020-7405 0338
E info@pen-international.org W www.pen-international.org
President, Jennifer Clement

PENSIONS ADVISORY SERVICE (1983), 11 Belgrave Road,
London SW1V 1RB T 0800-011 3797
W www.pensionsadvisoryservice.org.uk
Chief Executive, Caroline Siarkiewicz (acting)

PERENNIAL (1839), 115–117 Kingston Road, Leatherhead
KT22 7SU T 0800-093 8510 E info@perennial.org.uk
W www.perennial.org.uk
Chief Executive, Peter Newman

PHYSIOLOGICAL SOCIETY (1876), Hodgkin Huxley House,
30 Farringdon Lane, London EC1R 3AW T 020-7269 5710
E contactus@physoc.org W www.physoc.org
Chief Executive, Dariel Burdass

PILGRIM TRUST (1930), 23 Lower Belgrave Street, London
SW1W 0NR T 020-7834 6510 E info@thepilgrimtrust.org.uk
W www.thepilgrimtrust.org.uk
Director, Georgina Nayler

PLAIN ENGLISH CAMPAIGN (1979), 20 Union Road, High
Peak Sk22 3ES T 01663-744409 E info@plainenglish.co.uk
W www.plainenglish.co.uk
Director, Ms C. Maher, OBE

POETRY SOCIETY (1909), 22 Betterton Street, London
WC2H 9BX T 020-7420 9880 E info@poetrysociety.org.uk
W www.poetrysociety.org.uk
Director, Judith Palmer

POTENTIAL PLUS UK (1967), The Mansion, Bletchley Park,
Sherwood Drive, Milton Keynes MK3 6EB T 01908-646433
W www.potentialplusuk.org
Chief Executive, Julie Taplin

PRAYER BOOK SOCIETY (1975), The Studio, Copyhold
Farm, Reading RG8 7RT T 01189-842582
E pbs.admin@pbs.org.uk W www.pbs.org.uk
Chairman, Prudence Dailey

PRINCE'S TRUST (1976), 9 Eldon Street, London EC2M 7LS
T 0800-842 842 E webinfops@princes-trust.org.uk
W www.princes-trust.org.uk
Chief Executive, Dame Martina Milburn, DCVO, CBE

PRISONERS ABROAD (1978), 89–93 Fonthill Road, London
N4 3JH T 020-7561 6820 E info@prisonersabroad.org.uk
W www.prisonersabroad.org.uk
Chief Executive, Pauline Crowe, OBE

PRIVATE LIBRARIES ASSOCIATION (1956), Ravelston,
South View Road, Pinner HA5 3YD E info@plabooks.org
W www.plabooks.org
Hon. Secretary, Jim Maslen

PROFESSIONAL ASSOCIATION FOR CHILDCARE
AND EARLY YEARS (1971), Northside House, Third Floor,
69 Tweedy Road, Bromley BR1 3WA T 0300-003 0005
E info@pacey.org.uk W www.pacey.org.uk
Chief Executive, Liz Bayram

PROFESSIONAL PUBLISHERS ASSOCIATION (1970),
White Collar Factory, 1 Old Street Yard, London EC1Y 8AF
T 020-7404 4166 E info@ppa.org.uk W www.ppa.co.uk
Chief Executive, Barry McIlheney

PROSTATE CANCER UK (1996), Fourth Floor, The Counting
House, 53 Tooley Street, London SE1 2QN T 020-3310 7000
E info@prostatecanceruk.org W www.prostatecanceruk.org
Chief Executive, Angela Culhane

QUAKER PEACE AND SOCIAL WITNESS (2000),
Friends House, 173–177 Euston Road, London NW1 2BJ
T 020-7663 1000 E enquiries@quaker.org.uk
W www.quaker.org.uk
General Secretary, Oliver Robertson

QUEEN ELIZABETH'S FOUNDATION FOR DISABLED
PEOPLE (1934), Leatherhead Court, Woodlands Road,
Leatherhead KT22 0BN T 01372-841100 E info@qef.org.uk
W www.qef.org.uk
Chief Executive, Karen Deacon

QUEEN'S NURSING INSTITUTE (1887), 1A Henrietta Place,
London W1G 0LZ T 020-7549 1400 E mail@qni.org.uk
W www.qni.org.uk
Chief Executive, Dr Crystal Oldman, CBE

RAILWAY BENEFIT FUND (1858), 1st Floor, Millennium
House, Crewe CW2 6AD T 0345-241 2885
E info@railwaybenefitfund.org.uk
W www.railwaybenefitfund.org.uk
Chief Executive, Jason Tetley

RAMBLERS' ASSOCIATION (1935), 2nd Floor, Camelford
House, 87–90 Albert Embankment, London SE1 7TW
T 020-3961 3300 E ramblers@ramblers.org.uk
W www.ramblers.org.uk
Chief Executive, Vanessa Griffiths

RARE BREEDS SURVIVAL TRUST (1973), Stoneleigh Park,
Nr. Kenilworth CV8 2LG T 024-7669 6551
E enquiries@rbst.org.uk W www.rbst.org.uk
CEO, Christopher Price

REFUGEE COUNCIL (1951), PO Box 68614, London E15 9DQ
T 020-7346 6700 E info@refugeecouncil.org.uk
W www.refugeecouncil.org.uk
Chief Executive, Maurice Wren

REGIONAL STUDIES ASSOCIATION (1965), Sussex
Innovation Centre, Falmer Brighton BN1 9SB T 01273-698017
E office@regionalstudies.org W www.regionalstudies.org
Chief Executive, Sally Hardy

RELATE (1938), Premier House, Carolina Court, Doncaster
DN4 5RA T 0300-100 1234 E relate.enquiries@relate.org.uk
W www.relate.org.uk
Chief Executive, Aidan Jones, OBE

RETHINK (1972), 89 Albert Embankment, London SE1 7TP
T 0121-522 7007 E info@rethink.org W www.rethink.org
Chief Executive, Mark Winstanley

RFEA (REGULAR FORCES EMPLOYMENT
ASSOCIATION LTD) (1885), 1st Floor, Mountbarrow
House, 12 Elizabeth Street, London SW1W 9RB
T 0121-262 3058 E info@rfea.org.uk W www.rfea.org.uk
Chief Executive, Alistair Halliday

RICHARD III SOCIETY (1924), 18 Berberis Close, Milton
Keynes MK7 7DZ E secretary@richardiii.net W www.richardiii.net
Chair, Dr Phil Stone

ROYAL AERONAUTICAL SOCIETY (1866),
4 Hamilton Place, London W1J 7BQ T 020-7670 4300
E raes@aerosociety.com W www.aerosociety.com
President, Prof. Jonathan Cooper, MBE

ROYAL AGRICULTURAL BENEVOLENT INSTITUTION
(1860), Shaw House, 27 West Way, Oxford OX2 0QH
T 01865-724931 E info@rabi.org.uk W www.rabi.org.uk
Chief Executive, Alicia Chivers

ROYAL AGRICULTURAL SOCIETY OF THE
COMMONWEALTH (1957), c/o Royal Norfolk Agricultural
Association, Norfolk Showground, Norwich NR5 0TT
T 01603-731977 E info@therasc.com W www.therasc.com
Hon. Secretary, Michael Lambert

ROYAL AIR FORCE BENEVOLENT FUND (1919), 67
Portland Place, London W1B 1AR T 020-7580 8343
E mail@rafbf.org.uk W www.rafbf.org
Controller, Air Vice-Marshal Hon. David Murray, CVO, OBE

ROYAL AIR FORCES ASSOCIATION (1943), Atlas House,
41 Wembley Road, Leicester LE3 1UT T 0800-018 2361
W www.rafa.org.uk
Secretary General, Nick Bunting

ROYAL ARTILLERY ASSOCIATION (1920), Artillery
House, Royal Artillery Barracks, Salisbury SP4 8QT
T 01980-845233 E sarah.davies119@mod.gov.uk
W www.thegunners.org.uk
General Secretary, Lt.-Col. I. A. Vere Nicoll, MBE

ROYAL ASIATIC SOCIETY (1823), 14 Stephenson Way,
London NW1 2HD T 020-7388 4539
E info@royalasiaticsociety.org W www.royalasiaticsociety.org
President, Dr. A. Stockwell

ROYAL ASSOCIATION FOR DEAF PEOPLE (1841),
Block F, Parkside Office Village, Nesfield Road, Colchester
CO4 3ZL T 0300-688 2525 E info@royaldeaf.org.uk
W www.royaldeaf.org.uk
Chief Executives, A. Casson-Webb; L. Frearson; S. Mountford

ROYAL ASTRONOMICAL SOCIETY (1820), Burlington
House, London W1J 0BQ T 020-7734 4582 W www.ras.ac.uk
Executive Director, Philip Diamond

ROYAL BRITISH LEGION (1921), 199 Borough High Street,
London SE1 1AA T 0808-802 8080 E info@britishlegion.org.uk
W www.britishlegion.org.uk
Director-General, Charles Byrne

ROYAL BRITISH LEGION SCOTLAND (1921), New Haig
House, Logie Green Road, Edinburgh EH7 4HQ T 0131-550 1586
E info@legionscotland.org.uk W www.legionscotland.org.uk
Chief Executive Officer, Claire Armstrong

ROYAL CAMBRIAN ACADEMY (1882), Crown Lane,
Conwy LL32 8AN T 01492-593413 E rca@rcaconwy.org
W www.rcaconwy.org
President, Jeremy Yates

ROYAL CELTIC SOCIETY (1820), 25 Rutland Street,
Edinburgh EH1 2RN T 0131-228 6449
E info@royalcelticsociety.scot W www.royalcelticsociety.scot
Secretary, J. Gordon Cameron, WS

ROYAL COMMISSION FOR THE EXHIBITION OF 1851
(1850), 453 Sherfield Building, Imperial College SW7 2AZ
T 020-7594 8790 E royalcom1851@imperial.ac.uk
W www.royalcommission1851.org.uk
Secretary, Nigel Williams, CENG

ROYAL GEOGRAPHICAL SOCIETY (WITH THE INSTITUTE OF BRITISH GEOGRAPHERS) (1830), 1 Kensington Gore, SW7 2AR T 020-7591 3000 W www.rgs.org
Director, Prof. Joe Smith

ROYAL HIGHLAND AND AGRICULTURAL SOCIETY OF SCOTLAND (1784), Ingliston House, Royal Highland Centre, Edinburgh EH28 8NB T 0131-335 6200
E info@rhass.org.uk W www.rhass.org.uk
Chief Executive, Alan Laidlaw

ROYAL HISTORICAL SOCIETY (1868), University College London, Gower Street, WC1E 6BT T 020-7387 7532
E enquiries@royalhistsoc.org W www.royalhistsoc.org
Executive Secretary, Dr S. E. Carr

ROYAL HORTICULTURAL SOCIETY (1804), 80 Vincent Square, London SW1P 2PE T 020-3176 5800 W www.rhs.org.uk
Director-General, Sue Biggs

ROYAL HOSPITAL FOR NEURO-DISABILITY (1854), West Hill, London SW15 3SW T 020-8780 4500
E info@rhn.org.uk W www.rhn.org.uk
Chief Executive, Paul Allen

ROYAL HUMANE SOCIETY (1774), 50–51 Temple Chambers, 3–7 Temple Avenue, London EC4Y 0HP
T 020-7936 2942 E info@royalhumanesociety.org.uk
W www.royalhumanesociety.org.uk
Secretary, Lt-Col. Andrew Chapman

ROYAL INSTITUTE OF NAVIGATION (1947), 1 Kensington Gore, SW7 2AT T 020-7591 3134
E admin@rin.org.uk W www.rin.org.uk
Director, J R Pottle, BSC, MBA, FIET

ROYAL INSTITUTE OF OIL PAINTERS (1882), 17 Carlton House Terrace, London SW1Y 5BD T 020-7930 6844
E enquiries@theroi.org.uk W www.theroi.co.uk
President, Tim Benson

ROYAL INSTITUTE OF PAINTERS IN WATER COLOURS (1831), 17 Carlton House Terrace, London SW1Y 5BD T 020-7930 6844
W www.royalinstituteofpaintersinwatercolours.org
President, Rosa Sepple

ROYAL INSTITUTE OF PHILOSOPHY (1925), 14 Gordon Square, London WC1H 0AR T 020-7387 4130
W www.royalinstitutephilosophy.org
Managing Director, Dr James Garvey

ROYAL INSTITUTION OF GREAT BRITAIN (1799), 21 Albemarle Street, London W1S 4BS T 020-7670 2955
E ri@ri.ac.uk W www.rigb.org
Director, Dr Shaun Fitzgerald

ROYAL LIFE SAVING SOCIETY UK (1891), Red Hill House, 227 London Road, Worcester WR5 2JG T 0300-323 0096
E info@rlss.org.uk W www.rlss.org.uk
Chief Executive Officer, Robert Gofton

ROYAL LITERARY FUND (1790), 3 Johnson's Court, off Fleet Street, London EC4A 3EA T 020-7353 7150
W www.rlf.org.uk
Chief Executive, Eileen Gunn

ROYAL MEDICAL BENEVOLENT FUND (1836), 24 Kings Road, London SW19 8QN T 020-8540 9194 E info@rmbf.org
W www.rmbf.org
Chief Executive, Steve Crone

ROYAL MICROSCOPICAL SOCIETY (1839), 37–38 St Clements, Oxford OX4 1AJ T 01865-254760 E info@rms.org.uk
W www.rms.org.uk
Chief Executive, Allison Winton

ROYAL MUSICAL ASSOCIATION (1874), 4 Chandos Road, Chorlton-cum-Hardy M21 0ST T 0161-861 7542
E exec@rma.ac.uk W www.rma.ac.uk
President, Prof. Simon McVeigh

ROYAL NATIONAL COLLEGE FOR THE BLIND (1872), Venns Lane, Hereford HR1 1DT T 01432-265725
E info@rnc.ac.uk W www.rnc.ac.uk
Principal, Mark Fisher

ROYAL NATIONAL INSTITUTE OF BLIND PEOPLE (1868), 105 Judd Street, London WC1H 9NE T 030-3123 9999
E helpline@rnib.org.uk W www.rnib.org.uk
Chief Executive, Matt Stringer

ROYAL NATIONAL LIFEBOAT INSTITUTION (1824), West Quay Road, Poole BH15 1HZ T 0300-300 9990
W www.rnli.org
Chief Executive, Mark Dowie

ROYAL NAVAL ASSOCIATION (1949), Room 209, Royal Semaphore Tower, PP70, HM Naval Base, Portsmouth PO1 3LT
T 023-9272 3747 E admin@royalnavalassoc.com
W www.royal-naval-association.co.uk
General Secretary, Capt. Bill Oliphant, RN

ROYAL NAVAL BENEVOLENT TRUST (1922), Castaway House, 311 Twyford Avenue, Portsmouth PO2 8RN
T 023-9269 0112 E rnbt@rnbt.org.uk W www.rnbt.org.uk
Chief Executive, Cdr Rob Bosshardt, RN

ROYAL OSTEOPOROSIS SOCIETY (1986), Bath BA2 0PJ
T 01761-471771, **Helpline** 0808-800 0035
E info@theros.org.uk W www.theros.org.uk
Chief Executive, Claire Severgnini

ROYAL PHILATELIC SOCIETY LONDON (1869), 41 Devonshire Place, London W1G 6JY T 020-7486 1044
E secretary@rpsl.org.uk W www.rpsl.org.uk
President, Richard Stock

ROYAL PHILHARMONIC SOCIETY (1813), 48 Great Marlborough Street, London W1F 7BB T 020-7289 0019
E web@royalphilharmonicsociety.org.uk
W www.royalphilharmonicsociety.org.uk
Chief Executive, James Murphy

ROYAL PHOTOGRAPHIC SOCIETY (1853), RPS House, 337 Paintworks, Bristol BS4 3AR T 0117-316 4450
E FrontofHouse@rps.org W www.rps.org
President, Robert Albright, HONFRPS

ROYAL SCHOOL OF CHURCH MUSIC (1927), 19 The Close, Salisbury SP1 2EB T 01722-424848 E enquiries@rscm.com
W www.rscm.org.uk
Director, Hugh Morris

ROYAL SCHOOL OF NEEDLEWORK (1872), Apartment 12A, Hampton Court Palace KT8 9AU T 020-3166 6932
E enquiries@royal-needlework.org.uk
W www.royal-needlework.org.uk
Chief Executive, Dr Susan Kay-Williams

ROYAL SOCIETY FOR ASIAN AFFAIRS (1901), 1a St Martin's House, Polygon Road, London NW1 1QB
T 020-7235 5122 E info@rsaa.org.uk W www.rsaa.org.uk
Chief Executive, Michael Ryder, CMG

ROYAL SOCIETY FOR BLIND CHILDREN (1838), 52–58 Arcola Street, London E8 2DJ T 020-3198 0225
E enquiries@rsbc.org.uk W www.rsbc.org.uk
Chief Executive, Dr Tom Pey

ROYAL SOCIETY FOR THE ENCOURAGEMENT OF ARTS, MANUFACTURES AND COMMERCE (RSA) (1754), 8 John Adam Street, London WC2N 6EZ
T 020-7930 5115 E general@rsa.org.uk W www.thersa.org
Chief Executive, Matthew Taylor

THE ROYAL SOCIETY FOR THE PREVENTION OF ACCIDENTS (1916/17), 28 Calthorpe Road, Birmingham B15 1RP T 0121-248 2000 E help@rospa.com
W www.rospa.com
Chief Executive, Errol Taylor

ROYAL SOCIETY FOR THE PREVENTION OF CRUELTY TO ANIMALS (1824), Wilberforce Way, Horsham RH13 9RS T 0300-123 0346 W www.rspca.org.uk
Chief Executive, Chris Sherwood

ROYAL SOCIETY FOR THE PROTECTION OF BIRDS (1889), The Lodge, Potton Road, Sandy SG19 2DL
T 01767-680551 W www.rspb.org.uk
Chief Executive, Beccy Speight

ROYAL SOCIETY OF BIOLOGY (2009), 1 Naoroji Street, London WC1X 0GB **T** 020-3925 3440 **E** info@rsb.org.uk
W www.rsb.org.uk
Chief Executive, Dr Mark Downs

ROYAL SOCIETY OF CHEMISTRY (1841), Burlington House, London W1J 0BA **T** 020-7437 8656 **W** www.rsc.org
Chief Executive, Dr Robert Parker

ROYAL SOCIETY OF LITERATURE (1820), Somerset House, London WC2R 1LA **T** 020-7845 4679
E info@rsliterature.org **W** www.rsliterature.org
President, Dame Marina Warner, DBE, FRSL

ROYAL SOCIETY OF MARINE ARTISTS (1939), 17 Carlton House Terrace, London SW1Y 5BD **T** 020-7930 6844
E rsma.contact@gmail.com **W** www.rsma-web.co.uk
President, Benjamin Mowll

ROYAL SOCIETY OF MEDICINE (1805), 1 Wimpole Street, London W1G 0AE **T** 020-7290 2900 **E** info@rsm.ac.uk
W www.rsm.ac.uk
Chief Executive, Michele Acton

ROYAL SOCIETY OF MINIATURE PAINTERS, SCULPTORS AND GRAVERS (1895), 89 Roseberry Road, Dursley GL11 4PU **T** 01454-269268
E info@royal-miniature-society.org.uk
W www.royal-miniature-society.org.uk
President, Elizabeth Meek, MBE

THE ROYAL SOCIETY OF MUSICIANS OF GREAT BRITAIN (1738), 26 Fitzroy Square, London W1T 6BT
T 020-7629 6137 **E** enquiries@royalsocietyofmusicians.org
W www.royalsocietyofmusicians.org
President, Judith Weir, CBE

ROYAL SOCIETY OF PAINTER-PRINTMAKERS (1880), Bankside Gallery, 48 Hopton Street, SE1 9JH **T** 020-7928 7521
E banksidegallery.com **W** www.re-printmakers.com
President, David Ferry

ROYAL SOCIETY OF PORTRAIT PAINTERS (1891), 17 Carlton House Terrace, London SW1Y 5BD **T** 020-7930 6844
E enquiries@therp.co.uk **W** www.therp.co.uk
President, Richard Foster

ROYAL SOCIETY OF ST GEORGE (1894), PO Box 397, Loughton IG10 9GN **T** 020-3225 5011 **E** info@rssg.org.uk
W http://rssg.org.uk
Chairman, Joanna M. Cadman

ROYAL SOCIETY OF TROPICAL MEDICINE AND HYGIENE (1907), Northumberland House, 303–306 High Holborn, London WC1V 7JZ **T** 020-7405 2628
E amelia.fincham@rstmh.org **W** www.rstmh.org
Chief Executive, Tamar Ghosh

ROYAL STAR AND GARTER HOMES (1916), 15 Castle Mews, Hampton TW12 2NP **T** 020-8481 7676
E general.enquiries@starandgarter.org
W www.starandgarter.org
Chief Executive, Andy Cole, OBE

ROYAL THEATRICAL FUND (1839), 11 Garrick Street, London WC2E 9AR **T** 020-7836 3322 **E** admin@trtf.com
W www.trtf.com
President, Robert Lindsay

ROYAL UNITED SERVICES INSTITUTE FOR DEFENCE AND SECURITY STUDIES (1831), Whitehall, London SW1A 2ET **T** 020-7747 2600 **W** www.rusi.org
Director-General, Dr Karin von Hippel

ROYAL VOLUNTARY SERVICE (1938), Beck Court, Cardiff Gate Business Park, Cardiff CF23 8RP **T** 0330-555 0310
W www.royalvoluntaryservice.org.uk
Chief Executive, Catherine Johnstone, CBE

ROYAL WATERCOLOUR SOCIETY (1804), Bankside Gallery, 48 Hopton Street, London SE1 9JH **T** 020-7928 7521
E info@royalwatercoloursociety.com
W www.royalwatercoloursociety.co.uk
President, Jill Leman

ROYAL ZOOLOGICAL SOCIETY OF SCOTLAND (1909), Edinburgh Zoo, 134 Corstorphine Road, Edinburgh EH12 6TS **T** 0131-334 9171 **E** info@rzss.org.uk
W www.rzss.org.uk
Chief Executive, Barbara Smith

ST JOHN AMBULANCE (1877), St John's Gate, 27 St John's Lane, London EC1M 4BU **T** 0870-010 4950 **W** www.sja.org.uk
Chief Executive, Martin Houghton-Brown

SALTIRE SOCIETY (1936), 9 Fountain Close, 22 High Street, Edinburgh EH1 1TF **T** 0131-556 1836
E saltire@saltiresociety.org.uk **W** www.saltiresociety.org.uk
Convener, Prof Alan Riach

SAMARITANS (1953), The Upper Mill, Ewell KT17 2AF
T 020-8394 8300, **Helpline** 116 123 **E** admin@samaritans.org
W www.samaritans.org
Chief Executive, Ruth Sutherland

SANE (1986), St Mark's Studios, 14 Chillingworth Street, London N7 8QJ **T** 020-3805 1790, **Helpline** 0300-304 7000
E info@sane.org.uk **W** www.sane.org.uk
Chief Executive, Marjorie Wallace, CBE

SAVE THE CHILDREN (1919), 1 St John's Lane, London EC1M 4AR **T** 020-7012 6400
E supportercare@savethechildren.org.uk
W www.savethechildren.org.uk
Chief Executive, Kevin Watkins

SCHOOL LIBRARY ASSOCIATION (1937), 1 Pine Court, Swindon SN2 8AD **T** 01793-530166 **E** info@sla.org.uk
W www.sla.org.uk
Director, Alison Tarrant

SCOPE (1952), Here East Press Centre, 14 East Bay Lane, London E15 2GW **T** 020-7619 7100, **Helpline** 0808-800 3333
E supportercare@scope.org.uk **W** www.scope.org.uk
Chief Executive, Mark Atkinson

SCOTTISH ASSOCIATION FOR MARINE SCIENCE (1884), Scottish Marine Institute, Argyll PA37 1QA
T 01631-559000 **E** info@sams.ac.uk **W** www.sams.ac.uk
Director, Prof. Nicholas Owens

SCOTTISH ASSOCIATION FOR MENTAL HEALTH (1923), Brunswick House, 51 Wilson Street, Glasgow G1 1UZ
T 0141-530 1000 **E** enquire@samh.org.uk **W** www.samh.org.uk
Chief Executive, Billy Watson

SCOTTISH CHAMBERS OF COMMERCE (1948), Strathclyde Business School, 199 Cathedral Street, Glasgow G4 0QU **T** 0141-444 7500 **E** admin@scottishchambers.org.uk
W www.scottishchambers.org.uk
Chief Executive, Liz Cameron, OBE

SCOTTISH COUNCIL FOR VOLUNTARY ORGANISATIONS (1943), Mansfield Traquair Centre, 15 Mansfield Place, Edinburgh EH3 6BB **T** 0131-474 8000
E enquiries@scvo.org.uk **W** www.scvo.org.uk
Chief Executive, Anna Fowlie

SCOTTISH LAND AND ESTATES (1906), Stuart House, Eskmills Business Park, Musselburgh EH21 7PB **T** 0131-653 5401
E info@scottishlandandestates.co.uk
W www.scottishlandandestates.co.uk
Chief Executive, Sarah-Jane Laing

SCOTTISH SOCIETY FOR THE PREVENTION OF CRUELTY TO ANIMALS (1839), Kingseat Road, Dunfermline KY11 8RY **T** 03000-999 999
E info@scottishspca.org **W** www.scottishspca.org
Chief Executive, Kirsteen Campbell

SCOTTISH WILDLIFE TRUST (1964), Harbourside House, 110 Commercial Street, Edinburgh EH6 6NF **T** 0131-312 7765
E enquiries@scottishwildlifetrust.org.uk
W www.scottishwildlifetrust.org.uk
Chief Executive, Jo Pike

SCOUT ASSOCIATION (1907), Gilwell Park, Chingford, London E4 7QW **T** 0345-300 1818 **E** info.centre@scouts.org.uk
W www.scouts.org.uk
Chief Executive, Matt Hyde

SEEABILITY (1799), Newplan House, 41 East Street, Epsom KT17 1BL T 01372-755000 E enquiries@seeability.org
W www.seeability.org
Chief Executive, Lisa Hopkins

SELDEN SOCIETY (1887), School of Law, Queen Mary, London E1 4NS T 020-7882 3968 E selden-society@qmul.ac.uk
W www.selden-society.ac.uk
Secretary, Prof. Michael Lobban

SENSE (1955), 101 Pentonville Road, N1 9LG T 0300-330 9256
E info@sense.org.uk W www.sense.org.uk
Chief Executive, Richard Kramer

SHELTER (NATIONAL CAMPAIGN FOR HOMELESS PEOPLE) (1966), 88 Old Street, London EC1V 9HU
T 0300-330 1234, **Helpline** 0808-800 4444
E info@shelter.org.uk W www.shelter.org.uk
Chief Executive, Polly Neate

SIGHTSAVERS (ROYAL COMMONWEALTH SOCIETY FOR THE BLIND) (1950), Bumpers Way, Bumpers Farm, Chippenham SN14 6NG T 01444-446600 E info@sightsavers.org
W www.sightsavers.org
Chief Executive, Dr Caroline Harper, CBE

SOCIÉTÉ JERSIAISE (1873), 7 Pier Road, St Helier JE2 4XW
T 01534-758314 E info@societe-jersiaise.org
W www.societe-jersiaise.org
Administrative Secretary, Ms C. Cornick

SOCIETY FOR PROMOTING CHRISTIAN KNOWLEDGE (SPCK) (1698), 36 Causton Street, London SW1P 4ST T 020-7592 3900 E spck@spck.org.uk
W www.spckpublishing.co.uk
CEO, Sam Richardson

SOCIETY FOR THE PROMOTION OF HELLENIC STUDIES (1879), Senate House, Malet Street, London WC1E 7HU T 020-7862 8730 E secretary@hellenicsociety.org.uk
W www.hellenicsociety.org.uk
President, Prof. Judith Mossman

SOCIETY FOR THE PROMOTION OF ROMAN STUDIES (1910), Senate House, Malet Street, London WC1E 7HU T 020-7862 8727 E office@romansociety.org
W www.romansociety.org
President, Prof. Tim Cornell

SOCIETY OF ANTIQUARIES OF LONDON (1707), Burlington House, London W1J 0BE T 020-7479 7080
E admin@sal.org.uk W www.sal.org.uk
General-Secretary, John S. C. Lewis, FSA

SOCIETY OF ANTIQUARIES OF NEWCASTLE UPON TYNE (1813), Great North Museum: Hancock, Barras Bridge, Newcastle upon Tyne NE2 4PT T 0191-231 2700
E admin@newcastle-antiquaries.org.uk
W www.newcastle-antiquaries.org.uk
President, Nick Hodgson

SOCIETY OF ANTIQUARIES OF SCOTLAND (1780), National Museums Scotland, Chambers Street, Edinburgh EH1 1JF T 0131-247 4133 E info@socantscot.org
W www.socantscot.org
Director, Dr Simon Gilmour, FSA, FSA SCOT, MIFA

SOCIETY OF BOTANICAL ARTISTS (1985), 1 Knapp Cottages, Gillingham SP8 4NQ T 01747-825718
E info@soc-botanical-artists.org
W www.soc-botanical-artists.org
Executive Secretary, Pam Henderson

SOCIETY OF EDITORS (1999), University Centre, Granta Place, Cambridge CB2 1RU T 01223-304080
E office@societyofeditors.org W www.societyofeditors.org
Executive Director, Ian Murray

SOCIETY OF GENEALOGISTS (1911), 14 Charterhouse Buildings, Goswell Road, London EC1M 7BA T 020-7251 8799
E genealogy@sog.org.uk W www.sog.org.uk
Chief Executive, June Perrin

SOCIETY OF GLASS TECHNOLOGY (1917), 9 Churchill Way, Sheffield S35 2PY T 0114-263 4455 E info@sgt.org
W www.sgt.org
Managing Editor, David Moore

SOCIETY OF INDEXERS (1957), Woodbourn Business Centre, 10 Jessell Street, Sheffield S9 3HY T 0114-244 9561
E admin@indexers.org.uk W www.indexers.org.uk
Chair, Nicola King

SOCIETY OF LEGAL SCHOLARS (1908), School of Law, Southampton University, Southampton SO17 1BJ
T 023-8059 4039 E admin@legalscholars.ac.uk
W www.legalscholars.ac.uk
Hon. Secretary, Prof. Paula Giliker

SOCIETY OF SCRIBES AND ILLUMINATORS (1921), Art Workers Guild, 6 Queen Square, London WC1N 3AT
E honsec@calligraphyonline.org W www.calligraphyonline.org
Chair, Julie Chaney

SOCIETY OF SOLICITORS IN THE SUPREME COURT OF SCOTLAND (1784), SSC Library, Parliament House, Edinburgh EH1 1RF T 0131-225 6268
E enquiries@ssclibrary.co.uk W www.ssclibrary.co.uk
Secretary, Robert Shiels

SOCIETY OF WOMEN ARTISTS (1855), The Mall Galleries, The Mall, London T 07528-477002
E info@society-women-artists.org.uk
W www.society-women-artists.org.uk
Executive Secretary, Rebecca Cotton

SOCIETY OF WRITERS TO HM SIGNET (1594), The Signet Library, Parliament Square, Edinburgh EH1 1RF
T 0131-220 3249 E reception@wssociety.co.uk
W www.wssociety.co.uk
Chief Executive, Robert Pirrie

SOIL ASSOCIATION (1946), Spear House, 51 Victoria Street, Bristol BS1 6AD T 0300-330 0100 W www.soilassociation.org
Chief Executive, Helen Browning, OBE

SOMERSET ARCHAEOLOGICAL AND NATURAL HISTORY SOCIETY (1849), Somerset Heritage Centre, Brunel Way, Taunton TA2 6SF T 01823-272429
E office@sanhs.org W www.sanhs.org
Chair, Christine Jessop

SOUND AND MUSIC (1967), 3rd Floor, South Wing, Somerset House, London WC2R 1LA T 020-7759 1800
E info@soundandmusic.org W www.soundandmusic.org
Chief Executive, Susanna Eastburn, MBE

SOUND SEEKERS (1959), The Green House, 244-254 Cambridge Heath Road, London T 020-35596673
E help@sound-seekers.org.uk W www.sound-seekers.org.uk
Chief Executive, Kavita Prasad

SPURGEONS (1867), 74 Wellingborough Road, Rushden NN10 9TY T 01933-412412 E info@spurgeons.org
W www.spurgeons.org
Chief Executive, Ross Hendry

STANDING COUNCIL OF THE BARONETAGE (1903), 1 Tarrel Farm Cottages, Tain IV20 1SL T 01862-870177
E secretary@baronetage.org W www.baronetage.org
Chair, Sir Henry Bedingfeld, BT.

STOLL (SIR OSWALD STOLL FOUNDATION) (1916), 446 Fulham Road, London SW6 1DT T 020-7385 2110
E info@stoll.org.uk W www.stoll.org.uk
Chief Executive, Ed Tytherleigh

SUFFOLK INSTITUTE OF ARCHAEOLOGY AND HISTORY (1848), 116 Hardwick Lane, IP33 2LE
T 01284-753228 E generalsecretary@suffolkinstitute.org.uk
W www.suffolkinstitute.org.uk
Hon. Secretary, Jane Carr

SURREY ARCHAEOLOGICAL SOCIETY (1854), Castle Arch, Guildford GU1 3SX T 01483-532454
E info@surreyarchaeology.org.uk
W www.surreyarchaeology.org.uk
Hon. Secretary, David Calow

SUSSEX ARCHAEOLOGICAL SOCIETY (1846), Bull House, 92 High Street, Lewes BN7 1XH **T** 01273-486260 **E** adminlewes@sussexpast.co.uk **W** www.sussexpast.co.uk
Chief Executive, Tristan Bareham

SUSTRANS (1977), Head Office, 2 Cathedral Square, Bristol BS1 5DD **T** 0117 926 8893 **E** reception@sustrans.org.uk **W** www.sustrans.org.uk
Chief Executive, Xavier Brice

SUZY LAMPLUGH TRUST (1986), 17 Oval Way, London SE11 5RR **T** 020-7091 0014 **E** info@suzylamplugh.org **W** www.suzylamplugh.org
Chief Executive, Rachel Griffin

SWEDENBORG SOCIETY (1810), 20–21 Bloomsbury Way, London WC1A 2TH **T** 020-7405 7986
E admin@swedenborg.org.uk **W** www.swedenborg.org.uk
Executive Director, Stephen McNeilly

TAVISTOCK INSTITUTE (1947), 30 Tabernacle Street, London EC2A 4UE **T** 020-7417 0407 **E** hello@tavinstitute.org **W** www.tavinstitute.org
Chief Executive, Dr Eliat Aram

TERRENCE HIGGINS TRUST (1982), 314–320 Gray's Inn Road, London WC1X 8DP **T** 020-7812 1600 **E** info@tht.org.uk **W** www.tht.org.uk
Chief Executive, Ian Green

THEATRES TRUST (1976), 22 Charing Cross Road, London WC2H 0QL **T** 020-7836 8591 **E** info@theatrestrust.org.uk **W** www.theatrestrust.org.uk
Director, Jon Morgan

THORESBY SOCIETY (1889), The Leeds Library, 18 Commercial Street, Leeds LS1 6AL **E** secretary@thoresby.org.uk **W** www.thoresby.org.uk
President, Mrs E. Bradford

TOGETHER FOR MENTAL WELLBEING (1879), 52 Walnut Tree Walk, London SE11 6DN **T** 020-7780 7300 **E** contact-us@together-uk.org **W** www.together-uk.org
Chief Executive, Linda Bryant

TOWN AND COUNTRY PLANNING ASSOCIATION (1899), 17 Carlton House Terrace, London SW1Y 5AS **T** 020-7930 8903 **E** tcpa@tcpa.org.uk **W** www.tcpa.org.uk
Chief Executive, Fiona Howie

TREE COUNCIL (1974), 4 Docks Offices, Surrey Quays Road, London SE16 2XU **T** 020-7407 9992 **E** info@treecouncil.org.uk **W** www.treecouncil.org.uk
Chief Executive, Sarah Lom

TURN2US (1897), Hythe House, 200 Shepherds Bush Road, London W6 7NL **T** 020-8834 9200 **W** www.turn2us.org.uk
Chair, Sally O'Sullivan

UK YOUTH (1911), 8th Floor, Kings Buildings, 16 Smith Square, London SW1P 3HQ **T** 0203-137 3810 **E** info@ukyouth.org **W** www.ukyouth.org
Chief Executive, Anna Smee

UNDERSTANDING ANIMAL RESEARCH (2008), Abbey House, 74–76 St John Street, London EC1M 4DZ **E** office@uar.org.uk **W** www.uar.org.uk
Chief Executive, Wendy Jarrett

UNITED GRAND LODGE OF ENGLAND (1717), Freemasons' Hall, 60 Great Queen Street, London WC2B 5AZ **T** 020-7831 9811 **E** enquiries@ugle.org.uk **W** www.ugle.org.uk
Grand Master, HRH the Duke of Kent, KG, GCMG, GCVO

UNITED REFORMED CHURCH HISTORY SOCIETY (1972), Westminster College, Madingley Road, Cambridge CB3 0AA **T** 01223-330620 **E** mt212@cam.ac.uk **W** www.westminster.cam.ac.uk/rcl/about/urc-history-society
Hon. Secretary, Mrs M. Thompson

UNIVERSITIES FEDERATION FOR ANIMAL WELFARE (1926), The Old School, Brewhouse Hill, Wheathampstead AL4 8AN **T** 01582-831818 **E** ufaw@ufaw.org.uk **W** www.ufaw.org.uk
Chief Executive & Scientific Director, Dr R. C. Hubrecht

UNIVERSITIES UK (2000), Woburn House, 20 Tavistock Square, London WC1H 9HQ **T** 020-7419 4111
E info@universitiesuk.ac.uk **W** www.universitiesuk.ac.uk
Chief Executive, Alistair Jarvis

VEGAN SOCIETY (1944), Donald Watson House, 34–35 Ludgate Hill, Birmingham B3 1EH **T** 0121-523 1730 **E** info@vegansociety.com **W** www.vegansociety.com
Chief Executive, George Gill

VEGETARIAN SOCIETY OF THE UNITED KINGDOM LTD (1847), Parkdale, Dunham Road, Cheshire WA14 4QG **T** 0161-925 2000 **E** hello@vegsoc.org **W** www.vegsoc.org
Chair, Dale Hoyland

VERNACULAR ARCHITECTURE GROUP (1952), Kangaroo House, Colby, Appleby-in-Westmorland CA16 6BD **E** secretary@vag.org.uk **W** www.vag.org.uk
President, Dr Adam Menuge

VERSUS ARTHRITIS (1947), Copeman House, St Mary's Court, St Mary's Gate, Chesterfield S41 7TD **T** 0300-790 0400 **E** enquiries@versusarthritus.org **W** www.versusarthritis.org
Chief Executive, Liam O'Toole

VICTIM SUPPORT (1979), Octavia House, 50 Banner Street, London EC1Y 8ST **T** 020-7268 0200, **Helpline** 0808-1689 111 **W** www.victimsupport.org.uk
Chief Officer, Diana Fawcett

VICTIM SUPPORT SCOTLAND (1985), 15–23 Hardwell Close, Edinburgh EH8 9RX **T** 0131-668 4486 **E** info@victimsupportsco.org.uk **W** www.victimsupportsco.org.uk
Chief Executive, Kate Wallace

VICTORIA CROSS AND GEORGE CROSS ASSOCIATION (1956), Horse Guards, Whitehall, London SW1A 2AX **T** 020-7930 3506 **E** secretary@vcandgc.org **W** vcgca.org
Secretary, Rebecca Maciejewska

VICTORIAN SOCIETY (1958), 75 Cowcross Street, EC1M 6EJ **T** 020-8994 1019 **E** admin@victoriansociety.org.uk **W** www.victoriansociety.org.uk
Director, Christopher Costelloe

VOLUNTEERING MATTERS (1962), The Levy Centre, 18–24 Lower Clapton Road, London E5 0PD **T** 020-3780 5870 **W** www.volunteeringmatters.org.uk
Chief Executive, Oonagh Aitken

VSO (VOLUNTARY SERVICE OVERSEAS) (1958), 100 London Road, Kingston-Upon-Thames KT2 6QJ **T** 020-8780 7500 **E** enquiry@vso.org **W** www.vsointernational.org
Chief Executive, Dr Philip Goodwin

WAR WIDOWS ASSOCIATION OF GREAT BRITAIN (1971), 199 Borough High Street, SE1 1AA **T** 0845-241 2189 **E** info@warwidows.org.uk **W** www.warwidows.org.uk
Chairman, Mary Moreland

WELLBEING OF WOMEN (1965), First Floor, Fairgate House, 78 New Oxford Street, WC1A 1HB **T** 020-3697 7000 **E** hello@wellbeingofwomen.org.uk **W** www.wellbeingofwomen.org.uk
Chief Executive, Janet Lindsay

WESTMINSTER FOUNDATION FOR DEMOCRACY (1992), Artillery House, 11–19 Artillery Row, London SW1P 1RT **T** 020-7799 1311 **W** www.wfd.org
Chief Executive, Anthony Smith, CMG

WHICH? (1957), 2 Marylebone Road, London NW1 4DF **T** 020-7770 7000 **W** www.which.co.uk
Chair, Tim Gardam

WILDFOWL AND WETLANDS TRUST (1946), Slimbridge GL2 7BT **T** 01453-891900 **E** enquiries@wwt.org.uk **W** www.wwt.org.uk
Chief Executive, Martin Spray, CBE

WILLIAM MORRIS SOCIETY AND KELMSCOTT
FELLOWSHIP (1955), Kelmscott House, 26 Upper Mall,
London W6 9TA T 020-8741 3735
E info@williammorrissociety.org.uk
W www.williammorrissociety.org.uk
Hon. Secretary, Natalia Martynenko-Hunt

WILTSHIRE ARCHAEOLOGICAL AND NATURAL
HISTORY SOCIETY (1853), Wiltshire Heritage Museum, 41
Long Street, Devizes SN10 1NS T 01380-727369
E hello@wiltshiremuseum.org.uk
W www.wiltshiremuseum.org.uk/society
Director, David Dawson

WOMEN'S ENGINEERING SOCIETY (1919), c/o The IET,
Michael Faraday House, Stevenage SG1 2AY T 01438-765506
E info@wes.org.uk W www.wes.org.uk
President, Dawn Childs

WOMEN'S ROYAL NAVAL SERVICE BENEVOLENT
TRUST (1941), Castaway House, 311 Twyford Avenue,
Portsmouth PO2 8RN T 023-9265 5301
E generalsecretary@wrnsbt.org.uk W www.wrnsbt.org.uk
General Secretary, Sarah Ayton

WOODLAND TRUST (1972), Kempton Way, Grantham
NG31 6LL T 0330-333 3300 E england@woodlandtrust.org.uk
W www.woodlandtrust.org.uk
Chief Executive, Beccy Speight

WORKING FAMILIES (2003), Spaces, City Point, London
EC2Y 9AW T 020-7153 1230 E office@workingfamilies.org.uk
W www.workingfamilies.org.uk
Chief Executive, Jane van Zyl

YMCA (1844), 10–11 Charterhouse Square, London EC1M 6EH
T 020-7186 9500 E enquiries@ymca.org.uk
W www.ymca.org.uk
Chief Executive, Denise Hatton

YORKSHIRE ARCHAEOLOGICAL AND HISTORICAL
SOCIETY (1863), Stringer House, 34 Lupton Street, Leeds
LS10 2QW T 0113-245 7910 E yahs.office@gmail.com
W www.yas.org.uk
President, David Asquith

YOUNG WOMEN'S TRUST (1855), Unit D, 15–18 White Lion
Street, London N1 9PD T 020-7837 2019
E contact@youngwomenstrust.org
W www.youngwomenstrust.org
Chief Executive, Sophie Walker

YOUTH HOSTELS ASSOCIATION (ENGLAND &
WALES) (1930), Trevelyan House, Dimple Road, Matlock
DE4 3YH T 01629-592700 E customerservices@yha.org.uk
W www.yha.org.uk
Chief Executive, James Blake

ZOOLOGICAL SOCIETY OF LONDON (1826), Outer
Circle, Regent's Park, London NW1 4RY T 0344-225 1826
E generalenquiries@zsl.org W www.zsl.org
Director-General, Dominic Jermey, CVO, OBE

SCIENCE AND SPACE

SCIENCE AND DISCOVERY IN 2019–20

ASTRONOMY

SCIENCE AND DISCOVERY IN 2019–20

By Storm Dunlop

CAN AXIONS SOLVE THREE PROBLEMS?
In March 2020, in *Physical Review Letters*, Raymond Co of the University of Michigan and Keisuke Harigaya of the Institute for Advanced Study suggested that an extremely light hypothetical particle known as the axion that hardly reacts with ordinary matter may solve three of the major questions that are not satisfactorily addressed by the Standard Model of particle physics. The axion was originally suggested in 1977 as a possible solution for a problem – known as the strong CP problem – with the properties of the neutron. Then in 1982 it was found to be capable of explaining the existence of dark matter. In the latest study, it is suggested that axions were present at the formation of the universe and that 'rotation' of axions could account for an imbalance between matter and antimatter, sufficient to account for the existence of just matter today.

HOW CAN MATTER EXIST?
In February 2020, an international team led by researchers at the University of Sussex, and including scientists from the Rutherford Appleton Laboratory and the Paul Scherrer Institute in Switzerland, reported in *Physical Review Letters* that they had finally succeeded in accurately measuring one specific property of the neutron. The particular property of interest is known as the 'electric dipole moment' (EDM): a slight difference in electrical charge at opposite sides of a neutron. This asymmetry is of fundamental importance in understanding the structural asymmetry that is thought to determine why matter exists in the universe. The current Standard Model of particle physics suggests that equal quantities of matter and antimatter were created at the origin of the universe (in the Big Bang), and that these would be expected to annihilate one another. EDM is a minute effect and the measurements required the use of highly sophisticated instrumentation and methods. The effect found is smaller than predicted, and rules out certain theories that attempt to explain the presence of matter in the universe.

CONFIRMATION OF THE EXISTENCE OF ANYONS
In our 3D space, there are two types of fundamental particles: fermions and bosons. Examples of each are, respectively an electron and a photon. In a 2D system, however, a third class of 'quasiparticle', known as an 'anyon' may exist. Anyons result from the collective motion of large numbers of electrons, which behave as a single particle. The quasiparticles are found in quantum effects. In June 2020 it was announced that experiments had revealed the existence of one property (known as 'braiding') of such quasiparticles. Braiding involves the change in the wave function of two anyons, preserving a history of their interaction, something impossible with fermions and bosons in a three-dimensional system. Knowledge of such 2D systems is considered to be important in the development of quantum computing.

THE EARLY CATACLYSMIC HISTORY OF THE SOLAR SYSTEM
In August 2019, a study by scientists at the University of Colorado at Boulder, aided by scientists at the University of Oslo, suggested that the Solar System was subjected to a series of cataclysmic collisions at a very early epoch – far earlier than previously thought. The bombardment by comets, asteroids, and proto-planets took place about 44,800 million years ago, shortly after the formation of the Sun, and was initiated by a period of 'giant planet migration'. This migration is necessary to account for the Solar System's current structure. Previous evidence from the Moon suggested that the heavy bombardment occurred much later, at around 3,900 million years ago. The earlier age has implications for the emergence of life on Earth, which would have been able to develop as long ago as 4,400 million years.

PLATE TECTONICS STARTED EARLIER THAN PREVIOUSLY THOUGHT
In early August 2019, a team, based at the University of Witwatersrand, revealed that plate tectonics had started earlier in the Earth's history than previously thought. The study showed that sea water had been transported by plate tectonics deep into the Earth's interior and subsequently trapped in ancient lavas. The research showed that plate tectonics was active 3,300 million years ago, about 600 million years earlier than previously believed. This date is approximately the same as the age when lifeforms first emerged on Earth.

GRAVITATIONAL WAVES BECOME ALMOST COMMONPLACE
The detection of gravitational waves has now become more-or-less routine, particularly since the VIRGO detector at Pisa in Italy entered service in August 2017 alongside the LIGO installations in the USA. Waves are now detected almost daily and the range of different masses of the objects that are merging is extremely wide. In August 2017 the first merger of two low-mass neutron stars (masses 1.46 and 1.27 solar masses) was observed. Detection of this exceptionally low-mass event is particularly significant for the study of neutron stars, and an indication of the potential for this method of observation (a second neutron-star merger has since been detected.) To date, observed black-hole mass pairs range from 10.9 and 7.6 solar masses to 85 and 66 solar masses. (The latter produced an extremely massive remnant at about 140 solar masses.) Events involving very unequal masses (eg 29.7 and 8.4 solar masses) have also been detected. There appears to be a 'mass gap' – a lack of intermediate-mass objects – but this has yet to be confirmed.

LOSS OF A MAJOR ASTRONOMICAL FACILITY
In August 2020, at the Arecibo Observatory in Puerto Rico, one of the main cables suspending the instrumentation platform some 450ft (137m) above the 1,000ft (305m) reflecting dish snapped. A second support cable snapped in November. It was decided that repair would be too dangerous and the instrument was due to be dismantled. On 1 December, yet another cable snapped, causing the instrument platform to fall and create catastrophic damage.

The radio telescope was originally completed in November 1963 and intended to study the upper atmosphere. It was soon employed in fundamental radio-astronomy studies, and had many improvements and additional equipment over the years. It remained the largest radio telescope in the world until July 2016, when the 500m Aperture Spherical Telescope (FAST) was completed in Guizhou, China. The newer telescope will not be fully commissioned for about three years, and, currently, does not have the radar capacity that was so successfully used at Arecibo. Astronomers have already revived a 'dormant' radio telescope in Argentina to see if it is able to continue the series of pulsar timings that was carried out so successfully at Arecibo. One casualty of the collapse is the radar study of minor planets, where the telescope had been particularly successful and uniquely placed to carry out such work.

WHAT HAVE WE FOUND?

In late 2019, an astronomer examining data from the Australian Square Kilometre Array Pathfinder (ASKAP) radio telescope array, detected a strange circular feature. Circular features are well-known in astronomy, and usually represent spherical shells produced by violent events. However, this was so large that if it originated in a central outburst, that must have occurred an extremely long time ago. Subsequent studies have revealed three (and possibly nine) more, similar objects, which are now known as 'Odd Radio Circles' (ORC). Despite numerous attempts to explain their occurrence, no process has been found to be suitable, so, for the present, they remain unexplained.

ANOTHER INTERSTELLAR INTERLOPER

After the detection of the first object ('Oumuamua) that originated outside the Solar System, on 30 August 2019, the amateur astronomer Gennady Borisov, from MARGO observatory in the Crimea, using a homemade 0.65-metre telescope, discovered another object arriving from interstellar space. (This is the eighth comet discovered by Borisov.) Given the initial provisional designation of C/2019 Q$_6$ (a comet) was formally named 2I/Borisov by the International Astronomical Union.

2I/Borisov reached perihelion (the closest point to the Sun) at a distance just outside the orbit of Mars on 7 December 2019. In March 2020, a large outburst with release of a major fragment occurred, although by April 2020 the fragment had disappeared. Unlike 1I/'Oumuamua, which was effectively inert and could have been an asteroidal body, 2I/Borisov is undoubtedly a comet, both dust and gases having been observed originating from the nucleus, the upper size of which is about 0.4km. The gases have been identified as revealing cyanide (CN), diatomic carbon (C$_2$), amine (NH$_2$) bands, atomic oxygen (suggesting the outgassing of water), and OH lines.

All this indicates that the way in which comets form is common to all stellar systems. It has been suggested that it would be possible to send a spaceprobe to fly by the comet in 2045, but this would require use of an (untried) major rocket and various gravity assists from the Sun and Jupiter, so is unlikely to go ahead. Estimates put the number of interstellar interlopers within the Solar System as hundreds, if not thousands, at any one time, although the majority are far too faint to be detectable.

SAMPLING MINOR PLANETS

In April 2019, the Japanese *Hayabusa 2* spaceprobe obtained a sample of the surface material from the minor planet (asteroid) 162173 Ryugu. Ryugu is a potentially hazardous body of the Apollo group and is a primitive body with characteristics of both what are known as B-type and C-type asteroids. On 11 July 2019, the spaceprobe touched down at the same site, extended a sampling tube, and fired a small tungsten projectile to break the surface. It collected some of the resulting debris, which should have originated from the interior of the body. It then returned to Earth and on 5 December 2020 dropped the sample capsule at the Woomera range in Australia, where both samples were successfully recovered. The spaceprobe itself has plenty of fuel and has been redirected to a flyby of another Apollo body, known provisionally as 2001 CC$_{21}$ in July 2026 and then on to 1998 KY$_{26}$, which it will reach in July 2031.

On 20 October 2020, the Touch-And-Go Sample Acquisition Mechanisms (TAGSAM) on the NASA probe OSIRIS-Rex obtained samples from the primitive, carbonaceous chondritic, minor planet 01955 Bennu. It is expected to return its samples to Earth on 24 September 2023.

THE MYSTERIOUS FAST RADIO BURSTS AND MAGNETARS

The origins of the long-enigmatic fast radio bursts (FRBs), discovered in 2007, may have been found. These events are so transient, lasting just milliseconds, that they have been difficult to track down, even though a few of them are known to repeat. Now, at long last, a signal has been observed coming from a magnetar, a dense neutron star with an extremely strong magnetic field. This field is thought to be as high as one thousand trillion Gauss.

In May 2020, it was announced that the known magnetar, SGR 1935+2154, which is in our own galaxy, had emitted a pulse of radio waves with all the characteristics of an FRB. Magnetars are known to produce emit X-rays and gamma-rays, including bursts of such radiation.

In a separate development, in November 2020 a team, led by astrophysicists from Northwestern University in Evanston, Illinois, announced that they believed that they had observed the birth of a magnetar. On 22 May 2020, the light from a kilonova (a brilliant outburst some 1000 times brighter than a classical nova) arrived from a distant galaxy as a burst of gamma-rays. The amount of energy radiated in gamma-rays in just half a second was enormous. It amounted to more than the total energy output of the Sun over its whole lifetime of about 10,000 million years. The initial gamma-ray burst was detected by NASA's Swift space observatory. Many other telescopes then observed the object, including the Hubble Space Telescope, which detected anomalous near-infrared radiation.

It is believed that this event was the result of the merger of two neutron stars. Although such an event is thought to normally result in an object that immediately collapses into a black hole, in this instance it is believed that a supermassive neutron star (the magnetar) resulted from the merger. Rotating at some 1,000 times per second, the exceptionally strong magnetic field pumped energy into the ejecta left by the original explosion, giving rise to the large infra-red excess detected by the Hubble telescope.

GROUND-BASED ASTRONOMY UNDER THREAT

It has become obvious that commercial plans to launch thousands of satellites into orbit pose a very serious threat to certain astronomical studies. The SpaceX company has already launched many hundreds of small satellites, designed to provide fast broadband access anywhere on Earth. Other companies similarly intend to launch 'mega-constellations' of satellites, and a total of some 100,000 is likely if all plans go ahead. The threat to ground-based astronomy is extreme. Certain research activities are likely to be particularly affected. The search for near-Earth asteroids (the ones likely to pose a threat of impact) will be one of the worst affected. There are also concerns over the way in which radiation from the satellites will drown out faint radio signals from the cosmos. Certain surveys, such as that expected to be carried out by the Vera Rubin Telescope (formerly known as the Large Synoptic Survey Telescope) that is under construction in Chile, will be severely hampered and will lose up to 40 per cent of observing time at certain periods of the day. With no governmental restraints, commercial interests appear likely to prevent many serious scientific studies.

PLATE TECTONICS STARTED EARLIER THAN PREVIOUSLY THOUGHT

In early August 2019, a team, based at the University of Witwatersrand revealed that plate tectonics had started earlier in the Earth's history than previously thought. The study showed that sea water had been transported by plate tectonics deep into the Earth's interior and subsequently trapped in ancient lavas. The research showed that plate tectonics was active 3,300 million years ago, about 600 million years earlier than previously believed. This date is approximately the same as the age when lifeforms first emerged on Earth.

EXTREMELY EARLY BIPEDAL APES FROM EUROPE

In November 2019, it was announced by a team from the University of Tübingen in Germany that bones recovered from a site in Bavaria showed that the first apes to walk upright may have evolved in Europe, not Africa. The bones from the newly described species, *Danuvius guggenmosi*, are dated to an astonishing age of 11.6 million years. This is more than 5 million years earlier than the dates for *Sahelanthropus tchadensis* and *Orrorin tugenensis*, previously thought to be the earliest bipedal hominins. There are extreme implications for our view of human evolution and where this took place.

AN EARLY USE OF FIRE
In July 2019, evidence was presented that hominins in Kenya made use of fire as long ago as 1.5 million years. This extends evidence for the use of fire by several thousands of years and has re-opened debate about whether the consumption of more efficient food (ie, cooked meat) assisted the evolution of large-brained hominins.

The team, led by Sarah Hlubik of Rutgers University in New Jersey, found thousands of fragments of stone tools and burned bones at the site in the Kobe Fora region. In many cases the finds occurred around patches of burned ground, suggesting that tool-making (and perhaps cooking) were taking place close to open fires.

DID HOMININS ARISE IN EUROPE?
At a conference of the American Association of Physical Anthropologists in Cleveland, Ohio, in March 2019. David Begun of the University of Toronto presented evidence of a potential hominin ancestor found in southeastern Europe. The fragments of upper and lower jaw (initially assigned to the extinct ape *Ouranopithecus*), from Nikiti in northern Greece, are dated to 8 to 9 million years ago. They contained small, pointed canines (an attribute of hominins), and may belong to a formerly unrecognized species.

Previously the team had examined fossils of an ape known as *Graecopithecus*, that also lived in Greece, at 7.2 million years ago, and come to the tentative conclusion that they represented a hominin. These fossils also exhibited small canines, and additionally, the fused root to the premolars (another hominin attribute). It is therefore now suggested that the Nikiti form may have been the ancestor of the hominin, *Graecopithecus*, and that hominins migrated to Africa, where they evolved developed into several species and, eventually, into *Homo sapiens*.

WHO WAS OUR ANCESTOR?
In August 2019, the discovery by Professor Haile-Selassie (affiliated to the Cleveland Museum of Natural History in Ohio) was announced in Nature of a well-preserved and extremely old fossil of an ape-like species that may be the earliest human ancestor. The find was at Miro Dor, in the Mille District of Ethiopia's Afar Regional State. The fossil is of *Australopithecus anamensis*, which may have existed as long ago as 4.2 million years. *A. amanensis* was previously thought to be the direct ancestor of *Australopithecus afarensis*, (nicknamed 'Lucy'), believed to be a direct human ancestor. It is now obvious that the two species existed at the same time. This suggests that other advanced ape-like species may have co-existed, increasing the potential evolutionary routes to our eventual *Homo sapiens* species. This agrees with the recent acceptance that multiple hominin species existed at the same time and in the same locations.

THREE SPECIES OF HOMININS IN ONE PLACE
In April 2020, a team of 30 scientists from five countries revealed the discovery of *Homo erectus* remains at Drimolen, northwest of Johannesburg in South Africa. *H. erectus* is considered to be an ancestor of our species, *Homo sapiens*. The new remains are securely dated to 2 million years old. The same site also contained remains of a second ancestral species, *Paranthropus robustus*, also known from other local sites of the

same geological age. A third species, *Australopithecus sebida*, occurs in nearby deposits of the same age. The existence of three hominin species in essentially the same place at the same time is highly significant and contradicts the conventional view of one species replacing another, more primitive, form.

WE ARE A MIXED LOT
In July 2019 it was announced in *Proceedings of the National Academy of Sciences* by researchers from the University of Adelaide's Australian Centre for Ancient DNA (ACAD), that genetic analysis has revealed that modern-day *Homo sapiens* has interbred with at least five different archaic groups of humans. We have known for some time that the human genome contains elements from Neanderthals and the species known as Denisovans, but the other (currently unnamed) species are detected only as traces of DNA. The diversity appears to increase towards the east. Interbreeding with Neanderthals appears to have occurred soon after humans left East Africa around 60,000 years ago and that probably happened in the Middle East (possibly around 50,000 to 55,000 years ago). As the ancestral humans travelled east, they seem to have interbred with at least four other distinct groups (one being the Denisovans). The islands of Southeast Asia appear to have harboured several distinct groups of ancient (now extinct) humans. It seems that these groups existed in isolation from one another until modern human ancestors arrived.

LATE SURVIVAL OF *HOMO ERECTUS*
The hominin species *Homo erectus* is believed to be a direct ancestor of our own species, *Homo sapiens*, and the first to walk fully upright. It has long been thought that *H. erectus* became extinct in eastern Asia about 400,000 years ago. In December 2019, a team from the University of Iowa announced a dating of between 117,000 and 108,000 years for numerous specimens of *H. erectus* from Ngandong on the Solo River in Java. The individuals are thought to have died at the same time, perhaps as a result of a lahar created by a nearby volcano. This dating raises the possibility that *H. erectus* may have been present when the ancestors of *H. sapiens* arrived on the island.

EARLIEST EUROPEAN BONE TOOLS DISCOVERED
In August 2020, researchers from University College London Institute of Archaeology and the London Natural History Museum announced the discovery of some of the earliest organic (ie, not stone) tools in the world and certainly the earliest known from Europe. They came from the Boxgrove site in Sussex and appear to have been used in the manufacture of the numerous flint tools found at the site. The hominins using the site (dated to 500,000 years ago) were members of *Homo heidelbergensis*, a possible *Homo sapiens* ancestor.

DENISOVAN ART?
In July 2019, bones were excavated at Lingjing in Henan Province, China, at a site where ancient hominins, believed to be Denisovans, lived. The site was occupied between 125,000 and 105,000 years ago. The bones bore engravings of lines, created with a sharp point and rubbed with red ochre to make them more visible. Although the marks are geometrically simple, there are profound implications for the cognitive skills of the hominins who produced them. Similarly, despite there being some doubt about who created these signs, because modern humans arrived in the area at about 100,000 years ago, there is a good probability that these were actually created by the mysterious Denisovans.

A MUCH EARLIER DATE FOR HUMANS IN THE AMERICAS
In July 2020, an international team from Universidad Autónoma de Zacatecas, Mexico, the University of Oxford, and others announced the discovery of artefacts from Chiquihuite Cave, a rock shelter in Zacatecas, Mexico. The stone tools are

reliably dated to 33,000 years old by the Oxford Radiocarbon Accelerator Unit, using two, completely different, dating techniques. This date is more than twice the age of 11,500 years for the Clovis Culture, often regarded as the first inhabitants of the Americas, although in recent years discoveries at Mesa Verde in Chile and Buttermilk Creek in Texas, in particular, have thrown this into doubt.

The distribution of the stone tools (about 1,900 in number) suggests that the Chiquihuite Cave site was used for at least 2,000 years. Some archaeologists, however, have claimed that the finds are naturally shaped stones, not human artefacts. It was announced in August 2019 that a site at Coopers Ferry in western Idaho was occupied some 16,000 years ago, and this date is accepted by some as being the earliest settlement of the Americas by peoples using the coastal route from Siberia.

THE EARLIEST MODERN BIRD

In March 2020, the discovery was announced in the journal Nature of the remains of the earliest modern bird. The fossil was discovered in marine sedimentary rocks from Belgium, and has been named *Asteriornis maastrichtensis* (nicknamed 'Wonderchicken'). The skull, the most important part, was found by Daniel Field of the University of Cambridge and his team by the use of X-ray computed tomography. The extinct bird lived some 66.7 million years ago, thus well before the asteroidal impact that may have resulted in the extinction of the dinosaurs, which occurred 65 to 66 million years ago. The fossil displays features that relate it to the most common ancestor of modern birds. The skull exhibits features resembling those of modern chicken and also those of the duck family. The fragmentary limb bones suggest that the bird had long legs, which, together with the discovery site, suggest that it may have been a shorebird.

ENORMOUS PREHISTORIC CIRCLE DISCOVERED NEAR STONEHENGE

In late June 2020, archaeologists announced the discovery of an enormous circle of shafts, about 2km in overall diameter, enclosing the henge at Durrington Walls. The structure is larger than any other ever found in Britain. The discovery was made after a geophysical survey as part of the Stonehenge Hidden Landscape Project. The individual shafts are about 10m in diameter, and 5m deep. Archaeologists believe that the circle represents a boundary surrounding the religious site and thus warning people not to attempt to trespass on the sacred area but to use specific entrances.

DISCOVERY OF THE EARLIEST AND LARGEST MAYAN CONSTRUCTION

The largest Mayan complex was described in *Nature* in June 2020 by researchers from the University of Arizona. The previously unknown site in Mexico, called Aguada Fénix, was discovered by the use of airborne lidar instrumentation and reveals, amongst other features, a giant, raised ceremonial plaza, about 1,400m long and 400m wide. This enormous construction was built in the very early Mayan period, between 1,000 and 800 BC. No evidence has yet been found at Aguada Fénix of the existence of a powerful elite class that would oversee such a giant construction and other works in the surrounding area, suggesting that the works were carried out by the combined forces from small local settlements. Large Mayan cities and kingdoms did not develop in Southern Mexico and elsewhere in Central America until much later, around AD 250 to 900.

USA RETURNS TO MANNED SPACE FLIGHT

The United States returned to manned space flight in 2020, with the launch on 20 May 2020 by a Falcon 9 rocket of the SpaceX company's *Dragon 2* capsule (named *Endeavour*), with two astronauts, bound for the International Space Station (ISS).

The capsule later returned the astronauts safely to Earth on 2 August 2020. A second launch on 15 November carried four astronauts to the ISS. A test flight of Boeing's *Starliner* capsule in December 2019 failed to reach the ISS. A further flight is scheduled for 29 March 2021.

SPACEX COMPANY'S STARSHIP SPACECRAFT

In December 2020, the SpaceX company carried out the first major test of its reusable spacecraft design (known as *Starship*), in a sub-orbital flight from its Boca Chica facility in south Texas. *Starship* is a large vehicle (50m long), able to carry large numbers of passengers (with up to 40 individual cabins) or a heavy payload, to orbit and beyond. It uses its own, SpaceX-designed, Raptor engines and an unconventional horizontal attitude ('belly flop') method of atmospheric braking, before turning to the vertical for landing. In the first test, all stages were satisfactory, including the atmospheric braking, save that the vehicle landed too fast and suffered a catastrophic failure and explosion. The performance in all other stages were considered a great success.

In major missions, it would be teamed with the huge, reusable, SpaceX *Super Heavy* booster rocket, some 70m long, which has up to 28 Raptor engines and is actually more powerful than the *Saturn V* rocket used for the Apollo missions. It is capable of placing some 100,000kg of payload into low Earth orbit.

RETURN TO THE MOON

On 22 July 2019, the Indian Space Research Organisation launched the *Chandrayaan-2* spacecraft, which was inserted into lunar orbit on 20 August 2019. However, as a result of a software problem, the lunar lander (*Vikram*) crashed onto the lunar surface on 6 September 2019. A duplicate mission may be undertaken in 2021.

On 23 November 2020, the Chinese Lunar Exploration Programme launched the *Chang'e-5* lunar sample return spacecraft. This made a landing on the Mons Rümker area of Oceanus Procellarum, an area thought to be much younger than other regions of the Moon that have been sampled, most of which were affected by the giant Mare Imbrium impact at 3,900 million years ago. The probe rapidly obtained approximately 2kg of specimens, both scooped from the surface and drilled from a lower layer. The specimens were returned to Earth at a landing site in Inner Mongolie on 16 December 2020.

In November 2019 and December 2020, NASA designated six companies as potential suppliers of the Commercial Lunar Payload Services for various modules as part of its overall *Artemis* programme to return humans to the Moon. (Three contracts had previously been awarded to commercial companies for landers capable of delivering at least 10kg of scientific instrumentation by the end of 2021. Heavier payloads are being considered for delivery in 2023.) On 21 February 2019, NASA announced details of the first 12 payloads and on 1 July 2020 information on a further 12 payloads. The first of the small landers, *Peregrine Mission One*, is due for launch in July 2021.

MISSIONS TO MARS

Three missions to Mars were launched in July 2020 to take advantage of a favourable launch window. On 20 July, the United Arab Emirates launched the Emirates Mars Mission (named *Hope*) from Tanegashima Island in Japan. The spacecraft will be inserted into Mars orbit in February 2021 and then begin observations of the Martian atmosphere.

On 25 July 2020, China launched its *Tianwen-1* ('Questions to Heaven') Martian rover. The spacecraft was lifted off by a Long March 5 rocket from Wenchang spaceport on Hainan Island and is expected to enter Martian orbit in February 2021. The lander/rover is scheduled to reach the surface of Mars some two to three months later.

On 30 July 2020, NASA launched the spacecraft (*Mars 2020*) carrying the advanced *Perseverance* rover to Mars. This is scheduled to land at Jezero crater on 18 February 2021. The rover incorporates improvements made as a result of slight problems with NASA's highly successful *Curiosity* rover, and also includes more advanced instrumentation. The rover is accompanied by the simple helicopter *Ingenuity*, which, apart from being able to conduct scouting missions around the rover, has a primary objective of determining whether such drones can operate properly in the thin Martian atmosphere. The rover has a drill and can collect samples of rock, and store these in suitable containers. The overall aim is for a later mission to recover these containers and return them to Earth for study.

A CHANCE TO TACKLE PLASTIC POLLUTION
In September 2020, a team from the University of Portsmouth in the UK and the National Renewable Energy Laboratory (NREL) in the USA announced in *Proceedings of the National Academy of Sciences* that they had created a 'super-enzyme', by combining the PETase enzyme with another, called the MHETase enzyme, to obtain an enzyme that breaks down the PET plastic into its component parts, which can then be reused in other processes and materials. The original PETase enzyme, discovered at the Portsmouth Centre for Enzyme Innovation, broke down PET (the most ubiquitous plastic) at a rate far exceeding natural processes, but not fast enough for commercial use. The 'super-enzyme' acts six times faster, so that commercial applications and a solution to some of the problem of plastic pollution become practical.

MAJOR DEVELOPMENTS IN ELECTRON MICROSCOPY
In July 2019 it was announced that developments in cryo-electron microscopy (cryo-EM), giving exceptional increases in resolution was revolutionising biological research. The technique has been so refined that it has now been termed 'ultra-high-definition-3D-video-ology'. It is now possible to see the shape and structure of biological molecules in detail and the processes actually occurring inside cells. This is a major step forward in the development of drugs, especially for infectious diseases, and including problems such as those posed by Alzheimer's and Parkinson's diseases.

The technique involves freezing molecules (or viruses) within cells, and then making thousands of images from different angles and at different stages of a biological process. These images may then be used to create a video of the process in action.

EDITING DNA
In October 2019, the journal *Nature* carried details of a new method of editing DNA.

Although DNA may be edited with the Crispr-Cas9 technique, this depends on 'cutting' the strand of DNA and splicing in a suitable fragment. Unfortunately, the cuts are sometimes imperfect, occurring in the wrong place, so additional care needs to be taken to ensure that the final result is desirable.

In the new process, known as 'prime editing', the process allows one to search for a precise piece of the DNA sequence, and replace this with a known, required sequence. When used in combination with a specific enzyme, known as reverse transcriptase, the relevant 'edits' are incorporated into the DNA.

Prime editing has been used *in vitro* (in human cells) in the laboratory to reverse the effects of errors in various forms of disease, including one in the rare Tay-Sachs disease, and one in a form of sickle-cell anaemia.

It is estimated that prime editing has the potential to correct some 89 per cent of the approximately 75,000 mutations that may cause disease in people. As with all similar procedures much more work, likely to take years, is required before any benefit can be made available to individuals.

VACCINES AGAINST COVID-19
By mid-December 2020, as many as 57 vaccines against the COVID-19 coronavirus (coronavirus 2 or SARS-CoV-2) were in clinical trials, 40 in Phase I or II trials and 17 in Phase II to III trials. Those vaccines currently administered (except only the Russian Sputnik-5 vaccine) are known to have completed satisfactory Phase III trials.

The Oxford-AstraZeneca vaccine (AZD1222) is produced by what is known as a virus-vector method. In this, a virus, normally producing common-cold symptoms in chimpanzees, has been modified so that it will not reproduce in humans. In addition, changes cause the virus to produce 'spike' proteins like those by which the COVID-19 infects human cells. With vaccination, the body recognises these foreign proteins and produces antibodies against them. It also activates special T-cells that destroy any cells with the 'spike' protein. The body is thus primed against any future infection, although at present it is not known how long (in terms of months or years) such resistance persists.

The Pfizer-Biontech vaccine (tozinameran) is of a new type known as an RNA vaccine. It uses a small fragment of the genetic code of the virus. When injected, this causes just a part of the virus to be produced within the body, which then recognises this as foreign and attacks it.

The Moderna vaccine (mRNA-1273) uses a similar method to that in the Pfizer-BioNTech vaccine.

No details are available of the Russian 'Sputnik-5' vaccine, administered before final trials had been concluded, and which is believed to be similar to the Oxford-AstraZeneca vaccine. Other vaccines are being developed in China by Wuhan Biological Products and Sinopharm (an inactivated virus vaccine) and in Russia by Gamaleya Research Institute (Gam-COVID-Vac, produced in a way similar to the Oxford-AstraZeneca method). All are in final trials. A trial in Brazil of an inactivated virus vaccine from the Chinese company, Sinovac, was halted after an unspecified adverse reaction.

ASTRONOMY 2021

The following pages give astronomical data for each month of the year 2021. There are three pages of data for each month. All data are given for 0h Greenwich Mean Time (GMT), ie at the midnight at the beginning of the day named. This applies also to data for the months when British Summer Time is in operation (for dates, *see* below).

The astronomical data are given in a form suitable for observation with the naked eye, binoculars or with a small telescope. These data do not attempt to replace the *Astronomical Almanac* for professional astronomers. A fuller explanation of how to use the astronomical data is given after the data for the months.

CALENDAR FOR EACH MONTH

The calendar for each month comprises dates of general interest plus the dates of birth or death of well-known people. For key religious, civil and legal dates *see* page 9. For details of flag-flying days *see* page 23. For royal birthdays *see* pages 23 and 24–5. For public The Year 2021.

Fuller explanations of the various calendars can be found under Time Measurement and Calendars.

The zodiacal signs through which the Sun is passing each month are illustrated.

JULIAN DATE

Julian dates are a continuous count of days since the beginning of the Julian Period and is used primarily by astronomers for calculating elapsed days between two events. Julian Day Number 0 is assigned to the day starting at noon on Monday, 1 January 4713 BCE as it precedes any dates in recorded history. The Julian date (JD) of any instant is the Julian day number plus the fraction of a day since the preceding noon in Universal Time. Julian dates are expressed as a Julian day number with a decimal fraction added.

The Julian date on 2021 January 0.0 is 2459214.5. To find the Julian date for any other date in 2021 (at 0h GMT), add the day of the year number on the extreme right of the calendar for each month to the Julian date for 0.0 given above.

BRITISH SUMMER TIME

British Summer Time is the legal time for general purposes during the period in which it is in operation (*see also* Time, British Summer Time). During this period, clocks are kept one hour ahead of Greenwich Mean Time. The hour of changeover is 01h Greenwich Mean Time. The duration of Summer Time in 2021 is from 28 March 01h GMT to 31 October 01h GMT.

SEASONS

The seasons are defined astronomically as follows:

Spring from the vernal equinox to the summer solstice
Summer from the summer solstice to the autumnal equinox
Autumn from the autumnal equinox to the winter solstice
Winter from the winter solstice to the vernal equinox

The times when the seasons start in 2021 (to the nearest hour) are:

Northern Hemisphere
Vernal Equinox	March 20d 10h GMT
Summer Solstice	June 21d 04h GMT
Autumnal Equinox	September 22d 19h GMT
Winter Solstice	December 21d 16h GMT

Southern Hemisphere
Autumnal Equinox	March 20d 10h GMT
Winter Solstice	June 21d 04h GMT
Vernal Equinox	September 22d 19h GMT
Summer Solstice	December 21d 16h GMT

The longest day of the year, measured from sunrise to sunset, is at the summer solstice. The longest day in the UK will fall on 21 June in 2021.

The shortest day of the year is at the winter solstice. The shortest day in the UK will fall on 21 December in 2021.

The equinox is the point at which day and night are of equal length all over the world.

In popular parlance, the seasons in the northern hemisphere comprise the following months:

Spring	March, April, May
Summer	June, July, August
Autumn	September, October, November
Winter	December, January, February

The March equinox can fall as early as 19 March but this has not happened since 1796 and it will not happen again until 2044. This equinox in 2007 was on 21 March, however in 2008 it occurred on 20 March and will not revert to 21 March again until 2102.

In 2008 the June solstice occurred on 20 June, the first time since 1897. The June solstice in 1975 was on 22 June, but it will not occur on this date again until 2203.

 # January 2021

FIRST MONTH, 31 DAYS. *Janus,* god of the portal, facing two ways, past and future

1	*Friday*	Euro notes and coins entered circulation in twelve European Union countries 2002	day 1
2	*Saturday*	In Paris, Louis Daguerre took the first photograph of the moon 1839	2
3	*Sunday*	General Washington's revolutionary forces defeated the British at the battle of Princeton 1777	3
4	*Monday*	Sir Isaac Newton, physicist and mathematician who discovered the law of gravitation *b*. 1642	week 1 day 4
5	*Tuesday*	The German Worker's Party, predecessor of the Nazi party, is founded in Munich 1919	5
6	*Wednesday*	Demonstration by Samuel Morse of the first electric telegraph system 1838	6
7	*Thursday*	The inventor Henry Mill obtains a patent for the first typewriter 1714	7
8	*Friday*	Stephen Hawking *b*. 1942. Galileo Galilei *d*. 1642	8
9	*Saturday*	280,000 coal miners began a seven-week strike against the government 1972	9
10	*Sunday*	The Metropolitan line, the world's first underground railway, opens to passengers in London 1863	10
11	*Monday*	Insulin was first administered to a diabetic patient in Canada 1922	week 2 day 11
12	*Tuesday*	The Royal Aeronautical Society of Great Britain was founded 1866	12
13	*Wednesday*	The National Geographic Society is founded in Washington DC 1888	13
14	*Thursday*	The American War of Independence ended 1784	14
15	*Friday*	The British Museum opened to the public in Montagu House, Bloomsbury, London 1759	15
16	*Saturday*	Prohibition, the attempt to ban alcohol sale and consumption, began in the USA 1920	16
17	*Sunday*	Benny Goodman and his orchestra performed the first jazz concert at Carnegie Hall 1938	17
18	*Monday*	Airbus' 840-passenger A380, the world's biggest passenger jet, was unveiled in France 2005	week 3 day 18
19	*Tuesday*	The US senate votes against participation in the League of Nations 1920	19
20	*Wednesday*	The House of Commons assembled for the first time 1265	20
21	*Thursday*	Concorde's first commercial flights take off simultaneously from London and Paris 1976	21
22	*Friday*	Roberta Bondar becomes the first Canadian woman in space 1992	22
23	*Saturday*	A disguised King Henry VIII jousts in Richmond and is applauded before revealing his identity 1510	23
24	*Sunday*	The Macintosh 128K, the first computer built by Apple Macintosh, was released 1984	24
25	*Monday*	Karel Capek's play R.U.R., which introduced the word 'robot', premiered in Prague 1921	week 4 day 25
26	*Tuesday*	The Republic of India was proclaimed with Rajendra Prasad as president 1950	26
27	*Wednesday*	Soviet troops liberated the Auschwitz concentration camp 1945	27
28	*Thursday*	Jane Austen's romantic novel Pride and Prejudice is published 1813	28
29	*Friday*	Edgar Allan Poe's poem 'The Raven' was published in the New York Evening Mirror 1845	29
30	*Saturday*	The Beatles gave their last public performance on top of their London recording studio 1969	30
31	*Sunday*	The 100th British soldier was killed in the Iraq conflict 2006	31

ASTRONOMICAL PHENOMENA

d	h	
2	14	Earth at perihelion (0.98326 AU)
2	22	Regulus 4.7°S of the Moon
3	15	Quadrantid meteor shower
6	10	Last Quarter Moon
10	05	Mercury 1.6°S of Saturn
11	11	Mercury 1.5°S of Jupiter
11	20	Venus 1.5°N of the Moon
13	05	New Moon
13	21	Saturn 3.2°N of the Moon
14	01	Jupiter 3.3°N of the Moon
14	08	Mercury 2.3°N of the Moon
14	-	Pluto solar conjunction
20	PM	Mars 1.6° from Uranus
20	21	First Quarter Moon
20	-	Sun crosses into Capricornus
21	05	Mars 5.0°N of the Moon
24	-	Mercury at greatest elongation (18° 34' E)
24	-	Saturn solar conjunction
28	19	Full Moon
28	-	Jupiter solar conjunction

CONSTELLATIONS

The following constellations are visible at midnight throughout the month:
Draco (below the Pole), Ursa Minor (below the Pole), Camelopardalis, Perseus, Auriga, Taurus, Orion, Eridanus and Lepus

PHASES OF THE MOON

Phase, Apsides and Node	d	h	m
◖ Last Quarter	6	9	37
● New Moon	13	5	0
◑ First Quarter	20	21	2
○ Full Moon	28	19	16
Perigee (367,387 km)	9	15	37
Apogee (404,360 km)	21	13	11

SUNRISE AND SUNSET

	London				Bristol				Birmingham				Manchester				Newcastle				Glasgow				Belfast			
	0° 05'		51° 30'		2° 35'		51° 28'		1° 55'		52° 28'		2° 15'		53° 28'		1° 37'		54° 59'		4° 14'		55° 52'		5° 56'		54° 35'	
d	h	m	h	m	h	m	h	m	h	m	h	m	h	m	h	m	h	m	h	m	h	m	h	m	h	m	h	m
1	8	06	16	02	8	16	16	12	8	18	16	05	8	25	16	01	8	31	15	49	8	47	15	54	8	46	16	09
2	8	06	16	03	8	16	16	14	8	18	16	06	8	25	16	02	8	31	15	51	8	47	15	56	8	46	16	10
3	8	06	16	05	8	15	16	15	8	18	16	07	8	24	16	03	8	31	15	52	8	47	15	57	8	45	16	11
4	8	05	16	06	8	15	16	16	8	17	16	08	8	24	16	04	8	30	15	53	8	46	15	58	8	45	16	13
5	8	05	16	07	8	15	16	17	8	17	16	09	8	24	16	06	8	30	15	55	8	46	16	00	8	45	16	14
6	8	05	16	08	8	14	16	18	8	17	16	11	8	23	16	07	8	29	15	56	8	45	16	01	8	44	16	16
7	8	04	16	09	8	14	16	20	8	16	16	12	8	23	16	08	8	29	15	57	8	44	16	03	8	44	16	17
8	8	04	16	11	8	14	16	21	8	16	16	13	8	22	16	10	8	28	15	59	8	44	16	04	8	43	16	18
9	8	03	16	12	8	13	16	22	8	15	16	15	8	22	16	11	8	27	16	00	8	43	16	06	8	42	16	20
10	8	03	16	14	8	13	16	24	8	15	16	16	8	21	16	13	8	27	16	02	8	42	16	07	8	42	16	22
11	8	02	16	15	8	12	16	25	8	14	16	18	8	20	16	14	8	26	16	04	8	41	16	09	8	41	16	23
12	8	01	16	16	8	11	16	27	8	13	16	19	8	19	16	16	8	25	16	05	8	40	16	11	8	40	16	25
13	8	01	16	18	8	10	16	28	8	12	16	21	8	19	16	17	8	24	16	07	8	39	16	13	8	39	16	26
14	8	00	16	19	8	10	16	30	8	12	16	22	8	18	16	19	8	23	16	09	8	38	16	14	8	38	16	28
15	7	59	16	21	8	09	16	31	8	11	16	24	8	17	16	21	8	22	16	11	8	37	16	16	8	37	16	30
16	7	58	16	23	8	08	16	33	8	10	16	26	8	16	16	22	8	21	16	12	8	36	16	18	8	36	16	32
17	7	57	16	24	8	07	16	34	8	09	16	27	8	15	16	24	8	20	16	14	8	35	16	20	8	35	16	33
18	7	56	16	26	8	06	16	36	8	08	16	29	8	14	16	26	8	18	16	16	8	33	16	22	8	34	16	35
19	7	55	16	27	8	05	16	38	8	07	16	31	8	12	16	28	8	17	16	18	8	32	16	24	8	32	16	37
20	7	54	16	29	8	04	16	39	8	06	16	32	8	11	16	29	8	16	16	20	8	31	16	26	8	31	16	39
21	7	53	16	31	8	03	16	41	8	04	16	34	8	10	16	31	8	14	16	22	8	29	16	28	8	30	16	41
22	7	52	16	32	8	02	16	43	8	03	16	36	8	09	16	33	8	13	16	24	8	28	16	30	8	28	16	43
23	7	51	16	34	8	01	16	44	8	02	16	38	8	07	16	35	8	12	16	26	8	26	16	32	8	27	16	45
24	7	50	16	36	7	59	16	46	8	01	16	40	8	06	16	37	8	10	16	28	8	25	16	34	8	26	16	47
25	7	48	16	38	7	58	16	48	7	59	16	41	8	05	16	39	8	09	16	30	8	23	16	36	8	24	16	49
26	7	47	16	39	7	57	16	50	7	58	16	43	8	03	16	41	8	07	16	32	8	22	16	38	8	23	16	51
27	7	46	16	41	7	56	16	51	7	57	16	45	8	02	16	42	8	05	16	34	8	20	16	40	8	21	16	53
28	7	44	16	43	7	54	16	53	7	55	16	47	8	00	16	44	8	04	16	36	8	18	16	42	8	19	16	55
29	7	43	16	45	7	53	16	55	7	54	16	49	7	59	16	46	8	02	16	38	8	16	16	45	8	18	16	57
30	7	41	16	47	7	51	16	57	7	52	16	51	7	57	16	48	8	00	16	40	8	15	16	47	8	16	16	59
31	7	40	16	48	7	50	16	58	7	51	16	52	7	55	16	50	7	59	16	42	8	13	16	49	8	14	17	01

THE MOON

Day	Diam '	Phase %	Age d	Rise 52° h	Rise 52° m	Rise 56° h	Rise 56° m	Transit h	Transit m	Set 52° h	Set 52° m	Set 56° h	Set 56° m
1	31.0	96	16.8	18	21	18	0	1	44	10	7	10	31
2	31.2	91	17.8	19	39	19	22	2	37	10	37	10	54
3	31.4	84	18.8	21	0	20	48	3	29	10	59	11	13
4	31.6	76	19.8	22	20	22	14	4	18	11	19	11	27
5	31.8	66	20.8	23	41	23	41	5	7	11	37	11	39
6	32.0	55	21.8	-	-	-	-	5	55	11	53	11	51
7	32.2	43	22.8	1	3	1	8	6	44	12	11	12	4
8	32.4	32	23.8	2	27	2	38	7	36	12	31	12	19
9	32.6	22	24.8	3	52	4	9	8	30	12	57	12	38
10	32.6	13	25.8	5	18	5	41	9	27	13	29	13	6
11	32.4	6	26.8	6	38	7	5	10	27	14	14	13	45
12	32.2	2	27.8	7	46	8	16	11	29	15	12	14	42
13	32.0	0	28.8	8	40	9	7	12	28	16	21	15	55
14	31.6	1	0.3	9	19	9	42	13	25	17	38	17	16
15	31.2	4	1.3	9	48	10	5	14	17	18	56	18	40
16	30.8	9	2.3	10	10	10	23	15	5	20	12	20	2
17	30.4	16	3.3	10	28	10	35	15	50	21	25	21	19
18	30.2	24	4.3	10	43	10	46	16	32	22	35	22	34
19	29.8	33	5.3	10	57	10	56	17	13	23	44	23	47
20	29.6	42	6.3	11	11	11	5	17	54	-	-	-	-
21	29.6	51	7.3	11	25	11	16	18	35	0	52	1	0
22	29.6	61	8.3	11	42	11	28	19	19	2	1	2	14
23	29.6	70	9.3	12	4	11	45	20	5	3	11	3	29
24	29.8	78	10.3	12	30	12	7	20	53	4	20	4	43
25	30.0	85	11.3	13	6	12	38	21	45	5	28	5	54
26	30.4	92	12.3	13	53	13	23	22	39	6	30	6	58
27	30.8	96	13.3	14	53	14	24	23	34	7	23	7	51
28	31.0	99	14.3	16	5	15	39	-	-	8	5	8	31
29	31.4	100	15.3	17	22	17	4	0	29	8	38	8	57
30	31.6	98	16.3	18	44	18	31	1	22	9	3	9	19
31	32	94	17.3	20	7	20	0	2	14	9	25	9	34

THE PLANETS

MERCURY

Day	R.A.			Dec.	Mag.	Diam.	Phase	Rise			Transit			Set		
	h	m	s	°		"	%	h	m	s	h	m	s	h	m	s
1	19	18	2	-24.3	-1.0	4.8	98	9	1	59	12	34	34	16	7	25
6	19	53	18	-23.1	-0.9	5.0	95	9	7	16	12	50	3	16	33	19
11	20	27	41	-21.1	-0.9	5.3	90	9	7	20	13	4	31	17	2	22
16	20	59	55	-18.6	-0.9	5.8	82	9	2	0	13	16	37	17	32	1
21	21	27	43	-15.8	-0.8	6.4	68	8	50	43	13	23	50	17	57	40
26	21	47	1	-12.9	-0.3	7.4	47	8	32	20	13	21	53	18	11	45
31	21	52	22	-11.0	+0.8	8.6	23	8	5	36	13	5	20	18	4	34

VENUS

Day	R.A.			Dec.	Mag.	Diam.	Phase	Rise			Transit			Set		
	h	m	s	°		"	%	h	m	s	h	m	s	h	m	s
1	17	18	31	-22.4	-3.9	11.5	94	6	47	51	10	34	32	14	21	2
6	17	45	36	-23.2	-3.9	11.4	95	6	59	2	10	41	55	14	24	41
11	18	12	50	-23.2	-3.9	11.3	95	7	8	12	10	49	27	14	30	41
16	18	40	7	-23.1	-3.9	11.1	96	7	15	8	10	57	1	14	38	57
21	19	7	19	-22.7	-3.9	11.0	97	7	19	44	11	4	29	14	49	22
26	19	34	17	-22.1	-3.9	11.0	97	7	22	0	11	11	44	15	1	42
31	20	0	57	-21.1	-3.9	10.9	98	7	22	1	11	18	40	15	15	37

MARS

Day	R.A.			Dec.	Mag.	Diam.	Rise			Transit			Set		
	h	m	s	°		"	h	m	s	h	m	s	h	m	s
1	1	40	19	+11.3	-0.2	10.4	11	47	9	18	55	57	2	5	7
6	1	48	38	+12.2	-0.1	9.9	11	30	29	18	44	27	1	59	0
11	1	57	26	+13.1	0.0	9.5	11	14	8	18	33	27	1	53	31
16	2	6	40	+14.0	+0.1	9.0	10	58	7	18	22	54	1	48	36
21	2	16	19	+14.9	+0.2	8.6	10	42	25	18	12	46	1	44	11
26	2	26	20	+15.8	+0.3	8.3	10	27	2	18	3	0	1	40	11
31	2	36	41	+16.7	+0.4	7.9	10	11	59	17	53	36	1	36	32

JUPITER

Day	R.A.			Dec.	Mag.	Diam.	Rise			Transit			Set		
	h	m	s	°		"	h	m	s	h	m	s	h	m	s
1	20	20	47	-20.0	-2.0	32.9	9	31	17	13	35	15	17	39	22
6	20	25	32	-19.7	-1.9	32.7	9	14	32	13	20	19	17	26	16
11	20	30	20	-19.5	-1.9	32.6	8	57	46	13	5	27	17	13	16
16	20	35	10	-19.2	-1.9	32.6	8	40	58	12	50	36	17	0	22
21	20	40	0	-18.9	-1.9	32.5	8	24	8	12	35	46	16	47	31
26	20	44	51	-18.6	-1.9	32.5	8	7	16	12	20	56	16	34	43
31	20	49	41	-18.3	-2.0	32.5	7	50	21	12	6	6	16	21	57

Diam. = Equatorial. Polar Diam. is 94% of Equatorial Diam.

SATURN

Day	R.A.			Dec.	Mag.	Diam.	Rise			Transit			Set		
	h	m	s	°		"	h	m	s	h	m	s	h	m	s
1	20	15	53	-20.2	+0.6	15.2	9	27	29	13	30	15	17	33	9
6	20	18	16	-20.0	+0.6	15.2	9	9	21	13	12	58	17	16	44
11	20	20	42	-19.9	+0.6	15.2	8	51	12	12	55	44	17	0	23
16	20	23	9	-19.8	+0.6	15.2	8	33	4	12	38	31	16	44	4
21	20	25	36	-19.7	+0.6	15.2	8	14	56	12	21	18	16	27	47
26	20	28	4	-19.5	+0.6	15.2	7	56	47	12	4	6	16	11	31
31	20	30	31	-19.4	+0.6	15.2	7	38	37	11	46	53	15	55	15

Diam. = Equatorial. Polar Diam. is 90% of Equatorial Diam.
Rings – major axis 34", minor axis 12", Tilt 20°

URANUS

Day	R.A.			Dec.	Mag.	Diam.	Rise			Transit			Set		
	h	m	s	°		"	h	m	s	h	m	s	h	m	s
1	2	18	28	+13.4	+5.7	3.6	12	12	30	19	31	49	2	55	2
6	2	18	17	+13.3	+5.7	3.6	11	52	44	19	11	58	2	35	7
11	2	18	11	+13.3	+5.7	3.6	11	33	1	18	52	13	2	15	19
16	2	18	10	+13.3	+5.7	3.6	11	13	20	18	32	32	1	55	39
21	2	18	14	+13.3	+5.8	3.6	10	53	41	18	12	57	1	36	6
26	2	18	23	+13.4	+5.8	3.6	10	34	5	17	53	26	1	16	42
31	2	18	38	+13.4	+5.8	3.6	10	14	31	17	34	1	0	57	25

NEPTUNE

Day	R.A.			Dec.	Mag.	Diam.	Rise			Transit			Set		
	h	m	s	°		"	h	m	s	h	m	s	h	m	s
1	23	19	20	-5.6	+7.9	2.3	11	0	53	16	33	9	22	5	25
6	23	19	42	-5.5	+7.9	2.2	10	41	22	16	13	51	21	46	21
11	23	20	6	-5.5	+7.9	2.2	10	21	52	15	54	36	21	27	21
16	23	20	34	-5.4	+7.9	2.2	10	2	23	15	35	23	21	8	25
21	23	21	3	-5.4	+7.9	2.2	9	42	54	15	16	13	20	49	33
26	23	21	35	-5.3	+7.9	2.2	9	23	27	14	57	6	20	30	44
31	23	22	9	-5.2	+7.9	2.2	9	4	1	14	38	0	20	11	59

THE NIGHT SKY

Mercury moves into the evening sky following its superior conjunction last December but is not favourably placed for viewing until towards the end of the second week of January.

By the time it becomes visible, the innermost planet fits within a 5° circle with Jupiter and Saturn on the evening of the 9th. All are low in the southwest though, so find an unobstructed horizon in that direction.

Mercury closes to within 1½° of Saturn on the 10th and is the same distance from brighter Jupiter the next evening. The one-day old moon lies near the trio on the 14th and binoculars will help you follow the drama in the dusk.

Mercury's altitude then improves so that it does not set until nearly 1½ hours after the Sun mid-month. It reaches greatest elongation east on the 24th when Mercury climbs to almost 8° above the local horizon towards the end of civil twilight. Thereafter, it slides a little lower each evening, but remains reasonably easy pick out as a magnitude -0.7 spark.

Venus rises 1½ hours before the Sun at the beginning of January, but that interval rapidly diminishes, and we lose sight of the planet soon after the 21st as it is overwhelmed by the morning glow. We then do not see Venus again until April. The Moon is only two days before new when it is near the brilliant morning star on the 11th.

Mars continues to recede from Earth and dims from magnitude -0.2 to 0.4. The planet remains visible until the early hours though and does not set until the early hours all month. Mars crosses into Aries from Pisces on the 5th.

The Red Planet lies in the same binocular field as pea green *Uranus* (magnitude 5.7) during the second half of January, offering an ideal opportunity to spy the distant ice giant. The two are closest on the 20th when they are 1½° apart. The just past first quarter moon is in the area on the next night.

Jupiter (magnitude -1.9) is a bright evening object in Capricornus and can be found low in the southwest, setting about 100 minutes after the Sun at the beginning of the year.

Jupiter and Saturn are separated by 1° on January 1st following their recent Great Conjunction, but that gap widens daily due to Jupiter's more rapid motion on the celestial sphere. Both soon disappear into the Sun's glare, with Jupiter lost to view near the end of January as it reaches solar conjunction on the 29th.

Saturn (magnitude 0.6) can also be found in Capricornus but slips into the solar glare around mid-month and is at solar conjunction on the 24th.

The first of the major annual meteor showers are the Quadrantids that peak during the early hours of January 3rd. The light of the waning gibbous moon interferes somewhat this year.

February 2021

SECOND MONTH, 28 or 29 DAYS. *Februa*, Roman festival of Purification

1	*Monday*	The space shuttle *Columbia* breaks up as it re-enters the Earth's atmosphere 2003	week 5 day 32
2	*Tuesday*	The US supreme court convened for the first time 1790	33
3	*Wednesday*	Johannes Gutenberg, German publisher who invented movable type printing *d.* 1468	34
4	*Thursday*	Slavery was banned in the French Republic 1794	35
5	*Friday*	Sweet rationing ended in Great Britain 1953	36
6	*Saturday*	Alan Shepard became the first man to hit a golf ball on the Moon 1971	37
7	*Sunday*	The EU became official with the signing of the Maastricht Treaty 1991	38
8	*Monday*	The astronaut crew of the final Skylab mission returned to Earth 1974	week 6 day 39
9	*Tuesday*	Actor Joanne Woodward received the first star on the Hollywood Walk of Fame 1960	40
10	*Wednesday*	Wedding of Queen Victoria and Prince Albert at St James's Palace 1840	41
11	*Thursday*	Voltaire received 300 visitors in Paris the day after returning from 28 years in exile 1778	42
12	*Friday*	Lady Jane Grey was beheaded 1554	43
13	*Saturday*	The last 'Peanuts' comic strip appeared in newspapers, the day after Charles M. Schulz died 2000	44
14	*Sunday*	New York hosted the 'Boz' Ball, a lavish party in honour of Charles Dickens 1842	45
15	*Monday*	Galileo Galilei, mathematician and astronomer, the first man to use a telescope to study the skies *b.* 1564	week 7 day 46
16	*Tueday*	Fidel Castro became prime minister of Cuba 1959	47
17	*Wednesday*	The Blaine Act ends 13 years of prohibition in the USA 1933	48
18	*Thursday*	Mark Twain's *The Adventures of Huckleberry Finn* was first published 1885	49
19	*Friday*	The phonograph was patented by Thomas Edison 1878	50
20	*Saturday*	The New York Metropolitan Museum of Art opened 1872	51
21	*Sunday*	The Battle of Verdun, the longest battle of the First World War, began 1916	52
22	*Monday*	The American short story writer Raymond Chandler's *Will You Please Be Quiet, Please?* is published 1976	week 8 day 53
23	*Tuesday*	Passenger railway service linking Perth with Sydney (3,961km) opened 1970	54
24	*Wednesday*	Vladimir Putin dismissed the entire Russian government 2004	55
25	*Thursday*	Sylvia Plath and Ted Hughes first met at a party in Cambridge 1956	56
26	*Friday*	First factory for production of Volkswagen *Beetle*, the 'people's car', is opened by Adolf Hitler 1936	57
27	*Saturday*	Nigeria elected a civilian president, ending 15 years of military rule 1999	58
28	*Sunday*	James Watson and Francis Crick announced their discovery of the structure of DNA 1953	59

ASTRONOMICAL PHENOMENA

d	h	
1	-	Mars eastern quadrature
4	17	Last Quarter Moon
6	5	Venus 0.4°S of Saturn
8	-	Mercury inferior conjunction
10	21	Jupiter 3.7°N of the Moon
10	11	Saturn 3.5°N of the Moon
10	20	Venus 3.2°N of the Moon
11	12	Jupiter 0.4°N of Venus
11	19	New Moon
12	17	Mercury 4.8°N of Venus
13	19	Mercury 4.2°N of Jupiter
17	-	Sun crosses into Aquarius
18	23	Mars 3.7°N of the Moon
19	19	First Quarter Moon
20	-	Venus at aphelion
23	08	Mercury 4.0°N of Saturn
26	14	Regulus 4.6°S of the Moon
27	08	Full Moon
28	-	Mars 3°S of the Pleiades

CONSTELLATIONS

The following constellations are visible at midnight throughout the month:
Draco (below the Pole), Camelopardalis, Auriga, Taurus, Gemini, Orion, Canis Minor, Monoceros, Lepus, Canis Major and Puppis

PHASES OF THE MOON

Phase, Apsides and Node	d	h	m
◐ Last Quarter	4	17	37
● New Moon	11	19	6
◑ First Quarter	19	18	47
○ Full Moon	27	8	17
Perigee (370,116 km)	3	19	3
Apogee (404,467 km)	18	10	22

SUNRISE AND SUNSET

	London		Bristol		Birmingham		Manchester		Newcastle		Glasgow		Belfast	
	0° 05'	51° 30'	2° 35'	51° 28'	1° 55'	52° 28'	2° 15'	53° 28'	1° 37'	54° 59'	4° 14'	55° 52'	5° 56'	54° 35'
d	h m	h m	h m	h m	h m	h m	h m	h m	h m	h m	h m	h m	h m	h m
1	7 38	16 50	7 48	17 00	7 49	16 54	7 54	16 52	7 57	16 44	8 11	16 51	8 13	17 03
2	7 37	16 52	7 47	17 02	7 47	16 56	7 52	16 54	7 55	16 46	8 09	16 53	8 11	17 05
3	7 35	16 54	7 45	17 04	7 46	16 58	7 50	16 56	7 53	16 48	8 07	16 55	8 09	17 07
4	7 34	16 56	7 43	17 06	7 44	17 00	7 49	16 58	7 51	16 50	8 05	16 57	8 07	17 09
5	7 32	16 57	7 42	17 08	7 42	17 02	7 47	17 00	7 49	16 52	8 03	17 00	8 05	17 11
6	7 30	16 59	7 40	17 09	7 40	17 04	7 45	17 02	7 47	16 54	8 01	17 02	8 03	17 13
7	7 29	17 01	7 38	17 11	7 39	17 06	7 43	17 04	7 45	16 57	7 59	17 04	8 01	17 15
8	7 27	17 03	7 37	17 13	7 37	17 08	7 41	17 06	7 43	16 59	7 57	17 06	7 59	17 17
9	7 25	17 05	7 35	17 15	7 35	17 09	7 39	17 08	7 41	17 01	7 55	17 08	7 57	17 19
10	7 23	17 07	7 33	17 17	7 33	17 11	7 37	17 10	7 39	17 03	7 53	17 11	7 55	17 21
11	7 21	17 08	7 31	17 19	7 31	17 13	7 35	17 12	7 37	17 05	7 50	17 13	7 53	17 23
12	7 20	17 10	7 29	17 20	7 29	17 15	7 33	17 14	7 35	17 07	7 48	17 15	7 51	17 26
13	7 18	17 12	7 28	17 22	7 27	17 17	7 31	17 16	7 33	17 09	7 46	17 17	7 49	17 28
14	7 16	17 14	7 26	17 24	7 25	17 19	7 29	17 18	7 31	17 11	7 44	17 19	7 47	17 30
15	7 14	17 16	7 24	17 26	7 23	17 21	7 27	17 20	7 29	17 13	7 41	17 21	7 45	17 32
16	7 12	17 18	7 22	17 28	7 21	17 23	7 25	17 22	7 26	17 15	7 39	17 24	7 43	17 34
17	7 10	17 19	7 20	17 29	7 19	17 25	7 23	17 24	7 24	17 18	7 37	17 26	7 40	17 36
18	7 08	17 21	7 18	17 31	7 17	17 27	7 21	17 26	7 22	17 20	7 35	17 28	7 38	17 38
19	7 06	17 23	7 16	17 33	7 15	17 28	7 19	17 28	7 20	17 22	7 32	17 30	7 36	17 40
20	7 04	17 25	7 14	17 35	7 13	17 30	7 17	17 30	7 17	17 24	7 30	17 32	7 34	17 42
21	7 02	17 27	7 12	17 37	7 11	17 32	7 14	17 32	7 15	17 26	7 27	17 35	7 31	17 44
22	7 00	17 28	7 10	17 38	7 09	17 34	7 12	17 34	7 13	17 28	7 25	17 37	7 29	17 46
23	6 58	17 30	7 08	17 40	7 07	17 36	7 10	17 35	7 10	17 30	7 23	17 39	7 27	17 48
24	6 56	17 32	7 06	17 42	7 05	17 38	7 08	17 37	7 08	17 32	7 20	17 41	7 25	17 50
25	6 54	17 34	7 04	17 44	7 03	17 40	7 06	17 39	7 06	17 34	7 18	17 43	7 22	17 52
26	6 52	17 36	7 02	17 46	7 00	17 42	7 03	17 41	7 03	17 36	7 15	17 45	7 20	17 54
27	6 50	17 37	6 59	17 47	6 58	17 43	7 01	17 43	7 01	17 38	7 13	17 47	7 17	17 56
28	6 47	17 39	6 57	17 49	6 56	17 45	6 59	17 45	6 59	17 40	7 10	17 50	7 15	17 58

THE MOON

Day	Diam '	Phase %	Age d	Rise 52° h	Rise 52° m	Rise 56° h	Rise 56° m	Transit h	Transit m	Set 52° h	Set 52° m	Set 56° h	Set 56° m
1	32.0	88	18.3	21	29	21	28	3	4	9	43	9	47
2	32.2	80	19.3	22	52	22	55	3	53	10	0	9	59
3	32.2	70	20.3	-	-	-	-	4	42	10	17	10	11
4	32.2	59	21.3	0	15	0	25	5	32	10	36	10	25
5	32.2	47	22.3	1	39	1	54	6	25	11	0	10	42
6	32.2	36	23.3	3	2	3	25	7	20	11	28	11	7
7	32.0	25	24.3	4	23	4	49	8	18	12	7	11	40
8	32.0	16	25.3	5	34	6	3	9	17	12	59	12	28
9	31.8	9	26.3	6	32	6	59	10	16	14	3	13	34
10	31.6	4	27.3	7	16	7	41	11	13	15	16	14	52
11	31.2	1	28.3	7	48	8	7	12	6	16	33	16	15
12	31.0	0	29.3	8	12	8	27	12	56	17	50	17	37
13	30.6	2	0.7	8	31	8	41	13	42	19	5	18	57
14	30.4	5	1.7	8	47	8	52	14	26	20	17	20	14
15	30.0	10	2.7	9	2	9	2	15	8	21	28	21	29
16	29.8	17	3.7	9	15	9	12	15	48	22	37	22	43
17	29.6	25	4.7	9	30	9	22	16	30	23	46	23	56
18	29.6	34	5.7	9	46	9	33	17	12	-	-	-	-
19	29.6	43	6.7	10	5	9	48	17	57	0	55	1	11
20	29.6	52	7.7	10	28	10	7	18	43	2	4	2	25
21	29.8	62	8.7	11	0	10	33	19	33	3	12	3	38
22	30.2	71	9.7	11	40	11	12	20	26	4	16	4	45
23	30.4	79	10.7	12	34	12	6	21	21	5	13	5	43
24	31.0	87	11.7	13	41	13	14	22	16	5	59	6	27
25	31.4	93	12.7	14	58	14	35	23	10	6	36	6	58
26	31.8	98	13.7	16	19	16	4	-	-	7	4	7	22
27	32.2	100	14.7	17	44	17	34	0	3	7	28	7	39
28	32.4	99	15.7	19	9	19	5	0	55	7	47	7	53

THE PLANETS

MERCURY

Day	R.A. h	R.A. m	R.A. s	Dec. °	Mag.	Diam. "	Phase %	Rise h	Rise m	Rise s	Transit h	Transit m	Transit s	Set h	Set m	Set s
1	21	51	22	-10.8	+1.1	8.9	18	7	59	16	12	59	57	17	59	55
6	21	36	44	-10.7	+3.6	10.0	3	7	24	41	12	24	1	17	21	46
11	21	13	53	-12.2	+3.8	10.4	3	6	51	4	11	41	45	16	30	33
16	20	56	32	-14.0	+1.8	10.0	14	6	25	42	11	6	14	15	45	9
21	20	51	28	-15.3	+0.9	9.1	28	6	10	6	10	43	3	15	14	50
26	20	57	47	-16.0	+0.4	8.3	40	6	1	25	10	30	51	14	59	29

VENUS

Day	R.A. h	R.A. m	R.A. s	Dec. °	Mag.	Diam. "	Phase %	Rise h	Rise m	Rise s	Transit h	Transit m	Transit s	Set h	Set m	Set s
1	20	6	15	-20.9	-3.9	10.9	98	7	21	46	11	20	1	15	18	33
6	20	32	26	-19.7	-3.9	10.8	98	7	19	21	11	26	28	15	33	57
11	20	58	10	-18.2	-3.9	10.7	98	7	15	8	11	32	27	15	50	11
16	21	23	25	-16.5	-3.9	10.6	99	7	9	24	11	37	58	16	6	59
21	21	48	9	-14.6	-3.9	10.6	99	7	2	22	11	42	58	16	24	5
26	22	12	26	-12.5	-3.9	10.5	99	6	54	17	11	47	30	16	41	17

MARS

Day	R.A. h	R.A. m	R.A. s	Dec. °	Mag.	Diam. "	Rise h	Rise m	Rise s	Transit h	Transit m	Transit s	Set h	Set m	Set s
1	2	38	48	+16.8	+0.4	7.9	10	9	1	17	51	45	1	35	50
6	2	49	31	+17.7	+0.5	7.5	9	54	22	17	42	43	1	32	32
11	3	0	32	+18.5	+0.6	7.3	9	40	5	17	34	0	1	29	28
16	3	11	50	+19.3	+0.7	7.0	9	26	11	17	25	33	1	26	34
21	3	23	23	+20.0	+0.8	6.7	9	12	41	17	17	22	1	23	48
26	3	35	11	+20.8	+0.9	6.5	8	59	36	17	9	26	1	21	5

JUPITER

Day	R.A. h	R.A. m	R.A. s	Dec. °	Mag.	Diam. "	Rise h	Rise m	Rise s	Transit h	Transit m	Transit s	Set h	Set m	Set s
1	20	50	39	-18.2	-2.0	32.5	7	46	58	12	3	7	16	19	24
6	20	55	28	-17.9	-2.0	32.5	7	30	0	11	48	16	16	6	38
11	21	0	15	-17.6	-2.0	32.6	7	12	58	11	33	22	15	53	52
16	21	4	59	-17.3	-2.0	32.7	6	55	53	11	18	26	15	41	5
21	21	9	40	-16.9	-2.0	32.8	6	38	44	11	3	26	15	28	14
26	21	14	17	-16.6	-2.0	32.9	6	21	32	10	48	23	15	15	19

Diam. = Equatorial. Polar Diam. is 94% of Equatorial Diam.

SATURN

Day	R.A. h	R.A. m	R.A. s	Dec. °	Mag.	Diam. "	Rise h	Rise m	Rise s	Transit h	Transit m	Transit s	Set h	Set m	Set s
1	20	31	0	-19.4	+0.6	15.2	7	34	59	11	43	26	15	52	0
6	20	33	26	-19.2	+0.6	15.2	7	16	48	11	26	12	15	35	43
11	20	35	51	-19.1	+0.7	15.2	6	58	35	11	8	56	15	19	24
16	20	38	13	-18.9	+0.7	15.2	6	40	20	10	51	38	15	3	2
21	20	40	32	-18.8	+0.7	15.3	6	22	4	10	34	17	14	46	37
26	20	42	47	-18.7	+0.7	15.3	6	3	44	10	16	53	14	30	7

Diam. = Equatorial. Polar Diam. is 90% of Equatorial Diam.
Rings – major axis 34", minor axis 11", Tilt 19°

URANUS

Day	R.A. h	R.A. m	R.A. s	Dec. °	Mag.	Diam. "	Rise h	Rise m	Rise s	Transit h	Transit m	Transit s	Set h	Set m	Set s
1	2	18	41	+13.4	+5.8	3.6	10	10	37	17	30	8	0	53	34
6	2	19	1	+13.4	+5.8	3.5	9	51	6	17	10	49	0	34	26
11	2	19	26	+13.5	+5.8	3.5	9	31	37	16	51	34	0	15	26
16	2	19	56	+13.5	+5.8	3.5	9	12	11	16	32	24	23	52	41
21	2	20	30	+13.6	+5.8	3.5	8	52	47	16	13	19	23	33	54
26	2	21	9	+13.6	+5.8	3.5	8	33	25	15	54	18	23	15	14

NEPTUNE

Day	R.A. h	R.A. m	R.A. s	Dec. °	Mag.	Diam. "	Rise h	Rise m	Rise s	Transit h	Transit m	Transit s	Set h	Set m	Set s
1	23	22	16	-5.2	+7.9	2.2	9	0	8	14	34	11	20	8	14
6	23	22	52	-5.2	+8.0	2.2	8	40	43	14	15	7	19	49	32
11	23	23	29	-5.1	+8.0	2.2	8	21	18	13	56	5	19	30	53
16	23	24	8	-5.0	+8.0	2.2	8	1	54	13	37	4	19	12	15
21	23	24	48	-5.0	+8.0	2.2	7	42	31	13	18	5	18	53	39
26	23	25	29	-4.9	+8.0	2.2	7	23	8	12	59	6	18	35	5

THE NIGHT SKY

Mercury might be noticed very low in the south-western evening sky the first few days of the month but is getting a little fainter each day, which makes it more difficult to pick out of the twilight.

Mercury then switches to the morning sky for the second half of February following inferior conjunction on the 8th but struggles to only just 3° above the south-eastern horizon at the beginning of civil twilight on the 28th. The magnitude 0.5 planet is 4° from Saturn on the morning of the 23rd but they will be a challenge in a brightening sky.

Venus is too close to the Sun to be seen this month, but at more southerly latitudes it may be possible to glimpse it just 0.4° from Jupiter on the morning of February 11th. The pair only rise 20 minutes before the Sun from the UK that day, so any chance sighting is unlikely.

Mars continues its slow fade from magnitude 0.4 to 0.9 but is still not setting until just before 2am. The planet is at eastern quadrature on the 1st when the phase looks gibbous in a telescope. The Moon is then nearby on the evening of the 18th.

Mars moves into Taurus from Aries on the 24th and ends February close to the Pleiades star cluster. French astronomer Charles Messier (1730-1817) submitted the first draft of his famed catalogue of nebulous deep-sky objects 250 years ago this month, and the Pleiades were the last entry on that initial list, as number 45.

Missions from the United Arab Emirates, NASA, and the Chinese Space Agency all reach Mars this month. China's Tianwen-1 enters orbit on February 11th, from where it will study the Martian atmosphere and produce global maps. An onboard rover will land on the planet's surface two months later.

The UAE's Al-Amal ('Hope') arrives on the 15th, with the goal of investigating the Martian climate and atmosphere over a period of two years.

The last to make orbit is the US Mars 2020 from where it will release the Perseverance rover to land on February 18th in the 49 km diameter Jezero crater. The vehicle is designed for astro-biological and geological studies of the area and will cache material for a future Mars sample-return mission. Perseverance will also deploy the Ingenuity helicopter drone.

Jupiter (magnitude -2.0) emerges into the morning sky after conjunction with the Sun but is still a tough catch as it is only 1° up at the beginning of civil twilight at the end of the month.

Saturn (magnitude 0.7) also moves into the morning sky this month. It can be picked up low in the southeast during the last week of February when it rises an hour or so before the Sun. The northern aspect of its magnificent ring system is currently tilted a little more than 19° towards us.

March 2021

THIRD MONTH, 31 DAYS. *Mars,* Roman god of battle

1	*Monday*	The first recorded performance of Shakespeare's *Romeo and Juliet* occured at Lincoln's Inn Fields 1662	week 9 day 60
2	*Tuesday*	NASA launched *Pioneer 10,* which became the first space probe to exit the solar system 1972	61
3	*Wednesday*	The first edition of *Time* magazine was published, with Joseph G. Cannon on its cover 1923	62
4	*Thursday*	The Royal National Lifeboat Institution was founded 1824	63
5	*Friday*	Churchill claimed an 'iron curtain has descended across the continent' of Europe 1946	64
6	*Saturday*	German pharmaceutical company Friedrich Bayer & Co patented aspirin 1899	65
7	*Sunday*	Napoleon Bonaparte led France to victory against Prussian and Russian forces at Craonne 1814	66
8	*Monday*	BBC Radio 4 first broadcasts Douglas Adams' comic series *The Hitchhiker's Guide to the Galaxy* 1978	week 10 day 67
9	*Tuesday*	Northern Ireland votes to remain part of the UK in the sovereignty referendum 1973	68
10	*Wednesday*	The French Foreign Legion was established 1831	69
11	*Thursday*	Cai Lun, a Chinese eunuch, revolutionised papermaking, allowing it to be mass produced AD 105	70
12	*Friday*	Germany annexed Austria in the *Anshluss* 1938	71
13	*Saturday*	The German astronomer William Herschel discovers the planet Uranus 1781	72
14	*Sunday*	The first patient was successfully treated with penicillin 1942	73
15	*Monday*	Jesse Reno, an engineer, received a patent for the first escalator – the Reno Inclined Elevator 1892	week 11 day 74
16	*Tuesday*	The Lyttelton Theatre in London officially opened with Albert Finney as Hamlet 1976	75
17	*Wednesday*	A Van Gogh exhibition in Paris caused a sensation, 11 years after the artist's death 1901	76
18	*Thursday*	Cosmonaut Aleksey Leonov becomes the first person to walk in space 1965	77
19	*Friday*	Argentines hoisted a flag on South Georgia Island precipitating the Falklands War 1982	78
20	*Saturday*	Harriet Beecher Stowe's anti-slavery novel *Uncle Tom's Cabin* was published 1852	79
21	*Sunday*	The first driverless trains on the London Underground were demonstrated to the public 1963	80
22	*Monday*	The Football League was formed 1888	week 12 day 81
23	*Tuesday*	US President Ronald Reagan announced plans for a space-based defence system 1983	82
24	*Wednesday*	Union of English and Scottish crowns after Queen Elizabeth I's death 1603	83
25	*Thursday*	Christiaan Huygens discovered Saturn's largest moon, which was named Titan, 1655	84
26	*Friday*	Women were admitted to the London Stock Exchange 1973	85
27	*Saturday*	The European fighter jet made its maiden flight 1994	86
28	*Sunday*	Virginia Woolf commits suicide by filling her pockets with stones and walking into the River Ouse 1941	87
29	*Monday*	Queen Victoria opened the Royal Albert Hall 1871	week 13 day 88
30	*Tuesday*	Anaesthesia was used for the first time during an operation, in Georgia, USA 1842	89
31	*Wednesday*	The Greater London Council was abolished 1986	90

ASTRONOMICAL PHENOMENA

d	h	
4	-	Mars 2.6°S of Pleiades
5	07	Mercury 0.3°N of Jupiter
6	-	Mercury at greatest elongation (27° 16' W)
6	01	Last Quarter Moon
8	-	(4) Vesta at opposition
9	23	Saturn 3.7°N of the Moon
10	15	Jupiter 4.0°N of the Moon
11	01	Mercury 3.7°N of the Moon
11	-	Neptune solar conjunction
13	10	New Moon
13	-	Sun crosses into Pisces
13	00	Venus 3.9°N of the Moon
14	01	Venus 0.4°S of Neptune
19	18	Mars 1.9°N of the Moon
20	10	Vernal (Spring) equinox
21	15	First Quarter Moon
26	01	Regulus 4.7°S of the Moon
26	-	Venus at superior conjunction
28	19	Full Moon
30	19	Mercury 1.4°S of Neptune

CONSTELLATIONS

The following constellations are visible at midnight throughout the month:

Cepheus (below the Pole), Camelopardalis, Lynx, Gemini, Cancer, Leo, Canis Minor, Hydra, Monoceros, Canis Major and Puppis

PHASES OF THE MOON

Phase, Apsides and Node	d	h	m
◑ Last Quarter	6	1	30
● New Moon	13	10	21
◐ First Quarter	21	14	40
○ Full Moon	28	18	48
Perigee (365,423 km)	2	5	18
Apogee (405,253 km)	18	5	3
Perigee (360,309 km)	30	6	16

SUNRISE AND SUNSET

d	London 0° 05' rise h m	London 51° 30' set h m	Bristol 2° 35' rise h m	Bristol 51° 28' set h m	Birmingham 1° 55' rise h m	Birmingham 52° 28' set h m	Manchester 2° 15' rise h m	Manchester 53° 28' set h m	Newcastle 1° 37' rise h m	Newcastle 54° 59' set h m	Glasgow 4° 14' rise h m	Glasgow 55° 52' set h m	Belfast 5° 56' rise h m	Belfast 54° 35' set h m
1	6 45	17 41	6 55	17 51	6 54	17 47	6 56	17 47	6 56	17 42	7 08	17 52	7 13	18 00
2	6 43	17 43	6 53	17 53	6 52	17 49	6 54	17 49	6 54	17 44	7 05	17 54	7 10	18 02
3	6 41	17 44	6 51	17 54	6 49	17 51	6 52	17 51	6 51	17 47	7 03	17 56	7 08	18 04
4	6 39	17 46	6 49	17 56	6 47	17 53	6 50	17 53	6 49	17 49	7 00	17 58	7 06	18 06
5	6 37	17 48	6 47	17 58	6 45	17 54	6 47	17 55	6 46	17 51	6 58	18 00	7 03	18 08
6	6 34	17 50	6 44	18 00	6 43	17 56	6 45	17 57	6 44	17 53	6 55	18 02	7 01	18 10
7	6 32	17 51	6 42	18 01	6 40	17 58	6 42	17 58	6 41	17 55	6 53	18 04	6 58	18 12
8	6 30	17 53	6 40	18 03	6 38	18 00	6 40	18 00	6 39	17 57	6 50	18 06	6 56	18 14
9	6 28	17 55	6 38	18 05	6 36	18 02	6 38	18 02	6 36	17 59	6 48	18 08	6 53	18 16
10	6 25	17 57	6 35	18 07	6 33	18 03	6 35	18 04	6 34	18 01	6 45	18 10	6 51	18 18
11	6 23	17 58	6 33	18 08	6 31	18 05	6 33	18 06	6 31	18 03	6 42	18 12	6 48	18 20
12	6 21	18 00	6 31	18 10	6 29	18 07	6 31	18 08	6 29	18 05	6 40	18 15	6 46	18 22
13	6 19	18 02	6 29	18 12	6 26	18 09	6 28	18 10	6 26	18 07	6 37	18 17	6 43	18 24
14	6 16	18 03	6 26	18 13	6 24	18 10	6 26	18 12	6 24	18 08	6 35	18 19	6 41	18 26
15	6 14	18 05	6 24	18 15	6 22	18 12	6 23	18 13	6 21	18 10	6 32	18 21	6 38	18 28
16	6 12	18 07	6 22	18 17	6 19	18 14	6 21	18 15	6 19	18 12	6 29	18 23	6 36	18 30
17	6 10	18 09	6 20	18 19	6 17	18 16	6 19	18 17	6 16	18 14	6 27	18 25	6 33	18 32
18	6 07	18 10	6 17	18 20	6 15	18 18	6 16	18 19	6 14	18 16	6 24	18 27	6 31	18 34
19	6 05	18 12	6 15	18 22	6 12	18 19	6 14	18 21	6 11	18 18	6 21	18 29	6 28	18 36
20	6 03	18 14	6 13	18 24	6 10	18 21	6 11	18 23	6 09	18 20	6 19	18 31	6 26	18 38
21	6 01	18 15	6 11	18 25	6 08	18 23	6 09	18 24	6 06	18 22	6 16	18 33	6 23	18 39
22	5 58	18 17	6 08	18 27	6 05	18 25	6 06	18 26	6 03	18 24	6 14	18 35	6 21	18 41
23	5 56	18 19	6 06	18 29	6 03	18 26	6 04	18 28	6 01	18 26	6 11	18 37	6 18	18 43
24	5 54	18 20	6 04	18 30	6 01	18 28	6 02	18 30	5 58	18 28	6 08	18 39	6 16	18 45
25	5 51	18 22	6 01	18 32	5 58	18 30	5 59	18 32	5 56	18 30	6 06	18 41	6 13	18 47
26	5 49	18 24	5 59	18 34	5 56	18 32	5 57	18 34	5 53	18 32	6 03	18 43	6 11	18 49
27	5 47	18 25	5 57	18 35	5 54	18 33	5 54	18 35	5 51	18 34	6 01	18 45	6 08	18 51
28	5 45	18 27	5 55	18 37	5 51	18 35	5 52	18 37	5 48	18 36	5 58	18 47	6 06	18 53
29	5 42	18 29	5 52	18 39	5 49	18 37	5 49	18 39	5 46	18 38	5 55	18 49	6 03	18 55
30	5 40	18 30	5 50	18 40	5 47	18 39	5 47	18 41	5 43	18 40	5 53	18 51	6 01	18 57
31	5 38	18 32	5 48	18 42	5 44	18 40	5 45	18 43	5 41	18 42	5 50	18 53	5 58	18 59

THE MOON

Day	Diam '	Phase %	Age d	Rise 52° h	Rise 52° m	Rise 56° h	Rise 56° m	Transit h	Transit m	Set 52° h	Set 52° m	Set 56° h	Set 56° m
1	32.6	96	16.7	20	34	20	36	1	46	8	5	8	6
2	32.6	91	17.7	22	0	22	8	2	36	8	22	8	18
3	32.6	83	18.7	23	27	23	40	3	28	8	40	8	31
4	32.6	73	19.7	-	-	-	-	4	20	9	3	8	47
5	32.4	62	20.7	0	52	1	12	5	16	9	29	9	9
6	32.2	51	21.7	2	14	2	40	6	13	10	6	9	38
7	31.8	40	22.7	3	29	3	57	7	11	10	52	10	22
8	31.6	29	23.7	4	30	4	58	8	10	11	52	11	22
9	31.4	20	24.7	5	16	5	43	9	6	13	2	12	35
10	31.0	12	25.7	5	51	6	13	10	0	14	17	13	57
11	30.8	6	26.7	6	17	6	33	10	50	15	33	15	18
12	30.6	2	27.7	6	37	6	48	11	37	16	48	16	38
13	30.2	0	28.7	6	53	7	0	12	21	18	1	17	56
14	30.0	0	0.2	7	7	7	10	13	3	19	12	19	12
15	29.8	2	1.2	7	21	7	19	13	44	20	22	20	27
16	29.6	6	2.2	7	35	7	28	14	25	21	32	21	41
17	29.6	12	3.2	7	50	7	39	15	7	22	41	22	55
18	29.4	18	4.2	8	7	7	52	15	51	23	50	-	-
19	29.6	26	5.2	8	28	8	8	16	36	-	-	0	10
20	29.6	35	6.2	8	56	8	30	17	25	0	58	1	24
21	29.8	44	7.2	9	31	9	4	18	16	2	4	2	33
22	30.2	54	8.2	10	19	9	49	19	8	3	3	3	34
23	30.4	64	9.2	11	19	10	50	20	2	3	53	4	23
24	31.0	73	10.2	12	30	12	6	20	55	4	34	4	58
25	31.4	82	11.2	13	49	13	30	21	48	5	4	5	25
26	32.0	90	12.2	15	12	15	0	22	41	5	29	5	44
27	32.4	96	13.2	16	38	16	31	23	32	5	50	5	58
28	32.8	99	14.2	18	5	18	4	-	-	6	8	6	11
29	33.0	100	15.2	19	33	19	38	0	24	6	25	6	23
30	33.2	98	16.2	21	2	21	14	1	16	6	43	6	36
31	33.2	93	17.2	22	33	22	50	2	10	7	4	6	51

THE PLANETS

MERCURY

Day	R.A.			Dec.	Mag.	Diam.	Phase	Rise			Transit			Set		
	h	m	s	°		"	%	h	m	s	h	m	s	h	m	s
1	21	5	42	-16.1	+0.3	7.8	47	5	58	7	10	27	27	14	56	12
6	21	23	46	-15.7	+0.2	7.2	56	5	53	58	10	26	25	14	58	36
11	21	46	4	-14.7	+0.1	6.7	63	5	50	4	10	29	25	15	8	46
16	22	11	11	-13.0	0.0	6.2	69	5	45	33	10	35	8	15	24	59
21	22	38	20	-10.9	-0.1	5.9	75	5	40	2	10	42	47	15	46	3
26	23	7	4	-8.2	-0.2	5.6	80	5	33	31	10	52	0	16	11	15
31	23	37	16	-5.0	-0.4	5.4	85	5	26	8	11	2	40	16	40	14

VENUS

Day	R.A.			Dec.	Mag.	Diam.	Phase	Rise			Transit			Set		
	h	m	s	°		"	%	h	m	s	h	m	s	h	m	s
1	22	26	47	-11.2	-3.9	10.5	99	6	49	0	11	50	1	16	51	36
6	22	50	24	-8.9	-3.9	10.5	100	6	39	39	11	53	54	17	8	46
11	23	13	41	-6.5	-3.9	10.5	100	6	29	43	11	57	27	17	25	51
16	23	36	43	-4.1	-3.9	10.4	100	6	19	21	12	0	45	17	42	50
21	23	59	34	-1.6	-3.9	10.4	100	6	8	42	12	3	52	17	59	46
26	0	22	18	0.0	-3.9	10.4	100	5	57	53	12	6	54	18	16	41
31	0	45	3	+3.4	-3.9	10.4	100	5	47	2	12	9	55	18	33	38

MARS

Day	R.A.			Dec.	Mag.	Diam.	Rise			Transit			Set		
	h	m	s	°		"	h	m	s	h	m	s	h	m	s
1	3	42	22	+21.2	+0.9	6.4	8	51	58	17	4	46	1	19	27
6	3	54	30	+21.8	+1.0	6.2	8	39	37	16	57	10	1	16	40
11	4	6	50	+22.4	+1.0	6.0	8	27	47	16	49	47	1	13	48
16	4	19	22	+22.9	+1.1	5.8	8	16	28	16	42	35	1	10	46
21	4	32	3	+23.4	+1.2	5.6	8	5	44	16	35	33	1	7	31
26	4	44	54	+23.8	+1.2	5.5	7	55	34	16	28	40	1	3	58
31	4	57	52	+24.2	+1.3	5.3	7	46	0	16	21	55	1	0	5

JUPITER

Day	R.A.			Dec.	Mag.	Diam.	Rise			Transit			Set		
	h	m	s	°		"	h	m	s	h	m	s	h	m	s
1	21	17	1	-16.4	-2.0	33.0	6	11	10	10	39	18	15	7	32
6	21	21	31	-16.1	-2.0	33.2	5	53	51	10	24	8	14	54	29
11	21	25	55	-15.7	-2.0	33.5	5	36	28	10	8	51	14	41	20
16	21	30	13	-15.4	-2.0	33.7	5	19	0	9	53	29	14	28	3
21	21	34	24	-15.1	-2.0	34.0	5	1	28	9	38	0	14	14	36
26	21	38	28	-14.8	-2.0	34.3	4	43	52	9	22	23	14	1	0
31	21	42	24	-14.4	-2.1	34.7	4	26	10	9	6	39	13	47	12

Diam. = Equatorial. Polar Diam. is 94% of Equatorial Diam.

SATURN

Day	R.A.			Dec.	Mag.	Diam.	Rise			Transit			Set		
	h	m	s	°		"	h	m	s	h	m	s	h	m	s
1	20	44	7	-18.6	+0.7	15.4	5	52	43	10	6	24	14	20	11
6	20	46	16	-18.5	+0.7	15.5	5	34	20	9	48	53	14	3	32
11	20	48	20	-18.3	+0.7	15.5	5	15	53	9	31	18	13	46	47
16	20	50	19	-18.2	+0.7	15.6	4	57	23	9	13	36	13	29	55
21	20	52	12	-18.1	+0.7	15.7	4	38	49	8	55	50	13	12	54
26	20	53	58	-18.0	+0.8	15.8	4	20	12	8	37	56	12	55	45
31	20	55	38	-17.9	+0.8	15.9	4	1	30	8	19	56	12	38	26

Diam. = Equatorial. Polar Diam. is 90% of Equatorial Diam.
Rings – major axis 35", minor axis 11", Tilt 18°

URANUS

Day	R.A.			Dec.	Mag.	Diam.	Rise			Transit			Set		
	h	m	s	°		"	h	m	s	h	m	s	h	m	s
1	2	21	34	+13.6	+5.8	3.5	8	21	48	15	42	55	23	4	4
6	2	22	19	+13.7	+5.8	3.5	8	2	29	15	24	0	22	45	34
11	2	23	7	+13.8	+5.8	3.5	7	43	12	15	5	9	22	27	8
16	2	23	59	+13.9	+5.8	3.4	7	23	57	14	46	21	22	8	48
21	2	24	54	+13.9	+5.9	3.4	7	4	43	14	27	36	21	50	32
26	2	25	52	+14.0	+5.9	3.4	6	45	31	14	8	54	21	32	20
31	2	26	52	+14.1	+5.9	3.4	6	26	20	13	50	15	21	14	12

NEPTUNE

Day	R.A.			Dec.	Mag.	Diam.	Rise			Transit			Set		
	h	m	s	°		"	h	m	s	h	m	s	h	m	s
1	23	25	54	-4.8	+8.0	2.2	7	11	30	12	47	43	18	23	56
6	23	26	36	-4.8	+8.0	2.2	6	52	7	12	28	45	18	5	23
11	23	27	18	-4.7	+8.0	2.2	6	32	45	12	9	48	17	46	50
16	23	27	60	-4.6	+8.0	2.2	6	13	23	11	50	50	17	28	17
21	23	28	42	-4.5	+8.0	2.2	5	54	1	11	31	52	17	9	44
26	23	29	23	-4.5	+8.0	2.2	5	34	38	11	12	54	16	51	10
31	23	30	4	-4.4	+8.0	2.2	5	15	16	10	53	55	16	32	34

THE NIGHT SKY

Mercury can be seen low in the southeast prior to sunrise up to the end of the first week of March, with the magnitude 0.2 sun-baked world rising 45 minutes before the Sun on the 1st. It reaches greatest western elongation on the 6th but morning apparitions at more northerly latitudes in the springtime are generally poor. Mercury quickly slips back into the solar glare soon after elongation and is lost to view for the rest of the month.

Venus is not visible during February as it will be on the far side of the Sun when it passes through superior conjunction on the 26th.

Mars makes its way across Taurus this month and remains on view until well after local midnight. The planet's disk continues to dwindle in size for telescope users though, and at 5½ arc-seconds across, it is now only half as wide as it was at the start of the year.

Mars (magnitude 0.9) is closest to the Pleiades star cluster on the 4th when it is 2½° from the group's centre. They are one of the loveliest sights in the sky for binocular users, and any instrument reveals dozens of jewels scattered across the field. The cluster is roughly 115 million years old and lies about 445 light years away.

The Moon then passes by Mars on the 19th when they are less than 3° apart, while two days later, there is a chance contrast the tints of magnitude 1.2 Mars and the magnitude 0.8 orange-hued giant Aldebaran when the two are separated by 7°. As the month ends, Mars is in the same binocular field as the cluster NGC 1746.

Jupiter (magnitude -2.0) rises 45 minutes before the Sun at the beginning of March and heaves itself over the south-eastern skyline an hour beforehand by the 31st. Try to catch it close to magnitude 0.1 Mercury on the morning of the 5th when they are less than a half degree apart. The two are barely up at the start of civil twilight though for observers in the UK.

Saturn (magnitude 0.7) rises an hour before the Sun on March 1st but tacks an extra half hour onto that time by the end of the month.

For a few days either side of the new moon you can see the rest of the lunar disk faintly lit and nestling in the bright crescent. The phenomenon is known as earthshine and is due to sunlight bouncing off the day side of Earth on to the night side of the Moon, then back to the observer.

Leonardo da Vinci first correctly explained its cause, and spring evenings are a good opportunity to notice the glow. Look for an effect that is often called 'The Old Moon in the New Moon's arms' when the slender 32.5-hour old crescent lies in the western evening sky on the 14th.

April 2021

FOURTH MONTH, 30 DAYS. *Aperire*, to open; Earth opens to receive seed.

1	*Thursday*	VAT was introduced in the UK 1973	day 91
2	*Friday*	Charlie Chaplin returned to the USA for the first time in 20 years to collect an Oscar 1972	92
3	*Saturday*	The world's first mobile telephone call was placed in New York 1973	93
4	*Sunday*	NATO was established by 12 countries 1949	94

5	*Monday*	Julie Andrews won Best Actress at the Oscars for her role in *Mary Poppins* 1965	week 14 day 95
6	*Tuesday*	The modern Olympic Games were revived at Athens 1896	96
7	*Wednesday*	The unmanned *Mars Odyssey* spacecraft was launched from Cape Canaveral, Florida 1942	97
8	*Thursday*	The Venus de Milo was discovered on the Aegean island of Melos 1820	98
9	*Friday*	Captain Cook landed in Australia 1770	99
10	*Saturday*	The Titanic embarked on her maiden voyage 1912	100
11	*Sunday*	The *Ryan X-13 Vertijet*, the first jet to take off and land vertically, completed a full flight 1957	101

12	*Monday*	Yuri Gagarin became the first man to travel in space; the Soviet Union declared the space race won 1961	week 15 day 102
13	*Tuesday*	Ian Fleming's first James Bond novel, *Casino Royale*, adapted for cinema in 2006, was published 1953	103
14	*Wednesday*	The House of Lancaster won the Battle of Barnet in the War of the Roses 1471	104
15	*Thursday*	J. M. Barrie presents the copyright of his Peter Pan works to Great Ormond Street Hospital 1929	105
16	*Friday*	The Rolling Stones released their eponymous debut album 1964	106
17	*Saturday*	Geoffrey Chaucer first recited his Canterbury Tales 1397	107
18	*Sunday*	Over 60,000 people demonstrated against the hydrogen bomb in Trafalgar Square 1960	108

19	*Monday*	The American War of Independence began in Lexington, Mass. 1775	week 16 day 109
20	*Tuesday*	Edgar Allan Poe's 'The Murders in the Rue Morgue' was published 1841	110
21	*Wednesday*	Women in France received the right to vote 1944	111
22	*Thursday*	Germany first used poison gas against British troops 1915	112
23	*Friday*	The first decimal coins, 5p and 10p pieces, were issued 1968	113
24	*Saturday*	The Hubble space telescope was launched by the space shuttle Discovery 1990	114
25	*Sunday*	Scientists announced the discovery of the structure of DNA 1953	115

26	*Monday*	William Shakespeare was baptised at Holy Trinity Church, Stratford 1564	week 17 day 116
27	*Tuesday*	Betty Boothroyd became the first female Speaker of the House of Commons 1992	117
28	*Wendesday*	The League of Nations was founded 1919	118
29	*Thursday*	Women were admitted to Oxford University examinations 1885	119
30	*Friday*	New York opened its first World's Fair, attracting 44 million people over two seasons 1939	120

ASTRONOMICAL PHENOMENA

d	h	
4	10	Last Quarter Moon
6	08	Saturn 4.0°N of the Moon
7	07	Jupiter 4.4°N of the Moon
11	06	Mercury 3.0°N of the Moon
12	03	New Moon
12	10	Venus 2.9°N of the Moon
17	12	Mars 0.1°N of the Moon: Occultation
19	-	Sun crosses into Aries
20	07	First Quarter Moon
22	12	Lyrid meteor shower
22	10	Regulus 4.9°S of the Moon
22	23	Venus 0.25°S of Uranus
24	10	Mercury 0.8°N of Uranus
26	09	Mercury 1.3°N of Venus
26	PM	Mars very near M35
27	04	Full Moon
30	PM	Mercury 5° from the Pleiades

CONSTELLATIONS

The following constellations are visible at midnight throughout the month:
Cepheus (below the Pole), Cassiopeia (below the Pole), Ursa Major, Leo Minor, Leo., Sextans, Hydra and Crater

PHASES OF THE MOON

Phase, Apsides and Node	d	h	m
◐ Last Quarter	4	10	2
● New Moon	12	2	31
◑ First Quarter	20	6	59
○ Full Moon	27	3	32
Apogee (406,119 km)	14	17	46
Perigee (357,378 km)	27	15	22

SUNRISE AND SUNSET

	London		Bristol		Birmingham		Manchester		Newcastle		Glasgow		Belfast	
	0°	05' 51° 30'	2°	35' 51° 28'	1°	55' 52° 28'	2°	15' 53° 28'	1°	37' 54° 59'	4°	14' 55° 52'	5°	56' 54° 35'
d	h m	h m	h m	h m	h m	h m	h m	h m	h m	h m	h m	h m	h m	h m
1	5 36	18 34	5 46	18 44	5 42	18 42	5 42	18 45	5 38	18 44	5 47	18 55	5 56	19 01
2	5 33	18 36	5 43	18 46	5 40	18 44	5 40	18 46	5 35	18 46	5 45	18 57	5 53	19 02
3	5 31	18 37	5 41	18 47	5 37	18 46	5 37	18 48	5 33	18 48	5 42	18 59	5 51	19 04
4	5 29	18 39	5 39	18 49	5 35	18 47	5 35	18 50	5 30	18 50	5 40	19 01	5 48	19 06
5	5 26	18 41	5 37	18 51	5 33	18 49	5 33	18 52	5 28	18 52	5 37	19 03	5 46	19 08
6	5 24	18 42	5 34	18 52	5 30	18 51	5 30	18 54	5 25	18 54	5 34	19 05	5 43	19 10
7	5 22	18 44	5 32	18 54	5 28	18 53	5 28	18 56	5 23	18 55	5 32	19 07	5 41	19 12
8	5 20	18 46	5 30	18 56	5 26	18 54	5 25	18 57	5 20	18 57	5 29	19 09	5 38	19 14
9	5 18	18 47	5 28	18 57	5 23	18 56	5 23	18 59	5 18	18 59	5 27	19 11	5 36	19 16
10	5 15	18 49	5 25	18 59	5 21	18 58	5 21	19 01	5 15	19 01	5 24	19 14	5 33	19 18
11	5 13	18 51	5 23	19 01	5 19	19 00	5 18	19 03	5 13	19 03	5 22	19 16	5 31	19 20
12	5 11	18 52	5 21	19 02	5 17	19 01	5 16	19 05	5 10	19 05	5 19	19 18	5 29	19 22
13	5 09	18 54	5 19	19 04	5 14	19 03	5 14	19 06	5 08	19 07	5 17	19 20	5 26	19 24
14	5 07	18 56	5 17	19 06	5 12	19 05	5 11	19 08	5 06	19 09	5 14	19 22	5 24	19 25
15	5 04	18 57	5 15	19 07	5 10	19 07	5 09	19 10	5 03	19 11	5 11	19 24	5 21	19 27
16	5 02	18 59	5 12	19 09	5 08	19 08	5 07	19 12	5 01	19 13	5 09	19 26	5 19	19 29
17	5 00	19 01	5 10	19 10	5 05	19 10	5 05	19 14	4 58	19 15	5 06	19 28	5 17	19 31
18	4 58	19 02	5 08	19 12	5 03	19 12	5 02	19 16	4 56	19 17	5 04	19 30	5 14	19 33
19	4 56	19 04	5 06	19 14	5 01	19 14	5 00	19 17	4 54	19 19	5 02	19 32	5 12	19 35
20	4 54	19 06	5 04	19 15	4 59	19 15	4 58	19 19	4 51	19 21	4 59	19 34	5 10	19 37
21	4 52	19 07	5 02	19 17	4 57	19 17	4 56	19 21	4 49	19 23	4 57	19 36	5 07	19 39
22	4 50	19 09	5 00	19 19	4 55	19 19	4 53	19 23	4 47	19 25	4 54	19 38	5 05	19 41
23	4 48	19 11	4 58	19 20	4 53	19 20	4 51	19 25	4 44	19 27	4 52	19 40	5 03	19 43
24	4 46	19 12	4 56	19 22	4 50	19 22	4 49	19 26	4 42	19 29	4 50	19 42	5 00	19 45
25	4 44	19 14	4 54	19 24	4 48	19 24	4 47	19 28	4 40	19 30	4 47	19 44	4 58	19 47
26	4 42	19 16	4 52	19 25	4 46	19 26	4 45	19 30	4 37	19 32	4 45	19 46	4 56	19 48
27	4 40	19 17	4 50	19 27	4 44	19 27	4 43	19 32	4 35	19 34	4 42	19 48	4 54	19 50
28	4 38	19 19	4 48	19 29	4 42	19 29	4 40	19 34	4 33	19 36	4 40	19 50	4 52	19 52
29	4 36	19 21	4 46	19 30	4 40	19 31	4 38	19 35	4 31	19 38	4 38	19 52	4 49	19 54
30	4 34	19 22	4 44	19 32	4 38	19 33	4 36	19 37	4 28	19 40	4 36	19 54	4 47	19 56

THE MOON

Day	Diam '	Phase %	Age d	Rise 52° h	Rise 52° m	Rise 56° h	Rise 56° m	Transit h	Transit m	Set 52° h	Set 52° m	Set 56° h	Set 56° m
1	33.0	86	18.2	23	59	-	-	3	6	7	29	7	10
2	32.6	76	19.2	-	-	0	25	4	5	8	3	7	37
3	32.2	66	20.2	1	20	1	49	5	5	8	46	8	17
4	31.8	55	21.2	2	27	2	57	6	5	9	43	9	13
5	31.6	44	22.2	3	18	3	47	7	2	10	51	10	23
6	31.2	33	23.2	3	55	4	20	7	57	12	6	11	42
7	30.8	24	24.2	4	24	4	42	8	48	13	21	13	5
8	30.4	16	25.2	4	44	4	57	9	35	14	36	14	25
9	30.2	9	26.2	5	1	5	9	10	19	15	49	15	43
10	30.0	4	27.2	5	15	5	19	11	1	17	0	16	58
11	29.8	1	28.2	5	29	5	28	11	42	18	10	18	13
12	29.6	0	29.2	5	42	5	37	12	23	19	20	19	27
13	29.6	1	0.7	5	56	5	47	13	5	20	29	20	42
14	29.4	3	1.7	6	12	5	59	13	47	21	39	21	56
15	29.4	7	2.7	6	31	6	13	14	32	22	48	23	11
16	29.4	13	3.7	6	56	6	32	15	20	23	55	-	-
17	29.6	20	4.7	7	28	7	1	16	9	-	-	0	23
18	29.8	28	5.7	8	11	7	39	17	0	0	56	1	28
19	30.0	37	6.7	9	5	8	33	17	52	1	49	2	20
20	30.4	47	7.7	10	10	9	42	18	44	2	32	2	59
21	30.8	57	8.7	11	23	11	3	19	36	3	5	3	29
22	31.4	68	9.7	12	43	12	27	20	28	3	32	3	49
23	31.8	77	10.7	14	6	13	56	21	18	3	53	4	4
24	32.4	86	11.7	15	31	15	27	22	9	4	11	4	18
25	32.8	93	12.7	16	58	17	0	23	0	4	28	4	29
26	33.2	98	13.7	18	28	18	36	23	53	4	45	4	41
27	33.4	100	14.7	19	59	20	14	-	-	5	4	4	54
28	33.4	99	15.7	21	32	21	53	0	50	5	27	5	11
29	33.2	95	16.7	22	59	23	28	1	49	5	57	5	34
30	33.0	88	17.7	-	-	-	-	2	51	6	37	6	9

THE PLANETS

MERCURY

Day	R.A. h	m	s	Dec. °	Mag.	Diam. "	Phase %	Rise h	m	s	Transit h	m	s	Set h	m	s
1	23	43	30	-4.3	-0.5	5.3	86	5	24	34	11	4	59	16	46	29
6	0	15	38	0.0	-0.8	5.2	91	5	24	29	11	17	35	17	20	6
11	0	49	42	+3.5	-1.2	5.1	96	5	8	9	11	32	9	17	57	52
16	1	26	2	+7.9	-1.8	5.0	99	4	59	59	11	49	0	18	40	4
21	2	4	45	+12.4	-2.0	5.1	100	4	52	29	12	8	10	19	26	10
26	2	45	10	+16.6	-1.6	5.3	95	4	46	14	12	28	54	20	13	51

VENUS

Day	R.A. h	m	s	Dec. °	Mag.	Diam. "	Phase %	Rise h	m	s	Transit h	m	s	Set h	m	s
1	0	49	36	+3.9	-3.9	10.4	100	5	44	52	12	10	32	18	37	2
6	1	12	27	+6.4	-3.9	10.4	100	5	34	7	12	13	40	18	54	6
11	1	35	29	+8.8	-3.9	10.4	100	5	23	35	12	17	0	19	11	18
16	1	58	47	+11.2	-3.9	10.4	100	5	12	26	12	20	36	19	28	40
21	2	22	24	+13.4	-3.9	10.5	99	5	3	49	12	24	31	19	46	9
26	2	46	24	+15.5	-3.9	10.5	99	4	54	55	12	28	50	20	3	41

MARS

Day	R.A. h	m	s	Dec. °	Mag.	Diam. "	Rise h	m	s	Transit h	m	s	Set h	m	s
1	5	0	28	+24.2	+1.3	5.3	7	44	10	16	20	34	0	59	15
6	5	13	34	+24.5	+1.3	5.2	7	35	21	16	13	57	0	54	53
11	5	26	46	+24.7	+1.4	5.1	7	27	11	16	7	26	0	50	3
16	5	40	3	+24.8	+1.4	4.9	7	19	39	16	0	59	0	44	44
21	5	53	22	+24.9	+1.5	4.8	7	12	46	15	54	35	0	38	53
26	6	6	44	+24.9	+1.5	4.7	7	6	31	15	48	14	0	32	29

JUPITER

Day	R.A. h	m	s	Dec. °	Mag.	Diam. "	Rise h	m	s	Transit h	m	s	Set h	m	s
1	21	43	10	-14.4	-2.1	34.7	4	22	37	9	3	29	13	44	26
6	21	46	56	-14.1	-2.1	35.1	4	4	50	8	47	34	13	30	23
11	21	50	32	-13.8	-2.1	35.5	3	46	58	8	31	30	13	16	8
16	21	53	58	-13.5	-2.1	35.9	3	29	0	8	15	16	13	1	37
21	21	57	13	-13.2	-2.2	36.4	3	10	57	7	58	51	12	46	50
26	22	0	17	-13.0	-2.2	36.9	2	52	48	7	42	14	12	31	46

Diam. = Equatorial. Polar Diam. is 94% of Equatorial Diam.

SATURN

Day	R.A. h	m	s	Dec. °	Mag.	Diam. "	Rise h	m	s	Transit h	m	s	Set h	m	s
1	20	55	57	-17.9	+0.8	15.9	3	57	46	8	16	19	12	34	57
6	20	57	28	-17.8	+0.7	16.0	3	38	59	7	58	11	12	17	26
11	20	58	52	-17.7	+0.7	16.1	3	20	9	7	39	54	11	59	43
16	21	0	7	-17.6	+0.7	16.3	3	1	14	7	21	30	11	41	49
21	21	1	14	-17.5	+0.7	16.4	2	42	15	7	2	57	11	23	42
26	21	2	12	-17.5	+0.7	16.6	2	23	10	6	44	15	11	5	23

Diam. = Equatorial. Polar Diam. is 90% of Equatorial Diam.
Rings – major axis 37", minor axis 11", Tilt 17°

URANUS

Day	R.A. h	m	s	Dec. °	Mag.	Diam. "	Rise h	m	s	Transit h	m	s	Set h	m	s
1	2	27	4	+14.1	+5.9	3.4	6	22	30	13	46	31	21	10	34
6	2	28	7	+14.2	+5.9	3.4	6	3	20	13	27	54	20	52	30
11	2	29	11	+14.3	+5.9	3.4	5	44	12	13	9	17	20	34	28
16	2	30	17	+14.4	+5.9	3.4	5	25	4	12	50	44	20	16	27
21	2	31	23	+14.5	+5.9	3.4	5	5	56	12	32	11	19	58	29
26	2	32	31	+14.6	+5.9	3.4	4	46	50	12	13	39	19	40	31

NEPTUNE

Day	R.A. h	m	s	Dec. °	Mag.	Diam. "	Rise h	m	s	Transit h	m	s	Set h	m	s
1	23	30	12	-4.4	+8.0	2.2	5	11	23	10	50	7	16	28	51
6	23	30	52	-4.3	+8.0	2.2	4	52	0	10	31	7	16	10	14
11	23	31	30	-4.3	+8.0	2.2	4	32	37	10	12	6	15	51	35
16	23	32	7	-4.2	+7.9	2.2	4	13	13	9	53	3	15	32	53
21	23	32	42	-4.1	+7.9	2.2	3	53	49	9	33	59	15	14	9
26	23	33	15	-4.1	+7.9	2.2	3	34	24	9	14	53	14	55	22

THE NIGHT SKY

Mercury emerges into the evening sky after superior conjunction on the 19th and may be seen hugging the west-northwest horizon during the last week or so of April. The planet's altitude improves daily though up to the end of the month when it is nearly 5° high at the end of civil twilight and setting more than an hour after the Sun. Look for Mercury's magnitude -1.1 glint about 5° below the Pleiades on the evening of the 30th.

Venus (magnitude -3.9) reappears this month and can be found low in the west-northwest from the second half of April. Venus and Mercury (magnitude -1.6) are less than one degree apart on the evening of the 25th but are sinking fast in the twilight. Once you find Venus, use binoculars to glimpse fainter Mercury nearby.

Mars hangs around until the early hours – especially with summertime now in effect. It has now faded a little more to magnitude 1.7 but is still a reasonably bright object as it charges through Taurus, before crossing into Gemini on the 25th.

A line drawn between Zeta and Beta Tauri, marking the horns of the celestial bull, is bisected by Mars on the night of the 13th. The Moon is then near the planet on the 17th, and Mars can be found very close to the open cluster M35 in the feet of Gemini on the 26th.

Jupiter (magnitude -2.1) rises just over an hour before the Sun at the beginning of April but appears nearly two hours beforehand by the end of the month. It can be found in the east-southeast at this time amongst the dim stars of Capricornus. The shallow angle the ecliptic makes with the morning horizon from northern temperate latitudes at this time of year means the planet will appear low, despite its early appearance.

Jupiter is extremely close to 44 Capricorni (magnitude 5.9) on the 2nd, when the star looks like an extra Jovian moon but is slightly outside their orbital plane. It will appear nearer to the planet's disk than some of the Galilean satellites that morning, but a predicted occultation of the star by Jupiter is after sunrise from the UK.

The waning Moon is close to Jupiter on the morning of April 7th and later in the month, on the 26th, the planet crosses into Aquarius. Beforehand though, on the 16th, Mu Capricorni (magnitude 5.0) also masquerades as an attendant of the gas giant as Jupiter drags his entourage of 79 moons across the sky.

Saturn (magnitude 0.7), in Capricornus, rises 1½ hours before the Sun on the 1st with that interval almost doubling by the end of April. Like Jupiter, it too remains rather poorly placed in the morning sky from the UK. The moon is a couple of days after last quarter when it is near Saturn on the 6th.

May 2021   ♊

FIFTH MONTH, 31 DAYS. *Maia*, goddess of growth and increase

1	*Saturday*	Queen Victoria opened the Great Exhibition at Hyde Park, celebrating the Industrial Revolution 1851	day 121
2	*Sunday*	The King James version of the Bible was published 1611	122

3	*Monday*	Lord Byron swam from Europe to Asia across the Hellespont Strait 1810	week 18 day 123
4	*Tuesday*	Margaret Thatcher became UK's first woman prime minister 1979	124
5	*Wendesday*	*The Examiner* published the Romantic poet John Keats' sonnet 'O Solitude' 1816	125
6	*Thursday*	Postage stamps were introduced 1840	126
7	*Friday*	Native Americans rebelled against British forces at Fort Detroit during Pontiac's War 1763	127
8	*Saturday*	The Irish Literary Theatre opened with a performance of Yeats' play *The Countess Cathleen* 1899	128
9	*Sunday*	*Sam and Friends*, Jim Henson's first puppet TV show, aired in Washington DC 1955	129

10	*Monday*	Nelson Mandela became South Africa's first black president 1994	week 19 day 130
11	*Tuesday*	The Academy of Motion Picture Arts and Sciences held its inaugural banquet 1927	131
12	*Wednesday*	The USSR lifted its blockade on Berlin 1949	132
13	*Thursday*	Marie Curie, Nobel prize winning physicist, became the first female professor at the Sorbonne 1906	133
14	*Friday*	The USA's first space station was launched; *Skylab* spent over six years orbiting Earth 1973	134
15	*Saturday*	The Royal Opera House in Covent Garden opened 1858	135
16	*Sunday*	Mao Zedong launched the Cultural Revolution in the People's Republic of China 1966	136

17	*Monday*	Compact discs were introduced by Phillips 1978	week 20 day 137
18	*Tuesday*	Napoleon Bonaparte was proclaimed emperor of France 1804	138
19	*Wednesday*	Balamurali Ambati, aged 17 years and 294 days, graduated to become the world's youngest doctor 1995	139
20	*Thursday*	Levi Strauss and Jacob Davis received a patent to create 'waist overalls', now known as blue jeans 1873	140
21	*Friday*	Daylight saving time was first used in Britain 1916	141
22	*Saturday*	Apollo 10's lunar module flew within 14 miles of the Moon's surface in a rehearsal for Apollo 11 1969	142
23	*Sunday*	The New York Public Library was dedicated by President Howard Taft 1911	143

24	*Monday*	Samuel Morse sent the first electric telegram from Washington DC to Baltimore 1844	week 21 day 144
25	*Tuesday*	Gilbert and Sullivan's comic opera *HMS Pinafore* opened in London 1878	145
26	*Wednesday*	The last Confederate army in the American Civil War surrendered near New Orleans 1865	146
27	*Thursday*	British and French troops began to evacuate from Dunkirk in Operation Dynamo 1940	147
28	*Friday*	Two monkeys, Able and Baker, became the first living creatures to survive space flight 1959	148
29	*Saturday*	Edmund Hillary and Tenzing Norgay reached the summit of Mount Everest 1953	149
30	*Sunday*	Joan of Arc was burnt at the stake 1431	150

31	*Monday*	John Harvey Kellogg applied for a patent for 'flaked cereal', now known as Corn Flakes 1884	week 22 day 151

ASTRONOMICAL PHENOMENA

d	h	
3	20	Last Quarter Moon
3	17	Saturn 4.2°N of the Moon
4	03	Mercury 2.1°S of Pleiades
4	21	Jupiter 4.6°N of the Moon
5	01	Eta-Aquarid meteor shower
11	19	New Moon
13	18	Mercury 2.1°N of the Moon
15	05	Mars 1.5°S of the Moon
15	-	Sun crosses into Taurus
17	-	Mercury at greatest elongation (22° 01' E)
19	19	First Quarter Moon
19	18	Regulus 5.0°S of the Moon
21	-	Jupiter at western quadrature
26	11	Total Lunar Eclipse; mag=1.009
26	11	Full Moon
28	06	Mercury 0.4°S of Venus
31	01	Saturn 4.2°N of the Moon

CONSTELLATIONS

The following constellations are visible at midnight throughout the month:

Cepheus (below the Pole), Cassiopeia (below the Pole), Ursa Minor, Ursa Major, Canes Venatici, Coma Berenices, Bootes, Leo, Virgo, Crater, Corvus and Hydra

PHASES OF THE MOON

Phase, Apsides and Node	d	h	m
◑ Last Quarter	3	19	50
● New Quarter	11	19	0
◐ First Moon	19	19	13
○ Full Quarter	26	11	14
Apogee (406,512 km)	11	21	53
Perigee (357,311 km)	26	1	50

SUNRISE AND SUNSET

	London				Bristol				Birmingham				Manchester				Newcastle				Glasgow				Belfast			
	0°	05'	51°	30'	2°	35'	51°	28'	1°	55'	52°	28'	2°	15'	53°	28'	1°	37'	54°	59'	4°	14'	55°	52'	5°	56'	54°	35'
d	h	m	h	m	h	m	h	m	h	m	h	m	h	m	h	m	h	m	h	m	h	m	h	m	h	m	h	m
1	4	32	19	24	4	42	19	34	4	36	19	34	4	34	19	39	4	26	19	42	4	33	19	56	4	45	19	58
2	4	30	19	25	4	40	19	35	4	34	19	36	4	32	19	41	4	24	19	44	4	31	19	58	4	43	20	00
3	4	28	19	27	4	39	19	37	4	32	19	38	4	30	19	43	4	22	19	46	4	29	20	00	4	41	20	02
4	4	27	19	29	4	37	19	39	4	31	19	39	4	28	19	44	4	20	19	48	4	27	20	02	4	39	20	03
5	4	25	19	30	4	35	19	40	4	29	19	41	4	26	19	46	4	18	19	50	4	25	20	04	4	37	20	05
6	4	23	19	32	4	33	19	42	4	27	19	43	4	24	19	48	4	16	19	52	4	22	20	06	4	35	20	07
7	4	21	19	34	4	31	19	43	4	25	19	44	4	23	19	50	4	14	19	53	4	20	20	08	4	33	20	09
8	4	20	19	35	4	30	19	45	4	23	19	46	4	21	19	51	4	12	19	55	4	18	20	10	4	31	20	11
9	4	18	19	37	4	28	19	47	4	22	19	48	4	19	19	53	4	10	19	57	4	16	20	12	4	29	20	13
10	4	16	19	38	4	26	19	48	4	20	19	49	4	17	19	55	4	08	19	59	4	14	20	14	4	27	20	14
11	4	15	19	40	4	25	19	50	4	18	19	51	4	15	19	57	4	06	20	01	4	12	20	16	4	25	20	16
12	4	13	19	41	4	23	19	51	4	16	19	53	4	14	19	58	4	04	20	03	4	10	20	18	4	23	20	18
13	4	11	19	43	4	22	19	53	4	15	19	54	4	12	20	00	4	02	20	04	4	08	20	19	4	21	20	20
14	4	10	19	44	4	20	19	54	4	13	19	56	4	10	20	02	4	01	20	06	4	06	20	21	4	20	20	22
15	4	08	19	46	4	19	19	56	4	12	19	57	4	09	20	03	3	59	20	08	4	05	20	23	4	18	20	23
16	4	07	19	47	4	17	19	57	4	10	19	59	4	07	20	05	3	57	20	10	4	03	20	25	4	16	20	25
17	4	06	19	49	4	16	19	59	4	09	20	00	4	05	20	06	3	55	20	12	4	01	20	27	4	15	20	27
18	4	04	19	50	4	14	20	00	4	07	20	02	4	04	20	08	3	54	20	13	3	59	20	29	4	13	20	28
19	4	03	19	52	4	13	20	02	4	06	20	03	4	02	20	10	3	52	20	15	3	58	20	30	4	11	20	30
20	4	01	19	53	4	12	20	03	4	04	20	05	4	01	20	11	3	51	20	17	3	56	20	32	4	10	20	32
21	4	00	19	55	4	10	20	04	4	03	20	06	4	00	20	13	3	49	20	18	3	54	20	34	4	08	20	33
22	3	59	19	56	4	09	20	06	4	02	20	08	3	58	20	14	3	47	20	20	3	53	20	36	4	07	20	35
23	3	58	19	57	4	08	20	07	4	00	20	09	3	57	20	16	3	46	20	21	3	51	20	37	4	06	20	36
24	3	57	19	59	4	07	20	08	3	59	20	11	3	56	20	17	3	45	20	23	3	50	20	39	4	04	20	38
25	3	55	20	00	4	06	20	10	3	58	20	12	3	54	20	19	3	43	20	25	3	48	20	40	4	03	20	39
26	3	54	20	01	4	05	20	11	3	57	20	13	3	53	20	20	3	42	20	26	3	47	20	42	4	02	20	41
27	3	53	20	02	4	04	20	12	3	56	20	15	3	52	20	21	3	41	20	28	3	46	20	44	4	00	20	42
28	3	52	20	04	4	03	20	13	3	55	20	16	3	51	20	23	3	39	20	29	3	44	20	45	3	59	20	44
29	3	51	20	05	4	02	20	15	3	54	20	17	3	50	20	24	3	38	20	30	3	43	20	47	3	58	20	45
30	3	51	20	06	4	01	20	16	3	53	20	18	3	49	20	25	3	37	20	32	3	42	20	48	3	57	20	47
31	3	50	20	07	4	00	20	17	3	52	20	20	3	48	20	26	3	36	20	33	3	41	20	49	3	56	20	48

THE MOON

Day	Diam '	Phase %	Age d	Rise 52° h	Rise 52° m	Rise 56° h	Rise 56° m	Transit h	Transit m	Set 52° h	Set 52° m	Set 56° h	Set 56° m
1	32.6	80	18.7	0	16	0	47	3	54	7	30	7	0
2	32.0	70	19.7	1	15	1	45	4	55	8	37	8	8
3	31.6	59	20.7	1	58	2	25	5	52	9	52	9	26
4	31.2	48	21.7	2	30	2	49	6	45	11	10	10	50
5	30.6	38	22.7	2	52	3	7	7	33	12	25	12	12
6	30.4	28	23.7	3	10	3	20	8	18	13	39	13	31
7	30.0	20	24.7	3	25	3	30	9	1	14	50	14	47
8	29.8	13	25.7	3	38	3	39	9	42	16	0	16	1
9	29.6	7	26.7	3	50	3	47	10	22	17	9	17	15
10	29.4	3	27.7	4	4	3	56	11	3	18	19	18	30
11	29.4	1	28.7	4	19	4	7	11	45	19	29	19	45
12	29.4	0	0.1	4	37	4	20	12	30	20	39	20	59
13	29.4	1	1.1	5	0	4	37	13	16	21	47	22	13
14	29.6	4	2.1	5	28	5	3	14	5	22	50	23	21
15	29.6	9	3.1	6	7	5	36	14	55	23	46	-	-
16	29.8	15	4.1	6	57	6	25	15	47	-	-	0	18
17	30.0	23	5.1	7	58	7	28	16	39	0	32	1	0
18	30.4	32	6.1	9	8	8	43	17	30	1	8	1	33
19	30.8	42	7.1	10	23	10	6	18	20	1	36	1	55
20	31.2	52	8.1	11	42	11	30	19	9	1	57	2	12
21	31.8	63	9.1	13	4	12	57	19	57	2	16	2	25
22	32.2	73	10.1	14	27	14	26	20	46	2	33	2	36
23	32.6	83	11.1	15	53	15	58	21	37	2	49	2	47
24	33.0	91	12.1	17	23	17	34	22	31	3	6	2	59
25	33.4	97	13.1	18	54	19	13	23	29	3	26	3	13
26	33.4	100	14.1	20	27	20	51	-	-	3	52	3	32
27	33.4	100	15.1	21	51	22	22	0	30	4	26	4	1
28	33.2	96	16.1	23	1	23	34	1	34	5	14	4	43
29	32.8	91	17.1	23	54	-	-	2	38	6	16	5	45
30	32.2	83	18.1	-	-	0	23	3	40	7	31	7	4
31	31.8	74	19.1	0	31	0	53	4	37	8	51	8	29

THE PLANETS

MERCURY

Day	R.A. h m s	Dec. °	Mag.	Diam. "	Phase %	Rise h m s	Transit h m s	Set h m s
1	3 25 32	+20.2	-1.1	5.7	83	4 41 56	12 49 16	20 58 30
6	4 3 22	+22.9	-0.7	6.2	68	4 40 3	13 6 46	21 34 46
11	4 36 30	+24.5	-0.2	6.9	53	4 40 22	13 19 18	21 58 54
16	5 3 23	+25.2	+0.3	7.8	40	4 41 38	13 25 24	22 9 15
21	5 22 54	+25.1	+0.9	8.9	28	4 41 56	13 23 57	22 5 37
26	5 34 11	+24.4	+1.7	10.0	18	4 39 3	13 14 12	21 48 34
31	5 36 51	+23.2	+2.6	11.0	9	4 31 9	12 55 58	21 19 32

VENUS

Day	R.A. h m s	Dec. °	Mag.	Diam. "	Phase %	Rise h m s	Transit h m s	Set h m s
1	3 10 51	+17.4	-3.9	10.6	99	4 46 58	12 33 35	20 21 8
6	3 35 45	+19.2	-3.9	10.6	98	4 40 12	12 38 47	20 38 17
11	4 1 7	+20.7	-3.9	10.7	98	4 34 54	12 44 28	20 54 53
16	4 26 55	+22.0	-3.9	10.8	97	4 31 21	12 50 34	21 10 34
21	4 53 7	+23.0	-3.9	10.8	97	4 29 51	12 57 4	21 24 57
26	5 19 37	+23.8	-3.9	10.9	96	4 30 36	13 3 52	21 37 40
31	5 46 20	+24.3	-3.9	11.0	95	4 33 47	13 10 53	21 48 20

MARS

Day	R.A. h m s	Dec. °	Mag.	Diam. "	Rise h m s	Transit h m s	Set h m s
1	6 20 7	+24.8	+1.6	4.6	7 0 53	15 41 53	0 23 10
6	6 33 29	+24.7	+1.6	4.5	6 55 50	15 35 33	0 15 28
11	6 46 51	+24.4	+1.6	4.5	6 51 21	15 29 12	0 7 12
16	7 0 11	+24.1	+1.7	4.4	6 47 24	15 22 49	23 58 20
21	7 13 29	+23.8	+1.7	4.3	6 43 56	15 16 23	23 48 53
26	7 26 42	+23.3	+1.7	4.2	6 40 56	15 9 53	-23 38 51
31	7 39 51	+22.8	+1.7	4.2	6 38 19	15 3 20	23 28 17

JUPITER

Day	R.A. h m s	Dec. °	Mag.	Diam. "	Rise h m s	Transit h m s	Set h m s
1	22 3 8	-12.7	-2.2	37.4	2 34 33	7 25 26	12 16 24
6	22 5 47	-12.5	-2.2	38.0	2 16 12	7 8 25	12 0 42
11	22 8 13	-12.3	-2.3	38.5	1 57 45	6 51 10	11 44 39
16	22 10 23	-12.1	-2.3	39.1	1 39 12	6 33 41	11 28 14
21	22 12 19	-12.0	-2.3	39.8	1 20 32	6 15 57	11 11 26
26	22 13 60	-11.9	-2.4	40.4	1 1 45	5 57 57	10 54 14
31	22 15 24	-11.7	-2.4	41.1	0 42 51	5 39 41	10 36 36

Diam. = Equatorial. Polar Diam. is 94% of Equatorial Diam.

SATURN

Day	R.A. h m s	Dec. °	Mag.	Diam. "	Rise h m s	Transit h m s	Set h m s
1	21 3 1	-17.4	+0.7	16.7	2 4 1	6 25 24	10 46 50
6	21 3 40	-17.4	+0.7	16.8	1 44 47	6 6 24	10 28 3
11	21 4 10	-17.4	+0.7	17.0	1 25 28	5 47 14	10 9 3
16	21 4 30	-17.4	+0.6	17.1	1 6 4	5 27 55	9 49 48
21	21 4 41	-17.4	+0.6	17.3	0 46 35	5 8 25	9 30 19
26	21 4 41	-17.4	+0.6	17.4	0 27 0	4 48 46	9 10 35
31	21 4 42	-17.4	+0.6	17.5	0 3 32	4 28 57	8 50 37

Diam. = Equatorial. Polar Diam. is 90% of Equatorial Diam.
Rings – major axis 39", minor axis 11", Tilt 17°

URANUS

Day	R.A. h m s	Dec. °	Mag.	Diam. "	Rise h m s	Transit h m s	Set h m s
1	2 33 39	+14.6	+5.9	3.4	4 27 43	11 55 7	19 22 33
6	2 34 47	+14.7	+5.9	3.4	4 8 37	11 36 35	19 4 36
11	2 35 54	+14.8	+5.9	3.4	3 49 31	11 18 3	18 46 38
16	2 37 1	+14.9	+5.9	3.4	3 30 25	10 59 30	18 28 38
21	2 38 7	+15.0	+5.9	3.4	3 11 18	10 40 57	18 10 38
26	2 39 12	+15.1	+5.9	3.4	2 52 11	10 22 22	17 52 35
31	2 40 15	+15.2	+5.9	3.4	2 33 3	10 3 45	17 34 30

NEPTUNE

Day	R.A. h m s	Dec. °	Mag.	Diam. "	Rise h m s	Transit h m s	Set h m s
1	23 33 48	-4.0	+7.9	2.2	3 14 58	8 55 45	14 36 32
6	23 34 17	-4.0	+7.9	2.2	2 55 32	8 36 35	14 17 38
11	23 34 45	-3.9	+7.9	2.2	2 36 5	8 17 23	13 58 41
16	23 35 10	-3.9	+7.9	2.2	2 16 36	7 58 8	13 39 40
21	23 35 32	-3.8	+7.9	2.3	1 57 7	7 38 51	13 20 35
26	23 35 52	-3.8	+7.9	2.3	1 37 37	7 19 31	13 1 25
31	23 36 9	-3.8	+7.9	2.3	1 18 5	7 0 8	12 42 11

THE NIGHT SKY

Mercury can be seen almost to the end of May in the evening sky and soars 10° above the northwest skyline on the 12th when the magnitude -0.2 world is setting around two hours after the Sun. Greatest elongation is reached on the 17th.

Mercury passes 2° from the Pleiades star cluster on May 4th, and is less than 3° from the two-day old moon on the evening of the 13th. Watch the fleet-footed world and Venus converge towards the end of the month - the two are closest on the 28th when they are a ½° apart.

Venus (magnitude -3.9) remains quite low above the northwest horizon these evenings, but its brilliance catches the eye. It is setting 1½ hours after the Sun at the end of the month. Venus passes about 4½° from the Pleiades on the 9th but you will almost certainly need binoculars and a clear horizon to spot the cluster in the lingering twilight.

Mars (magnitude 1.6) continues to dwindle in size for telescope users and sets close to 1am summer time at the end of May. The planet dwells in the western sky presently and sits at the tip of an isosceles triangle with Castor and Pollux in Gemini on the 17th but is now dimmer than those two stars. Mars can be found to the upper left of the Moon on the evening of May 15th.

Jupiter (magnitude -2.3) rises two hours before the Sun at the beginning of May and three hours beforehand by the 31st. The Moon lies between Jupiter and Saturn on the morning of the 4th.

Saturn (magnitude 0.6) rises well before the Sun all month and telescope users can view the shadow of the planet's globe on the rings as it reaches western quadrature on the 3rd. The rings are currently tipped a little less than 17° earthward, their minimum for the year. On the morning of the 31st you will find Saturn to the upper left of the waning gibbous Moon as it rises.

Saturn is stationary on the 23rd and then begins to retrograde, travelling slowly westward across Capricornus to pass through opposition on August 2nd and then reaching its westernmost stationary point on October 11th.

A total lunar eclipse on May 26th is visible from Asia, Australia, New Zealand, Pacific countries, and the western parts of the Americas. The same night is also the biggest full moon of the year, and these are now popularly called supermoons.

May 26th's event is the shortest totality of the 21st century, as at maximum eclipse the northern limb of the Moon will touch the outer edge of Earth's umbra. The total phase will be just 14½ minutes long, and the southern part of the Moon's disk will appear deeper coloured due to it being nearer the centre of Earth's shadow cast in space.

 II June 2021

SIXTH MONTH, 30 DAYS. *Junius,* Roman *gens* (family)

1	*Tuesday*	Anne Boleyn, mother of Elizabeth I, was crowned Queen Consort of England 1533	152
2	*Wednesday*	Joan of Arc was burnt at the stake 1431	153
3	*Thursday*	The Tiananmen Square massacre took place in Peking (Beijing), China 1989	154
4	*Friday*	Allied forces completed their evacuation from Dunkirk 1940	155
5	*Saturday*	The Montgolfier Brothers demonstrated their hot air balloon in public for the first time 1783	156
6	*Sunday*	D-day: the Allied forces landed in Normandy 1944	157

7	*Monday*	Queen Elizabeth II's Silver Jubilee procession 1977	week 23 day 158
8	*Tuesday*	Margaret Bondfield became Britain's first woman cabinet minister 1929	159
9	*Wednesday*	A revamped Gatwick airport, costing £7.8m to build, was opened by Queen Elizabeth II 1958	160
10	*Thursday*	The first Oxford and Cambridge boat race took place 1829	161
11	*Friday*	The UN officially declared a famine in Sudan with over a million people facing starvation 1998	162
12	*Saturday*	Anne Frank was given a diary for her thirteenth birthday 1942	163
13	*Sunday*	The Beatles achieved their final US number one, 'The Long and Winding Road' 1970	164

14	*Monday*	English Civil War: parliamentarians defeated the royalists at the Battle of Naseby 1645	week 24 day 165
15	*Tuesday*	King John signed the Magna Carta at Runnymede in Surrey 1215	166
16	*Wednesday*	US aviation pioneer Henry Berliner conducted the first manned, controlled helicopter flight 1922	167
17	*Thursday*	The Statue of Liberty, a gift from France, arrived in New York 1885	168
18	*Friday*	The 1970 general election allowed people to vote from the age of 18 for the first time	169
19	*Saturday*	The first five-cent cinema, or 'nickelodeon', opened in Pittsburgh, USA 1905	170
20	*Sunday*	Queen Victoria became Queen of England at the age of 18 1837	171

21	*Monday*	The first stored-program computer, the Small-Scale Experimental Machine, ran its first program 1948	week 25 day 172
22	*Tuesday*	The Royal Greenwich Observatory, a centre for practical astronomy, was created by Royal Warrant 1675	173
23	*Wednesday*	Treatises attributed to John Frith were found in the belly of a cod at Cambridge market 1626	174
24	*Thursday*	Robert Bruce defeated Edward II at Bannockburn, securing Scottish independence 1314	175
25	*Friday*	Sioux Native Americans defeated General Custer and his men at the Battle of Little Bighorn 1876	176
26	*Saturday*	Representatives of 50 countries signed the United Nations Charter 1945	177
27	*Sunday*	The world's first atomic power station began producing electricity in Obninsk, Russia 1954	178

28	*Monday*	Archduke Franz Ferdinand of Austria was assassinated by Gavrilo Princip in Sarajevo 1914	week 26 day 179
29	*Tuesday*	The Globe Theatre burned down after fire broke out during a performance of Henry VIII 1613	180
30	*Wednesday*	Hitler ordered the assassination of hundreds of Nazis; now known as the Night of the Long Knives 1934	181

ASTRONOMICAL PHENOMENA

d	h	
1	09	Jupiter 4.6°N of the Moon
2	07	Last Quarter Moon
8	-	Juno at opposition
10	11	Annular solar eclipse; mag=0.943 (partial from the UK)
10	13	Mercury 4.0°S of the Moon
10	11	New Moon
11	-	Mercury at inferior conjunction
12	-	Venus at perihelion
12	07	Venus 1.5°S of the Moon
13	20	Mars 2.8°S of the Moon
15	23	Regulus 5.0°S of the Moon
18	04	First Quarter Moon
21	04	Summer solstice
21	-	Jupiter stationary, begins to retrograde
22	-	Sun crosses into Gemini
24	05	Mars 0.3°S of the Beehive star cluster in Cancer
24	19	Full Moon
26	09	Saturn 4.0°N of the Moon
28	18	Jupiter 4.5°N of the Moon

CONSTELLATIONS

The following constellations are visible at midnight throughout the month:

Cassiopeia (below the Pole), Ursa Minor, Draco, Ursa Major, Canes Venatici, Bootes, Corona, Serpens, Virgo and Libra

PHASES OF THE MOON

Phase, Apsides and Node	d	h	m
◑ Last Quarter	2	7	24
● New Moon	10	10	53
◐ First Quarter	18	3	54
○ Full Moon	24	18	40
Apogee (406,228 km)	8	2	27
Perigee (359,956 km)	23	9	55

SUNRISE AND SUNSET

	London				Bristol				Birmingham				Manchester				Newcastle				Glasgow				Belfast			
	0°	05'	51°	30'	2°	35'	51°	28'	1°	55'	52°	28'	2°	15'	53°	28'	1°	37'	54°	59'	4°	14'	55°	52'	5°	56'	54°	35'
d	h	m	h	m	h	m	h	m	h	m	h	m	h	m	h	m	h	m	h	m	h	m	h	m	h	m	h	m
1	3	49	20	08	3	59	20	18	3	51	20	21	3	47	20	28	3	35	20	34	3	40	20	51	3	55	20	49
2	3	48	20	09	3	58	20	19	3	50	20	22	3	46	20	29	3	34	20	36	3	39	20	52	3	54	20	50
3	3	47	20	10	3	58	20	20	3	50	20	23	3	45	20	30	3	33	20	37	3	38	20	53	3	53	20	51
4	3	47	20	11	3	57	20	21	3	49	20	24	3	44	20	31	3	32	20	38	3	37	20	54	3	52	20	53
5	3	46	20	12	3	56	20	22	3	48	20	25	3	44	20	32	3	32	20	39	3	36	20	56	3	52	20	54
6	3	46	20	13	3	56	20	23	3	48	20	26	3	43	20	33	3	31	20	40	3	35	20	57	3	51	20	55
7	3	45	20	14	3	55	20	24	3	47	20	27	3	42	20	34	3	30	20	41	3	35	20	58	3	50	20	56
8	3	45	20	15	3	55	20	25	3	46	20	27	3	42	20	35	3	30	20	42	3	34	20	59	3	50	20	57
9	3	44	20	16	3	54	20	25	3	46	20	28	3	41	20	36	3	29	20	43	3	33	21	00	3	49	20	57
10	3	44	20	16	3	54	20	26	3	46	20	29	3	41	20	36	3	29	20	44	3	33	21	01	3	49	20	58
11	3	43	20	17	3	54	20	27	3	45	20	30	3	41	20	37	3	28	20	45	3	32	21	01	3	48	20	59
12	3	43	20	18	3	53	20	27	3	45	20	30	3	40	20	38	3	28	20	45	3	32	21	02	3	48	21	00
13	3	43	20	18	3	53	20	28	3	45	20	31	3	40	20	38	3	27	20	46	3	32	21	03	3	48	21	01
14	3	43	20	19	3	53	20	29	3	45	20	32	3	40	20	39	3	27	20	47	3	31	21	04	3	47	21	01
15	3	43	20	19	3	53	20	29	3	44	20	32	3	40	20	40	3	27	20	47	3	31	21	04	3	47	21	02
16	3	43	20	20	3	53	20	30	3	44	20	33	3	40	20	40	3	27	20	48	3	31	21	05	3	47	21	02
17	3	43	20	20	3	53	20	30	3	44	20	33	3	40	20	41	3	27	20	48	3	31	21	05	3	47	21	03
18	3	43	20	20	3	53	20	30	3	44	20	33	3	40	20	41	3	27	20	49	3	31	21	05	3	47	21	03
19	3	43	20	21	3	53	20	31	3	45	20	34	3	40	20	41	3	27	20	49	3	31	21	06	3	47	21	03
20	3	43	20	21	3	53	20	31	3	45	20	34	3	40	20	41	3	27	20	49	3	31	21	06	3	47	21	04
21	3	43	20	21	3	53	20	31	3	45	20	34	3	40	20	42	3	27	20	49	3	31	21	06	3	47	21	04
22	3	43	20	22	3	53	20	31	3	45	20	34	3	40	20	42	3	27	20	49	3	32	21	06	3	48	21	04
23	3	44	20	22	3	54	20	31	3	45	20	34	3	41	20	42	3	28	20	50	3	32	21	07	3	48	21	04
24	3	44	20	22	3	54	20	31	3	46	20	35	3	41	20	42	3	28	20	50	3	32	21	07	3	48	21	04
25	3	44	20	22	3	54	20	31	3	46	20	34	3	41	20	42	3	29	20	50	3	33	21	06	3	49	21	04
26	3	45	20	22	3	55	20	31	3	47	20	34	3	42	20	42	3	29	20	49	3	33	21	06	3	49	21	04
27	3	45	20	21	3	55	20	31	3	47	20	34	3	42	20	42	3	30	20	49	3	34	21	06	3	50	21	04
28	3	46	20	21	3	56	20	31	3	48	20	34	3	43	20	42	3	30	20	49	3	34	21	06	3	50	21	04
29	3	46	20	21	3	57	20	31	3	48	20	34	3	43	20	41	3	31	20	49	3	35	21	06	3	51	21	03
30	3	47	20	21	3	57	20	31	3	49	20	34	3	44	20	41	3	32	20	48	3	36	21	05	3	52	21	03

THE MOON

Day	Diam '	Phase %	Age d	Rise 52° h	Rise 52° m	Rise 56° h	Rise 56° m	Transit h	Transit m	Set 52° h	Set 52° m	Set 56° h	Set 56° m
1	31.2	64	20.1	0	57	1	14	5	28	10	10	9	55
2	30.8	53	21.1	1	17	1	29	6	16	11	26	11	16
3	30.4	43	22.1	1	33	1	40	7	0	12	39	12	34
4	30.0	33	23.1	1	46	1	49	7	41	13	50	13	50
5	29.8	25	24.1	1	59	1	57	8	22	14	59	15	4
6	29.6	17	25.1	2	12	2	6	9	3	16	8	16	18
7	29.4	10	26.1	2	26	2	16	9	44	17	18	17	33
8	29.4	5	27.1	2	43	2	27	10	28	18	28	18	48
9	29.4	2	28.1	3	4	2	43	11	13	19	38	20	1
10	29.6	0	29.1	3	30	3	6	12	2	20	43	21	12
11	29.6	0	0.6	4	7	3	36	12	52	21	42	22	14
12	29.8	2	1.6	4	53	4	21	13	43	22	32	23	0
13	30.0	6	2.6	5	50	5	20	14	35	23	10	23	37
14	30.2	12	3.6	6	59	6	32	15	27	23	40	-	-
15	30.6	19	4.6	8	12	7	52	16	17	-	-	0	1
16	30.8	28	5.6	9	29	9	14	17	5	0	3	0	19
17	31.2	37	6.6	10	47	10	38	17	52	0	23	0	33
18	31.6	48	7.6	12	7	12	4	18	39	0	39	0	44
19	32.0	59	8.6	13	29	13	31	19	28	0	54	0	55
20	32.4	70	9.6	14	54	15	2	20	18	1	10	1	6
21	32.8	80	10.6	16	22	16	36	21	12	1	28	1	18
22	33.0	89	11.6	17	52	18	14	22	11	1	50	1	34
23	33.2	95	12.6	19	21	19	48	23	13	2	19	1	57
24	33.2	99	13.6	20	40	21	10	-	-	3	0	2	30
25	33.0	100	14.6	21	42	22	11	0	17	3	55	3	22
26	32.6	98	15.6	22	27	22	51	1	21	5	5	4	34
27	32.2	93	16.6	22	57	23	17	2	22	6	24	6	1
28	31.8	86	17.6	23	21	23	35	3	17	7	47	7	29
29	31.2	78	18.6	23	38	23	47	4	8	9	7	8	55
30	30.8	69	19.6	23	53	23	57	4	54	10	23	10	17

THE PLANETS

MERCURY

Day	R.A.			Dec.	Mag.	Diam.	Phase	Rise			Transit			Set		
	h	m	s	°		"	%	h	m	s	h	m	s	h	m	s
1	5	36	24	+23.0	+2.9	11.2	8	4	28	53	12	51	22	21	12	31
6	5	29	58	+21.5	+4.3	12.0	2	4	14	6	12	24	33	20	33	21
11	5	19	10	+20.0	+5.4	12.2	0	3	54	35	11	54	4	19	51	59
16	5	8	30	+18.8	+4.1	11.9	3	3	32	35	11	24	26	19	15	11
21	5	2	18	+18.3	+2.7	11.0	8	3	10	39	10	59	38	18	48	12
26	5	3	12	+18.5	+1.7	9.9	17	2	50	55	10	42	1	18	33	23

VENUS

Day	R.A.			Dec.	Mag.	Diam.	Phase	Rise			Transit			Set		
	h	m	s	°		"	%	h	m	s	h	m	s	h	m	s
1	5	51	42	+24.3	-3.9	11.1	95	4	34	44	13	12	18	21	50	12
6	6	18	32	+24.4	-3.9	11.2	95	4	40	54	13	19	24	21	58	4
11	6	45	19	+24.3	-3.9	11.3	94	4	49	30	13	26	27	22	3	25
16	7	11	55	+23.8	-3.9	11.5	93	5	0	18	13	33	19	22	6	11
21	7	38	13	+23.0	-3.9	11.6	92	5	13	1	13	39	53	22	6	25
26	8	4	8	+22.0	-3.9	11.8	91	5	27	16	13	46	2	22	4	20

MARS

Day	R.A.			Dec.	Mag.	Diam.	Rise			Transit			Set		
	h	m	s	°		"	h	m	s	h	m	s	h	m	s
1	7	42	29	+22.7	+1.7	4.2	6	37	50	15	2	0	23	26	7
6	7	55	32	+22.2	+1.8	4.1	6	35	39	14	55	21	23	13	10
11	8	8	30	+21.5	+1.8	4.0	6	33	46	14	48	36	23	3	17
16	8	21	23	+20.8	+1.8	4.0	6	32	4	14	41	45	22	51	11
21	8	34	9	+20.1	+1.8	3.9	6	30	44	14	34	49	22	38	41
26	8	46	49	+19.2	+1.8	3.9	6	29	29	14	27	46	22	25	48

JUPITER

Day	R.A.			Dec.	Mag.	Diam.	Rise			Transit			Set		
	h	m	s	°		"	h	m	s	h	m	s	h	m	s
1	22	15	38	-11.7	-2.4	41.2	0	39	3	5	36	0	10	33	1
6	22	16	42	-11.7	-2.5	41.9	0	20	0	5	17	23	10	14	52
11	22	17	28	-11.6	-2.5	42.6	23	57	3	4	58	30	9	56	15
16	22	17	56	-11.6	-2.5	43.2	23	37	44	4	39	18	9	37	10
21	22	18	6	-11.6	-2.6	43.9	23	18	18	4	19	48	9	17	37
26	22	17	57	-11.6	-2.6	44.6	22	58	43	3	59	59	8	57	35

Diam. = Equatorial. Polar Diam. is 94% of Equatorial Diam.

SATURN

Day	R.A.			Dec.	Mag.	Diam.	Rise			Transit			Set		
	h	m	s	°		"	h	m	s	h	m	s	h	m	s
1	21	4	29	-17.4	+0.6	17.6	23	59	35	4	24	59	8	46	36
6	21	4	8	-17.4	+0.5	17.7	23	39	50	4	4	58	8	26	21
11	21	3	38	-17.5	+0.5	17.8	23	19	59	3	44	49	8	5	52
16	21	2	59	-17.5	+0.5	18.0	23	0	4	3	24	30	7	45	10
21	21	2	12	-17.6	+0.4	18.1	22	40	3	3	4	3	7	24	16
26	21	1	16	-17.7	+0.4	18.2	22	19	59	2	43	28	7	3	10

Diam. = Equatorial. Polar Diam. is 90% of Equatorial Diam.
Rings – major axis 40", minor axis 12", Tilt 17°

URANUS

Day	R.A.			Dec.	Mag.	Diam.	Rise			Transit			Set		
	h	m	s	°		"	h	m	s	h	m	s	h	m	s
1	2	40	28	+15.2	+5.9	3.4	2	29	13	10	0	2	17	30	52
6	2	41	29	+15.3	+5.9	3.4	2	10	5	9	41	23	17	12	43
11	2	42	27	+15.3	+5.9	3.4	1	50	55	9	22	42	16	54	31
16	2	43	23	+15.4	+5.8	3.4	1	31	44	9	3	58	16	36	15
21	2	44	17	+15.5	+5.8	3.4	1	12	32	8	45	12	16	17	54
26	2	45	7	+15.5	+5.8	3.5	0	53	18	8	26	22	15	59	29

NEPTUNE

Day	R.A.			Dec.	Mag.	Diam.	Rise			Transit			Set		
	h	m	s	°		"	h	m	s	h	m	s	h	m	s
1	23	36	12	-3.8	+7.9	2.3	1	14	11	6	56	15	12	38	20
6	23	36	25	-3.8	+7.9	2.3	0	54	38	6	36	49	12	19	0
11	23	36	36	-3.7	+7.9	2.3	0	35	4	6	17	20	11	59	36
16	23	36	43	-3.7	+7.9	2.3	0	15	29	5	57	48	11	40	7
21	23	36	48	-3.7	+7.9	2.3	23	51	57	5	38	13	11	20	34
26	23	36	50	-3.7	+7.9	2.3	23	32	19	5	18	35	11	0	55

THE NIGHT SKY

Mercury is not visible this month as it passes between us and the Sun when at inferior conjunction on the 11th.

Venus (magnitude -3.8) continues to dominate the evening sky despite its low altitude and does not set until 1½ hours after the Sun all month. Telescope users will note the planet's phase is presently almost full.

Venus is very close to the star cluster M35 in Gemini on the 3rd, but they are low at the time. The planet is then beautifully paired with the 35-hour old lunar crescent on the evening of the 11th, after which Venus makes rapid progress across the sky to end June not far from M44 in Cancer.

Mars is quite low in the dusk, but its eastward pace keeps it out of the solar glare a little longer. The ochre-hued world has now dimmed to magnitude 1.8 and is setting roughly three hours after the Sun for most of June.

Mars is near the Moon on the evening of the 13th, and it then passes directly in front of the Beehive star cluster (M44) in Cancer on the 23rd and 24th when binoculars reveal the swarm. About 7½° separate Mars and Venus when they lie either side of the Beehive on the 30th.

Jupiter (magnitude -2.5) rises in the early hours at the beginning of June and is up just after midnight at the end of the month. It easily dominates the southern sky during the brief night this time of year. Jupiter is near the Moon both on June 1st and 28th as it makes its appearance over the horizon.

Jupiter reaches its easternmost stationary point in Aquarius on June 21st and then begins to retrograde, moving southwest towards the constellation's border with Capricornus, which it will cross back into mid-August.

Saturn (magnitude 0.5), in Capricornus, rises not long after the witching hour on June 1st but is visible just before midnight by the end of June. Saturn is to the upper left of the Moon on the night of the 26th.

An annular solar eclipse visible across Arctic regions of Canada and Russia, as well as Greenland, on June 10th is partial that morning from the UK. It will take about an hour from the time you notice the first nick out of the Sun's edge until greatest eclipse.

The maximum obscuration of the solar disk ranges from almost 32% in Glasgow to 20% from London. The websites astro.ukho.gov.uk/eclipse/0232021/ or www.timeanddate.com/eclipse will give the local circumstances.

Great care should be taken if you try observing the event. The only suitable method for the general observer is to project the Sun's image with a telescope or binocular onto a piece of white card. Eclipse glasses will let you see it safely with the unaided eye but discard them if their filter material is damaged in any way.

July 2021

SEVENTH MONTH, 31 DAYS. *Julius* Caesar, formerly *Quintilis*, fifth month of Roman pre-Julian calendar

1	*Thursday*	The Montgolfier Brothers demonstrated their hot air balloon in public for the first time 1783	day 182
2	*Friday*	Live 8 concerts were held around the globe to persuade political leaders to tackle poverty in Africa 2005	183
3	*Saturday*	After being stolen in 1296, the Stone of Scone is returned to Scotland by the British government 1996	184
4	*Sunday*	Marie Curie died, almost certainly due to her exposure to radiation 1934	185
5	*Monday*	The National Health Service Act came into effect 1948	week 27 day 186
6	*Tuesday*	Louis Pasteur began the modern era of immunisation by vaccinating a boy bitten by a rabid dog 1885	187
7	*Wednesday*	The Yardbirds broke up, leading to the creation of Led Zeppelin 1968	188
8	*Thursday*	The National Society for the Prevention of Cruelty to Children (NSPCC) was founded 1884	189
9	*Friday*	Michael Fagan breaks into Buckingham Palace and spends ten minutes talking to Queen Elizabeth II 1982	190
10	*Saturday*	*Telstar 1*, the first satellite to relay TV and telephone signals across the Atlantic, was launched 1962	191
11	*Sunday*	US space station *Skylab* re-entered Earth's atmosphere and disintegrated 1979	192
12	*Monday*	Ranjit Singh founds the Sikh Empire, based in the Punjab region 1799	week 28 day 193
13	*Tuesday*	Ruth Ellis, the last woman to be executed in Britain, was hanged 1955	194
14	*Wednesday*	*Mariner 4* takes the first up-close photos of another planet as it passes Mars 1965	195
15	*Thursday*	Emmeline Pankhurst, suffragette who helped women win the right to vote *b.* 1858	196
16	*Friday*	J. D. Salinger's seminal novel *The Catcher in the Rye* is published 1951	197
17	*Saturday*	Allied leaders held a conference in Potsdam to decide on the future of Germany 1945	198
18	*Sunday*	The Ballot Act 1872, requiring that elections are held by secret ballot, received royal assent	199
19	*Monday*	A French soldier uncovers the Rosetta Stone during Napoleon's Egyptian campaign 1799	week 29 day 200
20	*Tuesday*	US magazine *Billboard* published its first 'Music Popularity Chart' 1940	201
21	*Wednesday*	Neil Armstrong became the first man to walk on the Moon 1969	202
22	*Thursday*	The Tate Gallery opened 1897	203
23	*Friday*	Caravaggio received his first public commission, for the Contarelli Chapel in Rome 1599	204
24	*Saturday*	Amelia Earhart, who in 1932 became the first woman to fly solo over the Atlantic *b.* 1897	205
25	*Sunday*	Bob Dylan switched to an electric guitar at the Newport Folk Festival 1965	206
26	*Monday*	Apollo 15 launched, the first mission to the Moon which used the lunar rover 1971	week 30 day 207
27	*Tuesday*	Queen Elizabeth II declared the London 2012 Olympic Games open, after acting with James Bond 2012	208
28	*Wednesday*	Percy Bysshe Shelley and Mary Wollstonecraft eloped to France 1814	209
29	*Thursday*	The BBC Light Programme radio station began broadcasting 1945	210
30	*Friday*	US settlers and Shoshoni Native Americans signed the Treaty of Box Elder, Utah 1863	211
31	*Saturday*	Britain announced a total ban on the use of landmines 1998	212

ASTRONOMICAL PHENOMENA

d	h	
1	21	Last Quarter Moon
3	PM	Venus 0.1°N of Beehive
4	-	Mercury at greatest elongation (21° 33' W)
5	22	Earth is at aphelion
8	5	Moon 3°N of Mercury
10	1	New Moon
12	21	Moon 5°N of Mars and Venus
12	21	Venus 0.5°NW of Mars
13	-	Mars is at aphelion (1.66596 AU))
13	21	Venus 28' N of Mars
17	10	First Quarter Moon
17	-	Pluto at opposition (4.983 billion km distant)
21	-	Sun crosses into Cancer
21	PM	Venus 1°N of Regulus (daylight)
24	3	Full Moon
25	0	Jupiter, Saturn and Moon form a triangle
28	3	Delta-Aquarid meteor shower
29	PM	Mars 38'N of Regulus (daylight)
31	13	Last Quarter Moon

CONSTELLATIONS

The following constellations are visible at midnight throughout the month:

Ursa Minor, Draco, Corona, Hercules, Lyra, Serpens, Ophiuchus, Libra, Scorpius and Sagittarius

PHASES OF THE MOON

Phase, Apsides and Node		d	h	m
◗	Last Quarter	1	21	11
●	New Moon	10	1	17
◐	First Quarter	17	10	11
○	Full Moon	24	2	37
		31	13	16
Apogee (405,341 km)		5	14	47
Perigee (364,520 km)		21	10	24

SUNRISE AND SUNSET

	London				Bristol				Birmingham				Manchester				Newcastle				Glasgow				Belfast			
	0°	05'	51°	30'	2°	35'	51°	28'	1°	55'	52°	28'	2°	15'	53°	28'	1°	37'	54°	59'	4°	14'	55°	52'	5°	56'	54°	35'
d	h	m	h	m	h	m	h	m	h	m	h	m	h	m	h	m	h	m	h	m	h	m	h	m	h	m	h	m
1	3	48	20	21	3	58	20	30	3	49	20	33	3	45	20	41	3	32	20	48	3	37	21	05	3	52	21	03
2	3	48	20	20	3	59	20	30	3	50	20	33	3	46	20	40	3	33	20	47	3	37	21	04	3	53	21	02
3	3	49	20	20	3	59	20	30	3	51	20	32	3	46	20	40	3	34	20	47	3	38	21	04	3	54	21	02
4	3	50	20	19	4	00	20	29	3	52	20	32	3	47	20	39	3	35	20	46	3	39	21	03	3	55	21	01
5	3	51	20	19	4	01	20	29	3	53	20	31	3	48	20	39	3	36	20	46	3	40	21	02	3	56	21	00
6	3	52	20	18	4	02	20	28	3	54	20	31	3	49	20	38	3	37	20	45	3	41	21	01	3	57	21	00
7	3	52	20	18	4	03	20	27	3	55	20	30	3	50	20	37	3	38	20	44	3	42	21	01	3	58	20	59
8	3	53	20	17	4	04	20	27	3	56	20	29	3	51	20	36	3	39	20	43	3	44	21	00	3	59	20	58
9	3	54	20	16	4	05	20	26	3	57	20	29	3	52	20	36	3	40	20	42	3	45	20	59	4	00	20	57
10	3	55	20	15	4	06	20	25	3	58	20	28	3	53	20	35	3	41	20	42	3	46	20	58	4	01	20	56
11	3	56	20	15	4	07	20	24	3	59	20	27	3	54	20	34	3	43	20	41	3	47	20	57	4	03	20	55
12	3	58	20	14	4	08	20	24	4	00	20	26	3	56	20	33	3	44	20	39	3	49	20	56	4	04	20	54
13	3	59	20	13	4	09	20	23	4	01	20	25	3	57	20	32	3	45	20	38	3	50	20	54	4	05	20	53
14	4	00	20	12	4	10	20	22	4	02	20	24	3	58	20	31	3	47	20	37	3	51	20	53	4	06	20	52
15	4	01	20	11	4	11	20	21	4	03	20	23	3	59	20	30	3	48	20	36	3	53	20	52	4	08	20	51
16	4	02	20	10	4	12	20	20	4	05	20	22	4	01	20	29	3	49	20	35	3	54	20	51	4	09	20	50
17	4	03	20	09	4	14	20	19	4	06	20	21	4	02	20	27	3	51	20	33	3	56	20	49	4	11	20	48
18	4	05	20	08	4	15	20	18	4	07	20	20	4	03	20	26	3	52	20	32	3	58	20	48	4	12	20	47
19	4	06	20	07	4	16	20	16	4	09	20	19	4	05	20	25	3	54	20	31	3	59	20	46	4	13	20	46
20	4	07	20	05	4	17	20	15	4	10	20	17	4	06	20	24	3	55	20	29	4	01	20	45	4	15	20	44
21	4	09	20	04	4	19	20	14	4	11	20	16	4	08	20	22	3	57	20	28	4	02	20	43	4	17	20	43
22	4	10	20	03	4	20	20	13	4	13	20	15	4	09	20	21	3	59	20	26	4	04	20	42	4	18	20	41
23	4	11	20	02	4	21	20	11	4	14	20	13	4	11	20	19	4	00	20	25	4	06	20	40	4	20	20	40
24	4	13	20	00	4	23	20	10	4	16	20	12	4	12	20	18	4	02	20	23	4	07	20	38	4	21	20	38
25	4	14	19	59	4	24	20	09	4	17	20	10	4	14	20	16	4	04	20	21	4	09	20	37	4	23	20	37
26	4	15	19	57	4	26	20	07	4	19	20	09	4	15	20	15	4	05	20	20	4	11	20	35	4	25	20	35
27	4	17	19	56	4	27	20	06	4	20	20	07	4	17	20	13	4	07	20	18	4	13	20	33	4	26	20	33
28	4	18	19	54	4	28	20	04	4	22	20	06	4	18	20	11	4	09	20	16	4	14	20	31	4	28	20	31
29	4	20	19	53	4	30	20	03	4	23	20	04	4	20	20	10	4	10	20	14	4	16	20	29	4	30	20	30
30	4	21	19	51	4	31	20	01	4	25	20	03	4	22	20	08	4	12	20	13	4	18	20	27	4	31	20	28
31	4	23	19	50	4	33	20	00	4	26	20	01	4	23	20	06	4	14	20	11	4	20	20	25	4	33	20	26

THE MOON

Day	Diam '	Phase %	Age d	Rise 52° h	Rise 52° m	Rise 56° h	Rise 56° m	Transit h	Transit m	Set 52° h	Set 52° m	Set 56° h	Set 56° m
1	30.4	59	20.6	-	-	-	-	5	38	11	36	11	34
2	30.0	49	21.6	0	6	0	6	6	19	12	47	12	50
3	29.8	39	22.6	0	19	0	15	7	0	13	57	14	4
4	29.6	30	23.6	0	33	0	24	7	42	15	6	15	19
5	29.4	22	24.6	0	49	0	35	8	25	16	16	16	34
6	29.4	15	25.6	1	8	0	50	9	10	17	26	17	49
7	29.6	9	26.6	1	32	1	9	9	57	18	34	19	0
8	29.6	4	27.6	2	6	1	36	10	46	19	36	20	6
9	29.8	1	28.6	2	48	2	17	11	38	20	29	20	58
10	30.0	0	0.1	3	42	3	12	12	31	21	11	21	39
11	30.2	1	1.1	4	48	4	21	13	23	21	44	22	6
12	30.6	4	2.1	6	2	5	39	14	14	22	9	22	26
13	30.8	9	3.1	7	18	7	3	15	3	22	29	22	41
14	31.0	16	4.1	8	37	8	26	15	50	22	46	22	53
15	31.4	24	5.1	9	56	9	51	16	37	23	1	23	3
16	31.6	34	6.1	11	15	11	16	17	24	23	17	23	14
17	32.0	45	7.1	12	37	12	43	18	12	23	33	23	25
18	32.2	57	8.1	14	1	14	13	19	3	23	52	23	38
19	32.4	68	9.1	15	28	15	47	19	58	-	-	23	58
20	32.6	78	10.1	16	55	17	20	20	57	0	17	-	-
21	32.8	87	11.1	18	17	18	47	21	59	0	51	0	24
22	32.8	94	12.1	19	26	19	56	23	2	1	37	1	8
23	32.6	98	13.1	20	18	20	46	-	-	2	40	2	10
24	32.4	100	14.1	20	54	21	17	0	4	3	57	3	29
25	32.0	99	15.1	21	22	21	38	1	3	5	19	4	59
26	31.6	95	16.1	21	42	21	52	1	56	6	42	6	27
27	31.2	90	17.1	21	58	22	4	2	45	8	2	7	53
28	30.8	83	18.1	22	12	22	13	3	31	9	18	9	14
29	30.4	74	19.1	22	25	22	22	4	14	10	31	10	32
30	30.0	65	20.1	22	39	22	31	4	56	11	42	11	48
31	29.8	55	21.1	22	54	22	41	5	37	12	52	13	3

THE PLANETS

MERCURY

Day	R.A.			Dec.	Mag.	Diam.	Phase	Rise			Transit			Set		
	h	m	s	°		"	%	h	m	s	h	m	s	h	m	s
1	5	12	14	+19.2	+1.0	8.8	27	2	35	3	10	32	26	18	30	40
6	5	29	31	+20.4	+0.3	7.8	40	2	24	31	10	30	58	18	38	38
11	5	54	53	+21.6	-0.2	6.9	54	2	21	13	10	37	30	18	55	4
16	6	27	60	+22.6	-0.7	6.1	69	2	27	35	10	51	42	19	16	44
21	7	7	45	+22.8	-1.2	5.6	84	2	45	50	11	12	22	19	39	3
26	7	51	38	+22.1	-1.6	5.2	95	3	16	5	11	36	53	19	56	55
31	8	36	7	+20.3	-2.0	5.0	100	3	54	44	12	1	39	20	7	9

VENUS

Day	R.A.			Dec.	Mag.	Diam.	Phase	Rise			Transit			Set		
	h	m	s	°		"	%	h	m	s	h	m	s	h	m	s
1	8	29	33	+20.7	-3.9	12.0	90	5	42	42	13	51	42	22	0	8
6	8	54	28	+19.2	-3.9	12.2	89	5	58	55	13	56	51	21	54	7
11	9	18	50	+17.4	-3.9	12.5	88	6	15	35	14	1	26	21	46	34
16	9	42	38	+15.5	-3.9	12.7	86	6	32	27	14	5	29	21	37	45
21	10	5	55	+13.4	-3.9	13.0	85	6	49	18	14	9	0	21	27	54
26	10	28	42	+11.1	-3.9	13.2	84	7	5	59	14	12	1	21	17	15
31	10	51	2	+8.8	-3.9	13.6	82	7	22	27	14	14	35	21	5	56

MARS

Day	R.A.			Dec.	Mag.	Diam.	Rise			Transit			Set		
	h	m	s	°		"	h	m	s	h	m	s	h	m	s
1	8	59	22	+18.4	+1.8	3.9	6	28	23	14	20	37	22	12	34
6	9	11	50	+17.5	+1.8	3.8	6	27	23	14	13	22	21	59	3
11	9	24	11	+16.5	+1.8	3.8	6	26	27	14	6	1	21	45	15
16	9	36	27	+15.5	+1.8	3.7	6	25	35	13	58	34	21	31	13
21	9	48	38	+14.4	+1.8	3.7	6	24	45	13	51	2	21	16	59
26	10	0	43	+13.4	+1.8	3.7	6	23	56	13	43	25	21	2	33
31	10	12	43	+12.2	+1.8	3.7	6	23	7	13	35	43	20	47	57

JUPITER

Day	R.A.			Dec.	Mag.	Diam.	Rise			Transit			Set		
	h	m	s	°		"	h	m	s	h	m	s	h	m	s
1	22	17	30	-11.7	-2.6	45.3	22	39	1	3	39	53	8	37	5
6	22	16	45	-11.8	-2.7	45.9	22	19	10	3	19	28	8	16	6
11	22	15	43	-11.9	-2.7	46.5	21	59	12	2	58	46	7	54	40
16	22	14	23	-12.1	-2.7	47.1	21	39	5	2	37	47	7	32	49
21	22	12	48	-12.2	-2.8	47.6	21	18	51	2	16	32	7	10	33
26	22	10	59	-12.4	-2.8	48.0	20	58	31	1	55	3	6	47	56
31	22	8	56	-12.6	-2.8	48.4	20	38	3	1	33	21	6	25	0

Diam. = Equatorial. Polar Diam. is 94% of Equatorial Diam.

SATURN

Day	R.A.			Dec.	Mag.	Diam.	Rise			Transit			Set		
	h	m	s	°		"	h	m	s	h	m	s	h	m	s
1	21	0	13	-17.8	+0.4	18.3	21	59	50	2	22	45	6	41	54
6	20	59	3	-17.9	+0.3	18.4	21	39	38	2	1	56	6	20	28
11	20	57	47	-18.0	+0.3	18.4	21	19	21	1	41	1	5	58	54
16	20	56	26	-18.1	+0.3	18.5	20	59	2	1	20	0	5	37	13
21	20	55	2	-18.2	+0.2	18.6	20	38	41	0	58	56	5	15	26
26	20	53	34	-18.3	+0.2	18.6	20	18	17	0	37	49	4	53	36
31	20	52	5	-18.4	+0.2	18.6	19	57	52	0	16	41	4	31	44

Diam. = Equatorial. Polar Diam. is 90% of Equatorial Diam.
Rings – major axis 42", minor axis 13", Tilt 17°

URANUS

Day	R.A.			Dec.	Mag.	Diam.	Rise			Transit			Set		
	h	m	s	°		"	h	m	s	h	m	s	h	m	s
1	2	45	54	+15.6	+5.8	3.5	0	34	2	8	7	29	15	40	59
6	2	46	37	+15.6	+5.8	3.5	0	14	45	7	48	33	15	22	23
11	2	47	16	+15.7	+5.8	3.5	23	55	26	7	29	32	15	3	41
16	2	47	52	+15.7	+5.8	3.5	23	36	5	7	10	28	14	44	53
21	2	48	22	+15.8	+5.8	3.5	23	16	42	6	51	19	14	25	59
26	2	48	49	+15.8	+5.8	3.5	22	57	16	6	32	6	14	6	58
31	2	49	11	+15.8	+5.8	3.6	22	37	49	6	12	49	13	47	51

NEPTUNE

Day	R.A.			Dec.	Mag.	Diam.	Rise			Transit			Set		
	h	m	s	°		"	h	m	s	h	m	s	h	m	s
1	23	36	48	-3.7	+7.9	2.3	23	12	41	4	58	54	10	41	12
6	23	36	44	-3.8	+7.9	2.3	22	53	1	4	39	10	10	21	24
11	23	36	37	-3.8	+7.9	2.3	22	33	19	4	19	23	10	1	32
16	23	36	26	-3.8	+7.9	2.3	22	13	37	3	59	34	9	41	35
21	23	36	14	-3.8	+7.8	2.3	21	53	54	3	39	42	9	21	34
26	23	35	23	-3.8	+7.8	2.3	21	34	9	3	19	47	9	1	28
31	23	35	40	-3.9	+7.8	2.3	21	14	24	2	59	49	8	41	19

THE NIGHT SKY

Mercury is low in the morning at the beginning of July and can be found just above the eastern horizon as the sky begins to lighten. The magnitude 0.6 planet reaches greatest elongation west on the 4th but is best picked up towards the end of the second week of the month as its altitude improves.

Mercury is to the lower right of the very old Moon on the morning of July 8th when the planet is also near the star Zeta Tauri. The innermost world remains on view up to the start of the last week of July but will have become difficult to see by then.

Venus is low in the evening twilight all month and sets 1½ hours after the Sun. Binoculars will show Venus skirting the edge of the Beehive star cluster (M44) on the 3rd.

Venus quickly catches up with Mars as the month progresses, and the two are closest on the 13th when they are a ½° apart. The young lunar crescent nearby adds to the scene on the evenings of the 11th and 12th. Venus then passes a degree from Regulus in Leo on the 21st, a star that is occasionally occulted by a planet due to its proximity to the ecliptic.

Mars (magnitude 1.8) is setting about an hour after the Sun this month and crosses into Leo on the 11th. It has a dramatic encounter with much brighter Venus mid-month, but also will pass close to Regulus on the 29th. The two are quite low at the time though above the west-northwest skyline.

Jupiter (magnitude -2.7) rises late evening and is visible throughout most of the night. An app like Gas Giants (iOS) or Moons of Jupiter (Android) will let you follow the changing aspect of the Galilean moons daily. You can find Jupiter to the upper left of the Moon on the evening of July 25th.

NASA's Juno spacecraft currently circling Jupiter is due to be de-orbited this month after a five year mission. As its manoeuvring fuel is exhausted, the probe will be commanded to burn up in the Jovian atmosphere to avoid the risk of it crashing uncontrollably into - and contaminating - a moon like Europa, which may have a sub-surface ocean.

Juno has returned a treasure trove of science from Jupiter and made significant studies of its atmosphere, and gravity and magnetic fields. The powerful radiation belts surrounding Jupiter meant Juno was placed in a highly elliptical polar orbit to limit exposure of its delicate instruments. ESA will launch the JUpiter ICy moons Explorer (JUICE) in 2022 and it reaches the gas giant in 2029 to study Ganymede, Callisto, and Europa.

Saturn (magnitude 0.3) rises slightly earlier than Jupiter these evenings and its slightly yellowish tint is unmistakable. Saturn is directly above the full moon as it rises on the 24th.

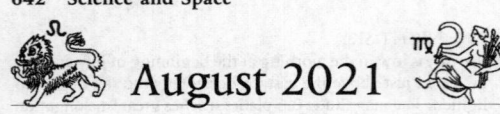

August 2021

EIGHTH MONTH, 31 DAYS. *Augustus*, formerly *Sextilis*, sixth month of Roman pre-Julian calendar

1	*Sunday*	MTV ('Music Television') began broadcasting with 'Video Killed the Radio Star' 1981	day 213

2	*Monday*	George Eliot began writing her masterpiece *Middlemarch* 1869	week 31 day 214
3	*Tuesday*	The Italian opera house La Scala opened 1778	215
4	*Wednesday*	President Woodrow Wilson proclaimed US neutrality from the war in Europe 1914	216
5	*Thursday*	The UK, USA and USSR signed the Nuclear Test Ban Treaty to prohibit above-ground nuclear tests 1963	217
6	*Friday*	The first atomic bomb was dropped by the USA on Hiroshima 1945	218
7	*Saturday*	An act was passed to make it illegal to employ anyone aged under 21 to sweep chimneys 1840	219
8	*Sunday*	President Nixon announced his resignation 1974	220

9	*Monday*	US writer Henry David Thoreau's book *Walden* was published 1854	week 32 day 221
10	*Tuesday*	The foundation stone was laid for the Royal Observatory at Greenwich 1675	222
11	*Wednesday*	The first Royal Ascot horse race took place 1711	223
12	*Thursday*	IBM introduced its personal computer for $1,600, which quickly came to dominate the market 1981	224
13	*Friday*	Barbed wire fences were put up overnight dividing East and West Berlin 1961	225
14	*Saturday*	Arthur Sullivan's *The Lost Chord* was used to demonstrate the newly perfected phonograph 1888	226
15	*Sunday*	The original Woodstock Music & Art Fair began in Bethel, New York 1969	227

16	*Monday*	The Peterloo Massacre takes place in Manchester, when cavalry charged a crowd 1819	week 33 day 228
17	*Tuesday*	Charles Blondin crossed the Niagara Falls on a tightrope 1859	229
18	*Wednesday*	Astronomer Pierre Janssen discovered helium in the solar spectrum 1868	230
19	*Thursday*	Mary Queen of Scots returned to Scotland aged 18 after spending 13 years in France 1561	231
20	*Friday*	The first round-the-world telegram was sent; it read 'This message sent around the world' 1911	232
21	*Saturday*	The *Mona Lisa* was stolen by Vincenzo Peruggia, a Louvre employee, who kept it for two years 1911	233
22	*Sunday*	The BBC performed its first experimental TV broadcast from Broadcasting House 1932	234

23	*Monday*	Film premiere of *The Big Sleep*, adapted from Raymond Chandler's novel 1946	week 32 day 235
24	*Tuesday*	Tom Stoppard's *Rosencrantz and Guildenstern are Dead* debuted 1966	236
25	*Wednesday*	The *Voyager 2* spacecraft reached Neptune after travelling for 12 years 1989	237
26	*Thursday*	US writer Ralph Waldo Emerson first met the influential writer Thomas Carlyle 1838	238
27	*Friday*	The first flight of a jet aircraft (*Heinkel He 178*) took place in Germany 1939	239
28	*Saturday*	Martin Luther King, Jr. delivered his 'I Have a Dream' speech, calling for an end to racism 1963	240
29	*Sunday*	Britain and China signed the Treaty of Nanking, ending the first Opium War 1842	241

30	*Monday*	Henry James returned to the USA after two decades in Europe 1904	week 35 day 242
31	*Tuesday*	Edvard Munch's *The Scream* was recovered by police, two years after its theft 2006	243

ASTRONOMICAL PHENOMENA

d	h	
2	-	Saturn at opposition
8	14	New Moon
9	12	Regulus 4.8°S of the Moon
9	03	Mercury 3.4°S of the Moon
10	00	Mars 4.3°S of the Moon
11	-	Sun crosses into Leo
11	07	Venus 4.3°S of the Moon
12	18	Mercury 1.2°N of Regulus
12	19	Perseid meteor shower
15	-	Jupiter without a visible Galilean moon
15	15	First Quarter Moon
16	18	Antares 4.5°S of the Moon
19	04	Mercury 0.1°S of Mars
20	-	Jupiter at opposition
20	22	Saturn 3.7°N of the Moon
21	05	Jupiter 4.0°N of the Moon
22	12	Full Moon
30	07	Last Quarter Moon

CONSTELLATIONS

The following constellations are visible at midnight throughout the month:
Draco, Hercules, Lyra, Cygnus, Sagitta, Ophiuchus, Serpens, Aquila and Sagittarius

PHASES OF THE MOON

Phase, Apsides and Node	d	h	m
● New Moon	8	13	50
◐ First Quarter	15	15	20
○ Full Moon	22	12	2
◑ Last Quarter	30	7	13
Apogee (404,410 km)	2	7	35
Perigee (369,124 km)	17	9	16
Apogee (404,100 km)	30	2	22

SUNRISE AND SUNSET

	London		Bristol		Birmingham		Manchester		Newcastle		Glasgow		Belfast	
	0° 05'	51° 30'	2° 35'	51° 28'	1° 55'	52° 28'	2° 15'	53° 28'	1° 37'	54° 59'	4° 14'	55° 52'	5° 56'	54° 35'
d	h m	h m	h m	h m	h m	h m	h m	h m	h m	h m	h m	h m	h m	h m
1	4 24	19 48	4 34	19 58	4 28	19 59	4 25	20 05	4 16	20 09	4 22	20 23	4 35	20 24
2	4 26	19 46	4 36	19 56	4 29	19 57	4 27	20 03	4 17	20 07	4 24	20 21	4 36	20 22
3	4 27	19 45	4 37	19 55	4 31	19 56	4 28	20 01	4 19	20 05	4 26	20 19	4 38	20 20
4	4 29	19 43	4 39	19 53	4 33	19 54	4 30	19 59	4 21	20 03	4 27	20 17	4 40	20 18
5	4 30	19 41	4 41	19 51	4 34	19 52	4 32	19 57	4 23	20 01	4 29	20 15	4 42	20 16
6	4 32	19 39	4 42	19 49	4 36	19 50	4 33	19 55	4 25	19 59	4 31	20 13	4 44	20 14
7	4 33	19 38	4 44	19 48	4 37	19 48	4 35	19 53	4 26	19 57	4 33	20 11	4 45	20 12
8	4 35	19 36	4 45	19 46	4 39	19 46	4 37	19 51	4 28	19 55	4 35	20 09	4 47	20 10
9	4 37	19 34	4 47	19 44	4 41	19 45	4 38	19 49	4 30	19 53	4 37	20 07	4 49	20 08
10	4 38	19 32	4 48	19 42	4 42	19 43	4 40	19 47	4 32	19 50	4 39	20 04	4 51	20 06
11	4 40	19 30	4 50	19 40	4 44	19 41	4 42	19 45	4 34	19 48	4 41	20 02	4 53	20 04
12	4 41	19 28	4 51	19 38	4 46	19 39	4 44	19 43	4 36	19 46	4 43	20 00	4 54	20 02
13	4 43	19 26	4 53	19 36	4 47	19 37	4 45	19 41	4 38	19 44	4 45	19 57	4 56	20 00
14	4 44	19 24	4 55	19 34	4 49	19 35	4 47	19 39	4 39	19 42	4 47	19 55	4 58	19 57
15	4 46	19 22	4 56	19 32	4 51	19 33	4 49	19 37	4 41	19 39	4 49	19 53	5 00	19 55
16	4 48	19 20	4 58	19 30	4 52	19 30	4 51	19 35	4 43	19 37	4 51	19 50	5 02	19 53
17	4 49	19 18	4 59	19 28	4 54	19 28	4 52	19 33	4 45	19 35	4 53	19 48	5 04	19 51
18	4 51	19 16	5 01	19 26	4 56	19 26	4 54	19 30	4 47	19 32	4 54	19 46	5 05	19 48
19	4 52	19 14	5 02	19 24	4 57	19 24	4 56	19 28	4 49	19 30	4 56	19 43	5 07	19 46
20	4 54	19 12	5 04	19 22	4 59	19 22	4 57	19 26	4 51	19 28	4 58	19 41	5 09	19 44
21	4 56	19 10	5 06	19 20	5 00	19 20	4 59	19 24	4 52	19 25	5 00	19 38	5 11	19 42
22	4 57	19 08	5 07	19 18	5 02	19 18	5 01	19 22	4 54	19 23	5 02	19 36	5 13	19 39
23	4 59	19 06	5 09	19 16	5 04	19 15	5 03	19 19	4 56	19 21	5 04	19 33	5 15	19 37
24	5 00	19 04	5 10	19 14	5 05	19 13	5 04	19 17	4 58	19 18	5 06	19 31	5 16	19 34
25	5 02	19 02	5 12	19 12	5 07	19 11	5 06	19 15	5 00	19 16	5 08	19 29	5 18	19 32
26	5 04	19 00	5 14	19 09	5 09	19 09	5 08	19 12	5 02	19 13	5 10	19 26	5 20	19 30
27	5 05	18 57	5 15	19 07	5 10	19 07	5 10	19 10	5 04	19 11	5 12	19 23	5 22	19 27
28	5 07	18 55	5 17	19 05	5 12	19 04	5 11	19 08	5 06	19 08	5 14	19 21	5 24	19 25
29	5 08	18 53	5 18	19 03	5 14	19 02	5 13	19 05	5 07	19 06	5 16	19 18	5 26	19 22
30	5 10	18 51	5 20	19 01	5 15	19 00	5 15	19 03	5 09	19 04	5 18	19 16	5 27	19 20
31	5 11	18 49	5 22	18 59	5 17	18 58	5 17	19 01	5 11	19 01	5 20	19 13	5 29	19 17

THE MOON

Day	Diam '	Phase %	Age d	Rise 52° h	Rise 52° m	Rise 56° h	Rise 56° m	Transit h	Transit m	Set 52° h	Set 52° m	Set 56° h	Set 56° m
1	29.6	46	22.1	23	12	22	55	6	20	14	2	14	19
2	29.6	37	23.1	23	33	23	12	7	4	15	13	15	34
3	29.6	28	24.1	-	-	23	36	7	50	16	22	16	48
4	29.6	20	25.1	0	4	-	-	8	39	17	26	17	55
5	29.8	13	26.1	0	41	0	11	9	31	18	23	18	53
6	30.0	7	27.1	1	32	1	2	10	23	19	8	19	38
7	30.4	3	28.1	2	34	2	7	11	16	19	45	20	9
8	30.6	0	29.1	3	47	3	23	12	8	20	13	20	32
9	31.0	0	0.5	5	4	4	46	12	58	20	35	20	48
10	31.2	2	1.5	6	24	6	12	13	47	20	52	21	0
11	31.4	7	2.5	7	44	7	37	14	35	21	8	21	12
12	31.8	13	3.5	9	4	9	4	15	22	21	23	21	22
13	32.0	22	4.5	10	26	10	31	16	10	21	39	21	32
14	32.0	32	5.5	11	49	11	59	17	0	21	57	21	45
15	32.2	43	6.5	13	14	13	31	17	52	22	19	22	2
16	32.4	54	7.5	14	40	15	2	18	48	22	49	22	24
17	32.4	66	8.5	16	1	16	31	19	48	23	29	23	1
18	32.4	76	9.5	17	14	17	45	20	49	-	-	23	53
19	32.2	85	10.5	18	10	18	41	21	50	0	24	-	-
20	32.2	92	11.5	18	52	19	18	22	49	1	34	1	6
21	32.0	97	12.5	19	23	19	42	23	44	2	54	2	30
22	31.6	100	13.5	19	45	19	57	-	-	4	17	4	0
23	31.4	100	14.5	20	2	20	10	0	35	5	38	5	26
24	31.0	97	15.5	20	17	20	20	1	22	6	56	6	50
25	30.6	93	16.5	20	30	20	29	2	7	8	12	8	11
26	30.2	87	17.5	20	44	20	38	2	50	9	24	9	28
27	30.0	80	18.5	20	58	20	47	3	32	10	36	10	45
28	29.8	71	19.5	21	14	21	0	4	14	11	47	12	1
29	29.6	62	20.5	21	34	21	14	4	58	12	58	13	18
30	29.6	53	21.5	22	1	21	35	5	43	14	7	14	33
31	29.6	43	22.5	22	34	22	6	6	31	15	14	15	43

THE PLANETS

MERCURY

Day	R.A.			Dec.	Mag.	Diam.	Phase	Rise			Transit			Set		
	h	m	s	°		"	%	h	m	s	h	m	s	h	m	s
1	8	44	48	+19.8	-2.0	5.0	100	4	2	59	12	6	21	20	8	14
6	9	26	19	+16.9	-1.5	5.0	98	4	44	35	12	27	53	20	9	27
11	10	4	7	+13.6	-1.0	5.0	94	5	24	20	12	45	37	20	5	11
16	10	38	15	+9.9	-0.6	5.1	90	6	0	36	12	59	41	19	57	10
21	11	9	10	+6.2	-0.4	5.3	85	6	33	4	13	10	34	19	46	39
26	11	37	21	+2.5	-0.2	5.5	80	7	1	53	13	18	44	19	34	20
31	12	3	9	0.0	-0.1	5.8	75	7	27	16	13	24	30	19	20	41

VENUS

Day	R.A.			Dec.	Mag.	Diam.	Phase	Rise			Transit			Set		
	h	m	s	°		"	%	h	m	s	h	m	s	h	m	s
1	10	55	28	+8.3	-3.9	13.6	82	7	25	43	14	15	4	21	3	37
6	11	17	22	+5.8	-4.0	14.0	81	7	41	55	14	17	12	20	51	43
11	11	38	59	+3.3	-4.0	14.3	79	7	57	54	14	19	3	20	39	28
16	12	0	23	0.0	-4.0	14.7	78	8	13	44	14	20	42	20	26	58
21	12	21	38	-1.8	-4.0	15.1	76	8	29	26	14	22	12	20	14	18
26	12	42	50	-4.4	-4.0	15.6	75	8	45	5	14	23	39	20	1	33
31	13	4	2	-6.9	-4.0	16.1	73	9	0	45	14	25	6	19	48	50

MARS

Day	R.A.			Dec.	Mag.	Diam.	Rise			Transit			Set		
	h	m	s	°		"	h	m	s	h	m	s	h	m	s
1	10	15	7	+12.0	+1.8	3.7	6	22	58	13	34	10	20	45	1
6	10	27	2	+10.8	+1.8	3.6	6	22	9	13	26	23	20	30	16
11	10	38	54	+9.7	+1.8	3.6	6	21	21	13	18	34	20	15	24
16	10	50	44	+8.4	+1.8	3.6	6	20	33	13	10	41	20	0	27
21	11	2	31	+7.2	+1.8	3.6	6	19	45	13	2	46	19	45	26
26	11	14	16	+5.9	+1.8	3.6	6	18	57	12	54	49	19	30	21
31	11	26	1	+4.7	+1.8	3.6	6	18	10	12	46	52	19	15	14

JUPITER

Day	R.A.			Dec.	Mag.	Diam.	Rise			Transit			Set		
	h	m	s	°		"	h	m	s	h	m	s	h	m	s
1	22	8	31	-12.7	-2.8	48.5	20	33	57	1	28	59	6	20	23
6	22	6	16	-12.9	-2.8	48.8	20	13	23	1	7	5	5	57	8
11	22	3	53	-13.1	-2.9	49.0	19	52	45	0	45	2	5	33	42
16	22	1	25	-13.4	-2.9	49.1	19	32	3	0	22	55	5	10	9
21	21	58	54	-13.6	-2.9	49.1	19	11	18	0	0	44	4	46	32
26	21	56	23	-13.8	-2.9	49.1	18	50	33	23	35	3	4	22	57
31	21	53	55	-14.0	-2.9	48.9	18	29	47	23	12	56	3	59	28

Diam. = Equatorial. Polar Diam. is 94% of Equatorial Diam.

SATURN

Day	R.A.			Dec.	Mag.	Diam.	Rise			Transit			Set		
	h	m	s	°		"	h	m	s	h	m	s	h	m	s
1	20	51	47	-18.4	+0.2	18.6	19	53	47	0	12	27	4	27	21
6	20	50	17	-18.5	+0.2	18.6	19	33	20	23	47	29	4	5	28
11	20	48	47	-18.6	+0.2	18.6	19	12	54	23	26	20	3	43	37
16	20	47	20	-18.7	+0.2	18.5	18	52	28	23	5	13	3	21	49
21	20	45	56	-18.8	+0.3	18.5	18	32	4	22	44	9	3	0	5
26	20	44	35	-18.9	+0.3	18.4	18	11	41	22	23	10	2	38	29
31	20	43	20	-19.0	+0.3	18.4	17	51	21	22	2	15	2	16	59

Diam. = Equatorial. Polar Diam. is 90% of Equatorial Diam.
Rings – major axis 42", minor axis 13", Tilt 18°

URANUS

Day	R.A.			Dec.	Mag.	Diam.	Rise			Transit			Set		
	h	m	s	°		"	h	m	s	h	m	s	h	m	s
1	2	49	15	+15.8	+5.8	3.6	22	33	55	6	8	56	13	44	0
6	2	49	31	+15.9	+5.8	3.6	22	14	24	5	49	33	13	24	44
11	2	49	42	+15.9	+5.8	3.6	21	54	51	5	30	5	13	5	21
16	2	49	49	+15.9	+5.7	3.6	21	35	15	5	10	32	12	45	50
21	2	49	50	+15.9	+5.7	3.6	21	15	36	4	50	54	12	26	13
26	2	49	47	+15.9	+5.7	3.6	20	55	56	4	31	11	12	6	27
31	2	49	39	+15.9	+5.7	3.6	20	36	12	4	11	23	11	46	35

NEPTUNE

Day	R.A.			Dec.	Mag.	Diam.	Rise			Transit			Set		
	h	m	s	°		"	h	m	s	h	m	s	h	m	s
1	23	35	37	-3.9	+7.8	2.3	21	10	26	2	55	50	8	37	17
6	23	35	16	-3.9	+7.8	2.3	20	50	39	2	35	49	8	17	4
11	23	34	53	-4.0	+7.8	2.3	20	30	52	2	15	47	7	56	47
16	23	34	29	-4.0	+7.8	2.4	20	11	3	1	55	43	7	36	28
21	23	34	3	-4.1	+7.8	2.4	19	51	14	1	35	38	7	16	6
26	23	33	35	-4.1	+7.8	2.4	19	31	24	1	15	31	6	55	42
31	23	33	6	-4.2	+7.8	2.4	19	11	33	0	55	22	6	35	16

THE NIGHT SKY

Mercury is at superior conjunction on the 1st but remains too deep in the bright twilight to be seen this month after it emerges into the evening sky.

Venus (magnitude -4.0) shines brightly low in the western sky these evenings and is presently setting an hour after the Sun. The young moon is nearby both on the 9th and 10th. Telescope users will notice Venus shows a gradually narrowing gibbous phase at present.

Mars (magnitude 1.8) is setting only 40 minutes after the Sun mid-month and so it will likely become lost to view for us around this time.

Jupiter (magnitude -2.9) is at opposition on the 20th in Capricornus when it rises around sunset and is visible throughout the night. The planet's annually improving position on the celestial sphere means better opportunities to come for northern hemisphere observers scrutinising detail in the gas giant's turbulent atmosphere through a telescope. Jupiter lies to the upper left of the almost full moon on the night of the 21st.

Jupiter is without a visible Galilean satellite on August 15th but they are absent during daylight from the UK. In the Americas, observers will see Io eclipsed and the shadows of the other three in transit – the next triple shadow crossing is not until December 2026 from the UK.

Saturn (magnitude 0.2) is also at opposition this month, but on the 2nd in Capricornus when the butterscotch-hued planet can be seen in the eastern sky as soon as twilight fades. Saturn does not show the same swirls and patterns in its atmosphere as Jupiter, but the magnificent ring system compensates. The nearly full moon is within 4° of Saturn on the 20th.

Saturn's largest moon Titan can be seen in steadily held binoculars, while a half dozen in total of its biggest satellites are within reach of most amateur telescopes. Note how much the ring system is tipped over the next few years as it slowly narrows until it becomes briefly edge-on from our perspective in 2025.

The four-day old Moon sets during the late evening on August 12th and so will not interfere with the maximum of the Perseid meteor shower. The radiant, or point of origin of the meteors when their paths are traced backward, lies in the constellation Perseus that is low in the northeast after dark. As the night progresses, rates improve as Perseus rises higher in the sky. Away from lit areas, you may see a meteor every couple of minutes.

Besides trying to glimpse the youngest moon, some observers like the challenge of sighting opposing crescents. This is where you can try for the shortest time between sightings of the Moon just before and after New. The Moon is 33 hours before New if spotted on the morning of the 7th, and less than 31 hours old on the evening of the 9th.

 # September 2021

NINTH MONTH, 30 DAYS. *Septem* (seven), seventh month of Roman pre-Julian calendar

1	*Wednesday*	A solar flare is observed for the first time by astronomer Richard Carrington 1859	day 244
2	*Thursday*	The original *Star Trek* was cancelled after its third season 1969	245
3	*Friday*	Oliver Cromwell's parliamentarians defeated Charles II's royalists at the second Battle of Worcester 1651	246
4	*Saturday*	Beatrix Potter wrote a letter containing the first incarnation of Peter Rabbit 1893	247
5	*Sunday*	James Glaisher and Henry Coxwell set a new altitude record when their balloon ascended 11km 1862	248
6	*Monday*	John Derry, piloting a de Havilland DH 108, became the first Briton to break the sound barrier 1948	week 36 day 249
7	*Tuesday*	The French poet Guillaume Apollinaire was mistakenly arrested for stealing the *Mona Lisa* 1911	250
8	*Wednesday*	Frank Sinatra, 19, appeared on the radio talent show *Major Bowes' Amateur Hour* 1935	251
9	*Thursday*	Scientists stated that the hole in the ozone layer had reached record size (28 million sq. km) 2000	252
10	*Friday*	Pablo Picasso's monumental painting, *Guernica*, was returned to Spain 1981	253
11	*Saturday*	The Siege of Drogheda ends with Oliver Cromwell's Roundheads massacring the defending Royalists 1649	254
12	*Sunday*	Four rail teenagers discovered paleolithic artwork on the walls of caves at Lascaux in south-west France 1940	255
13	*Monday*	A rail detector car which found faults in railroad tracks was demonstrated in New York, USA 1928	week 37 day 256
14	*Tuesday*	The Soviet Union's *Luna 2* became the first spacecraft to land on the Moon 1959	257
15	*Wednesday*	Allied nations celebrated Victory in Japan Day 1945	258
16	*Thursday*	The United Shakespeare Company bought the poet's childhood home in Stratford-upon-Avon 1847	259
17	*Friday*	*Lord of the Flies*, Nobel Prize winner William Golding's dystopian debut novel, was published 1954	260
18	*Saturday*	King George I sailed up the Thames to Greenwich, setting foot in England for the first time 1714	261
19	*Sunday*	Nikita Khrushchev was barred from visiting Disneyland 1959	262
20	*Monday*	The first Cannes film festival took place 1946	week 38 day 263
21	*Tuesday*	Great Britain abandoned the gold standard 1931	264
22	*Wednesday*	Charlotte Cooper, the first woman to win an Olympic gold medal, at the 1900 Olympic Games *b.* 1870	265
23	*Thursday*	Johan Galle discovered Neptune after using calculations predicting the planet's location 1846	266
24	*Friday*	Dougal Haston and Doug Scott became the first Britons to climb Everest 1975	267
25	*Saturday*	Diarist Samuel Pepys drank a cup of 'tee' for the first time 1660	268
26	*Sunday*	*West Side Story* premiered on Broadway 1957	269
27	*Monday*	SMART-1, the European Space Agency's first mission to the Moon, was launched from French Guiana 2003	week 39 day 270
28	*Tuesday*	William the Conqueror invaded England 1066	271
29	*Wednesday*	The Babi Yar massacre of nearly 34,000 Jews began in Nazi-occupied Ukraine 1941	272
30	*Thursday*	Neville Chamberlain declared 'peace for our time' after signing the Munich Agreement 1938	273

ASTRONOMICAL PHENOMENA

d	h	
4	04	Moon 2.9°N of the Beehive cluster
5	20	Regulus 4.8°S of the Moon
7	16	Mars 4.24°S of the Moon
7	00	New Moon
8	20	Mercury 6.5°S of the Moon
10	02	Venus 4.1°S of the Moon
13	21	First Quarter Moon
14	19	Mercury at greatest elongation (26° 46' E)
14	-	Neptune at opposition
17	02	Saturn 3.8°N of the Moon
17	-	Sun crosses into Virgo
18	07	Jupiter 4.0°N of the Moon
21	00	Full Moon (Harvest Moon)
21	02	Mercury 1.2°S of Spica
22	19	Autumnal equinox
29	02	Last Quarter Moon
30	15	Mercury 1.7°S of Spica

CONSTELLATIONS

The following constellations are visible at midnight throughout the month:

Draco, Cepheus, Lyra, Cygnus, Vulpecula, Sagitta, Delphinus, Equuleus, Aquila, Aquarius and Capricornus

PHASES OF THE MOON

Phase, Apsides and Node	d	h	m
● New Moon	7	0	52
◗ First Quarter	13	20	39
○ Full Moon	20	23	55
◗ Last Quarter	29	1	57
Perigee (368,461 km)	11	10	3
Apogee (404,640 km)	26	21	44

SUNRISE AND SUNSET

	London 0° 05' 51° 30'				Bristol 2° 35' 51° 28'				Birmingham 1° 55' 52° 28'				Manchester 2° 15' 53° 28'				Newcastle 1° 37' 54° 59'				Glasgow 4° 14' 55° 52'				Belfast 5° 56' 54° 35'			
d	h	m	h	m	h	m	h	m	h	m	h	m	h	m	h	m	h	m	h	m	h	m	h	m	h	m	h	m
1	5	13	18	46	5	23	18	56	5	19	18	55	5	18	18	58	5	13	18	59	5	22	19	11	5	31	19	15
2	5	15	18	44	5	25	18	54	5	20	18	53	5	20	18	56	5	15	18	56	5	24	19	08	5	33	19	13
3	5	16	18	42	5	26	18	52	5	22	18	51	5	22	18	54	5	17	18	54	5	26	19	06	5	35	19	10
4	5	18	18	40	5	28	18	50	5	24	18	48	5	24	18	51	5	19	18	51	5	28	19	03	5	37	19	08
5	5	19	18	37	5	30	18	47	5	25	18	46	5	25	18	49	5	20	18	49	5	29	19	00	5	38	19	05
6	5	21	18	35	5	31	18	45	5	27	18	44	5	27	18	46	5	22	18	46	5	31	18	58	5	40	19	03
7	5	23	18	33	5	33	18	43	5	29	18	41	5	29	18	44	5	24	18	43	5	33	18	55	5	42	19	00
8	5	24	18	31	5	34	18	41	5	30	18	39	5	31	18	42	5	26	18	41	5	35	18	53	5	44	18	58
9	5	26	18	28	5	36	18	38	5	32	18	37	5	32	18	39	5	28	18	38	5	37	18	50	5	46	18	55
10	5	27	18	26	5	37	18	36	5	34	18	34	5	34	18	37	5	30	18	36	5	39	18	47	5	48	18	53
11	5	29	18	24	5	39	18	34	5	35	18	32	5	36	18	34	5	32	18	33	5	41	18	45	5	49	18	50
12	5	31	18	21	5	41	18	31	5	37	18	30	5	37	18	32	5	33	18	31	5	43	18	42	5	51	18	48
13	5	32	18	19	5	42	18	29	5	39	18	27	5	39	18	29	5	35	18	28	5	45	18	39	5	53	18	45
14	5	34	18	17	5	44	18	27	5	40	18	25	5	41	18	27	5	37	18	26	5	47	18	37	5	55	18	42
15	5	35	18	15	5	45	18	24	5	42	18	22	5	43	18	24	5	39	18	23	5	49	18	34	5	57	18	40
16	5	37	18	12	5	47	18	22	5	44	18	20	5	44	18	22	5	41	18	20	5	51	18	31	5	58	18	37
17	5	39	18	10	5	49	18	20	5	45	18	18	5	46	18	20	5	43	18	18	5	53	18	29	6	00	18	35
18	5	40	18	08	5	50	18	18	5	47	18	15	5	48	18	17	5	45	18	15	5	55	18	26	6	02	18	32
19	5	42	18	05	5	52	18	15	5	49	18	13	5	50	18	15	5	47	18	13	5	57	18	24	6	04	18	30
20	5	43	18	03	5	53	18	13	5	50	18	11	5	51	18	12	5	48	18	10	5	59	18	21	6	06	18	27
21	5	45	18	01	5	55	18	11	5	52	18	08	5	53	18	10	5	50	18	08	6	00	18	18	6	08	18	25
22	5	47	17	58	5	57	18	08	5	54	18	06	5	55	18	07	5	52	18	05	6	02	18	16	6	09	18	22
23	5	48	17	56	5	58	18	06	5	55	18	03	5	57	18	05	5	54	18	02	6	04	18	13	6	11	18	20
24	5	50	17	54	6	00	18	04	5	57	18	01	5	58	18	00	5	56	18	00	6	06	18	10	6	13	18	17
25	5	51	17	52	6	01	18	01	5	59	17	59	6	00	18	00	5	58	17	57	6	08	18	08	6	15	18	15
26	5	53	17	49	6	03	17	59	6	00	17	56	6	02	17	58	6	00	17	55	6	10	18	05	6	17	18	12
27	5	55	17	47	6	05	17	57	6	02	17	54	6	04	17	55	6	02	17	52	6	12	18	02	6	19	18	10
28	5	56	17	45	6	06	17	55	6	04	17	52	6	05	17	53	6	03	17	50	6	14	18	00	6	21	18	07
29	5	58	17	42	6	08	17	52	6	06	17	49	6	07	17	50	6	05	17	47	6	16	17	57	6	22	18	04
30	6	00	17	40	6	10	17	50	6	07	17	47	6	09	17	48	6	07	17	45	6	18	17	55	6	24	18	02

THE MOON

Day	Diam '	Phase %	Age d	Rise 52° h	Rise 52° m	Rise 56° h	Rise 56° m	Transit h	Transit m	Set 52° h	Set 52° m	Set 56° h	Set 56° m
1	29.8	34	23.5	23	20	22	49	7	22	16	14	16	45
2	30.0	25	24.5	-	-	23	47	8	14	17	3	17	35
3	30.2	17	25.5	0	18	-	-	9	6	17	44	18	11
4	30.6	10	26.5	1	26	1	1	9	58	18	14	18	36
5	31.0	5	27.5	2	43	2	22	10	50	18	38	18	54
6	31.4	1	28.5	4	3	3	48	11	40	18	57	19	8
7	31.6	0	0.0	5	25	5	16	12	29	19	14	19	19
8	32.0	1	1.0	6	47	6	44	13	17	19	29	19	29
9	32.2	5	2.0	8	11	8	13	14	6	19	45	19	40
10	32.4	11	3.0	9	35	9	44	14	56	20	2	19	52
11	32.4	19	4.0	11	1	11	17	15	48	20	23	20	7
12	32.4	29	5.0	12	29	12	50	16	44	20	50	20	27
13	32.4	40	6.0	13	52	14	21	17	42	21	26	20	59
14	32.2	52	7.0	15	7	15	40	18	43	22	16	21	44
15	32.0	63	8.0	16	8	16	40	19	43	23	20	22	50
16	32.0	74	9.0	16	53	17	21	20	42	-	-	-	-
17	31.6	83	10.0	17	26	17	47	21	37	0	36	0	10
18	31.4	90	11.0	17	49	18	5	22	28	1	58	1	37
19	31.2	96	12.0	18	8	18	18	23	16	3	18	3	4
20	31.0	99	13.0	18	23	18	28	-	-	4	37	4	28
21	30.6	100	14.0	18	36	18	37	0	1	5	53	5	50
22	30.4	99	15.0	18	49	18	45	0	44	7	7	7	9
23	30.0	96	16.0	19	3	18	54	1	26	8	19	8	26
24	29.8	91	17.0	19	18	19	5	2	9	9	31	9	43
25	29.6	85	18.0	19	36	19	18	2	52	10	43	11	0
26	29.6	78	19.0	20	0	19	35	3	37	11	53	12	17
27	29.6	69	20.0	20	29	20	2	4	24	13	1	13	30
28	29.6	60	21.0	21	10	20	38	5	13	14	4	14	36
29	29.8	51	22.0	22	3	21	29	6	4	14	57	15	31
30	30.0	41	23.0	23	6	22	36	6	55	15	42	16	11

THE PLANETS

MERCURY

Day	R.A. h	m	s	Dec. °	Mag.	Diam. ''	Phase %	Rise h	m	s	Transit h	m	s	Set h	m	s
1	12	8	2	-1.7	0.0	5.9	74	7	31	56	13	25	22	19	17	49
6	12	31	7	-5.0	+0.1	6.2	68	7	53	6	13	28	23	19	2	52
11	12	51	42	-7.9	+0.1	6.7	62	8	10	9	13	28	48	18	46	55
16	13	9	8	-10.4	+0.2	7.2	54	8	21	44	13	25	56	18	29	54
21	13	22	8	-12.3	+0.4	7.9	44	8	25	18	13	18	23	18	11	42
26	13	28	35	-13.3	+0.7	8.7	32	8	16	42	13	3	59	17	52	13

VENUS

Day	R.A. h	m	s	Dec. °	Mag.	Diam. ''	Phase %	Rise h	m	s	Transit h	m	s	Set h	m	s
1	13	8	17	-7.4	-4.0	16.2	73	9	3	54	14	25	24	19	46	18
6	13	29	37	-9.9	-4.1	16.7	71	9	19	38	14	26	58	19	33	43
11	13	51	6	-12.3	-4.1	17.3	70	9	35	29	14	28	42	19	21	23
16	14	12	48	-14.6	-4.1	17.9	68	9	51	24	14	30	39	19	9	23
21	14	34	45	-16.8	-4.1	18.6	66	10	7	19	14	32	49	18	57	53
26	14	56	58	-18.8	-4.2	19.4	64	10	23	6	14	35	15	18	47	1

MARS

Day	R.A. h	m	s	Dec. °	Mag.	Diam. ''	Rise h	m	s	Transit h	m	s	Set h	m	s
1	11	28	22	+4.4	+1.8	3.6	6	18	1	12	45	17	19	12	12
6	11	40	7	+3.1	+1.8	3.6	6	17	16	12	37	20	18	57	4
11	11	51	53	+1.8	+1.8	3.6	6	16	33	12	29	24	18	41	55
16	12	3	40	0.0	+1.7	3.6	6	15	53	12	21	30	18	26	47
21	12	15	30	0.0	+1.7	3.5	6	15	16	12	13	38	18	11	41
26	12	27	24	-2.2	+1.7	3.6	6	14	43	12	5	50	17	56	38

JUPITER

Day	R.A. h	m	s	Dec. °	Mag.	Diam. ''	Rise h	m	s	Transit h	m	s	Set h	m	s
1	21	53	26	-14.1	-2.9	48.9	18	25	38	23	8	31	3	54	47
6	21	51	5	-14.3	-2.8	48.6	18	4	54	22	46	30	3	31	30
11	21	48	52	-14.5	-2.8	48.3	17	44	13	22	24	38	3	8	27
16	21	46	2	-14.7	-2.8	47.9	17	23	36	22	2	57	2	45	43
21	21	45	4	-14.8	-2.8	47.4	17	3	4	21	41	30	2	23	21
26	21	43	32	-14.9	-2.7	46.9	16	42	39	21	20	18	2	1	22

Diam. = Equatorial. Polar Diam. is 94% of Equatorial Diam.

SATURN

Day	R.A. h	m	s	Dec. °	Mag.	Diam. ''	Rise h	m	s	Transit h	m	s	Set h	m	s
1	20	43	6	-19.0	+0.3	18.3	17	47	17	21	58	5	2	12	43
6	20	41	58	-19.1	+0.3	18.2	17	27	0	21	37	17	1	51	25
11	20	40	57	-19.2	+0.4	18.1	17	6	47	21	16	37	1	30	17
16	20	40	4	-19.2	+0.4	18.0	16	46	38	20	56	5	1	9	21
21	20	39	20	-19.3	+0.4	17.9	16	26	34	20	35	41	0	48	38
26	20	38	45	-19.3	+0.4	17.8	16	6	35	20	15	26	0	28	8

Diam. = Equatorial. Polar Diam. is 90% of Equatorial Diam.
Rings – major axis 41", minor axis 13", Tilt 19°

URANUS

Day	R.A. h	m	s	Dec. °	Mag.	Diam. ''	Rise h	m	s	Transit h	m	s	Set h	m	s
1	2	49	36	+15.9	+5.7	3.7	20	32	15	4	7	25	11	42	36
6	2	49	22	+15.8	+5.7	3.7	20	12	29	3	47	31	11	22	35
11	2	49	3	+15.8	+5.7	3.7	19	52	40	3	27	33	11	2	27
16	2	48	40	+15.8	+5.7	3.7	19	32	48	3	7	30	10	42	13
21	2	48	13	+15.7	+5.7	3.7	19	9	3	2	47	23	10	21	52
26	2	47	41	+15.7	+5.7	3.7	18	49	8	2	27	12	10	1	26

NEPTUNE

Day	R.A. h	m	s	Dec. °	Mag.	Diam. ''	Rise h	m	s	Transit h	m	s	Set h	m	s
1	23	33	1	-4.2	+7.8	2.4	19	7	35	0	51	21	6	31	10
6	23	32	31	-4.2	+7.8	2.4	18	47	44	0	31	12	6	10	43
11	23	32	1	-4.3	+7.8	2.4	18	27	53	0	11	2	5	50	15
16	23	31	30	-4.4	+7.8	2.4	18	8	1	23	50	57	5	29	47
21	23	31	0	-4.4	+7.8	2.4	17	48	10	23	26	47	5	9	19
26	23	30	30	-4.5	+7.8	2.4	17	28	18	23	6	38	4	48	52

THE NIGHT SKY

Mercury should be visible mid-month in the evening sky when it reaches greatest elongation east on the 14th. The elusive magnitude 0.1 planet is setting about 45 minutes after the Sun at this time. Mercury's spark will be low in the west-southwest though, and well to the lower right of Venus.

Venus (magnitude -4.1) hangs above the western skyline for about an hour after sunset. The disk is 68% illuminated mid-month for telescope users and is slowly growing less fat while also swelling in apparent size. The two-day old moon is close to Venus on the evening of the 9th but they will be low in the west-northwest.

Mars is too close to the Sun to be seen this month. However, it moves into Virgo from Leo on the 6th and then crosses the celestial equator, moving from north to south, on the 18th.

Jupiter (magnitude -2.8) can be seen in the eastern sky after sunset and is on view until the early hours. It can be found 8° to the upper right of the Moon on the 18th.

Saturn (magnitude 0.4) is similarly already up in the east as night falls but sets soon after 1am summertime at the end of the month. The waxing Moon is near Saturn on the evening of the 16th.

Neptune (magnitude 7.8) is at opposition on the 14th in eastern Aquarius and not far from magnitude 4.2 Phi Aquarii. Steadily held binoculars are sufficient to spot the distant world when used with a chart of the planet's location.

The full moon on September 20th is the Harvest Moon as it falls closest to the autumn equinox. On average, the Moon rises around one hour later each night. What marks out the Harvest Moon as special is that it appears to rise around sunset for several successive evenings due to the shallow angle the ecliptic makes with the horizon from temperate latitudes in the northern hemisphere.

In binoculars at time of full moon you can make out bright spoke-like features radiating from some lunar craters. One of the most prominent ray systems is that centred on the 90-kilometre-wide crater Tycho that lies towards the Moon's southern highlands. When the moon is full you can see its rays extending for hundreds of kilometres across the lunar maria.

Tycho is one of the youngest major craters with an estimated age of 110 million years and so its rays are relatively fresh. Two large craters on Oceanus Procellarum - the Ocean of Storms is the large 'sea' on the left side of the Moon's disk - are also major ray centres. Copernicus and the slightly smaller crater Kepler both have complex patterns of material splattered around them. Further north, you will see Aristarchus - the brightest feature on the Moon and the result of an ancient impact that excavated highly reflective material.

October 2021

TENTH MONTH, 31 DAYS. *Octo* (eighth), eighth month of Roman pre-Julian calendar

1	*Friday*	The People's Republic of China was formally established 1949	day 274
2	*Saturday*	Charles Darwin returned from his momentous voyage to the Pacific aboard *HMS Beagle* 1836	275
3	*Sunday*	The reunification of East and West Germany was formerly completed and celebrated 1990	276

4	*Monday*	The Soviet Union launched *Sputnik 1*, the first man-made satellite, into orbit around the Earth 1957	week 40 day 277
5	*Tuesday*	*Monty Python's Flying Circus* first aired on BBC1 1969	278
6	*Wednesday*	The first feature-length 'talkie', *The Jazz Singer*, premiered in New York 1927	279
7	*Thursday*	The Soviet space probe *Luna 3* photographed the far side of the Moon for the first time 1959	280
8	*Friday*	The Post Office Tower, then the tallest building in London, was officially opened 1965	281
9	*Saturday*	Breathalyser tests came into force 1967	282
10	*Sunday*	William Lassell discovers Triton, Neptune's largest moon 1846	283

11	*Monday*	Kathryn D. Sullivan, a NASA astronaut, became the first woman to walk in space 1984	week 41 day 284
12	*Tuesday*	Oktoberfest took place in its original form: a celebration of a Bavarian royal wedding 1810	285
13	*Wednesday*	At the International Meridian Conference, Greenwich was adopted as the universal meridian 1884	286
14	*Thursday*	The first of A. A. Milne's *Winnie-the-Pooh* books was published 1926	287
15	*Friday*	The Black Panther Party, a black nationalist organisation, was formed in California 1966	288
16	*Saturday*	Samuel Franklin Cody completed the first aeroplane flight in the UK 1908	289
17	*Sunday*	British troops surrendered to American colonists at the Battle of Saratoga in New York 1777	290

18	*Monday*	The British Broadcasting Company, later the British Broadcasting Corporation, was founded 1922	week 42 day 291
19	*Tuesday*	The first battle of Ypres began marking the end of the 'Race to the Sea' 1914	292
20	*Wednesday*	Sydney Opera House was formally opened by Queen Elizabeth II 1973	293
21	*Thursday*	The Guggenheim museum opened in New York 1959	294
22	*Friday*	US president John F. Kennedy announced the discovery of Soviet nuclear weapons in Cuba 1962	295
23	*Saturday*	Edgehill, the first major battle of the English Civil War, ended indecisively 1642	296
24	*Sunday*	The United Nations formally came into existence 1945	297

25	*Monday*	The Charge of the Light Brigade, commemorated in Tennyson's famous poem, took place 1854	week 43 day 298
26	*Tuesday*	The leaders of Israel and Jordon signed a peace treaty, ending 46 years of war 1994	299
27	*Wednesday*	The Abortion Act was passed, allowing abortion for medical reasons 1967	300
28	*Thursday*	Jonathan Swift's classic novel *Gulliver's Travels* was published 1726	301
29	*Friday*	The US stock market collapsed, later known as the Wall Street Crash 1929	302
30	*Saturday*	Orson Welles' radio production of *War of the Worlds* first aired, inciting panic and complaints 1938	303
31	*Sunday*	The first collection of Arthur Conan Doyle's *The Adventures of Sherlock Holmes* was published 1892	304

ASTRONOMICAL PHENOMENA

2	-	Venus at aphelion
6	11	New Moon
8	-	Mars at solar conjunction
9	-	Mercury at inferior conjunction
9	08	Mercury 2.8°S of Mars
9	18	Venus 2.9°S of the Moon
13	03	First Quarter Moon
13	07	Saturn 3.9°N of the Moon
15	10	Jupiter 4.1°N of the Moon
16	14	Venus 1.4°N of Antares
18	-	Jupiter stationary, prograde motion resumes
20	15	Full Moon
21	11	Orionid meteor shower
25	-	Mercury at greatest elongation (18° 24' W)
28	20	Last Quarter Moon
28	-	Venus Dichotomy (half phase in a scope)
29	-	Venus at greatest elongation (47° 03' E)
30	-	Saturn at eastern quadrature

CONSTELLATIONS

The following constellations are visible at midnight throughout the month:

Ursa Major (below the Pole), Cepheus, Cassiopeia, Cygnus, Lacerta, Andromeda, Pegasus, Capricornus, Aquarius and Piscis Austrinus

PHASES OF THE MOON

Phase, Apsides and Node	d	h	m
● New Moon	6	11	5
◑ First Quarter	13	3	25
○ Full Moon	20	14	57
◐ Last Quarter	28	20	5
Perigee (363,386 km)	8	17	28
Apogee (405,615 km)	24	15	28

SUNRISE AND SUNSET

	London				Bristol				Birmingham				Manchester				Newcastle				Glasgow				Belfast		
	0°	$05'$	51°	$30'$	2°	$35'$	51°	$28'$	1°	$55'$	52°	$28'$	2°	$15'$	53°	$28'$	1°	$37'$	54°	$59'$	4°	$14'$	55°	$52'$	5°	$56'$	54°	$35'$
d	h	m	h	m	h	m	h	m	h	m	h	m	h	m	h	m	h	m	h	m	h	m	h	m	h	m	h	m
1	6	01	17	38	6	11	17	48	6	09	17	45	6	11	17	45	6	09	17	42	6	20	17	52	6	26	17	59
2	6	03	17	36	6	13	17	46	6	11	17	42	6	13	17	43	6	11	17	39	6	22	17	49	6	28	17	57
3	6	04	17	33	6	14	17	43	6	12	17	40	6	14	17	41	6	13	17	37	6	24	17	47	6	30	17	54
4	6	06	17	31	6	16	17	41	6	14	17	38	6	16	17	38	6	15	17	34	6	26	17	44	6	32	17	52
5	6	08	17	29	6	18	17	39	6	16	17	35	6	18	17	36	6	17	17	32	6	28	17	42	6	34	17	50
6	6	09	17	26	6	19	17	37	6	18	17	33	6	20	17	33	6	19	17	29	6	30	17	39	6	36	17	47
7	6	11	17	24	6	21	17	34	6	19	17	31	6	22	17	31	6	21	17	27	6	32	17	36	6	37	17	45
8	6	13	17	22	6	23	17	32	6	21	17	28	6	23	17	29	6	22	17	24	6	34	17	34	6	39	17	42
9	6	14	17	20	6	24	17	30	6	23	17	26	6	25	17	26	6	24	17	22	6	36	17	31	6	41	17	40
10	6	16	17	18	6	26	17	28	6	24	17	24	6	27	17	24	6	26	17	19	6	38	17	29	6	43	17	37
11	6	18	17	15	6	28	17	25	6	26	17	22	6	29	17	22	6	28	17	17	6	40	17	26	6	45	17	35
12	6	19	17	13	6	29	17	23	6	28	17	19	6	31	17	19	6	30	17	15	6	42	17	24	6	47	17	32
13	6	21	17	11	6	31	17	21	6	30	17	17	6	32	17	17	6	32	17	12	6	44	17	21	6	49	17	30
14	6	23	17	09	6	33	17	19	6	32	17	15	6	34	17	15	6	34	17	10	6	46	17	19	6	51	17	28
15	6	24	17	07	6	34	17	17	6	33	17	13	6	36	17	12	6	36	17	07	6	48	17	16	6	53	17	25
16	6	26	17	05	6	36	17	15	6	35	17	10	6	38	17	10	6	38	17	05	6	50	17	14	6	55	17	23
17	6	28	17	03	6	38	17	13	6	37	17	08	6	40	17	08	6	40	17	03	6	52	17	11	6	57	17	21
18	6	30	17	00	6	40	17	11	6	39	17	06	6	42	17	06	6	42	17	00	6	54	17	09	6	59	17	18
19	6	31	16	58	6	41	17	08	6	40	17	04	6	44	17	03	6	44	16	58	6	56	17	06	7	01	17	16
20	6	33	16	56	6	43	17	06	6	42	17	02	6	46	17	01	6	46	16	55	6	59	17	04	7	03	17	14
21	6	35	16	54	6	45	17	04	6	44	17	00	6	47	16	59	6	48	16	53	7	01	17	02	7	04	17	11
22	6	37	16	52	6	46	17	02	6	46	16	58	6	49	16	57	6	50	16	51	7	03	16	59	7	06	17	09
23	6	38	16	50	6	48	17	00	6	48	16	56	6	51	16	55	6	52	16	49	7	05	16	57	7	08	17	07
24	6	40	16	48	6	50	16	58	6	49	16	53	6	53	16	53	6	54	16	46	7	07	16	54	7	10	17	05
25	6	42	16	46	6	52	16	56	6	51	16	51	6	55	16	50	6	56	16	44	7	09	16	52	7	12	17	02
26	6	44	16	44	6	53	16	54	6	53	16	49	6	57	16	48	6	58	16	42	7	11	16	50	7	14	17	00
27	6	45	16	42	6	55	16	52	6	55	16	47	6	59	16	46	7	00	16	40	7	13	16	48	7	16	16	58
28	6	47	16	41	6	57	16	51	6	57	16	45	7	01	16	44	7	02	16	37	7	15	16	45	7	18	16	56
29	6	49	16	39	6	59	16	49	6	59	16	43	7	03	16	42	7	04	16	35	7	17	16	43	7	20	16	54
30	6	51	16	37	7	00	16	47	7	00	16	42	7	04	16	40	7	06	16	33	7	19	16	41	7	22	16	52
31	6	52	16	35	7	02	16	45	7	02	16	40	7	06	16	38	7	08	16	31	7	22	16	39	7	24	16	50

THE MOON

Day	Diam	Phase	Age	Rise		Rise		Transit		Set		Set	
	'	%	d	52°	52°	56°	56°			52°	52°	56°	56°
				h	m	h	m	h	m	h	m	h	m
2	30.6	23	25.0	0	18	–	–	8	38	16	41	16	59
3	31.2	15	26.0	1	36	1	19	9	28	17	1	17	15
4	31.6	8	27.0	2	58	2	46	10	18	17	19	17	26
5	32.0	3	28.0	4	20	4	15	11	7	17	34	17	37
6	32.4	0	29.0	5	45	5	45	11	56	17	50	17	47
7	32.6	0	0.5	7	11	7	18	12	46	18	6	17	58
8	32.8	3	1.5	8	40	8	52	13	40	18	25	18	11
9	32.8	9	2.5	10	10	10	30	14	36	18	50	18	29
10	32.8	17	3.5	11	39	12	5	15	35	19	24	18	57
11	32.6	26	4.5	12	59	13	32	16	36	20	10	19	37
12	32.4	37	5.5	14	6	14	39	17	38	21	11	20	38
13	32.0	49	6.5	14	55	15	25	18	37	22	24	21	56
14	31.8	60	7.5	15	31	15	54	19	33	23	44	23	21
15	31.4	70	8.5	15	56	16	14	20	25	–	–	–	–
16	31.0	79	9.5	16	15	16	28	21	13	1	4	0	48
17	30.8	87	10.5	16	31	16	38	21	58	2	22	2	12
18	30.6	93	11.5	16	44	16	46	22	40	3	38	3	33
19	30.2	97	12.5	16	57	16	54	23	23	4	52	4	52
20	30.0	100	13.5	17	10	17	3	–	–	6	4	6	9
21	29.8	100	14.5	17	24	17	12	0	5	7	16	7	27
22	29.6	98	15.5	17	40	17	23	0	47	8	29	8	44
23	29.6	95	16.5	18	2	17	39	1	32	9	40	10	0
24	29.4	90	17.5	18	28	18	2	2	18	10	50	11	17
25	29.4	84	18.5	19	5	18	32	3	6	11	54	12	27
26	29.6	76	19.5	19	51	19	18	3	56	12	52	13	26
27	29.6	68	20.5	20	49	20	18	4	47	13	39	14	10
28	30.0	58	21.5	21	58	21	30	5	38	14	16	14	43
29	30.2	49	22.5	23	12	22	51	6	28	14	44	15	5
30	30.6	39	23.5	–	–	–	–	7	18	15	5	15	21
31	31.2	29	24.5	0	30	0	15	8	6	15	23	15	34

THE PLANETS

MERCURY

Day	R.A. h	m	s	Dec. °	Mag.	Diam. "	Phase %	Rise h	m	s	Transit h	m	s	Set h	m	s
1	13	25	46	-12.9	+1.5	9.5	17	7	50	31	12	40	9	17	31	43
6	13	12	24	-10.8	+3.3	10.2	4	7	3	53	12	6	12	17	11	28
11	12	53	14	-7.3	+4.7	10.0	1	6	5	21	11	27	46	16	53	31
16	12	39	58	-4.1	+1.7	9.1	13	5	16	16	10	56	32	16	39	16
21	12	41	23	-2.9	+0.1	7.8	36	4	53	2	10	40	4	16	28	9
26	12	56	42	-3.9	-0.6	6.7	59	4	55	4	10	36	54	16	18	39
31	13	20	35	-6.2	-0.8	6.0	76	5	13	2	10	41	44	16	9	45

VENUS

Day	R.A. h	m	s	Dec. °	Mag.	Diam. "	Phase %	Rise h	m	s	Transit h	m	s	Set h	m	s
1	15	19	27	-20.6	-4.2	20.2	62	10	38	35	14	37	57	18	37	0
6	15	42	11	-22.3	-4.2	21.1	60	10	53	30	14	40	52	18	28	1
11	16	5	6	-23.7	-4.3	22.1	58	11	7	32	14	43	58	18	20	17
16	16	28	8	-24.9	-4.3	23.2	56	11	20	16	14	47	8	18	14	0
21	16	51	7	-25.9	-4.3	24.4	54	11	31	17	14	50	14	18	9	18
26	17	13	54	-26.6	-4.4	25.7	51	11	40	11	14	53	7	18	6	15
31	17	36	19	-27.0	-4.4	27.2	48	11	46	37	14	55	33	18	4	49

MARS

Day	R.A. h	m	s	Dec. °	Mag.	Diam. "	Rise h	m	s	Transit h	m	s	Set h	m	s
1	12	39	21	-3.5	+1.7	3.6	6	14	14	11	58	6	17	41	39
6	12	51	24	-4.8	+1.6	3.6	6	13	52	11	50	27	17	26	44
11	13	3	33	-6.1	+1.6	3.6	6	13	35	11	42	54	17	11	56
16	13	15	48	-7.4	+1.6	3.6	6	13	24	11	35	28	16	57	15
21	13	28	11	-8.6	+1.6	3.6	6	13	19	11	28	9	16	42	43
26	13	40	42	-9.9	+1.7	3.6	6	13	21	11	20	59	16	28	21
31	13	53	23	-11.1	+1.7	3.6	6	13	30	11	13	58	16	14	10

JUPITER

Day	R.A. h	m	s	Dec. °	Mag.	Diam. "	Rise h	m	s	Transit h	m	s	Set h	m	s
1	21	42	16	-15.0	-2.7	46.3	16	22	20	20	59	22	1	39	50
6	21	41	18	-15.1	-2.7	45.7	16	2	10	20	38	44	1	18	45
11	21	40	40	-15.1	-2.6	45.0	15	42	8	20	18	25	0	58	10
16	21	40	20	-15.2	-2.6	44.4	15	22	15	19	58	26	0	38	4
21	21	40	22	-15.1	-2.6	43.7	15	2	31	19	38	46	0	18	29
26	21	40	40	-15.1	-2.5	43.0	14	42	53	19	19	26	23	59	24
31	21	41	20	-15.0	-2.5	42.3	14	23	30	19	0	25	23	37	27

Diam. = Equatorial. Polar Diam. is 94% of Equatorial Diam.

SATURN

Day	R.A. h	m	s	Dec. °	Mag.	Diam. "	Rise h	m	s	Transit h	m	s	Set h	m	s
1	20	38	20	-19.3	+0.5	17.7	15	46	41	19	55	21	0	7	52
6	20	38	4	-19.3	+0.5	17.5	15	26	52	19	35	26	23	47	50
11	20	37	59	-19.3	+0.5	17.4	15	7	9	19	15	41	23	24	23
16	20	38	4	-19.3	+0.5	17.2	14	47	32	18	56	4	23	4	51
21	20	38	19	-19.3	+0.6	17.1	14	28	1	18	36	42	22	45	33
26	20	38	45	-19.3	+0.6	16.9	14	8	36	18	17	28	22	26	30
31	20	39	21	-19.3	+0.6	16.8	13	49	17	17	58	24	22	7	41

Diam. = Equatorial. Polar Diam. is 90% of Equatorial Diam.
Rings – major axis 39", minor axis 13", Tilt 19°

URANUS

Day	R.A. h	m	s	Dec. °	Mag.	Diam. "	Rise h	m	s	Transit h	m	s	Set h	m	s
1	2	47	6	+15.7	+5.7	3.7	18	29	10	2	6	58	9	40	54
6	2	46	28	+15.6	+5.7	3.7	18	9	11	1	46	40	9	20	17
11	2	45	47	+15.6	+5.7	3.7	17	49	10	1	26	19	8	59	36
16	2	45	3	+15.5	+5.7	3.7	17	29	8	1	5	56	8	38	52
21	2	44	17	+15.5	+5.7	3.8	17	9	5	0	45	30	8	18	4
26	2	43	30	+15.4	+5.7	3.8	16	49	2	0	25	3	7	57	14
31	2	42	41	+15.3	+5.6	3.8	16	28	57	0	4	36	7	36	23

NEPTUNE

Day	R.A. h	m	s	Dec. °	Mag.	Diam. "	Rise h	m	s	Transit h	m	s	Set h	m	s
1	23	30	1	-4.5	+7.8	2.4	17	8	27	22	46	29	4	28	26
6	23	29	32	-4.6	+7.8	2.4	16	48	35	22	26	21	4	8	1
11	23	29	5	-4.6	+7.8	2.4	16	28	45	22	6	14	3	47	39
16	23	28	40	-4.7	+7.8	2.3	16	8	54	21	46	9	3	27	19
21	23	28	16	-4.7	+7.8	2.3	15	49	5	21	26	6	3	7	2
26	23	27	54	-4.7	+7.8	2.3	15	29	16	21	6	5	2	46	48
31	23	27	34	-4.8	+7.8	2.3	15	9	28	20	46	5	2	26	38

THE NIGHT SKY

Mercury moves into the morning sky after inferior conjunction on the 9th and should be picked up around October 15th. However, your best chance of spotting the fleet-footed world is towards the end of the month as it gains in height daily and rapidly brightens then too.

Mercury is at greatest elongation west on the 25th and rises about an hour before the Sun. The magnitude -0.5 planet is then almost 10° above the eastern horizon at the beginning of civil twilight.

Venus is at greatest eastern elongation on the 29th and brightens a little in the evening sky. The main changes will require a scope though as the phase narrows from 62% illuminated on the 1st to 48% lit by Halloween.

Venus will be an exact half phase (dichotomy) on the 28th and reaches greatest elongation east a day later. Look for the glittering planet near the crescent moon on October 9th and close to Antares around the middle of the month.

Mars (magnitude 1.6) rises 50 minutes before the Sun at the end of October but is still too deep in the dawn glow to be visible. It passes through superior conjunction on the 8th.

Jupiter and Saturn both reach their stationary points this month and then go prograde, when their eastward motion on the celestial sphere resumes. Jupiter (magnitude -2.6) is setting at midnight by the end of October, but look for it near the Moon on the evening of the 15th.

NASA's Lucy mission to Jupiter's Trojan satellites is due to be launched this month. The targets are asteroids that cluster at a Lagrange point both ahead and behind Jupiter in its orbit by 60°. Lucy will use a series of complex manoeuvres to visit one Main Belt asteroid and seven Trojans over a 12 year mission.

Saturn (magnitude 0.5) slips from view even earlier than Jupiter and dips below the horizon by late-evening on the 31st. The Moon is a distant 9° from Saturn on the night of the 13th and the planet is at eastern quadrature on the 30th when telescope users again can see the globe's shadow cast on the rings.

The long awaited James Webb Space Telescope (JWST) is currently slated for launch on October 31st this year. Cost over-runs and technology challenges nearly scuppered the project, but JWST will be a worthy successor to the Hubble Space Telescope.

JWST has a 6.5-metre segmented primary mirror that will unfold as flower petals when it reaches its working orbit 1.2 million kilometres from Earth. Observations will largely be conducted in the infrared, allowing JWST to search for the first stars and infant galaxies, as well as study the evolution of proto-solar systems. The telescope will also be able to reveal more about the atmospheres of known extra-solar planets, maybe even finding they contain the building blocks of life.

November 2021

ELEVENTH MONTH, 30 DAYS. *Novem* (nine), ninth month of Roman pre-Julian calendar

1	*Monday*	Greenwich Mean Time was adopted as the standard against which the world's time zones were set 1884	week 44 day 305
2	*Tuesday*	Howard Hughes flew his eight-engine wooden aeroplane *Spruce Goose* for one minute 1947	306
3	*Wednesday*	The Soviet Union launched the first living creature into space, a dog named Laika 1957	307
4	*Thursday*	The entrance to Tutankhamun's tomb was discovered by the British archaeologist Howard Carter 1922	308
5	*Friday*	Guy Fawkes was found guarding explosives beneath the House of Lords during the Gunpowder Plot 1605	309
6	*Saturday*	George Eliot's first story, one of the *Scenes of Clerical Life*, was submitted for publication 1856	310
7	*Sunday*	Marie Curie, chemist and physicist who discovered radium and won two Nobel prizes *b.* 1867	311
8	*Monday*	The Bodleian library opened to scholars at Oxford University 1602	week 45 day 312
9	*Tuesday*	Physicist Gordon Gould wrote down the principles for the laser, but failed to patent his idea 1957	313
10	*Wednesday*	Fred Cohen presented his creation, the computer virus, to a security seminar in the USA 1983	314
11	*Thursday*	The signing of the Armistice at 11am marked the end of the First World War 1918	315
12	*Friday*	The Abbey Road recording studios in London were opened by Sir Edward Elgar 1931	316
13	*Saturday*	An aeroplane spread pellets of dry ice at 4,000m creating artificial snow for the first time 1946	317
14	*Sunday*	The Scottish Nationalist Party contested its first general election 1935	318
15	*Monday*	Brazil became a republic when the second and last emperor, Pedro II, was deposed in a military coup 1889	week 46 day 319
16	*Tuesday*	The discovery of Americium (atomic number 95) and curium (96), two new elements, was announced 1945	320
17	*Wednesday*	English-language bookshop and lending library Shakespeare and Company opened in Paris 1919	321
18	*Thursday*	Russia ratified the Kyoto Protocol on climate change 2004	322
19	*Friday*	The first National Lottery draw took place 1994	323
20	*Saturday*	Russia launcheed the first module of the International Space Station from Kazakhstan 1998	324
21	*Sunday*	Voltaire spent his 23rd birthday incarcerated in the Bastille 1717	325
22	*Monday*	Concorde began operating flights between New York and Europe with a flight time under 3.5 hours 1977	week 47 day 326
23	*Tuesday*	John Milton's *Areopagitica*, a pamphlet condemning pre-publication censorship, was published 1644	327
24	*Wednesday*	Charles Darwin's *On the Origin of Species* was published 1859	328
25	*Thursday*	Agatha Christie's murder mystery play *The Mousetrap* opens in London and is still running today 1952	329
26	*Friday*	The first Thanksgiving Day was celebrated nationally in America 1789	330
27	*Saturday*	US author Ken Kesey held his first all night 'acid test' party in California 1965	331
28	*Sunday*	The first female voters were allowed at a general election in New Zealand 1893	332
29	*Monday*	Rossini's *The Barber of Seville* became the first opera to be sung in Italian in the USA 1825	week 48 day 333
30	*Tuesday*	Production began on Alfred Hitchcock's film *Psycho* 1959	334

ASTRONOMICAL PHENOMENA

1	-	Sun crosses into Libra
3	19	Mercury 1.2°S of the Moon: Occultation
4	05	Mars 2.3°S of the Moon
4	21	New Moon
4	-	Uranus at opposition
8	05	Venus 1.1°S of the Moon: Occultation
10	04	Mercury 1.0°N of Mars
10	14	Saturn 4.1°N of the Moon
11	17	Jupiter 4.4°N of the Moon
11	13	First Quarter Moon
15	-	Jupiter is at eastern quadrature
17	18	Leonid meteor shower
19	09	Full Moon
19	09	Partial lunar eclipse; mag=0.974
24	-	Sun crosses into Scorpius
26	22	Regulus 5.2°S of the Moon
27	-	Ceres at opposition
27	12	Last Quarter Moon
29	-	Mercury at superior conjunction
30	-	Sun crosses into Ophiuchus

CONSTELLATIONS

The following constellations are visible at midnight throughout the month:

Ursa Major (below the Pole), Cepheus, Cassiopeia, Andromeda, Pegasus, Pisces, Aquarius and Cetus

PHASES OF THE MOON

Phase, Apsides and Node	d	h	m
● New Moon	4	21	15
☽ First Quarter	11	12	46
○ Full Moon	19	8	57
☾ Last Moon	27	12	28
Perigee (358,844 km)	5	22	18
Apogee (406,279 km)	21	2	13

SUNRISE AND SUNSET

	London				Bristol				Birmingham				Manchester				Newcastle				Glasgow				Belfast			
	0°	05'	51°	30'	2°	35'	51°	28'	1°	55'	52°	28'	2°	15'	53°	28'	1°	37'	54°	59'	4°	14'	55°	52'	5°	56'	54°	35'
d	h	m	h	m	h	m	h	m	h	m	h	m	h	m	h	m	h	m	h	m	h	m	h	m	h	m	h	m
1	6	54	16	33	7	04	16	43	7	04	16	38	7	08	16	36	7	10	16	29	7	24	16	37	7	26	16	48
2	6	56	16	31	7	06	16	41	7	06	16	36	7	10	16	34	7	12	16	27	7	26	16	34	7	28	16	45
3	6	58	16	30	7	07	16	40	7	08	16	34	7	12	16	32	7	14	16	25	7	28	16	32	7	30	16	43
4	6	59	16	28	7	09	16	38	7	10	16	32	7	14	16	30	7	16	16	23	7	30	16	30	7	32	16	42
5	7	01	16	26	7	11	16	36	7	11	16	30	7	16	16	29	7	18	16	21	7	32	16	28	7	34	16	40
6	7	03	16	24	7	13	16	35	7	13	16	29	7	18	16	27	7	21	16	19	7	34	16	26	7	36	16	38
7	7	05	16	23	7	15	16	33	7	15	16	27	7	20	16	25	7	23	16	17	7	36	16	24	7	38	16	36
8	7	06	16	21	7	16	16	31	7	17	16	25	7	22	16	23	7	25	16	15	7	39	16	22	7	40	16	34
9	7	08	16	20	7	18	16	30	7	19	16	24	7	23	16	22	7	27	16	13	7	41	16	20	7	42	16	32
10	7	10	16	18	7	20	16	28	7	20	16	22	7	25	16	20	7	29	16	11	7	43	16	18	7	44	16	30
11	7	12	16	17	7	22	16	27	7	22	16	20	7	27	16	18	7	31	16	10	7	45	16	16	7	46	16	29
12	7	13	16	15	7	23	16	25	7	24	16	19	7	29	16	17	7	33	16	08	7	47	16	15	7	48	16	27
13	7	15	16	14	7	25	16	24	7	26	16	17	7	31	16	15	7	35	16	06	7	49	16	13	7	50	16	25
14	7	17	16	12	7	27	16	22	7	28	16	16	7	33	16	13	7	37	16	05	7	51	16	11	7	52	16	24
15	7	19	16	11	7	28	16	21	7	29	16	15	7	35	16	12	7	39	16	03	7	53	16	09	7	54	16	22
16	7	20	16	09	7	30	16	20	7	31	16	13	7	37	16	10	7	41	16	01	7	55	16	08	7	56	16	20
17	7	22	16	08	7	32	16	18	7	33	16	12	7	38	16	09	7	43	16	00	7	57	16	06	7	58	16	19
18	7	24	16	07	7	34	16	17	7	35	16	10	7	40	16	08	7	44	15	58	7	59	16	05	8	00	16	17
19	7	25	16	06	7	35	16	16	7	37	16	09	7	42	16	06	7	46	15	57	8	01	16	03	8	02	16	16
20	7	27	16	05	7	37	16	15	7	38	16	08	7	44	16	05	7	48	15	55	8	03	16	02	8	04	16	15
21	7	29	16	03	7	38	16	14	7	40	16	07	7	46	16	04	7	50	15	54	8	05	16	00	8	06	16	13
22	7	30	16	02	7	40	16	12	7	42	16	06	7	47	16	03	7	52	15	53	8	07	15	59	8	07	16	12
23	7	32	16	01	7	42	16	11	7	43	16	05	7	49	16	01	7	54	15	52	8	09	15	57	8	09	16	11
24	7	33	16	00	7	43	16	10	7	45	16	03	7	51	16	00	7	56	15	50	8	11	15	56	8	11	16	10
25	7	35	15	59	7	45	16	10	7	47	16	02	7	52	15	59	7	57	15	49	8	13	15	55	8	13	16	08
26	7	36	15	59	7	46	16	09	7	48	16	02	7	54	15	58	7	59	15	48	8	14	15	54	8	14	16	07
27	7	38	15	58	7	48	16	08	7	50	16	01	7	56	15	57	8	01	15	47	8	16	15	53	8	16	16	06
28	7	40	15	57	7	49	16	07	7	51	16	00	7	57	15	56	8	03	15	46	8	18	15	51	8	18	16	05
29	7	41	15	56	7	51	16	06	7	53	15	59	7	59	15	55	8	04	15	45	8	20	15	50	8	19	16	04
30	7	42	15	55	7	52	16	06	7	54	15	58	8	00	15	55	8	06	15	44	8	21	15	49	8	21	16	04

THE MOON

Day	Diam	Phase	Age	Rise		Rise		Transit		Set		Set	
		%	d	52°	52°	56°	56°			52°	52°	56°	56°
	'			h	m	h	m	h	m	h	m	h	m
1	31.6	20	25.5	1	50	1	42	8	54	15	39	15	44
2	32.2	11	26.5	3	13	3	10	9	42	15	54	15	54
3	32.6	5	27.5	4	38	4	41	10	32	16	9	16	4
4	33.0	1	28.5	6	6	6	16	11	24	16	27	16	16
5	33.2	0	29.5	7	38	7	54	12	20	16	49	16	31
6	33.2	2	0.9	9	11	9	35	13	20	17	19	16	55
7	33.2	6	1.9	10	40	11	10	14	23	18	1	17	29
8	33.0	14	2.9	11	55	12	30	15	27	18	59	18	24
9	32.6	23	3.9	12	53	13	25	16	30	20	10	19	38
10	32.2	33	4.9	13	35	13	59	17	28	21	29	21	6
11	31.8	44	5.9	14	2	14	23	18	22	22	52	22	33
12	31.4	55	6.9	14	24	14	37	19	11	-	-	23	59
13	31.0	66	7.9	14	40	14	48	19	57	0	11	-	-
14	30.6	75	8.9	14	53	14	57	20	40	1	27	1	21
15	30.2	83	9.9	15	6	15	5	21	22	2	41	2	39
16	30.0	90	10.9	15	18	15	13	22	3	3	53	3	56
17	29.8	95	11.9	15	31	15	21	22	45	5	4	5	13
18	29.6	98	12.9	15	47	15	31	23	29	6	16	6	30
19	29.6	100	13.9	16	6	15	45	-	-	7	28	7	47
20	29.4	100	14.9	16	30	16	5	0	14	8	39	9	2
21	29.4	98	15.9	17	3	16	32	1	2	9	46	10	16
22	29.4	94	16.9	17	45	17	13	1	51	10	46	11	20
23	29.6	89	17.9	18	39	18	8	2	41	11	37	12	9
24	29.6	82	18.9	19	43	19	15	3	32	12	17	12	45
25	29.8	74	19.9	20	55	20	32	4	23	12	47	13	10
26	30.2	65	20.9	22	10	21	53	5	11	13	10	13	28
27	30.6	56	21.9	23	27	23	16	5	58	13	29	13	41
28	31.0	45	22.9	-	-	-	-	6	45	13	44	13	52
29	31.4	35	23.9	0	46	0	40	7	31	13	59	14	1
30	32.0	25	24.9	2	7	2	7	8	18	14	13	14	10

THE PLANETS

MERCURY

Day	R.A.			Dec.	Mag.	Diam.	Phase	Rise			Transit			Set		
	h	m	s	°		"	%	h	m	s	h	m	s	h	m	s
1	13	25	58	-6.8	-0.8	5.8	79	5	17	45	10	43	15	16	8	0
6	13	54	33	-9.9	-0.9	5.4	89	5	44	24	10	52	24	15	59	28
11	14	24	46	-13.0	-0.9	5.1	94	6	13	37	11	3	2	15	51	30
16	14	55	51	-16.0	-0.9	4.9	98	6	43	32	11	14	27	15	44	29
21	15	27	33	-18.6	-1.0	4.7	99	7	13	12	11	26	30	15	39	0
26	15	59	54	-21.0	-1.2	4.7	100	7	41	57	11	39	10	15	35	43

VENUS

Day	R.A.			Dec.	Mag.	Diam.	Phase	Rise			Transit			Set		
	h	m	s	°		"	%	h	m	s	h	m	s	h	m	s
1	17	40	44	-27.1	-4.4	27.5	48	11	47	35	14	55	58	18	4	42
6	18	2	23	-27.2	-4.5	29.2	46	11	50	40	14	57	37	18	4	59
11	18	23	8	-27.2	-4.5	31.2	43	11	50	42	14	58	17	18	6	21
16	18	42	40	-26.8	-4.6	33.3	40	11	47	33	14	57	40	18	8	18
21	19	0	40	-26.3	-4.6	35.8	36	11	41	6	14	55	25	18	10	15
26	19	16	46	-25.6	-4.6	38.6	33	11	31	20	14	51	11	18	11	31

MARS

Day	R.A.			Dec.	Mag.	Diam.	Rise			Transit			Set		
	h	m	s	°		"	h	m	s	h	m	s	h	m	s
1	13	55	56	-11.4	+1.7	3.6	6	13	33	11	12	35	16	11	22
6	14	8	49	-12.6	+1.6	3.6	6	13	50	11	5	47	15	57	28
11	14	21	52	-13.7	+1.6	3.7	6	14	13	10	59	8	15	43	49
16	14	35	7	-14.8	+1.6	3.7	6	14	41	10	52	41	15	30	28
21	14	48	33	-15.9	+1.6	3.7	6	15	13	10	46	26	15	17	27
26	15	2	11	-16.9	+1.6	3.7	6	15	47	10	40	23	15	4	48

JUPITER

Day	R.A.			Dec.	Mag.	Diam.	Rise			Transit			Set		
	h	m	s	°		"	h	m	s	h	m	s	h	m	s
1	21	41	30	-15.0	-2.5	42.2	14	19	38	18	56	39	23	33	47
6	21	42	32	-14.9	-2.5	41.5	14	0	23	18	38	1	23	15	46
11	21	43	53	-14.8	-2.4	40.8	13	41	16	18	19	41	22	58	13
16	21	45	32	-14.6	-2.4	40.2	13	22	18	18	1	40	22	41	8
21	21	47	27	-14.5	-2.4	39.5	13	3	28	17	43	55	22	24	28
26	21	49	38	-14.3	-2.3	38.9	12	44	45	17	26	26	22	8	12

Diam. = Equatorial. Polar Diam. is 94% of Equatorial Diam.

SATURN

Day	R.A.			Dec.	Mag.	Diam.	Rise			Transit			Set		
	h	m	s	°		"	h	m	s	h	m	s	h	m	s
1	20	39	29	-19.2	+0.6	16.8	13	45	25	17	54	36	22	3	57
6	20	40	17	-19.2	+0.6	16.6	13	26	13	17	35	44	21	45	25
11	20	41	14	-19.1	+0.6	16.5	13	7	5	17	17	2	21	27	7
16	20	42	21	-19.1	+0.7	16.4	12	48	3	16	58	29	21	9	3
21	20	43	36	-19.0	+0.7	16.2	12	29	6	16	40	4	20	51	11
26	20	45	0	-18.9	+0.7	16.1	12	10	13	16	21	48	20	33	32

Diam. = Equatorial. Polar Diam. is 90% of Equatorial Diam.
Rings – major axis 37", minor axis 12", Tilt 19°

URANUS

Day	R.A.			Dec.	Mag.	Diam.	Rise			Transit			Set		
	h	m	s	°		"	h	m	s	h	m	s	h	m	s
1	2	42	31	+15.3	+5.6	3.8	16	24	56	0	0	30	7	32	12
6	2	41	42	+15.3	+5.6	3.8	16	4	52	23	36	8	7	11	20
11	2	40	53	+15.2	+5.7	3.8	15	44	47	23	15	39	6	50	28
16	2	40	5	+15.1	+5.7	3.8	15	24	43	22	55	12	6	29	37
21	2	39	18	+15.1	+5.7	3.8	15	4	39	22	34	45	6	8	47
26	2	38	33	+15.0	+5.7	3.7	14	44	36	22	14	20	5	48	1

NEPTUNE

Day	R.A.			Dec.	Mag.	Diam.	Rise			Transit			Set		
	h	m	s	°		"	h	m	s	h	m	s	h	m	s
1	23	27	31	-4.8	+7.8	2.3	15	5	30	20	42	6	2	22	36
6	23	27	14	-4.8	+7.8	2.3	14	45	43	20	22	10	2	2	31
11	23	26	60	-4.8	+7.9	2.3	14	25	57	20	2	16	1	42	30
16	23	26	49	-4.8	+7.9	2.3	14	6	12	19	42	25	1	22	33
21	23	26	41	-4.9	+7.9	2.3	13	46	29	19	22	38	1	2	42
26	23	26	35	-4.9	+7.9	2.3	13	26	46	19	2	53	0	42	55

THE NIGHT SKY

Mercury is visible in the morning sky up to around mid-month but is best seen in the first week when the planet rises nearly two hours before the Sun and glimmers at mag. -0.8.

Mercury passes about 4° from Spica in Virgo on November 2nd and the lunar crescent is 38 hours from New when 6° to the upper right of the planet on the 3rd. Mercury is then at superior conjunction with the Sun on the 29th when it will not be visible.

Venus (magnitude -4.9) is a brilliant 'star' in the southwest these evenings and sets 2½ hours after the Sun on the 30th. The planet passes below M8, the Lagoon Nebula, in Sagittarius on the 5th, and can be found to the lower right of the Moon on the 8th. The phase is now narrowing towards a plump crescent that can be seen towards the end of the month in a telescope.

Mars (magnitude 1.6) gradually pulls clear of the solar glare in the morning sky and rises 1½ hours before the Sun by the end of the month. On the morning of the 4th the Moon is only 14½ hours from New when it is 2° from Mars. It will be a challenge to see such a thin lunar crescent but it is possible given a clear east-southeast horizon.

Mars and magnitude -0.9 Mercury lie just 1° apart on the morning of the 10th, but separate quite quickly. The Red Planet then passes quite close to the magnitude 2.8 star Alpha Librae on the 22nd.

Jupiter (magnitude -2.4) is at eastern quadrature on the 15th when the planet's disk looks gibbous. It is an evening sky object setting at midnight on the 1st and 1½ hours earlier at the end of November. Jupiter is 5° above the first quarter moon on the 11th.

Saturn (magnitude 0.7) can also be found in Capricornus, and is on view until late evening. The Moon is near Saturn on the 10th.

Uranus (magnitude 5.6) is at opposition on November 5th in the southern part of Aries. That night, it is the rightmost 'star' of three-in-a-row similarly bright points of light comprising Sigma and Omicron Arietis, along with Uranus. All fit in the same low power field of view of standard binoculars. On a night of good clear skies, try spot Uranus with the unaided eye from a dark site.

A partial lunar eclipse on the morning of the 19th is in progress at moonset from the UK so we only see the initial stages of the event. The Moon passes south of Earth's shadow, so the northern part of the disk is more dimmed.

See **W** eclipsewise.com/lunar/lunar.html and **W** timeanddate.com for timings. The eclipsed Moon is about 6° below the Pleiades star cluster as they sink in the west, adding some drama to photographs of the event.

December 2021

TWELFTH MONTH, 31 DAYS. *Decem* (ten), tenth month of Roman pre-Julian calendar

1	*Wednesday*	British and French workers joined the two halves of the Channel tunnel 1990	day 335
2	*Thursday*	St Paul's Cathedral opened 1697	336
3	*Friday*	The Malta summit brought the Cold War to a close 1989	337
4	*Saturday*	Treaty of Paris, made by King Henry III and King Louis IX of France, ends 100 years of conflict 1259	338
5	*Sunday*	The *Mary Celeste* was found abandoned 1872	339

6	*Monday*	Johann Palisa, Austrian astronomer known for his discovery of 122 asteroids *b.* 1848	week 49 day 340
7	*Tuesday*	NASA launches *Apollo 17*, the sixth and last mission to land on the Moon 1972	341
8	*Wednesday*	The first female actor appeared in a Shakespeare production, as Desdemona in *Othello* 1660	342
9	*Thursday*	The *American Minerva*, New York City's first daily newspaper, was founded 1793	343
10	*Friday*	US president Woodrow Wilson won the Nobel Peace Prize 1920	344
11	*Saturday*	The first dental anaesthetic, nitrous oxide ('laughing gas'), was used for a tooth extraction 1844	345
12	*Sunday*	Kenya became independent from the United Kingdom 1963	346

13	*Monday*	Gordo, a monkey, was lost in the Atlantic due to a technical problem after a 482km space journey 1958	week 50 day 347
14	*Tuesday*	Max Planck presents his quantum theory to the German Physical Society in Berlin 1900	348
15	*Wednesday*	The Chernobyl nuclear plant in Ukraine was shut down, 14 years after the infamous disaster 2000	349
16	*Thursday*	The Boston Tea Party in protest against taxation brought in by the British parliament took place 1773	350
17	*Friday*	Orville Wright made the first powered flight 1903	351
18	*Saturday*	The first two volumes of Laurence Sterne's humorous novel *Tristram Shandy* were published 1759	352
19	*Sunday*	Charles Dickens' novella *A Christmas Carol*, featuring the miserly Ebenezer Scrooge, was published 1843	353

20	*Monday*	New York's Broadway became known as the 'Great White Way' after being lit by electricity 1880	week 51 day 354
21	*Tuesday*	The 11-member Commonwealth of Independent States was formed 1991	355
22	*Wednesday*	Electric lights were first used to decorate Christmas trees by Edward Johnson 1882	356
23	*Thursday*	Vincent Van Gogh cut off part of his right ear 1888	357
24	*Friday*	US General Dwight D. Eisenhower was appointed Supreme Allied Commander 1943	358
25	*Saturday*	King George V made the first royal Christmas day broadcast 1932	359
26	*Sunday*	Marie Curie, and her husband Pierre, announced the discovery of radium 1898	360

27	*Monday*	HMS *Beagle* set sail from Plymouth with a young Charles Darwin on board 1831	week 52 day 361
28	*Tuesday*	The first commercial movie screening, *Workers Leaving The Lumière Factory in Lyon*, took place 1895	362
29	*Wednesday*	London experienced its worst night of bombing in the Blitz 1940	363
30	*Thursday*	Percy Bysshe Shelley married writer Mary Wollstonecraft Godwin in London 1816	364
31	*Friday*	The farthing ceased to be legal tender 1960	365

ASTRONOMICAL PHENOMENA

3	00	Mars 0.7°S of the Moon
4	08	Total solar eclipse; mag=1.037
4	08	New Moon
7	01	Venus 1.9°N of the Moon
8	02	Saturn 4.2°N of the Moon
9	06	Jupiter 4.5°N of the Moon
9	18	Venus at greatest brilliancy
11	02	First Quarter Moon
11	18	Venus 0.08°N of Pluto
14	07	Geminid meteor shower
19	05	Full Moon
19	-	Sun crosses into Sagittarius
21	16	Winter solstice
22	15	Ursid meteor shower
24	05	Regulus 5.1°S of the Moon
27	09	Mars 4.5°N of Antares
27	02	Last Quarter Moon
29	01	Mercury 4.2°S of Venus
31	20	Mars 1.0°N of Moon: Occultation

CONSTELLATIONS

The following constellations are visible at midnight throughout the month:
Ursa Major (below the Pole), Ursa Minor (below the Pole), Cassiopeia, Andromeda, Perseus, Triangulum, Aries, Taurus, Cetus and Eridanus

PHASES OF THE MOON

Phase, Apsides and Node	d	h	m
● New Moon	4	7	43
◑ First Quarter	11	1	36
○ Full Moon	19	4	35
◑ Last Quarter	27	2	24
Perigee (356,794 km)	4	10	4
Apogee (406,320 km)	18	2	15

SUNRISE AND SUNSET

	London				Bristol				Birmingham				Manchester				Newcastle				Glasgow				Belfast			
	0°	05'	51°	30'	2°	35'	51°	28'	1°	55'	52°	28'	2°	15'	53°	28'	1°	37'	54°	59'	4°	14'	55°	52'	5°	56'	54°	35'
d	h	m	h	m	h	m	h	m	h	m	h	m	h	m	h	m	h	m	h	m	h	m	h	m	h	m	h	m
1	7	44	15	55	7	54	16	05	7	56	15	58	8	02	15	54	8	08	15	43	8	23	15	49	8	23	16	03
2	7	45	15	54	7	55	16	04	7	57	15	57	8	03	15	53	8	09	15	42	8	25	15	48	8	24	16	02
3	7	47	15	54	7	56	16	04	7	58	15	56	8	05	15	53	8	11	15	42	8	26	15	47	8	26	16	01
4	7	48	15	53	7	58	16	03	8	00	15	56	8	06	15	52	8	12	15	41	8	28	15	46	8	27	16	01
5	7	49	15	53	7	59	16	03	8	01	15	55	8	08	15	52	8	14	15	40	8	29	15	46	8	29	16	00
6	7	50	15	52	8	00	16	02	8	02	15	55	8	09	15	51	8	15	15	40	8	31	15	45	8	30	16	00
7	7	52	15	52	8	01	16	02	8	04	15	55	8	10	15	51	8	16	15	39	8	32	15	45	8	31	15	59
8	7	53	15	52	8	02	16	02	8	05	15	54	8	11	15	50	8	18	15	39	8	34	15	44	8	33	15	59
9	7	54	15	52	8	04	16	02	8	06	15	54	8	13	15	50	8	19	15	39	8	35	15	44	8	34	15	58
10	7	55	15	51	8	05	16	02	8	07	15	54	8	14	15	50	8	20	15	38	8	36	15	43	8	35	15	58
11	7	56	15	51	8	06	16	01	8	08	15	54	8	15	15	50	8	21	15	38	8	37	15	43	8	36	15	58
12	7	57	15	51	8	07	16	01	8	09	15	54	8	16	15	50	8	22	15	38	8	38	15	43	8	37	15	58
13	7	58	15	51	8	08	16	01	8	10	15	54	8	17	15	50	8	23	15	38	8	39	15	43	8	38	15	58
14	7	59	15	51	8	09	16	01	8	11	15	54	8	18	15	50	8	24	15	38	8	40	15	43	8	39	15	58
15	8	00	15	51	8	09	16	02	8	12	15	54	8	19	15	50	8	25	15	38	8	41	15	43	8	40	15	58
16	8	00	15	52	8	10	16	02	8	13	15	54	8	20	15	50	8	26	15	38	8	42	15	43	8	41	15	58
17	8	01	15	52	8	11	16	02	8	13	15	54	8	20	15	50	8	27	15	38	8	43	15	43	8	42	15	58
18	8	02	15	52	8	12	16	02	8	14	15	55	8	21	15	50	8	28	15	39	8	44	15	43	8	42	15	58
19	8	02	15	53	8	12	16	03	8	15	15	55	8	22	15	51	8	28	15	39	8	45	15	44	8	43	15	59
20	8	03	15	53	8	13	16	03	8	15	15	55	8	22	15	51	8	29	15	39	8	45	15	44	8	44	15	59
21	8	04	15	53	8	13	16	04	8	16	15	56	8	23	15	52	8	29	15	40	8	46	15	45	8	44	16	00
22	8	04	15	54	8	14	16	04	8	16	15	56	8	23	15	52	8	30	15	40	8	46	15	45	8	45	16	00
23	8	05	15	55	8	14	16	05	8	17	15	57	8	24	15	53	8	30	15	41	8	47	15	46	8	45	16	01
24	8	05	15	55	8	15	16	05	8	17	15	57	8	24	15	53	8	31	15	42	8	47	15	46	8	46	16	01
25	8	05	15	56	8	15	16	06	8	18	15	58	8	24	15	54	8	31	15	42	8	47	15	47	8	46	16	02
26	8	05	15	57	8	15	16	07	8	18	15	59	8	25	15	55	8	31	15	43	8	47	15	48	8	46	16	03
27	8	06	15	57	8	16	16	08	8	18	16	00	8	25	15	56	8	31	15	44	8	48	15	49	8	46	16	04
28	8	06	15	58	8	16	16	08	8	18	16	01	8	25	15	56	8	32	15	45	8	48	15	50	8	46	16	05
29	8	06	15	59	8	16	16	09	8	18	16	01	8	25	15	57	8	32	15	46	8	48	15	51	8	46	16	06
30	8	06	16	00	8	16	16	10	8	18	16	02	8	25	15	58	8	31	15	47	8	48	15	52	8	46	16	07
31	8	06	16	01	8	16	16	11	8	18	16	03	8	25	15	59	8	31	15	48	8	47	15	53	8	46	16	08

THE MOON

Day	Diam	Phase	Age	Rise		Rise		Transit		Set		Set	
	'	%	d	52°	52°	56°	56°			52°	52°	56°	56°
				h	m	h	m	h	m	h	m	h	m
1	32.6	16	25.9	3	31	3	37	9	8	14	29	14	21
2	33.0	8	26.9	4	59	5	12	10	1	14	48	14	34
3	33.4	3	27.9	6	32	6	51	10	58	15	13	14	53
4	33.4	0	28.9	8	5	8	32	12	1	15	48	15	20
5	33.4	1	0.4	9	31	10	2	13	6	16	38	16	7
6	33.2	4	1.4	10	41	11	13	14	12	17	46	17	14
7	33.0	10	2.4	11	31	11	58	15	15	19	7	18	39
8	32.4	19	3.4	12	4	12	27	16	14	20	32	20	11
9	32.0	28	4.4	12	29	12	45	17	6	21	56	21	41
10	31.4	39	5.4	12	47	12	57	17	54	23	15	23	6
11	31.0	49	6.4	13	1	13	7	18	39	-	-	-	-
12	30.6	60	7.4	13	14	13	15	19	21	0	30	0	27
13	30.2	69	8.4	13	26	13	22	20	2	1	43	1	45
14	29.8	78	9.4	13	39	13	31	20	44	2	54	3	1
15	29.6	85	10.4	13	54	13	40	21	27	4	5	4	17
16	29.6	91	11.4	14	12	13	53	22	11	5	17	5	34
17	29.4	96	12.4	14	33	14	10	22	58	6	28	6	50
18	29.4	99	13.4	15	4	14	34	23	47	7	37	8	4
19	29.4	100	14.4	15	43	15	11	-	-	8	40	9	12
20	29.4	99	15.4	16	33	16	2	0	37	9	34	10	6
21	29.6	97	16.4	17	35	17	6	1	29	10	17	10	47
22	29.8	93	17.4	18	44	18	20	2	19	10	50	11	16
23	30.0	87	18.4	19	58	19	39	3	8	11	15	11	35
24	30.2	80	19.4	21	13	21	1	3	55	11	35	11	49
25	30.6	71	20.4	22	29	22	22	4	41	11	51	12	0
26	31.0	62	21.4	23	47	23	45	5	26	12	5	12	9
27	31.4	51	22.4	-	-	-	-	6	11	12	19	12	18
28	31.8	40	23.4	1	6	1	10	6	57	12	33	12	27
29	32.2	30	24.4	2	29	2	39	7	46	12	50	12	38
30	32.6	20	25.4	3	56	4	12	8	40	13	11	12	53
31	33.0	11	26.4	5	28	5	50	9	38	13	39	13	15

THE PLANETS

MERCURY

Day	R.A. h	m	s	Dec. °	Mag.	Diam. "	Phase %	Rise h	m	s	Transit h	m	s	Set h	m	s
1	16	32	56	-22.8	-1.2	4.6	100	8	9	7	11	52	32	15	35	23
6	17	6	40	-24.2	-1.0	4.7	99	8	33	55	12	6	34	15	38	49
11	17	40	60	-25.1	-0.8	4.7	98	8	55	27	12	21	13	15	46	44
16	18	15	44	-25.4	-0.8	4.9	96	9	12	48	12	36	13	15	59	36
21	18	50	30	-25.1	-0.7	5.1	93	9	25	8	12	51	11	16	17	24
26	19	24	34	-24.2	-0.7	5.4	88	9	31	43	13	5	21	16	39	22
31	19	56	43	-22.7	-0.7	5.8	80	9	31	52	13	17	22	17	3	26

VENUS

Day	R.A. h	m	s	Dec. °	Mag.	Diam. "	Phase %	Rise h	m	s	Transit h	m	s	Set h	m	s
1	19	30	35	-24.8	-4.7	41.7	29	11	18	11	14	44	34	18	11	21
6	19	41	43	-23.8	-4.7	45.2	25	11	1	36	14	35	7	18	8	58
11	19	49	38	-22.8	-4.7	49.0	20	10	41	23	14	22	20	18	3	29
16	19	53	48	-21.8	-4.6	53.2	16	10	17	22	14	5	43	17	54	7
21	19	53	45	-20.7	-4.6	57.5	11	9	49	23	13	44	51	17	40	16
26	19	49	17	-19.7	-4.5	61.6	7	9	17	31	13	19	41	17	22	4
31	19	40	41	-18.8	-4.3	65.0	3	8	42	23	12	50	43	16	58	51

MARS

Day	R.A. h	m	s	Dec. °	Mag.	Diam. "	Rise h	m	s	Transit h	m	s	Set h	m	s
1	15	16	3	-17.9	+1.6	3.8	6	16	22	10	34	33	14	52	34
6	15	30	7	-18.8	+1.6	3.8	6	16	55	10	28	56	14	40	48
11	15	44	24	-19.7	+1.6	3.8	6	17	23	10	23	32	14	29	34
16	15	58	54	-20.5	+1.6	3.9	6	17	42	10	18	20	14	18	52
21	16	13	37	-21.2	+1.6	3.9	6	17	49	10	13	21	14	8	48
26	16	28	31	-21.8	+1.6	3.9	6	17	41	10	8	34	13	59	24
31	16	43	38	-22.4	+1.5	4.0	6	17	13	10	3	59	13	50	44

JUPITER

Day	R.A. h	m	s	Dec. °	Mag.	Diam. "	Rise h	m	s	Transit h	m	s	Set h	m	s
1	21	52	5	-14.0	-2.3	38.4	12	26	9	17	9	12	21	52	21
6	21	54	46	-13.8	-2.3	37.8	12	7	40	16	52	12	21	36	51
11	21	57	40	-13.5	-2.2	37.3	11	49	16	16	35	26	21	21	42
16	22	0	47	-13.2	-2.2	36.8	11	30	58	16	18	52	21	6	52
21	22	4	4	-12.9	-2.2	36.3	11	12	45	16	2	29	20	52	19
26	22	7	32	-12.6	-2.2	35.9	10	54	35	15	46	17	20	38	4
31	22	11	10	-12.3	-2.1	35.5	10	36	30	15	30	14	20	24	3

Diam. = Equatorial. Polar Diam. is 94% of Equatorial Diam.

SATURN

Day	R.A. h	m	s	Dec. °	Mag.	Diam. "	Rise h	m	s	Transit h	m	s	Set h	m	s
1	20	46	32	-18.8	+0.7	16.0	11	51	25	16	3	40	20	16	4
6	20	48	12	-18.7	+0.7	15.9	11	32	41	15	45	40	19	58	47
11	20	49	58	-18.6	+0.7	15.8	11	14	0	15	27	46	19	41	40
16	20	51	51	-18.5	+0.7	15.7	10	55	23	15	9	59	19	24	43
21	20	53	49	-18.3	+0.7	15.6	10	36	48	14	52	17	19	7	54
26	20	55	53	-18.2	+0.7	15.5	10	18	14	14	34	41	18	51	13
31	20	58	1	-18.0	+0.7	15.5	9	59	46	14	17	9	18	34	39

Diam. = Equatorial. Polar Diam. is 90% of Equatorial Diam.
Rings – major axis 36", minor axis 11", Tilt 18°

URANUS

Day	R.A. h	m	s	Dec. °	Mag.	Diam. "	Rise h	m	s	Transit h	m	s	Set h	m	s
1	2	37	50	+15.0	+5.7	3.7	14	24	34	21	53	58	5	27	17
6	2	37	9	+14.9	+5.7	3.7	14	4	34	21	33	38	5	6	38
11	2	36	32	+14.9	+5.7	3.7	13	44	35	21	13	21	4	46	3
16	2	35	58	+14.8	+5.7	3.7	13	24	38	20	53	8	4	25	34
21	2	35	29	+14.8	+5.7	3.7	13	4	42	20	32	59	4	5	10
26	2	35	3	+14.8	+5.7	3.7	12	44	49	20	12	54	3	44	53
31	2	34	42	+14.7	+5.7	3.7	12	24	58	19	52	53	3	24	43

NEPTUNE

Day	R.A. h	m	s	Dec. °	Mag.	Diam. "	Rise h	m	s	Transit h	m	s	Set h	m	s
1	23	26	33	-4.9	+7.9	2.3	13	7	5	18	43	11	0	23	13
6	23	26	34	-4.9	+7.9	2.3	12	47	25	18	23	33	0	3	36
11	23	26	39	-4.8	+7.9	2.3	12	27	46	18	3	58	23	40	10
16	23	26	46	-4.8	+7.9	2.3	11	48	32	17	24	57	23	1	22
21	23	26	57	-4.8	+7.9	2.3	11	28	58	17	5	31	22	42	5
26	23	27	11	-4.8	+7.9	2.3	11	9	24	16	46	8	22	22	53
31	23	27	28	-4.7	+7.9	2.3	11	9	24	16	46	8	22	22	53

THE NIGHT SKY

Mercury may be spotted low in the southwest evening sky during the last few days of December when it sets about 1½ hours after the Sun.

Venus climbs to greatest brilliancy (magnitude -4.9) in the evening sky this month as its phase slims to a thin crescent. It sets 2½ hours after the Sun to begin with, but gradually slips from view earlier as the month progresses.

Venus is to the upper left of the crescent moon on the evening of December 6th and the planet - which has faded slightly to magnitude -4.3 at the time - is within 4½° of Mercury on the 28th.

Mars (magnitude 1.6) rises roughly an hour before the Sun all month but will be still somewhat low as twilight brightens. The disk currently measures less than four arc-seconds so is too small to make out any surface detail.

Mars crosses from Libra into Scorpius on the 16th, and then moves into Ophiuchus on Christmas Day. The planet is about 4½° from the red giant star Antares in Scorpius on the morning of the 27th.

The Moon is just 23½ hours from New when it is near Mars on December 2nd. There is then another more distant encounter with the Moon on the morning of the 31st.

Jupiter (magnitude -2.2) and *Saturn* (magnitude 0.7) both set a few hours after the Sun these evenings and remain a fine sight through the telescope during December. Jupiter is near the Moon on the 9th and moves into Aquarius on the 15th. Saturn is about 8° from the Moon on the 7th.

The gibbous moon does not set until just after 3am on the night of the Geminids peak on December 13/14 and so will wash out all but the brighter meteors.

The Geminids are bright and leave persistent trails, possibly due to the nature of the material shed by the asteroid 3200 Phaethon, which is the shower's parent body. The object is sometimes dubbed a 'rock comet' and solar heating at perihelion cracks its surface, causing dust and other particles to be ejected. The composition of a Geminid meteor is therefore a little harder than the fluff from most comets.

The stream is inclined to Earth's orbit and we are presently fording its more dense regions. But that situation will not last as gravitational perturbations by Jupiter shifts the dust trail. In only a few hundred years our encounters with the Geminids will be no more.

Japan's space agency JAXA is developing a mission to be launched towards Phaethon in 2024. DESTINY+ will fly by a number of near-Earth objects, before an encounter with Phaethon in 2028.

The path of the total solar eclipse on December 4th crosses the Antarctic, eighteen years after one from the same saros (152) which was seen by a number of people on various chartered flights.

ECLIPSES 2021

During 2021 there will be four eclipses, two of the Sun and two of the Moon (all times are in GMT):

1. Total Lunar Eclipse on 26 May beginning 11h 19m will be visible from eastern Asia, Australia, Pacific, Americas. Not visible from the UK and Europe.
2. Annular Solar Eclipse on 10 June beginning at 10h 36m. This will be visible as an Annular Eclipse from parts of north Canada, Greenland, eastern Russia, and as a partial eclipse: north North America, UK, Europe, Asia. From the UK it will have a magnitude of 30 per cent in the south and 50 per cent in north Scotland. Member 23 of 80 of Saros 147. Maximum duration 3m 51s.
3. Partial Lunar Eclipse (97 per cent) on 19 November beginning at 9h 04m. Visible Americas, North Europe including UK, eastern Asia, Australia, Pacific. In the UK it is a morning eclipse maximum at 9h 03m, but Moon sets at 7h 30m.
4. Total Solar Eclipse on 4 December beginning at 7h 35m. Visible from the Antarctic peninsula, southern Atlantic and southern Pacific. Member 13 of 70 of Saros 152. Maximum duration 1m 54s.

EXPLANATION OF ASTRONOMICAL DATA

Positions of the heavenly bodies are given only to the degree of accuracy required by amateur astronomers for setting telescopes, or for plotting on celestial globes or star atlases. Where intermediate positions are required, linear interpolation may be employed.

Detailed definitions of the terms used cannot be given here. They must be sought in astronomical literature, the internet or textbooks.

For the Moon, two columns calculated for latitudes 52° and 56°, are devoted to risings and settings, so the range 50° to 58° can be covered by interpolation and extrapolation. The times given in these columns are Greenwich Mean Times for the meridian of Greenwich. An observer west of this meridian must add their longitude (in time) and vice versa.

In accordance with the usual convention in astronomy, + and − indicate respectively north and south latitudes or declinations.

All data are, unless otherwise stated, for 0h Greenwich Mean Time (GMT), ie at the midnight at the beginning of the day named. Allowance must be made for British Summer Time during the period that this is in operation.

PAGE ONE OF EACH MONTH

Under the heading *Astronomical Phenomena* will be found particulars of the more important conjunctions of the Sun, Moon and planets with each other, and also the dates of other astronomical phenomena of special interest.

The Constellations listed each month are those that are near the meridian at the beginning of the month at 22h local mean time. Allowance must be made for British Summer Time when appropriate. The fact that any star crosses the meridian 4m earlier each night or 2h earlier each month may be used, in conjunction with the lists given each month, to find which constellations are favourably placed at any moment.

The principal phases of *the Moon* are the GMTs when the difference between the longitude of the Moon and that of the Sun is 0°, 90°, 180° or 270°. TThe times of perigee and apogee are those when the Moon is nearest to, and farthest from, the Earth, respectively. The nodes or points of intersection of the Moon's orbit and the ecliptic make a complete retrograde circuit of the ecliptic in about 19 years. From a knowledge of the longitude of the ascending node and the inclination, whose value does not vary much from 5°, the path of the Moon among the stars may be plotted on a celestial globe or star atlas.

PAGE TWO OF EACH MONTH

SUNRISE AND SUNSET

The GMTs of sunrise and sunset for seven cities, whose positions in longitude (W.) and latitude (N.) are given immediately below the name.

The times of sunrise and sunset are those when the Sun's upper limb, as affected by refraction, is on the true horizon of an observer at sea-level. Assuming the mean refraction to be 34', and the Sun's semi-diameter to be 16', the time given is that when the true zenith distance of the Sun's centre is 90°+34'+16' or 90° 50', or, in other words, when the depression of the Sun's centre below the true horizon is 50'. The upper limb is then 34' below the true horizon, but is brought there by refraction. An observer on a ship might see the Sun for a minute or so longer, because of the dip of the horizon, while another viewing the sunset over hills or mountains would record an earlier time. Nevertheless, the moment when the true zenith distance of the Sun's centre is 90° 50' is a precise time dependent only on the latitude and longitude of the place, and independent of its altitude above sea-level, the contour of its horizon, the vagaries of refraction or the small seasonal change in the Sun's diameter; this moment is suitable in every way as a definition of sunset (or sunrise) for all statutory purposes.

LIGHTING-UP TIME

The legal importance of sunrise and sunset is that the Road Vehicles Lighting Regulations 1989 (SI 1989 No. 1796) as amended, make the use of front and rear position lamps on vehicles compulsory during the period between sunset and sunrise. Headlamps on vehicles are required to be used during the hours of darkness on unlit roads, on lit roads with a speed limit exceeding 30mph, or whenever visibility is seriously reduced. The hours of darkness are defined in these regulations as the period between half an hour after sunset and half an hour before sunrise.

In all laws and regulations 'sunset' refers to the local sunset, ie the time at which the Sun sets at the place in question. This common-sense interpretation has been upheld by legal tribunals.

MEAN REFRACTION

Alt.	Ref.	Alt.	Ref.	Alt.	Ref.
° ′	′	° ′	′	° ′	′
1 20	21	3 12	13	7 54	6
1 30	20	3 34	12	9 27	5
1 41	19	4 00	11	11 39	4
1 52	18	4 30	10	15 00	3
2 05	17	5 06	9	20 42	2
2 19	16	5 50	8	32 20	1
2 35	15	6 44	7	62 17	0
2 52	14	7 54		90 00	
3 12					

THE MOON

The GMT for moonrise, transit and moonset are given for each day. These times are independent of latitude but must be corrected for longitude. For places in the British Isles it suffices to add the longitude if west, and vice versa bearing in mind that 1° = 4m and 15' = 1m.

Diameter (Diam) indicates the apparent size of the Moon. The Moon's orbit around the Earth is an ellipse and this makes the Moon appear larger or smaller. In popular parlance Super Moons are when the Moon is full and also closest (perigee). The Moon's apparent size can vary from 29.4' to 33.5'. Note that the Sun's diameter can also vary from 31.4' in July to 32.5' in January. These values are important in determining whether a solar eclipse can be total or annular.

The Phase column shows the percentage of the area of the Moon's disk illuminated, this is also the illuminated percentage of the diameter at right angles to the line of cusps. The terminator is a semi-ellipse whose major axis is the line of cusps, and whose semi-minor axis is determined by the tabulated percentage, from New Moon to Full Moon the east limb is dark, and vice versa.

The Age of the Moon is the number of days elapsed since the last full Moon. There are 29.53 days between successive full Moons.

PAGE THREE OF EACH MONTH

THE PLANETS

Positions of Mercury are given for every second day, and those of Venus and Mars for every fifth day; linear interpolation can be used to give intermediate values to the same precision. The diameter (Diam.) is given in seconds of arc. The phase is the illuminated percentage of the disk. In the case of the inner planets this approaches 100 per cent at superior conjunction and zero at inferior conjunction. When the phase is less than 50 per cent the planet is crescent-shaped or horned; for greater phases it is gibbous. In the case of the exterior planet Mars, the phase approaches 100 per cent at conjunction and opposition, and is a minimum at the quadratures.

The particulars for the four outer planets resemble those for the planets Mercury and Venus, except that, because of the dimness of Uranus and Neptune, these two planets require an optical aid, such as binoculars or a small telescope, to be seen. The diameters given for the rings of Saturn are those of the major axis (in the plane of the planet's equator) and the minor axis respectively. The former has a small seasonal change due to the slightly varying distance of the Earth from Saturn, but the latter varies from zero when the Earth passes through the ring plane every 15 years to its maximum opening half-way between these periods. The rings were last open at their widest extent (and Saturn at its brightest) in 2017. The Earth passed through the ring plane in 2009.

The GMT at which planets transit the Greenwich meridian is also given. The times of transit may be corrected to local meridians, as described above. To determine if a planet is visible or not, the transit time should be examined. If the transit time coincides with hours of darkness the planet should be easy to find, provided it is bright enough. If the time of transit is between 00h and 12h the planet should be visible above the eastern horizon; if between 12h and 24h, above the western horizon. The closer the transit time to midnight (0h) the longer it will be visible. The inner planets - Mercury and Venus can never transit at midnight because they are, from Earth, seen to be too close to the Sun. If they transit close to noon (12h) then they will be too close to the Sun to be visible except during a total solar eclipse or if the planet passes in front of the Sun (known as a *transit*). The rise or set times should be examined to see if either is near sunrise or sunset. If this also coincides with a large positive declination (Dec.) then conditions are favourable for viewing in the northern hemisphere. A negative (southern) declination favours observations in the southern hemisphere.

Consulting *The Night Sky* paragraphs will also help determine observability. Under this heading will be found notes describing the position and visibility of the planets and other phenomena.

OTHER INFORMATION

MAGNITUDE

Magnitudes of astronomical objects are measured in what may be considered the reverse to the obvious. Magnitude +3 is brighter than +4, magnitude -2 is brighter than magnitude -1. So from brighter to dimmer: -4, -3, -2, -1, 0, +1, +2, +3

etc, with +6 being the dimmest considered visible with the naked eye in very dark skies. Each magnitude is roughly 2.5 times brighter than the next, so a magnitude +1 object is 100 times brighter than a magnitude +6 object.

TIME

From the earliest ages, the natural division of time into recurring periods of day and night has provided the practical time-scale for the everyday activities of the human race. Indeed, if any alternative means of time measurement is adopted, it must be capable of adjustment so as to remain in general agreement with the natural time-scale defined by the diurnal rotation of the Earth on its axis. Ideally the rotation should be measured against a fixed frame of reference; in practice it must be measured against the background provided by the celestial bodies. If the Sun is chosen as the reference point, we obtain Apparent Solar Time, which is the time indicated by a sundial. It is not a uniform time but is subject to variations which amount to as much as a quarter of an hour in each direction. Such wide variations cannot be tolerated in a practical time-scale, and this has led to the concept of Mean Solar Time in which all the days are exactly the same length and equal to the average length of the Apparent Solar Day. The positions of the stars in the sky are specified in relation to a reference point in the sky known as the First Point of Aries (or the Vernal Equinox). It is therefore convenient to adopt this same reference point when considering the rotation of the Earth against the background of the stars. The time-scale so obtained is known as Apparent Sidereal Time.

GREENWICH MEAN TIME

The daily rotation of the Earth on its axis causes the Sun and the other heavenly bodies, which are not circumpolar, to appear to cross the sky from east to west. Circumpolar objects (mostly stars) are close enough to the celestial pole that they never set. It is convenient to represent this relative motion as if the Sun really performed a daily circuit around a fixed Earth. Noon in Apparent Solar Time may then be defined as the time at which the Sun transits across the observer's meridian. In Mean Solar Time, noon is similarly defined by the meridian transit of a fictitious Mean Sun moving uniformly in the sky with the same average speed as the true Sun. Apparent Solar Time used to be observed on the meridian of the transit circle telescope of the Royal Observatory at Greenwich. Modern measurements are made from similar instruments across the world. Greenwich Mean Time (GMT) is derived from these observations. The mean solar day is divided into 24 hours and, for astronomical and other scientific purposes, these are numbered 0 to 23, commencing at midnight. Civil time is usually reckoned in two periods of 12 hours, designated am (*ante meridiem*, ie before noon) and pm (*post meridiem*, ie after noon), although the 24 hour clock is increasingly being used.

UNIVERSAL TIME

Before 1925 January 1, GMT was reckoned in 24 hours commencing at noon; since that date it has been reckoned from midnight. To avoid confusion in the use of the designation GMT before and after 1925, since 1928 astronomers have tended to use the term Universal Time (UT) or Weltzeit (WZ) to denote GMT measured from Greenwich Mean Midnight.

In precision work it is necessary to take account of small variations in Universal Time. These arise from small irregularities in the rotation of the Earth. Observed astronomical time is designated UT0. Observed time corrected for the effects of the motion of the poles (giving rise to a 'wandering' in longitude) is designated UT1. There is also a seasonal fluctuation in the rate of rotation of the Earth arising from meteorological causes, often called the annual fluctuation.

UT1 corrected for this effect is designated UT2 and provides a time-scale free from short-period fluctuations. It is still subject to small secular and irregular changes.

APPARENT SOLAR TIME

As mentioned above, the time shown by a sundial is called Apparent Solar Time. It differs from Mean Solar Time by an amount known as the Equation of Time, which is the total effect of two causes which make the length of the apparent solar day non-uniform. One cause of variation is that the orbit of the Earth is not a circle but an ellipse, having the Sun at one focus. As a consequence, the angular speed of the Earth in its orbit is not constant; it is greatest at the beginning of January when the Earth is nearest the Sun.

The other cause is due to the obliquity of the ecliptic; the plane of the equator (which is at right angles to the axis of rotation of the Earth) does not coincide with the ecliptic (the plane defined by the apparent annual motion of the Sun around the celestial sphere) but is inclined to it at an angle of about 23.4°. As a result, the apparent solar day is shorter than average at the equinoxes and longer at the solstices. From the combined effects of the components due to obliquity and eccentricity, the equation of time reaches its extreme values in February (-14 minutes) and early November (+16 minutes). It has a zero value on four dates during the year, and it is only on these dates (approximately April 15, June 14, September 1 and December 25) that a sundial shows Mean Solar Time.

SIDEREAL TIME

A sidereal day is the duration of a complete rotation of the Earth with reference to the First Point of Aries. The length of a sidereal day in mean time is 23h 56m 04s.09. The term sidereal (or 'star') time is a little misleading since the time-scale so defined is not exactly the same as that which would be defined by successive transits of a selected star, as there is a small progressive motion between the stars and the First Point of Aries due to the precession of the Earth's axis. This makes the length of the sidereal day shorter than the true period of rotation by 0.008 seconds. Superimposed on this steady precessional motion are small oscillations (nutation), giving rise to fluctuations in apparent sidereal time amounting to as much as 1.2 seconds. It is therefore customary to employ Mean Sidereal Time, from which these fluctuations have been removed.

EPHEMERIS TIME

An analysis of observations of the positions of the Sun, Moon and planets taken over an extended period is used in preparing ephemerides. (An ephemeris is a table giving the apparent position of a heavenly body at regular intervals of time, eg one day or ten days, and may be used to compare current observations with tabulated positions.) Discrepancies between the positions of heavenly bodies observed over a 300-year period and their predicted positions arose because the time-scale to which the observations were related was based on the assumption that the rate of rotation of the Earth is constant. It is now known that this rate of rotation is variable. A revised time-scale, Ephemeris Time (ET), was devised to bring the ephemerides into agreement with the observations.

The second of ET is defined in terms of the annual motion of the Earth in its orbit around the Sun (1/31556925.9747 of the tropical year for 1900 January 0d 12h ET). The precise determination of ET from astronomical observations is a lengthy process as the requisite standard of accuracy can only be achieved by averaging over a number of years.

'In 1976 the International Astronomical Union adopted Terrestrial Dynamical Time (TDT), a new dynamical time-scale for general use whose scale unit is the SI second (see Atomic Time, below). TDT was renamed Terrestrial Time (TT) in 1991. ET is now of little more than historical interest.

TERRESTRIAL TIME

The uniform time system used in computing the ephemerides of the solar system is Terrestrial Time (TT), which has replaced ET for this purpose. Except for the most rigorous astronomical calculations, it may be assumed to be the same as ET. In June 2021 the difference TT − UT is estimated to be 69.5 seconds. This is known as Delta T.

ATOMIC TIME

The fundamental standards of time and frequency must be defined in terms of a periodic motion which is adequately constant, enduring and measurable. Progress has made it possible to use natural standards, such as atomic or molecular oscillations. Continuous oscillations are generated in an electrical circuit, the frequency of which is then compared or brought into coincidence with the frequency characteristic of the absorption or emission by the atoms or molecules when they change between two selected energy levels. Since the 13th General Conference on Weights and Measures in October 1967, the unit of time, the second, has been defined in the International System of units (SI) as 'the duration of 9,192,631,770 periods of the radiation corresponding to the transition between the two hyperfine levels of the ground state of the caesium-133 atom'.

In the UK, the national time scale is maintained by the National Physical Laboratory (NPL), using an ensemble of atomic clocks based on either caesium or hydrogen atoms. In addition the NPL (along with several other national laboratories) has constructed and operates caesium fountain primary frequency standards, which utilise the cooling of caesium atoms by laser light to determine the duration of the SI second at the highest attainable level of accuracy. Caesium fountain primary standards typically achieve an accuracy of around 2 parts in 10,000,000,000,000,000, which is equivalent to one second in 158 million years.

Timekeeping worldwide is based on two closely related atomic time scales that are established through international collaboration. International Atomic Time (TAI) is formed by combining the readings of more than 400 atomic clocks located in more than 70 institutes and was set close to the astronomically based Universal Time (UT) near the beginning of 1958. It was formally recognised in 1971 and since 1988 January 1 has been maintained by the International Bureau of Weights and Measures (BIPM). Civil time in almost all countries is now based on Coordinated Universal Time (UTC), which differs from TAI by 37 seconds and was designed to make both atomic time and UT available with accuracy appropriate for most users. On 1 January 1972 UTC was set to be exactly 10 seconds behind TAI, and since then the UTC time-scale has been adjusted by the insertion (or, in principle, omission) of leap seconds in order to keep it within ±0.9s of UT. These leap seconds are introduced, when necessary, at the same instant throughout the world, either at the end of December or at the end of June. The last leap second occurred immediately prior to 0h UTC on 2017 January 1, and was the 27th leap second. All leap seconds so far have been positive, with 61 seconds in the final minute of the UTC month. The time 23h 59m 60s UTC is followed one second later by 0h 0m 00s of the first day of the following month. Notices concerning the insertion of leap seconds are issued by the International Earth Rotation and Reference Systems Service (IERS).

The computation of UTC is carried out monthly by the BIPM and takes place in three stages. First, a weighted average known as Echelle Atomique Libre (EAL) is calculated from all of the contributing atomic clocks. In the second stage, TAI is generated by applying small corrections, derived from the results contributed by primary frequency standards, to the scale interval of EAL to maintain its value close to that of the SI second. Finally, UTC is formed from TAI by the addition of an integer number of seconds. The results are published monthly in the BIPM Circular T in the form of offsets at 5-day intervals between UTC and the time scales of contributing organisations.

RADIO TIME-SIGNALS

UTC is made generally available through time-signals and standard frequency broadcasts such as MSF in the UK, CHU in Canada and WWV and WWVH in the USA. These are based on national time-scales that are maintained in close agreement with UTC and provide traceability to the national time-scale and to UTC. The markers of seconds in the UTC scale coincide with those of TAI.

To disseminate the national time-scale in the UK, special signals (call-sign MSF) are broadcast by the National Physical Laboratory. From April 1, 2007 the MSF service, previously broadcast from British Telecom's radio station at Rugby, has been transmitted from Anthorn radio station in Cumbria. The signals are controlled from a caesium beam atomic frequency standard and consist of a precise frequency carrier of 60 kHz which is switched off, after being on for at least half a second, to mark every second. The first second of the minute begins with a period of 500 ms with the carrier switched off, to serve as a minute marker. In the other seconds the carrier is always off for at least one tenth of a second at the start and then it carries an on-off code giving the British clock time and date, together with information identifying the start of the next minute. Changes to and from summer time are made following government announcements. Leap seconds are inserted as announced by the IERS and information provided by them on the difference between UTC and UT is also signalled. Other broadcast signals in the UK include the BBC six pips signal, the BT Timeline ('speaking clock'), the NPL telephone and internet time services for computers, and a coded time-signal on the BBC 198 kHz transmitters which is used for timing in the electricity supply industry. From 1972 January 1 the six pips on the BBC have consisted of five short pips from second 55 to second 59 (six pips in the case of a leap second) followed by one lengthened pip, the start of which indicates the exact minute. From 1990 February 5 these signals have been controlled by the BBC with seconds markers referenced to the satellite-based US navigation system GPS (Global Positioning System) and time and day referenced to the MSF transmitter. Formerly they were generated by the Royal Greenwich Observatory. The NPL telephone and internet time services are directly connected to the national time scale.

Due to digital latency, time pips received via Digital Audio Broadcasting (DAB) radio and internet streaming are received late by significant and variable amounts, rendering them inaccurate if received in this way.

Accurate timing may also be obtained from the signals of international navigation systems such as the ground-based eLORAN, or the satellite-based American GPS or Russian GLONASS systems.

STANDARD TIME

Since 1880 the standard time in Britain has been Greenwich Mean Time (GMT); a statute that year enacted that the word 'time' when used in any legal document relating to Britain meant, unless otherwise specifically stated, the mean time of the Greenwich meridian. Greenwich was adopted as the universal meridian on 13 October 1884. A system of standard time by zones is used worldwide, standard time in each zone differing from that of the Greenwich meridian by an integral number of hours or, exceptionally, half-hours or quarter-hours,

either fast or slow. The large territories of the USA and Canada are divided into zones approximately 7.5° on either side of central meridians.

Variations from the standard time of some countries occur during part of the year; they are decided annually and are usually referred to as Summer Time or Daylight Saving Time.

At the 180th meridian the time can be either 12 hours fast on Greenwich Mean Time or 12 hours slow, and a change of date occurs. The internationally recognised date or calendar line is a modification of the 180th meridian, drawn so as to include islands of any one group on the same side of the line, or for political reasons.

Lat.	Long	Lat.	Long
90° S.	180°	48° N.	180°
51° S.	180°	53° N.	170° E.
45° S.	172.5° W.	65.5° N.	169° W.
15° S.	172.5° W.	68° N.	169° W.
5° S.	180°	90° N.	180°

Changes to the date line require an international conference.

BRITISH SUMMER TIME

In 1916 an Act ordained that during a defined period of that year the legal time for general purposes in Great Britain should be one hour in advance of Greenwich Mean Time. The Summer Time Acts 1922 and 1925 defined the period during which Summer Time was to be in force, stabilising practice until the Second World War.

During the Second World War (1941–5) and in 1947 Double Summer Time (two hours in advance of Greenwich Mean Time) was used for the period in which ordinary Summer Time would have been in force. During these years clocks were also kept one hour in advance of Greenwich Mean Time in the winter. After the war, ordinary Summer Time was invoked each year from 1948–68.

Between 1968 October 27 and 1971 October 31 clocks were kept one hour ahead of Greenwich Mean Time throughout the year. This was known as British Standard Time.

The most recent legislation is the Summer Time Act 1972, which enacted that 'the period of summer time for the purposes of this Act is the period beginning at two o'clock, Greenwich Mean Time, in the morning of the day after the third Saturday in March or, if that day is Easter Day, the day after the second Saturday in March, and ending at two o'clock, Greenwich Mean Time, in the morning of the day after the fourth Saturday in October.'

The duration of Summer Time can be varied by Order in Council and in recent years alterations have been made to synchronise the period of Summer Time in Britain with that used in Europe. The rule for 1981–94 defined the period of Summer Time in the UK as from the last Sunday in March to the day following the fourth Saturday in October and the hour of changeover was altered to 01h GMT.

There was no rule for the dates of Summer Time between 1995–7. Since 1998 the 9th European Parliament and Council Directive on Summer Time has harmonised the dates on which Summer Time begins and ends across member states as the last Sundays in March and October respectively. Under the directive Summer Time begins and ends at 01hr Greenwich Mean Time in each member state. Amendments to the Summer Time Act to implement the directive came into force on 11 March 2002.

The duration of Summer Time in 2021 is:
March 28 01h GMT to October 31 01h GMT

ASTRONOMICAL CONSTANTS

Solar parallax	8.794″
Astronomical unit	149,597,870 km
Annual precession in longitude	50.288″
Precession in right ascension	3.075s
Precession in declination	20.043″
Constant of nutation	9.202″
Constant of aberration	20.496″
Mean obliquity of ecliptic (2018)	23° 26′ 13″
Moon's mean equatorial hor parallax	57′ 02.70″
Velocity of light in vacuo	299,792.5 km/s
Equatorial radius of the Earth	6,378 km
Polar radius of the Earth	6,356 km
North galactic pole	
(IAU standard)	RA 12h 51m Dec + 27.1° N.
Solar apex	RA 18h04m Dec.+30°
Solar motion	20.0 km/s

Length of year (in mean solar days)

Tropical	365.24217
Sidereal	365.25636
Anomalistic (perihelion to perihelion)	365.25964
Eclipse	346.62008

Length of month (mean values)	d	h	m	s
Synodic (new Moon to new Moon)	29	12	44	02.8
Sidereal	27	07	43	11.6
Anomalistic (perigee to perigee)	27	13	18	33.2

THE EARTH

The shape of the Earth is that of an oblate spheroid or solid of revolution whose meridian sections are ellipses not differing much from circles, while the sections at right angles are circles. The length of the equatorial axis is about 12,756 km, and that of the polar axis is 12,714 km. The mean density of the Earth is 5.5 times that of water. Density increases from about 3.3g/cc near to the surface to about 17g/cc at the centre. The Earth and Moon revolve about their common centre of gravity in a lunar month; this centre in turn revolves round the Sun in a plane known as the ecliptic, that passes through the Sun's centre. The Earth's equator is inclined to this plane at an angle of 23.4°. This tilt is the cause of the seasons. In mid-latitudes, and when the Sun is high above the Equator, not only does the high noon altitude make the days longer, but the Sun's rays fall more perpendicularly on the Earth's surface; these effects combine to produce summer. In equatorial regions the noon altitude is large throughout the year, and there is little variation in the length of the day. In higher latitudes the noon altitude is lower, and the days in summer are appreciably longer than those in winter.

The average velocity of the Earth in its orbit is 30km/s. It makes a complete rotation on its axis in about 23h 56m of mean time, which is the sidereal day. Because of its annual revolution round the Sun, the rotation with respect to the Sun, or the solar day, is more than this by about four minutes. The extremity of the axis of rotation, or the North Pole of the Earth, is not rigidly fixed, but wanders over an area roughly 20 metres in diameter.

Perihelion is when the Earth is closest to the Sun, and *aphelion* when the Earth is furthest from the Sun:

Perihelion January 2021	2d 13h 15m	
	(147,093,162km, 0.983257060au)	
Aphelion July 2021	5d 22h 27m	
	(152,100,526km, 1.016729924au)	

GEOMAGNETISM AND SPACE WEATHER

The geomagnetic field is generated in the Earth's partially molten core. The movement of molten iron creates electrical current, and this in turn generates magnetic field that reaches far out into space in a region called the magnetosphere. The field varies in strength and direction from place to place, but also with time. It is stronger at the poles, though not exactly at the geographic poles, and is weaker in the equatorial region, particularly in S. America. The strength of the magnetic field in 2021 in microTeslas ranges from a minimum of about 22 µT in N. Argentina to 67 µT at the S. magnetic dip-pole (see figure). Superimposed on the field from the core are local anomalies; these are due to the influence of mineral deposits in the Earth's crust.

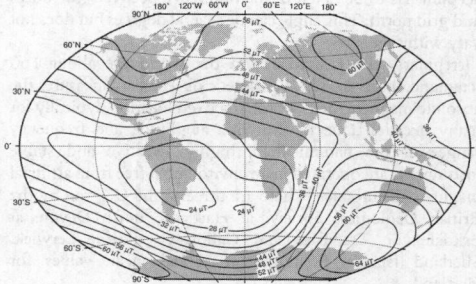

A small but highly dynamic proportion of the field is of external origin, associated with electrical current in the ionosphere and magnetosphere. The ionisation of the upper atmosphere depends on the incident particle and radiation flux, ultimately controlled by the Sun and the configuration of the internal magnetic field. There are short-term irregular storm events as well as regular daily, 27-day, seasonal and approximate 11-year variations in the external magnetic field. The term space weather refers to conditions on the Sun, in the solar wind and inside the magnetosphere that result in storm events which influence the performance and reliability of space-borne and ground-based technological systems.

A magnetic compass points along the horizontal component of a conceptual magnetic line of force. These lines of force converge on the magnetic dip-poles, the places where the Earth's magnetic field is vertical. These poles move with time, and their present (2021.0) approximate adopted mean positions are 86.4° N., 156.8° E. and 64.0° S., 135.7° E. It is important to realise that compasses do not point directly, ie via great circle routes, to the dip-poles.

There is also a 'magnetic equator', at all points of which the vertical component of the Earth's magnetic field is zero and a magnetised needle of a dip meter remains horizontal. This line, also called the dip equator, runs between 12° south and north of the geographical equator. North of the equator the dip meter needle points below the horizontal and south of the equator it points above the horizontal.

The following table indicates changes in magnetic declination (or variation of the compass relative to true north) at Greenwich over four centuries. Similar, though much smaller, changes have occurred in dip or magnetic inclination. These changes differ throughout the world.

London (Greenwich)

1580	11°	15′	E.		1873	19°	35′	W.
1665	01°	22′	W.		1925	13°	10′	W.
1730	13°	00′	W.		1950	09°	07′	W.
1773	21°	09′	W.		1975	06°	39′	W.
1823	24°	23′	W.(max)		1998	03°	32′	W.

In Great Britain, lines of equal declination (isogonics) now run approximately north–northeast to south–southwest. Though there are considerable local deviations due to geological causes, an approximate value of magnetic declination may be obtained by assuming that at 50° N. on the meridian of Greenwich (longitude 0°), the value in 2021 is 0° 44′ east. Easterly declination is now being sensed for the first time in over 350 years as the zero isogonic line (the agonic line) passes westwards across the country. Allowing for 8′ west for each degree of latitude northwards and one of 25′ west for each degree of longitude westwards. For example, at 53° N., 5° W., declination will be about 0° 44′ east + 24′ west + 125′ west, i.e. 1° 45′ west. The average annual change at the present time is about 13′ to the east. For navigation by compass using maps with the north lines from the British National Grid (as opposed to lines of equal longitude), account has to be taken of the difference between true north and grid north. This angle can be several degrees but does not vary with time.

Irregularly distributed around the world are about 160 magnetic observatories. A magnetic observatory measures the absolute magnetic field vector at a fixed location, typically for many decades. Due to the wide amplitude and frequency ranges of the natural field, highly sensitive and stable instruments are operated in an environment free from artificial magnetic disturbance. There are three in the UK, run by the British Geological Survey: at Hartland, north Devon; at Eskdalemuir, Dumfries and Galloway; and at Lerwick, Shetland Islands. Some recent annual mean values for Hartland:

Year	Declination West		Dip or inclination		Horizontal intensity	Vertical intensity
	°	′	°	′	nT	nT
1960	9	58.8	66	43.9	18.707	43.504
1970	9	06.5	66	26.1	19.033	43.636
1980	7	43.8	66	10.3	19.330	43.768
1990	6	15.0	66	09.7	19.539	43.896
2000	4	43.6	66	06.9	19.508	44.051
2019	1	31.9	65	58.5	19.809	44.438

nT = nanoTesla

The magnetic field is also observed by a series of specialised satellites, the current being a mission called Swarm. Three satellites launched by the European Space Agency in 2013, each equipped with magnetometers and star cameras for orientation, in 2020 continued to return accurate measurements of the Earth's magnetic field.

Reliance on the Earth's magnetic field for navigation by compass is not restricted to land, maritime or aeronautical navigation (in the latter two usually in as a fail-safe back-up system). It also extends underground with the oil industry using magnetic survey tools when drilling well-bores. Very accurate estimates of the local magnetic field are required for this, taking into account the crustal and external fields. Modern smartphones include miniature magnetometers and tables of declination values for orientation of maps.

SPACE WEATHER

Occasionally, sometimes with great suddenness, the Earth's magnetic field is subject for several hours to marked disturbance. In many instances such storm events are accompanied by widespread displays of auroras, marked changes in the incidence of cosmic rays, an increase in the reception of 'noise' from the Sun at radio frequencies, and rapid changes in the ionosphere and induced electric currents within the Earth. These can adversely affect satellite operations, telecommunications and electric power transmission systems. The storm events are caused by changes in the solar wind, a stream of ionised particles which emanates from the Sun and through which the Earth is continuously passing. Some of these changes are associated with visible eruptions on the Sun, usually in the region of sun-spots for which there is an approximate 11-year cycle of occurrence. There is some tendency for storm events to recur after intervals of about 27 days, the period of rotation of the Sun on its axis as seen from the Earth but the sources of many events are shorter lived than this. Predicting such storm events with any useful accuracy remains challenging but the year 2021, at the start of the ascending phase of solar cycle 25, is generally expected to be quiet.

ELEMENTS OF THE SOLAR SYSTEM

Orb	Mean distance from Sun (Earth = 1)	km 10⁶	Sidereal period days	Synodic period days	Incl. of orbit to ecliptic ° '	Diameter km	Mass (Earth = 1)	Period of rotation on axis days
Sun	—	—	—	—	—	1,392,000	332,981	25–35*
Mercury	0.39	58	88.0	116	7 00	4,879	0.0553	58.646
Venus	0.72	108	224.7	584	3 24	12,104	0.8150	243.019r
Earth	1.00	150	365.3	—	—	12,756e	1.0000	0.997
Mars	1.52	228	687.0	780	1 51	6,794e	0.1074	1.026
Jupiter	5.20	778	4,331.0	399	1 18	{ 142,984e 133,708p	317.83	{ 0.410e
Saturn	9.58	1433	10,747	378	2 29	{ 120,536e 108,728p	95.16	{ 0.446e
Uranus	19.22	2875	30,589	370	0 46	51,118e	14.54	0.718r
Neptune	30.11	4504	56,800	367	1 46	49,528e	17.15	0.671
Pluto†	39.48	5906	90,560	367	17 10	2,390	0.002	6.387r

e equatorial, p polar, r retrograde, * depending on latitude, † reclassified as a dwarf planet since August 2006

THE SATELLITES

Name		Star mag.	Mean distance from primary km	Sidereal period of revolution d	Name		Star mag.	Mean distance from primary km	Sidereal period of revolution d
EARTH					SATURN				
I	Moon	—	384,400	27.322	VII	Hyperion	14	1,481,000	21.277
					VIII	Iapetus	11	3,561,300	79.330
MARS					IX	Phoebe	16	12,952,000	550.48r
I	Phobos	11	9,378	0.319					
II	Deimos	12	23,459	1.262	URANUS				
					VI	Cordelia	24	49,770	0.335
JUPITER					VII	Ophelia	24	53,790	0.376
XVI	Metis	17	127,960	0.295	VIII	Bianca	23	59,170	0.435
XV	Adrastea	19	128,980	0.298	IX	Cressida	22	61,780	0.464
V	Amalthea	14	181,300	0.498	X	Desdemona	22	62,680	0.474
XIV	Thebe	16	221,900	0.675	XI	Juliet	21	64,350	0.493
I	Io	5	421,600	1.769	XII	Portia	21	66,090	0.513
II	Europa	5	670,900	3.551	XIII	Rosalind	22	69,900	0.558
III	Ganymede	5	1,070,000	7.155	XIV	Belinda	22	75,260	0.624
IV	Callisto	6	1,883,000	16.689	XV	Puck	20	86,010	0.762
XIII	Leda	20	11,165,000	240.92	V	Miranda	16	129,900	1.413
VI	Himalia	15	11,460,000	250.57	I	Ariel	14	191,020	2.520
X	Lysithea	18	11,717,000	259.22	II	Umbriel	15	266,300	4.144
VII	Elara	17	11,741,000	259.65	III	Titania	14	435,910	8.706
XII	Ananke	19	21,276,000	629.77r	IV	Oberon	14	583,520	13.463
XI	Carme	18	23,404,000	734.17r	XVI	Caliban	22	7,230,000	579.5r
VIII	Pasiphae	17	23,624,000	743.68r	XX	Stephano	24	8,002,000	676.5r
IX	Sinope	18	23,939,000	758.90r	XVII	Sycorax	21	12,179,000	1,283.4r
					XVIII	Prospero	23	16,256,000	1,977.3r
SATURN					XIX	Setebos	23	17,418,000	2,234.8r
XVIII	Pan	20	133,583	0.575					
XV	Atlas	18	137,640	0.602	NEPTUNE				
XVI	Prometheus	16	139,353	0.613	III	Naiad	25	48,230	0.294
XVII	Pandora	16	141,700	0.629	IV	Thalassa	24	50,080	0.311
XI	Epimetheus	15	151,422	0.694	V	Despina	23	52,530	0.335
X	Janus	14	151,472	0.695	VI	Galatea	22	61,950	0.429
I	Mimas	13	185,520	0.942	VII	Larissa	22	73,550	0.555
II	Enceladus	12	238,020	1.370	VIII	Proteus	20	117,650	1.122
III	Tethys	10	294,660	1.888	I	Triton	13	354,760	5.877
XIII	Telesto	19	294,660	1.888	II	Nereid	19	5,513,400	360.136
XIV	Calypso	19	294,660	1.888					
IV	Dione	10	377,400	2.737	PLUTO				
XII	Helene	18	377,400	2.737	I	Charon	17	19,596	6.387
V	Rhea	10	527,040	4.518					
VI	Titan	8	1,221,850	15.945					

The total number of satellites known so far for the outer planets are: Jupiter 79, Saturn 62, Uranus 27, Neptune 14, Pluto 5.

ABBREVIATIONS AND ACRONYMS

A

ABA	Amateur Boxing Association
abr	abridged
ac	alternating current
AC	*ante Christum* before Christ
	Companion, Order of Australia
ADC	Aide-de-Camp
ADC (P)	Personal ADC to the Queen
Adj.	Adjutant
Adj. Gen.	Adjutant General
Adm.	Admiral
AE	Air Efficiency award
AEM	Air Efficiency Medal
aet	after extra time
AFC	Air Force Cross
AFM	Air Force Medal
AG	Attorney-General
AH	*anno Hegirae* in the year of the Hegira
AM	Assembly Member (Wales)
ANC	African National Congress
AO	Air Officer
	Officer, Order of Australia
AOC	Air Officer Commanding
apptd	appointed
APR	annual percentage rate
AUC	*ab urbe condita* from the foundation of Rome
	anno urbis conditae from the founding of the city

B

b.	born
	bowled (cricket)
BAFTA	British Academy of Film and Television Arts
BAS	Bachelor in Agricultural Science
	British Antarctic Survey
BBFC	British Board of Film Classification
BCE	Before the Common (or Christian) Era
BCH (D)	Bachelor of (Dental) Surgery
BCL	Bachelor of Civil Law
BCOM	Bachelor of Commerce
BD	Bachelor of Divinity
BDA	British Dental Association
BDS	Bachelor of Dental Surgery
BED	Bachelor of Education
BEM	British Empire Medal
BENG	Bachelor of Engineering
BFPO	British Forces Post Office
BLIT	Bachelor of Literature
BLITT	Bachelor of Letters
BM	Bachelor of Medicine
BMA	British Medical Association
BMUS	Bachelor of Music
Bp	Bishop
BPHARM	Bachelor of Pharmacy
BPHIL	Bachelor of Philosophy
BPS	British Psychological Society
Brig.	Brigadier
BSI	British Standards Institution
BST	British Summer Time
Bt.	Baronet
BTEC	Business and Technology Education Council
BVMS	Bachelor of Veterinary Medicine and Surgery

C

c.	*circa* about
C.	Conservative
Cantuar:	of Canterbury (Archbishop)
Capt.	Captain
Carliol:	of Carlisle (Bishop)
CB	Companion, Order of the Bath
CBE	Commander, Order of the British Empire

CC	Companion, Order of Canada
CCHEM	chartered chemist
CD	Civil Defence
	Corps Diplomatique
Cdr	Commander
Cdre	Commodore
CDS	Chief of the Defence Staff
CE	civil engineer
	Common (or Christian) Era
CENG	chartered engineer
Cestr:	of Chester (Bishop)
CET	Central European Time
cf	*confer* compare
CGC	Conspicuous Gallantry Cross
CGEOL	chartered geologist
CGM	Conspicuous Gallantry Medal
CGS	Chief of General Staff
CH	Companion of Honour
CHB/M	Bachelor/Master of Surgery
CI	Channel Islands
Cicestr:	of Chichester (Bishop)
C-in-C	Commander-in-Chief
CILIP	Chartered Institute of Library and Information Professionals
CIPFA	Chartered Institute of Public Finance and Accountancy
CIS	Commonwealth of Independent States
CLJ	Commander, Order of St Lazarus of Jerusalem
CM	*Chirurgiae Magister* Master of Surgery
CMG	Companion, Order of St Michael and St George
CO	Commanding Officer
C of E	Church of England
Col.	Colonel
cons.	consecrated
Cpl.	Corporal
CPS	Crown Prosecution Service
CVO	Commander, Royal Victorian Order

D

d	*denarius* penny
d.	died
DAB	Digital Audio Broadcasting
DBE	Dame Commander, Order of the British Empire
DCB	Dame Commander, Order of the Bath
D CH	*Doctor Chirurgiae* Doctor of Surgery
DCL	Doctor of Civil Law
DCM	Distinguished Conduct Medal
DCMG	Dame Commander, Order of St Michael and St George
DCVO	Dame Commander, Royal Victorian Order
DD	Doctor of Divinity
DDS	Doctor of Dental Surgery
DFC	Distinguished Flying Cross
DFM	Distinguished Flying Medal
DHL	*Doctor Humaniorum Literarum* Doctor of Humane Letters/Literature
DIP ED	Diploma in Education
DIP HE	Diploma in Higher Education
DL	Deputy Lieutenant
DLIT	Doctor of Literature
DLITT	Doctor of Letters
DLR	Docklands Light Railway
DLS	Duckworth–Lewis–Stern method (cricket)
DMUS	Doctor of Music
DNA	deoxyribonucleic acid
DPH *or* DPHIL	Doctor of Philosophy
DPP	Director of Public Prosecutions
DSC	Distinguished Service Cross
DSc	Doctor of Science
DSM	Distinguished Service Medal

DSO	Companion, Distinguished Service Order
Dunelm:	of Durham (Bishop)
DUP	Democratic Unionist Party

E

Ebor:	of York (Archbishop)
EC	Elizabeth Cross
	European Community
ECG	electrocardiogram
ED	Efficiency Decoration
EEA	European Economic Area
EEG	electroencephalogram
EIB	European Investment Bank
ER	*Elizabetha Regina* Queen Elizabeth
ERM	exchange rate mechanism
ESA	European Space Agency
et seq	*et sequentia* and the following
Exon:	of Exeter (Bishop)

F

FAQ	frequently asked questions
FBA	Fellow, British Academy
FBS	Fellow, Botanical Society
FBU	Fire Brigades Union
FCA	Fellow, Institute of Chartered Accountants in England and Wales
FCCA	Fellow, Chartered Association of Certified Accountants
FCIB	Fellow, Chartered Institute of Bankers
	Fellow, Corporation of Insurance Brokers
FCII	Fellow, Chartered Insurance Institute
FCIPS	Fellow, Chartered Institute of Purchasing and Supply
FCIS	Fellow, Institute of Chartered Secretaries and Administrators
FCIT	Fellow, Chartered Institute of Transport
FCMA	Fellow, Chartered Institute of Management Accountants
FCP	Fellow, College of Preceptors
FD	*Fidei Defensor* Defender of the Faith
FE	further education
FFA	Fellow, Faculty of Actuaries (Scotland)
	Fellow, Institute of Financial Accountants
FFAS	Fellow, Faculty of Architects and Surveyors
FFCM	Fellow, Faculty of Community Medicine
FFPHM	Fellow, Faculty of Public Health Medicine
FGS	Fellow, Geological Society
FHS	Fellow, Heraldry Society
FHSM	Fellow, Institute of Health Service Management
FIA	Fellow, Institute of Actuaries
FIBIOL	Fellow, Institute of Biology
FICE	Fellow, Institution of Civil Engineers
FICS	Fellow, Institution of Chartered Shipbrokers
FIEE	Fellow, Institution of Electrical Engineers
FIM	Fellow, Institute of Metals
FIMGT	Fellow, Institute of Management
FIMM	Fellow, Institution of Mining and Metallurgy
FLS	Fellow, Linnean Society
FMEDSCI	Fellow, Academy of Medical Sciences
fo	folio
FPHS	Fellow, Philosophical Society
FRAD	Fellow, Royal Academy of Dancing
FRAES	Fellow, Royal Aeronautical Society
FRAGS	Fellow, Royal Agricultural Societies
FRAM	Fellow, Royal Academy of Music
FRAS	Fellow, Royal Asiatic Society
	Fellow, Royal Astronomical Society
FRBS	Fellow, Royal Botanic Society
	Fellow, Royal Society of British Sculptors
FRCA	Fellow, Royal College of Anaesthetists
FRCGP	Fellow, Royal College of General Practitioners
FRCM	Fellow, Royal College of Music
FRCO	Fellow, Royal College of Organists
FRCOG	Fellow, Royal College of Obstetricians and Gynaecologists

FRCP	Fellow, Royal College of Physicians, London
FRCPATH	Fellow, Royal College of Pathologists
FRCPE *or* FRCPED	Fellow, Royal College of Physicians, Edinburgh
FRCPI	Fellow, Royal College of Physicians, Ireland
FRCPSYCH	Fellow, Royal College of Psychiatrists
FRCR	Fellow, Royal College of Radiologists
FRCS	Fellow, Royal College of Surgeons of England
FRCSE *or* FRCSED	Fellow, Royal College of Surgeons of Edinburgh
FRCSGLAS	Fellow, Royal College of Physicians and Surgeons of Glasgow
FRCSI	Fellow, Royal College of Surgeons in Ireland
FRCVS	Fellow, Royal College of Veterinary Surgeons
FRENG	Fellow, Royal Academy of Engineering
FRGS	Fellow, Royal Geographical Society
FRHISTS	Fellow, Royal Historical Society
FRHS	Fellow, Royal Horticultural Society
FRIBA	Fellow, Royal Institute of British Architects
FRICS	Fellow, Royal Institution of Chartered Surveyors
FRMETS	Fellow, Royal Meteorological Society
FRMS	Fellow, Royal Microscopical Society
FRNS	Fellow, Royal Numismatic Society
FRPHARMS	Fellow, Royal Pharmaceutical Society
FRPS	Fellow, Royal Photographic Society
FRS	Fellow, Royal Society
FRSA	Fellow, Royal Society of Arts
FRSC	Fellow, Royal Society of Chemistry
FRSE	Fellow, Royal Society of Edinburgh
FRSH	Fellow, Royal Society of Health
FRSL	Fellow, Royal Society of Literature
FSA	Fellow, Society of Antiquaries
FTII	Fellow, Chartered Institute of Taxation
FZS	Fellow, Zoological Society

G

GBE	Dame/Knight Grand Cross, Order of the British Empire
GC	George Cross
GCB	Dame/Knight Grand Cross, Order of the Bath
GCLJ	Knight Grand Cross, Order of St Lazarus of Jerusalem
GCMG	Dame/Knight Grand Cross, Order of St Michael and St George
GCVO	Dame/Knight Grand Cross, Royal Victorian Order
Gen.	General
GHQ	general headquarters
GLA	Greater London Authority
GM	George Medal
GMB	Britain's General Union
GMT	Greenwich Mean Time
GOC	General Officer Commanding
Gp Capt.	Group Captain
GPS	Global Positioning System
GRU	*Glavnoje Razvedgvatel'noje Upravlenijie* Russian military intelligence agency

H

HB	His Beatitude
HBM	Her/His Britannic Majesty('s)
HE	Her/His Excellency
	higher education
	His Eminence
HH	Her/His Highness
	Her/His Honour
	His Holiness
HIM	Her/His Imperial Majesty
HM	Her/His Majesty('s)
HMAS	Her/His Majesty's Australian Ship
HMC	Headmasters' and Headmistresses' Conference
HMI	Her/His Majesty's Inspector
HMS	Her/His Majesty's Ship
Hon.	Honorary
	Honourable
HRH	Her/His Royal Highness

HRT	hormone replacement therapy	MCH(D)	Master of (Dental) Surgery
HSE	*hic sepultus est* here is buried	MDS	Master of Dental Surgery
HSH	Her/His Serene Highness	ME	Middle English
			myalgic encephalomyelitis
		MED	Master of Education
I		Mgr	Monsignor
IB	International Baccalaureate	MIT	Massachusetts Institute of Technology
ICC	International Cricket Council	MLA	Member of Legislative Assembly (NI)
	International Criminal Court	MLITT	Master of Letters
ICJ	International Court of Justice	Mlle	Mademoiselle
id	*idem* the same	MM	Military Medal
IP	intellectual property	Mme	Madame
	internet protocol	MMR	measles, mumps and rubella (vaccine)
IPSA	Independent Parliamentary Standards Authority	MN	Merchant Navy
IRA	Irish Republican Army	MPHIL	Master of Philosophy
IRC	International Rescue Committee	MR	Master of the Rolls
Is	Islands	MRI	magnetic resonance imaging
IS	Islamic State	MRSA	methicillin-resistant staphylococcus aureus
ISO	Imperial Service Order	MS	manuscript (*pl* MSS)
	International Organisation for Standardisation		Master of Surgery
ISP	internet service provider		multiple sclerosis
ISSN	International Standard Serial Number	MSP	Member of Scottish Parliament
ITU	International Telecommunication Union	MUSB/D	Bachelor/Doctor of Music
		MVO	Member, Royal Victorian Order
J			
JP	Justice of the Peace	**N**	
		NAAFI	Navy, Army and Air Force Institutes
		NAFTA	North American Free Trade Agreement
K		NAO	National Audit Office
KBE	Knight Commander, Order of the British Empire	NCO	non-commissioned officer
KCB	Knight Commander, Order of the Bath	NDPB	non-departmental public body
KCLJ	Knight Commander, Order of St Lazarus of Jerusalem	NFU	National Farmers' Union
		non seq	*non sequitur* it does not follow
KCMG	Knight Commander, Order of St Michael and St George	Norvic:	of Norwich (Bishop)
		NP	Notary Public
KCVO	Knight Commander, Royal Victorian Order	NSW	New South Wales (Australia)
KG	Knight of the Garter	NUJ	National Union of Journalists
KLJ	Knight, Order of St Lazarus of Jerusalem	NUS	National Union of Students
KP	Knight, Order of St Patrick	NUT	National Union of Teachers
KStJ	Knight, Order of St John of Jerusalem		
Kt.	Knight	**O**	
KT	Knight of the Thistle	Ob *or* obit	died
		OBE	Officer, Order of the British Empire
		OBR	Office for Budget Responsibility
L		OE	Old English
Lab.	Labour	OED	*Oxford English Dictionary*
Lat.	Latitude	OHMS	On Her/His Majesty's Service
lbw	leg before wicket (cricket)	OM	Order of Merit
lc	lower case (printing)	ono	or near(est) offer
LD	Liberal Democrat	op	*opus* work
LDS	Licentiate in Dental Surgery	op cit	*opere citato* in the work cited
LHD	*Literarum Humaniorum Doctor* Doctor of Humane Letters/Literature	OS	Ordnance Survey
		OStJ	Officer, Order of St John of Jerusalem
Lib.	Liberal		
LITT D	Doctor of Letters	**P**	
LLB	Bachelor of Laws	PC	Plaid Cymru
LLD	Doctor of Laws		Police Constable
LLM	Master of Laws		Privy Counsellor
loc cit	*loco citato* in the place cited	Petriburg:	of Peterborough (Bishop)
Londin:	of London (Bishop)	PG	parental guidance
Long.	longitude		postgraduate
lsd	*librae, solidi, denarii* pounds, shillings and pence	PHD	Doctor of Philosophy
Lt.	Lieutenant	pl	plural
LTA	Lawn Tennis Association	PLO	Palestine Liberation Organisation
LVO	Lieutenant, Royal Victorian Order	PM	post mortem
			Prime Minister
M		PO	Petty Officer
m.	married		Pilot Officer
M	Monsieur		postal order
Maj.	Major	PPS	Parliamentary Private Secretary
MB	*Medicinae Baccalaureus* Bachelor of Medicine	PR	proportional representation
MBA	Master of Business Administration	PRA	President of the Royal Academy
MBE	Member, Order of the British Empire	pro tem	*pro tempore* for the time being
MC	Master of Ceremonies	prox	*proximo* next month
	Military Cross	PRS	President of the Royal Society
MCB	Muslim Council of Britain		
MCC	Marylebone Cricket Club		

PRSE	President of the Royal Society of Edinburgh
Pte.	Private

Q

QBD	Queen's Bench Division
QC	Queen's Counsel
QE	quantitative easing
QED	*quod erat demonstrandum* which was to be proved
QGM	Queen's Gallantry Medal
QHC	Queen's Honorary Chaplain
QHDS	Queen's Honorary Dental Surgeon
QHNS	Queen's Honorary Nursing Sister
QHP	Queen's Honorary Physician
QHS	Queen's Honorary Surgeon
QMG	Quartermaster-General
QPM	Queen's Police Medal
QSO	quasi-stellar object *(quasar)*
	Queen's Service Order
quango	quasi-autonomous non-governmental organisation
qv	*quod vide* which see

R

r.	*recto* on the right-hand page
R	*Regina* Queen
	Rex King
RA	Royal Academy/Academician
	Royal Artillery
RAC	Royal Armoured Corps
RADA	Royal Academy of Dramatic Art
RADC	Royal Army Dental Corps
RAEC	Royal Army Educational Corps
RAES	Royal Aeronautical Society
	Royal Academy of Music
RAMC	Royal Army Medical Corps
RAVC	Royal Army Veterinary Corps
RC	Red Cross
	Roman Catholic
RCN	Royal College of Nursing
RD	Royal Naval and Royal Marine Forces Reserve Decoration
REME	Royal Electrical and Mechanical Engineers
Rep	Republican
Rep.	Republic
Revd	Reverend
RGS	Royal Geographical Society
RHS	Royal Horticultural Society
RI	Royal Institute of Painters in Watercolours
	Royal Institution
RIR	Royal Irish Regiment
RM	Royal Marines
RMA	Royal Military Academy
RMT	National Union of Rail, Maritime and Transport Workers
RNIB	Royal National Institute of Blind People
RNID	Royal National Institute for Deaf People
RNR	Royal Naval Reserve
Roffen:	of Rochester (Bishop)
RPA	Rural Payments Agency
RSA	Royal Scottish Academician
	Royal Society of Arts
RSC	Royal Shakespeare Company
RSE	Royal Society of Edinburgh
Rt. Hon.	Right Honourable
RVS	Royal Voluntary Service

S

s	section (Public Acts)
	solidus shilling
Salop	Shropshire

Sarum:	of Salisbury (Bishop)
SCD	Doctor of Science
SDLP	Social Democratic and Labour Party
SEAQ	Stock Exchange Automated Quotations system
SEN	special educational needs
SF	Sinn Fein
SFO	Serious Fraud Office
SI	statutory instrument
	Système International d'Unités International System of Units
sic	*sic* so written
sig	signature
	Signor
SOE	Special Operations Executive
sp	*sine prole* without issue
Sr	Senior
	Sister (title)
SS	steamship
stet	*stet* let it stand (printing)
Sub Lt.	sub-lieutenant

T

TEFL	teaching English as a foreign language
TNT	trinitrotoluene (explosive)
trans.	translated
TRH	Their Royal Highnesses
trs	transpose (printing)

U

U	Unionist
uc	upper case (printing)
UDA	Ulster Defence Association
UG	undergraduate
UNESCO	United Nations Educational, Scientific, and Cultural Organization
USB	universal serial bus
USMCA	United States-Mexico-Canada Agreement
UTC	*Temps Universel Coordonné* coordinated universal time
UVF	Ulster Volunteer Force

V

v	*versus* against
v.	*verso* on the left-hand page
VC	Victoria Cross
Ven	Venerable
VR	Volunteer Reserves Service Medal
VSO	Voluntary Service Overseas

W

w.	widowed
WBC	World Boxing Council
WBO	World Boxing Organisation
WCC	World Council of Churches
WFTU	World Federation of Trade Unions
Winton:	of Winchester (Bishop)
WO	Warrant Officer
WRAC	Women's Royal Army Corps
WRAF	Women's Royal Air Force
WRNS	Women's Royal Naval Service
WS	Writer to the Signet

Y

YMCA	Young Men's Christian Association
YWCA	Young Women's Christian Association

Z

ZANU-PF	Zimbabwean African National Union-Patriotic Front

INDEX

THE
FINAL
TWIST

Jeffery Deaver is the No.1 international bestselling author of more than forty novels, three collections of short stories, and a nonfiction law book. His books are sold in 150 countries and translated into twenty-five languages. His first novel featuring Lincoln Rhyme, *The Bone Collector*, was made into a major motion picture starring Denzel Washington and Angelina Jolie. It has also been adapted into a blockbuster television series called *Lincoln* starring Russell Hornsby, due to premier on NBC in 2020. Jeffery Deaver has received or been shortlisted for a number of awards around the world. A former journalist, folksinger, and attorney, he was born outside Chicago and has a bachelor of journalism degree from the University of Missouri and a law degree from Fordham University. You can visit his website at www.JefferyDeaver.com.

@JefferyDeaver
/JefferyDeaverInt

Stand-Alones

The October List

No Rest for the Dead *(Contributor)*

Carte Blanche *(A James Bond Novel)*

Watchlist *(Contributor)*

Edge

The Bodies Left Behind

Garden of Beasts

The Blue Nowhere

Speaking in Tongues

The Devil's Teardrop

A Maiden's Grave

Praying for Sleep

The Lesson of Her Death

Mistress of Justice

Short Fiction

COLLECTIONS

Trouble in Mind

More Twisted

Twisted

ANTHOLOGIES

Nothing Good Happens After Midnight *(Editor and Contributor)*

A Hot and Sultry Night for Crime *(Editor and Contributor)*

Ice Cold *(Editor and Contributor)*

Books to Die For *(Contributor)*

The Best American Mystery Stories 2009 *(Editor)*

STORIES

Forgotten

Turning Point

Verona

The Debriefing

The Second Hostage

Ninth and Nowhere

Captivated

The Victims' Club

Surprise Ending

Double Cross

The Deliveryman

A Textbook Case

As he stared into the murk, he noted three wires dangling from the rafters. One, near the stairs, ended in a fixture and a small bulb. The wires in the middle and far end had been cut and the ends were wrapped with electrician's tape.

Shaw knew why the two had been operated on: to keep someone from getting a good view of the end of the cellar.

Shining the beam over the back wall, he stepped close.

Got it, Ash.

As with the rest of the basement, this wall was constructed of four-by-eight plywood sheets nailed to studs, floor to ceiling, painted flat black. But an examination of the seams of one panel revealed a difference. It was a hidden door, opening onto a secure room. He took the locking-blade knife from his pocket and flicked it open. After scanning the surface a moment longer, he located a slit near the bottom. He pushed the blade inside and heard a click. The door sprung outward an inch. Replacing the knife and drawing his gun, he crouched, shining the beam inside, holding the flashlight high and to the left to draw fire, if an enemy were present and armed.

He reached inside and felt for tripwires. None.

He slowly drew the door toward him with his foot.

It had moved no more than eighteen inches when the bomb exploded with a searing flash and a stunning roar and a piece of shrapnel took him in the chest.

2

The risk in detonations is usually not death.

Most victims of an IED are blinded, deafened and/or muti-lated. Modern bomb materials move at more than thirty thou-sand feet per second; the shock wave could travel from sea level to the top of Mount Everest in the time it takes to clear your throat.

Shaw lay on the floor, unable to see, unable to hear, coughing, in pain. He touched the spot where the shrapnel had slammed into him. Sore. But no broken-skin wound. For some reason the skin hadn't broken. He did a fast inventory of the rest of his body. His arms, hands and legs still functioned.

Now: find his weapon. A bomb is often a prelude to an attack.

He could see nothing but, on his knees, he patted the damp con-crete in a circular pattern until he located the gun.

Squinting, but still seeing nothing. You can't *will* your vision to work.

No time for panic, no time for thinking of the consequences to his lifestyle if he'd been permanently blinded or deafened. Rock climbing, motorbiking, traveling the country—all endangered, but not something to worry about right now.

But how could he tell where the assault was coming from? In a crouch he moved to where he thought the coal bin was. It would at least provide some cover. He tried to listen but all he could hear was a tinnitus-like ringing in his ears.

After five desperate minutes he was aware of a faint glow co-alescing at the far end of the cellar. Light from the kitchen above.

So his vision wasn't gone completely. He'd been temporarily blinded by the brilliance of the explosion. Finally he could make out the beam of his tac light. It was ten feet away. He collected it and shone the bright light throughout the basement and into the room on the other side of the hidden door.

No attackers.

He holstered his weapon and snapped his fingers beside each ear. His hearing was returning too.

Then he assessed.

What had just happened?

If the bomber had wanted an intruder dead, that could've easily been arranged. Shaw shone his light on the frame of the hidden door and found the smoking device, gray metal. It was a large flash-bang—designed with combustible materials that, when detonated, emitted blinding light and a stunning sound but didn't fling deadly projectiles; its purpose was to serve as a warning.

He looked carefully to see why he'd missed it. Well, interesting. The device was a projectile. It had been launched from a shelf near the hidden door, rigged to explode after a half second or so. This is what had hit him in the chest. The trigger would be a motion or proximity detector. Shaw had never heard of a mechanism like this.

He carefully scanned the room for more traps. He found none.

Who had set it? His father and his colleagues had likely made the secret room, but they probably would not have left the grenade.

Ashton Shaw never worked with explosives. Possessing them without a license was illegal, and, for all his father's serious devotion to survivalism and distrust of authority, he didn't break the law.

Never give the authorities that kind of control over you.

Then Shaw confirmed his father could not have created the trap. When he examined the device more closely under the searing white beam, he noted that it was military-issue and bore a date stamp of last year.

Shaw flicked on an overhead light and tucked his flashlight away. He saw a battered utility table in the center of the twenty-by-twenty space, an old wooden chair, shelves that were largely bare but held some papers and clothes. Other stacks of documents sat against the wall. A large olive-drab duffel bag was in the corner.

On the table were scores of papers.

Was this it? The hidden treasure that others—his father among them—had died for?

He walked around the table, so he was facing the doorway to the secret room, and bent forward to find out.

3

Colter Shaw was here because of a discovery he'd made on his family's Compound in the soaring peaks of eastern California. There, on high and austere Echo Ridge, where his father had died, Shaw had found a letter the man had written and hidden years ago.

A letter that would change Shaw's life.

Ashton began the missive by saying that over his years as a professor and amateur historian and political scientist, he'd come to distrust the power of large corporations, institutions, politicians and wealthy individuals "who thrive in the netherworld between legality and illegality, democracy and dictatorship." He formed a circle of friends and fellow professors to take on and expose their corruption.

The company that they first set their sights on was BlackBridge Corporate Solutions, a firm known for its work in the shadowy field of corporate espionage. The outfit was behind many questionable practices, but the one that Ashton and his colleagues found the most reprehensible was their "Urban Improvement Plan," or "UIP." On the surface it appeared to help developers locate real estate. But

BlackBridge took the brokerage role one step further. Working with local gangs, BlackBridge operatives flooded targeted neighborhoods with free and cheap opioids, fentanyl and meth. Addiction soared. As the neighborhoods became unlivable, developers swooped in to buy them up for next to nothing.

This same tactic won results for political clients: PACs, lobbyists and candidates themselves. The infestation of illegal drugs would cause a shift in population as residents moved out, affecting congressional districting. The UIP was, in effect, gerrymandering by narcotics.

BlackBridge's schemes became personal for Ashton Shaw when a friend and former student of his—then a San Francisco city councilman—began looking into the UIP operation. Todd Zaleski and his wife were found murdered, a close-range gunshot for each of them. It appeared to be a robbery gone bad, but Ashton knew better.

He and his colleagues looked for evidence against the company, hoping to build a case for authorities. Nearly all BlackBridge workers refused to talk to them but he managed to learn of an employee who felt the UIP had crossed a line. A researcher for BlackBridge, Amos Gahl, found some evidence and smuggled it out of the company. The man hid what he'd stolen somewhere in the San Francisco area. But before he could contact Ashton or the authorities, he too was dead—the victim of a suspicious car crash.

Ashton had written in his letter: *It became my obsession to find what Gahl had hidden.*

Then BlackBridge learned of Ashton and those who shared his obsession. Several died in mysterious accidents, and the others dropped out of the mission, fearful for their lives. Soon, Ashton was alone in his quest to bring down the company that had killed his student and so many others in the City by the Bay—and, likely, untold other cities.

Then on a cold October night, Colter Shaw, sixteen years old, discovered his father's body in desolate Echo Ridge.

Since then, he'd become well aware of the shady figures he was up against:

Ian Helms, founder and CEO of BlackBridge. Now in his mid-fifties and movie-star handsome, he had had some national defense or intelligence jobs in the past and had worked in politics and lobbying.

Ebbitt Droon, a "facilitator" for the company, which is to say a hitman, was wiry with rat-like features. After several personal run-ins with the man, including one that featured a Molotov cocktail hurled in Shaw's direction, he was sure that Droon was a certifiable sadist.

Crema Braxton, BlackBridge operative in charge of stopping Ashton—and now stopping his son. Of her Ashton had written:

She may look like somebody's grandmother but oh, my, no.
She's the picture of ruthlessness and will do what needs to be
done.

She was an external relations supervisor, a euphemistic job description if ever there was one.

Ashton had concluded his letter with this:

Now, we get around to you.

You've clearly followed the breadcrumbs I've left leading you
to Echo Ridge and now know the whole story.

I can hardly in good conscience ask you to take on this
perilous job. No reasonable person would. But if you are so
inclined, I will say that in picking up where my search has

ended, you'll be fighting to secure justice for those who have perished or had their lives upended by BlackBridge and its clients, and you'll be guaranteeing that thousands in the future will not suffer similar fates.

The map included here indicates the locations in the city that might contain—or lead to—the evidence Gahl hid. After leaving this letter and accompanying documents, I will be returning to San Francisco and I hope I will have found more leads. They can be found at 618 Alvarez Street in San Francisco.

Finally, let me say this:

Never assume you're safe.

A.S.

4

This was Colter Shaw's mission. To check out each of the locations on his father's map—there were eighteen of them—and find the evidence Amos Gahl had hidden.

As he now looked over the documents in the secret room of the safe house's basement, he realized they had nothing to do with BlackBridge. They had to do with engineering projects and shipping. Some in English, some in Russian or perhaps another language using Cyrillic characters. Other printouts were in Spanish, a language that he could speak, and they related to shipping and transportation too. There were a number in Chinese as well.

Someone was using the secret room as a base of operations. One of the original members of his father's circle? Or, like Shaw, second generation? A man or a woman? Young? Middle-aged? Some of these materials were dated recently. He turned to the duffel bag on the floor and—after an examination for a tripwire—unzipped it.

Inside was the answer to the question of gender. The clothing was a man's, of larger-than-average physique. T-shirts, work shirts, cargo pants, jeans, sweaters, wool socks, baseball caps, gloves, casual jackets. Everything was black, charcoal gray or dark green.

Then he saw in the shadows against the back wall another stack of papers. Ah, here was his father's material. It was Ashton from whom Shaw had learned the art of calligraphy, and the man wrote in a script even more elegant—and smaller—than Shaw's.

His heart beat just a bit faster, seeing these.

Shaw carried the stack upstairs and set the papers on the rickety kitchen table. He sat down in an equally uncertain chair and began to read. There were more details about the UIP, and references to other schemes the company engaged in: dodgy earthquake inspections of high-rises (some located *on* the San Andreas Fault, no less), government contract kickbacks, land-use and zoning ploys, stock market manipulations, money laundering.

There was a clipping about the death of a California state assemblyman, with two question marks beside the victim's picture. The man had died in a car crash on the way to meet with a state attorney general. The resulting fire had destroyed his auto and boxes of records he had with him. The crash was curious but no criminal investigation was begun.

He found as well articles about Todd Zaleski, his father's former student turned city councilman whom Ashton believed was murdered by BlackBridge.

Everything he found hinted at the company's guilt. But this wasn't evidence—at least not enough for a prosecutor. Shaw had some experience on the topic of criminal law. After college he'd worked in a law firm, while deciding whether to take the LSATs and apply to law school. He'd been particularly inspired to study the subject by one Professor Sharphorn at the University of Michigan and thought he might take up the profession. In the end, his restless nature put the kibosh on a desk job, but an interest in the law stayed with him and he often read up on the subject; it was also helpful in his reward-seeking job.

No, nothing his father had found would interest the D.A.'s office.

Shaw then found a note, presumably from a colleague of Amos Gahl, intended for Ashton. It was a small sheet of paper folded many times. This no doubt meant it would have been left in a dead-drop, a spy technique of hiding communiqués under park benches or cracks in walls, avoiding the risk of electronic intercepts.

> *Amos is dead. It's in a BlackBridge courier bag. Don't know where he hid it. This is my last note. Too danger-ous. Good luck.*

So "it"—the evidence—was in a company bag hidden in one of the eighteen locations Ashton had identified as a likely spot. An arduous task, but there was no way around it. He'd have to start with the first and keep going until he found the courier bag—or give up after none of them panned out.

But he soon learned he wouldn't have to investigate eighteen locations. In fact, he didn't need to check out any.

He discovered in the stack a map identical to the one he'd found in Echo Ridge—well, identical except for one difference. All eighteen of the locations were crossed off with bold red Xs.

After leaving the map at the Compound, Ashton, as he'd written, had returned here and searched the sites himself, eliminating them all.

Shaw sighed. This meant that the evidence that would destroy BlackBridge could be squirreled away anywhere within the entire San Francisco Bay Area, which had to embrace thousands of square miles.

Maybe Ashton had discovered other possible sites. Shaw returned to the material to look for more clues, but his search was interrupted at that moment.

From Alvarez Street, out in front of the safe house, a woman called out. "Please!" she cried. "Somebody! Help me!"

5

Shaw looked out the bay window to see two people struggling in front of the chain-link gate that opened onto a scruffy lot containing the remnants of a building that had been partly burned years ago.

The dark-haired woman was in her thirties, he guessed. Dressed in faded jeans, a T-shirt, a scuffed dark blue leather jacket, running shoes. A white earbud cord dangled. She was looking around frantically as a squat man, dressed in a dusty, tattered combat jacket and baggy pants, gripped her forearm. The man was white and had a grimy look about him. Homeless, Shaw guessed, and, like many, possibly schizophrenic or a borderline personality. The man held a box cutter and was pulling the woman toward the gate. He seemed strong, which wasn't unusual; life on the street was physically arduous; to get by you needed to practice a version of survivalism. Even from this distance, Shaw could see veins rising high on the man's hands and forehead.

Through the front door and down the concrete steps fast, then approaching the two of them. Her face desperate, eyes wide, the woman looked toward him. "Please! He's hurting me!"

The attacker's eyes cut to Shaw. At first there was a mad defiance on the man's face, which struck Shaw as impish. With his short height and broad chest, he might be cast as a creature in a fantasy or mythological movie. His hands indeed looked strong.

"Oh, yeah, skinny boy, you want some of this? Fuck off."

Shaw kept coming.

The man waved the weapon dramatically. "You think I'm kidding?"

Shaw kept coming.

You'd think the guy wouldn't be in a carnal mood any longer, given the third-party presence. But he gripped the woman just as insistently as a moment ago, as if she were a home-run ball he'd caught in the stadium and wasn't going to give up to another fan. Without loosening his hold he stepped closer toward Shaw.

Who kept coming.

"Jesus! You deaf, asshole?"

In the Shaw family's Sierra Nevada enclave, where he had taught his children survival skills, Ashton had spent much time on firearms, those confounding inventions that are both blessings and curses. One of his father's rules was borrowed—straight from Shooting Practices 101.

Never draw a gun unless you intend to use it.

Shaw drew the Glock and pointed it at the attacker's head.

The man froze.

Shaw was taking his father's rule to heart, as he usually did with the man's lengthy list of don'ts. He believed, however, that the definition of *use* was open to interpretation. His was somewhat broader than Ashton's. In this case it meant not pulling the trigger but instead scaring the shit out of someone.

It was working.

"Oh . . . No, man . . . no, don't! Please! I didn't mean anything. I was just standing here. Asked her for some money. I ain't ate in a week. Then she starts coming on to me."

Shaw didn't say anything. He wasn't someone who negotiated or bantered. He kept the gun steady as he gazed coolly at the puckish face, which was encircled with damp, swept-back hair in a style that, Shaw believed, mercifully ceased to exist around 1975.

After a brief moment, the attacker released the woman. She stepped away, leaning against a segment of chain-link fence, breathing hard. Eyes were wide in her stricken face.

The building must have burned five years ago but, with the weighty moisture in the air, you could still detect burnt wood.

The man retracted the blade on the box cutter and started to put it away.

"No. Drop it."

"I—"

"Drop. It."

The gray tool clattered onto the gravelly sidewalk.

"Out of here now."

The man held up both his hands and backed away. Then he paused. He cocked his head and, with narrowed eyes and a hint of hope in his face, he asked, "Any chance you can spare a twenty?"

Shaw grimaced. The man ambled up the street.

Shaw holstered the gun and scanned the area. Only one other person was on the street—a bearded man in a thigh-length black coat and dark slacks, a stocking cap and an Oakland A's backpack. He wasn't nearby and was facing away. If he'd seen the incident, he had no interest in the participants or what had happened. The man stepped into an independent coffee shop. San Francisco, with its Italian roots, had many of these.

"My God," the woman whispered. "Thank you!" She was a little shorter than Shaw's six feet even, but not much, with an athletic build, toned legs and thighs under her tight-fitting distressed jeans. She had slim hips and lengthy arms. The veins were prominent in the backs of her hands too, just like her attacker's. Her brown hair was loose. She wore no makeup on her face, which seemed weather-toughened. A scar started near her temple and disappeared into her hairline.

"I don't know what to say. Are you, umm, police?" She glanced toward the weapon on his right hip and then perused him. She was wary.

With his short blond hair, muscular build and taciturn manner, Colter Shaw could easily be mistaken for law enforcement, a fed or a detective running complex homicides—the stuff of anti-terror cases. Today, she'd think, he was undercover, as he'd ridden here on the Yamaha in his biker gear: the jacket, navy-blue shirt under a black sweater to conceal his weapon, blue jeans and black Nocona boots.

"Kind of a private eye."

"I'm Tricia," she said.

He didn't give his, either real or a cover.

She shook her head, apparently at her own behavior. "Stupid, stupid . . ."

Shaw said, "Find a better quality of dealer. Or don't use at all." But he shrugged. "Easy for me to say."

Her lips tightened; she looked down. "I know. I try. This program, that program. Maybe this's a wake-up call." She offered him a wan smile. "Thank you, really."

And, in the opposite direction of the creature from Middle-earth, she walked off.

6

Shaw returned to the safe house, headed for the kitchen and the documents, but he got no farther than the living room.

He stopped, staring at a shelf on which sat a six-inch statuette, a bronze bald eagle. Wings spread, talons out, predator's eyes focused downward.

Shaw picked it up and turned it over in his hand, righted it once more.

To the casual observer, what he was holding looked to be a competently sculpted souvenir from a wildlife preserve gift shop, one of the more expensive behind-the-counter items.

But it was significantly more than that to Colter Shaw.

He had last seen it on a shelf in his bedroom in the Compound many years ago. Before it went missing. He had from time to time wondered where it had ended up. Had he stored it away himself when he'd cleaned his room to make space for gear or weapons he'd made or discoveries from his endless hikes through the mountains surrounding the Compound: rocks, pinecones, arrowheads, bones?

Finding it here gave him considerable pleasure, at last understanding the artwork's fate. His father must have brought it with him here as a reminder of his middle child. Shaw was thankful too it was not lost forever; how he'd come into possession of the sculpture was an important aspect of his childhood, a memento of an incident that had undoubtedly launched him into his present career and lifestyle.

The Restless Man . . .

But this icon of a bird in muscular flight brought sorrow too. It resurrected other memories of his childhood: specifically of his older brother, Russell.

Years ago, during a bad spell, Ashton Shaw had insisted that Dorion, then thirteen, make a one-hundred-foot free-climb up a sheer rock face in the middle of the night. This was a test. All of his children had to make the ascent when they became teenagers.

Russell and Colter already had done so. But had come to believe that the rite of passage was pointless, especially for their sister. Dorie was as talented athletically as her brothers with chalk and rope, and more so than Ashton himself. She'd already proved her ascent skills, including night climbs.

With a mind of her own even then, Dorion had simply decided she didn't need to . . . or want to. "Ash. No." The girl never shied.

But her father wouldn't let it go. He grew more and more riled and persistent.

The older brother intervened. Russell also said no.

The confrontation turned ugly. A knife was involved—on Ashton's part. And Russell, using skills his father himself had taught, prepared to defend his sister and take the weapon away from the wild-eyed man.

Mary Dove, her husband's psychiatrist and med-dispenser in chief—had been away on a family emergency, so there was no adult present to defuse the situation.

After a boilingly tense moment their father backed down and retreated to his bedroom, muttering to himself.

Not long after, Ashton had died in a fall from Echo Ridge.

The circumstances were suspicious, and more troubling, Shaw learned that his brother had lied about his whereabouts at the time of Ashton's death. He was, in fact, not far from Echo Ridge. Shaw believed that Russell had murdered the man. He was sure it had been agonizing, an impossible decision on his brother's part. But he guessed that at some point Russell had come to believe it was Dorie's life or Ashton's, and Russell made his choice. By then Ashton Shaw had become someone very different from the kind and witty man and teacher the children had known growing up.

Shaw had made his own impossible decision: accepting that his brother was guilty of patricide. The thought tore at him for years, and tore him and Russell apart.

Then, just weeks ago, the truth: Russell had had nothing to do with Ashton's death. It was a BlackBridge operative responsible, trailing their father to Echo Ridge on that cold, cold night in October.

Ebbitt Droon himself had told Shaw the story. "Your father . . . Braxton wanted him dead—but not yet, not till she had what she wanted. She sent somebody to, well, talk to him about the documents."

"Talk" meant torturing Ashton into giving up what he knew about Amos Gahl's theft of company secrets and evidence.

Droon had explained, "Near as we can piece it together, your father knew Braxton's man was on his way to your Compound. Ashton tipped to him and led him off, was going to kill him somewhere in the woods. The ambush didn't work. They fought. Your father fell."

But until that revelation, Shaw had indeed believed in his heart that Russell was their father's murderer. Devastated by false accusation, even if unspoken, Russell had vanished from the family's life.

No one had heard from him since Ashton's funeral, more than a decade ago.

Colter Shaw made his living finding people—good ones and bad, those lost because of fate and circumstance and those lost because they chose to be lost. He had devoted considerable time and money and effort to tracking down his brother. What he would say when he found him, Shaw had no idea. He'd practiced a script of one brother talking to the other, explaining, seeking forgiveness, trying to find a path out of estrangement.

But all his efforts had come to nothing. Russell Shaw had vanished, and he'd vanished very, very well.

Shaw recalled discussing this very subject with someone just last week, describing the impact.

The man had asked, "What would you say was the greatest minus regarding your brother? What hurts the most?"

Shaw had answered, "He'd been my friend. I was his. And I ruined it."

Seeing this eagle now made him feel Russell's absence all the more.

He set the statue on the kitchen table and returned to the stack of his father's materials. For an hour he pored over the documents. He found two notes in his father's fine hand. They didn't relate to the eighteen locations, which meant he'd discovered these spots after completing the scavenger hunt of the map.

One note was about a commercial building in the Embarcadero, the district along the eastern waterfront of San Francisco: the Hayward Brothers Warehouse.

The other was an address in Burlingame, a suburb south of the city, 3884 Camino.

Shaw now texted his private eye, requesting information. Mack McKenzie soon replied that she could find little more about the warehouse beyond that it was a historic building dating to the late

1800s, was not open for business to the public, and was presently for sale. The Burlingame address was a private home, owned by a man named Morton T. Nadler.

Shaw also found a business card, which represented a third possible location as well, the Stanford Library of Business and Commerce.

The library was located not in Palo Alto, where the university was situated, but in a part of town known as South of Market. Maybe it had nothing to do with Gahl's stolen evidence; it would be an odd place to hide a courier bag. Possibly Ashton Shaw had used it for research. He had never owned a computer, and certainly had never allowed one in any residence of his, so maybe he'd gone to the library to use one of its public workstations.

Shaw decided the library would be his first stop. It was the closest to the safe house. If that didn't pan out he would try the house in Burlingame and then the warehouse.

First, though, some security measures.

San Francisco was BlackBridge's turf. Odds were ninety percent that they didn't know he was here. But that dark ten percent required some due diligence.

He called up an app on his phone.

It happened to be tracing the whereabouts of Irena Braxton and Ebbitt Droon at that very moment.

Just the other day—under a fake identity—Braxton had talked her way into Shaw's camper and stolen what she thought was Ashton's map marking the places were Gahl's evidence was hidden and other materials.

Shaw had tipped to who she really was. What he'd intentionally left for her to steal was a map with eighteen phony locations marked and a copy of Henry David Thoreau's *Walden*, filled with code-like gibberish in the margins. A GPS tracker was hidden in the book's spine.

In the past two days the tracker had meandered over various

locations he'd marked on the map and spent time in a commercial skyscraper in downtown San Francisco, on Sutter Street, probably BlackBridge's satellite office. This was its present location.

He now shifted to Google Maps and examined the neighborhood in which the Stanford library was located. He hardly expected trouble but it was a procedure he followed with every reward job. Information was the best weapon a survivalist could have.

Which didn't mean hardware should be neglected.

Shaw checked his gun once more.

Never assume your weapon is loaded and hasn't been damaged or sabotaged since the last time you used it.

The .380 was indeed loaded, one in the bedroom and six in the mag. It was a good dependable pistol—as long as you held it firmly while firing. The model had a reputation for limp wrist failure to eject: spent brass hanging in the receiver. Colter Shaw had never had this problem.

He seated the gun in his gray plastic inside-the-waistband holster and made sure it was hidden. The rule was that if you're carrying concealed, you should keep it concealed, lest a concerned citizen spot the weapon, panic and call the cops.

There was another reason too.

Never let the enemy know the strength of your defenses . . .

7

A new threat.

As he stood beside his bike Shaw was aware that someone was watching him.

Slight build, leather jacket, baseball cap.

The giveaway was the sunglasses. Hardly necessary this morning. The day was typically foggy—sometimes the cloak burned off, sometimes it remained, sluggish and dull, like an irritating houseguest. Now the haze hung thickly in air redolent of damp pavement, exhaust, a hint of trash and the sea. In San Francisco, you were never far from water.

Shaw had examined the street subtly after leaving and locking the safe house. At first he saw no one other than the bearded man he'd spotted earlier, in the thigh-length black coat and stocking cap, Oakland A's backpack at his feet. He was at a table outside the coffee shop, sipping from a cup and texting. Then Shaw glanced into the Yamaha motorbike's rearview mirror and spotted the spy, a block and a half away.

Odds he was mistaken? Fifty percent.

He casually turned, checking out the rear tire of the Yamaha and looking back while not exactly looking.

The man disappeared behind the corner of the building where he'd been standing.

Bringing the answer to the surveillance question to nearly one hundred percent.

Who could it have been?

He was built like Droon—but if it were anyone from BlackBridge, how could they have learned about the safe house? Besides, in that case, they would have been on him the instant he stepped outside. A team would have forced him back into the safe house to have a "discussion" about what he was doing here in the city and where he believed Gahl's evidence was hidden.

Instead, he suspected it was the Russian- and Chinese-speaking inhabitant of the safe house, the man who was so adept at loud and blinding booby traps. Make that sixty percent.

And the odds that the man wasn't happy Shaw was now in residence and had likely examined charts and graphs he'd gone to great lengths to keep secret? An easy ninety-nine percent on that one.

Was it one of his father's colleagues? Or a successor in interest, like Shaw himself?

Possibly. No way to estimate the odds without any more information.

Dalton Crowe? The lug of a bounty hunter had crossed paths and traded blows with Shaw over the years. He was presently under the erroneous impression that Shaw had cheated him out of tens of thousands of dollars of reward money. Crowe didn't live anywhere near here but the man was a bully bordering on psychopathy. A drive of a thousand miles or so to collect a debt, even mistakenly, was well within his wheelhouse.

True, Crowe sported a refrigerator's physique, twice the size of the spy. But that didn't mean he hadn't recruited an underling. When you believe in your heart a man owes you $50K, you'll spend some capital to get it back.

Someone from a past job out for revenge? Absolutely a possibility. Just a few weeks ago, Shaw had made some enemies in Silicon Valley when a simple reward job turned into something considerably darker. The foes he'd made in the tech world of video gaming were particularly resourceful and, he had to assume, vindictive.

He thought of the squat, broad-chested man he'd confronted earlier, Tricia's attacker. Unlikely he'd return but people bested in a fight had been known to come back with superior firepower for a touch of revenge. It would be stupid and pointless, but those two words described more than a little slice of decisions made by the general population. He dismissed this, though, on the basis of the difference in physique.

He turned back to the front of the bike and unhooked it from the lamppost, stowing the impressive chain and lock. As he did, he took another glance in the rearview mirror and noted that his shadow had eased back into observing position.

Shaw tugged on his helmet and black leather gloves.

He unzipped his jacket and lifted the sweater for easy access to his weapon. Then, in an instant, the engine clattered to life and Shaw's boot tip tapped into first gear. He twisted the throttle hard. The rear tire swirled and smoked and he spun the bike one hundred and eighty degrees, launching into the street.

The figure vanished.

Shaw hit forty. As he neared the intersection where he'd turn to the right to confront the spy, he downshifted and eased off the gas, skidding to a fast stop. Shaw had to assume that the watcher was armed and targeting where he would spin around the corner, so without presenting himself as a target, he leaned the bike to the right and used the rearview mirror to view the cross street.

There was no threat but, damn it, he could see a car speeding away.

He gunned the engine again and pursued.

For about thirty feet.

Oh hell . . .

He slammed the rear brake hard, then gripped the front, the trickier of the two, the one that could send you over the handlebars. He managed to control the skid and bring the bike to stop just in time, before he ran through the bed of nails that the spy apparently had tossed onto the cobblestones before climbing into his car and speeding away. It was a clever trick, an improvised version of the nail strip that the police use to end high-speed chases. If the watcher had more in mind than just spying, he'd return with a weapon the minute Shaw set the bike down.

He caught a glimpse of the vehicle—a dark green Honda Accord with California plates. He couldn't make out the number. It vanished to the left, speeding toward the entrance ramp to the freeway.

Now that the spy had been made, would that be the end of him?

Shaw thought: ninety-nine-point-five percent no. But he had no facts for this number, just intuition.

He dismounted, found a piece of cardboard and swept the nails into a storm drain—concerned for fellow bikers' safety, of course, but also because, if there was an accident, he wouldn't want emergency vehicles in the area, their lights and sirens attracting attention and the police might go door by door to ask for witnesses.

He couldn't go on to the library just yet. Somebody—clearly a hostile—now knew about the safe house. He climbed onto the bike and sped back to the safe house. There he photographed every one of his father's documents and encrypted and uploaded them to his secure cloud storage system, copying Mack.

Returning then to the Yamaha, he fired the bike up once more and sped into the street, accelerating hard, as he headed for the main road that would take him to the Stanford library.

Suddenly, thoughts about the spy's identity and purpose were gone. It took only a few yards for the exhilaration to wrap its arms around him. Rock climbing was a complex, intellectual joy. Low-gear, high-throttle racing around corners on slidey tires, powering up and over hills . . . well, that was a pure, raw high.

Shaw had seen the police thriller *Bullitt*, from the '60s, in which the actor Steve McQueen—to whom, Shaw was regularly reminded, bore more than a passing resemblance—had muscled his Ford Mustang through the winding and hilly streets of San Francisco in pursuit of two hitmen in a Dodge Charger—the best car-chase scene ever filmed. When in town here, on his bike, Shaw never missed the chance to exploit the tricky and exhilarating geography of the city just like Detective Frank Bullitt, occasionally going airborne and enjoying lavish skids.

He now plowed through the neighborhood the safe house was located in: the Mission.

Shaw had some affection for the area, where he'd spent weeks on a reward job a few years back. The district had been sparsely populated until the infamous 1906 earthquake, which destroyed much of San Francisco. Because there was more open land and therefore less quake and fire damage in the Mission, residents began to move here to start life anew. These newcomers were Anglo—largely Polish and German—as well as Chicano and Latino. In the early to mid-twentieth century, the neighborhood was tawdry and rough-and-tumble and more than a little lawless. So it remained until the '70s, when counterculture hit.

The Mission was the epicenter of the punk music scene in the city, and of the gay, lesbian and trans communities as well.

Shaw had learned too, in his search for the Benson twins, that one of the more interesting aspects of the district was the number of inhabitants whose families came from the Yucatan. In the portion of the Mission he was driving through now, the Mayan language—expressive and complex—was the main tongue of many residents. He sped past grassy In Chan Kaajal Park, which in Mayan means "My Little Town."

As he traveled north he left the Mission behind and cruised into SoMa, the silly urbanized abbreviation of "South of Market." It was also known—mostly among the old-timers—by the more interesting nic "South of the Slots," after a now-defunct cable car that had run along Market. Like the Mission, SoMa had a colorful history but now that color was giving way to enterprise. This was home to scores of corporate headquarters, museums, galleries and traditional performing venues. What would the punksters have said?

Shaw soon arrived at the library, which was located on the north border of SoMa, the more affluent portion of the neighborhood. This portion of SoMa was close to the financial district and the legal firms and corporations that would use the services of a university business library.

Shaw pulled to the curb and idled his bike across the street from the library, which was a functional two-story structure constructed of glass and aluminum framing. Architecturally, the place didn't approach interesting. But Shaw observed it closely. He saw people were coming and going, dressed in conservative business attire for the most part. Some messengers, a few delivery people.

He pretended to make a phone call as he observed the entry procedures.

There was one entrance into a large lobby and inside were two doorways. One, to the left facing the guard station, was for visitors. The other, to the right, was members only. Visitors to the public side had to walk through a metal detector and dump pocket litter into a basket for examination. You also needed to display an ID, and your name was jotted down on a clipboard sheet, but there was no confirmation of your identity.

He dropped the bike into gear and drove up the block to a space reserved for cycles and scooters. He locked the Yamaha to a post with a snaky cable. He affixed his helmet too. Looking around, he slipped the holstered gun and blade into a locked compartment, under the seat, he'd built for this purpose. He'd made sure the hidden GPS transmit system, like a LoJack, was active—even a double-chained motorcycle can be stolen by a determined thief.

Colter Shaw didn't like leaving the weapons but there was no option. Then he reminded himself not to let his father's paranoia enwrap him entirely. After all, how much trouble could he possibly get himself into in a library?

8

He had his story ready.

Legal associate Carter Skye, of the law firm Dorion & Dove, had been sent by his firm to look up an insurance law issue. This cover was not made up entirely out of whole cloth. When he was a legal assistant years ago, he'd had to do some research on the topic for one of the partners. It was a tricky question of subrogation—when an insurance company pays off a claim and then earns the right to sue in the insured's name.

The pleasant Latino guard, however, had no interest in what Skye/Shaw's purpose might be, and Shaw had been undercover enough times to know never to make an otherwise innocent story seem suspicious by volunteering information.

"There a charge?" he asked.

The man explained that if you weren't affiliated with a school, entrance was ten dollars, which Shaw handed over in cash. Then, on request, he displayed his ID, which happened to feature his picture, height, weight and eye color, but the name, Skye, was his cover from his most recent undercover role. Mack was an expert at ginning up new identities. (This was completely legal as long as you didn't try to trick the law or scam someone.)

A machine hummed and out eased a sticky-backed badge with his picture on it. He plastered it onto his chest.

Shaw debated about showing the picture of Amos Gahl—he'd taken a shot with his phone from the article about the man's death—and asking if the guard remembered his being in here. The man, though, was young and if Gahl had used the library it would have been years ago.

"What's over there?" Shaw pointed to the double doors to the right.

MEMBERS ONLY

"Historical documents mostly."

"Legal?"

"Some. And planning and zoning, real estate, government filings."

"That right? My partners're handling a case with some issues going back thirty, forty years. I'm looking for some old housing rulings that city hall doesn't have. Is there any way I can get in?"

He hoped a senior librarian wouldn't pop out and ask what, specifically, he wanted.

"You gotta make an appointment. Call this number." The man handed Shaw a card, which vanished into his jeans pocket. It was more likely that his father or Gahl had used the public side of the place. If he found nothing there, maybe he'd bone up on old California real estate law and try to get inside the private portion.

Shaw thanked the man and then walked through the unresponsive metal detector into the spacious and well-lit open-to-the-public portion of the library.

Now, where to go from here?

It was an upscale facility, as you might expect, being attached to one of the best endowed universities in the country. In the center was a librarian's station, circular. A Black man of about thirty-five in a beige suit sat there, focused on his computer monitor.

Radiating outward from the center were rows of tables and spacious computer workstations with large monitors. The screen saver—a moving block of the name of the library—ricocheted in a leisurely fashion around each monitor. The desks and cubicles offered office supplies: pens, pads of paper, Post-it notes and paper clips. Ringing this open space were the stacks, containing books and periodicals. There were floor-to-ceiling windows in the front and on the side. Against the back wall were what seemed to be a dozen offices or conference rooms. Circling the second-floor balcony was a series of stacks and rooms, just as down here.

There weren't many patrons in this portion of the first floor. Two older businessmen who'd doffed their suit jackets pored over old books. A young woman in a plaid dress and a slim man in a dark suit and white shirt—both looked to be mid-thirties—were on computers.

Instinctively Shaw examined the library for escape routes. He sensed no threat, of course, but scanning for exits was a survival thing. He did it everywhere he went, automatically.

Never lose your orientation . . .

There was the front door, of course, and a stairway that led to the second floor. An elevator. A glass door in the back of the stacks led to the members-only side of the library. It opened onto a conference room, which might lead to other exits in the back of the structure, though it was presently occupied; a middle-aged businesswoman in a suit and a lean man in dark casual jacket sat with their backs to the glass door. A somber-faced man with bright blond hair sat across the table from them. The door had a latch but Shaw had no way of knowing whether or not it was now locked.

The left-side floor-to-ceiling windows featured a fire door, fitted with an alarm. It exited onto a side street. There were men's and women's restrooms, and a door on which was a sign: SUPPLIES.

He tucked this information away and got to work. Assuming that his father had identified the library as a place where Gahl might have hidden the evidence, where would the man have concealed it?

Shaw guessed that he probably had not stashed the entire courier bag, which he guessed from the name was not a slim piece of luggage; it would be conspicuous. He would probably have emptied it and put the contents—copies of incriminating emails, correspondence, spreadsheets, computer drives or disks, whatever it might be—in an out-of-the-way place. Maybe in the pages of a book or journal, maybe in the shadowy areas behind the volumes in the stacks or on top of the racks, maybe in the spaces beneath drawers in a workstation.

He strolled through the stacks, filled with such titles as *Liability in Maritime Collision Claims: Bays and Harbors*; *Piercing the Corporate Veil*; *Incorporation Guide for Nonprofits*. Easily four or five thousand books. He noted that many were outdated, like *Who's Who of San Francisco Commerce: 1948*. What better hiding place for documents or a CD or thumb drive than a book of that sort? In plain sight, yet inside a volume that no one would possibly need to refer to.

Yet Shaw calculated it would take a month to go through all the volumes. And it would be impossible to do that without arousing suspicion . . . No, Gahl was not a stupid man. He hid the evidence because he knew there was a chance he would be killed. It would be hidden in a place that somebody, a colleague, the police, could deduce.

Shaw noticed the librarian was looking his way.

He nodded a friendly greeting to the man, walked to one of the workstations and sat down. A swipe of the mouse revealed the main screen to be an internal database of the library's contents. Just what he wanted. He typed in *Gahl, Amos*. Nothing. Then *Shaw, Ashton*. Negative on that too.

But with *BlackBridge*, he had a hit.

The reference was to a book titled *California Corporate Licenses, Volume I.*

Had Gahl reasoned that Ashton Shaw or someone would do this very thing, run a computer search for the company, and accordingly hidden the evidence in the book?

An elegant and simple clue.

The listing sent Shaw to a stack near the librarian station. Yes, there was the book: thick and bound in dark red faux leather. He lifted the tome off the shelf and set it on the floor. Then he removed the adjoining volumes and examined the space behind them. Seeing nothing, he reached in and felt along the cool metal. Nothing. He returned the other books and took *Corporate Licenses* back to the workstation.

He began his examination, first opening up the book to see if Gahl had hollowed out a portion and slipped a thumb drive or chip inside. No, he hadn't. Nor were there any folded documents or notes between pages. The book was simply a listing of corporations with licenses to do business in the state. Shaw turned next to the Black-Bridge entry, thinking that would be a logical place to hide something or to leave a message about where the material was. Nothing. Shaw read the listing. The company was merely mentioned by name, without any other information. The headquarters was given as being in Los Angeles, which Shaw already knew, with offices in San Francisco and other cities.

He examined the hefty volume page by page. No evidence, no notes, no margin jottings. He probed into the spine too.

Nothing.

Hell. He re-shelved it and returned once more to the computer.

More searches. The councilman who'd been killed by Black-Bridge: *Zaleski, Todd.* No hits there. Had Gahl been clever with anagrams or other subtle clues? He typed in variations on the search terms.

He tried *UIP* and *Urban Improvement Plan.*

Without success.

He deleted his search history then swiped the computer to sleep, deciding that it was likely the library *wasn't* a possible hiding space for Gahl's materials after all. Maybe Shaw's other theory was correct. His father simply had used the library's computers to do online searches.

So, a waste of time.

Colter Shaw, however, corrected himself. No, that wasn't true; *eliminating* a possible lead is never a waste; the visit had gotten him one step closer to his goal. He'd learned to embrace this attitude in the reward-seeking business. Step by step by step.

It was time to get to the warehouse in the Embarcadero and the home in Burlingame, the last best chances for finding the evidence.

Before he left, though, he pulled out his phone and called up the tracking app, receiving data from the device he'd hidden in the copy of *Walden*, which Braxton and Droon presumably still had with them.

He was disappointed to see that the tracker was malfunctioning. The map that popped up showed Shaw's, not the book's, location. Well, he hadn't believed the device would last forever. He then frowned and noticed that the pinging circle indicating the whereabouts of the tracker was coming not exactly from where Shaw sat but about thirty or so feet away.

A refresh of the system. The ping remained in the exact position it had been a moment ago.

No, impossible . . .

His breathing coming quickly, pulse tapping hard, he sent a text to Mack, including the code they used for immediate attention, asking her about the library.

In sixty seconds—the woman seemed always to be on duty—her response was:

Library has no affiliation with Stanford or any other university.
Owned by an offshore corporation. CEO is Ian Helms, head of
BlackBridge. R U there now?

He texted:

Yes.

Two seconds later his phone hummed with her reply.

GTFO.

This was a variation on the emergency plan all survivalists have,
to escape when an enemy is coming for you. The more common, and
less coarse, version is: Get the Hell Out.

9

The library was a cover.

It was the members-only portion of the building and not the high-rise on Sutter Street downtown that was BlackBridge's base of operation in San Francisco.

Shaw gazed in the direction where the tracker indicated the book was, and he realized that Irena Braxton and Ebbitt Droon were the very people whose backs he'd noted through the glass door that opened onto the other side of the building.

He glanced once more that way and saw a fourth man in the conference room. He was pacing, arms crossed, as he appeared to be debating something. He posed a question, it seemed—his hands were raised and his face appeared irritated. Then, when someone must have answered, he nodded and he paced some more, gazing absently into the public side of the library.

It was the CEO, Ian Helms. The athletic, handsome man wore a well-tailored suit and a Rolex on one wrist, a bracelet on the other, both gold.

This was the first time Colter Shaw had glimpsed the man responsible for his father's death.

Helms would probably have no idea what Shaw looked like but it was not the time to take any chances. He slipped from the workstation and disappeared into the far reaches of the stacks.

GTFO . . .

He started to circle around the perimeter of the library to the front door. He kept his head down, moving steadily but not too fast through the stacks.

Only twenty feet later he stopped.

He'd been busted.

From the shadows of the rows of books, Shaw saw a large security guard in a dark suit enter the public side of the building from the lobby. The well-tanned man's head was cocked and he appeared to be listening to the Secret Service–type earpiece with a curly wire that disappeared into his jacket. He walked to the librarian at the central station. They shared some words, both of them looking around. The guard's jacket parted and the grip of a pistol showed. A second guard joined them. He was slimmer and more pale than the first, but tall too. Also armed. Shaw noted his hand was near his own pistol.

How would they have learned about him?

Then he got his answer:

The taller guard, more a bouncer than your average rent-a-cop, strode forward to the terminal where Shaw had sat and gazed about. The slimmer one joined him.

Shaw had just typed in a smorgasbord of words that would turn the bots within the system into frenzied hounds.

Shaw . . . Gahl . . . BlackBridge.

Some software had been programmed to report in when keywords were searched. The computer had dimed him out.

And it got even better, Shaw thought sardonically. Peering

through the stacks, he noted that right above the volume in which he'd found BlackBridge's name was a security camera. The book might've been placed there for that very reason: to get a picture of anyone with an interest in the company. The bigger guard was now looking at a monitor at the librarian's station. Both security people turned to the spot where the volume had been shelved.

Okay, escape plans.

Toss a book in the opposite direction and when the guards moved toward it, just sprint out the front?

No, that wouldn't work. Droon, Braxton and the BlackBridge op with the bleached blond hair had now joined in. They were in the lobby and headed for the public section of the library. Alarm showed in Braxton's face. Droon and Blond were as focused as hunters closing in on an elk. They were accompanied by Ian Helms.

Shaw slipped toward the back wall, hidden by the rows upon rows of books. As he moved to the rear of the facility he noted that many of the titles were duplicated. Two, three, a dozen times. This added to the supposition that while one might do some legitimate research in this portion of the library it was also a trap.

BlackBridge security people would have come up with the tactic. Anyone with an interest in the company—investigators, competitors, those with a grudge or out for revenge—might find clues that led to the library. There would be minimal security to get inside. Then the interloper would ask some questions of the librarian or, like Shaw, type in a computer search, and he'd get tagged as a threat.

They would then use sophisticated facial recognition and other techniques to identify the person and decide what kind of risk they were, or—depending on what they browsed—that they were no threat at all. He wouldn't have been surprised to find that Black-Bridge had some DNA scanner on doorknobs and computer keypads. Certainly devices would be capturing fingerprints and retinal patterns.

The offenders would then leave, having conveniently deposited their names in the database that BlackBridge was sure to maintain.

Or, perhaps, the inquisitive customers would not leave at all.

Maybe Ashton had suspected this was a BlackBridge facility and was going to check it out but was killed before he had a chance. That might have been how his father came by the business card Shaw had found in the secret room on Alvarez Street.

The bigger guard was glancing back at Irena Braxton and pointing his finger directly at the chair in front of the computer where Shaw had been sitting a few minutes ago.

Shaw evaluated the enemy. Ian Helms appeared fit enough, but Shaw assessed that there was less than a twenty percent chance he'd want to get his hands dirty, especially with armed minders present. Braxton was a stocky, middle-aged woman. She might be ruthless but she wasn't much of a physical threat unless she had a weapon in her many-hued shoulder bag.

In addition to the security guards, the other two threats were Ebbitt Droon and the bright-haired, sullen-faced minder, Blond. Droon, though of small stature, was wiry and strong and was likely carrying the same .40 pistol he'd threatened Shaw with previously. It was probably silenced so that the cries resulting from the bone-shattering impact would be louder than the report of the weapon itself.

Blond looked to be pure muscle and would likely also be armed.

On the other hand, Shaw had the benefit of witnesses: the four patrons, the three men and the woman. He doubted they were involved. This meant BlackBridge probably couldn't take Shaw down the easy way—with a gunshot.

If he could dodge the hostiles and work his way to the front, as they sought him in the stacks, maybe he could make the sprint after all.

But then Shaw's safety net vanished. The librarian approached the four potential witnesses and apparently asked them to leave, and to leave quickly. Which they did, concern on their faces. They had probably been told that there was some security issue. In this day and age, a brief warning was all the information people needed to evacuate. Thinking: terrorists, a crazy man with a gun, a bomb.

Eyes still on the front door, Shaw noted Ian Helms walk quickly outside; he wouldn't want to be connected to whatever was going to happen.

Braxton stationed herself at the front door, while rodent-faced Droon spoke urgently to the two security men, who towered over him. They hurried to the central station where the librarian pointed to a large monitor, which was probably now in security camera mode. They'd be scanning the vids recorded in the past half hour and would soon know that he was still on the main floor.

Shaw noted that the elevator light went out. It had been shut down.

And what about a run to the stairs and then out the upper floor windows?

Shaw dismissed it as having only a twenty percent chance of success, at best. A leap from a second story isn't impossible, given a landing zone of grass or trash, but Shaw had observed that the surfaces on all four sides of the building were sidewalk, asphalt or cobblestones. That would have meant a likely sprained ankle. The resulting pain wasn't the problem—he'd suffered worse—but that injury would have limited his ability to flee and left him a sitting target for Droon and the others. And you had to land perfectly to avoid a broken bone, and *that* pain was debilitating. Besides, the windows were probably sealed, as they were on this floor.

A jump from the roof was not an option at all.

Keeping in the shadows against the back wall, he considered the front door once more. Five to ten percent. To reach it he'd have to go past Droon, Blond and the two armed guards. Maybe the librarian was armed too. And he supposed that that exit was now locked down.

The windows? He gave that escape route ten percent tops. The glass was thick, intruder-proof. A chair would take multiple blows and Droon and the others would be on him well before the pane shattered.

A 911 call?

Ashton certainly was unreasonably paranoid about many things, but Shaw recalled the note the man had left in the safe house:

> Don't trust anyone. Some local authorities—SFPD, others—on BlackBridge payroll. Evidence should go to D.C. or Sacramento.

Besides, even if the police officers who showed up were legit, Shaw would have to explain what his suspicions about the company were, and at this point he wasn't able to expose BlackBridge—not without Gahl's hard evidence.

He'd also have to answer for making an emergency call when there was no apparent threat of violence, and Braxton would deny everything. She'd report him as a dangerous trespasser.

He'd put a call to police/fire down as a last resort and try some other way to get out.

He decided that he would get to the fire exit. He put this at a seventy percent chance of success. Since the door opened onto that side street, he couldn't run directly to his cycle; that would mean crossing in front of the library. The hostiles would see and simply hurry from the front door to intercept him.

No, once on the side street he would turn right, away from his Yamaha. A half block away he'd turn right again onto another narrow street he recalled from the map he'd studied earlier. He'd continue on this for three or four blocks, where he'd come to a park surrounded by businesses and restaurants. There he could vanish into crowds and continue north, then cut east and finally south and get to the motorbike without approaching the library.

Shaw was a good runner. Ashton had trained the children in the art of both sprinting and long-distance running, using as models the famed tribal runners, the Tarahumara in Mexico and the Sierra Madres.

He was sure he could out-sprint scrawny Droon and the muscle-bound Blond.

The other guards? The tall one couldn't be a runner; he was too stocky. The slighter one? Maybe he was fast.

Shaw couldn't dodge their bullets of course, and the big unknown factor was: Would they risk drawing and using their weapons in public? Probably.

Which is why the fire door escape offered only a seventy percent chance of success.

He looked through a gap in a row of insurance industry books. Braxton stood at the door to the lobby, scanning the first floor, arms crossed. Droon and Blond started walking toward the stacks on Shaw's left, as he faced them. The security guards remained together and began the right-side flanking movement.

Shaw slipped to the fire door.

PUSH BAR. ALARM WILL SOUND.

Shaw hoped it wasn't like the emergency exits at airports; with those, pushing the bar resulted in a blaring alarm, but the lock didn't unlatch for fifteen seconds—to give security a chance to approach and see who wanted to get out onto the tarmac.

He took a deep breath, readying himself for the sprint.

A firm push on the bar of the fire door.

The bar traveled all the way to the base of the device, without resistance. Nothing happened. There was no alarm, and the lock didn't disengage.

The mechanism had been disabled.

Shaw fished the safe house keys from his pocket and tried to jimmy the lock. It didn't work. He tried the slimmer motorcycle key. Nothing.

He slipped into a workstation and looked out from underneath. The net was closing. He could see legs and shoes. The four hunters would converge on him in minutes.

Time for the last resort. He glanced at a nearby wall and, in a crouch, hurried to it and knelt, directly underneath the fire alarm box.

His right hand snaked upward aiming for the alarm.

"Now, lookee here." The voice behind him was singsongy, eerie because of its phony cheer. Ebbitt Droon continued, "We shut that little old alarm thing down too, don'tcha know? All in honor of you, Mr. Colter Shaw."

10

Droon and Blond were now joined by the two security men.

Rising, Shaw looked over Blond, whose cold eyes were the shade of ebony, suggesting that the shocking yellow of his hair came not from genes but a bottle. Shaw had seen eyes like that before: he'd earned a reward of twenty thousand dollars by tracking down an escaped serial killer near Tulsa. Once in handcuffs the man had stared at Shaw with a look that said: If I ever escape again, you're next on my list. Blond's gaze was of the same species.

Droon said, "So here you are, Mr. Didn't Listen to What I Told Him. And not more than a couple of weeks ago, wasn't it? Heavens. You are something else."

Shaw fired a focused gaze at Droon. The scrawny man—the gangs would describe him as a *skel*—wasn't the one who had grappled with his father on Echo Ridge, combat that resulted in Ashton's death, but he worked for the organization that was responsible and this made him as guilty as the killer, in Shaw's mind.

Droon squinted back and his haughty impishness vanished. He looked away.

Shaw surveyed the area, checking left then right. His eyes made a leisurely circuit. Sizing up the guards and Blond.

Droon's confidence returned. He repeated, "Coupla weeks. During which you had plentya time to muse over what I said, about you keeping out of our matters here. But didn't take, looks like. How come?"

The upper Midwest patois was pronounced and what he brought to the sound was the tone of the unstable.

"Who's getting into whose space, Droon? Answer me this. You *were* in Tacoma just a few days ago, setting fire to somebody's perfectly nice SUV, just so your boss could rob me."

The fire, which had engulfed a Nissan Pathfinder, had been initiated to distract Shaw, so that Irena Braxton could steal the phony map and the GPS-rigged copy of *Walden*. Shaw now feigned irritation. He needed to keep on life support the façade that the map and book weren't a setup.

Droon said, "Oh, think I'll plead my Fifth Amendment right on that one, son, don'tcha know?" He looked Shaw up and down. "Do say I'm sorry we didn't get to go one-on-one. That would be a most enjoyable five minutes." He glanced at Blond with a wink. The big man beside him said nothing, those dark marbles of eyes peering at Shaw. His arms, and they were substantial, dangled.

The two security guards remained back five or six feet.

Droon said to Blond, "The one I was telling you about. Doesn't look so balls-out, does he? Told you." A laugh. His bravado was fully recovered. Another sweep over Shaw. "Now. Listen here. I see what you're up to, the way you're calculating, looking 'round. Well, no cavalry's riding out of the hills to save you. You're solo, and there it is.

"Now, without givin' too much away—always a good rule in

this life, don'tcha know? Without givin' too much away, we're looking for a certain . . . *thing*, let's call it. A thing that your daddy was looking for too. And before he went to meet his sweet Maker I think he found out where it was. Since you're here, we're suspecting you've got some sound thoughts on where it is."

Irena Braxton approached them, slipping away her phone. He wondered whom she'd rung up so urgently—and triumphantly—about his capture.

Droon nodded to her and continued, "We've been visiting all sorts of fun and exciting places on Daddy's map but we're not finding a single pearl in the oyster. So we need some help-out, you know what I'm saying?"

Shaw frowned. "What exactly is it you're looking for, Droon? Tell me and maybe I can help."

Droon clicked his tongue. "For me to know and you to find out. Just fill in the details. Is there another map? Did Daddy find something else?"

"How can I tell you anything about the map since you stole it?"

"You made a copy, didn't you? Sure you did, a buttoned-up boy like you. You're on the treasure hunt too!"

He looked around the library. "You really think people don't know I'm here?"

Irena Braxton joined in. "No," she said. "Nobody knows you're here. Now, Colter." She was condescending in both tone of voice and her use of his given name, assuming the role of a mother or schoolteacher none too pleased with a youngster's behavior. "Stop the nonsense. Of *course* you made a copy. And we have your history." A nod at the computer terminal. "You searched *Amos Gahl.* So, no more games. We both know what's going on here. You've got some other leads. A man like you, a professional tracker after all. What do you people say? 'Hot on the scent.' So, tell me about those notes in your father's book. They're codes. We know they are."

Actually they were gibberish. But Shaw said, "The book you stole." Summoning faux indignity.

She offered a perplexed frown. "We can't make heads or tails of it. We need you to decipher them. Your father writes in riddles."

"He's not writing anything now," Shaw said evenly.

Irritated, Braxton said, "As you've been informed, his death wasn't our intent. And the person responsible is no longer of this earth." She crossed her arms over her broad chest.

"That doesn't bring him back."

"This won't do, Colter. We've still got a half-dozen locations on the map to check out and you're going to help us. Amos Gahl stole something, and we have a right to it. He was our employee. You're aiding and abetting that crime."

"You got me. I confess."

Her eyes narrowed.

"Let's call nine-one-one. I'll give myself up."

The headmistress smiled kindly. "Once we have it, all the rough stuff goes away. And we're out of your life forever."

Shaw was eyeing his opponents even more closely than the matronly Braxton was studying him.

Droon displayed the want-to-smack-it-off grin. Blond was expressionless. He had a habit of flexing his fists. He'd been a boxer. But then, noting scars, Shaw decided that since boxing wasn't chic anymore, he'd probably be into bare-knuckle boxing or mixed martial arts. And when he killed—there was no doubt in Shaw's mind that he was a murderer—he did so without conversation. It was a job to complete; he'd kill, collect his check and get home, turning the pits of his eyes to TV or computer porn.

The other two, the guards in the suits, were uneasy. They didn't smack of military and had probably never seen combat. They were a threat, certainly, given their weapons, but they would be second-tier risks.

Braxton, as he'd decided before, was probably not a danger—unless that colorful purse of hers, macramé, of all things, held a Glock or Smith & Wesson.

The woman said to Droon, "We have that meeting tomorrow. I want to tell him something. Something concrete." She nodded to Shaw.

The petite, wiry man said, "Oh, I'll get something. He may not be in a talkative mood now. But that's gonna change. I guarantee it."

Braxton looked over Shaw. "Here's what's going to happen. We're going down to the basement and . . ."

Her voice faded as Shaw rubbed his eyes, shook his head slowly. He winced.

She gazed at him with curiosity, frowning.

"Not feeling all that great."

Droon muttered, "Why's that our concern, son, what you're feeling, what you aren't?"

Shaw closed his eyes and leaned against the wall.

"What's he doing?" one of the security men asked, the bigger one.

"Watch him," Braxton said.

"Let's get him downstairs," Droon said. He looked around. "This's gone on for too long." A glance at Blond. "You want a piece of him?"

The man with the bleached hair and the inky eyes said nothing but gave a brief nod.

Droon said to Braxton, "My man here gets good results."

She said to the security guards, "We'll be down there for an hour or two. No disturbances. Open the library back up. If anyone asks what happened, tell them it was a medical emergency. Nothing more than that."

"Yes, ma'am," said the bigger one. "We'll make sure."

Staring at Shaw, Droon asked no one, "The hell is he about?"

Shaw said, "Just . . . light . . . headed. Not feeling too well." He sagged and rubbed his eyes again.

"Jesus," Braxton said, angry. "Is he sick?"

"What're you doing?" Droon snapped. "What's he doing?"

"I'm dizzy."

Which wasn't an answer to the question. The true response was that Colter Shaw was engaging in the art of misdirection: keeping everyone's attention focused on his eyes, shoulders, torso, arms.

Not on his left foot.

Which was presently easing up the wall to the electrical outlet near the floor.

A paper clip protruded from one slot in the outlet, another from the second slot, millimeters apart. He had taken them from the cubicle where he'd been just before he'd run to the wall. He had no intention of pulling the alarm, which he'd figured had been disabled too. What he wanted was to get to the wall and stick the paper clips, which he'd unfolded to triple their length, into the outlet.

Droon started toward him.

Still leaning against the wall, Shaw held up his hand. "Just give me a minute . . ."

Frowning, Droon paused.

Shaw pressed one paper clip into the other with the upper part of his left shoe.

The resulting spark and staccato bang, impressive, were like a firecracker detonating. Instantly the library went dark.

11

roon and the security guards dropped into a crouch, looking around, not understanding what had happened.

"Shots!" the skinny man cried and ducked.

Shaw, protected from the current by his rubber soles, sprinted to the fire door.

"Wasn't a shot, you idiot," Braxton raged.

Shaw had taken a gamble—that the system overriding the latching mechanism of the emergency door would deactivate when power was lost.

Before Droon and the others could recover and pursue, Shaw grabbed a chair and then slammed into the exit bar with his hip. The door crashed open. He shoved it closed and wedged the chair back against the door handle, bracing it.

A shout. Shaw believed it was "Stop him!" He knew for sure it was Braxton's voice.

Shaw was tempted to run straight to his cycle but he kept to his original plan, turning to the right, away from the Yamaha, and sprinted full-out for the cross street. He heard a crash. It would be the fire exit door being muscled open and the chair that barred it flying into the street.

"Shaw!" Droon was shouting.

Shaw sprinted harder. At the side street, Morrison Lane, he turned to the right again.

And learned he'd made a mistake. Morrison did end at a park, but it was filled with people, who'd be in the direct path of any shots.

Then Shaw noted ahead of him an alley, on his left. He knew from the map that it would lead him to several parking garages, which he could weave through, giving him the chance to shake Droon and Blond. Shaw could then emerge and circle around to his bike—and his weapon.

Thirty yards until the alley.

Twenty, fifteen . . .

A glance back. No pursuers in sight yet.

Ten.

Five.

Before he got to the alley, he stopped and ducked behind a dumpster. He looked back at Droon and Blond moving in his direction. They were alone. The black-suited security people would have continued along the street on which the library was located.

Okay, into the alley . . .

He sprinted around the corner.

And stopped fast.

A dead end.

The alley was completely blocked by a construction site wall, ten feet high, plywood. The paint job—dark blue—was relatively new; only a few graffitied obscenities and gang tags marred the surface. This explained why the barricade had not been depicted on the map he'd examined in the safe house.

Shaw didn't bother to look for alternative forms of escape. The alley was doorless and windowless and though his father had taught him how to ascend walls of various heights and configurations, the technique for surmounting a ten-foot sheer surface was not part of the repertoire, not without rope or timber.

He'd no more than turned around when Droon and Blond stepped into the mouth of the alleyway.

Both were breathing hard and Blond winced with an apparent stitch in his side. He wasn't happy for the exercise.

Droon might have had a pain somewhere but he was also smiling broadly, as if Shaw's irritating attempt to escape had given the crazy man license to be particularly hearty—and creative—when it came to the torture that would follow.

12

Noting the absence of doors and windows opening onto the alley, Droon returned to the mouth and peered out. He looked up and down the street. His face revealed a hint of satisfaction, which meant no traffic, no pedestrians.

No witnesses.

He joined Blond once more. The two stood about twenty feet from Shaw. Neither was holding a weapon. They knew Shaw wasn't armed; he'd been through the metal detector. Blond now drew a silenced pistol. The SIG Sauer—a big, expensive and accurate gun—was pointed at the ground.

Blond: "We need a car."

Droon: "I'll text the Men in Black. They'll get one."

"Soon. Out in the open here. Don't like it."

Droon sent the message. He was grinning. "But maybe he'll cooperate 'fore they get here. And we'll just leave him be." He gestured toward Blond. They rolled the dumpster into the mouth of the alley, largely protecting them from view. Blond used only his left hand and kept the gun trained near Shaw. The safety was off, the finger outside the trigger guard. He knew what he was doing.

Shaw's impression was that neither man reported to the other. Blond, a facilitator like Droon, would also work for Braxton.

"Now, son, let's have ourselves a confab, don'tcha know?" He reached under his jacket and withdrew a knife from a camo scabbard. Shaw recognized it. Long, serrated. It was a SOG SEAL Team Elite fixed blade.

Looking around, Shaw judged angles and distances.

No good defensive solution presented itself, let alone an offensive one.

"Number one, that manuscript of your daddy's you so kindly let me have down in Silicon Valley coupla weeks ago, that was just a waste of good tree, wasn't it?"

Not for Colter Shaw, it wasn't. The four-hundred-some-odd-page stack of notes, maps, drawings and articles that Ashton had assembled was ninety-nine percent misdirection. But it contained the code that had directed Shaw to Echo Ridge, where he found the map and the letter that led to the Alvarez Street safe house and started Shaw on his mission here.

"I wouldn't know. You stole that from me too, didn't you? I never had a chance to read it. Did it have anything interesting in it?"

Shaw wondered if a passerby, someone in a window or on a rooftop, seeing a man with a gun, would call the police.

Droon was pointing the wicked blade Shaw's way. "How'd you find our library? Your daddy knew about it, did he?"

"Think he mentioned it."

"And you remembered that? From all those years ago?"

Blond said nothing. He was a block of wood, if wood could be attentive, suspicious and deadly.

Shaw told Droon, "I have a good memory. I'm lucky that way."

"Naw, naw. There's someplace here. Your daddy'd have a buddy in town you're staying with." He looked him over closely. "Or maybe a safe house all his own. Yep, betcha."

Somebody *must* have seen the pursuit and called 911.

But not a siren to be heard.

Not a ripple of flashing light to be seen.

Shaw was watching Blond. The big man's face was completely placid, as if were he to have any emotion that might distract him, that would lower his defenses. The eyes scanned constantly, the coal-black dots complementing the swarthy face, jarring with the sun-burst of yellow hair.

Droon was a wild card. Blond was a pro.

Blond asked, "Where should we take him? The basement?"

"Library's compromised. I'd say the Tannery."

Not, of course, a place where you morphed into a beach bum under UV rays.

Droon sent another text and read the reply. He told Blond: "Irena'll meet us."

Shaw leaned toward the scrawny man. "Will Helms be there too? I hope so."

Droon was silent for a moment, unmoving, as if trying to pro-cess Shaw's interest and intent. "He went back to the hotel."

Not getting his hands dirty in sports like torture.

"But Irena's lookin' forward to our chat. As much as I am. Prob-ably more. I do assure you, friend, that you will not like what's going to happen." He mimicked stabbing and twisting motions with the blade.

Shaw shrugged.

Droon thumbed the steel. "Everybody breaks, don'tcha know? Tell us what you've found out about Gahl and what he stole from us. You do that, and you're free to go. Get yourself a gelato."

"I don't like it," Blond said.

The rattish man glanced not toward his companion but toward Shaw.

"His eyes. He's working something. Doesn't look that bothered."

Droon said, "Checking stuff out, is all. He does that. The first time we met . . . Remember that, Shaw? I was having a laugh with a harmless little firebomb and you were sizing me up—and down and sideways. Every whichaway."

Blond muttered: "He's planning a move." He removed something from his inside jacket pocket. It appeared to be a thick rod of black metal, about a foot long. He said, "I cover him. You break something. Take him out of commission." He offered the bludgeon to Droon.

The man took it and slipped the knife back in its sheath. He nodded to the gun that Blond was holding. "Why not?"

"You need him alive. Don't want to risk a bleeder."

A pro's pro . . .

Droon seemed to agree. He hefted the rod and his expression reported that he liked the idea of breaking bones.

"Shaw, sorry t'have to do this. But, fact is, you just don't look desperate. You know what I'm saying? My word, you are the *least* desperate-looking person I have ever seen on this earth. You're not wasting time on worry; you're running through a big list. What can I do with this, what can I do with that?"

Pretty much.

There's not a lot an unarmed man can do in combat against two opponents when one of them is holding a gun and the other a bone-breaking rod with a knife on his belt.

With some cheer, Droon said, "Man up. Hold your hand out and let's do this fast . . ." He cocked his head and gave an odd grin, which pinched his face. "Or, better idea, you can tell us what you know. And waltz around an icky bout of pain now followed by the main course—a trip to the Tannery with my knife."

"I don't know what you're talking about."

"Okay, hand out."

Shaw held his right arm out.

"Nup. Other one. You may need to write down your ABCs for us, draw a pretty map, or some such."

Shaw did as instructed.

He now incrementally shifted his balance, so that most of his weight was on his right leg. When Droon swung the bar, Shaw's right hand would move in an arc and clamp down on the man's wrist. The mass of the heavy rod meant the slim man's arm would be driven toward the ground and he'd be off-kilter. Shaw would then spin him sideways, turning him into a shield against Blond's weapon and executing a choke hold, rendering Droon largely nonresponsive.

Shaw's right hand would dip into the jacket for the pistol he hoped the man still had on him and draw. He wouldn't threaten Blond, tell him to drop the SIG. He'd just fire away. He'd aim for the gun arm and hand. He recalled where the safety was located on Droon's Beretta.

If Droon didn't have the gun, or if Shaw couldn't get to it instantly, he'd rip the bar from Droon's hand and fling it toward Blond's face, then break a wrist and pull the knife.

He and his siblings had been taught the art of knife throwing by Ashton. It was hard to hit your target with the point, but you could count on your enemy to be distracted by a spiraling razor-sharp blade. Shaw would charge Blond when he ducked and try to wrestle the SIG from his hand.

If not, as a last resort, he'd vault the dumpster. The other men didn't look like they could follow him in a leap. It would take some seconds to push the unit out of the way. He would turn back toward the library—the direction they would least expect him to run, and the one with the fewest innocents on the street.

Shaw plastered an expression of dread on his face as Droon stepped forward, hefting the metal. The facilitator's gaze was one of pleasant anticipation.

Four feet away, three feet . . .

Playacting again, Shaw said, "Look, let's work this out, can't we? Money. You want money?"

Droon was drawing back with the bar.

"Wait."

Droon was beaming. "Don't you go whining, there, boy."

Shaw was perfectly balanced, ready to move, awash with the exhilaration that comes just before combat. Irrational, mad, intoxicating.

Which is when Blond said, "Stop."

Pausing, Droon turned.

"Get back. He's going to move on you. We'll do it this way." He looked down at his pistol.

13

D roon frowned. He clearly didn't see what Blond saw. "He'd take you," the big man offered.

"I wouldn't be so sure about that, my friend." But Droon stepped away from Shaw.

Blond said, "I'd risk a bullet. Top of the foot shouldn't be much bleeding."

Shaw sighed.

Droon walked back to Blond, who lifted the gun and pointed it at Shaw's foot. Now, he really meant it when he said, "We can work something out. You want information. I'll get you information."

Blond aimed carefully.

Even if he survived the Tannery, what would a bullet wound do to his foot? Shattering the complex bones of the appendage would render the Restless Man disabled for a very long time.

Silencers do not, in fact, make a weapon completely mute. There's a distinctive *phhhht*, followed by the click of the gun's slide snapping back and then returning into position. Often you can hear the ring of the spent shell jittering on the floor or concrete or cobblestone, like what the men were standing on now.

Colter Shaw heard the first two of these, the muted gunshot and the click of the pistol as the gun reloaded for a second shot. He did not hear the dancing of the spent brass.

He did, however, hear another sound. The wet, smacking snap of a bullet hitting Blond's forehead. The big man gave no facial reaction to the impact. He simply dropped.

Shaw crouched. The gunshot had come from above and behind him—the shooter was in the air, maybe on some scaffolding on the other side of the wooden construction fence.

Droon's sense of survival kicked in. Not waiting to parse the situation he tore back to the street—and proving Shaw wrong—easily vaulted the dumpster. He landed and rolled, then righted himself and sprinted back toward the library.

Shaw immediately thought of the green Honda Accord, his shadow. Had the driver followed him here and been aiming at Shaw, but hit Blond by mistake? He leapt forward and rolled through the grimy alley, snatching up Blond's SIG Sauer pistol.

Rising, in a crouch, Shaw glanced at Blond—he was dead—and drew back the slide of the SIG a quarter inch to make sure a round was chambered, something you always did with a weapon not your own.

He went prone behind the man's body—the only cover in the alley—and trained the weapon on the plywood construction site wall.

A man's voice called, "I'm not a hostile." Then to Shaw's surprise, the caller added, "Colter, I'm coming over the fence. Don't shoot."

He knows my name?

Something fell to the ground with a thud. It was a backpack, Oakland A's.

This would have to be the man he'd seen at the coffee shop up the street from the safe house on Alvarez—the bearded man in the thigh-length black coat and stocking cap. He climbed over the fence and landed lithely on the cobblestones, his low combat boots dampening the force.

Colter Shaw gasped. Which was something he had not done for years—since a piton gave way and he dropped twenty feet on a half-mile-high rock face before the safety rope arrested the fall.

He was not sure which shocked him the most at the moment: That he'd been saved from the fate of being shot with only seconds to spare.

Or that the man who'd done the saving was his long-lost brother, Russell.

14

Russell said, "I understand. You have questions. I do too. Later. First, this."

He was then on his phone, speaking in modulated yet commanding tones.

His brother was nearly identical in appearance to the man Shaw had last seen years ago at their father's funeral. He'd had a beard then, though it was shorter than this, as was his hair. These were two reasons Shaw hadn't recognized him near the safe house. Also, who the hell would expect the Reclusive One to be in San Francisco at the same time Shaw was?

The skin around the eyes was more weathered and ruddier. The beard was a uniform brown, without a touch of white or gray. The same was true for the tufts of straight hair protruding from the stocking cap.

One other difference between then and now: his eyes were presently cold, utterly inexpressive about the fact he'd just killed someone. Remorse, or even concern, let alone guilt, did not register.

"Help me here," Russell said, nodding toward the dumpster. Shaw noted his brother's voice was reminiscent of their father's. He was startled by the near mimicry, though he supposed he shouldn't be.

Shaw kept the muzzle of the SIG pointed away as he clicked the safety on and slipped the gun into his waistband—Russell glancing at him as he did so, apparently taking note that his younger brother had not forgotten their father's endless lessons and drills about weapons.

They pushed the dumpster out of the mouth of the alley.

Shaw was wondering why his brother had wanted to move the big contraption; doing so would expose Blond's body for any pass-erby to see. But the minute the dumpster was pushed aside and the alley was clear, a white van skidded to a stop in front of them and the side door slid open quickly.

Growing cautious, Shaw lifted the gun.

"They're mine," Russell said.

Three people climbed out.

Had the moment been less fraught—and confusing—Shaw might've smiled. He'd seen two of the trio earlier. One was Tricia, the woman in the street in front of the Alvarez Street safe house, and the man who'd attacked her—a verb Shaw put into mental quotation marks, since there'd been no assault at all, he now understood. Her screams for help had been merely a strategy to force Shaw outside and learn if he were a threat or not.

The broad-chested man had cleaned up considerably from his role as Homeless Man One. Russell introduced him as Ty. He glanced at Shaw without comment or other acknowledgment.

The third, whose name was Matt, was a slim, somber man of mixed race, with dark hair. His eyes scanned the alley and the street where the van was parked.

All three wore dark green jogging outfits and blue latex gloves.

A driver, whom Shaw could see only in silhouette, remained behind the wheel.

As Russell and Matt kept an eye on the side street, hands near their hips, Ty and Tricia—introduced now as Karin—stepped quickly to Blond's corpse.

Shaw said, "There're two other security people from the library. White. One heavy, one thin. Both armed. In dark suits, and—"

Karin said, "We know. They're in the parking garage on Harrison, picking up wheels. We have two minutes before they're here."

The phony attacker unfurled a body bag and he and Karin got to work with Blond. Soon the body was inside, zipped up tight.

"One, two . . . lift," the man said. The pair grunted simultaneously and hefted the weighty bag by the handles and began shuffling back to the van. Shaw thought about asking if they needed help but they didn't seem to. They were both quite strong, and—it appeared—had done this before. They got the bag to the van and muscled it inside.

Matt reached into the van and removed a broom and a spray bottle. He returned to the site of the shooting and spritzed liquid onto the bloodstain. The bullet would have been a hollow point, designed to expand in the brain, causing instantaneous lethal damage but remaining within the skull. Exit wounds created the biggest leaks.

He slipped the bottle into his slacks pocket and swept dirt and gravel over where the body had lain. This had some sort of procedural precision to it and was done to confound a crime scene crew, though Shaw doubted any police would ever investigate. Certainly Droon and Braxton would not be calling 911 to report that the BlackBridge employee had met his end.

"Give her the SIG."

Shaw withdrew the weapon and handed it to Karin grip first. She removed the magazine and the round in the chamber. She locked the slide back and then deposited the gun, the mag and the solo slug in a thick plastic bag. She put what seemed to be a damp cloth inside and sealed it up.

"My prints are on it," Shaw told her.

A faint, amused squint. Meaning: They won't be for long. Shaw wondered what the magic material was.

Broad Ty said, "Behind us. Hostiles."

An SUV was speeding toward them. Shaw could not see through the glary windshield but he supposed that Droon had been picked up by the two black-suited security guards earlier than he'd originally anticipated. The vehicle skidded to a stop and all three got out. They were trotting forward, cautiously, hands inside their jackets.

Russell nodded to Matt, who replaced the broom with an H&K submachine gun, mounted with a silencer. The man pulled the slide to chamber a round. He aimed toward Droon, who, with the others, fanned out, seeking cover behind trashcans.

Russell said, "No personnel. Vehicle only."

A muted chain saw of firing, and the slugs shredded the vehicle's grill. He'd been careful to group the rounds so that they didn't spill past the car and endanger anyone in the park.

Matt then joined the others, who were already in the van. Shaw slid the side door shut. He noted that it was particularly heavy and wondered if the panel was bulletproof. The vehicle's tires squealed loudly as the male driver, lean and dark-complected, steered, skidding, into the side street, away from the alley and the smoking SUV, and accelerated fast. Shaw held on tight. Russell made his way to the front passenger seat. Shaw and those in the back were benched against the wall. Matt was looking over a tablet. "No activity. We're good."

Russell said, "First his bike. Then the safe house on Alvarez."

I understand. You have questions . . .

An understatement, if ever there was one.

15

ow'd you place me at the library? From the air?"

There were so many questions to ask. Shaw wondered why he led with one of the least significant.

The two of them were alone in the safe house's dining room, illuminated with an ethereal glow from the windows, as the sunlight knuckled away the pale pastel fog. They sat at a maple table, dinged and scraped, a wedge under one leg for stability.

Reading a text or email on his phone, Russell said absently, "Use drones some. Not in cities usually. FAA and Homeland Security're problems."

"That right?"

His older brother seemed to be debating what to say and what he shouldn't. "Mostly, we had you on traffic and security cams. Algorithms. Handoffs." A shrug. Meaning he didn't want to—or legally couldn't—be more specific.

Russell finished sending a message and rose and looked out the bay window in the front of the living room. Then he moved to the side windows and examined the view from there. It was limited. They admitted light only, as they faced a solid brick wall about ten feet away. Russell made a circuit to the back, where another bay overlooked the small garden, the alley and, beyond, an apartment that resembled Soviet-era housing. Shaw realized that there were no windows in any adjoining buildings—front, side or back—that faced the safe house. This would be one of the reasons why their father had selected it.

Shaw walked to the front window and peered outside. He could see quiet Alvarez Street and the burnt-down building across the way, the site of Tricia's, well, Karin's, supposed attack. He reflected that it was surprising no one had bought the lot and constructed residential property. The Mission was vastly popular and developers could make a killing. Then again, *could* was the operative word; San Francisco was a pressure cooker of a real estate market. You could go bust as fast as you could make ten-figure profits.

Shaw's eyes moved from the building to the streets nearby. He was scanning both for BlackBridge ops, despite Russell's associate's reassurance they were clear, and for the Honda, his tail.

His brother returned to the table. The stocking cap was off and his dark hair wasn't *longish*; it was long, period.

"Does one of your people drive a dark green Honda Accord?" Shaw asked.

"No. Why?"

"Somebody was tailing me. They placed me here."

"No, not us, not part of my operation. You get the tag?"

"No."

Silence descended and now it was time for explanations.

Russell said, "Back there. Why were you targeted?"

"They weren't trying to kill me. They needed me alive. For the time being."

"Could see that. Angle of his aim. Still."

"They wanted information. I'll show you."

Shaw rose and from the kitchen gathered the material Ashton had left in the basement.

"This was in the secure room."

"Did you know about it before?"

"The room? No. All I had was the address."A glance around the living room. "But I knew what to look for. Remember, Ash taught us how to build one, make it blend in and dim the outside lights. He called it 'the camo of murk.'"

Russell's eyes narrowed, as a recollection arose—probably of the time Ashton had taught the three Shaw children how to build a disguised door for a hiding spot in the shed behind the cabin. He had told them, "Anybody can hide hinges and latches. The most important thing in fooling intruders is the *dust*. Dusty walls don't move." He taught them how to use rubber cement spray on the disguised door and surrounding panels and then shake a feather duster over the adhesive. Six-year-old Dorion had done the best job.

Russell said, "You missed the flash-bang. I got an alert."

"Careless. But at that point I didn't know anybody else had been here, and Ashton wasn't the IED sort."

"No. He wasn't."

"You know, some people use Ring or Nest for home security—not explosives."

Unsmiling, Russell shrugged, then nodded to the material on the table. "Saw that when I was here back a couple of years. Didn't mean anything to me. Assumed it was Ash's but you know . . . his rambling, the paranoia."

"Wouldn't mean anything without this." Shaw dug into his backpack and retrieved the letter their father had written about BlackBridge.

Russell read. "So BlackBridge's a dirty-tricks outfit. Never come across them before." Spoken in a tone that suggested he was more than familiar with such operations. "Where did this come from?" A nod at the letter.

Shaw hesitated. "He hid it on Echo Ridge."

The location where Shaw had convinced himself Russell had murdered their father.

His brother gave no reaction. "In the alley, they were all BlackBridge?"

"Right. The library was a front."

"I know that. When you went inside, I checked. Found out it wasn't connected to the university. And offshores don't own libraries. Not legitimate ones."

His resources were probably as good as Mack's. Most likely considerably better.

Russell looked over the letter once more. "Half of Ashton's worries were smoke."

"At least."

"Not this."

"No."

Shaw handed him the dead-drop note, written to their father by a sympathetic employee of BlackBridge.

Amos is dead. It's in a BlackBridge courier bag. Don't know where he hid it. This is my last note. Too dangerous. Good luck.

"'It'? The evidence Ashton was talking about."

"That's right." Shaw waved at the rest of the material he'd brought up from the basement. "Not like this, not supposition and suggestion. Whatever Gahl found is enough to get indictments."

"Ash told us 'Never go to Echo Ridge. Terrain's not so kind.' But it wasn't any worse than anywhere else in the high country. Maybe he didn't want us going there because it was a dead-drop for him and his circle." Russell glanced at Shaw, who nodded his understanding of the spy term. His brother continued, "The letter was meant for one of his colleagues. How'd you find it?"

"Long story. Came across some clues that led me there."

"Any of the friends still around?"

"Maybe, but most are dead or in hiding. BlackBridge is good at arranging accidents."

Shaw didn't tell his brother that he believed the letter had been left not for a colleague but for him. It was he who had been given, and who deciphered, the clues that led to Echo Ridge—and ultimately to the safe house. It wouldn't have been impossible for a colleague of Ashton's to deduce where the letter and map had been hidden. But why situate a dead-drop three hundred miles from San Francisco, where most of their father's associates were?

"And BlackBridge, they're behind Ash's death?" Russell eyed Shaw closely. "At the funeral, the word was 'accident.' But back then I got the feeling you didn't think so."

Was there something in his brother's tone? Did he or did he not know Shaw had silently accused him of murdering their father?

A chill flowed through him. "No, I didn't." He hesitated. "Some things didn't add up. His shotgun, the Benelli, was nowhere near where he fell. And did you ever know him to lose his footing on rock, ice, snow, sand, gravel?" He was speaking quickly. Did he sound defensive as he threw out some of the reasons why he'd formulated the theory of patricide?

He felt Russell's eyes on him still, and he chose to meet the man's gaze. Shaw said, "A couple of weeks ago I learned for sure it was BlackBridge." He explained what Ebbitt Droon had told him about the company's operative coming to the Compound to "talk" with their father. "That is, *torture* him and get him to tell them where the evidence was hidden. Ashton tipped to the op and ambushed him. But he was no match for the BlackBridge man."

"Hmm."

Shaw wanted so badly to grab his brother by the shoulders and shout: *I* was young, *you* were secretive. I saw the fight you and Ash had. And you were evasive about where you were on the night he was killed. I was wrong. But was what I did reason enough for you to vanish from the family altogether? Do you know what that did to our mother, our sister?

To me . . .

But of course, Colter Shaw couldn't ask that question because the answer might very well be what he feared: Because I can't forgive you.

Before he could stop himself he said, "The Reclusive One." Was it a subconscious jab at his brother's disappearance?

"What?"

"Looks like your profession, whatever it is, it's kept you true to your name."

Russell squinted. "The nicknames. When we were kids. Reclusive. You were restless. Dorie was clever."

"You're using the house for some kind of operation. How did you know about it?"

"I was in San Francisco for some training, long time ago, and Ash said there was a house he used when he was in town. We met here. He gave me a key. My group has operations here from time to time, so I use it as a command post."

"Group?"

Russell said nothing.

It would handle government security of some kind, he guessed. But out of the mainstream. The FBI, CIA, DoD, NSA and most of the rest of the alphabet soup of government entities couldn't get away with shooting someone with a silenced pistol and making the body and accessories go away as if you were cleaning up a broken jar of pickles dropped on a kitchen tile floor.

Shaw said, "I looked at the paperwork in the secure room. It's classified?"

"Not anymore, I guess."

"That a problem?"

A pause. "Not really."

"You speak Chinese, Russian?"

He didn't answer, but obviously he did. Russell had had years to learn quite a few skills since Shaw had seen him last.

"We have a full security setup when we're active but we closed the file on that op early this morning. All the cameras and mics were packed up and gone."

Shaw could only laugh. "That was smooth. The assault outside. Karin and Ty."

"When the device went off I got a message. The secure room was compromised. And we had to find out who."

"You, Karin and Ty, you put the whole set together in minutes? The costumes, makeup."

Russell lifted an eyebrow. "What we do. We train for things like that. Improvise. And they were nearby. She was wearing a body cam. She started to run your picture through our facial recognition database, but . . ." He shrugged. "I saw the image. After, I put together a surveillance package on you."

Why? Shaw wondered.

A moment later, Russell asked, "So you're here because of Ashton and BlackBridge? There's no reward?"

Shaw must've reacted.

"You're in the news some."

So he was curious about me. But not curious enough to pick up the phone and give me or our mother a call.

"No reward. It's all about BlackBridge."

Russell's look conveyed a question: But why?

Shaw: "I know what Ashton said. 'Never pursue revenge. It goes against the grain of survivalism.'"

"Was thinking that, yes."

"Well, this isn't revenge. It's finishing what he started. His mission."

There was really nothing more to add.

16

Russell sent a text on his elaborate phone. It was a brand that Shaw had never seen before.

He regarded his brother's luxurious beard. You'd think it would be a problem in clandestine work, if that's what Russell engaged in. He'd be instantly recognizable. Maybe he was famous in his field, though, and he sported the facial hair as a trademark.

His brother's phone hummed.

"Nothing in our system about Urban Improvement Plan or Amos Gahl," said Russell. He put the phone away. "Basic information about BlackBridge but they're not flagged with any red notices."

Shaw imagined his brother had access to a database that was exceedingly robust.

"Appreciate you checking. This group of yours . . . can you tell me?"

"No."

"Just 'group' with a lowercase 'g.'"

"What we go by." After a pause Russell asked, "You always use the Yamaha in your work?"

Shaw explained about living in the Winnebago but renting cars on his jobs to stay unobtrusive. Much of the rewards business is surveillance and questioning witnesses, and nothing blended better than a black Avis or Hertz (he picked that color because it gave the impression he was law enforcement, though he never said he was). "Still might rent a car here. Depends on the weather."

Russell took a call. He listened for a moment. He said, "That's right. Tell them it's closed permanently." He disconnected.

Silence drifted between them.

Shaw asked, "You have a family? Anyone in your life?"

"No. You?"

He thought of Victoria. "No."

"I heard you were married."

He thought of Margot. "No."

Roiling silence. Russell checked his phone once more.

"Dorion's good," Shaw told him.

"I know. I saw her and the girls last month."

"*Saw* them?" Shaw couldn't keep the surprise from his voice.

"I saw *them*. They didn't see me."

"Last I heard, at the funeral, you were in L.A."

"Based there. Near there."

The chitchat depressed Shaw and appeared to bore Russell.

All these years they hadn't seen each other, and this was the best they could do?

"Another question," Shaw asked.

Russell lifted his eyebrow.

"Why the hell the Oakland A's?" Shaw glanced at his brother's backpack.

No response to the levity.

The children had laughed a lot growing up. With very few other friends their age, they relied on one another for amusement and diversion.

Another blister of silence, then Russell said, "Need to get my team out of here."

"So you're leaving." Shaw had tried to keep his expression neutral. He wasn't sure he was successful.

"Assignments we're scheduled for. It's a busy time."

Spoken like a department store buyer planning for Christmas shopping season.

"Sure."

Russell walked down to the cellar and returned a moment later with the duffel bag. The sun had burned away the last tatters of fog by now and the water bottles bent the light, pasting fracturing shapes of brilliant white on the plaster walls.

His silent message resonated like a siren through the pleasant, yellow room: Your fight with BlackBridge isn't my fight, even if the company killed our father.

Shaw tipped his head. "Don't need to say I appreciate you showing up when you did."

Russell reciprocated the nod.

Shaw tried: "You want to give me a phone number?"

"We get randomly generated ones once a month."

Shaw wrote down his number in one of his notebooks. He didn't tear off the page and hand it to his brother. He held it up.

Russell looked for about ten seconds. He nodded.

Was it memorized, or discarded?

Shaw thought once more: Confess now. Tell him that I was wrong to accuse him of murder . . .

But no. This connection with his sibling might grow into something in the future—maybe Russell had indeed tucked the phone number away. But right here, right now, it was so very fragile. Gram for gram, the strands of a spider's web are stronger than steel. But it takes no more than a gust of wind, not even one so fierce, or the transit of a broom in the hands of a busy housekeeper to bring the creature's home, world and perhaps life to an abrupt end.

Shaw said, "It's good to see you're okay. I'll tell Mary Dove."

"Do that." His brother walked to the door and let himself out.

17

S haw fished in his backpack. He left his personal iPhone there and pulled out a burner. If he was concerned that his calls might be monitored, he used this one—an Android with some Linux kernel modifications for added encryption and security.

The call he was making now had nothing to do with BlackBridge or the UIP or Amos Gahl. Still, under the circumstances he wanted all the security he could get.

"Hello?"

"It's me."

"Colt." The woman's voice was, as always, low, steady. "You're at the house?"

"That's right. It's a safe house. Ash had a hidey-hole in the basement. I found more relevant material. Haven't made too much headway yet."

There was a pause. His mother was in effect saying: What else? Because there was obviously something else.

"I wanted to let you know. I saw him today. Russell."

"My God . . ." Mary Dove's whisper tapered to silence. She was a woman to whom the word *surprised* could rarely be applied. "He's all right?"

"Yes." Shaw was sipping coffee, tamed with milk, slowly. It was very hot.

"That answers the big question. He's alive."

All these years the family had not known whether Russell was still of this earth.

"How'd that come about?"

He explained that his older brother too had known about the house on Alvarez and used it occasionally.

"Yes, that's right. Ash mentioned he'd seen Russell in San Francisco once or twice."

"He's with the government, it looks like. CIA sort of operation, though not them."

"What does he do for them?"

"Intelligence of some sort."

He did not tell his mother about Blond's fate.

Her lack of response might have been a hum of skepticism about his answer.

"It's called the group. Not a formal name." Silence again. Then: "He seemed . . . okay. Good at his job."

"And he's—"

"Gone. An assignment. Couldn't tell me what."

A very rare sigh. "That boy . . . I never knew exactly what was going on in his mind. Remember? He'd spend days in the woods? And not part of Ash's training. I'd wake up, get the coffee and biscuits going and find that he'd left before first light, with rations and his weapon."

Her resonant voice was painted with discontent and for a moment Shaw regretted telling her about crossing paths with his brother. Maybe her hopes had been up momentarily that he'd return for a visit. "Well. He's who he is. But . . . did he say *why* he vanished, all these years?"

In honesty Colter Shaw could tell his mother, "No, he didn't." Because Russell had not spoken of his profound disappointment that the younger brother had silently accused the older of murder.

"It's going well, the search?"

"Good."

"A mother's got to say, 'Be careful.'"

Shaw chuckled.

Then Mary Dove said, "Glad you told me about your brother. Imagine you were debating letting me know. But it was the right thing." Then her tone changed and she said, "Anybody else you want to say hey to?"

"Matter of fact . . ."

"Hold on."

18

H i." Victoria Lesston's voice was also low, and there was a particular tone about it. Shaw tried to think of what the analogy to describe it might be. Then it occurred to him: a musical instrument. In particular, he refined: a cello, rich and resonant. In the middle strings range only.

"Tacoma was interesting. Got robbed and I'm responsible for a Nissan Pathfinder burning down to the rims. No injuries."

"Never dull with you, is it, Colt? What'd they get?"

"I'll go into it later. In person."

She laughed airily. "Sooner, not later, I hope."

Shaw pictured her deep-gray eyes and her ringlets of hair, which morphed from pale brunette to dark blond according to the whim of the sun or moon.

"The big news: my brother surfaced."

"Really? You said you weren't even sure he was alive."

"He's doing some kind of clandestine work. Think he needed to stay undercover."

"Like those KGB agents."

"Maybe something like that."

"When you're finished, will he come down here with you to see your mother?"

Thinking no, he said, "Maybe."

Her voice lowered. "How are you dealing with it?"

Not a question he was prepared to respond to. "Still surprised." He asked how she was feeling.

The beat told him she recognized, and respected, the deflection. "All good here. Your mother is pretty much amazing."

He had met Victoria a week ago, on a mission he'd had to the wilds of Washington State. The incident had started as a reward assignment but had soon turned into an undercover operation, which he'd undertaken, in part, to save Victoria from an enigmatic organization that might or might not have been a dangerous cult.

She'd been injured in a fall from a cliff's edge into a lake. A former Delta Force officer, Victoria was in fit shape and while the fall might have killed another person, she survived with only minor harm. Shaw had suggested she might want to return to the Compound where his mother, a general practitioner MD, as well as a psychiatrist, could help her with physical therapy.

Shaw had another reason to ask her to the homestead, and she apparently had a similar motive in accepting his invitation; he remembered their lengthy kiss outside her bedroom the night before he left on the drive that ultimately led him here to the safe house.

"Where are you?"

"The Western Hemisphere. Maybe."

Even with the encryption, he was reluctant to be too specific. *Never assume your conversations are private . . .*

"You're a stitch, Colter. Your mother sometimes calls you 'Colt.' Which do you like?"

Their courtship, if you could call it that, had been intense (a knife fight—between them—had figured) but they really hadn't known each other all that long.

"Either's good."

"Any excitement yet?"

"Not so much."

"Keep me posted on that."

"Most definitely."

"How do you like your pheasant?" Victoria asked.

"Never been asked that before." This was true. He considered. "Probably rarer than weller."

"I agree. Mary Dove and I're cooking tonight. A bird she got last season."

"You hunt?"

"I have but the last time I got pheasant was a couple years ago."

"What's your scattergun?" He was thinking of his father's wonderful Benelli Pacific Flyway, with a chrome receiver. An elegant weapon.

"I don't have one."

"What'd you borrow?"

"I didn't use a shotgun," she said.

"I don't think you can legally use a rifle on birds. Not in California."

"It wasn't in California and I didn't use a rifle."

"You didn't use a rifle?"

"Colter, how many times are you going to keep asking me questions I've already answered."

"Well, what did you use?"

"My Glock. The seventeen."

"In the air?"

"Of course, you can't shoot a bird on the ground. And it wasn't quick-draw Annie Oakley or anything like that. I was already holding the weapon."

"How many . . ." His voice faded.

"Rounds did I use, you were going to ask?"

He'd stifled the insulting question, but yes, that was what he was going to ask. Her Glock would hold seventeen rounds and you could probably get off three a second, aiming carefully.

Then he noticed she was silent once again.

Finally Victoria said, "It was one."

He reminded himself not to ask: A single shot?

Shaw was talented with sidearms but he didn't think he could hit a flying bird with either of his pistols and never with one shot.

"I mean, I aimed. I wasn't firing from the hip. Anyway, I agree: rare is best. Pheasant's lean. Dries out when you cook it too long. When are you back?"

"Hope it's not more than a couple of days."

"You need any help, I'm feeling better."

Victoria ran her own security consulting firm, based out of Southern California.

"I'll keep that in mind."

"You know, Colt, there are two kinds of people in the world."

Living/dead. Blond/brunette. Short/tall. Liberal/Conservative. Sexy/not so much. He did not, of course, say this, but replied with: "Okay?"

"Those who keep something in mind when they say they're going to keep something in mind. And those who have no intention of keeping something in mind when they say they're keeping something in mind."

"I'm the first type."

"I had a feeling you were. But I liked hearing you say so."

They made conversation for ten minutes or so, then he was eager to get on the trail of the BlackBridge evidence. He told her he'd better go. "I'll call you soon."

"You know, Colt, there are two types of people in the world . . ."

He laughed and said goodbye and they disconnected.

The two of them were similar in many ways. She was nearly as itinerant as he was, and as much of a calculated risk-taker. They shared a wry humor and an intolerance for bullying and stupidity. They'd certainly developed a rapport in Washington State and it didn't hurt that not only had he saved her life, but that she'd saved his.

And that kiss . . .

The relationship had a way to progress on that slippery, serpentine road on which matters of the heart pace before certain things could be said and asked.

This was fine with him. He was in no hurry. Velocity in love, like velocity on the motocross course, had in the past occasionally gotten Colter Shaw into trouble.

Best for restless men to take things slowly.

19

S haw told himself: assess.

He was in the kitchen of the safe house. He'd supplemented Mack's research on the two leads as to where Amos Gahl might have hidden the BlackBridge evidence. Morton Nadler, who owned the house in Burlingame that his father had been interested in, was retired. He had spent most of his working life as a management-level employee at San Francisco airport. What was his connection to Gahl? Would he have left Nadler the evidence to keep safe? Or was Nadler the *source* for incriminating information about BlackBridge, maybe because of his connection to the airlines and private aircraft?

The other spot, the Haywood Brothers Warehouse in the Embarcadero, had survived the Great San Francisco Earthquake of 1906. It had not been a functioning warehouse for some years, which did not bode well for Shaw's mission. Probably the building had been emptied out and if Gahl had hidden anything there the evidence would likely be in some other facility or, more likely, a landfill.

Because the building was for sale, there was a representative on-site, from whom Shaw might learn something.

His Android hummed. He pressed ANSWER and before he could say a word there came: "You into coincidences, Colt?"

The voice was a grumbling baritone. Caller ID told Shaw who the person on the other end was but even if it hadn't he would've known with the first syllable. Teddy Bruin was a former Marine who—along with his wife, former soldier Velma—ran the business side of Shaw's reward operation. They lived beside Shaw's property in Florida, though he'd seen them just the other day; they were on a road trip out West and had spent a few days at the Compound with Shaw, Victoria and Mary Dove.

A call from the Bruins meant one of two things: He had failed to collect a reward check, which usually happened because the offeror turned out to be on hard times.

Or they'd just learned of an offer.

"Coincidences?" Shaw queried.

"Three weeks ago, give or take, that offer in Silicon Valley, that girl? Father worried about her?"

"Right."

The reward that sent him deep into the world of the video gaming industry. A missing student had been kidnapped, it appeared, by a perp who was acting out a violent video game in real life.

"Well, we got a replay." Teddy chuckled. A joke on the game motif, Shaw noted. Teddy looked and sounded scary but he had quite the sense of humor.

"Hi, Colter." A woman's voice, as melodious as her husband's was raw.

"Velma. Where are you two?"

"Reno. I have a roll of quarters and I'm not coming home until I win back all the gas we spent on the drive here."

The couple owned a Winnebago that was the size of Shaw's—a

thirty-footer. It would take a string of jackpots to make that miracle happen.

"She's convinced that the odds're better with the slots in Reno than Vegas. You know, to attract tourists. Second-city kinda thing."

Shaw wouldn't know. He didn't gamble.

His eyes on his father's documents, he said, "Replay?"

Teddy: "Single *mom* this time, not dad. But another missing daughter. Mother's a widow. And the girl's older than the one a couple weeks ago. Twenty-two or -three."

Not only did the Bruins themselves scan social media and law enforcement posts for announcements of rewards, but they supervised a software program that sniffed out offers too. Velma had named it Algo after *algorithm*. "Where?"

"Why we're a-calling. San Francisco."

"Got a lot on the platter here."

"I know, Colt," Teddy said. "But a couple things. I'll just throw 'em out there. The reward? It's for seventeen fifty."

"You mean seventeen thousand, five hundred."

"No, I mean seventeen *hundred* and fifty buckaroos."

Very low for a missing child. And the low sum meant the mother had scraped together every penny she could.

"The other thing?"

"The offer," Velma told him. "Listen to what she posted online. I'm quoting: 'Please, please, please help!!!' A bunch of exclamations here. 'Tessy, love of my life, has gone missing in San Francisco. I'm sick with worry over her. I'm offering a Reward. I've started a Go-FundMe page to raise more. Please.' More exclamation points. Then a picture of her. Sweet kid."

Shaw's experience was that parents rarely posted a shot of demonic-looking children. "That kind of money, nobody'll go to the trouble to look for her."

"Exactly."

Shaw looked at his father's map with the eighteen red Xs on it.

"When was it posted?"

"Couple days ago."

Before BlackBridge knew he was in town, so it wouldn't be a trap.

He looked at the notes in such delicate and perfect script:

Haywood Brothers Warehouse, the Embarcadero
3884 Camino, Burlingame

After a moment he said, "Send me the offer."

They said goodbyes and a few seconds later his phone dinged with Maria Vasquez's reward notice. He read through it once. Shaw started to read it once more and put the mobile down. He thought: Why bother? Either you're going to do it or you're not.

Please, please, please help

Followed by a bunch of exclamation points.

20

O ne question was answered.

Maria Vasquez, mother of the missing woman, lived in the heart of the TL.

This explained the low sum she was offering for information about her daughter. Very few residents of San Francisco's Tenderloin would be able to come up with a big enough reward to snag anyone's attention.

The neighborhood, in the central part of the city, was infamous. Seedy, dilapidated, graffitied, marred by trash-filled streets and side-walks, the TL was home to street people, those working in the sex trade—traffickers among them—gangs and those involved in all phases of drug enterprises: manufacturers, transporters, sellers and, of course, consumers. The SFPD has defined more than six hundred "plots," small geographic areas of the city, for the purpose of analyz-ing crime stats. Seven of the ten most dangerous plots in San Fran-cisco were in the TL.

Shaw hadn't been here for years. Back then the place was filled with single-room occupancy hotels and small shabby apartments,

adult bookshops, massage parlors, bodegas, Asian and Filipino grocery stores, tobacco/vaping places, cell phone card and wig shops
and nail salons.

Much of that atmosphere persisted to this day but Shaw now saw
a few nods toward improvement. Outreach programs operated out of
storefronts, helping runaways, trafficking victims, addicts. There was
even some gentrification, albeit modest. Across the street from Maria
Vasquez's walk-up was a ten-story apartment building that offered
studio and one-bedroom units, which the poster described, with an
inexplicable hyphen, as DE-LUXE. There was a Starbucks wannabe on
the ground floor, along with an art gallery and a wine bar. Changing . . .
but not changed: the windows on the first two floors of most buildings
along this block were covered with thick iron security bars.

He chained his bike and helmet to a lamppost then walked to the
door of the apartment building. He pressed the intercom and, when
a woman answered, he said, "I called earlier. About the reward you
posted."

"You're—"

"Colter."

The door buzzer sounded and he stepped inside and climbed to
the third floor, smelling fresh paint, garlic and pot. He knocked on
the door of 3C. He heard the creak of footsteps and she answered.

Maria Vasquez looked him over cautiously, eyeing the leather
jacket and jeans and boots.

In most assignments, when meeting with offerors he wanted
them to see him as a professional—part lawyer, part detective, part
psychologist. His garb would be sport coat, laundered jeans, polished shoes, dress shirt in dark shades. Not an option now, not with
the Yamaha.

She'd have to deal with the reward-seeker as biker.

Something about his face, perhaps, put her at ease, though.
"Come in. Please, come in."

Vasquez, in her forties, was about five eight or nine, a pretty face and trim figure. Her dark features suggested blood from Mexico.

The one-bedroom apartment was nicer than he'd expected. The furniture was cheap but the walls had been painted recently—and were hung with bold floral posters and a half-dozen fine-arts photographs, reminiscent of the work of the famous West Coast photographers of the mid-twentieth century: Ansel Adams, Edward Weston, Imogen Cunningham.

She asked if he wanted anything to drink and he declined. They sat and the woman held her hands to her face. "Oh, it has been a terrible year. Such a terrible year. My husband, he died without insurance, and I lost my job. I was a receptionist at a tech company." A cynical grimace. "Big start-up! Oh, we were going to all be millionaires. They promised everything. Stock bonuses. All that. It went under. I've been doing *that* since then." She waved toward a pink waitress's uniform. "We lost our house. And the bank owns it and still they're suing us! I never wanted a big house in the first place. But Eduardo . . ." She shook her head, as if exhausted at replaying the car crash of her last twelve months. "And now this."

Tears formed, and she found a tissue in a battered, cracked beige purse with an old-style clasp on top. She blotted her eyes.

From a pocket in his leather jacket, Shaw extracted one of the 5-by-7-inch notebooks in which he jotted information during interviews like this. His handwriting, like his father's, was extremely small and precise. The notebooks were not ruled but each line of his script was perfectly horizontal.

He used a Delta Titanio Galassia fountain pen. The barrel was black and it featured three orange rings toward the nib. Occasionally an offeror or a witness might glance at the pen, which was not inexpensive, as if using it were pretentious or showy. But this wasn't the case. The pen was largely practical; filling page after page of notes in Shaw's minuscule script was tough on the hand and the gold-tipped fountain pen eased words onto the paper smoothly and with less effort than the best ballpoint. It was also a pleasure to use the fine device.

Someone once asked him why he didn't just use a tape recorder or at least type answers into a computer or tablet. His response: Speaking or typing creates just a glancing relationship with the words. Only when you write by hand do you truly possess them.

Shaw said, "Let me tell you who I am and what I do. You can look at me like a private investigator that you don't pay until I'm successful. I'll try to find your daughter. If I do that, you pay me your reward. You don't have to pay for any expenses."

A reward is, under the law, a unilateral contract. The offer is made but there is no enforceable bargain until one party—the reward-seeker—successfully completes the job. Then an enforceable contract comes into existence.

Vasquez nodded. "Yes, sir."

"Tell me what happened."

"Two days ago Tessy was gone when I got home from my shift. She was supposed to be at work at six but she didn't show up. Her phone doesn't ring. It just goes to voice mail. She didn't show up for work that night. I called her friends . . . Nobody's heard from her."

"Was she going someplace before work?"

"I don't know. She played guitar with friends some."

He asked if she'd talked to the police.

At this she grew silent for a moment. "Not yet. I heard with someone who's older, the police won't be interested for a few days."

They *might* be interested. But what she was really saying was: mother and daughter were undocumented and the cops might report them to Immigration and Customs Enforcement. That was a big concern he'd found in the immigrant community; while some police departments might not report them, by federal law they were required to.

"Did you have a fight? Did she run off?" The most common cause of missing youngsters.

"Oh, no, no. We are very close. We never fight. She's the love of my life!"

Parental kidnappings were the most common form of abduction. Even with children above the age of majority, like Tessy, a mother or father might coerce the youngster to come live with him or her. More and more were living at home until later in life nowadays. Vasquez was a widow but the general principle could apply.

"Have you had a partner or someone you're seeing who might've had an interest in her?"

She gave a laugh. "I work twelve-hour days, two shifts. That is the *last* thing on my mind."

"So you think someone forced her to come with them."

She sat forward, her hands shredding the tissue. "Here's what I'm worried about, sir. Tessy had some drug problems a few years ago. She fought it and won. She goes to meetings. She's a good girl. But there was this man, older. They dated. Mostly she went out with him because he supplied her. After she got sober, her sponsor told her she couldn't see him anymore. She broke up with him. He got furious. He stalked her."

"When?"

"Six months ago."

"What's his name?"

"All I know is Roman. I think it's a nickname."

"Address?"

Vasquez shook her head.

"Arrests?"

"Probably. I think so."

"Describe him."

"He's about thirty, no, probably more. Not tall, slim. Has a shaved head. Or he did. He's white but has a darker skin. There's a tattoo of a cross on his neck. An old-fashioned cross. Like the ancient times."

Shaw took a few moments to jot these notes. Then he asked, "Where does she work?"

"In a folk music club, in North Beach."

Shaw got the name.

"Every time I look at those, I want to cry." She waved at the photographs on the wall.

"She took those? She's talented."

A nod. "She studied, art school. And she can sing too. She has a nice voice."

She looked out the window. Her jaw was tight. "I wasn't there for her like I should have been. So expensive here . . . Working two jobs, both Eduardo and me. We weren't there . . . She got into trouble." She touched a finger to a lower lid and examined it—for running mascara. Of which there were some streaks. She grimaced and, taking a compact mirror from her purse, examined the damage and blotted some of the stain away.

Her hands were delicate, her skin smooth. She must have been in her early twenties when the girl was born.

Shaw asked questions he'd developed over the years in cases involving missing young people and jotted down her answers in his distinctive handwriting.

Friends' names and numbers. There was no find-my-phone app on her mobile. The phone was in her name, so her mother couldn't have the phone company ping it; only the police could and even then only with a warrant. Tessy had one of her mother's credit cards, but she hadn't used it.

"When was your last contact?"

"A phone call. She left a message. I couldn't pick up." Her lip trembled. She'd be thinking that maybe it was the last chance she would have had to speak to her daughter.

"Play it."

She did. They heard a light, cheerful voice chatting briefly and saying she'd call later. She was outdoors, on a noisy street.

Shaw asked, "Can you send it to me?"

She didn't understand. "Send . . . ?"

He explained, "You can save a voice mail as a WAV file."

"A wave?"

"*W-A-V.* It's a sound-recording format. You can save it on your phone. Google it. It's easy to do. Then email the recording to me." He gave her his address: ColterShawReward@gmail.com.

She said she would.

"I'd like to see her room."

"She doesn't have one. She sleeps here—on the pullout."

"Any personal effects? Papers, computer?"

She waved around the sparsely furnished place. "Most everything of ours is in storage in Mountain View. Where we had the house that was foreclosed."

"I think I have enough to get started. I'll need a photo. A better one than you posted online."

She didn't have any hard copies but she uploaded one to his phone.

The young woman, with long dark hair, was striking. High cheekbones, broad lips and big eyes, deep brown.

"Has anyone else called about the reward?"

"A couple of people." Her voice lowered. "They were just assholes. They didn't know anything. Just making stuff up about her being here or there so they could get the money."

"That happens. All right. I have other projects going on. But I'll do what I can."

She shook his hand warmly. "Thank you, Mr. Shaw."

"Colter."

"Thank you. Bless you." She touched the silver crucifix at her throat. Then said brightly, "It's more now."

"More?"

"What I can offer. I looked at the GoFundMe page an hour ago. People've contributed another $234. And I'm praying that there'll be more."

Shaw said, "Let's find her first. We'll worry about that later."

21

ever be blunt when subtle will do . . .

Colter Shaw was adept at guile. He liked outthinking the criminals he was pursuing, liked strategizing against the geography, the elements, the forces that conspired to keep him from finding a missing person.

But sometimes you just had to throw clever to the wind and go for it.

Blunt . . .

When he stepped out onto the pungent street in front of Maria Vasquez's apartment he caught a glimpse of the green Honda.

In one sense, there *was* some subtlety involved, in spotting the car. The driver had not parked directly on Vasquez's street, but around the corner. As he scanned around him he saw the Honda in a reflection—a newly washed plate-glass window was at the apex of a triangle, which also included Shaw and the green car.

Since there was no direct view of Shaw's bike from the car, that meant that the driver wasn't now in the vehicle but was one of dozens of people on the street, lying low and surveilling him. That

population included shoppers, folks delivering packages and envelopes and restaurant provisions, shopkeepers hard at work in the
never-ending job of scrubbing the sidewalks, some women and men
who were probably sex workers, a few pushers hawking their wares,
and their consumers, those just standing around, talking to others
in person or on cell phones and a few talking exclusively, and with
animation, to themselves.

Only one way to find out who.

Shaw made sure his holster was snug and turned in the direction
of the cross street walking quickly toward the side street where the
green Honda was parked.

He flushed the spy in one second.

Dressed in black jeans and a gray windbreaker, head covered
with a black baseball cap, the spy—about two hundred feet from
Shaw—turned instantly and ran back toward the car. It began as a
fast gait, then a sprint, though he paused briefly to speak to two
large workers, in T-shirts, one with a shock of curly red hair, the
other with a black, unwashed ponytail. Colleagues? Shaw didn't see
how. They were unloading supplies from a battered cab truck,
double-parked at the intersection around the corner of which sat the
green Honda.

The driver continued sprinting, Shaw was closing in. He'd catch
up before the man could leap into the car and speed off.

Or that *would* have happened, if not for one problem.

As he approached the delivery truck, the two men stepped directly into his path and held out hands. Curly growled, "Not so
fucking fast, asshole."

Shaw tried to dodge but Ponytail jogged in front and grabbed
him by the arm.

"Out of my way." Shaw lowered his center of gravity and got
ready to grapple him to the ground.

Curly took the other arm and they pushed Shaw up against the
truck. He was pinned.

"Going to break more bones? Lemme ask. That make you feel like a man?"

Ponytail, who bathed as infrequently as he shampooed, growled, "Me and him oughta break a few of yours. See how *you* like it."

"Okay. Take it easy." Since Shaw had no idea what was going on, he only offered those generic words. He relaxed a bit and when Ponytail did too, Shaw yanked his right arm free and got the man's meaty wrist in a come-along grip, dropping him to his knees.

"Fuck no." Curly casually slugged Shaw in the belly, and he too went down.

Shaw caught his breath, slowly rose and backed away.

He heard, from around the corner, a car start and tires cry.

Hell . . .

The men started toward him. Shaw backed up farther and lifted his left hand toward them, palm up, and with his right, pulled his jacket open and sweater up, revealing the gun.

"Fuck, you a cop?"

"Look, man . . . We didn't know."

The nausea faded. He snapped, "What'd he say to you?"

"Who?"

"The man I was chasing."

The workers regarded each other.

"You got it wrong, mister," Curly said.

"Wasn't no man. Was a girl."

"And hot, you ask me."

He spent several hours in his search for Tessy Vasquez.

The music club where she worked didn't serve lunch but Shaw was able to talk to the manager, a skinny young man in clothes two sizes too big and with a droopy Vietnam War–era mustache. He wore a stocking cap not unlike Russell's, but in green. He couldn't provide any helpful information and had never seen anyone fitting

Roman's description interacting with Tessy, who was a waitress and occasional performer at the club.

"I've asked the staff if they know anything about where she is," the guy said, "and nobody does. She just didn't show up for work. That's when I called her mother."

Outside the place, Shaw called the friends whose names Maria Vasquez had given him—at least those whose numbers he could find. Three answered but no one had any knowledge of where Tessy might be. One young woman, though, did tell him that Tessy was really into busking—street singing—lately. She'd mentioned she'd worried about some of the "pervs" in the parks and the squares she sang in, but she could provide nothing specific.

Shaw biked back to the safe house.

The place, which had seemed alive thanks to Russell's presence, was now stark. A newly formed fog didn't help much.

June gloom . . .

Shaw hung his leather jacket on a rack near the front door and tugged off his sweater, draping it on the rack too. The house was warm. He walked into the kitchen and pulled out a bag of ground Honduran coffee from the cupboard. He brewed a pot through a filter and poured a cup for himself. He hadn't brought the milk from the Winnebago, but he found some powdered Carnation in the refrigerator. Apparently his brother liked coffee the same way he did.

And where was the man now?

On a private jet to Singapore?

In a bunker in Utah?

Tracking down a terrorist in Houston?

The survivalist skills that Ashton had taught the family were a double-edged weapon. They could keep you safe from intrusion. But they could also be used to get close to your enemies, eliminate them and then evade detection as you escaped.

He recalled the matter-of-fact expression in his brother's eyes after he'd killed Blond in the alley. The only concerns were practical—getting his team there efficiently and quickly for the cleanup and getting away.

He sat on the couch and stretched back, boots out in front of him.

Thinking of the driver of the green Honda.

A girl . . .

And hot . . .

But who the hell was she? What was *her* mission?

One thing about her was clear. She was smart about keeping him from catching her: pitching the nails into his path. Smart too in using the two Neanderthals on the street in the TL. They'd said she'd been panicked and begged them to help; the man chasing her was an abusive ex, who'd put her in the hospital a dozen times. He'd broken her arm twice.

"You believed her?" Shaw had muttered.

Curly had shrugged. "'Course. She was like, yeah, you know, beautiful."

Ah, beauty. A lie detector that Shaw had heard of before.

They knew nothing else and had not seen the Honda's tag, so he'd left them to their labors. He'd made a brief canvass of the street where she'd parked the Honda. No one had noticed the woman or the car—at least that was everyone's story.

He wondered how her presence here would play out.

In the absence of fact, any theories were speculation, and trying to formulate any deductions was a waste of time.

His eyes strayed to something on the shelf nearby: the dark statuette of the eagle he'd seen earlier.

Colt, no. Don't! It's not our job . . .

22

"Are they crazy? They're going to die."

Russell is peering up the side of a steep snow-covered mountain, as he speaks these words to his younger brother. Colter is fourteen, his brother twenty. Russell is visiting his family in the Compound over semester break.

They are in snowshoes and dressed for the January cold, which is cold indeed at this elevation. They've been looking, unsuccessfully, for bighorn sheep, whose season is the latest of any game in the state. You can hunt them well into February.

Colter follows his brother's gaze to watch two people snowshoeing across a steep slope. One is in navy-blue overalls and stocking cap, the other wears lavender with a white head covering. The build of the latter tells Colter it is a woman. They are hiking from one side of the angular hillside to the other, about a hundred yards below the crest.

The land here is Shaw property but this particular location is about three miles from a public preserve. Ashton posted much of the land but generally doesn't make an issue out of trespassing unless there are firearms involved, which might include hunters or—as

Colter learned just last year in an armed standoff—an ominous intruder, overly interested in Ashton Shaw and his property.

His concern at the moment is not their legal right to be here, though. It's that the couple—apparently on a photographic safari—are at serious risk.

The pair is trudging through the heart of an avalanche field. They've come from Fresno or Bakersfield or Sacramento to record in pixels the soaring whitewashed mountains after several days of impressive blizzarding.

"City slickers," Russell mutters, using a term Colter understands though he's never heard it. Russell has spent two years away from the monastery of the Compound and has been exposed to many, many things that Colter cannot even imagine, new words and expressions among them.

"Don't know what the hell they're doing. Got to warn them."

A hissing wind lifts powder from the crest and continues down the slope. Upwind, the couple couldn't hear them from where they stood.

"We have to go up, get closer."

Russell nods. "But stay out of that field. It's a land mine."

In his survivalist training sessions, Ashton spent hours lecturing the children about avalanches. And Colter sees instantly how dangerous these conditions are. Snow is at its least stable immediately after a storm, as now. And it's particularly erratic on north faces, like this. The south sides of mountains get more sun, which melts and packs the fall. North side snow is *hoar*, as in hoarfrost, unpacked, loose and slippery as grains of sugar. Another factor: any incline above thirty degrees makes a mountain avalanche prone, and this slope is easily that.

Colter and Russell trek as quickly as one can on snowshoes and burdened by their rifles and backpacks.

The couple pauses, balancing on the tricky angle, and shoots some pictures that are surely magnificent and that also might represent their last view of this planet.

Of fatalities in avalanches, seventy percent are due to suffocation, thirty to blunt trauma. Few snowslides are exclusively of fine powder; most torrents are filled with sharp slabs of gray dirty pack and crushing ice like blocks of concrete.

The boys are about a hundred yards below and twenty behind the couple. They are breathless from the altitude and from the effort of climbing quickly uphill.

Finally Russell gestures his younger brother back and continues forward about ten feet, stopping on a high drift. He's right on the edge of the field, though how safe he and Colter truly are is unknown. Snow travels in any direction snow wants to travel. It can even go uphill.

Cupping his hands to his mouth, Russell shouts, "Hikers! It's dangerous! Avalanche!"

The wind—which happens to be another risk factor—whips his words back behind him; they didn't hear.

Both boys are now shouting.

No response. The man points into the distance and they take more pictures.

Russell starts uphill once more and edges into the field, telling his younger brother, "Stay back."

He stops and calls again, "It's dangerous! Get back! The way you came!"

A high rocky path led the couple to the mountainside. Once on it again they'd be safe.

Colter notices tiny white rivulets rolling down the hill from where the trespassers stand. Like white-furred animals scurrying from danger. The bundles travel fast and they travel far.

He wonders about using his rifle to fire into a tree and get their attention. Ashton lectured that most experts don't believe that sounds, even a big-caliber rifle shot, will start an avalanche, but he isn't going to take the chance. Also, indicating your location by firing a weapon is usually useless, thanks to echoing.

Russell moves closer yet to the couple. "It's dangerous!"

"Avalanche!" Colter shouts and waves his arms.

Finally the two look down and wave. "What?" The man's shout carries easily on the wind.

"Avalanche. You're in an avalanche field!"

The man and woman look at each other. He lifts his arms and shakes his head broadly. Meaning he doesn't hear. They plod along the difficult slope in the ungainly shoes.

Russell hurries back to his brother and they climb onto a rocky ledge on the border of the field. "We'll go up through the trees."

Just as the brothers start uphill, Colter hears a faint scream. The woman has lost her balance. Her legs go out from under her and she begins sliding on her back, arms splaying to stop the descent. There's a technique to slow yourself using snowshoes but she doesn't know it or, in panic, has forgotten.

Here it comes, Colter thinks.

But there is no avalanche.

The woman slides downward amid a cloud of powder and comes to a stop about even with the brothers, thirty, forty feet away from them. She struggles upright in the thigh-high powder, anchored by her wide mesh shoes. She checks her camera and other gear. She touches her pocket, shouting uphill. "Phone's okay!" She actually laughs.

Her friend gives a thumbs-up.

The woman is now in hearing range and Russell explains the danger. "You have to get out of there now! Both of you! It's an avalanche field. Dangerous!"

"Avalanche?"

"Now!" Colter calls. He thought her tumble would start one. People are the number-one cause of avalanches: skiers, snowmobilers and snowshoers, who go carelessly where they should not. But so far the massive ledge holds.

Russell says, "Get over here, off the slope! Unhook the snow-shoes and pull them out. And your friend, he needs to go back to the trees, the path you were on. He needs to turn around!"

She looks up and waves to him and then points to his left, mean-ing to return to the path. He gives yet another raised arm of incom-prehension.

She pulls her gloves off and digs out her phone. She makes a call. Colter sees him answer.

"Brad, honey, these boys say it's an avalanche area. Go back to the trees. That path we were on before we started across the hill."

Russell says, "Tell him to move very slowly. Really."

She relays this information, puts the phone away and bends down to unhook her shoes. She gets one undone and, after a strug-gle, yanks it out.

Can't she go any faster?

Uphill, Colter sees, the man starts toward the safety of the path.

He glances down and sees the trickles of snow accelerating away from beneath his feet.

More and more of them.

He panics and charges forward, slamming the oval snowshoes hard on the surface.

"No!" Colter and his brother shout simultaneously.

Just as the man scrambles out of the field, literally diving to safety, a shelf of snow breaks away and cascades downward. It is only ten feet wide or so and shallow but avalanches are a chain reac-tion. Colter knows this will trigger a much bigger fall.

The woman evidently hears the *whoosh* too and looks up at the wall sliding toward her. A brief scream. She is still forty feet from the safety of the high ground where the boys are. She's trapped in place by the remaining snowshoe. She bends down into the froth and frantically tries to undo the strap.

Colter assesses:

Odds that the whole field will give way? Eighty percent.

Survival of somebody who has no deep-snow training? Five percent.

Somebody who had *some* training? Unknown but better than that.

He drops his backpack and discards his weapons.

Russell is staring at his younger brother.

"Colt, no. Don't! It's not our job."

No time for discussion. Colter leaps off the ridge and runs quickly across the field, in the ungainly lope of a snowshoe jogger.

Just as he reaches her, the rest of the mountain cuts loose, a vast swath of snow, fifty or sixty yards wide, dropping, tumbling, picking up speed. Tides like this can easily exceed a hundred miles an hour.

As he pops the quick release of his shoes and steps out of them he sees her panicked face, tears streaming. She has large dark eyes, an upturned nose and lipstick, or sunscreen, that matches her violet snowsuit.

"Your other shoe?"

"What's going to happen?" she cries.

"Shoe?" he snaps.

"Undone." She straightens up and tries to pull it out. She blinks as she looks him over, maybe realizing for the first time how young he is.

"Leave the shoe!" Colter orders.

He lifts her camera off and tosses it away. In the turbulence of an avalanche, solid objects, even small ones, can maim and kill.

A glance crestward. They have thirty seconds.

"Listen to me. When it hits, don't fight it. Pretend you're swimming, kick with your arms and legs. Swim *with* it, like you're in the surf. Got that?"

No answer.

"Have you *got* it?" he insists.

"Yes, swimming."

Twenty seconds till the tide slams into them.

"When you feel yourself slowing, curl up and take a deep breath, as deep as you can. And with one hand clear a space around your mouth for air. Lift the other arm up as high as you can, so the searchers know where you are. Make a big space around your mouth. There'll be enough air for a half hour."

"I'm scared!"

Ten seconds. The wave is six feet high, now seven, now eight and accelerating. It's trailed by dust swirling and thick as forest fire smoke.

"You'll do fine. Swim, hand to mouth, arm up."

It's a slough avalanche—more loose snow than slabs. If they died it would be by suffocation, not a blow to the head. Colter doesn't know which is worse. Suffocation probably.

She stares at the wave. Colter turns her around so that she's facing downhill.

Five seconds.

Colter shuffles away so their bodies don't become bludgeons.

"Swim!"

She does. He does too and takes a deep breath.

In the time it takes to fill his lungs, the world turns black.

23

Mary Dove finishes tending to the wounds on her fourteen-year-old son's neck and cheek.

While *most* of the avalanche was slough—granular hoar snow—Colter didn't escape a chunk of sharp ice. Or possibly a rock.

The damage isn't severe.

They are in her office, which is a typical physician's, except for the walls, which are—as everything in the cabin—made of hand-hewn logs.

"Anywhere else?" she asks.

"No," Colter says. "Just a little sore."

"How far did it sweep you?"

"Football field," Colter says, though he doesn't have much frame of reference, only pictures in newspapers or magazines. He's never seen a game. In a home with no TV and no internet, one doesn't have a chance to view broadcast spectator sports, and the nearest teams are those of the colleges and high schools around Fresno. When the family went there, they always had errands to run or acquaintances and family to see. None of the children had much inclination anyway. If parents aren't excited about sports, their youngsters probably won't be either.

Mary Dove executes some range-of-motion tests, arms and legs, which her son seems to pass. More or less.

He goes into his bathroom and takes a very hot shower, minding the rule to keep the bandages dry. He towels off, dresses and lies down on his blanket, which is brown and woven in a Native American design.

He closes his eyes briefly, picturing the torrent of snow enwrapping him.

He followed the same advice he'd given the woman.

When he slowed, though, he realized that extending his arm to signal his whereabouts would do no good. He was too far under the surface, so he'd pulled his arm back, and taken another deep breath and, using both hands, cleared a large air reservoir in front of his face.

Finally he stopped sliding and he wasted no time in attempting to free himself, kneeing and punching and elbowing. The space he opened up before him was completely black, and he was disoriented as to where the surface might be. He recalled his father's lesson and made small snowballs and dropped them near his face and hands to see where they landed, so he could tell which way was down.

Never question gravity . . .

Then came the digging—scooping the snow down, packing it and then pushing upward with his feet and arms. Inches at a time.

Finally there was slight illumination over his head and he broke through, sucking in the air, which as in all snowfields gave off a sweet electrical scent.

He climbed out and rolled onto the snow surface, catching his breath. He called to his brother, who was probing the field nearby with a long branch. He dropped it and ran to Colter to help him up.

"The woman?" Colter asked. "She all right?"

His brother pointed.

The man who'd been with her, Brad, was digging her out of a deep pile of snow near the avalanche's toe—the end. She'd been swept much farther than he'd been. Colter saw that she had survived and was helping to dig herself out. She was unhurt.

Colter struggled to his feet, with Russell helping. His brother looked up the mountain and said, "The whole pack didn't come down. There's more that's unstable, a lot more. We should get them out and into the trees."

They walked to the couple.

"We spotted her arm," Russell said. "That's how we found where she was. You told her that."

Shaw nodded, and the foursome made their way to safety.

Now, in the Compound's rustic cabin, Colter is finally warm once more, inner core warm, and in only slight pain. He rises from his bed and walks into the living room where Russell and Dorion are sitting near a soothing dance of flames in the stacked-stone fireplace. They are both reading. When Colter enters the room, Dorion, eleven, leaps up and hugs him. He tells himself to give no reaction to the pain and he doesn't. She regards the bandage with still eyes, which means she's troubled.

"It's all right. A scratch."

"Okay," she says.

"Hey," Russell says and goes back to his book.

"Hey."

Dorion sits once more. "You know what the biggest one in the world was?"

She'd be talking about old-time locomotives, which, for some reason, she is passionate about.

"No clue."

"Union Pacific's Big Boy. Come on, Colter, look!" She shows him the book. According to the caption, the engine depicted was Locomotive Number 4014, and was an impressive piece of machinery. It had a 4-8-8-4 wheel arrangement, which, she explained to him a few years ago, was the number of locomotive wheels from front to back; it's how the machines are classified.

"Biggest expansion engine there ever was. It weighed more than a million pounds. It's in a museum in Los Angeles. I want to see it someday."

"We'll make sure that happens."

"You'll come too, Russell?" she asks.

"Sure." The older brother doesn't look up from his book. Colter wonders what he's reading. Russell has been into spy thrillers lately.

Mary Dove is in the kitchen, preparing dinner, while Ashton is in his study, the door closed, where he disappeared an hour ago after learning that his sons were all right.

Colter stretches and happens to glance to the mantel, where he sees a trio of framed pictures—two artist renderings and one photograph. The picture to the left is a sketch of a woman who has some Native American features. A handsome face, black hair parted severely in the middle, the sides dangling to her shoulders. She is Marie Aioe Dorion, the nation's first mountain woman. She was of Métis heritage, indigenous people in the central part of the United States and southern Canada. Widowed early, Dorion survived in the wilderness for months with two small children, in hostile territory.

The center picture is a reproduction of a painting of a handsome, rugged man wearing leather and a raccoon hat that encompasses much of his head. He is John Colter, an explorer with the Lewis and Clark Expedition.

The photograph on the right is of Osborne Russell, the explorer, politician and judge, who was in part responsible for founding the Oregon Territory. He is the most recent of the three, surviving into the late 1800s; hence the photographic image.

These three individuals were the sources for the Shaw children's names.

The study door opens and Ashton walks into the living room. He has changed a lot, Colter thinks, in the years since the family left the Bay Area for the Compound—to escape some threats that troubled him greatly but that he hasn't discussed much with the children, other than to warn them to be on the lookout for strangers on the Compound. His hair has gone mostly white and is often, like now, mussed. He wears jeans, a white shirt with pearl buttons—Mary Dove made it—and a leather vest. On his feet, tactical boots, the sort a soldier might wear.

He is carrying a cardboard box.

"Everyone," he says.

The three children look up. Mary Dove remains in the kitchen. The word was uttered in his speaking-to-the-children tone.

When they settle he looks at them one by one. Finally he says, "Never deny the power of ritual. Do you know what I mean?"

"Like in Harry Potter? The ceremonies at Hogwarts?" Dorie is a fan, to put it mildly.

"Exactly, Button."

Colter is thinking of the Lord of the Rings trilogy but he doesn't say anything.

Russell seems to be thinking of nothing in response. He just watches his father and the box he is holding.

"A general rule of survivalism is: 'Never risk yourself for a stranger.' But that's not what I believe. What's the good of learning our skills if we can't put them to use and help somebody else?"

The three of them—his children, his students—sit motionless on couch or chair, looking up at the intense eyes of their father.

"Colter saved somebody's life today. And I thought we should have a ritual."

The boy's face burns and he's sure it turns red. Dorion's, on the other hand, blossoms with happiness as she looks Colter's way. He gives her a smile. Russell now gazes at the fireplace, where the flames had turned from energetic blue to subdued orange.

Ashton reaches into the box and extracts a small statuette of an eagle in flight. He hands it to Colter, who takes it. It's heavy, metal.

He's worried that his father will expect him to make a speech. At fourteen he has rappelled down hundred-foot cliffs and borrowed a motorcycle from a friend in White Sulfur Springs, the nearest town, and hit ninety miles an hour on a road of imperfect asphalt. He has also pulled a pistol on an intruder in the Compound—that incident last year—and sent him on his way.

He would do any of those again rather than make a speech, even to this small audience.

"But he couldn't have done that without the love and support of his brother and sister. So our ritual includes both of you too." Ashton reaches into the box once more and takes out a statuette of a fox and hands it to Dorion. Her eyes ignite with pleasure. The only thing she likes more than locomotives is animals.

"And here's yours." He hands Russell a bear statuette. His brother says nothing but stares at the bronze, weighs it in his hand.

Shaw suddenly has a snap of understanding. The statues echo the nicknames of the children. Dorie is the clever one. Russell the reclusive one. And Colter the restless one.

Then the ritual is over—no speeches required—and Mary Dove announces that it's time to eat.

After dinner—which would have been bighorn sheep but is now elk—Colter takes the statuette into his bedroom and sets it on a shelf beside his copies of the Lord of the Rings trilogy, Ray Bradbury's short stories and a half-dozen law books, which for some reason he enjoys reading.

Now, years later, in the kitchen of the Alvarez Street safe house, Colter Shaw was looking at the same statue as intently as he was the night of the avalanche.

He recalled that when he left home to attend the University of Michigan and was packing his duffel bag for the trip he had noticed that the eagle statue was nowhere in his room.

Yet here it was now.

There was only one possible explanation for its appearance. His father had taken it with him when he'd come to the safe house. It was, maybe, a sentimental reminder of his son, something that Ash wanted to have with him. To make him feel close to home.

A perfectly reasonable, heartwarming explanation.

But Shaw believed there was another reason, a more important one, that Ashton had brought the eagle to San Francisco. It was the clearest message yet that Father wanted Colter, of all his children, to carry on his mission.

24

S haw's phone pinged with the sound of an incoming text. It was from his private investigator, in Washington, D.C., to whom he'd sent an encrypted email before his bike ride from the Tenderloin back here.

Charlotte "Mack" McKenzie might have been a model. With steely gray eyes, she was an even six feet tall, her complexion pale and her brown hair long. This was a problem for her in street work. Like a spy, PIs benefit from being inconspicuous. And no one could ever say that of Mack McKenzie. Her days of tailing people, though, were long past. She had put together a security and investigative operation that hummed, and she had a talented crew of staff and contractors to do the sweat labor.

Maria and Tessy Vasquez. Largely under the radar—likely undocumented—but social media and level-one governmental data confirm their identities. No criminal records. Probably legit. No AKA "Roman" in CA or U.S. criminal databases in SF area.

Mack was a woman after Shaw's own heart. In keeping with Shaw's approach to life, little was ever zero percent or one hundred percent with her, even if she wasn't quite as quick to assign a precise number as he was.

Probably legit . . .

She finished with:

Your requested analysis presently underway.

He replied, thanking her, and looked over the notes he'd taken at Maria Vasquez's apartment, a decent place in a modest building surrounded by the complex 'hood of the TL. He was concerned about the young woman, the talented singer and photographer.

For-profit kidnapping? Near zero percent.

The odds she'd been murdered and the body disposed of? Not great. Ten percent. That wasn't as common as cable TV would have us believe.

And what about her being in a meth house somewhere, strung out, after having relapsed? Thirty percent. She seemed to be making good on a fresh start. But add Roman into this equation and that boosted the number to sixty percent.

He suddenly saw his BlackBridge mission as a distraction from the reward job, which was, after all, his main profession. But he'd make it work. He'd do whatever was necessary to find the girl, or at least get some answer for her mother.

It just then happened that his phone hummed, and he took a call from one of Tessy's friends. The young woman couldn't provide any information about the missing girl. But in response to his question about Roman said, "Is he involved? Shit."

"I don't know. Her mother thinks it's possible."

"He's trouble. I think he's crazy. I mean, really, like a psycho-path."

Shaw asked if she had any specific information on him.

"No, I never really knew him. He didn't want Tessy hanging with us. He wanted her all to himself. He's dangerous, mister. He hangs with some really bad people. You know, gangs, that kind of thing. I heard he killed somebody. Jesus, I hope she didn't go back to him."

He tried the people he'd called earlier and, when none of them answered, left new messages. This was all he could do on the reward assignment for the time being, until Mack got back to him with his earlier request.

Back to the scavenger hunt of Amos Gahl's stolen evidence.

Glancing at his phone, he checked the tracker app. The chipped copy of *Walden* was still at the library.

He wondered what Helms, Braxton and Droon would be thinking about Blond's death. Was the mysterious bearded shooter a friend of Shaw's or was the incident merely a coincidence? Had Blond, who reeked of hired killer, been gunned down in retaliation for some earlier offense?

Shaw sat back, stared at the ceiling and silently asked Amos Gahl: What did you find?

And where is your courier bag hidden?

It was time to look at the two leads that might hold the answers to those questions: the house on Camino in Burlingame and the warehouse in the Embarcadero.

The coffee cup froze halfway to Shaw's mouth when he heard the doorbell ring.

He turned fast, hand near his pistol. He stood.

A voice called, "Me. I'm coming in."

The front door opened and Russell stepped inside. Still in the black hat, still in the dark, thigh-length coat, the tactical boots.

He walked into the kitchen.

"There's an issue." He took off his coat, revealing a green T-shirt. The muscles of his arms were pronounced. His jeans were held up by dark red suspenders. He sat. "Man in the alley?"

"Droon or the other one?"

"The dead one. Karin was handling disposal. She found a note, handwritten. In his pocket."

His brother displayed a photo on his phone.

Confirmation from Hunters Point crew.
6/26, 7:00 p.m. SP and family. All ↓

Russell remained stone-faced as his brother looked over the screen, then sat back.

Shaw said, "Does the 'All' and the arrow mean what I think it does?"

A nod. "It's a kill order. A hit on someone with the initials SP and his family. Or *her* family."

Shaw noticed that it had been folded many times, like the notes Amos Gahl's colleague had left for their father.

"Dead-drop," Shaw said.

"Some messages you don't send electronically no matter how good the encryption. We do it too."

Used dead-drops?

Or issued kill orders?

"Did Karin find his ID? Anything else?"

"Not yet. Running prints and DNA and facial recognition. May get it right away, may take a while. May never find out. People in this line of work do a lot of track covering."

Shaw asked, "With Blond gone, will they still go ahead with the hit?"

"Who?"

"The guy in the alley. My nic for him."

"Have to assume it's still a go. Handwritten KO, dead-drop, the arrow on the whole family. They'll assume that Blond got disappeared for some reason unrelated to this. That woman Braxton'll just find another triggerman."

"Thanks for telling me. But I can't go to the police. Ashton didn't trust them."

"Wouldn't want them anyway."

Of course. The note would be accompanied by a question: How did Shaw come by it? And the disquieting answer to that inquiry was: because his brother had shot someone in the head.

Russell looked at his watch; it was an analog model, brushed steel or titanium. "Two days until they die. We need to figure out a plan."

Had Shaw heard right? "'We'? You don't want to get involved in this, Russell."

His older brother clearly wasn't happy. "I do not, that's true. But what this's become, it isn't your thing. It's not a reward job, Colt. You can't do it on your own." He stalked up the stairs. "I've got reports to file. We'll talk strategy in the morning."

THE STEELWORKS

After the third guard draws his weapon and fires, Shaw returns one shot, missing, and he and Nita step into one of the empty storerooms. Shaw looks out occasionally, Glock ready. One or two of the men near the office will fire his way, but casually without aiming. It's covering fire only, to keep them down, to keep them back.

And it's working.

Shaw called 911 and reported the shots.

Why, though, are the three not charging him? Moving forward, shooting . . . They could overwhelm Shaw and the young woman. She's crying, shivering.

Rock, Paper, Scissors . . .

Still not charging them. Shaw then looks around the corner and sees why.

A man walks down the stairs, listing under the weight of a five-gallon gasoline can. He takes it into the TV room.

Because he's armed, they must assume that Shaw is an undercover cop, or at the least he's called the police. So the order has *come from the owner of the place to destroy the physical evidence, the computer files.*

Everything has to disappear.

Including the witnesses.

And in the process, they can avoid getting shot by charging Shaw.

With a crisp whoosh, the massive fireball fills the office and rolls into the corridor. Orange, black, yellow. Uncontrolled boiling, mesmerizing if it weren't so deadly. The men vanish.

Down here, Shaw notes, there are no sprinklers.

Shaw calls 911 again and reports there's now a fire.

For what good it will do. The entire building will be a pile of cinders in twenty minutes.

The stampede above them is a roar and is accompanied by muted screams. He believes he hears, "We have to get out. Help us!" The smoke will be rising to the dance floor.

The flames illuminate the basement. Shaw hopes he'll be able to see another exit. There is one but it's chained, and his lock-picking skills only go so far.

There's one way out.

"Come on." He takes Nita by the arm and leads her straight toward the conflagration.

"No!" she screams.

He tugs her more firmly. "Our only chance." She comes along.

They approach the turbulent flames, the heat scraping their skin. Just before it becomes unbearable, Shaw turns to the right, into the storeroom across from the office. The flames are lapping at the outer wall but have not yet eaten through.

He moves to the side facing the stairs and begins to kick the Sheetrock. This wouldn't work if he were in his rubber-soled Eccos but his boots' leather soles, the heels in particular, make indentations in the wall. Again, again. Finally he breaks through. It's a small hole. He ducks and looks through it. Yes, the area at the foot of the stairs—only ten feet away—is empty of hostiles. But soon it will be engulfed in flame.

More kicking. The hole grows slowly larger.

Nita helps. She's strong. When Shaw cracks a piece, she pulls it free. The hole is now about eighteen inches around. Almost big enough to fit through.

Kick, pull.

Both are coughing. His eyes sting and stream. The fire is stealing the oxygen. He feels light-headed.

Kick, pull . . .

Now, finally, it's big enough for them to fit through.

"Go on."

She wriggles through and collapses on the other side.

The pounding feet on the dance floor above them have stopped. Everyone has evacuated. The roar of the flames is the only sound.

Shaw turns to the hole they broke open in the Sheetrock and says to Nita, "Up the stairs now, fast. There'll be police."

"But . . . what about you?"

He smiles to her. "Not yet."

And turns back, jogging to the far end of the corridor.

PART TWO

JUNE 25

THE GREAT EARTHQUAKE

Time until the family dies: thirty-two hours.

25

The Shaw brothers had two missions, interwoven like ropes in a Gordian knot.

One, saving the SP family from the hitman who would replace Blond; the other, bringing down BlackBridge. In saving the family, they might find hard evidence linking the hit back to Braxton, Droon and maybe even Ian Helms himself. Or, finding that evidence in the first place might allow them to identify and save the family.

Their initial task was to try to identify Blond, and so after leaving the safe house they drove to Hunters Point, a neighborhood on the eastern edge of the city, jutting into the Bay.

Hunters Point and neighboring Bayview were among the toughest parts of the city, and the most densely populated with gangs.

Confirmation from Hunters Point crew.
6/26, 7:00 p.m. SP and family. All ↓

Which gang could the hit order mean?

Shaw had enlisted some help and this morning had sent a text to his friend and rock-climbing buddy, Tom Pepper, who, at the FBI, had worked terrorism and organized crime.

As Russell's SUV—a Lincoln Navigator—idled in a parking lot, Shaw's phone hummed. He answered, "Tom."

"Colt."

"You're on speaker here with my brother, Russell."

A pause. Shaw wondered what the man would be thinking. He knew of the estrangement, though not its basis. "Hello, Russell."

"Tom."

"Here's what I've got. Two main crews in Hunters Point—Bayview. One's Anglo. The Bayneck Locals. You know the Pecker-wood Movement?"

Shaw replied, "Vaguely. White supremacists, prison culture, drugs. Started in the South, right?"

"In the thirties. Then spread, lot of the members ended up in California. Skinheads, yeah, but they have some alliances with Latinx gangs. The Baynecks aren't technically Peckerwoods—there was some falling-out—but they're cut from the same cloth.

"The second main gang in that area is Black. The Hudson Kings. It's rap based, like the old Westmob and the rival Big Block. Okay, listen. They're all businessmen first—drugs and guns mostly—but that doesn't mean they're not violent and territorial and will take out a threat in an instant. I'm saying: They won't be inclined to cooperate."

Shaw said, "I'm going to appeal to their better nature."

Pepper chuckled. "Whatever you're doing, make sure it's during the daylight hours."

"We're here now," Russell said. "They have a social club, hang someplace?"

"The Kings had an HQ in a storefront on Northridge. I think near Harbor. The Baynecks used to operate out of a biker bar on Ingalls. Bayview and Hunters Point have complicated boundaries, so I'm not sure which 'hood they're in. I don't know anybody in the

Baynecks but there's an O.G. high up in the Kings. Kevin Miller. He was a stand-up guy. Didn't exactly cooperate, but he kept things calm. Nobody got shot. And that's saying something."

Russell was on his phone, checking GPS.

Pepper said, "I hope it's a damn big reward you're after."

"No reward."

"So. Last week you nearly got killed in a cult and there was no reward. And now you're tap-dancing with the crews in Hunters Point, and there's no reward."

Shaw said, "Sums it up."

"Good luck. Nice meeting you, Russell."

"Same."

Shaw disconnected. "Which first?"

"Hmm. Bikers're closer."

26

As they drove through the streets, both residential and commercial, Shaw looked around him. Hunters Point had always borne the brunt of commerce unwelcome in other parts of the city. At one time it was acres upon acres of slaughterhouses, power plants, tanneries and shipyards, all of which dumped waste into the land, the air and the water of the western Bay.

A hard place, battered and grubby, the Point was only somewhat improved over its nineteenth-century incarnation. Part workaday industrial, part slowly emerging residential and retail redevelopment, part weedy fields and labyrinthine foundations cleared of superstructure. Quite the mix: they drove by a series of vacant lots and a burned-out building right next to which was a small, Victorian-style opera house, painted bright green. Just past that was a construction site on which a sign announced this would be the future home of a division of a well-known internet company, whose headquarters was about fifteen miles south, on the eastern edge of Silicon Valley.

They soon spotted their destination. Lou's was the name of the bar and it was right out of central set design for a 1960s chopped-cycle movie. Peeling paint, grimy windows, a few unsteady tables and less steady chairs out in front, presently unoccupied. Two Harleys and a Moto Guzzi cycle leaned at the curb.

Russell parked and the two men got out, adjusting jacket and coat to make sure their pistols were invisible.

The interior of the bar was dim and smelled of Lysol and cigarette smoke. The only décor, aside from the ignored NO SMOKING sign, was old and fly-specked posters of surfers—more women than men—along with a wooden Nazi iron cross and a picture of Berchtesgaden, Hitler's mountain retreat.

There were a half-dozen Bayneck crew sitting at three tables. They'd been talking, before they turned en masse to gape at the newcomers. Breakfast beers, in bottles, and coffee mugs clustered on the scarred table. Four of them were classic bikers: huge and inked, with long frizzy beards and hair to the shoulders or in ponytails. Their cloth of choice was denim. The remaining two—slimmer—had shaved heads. One wore a Pendleton flannel shirt, the other a T-shirt under a bomber jacket. Both were in Doc Martens boots. One had a skateboard at his feet. Shaw knew that in this gang culture, extreme sports like boarding and, his own, motocross, were popular.

The smallest of the bearded men—marginally the oldest, Shaw estimated—looked them over and said in a gravelly voice, "Well, you're here for some reason. They don't letcha wear face hair like that in the Bureau or SFPD so this's about something else. Maybe you're with an organization"—he rolled the word out, adding an extra syllable or two—"that might have a contrary interest to ours."

Shaw noticed the bartender, a stocky man, balding, drop his hands below the level of the bar. And one of the shaved-headed men casually put his hand on his thigh. "This's a private club. Why don't you get the fuck out?"

Russell unbuttoned his jacket.

Shaw said, "Who's got the MGX-21?"

It was a top-of-the-line Moto Guzzi, and a beautiful cycle. The body was black and the cylinder head and front brake pad bright red.

The leader of the gang cut a glance to the bartender, whose hands became visible once more.

"Mine," said the biggest of the bikers.

"Hundred horses?" Shaw asked.

"Close enough. You ride?"

"I do."

"Bike?"

Shaw said, "Yamaha."

"XV1900?"

This was the largest Yamaha in production.

"Smaller."

"Figured," the leader said, both grunting and snickering simultaneously.

The leader said, "Now that we're done comparing dicks, why don't you take my young associate's advice." He nodded to the door.

Russell said, "We're looking for somebody. If you can help us it'll be worth something for you."

"Explain yourself."

Russell said, "I'm reaching for my phone." He did this very slowly. He held out the picture of Blond.

The man wouldn't know he was looking at a dead man. Karin had yet another talent apparently: Photoshop. She'd removed the bullet hole and adjusted the eyes a bit. Apparently there was a filter called "Liquify," Russell had explained, which gave the deceased man a bit of a smile. The image was grotesque only if you knew the truth.

"He scammed our mother out of twenty K," Russell added.

The brothers had prepared what they thought was a credible story, Russell providing most of the material. After all, he was the one who had been the director of the "mugging" theater outside of the safe house yesterday morning.

The leader frowned. Whatever this gang did for a living, robbing mothers was apparently off the table.

Shaw said, "We know he's some connection with a crew here. You get us his real name and who he runs with, there's a thousand in it for you. So, he wear your colors?"

The six men looked at the picture again, then regarded one another.

The leader said, "Not one of us. Never seen him."

The others agreed. Shaw believed they were telling the truth. There had not been a single flash of recognition in any eye.

Russell put his phone away.

The Bayneck in the flannel shirt—a twitchy man—said, "I think our looking was worth something." It was he who'd placed his hand on his thigh earlier, and the fingers now moved closer to where his weapon would rest.

For a very long moment not a soul moved.

Then the biggest of the bikers said, "Naw, forget it. Too early for that kind of shit. And I ain't finished but one beer yet. So I'm not in any mood."

The leader said, "All I'll say is why weren't you looking after your mother? Two grown men like you. Sad. Now, get on out."

27

Now the SUV was cruising through a different part of the district.

They were on their way to the Hudson Kings' head-quarters.

They were near the waterfront and Shaw looked out on the dark water at the decommissioned Hunters Point Naval Shipyard, dominated by the massive gantry crane that bore a skeletal resemblance to the battleships whose turrets it lifted off so that the cannon could be replaced fast. A huge civilian and naval shipbuilding and repair facility for more than a hundred years, the yard was now closed and parcels were being sold off for condominiums and commercial buildings—that is, if and when the land was decontaminated. The place was a Superfund toxic waste site and much of it was still tainted, including by radioactive materials. It was from this shipyard that the USS *Indianapolis* sailed to the Mariana Islands, its cargo parts for Little Boy and Fat Man, the atomic bombs that were dropped on Hiroshima and Nagasaki in August of 1945.

Cleanup was a big business here. Many small craft operated by a company called BayPoint Enviro-Sure Solutions were collecting drums with hazard warnings stenciled on the sides. The workers were wearing so much protective gear, they looked like astronauts laboring on the moon.

Russell turned and steered away from the water. A moment later he pointed to a storefront. "That's it."

There was nowhere to park nearby so he drove a block and a half farther, and pulled to the curb. The brothers climbed out and started to walk toward the storefront.

A trio of rats slipped from an abandoned warehouse nearby and nonchalantly vanished into a drain.

"Yo, you buying, man?"

The voice belonged to a skinny young man sitting on an unsteady chair in front of a dubious shop selling prepaid phones and minutes cards, along with vaping paraphernalia. Two figures inside were speaking into flip cells.

The brothers moved on without responding.

Some kids, from teens to mid-twenties, were clustered together on the corner between the brothers and the social club. They were smoking joints, a few cigarettes. The clothing was hoodies and T-shirts and baggy slacks. Their running shoes were nice, and the hairstyles ranged from shaved to elaborate works of art. A few wore medallions, chains and other bling. They looked over the white men walking slowly past and grew energized, whispering and snickering. They were assessing the men as easy targets: beard on one, slim build on another.

Three of the crew broke from the clutch and strode up the side-walk, stepping in front of and stopping Shaw and his brother.

"You need directions? I give you directions. You know what I'm saying? C-note, and I give you directions."

"You lost? They lost."

"What you about, man?" A young man got right in Shaw's face.

The brothers had no time for a fight.

Never resort to violence unless you have no alternative.

Ashton might have added: especially with foolish teenagers.

Two others joined the trio. The newcomers postured, gesturing broadly with bony hands. The grins were cold.

Courage in numbers isn't courage.

"I'm talking to you an' you ignoring me. That rude."

"Is Kevin Miller around?" Russell asked.

They fell silent.

Shaw said, "It's all good. We've got money for him."

The skinniest of them—a boy of about fifteen or sixteen—said, "I'll take it to him. Save you the trouble, you know what I'm saying?"

It was then someone else joined the clutch. A tall, lanky man in his mid-thirties. His face was wrinkled and he bore tats in the shape of teardrops near his eyes. They could signify either a long prison term or that he'd committed murder.

The boys glanced at him with a measure of respect.

"Yo, Kevin!"

"What up, Kevin?"

Signs were flashed, fists bumped.

So this was Tom Pepper's O.G.—original gangster—one who had earned his colors years ago and managed to survive life on the street.

"My man."

"Dog."

Both Shaw and Russell looked at him, holding his gaze steadily. Neither of the brothers said anything. Eyes still on the interlopers, Kevin said to the crew, "Right. Everybody, move off."

"But . . ." one protested.

A brief glance was all it took. The kids cast murderous looks toward Shaw and Russell but headed down the sidewalk.

"You wanted me, you got me." Kevin swiveled back, smooth, looking them over. "You L.E.?"

"We're not law."

A squinting assessment. "No. You don't smell law. How'd you get my name?"

"Tom Pepper vouched."

Kevin nodded. The teardrop beneath his eye was inked well. A bit of skin showed through the black and gave the image three dimensions.

Russell displayed Blond's doctored picture. "We're trying to find this man. He's got a connection with a crew here, Hunters Point, Bayview."

"That hair, it ain't normal."

Blond's complexion had grown lighter in death but the hairdo remained as brightly jaundiced as ever.

"I've got a thousand, if you help us out."

"Why here? He's white."

Shaw asked, "Don't you do business with everybody—regardless of race, creed, et cetera."

Kevin chuckled. "Talk to the rednecks."

"We did. They don't know him."

"Lemme see that picture again."

Russell displayed it.

The O.G. nodded with a thoughtful frown. "Sorry, brother. No idea. And I'm as connected as they come."

"Any other crews here?" Russell asked.

"Nothing righteous. Some franchises from Salinas keep flirting with the shorefront, north. They show up, we discourage them. They go away. They come back. You know what it is. All right. I got business." He looked at Shaw. "Tom Pepper. He was okay. Fair man. Good thing he still with us."

Kevin returned to the social club, and the men to the SUV. "We could canvass here a week and that's the only answer we're ever going to get. There's got to be a better way," Shaw said.

"Yeah. Find the courier bag. Use it as leverage to stop Black-Bridge." Russell started the big engine.

Shaw looked out the passenger window. He saw one of the young men who'd confronted them on the street—one of the skinnier, with a shaved head. The kid stood on a pile of rubble about thirty feet away. He reached up under his burgundy hoodie as he stared toward the vehicle with a demeaning smile.

Shaw tensed and his hand went toward his hip.

Russell glanced his brother's way.

Suddenly, the kid's hand zipped from under the sweatshirt and, with his fingers formed like a pistol, pointed at Shaw and mimicked firing, the hand jerking back in recoil. The smile vanished. His hand tightened into a fist and the next gesture involved a single finger. He clambered down the rubble heap and vanished.

Shaw said, "Let's pick up on Ashton's leads. Burlingame first."

"Put it in GPS."

Shaw pulled out his phone, then paused as he looked over the screen. "Not yet. Braxton and Droon are on the move."

28

The GPS tracker hidden in the spine of Henry David Thoreau's meditation on self-sufficiency had led them back to the Tenderloin.

They were not far from where Shaw's unexpected reward job— to locate Tessy Vasquez—had begun.

Russell parked the SUV in a spot in front of a dilapidated retail storefront, closed now. The window bills pleaded for lessees. A homeless man, wrapped in a gray blanket, slept in the doorway. A few dollar bills peeked from under the corner of his covering. Russell knelt and pushed them out of sight. Shaw had been about to do the same.

Orienting himself, glancing around the neighborhood, then at the GPS app, Shaw pointed to an alley.

The brothers declined an offer from a pale young woman in her early twenties and they stepped over another man, about the same age, unconscious and lying in the mouth of the alley. He too was presumably homeless, though his clothes were more or less clean and he didn't have any of the accoutrements that most street people possess: bags, shopping cart, blankets, extra clothing. Was he dead?

Russell apparently caught his brother's thought. He nudged the man's arm with his shoe and got a reaction. Three doors away was a storefront of a community outreach service. Shaw walked to it and stepped inside. A thin man of about fifty in a clerical collar looked up and offered a pleasant smile. "Help you?"

"There're two men, up the street, passed out. Maybe you've got somebody who could help. One's drunk, I think, but the other one might've OD'd. Out the door to the right."

He rose and called into the back room, "Rosie, come on and bring your bag." He said to Shaw, "Terrible. Overdoses're up fifty percent in the past couple months, and we've got a gang injunction here. I don't know what's going on."

The Urban Improvement Plan is what's going on.

Shaw returned to his brother and they proceeded down the alley, with Russell behind, checking for threats from that direction, just as Shaw did in the front. This was instinctive.

Never believe your enemies aren't pursuing you.

At the far end of the moist, soiled passage, they found themselves on the edge of a large area—taking up several blocks—that was in the process of being cleared. Bulldozers and backhoes, their yellow and black paint jobs spattered with mud, sat unoccupied, parked in the north section of the space. The site was a mix of partially demolished buildings and vacant ground. Pits of oily standing water shimmered and modest mountains of scrap materials from the destroyed buildings dotted the landscape. The terrain was light in color, almost beige. The soil would be clay.

In the center of the flattened area sat a black SUV, a Cadillac Escalade. The GPS indicated that it was the source of the pings. Braxton probably had with her a briefcase or backpack containing the material she'd stolen from Shaw's camper the other day, including the bugged book.

The Escalade's doors opened and Droon, who was the driver, and Braxton climbed out. They looked around—Russell and Shaw crouched behind a pile of scrap wood and plasterboard. When they rose and looked again, the pair from BlackBridge was in a heads-down conversation. Droon was nodding.

Another car pulled in and the two BlackBridge employees looked up. It was a Rolls-Royce, dark red. The sleek vehicle eased slowly over the uneven ground and parked, side by side with the Caddie.

No doors opened.

Braxton took a phone call.

Droon stretched and lit a cigarette.

Russell took out his phone, snapped some pictures, then put it back. "Look at the tags."

On the Rolls there was a sheet of white cardboard or plastic over the license plate. The illegal obfuscation would be only temporary; as soon as they hit the street, the driver would pause and pull off the rectangle.

Who was the visitor?

Braxton disconnected and the driver of the Rolls, a huge Asian man in a black suit, got out. He looked around, necessitating another dodge by the brothers. Then he opened the back passenger side door. The man who climbed out was of fair complexion, short, balding and round. He wore a pinstripe suit, navy blue, a pink shirt and a wide burgundy tie. A white handkerchief exploded from the breast pocket. His white-rimmed glasses were oversize and the lenses square—maybe stylish, maybe necessary for a serious vision malady. His expression suggested irritation or impatience.

Russell's phone appeared again and he took pictures of the newcomer.

Braxton and Droon joined him, rather than he them, which meant he was a BlackBridge client and, given the wheels, a valued one.

Shaw recalled what the woman had told her lieutenant earlier, in the Stanford library.

We have that meeting tomorrow. I want to tell him something. Something concrete . . .

That something would have been what they'd tortured out of Colter Shaw—the location of Gahl's evidence. Shaw guessed that where they now were was an example of the UIP. He thought of the unfortunate addicts on the street they'd just walked around, and all the clearing going on before them. The man in the Rolls was prob-ably a developer who'd bought the land for a song.

Braxton and Droon would now have to share that Shaw had not, in fact, led them to the evidence, which would implicate Mr. Rolls too.

How chilly would the meeting be?

The body language suggested that the BlackBridge duo felt something other than respect for a wealthy client. Shaw was looking at two very intimidated people, and to see Irena Braxton this way—an ice queen, if ever there was one—was oddly unsettling. As the chubby man spoke with them, unsmiling and gesticulating with his stubby hands often and broadly, she nodded and gave a polite, at-tentive frown, like a schoolgirl who'd flubbed a homework assign-ment. This attitude was, Shaw had no doubt, wholly alien to the woman.

But after what seemed to be her breathless reassurance, the client calmed. He gave them a smile of the sort you might affect when you hand a dollar to a homeless man, and his hands began to fidget less.

They were moving on to other business. Droon unfolded a map and held it up against the side of their SUV. Why not the hood? Shaw wondered. Oh, because the client was too short to see the map there. Everyone consulted the fluttering sheet.

"Who uses a paper map instead of a computer or tablet?" Rus-sell asked.

Shaw nodded at the rhetorical question. Someone who doesn't want electronic evidence, that's who. You can set fire to paper and it's gone forever, unlike digital data, which will last as long as bones from the Jurassic era. Russell produced a range-finder telescope. He looked, then handed it to Shaw.

After five minutes of discussion, the fat man pointed to several locations on the map and Droon marked them with a Sharpie. Then heads nodded and hands were shaken. Braxton and Droon remained where they were while the client stepped to the door of his Rolls. The driver swung the back passenger door open once more. Shaw got a look at two tanned legs, protruding from a short red skirt. Also: impressively high heels, which he thought odd for a woman to wear in the company of a short man like this, who, given the vehicle and his clothing had a surplus of ego. But, of course, there was no accounting for taste . . . or desire.

Before he got into the Rolls he turned and, no longer smiling, fired off more words, accentuated by the curious, jittery hand gestures. Braxton and Droon responded with scolded-dog nods. The man climbed into his sumptuous vehicle. The driver too, and the car sagged under his weight. The car rocked away over the packed construction site dirt.

29

Standing beside their SUV, Irena Braxton lifted a phone from her purse and made another call.

The vibrant handbag was similar to one of Margot's, Shaw recalled from their time together. Hers had been made by indigenous people in South America. It wasn't inexpensive but much of the purchase price went to a nonprofit organization that opposed the burning of the Amazon rain forest. Had Braxton, a known killer, bought hers from the same seller and for the same purpose? In his rewards business, Shaw had learned that the values and priorities people embraced were infinitely contradictory and enigmatic.

She replaced the phone and she and Droon fell silent. Less than a minute later a white van, with no markings on the side, pulled up. Out climbed two men, both white, both in good shape. Their outfits were similar: dark gray slacks and jackets, zippered up. One was tall and bareheaded, with a crew cut, the other short and crowned with a black baseball cap. They were unsmiling and cautious, but didn't scan the surroundings, perhaps assuming if Braxton and Droon were here, the place was safe. Their right hands, though, stayed gyroscopically close to their right hips, where their guns would reside.

They joined Braxton and Droon, who opened the map he'd had moments before and spread it out on the hood of the Escalade. The discussion among them was brief and ended with a nod from the two newcomers, one of whom kept the map. Then Braxton and Droon climbed back into the SUV. The vehicle left.

The brothers, however, remained. The BlackBridge ops were waiting for something and Shaw and Russell wanted to see what it might be.

The answer arrived about five minutes later: two slim men, in shorts and T-shirts, one of them loud red, the other white. The shirts were untucked—a likely indication of concealed weapons. They had light blue vinyl shoulder bags slung over their shoulders. Their heads were shaved and their complexions dark. The TL was the home to several pan-Asian gangs, most notably the notorious Filipino Bahala Na Gang, more ruthless than the Mafia or the Mexican cartels, Shaw had heard. The BNG's heyday was the end of the last century but many of the murderous crew still were active up and down the West Coast. San Francisco was their primary turf.

"Cutouts," Russell said. "The white-van men. They're insulating the man in the Rolls and Braxton and Droon. The actors never know who they're ultimately acting for. This is pro."

Among the men on the ground a discussion ensued. One of the van men pulled open the side door and took out two clear plastic bags, appearing to weigh two pounds each—maybe a kilo. Russell looked through the telescope again. He then gave it to Shaw, who scanned the clearing. He could see that the bags contained small packets of pills. These they handed over to the gangsters. The van man who'd kept the map now unfurled it.

"UIP," Shaw said. "Ashton's letter I showed you?"

His brother nodded, understanding blossoming in his face. He'd be recalling the Urban Improvement Plan, the cruelly ironic name for the BlackBridge operation that dumped hundreds of pounds of drugs on the streets of neighborhoods to destroy them.

Shaw said, "Monkey wrench." He dialed 911.

The woman's calm voice: "What's the nature of your emergency?"

"There's a drug deal in the construction site behind Turk at Simpson. I think they might have guns . . . wait, yes, they do!" He put some urgent dismay into his voice, a rattled citizen. He described the men and then disconnected without giving the requested identifying information about himself. Dispatchers were often skeptical about anonymous calls, but with a big drug deal, they'd definitely send a patrol cruiser.

And indeed they did. Almost immediately Shaw heard a vehicle approaching over the gravel. It was an SFPD car with two officers inside.

"That was fast," Russell said, frowning.

The squad car drove right up to the van and the cops climbed out. The driver was a Latino patrol uniform. The other, a tall Anglo, was a detective, wearing a light gray suit, a badge on his belt. They looked over the van men and the two Filipinos. Shaw found himself tensing in anticipation of a firefight. He and Russell would not want to get involved, but he dropped his hand near his gun, in case any of the crew charged their way to escape up the alley, with their own weapons drawn.

The foursome turned toward the cops. One of the men from the van nodded a greeting. The detective smiled back.

"Hell." A whisper from Shaw.

The gold shield had a discussion with the van men. Then all six in the construction zone turned and gazed around them, as Shaw and his brother ducked once more.

"Why they were here so fast," Russell said. "The cops were up the street standing guard."

"They going to come looking?"

But no. The men in the center of the cleared land stopped scanning; they'd apparently decided that whoever had dimed them out via the 911 call had, like most concerned citizens, hightailed it away. The two officers gave some words of farewell, maybe including the advice: pick a less visible place to meet next time. The taller of the van men gestured to one of the BNGs who fished some packets of Oxy or fent out of his bag and handed them to the officers, who nodded thanks then drove away.

The bangers and the BlackBridge duo pored over the map once more, so the distributors knew what neighborhood they were to poison today.

"How much?" Shaw asked.

"Value? At the group we don't get into that much. Guess a hundred K."

Scattering it on the street for free or at a bargain price. But, of course, Mr. Rolls would be making a thousand times that in the real estate deal.

The business was concluded—thick envelopes were handed out to the BNG men, who placed them, along with the drugs, into the shoulder bags. The van men returned to their vehicle, which was soon speeding away, leaving a trail of dust.

It was only then that Shaw realized it was a workday, and construction equipment and supplies were present, yet the site was completely devoid of workers. The owner—presumably Mr. Rolls—would have ordered the place closed down for the meeting.

And who are you? Shaw wondered of the man in the Rolls. Did you ever hear the name Ashton Shaw? Did your hands twitch and your mouth smile as Irena Braxton told you that one of her men was on the way to the Shaw Compound to have a "conversation" about what he'd discovered?

They didn't have license tags for an ID, but maybe Karin could get a facial recognition hit.

The BNGs donned flashy wraparound sunglasses—the lenses orange—and started out of the site.

The brothers rose.

As Shaw started after the gangbangers Russell turned the other way—back to the alley where they'd parked their SUV.

Both men realized they were on opposite courses and looked back to regard the other.

Shaw whispered, "We've got to stop them. This way." Nodding toward the BNGs.

Russell said, "No."

Shaw flashed back immediately to the avalanche field of their youth so many years ago, when he had sped out to save the life of the woman photographer on the steep and dangerous slope—and Russell had held back.

It's not our job . . .

He was about to lay out the urgent case for stopping the BNGs when his brother said tersely, "You thought I was leaving?"

Shaw didn't reply.

"Hawker's Pass," his brother muttered, seemingly irritated, and continued on his way.

Shaw said, "Oh."

30

In the shadows, close to the brick walls in the alley, Shaw followed the slim men who stalked up the cobblestones out of the demolition zone. He stepped over several dead rats and two more men, sprawled on their sides. They were breathing.

Where were the two Filipinos going to scatter their goods like farmers sowing corn seeds in the spring? What property did Mr. Rolls have his eye on?

He picked up his pace; the men ahead of him were walking quickly.

When they were nearly to the end of the alley, one glanced down and touched his partner on the arm. They stopped, removed the gaudy sunglasses and glanced at the wallet, lying on the cobblestones. They looked up and down the alley and spotted Shaw. He was strolling along in the same direction as they, paying the two no mind, pretending to talk on his cell phone as if in the middle of a pleasant conversation, perhaps a romantic one. Their looks revealed they didn't consider him a threat.

Red Shirt took a packet of drugs from his bag. While they were being paid to scatter the product on sidewalks and in alleys, what harm could there be in selling a bit? A little double-dipping never hurt anyone. As White Shirt bent and lifted the wallet and started to go through it, Red Shirt offered the packet toward Shaw.

He said, "I'll call you back." And slipped the phone away.

Shaw gave an intrigued smile as he stared at the drugs. He approached to within six feet and stopped. BNG crew were often skilled at the devastating forms of martial arts known as Suntukan and Sikaran, punching and kicking. The Philippines were also home to several grappling styles of combat.

The banger could be thinking to lure Shaw close and mug him. After all, why sell your product when you can make off with both the cash and the drugs?

"What is it?" Shaw asked.

"Oxy."

"How much?" He squinted at the bag.

"Twenty."

"How many pills? I can't see."

The BNG held the packet higher.

Which is when Russell stepped into the mouth of the alley and came up behind White Shirt and Tased him in the kidney. He groaned, shivered and dropped.

Red Shirt spun and reached for his weapon, which Shaw, lunging forward, snagged with his left hand, while seating the muzzle of his Glock against the man's ear.

"*Mapanganib ito* . . . Dangerous what you do!"

Shaw pulled Red Shirt's silver revolver from his hand. His confrere had a Glock and a switchblade knife, both of which Russell pocketed. They took the men's phones too.

Rising unsteadily and wincing against the pain in his back, White Shirt said in a thick accent, "You fucker, you die. You aren't know."

Russell picked up his wallet—emptied of ID and containing only cash—and slipped it back into his hip pocket. While Shaw covered both men, his brother plucked the barbs from White Shirt's skin. Then he collected the man's shoulder bag. Shaw gripped the strap of Red Shirt's tote but the man held on to it hard and turned, looking up at Shaw with furious eyes. "You stupid. This danger shit. It get you cut."

Russell had reloaded the Taser and was aiming. The man slumped and Shaw pulled the bag away.

"Run," Shaw whispered.

The man glared once more and, after White Shirt picked up his sunglasses—as enraged at the scratches on the lenses as at the theft of the drugs and money—they strode off, looking back. For the second time that day the brothers received a single-finger salute.

"They'll be stealing burners in five minutes and calling it in. We've got to go." Russell nodded up the alley. They walked to the SUV and climbed in. Russell pulled into traffic and the heavy vehicle sped out of the TL.

Hawker's Pass . . .

A battle between a settlement and a group of claim jumpers in Northern California during the Silver Rush days. The settlers planted a half-buried strongbox on the back road into the camp, and when the outlaws found it and started to dig it up, one group of settlers came in from the north side of the road, the other from the south and easily took the distracted jumpers. Shaw remembered sitting beside his father and brother and watching Ashton draw a map of the battle, as he lectured the boys about tactics.

Never attack an enemy directly when you can distract and flank . . .

So, no, Russell had not intended to leave. He had made stopping the BNGs his fight, as well as Shaw's, and had come up with a good strategy to do it with no bloodshed.

They left the TL and Russell drove back to the waterfront at Hunters Point, where they pitched the drugs and the BNGs' guns and phones and the knife into the Bay.

They returned to the safe house on Alvarez. Russell ran the plate of the van—it was not obscured, like the Caddy's and the Rolls's—and the information came back that it was registered to a corporation that was undoubtedly owned by an offshore entity. Russell sent the picture he'd taken of Mr. Rolls to someone—presumably Karin. Soon he received a text in return.

"Too far away for facial recognition."

"Burlingame now. Nadler's house." The town was south of San Francisco, a working-class and commuter community, the home of San Francisco airport. Shaw had seen a picture of the house, which Mack had sent. It was a tidy one-story dwelling, painted yellow and set amid a small but well-tended garden.

Shaw was calling up the address when his phone dinged with an incoming email.

It was from Mack McKenzie. He read the message.

He said, "We have to make a stop on the way."

31

Ghirardelli Square—part of the tourist magnet Fisherman's Wharf—wasn't busy on this cloudy day. Rain threatened.

Shaw and Russell were in the SUV, parked near the corner on which a man strummed a guitar. His case was open and people would occasionally toss coins or bills in. He was tall and lean and long blond hair flowed from beneath a cowboy hat with a tightly curled brim.

You could smell chocolate, exuding by chance or design from the Ghirardelli building. He explained to Russell how he'd come to take on the reward job to find Tessy Vasquez.

He then told him that his private investigator had, among her contractors, an audio analyst, to whom she'd sent Tessy's message. The expert had filtered out the young woman's voice and analyzed every sound on it.

The email Shaw had just received in the Tenderloin contained the results of that analysis. He called it up and the men read.

Music: Ambient music from outdoor café, recorded.

Music: Performers, including live guitar, drums, rap music and applause, possibly accompanying hip-hop dancers. Occasional breaks in vocal performances to say "Thanks" or "Thank you," presumably in response to tips. Hence, street performers.

Sounds of children laughing and occasionally breathless: Playground.

Foghorns, decibel level suggesting distance of three to four miles. Echoing off tall structure nearby. Possibly Avnet Tower on California Street.

Ship horn 1: This matches the tone of the *Marin Express*, ferry with service from Pier 41 in the Embarcadero to Sausalito, approximately one mile away.

Ship horn 2: This matches the *Alcatraz Cruiser*, a ship operated by Bay Cruise Tours, approximately one mile away.

Ship horn 3. This matches the tone of the *Sea Maid III*, operated by Cruise Tours Unlimited, docked at Eureka Promenade, approximately 300+ feet away.

Cable car bells, from opposite directions, probably the north terminus of the Powell/Mason line to the east, and Powell/Hyde line to the west. Powell/Mason is closer.

Correlating these data, I think the location is the southwest Fisherman's Wharf area, likely Ghirardelli Square.

"Whoever did it is good," Russell said.

Shaw was looking around. "I'll be back in a minute." He climbed out of the vehicle and approached the guitarist. He pulled a twenty from his pocket and dropped it into the guitar case.

"Hey, man, thanks." His eyes were wide.

"Got a question."

"Sure." Maybe hoping: Was he free to sign a multimillion-dollar recording contract?

"Do you know this girl? She's gone missing. I'm helping her mother try to find her."

"Oh, yeah. Tessy. Jesus. Missing?"

"When did you see her last?"

"I just got back from Portland. Before that. A week maybe."

"You know her well?"

"No. Talked about music some. Mostly just to divide up the corners, you know. So we didn't sing over each other. This sucks. I hope she's okay."

"You ever know if she had trouble with anyone?"

"Never saw it. Guys'd flirt. You know. She could handle it."

"Was she ever with a man named Roman?" Shaw described him.

"Doesn't sound familiar."

Shaw thanked him. He studied the block, turning in a slow circle. His eyes came to rest on a gift shop, specializing in saltwater taffy and objets d'art based on cable cars, the Golden Gate Bridge and Alcatraz.

He caught his brother's eye and nodded at the store. Russell joined him.

"Video?" his brother asked.

"It's right in the line of sight. Hope so."

The two men greeted the manager of the store, dressed for some reason like a clerk in an Old West general store. Straw hat, candy-striped shirt, suspenders and a sleeve garter. When they explained why they were here, he said, "Oh, no. Terrible." He added that he knew Tessy. She occasionally would come into the store and exchange the tip coins she'd received from performing for bills.

He handed over the counter to another worker, and the men followed him into the back room.

He logged on to a cloud server and typed in the date and time from the call Tessy had made to her mother. Scrubbing back and forth . . . Finally, in fast motion, Tessy walked into view, removed her guitar from the case, which she opened for the tips, and then slung the instrument over her neck. She was in a red blouse and a black gypsy skirt. Her dark hair was loose.

She began to sing, smiling to passersby. The chord changes seemed efficient. No fancy jazz riffs. He'd heard that a guitar had never been intended as a lead instrument, but a rhythm one. That came from his distant past, from Margot, who'd been a source of much of his popular cultural knowledge. The woman had then added, "But tell that to Jimi Hendrix."

Shaw's own personal favorite guitarist was the Australian Tommy Emmanuel, who seemed to pry an entire orchestra from his git-fiddle.

Shaw was amused that her guitar was a Yamaha, the same brand as his motorbike. He supposed they were the same company—though that was about as diversified a manufacturing operation as you would find.

"Can you scrub to where she leaves?"

The man did. They saw her put her guitar away and pull a phone from her pocket. She made a brief call—probably the one to her mother. She then picked up the guitar case, slung a purse over her shoulder and started up the street away from the store. She walked to the corner and turned right.

"You catch that?" Shaw asked.

"The van," Russell said.

A gray minivan, which had been parked on the same side of the street as Tessy was on, pulled into traffic as she walked by and proceeded slowly, as if following her. It made the same turn she did.

"Christ, you think they did . . . I mean, did something to her?" The manager's face radiated concern.

"Scrub back to where it arrives."

That was about twenty minutes before she left.

"Let it play in normal time."

Yes, it was suspicious. After the van parked, no one got out. And no one got in; it wasn't there to pick someone up. Then the passenger side doors opened and two men got out. They were Anglo, pale with thick black hair—one's was slicked back, the other's was a disorderly mop. They were in dress shirts and slacks. The one from the front seat removed a phone from his pocket and took a picture of the square, then fiddled with the screen.

"He's sending the picture."

A moment later, after what seemed to be a text exchange, Slick put the phone away. He lit a cigarette and the two climbed back into the van.

"We should call the police."

Russell said, "We will. Any way we can get a copy of that vid?"

"Sure." He rummaged in the desk and found an SD card. "From the time she arrived?"

"If you would, yes."

He typed some commands and within a minute the video, in the form of an MP4 file, was on the card.

Shaw said, "We'll pay you for it."

"No, no. Just get it to the police right away. God, I hope she's okay."

Shaw described Tessy's ex, Roman. "Was she ever in here with somebody who looked like him?"

"Not that I remember."

They thanked him. He handed them a business card. "Please let me know what happens."

Russell said they would and the men returned to the SUV.

As his brother fired up the big vehicle, Shaw sent a text to Mack, with the priority code, requesting information on a vehicle. He'd memorized the van's California license tag.

"Let's look at the cross street." Russell pulled into traffic and, following the same route as the gray van, turned the corner. The street was not much more than an alley—it was lined by the backs of buildings and loading docks, no storefronts or residences.

"Couldn't've picked a better place for a snatch," Russell said, "if we'd planned it out ahead of time."

32

S haw's phone hummed with a text.

Gray van is registered to a California corporation, Specialty
Services, LLC. No physical address. P.O. box. Specialty
Services is owned by an offshore. Have lawyers in St. Kitts
and Sacramento looking into ultimate ownership.

Shaw read this to his brother, as he piloted the SUV to
Burlingame.

"Doesn't look good. Police? This isn't a BlackBridge thing."

"They're undocumented. Tessy and her mother. They'll be de-
ported. Or Maria will be, by herself, if I can't find Tessy. Anyway,
the police won't get on board with what we have."

He couldn't tell his brother's reaction.

After fifteen minutes of silence, Russell asked, "It's like PI work
then?"

"The rewards? Pretty much. Looking for escapees, suspects.
Some private. Like Tessy."

"You do BEA?"

"No." Bond enforcement agents pursued bail skippers and FTAs—"failures to appear" at hearings or trials. The criminals whom bond agents pursued were invariably punks and drunks and could usually be located with minimal mental effort—in places like their girlfriends' or parents' basements or in the same bar where they got wasted the night they committed the crime they'd been hauled to jail for in the first place. He explained this.

"You want a better quality perp."

"A more *challenging* perp."

More silence.

"What're the rewards like?"

"You mean, amounts?"

Russell nodded.

"From a couple of thousand. To twenty million or so."

"Million?"

"Not my kind of work, generally. It's a State Department reward. The way those work is somebody in the bad guy's organization gets location information to the CIA. Then it's time for SEAL Team Six."

"Who's the twenty million?"

"Guy named Idrees Ayubi . . . He's a . . ." Shaw's voice faded as he saw his brother nodding knowingly. Given his profession, it wasn't surprising that he'd know the name of the terrorist with the highest bounty offered by the U.S. government.

After some silence Shaw said, "But it's not about the money. What I like about a reward is it's a flag. It means there's a problem that nobody's been able to solve. Never be bored."

"Was that one of Ash's? I don't remember it."

"No."

The boys had once asked their father—whom Russell dubbed the King of Never—why he phrased his rules beginning with the negative. The man's answer: "Gets your attention better."

Russell fell silent once again. Shaw wondered if he was still angry at the suggestion that he was running away from confronting the BNGs.

"A cult? Tom Pepper was saying?"

"Last week. Washington State."

"Somebody posted a reward to get a follower out of the place?"

Shaw explained that, no, he had learned about the cult on a reward job and he'd been troubled by the cult leaders' sadistic and predatory behavior. "I went in undercover, found a lot of vulnerable people—there were a hundred members altogether. I did what I could to save some of them. Made some enemies."

Shaw now realized two things: One, he was rambling, and he was doing it for the purpose of encouraging his brother to engage, to dive beneath the surface of their cocktail-party small talk.

And, two, Russell was simply filling the thorny pits of silence; he evidently had little interest in Shaw's narrative.

Finally Shaw said, "Something on your mind?" He didn't think he'd ever asked his brother this question.

Russell hesitated then said, "An assignment I have to get to."

"Here?"

"No. Can't say where."

"You don't want to be doing this, do you?" Shaw asked. He gestured toward the pleasant street they were coursing along in Burlingame but meant the pursuit of BlackBridge.

"Just, we should get it done."

Another voice ended the conversation: the woman within the GPS announced that their destination was on the left.

M a'am, I wonder if you'd be willing to help us out," Shaw said.

The woman in the doorway was early seventies, he estimated. She looked at them with a smile but with still eyes, as one will do with doorbell ringers who seem polite but are wholly unexpected. She'd be wondering about this pair in particular, who bore a very slight resemblance to each other. She wore an apron, not the sort serious chefs donned like body armor, but light blue, with frills and lace, insubstantial. A garment from a bygone era.

"My husband will be back soon."

Offered as a reason that she might be less helpful to them now, being only half the complement. And spoken too as a shield. Reinforcements would arrive momentarily.

Her name, they'd learned thanks to Mack's research, was Eleanor.

Shaw introduced himself and Russell and then said, "My brother and I are looking into some family history."

This was indisputable. Not the whole truth, but how often is *that* really necessary?

"We were going through some old family papers and found out our father had some interest in this house or whoever lived here."

Russell qualified, "A long time ago."

"Well, this's my husband's family's house. He's lived here thirty years. Who's your father? Oh, you said 'had.' Does that mean he's not with us any longer?"

"No, he's not," Shaw told her.

"I'm sorry." Her face exuded genuine sorrow. This was a woman who had experienced loss herself.

"What was your father's name?"

"Ashton Shaw."

A squint, and faint lines appeared in the powdery face. "I don't think I know the name. Maybe Mort does. You have a picture? Maybe it'll jog my memory?" She was more comfortable now, since the men weren't trying to talk their way inside and sell her insurance or aluminum siding.

Shaw was irritated with himself for not thinking to bring a picture of their father. He was surprised when Russell produced a small photo—and not on his camera but from the location where family pictures used to be kept: his wallet. Shaw was stung even deeper at

the thought that he had accused his older brother—even if silently—
of killing a man whose picture he carried around with him after all
these years.

Glancing down at the faded rectangle, he was more surprised yet
to find that the shot was not of Ashton alone, but of the three Shaw
men: father and sons. Ashton was behind, the boys in front. Shaw
was about twelve. They were rigged for rappelling in the high
country.

He turned back to Eleanor, expecting her to say, *My, I can see
the resemblance*, or something similar.

Instead she was frozen, gaping at the picture.

"Ma'am?" Russell asked.

"I *do* know him."

Shaw's pulse picked up. "How?"

"Years ago, ages. He was older than in your picture and his hair
was wilder. And whiter. But I remember him clearly. It was at the
funeral. He was looking very distraught. Well, we all were, of course.
But he seemed especially troubled. We thought that was odd since
no one in the family had a clue who he was."

Shaw: "Whose funeral was it?"

"My son. Amos."

"Amos Gahl?"

"That's right. I'm Eleanor Nadler now. I remarried after my first
husband passed."

She tilted her head and looked each of them over, and it was a
coy, conspiratorial gaze. "Why don't you come in? I'll make some
coffee. And you boys can tell me why you're really here."

33

The house smelled of mothballs, which, Shaw supposed, most people associate with grandparents' homes and old clothing in odd cuts and colors stored away forever.

Shaw's thought, though, was of snakes: during one particularly dry, infestive year, Ashton and the children had ringed the cabin and gardens with pungent spheres of naphthalene to ward off persistent rattlers searching for water and mice.

Eleanor nodded to a floral couch, and the Shaw brothers sat. She disappeared into the kitchen. Given his childhood, Shaw had no reference point for television sitcoms but he and Margot had occasionally lain on inflatable mattresses during one of her archeological digs and, on a tablet or computer, watched the shows her parents and grandparents had loved. Surreal to have just made love to a sultry woman, in the wilderness of Arizona, your pistol handy in case of coyotes, and be watching *The Andy Griffith Show* (funny) or *Bewitched* (not his style).

This home was immaculate, well dusted, pastel. There were

many objects sitting on many surfaces. China figurines were out-numbered only by family photographs.

Five minutes later the woman returned with a silver tray on which sat three delicate porcelain cups, filled with black coffee, on saucers. A sugar bowl and pitcher filled with viscous cream, not milk, sat beside them. Also, three spoons and three napkins folded into triangles. She passed out one cup each to Shaw and Russell and took one for herself. The brothers doctored with cream. The coffee was rich. African. Kenyan, Shaw was pretty sure.

In her soft voice she said, "I have a feeling that this isn't about 23andMe genealogy, is it?"

"No, Ms. Nadler—?" Russell began.

"Eleanor," she corrected. "I have a feeling we have something important in common. First names seem appropriate."

"Eleanor," Shaw said, sipping again and putting the cup down. The clink seemed loud. "We're here looking into how our father died." He had to say the next part. "We think he was killed under circumstances similar to your son's death."

"It was no accident," she muttered. "I know that."

Russell said, "Not long before he died, our father was in touch with some coworkers who knew Amos."

"At BlackBridge." Her lips tightened.

A nod. "They think Amos smuggled some evidence out of the company. Evidence of crimes they'd committed."

Shaw went on to explain about the Urban Improvement Plan and other illegal activities that the company was involved in: the stock manipulation, the kickbacks, the phony earthquake inspections.

She didn't know UIP or other specifics—Shaw supposed her son intentionally didn't tell her too much, to protect her—but she said, "There was always something wrong about that place. He was never comfortable there." Her eyes strayed to a picture on the wall. It depicted Gahl in his early twenties. He was in a soccer kit. Curly dark hair, a lean face. "He was such a good boy. Smart. Good-looking . . . Oh, he was a catch. I'd thought he'd bring home the most beautiful girl in college." A laugh. "He brought home some beautiful *boys* . . . That was the way he went. Fine with me." A sigh. "My son was happy. He loved academia."

"Where did he teach?" Russell asked.

"San Francisco State. He was happy there." Her face tightened. "Then he joined that company. It wasn't a good place. It was dark. But he got tempted. Where else could somebody with a history degree make the kind of money they paid him?"

Shaw: "Are you comfortable telling us more about his death?"

She was silent for a long moment, her eyes fixed on a ceramic statue of a bird, a mourning dove on the coffee table.

"Officially it was a car crash. He went off Highway One. You know how bad that can be south of the city?"

Both men nodded, and Shaw thought of the article in Ashton's secret room about the state assemblyman's crash and the ensuing fire that destroyed some records he had with him.

"It was near Maverick. The beach." The extreme surfing capital of the state.

"Only he had no reason to be driving that way. He'd left Black-Bridge and was spending all his time in the city on some project of his. That was odd—why he was fifty miles south of the city. And then . . ." She took a moment to compose herself. "And then there was the mortician."

Shaw encouraged her with a nod.

"He asked me if the police found who attacked him. I was dumbfounded. Attacked him? What did he mean? Oh, the poor man was beside himself. He thought I knew. You see, the body was badly burned but in getting it ready for the crematorium, he noticed stab wounds, deep ones. Someone had . . ." She steadied herself. A few breaths. "Someone had stabbed him and then twisted the knife. To cause more pain."

Shaw pictured the SOG knife, recalled Droon's gesturing with the blade yesterday morning.

Insert, twist . . .

His torture method of choice.

With her jaw tightly set, she whispered, "He said it looked like he was stabbed in the leg and the blade hit the femoral artery. *That* would be an accident. They wanted to keep him alive—I guess to find out where the evidence you mentioned was."

Had they caught him at the library yesterday Shaw too would have been strapped down and the SOG knife plunged into his arm or leg.

And with each question would have come another twist of the blade.

"Did Amos leave anything here? Records, files, computers, hard drives? Maybe a briefcase? He called it a courier bag."

She sipped from the cup and thought for a moment. "No. And near the end he didn't come by very often. He seemed paranoid. He believed he was being watched. But he would meet a friend here. At first, I thought it was sweet. Bringing a boyfriend home to meet Mom and Stepdad. They were . . . well, it was easy to see they were close. He was a coworker at BlackBridge, though I think he'd quit by the time he came here. But they weren't completely social get-togethers. We'd have a meal and then they'd go down to the cellar to talk. I think they wanted a place that was completely private and secure." Her eyes darkened. "Maybe Amos and his friend thought their own houses were bugged."

"Do you remember his friend's name?"

"I do. Because it was one you don't hear very much. A pretty name. La Fleur. Last name. It means 'flower' in French. I don't re-member his first."

"Do you know where he lives?"

"Marin, I think he said at dinner. Nothing more than the county. Maybe he was paranoid too. Even here."

"And you think La Fleur had quit BlackBridge?"

"I'm pretty sure so." A scornful laugh. "He probably had a conscience."

"Anyone else Amos met with from the company?"

"La Fleur's the only one I remember." She chuckled. "If I thought Amos was paranoid, you should have seen the friend. During dinner, he asked what kind of encryption our phones used. Mort and I laughed. Heavens! We thought it was a joke. But he was serious. When we said we didn't have an idea Amos made us shut our phones off. We thought he was humoring his friend. I suppose not. Sometimes it's not really paranoia at all, is it?"

Again, the brothers shared a glance.

They rose and thanked her for her time. Shaw said he'd be in touch if they learned anything else.

She walked them to the door. She looked out into the front yard, a pleasant setting. A Japanese maple dominated. Some bright flowers, purple and blue, lorded over recently mulched beds. Shaw, like all survivalists, knew some plants well—those that are edible, that are toxic, that can be used as medicines and antiseptics. Of flowers that were merely decorative he was largely ignorant.

Eleanor said, "Amos wasn't a fool. He'd know there was a chance that he'd get found out. And that means he wouldn't hide the evidence, this bag, so far out of sight that it couldn't be found by somebody else after he was gone."

Which echoed Shaw's very thought when he was searching for the bag in the Stanford library yesterday morning.

The woman continued, "You two are that somebody else."

She looked from one brother to the other, then tugged tight the drawstring of her frilly apron, not a stain upon it. Her placid, sitcom-grandmother face grew hard. Her eyes locked onto Shaw's. "Find it. And take those motherfuckers down."

34

Sausalito is a quaint bay- and cliffside suburb north of the Golden Gate Bridge.

The demographics are artists and craftspeople and, given the views, the fine scone and muffin bakeries, and the high-speed ferries to downtown, well-heeled professionals.

In Russell's SUV the brothers were presently rocking through the winding and hilly streets, which were lined with dense foliage.

The inimitable Karin had tracked down La Fleur—first name Earnest, spelled the nontraditional way—and gotten his address but, interestingly, the group's databases offered little other information about him.

The man was off the grid. No phone, no social media. Amos Gahl's mother had said that La Fleur had been an employee of Black-Bridge but even that assertion, which Shaw had every reason to believe, was not available for confirmation. Shaw suspected his identity had been scrubbed to vapor.

Learning this about La Fleur, Shaw reflected how his father had come up with perhaps the best form of scrubbing in existence— never entrusting a single fact about himself, his work, his family, to the digital world.

"That's it," Russell said, nodding ahead of them to a cul-de-sac.

The narrow street, on which there were no sidewalks, was bounded by old-growth trees and interwoven tangles of foliage. In this part of town were few houses and the ones they'd passed were fronted with short picket fences through which grew thick greenery. La Fleur's property was different. It was protected by a solid pressure-treated stockade fence, eight feet tall, aged to gray. The slats topped with strands of barbed wire.

Russell parked and they walked to the gate, which was locked.

"No intercom," he said.

Shaw knelt and looked through a foot-round hole that had been cut in the wood for mail. All he could see was more foliage.

Russell took a small flat object from his pocket—like a black metal fingernail file—and, after examining the crack between gate and fence, slipped the latch in with a swift move and pushed the gate open. They stepped inside and looked over La Fleur's house. The rambling residence, an architectural mess in Cape Cod gray, was on a steep hillside, with stilts holding it aloft, forty feet above the rocks below. This entire area was subject to tremors of varying magnitude and Shaw would not have lived in a stilt house here for any money, whatever the view.

On the other hand, the building was at least three-quarters of a century old and had clearly survived various past shakings, perhaps damaged but suffering no mortal injury.

The men started toward the structure down a serpentine path, which was, curiously, interrupted every ten feet or so with oil drums filled with concrete. They were a version of what you saw in front of embassies and government security agencies overseas, to prevent suicide bombers from plowing their explosive-filled Toyota pickups straight into the front door.

"Hmm," Russell said.

As they approached the last drum, Shaw suddenly tilted his head. Russell too.

Both men dropped fast, taking cover behind one barricade.

Nothing is more distinctive than the creaking sound of a homemade bow being drawn.

The arrow hissed over their heads and lodged in a tree to the left, fired by a figure standing just inside the front door of the house. They couldn't see clearly but his garment appeared to be a variation on nighttime camo—various shades of blue and black. He wore dark brown leather gloves.

The arrow was a crude projectile, also homemade, but it still traveled at typical arrow velocity—around two hundred feet per second—and embedded itself neatly in a eucalyptus, which is not a soft wood.

"That's a warning shot. Get the hell out of here!" The voice was raspy and manic.

"Mr. La Fleur," Shaw called. "We just want to talk!"

"You're trespassing!"

Russell: "You don't have an intercom."

Shaw said, "And you don't have a phone either."

"How the fuck did you know that?"

Another arrow banged into the steel drum to their right.

The men surveyed the field of fire. Shaw estimated: fifteen feet to the bottom step, then three up to the narrow porch, three more to the door.

Shaw tried to calculate the odds. A crossbow, which takes some effort and time to cock and fit with a bolt, would have been no problem. They could easily cover the ground in the time it took to reload. But a recursive bow like this? One could fire about eight arrows a minute, if the archer were aiming carefully.

A *skilled* archer, that is. It didn't seem that La Fleur was. He dropped another arrow as he tried to notch it. Then he got it ready to launch. Shaw noted that his hands were trembling.

"Sir, we're not a threat!" Russell called. "We'd just like to talk to you about—"

Clunk . . .

This arrow hit the drum they were behind.

Shaw was getting irritated. "Hey, cut it out! You could hurt bystanders doing that!"

"No, I could fucking hurt *you!*"

The brothers regarded each other again and nodded.

Another arrow hissed in their direction. As it flew by, Shaw and Russell were instantly on their feet, sprinting to the door. Shaw slammed into the heavy panel with his shoulder. The door in turn bowled the man to the floor.

La Fleur howled, dropped the weapon and held his hands up.

Russell pushed into the foyer just after Shaw, his pistol drawn, in case La Fleur chose to attack with a knife or, who knew, a broadsword or battle-axe.

But the skirmish was over as fast as it had begun.

He skittered over the oak to a corner, huddling and crying out, "Bastards!"

The man had wild white hair, not unlike Ashton's toward the end, though La Fleur's was pulled into a sloppy ponytail. He had lengthy blanched eyebrows. He was gaunt. Beneath the camo, he wore a red floral shirt and on his feet were sandals with tie-dye straps. Bronze earrings dangled. The man was a combat-ready hippie.

"Nazis! Fascists! I have rights!"

"Calm down," Shaw said, pulling the man's gloves off and zip-tying his hands behind him. He noted he hadn't trimmed his nails in ages. They were yellow.

"No!"

Shaw: "I'm just doing this so everybody's safe. We're not going to hurt you."

"You already did. My butt aches."

"Calm. Down."

The volume of the muttering diminished some and La Fleur nodded, as if he were afraid of the consequences of even speaking to the two home invaders.

Shaw re-latched the many locks.

"Anybody else in the house?"

A negative twisting of neck and head.

Guns drawn, the brothers went about clearing the place anyway. Though they hadn't seen—let alone trained with—each other since they were children, they fell instantly into the procedure that Ashton Shaw had taught. "Door closed, left . . . Bathroom, half-open right . . . Clear. Breeze from second bedroom, window open. Barred . . . No hostiles. Clear! . . . No cellar . . . Attic sealed . . ."

They returned to the living room. Shaw looked over the place, which was perfumed with three distinctive smells: damp fireplace ash, rich pot and ocean. Two windows faced east, the direction of San Francisco Bay. These would have offered stunning views had they not been covered with thick metal shutters. Shaw knew their make and model. They were bulletproof, expensive and a favorite of cartel bosses. He knew of these qualities from a reward job a few years ago. He could also attest to the fact that when hit by automatic gunfire, the resulting bang was as loud as the muzzle burst itself.

The house could have been outfitted by a survivalist. There were stacks upon stacks of sandbags, piled halfway up the walls, enough to stop a fusillade of bullets. Ports had been cut into the wall through which he could pepper attacking hordes with his caveman arrows. La Fleur also had medical supplies aplenty, including a satchel labeled SELF-SURGERY KIT.

Also fifty-gallon drums of drinking water and hundreds of

pounds of MRE. Meals ready to eat were a staple for the armed services . . . and for gullible pseudo-survivalists who listened to paranoia-dishing talk radio hosts.

Ashton Shaw had taught the children that true survivalism means learning how to grow, gather and hunt for your own food.

One difference between this cliffside dwelling and the Compound: La Fleur had a computer and a TV. In the Compound there'd been no electronics whatsoever, except an emergency cell phone. It was kept charged but shut off. The only time Shaw remembered its being used was the cold October morning when he went off to look for his father on Echo Ridge, after the man had gone missing.

35

The brothers helped La Fleur into an indented armchair of faded green fabric and Shaw cut the restraint off. Now the grizzled man was trying a different tack; he was contrite. "It's all a mistake. Me shooting at you? I thought you were burglars. Really. There's been a string of robberies in the neighborhood. I have clippings. Do you want to see them? I would never have shot you if I'd known you weren't burglars. Don't hurt me!"

Russell frowned. "Burglars? Hmm."

"Who'd you really think we were?" Shaw asked.

"From BlackBridge?" Russell asked.

The man froze and then looked down. It was as if the very word paralyzed him. He gave the faintest of nods.

"We're not," Shaw said.

Russell tapped the grip of his SIG Sauer. "If we were BlackBridge, you'd be dead. Right?"

La Fleur rubbed his wrists. He reached for a bong and a lighter on the chair-side table.

"No," Russell said.

"You want some?" he offered the stained glass tube. Both men ignored him. He put it down.

"Amos Gahl's mother told us about you."

His face softened "Eleanor! How is she?"

"She's fine."

"And her husband? Mort."

"Apparently okay," Shaw said. "He was out. Now, Earnest. We need your help. Amos found some evidence against BlackBridge. We think it's proof about the Urban Improvement Plan. You know about it?"

He frowned, taking this in. He remained cautious. "Who are you?"

"Our father," Shaw said, "was killed by Irena Braxton and Ebbitt Droon. Ian Helms too."

"Your father?"

"Ashton Shaw. Did you know him?"

"I don't remember the name. But there was somebody . . . wild-eyed, like a cowboy."

Russell displayed the picture.

"That's him. He stopped me outside where I was living. He told me he was a professor and one of his students had been killed by BlackBridge."

"Todd Zaleski, a city councilman."

La Fleur squinted. "That was it, yes! Supposedly a robbery but your dad didn't believe it. Like you guys—he was looking for what Ame had taken from BlackBridge. I told him I couldn't help him. He left and I never heard from him again."

"You were close to Amos, his mother told us."

A nod and his weathered lips drew taut.

"Will you help us? Whatever Amos found is in a courier bag. He hid it somewhere in the Bay Area."

Eyes again on the floor, La Fleur mumbled, "I don't know anything. I swear to God."

In the rewards business, Shaw had done a fair amount of kine-sics analysis—using body language to spot deception. Included in that fine art was noting verbal tics. Anyone who ends a sentence with the assurance that they're not lying probably is, and it's a dou-ble hit if a deity is invoked.

Shaw stared at him until La Fleur added, in a whisper, "Black-Bridge is the devil—the whole company. Everybody. Not just Helms and Braxton. It's like the buildings are evil, the walls are evil . . . It's so dangerous. Why do you think I'm living like this?"

"Don't you want Helms to go to prison for what they did to your friend?" Shaw asked.

The man looked away.

Shaw felt frustration. This man knew something. He said, "There's a family that Droon and Braxton are going to kill tomor-row."

La Fleur's face revealed some concern at this. "Why?"

Russell: "We don't know."

"We find Amos's evidence and go to the FBI. They arrest Ian Helms and Braxton and Droon. We stop the killing. Help us save them."

Russell stirred impatiently. Shaw had refined his interviewing and interrogation skills over the years in seeking rewards. Though he could be firm, he generally used logic, empathy and humor to win over the subjects. He suspected his brother took a somewhat differ-ent approach.

Shaw persisted. "You and Amos met at Eleanor's house a few times. You met there because she hadn't been 'Gahl' for years. She'd remarried and changed her name. So Braxton and Droon wouldn't know about her."

Shaw studied La Fleur patiently until he decided, it seemed, it wasn't too incriminating to answer. "That's right."

"What did Amos tell you when you were over at his mother's, the last time you met?"

He fidgeted, played with the bong. "Nothing. Really! We just chatted. Chewed the fat." His evasive face gave a smile. "My grandmother used to say that. When I was a kid I never knew what it meant. I still—"

Russell snapped, "What did Amos tell you?"

Shaw said patiently, yet in a firm voice, "They're going to murder a *family*. There was a note we found, a kill order. It didn't say 'target' singular or 'couple.' Husband and wife. It said 'family.' That means children. We have no idea who they are and we've only got twenty-four hours to find out and save them."

Russell said nothing more. With dark, threatening eyes he stared at the man.

Good cop, bad cop.

"The evidence," Shaw said. "Amos was going to hide it. I think you know where."

La Fleur shook his head vehemently. "No, no, no! We didn't talk about anything like that. We talked about plants, fertilizer."

"At midnight?"

"How did you know that's when we met?" The man's eyes grew alarmed.

Shaw hadn't, but it was logical.

"I'm a gardener. Look outside!" He uttered a forced laugh. "My last name, you know. 'Flower' in French. Amos was into plants too. We had some wine and talked about gardening." The sadness returned.

Russell shot a glance to his younger brother, who handed off the interview to him, easing back and falling silent.

As Russell leaned close, La Fleur shied, kneading his hands into fists then opening his fingers. Over and over. "I'll send an anonymous text to BlackBridge, attention Braxton and Droon. It'll have two items in it. One, your name. Two, your address."

"*What?*" A horrified whisper.

"When they come at you with their M4 assault rifles, your arrows aren't going to do anything but piss them off."

Bad cop had become worse cop.

His shoulders slumped. He sighed. "I'm probably screwed anyway. They tracked you on your phones."

"We have shielded and encrypted burners," Shaw said.

He didn't seem to believe them. "Oh yeah? What's your algorithm?"

"AES, Twofish and Scorpion."

With a glance toward Shaw, Russell said, "That's mine too." Curiously the brothers had, on their own, picked the same encryption package.

La Fleur snapped, "Let me see."

Russell offered his phone. La Fleur grabbed and studied it, then for some reason shook the mobile as if to see what kind of data would rattle out. He examined the screen once more. He handed it back. He seemed marginally relieved and didn't bother with Shaw's unit.

The man's zipping eyes settled on the knotty-pine floor. He rose and walked to a shuttered window. He opened the metal slat a few inches, ducking—as if to slip out of a sniper's crosshairs. After a moment he stood, crouching, and looked out.

Apparently satisfied there were no surveillance devices, or rifles, trained his way, he closed and re-latched the shutter. Walking to a far corner of the room, he turned on an elaborate LP record player and, pulling on latex gloves, removed an old-time album from its sleeve. He set the black disk gingerly on the turntable and, with infinite care, set the needle in the groove of the first track.

Music pounded into the room, some rock group. Anyone trying to listen in would hear only raging guitar and fierce drums.

La Fleur removed the gloves and replaced them in the box. He looked his intruders over. "You two really have no clue what's going on."

And with a defiant look at Russell, he grabbed the bong, lit up and inhaled long.

36

The smoke spiraled upward, dissolving at its leisure.

Never into recreational drugs, Shaw nonetheless found the rich smell of pot pleasant. He waited until La Fleur exhaled and sat back. A twitching tilt of his head like a squirrel assessing a tree. The man put the blue tube down.

"Oh, yes, Amos found something, and he hid it. But it had nothing to do with the Urban Improvement Plan. I have no idea why you're harping on that. Your father was wrong: there *is* no evidence against the company. If there were, Ame would have found it. He searched and searched. But there wasn't and there'll *never* be any evidence. Helms and his people're too smart to leave anything incriminating. They used cutout after cutout, encoding, anonymous servers, shell companies, encryption. The CIA should be as good as BlackBridge."

"Facts," Russell said. "Not drama."

La Fleur shot him a look that managed to be simultaneously hurt and defiant.

"My poor Ame . . . He got himself in over his head, didn't he? He took it upon himself to end the UIP. Helms had something his main client wanted desperately. It was code-named the Endgame

Sanction. Braxton and some thug had found it in the Embarcadero. Maybe Droon. Looks like a rat, doesn't he?"

Shaw said, "The Hayward Brothers Warehouse?"

"I don't know. But she found it and it was like . . . the ring of power. The client had wanted it forever, was paying a retainer of millions to track it down." A faint chuckle. "And you'll never guess what Ame did. He heard Helms talking about it, about how it was the end-all and be-all . . . and when the big boss stepped out of his office, my Ame simply waltzed in and nicked it! Dropped it in his courier bag and walked out the front door with a nighty-night to the guards."

"Why?"

"He was going to use it as leverage, get the company to shut down the UIP program. Or maybe stealing it, he thought the client would fire Helms, and then BlackBridge'd go out of business. I don't think he had a plan. He was just sick of working for such a vile bunch of men and women."

"What was this thing?"

"He never had a chance to tell me." His voice went soft. "He stole it about five p.m. He hid it about an hour later. Then at ten that night he called me. I'd never heard him so panicked. He said he'd done some research and found out what the Sanction was, and it needed to be destroyed. It was devastating. The client could never get it, no one could. He was going to destroy it himself but he couldn't get back to where he'd hidden it. He knew BlackBridge ops were searching for him. If anything happened to him, I was supposed to find it and get rid of it."

Shaw looked toward his brother, who frowned. What on earth was it?

"And he died while they were torturing him to find out where it was?" Shaw asked.

"That's right, I'm sure."

A new track came on, louder. The men had to huddle close to hear and be heard.

Russell asked, "Where did he hide it?"

"He was afraid of the phone lines, so he gave me two clues. One was the 'dog park.' He meant Quigley Square. A friend of ours lived there and we'd walk her dog if she was traveling."

Shaw knew the place, a transitional neighborhood in the city.

"The other clue was 'It's hidden underground, someplace you'd be expecting.'"

Great, thought Shaw. More scavenger hunt.

Another hit of the weed. "Then I heard a shout. It sounded like he dropped the phone. Then it seemed like there was a scuffle." He grew silent for a moment. "That was the last time I heard his voice."

"Any guesses where he meant?"

"No."

Russell: "You ever think about going to Quigley Square and doing what he wanted to? Destroying it?"

His eyes, more tearful, looked down at the dimpled wood floor. "I thought, yes, but I didn't. I'm a coward! Helms and Irena and Droon . . . they didn't know I existed anymore. I erased myself. I thought about it, finding whatever it was, doing what Amos wanted. But in the end, I balked. They're so powerful, so dangerous. They've got all the power of the police and the CIA!" His eyes grew wild— the way their father's occasionally had. "You just don't know . . . Besides, he died before he told them, so hidden it was and hidden it would remain. Forever. It was *like* being destroyed."

"Except," Shaw said, "they're still after it. And we have to get to it first."

"To save that family." La Fleur's voice was low.

"That's right." Russell called up a map of San Francisco on his phone. He focused in on Quigley Square. There were dozens of buildings bordering the park. Presumably they'd all have undergrounds—cellars or maybe tunnels.

Shaw asked, "Would it be in the friend's house? The dog friend?"

"Amos would never endanger anyone. In any case, she moved years ago."

Shaw wondered aloud: "Sewers? Transit system?"

"No BART station there," Russell noted. "Where would we *expect* it to be hidden, when we don't know what it is?" he muttered.

Shaw offered, "Maybe he hides it in a book and puts it in a cellar of a library or bookstore. He's got a CD or tape, he hides it in a music store basement. It's a computer disk, so it's in the basement of a school with a computer science lab." He shook his head. "We can't keep throwing out ideas. 'Never speculate.'"

Russell finished their father's rule: "'Make decisions from facts.'"

Shaw asked, "Who's the client that wanted the Sanction?"

La Fleur said, "Banyan Tree Inc. It's a big conglomerate. International. Into healthcare, medical equipment, transportation, communications, environmental work, real estate—"

"Real estate," Shaw said. "UIP."

Russell nodded.

Shaw asked where Banyan's headquarters was.

"In the city here. It's a skyscraper downtown."

"Four hundred block of Sutter?"

"Could be, yeah. That sounds right."

He said to Russell, "The tracker I tagged Braxton with placed her there."

Shaw had a thought. "Who's the head of Banyan Tree?"

"Jonathan Stuart Devereux."

Russell fished out his phone and displayed the picture he'd shot of the round bald man with the busy hands and the fancy British car at the site of the drug handover in the Tenderloin.

La Fleur examined the screen. "That's Devereux, yeah. Oh, he's a son of a bitch. Ruthless. He just drove a competitor into bankruptcy. Devereux's industrial spies—BlackBridge probably—found out they were breaking some laws or regulations and turned them in to the feds. It broke them. The CEO committed suicide."

La Fleur angrily exhaled a wad of smoke. "You know what a banyan tree is?"

Shaw said, "It's a fig. It strangles any tree competing with it for light."

La Fleur nodded. "And it's got the longest root spread of any tree on earth. Any doubt why Devereux picked the name?"

Russell said, "Endgame Sanction . . . Wonder in what sense."

Sanction was one of those odd words that had contradictory meanings: it could be either permission—as in you're sanctioned to attack—or punishment, as in imposing sanctions.

La Fleur said, "Or it might mean nothing. BlackBridge uses code names a lot." He grew thoughtful. And tugged at his ponytail, then picked up the bong and lighter once again.

Shaw wanted to get to Quigley Square and get started on the search. He rose. Russell too.

La Fleur inhaled deep, let the smoke amble from his mouth. Then he rose, shut the music off, and walked to the door with the brothers. He began to unhitch the various latches and locks. "I gave Amos some advice. It's one of those old clichés, but it's true. When you aim for an emperor, you better not miss. He aimed and he missed. I guess the same happened to your father. You two? You can still walk away."

He cracked the door, looked out and then pulled it fully open.

Russell eyed him sternly. "La Fleur, let me give *you* some advice." The man eased back, his face revealing alarm at the brother's fierce, dark eyes.

"First, never provide your enemy with cover." He nodded at the drums sitting staggered along the path to the street. "Get rid of them or move them. Second, never use inferior materials in your weapons. Make a new bow. Use locust, lemonwood or yew. It should be a foot longer. And fletch your arrows with short, parabolic feathers. You don't need accuracy at distance on a shooting zone this short. You need velocity. And order some parachute cord for the string. You got that?"

"Yessir," La Fleur whispered. "I'll get right on it."

37

Endgame Sanction. The hell you think it is?" Russell was piloting the SUV through the roller-coaster streets of San Francisco, on their way to Quigley Square.

Shaw only shook his head. He received an email from Mack McKenzie. He'd requested a profile of Devereux and Banyan Tree.

Shaw read her response aloud to his brother:

"Jonathan Stuart Devereux. Estimated worth, $1.4 billion. CEO and majority shareholder of Banyan Tree Inc. BT is solely a holding company. Devereux is known in the business world as the king of subsidiaries, which run all of the company's business. This is done to protect Banyan Tree and Devereux from liability. One reporter said, 'Nobody hides behind the corporate veil better than Jonathan Devereux.'"

Shaw looked at his brother. "She gives a list of everything he's into, which La Fleur told us. But there are some others. Data collection, information processing, media."

He returned to the email. "Recent incidents that have made the news: A subsidiary in the UK, Southampton Analytics, is being investigated by MI5, the domestic criminal investigation division, for hacking and interference with elections in the UK, France, Germany and the U.S. One of the board members is a Russian national who had been a military intelligence officer. There was no evidence that Banyan Tree was directly involved. Devereux either.

"Another one: Police in New Delhi arrested the managers of a huge call center after a fire killed twenty-four workers, on the grounds of failing to maintain a safe workplace. The company was owned by layers of shell corporations, set up by Banyan Tree. But, again, Devereux and the company weren't implicated.

"I found at least six similar incidents. Let me know if you want details.

"Banyan Tree has been in the news in California. The *Pacific Business Review* reported that over the past few years it's acquired one hundred and forty-seven small companies in the state. He's fired all the employees and's keeping them as shells. In the filings the stated purpose of them is to quote 'engage in various services for the public.'"

The king of subsidiaries . . .

"Mack has some things on Devereux's personal life. Born in England, U.S. citizen now. He's fifty-one. Married. His wife's fifty-six. I have a feeling she was not the miniskirted one in the Rolls at the UIP drop."

"Hmm."

Shaw summarized: Devereux had two teenage sons. His homes were in San Francisco, L.A., Miami Beach, London, Nice and Singapore. He was described as tireless, obsessed, always in motion.

Shaw remembered the constantly moving hands when the brothers had spied on him at the drug exchange.

Russell asked, "Anything about a relationship with Black-Bridge?"

"No."

Shaw continued to read. "It's disputed by genealogists, but

Devereux claims he's descended from Robert Devereux, Second Earl of Essex. It was during Elizabeth the First's reign, the fifteen hundreds. He was a favorite. And then he led a coup against the throne."

"Assume that was a bad idea."

"Beheaded in the Tower of London. The executioner wasn't exactly a pro. Took him three swings to get the job done."

38

Underground, *where you'd be expecting.*

Not much in the clue department.

"Think," Russell said. He brushed his beard absently.

The brothers looked around modest Quigley Square, at the center of which was a pleasant urban park—half concrete walks and benches and half trim lawns, bushes and trees. The surrounding streets echoed the San Francisco of the 1960s and '70s. Head shops and stores offering LP albums, souvenir tie-dye shirts and windup cable cars. You could even buy cassettes of classic thirty-five-millimeter adult films from that era.

Shaw looked over his phone. "The tracker's dead."

"In the *Walden* book?"

He nodded. "To fit in the spine, it was a small battery. Lasted longer than I thought. Or they might've found it."

Russell said, "So, we're black on hostiles. Act accordingly."

Shaw slipped the unit away and turned his attention back to the neighborhood.

Trying to guess Amos Gahl's clue—"underground, where you'd

be expecting"—the brothers noted the retail shops, as well as an old red-brick hospital, a classic diner, bodegas, a sushi restaurant that Shaw would avoid at all costs, dilapidated industrial buildings, car repair shops.

"Where would we *expect* something to be hidden?"

"And underground." Shaw pointed to a small regional bank. "Safe deposit box? A downstairs vault?"

"Need a key and ID."

They walked half a block to a warehouse. The building was huge and, they could see through the barred doors and windows, filled with construction equipment. If Amos Gahl had hidden the Endgame Sanction in the basement, it would take eons to find it.

Besides, why would they *expect* it to be hidden there?

"Underground," Shaw repeated absently, eyes on a sign in the concrete at his feet.

NO DUMPING

FLOWS TO BAY

The words were stenciled beside a storm drain grate. There were dozens of them. But nothing could have survived after all these years down there. You heard much about California's droughts and Shaw recalled the lessons his father gave the children in distilling salt water to make it drinkable. But the winter season here could still be counted on to dump a billion gallons on the city. Anything in the drains would have disintegrated and slushed into the Bay years ago. How did one get into a storm drain anyway?

"Where you'd be expecting . . ."

Shaw and Russell walked around the square, side by side. Homeless, always the homeless in San Francisco. Shaw could hardly blame them. Why live on the street in Minnesota or Anchorage? He would have come to San Francisco, the home of a warmer clime and wealthy executives, ready to toss a coin or bill into an inverted baseball cap.

He observed that none of these street people seemed strung out, unlike those he and Russell had seen that morning in the TL. Apparently, BlackBridge hadn't targeted Quigley Square for the Urban Improvement Plan. At least, not yet. But he could see it coming: two blocks away was a long expanse of glittery, glass-fronted high-rises. A developer standing on the soaring roof might look down at Quigley Square and think, "That's my next conquest. Get the BNG to work."

More scanning.

Then Shaw stopped fast, looking up.

No, couldn't be.

A glance to his right. He wasn't surprised to see that Russell was looking at exactly the same thing he was.

"It possible?" Russell said.

Where you'd be expecting . . .

They were looking at the hospital.

BETH ISRAEL OBSTETRICS AND MATERNITY CENTER

There was no doubt a good portion of the patients inside would certainly be *expecting*.

"Hmm." Again Russell almost smiled. He pulled out his phone and sent a text as they walked to the looming structure.

At the receptionist's station in the lobby, Russell slipped his phone away and stepped in front of Shaw and said, "We're here to visit a patient. Abigail Hanson. She had a C-section."

A computer screen was consulted. "Room seven-forty-two," she told them.

"Thanks," Shaw said.

So that was the text Russell had sent. As they walked to the elevators, Shaw asked, "Karin?"

"Hmm."

She was good.

In the basement Shaw had expected locked doors or gates. But no. The cellar was an easily accessed storage area. Lights were, how-ever, a problem. Only two of the twenty overhead bulbs were func-tional. Shaw had not brought his tac flashlight. After a search for more switches, Russell cocked his head, looking up, and gripped one of the darkened spheres in his substantial fingers and twisted. It came to life. Maintenance staff had apparently been ordered to partly unscrew the bulbs to keep utility costs down.

The men executed the same maneuver a dozen or so times and the place was soon awash in glare.

Shaw noted that the diminutive size of the room did not mean their task would be an easy one. It was packed with cabinets, car-tons, wooden boxes, cases of what seemed to be antiquated medical instruments—even, he was amused to see, the same fifty-gallon drums of civil defense water they'd found at La Fleur's sanctuary. Shelves were filled to overflowing with books, files and—eerily—organ and tissue samples in jars of what was probably formalin. Hearts and kidneys were especially popular.

The brothers paused. Footsteps sounded not too far away. A creak too, like a janitor's cart whose wheels needed oiling. It faded.

They resumed their search.

Where would Amos Gahl have hidden his courier bag?

While Russell began with filing cabinets—easily picking the simple locks—Shaw stepped back against the wall and gazed over the room.

The trick to finding something that's been hidden in plain sight is to look for what's just a bit out of order. Like those puzzles in the magazines he and his siblings would read when they were children: Spotting what was the difference between two adjacent cartoons or drawings. What's wrong with this picture?

What was out of place in this chamber of outmoded instru-ments, cold soggy organs and dusty faded treatises on medical prac-tices and procedures that had most likely become outmoded a year after they were published?

He circled slowly.

What's wrong with this picture?

Shaw stopped.

"Russell."

His brother looked toward him and then at what Shaw was gesturing toward.

High on a sturdy gray shelf containing scores of medical treatises, one object stood out. It appeared to be the spine of a book, though wider and taller than the others. Yet the brown leather did not bear any title, author or other information.

Russell, the taller of the two, slipped it from the shelf.

Was this the pot of gold?

It turned out to be a large briefcase that opened from the top.

"Courier bag?" Shaw asked.

"Hmm."

He started to open the bag, but his brother touched his arm. "No." The creaking had resumed. "Not here."

39

As soon as the brothers had left the hospital, they walked to the Quigley Square Diner, not far away. It was a please-seat-yourself establishment and soon they were sitting across from each other in a booth. They'd bought sandwiches neither was interested in—rent for the booth.

In the deserted back portion of the place, Russell ran a nitrate detector over the case to sense for explosives.

Never assume an object that's been in your enemy's possession is harmless.

No unstable substances were present.

Then he scanned it for transmitters. This too was negative.

Russell picked the lock securing the top flap of the case in five seconds and popped it open.

A laminated card was inside.

Property of BlackBridge Corporate Solutions, Inc.

And there was a number below with the request to please return if found.

The brothers shared a look.

Then they began to unearth the contents.

The top layers consisted of folded copies of *San Francisco Chronicles* and *Peoples* and *Times* from years ago.

Then, like the archeological sites Margot Keller was so adept at excavating, things got more interesting the farther down you went.

Beneath the innocuous periodicals were hundreds of documents—both photocopies and originals. Most were corporate or financial in nature: spreadsheets, balance sheets, contracts for services and goods, maps, memos about cash transfers, real estate plots, shipping schedules, accounts receivable, along with various contracts.

They found a series of draft bills for some bodies of legislature, something that Gahl, the historian, had discovered in his job as a researcher for BlackBridge, Shaw guessed. Probably they'd been drafted for a governmental client of the company, one who—they gathered as they read through the papers—favored eliminating regulations on the environment, manufacturing and banking. Shaw read one that proposed redefining *probable cause* in criminal matters to make it far easier for the police to get warrants and detain suspects. Another proposed bill eased the burden of getting permission for surveillance. The authoritarian nature of the documents was troubling.

They continued to dig, briefly examining each piece of paper: more spreadsheets, some documents that were quite old, one more than a hundred years.

Shaw finally came to the bottom of the courier bag.

Nothing referred to the "Endgame Sanction."

He did note, though, a bulge on the inside of the case—there was what seemed to be a hidden compartment, sealed at the top with Velcro. Shaw looked at Russell, who nodded.

Shaw pulled the flap open with a tearing sound, and looked into the space.

Bingo . . .

He extracted an old-style cassette player. Inside was a tape of the sort that could be played in a Walkman or similar device from the 1980s. There were no batteries, which was fortunate. After all these years, they would have corroded and chemical leakage might have destroyed the tape itself.

Russell left Shaw and walked across the street to a bodega. He returned with a package of AA batteries. Shaw loaded them in and, glancing once at his brother, hit REWIND. The unit worked.

So. This was the moment.

What was on the tape? Was it the Endgame Sanction itself? A recording of a secret meeting about it? The contents might put all the other documentation in the bag in context, answer clues, tie everything together.

Devastating . . .

When the tape was at the beginning and the REWIND button popped up, Russell hesitated a moment and pushed the PLAY button.

40

Suddenly rock music poured out, loud. And tinny, given the small speaker.

A few customers glanced their way.

Russell turned the volume down. "Black Eyed Peas," he said.

"That's a group?"

A nod.

Fast-forward.

"Beyoncé."

Fast-forward.

"Ludacris."

"What's ludicrous?" Shaw asked.

Russell eyed his brother. "You don't get out much, do you?"

Fast-forward.

"Mariah Carey."

Shaw: "I know her. Some Christmas song, right?"

On and on. Pausing at the end of each tune to listen for a voice explaining what the Sanction was, why it would be disastrous if it were to come into Jonathan Devereux's possession.

But no, there was just a gap of static and then the next song would begin.

Russell's still eyes gazed at the player.

They listened to the entire tape, both sides. Russell let it run all the way to the end and snap loudly off.

"Hmm."

Shaw said, "What's that technique called for hiding information in pictures and music?"

"Steganography." He was stroking his beard. "But that only works with digital media. Bytes of data. Analog?" A nod at the tape player. "No."

Shaw asked, "What about tracking? Something recorded over or under the music? Something we can't hear, like a dog whistle. Can that be done?"

Russell considered this. "Don't know. I'll see." He looked up a number on his phone and called.

A moment later he was saying, "It's me . . . You free? . . . I'm going to play some music clips. Tell me if there's anything out of detectable audio range." He listened for a moment. Then: "No project number . . . I know. I'll work it out later."

Perhaps a reference to the fact he was using the group's resources for a very non-group operation.

He set the phone beside the speaker and pressed PLAY. It was a country western song. After a minute he stopped and fast-forwarded the tape. He played another sixty seconds or so of a different song. He did this a half-dozen more times.

"You got that?" Russell said into his phone. Then he was listening to the person on the other end of the line. "'K." He disconnected. "She'll get back to us."

Five minutes later, after the brothers had gone through the contents of the courier bag once more and found nothing that even suggested the words *endgame* or *sanction*, Russell's phone hummed. He took the call. As usual, his face gave nothing away. When he disconnected he told his brother, "Nothing she could pick up. She's going to try a deeper analysis. But it doesn't look likely. High frequency on analog is not a known technique."

Shaw suspected Russell's group was quite well versed in *all* the known techniques.

"Karin?"

"No."

Shaw asked, "Could the names of the music groups spell out something? Or the songs."

The suggestion even *sounded* lame. But they tried. Russell knew most of the groups, though only about half of the songs. After five minutes of playing the anagram game, they gave up.

"The lining?"

A nod.

Shaw set the bag in his lap and, after making sure no one was near, opened his razor-sharp locking-blade knife. He cut into the cloth linings. He put the knife away and reached inside. The search was in vain.

"Microchip?" Shaw asked his brother.

"Hmm. I can order a scan. Doubt it."

The men found themselves looking at the please-call-if-found tag.

They shared a glance.

"Maybe," Russell said. His own knife appeared. It seemed the brothers both owned Benchmade folding knives, among the best on the market. Shaw's was a Bugout. Russell's was the Anthem model, costing about three hundred dollars more.

Russell used the blade to slit the tag and slowly pulled the lamination away from the cardboard.

He found nothing.

He dropped the tag and wire inside the courier bag and folded up the knife, put it away.

Shaw suggested, "The newspapers and magazines?" He explained:

maybe there was something marked in an article, or several of them, that could point them in some direction.

"Possible."

"But back at the safe house," Shaw said, looking around. "We've been here too long."

"Agree."

The men gathered up their booty and left the diner.

On the way to Russell's SUV, Shaw voiced what had been in the back of his mind from the moment the first arrows hissed their way from Earnest La Fleur's bow: "Percentage chance that Gahl was unstable and paranoid? He never had the Sanction at all. Ash—and Braxton and Droon—just *thought* he did."

Russell didn't put a number on it but he said the exact word that Shaw was thinking: "High. Too high."

Which meant that what their father had perished for was not evidence to bring down one of the most ruthless corporations on earth, or this mysterious Endgame Sanction.

Ashton Shaw had died for a greatest-hits mixtape.

41

Was that the car? The green Honda?

"Turn left. Fast."

Russell, behind the wheel of the big SUV, apparently trusted his brother's instincts. He spun the wheel hard, braking a little. Shaw would have gone faster.

Ahead, two blocks away he saw a green car reverse fast into an alley.

"There. I think that's her. Catch her."

"Her?" Russell asked.

Shaw hadn't told him that the driver following him was a blond woman. He mentioned this now, leaving out the "hot" part.

The SUV picked up speed and approached the alley the Honda had zipped into.

"When you get to the mouth, turn but don't drive in."

"Why?"

"She may have left a booby trap."

"These windows are bulletproof."

"What about the tires?" Shaw explained about the nails the woman had scattered earlier.

Russell lifted an eyebrow then skidded the vehicle to a stop.

Yes, a blanket of nails littered the front of the alley. Ahead of them, several blocks away, the car vanished into traffic.

"They have big heads," Russell said.

Shaw looked at his brother.

"The nails. They're roofing nails. You run over average nails, they stay flat. These, when the tire hits them, the points turn up, and into the tread." He knocked the Navigator into reverse. "You have no idea who she is?"

"Might be related to a job I did in Silicon Valley a couple of weeks ago. Made some enemies in the high-tech world."

Russell backed up and turned toward Alvarez.

"Keep an eye out when you're on your bike. She throws some in front of you, at speed, you'll set it down. Won't be good."

"I'll keep that in mind."

He parked two blocks away, not far from the coffee shop where Shaw had first seen Russell, though he hadn't known it at the time. Shaw was keeping his cycle locked here too, away from the safe house—in case someone had made one of the vehicles and traced it.

Inside, Shaw lifted Amos Gahl's courier bag onto the kitchen table and divided its contents into two piles.

He pushed one toward Russell and kept the other. The two men began reading through each sheet of paper carefully once more. Were there helpful notes in the margin? Were passages circled? Was a magazine opened to a certain article, a newspaper folded in a particular way?

Had Amos Gahl, who apparently loved his puzzles, been cautious and coy once again, using these publications and other documents to send a message about what the Sanction was?

Shaw thought again about the word *sanction*.

Permission. Punishment.

Or just a meaningless code name?

But poring over the contents uncovered no clues, no codes, no secrets subtle or obvious.

After an hour, both men sat back. "Maybe he just liked to read the news," Shaw said.

They sat in silence for a moment. Shaw gazed at the cassette recorder and, after collecting his tool kit from his backpack, unscrewed the back. Nothing inside but solid state electronics. He used a magnifier on the cassette itself but could see no writing or code. The labels on each side, which were blank, were glued tightly to the plastic; they couldn't be pried up to reveal a message hidden beneath them without tearing the paper.

Nodding at the stack of papers, Shaw said, "I'm not accepting it."

Russell glanced his way.

"That this is just somebody's imagination. It's real, the Sanction. And it's here." Pointing at the material on the table.

"You making that assumption?"

"Call it that."

After a pause Russell said, "I agree."

"So. We'll have to go through everything—"

Just then a persistent beep came from Russell's phone.

Instantly he was on his feet. His hand was near his weapon. "Have a sensor, front door. Somebody's picking the lock."

Shaw drew his Glock and crept to the closest window. "Droon, plus an entry team, five, six. Long guns too. How'd they make us?"

His brother shook his head.

Shaw saw one of the attackers standing at the open tailgate of an SUV. The men looked up and down the street. He then pulled something from the vehicle, turned and eyed the front of the safe house. He squinted directly toward Shaw. Then raised to his shoulder what looked like a large shotgun with a blunt object protruding from the muzzle. He pulled the trigger.

"Grenade!" Shaw shouted.

The brothers dove to the floor.

42

rena Braxton, wearing a staid gray suit, stood with her arms crossed over her chest, surveying the interior of the safe house, as if she were waiting for her grown son and daughter-in-law and the brood of grandchildren to arrive for Sunday supper.

Other BlackBridge workers—a lean, unsmiling blond woman in a black tac outfit and a solidly built Latino—were tossing the living and dining rooms. *Tossing.* That was the technical term for searching a home or office, though there was in fact nothing sloppy about the process. They were meticulous and careful and breaking or destroying nothing. Drawers were opened, cabinets, the refrigerator and freezer, the microwave, the closets, the spaces under cushions, under couches, under chairs.

Another man from the team was examining the empty Black-Bridge courier bag. He was the one who'd fired the grenade launcher. He had set down the weapon but like the others—aside from Braxton—he wore a sidearm, another expensive SIG Sauer.

One of the ops, a tall brunette woman, was in the living room. Hands on hips, she called, "Nothing. The Sanction's not here."

"What?" Braxton snapped, turning on her. "Is your search *finished*? How can you say it's not here if you're not finished?"

"Yes, ma'am. The case was empty, I assumed they took it with them."

"Oh, they didn't hide it here maybe? Do you think that's a possibility?"

The woman scurried back to work.

The others kept quiet and continued their tasks.

Ebbitt Droon came down from upstairs. "Didn't get out that way. Windows locked from the inside. Clothes, ammunition. Nothing helpful."

This scene was unfolding on Russell's laptop, four split screens. And remotely. The brothers were a block away—in the coffee shop where Shaw had first seen the man with the thigh-length coat, stocking cap and the A's backpack, the texting customer who had turned out to be his brother.

The grenade had not been a deadly fragmentation model, just a large flash-bang to stun and deafen, similar to the one Russell had used as an alarm on the door to the secure room in the cellar. The projectile had been fired accurately. But what the BlackBridge assault team didn't know—nor did Russell or Colter Shaw—was that in fitting out the safe house years ago Ashton had installed bullet-deflecting windows. The grenade would have hit the plexiglass at about four hundred feet per second, slow enough so that the device merely bounced off. This bought the brothers a little time, since the tables were turned and the device flashed and banged outside.

Upon learning they were under attack, the Shaw brothers knew they weren't in any position to engage four heavily armed tac ops. They chose to escape. Shaw shoveled the contents of the courier bag into his backpack, as Russell grabbed their computers.

"Basement," Russell said, at the same time as Shaw said, "Cellar."

So his brother had seen the coal bin too. Shaw had recognized right away that it was fake; the house wasn't more than fifty years old. No urban dwelling of that age had ever used coal for heat.

Ever the survivalist, weren't you, Ashton?

As they heard footsteps above them, they'd pulled the bin away and slipped into the four-foot-wide tunnel, then pulled the bin back in place behind them.

Never use a safe house that doesn't have a trapdoor . . .

A moment later they'd heard: "Cellar clear" and the thud of footsteps up the stairs.

The brothers had continued through the tunnel for about thirty feet and come to another wooden panel. They'd muscled it aside and, guns ready, stepped into the basement of the Soviet-bloc apartment building across the alley from the safe house. The large, mold-scented room was empty. They left via the service entrance and five minutes later were in the coffee shop, more unwanted food and drink at hand, just any other customers, watching Braxton, Droon and the others.

When Russell had returned to the safe house with the news about the text ordering the hit on the SP family, he'd brought with him surveillance equipment. The four cameras, fitted with sensitive microphones, were in household objects—lamps, a clock, a picture frame. They were wireless but transmitted on the same frequency as Russell's internet router in the closet in the front hall—so anyone scanning the house for surveillance, as Droon had done, would see only the server transmissions, not the spy cams.

Shaw said he was impressed, and Russell said his group had some people who came up with "clever ideas."

On the computer screen it was easy to see that Braxton was growing angrier. "We had eyes on them. They were here. How'd they get out?"

"Back window?" one of the male operatives said.

"And then why weren't any of you in the back?"

No one had an answer for that, and the searching continued.

"Look," Shaw said.

He was referring to Droon, who was only marginally interested in the cassette player. He punched a button, listened to a few seconds of a tune, then fast-forwarded and did the same several more times. He shut the unit off, shrugged toward Braxton and continued searching the room, leaving the device on the table.

Shaw continued, "They'd have to have audio engineers too, like your group. It means the Sanction's not electronic."

"Hmm."

Droon then took over examining the courier bag. He did so as closely as Shaw and Russell had done. He could see that the lining was cut but he was taking no chances. Maybe he was searching this carefully because it was his nature. Maybe it was self-preservation, so desperate were the minions to please Devereux.

Russell said, "Be helpful if they said what they're looking for. Help us narrow it down."

If anyone from BlackBridge mentioned a keyword, it might be possible for the brothers to identify the Endgame Sanction in the stack of material sitting in Shaw's backpack.

Russell typed. A camera scanned to the left, taking in the blond woman operative. Then to the right.

Shaw then said, "Notice a pattern?"

Russell nodded. "All they want is paperwork. That's why they don't care about the cassette. It's definitely paper, and probably—the way they're fanning pages—a single sheet."

After five minutes Droon muttered, "Bastards took it with 'em, don'tcha know?"

Braxton now seemed to accept this possibility. She nodded. "We found it once. We'll find it again. Devereux brings in ten million a year. And you know what the bonus'll be when we get it."

Braxton's attention turned to the window. The doorbell buzzed and one of the ops walked into the front alcove.

Then, just barely audible through the microphone, came the sounds of a creaking floor as a large man in a black suit stepped into sight. Shaw recognized him. He was Devereux's Asian American bodyguard and driver. Shaw recalled him from the construction site in the Tenderloin, where the BNG gangbangers had gotten their Johnny Appleseed bags of drugs to plant around the community as part of the UIP program.

The man looked around and, apparently after verifying that it was safe, he eased back into the alcove.

Jonathan Stuart Devereux stepped into the living room.

"You all right?" he asked in his cheery prime minister accent.

Braxton nodded in return.

Devereux sighed. "Your look, I can see your look. Your face. Don't faces tell us everything? We don't need words. Words lie, people lie. Faces don't. It's not here, is it?"

"We're on course. We're moving in." Braxton added, "We found the courier bag Gahl stole."

"All those many years ago."

"It had that tape recorder inside." She nodded toward the unit.

"But I'm not so very interested in a tape recorder, am I?"

Devereux examined the courier bag, peering inside, pulling it open wide. He paced through the house, gazing around him. Not looking for the Sanction, it seemed, just assessing what kind of lair his enemies had. In the kitchen he opened the refrigerator, plucked out a bottle of water and drank down half of it. He strolled back to the living room, picked up some of the items that the ops had searched. He studied magazines that had been here since Ashton's time. "My. Look, a cover story about that young, fresh unknown Taylor Swift." He dropped it. "And Prince Charles." Then he said, a hint of mocking in his voice, "But you're on course, you're moving in."

Braxton cast a taut glance to Droon.

A red-haired woman, twenty years younger and six inches taller than Devereux, stepped into the front hallway. Was it the same one as in the Rolls earlier? Her skirt and shoes were different. She was in a clinging white dress, hem high, top low. It clearly wasn't his fifty-six-year-old wife.

Braxton's glance toward her gave away nothing, but she couldn't be happy that he'd brought the woman to a professional endeavor. Devereux looked back at her with a grimace and he shooed her off with a wave of his hardworking fingers. She vanished.

The CEO of Banyan Tree walked in a slow circle. At a shelf he picked up some figures and examined them one by one. "This is cute, isn't it? A cat. Is it a cat? Bit dodgy. Maybe a dog with unfortunate ears. Yes, I think that's it."

He set it down and his hands went back to being energetic.

The grenade shooter continued his search, looking up under the furniture, until Braxton waved at him to stop.

"Was there anything else in the bag?"

"It was empty when we got inside."

"And they were here when you came knock, knock, knocking on the door?"

"We saw them, yes."

"And the sentence that would accompany that one is: But we don't know how they got out."

"That's right."

"With my prize, my prize . . . What's on the recorder? My, it's quite the old one, isn't it? Don't see those outside of movies."

"Just music."

"Was Gahl a music lover?"

"Apparently so," Braxton said.

"And you've explored every place that he had a connection with, *everywhere* he could have hidden it?"

"Yes."

His expression perplexed, Devereux said in a snide voice, "Oh, but wait. Wait. That can't be right."

She looked at him, lips tight.

"It appears you *didn't* explore one place. The one where Mr. Colter *Shaw* found it and you did not." He looked at the woman, eye to eye. They were the same height. "Do you suppose he gamed you, Irena? That map you stole? Do you think it was fake?"

Her face went still. She didn't answer.

"What is our only priority? Mine and yours and Ian's?"

"The Endgame Sanction."

"Ex-actly," purred the man.

"We'll find it, Mr. Devereux."

He could see it pained her to use his last name. He'd probably done some whip-cracking about protocols when he signed on as a client of BlackBridge. He'd want to be worshipped. He was the heir to sloppily beheaded royalty. His company was in better economic shape than Spain. And as his minions had not delivered the precious Sanction, he could snap a vicious whip whenever he wanted.

She offered, "It's a minor setback. Shaw did most of the work for us. He found the courier bag. Now we just have to get the Sanction from him."

A hurry-up gesture of Devereux's hands. "But he got away from you here."

"He did. But I'm sure he doesn't even know what it is. He'd never recognize it."

Shaw shook his head. He'd hoped they would say something more about it, so they could identify it in the contents of the courier bag—or know for certain that it wasn't there and begin a new search.

Devereux glanced back toward the street, where the woman in the white dress would be waiting for him. Then his eyes took in the blond BlackBridge op, looking her up and down. The gaze was the same as that in the faces of Shaw's nieces when they were about to devour ice cream sundaes.

"Who's the other one? The one with the beard?"

"We don't know. Maybe the son of another one of Ashton's colleagues."

Devereux examined another ceramic figurine. "How do you propose to find him?"

"Oh. He'll come to us."

His flitty British accent seemed more exaggerated than earlier as he asked, "And that will happen how?"

The woman pulled a piece of lint off her sweater and let it spiral to the floor. She didn't answer Devereux but said to Droon, "Get some people to Bethesda. And find somebody in Fresno. Somebody good."

"I'll do it now."

His heart pounding, Shaw looked at Russell, whose face had gone cold.

Their sister, Dorion, lived in Bethesda, Maryland.

And Fresno was the closest large city to the Compound, where their mother, Mary Dove Shaw, was at that very moment.

43

ello?" the woman on the other end of the phone line asked. Her voice was melodious.

Colter Shaw said, "The roses arrived. They look good."

There was silence, as he knew there would be. Dorion Shaw was processing the words.

"Anything I should know about them?"

"No details at this time."

"Thanks. Good talking to you." Dorion hung up.

Those words put in motion Escape Plan B. This involved the recipient's dropping everything and leaving the premises instantly—along with other family members. In Dorion's case that would include her husband and the ice-cream-loving daughters.

Before Dorion married, she'd told her fiancé about certain irregularities of her life growing up, and that there might be the occasional threat, some worse than others. Plan B meant that they were in imminent danger. It was one of Ashton Shaw's two most serious alerts, and one that nobody in the family ever questioned.

The sturdy woman in her late twenties would by now already be marshalling children and spouse and grabbing GTFO bags from the cellar and heading, via a circuitous route and a cutout car or two to a "vacation house," which is what the girls would think of it as. They were out of school and they might feel some pique that they had to miss photo camp or soccer practice. But they too would have received some lessons in what life might be like if you were a Shaw.

His next call was to his mother. His message to Mary Dove was different. He said, "Dinner will be late tonight."

"I'm sorry to hear that."

"But the guests'll be arriving soon."

"I'll look forward to seeing them."

Both hung up simultaneously.

This message invoked Plan A. It did not signal escape, but defense. Dorion lived in a vulnerable suburban setting, while Mary Dove was on the Compound, a place she would never be forced from—especially in the case of invaders responsible for her husband's death. The whole point of Ashton's survivalism was to prepare for threats like this. His mother was the best shot in the family, and she had a go bag ready in case she needed a temporary retreat into the wilderness—and pity any BlackBridge op who followed her there.

But against this crew it would be wise for her to have allies. Hence, the soon-to-arrive "guests." Of course, she had one ally in Victoria Lesston, the decorated former Delta Force officer who could bring down a game bird with a single shot from a handgun. But Shaw wanted more, so he called Tom Pepper and told the former FBI agent specifically what the concern was. He said he'd have two armed former special services ops at the Compound in a half hour.

"Would Mary Dove mind a helicopter landing in her backyard?" Pepper asked.

Shaw considered this. "Just tell them not to use the garden as a landing zone if they can avoid it. She just planted the root vegetables and she's especially partial to them."

44

The Embarcadero.

This was the name of both a lengthy road that runs along the northeast waterfront of San Francisco and the district for which that highway is a spine.

The two-mile-long strip was for years associated with transportation: the roadway itself, of course; a Belt Railroad, lugging products and produce north and south; an impressive pedestrian footbridge; and a second subterranean road.

It was, however, vessels that defined the Embarcadero. Liners, cargo, ferries. The ships operating out of Piers 1, 1½, 3 and 5, in the central Embarcadero, would transport thousands of passengers and untold tons of freight daily to ports foreign and domestic, including the picturesque waterway up to Sacramento. During the Second World War, the Bayfront became a de facto naval base.

Then came the Bay Bridge, connecting San Francisco to Oakland.

And almost immediately the Embarcadero began to die. Not

helping the vitality of the neighborhood was the transition from the old-style break-bulk vessels to enormous container ships, which needed massive piers and cranes and warehouses for which only Oakland had the space—and aesthetic tolerance.

The dilapidation of the Embarcadero lasted only so long, however. Given that much of the neighborhood was flanked by upscale Telegraph Hill to the north and the spreading financial district to the west, it was only a matter of time until the neighborhood began to recuperate. It was now largely gentrified and farmers-marketed, though its original blunt scruffiness could still be found in the southern regions.

It was in one of these neighborhoods that Russell parked his SUV, near Rincon Park, in which Shaw could see the Cupid's Span sculpture, a huge bow facing downward with an arrow buried in the ground. Supposedly this was a nod toward San Francisco's reputation as the City of Eros, or something like that. Shaw wasn't sure he got it, and the sculpture now brought to mind not art but Earnest La Fleur's sharp-tipped greeting in Sausalito.

The brothers climbed from the vehicle and walked half a block to an ancient three-story red-brick building. Above the arched doorway was etched in sandstone: HAYWOOD BROTHERS WAREHOUSING & STORAGE.

"Optimistic," Shaw said.

Russell looked at him with a frown of curiosity. Shaw nodded at the lintel over the door.

"Warehousing and storage. Their business plan was set in stone. Literally. Never thought they might have to diversify."

"Hmm."

Russell was simply not going to fall victim to humor.

They walked into the scuffed lobby with checkerboard tile for flooring. The walls were yellow stucco and the crown molding featured grizzly bears, the state animal of California.

Which, of course, put Shaw in mind of the statuette his father had given his brother, following the incident on the avalanche field so many years ago.

The Reclusive One . . .

A double door at the back of the lobby was chained and padlocked. To the right was a glass door on which a stenciled sign read: MANAGER.

Inside, a round man in a white short-sleeved shirt sat hunched over a computer. Shaw noted that when he and Russell entered, the man's right hand had strayed toward a drawer before assessing there wasn't much threat these two presented. The Embarcadero was not completely tamed.

"Help you?"

They had a cover story, which was similar to the fiction they'd spun upon first meeting Eleanor Nadler, Amos Gahl's mother. They were brothers researching their late aunt's life—she was a well-known professor at Cal—for a self-published book. It would be a Christmas present for their mother—the woman's sister.

"Mom'll love it," Shaw said.

The manager said, "Women do seem to like that family stuff, don't they? More'n us guys, I'd say."

Russell said with a faint, utterly uncharacteristic laugh. "You got that right." He really was quite the actor.

"We found a reference to the warehouse here in one of her diaries," Shaw told him. "We're curious what the connection was. Has this always been a working warehouse?"

"Not a working anything now. We're closed up." He nodded at the computer. "I'm making appointments for prospective buyers. The partnership owns it is putting it up on the block. This neighborhood is changing, you can see. Going to be condos and retail, probably."

The air was close, the temperature hot in the office—a renegade boiler, it seemed—and the man mopped his brow with a Kleenex, which he'd taken from his pocket, unfolded, used and then replaced.

"Only thing is, unless your aunt was connected with the government somehow, I doubt she would've had much to do with the place."

Shaw said, "Yessir, she did some government work."

"On occasion," Russell said, looking toward the door that seemed to lead to the warehouse proper. "What was stored here?"

The manager continued, "You know the earthquake, nineteen oh-six?"

The brothers nodded. The estimated 7.8- or 7.9-level event had destroyed about eighty percent of the city, killing three thousand.

"The quake was bad enough but it was the fires that did the most damage. Stop me if I'm telling you something you already know."

"Please." Shaw gestured with his hand for the man to continue. He seemed happy for the visitors. Shaw noted it was not an appointment calendar but a game of solitaire that was on his computer.

"The fire chief was killed in the initial quake and no one knew back then how to fight blazes that big, you know, ruptured gas lines and all. They dynamited buildings to make firebreaks but didn't do it right. That just started more fires. Worst part was that insurance companies wouldn't write earthquake policies but they would for fire damage. So people started setting fire to their own houses for the coverage—and most of them were wood. You can imagine.

"Anyway, there was fire in the Embarcadero, a lot of buildings went, but not these blocks, so the government workers loaded up all the official documents and records and drove them down here for safekeeping. Drove hell for leather, with the blaze right on their heels. The city and state removed a lot of the crap over the next decade. Went to the new city hall and the state and federal buildings. But they still left the warehouse half full. Millions of documents."

Shaw regarded Russell. "So, that's what she was doing, I'll bet. Researching something in the archives."

Shaw assessed that their acting was acceptable. Not Broadway, but superior community theater. To the manager: "She was a history prof."

"Was she now?"

"Can we show you a picture of her?" Russell asked.

He frowned. "Would this've been in the last two years? That's as long as I've been here."

"Lot longer than that."

"Well, I took over from a guy'd been at this desk for twenty years. Jimmy Spilt. I know, the name's a burden."

"You in touch with him?" Shaw asked.

"On and off."

"What's your name?"

"Barney Mellon."

Russell shook his hand. "I'm Peter and this's Joe."

Shaw gripped Barney's palm too.

"Say, Barney, any chance we could send Mr. Spilt a picture? See if he recognizes her?"

Russell added, "Tall order, but we'd appreciate it."

"You boys sure must love your mom."

"That's the truth," Shaw said.

Russell asked for Barney's phone number and sent the picture, which was of Irena Braxton.

Colter Shaw didn't have enough information to assess the odds of success. The best he could come up with was: Long shot, but let's hope.

Barney sent the photo off to the oddly surnamed former manager and it was no more than thirty seconds later that his mobile hummed. He regarded the screen and answered. "Heya, Jimmy, how's it hanging? . . . You still getting out to the mountains? Uh-huh . . . Heard it was bad, lost twenty thousand acres . . . Now, about that picture . . . These two fellows are here, doing something up nice for their mother." He listened for some moments, nodding broadly. "Sure, I'll let 'em know. So, what're you doing on Wednesday? . . . Good, good . . ." A fierce grin was on his face. He sat back, made the used Kleenex reappear and mopped his brow.

Russell and Shaw shared a glance. Russell's eyes dipped to the drawer, then the phone in the man's hand. Shaw gave a slight nod.

Russell stepped forward fast and clamped a hand on the drawer, an instant before the manager got to it. Simultaneously Shaw plucked the phone from his hand and disconnected.

Barney's chair rolled four feet and hit the wall. "Please, don't hurt me!"

Russell opened the drawer and removed the little .25 semiauto, ejected the round in the chamber and pushed out the bullets from the mag one by one. He pocketed them.

"What'd he tell you?" Russell asked bluntly.

When Barney didn't answer, Russell drew his own weapon.

Barney eyed the SIG and, vacillating between fear and rage, said breathlessly, "You didn't goddamn tell me your aunt was a psychopath. Now, what the hell do you really want?"

45

So," Shaw said, "Spilt recognized the picture."

"Of course he did. Wouldn't *you* remember somebody who handcuffs you, drags you through the archives and threatens to shoot you if you don't cooperate?"

"What was she looking for?" Russell said.

"I don't know. How would I know?"

Shaw said, "Call him back."

"What?"

"Call Spilt back." Shaw nodded impatiently, and Barney did as told.

Shaw took the phone from him.

"Barney," came the urgent voice on the other end. "Are you okay? What's going on?"

"Jimmy," Shaw snapped. "Listen to me. Barney's okay. So far."

"Oh, Jesus," the manager gasped.

Russell touched his own ear, and Shaw too heard the siren in the distance.

Goddamn it.

"Jimmy, I need you to do two things."

"The fuck're you? You the nephew of that bitch who—"

Shaw put the phone on speaker and glanced at the manager. "Two things, Jimmy, if you want your friend to be okay."

Barney called, "Please, Jimmy. Do whatever he asks."

"Okay, okay," came the voice.

"First, we're going to hang up and you call nine-one-one back and tell them it was a mistake. Somebody was playing a joke on you. Or something. Be credible. Then call me back."

Russell was on his phone. He lifted it toward Shaw.

"And, Jimmy," Shaw said, "we've got a scanner here, police scanner. We'll know if you don't do it. And that means you can say goodbye to Barney, and we'll come visit you too."

"Jesus, no, no, no! I'll do it. I'll do it!"

"Call. The. Police." Shaw disconnected.

What Russell was displaying probably wasn't a scanner app. More likely, Shaw guessed, he'd be speaking with Karin, but *she* would be patched into the city's emergency frequencies.

Fifteen, twenty seconds later the sirens stopped and Russell, listening into his mobile, nodded.

Just after that, Barney's phone hummed.

Shaw glanced at it and answered, punching the speaker button once more. "Okay, Jimmy, good job. The second thing you need to do. Answer some questions. Then we'll leave you and your buddy alone. Are we happy with that?"

"Yes, yes, anything."

"Tell us exactly what happened that day our aunt came to the warehouse."

"The hell *are* you?"

Barney cried, "Jesus, Jimmy! Answer the man's question. He's got a gun. Are you fucking crazy?"

"All right, all right. It was some weekday morning, I was the only one working. You know for the past fifty years the place's just been a repository. Nobody brings stuff in or takes it out. Your aunt comes in and asks for some records. I tell her it's not like a library. Only polite. I was real polite to her. Before I can release anything, I need a form filled out at city hall. She says she doesn't have time. And she's with this guy who's acting weird, twitchy, you know. They both scared me."

"Did he look like a rat?" Shaw asked.

"Yeah, kinda."

Russell: "What did she want?"

"Judicial records, she said. Judges' files. I tell her again I can't do anything without the form from city hall or the state, filled out proper. I tell her to leave and that's when she pulls a gun. The guy with her puts handcuffs on me.

"I tell them I don't know where judicial files'd be. She asks me how they're organized and I tell her by year. She says that's good enough. So, we go in the back and, and I point them to the year she wants, nineteen oh-six. And they both start going through everything, throwing stuff all over the floor. This goes on for an hour, maybe less but it *seemed* like an hour. Then she finds something and is like, 'Goddamn. At last,' or something.

"They look at me like they're deciding to kill me, not to kill me . . . Jesus. I'm begging them. She says, 'We were never here.' I just nod. I can't even speak. Then they leave."

"What was it she found?" Shaw took over the questioning.

"I have no idea. I didn't ask. They were ready to shoot me!"

"Was it a single sheet of paper or a bound document?"

"One page."

"Judicial records. So, a court decision?"

"No, we don't have those. They're published anyway. They could've found those in a law library or online. She wanted correspondence, notes, anything in judges' individual files."

"You call the police?" Russell asked.

"Of course not. They knew where I worked. They might come back."

Shaw said, "Listen, Jimmy. Just forget we talked to you."

"You fucking bet I'll forget."

Shaw disconnected and set Barney's phone on the desk.

Russell held up the peashooter of a gun. He hit a button and pulled the slide off. "This'll be in one trashcan outside, the magazine in another."

Shaw was amused. Maybe this was playbook procedure in some circles. Ebbitt Droon had done the same thing with Shaw's weapons in Silicon Valley not three weeks ago.

As the brothers walked to the door Shaw looked back.

Barney held up his hands, as if he were a surrendering soldier. "I get it. I get it. Just like your aunt—you were never here."

46

The new safe house wasn't bad; it certainly was in a better neighborhood than the one in the Mission.

Located in picturesque Pacific Heights, in the northern part of the city, the two-bedroom suite was in a sandstone apartment building whose front windows offered views of the Bay, Alcatraz, the Golden Gate Bridge and Sausalito, where some of the faint, distant greenery might have been Earnest La Fleur's yard.

The building was three stories high and represented classic 1960s architectural style, no frills, functional, uninspired.

The suite featured three escape routes—front stairs, back stairs and windows overlooking the roof of the one-story bicycle shop next door. Neither Shaw nor his brother had studied parkour—the leaping, sprinting and diving art of urban gymnastics—but they practiced tumbling and how to land safely when jumping from heights. Shaw was inspecting this particular exit now: out the open window he could look down and see tarred roof about eight feet below.

The safe house complied with Ashton's rule: *Never be without an escape plan.* (The accompanying dictum, *Never be without access to a weapon*, was taken care of, given the firepower the brothers carried.)

"Here," Shaw said, handing his brother a box of nine-millimeter ammunition.

Russell glanced down.

They were safety slugs, specially made to penetrate flesh but not exit and continue their path, injuring bystanders. The bullets would go through a piece of Sheetrock, if you missed your human target, but they lost deadly muzzle velocity soon after. In a setting like this new structure, where innocents might be just feet away behind walls and doors, they were a necessity.

Russell, though, looked at the ammo with a frown. Maybe he was thinking he was a good enough shot that he wouldn't miss and endanger anyone else. Maybe he found it helpful to shoot through walls and doors sometimes, in spite of Ashton's proscription:

Never fire a weapon when you don't have clear sight of your target . . .

"We have to," Shaw said.

"Not a firing solution I'm comfortable with. That's not standard procedure."

And his brother did not reload.

"Up to you." Shaw himself ejected the rounds and replaced them with the blue-tipped bullets. He was thinking: The brothers had worked well together on the investigation so far—especially their choreographed performances at the warehouse. Now tension seemed to have returned.

You don't want to be doing this, do you?

Just, we should get it done . . .

Shaw wondered if the resentment about Shaw's tacit accusation regarding Russell's role in Ashton's death was surfacing.

And, if so, where would it lead?

Shaw opened his backpack and emptied the BlackBridge courier bag's contents onto the table. Once again he and Russell divided it up and flipped through the documents, now knowing that the End-game Sanction was judicial in nature and from 1906.

"Got it," Shaw said. "I saw it before but didn't think anything of it."

He set the aging sheet of paper on the table.

So here it was: the Endgame Sanction.

> In the matter of the Voting Tally in the Twelfth Con-gressional District, regarding Proposition 06, being a referendum put before the People of the State, I, the Right Honorable Selmer P. Clarke, Superior Court, do find as a matter of fact the following:
>
> The initial ballot results as reported were in error. The correct vote tally was 1,244 in favor of the Propo-sition, 1,043 against.
>
> Accordingly, I order that the Vote Tally as amended to reflect the yea and nay ballots set forth herein, be entered into the record in the State Assembly and Sen-ate, effective as of this date, April 17, 1906.

An elaborate signature was beneath the text.

Russell picked up the sheet and turned it over. The back was empty. He then held it up to the light to look for hidden, or ob-scured, messages.

"Nothing." Russell rubbed the back. "It's an original, not a copy." A typewriter had been used to produce the document and you could just feel indentations from the keys.

Shaw read it once more. "I don't see how 'sanction' fits."

"La Fleur said it might be just a code. Maybe Helms and De-vereux didn't want anyone to use the words 'tally' or 'ruling' in public. They wanted to keep this secret."

Shaw shook his head. "Devereux is desperate to find it." He

recalled that La Fleur said if the Sanction were found the consequences would be disastrous.

Russell asked, "What's Proposition Oh-Six?"

Shaw booted up his computer and logged on through an encrypted server. He Googled the question. There was nothing in Wikipedia but he found a reference in an archive of California State constitutional and legislative measures. "It was a referendum in nineteen oh-six to amend the state constitution." He turned the Dell so both he and Russell could read. They scrolled through paragraph after paragraph of legalese, having to do with taxation, immigration and trade mostly.

Why was Gahl as desperate to destroy this document as Devereux was to get his hands on it?

Then an idea occurred to Shaw. He pulled out his Android and placed a call to her equally shielded burner phone.

Mary Dove answered on the second ring.

"How is it there?"

"We're good. Tom Pepper's men are here. They've set up a perimeter. Electronic warning. And, Colt, they have a machine gun. I mean, a big one, on a bipod. Can you imagine?"

"Good. I don't think it'll come to that."

"Hope not. We don't want to disturb the bears. We're right in the heart of mating season. Are you all right?"

"We're both good, Russell and I."

"Russell?"

"He came back to help me on Ashton's job."

"Well."

"I just have a minute. But I've got a question. And you're the only one who can answer it."

47

After a complicated drive, to make sure no one was following—and a scan for drones in the area by the resourceful Karin—they arrived in Berkeley, across the Bay, north of Oakland.

They were on their way to meet one of Ashton Shaw's academic colleagues, who lived near campus: Steven Field. He was a semi-retired professor of political history. When Shaw had called his mother a half hour ago, he'd asked if she knew of any of Ashton's associates who had this specialty. Mary Dove immediately mentioned Field.

Shaw had a vague recollection of seeing the man several times years back. Field had come to visit at the Compound. Those were the days when Ashton was at his peak. Oh, Shaw could remember a few bouts of bizarre behavior but Mary Dove would put on her psychiatrist's hat and make sure he got the right meds and monitored his behavior and he'd soon return to his animated, witty self.

One of the hardest parts of the move from the Bay Area to the Compound was the severing of social contacts. This was true for Colter and, particularly, his older brother; Dorion was just a toddler. Looking back, Shaw was sure it had been tough on Ashton and his wife too. They had both been professors and she had had the additional job of university principal investigator. Those vocations were callings that came with daily contact with colleagues, administrators, corporate executives and students. All of that vanished abruptly when he took the family to the Sierra Nevadas.

He would, however, encourage a few, select colleagues from the Bay Area to come for visits. Young Colter could recall men and women sitting in the living room in front of the huge fireplace, talking far into the night. Like all children, he paid little attention to the words but from time to time he would note the adults' animation, and feel, rather than hear, the laughter. As a child he didn't grasp all the nuances, but he enjoyed the animated talk about political science, law, government, American history and—Ashton's odd hobby—advanced physics.

Though invariably as the night grew later, the restless boy would become bored and head outside to listen to owls and wolves and gaze at the radiant canopy of stars.

Sometimes he'd take short nighttime hikes.

Often, with Russell.

His brother now asked, "You think Field was part of Ash's circle—to take on BlackBridge?"

Shaw had wondered that himself. Then, considering the matter, he said, "Doubt it. Those people're all gone now. I'd say they were just friends, fellow professors."

Earlier, Shaw had called Field and arranged to meet him in the privacy of his home.

But with a stipulation.

"We'd like to come in through your back door, off the alley."

The man's cheerful voice had said, "You must be a Shaw. You sound just like your father. He was always going on: They're watching me." Then he paused and laughed. "I was going to give you my address but if you know there's an alley—I won't even ask how you found that out—I guess you don't need it."

Shaw was aware of an urgency—the attack on the SP family was now a little more than twenty-four hours away. But they had to be careful and were taking a long route to Field's house, looking out for any sign of Droon or Braxton, as well as the mysterious green Honda.

They registered no threats, and Russell turned onto the street that would take them to the professor's home.

He found they had to divert, though. A protest was underway and the street was blocked.

Ashton had read his children plenty of fiction as bedtime approached in the Compound, but he also read them the news and history too—among those the rich history of demonstrations at the university and in the town itself. Civil rights, the Vietnam War and free speech were the main topics in the mid-sixties protests. Recently there'd been a series of violent clashes, mostly political and often involving free speech.

Shaw caught a glimpse of one of the signs.

CORPORATE SELLOUTS—NO!

That seemed to be the theme of the past few days.

Russell parked the SUV on the street two blocks from Field's house, standard procedure within his group, Shaw guessed. The huge vehicle was a sore thumb at the curb. Most of the modes of transportation here were hybrids, electric or human powered. Shaw even noted a few of the now-discontinued Smart cars.

Berkeley. Say no more.

The men proceeded into the alley. They continued along the pebbly lane for about fifty yards and then slipped through the gate in the picket fence into Field's backyard, where they followed a gently curving, moss-dotted flagstone path to the back door. The house might have been transplanted from a small English Midlands village. Clapboard siding in brown, forest-green windows, trim and doors. The garden was more lush and meticulously tended than the garden of Eleanor Nadler—Amos Gahl's mother.

Goateed Steven Field invited them into the kitchen, fragrant with the scents of baking. He was thin, balding and of grayish pallor—though he didn't seem unhealthy. He probably didn't get outside very much. He certainly had plenty to occupy him here. There must have been five thousand books neatly arranged on shelves in all the visible rooms—which didn't include the bedrooms. Even the kitchen was filled with reading matter.

Field wore pressed gray wool slacks, a white shirt and tie and a gray cardigan sweater. Shaw had a sense that he dressed this way every day, whether he was teaching or staying home.

He was sorry they couldn't meet his wife. She was teaching a class.

"Gertie's a professor at Cal too." His eyes crinkled. "Last year, I got married. A younger woman . . . One month younger!" He chuckled.

The three men sat in overstuffed chairs in the library, Field, against a dark wood-paneled wall, on which were mounted delft blue plates, pastoral scenes of Dutch farmhouses, windmills and level countryside.

Shaw and Russell opted out of any offered refreshments. Field was drinking tea from a cup that still had the bags—two of them—inside. The aroma was of herbs.

He looked them over. Now came the resemblance comment, how each brother bore some characteristics of his father, and how they differed. "I was so sorry to hear about Ash. An accident of some kind?"

"That's right." There was no time for details. To explain what had happened at Echo Ridge could take hours, and the clock was ticking down on SP and their family.

"Unfortunate. And Mary Dove, and Dorion?"

"They're doing well."

As well as can be expected while hunkering down in survival mode.

"Dorion's married and has two girls."

"Ah, wonderful." He looked them over carefully. "Now what can I do you gentlemen for?"

Shaw explained that they'd found a document, an old one. "A lot of people want to get their hands on it. I remember you and Ashton would spend hours talking political science and law and government. We thought maybe you could help us figure out what it is, why it's so important."

"Ash didn't teach poli sci, I believe, but it was one of his passions. And with your father, that's passion with an uppercase 'P.'"

Shaw took the ruling from his backpack and handed it to the professor.

Before he read, Field turned it over in his hand, held it up to the light. "Original."

"That's right. Nineteen oh-six."

"Typewritten. Most official documents were, back then. People think typewriters're a modern invention." Field produced glasses and pulled it closer, pushing aside the teacup so there'd be no accidents. He began to read, speaking absently. "Did you know the first electric typewriter was invented by Edison in the eighteen seventies? It became the ticker tape for the stock market and—"

He stopped speaking abruptly and his eyes grew wide as he stared at the words.

"Professor Field?" Shaw asked.

The man didn't seem to hear. He leapt to his feet and pulled down an old leather-bound book from the shelf. He cracked it open and read, his face a knot of concentration. He closed this volume and found another. He flipped pages again and, still standing, traced a passage with his finger.

Then he uttered a gasp of shock and whispered, "Holy Jesus."

Field ushered the brothers into the kitchen. "Bigger table. We need a bigger table."

The professor cleared the round piece of furniture of flowers and cookbooks. Then he set about gathering books from the library and stacking them here.

"Can we help?" Shaw asked.

Field didn't answer. He was lost in thought—and clearly dismayed.

Russell ran the back of his hand over the beard and he and his brother eyed the titles of the books the professor had plucked from shelves, all of which seemed to have to do with California history.

The last batch involved law books, California reporters and treatises. A U.S. *Supreme Court Reporter* too.

The professor didn't say a word. He kept skimming passages, marking some with a Post-it note and, in other instances, apparently synopsizing them on a yellow pad. Finally he sat back and muttered to himself. "It's true. It can't be but it is . . ."

"Professor?" Shaw was getting impatient. It was clear that Russell was too.

Staring at the tally certificate as if it were a land mine, Field said, "California's always had direct democracy—where citizens themselves approve or reject a certain law, including constitutional amendments. The governor and legislature approve a measure and then it goes to the people directly for a vote. If the majority approves, it changes the constitution. No further action's required.

"Enter Roland C. T. Briggs. Nineteen oh-six." Field tapped a thin, leather-bound volume with the man's name embossed in gold on the cover and spine. "He commissioned this biography himself. It wasn't exactly a bestseller. The subject was, let's say, unappealing. He should have had a co-author byline: written with his ego. Briggs was a real estate and railroad baron. Typical of the time: stole Native American land, worked his employees to death, drove competitors out of business illegally, monopolized industries. And I won't even get into his personal peccadillos."

Shaw thought immediately of Devereux.

"His team of lawyers drafted Proposition Oh-Six. It was full of obscure changes to trade and taxation. Briggs and his operatives managed to coerce and cajole—and bribe—the state assembly and the governor into approving the referendum vote. And it went on the ballot.

"His bludgeoning didn't stop there. He and his political machine pressured the people to vote for the referendum and it nearly made it. But it failed by a hairsbreadth. Everyone thought that was the end of the matter. But—according to this—no. It actually passed." He nodded at the tally.

"I guess someone noticed irregularities in voting in the Twelfth Congressional District. That's San Francisco. Maybe new ballots were discovered or there was evidence some were forged or duplicates. Anyway, a complaint must have been lodged and a state court judge reviewed the ballots and certified the new count—which was enough for the measure to pass and amend the constitution. Except that never happened."

"Why?"

"Because of the earthquake. Look at the date on the certified vote tally. April seventeenth. The earthquake was at five in the morning the next day. A number of government buildings and records were destroyed, and dozens of officials were killed. The judge, this Selmer Clarke, was one of the fatalities. In the chaos and destruction after the earthquake, the recount was forgotten—and no one knew the proposition had in fact passed. Briggs probably wanted to put the matter on the ballot again but he died not long after—of syphilis, it seems—and the whole question of the amendment went away."

Shaw asked, "What's the 'Holy Jesus' factor?"

"Proposition Oh-Six was dozens of pages long, but Briggs didn't care about ninety-nine percent of the measure. That was all smoke screen—so no one would focus on the only provision he cared about. Paragraph Fifteen."

Field opened a book and thumbed through musty pages. "Here." He pushed the volume toward the brothers.

Proposition 06

Paragraph 15. That section of the Constitution of the State of California which sets forth the requirements to hold office in the State shall be amended by the following:

To hold any public office in this State, all persons:

1. *must have been a resident of California for the five years preceding their election or appointment,*

2. *must have attained the age of 21 years, and*

3. *must have been a citizen of these United States for 10 years, if a natural person.*

242 : JEFFERY DEAVER

Shaw and Russell read the passage then both looked toward the professor questioningly.

"Let me explain. Like all business tycoons of the day Briggs hated Marxism, and the growing communist movement, which said basically all the woes of the earth come from the elite owning the means of production and oppressing the working class. Lenin wouldn't start the revolution in Russia for another ten years but there was plenty of evidence that communism as a form of government was coming.

"Briggs—and more than a few of his 'comrades,' if I may use the word—wanted to start an opposing movement. He wanted *capitalism* intertwined with government. And so—this."

Another tap of the book containing the language of Proposition 06.

Field said, in a whisper, "Does anything strike you as odd about those words? Anything bizarre? Anything revolutionary?"

Russell looked his way impatiently.

"Maybe in the *third* qualification," Field prompted.

Shaw suddenly understood. "Can't be," he whispered.

Field replied, "Oh, yes. This amendment gives a corporation the right to run for and hold office in California."

49

mpossible," Russell said.

The professor said, "Not impossible at all. It's one of the smartest political coups of all time. Most subversive too."

His finger traced the tally, then perhaps realizing it was an original, historic document he quickly removed his hand.

Russell said, "It doesn't say anything about corporations."

It was Shaw's legal experience that had given him a rough understanding of the implication. "Yes, it actually does."

Field nodded. "You're right, Colter. Let me explain." Field's eyes shone, both troubled and exhibiting a hint of admiration, as he stared at the paragraph. "Read it again."

The brothers both did.

"One, to hold office a person must have been a California resident for five years. The law is well settled that corporations can be residents of states. For tax purposes, they *must* be. Two, the person must have attained the age of twenty-one. It's an easy argument to make that a corporation begins to age from the date of incorporation.

"Ah, but the third line . . ." Field said this as if the words he was referring to were a magical incantation. "The third line is the key. To hold office a person must have been a U.S. citizen for ten years, but *only* if you're a *natural* person, not a *corporate* one. Corporations are excluded from that requirement. So to hold office in California, a company need only be a resident of the state for five years and incorporated at least twenty-one years ago."

His eyes on the judge's order, Russell said, "But this thing is over a hundred years old. It can't become law."

Field said, "It *is* the law. Now."

Shaw frowned. This was beyond his legal ken.

"In nineteen oh-six, the minute it passed, the constitution was amended. The governor, the state assembly—they don't need to approve anything. This has been the law for a hundred and ten years. It's just that nobody knows it."

Russell's face was still, as he stared out the window.

"And there's more." The man's visage revealed how unnerved he was.

"Go on," Shaw encouraged.

"Now, *any* U.S. citizen can run for office in California, unless you're a convicted felon or disqualified by term limits. The law doesn't require you to have been a citizen for a certain amount of time." A tap near the voting tally. "This, though, requires you to be a citizen for ten years."

Shaw said, "Which has the effect of ousting, what? Hundreds of people holding office now?"

Field nodded. "There'll have to be special elections or appointments for all the seats."

Shaw looked at Russell, who apparently had Shaw's very thought in mind.

To Field, Shaw said, "There's a man who's been looking for this: Jonathan Stuart Devereux."

Field's face filled with understanding. "Devereux, of course—

mastermind of multinational conglomerates and corporate acquisitions. What's his company again? I can't recall."

"Banyan Tree."

"That's right, sure. So he's the Roland C. T. Briggs of today. Of course he'd want the tally. Devereux can enter his company in any elections in the state . . . And he can bring all the company's resources to the campaign. You can spend as much money as you want on your own election. Campaign finance limits are on third-party donations. How can anyone win against an opponent who can spend a billion dollars?"

The professor was shaking his head. "And the language of Prop Oh-Six says 'hold' office, not just run in an election. The corporation could be appointed as head of the state environmental board, taxing authorities, immigration board, planning and zoning, financial regulation, sheriff, judges. My God. He could spin off subsidiaries and each one could run for office. Devereux could eventually control the legislature, judgeships, the state supreme court. And even if his companies didn't run for office, he could threaten other candidates, get them to agree to positions he wants in exchange for not crushing them at the polls."

Russell said, "Afraid there's something else."

Field sighed and seemed to prepare himself.

Shaw delivered the news: "Over the last few years, Devereux has been on a buying spree. He's acquired nearly one hundred and fifty subsidiaries in California. I'm sure they were incorporated more than twenty-one years ago—to meet the 'age' requirement."

"My God. He knows that those assemblymen and senators will be out of office. His companies'll run for the seat and bring all of Banyan Tree's money to the game. And of course, because of the new citizenship requirement, the politicians who'll be ousted are minorities. Asian and Latinx. People who fought for equal rights in the state. With them gone and Devereux calling the shots . . . I can't imagine what'll happen. It's like going back to the days before the Civil Rights Act."

It now occurred to Colter Shaw that the phrase *Endgame Sanction* was not a randomly picked code name at all. The first word could describe Devereux's companies coming into political power. And *sanction* ironically could be read in both senses. Banyan Tree would have permission to do what it wanted . . . and the power to punish.

"But how would it work? Who would actually sit in the assembly?"

Field said, "There are some practical issues, yes. But that could be worked out. The CEO or shareholders could appoint a representative."

Shaw said, "There'll be a court challenge."

Russell sat back in the chair. "Has to be struck down."

Field was looking out the window at some striking red flower. The Bay Area was a perpetual greenhouse. "I wish that were the case. But I wouldn't be too sure. At one point in our history, that would have been true. The founding fathers were smart enough to draw a distinction between corporations that ran cities and performed civic duties, on the one hand, and, on the other, those that were purely for profit, which they knew could be predatory. They looked at the British East India Company and called it '*imperium in imperio*,' an empire within an empire. They distrusted that.

"But eventually corporations began to grow in power and the owners and their lawyers found it helpful to, quote, 'impersonate' humans—so they could bring lawsuits in their own names. Eventually the federal government and all of the states enacted legislation that defined 'person' as including corporations for all legal purposes.

"And the expansion continues: A few years ago, we had the 'Citizens United' case. The Supreme Court ruled that corporations had a First Amendment right, just like humans, to make campaign contributions.

"Some think the decision might open the door for corporations to do more than just exercise freedom of speech." Field browsed his shelves and lifted a *Supreme Court Reporter,* a large hardcover bound in yellow, and thumbed through the densely packed pages. "I'm going to read you something. This is from Justice Stevens's dissent in 'Citizen's United.'

"'Corporations have no consciences, no beliefs, no feelings, no thoughts, no desires . . . They are not themselves members of "We the People" by whom and for whom our Constitution was established . . . At bottom, the Court's opinion is thus a rejection of the common sense of the American people, who have recognized a need to prevent corporations from undermining self-government since the founding, and who have fought against the distinctive corrupting potential of corporate electioneering since the days of Theodore Roosevelt.'"

Field closed the book.

Shaw said, "So, some sharp lawyer might claim that holding office is a form of expression and a First Amendment right."

"Oh, I could see that argument being made. There'd be others too." He looked at Russell. "So would it be struck down? Who knows? But I guarantee that Devereux'll throw massive amounts of money into lobbying for his side. I wouldn't put it past him to bribe or threaten to make sure the amendment stands."

That would be just the job for BlackBridge.

"And this is only the start. Devereux has to have plans to move into other states too."

"The man who would be king," Shaw said. Russell caught his eye, nodding.

Before they left the Bay Area for the media-free Compound, the young brothers had watched television. One night they'd seen an old movie, *The Man Who Would Be King.* Based on a Rudyard Kipling novella. It was about a couple of former British soldiers who set off to India and Afghanistan, aspiring to become just what the title suggested.

"That's Devereux," Field muttered.

Russell said, "We know what his agenda is too—his company gets elected."

Shaw recalled the memos in the courier bag: legislation and regulations to eliminate protections on the environment, banking, working conditions, civil rights. They hadn't made much sense at the time. Now the purpose was terribly clear. He explained this to Field, who took the news with an expression of disgust.

"Our country's two hundred and fifty years old. That's a long time by some standards. No country lasts forever, and there have been more governments overturned from within than by invasions." A scornful look at the tally.

Shaw slipped it into an envelope and placed that in his backpack.

"What . . ." Field cleared his throat. "What are you going to do with it?"

Shaw had not yet thought about this. He glanced at his brother, who shrugged.

Field walked them to the rear door. Before he opened it, he eyed Shaw closely, then Russell. His eyes were focused. His brows furrowed. "Does Devereux know you have it?"

"Not for certain."

"Then I see you have two options. One: Convince him that you never unearthed it. Hide it somewhere. Pray he gives up looking and never finds it."

"What's the other option?"

"It's an amendment that passed, yes. But I imagine that the people wouldn't have voted for it if they'd known the truth. So, I say: as Americans and lovers of democracy, you should light a bonfire and throw the damn thing in."

50

North Beach.

This neighborhood, the jewel in the crown above Chinatown, was one of the main Italian American portions of the city. The seashore part of the name came from one end of the district, the Barbary Coast, maybe the most notorious red-light district of any city along the Pacific coastline.

More sustaining was the Bohemian culture that developed in the 1950s and early '60s. North Beach was folk music at the hungry i and pot and *Mad* magazine wit. It was the half-century-old City Lights bookshop, owned and managed by poet Lawrence Ferlinghetti, making it the epicenter of the Beat movement. It had a tastefully risqué side too. North Beach was home to the Condor Club, a gentlemen's establishment that morphed through many iterations and was known internationally as the venue were the famed Carol Doda performed.

Shaw paused at the crest and caught his breath. Grant was not the steepest street in hilly San Francisco but it was one of them. He turned to his right and continued several blocks until he came to a storefront, Davis & Sons Rare Books and Antiquities.

Walking inside—his presence announced by an actual bell, mounted to the door—Shaw was greeted with a smell that took him back immediately to the wilderness cabin where he and his siblings had grown up. In the escape from the Bay Area to the Sierra Nevadas, Ashton and Mary Dove had carted with them a ton—quite literally—of books of all sorts. Hardbound mostly. That perfume of paper, cardboard, leather, glue and must was unforgettable and present in abundance here.

He looked around the large, jam-packed store. Every shelf was filled with volumes, organized according to curious categories.

Fiction, Scottish, 1700–1725
Nonfiction, British Literary Criticism, 1800–1810
Poetry, Caribbean, 1850–1875

On and on.

A young man behind the counter was on the phone and he smiled at Shaw and held up a just-be-a-sec finger.

Shaw nodded and browsed. In addition to books the store also offered writing and drawing implements and supplies going back hundreds of years. He walked to a case in which were fountain pens, holders and nibs, even quills. Antique notebooks too, early-era versions of the one he'd used in his meeting with Maria Vasquez in the reward job to find Tessy.

The man hung up and joined him.

"Hi."

Shaw nodded. The shop was Dickensian, to be sure, but the clerk wasn't Oliver or Pip. His stylish hair was moussed up, he bore an earring, and if his white shirt, floral tie and black slacks had been purchased with proceeds from the shop, then the antiquarian book business was doing exceedingly well.

"You interested in anything in the case?" He produced a key.

"I might be. But first, I'm interested in framing."

From his backpack he extracted a manila folder. Inside was a sketch he had drawn of Sierra Nevada mountain peaks as seen from Echo Ridge. He'd inherited his father's penmanship and skills at cartography, so he was not a bad artist.

Donning white cloth gloves, the man picked it up. "Not bad."

He turned it over, glancing at the typewritten words on the back.

In the matter of the Voting Tally in the Twelfth Congressional District, regarding Proposition 06, being a referendum put before the People of the State, I, the Right Honorable Selmer P. Clarke, Superior Court, do find as a matter of fact the following:

"Oh, that's nothing. Some scrap paper my father found at work and did the sketch on."

The Maybe-Davis turned it over without finishing the earth-shattering words.

He then took a loupe and examined the sheet. Finally he set it down. "You want it framed but also protected."

"Do I?"

"Of course you do. Now, before the mid–eighteen hundreds, most paper was made from cloth, usually by mechanical means. This meant that the stock was composed of long fibers. It was strong and chemical free. After that, manufacturing shifted to chemical pulping and the use of alum-rosin sizing—that led, of course, to sulfuric acid. Then too you've got your nitrogen oxides, formic, acetic, lactic and oxalic acids. Generated by cellulose itself. And, heavens, we haven't even gotten to pollutants in the air and the water in the factory."

Shaw took this in, nodding, having no idea what the point of the lecture might be.

"In other words, for framing, I can do some things to protect it but your basic plastic won't keep it from disintegrating. That would require a complete acid reduction or removal process."

"How long would I have?"

"I'm sorry?"

"I'm in a hurry, so if you just mounted it in a normal frame, how long until it disintegrated?"

The young man's face screwed up, as he prepared to deliver the bad news. A breath. "Your best-case scenario? I'd give it two hundred years."

Which, Shaw supposed, in the world of antiquarian documents, might be like a doctor looking up from an MRI scan and saying, "You'll be dead by Tuesday."

"I'll go with the plastic."

"Ah. Well. The customer is always right."

Though what he was really saying was: It's your funeral.

51

At 9:15 that evening, Colter Shaw braked the Yamaha to a stop. He was in the heart of Haight-Ashbury. It was ironic in the extreme that the area, named after two ardent nineteenth-century capitalists, was the birthplace of the Diggers, one of the most successful socialist movements in the history of the country. It was also where hippies first appeared and was ground zero for the Summer of Love in 1967.

A Whole Foods was not far away but the street where Shaw parked didn't reflect such recent aesthetic and economic enlightenment. Metal shutters as thick with layers of paint as a Leonardo da Vinci canvas were ratcheted down, protecting a tattoo parlor, a nail salon, a bodega and, of all things, what seemed to be an old-fashioned cobbler. A sepia painting of a woman's buttonhook boot was above the door.

Shaw parked and chained. Then stood and looked up at a huge red-brick building, which was old, and at the painted metal sign on the front, which was new.

THE STEELWORKS

The club was housed in a three-story former factory, constructed of smudged and soiled red brick, in whose walls were set windows that were painted over. As the name explained, it had in the early twentieth century been a steel-fabricating operation.

The only clues as to what was occurring inside were the line of people outside waiting admittance, and the resonating bass beats that assaulted anyone within fifty feet of the building. Colter Shaw looked the place over clinically and decided: pure hell.

In the days when he might have clubbed he was working out for the wrestling team at the University of Michigan, studying for classes, and engaging in orienteering competitions in the Upper Peninsula or camping with one of several equally outdoor-minded girlfriends.

He zipped his leather jacket up, then walked past the crowd to the front door, where a skinny man, lanky and sporting a mop of unruly red hair, sat on a stool.

Some in the queue of about thirty or forty also studied him, with glares. They were mostly in their twenties. The dress code was jeans or cargo pants, sweats, tank tops, faded loafers and boots. Impressive beards, though, unlike Russell's, they were overly topiaried. Tattoo artists had made thousands of dollars inking and modifying this crowd. Shaw sensed bathing was not a priority.

He said to the bouncer, "I need to find somebody in there."

"You gotta wait. We're at capacity."

Shaw laughed.

The skinny guy looked at him quizzically.

"No. You're *over* capacity. How many fire doors you have?"

Exits are vital to survivalists, fire exits in particular. The odds of having to escape from murderers, terrorists, kidnappers or black bears were infinitely small. Fleeing a tall wave of speedy, thousand-degree flames, however, was well within the realm of possibility.

"The hell *are* you?"

"I won't be long." Shaw started inside. The man who was next in line for entrance shouted, "There's a line here! No budging!" He lunged and went for Shaw's arm. Shaw stopped and stared. The man froze.

Shaw frowned. "Did you really say 'budging'?" He turned to the man's girlfriend. "Did he really say 'budging'? Are we in the high school lunch line?"

Blushing, the man grimaced and backed off. His girlfriend muttered to him acerbically, "Told you not to be an asshole."

The bouncer took over the defense of the castle. "You can't come in. I told you." He stood up. He wore an expandable baton on his hip. Shaw had been whipped by one. They really hurt.

He looked over the man. "I'm going inside to get my niece and then we're going to leave. She's sixteen."

The bouncer paused. His eyes swept the sidewalk. "She's *what*?"

The man, trying not to look stricken, glanced inside. Then back to Shaw. "All right. Go in. Get her. Just make it fast."

Shaw strode into the packed, sweaty crowd. He wasn't exactly sure what the point of the place was. There was a disc jockey and some people were dancing, or gyrating, on a large hardwood floor. Many sat on mismatched chairs and couches or were perched on stairways or wooden crates. They were shouting and drinking and vaping and smoking pot. Some were passed out. A few had thrown up; he navigated carefully.

No, this wasn't just hell, Shaw thought. It was Dante's Ninth Level—an appropriate metaphor, considering that a man named Dante Mladic was the owner of the club.

He made a circuit of the mad place, making his way through the sweating bodies, avoiding jostling, avoiding several drunk women and one man who came on to him.

Then, in the back, he noted two doors.

It was the one on the right he wanted because a guard sat on the chair just beside it. He was lean and about thirty, with curly blond hair and razor-sharp features—his nose, cheekbones, his chin. He was hunched over, reading something on his phone.

Shaw staggered up and tried the door. It was open, but instantly the man was on his feet, pushing it closed. "What're you doing?"

"Bathroom." Shaw's speech was slurred. He thought he was doing a pretty good job. The rewards business from time to time required a bit of acting.

"S'over there." The big man gestured with a thumb.

"No, it's broken. Something's broken. A pipe."

"Get the fuck out of here. I'll have you thrown out." The Balkan accent was faint.

"Bathroom," Shaw said again and walked to the second door, and stepped into a business office, which was empty and dark.

"The fuck," the man said and followed him in.

"Bathroom." Shaw kept with his preferred line of dialogue.

When the guard's fist drove forward toward Shaw's solar plexus, he easily sidestepped and dropped his center of gravity. He executed a fair wrestling takedown, his right arm going between the man's legs and around to his spine. In college his coach had said, "Can't be shy in this sport. You queasy about going for the jewels, take up fencing."

Shaw leveraged up and, gripping the man's collar with his left hand, he took him off the floor entirely and dropped him hard on the oak. Factories made very hard floors and his head banged with a sound you could hear over the music.

Still he needed to debilitate the man, so he dropped his fist into his gut. Hard but nothing broke.

He got out of the way in time to avoid the vomiting.

It was one hundred percent certain that Colter Shaw had just committed an unprovoked assault (the fear of an attack) and battery (an unwanted touching and, in this case, head banging and gut punching).

The question remained: Was it justifiable?

He believed it was.

Shaw was here because Mack McKenzie had finally traced the gray van into which Tessy Vasquez had possibly disappeared near Ghirardelli Square. Through several layers of offshore corporations, she'd learned that it was ultimately owned by a company controlled by Mladic, a San Francisco club owner. And suspected drug dealer and sex trafficker.

His base of operations was this club, the Steelworks.

If the man presently gasping for breath in front of him was not involved in crimes, Shaw would have some consequences to face. But he'd seen no option.

So he searched the man.

And discovered two things. One was a Glock 17 semiauto pistol, which he slipped into his waistband. The other was some information. His driver's license indicated he was Gregor Mladic, presumably Dante's son or nephew.

Make that three things.

In his rear pocket was a packet of zip ties.

Two of which Shaw used to bind his wrists and ankles.

Now, for the door on the right.

He opened it.

Colter Shaw drew his gun and started silently down the stairs descending into the old building's massive, pungent basement, redolent of mold and heating oil.

52

The pounding feet on the dance floor above them had stopped. Everyone had evacuated. The roar of the flames was the only sound encircling them.

Shaw turned to the hole they broke open in the Sheetrock and said to Nita, "Up the stairs now, fast. There'll be police."

"But . . . what about you?"

He smiled to her. "Not yet."

And turned back, jogging to the far end of the corridor.

It had been twenty minutes since Shaw had descended the stairs from the door on the right down to the cellar of the Steelworks club, and the blaze was growing by the minute—the blaze set by the men in the TV room, under what was surely Dante Mladic's order to destroy incriminating evidence in the office.

The TV men were gone, Nita was gone.

But Colter Shaw knew that he was not alone down here.

Choking, his mouth covered with his untucked shirt, he made his way down the main corridor, toward the far end.

Shaw believed he heard sirens, though it was hard to say over the raging fire.

At the end of the main corridor he turned down the hallway to the right. He drew his flashlight and hurried forward. Now that the footsteps above were gone and he was around the corner from the flames, he could hear thuds and the muffled cries of "Help" and "Get me out! Please!"

Shaw couldn't kick the door in—it opened outward—so as quickly as he could, he used the knife trick once more. In thirty seconds it was open.

He lifted his flashlight and played the beam over Tessy Vasquez. She gave a brief scream and huddled away. She was still wearing the outfit that she'd worn in the variety shop security video: the red blouse and gypsy skirt.

"Tessy, it's all right. Your mother sent me."

"Mother?"

"I'm going to get you out."

His knife was still open and with it he cut the restraints around her ankle.

"This way. Come on."

Heads down, coughing, both of them returned to the corridor.

"There are men, they have guns."

"They're gone."

She staggered along behind him, her legs not used to activity during her imprisonment.

They came to the turn and stepped into the main corridor.

Where Shaw saw that the escape route no longer existed.

The fire now spread from wall to wall. The two of them faced a roiling sheet of flame, floor to ceiling, slowly moving their way.

Soon, they'd be unconscious from lack of oxygen.

Shaw glanced at Tessy, who was crying.

He pointed toward the storeroom that had been Nita's cell.

"Find some cloth or paper towels, soak them with the bottled water and cover your face. Get low."

Ashton had taught the children that a wet cloth was good protection against smoke, but it was a myth that urine was a better liquid to dampen the cloth. That was only helpful, and marginally, in protecting against chlorine gas.

"We're going to die!"

"Do what I told you. Now."

She shuffled into the room, coughing hard.

Shaw got as close as he could to the flames, until he could hardly bear the searing heat. He drew from his waistband the Glock the guard upstairs had been carrying. It was a larger caliber, with a longer barrel, and the magazine contained more rounds.

He squinted into the fire and fired a shot.

A second, third.

Fourth, fifth, sixth.

It was on the seventh that the bullet found its target: the building's boiler. A stunning explosion rocked the basement accompanied by the banshee cry of escaping steam.

Shaw dove for cover in Nita's cell. They were some distance from the explosion, but still were hit with a blast of the moist heat that shot into the corridor and filled the rooms. Superheated steam, in a closed container, can reach extraordinarily high temperatures—900 degrees Fahrenheit. Had that been the case the steam could have melted the Sheetrock like newsprint and Shaw and Tessy might have been scalded to death. But he was ninety percent sure that a boiler this age was probably heated only to the standard 212.

Shaw rose and looked into the corridor. Some flames still flickered, but the path was clear.

"Let's go," he told Tessy and helped her to her feet. He went in lead, having replaced the guard's gun with his own, in case the traffickers returned, which he doubted would happen. The police and firemen would be there soon if they weren't already present.

Shaw glanced in the office and noted that not everything was destroyed. Crime Scene should probably find enough evidence to convict Mladic.

As they got to the stairs, they stopped. Footsteps were coming down. Shaw lifted his gun.

His tear-filled eyes peered through the smoke.

The heavy steps came closer.

Shaw got the gun into his pocket just before firemen arrived. The large men, fitted with their bulky equipment, plodded down the stairs.

One pulled his oxygen mask off. "Anyone else down here?"

"No. There's still some fire in the office. First door on your right."

Another fireman surveyed the scene. "What happened?"

"Boiler blew. Put out the flames."

"Lucky you."

As they started past, Shaw said, "Save the files and computers. The district attorney'll want to see them."

Shaw felt a fireman's head turn his way, then he and the young woman were climbing the stairs.

53

They sat on the couch of the Pacific Heights safe house.

Shaw and Tessy were alone. Russell was presently conducting surveillance at the Alvarez Street safe house, trying to spot and identify the blonde in the green Honda. He'd reported seeing nothing. Shaw texted his brother that he'd found and rescued the young woman.

The two had taken respective turns in the bathroom, scrubbing away sweat and soot, though the aroma of smoke was embedded in hair and clothing.

Tessy was sipping tea. Ashton was a big tea drinker, he recalled, and apparently so was his older son. The house had come with a supply of staples, including English breakfast and some herbals. Tessy had picked chamomile. Shaw didn't believe he'd had a cup of tea in five or six years.

The young woman's eyes were hollow as she explained what had happened. As Shaw and Russell had deduced, the men in the gray van had grabbed her.

"Was Roman involved?"

Her face screwed up with disgust. "Yes, he was behind it. He was so angry I told him I wasn't going out with him unless he got sober. I didn't want to be with him, but I thought maybe he'd stop using and become a better person. But he was just a psycho. He likes to hurt people."

"He was involved in the human trafficking himself?"

"I'm sure he was. He and the owner, Dante, hung out together."

There'd be records about Roman, probably, in the Steelworks. But to make sure the authorities learned of him, Shaw would also get his full name and particulars from Tessy and send them to his former FBI agent friend, Tom Pepper. He, in turn, would relay the information to SFPD and the Bureau field office here. That way Tessy would remain anonymous and wouldn't have to worry about Immigration and Customs.

"I . . . thank you for what you did. It was terrible. So terrible. There were some men who came to look at me. Like they were buying cattle or hogs at market. I would have died first."

He nodded. Colter Shaw had never been comfortable with gratitude. He didn't discount his contribution, but in most rewards jobs, he was merely returning life to the status quo.

After a minute, Tessy asked, "You have a girlfriend?"

Do I? he wondered. He nodded. A good way to end whatever she was thinking of.

"Good. I'm happy for you."

The doorbell rang. He went to the intercom, spoke with Maria Vasquez and buzzed her in.

She flung her arms around her daughter.

"*Ay*, all the smoke."

"He saved me, Mama. These men kidnapped me."

"It was that club? On TV?"

Shaw nodded. He asked, "Any casualties? I haven't seen the news."

"Some people were hurt. Nobody got killed. The police arrested people there, the owner. Human trafficking. Drugs." She began to sob. Her daughter held her tightly.

When he'd called 911 he'd mentioned he'd seen somebody in an office in the back of the club. "He seemed to be tied up. I don't know what that's about." He hoped Mladic's son was one of those who'd been collared.

Shaw said, "I got her out of there fast. We didn't talk to the police. They don't know your name."

He didn't tell her that he was no more eager to get the police involved than they were.

"I don't have the money with me now."

Shaw said, "Keep it. You can pay me when times are better for you."

"Bless you, bless you." She hugged him hard. Tessy did as well.

After they left, Shaw took his typical hot-then-cold shower and, when he'd dressed again, he drank down a whole bottle of mineral water, then opened a beer.

He caught a whiff of smoke, arising from the pile of clothes he stripped off. Into the trash. No time for dry cleaning.

He lifted his Android off the table and loaded the browser. At the website he sought, he had to scroll through a dozen numbers until he found one he thought might be helpful. He dialed and, despite the late hour, someone answered, a pleasant woman. He gave the name of the person he wanted to speak to and then his own.

It took no more than ten seconds to be connected.

PART THREE

JUNE 26

THE MAN WHO WOULD BE KING

Time until the family dies: eight hours.

54

The water was a chameleon.

Back on the Embarcadero, Colter Shaw was looking over the Bay. One thing he recalled from living here ages ago: the hue of the rocking waves would change from day to day. A riveting blue, rich as an empress's sapphire. Then a matte gray. Sometimes tropical green.

Today, under yet another June gloom overcast, the Bay was dun, the color—he couldn't help but think—of a newly turned grave in a cemetery rich with clay.

He kept his eye on the street, the traffic. Russell hadn't seen the green Honda or its blond driver recently but Shaw decided that she was too persistent to have given up.

He also suspected she'd rented a new car, now that he'd made her. It's what he would've done.

But that sedan wasn't the only vehicle he was interested in. There was another one he kept looking for.

And it happened to pull up to the curb now near him.

You didn't see many Rolls-Royces in the Bay Area. Of course, there was plenty of money to buy everything from Teslas to Ferraris to Bugattis, but the Rolls—and sibling Bentley—marque was not the sort that appealed to the Silicon Valley crowd, it seemed. Maybe the recent designs—you could mistake them for a Dodge at a distance—were not showy or distinctive enough. Maybe they signified old money, which Google, Facebook and YouTube decidedly were not.

Slinging his backpack over his shoulder, Shaw stood and walked to the ruddy-colored vehicle.

The driver, who'd exited the car, was the same man he and his brother had seen at the Tenderloin UIP meeting and the safe house. He was armed, a large 1911 Colt automatic on his hip.

Shaw walked around the car to the driver's side. The man said, "Mr. Shaw. I'm wearing a recording device, which will be running throughout this meeting." He spoke in unaccented American English.

"Are you now?"

"So the record will show that there's been no coercion. I'm inviting you into the car. And you're free to get in or not."

This was curious, since Shaw himself had arranged the get-together. There perhaps was a history of people being "encouraged" to get into Devereux's car when they were not wholly inclined to do so.

"Fair enough. And since we're setting ground rules, I'll tell *you* that I just texted my associate a photo of your car and its license tag. If I don't text her again in thirty minutes, she'll alert the police that there's been a kidnapping."

Shaw heard a high-pitched chuckle from inside. When the driver looked into the back, apparently getting the okay sign, he opened the door.

Sitting in the driver's side backseat was a gorgeous blonde with teased-up and sprayed-down hair. She was beautiful, no doubt, but would have been more so had she lost the heavy makeup, which favored purples and blues. She was not the woman Shaw and Russell had seen accompanying Devereux in the safe house on Alvarez, though in line with the dress code her skirt was just as short and her blouse just as low.

Devereux slipped his hand into a pocket and extracted several hundred dollar bills. "Get yourself some coffee or a glass of wine. Have some lunch. There's a good girl." The condescension dripped.

"Girl." She huffed but took the money. "Can't I come with?"

"Cassie, please."

"It's *Carrie*."

"I do beg forgiveness. I was distracted." His eyes scanned her figure.

Did men really get away with this crap? Shaw wondered.

She offered a forced smile to Shaw and climbed out, walking away on clattering heels.

He called after her, "If you get lunch, no garlic."

Shaw bent down and looked at Jonathan Stuart Devereux. "Droon and Braxton? Anyone from BlackBridge?"

"They don't even know I'm here, do they? I'm adhering to your requirements, Mr. Shaw. You've set the agenda."

Shaw got into the seat Carrie had occupied. He was enveloped in the cloud of her perfume. He dropped his backpack on the spacious floor before him. He glanced around. Bird's-eye maple, luxurious carpet, polished chrome. This really was a marvelous vehicle. There was a control on the door for what seemed to be a back massager.

The Rolls pulled away from the curb and moved silently and smoothly through the streets. It had to be one hell of a suspension system; some roads in the Embarcadero were cobblestoned.

Shaw had seen Devereux from a distance, in the Tenderloin and through Russell's security camera at the safe house. Up close, observing the man clearly, Shaw decided he could be an ambassador. This suit was gray with darker gray stripes. Maybe he felt the vertical lines made him look thinner. Today's explosive handkerchief was pale blue. Shaw caught a glimpse of a Ferragamo label inside his jacket. Did he keep it unbuttoned to show off the name? How much wealthier would he be if his corporation began holding office in the state? He suspected after a certain decimal place, you begin to focus on power, not gold.

"Mr. Shaw. I was, as you can imagine, surprised when I got your message."

Before they got to business, though, Devereux's phone hummed. He looked at the screen. "Yes?" Upon listening to a caller Shaw could not hear, Devereux grew motionless, his face stilled. "That will hardly work, now, will it?" His face was the epitome of calm but the voice was filled with ice. *"Mais, non."* And launched into what Shaw assumed was perfect French. Shaw had known a number of people from the UK who were multilingual. It was only a fifty-dollar BudgetAir ticket from London to any number of exotic locales. Very different in faraway America.

After five minutes he reverted to English once more, apparently addressing the original speaker. He wiped his brow and shiny head with a handkerchief. "You better do."

He disconnected and turned his attention back to Shaw, who suspected that he had not needed to take the call at all but—like with the suit jacket label—it was a show of power. He'd also like to keep people waiting; he had arrived at the Embarcadero fifteen minutes late. "So. The floor is yours."

"I have something you're after. I want to negotiate a deal. That's why I called you, and not Droon or Braxton. I don't trust them. All of their strong-arm crap. It's not helpful."

Devereux was silent for a moment but the pleasure was obvious in his face. "Always good to eliminate the middleman, if possible. Cheaper in the long run." He added, "Safer too in most instances."

Shaw continued, "You and the people from BlackBridge broke into a house of my father's. Alvarez Street."

The driver glanced in the rearview mirror.

Devereux reassured him with a shake of the head.

To Shaw he said, "That's not accurate. They were already there. I have no idea how they got in. They invited me to join them. I didn't know whose house it was." His fingers were flying, twitchy. It wasn't a palsy; he could control it. "Not at that time."

"My family's in danger."

Devereux nodded. "I see. You heard us. You were bugging the house."

"I don't believe it's bugging if it's your house."

"Well taken. Go on."

Shaw said, "My mother and sister are safe. But I want to make sure they stay safe. I'll give you what you want and you call off Droon and Braxton."

"I'm intrigued. So it *was* in Gahl's courier bag."

"That's right."

"And you want a guarantee of your family's safety for it, of course. But there's more in it for you. Do you know, Mr. Shaw, that one could argue that money dates back more than forty thousand years—to the Upper Paleolithic era. It took the form of barter but look at it this way: there were undoubtedly humans back then who did not need the flint arrowhead they traded ears of corn for. That makes the arrowhead a form of currency. A stone tuppence, you could say.

"Then there's the Mesopotamian shekel. I have one from five thousand years ago. That was among the first coins. The first mints were built in the first millennium B.C. They stamped gold and silver coins for the Lydians and Ionians to use to pay for armies."

"Hobby of yours?"

"Bloody well is!" Devereux blustered. He seemed delighted. "Now, back to business. I get what I want and I'll write you a check—well, you'll want a wire transfer, of course—for quite the pretty sum. You can move your family wherever you want. They'll be completely out of harm's way. What proof could you give me that you have it?"

Shaw said, "Why don't I show it to you." He lifted his backpack to his lap.

The fingers stopped moving, the arms stopped waving. Surprise— what seemed like an alien expression—blossomed in his face, followed by greedy anticipation.

Shaw unzipped the backpack and handed Devereux a thick plastic binder.

Devereux took it and emptied the contents onto his lap. He eagerly began flipping through the sheets of paper inside.

Shaw said, "Of course, these are copies. I have the originals."

Devereux frowned when he'd finished. "What's this?"

Shaw was hesitating, a confused look on his face. "It's what you're looking for."

"No, it's not. I don't know what this is."

"It's what Amos Gahl stole from BlackBridge. What was in the courier bag. Proof about the Urban Improvement Plan. It's evidence for the police."

Devereux shook his head. "Where's the voting tally?"

"What's that?"

He eyed Shaw closely. "The legal ruling from nineteen oh-six? A single sheet of paper signed by a judge?"

Shaw looked toward the papers in Devereux's hand. "That's all that was in the bag. I mean, some magazines and newspapers, some memos, but all dated within the past ten years. I went through every single page. Nothing a hundred years old." Shaw's body language skills came into play again, though in reverse. He made certain that now, when he was lying, he kept his mannerisms and expressions unchanged from a moment ago when he'd been telling the truth. "I thought that's what you wanted. To destroy the evidence about the UIP."

Devereux sighed. The hands began to twitch again. "I don't know what the UIP is."

"Really?"

"No," he muttered.

"BlackBridge's Urban Improvement Plan. Seeding drugs into neighborhoods to lower property values. So people like you can buy up the land for cheap."

The man's face grew rosier, and not in a good way. His jaw was tight. "I have no knowledge of that whatsoever. I hire BlackBridge to help me identify properties to buy, yes, but I know nothing about any drugs. What a horrific idea."

"It is. But it's not my issue. I'm not going on a crusade if it puts my family in danger."

Devereux would be wondering if Shaw was right. Maybe the courier bag *didn't* have the tally in it. But if not, then where was it? His eyes grew cold, and under those small fingers the copies of the UIP documents shivered. He read through them again. "I've dealt with enough solicitors and barristers in my day to know this hardly amounts to evidence, Mr. Shaw."

Silence for a moment as the Rolls climbed California Street and swerved around a cable car, bristling with enthusiastic tourists.

"I don't think I believe you, Mr. Shaw. You're playing hard to get. I'm going to assume you found the vote tally certificate. You hid it somewhere. And you're holding out for more."

Shaw appeared exasperated. He tried not to overdo it. "Voting about what? Why's it so important?"

"It just is." Devereux was growing irritated. Finally the man controlled his pique. "I would be willing to pay seven figures to you, in cash, untraceable, for the certificate. You will never want for anything again."

Curious phrase, archaic. And an odd concept; Colter Shaw had not wanted for anything for a long time. Maybe since birth, and money had nothing to do with it.

"This tally, whatever it is, wasn't in the courier bag. What do you want it for?"

The man who would be king . . .

Devereux didn't answer. He looked out the window. Very few people disappointed Jonathan Stuart Devereux, Shaw supposed. And fewer still did not do what he wished them to.

If this were Ebbitt Droon, of course, Shaw would probably be on his way to a warehouse in a deserted part of the city. Maybe across the Bay Bridge to Oakland, a city where there would be far more industrial spaces practically designed for torture and body disposal.

The Tannery . . .

When they had met once earlier in the month, Droon had tried to extract information by threatening him with a .40 pistol—a big, nasty bullet—targeting joints, which would have the effect of altering them forever. Now, apparently he'd returned to the twisting knife—what he'd used on Amos Gahl.

Devereux turned back to him. "All right. Eight figures."

Shaw wondered where on the scale between ten million and ninety-nine the man was thinking. He guessed the payoff would be on a low rung of the ladder.

"A higher number isn't going to miraculously produce something I didn't have two minutes ago. In exchange for leaving my family alone, I'll give you the Urban Improvement Plan evidence, whether or not you say you don't know what it is." He shrugged. "If it's not enough for the prosecutor, then it might at least point the police in a . . . helpful direction."

Sullen, Devereux muttered. "I doubt that will be a very productive endeavor, Mr. Shaw."

They had arrived back at the place where they had picked Shaw up. Carrie was nowhere to be seen.

The CEO looked around for her.

Perhaps it had been one jab too many.

Devereux shrugged. "It happens. Those girls . . ."

Shaw thought: Good for you, Carrie.

Devereux tapped the driver on the shoulder. The man shut the recorder off. The tape was soon to be erased.

A sigh. "I would hate to have to turn this matter back to Ian Helms and Irena Braxton. They're so . . . unsubtle. Let me encourage you to have another look at the contents of the courier bag. Discuss it with your bearded friend. Eight figures is, after all, eight figures."

He handed the copies back and Shaw slipped them into his backpack.

The driver was out of the car and opening the door. Shaw stepped out onto the sidewalk.

Shaw heard Devereux's voice. "I would look very carefully for that tally, Mr. Shaw. It would be good for everyone."

55

ow is it there?" Shaw asked.

Victoria Lesston said through the speaker on Shaw's Android, "We're vigilant. Carrying sidearms. Your friend's guys brought a machine gun."

"Mary Dove told me."

"What're you up to?"

Back in the Pacific Heights safe house, sitting beside an open window and letting a pleasant breeze breathe past him. "Just hung out with a lecherous billionaire."

"You have all the fun."

His eyes were on the sketch he'd done of Echo Ridge, in the Davis & Sons frame, hanging on the wall. Even though it was in save-a-few-bucks plastic, the art didn't look at all bad.

"Your mother," she said, "was telling me about Ash. Sorry I never got a chance to meet him."

"He was quite a man. Troubled, complicated, compassionate. Nobody like him in the world. He was a crusader."

"This thing you found? So, you think it's true?"

He said, "It is, yes. A real voting tally from nineteen oh-six. If it got out in public, it'll change . . . well, it'll change everything."

"Is it safe? The tally."

"I hid it in a picture frame."

"In plain sight?"

"Not really. It's facing backward."

"A framed blank page—isn't that a little obvious?"

"There's a sketch I drew on the back. A landscape."

"But it's not what your father was looking for?"

"The tally? No. He didn't even know it existed." His voice grew terse. "He was looking for evidence to bring down BlackBridge and get the president—this guy named Helms—arrested. But there never was any. Only the vote tally. Oh, he had a mixed tape too."

"A what?"

"Another story for when I see you again." He wished they could have a longer conversation, but this wasn't the time or place.

A pause. "Which will be when?"

Shaw nearly said as soon as possible. He missed her. But chose: "A few days. Just some loose ends here."

The front door opened and Russell walked into the living room.

"My brother's here. I better go."

"Say hi to the mystery man for me."

Shaw liked the lilt in her voice.

They disconnected.

Russell asked, "How did it go with Devereux?"

"He had an idea we'd found the tally. But he wasn't sure. He might think Gahl hid it somewhere else. He offered to pay us a little money for it."

"Little? Six figures?"

Silence.

"Seven?"

"More."

"Hmm." Russell's go-to response. The accompanying facial expression was: easy come, easy go.

"He suggested that Braxton and Droon were going to step up to bat again."

"Used a baseball analogy?"

"No, that was mine. He collects money. Devereux."

"Who doesn't?"

"No. I mean, he's a real collector. Old coins and bills. Ancient. A hobby. Does that make him a numismatist?"

"Couldn't tell you." Russell walked close to the frame and examined his brother's sketch.

It was only then that Shaw realized that it might be titled *View from Echo Ridge*. Which was, of course, the very spot where Colter had believed his brother had murdered Ashton. What had subconsciously motivated him to pick that scene for the drawing?

His brother studied it closely.

Would he remark on Shaw's choice?

"You can't see the typewriting on the other side" was all he offered. He turned away.

"They used thick paper back then."

Shaw was about to say something but then tensed, cocking his head.

"Colt?" Russell asked.

Shaw held up a finger. He rose and stepped to the front door. He peered through the peephole.

He stepped outside, hand on his gun. He noticed a woman in a maid's uniform, sorting towels on a cart, facing away. He returned a moment later and closed the door. "Maid."

It was then that a brilliant white flash from outside filled the room and an instant later the staccato crack of an explosion rattled windows. Car alarms were wailing.

Both brothers drew their guns and looked out.

Two men in tactical black and ski masks had blown open the door of Russell's SUV. Apparently the vehicle had extra reinforcement and the bang had not completely breached the vehicle. One of them was trying to pull the door open all the way.

Russell muttered, "You flank, the alley."

Shaw nodded.

His brother didn't bother with the subtle approach. He went for a frontal assault. He stepped out the window and balanced briefly on a ledge. He then judged angles and leapt onto the roof of the one-story building below.

Hiding his gun under his jacket, so as not to startle residents in the building and earn a 911 report, Shaw closed and locked the window his brother had just climbed through and then walked into the hallway, now empty. He was in a hurry, yes, but took the time to double-lock the door. He jogged to the stairwell that would take him to the exit in the basement.

On the street it was soon obvious that a firefight was not forthcoming.

The two tactical ops were gone.

Shaw joined Russell, standing beside the car and examining the damage, which was considerable. A six-inch hole had been blown in the door near the lock. It seemed like an efficient, if messy, way to enter a vehicle, but they hadn't known about the extra steel plates. The door held.

"What happened?" Shaw asked.

"They saw me and my weapon and decided not to engage. They had a van waiting up the street."

"BlackBridge? Or one of your customers from the Oakland operation?" Shaw was thinking of the hidden room in the safe house and his brother's maps of the docks across the Bay—which had a decidedly tactical theme about them.

"BlackBridge or Devereux. My other project? No one is a risk anymore."

"How'd they make us?" Shaw asked.

"I've got some thoughts on that."

But he didn't explain just now. He tilted his head, listening.

Sirens wailed in the distance.

"I'll have to talk to the cops." Russell was the epitome of calm.

"You have weapons inside?"

"Won't be a problem."

"Who's it registered to?" The smoke was acrid, Shaw's eyes burned. The breaching charge involved manganese or phosphorus.

"A company. Offshore. Done this before. Go back upstairs."

Shaw nodded.

He turned and left, walking back to the front door of the residence. The back one, through which he'd exited, was self-locking. And while he could jimmy it, there was no reason to. Shaw entered the building and climbed the stairs. Survivalists tended to avoid elevators. For one thing, he recalled his father's rule:

Never miss the opportunity to strengthen limbs in everyday life.

For another, in an elevator you're subject to someone else's control.

On the second floor, he walked to their unit and undid both locks.

He stepped in and closed the door behind him. He was only three or four feet inside when he glanced up to where he'd hung the Davis & Sons frame, containing the halfway decent sketch of the stark view from Echo Ridge.

The wall was now bare.

56

They'd tagged him.

That's how Droon and Braxton had found the new safe house.

Tagging.

"Got the back of your jacket." Russell scanned the garment with a handheld device that looked like a noncontact thermometer. The display lit up with little yellow dots.

"How?"

"Where were you when you met with Devereux?"

"The backseat of the Rolls."

"They coated it. RFID dust."

Radio frequency identification.

In the Compound, where there was no high-tech, the three children were not exposed to the basic internet, much less the universe of other digital esoterica. In the years since he'd been out in the real world, as a reward-seeker, Shaw had embraced much that was electronic and he'd heard of RFID dust. It was a common technique used by security and military forces—those from countries with sophisticated SIGINT—signals intelligence—operations, and sizable budgets. Radio frequency tracking systems were complicated and worked only with state-of-the-art equipment. Satellites and drones were involved.

Once tagged, you could be trailed even when you ducked out of sight and moved via underground passages. Algorithms compared geographic mapping systems to predict where you would emerge. When you did, another sensor would pick you up again, then hand off to others.

Really remarkable.

"There was a passenger in the seat before me, one of Devereux's dates."

"She got tagged too but there was plenty to go around." Russell added, "He maybe brought her along so you wouldn't be suspicious."

"You'll have to dump your jacket and jeans. Dry cleaning doesn't kill them. Your boots'll be okay."

So Devereux had indeed been lying. Braxton and Droon knew about his meeting and had arranged for the dust in anticipation of it.

Well, Shaw himself hadn't been the model of honesty with the billionaire.

Shaw went into the bedroom, stripped and tossed his clothes into a garbage bag—the second set of clothing he'd lost in the space of twenty-four hours. He changed into new jeans and a black polo shirt, untucked to keep his Glock concealed.

He found his brother on the phone. Russell nodded to a spot by the door and Shaw dropped the bag there. When he disconnected, his brother said, "I'm going to swap out the SUV. There's a place in South San Francisco we use. I'll take care of this." He picked up the bag. "I'll let you know if Karin gets anything on Blond." With that, he was out the door.

He didn't bother to call the management of the Pacific Heights residence. Shaw was sure that there was no maid service in this particular building at this particular time of day. The woman in the hall was no maid, but a BlackBridge employee.

The brothers could now return to the safe house on Alvarez Street. Why not? They weren't at risk any longer, since Devereux, Ian Helms and Braxton had the document in the plastic frame.

And what was happening with the vote tally now?

Shaw guessed it was already en route to Sacramento, probably via private helicopter or jet. The legal department of the state assembly would be gearing up to consider how to handle an issue that none of them had ever had to face in their collective years as legislators: a century-old amendment to the state constitution that allowed corporations to hold public office. There would be the matter of authentication and a flurry of behind-the-scenes meetings. Shaw had no doubt that Devereux was pulling strings and disbursing cash to key players in the legislative and judicial branches of government. Wielding threats too. BlackBridge would be putting its skills at blackmail and extortion to work to gin up support for the amendment.

He sat down at his laptop. A fast search of the internet revealed that Devereux, the governor, and the chief justice of the California supreme court played golf together with some frequency, and Banyan Tree employed one of the largest lobbying firms in the state.

He wondered what the reaction would be—in California, the United States, the world.

The intercom buzzer hummed. Police, canvassing after the shoot-out? Had somebody followed him from the Steelworks club last night?

"Yes?"

"Mr. Shaw?"

"Who's this?"

"Connie . . . Consuela Ramirez. Maria Vasquez's my dear friend. I'm Tessy's godmother. I'm sorry to trouble you. Can I see you for a few minutes? I won't be long."

He hit the entry button, then pulled his jacket on and lifted his shirt hem over the gun's grip. He could draw faster this way, rather than the two-step, which involved lifting a garment with one hand and drawing with the dominant. Sometimes seconds mattered.

He wasn't, however, too concerned. BlackBridge and Devereux had the document. Why draw attention by racking up bodies? Besides, the visitor had dropped Tessy's and her mother's names.

When the doorbell rang, he looked through the peephole and noted a dark-haired, attractive woman in her early thirties. She was in a nicely cut business suit. For some long seconds, Shaw watched her dark eyes through the lens. If she were with anyone, not visible, she would have glanced to the side. This did not happen.

Finally he let her in, tugging his shirt back down over his weapon.

"I'm Colter."

They shook hands.

"Would you like to sit?"

She picked the couch and Shaw a nearby chair. He detected an ambivalent floral scent, not jasmine, not lilac, not rose. Pleasant, though.

"Only a minute of your time."

"Please."

"Maria told me what you did. You saved Tessy's life." Her voice was breathless. "I don't know what we would have done . . . if . . ." She choked back a sob and wiped at her eyes, which were tearing. She looked in her purse.

Shaw asked if she wanted a tissue and she nodded. He got her a napkin from the kitchen.

She dabbed and tried to wipe the damaged mascara, much as Vasquez had done in her Tenderloin apartment. "Maria said you were a kind man. You would not take any money, the reward."

"She told me her situation, being laid off. I don't need the reward. I sometimes do that in my business."

More often than Velma Bruin liked.

"I don't have any more money than she does, but I do have this."
She opened her purse and handed him a black velvet bag. "This was
a gift from my mother. Diamond and gold."

Shaw looked inside and shook out a necklace. It was a flower petal,
a rose, he thought, with a diamond set in the center.

"I can't take this."

A firm smile crossed her face. "In this life, Mr. Shaw, there is not
much good. I would say good with a capital 'G,' you know. I think
good must be rewarded. I could not sleep if you didn't accept it. You
saved my goddaughter's life."

He had received stocks and bonds on his reward jobs, in lieu of
cash. Original art too. Never jewelry.

He hesitated. "Then thank you. I will." He put the piece back in
the bag and slipped that into his jacket pocket.

And walked her to the door.

She turned. "One favor? Maria's proud. She would be embarrassed if she knew what I did."

"A secret, sure."

She shook his hand with both of hers. "Good, with a capital 'G.'"

57

Colter Shaw had returned to Hunters Point.

He was all too aware that the clock was counting down on the SP family's murders, and could think of nothing else to do. Kevin Miller, the O.G. with the Hudson Kings, had told him that crews from Salinas were making forays into this part of Hunters Point.

For two hours he canvassed people on the shabby streets, flashing Blond's altered picture and asking if anybody knew him.

He wanted to believe that somewhere here was a lead to the identity of the family that BlackBridge had targeted to die.

A belief that was stubbornly, however, not becoming a reality.

As he walked back to the Yamaha, chained to a light pole in a large, deserted parking lot, he spotted some construction workers, jeans and T-shirts, tan or gray jackets. They'd just finished boarding up a building to the north side of the lot, the direction where the city proper lay. It was impossible to tell from the faded paint on the side of the place what the single-story structure might once have been. It seemed to say FRESH EGGS though that seemed plain odd.

He waved and walked toward the workers along the waterfront.

He noted that the bay near the shoreline was coagulated with grease and probably toxic runoff from the old shipyard. He could see, far away, the massive battleship turret crane, an unobstructed view, and even from this distance it was impressive, a monument to ingenuity and muscle and industry.

The Egg building was masterfully sealed. Substantial plywood boards and many Sheetrock screws had been involved. Maybe the place had fallen into the hands of crack or meth users and the owner wanted to secure it permanently.

Shaw walked up, smiled and nodded.

The six men, half of them Anglo, half Latino, glanced his way, then their eyes slipped to the asphalt.

"You work around here mostly?"

One of them said, "The Point, Bayview." The others remained cautious. Was he a cop? Immigration and Customs Enforcement?

"By any chance, you seen this guy? He was a buddy of mine in the Army. He's gone missing."

Offering his phone, Shaw continued to spin his tall tale. "Got into some drug trouble and ended up in Hunters Point somewhere. I want to find him, get him some help."

They seemed to buy his story. All looked at the picture, then at one another, but finally shook their heads. Shaw's sense was that they—unlike him—were being honest.

He thanked them and they piled into the vehicles and drove out of the parking lot, leaving the whole area deserted, except for Shaw.

It had been a long shot. As he walked back to his bike he wondered, Who are you, SP? And who are the children? How many? Were they sons, daughters, both? What was there about the gangs in Hunters Point that was central to your death sentence?

Questions, questions, questions . . .

And Colter Shaw was filled with anger that he couldn't seem to get a single answer.

He pulled on his helmet, started the bike, tapped it into gear and eased forward. He accelerated and was about a hundred feet from the exit when a battered gray pickup truck shot out from between two small, abandoned warehouses and aimed right for him, speeding with a gassy roar.

The Ford bore down on him at thirty, forty, fifty miles an hour. He had no choice but to brake and spin the bars. The pickup passed within two feet of his front fender.

Shaw tried to steer into the skid, but like much of the parking lot the surface here was sand and disintegrated asphalt. The Yamaha went down and he tumbled off with the bike pinning his right leg and arm under its two hundred pounds of metal. Not a huge weight but he could get no leverage to rise or to reach his weapon.

Which he now saw he needed.

The driver and the passenger had climbed from the pickup and were walking toward him.

Shaw recognized them.

The BNG gangbangers he and Russell had relieved of their drugs, money and guns in the TL yesterday.

They reached under their untucked shirts and pulled out their new weapons and approached the bike.

58

A*ng malaking tao,*" Red Shirt muttered.

White Shirt laughed. "*Hindi ganoon kalaki ngayon.*"

Which got a smile in return.

They were thirty feet away. Shaw struggled to shift the bike. It moved a bit, an inch.

Two inches.

Then the skinny men were twenty feet away. "Hey, asshole? Where what you stole?" The accent was thick, the words nearly imperceptible.

"Yeah, where?"

Just a little more and he could grab the Glock. A round was chambered, no safety to click. Point and shoot: the proud legacy of this brand of weapon.

Shaw muscled the bike a little farther off himself. Two more inches.

Come on, push it, come on . . .

Fifteen feet away.

He touched the grip of his weapon.

With one finger.

The men stopped. One whispered to the other. They shared another laugh.

Now two fingers.

White Shirt pulled a knife out of his pocket. It was spring operated and he flicked the black blade out.

Shaw thought: *Insert, twist . . .*

"I don't have the drugs here. I can get them," he said, stalling for time.

His fingers closed around the weapon's grip.

"Where?"

"They're back there." Shaw gestured toward the Egg building.

As they looked, he shouldered the bike up and crouched. The two BNGs turned, guns rising. Shaw's did too. He'd take one out at least, but where would the other one shoot him to wound. Maybe just to wound. They would really want their drugs back.

Weapons rose, fingers on the triggers . . .

At that moment a roar filled the parking lot.

It was a car engine. The vehicle was coming from the side, behind the Egg building.

The smiles vanished from the men's faces and they spun around, lifting the guns.

But they were too late.

The white Chevy Impala slammed into them at speed. One flew against the wall and the other caromed off the hood. They lay still, eyes closed, though breathing.

The car skidded to a stop.

Shaw glanced at the driver, getting out, the blond woman in sunglasses and baseball cap. So she *had* swapped out the green Honda.

She pulled the glasses off and looked at Shaw.

He squinted. *"You?"*

59

He knew her name only as Adelle.

Or more formally, Journeyman Adelle.

"Are you all right?"

Shaw ignored the scraped knee. It was bleeding. Not bad.

He nodded, scanning the area for other hostiles. He saw none. He pulled off his helmet. Shaw walked to the BNGs and collected their guns. He put them into one man's shoulder bag and set it by the motorcycle. He looked the men over. Neither was bleeding badly.

She glanced at the two Filipinos. Her gaze was clinical. Emotionless.

The woman, late twenties, had been a member and employee of the cult in Washington State where he had met Victoria Lesston—the cult he was just telling his brother about the charismatic—and dangerously narcissistic—clan leader had brainwashed her, and her fellow followers. She came to believe that if she were to kill herself, she would be reunited in the next life with her young daughter, who had died several years earlier.

There was no one near enough to have seen the incident. But

they'd have to clean up quickly. He sent Russell a text telling him he was needed urgently, giving the GPS coordinates. He concluded:

Déjà vu alley two days ago, near library. Two injured this time.

Need Karin/Ty with van.

The reply was nearly instantaneous.

K.

Slipping his phone away, Shaw said to her, "Thank you."

She nodded, still seemingly indifferent to what she'd just done. He wasn't surprised at her reaction, nor with the vehicular assault in the first place. When he'd first seen her, last week, she had observed with no emotion the brutal beating of a reporter by the sadistic head of the cult's security department. Shaw could still picture the three dots of the man's blood on her blouse.

She walked the fifteen feet to the water's edge and looked down. He joined her. He had plenty of questions, of course, but remained silent for a moment. Then:

"You got rid of the Honda."

She nodded. "You spotted me. I had to."

"So. How'd you get to San Francisco?"

After a moment she said, "At the camp? I talked to Journeyman Frederick and found out who you really were, that you'd been after this reward for Journeyman Adam, some crime they said he'd done. You were with him when he graduated."

The cult's troublingly sanitized term for suicide.

"He told me you had Adam's notebook and that you were going to give it to his father, Mr. Harper. I drove to his shipping business in Gig Harbor and waited for you."

Shaw couldn't help but appreciate her clever, industrious detective work. And as for following him to San Francisco, if you're going to be tailing a vehicle, when your subject is driving a thirty-foot motor home, your job is pretty damn easy.

"I was going to kill you. I didn't have a gun. But I had my car. I was going to drive you off the road. I felt you ruined my life. You destroyed it. Everything he taught about coming back, it seemed so true. I believed it." A sigh. "I remembered her face, her laugh, her little fingers—Jamie's. My daughter's . . . And all I could think was that you took away my chance to see her again. I wanted you to die. I was working up my courage. A couple times I almost hit you."

"Eli did nothing but lie to you, to everybody. He wanted money and he wanted sex and he wanted power. Trying to sell immortality. It was all fake."

"I know that now. Maybe I knew all along." A sad smile. "Eli was pretty sharp. You can't prove what he taught us doesn't work."

This was true. The only way to know for certain if there was an afterlife was to die, and nobody was going to send back social media pix from there, confirming the theory.

"The nails you threw into the street. You learn that from Journeyman Hugh?" The cult's head of security.

"He said we needed to know how to stop enemies coming after us."

"Why the change of heart, Adelle?"

She blinked, maybe at the use of her given name alone. In the cult you always used a prefix: at first "Novice," then "Apprentice" and finally the coveted "Journeyman."

Shaw had no idea what her last name was. Withholding those from members of the cult had been a way for the leader to control his sheep.

"I can't really say. Maybe . . . Eli's spell wore off."

She'd hesitated again before mentioning the cult leader's name.

It was a serious breach of the rules to fail to refer to him as "Master Eli."

She turned her eyes his way. "I kept thinking, you had to die . . . But I couldn't get out of my head that you *helped* people. You saved lives. Hugh and Eli would have poisoned them. And you nearly got killed . . . So I couldn't hurt you. It would just be wrong."

Noise from the highway. A Lincoln Navigator appeared, paused and then drove to where Adelle and Shaw stood. Russell got out.

"This is Adelle. Russell."

They nodded to each other and Russell looked over the BNGs. "How'd they make you?"

"Been here, asking about Blond. Maybe word got back."

Now the same white van Shaw remembered from several days ago pulled up, and Karin and Ty got out. The other group ops weren't present. Ty assessed one of the injured Filipinos and gave him an injection.

Shaw stirred.

Russell said, "Just a painkiller."

The second man too was treated.

"We'll drop them off at a hospital, take a picture of their licenses and tell them to get amnesia."

Shaw said, "She needs to be safe. Out of the area. Where can you go?"

"My sister's in Vegas."

Russell said, "We'll get you on a plane. It has to happen now."

Adelle nodded.

"I'll drive you to SFO." He nodded at her Impala. "Report it stolen to the rental company."

"But—"

"Report it stolen."

"Okay."

The car would be cubed within the day and in a scrapyard by tomorrow.

Russell asked, "You have things somewhere? A hotel?"

"Motel Six. Near the airport."

Karin took a call, listened then disconnected. "Possible facial recognition hit on Blond from the alley. Came up at a joint OC task force in San Leandro. They're cross-referencing. We should know soon."

The brothers shared a glance. If they could get his ID, that might be enough to crack the code of the Hunters Point gang, which would lead to finding out who the SP family was and stopping the hit.

Shaw checked his motorcycle for damage—there was little.

He said to Adelle, "You know you'll meet somebody, you'll have children. You'll never forget Jamie. But you can move on. Not in a cult. In the real world. We're diminished by things that happen to us in life. But we *can* find a separate happiness."

In his rewards business, Colter Shaw had on occasion had to counsel the grieving. Not all jobs ended happily.

There was a salute that was used in the cult, an open palm touching the opposite shoulder. By reflex Adelle started to do this now. Then stopped herself and gave a small smile and hugged Shaw hard.

60

After stopping along the way to make a purchase, Shaw returned to Pacific Heights to pack up. The brothers could now return to Alvarez Street, as the safe house was indeed safe once again. Mary Dove and Dorie and her family would not be in danger any longer either. There'd be no point in targeting them, though out of prudence Shaw texted them to keep Plans A and B in place for the time being.

Shaw brewed another cup of coffee, this one Guatemalan, and a fine brew it was, deriving from a grower that, in his opinion, had been sadly overlooked for years. He and the farmer knew each other. The man had suggested Shaw come to Central America, where abductions were common, and said, "You, Mr. Colter, can make a great deal of money, I would think, at rewards."

Shaw had explained that he was familiar with Latin American kidnappings. They occurred for two reasons. One was snatching corporate execs. The bad guys throw a CEO or general manager into the back of a van, submit a demand for a quarter million and release him or her when the money is dropped. The victim's company and family never post a reward offer; they buy kidnap insurance and in ninety-five percent of those cases the victim is returned largely unharmed.

The other reason people are kidnapped down there is because of politics or cartel business, in which case the vics are dead five minutes after they vanish and rescue is not an option.

This put Shaw in mind of SP and his, or her, family once again.

Confirmation from Hunters Point crew.
6/26, 7:00 p.m. SP and family. All ↓

Did SP have some connection with the voting tally? If so, the kill order might have been rescinded, now that the document was in Devereux's possession. But Shaw and Russell couldn't make that assumption. It seemed more likely that since the gangs in Hunters Point were involved, SP was targeted because they knew something about the Urban Improvement Plan. Maybe they had discovered the source of the opioids and other drugs being strewn around the city by BlackBridge and its subcontracting gangs.

He was lifting the cup to his lips when a knocking on the door resounded.

A man's low, threatening voice shouted, "Police! Warrant. Open the door!"

61

Colter Shaw stood, leaning forward, with his hands against the yellow-painted living room wall of the residence, a pleasant shade. His feet were back and spread. His palms were in roughly the same spot that the Davis & Sons Rare Books frame had rested before it had been stolen. He was looking at the nail, eight inches away from his face, on which it had hung.

"Don't move," the voice instructed. It belonged to a large Black SFPD officer, uniformed.

"I won't."

"Don't turn around."

"I won't."

Shaw knew the drill. He'd been arrested before. Detained too, which was arrest lite. He'd never been convicted, but that didn't mean there wouldn't be a first time.

"I'm armed." It was always a good idea to tell this to law enforcers when they were confronting or arresting/detaining you. In some jurisdictions it was required to so inform them.

"Okay."

Police always said that. Every single cop who'd arrested or de-tained him had said "Okay" pretty frequently.

He lifted Shaw's untucked shirt and plucked the Glock 42 from the Blackhawk holster. The gun would be tiny in his hand. The man was massive.

The cop wore a Glock 17, the full size, double-stack model, with seventeen rounds to play with. Nine-millimeter. Shaw's was a .380, and had only six in the mag.

It's never the number of rounds you have; it's where you put them.

The gun, Shaw's knife and the black velvet bag went on the cof-fee table.

Another cop—a short man, Anglo, with similar close-cropped hair, though blond in his case—was going through Shaw's wallet.

"He's got a conceal carry. California. Up to date."

"Okay." The big cop, named Q. Barnes according to the tag, was the one in charge. He un-holstered his cuffs and stepped closer. Shaw knew this was coming.

"I'm going to cuff you now for my safety and for yours."

More or less exactly what he'd told Earnest La Fleur in Sausalito.

"Put your hands behind your back, please."

Polite.

Shaw did and he felt the cuffs ratchet on. The man did a good job. They were tight enough so he couldn't get free but there was no pain.

"You're not under arrest at this point."

Because I haven't done anything that I can be arrested for. Shaw did not verbalize this, however. He said, "Okay."

The man turned Shaw around.

That was when he saw her.

Consuela Ramirez.

The young woman was walking into the safe house suite with a policewoman, an intensely focused redhead, hair in a tight ponytail. Makeup-free, save for a little blue eye shadow. She was petite but stood perfectly erect, even with all the cop accessories she wore: gun, mags, Taser, cuffs, pepper spray. You needed to be in good shape to do public safety. The bulletproof plate alone had to weigh ten pounds.

"Consuela," said Shaw. "What is this?"

She cocked her head with a faint frown. But she said nothing.

"This is the man you told us about?"

"Consuela . . ." Shaw repeated.

"Yessir," she said.

"It's okay, miss. Don't worry. You're okay. He's not going to hurt you."

"Hurt you?" Shaw said, frowning. "What's going on? What did she say?"

"Ms. Ramirez filled out an affidavit saying that she saw you with a significant quantity of narcotics. She had a relative who overdosed and was doing her civic duty to get them off the street. Now, you can help yourself here by cooperating. And I'll tell you, sir, it'll go a long way if you do."

"I don't know what's going on. I've never done drugs, let alone sold them."

"Cooperation?" Barnes reminded, steering back to his theme.

"Of course. Sure."

Barnes's face registered some relaxation. "So," he said. "The drugs?"

Shaw frowned broadly. "I don't know anything about any drugs. I assume you've looked my name up in NCIC. Nothing there, right?" His eyes were fixed on the young woman's, which were cast defiantly toward Shaw. She really was quite beautiful.

Barnes asked, "How do you know each other?"

Shaw beat her to whatever she was going to say, "I don't really know her. We have a mutual friend."

To Shaw, he said, "Tell me about the drugs."

"There are no drugs."

"Ms. Ramirez tells a different story." Barnes sighed, as if auto-
nomically responding to what he'd heard a thousand times before.
The officer returned to his favorite subject with: "You should be
more cooperative than you're being."

"Doesn't get any more cooperative than this. I'm telling you the
truth."

"All right."

A variation on "Okay."

Shaw shrugged. The cuffs jingled.

Barnes asked Connie, "Where?"

She pointed to the end table beside the couch, where she'd sat
earlier. "The drawer."

Barnes jerked his head toward another patrolman, an underling,
a short, uniformed cop with a shaved head and the complexion of
mixed races. He fit the description of Roman, Tessy's stalker former
boyfriend. The man opened the drawer. "Got something." After
donning blue latex gloves, he removed the bag and set it on the table,
near Shaw's accessories.

The woman's look of vindication was smug.

"About eight ounces, Quentin," the woman officer said, eyeing
the bag. "Way over felony."

Barnes sized up Shaw, assessing the offense not of drugs but of
failure to cooperate. He nodded to the underling who'd discovered the
bag. The officer removed a folding-blade knife and cut a small slit in
the top of the bag. From one of the many pockets in his service vest he
extracted a small bottle. He broke a liquid capsule inside and added a
bit of the white powder. He shook it. There was no color change.

"More," Barnes said.

The young officer added powder. It still didn't turn blue or green
or red, whatever it was supposed to.

"What?" Connie whispered. Her expression registered a minor Richter number of concern.

Shaw said, "It's not drugs."

Barnes asked, "No? What is it?"

"Chalk. I rock climb. This is just a misunderstanding. I appreciate her concern. Drugs are terrible." He looked into her lovely eyes. "I see why you'd think that, of course, but I'd never have anything to do with narcotics."

Barnes took the knife and sniffed. He handed the blade back to the other officer. He looked from one to the other. "Whole room," Barnes ordered. "Search it."

The others—four cops in total—began searching. They were good. Every place where a four-by-eight-by-two-inch pouch of cocaine could be hidden was examined.

After the dining room came the kitchen then the two bedrooms, the living room. All of the closets, of which there were a fair number, and they were big ones. For a last-minute safe house, it really offered some nice features.

Barnes was frustrated. He snapped, "Dog," to the patrolman who'd searched Shaw's wallet.

A moment later the canine made his appearance with a young Latina handler. He was a lithe and focused Malinois, one of the four Belgian herding breeds, the others being the Tervuren, Laekenois and the Belgian sheepdog. The Malinois was smaller and wirier than the German shepherd and had largely taken over law enforcement duties from the latter around the country.

The dog—whose name was Beau or Bo—zipped up and down the floor twitchily. Nose up, nose down, turning corners fast, sticking the lengthy muzzle into cushions and the gap between cabinets. Everywhere.

But he never once sat. Sitting is the signal that police K9s learn to indicate that they've found what they were searching for: the drugs, the explosives, the body. They don't point or bark and they never bring a treasure back to their handler in their eager and powerful jaws.

They sit.

But Beau or Bo didn't.

Barnes was no longer relaxed. And he definitely wasn't happy.

The handler gave the dog a dried meat treat. His confirmation that the suite was drug free was as much a win for the muscular animal as if he'd found a thousand pounds of smack.

"Officer Barnes?" Shaw asked.

The man continued to scan the residence, then finally looked toward Shaw. His massive, round face displayed no expression whatsoever. "Yes?"

"In your experience how many people who have CCPs are involved in criminal activity?"

To get a concealed carry permit you undergo an extensive background check. If a criminal past shows up, you're disqualified. If you can legally carry a sidearm—especially in California, where the requirements are more rigorous than in any other state in the union—that means you've been vetted about as well as a civilian can be.

Barnes looked at Connie. "Ms. Ramirez?"

"I'm sorry. I saw the package. I just thought . . ."

Barnes stepped away to make a radio call. This left Shaw and Connie in the living room, standing near each other. The woman officer with the taut hair was nearby, keeping an eye on them but she was out of earshot.

Shaw whispered, "Here's the deal, whoever you are. You come back here later. Alone. If you don't, I give the cop the video of you planting the real drugs in the drawer when I was getting you that tissue. I saw you wipe it, so it may not have your fingerprints on it, but it still has your DNA. Roll you up for felony possession."

The tears had been real, but a little Tabasco on the fingertips does the same thing as true sorrow or method acting.

"Do you understand?"

Silence. Her lip trembled. A nod.

Barnes and the others returned. The blond male cop took the cuffs off Shaw.

"Chalk," the big officer muttered. As the men and women in blue left, he added, "You should leave too, Ms. Ramirez."

"I'm sorry," she said. "I was worried. All those drugs . . . I did it for the children."

Which, Shaw reflected, was rather a nice touch.

62

Shaw opted for an Altamont Beer Works IPA and drank long.
Typically, he'd been cautious about the Maria Vasquez reward offer.

From Teddy Bruin's starting the conversation with "coincidence" to Mack McKenzie's assessment—"probably legit"—he had remained wary. There were too many people in the San Francisco area—from a video gaming exec in Silicon Valley to BlackBridge—who were not pleased with his recent visits here.

He was always skeptical of those posting rewards and he generally spent hours, sometimes days, researching the offerors. It was not unheard of, for example, for a murderer to post a reward for the "loved one" they themselves had dispatched, in a numb-headed attempt to appear blameless. Tessy's disappearance, though, had happened fast. He was no less cautious than on any other job but he didn't have the luxury of in-depth research. And, if her mother *was* telling the truth, she could have been in real danger from her abusive ex, Roman.

Of course, the girl's disappearance and the reward offer turned out to be one hundred percent genuine.

The "dear friend," though? He just didn't quite trust that scenario. Why hadn't Maria given him her name as someone whom Tessy might contact?

So he'd simply ignored the keep-it-between-us plea and called Maria, asked her about Tessy's godmother.

Alarmed, Vasquez had said, "*Dios mio!* Did something happen in Guadalajara?"

Answering his question.

Then he'd inquired: Had anybody called and asked her about the reward? Yes, a woman had seen the offer and called her and said that she too had a missing child, a son; did someone answer Maria's ad?

Yes, someone named Colter Shaw, Maria had explained to the woman. She had given her Shaw's number and address. "I'm sorry. I shouldn't have . . . I thought, maybe she has more money to pay you than I do."

"It's all right."

"This person, is she a problem?"

"I'll handle it." Shaw had told her, "It's probably nothing, but I'd recommend you go stay someplace else for a few days."

"Yes, of course. Okay, we'll leave now. And, Mr. Shaw, again, bless you!"

Immediately after disconnecting, he'd called up the security camera recording and watched "Connie" planting the drugs. Using a plastic bag, to avoid transferring his fingerprints, he'd collected the coke and put it, and the necklace, in another bag and hid them some blocks away in a vacant lot. Then on the way back from Hunters Point, he'd stopped at a sporting goods store and bought a bag of hand chalk. He returned to the Pacific Heights safe house and awaited the law. He was sure officers would descend at some point. What he didn't know was what the woman's game was.

Now, sipping more beer, he heard the buzzer.

"Yes?"

"It's me," came the sullen voice through the intercom.

When she arrived at the door upstairs, he checked her eye movement once more, hand on the gun.

She was alone now too.

He let her in and told her to stop. His voice was abrupt. "Hands."

"Come on," she whined.

"Up."

She grudgingly complied and he frisked her. She was clean. "Sit down." Pointing to the couch.

The woman complied. He pulled up a chair across from her.

"Did you really think I wouldn't call Maria?"

"You said you wouldn't." As if he'd cheated at checkers.

"Is this something you *do*? In addition to tricks? Planting drugs and getting people busted?"

He suspected she was a call girl.

She tried to look offended but it didn't work, and that answered his question. Shaw was continually amused at how the guilty can look so indignant when they get caught.

He opened her purse and shook out the contents. He pushed the pepper spray out of reach. There were no other weapons.

He shuffled through three driver's licenses, same picture, different names. One read "Consuela Ramirez."

"Which is real?"

"Sophia Ionescu."

"That's Romanian?"

She nodded.

Shaw asked, *"¿Y si te hubiera preguntado algo en español?"*

"I speak Spanish too."

He took a picture of the Sophia license and sent it to Mack. Less than thirty seconds later:

That's her. Two arrests for prostitution in California. One in Florida.

"You didn't answer my question. Is this something you do? A franchise?"

"A guy wanted to take you down. Get you in the system. He had this idea. He knew what you did for a living so he checked for people around here who'd posted rewards for missing kids or wives. He gave me the numbers and I called them up. Maria Vasquez told me you'd saved her daughter. You were so nice, you didn't even take the reward. This guy told me to pretend to be the girl's godmother. I do some acting too." Sophia said this with a wisp of pride.

"Yeah, you'd get an Oscar. Who hired you?"

"This guy I have dates with."

A phrase he figured meant something different from "This guy I date."

Shaw said, "That's half an answer."

"Ian. Ian Helm. Or Helms. Maybe an 's.' I don't know. He's rich, has some consulting company, he says."

Well. Interesting, but not utterly surprising, news.

"What'd he pay?"

"Ten thousand."

"You get along with him? Helms?"

"We fuck."

"Would you testify against him?"

Sophia laughed at Shaw's naivete.

He considered the issue but decided that this wasn't the way to go. Even if the woman cooperated, what could Helms be busted for? Nothing serious. Shaw didn't want to swipe at the men. He wanted to take the entire BlackBridge operation down permanently and send Helms to prison for decades.

Shaw leaned close, staring. He saw uneasiness cloud her eyes. He was using Russell's approach. "Is there any risk to Maria or Tessy?"

"No, no. We just wanted information."

"Because if there is . . ." He tapped her authentic driver's license.

"No, I swear. I told Ian no way would I help if anybody'd get hurt. I don't get involved in anything like that. I'm a three-G-a-night girl."

Offered, he guessed, as proof of her moral caliber.

"Give me your number. Your real one. And keep the phone alive. I may need to be in touch with you. If it goes out of service, a friend of mine comes to pay a visit at Eight Five Four Sumner Street. Or wherever you've moved. I will find you. You're in our system now."

Which meant nothing but sounded good, and certainly unnerved her.

"Jesus."

Shaw raised an eyebrow.

A tight-lipped nod, still looking victimized. She recited her cell number and Shaw memorized it.

"How much was the necklace?"

A shrug. "Fifty-nine ninety-nine. It's not a real diamond."

She looked at the pepper spray.

Shaw laughed and ushered her out the door.

63

The Alvarez Street safe house once again.

Karin and Ty were handling cleanup. The Filipino BNGs' pickup truck and the weapons were gone. The injured men, now practicing vows of silence, were in the hospital. Adelle was on her way to Vegas. And somewhere in Oakland a perfectly fine Chevrolet Impala, if somewhat bloodstained, was soon to become a two-ton block of scrap.

He wondered if Karin was having any luck finding the identity of Blond, with the task force in San Leandro.

Once they knew who he was, they could deep-background him and, ideally, find out where he'd been recently, whom he associated with, where he lived, what division of BlackBridge he worked for, which gang in Hunters Point he had a connection to.

And who SP was, and why he or she had been targeted for death.

Once those unknowns were brought to light, they would have a chance to save the family.

The time was 1:10 p.m. The kill order would go into effect in less than six hours.

His phone hummed with a text from Professor Steven Field.

It's on the news.

He flipped to a live TV streaming app on his phone and turned the unit horizontal.

The woman newscaster looked calm and in control and did a fine job reading the words that scrolled up on the teleprompter, but Shaw could see that she was having a bit of trouble understanding the concept. Then again, who wouldn't?

". . . *government document from more than a hundred years ago has been discovered in San Francisco. It's a voting tally of a recount in a statewide referendum in nineteen oh-six where the citizens of the state voted to allow . . .*" A dramatic pause. "*. . . corporations to run for public office. Officials say that the tally was lost among hundreds of thousands of documents that went missing after the earthquake that year, which destroyed three-quarters of the city. It's believed that the judge certifying the recount was killed in the disaster, which is why no one learned of it at the time.*"

Well. That didn't take long. Shaw supposed this was no surprise. Devereux had waited years to find his magic document. He'd move as quickly as possible to use his ring of power.

"*Joining us now is University of Utah business law professor, C. Edward Hobbs. Welcome, Dr. Hobbs. Explain how this amendment could become law after more than a hundred years.*"

"*Hello. Thank you for having me. There's no time limit on amendments going into effect once they've been approved. No statute of limitations, you might say. A proposition for an amendment doesn't need to be signed by the governor; it's not like a bill. Once a majority of the people have voted in favor, it becomes law.*"

"*So it's true then. This amendment will allow corporations to run for office?*"

"*Yes. And, we should say, not just run in an election. A*"

corporation could be appointed to a position too. Judges, sheriffs, regulatory board presidents."

"Will it be challenged?"

"No doubt it will. The tally itself will have to be authenticated. I'm sure there are experts doing that right now. But we have to remember there's been a groundswell of support lately to expand the rights of corporations. Look at 'Citizens United'—the 2010 case that extended the First Amendment right of free speech to corporations.

"The majority of Americans support that. And many professors and politicians I've spoken with consider the movement a good one—good for the country, good for democracy. If a corporation holds office, the authority is decentralized. There'll be an automatic system of checks and balances with the shareholders, the board and the CEO. Remember that the greatest innovations in the past century have come from corporate research. Corporations represent the best brain trusts in the world."

The shill—on Devereux's payroll, of course—gave no mention of the man's troubling policies described in the documents that Shaw and Russell had found in the courier bag, undermining human rights.

"So Facebook or Apple or Amazon could one day be governor of California."

"In theory, yes."

"But a corporation couldn't run for president of the United States?"

"No, the U.S. Constitution is clear on that. The amendment doesn't apply to federal elections or appointments either. Only state and local. But this is an important precedent. In law, we say, as California goes, so goes the nation . . ."

Shaw shut the broadcast off. He glanced around the safe house. In a windowless corner sat a brown Naugahyde armchair facing the bay window that overlooked the street. This would have been where his father sat—his back was never exposed to door or window.

Beside the chair was a scuffed and unsteady side table. Shaw walked to the chair and sat in it. He ran his hand over the arms, torn and scuffed. His father had been in San Francisco, just before he returned to the Compound, and not long after that he'd died. Maybe it was here that he'd sat as he assembled the clues that would lead someone—his son, as it turned out—to continue the quest to bring down BlackBridge Corporate Solutions, if he couldn't finish the job.

Maybe it was in this chair that he'd written the letter and circled the eighteen magic locations on the map that he'd hidden on Echo Ridge.

It was then that his phone hummed with a text from Russell.

Karin: Negative on San Leandro lead to Blond identity. If we don't find something in a few hours, the family's gone.

64

At three that afternoon, Shaw's iPhone trilled. He answered, "Hello?"

"Is this Colter Shaw?" The woman's voice was low, matter-of-fact.

"That's right."

"I was just speaking to your brother, Russell. I'm Julia Callahan. I'm with Systems Support in Bayshore Heights. He called me earlier about an analysis of an old cassette audiotape."

"I was with him then. You work with Russell, right? He never said exactly."

"My company does contract work for his organization. He told me to call you ASAP."

"Russell said you were going to do a deeper analysis. You find something else on the tape?"

"I did. They were smart, whoever made it. The first run through the analyzer showed only music tracks. But the more I listened to it I decided there was a pattern of sounds within the static between the tracks." Her voice was excited.

"Static?"

"Which wasn't static at all. I isolated it and slowed it down. Way down."

"What was on it?"

"A man's voice, reciting account numbers, routing instructions to offshore corporations and banks, wire transfers to individuals. The man specifically mentioned that the purpose of the transfers was to evade taxes. And some payments were made to outside contractors. And by contractors, it sounded like he meant . . . well . . ."

"Hitmen?"

"That was my impression. I'm just an audio analyst. But we work with companies that do security consulting, so I've got experience in the subject. He also mentioned some names. Braxton, Droon—I think that's a name. And the company they worked for, BlackBridge. And something called UIP was mentioned a half-dozen times. He gave sources for what he called 'product.'"

"Drugs."

"I figured."

Shaw asked, "So you've extracted what was said?"

"Yes, it's a separate recording. An MP3 file."

"Good. I need to get a copy. I can use it as leverage in an operation Russell and I are running."

"Give me an email address and I'll upload it."

Shaw said, "No. We need to keep it off the internet. Can you get me a physical copy? Maybe on a thumb drive?"

"I can."

"We only have a few hours. Bayshore's south of the city?"

"That's right."

"You know San Bruno state park?"

"Sure. I jog there some."

Shaw asked, "Is there a deserted place we can meet?"

"The south entrance, off McGuire Road. Nobody ever uses it."

"A half hour?"

"Okay."

"I'll be on a motorcycle. Black leather jacket."

"I've got a Toyota Camry. Blue."

"I'll bring the original tape."

"Good. I can do some deeper analysis."

Shaw paused. He whispered, "Evidence against them . . . So Ashton was right after all."

"What was that?"

"Oh. Just thinking out loud. I'll see you soon."

65

M any years ago, San Bruno, south of San Francisco, was an Ohlone village.

The Ohlones lived in scores of indigenous settlements from San Francisco down to Big Sur in precolonial America. Numbering in the tens of thousands, they were hunters, fishers and gatherers, and did some farming too. They were the first people in America to learn how to make bitter acorns into food. The Ohlone practiced the Kuksu religion, heavy into rites and rituals, usually practiced in secretive underground chambers.

Life was fine among these people until the conquistadores arrived and, with the Franciscans, set to work "missionizing" the tribes, moving them off their lands and forcing conversion to Christianity. The population was reduced by three-quarters on account of European diseases, against which the Ohlone had no natural immunity. The coup de grâce for the tribes, however, was not the missions, the Spanish or bacteria, but the state of California itself, whose first governor, Peter Burnett, said, in an address to the legislature in

1851, he would wage a war of extermination against the native people "until the Indian race becomes extinct." He pursued that policy to grim effect, though several Ohlone tribes still existed in the Central Coastal region.

Shaw knew this because he had some Ohlone blood in his veins, through Mary Dove, who'd taught him about their distant ancestry. San Bruno park, which had been in the heart of their territory, was a sample of what their home had been like two hundred and fifty years ago, before the gold, silver and silicon rushes: Lush and rich and verdant, covered with undulating hills.

It was into a small parking lot here that Colter Shaw now steered his Yamaha. He traversed the smooth asphalt, stopping in the center. He looked with some envy at nearby hiking trails, which would make for an exhilarating dirt bike ride.

That diversion would, of course, have to wait.

The place was not quite deserted. On one side of the small parking lot was a commercial van—a plumbing company. The driver, in overalls, was eating a sandwich and sipping from a very large soda cup. Also present was a California State Parks service pickup, its driver—in an oversize Smokey-the-Bear hat—making a call and referring to a clipboard. No joggers or hikers or sightseers were present. The gray sky shed mist and teased with the promise of rain.

A blue Toyota sedan pulled into the lot and edged slowly toward him. The car stopped and the door opened.

Shaw nodded to the woman in black leggings and sweater and a navy-blue windbreaker. "Julia?"

"Colter."

He joined her. "You weren't followed?"

"No. I'm sure. You?"

"I have an anti-tailing device."

She frowned. "What's that?"

He nodded to the Yamaha.

"In your motorcycle?" she asked.

"It *is* my motorcycle. You drive on the lane stripes seven miles over the limit and nobody can follow."

"I might try that someday."

"You ride?"

"No. But I always wanted to. I'd need somebody to teach me how. You have to take a test, don't you? To get a license."

"Piece of cake. You'll pass with flying colors."

She pursed her lips. "What *are* flying colors exactly? I'm always curious where expressions come from."

Shaw didn't know and he told her so.

She pulled a hair elastic off her wrist and tied her tangle of dark-blond hair up into a ponytail, centered high on the back of her head. "Where's Russell?"

"He's back at the safe house. Following up on some other leads for our operation." He looked her over, frowning. "You're not armed, are you?"

"Me?" She gave a laugh as if this were an absurd idea. "I work for a tech company. We don't carry guns. Why?"

Shaw nodded at the state park pickup. "Government property. Weapons aren't allowed."

"Are *you* armed?"

Shaw shrugged. "I am but I've had plenty of practice keeping mine out of sight."

The parks department truck's engine fired up and the unsmiling driver touched the brim of his hat as he pulled past them. Shaw nodded in reply. The truck vanished up a dirt trail into the woods.

She said, "I've got a thumb drive but I also ran a transcription program. It printed out everything. I got about a hundred pages." She retrieved a large white envelope from the front seat of her car.

"Excellent."

"I might pick up something more from the original. Second generation there's always some fallout. I was thinking . . ." Her voice faded, then she gasped, looking past Shaw.

The front door of the plumbing van was swinging open and the driver, a pale-faced man, climbed out. Blond as the dead man in the alley. He was huge, dressed in black tactical gear and was holding a pistol.

Then the side panel slid open and two others stepped to the ground: Ebbitt Droon, armed as well, and—looking every inch the harmless grandmother—Irena Braxton.

When they were out, standing on the ground, another figure emerged and joined them.

The head of BlackBridge, Ian Helms, stared his way. In a voice that was a rich, resonant baritone—as one might expect, coming from such a handsome leading man—he said, "Well, Colter Shaw."

66

Arms crossed, studying Shaw, Helms said, "Would've been in your best interest not to outsmart my friend."

Shaw supposed Helms was referring to Sophia/Connie and his dodging the bust at the Pacific Heights safe house.

I was worried. All those drugs . . . I did it for the children . . .

At least there he wouldn't be facing that fate they now had planned for him here in the park.

Droon took over. "Okay, Shaw, pull your shirt up. Slow, don'tcha know?"

"Just take it easy, Droon."

"What is this? What's going on?"

"Hush, there, Miss Julia," Droon scolded.

"How do you . . ." Her voice faded.

"Sit tight. I'll get to you in a minute, Lovely." He turned to Shaw. "Now, Righty, use that *left* hand of yours and pluck that sissy Glock off your hip and toss it in the bushes there. I want to see fingers out, like you're sipping tea from a dainty little cup."

"If I do that, it might go off and hurt someone."

"Now, now, you know better'n that. Those Austrians're too clever for accidents. Be a good boy and behave. Miss Julia's looking a little queasy. We don't want to upset her. Be a sorrow and shame. Go on, go on."

"What *is* this?" she repeated, her voice quavering.

Droon snapped to Shaw, "*Pistole*, son."

Shaw did as he'd been told, tugging his shirt up, revealing the weapon.

"Look at those abs. You must work out till the cows come home."

Shaw pitched the gun to the ground.

"Pull those jeans cuffs up too, would'ya, boy? You look like an ankle holster kind of guy."

Shaw complied.

"Goody good. Now. You, Miss Julia, you can stay fully clothed, much to my disappointment, don'tcha know? I heard you say you're not packing heat."

"You heard?"

Shaw glanced at the plumbing van. "They were listening. They know about the cassette. The analysis." He looked to Braxton. "After you stole the voting tally I thought you'd forget about us."

"We couldn't afford to do that."

Droon said, "You're our favorite number-one reward-seeker, Mr. Colter Shaw." He chuckled. "It'd hurt too much to say goodbye."

Helms waved his hand to silence the irritating man and stepped forward. "I wanted to see you in person, Shaw." He looked him over, and the man seemed enormously unimpressed. This was mutual. "The Shaw family . . . you've caused me nothing but grief."

"Grief?" Shaw laughed cynically. "My mother's a widow, thanks to you."

He sighed. "That again. It wasn't supposed to happen the way it did. We thought Ashton had found the vote tally certificate. Our man was simply going to pay him a lot of money for it."

"Your representative for those quote 'negotiations' was an armed trespasser on our property at three in the morning, tracking my father in the woods. What you meant to say was torture him until he told you where it was hidden, and *then* kill him. You're tedious, Helms."

"Tedious?" The handsome face darkened. The word had insulted him. Shaw realized whom he resembled: a younger Warren Beatty. His voice honed: "The Endgame Sanction. It's going to change the country fundamentally."

"Stalin changed Russia fundamentally. I don't think that's the kind of standard you want to be touting."

"BlackBridge didn't vote on Proposition Oh-Six. Mr. Devereux didn't vote on it. We were hired to locate a document that'd been duly passed by the citizens of the state in a legal election. We're just enabling the will of the people."

The words sounded like they came from a spokesperson at a press conference.

Helms continued, "Just think, Shaw. The amendment gives *any* corporation the right to run for office. A do-good nonprofit."

"You're not the shining light of social conscience, Helms. You're destroying neighborhoods with your Urban Improvement Plan."

Helms shrugged. "I never held a gun to anybody's head and said, 'Here. Take these drugs. Or else.'"

The big man with pale skin, the van driver, just watched everything quietly. Maybe he was the hitman who'd been brought in to replace Blond. The man who had his sights on the SP family.

Irena Braxton appeared impatient. "We knew that Gahl had found the voting tally and hid it." She glanced toward the white envelope. "We never knew he was sucking up evidence too."

"The tape recorder was in our safe house when you broke in," Shaw said. "You had a chance to get it then."

Helms muttered, "Well, better late . . ."

A nod toward Droon, who said, "Now, Miss Julia. Here's what's going to happen. You're going to give us that envelope and your purse—or wallet, if 'purse' is too sexist a thing to say. Sorry for the offense. I'm going to get your partic'lars, find out where you live and your family or, if you prefer, *loved ones* live."

"No, please!"

"Yes, please!" he mocked. "Then you're going back to the office and you're overwriting every single bit of that digital copy of that cassette. 'Overwrite' is the key word. 'Member that. Nothing really gets deleted 'less you overwrite it, as you probably know, being in this business."

Braxton said, "No calls to the police. Or my associates'll drive straight to your house."

"No!" Her voice choked. "I have children!" Her hand kneaded the envelope manically.

Droon said, "Settle there, Lovely. You make sure everything's gone and . . . promise never to say a word about this again. And your little ones and hubby'll be fine."

"How could you do this?" she raged.

Droon frowned as if he didn't understand the question. He turned to Shaw. "I want the original cassette too, don'tcha know? Where is it? And don't be playful. We don't have all day here."

Shaw's face darkened. "All right." He held up his right hand—indicating no threat—and reached into his jacket pocket with his left, removed the cassette.

"Lookee. Wasn't that easy and painless? Toss it here."

Shaw did and the man picked it up.

In that giddy, grating tone, Droon said, "All right, Miss Julia, the sooner you hightail to the office, the sooner—"

"Wait." The urgent word came from Braxton. Her head was angled, eyes squinting. "Wait."

Helms was frowning, and Droon turned toward her.

"You were scanning his safe house when you picked up the call from Julia, right?" Braxton asked.

Droon said, "Well, yup." There was an uneasiness in his voice, as he looked at his boss's powdered, troubled face.

"What phone did he pick up on? What was the number?"

"I . . ." Droon was thinking. "It started with eight-four-five or eight-four-something, I'm pretty sure. I can look up—"

"Jesus Christ!" Braxton's voice raged. "That's his iPhone!"

The woman would know that Shaw had been using his encrypted burner—the Android platform—since he'd been in San Francisco because he knew BlackBridge could listen in on the iPhone, which was unprotected.

If Shaw had picked up the call about the audiotape on the Apple, it was because he *wanted* them to hear the conversation.

"It's a trap! There's nothing on the tape. The static? That was just bullshit. He's got people here."

The pale man and Droon lowered their stances and scanned around them, weapons extended.

Shaw was disappointed. He had hoped to play the game out a little longer to get more information from Droon and Braxton—and more incriminating admissions.

Braxton whispered to Helms, "Get back in the truck, Ian. Now."

Colter Shaw then gave a nod.

From the woods nearby, the "park ranger," who was, in reality, Ty, Russell's associate from his group, called, "You with Black-Bridge, hands where I can see them! Drop the weapons. Lie face-down on the ground! If you present with a weapon or any threat, you will be fired on." He let loose a burst of rounds from his silenced H&K submachine gun. Dirt kicked up ten feet in front of the Black-Bridge crew. "Now!"

The pale op did exactly as told, tossing his pistol away as if it were burning his skin. Braxton, grimacing, unhooked her macramé hippie purse from her shoulder and dropped it. She began kneeling. When finally down, she eased face forward to the dirt. Ian Helms followed suit.

Ebbitt Droon began to do the same, making a show of reaching out to set his gun gingerly on the ground. But he suddenly reared backward, putting the plumbing van between himself and Ty. He looked right at Shaw, his eyes both sadistic and amused. "No, sir, no, sir."

He began to lift his gun toward him. Shaw instinctively crouched, hands forward in a defensive posture.

Which is when the woman beside him—not audio expert Julia but Shaw's friend Victoria Lesston—pulled the trigger of Shaw's Colt Python .357, which was in the white envelope. Because she wasn't able to aim, the big round missed Droon by a few inches and blew apart the side-view mirror of the plumbing van. Droon stumbled backward and fell, his gun flying into the brush. He rose and fled into the woods.

Victoria offered Shaw the Colt, but he said, "No, cover them." Nodding toward the BlackBridge crew. He didn't waste time searching for his Glock. Shaw turned toward the well-trod footpath Droon had disappeared down and sprinted after him.

67

Shaw caught up with the wiry man fifty yards away.

Breathing hard, Droon turned back, drawing the SOG knife from the scabbard on his belt.

"Okay, Reward Man. Pretty much had it with you, don'tcha know?"

Shaw ignored the words and assessed the terrain. A flat grass-covered clearing. Fair ground for both of them.

Never fight from a downhill position.

Droon moved quickly, dancing back and forth, the knife hand—his right—always in motion.

Shaw tried, and he only tried once. "It's over, Droon. You know it. Don't make it harder on yourself."

"Haw, you're a funny man to speak, Shaw." He lunged and swept the blade back and forth. Shaw easily dodged. "We debated finishing you in the camper in Tacoma. I was for that. But Irena said you might have something else for us. Something helpful." Another swipe. "And damn if you didn't. You found that certificate. That made her day, my oh my."

Shaw was paying no attention to the words. Let him talk, let him use up oxygen. What he was doing was studying Droon's arms and hands. That's what you always watched in a knife fight. He kept his own in front and kept dancing away from Droon, making the small man come to him, then backing off.

Instinctively, Shaw was thinking of the rules of combat with blade.

Rule One: If you're attacked by someone with a knife and you're unarmed, run.

Not an option here.

Droon, laughing, giddy, eyes filled with glittery light, kept jogging forward and back, sweeping the knife between the men. Shaw moved back, but returned immediately, keeping his own hands up and open—to avoid breaking a finger—and slammed them into Droon's right arm, knocking it aside. As soon as the blade was past, Shaw cuffed Droon painfully in the face. Then moved back.

This infuriated the man, and his resulting expression accentuated his rodent features.

At one point Shaw, thinking the ground behind him was flat, stumbled on a root he hadn't seen. He didn't fall, but lost balance momentarily. Droon sprung and Shaw felt pain as the blade slashed the back of his hand.

Rule Two: You will be stabbed in a knife fight. Accept it and try to present non-vital portions of your body.

Shaw continued to dance away every time Droon lunged. Shaw kept up the palm slugging at his opponent's face, stunning him.

He didn't go for the knife.

Rule Three: Do not try to get the knife away from the attacker. He has a religious connection with it and no martial arts move will cause him to drop it.

Droon was no longer smiling. Shaw was not playing fair, dancing in and out, cuffing ears and eyes. Another slash to the upper arm. The jacket took the brunt.

Droon would pounce and Shaw would leap back, but every time he did so his right palm or left would connect with Droon's face, which was now red in places and bleeding. That was his only target. In fast, out fast.

"How'd you like . . ." Droon took a deep breath. ". . . to be blind, son? That suit your way of life?" Like a fencer he thrust the knife forward. Shaw saw it coming. He stunned Droon with a blow to the ear. Hard enough and such a move can render your opponent unconscious. This strike didn't do that but it disoriented him.

"I'm tired of you, Shaw. Let's finish this."

Rule Four: When the attacker draws back, counterattack to the eyes and throat.

Droon leapt forward, and the blade missed Shaw's chest by inches. The second that the scrawny man turned slightly and drew the blade back, Shaw was on him, gripping the knife wrist in his left hand and clawing at the eyes. The man howled.

Shaw pressed his advantage and, still holding the knife hand, gripped the man under his right knee, lifted him into the air and slammed him onto his back on the hard, rock-strewn ground. His breath went out of his lungs.

The knife tumbled to the ground.

"No, son, no." Droon held up his hands, as if for mercy, but then pressed forward and seized Shaw's throat. Though he wasn't a large man, there was formidable strength in the grip.

As his vision began to fade, Shaw picked up the SOG knife and, holding it firmly in his right hand, plunged it into Droon's neck.

"No, wait, no." He seemed surprised. Maybe he thought that for some odd cosmic reason Colter Shaw didn't have the right, or wasn't able, to stab him with his own blade.

The pressure on Shaw's neck continued.

Colter Shaw thought of his father.

Thinking of one word:

Survival . . .

He twisted the blade, opening the rent in the man's neck wider. Blood propelled.

"Look . . . No . . . I . . ."

The arms dropped.

In no more than ten seconds, the man had gone limp.

Breathing hard, Shaw rolled off him, rose and stepped away ten feet. He kept a firm grip on the knife.

Never assume even a downed enemy is no threat . . .

Droon coughed once. Then his breathing ceased. Shaw watched him, motionless, his unblinking eyes staring upward. They were aimed toward an oak bough, not far overhead, stark in the gray sky, thick with clusters of early-season acorns, which were a pleasant green in color, a deep shade.

Colter Shaw thought: Not a bad image to carry with you in your last moments on earth.

68

G ot 'em on the wire," Ty said to Shaw. "Listen."

The operative, no longer in the park ranger hat, was playing the recording he'd made of the conversation among the BlackBridge crew as they'd waited in the plumbing truck.

BRAXTON: *We can't do anything with a damn ranger there.*
DROON: *We'll hope he leaves. If he doesn't, well, accidents happen, don'tcha know?*
BRAXTON: *No. We wait till he's gone. I want it as clean as possible.*
DROON: *We're going to have two bodies 'ventually. Three can't gum up the works any more.*
HELMS: *Not the ranger.*

A third voice was that of the pale man, whose name turned out to be George Stone, a BlackBridge employee. He'd been a mercenary in Africa and the Balkans, Ty had learned.

STONE: *We kill Shaw now?*

DROON: *Does that make sense? Don't you think it might be better to wait till she comes back from the office, then take them out together?*

HELMS: *All right, all right . . . Maybe make it look, murder-suicide.*

DROON: *Now there's an idea for you.*

HELMS: *Gahl. That son of a bitch. How did he even know about the money laundering? He was research.*

STONE: *He overheard something. Was in the old building. No-body was separate then.*

BRAXTON: *Right. Was years ago.*

HELMS: *At least half the finance infrastructure's still in place. Most of the banks're the same. And the contractors? Maybe he knew about taking out the councilman. Maybe there's an email, a note. Jesus, that info could burn us to the ground.*

DROON: *Yeah, the councilman. Todd Zaleski. Forgot all about that. Now that job went smooth as oil.*

HELMS: *Droon. Jesus. This isn't a performance review.*

DROON: *Sure, sir. Sorry. Oh, lookee here. S'that woman. Julia. Get ready to move.*

Ty shut the recorder off.

"That should be enough for the Bureau to get started," Shaw said.

"I'd think. Conspiracy to commit murder, extortion. *Admission* of murder. That's a sweet one. The councilman."

Shaw told him that the death of Zaleski, his father's protégé, was what had started Ashton Shaw on the trail of BlackBridge, all those many years ago.

Helms snapped, "Did you have a warrant for that recording?" His wrists, like those of the others, were zip-tied behind him.

Ty glanced at him briefly, the way you'd regard a fly that buzzed a bit close. "You just executed an illegal wiretap, you extorted Mr. Shaw and Ms. Lesston here under threat of force and your associate tried to kill two people and got killed himself. That means *you're* guilty of felony murder. And I haven't even got near conspiracy yet. Oh, by the way, we didn't trespass in your vehicle to plant a listening device. Your window was open, and my microphone just happens to be very good. So, no warrant needed."

Shaw gazed over at Braxton. He took satisfaction in the fact that the woman who was responsible for his father's death looked truly stricken. Her overly made-up face was taut. She was no longer grandmotherly, but ghostly.

Helms muttered, "I want an attorney."

Ty said in an oddly formal voice, "That will be arranged, I'm sure."

The takedown operation had been improvised and more than a little rushed. But no matter. It had worked. They now had everything they needed to get BlackBridge. Shaw texted Russell then walked up to Victoria, who was rubbing her shoulder—the one she'd injured last week. "You okay?"

"Just sore is all."

Her eyes widened slightly as she saw the slash on his hand, the messy blood.

"It's okay." He walked to his bike, lifted the seat and got a bottle of alcohol. He poured it over the wound, exhaling at the hot pain that radiated up to his jaw. She tore open the bandage he'd taken out, and when the liquid had evaporated off, she pressed on the skin and smoothed the edges.

"Droon?" She nodded toward the woods.

Shaw shook his head.

"I was going to say sorry I missed him. But worked out better this way, right?" she asked, in a soft voice.

Yes, Droon had been his. It couldn't end any differently.

He was about to ask her a question, when he suddenly sensed that the ambient sound had changed.

The parking lot had been filled with the white noise of traffic. San Bruno is bordered by the 101 and 280, both multilane Silicon Valley arteries and as busy as can be at all hours.

He'd been aware of the sticky rush of traffic. Been aware of the guttural whine of aircraft descending toward or departing from San Francisco and San Jose airports. Been aware of the wind in the pine and maples, a distant dog complaining.

Then, rising, rising, was the sound of a vehicle engine, growing louder.

Insistent.

He found his Glock in the brush, and he thought: Helms, Stone and Braxton had had their phones in the chaotic moments after she figured out the trap. She might have a speed-dial button on her mobile: NEED BACKUP or DISTRESS.

Shaw's team had a good defensive position where they were.

But the black Escalade was plowing unexpectedly over a pedestrian trail.

"Ty!" Shaw called. "Hostiles."

The big man nodded and clicked off the safety of his H&K.

He glanced at the Colt in Victoria's grip and, digging into his pocket, handed her ten loose shells. She reloaded and slipped the live shells in her pocket, then crouched, looking toward the approaching SUV.

A smoke grenade spiraled from the window of the SUV and popped, filling the area with dense gray cover. Shaw couldn't see for certain but he believed at least two men were out, firing automatic weapons—loud, unsilenced—in three-shot bursts. Shaw and Victoria rolled to cover behind a fallen tree. Ty was behind a low berm of grassy earth.

But he and Shaw lowered their weapons. It was impossible to

acquire a target. Shaw squinted through the raw, pungent smoke, Victoria too. She said, "Flank them?"

A nod. He started left, she right.

But they got only a few feet before the relentless machine-gun fire tore into the air and ground around them, spitting dirt and rocks and branches high into the air. The stream of slugs swept toward her.

"Victoria!" Shaw called, as he saw her go down.

69

Too much incoming fire, too much smoke to acquire targets.

Angry shouts from the attackers. "Move it, move it!"

Both Victoria and Ty were hidden from sight by the smoke. "Victoria!"

No response. Shaw's heart was slamming.

He tried to find a target. But it was impossible to see anything clearly through the thick, creamy cloud.

He knew they were in the SUV because the machine-gun spray had ceased. Shaw couldn't hear the doors slam—the weapons fire had partially deafened him—but he knew the Escalade was speeding away along another trail, a narrow one.

He stared in that direction but holstered his Glock.

Never discharge your weapon without a clear target . . .

He turned back. "Victoria!"

Still no response.

Jesus . . .

He'd gotten her into this.

Coughing, spitting out the vile fumes, he strode through the cloud to where he'd seen her fall.

"Victoria!"

Still nothing.

Come on, come on . . . Please.

He pushed through the smoke.

No body, no blood trail.

Had she been wounded and then snatched by one of the attackers?

Then . . . Did he hear a voice?

Again: "Here."

"Victoria."

A bout of coughing.

"Here!"

Then he saw her on her knees in a clump of sedge grass. He ran to her and helped her up. She clutched her torso. Then lowered her hands. No blood. No bullet wounds. She'd fallen hard to the ground, it seemed, the breath knocked from her lungs.

Arm around her shoulders, he helped her out of the haze. They were both coughing and wiping tears from the smoke, which wasn't the sort from wood or paper; the grenades spewed corroding, chemical fumes created by burning potassium chlorate or hexachloroethane and zinc. While not intended to debilitate, the thick clouds stung and choked.

"Ty!" Shaw called, looking around.

The broad-chested man was staggering from the berm behind which he'd taken cover, coughing and spitting as well.

Now that the smoke was drifting away on the breeze, they could see, probably a hundred yards away, the SUV was rocking along the pedestrian trail, about to turn out of sight.

Shaw said to Victoria, "You okay to go after them with me?"

She nodded. Shaw looked to Ty, who did the same.

The three of them started out of the dissipating cloud.

Then, suddenly, the Escalade lurched hard to the left, narrowly missing a tree. Something had flown from the right front tire.

A muted boom rolled over the landscape. Shaw knew it would have been much louder had his ears been functioning better. Then the windshield of the SUV blew to pieces. Another boom.

The Escalade stopped entirely. Several more booms, several more lurches.

Shaw said, "Engine's gone. It's dead."

You can't shoot a car motor by hitting the block, not with ordinary rounds. But all it takes is one well-placed bullet to destroy the delicate electronics under the hood that make today's cars such miracles of modern transportation—and so vulnerable to hackers.

Ty, Victoria and Shaw moved forward slowly, using trees for cover.

Shaw called, "Everyone, out of the vehicle now!"

Ty: "This is your last warning. Weapons on the ground. Step out with your hands raised. Now!"

A moment passed.

A huge ring as another rifle slug hit the driver's side door, low, tearing into the seat just beneath where he sat.

As the echoing report of the shot from the rifle rolled over them, all at once the doors opened and guns flew out. Soon everyone was on the ground.

"Let's get them bundled up."

While Victoria covered them with the Python, Shaw and Ty searched the whole crew: the Latino driver and another BlackBridge op, a redheaded, muscular ex-military sort, as well as Braxton, Helms and George Stone. Zip ties for the newcomers. The other three remained bound.

More vehicle noise, another SUV approaching, coming down the trail. This one was a Lincoln.

Its arrival didn't trouble Shaw in the least. Or surprise him.

The driver climbed out and walked toward Shaw and the others, leaving in the vehicle the McMillan TAC-338 sniper rifle he'd been using as he covered the takedown. He now had his own pistol in hand. He saw that the hostiles were down and slipped away his gun.

Shaw introduced Victoria to his brother.

70

Two hours earlier, as Shaw had sat in his father's Naugahyde chair, having learned that the San Leandro lead to finding the identity of the SP family had not panned out, he had glanced around the safe house and his eyes rested on the tape recorder.

With little time left until the family died, he'd forged a plan to ensnare Braxton and Droon and force them to abort the attack on the SP family.

He'd needed someone he could trust, a woman, and someone who wasn't afraid of combat. Russell's resourceful Karin was not a tactical op, and his group had none available. So Shaw had called Victoria Lesston and wondered if she'd help him out in an operation he was putting together.

She'd replied, "There're two types of people, Colter."

He'd laughed.

She said, "I'll get the next flight out."

"No time. My brother's organization'll send a chopper for you."

"Organization. What is it?"

"Don't know. He's tight-lipped."

"Have to say, Colter, with you not here, I've been feeling antsy. Not used to staying in one place for very long."

A Restless Woman . . .

He explained what he had in mind. Her role was to pretend to be Julia, the audio analyst Russell had called from the diner in Quigley Square. Victoria would call Shaw on his iPhone, which was compromised. If Braxton didn't tip to the fact he was using this phone, and not the encrypted Android, she would learn that there was incriminating evidence on the cassette and about the furtive meeting between Shaw and "Julia" at the park in San Bruno. She'd learn too that Russell was elsewhere—an assurance that only Shaw and the audio engineer would be present.

And the "evidence"? None of the science, which Victoria had fabricated on the fly, was real. There was no such thing as hiding voices in static.

But Shaw had figured, rightly as it turned out, that Ian Helms, Braxton and Droon were so desperate to make sure that the lurid details of BlackBridge's operations went undiscovered that they couldn't take any chances; they *had* to assume the evidence was real and destroy it, then kill the audio analyst and Shaw.

He had considered bringing in the law but still didn't know the extent of BlackBridge and Devereux's reach. He'd called Tom Pepper once again and told him his concerns. The former agent didn't know anyone in the San Francisco FBI field office, and so he couldn't vouch for them. But he did have some trusted agent friends in Denver. A team was being assembled. But Shaw and Russell needed to move fast to nail Braxton and Droon and stop the assault on the SP family. So he and Russell and Victoria put together their own private takedown.

"Citizen's arrest, you could call it," Shaw had told his brother.

Russell's response: "Hmm." Then: "It's a good plan, Colt."

And for the first time since they'd been in each other's company, the dourness had faded from his brother's face, replaced by what could pass for enthusiasm.

Russell had enlisted Ty to play the part of a state ranger; it wouldn't be suspicious for him to be in the park just making the rounds, spending time on his mobile, which was connected to sophisticated recording equipment that would suck up the conversation of the BlackBridge ops who came to meet Shaw and Victoria— certainly Braxton and Droon, perhaps others. He hadn't hoped for the other fish they caught: Ian Helms himself.

Russell took a high-cover position in the park with the sniper rifle on a bipod and covered them for the takedown. They hadn't expected a backup SUV, which, in any case, arrived via a tree-covered pedestrian trail; he'd had to move fast to get into a new position to sight in on the Cadillac and disable it.

When the FBI arrived from Denver, in about an hour, they could take this crew into custody, along with the tape and statements from Shaw, Russell, Victoria and Ty.

Shaw said to his brother, "Let's do some horse-trading."

Russell looked around and said, "We're black on the perimeter here." He looked to Ty and Victoria. "I'd get on the west and south."

"That's a go," Victoria said. She snagged one of the machine guns, checked it and scouted out a position to the west. Ty took the south.

Shaw and his brother walked to where Braxton and Helms were sitting on the ground, hands in restraints. Legs in front of them. Braxton surprised Shaw by saying in a raw, wounded voice, "You didn't need to kill him. He would have surrendered."

Shaw didn't respond. It would have been a push-pull conversation, since, no, Droon would not have surrendered and was a second away from shooting Shaw, in the first case, and stabbing him in the heart, in the second. The strangulation too.

The woman was clearly shaken by Droon's loss. This seemed out of character for her, a person who'd ordered the torture or handled the execution of any number of people. Maybe there'd been more to their relationship. Shaw had to admit that he found it bordered on unpleasant to picture romance between them, but who was he to judge when it came to matters of the heart, thought the Restless Man, whose track record in love was not stellar.

As Russell remained standing, a guard of sorts, Shaw crouched in front of Braxton and Helms, who said, "I'm not saying another word without my lawyer."

"We're not cops. We're not recording anymore. This isn't about evidence."

"Then?" Braxton muttered.

"We assume the SP hit is off now. Can you confirm that?"

A pause. "The what?" she asked.

Shaw looked from her to Helms. "If that family dies, it'll come back on you. We'll make sure of that. If the motive is to kill a witness, that's capital murder. Death penalty in California."

Helms appeared perplexed.

Russell said, "Give us the name."

Shaw, again in the good-cop role: "We'll tell the U.S. attorney you cooperated. That'll go a long way in your favor."

"Who the hell is SP?" Helms muttered. He turned to Braxton, who shook her head. She too seemed confused.

Shaw glanced at Russell. "Show them."

Russell took his phone and displayed the picture of the note that Karin had found on Blond's body, the kill order.

Confirmation from Hunters Point crew.
6/26, 7:00 p.m. SP and family. All ↓

Helms muttered, "I have no idea what that is."

Braxton shook her head yet again.

Russell said, "The Stanford library the other day? The man with Droon? This kill order was in his pocket."

Braxton said, "He was just a friend of Ebbitt Droon's. He was meeting him at the library to drop something off. Whatever that's about, the note isn't about one of our projects."

"He didn't work for BlackBridge?"

Helms said, "No."

The words—and the timbre of their voices—had moved Shaw from ten percent alert to ninety percent. He was in set mode.

Shaw asked Braxton, "Who is he?"

"Security. Works for a subsidiary of Banyan Tree."

"Name. Give me his name."

Russell crouched and leaned very close. His brother's chosen method for retrieving information.

"He's . . ." Braxton thought for a moment. "I think it's Richard Hogan."

Russell rose and said to his brother, "We got it wrong. Devereux's the one that wants SP dead, not BlackBridge."

"So the hit's still on." Shaw looked at his phone.

Three hours until the family died.

71

The brothers obtained Richard Hogan's address nearly simultaneously.

Shaw had sent a request to Mack, Russell to Karin.

Shaw's phone dinged first, but only seconds before his brother's.

The place where the hitman had lived was a yellow Victorian-façaded townhome in the shadow of Coit Tower on Telegraph Hill. An upmarket neighborhood. At first Shaw found this surprising, given Hogan's career—muscle work and kill orders—but Shaw supposed that Jonathan Stuart Devereux paid well.

Russell parallel parked on a steep incline and spun the wheel to chock the tire against the curb. Signs warned drivers to do this. Shaw supposed that the odds of a vehicle with an automatic transmission slipping out of park were minimal, but why not go the extra step? The incline had to be twenty degrees.

They climbed out of the SUV and Shaw dipped his head as two red-masked parrots zipped past. He noted several more, twitchily observing the street from the branches of a maple tree. Another pair was perched nearby too. The birds had made this neighborhood their own.

He and Russell crossed the street and approached the front door slowly, in a tactical formation, away from windows and the door itself. Hogan was no more, and Karin's information revealed he was single, but he might have had roommates, who were fellow Devereux employees. Or a lover in the same line of murderous work that he had pursued.

It was just the two of them now. Ty and Victoria had to keep an eye on Helms, Braxton and the other ops until the agents arrived from Denver.

Shaw and his brother looked through the windows, fast and carefully. The living space appeared unoccupied.

"I can't pick these."

Russell too examined the two deadbolts. He tapped his own shoulder and Shaw nodded.

Stepping three feet back, the brothers paused and looked around. The street was deserted.

Russell charged forward and crashed into the wood. The heavy panel slammed inward as if the hardware were skimpy tin.

The men fanned out, guns drawn, clearing the sparse place. Lacking in furniture, that is, but there were weapons and ammunition aplenty, computers, tactical gear, phones—cellular and satellite, clothing and body armor.

Russell held up an ID badge with Hogan's picture on it. The subsidiary he worked for within the Banyan Tree family was Sequoia Pest Removal.

The computers were passcode protected, as were the phones. Not impossible for an outfit like Russell's group to hack, Shaw supposed, but SP's family had only hours to live. Cracking the electronics would have taken too long.

Shaw said, "The kill order was handwritten. Let's look for paper."

They began rifling through stacks of documents that sat on Hogan's kitchen table and a precarious card table that served as a makeshift desk.

Shaw's pile was mostly receipts, maps, instruction booklets for newly purchased weapons, company memos that had nothing to do with the kill order, checkbooks and ledgers that showed transfers into banks in the Caribbean.

"Got something here," Russell said. Shaw joined him as he spread a sheet of paper flat on the desk.

It has come to my attention that a whistleblower, SP, has discovered the purpose of our Waste Management program. Following was found on his personal computer through a deep-hack:

"Banyan Tree is enlisting a subsidiary to dredge up toxic waste. Operatives then use unmarked vehicles to transport it to a competitor's facility, where it is dumped, as if the competitor were guilty of the pollution. This has resulted in the competitors being sued and fined, often going out of business, or losing so much money they are no longer players in the market. The plan is smart. Banyan's subsidiary analyzes each competitor's operation and determines what sort of dangerous materials those companies generate. Engineers then extract only those chemicals from the waste they dredge up. That is what is planted on the competitor's property, giving credence to their 'guilt.'"

As of now SP is still compiling information and trying to develop proof of our program. It's anticipated that he will probably have enough facts to go public within the next few weeks.

You'll be receiving further instructions.

"So that's what it's about," Russell said.

Shaw recalled what La Fleur had told them: about the CEO of one of Devereux's competitors committing suicide after going bankrupt—following Devereux's reporting him to the feds. La Fleur hadn't told them what regulations or laws had been broken, but it was now clear that they would have been environmental.

They dug through the rest of the documents and searched Hogan's clothes, looking for anything that might give them more information about SP.

Nothing.

Shaw: "Whistleblower. Means he's got some connection to the subsidiary, maybe he's a contractor, maybe an employee."

Russell went online and searched for Banyan Tree. It had been much in the news over the years and hundreds of employees were mentioned but there was no fast search filter that let him find workers with the potential victim's initials.

And because the company was privately owned, no employee records were available.

"Karin?" Shaw proposed.

"If we had a week or two, we could probably get somebody inside. Not on this time frame."

Shaw was musing, "Dredge. Waste."

The thought struck him almost like a slap on the back. He barked a quick laugh.

Russell looked toward him.

Shaw said, "We got it wrong."

72

Hunters Point yet again.

The vile smells, the trash, the dilapidated buildings, the lots where the skeletons of enterprises were all that remained of capitalist dreams from so many years ago. Seagulls quarreled over the slimmest remnants of garbage. Rats prowled silently but without caution.

The place was as tired as a car abandoned in the woods, not even worth scavenging for parts.

One structure here, though, shone. A white and green one-story building, recently painted. It sat on the water's edge and was surrounded by a parking lot in which a variety of modest vehicles sat.

BAYPOINT ENVIRO-SURE SOLUTIONS, INC.

A BANYAN TREE COMPANY

As the brothers sped into the lot in Russell's SUV, Shaw could see the thirty-foot transport boats they'd seen earlier: the ones leaving the island that had been part of the Hunters Point shipyard, filled with fifty-five-gallon drums, riding low. They would slog their way to the wide pier behind the building, where workers would offload the drums and use forklifts to load them onto long flatbed trucks.

The empty boats, with high drafts, would then return to the dismantled ship works for another load. Shaw wondered where the waste he was looking at was bound for: What competitor did Devereux have in his sights? How many employees and residents living nearby would be poisoned? How many animals? How much land would be tainted for decades to come? He wondered too if the idea of using waste as a weapon had come from the CEO of Banyan Tree himself? Or, like the Urban Improvement Plan, had it been the brainchild of Ian Helms?

Russell braked to a stop near the office and the men climbed out.

They had come back to the waterfront because of Shaw's thought after reading about "dredging" up waste, which is usually performed by a boat. That meant that the word *crew* in the text authorizing the killing of SP probably did not mean crew as in gang, despite the fact that there were plenty of those in Hunters Point. The word was meant in its original sense: those operating vessels.

Confirmation from Hunters Point crew.
6/26, 7:00 p.m. SP and family. All ↓

They walked over the parking lot of inky, newly laid asphalt to the office. Shaw noted on the side of one of the trucks was the name of the company, along with the tagline:

MAKING THE WORLD A BETTER PLACE TO BE . . .

Shaw wondered about the ellipses at the end. That form of punctuation sometimes was meant to suggest forward motion: Now get out there and live that clean life! But ellipses also were used to indicate that something had been omitted from the sentence. Like: "Making the world a better place to be . . . for our company, our shareholders and our illustrious CEO."

They looked through the window into the office, where a woman sat at a desk and several men in gray uniforms and orange vests stood in a cluster, sipping from coffee cups. The pier itself held a dozen workers.

"There," Russell said. He was glancing toward a man in a navy-blue windbreaker, matching slacks with a stripe up the side and headgear you rarely saw: a real captain's hat, the sort sometimes sitting atop lean and fake-tanned women in short blue skirts and tight white blouses, on the arms of rich businessmen.

The man was out of sight of the office and the pier, on the other side of a large rust-scarred fuel tank, where four empty flatbeds sat. He was scanning their license plates with a tablet, then tapping in notes. On his chest was a BayPoint Enviro-Sure Solutions ID badge.

They bypassed the office and, when no one was looking their way, stepped over a gray-painted chain and walked along the stone wall at waterside toward the man. The smell was of white gas—kerosene—and diesel fumes, generic ocean, and some truly foul chemical. The rocking water beside the dock was coated in concentric blue and purple and red circles of oil.

The grizzled man in the captain's hat made a call on his walkie-talkie, then strolled to another truck. He glanced back, seeing the brothers. He looked them up and down. "This's private property." The voice was a growl.

Shaw and Russell continued forward and stopped when they were about fifteen feet away.

His weathered face soured. "I said, case you didn't hear, private property. You get the fuck out of here."

Russell said, "We have some questions."

"Leave! Or you don't know the kind of hurt you'll have. I've whipped Somalian pirates, I've put down mutinies. I whaled on a carjacker so bad he needed his jaw rebuilt. Now!" The head, beneath its jaunty hat, turned toward the exit.

Russell said, "There's an employee—"

"What's with that beard? Are you some kind of Amish person?" His face grew even more fierce. "Or a Muslim?"

Shaw: "An employee at BayPoint Enviro-Sure. His—"

"I'm not telling you again." His cheeks reddened; his temperature must have risen a few degrees. Soon the shade was actually livid.

"—initials are S.P. He has some connection with this facility. We need his name and address. It's important. We'll pay you. A thousand."

"Why would I care what you need and don't need? Fuck-fancy. Get off this property now."

Fuck-fancy. Not a phrase Shaw was familiar with. He kind of liked it.

He continued, "I'm a spit away from calling security."

The expressions got better and better.

"All right. That's it." Up came the radio. Apparently the old salt hadn't whipped those pirates without backup.

But before the call went out, Russell smoothly drew his silenced pistol and blew a nearby rat to eternity.

Not the approach Colter Shaw would have taken.

Then again, as he'd learned very well over the past few days, it wasn't unusual for two siblings to solve a problem in significantly different ways.

73

At 6:45, fifteen minutes before the family was to die, Colter
Shaw was sitting, alone, in the front seat of Russell's Lincoln
Navigator. He was looking over the house of Samuel Prescott,
the BayPoint Enviro-Sure Solutions whistleblower. Shaw watched
the garage door rolling down, hiding from view the family's sedan,
a red Volvo.

Trevor Little—the belligerent pseudo captain on the Hunters
Point dock—had glanced in horror at Russell's gun and quickly told
the brothers Prescott's name. It seemed the employee and his family
had been out of town at a funeral but were due back today.

This would be the reason for the specific time and date of the hit
in the kill order; the murderer would have to wait until the family
returned to their home from the airport. Karin had checked passenger manifests and flight schedules. The Prescotts were due back at
about 4:30 and would be home about fifty minutes later—the time
it would take them to collect luggage and travel from San Francisco
International Airport to their home in Forest Hill, a suburb of San
Francisco.

Shaw, Russell and Ty had met the family's flight.

A scheduler at BayPoint Enviro-Sure Solutions, Prescott was in his forties, stocky and tanned, with sandy-colored hair. His wife, Bette, was blond and willowy. Their son and daughter were twins and had their mother's pallor and hair, freckled both. They were twelve.

At SFO, Ty had displayed an ID card, which Shaw caught a fast glimpse of. He saw the initials *U.S.* and a round emblem similar to, but not the same as, the Justice Department's. Shaw wondered if it was real. In any case, it took no convincing for Prescott to believe that he and his family were in danger.

Prescott had been surprised Devereux had learned of his espionage. He'd taken care to hide the fruits of his spying on his computer with sophisticated encryption.

He was not, however, surprised that the CEO had issued an order to have him killed. "He's murdering people with toxic waste. Why not kill somebody with a bullet?"

Explaining to the brothers how he'd discovered Devereux's toxic waste scheme, Prescott said, "The numbers, always the numbers. They never lie. I'm a scheduler, right? I keep an eye on transport down to the hour, the *minute*. I noticed that the timing of some of our trucks was off. When they went out and when they came back wasn't right. I knew how far they had to travel to the sites—the legitimate ones—and they were coming back to the dock too soon.

"Not a huge time difference, but it was suspicious. I called in sick one day and followed one of the trucks. It didn't go to the site it was supposed to. It went to a vacant lot in Oakland. The waste was pumped into an unmarked tanker. I followed it to a factory owned by one of Devereux's competitors. These men got out—like special forces, all in black. They dumped the waste into a creek downstream from the factory. I got pictures and samples. I was going to the EPA and the U.S. attorney this week. I just wanted to find a few more target locations."

Shaw looked over the street the family lived on. It was a quiet avenue in Forest Hill, with houses set back behind small front yards of grass or gardens. It was one of the least densely populated parts of the city and, as the name suggested, more arboreal than most. Their house was modest. Prescott made good money at his job and Bette was the senior bookkeeper for a chain of urgent-care clinics. But even with double incomes, this was all they could afford. Home prices in the Bay were crushing.

Though the blinds were drawn, Shaw noted the flickering light from the TV in the living room.

He scanned the street again and saw no threat. He also was watching the rooftops to the east, looking for rifle muzzles or scope flares.

Russell and Ty were in the latter's car, behind the house, scanning Hawk Hill Park, which is where a sniper targeting the Prescott house from the west would be. Those two had already swept the home for IEDs and found no traces of explosives. Drive-bys wouldn't be the order of the day either. To kill the family the team needed to get inside. The two pros in the business, Russell and Ty, believed the attack would be a dynamic entry, two or three ops kicking in the door and charging through the house. They would likely be supported by a sniper.

Why did the kill order include the entire family? he wondered.

Maybe just being meticulous. Maybe Devereux was worried that Prescott had explained what he'd found to his wife, and the children might have overheard.

Maybe to send a message to the rest of the thousands of employees at BayPoint Enviro-Sure Solutions and Banyan Tree, reminding them of where their loyalty should be.

5:56.

He called his brother and asked in a soft voice, "Zero here. Anything in the back?"

"Thought I saw a hostile. Just a jogger. No threat."

356 : JEFFERY DEAVER

"'K." They disconnected.

Would the ops come in an SUV, a couple of jeeps? He doubted a helicopter but supposed with Devereux's money that wasn't impossible.

Shaw was armed with both his Glock and his Colt Python, and, in the backseat, his Enfield .303—the World War One British infantry rifle, old and battered but perfectly accurate. He really hoped he didn't need to fire any weapons; he'd already been present at a fair number of incidents here. At some point the cops would have to get involved and, even if the firefight was justified, he wouldn't want that hassle.

Besides, he needed a shooter alive. He wanted witnesses to testify against Devereux. Sam Prescott had proof that would bring down BayPoint Enviro-Sure Solutions and its executives, but the parent company—and Devereux himself—would be insulated from liability. A hired killer, even working for one of Devereux's subsidiaries, might have evidence leading directly to the arrogant CEO himself.

A motor scooter went by, a young Asian man on the saddle. It vanished around the corner at the end of the block. An SUV, driven by a middle-aged woman, cruised up the hill, and likewise disappeared. A woman bicyclist, in a bold, floral athletic outfit, pedaled past and started up the steep hill, her feet moving rapidly, the gears in low.

At 7:10 his phone hummed.

Shaw answered and told his brother, "They're late." He said he'd seen a few vehicles. Nobody suspicious and none of the drivers—or the cyclist—had been interested in the Prescott house. "Sniper action? There's nothing in the front."

"No one presenting in the back, and any sniper and his spotter'd need time to set up, adjust for wind, humidity. We would've seen them by now."

"Are they just in good camo?"

"No. Got eyes on every usable nest. Couple of them're perfect . . . Hmm. They would've known the Prescotts landed an hour and a half ago."

Shaw said, "With Hogan disappearing, they're being cautious maybe."

"Think they called it off?"

"Ten percent chance of that. Tops."

"Agree."

They disconnected.

7:15.

Shaw noted the light from the Prescotts' living room change as a commercial came on the TV.

He was checking his phone for the time—it was 7:19—when the gut-punching explosion rocked the SUV. He looked up at the Prescott house to see flame boiling from each shattered window. Shaw climbed from the vehicle and ran toward the structure. He could get no closer than forty or fifty feet. Already the entire home was ablaze.

The device—whatever it was—had been perfectly designed. Not a soul could have gotten out of a trap like that alive.

74

They drove back in silence to the safe house, Colter Shaw and his brother.

Both men were stung by their failure.

"Goddamn it." Shaw's voice was bitter.

What a loss . . .

They had expected an assault. They had expected a C-4 or another nitrate-based bomb.

They weren't prepared for a very different improvised explosive device—and a particularly clever one. Devereux's new kill team had run a gas line disguised as a water pipe into the house and starting about 7:00 or so the timed system had begun filling the place with natural gas—but it was the original substance, before the foul rotten egg smell odorant, to warn of leaks, was added. No one could have detected it.

After a half hour, some type of timed igniter clicked to life. The resulting explosion had destroyed the house.

If no one had known the family was targeted for death, the incident would have been reported as an accident. The intense heat and flames would melt most of the parts of the device. Investigators would assume the real public utility pipe—now destroyed too—had cracked or suffered from a leak. The igniter would be vaporized as well.

Shaw and his brother, though, explained to the fire marshal that the explosion was meant to murder a whistleblower and his family.

"Why the hell didn't you tell anybody?" the marshal had demanded.

Because it never occurred to them that Devereux's men would try something like this.

And also because Shaw and Russell had inherited enough of their father's paranoia to not trust your average civic official—at least not in the case of BlackBridge.

They now arrived at the safe house and Russell parked. He had a good touch behind the wheel of a motor vehicle. All the children did. Homeschooling didn't provide the chance for official driver's ed classes, but Ashton had taught Russell, Colter and Dorion the skills needed to pilot vehicles from cycles to sedans to trucks from age twelve or so. It was curious that Russell drove so conservatively. In his work for the group, he was the blunter of the two brothers; Shaw, whose Yamaha occasionally went airborne vertical and returned to earth horizontal, had an approach to his own profession that was far more cerebral.

The brothers walked to the pale blue safe house on Alvarez and into the entry hall, where the FBI's Denver contingent was standing. Shaw nodded and introduced himself. Russell did too.

Shaw then walked into the living room and up to the four people sitting stiffly on the couch. He said to the four members of the Sam Prescott family, "We were wrong. There weren't any shooters. It was a firebomb. Your house is gone, your car, everything. I'm sorry."

75

Their failure was that they'd missed the chance to apprehend a single member of a dynamic entry team—someone who might be willing to testify against Devereux.

There was, of course, never any question about the family's going home from the airport; Russell, Shaw and Ty had transported them directly to the Alvarez safe house and then sped to Forest Hill to set up the bait and arrange the takedown of the assault team.

Russell had driven the Prescotts' sedan from the airport and had parked it in the garage so spotters would think the family was home. Ty, in his own car, parked behind the property. The men had checked the house for IEDs. When they were finished, they turned the TV and lights on to simulate occupancy, then left via the back door to wait for the attack.

A house destroyed and not a single suspect who might be willing to testify against Jonathan Stuart Devereux.

What a loss . . .

Shaw and Russell had done all they could do and now the case was in the hands of the FBI. The scrubbed, somber agent from the

Denver office was named Darrel Gardiner. He and his team would be temporary; the agents would review BlackBridge's records and interrogate suspects to find out if any San Francisco FBI personnel had been compromised. If not, Gardiner would hand over the case to the field office here.

With Victoria Lesston at his side, Shaw sat at the kitchen table in the safe house, as the FBI agent finished his interview with him. The agent had already spoken to Victoria, Russell and Ty.

Karin, it seemed, was the invisible woman. Her name never came up, and Shaw wasn't going to volunteer anything about her.

Looking over his notes, Special Agent Gardiner shook his head, topped with a blond businessman's severe trim. "Extortion, murder, attempted murder and conspiracy, burglary, hacking, eavesdropping . . . Well."

Shaw got the impression there was a stronger word he wished to use but couldn't bring himself to. Religious maybe. Or just the rigorous standards of the profession.

"Urban Improvement Plan?" A shake of his head. "They must've dumped thousands of kilos of drugs over the years."

Shaw said, "Tip of the iceberg. BlackBridge's got clients all over the world and the UIP was just one of their tactics."

The company was being shut down, and all the facilities were being seized and searched presently. Other warrants would follow. A U.S. congressman and a congresswoman from California were already looking into voting fraud allegations because of the UIP-manipulated congressional districts in the state. The woman legislator issued a statement condemning the gerrymandering and was calling for an investigation of the politicians who had benefited from the redistricting.

One problem remained, however, a serious one. All of the offenses that Gardiner had just recited had been committed by Helms, Braxton and the BlackBridge crew. Not a bit of evidence could be laid at the feet of Jonathan Stuart Devereux or Banyan Tree Holdings.

"The best insulation I've ever seen," Gardiner told Shaw and Victoria. "It's early, I understand, but so far Banyan Tree is driven snow."

Shaw asked the special agent about BayPoint Enviro-Sure Solutions, whose offices were presently being searched too. "Their execs and staff'll go down, but there's no evidence that the parent company or Devereux himself even knew anything about dumping toxic waste on competitors' land. No emails, no memos. We have phone records, but that's just who called who and when. We don't know the content."

"Devereux was the one who ordered it, right?" Victoria asked, her lips tight in anger.

Gardiner answered, "Of course. But the head of Enviro's taking the fall for the whole thing. Claims his boss was in the dark."

Gardiner closed his notebook and shut off the recorder. He slipped them away and handed both Shaw and Victoria his business card.

Other agents—a woman and a man, Latinx—were helping the Prescott family gather their luggage. They would be taken to a federal safe house, where they'd stay during the course of the BayPoint Enviro-Sure Solutions investigation. Shaw wondered if they'd go into witness protection. If Devereux remained free, they would have to.

The family still seemed dazed by what had hit them.

Sam Prescott said, "I don't know what to say, Mr. Shaw. We're alive because of you. And what they did, with that bomb in the house . . . Lord. I can't imagine being in there when the thing went off."

Shaw responded with, "Good luck." The gratitude matter again.

"Thank your brother too."

Russell was in the safe house, but not present with the family. He was assembling the surveillance gear he'd planted upon his return.

"I'll do that," Shaw said.

Prescott and his family then followed the watchful agents out the door.

Ty stepped inside. "Have to leave, Colter. Got a little bit of paperwork to take care of. Oh, I got a call from SFPD. They responded to a complaint in Hunters Point. Man said an Amish Muslim and his buddy threatened to shoot him and then zip-tied him to a radiator in an old warehouse. He said he's whaled on pirates and if he gets a chance he's going to punch those guys out too. Just a heads-up."

"I'll keep my eye out," Shaw said with a smile.

"You two make a good team. You brothers. You work together in the past?"

"Trained, ages ago. Never worked."

"Looks like it all came back to you. Russ was saying you climb mountains?"

"I do."

"For the fun of it?"

"You should try it some time."

"Jesus." Ty shook his hand.

"Oh. And one thing?" Shaw said, reflecting on meeting Ty for the first time in front of the safe house.

The squat man lifted a gear bag that had to weigh fifty pounds as if it contained pillows, and glanced Shaw's way.

"Be careful with those box cutters."

PART FOUR

JUNE 27

FLAME

76

t's safe."

"You say that. It's easy to *say* it's safe. Anybody can *say* it's safe. It's easy for me to say I can soar like a seagull but I can't."

Colter Shaw stood at the base of the porch and continued speaking to the shadows on the other side of the half-open door of Earnest La Fleur's Sausalito home.

No arrows had been launched, though the man might have gotten a piece of Shaw if he'd been inclined. He'd moved the oil-drum barricades, as Russell had suggested.

Shaw said, "Droon's dead. Braxton and Ian Helms're in jail, and the FBI and state police have locked down all the BlackBridge offices. ATF and SEC're after them too, I heard."

"Okay, okay, given that's true, which I still have to confirm," La Fleur offered by way of meager rebuttal, "what about the chief boilermaker, Devereux?"

Shaw's brow creased. "Nothing to nail him on yet."

"Told you. Man's elusive as a drop of mercury and just as toxic."

"Earnest," Shaw stretched out his unusual name. "Let me in. And could you point the arrow elsewhere?"

"How'd you know I was locked and loaded?"

Shaw exhaled loudly, not bothering to explain that he'd heard the creak of the bow once again—and not troubling either to correct the man, as he had others, by telling him that the "lock and load" phrase applied only to the M1 Garand rifle. And until you *unlocked* the weapon—which slipped a round into the chamber—it was only as dangerous as a baseball bat.

"All right. Come on in."

Shaw stepped into the man's cluttered house, still redolent of ocean and pot.

The scrawny hermit, gripping the bow and a de-notched arrow, pushed past Shaw and strode into the yard. There he stood for a moment and then disappeared into the complicated growth of plants most of whose genus and species Shaw did not know. Beyond them, however, was a landscape of plants featuring rich green leaves pointing outward like splayed fingers. Shaw knew what *this* crop was.

Returning, La Fleur said, "You might've been followed. It looked clear. But, listen to me: never assume you're safe."

Shaw nearly smiled. That was the last line of the letter his father had left in Echo Ridge.

La Fleur re-latched the door. There was a chain—that most insubstantial of protective devices. But it wasn't alone. The other security mechanisms were a knob lock, a massive deadbolt, a crossbar like you'd see in a Middle Ages castle and an iron rod tilting upward at a forty-five-degree angle from floor to door. Shaw wondered if he had a rope ladder somewhere in the place for a fast emergency descent down the cliffside. As a matter of fact, he did: a glance toward the windows revealed a coil of rope, one end of which was tied to a radiator.

"You want coffee, anything?" He was sipping from a chipped mug, as bulletproof as those in the diner where Shaw and his brother dissected the courier bag containing the mixtape and the ancient document that could change the face of American politics forever.

Shaw declined. "Brought you a present." He handed over one of the envelopes he and Russell had taken from the BNG gangbangers at the site of the Urban Improvement Plan meeting in the Tenderloin. "Ten K. Laundered and unmarked. Amos Gahl's mother got one too."

He peered inside and pulled the money out. "Okay, okay. Can't say I can't use it." He walked to a painting of an old-time sailing ship and lifted it down, revealing a wall safe. After turning his back so Shaw couldn't see the combination, he opened the door and slipped the cash inside. Upon closing it, he spun the dial a number of times and reseated the painting.

"Well, thankee." His face grew troubled. "So that son of a bitch Devereux still got what he wanted. Corporations running for office? What does he want more power for, more money? He's got a company worth a couple trillion dollars."

"Just one point two."

"This ain't funny, Shaw. That's bigger than Spain's gross domestic product. Banyan Tree's going to run for office, and then the world goes to shit with his new policies you were telling me about: fucking the environment, civil rights, immigration. Jesus my Lord, just occurred to me: Devereux could start his own schools. They can teach what they want. Indoctrinate the youth. Hitler did that. 'The Future Belongs to Me.'"

"The man who would be king."

La Fleur tilted his head slightly. "That was quite a flick. There was justice in the movie. You remember how it ended? But not here. Devereux? Hell, if he gets enough power he could change the U.S. Constitution and a company could become president of the United States."

"You think it'd come to that?"

A smile, both coy and troubled, spread over La Fleur's face. "But you don't have to look back too far into U.S. politics to see that pretty damn weird things can happen." He opened one of the metal blinds and looked out. The view of the city was indeed spectacular. And dominating the skyline was the massive office building that housed Banyan Tree. "It's like the missiles have been launched. I'm enjoying the last view of the country before the nukes hit." He gazed back to find Shaw looking at the same scene.

La Fleur was sizing him up. "You seem . . . what'sa word I'm looking for here, Shaw? Detached. Like you don't care about the cataclysm." The man squinted. "Yep, I'm sure of it. De-tached. How come's that? *Don't* you care?"

"Let's put on the TV. Something you might want to see."

La Fleur nodded toward the ancient set. "This one's safe, terrestrial. The only kind I'd ever have. You can't work for BlackBridge and not get this sense of how efficiently electrons can fuck you."

This was a man Ashton Shaw would've counted as a friend.

Shaw clicked the unit on. It had to warm up before the picture crisped into view.

The crawl at the bottom of the screen said BREAKING NEWS . . .

A brunette anchorwoman in a bright red dress was looking out at her invisible audience.

"Repeating this afternoon's top story, three independent forensic examiners have concluded that a recently discovered California Constitution amendment, to allow corporations to hold office in the state, is a forgery. The tally was dated April seventeenth, nineteen oh-six, but all three examiners found that the paper and ink dated to the nineteen twenties.

"Professor Anthony Rice of the University of California had this to say earlier . . ."

The scene cut to a recorded in-office interview. One shot revealed a large, pale man in a navy suit and a white shirt. His graying hair was thinning and curly.

"Hello, Professor Rice."

He tapped his round glasses higher on a lengthy nose and nodded to the camera.

"Afternoon."

"Tell us about this voting tally."

Rice repeated the story about the implications of Proposition 06 and then added:

"Over the years the voting tally became a kind of Holy Grail for big corporations, which would love nothing more than to hold office in the state."

"But the experts are saying it isn't real."

"I believe what happened is that a businessman in the nineteen twenties hired someone to forge it and hide it in government archives with other documents from around nineteen oh-six. His plan was probably to quote 'miraculously' discover it. Why didn't he? One reason might be the timing. Maybe he went bust in the Depression and his corporation went bankrupt. He faded off into obscurity."

"Do you think there really is a legitimate copy of the voting tally somewhere?"

"No, no. I'm sure there isn't. The tally was just a legal legend. It would be impossible for one to exist. The recount was a long time ago but it was in the twentieth century. As soon as the judge signed it, word would have spread . . . There were telephones, telegraphs, daily press and as many reporters per capita as we have nowadays. If a recount meant the proposition passed, that would have been front-page news. No, Prop Oh-Six was defeated by the people."

"Professor, has a corporation ever run for office?"

"A few have tried, as public relations stunts, but they never got very far. All legal scholars and political historians I know think it would be disastrous for democracy."

"Thank you, Professor. In other news—"

Shaw shut the TV off. It crackled to darkness.

"Well," La Fleur said. "That's one kettle of fish . . . You think it's for real? About the thing being forged?"

"It's real."

"You say that like a man who knows."

"I do. Because I was the forger."

77

So, I say: as Americans and lovers of democracy you should light a bonfire and throw the damn thing in . . .

Just after Shaw and Russell had left Professor Steven Field's house in Berkeley, with an understanding of just what Proposition 06 meant, Shaw had made a decision.

He'd considered the academic's advice—either hide or destroy the tally.

But Shaw had concluded that neither of those would work. BlackBridge, on Devereux's orders, would continue to search and would undoubtedly rack up more dead bodies in the scavenger hunt. The businessman had been searching for the tally certificate for years. Why would he stop now? But if it appeared that the tally never existed in the first place—that the rumors were based on a forgery— then he might lick his wounds and forget the matter.

Shaw would create a forgery himself. He would make sure Braxton and Droon stole it from the Pacific Heights safe house. Devereux would then send it to Sacramento to present to the state assembly, where forensic experts would determine it was a fake.

Shaw was confident he could pull it off. He had on occasion in the course of his business needed to track down documents for which people had offered rewards. Usually these were last wills and testaments, corporate purchase documents, adoption papers. Those jobs would occasionally land him square in the esoteric world of document examination and forgery.

He needed help, though, to make sure it was a solid job. And he knew whom to call. An expert skilled at *detecting* forgeries would also have to be an expert on how to create them. He called a friend. Parker Kincaid was a former FBI forensic document examiner. Based outside of Washington, D.C., he was now a consultant.

"Parker."

"Colt. How's it going?"

They caught up with small talk. Kincaid's son, Robby, was now an accomplished martial artist and he'd just won a big competition.

"Congratulations."

"What can I do for you?"

"Let's say I was tracking down some materials someone might use to create a forged document. I'm talking San Francisco."

"Okay."

Ah, the cop word again. Kincaid, after all, had been one.

"I'm speaking hypothetically."

"Hypothetically."

Shaw was amused. Kincaid's repetition suggested suspicion. On the other hand, he knew all about Shaw's rewards business and the number of people he'd rescued and the number of perps he'd collared. If Shaw was being coy, it was for a legitimate reason. Still, Parker had to ask, "I assume my former employer in Washington, D.C., would not have any reason to be concerned by *someone's* document?"

"Absolutely not."

"Good. Are we thinking modern day?"

"No. Nineteen twenties."

"Pen and ink?"

"And typewriter."

Kincaid didn't hesitate. "In the Bay Area, there's only one place a forger would go for supplies. Davis and Sons Rare Books and Antiquities."

"Thanks, Parker. Helpful."

"You ever get reward assignments in Northern Virginia?"

"Haven't yet. My sister lives in Maryland. I've been meaning to visit. I've got your number."

"Tell *someone* good luck."

The men had disconnected and Shaw had headed up to North Beach to the bookstore.

There, he had paid to have the original voting tally, with the sketch on the back, mounted in the cheap plastic frame.

He had bought a few other things too—out of the case he'd studied when he first arrived.

Among his purchases was a ninety-year-old Underwood No. 5 typewriter, the most common of the era. It was a high-standing classic, the workhorse of secretaries and reporters throughout the first half of the twentieth century. He also selected a notebook that dated to the 1920s, containing blank sheets similar in color and weight to the paper of the original tally, and pen-point nibs and holders. Most important, he was able to purchase a bottle of actual ink that was nearly one hundred years old. That had been his biggest concern. Shaw, though, had been surprised to find that there was quite the market among collectors for unopened ink bottles from the past.

No accounting for passions and hobbies . . .

Back in the safe house, he'd saturated the ribbon of the typewriter with the old ink, cranked in a piece of paper he'd cut from the notebook and typed out a voting tally certification identical to the original.

He'd examined it carefully. Nope. Didn't work; the ink wasn't as consistently dark as the original. He prepped the typewriter again.

This one was better, but he still wasn't satisfied. Now it was consistent, but too dark for a document that age.

The third one hit the mark. He let it dry then assembled a nib and holder to practice the signature of the Right Honorable Selmer P. Clarke—a wonderful name for a judge. He did what all professional forgers do when faking signatures: not attempt to actually sign the document, mimicking the original signatory, but to turn the page upside down and "draw" the signature, as if he were sketching a landscape or portrait.

After a dozen attempts he was confident, and he inked the man's scrawl onto the phony tally.

He heated the document briefly in the oven to make sure the ink was dry and to give the sheet additional distress and patina of age.

He took apart the frame, extracted the real tally, which went into the lining of his backpack. He drew another sketch on the back of the forgery and mounted that one into the frame, sketch side out. Onto the wall it went.

Shaw had then called Devereux and they met about his proposition to buy his family's safety with the "evidence" against BlackBridge and Banyan Tree. He'd arranged the get-together to give Droon or another op the chance to put a tracker on his bike (not guessing they would take the more sophisticated approach of the RFID dust), which led them back to Pacific Heights. At the safe house he'd purposefully left the window open, knowing that a surveillance outfit from BlackBridge was now eavesdropping. Shaw had made a pre-arranged call to Victoria Lesston and purposely sat near the open window to explain about the tally being hidden in the frame on the wall. He was pretty sure that the woman in the hall, dressed like a maid, was the op whose job it was to steal the document when her partners created a distraction by trying to blow the door off Russell's SUV.

Shaw knew the document examiners in Sacramento would find his creation to be fake but he wanted some insurance. He had contacted Professor Steven Field and told him of his plan.

The professor had laughed. "Well, aren't *you* your father's sons?"

"When the story breaks that it's fake I want a nail in the coffin—some expert to say that the tally was just a pipe dream. It'd be next to impossible for there really to've been one."

Field knew just whom to call. He got in touch with a colleague, Professor Anthony Rice, who had known Ashton Shaw too. He was more than happy to back up the story. Rice put out a tweet on the topic—that it was almost certain that there was no real voting tally. Media networks picked it up and invited the articulate, airtime-ready professor to be interviewed on the topic.

The entire world would get the word the tally was a myth.

Shaw now said to La Fleur, "You told us that when Amos found out that the tally was real, he was going to destroy it."

La Fleur nodded. "I know it would've been tough for him. He was a historian. Against his training to destroy an original document."

Never deny history . . .

One of Ashton's rules.

Shaw told La Fleur this.

"Good advice."

Shaw said, "Hitler's and Goebbels's and Himmler's writings were despicable but we don't burn them. That's different, though, from the Nuremberg Laws—nineteen thirty-five. Took away citizenship of Jews in Nazi Germany and became the justification for the death camps. What if there was the same voting tally controversy then? The law was passed but the tally went missing, and you found it. You could submit it and have the law go into effect, or you could burn it. What's your moral duty?"

"No doubt in my mind."

"That's why I'm here."

La Fleur frowned. His fingers drummed.

Shaw dug into his backpack and extracted the original tally. He handed it to La Fleur, who gazed at the document. "Heh. Short, isn't it? Doesn't seem so scary up close." He looked up. "You ever read *Lord of the Rings*?"

Shaw nodded.

La Fleur mused, "This is the ring of power." Then he lit up his bong, took a hit and laughed, as the smoke floated. "I'm an old man. I can be as goddamn melodramatic as I want."

Shaw rose and walked to La Fleur's fireplace. He opened the grate. He took the tally and placed it inside. "You want to do the honors?" Shaw asked, picking up a cigarette lighter and handing it to the man.

"Me?"

"BlackBridge killed your friend for this. Tortured him."

The man thought briefly. "And they killed *your* father. Let's both do it." He produced another lighter.

Shaw debated. It seemed sentimental, contrary to his theory of navigating your way through life by calculation and analysis. But then he recalled the day young Colter had saved the woman in the avalanche and his father had given him and his siblings their respective statuettes.

Never deny the power of ritual . . .

The men crouched before the pungent fireplace. Two clicks of two lighters, and they each touched the blue flame to opposite corners of the tally. They sat back and watched the document ignite and curl under the bright orange blaze, sending embers flitting upward into the flue like bugs curiously repelled by, rather than drawn to, a bright lamp on a gentle summer's dusk.

78

While San Francisco is home to more than forty geographic elevations, the A-list celebrities are the famed Seven Hills, just like in Rome. They are Telegraph Hill, Russian Hill, Rincon Hill, Twin Peaks, Mount Davidson, Lone Mountain, and the most luxurious, Nob Hill.

The name derives from *nabob*, the term referring to a rich and conspicuous businessman, and it was applied to this summit because it was here that the Big Four—the tycoons involved in the creation of the Central Pacific Railroad—had mansions: Leland Stanford, Collis Potter Huntington, Mark Hopkins and Charles Crocker. The men modestly referred to themselves as "the Associates."

Colter Shaw was now enjoying the unstoppable sun and the cool air in this lofty neighborhood, sitting in a rooftop bar and café. The view was fabulous. When the June gloom descends, or the autumn rainy season brings downpours for weeks upon end, San Francisco can be unbearably glum. But on days like this, the sun fully unfurled, the I-left-my-heart town can turn the wordless into Beat-era poets, the tone-deaf into chanteurs.

Shaw was sipping an Anchor Steam, the essential San Francisco beer. In his travels, which took him far afield, he always tended to pick local brews and this was one of his favorites.

Much of his day had been taken up with interviews with the San Francisco FBI agents who were running the BlackBridge case. All of the agents in the Bay Area field offices had been vetted and were clean. Ashton Shaw's concerns had proven to be a bit excessive in that while there was some SFPD corruption, only five patrolmen and brass were in BlackBridge's pocket, out of thousands of officers.

Shaw was sipping the beer and, mostly from curiosity, perusing a menu that was heavy with tourist fare—though of the Nob Hill variety: Manchego cheese, serrano ham, bruschetta, lobster rolls. Also a kids' menu, evidence that trust-fund youngsters enjoyed the same chow as their common counterparts did: cheese sticks, pizza, and potatoes and onion rings that had met their crispy fate in boiling oil.

He was not here for the food, though. He and Victoria would meet later and go to a back alley in Chinatown. He hoped he could find one of the places where, years ago, Ashton Shaw had had meetings over lunch with local Chinese businessmen, art dealers and professors. Occasionally Ash would bring along one or more of the children. Even Dorion too, at the time younger than three years old. His sister had eaten her noodles by hand, one at a time. Young Colter had been mesmerized by the quiet, observant Chinese men who treated Ashton with respect and seemed subtly impressed with the man's ability to discuss Asian philosophy and politics and wield chopsticks as if he'd been weaned from bottle to the lacquered rods at a single-digit age.

The memory faded, and it was on his third sip of Anchor Steam that he noted he was being watched.

A large man, Anglo, in a dark suit and slightly less dark shirt, was standing immobile near the hostess station outside and had been there for more time than seemed normal. Tables were available but he simply stood in one spot, with arms crossed. Through sun-glasses he was eyeing the patio, but mostly he was eyeing Colter Shaw.

Shaw's right hand set the bottle down and continued casually to the napkin in his lap and thereafter to the grip of the Glock 42 in the holster, tucked in the waistband of his black jeans and hidden by the shirt, which was roughly the same shade as that of the behemoth man's at the hostess station.

Well, there's the minder.

But where is the mindee?

The answer arrived a moment later like a foraging pigeon.

"No need for that," came the man's voice behind him. It had a delicate English lilt.

Shaw turned.

At a nearby table Jonathan Stuart Devereux lifted a glass of wine Shaw's way. Apparently he'd been observing Shaw observe the admirable scenery—and the substantial bodyguard.

"He's safe." As if talking about a dog. Then: "Join me, join me."

Shaw dropped his own menu on the table. He swiveled his chair, the metal legs gritting unpleasantly on the concrete floor. He easily lifted the heavy piece of furniture and plopped it down across from Devereux. The man was in a garish light blue suit—no stripes today—and pink shirt. The groping octopus of a handkerchief was cream-colored today. The shoes were polished to black mirrors.

"You followed me," Shaw said. "Not easy to miss a Rolls. I wasn't paying attention."

Devereux looked over his guest from behind those large, rectangular TV-screen glasses. Today the frames were baby blue. "Ah, but why here, Mr. Shaw? My word."

"The view. The beer."

"Don't have the soup, whatever you're leaning toward. Fair warning. It's watery and the onions grew from cans."

The man looked around, his hands gesturing before him, fingers bending and straightening, palms up, palms down. The digits adjusted his busy handkerchief. Why this look? What impression was he trying to convey? The word *dandy* came to mind.

The melodious voice, with its suave over-the-Pond modulation, offered, "Quite the adventure you've had in this town, haven't you, Shaw? You were born here."

This was not a question.

"Technically Berkeley."

"Cal. That's what the University of California at Berkeley is called. Yes. Berkeley's the town, Cal is the school. Your mother was a professor, a physician, but you were born off campus. *Not* at the medical center where she taught. She did quite the work as a principal investigator too, now, didn't she?"

Again, this was certain information that Devereux had found and kept, like acorns buried by fat-cheeked squirrels in late summer. Meant of course to intimidate.

"Quite the adventure," the man repeated, his voice now an ominous whisper.

"What can I do for you, Devereux?"

His hands became spirited once more and he muttered angrily, "I had such a fine plan. Such a pure design. We'd find the voting certificate, my companies would run for office, we'd win, of course. And then, bang." A palm struck the tabletop and drew attention. "Onward to the new world."

Shaw thought once more of the protests in Berkeley.

CORPORATE SELLOUTS—NO!

Devereux took a sip of yellow wine. "Oaky chardonnay. The sort that makes you shiver. The vintners in California need to work on that. But it's the best they have here."

Devereux would be a man who had to order from the right side of the menu.

"If you hadn't followed me here," Shaw said blandly, "you could've gone someplace with a better list."

Devereux's eyes strayed to a nearby table: two attractive women in business attire—white suit, lime-green dress, both form-fitting. He pushed the lenses higher, the better to study them. Which he did for a moment.

Shaw said, "I saw your political plans once Banyan Tree got into office. It was in Amos Gahl's courier bag. Deregulation was the theme. Environment, banking, healthcare and insurance. Cutting social programs to the bone. Private police. I smelled human rights issues."

Devereux turned away from visually molesting the two women diners.

"Ah, we could argue till the early hours, couldn't we? I could respond that deregulation leads to corporate success, which leads to more employment and a better economy. One could also contend that corporations are far more efficient and ethical than a mere mortal politician: a company would never be caught with its fly open. But you would come up with a counterargument. I would counter-counter. It would become oh-so tedious . . ." Another sip of the wine he was going to finish despite himself. "It would have been a noble experiment . . . But let's not quibble. Do you ride the cable cars?"

"I have."

"You know what the engineer's called."

Shaw answered, "A gripman." He seemed disappointed that Shaw had known. "And they have to be replaced every three days. The grips, not the men." A chuckle.

Shaw had another hit of beer. The leisurely tip of the bottle, accompanied by a glance into Devereux's eyes, was meant also to convey impatience.

The billionaire's face flared with anger. He leaned forward. In a low voice he drew the words out. "Something very wrong went down here, Shaw. I'm not sure what or how. But you were at the epicenter."

This was Devereux's show. There was nothing to do but listen.

"There's no record that we could find of any industrialist or financier in the nineteen twenties interested in a voting tally about Proposition Oh-Six."

"Is that right?" Shaw frowned in confusion.

"Oh, yes it is." Hands zipping here, hands zipping there. "And, from what I heard, the forgery was rather clumsily done. Not clumsy in the sense of technique or penmanship. It got the judge's handwriting down perfectly."

"You checked that too, did you?"

"I mean clumsy in terms of the materials, the supplies. One would think that a millionaire in the nineteen twenties would have hired a forger who'd use inks and paper that dated to nineteen oh-six. Easily come by back then."

"One would think."

Devereux extracted a monogrammed handkerchief. He patted his bald brow. "Of course, we're not here to debate. The people involved, all those many years ago, they know the truth." He couldn't resist adding, with a sardonic grin, "*If* they existed."

Shaw remained silent.

"A forgery it's been declared and that's tainted the whole barrel of apples. The army I had marshalled in Sacramento—quite the array—were enough to stop a court challenge. But now they've got cold feet. All those liberal, human-rights pundits and professors railing against capitalism . . . Yes, if we'd struck fast, we could've pushed it through and made sure it stuck. But t'was not to be." Hands jittering in the air. The waitress thought it was a summons. "No, no, no," he said darkly, and she retreated.

"So, it's fallen out the way it has." Then his fake thin-lipped smile vanished. "BlackBridge is gone. But I am CEO of one of the wealthiest corporations on the face of the earth, aren't I?"

"I suppose so. Hadn't actually heard of you until a few days ago."

His fingers froze briefly. With a smile on his moonish face, he said, "The voting tally, BayPoint Enviro-Sure Solutions . . . You've crossed me, Shaw. And that means your family has crossed me as well. Bad thing to do."

"I think it's time to say goodbye, Devereux."

"Oh, from your perspective, maybe. Not from mine."

Shaw rose, put a twenty down beside his empty beer bottle.

Devereux's eyes held his for a moment, then swiveled to the menu. He perused. "What to have, what to have . . ."

79

S haw descended from the rooftop restaurant to the lobby and stepped out into the garish décor, then proceeded outside, putting his phone away, having made two calls.

He waited in front of the hotel, in the shade of an arching, dark red awning, as the intense sunlight made the unshaded portion of the street glow surreally. In ten minutes, a dark-skinned man on a Vespa rolled up and spotted Shaw, braking to a stop. Shaw joined him. "From Mack." Shaw took the slim 4-by-5-inch envelope and instantly the courier was gone.

No more than five minutes later a cab pulled up and the second person he had called after meeting with Devereux climbed out, as the uniformed doorman scuttled forward.

Sophia Ionescu, aka Consuela Ramirez, aka Ksenia Vlanova, was really quite attractive.

Her shades were similar in shape to Devereux's eyeglasses. Hers were pricey too; they bore the Chanel logo. She wore a short white skirt, blue silk blouse, white cotton jacket, and very little else, it seemed. Over her shoulder was a black purse on a chain, also Chanel.

Well, she *was* a three-G-a-night girl.

She appeared glum, an expression that did nothing to diminish her beauty—as she muttered, "You said it was dues time."

Shaw nodded. "Take care of this, and I throw out the drugs you tried to plant. And erase the tape."

"Take care of what?"

"There's a man upstairs on the patio, having lunch." He showed her a picture of Jonathan Stuart Devereux. "You'll go up there, make contact and then take him to the Sherry-Nelson Arms Hotel. It's up the street."

"I know it." A shrug. "He looks like the Wizard of Oz. How do I know he'll come on to me?"

"He will." Shaw wasn't sure his entire plan would work but he had no doubt that Devereux would go for the bait.

After a drink or two, with conversation steeped in flirtation and wine, Devereux would make the offer.

"What if he wants to take me to his house?"

"He's married."

"Pig." But spoken as if identifying a species, not offering an insult.

Shaw opened the paper bag that Mack's delivery man had given him. He took out a plastic bag holding what looked like a credit card, slightly thicker than normal. On the front was printed the name of an airline and below that *Prestige Club* and a meaningless account number. He handed it to her. "Here's what's going to happen. You go up to the room with him. When you're inside, take his jacket off and kiss him."

"Do I have to?"

Shaw said, "Yes. Then tell him to go brush his teeth."

"Oh, that's why."

He'd told her to bring paste and a brush.

"When he's in the bathroom slip this into his wallet. He keeps it in his jacket pocket."

"And?

"You leave. You got cold feet."

"That's it?"

"That's it."

"Okay."

"Once I know you've done that, I'll dump the tape and drugs."

"How do I know you'll do it?"

Shaw shook his head, offering a tight-lipped smile.

A glance at the Prestige Club card. "It's not a bomb or poison or anything?"

"No."

She looked up at the hotel. "What did this guy do to you? I mean, to deserve this?"

Shaw kept to himself that his father, Todd Zaleski, other colleagues and Amos Gahl were dead because of Jonathan Stuart Devereux's quest for the Holy Proposition. He settled for: "A story for another day."

Then the three-G girl stepped toward the entrance of the building and fired a faintly impatient glance at the doorman, who had fallen in love in the past five minutes, and he adoringly pushed open the heavy door for her.

80

Devereux's still a problem."

Shaw had just walked into the safe house on Alvarez.

He continued speaking to Russell. "Mary Dove and Dorie . . . They're still at risk. We are too."

"Didn't figure him for the revenge sort. Thought he'd put his energies elsewhere."

"Yeah, well, we blew up his Grail."

Sitting at the coffee table, Shaw opened his laptop. He typed. "I'm tracing him."

"You got a device on him?"

"Correct."

Russell seemed impressed.

Shaw continued, "He can't operate the Urban Improvement Plan without another group like BlackBridge. I'm hoping he'll find some other dirty-tricks outfit. I'll let our Bureau contacts here know. Let's hope he stumbles."

"Hmm." On the screen Russell was watching the glowing dot

representing the Rolls-Royce, which had left Nob Hill and was making its way south. "How long will it last?"

"Four days, five."

"You know it's a long shot, finding a meeting, identifying principals."

"It is. But I'm hoping to find another UIP drop-off point, and the Bureau can get eyes and ears there in time."

"What system are you using?"

"MicroTrace."

"It's a good one. We use it. Send me the number of that unit. I'll have Karin keep eyes on him too."

Shaw sent the text to Russell's phone.

Both men watched the dot.

Then Shaw noted his brother's duffel bag and backpack sitting near the stairs.

Why the hell the Oakland A's? . . .

"Come back to the Compound. Victoria and I are driving down there. Until I can get some evidence on Devereux, I want to keep an eye on Mary Dove. Maybe have Dorie come too."

"Can't. There's that problem in Alaska. I told you about it."

Shaw said, "You can't be the only one with a beard and a SIG Sauer."

He thought this might, at last, raise a smile. No. His brother shook his head.

"Mary Dove'd love it." He hesitated then added, "Been forever."

Another pause. "Just can't."

"Sure."

You make a good team . . .

Well, after a rocky start, they had. He was thinking of Russell's enthusiastic embrace of his brother's plan to finally nail the Black-Bridge crew at San Bruno park.

Which made his brother's abrupt departure now all the more painful.

Shaw was looking down at the floor. There was a black scuff mark in the shape of a crescent moon. Had it been left by Shaw or Russell? Maybe Droon or one of the ops when they'd assaulted the safe house in search of the tally. Maybe by Ashton Shaw himself, if the mark was indelible enough to survive polishings over the years.

"Better go."

When it came to his brother there was no true north, there was not even a constellation to help Colter Shaw navigate through the words he wanted to say. He and Russell had never had serious conversations. They talked about how to cure pike for longest storage or which caliber and load were best for charging mountain lions. And for human intruders, armed and with intent. But never words about themselves.

That wasn't acceptable to Colter Shaw, not after all that had happened over the past few days. "Wait."

His brother turned back.

"Why . . . Why'd you disappear? All these years. We're blood. I've got a right to know."

A long moment passed. "What Ash taught us: survival."

Shaw could only shake his head.

"Survival for you, for everyone in the family. You have an idea of my job. I do bad things. I was afraid I'd put everybody at risk. There're prices on my head—sort of like a reward, if you think about it."

Just last week, in the cult in Washington State, one of the self-help gurus had told Shaw much the same.

I think he didn't want to leave. He felt he had no choice. If you pursue him now, and find him, he's just going to keep running . . . A protector sometimes protects best by leaving those in his care. The way a bird leads predators away from their young.

"Russell, we all know how to handle risks. It's what Ashton taught us. From day one in the Compound."

"All right." His brother inhaled twice before continuing: "It was survival for me too." The white noise roared like a deadly wave. "You really believed I'd hurt Ash?"

So we get to it. At last.

"I looked at the facts—the fight you two had about Dorie, the knife. Then you lied, you said you were in L.A. when he died. You were near the Compound."

"It was one of my first assignments. An op near Fresno. They gave it to me because I knew the territory. Nobody could know about it. Okay, Ashton taught us to look at facts. 'Never make decisions based on emotion.' But who somebody is, that's a fact too, isn't it? What you thought, what you accused me of . . . That was tough. It was easier to go away."

"I was wrong."

Was this a transgression that could be remedied by apology? Colter Shaw simply couldn't tell.

Russell's eyes went to the statue of the soaring eagle.

"Remember that?" Shaw asked, nodding at it. "Do you have the bear?"

"No."

Had he thrown it away because Ashton's ritual gave first prize to Colter? Russell's was for the supporting role.

His brother surprised him by saying, "I'd been meaning to send it back. Never got around to it."

Shaw considered this. "*You* had it, not Ash?"

"I took it, after the funeral."

"Why?"

Russell was silent for a moment. "I couldn't tell you."

"Keep it," Shaw said.

"No, it's yours."

Silence flowed and within it, this thought: the words he'd rehearsed for so long had finally been spoken . . . but had done nothing to bridge the chasm between them.

"Okay. Got to get the team up north. I'm glad this reward thing's working out. It suits you. The Restless Man."

"You were right. This BlackBridge operation, it wasn't what I do. I needed you."

A nod. There was no question of a handshake, much less an embrace. With backpack on his shoulder and duffel bag in hand, his older brother was out the door.

81

A t ten that evening, Shaw and Victoria were returning to the Alvarez Street safe house from a fine Italian dinner in the Embarcadero. The day had been rainy and the streets slick, so they had taken her rental, the car that had been at the scene of the takedown in San Bruno park. They both were curious what Avis would make of the bullet hole in the fender. At least she'd bought the loss-damage waiver, so she would not be charged, though Shaw wondered if gunfire invalidated the coverage.

They paused outside.

"Anything?" Victoria asked.

Shaw was looking at the security app on his phone. Russell had left several cameras in the house. With Devereux still a wild card, and with him knowing where the safe house was located, they were being cautious, though Shaw believed the man would play the long game. Nothing would happen to Shaw or the family just yet. That would be too suspicious. The descendant of the beheaded member of English royalty was dangerous, greedy and narcissistic, but not stupid.

"Clear." Shaw put the phone away.

They went inside, set the security system to at-home mode and opened wine and beer. "Think the fireplace works?" she asked.

"I checked. It's sealed. My father and his colleagues? Didn't want any surprise packages dropping in."

"Your mother and I had a conversation about him. He had a reputation for being paranoid," she said.

"That's right."

"But I guess after all this, he was just being cautious."

"Russell said some of his concerns were smoke. That was true. But what he really was? A survivalist before anything else. That's how I think of him now."

Shaw had some beer and called up the tracking program on his laptop. The red dot that was Devereux pulsed, but didn't move. Shaw panned in and saw that he was in a developed area off Highway 1, south of the city. He'd probably stopped off for a meal at one of the many seafood places along that sidewinding road. Perhaps he was on his way to Carmel, the magical kingdom on the Monterey Peninsula— it was the sort of place where he would have one of his mansions. And if so, was he accompanied by a tall, picturesque woman?

It was then that he heard Victoria's alarmed voice, "Well."

He noted her attention was on her phone.

"You have a news feed?"

Shaw asked, "Which one?"

"*Any* of them."

He picked one at random. And read.

BILLIONAIRE BUSINESSMAN JONATHAN STUART DEVEREUX, CEO OF BANYAN TREE HOLDINGS, WAS SHOT AND KILLED TONIGHT IN THE TOWN OF HALF MOON BAY, SOUTH OF SAN FRANCISCO.

MR. DEVEREUX WAS LEAVING AN EXCLUSIVE GOLF RESORT WHEN HE WAS FELLED BY A SINGLE SNIPER SHOT FROM THE HIGHWAY. HE WAS LEAVING THE RESTAURANT IN THE COMPANY OF EXECUTIVES OF ABERNATHY CONSULTING, SANTA CRUZ, AND A BODYGUARD. NO ONE ELSE WAS INJURED.

THE SAN FRANCISCO DAILY HERALD REPORTED THAT AN ANONY-
MOUS CALLER TO THE PAPER STATED THAT A LOCAL GANG WAS
BEHIND THE DEATH BECAUSE OF DEVEREUX'S INVOLVEMENT IN
ILLEGAL DRUG OPERATIONS THROUGHOUT THE BAY AREA. A SAN
MATEO COUNTY SHERIFF'S OFFICE SPOKESPERSON SAID THE
INVESTIGATION WAS ONGOING.

"God," Victoria said. "The UIP thing."

Shaw was doubtful. "He was insulated. That was BlackBridge's thing. Nobody'd know that he was the ultimate client. He was careful about that."

Dangerous, greedy and narcissistic, but not stupid . . .

It was then that his phone hummed with a text, and he read the brief message from an unknown number.

Delete the tracking app.

He stared at the words for a moment. Then the meaning hit him. Jesus. He did as the message instructed. Shaw replied.

Done.

A moment went by. Shaw debated. He sent another.

Take care . . .

Shaw wondered if he would get a response. Seconds later the phone vibrated again.

The number you are trying to reach is no longer in service.

PART FIVE

JULY 3

ASH

82

One of those stainless-steel afternoons, when humidity, temperature, clarity of the air and a show-off of a sun conspire to make the setting as perfect as a setting can be.

Colter Shaw parked the Winnebago near the cabin and climbed out, stretching after the seven-plus-hour drive from the north, eyeing the craggy and soaring peaks to the west of the property, the dense pelt of pine and oak to the east and south. Sun danced off the pond where he and Russell had fished for hours upon hours.

There'd been several days of matters to attend to in San Francisco, answering more questions—and there'd been quite a few—about the San Bruno shootout, Droon's death and the explosion of the Prescott home, the Urban Improvement Plan, BlackBridge. Yes, the various authorities had quite the list. Unfortunately Shaw could offer no insights into the tragic death of Devereux, but he said there was some credibility to the drug claim, since he knew for a fact that the man was one of the chief beneficiaries of the UIP.

Shaw had spent a day closing up the safe house on Alvarez, feeling his brother's absence even more keenly than he had after Russell had departed the first time, following the rescue at the library. He thought back to his surprise and pleasure when the man had returned to explain that he would be helping Shaw identify the victims of the kill order.

It's not a reward job, Colt. You can't do it on your own . . .

Then he'd tucked the feeling away and finished filling his backpack. He had hopped onto the Yamaha for the zipping ride to the RV camp to pick up the Winnebago.

Upon leaving the park, Shaw had not headed south toward the Sierra Nevadas. And the reason for this was that he was not alone in the camper. Beside him in the passenger seat was Victoria Lesston. It turned out that she found the idea of a vacation as alien as he, but they decided to take the plunge and spend some R & R in wine country.

They had found a charming bed-and-breakfast nestled into a verdant quadrant of a vineyard. The place was long on views and complex, tasty meals, and—thank God—short on gingham and plaques of ducks and geese in bonnets.

Those days—in the safe house and then in Napa—were the first time in ages that he had spent several contiguous nights in the company of a woman. Oh, he'd been wary of the trip at first, very wary, but Shaw soon found there was nothing to worry about; all the vineyards they toured offered good beer.

The amount of time in each other's company had been just right. At almost exactly the same moment, silence materialized between them, like a summoned spirit at a seance. It was benign, but it was silence nonetheless and they'd smiled, both understanding simultaneously that it was time to get back to their real worlds.

Now, in the Compound, Victoria climbed out of the camper too and stretched, somewhat more carefully than Shaw, given her hundred-foot high dive from a cliff not long ago—and the tumble to cover in San Bruno park. Together they walked toward the cabin, where they saw Mary Dove approaching from a field. She carried a heavy basket of vegetables.

Smiling, she nodded toward them, then the house, meaning she would off-load the provisions and then join them.

Victoria pulled off her sweater—Napa and Sonoma had been far more damp and chill than the weather here. Beneath she wore a gray silk blouse. And beneath that was a pale blue, lacey garment, not presently visible, though Shaw was by now quite familiar with its construction and the mechanics of the clasps.

She wore blue jeans, as did Shaw. He was in a black T-shirt and the leather jacket that still bore evidence of damage various skirmishes in the past few days, most notably the cuts from the knife duel with Droon. He had examined the marks and decided to leave the blemishes. He had no clue how to go about mending a garment that had come from a department store. His expertise in leather was limited to hides and skins that he had fleshed, salted and tanned.

They carried their bags to their respective rooms. Shaw stripped and took a scorching hot, then a freezing shower. He toweled off and dressed in clean jeans and a dress shirt. Then digging through his bag, he removed the eagle statue and replaced it on the shelf from which Russell had taken it so many years ago. He'd thought about keeping it in the camper but for some reason it seemed more appropriate here.

He joined Victoria on the front porch. Mary Dove now brought out three cups of coffee, along with the milk and sugar service, which she set on the table.

All three sat, fixed up the beverages to their liking and sipped.

Victoria had dozed for a portion of the trip but had apparently been aware of several calls Shaw had taken and made on the drive.

She mentioned this now and asked, "Status?"

"Bail denied for everybody."

"I noticed the streaks," Mary Dove said, nodding at his jacket. "And that." Now she looked to his hand, still bandaged following the slash from Droon's knife. "I do hope you wear your body armor when you ought to." Spoken in the same casual way another parent might say, "Wear your raincoat and galoshes; it's going to pour."

Shaw added, "The Bureau rolled up all the BayPoint Enviro-Sure Solutions executives and some BlackBridge people in L.A., Miami and New York. The company's gone."

The reason for this, of course, was ultimately Ashton Shaw's mission. Had he not started on his quest years ago to bring the outfit down, it would still be going full force, addicting people to drugs, engaging in dirty-tricks operations and leveraging companies like Devereux's into the pilot's seat of political office.

Mary Dove asked, "That wouldn't really have worked, would it? A corporation running for office?"

"I wouldn't have thought so, but who knows?" Shaw told her what Professor Field had said.

Mary Dove said, "That's a question Ash would've loved to think about—and debate until the wee hours." She looked toward Victoria. "He was quite the historical and political scientist, you know."

"Colt told me." Victoria said, "I wish I'd known him."

"He would've liked you," Mary Dove said. "He enjoyed his rappelling buddies."

The woman looked Victoria over. "You're free to stay as long as you like. I'm hosting a women's health retreat next week. Some good people."

"I need to leave in a day or so. I have a job interview on the East Coast."

They'd talked about this on the drive here. The job interview was not exactly that, but, like Russell's, Victoria's line of work required the occasional euphemism.

Her eyes were on his when she added, "But I'd like to come back."

"Always welcome," Mary Dove said and pressed Victoria's arm.

Shaw's glance seconded the motion.

"Tell me about him?" Mary Dove asked.

He knew that she was speaking of Russell.

"Mysterious, doesn't say much, sharp as a whip. Looks exactly the same—well, aside from the beard. It's longer now. His hair too. Still couldn't find out where he's working. Government, deep cover."

Victoria said, "Has or had some Pentagon connection. DoD."

"Why's that?"

"In San Bruno, after the shoot-out, he said we were 'black on backup.' That's Army talk. We used that on operations in Delta."

Shaw thought, Oh, yeah, Ashton Shaw would have loved this woman.

Mary Dove gave a soft smile, and gentle wrinkles folded around her mouth and eyes. "Did Russell say anything about a family?"

"Said he didn't have one."

There was a pause as Mary Dove's eyes fixed on a sunlit peak. "Did you ask him about visiting?"

One never evaded, much less lied, within the Shaw family. "I did. He said he couldn't. An assignment. Important."

"It's his job and his life."

"He's hard to read but I could tell he's content."

Leaving another thought understood, but unstated: both she and Ash had made the right decision in plotting out and executing the most difficult task in the world: their children's upbringing.

His mother said, "I've got to get dinner going. Venison with blackberry glaze. It's been soaking all day."

Her habit was to steep the meat in buttermilk, which eliminated the gamey flavor.

Motion in the corner of Shaw's eye. A nighthawk jotted above the field in his buoyant, erratic path. These particular birds have among the most complicated markings of any avian—their camo makes them virtually invisible during the day, but now, in approaching dusk, they're easily spotted as they hunt for flying insects. They're easily heard too: they issue a repetitive, raspy *creek-creek* when on wing. Colter had once been attacked by one when he had unknowingly trod too close to a nest. Both man and bird disengaged unharmed.

Looking away from the spirited bird, Shaw said, "Have a thought. What do you say about the three of us hiking Echo Ridge tomorrow."

"Lovely idea," said Mary Dove.

"Sounds good to me," Victoria said. Then after a brief pause she turned her head slightly and squinted. "But I think it's going to be four."

Shaw glanced at her and noted she was looking past him. Both he and his mother turned.

A figure stepped from the dirt road onto the driveway. The man was dressed in black and wearing a stocking cap. He carried a duffel bag in one hand, and a backpack was over his right shoulder. He paused, looking at the house and, seeing the trio on the porch, he brushed at his long beard with the back of his left hand and continued in a slow lope toward them.

"My," Mary Dove whispered, a hint of uncharacteristic emotion in her voice. She stepped off the planks, into the grass, to greet her eldest son.

Acknowledgments

Novels are not one-person endeavors. Creating them and getting them into the hands and hearts of readers is a team effort, and I am beyond lucky to have the best team in the world. My thanks to Sophie Baker, Felicity Blunt, Berit Böhm, Dominika Bojanowska, Penelope Burns, Annie Chen, Julia Wisdom, Sophie Churcher, Francesca Cinelli, Isabel Coburn, Luisa Collichio, Jane Davis, Liz Dawson, Julie Reece Deaver, Danielle Dieterich, Jenna Dolan, Mira Droumeva, Jodi Fabbri, Cathy Gleason, Alice Gomer, Iven Held, Ashley Hewlett, Sally Kim, Hamish Macaskill, Cristina Marino, Ashley McClay, Emily Mlynek, Nishtha Patel, Seba Pezzani, Rosie Pierce, Abbie Salter, Roberto Santachiara, Deborah Schneider, Sarah Shea, Mark Tavani, Madelyn Warcholik, Claire Ward, Alexis Welby, Sue and Jackie Yang. You're the best!

Jeffery Deaver

THE MIDNIGHT LOCK

THE
NEW
L

COMING NOVEMBER 2021

Active ACCOUNTING

Janet Brammer

David Cox

Michael Fardon

Aubrey Penning

OSBORNE BOOKS

Published by Osborne Books Limited
Unit 1B Everoak Estate
Bromyard Road
Worcester WR2 5HP
Tel 01905 748071
Email books@osbornebooks.co.uk
Website www.osbornebooks.co.uk

Graphic design by Jon Moore

Printed by the Bath Press, Bath

British Library Cataloguing in Publication Data
A catalogue record for this book is available from the British Library

ISBN 1 872962 37 8

CONTENTS

INTRODUCTION

Active Accounting has been written to cater for the needs of students who require a full understanding of financial and management accounting, but who may have no prior accounting knowledge. The text is suitable for:

- A/S and A2 Accounting courses
- AVCE accounting units
- Higher National
- first-year degree accounting modules
- the general reader who needs a simple explanation of a demanding subject

Active Accounting is divided into three sections:

1 'Accounting in Context' provides an introduction to accounting and accountants and the numerical 'language' that accountants speak.

2 'Financial Accounting' explains manual and computerised accounts and examines in detail the format and interpretation of financial statements.

3 'Management Accounting' adopts a practical approach to costing and budgeting and discusses the way business performance can be measured.

The chapters of **Active Accounting** contain:

- an opening Case Study which sets the chapter subject in a real-life 'active' context
- a clear 'down-to-earth' text with worked examples and further illustrative Case Studies
- a chapter summary and key terms to help with revision
- a range of activities – with answers to selected questions at the end of the book (Appendix 1)

An **Active Accounting Tutor Pack** contains the answers to the remainder of the activities. Details of the Tutor Pack are available from Osborne Books on 01905 748071.

Active Accounting is only one of a number of accounting and business texts produced by Osborne Books. If you would like to find out more, telephone our Sales office on 01905 748071 or visit us at www.osbornebooks.co.uk

Janet Brammer, David Cox, Michael Fardon, Aubrey Penning

Spring 2002

ACKNOWLEDGEMENTS

The publisher wishes to thank Mike Gilbert, Jon Moore and Carsten Zuntzt for their help with the reading and production of this book. Particular thanks must go to Roger Petheram of Worcester College of Technology for his role as lead editor of the text.

Thanks are also due to Tesco PLC for permission to use extracts from their Annual Report and Accounts and to Microsoft UK and Sage PLC for their permission to use screen images from their software in the text.

THE AUTHORS

Janet Brammer has over ten years experience lecturing on accountancy courses at Norwich City College. She is a Certified Accountant and previously worked in accountancy practice for a number of years. She has also tutored for the Open University and has written and contributed to a number of texts for Osborne Books and for ACCA.

David Cox is a Certified Accountant with more than twenty years experience teaching accountancy students. Formerly with the Management and Professional Studies Department at Worcester College of Technology, he now lectures on a freelance basis and carries out educational consultancy work in accountancy studies. He is author and joint author of a number of textbooks in the areas of accounting, finance and banking.

Michael Fardon has had extensive teaching experience of a wide range of banking, business and accountancy courses at Worcester College of Technology where he also set up and ran computer accounting courses. He now specialises in writing business and financial texts for Osborne Books.

Aubrey Penning has taught accounting on a wide variety of courses at Worcester College of Technology. He has fourteen years experience of teaching accountancy on a variety of courses in Worcester and Gwent. He is a Certified Accountant, and before his move into full-time teaching he worked for the health service, a housing association and a chemical supplier. He has written and contributed to a number of texts for Osborne Books.

section 1
accounting in context

CASE STUDY
Energy company collapses

The need for effective accounting was highlighted in the well-publicised collapse of Enron, a large US energy company which went bust causing shareholders to lose their money, employees their jobs and accountants their credibility. How did it happen? Who allowed it to happen? Read on . . .

Enron collapse blamed on lax accounting

From James Sargent New York Correspondent

The circumstances surrounding the collapse of Enron, the US energy company, continue to enrage all those who lost out.

New evidence has emerged about extravagances at the company ten months before it filed for bankruptcy. Bonuses of $320 million were paid to executives, including $3.6 million paid to the former chief executive.

All this was at the same time that the corporation was using 4,000 'off-balance-sheet' partnerships which allowed to it to report false profit and debt figures.

News that the corporation twice brought in a live elephant to liven up an employee meeting and hired the 85 acre Astroworld amusement park for an employee's family picnic will do little to console Enron's shareholders and lenders.

'What were the accountants doing when all this was going on?' asked a former employee. 'Did they have their heads buried in the sand?'

learning objectives

When you have studied this chapter, you will be able to:

■ appreciate the importance of providing accurate accounting information to the stakeholders of an organisation

■ distinguish between financial accounting and management accounting

■ describe the different types of accountant and the roles that they fulfil

THE DEVELOPING FUNCTIONS OF ACCOUNTING

the oldest profession in the world?

Accounting has sometimes been described as one of the oldest professions in the world.

The word **accounting** involves a number of concepts which have been in use since the Egyptian Pharoahs built the pyramids:

- keeping financial records – 'accounts' – of money spent and money received in relation to a project or a business

- using this information to 'account' to people who have interest in the project or business, for example the owners or the people providing the money – giving estimates of income, spending (expenses), profit or loss, money owed and money due

keeping records – medieval book-keeping

The mechanical task of keeping records of financial transactions such as income and expenses forms the 'nuts and bolts' of accounting. Traditionally known as **book-keeping**, it developed in medieval times into a double-entry system which involved every transaction being recorded in two separate 'accounts'. If, for example a medieval merchant bought a camel for a hundred pieces of gold, an entry would be marked in two accounts: a 'Camel' account and a 'Gold' account. We do not need to explore the intricacies of double-entry in this book, but you should at least have an appreciation of what it involves; please see Chapter 3 for further details.

accounting in the third Millennium

The differences between the medieval merchant and the modern organisation are those of scale and complexity. The modern organisation may be owned and run by the State (the public sector) or may be in private hands (the private sector) or may be a combination of the two.

The modern organisation is accountable in financial terms not only to its owners but also to a wide variety of people and organisations who have an interest in it – these are its **stakeholders** – for example shareholders, employees, managers, customers, suppliers, lenders and government.

The Case Study of Enron on the previous page points to a far more sophisticated set of functions of accounting than was used in medieval times. The failure of accountants to point out the warning signs of catastrophic failure and corruption suggests that they are nowadays more than just book-keepers.

The present-day functions of accounting include:

■ recording financial transactions

■ presenting financial data to the people who have an interest in the business – the stakeholders

Stakeholders need to know what is going on in a business, and this is precisely what went wrong with Enron in the Case Study: a great many people had the 'wool pulled over their eyes'.

The diagram below shows the stakeholders of a large organisation and the ways in which they are affected by the financial state of the organisation. For example is it . . .

■ providing shareholders a sufficient return on their investment?

■ able to repay its bank loans?

■ making enough money to pay its suppliers regularly?

■ paying the right level of taxes to the government?

■ helping society by donating money to charity?

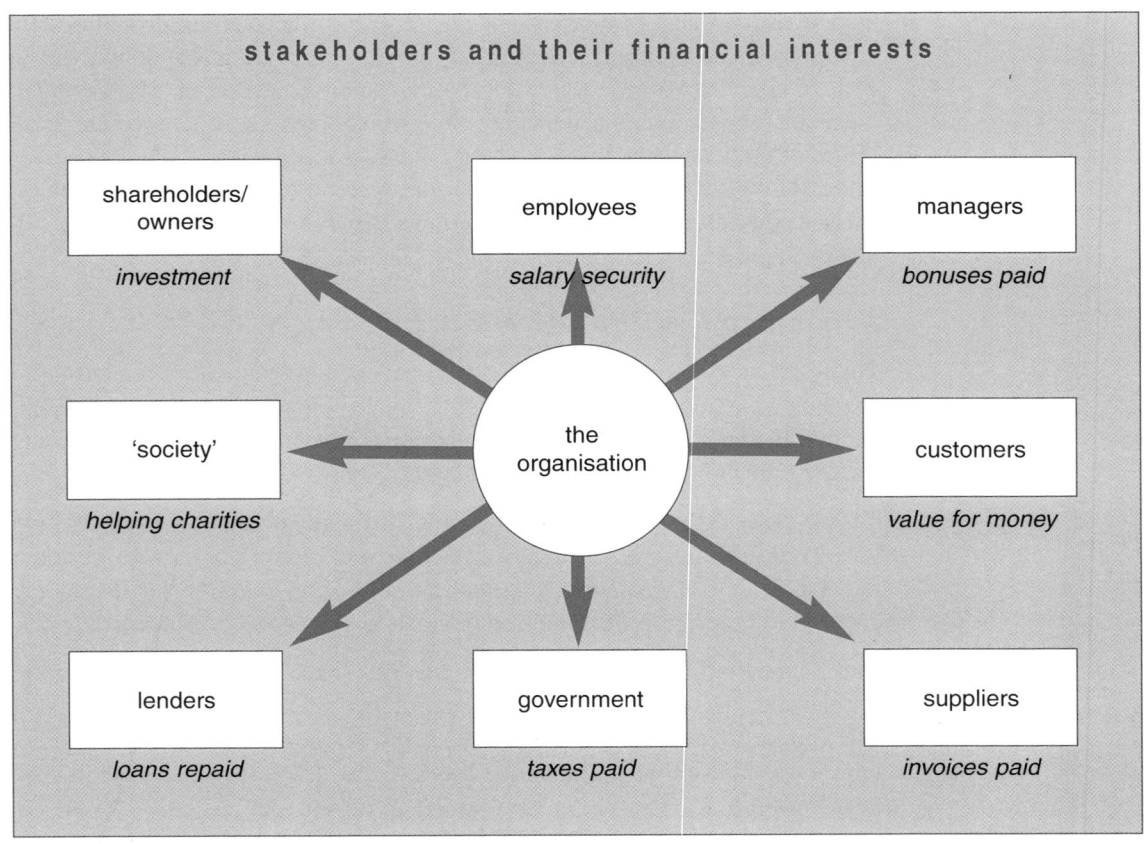

present-day functions of accounting

In order to act in the interests of stakeholders, present-day accountants have to carry out a wide range of functions, including:

- **recording and reporting**
  recording data and preparing financial reports about what has happened in the past – sales figures, profit statements, tax calculations, VAT returns

- **forecasting**
  preparing financial forecasts and budgets – these are estimates of what is expected to happen in the future

- **monitoring and control**
  comparing the figures in forecasts and budgets with what actually happens and then taking corrective action if the figures are off target

- **external auditing**
  checking by external and independent accountants that the recording of financial transactions within the organisation is accurate and in accordance with rules laid down by external regulatory bodies

- **internal auditing**
  checking by the organisation's own staff that the recording of financial transactions is accurate and in accordance with internal rules

In short, accounting is concerned with:

- **recording** financial data
- **reporting** financial data
- **planning** for the organisation's future – setting objectives and targets
- **managing** the organisation – taking action if the targets are not met

Now study the diagram below and see how the accounting functions relate either to **internal** use or to **external** reporting.

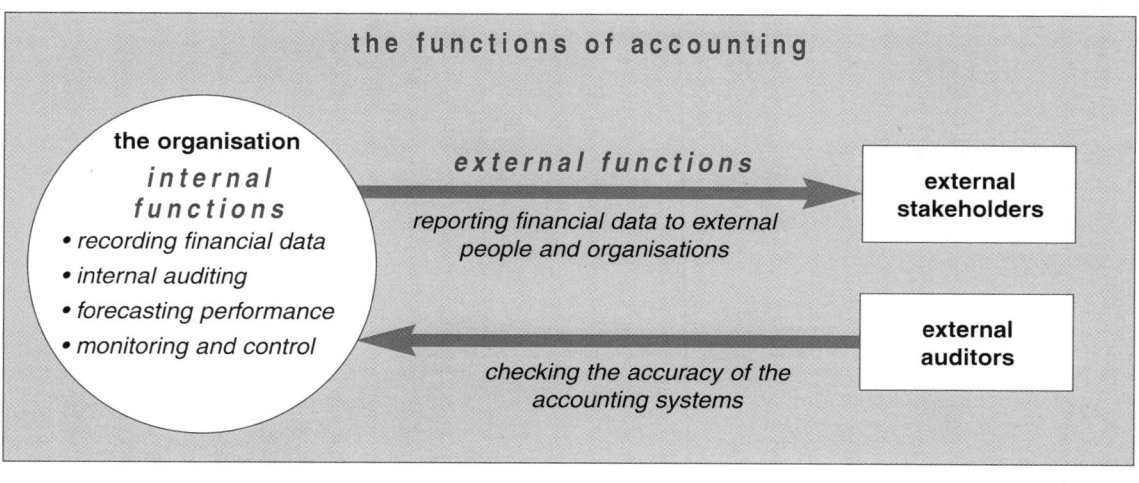

FINANCIAL AND MANAGEMENT ACCOUNTING

Accounting is often divided into two types: **financial accounting** and **management accounting**. This book has been written as a guide to these two different types of accounting, which can be described as follows:

■ **financial accounting** is involved with financial transactions that have already happened and with the preparation and interpretation of financial statements for the benefit of managers, the owners and, in some cases, the external stakeholders of an organisation

■ **management accounting** deals with all aspects of providing financial data to management (eg future income and costs) so that planning can take place and decisions be made, eg reducing or increasing selling prices or switching resources from one product or service to another

The differences between the two are shown in the table set out below . . .

financial accounting	management accounting
historical Records past financial transactions; covers the previous year's trading; looks backwards to analyse performance.	**recent past and future** Performance reports containing financial information on recent past, and projections for the future.
for outsiders Financial statements prepared mainly for shareholders, suppliers, the bank, the Inland Revenue, the Registrar of Companies.	**for insiders** Available only to managers, directors, and owners – and occasionally also to lenders such as banks.
outsiders make the rules The Companies Act specifies the accounting information that must be prepared; the Inland Revenue sets down requirements; the accountancy professional bodies publish standards of accounting practice.	**insiders make the rules** The content of reports and the principles used can be suited to the activities of the business and the requirements of its managers.
a 'true and fair' view Financial accounting is required to present a 'true and fair' view of the financial affairs of the business or organisation.	**a useful report** The main requirement of management accounting is to produce information that will enable the business or organisation to conduct its activities more effectively.
timing Generally there is little urgency to produce financial accounts for outsiders; financial statements are often produced and made available only once a year.	**timing** Management accounting information is prepared as frequently as circumstances demand; speed is often vital as information may go out-of-date very quickly.

TYPES OF ORGANISATION AND THE NEED FOR ACCOUNTING

In this chapter we have used a large limited company business with shareholders as an example to illustrate the importance of accounting to an organisation and to its stakeholders.

It must be appreciated, however, that there are many different types of organisation that will need to carry out accounting processes: some large, many small, some state-owned or state-controlled and many privately owned. These are described below and shown in the diagram on the next page, which you should study carefully.

Whatever the organisation, the accounting function must still take place. Generally speaking the larger the organisation – as we have seen from the Case Study – the greater the need for control and accountability to stakeholders. In a smaller business – a sole trader local taxi service, for example – the accounting records are far less complex and a smaller number of stakeholders is likely to be involved: possibly the Inland Revenue (for tax) and the bank (if the business has an overdraft).

public and private sectors

Public sector organisations are owned directly or indirectly by central or local government. They are not all businesses as such, although the trends for business goals such as profit and efficiency are becoming more dominant. Examples of public sector organisations include services such as the National Health Service and public corporations such as the BBC.

Local government also runs enterprises such as car parks, waste disposal and leisure facilities.

Private sector organisations are owned by private individuals in the form of companies, partnerships and sole trader businesses. Examples include well-known names such as BT, W H Smith and Virgin.

public-private partnerships

A more recent development is the trend for private sector businesses to invest in or to run public sector services. The Private Finance Initiative (PFI) is a Government-sponsored scheme which has involved the private sector in providing facilities such as prisons, barracks and hospitals. The new Worcester Royal Hospital, for example, is a result of companies in private ownership financing a public service run by the NHS. The revamp of the London Underground is another example.

On a smaller scale you may well find that your local leisure centre is owned by the local authority but run by a private sector company.

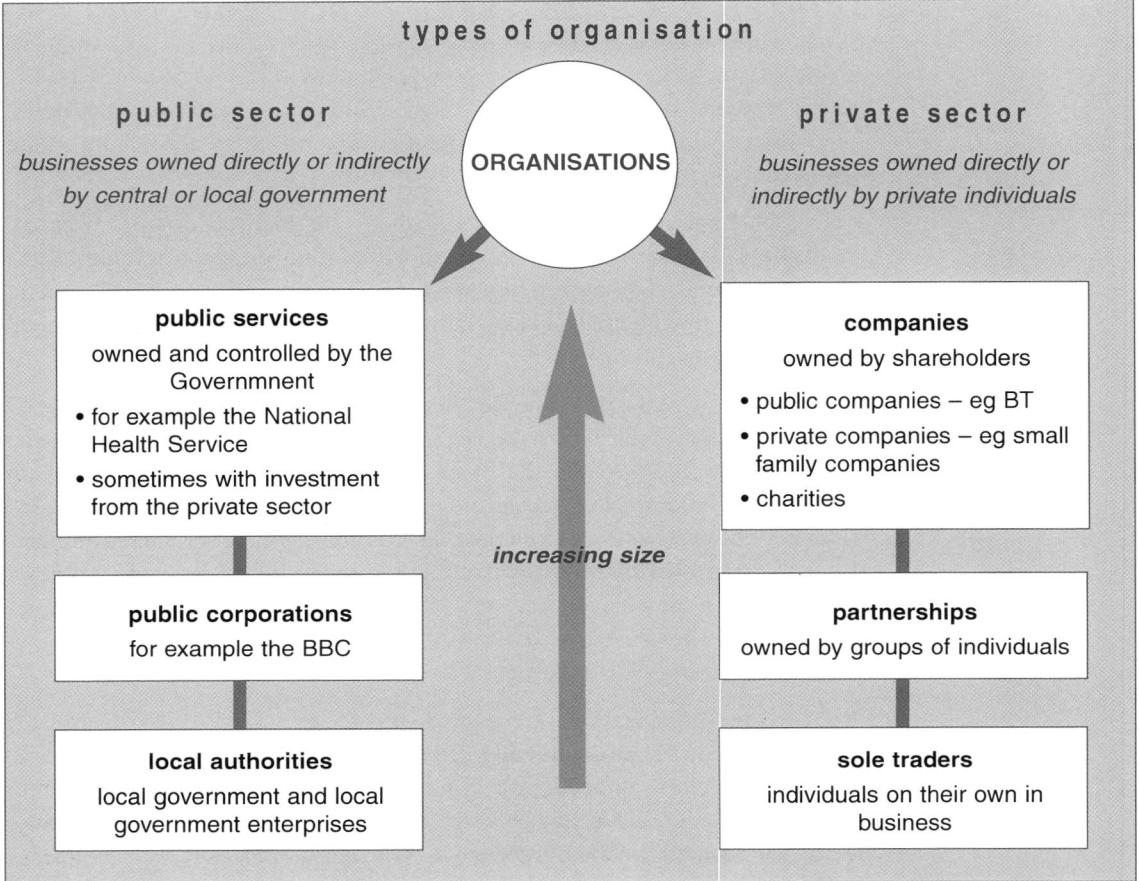

ACCOUNTING PERSONNEL

In this section we look at the different roles carried out by people working in accounting jobs. As we have seen, different organisations have different requirements. If you are thinking of a career in accounting, these descriptions should prove helpful.

book-keepers, accounts assistants

Anyone can keep the 'books' of a business; the important point is that they must be kept – by the owner, or by a full or part-time **book-keeper** or accounts assistant employed for the purpose. Book-keepers do not have to be qualified, although many are. The role will vary from someone coming in for half-a-day a week to write up the books of a small business, to hundreds of people being employed by larger companies as accounts assistants and using powerful computer systems.

The 'books' will vary from handwritten records (stationery shops sell accounting books designed especially for the smaller business) to computer accounting systems. Computer accounting is explained in more detail in Chapter 5.

accountants

The role of the accountant – who will, invariably, be professionally qualified – is to check, summarise, present, analyse and interpret the accounts for the benefit of the owner/owners and other interested parties. There are two types of specialist accountant that individually cover the two areas we have already described on page 12:

- **financial accountant**, mainly concerned with external reporting
- **management accountant**, mainly concerned with internal reporting

However, in medium-sized businesses, the two roles are often combined and the work undertaken by one accountant. In small businesses the roles are often undertaken by the owner, who is very often unqualified in accounting, which is one reason why small businesses sometimes run into financial trouble – the owner does not have his or her finger on the financial pulse.

financial accountant

The function of the **financial accountant** is very much concerned with financial transactions, and with using the information produced by the book-keeper. The financial accountant extracts information from the accounting records in order to provide a method of control, for instance over customers who buy on credit, suppliers and other outstanding bills, and cash and bank balances.

The role of a financial accountant also requires the preparation of year-end financial statements, and may also include negotiation with the Inland Revenue on tax matters for the business. Limited companies, in particular, must comply with the accounting requirements of the Companies Acts, and with the relevant Accounting Standards (see page 273). Company legislation, for example, requires the directors of a company to report annually to shareholders, and to disclose certain minimum financial accounting information.

management accountant

The **management accountant** obtains information about costs – eg the cost of labour, materials, overheads – and interprets it and prepares reports for the owners or managers of the business. In particular, the management accountant is concerned with financial decision-making, planning and control of the business.

auditors

Auditors are accountants whose role is to check that accounting procedures have been followed correctly. There are two types of auditors:

■ external auditors

■ internal auditors

External auditors are independent of the firm whose accounts are being audited, but work within a framework of Auditing Standards (issued by the Auditing Practices Board). The most common type of audit conducted by external auditors is the statutory audit of larger limited companies. In this, the auditors are reporting to the shareholders of a company, stating that the legal requirements laid down in the Companies Act have been complied with, and that the accounts represent a 'true and fair view' of the state of the business.

Internal auditors are employees of the business which they audit. Their duties are concerned with the internal check and control procedures of the business, for example setting down the procedures for the control of cash, authorisation of purchases, and disposal of property. The nature of their work requires that they should have a degree of independence within the company; they often report direct to the finance director.

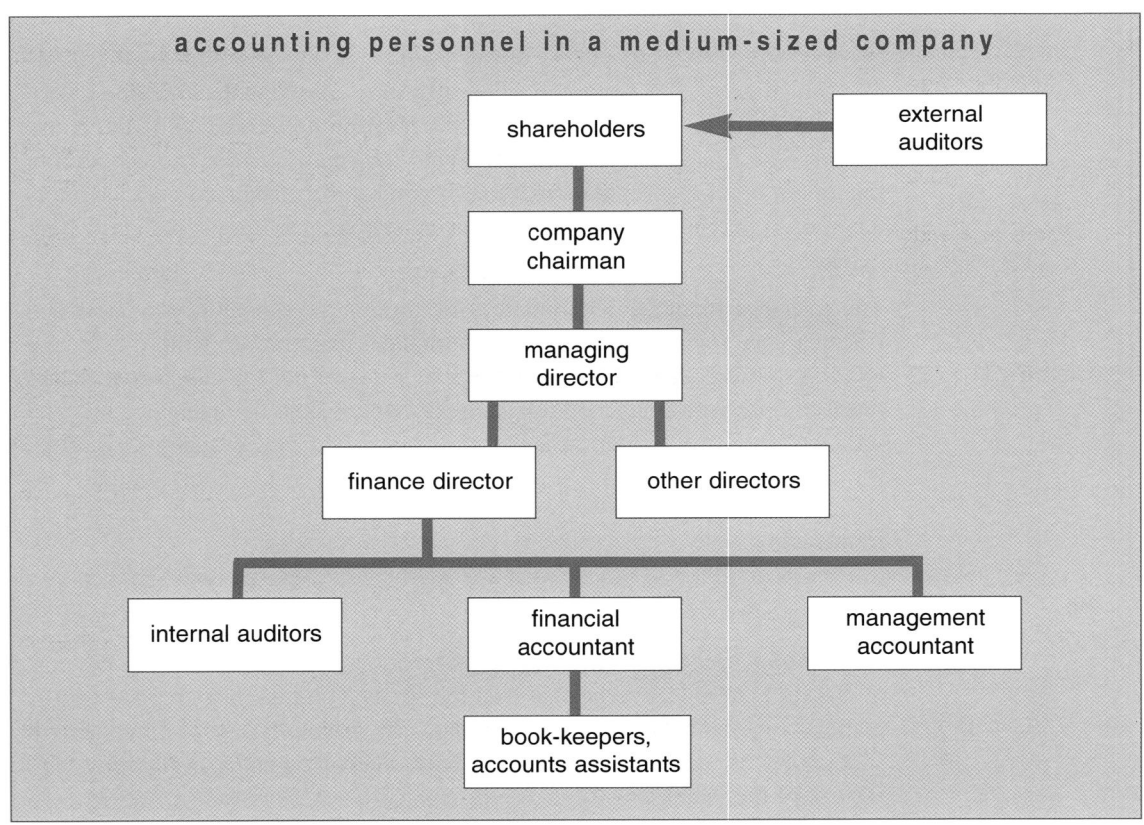

chapter summary

- The origins of accounting involved people maintaining financial records and communicating that information to others who needed to know about levels of income, spending, profits and debts.

- Book-keeping involves the recording of financial transactions; it developed over time into a 'double-entry' system which still forms the basis of many accounting systems, including computer accounting.

- The growth in scope and complexity of organisations, typified by the modern large public company, has meant that the role of accounting has expanded with the growth of stakeholders – people and organisations who have an interest in an organisation.

- The present-day functions of accounting include: recording data, reporting data, auditing, forecasting, and monitoring. Accounting is a discipline which is an essential tool of the business manager who needs to make decisions.

- Accounting can be classified into two main areas: financial accounting, which involves the reporting of financial information (past events), and management accounting, which involves forecasting and monitoring (future events). Financial accounting often reports data to people outside the organisation; management accounting is for internal use to enable managers to make decisions.

- The scope of the accounting functions in an organisation will depend on the size of the organisation. Often, the larger the organisation, the more complex the scope of the accounting functions.

- It is important to appreciate the variety and accounting needs of different organisations, for example public and private sector organisations, large public companies and small sole trader businesses.

- There is a wide variety of accounting jobs, all calling for different skills and qualifications: book-keepers, accounts assistants, financial accountants, management accountants, auditors.

key terms

accounting	recording financial transactions in 'accounts' and reporting the data to people who have an interest in it
book-keeping	maintaining records of financial transactions in accounts
stakeholders	people and organisations who have an interest (including a financial interest) in an organisation
financial accounting	the maintenance, interpretation and reporting of financial data concerned with past transactions to managers, owners and other stakeholders

management accounting	internal reporting to management of past and forecast financial and other data to provide the basis for decision-making, planning and control
public sector	organisations that are owned or controlled by central or local government
private sector	organisations that are owned directly or indirectly by private individuals and organisations
auditors	checking the accuracy of records of financial transactions and correctness of accounting procedures

activities

Note: an asterisk (*) after an activity number means that an answer is provided in Appendix 1.

1.1* Explain the difference between book-keeping and accounting.

1.2* Define the term 'stakeholder'.

1.3 Describe the difference between public sector and private sector organisations.

Find examples of organisations which operate in the public sector but which are wholly or partly owned by private sector organisations.

Comment on whether you think this arrangement benefits the customers of the organisations you have identified.

1.4* Read the following cutting from the financial press. Then answer the questions which follow.

Profits warning at Imperio Cars

From Ivor Pound Financial Correspondent

The share price of Imperio Cars, the car retailing group, dipped sharply yesterday to 456p from its high of 587p last month following a profits warning from the company.

'Trading conditions have been difficult in the last quarter,' commented Chairman Ian Router, 'cheap car imports have hit our forecourt sales and the recall of a number of Piranello models has not improved confidence in the market.'

Car manufacturers have also reported flat trading and erosion of margins as dealers have been offered extra discounts in order to shift excess production.

How might the following stakeholders be affected if Imperio Cars does, in fact, make a loss?

(a)   shareholders

(b)   employees

(c)   managers

(d)   customers

(e)   suppliers

(f)   banks

1.5   What type of accountant would have been responsible for reporting Imperio Cars' profits warning?

1.6   What type of accountant would have drawn up internal performance reports for Imperio Cars' sales?

1.7   What type of accountant would have been responsible for checking the financial records of Imperio Cars?

1.8*   Read again the press cutting which appeared in the opening Case Study of this chapter and is reproduced below. Answer the questions that follow.

Enron collapse blamed on lax accounting

From James Sargent New York Correspondent

The circumstances surrounding the collapse of Enron, the US energy company, continue to enrage all those who lost out.

New evidence has emerged about extravagances at the company ten months before it filed for bankruptcy. Bonuses of $320 million were paid to executives, including $3.6 million paid to the former chief executive.

All this was at the same time that the corporation was using 4,000 'off-balance-sheet' partnerships which allowed to it to report false profit and debt figures.

News that the corporation twice brought in a live elephant to liven up an employee meeting and hired the 85 acre Astroworld amusement park for an employee's family picnic will do little to console Enron's shareholders and lenders.

'What were the accountants doing when all this was going on?' asked a former employee. 'Did they have their heads buried in the sand?'

(a)   Explain how the company's collapse has affected the stakeholders of the business.

(b)   Describe the areas of accounting which appear to have been 'lax' in Enron's case.

CASE STUDY
Vector Stars Limited sales summary

Jay Vector, the Chief Executive of Vector Stars Limited, a company which sells compact discs and DVDs, is concerned about a downturn in sales and wants to look at the last few years' sales figures. He sends an email to the Sales Manager, Rob Dixon, who replies to the questions, inserting the answers into the message, as follows:

Reply to jvector@vectorstars.co.uk

>What were the total sales for the year 2002?

      About £6.7 million. About £600 thousand down on 2001.

>How do UK and overseas sales compare over the last three years?

      UK sales have continued to go up, but overseas sales have dropped by about a third last year, and that's the main reason for the downturn in total sales.

>We expected sales to grow over 2000 to 2002. How do actual sales compare with our forecasts?

      They were just above in 2000 and 2001, but have dropped back in 2002. The forecast for 2002 was £7.1 million.

Rob Dixon, the Sales Manager, has answered the questions, but he could probably have made the position a lot clearer if he had presented all the relevant figures for the three years in the form of a table such as you can see on page 23.

In this chapter we are going to study ways of presenting information to users.

---

learning objectives

When you have studied this chapter, you will be able to:

- *prepare information which satisfies the needs of users and the purpose for which it is required*
- *present information in a clear format, using tables*
- *add to the usefulness of information by calculating percentages and averages*
- *prepare and interpret line graphs, bar charts and pie charts*
- *understand the value of computers in the processing and presentation of information, in particular using tables, graphs and charts*

PRODUCING INFORMATION

The main work of financial and management accountants is to produce information.

All kinds of information must be set out in a way which actually 'informs' those who need to use it. The way it is set out will depend on the purpose for which the information is needed. Users require:

- all the relevant information for the purpose

- information which is free from bias

- information which is accurate and is presented clearly and concisely

- receipt of the required information in time to take action on it

Computers are ideal for most of the work involved in sorting and presenting information. Using a computer, calculations can be done quickly and accurately, even with very large quantities of data. 'User-friendly' information can be printed out, with charts and diagrams to highlight the main points.

PRESENTING INFORMATION IN TABLES

One of the simplest, but most useful, ways of presenting numerical information is to set it out in rows and columns, in the form of a table. This layout is used for all kinds of information, for example:

- bus timetables

- football league tables

- menu boards with prices in fast-food outlets

A table format makes it easy to see how figures compare with each other and to carry out further calculations.

Tables are used to show many kinds of financial accounting and management accounting information, for example:

- amounts of money received by a business from its customers

- amounts of money still owed to the business by its customers

- payments analysed into different kinds of expenditure

- profit and loss accounts

- budgets

constructing a table

Whether you are writing out a table or preparing it on a computer (as in the Case Study opposite), it must have:

■ a title to show what it is about

■ a heading to each column

■ a label on each row

■ vertical or horizontal lines separating the figures if these make the table easier to read

■ an indication of the units being used, usually just below the headings at the tops of columns – for example, large numbers are often given in thousands or even millions to save cluttering up the table with unnecessary zeros – it must be made clear if this is being done (eg £ or £000 or £M) because it makes a big difference to the actual figures!

Study the table on the opposite page.

using computer spreadsheets

Many computer programs can be used to present information in the form of a table and to carry out calculations on the data.

Spreadsheets are programs designed for this work.

When using a spreadsheet, the computer screen is divided into boxes or 'cells' formed by the rows and columns. Text or numbers can be entered into the cells and formatted as required, for example:

■ text can be centred within the box

■ numbers can be rounded to a chosen level of accuracy

■ numbers can be put into an appropriate format such as pounds and pence (or euros and cents)

The most useful feature of a spreadsheet is probably using it to perform calculations by inputting a formula in the cell where you want the result to appear. For example, you can instruct the program to display the total of a column of figures in a particular cell by inputting an 'adding up' formula in the cell that shows the total. What is particularly useful is that the total will be recalculated whenever figures are changed or when more data is entered in the column.

Much more complex calculations can be done – it is all down to inputting the correct formulas in the appropriate cells. Clearly this makes the spreadsheet a very powerful tool for the processing of large tables of information.

CASE STUDY
Vector Stars Limited

In the Case Study at the beginning of this chapter (page 20), the Sales Manager of Vector Stars Limited answered the Chief Executive's questions with approximate figures set within text. More accurate information could have been given clearly and concisely by producing a table of figures.

Note that it is clearly stated that all the figures in this table are in thousands of pounds, the table has a title and everything in the table is labelled.

Vector Stars Limited Forecast and Actual Sales	2000 £000s	2001 £000s	2002 £000s
UK Sales	3,102	3,593	4,239
Overseas Sales	3,815	3,692	2,470
Total Sales	6,917	7,285	6,709
Forecast Sales	6,800	6,950	7,100

using a spreadsheet

The Sales Department could alternatively enter the data on a spreadsheet ready for carrying out calculations to produce more information. For example, the Chief Executive may wish to know the percentage changes in sales from one year to the next. (Percentage calculations are explained on pages 25 to 27). The sales information, when entered on a spreadsheet, would look something like this:

CALCULATIONS TO MAKE INFORMATION MORE USEFUL

Starting with a table of figures such as the Vector Stars Limited Sales Summary in the Case Study above, it is often necessary to provide extra information by carrying out some calculations on the figures. More columns or rows can be added to the table. The calculations we will consider are:

- totals
- percentages
- averages

TOTALS

Totals of either rows or columns may be put in if they provide useful information.

Total Sales figures, made up of UK Sales and Overseas Sales, have already been entered in the table for Vector Stars Limited in the Case Study above.

The totals of the rows in this table would give the figures for the whole three-year period and an extra column could be used to show them if required.

PERCENTAGES

Information is often required by the management of a business in order to answer questions which involve making **comparisons**. For example:

- How does profit compare with sales revenue?
- How does actual expenditure on wages compare with the budget?
- How do this year's total sales compare with last year's?
- What proportion of our sales are exports?
- How do our actual sales compare with our forecast sales?

A key advantage of tables is that rows or columns of figures can easily be compared with one another.

Percentages are often used to help with comparisons, because they express a proportion in a standard way.

A percentage is the expression of a proportion as a number 'out of 100'.

examples of percentages

statement using a percentage	means the same as
5% of the output of T-shirts is faulty	5 out of every 100 T-shirts produced are faulty
The profit is 5% of sales	£5 profit has been made from every £100 of sales
20% of students have joined the Student Union	20 out of every 100 students have joined the Student Union

We will show by worked examples how to calculate:

◼ one number as a percentage of another

◼ parts of a total as percentages

◼ the percentage change from one figure to another

calculating one number as a percentage of another

This is a way of comparing numbers using percentages.

$$\text{Item A as a percentage of Item B is} \quad \frac{\text{Item A}}{\text{Item B}} \quad x \quad 100$$

WORKED EXAMPLE
one number as a percentage of another

180 students out of 900 in a college have joined the Student Union. To calculate 180 students as a percentage of 900 the method is as follows:

180 out of 900 people as a proportion is 180/900.

This is changed to a percentage either by multiplying by 100 or using the % function on a calculator. It is written as 'x 100%', but remember you do not have to multiply by 100 if you are using a % button on your calculator.

Therefore 180 as a percentage of 900 is (180/900) x 100 = 20%.

We could then state, for this college, '20% of the students have joined the Student Union' or '20 out of every 100 students have joined the Student Union.'

The percentage is useful for comparison with the previous year's percentage or with that of another college.

calculating the parts of a total as percentages

If we have a total which is split up into several parts, we can calculate each part as a percentage of the total. The total is 100%.

The calculation for each part uses the same method as in the worked example on the previous page.

Each part as a percentage of the total is $\dfrac{Part}{Total}$ *x 100*

WORKED EXAMPLE
parts of a total as percentages

The 900 students in a college are split into sections as follows:

First year students	360
Second year students	270
Third year students	270
Total	900

The number of first year students as a percentage of the total is

(360/900) x 100   = 40%

(360/900) is changed to a percentage either by multiplying by 100 or by using the % button on your calculator.

Similarly, for each of the other two years, 270 as a percentage of 900 is

(270/900) x 100   = 30%

We can then show the percentages with the original data in a table:

	Student numbers	%
First year students	360	40
Second year students	270	30
Third year students	270	30
Total	900	100

---

a note on rounding

Note that in this case the rounded percentages total exactly 100%, but sometimes **rounded** figures for the percentage parts of a total may add up to slightly less or slightly more than 100. This is called a **rounding difference**.

calculating percentage changes

It is often useful to calculate the percentage change from one figure to the next, for example a percentage wage increase or the percentage decrease in sales from one year to the next.

To calculate a percentage change from one figure to the next:

- calculate the difference between the figures

- calculate the difference as a percentage of the **first** figure, using the same method as in the worked example on page 25

The percentage change from number A to number B is $\dfrac{(B-A)}{A} \times 100$

WORKED EXAMPLE
calculating percentage changes

example 1: a percentage increase

If monthly wages costs for a business increase from £28,000 to £32,200, the percentage increase is the difference expressed as a percentage of the first figure.

The wages cost has increased by £32,200 − £28,000 = £4,200

4,200 as a percentage of the first figure 28,000 is

(4,200/28,000) x 100

= 15%

Therefore there has been a 15% increase in wages costs for the business.

example 2: a percentage decrease

If the number of staff in a department decreases from 40 to 35, this is a difference of 5.

The percentage decrease is

(5/40) x 100

= 12.5%.

Therefore there has been a 12.5% decrease in the number of staff in the department.

Note in this second example that the change is still compared with the first figure.

AVERAGES

It is important for the management of a business to be able to obtain the answers to such questions as:

- How much credit are we being given by our suppliers?

- What sales are we likely to achieve in December?

- How long do we normally keep stock in the warehouse before it is sold?

- How long do our customers usually take to pay us?

Only by keeping control over areas such as these does the business increase efficiency and profitability. Control is only possible when reliable information is available. It would be an easy option to give answers such as 'about . . .' or 'approximately . . .' based on opinions or impressions rather than facts. More accurate and useful information can be provided by collecting the relevant data and calculating **averages**.

An average is a way of measuring the 'centre' of a set of numbers.

The numbers may be amounts of money, such as:

- prices of products

- values of sales orders

- total sales income per month

Alternatively, we may have non-financial data, such as:

- numbers of days taken to pay invoices

- numbers of items held in stock at the close of each day

We will consider three ways of finding the 'centre' of a set of numbers:

- the **mean**

- the **median**

- the **mode**

which average?

Suppose the finance manager of a kitchen installation business wants to know for budgeting purposes the average job completion time in days, from initial enquiry through to final installation. He has just received the figures for the jobs completed last month. The figures are (in days):

  20, 25, 35, 35, 35, 36, 37, 55, 60, 65, 65

What is the average job completion time? We will look in turn at the mean, median and mode averages.

the mean

The arithmetic mean is probably the most commonly used and statistically reliable form of average. In everyday language the word 'average' generally refers to the mean.

The arithmetic mean is the sum of all the figures divided by the number of figures.

The sum of 20, 25, 35, 35, 35, 36, 37, 55, 60, 65, 65 = 468

$$\text{The arithmetic mean} \quad = \quad \frac{468}{11} \quad = \quad 42.6 \text{ days}$$

This tells the manager that, on average, a job takes approximately 43 days to complete. This will help him in the planning and budgeting process. Note:

- the result is not a whole number of days

- the result takes into account all values – if there had been an exceptional job taking 165 days instead of 65, the result would have been a mean average of 568 ÷ 11 = 51.6 days

the median

The median is the value of the middle figure in a series of figures (arranged in order of size).

Note that if there is no middle figure, as with an even number of values, the median is the arithmetic mean of the two figures nearest to the middle.

Here the median is 20, 25, 35, 35, 35, **36**, 37, 55, 60, 65, 65 = 36 days.

This indicates that half the jobs took 36 days or less and half the jobs took 36 days or more.

This will not be as helpful to the manager as the mean in this context; it is useful because it is not distorted by extreme values (eg 165 days).

the mode

The mode is the value that occurs most often in a series.

In this case the most common period is 35 days (3 jobs), followed closely by 65 days (2 jobs). Note that these two time periods are very widely dispersed. This would suggest that this type of average is not as helpful in the planning process. The mode is more useful in areas such as market research in answering questions such as:

'How much do people on average spend on a meal?'

'What is the most commonly occurring size of shirt?'

Note that there may not be a mode or there may be two or more equally common values.

CASE STUDY

Rose Limited – finding the 'average' order

situation

Rose Limited is a manufacturing company. During March 2002, 14 orders were received by Rose Ltd for its products. The values of the orders are listed below.

Rose Ltd: Sales orders March 2002	
Sales order number	Amount (£)
2201	4,350
2202	3,300
2203	5,150
2204	2,800
2205	5,000
2206	3,300
2207	2,950
2208	4,050
2209	2,700
2210	5,200
2211	3,650
2212	3,300
2213	2,950
2214	3,500

required

For the month of March 2002:

(a) Calculate the arithmetic mean of the values of Rose Ltd's Sales orders.

(b) By re-arranging the values in order of size, identify the Median and the Mode of the values of Sales orders.

(c) Comment on Rose Ltd's sales order summary for the month. Include comments relating to the meaning and usefulness of the three kinds of averages shown.

suggested solution

(a) There are 14 orders in March.
Total of the column of values = £52,200
Mean value of sales order = £52,200 ÷ 14
= £3,729 to the nearest £.

(b) When the orders are re-arranged in size order, we have:

Sales order number	Amount (£)
2209	2,700
2204	2,800
2207	2,950
2213	2,950
2202	3,300
2206	3,300
2212	3,300
2214	3,500
2211	3,650
2208	4,050
2201	4,350
2205	5,000
2203	5,150
2210	5,200

We can then see that the two middle items have values £3,300 and £3,500. Therefore the **median** value is £(3,300 + 3,500) ÷ 2 = £3,400.

We can also pick out the most common order value, which is £3,300 and this is the **mode**.

(c) Because the **mean** is calculated using all the values, it gives the best indication of the 'average' size of orders in each month.

Looking at the **median** value could help in decision-making situations, such as considering the level above which customers may be offered discounts.

The **mode** shows that the most common size of order is usually between £3,000 and £3,500. It is in the area of market research that the mode is most useful.

USING COMPUTERS FOR PERCENTAGES AND AVERAGES

Earlier in the chapter, we discussed the usefulness of **spreadsheet** programs for the processing and presentation of information in rows and columns.

We noted that a given calculation can be carried out on data in specified cells, provided that a formula is put into a separate cell of the spreadsheet, where the answer will appear.

The calculations of percentages which we have used above could be carried out in this way. Of the three types of average which we have discussed above, the mean could be calculated on a spreadsheet, because it is the result of a calculation which can be expressed in a formula, whereas the median and the mode are not.

Spreadsheets have many more advanced features which can be used in both financial and management accounting, for example:

- A sequence of calculations set up on a spreadsheet can easily be applied to more than one set of data. This is particularly beneficial for regular reports, such as quarterly sales analyses.

- Spreadsheets are invaluable for decision-making situations, when forecast results can easily be re-calculated with different assumptions, for example assuming different levels of sales volumes. This is sometimes referred to as 'What if?' analysis. Questions such as 'What if sales only increase by 1% per quarter rather than 2%?' can be answered immediately, once the spreadsheet has been set up.

If you have access to a computer with spreadsheet software, you may wish to practise the use of simple formulas with some of the calculations of percentages and means in this chapter.

PRESENTING INFORMATION USING GRAPHS AND CHARTS

When a large public company announces its annual results, it will publish details of the figures in a number of forms:

- the published annual report and accounts sent to shareholders
- press releases for the financial newspapers and magazines
- employee reports distributed to the workforce and management of the company, and sometimes also to the shareholders

In all these written reports, the information is usually presented in tables and illustrated using diagrams. This is because it is generally recognised that a diagram or picture has more impact and can show people the main points from all the information much more quickly and clearly than paragraphs of text. It must be remembered that the users of financial reports are not necessarily accountants.

There are two main types of information which can be shown particularly well in diagrams: time series information and proportional analysis.

Time series: information relating to regular intervals of time, for example:

- annual sales figures, as in the Case Study Vector Stars Limited
- monthly sales orders, as in the Case Ctudy Rose Limited

Time series are often presented as line graphs or bar charts:

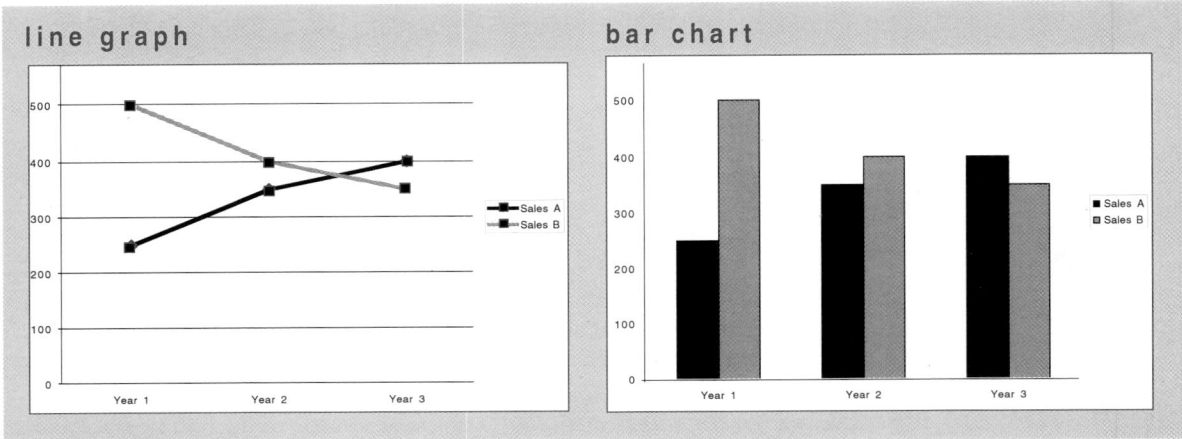

Proportional analysis: information relating to how a total is split up into parts, for example how a company's total sales are split between regions. Proportional analysis is often shown in a Pie Chart (a single year's figures) or a Component Bar Chart (which shows a split over a period of time).

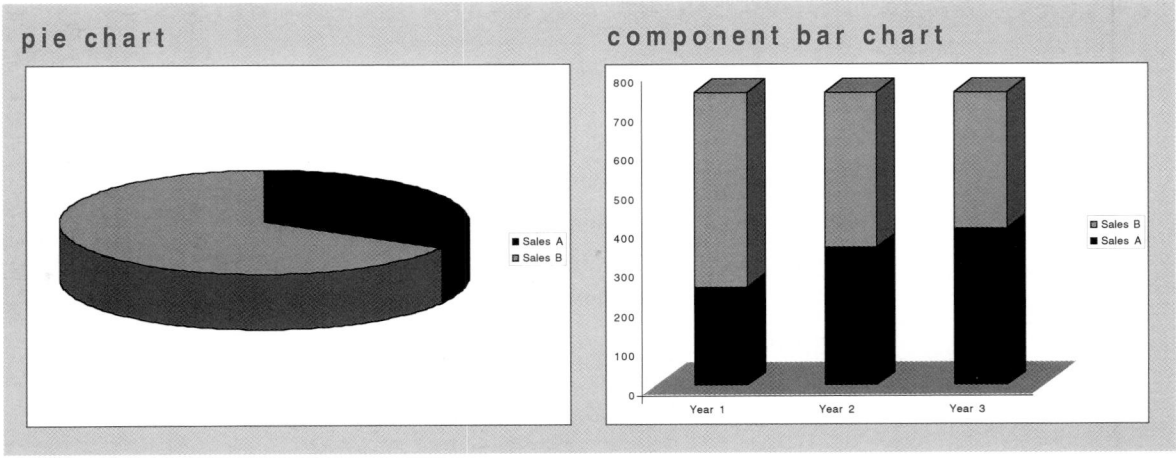

a note on graphs and variables

A line graph – which can be made up of straight lines or curves – shows the relationship between two variables. One variable will always depend on the other:

- the **independent variable** – the measurement that is at a fixed interval
- the **dependent variable** – the figure that will depend on the independent variable

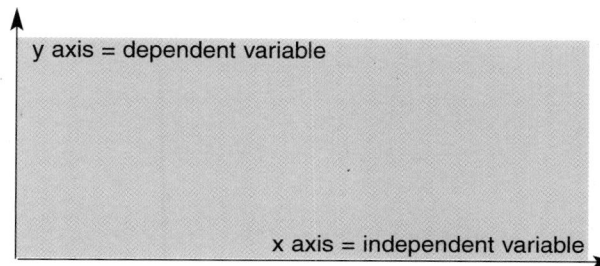

A common independent variable is time, but as you will see from the table shown below, it is not the only fixed measurement. You can also see that the dependent variable may be in terms of money or other units.

independent variable (horizontal)	dependent variable (vertical)
time (years)	sales (£)
units produced	costs of production (£)
income level (£)	number of holidays per year
working out in gym (minutes)	calories burned up

CASE STUDY
Vector Stars Limited

For the purpose of illustrating graphs and charts we will take as an example the sales figures for Vector Stars Limited, which we have looked at earlier in this chapter.

We have sales figures:

- for three years (the time series)
- broken down into home sales and overseas sales (proportional analysis)
- in comparison with the total sales projections for the three years

The following diagrams illustrate the information shown in this table

Vector Stars Ltd: Forecast and Actual sales	2000 £000s	2001 £000s	2002 £000s
UK Sales	3,102	3,593	4,239
Overseas Sales	3,815	3,692	2,470
Total Sales	6,917	7,285	6,709
Forecast Sales	6,800	6,950	7,100

line graph

The graph below shows clearly the trends in the UK and overseas sales figures and the way they compare with each other.

The independent variable is time, measured horizontally.

The different sales figures are the dependent variable, measured vertically in £000s.

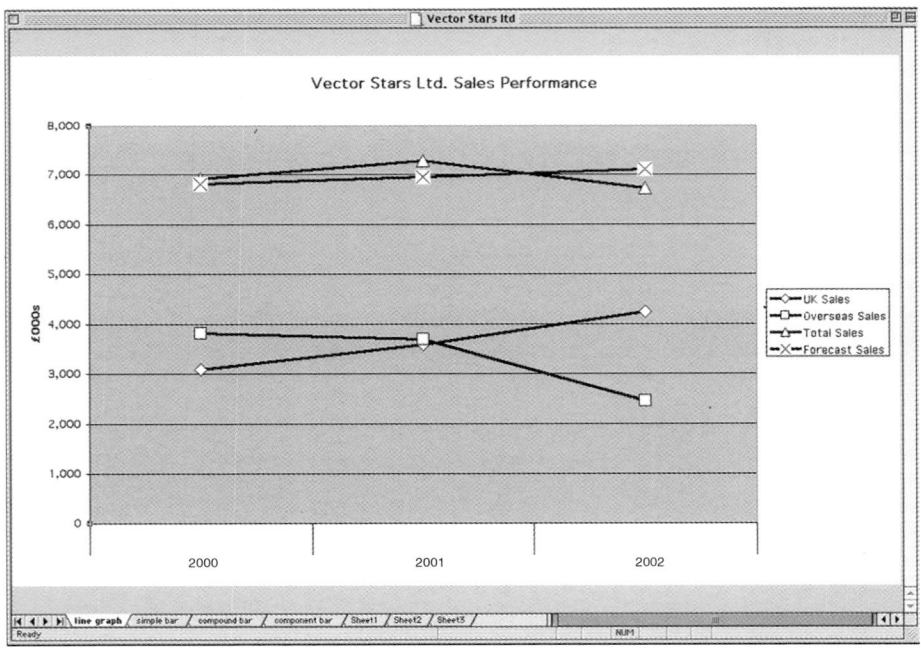

simple bar chart

The bar chart is a series of bars drawn such that the height of the bars represents the amount of the dependent variable.

The following bar chart shows the total sales for Vector Stars Ltd over the three years.

The simple bar chart is limited because it can only compare individual items from one set of data, in this case the total sales of Vector Stars Ltd. Its visual impact is strong, and it is consequently very popular. Note that it is the height of the bar that must be accurately charted. The width is of no significance, but the bars should all be of equal width.

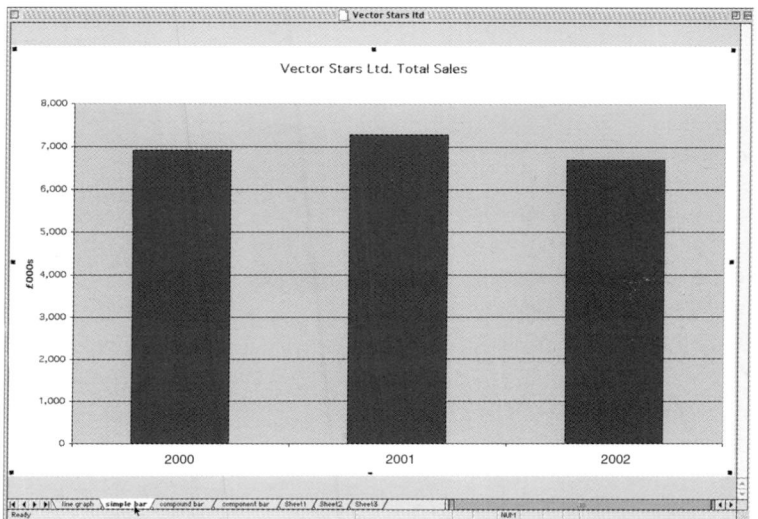

compound bar chart

A compound bar chart is a bar chart which sets out more than one variable by using groups of two or more bars.

The following compound bar chart sets out the total sales and forecast total sales for Vector Stars Ltd.

Note that the two separate bars should be clearly distinguished.

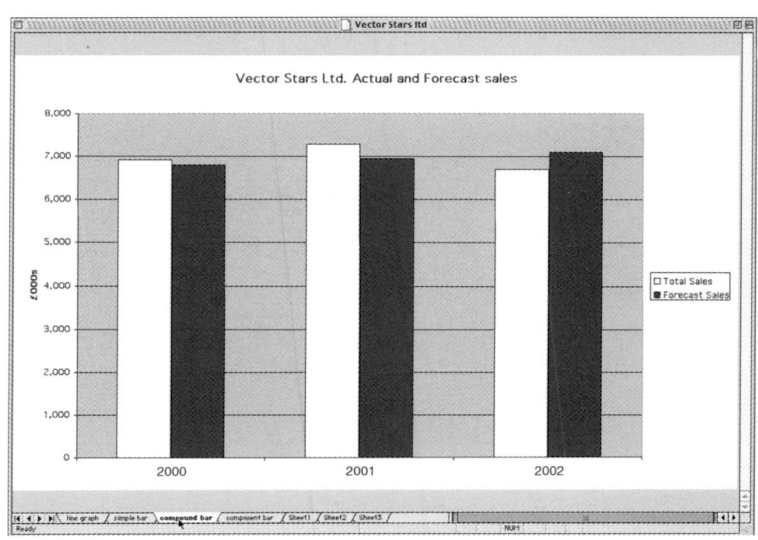

component bar chart

A component bar chart is a bar chart which subdivides each bar into its component parts.

This type of chart is useful in showing the make-up of variable totals. In the example below total sales for Vector Stars Ltd are subdivided into UK and overseas sales. It is very evident from this chart that the disappointing figure for 2002 is directly a result of the fall in overseas sales. Note the different shading of the components of the individual bars.

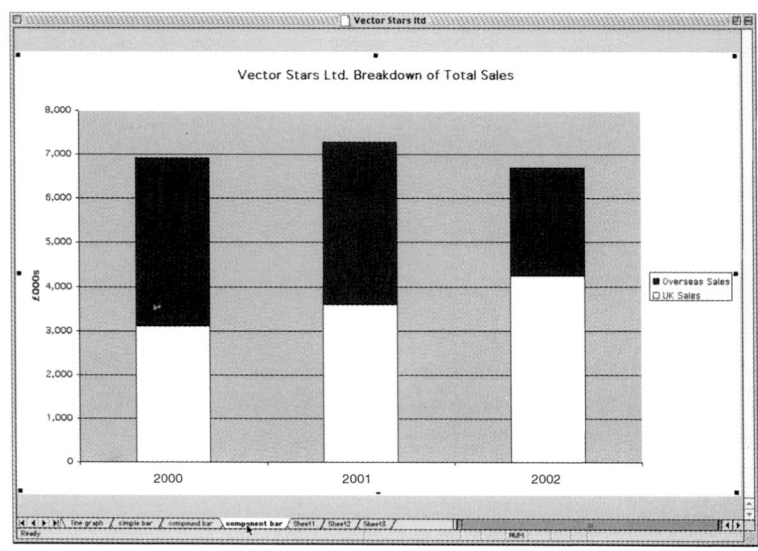

The component bar chart has the advantage that it can show both the changes in the total and the parts within the total.

pie chart

A pie chart is a circle divided into sectors to represent proportionally the parts of a whole.

A pie chart is a visually impressive way of illustrating the parts of a whole, but it has a number of shortcomings, including the fact that it cannot show a trend, and that it does not show clearly the relative sizes of small parts of the total.

calculating the sectors of a pie chart

A pie chart might be used to show the breakdown by area of the sales of Vector Stars Ltd. The starting point is the accounting data, for example:

Sales by area: Vector Stars Ltd in 2002	
Area	*£000s*
UK	4,239
Europe	1,040
North America	912
Japan	518
Total Sales	6,709

The total sales of £6,709,000 will become the whole circle of the pie divided into 'slices' or sectors, each of which will proportionally represent a geographical sales figure. As the angle at the centre of a circle is 360° it is necessary to work out the angle for each sector individually. The formula is as follows:

$$\frac{\textit{Figure for the part of the whole}}{\textit{Figure for the whole}} \times 360° \ = \ \textit{the angle at the centre for the sector (°)}$$

Applying the formula to the geographical sales figures for Vector Stars Limited, the calculation is:

Area of Sales	Calculation	Angle of sector (°)
UK	$\frac{4{,}239}{6\ 709} \times 360° =$	227
Europe	$\frac{1{,}040}{6{,}709} \times 360° =$	56
North America	$\frac{912}{6{,}709} \times 360° =$	49
Japan	$\frac{518}{6{,}709} \times 360° =$	28

The pie chart is set out below. Note the labelling and shading, and the fact that the degrees are *not* indicated (they are of no interest to the reader). Percentages could be calculated and added to the chart if required.

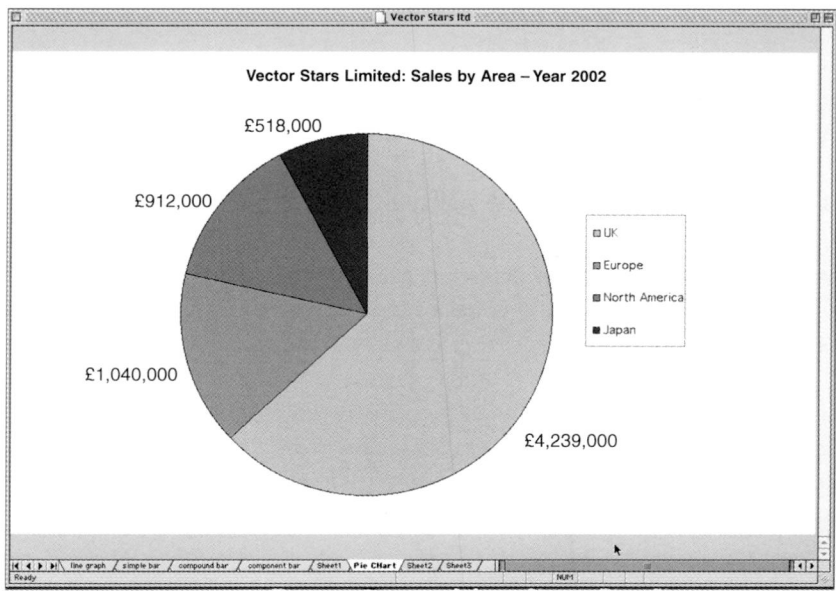

a note on using tables, graphs and charts

Earlier in this chapter we noted that information presented in a table must have a heading and the rows and columns must be clearly labelled. When using a diagram to present information it is essential to make it 'user-friendly' by including:

- a heading

- labels or a key

- numbers on the diagram or a numerical scale

- a statement, where appropriate, of the source of the data used

If you are using a computer to make charts, you will need to find out how to use the program to create different headings, labels and general format.

chapter summary

- Numerical information can be presented clearly and concisely in the form of a table.

- To be useful, a table must have a title and clearly labelled rows and columns.

- Depending on the purpose for which the information is required, additional rows or columns can be added to a table, to show totals, percentages and averages.

- Three kinds of average are the arithmetic mean, the median and the mode. They show different aspects of the original data. The mean is the calculated average and therefore most likely to be used where further calculations are to be carried out.

- The results of calculations should be rounded to a suitable level of accuracy for the purpose.

- Diagrams can be used to illustrate numerical information and have the advantage that they give an instant picture of the behaviour of the figures (eg increasing or decreasing trends, relative sizes of parts of a total, and so on).

- Computers can be used to process data very quickly and accurately and to present information in table format and in charts and diagrams. Spreadsheet software is particularly useful for numerical information which can be arranged in rows and columns, especially when the same sequence of calculations is to be carried out on more than one set of data.

key terms

spreadsheet	a computer program designed for processing numerical data arranged in rows and columns – a powerful tool for preparing and presenting information
percentage	the expression of a proportion as a number 'out of 100', eg a mark of 56% in an examination is the same as 56 out of 100 marks
average	a measure of the centre of a set of data
arithmetic mean	the average calculated as the sum of all the figures divided by the number of figures
median	the average identified as the middle figure of a series or the mean of the middle two figures (when the series is arranged in order of size)
mode	the average identified as the most frequently occurring value in a series (there may not be a mode, or there may be more than one equally frequent value)
variable	a measurement which can take different values, for example time, weight, temperature, monthly sales of a business, daily takings in a shop, and so on
independent variable	the horizontal measurement at regular intervals on a graph, for example time, measured in months or years
dependent variable	the vertical measurement on a graph, whose value depends on the value of the independent variable
line graph	a graph on which the corresponding value of the dependent variable is measured vertically and marked with a point for each of the regular measurements of the independent variable. The points marked in this way are then joined by straight lines
bar chart	a diagram in which numbers are represented by bars of equal width, and the height of each vertical bar corresponds to a number according to a given scale
simple bar chart	a bar chart representing one set of numbers by single bars
compound bar chart	a bar chart representing several sets of numbers by groups of bars
component bar chart	a bar chart representing totals together with the split of the totals into parts, by bars representing the totals and divided into sections representing the parts
pie chart	a chart in which the split of a total into parts is represented by the split of a circle into sectors

activities

Note: an asterisk (*) after an activity number means that an answer is provided in Appendix 1.

2.1*   (a)   Express 36 hours as a percentage of 150 hours.

    (b)   Express £490 as a percentage of £1,300.

    (c)   Express £2,500 as a percentage of £2 million.

2.2*   Calculate the percentage change in each of the following cases:

    (a)   A wage rate increases from £4.70 per hour to £4.90 per hour.

    (b)   The cost of administration per year in a business increases from £267,800 to £301,000.

    (c)   The number of students on a course decreases from 132 to 125 students.

    (d)   Total annual sales for a company decrease from £1.3 million to £980,000.

2.3*   Work out the arithmetic mean, median and mode of the following sets of numbers:

    (a)   1,2,3,3,4,5,6,7,8,9,10.

    (b)   1,7,9,12,13,15,15,16,19.

    (c)   201,230,289,701,823,832,832,849.

2.4   Red plc is a company which owns a chain of fast-food restaurants. The following data is available for five years (Year 5 being the most recent). Note that Turnover means the same as Sales or Sales Revenue.

Red plc Annual Statistics

Year	1	2	3	4	5
Turnover £millions	35.5	46.2	54.8	65.1	66.3
Number of restaurants	28	39	45	53	55
Number of employees	490	680	750	940	965

    (a)   Calculate the following, for each of the five years, giving your answers in a table:
        (i)   Average (Mean) Turnover per restaurant.
        (ii)   Average (Mean) Turnover per employee.
        (iii)   Average (Mean) number of employees per restaurant.
        (iv)   Year-on-year percentage changes in the Turnover and in the number of restaurants.

    (b)   Draw separate line graphs to illustrate the Turnover figures and the number of restaurants for the five years given.

    (c)   Comment briefly on the trends highlighted by your calculations and graphs.

2.5* Complete the gaps in the following table of financial data for Dales Sports and Leisure Club. Comment on the results that you produce.

Dales Sports and Leisure Club			
	2000	*2001*	*% change*
Number of members	273	328	
Total number of member visits	9,120	11,590	
Opening hours per week	60 hours	72 hours	
Total hours per year (50 weeks per year)			
Average number of visits per member			
Average number of visits per hour			
Average number of visits per week			

2.6 The table below shows the divisional sales figures for Newbury Products PLC.

Newbury Products PLC Sales by Division				
	Year 1 *£000s*	**Year 2** *£000s*	**Year 3** *£000s*	**Year 4** *£000s*
Sales Division A	400	500	550	600
Sales Division B	100	250	350	400
Sales Division C	350	300	250	300
Total Sales	850	1,050	1,150	1,300

You are to:

(a) Construct a compound bar chart showing the sales for all three divisions over the four years. Make brief comments on the trends shown. Is this the best form of chart to use to show these trends?

(b) Construct a component bar chart using the same data. Comment on the differences between the charts in (a) and (b) and state in what circumstances you would each one.

(c) Construct pie charts for Year 1 and Year 4 and comment on what they do and do not show.

2.7 You work in the finance department of Hyzaku Limited, the UK subsidiary of a Japanese car manufacturer which has made substantial inroads into the UK market with its revolutionary 'Trojan' multi-purpose vehicle, manufactured in the UK. You are given three sets of statistics and are asked to present them to the board of directors and to comment on the results.

Market Share: UK Market for MPVs (multi-purpose vehicles)

	Year 1	Year 2	Year 3
	£M	£M	£M
MPVs manufactured in the EU, imported into the UK	295	280	275
Hyzaku MPVs (manufactured in the UK)	150	195	250
US MPVs imported into the UK	140	130	115

(a) present this data in the form of a line graph

(b) comment on the trends shown

Actual and Projected Sales of Hyzaku MPVs (multi-purpose vehicles) in the UK Market

	Year 1	Year 2	Year 3
	£M	£M	£M
Actual Sales	150	195	250
Projected Sales	140	180	220

(c) present this data in the form of a compound bar chart

(d) comment on the trend shown

Breakdown of UK Sales by Area

	Year 1	Year 2	Year 3
	£M	£M	£M
South East	100	125	175
Midlands	25	45	25
Other Areas	25	25	50
Total Sales	150	195	250

(e) present this data in the form of a component bar chart

(f) comment on the regional trends; what should be done about the Midlands?

(g) one of your directors doesn't like your bar chart; present the data in another form that will show the trends clearly

(h) take the figures for the UK sales of Hyzaku vehicles in Year 3 and draw up a pie chart showing the breakdown of sales by area

section 2
financial accounting

CASE STUDY
Setting up shop

Gina Ricci is a friend of yours who is setting up a designer label clothes store in town. She has been told by her bank business adviser that she needs to keep accurate accounting records. One of the reasons for this is that she will have to show her accounts to the bank from time to time. She has also been told that she needs to keep accurate accounts because the tax authorities may want to see them and because she needs to keep track of what she owes and what she is owed.

She seems unsure of the way in which all the financial transactions, documents, records and reports all 'fit together'. She asks you:

'What do I do with all the invoices I receive from my suppliers? How do I record them?'

'How do I record all my shop takings?'

"How do I know if I am making a profit or not?'

There are clearly a lot of issues that need resolving before Gina can start trading.

A further complication is the question of computers. She says:

'I have heard that using a computer for the accounts will help – it will handle the documentation and will simplify the recording process – once the transaction is in the computer – that is it!'

This chapter looks at the way an accounting system works and introduces you to the workings of computer accounting (covered in more detail in Chapter 5).

learning objectives

When you have studied this chapter, you will be able to:

- ■ *describe the processes which make up an accounting system*
- ■ *distinguish between the workings of a manual accounting system and a computer-based accounting system*
- ■ *understand the concepts behind the workings of the double-entry accounting system, including the 'accounting equation'*
- ■ *carry out simple exercises in double-entry book-keeping*

THE ACCOUNTING SYSTEM

an overview

The **accounting system** as it relates to both manual and computer accounting is a series of simple stages. It starts off with financial transactions such as sales and purchases, and concludes with information used by management such as profit and loss statements. The stages are summarised in the diagram that follows:

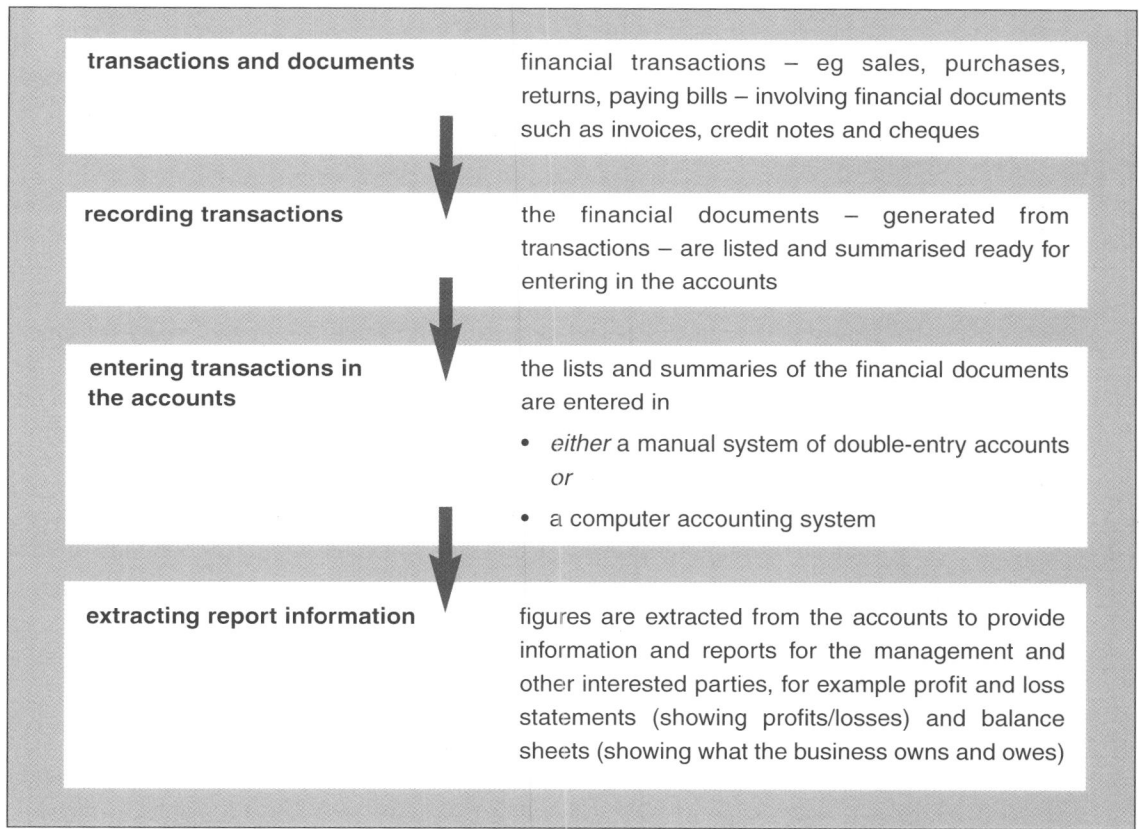

transactions and documents	financial transactions – eg sales, purchases, returns, paying bills – involving financial documents such as invoices, credit notes and cheques
recording transactions	the financial documents – generated from transactions – are listed and summarised ready for entering in the accounts
entering transactions in the accounts	the lists and summaries of the financial documents are entered in • *either* a manual system of double-entry accounts *or* • a computer accounting system
extracting report information	figures are extracted from the accounts to provide information and reports for the management and other interested parties, for example profit and loss statements (showing profits/losses) and balance sheets (showing what the business owns and owes)

We will now look at these stages individually to provide an overview of the system before explaining double-entry book-keeping in more detail.

STAGE 1 – TRANSACTIONS AND DOCUMENTS

Financial transactions involve financial documents. You may already be familiar with some of these.

sales and purchases – the invoice

When a business buys or sells goods or a service, the seller prepares an invoice which sets out the details of the goods sold or the service provided, the amount owing, and the date on which it should be paid.

refunds – the credit note

If the buyer returns goods which are bought on credit or has a problem with a service supplied on credit, the seller may agree to a refund and issue a credit note which is sent to the buyer, reducing the amount of money owed.

paying-in slips and cheques

Businesses need to pay money into the bank account, and take out cash and make payments by using cheques and other transfers. Money can be paid in on paying-in slips or sent electronically.

STAGE 2 – RECORDING TRANSACTIONS

Businesses need to list and summarise financial documents ready for entry into the accounting records. Manual systems often use **cash books** for bank and cash transactions and **day books** for listing sales, purchases and returned goods. Each day book will normally be totalled at regular intervals – daily, weekly or monthly, depending on the needs of the business.

Computer programs often use the batch system, which is a listing of the items with an overall total to check against the computer input. It is common to find batches for sales, purchases, returns, cheques received, cheques issued.

STAGE 3 – ENTERING TRANSACTIONS IN THE ACCOUNTS

When the financial documents have been listed in a day book or batch they are then entered in the accounts of the business. The format of a manual **double-entry account** for wages is shown at the top of the next page.

As you will see, this double-entry account is only half the story – an entry has also been made in another account – here it is the bank account. All this will be explained in detail later in this chapter, on page 49.

A computer system, on the other hand, needs only one entry to be made for each transaction, but will require the account details of the other entry (normally a numerical code) when that single entry is made. This is covered in more detail in Chapter 5.

double-entry account recording payment of wages of £4,250, paid by cheque								
Debit			Wages Account					Credit
Date	Details	Folio	£ p	Date	Details	Folio	£ p
01 Feb	Bank	CB007	4,250.00				
↑	↑	↑	↑				
date of the trans-action	name of the account in which the other entry is made	page or reference number of the other account	amount of the trans-action				

the ledger

Most accounting systems use the **ledger** system to organise the accounts. The word 'ledger' means 'book' but is used freely by both manual and computer systems to represent a section of the accounts kept on paper or on the computer. The ledgers can be summarised as follows:

■ **sales ledger**

the accounts of customers who have bought on credit (ie they have bought goods or services but will pay later) – these customers are known as 'debtors'

■ **purchases ledger**

the accounts of suppliers who have sold to the business on credit – these suppliers are known as 'creditors'

■ **cash book**

the book which records cash held by the business and bank accounts in the name of the business

■ **general or nominal ledger**

all the other accounts – expenses, income, assets (items owned) and liabilities (items owed) – this is also referred to as the 'main' ledger

STAGE 4 – EXTRACTING REPORT INFORMATION

Financial data held in the accounts is only useful when it can be extracted and used by the management of the business or presented to outsiders such as shareholders. The advantage of computer accounting systems is that reports can be generated automatically from a menu and printed out. You will encounter a number of different reports in your studies, including:

- **trial balance**

  which lists the balances of the double-entry accounts in two separate columns – this is a check on the accuracy of the book-keeping

- **profit and loss account**

  which shows the amount of profit or loss made by the business

- **balance sheet**

  which shows what the business owns (assets) what it owes (liabilities) and how it is financed (capital)

Now study the diagram below which summarises what we have covered so far in this chapter.

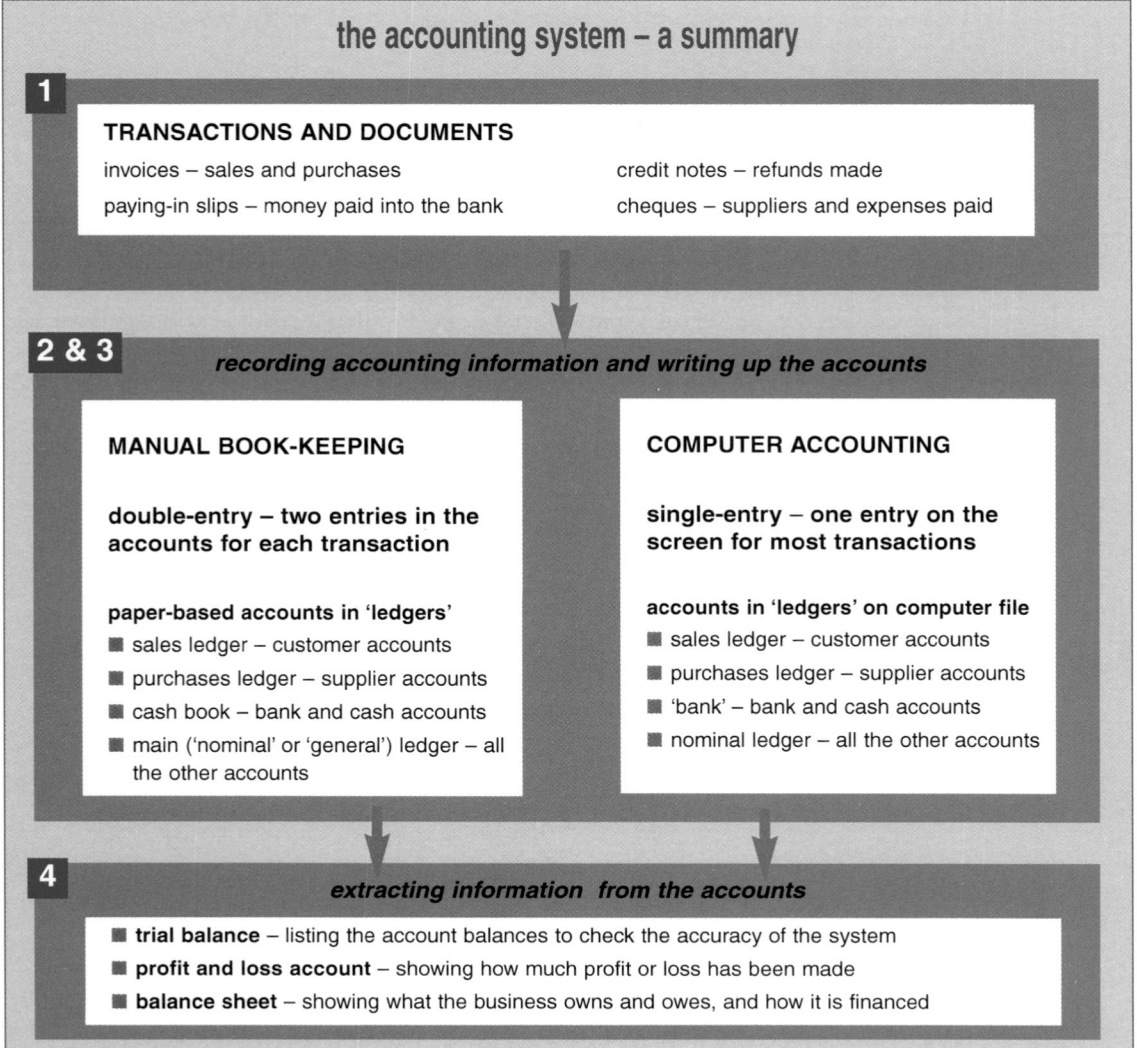

the accounting system – a summary

1

TRANSACTIONS AND DOCUMENTS

invoices – sales and purchases

paying-in slips – money paid into the bank

credit notes – refunds made

cheques – suppliers and expenses paid

2 & 3

recording accounting information and writing up the accounts

MANUAL BOOK-KEEPING

double-entry – two entries in the accounts for each transaction

paper-based accounts in 'ledgers'
- sales ledger – customer accounts
- purchases ledger – supplier accounts
- cash book – bank and cash accounts
- main ('nominal' or 'general') ledger – all the other accounts

COMPUTER ACCOUNTING

single-entry – one entry on the screen for most transactions

accounts in 'ledgers' on computer file
- sales ledger – customer accounts
- purchases ledger – supplier accounts
- 'bank' – bank and cash accounts
- nominal ledger – all the other accounts

4

extracting information from the accounts

- **trial balance** – listing the account balances to check the accuracy of the system
- **profit and loss account** – showing how much profit or loss has been made
- **balance sheet** – showing what the business owns and owes, and how it is financed

DOUBLE-ENTRY ACCOUNTS

Double-entry book-keeping in a manual accounting system involves entries being made in accounts for each transaction – debit entries (on the left-hand side of the account) and credit entries (on the right-hand side of the account).

If a transaction does not involve VAT (Value Added Tax) there will be two entries: an equal debit and credit. If VAT is involved there will be three entries, but the debit(s) must always equal the credit(s).

To make things simple we will ignore VAT in this chapter.

The decisions faced by anyone operating the double-entry system are:

- deciding which two accounts should be used for each transaction, and more critically . . .

- deciding which entry is the debit and which is the credit

There are simple rules which guide you, but, as with learning to drive a car, the early stages require both thought and concentration!

We will first look at the layout of a typical double-entry account. The illustration here shows an account for computer equipment recording a computer purchased for £450 and paid for by cheque from the bank account.

Debit				Computer Account			Credit
Date	Details	Folio	£ p	Date	Details	Folio	£ p
2002 01 Feb	Bank	CB007	450.00				
date of the trans- action	name of the account in which the other entry is made	page or reference number of the other account	amount of the trans- action				

Note the following:

- the name of the account – Computer Account – is written at the top

- the account is divided into two identical halves, separated by a central double vertical line: the left-hand side is called the 'Debit' side ('debit' is abbreviated to 'Dr'), the right-hand side is called the 'Credit' (or 'Cr') side
  A note for UK drivers! – **Dr**ive on the left   **Cr**ash on the right

- the date, details and amount of the transaction are entered in the columns:
  – in the 'Details' column is entered the name of the other account involved in the book-keeping transaction – here it is the Bank Account

– the 'Folio' column is used as a cross-referencing system to the other entry of the double-entry book-keeping transaction – here CB007 stands for page 7 in the Cash Book where the Bank Account entry is made

In a manual book-keeping system each account occupies a whole page or more, but in textbooks it is usual to simplify the format to save space and to put several accounts on a single page. The Computer Account set out in this simplified format is shown at the top of the next page.

You will see that the Folio column has gone and the column divisions have also disappeared. It is all much simpler, with just a single vertical line dividing the debit and credit sides.

The problem remains: if you are given a transaction to enter, how do you decide which is the debit entry and which is the credit entry?

dual aspect theory of double-entry

The principle of double-entry book-keeping is that every business transaction has a dual aspect:

■ one account receives value (the debit)

■ the other account gives value (the credit)

The Computer Account in the example here shows a gain in value (the debit) for the business, ie the new computer, while the Bank Account will give value (the credit) as the purchase price is paid to the seller.

practical aspects of double-entry

If this sounds too theoretical, look at the practical aspects of the system. For each double-entry transaction (ignoring any VAT for the sake of simplicity):

■ one account is debited (entry on the left of the account)

■ another account is credited (entry on the right of the account)

The practical rules for debits and credits are:

debit entry	**credit entry**
■ money paid into the bank	■ money paid out of the bank
■ purchases made, expenses paid	■ income items received
■ an asset (item owned) is acquired or increased	■ a liability (item owed) is incurred or increased

Look at the example on the next page and read the text in the blue boxes.

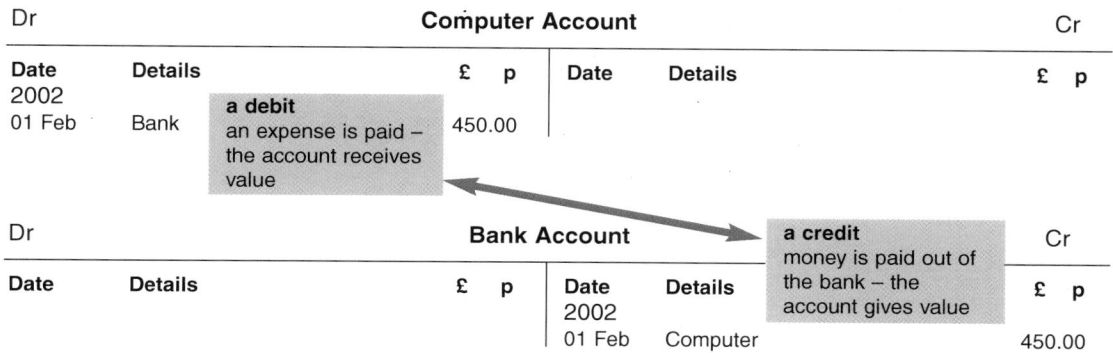

We will now put these double-entry book-keeping principles into practice by means of a Case Study.

CASE STUDY

Harry Smith Limited — double-entry book-keeping

situation

Harry Smith runs a magic and jokes shop. During the first week of September 2002 he has five transactions to enter in his double-entry accounts:

2 Sep 2002   Sale of goods for £12,000, a cheque received.

3 Sep 2002   Payment of wages of £1,200 by cheque.

4 Sep 2002   Purchase of goods for £3,000, paid for by cheque.

5 Sep 2002   Received loan of £5,000 from D B Dore, and paid cheque into bank.

6 Sep 2002   Purchase of computer costing £4,000, paid for by cheque.

Again, for the sake of simplicity we have ignored any VAT.

If you look at these five transactions for Harry Smith Limited, you will see that they all involve the bank account. One invariable rule for the bank account is that money received is recorded on the left-hand (debit) side, and money paid out is recorded on the right-hand (credit) side. By applying this rule, you can say that for a bank account:

Money in is a debit (on the left); money out is a credit (on the right)

Using this rule, the bank account for Harry Smith Limited, after entering the five transactions, appears as follows (see next page):

Dr				Bank Account			Cr
Date	Details		£ p	Date	Details		£ p
2002		money in		2002		money out	
02 Sep	Sales		12,000.00	03 Sep	Wages		1,200.00
05 Sep	D B Dore Loan		5,000.00	04 Sep	Purchases		3,000.00
				06 Sep	Computer		4,000.00

It is now a simple step to work out onto which side, debit or credit, the entries are recorded in the other accounts involved. If you bear in mind that money received is a debit (left-hand side) and money paid out is a credit (right-hand side), by looking at any double-entry transaction which involves the bank account you should:

- identify on which side of the bank account, debit (money in) or credit (money out), the item is recorded
- record the other double-entry item on the other side of the appropriate account

We are now in a position to set out the other accounts involved in the five transactions entered in the bank account. Note that in each case the description in the account is 'Bank'.

transaction
2 September 2002: sale of goods for £12,000, a cheque received

double-entry
Debit Bank Account (money in); Credit Sales Account (an income item)

Dr				Sales Account			Cr
Date	Details		£ p	Date	Details		£ p
2002				2002			
				02 Sep	Bank		12,000.00

transaction
3 September 2002: payment of wages of £1,200 by cheque

double-entry
Debit Wages Account (an expense); Credit Bank Account (money paid out)

Dr				Wages Account			Cr
Date	Details		£ p	Date	Details		£ p
2002				2002			
03 Sep	Bank		1,200.00				

transaction

4 September 2002: purchase of goods for £3,000, paid for by cheque

double-entry

Debit Purchases Account (an expense); Credit Bank Account (money paid out)

Dr				Purchases Account			Cr
Date	**Details**	**£**	**p**	**Date**	**Details**	**£**	**p**
2002				2002			
04 Sep	Bank	3,000.00					

transaction

5 September 2002: received loan of £5,000 from D B Dore and paid cheque into bank

double-entry

Debit Bank Account (money in); Credit D B Dore Loan Account (a liability)

Dr				D B Dore Loan Account			Cr
Date	**Details**	**£**	**p**	**Date**	**Details**	**£**	**p**
2002				2002			
				05 Sep	Bank	5,000.00	

transaction

6 September 2002: purchase of computer costing £4,000, paid for by cheque

double-entry

Debit Computer Account (asset acquired); Credit Bank Account (money paid out)

Dr				Computer Account			Cr
Date	**Details**	**£**	**p**	**Date**	**Details**	**£**	**p**
2002				2002			
06 Sep	Bank	4,000.00					

Note that the acquisition of a computer is the purchase of an item which will be retained for use in the business. It is therefore a fixed asset* and will be recorded in a separate account, and not in Purchases Account, which is used solely for recording the purchase of goods which the business is going to sell – ie magic and joke products in the case of Harry Smith Limited.

*An 'asset' is an item owned by a business. A 'fixed asset' is an asset which the business intends to keep for the foreseeable future.

DOUBLE-ENTRY FOR CREDIT SALES AND CREDIT PURCHASES

So far in this chapter we have looked at the treatment of double-entry transactions involving the bank account, and have used the bank account as a guide to working out which entry is a debit and which is a credit. In business many entries will involve the bank account, because cash and cheques are a common method of payment.

There will, however, be some transactions which do not involve the bank account. Purchases and sales on credit (ie where payment is made later) are the most common, and the double-entry rules for these follow the same logic: the book-keeper, on entering a credit purchase or credit sale, records the item in the sales account or purchases account as normal, but then records the second entry in the relevant account in the name of either the customer or the supplier, instead of in the bank account, because no money has yet changed hands. The entries (again ignoring any VAT) are therefore:

- **credit sale**   Debit   Customer's Account

                       Credit Sales Account

- **credit purchase** Credit Supplier's Account

                       Debit   Purchases Account

Let us now take an example of a credit sale made by Harry Smith Limited, and payment received after thirty days. On 10 September 2002 Harry Smith Limited sells goods invoiced at £5,000 on credit to Owl Promotions. The account entries are: debit Owl Promotions' Account; credit Sales Account.

Dr			Owl Promotions			Cr
Date	**Details**	**£ p**	**Date**	**Details**		**£ p**
2002			2002			
10 Sep	Sales	5,000.00				

Dr			Sales Account			Cr
Date	**Details**	**£ p**	**Date**	**Details**		**£ p**
2002			2002			
			10 Sep	Owl Promotions		5,000.00

On 10 October, thirty days after this sale has been made, Harry Smith Limited receives a cheque for £5,000 from Owl Promotions in settlement of the amount due; the cheque is paid into the bank. Harry Smith Limited's book-keeper will:

■ debit Bank Account £5,000 (money received)

■ credit the account of Owl Promotions £5,000

The accounts will appear as set out below. Note the existing entry from 10 September on the account of Owl Promotions.

Dr			Bank Account			Cr
Date	**Details**	**£ p**	**Date**	**Details**		**£ p**
2002			2002			
10 Oct	Owl Promotions	5,000.00				

Dr			Owl Promotions			Cr
Date	**Details**	**£ p**	**Date**	**Details**		**£ p**
2002			2002			
10 Sep	Sales	5,000.00	10 Oct	Bank		5,000.00

double-entry and credit purchases

Credit purchases made by a business are recorded in a similar way. If Harry Smith Limited purchases £2,500 of goods from H A Gridd Supplies on 12 September, and is given 30 days in which to pay, the entries in the books will be:

■ debit Purchases Account £2,500

■ credit H A Gridd Supplies' Account £2,500

Dr			Purchases Account			Cr
Date	**Details**	**£ p**	**Date**	**Details**		**£ p**
2002			2002			
12 Sep	H A Gridd Supplies	2,500.00				

Dr			H A Gridd Supplies			Cr
Date	**Details**	**£ p**	**Date**	**Details**		**£ p**
2002			2002			
			12 Sep	Purchases		2,500.00

Settlement of the invoice by Harry Smith Limited in thirty days' time will be recorded by the book-keeper with the following entries:

- debit H A Gridd Supplies Account £2,500
- credit Bank Account £2,500 (money paid out)

Dr			H A Gridd Supplies			Cr
Date	**Details**	**£ p**	**Date**	**Details**		**£ p**
2002			2002			
12 Oct	Bank	2,500.00	12 Sep	Purchases		2,500.00

Dr			Bank Account			Cr
Date	**Details**	**£ p**	**Date**	**Details**		**£ p**
2002			2002			
			12 Oct	H A Gridd Supplies		2,500.00

balancing off accounts

You will probably have noticed that in the above examples, the accounts of the customer (Owl Promotions) and the supplier (H A Gridd Supplies) have finished up with the same amounts on each side. In these cases, nothing is owing to Harry Smith Limited, or is owed by Harry Smith Limited.

In practice, as the business trades, there will be many entries on both sides of customer and supplier accounts. It is a useful exercise to balance off each account periodically, to see how much in total each customer owes, and how much is owed to each supplier of the business. This balancing off procedure is also applied to other accounts in the books of the business. A computer accounting system will, of course, do this balancing automatically.

Balancing accounts is covered in full in the next chapter.

THE ACCOUNTING EQUATION

Another way of understanding double-entry book-keeping is to look at the **accounting equation**.

Here the dual aspect of the debit and credit entries for each transaction are related to what happens in an equation. As your mathematical skills tell you, if you do something to one side of an equation you must do the same to the other side too, in order for it to remain balanced and have an equal amount on each side.

The equation involves the **balance sheet** of a business or any organisation. A balance sheet, is a financial statement extracted from the accounting records, setting out what a business or organisation owns and owes, and the way in which it is financed.

Suppose you are starting a business, you will need to acquire assets and will also need to raise and invest money in order to buy them. One form of the equation is therefore:

assets (items owned)

= liabilities (money borrowed) plus capital (the owner's money)

In order to explain this equation we need to define exactly what we mean by these terms . . .

- **assets** are items the business owns such as property and equipment, money in the bank and money owed to the business by debtors
- **liabilities** are the 'other side of the coin' to assets – they are amounts that the business owes: money borrowed and amounts due to suppliers (creditors) for assets acquired
- **capital** is the money which the owner has put into the business from his or her own pocket – it is the owner's investment

Using mathematics and moving the liabilities figure onto the other side (changing the liabilities to a minus), the equation:

assets = liabilities + capital

can be restated as:

assets *minus* liabilities = capital

This is the basis of the balance sheet.

assets	minus	**liabilities**	equals	**capital**
what a business owns		what a business owes		the owner's investment

Let us now look at how this equation is affected as financial transactions are carried out.

workings of the accounting equation

Business transactions will have an effect on the balance sheet and the equation, as each transaction has a dual effect on the accounts. The equation will always balance. For example, if the owner of a business pays in £10,000 of new capital in the form of a cheque, the assets (bank account) will increase by this amount, and so will capital (capital account).

The diagram below shows a number of transactions which might pass through the business bank account. Note in each case:

■ how the transaction has a twofold effect (the 'dual aspect')

■ what those effects are

■ how the equation (and hence the balance sheet) changes

■ the equation always balances after the changes

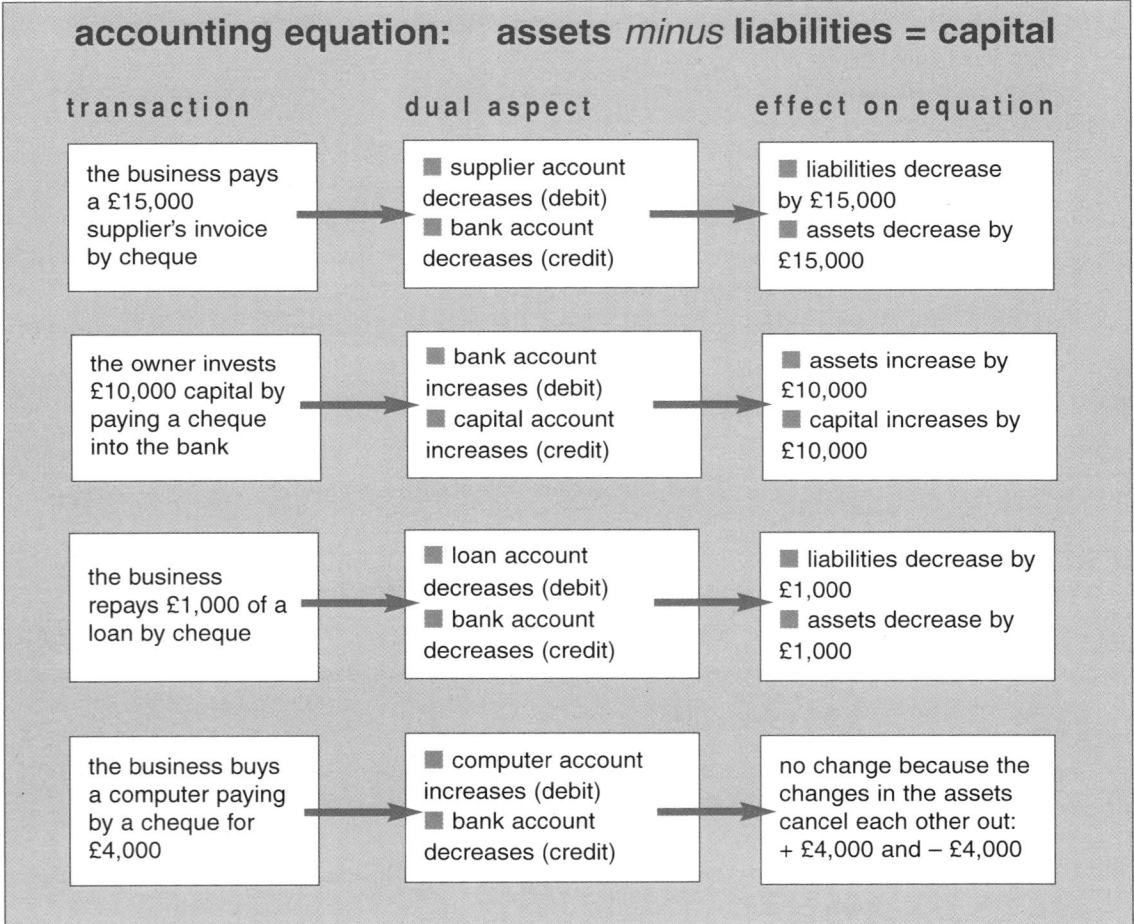

As you can see from the double-entry transactions, the equation always balances, and so will the balance sheet of a business. It is also worth noting that the balance sheet of a business will never stay static – unless, of course, all activity ceases. It will change from day to day as the business buys and sells, pays expenses and receives income. We will look at the balance sheets of different types of business in more detail in later chapters.

chapter summary

● The accounting system in an organisation forms a series of consecutive stages: financial transactions and documents, summaries of the transactions and documents, entering them into accounts kept in ledgers, using the data to produce financial reports for managers and owners.

● The accounting system can be manual (handwritten) or computerised; the same basic principles apply to both types.

● The double-entry system used by most organisations is based on the principle of there being two entries in separate accounts for each transaction – a debit and a credit. These reflect the dual aspect of accounting which states that for each transaction one account gives value and another account receives value.

● The accounting equation is based on the balance sheet of a business and can be stated in two ways:

$$assets \ = \ liabilities \ + \ capital$$
$$assets \ - \ liabilities \ = \ capital$$

The concept of the accounting equation principle is that for each financial transaction there are two entries (the double-entry system) which means that the equation always balances.

key terms

day book	a listing of financial transactions in the accounting system ready for entry in the double-entry accounts
double-entry account	an account into which financial transactions are entered – entries are made in two accounts for each transaction
ledger	an accounting book or section which contains specific types of account, for example the 'sales ledger' for customers who have bought on credit terms
assets	items which an organisation owns or is owed, eg vehicles or money due from customers (debtors)
liabilities	items which an organisation owes, eg loans or money due to suppliers (creditors)
capital	the investment of the owner(s) in an organisation
balance sheet	the financial statement which 'balances' assets with liabilities and capital: *assets – liabilities = capital*

activities

Note: an asterisk (*) after an activity number means that an answer is provided in Appendix 1.

3.1   Draw a flow diagram setting out the main stages in the accounting system of a business.

3.2   Describe the main function of a day book.

3.3*   Write short notes on the functions of the main four ledgers in an accounting system.

3.4*   State why a business will want to produce a trial balance.

3.5*   Describe the main purposes of a profit and loss account and a balance sheet.

3.6   Give an example of the way the dual aspect of accounting works in practice.

3.7*   The accounting equation is normally stated as

        assets – liabilities = capital

        State how the accounting equation is affected by the following transactions:

        (a)   the owner of a business pays a cheque for £10,000 (for capital) into the bank

        (b)   a business buys a Mercedes for the Managing Director for £45,000, paying by cheque

        (c)   the business pays by cheque a supplier's invoice for £3,500

        (d)   the bank lends the business £20,000 and transfers the money to the business bank account

questions 3.8 – 3.10

You are a trainee accountant in the firm of Anthony Blurr & Co. Your job is to assist with the accounts of start-up businesses, a number of which have no double-entry records. These are the tasks that you have to carry out.

3.8*   Will Abbott has kept his bank account up-to-date, but has not got around to the other double-entry items. Draw up the other accounts for him, and make the appropriate entries.

Dr			Bank Account		Cr
2001		£	2001		£
1 Feb	Sales	5,000	1 Feb	Purchases	3,500
2 Feb	Sales	7,500	2 Feb	Wages	2,510
3 Feb	Bank Loan	12,500	3 Feb	Van purchased	12,500
5 Feb	Sales	9,300	3 Feb	Purchases	5,000
			4 Feb	Rent paid	780

3.9 Sarah Banks has opened up a health food shop 'Just Nuts', but has not yet started to write up the books. As she is inexperienced she asks you to set up an accounting system for her.

She provides you with the following list of transactions for the first week's trading, starting on Monday 8 June 2001. You are to draw up the double-entry accounts for her and are to make the appropriate entries.

Monday

Paid £5,000 cheque as capital into the bank; purchases of £4,000, paid by cheque.
Paid £750 sales into the bank; paid week's rent £75 by cheque.

Tuesday

Paid £500 sales into the bank; made purchases of £425 by cheque.

Wednesday

Paid £420 sales into the bank; bought computer £890 by cheque.

Thursday

Paid £550 sales into the bank; made purchases £510 by cheque.

Friday

Paid £925 sales into the bank; paid assistant's wages £75 by cheque.

3.10 Anu Sharma has run into trouble recording entries in the business bank account. You are to set out the bank account as it should appear, rule up the other double-entry accounts and make the appropriate entries.

Dr			**Bank Account**			**Cr**
2001		£	2001			£
1 Jan	Purchases	1,000	2 Jan	Sales		5,000
5 Jan	Wages paid	2,700	3 Jan	Sales		7,000
5 Jan	Rent paid	150	4 Jan	Bank Loan received		5,500
8 Jan	Rates paid	6,210	9 Jan	Machine purchased		4,000
9 Jan	Sales	5,205	10 Jan	Sales		9,520
10 Jan	Purchases	6,750	12 Jan	Wages paid		2,850
11 Jan	Car purchase	5,500	12 Jan	Rent paid		150

BALANCING THE BOOKS

CASE STUDY
Balancing the books

Gina Ricci has set up her designer label clothes store in town. She is operating as a sole trader – in other words she is the sole proprietor of the business and not trading as a partnership or a limited company. She has decided which accounts she needs for her double-entry system. She has made a list of some of these accounts . . .

- purchases account – to record purchases of clothes
- suppliers' accounts – to record what she owes when she buys clothes on credit
- sales account – to record her takings from clothes that she sells
- customers' accounts – for any customers to whom she sells on credit
- expenses accounts – for paying bills such as rent, rates, wages, electricity, telephone, insurance, advertising – in fact for all the running expenses of her business

But Gina also has a number of questions:

'What should I do about VAT – do I have to register?'

'How am I supposed to organise these accounts and be confident that I have done all the entries correctly?'

'How am I going to know what I owe to my suppliers at any one time?'

Gina clearly has some work to do before she can get the accounts to give her the information she needs.

This chapter looks at the way the accounts are organised in the ledger system and how they are balanced and listed in the trial balance. It also explains about Value Added Tax (VAT) and how control (summary) accounts are used to help with the information that Gina needs.

learning objectives

When you have studied this chapter, you will be able to:

- *understand about VAT registration and the workings of VAT in the accounts*
- *describe the ledger system and the role of control accounts in summarising data*
- *balance double-entry accounts to find their 'total'*
- *construct a trial balance from the account balances and confirm the accuracy of the book-keeping process*

VALUE ADDED TAX (VAT)

what is VAT?

Value Added Tax (VAT) is a Government tax on spending paid by the person or organisation that buys goods or services. It is administered and collected by a Government Agency, HM Customs & Excise, and is charged on most sales, exceptions being items such as food, books, children's clothes and cycle helmets. If you would like further information about VAT, the HM Customs & Excise website www.hmce.gov.uk is well set out and helpful.

Gina, in the Case Study, is right in asking about VAT. If she does not take any action about it her accounting system will not be complete, and she could end up owing money to HM Customs & Excise.

how does VAT affect businesses?

The main principle of VAT is that it is paid by the final consumer of a product – as you will well know when you shop. Businesses that have helped create the product you buy can claim back all the VAT they have paid – which is why accounting for VAT is so important. In other words, businesses act as tax collectors – charging their customers VAT, but keeping back the amount of VAT they pay themselves.

All businesses by law, whether they are sole traders, partnerships, or limited companies have to register with HM Customs & Excise if their sales (or anticipated sales) of goods or services exceed a certain annual amount. This amount is known as the 'VAT threshold' and is normally increased annually in the Government's Spring Budget. It affects all but the smallest businesses.

What does VAT registration involve? Once businesses are registered they are legally bound by a number of rules and regulations:

- They are given a VAT registration number which must be quoted on all invoices and other stationery.
- They must keep accounts for VAT.
- They must regularly send details to HM Customs & Excise, on a VAT Return form, of the VAT they have charged to customers (on sales made) less the VAT they have paid out (on their purchases) to other businesses.

  This means that they will *either* send a payment to HM Customs & Excise for VAT due (when they have received more VAT than they have paid) *or* they will reclaim VAT if they have paid more VAT than they have charged – if, for example they sell food, books or children's clothes.

As you can see from all these requirements, keeping an accurate account for VAT is very important. The accounting records may be examined at any time by HM Customs & Excise inspectors – so they have to be right!

accounting for VAT

Businesses normally keep a double-entry account running for VAT charged and paid. The entries to this account come from:

■ VAT amounts on purchases, eg supplier invoices and expenses – debits

■ VAT amounts on sales of goods – credits

The balance of this account will be the amount due to HM Customs & Excise (or a refund due from HM Customs & Excise). The account illustrated below shows that VAT £1,000 (ie £3,000 less £2,000) is due to be paid:

Dr				VAT Account			Cr	
Date 2002	**Details**	**£**	**p**	**Date** 2002	**Details**		**£**	**p**
30 Sep	Purchases	2,000.00		30 Sep	Sales VAT		3,000.00	
	VAT on purchases				**VAT on sales**			

We will return to VAT account later in the chapter when we look at the trial balance (page 71). First, however, we will look in more detail at the way in which the accounts are organised in the ledger system.

THE LEDGER SYSTEM OF ACCOUNTS

We saw in the last chapter that the double-entry accounting records of a business are divided into 'ledgers'. A ledger is a traditional word for a book. The term is used to apply to sections of a handwritten accounting system and also to divisions in some computer accounting programs (see page 89). The main divisions of the ledger are:

■ **sales ledger**

the personal accounts of customers who have bought on credit (ie they have bought goods or services but will pay later) – these customers are also known as 'debtors'

■ **purchases ledger**

the personal accounts of suppliers who have sold to the business on credit – these suppliers are also known as 'creditors'

■ **cash book**

the book which records bank accounts in the name of the business, and cash held by the business; this book can be supplemented by a separate petty cash book for small business cash purchases and expenses

■ **main 'general' ledger (also known as 'nominal' ledger)**

all the other accounts in the accounting system, the main ones being:

- – income from sales and other sources
- – purchases of materials and stock
- – business expenses paid, eg wages, rent, insurance, advertising
- – assets (items owned) and liabilities (items owed)
- – capital (the investment of the owners)
- – VAT
- – stock (normally valued and entered in the accounts at each year-end)
- – profit/loss (normally calculated for each year)

Remember that for each double-entry transaction there will be entries in two accounts in any of the ledgers.

The ledger system can be represented diagrammatically:

the division of the ledger

SALES LEDGER

accounts for customers who have bought on credit – 'debtors'
- sales made
- returned goods
- payments received
- cash discounts given

PURCHASES LEDGER

accounts for suppliers who have supplied on credit – 'creditors'
- purchases made
- returned goods
- payments made
- cash discounts received

CASH BOOK

money paid in and out of the business
- bank accounts
- cash accounts
- petty cash (separate book)

MAIN / GENERAL / NOMINAL LEDGER
all the other accounts

• sales	• assets	• liabilities	• purchases
• sales returns	• stock	• capital	• purchases returns
• other income	• VAT	• profit/loss	• other expenses

the 'ledger' in computer accounting

The same principles apply to the way the accounts are classified in a computer accounting program. The illustration below shows the way the commonly used Sage computer accounting program structures its functions. You will see that the four icons to the left are the four main divisions of the ledger and the remaining four are additional functions available on the program.

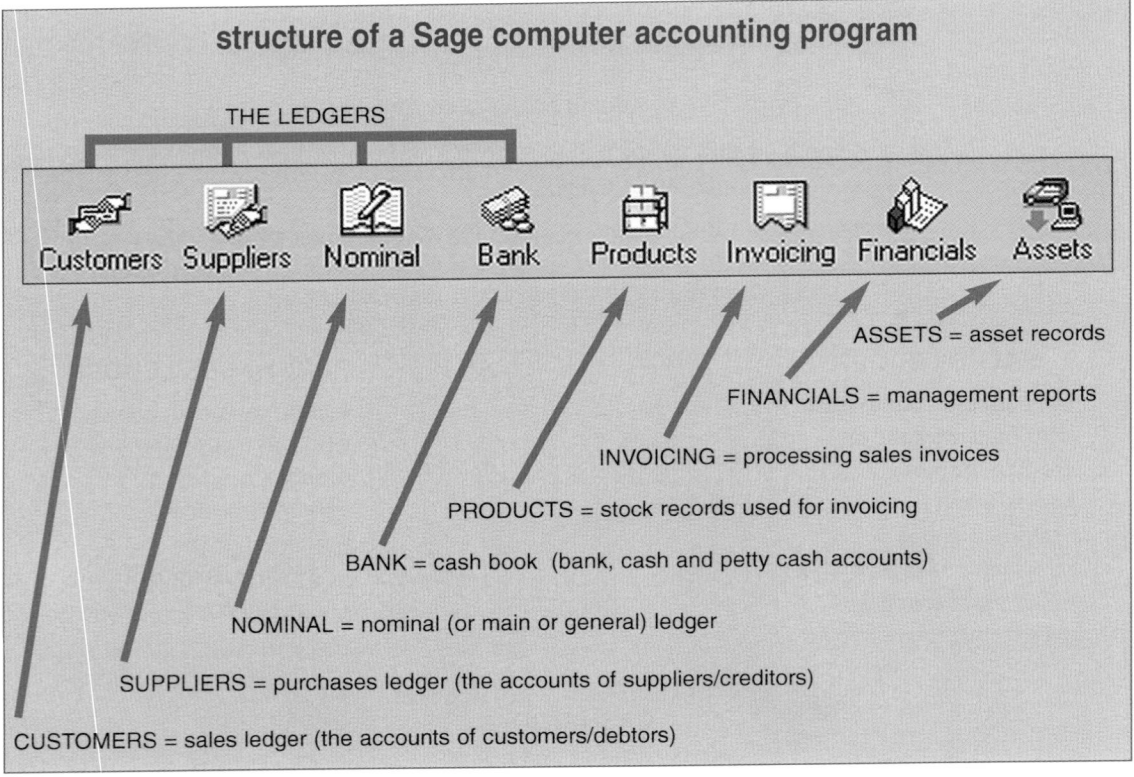

structure of a Sage computer accounting program

THE LEDGERS

Customers Suppliers Nominal Bank Products Invoicing Financials Assets

ASSETS = asset records

FINANCIALS = management reports

INVOICING = processing sales invoices

PRODUCTS = stock records used for invoicing

BANK = cash book (bank, cash and petty cash accounts)

NOMINAL = nominal (or main or general) ledger

SUPPLIERS = purchases ledger (the accounts of suppliers/creditors)

CUSTOMERS = sales ledger (the accounts of customers/debtors)

BALANCING THE ACCOUNTS AND THE TRIAL BALANCE

Double entry book-keeping involves the making of a debit entry and a credit entry for every transaction. It therefore follows that if the book-keeper has done his or her job accurately, the total of all the debit entries will equal the total of the credit entries for any given period. To test this accuracy the book-keeper will regularly, often on a monthly basis, check that the total of the debit entries equals the total of the credit entries by extracting a **trial balance**, which should show that these totals do, in fact, agree. A trial balance is illustrated on page 71.

balancing accounts

In order to provide the figures for a trial balance the book-keeper **balances** and calculates the running total of each account before setting out the trial balance.

Balancing of accounts is therefore regularly carried out both to speed up the preparation of the trial balance and also to provide the owner(s) of the business with valuable information about items such as sales, purchases, expenses and income.

The mechanics of balancing are straightforward, and have already been seen in their initial stages in our examination of the transactions of Harry Smith Limited in the last chapter.

When Harry Smith Limited issues an invoice for goods sold on credit, the book-keeper enters the amount on the debit (left-hand) side of the debtor's account in the Sales Ledger (with a corresponding credit to sales account). In the example of Owl Promotions set out below, the debit balance of the account is £5,000.

Dr				Owl Promotions			Cr
Date	Details	£	p	Date	Details	£	p
2002				2002			
10 Sep	Sales	5,000.00					

When Owl Promotions settles up by sending a cheque for £5,000, the amount is entered into Harry Smith Limited's bank account (a debit entry), and a corresponding credit entry is made to Owl Promotions' account:

Dr				Owl Promotions			Cr
Date	Details	£	p	Date	Details	£	p
2002				2002			
10 Sep	Sales	5,000.00		10 Oct	Bank	5,000.00	

Owl Promotions, according to the account, now owes nothing; the arithmetic difference between the debit side and the credit side is nil. If Owl Promotions on 25th October buys further goods from Harry Smith Limited for £10,000, simple arithmetic states that, as the invoice for £5,000 has been paid, they now owe £10,000, and the debit balance of their account will be £10,000. You will see from the account below that this £10,000 owing is the difference between the total of the debit side and the total of the credit side (£15,000 less £5,000 = £10,000).

Dr				Owl Promotions			Cr	
Date	**Details**		**£**	**p**	**Date**	**Details**	**£**	**p**
2002					2002			
10 Sep	Sales		5,000.00		10 Oct	Bank	5,000.00	
25 Oct	Sales		10,000.00					

On 31 October, at the month-end, the book-keeper balances off the double-entry accounts in preparation for the trial balance. Study the account below very carefully.

Dr				Owl Promotions				Cr	
Date	**Details**		**£**	**p**	**Date**	**Details**		**£**	**p**
2002					2002				
10 Sep	Sales		5,000.00		10 Oct	Bank		5,000.00	
25 Oct	Sales		10,000.00		31 Oct	Balance c/d	**2**	10,000.00	
		3	15,000.00				**3**	15,000.00	
1 Nov	Balance b/d	**4**	10,000.00						

The book-keeper, when balancing the account, takes the following steps, indicated (except for the first step) by the numbers in the blue shaded boxes in the account above.

1 The debit and the credit columns are separately added up and the totals noted in pencil. It is important to appreciate that nothing is entered in the account at this stage.

2 The difference between the two totals (the balance of the account) is entered in the account
- on the side of the smaller total
- on the next available line
- with the date of the balancing
- with the words 'Balance c/d', an abbreviation of 'Balance carried down'

The balance carried down of the above account is shown to be £10,000.

3 Both sides of the account are now added up and the totals (which should be identical and the higher of the two totals calculated) are entered on the same line in the appropriate column and double underlined. The double underlining indicates that the account is ruled off and the figures above the underlining should not be added to the figures below.

As we are dealing with double-entry book-keeping, the book-keeper must now – in order to complete the transaction of entering the difference (see Step 2) – enter the same amount on the other side of the account, below the totals entered in Step 3. In doing this, the book-keeper will have completed both a debit and a credit entry. The entry in this example reads '1 Nov Balance b/d £10,000.' This means that this is the amount owed by Owl Promotions to Harry Smith Limited on 31 October. The date here is not the month-end date (October 31) but the first day of the following month; the abbreviation 'b/d' stands for 'brought down'.

Here are two more examples of accounts which have been balanced:

Dr   **Wages Account**   **Cr**

Date	Details	£ p	Date	Details	£ p
2002			2002		
3 May	Bank	1,000.00	31 May	Balance c/d	5,150.00
10 May	Bank	1,200.00			
17 May	Bank	800.00			
24 May	Bank	1,000.00			
31 May	Bank	1,150.00			
		5,150.00			5,150.00
1 June	Balance b/d	5,150.00			

The balancing process above is carried out even if there are entries on only one side of the account.

Dr   **Bank Account**   **Cr**

Date	Details	£ p	Date	Details	£ p
2002			2002		
1 April	Balance b/d	1,000.00	1 April	Insurance	800.00
1 April	Sales	1,000.00	2 April	Rates	550.00
3 April	Sales	2,500.00	3 April	Purchases	4,500.00
5 April	Balance c/d	1,350.00			
		5,850.00			5,850.00
			6 April	Balance b/d	1,350.00

In the Bank Account there are entries on both sides and the balance brought down is the difference between them.

Note that if the balance brought down is on the debit side, this represents money in the bank; if the balance is on the credit side (as here), this would mean that the business has an overdraft from the bank.

CONTROL ACCOUNTS

There is one further type of account you need to know about before looking at the accounts listed in the trial balance - a **control account**.

A control account is a summary account or master account, which records the totals of entries to a particular set of accounts.

The Debtors Control Account, for instance, shows the total of all customers' accounts in the Sales Ledger and tells the owner of the business how much in total is owing from debtors.

The Creditors Control Account shows the total of all the suppliers' accounts in the Purchases Ledger and tells the owner of the business how much in total is owing to creditors.

The individual debtor and creditor accounts are known as 'memorandum' accounts.

control accounts and the trial balance

The trial balance (see next page) is the listing of all the account balances in two columns: debit balances on the left, credit balances on the right.

It is the balances of the control accounts which are taken to the trial balance rather than the individual customer and supplier balances, which would clutter it up and make it very long. The description of the control accounts in the trial balance is simply 'debtors' (a debit balance on the left) and 'creditors' (a credit balance on the right). Look at the diagram below.

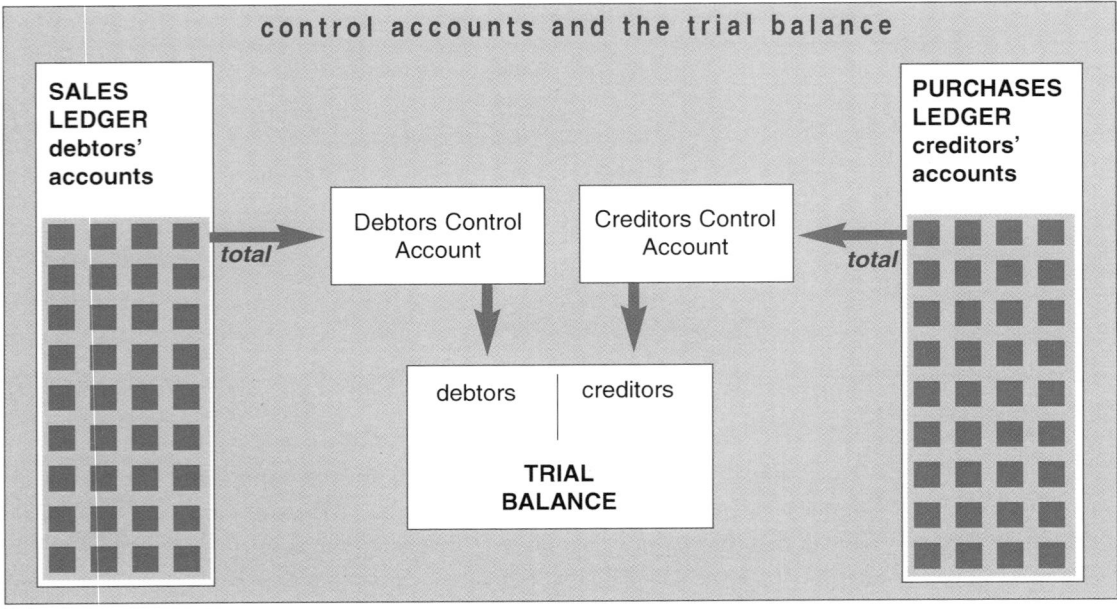

control accounts and the trial balance

TRIAL BALANCE

When the book-keeper has balanced the accounts and totalled up the control accounts, he or she can then draw up the trial balance.

A trial balance is a summary in two columns of the balances of all the accounts, listing debit balances on the left and credit balances on the right, and showing the total of each column. An example is shown below.

If the book-keeper has been accurate in the day-to-day recording of transactions, the total of the two columns should agree, as they do here.

The Case Study on the next page illustrates the practicalities of drawing up a trial balance from the double-entry accounts of a limited company.

the trial balance

TARA DOLCE
Trial balance as at 30 June 2002

	Dr £	Cr £
Premises	125,000	
Machinery	40,000	
Purchases	96,250	
Sales		146,390
Debtors	10,390	
Creditors		12,495
Administration expenses	18,740	
Wages	38,430	
Telephone	3,020	
Interest paid	2,350	
Travel expenses	1,045	
Bank overdraft		1,050
Cash	150	
Loan from bank		20,000
Capital		155,440
	335,375	335,375

CASE STUDY

Harry Smith Limited — the trial balance

situation

Harry Smith's book-keeper, Ron, has just completed balancing the double-entry accounts at the end of December 2002. He has listed them as follows, identifying them as debits or credits:

	£	
Capital	50,000	Cr
Bank	1,500	Dr
Purchases	95,000	Dr
Sales	179,000	Cr
Returns out	5,000	Cr
Returns in	4,000	Dr
Wages	37,000	Dr
Equipment	35,000	Dr
Vehicles	59,000	Dr
Debtors	58,500	Dr
Creditors	25,000	Cr
VAT due	21,000	Cr
Bank loan	10,000	Cr

Ron shows the list to Harry, who asks a number of questions:

questions

1   'How do you know whether the bank balance is money in the bank or an overdraft?'

2   'What are Returns in and Returns out?'

3   'What is the VAT due – is it something we have to pay, or is it being paid to us?'

4   'What are the Debtors and Creditors?'

5   'How do you know whether the figures are right or not?'

answers

Ron replies as follows:

1 The bank balance is a debit balance and therefore represents money in the bank. An overdraft would have been a credit balance. We do have a bank loan which is a credit balance.

2 'Returns in' are Sales returns. The account records all the goods that have been sent back to us. It is a debit balance because the refunds to our customers are effectively a cost to the business.

'Returns out' are Purchases returns. The account records all the goods that have been returned by us to our suppliers. It is a credit balance because it represents refunds made to us.

3 The VAT due is VAT we have to pay. It is a liability (we owe it to HM Customs & Excise) and so it is a credit balance.

4 Debtors is the balance of the Debtors Control Account, which is the total of all the debtor accounts in the Sales Ledger. It is a debit balance because it is money owed to us by our customers.

Creditors is the total of the Creditors Control Account, which is the total of all the creditor accounts in the Purchases Ledger. It is a credit balance because it is the money we owe to our suppliers.

5 We draw up a trial balance to show that the total of the debit balances (the left-hand column) equals the total of the credit balances (the right-hand column). As you can see we are correct here. If the columns did not have the same total we would have to investigate our arithmetic and the account entries in our ledgers. Of course, if we had a computerised accounting system I would not have to go to all this trouble – the system would produce a trial balance automatically – and it would balance!

The trial balance produced is shown below.

Trial Balance of Harry Smith Limited as at 31 December 2002

	Debit (£)	Credit (£)
Capital		50,000
Bank	1,500	
Purchases	95,000	
Sales		179,000
Returns out		5,000
Returns in	4,000	
Wages	37,000	
Equipment	35,000	
Vehicles	59,000	
Debtors	58,500	
Creditors		25,000
VAT due		21,000
Bank loan		10,000
	290,000	290,000

DEBIT AND CREDIT BALANCES – WHICH IS WHICH?

Certain accounts always have a debit balance, while others always have a credit balance. You may know a number of these already, but the lists set out below will help you when doing practical exercises.

debit balances

- cash account
- purchases account
- sales returns account (returns in)
- fixed asset accounts, eg premises, motor vehicles, machinery, office equipment, etc
- expense accounts, eg wages, telephone, rent paid, carriage
- drawings account
- debtors' accounts – often shown in the trial balance as a total – the debtors control account

credit balances

- sales account
- purchases returns account (returns out)
- income accounts, eg rent received, commission received, fees received
- capital account
- loan account
- VAT due to HM Customs & Excise
- creditors' accounts - often shown in the trial balance as a total – the creditors control account

bank account

Bank account can be either debit or credit – it will be debit when the business has money in the bank (an asset), and credit when it is overdrawn (a liability).

IF THE TRIAL BALANCE DOESN'T BALANCE . . .

If the trial balance fails to balance, ie the two totals are different, there is an error (or errors):

- either in the addition of the trial balance
- and/or in the double-entry book-keeping

The procedure for finding the error(s) is as follows:

■ check the addition of the trial balance

■ check that the balance of each account has been correctly entered in the trial balance, and under the correct heading, ie debit or credit

■ check the calculation of the balance on each account

■ calculate the amount that the trial balance is wrong, and then look in the accounts for a transaction for this amount: if one is found, check that the double-entry book-keeping has been carried out correctly

■ if the amount by which the trial balance is wrong is divisible by nine, then the error may be a reversal of figures, eg £65 entered as £56, or £45 entered as £54

ERRORS NOT SHOWN BY A TRIAL BALANCE

As mentioned earlier, a trial balance does not prove the complete accuracy of the accounting records. There are six types of error that are not shown by a trial balance.

error of omission

Here a business transaction has been completely omitted from the accounting records, ie both the debit and credit entries have not been made.

reversal of entries

With this error, the debit and credit entries have been made in the accounts but on the wrong side of the two accounts concerned.

mispost/error of commission

Here, a transaction is entered to the wrong person's account. For example, a sale of goods on credit to D Malfoy has been entered as debit to L Malfoy's account by mistake. The customer will soon pick up an error like this!

error of principle

This is when a transaction has been entered in the wrong type of account. For example, the cost of fuel for vehicles has been entered as a debit to motor vehicles account instead of motor vehicle expenses.

error of original entry (or transcription)

Here, the correct accounts have been used, and the correct sides. What is wrong is that the amount has been entered incorrectly in both accounts.

compensating error

This is where two errors cancel each other out. For example, if the balance of purchases account is calculated wrongly at £10 too much, and a similar error has occurred in calculating the balance of sales account, then the two errors will compensate each other, and the trial balance will not show the errors.

TRIAL BALANCES ON THE COMPUTER

Computers are very useful when it comes to producing trial balances and other reports for management: either in the form of a computer accounting program such as Sage, or failing that, a simple spreadsheet.

trial balance on a spreadsheet

A spreadsheet can easily be set up with columns for account names, debit balances, credit balances and totals for the columns. When the figures have been entered, they will automatically produce totals which should balance. Look at the example of a trial balance on a spreadsheet shown below.

	A	B	C	D	E	F
1		Dr	Cr			
2						
3						
4	Plant and machinery	35000				
5	Office equipment	15000				
6	Furniture and fixtures	25000				
7	Debtors control account	45500				
8	Bank current account	12450				
9	Creditors control account		32510			
10	Sales tax control account		17920			
11	Purchase tax control account	26600				
12	Loans		35000			
13	Ordinary Shares		75000			
14	Hardware sales		85000			
15	Software sales		15000			
16	Computer consultancy		2400			
17	Materials purchased	69100				
18	Advertising	12400				
19	Gross wages	16230				
20	Rent	4500				
21	General rates	450				
22	Electricity	150				
23	Telephone	275				
24	Stationery	175				
25						
26						
27	Total	262830	262830			

trial balance on a computer accounting program

If the business had been operating a computer accounting program such as Sage, the task of producing a trial balance would have been very simple. The computer would automatically keep a running balance of each ledger account and would transfer the balances (including the control accounts for debtors and creditors) to a trial balance report on the click of a mouse. The convenience of using a computer accounting program cannot be underestimated! The next chapter deals with this subject in more detail.

The report shown below is a printout of a Sage trial balance showing the figures from the spreadsheet on the previous page.

Pronto Supplies Limited
Period Trial Balance

To Period: Month 2, February 2001

N/C	Name	Debit	Credit
0020	Plant and Machinery	35,000.00	
0030	Office Equipment	15,000.00	
0040	Furniture and Fixtures	25,000.00	
1100	Debtors Control Account	45,500.00	
1200	Bank Current Account	12,450.00	
2100	Creditors Control Account		32,510.00
2200	Sales Tax Control Account		17,920.00
2201	Purchase Tax Control Account	26,600.00	
2300	Loans		35,000.00
3000	Ordinary Shares		75,000.00
4000	Sales Type A		85,000.00
4001	Sales Type B		15,000.00
4002	Sales Type C		2,400.00
5000	Materials Purchased	69,100.00	
6201	Advertising	12,400.00	
7000	Gross Wages	16,230.00	
7100	Rent	4,500.00	
7103	General Rates	450.00	
7200	Electricity	150.00	
7502	Telephone	275.00	
7504	Office Stationery	175.00	
	Totals:	**262,830.00**	**262,830.00**

THE TRIAL BALANCE – WHERE NEXT?

The trial balance, as well as being a check on the accuracy of the book-keeping, is often used as the starting point in the production of the final accounts of a business. These final accounts, which are often produced annually, comprise the profit and loss statement and balance sheet. They will be dealt with in Chapter 6.

chapter summary

- It is essential that a business runs an account for Value Added Tax (VAT) because the tax is charged on most goods and services. Businesses which reach the VAT threshold have to register for VAT.

- VAT is paid in full by the final consumer – so businesses act as tax collectors, charging VAT but claiming back the VAT that they themselves have paid.

- The double-entry system of accounts – manual and computerised – is normally divided up into four ledgers or 'books': sales ledger, purchases ledger, cash book and nominal ledger (also known as 'main' or 'general' ledger).

- Some ledgers such as purchases ledger and sales ledger (but not nominal) often contain a large number of accounts which are summarised in a control or 'total' account.

- The double-entry accounts – including the control accounts – are balanced regularly to find out the 'total' of each account. These totals are then regularly listed in a trial balance which sets out debit balances and credit balances in separate columns, the totals of which should be the same.

- The trial balance is an essential check of the accuracy of the double-entry book-keeping. If the columns of the trial balance do not agree, the error should be investigated and corrected.

- A computer accounting system produces an accurate and correct trial balance automatically, which is a substantial advantage of using a computer accounting system.

key terms

Value Added Tax (VAT)	a Government tax on spending paid by the person or organisation that buys goods or services
sales ledger	the personal accounts of customers who have bought on credit and owe money – the 'debtors' of the business
purchases ledger	the personal accounts of suppliers who have sold to the business on credit and who are owed money – the 'creditors' of the business
cash book	the book which contains the bank accounts together with accounts for any cash funds held by the business; it is often supplemented by a separate petty cash book
main, general or nominal ledger	the book which contains the remaining accounts of the business, such as income, expenses, assets, liabilities and capital

account balancing	the process of finding the total of each account and producing a debit or credit balance
control account	a summary or 'master' account which records the totals of a particular set of accounts
trial balance	a summary report, in two totalled columns, of the balances of all the accounts, listing debit balances on the left and credit balances on the right

activities

Note: an asterisk (*) after an activity number means that an answer is provided in Appendix 1.

4.1* VAT is a Government tax on spending.

    (a)   Who pays all the VAT when you buy a TV from an electrical store?

    (b)   What happens to the VAT which the electrical store is charged by the TV manufacturer when it buys the TV in the first place?

4.2* A business registers for VAT. Describe briefly what this means for the business.

4.3* (a)   Define a 'control' account.

    (b)   What does the balance of the Sales Ledger Control Account tell the business owner?

    (c)   What is the advantage of using a control account when you are drawing up a trial balance?

4.4 (a)   What does it imply about the ability of the book-keeper when the debit and credit totals of a trial balance are not the same figure?

    (b)   State two possible reasons why the debit and credit totals of a trial balance might not add up to the same total.

4.5* You are a trainee accountant with Porterhouse & Co. and have been called in to assist Robert Jefferson, a bookshop owner, who needs help with his double-entry book-keeping. You visit his premises and he hands you lists of items for the first two months of trading. He asks you to carry out a number of tasks for him. You are to ignore VAT.

    (a)*   You are to enter up the January transactions(see next page) in double-entry accounts and balance off each account as at 31 January.

    (b)*   You are to draw up a trial balance as at 31 January to prove your accuracy.

    (c)   You are to enter up the February transactions in the same accounts and balance off at the end of the month. (Note: answer in the Tutor Pack)

    (d)   You are to draw up a trial balance as at 28 February. (Note: answer in the Tutor Pack)

Transactions for January 2001

1 Jan   Introduced £5,000 capital, paid into bank account

2 Jan   Paid rent on premises £200 by cheque

4 Jan   Bought shop fittings £2,000 by cheque

5 Jan   Bought stock of books £2,500 on credit from Northam Publishers

8 Jan   Book sales £1,200 paid into bank

9 Jan   Book Sales £1,000 paid into bank

12 Jan   Bought books £5,000 on credit from Broadheath Books

15 Jan   Book sales £1,500 paid into bank

17 Jan   Book sales £1,250 paid into bank

19 Jan   Bought books from Financial Publications £2,500 by cheque

23 Jan   School returned books £580, unsuitable, cheque refund sent

30 Jan   Sold books on credit to Wyvern College, £1,095

Transactions for February 2001

3 Feb   Book sales £2,510 paid into bank

5 Feb   Paid rent on premises £200 by cheque

7 Feb   Bought shop fittings £1,385 by cheque

10 Feb   Book sales £3,875 paid into bank

11 Feb   Sent cheque £2,500 to Northam Publishers

13 Feb   Bought books £1,290 on credit Northam Publishers

14 Feb   Sent cheque £5,000 to Broadheath Books

17 Feb   Book sales £1,745 paid into bank

18 Feb   Wyvern College returned books £250

21 Feb   Book sales £1,435 paid into bank

24 Feb   Bought books £1,250 Associated Publishers on credit

28 Feb   Book sales £3,900 paid into bank

4.6   Produce the trial balance of Brian Montagu as at 28 February 2001.

	£
Cash	130
Sales	3,720
VAT due	250
Bank	720
Car	2,500
Machinery	1,500
Capital	5,000
Purchases	4,220
Debtors	192
Returns out	168
Creditors	254
Returns in	130

4.7   Produce the trial balance of Jane Greenwell as at 28 February 2001. Unfortunately, she has forgotten to open a capital account.

	£
Bank overdraft	1,250
Purchases	850
Cash	48
Sales	730
Returns out	144
Creditors	1,442
Equipment	2,704
Van	3,200
Returns in	90
Debtors	1,174
Wages	1,500
Capital	?

COMPUTER ACCOUNTING

CASE STUDY
Interlingo – computerising the accounts

Interlingo Translation Services provides translation services and also sells books and tapes.

Interlingo Translation Services is a sole trader business run by Jo Lane, a linguist who has worked as a translator with the European Commission in Brussels and has now settled back in her home town of Mereford. The business is very much a 'one person' business. Jo rents a small office in the town and does everything herself.

Larger clients, for example importers and exporters who need documents translated into English and sales literature translated into foreign languages, are supplied by Jo on credit terms (ie they are invoiced and pay later). Small local 'private' translating jobs which come about from local adverts are normally paid for on a cash basis (ie cash or cheque) and are not invoiced.

Jo has found that selling language books and tapes is a useful sideline. They are all sold for cash, but are bought on credit from the publishers.

Interlingo Translation Services was set up on 2 July 2001. The business is registered for VAT and after a month of using a manual accounting system Jo has decided to transfer her accounts to Sage Line 50 computer accounting software and sign up for a year's telephone technical support. Her main problem, common to so many sole traders, is that of time – finding time to process her accounts and to see how she is getting on in financial terms.

This chapter explains the principles of computer accounting and introduces you to the various functions contained in a Sage computer accounting program.

This is a very practical chapter: if you have access to a Sage computer accounting program you could try out the exercise which is available on www.osbornebooks.co.uk.

learning objectives

When you have studied this chapter, you will be able to:

- *describe the benefits of using a computer accounting system*

- *explain how a computer accounting system is set up*

- *explain how a computer accounting system processes and presents accounting transactions*

- *carry out simple exercises in computer accounting*

COMPUTER HARDWARE

Computer hardware is the equipment on which the programs will be run. There are two main ways of setting up the hardware – a standalone system and a network.

standalone system

A typical standalone system uses a single computer with a screen, mouse, a hard disk for data storage and a printer and scanner. This computer is likely be linked to the internet by telephone line. This type of system is useful for a small business when only one person needs to operate the computer at any one time.

networks (intranet)

A network (see diagram below) comprises a number of computer workstations linked to a central server (which holds all the data) and other

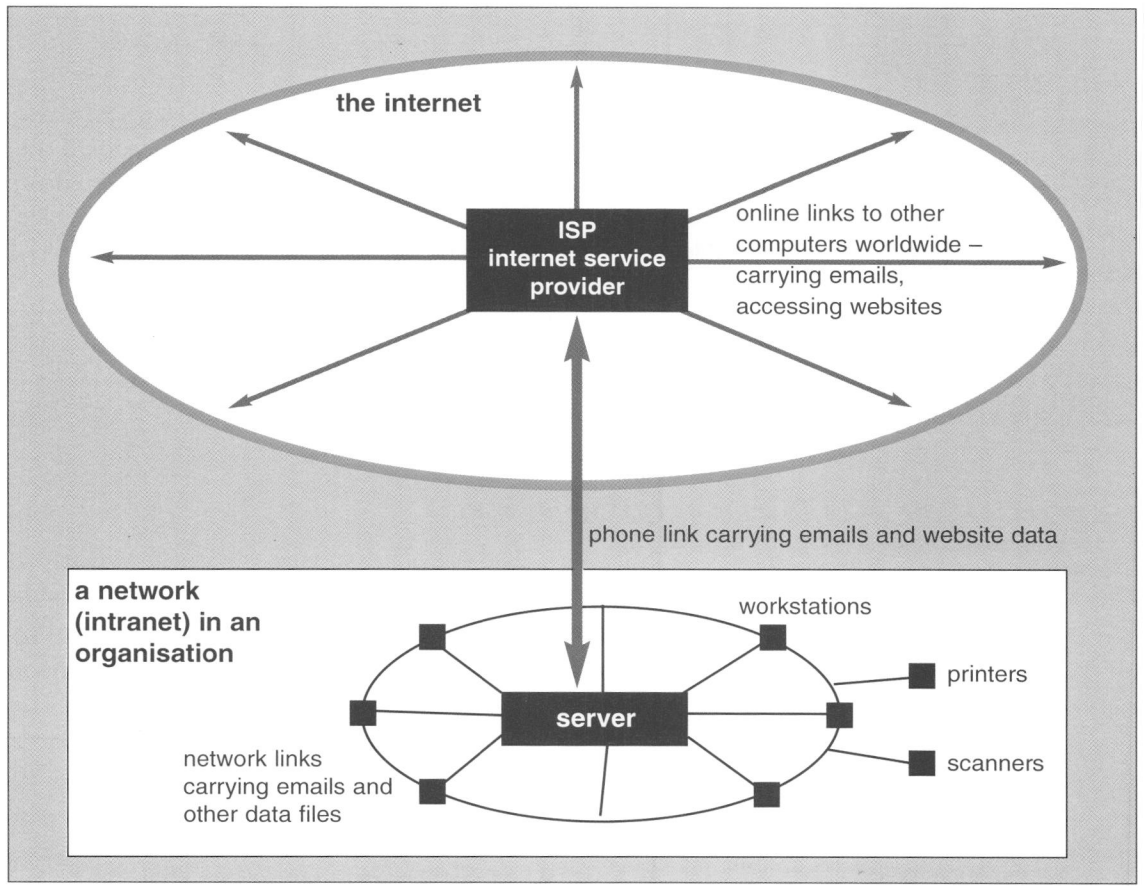

equipment such as printers and scanners – this type of system is likely to be used by a larger business or organisation (such as a College IT centre) where a number of operators need to access the system at the same time.

Data – including financial data from a computer accounting program – can be exchanged through the network and internal emails can be sent. This set-up is also known as an **intranet**. The system can also be linked up by phone line to an external internet service provider (ISP) so that the **internet** can be accessed and external emails sent and received.

printers

All computer systems need a printer to produce 'hard copy' such as letters, financial documents and management reports. The old-fashioned form of printer is the dot matrix printer which prints text as a series of dots using a printer head with pins. This is useful if you need multiple copies of documents such as invoices: the pins strike the paper with some force and can print the characters through a number of sheets of paper. If better quality printing is required an inkjet or laser printer can be used, but these types only print one copy at a time. They are also less noisy!

data storage and backup

It is very important that the data held by the computer is backed up regularly and stored away from the premises or transmitted to another location. Data can be backed up onto a variety of storage media, eg floppy disk, Zip disk, tape and CD. All systems should therefore have some form of data storage facility or be able to transmit data to another location.

COMPUTER SOFTWARE

Windows operating systems

The program – the software – that makes a computer work is known as the operating system. Most business computers are PCs (personal computers) which run the Windows operating system which is a Microsoft product. The main types of program used in business are:

■ word processing

■ databases

■ spreadsheets

■ email managers

■ accounting packages

Standard 'off-the-shelf' accounting programs such as Sage Line 50 are also designed for use on Windows, and it is this system which we will refer to and illustrate when explaining computer accounting in this chapter.

Before describing computer packages in detail we will first look at the computer spreadsheet, which is not only useful for handling data such as sales figures, but can also be adapted to handle the book-keeping entries.

SPREADSHEETS

A spreadsheet is a grid of boxes – 'cells' – set up on the computer, organised in rows and columns into which you can enter text and numbers. It enables you to make calculations with the figures. The computer program will work out the calculations automatically once you have entered an appropriate formula in the cell where the result of the calculations is required.

The major advantage of a spreadsheet is that if you change any of the figures the computer will automatically recalculate the total, saving you much time and effort.

Spreadsheets are used for a variety of functions in organisations:

- producing invoices – working out costs of products sold, calculating and adding on VAT and producing a sales total
- working out budgets for future expenditure
- working out sales figures for different products or areas

A commonly used spreadsheet program is Microsoft Excel. The example below shows regional sales figures input into Excel. Note that the rows are numbered and the columns have letter references. The total sales figure appears in the cell (box) which therefore has the reference of B11.

	A	B	C	D	E	F	G
1	REGIONAL SALES						
2							
3		AREA A	AREA B	AREA C			
4		£	£	£			
5							
6	January – March	67987	32423	54342			
7	April –June	83792	38383	62627			
8	July–September	76352	29872	54664			
9	October–December	87383	30982	52420			
10	Total Sales by Area	315514	131660	224053			
11	Total Sales	671227					

Regional Sales

producing graphs and charts

Another function of the spreadsheet is its ability to produce graphs and charts from the figures in the spreadsheet grid.

All that you need to do is to select the appropriate figures (see upper screen) and the computer does the rest through its charting function.

The bar chart produced is shown on the lower screen.

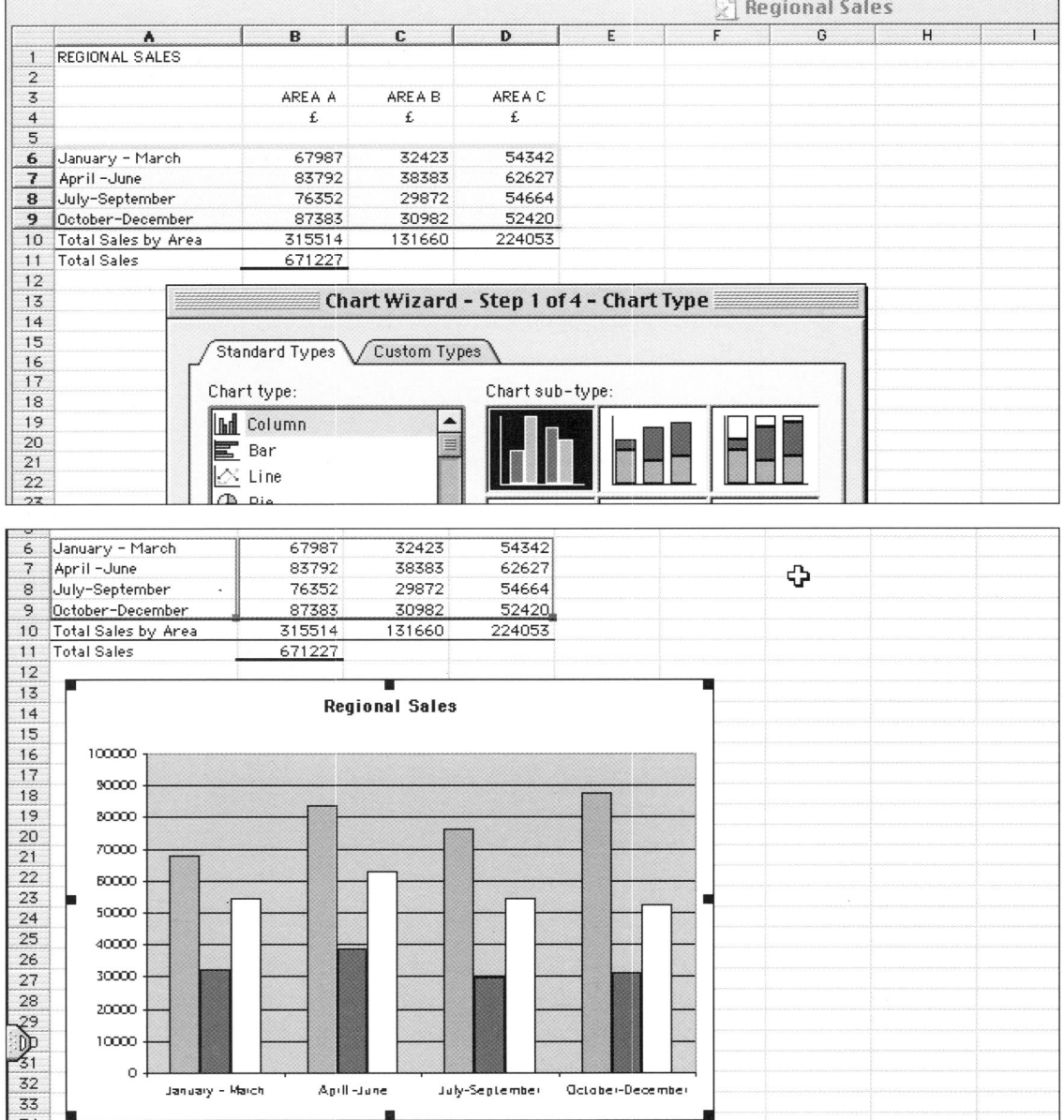

COMPUTER ACCOUNTING PROGRAMS

Although some organisations, particularly small businesses, still use paper-based accounting systems, an increasing number are now operating computerised accounting systems. Small and medium-sized businesses can buy 'off-the-shelf' accounting programs from suppliers such as Sage while larger businesses often have custom-designed programs. Computer accounting programs are easy to use and can automate operations such as invoicing which take so much time and effort in a manual system.

facilities

A typical computer accounting program will offer a number of facilities:

- on-screen input and printout of sales invoices and credit notes
- automatic updating of customer accounts with sales transactions
- recording of suppliers' invoices
- automatic updating of supplier accounts with details of purchases
- recording of money paid into the bank
- recording of payments to suppliers and for expenses

Payroll can also be computerised – normally using a separate program.

management reports

A computer accounting program can provide instant reports for management, for example:

- an aged debtors' summary – showing who owes you what and for what periods of time
- activity reports on customer and supplier accounts
- activity reports on expenses accounts
- VAT Return

advantages of a computer accounting program

Computer accounting programs are popular because they offer a number of distinct advantages over paper-based systems. They

- save time
- save money
- tend to be more accurate because they rely on single-entry input (one amount per transaction) rather than double-entry book-keeping
- provide the managers of the organisation with a clear and up-to-date picture of what is happening

computer accounting and ledgers

As we have seen in the last two chapters, the 'ledgers' of a business are basically the books of the business. 'The ledgers' is a term used to describe the way the accounts of a business are grouped into different sections.

To recap, there are four main ledgers in a traditional accounting system:

- **sales ledger** contains the accounts of debtors (customers)
- **purchases ledger** contains the accounts of creditors (suppliers)
- **cash book** contains the main cash book and the petty cash book
- **nominal ledger** (also called general or main ledger) contains the remaining accounts, eg expenses (including purchases), income (including sales), assets, loans, stock, VAT

A diagram illustrating these ledgers is shown on the next page. The structure of a computer accounting system is based on these ledgers. It may also include stock control and be linked to a payroll processing program.

A ledger-based computer accounting system is designed to be user-friendly in Windows software. You will already have seen the diagram below in the last chapter. Study the toolbar of the opening screen of the Sage Windows accounting system and read the notes printed underneath.

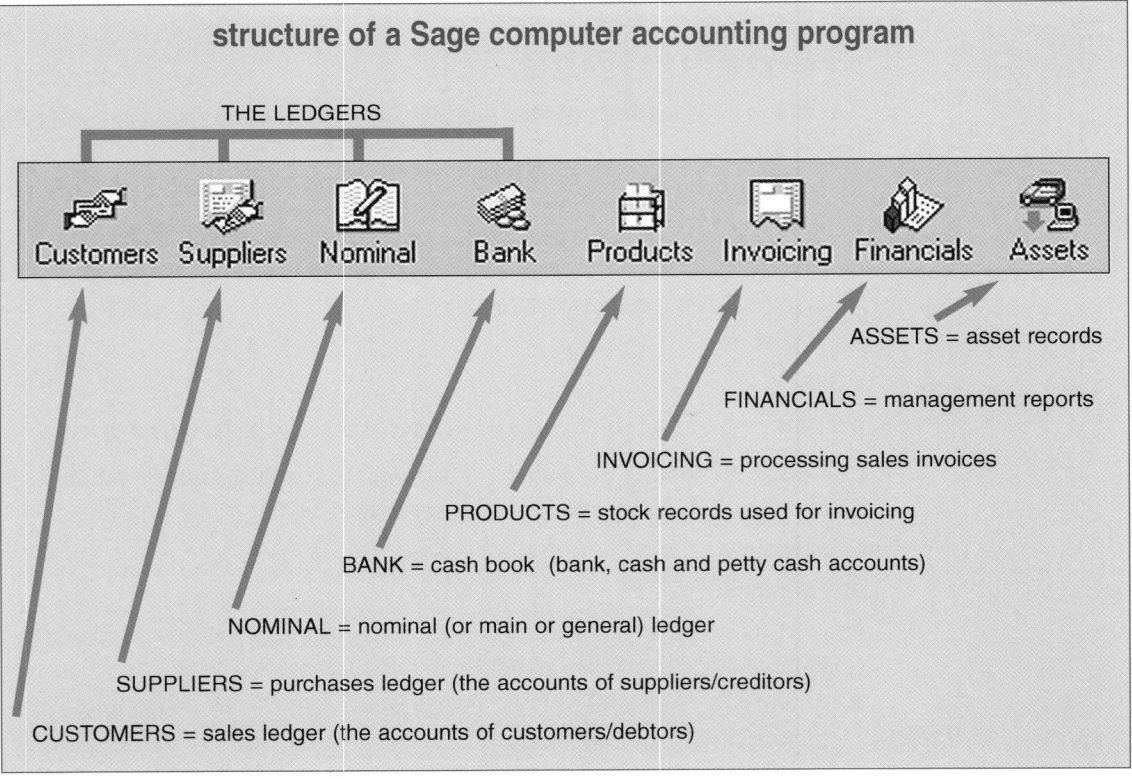

structure of a Sage computer accounting program

THE LEDGERS

Customers Suppliers Nominal Bank Products Invoicing Financials Assets

ASSETS = asset records

FINANCIALS = management reports

INVOICING = processing sales invoices

PRODUCTS = stock records used for invoicing

BANK = cash book (bank, cash and petty cash accounts)

NOMINAL = nominal (or main or general) ledger

SUPPLIERS = purchases ledger (the accounts of suppliers/creditors)

CUSTOMERS = sales ledger (the accounts of customers/debtors)

computerised ledgers – an integrated system

Before we look at the various functions on the toolbar, it is important to appreciate that a computerised ledger system is **fully integrated**. This means that when a business transaction is input on the computer it is normally recorded in two accounts at the same time, although only one amount is entered. Take the three transactions shown in the diagram below:

- a business buys from a supplier on credit (ie the business gets the goods but will pay later)

- a business sells to a customer on credit (ie the business sells the goods but will receive payment later)

- a business pays an advertising bill by cheque

At the centre of an integrated program is the nominal ledger which deals with all the accounts except customers' accounts and suppliers' accounts. It is affected one way or another by most transactions.

The diagram below shows how the three 'ledgers' can link with the nominal ledger. Note how an account in the nominal ledger is affected by each of these three transactions. This is the double-entry book-keeping system at work. The advantage of the computer system is that in each case only one entry has to be made. Life is made a great deal simpler by this!

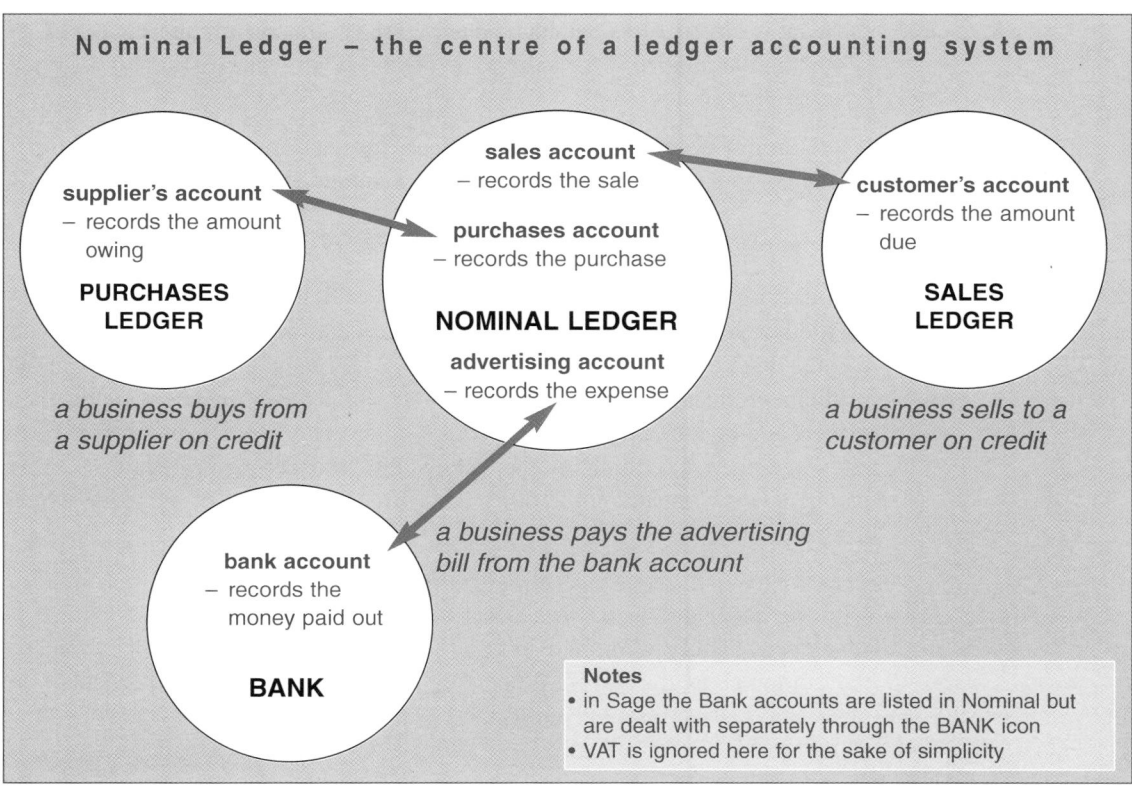

Nominal Ledger – the centre of a ledger accounting system

supplier's account – records the amount owing
PURCHASES LEDGER
a business buys from a supplier on credit

sales account – records the sale
purchases account – records the purchase
NOMINAL LEDGER
advertising account – records the expense

customer's account – records the amount due
SALES LEDGER
a business sells to a customer on credit

bank account – records the money paid out
BANK
a business pays the advertising bill from the bank account

Notes
- in Sage the Bank accounts are listed in Nominal but are dealt with separately through the BANK icon
- VAT is ignored here for the sake of simplicity

MANUAL OR ELECTRONIC INPUT?

manual input

Input into a computer accounting package is normally made direct on screen from source documents or other data. Typical transactions which form the 'bread and butter' of computer accounting input include:

- processing **sales invoices**, often in runs of several transactions known as 'batches' – the invoices are either written or typed out before input or, if a more advanced computer package is used, they can be input and printed out by the computer

- inputting **credit notes** from customers' debit notes or from authorised documentation which says why the credit note has to be issued and a refund made – again the credit notes may be produced separately and used as a basis for input, or they may be printed out by the computer

- inputting **bank receipts** (money paid into the bank) – for example cheques or BACS payments received from customers in settlement of accounts due; the source document in this case is the remittance advice which comes with the cheque or advises the BACS payment

- inputting details of new **customer accounts** – this is the input of text onto what is effectively a database screen in the computer accounting package; this might happen if the sales team has been very successful and obtained a number of new sales

There are, of course, many other types of transactions which you will input on the computer, but these are common examples.

electronic input and electronic trading

If you examine the mechanics of two computer-based businesses trading with each other you will often see an extraordinary combination of nineteenth and twenty-first century commercial practices. The financial data of the business selling a product is output in the form of a printed paper invoice which is then placed in an envelope and posted to the buyer who gets it a number of days later and then has to input the details into the computer (again) so that payment can be made on the due date – often in the form of a cheque which is again put in the post.

The twenty-first century solution to this problem is for the seller to link up with the buyer online and for electronic trading to take place: the invoice is sent electronically, often in response to an electronic purchase order, direct to the computer of the buyer. When the due date for payment is reached, an electronic instruction is given to the buyer's bank and a payment sent to the seller's bank – electronically.

So why are only a few businesses trading electronically? It is partly a problem of the cost of the equipment and software and partly a problem of compatibility of equipment and software. It is often the case of the biggest businesses calling the tune and dictating the systems that have to be used.

a guided tour

In this book we will assume that the trading is done using paper documentation. In the next few pages we will illustrate the main functions within a Sage computer accounting package. As you read this you will appreciate how computer accounting takes the 'hard slog' out of manual book-keeping. We will illustrate in turn the various functions on the main program toolbar:

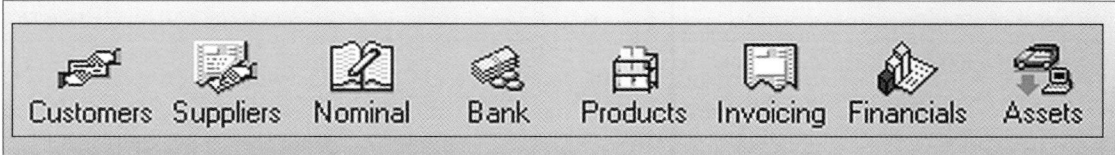

CUSTOMERS

'Customers' on the toolbar represents the sales ledger – the accounts of customers to whom the business sells its products.

The toolbar of 'Customers' is shown below.

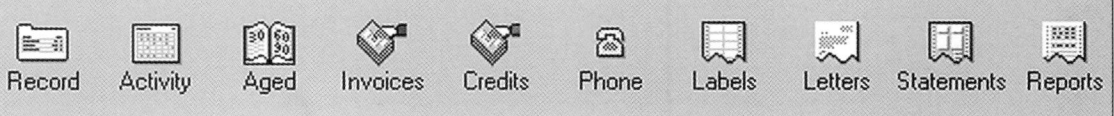

As you can see, there are a number of icons representing facilities available in 'Customers':

■ **Record** brings up the screen which enables you to add, view and edit customer names and addresses. A typical record screen is shown at the top of the next page.

■ **Activity** shows you the transactions – invoices, credit notes, payments – which have taken place on individual customer accounts.

■ **Aged** produces an aged debtors' summary, a list of customer account balances showing which accounts have been outstanding for 30 days, 60 days, 90 days or more. This is very useful in credit control (chasing up money that the business is owed).

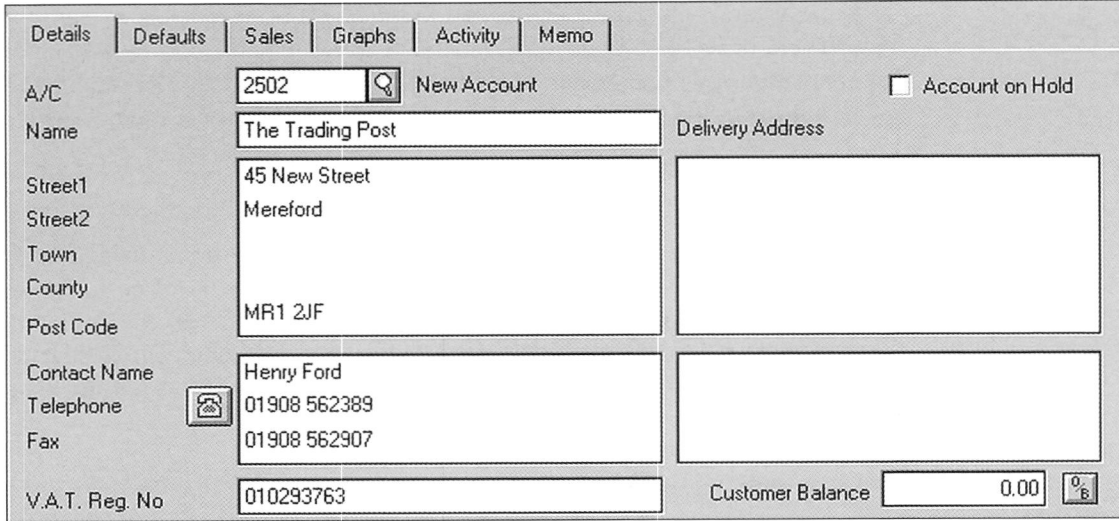

a customer screen

■ **Invoices** and **Credits** enable you to post to customer accounts invoices or credit notes that you have prepared by hand and which have not been generated by the computer accounting program. It is not used for producing documents which can be printed out.

■ If the computer is on-line, **Phone** enables the computer to dial automatically any customer you select from the screen.

■ **Labels**, **Letters**, **Statements** and **Reports** enable you to print these documents for any customers that you select. You may, for example, want to send chaser letters to customers whose accounts are overdue. If the computer has a standard letter text on file, mailmerged letters can be printed out automatically.

SUPPLIERS

'Suppliers' on the toolbar represents the purchases ledger – the accounts of suppliers from whom the business buys its materials and stock.

The toolbar of 'Suppliers' is shown below.

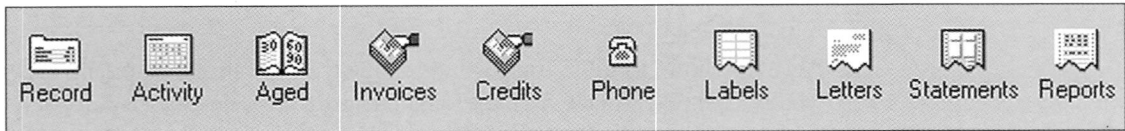

You will see that the icons on the Suppliers toolbar are exactly the same as the items on the 'Customers' toolbar and provide similar facilities. The supplier record screen is shown on the next page.

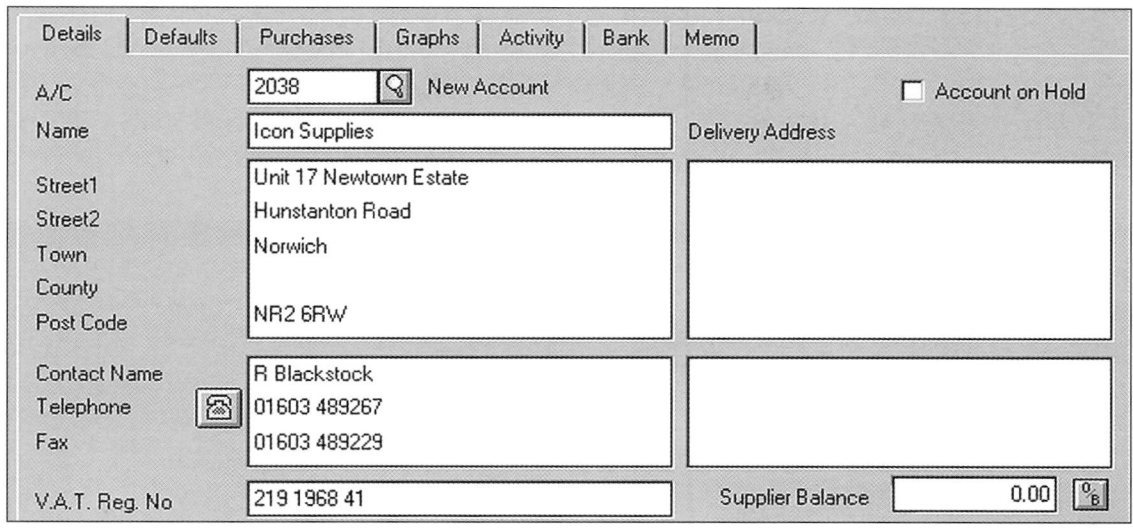

a supplier screen

NOMINAL

The Nominal icon on the opening toolbar represents the Nominal Ledger. Click on it and the Nominal Ledger toolbar will appear.

Remember that the Nominal Ledger contains many of the commonly used accounts, eg sales, purchases, expense accounts, assets, loans, capital, VAT.

■ **Record**, as with 'Customers' and 'Suppliers,' contains details of the accounts held. Most computer accounting programs will be supplied with the nominal accounts that you will need already installed and ready for use; these are known as the 'default accounts' and can be used or changed as you wish.

■ **Activity** provides details of the transactions on the individual accounts.

■ **Journals** allows you to make debit and credit journal entries (double-entry adjustments) between nominal accounts.

■ **Prepayments** and **Accruals** allow the accounts to be adjusted for prepaid bills (prepayments) or bills paid in arrears (accruals) so that the expense appears in the Profit and Loss Account for the correct period.

■ **Accounts** provides you with a 'Chart of Accounts' which places the nominal accounts in the correct part of the Ledger so that reports such as the Profit and Loss Account can be printed out with the accounts in the right section. When you set up the computer accounting system for the first time, the nominal accounts are normally already set up in the right place. Look at the illustration of the 'Chart of Accounts' below.

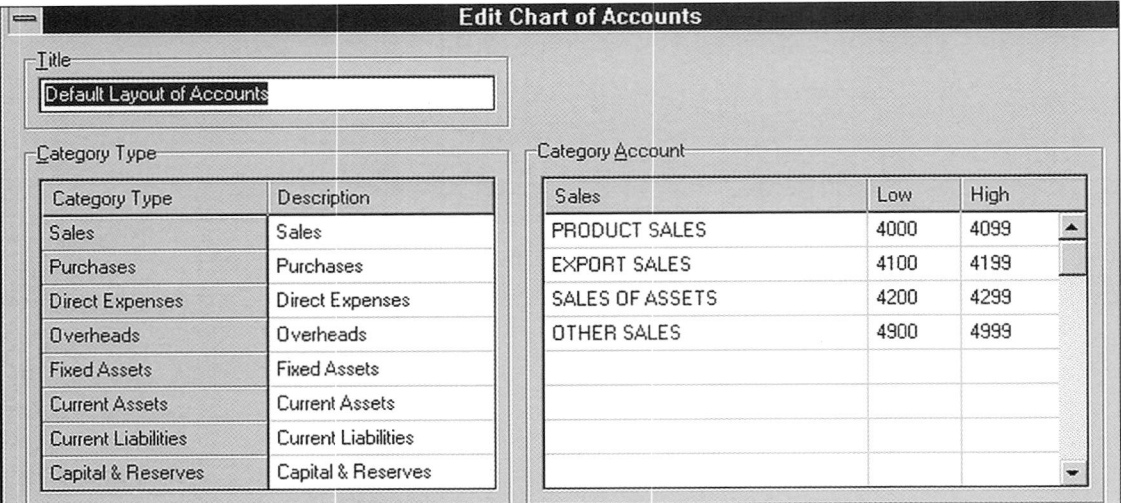

■ **Reports** available in the Nominal Ledger include budget and performance reports.

BANK

The bank icon on the opening toolbar enables you to process payments in and out of the bank account. It also enables you to carry out some of the regular accounting procedures involving the bank, such as reconciling the bank statement and making regular standing order payments.

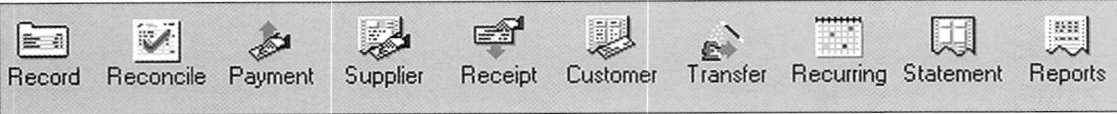

■ **Record** enables you to set up new bank accounts and edit existing ones
■ **Supplier** should be selected when you are making a payment for an outstanding invoice on an account in the purchases ledger
■ **Customer** should be selected when you are receiving payment into the bank account from one of your customers in the sales ledger

■ **Payment** and **receipt** are used to record payments you make and money received which do not involve invoices or which are cash (ie non-credit) transactions.

Note that when you input these payment and receipt transactions you are asked by the computer to enter a nominal account code which will analyse the payment for you, eg code 7211 when you pay a gas bill, 4900 when you receive interest on the bank account. The screen below shows a typical bank payment being made, in this case payment on Stationery Account 7500.

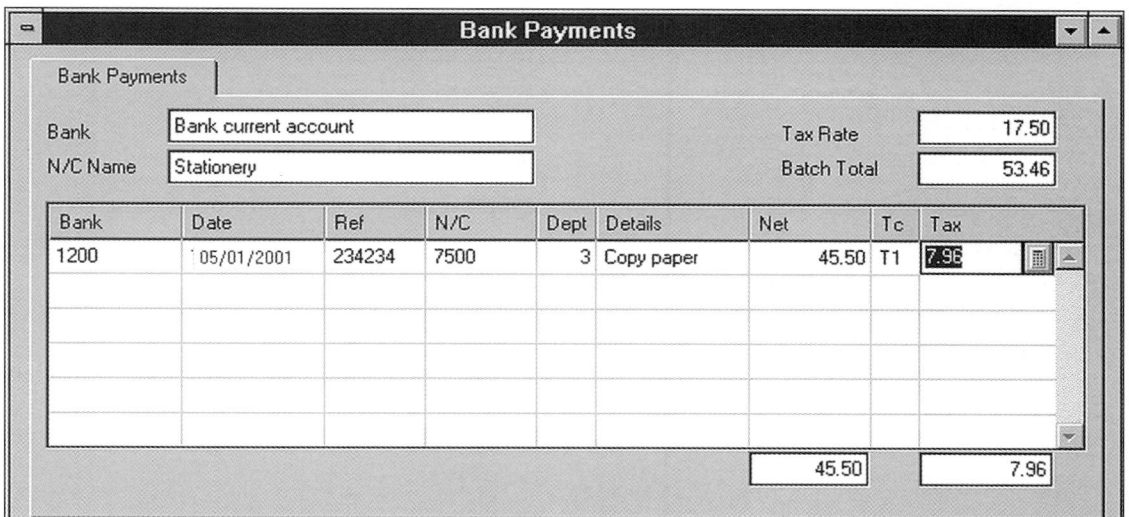

The other icons on the bank toolbar are straightforward. **Reconcile** enables you to agree the accounting records with the bank statement, **Transfer** enables you to carry out transfers between different bank accounts, **Recurring** enables you to process regular payments such as standing orders, **Statement** gives an up-to-date list of transactions on any of your bank accounts, and **Reports** provides summaries of payments and receipts.

PRODUCTS

The Products facility enables you to see what you have in stock and what has been sold.

The Products toolbar is shown below.

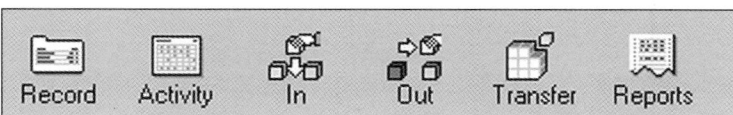

■ **Record** shows a screen which provides information about each item of stock. Each stock item is given a specific stock code and can be given a category number. Look at the screen shown below.

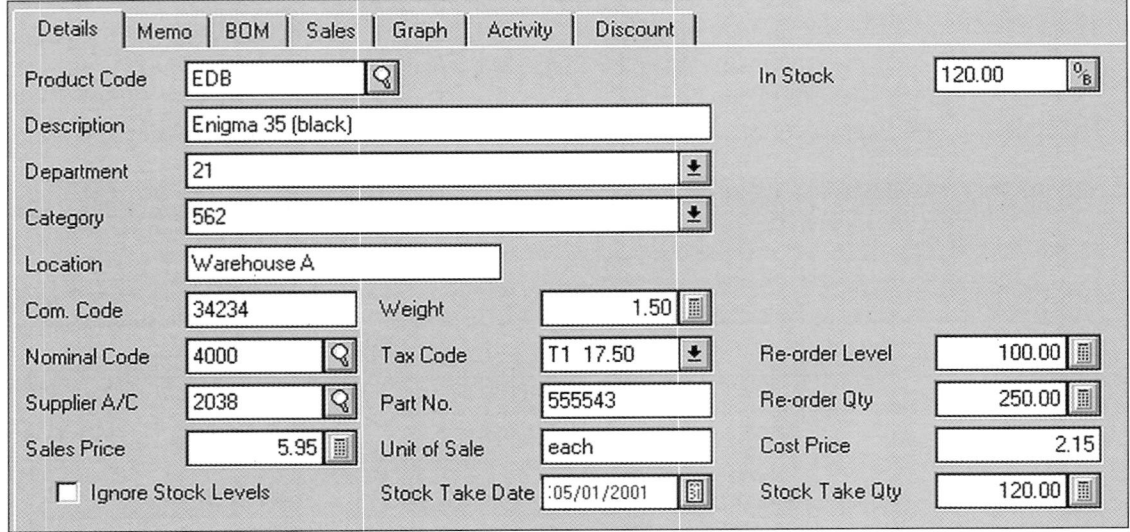

■ **Activity** enables you to view all the transactions for each stock code – eg sales, returns.

■ **In** and **Out** and **Transfer** enable you to adjust the recorded level of stock in situations which do not involve purchases or sales, eg writing off stock which has been flood damaged in the warehouse, adjusting the stock level following a stock count which shows that you have more stock than you thought.

■ **Reports** provide useful information such as stock levels, stock valuation, profits on sales of individual items.

INVOICING

Invoicing will allow you to enter invoice details on the computer screen and then to print out the invoices. Many businesses process invoices (and other documents) in batches: they will input a group (batch) of invoices and then print them out together in one run, ready for checking. The Invoicing toolbar is shown below.

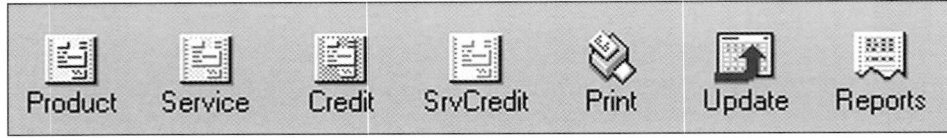

The toolbar shows that you can produce a **Product** invoice for an item sold which has a specific product code. If you are invoicing something which has no product code, for example a service or a 'one-off' item you use a **Service** invoice. The invoicing function **Credit** also allows you to produce credit notes for items such as returns. The function **SrvCredit** allows you to produce credit notes for service invoices, eg a refund for an overcharged service provided.

It is important to appreciate that invoicing is a function which requires a high degree of accuracy; it follows a number of distinct stages, many of which adjust other records held in the computer, and all of which require careful checking:

- input of details on screen – this uses data from the Customers file and the Products file

- printout of invoices, normally in batches with the **Print** function

- checking of invoices which have been printed out, both against the original documentation and a Day Book, which can be printed out from the **Reports** function to provide a listing of the input

- updating the ledgers in the Customer files with the **Update** function when all the invoices are found to be correct (or have been corrected) – this will post the invoice to the customer's account (Customers), reduce the level shown in the stock records (Products), and increase the amount shown in the Sales Account (Nominal)

An example of an invoice input screen is shown below; the printed invoice from this screen is illustrated on the next page.

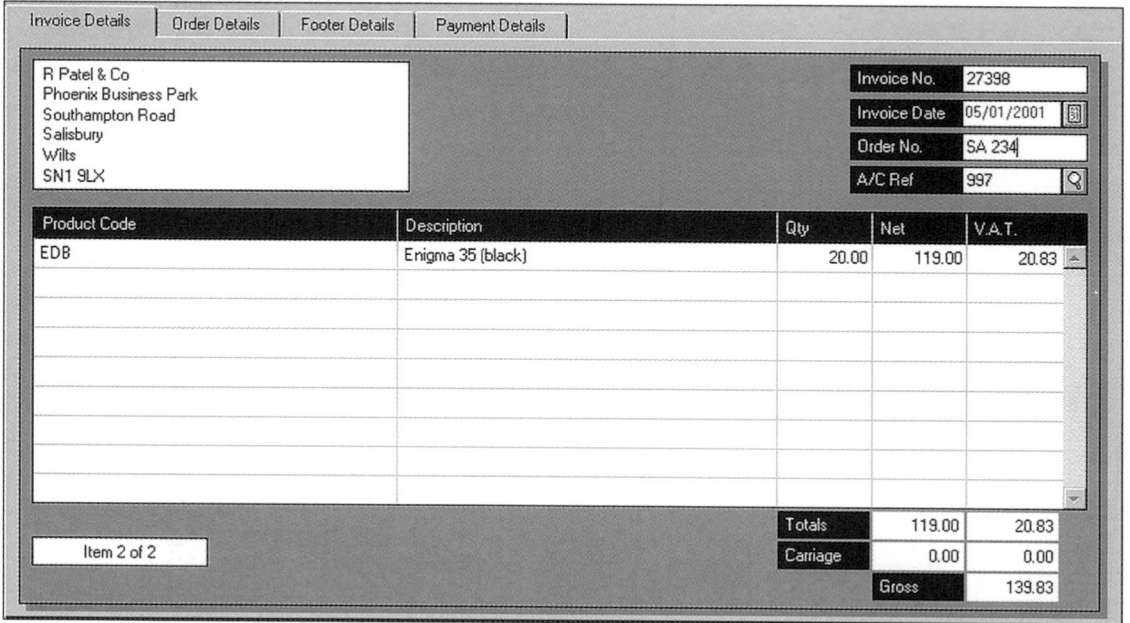

Enigma Limited

34 Packhorse Road
Mereford MR2 7YH
Tel 01908 433927 Fax 01908 433812 email edgar@goblin.co.uk
VAT Reg 727 7262 01

INVOICE

R Patel & Co
Phoenix Business Park
Southampton Road
Salisbury
Wilts
SN1 9LX

invoice no.	27398
invoice date	05/01/2001
order no.	SA234
account ref.	997

quantity	description	discount %	net amount	VAT amount
20	Enigma 35 (black)	0.00	119.00	20.83

Payment 30 days net

Total net	119.00
Total tax	20.83
Carriage	00.00
Invoice total	139.83

FINANCIAL REPORTS AND ASSET RECORDS

financials

The remaining icons on the main toolbar include **Financials** and **Assets**. Financials provides a variety of financial reports and statements, including

- the trial balance
- a profit statement and a balance sheet
- an on-screen VAT Return
- an audit trail (a comprehensive list of transactions – often needed by the accountant)

Because the computer produces these reports, statements and lists automatically, the business is saved much time and money. A typical VAT Return screen is shown below.

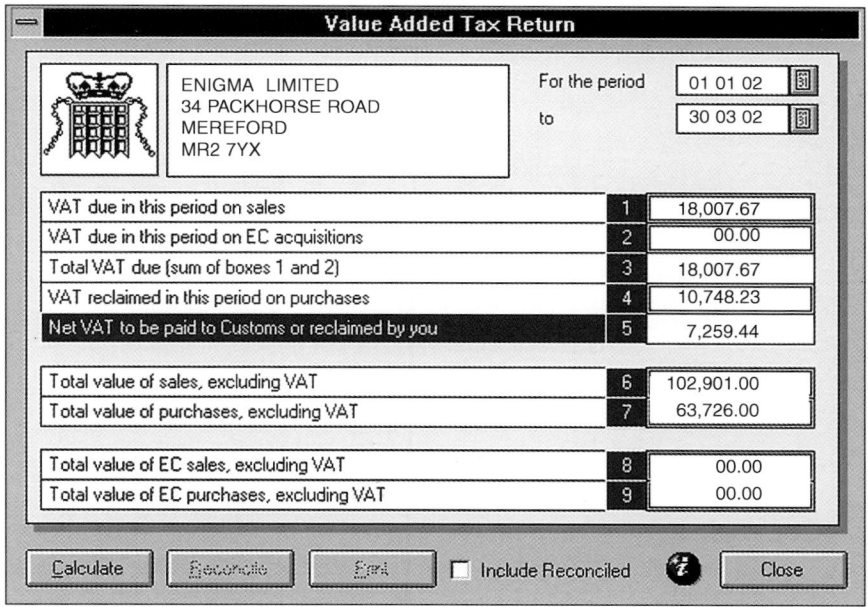

assets

These are fixed assets such as cars and computers, owned by the business. The asset records keep track of details such as cost, serial (or registration) number and date of purchase, all of which are needed by the business for accounting and insurance purposes.

COMPUTER ACCOUNTING SECURITY

The operation of a computer accounting program needs careful supervision and management by the business for two main reasons:

- **danger of fraud** – if someone gains unauthorised access to the system they could steal from the business by, for example, making large salary payments to a bank account and then pocketing the money

- **backing up** – if the data on the system is not backed up regularly and kept safely both on and off the premises, there could be a total loss of data if there was, for example, a fire or theft of the equipment

A number of sensible precautions can be taken to protect the business against these disasters.

the use of passwords

Most computer accounting programs require the user to key in the correct password before data can be accessed and transactions posted. The password should be known only by those staff authorised to use the program. The computer accounting program allows the password to be changed from time to time, and it is advisable to do this at regular intervals, although how often will vary, depending on the size of the business and the number of accounting staff.

It is also possible, when a number of employees use the accounting program, for different passwords to be issued for different functions and different levels of access to the system.

backing up procedures

It is a normal task in computer 'housekeeping' procedure to take back-up copies of all data files. Data can be stored on any reliable storage medium, eg floppy disk, Zip disk or writeable CD. At the end of each day when all the data files have been backed up, the back-up copy should be placed in a fire-proof safe for overnight storage or taken off-site by authorised staff.

Many businesses operate a set of five back-up disks so that, at any one time, they have a record of all the changes made to files in the last working week. At the end of each day, the oldest back-up is taken out and the latest files saved to it (and the date changed on the label). At the end of each month the end-of-month routines may be run and so it is advisable to keep a set of pre-update and post-update back-ups, ie a copy of the data before and after the routines.

At the end of each financial year, it is normal practice to keep a set of year-end disks, as they may be needed for audit purposes.

chapter summary

● Computer accounting systems save businesses time and money by automating many accounting processes, including the production of reports for management.

● Computer accounting systems can be set up on:
  - a single 'standalone' computer
  - a linked network of computer workstations linked to a server

● Most computer accounting programs are based on the Ledger system and integrate a number of different functions – one transaction will change the data in a number of different parts of the system.

● The different functions can include:
  - Customers – the sales ledger
  - Suppliers – purchases ledger
  - Nominal ledger – all the main accounts of the system
  - Bank – payments in and out
  - Products – stock control
  - Invoicing
  - Reports
  - Asset records

● An essential part of a computer accounting system is an efficient back-up and password procedure.

key terms

intranet	an internal linked network within an organisation
spreadsheet	a computer program designed for processing numerical data arranged in rows and columns – a powerful tool for preparing and presenting information
integrated system	a computer accounting system which generates two entries in the accounts each time an entry is made on screen
electronic trading	generation of documents on the computer, online transmission and computer-based payments
chart of accounts	the structure of the accounts in the nominal section of a computer accounting system, which enables the computer to produce reports based on those accounts

activities

a full-length Sage-based processing exercise is available free on the Osborne Books website: www.osbornebooks.co.uk – please call 01905 748071 if you need access details.

SOLE TRADER FINAL ACCOUNTS

CASE STUDY
Starting out in business

Olivia Boulton used to work as a buyer of kitchen and cookware goods for a large department store in central London. She was good at her job and knew the type of goods that sold well.

Two years ago, Olivia took the decision to set up in business on her own, selling a range of kitchen and cookware goods designed and manufactured in Italy. She decided to set up as a sole trader rather than taking on a partner or forming a limited company. She wanted the freedom of being her own boss, although she knew the financial risks involved in 'going it alone'.

In her first year of trading Olivia identified suitable rented premises in her home town of Brighton. She liked the premises so much that a year later she took the option of buying them and refitting the shop – all with the help of a bank loan.

Business has gone well since opening day. In fact, as well as selling to shop customers, she has also built up a small amount of wholesale trade, where she sells imported kitchen goods to other shops.

Now that the business is well established, Olivia feels that it is time she understood financial matters rather better. She employs a book-keeper to deal with day-to-day transactions and to write up the books. She has also taken on an accountant to prepare her year-end financial statements and deal with the tax calculations based on the profit she has made.

But she wants to know more about these financial statements: the trading and profit and loss account and the balance sheet . . .

learning objectives

When you have studied this chapter you will be able to:

■ understand the format of final accounts for sole traders

■ prepare final accounts for sole trader businesses from the book-keeper's trial balance

■ understand the link between double-entry book-keeping and final accounts

■ distinguish between capital expenditure and revenue expenditure

SOLE TRADERS

Sole traders are people who are in business on their own: they run shops, factories, farms, garages, local franchises, etc. The businesses are generally small because the owner usually has a limited amount of capital to invest. Profits are often small and, after the owner has taken out drawings, are usually ploughed back into the business.

People set up as sole traders for various reasons:

- the owner has independence and can run the business, by and large, without the need to involve others in decision making
- in a small business with few, if any, employees, personal service and supervision by the owner are available at all times
- the business is easy to establish legally – either using the owner's name, or a trading name such as 'Wyvern Plumbing Services'

The disadvantages of a sole-trader business are:

- the owner has unlimited liability for the debts of the business – this means that if the sole trader should become insolvent (unable to pay debts when they are due), the owner's personal assets may be sold to pay creditors
- expansion is limited because it can only be achieved by the owner ploughing back profits, or by borrowing from a lender such as a bank
- the owner usually has to work long hours and it may be difficult to find time to take holidays; if the owner should become ill the work of the business will either slow down or stop altogether

FINAL ACCOUNTS AND THE TRIAL BALANCE

final accounts

The final accounts (or financial statements) of a sole trader comprise:

- a **trading and profit and loss account** which shows the profit or loss of the business
- a **balance sheet**, which shows the assets and liabilities of the business together with the owner's capital

These final accounts can be produced more often than once a year in order to give information to the owner on how the business is progressing. However, it is customary to produce annual accounts for the benefit of the Inland Revenue, bank manager and other interested parties. In this way the trading and profit and loss account covers an accounting period of a financial year (which can end at any date – it doesn't have to be the calendar year), and the balance sheet shows the state of the business at the end of the accounting period.

trading and profit and loss account

income   minus   **expenses**   equals   **net profit (or loss)**

The trading and profit and loss account shows the income a business has received over a given period for goods sold or services provided (together with any small amounts of other income, eg rent received). It also sets out the expenses incurred – the cost of the product, and the overheads (eg wages, administration expenses, rent, and so on). The difference between income and expenses is the **net profit** of the business. If expenses are greater than income, then a loss has been made. The net profit (or loss) belongs to the owner(s) of the business.

balance sheet

assets   minus   **liabilities**   equals   **capital**

A balance sheet gives a 'snapshot' of the business at a particular date – the end of the financial year. A typical business balance sheet will show:

assets
What the business owns:
- fixed assets, eg premises, vehicles, computers
- current assets, eg stock of goods for resale, debtors (money owed by customers), bank and cash balances

liabilities
What the business owes:
- current liabilities, eg creditors, overdrafts, VAT due
- long-term liabilities, eg long-term bank loans

net assets
The total of fixed and current assets, less current and long-term liabilities. The net assets are financed by the owner(s) of the business, in the form of capital. Net assets therefore equals the total of the 'financed by' section – the balance sheet 'balances'.

capital
Where the money to finance the business has come from, eg the owner's investment, business profits.

TRIAL BALANCE

The starting point for preparing final accounts is the trial balance prepared by the book-keeper: all the figures recorded on the trial balance are used in the final accounts. The trading account and the profit and loss account are both 'accounts' in terms of double-entry book-keeping. By contrast, the balance sheet is not an account, but is simply a statement of account balances remaining after the trading and profit and loss accounts have been prepared.

To help us with the preparation of final accounts we will use the trial balance, shown in the Case Study on the next page. The trial balance has been produced by the book-keeper at the end of the financial year. In the Case Study we will present the final accounts:

■ before adjustments for items such as accruals, prepayments, bad debts and depreciation – these will be covered in the next chapter

■ in vertical format, ie in the column format used by accountants

On page 111 we will look at the double-entry book-keeping for amounts entered in the trading and profit and loss accounts.

CASE STUDY

Final accounts of Olivia Boulton from the trial balance

situation

Olivia Boulton runs a kitchen and cookware shop in Brighton. Her book-keeper has just extracted the year-end trial balance shown below and has drafted provisional final accounts for discussion with the accountant.

Note that the trial balance includes the stock value at the start of the year, while the end-of-year stock valuation is given after the trial balance. For the purposes of financial accounting, the stock of goods for resale is valued by the business at the end of each financial year, and the valuation is subsequently entered into the book-keeping system.

Trial balance of Olivia Boulton, as at 31 December 2002

	Dr £	Cr £
Stock at 1 January 2002	50,000	
Purchases	420,000	
Sales		557,500
Shop expenses	6,200	
Wages	33,500	
Rent paid	750	
Telephone expenses	500	
Interest paid	4,500	
Travel expenses	550	
Premises	200,000	
Shop fittings	40,000	
Debtors	10,100	
Bank	5,850	
Cash	50	
Capital		75,000
Drawings	27,000	
Loan from bank		150,000
Creditors		14,500
Value Added Tax		2,000
	799,000	799,000

Note: stock at 31 December 2002 was valued at £42,000

Trading account shows gross profit for the accounting period. **Profit and loss account** shows net profit for the accounting period. Note that 'profit and loss account' is often used as a general heading which includes both of these financial statements.

The amounts for **sales** and **purchases** include only items in which the business trades – eg a clothes shop buying clothes from the manufacturer and selling to the public. Note that items bought for use in the business, such as a new till for the shop, are not included with purchases but are shown as assets on the balance sheet.

Cost of sales represents the cost to the business of the goods which have been sold in this financial year. Cost of sales is:

	opening stock	(stock bought previously)
plus	purchases	(purchased during the year)
minus	closing stock	(stock left unsold at the end of the year)
equals	cost of sales	(cost of what has actually been sold)

Gross profit is calculated as:

sales – cost of sales = gross profit

If cost of sales is greater than sales, the business has made a gross loss.

Overheads, or expenses are the running costs of the business – known as *revenue expenditure*. The categories of overheads or expenses used vary according to the needs of each business.

Net profit is calculated as:

gross profit – overheads = net profit

If overheads are more than gross profit, the business has made a net loss.

The net profit is the amount the business earned for the owner during the year, and is subject to taxation. The owner can draw some or all of the net profit for personal use in the form of drawings. Part of the profit might well be left in the business in order to help build up the business for the future.

TRADING AND PROFIT AND LOSS ACCOUNT
of Olivia Boulton for the year ended 31 December 2002

	£	£
Sales		557,500
Opening stock (1 January 2002)	50,000	
Purchases	420,000	
	470,000	
Less Closing stock (31 December 2002)	42,000	
Cost of sales		428,000
Gross profit		129,500
Less overheads:		
Shop expenses	6,200	
Wages	33,500	
Rent paid	750	
Telephone expenses	500	
Interest paid	4,500	
Travel expenses	550	
		46,000
Net profit		83,500

Fixed assets comprise the long-term items owned by a business which are not bought with the intention of selling them off in the near future, eg premises, machinery, motor vehicles, office equipment, shop fittings, etc.

Current assets comprise short-term assets which change regularly, eg stock of goods for resale, debtors, bank balances and cash. These items will alter as the business trades, eg stock will be sold, or more will be bought; debtors will make payment to the business, or sales on credit will be made; the cash and bank balances will alter with the flow of money paid into the bank account, or as withdrawals are made.

Current liabilities are due for repayment within twelve months of the date of the balance sheet, eg creditors, and bank overdraft (which is repayable on demand, unlike a bank loan repayable over a period of years). VAT due to HM Customs & Excise is also listed as a current liability.

Working capital is the excess of current assets over current liabilities, ie current assets minus current liabilities = working capital. Without adequate working capital, a business will find it difficult to continue to operate. Working capital is also often referred to as *net current assets*.

Long-term liabilities are where repayment is due in more than one year from the date of the balance sheet; they are often described by terms such as 'bank loan,' 'long-term loan,' or 'mortgage.'

Net assets is the total of fixed and current assets, less current and long-term liabilities. The net assets are financed by the owner of the business, in the form of capital. Net assets therefore equals the total of the 'financed by' section – the balance sheet 'balances'.

Capital is the owner's investment, and is a liability of a business, ie it is what the business owes the owner.

BALANCE SHEET OF OLIVIA BOULTON

as at 31 December 2002

	£	£	£
Fixed Assets			
Premises			200,000
Shop fittings			40,000
			240,000
Current Assets			
Stock		42,000	
Debtors		10,100	
Bank		5,850	
Cash		50	
		58,000	
Less Current Liabilities			
Creditors	14,500		
Value Added Tax	2,000		
		16,500	
Working Capital			41,500
			281,500
Less Long-term Liabilities			
Loan from bank			150,000
NET ASSETS			131,500
FINANCED BY			
Capital			
Opening capital			75,000
Add net profit			83,500
			158,500
Less drawings			27,000
Closing capital			131,500

PREPARATION OF FINAL ACCOUNTS FROM A TRIAL BALANCE

The trial balance contains the basic figures necessary to prepare the final accounts but, as we shall see in the next section, the figures are transferred from the double-entry accounts of the business. Nevertheless, the trial balance is a suitable summary from which to prepare the final accounts. The information needed for the preparation of each of the final accounts needs to be picked out from the trial balance in the following way:

- go through the trial balance and write against the items the final account in which each appears
- 'tick' each figure as it is used – each item from the trial balance appears in the final accounts once only
- the year-end (closing) stock figure is not listed in the trial balance, but is shown as a note; the closing stock appears twice in the final accounts – firstly in the trading account, and secondly in the balance sheet (as a current asset)

If this routine is followed with the trial balance of Olivia Boulton, it appears as follows . . .

Trial balance of Olivia Boulton as at 31 December 2002				
	Dr	Cr		
	£	£		
Stock at 1 January 2002	50,000		T	✔
Purchases	420,000		T	✔
Sales		557,500	T	✔
Shop expenses	6,200		P & L (*expense*)	✔
Wages	33,500		P & L (*expense*)	✔
Rent paid	750		P & L (*expense*)	✔
Telephone	500		P & L (*expense*)	✔
Interest paid	4,500		P & L (*expense*)	✔
Travel expenses	550		P & L (*expense*)	✔
Premises	200,000		BS (*fixed asset*)	✔
Shop fittings	40,000		BS (*fixed asset*)	✔
Debtors	10,100		BS (*current asset*)	✔
Bank	5,850		BS (*current asset*)	✔
Cash	50		BS (*current asset*)	✔
Capital		75,000	BS (*capital*)	✔
Drawings	27,000		BS (*capital*)	✔
Loan from bank		150,000	BS (*long-term liability*)	✔
Creditors		14,500	BS (*current liability*)	✔
Value Added Tax		2,000	BS (*current liability*)	✔
	799,000	799,000		
Note: stock at 31 December 2002 was valued at £42,000			T	✔
			BS (*current asset*)	✔
Note: T = trading account; P & L = profit and loss account; BS = balance sheet				

DOUBLE-ENTRY BOOK-KEEPING AND FINAL ACCOUNTS

We have already noted earlier in this chapter that the trading and profit and loss account forms part of the double-entry book-keeping system. Therefore, each amount recorded in this account must have an opposite entry elsewhere in the accounting system. In preparing the trading and profit and loss account we are, in effect, emptying each account that has been storing up a record of the transactions of the business during the course of the financial year and transferring it to the trading and profit and loss account.

trading account

In the trading account of Olivia Boulton the balance of purchases account is transferred as follows (debit trading account; credit purchases account):

Dr		**Purchases Account**		Cr
2002		£	2002	£
31 Dec	Balance b/d (ie total for year)	420,000	31 Dec Trading account	420,000

The account now has a nil balance and is ready to receive the transactions for next year.

The balances of sales account (and also, where appropriate, sales returns and purchases returns account) will be cleared to nil in a similar way and the amounts transferred to trading account, as debits or credits as appropriate.

Stock account, however, is dealt with differently. Stock is valued for financial accounting purposes at the end of each year (it is also likely to be valued more regularly in order to provide management information). Only the annual stock valuation is recorded in stock account, and the account is not used at any other time. After the book-keeper has extracted the trial balance, but before preparation of the trading account, the stock account appears as follows:

Dr		**Stock Account**		Cr
2002		£	2002	£
1 Jan	Balance b/d	50,000		

This balance, which is the opening stock valuation for the year, is transferred to the trading account to leave a nil balance, as follows (debit trading account; credit stock account):

Dr			Stock Account			Cr
2002		£	2002			£
1 Jan	Balance b/d	50,000	31 Dec	Trading account		50,000

The closing stock valuation for the year – for Olivia Boulton it is £42,000 – is now recorded on the account as an asset (debit stock account; credit trading account):

Dr			Stock Account			Cr
2002		£	2002			£
1 Jan	Balance b/d	50,000	31 Dec	Trading account		50,000
31 Dec	Trading account	42,000	31 Dec	Balance c/d		42,000
2003						
1 Jan	Balance b/d	42,000				

The closing stock figure is shown on the balance sheet as a current asset, and will be the opening stock in next year's trading account.

profit and loss account

The overheads or expenses of running the business are transferred from the double-entry accounts to the profit and loss account. For example, the wages account of Olivia Boulton has been storing up information during the year and, at the end of the year, the total is transferred to profit and loss account (debit profit and loss account; credit wages account):

Dr			Wages Account		Cr
2002		£	2002		£
31 Dec	Balance b/d (ie total for year)	33,500	31 Dec	Profit and loss account	33,500

The wages account now has a nil balance and is ready to receive transactions for 2003, the next financial year.

net profit

After the profit and loss account has been completed, the amount of net profit (or net loss) is transferred to the owner's capital account. The book-keeping entries are:

- net profit:
  - debit profit and loss account
  - credit capital account
- net loss:
  - debit capital account
  - credit profit and loss account

A net profit increases the owner's stake in the business by adding to capital account, while a net loss decreases the owner's stake.

drawings

At the same time the account for drawings, which has been storing up the amount of drawings during the year is also transferred to capital account:
- debit capital account
- credit drawings account

In this way the total of drawings for the year is debited to capital account.

capital account

When these transactions are completed, the capital account of Olivia Boulton appears as:

Dr			Capital Account			Cr
2002		£	2002			£
31 Dec	Drawings for year	27,000	31 Dec	Balance b/d		75,000
31 Dec	Balance c/d	131,500	31 Dec	Profit and loss account		
				(net profit for year)		83,500
		158,500				158,500
2003			2003			
			1 Jan	Balance b/d		131,500

Note that it is the balance of capital account at the end of the year, ie £131,500, which forms the total for the capital section of the balance sheet. Although this figure could be shown on the balance sheet by itself, it is usual to show how it is calculated: capital at the start of the year *plus* net profit for the year, *minus* drawings for the year. In this way, the capital account is summarised on the balance sheet.

the balance sheet and double-entry

Unlike the trading and profit and loss account, the balance sheet is not part of the double-entry accounts. The balance sheet is made up of those accounts which remain with balances after the trading and profit and loss account transfers have been made. It consists of asset and liability accounts, the asset of closing stock, and the owner's capital and drawings.

SOLE TRADER FINAL ACCOUNTS: EXAMPLE LAYOUT

An example layout for the final accounts of a sole trader is reproduced in Appendix 2 and can also be downloaded from www.osbornebooks.co.uk. This format shows:

– an example layout for a trading and profit and loss account

– an example layout for a balance sheet

Note that when used for partnerships (see Chapter 10), the layout will need to be adjusted to take note of the appropriation of profits and of the partners' capital and current accounts.

ADDITIONAL ITEMS IN FINAL ACCOUNTS

As well as the adjustments to final accounts, there are a number of additional items that are shown in the trading and profit and loss account. These include:

- carriage in

- carriage out

- sales returns

- purchases returns

- discount received

- discount allowed

carriage in

This is the expense to a buyer of the carriage (transport) costs. For example, if an item is purchased by mail order, the buyer usually has to pay the additional cost of delivery.

In the trading account, the cost of carriage in is added to the cost of purchases. The reason for doing this is so that all purchases are at a 'delivered to your door' price.

carriage out

This is where the seller pays the expense of the carriage charge. For example, an item is sold to the customer and described as 'post free'.

In the profit and loss account, the cost of carriage out incurred on sales is shown as an expense of the business.

sales returns

Sales returns (or *returns in*) is where a debtor (a customer who has bought on credit) returns goods to the business. In final accounts, the amount of sales returns is deducted from the figure for sales in trading account.

purchases returns

Purchases returns (or *returns out*) is where a business returns goods to a creditor (a supplier).

In final accounts, the amount of purchases returns is deducted from the figure for purchases in trading account.

discount received

Discount received is an allowance offered by creditors on purchases invoice amounts for quick settlement, eg 2% cash discount for settlement within seven days.

In final accounts, the amount of discount received is shown in profit and loss account as income received.

discount allowed

This is an allowance offered to debtors on sales invoice amounts for quick settlement.

In final accounts, the amount of discount allowed is shown in profit and loss account as an expense.

CASE STUDY
Trading and profit and loss account – additional items

situation

An extract from the trial balance of Natasha Morgan, sole trader, is as follows:

Trial balance (extract) as at 30 June 2003

	Dr £	Cr £
Stock at 1 July 2002	12,350	
Sales		250,000
Purchases	156,000	
Sales returns	5,400	
Purchases returns		7,200
Carriage in	1,450	
Carriage out	3,250	
Discount received		2,500
Discount allowed	3,700	
Other expenses	78,550	

Note: stock at 30 June 2003 was valued at £16,300

Natasha asks for your help in the preparation of the trading and profit and loss account.

solution

There are a number of additional items to be incorporated into the layout of the trading and profit and loss account. In particular, the calculation of cost of sales is made in the following way:

    opening stock
    +   purchases
    +   carriage in
    –   purchases returns
    –   closing stock
    =   cost of sales

For Natasha Morgan's business, the trading and profit and loss account is as follows (note the use of three money columns):

TRADING AND PROFIT AND LOSS ACCOUNT OF NATASHA MORGAN

for the year ended 30 June 2003

	£	£	£
Sales			250,000
Less Sales returns			5,400
Net sales			244,600
Opening stock (1 July 2002)		12,350	
Purchases	156,000		
Add Carriage in	1,450		
	157,450		
Less Purchases returns	7,200		
Net purchases		150,250	
		162,600	
Less Closing stock (30 June 2003)		16,300	
Cost of sales			146,300
Gross profit			98,300
Add Discount received			2,500
			100,800
Less overheads:			
Discount allowed		3,700	
Other expenses		78,550	
Carriage out		3,250	
			85,500
Net profit			15,300

SERVICE SECTOR BUSINESSES

The final accounts of a service sector business – such as a secretarial agency, solicitor, estate agent, doctor – do not normally include a trading account. This is because the business, instead of trading in goods, supplies services. The final accounts of a service business consist of:

- profit and loss account
- balance sheet

The profit and loss account, instead of starting with gross profit from the trading account section, commences with the income from the business activity – such as 'fees', 'income from clients', 'charges', 'work done'. Other items of income – such as discount received – are added, and the overheads are then listed and deducted to give the net profit, or net loss, for the accounting period. An example of a service sector profit and loss account is shown below:

JEMMA SMITH, TRADING AS 'WYVERN SECRETARIAL AGENCY'
PROFIT AND LOSS ACCOUNT
for the year ended 31 December 2002

	£	£
Income from clients		110,000
Less overheads:		
Salaries	64,000	
Heating and lighting	2,000	
Telephone	2,000	
Rent and rates	6,000	
Sundry expenses	3,000	
		77,000
Net profit		33,000

The balance sheet layout of a service sector business is identical to that seen earlier (page 109); the only difference is that there is unlikely to be much stock, if any, in the current assets section.

CAPITAL EXPENDITURE AND REVENUE EXPENDITURE

When preparing final accounts, it is important to distinguish between **capital expenditure** and **revenue expenditure**.

capital expenditure

Capital expenditure can be defined as expenditure incurred on the purchase, alteration or improvement of fixed assets. For example, the purchase of a car for use in the business is capital expenditure. Included in capital expenditure are such costs as:

- delivery of fixed assets
- installation of fixed assets
- improvement (but not repair) of fixed assets
- legal costs of buying property

revenue expenditure

Revenue expenditure is expenditure incurred on running expenses. For example, the cost of petrol or diesel for the car (above) is revenue expenditure. Included in revenue expenditure are the costs of:

- maintenance and repair of fixed assets
- administration of the business
- selling and distributing the goods or products in which the business trades

capital expenditure and revenue expenditure – the differences

Capital expenditure is shown on the balance sheet, while revenue expenditure is an expense in the profit and loss account. It is important to classify these types of expenditure correctly in the accounting system. For example, if the cost of the car was shown as an expense in profit and loss account, then net profit would be reduced considerably, or a net loss recorded; meanwhile, the balance sheet would not show the car as a fixed asset – clearly this is incorrect as the business owns the asset.

Study the following examples; they show the differences between capital expenditure and revenue expenditure.

- **£30,000 cost of building an extension to the factory, which includes £1,000 for repairs to the existing factory**
  - capital expenditure, £29,000
  - revenue expenditure, £1,000 (because it is for repairs to an existing fixed asset)

- **a plot of land has been bought for £20,000, the legal costs are £750**

  - capital expenditure £20,750 (the legal costs are included in the capital expenditure, because they are the cost of acquiring the fixed asset, ie the legal costs are 'capitalised')

- **the business' own employees are used to install a new air conditioning system: wages £1,000, materials £1,500**

  - capital expenditure £2,500 (an addition to the property); note that, in cases such as this, revenue expenditure, ie wages and materials purchases, will need to be reduced to allow for the transfer to capital expenditure

- **own employees used to repair and redecorate the premises: wages £500, materials £750**

  - revenue expenditure £1,250 (repairs and redecoration are running expenses)

- **purchase of a new machine £10,000, payment for installation and setting up £250**

  - capital expenditure £10,250 (costs of installation of a fixed asset are capitalised)

Only by allocating capital expenditure and revenue expenditure correctly between the balance sheet and the profit and loss account can the final accounts reflect accurately the financial state of the business.

chapter summary

- The final accounts of a business comprise:

  - trading account, which shows gross profit

  - profit and loss account, which shows net profit (or loss)

  - balance sheet, which shows the assets and liabilities of the business at the year-end

- The starting point for the preparation of final accounts is the summary of the information from the accounting records contained in the book-keeper's trial balance.

- Each balance shown by the trial balance is entered into the final accounts once only.

- Any notes to the trial balance, such as the closing stock, affect the final accounts in two places.

- The trading account and profit and loss account form part of the double-entry book-keeping system – amounts entered must be recorded elsewhere in the accounts.

- The balance sheet is not part of the double-entry system; it lists the assets and liabilities at a particular date.

---

tutorial note

There is more material to cover in connection with final accounts, and the next few chapters deal with accruals and prepayments, depreciation of fixed assets, bad debts and provision for bad debts, and accounting concepts. In addition the more specialist final accounts of partnerships and limited companies (Chapters 10 and 12), will be studied. Final accounts can also be analysed and interpreted (Chapter 15) to give the user of the accounts information about the financial state of the business.

---

key terms

final accounts	accounting statements, comprising the profit and loss account and balance sheet, produced at least once a year, which give information to the owner(s) and other interested parties on how the business is progressing
profit and loss account	shows the net profit (or net loss) of the business for the accounting period
balance sheet	shows the assets, liabilities and capital of the business at the end of the accounting period
capital expenditure	expenditure incurred on the purchase, alteration or improvement of fixed assets
revenue expenditure	expenditure incurred on running expenses

activities

Note: an asterisk (*) after an activity number means that an answer is provided in Appendix 1.

6.1   Identify the main financial statements which comprise the final accounts of a sole trader. Explain the main sections contained within the statements.

6.2   Distinguish between:
(a)   gross profit and net profit
(b)   fixed assets and current assets
(c)   long-term liabilities and current liabilities
(d)   capital and loans

6.3*   The following information has been extracted from the business accounts of Matthew Lloyd for his first year of trading which ended on 31 December 2008:

	£
Purchases	94,350
Sales	125,890
Stock at 31 December 2008	5,950
Rates	4,850
Heating and lighting	2,120
Wages and salaries	10,350
Office equipment	8,500
Vehicles	10,750
Debtors	3,950
Bank balance (money at bank)	4,225
Cash	95
Creditors	1,750
Value Added Tax (due to HM Customs & Excise)	450
Capital at start of year	20,000
Drawings for year	8,900

You are to prepare the trading and profit and loss account of Matthew Lloyd for the year ended 31 December 2008, together with his balance sheet at that date.

6.4 Complete the table below for each item (a) to (g) indicating with a tick:
- whether the item would normally appear in the debit or credit column of the trial balance
- in which final account the item would appear at the end of the accounting period

| | TRIAL BALANCE | | FINAL ACCOUNTS | |
	Debit	Credit	TRADING & P& L	BALANCE SHEET
(a) Salaries				
(b) Purchases				
(c) Debtors				
(d) Sales returns				
(e) Discount received				
(f) Vehicle				
(g) Capital				

6.5* You are to fill in the missing figures for the following businesses:

	Sales	Opening Stock	Purchases	Closing Stock	Gross Profit	Expenses	Net Profit/(Loss)*
	£	£	£	£	£	£	£
Business A	20 000	5 000	10 000	3 000	....	4 000	....
Business B	35 000	8 000	15 000	5 000	....	....	10 000
Business C	....	6 500	18 750	7 250	18 500	11 750	....
Business D	45 250	9 500	....	10 500	20 750	....	10 950
Business E	71 250	....	49 250	9 100	22 750	24 450	....
Business F	25 650	4 950	13 750	....	11 550	....	(3 450)

* Note: a net loss is indicated in brackets

6.6* The following trial balance has been extracted by the book-keeper of John Adams at 31 December 2007:

	Dr £	Cr £
Stock at 1 January 2007	14,350	
Purchases	114,472	
Sales		259,688
Rates	13,718	
Heating and lighting	12,540	
Wages and salaries	42,614	
Vehicle expenses	5,817	
Advertising	6,341	
Premises	75,000	
Office equipment	33,000	
Vehicles	21,500	
Debtors	23,854	
Bank	1,235	
Cash	125	
Capital at 1 January 2007		62,500
Drawings	12,358	
Loan from bank		35,000
Creditors		17,281
Value Added Tax		2,455
	376,924	376,924

Stock at 31 December 2007 was valued at £16,280.

You are to prepare the trading and profit and loss account of John Adams for the year ended 31 December 2007, together with his balance sheet at that date.

6.7 The following trial balance has been extracted by the book-keeper of Clare Lewis at 31 December 2004:

	Dr £	Cr £
Debtors	18,600	
Creditors		12,140
Value Added Tax		1,210
Bank overdraft		4,610
Capital at 1 January 2004		25,250
Sales		144,810
Purchases	96,318	
Stock at 1 January 2004	16,010	
Salaries	18,465	
Heating and lighting	1,820	
Rent and rates	5,647	
Vehicles	9,820	
Office equipment	5,500	
Sundry expenses	845	
Vehicle expenses	1,684	
Drawings	13,311	
	188,020	188,020

Stock at 31 December 2004 was valued at £13,735.

You are to prepare the trading and profit and loss account of Clare Lewis for the year ended 31 December 2004, together with her balance sheet at that date.

6.8 Classify the following costs as either capital expenditure or as revenue expenditure

(a) purchase of vehicles

(b) rent paid on premises

(c) wages and salaries

(d) legal fees relating to the purchase of property

(e) redecoration of the office

(f) installation of air-conditioning in the office

(g) wages of own employees used to build extension to the stockroom

(h) installation and setting up of a new machine

ADJUSTMENTS TO FINAL ACCOUNTS

CASE STUDY
'Should these be recorded in the final accounts?'

It is the beginning of January 2003 and Olivia Boulton is having a meeting with her accountant. She has looked at the provisional final accounts her book-keeper prepared for her cookware shop for the year ended 31 December 2002 (see pages 107 and 109). She says that she now understands the difference between the trading and profit and loss account and the balance sheet.

In discussion with her accountant she mentions a number of points and wonders if they should be recorded in the final accounts in some way, as they may affect the profit position and the amounts she owes and is owed:

'On 5 January 2003, I received a 'phone bill for the shop for the calls made in December.'

'Towards the end of December I paid the rent for January for the storage space I use.'

'At the beginning of 2002 I bought my premises for £100,000 and I paid £20,000 for shop fittings – all with the help of a bank loan.'

'I sold £100 of goods to another kitchenware shop about six months ago. I've not been paid and I've heard recently that they've gone bust. I won't see my money now.'

'The wholesale side of the business is going well; I've got quite a few debtors – I hope they all pay up.'

Her accountant agrees that the provisional final accounts the book-keeper originally drew up should now be amended to take account of these factors.

In this chapter, we will look at each of these points mentioned by Olivia and will see how these adjustments are taken care of in the final accounts.

---

learning objectives

When you have studied this chapter you will be able to:

- *appreciate the concepts of accounting*
- *apply the adjustments for accruals and prepayments to final accounts*
- *understand the concept of depreciation and apply it to final accounts*
- *distinguish between bad debts written off and provision for bad debts and apply them to final accounts*

ACCOUNTING CONCEPTS

There are a number of **accounting concepts** – or 'rules' of accounting – which underlie the preparation of final accounts. They will help to decide what to do with the types of adjustments mentioned in the Case Study on the previous page. These concepts help to make final accounts relevant and reliable to users, and also enable them to be comparable and understandable.

The more important accounting concepts are illustrated in the diagram below.

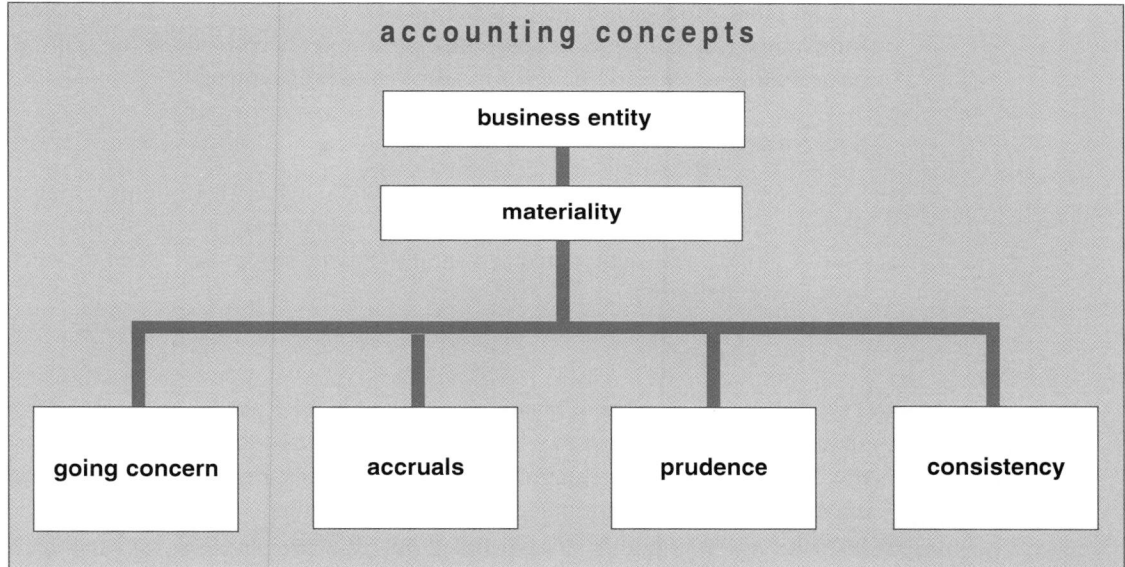

business entity

This refers to the fact that final accounts record and report on the activities of one particular business. They do not include the personal assets and liabilities of those who play a part in owning or running the business.

materiality

Some items are of such low value that it is not worth recording them separately, ie they are not 'material'. Examples include:

- small expense items grouped together as sundry expenses

- small end-of-year stocks of office stationery not valued for the purpose of final accounts

- low-cost fixed assets being charged as an expense in the profit and loss account

going concern

This presumes that the business to which the final accounts relate will continue to trade in the forseeable future, ie there is no intention to reduce significantly the size of the business or to liquidate it. If the business was not a going concern, assets could be worth a lot less, and the balance sheet could be affected considerably.

accruals

Expenses and income shown in the trading and profit and loss accounts should relate precisely to the time period of those accounts, even if it means, for example, including an expense that has not yet been paid for (an accrual) or excluding an expense paid for in advance (a prepayment).

prudence

This requires that final accounts should always, when there is any dounbt, report a conservative figure for profit or the valuation of assets. To this end, profits are not to be anticipated and should only be recognised when they can be reliably measured.

consistency

This requires that, when a business adopts particular accounting methods, it should normally continue to use such methods consistently. For example, the use of straight-line depreciation (see page 134) for a particular class of fixed asset would normally continue to be used in the future. Changes can be made provided there is a good reason for doing so, and a note of explanation is included in the financial statements. By application of consistency, comparability can be made between the final accounts of different years.

other accounting concepts

Other concepts followed when preparing final accounts include:

- **money measurement** – all items are expressed in the common denominator of money; only by using money can items be added together to give, for example, net profit or a balance sheet total

- **historical cost** – assets and liabilities are initially recorded in the final accounts at historical cost, ie the actual amount of the transaction (note that some businesses may adopt a policy of regular revaluation of assets)

- **dual aspect** – each business transaction is recorded by means of two opposite accounting entries (debit and credit), but of equal values; note that double-entry book-keeping is an example of the dual aspect concept in practice

- **realisation** – business transactions are recorded in the final accounts when the legal title passes between buyer and seller; this may well not be at the same time as payment is made, eg credit sales are recorded when the sale is made, but payment will be made at a later date

- **objectivity** – the presentation of financial statements should be objective, rather than subjective, and should not be influenced by the opinions or personal expectations of the owner of the business concerned, or the accountant preparing the accounts

ADJUSTMENTS TO FINAL ACCOUNTS

The six adjustments to final accounts are as follows:

- **closing stock** – incorporating the value of stock held at the financial year-end into the final accounts

- adjusting for **accruals** – expenses due in an accounting period which have not been paid for at the end of that period

- adjusting for **prepayments** – payments made in advance of the accounting period to which they relate

- **depreciation** of fixed assets – writing down the value of fixed assets over their useful economic lives

- **bad debts written off** – removing from the sales ledger the accounts of debtors who will not pay

- **provision for bad debts** – making provision for debtors who may not pay

Each of these adjustments is based on a number of accounting concepts, but the two main concepts which form the basis of these adjustments are the accruals concept (closing stock, accruals, prepayments) and the prudence concept (depreciation and the treatment of bad debts). The objective of the adjustments is to improve the relevance and reliability of final accounts in showing the profit, and the assets and liabilities of the business.

We will now look at each adjustment in turn and relate them to Olivia Boulton's business in the continuation of the Case Study on page 139.

CLOSING STOCK

At the end of each financial year a business must stock-take; this is where all stocks are physically counted and valued – normally at cost price. The problem facing a business is that 'cost price' may vary – normally it will rise during the year. Which 'cost price' should be taken to value the year-end stock? The most common of these methods is known as FIFO (first in, first out); this assumes that the oldest stock is issued first, so at the year-end the stock left will reflect the most recent cost prices.

So what adjustments should be made in the year-end accounts? When the closing stock at the year-end is valued, it represents that part of the year's purchases that have not been sold. The amount of closing stock is therefore

– deducted from purchases in the trading account to show what has been used in the year (called cost of sales)

– entered as a current asset in the year end balance sheet

We have already seen, in the Case Study in the previous chapter, how the closing stock value of £42,000 in Olivia Boulton's business was dealt with in her final accounts (see page 110).

SSAP 9: stocks and long-term contracts

Statement of Standard Accounting Practice (SSAP) no. 9, entitled 'Stocks and Long-term Contracts', is the accounting standard (see Chapter 14) which sets out how stocks should be valued. The principle of stock valuation, set out in SSAP 9, is that stocks should be valued at 'the lower of cost and net realisable value'. This valuation applies the prudence concept and is illustrated by the following diagram:

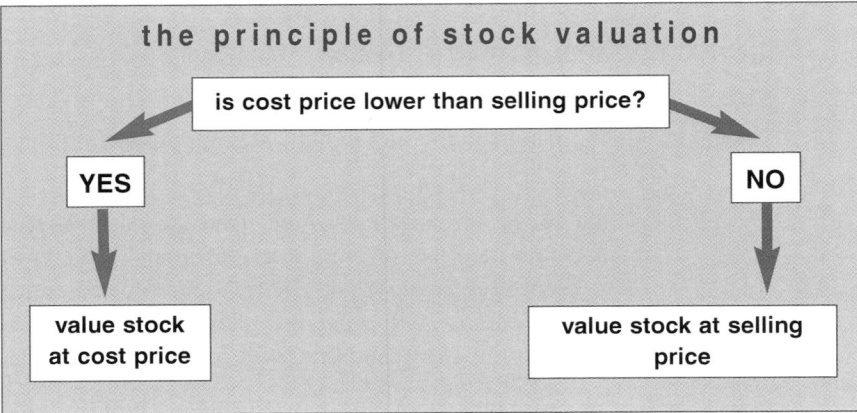

This diagram shows that two different stock values are compared:

■ **cost** – including additional costs to bring the product or service to its present location and condition

■ **net realisable value** – the expected selling price less any further costs such as selling and distribution

The lower of these two values is taken, and different items or groups are compared separately.

ACCRUAL OF EXPENSES

An accrual is an amount due in an accounting period which is unpaid at the end of that period.

In the final accounts, an accrued expense is:

▓ added to the expense amount shown in the trial balance before listing it in the profit and loss account

▓ shown as an accrual in the current liabilities section of the year end balance sheet

The reason for dealing with accruals in this way is to ensure that the profit and loss account records the cost that has been incurred for the year, instead of simply the amount that has been paid. In other words, the expense is adjusted to relate to the time period covered by the profit and loss account. The year-end balance sheet shows a liability for the amount that is due, but unpaid.

In this book, and generally in accounting exercises, details of accruals (and prepayments – see below) will usually appear as a note to the trial balance.

example of an accrued expense

The trial balance of Olivia Boulton (see page 105) shows a debit balance for telephone expenses of £500. Before preparing the final accounts, a telephone bill for £100 is received on 5 January 2003, ie at the beginning of the new financial year. As this bill is clearly for telephone calls made in 2002, an adjustment needs to be made in the final accounts for 2002 to record this accrued expense.

In the profit and loss account, the total cost of £600 (ie £500 from the trial balance, plus £100 accrued) will be recorded as an expense. In the balance sheet, £100 will be shown as a separate current liability of 'accruals'.

PREPAYMENT OF EXPENSES

A prepayment is a payment made in advance of the accounting period to which it relates.

A prepayment is, therefore, the opposite of an accrual: with a prepayment of expenses, some part of the expense has been paid in advance.

In the final accounts, a prepaid expense is:

▓ deducted from the expense amount shown in the trial balance before listing it in the profit and loss account

■ shown as a prepayment in the current assets section of the year end balance sheet

As with accruals, the reason for dealing with prepaid expenses in this way is to ensure that the profit and loss account records the cost incurred for the year, and not the amount that has been paid – the profit and loss account expense relates to the time period covered by the profit and loss account. The year end balance sheet shows an asset for the amount that has been prepaid.

example of a prepaid expense

Olivia Boulton tells you that the trial balance (see page 105) figure for rent paid of £750, includes £75 of rent paid in advance for January 2003. An adjustment needs to be made in the final accounts for 2002 to record this prepaid expense.

In the profit and loss account, the cost of £675 (ie £750 from the trial balance, less £75 prepaid) will be recorded as an expense. In the balance sheet, £75 will be shown as a separate current asset of 'prepayments'.

DEPRECIATION OF FIXED ASSETS

Depreciation is the estimate of the amount of the reduction in value of fixed assets over an estimated time period.

Fixed assets, for example machinery and vehicles, reduce in value – or depreciate – as time goes by, largely as a result of wear and tear. For example if you buy a new car on Thursday you will not be able to sell it for the same price the following Thursday; it will have dropped in value – depreciated – by a substantial amount in that time.

The aim of depreciation is to write down the value of fixed assets over their useful economic lives.

depreciation in final accounts

To provide a more accurate view of the financial state of a business, depreciation of fixed assets is recorded in the final accounts as follows:

■ the amount of depreciation for the year is included as an expense in profit and loss account; the effect of this is to reduce net profit

■ the value of fixed assets shown in the balance sheet is reduced to reflect the amount that they have depreciated since the assets were bought

The reason for making these adjustments for depreciation is because the business has had the use of the fixed assets during the year: the estimated fall in value of the assets is recorded in profit and loss account, which now shows a more accurate profit figure while, in the balance sheet, fixed assets are reduced in value to indicate their approximate 'true' value.

an example of depreciation in final accounts

Olivia Boulton tells you that she wishes you to show £10,000 for depreciation of shop fittings in her financial statements for 2002. As a result she will include an expense for depreciation of £10,000 in her profit and loss account (which will reduce her net profit). In the balance sheet the £10,000 will reduce the value of the shop fittings as shown below:

Balance sheet as at 31 December 2002

	£	£	£
Fixed assets	Cost	Depreciation to date	Net
Shop fittings	40,000	10,000	30,000

Notes:
- the left-hand money column is the original cost of the fixed asset
- the middle money column is depreciation from previous years (if any) – shown as a credit item **provision for depreciation** in the trial balance – added to this year's depreciation from profit and loss account
- the right hand money column is the **net book value** of the fixed asset, ie cost less depreciation to date equals net book value; this figure will be added to the net book value of other fixed assets to give the sub-total for this section of the balance sheet

depreciation – a non-cash expense

It is very important to understand that depreciation is a non-cash expense. Unlike most of the other expenses or overheads in profit and loss account, no cheque is written out, or cash paid, for depreciation. In cash terms, depreciation causes no outflow of money. As depreciation is a non-cash expense, it is not a method of providing the cash to replace the asset at the end of its life. (In order to do this, it would be necessary to create a separate fund into which cash is transferred at regular intervals; the fund needs to be represented by a separate bank account, eg a deposit account, which can be drawn against when the new fixed asset is purchased.)

depreciation methods

There are several different ways in which we can allow for the loss in value of fixed assets. All of these are estimates, and it is only when the asset is sold or scrapped that we will know the accuracy of the estimate.

The most common methods of calculating depreciation are:

▨ straight-line method

▨ reducing balance method

With the **straight-line method**, a fixed percentage is written off the original cost of the asset each year. For example, referring back to Olivia Boulton's shop fittings, straight-line depreciation of twenty-five per cent per annum will give depreciation amounts of:

2002	£10,000	ie £40,000 x 25%
2003	£10,000	ie £40,000 x 25%
		etc . . .

The formula to work out the amount of straight-line depreciation is as follows:

$$\frac{cost\ of\ fixed\ assets - resale\ value\ (if\ any)}{life\ of\ asset} = annual\ depreciation$$

With the **reducing balance method**, a fixed percentage is written off the reduced balance of the asset each year. The reduced balance is the cost of the asset, less depreciation to date. For example, with Olivia Boulton's shop fittings, reducing balance depreciation of twenty-five per cent per annum will give depreciation amounts of:

2002	£10,000	ie £40,000 x 25%
2003	£7,500	ie (£40,000 – £10,000) x 25%
		etc . . .

Straight-line depreciation is more often used for fixed assets that are likely to be kept for the whole of their expected lives, eg machinery, office equipment. Reducing balance depreciation is particularly appropriate for assets which depreciate more in their early years and which are not kept for the whole of their expected lives, eg vehicles.

sale of fixed assets

When a fixed asset is sold or disposed of, it is necessary to bring together:

▨ the original cost of the asset

▨ depreciation provided over the life of the asset

▨ sale proceeds

From these money amounts we can calculate the 'profit' or 'loss' on sale of the asset (more correctly the terms are 'over-provision' and 'under-provision' of depreciation, respectively). A profit on sale occurs when the asset is sold for more than its net book value at the date of sale; a loss on sale is when the sale proceeds are less than the net book value.

Small adjustments for under-provision or over-provision of depreciation will usually be needed because it is impossible, at the start of an asset's life, to predict exactly what it will sell for in a number of years' time.

WORKED EXAMPLES
Profit or loss on the sale of fixed assets

Example 1 – a loss on sale

A business bought a delivery van three years ago at a cost of £10,000. Depreciation has been £2,000 per year for three years. The van has just been sold for £3,500.

The calculations are:

	£	
original cost	10,000	
less depreciation to date of sale	6,000	(3 years x £2,000 per year)
net book value at date of sale	4,000	
sale proceeds	3,500	
∴ loss on sale	500	

The amount of the loss on sale is shown as an expense (overhead) in profit and loss account; in other words, it is like extra depreciation because the business under-provided for depreciation over the life of the asset. Note that the sale proceeds are a cash transaction (as opposed to the non-cash transactions of depreciation and loss on sale) and will be paid into the bank account.

Example 2 – a profit on sale

Using the details of the van, above, it is now sold for £4,500. The calculations are:

	£
original cost	10,000
less depreciation to date of sale	6,000
net book value at date of sale	4,000
sale proceeds	4,500
∴ profit on sale	500

The amount of the profit on sale is credited to profit and loss account as 'other income' (usually shown immediately below gross profit). Here the business has over-provided for depreciation over the life of the asset (ie too much has been charged) and so the non-cash adjustment of profit on sale is made. Note that the sale proceeds will be paid into the business bank account.

FRS 15: Tangible Fixed Assets

Financial Reporting Standard (FRS) no. 15, entitled 'Tangible Fixed Assets', is the accounting standard (see Chapter 14) which sets out the rules for dealing with depreciation in financial accounts. FRS 15 states that:

- fixed assets having a known useful economic life must be depreciated
- any acceptable depreciation method can be used to spread the cost of the fixed asset consistently over its useful economic life
- depreciation amounts are normally based on the cost of the fixed asset

BAD DEBTS WRITTEN OFF

A bad debt is a debt owing to a business which it considers will never be paid.

Credit control – the monitoring and collection of debts – is an important function in the efficient running of a business.

The prompt issue of invoices, statements and chaser letters, the sending of solicitors' letters, all bring an increasing pressure on the debtor to pay. If these fail, and court action is not economic because of the small size of the debt, the debt will be termed a 'bad debt' and will be *written off*; the debtor's account will be struck out of the Sales Ledger and the amount treated as an unfortunate but unavoidable expense to the business.

The double-entry treatment is to debit the amount to *bad debts written off account* in the General Ledger which records all debts written off during the year. Thus at the end of the year there will be a bad debts written off figure in the debit column of the trial balance which will be entered in the profit and loss account as an expense of the business.

If a note to a trial balance tells you that there is a bad debt which has not yet been written off in the Sales Ledger, then the accounting treatment in the final accounts is to:

- show the amount of the bad debt written off as an expense in profit and loss account
- deduct the amount from debtors in the balance sheet

Writing off bad debts is clearly a prudent measure as it reduces the debtors figure (Sales Ledger) to a reliable level. If a large bad debt was not written off, the debtors figure in the balance sheet would give an over-optimistic picture of the working capital position and net asset value of the business.

PROVISION FOR BAD DEBTS

Provision for bad debts is a separate procedure from writing off bad debts.

Provision for bad debts is an estimate by the business of the likely percentage of its debtors which may go bad during any one accounting period.

initial creation of a provision for bad debts

The procedure for provision for bad debts is very similar to that for the depreciation of assets. For example:

- A business at the end of the financial year estimates the percentage of its debtors which may go bad at 2.5%.
- The provision is calculated (£10,000 x 2.5% = £250) and
  - charged to the profit and loss account as an expense 'Provision for bad debts'
  - deducted from the debtors figure in the current assets section of the balance sheet in a separate column inset to the left from the listing of the other current assets:

Current Assets	£	£
Stock		42,000
Debtors	10,000	
Less provision for bad debts	250	
		9,750
Prepayments		75
Bank		5,850
Cash		50
		57,725

It must be emphasised that the £250 of debtors have not gone bad; if they did so, they would appear in the bad debts written off account and would already have been deducted from debtors before the balance sheet was drawn up, as we saw in the previous section. The business, in creating a provision for bad debts, is presenting a reliable estimate of its debtor position.

adjustments of provision for bad debts in subsequent years

Unlike depreciation of fixed assets, which is made at a fixed percentage each year, and which reduces the asset value, provision for bad debts usually remains as a static percentage of debtors, for example a fixed 5%. The only adjustments that need to be made to the money amount of the provision are:

- a change in provision policy, eg an increase in the fixed percentage from 2.5% to 5%
- arithmetic adjustment in the provision as a result of a change in the total of debtors (2.5% of £15,000 is going to be more than 2.5% of £10,000)

It follows that if either of these two situations arises, the adjustment to the existing provision will be either:

- upwards (increase in provision percentage or increase in debtor figure), or
- downwards (decrease in provision percentage or decrease in debtor figure)

An **increase in the provision** is dealt with in the final accounts as follows:

- show the increase as an expense in the profit and loss account
- Add the increase to the existing provision for bad debts figure and show the total on the balance sheet

A **decrease in the provision** is dealt with in the final accounts as follows:

- show the decrease as an income item in the profit and loss account (added below gross profit in the right-hand column
- subtract the decrease from the existing provision for bad debts figure, and show the total in the balance sheet

Note again that any provision for bad debts and the writing off of bad debts are completely separate adjustments; the two should never be confused. It is therefore quite common to see, in a profit and loss account, entries for both bad debts written off and provision for bad debts (creation or adjustment of the provision).

THE DUAL ASPECT OF ADJUSTMENTS – A SUMMARY

We saw in the previous chapter how each item from the trial balance appears in the final accounts once only (see page 110). With adjustments to the final accounts – closing stock, accruals and prepayments, depreciation of fixed assets, bad debts written off, and provision for bad debts – each adjustment has to be reflected in two aspects of the year-end accounts. The following is a summary of how the main adjustments are dealt with in the final accounts:

closing stock
- deduct from purchases in trading account
- current asset in balance sheet

accrual of expenses
- increase expense in profit and loss account
- current liability in balance sheet

prepayment of expenses
- decrease expense in profit and loss account
- current asset in balance sheet

provision for depreciation of fixed assets
- expense in profit and loss account
- fixed asset value reduced in balance sheet

bad debts written off
- expense in profit and loss account
- debtors' figure reduced in balance sheet*
  - * not required if bad debts written off account is already shown on the trial balance

creation of, or increase in, provision for bad debts
- expense in profit and loss account
- debtors' figure reduced in balance sheet by total amount of provision

decrease in provision for bad debts
- income in profit and loss account
- debtors' figure reduced in balance sheet by total amount of provision

CASE STUDY
Olivia Boulton: adjustments to final accounts

situation

Using the trial balance of Olivia Boulton at 31 December 2002 (see pages 105 and 110), the accountant will make adjustments to take account of the following:

■ after a stock-take at the end of December, closing stock was valued at £42,000

■ a telephone bill received on 5 January 2003 showed calls for £100 in 2002 (an accrual)

■ in December Olivia paid rent of £75 in advance for January (a prepayment)

■ Olivia's accountant advised her to depreciate the premises (which were bought during the year) at 2 per cent per annum, using the straight-line method

■ Olivia's accountant advised her to depreciate the shop fittings (which were bought during the year) at 25 per cent per annum, using the reducing balance method

■ Olivia incurred bad debts of £100 during 2002 which she had to write off

■ after writing off the bad debts, she created a provision for bad debts of 2.5% of debtors

solution

The final accounts incorporating these adjustments are shown on the next two pages. A summary of the effect of each adjustment is given below.

closing stock

As seen in the Case Study in Chapter 6 (page105), the adjustment for closing stock is to:

– deduct £42,000 from purchases in the trading account

– show stock valued at £42,000 as a current asset in the balance sheet

accrual of expenses

For the telephone expenses accrued:

– increase the profit and loss account expense by £100 to £600 (ie £500 from the trial balance, plus £100 accrued)

– show the £100 accrual as a current liability in the balance sheet

prepayment of expenses

For the rent prepaid:

– reduce the profit and loss account expense by £75 to £675 (ie £750 from the trial balance, less £75 prepaid)

– show the £75 prepayment as a current asset in the balance sheet

depreciation of fixed assets

The depreciation amounts are:

• premises: 2 per cent per annum straight-line, ie £4,000

• shop fittings: 25 per cent per annum reducing balance, ie £10,000

The depreciation is shown in the final accounts as follows:

– in the profit and loss account show (as expenses) provision for depreciation amounts for premises £4,000, and shop fittings £10,000

– in the balance sheet show the depreciation amounts being deducted from fixed assets to give net book values of £196,000 for premises and £30,000 for shop fittings

Note that, as this is the first year that Olivia Boulton has recorded depreciation, both depreciation for year and provision for depreciation amounts are the same.

bad debts written off

The adjustment to write off bad debts in the final accounts is as follows:

– record bad debts written off of £100 as an expense in profit and loss account

– reduce the debtors' figure by £100 to £10,000 and show this latter figure as a current asset in the balance sheet

provision for bad debts

Here Olivia Boulton is creating a new provision for bad debts of £250 (£10,000 x 2.5%); it is shown in the final accounts as follows:

– in profit and loss account record the £250 amount of the provision for bad debts as an expense

– in the balance sheet deduct £250 from the debtors' figure of £10,000 to give net debtors of £9,750 – it is this amount that is added in to current assets

Note that, where an existing provision for bad debts is to be increased, the above principles are followed with the balance sheet deduction being the total amount, ie existing provision plus increase. To reduce an existing provision, show the amount of the reduction as income in profit and loss account; the balance sheet deduction from debtors is the total amount of the provision remaining, ie existing provision less reduction.

final accounts

The final accounts of Olivia Boulton, incorporating the above adjustments, are shown below.

TRADING AND PROFIT AND LOSS ACCOUNT OF OLIVIA BOULTON

for the year ended 31 December 2002

	£	£
Sales		557,500
Opening stock (1 January 2002)	50,000	
Purchases	420,000	
	470,000	
Less Closing stock (31 December 2002)	42,000	
Cost of sales		428,000
Gross profit		129,500
Less overheads:		
Administration expenses	6,200	
Wages	33,500	
Rent paid	675	
Telephone	600	
Interest paid	4,500	
Travel expenses	550	
Provision for depreciation: premises	4,000	
shop fittings	10,000	
Bad debts written off	100	
Provision for bad debts	250	
		60,375
Net profit		69,125

BALANCE SHEET OF OLIVIA BOULTON
as at 31 December 2002

Fixed Assets	£ Cost	£ Dep'n to date	£ Net
Premises	200,000	4,000	196,000
Shop fittings	40,000	10,000	30,000
	240,000	14,000	226,000
Current Assets			
Stock		42,000	
Debtors	10,000		
Less provision for bad debts	250		
		9,750	
Prepayment		75	
Bank		5,850	
Cash		50	
		57,725	
Less Current Liabilities			
Creditors	14,500		
Accrual	100		
Value Added Tax	2,000		
		16,600	
Working Capital			41,125
			267,125
Less Long-term Liabilities			
Loan from bank			150,000
NET ASSETS			117,125
FINANCED BY			
Capital			
Opening capital			75,000
Add net profit			69,125
			144,125
Less drawings			27,000
Closing capital			117,125

PRIVATE EXPENSES AND GOODS FOR OWN USE

Adjustments also have to be made in the final accounts for the amount of any business facilities that are used by the owner for private purposes.

private expenses

Sometimes the owner of a business uses business facilities for private purposes, eg mobile phone or car. The owner will agree that part of the expense shall be charged to him or her as drawings, while the other part represents a business expense. For example, the balance of the telephone account is £600 at the year-end, and the owner agrees that this should be split as one-quarter private use, and three-quarters to the business. The book-keeping entries to record such adjustments are:

- debit drawings account with the amount of private use, £150
- credit telephone account with the amount of private use, £150
- debit profit and loss account with the amount of business use, £450
- credit telephone account with the amount of business use, £450

goods for own use

When the owner of a business takes some of the goods in which the business trades for his or her own use, the double-entry book-keeping is:

- debit drawings account
- credit purchases account

Note that where a business is VAT-registered, VAT must be accounted for on goods taken by the owner.

chapter summary

- The accounting concepts of business entity, materiality, going concern, accruals, prudence and consistency are fundamental to the relevance and reliability of final accounts.

- These concepts are applied by making certain adjustments to the figures from the trial balance when preparing the final accounts. The adjustments are for:

• closing stock	• accruals	• prepayments
• depreciation of fixed assets	• bad debts written off	• provision for bad debts

- Adjustments also need to be made in the final accounts for:
  - private expenses
  - goods for own use

key terms

accounting concepts	part of the 'rules' of accounting
business entity concept	final accounts record and report on the activities of one particular business
materiality concept	items with a low value are not worthwhile recording in the accounts separately
going concern concept	the presumption that the business to which the final accounts relate will continue to trade in the foreseeable future
accruals concept	expenses and revenues are matched so that they concern the same goods or services and the same time period
prudence concept	final accounts should always, where there is any doubt, report a conservative figure for profit or the valuation of assets
consistency concept	when a business adopts particular accounting methods, it should continue to use such methods consistently
accrual of expenses	an amount due in an accounting period which is unpaid at the end of that period
prepayment of expenses	a payment made in advance of the accounting period to which it relates
depreciation	the estimate of the amount of the reduction in value of fixed assets over an estimated time period
straight-line depreciation	a fixed percentage is written off the original cost of the asset each year
reducing balance depreciation	a fixed percentage is written off the reduced balance of the asset each year
bad debt	a debt owing to a business which it considers will never be paid
provision for bad debts	an estimate by a business of the likely percentage of its debtors which may go bad during any one accounting period
goods for own use	where the owner of a business takes some of the goods in which the business trades for his/her own use

activities

Note: an asterisk (*) after an activity number means that an answer is provided in Appendix 1.

7.1*   Explain the appropriate accounting concept in each of the following circumstances.

(a)   A business has a customer who owes £1,000. Despite sending numerous statements of account to the debtor, payment has not been received. It has been decided to make a provision for bad debts in respect of this customer.

(b)   From time-to-time a business buys a pack of blank video tapes in order to record business meetings. The tapes are re-used over a number of years and are sometimes kept as a permanent record of meetings. Accounting policy is to charge the cost of the tapes – £10 for a pack of five tapes – as an expense in profit and loss account.

(c)   As an accounting trainee you are instructed to prepare two sets of a business' final accounts for a particular year, one of which uses straight-line depreciation while the other uses reducing balance depreciation. The owner of the business says that he will use the set which shows the lower profit.

(d)   A business has a financial year end of 31 December 2007. In early February 2008, an electricity bill is received covering the period November 2007 – January 2008. It is decided to apportion two-thirds of the bill to the profit and loss account for 2007 and one-third to the profit and loss account for 2008.

7.2*   Explain how the following would be dealt with in the profit and loss account, and balance sheet of a business with a financial year end of 31 December 2002:

(a)   Wages and salaries paid to 31 December 2002 amount to £55,640. However, at that date, £1,120 is owing: this amount is paid on 4 January 2003.

(b)   Rates totalling £3,565 have been paid to cover the period 1 January 2002 to 31 March 2003.

(c)   A computer is rented at a cost of £150 per month. The rental for January 2003 was paid in December 2002 and is included in the total payments during 2002 which amount to £1,950.

7.3   The following information has been extracted from the accounts of Southtown Supplies, a wholesaling business, for the year ended 31 December 2009:

	£
Sales	420,000
Purchases	280,000
Stock at 1 January 2009	70,000
Stock at 31 December 2009	60,000

Rent and rates	10,250
Electricity	3,100
Telephone	1,820
Salaries	35,600
Vehicle expenses	13,750

Note: at 31 December 2009:

- rent prepaid is £550
- salaries owing are £450

You are to prepare the trading and profit and loss account of Southtown Supplies for the year ended 31 December 2009.

7.4* The following trial balance has been extracted by the book-keeper of John Barclay at 30 June 2009:

	Dr £	Cr £
Sales		864,321
Purchases	600,128	
Sales returns	2,746	
Purchases returns		3,894
Office expenses	33,947	
Salaries	122,611	
Vehicle expenses	36,894	
Discounts allowed	3,187	
Discounts received		4,951
Debtors and creditors	74,328	52,919
Value Added Tax		10,497
Stock at 1 July 2008	63,084	
Vehicles	83,500	
Office equipment	23,250	
Land and buildings	100,000	
Bank loan		75,000
Bank	1,197	
Capital		155,000
Drawings	21,710	
	1,166,582	1,166,582

Notes at 30 June 2009:

- stock was valued at £66,941
- vehicle expenses owing £1,250
- office expenses prepaid £346
- goods costing £250 were taken by John Barclay for his own use

You are to prepare the trading and profit and loss account of John Barclay for the year ended 30 June 2009, together with his balance sheet at that date.

7.5   The following trial balance has been extracted by the book-keeper of Hazel Harris at 31 December 2004:

	Dr £	Cr £
Bank loan		85,000
Capital		125,000
Purchases and sales	465,000	614,000
Building repairs	8,480	
Vehicles at cost	12,000	
Provision for depreciation on vehicles		2,400
Vehicle expenses	2,680	
Land and buildings at cost	120,000	
Provision for depreciation on buildings		10,000
Bank overdraft		2,000
Furniture and fittings at cost	25,000	
Provision for depreciation on furniture and fittings		2,500
Wages and salaries	86,060	
Discounts	10,610	8,140
Drawings	24,000	
Rates and insurance	6,070	
Debtors and creditors	52,130	38,730
Value Added Tax		3,120
General expenses	15,860	
Stock at 1 January 2004	63,000	
	890,890	890,890

Notes at 31 December 2004:

- Stock was valued at £88,000
- Wages and salaries outstanding: £3,180
- Rates and insurance paid in advance: £450
- Buildings are to be depreciated by £2,000
- Depreciate vehicles at 20 per cent using the straight-line method
- Depreciate furniture and fittings at 10 per cent using the straight-line method

You are to prepare her trading and profit and loss accounts for the year ended 31 December 2004, together with her balance sheet at that date.

7.6   Martin Hough, sole owner of Juicyburger, a fast food shop, operating from leased premises in the town, is suspicious of his accountant, Mr S Harris, whom he claims doesn't really understand the food business. On the telephone he asks Mr Harris why depreciation is charged on a rigid formula, as surely no-one really knows how much his equipment is worth, and in fact he might not get anything for it.

Draft a reply to Mr Hough from Mr Harris explaining the importance of depreciation and its application to final accounts.

7.7   You are the book-keeper at Waterston Plant Hire. At 31 December 2008, the end of the financial year, the business has gross debtors of £20,210. The owner decides to:

(a)   write off, as bad debts, the accounts of:

P Ross	£55
J Ball	£105
L Jones	£50

(b)   make a provision for bad debts of 2.5% of debtors (after writing off the above bad debts)

You are to explain how these transactions will be recorded in the final accounts at the end of the financial year.

7.8* The following trial balance has been extracted by the book-keeper of James Jenkins, who owns a patisserie and coffee lounge, as at 30 June 2009:

	Dr £	Cr £
Capital		36,175
Drawings	19,050	
Purchases and sales	105,240	168,432
Stock at 1 July 2008	9,427	
Debtors and creditors	3,840	5,294
Value Added Tax		1,492
Returns	975	1,237
Discounts	127	243
Wages and salaries	30,841	
Vehicle expenses	1,021	
Rent and rates	8,796	
Heating and lighting	1,840	
Telephone	355	
General expenses	1,752	
Bad debts written off	85	
Vehicle at cost	8,000	
Provision for depreciation on vehicle		3,500
Shop fittings at cost	6,000	
Provision for depreciation on shop fittings		2,400
Provision for bad debts		150
Cash	155	
Bank	21,419	
	218,923	218,923

Notes at 30 June 2009:

- stock was valued at £11,517
- vehicle expenses owing £55
- rent prepaid £275
- depreciate the vehicle at 25 per cent per annum, using the reducing balance method
- depreciate shop fittings at 10 per cent per annum, using the straight-line method
- the provision for bad debts is to be equal to 2.5 per cent of debtors

You are to prepare the trading and profit and loss account of James Jenkins for the year ended 30 June 2009, together with his balance sheet at that date.

INCOMPLETE RECORDS

You are working as a trainee for a firm of accountants and deal with a number of businesses. You have just been allotted a new client, Jack Perry, who runs a small stationery supplies business.

A client using a manual accounting system will often provide you at the year-end with a set of double-entry accounts and all the bank statements, cheque stubs, paying-in books, copies of invoices, VAT returns and so on. These are the easy clients. Easier still are the clients who run a computer accounting system and give you a set of disks and all the necessary paper-based back-up material.

Not so Jack Perry, who arrives at your office with a car boot full of box files and shoe boxes containing paid invoices and credit notes, copies of invoices issued, bank statements and other bank documentation, a cash book and other jottings and bits and pieces. But there are no double-entry accounts.

This is not uncommon. Many small businesses are like this. Although they do keep some records – 'incomplete records' – they do not run a double-entry system, but instead rely on a cash book to record income and expenses. At the financial year-end, it is the task of a book-keeper or accountant to use these incomplete records, to construct the final accounts so that the owner can see how much profit has been made and the tax bill can then be worked out.

In this chapter we will see how the 'incomplete' information provided by Jack Perry can be used to construct a set of final accounts.

learning objectives

When you have studied this chapter you will be able to:

- *identify the information required to construct final accounts from incomplete records*

- *calculate accounting figures from given information*

- *prepare final accounts from incomplete records*

- *use gross profit mark-up and margin to help with incomplete records accounting*

- *calculate stock losses – goods 'lost' as a result of fire, flood or theft – for insurance purposes*

WHAT ARE INCOMPLETE RECORDS?

Incomplete records' is the term used where the book-keeping system does not use double-entry principles and no trial balance is available. Some records are kept and the accountant will construct final accounts by:

- using the information available
- seeing what information may not be available, and how 'missing' figures can be calculated

information available to the accountant

The basic financial record kept by most businesses is a cash book, which records payments in and out. In practice, even if a cash book has not been kept, it is usually possible to reconstruct it from banking records, although this task can prove to be time-consuming. Other financial information will be available so that, in all, the accountant has the following to work from:

- cash book – the basic record for any single entry system
- banking details – statements, paying-in books, cheque counterfoils
- invoices – both received (for purchases) and sent (for sales) during the year
- expenses – during the year
- records of assets and liabilities – fixed and current assets, long-term and current liabilities, both at the beginning and end of the year
- details of fixed assets – bought or sold during the year

Information which may not be available, and will need to be calculated includes:

- capital at the beginning of the financial year
- purchases and sales for the year
- cash book summary
- profit for the year

the tools of accounting

In the two Case Studies which follow we shall see how to take the financial information that is available and, using the tools of accounting, construct the accounts that are required. The tools of accounting that may be needed are:

- the use of an opening trial balance, or statement of assets and liabilities
- the construction of a cash account and/or bank account
- the use of control accounts – sales ledger control account and purchases ledger control account

In addition, the following may be of use:

- the accounting equation (assets – liabilities = capital)
- gross profit mark-up and margin (see page 164)
- the format of the trading and profit and loss account and balance sheet

The two Case Studies make use of these tools of accounting, although it should be emphasised that no two incomplete records situations are the same. Practice is needed to help to develop your skills in this aspect of accounting.

CASE STUDY
Jack Perry – Stationery Supplies

The following information has been taken from the incomplete records of Jack Perry, who runs a small stationery supplies business.

LIST OF ASSETS AND LIABILITIES

	1 Jan 2008	31 Dec 2008
	£	£
Shop fittings	8,000	8,000
Stock	25,600	29,800
Debtors	29,200	20,400
Bank balance	5,000	not known
Creditors	20,800	16,000
Expenses owing	200	300

BANK SUMMARY FOR 2008

	£
Receipts from debtors	127,800
Payments to creditors	82,600
Drawings	12,500
Business expenses	30,600

In the text which follows we shall see how to construct the final accounts for 2008 from incomplete records. The information to be calculated is:

- opening capital, at the beginning of the financial year
- cash book summary for the year
- purchases and sales for the year
- profit for the year, and a year-end balance sheet

Note: for sake of simplicity we will ignore VAT on all transactions.

OPENING CAPITAL

Opening capital is needed in Jack Perry's case because a year-end balance sheet is to be prepared. In other situations with incomplete records, opening capital may be stated, being the difference between assets and liabilities. To calculate the capital at the beginning of the financial year, we use the formula: **assets − liabilities = capital**.

This is presented as a statement of assets and liabilities as follows:

	£	£
JACK PERRY STATEMENT OF ASSETS AND LIABILITIES as at 1 January 2008		
Assets		
Shop fittings		8,000
Stock		25,600
Debtors		29,200
Bank balance		5,000
		67,800
Less Liabilities		
Creditors	20,800	
Expenses owing	200	
		21,000
Capital at 1 January 2008		46,800

Notes:

- Here, the bank balance is an asset, ie money in the bank; if it was marked as an overdraft, it would be included amongst the liabilities.
- Look out for the opening bank balance or overdraft being stated elsewhere in the information; for example, a bank summary may be given which starts with the bank figure at the beginning of the year – this figure must be included in the statement of assets and liabilities, which is used to calculate opening capital.

CASH BOOK SUMMARY

A cash book summary enables us to find out the cash and bank balances at the year-end. (Sometimes this is not necessary, as a cash book may have been prepared already by the owner of the business.) In practice, the entries on the firm's bank statement can be used to produce a summary of receipts and payments for the year. In the case of Jack Perry's business, the cash book (bank columns) are:

Dr					Cash Book (bank columns)		Cr
2008			£	2008			£
1 Jan	Balance b/d		5,000		Payments to creditors		82,600
	Receipts from debtors		127,800		Drawings		12,500
					Expenses		30,600
				31 Dec	Balance c/d		7,100
			132,800		missing figure		132,800
2009				2009			
1 Jan	Balance b/d		7,100				

The bank balance of £7,100 on 31 December 2008 is calculated by filling in the missing figure (ie £132,800 minus the other three figures in the column).

Notes:

■ When preparing a cash book summary, look out for an opening bank balance that is overdrawn; this is entered on the credit side.

■ At the end of the cash book summary, a credit balance brought down is an overdraft.

PURCHASES AND SALES

In calculating purchases and sales, we need to take note of the creditors and debtors at both the beginning and the end of the year. The important point to note is that payments to creditors are not the same as purchases for the year (because of the change in the level of creditors). Likewise, receipts from debtors are not the same as sales (because of the change in debtors). Only in a business which trades solely on cash terms and has no debtors/creditors would the receipts and payments be the figures for sales and purchases.

calculating purchases and sales

The method of calculating the purchases and sales figures is:

■ purchases for year = payments to creditors in the year, less creditors at the beginning of the year, plus creditors at the end of the year

■ sales for year = receipts from debtors in the year, less debtors at the beginning of the year, plus debtors at the end of the year

When calculating purchases and sales, also take note of any cash discounts received and allowed and, for sales, bad debts written off.

The figures from Jack Perry's business are:

purchases	£82,600 – £20,800 + £16,000	= £77,800
sales	£127,800 – £29,200 + £20,400	= £119,000

use of control accounts

The use of control accounts (or totals accounts) is recommended for calculating purchases and sales in incomplete records questions. The information for purchases comes from the Case Study :

Dr		Purchases Ledger Control Account			Cr
2008		£	2008		£
31 Dec	Payments to creditors	82,600	1 Jan	Balances b/d	20,800
31 Dec	Balances c/d	16,000		Purchases (missing figure)	?
		98,600			98,600
2009			2009		
			1 Jan	Balances b/d	16,000

The missing figure of purchases for the year is calculated as:

$$£98,600 – £20,800 = £77,800$$

In a similar way, the sales figure can be calculated:

Dr		Sales Ledger Control Account			Cr
2008		£	2008		£
1 Jan	Balances b/d	29,200	31 Dec	Receipts from debtors	127,800
	Sales (missing figure)	?	31 Dec	Balances c/d	20,400
		148,200			148,200
2009			2009		
1 Jan	Balances b/d	20,400			

The missing figure of sales for the year is £148,200 – £29,200 = £119,000

The control account method, although its use is not essential in incomplete records questions, does bring a discipline to calculating the two important figures of purchases and sales. Do not forget that the control accounts give the figures for credit purchases and sales: cash purchases and sales need to be added, where applicable, to obtain total purchases and sales for the year.

purchases and sales – summary

Whichever method of calculating purchases or sales is used – calculation, or a control account – four pieces of information are usually required:

- opening balance
- closing balance
- payments or receipts for the year
- purchases or sales for the year

Provided that any three are known, the fourth can be calculated – the figure for purchases and sales was the missing figure in the examples above. However if, for example, we know the opening and closing debtors totals, together with sales for the year, then it is a simple matter to calculate the missing figure for receipts from debtors.

Remember that, if they are applicable, cash discounts allowed and received and, for sales, bad debts written off, should also be incorporated into the control accounts.

PREPARATION OF THE FINAL ACCOUNTS

trading and profit and loss account

Having calculated the figures for purchases and sales, we can now begin to prepare the trading and profit and loss account. The section as far as gross profit is:

JACK PERRY
TRADING AND PROFIT AND LOSS ACCOUNT
for the year ended 31 December 2008

	£	£
Sales		119,000
Opening stock	25,600	
Purchases	77,800	
	103,400	
Less closing stock	29,800	
Cost of sales		73,600
Gross profit		45,400

The profit and loss account follows but, before we are able to complete this, we need to know the figure for expenses for the year. The relevant information from the Case Study is:

- bank payments for expenses during year, £30,600
- expenses owing at 1 January 2008, £200
- expenses owing at 31 December 2008, £300

Like the calculation of purchases and sales, we cannot simply use the bank payments figure for expenses; we must take note of cash payments, together with accruals (and prepayments). The calculation is:

expenses for year = bank and cash payments less accruals at the beginning of the year (or plus prepayments), plus accruals at the end of the year (or less prepayments)

Thus the figure for Jack Perry's business expenses is:

£30,600 – £200 + £300 = £30,700.

Alternatively, expenses can be calculated by means of a control account:

Dr		**Expenses Control Account**		Cr
2008	£	2008		£
31 Dec Cash/bank	30,600	1 Jan Balance b/d		200
31 Dec Balance c/d	300	31 Dec Profit and loss account (missing figure)		?
	30,900			30,900
2009		2009		
		1 Jan Balance b/d		300

The missing figure is £30,900 – £200 = £30,700.

Jack Perry's profit and loss account concludes as follows:

	£
Gross profit	45,400
Less:	
Expenses	30,700
Net profit	14,700

balance sheet

The balance sheet can now be prepared using the assets and liabilities from the Case Study.

JACK PERRY

BALANCE SHEET

as at 31 December 2008

	£	£	£
Fixed Assets			
Shop fittings			8,000
Current Assets			
Stock		29,800	
Debtors		20,400	
Bank		7,100	
		57,300	
Less Current Liabilities			
Creditors	16,000		
Accruals	300		
		16,300	
Working Capital			41,000
NET ASSETS			49,000
FINANCED BY			
Capital			
Opening capital			46,800
Add net profit			14,700
			61,500
Less drawings			12,500
			49,000

CASE STUDY
Electroparts

We will now study a more comprehensive example of incomplete records accounting. This incorporates points on depreciation and the sale of a fixed asset. You may like to work through the Case Study before comparing your solution with the one shown.

situation

John Anstey owns a small business, Electroparts, which supplies spare parts for a wide range of electrical goods – cookers, fridges, freezers, kettles, dishwashers, etc. Most of his customers are self-employed repairers who buy parts for specific jobs from his trade counter – John allows them credit terms; some sales are made to members of the public carrying out 'do-it-yourself' repairs – these customers pay in cash at the time of sale. All purchases from suppliers are made on credit.

John does not keep a full set of accounting records; however, the following information has been produced for the year ended 31 December 2004:

	Assets and Liabilities of Electroparts at 1 January 2004		
		£	£
ASSETS	Buildings at cost	100,000	
	Less provision for depreciation	10,000	
			90,000
	Fixtures and fittings at cost	15,000	
	Less provision for depreciation	7,500	
			7,500
			97,500
	Stock	24,400	
	Debtors	21,650	
	Prepayment: general expenses	140	
	Cash	250	
			46,440
	Total Assets		143,940
LIABILITIES	Creditors	15,950	
	Bank overdraft	12,850	
	Total Liabilities		28,800
CAPITAL			115,140

Summary of the bank account (year ended 31 December 2004)

	£		£
Cash sales	45,280	Balance b/d	12,850
Receipts from debtors	177,410	Payments to creditors	149,620
Sale proceeds of fixtures and fittings	1,950	General expenses	17,340
		Wages	18,280
		Drawings	25,390
		Balance c/d	1,160
	224,640		224,640

other information

– On 31 December 2004, stock was valued at £28,400

– Depreciation is calculated at the rate of 2% on the cost of buildings and 10% on the cost of fixtures and fittings held at the end of the financial year. No depreciation is calculated in the year of sale/disposal

– Fixtures and fittings purchased on 1 January 2002 for £2,500 were sold on 30 September 2004, the purchaser paying by cheque

– The proceeds from cash sales are placed in the till and paid into the bank account at the end of the day, apart from a cash float which is retained in the till; the amount of the cash float was £250 until October, when it was increased to £500

– On 31 December 2004, creditors were £18,210, debtors were £23,840 and £210 was owing for general expenses

– During the year, bad debts of £870 have been written off

John Anstey asks you to:

1 Calculate the amount of credit sales during the year

2 Calculate the total sales during the year

3 Calculate the amount of purchases during the year

4 Calculate the profit or loss on the sale of fixtures and fittings

5 Calculate the figure for general expenses to be shown in the profit and loss account for the year ended 31 December 2004

6 Prepare the trading and profit and loss account for the year ended 31 December 2004

7 Prepare the balance sheet at 31 December 2004

Note: for the sake of simplicity, we will ignore VAT.

solution

1

Dr			Sales Ledger Control Account			Cr
2004		£	2004			£
1 Jan	Balances b/d	21,650		Receipts from debtors		177,410
	Credit sales			Bad debts written off		870
	(missing figure)	180,470	31 Dec	Balances c/d		23,840
		202,120				202,120

2

Dr			Sales Account		Cr
2004		£	2004		£
	Trading account			Credit sales (see above)	180,470
	(sales for year)	226,000		Cash sales	45,280
				Increase in cash float	250
		226,000			226,000

3

Dr			Purchases Ledger Control Account			Cr
2004		£	2004			£
	Payments to creditors	149,620	1 Jan	Balances b/d		15,950
31 Dec	Balance c/d	18,210		Purchases		
				(missing figure)		151,880
		167,830				167,830

4   **Profit or loss on disposal of fixtures and fittings**

Depreciation per year	£250	
Number of years' depreciation	2	(2002, 2003; no depreciation in year of sale)
Provision for depreciation	£500	

4

Dr	Disposals Account				Cr
2004		£	2004		£
30 Sep	Fixtures and fittings	2,500	30 Sep	Provision for depreciation	500
			30 Sep	Bank (sale proceeds)	1,950
			31 Dec	Profit and loss account (loss on sale)	50
		2,500			2,500

5

Dr	General Expenses Control Account				Cr
2004		£	2004		£
1 Jan	Balance b/d	140	31 Dec	Profit and loss account	
	Bank	17,340		(missing figure)	17,690
31 Dec	Balance c/d	210			
		17,690			17,690

6

JOHN ANSTEY, TRADING AS 'ELECTROPARTS'
TRADING AND PROFIT AND LOSS ACCOUNT
for the year ended 31 December 2004

	£	£
Sales		226,000
Opening stock	24,400	
Purchases	151,880	
	176,280	
Less Closing stock	28,400	
Cost of sales		147,880
Gross profit		78,120
Less overheads:		
General expenses	17,690	
Loss on sale of fixtures and fittings	50	
Provision for depreciation: buildings	2,000	
fixtures and fittings	*1,250	
Bad debts written off	870	
Wages	18,280	
		40,140
Net profit		37,980

*Note

Fixtures and fittings at cost on 1 January 2004	£15,000
Less cost price of fixtures and fittings sold 30 September 2004	£2,500
Fixtures and fittings at cost on 31 December 2004	£12,500
Depreciation at 10%	£1,250

7

JOHN ANSTEY, TRADING AS 'ELECTROPARTS'
BALANCE SHEET
as at 31 December 2004

	£	£	£
Fixed Assets	Cost	Dep'n to date	Net
Buildings	100,000	12,000	88,000
Fixtures and fittings	12,500	*8,250	4,250
	112,500	20,250	92,250
Current Assets			
Stock		28,400	
Debtors		23,840	
Bank		1,160	
Cash		500	
		53,900	
Less Current Liabilities			
Creditors	18,210		
Accrual: general expenses	210		
		18,420	
Working Capital			35,480
NET ASSETS			127,730
FINANCED BY			
Capital			
Opening capital (from assets and liabilities at 1 January 2004)			115,140
Add net profit			37,980
			153,120
Less drawings			25,390
Closing capital			127,730

*Note

Provision for depreciation of fixtures and fittings at 1 January 2004	7,500
Less provision for depreciation on asset sold	500
	7,000
Depreciation for year (see profit and loss account)	1,250
Provision for depreciation of fixtures and fittings at 31 December 2004	8,250

THE USE OF GROSS PROFIT MARK-UP AND MARGIN

It is often necessary to use accounting ratios and percentages in the preparation of final accounts from incomplete records.

The topic of ratios and percentages is covered fully in Chapter 15.

The two main percentages used for incomplete records accounting are:

- gross profit mark-up
- gross profit margin

It is quite common for a business to establish its selling price by reference to either a mark-up or a margin. The difference between the two is that:

- mark-up is a profit percentage added to buying or cost price
- margin is a percentage profit based on the selling price

For example, a product is bought by a retailer at a cost of £100; the retailer sells it for £125, ie

cost price	+	gross profit	=	selling price
£100	+	£25	=	£125

The **mark-up** is:

$$\frac{\text{gross profit}}{\text{cost price}} \quad \times \quad \frac{100}{1} \quad = \quad \frac{£25}{£100} \quad \times \quad \frac{100}{1} \quad = \quad \textbf{25\%}$$

The **margin** is:

$$\frac{\text{gross profit}}{\text{selling price}} \quad \times \quad \frac{100}{1} \quad = \quad \frac{£25}{£125} \quad \times \quad \frac{100}{1} \quad = \quad \textbf{20\%}$$

In incomplete records accounting, mark-up or the margin percentages can be used to calculate the sales figure, the purchases figure or the cost of sales. We will now study two examples.

WORKED EXAMPLES

example 1 – calculation of sales

- Cost of sales is £150,000

- Mark-up is 40%

- What are sales?

$$\text{Gross profit} \;=\; £150,000 \;\times\; \frac{40}{100} \;=\; £60,000$$

Sales = cost of sales + gross profit, ie £150,000 + £60,000 = **£210,000**

example 2 – calculation of purchases

- Sales are £450,000

- Margin is 20%

- Opening stock is £40,000; closing stock is £50,000

- What are purchases?

$$\text{Gross profit} = £450,000 \;\times\; \frac{20}{100} \;=\; £90,000$$

Cost of sales = sales – gross profit, ie £450,000 – £90,000 = £360,000

The purchases calculation is:

	Opening stock	£40,000
+	Purchases (missing figure)	?
–	Closing stock	£50,000
=	Cost of sales	£360,000
	Therefore purchases =	**£370,000**

STOCK LOSSES

A loss of stock may occur as a result of an event such as a fire, a flood or a theft. When such a loss occurs, an estimate of the value of the stock lost needs to be made in order for the business to make an insurance claim (always assuming that the stock was adequately insured). The value is calculated by preparing an accounting summary to the date of the event, and often making use of margins and mark-ups. The calculations are best carried out in three steps:

1 Opening stock
   +   purchases
   =   cost of stock available for sale

2 Sales
   –   gross profit (using normal gross profit margin)
   =   cost of sales

3 Cost of stock available for sale (from 1, above)
   –   cost of sales (2, above)
   =   estimated closing stock
   –   value of stock remaining or salvaged
   =   value of stock lost through fire, flood or theft

CASE STUDY
Clothing Supplies – theft of stock

situation

Peter Kamara runs Clothing Supplies, a small clothing wholesalers. Peter is convinced that various items of clothing have been stolen during the year and he asks you to calculate, from the accounting details, the value of stock stolen. The following information is available:

* sales for the year, £500,000

* opening stock at the beginning of the year, £15,000

* purchases for the year, £310,000

* closing stock at the end of the year, £22,000

* the gross profit margin achieved on all sales is 40 per cent

solution

CALCULATION OF STOCK LOSS FOR THE YEAR

	£	£
Opening stock		15,000
Purchases		310,000
Cost of stock available for sale		325,000
Sales	500,000	
Less normal gross profit margin (40%)	200,000	
Cost of sales		300,000
Estimated closing stock		25,000
Less actual closing stock		22,000
Value of stock loss		3,000

chapter summary

- Incomplete records is the term used where the book-keeping system does not use double-entry principles.

- In order to prepare final accounts, the accountant may well have to calculate:
  - capital at the beginning of the financial year
  - cash book summary
  - purchases and sales for the year
  - profit for the year

- On the basis of these calculations, the accountant can then construct the final accounts without recourse to a trial balance.

- Two ratios and percentages used in incomplete records accounting are:
  - gross profit mark-up
  - gross profit margin

- The value of stock losses caused by fire, flood or theft is calculated using margins and mark-ups.

key terms

incomplete records	a book-keeping system in which double-entry principles are not used
gross profit mark-up	profit percentage added to the buying price
gross profit margin	profit percentage based on the selling price
stock loss	loss of stock caused by fire, flood or theft

activities

Note: an asterisk (*) after an activity number means that an answer is provided in Appendix 1.

8.1* • Cost of sales for the year is £200,000.

   • Mark-up is 30%.

   What are sales for the year?

8.2* • Sales for the year are £100,000.

   • Gross profit margin is 25%.

   • Opening stock is £10,000; closing stock is £12,000.

   What are purchases for the year?

8.3* You are preparing accounts from incomplete records. Debtors at the start of the year were £2,500, and at the end were £3,250. Cheques received from debtors total £17,850; cash sales total £2,500. What is the sales figure for the year?

8.4* Jane Price owns a fashion shop called 'Trendsetters'. She has been in business for one year and, although she does not keep a full set of accounting records, the following information has been produced for the first year of trading, which ended on 31 December 2008:

Summary of the business bank account for the year ended 31 December 2008:

	£
Capital introduced	60,000
Receipts from sales	153,500
Payments to suppliers	95,000
Advertising	4,830
Wages	15,000
Rent and rates	8,750
General expenses	5,000
Shop fittings	50,000
Drawings	15,020

Summary of assets and liabilities as at 31 December 2008:

	£
Shop fittings at cost	50,000
Stock	73,900
Debtors	2,500
Creditors	65,000

Other information:

- Jane wishes to depreciate the shop fittings at 20% per year using the straight-line method

- At 31 December 2008, rent is prepaid by £250, and wages of £550 are owing

You are to:

(a) Calculate the amount of sales during the year.

(b) Calculate the amount of purchases during the year.

(c) Calculate the figures for

- rent and rates

- wages

to be shown in the profit and loss account for the year ended 31 December 2008

(d) Prepare Jane Price's trading and profit & loss account for the year ended 31 December 2008.

(e) Draw up Jane Price's balance sheet as at 31 December 2008.

Note: VAT is to be ignored on all transactions

8.5 James Hardy owns a business which sells computer supplies. Most of his customers are firms in the area, to whom he sells on credit terms. Although he does not keep a full set of accounting records, the following information is available in respect of the year ending 31 December 2009:

Summary of assets and liabilities;

	1 Jan 2009	31 Dec 2009
	£	£
Shop fittings (cost £10,000)	8,000	7,000
Stock	25,600	29,800
Bank balance	4,000	8,000
Cash	1,000	1,600
Debtors	29,200	20,400
Creditors	20,800	16,000
Accruals: business expenses	–	500

Summary of the business bank account for the year ended 31 December 2009:

	£
Receipts from customers	127,800
Payments to suppliers	82,600
Drawings	20,000
Business expenses	20,600

Other information:

Shop fittings are being depreciated at 10% per year, using the straight line method.

You are to

(a)   Calculate the amount of sales during the year

(b)   Calculate the amount of purchases during the year

(c)   Calculate the figure for business expenses to be shown in the profit and loss account for the year ended 31 December 2009

(d)   Prepare James Hardy's trading and profit and loss account for the year ended 31 December 2009

(e)   Draw up James Hardy's balance sheet as at 31 December 2009

Note: VAT is to be ignored on all transactions

8.6   Colin Smith owns a business which sells specialist central heating parts to trade customers. He has been in business for a number of years. Although he does not keep a full set of accounting records, the following information is available in respect of the year ended 30 June 2009:

Summary of assets and liabilities:

	1 July 2008	30 June 2009
	£	£
Assets		
Stock	25,000	27,500
Fixtures and fittings (cost £50,000)	40,000	35,000
Debtors	36,000	35,000
Bank	1,500	1,210
Liabilities		
Creditors	32,500	30,000
Accrual: business expenses	500	700

Summary of the business bank account for the year ended 30 June 2009

	£
Business expenses	30,000
Drawings	28,790
Receipts from debtors	121,000
Payments to suppliers	62,500

Other information:

•   Fixtures and fittings are being depreciated at 10% per year using the straight line method

•   Bad debts of £500 have been written off during the year

You are to

(a) Calculate the amount of sales during the year ended 30 June 2009

(b) Calculate the amount of purchases during the year ended 30 June 2009

(c) Calculate the figure for business expenses to be shown in the profit and loss account for the year ended 30 June 2009

(d) Prepare Colin Smith's trading and profit and loss account for the year ended 30 June 2009

(e) Draw up Colin Smith's balance sheet as at 30 June 2009

Note: VAT is to be ignored on all transactions

8.7   James Harvey runs a stationery supplies shop. He is convinced that one of his employees is stealing stationery. He asks you to calculate from the accounting records the value of stock stolen. The following information is available:

- sales for the year, £180,000

- opening stock at the beginning of the year, £21,500

- purchases for the year, £132,000

- closing stock at the end of the year, £26,000

- the gross profit margin achieved on all sales is 30 per cent

You are to calculate the value of stock stolen (if any) during the year.

8.8   Talib Zabbar owns a shop selling children's clothes. He is convinced that his customers are stealing goods from the shop. He asks you to calculate from the accounting records the value of stock stolen.

The following information is available:

- sales for the year, £160,000

- opening stock at the beginning of the year, £30,500

- purchases for the year, £89,500

- closing stock at the end of the year, £21,500

- the gross profit margin achieved on all sales is 40 per cent.

You are to calculate the value of stock stolen (if any) during the year.

CLUB AND SOCIETY ACCOUNTS

CASE STUDY
'We need a treasurer . . .'

If you belong to a club or a society, and admit to a knowledge of book-keeping or accounting, you are in danger – you may soon find yourself elected as the treasurer!

It is the job of the treasurer of a club or society to maintain proper accounting records. These will be audited once a year either by another member, or by an outside accountant.

The treasurer attends committee meetings of the club or society and reports on financial progress. At the end of the financial year, the treasurer prepares financial statements which are then presented to members at the annual general meeting. The accounting records of clubs and societies should be kept by the treasurer to the highest standards – at least that is the ideal.

The accounts of non-profit making organisations – such as clubs and societies – are different from those of businesses. Instead of having the primary objective of profit, clubs and societies are set up to provide facilities and services to members and their accounts reflect this difference

Now, let us assume that you have just been appointed as treasurer to the South Dempsey Sports Club . . .

In this chapter we will explain how you prepare the club's year-end accounts, and we will discuss the accounting treatment of the accounts of clubs and societies.

learning objectives

When you have studied this chapter you will be able to:

■   *appreciate the differences in accounting terminology between business and non-profit making organisations*

■   *prepare club/society year-end accounts*

■   *decide the appropriate accounting treatment for aspects of club/society accounts*

ACCOUNTING TERMINOLOGY

Businesses and non-profit making organisations – such as clubs and societies – differ in their aims and accounting terminology, as shown in the table below.

	Business	Non-profit making organisation
PRIMARY OBJECTIVE	To make a profit	To provide facilities and services to members
MAIN ACCOUNTING STATEMENTS	Trading and profit and loss account Balance sheet	Income and expenditure account Balance sheet
FINANCIAL PERFORMANCE	Profit Loss	Surplus of income over expenditure Deficit
FUNDING	Capital	Accumulated fund

ACCOUNTING RECORDS OF A CLUB OR SOCIETY

Few clubs and societies keep accounting records in double-entry form. For most clubs, the treasurer keeps a cash book, which is a simple version of the cash book used by businesses. It records receipts paid into the bank and payments made from the bank, together with cash receipts and payments. The cash book is ruled off and balanced at the end of the financial year.

Often a summary of the cash book is presented to members in the form of a **receipts and payments account** (see Case Study on page 177); for a very small club, this information forms the 'year-end accounts'. However, there are two accounting problems in using a receipts and payments account:

- accruals and prepayments cannot be made
- the distinction between capital and revenue expenditure cannot be made

Thus, whilst a receipt and payments account may be suitable for a small club which meets infrequently or deals in small amounts of money, a larger club needs to produce final accounts in the form of:

- income and expenditure account
- balance sheet

INCOME AND EXPENDITURE ACCOUNT

The income and expenditure account of a club or society lists the income and deducts the expenditure using a layout similar to a profit and loss account. The account will then show:

■ either a surplus of income over expenditure

■ or a deficit of expenditure over income

The income and expenditure account is prepared from the receipts and payments account, taking note of:

■ accruals

■ prepayments

■ provision for depreciation of fixed assets

Capital expenditure, eg the purchase of a new lawnmower for a cricket club, is not recorded in the income and expenditure account, although depreciation of the lawnmower will be shown.

A major source of income for a club is members' subscriptions. Some members will prepay subscriptions for the next financial year, while others will be late in paying, or may never pay at all, ceasing to be members. Unless the club has a different policy, the treasurer calculates the subscriptions that should have been received, as shown in the following formula:

	subscriptions received in year	**1**
add	subscriptions prepaid at start of year	**2**
less	subscriptions owing at start of year	**3**
less	subscriptions paid in advance at end of the year	**4**
add	subscriptions due but unpaid at end of the year	**5**
equals	subscription income for year to be shown in income and expenditure account	**6**

The subscriptions are best calculated by means of a control account, the format of which is shown on the next page. The numbers in the coloured boxes refer to the parts of the formula set out above.

Dr	Subscriptions Control Account				Cr
	£				£
Balance at start of year (subscriptions owing)	3		Balance at start of year (subscriptions prepaid)		2
Income and expenditure account (subscription income for year)	6		Subscriptions received in year	1	
Balance at end of year (subscriptions prepaid)	4		Balance at end of year (subscriptions owing)		5

In the balance sheet of the club, subscriptions in advance are recorded as a current liability, while subscriptions due but unpaid are a current asset – debtors for subscriptions. This method of handling subscriptions takes note of prepayments and accruals and is the way in which we would deal with such items in the accounts of a business. However, in practice, the treasurer of a club may decide not to record subscriptions due but unpaid as debtors because, unlike a business, the club will not sue for unpaid amounts. The most realistic approach is to ignore such subscriptions – if they are subsequently paid, they can be brought into that year's income.

Other sources of income for clubs or societies include:

■ trading activities, eg a bar, catering facilities

■ donations received

■ room lettings to other organisations

■ special activities, eg jumble sale, dinner dance

BALANCE SHEET

The balance sheet of a club or society is presented in a very similar way to that of a business. The major difference is that, instead of capital, a club has an accumulated fund. If the accumulated fund is not known at the start of the financial year, it is calculated as:

assets – liabilities = accumulated fund

In the balance sheet a surplus from the income and expenditure account is added to the accumulated fund, while a deficit is deducted.

TRADING ACTIVITIES

Although the primary objective of clubs and societies and other non-profit making organisations is to provide facilities and services to members, many organisations carry out an activity on a regular basis with the intention of making a profit. Examples of such trading activities include:

- a bar for the use of members

- provision of catering facilities for members

- the purchase of goods to sell to members on favourable terms, eg seeds and fertilisers by a gardening society

In the year-end accounts, the treasurer should prepare a separate account for such activities so as to show the profit or loss. The layout of this account is exactly the same as that for a trading business, with opening stock, closing stock, purchases and sales. Any direct costs associated with the trading activity – such as the wages of bar staff – will be included. The profit or loss on trading activities is then taken to the income and expenditure account.

FUND-RAISING EVENTS

Most clubs and societies organise fund-raising events from time-to-time, eg jumble sales, raffles, coffee mornings, etc. It is usual to show the separate profit or loss on such events within the income and expenditure account. This is done by linking the income and the expenses together, for example:

	£	£
Income		
Christmas Fayre		
takings	550	
less expenses	210	
profit		340

CASE STUDY
South Dempsey Sports Club

situation

You have been appointed as the treasurer of the South Dempsey Sports Club. At the beginning of the financial year, on 1 January 2002, the assets and liabilities of the club were:

- bank balance, £431
- furniture and fittings, £1,000
- sports equipment, £1,250
- bar stock, £210

For the year ended 31 December 2002, you prepare the following receipts and payments account :

RECEIPTS AND PAYMENTS ACCOUNT
for the year ended 31 December 2002

RECEIPTS	£	PAYMENTS	£
Balance b/d	431	Rent paid	2,500
Subscriptions	1,875	Electricity	295
Bar takings	3,700	Bar purchases	1,210
Donation	100	Bar wages	790
Sale of raffle tickets	310	Raffle prizes	120
		Sports equipment	500
		Secretary's expenses	730
		Sundry expenses	220
		Balance c/d	51
	6,416		6,416

The shortcomings of the receipts and payments account are that:

- It ignores the fact that subscriptions of £1,875 include £175 paid by members in advance for next year.
- There is bar stock of £320 at the end of the year.
- Rent of £500 has been paid for the first quarter of next year (a prepayment).
- The acquisition of sports equipment of £500 is shown along with other payments; it needs to be identified and listed on the balance sheet as a fixed asset.
- At the end of the year, furniture is valued at £800, and sports equipment is valued at £1,500.

As the receipts and payments account does not show an entirely true picture of the club's affairs for the year, you use the information in the preparation of the:

- income and expenditure account
- balance sheet

solution

The steps to prepare the year-end accounts of the club are:

- an opening trial balance – to calculate the accumulated fund at the start of the year
- a closing trial balance – incorporating amounts from the receipts and payments account (or summary of the club's cash book)
- year-end accounts, ie income and expenditure account and balance sheet

The opening trial balance is as follows:

SOUTH DEMPSEY SPORTS CLUB
Opening trial balance as at 1 January 2002

	Dr £	Cr £
Bank balance	431	
Furniture and fittings	1,000	
Sports equipment	1,250	
Bar stock at 1 January 2002	210	
Accumulated fund		*2,891
	2,891	2,891

* calculated as the 'missing figure'

The year-end trial balance incorporates the figures from the opening trial balance and the amounts from the receipts and payments account. Note that sports equipment is shown as £1,750 (ie £1,250 from the opening trial balance, plus additions of £500 shown in the receipts and payments account). The trial balance is as follows:

SOUTH DEMPSEY SPORTS CLUB
Trial balance as at 31 December 2002

	Dr £	Cr £
Bank balance	51	
Furniture and fittings	1,000	
Sports equipment (£1,250 + £500)	1,750	
Bar stock at 1 January 2002	210	
Accumulated fund		2,891
Subscriptions		1,875
Bar takings		3,700
Donations		100
Sale of raffle tickets		310
Rent paid	2,500	

Electricity	295	
Bar purchases	1,210	
Bar wages	790	
Raffle prizes	120	
Secretary's expenses	730	
Sundry expenses	220	
	8,876	8,876

In preparing the income and expenditure account, note is taken of the following adjustments:

- Provision for depreciation of fixed assets

  furniture, £1,000 − £800 = £200 depreciation

  sports equipment, £1,750 − £1,500 = £250 depreciation

- Subscriptions in advance of £175; thus the amount recorded in the income and expenditure account is £1,875 − £175 = £1,700. Note that subscriptions which are due but unpaid are often, in practice, ignored for the year's accounts – they are often paid late, if indeed they are paid at all.

- Rent prepaid £500; thus the amount recorded in the income and expenditure account is £2,500 − £500 = £2,000.

- Bar closing stock of £320, which is dealt with in the same way as the closing stock of a business.

The income and expenditure account and balance sheet are presented as shown on the next two pages. Note the following points:

- The profit on the bar has been calculated separately in a 'bar trading account' and then brought into the income and expenditure account. It is usual for clubs and societies to show the figures relating to main trading activities in a separate account.

- The donation received has been shown as income; as it is a relatively small amount this would seem to be the correct treatment (see also page 182). Had it been a much larger amount, it would have been taken directly to the balance sheet.

- The profit on the raffle has been disclosed within the income and expenditure account; an alternative treatment would be to show the cost of raffle prizes as expenditure.

- A surplus of income over expenditure (as here) is the equivalent of a business making a net profit, while a deficit is the equivalent of a net loss. The surplus is added to the accumulated fund – the equivalent of a business' capital – in the balance sheet (a deficit would be deducted).

SOUTH DEMPSEY SPORTS CLUB
BAR TRADING ACCOUNT
for the year ended 31 December 2002

	£	£
Bar takings		3,700
Opening stock	210	
Purchases	1,210	
	1,420	
Less Closing stock	320	
	1,100	
Bar wages	790	
		1,890
Profit on bar		1,810

SOUTH DEMPSEY SPORTS CLUB
INCOME AND EXPENDITURE ACCOUNT
for the year ended 31 December 2002

	£	£
Income		
Profit on bar		1,810
Subscriptions		1,700
Donation		100
Sale of raffle tickets	310	
Less raffle prizes	120	
Profit on raffle		190
		3,800
Less expenditure		
Rent	2,000	
Electricity	295	
Secretary's expenses	730	
Sundry expenses	220	
Provision for depreciation:		
furniture	200	
sports equipment	250	
		3,695
Surplus of income over expenditure		105

SOUTH DEMPSEY SPORTS CLUB
BALANCE SHEET
as at 31 December 2002

	£	£
Fixed Assets		
Furniture and fittings (at valuation)		800
Sports equipment (at valuation)		1,500
		2,300
Current Assets		
Bar stock	320	
Prepayment (rent)	500	
Bank	51	
	871	
Less Current Liabilities		
Subscriptions in advance	175	
Working Capital		696
NET ASSETS		2,996
REPRESENTED BY		
Accumulated fund		2,891
Surplus of income over expenditure		105
		2,996

CLUB ACCOUNTS: PROBLEM AREAS

There are a number of possible areas that need to be clarified by a newly appointed treasurer of a club or society. These are the club's policy on:

- overdue subscriptions
- life membership
- entrance/joining fees
- donations received
- depreciation

The club's rules should state how these are to be handled in the accounts; if not, a new treasurer will have to see how they were dealt with in previous years, or ask the committee for a decision.

overdue subscriptions

We have seen earlier that the practical policy adopted by most treasurers is to ignore overdue subscriptions (but an adjustment is made for prepaid subscriptions). However, in questions and assessments, unless instructed otherwise, overdue subscriptions should be treated as accruals, and subscriptions in advance as prepayments.

life membership

Some clubs and societies offer life membership in exchange for a one-off payment. The problem for the treasurer is whether to record this payment as income for the year in which it is received, or to credit it to a reserve account (eg Life Subscriptions Account), the balance of which is then transferred bit-by-bit over a number of years to the income and expenditure account. The time period for this will depend on the nature of the club: for example, the 'Over-eighties Gentleman's Dining Club' is likely to transfer its life subscriptions account to income rather more quickly than will a stamp collecting club.

A club of which the writer is a member has the following accounting policy:

'Three per cent of the life subscriptions account is released to income each year.'

The policy for accounting for life membership will normally be stated clearly in questions you are given to complete.

entrance or joining fees

Often a one-off charge is made in the year of joining a club as an entrance fee. It is possible to justify making such a charge by arguing that it covers the cost of processing new members' applications; on the other hand it gives extra income to the club and, once a person is a member, it acts as an incentive for them to remain a member (because, if their membership lapsed, the joining fee would be payable again upon rejoining).

The treasurer needs to know how to account for the joining fee:

- either, it is treated as income for the year of joining (but this could distort income if a membership 'drive' was held in one particular year)
- or, it is credited to an entrance fees account which is transferred to income over a number of years

donations received

There are two alternative accounting treatments which can be used for donations received:

- record the amount as income in the income and expenditure account, or
- record the amount as an addition to the accumulated fund in the balance sheet

The first method treats the donation as income for the year, while the second capitalises the amount (ie records it on the balance sheet). As to which is to be used depends very much on the amount of the donation in relation to the size of the club's activities – the accounting concept of materiality applies. For example, a £10 donation would normally be recorded as income; however, a legacy of several thousands of pounds from a deceased club member ought to be capitalised and added to the accumulated fund. If the club rules do not state how donations received are to be dealt with in the accounts, the treasurer must use his or her own judgement and will probably apply the materiality concept.

Remember that, in practice, donations will not always be cash amounts, other assets could be donated, eg a plot of land, a work of art. Here the asset will need to be valued and recorded in the accounts. In the case of assets other than cash, it is likely that they will need to be capitalised and recorded on the balance sheet.

depreciation

As in the final accounts of a business, fixed assets should be depreciated in club accounts; the same principles will apply (see Chapter 7). Provision for depreciation for the year is charged as an expense in the income and expenditure account, while the asset is shown in the balance sheet at cost less depreciation to date, to give the net book value.

Often clubs simply value fixed assets at the end of each financial year. The fall in value, subject to any acquisitions or sales, is the provision for depreciation for the year which is charged as an expense in the income and expenditure account. The fixed asset will then be shown at the reduced value in the year end balance sheet.

PRACTICAL POINTS FOR TREASURERS

As noted in the introduction to this chapter, the treasurer of a club or society is responsible for maintaining proper accounting records. The same high standards of financial recording as would be applied to the accounts of a business should be used by the club treasurer. Two areas are of particular importance:

authority to spend

Before making payments, the treasurer must ensure that he or she has the authority to spend the club's money. For 'one-off' transactions, eg the purchase of a new lawnmower by a cricket club, the minutes of the relevant committee meeting will show that the purchase was agreed. For regular activities, eg small expenses such as printing, electricity, the club's rules will authorise the treasurer to make payment against invoices received.

documentary evidence

The treasurer should ensure that there is documentary evidence for every transaction passing through the accounts of the club. For example, payments should only be made against invoices received in the name of the club, while a receipt should be given for all money received. In this way, an audit trail is created. All documents should be retained for the use of the club's auditor, who will check the accounting records after the end of each financial year. The documents should then be stored for at least six years in case there are subsequent queries.

chapter summary

- Unlike a business, a non-profit making organisation – such as a club or society – does not base its activities on profit, but operates for the benefit of its members.

- Many clubs and societies have large sums of money passing through their hands and, like businesses, need tight accounting controls.

- The year-end accounts of a club consist of
  - income and expenditure account
  - balance sheet

- Where a club carries out a trading activity with the intention of making a profit, a separate account is often prepared for the activity.

- Accounting policies on which the treasurer needs guidance from the club's committee are:
  - overdue subscriptions
  - life membership
  - entrance/joining fees
  - donations received
  - depreciation

key terms

receipts and payments account	summary of the cash book showing the main sources and uses of money
income and expenditure account	the equivalent of a business' profit and loss account
surplus of income over expenditure	the equivalent of a business' profit
deficit of expenditure over income	the equivalent of a business' loss
accumulated fund	assets less liabilities; the equivalent of the capital of a business

activities

Note: an asterisk (*) after an activity number means that an answer is provided in Appendix 1.

9.1 Distinguish between:

(a) receipts and payments account, and income and expenditure account

(b) profit, and surplus of income and expenditure

(c) capital, and accumulated fund

9.2* The following information is available to the treasurer of Wyemeadow Golf Club for the year ended 31 December 2009:

1 January	Subscriptions prepaid	£1,250
	Subscriptions owing	£2,750
31 December	Subscriptions received during the year	£25,500
	Subscriptions prepaid for 2010	£1,750
	Subscriptions owing for 2009	£3,250

Note: all subscriptions due at 1 January 2009 have now been paid and are included in the receipts for the year.

You are to calculate the amount of subscription income to be shown in the income and expenditure account for the year ended 31 December 2009.

9.3* Westside Sports Club was set up on 1 July 2008. You are the treasurer and, at the end of the first year, you prepare a receipts and payments account as follows:

RECEIPTS AND PAYMENTS ACCOUNT
for the year ended 30 June 2009

RECEIPTS	£	PAYMENTS	£
Subscriptions	1,540	Equipment	1,500
Competition entry fees	498	Postage and stationery	197
Sale of snacks	1,108	Rent	550
		Competition expenses	320
		Purchase of snacks	520
		Balance c/d	59
	3,146		3,146

Additional information at 30 June 2009:

- subscriptions paid in advance for next year, £80
- rent owing, £100
- stock of snacks is valued at £70
- equipment is to be depreciated at 20%

You are to prepare the income and expenditure account and balance sheet of Westside Sports Club for the year ended 30 June 2009.

9.4   You have recently taken over as the treasurer of the Hallow Choir. The accounts of the previous year (to 31 December 2008) have been prepared, but only as a receipts and payments account as follows:

RECEIPTS AND PAYMENTS ACCOUNT
for the year to 31 December 2008

RECEIPTS	£	PAYMENTS	£
Balance b/d	112	Concert costs	1,250
Subscriptions	750	Conductor's fee	300
Music festival prize	500	Music purchase	450
Concert ticket sales	825	Printing of programmes	60
Fund raising activities (raffles)	427	Balance c/d	554
	2,614		2,614

Additionally, you note that:

- £65 of subscriptions, included in the £750, are paid in advance for 2009
- the club owes £40 for programme printing
- stocks of music, which are treated as fixed assets, are lent to club members free of charge; in last year's balance sheet they were valued at £875; for the current year's balance sheet they are to be valued at £1,125

You are to prepare the income and expenditure account and balance sheet of Hallow Choir for the year ended 31 December 2008.

9.5   The assets and liabilities of the Southwick Social Club as at 1 July 2008 were:

- bank balance, £580
- furniture and equipment, £2,500
- bar stock, £540
- rent owing, £120

For the year ended 30 June 2009, the treasurer prepared the following receipts and payments account:

RECEIPTS AND PAYMENTS ACCOUNT
for the year ended 30 June 2009

RECEIPTS	£	PAYMENTS	£
Balance b/d	580	Bar purchases	3,975
Subscriptions	2,790	Dinner dance expenses	1,280
Bar takings	6,380	Secretary's expenses	890
Dinner dance ticket sales	790	Bar wages	1,530
		Rent	940
		Furniture and equipment	1,710
		Balance c/d	215
	10,540		10,540

Additional information at 30 June 2009:
- bar stocks are valued at £630
- furniture and equipment is valued at £3,500
- subscriptions prepaid for next year, £210
- rent owing, £190

You are to prepare the income and expenditure account and balance sheet of Southwick Social Club for the year ended 30 June 2009.

PARTNERSHIP FINAL ACCOUNTS

CASE STUDY
expanding the business...

Ramjit Singh has been running a CD music shop for a few years now. The specialist CDs that he imports from the USA and Japan sell well in his shop in Norwich. He would like to enlarge the sales area of the shop to display a wider range of albums. He has found out that the shop next door is empty and thinks it would be ideal for his expansion plans. In the longer term he thinks he could open other shops in other locations in the UK.

Ramjit is sure that there is a wider market for the products he sells. He is looking into the possibility of a mail order service and selling from a website, which will enable him to sell his speciality products worldwide. However, as a sole trader, he is aware of his limitations:

– he is responsible for every aspect of the business
– he can raise only limited amounts of finance
– he would need assistance to run an expanding business

A good friend of his, Veta Bix, has often helped out in the shop at short notice. Veta has suggested that she might like to become involved in the business on a more formal basis.

After discussions with their solicitors, the two of them have decided to form a business partnership. The advantages are that Veta will be able to put some finance into the business and will be able to take on some of the management responsibilities from Ramjit.

They have decided to rebrand the shop under the name of 'RaVe Music' – incorporating the first two letters of their first names, Ramjit and Veta.

They will also need to make a partnership agreement . . .

In this chapter we look at the accounting requirements of partnerships, together with the layout of partnership final accounts.

learning objectives

When you have studied this chapter you will be able to:

■ *define a partnership*
■ *appreciate the accounting requirements of a partnership*
■ *prepare the appropriation of partnership profits*
■ *draft final accounts for a partnership from appropriate information*

WHAT DOES A PARTNERSHIP INVOLVE?

The Partnership Act of 1890 defines a partnership as:

the relation which subsists between persons carrying on a business in common with a view of profit

Normally, partnerships consist of between two and twenty partners (exceptions being large professional firms, eg solicitors and accountants). Partnerships are often larger businesses than sole traders because, as there is more than one owner, there is likely to be more capital. A partnership may be formed to set up a new business or it may be the logical growth of a sole trader taking in partners to increase the capital.

advantages and disadvantages

Partnerships are cheap and easy to set up; their **advantages** are:
- there is the possibility of increased capital
- individual partners may be able to specialise in particular areas of the business
- with more people running the business, there is cover for illness and holidays

The **disadvantages** are:
- as there is more than one owner, decisions may take longer because other partners may need to be consulted
- there may be disagreements amongst the partners
- each partner is liable in law for the dealings and business debts of the whole firm (unless it is a 'limited liability partnership' set up under the Limited Liability Partnerships Act 2000)
- the retirement or death of one partner may adversely affect the running of the business

accounting requirements of a partnership

The accounting requirements of a partnership are:
- either to follow the rules set out in the Partnership Act 1890
- or – and more likely – for the partners to agree amongst themselves, by means of a partnership agreement (see page 191), to follow different accounting rules

Unless the partners agree otherwise, the Partnership Act 1890 states the following accounting rules:
- profits and losses are to be shared equally between the partners

■ no partner is entitled to a salary

■ partners are not entitled to receive interest on their capital

■ interest is not to be charged on partners' drawings

■ when a partner contributes more capital than agreed, he or she is entitled to receive interest at five per cent per annum on the excess

As noted above, the partners may well decide to follow different accounting rules – these will be set out in a partnership agreement (see the next page).

YEAR-END ACCOUNTS OF A PARTNERSHIP

A partnership prepares the same type of final accounts as a sole trader business:

■ profit and loss account

■ balance sheet

The main difference is that, immediately after the profit and loss account, follows an **appropriation section** (often described as an appropriation account). This shows how the net profit from profit and loss account is shared amongst the partners.

example of sharing profits

Jan, Kay and Lil are partners sharing profits and losses equally; their profit and loss account for 2002 shows a net profit of £60,000. The appropriation of profits appears as:

JAN, KAY AND LIL	
PROFIT AND LOSS APPROPRIATION ACCOUNT	
for the year ended 31 December 2002	
	£
Net profit	60,000
Share of profits:	
Jan	20,000
Kay	20,000
Lil	20,000
	60,000

The above is a simple appropriation of profits. A more complex appropriation account (see Case Study on page 194) deals with other accounting points from the partnership agreement (see next section).

PARTNERSHIP AGREEMENT

The accounting rules from the Partnership Act are often varied with the agreement of all partners, by means of a partnership agreement. In particular, a partnership agreement will usually cover the following:

- division of profits and losses between partners
- partners' salaries/commission
- whether interest is to be allowed on capital and at what rate
- whether interest is to be charged on partners' drawings, and at what rate

The money amounts involved for each of these points (where allowed by the partnership agreement) are shown in the partnership appropriation account (see Case Study on page 195).

division of profits and losses between partners

The Partnership Act states that, in the absence of an agreement to the contrary, profits and losses are to be shared equally. A partner's share of the profits is normally taken out of the business in the form of drawings. Clearly, if one partner has contributed much more capital than the other partner(s), it would be unfair to apply this clause from the Act. Consequently, many partnerships agree to share profits and losses on a different basis – often in the same proportions as they have contributed capital.

partners' salaries/commission

Although the Act says that no partner is entitled to a salary, it is quite usual in the partnership agreement for one or more partners to be paid a salary. The reason for doing this is that often in a partnership, one of the partners spends more time working in the partnership than the other(s). The agreement to pay a salary is in recognition of the work done. Note that partners' salaries are not shown as an expense in profit anf loss account; instead they appear in the partnership appropriation account (see Case Study on page 195).

Many professional partnerships, such as solicitors and accountants, have junior partners who receive a partnership salary because they work full-time in the business, but have not yet contributed any capital. In a partnership, there may not be a requirement to contribute capital, unless the partnership agreement states otherwise; however, most partners will eventually do so.

As an alternative to a salary, a partner might be paid a commission on sales. As with a salary, this is not shown as an expense in the profit and loss account, but appears in the partnership appropriation account.

interest allowed on capital

Many partnerships include a clause in their partnership agreement which allows interest to be paid on capital; the rate of interest will be stated also. This clause is used to compensate partners for the loss of use of their capital, ie it is not available to invest elsewhere. Often, interest is allowed on capital in partnerships where profits and losses are shared equally – it is one way of partly adjusting for different capital balances. As noted earlier, the Partnership Act does not permit interest to be paid on capital, so reference to it must be made in the partnership agreement.

When calculating interest on capital, it may be necessary to allow for part years. For example:

1 January 2002 capital balance	£20,000
1 July 2002 additional capital contributed	£4,000
the rate of interest allowed on capital	10% per annum
the partnership's financial year-end	31 December 2002

Interest allowed on capital is calculated as:

1 January - 30 June £20,000 x 10% (for 6 months)	£1,000
1 July - 31 December £24,000 x 10% (for 6 months)	£1,200
Interest allowed on capital for year	£2,200

interest charged on partners' drawings

In order to discourage partners from drawing out too much money from the business early in the financial year, the partnership agreement may stipulate that interest is to be charged on partners' drawings, and at what rate. This acts as a penalty against early withdrawal when the business may be short of cash. For example:

a partner's drawings for 2002	£24,000
withdrawal at the end of each quarter (31 March, 30 June, 30 September, 31 December)	£6,000
the rate of interest charged on partners' drawings	10% per annum
the partnership's financial year-end	31 December 2002

Interest charged is calculated as:

31 March: £6,000 x 10% x 9 months	£450
30 June: £6,000 x 10% x 6 months	£300
30 September: £6,000 x 10% x 3 months	£150
Interest charged on partner's drawings for year	£900

No interest is charged on the withdrawal on 31 December, because it is at the end of the financial year. The amount of interest charged on drawings for the year is shown in the partnership appropriation account (see Case Study on page 195), where it increases the profit to be shared amongst the partners.

other points – loans and interest

interest on loans to the partnership

If a partner makes a loan to the partnership, the rate of interest to be paid needs to be agreed, otherwise the rate specified in the Partnership Act 1890 applies – five per cent per annum.

Interest on loans is charged as an expense in the profit and loss account, and is not shown in the appropriation account.

interest on current accounts

The partnership agreement may state that interest is to be allowed at a specified rate on the credit balance of partners' current accounts (see below), and is to be charged on debit balances.

CAPITAL ACCOUNTS AND CURRENT ACCOUNTS

The important book-keeping difference between a sole trader and a partnership is that each partner usually has a **capital account** and a **current account**. The capital account is normally *fixed*, and only alters if a permanent increase or decrease in capital contributed by the partner takes place. The current account is *fluctuating* and it is to this account that:

- share of profits is credited

- share of loss is debited

- salary (if any), or commissions, are credited

- interest allowed on partners' capital is credited

- drawings and goods for own use are debited

- interest charged on partners' drawings is debited

- interest allowed on loans made by partners is credited

Thus, the current account is treated as a working account, while capital account remains fixed, except for capital introduced or withdrawn.

A partner's current account has the following layout:

Dr	**Partner Ali: Current Account**	Cr
£		£
Drawings/goods for own use	Balance b/d	
Interest charged on drawings*	Share of net profit	
	Salary (or commissions)*	
	Interest allowed on capital*	
Balance c/d	Interest allowed on loans*	

* if these items are allowed by the partnership agreement

Note that whilst the normal balance on a partner's current account is credit, when the partner has drawn out more than his or her share of the profits, then the balance will be debit.

CASE STUDY
Ali and Bob: appropriation of partnership profits

As we have seen earlier in this chapter, the appropriation section (often described as the appropriation account) follows the profit and loss account and shows how net profit has been divided amongst the partners. This Case Study shows a partnership salary (not to be shown in profit and loss account), interest allowed on partners' capital, and interest charged on partners' drawings.

situation

Ali and Bob are in partnership sharing profits and losses 60 per cent and 40 per cent respectively. Net profit for the year ended 31 March 2002 is £42,000.

At 1 April 2001 (the start of the year), the partners have the following balances:

	Capital account	Current account
	£	£
Ali	40,000	2,000 Cr
Bob	30,000	400 Cr

- There have been no changes to the capital accounts during the year; interest is allowed on partners' capitals at the rate of eight per cent per year.
- Bob is entitled to a salary of £16,000 per year.
- On 30 September 2001 (half-way through the financial year), partners' drawings were made: Ali £18,000, Bob £24,000; there were no other drawings. Interest is charged on partners' drawings at the rate of ten per cent per year.

solution

The appropriation of profits will be made as follows:

ALI AND BOB, IN PARTNERSHIP
PROFIT AND LOSS APPROPRIATION ACCOUNT
for the year ended 31 March 2002

	£	£
Net profit		42,000
Add interest charged on partners' drawings:		
Ali (£18,000 ÷ 2* x 10%)	900	
Bob (£24,000 ÷ 2* x 10%)	1,200	
* divided by two because interest is for 6 months		2,100
		44,100
Less appropriation of profits:		
Salary: Bob		16,000
Interest allowed on partners' capitals:		
Ali	3,200	
Bob	2,400	
		5,600
		22,500
Share of remaining profits:		
Ali (60%)	13,500	
Bob (40%)	9,000	
		22,500

Note that all of the available profit – after allowing for any salary, and interest charged and allowed – is shared amongst the partners, in the ratio in which they share profits and losses. The partners' current accounts for the year appear as follows:

Dr		Ali	Bob		Partners' Current Accounts	Ali	Bob	Cr
		Ali	**Bob**			**Ali**	**Bob**	
2001/2		£	£	2001/2		£	£	
31 Mar	Drawings	18,000	24,000	1 Apr	Balances b/d	2,000	400	
31 Mar	Interest on drawings	900	1,200		Salary	–	16,000	
31 Mar	Balance c/d	–	2,600	31 Mar	Interest on capital	3,200	2,400	
				31 Mar	Share of profits	13,500	9,000	
				31 Mar	Balance c/d	200	-	
		18,900	27,800			18,900	27,800	
2002/3				2002/3				
1 Apr	Balance b/d	200	–	1 Apr	Balance b/d	–	2,600	

Note: The above layout for the partners' current accounts uses a normal 'T' account but in a side-by-side format with a column for each partner on both the debit and credit sides. As an alternative, separate current accounts can be produced for each partner.

From the current accounts we can see that Ali has drawn more out than the balance of the account, and so at the end of the year has a debit balance of £200 on current account. By contrast, Bob has a credit balance of £2,600 on current account.

BALANCE SHEET

The balance sheet of a partnership must show the year-end balances on each partner's capital and current account. However, the transactions that have taken place on each account can be shown in summary form – in the same way that, in a sole trader's balance sheet, net profit for the year is added and drawings for the year are deducted.

The other sections of the balance sheet – fixed assets, current assets, current and long-term liabilities – are presented in the same way as for a sole trader.

The following is an example balance sheet layout for the 'financed by' section (the other sections of the balance sheet are not shown). It details the capital and current accounts of the partnership of Ali and Bob (see Case Study above).

ALI AND BOB, IN PARTNERSHIP

BALANCE SHEET (EXTRACT) as at 31 March 2002

FINANCED BY	£	£
Capital Accounts		
Ali	40,000	
Bob	30,000	
		70,000
Current Accounts		
Ali	(200)	
Bob	2,600	
		2,400
		72,400

Note: Only the closing balances of the partners' current accounts have been shown here – see the detailed double-entry accounts on the previous page.

– either, show detailed double-entry accounts, carrying the balances into the balance sheet

– or, show detailed current accounts on the face of the balance sheet (see Case Study on the next page)

PARTNERSHIP FINAL ACCOUNTS FROM THE TRIAL BALANCE

The procedures for preparing the final accounts of a partnership from a trial balance are exactly the same as for sole traders. The only differences to note are that partners' capital and current accounts are shown in the balance sheet. Transactions affecting the partners' current accounts – such as share of profits, partners' salaries, drawings, etc – can be shown either in the form of a double-entry 'T' account (as on the previous page), or directly on the face of the balance sheet (see the Case Study on the next page). Whichever is done, it is the closing balances of the current accounts that are added in to the 'financed by' section of the balance sheet.

CASE STUDY
Ramjit Singh and Veta Bix: partnership final accounts

situation

The trial balance for the partnership of Ramjit Singh and Veta Bix, trading as RaVe Music, at 31 December 2005 is shown below.

RAMJIT SINGH AND VETA BIX IN PARTNERSHIP, TRADING AS RAVE MUSIC
TRIAL BALANCE AS AT 31 DECEMBER 2005

		Dr £	Cr £
Stock at 1 January 2005		20,000	
Sales			250,000
Purchases		120,000	
Freehold land and buildings		200,000	
Provision for depreciation:	freehold land and buildings		9,000
Fixtures and fittings		20,000	
Provision for depreciation:	fixtures and fittings		8,000
Wages and salaries		35,000	
Shop expenses		20,000	
Debtors		3,000	
Creditors			7,000
Value Added Tax			4,000
Bank overdraft			2,000
Bank loan			80,000
Capital accounts:	Ramjit Singh		50,000
	Veta Bix		45,000
Current accounts:	Ramjit Singh		4,000
	Veta Bix		1,000
Drawings:	Ramjit Singh	24,000	
	Veta Bix	18,000	
		460,000	460,000

Notes at 31 December 2005:
- stock was valued at £30,000
- wages and salaries owing £1,700
- shop expenses prepaid £800
- depreciate the freehold buildings by £3,000, and the fixtures and fittings by 10 per cent (straight-line method)
- goods taken for own use, Ramjit £500, Veta £400
- the partners share profits and losses equally

solution

The final accounts of the Ramjit Singh and Veta Bix, trading as RaVe Music, are shown below.

RAMJIT SINGH AND VETA BIX IN PARTNERSHIP, TRADING AS RAVE MUSIC
TRADING AND PROFIT AND LOSS ACCOUNT
for the year ended 31 December 2005

	£	£	£
Sales			250,000
Opening stock		20,000	
Purchases	120,000		
Less Goods for own use	900		
		119,100	
		139,100	
Less Closing stock		30,000	
Cost of sales			109,100
Gross profit			140,900
Less overheads:			
Wages and salaries		36,700	
Shop expenses		19,200	
Provision for depreciation			
freehold buildings		3,000	
fixtures and fittings		2,000	
			60,900
Net profit			80,000
Share of profits:			
Ramjit Singh			40,000
Veta Bix			40,000
			80,000

RAMJIT SINGH AND VETA BIX IN PARTNERSHIP, TRADING AS RAVE MUSIC
BALANCE SHEET as at 31 December 2005

	£	£	£
Fixed Assets	Cost	Dep'n to date	Net
Freehold land and buildings	200,000	12,000	188,000
Fixtures and fittings	20,000	10,000	10,000
	220,000	22,000	198,000
Current Assets			
Stock		30,000	
Debtors		3,000	
Prepayments		800	
		33,800	
Less Current Liabilities			
Creditors	7,000		
Accruals	1,700		
Value Added Tax	4,000		
Bank	2,000		
		14,700	
Net Current Assets			19,100
			217,100
Less Long-term Liabilities			
Bank loan			80,000
NET ASSETS			137,100
FINANCED BY			
Capital Accounts			
Ramjit Singh		50,000	
Veta Bix		45,000	
			95,000

Current Accounts	R. Singh	V. Bix	
Opening Balance	4,000	1,000	
Add: share of profit	40,000	40,000	
	44,000	41,000	
Less: drawings	24,000	18,000	
goods for own use*	500	400	
	19,500	22,600	
			42,100
			137,100

* goods for own use can be incorporated into the amount for drawings: it is shown here separately so that the accounting treatment can be seen clearly.

chapter summary

- A partnership is formed when two or more (usually up to a maximum of twenty) people set up in business.

- The Partnership Act 1890 states certain accounting rules, principally that profits and losses must be shared equally.

- Many partnerships over-ride the accounting rules of the Act by making a partnership agreement which covers:
    - division of profits and losses between partners
    - partners' salaries/commissions
    - whether interest is to be allowed on capital, and at what rate
    - whether interest is to be charged on partners' drawings, and at what rate

- The usual way to account for partners' capital is to maintain a fixed capital account for each partner. This is complemented by a fluctuating current account which is used as a working account for share of profits, drawings, etc.

- The final accounts of partnerships are similar to those of sole traders, but incorporate:
    - an appropriation section, as a continuation of the profit and loss account, to show the share of profits and losses
    - individual capital and current accounts for each partner shown in the balance sheet

key terms

partnership	the relation which subsists between persons carrying on a business in common with a view of profit
Partnership Act 1890	legislation which includes the accounting rules of partnerships
partnership agreement	agreement between the partners which, amongst other things, often varies the accounting rules of the Partnership Act 1890
appropriation section	part of the profit and loss account which shows how the net profit is shared amongst the partners
capital account	account which records the amount of capital contributed by a partner; usually for a fixed amount, which only alters where a permanent increase or decrease takes place
current account	a fluctuating account to which is credited: share of profits, salary (if any), interest allowed on capital, and to which is debited: share of losses, drawings and interest charged on partner's drawings

activities

10.1 (a) Define a partnership.

(b) State three accounting provisions from the Partnership Act 1890 which will apply to a partnership where no partnership agreement exists.

10.2 Distinguish between:

(a) capital account and current account

(b) interest on capital and interest on drawings

10.3* Lysa and Mark are in partnership and own a shop, 'Trends', which sells fashionable teenage clothes. The following figures are extracted from their accounts for the year ended 31 December 2008:

	£	
Capital accounts at 1 January 2008:		
Lysa	50,000	Cr
Mark	40,000	Cr
Current accounts at 1 January 2008:		
Lysa	420	Cr
Mark	1,780	Cr
Drawings for the year:		
Lysa	13,000	
Mark	12,250	
Interest on capital for the year:		
Lysa	2,500	
Mark	2,000	
Share of profits for the year:		
Lysa	9,300	
Mark	9,300	

Notes:

• no partner is entitled to a salary

• there is no interest charged on drawings

You are to show the partners' capital and current accounts for the year ended 31 December 2008.

10.4* John James and Steven Hill are in partnership and own a wine shop called 'Grapes'. The following trial balance has been taken from their accounts for the year ended 31 December 2001, after the calculation of gross profit:

	Dr £	Cr £
Capital accounts:		
James		38,000
Hill		32,000
Current accounts:		
James	3,000	
Hill		1,000
Drawings:		
James	14,000	
Hill	18,000	
Gross profit		89,000
Rent and rates	7,500	
Advertising	12,000	
Heat and light	3,500	
Wages and salaries	18,000	
Sundry expenses	4,000	
Shop fittings at cost	20,000	
*Stock at 31 December 2001	35,000	
Bank	29,000	
Debtors	6,000	
Creditors		8,000
Value Added Tax		2,000
	170,000	170,000

*   Closing stock is included in the trial balance because gross profit for the year has already been calculated.

Notes at 31 December 2001:

* profits and losses are to be shared equally

* depreciation is to be charged on the shop fittings at 10% per year

You are to

(a)   prepare the partnership profit and loss account (incorporating the appropriation account) for the year ended 31 December 2001, together with the partnership balance sheet at that date

(b)   show the partners' capital and current accounts for the year ended 31 December 2001

10.5 Clark and Pearce are in partnership selling business computer systems. The following trial balance has been taken from their accounts for the year ended 30 June 2009, after calculation of gross profit:

	Dr £	Cr £
Gross profit		105.000
Salaries	30,400	
Electricity	2,420	
Telephone	3,110	
Rent and rates	10,000	
Discount allowed	140	
Office expenses	10,610	
Stock at 30 June 2009*	41,570	
Debtors and creditors	20,000	6,950
Value Added Tax		5,240
Bad debts written off	1,200	
Provision for bad debts		780
Office equipmant at cost	52,000	
Provision for depreciation on office equipment		20,800
Clark Capital account		60,000
Current account		430
Drawings	20,600	
Pearce Capital account		30,000
Current account		300
Drawings	15,700	
Bank	21,750	
	229,500	229,500

* Closing stock is included in the trial balance because gross profit for the year has been calculated already.

Notes at 30 June 2009:

- profits and losses are shared as follows: Clark two-thirds, Pearce one-third
- depreciate the office equipment at 20 per cent, using the straight line method

You are to

(a)   prepare the partnership profit and loss account (incorporating the appropriation account) for the year ended 30 June 2009, together with the partnership balance sheet at that date

(b)   show the partners' capital and current accounts for the year ended 30 June 2009

10.6 Sara and Simon Perry are in partnership running a catering service called 'Class Caterers'. The following trial balance has been taken from their accounts for the year ended 31 March 2009:

	Dr £	Cr £
Capital accounrts:		
Sara		10,000
Simon		6,000
Current accounts:		
Sara		560
Simon		1,050
Drawings:		
Sara	12,700	
Simon	7,400	
Pruchases	11,300	
Sales		44,080
Stock at 1 April 2008	2,850	
Wages	8,020	
Rent and rates	4,090	
Sundry expenses	1,390	
Equipment	8,000	
Debtors	4,500	
Creditors		5,850
Value Added Tax		1,350
Bank	8,640	
	68,890	68,890

Notes at 31 March 2009:

- stock was valued at £3,460

- sundry expenses owing, £110

- depreciation is to be charged on the equipment at 10% per year

- profits and losses are to be shared equally

You are to

(a) prepare the partnership profit and loss account (incorporating the appropriation account) for the year ended 31 March 2009, together with the partnership balance sheet at that date

(b) show the partners' capital and current accounts for the year ended 31 March 2009

10.7 Anne Adams and Jenny Beeson are partners in an electrical supplies shop called 'A & B Electrics'. They share profits and losses equally. The following trial balance has been taken from their accounts for the year ended 30 June 2009:

		Dr	Cr
		£	£
Capital accounts:	A Adams		30,000
	J Beeson		20,000
Current accounts:	A Adams		780
	J Beeson		920
Drawings	A Adams	14,000	
	J Beeson	12,000	
Stock at 1 July 2008		26,550	
Purchases and sales		175,290	250,140
Returns		1,360	850
Rent and rates		8,420	
Wages		28,700	
Vehicle expenses		2,470	
General expenses		6,210	
Vehicle at cost		12,000	
Fixtures and fittings at cost		4,000	
Provision for depreciation	vehicle		3,000
	fixtures and fittings		800
Debtors and creditors		6,850	12,360
Value Added Tax			2,410
Bank		22,009	
Cash		1,376	
Bad debts written off		175	
Provision for bad debt			150
		321,410	321,410

Notes at 30 June 2009:

- stock is valued at £27,750

- rates paid in advance £250

- wages owing £320

- provision for bad debt to be equal to 2 per cent debtors

- depreciation on fixtures and fittings to be provided at 10 per cent per annum using the straight line method

- depreciation on motor vehicles to be provided at 25 per cent per annum using the reducing balance method

You are to

(a)   prepare the partnership final accounts for the year ended 30 June 2009

(b)   show the partners' capital and current accounts for the year ended 30 June 2009

CHANGES IN PARTNERSHIPS

CASE STUDY
changing the partnership

Ramjit Singh and Veta Bix (who featured in the last chapter) are now well established as a partnership business selling specialist and mainstream music.

They have expanded the sales area of their Norwich shop by buying the next-door premises. The shop has been rebranded under the name 'RaVe Music', and they have developed their mail order business through their website. They now sell their specialist CDs worldwide.

At the moment they share the profits and losses of their partnership equally, but have wondered about making changes in the future as and when the business commitments of the two partners change.

At the same time, they have been giving thought to developing the business further, perhaps by expanding their operations and taking on another partner. They have made an appointment with their accountant, to ask for advice about the accounting implications of these changes.

In this chapter we look at the principles involved – and the accounting entries made – to deal with changes in partnerships. The areas covered include the profit-sharing ratio and the introduction of a new partner.

These changes also involve consideration of the 'goodwill' – the businesss name and reputation built up by businesses such as the partnership run by Ramjit and Veta.

learning objectives

When you have studied this chapter you will be able to:

- *explain the concept of goodwill*
- *understand the principles of:*
  - *admission of a new partner*
  - *retirement of a partner*
  - *death of a partner*
  - *changes in profit-sharing ratios*
  - *revaluation of assets*
  - *dissolution of a partnership*
- *prepare accounting entries to deal with these various situations*

GOODWILL

The balance sheet of a partnership, like that of many businesses, rarely indicates the true 'going concern' value of the business. Usually the recorded figures underestimate the worth of a business. There are two main reasons for this:

- **prudence** – if there is any doubt about the value of assets, they are stated at the lowest possible figure.

- **goodwill** – a going concern business will often have a value of goodwill, because of various factors, eg the trade that has been built up, the reputation of the business, the brand name, the location of the business, the skill of the workforce, and the success at developing new products

definition of goodwill

Goodwill can be defined formally in accounting terms as:

the difference between the value of a business as a whole, and the net value of its separate assets and liabilities.

For example, an existing business is bought for £500,000, with the separate assets and liabilities being worth £450,000 net; goodwill is, therefore, £50,000. Thus goodwill has a value as an 'intangible' fixed asset to the owner or owners of a going concern business, whether or not it is recorded on the balance sheet. (An 'intangible' asset is an asset which does not have a physical existence). As you will see in the sections which follow, a valuation has to be placed on goodwill when changes take place in a partnership.

valuation of goodwill

The valuation of goodwill is always subject to negotiation between the people concerned if, for instance, a partnership business is to be sold. It is, most commonly, based on the profits of the business – eg the average net profit over the last, say, three years and multiplied by an agreed figure, perhaps six times.

In a balance sheet, goodwill is shown as an intangible fixed asset. It is only recorded on the balance sheet when it has been purchased, eg a sole trader or a partnership purchasing goodwill when taking over another business. It should then:

- either, be depreciated (amortised) to profit and loss account over its estimated useful economic life (generally up to a maximum of 20 years)

- or, if the useful estimated economic life is deemed to be indefinite, the goodwill need not be amortised, provided that its continuing existence can be justified (by means of an annual 'impairment review')

We will now see how goodwill is used when changes are made to partnerships, eg the admission of a new partner or retirement of an existing partner. For these changes, a value for goodwill is agreed and this amount is temporarily debited to goodwill account, and credited to the partners' capital accounts in their profit-sharing ratio. After the change in the partnership, as you will see, the partners' capital accounts are debited and goodwill account is credited. Thus a 'nil' balance remains on goodwill account and, therefore, it is not recorded on the partnership balance sheet. This is a prudent approach, and is the method commonly followed when changes are made to partnerships.

ADMISSION OF A NEW PARTNER

A new partner – who can only be admitted with the consent of all existing partners – is normally charged a premium for goodwill. This is because the new partner will start to share in the profits of the business immediately and will benefit from the goodwill established by the existing partners. If the business was to be sold shortly after the admission of a new partner, a price will again be agreed for goodwill and this will be shared amongst all the partners (including the new partner).

To make allowance for this benefit it is necessary to make book-keeping adjustments in the partners' capital accounts. The most common way of doing this is to use a goodwill account which is opened by the old partners with the agreed valuation of goodwill and, immediately after the admission of the new partner, is closed by transfer to the partners' capital accounts, including that of the new partner.

The procedures on admission of a new partner are:

- **agree a valuation for goodwill**

- **old partners**
  - debit goodwill account with the amount of goodwill
  - credit partners' capital accounts (in their old profit-sharing ratio) with the amount of goodwill

- **old partners + new partner**
  - debit partners' capital accounts (in their new profit-sharing ratio) with the amount of goodwill
  - credit goodwill account with the amount of goodwill

The effect of this is to charge the new partner with a premium for goodwill.

CASE STUDY

Al and Ben: admission of a new partner

situation

Al and Ben are in partnership sharing profits and losses equally. Their balance sheet as at 31 December 2001 is as follows:

BALANCE SHEET OF AL AND BEN AS AT 31 DECEMBER 2001	
	£
Net assets	80,000
Capital accounts:	
Al	45,000
Ben	35,000
	80,000

On 1 January 2002 the partners agree to admit Col into the partnership, with a new profit-sharing ratio of 2:2:1. Goodwill has been agreed at a valuation of £25,000. Col will bring £20,000 of cash into the business as his capital, part of which represents a premium for goodwill.

solution

The accounting procedures on the admission of Col into the partnership are as follows:

- goodwill has been valued at £25,000
- old partners:
  - debit goodwill account   £25,000
  - credit capital accounts (in their old profit-sharing ratio)
    - Al   £12,500
    - Ben   £12,500
- old partners + new partner
  - debit capital accounts (in their new profit-sharing ratio)
    - Al   £10,000
    - Ben   £10,000
    - Col   £5,000
  - credit goodwill account   £25,000

The capital accounts of the partners, after the above transactions have been recorded, appear as (see next page):

Dr				**Partners' Capital Accounts**				Cr
	Al	Ben	Col		Al	Ben	Col
	£	£	£		£	£	£
Goodwill written off	10,000	10,000	5,000	Balances b/d	45,000	35,000	-
Balances c/d	47,500	37,500	15,000	Goodwill created	12,500	12,500	-
				Bank	-	-	20,000
	57,500	47,500	20,000		57,500	47,500	20,000
				Balances b/d	47,500	37,500	15,000

The balance sheet, following the admission of Col, appears as:

BALANCE SHEET OF AL, BEN AND COL AS AT 1 JANUARY 2002

	£
Net assets (£80,000 + £20,000)	100,000
Capital accounts:	
Al (£45,000 + £12,500 - £10,000)	47,500
Ben (£35,000 + £12,500 - £10,000)	37,500
Col (£20,000 - £5,000)	15,000
	100,000

In this way, the new partner has paid the existing partners a premium of £5,000 for a one-fifth share of the profits of a business with a goodwill value of £25,000.

Although a goodwill account has been used, it has been fully utilised with adjusting entries made in the capital accounts of the partners, as follows:

Dr		**Goodwill Account**		Cr
	£			£
Al goodwill created	12,500	Al goodwill written off		10,000
Ben	12,500	Ben		10,000
		Col		5,000
	25,000			25,000

note: goodwill – alternative treatment

As there is no remaining balance on goodwill account, it does not appear on the balance sheet. Whilst the write-off of goodwill is the most usual treatment in partnership accounts, it would be possible for goodwill account to be kept open with a debit balance, being the amount of the intangible fixed asset (in this example, for £25,000). The capital accounts would not, therefore, be debited with the goodwill written off (in this example, £10,000, £10,000 and £5,000). Questions will always state the accounting treatment of goodwill – invariably no account will remain open for goodwill, with all adjusting entries being passed through the partners' capital accounts.

RETIREMENT OF A PARTNER

When a partner retires it is necessary to calculate how much is due to the partner in respect of capital and profits. The partnership agreement normally details the procedures to be followed when a partner retires. The most common procedure requires goodwill to be valued and this operates in a similar way to the admission of a new partner, as follows:

- **agree a valuation for goodwill**

- **old partners**
  - debit goodwill account with the amount of goodwill
  - credit partners' capital accounts (in their old profit-sharing ratio) with the amount of goodwill

- **remaining partners**
  - debit partners' capital accounts (in their new profit-sharing ratio) with the amount of goodwill
  - credit goodwill account with the amount of goodwill

The effect of this is to credit the retiring partner with the amount of the goodwill built up whilst he or she was a partner. This amount, plus the retiring partner's capital and current account balances can then be paid out of the partnership bank account. (If there is insufficient money for this, it is quite usual for a retiring partner to leave some of the capital in the business as a loan, which is repaid over a period of time.)

CASE STUDY

Jan, Kay and Lil: retirement of a partner

situation

Jan, Kay and Lil are in partnership sharing profit and losses in the ratio of 2:2:1 respectively. Partner Jan decides to retire on 31 December 2001 when the partnership balance sheet is as follows:

BALANCE SHEET OF JAN, KAY AND LIL AS AT 31 DECEMBER 2001	
	£
Net assets	100,000
Capital accounts:	
Jan	35,000
Kay	45,000
Lil	20,000
	100,000

Goodwill is agreed at a valuation of £30,000. Kay and Lil are to continue in partnership and will share profits and losses in the ratio of 2:1 respectively. Jan agrees to leave £20,000 of the amount due to her as a loan to the new partnership.

solution

The accounting procedures on the retirement of Jan from the partnership are as follows:

- goodwill has been valued at £30,000
- old partners:
  - debit goodwill account   £30,000
  - credit capital accounts (in their old profit-sharing ratio of 2:2:1)

Jan	£12,000
Kay	£12,000
Lil	£6,000

- remaining partners
  - debit capital accounts (in their new profit-sharing ratio of 2:1)

Kay	£20,000
Lil	£10,000

  - credit goodwill account   £30,000

The capital accounts of the partners, after the above transactions have been recorded, appear as:

Dr	Jan £	Kay £	Lil £	Partners' Capital Accounts	Jan £	Kay £	Lil £	Cr
Goodwill written off	–	20,000	10,000	Balances b/d	35,000	45,000	20,000	
Loan account	20,000			Goodwill created	12,000	12,000	6,000	
Bank	27,000							
Balances c/d	–	37,000	16,000					
	47,000	57,000	26,000		47,000	57,000	26,000	
				Balances b/d	–	37,000	16,000	

Note: After recording goodwill, the balance of Jan's capital account is £47,000 (ie £35,000 + £12,000, being her share of the goodwill). Of this, £20,000 will be retained in the business as a loan, and £27,000 will be paid to her from the partnership bank account.

The balance sheet, after the retirement of Jan, appears as follows:

BALANCE SHEET OF KAY AND LIL AS AT 1 JANUARY 2002

	£
Net assets (£100,000 - £27,000 paid to Jan)	73,000
Less Loan account of Jan	20,000
	53,000
Capital accounts:	
Kay (£45,000 + £12,000 - £20,000)	37,000
Lil (£20,000 + £6,000 - £10,000)	16,000
	53,000

The effect of this is that the remaining partners have bought out Jan's £12,000 share of the goodwill of the business, ie it has cost Kay £8,000, and Lil £4,000. If the business was to be sold later, Kay and Lil would share the goodwill obtained from the sale in their new profit-sharing ratio.

DEATH OF A PARTNER

The accounting procedures on the death of a partner are very similar to those for a partner's retirement. The only difference is that the amount due to the deceased partner is placed in an account called 'Executors (or Administrators) of X deceased' pending payment.

CHANGES IN PROFIT-SHARING RATIOS

It may be necessary, from time-to-time, to change the profit-sharing ratios of partners. A partner's share of profits might be increased because of an increase in capital in relation to the other partners, or because of a more active role in running the business. Equally, a share of profits may be decreased if a partner withdraws capital or spends less time in the business. Clearly, the agreement of all partners is needed to make changes, and the guidance of the partnership agreement should be followed.

Generally, a change in profit-sharing ratios involves establishing a figure for goodwill, even if the partnership is to continue with the same partners; this is to establish how much goodwill was built up while they shared profits in their old ratios. Each partner will, therefore, receive a value for the goodwill based on the old profit-sharing ratio.

CASE STUDY
Col and Des: changes in proft-sharing ratios

situation

Col and Des are in partnership sharing profits and losses equally. Their balance sheet at 31 December 2001 is as follows:

BALANCE SHEET OF COL AND DES AS AT 31 DECEMBER 2001

	£
Net assets	60,000
Capital accounts:	
Col	35,000
Des	25,000
	60,000

The partners agree that, as from 1 January 2002, Col will take a two-thirds share of the profits and losses, with Des taking one-third. It is agreed that goodwill shall be valued at £30,000.

solution

The accounting procedures on the change in the profit-sharing ratio are as follows:

- goodwill has been valued at £30,000
- old profit-sharing ratio:
  - debit goodwill account   £30,000
  - credit capital accounts (in their old profit-sharing ratio of 1:1)

    Col   £15,000

    Des   £15,000
- new profit-sharing ratio:
  - debit capital accounts (in their new profit-sharing ratio of 2:1)

    Col   £20,000

    Des   £10,000
  - credit goodwill account   £30,000

The capital accounts of the partners, after the above transactions have been recorded, appear as:

Dr	Col £	Des £	Partners' Capital Accounts	Col £	Des £ Cr
Goodwill written off	20,000	10,000	Balances b/d	35,000	25,000
Balances c/d	30,000	30,000	Goodwill created	15,000	15,000
	50,000	40,000		50,000	40,000
			Balances b/d	30,000	30,000

The balance sheet at 1 January 2002 appears as:

BALANCE SHEET OF COL AND DES AS AT 1 JANUARY 2002

	£
Net assets	60,000
Capital accounts:	
Col (£35,000 + £15,000 − £20,000)	30,000
Des (£25,000 + £15,000 − £10,000)	30,000
	60,000

The effect is that Col has 'paid' Des £5,000 to increase his share of the profits from half to two-thirds. This may seem unfair but neither partner is worse off in the event of the business being sold, assuming that the business is sold for £90,000 (£60,000 assets + £30,000 goodwill). Before the change in the profit-sharing ratio they would have received:

Col £35,000 capital + £15,000 half-share of goodwill = £50,000

Des £25,000 capital + £15,000 half-share of goodwill = £40,000

After the change, they will receive:

Col £30,000 capital + £20,000 two-thirds share of goodwill = £50,000

Des £30,000 capital + £10,000 one-third share of goodwill   = £40,000

As far as the realisation amounts are concerned, the position remains unchanged: it is only the profit-sharing ratios that will be different as from 1 January 2002. Also, any increase in goodwill above the £30,000 figure will be shared in the new ratio.

REVALUATION OF ASSETS

So far in this chapter we have looked at the adjustments made for goodwill in various changes made to partnerships. Goodwill, however, reflects only one aspect of a partner's interest in the business. For example, some of the assets may have appreciated in value, but adjustments may not have been made in the accounts; other assets may have fallen in value, while provisions for depreciation and/or bad debts may have been too much or too little. With a change in the personnel of a partnership, a revaluation account may be needed to correct any discrepancies in values. The accounting procedure is:

- **increase in the value of an asset**
  - debit asset account with the amount of the increase
  - credit revaluation account with the amount of the increase

- **reduction in the value of an asset**
  - debit revaluation account the amount of the reduction
  - credit asset account the amount of the reduction

- **increase in provision for depreciation/bad debts**
  - debit revaluation account with the amount of the increase
  - credit provision account with the amount of the increase

- **reduction in provision for depreciation/bad debts**
  - debit provision account with the amount of the reduction
  - credit revaluation account the amount of the reduction

After these adjustments have been recorded in the books of account, the balance of the revaluation account is divided among the partners in their profit-sharing ratios.

CASE STUDY
Matt, Nia and Olly: revaluation of assets

situation

Matt, Nia and Olly are in partnership sharing profits and losses equally.

On 31 December 2001 their balance sheet is as follows:

BALANCE SHEET OF MATT, NIA AND OLLY AS AT 31 DECEMBER 2001

	£	£	£
Fixed Assets	Cost	Dep'n to date	Net
Land	100,000	-	100,000
Machinery	50,000	10,000	40,000
	150,000	10,000	140,000
Current Assets			
Stock		30,000	
Debtors		20,000	
Bank		5,000	
		55,000	
Less Current Liabilities			
Creditors		25,000	
Working Capital			30,000
NET ASSETS			170,000
FINANCED BY			
Capital accounts			
Matt			60,000
Nia			60,000
Olly			50,000
			170,000

Olly decides to retire at 31 December 2001; Matt and Nia are to continue the partnership and will share profits and losses equally. The following valuations are agreed:

Goodwill	£30,000
Land	£150,000
Machinery	£30,000
Stock	£21,000

A provision for bad debts equal to five per cent of debtors is to be made.

Olly agrees that the money owing on retirement are to be retained in the business as a long-term loan.

solution

The revaluation account and adjusted balance sheet appear as follows:

Dr		Revaluation Account		Cr
	£			£
Provision for depreciation:		Goodwill		30,000
Machinery	10,000	Land		50,000
Stock	9,000			
Provision for bad debts	1,000			
Surplus on revaluation c/d	60,000			80,000
	80,000			
Capital accounts:		Surplus on revaluation b/d		60,000
Matt (one-third)	20,000			
Nia (one-third)	20,000			
Olly (one-third)	20,000			
	60,000			60,000

Note that the amount of goodwill has been credited to revaluation account (and thus to the capital accounts); it will, later, be debited to the capital accounts of the two remaining partners at £15,000 each – in this way it will not feature on the balance sheet.

The capital accounts of the partners, after the above transactions have been recorded, appear as:

Dr				Partners' Capital Accounts				Cr
	Matt	Nia	Olly		Matt	Nia	Olly
	£	£	£		£	£	£
Goodwill written off	15,000	15,000	–	Balances b/d	60,000	60,000	50,000
Loan account			70,000	Revaluation acc*			
Balances c/d	65,000	65,000	–	surplus	20,000	20,000	20,000
	80,000	80,000	70,000		80,000	80,000	70,000
				Balances b/d	65,000	65,000	–

* Note that revaluation account includes goodwill created.

The balance sheet at 1 January 2002 appears as follows:

BALANCE SHEET OF MATT AND NIA AS AT 1 JANUARY 2002

	£	£	£
Fixed Assets	Cost	Dep'n to date	Net
Land	150,000	–	150,000
Machinery	50,000	20,000	30,000
	200,000	20,000	180,000
Current Assets			
Stock		21,000	
Debtors	20,000		
Less provision for bad debts	1,000		
		19,000	
Bank		5,000	
		45,000	
Less Current Liabilities			
Creditors		25,000	
Working Capital			20,000
			200,000
Less Long-term Liabilities			
Loan account of Olly (£50,000 + £20,000)			70,000
NET ASSETS			130,000
FINANCED BY			
Capital accounts			
Matt (£60,000 + £20,000 − £15,000)			65,000
Nia (£60,000 + £20,000 − £15,000)			65,000
			130,000

DISSOLUTION OF A PARTNERSHIP

There are various reasons why a partnership may come to an end:

- a partnership may be formed for a fixed term or for a specific purpose and, at the end of that term or when that purpose has been achieved, it is dissolved

- a partnership might be dissolved as a result of bankruptcy, or because a partner retires or dies and no new partners can be found to keep the firm going

- sales may fall due to changes in technology and product obsolescence, with the partners not feeling it is worthwhile to seek out and develop new products

- at the other end of the scale, the business might expand to such an extent that, in order to acquire extra capital needed for growth, the partnership may be dissolved and a limited company formed to take over its assets and liabilities.

Whatever the reason for dissolving the partnership, the accounts have to be closed. A **realisation account** is used to record the closing transactions, and this account shows the net gain or loss that is available for distribution among the partners. The Partnership Act 1890 requires that monies realised from the sale of assets are to be applied in the following order:

- firstly, in settlement of the firm's debts, other than those to partners

- then, in repayment of partners' loans

- then, in settlement of partners' capital and current accounts

steps to close the books of a partnership

1   Asset accounts (except for cash/bank) are closed by transfer to realisation account:

   – debit realisation account

   – credit asset accounts

2   Provisions accounts, eg depreciation, bad debts, are transferred to realisation account:

   – debit provision account

   – credit realisation account

3   As assets are sold, the proceeds are placed to cash/bank account, and the sum recorded in realisation account:

   – debit cash/bank account

   – credit realisation account

4 If a partner takes over any assets, the value is agreed and the amount is deducted from the partner's capital account and transferred to realisation account:

– debit partner's capital account

– credit realisation account

5 As expenses of realisation are incurred, they are paid from cash/bank account and entered in realisation account:

– debit realisation account

– credit cash/bank account

6 Creditors are paid off:

– debit creditors' accounts

– credit cash/bank account

7 The balance of realisation account, after all assets have been sold and all creditors have been paid, represents the profit or loss on realisation, and is transferred to the partners' capital accounts in the proportion in which profits and losses are shared. If a profit has been made, the transactions are:

– debit realisation account

– credit partners' capital accounts

Where a loss has been made, the entries are reversed.

8 Partners' loans (if any) are repaid:

– debit partners' loan accounts

– credit cash/bank account

9 Partners' current accounts are transferred to capital accounts:

– debit partners' current accounts

– credit partners' capital accounts

If a partner has a debit balance on current account, the entries will be reversed.

10 If any partner now has a debit balance on capital account, he or she must pay in money from private funds to clear the balance:

– debit cash/bank account

– credit partner's capital account

11 The remaining cash and bank balances are used to repay the credit balances on partners' capital accounts:

– debit partners' capital accounts

– credit cash/bank account

CASE STUDY

Dan, Eve and Fay: dissolution of a partnership

situation

Dan, Eve and Fay are in partnership, sharing profits and losses equally. As a result of falling sales they decide to dissolve the partnership as from 31 December 2002. The balance sheet at that date is shown below:

BALANCE SHEET OF DAN, EVE AND FAY AS AT 31 DECEMBER 2002

	£	£	£
Fixed Assets	Cost	Dep'n to date	Net
Machinery	25,000	10,000	15,000
Delivery van	10,000	5,000	5,000
	35,000	15,000	20,000
Current Assets			
Stock		12,000	
Debtors		10,000	
Bank		3,000	
		25,000	
Less Current Liabilities			
Creditors		8,000	
Working Capital			17,000
NET ASSETS			37,000
FINANCED BY			
Capital accounts			
Dan			13,000
Eve			12,000
Fay			12,000
			37,000

The sale proceeds of the assets are machinery £12,000, stock £8,000, debtors £9,000. Dan is to take over the delivery van at an agreed valuation of £3,000. The expenses of realisation amount to £2,000.

solution

The realisation account, partners' capital accounts and bank account to record the dissolution of the partnership are shown on the next page:

Dr		Realisation Account		Cr
	£			£
Machinery	25,000	Provisions for depreciation:		
Delivery van	10,000	machinery		10,000
Stock	12,000	delivery van		5,000
Debtors	10,000	Bank: machinery		12,000
Bank: realisation expenses	2,000	Bank: stock		8,000
		Bank: debtors		9,000
		Dan's capital account: van		3,000
		Loss on realisation c/d		12,000
	59,000			59,000
Loss on realisation b/d	12,000	Capital accounts:		
		Dan (one-third)		4,000
		Eve (one-third)		4,000
		Fay (one-third)		4,000
	12,000			12,000

Dr				Partners' Capital Accounts				Cr
	Dan	Eve	Fay		Dan	Eve	Fay	
	£	£	£		£	£	£	
Realisation account:				Balances b/d	13,000	12,000	12,000	
delivery van	3,000	-	-					
Realisation account:								
loss	4,000	4,000	4,000					
Bank	6,000	8,000	8,000					
	13,000	12,000	12,000		13,000	12,000	12,000	

Dr		Bank Account		Cr
	£			£
Balance b/d	3,000	Realisation account: expenses		2,000
Machinery	12,000	Creditors		8,000
Stock	8,000	Capital accounts:		
Debtors	9,000	Dan		6,000
		Eve		8,000
		Fay		8,000
	32,000			32,000

As can be seen from the above accounts, the assets have been realised, the liabilities paid, and the balances due to the partners have been settled; the partnership has been dissolved.

THE RULE IN GARNER V MURRAY

When a partnership is dissolved, any partner with a debit balance remaining on capital account must pay in monies from private funds to clear the balance. However, if such a partner is insolvent, then the other partners must share the loss in the ratio of their last agreed capital balances, ie the balances of their capital accounts before the dissolution began.

This rule was established in the legal case of Garner v Murray (1904) and is a departure from other changes to partnerships where the ratio in which profits or losses are shared has been used.

chapter summary

- Goodwill is an intangible fixed asset, ie it has value but no physical existence.

- Goodwill should only be shown in the balance sheet when it has been purchased; it should then be:
  - either, amortised to profit and loss account over its estimated useful economic life
  - or, if the estimated useful economic life is deemed to be indefinite, the goodwill need not be amortised, provided that its continuing existence can be justified

- With partnerships, goodwill is normally calculated for transactions involving changes in the structure of the business to cover:

  - admission of a new partner
  - retirement of a partner
  - death of a partner
  - changes in profit-sharing ratios

  A goodwill account is normally created just before the change, and then deleted immediately after the change, ie it does not appear on the partnership balance sheet.

- A revaluation account is used whenever assets are revalued prior to making changes to the personnel of the partnership.

- When a partnership is dissolved, a realisation account is used to record the sale proceeds of assets, and to calculate any profit or loss on realisation due to the partners.

---

key terms

goodwill	the difference between the value of a business as a whole, and the net value of its separate assets and liabilities
goodwill account	an account to which goodwill, an intangible fixed asset, is debited
premium for goodwill	amount charged to a new partner who joins an existing partnership
revaluation account	account used when assets are increased or decreased in value, eg when changes are made to a partnership
realisation account	account used when assets are realised, eg on the dissolution of a partnership

---

activities

Note: an asterisk (*) after an activity number means that an answer is provided in Appendix 1.

11.1 (a) Explain the concept of goodwill in partnership accounting.

(b) Using figures of your choice, demonstrate the accounting procedures that must be undertaken in order to admit a new partner to the business where goodwill is valued and then eliminated from the books of account.

11.2 Dave and Elsa are in partnership sharing profits and losses equally. Their balance sheet at 30 September 2003 is as follows:

BALANCE SHEET OF DAVE AND ELSA AS AT 30 SEPTEMBER 2003

	£
Net assets	130,000
Capital accounts:	
Dave	80,000
Elsa	50,000
	130,000

The partners agree that, as from 1 October 2003, Dave will take a two-thirds share of the profits and losses, with Elsa taking one-third. It is agreed that goodwill should be valued at £45,000.

You are to show the partners' capital accounts to record the change in the profit-sharing ratio, together with their balance sheet after the change.

11.3* Jim and Maisie are in partnership sharing profits and losses in the ratio 3:2. At 31 December 2001 the balances of their capital accounts are £60,000 and £40,000 respectively. Current accounts are not used by the partnership.

On 1 January 2002, Matt is admitted into the partnership, with a new profit-sharing ratio of 3:2:1. Goodwill has been agreed at a valuation of £48,000. Matt will bring £28,000 of cash into the business as his capital and premium for goodwill. Goodwill is to be eliminated.

For the year ended 31 December 2002, the partnership profits amount to £60,000, and the partners' drawings were:

	£
Jim	12,000
Maisie	12,000
Matt	8,000

Jim retired on 1 January 2003 and the firm's goodwill was then agreed to be worth £72,000. His capital and his share of the goodwill were left as a loan to the firm. Maisie and Matt agreed to share future profits and losses in the ratio 2:1. Goodwill is to be eliminated.

You are to show the partners' capital accounts for the period from 31 December 2001 to 1 January 2003.

11.4* Reena, Sam and Tamara are in partnership sharing profits in the ratio 4:2:2 respectively. Sam is to retire on 31 August 2001 and is to be paid the amount due to him in cash.

The balance sheet drawn up immediately before Sam's retirement was as follows:

	£
Fixed assets	50,000
Current assets	10,000
Cash at bank	25,000
	85,000
Creditors	(10,000)
	75,000
Capital accounts:	
Reena	33,000
Sam	12,000
Tamara	30,000
	75,000

Goodwill is to be valued at £16,000 and fixed assets are to be revalued at £74,000. No goodwill is to remain in the books after Sam's retirement.

In the new partnership Reena and Tamara are to share profits equally.

You are to prepare

(a)   the partners' capital accounts showing the amount Sam is to be paid upon retirement

(b)   the balance sheet immediately after Sam's departure from the business

11.5 Henry and Jenny are in partnership sharing profits and losses in a 3:2 ratio. Their balance sheet at 31 December 2008 is as follows:

BALANCE SHEET OF HENRY AND JENNY AS AT 31 DECEMBER 2008

	£	£
Fixed Assets		
Premises (net book value)		150,000
Vehicles (net book value)		30,000
		180,000
Current Assets		
Stock	20,000	
Debtors	25,000	
Bank	3,000	
	48,000	
Less Current Liabilities		
Creditors	28,000	
Working Capital		20,000
NET ASSETS		200,000
FINANCED BY		
Capital accounts		
Henry		100,000
Jenny		90,000
		190,000
Current accounts		
Henry	8,500	
Jenny	1,500	
		10,000
		200,000

On 1 January 2009 the partners decide to admit Kylie into the partnership. On this date:

- goodwill was valued at £40,000
- the premises were valued at £180,000
- the stock valuation includes £3,000 of stock which is obsolete and should be written off
- an amount of £2,000, owed by a debtor, is considered to be irrecoverable, and the balance was written off

The new partnership agreement states that Henry, Jenny and Kylie are to share profits and losses in a 2:2:1 ratio.

Kylie will pay £50,000 into the business by cheque as her capital, part of which represents a premium for goodwill.

You are to prepare the following:

- the revaluation account for Henry and Jenny in partnership

- the goodwill account for the partnership

- partners' capital accounts

- the balance sheet at 1 January 2009 for Henry, Jenny and Kylie in partnership

11.6 The following is the summarised balance sheet of Amy, Briony, Clarissa and Daljit who share profits and losses in the ratio of 4:3:2:1 respectively:

BALANCE SHEET AS AT 30 JUNE 2005

	£	£
Fixed Assets		
Premises (net book value)	100,000	
Plant and equipment (net book value)	30,000	
Vehicles (net book value)	20,000	
		150,000
Current Assets		
Stock	25,000	
Debtors	20,000	
Bank	5,000	
	50,000	
Less Current Liabilities		
Creditors	25,000	
Working Capital		25,000
NET ASSETS		175,000

FINANCED BY

Capital accounts

Amy	60,000
Briony	50,000
Clarissa	40,000
Daljit	25,000
	175,000

The partners decide to dissolve the business as from 30 June 2005. The following are the proceeds of sale:

- the premises, when sold, realised £160,000; the plant and equipment was sold at auction for £26,000

- the vehicles were sold to a garage for cash totalling £18,000

- the stock and debtors collectively realised £38,000; the creditors after discounts were settled for £23,000

- the costs of realisation and the auction amounted to £4,000 which was paid for by cheque

You are to draft the closing entries in the partnership books of account.

LIMITED COMPANY ACCOUNTS

CASE STUDY
'We've big plans for expansion...'

Ramjit and Veta have been trading very successfully for the last three years running their music business as a partnership. At the moment they have three shops and a mail order business trading under the 'RaVe' name. They have plans, as they say to their accountant:

'We've big plans for expansion and have identified suitable sites for new shops in the south east, nearer to London. Our problem, though, is finance; we will need a lot more capital. As a partnership, it is difficult to see how we can raise the money we will need. We are also concerned about our unlimited liability for the debts of the partnership.'

Their accountant suggests that they consider forming a private limited company which will enable them to issue shares to family, friends and to local investors. As the accountant says:

'We aren't talking about a company quoted on the Stock Market – although some small businesses have made it to that stage. Instead, forming a private limited company should enable you to raise the finance you need and you will still be able to retain control of the business.'

The accountant suggests they call the company RaVe Music Limited. He comments:

'Forming a company is a big change from a partnership. The company will have to produce formal annual accounts, which have to be filed at Companies House. The way you draw income from the company will also be different – a mix of salary and dividend payments. In terms of cost, it is quite an expensive option, but it would give you both the added protection of limited liability. You may also find that your tax bill is reduced.'

In this chapter we look at the form and structure of a limited company's final accounts.

learning objectives

When you have studied this chapter you will be able to:

- *appreciate the advantages of forming a limited company*
- *understand the differences between a private limited company, a public limited company, and a company limited by guarantee*
- *distinguish between ordinary shares and preference shares*
- *distinguish between capital reserves and revenue reserves*
- *prepare limited company profit and loss accounts and balance sheets*

ADVANTAGES OF FORMING A LIMITED COMPANY

A limited company is a separate legal entity, owned by shareholders and managed by directors.

The limited company is often chosen as the legal status of a business for a number of reasons:

limited liability

The shareholders (members) of a company can only lose the amount of their investment, being the money paid already, together with any money unpaid on their shares (unpaid instalments on new share issues, for example). Thus, if the company became insolvent (went 'bust'), shareholders would have to pay any unpaid instalments to help pay the creditors. As this happens very rarely, shareholders are usually in a safe position: their personal assets, unless pledged as security to a lender (as in the case of a director/shareholder), are not available to the company's creditors – they have **limited liability**.

separate legal entity

A limited company is a separate legal entity from its owners. Anyone taking legal action proceeds against the company and not the individual shareholders.

ability to raise finance

A limited company can raise substantial funds from outside sources by the issue of shares:

- for the larger public company – from the public and investing institutions on the Stock Exchange or similar markets
- for the smaller company – privately from venture capital companies, relatives and friends

Companies can also raise finance by means of debentures (see page 238).

membership

A member of a limited company is a person who owns at least one share in that company. The minimum number of members is two, but there is no upper limit. A member of a company is the same as a shareholder.

other factors

A limited company is usually a much larger business unit than a sole trader or partnership. This gives the company a higher standing and status in the business community, allowing it to benefit from economies of scale, and making it of sufficient size to employ specialists for functions such as production, marketing, finance and human resources.

THE COMPANIES ACT

Limited companies are regulated by the Companies Act 1985, as amended by the Companies Act 1989.

Under the terms of the 1985 Act there are two main types of limited company: the larger **public limited company** (abbreviated to 'Plc'), which is defined in the Act, and the smaller company, traditionally known as a **private limited company** (abbreviated to 'Ltd'), which is any other limited company. A further type of company is limited by guarantee.

public limited company (Plc)

A company may become a public limited company if it has:

- issued share capital of over £50,000
- at least two members (shareholders) and at least two directors

A public limited company may raise capital from the public on the Stock Exchange or similar markets – the new issues and privatisations of recent years are examples of this. A public limited company does not have to issue shares on the stock markets, and not all do so.

private limited company (Ltd)

The private limited company is the most common form of limited company. The term private is not set out in the Companies Act 1985, but it is a traditional description, and well describes the smaller company, often in family ownership. A private limited company has:

- no minimum requirement for issued share capital
- at least two members (shareholders) and at least one director

The shares are not traded publicly, but are transferable between individuals, although valuation will be more difficult for shares not quoted on the stock markets.

company limited by guarantee

A company limited by guarantee is not formed with share capital, but relies on the guarantee of its members to pay a stated amount in the event of the company's insolvency. Examples of such companies include charities, and artistic and educational organisations.

GOVERNING DOCUMENTS OF COMPANIES

There are a number of documents required by the Companies Act in the setting-up of a company. Two essential governing documents are the Memorandum of Association and the Articles of Association.

The **Memorandum of Association**, the constitution of the company, regulates the affairs of the company to the outside world and contains five main clauses:

1 the name of the company (together with the words 'public limited company' or 'limited', as appropriate)

2 capital of the company (the amount that can be issued in shares: the authorised share capital)

3 'objects' of the company, ie what activities the company can engage in; under the Companies Act the objects can be stated as being those of 'a general commercial company', ie the company can engage in any commercial activity

4 registered office of the company (not the address, but whether it is registered in England and Wales, or in Scotland)

5 a statement that the liability of the members is limited

The **Articles of Association** regulate the internal administration of the company, including the powers of directors and the holding of company meetings.

ACCOUNTING REQUIREMENTS OF THE COMPANIES ACT

The Companies Act 1985 (as amended by the Companies Act 1989) requires that companies produce sets of accounts. The Act seeks to protect the interests of shareholders, creditors, and lenders by requiring accounts to be presented in a standardised layout. This enables comparisons to be made with other companies so that users of accounts can understand and assess the progress being made. The Act also states the detailed information that must be disclosed.

For larger companies the accounts are audited by external auditors – this is a costly and time-consuming exercise (smaller and medium-sized companies are often exempt from audit). Nevertheless, the audit process enhances the reliability of the accounts for users.

The accounts must be sent to Companies House, where they are available for public inspection. The accounts are available to all shareholders, together with a report on the company's activities during the year.

In this chapter we will study the 'internal use' accounts, rather than being concerned with the accounting requirements of the Companies Act. Chapter 14 will look at such 'published accounts', as they are often known.

Before we examine the financial statements in detail we will look first at the principal ways in which a company raises finance: shares. There are different types of shares which appear in a company's balance sheet as the company's share capital.

TYPES OF SHARES ISSUED BY LIMITED COMPANIES

The **authorised share capital** is stated in the Memorandum of Association and is the maximum share capital that the company is allowed to issue. The authorised share capital may not be the same as the **issued share capital**; under company law the issued capital cannot exceed the amount authorised. If a company which has issued the full extent of its authorised share capital wishes to make an increase, it must first pass the appropriate resolution at a general meeting of the shareholders.

The authorised share capital is shown on the balance sheet (or as a note to the accounts) 'for information', but is not added into the balance sheet total, as it may not be the same amount as the issued share capital. By contrast, the issued share capital – showing the classes and number of shares that have been issued – forms a part of the 'financed by' section of the balance sheet of a limited company.

The authorised and issued share capital may be divided into a number of classes or types of share; the main types are **ordinary shares** and, less commonly, **preference shares.**

ordinary (equity) shares

These are the most commonly issued class of share which carry the main 'risks and rewards' of the business: the risks are of losing part or all of the value of the shares if the business loses money or becomes insolvent; the rewards are that they take a share of the profits – in the form of **dividends** – after allowance has been made for all expenses of the business, including loan and debenture interest, taxation, and after preference dividends (if any). When a company makes large profits, it will have the ability to pay higher dividends to the ordinary shareholders; when losses are made, the ordinary shareholders may receive no dividend.

Companies rarely pay out all of their profits in the form of dividends; most retain some profits as reserves. These can always be used to enable a dividend to be paid in a year when the company makes little or no profit, always assuming that the company has sufficient cash in the bank to make the payment. Ordinary shareholders, in the event of the company becoming insolvent, will be the last to receive any repayment of their investment: other creditors will be paid off first.

Ordinary shares usually carry voting rights – thus shareholders have a say at the annual general meeting and at any other shareholders' meetings.

preference shares

Whereas ordinary share dividends will vary from year-to-year, preference shares usually carry a fixed percentage rate of dividend – for example, ten per cent of nominal value. Their dividends are paid in preference to those of ordinary shareholders; but they are only paid if the company makes profits. In the event of the company ceasing to trade, the preference shareholders will also receive repayment of capital before the ordinary shareholders.

Preference shares do not normally carry voting rights.

nominal and market values of shares

Each share has a **nominal value** – or face value – which is entered in the accounts. Shares may be issued with nominal values of 5p, 10p, 25p, 50p or £1, or indeed for any amount. Thus a company with an authorised share capital of £100,000 might state in its Memorandum of Association that this is divided up into:

100,000 ordinary shares of 50p each	£50,000
50,000 ten per cent preference shares of £1 each	£50,000
	£100,000

The nominal value usually bears little relationship to the market value. The **market value** is the price at which issued – or 'secondhand' – shares are traded. Share prices of a quoted public limited company may be listed in the Financial Times.

issue price

This is the price at which shares are issued to shareholders by the company – either when the company is being set up, or at a later date when it needs to raise more funds. The issue price is either 'at par' (ie the nominal value), or above nominal value. In the latter case, the amount of the difference between issue price and nominal value is known as a **share premium** (see page 122): for example – nominal value £1.00; issue price £1.50; therefore share premium is 50p per share.

LOANS AND DEBENTURES

In addition to money provided by shareholders, who are the owners of the company, further funds can be obtained by borrowing in the form of loans or debentures:

- **Loans** are monies borrowed by companies from lenders – such as banks – on a medium or long-term basis. Generally repayments are made throughout the period of the loan, but can often be tailored to suit the needs of the borrower. Invariably lenders require security for loans so that, if the loan is not repaid, the lender has an asset – such as property – that can be sold.

  Smaller companies are sometimes also financed by directors' loans.

- **Debentures** are formal certificates issued by companies raising long-term finance from lenders and investors. Debenture certificates issued by large public limited companies are often traded on the Stock Exchange. Debentures are commonly secured against assets such as property that, in the event of the company ceasing to trade, could be sold and used to repay the debenture holders.

Loans and debentures usually carry fixed rates of interest that must be paid, just like other business overheads, whether a company makes profits or not. As loan and debenture interest is a business expense, this is shown in the profit and loss account along with all other overheads. In the event of the company ceasing to trade, loan and debenture-holders would be repaid before any shareholders.

TRADING AND PROFIT AND LOSS ACCOUNT

A limited company uses the same form of financial statements as a sole trader or partnership. However there are two overhead items commonly found in the profit and loss account of a limited company that are not found in those of other business types:

- **directors' remuneration** – ie amounts paid to directors; as directors are employed by the company, their pay appears amongst the overheads of the company

- **debenture interest** – as already noted, when debentures are issued by companies, the interest is shown as an overhead in the profit and loss account

A limited company follows the profit and loss account with an **appropriation section**. This shows how net profit has been distributed and includes:

■ corporation tax – the tax payable on company profits

■ dividends paid and proposed – on both ordinary and preference shares, including interim dividends (usually paid just over half-way through the financial year) and final dividends (proposed at the end of the year, and paid early in the next financial year)

■ transfers to and from reserves – see below

The diagram on pages 242 and 243 shows an example of a limited company's trading and profit and loss account for internal use.

BALANCE SHEET

Balance sheets of limited companies follow the same layout as those we have seen earlier, but the capital section is more complex because of the different classes of shares that may be issued, and the various reserves. The diagram on pages 244 and 245 shows the internal use balance sheet of RaVe Music Limited as an example (published accounts are covered in Chapter 14).

RESERVES

A limited company rarely distributes all its profits to its shareholders. Instead, it will often keep part of the profits earned each year in the form of reserves. There are two types of reserves:

■ capital reserves, which are created as a result of a non-trading profit

■ revenue reserves, which are retained profits from profit and loss account

capital reserves

Examples of capital reserves (which cannot be used to fund dividend payments) include:

■ **Revaluation reserve.** This occurs when a fixed asset, most probably property, is revalued (in an upwards direction) in the balance sheet. The amount of the revaluation is placed in a revaluation reserve where it increases the value of the shareholders' investment in the company. Note, however, that this is purely a 'book' adjustment – no cash has changed hands.

In the example on the next page a company revalues its property upwards by £250,000 from £500,000 to £750,000.

BALANCE SHEET (EXTRACTS)

	£
Before revaluation	
Fixed asset: property at cost	500,000
Share capital: ordinary shares of £1 each	500,000
After revaluation	
Fixed asset: property at revaluation	750,000
Share capital: ordinary shares of £1 each	500,000
Capital reserve: revaluation reserve	250,000
	750,000

■ **Share premium account.** An established company may issue additional shares to the public at a higher amount than the nominal value. For example, a company seeks finance for further expansion by issuing additional ordinary shares. The shares have a nominal value of £1 each, but, because it is a well-established company, the shares are issued at £1.50 each. Of this amount, £1 is recorded in the issued share capital section, and the extra 50p is the share premium.

revenue reserves

Revenue reserves are profits generated from trading activities; they have been retained in the company to help build the company for the future. Revenue reserves include the balance of the appropriation section of the profit and loss account: this balance is commonly described as 'profit and loss account balance' or 'balance of retained profits'. Alternatively, a transfer may be made from the appropriation section to a named revenue reserve account, such as general reserve, or a revenue reserve for a specific purpose, such as reserve for the replacement of machinery. Transfers to or from these named revenue reserve accounts are made in the appropriation section of the profit and loss account.

reserves: profits not cash

It should be noted that reserves – both capital and revenue – are not cash funds to be used whenever the company needs money, but are in fact represented by assets shown on the balance sheet. The reserves record the fact that the assets belong to the shareholders via their ownership of the company.

EXAMPLE ACCOUNTS

On the next four pages are set out the trading and profit and loss account and balance sheet for RaVe Music Limited, a private limited company. Note that these are the 'internal use' accounts – the detailed accounting requirements of the Companies Act are covered in Chapter 14.

Explanations of the financial statements are set out on the left-hand page.

ACCESSIBILITY OF ACCOUNTS

Limited company accounts are far more readily accessible to interested parties than the accounts of sole traders and partnerships:

■ all limited companies must submit accounts to Companies House where they are available for public inspection

■ a copy of the accounts is available to all shareholders, together with a report on the company's activities during the year

■ the profit statements and balance sheets of larger public limited companies are commented on and discussed in the media

■ the accounts of larger public limited companies are freely available to potential investors, lenders and other interested parties

The **appropriation section** (or account) is the part of the profit and loss account which shows how net profit is distributed. It includes corporation tax, dividends paid and proposed, and transfers to and from reserves.

The **overheads** of a limited company include directors' remuneration and interest paid on debentures (if debentures have been issued).

The company has recorded a **net profit** of £43,000 in its profit and loss account – this is brought into the appropriation section.

Corporation tax, the tax that a company has to pay, based on its profits, is shown in the appropriation section. We shall not be studying the calculations for corporation tax in this book. It is, however, important to see how the tax is recorded in the financial statements.

The company has already paid **interim dividends** on the two classes of shares it has in issue (ordinary shares and preference shares); these would, most probably, have been paid just over half-way through the company's financial year. The company also proposes to pay a **final dividend** to its shareholders: these will be paid in the early part of the next financial year. Note that a dividend is often expressed as an amount per share, based on the nominal value, eg 5p per £1 nominal value share (which is the same as a five per cent dividend).

Added to **net profit** is a **balance** of £41,000. This represents profits of the company from previous years that have not been distributed as dividends. Note that the appropriation section shows a balance of retained profits at the year-end of £50,000. Such retained profits form a revenue reserve of the company.

RAVE MUSIC LIMITED
TRADING AND PROFIT AND LOSS ACCOUNT
for the year ended 31 December 2008

	£	£
Sales		725,000
Opening stock	45,000	
Purchases	381,000	
	426,000	
Less closing stock	50,000	
Cost of sales		376,000
Gross profit		349,000
Less overheads:		
Directors' remuneration	75,000	
Debenture interest	6,000	
Other overheads	225,000	
		306,000
Net profit for year before taxation		43,000
Less corporation tax		15,000
Profit for year after taxation		28,000
Less interim dividends paid		
ordinary shares	5,000	
preference shares	2,000	
final dividends proposed		
ordinary shares	10,000	
preference shares	2,000	
		19,000
Retained profit for year		9,000
Add balance of retained profits at beginning of year		41,000
Balance of retained profits at end of year		50,000

Limited company balance sheets usually distinguish between:

intangible fixed assets, which do not have material substance but belong to the company and have value, eg goodwill (the amount paid for the reputation and connections of a business that has been taken over), patents and trademarks; intangible fixed assets are amortised (depreciated) in the same way as tangible fixed assets.

tangible fixed assets, which have material substance, such as premises, equipment, machinery, vehicles, fixtures and fittings.

As well as the usual **current liabilities**, for limited companies, this section also contains the amount of proposed dividends (but not dividends that have been paid in the year) and the amount of corporation tax to be paid within the next twelve months. The amounts for both of these items are also included in the appropriation section of the profit and loss account.

Long-term liabilities are those that are due to be repaid more than twelve months from the date of the balance sheet, eg loans and debentures.

Authorised share capital is included on the balance sheet 'for information', but is not added into the balance sheet total, as it may not be the same amount as the issued share capital.

Issued share capital shows the classes and number of shares that have been issued. In this balance sheet, the shares are described as being fully paid, meaning that the company has received the full amount of the value of each share from the shareholders. Sometimes shares will be partly paid, eg ordinary shares of £1, but 75p paid. This means that the company can make a call on the shareholders to pay the extra 25p to make the shares fully paid.

Capital reserves are created as a result of non-trading profit.

Revenue reserves are retained profits from profit and loss account.

The total for **shareholders' funds** represents the stake of the shareholders in the company. It comprises share capital (ordinary and preference shares), plus reserves (capital and revenue reserves).

RAVE MUSIC LIMITED
BALANCE SHEET AS AT 31 DECEMBER 2008

Fixed Assets	Cost £	Dep'n to date £	Net £
Intangible			
Goodwill	50,000	20,000	30,000
Tangible			
Freehold land and buildings	410,000	110,000	300,000
Fixtures and fittings	100,000	25,000	75,000
	560,000	155,000	405,000

Current Assets			
Stock		50,000	
Debtors		23,000	
Bank		32,000	
Cash		2,000	
		107,000	

Less Current Liabilities			
Creditors	25,000		
Proposed dividends	12,000		
Corporation tax	15,000		
		52,000	
Working Capital*			55,000
			460,000

Less Long-term Liabilities		
10% debentures		60,000
NET ASSETS		400,000

FINANCED BY

Authorised Share Capital	
100,000 10% preference shares of £1 each	100,000
600,000 ordinary shares of £1 each	600,000
	700,000

Issued Share Capital	
40,000 10% preference shares of £1 each, fully paid	40,000
300,000 ordinary shares of £1 each, fully paid	300,000
	340,000

Capital Reserve	
Share premium account	10,000

Revenue Reserve	
Profit and loss account	50,000
SHAREHOLDERS' FUNDS	400,000

chapter summary

- A limited company has a separate legal entity from its owners.

- A company is regulated by the Companies Act 1985 (as amended by the Companies Act 1989), and is owned by shareholders and managed by directors.

- A limited company may be either a public limited company or a private limited company.

- The liability of shareholders is limited to any money unpaid on their shares.

- The main types of shares that may be issued by companies are ordinary shares and preference shares.

- Borrowings in the form of loans and debentures are a further source of finance.

- The final accounts of a company include an appropriation section, which follows the profit and loss account.

- The balance sheet of a limited company is similar to that of sole traders and partnerships but the capital and reserves section reflects the ownership of the company by its shareholders:
  - a statement of the authorised and issued share capital
  - details of capital reserves and revenue reserves

key terms

limited company	a separate legal entity owned by shareholders and managed by directors
limited liability	shareholders of a company are liable for company debts only to the extent of any money unpaid on their shares
shareholder	person who owns at least one share in a limited company; a shareholder is also a member of a company
public limited company	a company, registered as a plc, with an issued share capital of over £50,000 and at least two members and at least two directors; it may raise funds on the stock markets
private limited company	any limited company with share capital other than a public limited company
Memorandum of Association	the document setting out the constitution of the company, which regulates the affairs of the company to the outside world
Articles of Association	the document regulating the internal administration of the company

ordinary shares	commonly issued type of shares which take a share in the profits of the company but which also carry the main risks
preference shares	shares which carry a fixed rate of dividend paid, subject to sufficient profits, in preference to ordinary shareholders; in event of repayment of capital, rank before the ordinary shareholders
debentures	issued by companies raising long-term finance; debenture interest is an overhead in profit and loss account
nominal value	the face value of the shares entered in the accounts
issue price	the price at which shares are issued to shareholders by the company
market value	the price at which shares are traded
directors' remuneration	amounts paid to directors as employees of the company; an overhead in profit and loss account
appropriation section	the part of profit and loss account which shows how net profit is distributed, and includes corporation tax, dividends paid and proposed, and transfers to and from reserves
dividends	amounts paid to shareholders from the profit of the company; an interim dividend is paid just over half-way through a financial year; a final dividend is paid early in the following year
authorised share capital	amount of share capital authorised by the company's Memorandum of Association
issued share capital	the classes and number of shares that have been issued by the company; cannot exceed the authorised share capital
reserves	profits retained by the company; two main types: – capital reserves, created as a result of a non-trading profit – revenue reserves, retained profits from profit and loss account
revaluation reserve	capital reserve created by the upwards revaluation of a fixed asset, most usually property; cannot be used to fund dividend payments
share premium account	capital reserve created by the issue of shares at a price higher than nominal value, the excess being credited to share premium; cannot be used to fund dividend payments

activities

Note: an asterisk (*) after an activity number means that an answer is provided in Appendix 1.

12.1   Distinguish between:

(a)   a public limited company and a private limited company

(b)   the Memorandum of Association and the Articles of Association

(c)   authorised share capital and issued share capital

(d)   ordinary shares and preference shares

(e)   nominal value and market value of shares

(f)   capital reserves and revenue reserves

12.2   Prepare a five-minute talk on the types of companies and the advantages of forming a limited company. The talk is to form part of your local radio station's business programme entitled 'Business Matters'. To accompany your talk, prepare a handout which can be distributed to listeners who contact the station.

12.3   Explain where the following items appear in a limited company's year-end financial statements:

(a)   debenture interest

(b)   directors' remuneration

(c)   corporation tax

(d)   dividends proposed

(e)   revaluation reserve

(f)   goodwill

12.4   Mason Motors Limited is a second-hand car business. The following information is available for the year ended 31 December 2001:

•   balance of retained profits from previous years stands at £100,000

•   net profit for the year was £75,000

•   it has been agreed that a transfer to a general reserve of £20,000 is to be made

•   corporation tax of £20,050 is to be paid on the year's profit

•   it has been agreed that a dividend of 10% is to be paid on the issued share capital of £100,000

You are to

(a)   Set out the appropriation section of the profit and loss account for Mason Motors Limited for the year ended 31 December 2001.

(b)   State how you would reply to one of the directors of the company who asks if the £20,000 being transferred to general reserve could be used to rebuild the garage forecourt.

12.5*   The following figures are taken from the accounting records of Jobseekers Limited, a recruitment agency, at the end of the financial year on 31 December 2006:

	£
Issued share capital (£1 ordinary shares)	100,000
Premises at cost	175,000
Depreciation of premises to date	10,500
Office equipment at cost	25,000
Depreciation of office equipment to date	5,000
Goodwill at cost	20,000
Amortisation of goodwill to date	6,000
Stock at 31 December 2006	750
Debtors	42,500
Creditors	7,250
Bank overdraft	13,950
Bank loan	55,000
Net profit for year before taxation	68,200
Corporation tax for the year	14,850
Interim ordinary dividend paid	10,000
Final ordinary dividend proposed	40,000
Retained profit at 1 January 2006	7,350

You are to prepare the appropriation section of the profit and loss account (starting with net profit) for the year ended 31 December 2006, together with a balance sheet at that date.

12.6*   The following trial balance was extracted from the books of Sidbury Trading Company Limited, a local stationery supplies firm, as at 31 December 2002:

	Dr £	Cr £
Share capital		240,000
Freehold land and buildings at cost	142,000	
Vans at cost	55,000	
Provision for depreciation on vans at 1 January 2002		21,800
Purchases and sales	189,273	297,462
Rent and rates	4,000	
General expenses	9,741	
Wages and salaries	34,689	
Bad debts written off	948	
Provision for bad debts at 1 January 2002		1,076
Directors' salaries	25,000	
Debtors and creditors	26,482	14,555
Value Added Tax		2,419
Retained profit at 1 January 2002		18,397
Stock at 1 January 2002	42,618	
Bank	65,958	
	595,709	595,709

You are given the following additional information:

- The authorised share capital is 300,000 ordinary shares of £1 each; all the shares which have been issued are fully paid.
- Wages and salaries outstanding at 31 December 2002 amounted to £354.
- The provision for bad debts is to be increased by £124.
- Stock at 31 December 2002 is valued at £47,288.
- Rent and rates amounting to £400 were paid in advance at 31 December 2002.
- It is proposed to pay a dividend of £8,000 for 2002.
- Depreciation on vans is to be charged at the rate of 20 per cent per annum on cost.
- Corporation tax of £12,000 is to be provided for.

You are to prepare appropriate final accounts for the year 2002, together with a balance sheet at 31 December 2002.

12.7 Playfair Ltd has an authorised share capital of 50,000 ordinary shares of £1 each and 10,000 8% preference shares of £1 each. At 31 December 2003, the following trial balance was extracted:

	Dr £	Cr £
Ordinary share capital		50,000
8% preference share capital		8,000
Plant and machinery at cost	34,000	
Motor vehicles at cost	16,000	
Debtors and creditors	34,980	15,900
Value Added Tax		1,970
Bank	14,505	
10% debentures		9,000
Stock at 1 January 2003	25,200	
General expenses	11,020	
Purchases and sales	164,764	233,384
Bad debts written off	2,400	
Debenture interest	900	
Discounts	325	640
Salaries	24,210	
Insurance	300	
Provision for depreciation:		
plant and machinery		16,000
motor vehicles		7,200
Directors' fees	17,000	
Interim preference dividend paid	320	
Profit and loss account at 1 January 2003		3,300
Provision for bad debts at 1 January 2003		530
	345,924	345,924

Additional information:
- Stock at 31 December 2003 is valued at £28,247.
- Depreciation on plant and machinery is to be provided for at the rate of 10 per cent per annum calculated on cost.
- Depreciation on motor vehicles is to be provided for at the rate of 20 per cent per annum using the reducing balance method.
- Insurance prepaid at 31 December 2003 amounted to £60.
- General expenses owing at 31 December 2003 amounted to £110.
- The provision for bad debts is to be increased to £750.
- The directors propose to pay an ordinary dividend of 6 per cent to the ordinary shareholders and to pay the remaining dividend due to the preference shareholders.
- £2,000 is to be transferred to General Reserve.
- Corporation tax of £4,000 is to be provided for.

You are to prepare appropriate final accounts for the year ended 31 December 2003, together with a balance sheet at that date.

13 CASH FLOW STATEMENTS

CASE STUDY
'Profit does not equal cash...'

The accountant been working on the accounts of Samantha Smith, a sole trader. Samantha runs a part-time business selling children's clothes. The profit and loss account prepared for the year ended 31 December 2002 shows a net profit of £4,080.

When discussing the accounts with the accountant, Samantha says:

'I am quite pleased with the profit figure. It is down a bit from the previous year, but trading was quite difficult for most of the period, although it picked up well in the run-up to Christmas. My main concern is that I cannot understand why I am overdrawn at the bank by £725 on 31 December 2002 when I made a profit of £4,080 during the year. Can you please explain this to me?'

The issue raised by Samantha is important. The profit and loss account shows profitability, and the balance sheet shows the asset strength of a business. Whilst these two financial statements give a great deal of information about the progress of a business during an accounting period, profit does not equal cash, and strength in assets does not necessarily mean a large balance at the bank.

In order to give a detailed answer to Samantha her accountant needs to prepare a cash flow statement. This links profit from the profit and loss account with changes in assets and liabilities in the balance sheet and the cash flows of the business over a period of time.

This chapter discusses the need for a cash flow statement and explains its structure and interpretation.

learning objectives

When you have studied this chapter you will be able to:

- ◼ *appreciate the need for a cash flow statement*

- ◼ *understand the cash flow for the main sections of the statement*

- ◼ *see how the cash flows relate to the main areas of business activity*

- ◼ *prepare cash flow statements to a recognised format*

- ◼ *interpret cash flow statements*

FUNCTION OF THE CASH FLOW STATEMENT

The **cash flow statement** links profit from the profit and loss account with changes in assets and liabilities in the balance sheet, and shows the effect on the cash of the business.

A cash flow statement uses information from the accounting records (including profit and loss account and balance sheet) to show an overall view of money flowing in and out of a business during an accounting period.

Such a statement explains to the owner or shareholders why, after a year of good profits for example, there is a reduced balance at the bank or a larger bank overdraft at the year-end than there was at the beginning of the year. The cash flow statement concentrates on the liquidity of the business: it is often a lack of cash (a lack of liquidity) that causes most businesses to fail. The importance of the cash flow statement is such that all but small limited companies must include the statement as a part of their accounts. For sole traders and partnerships, the information that the statement contains is of considerable interest to the owner(s) and to a lender, such as a bank.

The format used in this chapter for the cash flow statement follows the guidelines set out in Financial Reporting Standard No.1 'Cash flow statements'.

FORMAT OF THE CASH FLOW STATEMENT

FRS 1 provides a format for cash flow statements which is divided into eight sections:

1   Operating activities

2   Returns on investments and servicing of finance

3   Taxation

4   Capital expenditure and financial investment

5   Acquisitions and disposals

6   Equity dividends paid

7   Management of liquid resources

8   Financing

The cash flows for the year affecting each of these main areas of business activity are shown in the statement, although not every business will have cash flows under each of the eight sections. The final figure at the bottom of the cash flow statement shows the net cash inflow or outflow for the period.

The illustration on the next page shows the main cash inflows and outflows under each heading, and indicates the content of the cash flow statement. The first section – operating activities – needs a word of further explanation, particularly as it is the main source of cash inflow for most businesses.

operating activities

The net cash inflow from operating activities is calculated by using figures from the profit and loss account and balance sheet as follows:

operating profit (ie net profit, before deduction of interest)

add   depreciation for the year

add   loss on sale of fixed assets

deduct   profit on sale of fixed assets – see page 262

add   decrease in stock (or *deduct* increase in stock)

add   decrease in debtors (or *deduct* increase in debtors)

add   increase in creditors (or *deduct* decrease in creditors)

Note that depreciation is added to profit because depreciation is a non-cash expense, that is, no money is paid out by the business in respect of depreciation charged to profit and loss account.

LAYOUT OF A CASH FLOW STATEMENT

A cash flow statement uses a common layout which can be amended to suit the particular needs of the business for which it is being prepared. The example layout shown on page 256 (with specimen figures included) is commonly used – see also the cash flow statement for Tesco PLC shown on page 281.

Also in this chapter we will be looking at two Case Studies: the first (on page 257) shows how a cash flow statement is prepared for a sole trader business, the second (on page 260) is for a limited company.

CASH FLOW STATEMENT

Operating activities

- Operating profit (ie net profit, before deduction of interest)
- Depreciation charge for the year (see page 262 for treatment of a profit or a loss on sale of fixed assets)
- Changes in stock, debtors and creditors

Returns on investments and servicing of finance

- Inflows: interest received, dividends received
- Outflows: interest paid, dividends paid on preference shares (but not ordinary shares – see below)

Taxation

- Outflow: corporation tax paid by limited companies during the year

Capital expenditure and financial investment

- Inflows: sale proceeds from fixed assets and investments
- Outflows: purchase cost of fixed assets and investments

Acquisitions and disposals

- Inflows: sale proceeds from investments and interests in
    - subsidiary companies (where more than 50 per cent of the shares in another company is owned)
    - associated companies (where between 20 per cent and 50 per cent of the shares in another company is owned)
    - joint ventures (where a project is undertaken jointly with another company)
- Outflows: purchase cost of investments in subsidiary companies, associated companies, and of interests in joint ventures

Equity dividends paid

- Outflow: the amount of dividends paid to equity (ordinary) shareholders during the year (where the cash flow statement is for a sole trader or partnership, the amount of drawings will be shown here)

Management of liquid resources

- Inflows: sale proceeds from short-term investments that are almost as good as cash – such as treasury bills (a form of government debt), and term deposits of up to a year with a bank
- Outflows: purchase of short-term liquid investments

Financing

- Inflows: receipts from increase in capital /share capital, raising/increase of loans (note: no cash inflow from a bonus issue of shares – see page 287)
- Outflows: repayment of capital/share capital/loans

Contents of a cash flow statement

ORION LIMITED
CASH FLOW STATEMENT FOR THE YEAR ENDED 31 DECEMBER 2002

	£	£
Net cash inflow from operating activities		89,000
Returns on investments and servicing of finance:		
Interest received	10,000	
Interest paid	(5,000)	
		5,000
Taxation:		
Corporation tax paid (note: amount paid during year)		(6,000)
Capital expenditure and financial investment:		
Payments to acquire fixed assets	(125,000)	
Receipts from sales of fixed assets	15,000	
		(110,000)
Acquisitions and disposals:		
Purchase of subsidiary undertakings	(–)	
Sale of a business	–	
		–
Equity dividends paid: (note: amount paid during year)		(22,000)
Cash outflow before use of liquid resources and financing		(44,000)
Management of liquid resources:		
Purchase of treasury bills	(250,000)	
Sale of treasury bills	200,000	
		(50,000)
Financing:		
Issue of share capital	275,000	
Repayment of capital/share capital	(–)	
Increase in loans	–	
Repayment of loans	(90,000)	
		185,000
Increase in cash		91,000

Reconciliation of operating profit to net cash inflow from operating activities	
Operating profit (note: before tax and interest)	75,000
Depreciation for year	10,000
Decrease in stock	2,000
Increase in debtors	(5,000)
Increase in creditors	7,000
Net cash inflow from operating activities	89,000

notes on the cash flow statement

- The separate amounts shown for each section can, if preferred, be detailed in a note to the cash flow statement. The operating activities section is invariably set out in detail as a note below the cash flow statement (see example opposite), with just the figure for net cash flow from operating activities being shown on the statement (see blue line).

- Money amounts shown in brackets indicate a deduction or, where the figure is a sub-total, a negative figure.

- The changes in the main working capital items of stock, debtors and creditors have an effect on cash balances. For example, a decrease in stock increases cash, while an increase in debtors reduces cash.

- The cash flow statement concludes with a figure for the increase or decrease in cash for the period. This is calculated from the subtotals of each of the eight sections of the statement.

CASE STUDY

Samantha Smith: a sole trader cash flow statement

situation

Samantha Smith sells children's clothes as a part-time business at a local indoor market. Her balance sheets for the last two years are as follows:

BALANCE SHEETS AS AT 31 DECEMBER						
	2001			2002		
	£ Cost	£ Dep'n	£ Net	£ Cost	£ Dep'n	£ Net
Fixed Assets						
Display equipment	1,500	500	1,000	2,000	750	1,250
Current Assets						
Stock		3,750			4,850	
Debtors		625			1,040	
Bank		220			–	
		4,595			5,890	
Less Current Liabilities						
Creditors	2,020			4,360		
Bank	–			725		
		2,020			5,085	
Net Current Assets			2,575			805
			3,575			2,055
Less Long-term Liabilities						
Loan from husband			–			1,000
NET ASSETS			3,575			1,055

FINANCED BY		
Capital	£	£
Opening capital	3,300	3,575
Add net profit for year	5,450	4,080
	8,750	7,655
Less drawings	5,175	6,600
	3,575	1,055

Note: Interest paid on the loan and bank overdraft in 2002 was £450.

Samantha Smith says to you: 'I cannot understand why I am overdrawn at the bank by £725 on 31 December 2002 when I made a profit of £4,080 during the year'. She asks you to help her by explaining why this is.

solution
A cash flow statement will give Samantha Smith the answer:

CASH FLOW STATEMENT FOR THE YEAR ENDED 31 DECEMBER 2002		
	£	£
Net cash inflow from operating activities		5,605
Returns on investments and servicing of finance:		
Interest paid		(450)
Taxation:		
Corporation tax paid		not applicable
Capital expenditure and financial investment:		
Payments to acquire fixed assets		(500)
Equity dividends paid: (drawings)		(6,600)
Cash outflow before use of liquid resources and financing		(1,945)
Financing:		
Loan from husband		1,000
Decrease in cash		(945)

Reconciliation of operating profit to net cash inflow from operating activities	
Operating profit (before interest)	4,530
Depreciation for year	250
Increase in stock	(1,100)
Increase in debtors	(415)
Increase in creditors	2,340
Net cash inflow from operating activities	5,605

> **Tutorial note**
> When preparing a cash flow statement from financial statements, take a moment or two to establish which is the earlier year and which is the later year. In this Case Study they are set out from left to right, ie 2001 followed by 2002. In some question layouts you may find that the later year is shown first, ie 2002 followed by 2001.

points to note from the cash flow statement

- Net profit for the year (before interest) is calculated as:

net profit for 2002	£4,080
interest for 2002	£450
	£4,530

- Depreciation for the year of £250 is the amount of the increase in depreciation to date shown on the balance sheets, that is, £750 minus £500.

- An increase in stock and debtors reduces the cash available to the business (because stock is being bought, debtors are being allowed more time to pay). By contrast, an increase in creditors gives an increase in cash (because creditors are allowing Samantha Smith more time to pay).

- In this example there is no tax paid (because Samantha Smith is a sole trader who will be taxed as an individual, unlike a company which pays tax on its profits); however, the place where tax would appear is indicated on the cash flow statement.

- Payments to acquire fixed assets £500 is the amount of the increase in the cost of fixed assets shown on the balance sheets, that is, £2,000 minus £1,500.

- As this is a sole trader business, drawings are shown on the cash flow statement in place of equity dividends.

- The change in the bank balance is summarised as follows: from a balance of £220 in the bank to an overdraft of £725 is a 'swing' in the bank of minus £945, which is the amount of the decrease in cash shown by the cash flow statement.

> **your explanation to Samantha Smith**
> In this example, the statement highlights the following points for the owner of the business:
>
> - net cash inflow from operating activities is £5,605, whereas owner's drawings are £6,600; this state of affairs cannot continue for long
>
> - fixed assets costing £500 have been purchased
>
> - a long-term loan of £1,000 has been raised from her husband
>
> - over the year there has been a decrease in cash of £945, this trend cannot be continued for long
>
> - by the end of 2002 the business has an overdraft of £725, caused mainly by the excessive drawings of the owner
>
> - in conclusion, the liquidity position of this business has deteriorated over the two years, and corrective action will be necessary

CASE STUDY
Limited company cash flow statement

situation
The balance sheets of Newtown Trading Company Limited for 2001 and 2002 are as follows:

BALANCE SHEETS AS AT 31 DECEMBER

	2001			2002		
	£	£	£	£	£	£
	Cost	Dep'n	Net	Cost or reval'n	Dep'n	Net
Fixed Assets						
Land	75,000	–	75,000	125,000	–	125,000
Vehicles	22,200	6,200	16,000	39,000	8,900	30,100
	97,200	6,200	91,000	164,000	8,900	155,100
Current Assets						
Stock		7,000			11,000	
Debtors		5,000			3,700	
Bank		1,000			500	
		13,000			15,200	
Less Current Liabilities						
Creditors	3,500			4,800		
Proposed dividends	2,000			2,500		
Corporation tax	1,000			1,500		
		6,500			8,800	
Net Current Assets			6,500			6,400
			97,500			161,500
Less Long-term Liabilities						
Debentures			5,000			3,000
NET ASSETS			92,500			158,500
FINANCED BY						
Ordinary share capital			80,000			90,000
Share premium account			1,500			2,500
Revaluation reserve			–			50,000
Retained profits			11,000			16,000
SHAREHOLDERS' FUNDS			92,500			158,500

Prepare a cash flow statement for the year ended 31 December 2002 and comment on the main points highlighted by the statement. Note the following points:

- Extract from the profit and loss account for 2002:

	£
Operating profit	9,400
Interest paid	400
Net profit	9,000
Less: Corporation tax	1,500
Proposed ordinary dividend	2,500
Retained profit for year	5,000

- During 2002 the land was revalued at £125,000.

solution

NEWTOWN TRADING COMPANY LIMITED
CASH FLOW STATEMENT FOR THE YEAR ENDED 31 DECEMBER 2002

	£	£
Net cash inflow from operating activities		10,700
Returns on investments and servicing of finance:		
Interest paid		(400)
Taxation:		
Corporation tax paid		(1,000)
Capital expenditure and financial investment:		
Payments to acquire fixed assets (vehicles)		(16,800)
Equity dividends paid:		(2,000)
Cash outflow before use of liquid resources and financing		(9,500)
Financing:		
Issue of ordinary shares at a premium		
ie £10,000 + £1,000 =	11,000	
Repayment of debentures	(2,000)	
		9,000
Decrease in cash**		(500)

Reconciliation of operating profit to net cash inflow from operating activities	
Operating profit (before interest)	9,400
Depreciation for year*	2,700
Increase in stock	(4,000)
Decrease in debtors	1,300
Increase in creditors	1,300
Net cash inflow from operating activities	10,700

notes on the cash flow statement

* Depreciation charged: £8,900 – £6,200 = £2,700

** Decrease in cash: from £1,000 to £500 = £500

Both proposed dividends and corporation tax – which are current liabilities at 31 December 2001 – are paid in 2002. Likewise, the current liabilities for dividends and tax at 31 December 2002 will be paid in 2003 (and will appear on that year's cash flow statement).

The revaluation of the land (increase in the value of the fixed asset, and revaluation reserve recorded in the 'financed by' section) does not feature in the cash flow statement because it is a non-cash transaction.

how useful is the cash flow statement?

The following points are highlighted by the statement on the previous page:

* net cash inflow from operating activities is £10,700

* a purchase of vehicles of £16,800 has been made, financed partly by operating activities, and partly by an issue of shares at a premium

* the bank balance during the year has fallen by £500, ie from £1,000 to £500

In conclusion, the picture shown by the cash flow statement is that of a business which is generating cash from its operating activities and using them to build for the future.

PROFIT OR LOSS ON SALE OF FIXED ASSETS

a difference between book value and sale proceeds

When a business sells fixed assets it is most unlikely that the resultant sale proceeds will equal the net book value (cost price, less depreciation to date).

dealing with a profit or loss on sale

The accounting solution is to transfer any small profit or loss on sale – non-cash items – to profit and loss account. However, such a profit or loss on sale must be handled with care when preparing a cash flow statement because, in such a statement we have to adjust for non-cash items when calculating the net cash inflow from operating activities; at the same time we must separately identify the amount of the sale proceeds of fixed assets in the capital expenditure section.

CASE STUDY

Profit and loss on sale of fixed assets

situation

H & J Wells are electrical contractors. For the year ended 30 June 2002 their profit and loss account is as follows:

	£	£
Gross profit		37,500
Less expenses:		
General expenses	23,000	
Provision for depreciation: machinery	2,000	
vehicles	3,000	
		28,000
Net profit		9,500

profit on sale

During the course of the year they have sold the following fixed asset; the effects of the sale transaction have not yet been recorded in their profit and loss account:

		£
Machine:	cost price	1,000
	depreciation to date	750
	net book value	250
	sale proceeds	350

As the machine has been sold for £100 more than book value, this sum is shown in profit and loss account, as follows:

	£	£
Gross profit		37,500
Profit on sale of fixed assets		100
		37,600
Less expenses:		
General expenses	23,000	
Provision for depreciation: machinery	2,000	
vehicles	3,000	
		28,000
Net profit		9,600

The cash flow statement, based on the amended profit and loss account, will include the following figures:

CASHFLOW STATEMENT (EXTRACT) OF H & J WELLS
FOR THE YEAR ENDED 30 JUNE 2002

	£	£
Operating activities (this will be shown as a note)		
Operating profit (here, the same as net profit)	9,600	
Depreciation	5,000	
Profit on sale of fixed assets	(100)	
(Increase)/decrease in stock	. . .	
(Increase)/decrease in debtors	. . .	
Increase/(decrease) in creditors	. . .	
Net cash inflow from operating activities		14,500
Capital expenditure and financial investment:		
Payments to acquire fixed assets	(. . .)	
Receipts from sales of fixed assets	350	
		350

Note that profit on sale of fixed assets is deducted in the operating activities section because it is non-cash income. (Only the sections of the cash flow statement affected by the sale are shown above.)

loss on sale

If the machine in the Case Study had been sold for £150, this would have given a 'loss on sale' of £100. This amount would be debited to profit and loss account, to give an amended net profit of £9,400. The effect on the cash flow statement would be twofold:

1 In the operating activities section, loss on sale of fixed assets of £100 would be added; the net cash inflow from operating activities remains at £14,500 (which proves that both profit and loss on sale of fixed assets are non-cash items)

2 In the capital expenditure section, receipts from sales of fixed assets would be £150

conclusion: profit or a loss on sale of fixed assets

The rule for dealing with a profit or a loss on sale of fixed assets in cash flow statements is:

■ add the amount of the loss on sale, or deduct the amount of the profit on sale, to or from the operating profit when calculating the net cash flow from operating activities

■ show the total sale proceeds, ie the amount of the cheque received, as receipts from sales of fixed assets in the capital expenditure section

REVALUATION OF FIXED ASSETS

From time-to-time some fixed assets are revalued upwards and the amount of the revaluation is recorded in the balance sheet. The most common assets to be treated in this way are land and buildings. The value of the fixed asset is increased and the amount of the revaluation is placed to a revaluation reserve in the 'financed by' section of the balance sheet where it increases the value of the shareholders' investment in the company. As a revaluation is purely a 'book' adjustment, ie no cash has changed hands, it does not feature in a cash flow statement – see the Case Study of Newtown Trading Company Limited on pages 260 to 262.

USING THE CASH FLOW STATEMENT

The cash flow statement is important because it identifies the sources of cash flowing into the business and shows how they have been used. We need to read the statement in conjunction with the other two financial statements – profit and loss account and balance sheet – and also in the context of the previous year's statements. The following points should also be borne in mind:

■ Like the other financial statements, the cash flow statement uses the money measurement concept. This means that only items which can be recorded in money terms can be included; also we must be aware of the effect of inflation when comparing one year with the next.

■ We are looking for a reasonable cash flow from operating activities each year – this is the cash from the trading activities of the business.

■ Changes in the working items of stock, debtors and creditors need to be put into context. For example, it would be a warning sign if there were large increases in these items in a business with a falling operating profit, and such a trend would put a strain on the liquidity of the business.

■ The statement will show the amount of investment made during the year (eg the purchase of fixed assets). In general there should be a link between the cost of the investment and an increase in loans and/or capital – it isn't usual to finance fixed assets from short-term sources, such as a bank overdraft.

■ Where there has been an increase in loans and/or capital, look to see how the cash has been used. Was it to buy fixed assets or other investments, or to finance stocks and debtors, or other purposes?

■ The statement, as a whole, links profit with changes in cash. Both of these are important: without profits the business cannot generate cash (unless it sells fixed assets), and without cash it cannot pay bills as they fall due.

chapter summary

● The objective of a cash flow statement is to show an overall view of money flowing in and out of a business during an accounting period

● A cashflow statement is divided into eight sections:

    1   operating activities

    2   returns on investments and servicing of finance

    3   taxation

    4   capital expenditure and financial investment

    5   acquisitions and disposals

    6   equity dividends paid

    7   management of liquid resources

    8   financing

● Financial Reporting Standard No. 1 'Cash flow statements' provides a specimen layout.

● Larger limited companies are required to include a cash flow statement as a part of their published accounts. They are also useful statements for sole traders, partnerships and smaller limited companies.

key terms

| cash flow statement | shows an overall view of money flowing in and out of a business during an accounting period |

cash flow from operating activities — operating profit (before interest and tax), plus depreciation for the year, plus loss (or minus profit) on sale of fixed assets, together with changes in the working capital items (stock, debtors and creditors)

returns on investments and servicing of finance — interest received and paid; dividends received; dividends paid on preference shares

capital expenditure and financial investment — purchase and/or sale of fixed assets and investments

liquid resources — short term investments that are almost equal to cash

financing — issue or repayment of loans or share capital or capital

activities

Note: an asterisk (*) after an activity number means that an answer is provided in Appendix 1.

13.1 Explain why depreciation is added back to the operating profit in the operating activities section of a cash flow statement?

13.2 Raven Limited has an operating profit of £30,000 for 2005, and there were the following movements in the year:

	£
depreciation charge	10,000
increase in stock	5,000
decrease in debtors	4,000
increase in creditors	6,000

Calculate the net cash flow from operating activities.

13.3 Meadow Limited has an operating loss of £10,000 for 2006, and there were the following movements in the year:

	£
depreciation charge	8,000
decrease in stock	4,000
increase in debtors	5,000
decrease in creditors	3,000

Calculate the net cash flow from operating activities.

13.4 Explain five points that you would look for when analysing the cash flow statement of a business.

13.5* John Smith has been in business for two years. He is puzzled by his balance sheets because, although they show a profit for each year, his bank balance has fallen and is now an overdraft. He asks for your assistance to explain what has happened. The balance sheets are as follows:

BALANCE SHEET AS AT 31 DECEMBER

	2001 £ Cost	2001 £ Dep'n	2001 £ Net	2002 £ Cost	2002 £ Dep'n	2002 £ Net
Fixed Assets						
Fixtures and fittings	3,000	600	2,400	5,000	1,600	3,400
Current Assets						
Stock		5,500			9,000	
Debtors		750			1,550	
Bank		850			–	
		7,100			10,550	
Current Liabilities						
Creditors	2,500			2,750		
Bank overdraft	–			2,200		
		2,500			4,950	
Net Current Assets			4,600			5,600
NET ASSETS			7,000			9,000
FINANCED BY						
Capital			5,000			7,000
Add Net profit for year			8,750			11,000
			13,750			18,000
Less Drawings			6,750			9,000
			7,000			9,000

Note: Interest paid on the bank overdraft in 2002 was £250.

You are to prepare a cash flow statement for the year-ended 31 December 2002.

13.6   Richard Williams runs a stationery supplies shop; his balance sheets for the last two years are:

BALANCE SHEET AS AT 30 SEPTEMBER

	2005			2006		
	£	£	£	£	£	£
	Cost	Dep'n	Net	Cost	Dep'n	Net
Fixed Assets	60,000	12,000	48,000	70,000	23,600	46,400
Current Assets						
Stock		9,800			13,600	
Debtors		10,800			15,000	
		20,600			28,600	
Less Current Liabilities						
Creditors	7,200			14,600		
Bank overdraft	1,000			4,700		
		8,200			19,300	
Net Current Assets			12,400			9,300
			60,400			55,700
Less Long-term Liabilities						
Bank loan			10,000			15,000
NET ASSETS			50,400			40,700
FINANCED BY						
Capital			50,000			50,400
Add Net profit/(loss)			10,800			(1,500)
			60,800			48,900
Less Drawings			10,400			8,200
			50,400			40,700

Note: Loan and overdraft interest paid in 2006 was £2,200.

You are to prepare a cash flow statement for the year-ended 30 September 2006.

13.7 Using the balance sheets of Richard Williams in question 13.6, prepare revised cash flow statements for the year to 30 September 2006, to take note of the following:

Situation 1

A fixed asset with a cost price of £5,000 and depreciation to date of £3,000 was sold for £2,500.

Situation 2

A fixed asset with a cost price of £5,000 and depreciation to date of £3,000 was sold for £1,500.

Notes:

- two separate cash flow statements for the year ended 30 September 2006 are required
- assume that the balance sheet for 2006 already includes the sale transactions, ie do not adjust the net loss by the amount of the profit or loss on sale, or the bank account by the sale proceeds

13.8 Martin Jackson is a shareholder in Retail News Limited, a company that operates a chain of newsagents throughout the West Midlands. Martin comments that, whilst the company is making reasonable profits, the bank balance has fallen quite considerably. He provides you with the following information for Retail News Limited:

BALANCE SHEET AS AT 31 DECEMBER

	2004		2005		2006	
	£000	£000	£000	£000	£000	£000
Fixed Assets at cost		252		274		298
Add Additions during year		22		24		26
		274		298		324
Less Depreciation to date		74		98		118
		200		200		206
Current Assets						
Stock	50		64		70	
Debtors	80		120		160	
Bank	10		–		–	
	140		184		230	
Less Current Liabilities						
Creditors	56		72		78	
Bank	–		10		46	
Proposed dividends	16		20		16	
Corporation tax	4		5		8	
	76		107		148	
Net Current Assets		64		77		82
NET ASSETS		264		277		288
FINANCED BY						
Share Capital		200		210		210
Retained profits		64		67		78
		264		277		288

Note: Interest paid on the bank overdraft was: £3,000 in 2005, and £15,000 in 2006.
You are to prepare a cash flow statement for the years ended for 2005 and 2006.

13.9* Miller plc's profit and loss account for the year to 30 June 2003 and balance sheets for 2002 and 2003 were as follows:

Miller plc abridged Profit and Loss Account for the year to 30 June 2003

	£000
Operating profit	1,100
Interest payable	(100)
Profit before tax	1,000
Corporation tax	(200)
Profit after tax	800
Dividend proposed	(400)
Retained profit for the year	400

Miller plc Balance Sheets as at 30 June

	2002		2003	
Fixed Assets	£000	£000	£000	£000
At cost	13,600		16,300	
Less Depreciation to date	8,160	5,440	9,660	6,640
Current Assets				
Stock	300		340	
Debtors	1,200		1,300	
Prepayments	100		80	
Bank	40		20	
	1,640		1,740	
Less Current Liabilities				
Creditors	660		800	
Accruals	60		120	
Taxation	360		260	
Dividend proposed	400		200	
	1,480		1,380	
Net Current Assets		160		360
		5,600		7,000
Less Long-term Liabilities				
10% Debentures		–		(1,000)
		5,600		6,000
Capital and Reserves				
Ordinary share capital		4,000		4,000
Share premium account		600		600
Profit and loss account		1,000		1,400
		5,600		6,000

Notes to the accounts

During the year the company sold machinery which had cost £1,600,000 on which there was accumulated depreciation totalling £400,000. The net proceeds from the sale amounted to £1,400,000. Interest on debentures is paid to date.

You are to prepare a cash flow statement for Miller plc for the year to 30 June 2003 in accordance with FRS 1.

CASE STUDY
'How do I find out about a public limited company?'

Many people – 'stakeholders' – have an interest in public limited companies. Take a supermarket chain like Tesco PLC, for example: the company will have 'stakeholders' in the form of employees, managers, lenders, the Government and, of course, its shareholders.

Each shareholder owns a part of the company and is entitled to know its financial results. These are communicated in various reports which are available either on the company website (look at www.uk.tesco.com for example) or in paper format.

Take Flick O'Brien, who works for a chain of retail stores, set up as a public limited company. She owns shares in the company, bought through an employee scheme:

'I don't know everything about my employer, but each year I get an 'Annual Review and Financial Summary'. It gives me what they call 'Financial Highlights' which tells me how much profit has been made and what the annual sales figure is. They seem to be going up all the time, which is good news. It also contains information about new stores and new products.'

Then take Dai Trayder:

'I buy and sell company shares most weeks to try and make some money. I do all my trading on the internet. I like to get hold of the full glossy Annual Report and Accounts for each company if I can. Sometimes they can be downloaded from the company website – or they can be posted. They contain all the financial details I need to help me decide whether or not to invest – profit and loss account, balance sheet, cash flow statement. They are superbly presented with tables, charts and photographs. And they are free!'

This chapter illustrates extracts from a typical Annual Report and Accounts and explains the financial statements, auditors' report and the accounting policies adopted by a public limited company.

---

learning objectives

When you have studied this chapter you will be able to:

- *appreciate the need for published accounts*
- *understand the main financial statements required by the Companies Act*
- *interpret the auditors' report*
- *understand the accounting policies being followed by a particular company*
- *distinguish between a bonus issue of shares and a rights issue of shares*

COMPANY 'ACCOUNTS'

Every limited company, whether public or private, is required by law to produce financial statements, which are also available for anyone to inspect if they so wish. We need to distinguish between the *statutory accounts* and the *report and accounts*. The **statutory accounts a**re those which are required to be produced under company law, and a copy of these is filed with the Registrar of Companies. The **report and accounts** – often referred to as the **corporate report** – is available to every shareholder and contains:

- directors' report
- auditors' report (where required)
- profit and loss account
- balance sheet
- cash flow statement (where required)
- notes to the accounts, including a statement of the company's accounting policies

Company law not only requires the production of financial statements, but also states the detailed information that must be disclosed. The legal requirements are detailed in the relevant sections of the Companies Act 1985 (as amended by the Companies Act 1989).

STATEMENTS REQUIRED BY THE COMPANIES ACT

The financial statements required by the Companies Act are:

- profit and loss account
- balance sheet
- directors' report
- auditors' report
- consolidated accounts, where appropriate

When producing financial statements, companies also have to take note of the requirements of the accounting standards – Statements of Standard Accounting Practice (SSAPs) and Financial Reporting Standards (FRSs). These are issued by the Accounting Standards Board and set out acceptable accounting methods for various topics. Of particular note is FRS 1, which requires larger limited companies to include a cash flow statement (see previous chapter) as part of the published accounts.

PROFIT AND LOSS ACCOUNT

The published profit and loss account does not, by law, have to detail every single overhead incurred by the company – to do so would be to disclose important management information to competitors. Instead, the main items are summarised; however, the Companies Act requires that certain items must be detailed either in the profit and loss account itself, or in separate notes to the accounts (see page 284).

The profit and loss account must follow one of two standard formats set out in the Act, and the example on the next page shows the one that is most commonly used by trading companies, and is adapted to take note of the requirements of Financial Reporting Standard No. 3 – see below.

As mentioned above, much of the detail shown in profit and loss account is summarised. For example:

- turnover incorporates the figures for sales and sales returns
- cost of sales includes opening stock, purchases, purchases returns, carriage inwards and closing stock
- distribution costs include warehouse costs, post and packing, delivery drivers' wages, running costs of vehicles, depreciation of vehicles, etc
- administrative expenses include office costs, rent and rates, heating and lighting, depreciation of office equipment, etc.

A profit and loss account for Tesco PLC is shown on page 276. This gives the consolidated (or group) profit and loss account, together with the figures for the previous year. Group accounts are explained on page 289.

continuing and discontinued operations

Limited company profit and loss accounts are also required (by FRS 3 'Reporting Financial Performance') to show the financial results of any changes to the structure of the company, eg the purchase of another company, or the disposal of a section of the business. To this end the profit and loss account must distinguish between:

- results of continuing operations, ie from those parts of the business that have been kept throughout the year
- results of acquisitions, ie from businesses bought during the year
- results of discontinued operations, ie from parts of the business that have been sold or terminated during the year
- exceptional items (see below) of which the following are to be disclosed:
  - profits or losses on the sale or termination of an operation
  - costs of fundamental reorganisation
  - profits or losses on the disposal of fixed assets

continued on page 277 . . .

DURNING PLC

Profit and Loss Account for the year ended 31 December 2002

	£000s	£000s
Turnover		
Continuing operations	22,000	
Acquisitions	3,000	
	25,000	
Discontinued operations	2,000	27,000
Cost of sales		16,500
Gross profit		10,500
Distribution costs		4,250
Administrative expenses		4,000
Operating profit		
Continuing operations	2,000	
Acquisitions	200	
	2,200	
Discontinued operations	50	2,250
Profit on disposal of discontinued operations		250
		2,500
Other operating income		250
Income from shares in group undertakings		–
Income from participating interests		–
Income from other fixed asset investments		100
Other interest receivable and similar income		–
Amounts written off investments		–
Profit on ordinary activities before interest		2,850
Interest payable and similar charges		200
Profit on ordinary activities before taxation		2,650
Tax on profit on ordinary activities		725
Profit on ordinary activities after taxation		1,925
Extraordinary items		–
Profit for the financial year		1,925
Dividends		1,125
Retained profit for the financial year		800

GROUP PROFIT AND LOSS ACCOUNT
52 weeks ended 24 February 2001

	note	2001 £m	2000 £m
Sales at net selling prices	1	22,773	20,358
Value added tax		(1,785)	(1,562)
Turnover excluding value added tax	1/2	20,988	18,796
Operating expenses			
– Normal operating expenses		(19,770)	(17,712)
– Employee profit-sharing	3	(44)	(41)
– Integration costs	2	–	(6)
– Goodwill amortisation	11	(8)	(7)
Operating profit	1/2	1,166	1,030
Share of operating profit of joint ventures		21	11
Net loss on disposal of fixed assets		(8)	(9)
Profit on ordinary activities before interest and taxation		1,179	1,032
Net interest payable	7	(125)	(99)
Profit on ordinary activities before taxation	4	1,054	933
Profit before integration costs, net loss on disposal of fixed assets and goodwill amortisation		1,070	955
Integration costs		–	(6)
Net loss on disposal of fixed assets		(8)	(9)
Goodwill amortisation		(8)	(7)
Tax on profit on ordinary activities	8	(288)	(259)
Profit on ordinary activities after taxation		766	674
Minority interests		1	–
Profit for the financial year		767	674
Dividends	9	(340)	(302)
Retained profit for the financial year	24	427	372
		Pence	Pence
Earnings per share	10	11.29	10.07
Adjusted for integration costs after taxation		–	0.06
Adjusted for net loss on disposal of fixed assets after taxation		0.12	0.13
Adjusted for goodwill amortisation		0.12	0.10
Adjusted earnings per share	10	11.53	10.36
Diluted earnings per share	10	11.07	9.89
Adjusted for integration costs after taxation		–	0.06
Adjusted for net loss on disposal of fixed assets after taxation		0.12	0.13
Adjusted for goodwill amortisation		0.12	0.10
Adjusted diluted earnings per share	10	11.31	10.18
Dividend per share	9	4.98	4.48
Dividend cover (times)		2.27	2.27

Accounting policies and notes forming part of these financial statements are on pages 22 to 39.

Profit and loss account of Tesco PLC

(note that, for comparison, figures for both the current year and last year are shown)

continued from page 274 . . .

▓ extraordinary items (see below)

The objective of these requirements is to give more information to users of accounts.

non-recurring profits and losses

FRS 3 distinguishes between three categories of non-recurring profits and losses:

Exceptional items are defined as 'material items which derive from events or transactions that fall within the ordinary activities of the reporting entity and which individually or, if of a similar type, in aggregate, need to be disclosed by virtue of their size or incidence if the financial statements are to give a true and fair view'.

Extraordinary items are defined as 'material items possessing a high degree of abnormality which arise from events or transactions that fall outside the ordinary activities of the reporting entity and which are not expected to recur'. As extraordinary items are recorded in profit and loss account 'below the line' – ie after profit on ordinary activities – FRS 3 requires virtually all one-off transactions to be classified as exceptional items and shown 'above the line'.

Prior period adjustments are defined as 'material adjustments applicable to prior periods arising from changes in accounting policies or from the correction of fundamental errors'.

Any such adjustments are accounted for by restating the figures for the prior period and by adjusting the opening balance of retained profits for the current year.

statement of total recognised gains and losses

FRS 3 requires that a statement of total recognised gains and losses is included in the year-end financial statements and is given the same prominence as profit and loss account and balance sheet. As its name implies, it shows total recognised gains and losses – from profit and loss account, together with unrealised profits (for example, the revaluation of fixed assets) – to record the total movement in shareholders' funds for the accounting period.

The statement starts with the figure of profit for the financial year (from profit and loss account before deduction of dividends) and then adjusts for unrealised gains and losses, differences arising from changes in foreign currency exchange rates, and prior period adjustments. An example is given on the next page.

> **DURNING PLC**
>
> **Statement of Total Recognised Gains and Losses**
>
> **for the year ended 31 December 2002**
>
> | | £000s |
> |---|---|
> | Profit for the financial year | 2,650 |
> | Unrealised surplus on revaluation of properties | 1,000 |
> | Total recognised gains | 3,650 |
> | Prior year adjustment | (100) |
> | Total gains and losses for year | 3,550 |

BALANCE SHEET

The Companies Act 1985 sets out the standard formats for balance sheets. The example on the next page is presented in the layout most commonly used. As with the profit and loss account, extra detail is often shown in the notes to the balance sheet (see page 284).

The layout of the balance sheet follows that which we have used for limited companies in the previous chapter. However, some of the terms used need further explanation:

- **intangible fixed assets** – those assets which do not have material substance but belong to the company, eg goodwill (the amount paid for the reputation and connections of a business that has been taken over), patents and trademarks

- **tangible fixed assets** – those assets which have material substance, such as premises, equipment, vehicles

- **investments** – shares held in other companies, or government securities: classed as fixed asset investments if there is the intention to hold them for a long time, and as current asset investments where they are likely to be sold within twelve months of the balance sheet date

- **creditors: amounts falling due within one year** – the term used in company balance sheets to mean current liabilities, ie amounts that are due to be paid within twelve months of the balance sheet date

- **creditors: amounts falling due after more than one year** – the term used to mean long-term liabilities, ie amounts that are due to be paid more than twelve months from the balance sheet date, eg loans and debentures

■ **provisions for liabilities and charges** – an estimate of possible liabilities to be paid in the future.

DURNING PLC		
Balance Sheet as at 31 December 2002		
	£000s	£000s
Fixed assets		
Intangible assets		50
Tangible assets		6,750
Investments		1,000
		7,800
Current assets		
Stock	1,190	
Debtors	1,600	
Investments	–	
Cash at bank and in hand	10	
	2,800	
Creditors: amounts falling due within one year	1,800	
Net current assets		1,000
Total assets *less* current liabilities		8,800
Creditors: amounts falling due after more than one year		1,500
Provisions for liabilities and charges		100
		7,200
Capital and reserves		
Called up share capital		2,800
Share premium		400
Revaluation reserve		1,500
Profit and loss account		2,500
		7,200

A balance sheet for Tesco PLC is shown on the next page.

BALANCE SHEETS

24 February 2001

	note	Group 2001 £m	Group 2000 £m	Company 2001 £m	Company 2000 £m
Fixed assets					
Intangible assets	11	154	136	–	–
Tangible assets	12	9,580	8,140	–	–
Investments	13	101	79	5,774	5,200
Investments in joint ventures	13	203	172	146	124
		10,038	8,527	5,920	5,324
Current assets					
Stocks	14	838	744	–	–
Debtors	15	322	252	874	1,183
Investments	16	255	258	2	21
Cash at bank and in hand		279	88	–	–
		1,694	1,342	876	1,204
Creditors: falling due within one year	17	(4,389)	(3,487)	(2,518)	(2,525)
Net current liabilities		(2,695)	(2,145)	(1,642)	(1,321)
Total assets less current liabilities		7,343	6,382	4,278	4,003
Creditors: falling due after more than one year	18	(1,927)	(1,565)	(1,819)	(1,492)
Provisions for liabilities and charges	21	(24)	(19)	–	–
Total net assets		5,392	4,798	2,459	2,511
Capital and reserves					
Called up share capital	23	347	341	347	341
Share premium account	24	1,870	1,650	1,870	1,650
Other reserves	24	40	40	–	–
Profit and loss account	24	3,099	2,738	242	520
Equity shareholders' funds		5,356	4,769	2,459	2,511
Minority interests		36	29	–	–
Total capital employed		5,392	4,798	2,459	2,511

Accounting policies and notes forming part of these financial statements are on pages 22 to 39.

Terry Leahy

Andrew Higginson

Directors

Financial statements approved by the Board on 9 April 2001.

Balance sheet of Tesco PLC

(note that both the 'group' and 'company' balance sheets are shown – see also consolidated accounts on page 289)

GROUP CASH FLOW STATEMENT

52 weeks ended 24 February 2001

	note	2001 £m	2000 £m
Net cash inflow from operating activities	31	1,937	1,513
Returns on investments and servicing of finance			
Interest received		49	58
Interest paid		(206)	(188)
Interest element of finance lease rental payments		(4)	(1)
Net cash outflow from returns on investments and servicing of finance		(161)	(131)
Taxation			
Corporation tax paid		(272)	(213)
Capital expenditure and financial investment			
Payments to acquire tangible fixed assets		(1,953)	(1,296)
Receipts from sale of tangible fixed assets		43	85
Purchase of own shares		(58)	(18)
Net cash outflow from capital expenditure and financial investment		(1,968)	(1,229)
Acquisitions and disposals			
Purchase of subsidiary undertakings		(41)	(61)
(Invested in)/received from joint ventures		(35)	62
Net cash (outflow)/inflow from acquisitions and disposals		(76)	1
Equity dividends paid		(254)	(262)
Cash outflow before use of liquid resources and financing		(794)	(321)
Management of liquid resources			
Increase in short-term deposits		–	(68)
Financing			
Ordinary shares issued for cash		88	20
Increase in other loans		928	322
New finance leases		13	29
Capital element of finance leases repaid		(46)	(20)
Net cash inflow from financing		983	351
Increase/(decrease) in cash		189	(38)
Reconciliation of net cash flow to movement in net debt			
Increase/(decrease) in cash		189	(38)
Cash inflow from increase in debt and lease financing		(895)	(331)
Cash used to increase liquid resources		–	68
Amortisation of 4% unsecured deep discount loan stock and RPI bond		(7)	(4)
Other non-cash movements		(8)	(30)
Foreign exchange differences		(23)	(5)
Increase in net debt		(744)	(340)
Opening net debt	32	(2,060)	(1,720)
Closing net debt	32	(2,804)	(2,060)

Accounting policies and notes forming part of these financial statements are on pages 22 to 39.

Cash flow statement of Tesco PLC

DIRECTORS' REPORT

The report contains details of the following:

■ review of the activities of the company over the past year and of likely developments in the future, including research and development activity

■ directors' names and their shareholdings

■ proposed dividends

■ significant differences between the book value and market value of land and buildings

■ political and charitable contributions

■ policy on employment of disabled people

■ health and safety at work of employees

■ action taken on employee involvement and consultation

■ policy on payment of creditors

CASH FLOW STATEMENTS

All but the smaller limited companies must include, as part of their published accounts, a cash flow statement, which we described in detail in Chapter 13. Such a statement shows where the funds (money) have come from during the course of a financial year, and how such funds have been used. The statement also provides a direct link between the previous year's balance sheet and the current one. A recent cash flow statement for Tesco PLC is shown on the previous page.

AUDITORS' REPORT

Larger companies must have their accounts audited by external auditors, who are appointed by the shareholders to check the accounts. The auditors' report, which is printed in the published accounts, is the culmination of their work. The three main sections of the auditors' report are:

■ **respective responsibilities of directors and auditors** – the directors are responsible for preparing the accounts, while the auditors are responsible for forming an opinion on the accounts

■ **basis of opinion** – the framework of Auditing Standards (issued by the Auditing Practices Board) within which the audit was conducted, other assessments, and the way in which the audit was planned and performed

■ **opinion** – the auditors' view of the company's accounts

An 'unqualified' auditors' opinion will read as follows:

> *'In our opinion the financial statements give a true and fair view of the state of affairs of the Company at .... 20.., and of the profit, and cash flows of the Company for the year then ended, and have been properly prepared in accordance with the Companies Act 1985.'*

A 'qualified' auditors' report will raise points that the auditors consider have not been dealt with correctly in the accounts. Where such points are not too serious, the auditors will use phrases such as 'except for ...' or 'subject to ... the financial statements give a true and fair view'. Much more serious is where the auditors' statement says that the accounts 'do not show a true and fair view' or 'we are unable to form an opinion ...'. These indicate a major disagreement between the company and the auditors, and a person involved with the company – such as an investor or creditor – should take serious note.

Note that smaller private companies are exempt from audit requirements if their turnover (sales) for the year is below a certain figure.

ACCOUNTING POLICIES

The Companies Act requires companies to include a statement of their accounting policies in the published accounts. FRS 18 'Accounting policies' defines accounting policies as 'those principles, bases, conventions, rules and practices applied by an entity that specify how the effects of transactions and other events are to be reflected in its financial statements through

– recognising
– selecting measurement bases for, and
– presenting

assets, liabilities, gains, losses and changes to shareholders' funds'.

The objective of FRS 18 is to ensure that:

■ entities adopt the most appropriate accounting policies in order to give a true and fair view

■ accounting policies adopted are reviewed regularly to ensure that they remain appropriate, and changes are made as necessary

■ information is disclosed in the financial statements to enable users to understand the accounting policies adopted and their implementation

When selecting accounting policies, the four criteria of relevance, reliability, comparability and understandability need to be considered.

Estimation techniques – such as straight-line and reducing balance depreciation methods, discounting of expected cash flows, and provisions for bad debts – are not accounting policies but, instead, are ways in which money amounts are arrived at under accounting policies. An accounting policy may say 'we depreciate computers over five years', but an estimation technique – eg straight-line depreciation – is used to calculate the money amounts shown in the financial statements.

An extract from the accounting policies of Tesco PLC is shown on the next page.

NOTES TO THE ACCOUNTS

The Companies Act 1985, as well as requiring the presentation of financial statements in a particular layout, also requires additional information to be provided. These **notes to the accounts** include:

■ disclosure of accounting policies (see previous section)

■ details of authorised and allotted share capital

■ movements on fixed assets

■ details of listed investments

■ movements on reserves

■ provision for deferred tax

■ analysis of indebtedness

■ details of charges and contingent liabilities

■ details of interest or similar charges on loans and overdrafts

■ basis of computation of UK Corporation Tax and details of tax charge

■ directors' emoluments including Chairman's emoluments where necessary

■ auditor's remuneration

ACCOUNTING POLICIES

Basis of financial statements

These financial statements have been prepared under the historical cost convention, in accordance with applicable accounting standards and the Companies Act 1985.

The Group has adopted Financial Reporting Standard 18, 'Accounting Policies', during the year.

Basis of consolidation

The Group profit and loss account and balance sheet consist of the financial statements of the parent company, its subsidiary undertakings and the Group's share of interests in joint ventures. The accounts of the parent company's subsidiary undertakings are prepared to dates around 24 February 2001 apart from Global T.H., Tesco Polska Sp. z o.o., Tesco Stores ČR a.s., Tesco Stores SR a.s., Samsung Tesco Co. Limited, Tesco Taiwan Co. Limited and Ek-Chai Distribution System Co. Ltd which prepared accounts to 31 December 2000. In the opinion of the Directors it is necessary for the above named subsidiaries to prepare accounts to a date earlier than the rest of the Group to enable the timely publication of the Group financial statements.

The Group's interests in joint ventures are accounted for using the gross equity method. As a result of a change in its financial year end, the share of interests of joint ventures for the year to 24 February 2001 includes the results of the Tesco Personal Finance Group for the ten months to 31 December 2000.

Stocks

Stocks comprise goods held for resale and properties held for, or in the course of, development and are valued at the lower of cost and net realisable value. Stocks in stores are calculated at retail prices and reduced by appropriate margins to the lower of cost and net realisable value.

Money market deposits

Money market deposits are stated at cost. All income from these investments is included in the profit and loss account as interest receivable and similar income.

Fixed assets and depreciation

Fixed assets are carried at cost and include amounts in respect of interest paid on funds specifically related to the financing of assets in the course of construction.

Depreciation is provided on a straight-line basis over the anticipated useful economic lives of the assets. Following a review of the useful economic lives and the residual values of a number of classes of tangible fixed assets, these have been revised.

The principal changes have been to:

• Increase the period over which land premia is amortised from 25 years to 40 years.

• Provide additional depreciation where a decision has been made to replace a store, to write it down to its net realiseable value over its remaining useful economic life.

The net effect of these changes has not materially impacted the results for the year.

The following rates applied for the year ended 24 February 2001:

• Land premia paid in excess of the alternative use value – at 2.5% of cost.

• Freehold and leasehold buildings with greater than 40 years unexpired – at 2.5% of cost.

• Leasehold properties with less than 40 years unexpired are amortised by equal annual instalments over the unexpired period of the lease.

• Plant, equipment, fixtures and fittings and motor vehicles – at rates varying from 10% to 33%.

Goodwill

Goodwill arising from transactions entered into after 1 March 1998 is capitalised and amortised on a straight-line basis over its useful economic life, up to a maximum of 20 years.

All goodwill from transactions entered into prior to 1 March 1998 has been written off to reserves.

Impairment of fixed assets and goodwill

Fixed assets and goodwill are subject to review for impairment in accordance with Financial Reporting Standard 11, 'Impairment of Fixed Assets and Goodwill'. Any impairment is recognised in the profit and loss account in the year in which it occurs.

Extract from the accounting policies of Tesco PLC

SMALL AND MEDIUM-SIZED COMPANIES

The Companies Act allows small and medium-sized private companies to file modified accounts with the Registrar of Companies. However, accounts must still be prepared in full form for presentation to their members. A company qualifies to be treated as small or medium-sized if it satisfies any two or more of the following conditions:

	small	medium
turnover (sales) does not exceed	£2.8m	£11.2m
assets do not exceed	£1.4m	£5.6m
average number of employees does not exceed	50	250

small companies

A small company need not file a profit and loss account. The directors' report can be abbreviated and details of directors' emoluments need not be disclosed. The balance sheet can list only the main asset and liability headings, with notes to the accounts reduced to include only details of accounting policies, share capital, indebtedness, and figures for the previous year.

For taxation purposes, the Inland Revenue accepts a simple profit and loss account which is used to calculate the amount of corporation tax due.

medium-sized companies

Concessions for medium-sized companies are more limited: details of sales turnover and the make-up of cost of sales need not be given; instead, the profit and loss account starts with the figure for gross profit. In all other respects, a full set of accounts must be filed.

Note: the above concessions apply only to private limited companies; public limited companies of all sizes must file full accounts.

BONUS ISSUES AND RIGHTS ISSUES

Limited companies – and particularly plcs – quite often increase their capital by means of either **bonus issues** or **rights issues** of shares.

Whilst both of these have the effect of increasing the number of shares in issue, they have quite different effects on the structure of the company balance sheet.

bonus issues

A **bonus issue** is made when a company issues free shares to existing shareholders; it does this by using reserves that have built up and capitalising them (ie they are turned into permanent share capital). The bonus issue is distributed on the basis of existing shareholdings – for example, one bonus share for every two shares already held.

With a bonus issue no cash flows in or out of the company. The shareholders are no better off: with more shares in issue the stock market price per share will fall in proportion to the bonus issue, ie the company's net assets are now spread among a greater number of shares.

Bonus issues are made in order to acknowledge the fact that reserves belong to shareholders. Often a build-up of reserves occurs because a company hasn't the cash to pay dividends, so a bonus issue is a way of passing the reserves to shareholders.

Note that capital or revenue reserves can be used for bonus issues. If there is a choice, then capital reserves are used first – this is because it is one of the few uses of a capital reserve, which cannot be used to fund the payment of dividends.

rights issues

A **rights issue** is used by a company seeking to raise further finance through the issue of shares. Instead of going to the considerable expense of offering additional shares to the public, it is cheaper to offer shares to existing shareholders at a favourable price (usually a little below the current market price). As with a bonus issue the extra shares are offered in proportion to the shareholders' existing holding. The shareholder may take up the rights by subscribing for the shares offered; alternatively the rights can often be sold on the stock market.

CASE STUDY
Severn plc & Wye plc: bonus issues and rights issues

situation

The following are the summary balance sheets of Severn plc and Wye plc:

	Severn	Wye
	£	£
Fixed assets	300,000	300,000
Current assets (including bank)	100,000	100,000
	400,000	400,000
Ordinary shares of £1 each	200,000	200,000
Reserves (capital and revenue)	200,000	200,000
	400,000	400,000

Severn is planning a one-for-two bonus issue.

Wye is seeking finance for a capital expenditure programme through a one-for-two rights issue at a price of £1.80 per share (the current market price is £2.10).

solution

After the issues, the balance sheets appear as:

	Severn	Wye
	£	£
Fixed assets	300,000	300,000
Current assets (including bank)	100,000	280,000
	400,000	580,000
Ordinary shares of £1 each	300,000	300,000
Share premium account (capital reserve)	–	80,000
Reserves	100,000	200,000
	400,000	580,000

The changes are:

Severn   Reserves are reduced by £100,000, whilst share capital is increased by the same amount; the ordinary share capital is now more in balance with fixed assets; no cash has been received.

Wye   The bank balance has increased by £180,000, being 100,000 shares (assuming that all shareholders took up their rights) at £1.80; share capital has increased by £100,000, whilst 80p per share is the share premium, ie £80,000 in total. The company now has the money to finance its capital expenditure programme. There are also significant reserves which could be used for a bonus issue in the future.

ACCOUNTING STANDARDS

Since 1971 a number of accounting standards have been produced to provide a framework for accounting, and to reduce the variety of alternative accounting treatments which companies may use in their financial statements.

Statements of Standard Accounting Practice

Statements of Standard Accounting Practice (SSAPs) were issued by the Accounting Standards Committee between 1971 and 1990. Of the twenty-five SSAPs issued, a large number have now been withdrawn and replaced by Financial Reporting Standards.

Financial Reporting Standards

Financial Reporting Standards (FRSs) have been issued by the Accounting Standards Board (ASB) since 1991. A list of current accounting standards can be seen on the ASB's website at www.asb.org.uk. The ASB's aim has been to develop standards that are consistent with one another and to reduce the number of options allowed in the preparation of financial statements.

authority of accounting standards

Although not laws in themselves, accounting standards are defined in the Companies Act 1989. The Act requires directors of companies – other than small or medium-sized companies – to disclose whether the accounts have been prepared in accordance with applicable accounting standards, particulars of any material departure from those standards, and the reasons for any such departure.

CONSOLIDATED ACCOUNTS

In recent years many companies have been taken over by other companies to form groups. Each company within a group maintains its separate legal entity, and so a group of companies may take the following form:

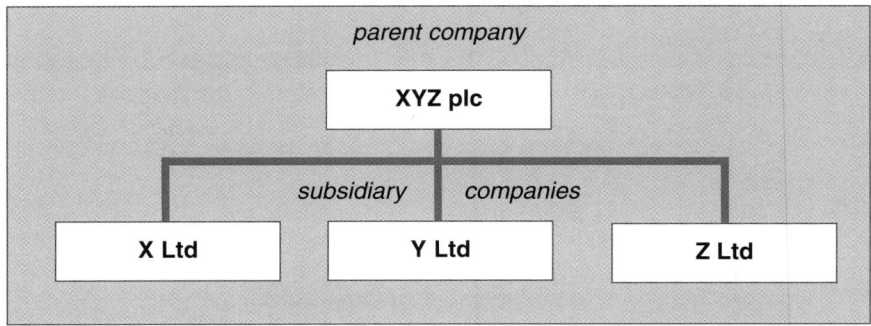

The Companies Act 1985 makes various provisions concerning groups of companies, including:

- a parent company and subsidiary company relationship generally exists where a parent company owns more than 50 per cent of another company's share capital, or controls the composition of its board of directors
- a parent company is required to produce group published accounts
- group accounts must include a consolidated profit and loss account and a consolidated balance sheet. Such consolidated accounts are designed to show the position of the group as if it were a single entity
- a parent company, which produces a consolidated profit and loss account, is not legally obliged to produce its own profit and loss account

It is likely that, when you are studying a set of published accounts, you will find that you need to use the consolidated accounts for the group.

chapter summary

- The Companies Act 1985 (as amended by the Companies Act 1989) requires a considerable amount of detail to be disclosed in the published accounts of limited companies.

- The Act requires all limited companies to produce:
  - a profit and loss account
  - a balance sheet
  - a directors' report
  - an auditors' report

- The Act lays down formats for profit and loss account and balance sheet.

- Besides the requirements of the Companies Act, companies must also abide by the Statements of Standard Accounting Practice (SSAPs) and Financial Reporting Standards (FRSs), as laid down by the Accounting Standards Board.

- Most companies also include in their published accounts a cash flow statement which shows where the funds (money) has come from during the course of the financial year, and how it has been used.

- For larger companies, external auditors report to the shareholders on the state of affairs of the company.

- The directors establish the accounting policies which the company will follow.

- Consolidated accounts are prepared for groups of companies.

key terms

statutory accounts	financial statements required by law, a copy of which is filed at Companies House, where it can be inspected
report and accounts	the corporate report of the company which is available to every shareholder
summary financial statement	a shorter version of the statutory accounts which, by agreement with individual shareholders, can be sent in place of the report and accounts
exceptional items	'material items which derive from events or transactions that fall within the ordinary activities of the reporting entity and which individually or, if of a similar type, in aggregate, need to be disclosed by virtue of their size or incidence if the financial statements are to give a true and fair view' (FRS 3)
extraordinary items	'material items possessing a high degree of abnormality which arise from events or transactions that fall outside the ordinary activities of the reporting entity and which are not expected to recur' (FRS 3)
prior period adjustments	'material adjustments applicable to prior periods arising from changes in accounting policies or from the correction of fundamental errors' (FRS 3)
auditors' report	gives the auditors' opinion on the company's financial statements as to whether they give a true and fair view of the state of affairs of the company
accounting policies	the specific accounting principles, bases, conventions, rules and practices that the directors of a company choose to follow
bonus issue	the capitalisation of reserves – either capital or revenue – in the form of free shares issued to existing shareholders in proportion to their holdings; no cash flows into the company
rights issue	the raising of cash by offering shares to existing shareholders, in proportion to their holdings, at a favourable pric
consolidated accounts	group accounts for a parent company and its subsidiary companies

---

activities

14.1   Explain what is contained within the report and accounts – or corporate report – of a public limited company.

14.2*   Distinguish between 'exceptional items' and 'extraordinary items', and explain where each appears in the profit and loss account. Where possible, give an example of each.

14.3*   List four items that have to be included in a directors' report.

14.4   From a set of published accounts, give an example of an unqualified auditors' report.

14.5   Select a public limited company of your choice and obtain the latest set of published accounts. (Write to the company asking for a set or look on the company's website; alternatively some financial newspapers offer a 'report and accounts service' whereby accounts for the larger plcs can be sent on request.)

Read the report and accounts and, from the financial statements, extract the following information for the current and previous year (if there is a choice of figures, use those from the consolidated accounts):

profit and loss account
- turnover
- profit on ordinary activities before taxation
- profit for the financial year
- earnings per share

balance sheet
- total of fixed assets
- total of current assets
- total of current liabilities (often shown as 'creditors: amounts falling due within one year')
- total of long-term liabilities (often shown as 'creditors: amounts falling due after one year')
- capital employed

cash flow statement
- cash flow from operating activities (noting any significant amounts)
- cash flow from
    - returns on investments and servicing of finance
    - taxation
    - capital expenditure and financial investment
    - acquisitions and dispersals
    - financing
    (note any significant amounts)

auditors' report (current year only)
- does it state that the financial statements show a 'true and fair view'?
- are there any 'qualifications' to the report

accounting policies (current year only)
- what method is used for valuing stocks?
- what depreciation policies are used?

Compile a short report – from the point of view of a private investor – which contains:
- an introduction to the selected plc; its structure, size, products, position in its own industry
- the information extracted from the published accounts
- a portfolio of your observations from the report and accounts, eg
  - is the company expanding/declining/remaining static?
  - has money been spent on major capital expenditure?
  - have the shareholders received higher/lower dividends?

14.6* The following trial balance has been extracted from the accounts of Trevaunance plc as at 31 March 2002:

	Dr	Cr
	£000	£000
Administration expenses	240	
Share capital (£1 ordinary shares)		600
Debtors	600	
Bank	75	
Accruals		15
Share premium account		100
Distribution costs	500	
Trade creditors		300
Other creditors		80
Plant and machinery at cost	1,000	
Accumulated depreciation at 31 March 2002		400
Profit and loss account		210
Purchases	1,800	
Stock at 1 April 2001	160	
Sales		2,670
	4,375	4,375

Additional information

- Stock at 31 March 2002 was valued at £280,000.

- Corporation tax charge based on the profits for the year is estimated to be £65,000.

- A final ordinary dividend of 20 pence per share is proposed.

Tutorial note

Depreciation for the year has already been provided for in the list of balances above and allocated to administration expenses and distribution costs accordingly.

You are to prepare the company's published profit and loss account for the year to 31 March 2002 and a balance sheet as at that date in accordance with the Companies Act and FRS 3, so far as the information permits. (Use the layout for the profit and loss account shown on the next page.)

14.7   The following list of balances was extracted from the books of Chapelporth plc on 31 December 2002:

	£
Sales	2,642,400
Administration expenses	220,180
Distribution costs	216,320
Interest paid on loan	10,000
Share premium account	40,000
Purchases	2,089,600
Stock at 1 January 2002	318,500
Cash at bank	20,640
Debtors	415,800
Provision for bad debts at 1 January 2002	10,074
Bad debts written off	8,900
Creditors	428,250
10% loan (repayable in 2005)	200,000
Office equipment (net book value at 31 December 2002)	130,060
Vehicles (net book value at 31 December 2002)	235,000
Share capital (£1 ordinary shares)	200,000
Profit and loss account at 1 January 2002	144,276

Notes

- Accrue for £10,000 loan interest due, which is payable on 1 January 2003.

- Provide for administration expenses of £12,200 paid in advance at 31 December 2002, and distribution costs of £21,300 owing at 31 December 2002.

- Provision for bad debts is to be maintained at 3% of debtors.

- Stock at 31 December 2002 was valued at £340,600.

- Provide for corporation tax of £45,000 which is payable on 30 September 2003.

- The directors propose a dividend of 10 pence per share.

- Depreciation for the year has already been provided for and has already been allocated to the respective expense accounts in the list of balances.

You are to prepare the company's published profit and loss account for the year ended 31 December 2002 and a balance sheet as at that date in accordance with the Companies Act and FRS 3, so far as the information permits.

(Use the layout for the profit and loss account shown below.)

SPECIMEN LAYOUT

PROFIT AND LOSS ACCOUNT FOR THE YEAR ENDED ....

Turnover (sales) – continuing operations	....
Cost of sales	....
Gross profit	....
Distribution costs	....
Administration expenses	....
Operating profit – continuing operations	....
Interest payable and similar charges	....
Profit on ordinary activities before taxation	....
Tax on profit on ordinary activities	....
Profit on ordinary activities after taxation	....
Dividends	....
Retained profit for the financial year	....

CASE STUDY
'Is this company any good?'

A friend says to you:

'You remember those company shares I've got? Well, the Annual Report and Accounts dropped through the letter box last week. I managed to find the profit and loss account and balance sheet. They look pretty dull to me and don't tell me much. To tell you the truth, I need to know if this company is doing all right and is any good as an investment.'

You explain to your friend:

'They may look dull but in fact the financial statements of businesses – profit and loss account, balance sheet, and cash flow statement – come in very useful. They are often interpreted by analysts by means of accounting ratios. This is so that they can assess strengths and weaknesses – and see if the business is doing well and is a good ongoing investment. They make comparisons between different years and different businesses to see how the business is doing compared with the industry as a whole.'

Your friend looks bored and says:

'But who wants to know all that?'

You reply:

'Well you do for a start, as an investor. Then there are the banks who lend money, businesses that might want to buy them out. A bit like prospecting for likely footballers to sign up for your team – you want to see them play first and know how they perform under pressure.'

In this chapter we examine the main accounting ratios and performance indicators as they relate to the areas of profitability, liquidity, efficient use of resources, financial position and investment potential.

learning objectives

When you have studied this chapter you will be able to:

- understand the importance of interpretation of financial statements
- calculate the main accounting ratios in the areas of profitability, liquidity, use of resources, financial position and investment potential
- comment on trends shown by the main accounting ratios
- report on the overall financial situation of a business
- appreciate the limitations of ratio analysis

INTERESTED PARTIES

Interpretation of financial statements is not always made by an accountant; interested parties include:

- **managers** of the business, who need to make financial decisions affecting the future development of the business

- **banks**, who are being asked to lend money to finance the business

- **creditors**, who wish to assess the likelihood of receiving payment

- **customers**, who wish to be assured of continuity of supplies in the future

- **shareholders**, who wish to be assured that their investment is sound

- prospective **investors**, who wish to compare relative strengths and weaknesses

- **employees** and **trade unions**, who wish to check on the financial prospects of the business

- **government** and **government agencies**, eg Inland Revenue, HM Customs and Excise, who wish to check they are receiving the amount due to them

From the financial statements the interested party will be able to calculate the main ratios, percentages and performance indicators. By doing this, the strengths and weaknesses of the entity will be highlighted and appropriate conclusions can be drawn.

TYPES OF ACCOUNTING RATIOS & PERFORMANCE INDICATORS

The general term 'accounting ratios' is usually used to describe the calculations aspect of interpretation of financial statements. The term 'ratio' is, in fact, partly misleading because the performance indicators include percentages, time periods, as well as ratios in the strict sense of the word.

Most ratios are applicable to sole traders, partnerships and limited companies; however, as we will see, there are a number which relate specifically to the share capital and reserves of limited companies.

The main themes covered by the interpretation of accounts are:

- **profitability** – the relationship between profit and sales turnover, assets and capital employed

- **liquidity** – the stability of the business on a short-term basis

- **use of resources** – the effective and efficient use of assets and liabilities

- **financial position** – the way in which the business has been financed

- **investment ratios** – the returns to shareholders (or potential shareholders) in companies

MAKING USE OF ACCOUNTING RATIOS

It is important when examining a set of financial statements and calculating accounting ratios to relate them to reference points or standards. These points of reference might be to:

- establish trends from past years, to provide a standard of comparison

- benchmark against another similar business in the same industry

- compare against industry averages

Above all, it is important to understand the relationships between ratios: one ratio may give an indication of the state of the business, but this needs to be supported by other ratios. Ratios can indicate symptoms, but the cause will then need to be investigated.

Another use of ratios is to estimate forward the likely profit or balance sheet of a business. For example, it might be assumed that the same gross profit percentage as last year will also apply next year; thus, given an estimated increase in sales, it is a simple matter to estimate gross profit. In a similar way, by making use of ratios, net profit and the balance sheet can be forecast.

Whilst all of the ratios calculated in this chapter use figures from the profit and loss account and balance sheet, the cash flow statement is important too. It assists in confirming the views shown by the accounting ratios and provides further evidence of the position.

ACCOUNTING RATIOS FOR PROFITABILITY

- Study the table and financial statements on the next two pages. They show the ways in which the profitability of a business is assessed.

- Then read the section entitled 'Profitability' which follows.

- Note that the accounting ratios from the financial statements of Wyvern Trading Company Limited shown here are calculated and discussed in the Case Study on pages 314 to 320.

PROFITABILITY

Gross profit/sales percentage $=$ $\dfrac{\text{Gross profit}}{\text{Sales}} \times \dfrac{100}{1}$

Expense/sales percentage $=$ $\dfrac{\text{Specified expense}}{\text{Sales}} \times \dfrac{100}{1}$

Operating profit/sales percentage $=$ $\dfrac{\text{Operating profit*}}{\text{Sales}} \times \dfrac{100}{1}$

* profit before interest and tax

Net profit/sales percentage $=$ $\dfrac{\text{Net profit}}{\text{Sales}} \times \dfrac{100}{1}$

Return on capital employed $=$ $\dfrac{\text{Operating profit}}{\text{Capital employed*}} \times \dfrac{100}{1}$

* share capital + reserves + long-term liabilities

Return on equity $=$ $\dfrac{\text{Profit after tax} - \text{preference dividend (if any)}}{\text{Equity*}} \times \dfrac{100}{1}$

* ordinary share capital + reserves

Earnings per share $=$ $\dfrac{\text{Profit after tax} - \text{preference dividend (if any)}}{\text{Number of issued ordinary shares}}$

Wyvern Trading Company Limited
TRADING AND PROFIT AND LOSS ACCOUNT
for the year ended 31 December 2002

	£000s	£000s
Sales		1,430
Opening stock	200	
Purchases	1,000	
	1,200	
Less Closing stock	240	
Cost of sales		960
Gross profit		470
Less overheads:		
Selling expenses	150	
Administration expenses	140	
		290
Operating profit		180
Less: Debenture interest		10
Net profit for year before taxation		170
Less: Corporation tax		50
Profit for year after taxation		120
Less:		
preference dividend paid	25	
ordinary dividend proposed	75	
		100
Retained profit for the year		20
Add balance of retained profits at beginning of year		180
Balance of retained profits at end of year		200

BALANCE SHEET (extract)

Capital employed (share capital + reserves + long-term liabilities)	1,550
Equity (ordinary share capital + reserves)	1,200
Number of issued ordinary shares (000s)	1,000

Note: Items used in the ratios on the previous page are shown in bold type on a grey background

PROFITABILITY

One of the main objectives of a business is to make a profit. Profitability ratios examine the relationship between profit and sales turnover, assets and capital employed. Before calculating the profitability ratios, it is important to read the profit and loss account in order to review the figures.

The key profitability ratios are illustrated on page 299. We will be calculating and discussing the accounting ratios from these figures in the Case Study on pages 314 to 320.

gross profit percentage

$$\frac{Gross\ profit}{Sales} \quad x \quad \frac{100}{1}$$

This expresses, as a percentage, the gross profit (sales minus cost of sales) in relation to sales. For example, a gross profit percentage of 20 per cent means that for every £100 of sales made, the gross profit is £20.

The gross profit percentage should be similar from year-to-year for the same business. It will vary between organisations in different areas of business, eg the gross profit percentage on jewellery is considerably higher than that on food. A significant change from one year to the next, particularly a fall in the percentage, requires investigation into the buying and selling prices.

Gross profit percentage, and also net profit percentage (see next page), need to be considered in context. For example, a supermarket may well have a lower gross profit percentage than a small corner shop but, because of the supermarket's much higher turnover, the amount of profit will be much higher. Whatever the type of business, gross profit – both as an amount and a percentage – needs to be sufficient to cover the overheads (expenses), and then to give an acceptable return on capital.

expense/sales percentage

$$\frac{Specified\ expense}{Sales} \quad x \quad \frac{100}{1}$$

A large expense or overhead item can be expressed as a percentage of sales: for example, the relationship between advertising and sales might be found to be 10 per cent in one year, but 20 per cent the next year. This could indicate that an increase in advertising had failed to produce a proportionate increase in sales.

Note that each expense falls into one of three categories of cost:

1   fixed costs, or

2   variable costs, or

3   semi-variable costs

Fixed costs remain constant despite other changes. Variable costs alter with changed circumstances, such as increased output or sales. Semi-variable costs combine both a fixed and a variable element, eg hire of a car at a basic (fixed) cost, with a (variable) cost per mile.

It is important to appreciate the nature of costs when interpreting accounts: for example, if sales this year are twice last year's figure, not all expenses will have doubled.

operating profit percentage

$$\frac{\text{Operating profit}^* \quad x}{\text{Sales}} \quad \frac{100}{1}$$

* profit before interest and tax

Net profit is calculated after loan and bank interest has been charged to profit and loss account. Thus it may be distorted when comparisons are made between two different businesses where one is heavily financed by means of loans, and the other is financed by owner's capital. The solution is to calculate the operating profit percentage which uses profit before interest and tax.

net profit percentage

$$\frac{\text{Net profit} \quad x}{\text{Sales}} \quad \frac{100}{1}$$

As with gross profit percentage, the net profit percentage should be similar from year-to-year for the same business, and should also be comparable with other firms in the same line of business. Net profit percentage should, ideally, increase from year-to-year, which indicates that the profit and loss account costs are being kept under control. Any significant fall should be investigated to see if it has been caused by

■   a fall in gross profit percentage

■   and/or an increase in one particular expense, eg wages and salaries, advertising, etc

return on capital employed (ROCE)

Return on capital employed expresses the profit of a business in relation to the capital employed. The percentage return is best thought of in relation to other investments, eg a bank or building society might offer a return of five per cent. A person running a business is investing a sum of money in that business, and the profit is the return that is achieved on that investment. However, it should be noted that the risks in running a business are considerably greater than depositing the money with a bank or building society, and an additional return to allow for the extra risk is needed.

For limited companies, the calculation of return on capital employed must take note of their different methods of financing. It is necessary to distinguish between the ordinary shareholders' investment (the equity) and the capital employed by the company, which includes preference shares and debentures/long-term loans.

The calculation for capital employed is:

	Ordinary share capital
add	*Reserves (capital and revenue)*
equals	*Equity*
add	*Preference share capital*
add	*Debentures/long-term loans*
equals	*Capital Employed*

The reason for including preference shares and debentures/long-term loans in the capital employed is that the company has the use of the money from these contributors for the foreseeable future, or certainly for a fixed time period.

The calculation of return on capital employed is:

$$\frac{Operating\ profit^*}{Capital\ employed^{**}} \times \frac{100}{1}$$

* profit before interest and tax

** ordinary share capital + reserves + preference share capital + debentures/long- term loans

return on equity

$$\frac{\textit{Profit after tax} - \textit{preference dividend (if any)}}{\textit{Equity*}} \quad x \quad \frac{100}{1}$$

* ordinary share capital + reserves

Whilst return on capital employed looks at the overall return on the long-term sources of finance (the capital employed), return on equity focuses on the return for the ordinary shareholders. Also known as 'return on ordinary shareholders' equity', return on equity indicates the return the company is making on their funds, ie ordinary shares and reserves. The decision as to whether they remain as ordinary shareholders is primarily whether they could get a better return elsewhere.

Note that, when calculating return on equity, use the profit after tax and preference dividends (if any), ie the amount of profit available to the ordinary shareholders after all other parties (corporation tax, preference share dividend) have been deducted.

earnings per share

$$\frac{\textit{Profit after tax} - \textit{preference dividend (if any)}}{\textit{Number of issued ordinary shares}}$$

Earnings per share (or EPS) measures the amount of profit – usually expressed in pence – earned by each ordinary share, after corporation tax and preference dividends. Comparisons can be made with previous years to provide a basis for assessing the company's performance.

ACCOUNTING RATIOS FOR LIQUIDITY, USE OF RESOURCES AND FINANCIAL POSITION

- Study the ratios table and financial statements on the next two pages. They show the ways in which the liquidity, use of resources, and financial position of a business are assessed.

- Then read the sections which follow.

- Note that the accounting ratios from the financial statements of Wyvern Trading Company Limited are calculated and discussed in the Case Study on pages 314 to 320.

LIQUIDITY

Working capital ratio =
(or current ratio)

$$\frac{\text{Current assets}}{\text{Current liabilities}}$$

Liquid capital ratio =
(or quick ratio/acid test)

$$\frac{\text{Current assets} - \text{stock}}{\text{Current liabilities}}$$

USE OF RESOURCES

Stock turnover (days) =

$$\frac{\text{Stock}}{\text{Cost of sales}} \times 365 \text{ days}$$

Debtors' collection period (days) =

$$\frac{\text{Debtors}}{\text{Sales}} \times 365 \text{ days}$$

Creditors' payment period (days) =

$$\frac{\text{Creditors}}{\text{Purchases}} \times 365 \text{ days}$$

Asset turnover ratio =

$$\frac{\text{Sales}}{\text{Net assets*}}$$

* fixed assets + current assets – current liabilities – long-term liabilities

FINANCIAL POSITION

Interest cover =

$$\frac{\text{Operating profit}}{\text{Interest paid}}$$

Gearing =

$$\frac{\text{Debt (long-term loans, including preference shares)}}{\text{Capital employed*}} \times \frac{100}{1}$$

* ordinary share capital + reserves + preference share capital + long-term loans

alternative calculation:

$$\frac{\text{Debt}}{\text{Equity*}} \times \frac{100}{1}$$

* ordinary share capital + reserves

Wyvern Trading Company Limited
BALANCE SHEET
as at 31 December 2002

Fixed Assets	Cost £000s	Dep'n to date £000s	Net £000s
Premises	1,100	250	850
Fixtures and fittings	300	120	180
Vehicles	350	100	250
	1,750	470	1,280

Current Assets			
Stock		240	
Debtors		150	
Bank/cash		135	
		525	

Less Current Liabilities			
Creditors	130		
Proposed ordinary dividend	75		
Corporation tax	50		
		255	
Net Current Assets			270
			1,550
Less Long-term Liabilities			
10% Debentures			100
NET ASSETS			1,450

FINANCED BY		
Authorised and Issued Share Capital		
1,000,000 ordinary shares of £1 each, fully paid		1,000
250,000 10% preference shares of £1 each, fully paid		250
		1,250
Revenue Reserve		
Profit and loss account		200
SHAREHOLDERS' FUNDS		1,450

PROFIT AND LOSS ACCOUNT (extract)

Cost of sales	960
Sales	1,430
Purchases	1,000

Note: Items used in ratios are shown in bold type with a grey background.

LIQUIDITY

Liquidity ratios measure the financial stability of a business, ie the ability of a business to pay its way on a short-term basis. Here we focus our attention on the current assets and current liabilities sections of the balance sheet.

The key liquidity ratios are shown on page 305; these are linked to the balance sheet of Wyvern Trading Company Limited. The ratios are calculated and discussed in the Case Study on pages 314 to 320.

working capital

Working capital = Current assets − Current liabilities

Working capital (often called 'net current assets') is needed by all businesses in order to finance day-to-day trading activities. Sufficient working capital enables a business to hold adequate stocks, allow a measure of credit to its customers (debtors), and to pay its suppliers (creditors) as payments fall due.

working capital ratio (or current ratio)

Working capital ratio = Current assets : Current liabilities

Working capital ratio uses figures from the balance sheet and measures the relationship between current assets and current liabilities. Although there is no ideal working capital ratio, an acceptable ratio is about 2:1, ie £2 of current assets to every £1 of current liabilities. However, a business in the retail trade may be able to work with a lower ratio, eg 1.5:1 or even less, because it deals mainly in sales for cash and so does not have a large figure for debtors. A working capital ratio can be too high: if it is above 3:1 an investigation of the make-up of current assets and current liabilities is needed: eg the business may have too much stock, too many debtors, or too much cash at the bank, or even too few creditors.

Note that the current ratio can also be expressed as a percentage. For example, a current ratio of 2:1 is the same as 200 per cent.

liquid capital ratio (or quick ratio, or acid test)

$$Liquid\ capital\ ratio = \frac{Current\ assets\ -\ stock}{Current\ liabilities}$$

The liquid capital ratio uses the current assets and current liabilities from the balance sheet, but stock is omitted. This is because stock is the least liquid current asset: it has to be sold, turned into debtors, and then the cash has to be collected from the debtors. Also, some of the stock included in the balance sheet figure may be unsaleable or obsolete. Thus the liquid ratio provides a direct comparison between debtors/cash/bank and short-term liabilities. The balance between liquid assets, that is debtors and cash/bank, and current liabilities should, ideally, be about 1:1, ie £1 of liquid assets to each £1 of current liabilities. At this ratio a business is expected to be able to pay its current liabilities from its liquid assets; a figure below 1:1, eg 0.75:1, indicates that the firm would have difficulty in meeting pressing demands from creditors. However, as with the working capital ratio, some businesses are able to operate with a lower liquid ratio than others.

The liquid capital ratio can also be expressed as a percentage, eg 1:1 is the same as 100%.

USE OF RESOURCES

Use of resources measures how efficiently the management controls the current aspects of the business – principally stock, debtors and creditors. Like all accounting ratios, comparison needs to be made either with figures for the previous year, or with a similar firm.

stock turnover

$$\frac{Stock}{Cost\ of\ sales} \quad x \quad 365\ days$$

Stock turnover is the number of days' stock held on average. This figure will depend on the type of goods sold by the business. For example, a market trader selling fresh flowers, who finishes each day when sold out, will have a stock turnover of one day. By contrast, a jewellery shop – because it may hold large stocks of jewellery – will have a much slower stock turnover, perhaps sixty or ninety days, or longer. Nevertheless, it is important for a business to keep its stock days as short as possible, subject to being able to meet the needs of most of its customers. A business which is improving in efficiency will generally have a quicker stock turnover comparing one year with the previous one, or with the stock turnover of similar businesses.

Stock turnover can also be expressed as number of times per year:

$$\frac{Cost\ of\ sales}{Stock} = Stock\ turnover\ (times\ per\ year)$$

A stock turnover of, say, twelve times a year means that about thirty days' stock is held. Note that stock turnover can only be calculated where a business buys and sells goods; it cannot be used for a business that provides a service.

debtors' collection period

$$\frac{Debtors}{Sales} \quad x \quad 365\ days$$

This calculation shows how many days, on average, debtors take to pay for goods sold to them by the business. The debt collection time can be compared with that for the previous year, or with that of a similar business. In the UK, most debtors should make payment within about 30 days; however, sales made abroad will take longer for the proceeds to be received. A comparison from year-to-year of the collection period is a measure of the firm's efficiency at collecting the money that is due to it and we are looking for some reduction in debtor days over time. Ideally debtor days should be shorter than creditor days (see below): this indicates that money is being received from debtors before it is paid out to creditors.

creditors' payment period

$$\frac{Creditors}{Purchases} \quad x \quad 365\ days$$

This calculation is the opposite aspect to that of debtors: here we are measuring the speed it takes to pay creditors. While creditors can be a useful temporary source of finance, delaying payment too long may cause problems. This ratio is most appropriate for businesses that buy and sell goods; it cannot be used for a business that provides a service; it is also difficult to interpret when a business buys in some goods and, at the same time, provides a service, eg an hotel. Generally, though, we would expect to see the creditor days period longer than the debtor days, ie money is being received from debtors before it is paid out to creditors. We would also be looking for a similar figure for creditor days from one year to the next: this would indicate a stable business.

Note that there is invariably an inconsistency in calculating both debtors' collection and creditors' payment periods: the figures for debtors and creditors on the balance sheet include VAT, while sales and purchases from the trading account exclude VAT. Strictly, therefore, we are not comparing like with like; however, the comparison should be made with reference to the previous year, or a similar company, calculated on the same basis from year-to-year.

asset turnover ratio

$$\frac{Sales}{Net\ assets^{*}}$$

* fixed assets + current assets – current liabilities – long-term liabilities

This ratio measures the efficiency of the use of net assets in generating sales. An increasing ratio from one year to the next indicates greater efficiency. A fall in the ratio may be caused either by a decrease in sales, or an increase in net assets – perhaps caused by the purchase or revaluation of fixed assets, or increased stockholding, or increased debtors as a result of poor credit control.

Different types of businesses will have very different asset turnover ratios. For example a supermarket, with high sales and relatively few assets, will have a very high figure; by contrast, an engineering business, with lower sales and a substantial investment in fixed and current assets, will have a much lower figure.

FINANCIAL POSITION

Financial position measures the strength and long-term financing of the business. Two ratios are calculated – interest cover and gearing. Interest cover considers the ability of the business to meet (or cover) its interest payments from its operating profit; gearing focuses on the balance in the long-term funding of the business between monies from loan providers and monies from ordinary shareholders.

Both ratios look at aspects of loan finance and it is important to remember that both interest and loan repayments must be made on time; if they are not the loan provider may well be able to seek payment by forcing the company to sell assets and, in the worst case, may well be able to force the company into liquidation.

interest cover

$$\frac{Operating\ profit}{Interest}$$

The interest cover ratio, linked closely to gearing, considers the safety margin (or cover) of profit over the interest payable by a business. For example, if the operating profit of a business was £10,000, and interest payable was £5,000, this would give interest cover of two times, which is a low figure. If the interest was £1,000, this would give interest cover of ten times which is a higher and much more acceptable figure. Thus, the conclusion to draw is that the higher the interest cover, the better (although there is an argument for having some debt).

gearing

$$\frac{Debt\ (long\text{-}term\ loans\ including\ any\ preference\ shares)}{Capital\ employed^*} \times \frac{100}{1}$$

* ordinary share capital + reserves + preference share capital + long-term loans

Whilst the liquidity ratios seen earlier focus on whether the business can pay its way in the short-term, gearing is concerned with long-term financial stability. Here we measure how much of the business is financed by debt (including any preference shares) against capital employed (debt + equity), defined above. The higher the gearing percentage, the less secure will be the financing of the business and, therefore, the future of the business. This is because debt is costly in terms of interest payments (particularly if interest rates are variable). It is difficult to set a standard for an acceptable gearing ratio: in general terms most investors (or lenders) would not wish to see a gearing percentage of greater than 50%.

Gearing can also be expressed as a ratio, ie debt:equity. Thus a gearing percentage of 50% is a ratio of 0.5:1.

An alternative calculation for gearing is to measure debt in relation to the equity of the business:

$$\frac{Debt}{Equity^*} \times \frac{100}{1}$$

* ordinary share capital + reserves

Usually in questions, either calculation is acceptable; both methods use similar components:

either $\dfrac{Debt}{Capital\ employed}$ or $\dfrac{Debt}{Equity}$

The first calculation will always give a lower gearing percentage than the second when using the same figures. For example:

$$\frac{£50,000\ (debt)}{£50,000\ (debt) + £100,000\ (equity)} = 33\%$$

$$\frac{£50,000\ (debt)}{£100,000\ (equity)} = 50\%$$

When making comparisons from one year to the next, or between different companies, it is important to be consistent in the way in which gearing is calculated in order for appropriate conclusions to be drawn.

INVESTMENT RATIOS

Investment ratios are used by existing or potential shareholders of companies. The ratios will help to assess the performance of the company in which they wish to invest.

dividend yield

$$\frac{\textit{Ordinary share dividend (in pence)}}{\textit{Market price of ordinary share (in pence)}} \times \frac{100}{1}$$

Investors in companies which are quoted on the stock market can obtain this information from the share price pages of the financial press. The dividend yield gives the investor the annual percentage return paid on a quoted share. However, dividend yield is an inadequate measure because it ignores the overall profits – or 'earnings' – available for the ordinary shareholders; retained profits (ie that part of profits not paid as dividends) should help to boost the share price, so giving investors capital growth rather than income.

earnings per share

$$\frac{\textit{Profit after tax – preference dividend (if any)}}{\textit{Number of issued ordinary shares}}$$

As noted earlier (page 304) earnings per share (or EPS) measures the amount of profit earned by each ordinary share, after corporation tax and preference dividends.

earnings yield

$$\frac{\textit{Earnings per ordinary share (in pence)}}{\textit{Market price of ordinary share (in pence)}} \times \frac{100}{1}$$

This compares, in percentage terms, the earnings per ordinary share (after corporation tax and preference dividends) with the market price per share. It is an important calculation for investors because it shows the return earned by the company on each ordinary share. Some part of the earnings will, most likely, have been paid to investors, while the rest will have been retained in the company and should help to increase the capital value of the shares.

price/earnings ratio

$$\frac{\textit{Market price of ordinary share (in pence)}}{\textit{Earnings per ordinary share (in pence)}} = \textit{Price/earnings ratio}$$

The price/earnings ratio (or P/E ratio, as it is often abbreviated) compares the current market price of a share with the earnings (after corporation tax) of that share. For example, if a particular share has a market price of £3, and the earnings per share in the current year are 30p, then the P/E ratio is 10. This simply means that a person buying the share for £3 is paying ten times the last reported earnings of that share.

Investors use the P/E ratio to help them make decisions as to the 'expensiveness' of a share. In general, high P/E ratios (ie a higher number) indicate that the stock market price has been pushed up in anticipation of an expected improvement in earnings: therefore, the share is now expensive. The reason for a low P/E ratio is usually that investors do not expect much (if any) growth in the company's earnings in the foreseeable future.

P/E ratio is simply a reciprocal of the earnings yield (see above). Thus a P/E ratio of 10 is the same as an earnings yield of 10 per cent; a P/E ratio of 20 is the same as an earnings yield of 5 per cent.

dividend cover

$$\frac{\textit{Profit after tax} - \textit{preference dividend (if any)}}{\textit{Ordinary dividends}}$$

This figure shows the margin of safety between the amount of profit a company makes and the amount paid out in dividends. The figure must be greater than 1 if the company is not to use past retained profits to fund the current dividend. A figure of 5 as dividend cover indicates that profit exceeds dividend by five times – a healthy sign. The share price pages in the financial press quote the figure under the column headed 'cover' or 'cvr'.

INTERPRETATION OF ACCOUNTS

Interpretation of accounts is much more than a mechanical process of calculating a number of ratios. It involves the analysis of the relationships between the figures in the financial statement and the presentation of the information gathered in a meaningful way to interested parties.

There now follow two Case Studies which put into practice the analytical approach explained earlier in this chapter:

1 **Wyvern Trading Company Limited**

In the first we look at limited company financial statements from the point of view of a potential investor (for clarity, one year's statements are given although, in practice, more than one year would be used to establish a trend). The comments given indicate what should be looked for when analysing and interpreting a set of financial statements.

2 **Surgdressings Limited**

In the second we consider financial statements from the point of view of a potential buyer of products from the company. The interpretation seeks to assess the risk of switching to the supplier, and to make comparisons with industry average figures.

CASE STUDY

Accounting ratios: Wyvern Trading Company Ltd

situation

The financial statements of Wyvern Trading Company Limited are shown in this Case Study. The business trades in office supplies and sells to the public through its three retail shops in the Wyvern area; it also delivers direct to businesses in the area from its modern warehouse on a local business park.

solution

The financial statements and accounting ratios are to be considered from the viewpoint of a potential investor.

All figures shown are in £000s. The analysis starts on page 317.

Wyvern Trading Company Limited
TRADING AND PROFIT AND LOSS ACCOUNT
for the year ended 31 December 2002

	£000s	£000s
Sales		1,430
Opening stock	200	
Purchases	1,000	
	1,200	
Less Closing stock	240	
Cost of sales		960
Gross profit		470
Less overheads:		
Selling expenses	150	
Administration expenses	140	
		290
Operating profit		180
Less: Debenture interest		10
Net profit for year before taxation		170
Less: Corporation tax		50
Profit for year after taxation		120
Less:		
preference dividend paid	25	
ordinary dividend proposed	75	
		100
Retained profit for the year		20
Add balance of retained profits at beginning of year		180
Balance of retained profits at end of year		200

Wyvern Trading Company Limited
BALANCE SHEET as at 31 December 2002

Fixed Assets	Cost £000s	Dep'n to date £000s	Net £000s
Premises	1,100	250	850
Fixtures and fittings	300	120	180
Vehicles	350	100	250
	1,750	470	1,280

Current Assets			
Stock		240	
Debtors		150	
Bank/cash		135	
		525	

Less Current Liabilities			
Creditors	130		
Proposed ordinary dividend	75		
Corporation tax	50		
		255	

Net Current Assets			270
			1,550

Less Long-term Liabilities			
10% debentures			100
NET ASSETS			1,450

FINANCED BY
Authorised and Issued Share Capital

1,000,000 ordinary shares of £1 each, fully paid	1,000
250,000 10% preference shares of £1 each, fully paid	250
	1,250

Revenue Reserve

Profit and loss account	200
SHAREHOLDERS' FUNDS	1,450

Note: the current market price of the ordinary shares is £1.25

PROFITABILITY

Gross profit/sales percentage

$$\frac{£470}{£1,430} \quad \times \quad \frac{100}{1} \qquad\qquad = \quad 32.87\%$$

Selling expenses to sales

$$\frac{£150}{£1,430} \quad \times \quad \frac{100}{1} \qquad\qquad = \quad 10.49\%$$

Operating profit/sales percentage

$$\frac{£180}{£1,430} \quad \times \quad \frac{100}{1} \qquad\qquad = \quad 12.59\%$$

Net profit/sales percentage

$$\frac{£170}{£1,430} \quad \times \quad \frac{100}{1} \qquad\qquad = \quad 11.89\%$$

Return on capital employed

$$\frac{£180}{£1,000 + £250 + £200 + £100} \quad \times \quad \frac{100}{1} \qquad = \quad 11.61\%$$

Return on equity

$$\frac{£120 - £25}{£1,000 + £200} \quad \times \quad \frac{100}{1} \qquad\qquad = \quad 7.92\%$$

Earnings per share

$$\frac{£120 - £25}{1,000} \qquad\qquad = \quad 9.5\text{p per ordinary share}$$

The gross and net profit percentages seem to be acceptable figures for the type of business, although comparisons should be made with those of the previous accounting period. A business should always aim at least to hold its percentages and, ideally, to make a small improvement. A significant fall in the percentages may indicate a poor buying policy, poor pricing (perhaps caused by competition), and the causes should be investigated.

Selling expenses seem to be quite a high percentage of sales. As these are likely to be a relatively fixed cost, it would seem that the business could increase sales turnover without a corresponding increase in sales expenses.

The small difference between net profit percentage and operating profit percentage indicates that finance costs are relatively low.

Return on capital employed is satisfactory, but could be better. At 11.61% it is less than two percentage points above the ten per cent cost of the preference shares and debentures (ignoring the taxation advantages of issuing debentures). Return on equity is 7.92%; a potential shareholder needs to compare this with the returns available elsewhere.

The figure for earnings per share indicates that the company is not highly profitable for its shareholders; potential shareholders will be looking for increases in this figure.

LIQUIDITY
Working capital (or current) ratio

$$\frac{£525}{£255} \qquad = 2.06:1$$

Liquid capital ratio (or quick ratio/acid test)

$$\frac{(£525 - £240)}{£255} \qquad = 1.12:1$$

The working capital and liquid capital ratios are excellent: they are slightly higher than the expected 'norms' of 2:1 and 1:1 respectively (although many companies operate successfully with lower ratios); however, they are not too high which would be an indication of inefficient use of assets.

These two ratios indicate that the company is very solvent, with no short-term liquidity problems.

USE OF RESOURCES
Stock turnover

$$\frac{£240 \times 365}{£960} \qquad = \ 91 \text{ days (or 4 times per year)}$$

Debtors' collection period

$$\frac{£150 \times 365}{£1,430} \qquad = 38 \text{ days}$$

Creditors' payment period

$$\frac{£130 \times 365}{£1,000} \qquad = 47 \text{ days}$$

Asset turnover ratio

$$\frac{£1,430}{£1,450^*} \qquad = \ 0.99:1$$

* fixed assets + current assets – current liabilities – long-term liabilities

This group of ratios shows the main weakness of the company: not enough business is passing through for the size of the company.

Stock turnover is very low for an office supplies business: the stock is turning over only every 91 days – surely it should be faster than this?

Debtors' collection period is acceptable on the face of it – 30 days would be better – but quite a volume of the sales will be made through the retail outlets in cash. This amount should, if known, be deducted from the sales turnover before calculating the debtors' collection period: thus the collection period is, in reality, longer than that calculated.

Creditors' payment period is quite leisurely for this type of business – long delays could cause problems with suppliers in the future.

The asset turnover ratio says it all: this type of business should be able to obtain a much better figure:

- either, sales need to be increased using the same net assets

- or, sales need to be maintained, but net assets reduced

FINANCIAL POSITION

Interest cover

$$\frac{£180}{£10} = 18 \text{ times}$$

Gearing

$$\frac{£250 + £100}{£1,000 + £200 + £250 + £100} \times \frac{100}{1} = 23\% \text{ or } 0.23:1$$

The interest cover figure of 18 is very high and shows that the company has no problems in paying interest.

The gearing percentage is low: anything up to 50% (0.5:1) could be seen. With a low figure of 23% this indicates that the company could borrow more money if it wished to finance, say, expansion plans (there are plenty of fixed assets for a lender – such as a bank – to take as security for a loan). At the present level of gearing there is only a low risk to potential investors.

Note that the alternative calculation for gearing is:

$$\frac{£250 + £100}{£1,000 + £200} \times \frac{100}{1} = 29\% \text{ or } 0.29:1$$

INVESTMENT RATIOS

Dividend yield*

$$\frac{£75}{(1,000 \times £1.25)} \times \frac{100}{1} = 6\%$$

* like a number of investment ratios, this can be calculated either per share, or on the total shares in issue (as here).

Earnings per share

$$\frac{(£170 - £50 - £25)}{1,000} \qquad = 9.5 \text{ pence per share}$$

Earnings yield

$$\frac{9.5p}{125p} \times \frac{100}{1} \qquad = 7.6\%$$

Price/earnings ratio

$$\frac{125p}{9.5p} \qquad = 13.16 \text{ times}$$

Dividend cover

$$\frac{(£170 - £50 - £25)}{£75} \qquad = 1.27 \text{ times}$$

These ratios indicate that the company is not highly profitable for its shareholders (although shares are often bought for potential capital gains rather than income). The dividend yield is only 6 per cent, and the dividend is covered just 1.27 times: if profits were to fall, it is unlikely that the current level of dividend could be sustained. The lower price/earnings ratio seems appropriate for this company.

CONCLUSION

This appears to be a profitable business, although there may be some scope for cutting down somewhat on the profit and loss account selling expenses (administration expenses could be looked at too). The business offers a reasonable return on capital, although things could be improved.

The company is solvent and has good working capital and liquid capital ratios. Interest cover is high and gearing is low – a good sign during times of variable interest rates.

The main area of weakness is in asset utilisation. It appears that the company could do much to reduce the days for stock turnover and the debtors' collection period; at the same time creditors could be paid faster. Asset turnover is very low for this type of business and it does seem that there is much scope for expansion within the structure of the existing company. As the benefits of expansion flow through to the financial statements, the investment ratios should show an improvement from their present modest performance. However, a potential investor will need to consider if the directors have the ability to focus on the weaknesses shown by the ratio analysis and to take steps to improve the business.

CASE STUDY
Accounting ratios: assessing a supplier – Surgdressings Ltd

situation

You work for the Wyvern NHS Trust, which runs Wyvern Hospital. The Trust has been approached by a supplier of surgical dressings, Surgdressings Limited, which is offering its products at advantageous prices.

The Surgical Director of Wyvern NHS Trust is satisfied with the quality and suitability of the products offered and the Finance Director, your boss, has obtained the latest financial statements from the company which are set out on the next page.

You have been asked to prepare a report for the Finance Director recommending whether or not to use Surgdressings Limited as a supplier of surgical dressings to the Trust. You are to use the information contained in the financial statements of Surgdressings Limited and the industry averages supplied. Included in your report should be:

* comments on the company's
  – profitability
  – liquidity
  – financial position

* consideration of how the company has changed over the two years

* comparison with the industry as a whole

The report should include calculation of the following ratios for the two years:
  – return on capital employed
  – net profit percentage
  – quick ratio/acid test
  – gearing

The relevant industry average ratios are as follows:

	2001	2000
Return on capital employed	11.3%	11.1%
Net profit percentage	16.4%	16.2%
Quick ratio/acid test	1.0:1	0.9:1
Gearing (debt/capital employed)	33%	35%

SURGDRESSINGS LIMITED
Summary profit and loss accounts for the year ended 31 December

	2001	2000
	£000s	£000s
Turnover	4,600	4,300
Cost of sales	2,245	2,135
Gross profit	2,355	2,165
Overheads	1,582	1,491
Net profit before tax	773	674

Summary balance sheets as at 31 December

	2001 £000s	2001 £000s	2000 £000s	2000 £000s
Fixed Assets		5,534		6,347
Current Assets				
Stock	566		544	
Debtors	655		597	
Bank	228		104	
	1,449		1,245	
Current Liabilities				
Trade creditors	572		504	
Taxation	242		288	
	814		792	
Net Current Assets		635		453
Long-term loan		(1,824)		(3,210)
NET ASSETS		4,345		3,590
Share capital (ordinary shares)		2,300		2,000
Share premium		670		450
Profit and loss account		1,375		1,140
SHAREHOLDERS' FUNDS		4,345		3,590

solution

REPORT

To: Finance Director, Wyvern NHS Trust

From: A Student

Date: today's date

Re: Analysis of Surgdressings Limited's financial statements 2000/2001

Introduction

The purpose of this report is to analyse the financial statements of Surgdressings Limited for 2000 and 2001 to determine whether the Trust should use the company as a supplier of surgical dressings.

Calculation of ratios

The following ratios have been calculated:

	2001			2000		
	company		*industry average*	*company*		*industry average*
Return on capital employed	$\dfrac{773}{6,169}$	=12.5%	11.3%	$\dfrac{674}{6,800}$	= 9.9%	11.1%
Net profit percentage	$\dfrac{773}{4,600}$	=16.8%	16.4%	$\dfrac{674}{4,300}$	= 15.7%	16.2%
Quick ratio/acid test	$\dfrac{883}{814}$	= 1.1:1	1.0:1	$\dfrac{701}{792}$	= 0.9:1	0.9:1
Gearing	$\dfrac{1,824}{6,169}$	= 30%	33%	$\dfrac{3,210}{6,800}$	= 47%	35%

Comment and analysis

▨ In terms of profitability, the company has improved from 2000 to 2001.

▨ Return on capital employed has increased from 15.7% to 16.8% – this means that the company is generating more profit in 2001 from the available capital employed than it did in 2000. The company has gone from being below the industry average in 2000 to being better than the average in 2001.

▨ Net profit percentage has also improved, increasing from 15.7% in 2000 to 16.8% in 2001. This means that the company is generating more profit from sales in 2001 than it did in the previous year. In 2000 the company was below the industry average but in 2001 it is better than the average. As it is now performing better than the average, this suggests that it may continue to be successful in the future.

■ The liquidity of the company has improved during the year.

■ The quick ratio (or acid test) has gone up from 0.9:1 to 1.1:1. This indicates that the liquid assets, ie debtors and stock, are greater than current liabilities in 2001. The company has gone from being the same as the industry average in 2000 to better than average in 2001. Thus, in 2001, Surgdressings Limited is more liquid than the average business in the industry.

■ The financial position of the company has improved considerably during the year.

■ In 2000 the gearing ratio was a high 47%. In 2001 the percentage of debt finance to capital employed declined to 30%. A high gearing ratio is often seen as a risk to a company's long-term survival: in times of economic downturn, when profits fall, a high-geared company will have increasing difficulty in making interest payments on debt – in extreme cases, a company could be forced into liquidation. In 2000, the gearing ratio of Surgdressings Limited was much higher than the industry average, making it relatively more risky than the average of companies in the industry. The much improved ratio in 2001 is now below the industry average, making it less risky than the average of other companies in the industry.

CONCLUSION

■ Based solely on the information provided in the financial statements of Surgdressings Limited and the ratios calculated, it is recommended that the company is used by the Trust as a supplier of surgical dressings.

■ The company has increasing profitability, liquidity and financial position in 2001 when compared with 2000. It also compares favourably with other companies in the same industry and appears to present a lower risk than the average of the sector.

LIMITATIONS IN THE INTERPRETATION OF ACCOUNTS

Although accounting ratios can usefully highlight strengths and weaknesses, they should always be considered as a part of the overall assessment of a business, rather than as a whole. We have already seen the need to place ratios in context and relate them to a reference point or standard. The limitations of ratio analysis should always be borne in mind.

retrospective nature of accounting ratios

Accounting ratios are usually retrospective, based on previous performance and conditions prevailing in the past. They may not necessarily be valid for making forward projections: for example, a large customer may become insolvent, so threatening the business with a bad debt, and also reducing sales in the future.

differences in accounting policies

When the financial statements of a business are compared, either with previous years' figures, or with figures from a similar business, there is a danger that the comparative statements are not drawn up on the same basis as those currently being worked on. Different accounting policies, in respect of depreciation and stock valuation for instance, may well result in distortion and invalid comparisons.

inflation

Inflation may prove a problem, as most financial statements are prepared on an historic cost basis, that is, assets and liabilities are recorded at their original cost. As a result, comparison of figures from one year to the next may be difficult. In countries where inflation is running at high levels any form of comparison becomes practically meaningless.

reliance on standards

We have already mentioned guideline standards for some accounting ratios, for instance 2:1 for the working capital ratio. There is a danger of relying too heavily on such suggested standards, and ignoring other factors in the balance sheet. An example of this would be to criticise a business for having a low current ratio when the business sells the majority of its goods for cash and consequently has a very low debtors figure: this would in fact be the case with many well-known and successful retail companies.

other considerations

Economic: The general economic climate and the effect this may have on the nature of the business, eg in an economic downturn retailers are usually the first to suffer, whereas manufacturers feel the effects later.

State of the business: The chairman's report for a limited company should be read in conjunction with the financial statements (including the cash flow statement) to ascertain an overall view of the state of the business. Of great importance are the products of the company and their stage in the product life cycle, eg is a car manufacturer relying on old models, or is there an up-to-date product range which appeals to buyers?

Comparing like with like: Before making comparisons between 'similar' businesses, we need to ensure that we are comparing 'like with like'. Differences, such as the acquisition of assets – renting premises compared with ownership, leasing vehicles compared with ownership – will affect the profitability of the business and the structure of the balance sheet; likewise, the long-term financing of a business – the balance between debt finance and equity finance – will also have an effect.

chapter summary

> **Tutorial note**
>
> The formulas for accounting ratios are summarised in this chapter on pages 299 and 305.

- Accounting ratios are numerical values – percentages, time periods, ratios – extracted from the financial statements of businesses.

- Accounting ratios can be used to measure:
  - profitability
  - liquidity
  - use of resources
  - financial position
  - investment potential

- Comparisons need to be made with previous financial statements, or those of similar companies.

- There are a number of limitations to be borne in mind when drawing conclusions from accounting ratios:
  - retrospective nature, based on past performance
  - differences in accounting policies
  - effects of inflation when comparing year-to-year
  - reliance on standards
  - economic and other factors

key terms

profitability

measures the relationship between profit and sales turnover, assets and capital employed; ratios include:

- gross profit percentage
- expenses/sales percentage
- operating profit percentage
- net profit percentage
- return on capital employed
- return on equity
- earnings per share

liquidity

measures the financial stability of a business, ie the ability of a business to pay its way on a short-term basis; ratios include:

- working capital (current) ratio
- liquid capital ratio (or quick ratio/acid test)

use of resources

measures how efficiently the management controls the current aspects of the business – principally stock, debtors and creditors; ratios include:

- stock turnover
- debtors' collection period
- creditors' payment period
- asset turnover ratio

financial position

measures the strength and long-term financing of the business; ratios include:

- gearing
- interest cover

investment potential

measures the returns to shareholders (or potential shareholders) in companies; ratios include:

- dividend yield
- earnings per share
- earnings yield
- price/earnings ratio
- dividend cover

activities

Note: an asterisk (*) after an activity number means that an answer is provided in Appendix 1.

15.1 Select four groups of interested parties who may wish to interpret the financial statements of a public limited company. For each group, explain why they are interested in the financial statements.

15.2* The following information is taken from the profit and loss accounts of two plcs:

	Alpha plc £m	Beta plc £m
Sales	55.7	22.3
Cost of sales	(49.1)	(10.2)
Gross profit	6.6	12.1
Expenses	(4.4)	(6.3)
Operating profit	2.2	5.8
Interest paid	(0.6)	(1.1)
Net profit before tax	1.6	4.7
Note: Capital employed	£8.8m	£34.3m

You are to calculate, for each company:
- gross profit percentage
- net profit percentage
- operating profit percentage
- return on capital employed

15.3* The following is taken from the balance sheets of two plcs:

	Capa plc £m	Delta plc £m
Stock	3.8	4.1
Debtors	4.5	0.7
Bank/(bank overdraft)	(0.4)	6.3
Creditors	5.1	10.7
Long-term loans	3.2	2.1
Ordinary share capital	4.5	8.4
Reserves	1.4	4.7
Notes:		
Sales for year	43.9	96.3
Purchases for year	32.4	85.1
Cost of sales for year	33.6	84.7

You are to calculate, for each company:

- working capital ratio
- liquid capital ratio
- debtors' collection period
- creditors' payment period
- stock turnover
- gearing ratio

One company runs department stores, the other is a chemical manufacturer. Which is which? Why is this?

15.4 The following is taken from the balance sheets of two plcs:

	ABC plc	XYZ plc
Ordinary dividend for year	£750,000	£1,250,000
Number of issued ordinary shares of £1 each	5,000,000	15,000,000
Current market price per share	£1.50	£6.00
Net profit after corporation tax and preference dividends	£1,500,000	£5,500,000

Note: both companies are in the same industry.

For each business, calculate:

- dividend yield
- earnings per share
- earnings yield
- price/earnings ratio
- dividend cover

You are to state in which company would you invest for (a) capital growth, (b) income.

15.5 Below is the balance sheet of Mithian plc for the year ended 30 September 2003.

	£000	£000
Fixed Assets at net book value		500
Current Assets		
Stock	150	
Debtors	95	
Bank	5	
	250	

continued on next page . . .

Creditors: amounts falling due within one year

Creditors	175
Bank overdraft	25
	200

NET CURRENT ASSETS	50
	550

Creditors: amounts falling due after more than one year

Bank loan	100
	450

Capital and Reserves

Ordinary share capital	300
Share premium account	50
Profit and loss account	100
	450

1   Which is the liquid capital (acid test) ratio for Mithian plc?
   (a)   1.25:1
   (b)   0.5:1
   (c)   1:1
   (d)   5:1

2   Which is the calculation for the gearing ratio of Mithian plc?
   (a)   300/450 x 100
   (b)   350/450 x 100
   (c)   125/550 x 100
   (d)   100/550 x 100

3   If Mithian plc's sales for the year were £405,000, which is the asset turnover ratio?
   (a)   0.9:1
   (b)   0.74:1
   (c)   0.81:1
   (d)   1.11:1

4   Which is the debtor collection period in days if the credit sales of the company are £405,000 for the year? (Round up to whole days).
   (a)   86 days
   (b)   68 days
   (c)   158 days
   (d)   61 days

5 Which of the following is the correct calculation for interest cover?
(a) total debt/interest payable
(b) interest payable/total debt
(c) operating profit/interest payable
(d) interest payable/operating profit

15.6 The following information relates to two businesses, A and B:

	business A £000s	business B £000s
PROFIT AND LOSS ACCOUNT (EXTRACTS)		
Sales	3,057	1,628
Cost of sales	2,647	911
Gross Profit	410	717
Overheads	366	648
Net Profit	44	69

	business A £000s	£000s	business B £000s	£000s
SUMMARISED BALANCE SHEETS				
Fixed Assets		344		555
Current Assets				
Stock	242		237	
Debtors	6		269	
Bank	3		1	
	251		507	
Less Current Liabilities	195		212	
Working Capital		56		295
NET ASSETS		400		850
FINANCED BY				
Capital		400		850

One business operates a chain of grocery supermarkets; the other is a heavy engineering company. You are to calculate the following accounting ratios for both businesses:

(a)   gross profit percentage

(b)   net profit percentage

(c)   stock turnover (use balance sheet figure as average stock)

(d)   working capital ratio

(e)   liquid capital ratio

(f)   debtors' collection period

(g)   return on capital employed

Indicate which company you believe to be the grocery supermarket chain and which the heavy engineering business. Briefly explain the reasons for your choice based on the ratios calculated and the accounting information.

15.7*   The following summarised information is available to you:

J D ROWLES: TRADING AND PROFIT AND LOSS ACCOUNT (extracts)
for the years ended 30 April 2005 and 30 April 2006

	2005	2006
	£	£
Sales (all on credit)	120,000	200,000
Cost of sales	80,000	150,000
Gross profit	40,000	50,000
Expenses	10,000	15,000
Net profit	30,000	35,000

BALANCE SHEET (EXTRACTS) AS AT 30 APRIL 2005 AND 30 APRIL 2006

	2005 £	2005 £	2005 £	2006 £	2006 £	2006 £
Fixed Assets			15,000			12,000
Current Assets						
Stock		7,000			18,000	
Debtors		12,000			36,000	
Bank		1,000			–	
		20,000			54,000	
Less Current Liabilities						
Creditors	6,000			15,000		
Bank overdraft	–			10,000		
		6,000			25,000	
Net Current Assets			14,000			29,000
NET ASSETS			29,000			41,000
FINANCED BY						
Capital						
Opening capital			22,000			29,000
Add net profit			30,000			35 000
			52,000			64,000
Less drawings			23,000			23,000
			29,000			41,000

Notes:

- there were no purchases or disposals of fixed assets during the year

- during 2005 and 2006 selling prices were reduced in order to stimulate sales

- assume that price levels were stable

You are to use accounting ratios to analyse and assess the profitability, liquidity and use of resources of the business over the two years.

15.8   Select a public limited company of your choice and obtain the latest set of published accounts.

Calculate accounting ratios for the last two years which examine:

- profitability
- liquidity
- use of resources
- investment ratios

Write a report which presents an overall assessment of the progress (or otherwise) made by the plc over the last two years.

Note: This Activity could be expanded to include: share price movements over the last six months, consideration of the place of the company within its industry and expectations for the future.

section 3

management accounting

COST ACCOUNTING

Thyme plc is a manufacturer of TV sets. Each TV set is made from a large number of components – the raw materials for making the product. Production staff, using machinery and equipment, make the TV sets as they move along the production line.

Production staff are not the only employees of Thyme plc. There are also accountants, secretaries, fork-lift truck drivers and many others. These other employees all use different materials and equipment to do their work. For example, the accountants and secretaries use:

■ office materials, such as stationery, computer disks and printer cartridges

■ office equipment, such as telephones, computers, printers and photocopiers

All these people and items have to be paid for and are therefore costs to the company. There are many different kinds of costs: just a few examples are given above. The managers of Thyme plc will need the costs to be analysed in different ways, to give them the answers to such questions as:

■ how much does it cost to make one TV set?

■ do we need to increase our selling prices?

■ which models make the highest profits?

In this chapter we will consider different ways of analysing or classifying the costs incurred by an organisation, so that useful information can be produced for managers.

learning objectives

When you have studied this chapter you will be able to:

■ understand the importance of cost and management accounting

■ suggest cost units and cost centres for different types of business

■ identify the materials costs, labour costs and expenses of an organisation

■ identify the direct costs and indirect costs (overheads) of an organisation

■ analyse costs by function: production, administration and so on

■ define Total Production Cost and Production Cost per unit in manufacturing organisations

COST AND MANAGEMENT ACCOUNTING

the purpose of cost and management accounting

In the Case Study Thyme plc on the previous page, we saw that costs need to be analysed to provide information for managers. Managers need answers to detailed questions about costs. The answers will assist them with:

- planning for the future
- control of expenditure within the organisation
- decision-making

This is the purpose of Cost and Management Accounting.

The dividing line between Cost Accounting and Management Accounting is not always clear. Usually the cost accountant is the person who obtains and analyses information about costs. The management accountant then interprets the information and prepares reports for management purposes.

financial accounting and management accounting

Financial accounting starts with the financial data relating to transactions carried out over a period of time. This information is processed through the accounting records and extracted and presented in the form of a Trading and Profit and Loss Account and Balance Sheet.

It is important to emphasise that, although financial accounting and management accounting produce different types of reports and statements, the basic data from which the information comes is the same set of transactions, carried out by the business over the given period. This is illustrated in the diagram below.

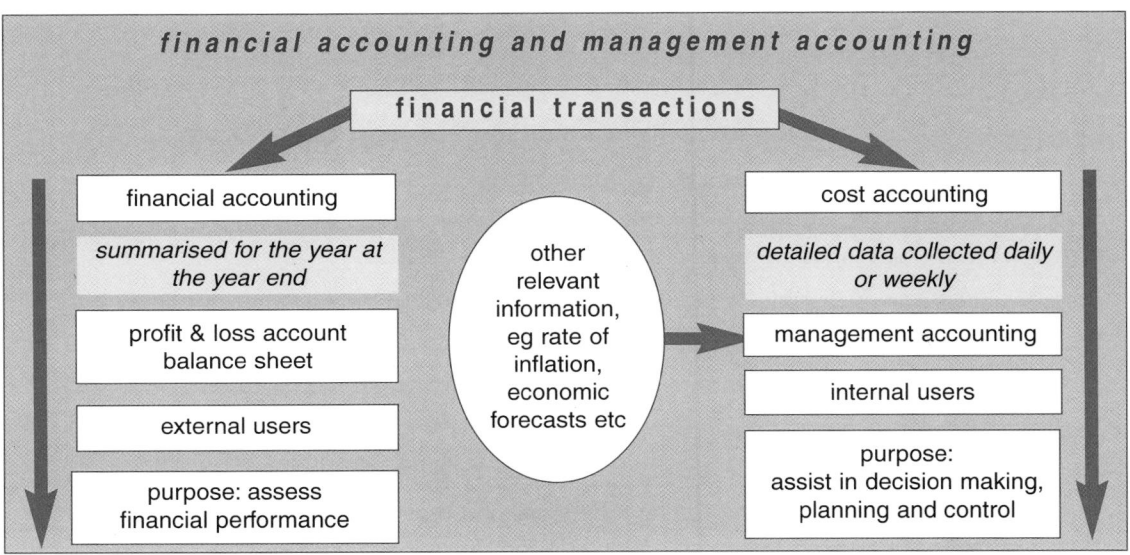

using computers for accounting

Computerised accounting systems allow the financial accounting and cost accounting systems to be integrated into one double-entry system. The transaction data is input to the system only once. Both financial accounts and cost accounts can be produced from this same set of data. The speed with which computers can sort data makes it possible to obtain very quickly the information that is needed.

COST UNITS AND COST CENTRES

Cost accounting enables the managers of a business to know the cost of the firm's output – whether it is a product or a service. Once costing information is available, managers can use it to help with decision-making, planning and control.

Cost accounting is widely used by all types of business – the cost of a hospital operation, the cost of tuition to a student, the cost of a swim at a sports centre, the cost of a passenger's bus journey are all just as important as the cost of making a product. A business – whether it provides a service or makes a product – needs to keep its costs under review; in order to do this it needs accurate cost information. Thus a cost accounting system will provide answers to questions such as:

'What does it cost us to provide a student with a day's accountancy course?'

'What does it cost us to carry out a hip replacement operation?'

'What does it cost us to make a pair of trainers?'

'What does it cost us to serve a cheeseburger and fries?'

'What does it cost us to provide a week's holiday in the Canaries?'

These questions illustrate the idea of finding the cost of a 'cost unit'.

Cost units are units of output to which costs can be charged.

A cost unit can be:

■ a unit of production from a factory such as a car, a television, an item of furniture

■ a unit of service, such as a passenger-mile on a bus, a transaction on a bank statement, an attendance at a swimming pool, a call unit on a telephone

Care should be taken in choosing the appropriate cost unit. Within a business – particularly in the service industry – there may well be several cost units that can be used. For example, in a hotel the cost units in the restaurant will be meals, and for the rooms, the cost units will be guest nights.

The main purpose of cost accounting is to determine the cost of a cost unit, eg to answer the question, 'How much does it cost to make one TV?'

Costs also need to be charged to a specific part of a business – a **cost centre**.

Cost centres are sections of a business to which costs can be charged.

A cost centre in a manufacturing business, for example, is a department of a factory, a particular stage in the production process, or even a whole factory. In a college, examples of cost centres are the teaching departments, or particular sections of departments such as the college's administrative office. In a hospital, examples of cost centres are the hospital wards, operating theatres, specialist sections such as the X-ray department, pathology department.

Collecting costs together in cost centres assists with control of the business. The manager of a cost centre can be held responsible for its costs.

CLASSIFICATION OF COSTS: MATERIALS, LABOUR AND EXPENSES

In the Case Study Thyme plc at the beginning of this chapter, there are examples of many different kinds of cost. In order to prepare information for the managers of the company, the costs must be **classified**, ie organised into sets in a way which the managers will find useful.

The most basic way of splitting up costs is according to the type of expenditure under the headings:

■ materials, for example the components to make a television set

■ labour, for example the wages of an employee

■ expenses, for example rent and rates, telephone charges, insurance

Materials costs are the costs of all sorts of raw materials, components and other goods used.

Labour costs are the costs of employees' wages and salaries.

Expenses are other costs, which cannot be included in 'materials' or 'labour'.

Notice that the meaning of the term 'expenses' is different here from its everyday use and from its use in financial accounting.

Splitting costs into these three types of expenditure provides important information. Costs cannot be controlled unless managers can see the breakdown of the total into different kinds of cost.

CLASSIFICATION OF COSTS: DIRECT AND INDIRECT COSTS

We have seen above that costs can be split according to the three types of expenditure:

■ materials costs

■ labour costs

■ expenses

Within each of these categories, some costs can be identified directly with each unit of output. For example:

■ the cost of components used in making television sets

■ the wages of workers on a production line in a factory

These are termed **direct costs**. In manufacturing, the total of all the direct costs is called the **prime cost** of the output.

A direct cost is a cost that can be identified directly with each unit of output.

Prime cost is the total of all direct costs.

Costs which cannot be identified directly with each unit of output are **indirect costs** or overheads.

Indirect costs (overheads) are all costs other than those identified as 'direct costs'. They cannot be identified directly with specific units of output.

There are many examples of overheads, including:

■ telephone charges

■ insurance premiums

■ the cost of wages of non-production staff, such as managers, secretaries, cost accountants and so on

■ the running costs of delivery vehicles

■ the depreciation charge for fixed assets

Note particularly the last two examples. In cost accounting, as in financial accounting, we distinguish between capital and revenue expenditure. In our analysis of costs we are referring to revenue expenditure, and therefore include the running costs and depreciation of fixed assets, rather than the capital cost of their purchase.

We now have six possible classifications for costs, each of the three categories of materials, labour and expenses being split into direct and indirect costs. These are illustrated for a manufacturing business in the table on the next page.

	DIRECT COSTS	INDIRECT COSTS
MATERIALS	The cost of raw materials from which the finished product is made.	The cost of all other materials, eg grease for machines, cleaning materials.
LABOUR	Wages paid to those who work the machinery on the production line or who are involved in assembly or finishing of the product.	Wages and salaries paid to all other employees, eg managers and supervisors, maintenance staff, administration staff.
EXPENSES	Any expenses which can be attributed to particular units of output, eg royalties payable to the designer of a product, fees linked directly to specific output and paid to people who are not employees.	All other expenses, eg rent, rates, telephone, lighting and heating costs, depreciation of fixed assets, insurance, advertising, etc. These are costs which cannot be linked directly with units of output.
TOTAL	**TOTAL DIRECT COST = PRIME COST**	**TOTAL INDIRECT COST = TOTAL OVERHEADS**

The Case Studies that follow show how costs can be classified into the three categories of materials, labour and expenses in a manufacturing company and in a business that provides a service.

CASE STUDY 1
Severn Manufacturing Company Limited

Severn Manufacturing Company Limited makes chairs for school and college use. The chairs have plastic seats, and tubular steel legs.

required

The firm's cost accountant asks you to help her classify the costs into:

- direct materials
- direct labour
- direct expenses
- indirect materials
- indirect labour
- indirect expenses

The costs to be classified are:

(a) tubular steel

(b) factory foreman's salary

(c) wages of employee operating the moulding machine which produces the chair seats

(d) works canteen assistant's wages

(e) rates of factory

(f) power to operate machines

(g) factory heating and lighting

(h) plastic for making chair seats

(i) hire of special machinery for one particular order

(j) cost of oil for the moulding machine

(k) rent of administrative office

(l) depreciation of factory machinery

(m) depreciation of office equipment

solution

These costs can be classified in a table as follows:

	DIRECT COSTS	INDIRECT COSTS
Materials	(a) tubular steel (h) plastic for making chair seats	(j) cost of oil for the moulding machine
Labour	(c) wages of employee operating the moulding machine which produces the chair seats	(b) factory foreman's salary (d) works canteen assistant's wages
Expenses	(i) hire of special machinery for one particular order	(e) rates of factory (f) power to operate machines* (g) factory heating and lighting (k) rent of administrative office (l) depreciation of factory machinery (m) depreciation of office equipment

The cost unit in this case is a chair. This is the product made by the company.

*Note

In the above, the cost of power to operate machines was classified as an indirect expense. This is often the case because it is not worthwhile for the cost accountant to analyse the cost of power for each unit of production. An industry that uses a lot of power might well have meters fitted to each machine so that costs can be identified. Other, lesser users of power, are unlikely to calculate the separate cost and will consider power to be an indirect expense.

CASE STUDY 2

The Albion Restaurant – a service business

The Albion Restaurant is a large, independent restaurant. Some of the costs incurred by the Albion Restaurant are listed below:

(a)   wages of the cleaner

(b)   cost of heating the restaurant

(c)   wages of the chefs

(d)   telephone charges

(e)   paper table covers and napkins

(f)   cost of ingredients for meals

(g)   cleaning materials

(h)   advertising costs

(i)   maintenance contract for ovens

(j)   wages of waiters and waitresses

required

1 Suggest a suitable cost unit for a restaurant.

2 Classify the costs into the six categories shown in the table below. Give your answer by entering the costs into the table:

	DIRECT COSTS	INDIRECT COSTS
MATERIALS		
LABOUR		
EXPENSES		

solution

An appropriate cost unit for a restaurant would be one meal.

	DIRECT COSTS	INDIRECT COSTS
MATERIALS	(f) cost of ingredients for meals	(e) paper table covers and napkins (g) cleaning materials
LABOUR	(c) wages of the chefs (j) wages of waiters and waitresses*	(a) wages of the cleaner
EXPENSES		(b) cost of heating the restaurant (d) telephone charges (h) advertising costs (i) maintenance contract for ovens

*Note

You may have classified (j) 'wages of waiters and waitresses' as 'indirect wages'. This is an equally valid answer.

A cost accounting system is designed to suit a particular organisation. There are some costs that may be treated as either direct or indirect costs, depending on the particular situation and the information required from the system. Costs which could be linked directly to cost units may be treated as overheads if this is easier and saves time without losing any useful information. See also the note relating to the cost of power in Case Study 1, Severn Manufacturing Company Ltd.

CLASSIFICATION OF COSTS BY FUNCTION

In the previous section, we have studied in detail a basic method for classifying costs, but this is not the only possible way of grouping costs together. Another method is to look at the costs incurred in different sections of the organisation, according to their 'function' or the kind of work being done.

In manufacturing, the main function is **production** of the goods. The business could not be run, however, without secretaries, administrators, accountants, sales and delivery staff and so on. Look back at the Case Study Thyme plc at the beginning of this chapter, which includes several examples of **non-production** costs.

When costs are classified by function, the main headings generally used are:

- production
- administration
- selling and distribution ⎤
- finance ⎦ — non-production costs

Other functions can be added to suit the needs of a particular business. For example, a 'Research and Development' heading could be used if a company spent large sums of money in researching and developing new products.

Non-manufacturing organisations – such as a hospital or a college – may use other 'function' headings, according to the kind of work each section of the organisation carries out.

It is important to note that, in classifying costs by their function, we are looking at the same set of costs for the organisation as before. We are simply presenting them in different groupings.

It is an important function of accounting that information should be presented in the form most suitable for the purpose for which it is required. For some management purposes, a functional analysis provides better information.

The Case Study which follows, illustrates how the TV manufacturer Thyme plc classifies its costs by function.

CASE STUDY
Thyme plc – classification of cost by function

Some of the indirect costs incurred by Thyme plc are listed below:

(a) depreciation charge for delivery vehicles

(b) salary of the personnel manager

(c) materials used for maintaining factory machinery

(d) cost of computer disks for office computers

(e) interest payable on a bank overdraft

(f) salary of the sales manager

(g) cost of power used for running factory machinery

(h) maintenance contract for office photocopier

required

Classify the costs by function and give your answer by entering the costs into a table.

solution

PRODUCTION COSTS	(c) materials used for maintaining factory machinery
	(g) cost of power used for running factory machinery
SELLING AND DISTRIBUTION COSTS	(a) depreciation charge for delivery vehicles
	(f) salary of the sales manager
ADMINISTRATION COSTS	(b) salary of the personnel manager
	(d) cost of computer disks for office computers
	(h) maintenance contract for office photocopier
FINANCE COSTS	(e) interest payable on a bank overdraft

CALCULATING TOTAL PRODUCTION COST

The diagram on the next page shows the costs of the three main sections or 'areas' of a manufacturing business. These three separate sections are:

■ the **factory** – where production takes place and the product is 'finished' and made ready for selling

■ the **warehouse** – where finished goods are stored and from where they are despatched when they are sold

■ the **office** – where the support functions take place – marketing, sales, finance, administration and so on

In this section we concentrate on looking at the costs incurred by the factory, ie the total cost of production.

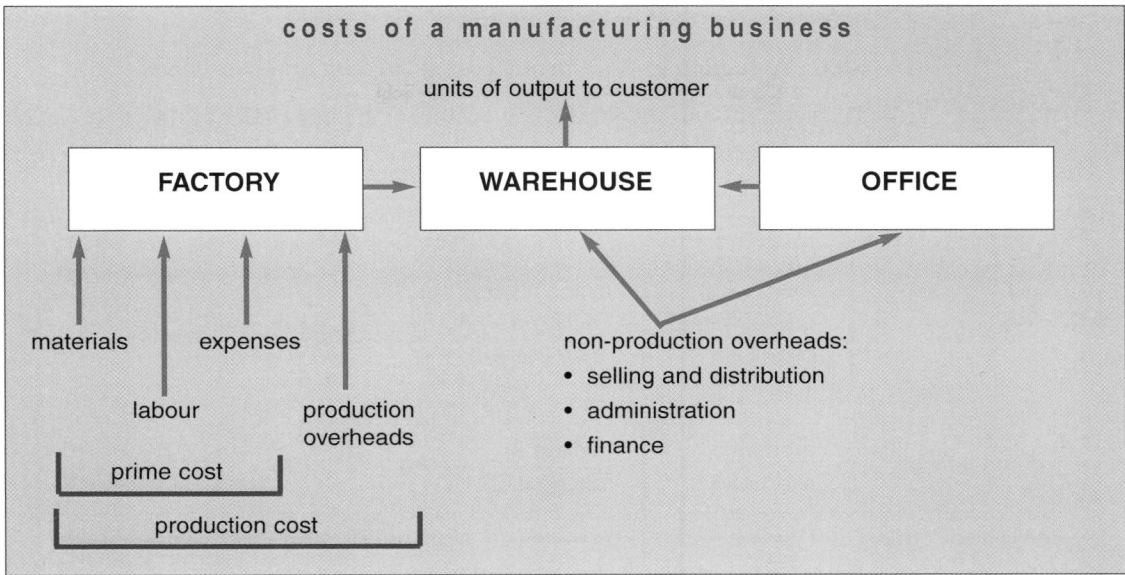

production cost

The diagram above shows the costs which go into **production** (the factory) of a manufacturing business. They are:

- ▢ direct materials
- ▢ direct labour
- ▢ direct expenses

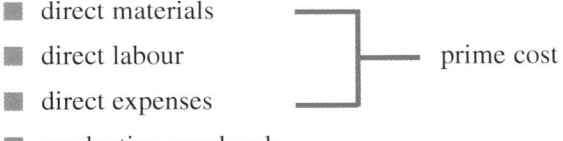

prime cost

- ▢ production overheads

The other costs involved relate to the warehouse and the office.

warehouse and office costs

The warehouse and office are **non-production** sections of the business. In the diagram, 'non-production overheads' include the costs of the functions other than production:

- ▢ selling and distribution
- ▢ administration
- ▢ finance

calculating total production costs

Looking at the diagram above we can therefore say:

total production cost = total direct costs + production overheads

We have also seen that total direct costs are known as 'prime cost'. The definition can therefore be restated as:

total production cost = prime cost + production overheads

The separation of the production cost from the remainder of the costs can be shown in a diagram:

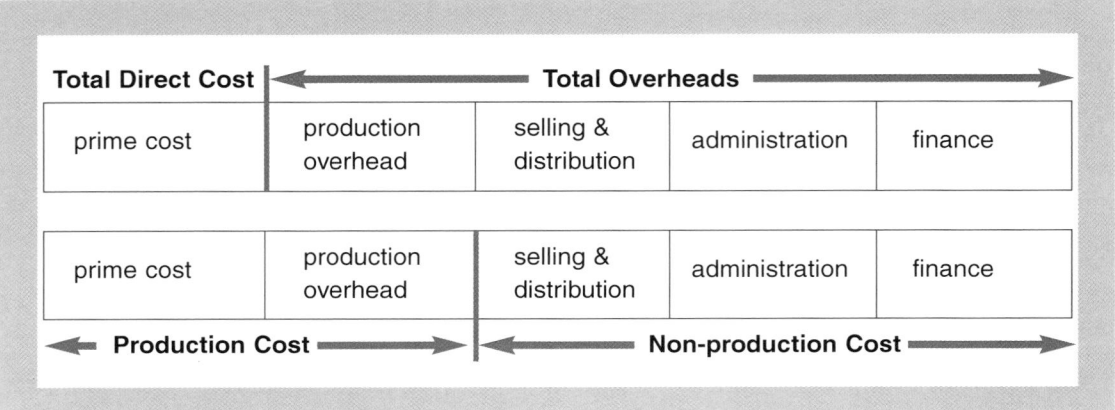

calculating unit cost

Using the formula shown above, the **total costs of production** can be collected together for a given time period. This enables us to answer the question:

'How much does it cost to make one unit of output?'

In the case of Thyme plc, a manufacturer of televisions sets, for example:

'How much does it cost to make one television set?'

We would need to know how many television sets had been made in the time period, and divide the total production cost by that number. The formula is:

cost of producing one unit of output   =

total costs of production for the period
number of units produced in the period

Calculating the total production cost of finished output in a manufacturing organisation is an essential part of the preparation of a Manufacturing Account, which we will study in the next chapter.

costs for a service business

While the units of 'output' of businesses that produce a service are not manufactured products, they still incur the costs of:

■ materials

■ labour

■ expenses

As in a manufacturing business, some of the costs can be linked directly to the 'output' or the cost units of the organisation, but others are classed as overheads.

chapter summary

● Cost and management accounting are essential to provide information for managers of organisations, to assist with decision-making, planning and control.

● Costs may be charged directly to cost units or to sections of the business defined as cost centres.

● Costs may be classified in different ways, depending on the purpose for which the information is required.

● The three categories of cost: materials costs, labour costs and expenses can each be split into direct costs and indirect costs. Indirect costs are also called 'overheads'. This gives a six-way split of costs (although sometimes there are no costs in the category of 'direct expenses'):

DIRECT MATERIALS	INDIRECT MATERIALS
DIRECT LABOUR	INDIRECT LABOUR
DIRECT EXPENSES	INDIRECT EXPENSES
TOTAL DIRECT COSTS or PRIME COST	TOTAL OVERHEADS

● Overheads may be classified by dividing them amongst the functions or sections of the business:
  – factory (or production)
  – selling and distribution
  – administration
  – finance
  – other section headings as appropriate to the organisation

● In manufacturing, total production cost is the total of direct costs together with the production (factory) overheads.

● Cost of producing one unit of output = $\dfrac{\text{total costs of production for the period}}{\text{number of units produced in the period}}$

key terms

cost unit	unit of output to which costs can be charged
cost centre	section of a business to which costs can be charged
materials costs	the costs of all sorts of raw materials, components and other goods used
labour costs	the costs of employees' wages and salaries
expenses	other costs, which cannot be included in 'materials' or 'labour'
direct cost	a cost that can be identified directly with each unit of output
indirect cost (overhead)	a cost that cannot be identified directly with each unit of output
prime cost	the total of all direct costs
production cost	the total of direct costs and production overheads, ie prime cost plus production overheads
cost of producing one unit of output	$\dfrac{\text{total costs of production for the period}}{\text{number of units produced in the period}}$

activities

Note: an asterisk (*) after an activity number means that an answer is provided in Appendix 1.

16.1* Suggest one cost unit and two cost centres for:

(a) a college of further education

(b) a mixed farm, growing crops and raising cattle

16.2 Suggest likely cost centres for each of the following:

A theatre in a provincial town, where touring productions are staged. The theatre has a bar and a confectionery counter. Ticket sales are dealt with by the theatre's own box office, and the plays are advertised locally.

A garage, which sells new and used cars of two different makes. Cars are also repaired, serviced and valeted.

16.3* The following are items of expenditure incurred in a company which manufactures clothing. Sort them and enter them into three columns, headed 'Materials costs', 'Labour costs' and 'Expenses'.

(a) Premium for the insurance of buildings

(b) Salaries of the office staff

(c) The cost of zip fasteners

(d) The cost of electricity

(e) Wages of storekeepers

(f) Overtime payments for machinists

(g) The cost of a consignment of blue denim

(h) The cost of pre-printed stationery

(i) The cost of television advertising

(j) The cost of cones of thread

(k) Road fund licences for vehicles

(l) The canteen chef's wages

16.4* Eveshore Pottery Company Limited manufactures a range of 'souvenir' mugs, cups and saucers, plates, etc, which sell well to visitors from abroad who are seeking a reminder of 'Olde England'. A number of different costs have been incurred during the last month, and you are asked to assist the cost accountant by classifying them into:

• Direct materials

• Indirect materials

• Direct labour

• Indirect labour

• Direct expenses

• Indirect expenses

The costs are:

(a) Cleaning materials for the machines

(b) Wages of factory foreman

(c) Clay from which the 'pots' are made

(d) 5p royalties payable to the designer for each 'Eveshore Plate' made

(e) Salary of office typist

(f) Electricity used to heat the kilns

(g) Rates of factory

(h) Depreciation of office typewriters

(i) Wages of production-line workers

(j) Salesman's salary

(k) Interest charged on bank overdraft

Of the overhead costs, ie indirect materials, indirect labour, and indirect expenses, you are to indicate which would be:

- factory overheads

- selling and distribution overheads

- administration overheads

- finance overheads

16.5   Wyvern Water Limited bottles natural spring water at its plant at Walcoll at the base of the Wyvern Hills. The natural spring is on land owned by a local farmer to whom a royalty is paid for each bottle of water produced.

You are working in the costing section of Wyvern Water and are asked to analyse the following cost items into the appropriate columns and to agree the totals:

Cost item	Total cost	Prime cost	Production overheads	Admin costs	Selling and distribution costs
	£	£	£	£	£
Wages of employees working on the bottling line	6,025				
Wages of employees in the stores department	2,750				
Cost of bottles	4,050				
Safety goggles for bottling line employees	240				
Advertisement for new employees	125				
Depreciation of bottling machinery	500				
Depreciation of sales staff's cars	1,000				
Royalty paid to local farmer	750				
Cost of trade exhibition	1,500				
Computer stationery	210				
Sales staff salaries	4,095				
TOTALS	21,245				

16.6　The following figures relate to the accounts of Hughes Limited, a manufacturing business, for the year ended 31 December 2003:

	£
Raw materials used in the factory	118,830
Rent and rates	16,460
Factory wages	117,315
Factory power	3,825
Factory heat and light	1,185
Factory expenses and maintenance	4,095
Salaries and wages of office staff	69,350
Advertising	11,085
Office expenses	3,930
Depreciation of factory plant and machinery	3,725
Sales revenue	426,350

Prepare a total cost statement for the year which shows:

* prime cost
* production cost
* total cost

Discuss any assumptions that you make and state if you need further information from the company.

MANUFACTURING ACCOUNTS

CASE STUDY
Thyme plc

Thyme plc is a manufacturer of TVs, which are made from a large number of components. At the end of its financial year, Thyme plc prepares a Trading and Profit and Loss Account and a Balance Sheet, just like any other business. The Balance Sheet shows a value for the 'closing stock' in amongst the current assets, as usual.

The sales and distribution manager of Thyme plc, who is not an accountant, comments at a meeting where the draft accounts are being presented:

'Why have one figure for closing stock when there are in fact a number of very different types of stock involved? I reckon there are three:

– components still sitting in the factory, not yet used

– partly finished television sets, where some of the components have been put together

– Completely finished television sets, ready to be sent out to customers

How are these dealt with in the accounts?'

In this chapter we will examine the ways in which these three kinds of stock are treated in the financial accounts. In particular we will study the preparation of a **Manufacturing Account**, which, as the name suggests, deals with the treatment of manufacturing costs, including stock.

learning objectives

When you have studied this chapter you will be able to:

- ■ *identify the three kinds of stock held in a manufacturing business*

- ■ *demonstrate how opening and closing values of the three kinds of stock are dealt with in the financial accounts of a manufacturing business*

- ■ *prepare a manufacturing account from given data*

- ■ *prepare a trading and profit and loss account for a manufacturing business*

ACCOUNTING IN A MANUFACTURING BUSINESS

stocks in a manufacturing business

At the end of the financial year, it is necessary for any business to value its closing stock. The value will appear on the balance sheet as a current asset and will also affect the cost of sales in the trading account.

In a manufacturing business, the **balance sheet value of stock** must include the values of three kinds of stocks:

- stocks of **raw materials** stored in the factory or elsewhere

- stocks of **work-in-progress**, ie products that are partly made; costs have been incurred in carrying out this work (in terms of materials, labour and production overheads) but the products are not finished and cannot yet be sold

- stocks of **finished goods**, ie completed products, ready to be sold

For example, in the Case Study of Thyme plc, above, the stocks consist of:

- stocks of components (raw materials for making the TVs)

- stocks of TVs that are 'work-in-progress', ie not finished – the production line has put together some of the components, but the work has not been completed

- stocks of finished TVs, ready to be sold to customers

The first distinction to be drawn is that stocks of raw materials and work-in-progress remain in the factory, ie the **manufacturing** side of the business, while stocks of finished goods are in the warehouse, ready to be sold, ie the **trading** side of the business.

Study the diagram below.

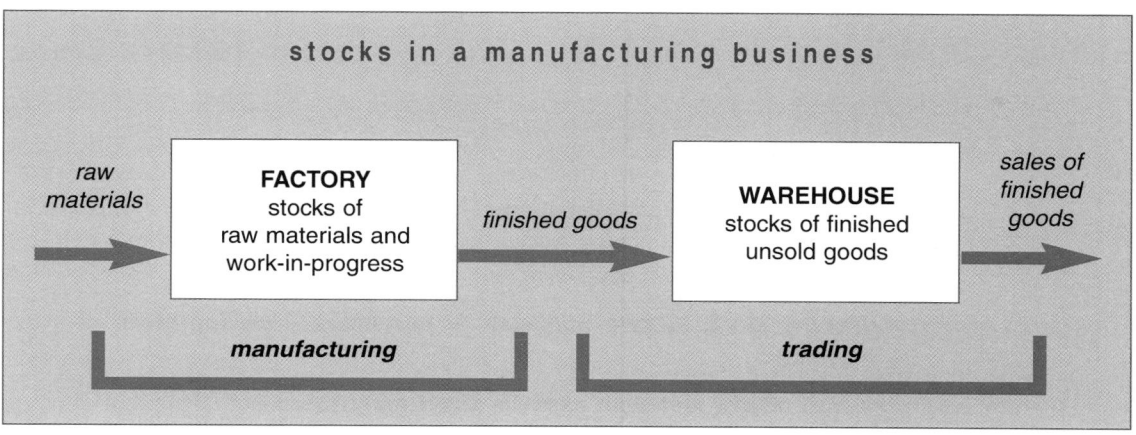

The diagram shows the distinction between the factory – **manufacturing** – side of the business and the selling – **trading** – side. It is important that the cost accounting system should be able to provide separate valuations for each of the three kinds of stock which will all appear in the balance sheet.

THE MANUFACTURING ACCOUNT

A manufacturing account must be prepared at the end of the financial year for a manufacturing business.

The bottom line of this financial statement provides **the total production cost of finished goods for the period.** Total production cost is defined as:

total production cost = direct costs (prime cost) + production overheads

The manufacturing account includes all the **direct costs** (prime cost) of making the products, together with the **production overheads**. Finished goods are sent from the factory to the warehouse, from which they are sold to customers. The accounts reflect this movement: the cost of producing the finished goods – adjusted for any work-in-progress not yet completed – is carried forward from the manufacturing account to the trading account. The calculations are explained step by step below.

	manufacturing account calculation
	cost of raw materials used
plus	direct labour costs and direct expenses
equals	prime cost
plus	production (factory) overheads
minus	cost of any work-in-progress
equals	cost of producing finished goods

calculating the total production cost of finished goods

step 1   raw materials used in the factory

The first step in the manufacturing account is to calculate the direct cost of the **raw materials** actually used. The closing stock (the stock not used) is deducted from the opening stock plus the purchases, and so it follows that the remainder must have been used (see diagram on the next page):

opening stock of raw materials + purchases – closing stock of raw materials

= cost of raw materials used = direct materials cost

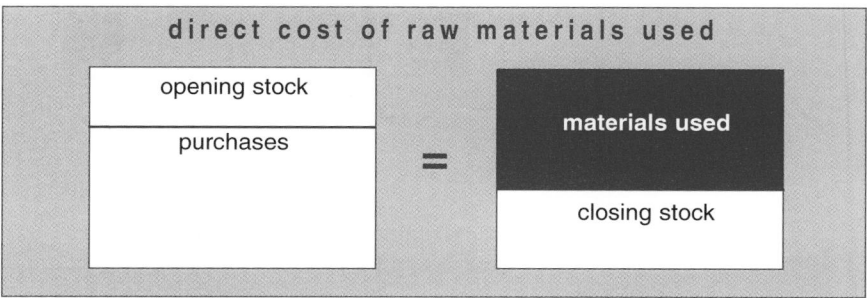

step 2   calculating prime cost

In addition to the direct cost of materials used, the cost of direct labour and any direct expenses must be added. The total of all the direct costs is the prime cost.

step 3   adding production overheads (factory overheads)

Production overheads are added to the prime cost to give the **Total Production Cost**. Production overheads are the overheads relating to the factory.

Note that some overheads – eg rent and rates – may be split between the factory and the office. The factory part of the total figure is included in the Manufacturing Account at this stage and the office part will be included in the Profit and Loss Account.

step 4   adjusting for work-in-progress

Remember that work-in-progress (eg half-made TV sets) remains in the factory – it cannot be sold because it is not complete. Therefore there is an adjustment at the end of the manufacturing account to ensure that the cost of closing work-in-progress is removed from the total of all production costs, leaving just the cost of producing the finished (completed) goods.

Note also that if there is any work-in-progress brought forward at the start of the period, its value must be included in the manufacturing account. The calculation for the production cost of goods completed is:

	total production cost
plus	**cost of the opening work-in-progress**
minus	**cost of the closing work-in-progress**
equals	**Production cost of goods completed**

This figure (production cost of goods completed) is the bottom line of the Manufacturing Account and is passed to the Trading Account.

The work-in-progress adjustment may be illustrated as follows:

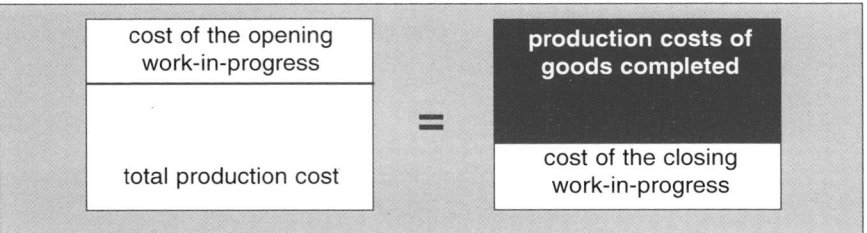

TRADING AND PROFIT AND LOSS ACCOUNTS

The trading and profit and loss accounts follow on from the manufacturing account.

the trading account

In the trading account the manufacturer sells its manufactured goods to its customers. It is also in effect 'buying' the finished goods from its own factory. Instead of 'purchases' of goods from outside suppliers, we now have the 'cost of production' of finished goods coming from the factory. This figure is brought forward from the manufacturing account as explained above.

The cost of sales (or 'cost of goods sold') is therefore calculated in the trading account as:

opening stock of finished goods

plus **production cost of goods completed**

less **closing stock of finished goods**

the profit and loss account

The profit and loss account of a manufacturing business is prepared in exactly the same way as for any other business. Notice that the **factory** costs have already been dealt with in the manufacturing account, so the profit and loss account deals only with **non-production** (usually warehouse and office) costs.

summary so far . . .

The diagram opposite illustrates how the Manufacturing, Trading and Profit and Loss Accounts are constructed and shows where the three stock adjustments – for raw materials, work-in-progress and finished goods – are made in the accounts.

The two Case Studies that follow put these principles into practice.

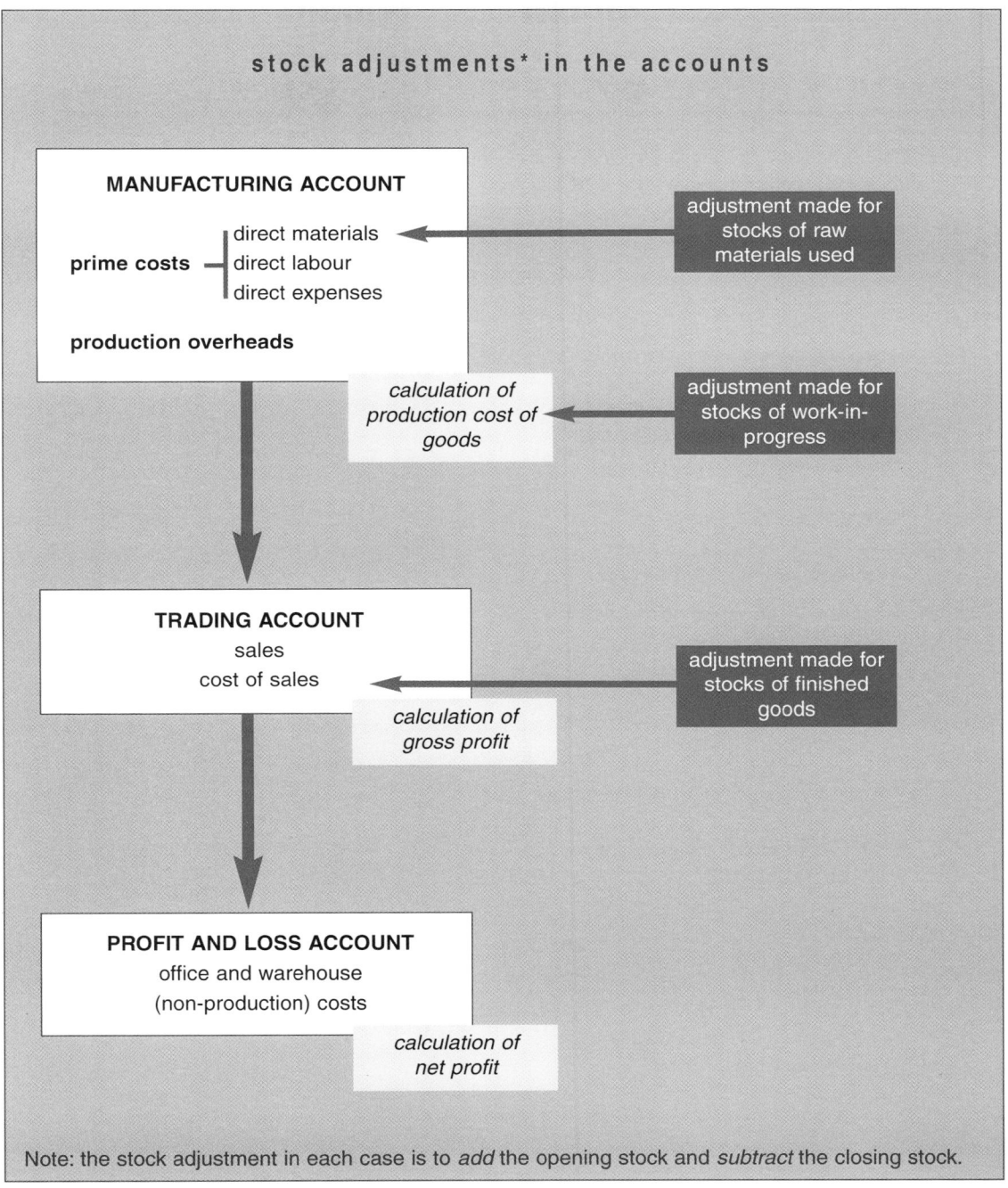

stock adjustments* in the accounts

MANUFACTURING ACCOUNT

prime costs — direct materials / direct labour / direct expenses

production overheads

adjustment made for stocks of raw materials used

calculation of production cost of goods

adjustment made for stocks of work-in-progress

TRADING ACCOUNT
sales
cost of sales

adjustment made for stocks of finished goods

calculation of gross profit

PROFIT AND LOSS ACCOUNT
office and warehouse
(non-production) costs

calculation of net profit

Note: the stock adjustment in each case is to *add* the opening stock and *subtract* the closing stock.

Now study the two Case Studies that follow. We will first show the layout of the accounts for a manufacturing business, together with notes highlighting important points. We will then illustrate the calculations required in order to prepare the accounts for a manufacturing company.

CASE STUDY 1
Severn Manufacturing Company Limited

Severn Manufacturing Company Limited makes office chairs. The layout of its manufacturing, trading, and profit and loss account for the year 2002 is as follows:

Manufacturing, trading, and profit and loss accounts for the year ended 31 December 2002

	£	£	
Opening stock of raw materials		5,000	
Add: Purchases of raw materials		50,000	
		55,000	
Less: Closing stock of raw materials		6,000	
COST OF RAW MATERIALS USED		49,000	
Direct labour		26,000	
Direct expenses		2,500	
PRIME COST		77,500	manufacturing account
Production (factory) overheads			
Indirect materials	2,000		
Indirect labour	16,000		
Rent of factory	5,000		
Depreciation of factory machinery	10,000		
Factory light and heat	4,000		
		37,000	
		114,500	
Add: Opening stock of work-in-progress		4,000	
		118,500	
Less: Closing stock of work-in-progress		3,000	
PRODUCTION COST OF GOODS COMPLETED		115,500	
SALES		195,500	
Opening stock of finished goods	6,500		
Add: Production cost of finished goods	115,500		
	122,000		
Less: Closing stock of finished goods	7,500		
COST OF SALES		114,500	
GROSS PROFIT		81,000	trading & profit & loss account
Office overheads			
Selling and distribution costs	38,500		
Administration costs	32,000		
Finance costs	3,500		
		74,000	
NET PROFIT		7,000	

points to note

1 The first step in the manufacturing account is to calculate the cost of the **raw materials used**.

2 The next step is to calculate the prime cost of the production.

3 The manufacturing account collects together all 'factory' costs, ie prime costs plus production overheads.

4 If there is any work-in-progress, an adjustment is made at the end of the manufacturing account. This ensures that the figure carried forward is the **cost of the goods completed in the period.**

5 'Sales' go into the top line of the Trading Account as usual.

6 The **cost of sales** is calculated in the normal way, except that the production or 'factory' cost replaces the 'purchases' of goods for sale. The production cost of the goods completed is brought down from the Manufacturing Account.

7 **Gross Profit = Sales – Cost of Sales,** as usual.

8 The Profit and Loss Account shows all **non-production** (non-factory) ie **warehouse and office costs**.

CASE STUDY 2

Swift Limited

Swift Ltd is a small company, specialising in the manufacture of surf-boards. The following information relates to the year ended 31 December 2002.

	Opening stock 1 January 2002	Closing stock 31 December 2002
	£	£
Stock of raw material (at cost)	15,275	14,385
Stock of work-in-progress (valued at factory cost)	3,800	3,250
Stock of finished goods	27,350	26,000

	£
Purchases of raw materials	43,850
Factory wages (direct)	22,725
Factory indirect expenses	12,500
Depreciation of factory machinery	1,500
Rent and rates *	6,000
General administration expenses	13,250
Sales of finished goods	168,000
Depreciation of vehicles	1,400
Vehicle running expenses	2,550
Selling expenses	13,090

* Rent and rates are three-quarters for the factory and one quarter for buildings housing the warehouse and office.

required

Prepare the manufacturing, trading and profit and loss accounts for Swift Ltd, for the year ended 31 December 2002.

solution

Hint: when preparing these accounts from given data, it is useful to mark against each item where it will go. Remember that the stocks of raw materials and work-in-progress are dealt with in the Manufacturing Account. The finished goods stocks appear in the Trading Account.

Purchases of raw materials and all 'factory' expenditure go into the manufacturing Account. In the case of rent and rates, the factory part must be calculated.

Factory rent and rates = 0.75 x £6,000 = £4,500 ⟶ manufacturing account

Non-production rent and rates = 0.25 x £6,000 = £1,500 ⟶ profit and loss account

All other costs relating to the office (administration) and selling and distribution (including vehicles) are also entered in the Profit and Loss Account.

Sales are part of the Trading Account.

SWIFT LTD: MANUFACTURING ACCOUNT FOR THE YEAR ENDED 31 DECEMBER 2002

	£	£
Opening stock of raw materials	15,275	
Add: Purchases of raw materials	43,850	
	59,125	
Less: Closing stock of raw materials	14,385	
COST OF RAW MATERIALS USED		44,740
Direct Labour (factory wages)		22,725
PRIME COST		67,465
PRODUCTION (factory) OVERHEADS		
Factory indirect expenses	12,500	
Factory machinery depreciation	1,500	
Factory rent & rates	4,500	18,500
		85,965
Add: Opening stock of work-in-progress		3,800
		89,765
Less: Closing stock of work-in-progress		3,250
PRODUCTION COST OF GOODS COMPLETED		86,515

TRADING AND PROFIT AND LOSS ACCOUNT FOR
SWIFT LTD FOR THE YEAR ENDED 31 DECEMBER 2002

	£	£
SALES		168,000
Opening stock of finished goods	27,350	
Add: Production cost of goods completed	86,515	
	113,865	
Less: Closing stock of finished goods	26,000	
COST OF SALES		87,865
GROSS PROFIT		80,135
Non-production overheads:		
Selling & distribution (working note 1 - see below)	17,040	
Administration (working note 2 - see below)	14,750	
		31,790
NET PROFIT		48,345

Working note 1: Selling and distribution costs include:

Depreciation of vehicles	1,400
Vehicle running expenses	2,550
Selling expenses	13,090
	17,040

Working note 2: Administration costs include

Rent and rates (one quarter)	1,500
General administration expenses	13,250
	14,750

chapter summary

● Manufacturing businesses have three types of stock:
  – raw materials
  – work-in-progress
  – finished goods

● The total value of all three kinds of stock is shown on the balance sheet of a manufacturing business.

● Raw materials and work-in-progress remain in the factory and are therefore dealt with in the manufacturing account:

opening stock of raw materials + purchases – closing stock of raw materials
= cost of raw materials used

total production cost + cost of the opening work-in-progress – cost of the closing work-in-progress
= production cost of finished goods

● Finished goods are transferred from the factory to the warehouse: their cost of production is similarly transferred from the manufacturing account to the trading account.

● For a manufacturing organisation, the manufacturing account collects together all the factory (production) costs, ie prime cost plus production overheads.

● In the trading account, the cost of sales or 'cost of goods sold' is calculated as follows:

    opening stock of finished goods
plus: *production cost of finished goods*
less: *closing stock of finished goods*

● The profit and loss account deals with non-production costs, such as warehouse and office costs.

key terms

prime cost	the total of all direct costs
production cost	the total of direct costs and production overheads, ie prime cost plus production overheads
work-in-progress	units of production that have been started but are not complete at the balance sheet date – a value must be attached to work-in-progress, to be included in the closing stock valuation along with the values of raw materials stocks and finished goods stocks.

activities

Note: an asterisk (*) after an activity number means that an answer is provided in Appendix 1.

17.1* The following figures relate to the accounts of Hughes Ltd, a manufacturing business, for the year ended 31 December 2001:

	£
Stocks of raw materials at 1 January 2001	15,930
Stocks of raw materials at 31 December 2001	22,395
Stocks of work-in-progress at 1 January 2001	6,250
Stocks of work-in-progress at 31 December 2001	6,980
Stocks of finished goods at 1 January 2001	21,320
Stocks of finished goods at 31 December 2001	48,255
Purchases of raw materials	118,830
Sales of finished goods	398,475
Rent and rates	16,460
Manufacturing wages	117,315
Manufacturing power	3,825
Manufacturing heat and light	1,185
Manufacturing expenses and maintenance	4,095
Salaries and wages	69,350
Advertising	11,085
Office expenses	3,930
Depreciation of plant and machinery	3,725

One-half of 'salaries and wages' and three-quarters of the 'rent and rates' are to be treated as a manufacturing charge.

You are to prepare manufacturing, trading and profit and loss accounts for the year to show clearly:

(a) prime cost

(b) production cost of goods completed

(c) cost of sales

(d) gross profit for the year

(e) net profit for the year

17.2* From the following figures, which relate to Martley Manufacturing Limited for the year ended 31 December 2001, prepare accounts in such a form as to show clearly:

(a) cost of raw materials used

(b) prime cost

(c) production cost of goods completed

(d) cost of sales

(e) gross profit

(f) net profit

	£
Stocks at beginning of year:	
Raw materials	105,000
Work-in-progress	24,000
Finished goods	43,000
Stocks at end of year:	
Raw materials	102,000
Work-in-progress	29,000
Finished goods	32,000
Expenditure during year:	
Purchases of raw materials	272,000
Direct factory wages	126,000
Rent and rates	12,000
Factory power	20,000
Depreciation of factory machinery	9,000
Repairs to factory buildings	3,000
Sundry factory expenses	9,000
Indirect wages and salaries	84,000
Advertising	38,000
Office expenses	31,000
Depreciation of office equipment	7,500
Sales during year	704,000

Additional information:

(a) indirect wages and salaries owing at year-end £4,000

(b) office expenses prepaid at year-end £2,000

(c) one-half of indirect wages and salaries to be treated as a manufacturing charge

(d) three-quarters of rent and rates to be treated as a manufacturing charge

17.3 The following figures relate to John Smith's manufacturing business for the year ended 31 March 2007:

	£
Capital	184,440
Light and heat	16,500
Manufacturing wages	99,010
Bank overdraft	50,870
Drawings	15,500
Office salaries	21,160
Royalties (paid to owners of patents)	42,930
Advertising	8,560
Stocks (1 April 2006):	
Raw materials	71,020
Finished goods	72,780
Commission paid to salesman	18,100
Premises (at cost)	58,750
Machinery and plant (cost £125,000)	76,000
Sales	715,800
Debtors	75,000
Provision for bad debts	2,000
Office machinery (cost £10,000)	5,000
Rates	1,700
Creditors	78,330
Purchases of raw materials	449,430

You are also given the following information at 31 March 2007:

(1) stocks: raw materials £70,640

finished goods £74,480

(2) light and heat is to be apportioned two-thirds to the factory, one-third to the office

(3) rates are to be divided equally between factory and office

(4) the provision for bad debts is to be 4% of debtors

(5) salaries due but unpaid amount to £490

(6) depreciation: machinery and plant 15% on reducing balance

office equipment 10% on cost

You are to prepare:

1   Accounts for the year ended 31 March 2007 to show clearly:

       (a)   prime cost

       (b)   production cost of goods completed

       (c)   cost of sales

       (d)   gross profit

       (e)   net profit

2   A balance sheet at 31 March 2007.

17.4   The following balances have been extracted from the accounting system of Eresham Manufacturing Company Limited, and relate to the year ended 31 December 2003:

	£
Share capital (£1 ordinary shares)	410,000
Retained profits at 1 January 2003	24,650
10% debentures	100,000
Freehold premises at cost	425,000
Factory machinery at cost	250,000
Office equipment at cost	45,000
Depreciation on factory machinery to 31 December 2002	68,500
Depreciation on office equipment to 31 December 2002	17,500
Sales	824,500
Purchases of raw materials	326,250
Manufacturing wages	236,650
Factory rates and insurance	17,285
Office rates and insurance	6,390
Factory power	12,250
Office heating and lighting	2,755
Factory expenses	3,210
Office expenses	4,865
Bank interest	2,315
Office salaries	65,950

Debtors	84,690
Creditors	47,610
Bank overdraft	80,740
Stocks at 1 January 2003:	
Raw materials	41,250
Work-in-progress	17,860
Finished goods	31,780

The following additional information is available:

(a)   Debenture interest for the year has not yet been paid and is to be provided for.

(b)   Depreciation on factory machinery and on office equipment is to be calculated at 10% per annum on cost.

(c)   Provision is to be made for an ordinary share dividend of 10p per share.

(d)   Office expenses owing at 31 December 2003 amount to £375.

(e)   Factory insurance prepaid at 31 December 2003 amounts to £510.

(f)   Stocks at 31 December 2003 amount to:

	£
Raw materials	47,680
Work-in-progress	24,310
Finished goods	30,620

You are to prepare:

1   Manufacturing, trading and profit and loss accounts for the year ended 31 December 2003.

2   A balance sheet at 31 December 2003.

18 ACCOUNTING FOR MATERIALS

CASE STUDY
How much did that cost?

'How much did that cost?' would seem to be an easy question to answer.

For a business, though, it is not always that easy to come to a firm conclusion about the cost of an item.

For example, suppose a supermarket bought 100 cans of orange drink at a cost of 25p each. Then a week later it purchased another 100 identical cans, but the price has increased to 30p a can. If you now ask the question *'How much did this can cost?'* . . . the reply may well be *'It depends.'*

It depends on how the business has chosen to account for its stocks.

They could, for example, keep details of all the different prices, or they could calculate an average. When the profit and loss account and balance sheet are being prepared at the end of the financial year, it will be necessary to know the cost of the cans that have been sold and the value of the cans remaining in stock.

In this chapter we will consider aspects of accounting for materials, and look at three methods of accounting for stocks of materials or goods – such as cans of orange – when they have been bought at differing prices.

learning objectives

When you have studied this chapter you will be able to:

- *calculate the value of stocks using information about costs and net realisable values*

- *identify and record the values to be attached to issues from stores of materials to be used (or goods to be sold), using different methods of valuation*

- *explain the effects of the different methods of valuing closing stock on the profit for a given period*

- *comment on the advantages and disadvantages of the three methods*

STOCK VALUATION

At any time, most businesses will hold materials in stock ready for use or resale. The diagram below examines the holding of stocks by three types of business: a manufacturing business (studied in the last chapter) which makes stock, a trading business such as a shop, which buys and sells stock and a service business.

Manufacturing Business	Trading Business	Service Business
raw materials and components	**goods for sale**	**consumable materials**
These stocks are held by a manufacturer to reduce the risk of production delays if a supplier fails to deliver on time. A vehicle manufacturer may hold a stock of plastic bumpers, for example.	These are items the retailer or wholesaler has bought in (eg from the manufacturer) and has available for sale to the customer.	These are materials that are either for use in the organisation or for sale to the customer as part of the service provided.
	For example:	For example:
work in progress	■ *retailers* a supermarket will have a stock of cans of orange drink for sale	■ *for use in the organisation* in a college there will be a stock of paper for the photocopiers
These are stocks of partly finished goods on the production line. In a car factory these would be cars partly assembled, for example.	■ *wholesalers* a timber merchant will have quantities of wood for sale to customers	■ *items for sale* an optician will sell reading glasses as part of the service provided
finished goods		
These are goods that have been completed and are ready for sale to customers. A vehicle manufacturer would have completed cars ready for sale, for example.		

stock valuation

The general rule is that stock can be valued at *either*:

■ what it cost the business to buy the stock (including additional costs to bring the product or service to its present location or condition, such as delivery charges) *or*

■ the net realisable value – the actual or estimated selling price (less any extra costs such as selling and distribution) – ie what you would get for it

Stock valuation is normally made at the *lower of cost and net realisable value.* This valuation is taken from Statement of Standard Accounting Practice (SSAP) No 9, entitled 'Stocks and long-term contracts'. This method of valuation applies the 'prudence' concept of accounting. It can be illustrated as follows:

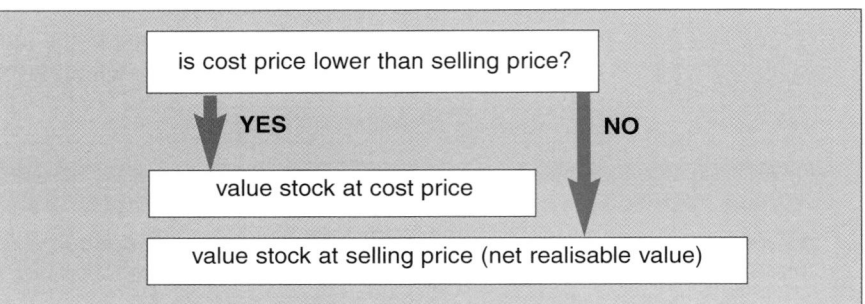

WORKED EXAMPLE
stock valuation

A shop bought in a range of 'designer' beachwear in the Spring, with each item costing £15 and selling for £30. Most of the stock is sold but in October ten items remain unsold. These are put onto the 'bargain rail' at £18 each. On 31 December, at the end of the shop's financial year, five items remain unsold. At what price will they be included in the year-end stock valuation?

Answer: They will be valued at cost of £15 each, ie 5 x £15 = £75.

Twelve months later three items still remain unsold, and have just been further reduced to £10 each. At what price will they now be valued in the year-end stock valuation?

Answer: They will now be valued at net realisable value of £10 each, ie 3 x £10 = £30.

Important Note: Stock is *never* valued at selling price when selling price is above cost price; this is because selling price includes profit.

CATEGORIES OF STOCK

Statement of Standard Accounting Practice No 9 requires that, in calculating the lower of cost and net realisable value, note should be taken of:

■ separate items of stock, or
■ groups of similar items

This means that the stock valuation 'rule' must be applied to each separate item of stock, or each group or category of similar stocks. The total cost cannot be compared with the total net realisable value, as is shown by the Case Study which follows.

CASE STUDY
Paint and Wallpaper Supplies

situation

The year-end stocks for the two main groups of stock held by the business Paint and Wallpaper Supplies are found to be:

	Cost	Net realisable value
	£	£
Paints	2,500	2,300
Wallpapers	5,000	7,500
	7,500	9,800

How will the stock be valued for the year-end accounts?

solution

The correct stock valuation is £7,300, which takes the 'lower of cost and net realisable value' for each group of stock, ie

	£
Paints (at net realisable value)	2,300
Wallpapers (at cost)	5,000
	7,300

You will also note that this valuation is the lowest possible choice, indicating that stock valuation follows the *prudence concept* in accounting.

STOCK VALUATION FOR MANUFACTURING BUSINESSES

We have seen that under SSAP 9, stock is normally valued at the lower of cost and net realisable value. This principle applies to a manufacturer for the three types of stock that may be held at the year-end:

- raw materials
- work-in-progress
- finished goods

For raw materials, the comparison is made between cost and net realisable value. We will see later in this chapter how 'cost' can be defined, if identical materials have been bought at different prices.

For stocks of both work-in-progress and finished goods, SSAP 9 requires that the cost valuation includes expenditure not only on direct materials but also on direct labour, direct expenses and production overheads. Thus for work-in-progress and finished goods, 'cost' means 'production cost', ie the total of:

■ direct materials

■ direct labour

■ direct expenses

■ production overheads (to bring the product to its present location or condition)

Such 'cost' is then compared with net realisable value – less any further costs necessary to complete the item or get it in a condition to be sold – and the lower figure is taken as the stock valuation. (Remember that different items or groups of stock are compared separately.)

CASE STUDY
ABC Manufacturing

situation

ABC Manufacturing started in business on 1 July 2000 producing security devices for doors and windows. During the first year 2,000 units were sold and, at the end of the year, on 30 June 2001, there were 200 units in stock which were finished and 20 units which were exactly half-finished as regards direct materials, direct labour and production overheads.

Costs for the first year were:

	£
Direct materials used	18,785
Direct labour	13,260
Production overheads	8,840
Non-production overheads	4,420
Total cost for year	45,305

At 30 June 2001 it was estimated that the net realisable value of each completed security device was £35. There were no stocks of direct materials.

required:

Calculate the stock valuation at 30 June 2001 for:

• work-in-progress

• finished goods

solution

WORK-IN-PROGRESS

To calculate the value of both work-in-progress and finished goods we need to know the production cost, ie direct materials, direct labour and production overheads. This is:

	£
Direct materials used	18,785
Direct labour	13,260
Production overheads	8,840
Production cost for year	**40,885**

All these costs are included because they have been incurred in bringing the product to its present location or condition. Non-production overheads are not included because they are not directly related to production.

Thus, a production cost of £40,885 has produced:

Units sold	2,000
Closing stock of completed units	200
Closing stock of work-in-progress –	
20 units exactly half-finished equals	
10 completed units	10
Production for year	**2,210**

The **cost per unit** is:

$$\frac{£40,885}{2,210} = \textbf{£18.50 per unit}$$

The 20 half-finished units have a cost of (20 ÷ 2) x £18.50 = **£185.**

They have a net realisable value of (20 ÷ 2) x £35 = **£350**.

The value of work-in-progress will, therefore, be shown in the accounts as **£185**, which is the lower of cost and net realisable value.

FINISHED GOODS

The completed units in stock at the end of the year have a production cost of 200 x £18.50 = £3,700, compared with a net realisable value of 200 x £35 = £7,000. Applying the rule of lower of cost and net realisable value, finished goods stock will be valued at the cost price, **£3,700.**

METHODS OF STOCK VALUATION

issuing of materials and goods

The costing process requires that a value is given to raw materials (for a manufacturer) and goods (for a shop) when they are 'issued'. This means the point at which they are handed over to the production line or placed on the shop shelves. Traditionally the materials and goods were issued from 'stores' – a storage area or stockroom – where they had been kept by the business since delivery from the supplier. The phrase 'issued from stores' is still used, although nowadays materials and stocks are often delivered at the very last minute to save storage and finance costs. This is known as Just In Time ordering (JIT).

The cost of the materials or goods at the time of issue is normally the purchase cost – ie the price the business paid the supplier. But, as we saw in the opening Case Study of this chapter), prices do vary – so which price do you take and what valuation do you give the materials or goods?

The three most commonly used methods for deciding which 'cost' to use for raw materials used in the production process or sold from shop shelves are:

FIFO (First In First Out)

In this method, the first (oldest) cost prices are used first when goods are issued from stores. This means that the remaining stock is valued at the most recent cost prices.

LIFO (Last In First Out)

In this method, the most recent (last) cost prices are used first when goods are issued from stores. This means that the remaining stock is valued at older cost prices.

AVCO (Average Cost)

In this method, an average cost is calculated for the goods in stock at a given time, using the formula:

average cost = $\dfrac{\textbf{total cost of goods in stock}}{\textbf{number of items in stock}}$

The average cost is then used to attach a value to issues from stores. A new average must be calculated each time that further purchases are made.

Having chosen a suitable stock valuation method, a business will continue to use that method unless there are good reasons for making the change. This is in line with the consistency concept of accounting.

recording stock values – stores ledger record

In order to be able to calculate accurately the price at which stocks of materials are issued and to ascertain a valuation of stock, a stores ledger record is used, as shown below. This method of recording stock data is also used in the Case Study which follows.

	STORES LEDGER RECORD								
Date	Receipts			Issues			Balance		
	Quantity	Price*	Value	Quantity	Price*	Value	Quantity	Price*	Value
		£	£		£	£		£	£

*price = cost price, not selling price

CASE STUDY

H Rashid computer supplies – stores ledger records

situation

H Rashid runs a computer supplies company. One of the items he sells is the 'Zap' data disk.

To show how the stores ledger records would appear under FIFO, LIFO and AVCO, and the closing stock valuation at 31 May 2002, the following data is used for each method:

January	Opening stock of 40 units at a cost of £3.00 each
February	Bought 20 units at a cost of £3.60 each
March	Sold 36 units for £6 each
April	Bought 20 units at a cost of £3.75 each
May	Sold 25 units for £6 each

What will be the profit for the period using each stock valuation method?

Note: In the first two methods, units issued at the same time may be valued at different prices. This is because the quantities received, with their prices, are listed separately and used in a specific order. There may be insufficient units at one price, eg see the May issue using both FIFO and LIFO methods.

FIFO

STORES LEDGER RECORD

Date	Receipts			Issues			Balance		
2002	Quantity	Price	Value	Quantity	Price	Value	Quantity	Price	Value
		£	£		£	£		£	£
Jan	Balance						40	3.00	120.00
Feb	20	3.60	72.00				40	3.00	120.00
							20	3.60	72.00
							60		192.00
March				36	3.00	108.00	4	3.00	12.00
							20	3.60	72.00
							24		84.00
April	20	3.75	75.00				4	3.00	12.00
							20	3.60	72.00
							20	3.75	75.00
							44		159.00
May				4	3.00	12.00			
				20	3.60	72.00			
				1	3.75	3.75	19	3.75	71.25

Note: In the 'Balance' columns, a new list of stock quantities and prices is started after each receipt or issue. When stock is issued, prices are used from the **top** of the list downwards.

LIFO

STORES LEDGER RECORD

Date	Receipts			Issues			Balance		
2002	Quantity	Price	Value	Quantity	Price	Value	Quantity	Price	Value
		£	£		£	£		£	£
Jan	Balance						40	3.00	120.00
Feb	20	3.60	72.00				40	3.00	120.00
							20	3.60	72.00
							60		192.00
March				20	3.60	72.00			
				16	3.00	48.00	24	3.00	72.00
April	20	3.75	75.00				24	3.00	72.00
							20	3.75	75.00
							44		147.00
May				20	3.75	75.00			
				5	3.00	15.00	19	3.00	57.00

Note: In the 'Balance' columns, a new list of stock quantities and prices is started after each receipt or issue. When stock is issued, prices are used from the **bottom** of the list upwards. However, the new balance list each time must be kept in date order.

AVCO

In this method, each quantity issued is valued at the average price per unit, and so is the balance in stock. The complete list of different prices does not have to be re-written each time.

STORES LEDGER RECORD

Date	Receipts			Issues			Balance		
2002	*Quantity*	*Price*	*Value*	*Quantity*	*Price*	*Value*	*Quantity*	*Price*	*Value*
		£	£		£	£		£	£
Jan	Balance						40	3.00	120.00
Feb	20	3.60	72.00				40	3.00	120.00
							20	3.60	72.00
							60	3.20	192.00
March				36	3.20	115.20	24	3.20	76.80
April	20	3.75	75.00				24	3.20	76.80
							20	3.75	75.00
							44	3.45	151.80
May				25	3.45	86.25	19	3.45	65.55

Note: Average cost is calculated by dividing the quantity held in stock into the value of the stock. For example, at the end of February, the average cost is £192 ÷ 60 units = £3.20, and at the end of April it is £151.80 ÷ 44 = £3.45.

The closing stock valuations at the end of May 2002 under each method show cost prices of:

FIFO   £71.25

LIFO   £57.00

AVCO   £65.55

There is quite a difference, and this has come about because different stock methods have been used.

effect on profit

In the example above, the selling price was £6 per unit. The effect on gross profit of using different stock valuations is shown on the next page.

		FIFO	LIFO	AVCO
		£	£	£
Sales: 61 units at £6		366.00	366.00	366.00
Opening stock:	40 units at £3	120.00	120.00	120.00
Purchases:	20 units at £3.60 and	147.00	147.00	147.00
	20 units at £3.75			
		267.00	267.00	267.00
Less Closing stock: 19 units		71.25	57.00	65.55
Cost of sales		195.75	210.00	201.45
Gross profit = Sales − Cost of Sales		170.25	156.00	164.55

Notice that the Cost of Sales figure in each case is also obtainable by adding up the values in the 'Issues' column. You can also check in each case that, both in Units and in Values:

opening stock + receipts − issues = closing stock

The Case Study shows that in times of rising prices, FIFO produces the highest reported profit, LIFO the lowest, and AVCO between the other two. However, over the life of a business, total profit is the same in total, whichever method is chosen: the profit is allocated to different years depending on which method is used.

The choice of method depends on which method is considered to give the most useful information for management purposes.

ADVANTAGES AND DISADVANTAGES OF FIFO, LIFO AND AVCO

FIFO (first in, first out)

advantages

- it is realistic, ie it assumes that goods are issued in order of receipt
- it is easy to calculate
- stock valuation comprises actual prices at which items have been bought
- the closing stock valuation is close to the most recent prices

disadvantages

- prices at which goods are issued are not necessarily the latest prices
- in times of rising prices, profits will be higher than with other methods (resulting in more tax to pay)
- the method is cumbersome as the list of different prices must be maintained

LIFO (last in, first out)

advantages

- goods are issued at the latest prices
- it is easy to calculate
- in manufacturing, materials are issued at more up-to-date prices, giving a more realistic production cost

disadvantages

- illogical, ie it assumes goods are issued in reverse order from that in which they are received
- the closing stock valuation is not usually at most recent prices
- when stocks are being run down, issues will 'dip into' old stock at out-of-date prices
- may not be acceptable to the Inland Revenue for taxation purposes as the method overstates cost of sales and understates profit
- the method is cumbersome as the list of different prices must be maintained

AVCO (average cost)

advantages

- over a number of accounting periods reported profits are smoothed, ie both high and low profits are avoided
- fluctuations in purchase prices are evened out so that issues do not vary greatly
- logical, ie it assumes that identical units, even when purchased at different times, have the same value
- closing stock valuation is close to current market values (in times of rising prices, it will be below current market values)
- the calculations can be computerised more easily than the other methods

disadvantages

- a new average has to be calculated after each receipt, and calculations may be to several decimal places
- issues and stock valuation are usually at prices which never existed
- issues may not be at current prices and, in times of rising prices, will be below current prices

The important point to remember is that a business must adopt a consistent stock valuation policy, ie it should choose one method of finding the cost price, and not change it without good reason. FIFO and AVCO are more commonly used than LIFO; in particular, LIFO usually results in a stock valuation for the final accounts which bears little relationship to recent costs – for this reason it is not favoured by SSAP 9.

Now study the table below to consolidate what you have learnt so far.

	FIFO	LIFO	AVCO
method	The costs used for goods sold or issued follow the order in which the goods were received.	The costs used for goods sold or issued are opposite to the order in which the goods were received.	This method does not relate issues to any particular batch of goods received, but uses an average cost.
calculation	It is easy to calculate costs because they relate to specific receipts of materials or goods.	It is easy to calculate costs because they relate to specific receipts of materials or goods.	More complex because of the need to calculate average costs.
stock valuation	Stock valuations are based on the most recent prices of materials or goods received.	Stock valuations are based on older prices of materials or goods received.	Average costs are used to value closing stock.
profits and taxation	In times of rising prices this method will result in higher reported profits than the other methods, resulting in more tax being payable. This method is acceptable for tax purposes.	In times of rising prices this method will result in lower reported profits than the other methods. This may not be acceptable for tax purposes.	The average method will smooth out some of the peaks and troughs of profit and loss. This method is acceptable for tax purposes.
administration	Use of this method will mean keeping track of each receipt until the goods are issued or sold.	Use of this method will mean keeping track of each receipt until the goods are issued or sold.	There is no need to track each receipt as an average cost is used. This also means it is easier to computerise the stock records.
cost of sales	In a time of rising prices this method will use older, out of date prices for cost of sales or goods issued.	In a time of rising prices this method will use more up-to-date prices for cost of sales or goods issued.	This method will give an average price for the cost of sales.

OTHER STOCK VALUATION METHODS

As well as the FIFO, LIFO and AVCO methods used to determine the valuation of closing stock, other methods which could be used include:

standard cost

This uses a pre-determined cost – the standard cost (see Chapter 23) – based on the business' estimates of expected cost levels. SSAP 9 stresses that standard costs should be reviewed frequently, to ensure that they bear a reasonable relationship to actual costs during the period.

replacement cost

This method considers the price at which the items of stock can be replaced, either by purchase or by manufacture. SSAP 9 considers this method unacceptable because replacement cost is not necessarily the same as actual cost. For example, in times of rising prices, replacement cost will be higher than actual cost, which means that a profit is taken before the stock is sold.

This method, similarly to LIFO, gives a more up-to-date production cost for the work done.

chapter summary

- At the end of the financial year, every organisation must value its stocks of materials or goods, in order to calculate the profit and to enter the stock figure on the balance sheet.

- In accordance with SSAP 9, stocks are to be valued at the lower of cost and net realisable value.

- In applying SSAP 9, comparison must be made between cost and net realisable value for each separate category of stock.

- In manufacturing organisations, there are three types of stock (raw materials, work-in-progress and finished goods) to be valued.

- The 'cost' of work-in-progress and finished goods in manufacturing is the production cost, which equals direct costs plus production overheads.

- The 'cost' of raw materials and goods when first acquired by the business is the purchase price.

- The raw materials and goods are 'issued' to the production line and to the shop shelves respectively, at the purchase price.

- The acquisition and issue of raw materials and goods is recorded on a 'Stores Ledger Record'.

- If materials or goods have been purchased at differing prices, the value attached to them as they are issued may be on the basis of:
    - first in first out (FIFO)
    - last in first out (LIFO)
    - average cost (AVCO)

- Each of the methods, FIFO, LIFO or AVCO, results in a different value for the closing stock, and hence a different reported profit in a given time period.

- Closing stock of one period becomes the opening stock of the next and therefore the method, once chosen, should be used consistently. Over a number of time periods, the differences in reported profits will cancel out.

- Possible alternatives to FIFO, LIFO and AVCO include standard costing and using replacement cost.

key terms

cost of stock	the amount it cost to buy the stock (including additional costs to bring the product to its present location and condition)
net realisable value	the selling price obtainable, less any further costs to be incurred such as selling and distribution costs
FIFO	'First in First out' method of attaching a value to each issue of materials or goods from stores, using the oldest cost prices first
LIFO	'Last in First out' method of attaching a value to each issue of materials or goods from stores, using most recent cost prices first
AVCO	'Average Cost' method of attaching a value to each issue of materials or goods from stores, using a weighted average of the cost prices of all items in stock at the date of issue
standard cost	a predetermined cost based on the business' estimates of expected cost levels – the standard cost of materials can be used as an alternative to FIFO, LIFO and AVCO for attaching a value to issues from stores and to closing stock
replacement cost	the cost price of replacing stock, either by purchase or by manufacture

activities

Note: an asterisk (*) after an activity number means that an answer is provided in Appendix 1.

18.1* Go Games Ltd sells computer games. At the end of the financial year, the company's stocks include:

300 copies of 'X1X' game that cost £40 each and will sell at only £30, because it is an out-of-date version.

260 copies of a newly-released game, 'X-TRA-G' that cost £56 each and will be sold for £90 each.

100 copies of a current version of 'X-TREME 2' game, which is expected to be up-dated to 'X-TREME 3' in the near future. These cost £35 each and normally sell for £55, but because they may soon be out of date, Go Games Ltd has reduced the price to £42 each.

Required:

Calculate the total value of the stock items described above, using the principles of SSAP 9.

18.2 A football club shop holds stocks of replica club strip as well as other goods and clothing. The club strip has recently been changed and the old version will have to be sold at greatly reduced prices. At the end of the financial year, the stocks in the shop include:

	Cost	Net realisable value
	£	£
Replica strip (old version)	3,800	2,500
Replica strip (new version)	8,400	11,000
	12,200	13,500

Required:

Determine the total value of the stock items above, according to the principles of SSAP 9.

18.3* From the following information prepare stores ledger records for product X using:

(a) FIFO

(b) LIFO

(c) AVCO

- 20 units of the product are bought in January 2002 at a cost of £3 each
- 10 units are bought in February at a cost of £3.50 each
- 8 units are sold in March
- 10 units are bought in April at a cost of £4.00 each
- 16 units are sold in May

Note: where appropriate, work to two decimal places.

18.4 XY Limited is formed on 1 January 2002 and, at the end of its first half-year of trading, the stores ledger records show the following:

2002	TYPE X		TYPE Y	
	Receipts (units)	**Issues (units)**	**Receipts (units)**	**Issues (units)**
January	100 at £4.00		200 at £10.00	
February		80	100 at £9.50	
March	140 at £4.20			240
April	100 at £3.80		100 at £10.50	
May		140	140 at £10.00	
June	80 at £4.50			100

At 30 June 2002, the net realisable value of each type of stock is:

type X	£1,750
type Y	£1,950
	£3,700

You are to:

•   Complete stores ledger records for products X and Y using (a) FIFO, (b) LIFO, (c) AVCO.
•   The business has decided to use the FIFO method. Show the amount at which its stocks should be valued on 30 June 2002 in order to comply with standard accountancy practice.

Note: where appropriate, work to two decimal places.

18.5* Leep Ltd. was incorporated in December 2003 to trade in a single product called 'Peel'. The company began trading on 1 January 2004. Purchases and sales for the five years to 31 December 2008 when the company discontinued 'Peel' in favour of a more profitable line, were as follows:

	PURCHASES		SALES	
	Units	*Price per unit*	*Units*	*Price per unit*
		£		£
2004	100	400	80	500
2005	100	450	80	550
2006	100	500	80	600
2007	100	550	80	650
2008	–	–	80	700

You are to:

(a)   Use the FIFO basis in order to calculate the gross profit of Leep Ltd for each of the five years to 31 December 2008.

(b)   Use the LIFO basis in order to calculate the gross profit for each of the five years to 31 December 2008.

(c)   Compare the results of your calculations and consider the relative merits of FIFO and LIFO as bases for valuing stock during a period of inflation.

18.6   Your friend, Gerry Gallagher, has recently set up in business selling plastic toys. The transactions for his first month of trading are:

1 April	Bought 500 toys at £1.50 each
3 April	Sold 250 toys at £2.50 each
7 April	Bought 1,000 toys at £1.40 each
14 April	Sold 600 toys at £2.60 each
20 April	Sold 300 toys at £2.70 each
27 April	Bought 1,000 toys at £1.60 each

At the end of April he asks you to help him to value his closing stock. He has heard that other firms in the toy trade value their stock on one of three methods: FIFO, LIFO or AVCO. He asks you to do the calculations for him, and also to work out his gross profit using each stock valuation method. He comments that he 'will use the stock valuation that gives the highest profit' because he wants to impress his bank manager.

You are to:

(a)   Calculate his closing stock valuation using each of the three methods.

(b)   Calculate the gross profit for the month, using each method.

(c)   Respond to his comment.

19 ACCOUNTING FOR LABOUR

CASE STUDY
Melita PLC – producing cans of orange drink

Cans of orange drink supplied to supermarkets are produced by a canning factory owned by Melita PLC. The price per can charged to the shops must be sufficient for the factory to make a profit. In the factory, therefore, the question is, *'How much does it cost to produce a can of orange?'*

The cost accountant of Melita PLC knows that the total production cost of a can of orange includes:

- direct materials
- direct labour
- direct expenses
- production overheads

The question at the moment facing the cost accountant is how much to charge for direct labour. The annual negotiations between management and factory workers over pay rates are currently taking place.

The cost of direct labour will depend on the level of wages of the factory workers and the way in which they are paid. For example, they could be paid by the hour or by the number of cans produced. All this will depend on the outcome of the negotiations.

In this chapter we will discuss aspects of accounting for labour, and look at three methods of calculation of employees' gross earnings.

learning objectives

When you have studied this chapter you will be able to:

- *calculate the gross earnings of employees using time rates, piecework rates and bonus systems*
- *comment on the advantages and disadvantages of the different methods of calculating earnings*
- *identify the part of the wages of direct workers normally treated as indirect costs: overtime premium and idle or non-productive time*

ACCOUNTING FOR LABOUR COSTS

We saw in Chapter 16 how costs may be classified as materials costs, labour costs and expenses. All businesses incur labour costs: the costs of wages and salaries of all their employees.

factors that affect labour costs

There are many factors that need to be considered by a business when deciding how much to pay employees. The starting point will always be the amount that is paid by other businesses in the area for similar grades of employees but, at the same time, the wider economic implications of supply and demand will affect wage rates.

The factors to consider include:
- wage rates paid by other local businesses
- comparisons with national average wage rates
- the national minimum wage rate imposed by government
- any government incentives to take on additional employees, such as young people or the long-term unemployed
- local employment conditions – high unemployment in the area will drive down wage rates; conversely, low unemployment, and especially a shortage of skilled labour, will increase wage rates
- for a new business, it might be prudent to choose to locate in an area of high unemployment – in addition to lower wage rates, there may be government incentives in the form of reduced rents and rates, training and other grants

Before taking on labour, a business must decide how to calculate gross pay for its employees. The methods of labour remuneration are looked at in detail on the next page.

Earnings are usually calculated according to time worked or work done, or a combination of both.

From time to time, employees will expect their pay rates to be reviewed and then, most probably, increased. Usually such a process takes place each year when wage rates are negotiated. In the negotiations, both the employer and the representatives of the employees will take into account such things as:
- the rise in the cost of living, for example, as measured by the Retail Price Index (RPI)
- the overall employment situation
- the profitability of the business – can it afford to pay increased wage rates?

While the employer will be seeking a package of measures that gives the business a more efficient workforce, employees will be looking for higher wages together with enhanced benefits.

LABOUR REMUNERATION

Direct labour cost is the wages paid to those who work on a production line, are involved in assembly, or are involved in the output of a service business.

The three main methods of direct labour remuneration are as follows:

time rate Time rate (sometimes known as a day rate) is where the employee is paid on the basis of time spent at work. Overtime may be paid for hours worked beyond a standard number of hours, or for work carried out on days which are not part of the working week, eg Saturdays or Sundays. Overtime is often paid at rates such as 'time-and-a-quarter', 'time-and-a-half', or even 'double-time'.

'Time-and-a-half', for example, means that 1.5 times the basic hourly rate is paid.

piecework rate The employee is paid an agreed sum for each task carried out or for each unit of output completed.

In some cases, employees may have a guaranteed minimum wage.

bonus system The employee is paid a time rate and then receives a bonus if output is better than expected. Such systems are often linked into standard costing – see Chapter 23 – where the quantity of work that can be achieved at a standard performance in an hour (a standard hour) is estimated; the bonus is then expressed as an agreed percentage of the standard hours saved.

Bonus systems base employees' earnings on a combination of time taken and work done.

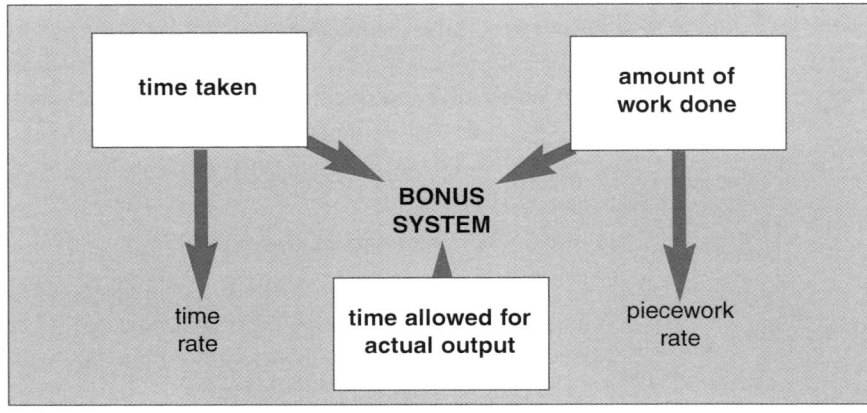

Most other employees, eg factory supervisors, sales staff, office staff, are usually paid on a weekly or monthly basis. Such wages and salaries – classed as indirect labour costs – may be increased by bonus payments; for example, a production bonus for factory supervisors, commissions for sales staff, a profit-sharing scheme for all employees.

There are many variations on the three methods outlined above and, indeed, changing patterns of employment create different remuneration methods from those that would have been the norm just a few years ago. For example, the contracting out of many business support services – such as cleaning, or security – means that the costing of such services by the provider may incorporate time rates and bonus systems whereas previously the employees would have been paid on a weekly or monthly basis.

In order to calculate gross wages, information about hours worked and/or work done must be recorded. The documents used include:

- **time sheets**, where employees record the hours they have worked

- **clock cards**, where employees 'clock in' at the start of work, and 'clock out' at the end – these are often computerised

- **piecework tickets**, completed by employees who work on a batch of output

- **job cards**, where each employee records the amount of time spent on each job

- **route cards** – which are used to follow a product through the production process – on which employees record the amount of time they spend working on the product

- **computer cards** – 'swipe' cards which link direct into the computerised payroll are increasingly being used by employers to record attendance

CASE STUDY

labour remuneration – Westmid Manufacturing

situation

Westmid Manufacturing Company has three factories in the West Midlands making parts for the car industry. Each factory was bought from the previous owners and, as a result, each has a different method for remunerating its direct labour workforce. The details of the method of remuneration in each factory, together with data on two employees from each factory, are as follows:

Walsall factory

In this factory, which is involved in heavy engineering, employees are paid on the basis of a time rate. Employees are required to 'clock in' and 'clock out' each day.

John Brown is a machine operator and his clock card for last week shows that he worked 39 hours; his hourly rate of pay is £8 per hour.

Stefan Wozniak is a skilled lathe operator and his clock card shows that he worked 42 hours; his hourly rate of pay is £10 per hour, with overtime at 'time-and-a-half' for hours worked beyond 40 hours.

Dudley factory

This factory operates a number of light engineering production lines making car components such as windscreen wiper blades, headlamp surrounds, and interior mirrors. The production line employees are all paid on a piecework basis; however, each employee receives a guaranteed time rate which is paid if the piecework earnings are less than the time rate. This may happen if, for example, there are machine breakdowns and the production line has to be halted.

Tracey Johnson works on the line making headlamp surrounds. For each one that passes through her part of the process, she is paid 30p; her guaranteed time rate is 37 hours each week at £6 per hour. Last week's production records show that she processed 870 units.

Pete Bronyah is on the line which makes interior mirrors. For his part of the process he receives £1.00 for each one, with a guaranteed time rate of 37 hours at £6 per hour. Last week there was a machine failure and he was only able to process 150 units.

Wolverhampton factory

In this factory a number of engineering production lines are operated. The direct labour force is paid on a time rate basis, but a bonus is paid if work is completed faster than the standard performance. Thus a standard time allowance is given for each task and, if it is completed in less time, a bonus is paid: the bonus in this factory is for the savings achieved, to be shared equally between employer and employee. Wages are, therefore, paid on the following basis: time rate + 50% of (time saved x time rate). If no bonus is due, then the time rate applies.

Martin Lee worked 38 hours last week; his time rate is £10 per hour. He is allowed a standard time of 30 minutes to carry out his work on each unit of production; last week he completed 71 units.

Sara King has a time rate of £11 per hour; last week she worked 40 hours. She is allowed a standard time of 15 minutes to carry out her work on each unit of production; last week she completed 184 units.

What were the gross earnings of each employee?

solution

Walsall factory

John Brown:	39 hours x £8.00 per hour	=	£312.00
Stefan Wozniak:	40 hours x £10.00 per hour = £400		
	2 hours x £15.00 per hour = £30	=	£430.00

Dudley factory

Tracey Johnson:	Piecework rate, 870 units x 30p per unit	=	£261.00
	Guaranteed time rate, 37 hours x £6.00 per hour	=	£222.00
	Therefore piecework rate of £261.00 is paid.		
Pete Bronyah:	Piecework rate, 150 units x £1.00 per unit	=	£150.00
	Guaranteed time rate, 37 hours x £6.00 per hour	=	£222.00
	Therefore guaranteed time rate of £222.00 is paid.		

Wolverhampton factory

Martin Lee:	Time rate, 38 hours x £10.00 per hour	=	£380.00
	Bonus: time allowed 71 units x 30 minutes each = 35 hours 30 minutes		
	Therefore no time saved, so no bonus payable.		
	Time rate of £380 paid.		
Sara King:	Time rate, 40 hours x £11.00 per hour	=	£440.00
	Bonus: time allowed 184 x 15 minutes each = 46 hours		
	Therefore time saved is 6 hours		
	Bonus is 50% of (6 hours x £11.00)	=	£33.00
	Therefore wages are £440.00 + £33.00	=	£473.00

The Case Study illustrates some of the direct labour remuneration methods in use, but it should be appreciated that there are many variations on these to be found.

DIRECT LABOUR REMUNERATION METHODS: ADVANTAGES & DISADVANTAGES

time rate

Time rate is often used where it is difficult to measure output, and where quality is more important than quantity. Variations include a high time rate, used to motivate employees where a higher standard of work is required.

advantages

- easy to understand and to calculate
- no requirement to establish time allowances and piecework rates
- the employee receives a regular wage, unaffected by fluctuations in output
- the employer pays a regular amount, making planning for cash flows easier
- can be used for all direct labour employees
- quality of the finished product does not suffer as a result of hurried work

disadvantages

- both efficient and inefficient employees receive the same wage
- no incentive is given to employees to work harder
- slower working will not affect basic wage, but may lead to overtime
- more supervisors are needed to ensure that output is maintained

piecework rate

Piecework rate is used where the quantity of output is important, and there is less emphasis on quality. Variations include:

- piecework with guaranteed time rate, which ensures that employees are paid if production is stopped through no fault of their own, eg machine breakdown, or shortage of materials
- differential piecework system, where a higher rate is paid for all output beyond a certain level, eg 50p per unit for the first 100 units each day, then 60p per unit thereafter; used to motivate employees to produce more than a basic level of output
- attendance allowances, paid to encourage employees on piecework to attend each day, thus ensuring that the production-line can be staffed and operated every working day

advantages

- payment of wages is linked directly to output
- more efficient workers earn more than those who are less efficient
- work is done more quickly and less time is wasted

disadvantages

- not suitable for all direct labour employees
- pay is reduced if there are production problems, eg machine breakdown or shortage of materials
- quality of the finished product may be low
- more inspectors may be needed
- control systems needed to check the amount produced by each worker
- more complex pay calculations
- may be difficulty in agreeing piecework rates with employees
- the employer cannot plan ahead for wages so easily, as they may be irregular amounts

bonus systems

Bonus systems are used to encourage employees to be more efficient in an environment where the work is not so repetitive. Variations include an accelerating premium bonus – which is an increased bonus paid for higher levels of output, and group bonuses paid to groups of employees who achieve increased output – the group could be as large as the entire workforce of a large company, or as small as a team of two or three people.

advantages

- wages linked to output, but minimum wage is guaranteed each week
- work is done more quickly and less time is wasted
- more efficient workers earn more
- a bonus system can often be applied to the entire workforce

disadvantages

- bonus is not paid if circumstances beyond employee's control prevent work, eg machine breakdown or shortage of materials
- quality of finished product may be low
- more inspectors may be needed and additional control procedures
- pay calculations may be more complex
- there may be difficulty in agreeing bonus rates with employees
- group bonus schemes may cause conflict within the group, if some workers consider that others are working too slowly

qualities of a good labour remuneration scheme

These include:

- reward should be related to effort and fair to all staff
- the scheme should be easy to manage and administer, and cheap and efficient to run
- it should be easy for employees to understand how pay is calculated

- payment should be made at regular intervals and soon after the event, eg employees on piecework should be paid in the week after the production has been achieved

- the principles of the scheme should remain constant, but there should be flexibility to deal with changes in production techniques

The three main methods of remuneration, together with some alternative systems are summarised in the table on the opposite page.

OVERTIME AND IDLE TIME

In Chapter 16 we divided labour costs between:

- **direct costs**, labour costs of production-line employees

- **indirect costs**, labour costs of other employees, such as supervisors, and office staff

Whilst this distinction appears clear enough, there are times when a proportion of the labour costs of production-line employees is classed as an indirect cost (rather than a direct cost) and is included amongst the overheads of the business. This is done if part of the cost of wages of the direct workers cannot be linked to specific work.

overtime payments

When production-line employees work overtime they are usually paid at a rate above the time rate. For example, overtime might be paid at 'time-and-a-half'; thus an employee with a time rate of £8 an hour will be paid overtime at £12 an hour. The additional £4 per hour is called **overtime premium**. For normal cost accounting purposes, any overtime worked is charged at £8 an hour to direct labour, and £4 an hour to indirect labour. In this way, the cost of overtime is spread across all output and is not charged solely to the output being worked on during the overtime period.

Basic pay for hours worked by direct workers is therefore a direct labour cost, whereas overtime premium is an indirect labour cost.

idle time

Idle time occurs when production is stopped through no fault of the production-line employees – for example, a machine breakdown, or a shortage of materials. Employees paid under a piecework or a bonus system will receive time rate for the period of the stoppage. Such wages costs are normally charged to overheads as indirect labour.

Similarly, time spent by direct workers on non-productive work would also usually be treated as an overhead.

methods of remuneration – a summary

	TIME RATE	PIECEWORK RATE	BONUS SYSTEM
situation	This system is used where it is difficult to measure the quantity of output and where quality is more important than volume of output.	This system is used where the work is repetitive and quantity of output is more important than quality.	This system is used to motivate employees, where the work is not so repetitive as in piecework but is measurable.
gross pay calculation	Hours worked x rate per hour This is easy to calculate and understand.	Number of items produced x rate per item This is easy to calculate and understand.	Basic pay + proportion of the time saved Time saved is the difference between time allowed and time taken to do a task. More complex to calculate and understand.
motivation	Pay is not linked to output and therefore there is no incentive to work hard. Slower workers may get paid overtime at higher rates.	Pay is related directly to output. There is a direct incentive to work as the amount of output determines the amount paid.	There is some incentive to work in order to earn a bonus as well as basic pay.
quality of output	There is no pressure on time and so quality should be maintained.	The fact that pay is related to output means it is important that quality standards of output are met.	The link between pay and output means that the quality of output needs to be checked.
control	It is important that the volume and quality of output is maintained.	It is important that the volume and quality of output is maintained.	It is important that the volume and quality of output is maintained.
administration	There is no need to set time allowances for output.	There is a need to set time allowances for work done and to keep these up to date.	There is a need to set time allowances for work done and to keep these up to date.
payment to employees	A regular amount is earned by the employee.	The amount earned by the employee varies with the output the employee produces.	There is some regular income but pay can be increased by additional effort.
ALTERNATIVE SYSTEMS	**High day rate** – employees are paid a higher than average rate per hour but agree to produce a given amount of output at a given quality.	**Attendance allowance** – to ensure employees turn up. **Guaranteed day rate** – to give employees a minimum payment. **Differential piecework** – to pay efficient workers more for output beyond a given level of output, ie an extra amount per unit.	**Group bonus schemes** – used where employees work as a group. This can include all workers, eg cleaners. This may create problems as the most efficient workers may be held back by the less efficient workers.

chapter summary

- Labour costs are incurred in every kind of business and are influenced by levels of wages and by the method of remuneration.

- Levels of wage rates paid to employees are influenced by a number of factors including the rates paid by similar local businesses, compulsory minimum rates and national averages.

- The main methods of remuneration are based either on time or amounts of work done or on a combination of both.

- Different methods of remuneration have advantages and disadvantages for the employer and the employee. The employer needs to control the cost of wages, but also to motivate employees to produce work of suitable quality within a reasonable time.

- A good remuneration scheme should be fair, easy to understand and efficiently managed.

- Certain wages costs of the direct workers may be classed as indirect labour costs: these include overtime premium and payment for idle or non-productive time.

key terms

time rate	a method of payment based on the time worked by an employee, giving the formula: gross earnings = hours worked x rate per hour
piecework rate	a method of payment based on the work done by an employee, giving the formula: gross earnings = units produced x rate per unit
bonus system	a method of payment in which an employee may earn a bonus by completing work in less time than the time allowed – usually the bonus is calculated as a share of the hours saved, multiplied by the rate per hour
standard hour	the quantity of work that can be achieved by one worker in one hour, at a standard level of performance
overtime premium	the additional pay above normal rates which is paid to employees working overtime, for example, the premium part of 'time-and-a-half' is the extra 'half' of the hourly rate
idle time	time during which work is stopped, due to reasons such as machine breakdown or shortage of materials

activities

Note: an asterisk (*) after an activity number means that an answer is provided in Appendix 1.

19.1* A manufacturing business pays its production workers on a time rate basis. A bonus is paid where production is completed faster than the standard hour output; the bonus is paid at half of the time rate for production time saved. How much will each of the following employees earn for the week?

Employee	Time rate	Hours worked	Standard hour output	Actual production
N Ball	£8.00 per hour	35	30 units	1,010 units
T Smith	£9.00 per hour	37	40 units	1,560 units
L Lewis	£10.00 per hour	40	20 units	855 units
M Wilson	£7.00 per hour	38	24 units	940 units

19.2 Harrison & Company is a manufacturing business. Currently it pays its production-line workers on a time rate basis. The employee representatives have recently approached the management of the company, with a view to seeking alternative methods of remuneration. Suggestions have been made that either a piecework system, or a time rate with a production bonus system would be more appropriate.

The office manager has asked you, as an accounts assistant, to draft a memorandum to the management giving advantages and disadvantages of:

- time rate
- piecework
- time rate, plus production bonus

as methods of remunerating production-line employees. In particular, you are asked to describe two circumstances under which the piecework basis would not be in the interests of employees.

19.3* (a) A company pays its production-line employees on a piecework basis, but with a guaranteed time rate. How much will each of the following employees earn during the week?

Employee	Time rate	Hours worked	Production	Piecework rate
L Fry	£10.00 per hour	40	1,200 units	30p per unit
R Williams	£8.00 per hour	37	450 units	70p per unit
P Grant	£9.50 per hour	36	725 units	50p per unit

(b) What are the problems a company might face in operating a piecework system of remuneration?

19.4   Print 'n Go is a print shop that specialises in printing headed notepaper for businesses. It employs two printers, Steve Kurtin and Pete Singh. Both are paid a basic rate per hour for a 35-hour week with two overtime rates: time-and-a-third for weekdays (rate 1), and time-and-a-half for week-ends (rate 2). In addition, a production bonus is paid of 25p per 1,000 copies printed.

Details for last week are as follows:

	Steve Kurtin	Pete Singh
Basic rate per hour	£5.50	£6.50
Total hours worked	39	42
Overtime: rate 1	4	3
rate 2	–	4
Number of copies printed	45,000	57,000

You are to:

(a)   calculate the gross wages earned by each employee for last week

(b)   calculate the piecework rate per 1,000 copies printed that would be equal to the gross wages earned by Steve Kurtin for the week, assuming the same output level of 45,000 copies

19.5   Wyvern Fabrication Company has two departments – moulding and finishing. Data relating to labour for a four-week period is given on the labour cost card shown below.

The company uses a bonus scheme whereby employees receive 50 per cent of the standard hours saved in each department, paid at the actual labour rate per hour. This is not included in the actual wages cost, which shows actual hours multiplied by the actual wage rate.

LABOUR COST CARD		
for the four weeks ended 26 February 2002		
	MOULDING	FINISHING
Actual wages cost (£)	31,160	36,450
Standard hours	4,000	5,000
Actual hours	4,100	4,500
Standard hours saved		
Bonus (£)		
Total labour cost (£)		

You are to calculate the total labour cost for each department.

19.6* The direct workers in Haven Ltd are paid a basic wage of £6.20 per hour. For time worked above 40 hours per week, they receive overtime pay at time-and-a-half. For two particular weeks, we have the following information for a team of 10 direct workers:

Week 1: Total hours worked = 450 hours, including 50 hours of overtime.

Week 2: Total hours worked = 400 hours, including 20 hours of non-production work, clearing up and re-organising a section of the factory during a machine breakdown.

Required: For each of the two given weeks:

(a) Calculate the gross earnings in total for the team of 10 employees.

(b) State how much of the gross earnings calculated in (a) would normally be treated as an indirect labour cost.

20 OVERHEADS

CASE STUDY
CoolHeads – a hairdressing business

CoolHeads is a new hairdressing business, being set up by Nathan and Morgan in a rented shop.

Nathan and Morgan are preparing their price list. They must set the prices sufficiently high to cover all their costs and to give them a profit.

They have details of the costs of all the materials they need (shampoos, colourings and so on) from a specialist supplier. Nathan and Morgan have decided the rate to charge to the business for their own work and they do not intend to employ anyone else for the time being.

But there are other costs which they will also incur – their overheads – and they are not so sure how they will work these into their pricing structure. Nathan asks:

'What about the shop rent and the business rates we have to pay? What about the electricity, the insurance, the telephone bill and all the advertising we have to do? How are we going to cover these costs?'

'How much will it cost us in total to deal with each customer?'

'How do we make sure that we are going to make a profit?'

In this chapter we will examine how 'overhead' costs are calculated for a product or service and are added to the direct costs incurred. We will also see how these costs relate to the price charged for the product or service.

learning objectives

When you have studied this chapter you will be able to:

- appreciate the importance of collecting overhead costs together in cost centres
- understand how some overheads can be allocated to particular cost centres
- calculate the apportionment of overheads to cost centres
- re-apportion the total overheads from service cost centres to production cost centres
- calculate overhead absorption rates for production cost centres based on units, direct labour hours or machine hours
- apply overhead absorption rates to actual work done
- calculate over/under-absorption of overheads

OVERHEADS

In Chapter 16 'Cost Accounting' we saw that costs could be classified as follows:

	DIRECT MATERIALS		INDIRECT MATERIALS
+	DIRECT LABOUR	+	INDIRECT LABOUR
+	DIRECT EXPENSES	+	INDIRECT EXPENSES
=	TOTAL DIRECT COSTS (PRIME COST)	=	TOTAL OVERHEADS

Direct costs can be identified directly with each unit of output, but indirect costs (overheads) cannot be identified directly with each unit of output.

Overheads do not relate to particular units of output but must, instead, be shared amongst all the cost units (units of output to which costs can be charged) to which they relate. For example, the cost of the factory rent must be included in the cost of the firm's output.

The important point to remember is that all the overheads of a business, together with the direct costs (materials, labour and expenses) must be covered by money flowing in from the firm's output – the sales of products or services.

CASE STUDY
CoolHeads – continued

The Case Study of the hairdressers CoolHeads was introduced on the opposite page. For pricing purposes, Nathan and Morgan need to include overheads in the cost of each item on their list.

In a small business like this, the whole business could be a single cost centre. All the overheads could be allowed for in a single rate to charge for a hair cut.

Suppose Nathan and Morgan estimate that their total overheads for the first year of trading will be £27,000. They expect to be working on hairstyling for 1,500 hours each during the year, ie a total of 3,000 hours between them.

Therefore, they could decide in advance that each hour of their work should be charged £27,000 ÷ 3,000 = £9 for overheads. A job that takes two hours to complete would then be charged 2 x £9 = £18 for overheads.

Notice that in a service business such as hairdressing, direct materials costs are likely to be relatively small in comparison with the cost of direct labour and overheads. It is essential for Nathan and Morgan to consider the cost of overheads when they are setting their prices and the hourly rate is one possible way of doing this. This is called an 'overhead absorption rate' and we will look in more detail at this idea later in this chapter (see page 412).

In larger organisations, overheads are usually classified by function under headings such as:

- **factory** or **production**, eg factory rent and rates, indirect factory labour, indirect factory materials, heating and lighting of factory

- **selling and distribution**, eg salaries of sales staff, vehicle costs, delivery costs

- **administration**, eg office rent and rates, office salaries, heating and lighting of office, indirect office materials

- **finance**, eg bank interest

Each of these functions or sections of the business is likely to be what is known as a **cost centre**, a term which was defined in Chapter 16 as follows:

Cost centres are sections of a business to which costs can be charged.

In order to deal with the overheads we need to know how the whole organisation is split into cost centres. This will depend on the size of the business and the way in which the work is organised.

COLLECTING OVERHEADS IN COST CENTRES

allocation of overheads

Some overheads belong entirely to one particular cost centre, for example:

- the salary of a supervisor who works in only one cost centre

- the rent of a separate building in which there is only one cost centre

- the cost of indirect materials that have been issued to one particular cost centre

Overheads like these can therefore be allocated to the cost centre to which they belong.

Allocation of overheads is the charging to a particular cost centre of overheads that are incurred entirely by that cost centre.

apportionment of overheads

Overheads that cannot be allocated to a particular cost centre have to be shared or **apportioned** between two or more cost centres.

Apportionment of overheads is the sharing of overheads over a number of cost centres to which they relate. Each cost centre is charged with a proportion of the overhead cost.

For example, a department which is a cost centre within a factory will be charged a proportion of the factory rent and rates. Another example is where a supervisor works within two departments, both of which are separate cost centres: the indirect labour cost of employing the supervisor is shared between the two cost centres.

With apportionment, a suitable **basis** must be found to apportion overheads between cost centres; the basis selected should be related to the type of cost. Different methods might be used for each overhead. For example:

OVERHEAD	BASIS OF APPORTIONMENT
rent, rates	floor area (or volume of space) of cost centres
heating, lighting	floor area (or volume of space) of cost centres
buildings insurance	floor area (or volume of space) of cost centres
buildings depreciation	floor area (or volume of space) of cost centres
machinery insurance	cost or net book value of machinery and equipment
canteen	number of employees in each cost centre
supervisory costs	number of employees in each cost centre, or labour hours worked by supervisors in each cost centre

It must be stressed that apportionment is used for those overheads that cannot be allocated to a particular cost centre. For example, if a college's Business Studies Department occupies a building in another part of town from the main college building, the rates for the building can clearly be allocated to the Business Studies cost centre. By contrast, the rates for the main college building must be **apportioned** amongst the cost centres on the main campus.

apportionment and ratios

It is important to understand the method of apportionment of overheads using ratios. For example, overheads relating to buildings are often shared in the ratio of the floor area used by the cost centres.

Now read through the Worked Example and the Case Study which follow.

WORKED EXAMPLE
apportionment using ratios

A business has four cost centres: two production departments, A and B, and two non-production cost centres, stores and maintenance. The total rent per year for the business premises is £12,000. This is to be apportioned on the basis of floor area, given as:

	Production Dept A	Production Dept B	Stores	Maintenance
Floor area (square metres)	400	550	350	200

Step 1

Calculate the total floor area: 400 + 550 + 350 + 200 = 1,500 square metres

Step 2

Divide the total rent by the total floor area: £12,000 ÷ 1,500 = £8

This gives a rate of £8 per square metre.

Step 3

Multiply the floor area in each cost centre by the rate per square metre. This gives the share of rent for each cost centre. For example, in Production Department A, the share of rent is 400 x £8 = £3,200. The results are shown in the table:

	Production Dept A	Production Dept B	Stores	Maintenance
Floor area (square metres)	400	550	350	200
Rent apportioned	£3,200	£4,400	£2,800	£1,600

Step 4

Check that the apportioned amounts agree with the total rent:

£3,200 + £4,400 + £ 2,800 + £1,600 = £12,000.

CASE STUDY

Pilot Engineering Ltd – overhead allocation & apportionment

situation

Pilot Engineering Limited, which makes car engine components, uses some of the latest laser equipment . in one department, while another section of the business continues to use traditional machinery. Details of the factory are as follows:

Department X is a 'hi-tech' machine shop equipped with laser-controlled machinery which cost £80,000. This department has 400 square metres of floor area. There are three machine operators: the supervisor spends one-third of the time in this department.

Department Y is a 'low-tech' part of the factory equipped with machinery which cost £20,000. The floor area is 600 square metres. There are two workers who spend all their time in this department: the supervisor spends two-thirds of the time in this department.

The overheads to be allocated or apportioned are as follows:

1	Factory rates	£12,000
2	Wages of the supervisor	£21,000
3	Factory heating and lighting	£2,500
4	Depreciation of machinery	£20,000
5	Buildings insurance	£2,000
6	Insurance of machinery	£1,500
7	Specialist materials for the laser equipment	£2,500

How should each of these be allocated or apportioned to each department?

solution

The recommendations are:

1   Factory rates – apportioned on the basis of floor area.

2   Supervisor's wages – apportioned on the basis of time spent, ie one-third to Department X, and two-thirds to Department Y. If the time spent was not known, an alternative basis could be established, based on the number of employees.

3   Factory heating and lighting – apportioned on the basis of floor area.

4   Depreciation of machinery – apportioned on the basis of machine value.

5   Buildings insurance – apportioned on the basis of floor area.

6   Insurance of machinery – apportioned on the basis of machine value.

7   Specialist materials for the laser equipment – allocated to Department X because this cost belongs entirely to Department X.

It is important to note that there are no fixed rules for the apportionment of overheads – the only proviso is that a fair proportion of the overhead is charged to each department which has some responsibility for the cost being incurred.

The apportionment of overheads for Pilot Engineering Limited is as follows:
(sample workings are shown below the table)

overhead	basis of apportionment	total £	dept X £	dept Y £
Factory rates	Floor area	12,000	4,800	7,200
Wages of supervisor	Time spent	21,000	7,000	14,000
Heating and lighting	Floor area	2,500	1,000	1,500
Dep'n of machinery	Machine value	20,000	16,000	4,000
Buildings insurance	Floor area	2,000	800	1,200
Machinery insurance	Machine value	1,500	1,200	300
Specialist materials	Allocation	2,500	2,500	–
		61,500	33,300	28,200

workings

For example, the floor areas of the two departments are:

Dept X	400	square metres
Dept Y	600	square metres
Total	1,000	square metres

Factory Rates are apportioned as follows:

$$\frac{£12,000}{1,000} = £12 \text{ per square metre}$$

Dept X Rates:	£12 x 400 =	£4,800
Dept Y Rates	£12 x 600 =	£7,200
Total (check)		£12,000

Note that overhead apportionment is often, in practice, calculated using a computer spreadsheet.

SERVICE DEPARTMENTS

Many businesses have departments which provide services within the business; for example, maintenance, transport, stores or stationery. Each service department is likely to be a cost centre, to which a proportion of overheads is charged. As service departments do not themselves have any cost units to which their overheads may be charged, the costs of each service department must be re-apportioned to the production departments (which do have cost units to which overheads can be charged). A suitable basis of re-allocation must be used, for example:

- the overheads of a maintenance department might be re-apportioned to production departments on the basis of value of machinery or equipment, or on the basis of time spent in each production department

- the overheads of a stores or stationery department could be re-apportioned on the basis of value of goods issued to production departments

- the overheads of a subsidised canteen could be re-apportioned on the basis of the number of employees

Re-apportionment of service department overheads is considered in the next section.

RE-APPORTIONMENT OF SERVICE DEPARTMENT OVERHEADS

The overheads of service departments are charged to production cost centres using different techniques depending on the complexity of the business:

- **direct apportionment** is used where service departments provide services to production departments only

- the **step-down method** is used where service departments provide services to production departments and to some other service departments

- the **reciprocal method** is used where service departments provide services to production departments and to all other service departments

To illustrate this, we will apply these techniques to a business with two production departments, A and B, and two service departments, stores and maintenance. After allocation and apportionment of production overheads, the totals are:

	total	production dept A	production dept B	stores	maintenance
	£	£	£	£	£
Overheads	20,400	10,000	5,000	2,400	3,000

direct apportionment

Here the service departments do not provide services to one another. Their costs are directly apportioned to production departments using a suitable basis. In the example above:

■ stores overheads are re-apportioned on the basis of the number of stores requisitions – department A has made 150 requisitions; department B has made 50

■ maintenance overheads are re-apportioned on the value of machinery – department A has machinery with a net book value of £20,000, department B's machinery has a value of £10,000

Using direct apportionment, the overheads of the service departments are re-apportioned as shown in the table below. The method of calculation using ratios is the same as we used for apportionment.

Notice that the total is taken out of the service cost centre column when it is shared between the production cost centres.

	total	production dept A	production dept B	stores	maintenance
	£	£	£	£	£
Overheads	20,400	10,000	5,000	2,400	3,000
Stores	–	1,800	600	(2,400)	–
Maintenance	–	2,000	1,000	–	(3,000)
	20,400	13,800	6,600	–	–

Thus all the overheads have now been charged to the production departments where they can be 'absorbed' into the cost units which form the output of each department. We will see how the absorption is carried out later in this chapter.

step-down method

This is used where, as well as to production departments, one service department provides services to another. Using the example, the stores department deals with requisitions from the maintenance department, but no maintenance work is carried out in the stores department. Under the step-down method we re-apportion firstly the overheads of the stores department (because it does not receive any services from the maintenance department), and secondly the overheads of the maintenance department:

- stores requisitions – department A, 150; department B, 50; maintenance, 50

- value of machinery – department A, £20,000; department B, £10,000

The re-apportionment of the production overheads of the service departments, using the step-down method, is as follows:

	total	production dept A	production dept B	stores	maintenance
	£	£	£	£	£
Overheads	20,400	10,000	5,000	2,400	3,000
Stores	–	1,440	480	(2,400)	480
				–	*3,480
Maintenance	–	2,320	1,160	–	(3,480)
	20,400	13,760	6,640	–	–

* Note that a new total is calculated for the maintenance department before it is re-apportioned. £480 from stores is added to the original £3,000 overheads in the maintenance department.

All the overheads have now been charged to the production departments.

reciprocal method

This is used where service departments provide services to all other departments, including other service departments. Thus, in the example, the stores department deals with requisitions from the maintenance department, and there is a maintenance service provided to stores. The apportionment of production overheads to production departments is carried out by repeating the re-apportionment of service department overheads:

- stores requisitions – department A, 150; department B, 50; maintenance, 50

- value of machinery – department A, £20,000; department B, £10,000; stores, £10,000

With this method, some rounding of money amounts is necessary. Once the repeated re-apportionment brings service department overheads to small amounts, it is best to make one final re-apportionment to production departments only (as has been done here with stores).

	total	production dept A	production dept B	stores	maintenance
	£	£	£	£	£
Overheads	20,400	10,000	5,000	2,400	3,000
Stores	–	1,440	480	(2,400)	480
				–	3,480
Maintenance	–	1,740	870	870	(3,480)
Stores	–	522	174	(870)	174
Maintenance	–	87	44	43	(174)
Stores	–	32	11	(43)	–
	20,400	13,821	6,579	–	–

All the overheads have now been charged to the production departments:

	£
department A	13,821
department B	6,579
	20,400

OVERHEAD ABSORPTION

Once overheads have been allocated or apportioned to production cost centres, the final step is to ensure that the overheads are charged to cost units. In the language of cost accounting this is known as 'absorption' or 'recovery', ie the cost of overheads is charged to the cost units which pass through that particular production department.

We saw in the Case Study CoolHeads at the beginning of this chapter, how overheads could be allowed for when deciding on selling prices.

Similarly, if you take a car to be repaired at a garage, the bill may be presented as follows:

Parts	£70.00
Labour: 3 hours at £30 per hour	£90.00
Total	£160.00

Within this bill are the three main elements of cost: materials (parts), labour and overheads. The last two are combined as labour – the garage mechanic is not paid £30 per hour; instead the labour rate might be £10 per hour, with the rest, ie £20 per hour, being a contribution towards the overheads and profit of the garage. Other examples are accountants and solicitors, who charge a 'rate per hour', part of which is used to contribute to the cost of overheads and profit.

To be profitable, a business must ensure that its selling prices more than cover all its costs:

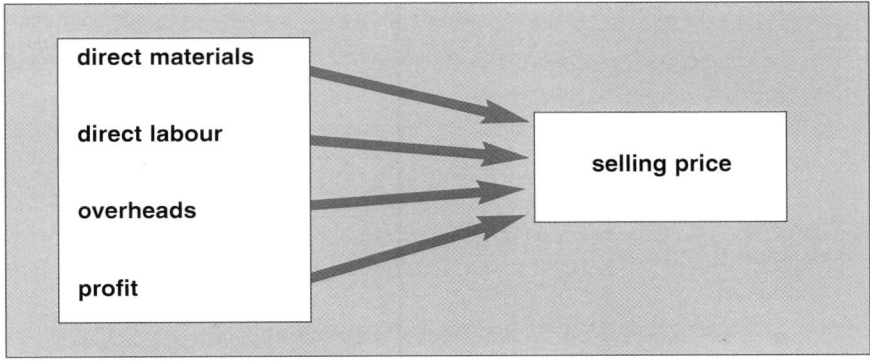

calculating overhead absorption rates

In order to absorb the overheads of a department, there are two steps to be followed:

1 calculation of the overhead absorption rate (OAR)

2 application of this rate to actual work done

The overhead absorption rate is calculated using estimated or budgeted figures as follows, for a given time period:

$$OAR = \frac{\textit{total budgeted cost centre overheads}}{\textit{total planned work in the cost centre}}$$

The amount of work must be measured in a suitable way, usually:

▪ units of output, or

▪ direct labour hours, or

▪ machine hours

Each of these methods is illustrated below.

units of output method of calculation

Using this method, production overhead is absorbed on the basis of each unit of output.

1 Calculation of the overhead absorption rate, using budgeted (expected) figures:

$$\frac{\textit{total cost centre overheads}}{\textit{total cost units}} = \textit{cost per unit}$$

2 Application of the rate:

cost units x overhead absorption rate = overhead absorbed

> **Example**
>
> Department A total budgeted cost centre overheads for year   £100,000
>
> expected total output for year   20,000 units
>
> output in March   1,500 units
>
> 1 Overhead absorption rate:
>
> $$\frac{£100,000}{20,000 \text{ units}} = £5 \text{ per unit}$$
>
> 2 Application of the rate:
>
> 1,500 units x £5 = £7,500 of overhead absorbed in March

direct labour hour method of calculation

With this method, production overhead is absorbed on the basis of the number of direct labour hours worked.

1 Calculation of the overhead absorption rate, using budgeted (expected) figures:

$$\frac{\textit{total cost centre overheads}}{\textit{total direct labour hours (in cost centre)}} = \textit{cost per direct labour hour}$$

2 Application of the rate:

direct labour hours worked x overhead absorption rate

= overhead absorbed

> *Example*
>
> | Department B | total budgeted cost centre overheads for year | £40,000 |
> |---|---|---|
> | | expected direct labour hours for year | 5,000 |
> | | actual direct labour hours in March | 450 |
>
> 1 Overhead absorption rate:
>
> $$\frac{£40,000}{5,000 \text{ hours}} = £8 \text{ per direct labour hour}$$
>
> 2 Application of the rate:
>
> 450 hours x £8 = £3,600 of overhead absorbed in March

machine hour method of calculation

Here the production overhead is absorbed on the basis of machine hours.

1 Calculation of the overhead absorption rate, using budgeted (expected) figures:

$$\frac{total\ cost\ centre\ overheads}{total\ machine\ hours\ (in\ cost\ centre)} = cost\ per\ machine\ hour$$

2 Application of the rate:

machine hours worked x overhead absorption rate

= overhead absorbed

> *Example*
>
> | Department C | total budgeted cost centre overheads for year | £216,000 |
> |---|---|---|
> | | expected machine hours for year | 36,000 |
> | | actual machine hours in March | 3,500 |
>
> 1 Overhead absorption rate:
>
> $$\frac{£216,000}{36,000 \text{ hours}} = £6 \text{ per machine hour}$$
>
> 2 Application of the rate:
>
> 3,500 hours x £6 = £21,000 of overhead absorbed in March

which method to use?

Only one overhead absorption rate will be used in a particular department, and the method selected must relate to the reason why the costs are incurred. For example, a cost centre which is machine based, where most of the overheads incurred relate to machinery, will use a machine hour basis.

Where units of production are identical, eg in a factory, the units of output method is appropriate. However, it would be entirely unsuitable where different types and sizes of product pass through the same department, because each unit would be charged the same rate.

The direct labour hour method is a very popular method (eg the garage mentioned earlier) because overheads are absorbed on a time basis. Thus the cost unit that requires twice the direct labour of another cost unit will be charged twice the overhead. However this method will be inappropriate where some units are worked on by hand while others quickly pass through a machinery process and require little direct labour time.

A machine hour rate is particularly appropriate where expensive machinery is used in the department. However, it would be unsuitable where not all products pass through the machine but some are worked on by hand: in the latter case, no overheads would be charged to the cost units.

It is important to select the best method of overhead absorption for the particular business, otherwise wrong decisions will be made on the basis of the costing information.

In this chapter, we have calculated overhead absorption rates based on:

■ units of output

■ direct labour hours

■ machine hours

There are other possible bases which could be used. For example, overheads could be charged as a percentage of:

■ direct material cost

■ direct labour cost

■ prime cost

The principles are the same for any method of absorption:

■ the rate to use is calculated in advance using estimates

■ the rate is applied to the actual work done

For example, if the estimates showed that it would be necessary to add 20% on to prime cost for overheads, then a job having a prime cost of £6,000 would absorb £6,000 x 20% = £1,200 of overheads.

OVER OR UNDER-ABSORPTION OF OVERHEADS

We saw on page 403 that Nathan and Morgan estimated that their total overheads for the first year of trading would be £27,000. They expected to be working on hairstyling for 1,500 hours each during the year, ie a total of 3,000 hours between them.

Therefore, they could have decided in advance that each hour of their work should be charged £27,000/3,000 = £9 for overheads. A job taking two hours to complete would then be charged 2 x £9 = £18 for overheads. This is a simple example of the absorption of overheads using a pre-determined rate. (The word 'recovery' is sometimes used instead of 'absorption' – it means the same.)

At the end of CoolHeads' first year, it is most unlikely that Nathan and Morgan will find that everything went exactly according to plan. They may have spent more or less on the overheads than £27,000. They may have worked on styling for more or less than 3,000 hours in total.

They will find, therefore, that the amount of overheads they have absorbed into the cost of their actual work during the year is not the same as the amount they have spent. If the amount absorbed is the greater, the difference is called 'over-absorption' or 'over-recovery' of overheads. If the amount absorbed is less than the amount spent, the difference is called 'under-absorption' or 'under-recovery'.

Over-absorption or under-absorption (recovery) is the difference between the total amount of overheads absorbed (recovered) in a given period and the total amount spent on overheads.

The following worked example shows the calculation when the overhead absorption rate is based on units of output.

Example

Department D

overhead absorption rate (based on units of output)	£6.00 per unit
actual output in year	6,300 units
actual overheads for year	£36,000

- actual overheads for the department are £36,000

- actual overhead absorbed: 6,300 units x £6.00 per unit = £37,800

- over-absorption of overhead: £37,800 – £36,000 = £1,800

At the end of the financial year, an adjustment is made in the accounts for the total over-absorbed or under-absorbed overhead.

Where there is over-absorption of overheads, the amount is

- debited to production overheads account
- credited to profit and loss account

Thus over-absorption of overheads seems, on first impressions, to be a 'bonus' for a business – profits will be higher; however, it should be remembered that the overhead rate may have been set too high. As a consequence, sales might have been lost because the selling price has been too high.

Under-absorption of overheads is

- credited to production overheads account
- debited to profit and loss account

Here the amount of under-absorbed overheads adds to the total cost of production, and so reduces profits.

chapter summary

- Direct costs can be charged directly to cost units.

- Indirect costs (overheads) cannot be charged to cost units immediately.

- Overheads are:
    - allocated to a specific cost centre, if they belong entirely to that cost centre
    - apportioned between cost centres, if they are shared

- Apportionment is done on a suitable basis, using ratios of floor area, numbers of employees and so on.

- The total overheads allocated and apportioned to the service cost centres are then re-apportioned to the production cost centres.

- After re-apportionment of the service cost centre overheads, the total overheads in each production cost centre can be calculated.

- All the above steps can be carried out using expected or budgeted overhead amounts.

- Overhead absorption rates are calculated using the total expected or budgeted overheads in each cost centre.

- An overhead absorption rate is calculated as follows:

$$\textit{overhead absorption rate} \quad = \quad \frac{\textit{total budgeted cost centre overheads}}{\textit{total planned work in cost centre}}$$

where the planned amount of work may be measured in terms of product units, direct labour hours or machine hours.

- Overhead absorption rates are applied to the actual work carried out. A direct labour hour absorption rate is applied as follows, for example:

Direct labour hours worked x overhead absorption rate = overhead absorbed

- At the end of a given period, the amount of overhead absorbed may differ from the amount actually spent on the overheads. The difference is either an over-absorption (when the amount absorbed is greater than the amount spent) or an under-absorption (when the amount absorbed is less than the amount spent).

- An adjustment is made for the total over-absorption or under-absorption of overheads for a period in the profit and loss account for the period.

key terms

overheads	indirect costs, made up of
	indirect materials + indirect labour + indirect expenses
cost centres	sections of a business to which costs can be charged
allocation of overheads	the charging to a particular cost centre of overheads that are incurred entirely by that cost centre
apportionment of overheads	the sharing of overheads over a number of cost centres to which they relate – each cost centre is charged with a proportion of the overhead cost
service department	a non-production cost centre that provides services to other cost centres in the business
re-apportionment of service department overheads	the sharing of the total overheads from a service department, a proportion being charged to each cost centre it serves; after all re-apportionment has been carried out, the overheads will be charged to production cost centres only
absorption (recovery) of overheads	the charging of overheads to cost units (units of output)
overhead absorption rate (OAR)	the rate used to charge overheads to cost units – calculated in advance, as:
	budgeted total overhead ÷ planned amount of work
basis of absorption	the measurement of work used to calculate the overhead absorption rate, for example: • units of output • direct labour hours • machine hours
over- or under-absorption (recovery)	the difference between the total amount of overheads absorbed (recovered) in a given period and the total amount spent on overheads

activities

20.1* Distinguish between:
- allocation of overheads
- apportionment of overheads

20.2 Wyvern Fabrication Company has two production departments – moulding and finishing.

The company charges overheads on the basis of machine hours and the following overhead analysis information is available to you (note that service department overheads have already been apportioned to production departments):

OVERHEAD ANALYSIS SHEET		
	MOULDING	FINISHING
Budgeted total overheads (£)	9,338	3,298
Budgeted machine hours	1,450	680
Budgeted overhead absorption rate (£)		

Details of a particular job of work are as follows:

JOB OVERHEAD ANALYSIS SHEET		
	MOULDING	FINISHING
Job machine hours	412	154
Budgeted overhead absorption rate (£)		
Overhead absorbed by job (£)		

You are to:

(a) Calculate the overhead absorption rate for each of the two departments and complete the overhead analysis sheet.

(b) Calculate the production overhead absorbed by the job and complete the job overhead analysis sheet.

(c) Suggest two other overhead absorption rates that the company might use and comment on the circumstances that would make them appropriate.

20.3* ABC Limited is a manufacturing business with three cost centres: Departments A, B and C. The following are the expected factory overheads for the forthcoming year:

Rent and rates	£7,210
Depreciation of machinery	£10,800
Supervisor's salary	£12,750
Insurance of machinery	£750

Departmental information is:

	Dept A	Dept B	Dept C
Floor area (sq m)	300	150	250
Value of machinery	£25,000	£15,000	£10,000
Number of production-line employees	8	4	3

You are to:

(a)   Apportion the overheads to the cost centres, stating the basis of apportionment.

(b)   Calculate the overhead absorption rate (to two decimal places) of each department, based on direct labour hours. Note that the factory works a 37 hour week for 48 weeks in a year.

20.4 Wye Engineering Limited offers specialist engineering services to the car industry. It has two production departments – machining and finishing – and a service department which maintains the machinery of both departments. Expected production overheads for the forthcoming year are:

	£
Rent and rates	5,520
Buildings insurance	1,320
Insurance of machinery	1,650
Lighting and heating	3,720
Depreciation of machinery	11,000
Supervisory salaries	30,000
Maintenance department salary	16,000
Factory cleaning	4,800

The following information is available:

	Machining	Finishing	Maintenance
Floor area (square metres)	300	200	100
Number of employees	6	3	1
Value of machinery	£40,000	£15,000	–

The factory works a 35 hour week for 47 weeks each year.

You are to:

(a)   Prepare an analysis of production overheads showing the basis of allocation and apportionment to the three departments of the business.

(b)   Re-apportion the service department overheads to production departments on the basis of value of machinery.

(c)   Calculate an overhead absorption rate based on direct labour hours for each of the two production departments.

(d)   Discuss alternative overhead absorption rates that the company could use.

20.5*   Mercia Tutorial College has two teaching departments – business studies and general studies – and two service departments – administration and technical support. The overheads of each department are as follows:

	£
• business studies	40,000
• general studies	20,000
• administration	9,600
• technical support	12,000

The basis for re-apportioning the overheads of the service departments is:

- technical support, on the value of equipment in each department – business studies, £50,000; general studies, £25,000; administration, £25,000

- administration, on the number of students in the teaching departments – business studies, 500; general studies, 250

You are to use the step-down method to re-apportion the two service department overheads to the two teaching departments.

20.6   Cradley Cider Company has two production departments – Triple X and Scrumpy – and two service departments – stores and maintenance. The overheads of each department are as follows:

	£
Triple X	20,000
Scrumpy	10,000
Stores	5,000
Maintenance	6,000

The basis for re-apportioning the overheads of the service departments is:

- stores, on the number of requisitions – Triple X, 120; Scrumpy, 40; maintenance, 40

- maintenance, on the value of equipment in each department – Triple X, £25,000; Scrumpy, £20,000; stores, £5,000

You are to use the reciprocal method to re-apportion the two service department overheads to the two production departments.

20.7 Rossiter and Rossiter is a firm of chartered accountants, with two partners. Overhead costs for next year are estimated to be:

	£
Office rent	10,000
Secretarial salaries	30,000
Rates	4,800
Heating and lighting	2,400
Stationery	2,000
Postage and telephone	5,100
Car expenses	5,600

The two partners plan to work for 47 weeks next year. They will each be in the office for 40 hours per week, but will be working on behalf of their clients for 35 hours per week.

(a)   What is the overhead absorption rate per partner hour?

(b)   If each partner wishes to earn a salary of £30,000 per year, what is the combined hourly rate per partner, which includes overheads and their salaries?

(c)   If both partners actually work on their clients' behalf for 37 hours per week, what will be the total over-absorption of overheads for the year?

20.8 A friend of yours is about to start in business making garden seats. She plans to make two different qualities – 'Standard' and 'De Luxe'. Costs per unit for direct materials and labour are expected to be:

	Standard	De Luxe
	£	£
Direct materials	12.50	20.00
Direct labour:		
3 hours at £8.00 per hour	24.00	–
3.5 hours at £10.00 per hour	–	35.00
	36.50	55.00
Machine hours	1	2.5

Production overheads are expected to be £1,000 per month.

Production is expected to be 80 'Standard' seats and 40 'De Luxe' seats per month.

(a)   Suggest three different methods by which overheads can be absorbed.

(b)   Calculate the production cost of each of the two qualities of garden seats using the three different methods of overhead absorption.

(c)   Compare the results of your calculations and suggest to your friend the most appropriate method of overhead absorption for this business.

21 METHODS OF COSTING

CASE STUDY
Racers Ltd – manufacturing racing bikes

Otto Kranz, a former cycling champion, is setting up a company to manufacture racing bikes. The business is to be called Racers Ltd.

Otto is aware that he has two very distinct markets into which to sell his cycles:

■ Some of his cycles will be produced to the specific requirements of individual cyclists for international level competition racing – this is the area which really interests Otto. He can charge a premium price for these custom-built designs.

■ He also has to sell to the mass market for quality racing bikes which will be made in batches of 20 to standard designs. These will sold in specialist shops and are cheaper, both to manufacture and in terms of selling price.

But Otto is confused about how he is going to cost out these two different methods of production – the 'one-off' and the standard design. He says:

'I can record the costs of the direct materials and labour hours used to make the 'one-off' cycle and the batches of 20. But what about the overheads? Will I need more than one costing system here?'

In this chapter we consider the different methods of costing that may be applied in different situations, depending on the kind of work being done. In the case of Racers Ltd, two methods are likely to be adopted by Otto: job costing (for the one-off designs) and batch costing (for the mass-market bikes).

learning objectives

When you have studied this chapter you will be able to:

■ *understand the main principles relating to each method of costing*

■ *describe the methods of costing used for separate jobs: job costing, batch costing and contract costing*

■ *describe the methods of costing used when the work is continuous: service costing and process costing*

■ *identify the method of costing that would be used in various types of business*

■ *calculate job or batch costs and selling prices from given data*

■ *calculate average costs per cost unit in service costing and in process costing*

COSTING METHODS FOR SPECIFIC ORDERS

who decides the method?

One of the main aims of cost and management accounting is to establish the cost of one **cost unit** of work, whatever kind of work it is. The cost unit must be a suitable way of measuring the work of the organisation. In management accounting it is the people working inside the business who choose the method to suit the type of work being done.

types of specific order costing

The 'one-off' racing cycles in the Case Study Racers Ltd above illustrate one kind of work, where customers order what they want, before it is made. The work consists of specific orders. The customer agrees to buy the product before the work is done.

Many service businesses also carry out work to customers' requirements, for example, accountants and solicitors. Each piece of work is different and is kept separate from the others.

Costing methods which are used by business to collect costs and to calculate the total cost of their output include:

- job costing

- batch costing

- contract costing

Each of these is used in conjunction with absorption costing to recover the cost of overheads. Remember that businesses must recover their overheads in the total price charged to their customers – this applies both to manufacturing businesses and to service industries, such as banks, shops and transport companies.

JOB COSTING

Job costing is used where each job can be separately identified from other jobs and costs are charged to the job.

The job becomes the cost unit to which costs are charged.

Examples of job costing include engineering firms that produce 'one-offs' to the customer's specifications, printing businesses, vehicle repairs, jobbing builders, painters and decorators.

The diagram below shows the main steps involved in job costing. The important points are:

■ each job is given a number, in order to identify it

■ a separate job cost card (or sheet) is prepared for each job, listing the estimates of direct materials, direct labour, direct expenses and overheads (most businesses nowadays use a computer system to help with their costing and, in practice, the job cost card is held as a computer record on a database)

■ the actual costs incurred are compared with the estimated costs, and the differences (called 'variances') between the two are analysed (there is more on variance analysis in Chapter 23); action can then be taken to correct the variances, which will help when preparing future estimates

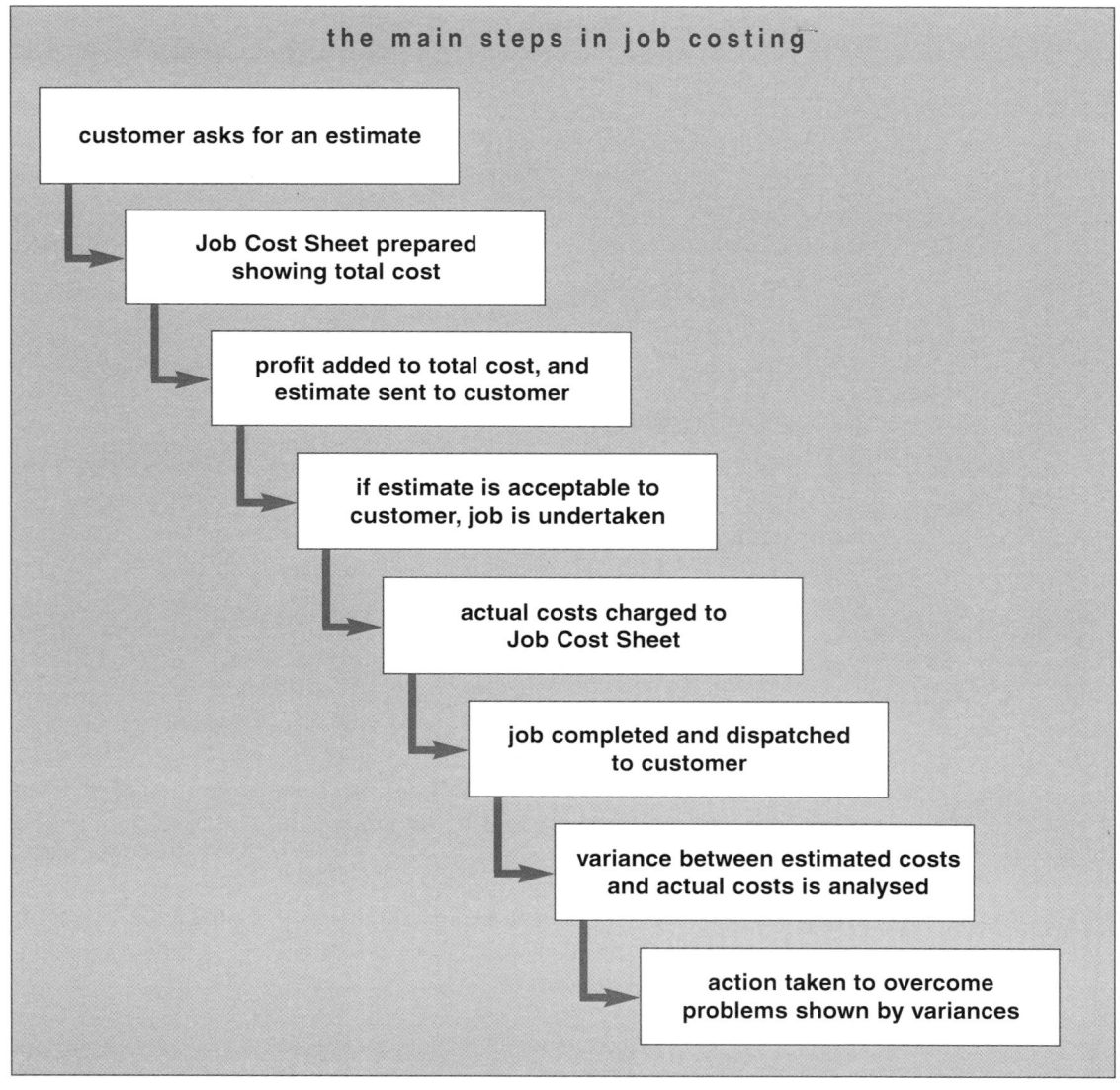

CASE STUDY
'FashionAid' – a charity programme

situation

The youth group at a local church has decided to organise an evening fashion show, to be called 'FashionAid'. The objective of the show is to raise money to send to a children's charity working in Central Africa. One of the organisers has asked for your help in arranging the printing of a programme for the evening's events. You approach Pearshore Printers for an estimate of the cost of printing 750 copies of a sixteen page programme.

solution

Pearshore Printers allocate a reference number to the job. They prepare a Job Cost Sheet on their computer database as follows:

JOB NO. 6789
'FashionAid' Programme: 750 copies

	£
Direct Materials	
Paper for text: white glossart paper code 135	82.00
Paper for cover: coated board code 235	55.00
Printing plates	15.00
Direct Labour	
Printing: 5 hours at £10.00 per hour	50.00
Finishing: 2 hours at £9.00 per hour	18.00
Overheads (based on direct labour hours)	
7 hours at £20.00 per hour	140.00
TOTAL COST	360.00
Profit (15% of total cost)	54.00
SELLING PRICE	414.00

These estimated costs will be obtained as follows:

- *direct materials,* from the stores ledger records for materials already in stock, and from the firm's Purchasing Department for items that need to be bought in especially for this job
- *direct labour,* from the payroll records of the different grades of labour to be employed on this job
- *overheads,* from the pre-determined overhead absorption rate based, for this job, on direct labour hours

Assuming that the price is acceptable to the customer, the job will go ahead and Pearshore Printers will charge the actual costs to the job, and will calculate any differences, or 'variances', as follows:

JOB NO. 6789
'FashionAid' Programme: 750 copies

	ESTIMATE	ACTUAL	VARIANCE*
	£	£	£
Direct Materials			
Paper for text	82.00	90.00	8 ADV
Paper for cover	55.00	50.00	5 FAV
Printing plates	15.00	15.00	–
Direct Labour			
Printing: actual 6 hours at £10.00 per hour	50.00	60.00	10 ADV
Finishing: actual 2 hours at £9.00 per hour	18.00	18.00	–
Overheads			
8 hours at £20.00 per hour	140.00	160.00	20 ADV
TOTAL COST	360.00	393.00	33 ADV
Profit	54.00	21.00	33 ADV
SELLING PRICE	414.00	414.00	–

---

* The variances are either adverse or favourable:

- – a favourable variance is where the actual cost is lower than the estimate
- – an adverse variance is where the actual cost is higher than the estimate

Pearshore Printers would need to analyse the reason for the variances (see Chapter 23), and to take corrective steps to overcome the problems caused by them.

BATCH COSTING

Batch costing is used where the output consists of a number of identical items which are produced together as a batch.

Examples of batch costing include a bakery producing a batch of standard white loaves, and then a batch of croissants; or a clothing factory producing a batch of jackets, and then a batch of trousers. Each batch is the cost unit to which the costs are charged. Once the batch has been produced, the cost per unit is calculated as follows:

$$\frac{\textit{total batch cost}}{\textit{number of units of output}} = \textit{cost per unit}$$

In essence, batch costing is very similar to job costing, but in a batch a number of identical units are produced.

CONTRACT COSTING

Contract costing is used by the construction industry and major engineering companies to cost large, complex projects which last for a long period of time (usually more than a year).

The principles followed are those of job costing but the length and complexity of contract work causes financial differences:

■ A large contract will often itself comprise a considerable number of smaller jobs (some of which may be sub-contracted) to be costed.

■ Invariably, building contracts are based at the construction site – this means that many costs that would otherwise be indirect become direct costs, eg supervisors' wages, site power and telephones, fuel for vehicles, depreciation of equipment.

■ As many contracts run for longer than one year, there is a need to calculate the profit or loss on the contract at the end of the financial year of the construction company, and to value the contract for balance sheet purposes. The contract is valued as follows:

–   if an overall **profit** is expected, the value equals costs to date plus attributable profit (depending on the stage reached in the contract)

–   if an overall **loss** is expected, the value equals costs to date, less the whole of the expected loss

Clearly the costing of a contract is a major task and one which can go spectacularly wrong, as a number of companies have found in the past.

The diagram below summarises the costing methods for specific orders.

SPECIFIC ORDERS		
separate pieces of work		
job costing	**batch costing**	**contract costing**
for example:	for example:	for example:
• making one racing cycle	• making a batch of cycles to a standard design	• building a bridge
• preparing one client's accounts	• printing a batch of leaflets	• building a ship
• putting a central heating system into one house	• baking a batch of loaves	• renovating a large house

CONTINUOUS WORK

In both manufacturing and service industries, work may be done continuously rather than in separate jobs. This requires specific costing methods appropriate to those types of business. For example:

■ a bus company runs a continuous service of buses, available for customers to use and customers pay for their use of the service – the business will be costed using the **service costing** method

■ in the manufacture of chocolate bars, production is a continuous process and the chocolate bars are available for customers to come along and choose to buy them, after they are made – the business will be costed using the **process costing** method

We will look at these two methods in turn.

SERVICE COSTING

This method of costing applies to service industries. By using service costing, the cost per passenger mile of a bus or train service, the cost of cleaning an office, and the cost per student hour at a school or college, can be calculated. (However, a bus company quoting for a trip to the seaside for a pensioners' group, or a college tendering for an in-house course, would use job costing.)

WORKED EXAMPLE
service costs

A nursing home has capacity for twenty residents at any one time. The home achieves an occupancy rate of 90%, ie an average of eighteen beds are occupied at any one time. Costs for last year were:

	£
direct costs	
food and other supplies	27,290
nursing and medical staff	116,340
other support services	22,650
indirect costs	
overheads	29,410
	195,690

The cost per day of each resident is calculated as follows:

- The occupancy in days is (20 residents x 365 days) x 90% = 6,570 days

- Cost per day per resident is:

$$\frac{\text{total cost}}{\text{number of days}} = \frac{£195,690}{6,570} = £29.79 \text{ per resident}$$

PROCESS COSTING

This method of costing is used for continuous manufacturing processes, such as the manufacture of chocolate bars, cider, paint, chemicals and so on. The process continually produces identical units of output.

The total costs of the process for a given time period are collected together. To obtain an average cost per unit of output, the total cost is divided by the number of units of output in the period.

$$\text{Cost per cost unit} = \frac{\text{Total costs of continuous work for the period}}{\text{Total cost units for the period}}$$

WORKED EXAMPLE
process costing

Chox Ltd manufactures chocolate bars in a continuous process. In a given time period 1,600,000 bars are made and the costs of the process are as follows:

Direct materials (ingredients)	£40,000
Direct labour (machine operators)	£24,000
Production overheads	£32,000
Total costs of production for period	£96,000

$$\text{Production cost per bar} \quad = \quad \frac{£96,000}{1,600,000} \quad = \quad £0.06$$

PROCESS COSTING AND WORK-IN-PROGRESS

Process costing is straightforward if all the items on the production line are completed at the end of the day. In a more complex environment there will be items that have been started but not completed. This is known as **work-in-progress**, which was explained in Chapter 17 (see page 357).

For example, the production line at a car factory will always have cars which vary from being only just started, to those nearing the end of the line which are almost complete.

In calculating the cost per unit, it is necessary to take into account the degree of completeness of the work-in-progress. This is done by making equivalent unit calculations:

number of units in progress x percentage of completeness
  = equivalent units

Thus, 100 units which are exactly 40% complete are equal to 40 completed units.

The formula for calculating the cost per unit now becomes:

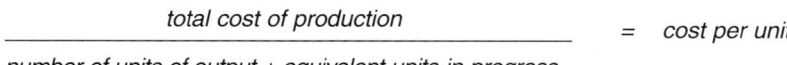

$$\frac{\textit{total cost of production}}{\textit{number of units of output + equivalent units-in-progress}} \quad = \quad \textit{cost per unit}$$

WORKED EXAMPLE
work-in-progress

Cradley Cider Company brews a popular local cider at its cider house in rural Herefordshire. The figures for the first month of the new season's production of its award-winning 'Triple X' variety are:

total cost of production	£8,500
units completed	800 barrels
units in progress	100 barrels

The units in progress are exactly half-finished. The equivalent units in progress, and the cost per barrel, for the month are as follows:

completed units		=	800 barrels
equivalent units	100 x 50%	=	50 barrels
cost per unit	$\frac{£8,500}{800 + 50}$	=	£10 per barrel

Although, in the example above, it was assumed that the work-in-progress was exactly half-finished, this may well not be the case for all the elements of cost. For example, while direct materials might be 100% complete, direct labour, and overheads might be 50% complete. Allowance has to be made for these differences in the calculation of the valuation of work-in-progress, and the layout used in the example below is one way in which the calculations can be made.

WORKED EXAMPLE
different cost elements

The Toy Manufacturing Company makes a plastic toy called a 'Humber-Wumber'. The figures for the first month's production are:

direct materials	£6,600
direct labour	£3,500
production overheads	£4,000
units completed	900
units in progress	200

The units in progress are complete as regards materials, but are 50% complete for direct labour and overheads.

continued on next page

Cost element	Costs	Completed Units	Work-in-progress			Total Equivalent Units	Cost per Unit	WIP value
			Units	% complete	Equivalent Units			
	A	B	C	D	E	F	G	H
					C x D	B + E	A ÷ F	E x G
	£			%			£	£
Direct materials	6,600	900	200	100	200	1,100	6.00	1,200
Direct labour	3,500	900	200	50	100	1,000	3.50	350
Production overheads	4,000	900	200	50	100	1,000	4.00	400
Total	14,100						13.50	1,950

Note: columns are lettered to show how calculations are made.

Using an average cost basis, the cost per unit of the first month's production, and the month-end valuation figure for work-in-progress (WIP) is as follows:

900 completed units at £13.50 each	=	£12,150
work-in-progress valuation	=	£1,950
total costs for month	=	£14,100

opening work-in-progress

When there is opening work-in-progress, the values of the different cost elements are added to the input costs of the period. For example, if in the month which follows the example above, direct labour costs are £4,000, the figure shown in the column costs for direct labour will be:

work-in-progress at start	=	£350
input costs (month's costs)	=	£4,000
total costs for the month	=	£4,350

The calculation of costs per unit and work-in-progress valuation at the month-end can then be made as follows:

value of opening work-in-progress   +   input costs for period

---

number of units of output + equivalent units in closing work-in-progress

= cost per unit

summary – continuous costing methods

The diagram below summarises the methods used for continuous work.

CONTINUOUS WORK	
service costing for example: • running a nursing home • providing a bus service • providing banking services	**process costing** for example: • making chocolate bars • brewing beer or cider • manufacturing paint or chemicals

chapter summary

● The method chosen for cost accounting within a business depends on the kind of work being done.

● In manufacturing and in service industries, work may consist of separately identifiable jobs or it may be continuous.

● Separately identifiable jobs are usually done to a customer's specific order.

● Costs are calculated for each separately identifiable job.

● The costing method to be used for specific orders (separate jobs) is:
  – job costing for a single unit of work
  – batch costing for a batch of identical units
  – contract costing for a long-term contract

● The costing method to be used for continuous work is:
  – process costing for continuous manufacturing processes
  – service costing for continuous services

● To obtain a cost per cost unit for continuous work, the total costs for a time period are first collected together, then divided by the number of cost units produced or provided in the time period, ie

cost per cost unit   = $\dfrac{\textit{total costs of continuous work for the period}}{\textit{total cost units for the period}}$

● If there is work-in-progress at the end of the period, the number of equivalent complete units is calculated, for example 500 units that are 50% complete are equivalent to 500 x 50% = 250 completed units.

● The value of opening work-in-progress is part of the total cost for the period.

key terms

costing method	a technique used to collect costs and to calculate the total cost of output
job/batch/contract costing	a form of specific order costing which applies costs to jobs/batches/contracts
service costing	a form of costing for service industries; costs are averaged to find the cost per unit
job cost card/sheet	card/sheet (or record on a computer database) which shows the estimated and actual direct and indirect costs for a particular job
variance	the difference between an estimated cost and an actual cost
favourable variance	where the actual cost is lower than the estimate
adverse variance	where the actual cost is higher than the estimate
process costing	method of costing applied to continuous manufacturing processes
work-in-progress (WIP)	partly completed goods at a particular time
equivalent units	number of units in progress x percentage of completeness
cost per unit	$\dfrac{\textit{total costs}}{\textit{number of units (including equivalent units)}}$

activities

Note: an asterisk (*) after an activity number means that an answer is provided in Appendix 1.

21.1   State, with reasons, the method of costing you think would be appropriate for:

   •   an accountant

   •   a bus company

   •   a baker

   •   a sports centre

   •   a hotel

   •   a construction company

21.2*   A clothing manufacturer has been asked to give a quotation for the supply of a batch of uniforms for a band. Materials for the uniforms will be:

   •   100 metres of cloth at £7.50 per metre

   •   75 metres of braiding at £4.00 per metre

It is estimated that the job will take the machinists a total of 35 hours.

They are paid at the rate of £6.00 per hour.

The overhead absorption rate is £8.50 per direct labour hour.

You are to:

(a)   calculate the cost of the job

(b)   calculate the selling price if the company is to make a profit of 20% on the cost price

21.3   Rowcester Engineering Limited is asked to quote for the supply of a replacement cylinder head for a large stationary engine installed in a local factory.

The item will need to be cast in the foundry and then passed to the finishing shop for machining to specification.

Materials needed will be a 100 kg ingot of high-strength steel, which costs £10 per kg.

Direct labour will be 10 hours in the foundry, and 15 hours in the finishing shop, of which 12 hours will be machine hours.

Foundry workers are paid £10 per hour, while machine operators in the finishing shop are paid £12 per hour.

Overheads are charged on the basis of 80% of direct labour cost in the foundry, and on the basis of £20 per machine hour in the finishing shop.

Profit is to be 25% of cost price.

You are to:

(a)   Prepare a Job Cost Sheet which shows the estimated cost of the job, and the selling price.

(b)   Prepare an actual cost statement on the basis of the following:

- the cost of materials was £11 per kg

- the job took 12 labour hours in the foundry (of which 11 were machine hours)

- the job took 14 labour hours in the finishing shop

- machine operators in the finishing shop are now paid £12.50 per hour

- machine time in the finishing shop was 11 hours

(c)   Show the variances (and whether they are adverse or favourable) and the actual profit (or loss) made on this job.

21.4* City Transit plc is a small train operating company which runs passenger rail services on a commuter line in a large city. The line links the docks area, which has been redeveloped with flats and houses, with the city centre, and then runs on through the suburbs. An intensive service is operated from early morning to late at night carrying people to and from work, schoolchildren, shoppers and leisure travellers.

The tracks that City Transit uses are leased from the track owner, Trakrail plc.

The modern fleet of six diesel trains is owned and maintained by City Transit.

The following information is available in respect of last year's operations:

	cost	estimated life
Diesel trains	£650,000 each	20 years

Depreciation is on a straight-line basis, assuming a residual value of £50,000 for each train.

Leasing charges for track	£500,000 pa
Maintenance charges for trains	£455,000 pa
Fuel for trains	£105,000 pa
Wages of drivers and conductors	£240,000 pa
Administration	£260,000 pa

There were 2.5 million passenger journeys last year with an average distance travelled of five miles.

You are to calculate the cost per passenger mile of operating the railway for last year.

21.5   A manufacturer of plastic toys has the following information concerning the first month of production:

Direct materials   £11,500

Direct labour   £9,000

Production overheads   £18,000

Toys completed   20,000

Toys in progress   5,000

The work-in-progress is complete as regards materials, but is 50% complete as regards direct labour and production overhead.

You are to:

(a)   Calculate the cost per toy of the first month's production

(b)   Calculate the month-end valuation for work-in-progress

MARGINAL COSTING

Jo and Mo are friends who think they have hit on a sound business idea. They have noticed the need for expert DJs in clubs, and believe that there is a market to teach people Disc Jockey skills. They plan to provide courses, calling the business the JoMo School for DJs.

They have hired a local club, sound equipment and experts to demonstrate DJ techniques. There are still a few issues that concern them.

Mo explains:

'We've researched the competition, and have a good idea of what we can charge for coming on the course. We have also estimated what it will all cost. What we need are some costing techniques so that we can answer some important questions, for example:

How many people do we need to take on our course in order to break-even?

How much profit would we make if more or less than that number signed up?

What would happen if we charged more, or less, or if we revised our costs?

What is the most we could make, or lose?'

In this chapter we will use the costing technique of marginal costing to help Mo answer her questions quickly and easily. We will return to the JoMo School for DJs and learn how to estimate key profit and output figures in given situations. We will also see how the same techniques can be applied to other organisations and businesses.

---

learning objectives

When you have studied this chapter you will be able to:

- *understand the ideas behind marginal costing, and how it differs from absorption costing*

- *calculate break-even points*

- *carry out 'what-if' analysis on projected figures*

- *use marginal costing to help with pricing*

- *understand the limitations of some marginal costing techniques*

- *understand the impact of using marginal costing on reported profit figures*

COST BEHAVIOUR AND MARGINAL COSTING

Before we can look at the specific techniques that we are going to use, it will be useful to see what the basic idea behind marginal costing is, and what some of the terms that are used mean.

marginal costing

It is important to understand that costs behave in different ways as the volume of activity changes. This is fundamental to marginal costing.

There are three ways that the costs could behave within a range of activity levels:

variable costs   These are the costs where the the cost varies in proportion to the activity level. For example, if a car manufacturer makes more cars it will use more sheet metal – a variable cost. Variable costs are also known as marginal costs.

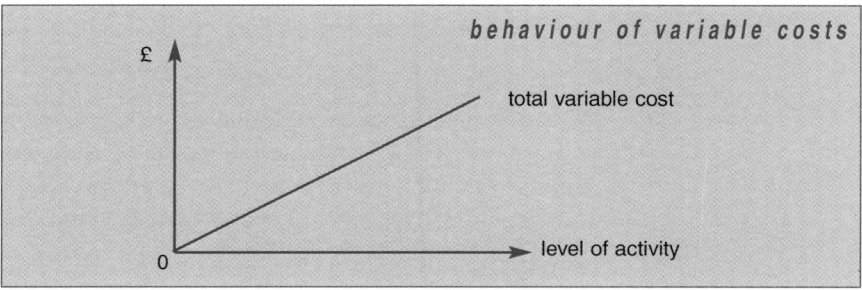

fixed costs   These are costs that do not normally change when the level of activity changes. The cost of insuring a car factory against business risks will not vary in line with the number of cars produced – it is a fixed cost.

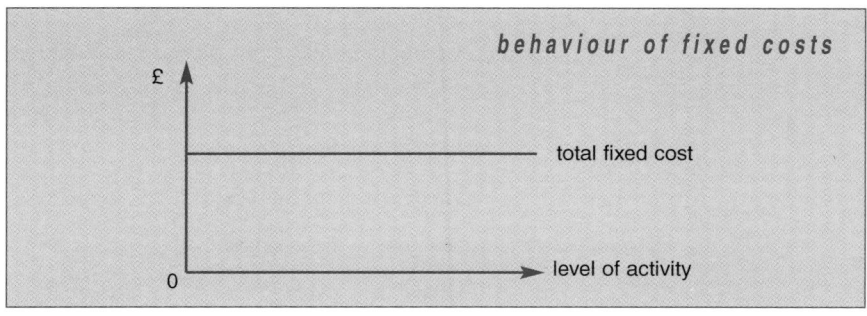

semi-variable costs   These are costs where a part of the cost acts as a variable cost, and a part acts as a fixed cost. Some fuel bills are semi-variable: there is a fixed 'standing charge' and a variable 'unit charge'.

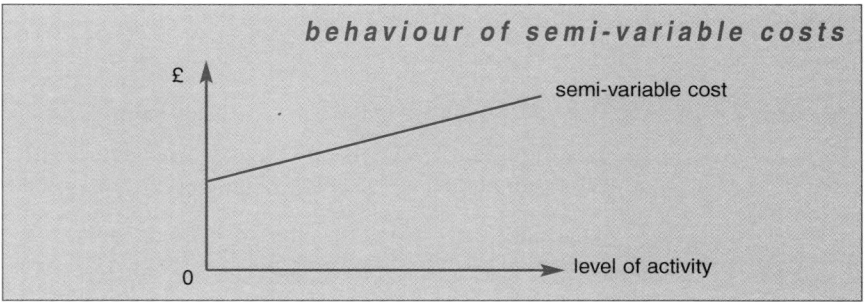

costs, contribution and profit

In marginal costing all costs need to be classifed as variable costs or fixed costs. As part of this exercise, semi-variable costs are divided into their fixed and variable components. For example, a car manufacturer will need to identify:

- the variable costs of each car
- the total fixed costs of a manufacturing business over a period of time

When the manufacturer sells a car it will receive the selling price, which it will use to cover the variable costs of the car. As the selling price is greater than the variable cost there will also be money available to pay off the fixed costs incurred. This amount is known as the **contribution**. The formula is:

contribution = selling price per unit *less* variable cost per unit

It follows that the difference between the sales income and the variable costs of the units sold in a period is the **total contribution** that the sales of all the units in the period make towards the fixed costs of the organisation.

A business can work out its profit for any given period from the fixed costs and total contribution figures:

profit = total contribution less total fixed costs

A marginal costing statement can be prepared using the following format:

	sales
less	variable costs
equals	contribution
less	fixed costs
equals	profit

CASE STUDY

The Marginal Company — marginal costing

The Marginal Company manufactures one product, the Marg. The following costs relate to a financial year, when 100,000 units of Marg are made:

Direct Materials	£350,000
Direct Labour	£230,000
Indirect Costs	£310,000

Investigations into the behaviour of the costs has revealed the following information:

- Direct Materials behave as variable costs.
- Direct Labour behaves as a variable cost.
- Of the Indirect Costs, £270,000 behaves as a fixed cost, and the remainder as a variable cost.

required

1 Calculate the cost of one unit of Marg using Marginal Costing.

2 If each unit of Marg sells for £10, and all the production of 100,000 units is sold, calculate the profit for the year using a marginal costing statement. Show the contribution per unit and total contribution.

solution

1 COSTING A UNIT OF MARG

Using only the variable (marginal) costs to cost one unit of Marg:

Direct Materials (£350,000 ÷ 100,000)	£3.50
Direct Labour (£230,000 ÷ 100,000)	£2.30
Variable Costs (£310,000 − £270,000 = £40,000 ÷ 100,000)	£0.40
Total marginal cost per unit	£6.20

2 MARGINAL COSTING STATEMENT FOR THE FINANCIAL YEAR.

	Per Unit £	For Year £
Sales	10.00	1,000,000
Less Variable Costs	6.20	620,000
Contribution	3.80	380,000
Less Fixed Costs*		270,000
Profit		110,000

*Note that the fixed costs are not calculated in unit terms, but are simply deducted in total from the total contribution.

COMPARING ABSORPTION COSTING AND MARGINAL COSTING

You will be familiar with the terminology of absorption costing from the earlier chapters in this book. The diagram below demonstrates how the terms in marginal costing can relate to the same costs as those categorised under absorption costing terms.

Note that when using marginal costing it is the behaviour of the cost that is important, not the origin of the cost.

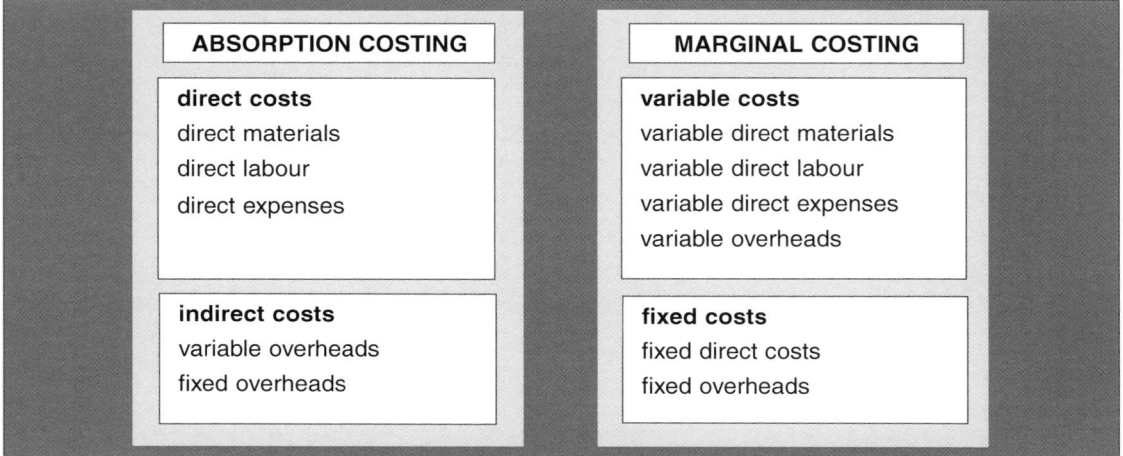

ABSORPTION COSTING

direct costs
direct materials
direct labour
direct expenses

indirect costs
variable overheads
fixed overheads

MARGINAL COSTING

variable costs
variable direct materials
variable direct labour
variable direct expenses
variable overheads

fixed costs
fixed direct costs
fixed overheads

BREAK-EVEN

The break-even point for a business is the output level (units manufactured or services provided) at which the income from sales is just enough to cover all the costs. Break-even is the point at which the profit (or loss) is zero. The output level can be measured in a way that is appropriate for the particular business. It is commonly measured in sales units. The formula for break-even in sales units is:

$$\text{break-even point (in sales units)} = \frac{\textit{fixed costs}}{\textit{contribution per unit}}$$

The JoMo School for DJs Case Study which follows, shows how this formula is used to calculate a break-even point.

CASE STUDY
JoMo School for DJs – break-even

Jo and Mo are planning to run a one-day introductory course to teach participants the basic techniques of being a DJ. All students will be charged a fee of £125 to include refreshments, lunch and all materials. The maximum number of students that can be comfortably accommodated on the course is 20. The estimated costs of running the course are as follows:

Hire of club	£150
Lunches	£ 10 per student
Advertising	£ 300
Equipment hire	£ 100
Refreshments	£ 5 per student
Fees for DJs	£ 400
Student materials	£ 10 per student
Insurance	£ 50

required

Calculate the break-even point in terms of the number of students signed up for a DJ course.

solution

The first thing to do is to divide the estimated costs into fixed and variable costs. Fixed costs will be incurred regardless of the number of participants on the course (up to the course capacity), while variable costs change in proportion to the number of students. This gives us the following analysis, with totals:

	Fixed Costs for the course £	Variable Costs per student £
Hire of club	150	
Lunches		10
Advertising	300	
Equipment hire	100	
Refreshments		5
Fees for DJs	400	
Student materials		10
Insurance	50	
Totals	1000	25

Since Jo and Mo will be charging each student £125 for the course, the 'contribution' that each student makes is:

selling price	£125 per student
less variable cost	£25 per student
= contribution	£100 per student.

Because the variable costs for the student have been taken into account, this 'contribution' is towards covering the fixed costs, and ultimately making a profit.

The break-even formula now makes sense – it is simply saying 'How many students' contributions of £100 each will it take to cover the fixed costs?' The fixed costs are £1000, and therefore will be covered by 10 students' contributions.

Using the formula, this calculation is carried out as follows:

Break-even point (in sales units) $\dfrac{\text{Fixed Costs}}{\text{Contribution per unit}}$ $\dfrac{£1000}{£100}$ = 10 students

We can see that if Jo and Mo enrol 10 students for a DJ course they will achieve break-even. Since they can accommodate up to 20 students, any number of students between 11 and 20 will generate a profit.

USING BREAK-EVEN CHARTS

Break-even calculations can also be demonstrated using a break-even chart. The chart at the top of the next page is based on the calculations from the Case Study. The chart makes the same assumption that costs within the range are either fixed or variable, and therefore uses straight lines to show how costs behave. Any semi-variable costs would be divided into their fixed and variable parts. Notice the similarity between the way that costs are shown on this chart, and the earlier individual cost behaviour diagrams (see pages 441 to 442). The chart which follows is constructed as follows:

■ The scales on the graph are chosen so that the horizontal axis measures output from 0 to 20 students, and the vertical axis represents the income and costs at those levels. This means that the maximum that the vertical axis will need to reach will be (20 x £125) = £2,500.

■ The fixed cost line is a horizontal line at the £1,000 level. It is horizontal since the fixed cost will remain the same no matter how many students enrol.

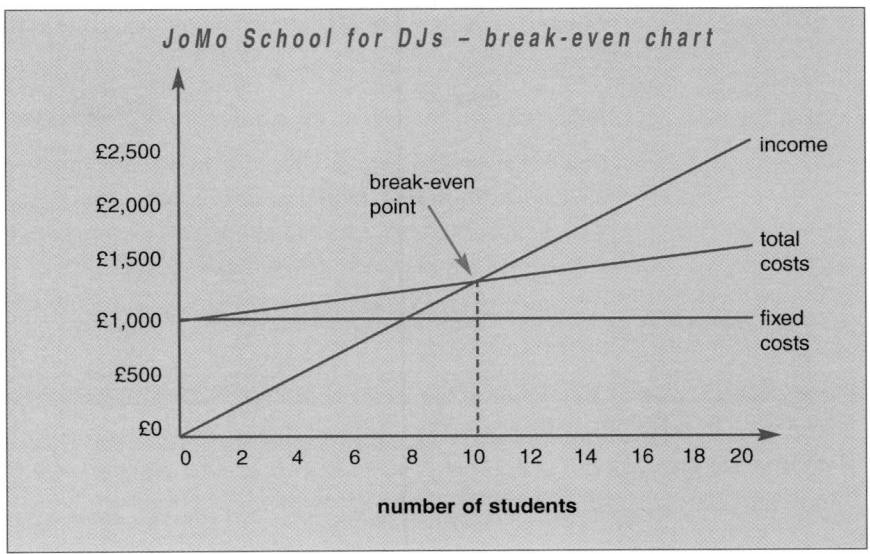

- The total cost line starts at the £1,000 point based on zero students. This is because if the course goes ahead with no students the fixed costs will still have to be paid. The line is drawn to a point of £1,500, situated at the 20 students level. This is based on a total cost of £1,500, ie fixed cost £1,000 plus variable costs of £500 (20 x £25) for 20 students.
- The income line is drawn from zero income (zero students), to the income of £2,500 that would be generated from 20 enrolments.

What we now find is that:

- the break-even point of 10 students is represented on the graph where the total cost line crosses the income line
- student numbers to the left of this point will result in losses since the income line is below the total cost line
- student numbers exceeding 10 will result in profit, since in the part of the graph to the right of the break-even point the income line is higher than the total cost line

WHAT-IF ANALYSIS

Marginal costing enables us to work out quickly and easily the profit or loss at any level of output if we already know the break-even point and the contribution per unit. This is because for every unit that is sold above the break-even point the profit will equal the contribution (ie income less variable costs) per unit. If we sell fewer than the break-even number, we will lose the contribution of that shortfall.

The profit or loss calculation can be expressed as a formula:

profit (or loss) =

(units sold – units needed for break-even) x contribution per unit

The 'what-if' scenario involves the management of a business wanting to see the effect of altering selling prices or any of the costs. If this is carried out it will be necessary to recalculate the revised break-even point and then apply the above formula to the revised sales level.

We will now rejoin Jo and Mo to see how these principles can be applied to their business.

CASE STUDY

JoMo School for DJs — 'what-if' analysis

Having established the break-even point as 10 students, Jo is keen to see what would happen to the profit or loss at various different numbers of students.

'I would like to know how much profit we would make if the maximum of 20 students signed up, or how much we would lose if only 5 enrolled.'

'What about if we charged £160 instead of £125, but spent an extra £10 per student on better materials?' asked Mo, *'or even reduced the price to £100, but cut advertising by £100?'*

required

1   Based on Jo's question, calculate the profit or loss if 20 or 5 students enrol, and use a break-even chart to demonstrate.

2   Based on Mo's two suggestions, calculate the new break-even points, and for each suggestion, the profit or loss if 20 or 5 students enrol.

solution

1   Based on the original figures, if 20 students enrol the profit would be:

number of courses sold – number of courses needed to break-even x contribution per unit

=   (20 – 10) x £100   =   £1,000 profit

If only 5 enrol the calculation would be:

=   (5 – 10) x £100   =   £500 loss (since the answer is negative)

Look at the break-even chart on the next page.

■   The profit when 20 students enrol is found by measuring the vertical distance between the income line and the total cost line at the 20 students point on the horizontal axis. This distance is read from the vertical scale to estimate the profit in £s.

■   The loss if only 5 students enrol can similarly be found by measuring the distance between the same two lines at the 5 students point on the horizontal axis.

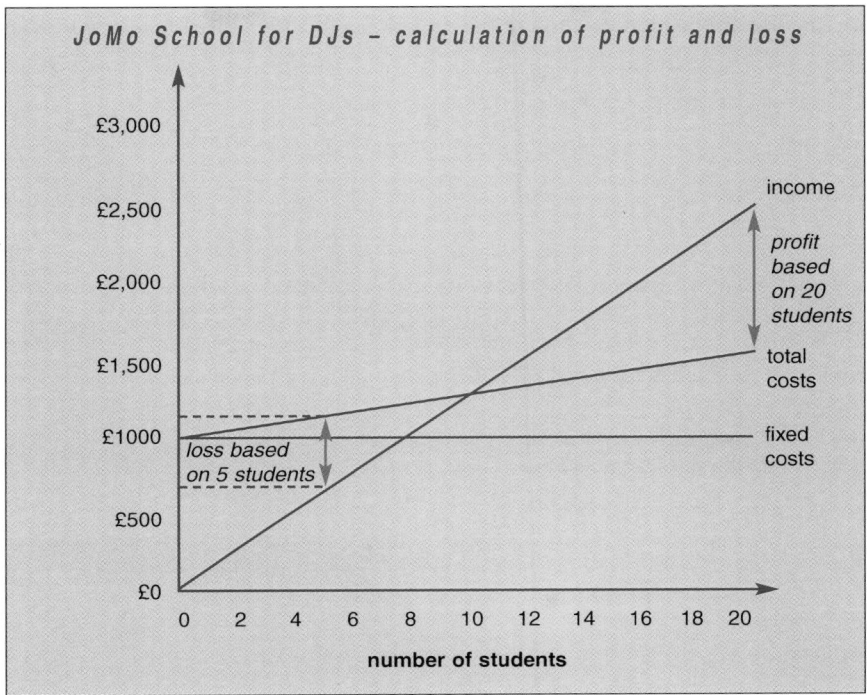

JoMo School for DJs – calculation of profit and loss

2 **Mo's first suggestion is to increase the course fee from £125 to £160 and spend an extra £10 per student on materials.** The revised contribution that each student makes would then be:

'selling price'	£160	per student
less variable cost (£25 + £10)	£35	per student
= contribution	£125	per student

Since the fixed costs are still £1000, this gives a revised break-even point of

£1000 ÷ £125   =   8 students

Based on these first revised figures, if 20 students enrol the profit would be:

=   number of courses sold – number of courses needed to break-even x contribution per unit

(20 – 8) x £125   =   £1,500 profit

If only 5 students enrol the position would be:

(5 – 8) x £125   =   £375 loss

Mo's second suggestion was to cut the course fee to £100 and reduce advertising costs by £100.

Here the revised contribution that each student makes is:

selling price	£100	per student
less variable cost	£25	per student
= contribution	£ 75	per student

Since the fixed costs are now £900 (£1000 – £100), this gives a revised break-even point of

£900 ÷ £75   =   12 students

Based on these revised figures, if 20 students enrol the profit would be:

(20 – 12) x £75   =   £600 profit

If only 5 enrol the position would be:

(5 – 12) x £75   =   £525 loss

PRICING DECISIONS

The question of what to charge customers is a complicated one, and depends on issues like:

■ what competitors are charging

■ the costs levels of the business

■ the level of sales the business can expect

■ what the business thinks its customers will be prepared to pay

One area in which marginal costing can help is in determining an absolute minimum price that could be charged. This can be particularly useful for pricing additional sales at a special reduced rate when sales have already been made at the normal selling price.

The rule is simple – you assume fixed costs have already been paid off and so all you have got to do is to cover the variable costs of any additional sales. If further sales are made at a price that is above the variable costs of each unit then that 'contribution' (ie sales price minus variable costs) will all be profit.

We will now see how this applies to the JoMo School for DJs.

CASE STUDY
JoMo School for DJs — minimum pricing decisions

The introductory course for DJs looks like being a success. The original costs and prices were agreed on as follows:

Selling Price	£125 per student
Variable costs	£ 25 per student
Fixed costs	£1,000 for the course

Twelve students have signed up and paid their fees, and the course is to run in a few days time.

At this point Mo gets a telephone call from a local activity holiday centre. They would like to book places for eight students who are interested in making the course a part of their holiday. The problem is that the holiday centre is on a tight budget; they are only prepared to pay £80 per student, and if that price is not acceptable they will send their holidaymakers go-karting instead.

required

Calculate whether by accepting these terms for the additional 8 students Mo and Jo will increase their overall profit, and if so by how much. List other factors that they may like to consider before making a final decision.

solution

The introductory course currently has the capacity (just) to take the extra eight students, without changing the existing fixed costs.

The additional income would be 8 x special price of £80	= £640
The additional costs incurred would be 8 x variable costs of £25	= £200
Therefore additional contribution would be made of	£440

Since fixed costs are unchanged this £440 will all represent additional profit.

Other factors to be considered by Jo and Mo include:

- Whether there may be last-minute demand from customers willing to pay the usual price. If they go ahead with the above proposal they would have to turn these customers (and their higher contributions) away.

- Whether the activity holiday centre would expect similar deals for any courses run in the future. While this could be a welcome source of additional students, it should not form a substitute for students paying the normal rate.

- Whether the students paying the normal rate may become aware of the cheap deal offered to the activity holiday centre, and demand a similar price. This seems unlikely in this case.

LIMITATIONS OF BREAK-EVEN ANALYSIS

Break-even analysis is a useful tool, and is easy to understand and apply. There are some limitations to its use which mean that it will not always work as well as it has in the Case Studies that we have looked at.

■ We should be careful that we do not assume that costs will behave the same at any level of output. Some fixed costs may increase if output goes beyond certain levels – for example if Jo and Mo needed a bigger venue or had to bring in more DJs to cope with the number of students. The variable costs might not stay exactly in proportion to sales either – there may be discounts available for large quantities that would distort the analysis.

■ Break-even analysis is at its simplest when the output is in a form that can be measured in units, and all the fixed costs relate to those outputs – just like the case studies we have examined. When organisations have several outputs and some fixed costs relate to more than one output, break-even becomes more complicated and difficult to apply. If Mo and Jo ran several courses at different prices, but using some of the same facilities, it would be more difficult to apply these techniques and produce meaningful results.

MARGINAL COSTING AND RECORDED PROFIT

We have seen in this chapter that marginal costing can be useful to organisations because it focuses on the way that costs behave. This means that techniques like break-even and 'what-if' analysis can be carried out to help plan and monitor costs and make decisions. The choice of costing system that an organisation uses will, however, have implications not only for the way that its profit statements are laid out, but also for the amount of profit that is recorded.

variations in stock valuation

One of the reasons that organisations use a costing system is so that the value of the stock of finished goods (and work in progress) can be calculated and incorporated into profit statements. Since the different approaches to costing that we have examined give different costs per unit, they will result in different valuations of stock. This will in turn affect the profit calculation when stock levels change. A marginal costing system will value stock at just the variable costs, but a system that absorbs fixed costs into the stock valuation can result in fixed costs being charged to a period other than the one in which they were incurred.

the effect of stock valuation on profit

The costs incurred in producing goods in a given period *plus* the cost of the opening stock at the beginning of that period *equals* the cost of sales for that period *plus* the cost of the closing stock. This can be seen as follows:

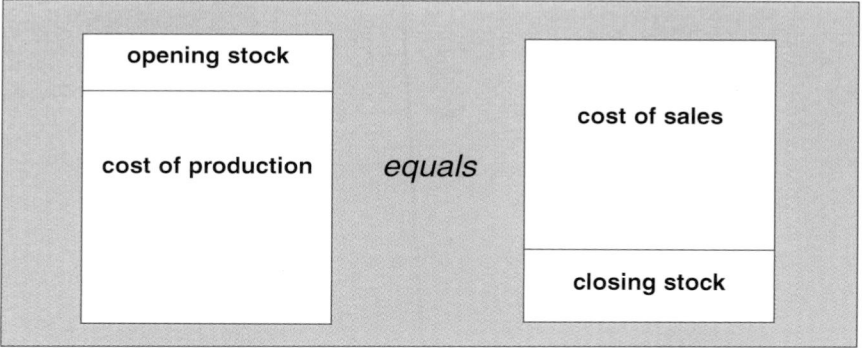

The method of *valuation* of the closing stock is therefore critical as it will affect both the cost of sales and also the level of recorded profit.

The Case Study below shows how the same data is treated using different costing systems.

CASE STUDY

The Alternative Company – costing methods and profit

The Alternative Company manufactures a single product, and produces monthly management accounts.

In each of Month 1 and Month 2, 10,000 units were produced, and the following costs were incurred:

Direct Material	£100,000
Direct Labour	£150,000
Fixed Overheads	£250,000
Total Costs	£500,000

Both the costs and the volume of output were in line with the budget.

Units were sold for £70 each, and in Month 1 the whole production of 10,000 units was sold, whereas in month 2 only 8,000 units were sold. There was no stock at the start of Month 1.

Direct Material and Direct Labour are both variable costs.

required

1 Calculate the cost per unit using:

    (a) absorption costing using units as an absorption base

    (b) marginal costing

2 Draft management accounts for each month using:

    (a) absorption costing

    (b) marginal costing

3 Comment on the reasons for any difference in profits.

solution

1 **Calculation of cost per unit**

    (a) Absorption Costing (using all costs)

        £500,000 ÷ 10,000   = £50 per unit

    (b) Marginal Costing (using variable costs only)

        £250,000 ÷ 10,000   = £25 per unit

2 **Producing management accounts**

    (a) **ABSORPTION COSTING**

	Month 1		Month 2	
	£	£	£	£
Sales		700,000		560,000
Less cost of sales:				
Opening stock	–		–	
Cost of production (10,000 x £50)	500,000		500,000	
Less closing stock (2,000 x £50)	–		100,000	
		500,000		400,000
Profit		200,000		160,000

(b)   **MARGINAL COSTING**

	Month 1		Month 2	
	£	£	£	£
Sales		700,000		560,000
Less variable cost of sales:				
opening stock	–		–	
Variable cost of production				
(10,000 x £25)	250,000		250,000	
less closing stock				
(2,000 x £25)	–		50,000	
		250,000		200,000
Contribution		450,000		360,000
Less fixed costs		250,000		250,000
Profit		200,000		110,000

3   Comments on the reasons for differences in profit

The profits are identical when there is no change in stock level, as in Month 1, when both opening and closing stocks are zero. However when the stock level changes between the start and end of the period (as in Month 2) the stock valuation has an impact on profit.

The additional reported profit of £50,000 (£160,000 compared with £110,000) by using the absorption system is due to £50,000 of the fixed costs being absorbed into the closing stock and effectively carried into the next period. If the stocks again fell to nil in Month 3 the profit difference would be reversed.

The differences in reported profits are only timing differences – the differences in profit are just reported in different periods.

conclusion

■   Where stock levels increase, absorption costing will record a higher profit than marginal costing, as more of the cost incurred is pushed into the next period.

■   Where stock levels decrease, absorption costing will record a lower profit than marginal costing, as more of the costs from the previous period are set against income.

■   Where stock levels are constant, then, providing there has been no change in unit costs, there will be no difference in recorded profit under either system.

You can therefore see that if an organisation uses absorption costing, significantly building up (or reducing) stock levels can distort profits.

chapter summary

- Marginal costing can be used as an alternative to absorption costing. It is based on analysing costs according to their behaviour at different output levels rather than their origin.

- Break-even analysis is one of the techniques that marginal costing enables us to use. It determines the output level that is required to just cover the costs. Break-even charts can be used to illustrate the situation.

- Marginal costing can help with analysing the outcome of various alternative output, pricing and cost scenarios. This is often called 'what-if' analysis.

- Marginal costing can help with pricing decisions, especially when a lowest price needs to be established or an additional order priced.

- Break-even analysis has its limitations. Care needs to be taken to make sure that it is applied appropriately.

- Using marginal costing instead of absorption costing will have an impact on reported profit for a period. The differences will be due to the exclusion of fixed costs from stock valuations under marginal costing.

key terms

variable costs	costs where the total amount varies in proportion to the activity level when the activity level changes; these costs are also known as marginal costs when using marginal costing
fixed costs	costs that do not change when the level of activity changes (within a certain range)
semi-variable costs	costs that contain elements that behave as variable costs and elements that behave as fixed costs; these costs are analysed into these elements for marginal costing purposes
marginal costing	this costing system categorises costs according to their cost behaviour, and divides them into variable and fixed costs; this system uses a cost for each unit of output based purely on the variable (or 'marginal') costs – all fixed costs are regarded as time based and are therefore linked to accounting periods rather than units of output
contribution	this is the difference between the selling price and the total variable costs, calculated for a single unit of output or for the output of a period of time – it provides the 'contribution' that the sale of a unit (or units) makes towards fixed costs and ultimately profit

break-even point	the level of sales (or output) that produces income that exactly covers costs, and where profit/loss is therefore zero
break-even chart (or graph)	a chart that illustrates the effect of various output levels in terms of income and costs, and shows the location of the break-even point
what-if analysis	a technique that demonstrates the effect of different output, price and cost scenarios on profit – it is usually based on the concept of marginal costing

activities

Note: an asterisk (*) after an activity number means that an answer is provided in Appendix 1.

22.1* Each of the following types of costs is incurred by Seedy Limited, a company that makes music CDs:

(a) factory rates

(b) CD cases

(c) production workers paid a basic wage plus a bonus per CD made

(d) production supervisors paid a fixed salary

(e) blank CDs

(f) factory rent

(g) cellophane for packaging individual CDs

(h) royalties paid to recording artists for each CD made

Required:

State whether each of the above costs behaves as a fixed, variable, or semi-variable cost.

22.2 You have been asked to organise a day of lectures on costing techniques for students. You will need to advertise the event, and hire a suitable room in a local hotel, and speakers. You will also need to provide lunch and course materials for each person who books a place, and decide how much to charge them each for the day.

Required:

Using your own estimates for the relevant costs and price, calculate the following:

(a) total fixed costs for the event

(b) total variable costs per delegate

(c) contribution per delegate

(d) break-even point in numbers of delegates

22.3 The Last Company Ltd. is famous for its 'Snowdon' range of hill-walking boots. The management of the company are considering the production for next year and have asked you, as cost clerk, to help with certain financial decisions.

The following information is available:

Wholesale selling price (per pair)   £30.00

Raw materials (per pair)   £7.50

Direct labour (per pair)   £5.50

Fixed costs   £150,000.00 per year

The company is planning to manufacture 12,500 pairs of boots next year.

(a)   You are asked to calculate:

- the marginal cost per pair

- the absorption cost per pair

- the break-even point (in pairs of boots)

- the profit or loss if 12,500 pairs of boots are sold

(b)   A mail order company, Salesbypost Ltd, has approached The Last Company Ltd. with a view to selling the 'Snowdon' boot through its catalogue. Salesbypost Ltd is prepared to guarantee to sell 2,500 pairs of boots each year but, in view of the large quantity, offers a price of £20 per pair. As The Last Company Ltd usually sells through specialist shops, it is not expected that 'normal' sales will be affected. This 'special order' is within the capacity of the factory, and fixed costs will remain unchanged. You are to advise the management as to whether this offer should be accepted.

(c)   A manufacturer in the Far East has offered to make the 'Snowdon' boot under licence at a price of £20 per pair up to 10,000 pairs, and then £15 per pair above this level. Quality is guaranteed and, if this option is taken, The The Last Company Ltd would cease manufacturing and would act as distributors: as a result, fixed costs would fall to £50,000 pa. You are to advise the company, in financial terms, if this offer should be taken up. Are there any other points, besides financial, that The Last Company Ltd should consider before making its decision?

22.4 The System Company manufactures one product, the Tem. Budgeted production is 4,000 Tems per week. During each of the first two weeks of this year it had costs as follows, exactly as budgeted.

Direct Materials   £5,000

Direct Labour   £9,000

Fixed Overheads   £6,000

The company had no finished goods in stock at the start of week 1. In both weeks it produced 4,000 units. Sales in week 1 were 3,000 units, and in week 2 were 5,000 units, all at £8 per Tem.

Both Direct Materials and Direct Labour behave as Variable Costs.

(a)   Produce profit statements for each of the two weeks, using:

      1   absorption costing, absorbing fixed overheads on a per unit basis

      2   marginal costing

(b)   Explain briefly the reason for the difference between recorded profits under the alternative costing systems.

22.5* Kings B & B is a bed and breakfast establishment that caters for individual travellers who want a good night's sleep in a clean bed with a hearty breakfast. There are 10 single bedrooms available, and bed and breakfast is priced at £16 per person per night. Kings B & B is open 7 nights a week.

The following are typical costs:

	Weekly Costs (for the whole place)	Costs Per Guest Night
Heating & lighting	£20	
Breakfast foods		£3
Cleaning staff – basic pay	£100	
Cleaning staff – bonus		£1
Administration	£10	
Laundry		£2
Breakfast staff	£70	
Other overheads	£80	

(a)   Calculate the fixed costs per week and the contribution per guest per night.

(b)   Calculate the average number of guests per night it would take to break-even.

(c)   Calculate the weekly profit or loss if there were 42 guest nights in a week (ie an average of 6 guests on each of the 7 nights).

STANDARD COSTING AND VARIANCES

CASE STUDY
Jean-E-Us — predicting and controlling costs

Jean-E-Us is a company that manufactures denim jeans for sale to fashion wholesalers. Its founder Gene Edwards had wide experience in the fashion trade, and could design the jeans just as the buyers wanted. To start with, all went well. Then the company profit performance became unpredictable. Gene commented to his accountant:

'I knew that everything wasn't quite right, but I couldn't put my finger on the problem.

I've been busy finalising the designs for the new range. I know that there have been some price rises in denim cloth, and that my current designs have taken longer to manufacture than expected. I thought that would be more than outweighed by the savings in labour costs because we've taken on a lot of trainees, and they're not paid the full rate yet.

The trouble is, I don't know how much difference to the profit each factor has made – how much is due to the material price rise, how much is down to the slower working.'

The accountant thought about it for a while and then replied:

'Your main problem is that you don't really know how much you expect each pair of jeans to cost. You had a pretty good idea when the business was started, but since then a lot has changed and you have lost track of the figures.

I suggest that we set up a Standard Costing system – then we can predict the cost of each pair of jeans that you make, and if things don't go quite to plan we can work out how the different factors that we identify have affected profit.'

In this chapter we will examine how standard costing can help businesses like Jean-E-Us to plan and control their costs. We will return to Jean-E-Us after we have explained the standard costing system, and have shown how the techniques work.

learning objectives

When you have studied this chapter you will be able to:

- *understand why standard costing is useful, and where the information to set standards can come from*
- *calculate direct cost variances*
- *identify possible causes for direct cost variances*
- *understand the implications of fixed overheads*
- *calculate the main fixed overhead variances*
- *reconcile standard and actual costs using variances*

BACKGROUND TO STANDARD COSTING

Standard costing was developed primarily in the manufacturing industry as a formal method for calculating the expected costs of products. It differs from general budget setting (which is normally concerned with the costs of sections of the organisation), because it focuses on the cost of what the organisation produces (the 'cost units').

Standard costing establishes in detail the standard cost of each component of a product, so that a total product cost can be calculated.

Standard costing is ideal for situations where components are identical and manufacturing operations are repetitive.

advantages of standard costing

The main advantages of operating with a standard costing system in place are that the standard costs can be used:

■ to help with **decision making**, for example as a basis for pricing decisions

■ to assist in **planning**, for example to plan the quantity and cost of the resources needed for future production

■ as a mechanism for **controlling** costs: standard costs can be compared with actual costs (by calculating variances) so that action can be taken when appropriate

In addition there may be other benefits to setting up and using a standard costing system:

■ the preliminary examination of current production techniques and resources may reveal hidden inefficiencies and unnecessary expenditure

■ the fact that costs are to be monitored may increase the cost consciousness of the workforce (and the management)

■ the system lends itself to exception reporting – this is a technique where results are only reported when they are outside a predetermined range so that action can be taken; for example a company may decide that only when costs are more than 2% away from the standard should the variances be investigated

There is therefore a variety of arguments for developing and using a standard costing system. The main uses that a particular organisation intends to make of the system will determine how it goes about setting standards. We will now see what a 'standard cost' consists of, what information we will need to set the standards and where it can be obtained.

COMPOSITION OF STANDARD COSTS

elements of standard costs

The composition of standard costs – whether you are calculating the standard cost of a rubber washer, an aeroplane, or a hip-replacement operation – can be analysed into common elements:

Direct Costs	Indirect Costs
Direct Materials	Variable Overheads
Direct Labour	Fixed Overheads
Direct Expenses	

We will concentrate on the standards and variances for direct materials, direct labour, and fixed overheads.

absorption costing and marginal costing models

The breakdown of costs (shown above) into direct and indirect costs is based on the **absorption costing** model, where a suitable portion of all production costs (indirect as well as direct) is absorbed into the product's cost. A great many standard costing systems use this approach.

Some organisations prefer to use standard costing based on the **marginal costing** model if that ties in with their other costing systems. We looked at some of the ways that marginal costing can be used to help with decision making in the last chapter. However, we will concentrate on examining standard costing using traditional absorption costing, since that is the most likely form that you will come across.

standard direct material costs

You can assume when developing a standard direct material cost (and calculating variances) that this cost behaves as a variable cost. For example, it is reasonable to expect that the material cost for 2,000 items will be twice the cost of 1,000 of the same item. This assumption allows us to work out the standard cost for individual units, so that we can then multiply it by the quantity produced. It also explains why the absorption and marginal versions of these standards are effectively the same.

The standard direct material cost for a product comprises two elements:

■ the amount of the material, and

■ the cost of the material

For example, a batch of 1,000 rubber washers may require 3 kilos of rubber, which costs £1 per kilo. If this data were accepted as the standard figures, then the standard direct material cost for each batch of washers would clearly be 3 kilos x £1 = £3.00.

The fact that the data needed to calculate a standard direct material cost is based both on the *amount* and also on the *cost* of the materials helps us to see:

- where the information will come from, and
- how the variances can be calculated

standard direct labour costs

The composition of the standard direct labour cost for a cost unit is very similar to the material cost. It is based on the assumption that this type of cost is variable, and so twice as many products will cost about twice as much. The standard direct labour cost for a product also consists of two elements:

- the amount of labour time to be used, and
- the labour cost per unit of time (the labour rate)

Using our example of a batch of rubber washers, if the standard direct labour time needed to manufacture them was 2 hours, and the standard labour cost was £8 per hour, then the standard direct labour cost would obviously be £16 per batch. Assuming there were no other direct costs, the total standard direct cost would be:

	£	
Materials	3.00	
Labour	16.00	
	19.00	for one batch of washers

SOURCES OF INFORMATION FOR STANDARD SETTING

Once we are familiar with the elements that make up a standard for direct cost, we can now look at the information sources for each of those elements. The way an organisation chooses to set standards will have an impact on how reliable and accurate they are, and for how long they can remain useful. There will be a range of values that could be used for each figure, and the organisation should have a policy that will guide managers in setting standards; this will also determine how any variances are ultimately interpreted.

The following examples of sources of information should not be learnt as lists. You are advised to think about each one so that you can see how it could be useful. In this way you can then suggest suitable information sources for a given situation.

the amount of material

The main information sources could be:

- product specifications (the 'recipe' for the product being made)
- technical data from the material supplier (eg recommended usage)
- historical data on quantities used in the past
- observation of manufacture

Standard setting may also need to take into account:

- estimates of wastage
- quality of material
- production equipment and machinery available, and its performance

the cost of material

The information sources could include:

- data from suppliers
- records of previous prices paid
- anticipated cost inflation (measured by general or specific price indices)
- anticipated demand for scarce supplies
- production schedules and bulk buying policy (in conjunction with availability of bulk discounts)
- seasonality of prices
- anticipated currency exchange rates

the amount of labour time

Information sources could include:

- data on previous output and efficiency levels
- results of formal observations (work study, or 'time and motion' study)
- anticipated changes in working practices or productivity levels
- the level of training of employees to be used

the labour cost per unit of labour time

Possible sources of data include:

- current pay rates
- anticipated pay rises
- the expected effects of bonus schemes

To establish an appropriate rate it may also be necessary to take into account:

- equivalent pay rates of other employers in the locality
- changes in legislation (eg minimum wage rates)
- general or industry-specific wage cost indices
- grade of labour (or subcontractors) to be used

THE CALCULATION OF DIRECT COST VARIANCES

When cost standards have been set we can compare them with the actual results as they become available. We do this by working out 'variances' – the difference in cost between standard cost and actual cost.

Variances are 'favourable' when the actual costs are lower than the standard and 'adverse' when the actual costs (or quantities) are higher than the standard.

We will first summarise the types of variance and then explain how to do the calculations. Set out below is a diagram showing the variances that we will be studying. This type of diagram is sometimes known as a 'variance tree'. (Direct expense variances and variable overhead variances have been ignored in these diagrams for simplicity.)

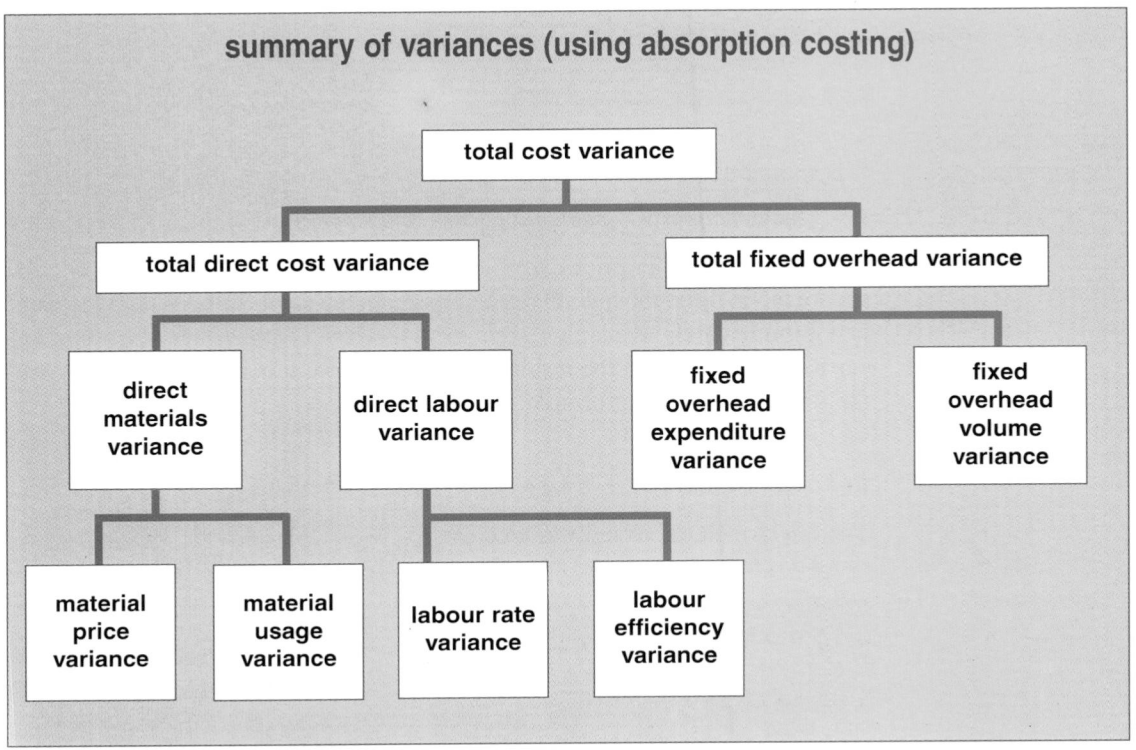

DIRECT MATERIAL VARIANCE

The total direct material variance is the difference between the standard cost of material and the actual cost of material for the actual production.

It would make no sense to compare the actual cost of what was produced with the standard cost of another quantity; we must compare like with like. Often the standard cost figure that we need can be arrived at by multiplying the standard cost for one unit by the quantity of units actually produced. The actual costs will of course already relate to the actual production level.

The total direct material variance can then be analysed into the **direct material price variance,** and the **direct material usage variance**. As their names suggest, the first sub-variance measures the amount of the cost difference due to the price of material, and the second, the cost difference due to the amount of material used.

direct material price variance

The direct material price variance =

the standard cost of the actual quantity of material used	minus	the actual cost of the actual quantity of material used

It is sometimes useful to express this as:

actual quantity x (standard price – actual price)

This will work if the prices are for a unit of material (for example a kilo or square metre), and the quantity is expressed in the same units. Where the data is not immediately available in this form there is a danger that any rounding carried out will distort the result of the calculation. It is then advisable to use the first version of the formula.

direct material usage variance

The direct material usage variance =

the standard quantity of material for the actual production at standard price	minus	the actual quantity of material used at standard price

This is often expressed as:

standard price x (standard quantity – actual quantity)

The information for this variance is usually available in this form, so the rounding problems associated with price variances are unlikely to arise.

All the above formulas have been presented so that numerically positive answers will give rise to favourable variances, and a negative answer will mean the variance will be adverse. However it is best to determine favourable or adverse from logic since formulas can be remembered incorrectly. Simply, if it costs more than standard, or the usage is more than standard, the direct variance must be adverse.

calculation of variances

The key to calculating the variances accurately is remembering the basis of the formulas. One method that may help is the mnemonic 'PAUS', based on:

Price variances are based on

Actual quantities, but

Usage variances are based on

Standard prices.

One explanation why the variances are calculated in this way is that purchases are sometimes converted to standard price (and a price variance calculated) when the materials are bought. This price variance would relate to the actual materials bought. The materials in stock would then be valued at standard price, and the usage variance would be calculated based on the amounts issued to production at standard price.

A diagram can be used to illustrate how direct material variances are linked. It can be a useful aid to explanation, but should not be used as a means of remembering how to calculate the variances, since when some variances are favourable the diagram can become less easy to follow.

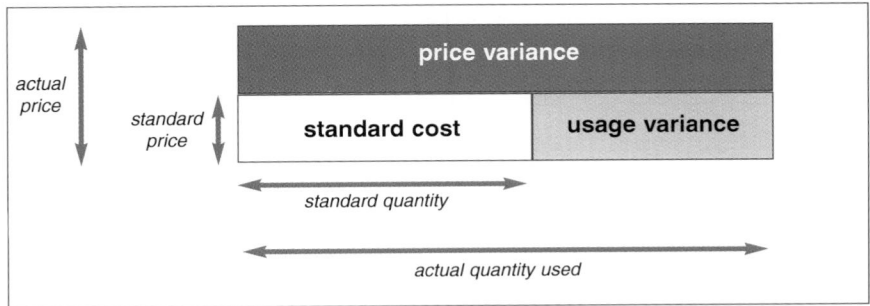

Also remember that the two sub-variances must add up to the total direct material variance. This is a useful check.

CASE STUDY
Jean-E-Us — Direct Material Variance

Jean-E-Us makes denim jeans that are sold to various clothing wholesalers. The company now uses standard costing to help plan and control its costs. Although it makes several styles and sizes of jeans, they all use the same grade of denim. This has a standard price of £2.50 per square metre. The standard quantity of denim to make an average pair of jeans has been set at 3 square metres, after allowing for wastage. This gives a standard material cost of £7.50 for every pair of jeans manufactured.

During November the company made 2,300 pairs of jeans. To do this they used 7,000 square metres of denim. The denim cost an average of £2.60 per square metre (£18,200 in total).

required

Calculate the total direct material variance for the November production, and analyse it into the direct material price variance and the direct material usage variance.

solution

Total direct material variance

All the variances will be based on the actual production that took place in November of 2,300 pairs of jeans. The first calculation is therefore to work out the standard material cost of this volume of production:

2,300 pairs of jeans x £7.50 per pair = £17,250.

We know that the material actually cost £18,200 (based on 7,000 square metres at £2.60 per square metre).

The total direct material variance is therefore:

£17,250 - £18,200 = £950 Adverse

This is based on the difference between the standard and the actual cost of material for the actual production. It is adverse since the material cost was more than expected.

Direct Material Price Variance

The direct material price variance shows the part of the total material variance that is due to the actual price per square metre differing from the standard price. Note that it is based on the actual quantity of material used. (Remember the PA part of PAUS):

Actual quantity x (standard price – actual price)
7,000 square metres x (£2.50 – £2.60)
= £700 Adverse.

The variance is adverse because we paid more per square metre than we expected.

If the actual price per square metre is not a round number, then we would use the other version of the formula as follows:

The standard cost of the actual quantity of material used minus the actual cost of the actual quantity of material used.

This would give the figures:

(7,000 square metres x £2.50) – £18,200
= £700 Adverse.

The answer is the same, but make sure that you can use both versions to calculate the material price variance.

Direct Material Usage Variance

The direct material usage variance shows the part of the total material variance that is due to the quantity of material that we used differing from the standard quantity.

We use the standard price per metre to value this difference in quantity. (Remember the US part of PAUS):

Standard price x (standard quantity – actual quantity)

We can calculate the standard quantity of denim for 2,300 pairs of jeans as:

2,300 x 3 square metres = 6,900 square metres.

This is then used with the other data that we already have:

£2.50 x (6,900 sq metres – 7,000 sq metres)   = £250 Adverse.

The variance is adverse since we used more material than the standard quantity.

We should now find that these two sub-variances

add back to the total direct material variance:

Direct Material Price Variance	**£700 Adv**
Direct Material Usage Variance	**£250 Adv**
Total Direct Material Variance	**£950 Adv**

This is a good indicator that our calculations are correct. If ithe total does not agree then we will know that we have made an error!

DIRECT LABOUR VARIANCE

The calculation of direct labour variances is very similar to that of direct material variances.

The total direct labour variance is the difference between the standard cost of labour and the actual cost of labour for the actual production.

This total labour variance can then be analysed into two sub-variances in a similar way to material variances. The direct labour rate variance measures the labour cost difference due to the rate paid, and the direct labour efficiency variance measures the cost difference due to the amount of labour time used. The concept of labour 'rate' is similar to material 'price', and labour 'efficiency' is similar to material 'usage'. This makes remembering the calculation method and interpreting the variances much easier.

direct labour rate variance

The direct labour rate variance =

the standard cost of the actual labour hours used	minus	the actual cost of the actual labour hours used

It is sometimes useful to express this as:

actual labour hours x (standard rate – actual rate)

Note how similar this is to the direct material price variance. This version of the formula will work if both rates are hourly. There is a risk of rounding errors if the actual hourly rate cannot be calculated exactly, in which case it is advisable to use the first version of the formula.

direct labour efficiency variance

The direct labour efficiency variance =

standard labour hours for actual production at standard rate	minus	actual labour hours used at standard rate

This is often expressed as:

standard rate x (standard hours – actual hours)

This also has a strong resemblance to the material usage variance; we are simply considering the quantity of labour hours instead of the quantity of material. We will usually have the information for this variance available in this form, so the rounding problems are unlikely to arise.

Provided we can remember the similarity of the labour sub-variances to the material ones, there is probably no need to use any other memory aid. The direct labour sub-variances must add up to the total direct labour variance.

CASE STUDY
Jean-E-Us – Direct Labour Variance

Jean-E-Us (see last Case Study) has the following standard labour data for producing one pair of jeans:

All types of jeans use the same grade of labour, and the standard rate of pay is £5.60 per hour.

The standard labour time to make a pair of jeans is 45 minutes, including cutting the material out and sewing and finishing the garment. This gives a standard labour cost of £4.20 for every pair of jeans manufactured.

During November the company made 2,300 pairs of jeans. The actual labour cost was £10,000, based on 2,000 actual hours worked at an average rate of pay of £5.00 per hour.

required

Calculate the total direct labour variance for the November production, and analyse it into the direct labour rate variance and the direct labour efficiency variance.

solution

Total Direct Labour Variance
The calculation starts with the standard labour cost for the November production of 2,300 pairs of jeans:

2,300 x £4.20 = £9,660

This means that the total labour variance is:

£9,660 – £10,000 = £340 Adverse

This is based on the difference between the standard and the actual cost of labour for the actual production. It is adverse since the labour cost was more than expected.

Direct Labour Rate Variance

The direct labour rate variance shows the part of the total labour variance that is due to the actual labour rate per hour differing from the standard rate. It is based on the actual number of hours worked.

Actual labour hours x (standard rate – actual rate)

2,000 labour hours x (£5.60 – £5.00) = £1,200 Fav

The variance is favourable because we paid less per labour hour than we expected.

In a similar way to material price variances, if the actual labour rate per hour is not a round number, then we would use the other version of the formula.

Direct Labour Efficiency Variance

The direct labour efficiency variance shows the part of the total labour variance that is due to the number of labour hours that were required differing from the standard number of hours to produce the actual production level. We use the standard labour rate per hour to value this time difference.

Standard labour rate x (standard hrs – actual hrs)

We can calculate the standard labour hours to make 2,300 pairs of jeans as:

2,300 x 45 minutes = 103,500 minutes =

1,725 standard labour hours

This is then used with the other data that we already have:

£5.60 x (1,725 standard labour hours – 2,000 actual hours)

= £ 1,540 Adverse

The variance is adverse since we took longer than the standard time.

We should now find that these two sub-variances add back to the total direct labour variance:

Direct Labour Rate Variance	**£1,200 Fav**
Direct Labour Efficiency Variance	**£1,540 Adv**
Total Direct Labour Variance	**£340 Adv**

THE MAIN CAUSES OF DIRECT VARIANCES

If you are familiar with the sources of data for creating variances, and what each variance means, it should not be necessary to learn lists of possible causes of variances. Instead it should be possible to think your way logically through each situation to assess its impact on variances. You may be given a scenario and asked to suggest the possible causes of variances. It is far better to use the facts given to you about the situation to develop a reasoned commentary, than to remember an 'all purpose' list of causes and simply regurgitate it.

interdependence of variables

Some situations may give rise to more than one variance. For example, purchasing cheaper material of lower quality could cause a favourable price variance but an adverse usage variance if there was higher wastage. This is often referred to as the **interdependence of variances**. It can result in unfair praise or blame if different managers are responsible for each variance.

The following table gives examples of possible causes of variances. Read it carefully, and ensure that you can appreciate the logic of including each item, and its effect. There may be situations where you can envisage the cause creating further variances, since the table is not intended to be exhaustive.

'A' or 'F' refers to whether adverse or favourable variances may result.

Direct Variance:	Material Price	Material Usage	Labour Rate	Labour Efficiency
Possible Cause:				
Poorly set standard	A or F	A or F	A or F	A or F
Different material supplier	A or F			
Different material quality	A or F	A or F		A or F
Different currency exchange rate	A or F			
Poor training		A		A
Higher grade staff		F	A	F
Unexpected pay increase			A	
High general inflation	A		A	
Improved production machinery		F		F
Unexpected bulk discounts	F			
Low bonus payments			F	A

FIXED OVERHEADS

the difference between variable and fixed costs

So far in this chapter we have examined the direct costs of materials and labour. We looked at how standard costing could be used to predict this part of a product's cost and how variances could be calculated to help analyse any differences between the standard cost and the actual cost. Since direct costs will often rise in proportion to the output of products there is logic in calculating a standard for the direct cost for one unit of production, and expecting it to remain the same when multiplied by the number of items produced. For example, it would seem fair to expect that the direct material for 2,000 widgets would cost about 2,000 times more than that for one widget.

You can assume that direct costs will behave in the same way as variable costs, ie they will change in line with the level of activity (the number of products produced). They are therefore different from fixed costs: **variable costs** are costs where the total amount varies in proportion to the activity level when the activity level changes; **fixed costs** are costs that do not normally change when the level of activity changes.

fixed overhead variances – absorption costing

One advantage that standard **absorption costing** can claim is that the standard cost for a product will be a 'full' cost, and incorporate a portion of *all* the costs of production. Incorporating fixed costs into the cost of the product means that an **absorption rate** must be used which will apply the fixed costs to each of the units of production. So, if the actual production level is close to the projected level, and all cost estimates are reasonably accurate, the standard cost of the product will be close to the actual full cost. However, the standard cost will give an inaccurate forecast of product cost:

■ if the costs are not as expected and

■ if the production volume is not in line with projections

For this reason the fixed overhead variances produced under standard absorption costing need to take account of:

■ overhead costs

■ production volumes

The variances analyse the differences between the amount of fixed overhead absorbed by a standard absorption costing system, and the actual cost of the fixed overheads.

total fixed overhead variances and expenditure and volume variances

The absorption rate is agreed before the period starts, and is arranged so that the planned level of output will cause enough overhead absorption to exactly match the expected overheads. If the absorption rate is based on units, then the output will be measured in units, but if the absorption base is labour hours or machine hours, then we must also measure the output in standard labour or machine hours.

If everything goes to plan there will be no under-absorption or over-absorption, and no fixed overhead variances! The plan could be thought of as a pair of weighing scales, as shown in this diagram:

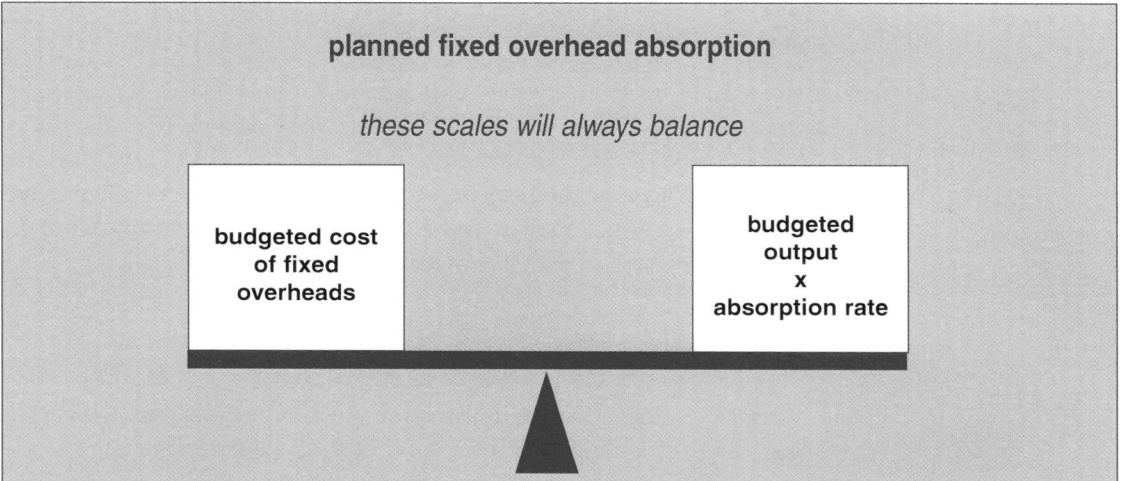

This diagram is based on the planned figures and so will always balance, since the figures are designed to agree. It would not make sense to plan for an imbalance!

will the plan work? – possible imbalances

Once actual figures are used there may be an imbalance due to either

- the fixed overheads not costing what was expected, or
- the output not turning out to be as planned, or – as usually happens –
- a combination of the two

Since the absorption rate is worked out in advance and used throughout, the rate itself will not be a source of any imbalance.

Once the results for the period are known, then the planned figures on the diagram shown above can be replaced by the actual figures in the diagram shown on the next page.

under-absorption – adverse variance

The scales in this diagram tip down on the left because actual costs are higher than the amount of cost absorbed and so there is under-absorption. This will result in the total fixed overhead variance being adverse.

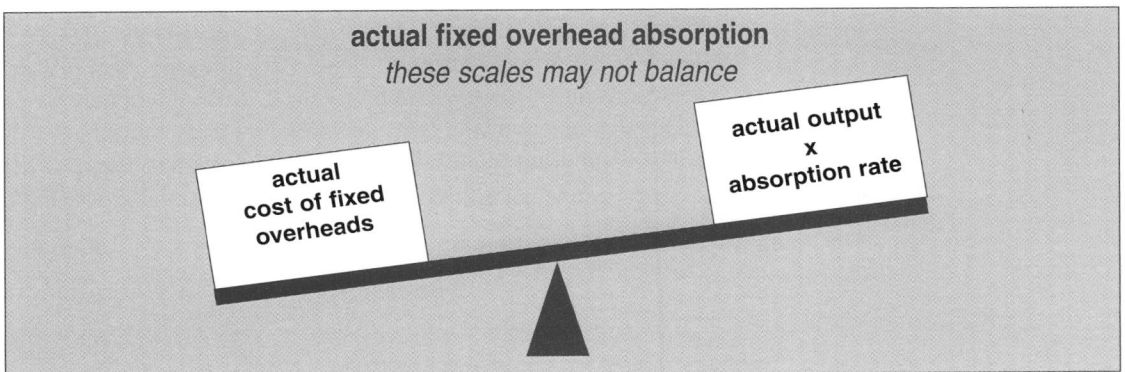

over-absorption – favourable variance

The scales in the next diagram tip down on the right because actual costs are lower than the amount of cost absorbed, and so there is over-absorption. This will result in the total fixed overhead variance being favourable.

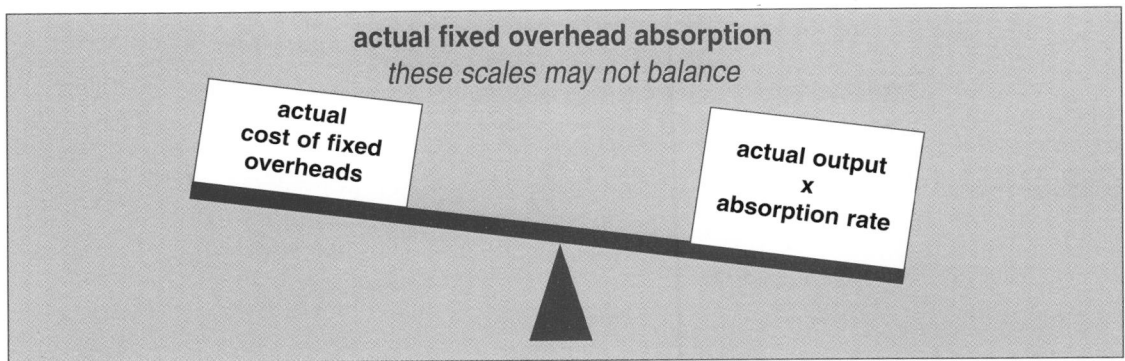

fixed overhead expenditure and volume variances

The imbalances shown in the last two diagrams measure the total fixed overhead variance – this is due to the difference between the plan and what actually happens. There are two reasons why the actual results could be different from the plan, and these two reasons combine to result in the total fixed overhead variance. They are:

1 The actual amount spent on fixed overheads may not be the same as the planned (or budgeted) fixed overheads. In the diagrams the left-hand sides of the scales – the actual cost – will be different from the planned figure. This difference is measured by the fixed overhead expenditure variance.

2 The actual volume of output may not be the same as the planned level of output. This will cause a different amount of fixed overhead to be absorbed than was expected. In the diagrams the figures in the right-hand sides of the scales will differ. This difference is measured by the fixed overhead volume variance.

In basic terms, the actual figures on both sides of the scales (last two diagrams) are likely to be different from the plan (first diagram) because of changes in expenditure and output volume levels. It is the combination of these two differences/variances which will decide which way the scales will tip and result in an overall total fixed overhead variance. A tip to the left will be an overall adverse variance, a tip to the right will be a favourable variance.

The main variances can be summarised when we bring the two diagrams together like this:

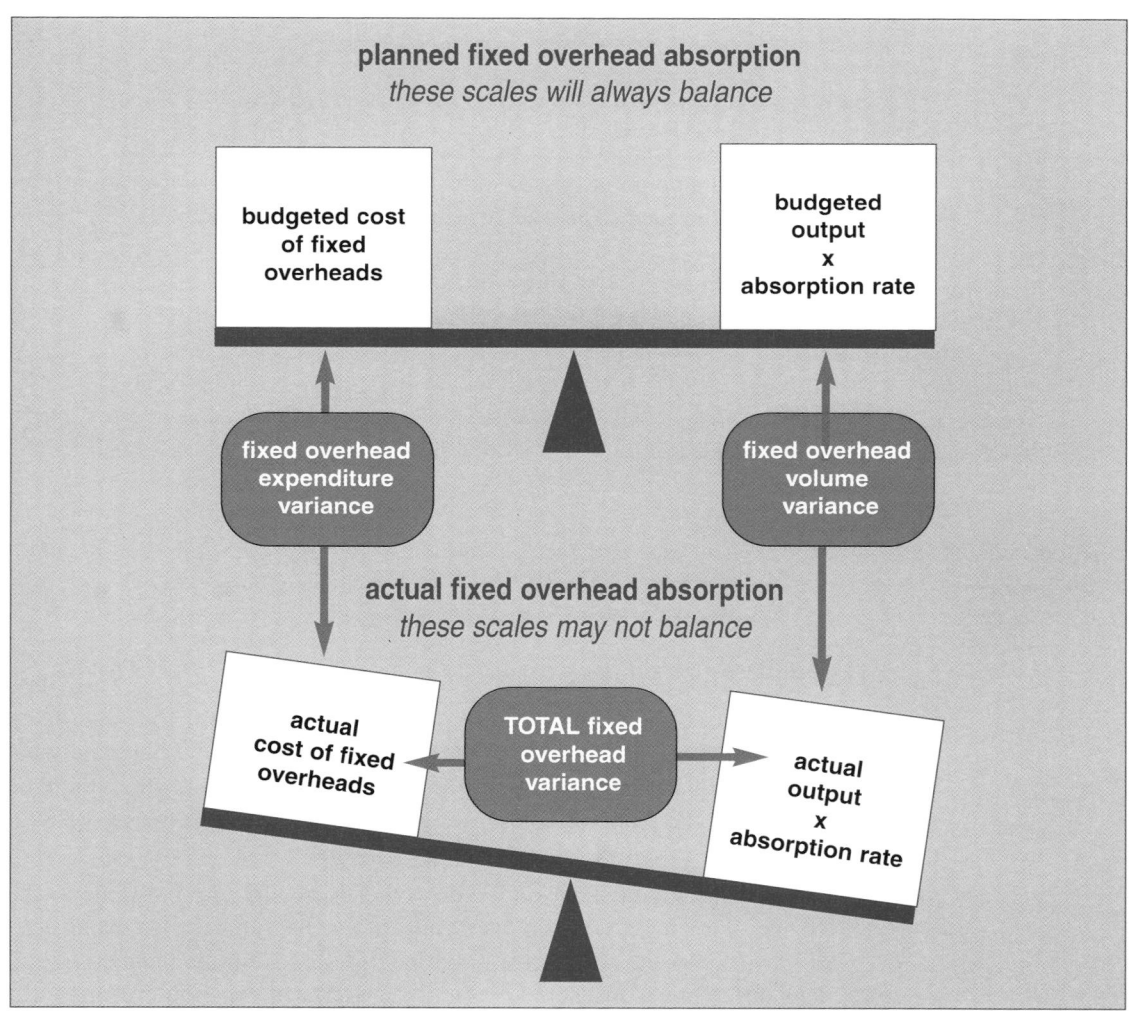

Total fixed overhead variance therefore equals:

fixed overhead absorbed – actual cost of fixed overhead

the absorption base

Remember that the amount of fixed overhead absorbed will be based on the actual output multiplied by the absorption rate. The way that the output is measured here will depend on the way that absorption is to take place (the absorption base). If the absorption base is production units, then the output needs to be measured in that form.

We will only use examples and case studies where the absorption base is the number of production units. You may come across situations where standard hours are used as an absorption base. This simply means that the two production levels (budgeted and actual) have been converted into standard hours for convenience. If this method is used, the volume variance can be further divided into two more variances – the fixed overhead capacity and efficiency variances. These additional sub-variances are not discussed further in this book.

calculation of fixed overhead expenditure and volume variances

The fixed overhead expenditure variance is shown on the left-hand side of the last diagram, and is calculated as follows:

Budgeted Cost of Fixed Overheads	*minus*	Actual Cost of Fixed Overheads

If the actual cost is less than the budgeted cost the variance is favourable, and if it is greater the variance is adverse.

The fixed overhead volume variance is shown on the right-hand side of the last diagram, and is calculated as follows:

absorption rate x (actual output – budgeted output)

CASE STUDY

Jean-E-Us – Fixed Overhead Variances

Jean-E-Us has the following standard fixed overheads data:

Each pair of jeans made absorbs £8.00 in fixed overheads. This was calculated based on the budgeted fixed overheads of £20,000 per month, divided by the budgeted production level of 2,500 pairs of jeans per month. In November the actual fixed overheads amounted to £21,000. The production was 2,300 pairs of jeans (as stated earlier).

required

Calculate the total fixed overhead variance for November, and analyse it into the fixed overhead expenditure variance and the fixed overhead volume variance.

solution

Using the diagram, we can insert the data from the Case Study:

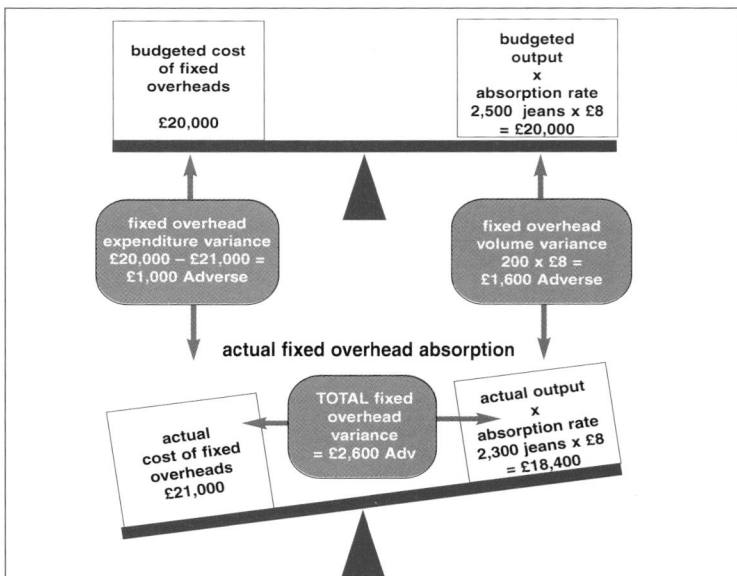

The expenditure variance is adverse because the costs were more than expected. The volume variance was adverse because the production volume was lower, therefore not absorbing enough overheads. The total adverse variance represents the shortfall of overheads absorbed compared with actual overheads.

We should now find that the two overhead sub-variances add back to the total fixed overhead variance:

Fixed Overhead Expenditure Variance	£1,000 Adverse
Fixed Overhead Volume Variance	£1,600 Adverse
Total Fixed Overhead Variance	£2,600 Adverse

USING VARIANCES TO RECONCILE ACTUAL WITH STANDARD COSTS

reconciliation statements

It is important that we can show how variances account for all the cost differences between the standard cost of the production and the actual cost. We can do this by using a **reconciliation statement**. Note that we must compare like with like and use the data for the standard cost of the actual production to compare with the actual cost. The actual cost will of course also relate to the actual production.

The reconciliation statement can start with either the standard or the actual cost, and will arrive, via the variances, at the other figure. We are accounting for the differences, in the same way that a bank reconciliation statement accounts for the differences between the cash book balance and the bank account balance.

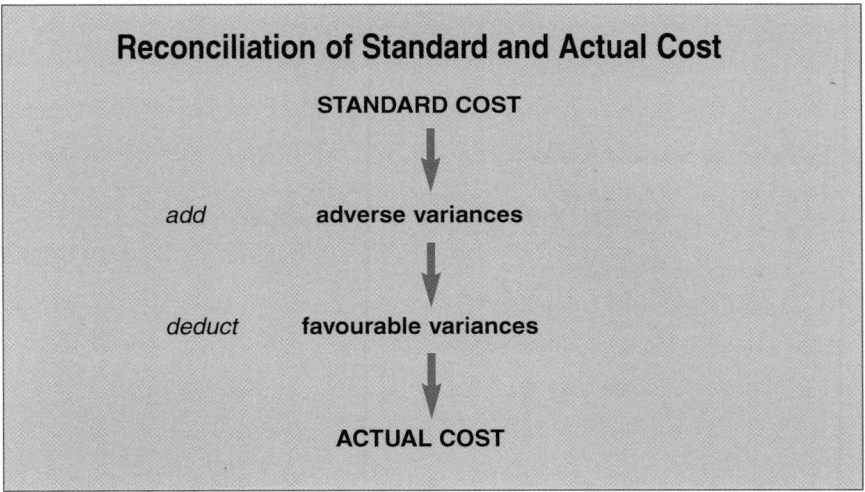

Reconciliation of Standard and Actual Cost

STANDARD COST

add **adverse variances**

deduct **favourable variances**

ACTUAL COST

If we start the statement with the standard cost of the production, then each adverse variance will be added to this amount, since the actual cost we are working towards will be higher. Any favourable variances will be deducted since this accounts for a lower actual amount. Since a reconciliation only takes a short time to prepare, it is often worth producing since it will show if any variances are inaccurate.

Remember that, like agreement of a trial balance, a satisfactory variance reconciliation is not a guarantee that the variances are correct! Also remember that sub-variances are part of main variances, so be careful not to double count them.

The various direct and overhead variances have been calculated for Jean-E-Us for the production of 2,300 pairs of jeans in November. The standard costs for one pair of jeans were:

		£
Direct Materials	3 square metres denim at £2.50 sq mt	7.50
Direct Labour	45 minutes labour at £5.60 hour	4.20
Fixed Overheads	£8.00 per pair of jeans	8.00
		19.70

The actual costs in November were:

Direct Materials	£18,200
Direct Labour	£10,000
Fixed Overheads	£21,000
	£49,200

The variances were calculated as:	£
Direct Material Price Variance	700 A
Direct Material Usage Variance	250 A
Direct Labour Rate Variance	1,200 F
Direct Labour Efficiency Variance	1,540 A
Fixed Overhead Expenditure Variance	1,000 A
Fixed Overhead Volume Variance	1,600 A

The following facts were also confirmed regarding the operations in November:

- A high number of trainees were used in the labour force. They were paid a lower rate than fully trained employees.

- There was an unexpected price increase in the cost of denim from the company's supplier.

- There was an unexpected rise in insurance costs that form part of the company's fixed overheads.

tasks required

1 Produce a statement that reconciles the standard cost of producing 2,300 pairs of jeans with the actual costs that were incurred in November.

2 Suggest how the different variances may be linked to the facts that have been confirmed.

solution

task 1

Our reconciliation statement will start with the standard cost of producing the jeans that were actually made – in other words how much we would predict the 2,300 jeans would cost. The variances that have been calculated are then used to explain the gap between that figure and the actual cost. Adverse variances are added to the standard cost (since they mean that the actual cost is greater), and favourable variances are deducted.

Reconciliation Statement for November

		£	£
Standard Cost of 2,300 jeans. £19.70 x 2,300 =			45,310
Variances:			
Add	Direct Material Price Variance	700 A	
Add	Direct Material Usage Variance	250 A	
Deduct	Direct Labour Rate Variance	(1,200 F)	
Add	Direct Labour Efficiency Variance	1,540 A	
Add	Fixed Overhead Expenditure Variance	1,000 A	
Add	Fixed Overhead Volume Variance	1,600 A	
			3,890
Actual Costs incurred			49,200

task 2

The facts about the November operations seem to link with the variances as follows:

- The direct material price variance is due to the unexpected price increase in denim from the company's supplier.

- The direct material usage variance shows that more than the standard amount of material was used. This may link to the trainee workers who may have wasted more material than usual.

- The favourable labour rate variance is due to the average lower rate being paid compared with the standard rate. This ties in with the fact that the trainees are paid a lower rate.

- The adverse labour efficiency variance is because work was slower than expected. This could also be due to the use of trainees.

- One of the reasons for the adverse fixed overhead expenditure variance would be the increased insurance cost that was not expected.

- The fixed overhead volume variance is caused by lower output than expected. The slower working by the trainees could be responsible for this.

We can see that the majority of the adverse variances may be linked to the use of trainees (£250 + £1,540 + £1,600 = £3,390). Set against this is the saving of £1,200 due to their lower pay rate. Provided the trainees improve their performance over time, these causes for variance will disappear.

chapter summary

- Standard costing was developed in the manufacturing industry as a method of predicting the cost of products. When comparing actual costs with the expected (standard) costs, it enables variances to be calculated that help explain differences in the costs. There are various other benefits from setting up and using a standard costing system.

- Standard costs can be used based on a traditional absorption costing system. The direct cost variances for materials and labour can be divided into sub-variances based on the cost per unit of the resource (Price or Rate variances) and the quantity of resource used (Usage and Efficiency variances).

- Information for setting standards can be derived from inside and outside the organisation. This information includes formal and informal historical data and technical specifications, and can be general or specific.

- Direct cost variances (including sub-variances) are calculated according to rules that help ensure uniformity. The variances can be used to reconcile the standard cost for the production with the actual costs.

- Fixed overhead variances differ from direct variances due to the way that fixed costs behave and the way the chosen costing system deals with them.

- When absorption costing is used, fixed overheads are absorbed into the output based on a predetermined rate. The total fixed overhead variance is the amount by which the amount of overhead absorbed differs from the overhead actually incurred. This can be due to the expenditure on overhead being different to what was planned, or the volume of output being different, or both.

- There can be many causes of variances, some influencing just one variance, while others affect several. The accurate calculation of a variance does not provide information on the cause itself, but the causes can often be deduced by examining the factors surrounding the situation.

key terms

standard costing	a formal method for predetermining the cost of cost units or products
variance analysis	the comparison of actual costs with standard costs and the calculation of variances which account for differences in the costs
absorption costing	a technique that values cost units based on a suitable part of all the costs of production, whether fixed or variable in behaviour
total direct material variance	the difference between the standard material cost for the actual production and the actual material cost

direct material price variance	the part of the total direct material variance due to differing material prices – it is based on the difference between standard and actual prices for the actual quantity of material used (or bought)
direct material usage variance	the part of the total direct material variance due to differing quantities of material used – it is based on the difference between the standard quantity of material for the actual production, and the actual quantity of material used, valued at standard price
total direct labour variance	the difference between the standard labour cost for the actual production and the actual labour cost
direct labour rate variance	the part of the total direct labour variance due to differing labour rates – it is based on the difference between the actual labour hours at standard rate and the actual labour cost
direct labour efficiency variance	the part of the total direct labour variance due to differing time being spent – it is based on the difference between the standard labour time for the actual production, and the actual labour time used, valued at standard rate
cost reconciliation statement	a statement reconciling the standard cost of the actual production with the actual cost by using relevant variances
fixed overheads	indirect costs which do not vary in proportion to the volume of production or other output
total fixed overhead variance (absorption costing)	the difference between the actual expenditure on fixed overheads, and the amount of fixed overhead absorbed by the actual output; the expenditure and volume variances will combine in this total variance
fixed overhead expenditure variance (absorption costing)	the difference between the budgeted expenditure and the actual expenditure on fixed overheads in a reporting period
fixed overhead volume variance (absorption costing)	the difference between the fixed overhead which would have been absorbed by the budgeted output and the fixed overhead which was absorbed by the actual output; the efficiency and capacity variance will combine in this variance

activities

Note: an asterisk (*) after an activity number means that an answer is provided in Appendix 1.

23.1* Quango Limited has set its direct standard costs for one unit of its product, the quango, as follows:

Direct Materials: 96 kg @ £ 9.45 per kilo

Direct Labour: 5 hours 6 minutes @ £6.30 per hour

During week 13 the company produced 700 units of quango, and incurred direct costs as follows:

Direct Materials: 71.5 tonnes were used, costing a total of £678,700

Direct Labour: 3,850 hours were worked, costing a total of £24,220

Note: there are 1,000 kilos in a tonne.

Required:

Calculate the relevant direct cost variances and use them to reconcile the standard cost for the actual production level with the actual costs.

23.2* A company has the following data on direct costs for the month of August.

		£
Production Units made		19,000
Actual Direct Materials	37,000 kg	278,000
Actual Direct Labour	9,800 hrs	58,600
Total Actual Direct Costs		336,600

Standard data is as follows for one unit of production:

Direct Materials	2 kg at £7.50 per kilo	=	£15.00
Direct Labour	0.5 hour at £6.00 per hour	=	£3.00

Required:

Calculate the relevant direct cost variances.

23.3* The following comments were made by an inexperienced trainee:

Required:

State which of the comments are valid, and which are false.

(a)   The likelihood of obtaining bulk discounts cannot be relevant when setting direct material price standards.

(b)   Work study is often used to assist in setting times for direct labour standards.

(c)   Material price standards must always be amended when a different supplier is used.

(d)   Two of the main reasons for using standard costing are to improve planning and control.

(e)   Standard costing can be used in conjunction with responsibility accounting. Using this technique each manager would be expected to control the variances occurring in his area of responsibility.

(f)   Interpretation of variances can help point to the reasons why costs are not in line with the plans.

(g)   Proposed bonus schemes should be taken into account when setting labour rate standards.

(h)   Reconciling standard cost with actual cost is difficult because when variances are a mixture of adverse and favourable, the statement may not agree.

(i)   If a reconciliation of standard cost for the actual production level with the actual cost agrees, this guarantees that all the variances are correct.

23.4* Jo is a self-employed haulage contractor who owns her articulated lorry. Her plans before the financial year started were to drive 50,000 miles in the next year, and absorb the budgeted annual fixed overheads of £10,000 using miles travelled as an absorption base.

In reality she travelled 45,000 miles, and the fixed overheads amounted to £12,000.

(a)   Calculate the budgeted absorption rate per mile.

(b)   Calculate the – fixed overhead expenditure variance

– fixed overhead volume variance

– total fixed overhead variance

(c)   State whether there has been under-absorption or over-absorption.

23.5 Cottage Doors Limited make doors by hand from reclaimed timber. The reclaimed timber is sometimes difficult to obtain. They only make one style of door, although it is made in different sizes. The following data and tasks relate to the operations of the business during October.

The reclaimed pine that the company uses is obtained from various second-hand pine suppliers. The standard cost of one square metre of suitable reclaimed pine is £28. During October the business used 350 square metres of reclaimed pine. This actually cost £10,500. Some of the pine that was delivered was delayed, and they were unable to obtain any more pine that month, and could not produce as many doors as they had planned.

The standard quantity of reclaimed pine to make one door is 2.5 square metres. This is based on an average-sized door, and allows for some wastage of wood. During October the company made 130 doors.

The standard time to make one door is 3 hours. The standard labour rate is £7.00 per hour. During October the company used 400 labour hours, which cost £3,000. The employees had received a pay rise since the standards were set.

The company had budgeted fixed overheads for October of £2,400, but the actual fixed overheads were £2,350. The business had planned to make 200 doors in October, and the standard fixed overhead absorption rate had therefore been agreed in advance at £12.00 per door. The weather was unusually mild for October, and this saved electricity costs.

Required

(a)   Using the standard data given, calculate the standard cost of one door.

(b)   Calculate the relevant direct and fixed overhead variances for the October production of doors.

(c)   Reconcile the standard cost of 130 doors with the actual costs incurred in October, using the variances that you have calculated.

(d)   Using the data given, suggest reasons for the variances that have occurred.

23.6 Jean-E-Us makes denim jeans that are sold to various clothing wholesalers. The company uses standard costing to help plan and control its costs.

Although it makes several styles and sizes of jeans, they all use the same grade of denim. This has a standard price of £2.50 per square metre. The standard quantity of denim to make an average pair of jeans has been set at 3 square metres, after allowing for wastage. This gave a standard material cost of £7.50 for every pair of jeans manufactured.

All types of jeans use the same grade of labour, and the standard rate of pay is £5.60 per hour. The standard labour time to make a pair of jeans is 45 minutes, including cutting the material out and sewing and finishing the garment. This gives a standard labour cost of £4.20 for every pair of jeans manufactured.

Each pair of jeans made absorbs £8.00 in fixed overheads. This was calculated based on the budgeted fixed overheads of £20,000 per month, divided by the budgeted production level of 2,500 pairs of jeans per month.

During December the company made 2,400 pairs of jeans. To do this they used 7,300 square metres of denim. The denim cost an average of £2.55 per square metre (£18,615 in total).

The actual labour cost was £10,450, based on 1,900 actual hours worked at an average rate of pay of £5.50 per hour.

In December the actual fixed overheads amounted to £20,800.

Required

1   Calculate the standard cost of one pair of jeans.

2   Calculate the standard cost of the December production of 2,400 pairs of jeans.

3   Calculate the total of the actual costs incurred in December.

4   Calculate all relevant variances for the December production.

5   Use the variances to reconcile the standard cost (calculated in [2]), with the total actual costs incurred (calculated in [3]).

CASE STUDY
LetzGo Holidays

LetzGo Holidays specialises in holidays to European destinations for the 18 to 25 age group. The company has to book its hotel rooms as much as a year in advance, and is finding it difficult to accurately predict the level of demand.

Charles Letz, the firm's founder, is explaining the current situation to his business adviser:

'We've been running for a few years now, and there seems to be a pattern of demand emerging.

Of course the holiday business is very seasonal, but there must be a way of analysing the past to help predict the future. I don't expect the results to be perfect, but I would like a logical basis on which I can build my forecasts.

I also know that our customers view the price that they pay as one of the most important features of a holiday. Although we've had to raise prices slightly most years, I think our holidays represent better value now than ever, but I'd like some data to be able to prove it.

Then perhaps we could have an advertising campaign showing how our prices have got better – but it must be accurate. Imagine having to withdraw the adverts if we couldn't prove our claims!'

The business adviser thought for a moment and then replied.

'There are two techniques that I think may help with your problems. They are **time series analysis** and using **index numbers**. Both are quite straightforward, and you may find that they can help with other aspects of the business as well.'

learning objectives

When you have studied this chapter you will be able to:

■ use time series analysis to use past data to generate a forecast of the future

■ use index numbers to show the effects of inflation on prices and costs, and apply the technique to other situations

TIME SERIES ANALYSIS

Time series analysis involves analysing numerical trends over a time period. It is often used to examine past and present trends so that future trends can be forecast. The term 'trend analysis' is used to describe the technique that we will now examine. At its simplest the concept is based on the assumption that data will continue to move in the same direction in the future as it has in the past.

Using the sales of a shoe shop as an example we will now look a range of techniques for dealing with trends.

an identical annual change

A shoe shop 'Comfy Feet' has sold the following numbers of pairs of shoes annually over the last few years:

Year 1	10,000
Year 2	11,000
Year 3	12,000
Year 4	13,000
Year 5	14,000
Year 6	15,000
Year 7	16,000

It does not require a great deal of arithmetic to calculate that if the trend continues at the previous rate – an increase of 1,000 pairs a year – then shoe sales could be forecast at 17,000 pairs in Year 8 and 18,000 pairs in Year 9. Of course this is a very simple example, and life is rarely this straightforward. For example, for how long can this rate of increase be sustained?

average annual change

A slightly more complex technique could have been used to arrive at the same answer for the shoe shop. If we compare the number of sales in Year 7 with the number in Year 1, we can see that it has risen by 6,000 pairs. By dividing that figure by the number of times the year changed in our data, we can arrive at an average change per year. The number of times that the year changes is 6, which is the same as the number of 'spaces' between the years (or alternatively the total number of years minus 1).

Shown as an equation this becomes:

Average Annual Sales Change =

$$\frac{(Sales\ in\ Last\ Year - Sales\ in\ First\ Year)}{(Number\ of\ Years - 1)} = \frac{(16,000 - 10,000)}{(7 - 1)}$$

= + 1,000, which is what we would expect.

The + 1,000 would then be added to the sales data in Year 7 of 16,000 (the last actual data) to arrive at a forecast of 17,000.

This technique is useful when all the increases are not quite identical, yet we want to use the average increase to forecast the trend. A negative answer would show that the average change is a reduction, not an increase. We will use this technique when estimating the trend movement in more complicated situations.

constructing a graph

The same result can be produced graphically. Using the same shoe shop example we can extend the graph based on the actual data to form a forecast line.

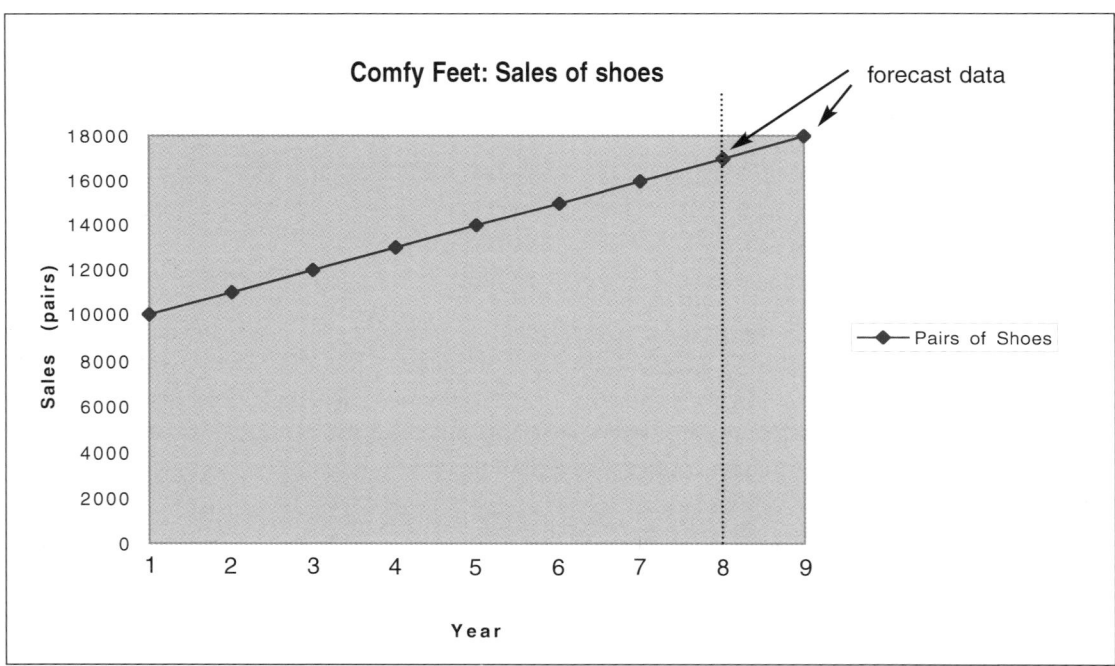

If, in another situation, the actual data does not produce exactly equal increases, the graph will produce the same answer as the average annual change provided the straight line runs through the first and last year's data points.

using a formula

The data in the example could have been expressed in the following formula:

$$y = mx + c$$

where

    y   is the forecast amount

    m is 1,000 (the amount by which the data increases each year)

    x   is the number of years since the start year (Year 1)

    c   is 10,000, which is the sales figure in the start year (Year 1)

If we wanted a forecast for Year 9, we could calculate it as:

Forecast	=	(1,000 x number of years since Year 1) + 10,000
y (the forecast)	=	(1,000 x 8) + 10,000
	=	18,000, which is what we would expect.

This formula works because the formula is based on the equation of a straight line.

TIME SERIES ANALYSIS AND SEASONAL VARIATIONS

There are four main factors that can influence data which is generated over a period of time:

■ **the underlying trend**

This is the way that the data is generally moving in the long term. For example the volume of traffic on our roads is generally increasing as time goes on.

■ **long-term cycles**

These are slow moving variations that may be caused by economic cycles or social trends. For example, when economic prosperity generally increases, this may increase the volume of traffic as more people own cars and fewer use buses. In times of economic depression there may be a decrease in car use as people cannot afford to travel as much or may not have employment which requires them to travel.

■ **seasonal variations**

This term refers to regular, predictable cycles in the data. The cycles may or may not be seasonal in the normal use of the term (eg Spring, Summer, etc). For example traffic volumes are always higher in the daytime, especially on weekdays, and lower at weekends and at night.

■ **random variations**

All data will be affected by influences that are unpredictable. For example flooding of some roads may reduce traffic volume along that route, but increase it on alternative routes. Similarly the traffic volume may be influenced by a temporary shortage of fuel in the country.

In the following type of numerical problems we will ignore the effects of long-term cycles (which will effectively be considered as a part of the trend) and random variations (which are impossible to forecast). We are therefore left with analysing data into underlying trends and seasonal variations, in order to create forecasts.

The technique that we will use follows the process in this diagram:

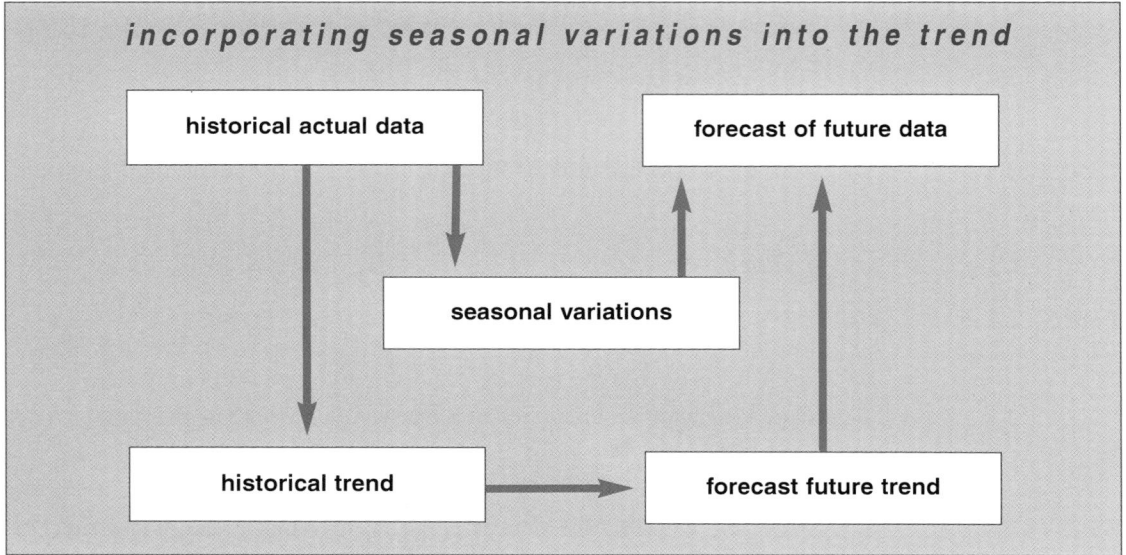

The process is as follows:

1 The historical actual data is analysed into the historical trend and the seasonal variations.

2 The historical trend is used to forecast the future trend, using the techniques examined in the last section.

3 The seasonal variations are incorporated with the forecast future trend to provide a forecast of where the actual data will be in the future.

analysing historical actual data

The trend can often be calculated by using 'moving averages'. If you are using moving averages it is important that:

■ your workings are laid out accurately

■ the number of pieces of data that are averaged corresponds with the number of 'seasons' in a cycle

■ where there is an even number of 'seasons' in a cycle, a further averaging of each pair of averages takes place

The Case Study on the next page shows the full process.

CASE STUDY

The Seasonal Company: moving averages and forecast trends

The Seasonal Company sells various products, including wellington boots for use in wet weather. The quarterly management accounts for recent quarters have revealed that the following numbers of these boots were sold:

	Quarter 1	Quarter 2	Quarter 3	Quarter 4
Year 1	4,000	1,600	2,200	4,800
Year 2	4,400	2,000	2,500	5,200
Year 3	4,800	2,400	3,100	5,600
Year 4	5,200	2,800	3,400	6,000

required

1 Use moving averages to analyse the historical data into the trend and the seasonal variations.

2 Use the data from (1) to forecast the sales for each quarter of Year 5 (next year).

solution

1 Calculating the trend and seasonal variations

Step 1 The first thing to do is to rearrange the historical data into a single column with spaces between each of the figures – this is to the right of the date column:

Year	Quarter	Step 1 Historical Sales Data	Step 2 4-point Moving Average	Step 3 Averaged Pairs (Trend)	Step 4 Seasonal Variation
1	1	4,000			
	2	1,600			
			3,150		
	3	2,200		3,200	−1,000
			3,250		
	4	4,800		3,300	+1,500
			3,350		
2	1	4,400		3,387.5	+1,012.5
			3,425		
	2	2,000		3,475	−1,475
			3,525		
	3	2,500		3,575	−1,075
			3,625		
	4	5,200		3,675	+1,525
			3,725		
3	1	4,800		3,800	+1,000
			3,825		
	2	2,400		3,925	−1,525
			3,925		
	3	3,100		4,025	−925
			4,075		
	4	5,600		4,125	+1,475
			4,175		
4	1	5,200		4,212.5	+987.5
			4,250		
	2	2,800		4,300	−1,500
			4,350		
	3	3,400			
	4	6,000			

Step 2 Calculate the 4-point moving averages. This is the average of each group of four figures, starting with Year 1 quarters 1 to 4, followed by Year 1 quarter 2 to Year 2 quarter 1, and so on. Place each moving average in the appropriate column, alongside the centre point of the figures from which it was calculated. We are using a 4-point average because there are 4 quarters in our data. This also means that the average will fall alongside gaps between our original data. Note that the shaded lines and arrows are drawn here for illustration only – to show where the figures come from.

Step 3 Calculate the average of each adjacent pair of moving averages. These are also known as 'centred moving averages'. This is carried out so that these figures can be placed alongside the centre of each pair, and will therefore fall in line with the original quarterly data (see shaded arrow). If there was an odd number of 'seasons' in a cycle (for example 13 four-weekly periods) then this stage would not be required. We have now calculated the trend figures. Notice that the first trend calculated is in quarter 3 of the first year, and the last one is in quarter 2 of the last year. This is inevitable when calculating a trend from quarterly data using moving averages.

Step 4 Calculate the seasonal variations, and insert them into the last column. These are the amounts by which the actual figures (left hand column) are greater or smaller than the trend figures. Be careful to use the correct + or – sign. The shaded arrows show the figures that are used.

2 Forecast the sales for each quarter of Year 5

In order to use the data that we have calculated for a forecast we will need to work out some average figures. This is because in this case study you will notice that:

• the trend is not increasing by exactly the same amount every quarter

• the seasonal variations are similar, but not quite identical for each of the same quarters

We can use the technique for calculating the average increase in the trend that we looked at earlier:

Average Trend Change =

$$\frac{(Last\ known\ trend - First\ known\ trend)}{(Number\ of\ Quarterly\ trends - 1)} = \frac{(4,300 - 3,200)}{11} = +100$$

We can also average the seasonal variations by grouping them together in quarters:

Year	Quarter 1	Quarter 2	Quarter 3	Quarter 4
1			– 1,000	+ 1,500
2	+ 1,012.5	– 1,475	– 1,075	+ 1,525
3	+ 1,000	– 1,525	– 925	+ 1,475
4	+ 987.5	– 1,500		
Totals	+ 3,000	– 4,500	– 3,000	+ 4,500
Averages	+ 1,000	– 1,500	– 1,000	+ 1,500

At this stage we should check that the average seasonal variations total zero. Here they do, but if they do not then minor adjustments will need to be made to the figures.

We can now use the average trend movements and the average seasonal variations to create a forecast. We start with the trend at the last point when it was calculated, and work out where it will be at future points by using the average movements. For example quarter 1 of Year 5 is 3 quarters past quarter 2 of Year 4, which is when we last knew the trend. We then incorporate the average seasonal variations to complete the forecast.

Forecast Workings:

		Forecast Trend		*Seasonal Variations*	*Forecast*
Year 5	Qtr 1	4,300 + (3 x 100)	= 4,600	+ 1,000	5,600
	Qtr 2	4,300 + (4 x 100)	= 4,700	− 1,500	3,200
	Qtr 3	4,300 + (5 x 100)	= 4,800	− 1,000	3,800
	Qtr 4	4,300 + (6 x 100)	= 4,900	+ 1,500	6,400

All the data and the solution to this Case Study can be shown on a graph, as follows:

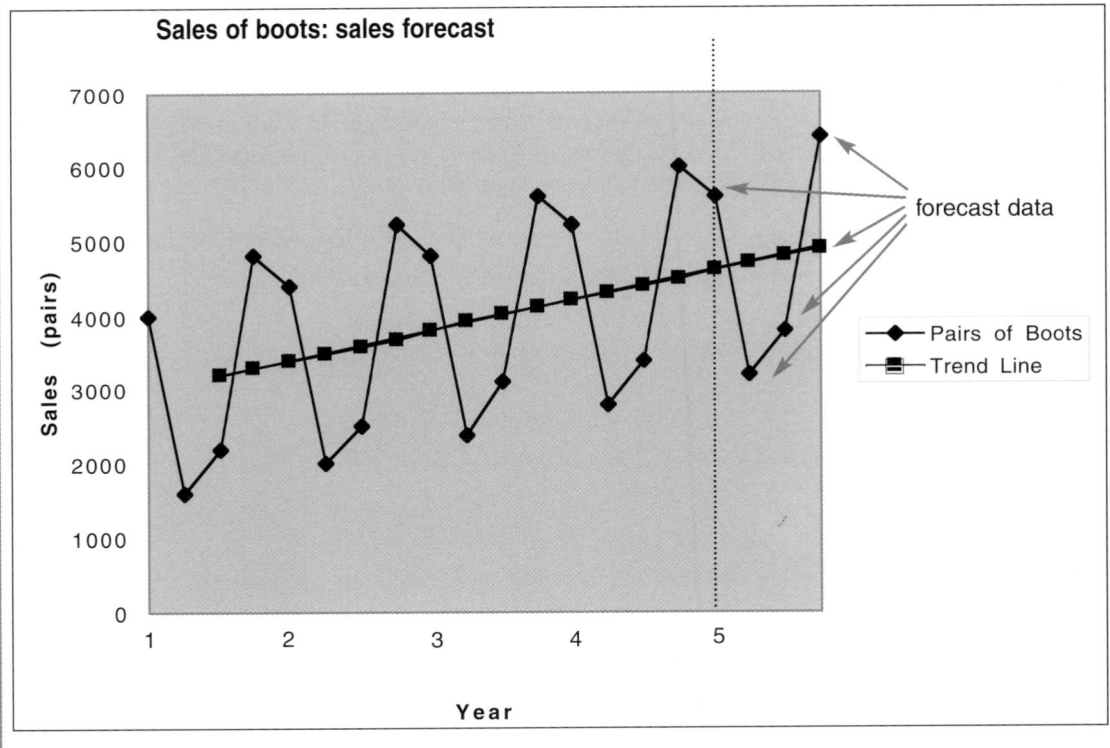

Let us now see how the technique of time series analysis can help LetzGo Holidays forecast its sales levels.

CASE STUDY
Forecasting demand: LetzGo Holidays

Charles Letz, the founder of LetzGo Holidays has provided the following historical data on numbers of holidays in Tunisia that the firm has sold over the last few years:

	Quarter 1	Quarter 2	Quarter 3	Quarter 4
2000	1,000	2,900	3,400	1,300
2001	1,400	3,300	3,800	1,700
2002	1,800	3,700	4,200	2,100
2003	2,200	4,100	4,600	2,500

required

1 Using suitable techniques, forecast the number of holidays that may be sold in each of the quarters of the years 2004 and 2005.

2 Suggest practical reasons, based on the Case Study situation, why the forecast may prove inaccurate.

solution

Before analysing the historical data into a trend and seasonal variations it is worth confirming that the data contains regular seasonal variations. The easiest way to check this is to draw the data onto a graph, and make sure that there are clear, regular patterns in the data:

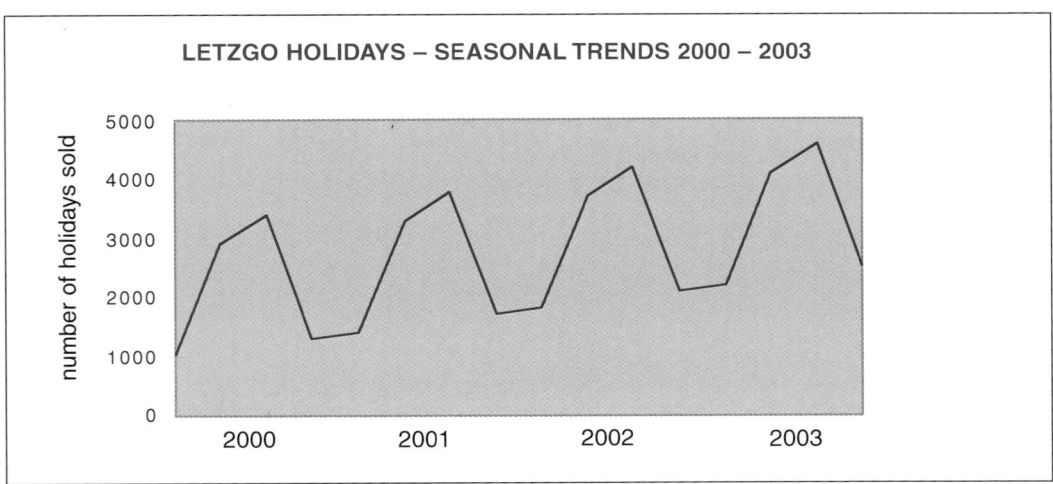

We can see the pattern quite clearly – number of holidays starts from a low figure each year in the first quarter, then rises and peaks in quarter 3 before falling back in the last quarter. We can now set out a working paper as we did in the 'Seasonal Company' case study to calculate the trend (by using moving averages) and the seasonal variations as follows:

Year	Quarter	Historical Data	4-point Moving Averages	Averaged Pairs (Trend)	Seasonal Variation
2000	1	1,000			
	2	2,900			
			2,150		
	3	3,400		2,200	+1,200
			2,250		
	4	1,300		2,300	−1,000
			2,350		
2001	1	1,400		2,400	−1,000
			2,450		
	2	3,300		2,500	+800
			2,550		
	3	3,800		2,600	+1,200
			2,650		
	4	1,700		2,700	−1,000
			2,750		
2002	1	1,800		2,800	−1,000
			2,850		
	2	3,700		2,900	+800
			2,950		
	3	4,200		3,000	+1,200
			3,050		
	4	2,100		3,100	−1,000
			3,150		
2003	1	2,200		3,200	−1,000
			3,250		
	2	4,100		3,300	+800
			3,350		
	3	4,600			
	4	2,500			

In this case study we can see that:

- the trend is rising by exactly 100 holidays every quarter, and
- the seasonal variations are identical for the same quarters in each year (quarter 1 is always − 1,000, quarter 2 is always + 800, quarter 3 is always + 1,200, and quarter 4 is always − 1,000)

This makes the final stage of forecasting straightforward. By the first quarter of 2004 the trend should have risen to 3,600 (it was 3,300 in quarter 2 of 2003, plus 3 rises of 100). The forecast for 2004 and 2005 can now be completed in a table as follows, and a graph of the results produced to illustrate the situation.

	Quarter	Forecast Trend	Seasonal Variations	Forecast
2004	1	3,600	− 1,000	2,600
	2	3,700	+800	4,500
	3	3,800	+1,200	5,000
	4	3,900	−1,000	2,900
2005	1	4,000	−1,000	3,000
	2	4,100	+800	4,900
	3	4,200	+1,200	5,400
	4	4,300	−1,000	3,300

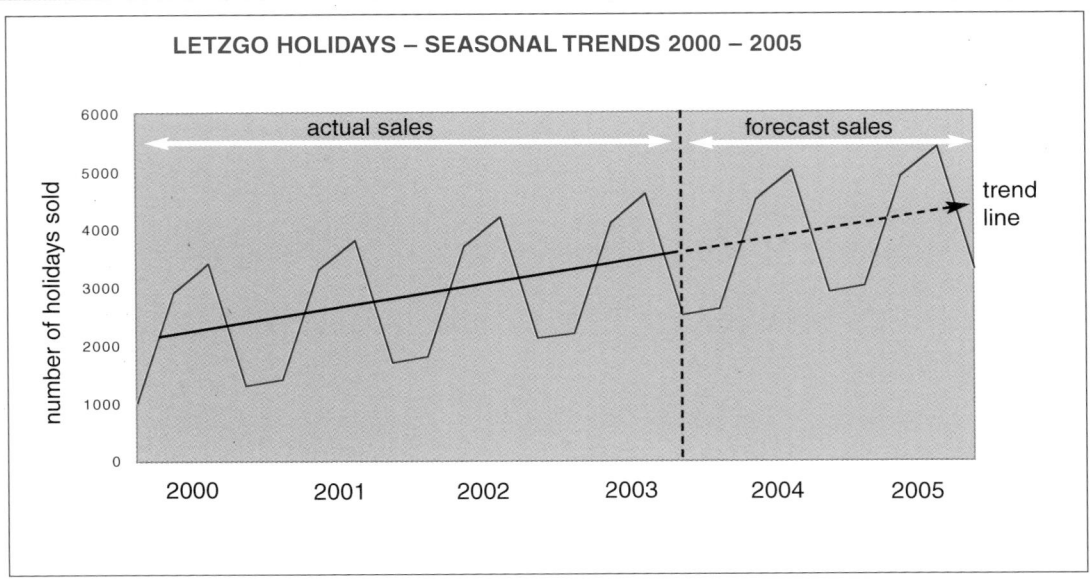

Reasons that the forecast could prove inaccurate include:

- The exchange rate between the UK and Tunisia could alter significantly, making the holidays more or less expensive. This would affect demand for holidays there.
- Other destinations that compete with Tunisia could improve their facilities or reduce their prices. This could reduce the demand for holidays in Tunisia.
- Tunisia could become a more (or less) fashionable destination for the young holidaymakers that LetzGo sells to.
- The economic situation in the UK could change. If it worsened then demand for holidays abroad could decrease.

ABSOLUTE OR PERCENTAGE SEASONAL VARIATIONS?

The examples that we have used so far have used the idea of absolute (or 'additive') seasonal variations – ones that are expressed in the same units as the actual data that is being analysed. Sometimes a more accurate forecast can be obtained when the seasonal variations are expressed as a percentage of the trend. This would make sense when the variations naturally become greater as the trend increases. This could occur, for example, if we were analysing the cost of domestic heating over a number of years: as the trend increased (due to cost inflation) the differences between the summer and winter heating costs would also increase at about the same rate.

CASE STUDY

UK ice cream consumption

An investigation into the quarterly amount an average UK household spends on ice cream has revealed an underlying trend and percentage variations as follows:

Each quarter the trend increased by £1, and by quarter 4 of 2000 it had reached £50 per quarter.

The seasonal variations, based on percentages of the trend in that quarter were calculated as:

Quarter 1	− 70%
Quarter 2	+ 40%
Quarter 3	+ 60%
Quarter 4	− 30%

required

Forecast the average quarterly spend on ice cream per household in each quarter of 2003.

solution

The calculation here is straightforward. Note that quarter 1 of 2003 is 9 quarters later than the quarter that we already know the trend for, ie quarter 4 of 2000.

		Forecast Trend		Seasonal Variations	Forecast
2003	Qtr 1	£50 + (9 x £1)	= £59	− 70%	£17.70
	Qtr 2	£50 + (10 x £1)	= £60	+ 40%	£84.00
	Qtr 3	£50 + (11 x £1)	= £61	+ 60%	£97.60
	Qtr 4	£50 + (12 x £1)	= £62	− 30%	£43.40

INDEX NUMBERS

Index numbers are used to assist in the comparison of numerical data over time. The most commonly used index is perhaps the Retail Price Index that gives an indication of inflation by comparing the cost of a group of expenses typically incurred by households in the UK from year to year. There are many other types of index numbers that have been created for specific purposes, for example:

- the average wage rate for a particular job, or for all employment
- the average house price either by region or throughout the UK
- the market price of shares (eg the FTSE 100 index)
- the quantities of specific items that are sold or used (eg litres of unleaded petrol)
- the quantities of a group of items that are sold or used (eg litres of all motor fuel)

Whatever type of index we need to use, the principle is the same. The index numbers represent a convenient way of comparing figures. For example, the RPI was 166.6 in January 2000, and it is estimated it will be 183.0 in January 2004. This means that average household costs will have gone up by about 10% in the four years between. We could also calculate that if something that cost £5.00 in January 2000 had risen exactly in line with inflation, it would have cost £5.49 in January 2004. This calculation is carried out by:

$$\text{historical price} \quad \times \quad \frac{\text{index of time converting to}}{\text{index of time converting from}}$$

ie   £5.00   x   (183.0 ÷ 166.6)   =   £5.49

You may be told that the 'base year' for a particular index is a certain point in time. This is when the particular index was 100. For example the current RPI index was 100 in January 1987. You do not need to know the base year to do the sort of calculations that are likely to be asked of you.

Index numbers referring to costs or prices are the most commonly used ones referred to in this book. If we want to use cost index numbers to monitor past costs or forecast future ones, then it is best to use as specific an index as possible. This will then provide greater accuracy than a more general index.

For example, if we were operating in the food industry, and wanted to compare our coffee cost movements with the average that the industry had experienced, we should use an index that analyses coffee costs in the food industry. This would be much more accurate than the RPI, and also better than a general cost index for the food industry.

We will now return to LetzGo Holidays and apply the technique of index numbers to the prices that it charges.

CASE STUDY
Using index numbers to adjust for inflation: LetzGo Holidays

The following data relates to holidays in Tunisia sold by LetzGo Holidays in August each year.

Year	Number of Holidays	Total Selling Price
2000	1190	£476,000
2001	1330	£537,320
2002	1470	£602,700
2003	1610	£668,150

Charles Letz (the firm's founder) believes that although the average price charged per holiday has risen each year, the rises are lower than UK inflation. If this is true, he is keen to use the data in an advertising campaign to stress that these holidays have become cheaper in real terms.

The following are the UK retail price index figures (August 2002 and 2003 have been estimated):

August 2000	170.5
August 2001	174.0
August 2002	179.0
August 2003	182.0

required

1 Calculate the average actual price of an August holiday for each of the years 2000 to 2003.

2 Restate these actual average prices based on the UK cost of living in August 2003. (i.e. in August 2003 prices).

3 Show both sets of figures on a suitable graph.

4 Write a statement that could be used in advertising literature to clearly reflect your findings.

solution

1 The average actual prices are calculated by dividing the total selling prices by the number of holidays:

2000:	£476,000 ÷ 1190	=	£400
2001:	£537,320 ÷ 1330	=	£404
2002:	£602,700 ÷ 1470	=	£410
2003:	£668,150 ÷ 1610	=	£415

2   These prices can be restated in August 2003 UK prices by multiplying by the RPI in August 2003 and dividing by the RPI at the time of the original prices:

2000:	£400 x 182 ÷ 170.5	=	£426.98
2001:	£404 x 182 ÷ 174.0	=	£422.57
2002:	£410 x 182 ÷ 179.0	=	£416.87
2003:	£415	=	£415.00

3   Graph to show average price for an August holiday in Tunisia with LetzGo.

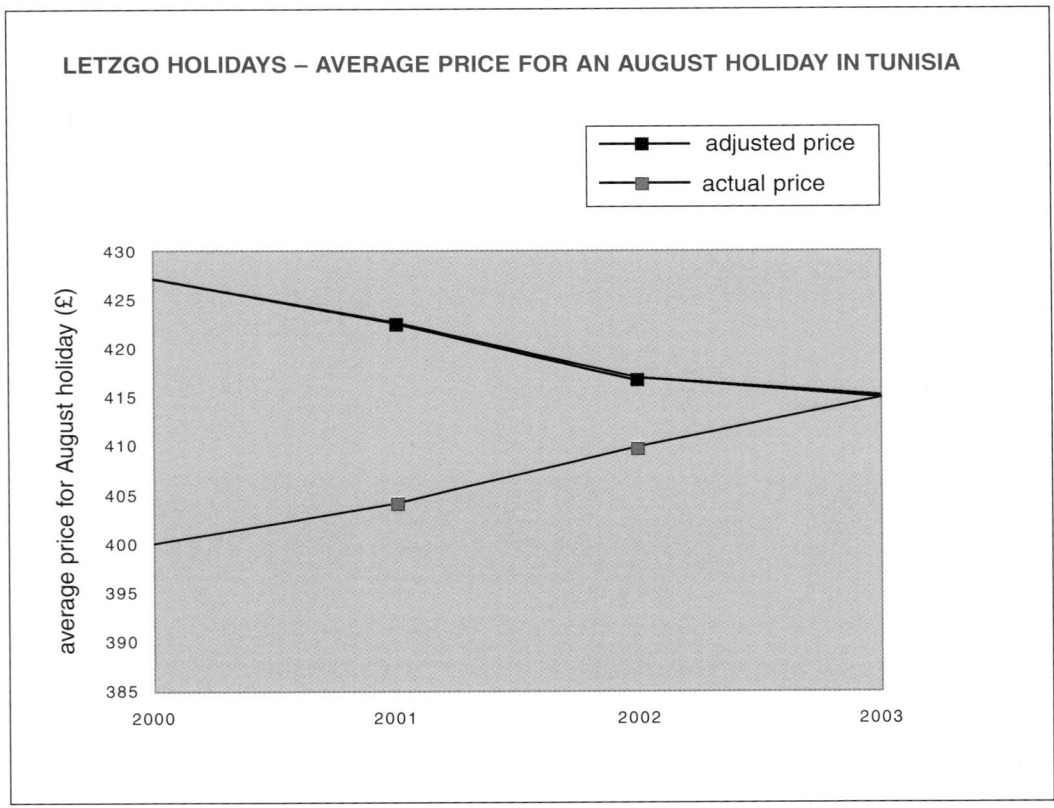

4   Statements could include:

• Each year the average price of a LetzGo August holiday in Tunisia fell in real terms (after allowing for UK inflation).

• LetzGo August holidays in Tunisia were cheaper in real terms in 2003 than in any of the previous three years.

chapter summary

- Time series analysis can be used to identify trends in past data so that future data can be forecast. The trend can often be established by using moving averages.

- Regular repeating patterns called seasonal variations may also be present in the data, and these patterns can be also used to develop the forecast.

- Index numbers are used to compare various sorts of data over time. Although the numbers themselves are not amounts of money or quantity, they can be used to represent their movements over time.

- The Retail Price Index is a common example of an index. It is used as a measure of inflation by comparing the costs incurred by UK households at different times.

- We can adjust actual figures (for example costs) by using the RPI or other index numbers. This provides us with information of how the cost would look once inflation or other specific effects have been taken into account.

key terms

time series analysis	the analysis of data that occurs over time – it can include the technique of trend analysis where the trend in the data is identified, often to facilitate forecasting
moving averages	a technique of calculating the averages of groups of data, so that each group overlaps with those groups preceding and following – it is often used to identify the trend in a time series
seasonal variations	a pattern of regular movements in data away from the underlying trend; these patterns repeat themselves over time, and may be due to various regular cycles as well as seasons
forecast	an estimation of data in the future, which may be generated by numerical techniques such as time series analysis, or modified or built up in other ways
index numbers	a series of numbers that are used to compare some attribute of data, for example prices or quantities of specific items or groups of items
retail price index (RPI)	the index most often used to measure the effect of UK inflation, the RPI regularly measures the cost of a range of products and services that are purchased by typical UK households

activities

Note: an asterisk (*) after an activity number means that an answer is provided in Appendix 1.

24.1*   The Supashop that is open 5 days per week has the following cash sales over a period.

	Tues	Wed	Thurs	Fri	Sat
Week 1	£1,830	£1,920	£2,080	£2,160	£2,160
Week 2	£1,880	£1,970	£2,130	£2,210	£2,210
Week 3	£1,930	£2,020	£2,180	£2,260	£2,260

Required

(a)   Using moving averages, analyse this data into the trend and seasonal variations.

(b)   Use the data from (a) to forecast the cash sales for each day of week 4.

24.2   A computer program has analysed the sales data of Pegasus Limited, a garden ornament manufacturer. Using quarter numbers (quarter 30 is the first quarter of year 2000) the sales trend has been determined as:

Sales Trend (in £) = (Quarter Number x £1,200) + £83,000

The Seasonal Variations have been determined as the following percentages of the trend:

Quarter 1   – 10%

Quarter 2   + 80%

Quarter 3   + 15%

Quarter 4   – 85%

Required

(a)   Use the above data to calculate the forecast of sales for Pegasus Limited in £ for each quarter of 2003.

(b)   Comment on any drawbacks of producing sales revenue forecasts directly in money amounts.

24.3 The following historical data relates to sales in units of the Enigma Company.

	Quarter 1	Quarter 2	Quarter 3	Quarter 4
Year 1	500	430	330	280
Year 2	460	390	290	240
Year 3	420	350	250	200
Year 4	380	310	210	160

Required

(a) Using moving averages, analyse this data into the trend and additive seasonal variations.

(b) Use the data to forecast the unit sales for each quarter of year 5.

24.4* An insurance company has analysed its sales of travel insurance over the last two years, and produced the following information:

Year	Quarter	Trend (Policies)	Seasonal Variation (Policies)
1	1	5,800	− 430
	2	5,870	− 350
	3	5,935	+ 880
	4	6,010	− 100
2	1	6,090	− 430
	2	6,165	− 350
	3	6,220	+ 880
	4	6,290	− 100

Required

(a) Calculate the average trend movement per quarter over the last two years.

(b) Use the average trend movement to forecast the expected sales (in numbers of policies) in quarters 3 and 4 of year 3.

24.5 Charles Letz, founder of LetzGo Holidays is concerned about the rising costs of hotel rooms in Goratia. The price of a hotel room is charged in local currency (Go$), and Charles then pays the invoices during the year, converting the cost into sterling at the relevant exchange rate. Although the cost in £ (sterling) is rising each year, the hotelier in Goratia has assured Charles that he has not increased his prices. Charles is concerned that if his costs continue to rise, the holidays in Goratia will become too expensive. Charles has provided the following sample costs for a single hotel room for a week in Goratia:

July 2000	£100
July 2001	£120
July 2002	£150

You have extracted the following information from the index of exchange rates between the UK and Goratia:

Date	Go$ to £1
July 2000	600
July 2001	500
July 2002	400

Required

(a) Calculate the price of a hotel room for each of the three dates in Go$ using the exchange rates operating at the time from the index numbers given.

(b) Calculate the percentage rise in £sterling costs of a hotel room between July 2001 and July 2002. Calculate what the cost would be in £sterling in July 2003 if this percentage rise was repeated between July 2002 and July 2003.

24.6 Charles Letz of LetzGo Holidays is planning the number and cost of self-catering rooms to be booked next year in Southern Horatia. He has compiled the following data on the number of rooms required in each quarter over the last few years:

Year	Quarter	Number of rooms
2000	1	3,200
	2	5,450
	3	7,400
	4	3,650
2001	1	3,000
	2	5,250
	3	7,200
	4	3,450
2002	1	2,800
	2	5,050
	3	7,000
	4	3,250
2003	1	2,600
	2	4,850
	3	6,800
	4	3,050

The rooms must be paid for in Horatian Dollars (H$), after exchanging £ for H$ at the appropriate rate. During 2003 the cost of each room for a week was H$240. The exchange rate in 2003 was H$4 = £1.

During 2004 the cost of a room for a week has been renegotiated at H$220. The exchange rate during 2004 is expected to be approximately H$3.5 = £1.

Required:

(a) Using moving averages, calculate the historical trend and seasonal variations for the number of rooms required for each quarter of 2000 - 2003.

(b) Use the data from (a) to forecast the number of rooms required in each quarter of 2004.

(c) Calculate the cost in £ of a room for one week in Southern Horatia during 2003 and estimate the equivalent cost in 2004.

(d) If the average retail price index in the UK during 2003 is 182.0 and in 2004 is 188.0, calculate whether the average cost of a room in £ has become more expensive, or less expensive, after taking UK inflation into account. Comment briefly on the reasons for your findings.

BUDGETING

CASE STUDY
Camper-Fans — planning for a new business

Kylie and Jed have spent a few years travelling together, and are now planning a new business where they can use some of their experience gained from their time on the road.

'We've been working our way around Europe, doing odd jobs here and there and catching the surf when it was right,' explained Kylie.

'We travelled in an old VW camper van, fixing it when it broke down and moving on when we got the urge. We realised that there are a lot of people out there doing (or planning) the same sort of thing — but what they need is cheap and reliable transport in the form of a camper van.'

Jed picked up the story:

'I approached a firm that hires out camper vans to holidaymakers, and they've agreed to sell their old models on to us. They'll have high mileage, but Kylie and I can recondition the main bits, and reckon we can sell them and make a reasonable profit. We've even got a workshop and sales area lined up, but we know we'll have to firm up our plans.

The bank won't even talk to us unless we've got budgets and cash-flow projections, but we don't know where to start, or whether such things will actually help us with our business, not just keep the bank happy!'

This chapter will explain the different types of budget used by organisations and show how they are coordinated and monitored.

---

learning objectives

When you have studied this chapter you will be able to:

- *explain the purposes of creating budgets*

- *identify the main steps in budget preparation*

- *create sets of profit and cash based budgets for new and existing businesses*

- *use flexed budgets to monitor and control businesses*

- *identify the main features of incremental and zero based budget setting*

THE PURPOSES OF BUDGETS

A budget is a financial plan for an organisation, prepared in advance.

In any organisation the budget provides the mechanism by which the objectives of the organisation can be achieved. In this way it forms a link between the current position and the position that the organisation's managers are aiming for. By using a budget firstly to plan and then to monitor, the managers can ensure that the organisation's progress is coordinated to achieve the objectives of the organisation.

The specific purposes and benefits of using budgets are as follows:

the budget assists planning

By formalising the agreed objectives of the organisation through a budget preparation system, an organisation can ensure that its plans are achievable. It will be able to decide what resources are required to produce the desired outputs, and to make sure that they will be available at the right time.

the budget communicates and coordinates

Because a budget will be agreed by an organisation, all the relevant personnel will be working towards the same ends.

During the budget-setting process any anticipated problems should be resolved and any areas of potential confusion clarified. All the organisation's departments should be in a position to play their part in achieving the overall goals. This objective of all parts of the organisation working towards the same ends is sometimes referred to as 'goal congruence'.

the budget can be used to monitor and control

An important reason for producing a budget is that management is able to monitor the actual results against the budget. This is so that action can be taken to modify the operation of the organisation as time passes, or possibly to change the budget if it becomes unachievable. This is similar to the way that standard costing is used to monitor and control costs, and can be used alongside that technique.

For organisations where control of activities is deemed to be a high priority the budget can be used as the primary tool to ensure conformity to agreed plans. Once the budget is agreed it can effectively become the authority to follow a particular course of action or spend a certain amount of money.

Public sector organisations, with their necessary emphasis on strict accountability, will tend to take this approach, as will some commercial organisations that choose not to delegate too much authority.

the budget can be used to motivate

A budget can be part of the organisation's techniques for motivating managers and other staff to achieve the organisation's objectives. The extent to which this happens will depend on how the budget is agreed and set, and whether it is perceived as fair and achievable. The budget may also be linked to rewards (for example, bonuses) where targets are met or exceeded.

THE INITIAL STEPS IN BUDGET PREPARATION

the aims of an organisation

Before an organisation's managers can begin to build a useful budget there are several initial steps that must be taken. These are based around the fundamental questions about the **aims** – the 'vision' – of the organisation:

'Where do we want it to go?'

'How do we get it there?'

These are essentially long-term issues, and once agreed upon would not tend to be changed very often.

objectives and strategy

For a budget to be of use to an organisation it must be a mechanism for helping the organisation achieve its **objectives**. The objectives are the targets that the managers of the organisation wish it to achieve. The way in which these objectives are expressed will depend upon the type of organisation and the way in which it operates. For example a pet food manufacturer may have the specific objective of obtaining sales penetration of 25% of the UK dog food market, whereas an independent TV production company may have the objective of achieving viewing ratings of over 25% on commercial UK TV.

The organisation must then develop a **strategy** for achieving those objectives. Several alternatives may need to be considered before the final strategy is decided upon. The pet food company mentioned in the above example may decide that it needs to develop and market a new food product for young dogs, to help it to achieve its objective. The independent TV production company may have a strategy of producing pilots for ten new programmes each year from which it can then develop the most promising.

limiting factors – the 'key' budget factor

When an organisation prepares a budget, it must first analyse its **limiting factors** – the issues that determine the level of its output. For a commercial organisation these could include:

- the size of its market

- capacity of its premises

- availability of raw material

- amount of working capital

- availability of skilled workers

One of these factors will be the main one that affects the activity level of the organisation – the **key budget factor.** This is the factor (sometimes known as the 'principal budget factor') that all the aspects of the operation depend upon. For most manufacturing or trading operations the key budget factor is sales; the assumptions that are made about the level of sales in the budget will affect all the other parts of the budget. This is because the organisation will plan to support the budgeted sales level and build the budgets and assumptions around this one issue.

Although sales level is the most common key factor, some commercial organisations may decide that a different factor is the most important in their particular circumstances. For example, if a manufacturer can sell all that it produces, but has production restricted by lack of skilled labour, then the assumed labour level would become the key budget factor. A similar situation would arise if there were production restrictions caused by shortages of raw materials, or limited machine capacity.

Non-commercial organisations will also need to identify their key budget factor, and build their budgets around their assumptions concerning it. Charities and government agencies may consider that there is a demand for their services that is virtually limitless; their principal budget (key) factor is the amount of money they receive to fund what they do. For example, the Government's healthcare provision is limited by the amount of funding it can get from the government spending allocation and from private enterprise. The demand for Oxfam's aid is very high, but its key budget factor is the amount of money it can expect to raise to fund that aid.

Later in the chapter we will continue the Camper-Fan Case Study and explain the 'nuts and bolts' of the way in which budgets are created.

the initial budgeting process

If we combine the ideas just discussed, the initial budget process for an established organisation would follow this pattern:

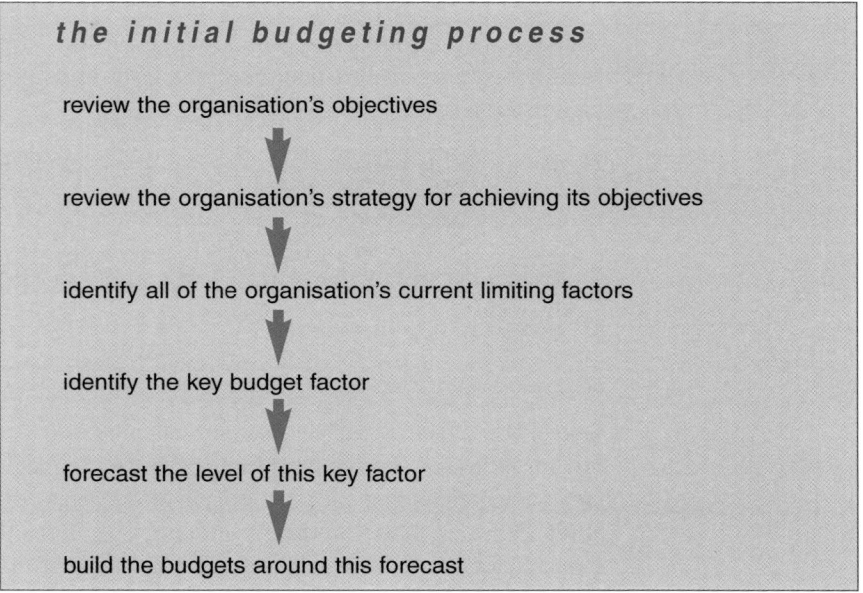

the initial budgeting process

review the organisation's objectives

review the organisation's strategy for achieving its objectives

identify all of the organisation's current limiting factors

identify the key budget factor

forecast the level of this key factor

build the budgets around this forecast

CREATING THE MAIN BUDGETS

There are three main budgets that most organisations ultimately need to create, and they must fit together and be based on common assumptions. These three budgets are:

budgeted profit & loss account

This is based on the same format as the historical profit and loss account. It contains a summary of the budgeted **income** and **expenditure** of the organisation for a future period, and the resulting budgeted profit or loss. It is not cash based, but uses the matching concept to set the expected costs to be incurred by the business against the expected income in any particular time period. It is often produced as a document for a financial year, although it can be broken into months or weeks if required.

cash budget (cash-flow forecast)

This is a projection of the **flow of money** in and out of the business, and therefore shows what will happen to the bank balance if everything goes according to plan. It is only concerned with movements of 'cash', and will include capital expenditure (eg purchases of equipment) as well as revenue expenditure (running costs of the business). It will exclude non-cash expenditure like depreciation. Because bank balances can fluctuate significantly within a business, this budget is usually produced for a series of months or weeks so that any peaks or troughs in the bank balance can be identified. The cash budget is also known as a 'cash-flow forecast'.

budgeted balance sheet

This is based on the same format as the historical balance sheet produced for financial accounting purposes, but is based in the future. It is a statement of the expected **assets**, **liabilities** and **capital** at the end of the budgeting period. Because this document will tie in with the other two main budgets, it will incorporate the profit generated in the budgeted profit and loss account, and the final bank balance as predicted in the cash budget.

The budgeted profit and loss account and the budgeted balance sheet are together known as the **master budget**. There are also a number of other budgets that often have to be created in order to build up sufficient information to create the master budget and the cash budget. We will look at these later in the chapter. First of all we will look at how a relatively simple set of budgets can be created.

We will now return to Kylie and Jed from our introductory Case Study to help them to prepare an initial set of budgets. The key budget factor in this case study is the projected sales level, and all the budgets will be based around this. Although this set of budgets is to be for only six months, the principle involved is identical to producing budgets for a longer period.

CASE STUDY
Camper-Fans – creating an initial set of budgets

situation

Kylie and Jed are planning to start a business selling used camper vans. They will buy their stock from a hire company, recondition the mechanicals, and sell them on to young travellers who want cheap but reliable transport and accommodation. They have agreed to buy at a fixed price of £3,000 for the high mileage vans, and the sellers can supply as many as they are likely to need, at least in the short term.

They plan to start the venture in January, and spend January and February preparing the first few vehicles for sale. They have then estimated as best they can the sales levels for the coming months as follows:

Estimated sales in:

March		2 camper vans
April		3 camper vans
May		4 camper vans
June & subsequent months		4 camper vans

The sales will all be on a cash basis for £5,000 each. Purchases of the vans will also be for cash, but the parts to recondition the mechanical bits (estimated at £400 per van) will be supplied on one month's credit. They will buy the necessary parts at the same time as the vans. They plan to buy 3 vans in January, and build up their stock so that by the end of February and each following month there will be enough vans ready for sale to satisfy the estimated demand of the following two months. In this way they hope to have enough on display to offer prospective customers a reasonable choice.

Kylie and Jed have found suitable premises with a small garage to work on the vehicles and a forecourt area. The rent is £4,000 per year, payable annually in advance. They will immediately equip the garage with tools costing £1,000, which should last about 4 years.

Other costs of running the business are estimated at £400 per month, all payable in the month that they are incurred.

Kylie and Jed have scraped together £20,000 cash as initial capital, and hope that any further finance required can be provided by a temporary bank overdraft facility. They will each draw £800 from the business per month in the first year, as they feel that this is the minimum amount that they can live on.

required

Draft a set of master budgets and a cash budget (cash-flow forecast) for the first six months of the business for Camper-Fans.

solution

The best place to start the calculations is to work out how many vans will need to be bought each month to comply with their stock requirements. This will be useful for all the main budgets, and will be vital to complete the cash budget. It can be carried out in the form of a table, as follows:

Numbers of Camper Vans:				
Month	*Opening Stock*	*Purchases*	*Sales*	*Closing Stock*
Jan	0	3	0	3
Feb	3	2	0	5
March	5	4	2	7
April	7	4	3	8
May	8	4	4	8
June	8	4	4	8
		21	13	

The figures in the table are worked out as follows. The sales figures for each month are inserted first. Then the January purchases are inserted from the Case Study. For each month the following will be true (in numbers of vans):

Opening Stock + Purchases – Sales = Closing Stock

Therefore the closing stock in January will be 3 vans, (0 + 3 – 0 = 3) which will also form the opening stock in February. Since the closing stock in February needs to be 5 vans to satisfy the demand in March and April, the February purchases must be 2. The closing and opening stocks are then calculated for each of the remaining months, and the purchases calculated accordingly.

Notice that totals of purchases and sales have been included, and that these also comply with the above equation for the six months as a whole:

Opening Stock + Purchases – Sales = Closing Stock (ie 0 + 21 – 13 = 8)

Now that the movements of camper vans have been worked out, the budgeted profit and loss account and cash-flow forecasts can be prepared. Workings have been shown to clarify the sources of the figures, together with references to the explanatory notes but these would normally be excluded from the finished document.

Camper-Fans
Budgeted Profit & Loss Account for 1st 6 months

	£	£
Sales (13 vans at £5,000)		65,000 (1)
Less cost of vans sold:		
(13 vans at (£3,000 + £400 parts))		44,200 (2)
Gross Profit		20,800 (3)
Less Expenses:		
Premises Rent (£4,000 x 6/12)	2,000 (4)	
Depreciation of Equipment		
(£1,000 x 25% x 6/12)	125 (5)	
Other Costs (£400 x 6 months)	2,400 (6)	
		4,525
Budgeted Net Profit		16,275

Notes

1   The sales figure relates to the income of the budgetary period. In this case the money from these sales would also be received in the period, but this would not necessarily be the case. Credit sales would also appear here, based on the date invoiced.

2   Here the cost of sales relates to the same 13 camper vans that will be sold in the period. This is an example of matching costs with income. An alternative form of presentation would have been to show the value of the purchases of vans plus parts, less the value of closing stock. This would provide the same cost of sales figure.

3   The gross profit represents the profit made on the 13 vans before deducting the running costs of the business. It therefore agrees with 13 x (£5,000 – (£3,000 + £400))= £20,800. The cost of labour has been excluded in this case since it is provided by the owners of the business (Kylie and Jed), and will therefore appear as drawings (money taken out by the owners).

4   Although £4,000 rent has been paid for, the full amount relates to a 12 month period. It is therefore fair to incorporate only 6 months rent in this budget. This is another example of the matching concept.

5   The £1,000 worth of equipment is estimated to last 4 years. The £125 therefore represents 6 months' depreciation (£1,000 x 6/48). The cost is spread over the expected useful life of the equipment.

6   The other costs are cash based running costs that will appear both in this budget and in the cash budget.

We can now move on to preparing the cash budget. This will be prepared as a table in months, so that any fluctuations in cash requirements can be seen clearly. The statement consists of three sections: the monthly receipts, payments, and summary with cash balances. The statement is easiest to construct one row at a time, with the arithmetic and the summary section completed last. In this statement the figures are explained in the notes that follow.

Camper-Fans
Cash budget for the first six months

Details	Jan	Feb	March	April	May	June
Receipts:						
Capital Invested	20,000					
Cash Sales (1)	0	0	10,000	15,000	20,000	20,000
Total Receipts	20,000	0	10,000	15,000	20,000	20,000
Payments:						
Camper Vans (2)	9,000	6,000	12,000	12,000	12,000	12,000
Parts (3)	0	1,200	800	1,600	1,600	1,600
Rent (4)	4,000					
Other Costs (5)	400	400	400	400	400	400
Equipment (6)	1,000					
Drawings (7)	1,600	1,600	1,600	1,600	1,600	1,600
Total Payments	16,000	9,200	14,800	15,600	15,600	15,600
Summary:						
Opening BankBalance	0	4,000	(5,200)	(10,000)	(10,000)	(6,200)
Add Receipts	20,000	0	10,000	15,000	20,000	20,000
Less Payments	(16,000)	(9,200)	(14,800)	(15,600)	(15,600)	(15,600)
Closing Bank Balance	4,000	(5,200)	(10,000)	(10,600)	(6,200)	(1,800)

Notes

1   Since all the sales are for cash, the receipt will occur in the month that the sale is made. The figures are based on the numbers of camper vans to be sold at £5,000 each.

2   The ex-hire vans are purchased for cash. The figures are taken from the table produced at the start of this solution, at £3,000 each.

3   The parts are bought at £400 for each van at the same time as the van is purchased. They are bought on 1 month's credit, and therefore the figures in the cash budget are lagged by one month (eg parts bought in January are paid for in February).

4   The year's rent is paid in January.

5   'Other Costs' are paid in the month that they relate to.

6   Equipment (a capital expenditure item) is paid for in January. Note that depreciation is not shown in the cash budget.

7   Drawings of £800 each for Kylie and Jed are taken monthly.

The final main budget statement to be completed is the budgeted balance sheet. This cannot be completed until the other two documents have been finished, since their results feed into it. The balance sheet is shown here, followed by explanatory notes.

Camper-Fans
Budgeted Balance Sheet as at the end of June

	£	£	£
Fixed Assets:			
	Cost	*Dep'n*	*Net*
Equipment (1)	1,000	125	875
Current Assets:			
Stock of Camper Vans (2)		27,200	
Debtors (3)		0	
Prepayments (4)		2,000	
		29,200	
Less Current Liabilities:			
Creditors for Parts (5)	1,600		
Bank Overdraft (6)	1,800		
		3,400	
			25,800
Total Net Assets			26,675
Financed by:			
Capital Invested			20,000
Add Budgeted Profit (7)			16,275
Less Budgeted Drawings (8)			(9,600)
			26,675

Notes

1   The equipment is shown at cost less accumulated depreciation. Here the only depreciation so far is that for the first 6 months.

2   The stock of camper vans at the end of June is valued at cost; (the buying price of £3,000 plus the parts of £400) x 8 camper vans. The labour cost has been excluded since it forms drawings in this Case Study. Other stock valuation bases are also possible.

3   There are no debtors since all sales are on a cash basis.

4   The prepayments figure of £2,000 represents the rent for the second six months that has already been paid. It was excluded from the budgeted profit and loss account, and is an asset in the business at the end of June.

5   The creditor for parts has arisen because the parts are bought on credit. This figure represents the amount of parts bought in June, but not to be paid for until July, and therefore not shown in the cash budget.

6   The bank overdraft figure is the closing June balance taken from the cash budget.

7   The budgeted profit is taken from the budgeted profit & loss account.

8   The budgeted drawings are the amounts taken from the business by Kylie and Jed in the six months. The figure is the same as the one shown in the cash budget.

USING ADDITIONAL BUDGETS IN MANUFACTURING ORGANISATIONS

The three budgets that we have already looked at form the basis for most organisations, but in complex businesses it is usual to develop additional budgets before completing the master budgets and cash budget. Some manufacturing businesses also use a budgeted version of the manufacturing account in the same format as the historical version described in Chapter 17. A comprehensive set of budgets for a manufacturing business (including the budgets already explained) would be as follows:

sales budget	usually generated directly from the key factor – the forecast sales figures
production budget	based on the sales budget together with the anticipated finished goods stock levels
materials usage budget	based on the production budget
materials purchase budget	based on the materials usage budget, together with the anticipated materials stock levels
labour utilisation budget	also based on the production budget
functional budgets	to support the operation (often based on departments), for example administration

	budget, finance budget; these may not be so dependent upon the sales level as other budgets that are linked more closely; (zero based budgeting, as discussed on page 529, can be used to develop this type of budget)
capital expenditure budget	this would also have to be developed in conjunction with the revenue budgets to ensure that the agreed spending on new or replacement equipment was in place
cash-flow budget	this would take account of all the other budgets and their effect on the organisation's liquidity
master budget	the calculations from all the revenue and capital budgets contribute to the **master budget** which takes the form of a budgeted profit and loss account and balance sheet

the effect of changing stock levels

You will have noticed several references in the list of budgets to **stock levels**. Where stock levels are to remain constant the situation is simple. For example the production budget will be identical to the sales budget if the finished goods stock level is to remain unchanged, ie the amount you will produce will be the amount you estimate you are going to sell. However if the stock level is to increase then the extra units of goods that will go into stock will need to be produced in addition to the units that are to be sold in the budget period. This is a concept that we will return to frequently.

creating the main additional budgets

The diagram on the next page shows how data feeds from the sales budget to the production budget and uses information on finished goods stocks. The production budget is then used to complete the labour utilisation budget and the materials usage budget. This in turn is used in combination with the raw material stock levels to create the materials purchases budget.

The information from these budgets together with functional budgets and the capital expenditure budget is then used in the cash-flow budgets and master budgets. We will use a Case Study of a manufacturing business to demonstrate how this all works. We will use the standard cost data (as developed in Chapter 23) to create the budget, but the procedure is exactly the same if data comes from a less formal source.

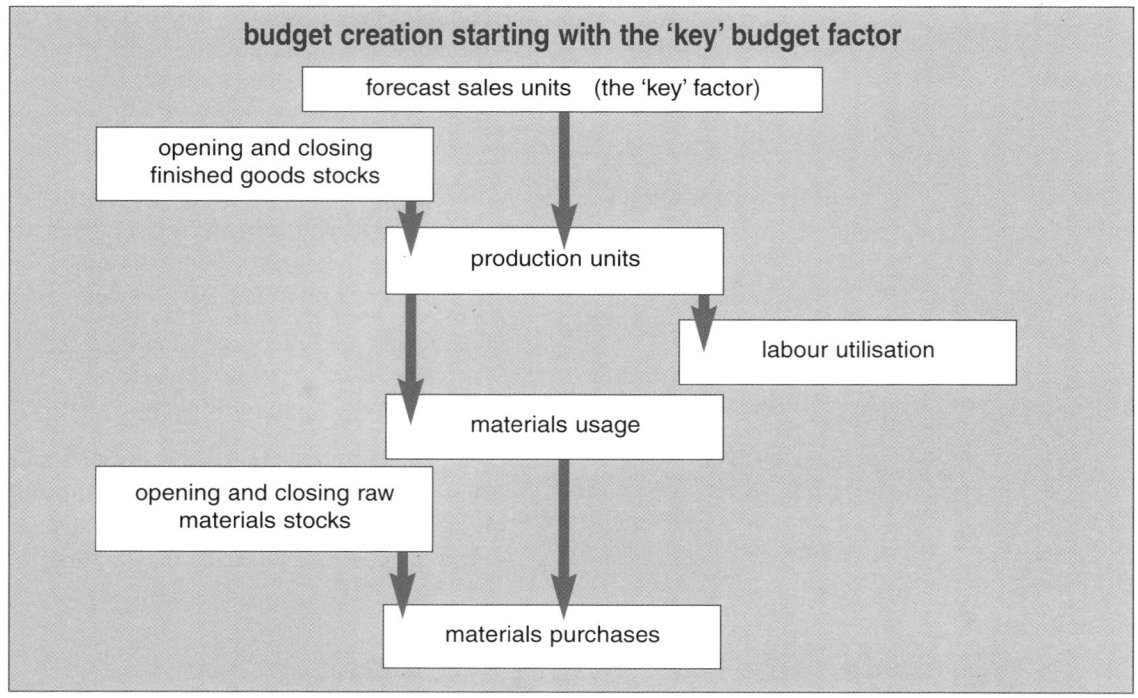

CASE STUDY

Jean-E-Us — creating budgets for a manufacturing business

situation

Jean-E-Us makes denim jeans that are sold to various clothing wholesalers. The company uses standard costing to help plan and control its costs.

The company is now preparing its budgets for the first three months of next year, and has provided the following data:

The standard cost of one pair of jeans is calculated as follows:

Direct materials: 3 square metres at £2.50 per square metre	£7.50
Direct labour: 45 minutes at £5.60 per hour	£4.20
Fixed overheads: £20,000 ÷ 2,500 pairs jeans per month	£8.00
Total standard cost per pair	£19.70

The jeans sell for £25.00 per pair to wholesalers on one month's credit.

Forecast sales levels are:

	January	2,200 units (pairs of jeans)
	February	2,500 units
	March	2,800 units
	April	2,200 units

The stock of finished jeans at the month-end is planned to equal half of the next month's forecast sales level. The stock of raw materials held at each month-end is to be sufficient for half of the following month's production. At the end of March this stock is to be 3,750 sq metres. Raw material purchases are made on one month's credit.

The fixed overheads of £20,000 per month include £3,000 depreciation on existing fixed assets. There are no planned purchases of further fixed assets. All the other fixed overheads are paid for in the month they are incurred. Direct labour is also paid for in the month that it is incurred.

The following is a summary of the balance sheet of Jean-E-Us at the end of December preceding the budget period, with workings where necessary.

JEAN-E-US: SUMMARY BALANCE SHEET AS AT 31 DECEMBER

	£	£
Fixed Assets: (Cost £144,000, cumulative depreciation £36,000)		108,000
Current Assets:		
Stocks: Finished goods (1,100 pairs at £19.70)	21,670	
Raw materials (3,525 square metres at £2.50)	8,813	
Debtors (re December sales)	62,500	
Bank	10,000	
	102,983	
Current Liabilities:		
Creditors (re December purchases)	18,750	
		84,233
Total Net Assets		192,233
Capital as at December 31		192,233

---

required

Prepare the following budgets for Jean-E-Us for the months of January, February and March, using standard costs.

- Production budget (in pairs of jeans)
- Labour utilisation budget (in hours and £)
- Materials usage budget (in square metres of denim)
- Materials purchases budget (in square metres and £)

Using the data from these budgets, prepare a set of master budgets for the quarter, together with a cash budget in months.

solution

The production budget is worked out in pairs of jeans, taking account of planned finished goods stock levels, as follows:

	January	February	March
Forecast Sales	2,200	2,500	2,800
Less opening stocks	(1,100)	(1,250)	(1,400)
Add closing stocks	1,250	1,400	1,100
Production Budget	2,350	2,650	2,500

The labour utilisation budget (or labour budget) uses the pairs of jeans from the production budget, and multiplies it by the time for each pair of jeans (45 minutes). This time is then valued at the standard hourly rate (£5.60).

	January	February	March
Labour Budget (hours)	1,762.5	1,987.5	1,875
Labour Budget (£)	£9,870	£11,130	£10,500

The materials usage budget uses the pairs of jeans from the production budget, and multiplies it by the standard amount of denim needed to make each pair of jeans (3 sq metres).

	January	February	March
Materials Usage Budget (square metres)	7,050.	7,950.	7,500.

The materials purchases budget is worked out in square metres of denim, starting with the materials usage budget, and taking account of the required levels of raw materials stocks.

	January	February	March
Materials Usage Budget	7,050	7,950	7,500
Less opening stock of Raw Materials	(3,525)	(3,975)	(3,750)
Add closing stock of Raw Materials	3,975	3,750	3,750
Materials Purchases In square metres	7,500	7,725	7,500
Materials Purchases (£)	£18,750	£19,312	£18,750

The budgeted profit and loss account can be prepared as follows:

Jean-E-Us – Budgeted Profit and Loss Account for January – March

	£	£
Sales (7,500 pairs of jeans at £25)		187,500
Less cost of goods sold: (7,500 pairs of jeans at £19.70)		147,750
Budgeted Profit		39,750

The budgeted profit and loss account has been prepared in summary form for simplicity, but could be shown in more detail by using the separate elements of the standard costs. Since the planned production is 7,500 pairs of jeans, each pair absorbing £8, this will exactly cover the quarter's fixed costs of £60,000.

The cash budget can now be prepared using data from the previous balance sheet and that produced in the separate additional budgets.

Jean-E-Us – Cash Budget for the period January – March			
	Jan £	Feb £	March £
Receipts:			
From Debtors / Sales (1)	62,500	55,000	62,500
Payments:			
Creditors / Purchases (2)	18,750	18,750	19,312
Labour (3)	9,870	11,130	10,500
Fixed Overheads (4)	17,000	17,000	17,000
Total Payments	45,620	46,880	46,812
Summary:			
Opening Balance (5)	10,000	26,880	35,000
Add Receipts	62,500	55,000	62,500
Less Payments	(45,620)	(46,880)	(46,812)
Closing Balance	26,880	35,000	50,688

Notes

1. The January receipts are the December sales that are shown as debtors in the balance sheet at the end of December. The receipts in February and March relate to the forecast sales at £25 per pair made in January and February respectively (to allow for the one month credit given on invoices).

2. The January payment is the creditor from the December balance sheet. The following two payments are from the materials purchases budget for January and February. Payments occur one month after purchase (again to allow for the one month credit terms).

3. The labour costs are taken from the labour utilisation budget. There is no time delay with these payments.

4. The fixed overheads relate to the monthly amount of £20,000, less the depreciation included of £3,000 per month.

5. The opening bank balance in January is taken from the balance sheet at the end of the preceding December.

We can now complete the final main budget statement – the budgeted balance sheet. The document is shown on the next page, followed by explanatory notes.

Jean-E-Us – Budgeted Balance Sheet as at 31 March

	£	£	£
Fixed Assets:			
	Cost	Dep'n	Net
Equipment (1)	144,000	45,000	99,000
Current Assets:			
Stocks: Finished Goods (2)		21,670	
Raw Materials (3)		9,375	
Debtors (4)		70,000	
Bank (5)		50,688	
		151,733	
Less Current Liabilities:			
Creditors for Purchases (6)		18,750	
			132,983
Total Net Assets			231,983
Financed by:			
Capital at 31 Dec			192,233
Add Budgeted Profit (7)			39,750
			231,983

Notes

1   The equipment depreciation is increased by the £3,000 x 3 months that relates to the budget period.

2   Finished goods stocks are based on those used in the production budget, valued at the standard cost of £19.70 per pair.

3   Raw material stocks are the 3,750 square metres given in the Case Study (and used in the workings for the material purchases budget), valued at standard cost of £2.50 per square metre.

4   The debtors figure relates to the forecast March sales of 2,800 pairs of jeans at £25 per pair.

5   The forecast bank balance is taken from the cash budget.

6   The creditors amount is taken from the March purchases budget, since the payments are made on one month's credit.

7   The budgeted profit is taken from the budgeted profit and loss account for the three months.

USING BUDGETS TO MONITOR PROGRESS

budget monitoring

As discussed at the start of the chapter, part of the purpose of budgets is to allow monitoring of actual activity against them, and comparisons to be made. If the actual result is different from the target budget figure, action may be taken to remedy the situation so that the actual result will be nearer to the budget figure in the future. Occasionally, if it is thought necessary, the budget can be altered to come in line with the actual situation.

The way in which budgets are used in an organisation is often laid down formally in a Budget Manual. In many organisations the responsibility for budget setting and control will rest with a Budget Committee. This will be made up of senior representatives of all major parts of the organisation to ensure full coordination.

fixed and flexed budgets

The budgets that we have prepared so far are called **fixed budgets**. They represent the best estimate of how the organisation sees the future, but are only based on one set of assumptions and so may be unsuitable when the activity level turns out to be quite different from the level that was planned.

For example, suppose that a taxi driver has a budget of £50 for fuel per week, based on the assumption that he would carry passengers 500 miles in the week. One week he spends £80 on fuel and is called into the office to explain his apparently excessive spending. 'I thought you'd be pleased,' he says to the manager, 'I did 850 miles last week earning you profits, and all I get is a ticking off for spending too much!'

This example is clearly not a fair way to use budgets, nor is it the best way to motivate staff. The alternative is to use **flexed budgets** (also known as flexible budgets) as a comparison with the actual position.

A flexed budget is one that is prepared in order to match the actual activity level.

A series of budgets could be prepared in advance at different levels of activity, or a flexed budget specially prepared once the actual activity level is known. The way that costs behave (as examined in Chapter 22 on marginal costing) is used to develop the budget, so that it forms a fair reflection of the income and costs at the specific activity level. In the above taxi example, the fuel budget would be £85 for a week when 850 miles were driven, since fuel is a variable cost, so in this case the actual cost was just below this budget.

We will now return to our Case Study scenario to see how this can be applied.

CASE STUDY
Camper-Fans — using a flexed budget

The first six months of the business have just finished, and Jed has produced this statement comparing the budgeted profit and loss account (as prepared earlier) with the actual figures, and showing the differences as variances: adverse (A) or favourable (F).

Camper-Fans – Budget and Actual Comparison for the first 6 months	Budget £	Actual £	Variances £
Sales	65,000	74,800	9,800 F
Less cost of vans sold	44,200	52,500	8,300 A
Gross Profit	20,800	22,300	
Less Expenses:			
Premises Rent	2,000	2,000	0
Depreciation of Equipment	125	125	0
Other Costs	2,400	2,900	500 A
	4,525	5,025	
Net Profit	16,275	17,275	1,000 F

Jed is pleased by the comparison, especially since they made £1,000 more profit than they had planned. Kylie is a little more cautious: *'It's good that we made a bit more profit, but don't forget we forecast sales of 13 camper vans, but actually sold 15 after spending an extra £500 on advertising. I would have expected more extra profit on that basis.'*

'Well we did have to sell two of the vans at £100 each less than the usual £5,000 each, and although we still bought all the vans at the agreed £3,000 each, the parts that we bought were a bit more expensive on average than we initially budgeted,' admitted Jed.

required

- Produce a revised statement comparing the actual income and expenditure with a flexed budget, based on selling 15 camper vans.

- Explain how the revised variances fit with the additional information given by Kylie and Jed.

solution

Camper-Fans – Flexed Budget and Actual Comparison for the first 6 months			
	Flexed Budget £	Actual £	Variances £
Sales	75,000	74,800	200 A
Less cost of vans sold:	51,000	52,500	1,500 A
Gross Profit	24,000	22,300	1,700 A
Less Expenses:			
Premises Rent	2,000	2,000	0
Depreciation of Equipment	125	125	0
Other Costs	2,400	2,900	500 A
	4,525	5,025	
Net Profit	19,475	17,275	2,200 A

The flexed budget is based on 15 camper vans, using a budgeted selling price of £5,000 each and cost of vans sold of £3,400 each,

This now shows that they made overall £2,200 less profit than they would have expected from selling the 15 camper vans. This difference can be accounted for as follows:

• The adverse sales variance of £200 is due to the two vans each sold at £100 less than usual.

• The cost of sales adverse variance of £1,500 is due to a higher than expected cost for parts. The parts actually cost an average of £500 per van, £100 more per van than budgeted.

• The other costs adverse variance of £500 is due to the additional advertising that was not budgeted for.

SPECIFIC WAYS OF SETTING FUNCTIONAL BUDGETS

Once a business is established it needs to reset its budgets year after year. The budgets for departments such as Administration or Finance do not depend heavily on the usual key budget factor of sales, and so require a different approach. There are two main ways that these can be tackled – **incremental budgeting** and **zero based budgeting**.

incremental budgeting

Incremental budgeting is a traditional method, widely used in commercial organisations and in the public sector. Incremental budgeting means:

Basing the budget for a department or function on that of the previous period, usually adjusting for inflation by a percentage increase.

Specific changes, such as a planned expansion or reduction in activities, would also be allowed for. In some cases the previous year's actual costs may be used as a starting point, rather than the budget, particularly if the actual costs were lower.

WORKED EXAMPLE
incremental budgeting

Quenchit Ltd is a water bottling company. Transport costs for last year amounted to £120,000. Planned expansion is expected to result in £10,000 additional transport costs (estimated at current prices). Inflation is expected to be 3%.

The transport budget for the next year could be based on:

£120,000 + £10,000 = £130,000 to allow for expansion,

then £130,000 x 103% = £133,900 to allow for inflation.

advantages of incremental budgeting

The advantages of the incremental budgeting method are:
- the budget is stable and change is gradual and planned
- managers can operate their departments on a consistent basis
- the system is relatively simple to operate and easy to understand
- conflicts should be avoided if departments can be seen to be treated similarly, and coordination between budgets is easier to achieve
- the impact of change can be seen quickly

disadvantages of incremental budgeting

There are, however, a number of criticisms of this method:

- incremental budgeting assumes activities and methods of working will continue in the same way, giving no incentive for developing new ideas

- there is no incentive to try to reduce costs – on the contrary, spending up to the budget is encouraged by this method, so that next year the level of budget is maintained

- the budgets may become out of date, and no longer relate to the level of activity or the type of work being carried out

- the priority for resources may have changed since the budgets were set originally

- there may be 'budgetary slack' built in to the budgets, which is never reviewed – this means that managers have overestimated their requirements in the past, in order to obtain a budget which is easier to work to, and which will allow them to achieve favourable results

ZERO BASED BUDGETING (ZBB)

Zero based budgeting is a method which was developed with a view to eliminating some of the problems of incremental budgeting.

Zero based budgeting takes the opposite view: instead of assuming everything will continue as before, the focus is on achieving the organisation's objectives in the most efficient way. Zero based budgeting works as follows:

The budget for each budget centre starts from a base of zero for each period. Budgets for proposed activities are then put forward, assessed and prioritised (in relation to the organisation's objectives) and allocated funds in order of priority.

The stages in the process are as follows:

- the functions of the organisation are analysed to identify the structure of departments to be used as budget centres

- the work of each department (budget centre) is then analysed to identify the activities actually carried out

- starting from a base of zero, budgets are prepared in each budget centre, showing the costs and benefits of the work of the department; these budgets show the expected results at several different levels of activity and are called 'decision packages'

- the decision packages must then be judged by managers and put in order according to how efficiently they contribute towards the organisation's objectives

- the total funds available are allocated to decision packages in order of priority, thus deciding which activities are to be carried out and at what level – if a particular activity is obsolete or contributing nothing, it will receive no funds and will be discontinued.

advantages of zero based budgeting

The advantages of the zero based budgeting method are:

- this system focuses the use of resources on achieving the organisation's objectives

- budget centre managers have to re-evaluate in detail the cost-effectiveness of the working methods and results achieved in their departments

- new projects are compared with existing work, so that innovation is encouraged, rather than assuming existing activities must continue

- allocation of resources is linked to the achievement of results

- wastage and budgetary slack should be eliminated, because budgets which are not cost-effective will not be given funds

- planning and budgeting is combined into a single process when the decision packages to be funded are chosen

disadvantages of zero based budgeting

Zero based budgeting is also criticised, because:

- the process itself is very complex and therefore costly to operate

- by separating different activities, links between them may not be allowed for, leading to an uncoordinated approach

- short-term benefits may be emphasised in the decision packages, to the detriment of long-term planning

- the process of judging and prioritising the decision packages may be extremely difficult and it may be affected by the internal politics of the organisation, so that it is not really objective

Zero based budgeting can only be applied where different levels of a particular type of work are possible and where the costs and benefits can be identified.

chapter summary

- Budgets can be used to assist planning, to communicate and co-ordinate ideas, and to monitor and control outcomes. They may also be used to help motivate managers and employees.

- Budgets must be in line with the objectives of the organisation, and the organisation's chosen strategy to achieve those objectives. Before starting to create a budget, the key budget factor must be recognised, and its numerical impact forecast. For most commercial organisations this factor is the sales level, but it could be based on specific resources or factors.

- The three main budgets are:

  - the profit and loss budget – which shows income and expenditure for a future period and hence the expected profit

  - the cash budget (cash-flow forecast) – which shows future inflows and outflows of money through the bank account and each month-end bank balance

  - the budgeted balance sheet – which includes figures from the profit and loss budget and the cash budget

  The budgeted profit and loss account and the budgeted balance sheet are together known as the master budget.

- Budgets that are prepared for manufacturing businesses typically include Sales, Production, Material Usage, Material Purchases, and Labour Utilisation, together with other budgets including various functional (including departmental) budgets, and capital expenditure budgets. These are co-ordinated and amalgamated to form a set of master budgets (see above).

- Budgets for manufacturing organisations can be created by working from the forecast sales data to the production level by using anticipated finished goods stock levels. From the production budget the materials usage can be ascertained, and by incorporating the anticipated materials stock levels, the materials purchases can be calculated. Other budgets can also be created from the production budget. Budgeted manufacturing accounts can also be generated and will link with the budgets.

- The way in which budgets are used in an organisation is often laid down in the Budget Manual. In many organisations the responsibility for budget setting and control will rest with the Budget Committee. This will incorporate senior representatives of all major parts of the organisation to ensure full co-ordination in budget planning.

- Flexed (or flexible) budgets can be used to monitor actual results. They are based on a budget for the actual activity level achieved, and therefore compare like with like.

- Incremental and zero based budgeting are techniques that are useful for setting budgets of functional areas or departments. They each have advantages and disadvantages.

key terms

budget	a financial plan for an organisation, prepared before the period starts
key (or principal) budget factor	the main factor (whether internal or external) that determines the planned activity level of the organisation
budgeted profit & loss account	a budget that contains a summary of the budgeted income and expenditure of the organisation for a future period, and the resulting budgeted profit or loss; it forms part of the master budget
cash budget (cash-flow forecast)	a budget that shows the flow of money in and out of the business, and the resulting future bank balances
budgeted balance sheet	a statement of the expected assets, liabilities and capital at the end of the budgeting period; it forms part of the master budget
production budget	a budget that plans how much should be produced in a particular period, to allow for anticipated sales and stock movements of finished goods
labour utilisation budget	a budget that details the labour input required to meet the needs of the production budget
materials usage budget	a budget that plans the amount of materials that is required to satisfy the production budget
materials purchases budget	a budget that plans for the level of purchases needed to meet the demands of the materials utilisation budget, after allowing for material stock levels
fixed budget	a budget which is set for a particular level of activity
flexed (or flexible) budget	a budget which is adjusted to allow for changes in costs (and income) resulting from a change in the level of activity
incremental budgeting	a method of budgeting in which budgets are based on the previous period's budgets, updated for developments and inflation
zero based budgeting	a method of budgeting in which budgets are set to zero at the start of each period – budgets for proposed activities are then judged and prioritised in relation to the organisation's objectives, and funds allocated accordingly

activities

25.1* Suggest the key (or principal) budget factors for the following organisations:

(a) A partnership of two craftsmen who make high-quality violins for leading musicians. The work is labour intensive and highly skilled. They are easily able to sell all they produce.

(b) A transport company that has a contract to work only for a major supplier of turkeys. The turkey supplier is currently expanding, but there is an agreement in place for all their transport requirements to be met by this one company for the next 12 months.

(c) A company whose team of engineers has a contract to maintain the Metro in Manchester. They have no plans to seek other contracts.

(d) A company that has opened a new baked potato outlet on a busy business park. The firm has the sole rights to supply potatoes to the 3,000 staff on the site, and has the capacity to cook and sell 100 baked potatoes per day.

25.2* A manufacturing company that makes kitchen chairs is planning its activities for month 5 in the current year. The following data is available:

Sales in month 5 are forecast at 1,800 units.

Each completed unit requires 4 kilos of raw material.

Planned stock levels are:

	Raw Materials	Finished Goods
At end of month 4	1,200 kilos	500 units
At end of month 5	1,500 kilos	400 units

Required

Calculate the following budgets for month 5:

- production budget (in units)
- raw materials usage (in kilos)
- raw materials purchases (in kilos)

25.3 Jim Smith has recently been made redundant; he has received a redundancy payment and this, together with his accumulated savings, amounts to £10,000. He has decided to set up his own business selling computer stationery and will start trading with an initial capital of £10,000 on 1 January. On this date he will buy a van for business use at a cost of £6,000. He has estimated his purchases, sales, and expenses for the next six months as follows:

	Purchases	Sales	Expenses
	£	£	£
January	4,500	1,250	750
February	4,500	3,000	600
March	3,500	4,000	600
April	3,500	4,000	650
May	3,500	4,500	650
June	4,000	6,000	700

He will pay for purchases in the month after purchase and expects his customers to pay for sales in the month after sale. All expenses will be paid for in the month in which they are incurred.

Jim realizes that he may need bank overdraft facilities before his business becomes established. He asks you to help him with information for the bank and, in particular, he asks you to prepare:

(a)   a month-by-month cash budget for the first six months

(b)   a budgeted trading and profit and loss account for the first six months – for this he tells you that his closing stock at 30 June is expected to have a value of £3,250, and that he wishes to depreciate the van at 20% per annum.

(c)   A budgeted balance sheet as at 30 June

25.4   Mayday Limited was recently formed and plans to commence trading on 1 June 2001. During May the company will issue 200,000 ordinary shares of £1 each at par and the cash will be subscribed at once. During the same month £130,000 will be spent on plant and £50,000 will be invested in stock, resulting in a cash balance on 1 June of £20,000.

Plans for the twelve months commencing 1 June 2001 are as follows:

•   Stock costing £40,000 will be sold each month at a mark-up of 25%. Customers are expected to pay in the second month following sale.

•   Month-end stock levels will be maintained at £50,000 and purchases will be paid for in the month following delivery.

•   Wages and other expenses will amount to £6,000 per month, payable in the month during which the costs are incurred.

•   Plant will have a ten-year life and no scrap value. Depreciation is to be charged on the straight line basis.

You are to prepare:

(a)   a month-by-month cash budget for Mayday Limited for the year to 31 May 2002

(b)   the company's budgeted trading and profit and loss accounts for the year ending 31 May 2002, together with a budgeted balance sheet at that date

25.5 The balance sheet of Antonio's Speciality Food Shop at 31 August 2001 was:

	£ Cost	£ Dep'n	£ Net
Fixed assets	15,000	3,000	12,000
Current assets			
Stocks		5,000	
Debtors		800	
		5,800	
Less current liabilities			
Creditors	3,000		
Bank overdraft	1,050		
		4,050	
Working capital			1,750
NET ASSETS			13,750
FINANCED BY			
Antonio's capital			13,750

On the basis of past performance, Antonio expects that his sales during the coming six months will be:

September	October	November	December	January	February
£8,000	£8,000	£10,000	£20,000	£6,000	£6,000

Antonio allows credit to some of his regular customers, and the proportions of cash and credit sales are usually:

	Cash sales	Credit sales
November	80%	20%
December	60%	40%
All other months	90%	10%

Customers who buy on credit normally pay in the following month. Antonio's gross profit margin is consistently 25 per cent of his selling price. He normally maintains his stocks at a constant level by purchasing goods in the month in which they are sold: the only exception to this is that in November he purchases in advance 50 per cent of the goods he expects to sell in December.

Half of the purchases each month are made from suppliers who give a 2 per cent cash discount for immediate payment and he takes advantage of the discount. He pays for the remainder (without discount) in the month after purchase.

Expenditure on wages, rent and other running expenses of the shop are consistently £2,000 per month, paid in the month in which they are incurred.

Fixed assets are depreciated at 10 per cent per annum on cost price.

You are to:

(a)   • prepare a cash budget showing Antonio's bank balance or overdraft for each month in the half-year ending 29 February 2002

   • prepare Antonio's balance sheet at 29 February 2002

(b)   If Antonio's bank manager considered it necessary to fix the overdraft limit at £3,500, explain what Antonio should do in order to observe the limit.

25.6 (a)   Explain what is meant by:

   • fixed budgets, and

   • flexible budgets

What is the main objective of preparing flexible budgets?

(b)   Seats Limited manufactures chairs which sell to schools and colleges throughout Britain. The company is currently producing budgets for the next year. The sales director is budgeting for sales of 90,000 chairs; the selling price is £10 each. Production costs are budgeted as being:

materials	£2.50 per chair
labour	£2.75 per chair
variable overheads	£0.50 per chair
fixed overheads	£242,000 per year

However, a general election was announced a few days ago, and conversation at today's board meeting of the company's directors goes as follows:

'The outcome of the election looks unpredictable'.

'If the government is re-elected, they are committed to a 10% cut in education spending.'

'On the other hand, if the opposition party win, they have pledged to increase education spending by 25%.'

'Until we get further information we had better assume that our sales will be affected by the same percentages.'

You are to:

(a) Prepare the fixed budget for the year based on sales of 90,000 chairs, to show budgeted profit.

(b) Prepare two flexible budgets based on the changes in educational spending proposed by each of the main political parties.

(c) Write a memorandum to the directors explaining the reason for the different budgeted profit figures.

25.7   Which one of the following is a feature of an incremental budget?

   (a)   all budgets are initially set at zero

   (b)   it is based on the previous year's budget initially

   (c)   it remains fixed and is not updated for inflation

   (d)   it is based on specific organisational programmes

25.8   Hoffmann PLC makes vacuum cleaners and other domestic appliances. It is well known for its Hoffmann 'DustIn' cleaner. The company is setting its budgets for next year for various functional departments. The credit control department is responsible for managing the organisation's debtors, including resolving invoice queries and ensuring that payments are received on time.

   (a)   The department had a budget of £130,000 last year, made up of £125,000 labour costs plus £5,000 other costs. The organisation is to budget for a 4% increase in the cost of labour, and to allow for general inflation on all other costs of 2%.

   Required

   Assuming incremental budgeting is to be used, calculate the total budget for the credit control department for the next year.

   (b)   The following additional data has been developed so that zero based budgeting can be applied to the department. There are three possible decision packages linked to levels of service that the credit control department can provide:

   Decision package 1 is a basic level of service that could be provided by the department for a total cost next year of £80,000. It would involve a reduction in staffing from the current level that would lead to longer times being taken to resolve invoice queries and less time available to be spent chasing overdue debtors. The average amount owed to the organisation would increase by £800,000, and this would cost an additional £64,000 per year in interest charges, based on 8% p.a.

   Decision package 2 is the current level of service, with costs as outlined in part (a) of the activity.

   Decision package 3 would provide a labour intensive level of service that would allow for the appointment of additional staff to closely monitor outstanding debtors and deal with queries as soon as they arose. The total cost of providing this level of service next year would be £160,000. This level of service would reduce the amount owing to the company by an average £400,000, and this would generate interest savings at 8% p.a.

   Required

   Assuming zero based budgeting is to be used next year:

   1   Calculate the costs and benefits of opting for either decision package 1 or decision package 3 compared to decision package 2.

   2   Recommend the decision package that should form the basis of the budget for the credit control department for next year.

MANAGING WORKING CAPITAL

Jean-E-Us: where's the money gone?

Jean-E-Us is a company that manufactures denim jeans for sale to various fashion wholesalers.

Gene Edwards, the manager, has implemented a standard costing system and is using budgets to plan his operations. He has now received accounting statements based on the company's performance, and is comparing them with the budget he prepared earlier. He is talking about these to his accountant:

'I can't understand it. Most things have turned out as we predicted in the budget, like selling prices, costs, and the number of jeans we sold, but there just isn't the money in the bank that we forecast.

I was hoping to use the surplus cash to buy a computer aided design system to streamline the creation and manufacture of new styles of jeans. Apart from the advantages the new system would bring to our current workload, I want to tender for a new large contract, but the new designs would be impossible to create in time without this new system.'

The accountant replies:

'Let's have a look at how your stock, debtors and creditors are being managed. If the money is not in the bank then too much may be tied up in stock in the warehouse and money owed by customers. If we can get these under control then we should be able to find the cash that you need. Mind you, we'll have to look at that new contract closely – if you stretch your resources too far that may bring you more problems.'

This chapter examines the management by an organisation of cash and the other components of working capital – stock, debtors and creditors.

---

learning objectives

When you have studied this chapter you will be able to:

- explain the importance of working capital and the cash cycle
- use ratios to measure liquidity and levels of stock, debtors and creditors
- identify the key issues in managing working capital
- calculate the benefits of granting or obtaining prompt payment discounts
- establish the effects on cash balances of various working capital strategies
- explain the implications of expanding a business with limited resources

WORKING CAPITAL AND THE CASH CYCLE

Working capital is the part of the capital of the business which circulates between the stock, debtors, cash and trade creditors. These current assets and liabilities are constantly changing, unlike the fixed assets which change only occasionally. The formula for working capital is:

working capital = current assets less current liabilities

The circulation of working capital can be illustrated by the **cash cycle**:

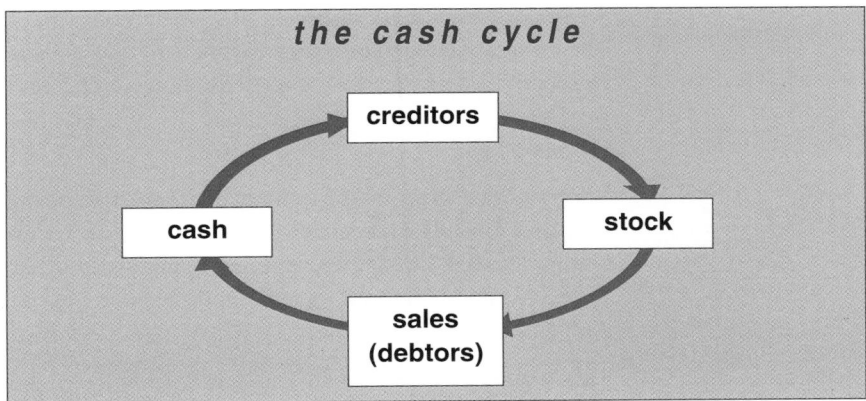

The diagram of the cash cycle above represents how creditors (suppliers) provide stock. When stock is sold it results in an increase in debtors. When debtors pay, the cash increases. When creditors are paid, the cash moves along to the creditors. This decreases the creditors' balance, but it will increase again when more stock is provided . . . and so on.

The same cycle applies to manufacturing organisations, except that the stock that is bought (ie materials) must be turned into finished goods before it can be sold.

The cash cycle is measured as the time from when payment is made for raw materials or stock until the time that payment is received for goods sold.

Example 1

A firm receives raw materials at the end of April, and pays for them one month later. The raw materials are processed during May, and the finished goods are held in stock until the end of August, when they are sold on two months credit. The customer pays on time.

We can show the cash cycle for this example in the form of a time line as illustrated on the next page.

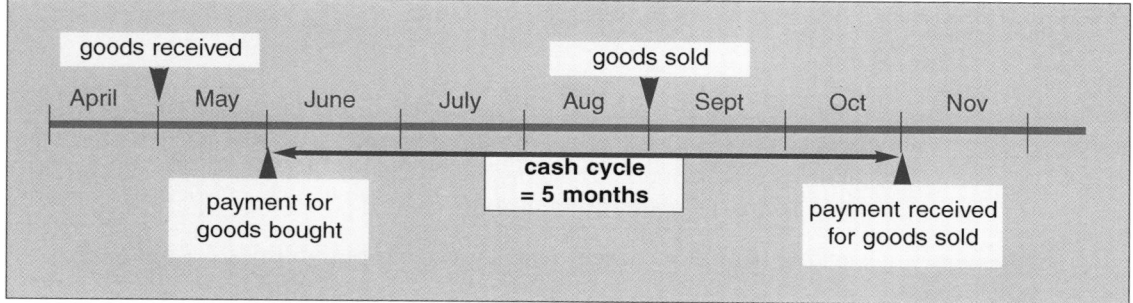

As we can see, the cash for the raw materials is paid out at the end of May. The money is received from the sale of the finished goods at the end of October. This gives a time for the cash cycle of 5 months.

Example 2

Suppose the firm in the above example had acted as follows: The raw materials that were received at the end of April were paid for on 2 months credit. The finished goods were held in stock until the end of July when they were sold on one month's credit, and the customer paid on time at the end of August.

This would give a cash cycle time of 2 months.

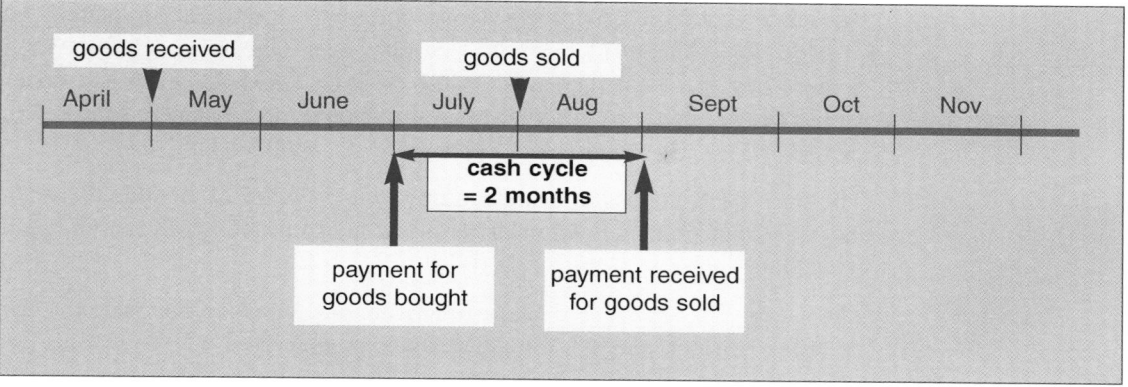

The business in Example 1 has to wait five months for the cycle to complete and to receive its cash. In the second example the wait is only two months.

The examples above show only sample information about one set of goods. Because firms operate continuously, the pattern would be repeating over and over again, and this would affect the amount of money that the firm would need to tie up in the cash cycle. The longer the cash cycle, the more money is tied up in working capital; the shorter the cash cycle, the less money is tied up.

WORKING CAPITAL IN THE BALANCE SHEET

The balance sheet is a statement that contains details of an organisation's assets and liabilities at a point in time. It is always prepared at the end of an accounting period as a financial accounting document, but can also be used for planning purposes as part of a budget and prepared at any time for management accounting purposes.

Working capital can easily be identified in a balance sheet, as it appears after the section on fixed assets – it is shown as the difference between current assets and current liabilities. It is described as 'working capital' or 'net current assets'. Although a balance sheet only gives the position at one point in time, it can be very useful way to examine the working capital, since it will often show a situation that is typical for the organisation.

The following is an example of the way that working capital data is shown in a balance sheet:

Cash Cycles Limited – Extract from Balance Sheet as at 31 December 2002

	£'000	£'000
Current Assets		
Stocks	300	
Debtors	400	
Bank	100	
	800	
Less Current Liabilities		
Creditors	200	
Working Capital		600

In this example Cash Cycles Limited has working capital of £600,000. Of that amount only £100,000 is in the business bank account; the rest is tied up in stock and debtors and is owed to creditors.

USING RATIOS TO EXAMINE WORKING CAPITAL

a balancing act

It is sometimes difficult to calculate the amount that needs to be invested in working capital. If there is too little working capital, the organisation may not be able to afford to have enough stock to supply its customers, or it may not have enough money to pay its creditors. If it has too much invested in working capital then its profitability may suffer: it may not be able to invest in the fixed assets it needs or take on other profitable projects.

liquidity

Liquidity is the ability of an organisation to pay its creditors as they become due.

The liquidity of an organisation results from the amount and composition of its working capital. Ratios can be calculated to help us examine various aspects of an organisation, including its working capital and liquidity.

The calculation of a ratio on its own can be of some use, but its use is often much greater if it is used to make comparisons. Ratios based on the actual position at a given moment can be compared with:

- the previous position for the same organisation
- the planned (or budgeted) position for the same organisation
- the position of another similar organisation or the average for organisations in the same industry

LIQUIDITY RATIOS

There are two main ratios that can be used to measure liquidity.

current ratio

The current ratio (also known as the working capital ratio) is simply a comparison between the value of current assets and the value of current liabilities:

Current Ratio = $\dfrac{\text{Current Assets}}{\text{Current Liabilities}}$

The calculation is expressed as a number that shows the relationship between current assets and current liabilities. To use the figures from the balance sheet on page 541 would give a current ratio of £800,000 ÷ £200,000 = 4. This could be expressed as 4:1. This simply means that Cash Cycles Limited has four times as much value in its current assets as it has in its current liabilities. This could be interpreted to show that the company has a high level of liquidity and should find it easy to pay its creditors. It has four times more resources in its current assets than the amount needed to pay the current liabilities. Of course, not all the money is in the bank yet, but as the creditors become due more money will have flowed from stock to debtors, and then into the bank in line with the cash cycle described on page 539.

Because the current ratio is such a simple measurement, the result can only be a crude indication of liquidity. Other ratios can give a fuller picture.

quick ratio (acid test or liquid capital ratio)

The quick ratio (also called the acid test or liquid capital ratio) is a development of the current ratio. The idea behind this ratio is that stock normally takes longer than debtors to turn into cash, and should be excluded from current assets in the comparison with current liabilities. The formula is:

$$Quick\ Ratio \quad = \quad \frac{(Current\ Assets - Stock)}{Current\ Liabilities}$$

The number obtained from this ratio will be lower than that obtained from the current ratio, unless there is no stock in the business. Using the data from Cash Cycles Limited would give a calculation of (£800,000 − £300,000) ÷ £200,000 = 2.5 (or 2.5:1). This shows that the company should be able to pay its liabilities easily since there is two and a half times more value in debtors and the bank than is owed to creditors. This is also demonstrating that Cash Cycles Limited has good (or high) liquidity. If a business had a quick ratio of less than 1 then it would owe more current liabilities than it had in the bank plus debtors. In such a situation it would have great difficulty in paying its bills as they became due, because of poor liquidity.

CASE STUDY
Current ratio: A Ltd, B Ltd, C Ltd

A Ltd, B Ltd and C Ltd are similar companies, which have current assets as shown:

	A Ltd £000	B Ltd £000	C Ltd £000
Stock	170	100	50
Debtors	90	140	110
Cash at bank and in hand	40	60	140
	300	300	300

Each of the three companies has current liabilities of £150,000.

required

Calculate (a) the current ratio and (b) the quick ratio for each of the three companies and compare the liquidity position of the three companies.

solution

The calculations are as follows:

(a) current ratio:

current assets = £300,000 and current liabilities = £150,000.

Each of the three companies therefore has a current ratio of 2 : 1.

(a) quick ratio:

A Ltd: $\dfrac{300 - 170}{150}$ = 0.87, giving a quick ratio of 0.87 : 1

B Ltd: $\dfrac{300 - 100}{150}$ = 1.33, giving a quick ratio of 1.33 : 1

C Ltd: $\dfrac{300 - 50}{150}$ = 1.67, giving a quick ratio of 1.67 : 1

comments

A Ltd has built up stocks to a high level and we cannot be sure that these can easily be sold, in order to convert them into debtors and then into cash. When the stocks are taken out, A Ltd's current assets do not cover its current liabilities.

B Ltd has a better liquidity position, provided the debtors are well controlled.

C Ltd has the most liquid current assets and could pay most of its creditors immediately.

RATIOS FOR EXAMINING THE INDIVIDUAL ELEMENTS OF WORKING CAPITAL

Using ratios like the current ratio and the quick (acid test) ratio will give a general picture of an organisation's liquidity, but it doesn't tell the whole story. An organisation must have sufficient liquidity to survive, but as mentioned earlier, too much value tied up in current assets may be wasteful. There are ratios that can be used to help judge whether the amounts of stock, debtors and creditors are reasonable for the business. They will also highlight any changes.

All these ratios use the idea that we saw in the cash cycle – the length of time that it takes to progress through the stages of the cycle until the cash that was paid out to suppliers comes back in again from debtors. Instead of looking at sample transactions as we did at the start of this chapter, we will use the data in the profit and loss account and the balance sheet to provide average times for each of the main elements of working capital.

Let us assume that Cash Cycles Limited has the following data in its profit & loss account and balance sheet.

Cash Cycles Limited – Extract from Profit & Loss Account for year ended 31 December 2002

	£'000	£'000
Sales		2,000
Less cost of sales:		
Opening stock	200	
Purchases	1,300	
	1,500	
Less closing stock	300	
Cost of Sales		1,200
Gross profit		800

Cash Cycles Ltd – Extract from Balance Sheet as at 31 December 2002

	£'000	£'000
Current Assets		
Stocks	300	
Debtors	400	
Bank	100	
	800	
Less Current Liabilities		
Creditors	200	
Working Capital		600

---

average stock

Stock can be examined by using a calculation of **stock days** as follows:

$$\textit{Stock Days} = \frac{\textit{Stock}}{\textit{Cost of Sales}} \times 365$$

This is an indication of how much stock is held, measured in how long it takes to sell. 'Cost of sales' is used since both this figure and stock are valued at cost, and the calculation is therefore consistent. If we want to measure the closing stock of Cash Cycles Limited we would get the calculation:

$$\frac{£300,000}{£1,200,000} \times 365 = 91 \text{ days}$$

This is saying that, assuming the sales continue at the same pace, the year-end stock would take an average 91 days to sell. A similar calculation could be made for the average stock for the year. The average stock figure is:

$$\frac{(£200,000 + £300,000) \div 2}{£1,200,000} \times 365 = 76 \text{ days}$$

debtors collection period

Debtors can be examined by using a calculation of **debtor days** as follows:

$$Debtor\ Days = \frac{Debtors}{Credit\ Sales} \times 365$$

This is an indication of how long debtors are taking to pay on average.

Assuming that all Cash Cycles Limited's sales are on credit, the calculation is:

$$\frac{£400,000}{£2,000,000} \times 365 = 73 \text{ days}$$

creditors payment period

Trade Creditors can be examined by using a calculation of **creditor days** as follows:

$$Creditor\ Days = \frac{Trade\ Creditors}{Purchases} \times 365$$

This is an indication of how long the organisation is taking to pay its trade creditors. Trade creditors are often all or most of the current liabilities of a trading organisation. Assuming that all Cash Cycles Limited's creditors are trade creditors, the calculation is:

$$\frac{£200,000}{£1,300,000} \times 365 = 56 \text{ days}.$$

Since creditors are liabilities rather than assets, the longer the creditor days, the less money is tied up in working capital. For Cash Cycles Limited a point to note would be that it is paying its creditors more quickly than its debtors are paying their bills.

MANAGING WORKING CAPITAL

The calculation of the above ratios is an effective tool in the management of working capital. The ratios can show when an organisation has working capital that is out of line with that held by its competitors, or when its working capital has slipped from the position established in the master budget. Ratios that act as comparisons or targets are also referred to as 'benchmarks'.

Each of the elements of working capital (stock, debtors, cash and creditors) needs to be managed effectively. We will look at each of these in turn.

managing stock

The management of stock is very much a balancing act. If stocks of raw materials are too low, the firm risks running out and production coming to a halt. If stocks of finished goods are too low, there is a risk that they will not be able to supply what customers want promptly, and they may purchase elsewhere. If stocks of either type are too high then it costs more in terms of storage, insurance, and interest on money borrowed as well as risking deterioration or obsolescence (becoming out of date). Key elements of good stock management are as follows:

- make sure there is a reliable system for knowing what the stock levels are – these can be manual or computerised, but with physical checks (stock-takes)
- keep an appropriate amount of 'buffer' stock to cover unexpected delays in deliveries or increased requirements
- re-order raw materials at appropriate times, taking into account lead times (times between placing an order and receiving goods) – some organisations use a predetermined 're-order level' to formalise this
- forecast demand levels using appropriate techniques, and feed this information into the production planning system
- monitor actual stock levels against budgeted levels to ensure that plans are being adhered to

managing debtors

The management of debtors is often referred to as **credit control,** and involves the granting of credit to suitable customers, monitoring the amounts outstanding and chasing payment where appropriate. Granting credit to customers can be seen as a method of increasing sales, but amounts outstanding need to be kept under control and late payments and bad debts minimised. Clearly, the more that is owed to a business, the less there will be in its bank account. Key elements of managing debtors are as follows:

■ the organisation should determine in advance how it decides whether to grant credit; for example what information will be required in terms of references and credit history

■ credit limits should be used to help limit the exposure to slow payers and help reduce bad debts

■ up-to-date information must be held on all amounts outstanding, and continually monitored

■ any queries must be dealt with swiftly and fairly

■ appropriate methods must be used to chase slow payers, including suspending further orders and threatening legal action where necessary

■ discounts may be used to encourage early payment (see below)

managing cash

The level of the cash (or bank) balance will result from the interaction of stock, debtors and creditors. The balance should be monitored to ensure that it is at a level as anticipated by the cash flow budget. Surplus funds should be invested appropriately to give a suitable combination of safety, liquidity, and profitability. Suitable borrowing facilities (for example bank overdraft) should be available and used for short-term cash shortages.

managing creditors

Managing creditors involves negotiating suitable credit terms with suppliers (ie as long as possible) and making payment according to those terms. Although making late payments will improve cash flow, it is a dangerous strategy if done too much, since a reputation for slow payment (and perhaps being a poor credit risk) would be easy to gain and difficult to lose. Discounts for prompt payment may be worth receiving, but are not always worthwhile, as discussed below.

making good use of discounts for prompt payment

Discounts may be offered to debtors or received from creditors as a way of rewarding early or prompt payment. Before offering or taking such a discount, organisations should ensure that the decision is of benefit to them. The two issues to consider are:

■ **the amount of cash available in the business (liquidity)**

If a business has poor liquidity and therefore little surplus cash then it may consider offering early payment discounts to its customers to speed up payment, but would be unlikely to take discounts offered to it by creditors. If the business has surplus cash then it can take discounts offered if they are worthwhile.

■ **the cost or benefit of the discount compared to other interest rates that are being paid or received**

The question here is how the discount rate offered compares with the current interest rates. Is it worth paying early if the money could earn more on deposit or cost more to be borrowed?

The calculation should take account of the change in date of payment that would result, and use this to calculate the effective interest rate of the discount. This applies whether the discount is being offered or received. The rate calculated can then be compared to other relevant rates for the organisation before making a decision.

For example, suppose a discount of 2% is being offered for payment in 7 days instead of the usual 45 days. Since this would bring forward the payment by 38 days, it is equivalent to an annual rate of:

2% x 365 ÷ 38 = 19% p.a.

The firm being offered the discount would gain by paying early provided it could not obtain that rate of return elsewhere (eg a deposit account at the bank). The firm offering that level of discount must realise that it is effectively paying 19% p.a. and compare that rate with how much it would cost to borrow elsewhere.

WHAT-IF CALCULATIONS WITH WORKING CAPITAL

The amount that a business has invested in its working capital is usually a fairly constant amount. It can be thought of as the part of the overall investment in the business that is 'left over' after the required investment in fixed assets. Although it will rise as a business generates profit, and fall as drawings or dividends are paid out, these changes are often small in relation to the overall amount.

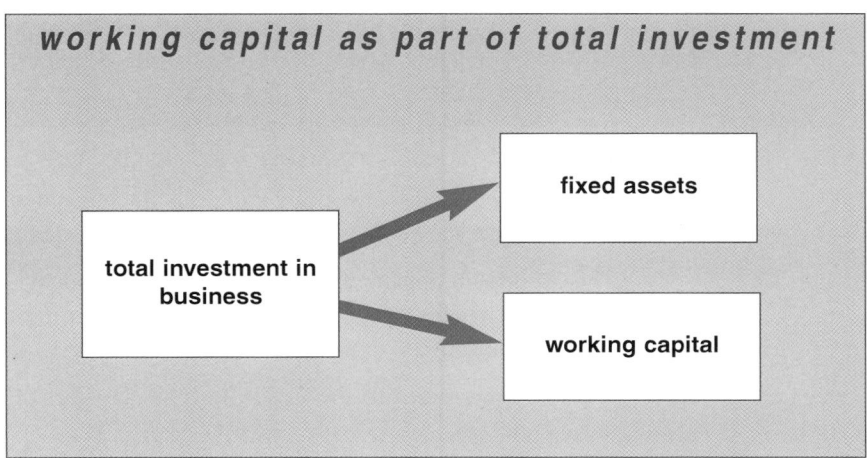

working capital as part of total investment

total investment in business

fixed assets

working capital

If we think of the working capital amount as a whole as constant, then we can see that changes in any one element will result in changes in the last part of the cash cycle – the bank or cash balance.

For example, if we look again at the working capital of Cash Cycles Limited, and assume that:

- stock could be reduced by £70,000 by careful control
- debtors could be reduced by £50,000 by tighter management
- creditors could be increased by £30,000 by renegotiating terms

Then these changes would feed through into more money in the bank as follows:

Cash Cycles Ltd – Extract from Balance Sheet as at 31 December 2002

	Original Position	Revised Position
	£'000	£'000
Current Assets		
Stocks	300	230
Debtors	400	350
Bank	100	250
	800	830
Less Current Liabilities		
Creditors	200	230
Net Current Assets	600	600

Note that the total for working capital is unchanged at £600,000, but that the bank balance has increased by £150,000 due to the three changes outlined.

This approach means that we can quickly calculate the likely effect of proposed changes in any of the elements of working capital, either singly or in combination.

We will now return to the Case Study at the start of the chapter and apply these concepts.

CASE STUDY
Jean-E-Us: managing working capital

Jean-E-Us is a company that manufactures denim jeans for sale to various fashion wholesalers. Gene Edwards, the manager, has now received accounting statements based on the company's performance, and is comparing them with the budget he prepared earlier. He is concerned that although many aspects of the performance are similar to the budgeted amounts, the bank balance is significantly lower than expected.

The following is a comparison of the working capital from the budgeted balance sheet with the actual figures as at 31 March.

		Budget £	Actual £
Current Assets:			
Stocks:	Finished Goods	21,670	21,670
	Raw Materials	9,375	29,375
Debtors		70,000	95,000
Bank		50,125	1,125
		151,170	147,170
Less Current Liabilities:			
Creditors for Purchases		18,187	14,187
		132,983	132,983

After discussions with various members of staff in the organisation, the following facts emerge:

- During February it was thought that there might be a problem in obtaining sufficient denim cloth for the company's needs because of threatened industrial action at the supplier's company. An additional 8,000 square metres of the cloth at £2.50 per square metre was ordered and received in February, and the invoice was paid during March. Other orders have been placed in line with the budget. It has now been confirmed that the threat of action has been withdrawn and all future supply requirements can be met.
- A major customer that bought 1,000 pairs of jeans in February (for £25 per pair) has not yet paid the amount due. The customer has promised to pay during April.

required

1. Identify the way that each of the two issues outlined will have changed the elements of working capital.

2. Identify a possible cause of any other difference between the budgeted and actual working capital.

3. Suggest appropriate action that the company should take during April to improve the cash position and avoid similar problems in the future.

solution

1 Changes in the elements of working capital

The issues identified will have affected the working capital as follows:

The additional purchase of 8,000 square metres of cloth at £2.50 per square metre, and the payment of the invoice will have:

- increased raw materials stocks by 8,000 x £2.50 = £20,000 – this accounts for all the difference in raw material stocks compared with the budget
- reduced the bank balance by £20,000

The delay in receiving payment from the customer for 1,000 pairs of jeans at £25.00 per pair will have:

- increased debtors by 1,000 x £25 = £25,000 from the figure expected – this accounts for all the difference in debtors compared with the budget
- reduced the bank balance by £25,000 from the figure expected

2 Causes of other differences between budget and actual figures

The two issues would account for a reduced bank balance of:

Budgeted bank balance	£50,125
Less stock difference	(£20,000)
Less debtors difference	(£25,000)
Balance accounted for	£ 5,125

This leaves differences of:

Bank	£4,000 (£5,125 as above compared with actual of £1,125)
Creditors	£4,000 (budget £18,187 compared with actual of £14,187)

This final difference of £4,000 would be accounted for by an early payment to creditors of £4,000, thereby reducing both creditors and the bank balance.

3 Suggested actions to imrove the cash position

The suggested action to improve the cash position is as follows:

- reduce the next order of raw materials by 8,000 square metres of cloth – this will reduce the stocks as the cloth is used up in line with the budget
- monitor the debtors to ensure that the delayed payment is made as promised, and that other payments are not delayed – if this delay is a result of cash flow difficulties experienced by the customer, it should act as a warning signal that there may be a risk of a future bad debt
- examine the position regarding the apparent early payment to creditors; monitor future payments made to creditors to ensure that they are in accordance with the credit terms agreed and the budget

THE EFFECTS OF BUSINESS EXPANSION ON WORKING CAPITAL

If a business expands by increasing its sales level, then this will also result in increased purchases and possibly other expenditure. A further implication that may be overlooked is that stock, debtors and creditors will also increase – typically in proportion to the increase in sales. This means that either

■ more investment will be needed in working capital as a whole, or

■ the cash or bank balance will be reduced as it is squeezed by the effect of the other elements of working capital

When a business expands without sufficient working capital this will cause liquidity problems, and possibly lead to the failure of the business. The rapid expansion of a business without sufficient working capital is known as overtrading, and is a problem often encountered by new businesses.

The effects on working capital of business expansion can be quite dramatic, as the following case study demonstrates.

CASE STUDY
Jean-E-Us: working capital for expansion

Jean-E-Us is a company that manufactures denim jeans for sale to various fashion wholesalers. Gene Edwards, the manager, is planning to tender for a new contact that will double the sales level of the company. He has solved his previous cash problem and spent some surplus cash on a new computer aided design system, and is now looking at the possible consequences of the new contract.

'Let's get a rough idea of the size of working capital we'll need,' said Gene's accountant as they were discussing the proposals. 'Here are approximate figures for the current working capital without the new contract – let's see how they would be changed by doubling sales.'

Current Working Capital

Current Assets:

Stocks:	Finished Goods	25,000
	Raw Materials	10,000
Debtors		70,000
Bank		25,000
		130,000

Less Current Liabilities:

Creditors for Purchases	20,000
Total Working Capital	110,000

required

Assuming that stock, debtors and creditors will all double as a result of the increased sales level, show the revised working capital position, assuming that:

(a) the bank balance is maintained at £25,000 and the total investment in working capital changes, or

(b) an overdraft is used to cover the increased requirements, assuming the total of working capital remains at £110,000

solution

		Current Position	Option (a)	Option (b)
		£	£	£
Current Assets				
Stocks:	Finished Goods	25,000	50,000	50,000
	Raw Materials	10,000	20,000	20,000
Debtors		70,000	140,000	140,000
Bank		25,000	25,000	–
		130,000	235,000	210,000
Less Current Liabilities:				
Creditors		20,000	40,000	40,000
Bank Overdraft		–	–	60,000
Total Working Capital		110,000	195,000	110,000

The additional working capital needed, (as demonstrated in option [a]) is £195,000 – £110,000 = £85,000. If this were not raised in some other way then it would change the bank balance from a positive £25,000 to an overdraft of £60,000.

Assuming the additional sales were profitable, there would eventually be positive cash flow from the operations that would help the working capital position, but this could take a considerable time to work through the cash cycle. In the meantime the cost of interest on the additional working capital (assuming it can be obtained) will reduce the profitability of the business.

chapter summary

- Working capital is the term used to describe the current assets minus the current liabilities of a business. It represents the value tied up in stocks, debtors and cash less short-term creditors.

- The cash cycle is the natural movement through working capital as payment is made for purchases of stock; these are processed and sold and generate debtors, that eventually replenish the cash. The longer the cash cycle takes to operate, the more working capital will be required.

- Ratios can be used to monitor liquidity and the main elements of working capital. The ratios based on the actual position can be used to compare with previous figures, budgeted figures, or benchmarks based on the performance of other organisations in the same sector.

- The total investment in working capital is often fairly static. This means that changes in the levels of stock, debtors and creditors will have an immediate effect on the cash or bank balance, and this effect can be predicted.

- Stock, debtors, cash and creditors all need careful managing to ensure that they remain at optimum levels. Discounts for prompt payment can be a useful tool in the management of debtors and creditors.

- Expanding a business by increasing sales requires additional working capital. Attempting to expand without sufficient working capital is known as overtrading.

key terms

working capital	the current assets minus the current liabilities of an organisation – also known as net current assets
cash cycle	the circulation of value through working capital as cash is paid out, and eventually received back again (the length of the cash cycle can be measured in days)
liquidity	the ability of an organisation to pay its liabilities as they become due – it involves keeping sufficient current assets in money or in a form that will quickly convert to money
current ratio	a ratio to measure liquidity – it is calculated by dividing current assets by current liabilities
quick ratio	a ratio to measure liquidity that ignores the value of stocks – it is calculated by dividing current assets minus stocks by current liabilities – it is also known as the acid test ratio

stock days	a ratio to help manage stock levels by converting the value of stock into the average length of time it should take to sell – it can be calculated by dividing the stock value by the year's cost of sales, and then multiplying the result by 365
debtor days	a ratio to help manage debtors by converting the value of debtors into the average length of time that they are taking to pay – it can be calculated by dividing debtors by the year's credit sales, and then multiplying the result by 365
creditor days	a ratio to help manage creditors by converting the value of creditors into the average length of time that the organisation is taking to pay them – it can be calculated by dividing trade creditors by the year's purchases, and then multiplying the result by 365
overtrading	the term used to describe expanding the sales level of a business without ensuring that there is sufficient working capital

activities

Note: an asterisk (*) after an activity number means that an answer is provided in Appendix 1.

26.1   A firm receives raw materials at the end of January on one month's credit, and pays for them on time. The raw materials are processed during February, and the finished goods are held in stock until the end of May, when they are sold on two month's credit. The customer pays on time.

(a)   Draw a line diagram and calculate the cash cycle in months.

(b)   Calculate the cash cycle in months if the firm bought on two months credit but sold on one month's credit.

26.2*   The working capital of an organisation is made up of:

	£'000
Stocks	200
Debtors	150
Bank	20
Creditors	210

Calculate:

(a)   the total working capital

(b)   the bank balance if stocks were reduced by 25% and debtors were reduced by 33.33%, but the remainder of the balance sheet was unchanged

26.3*   Kool Limited, a trading company, is comparing the working capital from the budgeted balance sheet with the actual figures.

	Budget	Actual
	£	£
Current Assets:		
Stocks:	20,000	50,000
Debtors	40,000	80,000
Bank	50,000	0
	110,000	130,000
Less Current Liabilities:		
Creditors for Purchases	30,000	50,000
	80,000	80,000

The following information has been obtained about the actual performance.

• The credit controller has been off sick, so no one has been chasing debtors for the past few weeks. This has doubled the debtors.

• An order of £20,000 worth of purchases was delivered before the above balance sheet date instead of afterwards as requested.

• An additional £10,000 worth of purchases was bought and paid for earlier in the year when a supplier offered a special price. The goods have not yet been sold.

Required

Explain how each of the above pieces of information help to account for the differences between the budgeted parts of working capital and the actual figures.

26.4 The following information relates to Greengrass Limited, a trading company.

Extract from Profit and Loss Account for year ended 31 December

	£'000	£'000
Sales		3,000
Less cost of sales:		
Opening stock	300	
Purchases	2,300	
	2,600	
Less closing stock	300	
		2,300
Gross profit		700

Extract from Balance Sheet as at 31 December

	£'000	£'000
Current assets		
Stocks	300	
Debtors	500	
Bank	100	
	900	
Less current liabilities:		
Creditors	400	
Working capital		500

All sales are on credit, and all creditors relate to purchases.

Required:

(a) Calculate the following ratios for Greengrass Limited:
  • current ratio
  • quick ratio
  • stock days (to the nearest day)
  • debtor days (to the nearest day)
  • creditor days (to the nearest day)

(b)   The company has proposed the following as part of its budget for the next year.

	£'000	£'000
Sales		4,000
Less cost of sales:		
Opening stock	300	
Purchases	3,170	
	3,470	
Less closing stock	400	
		3,070
Gross profit		930

Assuming that the total value of working capital remains the same as the previous year, and that both debtor days and creditor days remain unchanged, show how working capital would appear at the year-end.

(c)   Calculate the revised current and quick ratios based on your solution to part (b) and comment briefly on any change in the liquidity of the company.

MEASURING PERFORMANCE

CASE STUDY
Vector Stars Ltd

The chief executive of Vector Stars Ltd, Jay Vector, is studying a table in an internal memo showing the company's results for the last three years . . .

	Year 1	Year 2	Year 3
	£000s	£000s	£000s
Total Sales	6,917	7,285	6,709
Gross Profit	3,110	3,300	2,950
Net Profit	1,050	900	650

Jay says to his finance manager:

'I need more information. I can see that things are not going too well. I need to be able to identify the performance trends and see where the problem lies.'

The manager replies:

'We have the ratios we calculated from the profit and loss account and balance sheet. Here are some profit ratios to start with. As you can see the problem looks like an overheads one – gross profit keeps fairly constant but expenses are reducing the level of net profit . . .'

	Year 1	Year 2	Year 3
Gross Profit percentage	45%	45%	44%
Net Profit percentage	15%	12%	10%

In this chapter we examine the ways in which managers of an organisation can measure and analyse its financial data in order to remedy problems and improve performance.

learning objectives

When you have studied this chapter you will be able to:

■ consider ways of measuring and comparing the performance of organisations

■ use ratios to analyse the profit and loss account and the balance sheet

■ interpret ratios and appreciate the limitations of ratio analysis

■ suggest suitable measurements of performance for different kinds of work and different types of organisation

MEASURING THE PERFORMANCE OF ORGANISATIONS

performance indicators

Managers need to be able to measure the performance of their organisation to see where improvements can be made. In Chapter 23 we studied the analysis of cost variances. These are examples of performance measurements which can be used:

- to see how well materials and labour time have been used
- to help with control of the business
- to help with planning for the future

A list of variances for one cost centre for one time period is not particularly useful on its own. Managers need to be able to compare them with target levels, with the variances for other time periods or with those for other similar cost centres.

In this chapter we will consider different ways of measuring the performance of an organisation (or of a part of an organisation). For example, we can calculate profit as a percentage of sales, sales revenue per employee, the percentage of orders which are delivered late, and many other measures. An individual measurement is called a **performance indicator**. What we have seen above for variance analysis applies to any performance indicator.

A performance indicator may be used for:

- identifying problems
- controlling costs
- measuring the use of resources such as materials, labour and machines
- measuring an individual's performance
- planning

Examples of performance indicators include:

- the direct materials usage variance, which may identify a problem relating to wastage of materials
- the administration cost as a percentage of turnover, which may help with control of costs
- the number of hours of machine down time, which is relevant to how well resources are being used
- profit as a percentage of turnover, which may indicate how well a company has been managed
- the number of product units rejected on inspection, which may help with planning production levels and improving quality

The usefulness of a performance indicator depends on:

■ comparing with standards, budgets or targets

■ comparing with other periods of time

■ comparing with other similar organisations

making comparisons – benchmarking

Comparing performance indicators with standards or targets includes benchmarking.

Benchmarks are standards or targets which should be related to what is important to the organisation.

Benchmarks may be:

■ set internally and relate to a single aspect of the work, for example: all correspondence to be answered within three working days

■ set by external bodies, for example government targets relating to pollution of the environment

■ set (either internally or externally) with reference to similar organisations, for example the expected level of profitability calculated as an average for the industry

A single organisation may have a number of benchmarks, including all three types described above:

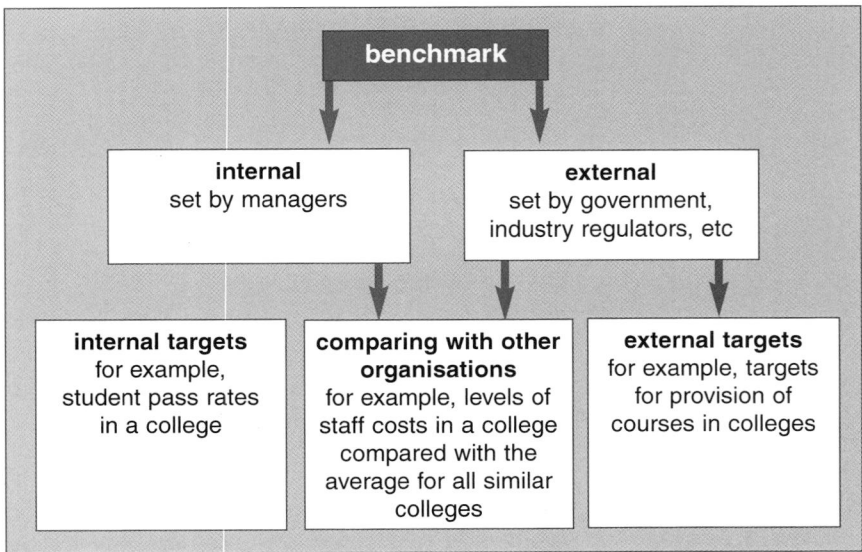

Measurement of how well an organisation (or a part of an organisation) has performed in achieving these aims means that it has to record the necessary data to compare with the benchmark.

making comparisons – time series

A time series is the comparison of data over a number of periods of time.

A time series is used to show a trend and possibly a pattern of variations around the trend. A performance indicator may show these features over a number of time periods, adding to the usefulness of the information.

For example, the number of customer complaints in a given time period can be a useful performance indicator for an organisation. An overall downward trend in the number of complaints shows improvement. An overall upward trend would have to be investigated.

When items measured in money terms, such as Sales Revenue or Profit, are being compared over a number of years, it may be necessary to take out the effect of inflation. This can be done using index numbers, as shown in Chapter 24.

making comparisons – consistency

Comparisons can give very useful information. However, we must be sure that figures being compared really are 'comparable'. In other words, they must have been prepared in a consistent way, so that we are comparing 'like with like'.

For example, the net profit figures for a business over a number of years can be compared, provided that the same accounting policies have been applied throughout. A change in the policy for depreciation, for example, would affect the profit figures and they would not be comparable.

data for performance measurement

The diagram on the next page shows that there are different kinds of data that may be used for performance measurement.

Quantitative data is data which can be stated in numbers, and this can be split into:

- financial or monetary data – ie expressed in terms of money, and
- non-financial or non-monetary data, which is in terms of units other than money, such as numbers of hours

Qualitative data is data which cannot be put in numerical terms. It can consist of people's opinions or judgements, for example the views of students about a teacher. This type of data is used for performance measurement, particularly in appraisal schemes for types of work where there is no clearcut numerical measure of performance. A combination of quantitative and qualitative data is often used.

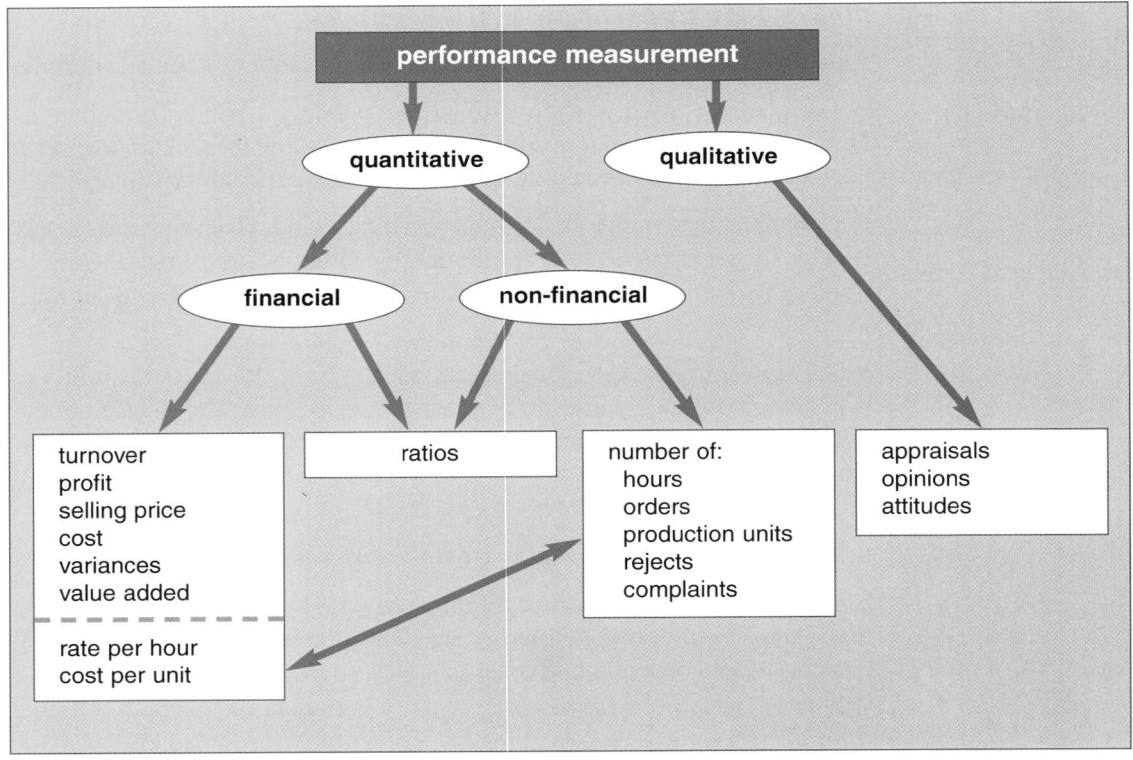

The examples shown in the diagram above include variances as an example of financial data. You have seen in your earlier studies that variances are given in money terms. The other point to note about variances is that each variance comes from two pieces of information and is the difference between them. An alternative way of comparing two pieces of information is to calculate a ratio or percentage, and this is one of the most common ways of arriving at a useful measure of performance. Percentages are particularly useful when comparisons are being made.

tutorial note

When turning a ratio into a percentage,

either multiply by 100

or   use the % button on your calculator.

For example, the ratio 1:4 or 1/4 becomes $\dfrac{1}{4}$ x 100 = 25%

CASE STUDY

Performance indicators as percentages: Little Ltd & Large Ltd

Little Ltd and Large Ltd are companies which operate in the same industry. For a given period, we have the following data:

	Little Ltd £000s	Large Ltd £000s
Turnover	465	2,550
Gross Profit	185	895

At a glance, it is not easy to compare these figures because of the difference in size. If we calculate the gross profit as a percentage of turnover, we obtain more useful information for comparison:

Little Ltd   Gross profit percentage $= \dfrac{185}{465} \times 100 = 39.8\%$

Large Ltd   Gross profit percentage $= \dfrac{895}{2{,}550} \times 100 = 35.1\%$

We can then see that Little Ltd is translating a greater proportion of its turnover into gross profit than Large Ltd. This is an example of a performance indicator.

RATIO ANALYSIS

Ratio analysis generally refers to the calculation of a set of ratios or percentages using data from the financial and management accounts of a business. The trading and profit and loss account and the balance sheet are used in the analysis, which can then be used to evaluate the performance of the business, particularly by:

- comparing with budgets or targets
- comparing with other periods of time
- comparing with other similar organisations

In the case of limited companies, people outside the company can look at the final accounts and calculate ratios, for example when deciding whether to buy shares in the company.

In order to make meaningful comparisons between organisations or between time periods, the accounts must have been prepared on the same basis – applying the principle of consistency by comparing like with like.

sources of data for ratios

In this chapter we consider some of the ratios which can be calculated from the profit and loss account and the balance sheet of a business. Some of these ratios have already been explained in the last chapter. We will do this in a number of stages:

1   We will consider first the ratios calculated from the profit and loss account separately, before linking sales and profits with the balance sheet.

2   The key measure of profit in relation to the assets shown on the balance sheet is Return on Capital Employed.

3   Our third section on ratio analysis will include ratios relating to the current assets and current liabilities of the organisation.

The diagram below illustrates these groups of ratios, the sources of data for their calculation, and the stages (shown by the numbers) in which we will look at them.

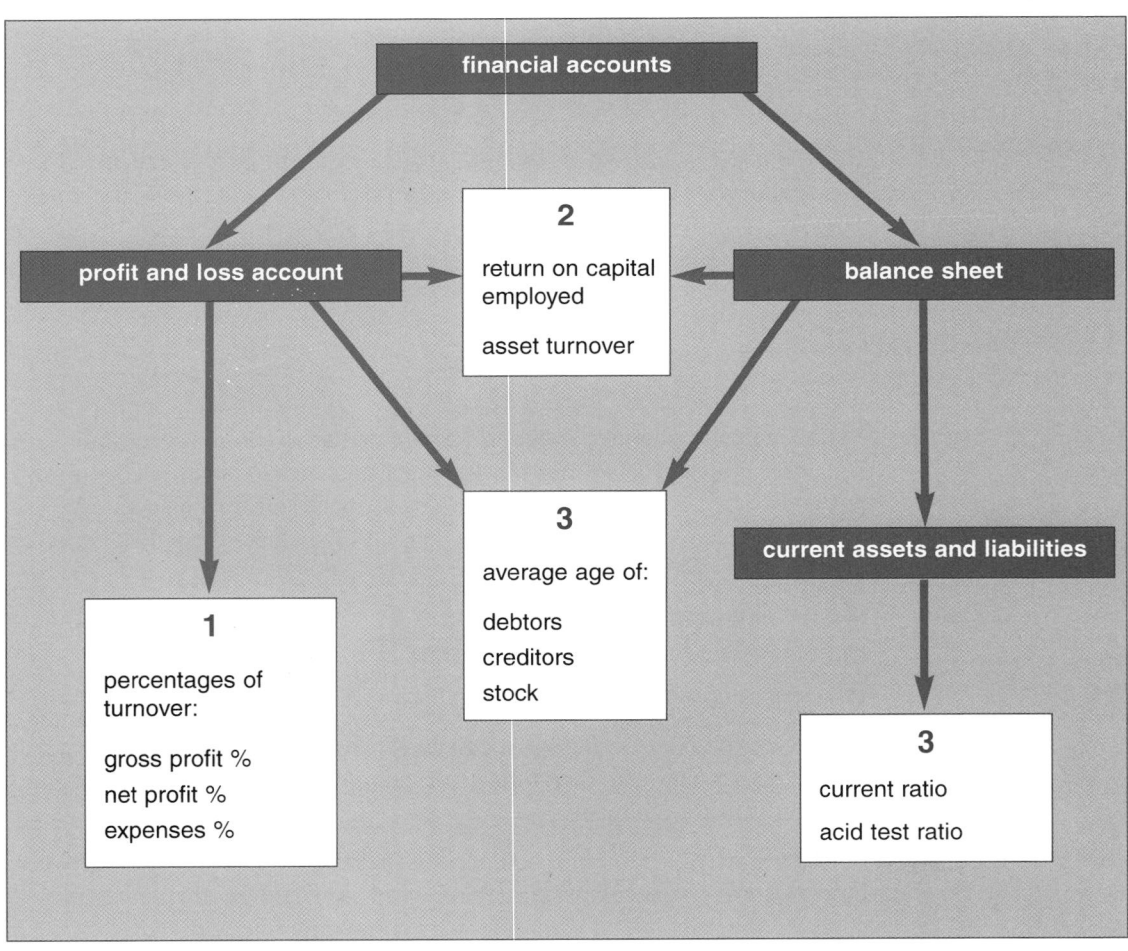

CALCULATION OF RATIOS: THE PROFIT AND LOSS ACCOUNT

Profit percentages are calculated on the basis of turnover (sales revenue). This can be done for gross profit and net profit. In the accounts of a company, several versions of profit are given, before and after interest and tax. To measure the performance of the company, the 'operating profit' or 'profit before interest and tax' is used for many ratios, because this is the profit from the main trading activities of the company. In the formulas below, the terms 'sales' and 'turnover' mean the same thing.

- *gross profit margin (percentage)* $= \dfrac{gross\ profit}{sales} \times 100$

- *net profit percentage* $= \dfrac{net\ profit}{sales} \times 100$

- *operating profit percentage* $= \dfrac{operating\ profit}{sales} \times 100$

Profit percentages are indicators of the profitability of the business.

Any other figure from the profit and loss account can also be calculated as a percentage of sales, particularly if it appears to need investigation. For example, if selling expenses have increased from one period to the next, it may be useful to calculate for each period

- *selling expenses as a percentage of sales* $= \dfrac{selling\ expenses}{sales} \times 100$

- *any type of expense as a percentage of sales* $= \dfrac{expense \times 100}{sales}$

Similarly, if details of the costs of materials and wages are available, we can calculate, for any type of cost:

- *Cost as a percentage of sales* $= \dfrac{cost}{sales} \times 100$

Whether costs behave as fixed or variable costs in relation to activity levels makes a difference to how we would expect the ratios to behave. A higher turnover figure often results from selling more products, which would mean that total variable costs would also be higher. Total fixed costs, however, would not be expected to change with the quantity of sales and production. In percentage terms, this means that we would expect:

■ a variable cost to remain at a similar level as a percentage of turnover

■ a fixed cost as a percentage of turnover to decrease as turnover increases

Calculation of the profit and loss account ratios will show how the revenue from sales has been split between the elements of cost and the profit. The following Case Study illustrates this.

CASE STUDY
Ratio analysis of the profit and loss account: Ayebridge Ltd

Ayebridge Limited is a manufacturer of electronic circuits used in domestic products. The following Profit and Loss Account for the year ended 30 June 2001 includes some detail of the cost of sales.

Ayebridge Ltd: Profit and Loss Account for the year ended 30 June 2001

	£000s	£000s
Sales		6,000
Less cost of sales:		
Materials	800	
Labour	900	
Production overheads	1,700	
Cost of sales		3,400
GROSS PROFIT		2,600
Selling and Distribution	813	
Administration	967	1,780
OPERATING PROFIT		820

required
Analyse the Ayebridge Limited Profit and Loss Account given above, using ratio analysis.

solution
Using the formulas listed in this chapter, we obtain:

Gross profit margin (percentage) = $\frac{\text{Gross profit} \times 100}{\text{Sales}} = \frac{2,600 \times 100}{6,000} = 43.3\%$

This shows that 43.3% of the Sales Revenue remains as Gross Profit after the Cost of Sales has been deducted (see diagram on the opposite page).
The Cost of Sales therefore represents 100% – 43.3% = 56.7% of the Sales Revenue. In this example it is possible to calculate percentages for the three elements of the cost of sales, as follows:

■ Materials cost as a percentage of sales = $\frac{800 \times 100}{6,000} =$ 13.3%

■ Labour cost as a percentage of sales = $\dfrac{900}{6,000}$ x 100 = 15.0%

■ Production overheads as a percentage of sales = $\dfrac{1,700}{6,000}$ x 100 = 28.3%

In order to draw any conclusions from these calculations, we would need more information for comparison. We would need the same format of Profit and Loss Account for Ayebridge Limited for other years, or as a budget for the year ended 30 June 2001. Alternatively, we could compare Ayebridge's figures with averages for the industry or with those for other similar businesses, if available. The same applies to the remaining percentages:

■ Operating profit percentage = $\dfrac{820}{6,000}$ x 100 = 13.7%

Each of the two categories of expense could also be calculated as a percentage of sales:

■ Selling and Distribution as a percentage of sales = 13.6%

■ Administration as a percentage of sales = 16.1%

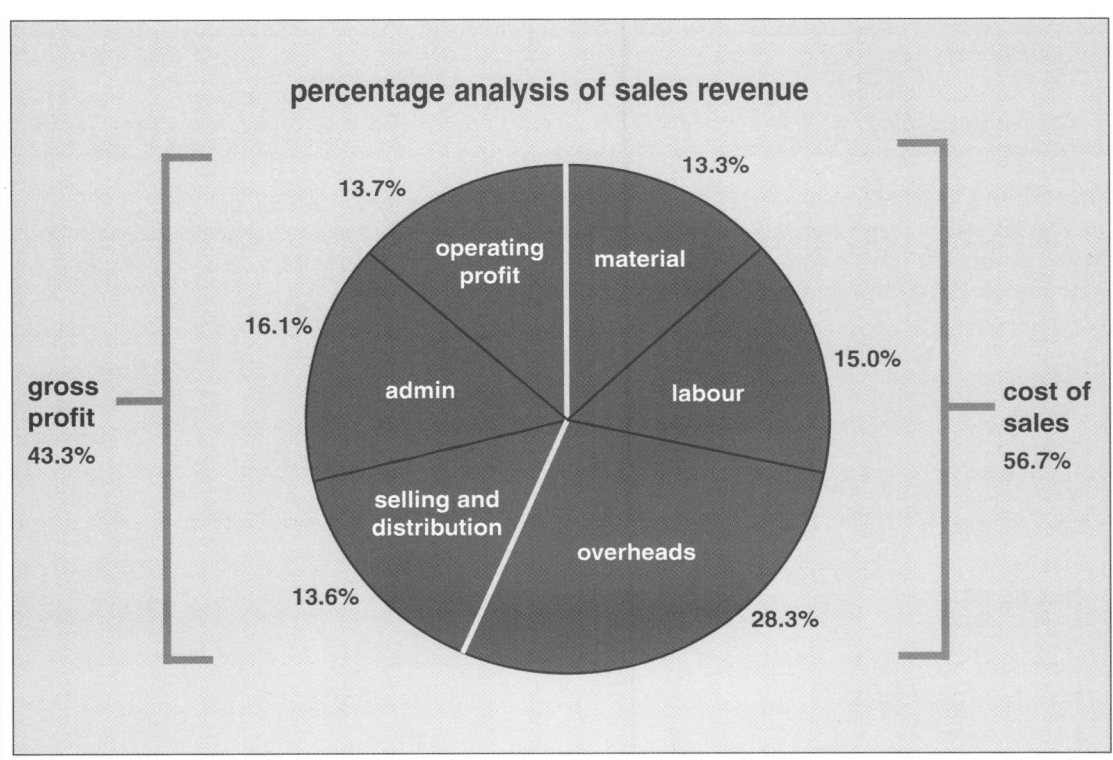

Case Study continued – comparison with the previous year

Consider the table below, which shows information for Ayebridge Limited for the year ended 30 June 2000, together with answers from our calculations for the year ended 30 June 2001.

	30 June 2000	30 June 2001
Gross profit percentage	41.0%	43.3%
Operating profit percentage	15.4%	13.7%

The Gross Profit percentage has therefore increased from 41% in the previous year, to 43.3% in the year ended 30 June 2001. This improvement means that a lower proportion of the Sales Revenue has been used for Cost of Sales. This could result from increasing selling prices or from reducing costs. With more detailed information for the previous year this could be analysed further.

The Operating Profit percentage, however, has decreased from 15.4% in the previous year to 13.7% in the year ended 30 June 2001. This could be because the expenses have increased, but it could also be due to a reduction in the total sales revenue, or both. Increased selling prices may reduce demand for the products, and this could result in lower total sales revenue.

These comments show that the calculated percentages alone are not enough. To see exactly what has happened, we would need to look back at the original data as well.

CASE STUDY
Ratio analysis of the profit and loss account: Beeton Ltd

The following information relates to Beeton Ltd, a chain of retail stationery shops.
Note: whenever you are given data for different time periods, make sure you check which is the earlier and which the later time period. Here the earlier year is on the right, but this is not always so. If you do not check, you may discuss a completely opposite case!

Beeton Ltd: Trading and Profit and Loss Account for the year ended:

	31 March 2001		31 March 2000	
Sales		4,200		3,400
Less cost of sales:				
Opening stock	450		410	
Purchases	2,896		2,250	
Less closing stock	(490)	2,856	(450)	2,210
GROSS PROFIT		1,344		1,190
Expenses:				
Selling and Distribution	157		128	
Administration	200	357	280	408
OPERATING PROFIT		987		782

required

Analyse the Profit and Loss Account, for each of the given years, by calculating (correct to one decimal place)

■ the gross profit margin on sales

■ the operating profit as a percentage of sales

■ two other percentages to aid your analysis

Identify where possible the reasons for changes in the profitability of Beeton Ltd.

solution

Year ended:	31 March 2001	31 March 2000
Gross profit margin on sales	32%	35%
Operating profit percentage	23.5%	23%
Expenses as % of sales:		
Selling and distribution	3.7%	3.8%
Administration	4.8%	8.2%

The **Gross Profit margin** on sales has decreased in the year to 31 March 2001. This may be due to having to reduce selling prices in order to increase sales demand. It could also be caused by increases in purchasing costs, or a combination of these reasons.

The **Operating Profit percentage** has increased slightly. It can be seen from the profit and loss accounts and from the expense percentages that this level of operating profit percentage has been maintained by cutting administration costs. This cost has been reduced by £80,000, even though sales have increased. The effect is to cut the administration costs as a percentage of sales from 8.2% to 4.8%. The selling and distribution costs are at a similar level as a percentage of sales in both years.

RATIOS LINKING TURNOVER AND PROFITS TO THE BALANCE SHEET

The balance sheet of an organisation represents the equation:

assets – liabilities = capital

and the capital represents the owners' interest in the business.

We can therefore look at the balance sheet from either side – as the net assets or as the capital provided by the owners. Note that:

■ 'assets' includes both fixed and current assets

■ 'liabilities' includes current and long-term liabilities

Long-term liabilities, such as loans, can be viewed as a long-term source of finance for the organisation by rearranging the equation as:

fixed and current assets – current liabilities

= long-term liabilities + capital

This version of the equation will be used in calculating the Return on Capital Employed on the next page and examples will show how it works.

---

tutorial note

The balance sheet of an organisation shows its assets, liabilities and owners' capital on a specific date.

It is important to remember, when using a balance sheet for ratio analysis, and when interpreting the ratios, that the position shown on that date may not be typical. A single transaction the next day, such as a payment to a creditor, will alter the position. Bearing this in mind, we calculate a number of ratios using the balance sheet.

RETURN ON CAPITAL EMPLOYED (ROCE)

Return on Capital Employed is a key ratio which shows how well the management of an organisation has used the assets (or the resources shown on the Balance Sheet) to generate profits.

To calculate ROCE, the profit is expressed as a percentage of the capital employed in the business.

The difficulty comes in deciding which 'profit' figure to use, and what is meant by 'capital employed'. If comparisons are being made between companies, for example, then the ROCE must be calculated in the same way for each company (as far as is possible from the available information).

Usually, the measurement of management performance would mean that the operating profit is used, and the capital employed would take account of the assets used in the main activities of the organisation.

The capital employed figure to use in straightforward cases is equal to the fixed assets plus the net current assets. By 'net current assets' we mean 'current assets less current liabilities', ie the working capital.

Referring back to the balance sheet equation above,

fixed assets plus net current assets

= fixed and current assets – current liabilities

= long-term liabilities + capital

We are looking at the 'capital employed' either as the assets being used to generate profits or the funds which are being used to finance those assets.

We therefore have the formulas:

$$ROCE = \frac{operating\ profit}{fixed\ assets\ +\ net\ current\ assets} \times 100$$

or

$$ROCE = \frac{operating\ profit}{capital\ on\ balance\ sheet\ +\ long\text{-}term\ liabilities} \times 100$$

You may find the term 'profit before interest and tax' instead of operating profit in some examples. It is advisable to make your method clear when calculating ROCE, because of the possible variations in the definitions.

CASE STUDY
Return on capital employed: John Kent

John Kent is a sole trader who runs a plumbing business employing two other people. He financed part of the purchase of his vans with a long-term loan from his father. We have the following simplified balance sheet:

Balance Sheet of John Kent as at 31 March 2001		
	£	£
Fixed Assets:		
Vehicles at cost	50,000	
Less: provision for depreciation	12,500	37,500
Equipment at cost	6,800	
Less: provision for depreciation	1,200	5,600
		43,100
Current Assets	8,400	
Current Liabilities	(3,900)	
Net current assets		4,500
Long term loan		(30,000)
		17,600
Capital as at 31 March 2001		17,600

required

Show the calculation of the Capital Employed as at 31 March 2001 for John Kent from the above balance sheet using:

■ fixed assets plus net current assets

■ capital on balance sheet plus long-term liabilities

solution

■ Fixed assets plus net current assets = £43,100 + £4,500 = £47,600

■ Capital on balance sheet plus long-term liabilities
   = £17,600 + £30,000 = £47,600

Note: These two views of the balance sheet give the same figure for capital employed (at 31 March 2001).

CASE STUDY

ROCE and the balance sheet of a limited company: Wing Ltd

This case study illustrates some of the features of a limited company balance sheet, using a simplified version.

Balance Sheet of Wing Ltd as at 31 March 2001		
	£000s	£000s
Fixed Assets (Net Book Value)		750
Current Assets	95	
Current Liabilities	68	
Net current assets		27
		777
Long term loans		150
		627
Capital and Reserves:		
£1 Ordinary Shares issued and fully paid		350
Reserves		200
Profit and Loss Account		77
		627

Note that the Balance Sheet total of £627,000 represents for Capital and Reserves:

- Share Capital which has been introduced into the company (by investors buying shares).

- Reserves, which represent amounts of capital or profits which have been set aside to be used in future.

- Profit and Loss Account, which represents accumulated profits retained within the business (other than those set aside in reserves).

required

Determine the Capital Employed for Wing Ltd as at 31 March 2001 and calculate the Return on Capital Employed. (Note: Operating Profit for the year was £233,100.)

solution

Wing Ltd has long-term loans of £150,000 which are being used, along with the accumulated total capital, to finance the operating activities of the company. Therefore the Capital Employed is:

Balance Sheet total + Long term loans = £627,000 + £150,000 = £777,000

or Fixed Assets + Net Current Assets = £750,000 + £27,000 = £777,000

Applying the formula:

$$\text{Return on Capital Employed} = \frac{\text{Operating profit}}{\text{Capital employed}} \times 100$$

$$= \frac{£233,100}{£777,000} \times 100 = 30\%$$

asset turnover

Asset turnover is another important ratio which links the balance sheet with the profit and loss account.

Asset turnover is the number of times the value of the assets has been obtained in turnover (sales).

Again there may be different definitions of the value of the assets, but we will use the fixed assets plus net current assets as above.

$$\text{asset turnover} = \frac{\text{turnover}}{\text{fixed assets + net current assets}}$$

CASE STUDY

Asset turnover: Wing Ltd

In the Wing Limited Case Study (see previous page), if the turnover for the year ended 31 March 2001 was £1,165,500, then:

asset turnover $= \dfrac{£1,165,500}{£750,000 + £27,000} = 1.5$ times

ROCE and operating profit margin

There is an important link between ROCE, Asset Turnover and the Operating Profit margin (ie Operating Profit as a percentage of Sales):

ROCE = operating profit margin x asset turnover

because

$$\frac{Operating\ Profit}{Fixed\ \&\ net\ current\ assets} = \frac{Operating\ Profit}{\cancel{Sales}}\ x\ \frac{\cancel{Sales}}{Fixed\ \&\ net\ current\ assets}$$

The sales (turnover) figure can be cancelled in the calculation of the right hand side of this equation (see lines).

The following diagram illustrates these connections:

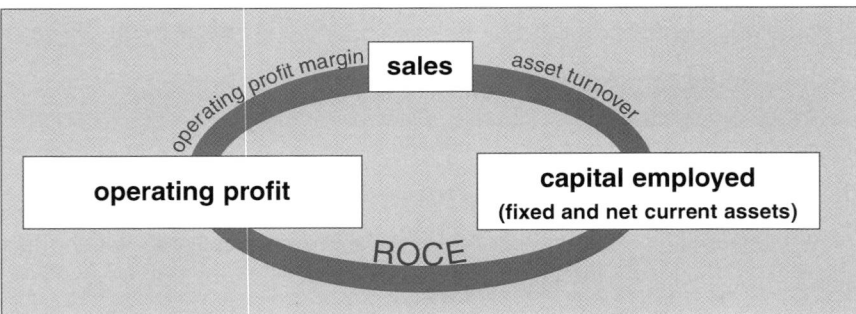

It is easiest to see this using the figures from the Wing Limited Case Study:

$$\frac{£233,100}{£777,000}\ x\ 100\% = \frac{£233,100}{£1,165,500}\ x\ 100\%\ x\ \frac{£1,165,500}{£777,000} = 20\%\ x\ 1.5 = 30\%$$

This relationship means that the ROCE can be increased either by increasing the operating profit margin or by improving the asset turnover or both. In other words, using the assets more effectively to generate sales or spending less of the sales revenue on operating costs can both improve ROCE.

CALCULATION OF RATIOS: CURRENT ASSETS AND LIABILITIES

The ratios and percentages usually calculated from the Balance Sheet include several which relate to the current assets and current liabilities. These can be grouped under the heading 'Working Capital Ratios' and have already been covered in detail in Chapter 26.

The performance indicators relating to current assets and current liabilities which you should know about are:

- current ratio
- quick ratio (acid test ratio)
- debtors collection period
- creditors payment period
- stock holding period
- stock turnover

If you are not familiar with these ratios, or do not know their formulas, you should turn back and read pages 542 to 546.

We will now look at a long Case Study which gives practice in calculating and interpreting all the ratios.

CASE STUDY
Ratio analysis: Bamberdale plc

Bamberdale plc is a large manufacturing company in the chemicals industry producing a range of different products. The following information is available for the years ended 30 September 2000 and 2001. (Note as before that the earlier year is shown on the right.)

The profit and loss account for a limited company is immediately followed by the appropriation account, showing the amount of dividends to be paid out of profits to shareholders. The remaining profit is retained within the business and is added to the retained profits, which are part of the capital of the company. The term 'Debentures' under long-term liabilities in this example refers to long term loans, (which are often secured on the assets in a similar way to a domestic mortgage). For ease of working, the information is shown in a simplified format.

Bamberdale plc Profit and Loss Account for the year ended 30 September

	2001 £m	2001 £m	2000 £m	2000 £m
Turnover		2,660		2,200
Opening stock	400		277	
Purchases	1,945		1,723	
Less closing stock	350		400	
Cost of sales		1,995		1,600
Gross profit		665		600
Selling and distribution	120		105	
Administration	240	360	210	315
Operating Profit		305		285
Interest charges		25		20
Profit before taxation		280		265
Taxation		84		62
Profit after taxation		196		203
Dividends		90		64
Retained profit for the year		106		139

Bamberdale plc Balance Sheet as at 30 September:

	2001 £m	2001 £m	2000 £m	2000 £m
Fixed assets at cost	1,370		763	
Provision for depreciation	770	600	500	263
Current assets:				
Stock	350		400	
Debtors	200		210	
Cash at bank	26		97	
	576		707	
Current liabilities:				
Trade creditors	236		224	
Taxation	84		62	
Dividends	90		64	
	410		350	
Net current assets		166		357
Long term liabilities:				
Debentures		200		160
		566		460
Financed by:				
Ordinary shares issued and fully paid		300		300
Retained profit		266		160
		566		460

required

Carry out an analysis of the ratios studied in this chapter (listed below) for Bamberdale plc and comment on the results.

The ratios to be used are:
1 Gross profit margin
2 Operating profit %
3 Selling and distribution % (of sales)
4 Administration % (of sales)
5 ROCE
6 Asset turnover
7 Current ratio
8 acid test ratio
9 Debtors collection period
10 Creditors payment period
11 Average age of stock (use average stock)

solution

The following indicators are calculated from the information given, using the formulas in this and the last chapter. (See if you can carry out these calculations, before looking at the workings on page 581).

		30 Sept 2001	30 Sept 2000
1	Gross profit margin	25.0%	27.3%
2	Operating profit %	11.5%	13.0%
3	Selling and distribution % (of sales)	4.5%	4.8%
4	Administration % (of sales)	9.0%	9.5%
5	ROCE	39.8%	46.0%
6	Asset turnover	3.47 times	3.55 times
7	Current ratio	1.4 : 1	2.0 : 1
8	acid test ratio	0.6 : 1	0.9 : 1
9	Debtors collection period	27 days	35 days
10	Creditors payment period	44 days	47 days
11	Average age of stock	69 days	77 days

comments

We can look first at the original figures, before considering the ratios. It is clear that, in the year ended 30 September 2001, turnover has increased, and so have the gross profit and operating profit figures. On the balance sheet, we can see that fixed assets have been purchased during the year, and there are also additional long term loans (debentures). Current assets have decreased, particularly the cash at bank. It seems that the extra loans have partly financed the new fixed assets, but cash has also been used for this. These assets have helped to generate higher sales and this has resulted in higher profits. However, the ratios will show how well the company has used its assets in comparison to the previous year, and what percentage of the higher sales has been translated into profits.

solution

1   Gross profit margin has decreased, which suggests that selling prices have been reduced (this could result in more demand for the products and therefore higher turnover). Alternatively, purchase costs may have gone up, or both.

2, 3 & 4   The expenses have increased approximately in line with turnover, being at similar percentage levels. Together with the lower gross profit margin, this has resulted in a decrease in the operating profit percentage. The increase in the amount of administration expenses could be investigated, as it might be expected that the majority of these costs would be fixed.

5   ROCE has decreased from 46.0% to 39.8%. This is due to the fact that the capital employed has increased. (The operating profit has also increased, but because we are dividing it by a much larger number, the resulting percentage has gone down.) We saw that we can look at the capital employed from the point of view of the fixed and net current assets being used or the financing of those assets. The fixed assets being used in the year ended 30 September 2000 were probably older and therefore the accumulated depreciation had considerably reduced their value on the balance sheet. In the following year, a significant factor is that there are new fixed assets included on the balance sheet as at 30 September. There is no information as to whether these were acquired early or late in the year, which would make a difference to the amount of profit they could generate.

     Looking at the increase in capital employed from the finance point of view, it is due to the £40m increase in debentures and the £106m retained profit for the year ended 30 September 2001.

6   The asset turnover has decreased slightly, but considering the effect of the additional fixed assets as discussed above, it seems that the company has continued to use its assets to generate sales at a similar level.

7 & 8   The current and acid test ratios have both deteriorated and may cause concern at these levels. The main reasons are the decrease in cash and the increase in current liabilities, particularly tax and dividends. Some of the cash may have been used for the purchase of fixed assets. Cash will be required to pay the tax and dividends when they fall due and this could prove to be a problem.

9,10 & 11   There has been an improvement in the collection of debts, and stock is being turned over slightly more quickly. The payment period for trade creditors has changed only slightly and the net effect is that the circulation of working capital has been speeded up.

More general discussion of this case study could include some of the following points:

- In general, the year ended 30 September 2001 has been one of expansion for Bamberdale plc.

- Sales have increased at a rate which corresponds with the expansion, and therefore to reverse the decline in profitability, opportunities for cost reduction should be investigated.

- It will be important to review the ROCE in the next year, ending 30 September 2002, to check that it does not continue a downward trend. The current year's decrease can be explained by the effect of increased capital employed and next year should see an improvement if the new assets generate sufficient profits.

- The main problem at 30 September 2001 is liquidity. As at the balance sheet date, the company appears to need more cash. The improvement in collection of debts is helpful, but the company may still have difficulty in paying its tax liability and the dividends. The dividend has increased by over 40% on the year before, and this is a policy decision on the part of the directors. They now need to obtain the necessary cash to cover it. Possible ways of doing this include selling fixed assets, issuing more shares or taking out more loans. What they choose to do will of course affect next year's results and ratios.

workings

		30 Sept 2001 (£m)	30 Sept 2000 (£m)
1	$\dfrac{\text{Gross Profit} \times 100}{\text{Sales}}$	$\dfrac{665 \times 100}{2{,}660}$	$\dfrac{600 \times 100}{2{,}200}$
2	$\dfrac{\text{Operating Profit} \times 100}{\text{Sales}}$	$\dfrac{305 \times 100}{2{,}660}$	$\dfrac{285 \times 100}{2{,}200}$
3	$\dfrac{\text{Selling \& Dist.} \times 100}{\text{Sales}}$	$\dfrac{120 \times 100}{2{,}660}$	$\dfrac{105 \times 100}{2{,}200}$
4	$\dfrac{\text{Administration} \times 100}{\text{Sales}}$	$\dfrac{240 \times 100}{2{,}660}$	$\dfrac{210 \times 100}{2{,}200}$
5	$\dfrac{\text{Operating profit} \times 100}{\text{Capital employed}}$	$\dfrac{305 \times 100}{566 + 200}$	$\dfrac{285 \times 100}{460 + 160}$
6	$\dfrac{\text{Turnover}}{\text{Fixed \& net current assets}}$	$\dfrac{2{,}660}{600 + 166}$	$\dfrac{2{,}200}{263 + 357}$
7	$\dfrac{\text{Current assets}}{\text{Current liabilities}}$	$\dfrac{576}{410}$	$\dfrac{707}{350}$
8	$\dfrac{\text{Current assets} - \text{Stock}}{\text{Current liabilities}}$	$\dfrac{226}{410}$	$\dfrac{307}{350}$
9	$\dfrac{\text{Debtors} \times 365}{\text{Credit sales}}$	$\dfrac{200 \times 365}{2{,}660}$	$\dfrac{210 \times 365}{2{,}200}$
10	$\dfrac{\text{Trade Creditors} \times 365}{\text{Credit purchases}}$	$\dfrac{236 \times 365}{1{,}945}$	$\dfrac{224 \times 365}{1{,}723}$
11	$\dfrac{\text{Average stock} \times 365}{\text{Cost of sales}}$	$\dfrac{0.5 \times (400+350) \times 365}{1{,}995}$	$\dfrac{0.5 \times (277+400) \times 365}{1{,}600}$

LIMITATIONS OF RATIO ANALYSIS

In the introduction to this section, it was emphasised that one set of ratios alone does not give very useful information. Ratios for other time periods or other organisations are useful for comparison, as are target ratios.

like with like?

The principle of comparing like with like should be applied in ratio analysis, but this is not always straightforward. Some of the ratios can be defined in different ways, so the particular definition used should be made clear. Even so, detailed information may not be given, for example to split sales into cash sales and credit sales.

When using the published accounts of companies, it is not possible to guarantee that we are comparing like with like, as different policies (including those regarding depreciation, stock valuation and goodwill, for example) will affect the results.

distortion

There is the possibility that the balance sheet does not show a typical position. Discussion of a particular case may include looking for ways in which the ratios could have been distorted. For example, high levels of spending on research, training or marketing may reduce profits in one period, but bring much greater benefits in a later period. The reverse is also true: cutting these costs may improve the profit ratios in the short-term, but in the long-term sales and profits would suffer.

Distortion can also occur if a business is seasonal and the balance sheet does not show a typical position, or even where 'window-dressing' occurs to impress investors and lenders. 'Window-dressing' is, of course, a highly dubious practice.

the effects of inflation

When making comparisons over different time periods, the ratios are based on historical costs as shown in the accounts. If there has been inflation during the time periods, a better comparison can be made by making adjustments for this before calculating the ratios. (See Chapter 24).

Before drawing firm conclusions from ratio analysis, these limitations should be borne in mind. However, the analysis can give useful information, particularly in showing how items in the financial statements relate to each other and in identifying trends.

FURTHER ASPECTS OF PERFORMANCE MEASUREMENT

financial Indicators: calculating averages

Although total amounts of money such as sales, profits and costs may be used for performance measurement, it is often useful to calculate an average (the mean) 'per employee', 'per hour', 'per unit of output' and so on. This is a simple calculation which relates the financial data to the size of the organisation in some way.

---

examples

1   If sales orders amount to £32 million for the year and there are 16 sales representatives, then

Average sales orders per representative = £32m ÷ 16 = £2m

2   If materials cost £87,000 in total for output of 29,000 units of a product, then

Average cost of materials per unit = £87,000 ÷ 29,000 = £3

3   If training costs for the year total £171,000 and there are 450 employees, then

Average expenditure on training per employee = £171,000 ÷ 450 = £380

---

unit cost

A particularly useful average is the cost per unit of output. This can be applied to products or services, provided the output achieved can be measured in some way.

'Cost per unit' may be calculated for the total cost, or for some particular element of cost, for example:

Production labour cost per unit   =

total cost of production labour divided by number of units of output

---

example

In a given period, the output of a division is 15,000 product units.

The costs of production are as follows:

Direct materials	£97,500
Direct labour	£63,750
Production overheads	£85,500
Total production cost	£246,750

Therefore, for these costs, the Unit Cost could be calculated as follows:				
Direct materials:	£97,500 ÷ 15,000	=	£6.50	per unit
Direct labour:	£63,750 ÷ 15,000	=	£4.25	per unit
Production overheads:	£85,500 ÷ 15,000	=	£5.70	per unit
Total production cost:	£246,750 ÷ 15,000	=	£16.45	per unit

NON-FINANCIAL INDICATORS

The diagram on page 564 of this chapter shows that numerical measurements may be in terms of money or other units. A non-financial indicator is a measurement which is expressed in numbers, but not in money terms, the possible units being very varied: for example hours, transactions, units of product, customers and so on.

Non-financial indicators can take many forms, because they can be designed to measure aspects of any kind of work. They are useful in manufacturing and service industries and can be applied in both profit-making and non-profit making organisations.

Some examples of non-financial indicators are given below. Several indicators may be used together for the same activity. You may be able to think of other examples.

Activity or aspect to be measured	Non-financial indicator
Automated production	Hours of machine down time
Absenteeism	Employee-days absence
Telephone helpline	Average time in seconds taken to answer calls
Quality of service	Number of customer complaints
Input of data to computer	Number of errors per 1,000 inputs
Customer satisfaction	Number of repeat orders
Quality of output	Number of units rejected per 1,000

Further examples of non-financial indicators will occur when different types of organisation are considered later in this chapter.

QUALITATIVE (NON-NUMERICAL) MEASURES

The diagram on page 564 shows that some measurements are not 'quantitive', but 'qualitative'. This refers to the fact that some aspects of work are very difficult to measure in terms of numbers, for example: motivation of others, team working, helpfulness to customers.

When numerical indicators are not suitable, opinions and attitudes have to be recorded, perhaps by customer surveys. Surveys often ask customers to give ratings, say on a scale of 1 to 5, but these are only an aid to obtaining an overall view, not an accurate measurement.

Appraisal schemes within an organisation may involve collecting people's opinions about someone else's work. For example, those present at a meeting may be asked their opinion as to how well the person chairing the meeting carried out that task. Work relationships can affect the judgements given (and vice versa), so the usefulness of this feedback may be limited.

PERFORMANCE MEASUREMENT IN SERVICE ORGANISATIONS

It is more difficult to measure the performance of a service organisation or department than one which produces tangible goods. Services cannot be checked before being provided in the same way as products can be inspected for faults.

The usual financial measures and ratios can be used for profit-making service organisations. (Non-profit-making organisations are considered on the next page.)

Non-financial and qualitative measures, discussed earlier in this chapter, are often applicable to services. For example:

■ Average waiting times for customers can be calculated and compared to a target.

■ The number of customer complaints indicates the level of customer satisfaction.

■ Analysis of customer opinions can be collected through surveys. Aspects such as 'Are the staff friendly and helpful?' can be judged in this way.

■ Services can also be assessed by internal observation. Telephone services are monitored by supervisors listening to samples of calls, for example.

The appropriate performance indicators to use depend on the type of service being provided and what its aims must be. From the organisation's point of view, financial indicators are likely to be important. If we then consider what features of the service would be important to customers, we can see which items of data are available to measure those features.

For example, in a Further Education College, comparisons of costs and incomes with budgets measure financial aspects. Customers' views may be more dependent on non-financial indicators such as average class size and pass rates or qualitative measures relating to the teachers and the classroom environment.

PERFORMANCE MEASUREMENT IN NON-PROFIT MAKING ORGANISATIONS

Non-profit making organisations include charities and clubs as well as some public sector organisations. Without the objective of profit, there may be no single aim by which 'success' can be measured.

Performance indicators need to be designed to measure how well the organisation has achieved its aims. Much of the section on service organisations above applies to non-profit making organisations, many of which do provide services. Instead of profit, value for money is the main financial criterion. This is usually defined as:

■ **economy**: controlling expenditure on costs

■ **efficiency**: relating 'outputs' to inputs, meaning that obtaining more from the money spent shows greater efficiency

■ **effectiveness**: relating 'outputs' to the aims of the organisation, so that achieving more of what it sets out to do shows greater effectiveness

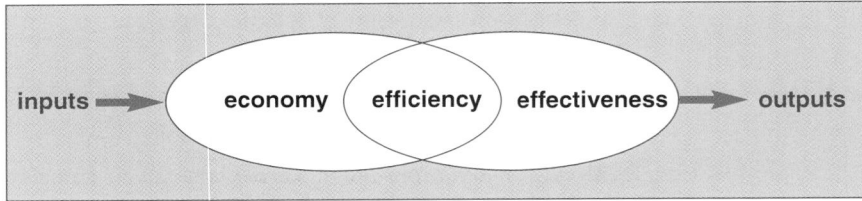

Economy can be measured in the same way as costs in businesses, by comparing with budgets and calculating variances for example.

A possible indicator for **efficiency** is the cost per unit, where units of output can be defined. For example, in a nursing home, the cost of a patient-day could be calculated.

Effectiveness may be measured by comparison with targets or with other similar organisations.

Some aspects of non-profit making activities can only be assessed by qualitative measures: opinions and judgements of experts, users or those who provide the funding. Representatives of government agencies or funding bodies may carry out observations or inspections, as in schools for example.

The general principles of performance measurement apply to these organisations as well as to businesses:

■ comparability – comparing like with like

■ comparison with standards, budgets or targets

■ comparison with similar organisations

■ comparison over time, to look for trends

chapter summary

● Numerical (quantitative) data can be used for performance measurement and this may be in terms of money or other units.

● Opinions and judgements which are not numerical (qualitative) are also important when measuring performance.

● Comparisons are more useful than single sets of data, provided the data being compared has been prepared on a consistent basis, to compare like with like. Comparison may be made:

– with standards, budgets or targets

– with other periods of time

– with other similar organisations

● Methods and techniques for performance measurement include:

– ratio analysis: the calculation of percentages and ratios from the financial accounts – the working capital ratios were explained in detail in the last chapter

– calculating averages per employee, per unit of output and so on – unit cost is an example of this

– using non-financial indicators to measure specific aspects of performance

– using qualitative (non-numerical) measures

● In service organisations, financial, non-financial and qualitative measures of performance may all be used, depending on the type of work and the aims of the organisation. Measurements should relate to what is important to customers.

● Financial performance measurement for non-profit making organisations is based on value for money, which is achieved through economy, efficiency and effectiveness.

key terms

performance indicator
an individual measurement used to evaluate the performance of an organisation or part of an organisation

benchmarking
the setting of standards or targets for the activities of an organisation

trend
the underlying behaviour of a series of figures over time

comparability
the principle of comparing like with like, that is, comparing data prepared on consistent bases

quantitative data
data which can be measured in numerical terms, including financial and non-financial data

qualitative data
data which cannot be measured in numerical terms, such as opinions and attitudes

ratio analysis
the analysis of the financial accounts of an organisation by calculating ratios and percentages

gross profit margin (percentage)
$$\frac{\text{gross profit}}{\text{sales}} \times 100$$

net profit percentage
$$\frac{\text{net profit}}{\text{sales}} \times 100$$

operating profit percentage
$$\frac{\text{operating profit}}{\text{sales}} \times 100$$

ROCE
(return on capital employed)
$$\frac{\text{operating profit}}{\text{fixed assets + net current assets}} \times 100$$

asset turnover (number of times)
$$\frac{\text{turnover}}{\text{fixed assets + net current assets}}$$

financial indicator
a performance indicator measured in money terms

non-financial indicator
a performance indicator measured in units other than money

activities

Note: an asterisk (*) after an activity number means that an answer is provided in Appendix 1.

27.1 Explain briefly what is meant by the following terms relating to performance measurement:

(a) consistency

(b) benchmarking

(c) qualitative data

27.2* The following information relates to Raven Ltd for a given period:

Sales revenue = £500,000

Gross profit margin = 24%

Operating profit = £50,000

Which of the following four statements is correct for Raven Ltd for the given period?

(a) Cost of sales = £620,000   Expenses = £170,000

(b) Cost of sales = £70,000   Expenses = £380,000

(c) Cost of sales = £380,000   Expenses = £70,000

(d) Cost of sales = £330,000   Expenses = £170,000

27.3 The following profit and loss accounts relate to a small retail shop selling stationery and gifts:

Toni Jones – Profit and Loss Account for the year ended:

	31 May 2001		31 May 2000	
	£000s	£000s	£000s	£000s
Sales		525		450
Less: Cost of Sales				
Opening stock	50		30	
Purchases	408		335	
Less: Closing Stock	(80)	378	(50)	315
Gross Profit		147		135
Less: Expenses:				
Administration	25		24	
Selling	38	63	30	54
Net Profit		84		81

Required

For Toni Jones for the given years, calculate:

(a) Gross Profit percentage

(b) Net Profit percentage

(c) each expense as a percentage of Sales

Comment briefly on the original figures and on the percentages calculated.

27.4* Ace plc is an electrical goods manufacturing group and the information below relates to one of its subsidiaries, Jack Limited.

Jack Ltd: Summary Profit and Loss Account for the year ended 30 June 2001

	£000s	£000s
Turnover		2,500
Less: Cost of Sales		
Opening Stock	30	
Cost of Production	650	
Less: Closing Stock	(90)	590
Gross Profit		1,910
Administration	780	
Selling and Distribution	505	1,285
Operating Profit		625

Jack Ltd: extract from Balance Sheet as at 30 June 2001:

	£000s	£000s	£000s
Fixed assets	Land and Buildings	Plant	Total
At cost	900	2,000	2,900
Additions	-	1,000	1,000
	900	3,000	3,900
Accumulated depreciation	-	1,380	1,380
	900	1,620	2,520
Current Assets:			
Raw materials stock	10		
Finished goods stock	90		
Debtors	160		
Cash at bank	110		
	370		
Current liabilities	(50)		320
Net Assets			2,840

Required:

(a)   Calculate the following ratios for subsidiary Jack Ltd for the financial year

- gross profit margin
- operating profit margin
- return on capital employed (ROCE)
- asset turnover
- the average age of debtors
- the average age of finished goods stock (using average stock)

(b)   The directors of Ace plc consider that ROCE and asset turnover are important performance measures, and subsidiary company Jack Ltd has failed to meet the group targets, which are:

Target ROCE   26%

Target asset turnover   1.5 times

Identify one factor which may have affected the performance of subsidiary company Jack Ltd in relation to these targets in the year ended 30 June 2001.

(c)   Calculate the turnover which Subsidiary Jack Ltd would have obtained if it had achieved the target level of asset turnover.

(d)   Assuming subsidiary Jack Ltd maintained the same operating profit margin, calculate the ROCE which would have resulted from the turnover calculated in (c) above.

27.5   Using formulas, calculate the answers to the following:

(a)   If the gross profit margin is 35% and the turnover is £200,000, what is the cost of sales?

(b)   If the stock is £4,200, the current liabilities total £7,000, and the acid test ratio is 0.9 : 1, what is the current ratio?

27.6* Give two examples of each of the following for a manufacturing company:

(a)   financial quantitative performance indicators

(b)   non-financial quantitative performance indicators

(c)   qualitative performance indicators

27.7 Wessit Housing Association is considering offering a contract for double-glazing its properties to one of two suppliers, Staylite Ltd and Temeglass Ltd. The following information has been extracted from the most recent annual report and accounts of the two companies.

	Staylite Ltd £000s	Temeglass Ltd £000s
Sales	7,660	9,500
Gross profit	3,467	4,522
Operating profit	403	627
Interest charges	45	2
Fixed assets (net book value)	600	800
Current assets	198	307
Stock included in current assets	82	120
Current liabilities	182	156
Debentures	450	0
Share capital and reserves	166	951
Average number of employees	16	18

Required

(a)   Calculate the following ratios for each of the two companies:

- gross profit margin
- operating profit percentage
- return on capital employed
- current ratio
- quick ratio
- asset turnover
- sales per employee
- operating profit per employee

(b)   Using the given information and the ratios you have calculated, comment on the profitability and financial position of the two suppliers.

(c)   Explain the limitations of the above analysis, in particular from the point of view of Wessit Housing Association's decision about the contract.

(d)   Suggest one further indicator which Wessit Housing Association should seek to obtain (not necessarily from the report and accounts) before making this decision.

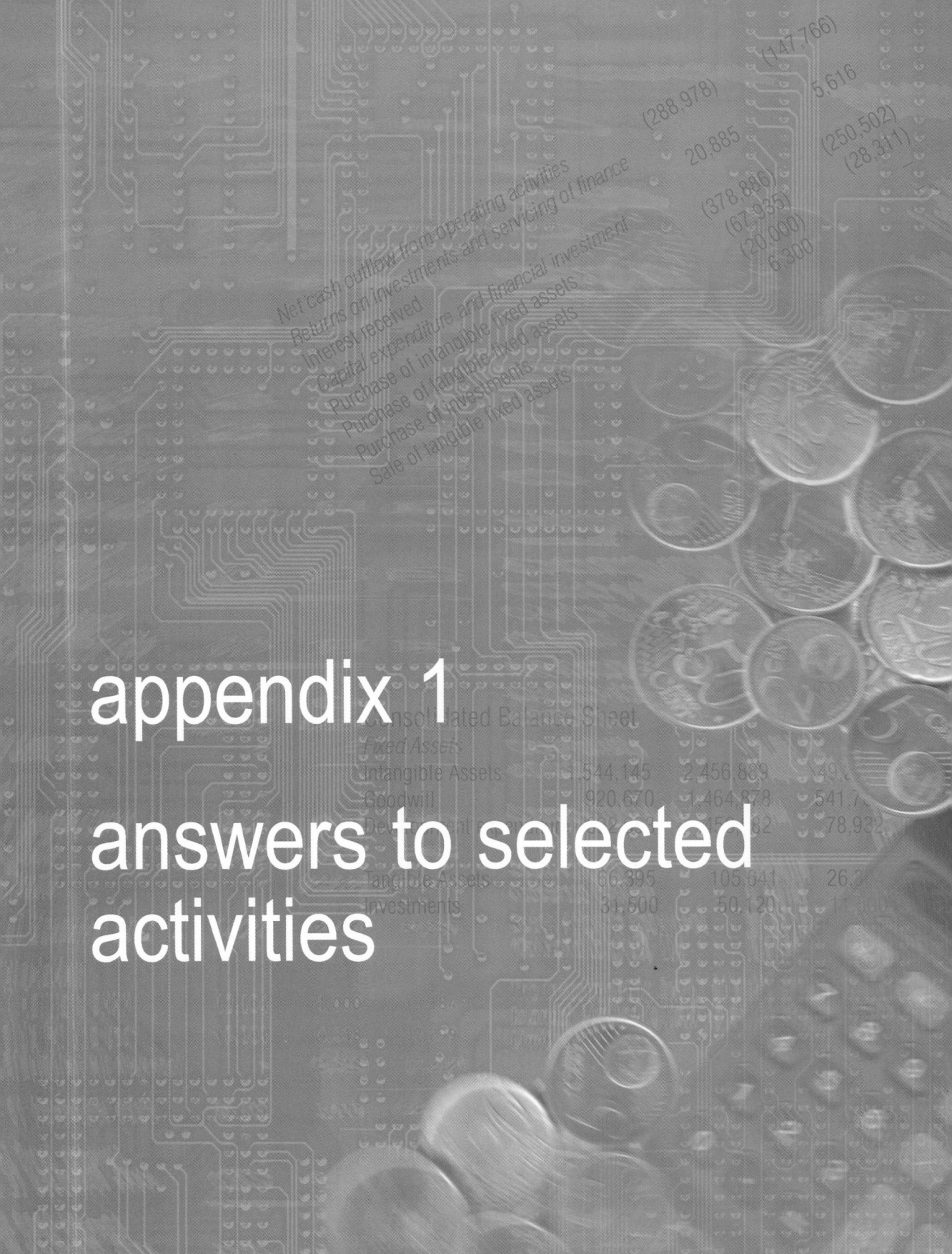

appendix 1

answers to selected activities

1.1 Book-keeping involves the maintenance of records of financial transactions in accounts whereas accounting has the wider functions of recording financial transactions and then reporting the data to people who have an interest in it.

1.2 A stakeholder is an individual or an organisation that has an interest in an organisation.

1.4
(a) reduced or no dividend
(b) job losses, cuts in salaries
(c) redundancies, cuts in bonuses
(d) drop in quality, longer waiting lists, association of car brand with lack of success
(e) longer payment periods, or no payment if the situation gets worse
(f) concern over ability of company to service borrowing, possible insolvency

1.8
(a) Shareholders lose their investment, employees and managers their jobs, lenders their loans, suppliers their money and business, customers their continuity of power supply.
(b) Financial accounting in presenting fairy tale financial statements, management accountants for not seeing what was happening, auditors for lax auditing. Depending on the currency of this Case Study, students might recall that the auditors were accused of putting the important documents through the shredder.

CHAPTER 2: Talking Money

2.1
(a) (36 ÷ 150) x 100 % = 24%
(b) (490 ÷ 1,300) x 100 % = 37.7% correct to one decimal place
(c) The figures must both be expressed in the same way:
(2,500 ÷ 2,000,000) x 100 % or (0.0025 ÷ 2.0) x 100 % = 0.125%

2.2
(a) 4.90 – 4.70 = 0.20.
(0.20 ÷ 4.70) x 100 % = 4.3% increase.
(b) 301,000 – 267,800 = 33,200
(33,200 ÷ 267,800) x 100 % = 12.4% increase.
(c) 132 – 125 = 7
(7 ÷ 132) x 100 % = 5.3% decrease.
(d) 1,300,000 – 980,000 = 320,000
(320,000 ÷ 1,300,000) x 100 % or (0.32 ÷ 1.3) x 100 % = 24.6%

2.3

	mean	median	mode
(a)	58 ÷ 11 = 5.3	5	3
(b)	107 ÷ 9 = 11.9	13	15
(c)	4757 ÷ 8 = 594.6	762	832

2.5 Dale Sports and Leisure Club: you may have calculated some of the figures shown in the following table with the original data:

Dale Sports and Leisure Club two-year summary

	2000	2001	% change
Number of members	273	328	20% increase
Total number of member visits	9,120	11,590	27% increase
Opening hours per week (50 weeks)	60 hours	72 hours	20% increase
Total hours per year	3,000 hours	3,600 hours	20% increase
Average number of visits per member	33.4	35.3	6% increase
Average number of visits per hour	3.0	3.2	7% increase
Average number of visits per week	182.4	231.8	27% increase

Comments: Your comments may include the following or other valid points:

- The membership increased by 20% from 2000 to 2001, and the club also increased its opening hours by 20%.

- The members made more use of the club in 2001, perhaps because of the increased opening hours. On average each member made 6% more visits to the club (35 instead of 33).

- Usage of the opening hours increased by 7% in 2001 as a result of having more members and of members making more visits.

CHAPTER 3: Accounting Records

3.3 *sales ledger* – the accounts of customers who have bought on credit (ie they have bought goods or services but will pay later) – these customers are also known as 'debtors'

purchases ledger – the accounts of suppliers who have sold to the business on credit – these suppliers are also known as 'creditors'

cash book – the book which records cash held by the business and bank accounts in the name of the business (and also the petty cash book)

general or nominal ledger – all the other accounts – expenses, income, assets (items owned) and liabilities (items owed) – also referred to as the 'main' ledger

3.4 To prove the accuracy of the double-entry book-keeping.

3.5 The profit and loss statement shows the profit (or loss) made by the business.
The balance sheet shows what the business owns (assets), what it owes (liabilities) and how it is financed (capital).

3.7 (a) both sides of equation increase: asset (bank account) increases £10,000 = capital increases £10,000

(b) equation unchanged as transaction cancels itself out: asset (vehicle account) increase of £45,000 cancelled out by decrease in asset (bank account) £45,000

(c) both assets and liabilities decrease: asset (bank account) reduced by £3,500, liability (supplier account) also reduced by £3,500

(d) both assets and liabilities increase: asset (bank account) increases £20,000, liability (bank loan) increases by £20,000

3.8 Will Abbott: 1 Feb Cr Sales £5,000, 1 Feb Dr Purchases £3,500, 2 Feb Cr Sales £7,500, 2 Feb Dr Wages £2,510, 3 Feb Cr Bank Loan £12,500, 3 Feb Dr Van £12,500, 3 Feb Dr Purchases £5,000, 4 Feb Dr Rent £780, 5 Feb Cr Sales £9,300.

CHAPTER 4: Balancing the Books

4.1 (a) You the final purchaser pay the whole VAT amount.

(b) It pays the VAT on the TV charged by the manufacturer and then claims this amount back by setting it off against the VAT it charges you. (which will be more) when it settles up with H M Customs & Excise.

4.2 Issue of a VAT registration number; use of number on invoices, letterheads etc; an account number must be kept for VAT; VAT must be charged on sales; VAT can be reclaimed on purchases; the difference to be accounted for to H M Customs & Excise on VAT Return; VAT records can be inspected at any time.

4.3 (a) a control account is a summary or 'total' account for a number of subsidiary accounts

(b) the total amount of money owing by credit customers ('debtors')

(c) it means that only the control account balance needs to be shown in the trial balance – not the balances of all the subsidiary accounts – this makes the trial balance clearer and more concise

---

4.5

(a)

Account	Debit Column £	Credit Column £
Bank	1 Jan Capital 5,000	2 Jan Rent 200
	8 Jan Sales 1,200	4 Jan Shop Fittings 2,000
	9 Jan Sales 1,000	19 Jan Purchases 2,500
	15 Jan Sales 1,500	23 Jan Returns in 580
	17 Jan Sales 1,250	Balance c/d 4,670
	Total 9,950	Total 9,950
Capital		1 Jan Bank 5,000
Rent	2 Jan Bank 200	
Shop fittings	4 Jan Bank 2,000	
Northam Publishers		5 Jan Purchases 2,500
Purchases	5 Jan Northam Publ. 2,500	
	12 Jan Broadheath B. 5,000	
	19 Jan Bank 2,500	31 Jan Balance c/d 10,000
Sales		8 Jan Bank 1,200
		9 Jan Bank 1,000
		15 Jan Bank 1,500
		17 Jan Bank 1,250
		30 Jan Wyvern Coll. 1,095
Broadheath Books	31 Jan Balance c/d 6,045	12 Jan Purchases 5,000
Returns in	23 Jan Bank 580	
Wyvern College	30 Jan Sales 1,095	

(b) Trial Balance of Robert Jefferson as at 31 January

	Dr £	Cr £
Bank	4,670	
Capital		5,000
Rent	200	
Shop Fittings	2,000	
Northam Publishers		2,500
Purchases	10,000	
Sales		6,045
Broadheath Books		5,000
Returns in	580	
Wyvern College	1,095	
	18,545	18,545

6.3

MATTHEW LLOYD

TRADING AND PROFIT AND LOSS ACCOUNT
FOR THE YEAR ENDED 31 DECEMBER 2008

	£	£
Sales		125,890
Opening stock	—	
Purchases	94,350	
Less Closing stock	5,950	
Cost of sales		88,400
Gross profit		37,490
Less overheads:		
Rates	4,850	
Heating and lighting	2,120	
Wages and salaries	10,350	
		17,320
Net profit		20,170

BALANCE SHEET AS AT 31 DECEMBER 2008

	£	£
Fixed Assets		
Office equipment		8,500
Vehicles		10,750
		19,250
Current Assets		
Stock	5,950	
Debtors	3,950	
Bank	4,225	
Cash	95	
	14,220	
Less Current Liabilities		
Creditors	1,750	
Value Added Tax	450	
	2,200	
Working Capital		12,020
NET ASSETS		31,270
FINANCED BY		
Capital		
Opening capital		20,000
Add Net profit		20,170
		40,170
Less Drawings		8,900
		31,270

6.5

Business A:	gross profit £8,000, net profit £4,000
Business B:	gross profit £17,000, expenses £7,000
Business C:	sales £36,500, net profit £6,750
Business D:	purchases £25,500, expenses £9,800
Business E:	opening stock £8,350, net loss £1,700
Business F:	closing stock £4,600, expenses £15,000

6.6

JOHN ADAMS

TRADING AND PROFIT AND LOSS ACCOUNT
FOR THE YEAR ENDED 31 DECEMBER 2007

	£	£
Sales		259,688
Opening stock	14,350	
Purchases	114,472	
	128,822	
Less Closing stock	16,280	
Cost of sales		112,542
Gross profit		147,146
Less overheads:		
Rates	13,718	
Heating and lighting	12,540	
Wages and salaries	42,614	
Vehicle expenses	5,817	
Advertising	6,341	
		81,030
Net profit		66,116

BALANCE SHEET AS AT 31 DECEMBER 2007

	£	£
Fixed Assets		
Premises		75,000
Office equipment		33,000
Vehicles		21,500
		129,500
Current Assets		
Stock	16,280	
Debtors	23,854	
Bank	1,235	
Cash	125	
	41,494	
Less Current Liabilities		
Creditors	17,281	
Value Added Tax	2,455	
	19,736	
Working Capital		21,758
		151,258
Less Long-term Liabilities		
Loan from bank		35,000
NET ASSETS		116,258
FINANCED BY		
Capital		
Opening capital		62,500
Add Net profit		66,116
		128,616
Less Drawings		12,358
		116,258

7.1

(a) Prudence: by making a provision for bad debts the business is recording the possibility that the debtor may not pay.

(b) Materiality: although the video tapes will be kept for a number of years they are not treated as a fixed asset and depreciated because their cost is not material to the business.

(c) Consistency: the owner of the business should use the most appropriate depreciation method for the type of asset, and apply it consistently from year-to-year. In this way the accounts of different years are comparable; the accounting policy can be changed – for example, from one method of depreciation to another – provided there are good reasons for so doing, with a note to the final accounts explaining what has happened.

(d) Accruals (or matching): here the expense of electricity is being matched to the time period in which the cost was incurred.

7.2

(a) Expense in profit and loss account of £56,760; balance sheet shows wages and salaries accrued (current liability) of £1,120.

(b) Expense in profit and loss account of £2,852; balance sheet shows rates prepaid (current asset) of £713.

(c) Expense in profit and loss account of £1,800; balance sheet shows computer rental prepaid (current asset) of £150.

7.4

JOHN BARCLAY

TRADING AND PROFIT AND LOSS ACCOUNT FOR THE YEAR ENDED 30 JUNE 2009

	£	£	£
Sales			864,321
Less Sales returns			2,746
Net sales			861,575
Opening stock (1 July 2008)		63,084	
Purchases (less £250 goods for own use)	599,878		
Less Purchase returns	3,894		
Net purchases		595,984	
		659,068	
Less Closing stock (30 June 2009)		66,941	
Cost of sales			592,127
Gross profit			269,448
Add Discount received			4,951
			274,399
Less overheads:			
Office expenses		33,601	
Salaries		122,611	
Vehicle expenses		38,144	
Discount allowed		3,187	
			197,543
Net profit			76,856

BALANCE SHEET AS AT 30 JUNE 2009

	£	£	£
Fixed Assets			
Land and buildings			100,000
Vehicles			83,500
Office equipment			23,250
			206,750
Current Assets			
Stock		66,941	
Debtors		74,328	
Prepayment		346	
Bank		1,197	
		142,812	
Less Current Liabilities			
Creditors	52,919		
Value Added Tax	10,497		
Accrual	1,250		
		64,666	
Working Capital			78,146
			284,896
Less Long-term Liabilities			
Bank loan			75,000
NET ASSETS			209,896
FINANCED BY:			
Capital			
Opening capital			155,000
Add net profit			76,856
			231,856
Less drawings (plus £250 goods for own use)			21,960
			209,896

JAMES JENKINS

TRADING AND PROFIT AND LOSS ACCOUNT FOR THE YEAR ENDED 30 JUNE 2009

	£	£	£
Sales			168,432
Less Sales returns			975
Net sales			167,457
Opening stock		9,427	
Purchases	105,240		
Less Purchases returns	1,237		
Net purchases		104,003	
		113,430	
Less Closing stock		11,517	
Cost of sales			101,913
Gross profit			65,544
Add income:			
Discount received			243
Reduction in provision for bad debts			54
			65,841
Less overheads:			
Discount allowed		127	
Wages and salaries		30,841	
Vehicle expenses		1,076	
Rent and rates		8,521	
Heating and lighting		1,840	
Telephone		355	
General expenses		1,752	
Bad debts written off		85	
Provision for depreciation:			
vehicle		1,125	
shop fittings		600	
			46,322
Net profit			19,519

BALANCE SHEET AS AT 30 JUNE 2009

	£ Cost	£ Dep'n to date	£ Net
Fixed Assets			
Vehicle	8,000	4,625	3,375
Shop fittings	6,000	3,000	3,000
	14,000	7,625	6,375
Current Assets			
Stock		11,517	
Debtors	3,840		
Less Provision for bad debts	96		
		3,744	
Prepayments		275	
Bank		21,419	
Cash		155	
		37,110	
Less Current Liabilities			
Creditors	5,294		
Value Added Tax	1,492		
Accruals	55		
		6,841	
Working Capital			30,269
NET ASSETS			36,644
FINANCED BY			
Capital			
Opening capital			36,175
Add Net profit			19,519
			55,694
Less Drawings			19,050
			36,644

8.1 £260,000

8.2 £77,000

8.3 £21,100

8.4

(a)
	£
receipts from sales	153,500
add debtors at year end	2,500
sales for year	156,000

(b)
payments to suppliers	95,000
add creditors at year end	65,000
purchases for year	160,000

(c)
payments for rent and rates	8,750
less rent prepaid at 31 Dec 2008	250
rent and rates for year	8,500

payments for wages	15,000
add wages accrued at 31 Dec 2008	550
wages for year	15,550

(d)

TRADING AND PROFIT AND LOSS ACCOUNT OF JANE PRICE
for the year ended 31 December 2008

	£	£
Sales		156,000
Purchases	160,000	
Less Closing stock	73,900	
Cost of sales		86,100
Gross profit		69,900
Less overheads:		
Advertising	4,830	
Rent and rates	8,500	
Wages	15,550	
General expenses	5,000	
Depreciation: shop fittings	10,000	
		43,880
Net profit		26,020

(e)

BALANCE SHEET OF JANE PRICE
as at 31 December 2008

	Cost £	Depreciation to date £	Net £
Fixed assets			
Shop fittings	50,000	10,000	40,000
Current assets			
Stock		73,900	
Debtors		2,500	
Prepayment: rent		250	
Bank*		19,900	
		96,550	
Less Current liabilities			
Creditors	65,000		
Accrual: wages	550		
		65,550	
Working capital			31,000
NET ASSETS			71,000

FINANCED BY

Capital

	£
Opening capital (introduced at start of year)	60,000
Add net profit	26,020
	86,020
Less drawings	15,020
Closing capital	71,000

* Cash book summary:

	£
• total receipts for year	213,500
• less total payments for year	193,600
• **balance at year end**	19,900

9.2

Subscriptions Control Account

Dr				£		Cr £
2009			2009			
1 Jan	Balance b/d (subscriptions owing)	2,750	1 Jan	Balance b/d (subscriptions prepaid)		1,250
31 Dec	Income and expenditure account (subscription income for year)	25,500	31 Dec	Subscriptions received in year		25,500
31 Dec	Balance c/d (subscriptions prepaid)	1,750	31 Dec	Balance c/d (subscriptions owing)		3,250
		30,000				30,000

Note: the subscription income for the year to be transferred to income and expenditure account, £25,500, is calculated as the 'missing figure'.

9.3

WESTSIDE SPORTS CLUB
INCOME AND EXPENDITURE ACCOUNT FOR THE YEAR ENDED 30 JUNE 2009

	£	£	£
Income			
Subscriptions			1,460
Competition entry fees			498
Sale of snacks		1,108	
Purchase of snacks	520		
Less Closing stock	70		
		450	
Profit on snacks			658
			2,616
Less Expenditure			
Postage and stationery		197	
Rent paid		650	
Competition expenses		320	
Provision for depreciation: equipment		300	
			1,467
Surplus of income over expenditure			1,149

BALANCE SHEET AS AT 30 JUNE 2009

	Cost £	Dep'n to date £	Net £
Fixed Assets			
Equipment	1,500	300	1,200
Current Assets			
Stock of snacks		70	
Bank		59	
		129	
Less Current Liabilities			
Subscriptions in advance	80		
Accrual for rent	100		
		180	
Working capital			(51)
NET ASSETS			1,149
REPRESENTED BY			
Accumulated fund			–
Surplus of income over expenditure			1,149
			1,149

10.3

Partners' Capital Accounts

Dr		Lysa £	Mark £			Cr Lysa £	Mark £
2008				2008			
31 Dec	Balances c/d	50,000	40,000	1 Jan	Balances b/d	50,000	40,000
				2009			
				1 Jan	Balances b/d	50,000	40,000

Partners' Current Accounts

Dr		Lysa £	Mark £			Cr Lysa £	Mark £
2008				2008			
31 Dec	Drawings	13,000	12,250	1 Jan	Balances b/d	420	1,780
31 Dec	Balance c/d	–	830	31 Dec	Interest on capital	2,500	2,000
				31 Dec	Share of profits	9,300	9,300
				31 Dec	Balance c/d	780	–
		13,000	13,080			13,000	13,080
2009				2009			
1 Jan	Balance b/d	780	–	1 Jan	Balance b/d	–	830

10.4 (a)

JOHN JAMES AND STEVEN HILL TRADING AS "GRAPES"
PROFIT AND LOSS ACCOUNT FOR THE YEAR ENDED 31 DECEMBER 2001

	£	£
Gross profit		89,000
Less overheads:		
Rent and rates	7,500	
Advertising	12,000	
Heat and light	3,500	
Wages and salaries	18,000	
Sundry expenses	4,000	
Provision for depreciation: shop fittings	2,000	47,000
Net profit		42,000
Share of profits:		
John James		21,000
Steven Hill		21,000
		42,000

BALANCE SHEET AS AT 31 DECEMBER 2001

	Cost £	Dep'n to date £	Net £
Fixed Assets			
Shop fittings	20,000	2,000	18,000
Current Assets			
Stock		35,000	
Debtors		6,000	
Bank		29,000	
		70,000	
Less Current Liabilities			
Creditors	8,000		
Value Added Tax	2,000	10,000	
Working Capital			60,000
NET ASSETS			78,000
FINANCED BY			
Capital Accounts			
John James		38,000	
Steven Hill		32,000	70,000
Current Accounts			
John James		4,000	
Steven Hill		4,000	8,000
			78,000

(b)

Partners' Capital Accounts

Dr		James £	Hill £			James £	Hill £	Cr
2001				2001				
31 Dec	Balances c/d	38,000	32,000	1 Jan	Balances b/d	38,000	32,000	
		38,000	32,000	2002		38,000	32,000	
				1 Jan	Balances b/d			

Partners' Current Accounts

Dr		James £	Hill £			James £	Hill £	Cr
2001				2001				
1 Jan	Balance b/d	3,000	–	1 Jan	Balance b/d	–	1,000
31 Dec	Drawings	14,000	18,000	31 Dec	Share of profits	21,000	21,000
31 Dec	Balances c/d	4,000	4,000					
		21,000	22,000			21,000	22,000	
				2002				
				1 Jan	Balances b/d	4,000	4,000	

CHAPTER 11: Changes in Partnerships

11.3

Partners' Capital Accounts

Dr		Jim £	Maisie £	Matt £			Jim £	Maisie £	Matt £	Cr
2001					2001					
					31 Dec	Balances b/d	60,000	40,000	–	
2002					2002					
1 Jan	Goodwill written off	24,000	16,000	8,000	1 Jan	Goodwill created	28,800	19,200	–	
31 Dec	Drawings	12,000	12,000	8,000	1 Jan	Bank			28,000	
31 Dec	Balances c/d	82,800	51,200	22,000	31 Dec	Share of profits	30,000	20,000	10,000	
		118,800	79,200	38,000			118,800	79,200	38,000	
2003					2003					
1 Jan	Goodwill written off	–	48,000	24,000	1 Jan	Balances b/d	82,800	51,200	22,000	
1 Jan	Loan account: Jim	118,800			1 Jan	Goodwill created	36,000	24,000	12,000	
1 Jan	Balances c/d	–	27,200	10,000						
		118,800	75,200	34,000			118,800	75,200	34,000	
					1 Jan	Balances b/d	–	27,200	10,000	

11.4 (a)

Revaluation Account

Dr	£		Cr	£
Surplus on revaluation c/d	40,000	Goodwill		16,000
		Fixed assets (£74,000 – £50,000)		24,000
	40,000			40,000
		Surplus on revaluation b/d		40,000
Capital accounts:				
Reena (4/8)	20,000			
Sam (2/8)	10,000			
Tamara (2/8)	10,000			
	40,000			40,000

Partners' Capital Accounts

Dr	Reena	Sam	Tamara		Cr	Reena	Sam	Tamara
	£	£	£			£	£	£
Goodwill w/off	8,000	–	8,000	Balances b/d		33,000	12,000	30,000
Bank		22,000		Revaluation acc surplus*		20,000	10,000	10,000
Balances c/d	45,000	–	32,000					
	53,000	22,000	40,000			53,000	22,000	40,000
				Balances b/d		45,000	–	32,000

(b)

Reena and Tamara: Balance Sheet as at 1 September 2001

	£
Fixed Assets (£50,000 + £24,000)	74,000
Current Assets	10,000
Cash at Bank (£25,000 – £22,000)	3,000
	87,000
Creditors	(10,000)
	77,000
Capital Accounts	
Reena	45,000
Tamara	32,000
	77,000

* Note that revaluation account surplus includes goodwill created

12.5

JOBSEEKERS LIMITED

PROFIT AND LOSS ACCOUNT (APPROPRIATION SECTION)
FOR THE YEAR ENDED 31 DECEMBER 2006

	£	£
Net profit for year before taxation		68,200
Less corporation tax		14,850
Profit for year after taxation		53,350
Less interim ordinary dividends paid	10,000	
final ordinary dividend proposed	40,000	
		50,000
Retained profit for year		3,350
Retained profit at 1 January 2006		7,350
Retained profit at 31 December 2006		10,700

BALANCE SHEET AS AT 31 DECEMBER 2006

Fixed Assets	Cost	Dep'n to date	Net
	£	£	£
Intangible			
Goodwill	20,000	6,000	14,000
Tangible			
Premises	175,000	10,500	164,500
Office equipment	25,000	5,000	20,000
	220,000	21,500	198,500
Current Assets			
Stock		750	
Debtors		42,500	
		43,250	
Less Current Liabilities			
Creditors	7,250		
Bank overdraft	13,950		
Proposed dividends	40,000		
Corporation tax	14,850		
	76,050		
Working Capital			(32,800)
			165,700

		£
Less Long-term Liabilities		
Bank loan		55,000
NET ASSETS		110,700
FINANCED BY		
Issued Share Capital		
100,000 ordinary shares of £1 each		100,000
Revenue Reserve		
Profit and loss account		10,700
SHAREHOLDERS' FUNDS		110,700

SIDBURY TRADING CO LTD
TRADING AND PROFIT AND LOSS ACCOUNT
FOR THE YEAR ENDED 31 DECEMBER 2002

	£	£
Sales		297,462
Opening stock	42,618	
Purchases	189,273	
	231,891	
Less Closing stock	47,288	
Cost of sales		184,603
Gross profit		112,859
Less overheads:		
Provision for depreciation on vans	11,000	
Rent and rates	3,600	
General expenses	9,741	
Wages and salaries	35,043	
Bad debts written off	948	
Increase in provision for bad debts	124	
Directors' salaries	25,000	
		85,456
Net profit for year before taxation		27,403
Less corporation tax		12,000
Profit for year after taxation		15,403
Less ordinary dividend proposed		8,000
Retained profit for year		7,403
Add balance of retained profits at beginning of year		18,397
Balance of retained profits at end of year		25,800

BALANCE SHEET AS AT 31 DECEMBER 2002

	£ Cost	£ Dep'n to date	£ Net
Fixed Assets			
Land and buildings	142,000	—	142,000
Vans	55,000	32,800	22,200
	197,000	32,800	164,200
Current Assets			
Stock		47,288	
Debtors	26,482		
Less Provision for bad debts	1,200		
		25,282	
Prepayment (rates)		400	
Bank		65,958	
		138,928	
Less Current Liabilities			
Creditors	14,555		
Value Added Tax	2,419		
Accrual (wages and salaries)	354		
Corporation tax	12,000		
Proposed ordinary dividend	8,000		
		37,328	
Working Capital			101,600
NET ASSETS			265,800
FINANCED BY			
Authorised Share Capital			
300,000 ordinary shares of £1 each			300,000
Issued Share Capital			
240,000 ordinary shares of £1 each, fully paid			240,000
Revenue Reserves			
Profit and loss account			25,800
SHAREHOLDERS' FUNDS			265,800

CHAPTER 13: Cash Flow Statements

13.5
CASH FLOW STATEMENT OF JOHN SMITH FOR THE YEAR ENDED 31 DECEMBER 2002

	£	£
Net cash inflow from operating activities		8,200
Returns on investments and servicing of finance:		
Interest paid	(250)	(250)
Taxation:		
Corporation tax paid		not applicable
Capital expenditure and financial investment:		
Payments to acquire fixed assets		(2,000)
Equity dividends paid: (drawings)		(9,000)
Cash outflow before use of liquid resources and financing		(3,050)
Financing:		–
Decrease in cash		*(3,050)

Reconciliation of operating profit to net cash inflow from operating activities

Operating profit (before interest)	11,250
Depreciation	1,000
Increase in stock	(3,500)
Increase in debtors	(800)
Increase in creditors	250
Net cash inflow from operating activities	8,200

* Bank balance at start of year	850
Bank balance at end of year	(2,200)
Decrease in cash	(3,050)

MILLER PLC
CASH FLOW STATEMENT FOR THE YEAR ENDED 30 JUNE 2003

	£000	£000
Net cash inflow from operating activities		2,880
Returns on investments and servicing of finance:		
Interest paid		(100)
Taxation:		
Corporation tax paid (see note 3)		(300)
Capital expenditure and financial investment:		
Payments to acquire fixed assets (see note 4)	(4,300)	
Receipts from sales of fixed assets	1,400	
		(2,900)
Equity dividends paid: (see note 5)		(600)
Cash outflow before use of liquid resources and financing		(1,020)
Financing:		
Issue of debentures		1,000
Decrease in cash		*(20)

Reconciliation of operating profit to net cash inflow from operating activities	
Operating profit (before interest)	1,100
Depreciation (see note 1)	1,900
Profit on sale of fixed assets (see note 2)	(200)
Increase in stock	(40)
Increase in debtors	(100)
Increase in creditors	140
Decrease in prepayments	20
Increase in accruals	60
Net cash inflow from operating activities	2,880

Bank balance at start of year	40
Bank balance at end of year	20
*Decrease in cash	(20)

Notes

		£000
1	Depreciation on fixed assets is calculated as follows:	
	Balance at 30 June 2002	8,160
	Less: Depreciation on assets sold during year	400
		7,760
	Depreciation for 2003 (balancing figure – to cash flow statement)	1,900
	Balance at 30 June 2003	9,660
2	Profit on sale of fixed assets is calculated as follows:	
	Cost price	1,600
	Less: Depreciation to date	400
		1,200
	Sale proceeds	1,400
	Profit on sale – to cash flow statement	200
3	Corporation tax paid is calculated as follows:	
	Balance at 30 June 2002	360
	Transfer from profit and loss account for 2003	200
		560
	Corporation tax paid in 2003 (balancing figure – to cash flow statement)	300
	Balance at 30 June 2003	260
4	Payments to acquire fixed assets is calculated as follows:	
	Balance at 30 June 2002	13,600
	Less: Cost price of assets sold during year	1,600
		12,000
	Payments made in 2003 (balancing figure – to cash flow statement)	4,300
	Balance at 30 June 2003	16,300
5	Equity dividends paid is calculated as follows:	
	Balance at 30 June 2002	400
	Transfer from profit and loss account for 2003	400
		800
	Dividends paid (balancing figure – to cash flow statement)	600
	Balance at 30 June 2003	200

14.2 **Exceptional items** are defined in Financial Reporting Standard no 3 as 'material items which derive from events or transactions that fall within the ordinary activities of the reporting entity and which individually or, if of a similar type, in aggregate, need to be disclosed by virtue of their size or incidence if the financial statements are to give a true and fair view'.

Extraordinary items are defined in FRS 3 as 'material items possessing a high degree of abnormality which arise from events or transactions that fall outside the ordinary activities of the reporting entity and which are not expected to recur'.

Profit and loss account:

- exceptional items are recorded before profit on ordinary activities
- extraordinary items are recorded after profit on ordinary activities

Examples:

- exceptional items
  - profits or losses on the sale or termination of part of the business
  - reorganisation costs
  - profits or losses on the disposal of fixed assets
- extraordinary items
  - no examples
  - FRS 3 requires virtually all one-off transactions to be classified as exceptional items and recorded before profit on ordinary activities

14.3 Items to be included in a directors' report (four items required for the question):

- review of the activities of the company over the past year and of likely developments in the future, including research and development activity
- directors' names and their shareholdings
- proposed dividends
- significant differences between the book value and market value of land and buildings
- political and charitable contributions
- policy on employment of disabled people
- health and safety at work of employees
- action taken on employee involvement and consultation
- policy on payment of creditors

14.6 TREVAUNANCE PLC
PROFIT AND LOSS ACCOUNT FOR THE YEAR ENDED 31 MARCH 2002

	£000
Turnover (sales) – continuing operations	2,670
Cost of sales (see note 1)	1,680
Gross profit	990
Distribution costs	500
Administration expenses	240
Operating profit – continuing operations	250
Interest payable and similar charges	—
Profit on ordinary activities before taxation	250
Tax on profit on ordinary activities	65
Profit on ordinary activities after taxation	185
Dividends	120
Retained profit for the financial year	65

BALANCE SHEET AS AT 31 MARCH 2002

	£000	£000
Fixed assets		
Tangible assets (1,000 – 400)		600
Current assets		
Stock	280	
Debtors	600	
Bank	75	
	955	
Creditors: amounts falling due within one year (see note 2)	580	
Net current assets		375
		975
Capital and reserves		
Called up share capital		600
Share premium account		100
Profit and loss account (210 + 65)		275
		975

Working notes

1 Cost of sales is calculated as follows:

	£000
opening stock	160
purchases	1,800
	1,960
less closing stock	280
	1,680

2 Creditors: amounts falling due within one year

	£000
trade creditors	300
other creditors	80
accruals	15
corporation tax payable	65
ordinary dividend payable	120
	580

Liquidity

	2005	2006
Working capital ratio	3.33:1	2.16:1
Liquid capital ratio	2.17:1	1.44:1

Both ratios have fallen, but are still very satisfactory and indicate that the business does not have liquidity problems. The business is nil geared.

Use of resources

	2005	2006
Stock turnover	32 days	44 days
Debtors' collection period	37 days	66 days
Creditors' payment period	27 days	37 days
Asset turnover ratio	4.14:1	4.88:1

Stock turnover has slowed; debtors' collection period has lengthened – Rowles may have relaxed debtors' terms in order to achieve higher sales; creditors' payment period has lengthened – the creditors may become reluctant to supply the business unless they are paid more promptly. The asset turnover ratio has increased, indicating the policy of increased sales.

Conclusion

A profitable and expanding business. The decision to reduce selling prices has increased turnover and profits. The expansion has not caused liquidity problems, but there are warning signs of possible future problems in the asset utilisation figures. The business provides an excellent return on capital employed.

CHAPTER 15: Interpretation of Financial Statements

15.2

	Alpha plc	Beta plc
• gross profit percentage	11.85%	54.26%
• net profit percentage	2.87%	21.08%
• operating profit percentage	3.95%	26.01%
• return on capital employed	25%	16.91%

15.3

	Capa plc	Delta plc
• working capital ratio	1.51:1	1.04:1
• liquid capital ratio	0.82:1	0.65:1
• debtors' collection period	37 days	3 days
• creditors' payment period	57 days	46 days
• stock turnover	41 days	18 days
• gearing ratio	0.35:1 or 0.54:1	0.14:1 or 0.16:1

Capa plc is the chemical manufacturer, while Delta plc runs department stores.

All of the ratios for Capa are close to the benchmarks for a manufacturing business: eg working capital and liquid ratios, although a little low, are near the 'accepted' figures of 2:1 and 1:1, respectively. Debtors, creditors and stock turnover show quite a high level of stock being held; debtors' turnover indicates that most sales are on credit; creditors' turnover is rather high. The gearing ratio is acceptable – medium-geared.

For Delta plc, the ratios indicate a business that sells most of its goods on cash terms: low working capital and liquid ratios, with minimal debtors' turnover. The stock turnover is speedy, whilst creditors are paid after one-and-a-half months. The gearing ratio is low, indicating that there is scope for future borrowing should it be required.

15.7 Profitability

	2005	2006
Gross profit/sales	33.3%	25.0%
Net profit/sales	25.0%	17.5%
Expenses/sales	8.3%	7.5%
Return on capital employed	136.0%*/103.4%§	120.0%*/85.4%§

* opening capital used   § closing capital used

Reduction in selling prices is shown by the fall in gross profit/sales percentage. The policy has been successful, as the sales increase has been sufficient to give higher gross and net profits. Expenses/sales percentage has fallen, showing that overheads are under control. The return on capital employed has been reduced, but is still very high.

16.1 Suggestions to include:

	COST UNIT	COST CENTRE
college of further education	student hour	teaching department learning resources administration
mixed farm	tonne of wheat head of cattle	field cattle shed

16.3

Materials Costs	Labour Costs	Expenses
The cost of zip fasteners	Salaries of office staff	Premium for insurance of buildings
Cost of a consignment of blue denim	Wages of storekeepers	The cost of electricity
The cost of preprinted stationery	Overtime payments for machinists	The cost of television advertising
The cost of cones of thread	The canteen chef's wages	Road fund licences for vehicles

16.4

(a) indirect materials, (b) indirect labour, (c) direct labour, (d) direct expenses, (e) indirect expenses, (f) indirect expense, (or direct expense), (g) indirect expense, (h) indirect expense. (i) direct labour, (j) indirect expenses, (k) indirect expenses.

Factory overheads: (b), (f), (g)   Selling and distribution overheads: (j)

Administration overheads: (e), (h)   Finance overheads: (k)

17.1 HUGHES LIMITED
MANUFACTURING, TRADING AND PROFIT AND LOSS ACCOUNT
for the year ended 31 December 2001

	£	£
Opening stocks of raw materials		15,930
Add purchases of raw materials		118,830
		134,760
Less closing stock of raw materials		22,395
COST OF RAW MATERIALS USED		112,365
Manufacturing wages		117,315
PRIME COST		229,680
Factory overheads		
Rent and rates (75%)	12,345	
Power	3,825	
Heat and light	1,185	
Expenses and maintenance	4,095	
Salaries and wages (50%)	34,675	
Depreciation of plant and machinery	3,725	
		59,850
		289,530
Add opening stock of work-in-progress		6,250
		295,780
Less closing stock of work-in-progress		6,980
PRODUCTION COST OF GOODS COMPLETED		288,800
Sales		398,475
Opening stock of finished goods	21,320	
Production cost of goods completed	288,800	
	310,120	
Less closing stocks of finished goods	48,255	
COST OF SALES		261,865
GROSS PROFIT		136,610
Less overheads		
Rent and rates (25%)	4,115	
Salaries and wages (50%)	34,675	
Advertising	11,085	
Office expenses	3,930	
		53,805
NET PROFIT		82,805

17.2 MARTLEY MANUFACTURING LIMITED
MANUFACTURING, TRADING AND PROFIT AND LOSS ACCOUNT
for the year ended 31 December 2001

	£	£
Opening stocks of raw materials		105,000
Add purchases of raw materials		272,000
		377,000
Less closing stock of raw materials		102,000
COST OF RAW MATERIALS USED		275,000
Direct factory wages		126,000
PRIME COST		401,000
Factory overheads		
Rent and rates (75%)	9,000	
Factory power	20,000	
Depreciation of factory machinery	9,000	
Repairs for factory buildings	3,000	
Sundry factory expenses	9,000	
Indirect salaries and wages (50%)	44,000	
		94,000
		495,000
Add opening stock of work-in-progress		24,000
		519,000
Less closing stock of work-in-progress		29,000
PRODUCTION COST OF GOODS COMPLETED		490,000
Sales		704,000
Opening stock of finished goods	43,000	
Production cost of goods completed	490,000	
	533,000	
Less closing stocks of finished goods	32,000	
COST OF SALES		501,000
GROSS PROFIT		203,000
Less overheads		
Rent and rates (25%)	3,000	
Indirect salaries and wages (50%)	44,000	
Advertising	38,000	
Office expenses	29,000	
Depreciation of office equipment	7,500	
		121,500
NET PROFIT		81,500

CHAPTER 18: Accounting for Materials

18.1 SSAP 9 states that each category of stock must be value at the lower of cost and net realisable value.

'X1X': cost = £40, net realisable value = £30, therefore they are valued at £30 each.

'X-TRA-G': cost = £56, net realisable value = £90, therefore they are valued at £56 each.

'X-TREME 2': Cost = £35, net realisable value = £42, therefore they are valued at £35 each.

The total value of these items is therefore:

'X1X'	300 at £30 each	=	£9,000
'X-TRA-G'	260 at £56 each	=	£14,560
'X-TREME 2'	100 at £35 each	=	£3,500
TOTAL VALUE		=	£27,060

18.3

FIFO

STORES LEDGER RECORD

Date	Receipts			Issues			Balance		
2002	Quantity	Price	Value	Quantity	Price	Value	Quantity	Price	Value
		£	£		£	£		£	£
January	20	3.00	60.00				20	3.00	60.00
February	10	3.50	35.00				20	3.00	60.00
							10	3.50	35.00
							30		95.00
March				8	3.00	24.00	12	3.00	36.00
							10	3.50	35.00
							22		71.00
April	10	4.00	40.00				12	3.00	36.00
							10	3.50	35.00
							10	4.00	40.00
							32		111.00
May				12	3.00	36.00	6	3.50	21.00
				4	3.50	14.00	10	4.00	40.00
							16		61.00

LIFO

STORES LEDGER RECORD

Date	Receipts			Issues			Balance		
	Quantity	Price £	Value £	Quantity	Price £	Value £	Quantity	Price £	Value £
2002									
January	20	3.00	60.00				20	3.00	60.00
February	10	3.50	35.00				20	3.00	60.00
							10	3.50	35.00
							30		95.00
March				8	3.50	28.00	20	3.00	60.00
							2	3.50	7.00
							22		67.00
April	10	4.00	40.00				20	3.00	60.00
							2	3.50	7.00
							10	4.00	40.00
							32		107.00
May				10	4.00	40.00	16	3.00	48.00
				2	3.50	7.00			
				4	3.00	12.00			

AVCO

STORES LEDGER RECORD

Date	Receipts			Issues			Balance		
	Quantity	Price £	Value £	Quantity	Price £	Value £	Quantity	Price £	Value £
2002									
January	20	3.00	60.00				20	3.00	60.00
February	10	3.50	35.00				20	3.00	60.00
							10	3.50	35.00
							30	3.17	95.00
March				8	3.17	25.33	22	3.17	69.67
April	10	4.00	40.00				22	3.17	69.67
							10	4.00	40.00
							32	3.43	109.67
May				16	3.43	54.84	16	3.43	54.83

Note: some figures have been rounded to the nearest penny

18.5 Gross profits

	FIFO £	LIFO £
2004	8,000	8,000
2005	9,000	8,000
2006	10,000	8,000
2007	11,000	8,000
2008	12,000	18,000
Total	50,000	50,000

Total profits, over the five-year period, are the same in both cases because the entire life of the product is being considered. Thus the method of stock valuation employed affects only the allocation of the profits between each of the five years.

When stock levels are rising, profits are lower if LIFO is used. This is because, under LIFO, the most recent costs are matched against sales proceeds for the purpose of calculating profit, while items in stock are valued at the earliest purchase prices. The lower profits during each of the first four years are compensated in year 5 when stocks are run down to zero and the 'old' costs are matched against current sales. The FIFO method shows profits increasing by £1,000

CHAPTER 19: Accounting for Labour

19.1

N Ball:	35 hours x £8.00 per hour = £280.00 (no bonus)
T Smith:	37 hours x £9.00 per hour = £333.00 + bonus £9.00 = £342.00
L Lewis:	40 hours x £10.00 per hour = £400.00 + bonus £13.75 = £413.75
M Wilson:	38 hours x £7.00 per hour = £266.00 + bonus £4.08 = £270.08

19.3 (a)
- L Fry: £400.00 (time rate)
- R Williams: £315.00 (piecework rate)
- P Grant: £362.50 (piecework rate)

(b)
- not suitable for all direct labour employees
- employees' pay is reduced if there are production problems
- quality of the finished product may be low
- more inspectors may be needed
- control systems needed to check the amount produced by each worker
- more complex pay calculations
- may be difficulty in agreeing piecework rates with employees

19.6 (a) Week 1: 400 hours at £6.20 per hour = £2,480
50 hours at 1.5 x £6.20 = 50 x £9.30 = £465
Total gross earnings for Week 1 = £2,480 + £465 = £2,945

Week 2: 400 hours at £6.20 per hour = £2,480 = Total gross earnings

(b) Week 1: Normally treated as Indirect Labour cost would be overtime premium on 50 hours, ie 50 x 0.5 x £6.20 = £155.

Week 2: Normally treated as Indirect Labour cost would be 20 hours of non-production work at basic pay, ie 20 x £6.20 = £124.

CHAPTER 20: Overheads

20.1
- allocation of overheads – the charging to a cost centre of those overheads that have been directly incurred by that cost centre
- apportionment of overheads – the charging to a cost centre of a proportion of overheads

20.3 (a)

cost	basis of apportionment	total	dept A	dept B	dept C
		£	£	£	£
Rent and rates	Floor area	7,210	3,090	1,545	2,575
Depn. of machinery	Value of machinery	10,800	5,400	3,240	2,160
Supervisor's salary	Production-line employees	12,750	6,800	3,400	2,550
Machinery insurance	Value of machinery	750	375	225	150
		31,510	15,665	8,410	7,435

(b)

37 hours x 48 weeks	= 1,776 direct labour hours per employee
Dept A: 8 employees	= 14,208 hours = £1.10 per direct labour hour
Dept B: 4 employees	= 7,104 hours = £1.18 per direct labour hour
Dept C: 3 employees	= 5,328 hours = £1.40 per direct labour hour

20.5

	total	business studies	general studies	administration	technical support
	£	£	£	£	£
Overheads	81,600	40,000	20,000	9,600	12,000
Technical support	–	6,000	3,000	3,000	(12,000)
				12,600	
Administration		8,400	4,200	(12,600)	–
	81,600	54,400	27,200	–	–

21.2

		£	£
Direct materials:	100m x £7.50	750.00	
	75m x £4.00	300.00	
			1,050.00
Direct labour:	35 hours x £6.00		210.00
Overheads:	35 hours x £8.50		297.50
(a) TOTAL COST			1,557.50
	Profit (20% of total cost)		311.50
(b) SELLING PRICE			1,869.00

21.4

Total costs:

	£
Depreciation of diesel trains £30,000* x 6 trains	180,000
Leasing charges for track	500,000
Maintenance charges for trains	455,000
Fuel for trains	105,000
Wages of drivers and conductors	240,000
Administration	260,000
	1,740,000

* (£650,000 – £50,000) ÷ 20 years = £30,000 per train per year

Cost per passenger mile:

$$\frac{£1,740,000}{2.5m \text{ journeys x 5 miles}} = £0.1392 \text{ per passenger mile}$$

22.1

(a) fixed
(b) variable
(c) semi-variable
(d) fixed
(e) variable
(f) fixed
(g) variable
(h) variable.

22.5

(a) Fixed Costs (£20 + £100 + £10 + £70 + £80) = £280 per week

(b) Contribution (£16 – (£3 + £1 + £2) = £10 per guest night

Break-even = £280 / £10 = 28 guest-nights per week.

This is 28÷ 7 = 4 guests per night.

(c) This is 6 – 4 = 2 more guests per night than break-even. The weekly profit would therefore be 2 x £10 x 7 nights = £140.

23.1 Direct Material Price Variance: (71,500 kg x £9.45) – £678,700 = £ 3,025 A

Direct Material Usage Variance: £9.45 x ((96 kg x 700 units) – 71,500 kg) = £ 40,635 A

Note: 5 hours 6 minutes = 5.1 hours.
Direct Labour Rate Variance: (3,850 hrs x £6.30) – £24,220 = £ 35 F
Direct Labour Efficiency Variance: £6.30 x ([5.1 hr x 700 units] – 3,850 hrs) = £ 1,764 A

Reconciliation:

Standard Cost for Actual Production Level

700 x ((96 x £9.45) + (5.1 x £6.30))	£ 657,531	
Add: Direct Material Price Variance	£3,025	A
Direct Material Usage Variance	£40,635	A
Less: Direct Labour Rate Variance	(£35)	F
Add: Direct Labour Efficiency Variance	£1,764	A
Actual Cost of Actual Production (£678,700 + £24,220)	£702,920	

23.2 Total Direct Material Variance:

Standard material cost of this volume of production:
19,000 units x £15.00 per unit = £285,000.

The total direct material variance is therefore
£285,000 – £278,000   = £7,000 Favourable

Direct Material Price Variance:
(37,000 kg x £7.50) – £278,000   = £500 Adverse

Direct Material Usage Variance
£7.50 x ((2kg x 19,000 units) – 37,000 kg)   = £7,500 Favourable

Total Direct Labour Variance:

Standard labour cost of this volume of production:

19,000 units x £3.00 per unit = £57,000.

The total direct labour variance is therefore:

£57,000 – £58,600   = £1,600 Adverse

Direct Labour Rate Variance:

(9,800 hours kg x £6.00) – £58,600   = £200 Favourable

Direct Labour Efficiency Variance

£6.00 x ((0.5 hour x 19,000 units) – 9,800 hrs)   = £1,800 Adverse

23.3 The following comments are valid: (b), (d), (e), (f), (g).
The remaining comments are false.

23.4 (a) £10,000 ÷ 50,000   = £0.20 per mile

(b) Exp £10,000 – £12,000   = £2,000 adverse
    Vol £0.20 x (45,000 – 50,000)   = £1,000 adverse

    Total absorbed amount – actual fixed overheads
    (£0.20 x 45,000) – £12,000   = £3,000 adverse (or £2,000 + £1,000)!

(c) Under-absorption.

CHAPTER 24: Forecasting Techniques

24.1 (a) As can be seen from the workings, this example has a regular trend, increasing by £10 each day, and seasonal variations that are consistent, with each set of 5 totalling zero.

(b) The forecast for week 4 is calculated as follows:

	Forecast Trend £		Seasonal Variations	Forecast £
Tues	2,130 + (3 x 10)	= 2,160	– 180	1,980
Wed	2,130 + (4 x 10)	= 2,170	– 100	2,070
Thurs	2,130 + (5 x 10)	= 2,180	+ 50	2,230
Fri	2,130 + (6 x 10)	= 2,190	+ 120	2,310
Sat	2,130 + (7 x 10)	= 2,200	+ 110	2,310

Workings

Week	Day	Sales £	5-Point Moving Average (Trend)	Seasonal Variations
Week 1	Tues	1830		
	Wed	1920		
	Thurs	2080	2030	+ 50
	Fri	2160	2040	+120
	Sat	2160	2050	+110
Week 2	Tues	1880	2060	–180
	Wed	1970	2070	–100
	Thurs	2130	2080	+ 50
	Fri	2210	2090	+120
	Sat	2210	2100	+110
Week 3	Tues	1930	2110	–180
	Wed	2020	2120	–100
	Thurs	2180	2130	+ 50
	Fri	2260		
	Sat	2260		

24.4 (a) Average trend movement is difference between last and first trend figures, divided by number of movements.

= (6,290 – 5,800) ÷ 7   = + 70

(b) If trend is increasing at an average 70 policies per quarter, then by

Year 3 quarter 3 it will be 6,290 + (3 x 70)   = 6,500, and by

Year 3 quarter 4 it will be 6,290 + (4 x 70)   = 6,570.

Adjusting these figures by the seasonal variations (which were identical for both years) gives:

Year 3 quarter 3 forecast of (6,500 + 880)   = 7,380

Year 3 quarter 4 forecast of (6,570 – 100)   = 6,470.

CHAPTER 25: Budgeting

25.1 (a) The speed at which the craftsmen work, and their working hours will determine their output. Since they can sell all that they produce their output will be the principal budget factor.

(b) The transport requirements of the turkey supplier will form the principal budget factor. The transport company and the turkey supplier will have a common activity level over the coming year.

(c) The maintenance requirements of the Manchester trams will form the principal budget factor. This will in turn depend upon maintenance schedules for the current fleet, plus that for any additional trams to be acquired.

(d) The demand from the staff at the business park for baked potatoes seems likely to easily outstrip supply, based on the figures given. The capacity of the outlet would therefore form the principal budget factor.

25.2 The production budget in units for month 5 equals:

Budgeted Sales Units	1,800	units
– Opening Stock of Finished Goods	(500)	units
+ Closing Stock of Finished Goods	400	units
Production budget	1,700	units

The raw materials usage budget is based on the raw material required to satisfy the production budget:

Raw Materials Usage   = (1,700 units x 4 kilos per unit)   ÷ 6,800 kilos.

The raw material purchases budget for month 5 will equal:

Raw materials usage budget   6,800 kilos
- opening stock of raw materials,   (1,200) kilos
+ closing stock of raw materials.   1,500 kilos
Raw materials purchases budget   7,100 kilos

CHAPTER 26: Managing Working Capital

26.2

	(a) Current Position	(b) Revised Position
	£'000	£'000
Stocks	200	150
Debtors	150	100
Bank	20	120 (bal figure)
Less Creditors	(210)	(210)
Total Working Capital	160	160

26.3

- The credit controller's absence accounts for an increase in debtors of £40,000, and an equal reduction in the bank balance.

- The early delivery accounts for increased stock of £20,000 and an increase in creditors of the same amount.

- The additional goods bought account for an increase in stock of £10,000, and a reduction in the bank balance of the same amount since the goods have been paid for.

These three issues together account for the differences between the budgeted and actual positions.

CHAPTER 27: Measuring Performance

27.2 Answer (c) is correct, because the gross profit = £500,000 x 24% = £120,000

Therefore £500,000 – Cost of sales = £120,000

And cost of sales = £500,000 – £120,000 = £380,000.

Gross profit – Expenses = Operating profit

Therefore £120,000 – expenses = £50,000

And hence expenses = £120,000 – £50,000 = £70,000

27.4

(a)

Gross Profit margin	= (1,910 ÷ 2,500) x 100%	= 76.4%
Operating profit margin	= (625 ÷ 2,500) x 100%	= 25.0%
Return on Capital Employed	= (625 ÷ 2,840) x 100%	= 22.0%
Asset turnover	= 2,500 ÷ 2,840	= 0.88 times
The average age of debtors	= (160 ÷ 2,500) x 365	= 23 days
Average finished goods stock	= 0.5 x (30 + 90)	= 60

The average age of finished goods stock (using average stock)

= (60 ÷ 590) x 365   = 37 days.

(b) Both ROCE and Asset turnover depend on the value of the net assets. During the year ended 30 June 2001, Subsidiary Jack Ltd has considerable additions to the fixed assets, but it is not known at what time of the year these were acquired. It is possible that these new assets have not yet generated additional sales (for asset turnover) or profits (for ROCE). These two measures would be lower as a result.

(c) If Subsidiary Jack Ltd had achieved the target Asset turnover of 1.5 times, its turnover would have been 1.5 x £2,840,000 = £4,260,000.

(d) Assuming Subsidiary Jack Ltd had maintained its operating profit margin of 25% on turnover of £4,260,000, its operating profit would be

25% x £4,260,000 = £1,065,000.

With this operating profit, its ROCE would be

(1,065 ÷ 2,840) x 100% = 37.5%.

27.6 You may have given examples including any of the following:

(a) Amount of gross profit, net profit, turnover, prices, variances, value added

(b) Ratios, number of machine hours used, number of units produced, number of rejected units, number of orders processed, number of customer complaints, etc

(c) Results of customer opinion surveys, peer reviews or appraisals

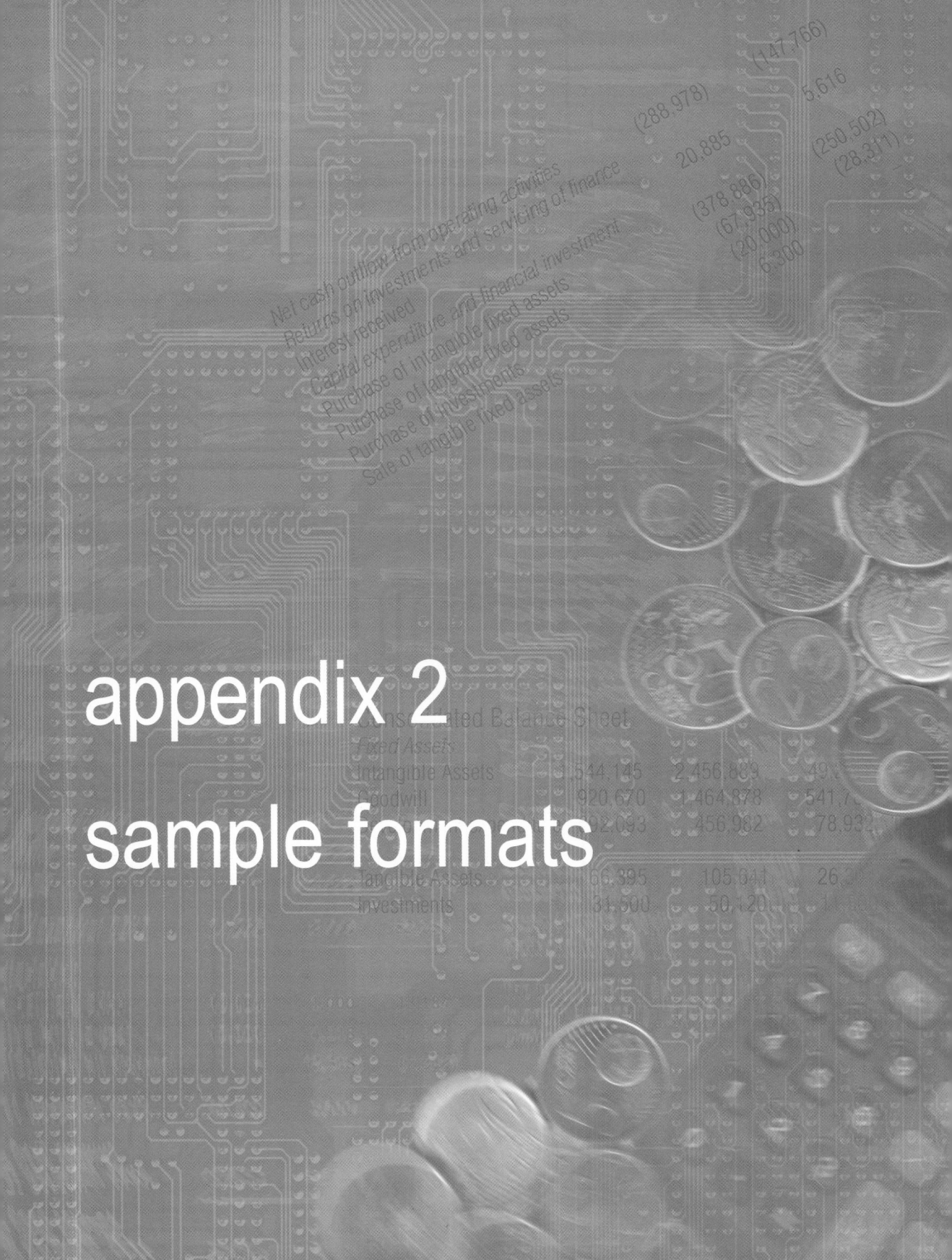

appendix 2

sample formats

APPENDIX CONTENTS

DOUBLE-ENTRY ACCOUNTS

Dr   Cr

Date	Details	Amount	Date	Details	Amount
		£			£

Dr   Cr

Date	Details	Amount	Date	Details	Amount
		£			£

Dr   Cr

Date	Details	Amount	Date	Details	Amount
		£			£

sole trader final accounts

TRADING AND PROFIT AND LOSS ACCOUNT OF ***name***
FOR THE YEAR/PERIOD ENDED ***date***

	£	£	£	
Sales			x	
Less Sales returns			x	
Net sales			x	(a)
Opening stock		x		
Purchases	x			
Carriage in	x			
Less Purchases returns	x			
Net purchases		x		
		x		
Less closing stock		x		
Cost of sales			x	(b)
Gross profit (a) − (b)			x	(c)
Add other income, eg				
Discount received			x	
Reduction in provision for bad debts			x	(d)
Profit on sale of fixed assets			x	
Other income			x	
(c) + (d)			x	(e)
Less expenses, eg				
Vehicle running expenses		x		
Rent		x		
Rates		x		
Heating and lighting		x		
Telephone		x		
Salaries and wages*		x		
Discount allowed		x		
Carriage out		x		
Other items, eg				
Provision for depreciation		x		
Loss on sale of fixed assets		x		
Bad debts written off		x		
Increase in provision for bad debts		x		
			x	(f)
Net profit (e) − (f)			x	(g)

TRADING ACCOUNT / *PROFIT AND LOSS ACCOUNT*

* Wages are sometimes listed as an expense in the trading account section

BALANCE SHEET OF * name *** AS AT *** date *****

		£	£	£	
Fixed Assets		Cost (a)	Dep'n to date (b)	Net	(a) – (b)
Intangible:	Goodwill	x	x	x	
Tangible:	Premises	x	x	x	
	Equipment	x	x	x	
	Vehicles	x	x	x	
	etc	x	x	x	
		x	x	x	(c)

	£	£	
Current Assets			
Stock (closing)		x	
Debtors	x		
Less Provision for bad debts	x		
		x	
Prepayments		x	
Bank		x	
Cash		x	
		x	(d)
Less Current Liabilities			
Creditors	x		
Accruals	x		
Bank overdraft	x		
		x	(e)
Working Capital (d)– (e)		x	(f)
(c) + (f)		x	(g)
Less Long-term Liabilities			
Loans		x	(h)
NET ASSETS (g) – (h)		x	(i)
FINANCED BY			
Capital			
Opening capital		x	
Add Net profit (from profit and loss account)		x	
		x	
Less Drawings		x	
		x	(i)

Note: Balance sheet balances at points (i)

Practical point: when preparing handwritten final accounts it is usual practice to underline all the headings and sub-headings shown in bold print in the example layout.

limited company final accounts

*** NAME OF COMPANY *** LIMITED
TRADING AND PROFIT AND LOSS ACCOUNT FOR THE YEAR/PERIOD ENDED *** DATE ***

	£	£	
Sales	X		(a)
Opening stock	X		
Purchases or production cost	X		
	X		
Less closing stock	X		
Cost of sales		X	(b)
Gross profit (a) − (b)		X	(c)
Less expenses:			
eg Selling and distribution costs	X		
Administration costs	X		
Finance costs	X		
		X	(d)
Net profit for year before taxation (c) − (d)		X	(e)
Less corporation tax		X	(f)
Profit for year after taxation (e) − (f)		X	(g)
Less interim dividends paid			
ordinary shares	X		
preference shares	X		
final dividends proposed			
ordinary shares	X		
preference shares	X		
		X	(h)
Retained profit for year (g) − (h)		X	(i)
Add balance of retained profits at beginning of year		X	(j)
Balance of retained profits at end of year (i) + (j)		X	(k)

Notes:
- for a manufacturing business, production cost (ie the factory cost of manufacturing the products) is shown instead of purchases
- depreciation of fixed assets is included in the costs for production, selling and distribution, and administration, as appropriate
- directors' remuneration and debenture interest is included in the expenses

*** NAME OF COMPANY *** LIMITED
BALANCE SHEET AS AT *** DATE ***

Fixed Assets	Cost (a) £	Dep'n to date (b) £	Net (a) – (b) £
Intangible			
Goodwill	x	x	x
Tangible			
Freehold land and buildings	x	x	x
Machinery	x	x	x
Fixtures and fittings	x	x	x
etc	x	x	x
	x	x	x (c)

Current Assets			
Stock *(closing)*		x	
Debtors		x	
Bank		x	
Cash		x	
		x	(d)

Less Current Liabilities			
Creditors	x		
Bank overdraft	x		
Proposed dividends	x		
Corporation tax	x		
		x	(e)

Working Capital (d) – (e)   x (f)

(c) + (f)   x (g)

Less Long-term Liabilities

Debentures   x (h)

NET ASSETS (g) – (h)   x (i)

FINANCED BY

Authorised share capital

x (number) preference shares of £x (nominal value) each	x
x (number) ordinary shares of £x (nominal value) each	x
	x

Issued share capital

x (number) preference shares of £x (nominal value) each, fully/partly paid	x
x (number) ordinary shares of £x (nominal value) each, fully/partly paid	x
	x

Capital reserves

Share premium account	x	
Revaluation reserve	x	x

Revenue reserves

Profit and loss account	x	
General reserve	x	x

SHAREHOLDERS' FUNDS   x (i)

Note: balance sheet balances at points (i)

profit and loss account for published limited company accounts (FRS 3)

PROFIT AND LOSS ACCOUNT FOR THE YEAR ENDED ....

Turnover (sales) – continuing operations ....

Cost of sales ....

Gross profit ....

Distribution costs ....

Administration expenses ....

Operating profit – continuing operations ....

Interest payable and similar charges ....

Profit on ordinary activities before taxation ....

Tax on profit on ordinary activities ....

Profit on ordinary activities after taxation ....

Dividends ....

Retained profit for the financial year ....

cash flow statement

CASH FLOW STATEMENT FOR THE YEAR ENDED *** DATE ***

	£	£
Operating activities:		
Operating profit (note: before tax and interest)	x	
Depreciation for year	x	
Increase or decrease in stocks	(x) or x	
Increase or decrease in debtors	(x) or x	
Increase or decrease in creditors	x or (x)	
Net cash inflow from operating activities		x
Returns on investments and servicing of finance:		
Interest and dividends received	x	
Interest and dividends paid		
(dividends on ordinary shares shown below)	(x)	
		x or (x)
Taxation:		
Corporation tax paid (note: amount *paid* during year)		(x)
Capital expenditure and financial investment		
Payments to acquire fixed assets and investments	(x)	
Receipts from sales of fixed assets and investments	x	
		x or (x)
Acquisitions and disposals		
eg purchase of subsidiary undertakings	(x)	
eg sale of a business	x	x or (x)
Equity dividends paid: (note: amount *paid* during year)		(x)
Cash inflow or outflow before use of liquid resources and financing		x or (x)
Management of liquid resources:		
eg purchase of treasury bills	(x)	
eg sale of treasury bills	x	
		x or (x)
Financing:		
Issue of share capital	x	
Repayment of share capital	(x)	
Increase in loans	x	
Repayment of loans	(x)	
		x or (x)
Increase or decrease in cash		x or (x)

Note: money amounts shown in brackets indicate a deduction or, where the figure is a sub-total, a negative figure

Accounting ratios worksheet

This worksheet will assist in calculating the main accounting ratios from a set of final accounts. Use it as follows:

- *enter the figures from the trading and profit and loss account and balance sheet against items 1 – 11*
- *calculate the ratios and percentages using the numbered figures, as indicated on the next page*

Note that this will assist in the calculation of the main accounting ratios; but it will not provide the interpretative aspects.

FIGURES FROM FINAL ACCOUNTS

Trading and profit and loss account

1	Sales (or turnover)	
2	Cost of goods sold (or cost of sales)	
3	Operating profit (or net profit + interest payable)	
4	Net profit (or profit on ordinary activities) before taxation	

Balance sheet

5	Current assets sub-total	
6	Stock	
7	Debtors	
8	Current liabilities sub-total (or creditors: amounts falling due within one year)	
9	Trade creditors	
10	Long-term liabilities (or creditors: amounts falling due after more than one year)	
11	Capital and reserves total	

ACCOUNTING RATIOS

	figures from the table on the previous page		previous year	current year
Profitability				
Gross profit/sales percentage	$\dfrac{1-2}{1}$	x $\dfrac{100}{1}$	%	%
Operating profit/sales percentage	$\dfrac{3}{1}$	x $\dfrac{100}{1}$	%	%
Net profit/sales percentage	$\dfrac{4}{1}$	x $\dfrac{100}{1}$	%	%
Return on capital employed	$\dfrac{3}{10+11}$	x $\dfrac{100}{1}$	%	%
Return on equity*	$\dfrac{4-\text{tax}}{11}$	x $\dfrac{100}{1}$	%	%
* less preference dividend (if any)				
Liquidity				
Working capital ratio	$\dfrac{5}{8}$		:1	:1
Liquid capital ratio	$\dfrac{5-6}{8}$		:1	:1
Financial position				
Capital gearing percentage†	$\dfrac{10}{11}$	x $\dfrac{100}{1}$	%	%
Use of resources				
Stock turnover (days)	$\dfrac{6\,*}{2}$	x 365	days	days
* ideally, this should be the average of opening stock and closing stock				
Debtors' collection period (days)	$\dfrac{7}{1}$	x 365	days	days
Creditors' payment period (days)	$\dfrac{9}{2*}$	x 365	days	days
* ideally, this should be the purchases figure				

† alternative gearing calculation: $\dfrac{10}{10+11}$

index

INDEX

---

*__Accounting ratios__: for ratios seen from the financial accounting perspective, refer to the ratios in the page range 297 to 313; for management accounting studies, refer to the ratios in the 565-582 page range.

636

notes

notes

notes